The Aunt Lute

ANTHOLOGY

of U.S.

Contributors

KEVIN DiPIRRO
BONNIE J. DOW
GEORGETTE ENRIQUEZ
ARMANDO GARCÍA
MARCY KNOPF-NEWMAN
MONICA MARTINEZ
JANET FRY REED
ELDA MARÍA ROMÁN

aunt lute books   SAN FRANCISCO

WOMEN
WRITERS

General Editors
LISA MARIA HOGELAND
AND SHAY BRAWN

Co-Editors
JULIANA CHANG, LINDA GARBER,
MICHELLE GIBSON, ANAHID KASSABIAN,
DEBORAH T. MEEM, RHONDA PETTIT,
MARÍA JOSEFINA SALDAÑA-PORTILLO

VOLUME TWO: *The 20th Century*

Quoted material on cover is taken from "How to Tame a Wild Tongue" by Gloria Anzaldúa, "Heritage" by Gwendolyn Bennett, "The Transformation of Silence into Language and Action" by Audre Lorde, and "Woman" by Ella Wheeler Wilcox.

Pages 1443 to 1453 constitute a legal extension of this copyright page.

Aunt Lute Books
P.O. Box 410687
San Francisco, CA 94141
www.auntlute.com

Executive Director: Joan Pinkvoss
Artistic Director: Shay Brawn
Managing Editor: Gina Gemello
Editorial Assistant: Ladi Youssefi
Permissions Director: Elisabeth Rohrbach
Production: Chelsea Adewunmi, Erica Bestpitch, KB Burnside, Marisa Crawford, Andrea de Brito, Noelle de la Paz, Maria DeLorenzo, Sarah Duni, Anisha K. Gidvani, Shahara Godfrey, Marielle Gomez, Riah Gouvea, Sarah Graham, Rashida Harmon, Laura Kramp, Merri Kwan, Claudia LaMar, Sarah Leavitt, Cloé-Mai Le Gall-Scoville, Cassie McGettigan, Soma Nath, Anna Neary, Sabrina Peterson, Kathleen Pullum, Riki García Rebel, Emily Ryan, Mona Lisa Safai, Aileen Suzara, Andrea Blythe Svendsen, Jenna Varden, Melissa Wong-Shing, and Ladi Youssefi.

Cover Design: Amy Woloszyn | amymade graphic design
Text Design: Kajun Graphics
Typesetting: Den Legaspi

This book was made possible through the support of the National Endowment for the Arts, the San Francisco Arts Commission, and the Vessel Foundation.

Library of Congress Cataloging-in-Publication Data
The Aunt Lute anthology of U.S. women writers / general editors, Lisa Maria Hogeland, Mary Klages.-- 1st ed.

   p. cm.
  Includes bibliographical references.
  ISBN 1-879960-68-0 (v. 1, pbk. : alk. paper)
 1. American literature--Women authors. 2. Women--United States--Literary collections. 3. United States--Literary collections. I. Hogeland, Lisa Maria. II. Klages, Mary.

  PS508.W7A96 2004
  810.8'09287--dc22

                    2004022106

Printed in the United States of America
10 9 8 7 6 5 4 3 2 1

Acknowledgments

A work of this scope would be impossible to complete without the support of many people.

Several individuals provided critical help in consulting about text selection, including Chelsea Adewunmi; Lisa Botshon, University of Maine at Augusta; Sharon Dean, University of Cincinnati; Annie Finch, University of Southern Maine; and Anneliese Truame. Important research was provided by Paige Eve Chant, while Leonard Garber offered translation assistance and innumerable historical minutiae were verified by Sabrina Peterson and Cloé-Mai Le Gall-Scoville.

The press and individual editors have also benefited from the generous material support of individuals and institutions, whom we gratefully acknowledge here: Brown University; Marta Drury; McMicken College of Arts and Sciences, University of Cincinnati; the National Endowment for the Arts; The San Francisco Arts Commission Cultural Equity Fund; Sara Paretsky; The College of Arts and Sciences, Santa Clara University; and the Vessel Foundation.

We want to thank the capable and generous staffs of the following libraries: Langsam Library, University of Cincinnati; the Public Library of Hamilton County and the City of Cincinnati; the Public Library of Nashville, Tennessee; and Green Library, Stanford University.

Preparing this manuscript for publication has involved thousands of hours of painstaking proofreading, copyediting, and fact-checking, most of which was accomplished through the efforts of a diligent and dedicated set of interns. We are profoundly thankful to them for the gift of their time, intelligence, and commitment: Chelsea Adewunmi, Erica Bestpitch, KB Burnside, Marisa Crawford, Andrea de Brito, Noelle de la Paz, Maria DeLorenzo, Sarah Duni, Anisha K. Gidvani, Riah Gouvea, Sarah Graham, Rashida Harmon, Laura Kramp, Merri Kwan, Claudia LaMar, Sarah Leavitt, Cloé-Mai Le Gall-Scoville, Cassie McGettigan, Anna Neary, Sabrina Peterson, Kathleen Pullum, Riki García Rebel, Elizabeth Rohrbach, Emily Ryan, Mona Lisa Safai, Aileen Suzara, Andrea Blythe Svendsen, Jenna Varden, Melissa Wong-Shing, and Ladi Youssefi.

We are also indebted to the many people—authors, publishers, agents, rights coordinators, and friends of friends—who helped us navigate the sometimes byzantine process of obtaining permissions to reprint the many pieces in this volume. We are particularly thankful to Christina Brianik at Rutgers University Press, Julie Graves at Firebrand Books, and Suzanna Tamminen at Wesleyan University Press, as well as David Kazanjian and Gerald Nicosia.

The editors wish to express particular thanks to the amazing Gina Gemello, who has overseen the production of both volumes of this anthology, for so ably and gracefully marshaling us all—editors and interns alike—through the complex and often messy task of putting all the pieces together.

Finally, the editors would like to thank Joan Pinkvoss, executive director and co-founder of Aunt Lute Books, not only for her unwavering support for this project, but for inspiring all of us with her commitment to bringing into print the work of women whose voices have long been marginalized and devalued.

The Aunt Lute ANTHOLOGY
of U.S. WOMEN WRITERS

CONTENTS

Preface

I.

The last thirty years have seen an enormous revision of the U.S. literary canon as it has expanded to include more works by women, working class people, and people of color. The kind of American literature survey course that many of the editors of this volume experienced as undergraduates (yes Emily Dickinson, maybe Anne Bradstreet, maybe Langston Hughes, no women of color writers) is, happily, a thing of the past (though perhaps unevenly so). The institutional success of that curricular transformation was perhaps best embodied in the publication of the now premier anthology of U.S. writing, *The Heath Anthology of American Literature,* which debuted in 1989 and has since set the standard for inclusiveness. Its reconstruction of the U.S. literary landscape with each succeeding edition both enlarges and destabilizes that landscape, helping students to see how fraught its major categories, "American" and "Literature," truly are.

What need is there, then, for the anthology you hold in your hands? What is still to be gained by considering U.S. *women's* writing as a separate tradition, apart from men's writing, given the increased representation of women? Part of the answer to that question lies in the fact that for the better part of the twentieth century, women writers were burdened by the repression of a women's tradition of writing. While there was an extraordinary amount of women's writing in the nineteenth century, most of that writing was either forgotten or dismissed as trivial (local, sentimental, domestic) by the emergent profession of American literary study. In the absence of that tradition, most women writing in the first several decades of the twentieth century experienced the category of "woman writer" itself as contradictory, and many women writers have felt compelled to take a position for or against themselves as women, whether it is to reject that categorization, as Laura (Riding) Jackson did, or to embrace it, as Amy Lowell did. From the vantage point of those of us writing and studying now, the history of American women's writing might appear to be an unbroken conversation stretching across generations and centuries. But that is to a great extent an illusion produced by the very success of women writers and feminist scholars in recovering, reconstructing, and joining in conversation with the lost voices of earlier women writers, a process we can see occurring up through the 1970s and 1980s in the works of such writers as Adrienne Rich and Alice Walker.

Apart from the historical significance of gender as a defining condition of women's writing, it is also the case that gender persists as an important axis of social and political identity, and thus remains a crucial lens through which to view cultural production. This is not to suggest, of course, that all women experience their gender in the same way. Indeed, it is to suggest quite the opposite: One of the reasons to assemble a women's tradition is to show precisely how complicated the category "women" is, a complexity which might be obscured in a non-gender-based anthology. While in the past few decades there have been many anthologies of U.S. women's writing published, those have been largely devoted to specific genres, themes, periods, or identity-based traditions. These anthologies have been and continue to be crucial in constructing and reconstructing important subfields in American literary study. However, we believe that it is also important to place these women's traditions side by side (by side by side). It is only when we place women writers in dialog with each other that we come to see how race, class, sexuality, ability, and other social determinants unsettle our thinking about what it means to be a woman or a woman writer. Women experience gender differently in relation to their cultural and social locations, and the nuances of those are rendered more apparent in a comprehensive anthology.

In keeping with Aunt Lute Books' founding mission, the works of women of color writers are squarely at the center of our vision of U.S. women's writing. That decision allows us to forward many of the primary issues these writers take up as crucial issues for the U.S. in the twentieth century—race, "race," racism, and racialization; difference, multiplicity, culture, and "culture;" diaspora, migration, immigration, and emigration; translation, code-switching, dialect, and creole. Additionally, it has allowed us to situate histories of oppression and resistance, violence and internalization, achievement and celebration, and heroism and collaboration at the center of U.S. history. Of course, other issues conventionally understood as "women's issues" (pregnancy and childbirth, domestic violence, marriage, romantic love, families, work, education, writing), also sit at the center of work by women of color, just as they do for white women. And issues not conventionally understood as "women's issues" (war, economics, medicine, labor, to name a few) are also at stake in works by women writers of all backgrounds. In making our selections, we have sought to convey to readers the amazing breadth and variety of women's contributions to the critical conversations of the twentieth century.

In addition to forwarding women writers of color, we have also included such little read white women writers as Edna Ferber, Dorothy Canfield Fisher, Fannie Hurst, and Zona Gale. Ferber and Hurst in particular were widely read and wildly popular writers, each lauded in her time as the most popular woman writer in America. One of our surprises in compiling this volume is how quickly (some) women writers have disappeared from critical conversations, even after the pervasive sexism of the earlier twentieth century has dissipated to some extent.

As with Volume I, we have been particularly interested in tracking the ways in which women writers "enter the conversation," which is often not by way of traditional literary genres. Thus we have included some samples of journalism, autobiography, and essay. We have also included a thread of music—from blues lyrics to protest songs to opera libretti. Blues, of course, are an important part of the poetics of Black women's literary tradition, and a significant resource from which contemporary African-American women writers draw. Like the blues, protest songs and women's folk music have often provided women with access to a public voice in a way that the institution of literature has not. And, given the rootedness of those genres in performance, they represent a form of women's writing that transcends the limits of literacy. Finally, it can be difficult to draw a bright line in contemporary practice between poetry, spoken word, and lyrics, and so we felt it important to include a strong offering of the more performative genres. In choosing opera libretti to represent two of the major writers of the twentieth century—Gertrude Stein and Toni Morrison—we mean to emphasize how important performance is and has been to the tradition of women's writing in the U.S.

Another line that can be difficult to draw is that between periods. All periodization of writers is arbitrary—Charlotte Perkins Gilman could have appeared in either volume, for example, and several of the turn-of-the-century poets from Volume I might have been in this volume along with Ella Wheeler Wilcox. Gilman's "The Yellow Wall-Paper," we felt, resonated better with the concerns raised by writers in Volume I; those turn-of-the-century poets helped pave the way for the discovery of Emily Dickinson, and so we wanted the majority of them to be in her volume. This general problem in literary scholarship is exacerbated in the women's tradition(s), not least because some women writers simply outlive their period designations. Thus, for example, Kay Boyle and Dorothy West—Modernist and Harlem Renaissance writers, respectively—wrote and published long after their movements or moments had ended. Literary history, it turns out, is messy, and its messiness is perhaps most obvious at the volume break.

This, then, is our vision of twentieth century U.S. women's writing: multicultural, multi-ethnic, multi-genre, transnation, transsex, sometimes in translation, the well known and the obscure, the fallen-out-of-favor and the Nobel Laureate. Once again, as we did in Volume I, we've omitted excerpts from novels, making room, we believe, for the most diverse collection of U.S. women's literary work ever assembled. We hope students, teachers, and scholars can find here—as we did—new works, new writers, new conversations, and new questions.

+ + +

Note on Texts and Dates

Nearly every text in this volume has been previously published in some form. Where possible, we used the earliest published version of each text to assure greatest accuracy. Where there were obvious typographical errors, we corrected them silently (and, when possible, in consultation with the authors). We did not, however, "correct" archaic usage, spellings, or punctuation. The dates for fiction, non-fiction prose, and drama are the dates of first publication. The dates for poetry reflect the poem's first publication in a collection. Where there is a substantial difference between the time a text was written and the time it was published, we have noted that gap in the annotations. We welcome any corrections or additional information about dates and versions that readers wish to supply.

ELLA WHEELER WILCOX (1850-1919)

The author of more than forty books of poetry, fiction, children's verse, and essays, Ella Wheeler was born November 5, 1850, in Johnstown, Wisconsin, to Marcus H. and Sarah Pratt Wheeler. She attended district school and later spent a term at Wisconsin University, which she considered a "waste of time." After her marriage in 1884 to Robert Wilcox, she moved to Connecticut, where she lived a conventional and highly productive life. The poet who penned "Laugh and the world laughs with you/Weep and you weep alone" became involved in the temperance movement, helped establish the New York Institute for Psychical Research, traveled widely, and became involved in the women's issues of her time.

The nature of her involvement, like that of her poetry, is marked by contradiction, particularly when her work is considered from a feminist perspective. Her 1883 volume, *Poems of Passion,* created a scandal—and consequently huge sales—because of its focus on female physical desire. She would later warn World War I soldiers against venereal disease, reciting her poem "Soldiers, Come Home Clean" during a European tour. Her interest in unions and the working classes became evident in *Poems of Progress* (1909). In combining marriage and a prolific career as a popular poet, Wilcox became a powerful role model for women. She believed poetry stemmed from feeling and should serve social rather than merely aesthetic purposes. Yet she also believed, like Lydia Huntley Sigourney, that a woman's highest calling was to be wife and mother, concluding her poem "Little Mothers of Men to Be" with the line *"We must better the mothers to better the race!"* She wrote anti-war poems as well as patriotic pro-war poems, divorce poems critical of women as well as men, and poems using racial stereotypes to sympathetically convey the plight of African Americans. These inconsistencies did not offend her many readers, but her conventionally rhymed and metered poems, often containing moral lessons and surface optimism, quickly fell out of favor with early twentieth century critics.

Solitude

Laugh, and the world laughs with you;
Weep, and you weep alone;
    For the sad old earth
    Must borrow its mirth,
It has trouble enough of its own.   5

Sing, and the hills will answer;
Sigh, it is lost on the air;
    The echoes bound
    To a joyful sound,
But shrink from voicing care.   10

Rejoice, and men seek you;
Grieve, and they turn and go;
    They want full measure
    Of all your pleasure,
But they do not want your woe.   15

Be glad, and your friends are many;
Be sad, and you lose them all;
    There are none to decline

Your nectared wine,
But alone you must drink life's gall.   20

Feast, and your halls are crowded;
Fast, and the world goes by;
    Succeed and give,
    And it helps you live,
But it cannot help you die.   25

There is room in the halls of pleasure
For a long and lordly train;
    But one by one
    We must all file on
Through the narrow aisles of pain.   30

                                  —1882

Communism

When my blood flows calm as a purling river
When my heart is asleep and my brain has sway,
It is then that I vow we must part forever,
That I will forget you, and put you away
Out of my life, as a dream is banished   5
Out of the mind when the dreamer awakes;
That I know it will be when the spell has vanished,
Better for both of our sakes.

When the court of the mind is ruled by Reason,
I know it is wiser for us to part;   10
But Love is a spy who is plotting treason,
In league with that warm, red rebel, the Heart.
They whisper to me that the King is cruel,
That his reign is wicked, his law a sin,
And every word they utter is fuel   15
To the flame that smolders within.

And on nights like this, when my blood runs riot
With the fever of youth and its made desires,
When my brain in vain bids my heart be quiet,
When my breast seems the center of lava-fires,   20
Oh, then is the time when most I miss you,
And I swear by the stars and my soul and say
That I will have you, and hold you, and kiss you,
Though the whole world stands in the way.

And like Communists, as mad, as disloyal,   25
My fierce emotions roam out of their lair;
They hate King Reason for being royal—
They would fire his castle, and burn him there.
O Love! they would clasp you, and crush you and kill you,
In the insurrection of uncontrol.   30

Across the miles, does this wild war thrill you
That is raging in my soul?

—1883

Woman

Give us that grand word "woman" once again,
And let's have done with "lady": one's a term
Full of fine force, strong, beautiful, and firm,
Fit for the noblest use of tongue or pen;
And one's a word for lackeys. One suggests   5
The Mother, Wife, and Sister! One the dame
Whose costly robe, mayhap, gives her the name.
One word upon its own strength leans and rests;
The other minces tiptoe. Who would be
The perfect woman must grow brave of heart   10
And broad of soul to play her troubled part
Well in life's drama. While each day we see
The "perfect lady" skilled in what to do
And what to say, grace in each tone and act
('Tis taught in schools, but needs some native tact),   15
Yet narrow in her mind as in her shoe.
Give the first place then to the nobler phrase,
And leave the lesser word for lesser praise.

—1902

FANNIE BARRIER WILLIAMS (1855-1944)

Reformer, lecturer, and writer Fannie Barrier was born in Brockport, New York, to Anthony Barrier, a barber and coal merchant, and Harriet Barrier, a Sunday school teacher. The Barrier family was well respected in their mostly white community, and young Fannie was insulated from the racism she would later encounter. In 1870, she was the first African American to graduate from the State Normal School. After the Civil War, Barrier took a teaching position in the South, but found the racism there unbearable. She studied piano at the New England Conservatory of Music, but ultimately left because Southern white students objected to her presence. Barrier then moved to Washington, D.C., to teach, where she met S. Laing Williams, a law student whom she married in 1887. The couple moved to Chicago, where they became leaders in the local and national African-American community, working with Booker T. Washington and W.E.B. DuBois. Williams became known across the country as a lecturer, advocating Black women's education, the integration of churches, and racial uplift. She worked as a journalist for several Black newspapers in Chicago, and founded women's clubs and institutions to help Black women. After her husband died in 1921, Williams continued her work. In 1926, she returned to Brockport to care for her sister. The Barrier family home is now a New York State historical site.

A Northern Negro's Autobiography

In THE INDEPENDENT[1] of March 17th last I read, with a great deal of interest, three contributions to the so-called race problem, to be found in the experiences of a Southern colored woman, a Southern white woman and a Northern white woman.

I am a Northern colored woman, a mulatto in complexion, and was born since the war in a village town of Western New York. My parents and grandparents were free people. My mother was born in New York State and my father in Pennsylvania. They both attended the common schools and were fairly educated. They had a taste for good books and the refinements of life, were public spirited and regarded as good citizens. My father moved to this Western New York village when he was quite a boy and was a resident of the town for over fifty years; he was married to my mother in this town and three children were born to them; he created for himself a good business and was able to take good care of his family. My parents were strictly religious people and were members of one of the largest white churches in the village. My father, during his membership in this church, held successively almost every important office open to a layman, having been clerk, trustee, treasurer and deacon, which office he held at the time of his death, in 1890. He was for years teacher of an adult Bible class composed of some of the best men and women of the village, and my mother is still a teacher of a large Bible class of women in the same Sunday school. Ours was the only colored family in the church, in fact, the only one in the town for many years, and certainly there could not have been a relationship more cordial, respectful and intimate than that of our family and the white people of this community. We three children were sent to school as soon as we were old enough, and remained there until we were graduated. During our school days our associates, schoolmates and companions were all white boys and girls. These relationships were natural, spontaneous and free from all restraint. We went freely to each other's houses, to parties, socials, and joined on equal terms in all school entertainments with perfect comradeship. We suffered from no discriminations on account of color or "previous condition," and lived in blissful ignorance of the fact that we were practicing the unpardonable sin of "social equality." Indeed, until I became a young woman and went South to teach I had never been reminded that I belonged to an "inferior race."

After I was graduated from school my first ambition was to teach. I could easily have obtained a position there at my own home, but I wanted to go out into the world and do something large or out of the ordinary. I had known of quite a number of fine young white women who had gone South to teach the freedmen, and, following my race instinct, I resolved to do the same. I soon obtained a situation in one of the ex-slave States. It was here and for the first time that I began life as a colored person, in all that that term implies. No one but a colored woman, reared and educated as I was, can ever know what it means to be brought face to face with conditions that fairly overwhelm you with the ugly reminder that a certain penalty must be suffered by those who, not being able to select their own parentage, must be born of a dark complexion. What a shattering of cherished ideals! Everything that I learned and experienced in my innocent social relationships in New York State had to be unlearned and readjusted to these lowered standards and changed conditions. The Bible that I had

---

[1] A popular journal.

been taught, the preaching I had heard, the philosophy and ethics and the rules of conduct that I had been so sure of, were all to be discounted. All truth seemed here only half truths. I found that, instead of there being a unity of life common to all intelligent, respectable and ambitious people, down South life was divided into white and black lines, and that in every direction my ambitions and aspirations were to have no beginnings and no chance for development. But, in spite of all this, I tried to adapt myself to these hateful conditions. I had some talent for painting, and in order to obtain further instruction I importuned a white art teacher to admit me into one of her classes, to which she finally consented, but on the second day of my appearance in the class I chanced to look up suddenly and was amazed to find that I was completely surrounded by screens, and when I resented the apparent insult, it was made the condition of my remaining in the class. I had missed the training that would have made this continued humiliation possible; so at a great sacrifice I went to a New England city, but even here, in the very cradle of liberty, white Southerners were there before me, and to save their feelings I was told by the principal of the school, a man who was descended from a long line of abolition ancestors, that it would imperil the interests of the school if I remained, as all of his Southern pupils would leave, and again I had to submit to the tyranny of a dark complexion. But it is scarcely possible to enumerate the many ways in which an ambitious colored young woman is prevented from being all that she might be in the higher directions of life in this country. Plainly I would have been far happier as a woman if my life up to the age of eighteen years had not been so free, spontaneous and unhampered by race prejudice. I have still many white friends and the old home and school associations are still sweet and delightful and always renewed with pleasure, yet I have never quite recovered from the shock and pain of my first bitter realization that to be a colored woman is to be discredited, mistrusted and often meanly hated. My faith in the verities of religion, in justice, in love and many sacredly taught sentiments has greatly decreased since I have learned how little even these stand for when you are a colored woman.

After teaching a few years in the South, I went back to my home in New York State to be married. After the buffetings, discouragements and discourtesies that I had been compelled to endure, it was almost as in a dream that I saw again my schoolmates gather around me, making my home beautiful with flowers, managing every detail of preparation for my wedding, showering me with gifts, and joining in the ceremony with tears and blessings. My own family and my husband were the only persons to lend color to the occasion. Minister, attendants, friends, flowers and hearts were of purest white. If this be social equality, it certainly was not of my own seeking and I must say that no one seemed harmed by it. It seemed all a simple part of the natural life we lived where people are loved and respected for their worth, in spite of their darker complexions.

After my marriage my husband and I moved to one of the larger cities of the North, where we have continued to live. In this larger field of life and action I found myself, like many another woman, becoming interested in many things that come within the range of woman's active sympathy and influence.

My interest in various reform work, irrespective of color, led me frequently to join hand in hand with white women on a common basis of fellowship and helpfulness extended to all who needed our sympathy and interest. I experienced very few evidences of race prejudice and perhaps had more than my share of kindness and recognition. However, this kindness to me as an individual did not satisfy me or blind me to the many inequalities suffered by young colored women seeking employment and other advantages of metropolitan life. I soon discovered that it was much easier for progressive white women to be considerate and even companionable to one colored woman whom they chanced to know and like than to be just and generous to colored young women as a race who needed their sympathy and influence in securing employment and recognition according to their tastes and ability. To this end I began to use my influence and associations to further the cause of these helpless young colored women, in an effort to save them to themselves and society, by finding, for those who must work, suitable employment. How surprisingly difficult was my task may be seen in the following instances selected from many of like nature:

I was encouraged to call upon a certain bank president, well known for his broad, humane principles and high-mindedness. I told him what I wanted, and how I thought he could give me some practical assistance, and enlarged upon the difficulties that stand in the way of ambitious and capable young colored women. He was inclined to think, and frankly told me, that he thought I was a little overstating the case, and added, with rather a triumphant air, so sure he was that I could not make good my statements as to ability, fitness, etc., "We need a competent stenographer right here in the bank now; if you will send to me the kind of a young colored woman you describe, that is thoroughly equipped, I think I can convince you that you are wrong." I ventured to tell him that the young woman I had in mind did not show much color. He at once interrupted me by saying, "Oh, that will not cut any figure; you send the young woman here." I did so and allowed a long time to elapse before going to see him again. When I did call, at the young woman's request, the gentleman said, with deep humiliation, "I am ashamed to confess, Mrs.——, that you were right and I was wrong. I felt it my duty to say to the directors that this young woman had a slight trace of negro blood. That settled it. They promptly said, 'We don't want her, that's all.'" He gave the names of some of the directors and I recognized one of them as a man of long prayers and a heavy contributor to the Foreign Mission Fund; another's name was a household word on account of his financial interest in Home Missions and Church extension work. I went back to the young woman and could but weep with her because I knew that she was almost in despair over the necessity of speedily finding something to do. The only consolation I could offer was that the president declared she was the most skillful and thoroughly competent young woman who had ever applied for the position.

I tried another large establishment and had a pleasant talk with the manager, who unwittingly committed himself to an overwhelming desire "to help the colored people." He said that his parents were staunch abolitionists and connected with the underground railway, and that he distinctly remembered that as a child he was not allowed to eat sugar that had been cultivated by the labor of the poor slave or to wear cotton manufactured by slave labor, and his face glowed as he told me how he loved his "black mammie," and so on *ad nauseam*. I began to feel quite elated at the correctness of my judgment in seeking him out of so many. I then said: "I see that you employ a large number of young women as clerks and stenographers. I have in mind some very competent young colored women who are almost on the verge of despair for lack of suitable employment. Would you be willing to try one of them should you have a vacancy?" The grayness of age swept over his countenance as he solemnly said: "Oh,

I wish you had not asked me that question. My clerks would leave and such an inno-vation would cause a general upheaval in my business." "But," I said, "your clerks surely do not run your business!" "No," he said, "you could not understand." Knowing that he was very religious, my almost forgotten Bible training came to mind. I quoted Scripture as to "God being no respecter of persons,"[2] and reminded him that these young women were in moral danger through enforced idleness, and quoted the anathema of offending one of "these little ones" whom Christ loved.[3] But he did not seem to fear at all condemnation from that high tribunal. His only reply was, "Oh, that is different," and I turned away, sadly thinking "Is it different?"

This still remains a sad chapter in my experience, even tho I have been successful in finding a few good positions for young colored women, not one of whom has ever lost her position through any fault of hers. On the contrary, they have become the prize workers wherever they have been employed. One of them became her employer's private secretary, and he told me with much enthusiasm that her place could scarcely be filled, she had become so efficient and showed such an intelligent grasp upon the requirements of the position. My plea has always been simply to give these girls a chance and let them stand or fall by any test that is not merely a color test.

I want to speak of one other instance. It sometimes happens that after I have suc-ceeded in getting these girls placed and their competency has been proved they are subjected to the most unexpected humiliations. A young woman of very refined and dignified appearance and with only a slight trace of African blood had held her posi-tion for some time in an office where she had been bookkeeper, stenographer and clerk, respectively, and was very highly thought of both by her employer and her fellow clerks. She was sitting at her desk one day when a man entered and asked for her employer. She told him to be seated, that Mr.—— would be back in a moment. The man walked around the office, then came back to her and said: "I came from a section of the country where we make your people know their places. Don't you think you are out of yours?" She merely looked up and said, "I think I know my place." He strolled about for a moment, then came back to her and said: "I am a Southern man, I am, and I would like to know what kind of a man this is that employs a 'nigger' to sit at a desk and write." She replied: "You will find Mr.—— a perfect gentleman." The proprietor came in, in a moment, and ushered the man into his private office. The Southern gentleman came out of the office very precipitately. It evidently only took him a few seconds to verify the clerk's words that "her employer was a perfect gentleman."

It may be plainly seen that public efforts of this kind and a talent for public speak-ing and writing would naturally bring to me a recognition and association independ-ent of any self-seeking on my own account. It, therefore, seemed altogether natural that some of my white friends should ask me to make application for membership in a prominent woman's club on the ground of mutual helpfulness and mutual interest in many things. I allowed my name to be presented to the club without the slightest dream that it would cause any opposition or even discussion. This progressive club has a membership of over eight hundred women, and its personality fairly represents the wealth, intelligence and culture of the women of the city. When the members of this great club came to know the color of its new applicant there was a startled cry that

---

[2] Acts 10:34.   [3] Mark 9:42.

seemed to have no bounds. Up to this time no one knew that there was any anti-negro sentiment in the club. Its purposes were so humane and philanthropic and its grade of individual membership so high and inclusive of almost every nationality that, my endorsers thought that my application would only be subject to the club's test of eligibility, which was declared to be "Character, intelligence and the reciprocal advantage to the club and the individual, without regard to race, color, religion or politics." For nearly fourteen months my application was fought by a determined minority. Other clubs throughout the country took up the matter, and the awful example was held up in such a way as to frighten many would-be friends. The whole anti-slavery question was fought over again in the same spirit and with the same arguments, but the common sense of the members finally prevailed over their prejudices. When the final vote was taken I was elected to membership by a decisive majority.

Before my admission into the club some of the members came to me and frankly told me that they would leave the club, much as they valued their membership, if I persisted in coming in. Their only reason was that they did not think the time had yet come for that sort of equality. Since my application was not of my own seeking I refused to recognize their unreasonable prejudices as something that ought to be fostered and perpetuated; beside, I felt that I owed something to the friends who had shown me such unswerving loyalty through all those long and trying months, when every phase of my public and private life was scrutinized and commented upon in a vain effort to find something in proof of my ineligibility. That I should possess any finer feeling that must suffer under this merciless persecution and unwelcome notoriety seemed not to be thought of by those who professed to believe that my presence in a club of eight hundred women would be at a cost of their fair self-respect. I cannot say that I have experienced the same kind of humiliations as recited in the pathetic story of a Southern colored woman in THE INDEPENDENT of March 17th, but I can but believe that the prejudice that blights and hinders is quite as decided in the North as it is in the South, but does not manifest itself so openly and brutally.

Fortunately, since my marriage I have had but little experience south of Mason and Dixon's line.[4] Some time ago I was induced by several clubs in different States and cities of the South to make a kind of lecture tour through that section. I knew, of course, of the miserable separations, "Jim Crow"[5] cars, and other offensive restrictions and resolved to make the best of them. But the "Jim Crow" cars were almost intolerable to me. I was fortunate enough to escape them in every instance. There is such a cosmopolitan population in some of the Southwestern States, made up of Spanish, Mexican and French nationalities, that the conductors are very often deceived; beside, they know that an insult can scarcely go further than to ask the wrong person if he or she be colored. I made it a rule always to take my seat in the first-class car, to which I felt I was entitled by virtue of my first-class ticket. However, adapting one's self to these false conditions does not contribute to one's peace of mind, self-respect or honesty. I remember that at a certain place I was too late to procure my ticket at the station, and the conductor told me that I would have to go out at the next station and buy my ticket, and then, despite my English book, which I was very ostentatiously

---

[4] A U.S. boundary line originally surveyed by Charles Mason and Jeremiah Dixon in the 1760s, which would later mark the division between the North and the South.

[5] Originally a character in minstrel shows, later a term naming practices and laws of racial segregation.

reading, he stepped back and quickly asked me, "Madame, are you colored?" I as quickly replied, "Je suis Français."[6] "Français?" he repeated. I said, "Oui."[7] He then called to the brakeman and said, "Take this lady's money and go out at the next station and buy her ticket for her," which he kindly did, and I as kindly replied, as he handed me the ticket, "Merci."[8] Fortunately their knowledge of French ended before mine did or there might have been some embarrassments as to my further unfamiliarity with my mother tongue. However, I quieted my conscience by recalling that there was quite a strain of French blood in my ancestry, and too that their barbarous laws did not allow a lady to be both comfortable and honest. It is needless to say that I traveled undisturbed in the cars to which my ticket entitled me after this success, but I carried an abiding heartache for the refined and helpless colored women who must live continuously under these repressive and unjust laws. The hateful interpretation of these laws is to make no distinction between the educated and refined and the ignorant and depraved negro.

Again, the South seems to be full of paradoxes. In one city of the far South I was asked to address a club of very aristocratic white women, which I did with considerable satisfaction to myself because it gave me an opportunity to call the attention of these white women to the many cultured and educated colored women living right there in their midst, whom they did not know, and to suggest that they find some common ground of fellowship and helpfulness that must result in the general uplift of all women. These women gave me a respectful and appreciative hearing, and the majority of them graciously remained and received an introduction to me after the address. A curious feature of the meeting was that, altho it had been announced in all the papers as a public meeting, not a colored person was present except myself, which shows how almost insurmountable a color line can be.

In another city I had a very different experience, which betrayed my unconscious fear of the treachery of Southern prejudice, tho following so closely upon the pleasant experience above related. I noticed, while on my way to the church where I was advertised to speak to a colored audience, that we were being followed by a half a dozen of what seemed to me the typical Southern "cracker," red shirt and all. I was not thinking of moonshiners, but of Ku-Klux clans, midnight lynching parties, etc. My fears were further increased when they suddenly stopped and separated, so that my friends and myself were obliged to pass between the lines of three so made. My friends tried to reassure me, but I fancied with trembling tones, but my menacing escort then closed up ranks and again followed on. Finally they beckoned to the only gentleman with us and asked him what I was going to talk about. He told them the subject and hastened to console me. When we got to the church and just before I rose to speak these six men all filed in and sat down near the platform, accompanied by another individual even more fierce in appearance than they were, whom I afterward learned was the deputy sheriff of the town. My feelings are better imagined than described, but I found myself struggling to hold the attention only of this menacing portion of my audience. They remained to the close of the lecture and as they went out expressed appreciation of my "good sense," as they termed it.

This recital has no place in this article save to show the many contrasts a brief visit

---

[6] (Fr.) I am French.
[7] (Fr.) Yes.

[8] (Fr.) Thank you.

to the Southland is capable of revealing. It is only just to add that I have traveled in the first-class—that is, white—cars all through the South, through Texas, Georgia and as far as Birmingham, Ala., but I have never received an insult or discourtesy from a Southern white man. While, fortunately, this has been my experience, still I believe that in some other localities in the South such an experience would seem almost incredible.

I want to refer briefly to the remarks of one of the writers in THE INDEPEN-DENT with reference to the character strength of colored women. I think it but just to say that we must look to American slavery as the source of every imperfection that mars the character of the colored American. It ought not to be necessary to remind a Southern woman that less than 50 years ago the ill-starred mothers of this ransomed race were not allowed to be modest, not allowed to follow the instincts of moral recti-tude, and there was no living man to whom they could cry for protection against the men who not only owned them, body and soul, but also the souls of their husbands, their brothers, and, alas, their sons. Slavery made her the only woman in America for whom virtue was not an ornament and a necessity. But in spite of this dark and painful past, I believe that the sweeping assertions of this writer are grossly untrue and unjust at least to thousands of colored women in the North who were free from the debasing influence of slavery, as well as thousands of women in the South, who instinctively fought to preserve their own honor and that of their unfortunate offspring. I believe that the colored women are just as strong and just as weak as any other women with like education, training and environment.

It is a significant and shameful fact that I am constantly in receipt of letters from the still unprotected colored women of the South, begging me to find employment for their daughters according to their ability, as domestics or otherwise, to save them from going into the homes of the South as servants, as there is nothing to save them from dishonor and degradation. Many prominent white women and ministers will verify this statement. The heartbroken cry of some of these helpless mothers bears no sug-gestion of the "flaunting pride of dishonor" so easily obtained, by simply allowing their daughters to enter the homes of the white women of the South. Their own mothers cannot protect them and white women will not, or do not. The moral feature of this problem has complications that it would seem better not to dwell on. From my own study of the question, the colored woman deserves greater credit for what she has done and is doing than blame for what she cannot so soon overcome.

As to the negro problem, the only things one can be really sure of is that it has a beginning, and we know that it is progressing some way, but no one knows the end. Prejudice is here and everywhere, but it may not manifest itself so brutally as in the South. The chief interest in the North seems to be centered in business, and it is in business where race prejudice shows itself the strongest. The chief interest in the South is social supremacy, therefore prejudice manifests itself most strongly against even an imaginary approach to social contact. Here in the Northern States I find that a colored woman of character and intelligence will be recognized and respected, but the white woman who will recognize and associate with her in the same club or church would probably not tolerate her as a fellow clerk in office....

The conclusion of the whole matter seems to be that whether I live in the North or the South, I cannot be counted for my full value, be that much or little. I dare not cease to hope and aspire and believe in human love and justice, but progress is painful and my faith is often strained to the breaking point.

CHICAGO, ILL.

—1904

JANE ADDAMS (1860-1935)

Jane Addams was born to well-to-do parents in Cedarville, Illinois. After her graduation from Rockford Seminary in 1882, she hoped to pursue a career in medicine, but was discouraged by her family, who feared she would never marry if she became a doctor. This disappointment, combined with the death of her father, plunged Addams into a depression which left her a semi-invalid for a time. After her recovery, she traveled to England with friends and visited Toynbee Hall, a settlement house in London. The settlement house movement was a radical concept that sent middle-class reformers to live where they worked, providing direct aid to the poor. Upon returning to the United States, Addams and her companion Ellen Gates Starr decided to establish a settlement house in Chicago; they founded Hull House in 1889. Within a few years, Hull House was serving thousands of newly arrived immigrants. It provided many services: child care, legal aid, medical care, meeting space for labor organizing, and adult education classes (including cooking, sewing, literacy, art, politics, homemaking, dance, theater, and citizenship). Addams became widely known for her work at Hull House, but she also courted controversy by focusing as much on the root causes of poverty as on philanthropy. She supported, for instance, the workers who had protested working conditions during the Haymarket Riots; she lobbied for worker protection and against child labor; she favored woman suffrage; her Woman's Peace Party opposed World War I; and, perhaps most controversial of all, she was a member of both the American Civil Liberties Union and the NAACP. Addams wrote many articles, books, and pamphlets. In recognition of her lifetime of achievement, she was awarded the Nobel Peace Prize in 1931.

Patriotism and Pacifists in Wartime

The position of the pacifist in time of war is most difficult, and necessarily he must abandon the perfectly legitimate propaganda he maintained before war was declared. When he, with his fellow countrymen, is caught up by a wave of tremendous enthusiasm and is carried out into a high sea of patriotic feeling, he realizes that the virtues which he extols are brought into unhappy contrast to those which war, with its keen sense of a separate national existence, places in the foreground.

Nevertheless, the modern peace movement, since it was inaugurated three hundred years ago, has been kept alive throughout many great wars and during the present war some sort of peace organization has been maintained in all of the belligerent nations. Our Woman's International Committee for Permanent Peace,[1] for instance, of which I have the honor to be chairman, is in constant communication with our branches organized since this war began in such fighting nations and colonies as Australia, Austria, Belgium, Canada, Finland, Germany, Great Britain, Ireland, Hungary, British

---

[1] The International Committee of Women for Permanent Peace was founded in 1915; four years later it became the Women's International League for Peace and Freedom.

India, Italy, France, Poland and Russia, in addition to the neutral countries of Europe and one or two of South America.

Surely the United States will be as tolerant to pacifists in time of war as those countries have been, some of which are fighting for their very existence, and fellow-citizens, however divided in opinion, will be able to discuss those aspects of patriotism which endure through all vicissitudes.

Before taking up the subject of this paper, it may be well to state that there are many types of pacifists, from the extreme left, composed of non-resistants, through the middle-of-the-road groups, to the extreme right, who can barely be distinguished from mild militarists; and that in our movement, as well as in many others, we must occasionally remind ourselves of Emerson's[2] saying, that the test of a real reformer is his ability to put up with the other reformers.

In one position, however, we are all agreed, and to this as to an abstract proposition, we must hold at all times, even after war has been declared: that war, although exhibiting some of the noblest qualities of the human spirit, yet affords no solution for vexed international problems; and that moreover after war has been resorted to, its very existence, in spite of its superb heroisms and sacrifices which we also greatly admire, tends to obscure and confuse those faculties which might otherwise find a solution.

In the stir of the heroic moment when a nation enters war, men's minds are driven back to the earliest obligations of patriotism, and almost without volition the emotions move along the worn grooves of blind admiration for the soldier and of unspeakable contempt for him who, in the hour of danger, declares that fighting is unnecessary. We pacifists are not surprised, therefore, when apparently striking across and reversing this popular conception of patriotism, that we should not only be considered incapable of facing reality, but that we should be called traitors and cowards. It makes it all the more incumbent upon us, however, to demonstrate, if we can that in our former advocacy we urged a reasonable and vital alternative to war, and that our position now does not necessarily imply lack of patriotism or cowardice.

To take up the three charges in order:

Pacifists and "Passivism"

First: The similarity of sound between the words "passive" and "pacifism" is often misleading, for most pacifists agree with such statements as that made by Mr. Brailsford[3] in *The New Republic* of March 17th—that wonderful journal, *The New Republic,* from which so many preachers are now taking their texts in preference to the New Testament. Mr. Brailsford, an Englishman, said: "This war was an act of insurgence against the death in life which acquiesces in hampered conditions and unsolved problems. There was in this concerted rush to ruin and death the force of a rebellious and unconquerable life. It was bent on a change, for it knew that the real denial and surrender of life is not a physical death but the refusal to move and progress." Agreeing substantially with this analysis of the causes of the present war, we pacifists, so far from passively wishing nothing to be done, contend on the contrary that this world crisis should be utilized for the creation of an international government able to make the

---

[2] Ralph Waldo Emerson (1803-82), American essayist.

[3] Henry Noel Brailsford (1873-1958), British author and early contributor to *The New Republic* after its founding in 1914.

necessary political and economic changes when they are due; we feel that it is unspeakably stupid that the nations should have failed to create an international organization through which each one, without danger to itself, might recognize and even encourage the impulse toward growth in other nations.

Pacifists believe that in the Europe of 1914, certain tendencies were steadily pushing towards large changes which in the end made war, because the system of peace had no way of effecting those changes without war, no adequate international organization which could cope with the situation. The conception of peace founded upon the balance of power or the undisturbed *status quo* was so negative that frustrated national impulses and suppressed vital forces led to war, because no method of orderly expression had been devised.

We are not advocating the mid-Victorian idea that good men from every country meet together at The Hague or elsewhere, where they shall pass a resolution, that "wars hereby cease" and that "the world hereby be federated." What we insist upon is that the world can be organized politically by its statesmen as it has been already organized into an international fiscal system by its bankers or into an international scientific association by its scientists. We ask why the problem of building a railroad to Bagdad, of securing corridors to the sea for a land-locked nation, or warm water harbors for Russia, should result in war. Surely the minds of this generation are capable of solving such problems as the minds of other generations have solved their difficult problems. Is it not obviously because such situations transcend national boundaries and must be approached in a spirit of world adjustment, while men's minds still held apart by national suspicions and rivalries are unable to approach them in a spirit of peaceful adjustment?

The very breakdown exhibited by the present war reinforces the pacifists' contention that there is need of an international charter—a Magna Charta[4] indeed—of international rights, to be issued by the nations great and small, with large provisions for economic freedom.

The Patriotism of Pacifists

In reply to the old charge of lack of patriotism, we claim that we are patriotic from the historic viewpoint as well as by other standards. American pacifists believe—if I may go back to those days before the war, which already seem so far away—that the United States was especially qualified by her own particular experience to take the leadership in a peaceful organization of the world. We then ventured to remind our fellow citizens that when the founders of this republic adopted the federal constitution and established the Supreme Court, they were entering upon a great political experiment of whose outcome they were by no means certain. The thirteen colonies somewhat slowly came into the federation, and some of them consented very reluctantly to the use of the supreme court. Nevertheless, the great political experiment of the United States was so well established by the middle of the 19th century, that America had come to stand to the world for the principle of federal government and for a supreme tribunal whose decisions were binding upon sovereign states.

We pacifists hoped that the United States might perform a similar service in the international field, by demonstrating that the same principles of federation and of an

---

[4] An English charter issued in 1215 stating that the king was subject to the rule of law. It is considered to be one of the most important legal documents in the history of democracy.

interstate tribunal might be extended among widely separated nations as they had already been established between contiguous states. Stirred by enthusiasm over the great historical experiment of the United States, it seemed to us that American patriotism might rise to a supreme effort. We hoped that the United States might refuse to follow the beaten paths of upholding the rights of a separate nationalism by war, because her own experience for more than a century had so thoroughly committed her to federation and to peaceful adjudication as to every-day methods of government. The President's speech before the Senate[5] embodied such a masterly restatement of these early American principles that thousands of his fellow citizens dedicated themselves anew to finding a method for applying them in the wider and more difficult field of international relationships.

The Task of Organization

We also counted upon the fact that this great war had challenged the validity of the existing status between nations as it had never been questioned before, and that radical changes were being proposed by the most conservative of men and of nations. As conceived by the pacifist, the constructive task laid upon the United States in the recent crisis called for something more than diplomacy and the old type of statesmanship.

It demanded a penetration which might discover a more adequate moral basis for the relationship between nations and the sustained energy to translate the discovery into political action. The exercise of the highest political intelligence, we hoped, might not only establish a new scale of moral values, but might hasten to a speedy completion for immediate use, that international organization which has been so long discussed and so ardently anticipated. For there is another similarity between the end of the 18th century and the present time; quite as the Declaration of Independence and the adoption of the Constitution had been preceded by much philosophic writing on the essential equality of all men and on the possibility of establishing self government among them, so the new internationalism has long had its thinkers who have laid a foundation of abstract principle. Then, as now, however, the great need was not for more writing, nor even for able propaganda, but for a sober attempt to put them into practice, to translate them into concrete acts.

American Precedents

We were more hopeful of this from the fact that the test of experience had already been applied by the United States to such a course of actions at least so far as to substitute adjudication for war. Four times before now has our country become involved in the fringe of European wars, and in three instances the difficulties were peacefully adjudicated.

In 1798, when the French Revolution had pulled most of Europe into war, George Washington, who was then President—perhaps because he was so enthusiastic over our Supreme Court—refused to yield to the clamor of his countrymen to go to war on the side of France, our recent friend, against Great Britain, our recent enemy, and sent Chief Justice John Jay over to London to adjust the difficulties which had arisen in connection with our shipping. Because John Jay was successful in his mission, George Washington became for the time so unpopular that he publicly expressed the

---

[5] On January 22, 1917, less than three months before the U.S. entered World War I, President Woodrow Wilson addressed the Senate, appealing for a settlement of the European war on the basis of "peace without victory."

wish that he had never been born although he does not seem to have permanently lost his place in the hearts of his countrymen.

Four years later, when France violated our neutral rights on the seas, John Adams, as President, sent commissioners to Paris who adjudicated the matter. Although keeping the peace made Adams so unpopular that he failed of his second term, many years later, as an old man, he said that his tombstone might well be inscribed with the words: "He kept the peace with France."

Adams' successor, Thomas Jefferson, encountered the same difficulty, and in spite of grave mistakes, succeeded in keeping the country out of war. He was finally rewarded by the peaceful acquisition of the vast Louisiana territory.

The War of 1812 was the result of a disregard of neutral rights incident to the Napoleonic upheaval and made the first break in the chain of international adjudications instituted by Chief Justice Jay, which had become known as the American plan.

Although both England and France had violated our rights at sea, the United States was drawn into war with England at the moment when she was in a death grapple with Napoleon, and so irrational is war, that in the final terms of peace, the treaty did not mention the very matter upon which war had been declared. Perhaps, however, three adjudications out of five instances in which the shipping of the United States has become involved in European war is as much as can be hoped for.

Pacifists Against Isolation

With such a national history back of us, as pacifists we are thrown into despair over our inability to make our position clear when we are accused of wishing to isolate the United States and to keep our country out of world politics. We are, of course, urging a policy exactly the reverse, that this country should lead the nations of the world into a wider life of coordinated political activity; that the United States should boldly recognize the fact that the vital political problems of our time have become as intrinsically international in character as have the commercial and social problems so closely connected with them; that modern wars are not so much the result of quarrels between nations as of the rebellion against international situations inevitably developed through the changing years, which admit of adequate treatment only through an international agency not yet created. The fact that such an agency has been long desired, the necessity for it clearly set forth by statesmen in all the civilized nations, and that a splendid beginning had already been made at The Hague, makes the situation only more acute.

America's Resources for Leadership

We had also hoped much from the varied population of the United States, for whether we will or not, our very composition would make it easier for us than for any other nation to establish an international organization founded upon understanding and good will did we but possess the requisite courage and intelligence to utilize it.

There are in this country thousands of emigrants from the Central Powers, to whom a war between the United States and the fatherland means exquisite torture. They and their inheritances are a part of the situation which faces us. They are a source of great strength in an international venture, as they are undoubtedly a source of weakness in a purely nationalistic position of the old-fashioned sort. These ties of blood, binding us to all the nations of the earth, afford a unique equipment for a great international task if the United States could but push forward into the shifting area of internationalism.

Modern warfare is an intimately social and domestic affair. The civilian suffering and, in certain regions, the civilian mortality, is as great as that endured by the soldiers. There are thousands of our fellow citizens who cannot tear their minds away from Poland, Galicia, Syria, Armenia, Serbia, Roumania, Greece, where their own relatives are dying from diseases superinduced by hardship and hunger. To such sore and troubled minds war had come to be a hideousness which belongs to Europe alone and was part of that privation and depression which they had left behind them when they came to America. Newly immigrated Austrian subjects of a dozen nationalities came to their American friends during the weeks of suspense, utterly bewildered by the prospect of war. They had heard not three months before that the President of the United States did not believe in war—for so the Senate speech has been interpreted by many simple minds—and they had concluded that whatever happened, some more American way would be found.

The multitude of German subjects who have settled and developed certain parts of the United States had, it seems to me, every right to be considered as important factors in the situation, before war was declared. President Wilson himself said, in February, after the U-boat campaign had been announced, that he was giving due weight to the legitimate rights of the American citizens of German descent. The men of '48[6] are as truly responsible for our national ideals as the Puritans of New England, the Quakers of Pennsylvania, or the Russian revolutionists of the '90s. How valuable that gallant spirit of '48, spreading as it did from one European country to another, could be made in an international venture it is difficult to estimate.

It has been said that this great war will prove the bloody angle at which mankind turns from centuries of warfare to the age of peace. But certainly this will not happen automatically nor without leadership founded upon clear thinking and international sympathies.

It is very easy to go to war for a well defined aim which changes imperceptibly as the war progresses, and to continue the war or even end it on quite other grounds. Shifting aims is one of the inherent characteristics of war as an institution.

Pacifists hoped that this revolution in international relationships, which has been steadily approaching for three hundred years and is long over-due might have been obtained without our participation in the war; but we also believe that it may be obtained after the war, if the United States succeeds in protecting and preserving the higher standards of internationalism.

National Unselfishness

Pacifists recognize and rejoice in the large element of national unselfishness and in the recognition of international obligation set forth by President Wilson as reasons for our participation in the great war. We feel that the exalted sense of patriotism in which each loses himself in the consciousness of a national existence has been enlarged by an alliance with nations across the Atlantic and across the Pacific with whom we are united in a common purpose. Let the United States, by all means, send a

---

[6] The so-called "March Rebellion" of 1848 in Germany was intended to overthrow the hereditary monarchy and install a constitutional republic. Ultimately it failed, and King Friedrich Wilhelm IV was offered the crown. Not until the Weimar Republic (after World War I) was a German parliament established.

governmental commission to Russia; plans for a better fiscal system to bewildered China; food to all nations wherever little children are starving; but let us never forget that the inspiring and overwhelming sense of a common purpose, which an alliance with fifteen or sixteen nations gives us, is but a forecast of what might be experienced if the genuine international alliance were achieved, including all the nations of the earth.

In so far as we and our allies are held together by the consciousness of a common enemy and the fear of a common danger, there is a chance for the growth of the animosity and hatred which may yet overwhelm the attempt at international organization to be undertaken after the war, as it has defeated so many high-hearted attempts in the past.

May we not say in all sincerity that for thirty-three months Europe has been earnestly striving to obtain through patriotic wars, that which can finally be secured only through international organization? Millions of men, loyal to one international alliance, are gallantly fighting millions of men loyal to another international alliance, because of Europe's inability to make an alliance including them all. Can the United States discharge her duty in this situation save as she finally makes possible the establishment of a genuine international government?

America's Sense of Failure

Ever since the European war began, the United States has been conscious of a failure to respond to a moral demand; she has vaguely felt that she was shirking her share in a world effort toward the higher good; she has had black moments of compunction and shame for her own immunity and safety. Can she hope through war to assuage the feverish thirst for action she has felt during all those three years? There is no doubt that she has made the correct diagnosis of her case, of her weariness with a selfish, materialistic life, and of her need for concerted, self-forgetting action. But is bloodletting a sufficiently modern remedy in such a diagnosis? Will she lose her sense of futility and her consciousness of moral failure, when thousands of her young men are facing the dangers of war? Will she not at the end of this war still feel her inadequacy and sense of failure unless she is able to embody in a permanent organization the cosmopolitanism which is the essence of her spirit? Will she be content, even in war time, to organize food supplies of one group of nations and to leave the women and children of any nation still starving?

Is not the government of the United States somewhat in the position of those of us who have lived for many years among immigrants? It is quite impossible for us to ask just now whether the parents of a child who needs food are Italians, and therefore now our allies, or Dalmatians and therefore now our "alien enemies." Such a question is as remote as if during the Balkan war[7] we had anxiously inquired whether the parents were Macedonians or Montenegrins, although that was then a distinction of paramount importance to thousands of our neighbors.

It has been officially declared that we are entering this war "to make the world safe for democracy."[8] While we are still free to make terms with our allies, are we not under

---

[7] During the First Balkan War (1912-13), the Balkan League (Serbia, Montenegro, Greece, and Bulgaria) succeeded in conquering the European provinces of the Ottoman Empire (Albania, Macedonia, and Thrace).

[8] On April 2, 1917, President Woodrow Wilson went before a joint session of Congress to seek a Declaration of War against Germany so that the world could "be made safe for democracy." Four days later, Congress voted to declare war, with six senators and fifty congressmen dissenting.

obligation to assert that the United States owes too much to all the nations of the earth whose sons have developed our raw prairies into fertile fields, to allow the women and children of any of them to starve?

It is told of the recent Irish uprising that after Sheehy Skeffington[9] had been arrested, an English soldier was placed on guard in the house lest Mrs. Skeffington and her little boy might destroy possibly incriminating papers; that the soldier, after standing for a long time in the presence of the woman and child, finally shifted his position and, looking uneasily at Mrs. Skeffington, said, "You see, I didn't enlist exactly for this."

Would it not be possible for the United States to tell her allies that she had not enlisted in this great war for the purpose of starving women and children? When the United States entered the war the final outcome was apparently to be decided by food supply rather than by force of arms. Could Germany hold out during the spring and early summer until the new crop was garnered? Could England feed herself were the U-boat campaign[10] in any degree successful, were the terrible questions in men's minds.

For decades civilized nations had confidently depended upon other nations for their supply of cattle and of grain until long continued war brought the primitive fear of starvation back into the world with so many other obsolete terrors.

National Boundaries and Food Supply

Such an international organization as the United States is now creating in connection with her allies for the control of their common food supply is clearly transcending old national bounds. It may be a new phase of political unification in advance of all former achievements, or it may be one of those shifting alliances for war purposes of which European history affords so many examples. Simply because food is so strategic, as it were, we lay ourselves open to the latter temptations. Could we not free ourselves from this and at the same time perform a great service if we urge that an international commission sit at Athens during the rest of this war, as an international commission sat in London during the Balkan wars? Such a commission might at once insist upon a more humane prosecution of the war, at least so far as civilian populations are concerned, a more merciful administration of the lands occupied, and distribution of foodstuffs to all conquered peoples.

Military Coercion or Social Control?

The United States has to her credit a long account of the spread of democratic institutions during the years when she was at peace with the rest of the world. Her own experiment as a republic was quickly followed by France, and later by Switzerland, and to the south of her a vast continent contains no nation which fails—through many vicissitudes though it be—to maintain a republican form of government.

It has long been the aim of this government of ours and of similar types of government the world over to replace coercion by the full consent of the governed, to educate and strengthen the free will of the people through the use of democratic

---

[9] Francis Sheehy-Skeffington (1878-1916), Irish suffragist, pacifist, and writer. "Skeffy" was murdered after admitting to sympathizing with the so-called "Easter Rising" against British colonial rule in Ireland in 1916.

[10] In the first years of World War I, German U-boats (submarines) established an effective blockade, preventing many military and humanitarian supplies from reaching England.

institutions, and to safeguard even the rights of minorities. This age-long process of obtaining the inner consent of the citizen to the outward acts of his government is of necessity violently interrupted and thrown back in war time; but we all realize that some day it must be resumed and carried forward again, perhaps on an international basis. Let us strive to keep our minds clear regarding it.

Some of us once dreamed that the cosmopolitan inhabitants of this great nation might at last become united in a vast common endeavor for social ends. We hoped that this fusing might be accomplished without the sense of opposition to a common enemy which is an old method of welding people together, better fitted for military than for social use. If this for the moment is impossible, let us at least place the spirit of cooperation above that of bitterness and remember the wide distinction between social control and military coercion.

It is easy for all of us to grow confused in a moment like this for the pacifist, like the rest of the world, has developed a high degree of suggestibility; we too share that sensitiveness to the feelings, the opinion, and the customs of our own social group which is said to be an inheritance from an almost prehuman past. An instinct which once enabled the man-pack to survive when it was a question of keeping a herd together, or of perishing off the face of the earth is perhaps not under-developed in any of us.

Are Pacifists Cowards?

When as pacifists we urge a courageous venture into international ethics, which will require a fine valor as well as a high intelligence, we experience a sense of anti-climax when we are told that because we do not want war, we are so cowardly as to care for "safety first," that we place human life, physical life, above the great ideals of national righteousness.

But surely that man is not without courage who, seeing that which is invisible to the majority of his fellow countrymen, still asserts his conviction, and is ready to vindicate its spiritual value over against the world. Each advance in the zigzag line of human progress has traditionally been embodied in small groups of individuals, who have ceased to be in harmony with the status quo and have demanded modifications. Such modifications did not always prove to be in the line of progress, but whether they were or not, they always excited opposition, which from the nature of the case was never so determined as when the proposed changes touched moral achievements which were greatly prized and had been secured with much difficulty.

Bearing in mind the long struggle to secure and maintain national unity, the pacifist easily understands why his theories seem particularly obnoxious just now, although in point of fact our national unity is not threatened, and would be finely consummated in an international organization.

Peace and Justice

With visions of international justice filling our minds, pacifists are always a little startled when those who insist that justice can only be established by war, accuse us of caring for peace irrespective of justice. Many of the pacifists in their individual and corporate capacity have long striven for social and political justice with a fervor perhaps equal to that employed by the advocates of force, and we realize that a sense of justice has become the keynote to the best political and social activity in this generation. Although this ruling passion for juster relations between man and man, group and group, or between nation and nation, is not without its sterner aspects, among those who dream of a wider social justice throughout the world there has developed a conviction that justice between men or between nations can be achieved only through understanding and fellowship, and that a finely tempered sense of justice, which alone is of any service in modern civilization, cannot be secured in the storm and stress of war. This is not only because war inevitably arouses the more primitive antagonisms, but because the spirit of fighting burns away all of those impulses, certainly towards the enemy, which foster the will to justice.

We believe that the ardor and self sacrifice so characteristic of youth could be enlisted for the vitally energetic role which we hope our beloved country will inaugurate in the international life of the world. We realize that it is only the ardent spirits, the lovers of mankind, who will be able to break down the suspicion and lack of understanding which has so long stood in the way of the necessary changes upon which international good order depends; who will at last create a political organization enabling nations to secure without war, those high ends which they now gallantly seek to obtain upon the battlefield.

With such a creed, can the pacifists of today be accused of selfishness when they urge upon the United States not isolation, not indifference to moral issues and to the fate of liberty and democracy, but a strenuous endeavor to lead all nations of the earth into an organized international life worthy of civilized men?

—1917

EDITH WHARTON (1862-1937)

Edith Jones was born in New York City, the youngest child of Lucretia Stevens (Rhinelander) and George Frederick Jones, members of New York's social elite. Her family's wealth meant that young Edith received an extensive education both from private tutors and from her family's travels through Europe. She started writing at a young age, secretly composing a novel at the age of fifteen, and publishing, privately, a collection of verse when she was sixteen. She was married in 1885 to Edward Wharton, a man considerably older than she, who suffered from ill health and had little interest in intellectual or artistic pursuits. Wharton spent the early years of her marriage acting as a hostess in New York's social scene; after her marriage ended in divorce in 1913, she moved to France. Her career as a writer began in earnest after a nervous breakdown in 1895, which resulted in a stay at a sanatorium. She published several short stories in periodicals, and her first fiction collection, *The Greater Inclination,* was published in 1899, earning praise from the prominent novelist Henry James. Wharton went on to produce several more volumes of short stories and over a dozen novels. Most of her fiction was in the realist mode, offering a carefully rendered insider's view of the lives and values of upper-class Americans, such as *The House of Mirth* (1905), *The Custom of the Country* (1913), *Summer* (1917), and *The Age of Innocence* (1920), for which she won a Pulitzer Prize. She also wrote a number of ghost stories, several of which were collected in the volume *Ghosts* (1937). Wharton died in 1937 of heart failure in St. Brice-sous-Foret, France. She is buried in Versailles.

The Other Two

Waythorn, on the drawing-room hearth, waited for his wife to come down to dinner.

It was their first night under his own roof, and he was surprised at his thrill of boyish agitation. He was not so old, to be sure—his glass gave him little more than the five-and-thirty years to which his wife confessed—but he had fancied himself already in the temperate zone; yet here he was listening for her step with a tender sense of all it symbolised, with some old trail of verse about the garlanded nuptial door-posts floating through his enjoyment of the pleasant room and the good dinner just beyond it.

They had been hastily recalled from their honeymoon by the illness of Lily Haskett, the child of Mrs. Waythorn's first marriage. The little girl, at Waythorn's desire, had been transferred to his house on the day of her mother's wedding, and the doctor, on their arrival, broke the news that she was ill with typhoid, but declared that all the symptoms were favourable. Lily could show twelve years of unblemished health, and the case promised to be a light one. The nurse spoke as reassuringly, and after a moment of alarm Mrs. Waythorn had adjusted herself to the situation. She was very fond of Lily—her affection for the child had perhaps been her decisive charm in Waythorn's eyes—but she had the perfectly balanced nerves which her little girl had inherited, and no woman ever wasted less tissue in unproductive worry. Waythorn was therefore quite prepared to see her come in presently, a little late because of a last look at Lily, but as serene and well-appointed as if her good-night kiss had been laid on the brow of health. Her composure was restful to him; it acted as ballast to his somewhat unstable sensibilities. As he pictured her bending over the child's bed he thought how soothing her presence must be in illness: her very step would prognosticate recovery.

His own life had been a gray one, from temperament rather than circumstance, and he had been drawn to her by the unperturbed gaiety which kept her fresh and elastic at an age when most women's activities are growing either slack or febrile. He knew what was said about her; for, popular as she was, there had always been a faint undercurrent of detraction. When she had appeared in New York, nine or ten years earlier, as the pretty Mrs. Haskett whom Gus Varick had unearthed somewhere—was it in Pittsburg or Utica?—society, while promptly accepting her, had reserved the right to cast a doubt on its own indiscrimination. Enquiry, however, established her undoubted connection with a socially reigning family, and explained her recent divorce as the natural result of a runaway match at seventeen; and as nothing was known of Mr. Haskett it was easy to believe the worst of him.

Alice Haskett's remarriage with Gus Varick was a passport to the set whose recognition she coveted, and for a few years the Varicks were the most popular couple in town. Unfortunately the alliance was brief and stormy, and this time the husband had his champions. Still, even Varick's stanchest supporters admitted that he was not meant for matrimony, and Mrs. Varick's grievances were of a nature to bear the inspection of the New York courts. A New York divorce is in itself a diploma of virtue, and in the semi-widowhood of this second separation Mrs. Varick took on an air of sanctity, and was allowed to confide her wrongs to some of the most scrupulous ears in town. But when it was known that she was to marry Waythorn there was a momentary reaction. Her best friends would have preferred to see her remain in the rôle of the injured wife, which was as becoming to her as crape to a rosy complexion. True, a decent time had elapsed, and it was not even suggested that Waythorn had supplanted his predecessor. People shook their heads over him, however, and one grudging friend, to whom he affirmed that he took the step with his eyes open, replied oracularly: "Yes—and with your ears shut."

Waythorn could afford to smile at these innuendoes. In the Wall Street phrase, he had "discounted" them. He knew that society has not yet adapted itself to the consequences of divorce, and that till the adaptation takes place every woman who uses the freedom the law accords her must be her own social justification. Waythorn had an amused confidence in his wife's ability to justify herself. His expectations were fulfilled, and before the wedding took place Alice Varick's group had rallied openly to her support. She took it all imperturbably: she had a way of surmounting obstacles without seeming to be aware of them, and Waythorn looked back with wonder at the trivialities over which he had worn his nerves thin. He had the sense of having found refuge in a richer, warmer nature than his own, and his satisfaction, at the moment, was humourously summed up in the thought that his wife, when she had done all she could for Lily, would not be ashamed to come down and enjoy a good dinner.

The anticipation of such enjoyment was not, however, the sentiment expressed by Mrs. Waythorn's charming face when she presently joined him. Though she had put on her most engaging teagown she had neglected to assume the smile that went with it, and Waythorn thought he had never seen her look so nearly worried.

"What is it?" he asked. "Is anything wrong with Lily?"

"No; I've just been in and she's still sleeping." Mrs. Waythorn hesitated. "But something tiresome has happened."

He had taken her two hands, and now perceived that he was crushing a paper between them.

"This letter?"

"Yes—Mr. Haskett has written—I mean his lawyer has written."

Waythorn felt himself flush uncomfortably. He dropped his wife's hands.

"What about?"

"About seeing Lily. You know the courts—"

"Yes, yes," he interrupted nervously.

Nothing was known about Haskett in New York. He was vaguely supposed to have remained in the outer darkness from which his wife had been rescued, and Waythorn was one of the few who were aware that he had given up his business in Utica and followed her to New York in order to be near his little girl. In the days of his wooing, Waythorn had often met Lily on the doorstep, rosy and smiling, on her way "to see papa."

"I am so sorry," Mrs. Waythorn murmured.

He roused himself. "What does he want?"

"He wants to see her. You know she goes to him once a week."

"Well—he doesn't expect her to go to him now, does he?"

"No—he has heard of her illness; but he expects to come here."

"Here?"

Mrs. Waythorn reddened under his gaze. They looked away from each other.

"I'm afraid he has the right....You'll see...." She made a proffer of the letter.

Waythorn moved away with a gesture of refusal. He stood staring about the softly lighted room, which a moment before had seemed so full of bridal intimacy.

"I'm so sorry," she repeated. "If Lily could have been moved—"

"That's out of the question," he returned impatiently.

"I suppose so."

Her lip was beginning to tremble, and he felt himself a brute.

"He must come, of course," he said. "When is—his day?"

"I'm afraid—to-morrow."

"Very well. Send a note in the morning."

The butler entered to announce dinner.

Waythorn turned to his wife. "Come—you must be tired. It's beastly, but try to forget about it," he said, drawing her hand through his arm.

"You're so good, dear. I'll try," she whispered back.

Her face cleared at once, and as she looked at him across the flowers, between the rosy candle-shades, he saw her lips waver back into a smile.

"How pretty everything is!" she sighed luxuriously.

He turned to the butler. "The champagne at once, please. Mrs. Waythorn is tired."

In a moment or two their eyes met above the sparkling glasses. Her own were quite clear and untroubled: he saw that she had obeyed his injunction and forgotten.

II

Waythorn, the next morning, went down town earlier than usual. Haskett was not likely to come till the afternoon, but the instinct of flight drove him forth. He meant to stay away all day—he had thoughts of dining at his club. As his door closed behind him he reflected that before he opened it again it would have admitted another man who had as much right to enter it as himself, and the thought filled him with a physical repugnance.

He caught the "elevated" at the employés' hour, and found himself crushed between two layers of pendulous humanity. At Eighth Street the man facing him wriggled out, and another took his place. Waythorn glanced up and saw that it was Gus Varick. The men were so close together that it was impossible to ignore the smile of recognition on Varick's handsome overblown face. And after all—why not? They had always been on good terms, and Varick had been divorced before Waythorn's attentions to his wife began. The two exchanged a word on the perennial grievance of the congested trains, and when a seat at their side was miraculously left empty the instinct of self-preservation made Waythorn slip into it after Varick.

The latter drew the stout man's breath of relief. "Lord—I was beginning to feel like a pressed flower." He leaned back, looking unconcernedly at Waythorn. "Sorry to hear that Sellers is knocked out again."

"Sellers?" echoed Waythorn, starting at his partner's name.

Varick looked surprised. "You didn't know he was laid up with the gout?"

"No. I've been away—I only got back last night." Waythorn felt himself reddening in anticipation of the other's smile.

"Ah—yes; to be sure. And Sellers's attack came on two days ago. I'm afraid he's pretty bad. Very awkward for me, as it happens, because he was just putting through a rather important thing for me."

"Ah?" Waythorn wondered vaguely since when Varick had been dealing in "important things." Hitherto he had dabbled only in the shallow pools of speculation, with which Waythorn's office did not usually concern itself.

It occurred to him that Varick might be talking at random, to relieve the strain of their propinquity. That strain was becoming momentarily more apparent to Waythorn, and when, at Cortlandt Street, he caught sight of an acquaintance and had a sudden vision of the picture he and Varick must present to an initiated eye, he jumped up with a muttered excuse,

"I hope you'll find Sellers better," said Varick civilly, and he stammered back: "If I can be of any use to you—" and let the departing crowd sweep him to the platform.

At his office he heard that Sellers was in fact ill with the gout, and would probably not be able to leave the house for some weeks.

"I'm sorry it should have happened so, Mr. Waythorn," the senior clerk said with affable significance. "Mr. Sellers was very much upset at the idea of giving you such a lot of extra work just now."

"Oh, that's no matter," said Waythorn hastily. He secretly welcomed the pressure of additional business, and was glad to think that, when the day's work was over, he would have to call at his partner's on the way home.

He was late for luncheon, and turned in at the nearest resturant instead of going to his club. The place was full, and the waiter hurried him to the back of the room to capture the only vacant table. In the cloud of cigar-smoke Waythorn did not at once distinguish his neighbours; but presently, looking about him, he saw Varick seated a few feet off. This time, luckily, they were too far apart for conversation, and Varick, who faced another way, had probably not even seen him; but there was an irony in their renewed nearness.

Varick was said to be fond of good living, and as Waythorn sat despatching his hurried luncheon he looked across half enviously at the other's leisurely degustation of his meal. When Waythorn first saw him he had been helping himself with critical deliberation to a bit of Camembert at the ideal point of liquefaction, and now, the cheese removed, he was just pouring his *café double* from its little two-storied earthen pot. He poured slowly, his ruddy profile bent above the task, and one beringed white hand steadying the lid of the coffee-pot; then he stretched his other hand to the decanter of cognac at his elbow, filled a liqueur-glass, took a tentative sip, and poured the brandy into his coffee-cup.

Waythorn watched him in a kind of fascination. What was he thinking of—only of the flavour of the coffee and the liqueur? Had the morning's meeting left no more trace in his thoughts than on his face? Had his wife so completely passed out of his life that even this odd encounter with her present husband, within a week after her remarriage, was no more than an incident in his day? And as Waythorn mused, another idea struck him: had Haskett ever met Varick as Varick and he had just met? The recollection of Haskett perturbed him, and he rose and left the restaurant, taking a circuitous way out to escape the placid irony of Varick's nod.

It was after seven when Waythorn reached home. He thought the footman who opened the door looked at him oddly.

"How is Miss Lily?" he asked in haste.

"Doing very well, sir. A gentleman—"

"Tell Barlow to put off dinner for half an hour," Waythorn cut him off, hurrying upstairs.

He went straight to his room and dressed without seeing his wife. When he reached the drawing-room she was there, fresh and radiant. Lily's day had been good; the doctor was not coming back that evening.

At dinner Waythorn told her of Sellers's illness and of the resulting complications. She listened sympathetically, adjuring him not to let himself be overworked, and asking vague feminine questions about the routine of the office. Then she gave him the chronicle of Lily's day; quoted the nurse and doctor, and told him who had called to inquire. He had never seen her more serene and unruffled. It struck him, with a curious pang, that she was very happy in being with him, so happy that she found a childish pleasure in rehearsing the trivial incidents of her day.

After dinner they went to the library, and the servant put the coffee and liqueurs on a low table before her and left the room. She looked singularly soft and girlish in her rosy pale dress, against the dark leather of one of his bachelor armchairs. A day earlier the contrast would have charmed him.

He turned away now, choosing a cigar with affected deliberation.

"Did Haskett come?" he asked, with his back to her.

"Oh, yes—he came."

"You didn't see him, of course?"

She hesitated a moment. "I let the nurse see him."

That was all. There was nothing more to ask. He swung round toward her, applying a match to his cigar. Well, the thing was over for a week, at any rate. He would try not to think of it. She looked up at him, a trifle rosier than usual, with a smile in her eyes.

"Ready for your coffee, dear?"

He leaned against the mantelpiece, watching her as she lifted the coffee-pot. The lamplight struck a gleam from her bracelets and tipped her soft hair with brightness. How light and slender she was, and how each gesture flowed into the next! She seemed a creature all compact of harmonies. As the thought of Haskett receded, Waythorn felt himself yielding again to the joy of possessorship. They were his, those white hands with their flitting motions, his the light haze of hair, the lips and eyes….

She set down the coffee-pot, and reaching for the decanter of cognac, measured off a liqueur-glass and poured it into his cup.

Waythorn uttered a sudden exclamation.

"What is the matter?" she said, startled.

"Nothing; only—I don't take cognac in my coffee."

"Oh, how stupid of me," she cried.

Their eyes met, and she blushed a sudden agonised red.

III

Ten days later, Mr. Sellers, still house-bound, asked Waythorn to call on his way down town.

The senior partner, with his swaddled foot propped up by the fire, greeted his associate with an air of embarrassment.

"I'm sorry, my dear fellow; I've got to ask you to do an awkward thing for me."

Waythorn waited, and the other went on, after a pause apparently given to the arrangement of his phrases: "The fact is, when I was knocked out I had just gone into a rather complicated piece of business for—Gus Varick."

"Well?" said Waythorn, with an attempt to put him at his ease.

"Well—it's this way: Varick came to me the day before my attack. He had evidently had an inside tip from somebody, and had made about a hundred thousand. He came to me for advice, and I suggested his going in with Vanderlyn."

"Oh, the deuce!" Waythorn exclaimed. He saw in a flash what had happened. The investment was an alluring one, but required negotiation. He listened quietly while Sellers put the case before him, and, the statement ended, he said: "You think I ought to see Varick?"

"I'm afraid I can't as yet. The doctor is obdurate. And this thing can't wait. I hate to ask you, but no one else in the office knows the ins and outs of it."

Waythorn stood silent. He did not care a farthing for the success of Varick's venture, but the honour of the office was to be considered, and he could hardly refuse to oblige his partner.

"Very well," he said, "I'll do it."

That afternoon, apprised by telephone, Varick called at the office. Waythorn, waiting in his private room, wondered what the others thought of it. The newspapers, at the time of Mrs. Waythorn's marriage, had acquainted their readers with every detail of her previous matrimonial ventures, and Waythorn could fancy the clerks smiling behind Varick's back as he was ushered in.

Varick bore himself admirably. He was easy without being undignified, and Waythorn was conscious of cutting a much less impressive figure. Varick had no experience of business, and the talk prolonged itself for nearly an hour while Waythorn set forth with scrupulous precision the details of the proposed transaction.

"I'm awfully obliged to you," Varick said as he rose. "The fact is I'm not used to having much money to look after, and I don't want to make an ass of myself—" He smiled, and Waythorn could not help noticing that there was something pleasant about his smile. "It feels uncommonly queer to have enough cash to pay one's bills. I'd have sold my soul for it a few years ago!"

Waythorn winced at the allusion. He had heard it rumoured that a lack of funds had been one of the determining causes of the Varick separation, but it did not occur to him that Varick's words were intentional. It seemed more likely that the desire to keep clear of embarrassing topics had fatally drawn him into one. Waythorn did not wish to be outdone in civility.

"We'll do the best we can for you," he said. "I think this is a good thing you're in."

"Oh, I'm sure it's immense. It's awfully good of you—" Varick broke off, embarrassed. "I suppose the thing's settled now—but if—"

"If anything happens before Sellers is about, I'll see you again," said Waythorn quietly. He was glad, in the end, to appear the more self-possessed of the two.

The course of Lily's illness ran smooth, and as the days passed Waythorn grew used to the idea of Haskett's weekly visit. The first time the day came round, he stayed out late, and questioned his wife as to the visit on his return. She replied at once that Haskett had merely seen the nurse downstairs, as the doctor did not wish any one in the child's sickroom till after the crisis.

The following week Waythorn was again conscious of the recurrence of the day, but had forgotten it by the time he came home to dinner. The crisis of the disease came a few days later, with a rapid decline of fever, and the little girl was pronounced out of danger. In the rejoicing which ensued the thought of Haskett passed out of Waythorn's mind, and one afternoon, letting himself into the house with a latch-key, he went straight to his library without noticing a shabby hat and umbrella in the hall.

In the library he found a small effaced-looking man with a thinnish gray beard sitting on the edge of a chair. The stranger might have been a piano-tuner, or one of those mysteriously efficient persons who are summoned in emergencies to adjust some detail of the domestic machinery. He blinked at Waythorn through a pair of gold-rimmed spectacles and said mildly: "Mr. Waythorn, I presume? I am Lily's father."

Waythorn flushed. "Oh—" he stammered uncomfortably. He broke off, disliking to appear rude. Inwardly he was trying to adjust the actual Haskett to the image of him projected by his wife's reminiscences. Waythorn had been allowed to infer that Alice's first husband was a brute.

"I am sorry to intrude," said Haskett, with his over-the-counter politeness.

"Don't mention it," returned Waythorn, collecting himself. "I suppose the nurse has been told?"

"I presume so. I can wait," said Haskett. He had a resigned way of speaking, as though life had worn down his natural powers of resistance.

Waythorn stood on the threshold, nervously pulling off his gloves.

"I'm sorry you've been detained. I will send for the nurse," he said; and as he opened the door he added with an effort: "I'm glad we can give you a good report of Lily." He winced as the *we* slipped out, but Haskett seemed not to notice it.

"Thank you, Mr. Waythorn. It's been an anxious time for me."

"Ah, well, that's past. Soon she'll be able to go to you." Waythorn nodded and passed out.

In his own room he flung himself down with a groan. He hated the womanish sensibility which made him suffer so acutely from the grotesque chances of life. He had known when he married that his wife's former husbands were both living, and that amid the multiplied contacts of modern existence there were a thousand chances to one that he would run against one or the other, yet he found himself as much disturbed by his brief encounter with Haskett as though the law had not obligingly removed all difficulties in the way of their meeting.

Waythorn sprang up and began to pace the room nervously. He had not suffered half as much from his two meetings with Varick. It was Haskett's presence in his own house that made the situation so intolerable. He stood still, hearing steps in the passage.

"This way, please," he heard the nurse say. Haskett was being taken upstairs, then: not a corner of the house but was open to him. Waythorn dropped into another chair, staring vaguely ahead of him. On his dressing-table stood a photograph of Alice, taken when he had first known her. She was Alice Varick then—how fine and exquisite he had thought her! Those were Varick's pearls about her neck. At Waythorn's instance they had been returned before her marriage. Had Haskett ever given her any trinkets—and what had become of them, Waythorn wondered? He realised suddenly that he knew very little of Haskett's past or present situation; but from the man's appearance and manner of speech he could reconstruct with curious precision the surroundings of Alice's first marriage. And it startled him to think that she had, in the background of her life, a phase of existence so different from anything with which he had connected her. Varick, whatever his faults, was a gentleman, in the conventional, traditional sense of the term: the sense which at that moment seemed, oddly enough, to have most meaning to Waythorn. He and Varick had the same social habits, spoke the same language, understood the same allusions. But this other man...it was grotesquely uppermost in Waythorn's mind that Haskett had worn a made-up tie attached with an elastic. Why should that ridiculous detail symbolise the whole man? Waythorn was exasperated by his own paltriness, but the fact of the tie expanded, forced itself on him, became as it were the key to Alice's past. He could see her, as Mrs. Haskett, sitting in a "front parlour" furnished in plush, with a pianola, and a copy of "Ben Hur"[1] on the centre-table. He could see her going to the theatre with Haskett— or perhaps even to a "Church Sociable"—she in a "picture hat" and Haskett in a black frock-coat, a little creased, with the made-up tie on an elastic. On the way home they would stop and look at the illuminated shop-windows, lingering over the photographs of New York actresses. On Sunday afternoons Haskett would take her for a walk, pushing Lily ahead of them in a white enamelled perambulator, and Waythorn had a vision of the people they would stop and talk to. He could fancy how pretty Alice must have looked, in a dress adroitly constructed from the hints of a New York fashion-paper, and how she must have looked down on the other women, chafing at her life, and secretly feeling that she belonged in a bigger place.

For the moment his foremost thought was one of wonder at the way in which she had shed the phase of existence which her marriage with Haskett implied. It was as if her whole aspect, every gesture, every inflection, every allusion, were a studied negation of that period of her life. If she had denied being married to Haskett she could hardly have stood more convicted of duplicity than in this obliteration of the self which had been his wife.

Waythorn started up, checking himself in the analysis of her motives. What right had he to create a fantastic effigy of her and then pass judgment on it? She had spoken vaguely of her first marriage as unhappy, had hinted, with becoming reticence, that Haskett had wrought havoc among her young illusions....It was a pity for Waythorn's peace of mind that Haskett's very inoffensiveness shed a new light on the nature of those illusions. A man would rather think that his wife has been brutalised by her first husband than that the process has been reversed.

IV

"Mr. Waythorn, I don't like that French governess of Lily's."

Haskett, subdued and apologetic, stood before Waythorn in the library, revolving his shabby hat in his hand.

Waythorn, surprised in his armchair over the evening paper, stared back perplexedly at his visitor.

"You'll excuse my asking to see you," Haskett continued. "But this is my last visit, and I thought if I could have a word with you it would be a better way than writing to Mrs. Waythorn's lawyer."

Waythorn rose uneasily. He did not like the French governess either; but that was irrelevant.

"I am not so sure of that," he returned stiffly; "but since you wish it I will give your message to—my wife." He always hesitated over the possessive pronoun in addressing Haskett.

The latter sighed. "I don't know as that will help much. She didn't like it when I

---

[1] *Ben-Hur: A Tale of the Christ* (1880), novel by Lew Wallace.

spoke to her."

Waythorn turned red. "When did you see her?" he asked.

"Not since the first day I came to see Lily—right after she was taken sick. I remarked to her then that I didn't like the governess."

Waythorn made no answer. He remembered distinctly that, after that first visit, he had asked his wife if she had seen Haskett. She had lied to him then, but she had respected his wishes since; and the incident cast a curious light on her character. He was sure she would not have seen Haskett that first day if she had divined that Waythorn would object, and the fact that she did not divine it was almost as disagreeable to the latter as the discovery that she had lied to him.

"I don't like the woman," Haskett was repeating with mild persistency. "She ain't straight, Mr. Waythorn—she'll teach the child to be underhand. I've noticed a change in Lily—she's too anxious to please—and she don't always tell the truth. She used to be the straightest child, Mr. Waythorn—" He broke off, his voice a little thick. "Not but what I want her to have a stylish education," he ended.

Waythorn was touched. "I'm sorry, Mr. Haskett; but frankly, I don't quite see what I can do."

Haskett hesitated. Then he laid his hat on the table, and advanced to the hearth-rug, on which Waythorn was standing. There was nothing aggressive in his manner, but he had the solemnity of a timid man resolved on a decisive measure.

"There's just one thing you can do, Mr. Waythorn," he said. "You can remind Mrs. Waythorn that, by the decree of the courts, I am entitled to have a voice in Lily's bringing up." He paused, and went on more deprecatingly: "I'm not the kind to talk about enforcing my rights, Mr. Waythorn. I don't know as I think a man is entitled to rights he hasn't known how to hold on to; but this business of the child is different. I've never let go there—and I never mean to."

The scene left Waythorn deeply shaken. Shamefacedly, in indirect ways, he had been finding out about Haskett; and all that he had learned was favourable. The little man, in order to be near his daughter, had sold out his share in a profitable business in Utica, and accepted a modest clerkship in a New York manufacturing house. He boarded in a shabby street and had few acquaintances. His passion for Lily filled his life. Waythorn felt that this exploration of Haskett was like groping about with a dark-lantern in his wife's past; but he saw now that there were recesses his lantern had not explored. He had never enquired into the exact circumstances of his wife's first matrimonial rupture. On the surface all had been fair. It was she who had obtained the divorce, and the court had given her the child. But Waythorn knew how many ambiguities such a verdict might cover. The mere fact that Haskett retained a right over his daughter implied an unsuspected compromise. Waythorn was an idealist. He always refused to recognise unpleasant contingencies till he found himself confronted with them, and then he saw them followed by a spectral train of consequences. His next days were thus haunted, and he determined to try to lay the ghosts by conjuring them up in his wife's presence.

When he repeated Haskett's request a flame of anger passed over her face; but she subdued it instantly and spoke with a slight quiver of outraged motherhood.

"It is very ungentlemanly of him," she said.

The word grated on Waythorn. "That is neither here nor there. It's a bare question of rights."

She murmured: "It's not as if he could ever be a help to Lily—"

Waythorn flushed. This was even less to his taste. "The question is," he repeated, "what authority has he over her?"

She looked downward, twisting herself a little in her seat. "I am willing to see him— I thought you objected," she faltered.

In a flash he understood that she knew the extent of Haskett's claims. Perhaps it was not the first time she had resisted them.

"My objecting has nothing to do with it," he said coldly; "if Haskett has a right to be consulted you must consult him."

She burst into tears, and he saw that she expected him to regard her as a victim.

Haskett did not abuse his rights. Waythorn had felt miserably sure that he would not. But the governess was dismissed, and from time to time the little man demanded an interview with Alice. After the first outburst she accepted the situation with her usual adaptability. Haskett had once reminded Waythorn of the piano-tuner, and Mrs. Waythorn, after a month or two, appeared to class him with that domestic familiar. Waythorn could not but respect the father's tenacity. At first he had tried to cultivate the suspicion that Haskett might be "up to" something, that he had an object in secur-ing a foothold in the house. But in his heart Waythorn was sure of Haskett's single-mindedness; he even guessed in the latter a mild contempt for such advantages as his relation with the Waythorns might offer. Haskett's sincerity of purpose made him invulnerable, and his successor had to accept him as a lien on the property.

Mr. Sellers was sent to Europe to recover from his gout, and Varick's affairs hung on Waythorn's hands. The negotiations were prolonged and complicated; they neces-sitated frequent conferences between the two men, and the interests of the firm forbade Waythorn's suggesting that his client should transfer his business to another office.

Varick appeared well in the transaction. In moments of relaxation his coarse streak appeared, and Waythorn dreaded his geniality; but in the office he was concise and clear-headed, with a flattering deference to Waythorn's judgment. Their business rela-tions being so affably established, it would have been absurd for the two men to ignore each other in society. The first time they met in a drawing-room, Varick took up their intercourse in the same easy key, and his hostess's grateful glance obliged Waythorn to respond to it. After that they ran across each other frequently, and one evening at a ball Waythorn, wandering through the remoter rooms, came upon Varick seated beside his wife. She coloured a little, and faltered in what she was saying; but Varick nodded to Waythorn without rising, and the latter strolled on.

In the carriage, on the way home, he broke out nervously: "I didn't know you spoke to Varick."

Her voice trembled a little. "It's the first time—he happened to be standing near me; I didn't know what to do. It's so awkward, meeting everywhere—and he said you had been very kind about some business."

"That's different," said Waythorn.

She paused a moment. "I'll do just as you wish," she returned pliantly. "I thought it would be less awkward to speak to him when we meet."

Her pliancy was beginning to sicken him. Had she really no will of her own—no theory about her relationship to these men? She had accepted Haskett—did she mean to accept Varick? It was "less awkward," as she had said, and her instinct was to evade difficulties or to circumvent them. With sudden vividness Waythorn saw how the instinct had developed. She was "as easy as an old shoe"—a shoe that too many feet had worn. Her elasticity was the result of tension in too many different directions. Alice Haskett—Alice Varick—Alice Waythorn—she had been each in turn, and had left hanging to each name a little of her privacy, a little of her personality, a little of the inmost self where the unknown god abides.

"Yes—it's better to speak to Varick," said Waythorn wearily.

V

The winter wore on, and society took advantage of the Waythorns' acceptance of Varick. Harassed hostesses were grateful to them for bridging over a social difficulty, and Mrs. Waythorn was held up as a miracle of good taste. Some experimental spirits could not resist the diversion of throwing Varick and his former wife together, and there were those who thought he found a zest in the propinquity. But Mrs. Waythorn's conduct remained irreproachable. She neither avoided Varick nor sought him out. Even Waythorn could not but admit that she had discovered the solution of the newest social problem.

He had married her without giving much thought to that problem. He had fancied that a woman can shed her past like a man. But now he saw that Alice was bound to hers both by the circumstances which forced her into continued relation with it, and by the traces it had left on her nature. With grim irony Waythorn compared himself to a member of a syndicate. He held so many shares in his wife's personality and his predecessors were his partners in the business. If there had been any element of passion in the transaction he would have felt less deteriorated by it. The fact that Alice took her change of husbands like a change of weather reduced the situation to mediocrity. He could have forgiven her for blunders, for excesses; for resisting Haskett, for yielding to Varick; for anything but her acquiescence and her tact. She reminded him of a juggler tossing knives; but the knives were blunt and she knew they would never cut her.

And then, gradually, habit formed a protecting surface for his sensibilities. If he paid for each day's comfort with the small change of his illusions, he grew daily to value the comfort more and set less store upon the coin. He had drifted into a dulling propinquity with Haskett and Varick and he took refuge in the cheap revenge of satirising the situation. He even began to reckon up the advantages which accrued from it, to ask himself if it were not better to own a third of a wife who knew how to make a man happy than a whole one who had lacked opportunity to acquire the art. For it *was* an art, and made up, like all others, of concessions, eliminations and embellishments; of lights judiciously thrown and shadows skilfully softened. His wife knew exactly how to manage the lights, and he knew exactly to what training she owed her skill. He even tried to trace the source of his obligations, to discriminate between the influences which had combined to produce his domestic happiness: he perceived that Haskett's commonness had made Alice worship good breeding, while Varick's liberal construction of the marriage bond had taught her to value the conjugal virtues; so that he was directly indebted to his predecessors for the devotion which made his life easy if not inspiring.

From this phase he passed into that of complete acceptance. He ceased to satirise himself because time dulled the irony of the situation and the joke lost its humour with its sting. Even the sight of Haskett's hat on the hall table had ceased to touch the springs of epigram. The hat was often seen there now, for it had been decided that it was better for Lily's father to visit her than for the little girl to go to his boarding-house. Waythorn, having acquiesced in this arrangement, had been surprised to find how little difference it made. Haskett was never obtrusive, and the few visitors who met him on the stairs were unaware of his identity. Waythorn did not know how often he saw Alice, but with himself Haskett was seldom in contact.

One afternoon, however, he learned on entering that Lily's father was waiting to see him. In the library he found Haskett occupying a chair in his usual provisional way. Waythorn always felt grateful to him for not leaning back.

"I hope you'll excuse me, Mr. Waythorn," he said rising. "I wanted to see Mrs. Waythorn about Lily, and your man asked me to wait here till she came in."

"Of course," said Waythorn, remembering that a sudden leak had that morning given over the drawing-room to the plumbers.

He opened his cigar-case and held it out to his visitor, and Haskett's acceptance seemed to mark a fresh stage in their intercourse. The spring evening was chilly, and Waythorn invited his guest to draw up his chair to the fire. He meant to find an excuse to leave Haskett in a moment; but he was tired and cold, and after all the little man no longer jarred on him.

The two were enclosed in the intimacy of their blended cigar-smoke when the door opened and Varick walked into the room. Waythorn rose abruptly. It was the first time that Varick had come to the house, and the surprise of seeing him, combined with the singular inopportuneness of his arrival, gave a new edge to Waythorn's blunted sensibilities. He stared at his visitor without speaking.

Varick seemed too preoccupied to notice his host's embarrassment.

"My dear fellow," he exclaimed in his most expansive tone, "I must apologise for tumbling in on you in this way, but I was too late to catch you down town, and so I thought—"

He stopped short, catching sight of Haskett, and his sanguine colour deepened to a flush which spread vividly under his scant blond hair. But in a moment he recovered himself and nodded slightly. Haskett returned the bow in silence, and Waythorn was still groping for speech when the footman came in carrying a tea-table.

The intrusion offered a welcome vent to Waythorn's nerves. "What the deuce are you bringing this here for?" he said sharply.

"I beg your pardon, sir, but the plumbers are still in the drawing-room, and Mrs. Waythorn said she would have tea in the library." The footman's perfectly respectful tone implied a reflection on Waythorn's reasonableness.

"Oh, very well," said the latter resignedly, and the footman proceeded to open the folding tea-table and set out its complicated appointments. While this interminable process continued the three men stood motionless, watching it with a fascinated stare, till Waythorn, to break the silence, said to Varick: "Won't you have a cigar?"

He held out the case he had just tendered to Haskett, and Varick helped himself with a smile. Waythorn looked about for a match, and finding none, proffered a light from his own cigar. Haskett, in the background, held his ground mildly, examining his cigar-tip now and then, and stepping forward at the right moment to knock its ashes into the fire.

The footman at last withdrew, and Varick immediately began: "If I could just say half a word to you about this business—"

"Certainly," stammered Waythorn; "in the dining-room—"

But as he placed his hand on the door it opened from without, and his wife appeared on the threshold.

She came in fresh and smiling, in her street dress and hat, shedding a fragrance from the boa which she loosened in advancing.

"Shall we have tea in here, dear?" she began; and then she caught sight of Varick. Her smile deepened, veiling a slight tremor of surprise.

"Why, how do you do?" she said with a distinct note of pleasure.

As she shook hands with Varick she saw Haskett standing behind him. Her smile faded for a moment, but she recalled it quickly, with a scarcely perceptible side-glance at Waythorn.

"How do you do, Mr. Haskett?" she said, and shook hands with him a shade less cordially.

The three men stood awkwardly before her, till Varick, always the most self-possessed, dashed into an explanatory phrase.

"We—I had to see Waythorn a moment on business," he stammered, brick-red from chin to nape.

Haskett stepped forward with his air of mild obstinacy. "I am sorry to intrude; but you appointed five o'clock—" he directed his resigned glance to the time-piece on the mantel.

She swept aside their embarrassment with a charming gesture of hospitality.

"I'm so sorry—I'm always late; but the afternoon was so lovely." She stood drawing off her gloves, propitiatory and graceful, diffusing about her a sense of ease and familiarity in which the situation lost its grotesqueness. "But before talking business," she added brightly, "I'm sure every one wants a cup of tea."

She dropped into her low chair by the tea-table, and the two visitors, as if drawn by her smile, advanced to receive the cups she held out.

She glanced about for Waythorn, and he took the third cup with a laugh.

—1904

SUI SIN FAR (EDITH EATON) (1865-1914)

Edith Eaton and her sister Winnifred Eaton have been called the first published writers of Chinese-North American descent. Edith Eaton published short stories and journalistic articles under the pen name Sui Sin Far, a childhood nickname meaning "Water Lily." Born in Macclesfield, England, Edith was the second of fourteen children born to Grace Trefusias, a Chinese woman raised in England, and Edward Eaton, a British silk merchant. When she was seven, her family moved first to Hudson City, New York, and then settled in Montreal, Quebec. The Eatons encouraged artistic expression in their children, and Edith and Winnifred both published poems, stories, and articles for their local newspaper while in their teens. As a journalist, Eaton reported on the Chinese communities of the various cities in which she lived: San Francisco, Los Angeles, Boston, and Seattle. Her collection of short stories, *Mrs. Spring Fragrance,* was published in 1912. Contemporary critics of Asian-American literature praise Eaton's sympathetic portrayals of the Chinese in North America during a time of strong anti-Chinese sentiment. Because Eaton could have passed for white, her identification with Chinese and Chinese Americans is seen as deliberate and courageous. Her memoir "Leaves from the Mental Portfolio of an Eurasian" is an early text articulating the experience of subjects with mixed white and Asian ancestry. She returned to Montreal in 1913, ill with rheumatism and general bad health. She died there on April 7, 1914.

The Americanizing of Pau Tsu

I

When Wan Hom Hing came to Seattle to start a branch of the merchant business which his firm carried on so successfully in the different ports of China, he brought with him his nephew, Wan Lin Fo, then eighteen years of age. Wan Lin Fo was a well-educated Chinese youth, with bright eyes and keen ears. In a few years' time he knew as much about the business as did any of the senior partners. Moreover, he learned to speak and write the American language with such fluency that he was never at a loss for an answer, when the white man, as was sometimes the case, sought to pose him. "All work and no play," however, is as much against the principles of a Chinese youth as it is against those of a young American, and now and again Lin Fo would while away an evening at the Chinese Literary Club, above the Chinese restaurant, discussing with some chosen companions the works and merits of Chinese sages— and some other things. New Year's Day, or rather, Week, would also see him, business forgotten, arrayed in national costume of finest silk, and color "the blue of the sky after rain," visiting with his friends, both Chinese and American, and scattering silver and gold coin amongst the youngsters of the families visited.

It was on the occasion of one of these New Year's visits that Wan Lin Fo first made known to the family of his firm's silent American partner, Thomas Raymond, that he was betrothed. It came about in this wise: One of the young ladies of the house, who was fair and frank of face and friendly and cheery in manner, observing as she handed him a cup of tea that Lin Fo's eyes wore a rather wistful expression, questioned him as to the wherefore:

"Miss Adah," replied Lin Fo, "may I tell you something?"

"Certainly, Mr. Wan," replied the girl. "You know how I enjoy hearing your tales."

"But this is no tale. Miss Adah, you have inspired in me a love—"

Adah Raymond started. Wan Lin Fo spake slowly.

"For the little girl in China to whom I am betrothed."

"Oh, Mr. Wan! That is good news. But what have I to do with it?"

"This, Miss Adah! Every time I come to this house, I see you, so good and so beautiful, dispensing tea and happiness to all around, and I think, could I have in my home and ever by my side one who is also both good and beautiful, what a felicitous life mine would be!"

"You must not flatter me, Mr. Wan!"

"All that I say is founded on my heart. But I will speak not of you. I will speak of Pau Tsu."

"Pau Tsu?"

"Yes. That is the name of my future wife. It means a pearl."

"How pretty! Tell me all about her!"

"I was betrothed to Pau Tsu before leaving China. My parents adopted her to be my wife. As I remember, she had shining eyes and the good-luck color was on her cheek. Her mouth was like a red vine leaf, and her eyebrows most exquisitely arched. As slender as a willow was her form, and when she spoke, her voice lilted from note to note in the sweetest melody."

Adah Raymond softly clapped her hands.

"Ah! You were even then in love with her."

"No," replied Lin Fo thoughtfully. "I was too young to be in love—sixteen years of age. Pau Tsu was thirteen. But, as I have confessed, you have caused me to remember and love her."

Adah Raymond was not a self-conscious girl, but for the life of her she could think of no reply to Lin Fo's speech.

"I am twenty-two years old now," he continued. "Pau Tsu is eighteen. Tomorrow I will write to my parents and persuade them to send her to me at the time of the spring festival. My elder brother was married last year, and his wife is now under my parents' roof, so that Pau Tsu, who has been the daughter of the house for so many years, can now be spared to me."

"What a sweet little thing she must be," commented Adah Raymond.

"You will say that when you see her," proudly responded Lin Fo. "My parents say she is always happy. There is not a bird or flower or dewdrop in which she does not find some glad meaning."

"I shall be so glad to know her. Can she speak English?"

Lin Fo's face fell.

"No," he replied, "but,"—brightening—"when she comes I will have her learn to speak like you—and be like you."

II

Pau Tsu came with the spring, and Wan Lin Fo was one the happiest and proud-est of bridegrooms. The tiny bride was really very pretty—even to American eyes. In her peach and plum colored robes, her little arms and hands sparkling with jewels, and her shiny black head decorated with wonderful combs and pins, she appeared a bit of Eastern coloring amidst the Western lights and shades.

Lin Fo had not been forgotten, and her eyes under their downcast lids discovered him at once, as he stood awaiting her amongst a group of young Chinese merchants on the deck of the vessel.

The apartments he had prepared for her were furnished in American style, and her birdlike little figure in Oriental dress seemed rather out of place at first. It was not long, however, before she brought forth from the great box, which she had brought over seas, screens and fans, vases, panels, Chinese matting, artificial flowers and birds, and a number of exquisite carvings and pieces of antique porcelain. With these she transformed the American flat into an Oriental bower, even setting up in her sleeping-room a little chapel, enshrined in which was an image of the Goddess of Mercy, two ancestral tablets, and other emblems of her faith in the Gods of her fathers.

The Misses Raymond called upon her soon after arrival, and she smiled and looked pleased. She shyly presented each girl with a Chinese cup and saucer, also a couple of antique vases, covered with whimsical pictures, which Lin Fo tried his best to explain.

The girls were delighted with the gifts, and having fallen, as they expressed themselves, in love with the little bride, invited her through her husband to attend a lunch party, which they intended giving the following Wednesday on Lake Washington.

Lin Fo accepted the invitation in behalf of himself and wife. He was quite at home with the Americans and, being a young man, enjoyed their rather effusive appreciation of him as an educated Chinaman. Moreover, he was of the opinion that the society of the American young ladies would benefit Pau Tsu in helping her to acquire the ways and language of the land in which he hoped to make a fortune.

Wan Lin Fo was a true son of the Middle Kingdom and secretly pitied all those who were born far away from its influences; but there was much about the Americans that he admired. He also entertained sentiments of respect for a motto which hung in his room which bore the legend: "When in Rome, do as the Romans do."

"What is best for men is also best for women in this country," he told Pau Tsu when she wept over his suggestion that she should take some lessons in English from a white woman.

"It may be best for a man who goes out in the street," she sobbed, "to learn the new language, but of what importance is it to a woman who lives only within the house and her husband's heart?"

It was seldom, however, that she protested against the wishes of Lin Fo. As her mother-in-law had said, she was a docile, happy little creature. Moreover, she loved her husband.

But as the days and weeks went by the girl bride whose life hitherto had been spent in the quiet retirement of a Chinese home in the performance of filial duties, in embroidery work and lute playing, in sipping tea and chatting with gentle girl companions, felt very much bewildered by the novelty and stir of the new world into which she had been suddenly thrown. She could not understand, for all Lin Fo's explanations, why it was required of her to learn the strangers' language and adopt their ways. Her husband's tongue was the same as her own. So also her little maid's. It puzzled her to be always seeing this and hearing that—sights and sounds which as yet had no meaning for her. Why also was it necessary to receive visitors nearly every evening?—visitors who could neither understand nor make themselves understood by her, for all their curious smiles and stares, which she bore like a second Vashti— or rather, Esther.[1] And why, oh! why should she be constrained to eat her food with clumsy, murderous looking American implements instead of with her own elegant and easily manipulated ivory chopsticks?

Adah Raymond, who at Lin Fo's request was a frequent visitor to the house, could not fail to observe that Pau Tsu's small face grew daily smaller and thinner, and that the smile with which she invariably greeted her, though sweet, was tinged with melancholy. Her woman's instinct told her that something was wrong, but what it was the light within her failed to discover. She would reach over to Pau Tsu and take within her own firm, white hand the small, trembling fingers, pressing them lovingly and sympathetically; and the little Chinese woman would look up into the beautiful face bent above hers and think to herself: "No wonder he wishes me to be like her!"

If Lin Fo happened to come in before Adah Raymond left he would engage the visitor in bright and animated conversation. They had so much of common interest

---

[1] In the Bible, Queen Vashti is banished for disobeying King Ahasuerus; Esther, a Jewish orphan, is made queen. Esther discovers a plot against the Jewish people and intervenes.

to discuss, as is always the way with young people who have lived any length of time in a growing city of the West. But to Pau Tsu, pouring tea and dispensing sweetmeats, it was all Greek, or rather, all American.

"Look, my pearl, what I have brought you," said Lin Fo one afternoon as he entered his wife's apartments, followed by a messenger-boy, who deposited in the middle of the room a large cardboard box.

With murmurs of wonder Pau Tsu drew near, and the messenger-boy having withdrawn Lin Fo cut the string, and drew forth a beautiful lace evening dress and dark blue walking costume, both made in American style.

For a moment there was silence in the room. Lin Fo looked at his wife in surprise. Her face was pale and her little body was trembling, while her hands were drawn up into her sleeves.

"Why, Pau Tsu!" he exclaimed, "I thought to make you glad."

At these words the girl bent over the dress of filmy lace, and gathering the flounce in her hand smoothed it over her knee; then lifting a smiling face to her husband, replied: "Oh, you are too good, too kind to your unworthy Pau Tsu. My speech is slow, because I am overcome with happiness."

Then with exclamations of delight and admiration she lifted the dresses out of the box and laid them carefully over the couch.

"I wish you to dress like an American woman when we go out or receive," said her husband. "It is the proper thing in America to do as the Americans do. You will notice, light of my eyes, that it is only on New Year and our national holidays that I wear the costume of our country and attach a queue. The wife should follow the husband in all things."

A ripple of laughter escaped Pau Tsu's lips.

"When I wear that dress," said she, touching the walking costume, "I will look like your friend, Miss Raymond."

She struck her hands together gleefully, but when her husband had gone to his business she bowed upon the floor and wept pitifully.

III

During the rainy season Pau Tsu was attacked with a very bad cough. A daughter of Southern China, the chill, moist climate of the Puget Sound winter was very hard on her delicate lungs. Lin Fo worried much over the state of her health, and meeting Adah Raymond on the street one afternoon told her of his anxiety. The kind-hearted girl immediately returned with him to the house. Pau Tsu was lying on her couch, feverish and breathing hard. The American girl felt her hands and head.

"She must have a doctor," said she, mentioning the name of her family's physician.

Pau Tsu shuddered. She understood a little English by this time.

"No! No! Not a man, *not* a man!" she cried.

Adah Raymond looked up at Lin Fo.

"I understand," said she. "There are several women doctors in this town. Let us send for one."

But Lin Fo's face was set.

"No!" he declared. "We are in America. Pau Tsu shall be attended to by your physician."

Adah Raymond was about to protest against this dictum when the sick wife, who had also heard it, touched her hand and whispered: "I not mind now. Man all right."

So the other girl closed her lips, feeling that if the wife would not dispute her husband's will it was not her place to do so; but her heart ached with compassion as she bared Pau Tsu's chest for the stethoscope.

"It was like preparing a lamb for slaughter," she told her sister afterwards. "Pau Tsu was motionless, her eyes closed and her lips sealed, while the doctor remained; but after he had left and we two were alone she shuddered and moaned like one bereft of reason. I honestly believe that the examination was worse than death to that little Chinese woman. The modesty of generations of maternal ancestors was crucified as I rolled down the neck of her silk tunic."

It was a week after the doctor's visit, and Pau Tsu, whose cough had yielded to treatment, though she was still far from well, was playing on her lute, and whisperingly singing this little song, said to have been written on a fan which was presented to an ancient Chinese emperor by one of his wives:

"Of fresh new silk,
All snowy white,
And round as a harvest moon,
A pledge of purity and love,
A small but welcome boon.

While summer lasts,
When borne in hand,
Or folded on thy breast,
'Twill gently soothe thy burning brow,
And charm thee to thy rest.

But, oh, when Autumn winds blow chill,
And days are bleak and cold,
No longer sought, no longer loved,
'Twill lie in dust and mould.

This silken fan then deign accept,
Sad emblem of my lot,
Caressed and cherished for an hour,
Then speedily forgot."

"Why so melancholy, my pearl?" asked Lin Fo, entering from the street.

"When a bird is about to die, its notes are sad," returned Pau Tsu.

"But thou art not for death—thou art for life," declared Lin Fo, drawing her towards him and gazing into a face which day by day seemed to grow finer and more transparent.

IV

A Chinese messenger-boy ran up the street, entered the store of Wan Hom Hing & Co. and asked for the junior partner. When Lin Fo came forward he handed him a dainty, flowered missive, neatly folded and addressed. The receiver opened it and read:

DEAR AND HONORED HUSBAND,—Your unworthy Pau Tsu lacks the courage to face the ordeal before her. She has, therefore, left you and prays you to obtain a divorce, as is the custom in America, so that you may be happy with the Beautiful One, who is so much your Pau Tsu's superior. This, she acknowledges, for she sees with your eyes, in which, like a star, the Beautiful One shineth. Else, why should you have your Pau Tsu follow in her footsteps? She has tried to obey your will and to be as an American woman; but now she is very weary, and the terror of what is before her has overcome.

Your stupid thorn,

Pau Tsu

Mechanically Lin Fo folded the letter and thrust it within his breast pocket. A customer inquired of him the price of a lacquered tray. "I wish you good morning," he replied, reaching for his hat. The customer and clerks gaped after him as he left the store.

Out in the street, as fate would have it, he met Adah Raymond. He would have turned aside had she not spoken to him.

"Whatever is the matter with you, Mr. Wan?" she inquired. "You don't look yourself at all."

"The density of my difficulties you cannot understand," he replied, striding past her.

But Adah Raymond was persistent. She had worried lately over Pau Tsu.

"Something is wrong with your wife," she declared.

Lin Fo wheeled around.

"Do you know where she is?" he asked with quick suspicion.

"Why, no!" exclaimed the girl in surprise.

"Well, she has left me."

Adah Raymond stood incredulous for a moment, then with indignant eyes she turned upon the deserted husband.

"You deserve it!" she cried, "I have seen it for some time: your cruel, arbitrary treatment of the dearest, sweetest little soul in the world."

"I beg your pardon, Miss Adah," returned Lin Fo, "but I do not understand. Pau Tsu is heart of my heart. How then could I be cruel to her?"

"Oh, you stupid!" exclaimed the girl. "You're a Chinaman, but you're almost as stupid as an American. Your cruelty consisted in forcing Pau Tsu to be—what nature never intended her to be—an American woman; to adapt and adopt in a few months' time all our ways and customs. I saw it long ago, but as Pau Tsu was too sweet and meek to see any faults in her man I had not the heart to open her eyes—or yours. Is it not true that she has left you for this reason?"

"Yes," murmured Lin Fo. He was completely crushed. "And some other things."

"What other things?"

"She—is—afraid—of—the—doctor."

"She is!"—fiercely—"Shame upon you!"

Lin Fo began to walk on, but the girl kept by his side and continued:

"You wanted your wife to be an American woman while you remained a Chinaman. For all your clever adaptation of our American ways you are a thorough Chinaman. Do you think an American would dare treat his wife as you have treated yours?"

Wan Lin Fo made no response. He was wondering how he could ever have wished his gentle Pau Tsu to be like this angry woman. Now his Pau Tsu was gone. His anguish for the moment made him oblivious to the presence of his companion and the words she was saying. His silence softened the American girl. After all, men, even Chinamen, were nothing but big, clumsy boys, and she didn't believe in kicking a man after he was down.

"But, cheer up, you're sure to find her," said she, suddenly changing her tone. "Probably her maid has friends in Chinatown who have taken them in."

"If I find her," said Lin Fo fervently, "I will not care if she never speaks an American word, and I will take her for a trip to China, so that our son may be born in the country that Heaven loves."

"You cannot make too much amends for all she has suffered. As to Americanizing Pau Tsu—that will come in time. I am quite sure that were I transferred to your country and commanded to turn myself into a Chinese woman in the space of two or three months I would prove a sorry disappointment to whomever built their hopes upon me."

Many hours elapsed before any trace could be found of the missing one. All the known friends and acquaintances of little Pau Tsu were called upon and questioned; but if they had knowledge of the young wife's hiding place they refused to divulge it. Though Lin Fo's face was grave with an unexpressed fear, their sympathies were certainly not with him.

The seekers were about giving up the search in despair when a little boy, dangling in his hands a string of blue beads, arrested the attention of the young husband. He knew the necklace to be a gift from Pau Tsu to the maid, A-Toy. He had bought it himself. Stopping and questioning the little fellow he learned to his great joy that his wife and her maid were at the boy's home, under the care of his grandmother, who was a woman learned in herb lore.

Adah Raymond smiled in sympathy with her companion's evident great relief.

"Everything will now be all right," said she, following Lin Fo as he proceeded to the house pointed out by the lad. Arrived there, she suggested that the husband enter first and alone. She would wait a few moments.

"Miss Adah," said Lin Fo, "ten thousand times I beg your pardon, but perhaps you will come to see my wife some other time—not today?"

He hesitated, embarrassed and humiliated.

In one silent moment Adah Raymond grasped the meaning of all the morning's trouble—of all Pau Tsu's sadness.

"Lord, what fools we mortals be!" she soliloquized as she walked home alone. "I ought to have known. What else could Pau Tsu have thought?—coming from a land where women have no men friends save their husbands. How she must have suffered under her smiles! Poor, brave little soul!"

—1912

Mary Hunter Austin (1868-1934)

Mary Hunter was born in Carlinville, Illinois, to lawyer George Hunter and Susan Savilla Graham. Both her father and her sister died when Austin was ten. In 1888, her mother moved the family to the San Joaquin Valley in California. In 1891, she married Stafford Wallace Austin; the couple's daughter, born the next year, had severe mental retardation and was eventually institutionalized. The American Southwest provided the material for most of Austin's writing—her first book, *The Land of Little Rain* (1903), was a series of sketches of the desert and its inhabitants. Austin separated from her husband the next year, and they were divorced in 1914. She continued writing about the Southwest, especially about Native American cultures, in such volumes as *Lost Borders* (1909) and *The Land of Journeys' Ending* (1924). Austin lived briefly in Carmel, California; Greenwich Village, New York; Italy; and, during the last decade of her life, Santa Fe, New Mexico. Austin wrote both fiction and nonfiction, including *A Woman of Genius* (1912), her most well-known novel, and the autobiographical *Earth Horizon* (1932). She also collected Native American stories for children. "The Man Who Was Loved by Women" is from *One Smoke Stories* (1934).

The Man Who Was Loved by Women

There was a man of the Navajo who, without deserving it, was much loved by women. It was not believed, in the beginning, that he had desired anything of the kind, or that he practiced any medicine to turn their hearts. He was handsome, which, as he said in a song he made about himself, was hardly his fault, and in one way and another was the source of a great deal of trouble to him.

If this Tsaysiki had married the first maiden who fixed her affections upon him, he would have had children and become an excellent tribesman; but before he had collected the proper number of horses for her dowry, he went with his father to the place of the Four Smokes to trade. There he met a Comanche woman, somewhat older than himself, who had a way of talking to men so that they believed her. She told Tsaysiki that it was a mistake for him to fasten a pack-strap to his back before he had proved himself against tribes other than his own. When a man has lived always among his own kin, who can say how much of what happens to him is pure kindness? So Tsaysiki sent a present to his girl at Peach Springs, and went North with the Comanche woman for the space of four moons, returning by way of Taos and the Tewa pueblos.

At first, being young and without experience, he told the women he met that he was betrothed to a girl at home, and got so much credit with them for his honesty that the way was opened for him to take what was offered without giving more than his pleasure in return. This is a mistake, for with women, no matter how free the giving, there is always something to pay for it in the end, and it is easiest paid where it is owed. The women of Taos were handsome, and proud givers, not asking for anything that is not bestowed, but the men of Taos are proud also, and though not so light on their feet, heavier than the Navajos. So Tsaysiki returned by way of Tesuque and the Keres towns, to his home camp under Carizal, to find that the girl he left had been married to somebody else in his absence.

Though he had forgotten her many times in the course of his journey, Tsaysiki felt himself injured. For his hurt's sake he had to make her sorry for herself by showing her how many other women cared for him. This he did so successfully that the Elders advised him that unless he felt disposed to marry one of them and devote himself to his duties as the father of a family, he would do better to join the remnant of his clan at Horizontal Water. But lest he should find himself in danger of again being pressed to take a wife, when he arrived there, Tsaysiki sought comfort from the women already married. He was always able to find one or two who believed him when he said he could not help what happened to him on account of women. But their husbands, on whom no doubt they had proved it, were even less kind than the fathers at Peach Springs, and in the end Tsaysiki found it more convenient to join an unimportant band that moved about a great deal in the neighborhood of Pelado Peak, and was dominated, not by a Head Man, but by a woman called Dysildji. There, in the course of a few weeks, he fell into serious trouble over a girl who had taken the Jesus Road by the advice of the missionaries, and, when she found herself with child, ate wild parsnip root and died of it.

This was hard on Tsaysiki, for she was a plain and simple girl to whom he had been kind merely from habit. Nevertheless, he was called before the Elders, for the band was a small one, and the death of a young and healthy woman was rated as more than twenty head of cattle. Besides, there were the missionaries who, notwithstanding they had put the idea into the girl's head that an unfathered child was a thing to eat wild parsnip over, would have laid her death to the Navajos. Before putting anything in execution against Tsaysiki, however, the Elders waited for Dysildji, who had gone down to Kayenta to oversee the shearing of her sheep of which she had three bands, as well as cattle and many horses which she had from her father. Dysildji was not altogether young, but well looking and of so free a fancy that, though she had tried several, she had not yet found a husband to suit her. But because she had always been constant to the rights of other women, and because of her great possessions, she was left unrebuked, and much respected.

Dysildji came in from her shearing with the red sun behind her and looked the young man over. She saw that he was handsome, and had a way with women which he did not hesitate to use with Dysildji as soon as he found her looking at him. For some reason this pleased her. Other men had been too much in fear of her sharp mind and her great wealth to play upon her, and that may have been what she wanted. But it must also be remembered that she had taken all women for her sisters, and the account of Tsaysiki's loves had followed him. She heard what the Elders said, and how Tsaysiki answered them, with his eye sidewise toward the Head Woman—how he was the sort of man who could not help what happened to him on account of women.

"Leave him to me," said the Head Woman, and the Elders were well satisfied to have it so. Dysildji took the young man to her house and explained that they should be married, "For we will make a handsome couple," she said, "and I mean to have several children. Also, since we are both the sort of people that other people cannot help falling in love with, we will understand that, when that happens, there will be no offense taken on either side."

Tsaysiki was as pleased as a stallion, for to be the husband of the richest woman of the Navajos and at the same time free in his affections was more than even a favorite of the Yei had a right to expect from them. Dysildji gave him a silver belt having conchos of a hand's breadth, necklaces set with great lumps of turquoise, and a different blanket for every occasion, so that when they walked abroad together they clinked pleasantly of silver, and were noticed by everybody. Dysildji introduced her husband to all her women friends explaining that there was an understanding between them that anybody who fell in love with either of them was to expect nothing but highness from the other. Then she asked him to sing the song he had made about himself some years earlier, and which ran thus:

> Blame not me but the Yei
> Who have brought handsomeness upon me.
> How can I help it if women love me?

At this the other women, instead of looking sympathetically as they had used, looked every other way, and even occasionally snickered.

If, however, Tsaysiki did not know it before, he found out very quickly that, though women will fight for a man they have marked for their own, they will not take him as a gift from another woman. He also discovered that, no matter what agreement he has with her, a man who is openly neglected by his wife for the head of the Four-Feather Band is made to seem ridiculous. But by the time he discovered how ridiculous it was, it was too late for him to do anything about it, either when the men complimented him on his forbearance or the other women consoled him. And a Navajo may not divorce his wife for conduct he has once tolerated.

In the course of time Dysildji's flocks increased, so that she brought up a young man of the Yaquis, whom she had met at the *fiesta* of San Carlos, to be head herder to them. He was a personable man, and knew how to make himself secure with his employer. It is told that the first time Dysildji brought him to the hogan, Tsaysiki came out to meet them.

"This is only my husband," she told the herder. "You need not pay any attention to what he thinks, and he will not say anything, because we have an agreement," and she gave him the horses to hold. Half an hour later the Yaqui, looking out of the window and seeing the husband still there, became a little uneasy, for the Yaquis are strict with their women. "You needn't be," Dysildji assured him. "My husband is the sort of man who cannot help what happens to him on account of a woman." And out of consideration for the Yaqui, she said it aloud so that Tsaysiki, holding the two horses, heard her.

—1934

EMMA GOLDMAN (1869–1940)

An anarchist whose feminism anticipated that of the second wave (1960s-1970s), Emma Goldman was born to Taube Bienowitch and Abraham Goldman, in the Kovno province of Czarist Russia (now Kaunas, Lithuania). Along with two brothers and two stepsisters, she endured a childhood of poverty and harsh discipline. Though an excellent student, her family's poverty prevented her from finishing her high school education; she developed her knowledge through both experience and reading. Goldman first learned about revolutionary women as a young girl, while working in a glove factory in St. Petersburg. After immigrating with one of her stepsisters to New York to avoid a marriage that her father attempted to arrange, she worked in a garment factory in Rochester, where she met and married Jacob A. Kersner, and became a U.S. citizen. When her marriage failed, she moved to New York City.

Goldman became firmly committed to anarchism and social revolution in the aftermath of the 1886 Haymarket Square labor demonstration against police brutality in Chicago. She worked as an organizer, public lecturer, and midwife, making women's reproductive issues and sexual independence cornerstones of her feminism. In 1908 her naturalization as a citizen was revoked due to her political activity. Yet Goldman disagreed with suffragists regarding the importance of the vote for women, insisting that liberation lay within the individual woman rather than a corrupt system of government. In 1906 she founded *Mother Earth* magazine, and edited it until 1917, when she was jailed for advocating pacifism during World War I. This sentence led to her deportation to Russia, a country she later rejected for its oppression. She moved briefly to England, where she married Welshman James Colton, and then lived in Spain, France, and Canada. In 1940, Goldman died of a stroke in Toronto. She is buried close to the Haymarket martyrs in Waldheim Cemetry, Chicago.

Was My Life Worth Living?

How much a personal philosophy is a matter of temperament and how much it results from experience is a moot question. Naturally we arrive at conclusions in the light of our experience, through the application of a process we call reasoning to the facts observed in the events of our lives. The child is susceptible to fantasy. At the same time he sees life more truly in some respects than his elders do as he becomes conscious of his surroundings. He has not yet become absorbed by the customs and prejudices which make up the largest part of what passes for thinking. Each child responds differently to his environment. Some become rebels, refusing to be dazzled by social superstitions. They are outraged by every injustice perpetrated upon them or upon others. They grow ever more sensitive to the suffering round them and the restrictions which authority places in their way. Others become rubber stamps, registering every convention and taboo imposed upon them.

I evidently belong to the first category. Since my earliest recollection of my youth in Russia I have rebelled against orthodoxy in every form. I could never bear to witness harshness whether on the part of our parents to us or in their dealings with the servants. I was outraged over the official brutality practiced on the peasants in our neighborhood. I wept bitter tears when the young men were conscripted into the army and torn from homes and hearths. I resented the treatment of our servants, who did the hardest work and yet had to put up with wretched sleeping quarters and the leavings of our table. I was indignant when I discovered that love between young people of Jewish and Gentile origin was considered the crime of crimes, and the birth of an illegitimate child the most depraved immorality.

On coming to America I had the same hopes as have most European immigrants and the same disillusionment, though the latter affected me more keenly and more deeply. The immigrant without money and without connections is not permitted to cherish the comforting illusion that America is a benevolent uncle who assumes a tender and impartial guardianship of nephews and nieces. I soon learned that in a republic there are myriad ways by which the strong, the cunning, the rich can seize power and hold it. I saw the many work for small wages which kept them always on the borderline of want for the few who made huge profits. I saw the courts, the halls of legislation, the press, and the schools—in fact every avenue of education and protection—effectively used as an instrument for the safeguarding of a minority, while the masses were denied every right. I found that the politicians knew how to befog every issue, how to control public opinion and manipulate votes to their own advantage and to that of their financial and industrial allies. This was the picture of democracy I soon discovered on my arrival in the United States. Fundamentally there have been few changes since that time.

This situation, which was a matter of daily experience, was brought home to me with a force that tore away shams and made reality stand out vividly and clearly by an event which occurred shortly after my coming to America. It was the so-called Haymarket riot,[1] which resulted in the trial and conviction of eight men, among them five Anarchists. Their crime was an all-embracing love for their fellow-men and their determination to emancipate the oppressed and disinherited masses. In no way had the State of Illinois succeeded in proving their connection with the bomb that had been thrown at an open-air meeting in Haymarket Square in Chicago. It was their Anarchism which resulted in their conviction and execution on the 11th of November, 1887. This judicial crime left an indelible mark on my mind and heart and sent me forth to acquaint myself with the ideal for which these men had died so heroically. I dedicated myself to their cause.

It requires something more than personal experience to gain a philosophy or point of view from any specific event. It is the quality of our response to the event and our capacity to enter into the lives of others that help us to make their lives and experiences our own. In my own case my convictions have derived and developed from events in the lives of others as well as from my own experience. What I have seen meted out to others by authority and repression, economic and political, transcends anything I myself may have endured.

I have often been asked why I maintained such a non-compromising antagonism to government and in what way I have found myself oppressed by it. In my opinion every individual is hampered by it. It exacts taxes from production. It creates tariffs, which prevent free exchange. It stands ever for the *status quo* and traditional conduct and belief. It comes into private lives and into most intimate personal relations, enabling the superstitious, puritanical, and distorted ones to impose their ignorant prejudice and moral servitudes upon the sensitive, the imaginative, and the free spirits. Government does this by its divorce laws, its moral censorships, and by a thousand petty persecutions of those who are too honest to wear the moral mask of respectability. In addition, government protects the strong at the expense of the weak, provides courts and laws which the rich may scorn and the poor must obey. It enables the predatory rich to make wars to provide foreign markets for the favored ones, with prosperity for the rulers and wholesale death for the ruled. However, it is not only government in the sense of the state which is destructive of every individual value and quality. It is the whole complex of authority and institutional domination which strangles life. It is the superstition, myth, pretense, evasions, and subservience which support authority and institutional domination. It is the reverence for these institutions instilled in the school, the church, and the home in order that man may believe and obey without protest. Such a process of devitalizing and distorting personalities of the individual and of whole communities may have been a part of historical evolution; but it should be strenuously combated by every honest and independent mind in an age which has any

---

[1] At a rally in Chicago's Haymarket Square on May 4, 1886, which took place after days of strikes and police violence, someone in the crowd threw a bomb that killed a police officer. Eight men connected with the rally and its organizers were arrested, seven of whom were sentenced to death. Four men were hanged; the other three were pardoned in 1893.

pretense to enlightenment.

It has often been suggested to me that the Constitution of the United States is a sufficient safeguard for the freedom of its citizens. It is obvious that even the freedom it pretends to guarantee is very limited. I have not been impressed with the adequacy of the safeguard. The nations of the world, with centuries of international law behind them, have never hesitated to engage in mass destruction when solemnly pledged to keep the peace; and the legal documents in America have not prevented the United States from doing the same. Those in authority have and always will abuse their power. And the instances when they do not do so are as rare as roses growing on icebergs. Far from the Constitution playing any liberating part in the lives of the American people, it has robbed them of the capacity to rely on their own resources or do their own thinking. Americans are so easily hoodwinked by the sanctity of law and authority. In fact, the pattern of life has become standardized, routinized, and mechanized like canned food and Sunday sermons. The hundred-percenter[2] easily swallows syndicated information and factory-made ideas and beliefs. He thrives on the wisdom given him over the radio and cheap magazines by corporations whose philanthropic aim is selling America out. He accepts the standards of conduct and art in the same breath with the advertising of chewing gum, toothpaste, and shoe polish. Even songs are turned out like buttons or automobile tires—all cast from the same mold.

II

Yet I do not despair of American life. On the contrary, I feel that the freshness of the American approach and the untapped stores of intellectual and emotional energy resident in the country offer much promise for the future. The War has left in its wake a confused generation. The madness and brutality they had seen, the needless cruelty and waste which had almost wrecked the world made them doubt the values their elders had given them. Some, knowing nothing of the world's past, attempted to create new forms of life and art from the air. Others experimented with decadence and despair. Many of them, even in revolt, were pathetic. They were thrust back into submission and futility because they were lacking in an ideal and were further hampered by a sense of sin and the burden of dead ideas in which they could no longer believe.

Of late there has been a new spirit manifested in the youth which is growing up with the depression. This spirit is more purposeful though still confused. It wants to create a new world, but is not clear as to how it wants to go about it. For that reason the young generation asks for saviors. It tends to believe in dictators and to hail each new aspirant for that honor as a messiah. It wants cut and dried systems of salvation with a wise minority to direct society on some one-way road to utopia. It has not yet realized that it must save itself. The young generation has not yet learned that the problems confronting them can be solved only by themselves and will have to be settled on the basis of social and economic freedom in co-operation with the struggling masses for the right to the table and joy of life.

As I have already stated, my objection to authority in whatever form has been derived from a much larger social view, rather than from anything I myself may have suffered from it. Government has, of course, interfered with my full expression, as it has with others. Certainly the powers have not spared me. Raids on my lectures during my thirty-five years' activity in the United States were a common occurrence,

---

[2] Extreme nationalist.

followed by innumerable arrests and three convictions to terms of imprisonment. This was followed by the annulment of my citizenship and my deportation. The hand of authority was forever interfering with my life. If I have none the less expressed myself, it was in spite of every curtailment and difficulty put in my path and not because of them. In that I was by no means alone. The whole world has given heroic figures to humanity, who in the face of persecution and obloquy have lived and fought for their right and the right of mankind to free and unstinted expression. America has the distinction of having contributed a large quota of native-born children who have most assuredly not lagged behind. Walt Whitman, Henry David Thoreau, Voltairine de Cleyre, one of America's great Anarchists, Moses Harman, the pioneer of woman's emancipation from sexual bondage, Horace Traubel, sweet singer of liberty,[3] and quite an array of other brave souls have expressed themselves in keeping with their vision of a new social order based on freedom from every form of coercion. True, the price they had to pay was high. They were deprived of most of the comforts society offers to ability and talent, but denies when they will not be subservient. But whatever the price, their lives were enriched beyond the common lot. I, too, feel enriched beyond measure. But that is due to the discovery of Anarchism, which more than anything else has strengthened my conviction that authority stultifies human development, while full freedom assures it.

I consider Anarchism the most beautiful and practical philosophy that has yet been thought of in its application to individual expression and the relation it establishes between the individual and society. Moreover, I am certain that Anarchism is too vital and too close to human nature ever to die. It is my conviction that dictatorship, whether to the right or to the left, can never work—that it never has worked, and that time will prove this again, as it has been proved before. When the failure of modern dictatorship and authoritarian philosophies becomes more apparent and the realization of failure more general, Anarchism will be vindicated. Considered from this point, a recrudescence of Anarchist ideas in the near future is very probable. When this occurs and takes effect, I believe that humanity will at last leave the maze in which it is now lost and will start on the path to sane living and regeneration through freedom.

There are many who deny the possibility of such regeneration on the ground that human nature cannot change. Those who insist that human nature remains the same at all times have learned nothing and forgotten nothing. They certainly have not the faintest idea of the tremendous strides that have been made in sociology and psychology, proving beyond a shadow of a doubt that human nature is plastic and can be changed. Human nature is by no means a fixed quantity. Rather, it is fluid and responsive to new conditions. If, for instance, the so-called instinct of self-preservation were as fundamental as it is supposed to be, wars would have been eliminated long ago, as would all dangerous and hazardous occupations.

Right here I want to point out that there would not be such great changes required as is commonly supposed to insure the success of a new social order, as conceived by Anarchists. I feel that our present equipment would be adequate if the artificial oppressions and inequalities and the organized force and violence supporting them were removed.

[3] Walt Whitman (1819-1892), American poet; Henry David Thoreau (1817-1862), American writer; Voltairine de Cleyre (1866-1912), American writer and anarchist; Moses Harman (1830-1910), American journalist and publisher of the anarchist magazine *Lucifer, the Light-Bearer;* Horace Traubel (1858-1919), American journalist and socialist.

Again it is argued that if human nature can be changed, would not the love of liberty be trained out of the human heart? Love of freedom is a universal trait, and no tyranny has thus far succeeded in eradicating it. Some of the modern dictators might try it, and in fact are trying it with every means of cruelty at their command. Even if they should last long enough to carry on such a project—which is hardly conceivable—there are other difficulties. For one thing, the people whom the dictators are attempting to train would have to be cut off from every tradition in their history that might suggest to them the benefits of freedom. They would also have to isolate them from contact with any other people from whom they could get libertarian ideas. The very fact, however, that a person has a consciousness of self, of being different from others, creates a desire to act freely. The craving for liberty and self-expression is a very fundamental and dominant trait.

As is usual when people are trying to get rid of uncomfortable facts, I have often encountered the statement that the average man does not want liberty; that the love for it exists in very few; that the American people, for instance, simply do not care for it. That the American people are not wholly lacking in the desire for freedom was proved by their resistance to the late Prohibition Law, which was so effective that even the politicians finally responded to popular demand and repealed the amendment. If the American masses had been as determined in dealing with more important issues, much more might have been accomplished. It is true, however, that the American people are just beginning to be ready for advanced ideas. This is due to the historical evolution of the country. The rise of capitalism and a very powerful state are, after all, recent in the United States. Many still foolishly believe themselves back in the pioneer tradition when success was easy, opportunities more plentiful than now, and the economic position of the individual was not likely to become static and hopeless.

It is true, none the less, that the average American is still steeped in these traditions, convinced that prosperity will yet return. But because a number of people lack individuality and the capacity for independent thinking I cannot admit that for this reason society must have a special nursery to regenerate them. I would insist that liberty, real liberty, a freer and more flexible society, is the only medium for the development of the best potentialities of the individual.

I will grant that some individuals grow to great stature in revolt against existing conditions. I am only too aware of the fact that my own development was largely in revolt. But I consider it absurd to argue from this fact that social evils should be perpetrated to make revolt against them necessary. Such an argument would be a repetition of the old religious idea of purification. For one thing it is lacking in imagination to suppose that one who shows qualities above the ordinary could have developed only in one way. The person who under this system has developed along the lines of revolt might readily in a different social situation have developed as an artist, scientist, or in any other creative and intellectual capacity.

III

Now I do not claim that the triumph of my ideas would eliminate all possible problems from the life of man for all time. What I do believe is that the removal of the present artificial obstacles to progress would clear the ground for new conquests and joy of life. Nature and our own complexes are apt to continue to provide us with enough pain and struggle. Why then maintain the needless suffering imposed by our present social structure, on the mythical grounds that our characters are thus strengthened, when broken hearts and crushed lives about us every day give the lie to such a notion?

Most of the worry about the softening of human character under freedom comes from prosperous people. It would be difficult to convince the starving man that plenty to eat would ruin his character. As for individual development in the society to which I look forward, I feel that with freedom and abundance unguessed springs of individual initiative would be released. Human curiosity and interest in the world could be trusted to develop individuals in every conceivable line of effort.

Of course those steeped in the present find it impossible to realize that gain as an incentive could be replaced by another force that would motivate people to give the best that is in them. To be sure, profit and gain are strong factors in our present system. They have to be. Even the rich feel a sense of insecurity. That is, they want to protect what they have and to strengthen themselves. The gain and profit motives, however, are tied up with more fundamental motives. When a man provides himself with clothes and shelter, if he is the money-maker type, he continues to work to establish his status—to give himself prestige of the sort admired in the eyes of his fellowmen. Under different and more just conditions of life these more fundamental motives could be put to special uses, and the profit motive, which is only their manifestation, will pass away. Even to-day the scientist, inventor, poet, and artist are not primarily moved by the consideration of gain or profit. The urge to create is the first and most impelling force in their lives. If this urge is lacking in the mass of workers it is not at all surprising, for their occupation is deadly routine. Without any relation to their lives or needs, their work is done in the most appalling surroundings, at the behest of those who have the power of life and death over the masses. Why then should they be impelled to give of themselves more than is absolutely necessary to eke out their miserable existence?

In art, science, literature, and in departments of life which we believe to be somewhat removed from our daily living we are hospitable to research, experiment, and innovation. Yet, so great is our traditional reverence for authority that an irrational fear arises in most people when experiment is suggested to them. Surely there is even greater reason for experiment in the social field than in the scientific. It is to be hoped, therefore, that humanity or some portion of it will be given the opportunity in the not too distant future to try its fortune living and developing under an application of freedom corresponding to the early stages of an anarchistic society. The belief in freedom assumes that human beings can co-operate. They do it even now to a surprising extent, or organized society would be impossible. If the devices by which men can harm one another, such as private property, are removed and if the worship of authority can be discarded, co-operation will be spontaneous and inevitable, and the individual will find it his highest calling to contribute to the enrichment of social well-being.

Anarchism alone stresses the importance of the individual, his possibilities and needs in a free society. Instead of telling him that he must fall down and worship before institutions, live and die for abstractions, break his heart and stunt his life for taboos, Anarchism insists that the center of gravity in society is the individual—that he must think for himself, act freely, and live fully. The aim of Anarchism is that every individual in the world shall be able to do so. If he is to develop freely and fully, he must be relieved from the interference and oppression of others. Freedom is, therefore, the cornerstone of the Anarchist philosophy. Of course, this has nothing in common with a much boasted "rugged individualism." Such predatory individualism is really flabby, not rugged. At the least danger to its safety it runs to cover of the state and wails for protection of armies, navies, or whatever devices for strangulation it has at its command. Their "rugged individualism" is simply one of the many pretenses the ruling class makes to unbridled business and political extortion.

Regardless of the present trend toward the strong-armed man, the totalitarian states, or the dictatorship from the left, my ideas have remained unshaken. In fact, they have been strengthened by my personal experience and the world events through the years. I see no reason to change, as I do not believe that the tendency of dictatorship can ever successfully solve our social problems. As in the past, so I do now insist that freedom is the soul of progress and essential to every phase of life. I consider this as near a law of social evolution as anything we can postulate. My faith is in the individual and in the capacity of free individuals for united endeavor.

The fact that the Anarchist movement for which I have striven so long is to a certain extent in abeyance and overshadowed by philosophies of authority and coercion affects me with concern, but not with despair. It seems to me a point of special significance that many countries decline to admit Anarchists. All governments hold the view that while parties of the right and left may advocate social changes, still they cling to the idea of government and authority. Anarchism alone breaks with both and propagates uncompromising rebellion. In the long run, therefore, it is Anarchism which is considered deadlier to the present regime than all other social theories that are now clamoring for power.

Considered from this angle, I think my life and my work have been successful. What is generally regarded as success—acquisition of wealth, the capture of power or social prestige—I consider the most dismal failures. I hold when it is said of a man that he has arrived, it means that he is finished—his development has stopped at that point. I have always striven to remain in a state of flux and continued growth, and not to petrify in a niche of self-satisfaction. If I had my life to live over again, like anyone else, I should wish to alter minor details. But in any of my more important actions and attitudes I would repeat my life as I have lived it. Certainly I should work for Anarchism with the same devotion and confidence in its ultimate triumph.

—1934

WILLA CATHER (1873-1947)

When Willa Cather was nine years old, her family moved from Virginia to Nebraska, a move that proved to be a life-shaping experience for Cather, who was instantly awestruck by the stark, beautiful, and unyielding Nebraska landscape. The Cathers lived in Red Cloud, a town where many Scandinavians, Bohemians, Germans, and French settled, hoping to prosper in a forbidding new land. Many characters based on these stubborn immigrants populated Cather's later fiction. As a young woman, Cather was a talented nonconformist. During her years at the University of Nebraska in the 1890s, she cropped her hair, dressed in men's clothing, and often referred to herself as "Dr. William Cather, M.D." She began her writing career as a theatre and literature critic in Lincoln, and then took a job as a journalist in Pittsburgh (PA). There she met Isabelle McClung, who became her close friend (and perhaps her lover, although at the time "lesbian" was not thought of as an identity). McClung urged Cather to write fiction, and in 1906 she joined the staff of *McClure's,* the most widely circulated general monthly in the U.S. Many felt that Cather was a brilliant magazine executive, but she felt unfulfilled in that position. Encouraged by her friend and mentor Sarah Orne Jewett, Cather resigned from *McClure's* and concentrated on fiction. She won a Pulitzer Prize for *One of Ours* (1922), and the Howells Medal for *Death Comes for the Archbishop* (1927), a quasi-historical novel set in New Mexico, which many critics have felt is her finest literary achievement. Today Cather is best known for her epic prairie novels *O Pioneers!* (1913) and *My Antonia* (1918). She wrote in a spare, unadorned style that she described as *démeublé* (unfurnished). Her insistence that a writer's only true creativity lies in evoking "the thing not named" has earned her a central place in American modernism.

Tommy, the Unsentimental

"Your father says he has no business tact at all, and of course that's dreadfully unfortunate."

"Business," replied Tommy, "he's a baby in business; he's good for nothing on earth but to keep his hair parted straight and wear that white carnation in his buttonhole. He has 'em sent down from Hastings twice a week as regularly as the mail comes, but the drafts he cashes lie in his safe until they are lost, or somebody finds them. I go up occasionally and send a package away for him myself. He'll answer your notes promptly enough, but his business letters—I believe he destroys them unopened to shake the responsibility of answering them."

"I am at a loss to see how you can have such patience with him, Tommy, in so many ways he is thoroughly reprehensible."

"Well, a man's likeableness don't depend at all on his virtues or acquirements, nor a woman's either, unfortunately. You like them or you don't like them, and that's all there is to it. For the why of it you must appeal to a higher oracle than I. Jay is a likeable fellow, and that's his only and sole acquirement, but after all it's a rather happy one."

"Yes, he certainly is that," replied Miss Jessica, as she deliberately turned off the gas jet and proceeded to arrange her toilet articles. Tommy watched her closely and then turned away with a baffled expression.

Needless to say, Tommy was not a boy, although her keen gray eyes and wide forehead were scarcely girlish, and she had the lank figure of an active half grown lad. Her real name was Theodosia, but during Thomas Shirley's frequent absences from the bank she had attended to his business and correspondence signing herself "T. Shirley," until everyone in Southdown called her "Tommy." That blunt sort of familiarity is not unfrequent in the West, and is meant well enough. People rather expect some business ability in a girl there, and they respect it immensely. That, Tommy undoubtedly had, and if she had not, things would have gone at sixes and sevens in the Southdown National. For Thomas Shirley had big land interests in Wyoming that called him constantly away from home, and his cashier, little Jay Ellington Harper, was, in the local phrase, a weak brother[1] in the bank. He was the son of a friend of old Shirley's, whose papa had sent him West, because he had made a sad mess of his college career, and had spent too much money and gone at too giddy a pace down East. Conditions changed the young gentleman's life, for it was simply impossible to

---

[1] 1 Corinthians 8:11.

live either prodigally or rapidly in Southdown, but they could not materially affect his mental habits or inclinations. He was made cashier of Shirley's bank because his father bought in half the stock, but Tommy did his work for him.

The relation between these two young people was peculiar; Harper was, in his way, very grateful to her for keeping him out of disgrace with her father, and showed it by a hundred little attentions which were new to her and much more agreeable than the work she did for him was irksome. Tommy knew that she was immensely fond of him, and she knew at the same time that she was thoroughly foolish for being so. As she expressed it, she was not of his sort, and never would be. She did not often take pains to think, but when she did she saw matters pretty clearly, and she was of a peculiarly unfeminine mind that could not escape meeting and acknowledging a logical conclusion. But she went on liking Jay Ellington Harper, just the same. Now Harper was the only foolish man of Tommy's acquaintance. She knew plenty of active young business men and sturdy ranchers, such as one meets about live western towns, and took no particular interest in them, probably just because they were practical and sensible and thoroughly of her own kind. She knew almost no women, because in those days there were few women in Southdown who were in any sense interesting, or interested in anything but babies and salads. Her best friends were her father's old business friends, elderly men who had seen a good deal of the world, and who were very proud and fond of Tommy. They recognized a sort of squareness and honesty of spirit in the girl that Jay Ellington Harper never discovered, or, if he did, knew too little of its rareness to value highly. Those old speculators and men of business had always felt a sort of responsibility for Tom Shirley's little girl, and had rather taken her mother's place, and been her advisers on many points upon which men seldom feel at liberty to address a girl.

She was just one of them; she played whist and billiards with them, and made their cocktails for them, not scorning to take one herself occasionally. Indeed, Tommy's cocktails were things of fame in Southdown, and the professional compounders of drinks always bowed respectfully to her as though acknowledging a powerful rival.

Now all these things displeased and puzzled Jay Ellington Harper, and Tommy knew it full well, but clung to her old manner of living with a stubborn pertinacity, feeling somehow that to change would be both foolish and disloyal to the Old Boys. And as things went on, the seven Old Boys made greater demands upon her time than ever, for they were shrewd men, most of them, and had not lived fifty years in this world without learning a few things and unlearning many more. And while Tommy lived on in the blissful delusion that her role of indifference was perfectly played and without a flaw, they suspected how things were going and were perplexed as to the outcome. Still, their confidence was by no means shaken, and as Joe Elsworth said to Joe Sawyer one evening at billiards, "I think we can pretty nearly depend on Tommy's good sense."

They were too wise to say anything to Tommy, but they said just a word or two to Thomas Shirley, Sr., and combined to make things very unpleasant for Mr. Jay Ellington Harper.

At length their relations with Harper became so strained that the young man felt it would be better for him to leave town, so his father started him in a little bank of his own up in Red Willow. Red Willow, however, was scarcely a safe distance, being only some twenty-five miles north, upon the Divide, and Tommy occasionally found excuse to run up on her wheel to straighten out the young man's business for him. So when she suddenly decided to go East to school for a year, Thomas, Sr., drew a sigh of great relief. But the seven Old Boys shook their heads; they did not like to see her gravitating toward the East; it was a sign of weakening, they said, and showed an inclination to experiment with another kind of life, Jay Ellington Harper's kind.

But to school Tommy went, and from all reports conducted herself in a most seemly manner; made no more cocktails, played no more billiards. She took rather her own way with the curriculum, but she distinguished herself in athletics, which in Southdown counted for vastly more than erudition.

Her evident joy on getting back to Southdown was appreciated by everyone. She went about shaking hands with everybody, her shrewd face, that was so like a clever wholesome boy's, held high with happiness. As she said to old Joe Elsworth one morning, when they were driving behind his stud through a little thicket of cotton-wood scattered along the sun-parched bluffs, "It's all very fine down East there, and the hills are great, but one gets mighty homesick for this sky, the old intense blue of it, you know. Down there the skies are all pale and smoky. And this wind, this hateful, dear, old everlasting wind that comes down like the sweep of cavalry and is never tamed or broken, O Joe, I used to get hungry for this wind! I couldn't sleep in that lifeless stillness down there."

"How about the people, Tom?"

"O, they are fine enough folk, but we're not their sort, Joe, and never can be."

"You realize that, do you, fully?"

"Quite fully enough, thank you, Joe." She laughed rather dismally, and Joe cut his horse with the whip.

The only unsatisfactory thing about Tommy's return was that she brought with her a girl she had grown fond of at school, a dainty, white, languid bit of a thing, who used violet perfumes and carried a sunshade. The Old Boys said it was a bad sign when a rebellious girl like Tommy took to being sweet and gentle to one of her own sex, the worst sign in the world.

The new girl was no sooner in town than a new complication came about. There was no doubt of the impression she made on Jay Ellington Harper. She indisputably had all those little evidences of good breeding that were about the only things which could touch the timid, harassed young man who was so much out of his element. It was a very plain case on his part, and the souls of the seven were troubled within them. Said Joe Elsworth to the other Joe, "The heart of the cad is gone out to the little muff, as is right and proper and in accordance with the eternal fitness of things. But there's the other girl who has the blindness that may not be cured, and she gets all the rub of it. It's no use, I can't help her, and I am going to run down to Kansas City for awhile. I can't stay here and see the abominable suffering of it." He didn't go, however.

There was just one other person who understood the hopelessness of the situation quite as well as Joe, and that was Tommy. That is, she understood Harper's attitude. As to Miss Jessica's she was not quite so certain, for Miss Jessica, though pale and languid and addicted to sunshades, was a maiden most discreet. Conversations on the subject usually ended without any further information as to Miss Jessica's feelings, and Tommy sometimes wondered if she were capable of having any at all.

At last the calamity which Tommy had long foretold descended upon Jay Ellington Harper. One morning she received a telegram from him begging her to intercede with her father; there was a run on his bank and he must have help before noon. It was then ten thirty, and the one sleepy little train that ran up to Red Willow daily had crawled out of the station an hour before. Thomas Shirley, Sr., was not at home.

"And it's a good thing for Jay Ellington he's not, he might be more stony hearted than I," remarked Tommy, as she closed the ledger and turned to the terrified Miss Jessica. "Of course we're his only chance, no one else would turn their hand over to help him. The train went an hour ago and he says it must be there by noon. It's the only bank in the town, so nothing can be done by telegraph. There is nothing left but to wheel for it. I may make it, and I may not. Jess, you scamper up to the house and get my wheel out, the tire may need a little attention. I will be along in a minute."

"O, Theodosia, can't I go with you? I must go!"

"You go! O, yes, of course, if you want to. You know what you are getting into, though. It's twenty-five miles uppish grade and hilly, and only an hour and a quarter to do it in."

"O, Theodosia, I can do anything now!" cried Miss Jessica, as she put up her sunshade and fled precipitately. Tommy smiled as she began cramming bank notes into a canvas bag. "May be you can, my dear, and may be you can't."

The road from Southdown to Red Willow is not by any means a favorite bicycle road; it is rough, hilly and climbs from the river bottoms up to the big Divide by a steady up grade, running white and hot through the scorched corn fields and grazing lands where the long-horned Texan cattle browse about in the old buffalo wallows. Miss Jessica soon found that with the pedaling that had to be done there was little time left for emotion of any sort, or little sensibility for anything but the throbbing, dazzling heat that had to be endured. Down there in the valley the distant bluffs were vibrating and dancing with the heat, the cattle, completely overcome by it, had hidden under the shelving banks of the "draws" and the prairie dogs had fled to the bottom of their holes that are said to reach to water. The whirr of the seventeen-year locust was the only thing that spoke of animation, and that ground on as if only animated and enlivened by the sickening, destroying heat. The sun was like hot brass, and the wind that blew up from the south was hotter still. But Tommy knew that wind was their only chance. Miss Jessica began to feel that unless she could stop and get some water she was not much longer for this vale of tears. She suggested this possibility to Tommy, but Tommy only shook her head, "Take too much time," and bent over her handle bars, never lifting her eyes from the road in front of her. It flashed upon Miss Jessica that Tommy was not only very unkind, but that she sat very badly on her wheel and looked aggressively masculine and professional when she bent her shoulders and pumped like that. But just then Miss Jessica found it harder than ever to breathe, and the bluffs across the river began doing serpentines and skirt dances, and more important and personal considerations occupied the young lady.

When they were fairly over the first half of the road, Tommy took out her watch. "Have to hurry up, Jess, I can't wait for you."

"O, Tommy, I can't," panted Miss Jessica, dismounting and sitting down in a little heap by the roadside. "You go on, Tommy, and tell him—tell him I hope it won't fail, and I'd do anything to save him."

By this time the discreet Miss Jessica was reduced to tears, and Tommy nodded as she disappeared over the hill laughing to herself. "Poor Jess, anything but the one thing he needs. Well, your kind have the best of it generally, but in little affairs of this sort my kind come out rather strongly. We're rather better at them than at dancing. It's only fair, one side shouldn't have all."

Just at twelve o'clock, when Jay Ellington Harper, his collar crushed and wet about his throat, his eyeglass dimmed with perspiration, his hair hanging damp over his forehead, and even the ends of his moustache dripping with moisture, was attempting to reason with a score of angry Bohemians, Tommy came quietly through the door, grip in hand. She went straight behind the grating, and standing screened by the bookkeeper's desk, handed the bag to Harper and turned to the spokesman of the Bohemians.

"What's all this business mean, Anton? Do you all come to bank at once nowadays?"

"We want 'a money, want 'a our money, he no got it, no give it," bawled the big beery Bohemian.

"O, don't chaff 'em any longer, give 'em their money and get rid of 'em, I want to see you," said Tommy carelessly, as she went into the consulting room.

When Harper entered half an hour later, after the rush was over, all that was left of his usual immaculate appearance was his eyeglass and the white flower in his buttonhole.

"This has been terrible!" he gasped. "Miss Theodosia, I can never thank you."

"No," interrupted Tommy. "You never can, and I don't want any thanks. It was rather a tight place, though, wasn't it? You looked like a ghost when I came in. What started them?"

"How should I know? They just came down like the wolf on the fold. It sounded like the approach of a ghost dance."[2]

"And of course you had no reserve? O, I always told you this would come, it was inevitable with your charming methods. By the way, Jess sends her regrets and says she would do anything to save you. She started out with me, but she has fallen by the wayside. O, don't be alarmed, she is not hurt, just winded. I left her all bunched up by the road like a little white rabbit. I think the lack of romance in the escapade did her up about as much as anything; she is essentially romantic. If we had been on fiery steeds bespattered with foam I think she would have made it, but a wheel hurt her dignity. I'll tend bank; you'd better get your wheel and go and look her up and comfort her. And as soon as it is convenient, Jay, I wish you'd marry her and be done with it, I want to get this thing off my mind."

Jay Ellington Harper dropped into a chair and turned a shade whiter.

"Theodosia, what do you mean? Don't you remember what I said to you last fall, the night before you went to school? Don't you remember what I wrote you—"

Tommy sat down on the table beside him and looked seriously and frankly into his eyes.

"Now, see here, Jay Ellington, we have been playing a nice little game, and now it's time to quit. One must grow up sometime. You are horribly wrought up over Jess, and why deny it? She's your kind, and clean daft about you, so there is only one thing to do. That's all."

Jay Ellington wiped his brow, and felt unequal to the situation. Perhaps he really

---

[2] [*Author's note.*] The ghost dance, a ritualistic worship of Wovoka, a self-appointed Indian Messiah, was associated with the so-called Sioux Uprising of 1890, which culminated in the battle of Wounded Knee, in South Dakota near the Nebraska border, on December 29, 1890.

came nearer to being moved down to his stolid little depths than he ever had before. His voice shook a good deal and was very low as he answered her.

"You have been very good to me, I didn't believe any woman could be at once so kind and clever. You almost made a man of even me."

"Well, I certainly didn't succeed. As to being good to you, that's rather a break, you know; I am amiable, but I am only flesh and blood after all. Since I have known you I have not been at all good, in any sense of the word, and I suspect I have been anything but clever. Now, take mercy upon Jess—and me—and go. Go on, that ride is beginning to tell on me. Such things strain one's nerve.... Thank Heaven he's gone at last and had sense enough not to say anything more. It was growing rather critical. As I told him I am not at all superhuman."

After Jay Ellington Harper had bowed himself out, when Tommy sat alone in the darkened office, watching the flapping blinds, with the bank books before her, she noticed a white flower on the floor. It was the one Jay Ellington Harper had worn in his coat and had dropped in his nervous agitation. She picked it up and stood holding it a moment, biting her lip. Then she dropped it into the grate and turned away, shrugging her thin shoulders.

"They are awful idiots, half of them, and never think of anything beyond their dinner. But O, how we do like 'em!"

—1896

LOLA RIDGE (1873-1941)

Rose Emily Ridge was born in Dublin, Ireland, in 1873. She spent part of her childhood in Australia and New Zealand, where her mother remarried. The family lived in poverty, with Ridge's stepfather vacillating between periods of kindness and drunken rages. Ridge married the manager of a gold mine in 1895, but left him and returned to Sydney to study art at Trinity College. In 1907 she emigrated to San Francisco, renaming herself Lola to prevent her husband from finding her. Three years later she moved to New York City, where she remained. In New York, Ridge supported herself with her writing and became active in labor and social issues. She married David Lawson in 1919. Although Ridge had been writing poetry since her youth, she did not publish her first book, *The Ghetto and Other Poems* (1918), until she was forty-five. Despite the anti-Semitism of many modernist artists and much of the public, *The Ghetto and Other Poems,* which explores the plight of Jewish immigrants in America, was met with popular success and launched Ridge's literary career.

Ridge served as the American editor for *Broom,* an international magazine of the arts, and continued writing poetry. Her *Sun-Up and Other Poems* (1920) contained autobiographical material, but literary and political themes were present in her next two volumes, *Red Flag* (1927) and *Firehead* (1929). Like Edna St. Vincent Millay, Dorothy Parker, and others, Ridge was arrested for protesting against the Sacco-Vanzetti executions (an event to which *Firehead* responded). During the 1930s, she made a difficult pilgrimage alone to Baghdad to write a long poem about the relationship between violence and the fire of creative spirit; *Dance of Fire* (1935), her last book, was the result. Ridge twice shared the Shelley Memorial Award from the Poetry Society of America: with Frances Frost in 1933 and with Marya Zaturenska in 1934. She also received a Guggenheim award in 1935, as well as other monetary prizes for her poetry. Plagued by health problems for most of her life, Ridge died in 1941.

Lullaby

Rock-a-by baby, woolly and brown…
(There's a shout at the door an' a big red light…)
Lil' coon baby, mammy is down…
Han's that hold yuh are steady an' white…

Look piccaninny—such a gran' blaze   5
Lickin' up the roof an' the sticks of home—
Ever see the like in all yo' days!
—Cain't yuh sleep, mah bit-of-honey-comb?

Rock-a-by baby, up to the sky!
Look at the cherries driftin' by—   10
Bright red cherries spilled on the groun'—
Piping-hot cherries at nuthin' a poun'!

Hush, mah lil' black-bug—doan yuh weep.
Daddy's run away an' mammy's in a heap
By her own fron' door in the blazin' heat   15
Outah the shacks like warts on the street…

An' the singin' flame an' the gleeful crowd
Circlin' aroun'…won't mammy be proud!
With a stone at her hade an' a stone on her heart,
An' her mouth like a red plum, broken apart…   20

See where the blue an' khaki prance,
Adding brave colors to the dance
About the big bonfire white folks make—
Such gran' doin's fo' a lil' coon's sake!

Hear all the eagah feet runnin' in town—   25
See all the willin' han's reach outah night—
Han's that are wonderful, steady an' white!
To toss up a lil' babe, blinkin' an' brown…

Rock-a-by baby—higher an' higher!
Mammy is sleepin' an' daddy's run lame…   30
(Soun' may yuh sleep in yo' cradle o' fire!)
Rock-a-by baby, hushed in the flame…

(An incident of the East St. Louis Race Riots, when some white women flung a living colored baby into the heart of a blazing fire.)

—1918

Emma Goldman[1]

How should they appraise you,
who walk up close to you

---

[1] Emma Goldman (1869-1940), Lithuanian-born anarchist, author, and activist who emigrated to the U.S.

as to a mountain,
each proclaiming his own eyeful
against the other's eyeful.   5

Only time
standing well off
shall measure your circumference
        and height.

—1920

Amy Lowell[2]

Your words are frost on speargrass,
Your words are glancing light
On foils at play,
Your words are shapely...buoyant as balloons,
They make brave sallies at the stars.   5
When your words fall and grow cold
Little greedy hands
Will gather them for necklets.

—1927

---

[2] Amy Lowell (1874-1925), American critic and poet, and a member of the prominent Lowell family of Boston.

ZONA GALE (1874-1938)

Born in Portage, Wisconsin, Zona Gale was the daughter of Eliza Beers, a teacher, and Charles Franklin Gale, a railroad worker. She attended the University of Wisconsin, receiving a B.A. in 1895 and an M.A. in 1899. Gale worked as a journalist for Milwaukee's *Evening Wisconsin* and *Journal,* and later for the *New York Evening World*. Her first novel, *Romance Island,* was published in 1906. Between 1903 and 1910 Gale published eighty-three stories, including the first of the "Friendship Village" stories chronicling small-town life in a place much like Portage, to which she had returned in 1909 to support her parents. Gale won the Pulitzer Prize for drama in 1921 (the first woman to do so) for the adaptation of her 1920 novel *Miss Lulu Bett,* reportedly in part because she modified the ending for the stage to lessen the story's feminism. Gale was a prolific writer, publishing nine volumes of stories, thirteen novels, and seven plays, in addition to several works of nonfiction. She was also an activist, supporting progressive causes such as woman suffrage, and opposing World War I and the execution of the Italian anarchists Nicola Sacco and Bartolomeo Vanzetti. In 1928 she married William L. Breese, a banker, and they adopted a child, Leslyn. "The Prodigal Guest" appeared in *Neighborhood Stories* in 1914.

The Prodigal Guest

Aunt Ellis wrote to me:

"DEAR CALLIOPE: Now come and pay me the visit. You've never been here since the time I had sciatica and was cross. Come now, and I'll try to hold my temper and my tongue."

I wrote back to her:

"I'll come. I was saving up to buy a new cook-stove next fall, but I'll bring my cook-stove and come in time for the parade. I did want to see that."

She answered:

"Mercy, Calliope, I might have known it! You always did love a circus in the village, and these women are certainly making a circus parade of themselves. However, we'll even drive down to see them do it, if you'll really come. Now you know how much I want you."

"I might have known," I said to myself, "that Aunt Ellis would be like that. The poor thing has had such an easy time that she can't help it. She thinks what's been, is."

She wrote me that she was coming in from the country an hour after my train got there, but that the automobile would be there for me. And I wrote her that I would come down the platform with my umbrella up, so's her man would know me; and so I done, and he picked me out real ready.

When we got to her big house, that somehow looked so used to being a big house, there was a little boy sitting on the bottom step, half asleep, with a big box.

"What's the matter, lamb?" I says.

"Beg pad', ma'am, he's likely waitin' to beg," says the chauf—— that word. "I'd go right by if I was you."

But the little fellow'd woke up and looked up.

"I can't find the place," he says, and stuck out his big box. The man looked at the label. "They ain't no such number in this street," says he. "It's a mistake."

The little fellow kind of begun to cry, and the wind was blowing up real bitter. I made out that him and his family made toys for the up-town shops, and somebody in our neighborhood had ordered some direct, and he was afraid to go home without the money. I didn't have any money to give him, but I says to the chauf——

"Ask him where he lives, will you? And see if we'd have time to take him home before Mis' Winthrop's train gets in."

The chauf—— done it, some like a prime minister, and he says, cold, he thought we'd have time, and I put the baby in the car. He was a real sweet little fellow, about seven. He told me his part in making the toys, and his mother's, and his two little sisters', and I give him the rest o' my lunch, and he knew how to laugh when he got the chance, and we had a real happy time of it. And we come to his home.

Never, not if I live till after my dying day, will I forget the looks of that back upstairs place he called home, nor the smell of it—the smell of it. The waxy woman that was his mother, in a red waist, and with a big weight of hair, had forgot how to look surprised—that struck me as so awful—she'd forgot how to look surprised, just the same as a grand lady that's learned not to; and there was the stumpy man that grunted for short instead of bothering with words; and the two little girls that might of been anybody's—if they'd been clean—one of 'em with regular portrait hair. I stayed a minute, and give 'em the cost of about one griddle of my cook-stove, and then I went to the station to meet Aunt Ellis. And I poured it all out to her, as soon as she'd give me her cheek to kiss.

"So you haven't had any tea!" she said, getting in the automobile. "I'm sorry you've been so annoyed the first thing."

"Annoyed!" I says over. "Annoyed! Well, yes," I says, "poor people is real annoying. I wonder we have 'em."

I was dying to ask her about the parade, but I didn't like to; till after we'd had dinner in front of snow and silver and sparkles and so on, and had gone in her parlor-with-another-name, and set down in the midst of flowers and shades and lace, and rugs the color of different kinds of preserves, and wood-work like the skin of a cooked prune. Then I says:

"You know I'm just dying to hear about the parade."

She lifted her hand and shut her eyes, brief.

"Calliope," she says, "I don't know what has come over women. They seem to want to attract attention to themselves. They seem to want to be conspicuous and talked about. They seem to want ——"

"They want lots o' things," says I, dry, "but it ain't any of them, Aunt Ellis. What time does the parade start?"

"You're bound to see it?" she says. "When I think of my dear Miss Markham—they used to say her school taught not manners, but manner—and what she would say to the womanhood of to-day....We'll drive down if you say so, Calliope—but I don't know whether I can bear it long."

"Manner," I says over. "Manner. That's just what we're trying to learn now, manner of being alive. We haven't known very much about that, it seems."

I kept thinking that over next day when we were drawn up beside the curb in the car, waiting for them to come. "We're trying to learn manner at last—the manner of being alive." There were lots of other cars, with women so pretty you felt like crying up into the sky to ask there if we knew for sure what all that perfection was for, or if there was something else to it we didn't know—yet. And thousands of women on foot, and thousands of women in windows.... I looked at them and wondered if they thought we were, and life was, as decent as we and it could be, and, if not, how they were preparing to help change it. I thought of the rest that were up town in colored nests, and them that were down town in factories, and them that were to home in the villages, and them that were out all along the miles and miles to the other ocean, just the same way. And here was going to come this little line of women walking along the street, a little line of women that thought they see new life for us all, and see it more abundant.

"Manner," I says, "we're just beginning to learn manner."

Then, way down the avenue, they began to come. By ones and by fours and by eights, with colors and with music and with that that was greater than all of them—the tramp and tramp of feet; feet that weren't dancing to balls, nor racking up and down in shops buying pretty things to make 'em power, nor just paddling around a kitchen the same as mine had always done—but feet that were marching, in a big, peaceful army, towards the place where the big, new tasks of to-morrow are going to be, that won't interfere with the best tasks of yesterday no more than the earth's orbit interferes with its whirling round and round.

"That's it," I says, "that's it! We've been whirling round and round, manufacturing the days and the nights, and we never knew we had an orbit too."

So they come, till they begun to pass where we were—some heads up, some eyes down, women, women, marching to a tune that was being beat out by thousands of hearts all over the world. I'd never seen women like this before. I saw them like I'd never seen them—I felt I was one of 'em like I'd never known that either. And I saw what they saw and I felt what they felt more than I ever knew I done.

Then I heard Aunt Ellis making a little noise in her breath.

"The bad taste of it—the bad taste of it, Calliope!" she said. "When I was a girl we used to use the word ladylike—we used to strive to deserve it. It's a beautiful word. But these ——"

"We've been ladylike," says I, sad, "for five or ten thousand years, and where has it got us to?"

"Oh, but, Calliope, they like it—they like the publicity and the notoriety and the ——"

I kept still, but I hurt all over me. I can stand anything only hearing that they like it—the way Aunt Ellis meant. I thought to myself that I bet the folks that used to watch martyrs were heard to say that martyrs prob'ly thought flames was becoming or they wouldn't be burnt. But when I looked at Aunt Ellis sitting in her car with her hand over her eyes, it come over me all at once the tragedy of it—of all them that watch us cast their old ideals in new forms—their old ideals.

All of a sudden I stood up in the car. The parade had got blocked for a minute, and right in front of the curb where we stood I saw a woman I knew; a little waxy-looking thing, that couldn't look surprised or exalted or afraid or anything else, and I knew her in a minute—even to the red calico waist and the big weight of hair, just as I had seen her by the toy table in her "home" the night before. And there she was, marching. And here was Aunt Ellis and me.

I leaned over and touched Aunt Ellis.

"You mustn't mind," I says; "I'm going too."

She looked at me like I'd turned into somebody else.

"I'm going out there," I says, "with them. I see it like they do—I feel it like they do. And them that sees it and feels it and don't help it along is holding it back. I'll find my way home...."

I ran to them. I stepped right out in the street among them and fell in step with them, and then I saw something. While I was making my way through the crowd to them the line had passed on, and them I was with was all in caps and gowns. I stopped still in the road.

"Great land!" I says to the woman nearest, "you're college, ain't you? And I never even got through high school."

She smiled and put out her hand.

"Come on," she says.

Whatever happens to me afterward, I've had that hour. No woman that has ever had it will ever forget it—the fear and the courage, the pride and the dread, the hurt and the power and the glory. I don't know whether it's the way—but what is the way? I only know that all down the street, between the rows of watching faces, I could think of that little waxy woman going along ahead, and of the kind of place that she called home, and of the kind of a life she and her children had. And I knew then and I know now that the poverty and the dirt and some of the death in the world is our job, it's our job too. And if they won't let us do it ladylike, we'll do it just plain.

When I got home, Aunt Ellis was having tea. She smiled at me kind of sad, as a prodigal guest deserved.

"Aunt Ellis," I says, "I've give 'em the rest of my cook-stove money, except my fare home."

"My poor Calliope," she says, "that's just the trouble. You all go to such hysterical extremes."

I'd heard that word several times on the street. I couldn't stand it any longer.

"Was that hysterics to-day?" I says. "I've often wondered what they're like. I've never had the time to have them, myself. Well," I says, tired but serene, "if that was hysterics, leave 'em make the most of it."

I looked at her, meditative.

"Miss Markham and you and the women that marched to-day and me," I says. "And a hundred years from now we'll all be conservatives together. And there'll be some big new day coming on that would startle me now, just the same as it would you. But the way I feel to-night, honest—I donno but I'm ready for that one too."

—1914

AMY LOWELL (1874-1925)

Born in Brookline, Massachusetts, Amy Lowell was the descendant of two prominent families. Her father was a member of the board at the Massachusetts Institute of Technology; her brother Percival, a noted astronomer, founded the Lowell observatory at Harvard; her brother Abbott was a president of Harvard; and a cousin of her grandfather's was the poet James Russell Lowell, the first editor of the *Atlantic Monthly*. Lowell's early life—a debut, tutors, travel—was typical of women in her class. She grew up on Sevenels, the family estate, which she later inherited; images from the estate's extensive gardens appear frequently in her poetry. In 1902, Lowell attended a play starring the Italian actress Eleanora Duse; she attended every subsequent night of the run, and discovered her new vocation: poetry. In 1912, the year that she published her first book of poems, *A Dome of Many-Coloured Glass,* Lowell met Ada Dwyer Russell, an actress with whom she spent the rest of her life. Lowell and Russell went to London in 1913 to meet the poets whose work Lowell had read in Harriet Monroe's magazine *Poetry*. In London, the couple met Ezra Pound (with whom Lowell would battle for leadership of the Imagist movement) and, on a trip the following year, they met H.D., Robert Frost, D. H. Lawrence, and others. Lowell's books of poems include *Sword Blades and Poppy Seeds* (1914), *Can Grand's Castle* (1918), and *Pictures of the Floating World* (1919). Lowell also wrote criticism; *Tendencies in Modern American Poetry* (1917) helped establish her reputation as a critic, as did the three Imagist anthologies she edited in 1915, 1916, and 1917. In addition to Imagism, Lowell was influenced by Asian poetic forms, folk tales, Romanticism (she wrote a two-volume biography of John Keats), and women poets. Her posthumous volume, *What's O'Clock,* won the Pulitzer Prize in 1926. After her death, critics savaged her work, at least in part because of her lesbianism. *The Complete Poetical Works of Amy Lowell* was published in 1955, and her work re-entered literary anthologies in the 1980s as part of a scholarly reconsideration of Modernism, and its women writers in particular.

Patterns

I walk down the garden paths,
And all the daffodils
Are blowing, and the bright blue squills.
I walk down the patterned garden-paths
In my stiff, brocaded gown.

5

With my powdered hair and jewelled fan,
I too am a rare
Pattern. As I wander down
The garden paths.

My dress is richly figured,   10
And the train
Makes a pink and silver stain
On the gravel, and the thrift
Of the borders.
Just a plate of current fashion,   15
Tripping by in high-heeled, ribboned shoes.
Not a softness anywhere about me,
Only whalebone and brocade.
And I sink on a seat in the shade
Of a lime tree. For my passion   20
Wars against the stiff brocade.
The daffodils and squills
Flutter in the breeze
As they please.
And I weep;   25
For the lime-tree is in blossom
And one small flower has dropped upon my bosom.

And the plashing of waterdrops
In the marble fountain
Comes down the garden-paths.   30
The dripping never stops.
Underneath my stiffened gown
Is the softness of a woman bathing in a marble basin,
A basin in the midst of hedges grown
So thick, she cannot see her lover hiding,   35
But she guesses he is near,
And the sliding of the water
Seems the stroking of a dear
Hand upon her.
What is Summer in a fine brocaded gown!   40
I should like to see it lying in a heap upon the ground.
All the pink and silver crumpled up on the ground.

I would be the pink and silver as I ran along the paths,
And he would stumble after,
Bewildered by my laughter.   45
I should see the sun flashing from his sword-hilt and the buckles
    on his shoes.
I would choose
To lead him in a maze along the patterned paths,
A bright and laughing maze for my heavy-booted lover.
Till he caught me in the shade,   50
And the buttons of his waistcoat bruised my body as he clasped me,

Aching, melting, unafraid.
With the shadows of the leaves and the sundrops,
And the plopping of the waterdrops,
All about us in the open afternoon—   55
I am very like to swoon
With the weight of this brocade,
For the sun sifts through the shade.

Underneath the fallen blossom
In my bosom,   60
Is a letter I have hid.
It was brought to me this morning by a rider from the Duke.
"Madam, we regret to inform you that Lord Hartwell
Died in action Thursday se'nnight."
As I read it in the white, morning sunlight,   65
The letters squirmed like snakes.
"Any answer, Madam," said my footman.
"No," I told him.
"See that the messenger takes some refreshment.
No, no answer."   70
And I walked into the garden,
Up and down the patterned paths,
In my stiff, correct brocade.
The blue and yellow flowers stood up proudly in the sun,
Each one.   75
I stood upright too,
Held rigid to the pattern
By the stiffness of my gown.
Up and down I walked,
Up and down.   80

In a month he would have been my husband.
In a month, here, underneath this lime,
We would have broke the pattern;
He for me, and I for him,
He as Colonel, I as Lady,   85
On this shady seat.
He had a whim
That sunlight carried blessing.
And I answered, "It shall be as you have said."
Now he is dead.   90
In Summer and in Winter I shall walk
Up and down
The patterned garden-paths
In my stiff, brocaded gown.
The squills and daffodils   95
Will give place to pillared roses, and to asters, and to snow.
I shall go
Up and down,
In my gown.

Gorgeously arrayed,   100
Boned and stayed.
And the softness of my body will be guarded from embrace
By each button, hook, and lace.
For the man who should loose me is dead,
Fighting with the Duke in Flanders,   105
In a pattern called a war.
Christ! What are patterns for?

—1916

Madonna of the Evening Flowers

All day long I have been working,
Now I am tired.
I call: "Where are you?"
But there is only the oak-tree rustling in the wind.
The house is very quiet,   5
The sun shines in on your books,
On your scissors and thimble just put down,
But you are not there.
Suddenly I am lonely:
Where are you?   10
I go about searching.

Then I see you,
Standing under a spire of pale blue larkspur,
With a basket of roses on your arm.
You are cool, like silver,   15
And you smile.
I think the Canterbury bells are playing little tunes.

You tell me that the peonies need spraying,
That the columbines have overrun all bounds,
That the pyrus japonica should be cut back and rounded.   20
You tell me these things.
But I look at you, heart of silver,
White heart-flame of polished silver,
Burning beneath the blue steeples of the larkspur,
And I long to kneel instantly at your feet,   25
While all about us peal the loud, sweet *Te Deums*[1] of the Canterbury bells.

—1919

The Sisters

Taking us by and large, we're a queer lot
We women who write poetry. And when you think
How few of us there've been, it's queerer still.
I wonder what it is that makes us do it,
Singles us out to scribble down, man-wise,   5

---

[1] (Lat.) Hymns.

The fragments of ourselves. Why are we
Already mother-creatures, double-bearing,
With matrices in body and in brain?
I rather think that there is just the reason
We are so sparse a kind of human being;   10
The strength of forty thousand Atlases[2]
Is needed for our every-day concerns.
There's Sapho,[3] now I wonder what was Sapho.
I know a single slender thing about her:
That, loving, she was like a burning birch-tree   15
All tall and glittering fire, and that she wrote
Like the same fire caught up to Heaven and held there,
A frozen blaze before it broke and fell.
Ah, me! I wish I could have talked to Sapho,
Surprised her reticences by flinging mine   20
Into the wind. This tossing off of garments
Which cloud the soul is none too easy doing
With us to-day. But still I think with Sapho
One might accomplish it, were she in the mood
To bare her loveliness of words and tell   25
The reasons, as she possibly conceived them,
Of why they are so lovely. Just to know
How she came at them, just to watch
The crisp sea sunshine playing on her hair,
And listen, thinking all the while 'twas she   30
Who spoke and that we two were sisters
Of a strange, isolated little family.
And she is Sapho—Sapho—not Miss or Mrs.,
A leaping fire we call so for convenience;
But Mrs. Browning[4]—who would ever think   35
Of such presumption as to call her "Ba."
Which draws the perfect line between sea-cliffs
And a close-shuttered room in Wimpole Street.[5]
Sapho could fly her impulses like bright
Balloons tip-tilting to a morning air   40
And write about it. Mrs. Browning's heart
Was squeezed in stiff conventions. So she lay
Stretched out upon a sofa, reading Greek
And speculating, as I must suppose,
In just this way on Sapho; all the need,   45
The huge, imperious need of loving, crushed
Within the body she believed so sick.
And it was sick, poor lady, because words
Are merely simulacra after deeds
Have wrought a pattern; when they take the place   50

---

[2] In Greek mythology, a Titan punished by Zeus, who made him hold up the sky.

[3] Sappho (ca. 630-ca. 570 B.C.E.), Greek poet whose work survives only in fragments.

[4] Elizabeth Barrett Browning (1806-1861), British poet. "Ba" was her family nickname.

[5] Barrett Browning's home, presided over by her tyrannical father.

Of actions they breed a poisonous miasma
Which, though it leave the brain, eats up the body.
So Mrs. Browning, aloof and delicate,
Lay still upon her sofa, all her strength
Going to uphold her over-topping brain.   55
It seems miraculous, but she escaped
To freedom and another motherhood
Than that of poems. She was a very woman
And needed both.
               If I had gone to call,   60
Would Wimpole Street have been the kindlier place,
Or Casa Guidi,[6] in which to have met her?
I am a little doubtful of that meeting,
For Queen Victoria was very young and strong
And all-pervading in her apogee   65
At just that time. If we had struck to poetry,
Sternly refusing to be drawn off by mesmerism
Or Roman revolutions, it might have done.
For, after all, she is another sister,
But always, I rather think, an older sister   70
And not herself so curious a technician
As to admit newfangled modes of writing—
"Except, of course, in Robert, and that is neither
Here nor there for Robert is a genius."
I do not like the turn this dream is taking,   75
Since I am very fond of Mrs. Browning
And very much indeed should like to hear her
Graciously asking me to call her "Ba."
But then the Devil of Verisimilitude
Creeps in and forces me to know she wouldn't.   80
Convention again, and how it chafes my nerves,
For we are such a little family
Of singing sisters, and as if I didn't know
What those years felt like tied down to the sofa.
Confound Victoria, and the slimy inhibitions   85
She loosed on all us Anglo-Saxon creatures!
Suppose there hadn't been a Robert Browning,
No "Sonnets from the Portuguese"[7] would have been written.
They are the first of all her poems to be,
One might say, fertilized. For, after all,   90
A poet is flesh and blood as well as brain
And Mrs. Browning, as I said before,
Was very, very woman. Well, there are two
Of us, and vastly unlike that's for certain.
Unlike at least until we tear the veils   95
Away which commonly gird souls. I scarcely think

[6] The house in Florence, Italy, where Barrett Browning lived with her husband, poet Robert Browning (1812-1889).

[7] An 1850 volume of love poems by Barrett Browning.

Mrs. Browning would have approved the process
In spite of what had surely been relief;
For speaking souls must always want to speak
Even when bat-eyed, narrow-minded Queens   100
Set prudishness to keep the keys of impulse.
Then do the frowning Gods invent new banes
And make the need of sofas. But Sapho was dead
And I, and others, not yet peeped above
The edge of possibility. So that's an end   105
To speculating over tea-time talks
Beyond the movement of pentameters
With Mrs. Browning.
                            But I go dreaming on,
In love with these my spiritual relations.   110
I rather think I see myself walk up
A flight of wooden steps and ring a bell
And send a card in to Miss Dickinson.[8]
Yet that's a very silly way to do.
I should have taken the dream twist-ends about   115
And climbed over the fence and found her deep
Engrossed in the doings of a humming-bird
Among nasturtiums. Not having expected strangers,
She might forget to think me one, and holding up
A finger say quite casually: "Take care.   120
Don't frighten him, he's only just begun."
"Now this," I will believe I should have thought,
"Is even better than Sapho. With Emily
You're really here, or never anywhere at all
In range of mind." Wherefore, having begun   125
In this strict centre, we could slowly progress
To various circumferences, as we pleased.
We could, but should we? That would quite depend
On Emily. I think she'd be exacting,
Without intention possibly, and ask   130
A thousand tight-rope tricks of understanding.
But, bless you, I would somersault all day
If by so doing I might stay with her.
I hardly think that we should mention souls
Although they might just round the corner from us   135
In some half-quizzical, half-wistful metaphor.
I'm very sure that I should never seek
To turn her parables to stated fact.
Sapho would speak, I think, quite openly,
And Mrs. Browning guard a careful silence,   140
But Emily would set doors ajar and slam them
And love you for your speed of observation.

Strange trio of my sisters, most diverse,

---

[8] Emily Dickinson (1830-1886), American poet.

And how extraordinarily unlike
Each is to me, and which way shall I go? 145
Sapho spent and gained; and Mrs. Browning,
After a miser girlhood, cut the strings
Which tied her money-bags and let them run;
But Emily hoarded—hoarded—only giving
Herself to cold, white paper. Starved and tortured, 150
She cheated her despair with games of patience
And fooled herself by winning. Frail little elf,
The lonely brain-child of a gaunt maturity,
She hung her womanhood upon a bough
And played ball with the stars—too long—too long— 155
The garment of herself hung on a tree
Until at last she lost even the desire
To take it down. Whose fault? Why let us say,
To be consistent, Queen Victoria's.
But really, not to over-rate the queen, 160
I feel obliged to mention Martin Luther,[9]
And behind him the long line of Church Fathers
Who draped their prurience like a dirty cloth
About the naked majesty of God.
Good-bye, my sisters, all of you are great, 165
And all of you are marvellously strange,
And none of you has any word for me.
I cannot write like you, I cannot think
In terms of Pagan or of Christian now.
I only hope that possibly some day 170
Some other woman with an itch for writing
May turn to me as I have turned to you
And chat with me a brief few minutes. How
We lie, we poets! It is three good hours
I have been dreaming. Has it seemed so long 175
To you? And yet I thank you for the time
Although you leave me sad and self-distrustful,
For older sisters are very sobering things.
Put on your cloaks, my dears, the motor's waiting.
No, you have not seemed strange to me, but near, 180
Frightfully near, and rather terrifying.
I understand you all, for in myself—
Is that presumption? Yet indeed it's true—
We are one family. And still my answer
Will not be any one of yours, I see. 185
Well, never mind that now. Good night! Good night!

—1925

---

[9] Martin Luther (1483-1546), German theologian and reformer.

GERTRUDE STEIN (1874-1946)

Gertrude Stein was born in Allegheny, Pennsylvania in 1874 to Jewish-Bavarian parents. During her childhood she visited Vienna and Paris, but most of her girlhood was spent in Oakland, California. Best known for her experimental, sometimes difficult, prose and poetry, the expatriate Stein is also renowned as the mistress of the Parisian salon at 27 Rue de Fleurus, where she entertained some of the most famous writers and visual artists of her day. Alice B. Toklas, Stein's romantic partner for more than forty years, worked as her secretary/typist and personal assistant throughout their entire relationship, carefully restricting access to Stein and shaping Stein's image. Stein, in turn, contributed to the mythology of their relationship in *The Autobiography of Alice B. Toklas* (1933), which is much more the author's story than that of her lover. Stein thought of (and referred to) herself as a genius, but did not enjoy much critical success during her lifetime. While a few saw her work as a legitimate attempt to create a cubist essence in writing, many others found it dense and often unnecessarily repetitive and incomprehensible. Nevertheless, she was enormously famous; her lecture tour in the 1930s, undertaken after the success of her first full-length opera, *Four Saints in Three Acts* (1934), made her a household name in the United States. *The Mother of Us All* (1947), Stein's second full-length opera, brings together characters from different periods of U.S. history to explore the legacy of suffragist Susan B. Anthony. Other works by Stein include *Three Lives* (1909), *Tender Buttons* (1914), and *The Making of Americans* (1925).

The Mother of Us All

Act I

Prologue sung by VIRGIL T.[1]

Pity the poor persecutor.
> Why,
If money is money isn't money money,
> Why,
Pity the poor persecutor,
> Why,
Is money money or isn't money money.
> Why.
Pity the poor persecutor.
Pity the poor persecutor because the poor persecutor
> always gets to be poor
> Why,
Because the persecutor gets persecuted
Because is money money or isn't money money,
> That's why,
When the poor persecutor is persecuted he has to cry,
> Why,
Because the persecutor always ends by being persecuted,
> That is the reason why.

VIRGIL T. *after he has sung his prelude begins to sit*

---

[1] Virgil Thomson (1896-1989) wrote the music for this and another of Stein's operas, *Four Saints in Three Acts*.

VIRGIL T.:	Begin to sit.
	Begins to sit.
	He begins to sit.
	That's why.
	Begins to sit.
	He begins to sit.
	And that is the reason why.

Act I
Scene 1

DANIEL WEBSTER:[2]	He digged a pit, he digged it deep
	he digged it for his brother.
	Into the pit he did fall in the pit
	he digged for tother.
ALL THE CHARACTERS:	Daniel was my father's name,
	My father's name was Daniel.
JO THE LOITERER:	Not Daniel.
CHRIS THE CITIZEN:	Not Daniel in the lion's den.[3]
ALL THE CHARACTERS:	My father's name was Daniel.
G.S.:[4]	My father's name was Daniel, Daniel
	and a bear, a bearded Daniel,
	not Daniel in the lion's den not
	Daniel, yes Daniel my father had
	a beard my father's name was Daniel,
DANIEL WEBSTER:	He digged a pit he digged it deep
	he digged it for his brother,
	Into the pit he did fall in the pit
	he digged for tother.
INDIANA ELLIOT:	Choose a name.
SUSAN B. ANTHONY:[5]	Susan B. Anthony is my name to choose a name is feeble,
	Susan B. Anthony is my name, a name can only be a name
	my name can only be my name, I have a name, Susan B.
	Anthony is my name, to choose a name is feeble.
INDIANA ELLIOT:	Yes that's easy, Susan B. Anthony is that kind of a name
	but my name Indiana Elliot. What's in a name.
SUSAN B. ANTHONY:	Everything.
G.S.:	My father's name was Daniel he had a black beard he was
	not tall not at all tall, he had a black beard his name was
	Daniel.
ALL THE CHARACTERS:	My father had a name his name was Daniel.
JO THE LOITERER:	Not Daniel.
CHRIS A CITIZEN:	Not Daniel not Daniel in the lion's den not Daniel.
SUSAN B. ANTHONY:	I had a father, Daniel was not his name.
INDIANA ELLIOT:	I had no father no father.

---

[2] Daniel Webster (1782-1852), American politician.
[3] Daniel 6.
[4] Stein herself.
[5] Susan B. Anthony (1820-1906), American feminist.

DANIEL WEBSTER:	He digged a pit he digged it deep he digged it for his brother, into the pit he did fall in the pit he digged for tother.

Act I
Scene 2

JO THE LOITERER:	I want to tell
CHRIS THE CITIZEN:	Very well
JO THE LOITERER:	I want to tell oh hell.
CHRIS THE CITIZEN:	Oh very well.
JO THE LOITERER:	I want to tell oh hell I want to tell about my wife.
CHRIS THE CITIZEN:	And have you got one.
JO THE LOITERER:	No not one.
CHRIS THE CITIZEN:	Two then
JO THE LOITERER:	No not two.
CHRIS:	How many then
JO THE LOITERER:	I haven't got one. I want to tell oh hell about my wife I haven't got one.
CHRIS THE CITIZEN:	Well.
JO THE LOITERER:	My wife, she had a garden.
CHRIS THE CITIZEN:	Yes
JO THE LOITERER:	And I bought one.
CHRIS THE CITIZEN:	A wife.
	No said Jo I was poor and I bought a garden. And then said Chris. She said, said Jo, she said my wife said one tree in my garden was her tree in her garden. And said Chris, Was it. Jo, We quarreled about it. And then said Chris. And then said Jo, we took a train and we went where we went. And then said Chris. She gave me a little package said Jo. And was it a tree said Chris. No it was money said Jo. And was she your wife said Chris, yes said Jo when she was funny, How funny said Chris. Very funny said Jo. Very funny said Jo. To be funny you have to take everything in the kitchen and put it on the floor, you have to take all your money and all your jewels and put them near the door you have to go to bed then and leave the door ajar. That is the way you do when you are funny.
CHRIS THE CITIZEN:	Was she funny.
JO THE LOITERER:	Yes she was funny.
	CHRIS *and* JO *put their arms around each other*
ANGEL MORE:	Not any more I am not a martyr any more, not any more. Be a martyr said Chris.
ANGEL MORE:	Not any more. I am not a martyr any more. Surrounded by sweet smelling flowers I

fell asleep three times.

Darn and wash and patch, darn and wash
and patch, darn and wash and patch
darn and wash and patch.

JO THE LOITERER: Anybody can be accused of loitering.

CHRIS BLAKE A CITIZEN: Any loiterer can be accused of loitering.

HENRIETTA M.: Daniel Webster needs an artichoke.

ANGEL MORE: Susan B. is cold in wet weather.

HENRY B.: She swore an oath she'd quickly come to any one to any one.

ANTHONY COMSTOCK:[6] Caution and curiosity, oil and obligation, wheels and appurtenances, in the way of means.

VIRGIL T.: What means.

JOHN ADAMS:[7] I wish to say I also wish to stay,
I also wish to go away, I also wish
I endeavor to also wish.

ANGEL MORE: I wept on a wish.

JOHN ADAMS: Whenever I hear any one say of course, do I deny it, yes I do deny it whenever I hear any one say of course I deny it, I do deny it.

THADDEUS S.:[8] Be mean.

DANIEL WEBSTER: Be there.

HENRIETTA M.: Be where

CONSTANCE FLETCHER:[9] I do and I do not declare that roses and wreaths, wreaths and roses around and around, blind as a bat, curled as a hat and a plume, be mine when I die, farewell to a thought, he left all alone, be firm in despair dear dear never share, dear dear, dear dear, I Constance Fletcher dear dear, I am a dear, I am a dear dear I am a dear, here there everywhere. I bow myself out.

INDIANA ELLIOT: Anybody else would be sorry.

SUSAN B. ANTHONY: Hush, I hush, you hush, they hush, we hush. Hush.

GLOSTER HEMING *and* ISABEL WENTWORTH: We, hush, dear as we are, we are very dear to us and to you we hush, we hush you say hush, dear hush. Hush dear.

ANNA HOPE:[10] I open any door, that is the way that any day is to-day, any day is to-day I open any door every door a door.

LILLIAN RUSSELL:[11] Thank you.

ANTHONY COMSTOCK: Quilts are not crazy, they are kind.

JENNY REEFER: My goodness gracious me.

---

[6] Anthony Comstock (1844-1915), postal inspector and originator of Comstock Laws, which criminalized sending materials deemed "obscene" by mail.

[7] Usually taken to be John Quincy Adams (1767-1848), U.S. president from 1825 to 1829.

[8] Thaddeus Stevens (1792-1868), anti-slavery politician.

[9] Julia Constance Fletcher (1859-1938), friend of Stein's, novelist and playwright; pseudo. George Fleming.

[10] Possibly painter Anna Hope "Nan" Hudson (1869-1957).

[11] Lillian Russell (1861-1922), singer and actress.

ULYSSES S. GRANT:[12]	He knew that his name was not Eisenhower.[13] Yes he knew it. He did know it.
HERMAN ATLAN:[14]	He asked me to come he did ask me.
DONALD GALLUP:[15]	I chose a long time, a very long time, four hours are a very long time, I chose, I took a very long time, I took a very long time. Yes I took a very long time to choose, yes I did.
T.T. AND A.A.:	They missed the boat yes did they did they missed the boat.
JO THE LOITERER:	I came again but not when I was expected, but yes when I was expected because they did expect me.
CHRIS THE CITIZEN:	I came to dinner.

They all sit down

Curtain

Act I
Scene 3

SUSAN B. ANTHONY *and* DANIEL WEBSTER *seated in two straight-backed chairs not too near each other.* JO THE LOITERER *comes in*

JO THE LOITERER:	I don't know where a mouse is I don't know what a mouse is. What is a mouse.
ANGEL MORE:	I am a mouse
JO THE LOITERER:	Well
ANGEL MORE:	Yes Well
JO THE LOITERER:	All right well. Well what is a mouse
ANGEL MORE:	I am a mouse
JO THE LOITERER:	Well if you are what is a mouse
ANGEL MORE:	You know what a mouse is, I am a mouse.
JO THE LOITERER:	Yes well, And she.

SUSAN B. *dressed like a Quakeress turns around*

SUSAN B.:	I hear a sound.
JO THE LOITERER:	Yes well
DANIEL WEBSTER:	I do not hear a sound. When I am told.
SUSAN B. ANTHONY:	Silence.

Everybody is silent

SUSAN B. ANTHONY:	Youth is young, I am not old.
DANIEL WEBSTER:	When the mariner has been tossed for many days, in thick weather, and on an unknown sea, he naturally avails

---

[12] Ulysses S. Grant (1822-1885), Civil War general and U.S. president from 1869 to 1877.
[13] Dwight D. Eisenhower (1890-1969), Supreme Commander of the Allied Forces in Europe during World War II; would go on to serve as President of the United States.

[14] French painter Jean-Michel Atlan (1913-1960), a one-time friend of Stein's.
[15] Donald Gallup (1913-2000), scholar, librarian, and a friend of Stein's.

	himself of the first pause in the storm.
SUSAN B. ANTHONY:	For instance. They should always fight. They should be martyrs. Some should be martyrs. Will they. They will.
DANIEL WEBSTER:	We have thus heard sir what a resolution is.
SUSAN B. ANTHONY:	I am resolved.
DANIEL WEBSTER:	When this debate sir was to be resumed on Thursday it so happened that it would have been convenient for me to be elsewhere.
SUSAN B.:	I am here, ready to be here. Ready to be where. Ready to be here. It is my habit.
DANIEL WEBSTER:	The honorable member complained that I had slept on his speech.
SUSAN B.:	The right to sleep is given to no woman.
DANIEL WEBSTER:	I did sleep on the gentleman's speech; and slept soundly.
SUSAN B.:	I too have slept soundly when I have slept, yes when I have slept I too have slept soundly.
DANIEL WEBSTER:	Matches and over matches.
SUSAN B.:	I understand you undertake to overthrow my undertaking.
DANIEL WEBSTER:	I can tell the honorable member once for all that he is greatly mistaken, and that he is dealing with one whose temper and character he has yet much to learn.
SUSAN B.:	I have declared that patience is never more than patient. I too have declared, that I who am not patient am patient.
DANIEL WEBSTER:	What interest asks he has South Carolina in a canal in Ohio.
SUSAN B.:	What interest have they in me, what interest have I in them, who holds the head of whom, who can bite their lips to avoid a swoon.
DANIEL WEBSTER:	The harvest of neutrality had been great, but we had gathered it all.
SUSAN B.:	Near hours are made not by shade not by heat not by joy, I always know that not now rather not now, yes and I do not stamp but I know that now yes now is now. I have never asked any one to forgive me.
DANIEL WEBSTER:	On yet another point I was still more unaccountably mis-understood.
SUSAN B.:	Do we do what we have to do or do we have to do what we do. I answer.
DANIEL WEBSTER:	Mr. President I shall enter on no encomium upon Massa-chusetts she need none. There she is behold her and judge for yourselves.
SUSAN B.:	I enter into a tabernacle I was born a believer in peace, I say fight for the right, be a martyr and live, be a coward and die, and why, because they, yes they, sooner or later go away. They leave us here. They come again. Don't forget, they come again.
DANIEL WEBSTER:	So sir I understand the gentleman and am happy to find I

	did not misunderstand him.
SUSAN B.:	I should believe, what they ask, but they know, they
DANIEL WEBSTER:	know.
	It has been to us all a copious fountain of national, social
SUSAN B.:	and personal happiness.
	Shall I protest, not while I live and breathe, I shall protest,
DANIEL WEBSTER:	shall I protest, shall I protest while I live and breathe.
	When my eyes shall be turned to behold for the last time
SUSAN B.:	the sun in heaven.
JO THE LOITERER:	Yes.
ANGEL MORE:	I like a mouse
JO THE LOITERER:	I hate mice.
	I am not talking about mice, I am talking about a mouse.
ANGEL MORE:	I like a mouse.
JO THE LOITERER:	I hate a mouse.
	Now do you.

Curtain

INTERLUDE

Susan B. A Short Story

Yes I was said Susan.

You mean you are, said Anne.

No said Susan no.

When this you see remember me said Susan B.

I do said Anne.

After a while there was education. Who is educated said Anne.

Susan began to follow, she began to follow herself. I am not tired said Susan. No not said Anne. No I am not said Susan. This was the beginning. They began to travel not to travel you know but to go from one place to another place. In each place Susan B. said here I am I am here. Well said Anne. Do not let it trouble you said Susan politely. By the time she was there she was polite. She often thought about politeness. She said politeness was so agreeable. It is said Anne. Yes said Susan yes I think so that is to say politeness is agreeable that is to say it could be agreeable if everybody were polite but when it is only me, ah me, said Susan B.

Anne was reproachful why do you not speak louder she said to Susan B. I speak as loudly as I can said Susan B. I even speak louder I even speak louder than I can. Do you really said Anne. Yes I really do said Susan B. it was dark and as it was dark it was necessary to speak louder or very softly, very softly. Dear me said Susan B., if it was not so early I would be sleepy. I myself said Anne never like to look at a newspaper. You are entirely right said Susan B. only I disagree with you. You do said Anne. You know very well I do said Susan B.

Men said Susan B. are so conservative, so selfish, so boresome and said Susan B. they are so ugly, and said Susan B. they are gullible, anybody can convince them, listen said Susan B. they listen to me. Well said Anne anybody would. I know said Susan B. I know anybody would I know that.

Once upon a time any day was full of occupation. You were never tired said Anne. No I was never tired said Susan B. And now, said Anne. Now I am never tired said Susan B. Let us said Anne let us think about everything. No said Susan B. no, no no, I know, I know said Susan B. no, said Susan B. No. But said Anne. But me no buts said Susan B. I know, now you like every one, every one and you each one and you they all do, they all listen to me, utterly unnecessary to deny, why deny, they themselves will they deny that they listen to me but let them deny it, all the same they do they do listen to me all the men do, see them said Susan B., do see them, see them, why not, said Susan B., they are men, and men, well of course they know that they cannot either see or hear unless I tell them so, poor things said Susan B. I do not pity them. Poor things. Yes said Anne they are poor things. Yes said Susan B. they are poor things. They are poor things said Susan B. men are poor things. Yes they are said Anne. Yes they are said Susan B. and nobody pities them. No said Anne no, nobody pities them. Very likely said Susan B. More than likely, said Anne. Yes said Susan B. yes.

It was not easy to go away but Susan B. did go away. She kept on going away and every time she went away she went away again. Oh my said Susan B. why do I go away, I go away because if I did not go away I would stay. Yes of course said Anne yes of course, if you did not go away you would stay. Yes of course said Susan B. Now said Susan B., let us not forget that in each place men are the same just the same, they are conservative, they are selfish and they listen to me. Yes they do said Anne. Yes they do said Susan B.

Susan B. was right, she said she was right and she was right. Susan B. was right. She was right because she was right. It is easy to be right, everybody else is wrong so it is easy to be right, and Susan B. was right, of course she was right, it is easy to be right, everybody else is wrong it is easy to be right. And said Susan B., in a way yes in a way yes really in a way, in a way really it is useful to be right. It does what it does, it does do what it does, if you are right, it does do what it does. It is very remarkable said Anne. Not very remarkable said Susan B. not very remarkable, no not very remarkable. It is not very remarkable really not very remarkable said Anne. No said Susan B. no not very remarkable.

And said Susan B. that is what I mean by not very remarkable.

Susan B. said she would not leave home. No said Susan B. I will not leave home. Why not said Anne. Why not said Susan B. all right I will I always have I always will. Yes you always will said Anne. Yes I always will said Susan B. In a little while anything began again and Susan B. said she did not mind. Really and truly said Susan B. really and truly I do not mind. No said Anne you do not mind, no said Susan B. no really and truly truly and really I do not mind. It was very necessary never to be cautious said Susan B. Yes said Anne it is very necessary.

In a little while they found everything very mixed. It is not really mixed said Susan B. How can anything be really mixed when men are conservative, dull, monotonous, deceived, stupid, unchanging and bullies, how said Susan B. how when men are men can they be mixed. Yes said Anne, yes men are men, how can they when men are men how can they be mixed yes how can they. Well said Susan B. let us go on they always listen to me. Yes said Anne yes they always listen to you. Yes said Susan B. yes they always listen to me.

Act II

ANDREW J.:[16]	It is cold weather.
HENRIETTA M.:	In winter.
ANDREW J.:	Wherever I am

THADDEUS S. *comes in singing a song*

THADDEUS S.: I believe in public school education, I do not believe in free masons I believe in public school education, I do not believe that every one can do whatever he likes because [*a pause*] I have not always done what I liked, but, I would, if I could, and so I will, I will do what I will, I will have my will, and they, when the they, where are they, beside a poll, Gallup the poll. It is remarkable that there could be any nice person by the name of Gallup, but there is, yes there is, that is my decision.

ANDREW J.: Bother your decision, I tell you it is cold weather.

HENRIETTA M.: In winter.

ANDREW J.: Wherever I am.

CONSTANCE FLETCHER: Antagonises is a pleasant name, antagonises is a pleasant word, antagonises has occurred, bless you all and one.

JOHN ADAMS: Dear Miss Constance Fletcher, it is a great pleasure that I kneel at your feet, but I am Adams, I kneel at the feet of none, not any one, dear Miss Constance Fletcher dear dear Miss Constance Fletcher I kneel at your feet, you would have ruined my father if I had had one but I have had one and you had ruined him, dear Miss Constance Fletcher if I had not been an Adams I would have kneeled at your feet.

CONSTANCE FLETCHER: And kissed my hand.

J. ADAMS: [*Shuddering*] And kissed your hand.

CONSTANCE FLETCHER: What a pity, no not what a pity it is better so, but what a pity what a pity it is what a pity.

J. ADAMS: Do not pity me kind beautiful lovely Miss Constance Fletcher do not pity me, no do not pity me, I am an Adams and not pitiable.

CONSTANCE FLETCHER: Dear dear me if he had not been an Adams he would have kneeled at my feet and he would have kissed my hand. Do you mean that you would have kissed my hand or my hands, dear Mr. Adams.

J. ADAMS: I mean that I would have first kneeled at your feet and then I would have kissed one of your hands and then I would still kneeling have kissed both of your hands, if I had not been an Adams.

CONSTANCE FLETCHER: Dear me Mr. Adams dear me.

---

[16] Andrew Johnson (1808-1875), U.S. president from 1865 to 1869.

ALL THE CHARACTERS:	If he had not been an Adams he would have kneeled at her feet and he would have kissed one of her hands, and then still kneeling he would have kissed both of her hands still kneeling if he had not been an Adams.
ANDREW J.:	It is cold weather.
HENRIETTA M.:	In winter.
ANDREW J.:	Wherever I am.
THADDEUS S.:	When I look at him I fly, I mean when he looks at me he can cry.
LILLIAN RUSSELL:	It is very naughty for men to quarrel so.
HERMAN ATLAN:	They do quarrel so.
LILLIAN RUSSELL:	It is very naughty of them very naughty.

JENNY REEFER *beings to waltz with* HERMAN ATLAN

A SLOW CHORUS:	Naughty men, they quarrel so Quarrel about what. About how late the moon can rise. About how soon the earth can turn. About how naked are the stars. About how black are blacker men. About how pink are pinks in spring. About what corn is best to pop. About how many feet the ocean has dropped. Naughty men naughty men, they are always always quarreling.
JENNY REEFER:	Ulysses S. Grant was not the most earnest nor the most noble of men, but he was not always quarreling.
DONALD GALLUP:	No he was not.
JO THE LOITERER:	Has everybody forgotten Isabel Wentworth. I just want to say has everybody forgotten Isabel Wentworth.
CHRIS THE CITIZEN:	Why shouldn't everybody forget Isabel Wentworth.
JO THE LOITERER:	Well that is just what I want to know I just want to know if everybody has forgotten Isabel Wentworth. That is all I want to know I just want to know if everybody has forgotten Isabel Wentworth.

Act II
Scene 2

SUSAN B.:	Shall I regret having been born, will I regret having been born, shall and will, will and shall, I regret having been born.
ANNE:	Is Henrietta M. a sister of Angel More.
SUSAN B.:	No, I used to feel that sisters should be sisters, and that sisters prefer sisters, and I.
ANNE:	Is Angel More the sister of Henrietta M. It is important that I know important.

SUSAN B.:	Yes important.
ANNE:	An Indiana Elliot are there any other Elliots beside Indiana Elliot. It is important that I should know, very important.
SUSAN B.:	Should one work up excitement, or should one turn it low so that it will explode louder, should one work up excitement should one.
ANNE:	Are there any other Elliots beside Indiana Elliot, had she sisters or even cousins, it is very important that I should know, very important.
SUSAN B.:	A life is never given for a life, when a life is given a life is gone, if no life is gone there is no room for more life, life and strife, I give my life, that is to say, I live my life every day.
ANNE:	And Isabel Wentworth, is she older or younger than she was it is very important very important that I should know
	just how old she is. I must have a list I must of how old
SUSAN B.:	every one is, it is very important.
ANNE:	I am ready.
	We have forgotten we have forgotten Jenny Reefer, I don't know even who she is, it is very important that I know
SUSAN B.:	who Jenny Reefer is very important.
	And perhaps it is important to know who Lillian Russell
ANNE:	is, perhaps it is important.
SUSAN B.:	It is not important to know who Lillian Russell is.
ANNE:	Then you do know.
SUSAN B.:	It is not important for me to know who Lillian Russell is. I must choose I do choose, men and women women and men I do choose. I must choose colored or white white or colored I must choose, I must choose, weak or strong, strong or weak I must choose.

All the men coming forward together

SUSAN B.:	I must choose
JO THE LOITERER:	Fight fight fight, between the nigger and the white.
CHRIS THE CITIZEN:	And the women.
ANDREW J.:	I wish to say that little men are bigger than big men, that they know how to drink and to get drunk. They say I was a little man next to that big man, nobody can say what they do say nobody can.
CHORUS OF ALL THE MEN:	No nobody can, we feel that way too, no nobody can.
ANDREW JOHNSON:	Begin to be drunk when you can so be a bigger man than a big man, you can.
CHORUS OF MEN:	You can.
ANDREW J.:	I often think, I am a bigger man than a bigger man. I often think I am.

ANDREW J. *moves around and as he moves around he sees himself in a mirror*

Nobody can say little as I am I am not bigger than anybody bigger bigger bigger [*and then in a low whisper*] bigger than him bigger than him.

JO THE LOITERER: Fight fight between the big and the big never between the little and the big.

CHRIS THE CITIZEN: They don't fight.

VIRGIL T. *makes them all gather around him*

VIRGIL T.: Hear me he says hear me in every way I have satisfaction, I sit I stand I walk around and I am grand, and you all know it.

CHORUS OF MEN: Yes we all know it. That's that.

and said VIRGIL T.: I will call you up one by one and then you will know which one is which, I know, then you will be known. Very well, Henry B.

HENRY B.: [*Comes forward*] I almost thought that I was Tommy I almost did I almost thought I was Tommy W. but if I were Tommy W. I would never come again, not if I could do better no not if I could do better.

VIRGIL T.: Useless. John Adams. [JOHN ADAMS *advances*] Tell me are you the real John Adams you know I sometimes doubt it not really doubt it you know but doubt it.

JOHN ADAMS: If you were silent I would speak.

JO THE LOITERER: Fight fight fight between day and night.

CHRIS THE CITIZEN: Which is day and which is night.

JO THE LOITERER: Hush, which.

JOHN ADAMS: I ask you Virgil T. do you love women, I do. I love women but I am never subdued by them never.

VIRGIL T.: He is no good. Andrew J. and Thaddeus S. better come together.

JO THE LOITERER: He wants to fight fight fight between.

CHRIS: Between what.

JO THE LOITERER: Between the dead.

ANDREW J.: I tell you I am bigger bigger is not biggest is not bigger. I am bigger and just to the last minute, I stick, it's better to stick than to die, it's better to itch than to cry, I have tried them all.

VIRGIL T.: You bet you have.

THADDEUS S.: I can be carried in dying but I will never quit trying.

JO THE LOITERER: Oh go to bed when all is said oh go to bed, everybody, let's hear the women.

CHRIS THE CITIZEN: Fight fight between the nigger and the white and the women.

ANDREW J. *and* THADDEUS S. *begin to quarrel violently*

Tell me said Virgil T. tell me I am from Missouri.

Everybody suddenly stricken dumb
DANIEL *advances holding* HENRIETTA M. *by the hand*

DANIEL: Ladies and gentleman let me present you let me present to you Henrietta M. it is rare in this troubled world to find a woman without a last name rare delicious and troubling, ladies and gentlemen let me present Henrietta M.

Curtain

Act II
Scene 3

SUSAN B.:   I do not know whether I am asleep or awake, awake or asleep, asleep or awake. Do I know.

JO THE LOITERER: I know, you are awake Susan B.

A snowy landscape.
a negro man and a negro woman

SUSAN B.:   Negro man would you vote if you only can and not she.

NEGRO MAN: You bet.

SUSAN B.:   I fought for you that you could vote would you vote if they would not let me.

NEGRO MAN: Holy gee.

SUSAN B.:   [*Moving down in the snow*] If I believe that I am right and I am right if they believe that they are right and they are not in the right, might, might, might there be what might be.

NEGRO MAN AND WOMAN: [*Following her*] All right Susan B. all right.

SUSAN B.:   How then can we entertain a hope that they will act differently, we may pretend to go in good faith but there will be no faith in us.

DONALD GALLUP: Let me help you Susan B.

SUSAN B.:   And if you do and I annoy you what will you do.

DONALD GALLUP: But I will help you Susan B.

SUSAN B.:   I tell you if you do and I annoy you what will you do.

DONALD GALLUP: I wonder if I can help you Susan B.

SUSAN B.:   I wonder.

ANDREW G., THADDEUS *and* DANIEL WEBSTER *come in together*

We are the chorus of the V.I.P.
Very important persons to every one who can hear and see, we are the chorus of the V.I.P.

SUSAN B.:   Yes, so they are. I am important but not that way, not that way.

THE THREE V.I.P.'S:	We you see we V.I.P. very important to any one who can hear or you can see, just we three, of course lots of others but just we three, just we three we are the chorus of V.I.P. Very important persons to any one who can hear or can see.
SUSAN B.:	My constantly recurring thought and prayer now are that no word or act of mine may lessen the might of this country in the scale of truth and right.
THE CHORUS OF V.I.P.:	
DANIEL WEBSTER:	When they all listen to me.
THADDEUS S.:	When they all listen to me.
ANDREW J.:	When they all listen to him, by him I mean me.
DANIEL WEBSTER:	By him I mean me.
THADDEUS S.:	It is not necessary to have any meaning I am he, he is me I am a V.I.P.
THE THREE:	We are the V.I.P. the very important persons, we have special rights, they ask us first and they wait for us last and wherever we are well there we are everybody knows we are there, we are the V.I.P. Very important persons for everybody to see.
JO THE LOITERER:	I wished that I knew the difference between rich and poor, I used to think I was poor, now I think I am rich and I am rich, quite rich not very rich quite rich, I wish I knew the difference between rich and poor.
CHRIS THE CITIZEN:	Ask her, ask Susan B. I always ask, I find they like it and I like it, and if I like it, and if they like it, I am not rich and I am not poor, just like that Jo just like that.
JO THE LOITERER:	Susan B. listen to me, what is the difference between rich and poor poor and rich no use to ask the V.I.P., they never answer me but you Susan B. you answer, answer me.
SUSAN B.:	Rich, to be rich, is to be so rich that when they are rich they have it to be that they do not listen and when they do they do not hear, and to be poor to be poor, is to be so poor they listen and listen and what they hear well what do they hear, they hear that they listen, they listen to hear, that is what it is to be poor, but I, I Susan B., there is no wealth nor poverty, there is no wealth, what is wealth, there is no poverty, what is poverty, has a pen ink, has it.
JO THE LOITERER:	I had a pen that was to have ink for a year and it only lasted six weeks.
SUSAN B.:	Yes I know Jo. I know.

Curtain

Act II
Scene 4

A Meeting.

SUSAN B. ON THE PLATFORM:	Ladies there is no neutral position for us to assume. If we say we love the cause and then sit down at our ease, surely does our action speak the lie.
	And now will Daniel Webster take the platform as never before.
DANIEL WEBSTER:	Coming and coming alone, no man is alone when he comes, when he comes when he is coming he is not alone and now ladies and gentlemen I have done, remember that remember me remember each one.
SUSAN B.:	And now Virgil T. Virgil T. will bow and speak and when it is necessary they will know that he is he.
VIRGIL T.:	I make what I make, I make a noise, there is a poise in making a noise.

An interruption at the door

JO THE LOITERER:	I have behind me a crowd, are we allowed.
SUSAN B.:	A crowd is never allowed but each one of you can come in.
CHRIS THE CITIZEN:	But if we are allowed then we are a crowd.
SUSAN B.:	No, this is the cause, and a cause is a pause. Pause before you come in.
JO THE LOITERER:	Yes ma'am.

All the characters crowd in. CONSTANCE FLETCHER *and* INDIANA ELLIOT *leading*

DANIEL WEBSTER:	I resist it to-day and always. Who ever falters or whoever flies I continue the contest.
CONSTANCE FLETCHER *and* INDIANA ELLIOT:	[*Bowing low say*] Dear man, he can make us glad that we have had so great so dear a man here with us now and now we bow before him here, this dear this dear great man.
SUSAN B.:	Hush, this is slush. Hush.
JOHN ADAMS:	I cannot be still when still and until I see Constance Fletcher dear Constance Fletcher noble Constance Fletcher and I spill I spill over like a thrill and a trill, dear Constance Fletcher there is no cause in her presence, how can there be a cause. Women what are women. There is Constance Fletcher, men what are men, there is Constance Fletcher, Adams, yes, Adams, I am John Adams, there is Constance Fletcher, when this you see listen to me, Constance, no I cannot call her Constance I can only call her Constance Fletcher.

INDIANA ELLIOT:	And how about me.
JO THE LOITERER:	Whist shut up I have just had an awful letter from home, shut up.
INDIANA ELLIOT:	What did they say.
JO THE LOITERER:	They said I must come home and not marry you.
INDIANA:	Who ever said we were going to marry.
JO THE LOITERER:	Believe me I never did.
INDIANA:	Disgrace to the cause of women, out.
	And she shoves him out.
JO THE LOITERER:	Help Susan B. help me.
SUSAN B.:	I know that we suffer, and we suffer we grow strong, I know that we wait and as we wait we are bold, I know that we are beaten and as we are beaten we win, I know that men know that this is not so but it is so, I know, yes I know.
JO THE LOITERER:	There didn't I tell you she knew best, you just give me a kiss and let me alone.
DANIEL WEBSTER:	I who was once old am now young, I who was once weak am now strong, I who have left every one behind am now overtaken.
SUSAN B.:	I undertake to overthrow your undertaking.
JO THE LOITERER:	You bet.
CHRIS THE CITIZEN:	I always repeat everything I hear.
JO THE LOITERER:	You sure do.

While all this is going on, all the characters are crowding up on the platform

THEY SAY:	Now we are all here there is nobody down there to hear, now if it is we're always like that there would be no reason why anybody should cry, because very likely if at all it would be so nice to be the head, we are the head we have all the bread.
JO THE LOITERER:	And the butter too.
CHRIS THE CITIZEN:	And Kalamazoo.
SUSAN B.:	[*advancing*] I speak to those below who are not there who are not there who are not there. I speak to those below to those below who are not there to those below who are not there.

Curtain

Act II
Scene 5

SUSAN B.:	Will they remember that it is true that neither they that neither you, will they marry will they carry, aloud, the right to know that even if they love them so, they are alone to live and die, they are alone to sink and swim they are

alone to have what they own, to have no idea but that they are here, to struggle and thirst to do everything first, because until it is done there is no other one.

JO THE LOITERER *leads in* INDIANA ELLIOT *in wedding attire, followed by* JOHN ADAMS *and* CONSTANCE FLETCHER *and followed by* DANIEL WEBSTER *and* ANGEL MORE. *All the other characters to follow after.* ANNE *and* JENNY REEFER *come and stand by* SUSAN B. ULYSSES S. GRANT *sits down in a chair right behind the procession*

ANNE:	Marriage.
JENNY REEFER:	Marry marriage.
SUSAN B.:	I know I know and I have told you so, but if no one marries how can there be women to tell men, women to tell men.
ANNE:	What
JENNY REEFER:	Women should not tell men.
SUSAN B.:	Men can not count, they do not know that two and two make four if women do not tell them so. There is a devil creeps into men when their hands are strengthened. Men want to be half slave half free. Women want to be all slave or all free therefore men govern and women know, and yet.
ANNE:	Yet.
JENNY REEFER:	There is no yet in paradise.
SUSAN B.:	Let them marry.

The marrying commences

JO THE LOITERER:	I tell her if she marries me do I marry her.
INDIANA ELLIOT:	Listen to what he says so you can answer, have you the ring.
JO THE LOITERER:	You did not like the ring and mine is too large.
INDIANA ELLIOT:	Hush.
JO THE LOITERER:	I wish my name was Adams.
INDIANA ELLIOT:	Hush.
JOHN ADAMS:	I never marry I have been twice divorced but I have never married, fair Constance Fletcher fair Constance Fletcher do you not admire me that I never can married be. I who have been twice divorced. Dear Constance Fletcher dear dear Constance Fletcher do you not admire me.
CONSTANCE FLETCHER:	So beautiful. It is so beautiful to meet you here, so beautiful, so beautiful to meet you here dear, dear John Adams, so beautiful to meet you here.
DANIEL WEBSTER:	When I have joined and not having joined have separated and not having separated have led, and not having led have thundered, when I having thundered have provoked

and having provoked have dominated, may I dear Angel More not kneel at your feet because I cannot kneel my knees are not kneeling knees but dear Angel More be my Angel More for evermore.

ANGEL MORE: I join the choir that is visible, because the choir that is visible is as visible.

DANIEL WEBSTER: As what Angel More.

ANGEL MORE: As visible as visible, do you not hear me, as visible.

DANIEL WEBSTER: You do not and I do not.

ANGEL MORE: What.

DANIEL WEBSTER: Separate marriage from marriage.

ANGEL MORE: And why not.

DANIEL WEBSTER: And.

Just at this moment ULYSSES S. GRANT *makes his chair pound on the floor*

ULYSSES S. GRANT: As long as I sit I am sitting, silence again as you were, you were all silent, as long as I sit I am sitting.

ALL TOGETHER: We are silent, as we were.

SUSAN B.: We are all here to celebrate the civil and religious marriage of Jo the Loiterer and Indiana Elliot.

JO THE LOITERER: Who is civil and who is religious.

ANNE: Who is, listen to Susan B. She knows.

THE BROTHER OF INDIANA ELLIOT: [*Rushes in*] Nobody knows who I am but I forbid the marriage, do we know whether Jo the Loiterer is a bigamist or a grandfather or an uncle or a refugee. Do we know, no we do not know and I forbid the marriage, I forbid it, I am Indiana Elliot's brother and I forbid it, I am known as Herman Atlan and I forbid it, I am known as Anthony Comstock and I forbid it, I am Indiana Elliot's brother and I forbid it.

JO THE LOITERER: Well well well, I knew that ring of mine was too large, It could not fall off on account of my joints but I knew it was too large.

INDIANA ELLIOT: I renounce my brother.

JO THE LOITERER: That's right my dear that's all right.

SUSAN B.: What is marriage, is marriage protection or religion, is marriage renunciation or abundance, is marriage a stepping-stone or an end. What is marriage.

ANNE: I will never marry.

JENNY REEFER: If I marry I will divorce but I will not marry because if I did marry, I would be married.

ULYSSES S. GRANT *pounds his chair*

ULYSSES S. GRANT: Didn't I say I do not like noise, I do not like cannon balls, I do not like storms, I do not like talking, I do not like

	noise. I like everything and everybody to be silent and what I like I have. Everybody be silent.
JO THE LOITERER:	I know I was silent, everybody can tell just by listening to me just how silent I am, dear General, dear General Ulysses, dear General Ulysses Simpson dear General Ulysses Simpson Grant, dear dear sir, am I not a perfect example of what you like, am I not silent.

ULYSSES S. GRANT's *chair pounds and he is silent*

SUSAN B.:	I am not married and the reason why is that I have had to do what I have had to do, I have had to be what I have had to be, I could never be one of two I could never be two in one as married couples do and can, I am but one all one, one and all one, and so I have never been married to any one.
ANNE:	But I have been. I have been married to what you have been to that one.
SUSAN B.:	No no, no, you may be married to the past one, the one that is not the present one, no one can be married to the present one, the one, the one, the present one.
JENNY REEFER:	I understand you undertake to overthrow their undertaking.
SUSAN B.:	I love the sound of these, one over two, two under one, three under four, four over more.
ANNE:	Dear Susan B. Anthony thank you.
JOHN ADAMS:	All this time I have been lost in my thoughts in my thoughts of thee beautiful thee, Constance Fletcher, do you see, I have been lost in my thoughts of thee.
CONSTANCE FLETCHER:	I am blind and therefore I dream.
DANIEL WEBSTER:	Dear Angel More, dear Angel More, there have been men who have stammered and stuttered but not, not I.
ANGEL MORE:	Speak louder.
DANIEL WEBSTER:	Not I.
THE CHORUS:	Why the hell don't you all get married, why don't you, we want to go home, why don't you.
JO THE LOITERER:	Why don't you.
INDIANA ELLIOT:	Why don't you.
INDIANA ELLIOT'S BROTHER:	Why don't you because I am here.

The crowd remove him forcibly

SUSAN B. ANTHONY:	[*Suddenly*] They are married all married and their children women as well as men will have the vote, they will they will, they will have the vote.

Curtain

Act II
Scene 6

SUSAN B. *doing her house-work in her house*

ANNE:	[*Enter*] Susan B. they want you.
SUSAN B.:	Do they
ANNE:	Yes. You must go.
SUSAN B.:	No.
JENNY REEFER:	[*Comes in*] Oh yes they want to know if you are here.
SUSAN B.:	Yes still alive. Painters paint and writers write and soldiers drink and fight and I I am still alive.
ANNE:	They want you.
SUSAN B.:	And when they have me.
JENNY REEFER:	Then they will want you again.
SUSAN B.:	Yes I know, they love me so, they tell me so and they tell me so, but I, I do not tell them so because I know, they will not do what they could do and I I will be left alone to die but they will not have done what I need to have done to make it right that I live lived my life and fight.
JO THE LOITERER:	[*At the window*] Indiana Elliot wants to come in, she will not take my name she says it is not all the same, she says that she is Indiana Elliot and that I am Jo, and that she will not take my name and that she will always tell me so. Oh yes she is right of course she is right it is not all the same Indiana Elliot is her name, she is only married to me, but there is no difference that I can see, but all the same there she is and she will not change her name, yes it is all the same.
SUSAN B.:	Let her in.
INDIANA ELLIOT:	Oh, Susan B. they want you they have to have you, can I tell them you are coming I have not changed my name can I tell them you are coming and that you will do everything.
SUSAN B.:	No but there is no use in telling them so, they won't vote my laws, there is always a clause, there is always a pause, they won't vote my laws.

ANDREW JOHNSON *puts his head in at the door*

ANDREW JOHNSON:	Will the good lady come right along.
THADDEUS STEVENS:	[*Behind him*] We are waiting, will the good lady not keep us waiting, will the good lady not keep us waiting.
SUSAN B.:	You you know so well that you will not vote my laws.
STEVENS:	Dear lady remember humanity comes first.
SUSAN B.:	You mean men come first, women, you will not vote my laws, how can you dare when you do not care, how can you dare, there is no humanity in humans, there is only law, and you will not because you know so well that there

is no humanity there are only laws, you know it so well that you will not you will not vote my laws.

SUSAN B. *goes back to her housework.*
All the characters crowd in

CHORUS: Do come Susan B. Anthony do come nobody no nobody can make them come the way you make them come, do come do come Susan B. Anthony, it is your duty, Susan B. Anthony, you know you know your duty, you come, do come, come.

SUSAN B. ANTHONY: I suppose I will be coming, is it because you flatter me, is it because if I do not come you will forget me and never vote my laws, you will never vote my laws even if I do come but if I do not come you will never vote my laws, come or not come it always comes to the same thing it comes to their not voting my laws, not voting my laws, tell me all you men tell me you know you will never vote my laws.

ALL THE MEN: Dear kind lady we count on you, and as we count on you so can you count on us.

SUSAN B. ANTHONY: Yes but I work for you I do, I say never again, never again, never never, and yet I know I do say no but I do not mean no, I know I always hope that if I go that if I go and go and go, perhaps then you men will vote my laws but I know how well I know, a little this way a little that way you steal away, you steal a piece away you steal your-selves away, you do not intend to stay and vote my laws, and still when you call I go, I go, I go, I say no, no, no, and I go, but no, this time no, this time you have to do more than promise, you must write it down that you will vote my laws, but no, you will pay no attention to what is written, well then swear by my hearth, as you hope to have a home and hearth, swear after I work for you swear that you will vote my laws, but no, no oaths, no thoughts, no decisions, no intentions, no gratitude, no convictions, no nothing will make you pass my laws. Tell me can any of you be honest now, and say you will not pass my laws.

JO THE LOITERER: I can I can be honest I can say I will not pass your laws, because you see I have no vote, no loiterer has a vote so it is easy Susan B. Anthony easy for one man among all these men to be honest and to say I will not pass your laws. Anyway Susan B. Anthony what are your laws. Would it really be all right to pass them, if you say so it is all right with me. I have no vote myself but I'll make them as long as I don't have to change my name don't have to don't have to change my name.

T. STEVENS: Thanks dear Susan B. Anthony, thanks we all know that

	whatever happens we all can depend upon you to do your best for any cause which is a cause, and any cause is a cause and because any cause is a cause therefore you will always do your best for any cause, and now you will be doing your best for this cause our cause the cause.
SUSAN B.:	Because. Very well is it snowing.
CHORUS:	Not just now.
SUSAN B. ANTHONY:	Is it cold.
CHORUS:	A little.
SUSAN B. ANTHONY:	I am not well
CHORUS:	But you look so well and once started it will be all right.
SUSAN B. ANTHONY:	All right

Curtain

Act II
Scene 7

SUSAN B. ANTHONY *busy with her housework*

ANNE:	[*Comes in*] Oh it was wonderful, wonderful, they listen to nobody the way they listen to you.
SUSAN B.:	Yes it is wonderful as the result of my work for the first time the word male has been written into the constitution of the United States concerning suffrage. Yes it is wonderful.
ANNE:	But
SUSAN B.:	Yes but, what is man, what are men, what are they. I do not say that they haven't kind hearts, if I fall down in a faint, they will rush to pick me up, if my house is on fire, they will rush in to put the fire out and help me, yes they have kind hearts but they are afraid, afraid, they are afraid, they are afraid. They fear women, they fear each other, they fear their neighbor, they fear other countries and then they hearten themselves in their fear by crowding together and following each other, and when they crowd together and follow each other they are brutes, like animals who stampede, and so they have written in the name male into the United States constitution, because they are afraid of black men because they are afraid of women, because they are afraid afraid. Men are afraid.
ANNE:	[*Timidly*] And women.
SUSAN B.:	Ah women often have not any sense of danger, after all a hen screams pitifully when she sees an eagle but she is afraid only for her children, men are afraid for themselves, that is the real difference between men and women.
ANNE:	But Susan B. why do you not say these things out loud.
SUSAN B.:	Why not, because if I did they would not listen they not

alone would not listen they would revenge themselves. Men have kind hearts when they are not afraid but they are afraid afraid afraid. I say they are afraid, but if I were to tell them so their kindness would turn to hate. Yes the Quakers are right, they are not afraid because they do not fight, they do not fight.

ANNE: But Susan B. you fight and you are not afraid.

SUSAN B.: I fight and I am not afraid, I fight but I am not afraid.

ANNE: And you will win.

SUSAN B.: Win what, win what.

ANNE: Win the vote for women.

SUSAN B.: Yes some day some day the women will vote and by that time.

ANNE: By that time oh wonderful time.

SUSAN B.: By that time it will do them no good because having the vote they will become like men, they will be afraid, having the vote will make them afraid, oh I know it, but I will fight for the right, for the right to vote for them even though they become like men, become afraid like men, become like men.

ANNE *bursts into tears.* JENNY REEFER *rushes in*

JENNY REEFER: I have just converted Lillian Russell to the cause of woman's suffrage, I have converted her, she will give all herself and all she earns oh wonderful day I know you will say, here she comes isn't she beautiful.

LILLIAN RUSSELL *comes in followed by all the women in the* CHORUS. *Women crowding around,* CONSTANCE FLETCHER *in the background*

LILLIAN RUSSELL: Dear friends, it is so beautiful to meet you all, so beautiful, so beautiful to meet you all.

JOHN ADAMS *comes in and sees* CONSTANCE FLETCHER

JOHN ADAMS: Dear friend beautiful friend, there is no beauty where you are not.

CONSTANCE FLETCHER: Yes dear friend but look look at real beauty look at Lillian Russell look at real beauty.

JOHN ADAMS: Real beauty real beauty is all there is of beauty and why should my eye wander where no eye can look without having looked before. Dear friend I kneel to you because dear friend each time I see you I have never looked before, dear friend you are an open door.

DANIEL WEBSTER *strides in, the women separate*

DANIEL WEBSTER: What what is it, what is it, what is the false and the true and I say to you you Susan B. Anthony, you know the false from the true and yet you will not wait you will not wait, I say you will you will wait. When my eyes, and I have eyes when my eyes, beyond that I seek not to penetrate the veil, why should you want what you have chosen, when mine eyes, why do you want that the curtain may rise, why when mine eyes, why should the vision be opened to what lies behind, why, Susan B. Anthony fight the fight that is the fight, that any fight may be a fight for the right. I hear that you say that the word male should not be written into the constitution of the United States of America, but I say, I say, that so long that the gorgeous ensign of the republic, still full high advanced, its arms and trophies streaming in their original luster not a stripe erased or polluted not a single star obscured.

JO THE LOITERER:	She has decided to change her name.
INDIANA ELLIOT:	Not because it is his name but it is such a pretty name, Indiana Loiterer is such a pretty name I think all the same he will have to change his name, he must be Jo Elliot, yes he must, it is what he has to do, he has to be Jo Elliot and I am going to be Indiana Loiterer, dear friends, all friends is it not a lovely name, Indiana Loiterer all the same.
JO THE LOITERER:	All right I never fight, nobody will know it's men, but what can I do, if am not she and I am not me, what can I do, if a name is not true, what can I do but do as she tells me.
ALL THE CHORUS:	She is quite right, Indiana Loiterer is so harmonious, so harmonious, Indiana Loiterer is so harmonious.
ALL THE MEN:	[*Come in.*] What did she say.
JO:	I was talking not she but nobody no nobody ever wants to listen to me.
ALL THE CHORUS MEN AND WOMEN:	Susan B. Anthony was very successful we are all very grateful to Susan B. Anthony because she was so successful, she worked for the votes for women and she worked for the vote for colored men and she was so successful, they wrote the word male into the constitution of the United States of America, dear Susan B. Anthony. Dear Susan B., whenever she wants to be and she always wants to be she is always so successful so very successful. So successful.

Curtain

Act II
Scene 8

SUSAN B.:	*The Congressional Hall, the replica of the statue of* SUSAN B. ANTHONY *and her comrades in the suffrage fight*

ANNE:

[*Alone in front of the statuary*] The Vote. Women have the vote. They have it each and every one, it is glorious glorious glorious.

SUSAN B. ANTHONY:

[*Behind the statue*] Yes women have the vote, all my long life of strength and strife, all my long life, women have it, they can vote, every man and every woman have the vote, the word male is not there any more, that is to say, that is to say.

Silence. VIRGIL T. *comes in very nicely, he looks around and sees* ANNE

VIRGIL T.:

Very well indeed, very well indeed, you are looking very well indeed, have you a chair anywhere, very well indeed, as we sit, we sit, some day very soon some day they will vote sitting and that will be a very successful day any day, every day.

HENRY B. *comes in. He looks all around at the statue and then he sighs*

HENRY B.:

Does it really mean that women are as white and cold as marble does it really mean that.

ANGEL MORE *comes in and bows gracefully to the sculptured group*

ANGEL MORE:

I can always think of dear Daniel Webster daily.

JOHN ADAMS *comes in and looks around, and then carefully examines the statue*

JOHN ADAMS:

I think that they might have added dear delicate Constance Fletcher I do think they might have added her wonderful profile, I do think they might have, I do, I really do.

ANDREW JOHNSON *shuffles in*

ANDREW JOHNSON:

I have no hope in black or white in white or black in black or black or white or white, no hope.

THADDEUS STEVENS *comes in, he does not address anybody, he stands before the statue and frowns*

THADDEUS S.:

Rob the cradle, rob it, rob the robber, rob him, rob whatever there is to be taken, rob, rob the cradle, rob it.

DANIEL WEBSTER:

[*He sees nothing else*] Angel More, more more Angel More, did you hear me, can you hear shall you hear me, when they come and they do come, when they go and they do go, Angel More can you will you shall you may you might you would you hear me, when they have lost and won, when they have won and lost, when words are bitter and snow is white, Angel More come to me and we will leave together.

ANGEL MORE: Dear sir, not leave, stay.

HENRIETTA M.: I have never been mentioned again. [*She curtseys*]

CONSTANCE FLETCHER: Here I am, I am almost blind but here I am, dear dear here I am, I cannot see what is so white, here I am.

JOHN ADAMS: [*Kissing her hand*] Here you are, blind as a bat and beautiful as a bird, here you are, white and cold as marble, beautiful as marble, yes that is marble but you you are the living marble dear Constance Fletcher, you are.

CONSTANCE FLETCHER: Thank you yes I am here, blind as a bat, I am here.

INDIANA ELLIOT: I am sorry to interrupt so sorry to interrupt but I have a great deal to say about marriage, either one or the other married must be economical, either one or the other, if either one or the other of a married couple are economical then a marriage is successful, if not not, I have a great deal to say about marriage, and dear Susan B. Anthony was never married, how wonderful it is to be never married how wonderful. I have a great deal to say about marriage.

SUSAN B. ANTHONY: [*Voice from behind the statue*] It is a puzzle, I am not puzzled but it is a puzzle, if there are no children there are no men and women, and if there are men and women, it is rather horrible, and if it is rather horrible, then there are children, I am not puzzled but it is very puzzling, women and men vote and children, I am not puzzled but it is very puzzling. I have only been a man who has a very fine name, and it

GLOSTER HEMING: must be said I made it up yes I did, so many do why not I, so many do, so many do, and why not two, when anybody might, and you can vote and you can dote with any name. Thank you.

ISABEL WENTWORTH: They looked for me and they found me, I like to talk about it. It is very nearly necessary not to be noisy not to be noisy and hope, hope and hop, no use in enjoying men and women no use, I wonder why we are all happy, yes.

ANNE HOPE: There is another Anne and she believes, I am hopey hope and I do not believe I have been in California and Kalamazoo, and I do not believe I burst into tears and I do not believe.

They all crowd closer together and LILLIAN RUSSELL *who comes in stands quite alone*

LILLIAN RUSSELL: I can act so drunk that I never drink, I can drink so drunk that I never act, I have a curl I was a girl and I am old and fat but very handsome for all that.

ANTHONY COMSTOCK *comes in and glares at her*

ANTHONY COMSTOCK: I have heard that they have thought that they would wish that one like you could vote a vote and help to let the ones who want do what they like, I have heard that even you, and I am through, I cannot hope that there is dope, oh yes a horrid word. I have never heard, short.

JENNY REEFER: I have hope and faith, not charity no not charity, I have hope and faith, no not, not charity, no not charity.

ULYSSES S. GRANT: Women are women, soldiers are soldiers, men are not men, lies are not lies, do, and then a dog barks, listen to him and then a dog barks, a dog barks a dog barks any dog barks, listen to him any dog barks.

He sits down

HERMAN ATLAN: I am not loved any more, I was loved oh yes I was loved but I am not loved any more, I am not, was I not, I knew I would refuse what a woman would choose and so I am not loved any more, not loved any more.

DONALD GALLUP: Last but not least, first and not best, I am tall as a man, I am firm as a clam, and I never change, from day to day.

JO THE LOITERER *and* CHRIS A CITIZEN

JO THE LOITERER: Let us dance and sing, Chrissy Chris, wet and not in debt, I am a married man and I know how I show I am a married man. She votes, she changes her name and she votes.

They all crowd together in front of the statue, there is a moment of silence and then a chorus

CHORUS: To vote the vote, the vote we vote, can vote do vote will vote could vote, the vote the vote.

JO THE LOITERER: I am the only one who cannot vote, no loiterer can vote.

INDIANA ELLIOT: I am a loiterer Indiana Loiterer and I can vote.

JO THE LOITERER: You only have the name, you have not got the game.

CHORUS: The vote the vote we will have the vote.

LILLIAN RUSSELL: It is so beautiful to meet you all here so beautiful.

ULYSSES S. GRANT: Vote the vote, the army does not vote, the general generals, there is no vote, bah vote.

THE CHORUS: The vote we vote we note the vote.

They all bow and smile to the statue.
Suddenly SUSAN B.'*s voice is heard*

SUSAN B.'S VOICE: We cannot retrace our steps, going forward may be the same as going backwards. We cannot retrace our steps, retrace our steps. All my long life, all my life, we do not retrace our steps, all my long life, but.

A silence a long silence

But—we do not retrace our steps, all my long life, and here, here we are here, in marble and gold, did I say gold, yes I said gold, in marble and gold and where—

A silence

Where is where. In my long life of effort and strife, dear life, life is strife, in my long life, it will not come and go, I tell you so, it will stay it will pay but

A long silence

But do I want what we have got, has it not gone, what made it live, has it not gone because now it is had, in my long life in my long life

Silence

Life is strife, I was a martyr all my life not to what I won but to what was done.

Silence

Do you know because I tell you so, or do you know, do you know.

Silence

My long life, my long life.

Curtain

—1945-46

WINNIFRED EATON (ONOTO WATANNA) (1875-1954)

Raised in Montreal, Quebec, Winnifred Eaton was the eighth of fourteen children born to Grace Trefusias, a Chinese woman raised in England, and Edward Eaton, a British silk merchant. Winnifred and her sister Edith are often considered the first published writers of Chinese-North American descent. The Eatons encouraged artistic expression in their children, and the sisters both published poems, stories, and articles for their local newspaper while in their teens. Eaton's first novel, *Mrs. Nume of Japan* (1899), was published when she was in her early twenties. She also wrote stories, screenplays, and screen adaptations for various film companies. Whereas her sister Edith published essays and stories depicting the Chinese sympathetically, the bulk of Winnifred Eaton's seventeen novels and numerous short stories were Japanese-themed romances published under the pen name "Onoto Watanna." Eaton's Japanese persona seemed designed to appeal to mainstream readers' sense of an exoticized Japan, which was held in higher regard than China at the time. The romances often featured Japanese or Eurasian heroines in socially inferior positions, paired with American or English men in influential positions. Unavailable for many years, a number of these books have been reissued recently. Some critics consider Eaton a "trickster" figure, noting, for example, that she has fictionalized her life story (such as in *Who's Who*), stating that she was born in Nagasaki, Japan, to a Japanese noblewoman. In fact, Eaton spent most of her life in New York, Hollywood, and Calgary. The excerpt below is taken from *Me: A Book of Remembrance* (1915), which details her experiences as a foreign correspondent in Jamaica when she was seventeen.

from Me

III

"Do you know," said my room-mate on the night before we reached Jamaica, "that that four-fifty you paid me for those waists just about covers my tips."

"Tips?" I repeated innocently. "What are tips?"

She gave me a long, amazed look, her mouth wide-open.

"Good heavens!" at last she said, "where *have* you lived all of your life?"

"In Quebec," I said honestly.

"And you never heard of tips—people giving tips to waiters and servants?"

I grew uncomfortably red under her amused and amazed glance. In the seven days of that voyage my own extraordinary ignorance had been daily brought home to me. I now said lamely:

"Well, we had only one servant that I can ever remember, a woman named Sung-Sung whom papa brought from China; but she was more like one of our family, a sort of slave. We never gave her tips, or whatever you call it."

Did I not know, pursued my American friend, that people gave extra money—that is, "tips"—to waiters at restaurants and hotels when they got through eating a meal?

I told her crossly and truthfully that I had never been in a hotel or restaurant in all my life. She threw up her hands, and pronounced me a vast object of pity. She then fully enlightened me as to the exact meaning of the word "tips," and left me to calculate painfully upon a bit of paper the division of two dollars and fifty cents among five people; to wit, stewardesses, cabin boys, waiters, etc.

I didn't tell her that that was the last of my money—that two-fifty. However, I did not expend any thought upon the subject of what was to become of me when I arrived in Jamaica sans a single cent.

We brought our bags and belongings out on deck before the boat docked next day. Every one was crowded against the rails, watching the approaching land.

A crowd seemed to be swarming on the wharves, awaiting our boat. As we came nearer, I was amazed to find that this crowd was made up almost entirely of negroes. We have few negroes in Canada, and I had seen only one in all my life. I remember an older sister had shown him to me in church—he was pure black—and told me he was the "Bogy man," and that he'd probably come around to see me that night. I was six. I never took my eyes once from his face during the service, and I have never forgotten that face.

It was, therefore, with a genuine thrill of excitement and fear that I looked down upon that vast sea of upturned black and brown faces. Never will I forget that first impression of Jamaica. Everywhere I looked were negroes—men and women and children, some half naked, some with bright handkerchiefs knotted about their heads, some gaudily attired, some dressed in immaculate white duck, just like the people on the boat.

People were saying good-by, and many had already gone down the gang-plank. Several women asked me for my address, and said they did not want to lose me. I told them I did not know just where I was going. I expected Mr. Campbell to meet me.

As Mr. Campbell had not come on board, however, and as Captain Hollowell and Mr. Marsden seemed to have forgotten my existence in the great rush of arrival, I, too, at last descended the gang-plank. I found myself one of that miscellaneous throng of colored and white people.

A number of white men and women were hurrying about meeting and welcoming expected passengers, who were soon disposed of in various vehicles. Soon not one of the boat's passengers remained, even my room-mate being one of a party that climbed aboard a bus marked, "The Crystal Springs Hotel."

I was alone on that Jamaica wharf, and no one had come to claim me!

It was getting toward evening, and the sky in the west was as red as blood. I sat down on my bag and waited. Most of the people left on the dock were laborers who were engaged in unloading the ship's cargo. Women with heavy loads on their heads, their hands on their shaking hips, and chattering in a high singsong dialect (I didn't recognize it for English at first!), passed me. Some of them looked at me curiously, and one, a terrifying, pock-marked crone, said something to me that I could not understand.

I saw the sun slipping down in the sky, but it was still as bright and clear as mid-day. Sitting alone on that Jamaica wharf, I scarcely saw the shadows deepening as I looked out across the Caribbean Sea, which shone like a jewel under the fading light. I forgot my surroundings and my anxiety at the failure of my employer to meet me; I felt no fear, just a vague sort of enchantment and interest in this new land I had discovered.

But I started up screaming when I felt a hand on my shoulder, and looking up in the steadily deepening twilight, I saw a smiling face approach my own, and the face was black!

I fled toward the boat, crying out wildly:

"Captain Hollowell! O Captain Hollowell!"

I left my little bag behind me. Fear lent wings to my feet, and I kept crying out to Captain Hollowell as I ran up that gang-plank, mercifully still down. At the end of it was my dear blond purser, and right into his arms unhesitatingly I ran. He kept saying: "Well! well! well!" and he took me to Captain Hollowell, who swore dreadfully when he learned that Mr. Campbell had not met me. Then my purser went to the dock wharf to get my bag, and to "skin the hide off that damned black baboon" who had frightened me.

I ate dinner with Captain Hollowell and the officers of the *Atlas* that night, the last remaining passenger on the boat. After dinner, accompanied by the captain and the purser, I was taken by carriage to the office of *The Lantern*.

I don't know what Captain Hollowell said to Mr. Campbell before I was finally called in, for I had been left in the outer office. Their voices were loud and angry, and I thought they were quarreling. I devoutly hoped it was not over me. I was tired and sleepy. In fact, when Captain Hollowell motioned to me to come in, I remember rubbing my eyes, and he put his arm about me and told me not to cry.

In a dingy office, with papers and books scattered about in the most bewildering disorder, at a long desk-table, likewise piled with books and journals and papers, sat an old man who looked exactly like the pictures of Ibsen.[1] He was sitting all crumpled up, as it were, in a big armchair; but as I came forward he sat up straight. He stared at me so long, and with such an expression of amazement, that I became uneasy and embarrassed. I remember holding on tight to Captain Hollowell's sleeve on one side and Mr. Marsden's on the other. And then at last a single sentence came from the lips of my employer. It came explosively, despairingly:

"My God!" said the owner of *The Lantern.*

It seems that our Quebec friend had been assigned to obtain for *The Lantern* a mature and experienced journalist. Mr. Campbell had expected a woman of the then approved, if feared, type of bluestocking, and behold a baby had been dropped into his lap!

The captain and Marsden had departed. I sat alone with that old man who looked like Ibsen, and who stared at me as if I were some freak of nature. He had his elbows upon his desk, and his chin propped up in the cup of his hands. He began to ask me questions, after he had literally stared me down and out of countenance, and I sat there before him, twisting my handkerchief in my hand.

"How old are you?"

"Seventeen. I mean—I'm going on eighteen." Eighteen was, in fact, eleven months off.

"Have you ever worked before?"

"I've written things."

After a silent moment, during which he glared at me more angrily than ever, he demanded:

"What have you written?"

"Poetry," I said, and stopped because he said again in that lost voice, "My God!"

"What else?"

"I had a story published in *The Star*," I said. "I've got it here, if you'd like to see it."

He made a motion of emphatic dissent.

"What else have you done?"

"I taught myself shorthand," I said, "and I can take dictation as fast as you can talk."

He looked frankly skeptical and in no wise impressed.

"How can you do that if you've had no experience as a stenographer?"

"I got a shorthand book," I said eagerly. "It's not at all hard to teach yourself after you learn the rudiments. My sister showed me that. She's secretary to the Premier of Canada. As soon as I had learned shorthand, I acquired practice and speed by going to church and prayer-meetings and taking down sermons."

After a moment he said grudgingly:

"Not a bad idea." And then added, "What do you think you are going to do here?"

"Write for your paper," I said as conciliatingly as I could.

"What?" he inquired curiously.

"Why—anything—poetry—"

[1] Henrick Ibsen (1828-1906), Norwegian playwright.

He waved his hand in such a dismissing manner that I got up, though it was my poetry, not I, he wished to be rid of just then. I went nearer to him.

"I know you don't want me," I said, "and I don't want to stay. I'm sorry I came. I wouldn't if I had known that this was a hot, beastly old country where nearly everybody is black. If you'll just get me back to the boat, I know Captain Hollowell will let me go back with him, even if I haven't the money for my fare."

"What about the money I paid for you to come here?" he snarled. "Think I'm going to lose that?"

I did not answer him. I felt enervated, homesick, miserable, and tired. He got up presently, limped over to another table,—he was lame,—poured a glass of water, brought it to me with a big fan, and said gruffly, "Sit!"

The act, I don't know why, touched me. In a dim way I began to appreciate his position. He was a lame old man running a fiery, two-sheet little newspaper in this tropical land far from his native Canada. There was no staff, and, indeed, none of the ordinary appurtenances of a newspaper office. He employed only one able assistant, and as he could not get such a person in Jamaica and could not afford to pay a man's salary, being very loyal to Canada, he had been accustomed to send there for bright and expert young women reporters to do virtually all the work of running his newspaper. Newspaper women are not plentiful in Canada. The fare to Jamaica is, or was then, about $55. Mr. Campbell must have turned all these things over in his mind as he looked at this latest product of his native land, a green, green girl of seventeen, whose promise that she would "look older next day," when her "hair was done up," carried little reassurance as to her intelligence or ability.

He did a lot of "cussing" of our common friend in Canada. Finally he said that he would take me over to the Myrtle Bank Hotel, where accommodations had been arranged for me, and we could talk the matter over in the morning.

While he was getting his stick and hat, the latter a green-lined helmet, I couldn't resist looking at some of his books. He caught me doing this, and asked me gruffly if I had ever read anything. I said:

"Yes, Dickens, George Eliot, and Sir Walter Scott;[2] and I've read Huxley and Darwin,[3] and lots of books on astronomy to my father, who is very fond of that subject." As he made no comment, nor seemed at all impressed by my erudition, I added proudly: "My father's an Oxford man, and a descendant of the family of Sir Isaac Newton."

There was some legend to this effect in our family. In fact, the greatness of my father's people had been a sort of fairy-story with us all, and we knew that it was his marriage with mama that had cut him off from his kindred. My Jamaica employer, however, showed no interest in my distinguished ancestry. He took me roughly by the arm, and half leaning upon, half leading me, hobbled with me out into the dark street.

It was about nine o'clock. As we approached the hotel, which was only a short distance from the office of *The Lantern*, it pleased me as a happy omen that somewhere within those fragrant, moonlit gardens a band began to play most beautifully.

---

[2] Charles Dickens (1812-1870), British novelist; George Eliot, pen name of British novelist Mary Ann Evans (1819-1880); Sir Walter Scott (1771-1832), Scottish novelist.

[3] Thomas Henry Huxley (1825-1895), British naturalist; Charles Darwin (1809-1882), British naturalist.

Mr. Campbell took me to the room of the girl whose place I was to take, and who was also from Quebec. She had already gone to bed, but she rose to let me in. Mr. Campbell merely knocked hard on the door and said:

"Here's Miss Ascough. You should have met her," and angrily shoved me in, so it seemed to me.

Miss Foster, her hair screwed up in curl-papers, after looking at me only a moment, said in a tired, complaining voice, like that of a sick person, that I had better get to bed right away; and then she got into bed, and turned her face to the wall. I tried to draw her out a bit while undressing, but to all my questions she returned monosyllabic answers. I put out the light, and crept into bed beside her. The last thing she said to me, and very irritably, was:

"Keep to your own side of the bed."

I slept fairly well, considering the oppressiveness of the heat, but I awoke once when something buzzed against my face.

"What's that?" I cried, sitting up in bed.

She murmured crossly:

"Oh, for heaven's sake lie down! I haven't slept a wink for a century. You'll have to get used to Jamaica bugs and scorpions. They ought to have screens in the windows!"

After that I slept with the sheet over my head.

IV

I was awakened at six the following morning. A strange, singsong voice called into the room:

"Marnin', missee! Heah's your coffee."

I found Miss Foster up and dressed. She was sitting at a table drinking coffee. She put up the shade and let the light in. Then she came over to the bed, where the maid had set the tray. I was looking at what I supposed to be my breakfast. It consisted of a cup of black coffee and a single piece of dry toast.

"You'd better drink your coffee," said Miss Foster, wearily. "It will sustain you for a while."

I got a good look at her, standing by my bed. The yellowness of her skin startled me, and I wondered whether it could be possible that she, too, was "colored." Then I remembered that she was from my home. Moreover, her eyes were a pale blue, and her hair a light, nondescript brown. She had a peevish expression, even now while she made an effort at friendliness. She sat down on the side of my bed, and while I drank my coffee and nibbled my piece of toast she told me a few things about the country.

Jamaica, she said, was the beastliest country on the face of the earth. Though for a few months its climate was tolerable, the rest of the year it was almost unbearable. What with the crushing heat and the dirty, drizzling rain that followed, and fell without ceasing for months at a time, all ambition, all strength, all hope were slowly knocked out of one. There were a score of fevers, each one as bad as the others. She was suffering from one now. That was why she was going home. She was young, so she said, but she felt like an old woman. She pitied me, she declared, for what was before me, and said Campbell had no right to bring healthy young girls from Canada without first telling them what they were coming up against.

I put in here that perhaps I should fare better. I said:

"I'm almost abnormally healthy and strong, you know, even if I look thin. I'm the wiry kind."

She sniffed at that, and then said, with a shrug:

"Oh, well, maybe you will escape. I'm sure I wish you better luck than mine. But one thing's certain: you'll lose that Canadian complexion of yours all right."

My duties, she said, would be explained to me by Mr. Campbell himself, though she was going to stay over a day or two to help break me in. My salary would be ten dollars a week and free board and lodging at the Myrtle Bank Hotel. I told her of the slighting reception I had received at the hands of Mr. Campbell, and she said:

"Oh, well, he's a crank. You couldn't please him, no matter what you did." Then she added: "I don't see, anyhow, why he objected to you. Brains are n't so much needed in a position like this as legs and a constitution of iron."

As the day advanced, the heat encroached. Miss Foster sat fanning herself languidly by the window, looking out with a far-away expression. I told her about my clothes, and how mortified I was to find them so different from those of the others on the boat. She said:

"You can have all my clothes, if you want. They won't do for Canada."

That suggested a brilliant solution of my problem of how I was to secure immediately suitable clothes for Jamaica. I suggested that as she was going to Canada, she could have mine, and I would take hers. The proposition seemed to give her a sort of grim amusement. She looked over my clothes. She took the woolen underwear and heavy, hand-knitted stockings (that Sung-Sung had made for an older brother, and which had descended to me after two sisters had had them!), two woolen skirts, my heavy overcoat, and several other pieces.

She gave me a number of white muslin dresses,—they seemed lovely to me,—an evening gown with a real low neck, cotton underwear, hose, etc.

I put my hair up for the first time that morning. As I curled it a bit, this was not difficult to do. I simply rolled it up at the back and held the chignon in place with four bone hair-pins that she gave me. I put on one of her white muslin dresses but it was so long for me that we had to make a wide tuck in it. Then I wore a wide Leghorn hat, the only trimming of which was a piece of cream-colored mull twisted like a scarf about the crown.

I asked Miss Foster if I looked all right, and was suitably dressed, and she said grudgingly:

"Yes, you'll do. You're quite pretty. You'd better look out."

Asked to explain, she merely shrugged her shoulders and said:

"There's only a handful of white women here, you know. We don't count the tourists. You'll have all you can do to hold the men here at arm's-length."

This last prospect by no means bothered me. I had the most decided and instinctive liking for the opposite sex.

The hotel was beautiful, built somewhat in the Spanish style, with a great inner court, and an arcade that ran under the building. Long verandas ran out like piers on each side of the court, which was part of the wonderful garden that extended to the shores of the Caribbean.

The first thing I saw as we came out from our room upon one of the long pier verandas was an enormous bird. It was sitting on the branch of a fantastic and incredibly tall tree that was all trunk, and then burst into great fan-like foliage at the top. Subsequently I learned that this was a cocoanut tree.

The proprietor of the hotel, who was dark, smiling, and deferential, came up to be introduced to me, and I said, meaning to pay a compliment to his country:

"You have fine-looking birds here."

He looked at me sharply and then snickered, as if he thought I were joking about something.

"That's a scavenger," he said. "There are hundreds, thousands of them here in Jamaica. Glad you like them."

I thought it an ugly name for a bird, but I said:

"It's a very interesting bird, I think."

Miss Foster pulled me along and said sharply that the birds were vultures. They called them scavengers in Jamaica because they really acted as such. Every bit of dirt and filth and refuse, she declared with disgust, was thrown into the streets, and devoured shortly by the scavengers. If a horse or animal died or was killed, it was put into the street. Within a few minutes it had completely disappeared, the scavengers having descended like flies upon its body. She darkly hinted, moreover, that many a human corpse had met a similar fate. I acquired a shuddering horror for that "interesting bird" then and there, I can tell you, and I thought of the unscreened windows, and asked Miss Foster if they ever had been known to touch living things. She shrugged her shoulders, which was not reassuring.

Miss Foster took me into the hotel's great dining-room, which was like a pleasant open conservatory, with great palms and plants everywhere. There we had breakfast, for it seems coffee and toast were just an appetizer. I never became used to Jamaica cooking. It was mushy, hot, and sweet.

After breakfast we reported at *The Lantern,* where Mr. Campbell, looking even fiercer in the day, impatiently awaited us. He wished Miss Foster to take me directly out to Government House and teach me my duties there, as the Legislative Council was then in session. He mumbled off a lot of instructions to Miss Foster, ignoring me completely. His apparent contempt for me, and his evident belief that there was no good to be expected from me, whetted my desire to prove to him that I was not such a fool as I looked, or, rather, as he seemed to think I looked. I listened intently to everything he said to Miss Foster, but even so I received only a confused medley of "Bills—attorney-general—Representative So and So—Hon. Mr. So and So," etc.

I carried away with me, however, one vivid instruction, and that was that it was absolutely necessary for *The Lantern* to have the goodwill of the Hon. Mr. Burbank, whom we must support in everything. It seemed, according to Mr. Campbell, that there was some newspaper libel law that was being pressed in the House that, if passed, would bring the Jamaica press down to a pusillanimous condition.

Mr. Burbank was to fight this bill for the newspapers. He was, in fact, our representative and champion. *The Lantern,* in return, was prepared to support him in other measures that he was fathering. Miss Foster and I were to remember to treat him with more than common attention. I did not know, of course, that this meant in our newspaper references to him, and I made a fervent vow personally to win the favor of said Burbank.

We got into a splendid little equipage, upholstered in tan cloth and with a large tan umbrella top, which was lined with green.

We drove for several miles through a country remarkable for its beautiful scenery. It was a land of color. It was like a land of perpetual spring—a spring that was ever green. I saw not a single shade that was dull. Even the trunks of the gigantic trees seemed to have a warm tone. The flowers were startlingly bright—yellow, scarlet, and purple.

We passed many country people along the road. They moved with a sort of languid, swinging amble, as if they dragged, not lifted, their flat feet. Women carried on their heads enormous bundles and sometimes trays. How they balanced them so firmly was always a mystery to me, especially as most of them either had their hands on their hips, or, more extraordinary, carried or led children, and even ran at times. Asses, loaded on each side with produce, ambled along as draggingly as the natives.

Miss Foster made only three or four remarks during the entire journey. These are her remarks. They are curious taken altogether:

"This carriage belongs to Mr. Burbank. He supplies all the vehicles, by the way, for the press."

"Those are the botanical gardens. Jamaica has Mr. Burbank to thank for their present excellent condition. Remember that."

"We are going by the Burbank plantation now. He has a place in Kingston, too, and a summer home in the mountains."

"If we beat that newspaper libel law, you'll have a chance to write all the funny things and rhymes you want about the mean sneaks who are trying to push it through."

Even during the long drive through the green country I had been insensibly affected by the ever-growing heat. In the long chamber of Government House, where the session was to be held, there seemed not a breath of air stirring. It was insufferably hot, though the place was virtually empty when we arrived. I had a shuddering notion of what it would be like when full.

Miss Foster was hustling about, getting "papers" and "literature" of various kinds, and as the legislators arrived, she chatted with some of them. She had left me to my own devices, and I did not know what to do with myself. I was much embarrassed, as every one who passed into the place took a look at me. We were the only two girls in the House.

There was a long table in the middle of the room, at which the members of Parliament and the elected members had their seats, and there was a smaller table at one side for the press. I had remained by the door, awaiting Miss Foster's instructions. The room was rapidly beginning to fill. A file of black soldiers spread themselves about the room, standing very fine and erect against the walls. At the council table, on one side, were the Parliament members, Englishmen, every one of whom wore the conventional monocle. On the other side were the elected members, who were, without an exception, colored men. I was musing over this when a very large, stout, and handsome personage (he was a personage!) entered ponderously, followed by several younger men. Every one in the room rose, and until he took his seat (in a big chair on a little elevated platform at the end of the room) they remained standing. This was his Excellency Sir Henry Drake, the Governor-General of Jamaica. The House was now in session.

By this time I experienced a natural anxiety to know what was to become of me. Surely I was not supposed to stand there by the door. Glancing across at the press table, I presently saw Miss Foster among the reporters. She was half standing, and beckoning to me to join her. Confused and embarrassed, I passed along at the back of one end of the council table, and was proceeding in the direction of the press table, when suddenly the room reverberated with loud cries from the soldiers of, "Order! order! order!"

I hesitated only a moment, ignorant of the fact that that call was directed against me, and, as I paused, I looked directly into the purpling face of the Governor of Jamaica. He had put on his monocle. His face was long and preternaturally solemn, but there was a queer, twisted smile about his mouth, and I swear that he winked at me through that monocle, which fell into his hand. I proceeded to my seat, red as a beet.

"Great guns!" whispered Miss Foster, dragging me down beside her, "you walked in *front* of the governor! You should have gone behind his chair. What will Mr. Campbell say when he knows you were called to order the first day! A fine reflection on *The Lantern!*" She added the last sentence almost bitterly.

What went on at that session I never in the world could have told. It was all like an incomprehensible dream. Black men, the elected members, rose, and long and eloquently talked in regard to some bill. White men (government) rose and languidly responded, sometimes with a sort of drawling good humor, sometimes satirically. I began to feel the effect of the oppressive atmosphere in a way I had not yet experienced. An unconquerable impulse to lay my head down upon the table and go to sleep seized upon me, and I could scarcely keep my eyes open. At last my head did fall back against the chair; my eyes closed. I did not exactly faint, but I succumbed slightly to the heat. I heard a voice whispering at my ear, for the proceedings went on, as if it were a common thing for a woman to faint in Government House.

"Drink this!" said the voice, and I opened my eyes and looked up into a fair, boyish face that was bending over mine. I drank that cool Jamaica kola, and recovered myself sufficiently to sit up again. Said my new friend:

"It'll be cooler soon. You'll get used to the climate, and if I were you, I wouldn't try to do any work today."

I said:

"I've got to *learn*. Miss Foster sails to-morrow, and after that—"

I'll show you after that," he said, and smiled reassuringly.

At one there was an adjournment for luncheon. I then became the center of interest, and was introduced by Miss Foster to the members of the press. Jamaica boasted three papers beside ours, and there were representatives at the Parliament's sessions from other West Indian islands. I was also introduced to several of the members, both black and white.

I went to luncheon with Miss Foster and two members of Parliament (white) and three reporters, one of them the young man who had given me the kola, and whose name was Verley Marchmont. He was an Englishman, the younger son in a poor, but titled, family. We had luncheon at a little inn hard by, and while there I made three engagements for the week. With one of the men I was to go to a polo match (Jamaica had a native regiment whose officers were English), with another I was to attend a ball in a lighthouse, and young Marchmont, who was only about eighteen, was to call upon me that evening.

At the end of the afternoon session, which was not quite so wearing, as it had grown cooler, I was introduced by Miss Foster to the governor's secretary, Lord George Fitzpatrick, who had been smiling at me from behind the governor's back most of the day. By him I was introduced to the governor, who seemed to regard me as a more or less funny curiosity, if I am to judge from his humorous expression. Lord George also introduced me to other government members, and he asked me if I liked candies. I said I did. He asked me if I played golf or rode horseback. I said I didn't, but I could learn, and he said he was a great teacher.

By this time I thought I had met everyone connected with the House, when suddenly I heard some one—I think it was one of the reporters—call out:

"Oh, all right, Mr. Burbank. I'll see to it."

Miss Foster was drawing me along toward the door. It was time to go. Our carriage was waiting for us. As we were going out, I asked her whether I had yet met Mr. Burbank, and she said she supposed so.

"I don't remember meeting him," I persisted, "and I want very specially to meet Mr. Burbank."

On the steps below us a man somewhat dudishly attired in immaculate white duck, and wearing a green-lined helmet, turned around and looked up at us. His face was almost pure black. His nose was large and somewhat hooked. I have subsequently learned that he was partly Hebrew. He had an enormous mouth, and teeth thickly set with gold. He wore gold-rimmed glasses with a chain, and these and his fine clothes gave a touch of distinction to his appearance. At least it made him stand out from the average colored man. As I spoke, I saw him look at me with a curious expression; then smiling, he held out his big hand.

"I am the Hon. Mr. Burbank," he said.

I was startled to find that this man I had been planning to cultivate was black. I do not know why, but as I looked down into that ingratiating face, I was filled with a sudden panic of almost instinctive fear, and although he held out his hand to me, I did not take it. For that I was severely lectured by Miss Foster all the way back. She reminded me that I could not afford to snub so powerful a Jamaican as Burbank, and that if I had the slightest feeling of race prejudice, I had better either kill it at once or clear out of Jamaica. She said that socially there was absolutely no difference between the white and colored people in Jamaica.

As a matter of fact, I had literally never even heard the expression "race prejudice" before, and I was as far from feeling it as any person in the world. It must be remembered that in Canada we do not encounter the problem of race. One color there is as good as another. Certainly people of Indian extraction are well thought of and esteemed, and my own mother was a foreigner. What should I, a girl who had never before been outside Quebec, and whose experience had been within the narrow confines of home and a small circle, know of race prejudice?

Vaguely I had a feeling that all men were equal as men. I do not believe it was in me to turn from a man merely because of his race, so long as he himself was not personally repugnant to me. I myself was dark and foreign-looking, but the blond type I adored. In all my most fanciful imaginings and dreams I had always been golden-haired and blue-eyed.

—1915

SARAH N. CLEGHORN (1876-1959)

Born in Norfolk, Virginia, Sarah Norcliffe Cleghorn was the daughter of John Dalton, a Scottish immigrant and investment broker, and Sarah Chestnut (Howley) Cleghorn. She met fellow Montessori-education advocate Dorothy Canfield Fisher during their childhood in Vermont; the two would later collaborate on three books: *Hillsboro People* (1915), *Fellow Captains* (1916), and *Nothing Ever Happens and How It Does* (1940). Cleghorn graduated from Radcliffe in 1896, and began publishing in major magazines at the turn of the century. Her publication slowed before the First World War because of her socialist and pacifist politics—she was engaged in many of the reform movements of her time, including anti-lynching, anti-vivisection, anti-child labor, as well as the woman suffrage movement. Her work includes two novels, *A Turnpike Lady* (1907) and *The Spinster* (1916); two collections of essays, *Poems of Peace and Freedom* (1945) and *The Seamless Robe* (1945); an autobiography, *Threescore* (1936); and the collection of poems *Portraits and Protests* (1917), from which these selections are taken.

The Golf Links Lie So Near the Mill

The golf links lie so near the mill
    That almost every day
The laboring children can look out
    And see the men at play.

—1916

Comrade Jesus

Thanks to Saint Matthew,[1] who had been
At mass-meetings in Palestine,
We know whose side was spoken for
When Comrade Jesus had the floor.

"Where sore they toil and hard they lie,   5
Among the great unwashed, dwell I.
The tramp, the convict, I am he:
Cold-shoulder him, cold-shoulder me."

By Dives' door, with thoughtful eye,
He did tomorrow prophesy:—   10
"The Kingdom's gate is low and small:
The rich can scarce wedge through at all."

"A dangerous man," said Caiaphas,
"An ignorant demagogue, alas.
Friend of low women, it is he   15
Slanders the upright Pharisee."

For law and order, it was plain,
For Holy Church, he must be slain.
The troops were there to awe the crowd:
Mob violence was not allowed.   20

---

[1] Most of the references here are to the Gospel of Matthew.

Their clumsy force with force to foil,
His strong, clean hands he would not soil.
He saw their childishness quite plain
Between the lightnings of his pain.

Between the twilights of his end   25
He made his fellow-felon friend.
With swollen tongue and blinded eyes
Invited him to Paradise.

Ah, let no Local[2] him refuse!
Comrade Jesus hath paid his dues.   30
Whatever other be debarred,
Comrade Jesus hath his red card.

—1917

Jane Addams[3]

Physician to the city and the state,
    For their infection-seeking cause and cure;
Of cheated maidenhood the advocate,
    Of childhood robbed, and old age premature;

Judge of the waste and wreckage of her time;   5
    Captain in Freedom's dim bewildered war;
Evangelist of the slow-rising prime
    The long-exploited many weary for;—

Americans! we are not all untrue
    To the high faith our forefathers professed,   10
While our young civic soldiers, not a few,
    Follow this Maid of Orleans[4] of the West.

—1917

---

[2] A chapter of a union.   [4] Joan of Arc.
[3] Jane Addams (1860-1935), social reformer.

SUSAN GLASPELL (1876-1948)

Susan Glaspell, whose keen critiques on capitalism contributed greatly to the American literary landscape during the first half of the twentieth century, was born in Davenport, Iowa. After earning a doctorate at Drake University in nearby Des Moines, she began work as a reporter for the *Des Moines Daily News* and the *Des Moines Capital*. Glaspell published her work regularly in various magazines with primarily female readerships, and she published her first novel, *The Glory of the Conquered*, in 1909. Following a 1910 tour of Europe, Glaspell returned to the U.S. and began a romance with a married writer, George Cram Cook. A few years later, Cook divorced his wife and moved with Glaspell to New York City. They began the seminal theatre group the Provincetown Players, which produced the works of promising new American playwrights, among them, famously, Eugene O'Neill. Glaspell's greatest dramatic success was *Alison's House* (1930), which won the Pulitzer Prize for drama; her other produced plays include *Suppressed Desires* (1915), *Close the Book* (1917), *Bernice* (1919), *Inheritors* (1921), *The Verge* (1921), and *The Comic Artist* (1927). Glaspell published over fifty short stories and nine novels, including *The Visioning* (1911), *Fidelity* (1915), *Brook Evans* (1930), *The Morning Is Near Us* (1939), *Norma Ashe* (1942), and *Judd Rankin's Daughter* (1945). Glaspell died in 1948 in Provincetown.

Trifles

SCENE: *The kitchen in the now abandoned farmhouse of* JOHN WRIGHT, *a gloomy kitchen, and left without having been put in order—unwashed pans under the sink, a loaf of bread outside the bread-box, a dish-towel on the table—other signs of incompleted work. At the rear the outer door opens and the* SHERIFF *comes in followed by the* COUNTY ATTORNEY *and* HALE. *The* SHERIFF *and* HALE *are men in middle life, the* COUNTY ATTORNEY *is a young man; all are much bundled up and go at once to the stove. They are followed by the two women—the* SHERIFF's *wife first; she is a slight wiry woman, a thin nervous face.* MRS HALE *is larger and would ordinarily be called more comfortable looking, but she is disturbed now and looks fearfully about as she enters. The women have come in slowly, and stand close together near the door.*

COUNTY ATTORNEY: [*rubbing his hands*] This feels good. Come up to the fire, ladies.

MRS PETERS: [*after taking a step forward*] I'm not—cold.

SHERIFF: [*Unbuttoning his overcoat and stepping away from the stove as if to mark the beginning of official business*] Now, Mr Hale, before we move things about, you explain to Mr Henderson just what you saw when you came here yesterday morning.

COUNTY ATTORNEY: By the way, has anything been moved? Are things just as you left them yesterday?

SHERIFF: [*looking about*] It's just the same. When it dropped below zero last night I thought I'd better send Frank out this morning to make a fire for us—no use getting pneumonia with a big case on, but I told him not to touch anything except the stove—and you know Frank.

COUNTY ATTORNEY: Somebody should have been left here yesterday.

SHERIFF: Oh—yesterday. When I had to send Frank to Morris Center for that man who went crazy—I want you to know I had my hands full yesterday. I knew you could get back from Omaha by today and as long as I went over everything here myself—

COUNTY ATTORNEY: Well, Mr Hale, tell just what happened when you came here yesterday morning.

HALE: Harry and I had started to town with a load of potatoes. We came along the road from my place and as I got here I said, 'I'm going to see if I can't get John Wright to go in with me on a party telephone.'[1] I spoke to Wright about it once before and he put me off, saying folks talked too much anyway, and all he asked was peace and quiet—I guess you know about how much he talked himself; but I thought maybe if I went to the house and talked about it before his wife, though I said to Harry that I didn't know as what his wife wanted made much difference to John—

COUNTY ATTORNEY: Let's talk about that later, Mr Hale. I do want to talk about that,

---

[1] A single telephone line that is shared among two or more households in the same neighborhood.

but tell now just what happened when you got to the house.

HALE: I didn't hear or see anything; I knocked on the door, and still it was all quiet inside. I knew they must be up, it was past eight o'clock. So I knocked again, and I thought I heard somebody say, 'Come in.' I wasn't sure, I'm not sure yet, but I opened the door—this door [*indicating the door by which the two women are still standing*] and there in that rocker—[*pointing to it*] sat Mrs Wright.

[*They all look at the rocker.*]

COUNTY ATTORNEY: What—was she doing?

HALE: She was rockin' back and forth. She had her apron in her hand and was kind of—pleating it.

COUNTY ATTORNEY: And how did she—look?

HALE: Well, she looked queer.

COUNTY ATTORNEY: How do you mean—queer?

HALE: Well, as if she didn't know what she was going to do next. And kind of done up.

COUNTY ATTORNEY: How did she seem to feel about your coming?

HALE: Why, I don't think she minded—one way or other. She didn't pay much attention. I said, 'How do, Mrs Wright, it's cold, ain't it?' And she said, 'Is it?'—and went on kind of pleating at her apron. Well, I was surprised; she didn't ask me to come up to the stove, or to set down, but just sat there, not even looking at me, so I said, 'I want to see John.' And then she—laughed. I guess you would call it a laugh. I thought of Harry and the team outside, so I said a little sharp: 'Can't I see John?' 'No,' she says, kind o' dull like. 'Ain't he home?' says I. 'Yes,' says she, 'he's home.' 'Then why can't I see him?' I asked her, out of patience. ''Cause he's dead,' says she. '*Dead?*' says I. She just nodded her head, not getting a bit excited, but rockin' back and forth. 'Why—where is he?' says I, not knowing what to say. She just pointed upstairs—like that [*himself pointing to the room above*] I got up, with the idea of going up there. I walked from there to here—then I says, 'Why, what did he die of?' 'He died of a rope round his neck,' says she, and just went on pleatin' at her apron. Well, I went out and called Harry. I thought I might—need help. We went upstairs and there he was lyin'—

COUNTY ATTORNEY: I think I'd rather have you go into that upstairs, where you can point it all out. Just go on now with the rest of the story.

HALE: Well, my first thought was to get that rope off. It looked...[*stops, his face twitches*]...but Harry, he went up to him, and he said, 'No, he's dead all right, and we'd better not touch anything.' So we went back down stairs. She was still sitting that same way. 'Has anybody been notified?' I asked. 'No,' says she, unconcerned. 'Who did this, Mrs Wright?' said Harry. He said it business-like—and she stopped pleatin' of her apron. 'I don't know,' she says. 'You don't *know?*' says Harry. 'No,' says she. 'Weren't you sleepin' in the bed with him?' says Harry. 'Yes,' says she, 'but I was on the inside.' 'Somebody slipped a rope round his neck and strangled him and you didn't wake up?' says Harry. 'I didn't wake up,' she said after him. We must 'a looked as if we didn't see how that could be, for after a minute she said, 'I sleep sound.' Harry was going to ask her more questions but I said maybe we ought to let her tell her story first to the coroner, or the sheriff, so Harry went fast as he could to Rivers' place, where there's a telephone.

COUNTY ATTORNEY: And what did Mrs Wright do when she knew that you had gone for the coroner?

HALE: She moved from that chair to this one over here [*pointing to a small chair in the corner*] and just sat there with her hands held together and looking down. I got a feeling that I ought to make some conversation, so I said I had come in to see if John wanted to put in a telephone, and at that she started to laugh, and then she stopped and looked at me—scared. [*the* COUNTY ATTORNEY, *who has had his notebook out, makes a note*] I dunno, maybe it wasn't scared. I wouldn't like to say it was. Soon Harry got back, and then Dr Lloyd came, and you, Mr Peters, and so I guess that's all I know that you don't.

COUNTY ATTORNEY: [*looking around*] I guess we'll go upstairs first—and then out to the barn and around there. [*to the* SHERIFF] You're convinced that there was nothing important here—nothing that would point to any motive.

SHERIFF: Nothing here but kitchen things.

[*The* COUNTY ATTORNEY, *after again looking around the kitchen, opens the door of a cupboard closet. He gets up on a chair and looks on a shelf. Pulls his hand away, sticky.*]

COUNTY ATTORNEY: Here's a nice mess.

[*The women draw nearer.*]

MRS PETERS: [*to the other woman*] Oh, her fruit; it did freeze. [*to the* LAWYER] She worried about that when it turned so cold. She said the fire'd go out and her jars would break.

SHERIFF: Well, can you beat the women! Held for murder and worryin' about her preserves.

COUNTY ATTORNEY: I guess before we're through she may have something more serious than preserves to worry about.

HALE: Well, women are used to worrying over trifles.

[*The two women move a little closer together.*]

COUNTY ATTORNEY: [*with the gallantry of a young politician*] And yet, for all their worries, what would we do without the ladies? [*the women do not unbend. He goes to the sink, takes a dipperful of water from the pail and pouring it into a basin, washes his hands. Starts to wipe them on the roller-towel, turns it for a cleaner place*] Dirty towels! [*kicks his foot against the pans under the sink*] Not much of a housekeeper, would you say, ladies?

MRS HALE: [*stiffly*] There's a great deal of work to be done on a farm.

COUNTY ATTORNEY: To be sure. And yet [*with a little bow to her*] I know there are some Dickson county farmhouses which do not have such roller towels. [*He gives it a pull to expose its length again.*]

MRS HALE: Those towels get dirty awful quick. Men's hands aren't always as clean as they might be.

COUNTY ATTORNEY: Ah, loyal to your sex, I see. But you and Mrs Wright were neighbors. I suppose you were friends, too.

MRS HALE: [*shaking her head*] I've not seen much of her of late years. I've not been in this house—it's more than a year.

COUNTY ATTORNEY: And why was that? You didn't like her?

MRS HALE: I liked her all well enough. Farmers' wives have their hands full, Mr Henderson. And then—

COUNTY ATTORNEY: Yes—?

MRS HALE: [*looking about*] It never seemed a very cheerful place.

COUNTY ATTORNEY: No—it's not cheerful. I shouldn't say she had the homemaking instinct.

MRS HALE: Well, I don't know as Wright had, either.

COUNTY ATTORNEY: You mean that they didn't get on very well?

MRS HALE: No, I don't mean anything. But I don't think a place'd be any cheerfuller for John Wright's being in it.

COUNTY ATTORNEY: I'd like to talk more of that a little later. I want to get the lay of things upstairs now. [*He goes to the left, where three steps lead to a stair door.*]

SHERIFF: I suppose anything Mrs Peters does'll be all right. She was to take in some clothes for her, you know, and a few little things. We left in such a hurry yesterday.

COUNTY ATTORNEY: Yes, but I would like to see what you take, Mrs Peters, and keep an eye out for anything that might be of use to us.

MRS PETERS: Yes, Mr Henderson.

[*The women listen to the men's steps on the stairs, then look about the kitchen.*]

MRS HALE: I'd hate to have men coming into my kitchen, snooping around and criticising. [*She arranges the pans under sink which the* LAWYER *had shoved out of place.*]

MRS PETERS: Of course it's no more than their duty.

MRS HALE: Duty's all right, but I guess that deputy sheriff that came out to make the fire might have got a little of this on. [*gives the roller towel a pull*] Wish I'd thought of that sooner. Seems mean to talk about her for not having things slicked up when she had to come away in such a hurry.

MRS PETERS: [*who has gone to a small table in the left rear corner of the room, and lifted one end of a towel that covers a pan*] She had bread set. [*Stands still.*]

MRS HALE: [*eyes fixed on a loaf of bread beside the bread-box, which is on a low shelf at the other side of the room. Moves slowly toward it*] She was going to put this in there. [*picks up loaf, then abruptly drops it. In a manner of returning to familiar things*] It's a shame about her fruit. I wonder if it's all gone. [*gets up on the chair and looks*] I think there's some here that's all right, Mrs Peters. Yes—here; [*holding it toward the window*] this is cherries, too. [*looking again*] I declare I believe that's the only one. [*gets down, bottle in her hand. Goes to the sink and wipes it off on the outside*] She'll feel awful bad after all her hard work in the hot weather. I remember the afternoon I put up my cherries last summer. [*She puts the bottle on the big kitchen table, center of the room. With a sigh, is about to sit down in the rocking-chair. Before she is seated realizes what chair it is; with a slow look at it, steps back. The chair which she has touched rocks back and forth.*]

MRS PETERS: Well, I must get those things from the front room closet. [*she goes to the door at the right, but after looking into the other room, steps back*] You coming with me, Mrs Hale? You could help me carry them.

[*They go in the other room; reappear,* MRS PETERS *carrying a dress and skirt,* MRS HALE *following with a pair of shoes.*]

MRS PETERS: My, it's cold in there. [*She puts the clothes on the big table, and hurries to the stove.*]

MRS HALE: [*examining the skirt*] Wright was close. I think maybe that's why she kept so much to herself. She didn't even belong to the Ladies Aid. I suppose she felt she couldn't do her part, and then you don't enjoy things when you feel shabby. She used to wear pretty clothes and be lively, when she was Minnie Foster, one of the town girls singing in the choir. But that—oh, that was thirty years ago. This all you was to take in?

MRS PETERS: She said she wanted an apron. Funny thing to want, for there isn't much to get you dirty in jail, goodness knows. But I suppose just to make her feel more natural. She said they was in the top drawer in this cupboard. Yes, here. And then her little shawl that always hung behind the door. [*opens stair door and looks*] Yes, here it is. [*Quickly shuts door leading upstairs.*]

MRS HALE: [*abruptly moving toward her*] Mrs Peters?

MRS PETERS: Yes, Mrs Hale?

MRS HALE: Do you think she did it?

MRS PETERS: [*in a frightened voice*] Oh, I don't know.

MRS HALE: Well, I don't think she did. Asking for an apron and her little shawl. Worrying about her fruit.

MRS PETERS: [*starts to speak, glances up, where footsteps are heard in the room above. In a low voice*] Mr Peters says it looks bad for her. Mr Henderson is awful sarcastic in a speech and he'll make fun of her sayin' she didn't wake up.

MRS HALE: Well, I guess John Wright didn't wake when they was slipping that rope under his neck.

MRS PETERS: No, it's strange. It must have been done awful crafty and still. They say it was such a—funny way to kill a man, rigging it all up like that.

MRS HALE: That's just what Mr Hale said. There was a gun in the house. He says that's what he can't understand.

MRS PETERS: Mr Henderson said coming out that what was needed for the case was a motive; something to show anger, or—sudden feeling.

MRS HALE: [*who is standing by the table*] Well, I don't see any signs of anger around here. [*she puts her hand on the dish towel which lies on the table, stands looking down at table, one half of which is clean, the other half messy*] It's wiped to here. [*makes a move as if to finish work, then turns and looks at loaf of bread outside the breadbox. Drops towel. In that voice of coming back to familiar things.*] Wonder how they are finding things upstairs. I hope she had it a little more red-up[2] up there. You know, it seems kind of *sneaking*. Locking her up in town and then coming out here and trying to get her own house to turn against her!

MRS PETERS: But Mrs Hale, the law is the law.

MRS HALE: I s'pose 'tis. [*unbuttoning her coat*] Better loosen up your things, Mrs Peters. You won't feel them when you go out.

[MRS PETERS *takes off her fur tippet,[3] goes to hang it on hook at back of room, stands looking at the under part of the small corner table.*]

MRS PETERS: She was piecing a quilt.

[*She brings the large sewing basket and they look at the bright pieces.*]

MRS HALE: It's log cabin pattern. Pretty, isn't it? I wonder if she was goin' to quilt it or just knot it?

[*Footsteps have been heard coming down the stairs. The* SHERIFF *enters followed by* HALE *and the* COUNTY ATTORNEY.]

SHERIFF: They wonder if she was going to quilt it or just knot it!

[*The men laugh, the women look abashed.*]

COUNTY ATTORNEY: [*rubbing his hands over the stove*] Frank's fire didn't do much up there, did it? Well, let's go out to the barn and get that cleared up.

---

[2] Tidied up.　　　　　　[3] A covering for the shoulders.

[*The men go outside.*]

MRS HALE: [*resentfully*] I don't know as there's anything so strange, our takin' up our time with little things while we're waiting for them to get the evidence. [*she sits down at the big table smoothing out a block with decision*] I don't see as it's anything to laugh about.

MRS PETERS: [*apologetically*] Of course they've got awful important things on their minds. [*Pulls up a chair and joins* MRS HALE *at the table.*]

MRS HALE: [*examining another block*] Mrs Peters, look at this one. Here, this is the one she was working on, and look at the sewing! All the rest of it has been so nice and even. And look at this! It's all over the place! Why, it looks as if she didn't know what she was about!

[*After she had said this they look at each other, then start to glance back at the door. After an instant* MRS HALE *has pulled at a knot and ripped the sewing.*]

MRS PETERS: Oh, what are you doing, Mrs Hale?

MRS HALE: [*mildly*] Just pulling out a stitch or two that's not sewed very good. [*threading a needle*] Bad sewing always made me fidgety.

MRS PETERS: [*nervously*] I don't think we ought to touch things.

MRS HALE: I'll just finish up this end. [*suddenly stopping and leaning forward*] Mrs Peters?

MRS PETERS: Yes, Mrs Hale?

MRS HALE: What do you suppose she was so nervous about?

MRS PETERS: Oh—I don't know. I don't know as she was nervous. I sometimes sew awful queer when I'm just tired. [MRS HALE *starts to say something, looks at* MRS PETERS, *then goes on sewing*] Well I must get these things wrapped up. They may be through sooner than we think. [*putting apron and other things together*] I wonder where I can find a piece of paper, and string.

MRS HALE: In that cupboard, maybe.

MRS PETERS: [*looking in cupboard*] Why, here's a bird-cage. [*holds it up*] Did she have a bird, Mrs Hale?

MRS HALE: Why, I don't know whether she did or not—I've not been here for so long. There was a man around last year selling canaries cheap, but I don't know as she took one; maybe she did. She used to sing real pretty herself.

MRS PETERS: [*glancing around*] Seems funny to think of a bird here. But she must have had one, or why would she have a cage? I wonder what happened to it.

MRS HALE: I s'pose maybe the cat got it.

MRS PETERS: No, she didn't have a cat. She's got that feeling some people have about cats—being afraid of them. My cat got in her room and she was real upset and asked me to take it out.

MRS HALE: My sister Bessie was like that. Queer, ain't it?

MRS PETERS: [*examining the cage*] Why, look at this door. It's broke. One hinge is pulled apart.

MRS HALE: [*looking too*] Looks as if someone must have been rough with it.

MRS PETERS: Why, yes. [*She brings the cage forward and puts it on the table.*]

MRS HALE: I wish if they're going to find any evidence they'd be about it. I don't like this place.

MRS PETERS: But I'm awful glad you came with me, Mrs Hale. It would be lonesome for me sitting here alone.

MRS HALE: It would, wouldn't it? [*dropping her sewing*] But I tell you what I do wish,

Mrs Peters. I wish I had come over sometimes when *she* was here. I—[*looking around the room*]—wish I had.

MRS PETERS: But of course you were awful busy, Mrs Hale—your house and your children.

MRS HALE: I could've come. I stayed away because it weren't cheerful—and that's why I ought to have come. I—I've never liked this place. Maybe because it's down in a hollow and you don't see the road. I dunno what it is, but it's a lonesome place and always was. I wish I had come over to see Minnie Foster sometimes. I can see now—[*shakes her head*]

MRS PETERS: Well, you mustn't reproach yourself, Mrs Hale. Somehow we just don't see how it is with other folks until—something comes up.

MRS HALE: Not having children makes less work—but it makes a quiet house, and Wright out to work all day, and no company when he did come in. Did you know John Wright, Mrs Peters?

MRS PETERS: Not to know him; I've seen him in town. They say he was a good man.

MRS HALE: Yes—good; he didn't drink, and kept his word as well as most, I guess, and paid his debts. But he was a hard man, Mrs Peters. Just to pass the time of day with him—[*shivers*] Like a raw wind that gets to the bone. [*pauses, her eye falling on the cage*] I should think she would 'a wanted a bird. But what do you suppose went with it?

MRS PETERS: I don't know, unless it got sick and died.

[*She reaches over and swings the broken door, swings it again, both women watch it.*]

MRS HALE: You weren't raised round here, were you? [MRS PETERS *shakes her head*] You didn't know—her?

MRS PETERS: Not till they brought her yesterday.

MRS HALE: She—come to think of it, she was kind of like a bird herself—real sweet and pretty, but kind of timid and—fluttery. How—she—did—change. [*silence; then as if struck by a happy thought and relieved to get back to everyday things*] Tell you what, Mrs Peters, why don't you take the quilt in with you? It might take up her mind.

MRS PETERS: Why, I think that's a real nice idea, Mrs Hale. There couldn't possibly be any objection to it, could there? Now, just what would I take? I wonder if her patches are in here—and her things.

[*They look in the sewing basket.*]

MRS HALE: Here's some red. I expect this has got sewing things in it. [*brings out a fancy box*] What a pretty box. Looks like something somebody would give you. Maybe her scissors are in here. [*Opens box. Suddenly puts her hand to her nose*] Why—[MRS PETERS *bends nearer, then turns her face away*] There's something wrapped up in this piece of silk.

MRS PETERS: Why, this isn't her scissors.

MRS HALE: [*lifting the silk*] Oh, Mrs Peters—it's—

[MRS PETERS *bends closer.*]

MRS PETERS: It's the bird.

MRS HALE: [*jumping up*] But, Mrs Peters—look at it! It's neck! Look at its neck! It's all—other side *to*.

MRS PETERS: Somebody—wrung—its—neck.

[*Their eyes meet. A look of growing comprehension, of horror. Steps are heard outside.* MRS HALE *slips box under quilt pieces, and sinks into her chair. Enter* SHERIFF *and* COUNTY ATTORNEY. MRS PETERS *rises.*]

COUNTY ATTORNEY: [*as one turning from serious things to little pleasantries*] Well ladies, have you decided whether she was going to quilt it or knot it?

MRS PETERS: We think she was going to—knot it.

COUNTY ATTORNEY: Well, that's interesting, I'm sure. [*seeing the birdcage*] Has the bird flown?

MRS PETERS: [*putting more quilt pieces over the box*] We think the—cat got it.

COUNTY ATTORNEY: [*preoccupied*] Is there a cat?

[MRS HALE *glances in a quick covert way at* MRS PETERS.]

MRS PETERS: Well, not *now*. They're superstitious, you know. They leave.

COUNTY ATTORNEY: [*to* SHERIFF PETERS, *continuing an interrupted conversation*] No sign at all of anyone having come from the outside. Their own rope. Now let's go up again and go over it piece by piece. [*they start upstairs*] It would have to have been someone who knew just the—

[MRS PETERS *sits down. The two women sit there not looking at one another, but as if peering into something and at the same time holding back. When they talk now it is in the manner of feeling their way over strange ground, as if afraid of what they are saying, but as if they can not help saying it.*]

MRS HALE: She liked the bird. She was going to bury it in that pretty box.

MRS PETERS: [*in a whisper*] When I was a girl—my kitten—there was a boy took a hatchet, and before my eyes—and before I could get there—[*covers her face an instant*] If they hadn't held me back I would have—[*catches herself, looks upstairs where steps are heard, falters weakly*]—hurt him.

MRS HALE: [*with a slow look around her*] I wonder how it would seem never to have had any children around. [*pause*] No, Wright wouldn't like the bird—a thing that sang. She used to sing. He killed that, too.

MRS PETERS: [*moving uneasily*] We don't know who killed the bird.

MRS HALE: I knew John Wright.

MRS PETERS: It was an awful thing was done in this house that night, Mrs Hale. Killing a man while he slept, slipping a rope around his neck that choked the life out of him.

MRS HALE: His neck. Choked the life out of him. [*Her hand goes out and rests on the bird-cage.*]

MRS PETERS: [*with rising voice*] We don't know who killed him. We don't know.

MRS HALE: [*her own feeling not interrupted*] If there'd been years and years of nothing, then a bird to sing to you, it would be awful—still, after the bird was still.

MRS PETERS: [*something within her speaking*] I know what stillness is. When we homesteaded in Dakota, and my first baby died—after he was two years old, and me with no other then—

MRS HALE: [*moving*] How soon do you suppose they'll be through, looking for the evidence?

MRS PETERS: I know what stillness is. [*pulling herself back*] The law has got to punish crime, Mrs Hale.

MRS HALE: [*not as if answering that*] I wish you'd seen Minnie Foster when she wore a white dress with blue ribbons and stood up there in the choir and sang. [*a look around the room*] Oh, I *wish* I'd come over here once in a while! That was a crime! That was a crime! Who's going to punish that?

MRS PETERS: [*looking upstairs*] We mustn't—take on.

MRS HALE: I might have known she needed help! I know how things can be—for women. I tell you, it's queer, Mrs Peters. We live close together and we live far apart. We all go through the same things—it's all just a different kind of the same thing. [*brushes her eyes, noticing the bottle of fruit, reaches out for it*] If I was you, I wouldn't tell her her fruit was gone. Tell her it *ain't*. Tell her it's all right. Take this in to prove it to her. She—she may never know whether it was broke or not.

MRS PETERS: [*takes the bottle, looks about for something to wrap it in; takes petticoat from the clothes brought from the other room, very nervously begins winding this around the bottle. In a false voice*] My, it's a good thing the men couldn't hear us. Wouldn't they just laugh! Getting all stirred up over a little thing like a—dead canary. As if that could have anything to do with—with—wouldn't they *laugh!*

[*The men are heard coming down stairs.*]

MRS HALE: [*under her breath*] Maybe they would—maybe they wouldn't.

COUNTY ATTORNEY: No, Peters, it's all perfectly clear except a reason for doing it. But you know juries when it comes to women. If there was some definite thing. Something to show—something to make a story about—a thing that would connect up with this strange way of doing it— [*The women's eyes meet for an instant. Enter* HALE *from outer door.*]

HALE: Well, I've got the team around. Pretty cold out there.

COUNTY ATTORNEY: I'm going to stay here a while by myself. [*to the* SHERIFF] You can send Frank out for me, can't you? I want to go over everything. I'm not satisfied that we can't do better.

SHERIFF: Do you want to see what Mrs Peters is going to take in? [*The* LAWYER *goes to the table, picks up the apron, laughs.*]

COUNTY ATTORNEY: Oh, I guess they're not very dangerous things the ladies have picked out. [*Moves a few things about, disturbing the quilt pieces which cover the box. Steps back.*] No, Mrs Peters doesn't need supervising. For that matter, a sheriff's wife is married to the law. Ever think of it that way, Mrs Peters?

MRS PETERS: Not—just that way.

SHERIFF: [*chuckling*] Married to the law. [*moves toward the other room*] I just want you to come in here a minute, George. We ought to take a look at these windows.

COUNTY ATTORNEY: [*scoffingly*] Oh, windows!

SHERIFF: We'll be right out, Mr Hale.

[HALE *goes outside. The* SHERIFF *follows the county attorney into the other room. Then* MRS HALE *rises, hands tight together, looking intensely at* MRS PETERS, *whose eyes make a slow turn, finally meeting* MRS HALE's. *A moment* MRS HALE *holds her, then her own eyes point the way to where the box is concealed. Suddenly* MRS PETERS *throws back quilt pieces and tries to put the box in the bag she is wearing. It is too big. She opens box, starts to take bird out, cannot touch it, goes to pieces, stands there helpless. Sound of a knob turning in the other room.* MRS HALE *snatches the box and puts it in the pocket of her big coat. Enter* COUNTY ATTORNEY *and* SHERIFF.]

COUNTY ATTORNEY: [*facetiously*] Well, Henry, at least we found out that she was not going to quilt it. She was going to—what is it you call it, ladies?

MRS HALE: [*her hand against her pocket*] We call it—knot it, Mr Henderson.

CURTAIN

—1916

ZITKALA-SÁ (GERTRUDE SIMMONS BONIN) (1876-1938)

Gertrude Simmons was born February 22, 1876, on the Yankton Sioux Reservation in South Dakota. Her mother was a Yankton Nakota Sioux and her father was white. As a child, she pursued her education by attending (against her mother's wishes) White's Manual Labor School, a Quaker missionary school in Wabash, Indiana. After leaving Earlham College in Richmond, Indiana, in 1897, Simmons accepted a teaching position at the Carlisle Indian Industrial School in Carlisle, Pennsylvania. She was disturbed by the rigid, militaristic approach to education there, and decided to quit her job. She briefly studied music at the Boston Conservatory of Music in 1899, but returned home to be near her family in 1901. Her first autobiographical essays and stories were published in 1900, appearing in *Harper's* and *Atlantic Monthly* under the Nakota name she chose for herself, Zitkala-Sá (Red Bird). Many of these writings were later published in book form, along with some new material, as *American Indian Stories* (1921). Her first book, *Old Indian Legends* (1901), was a collection of traditional Nakota stories. In 1902, she married Raymond Talestase Bonin, a Nakota, who worked for the Indian Service. Shortly thereafter, they moved to the Uintah and Ouray Reservation in Utah, where she worked as a clerk and as a teacher. During this time she became active in the Society of American Indians (SAI), an important pan-Indian organization that sought to address issues affecting all tribes. After she was elected secretary of the SAI, she and her husband moved to Washington, D.C., where she continued to be active on behalf of Native rights for the rest of her life. She lectured across the country and worked with multiple organizations, particularly in lobbying for Indian citizenship, a goal which came to fruition with the passage of the Indian Citizenship Act in 1924. She died in 1938, and was buried in Arlington National Cemetery.

The School Days of an Indian Girl

I.

The Land of Red Apples

There were eight in our party of bronzed children who were going East with the missionaries. Among us were three young braves, two tall girls, and we three little ones, Judéwin, Thowin, and I.

We had been very impatient to start on our journey to the Red Apple Country, which, we were told, lay a little beyond the great circular horizon of the Western prairie. Under a sky of rosy apples we dreamt of roaming as freely and happily as we had chased the cloud shadows on the Dakota plains. We had anticipated much pleasure from a ride on the iron horse, but the throngs of staring palefaces disturbed and troubled us.

On the train, fair women, with tottering babies on each arm, stopped their haste and scrutinized the children of absent mothers. Large men, with heavy bundles in their hands, halted near by, and riveted their glassy blue eyes upon us.

I sank deep into the corner of my seat, for I resented being watched. Directly in front of me, children who were no larger than I hung themselves upon the backs of their seats, with their bold white faces toward me. Sometimes they took their forefingers out of their mouths and pointed at my moccasined feet. Their mothers, instead of reproving such rude curiosity, looked closely at me, and attracted their children's further notice to my blanket. This embarrassed me, and kept me constantly on the verge of tears.

I sat perfectly still, with my eyes downcast, daring only now and then to shoot long glances around me. Chancing to turn to the window at my side, I was quite breathless upon seeing one familiar object. It was the telegraph pole which strode by at short paces. Very near my mother's dwelling, along the edge of a road thickly bordered with wild sunflowers, some poles like these had been planted by white men. Often I had stopped, on my way down the road, to hold my ear against the pole, and, hearing its low moaning, I used to wonder what the paleface had done to hurt it. Now I sat watching for each pole that glided by to be the last one.

In this way I had forgotten my uncomfortable surroundings, when I heard one of my comrades call out my name. I saw the missionary standing very near, tossing candies and gums into our midst. This amused us all, and we tried to see who could catch the most of the sweetmeats.

Though we rode several days inside of the iron horse, I do not recall a single thing about our luncheons.

It was night when we reached the school grounds. The lights from the windows of the large buildings fell upon some of the icicled trees that stood beneath them. We were led toward an open door, where the brightness of the lights within flooded out over the heads of the excited palefaces who blocked our way. My body trembled more from fear than from the snow I trod upon.

Entering the house, I stood close against the wall. The strong glaring light in the large whitewashed room dazzled my eyes. The noisy hurrying of hard shoes upon a bare wooden floor increased the whirring in my ears. My only safety seemed to be in keeping next to the wall. As I was wondering in which direction to escape from all this confusion, two warm hands grasped me firmly, and in the same moment I was tossed high in midair. A rosy-cheeked paleface woman caught me in her arms. I was both frightened and insulted by such trifling. I stared into her eyes, wishing her to let me stand on my own feet, but she jumped me up and down with increasing enthusiasm. My mother had never made a plaything of her wee daughter. Remembering this I began to cry aloud.

They misunderstood the cause of my tears, and placed me at a white table loaded with food. There our party were united again. As I did not hush my crying, one of the older ones whispered to me, "Wait until you are alone in the night."

It was very little I could swallow besides my sobs, that evening.

"Oh, I want my mother and my brother Dawée! I want to go to my aunt!" I pleaded; but the ears of the palefaces could not hear me.

From the table we were taken along an upward incline of wooden boxes, which I learned afterward to call a stairway. At the top was a quiet hall, dimly lighted. Many narrow beds were in one straight line down the entire length of the wall. In them lay sleeping brown faces, which peeped just out of the coverings. I was tucked into bed with one of the tall girls, because she talked to me in my mother tongue and seemed to soothe me.

I had arrived in the wonderful land of rosy skies, but I was not happy, as I had thought I should be. My long travel and the bewildering sights had exhausted me. I fell asleep, heaving deep, tired sobs. My tears were left to dry themselves in streaks, because neither my aunt nor my mother was near to wipe them away.

II.
The Cutting of My Long Hair

The first day in the land of apples was a bitter-cold one; for the snow still covered the ground, and trees were bare. A large bell rang for breakfast, its loud metallic voice crashing through the belfry overhead and into our sensitive ears. The annoying clatter of shoes on bare floors gave us no peace. The constant clash of harsh noises, with an undercurrent of many voices murmuring an unknown tongue, made a bedlam within which I was securely tied. And though my spirit tore itself in struggling for its lost freedom, all was useless.

A paleface woman, with white hair, came up after us. We were placed in a line of girls who were marching into the dining room. These were Indian girls, in stiff shoes and closely clinging dresses. The small girls wore sleeved aprons and shingled hair. As I walked noiselessly in my soft moccasins, I felt like sinking to the floor, for my blanket had been stripped from my shoulders. I looked hard at the Indian girls, who seemed not to care that they were even more immodestly dressed than I, in their tightly fitting clothes. While we marched in, the boys entered at an opposite door. I watched for the three young braves who came in our party. I spied them in the rear ranks, looking as uncomfortable as I felt.

A small bell was tapped, and each of the pupils drew a chair from under the table. Supposing this act meant they were to be seated, I pulled out mine and at once slipped into it from one side. But when I turned my head, I saw that I was the only one seated, and all the rest at our table remained standing. Just as I began to rise, looking shyly around to see how chairs were to be used, a second bell was sounded. All were seated at last, and I had to crawl back into my chair again. I heard a man's voice at one end of the hall, and I looked around to see him. But all the others hung their heads over their plates. As I glanced at the long chain of tables, I caught the eyes of a paleface woman upon me. Immediately I dropped my eyes, wondering why I was so keenly watched by the strange woman. The man ceased his mutterings, and then a third bell was tapped. Every one picked up his knife and fork and began eating. I began crying instead, for by this time I was afraid to venture anything more.

But this eating by formula was not the hardest trial in that first day. Late in the morning, my friend Judéwin gave me a terrible warning. Judéwin knew a few words of English; and she had overheard the paleface woman talk about cutting our long, heavy hair. Our mothers had taught us that only unskilled warriors who were captured had their hair shingled by the enemy. Among our people, short hair was worn by mourners, and shingled hair by cowards!

We discussed our fate some moments, and when Judéwin said, "We have to submit, because they are strong," I rebelled.

"No, I will not submit! I will struggle first!" I answered.

I watched my chance, and when no one noticed I disappeared. I crept up the stairs as quietly as I could in my squeaking shoes,—my moccasins had been exchanged for shoes. Along the hall I passed, without knowing whither I was going. Turning aside to an open door, I found a large room with three white beds in it. The windows were covered with dark green curtains, which made the room very dim. Thankful that no one was there, I directed my steps toward the corner farthest from the door. On my hands and knees I crawled under the bed, and cuddled myself in the dark corner.

From my hiding place I peered out, shuddering with fear whenever I heard footsteps near by. Though in the hall loud voices were calling my name, and I knew that even Judéwin was searching for me, I did not open my mouth to answer. Then the steps were quickened and the voices became excited. The sounds came nearer and nearer. Women and girls entered the room. I held my breath and watched them open closet doors and peep behind large trunks. Some one threw up the curtains, and the room was filled with sudden light. What caused them to stoop and look under the bed I do not know. I remember being dragged out, though I resisted by kicking and scratching wildly. In spite of myself, I was carried downstairs and tied fast in a chair.

I cried aloud, shaking my head all the while until I felt the cold blades of the scissors against my neck, and heard them gnaw off one of my thick braids. Then I lost my spirit. Since the day I was taken from my mother I had suffered extreme indignities. People had stared at me. I had been tossed about in the air like a wooden puppet. And now my long hair was shingled like a coward's! In my anguish I moaned for my mother, but no one came to comfort me. Not a soul reasoned quietly with me, as my own mother used to do; for now I was only one of many little animals driven by a herder.

III.
The Snow Episode

A short time after our arrival we three Dakotas were playing in the snowdrift. We were all still deaf to the English language, excepting Judéwin, who always heard such puzzling things. One morning we learned through her ears that we were forbidden to fall lengthwise in the snow, as we had been doing, to see our own impressions. However, before many hours we had forgotten the order, and were having great sport in the snow, when a shrill voice called us. Looking up, we saw an imperative hand beckoning us into the house. We shook the snow off ourselves, and started toward the woman as slowly as we dared.

Judéwin said: "Now the paleface is angry with us. She is going to punish us for falling into the snow. If she looks straight into your eyes and talks loudly, you must wait until she stops. Then, after a tiny pause, say, 'No.'" The rest of the way we practiced upon the little word "no."

As it happened, Thowin was summoned to judgment first. The door shut behind her with a click.

Judéwin and I stood silently listening at the keyhole. The paleface woman talked in very severe tones. Her words fell from her lips like crackling embers, and her inflection ran up like the small end of a switch. I understood her voice better than the things she was saying. I was certain we had made her very impatient with us. Judéwin heard enough of the words to realize all too late that she had taught us the wrong reply.

"Oh, poor Thowin!" she gasped, as she put both hands over her ears.

Just then I heard Thowin's tremulous answer, "No."

With an angry exclamation, the woman gave her a hard spanking. Then she stopped to say something. Judéwin said it was this: "Are you going to obey my word the next time?"

Thowin answered again with the only word at her command, "No."

This time the woman meant her blows to smart, for the poor frightened girl shrieked at the top of her voice. In the midst of the whipping the blows ceased abruptly, and the woman asked another question: "Are you going to fall in the snow again?"

Thowin gave her bad password another trial. We heard her say feebly, "No! No!"

With this the woman hid away her half-worn slipper, and led the child out, stroking her black shorn head. Perhaps it occurred to her that brute force is not the solution for such a problem. She did nothing to Judéwin nor to me. She only returned to us our unhappy comrade, and left us alone in the room.

During the first two or three seasons misunderstandings as ridiculous as this one of the snow episode frequently took place, bringing unjustifiable frights and punishments into our little lives.

Within a year I was able to express myself somewhat in broken English. As soon as I comprehended a part of what was said and done, a mischievous spirit of revenge possessed me. One day I was called in from my play for some misconduct. I had disregarded a rule which seemed to me very needlessly binding. I was sent into the kitchen to mash the turnips for dinner. It was noon, and steaming dishes were hastily carried into the dining-room. I hated turnips, and their odor which came from the brown jar was offensive to me. With fire in my heart, I took the wooden tool that the paleface woman held out to me. I stood upon a step, and, grasping the handle with both hands, I bent in hot rage over the turnips. I worked my vengeance upon them. All were so busily occupied that no one noticed me. I saw that the turnips were in a pulp, and that further beating could not improve them; but the order was, "Mash these turnips," and mash them I would! I renewed my energy; and as I sent the masher into the bottom of the jar, I felt a satisfying sensation that the weight of my body had gone into it.

Just here a paleface woman came up to my table. As she looked into the jar, she shoved my hands roughly aside. I stood fearless and angry. She placed her red hands upon the rim of the jar. Then she gave one lift and stride away from the table. But lo! the pulpy contents fell through the crumbled bottom to the floor! She spared me no scolding phrases that I had earned. I did not heed them. I felt triumphant in my revenge, though deep within me I was a wee bit sorry to have broken the jar.

As I sat eating my dinner, and saw that no turnips were served, I whooped in my heart for having once asserted the rebellion within me.

IV.
The Devil

Among the legends the old warriors used to tell me were many stories of evil spirits. But I was taught to fear them no more than those who stalked about in material guise. I never knew there was an insolent chieftain among the bad spirits, who dared to array his forces against the Great Spirit, until I heard this white man's legend from a paleface woman.

Out of a large book she showed me a picture of the white man's devil. I looked in horror upon the strong claws that grew out of his fur-covered fingers. His feet were like his hands. Trailing at his heels was a scaly tail tipped with a serpent's open jaws. His face was a patchwork: he had bearded cheeks, like some I had seen palefaces wear; his nose was an eagle's bill, and his sharp-pointed ears were pricked up like those of a sly fox. Above them a pair of cow's horns curved upward. I trembled with awe, and my heart throbbed in my throat, as I looked at the king of evil spirits. Then I heard the paleface woman say that this terrible creature roamed loose in the world, and that little girls who disobeyed school regulations were to be tortured by him.

That night I dreamt about this evil divinity. Once again I seemed to be in my mother's cottage. An Indian woman had come to visit my mother. On opposite sides of the kitchen stove, which stood in the center of the small house, my mother and her guest were seated in straight-backed chairs. I played with a train of empty spools hitched together on a string. It was night, and the wick burned feebly. Suddenly I heard some one turn our door-knob from without.

My mother and the woman hushed their talk, and both looked toward the door. It opened gradually. I waited behind the stove. The hinges squeaked as the door was slowly, very slowly pushed inward.

Then in rushed the devil! He was tall! He looked exactly like the picture I had seen of him in the white man's papers. He did not speak to my mother, because he did not know the Indian language, but his glittering yellow eyes were fastened upon me. He took long strides around the stove, passing behind the woman's chair. I threw down my spools, and ran to my mother. He did not fear her, but followed closely after me. Then I ran round and round the stove, crying aloud for help. But my mother and the woman seemed not to know my danger. They sat still, looking quietly upon the devil's chase after me. At last I grew dizzy. My head revolved as on a hidden pivot. My knees became numb, and doubled under my weight like a pair of knife blades without a spring. Beside my mother's chair I fell in a heap. Just as the devil stooped over me with outstretched claws my mother awoke from her quiet indifference, and lifted me on her lap. Whereupon the devil vanished, and I was awake.

On the following morning I took my revenge upon the devil. Stealing into the room where a wall of shelves was filled with books, I drew forth The Stories of the Bible. With a broken slate pencil I carried in my apron pocket, I began by scratching out his wicked eyes. A few moments later, when I was ready to leave the room, there was a ragged hole in the page where the picture of the devil had once been.

V.

Iron Routine

A loud-clamoring bell awakened us at half-past six in the cold winter mornings. From happy dreams of Western rolling lands and unlassoed freedom we tumbled out upon chilly bare floors back again into a paleface day. We had short time to jump into our shoes and clothes, and wet our eyes with icy water, before a small hand bell was vigorously rung for roll call.

There were too many drowsy children and too numerous orders for the day to waste a moment in any apology to nature for giving her children such a shock in the early morning. We rushed downstairs, bounding over two high steps at a time, to land in the assembly room.

A paleface woman, with a yellow-covered roll book open on her arm and a gnawed pencil in her hand, appeared at the door. Her small, tired face was coldly lighted with a pair of large gray eyes.

She stood still in a halo of authority, while over the rim of her spectacles her eyes pried nervously about the room. Having glanced at her long list of names and called out the first one, she tossed up her chin and peered through the crystals of her spectacles to make sure of the answer "Here."

Relentlessly her pencil black-marked our daily records if we were not present to respond to our names, and no chum of ours had done it successfully for us. No matter if a dull headache or the painful cough of slow consumption had delayed the absentee, there was only time enough to mark the tardiness. It was next to impossible to leave the iron routine after the civilizing machine had once begun its day's buzzing; and as it was inbred in me to suffer in silence rather than to appeal to the ears of one whose open eyes could not see my pain, I have many times trudged in the day's harness heavy-footed, like a dumb sick brute.

Once I lost a dear classmate. I remember well how she used to mope along at my side, until one morning she could not raise her head from her pillow. At her deathbed I stood weeping, as the paleface woman sat near her moistening the dry lips. Among the folds of the bedclothes I saw the open pages of the white man's Bible. The dying Indian girl talked disconnectedly of Jesus the Christ and the paleface who was cooling her swollen hands and feet.

I grew bitter, and censured the woman for cruel neglect of our physical ills. I despised the pencils that moved automatically, and the one teaspoon which dealt out, from a large bottle, healing to a row of variously ailing Indian children. I blamed the hard-working, well-meaning, ignorant woman who was inculcating in our hearts her superstitious ideas. Though I was sullen in all my little troubles, as soon as I felt better I was ready again to smile upon the cruel woman. Within a week I was again actively testing the chains which tightly bound my individuality like a mummy for burial.

The melancholy of those black days has left so long a shadow that it darkens the path of years that have since gone by. These sad memories rise above those of smoothly grinding school days. Perhaps my Indian nature is the moaning wind which stirs them now for their present record. But, however tempestuous this is within me, it comes out as the low voice of a curiously colored seashell, which is only for those ears that are bent with compassion to hear it.

VI.
Four Strange Summers

After my first three years of school, I roamed again in the Western country through four strange summers.

During this time I seemed to hang in the heart of chaos, beyond the touch or voice of human aid. My brother, being almost ten years my senior, did not quite understand my feelings. My mother had never gone inside of a schoolhouse, and so she was not capable of comforting her daughter who could read and write. Even nature seemed to have no place for me. I was neither a wee girl nor a tall one; neither a wild Indian nor a tame one. This deplorable situation was the effect of my brief course in the East, and the unsatisfactory "teenth" in a girl's years.

It was under these trying conditions that, one bright afternoon, as I sat restless and unhappy in my mother's cabin, I caught the sound of the spirited step of my brother's pony on the road which passed by our dwelling. Soon I heard the wheels of a light buckboard, and Dawée's familiar "Ho!" to his pony. He alighted upon the bare ground in front of our house. Tying his pony to one of the projecting corner logs of the low-roofed cottage, he stepped upon the wooden doorstep.

I met him there with a hurried greeting, and, as I passed by, he looked a quiet

"What?" into my eyes.

When he began talking with my mother, I slipped the rope from the pony's bridle. Seizing the reins and bracing my feet against the dashboard, I wheeled around in an instant. The pony was ever ready to try his speed. Looking backward, I saw Dawée waving his hand to me. I turned with the curve in the road and disappeared. I followed the winding road which crawled upward between the bases of little hillocks. Deep water-worn ditches ran parallel on either side. A strong wind blew against my cheeks and fluttered my sleeves. The pony reached the top of the highest hill, and began an even race on the level lands. There was nothing moving within that great circular horizon of the Dakota prairies save the tall grasses, over which the wind blew and rolled off in long, shadowy waves.

Within this vast wigwam of blue and green I rode reckless and insignificant. It satisfied my small consciousness to see the white foam fly from the pony's mouth.

Suddenly, out of the earth a coyote came forth at a swinging trot that was taking the cunning thief toward the hills and the village beyond. Upon the moment's impulse, I gave him a long chase and a wholesome fright. As I turned away to go back to the village, the wolf sank down upon his haunches for rest, for it was a hot summer day; and as I drove slowly homeward, I saw his sharp nose still pointed at me, until I vanished below the margin of the hilltops.

In a little while I came in sight of my mother's house. Dawée stood in the yard, laughing at an old warrior who was pointing his forefinger, and again waving his whole hand, toward the hills. With his blanket drawn over one shoulder, he talked and motioned excitedly. Dawée turned the old man by the shoulder and pointed me out to him.

"Oh, han!" (Oh, yes) the warrior muttered, and went his way. He had climbed the top of his favorite barren hill to survey the surrounding prairies, when he spied my chase after the coyote. His keen eyes recognized the pony and driver. At once uneasy for my safety, he had come running to my mother's cabin to give her warning. I did not appreciate his kindly interest, for there was an unrest gnawing at my heart.

As soon as he went away, I asked Dawée about something else.

"No, my baby sister, I cannot take you with me to the party tonight," he replied. Though I was not far from fifteen, and I felt that before long I should enjoy all the privileges of my tall cousin, Dawée persisted in calling me his baby sister.

That moonlight night, I cried in my mother's presence when I heard the jolly young people pass by our cottage. They were no more young braves in blankets and eagle plumes, nor Indian maids with prettily painted cheeks. They had gone three years to school in the East, and had become civilized. The young men wore the white man's coat and trousers, with bright neckties. The girls wore tight muslin dresses, with ribbons at neck and waist. At these gatherings they talked English. I could speak English almost as well as my brother, but I was not properly dressed to be taken along. I had no hat, no ribbons, and no close-fitting gown. Since my return from school I had thrown away my shoes, and wore again the soft moccasins.

While Dawée was busily preparing to go I controlled my tears. But when I heard him bounding away on his pony, I buried my face in my arms and cried hot tears.

My mother was troubled by my unhappiness. Coming to my side, she offered me the only printed matter we had in our home. It was an Indian Bible, given her some years ago by a missionary. She tried to console me. "Here, my child, are the white man's papers. Read a little from them," she said most piously.

I took it from her hand, for her sake; but my enraged spirit felt more like burning the book, which afforded me no help, and was a perfect delusion to my mother. I did not read it, but laid it unopened on the floor, where I sat on my feet. The dim yellow light of the braided muslin burning in a small vessel of oil flickered and sizzled in the awful silent storm which followed my rejection of the Bible.

Now my wrath against the fates consumed my tears before they reached my eyes. I sat stony, with a bowed head. My mother threw a shawl over her head and shoulders, and stepped out into the night.

After an uncertain solitude, I was suddenly aroused by a loud cry piercing the night. It was my mother's voice wailing among the barren hills which held the bones of buried warriors. She called aloud for her brother's spirits to support her in her helpless misery. My fingers grey icy cold, as I realized that my unrestrained tears had betrayed my suffering to her, and she was grieving for me.

Before she returned, though I knew she was on her way, for she had ceased her weeping, I extinguished the light, and leaned my head on the window sill.

Many schemes of running away from my surroundings hovered about in my mind. A few more moons of such a turmoil drove me away to the eastern school. I rode on the white man's iron steed, thinking it would bring me back to my mother in a few winters, when I should be grown tall, and there would be congenial friends awaiting me.

VII.
Incurring My Mother's Displeasure

In the second journey to the East I had not come without some precautions. I had a secret interview with one of our best medicine men, and when I left his wigwam I carried securely in my sleeve a tiny bunch of magic roots. This possession assured me of friends wherever I should go. So absolutely did I believe in its charms that I wore it through all the school routine for more than a year. Then, before I lost my faith in the dead roots, I lost the little buckskin bag containing all my good luck.

At the close of this second term of three years I was the proud owner of my first diploma. The following autumn I ventured upon a college career against my mother's will.

I had written for her approval, but in her reply I found no encouragement. She called my notice to her neighbor's children, who had completed their education in three years. They had returned to their homes, and were then talking English with the frontier settlers. Her few words hinted that I had better give up my slow attempt to learn the white man's ways, and be content to roam over the prairies and find my living upon wild roots. I silenced her by deliberate disobedience.

Thus, homeless and heavy-hearted, I began anew my life among strangers.

As I hid myself in my little room in the college dormitory, away from the scornful and yet curious eyes of the students, I pined for sympathy. Often I wept in secret, wishing I had gone West, to be nourished by my mother's love, instead of remaining among a cold race whose hearts were frozen hard with prejudice.

During the fall and winter seasons I scarcely had a real friend, though by that time several of my classmates were courteous to me at a safe distance.

My mother had not yet forgiven my rudeness to her, and I had no moment for letter-writing. By daylight and lamplight, I spun with reeds and thistles, until my hands were tired from their weaving, the magic design which promised me the white man's respect.

At length, in the spring term, I entered an oratorical contest among the various classes. As the day of competition approached, it did not seem possible that the event was so near at hand, but it came. In the chapel the classes assembled together, with their invited guests. The high platform was carpeted, and gayly festooned with college colors. A bright white light illumined the room, and outlined clearly the great polished beams that arched the domed ceiling. The assembled crowds filled the air with pulsating murmurs. When the hour for speaking arrived all were hushed. But on the wall the old clock which pointed out the trying moment ticked calmly on.

One after another I saw and heard the orators. Still, I could not realize that they longed for the favorable decision of the judges as much as I did. Each contestant received a loud burst of applause, and some were cheered heartily. Too soon my turn came, and I paused for a moment behind the curtains for a deep breath. After my concluding words, I heard the same applause that the others had called out.

Upon my retreating steps, I was astounded to receive from my fellow-students a large bouquet of roses tied with flowing ribbons. With the lovely flowers I fled from the stage. This friendly token was a rebuke to me for the hard feelings I had borne them.

Later, the decision of the judges awarded me the first place. Then there was a mad uproar in the hall, where my classmates sang and shouted my name at the top of their lungs; and the disappointed students howled and brayed in fearfully dissonant tin trumpets. In this excitement, happy students rushed forward to offer their congratulations. And I could not conceal a smile when they wished to escort me in a procession to the students' parlor, where all were going to calm themselves. Thanking them for the kind spirit which prompted them to make such a proposition, I walked alone with the night to my own little room.

A few weeks afterward, I appeared as the college representative in another contest. This time the competition was among orators from different colleges in our State. It was held at the State capital, in one of the largest opera houses.

Here again was a strong prejudice against my people. In the evening, as the great audience filled the house, the student bodies began warring among themselves. Fortunately, I was spared witnessing any of the noisy wrangling before the contest began. The slurs against the Indian that stained the lips of our opponents were already burning like a dry fever within my breast.

But after the orations were delivered a deeper burn awaited me. There, before that vast ocean of eyes, some college rowdies threw out a large white flag, with a drawing of a most forlorn Indian girl on it. Under this they had printed in bold black letters words that ridiculed the college which was represented by a "squaw." Such worse than barbarian rudeness embittered me. While we waited for the verdict of the judges, I gleamed fiercely upon the throngs of palefaces. My teeth were hard set, as I saw the white flag still floating insolently in the air.

Then anxiously we watched the man carry toward the stage the envelope containing the final decision.

There were two prizes given, that night, and one of them was mine!

The evil spirit laughed within me when the white flag dropped out of sight, and the hands which hurled it hung limp in defeat.

Leaving the crowd as quickly as possible, I was soon in my room. The rest of the night I sat in an armchair and gazed into the crackling fire. I laughed no more in triumph when thus alone. The little taste of victory did not satisfy a hunger in my heart. In my mind I saw my mother far away on the Western plains, and she was holding a charge against me.

—1900-01

ADELINE F. RIES (N.D.)

No biographical information is available for Adeline Ries. "Mammy: A Story" was originally published in January 1917 in the magazine *The Crisis*. Founded in 1910, *The Crisis* was (and is) the official publication of the National Association for the Advancement of Colored People (NAACP); W.E.B. DuBois was its first editor. Originally titled *The Crisis: A Record of the Darker Races,* the magazine published essays and articles about current events, but also served as a literature and arts review. It developed a wide readership among African Americans as well as whites, with a circulation of 50,000 in 1917, the year "Mammy: A Story" was published. Readership reached a peak of 100,000 in 1919, as the Harlem Renaissance was beginning.

Mammy
A Story

Mammy's heart felt heavy indeed when (the time was now two years past) marriage had borne Shiela, her "white baby," away from the Governor's plantation to the coast. But as the months passed, the old colored nurse became accustomed to the change, until the great joy brought by the news that Shiela had a son, made her reconciliation complete. Besides, had there not always been Lucy, Mammy's own "black baby," to comfort her?

Yes, up to that day there had always been Lucy; but on that very day the young Negress had been sold—sold like common household ware!—and (the irony of it chilled poor Mammy's leaden heart)—she had been sold to Shiela as nurse to the baby whose birth, but four days earlier had caused Mammy so much rejoicing. The poor slave could not believe that it was true, and as she buried her head deeper into the pillows, she prayed that she might wake to find it all a dream.

But a reality it proved and a reality which she dared not attempt to change. For despite the Governor's customary kindness, she knew from experience, that any interference on her part would but result in serious floggings. One morning each week she would go to his study and he would tell her the news from the coast and then with a kindly smile dismiss her.

So for about a year, Mammy feasted her hungering soul with these meagre scraps of news, until one morning, contrary to his wont, the Governor rose as she entered the room, and he bade her sit in a chair close to his own. Placing one of his white hands over her knotted brown ones, he read aloud the letter he held in his other hand:

"Dear Father:—

"I can hardly write the sad news and can, therefore, fully appreciate how difficult it will be for you to deliver it verbally. Lucy was found lying on the nursery floor yesterday, dead. The physician whom I immediately summoned pronounced her death a case of heart-failure. Break it gently to my dear old mammy, father, and tell her too, that the coach, should she wish to come here before the burial, is at her disposal.

"Your daughter,

"SHIELA."

While he read, the Governor unconsciously nerved himself to a violent outburst of grief, but none came. Instead, as he finished, Mammy rose, curtsied, and made as if to withdraw. At the door she turned back and requested the coach, "if it weren't asking too much," and then left the room. She did not return to her cabin; simply stood at the edge of the road until the coach with its horses and driver drew up and then she entered. From that time and until nightfall she did not once change the upright position she had assumed, nor did her eyelids once droop over her staring eyes. "They took her from me an' she died"—"They took her from me an' she died"—over and over she repeated the same sentence.

When early the next morning Mammy reached Shiela's home, Shiela herself came down the road to meet her, ready with words of comfort and love. But as in years gone by, it was Mammy who took the golden head on her breast, and patted it, and bade the girl to dry her tears. As of old, too, it was Mammy who first spoke of other things; she asked to be shown the baby, and Shiela only too willingly led the way to the nursery where in his crib the child lay cooing to itself. Mammy took up the little body and again and again tossed it up into the air with the old cry, "Up she goes, Shiela," till he laughed aloud.

Suddenly she stopped, and clasping the child close she took a hurried step towards the open window. At a short distance from the house rolled the sea and Mammy gazed upon it as if fascinated. And as she stared, over and over the words formed themselves: "They took her from me an' she died,"—"They took her from me an' she died."

From below came the sound of voices, "They're waiting for you, Mammy,"—it was Shiela's soft voice that spoke—"to take Lucy—you understand, dear."

Mammy's eyes remained fixed upon the waves,—"I can't go—go foh me, chile, won't you?" And Shiela thought that she understood the poor woman's feelings and without even pausing to kiss her child she left the room and joined the waiting slaves.

Mammy heard the scraping as of a heavy box upon the gravel below; heard the tramp of departing footsteps as they grew fainter and fainter until they died away. Then and only then, did she turn her eyes from the wild waters and looking down at the child in her arms, she laughed a low, peculiar laugh. She smoothed back the golden ringlets from his forehead, straightened out the little white dress, and then, choosing a light covering for his head, she descended the stairs and passed quietly out of the house.

A short walk brought Mammy and her burden to the lonely beach; at the water's edge she stood still. Then she shifted the child's position until she supported his weight in her hands and with a shrill cry of "Up she goes, Shiela," she lifted him above her head. Suddenly she flung her arms forward, at the same time releasing her hold of his little body. A large breaker caught him in its foam, swept him a few feet towards the shore and retreating, carried him out into the sea—

A few hours later, two slaves in frantic search for the missing child found Mammy on the beach tossing handfuls of sand into the air and uttering loud, incoherent cries. And as they came close, she pointed towards the sea and with the laugh of a madwoman shouted: "They took her from me an' she died!"

—1917

LUISA CAPETILLO (1879-1922)

Luisa Capetillo was born in Arecibo, Puerto Rico, to Margarita Perón and Luis Capetillo Echevarría, both members of the idealistic revolutionary tradition. Capetillo's parents passed their beliefs on to their only daughter; she was home schooled by her mother, who familiarized her with humanist authors such as Victor Hugo, Leo Tolstoy, and Emile Zola, as well as the philosophy of John Stuart Mill and Peter Kropotkin. As an adult, Capetillo supported herself and her two children by writing articles on socialism for newspapers and by working as a lectora (reader). She also worked in the Arecibo tobacco processing plants, reading the works of revolutionary theorists to the workers there. In 1907, her first published book, *Ensayos libertarios* (Libertarian Essays), professed anarchism and the principles of universal brotherhood as a liberatory way of life. Capetillo published her third book in 1911, *Mi Opinión sobre las Libertades, Derechos, y Deberes de la Mujer como Compañera, Madre y Ser Independiente* (My Opinion on the Freedom, Rights, and Duties of the Woman as Companion, Mother, and Independent Being), which is recognized as the first feminist manifesto in Puerto Rico. The book argues for the education of all women, explains her concept of "free love" (which advocates for people to form emotional and sexual contracts that are not sanctioned by the state or the church), and it also claims that social institutions help to perpetuate the subordinate status of women. In 1912, Capetillo moved to New York City and helped organize tobacco workers in Florida, as well as in Cuba. She advocated for women's independence (both social and economic), universal suffrage, and complete self-determination. Capetillo is recognized as a radical feminist, an anarchist, a labor organizer, and a foundational figure of Puerto Rican literature. While living in Rio Piedras, she contracted tuberculosis and died on April 10, 1922.

How Poor Women Prostitute Themselves
A One Act Play

Scene: A simple living room

WOMAN: [*Enters scene in a house dress, followed by a well-dressed man who gives her money.*]
YOUNG MAN: Are you happy with this life?
WOMAN: No, but what choice do I have?
YOUNG MAN: Work at a factory.
WOMAN: I don't know a trade, and besides, how much would I make?
YOUNG MAN: Enough to feed yourself.
WOMAN: You're telling me to go earn a miserable wage, to breathe bad air, and to listen to the impertinences of some vulgar foreman. That won't fix the harm done: we women will always be sacrificed in this infinite holocaust to a hypocritical social lie. It's all the same, for me or for someone else: it's human flesh that is humiliated or despised, that is sold and that atrophies, that is outraged, that is used and trampled on in the name of Christian morality. [*with energy*] What could you say to me that any other woman doesn't deserve to hear? It's all the same: treat me the

same. We can only vindicate ourselves as a whole, or not at all—I'm no better than any other woman.

YOUNG MAN: That's true, one person alone is powerless. All women have the right to be happy, to be respected.

WOMAN: Along with stupid courtesies, social respect is a farce. If it can't prevent a poor tubercular girl from getting sick, why should she give a damn? Would respect give her the means to live comfortably? Because of the rich people's virtue and decorum they'll give her an apology when her soul has been left twisted and her body in the factory; why doesn't respect guarantee health and get rid of deprivation? Useless words!

YOUNG MAN: You're selfishness incarnate in an ignorant lady.

WOMAN: Why isn't that virtue inaccessible to the poor people in the grave? Why doesn't it take the stench out of the fermentation in the ditch? If you buried two girls of equal size and age, one an immaculate virgin, the other surrounded by vice and misery, would the dirt respect one more than the other? Would the dirt free the virgin from the worms?

YOUNG MAN: No, Mother Nature doesn't make those choices. For her, the virgin is the same as the prostitute. She is the equalizer, the lever par excellence.

WOMAN: Then, friend, what's the sense of living one way or the other? It's all the same: social hypocrisies don't bother my soul or disturb my mind.

YOUNG MAN: I understand. But if those things don't matter to you, I should remind you that you're exposed to thousands of diseases, and you practice vices that pleasure the mob of degenerates that use you and then treat you with scorn.

WOMAN: All that is very splendid to say, but if you were in my circumstances you would surely accept it one way or the other. One day a drunk came, and my opinions meant nothing to him. I was disgusted to go near him. He usually comes every Friday; he'll surely come this evening. What can I do about it?

YOUNG MAN: Well, I need to go. Please excuse my questions. Until another day. [*He salutes her courteously with his hat.*]

WOMAN: [*Alone*] An excellent young man. But it is already very late—what can I do?—and besides, it's the same to do it with only one as to do it with many. Aren't they all brothers, like in the Bible and all other religions? All that mess of uselessness seems ridiculous and stupid to me. If everything is for sale, why worry so much because we charge a fee? If she who joins herself with a man—through civil marriage or through some religion—also sells herself, doesn't the husband have to cover all the costs? Very few of them go to the factories, but isn't that a kind of sale? They don't want to call it that, but it's a sale just like ours.

DRUNK MAN: Good evening!

WOMAN: Come in.

THE MAN: May I? Very good then, let's hurry, I have to go. [*Shaking*]

WOMAN: Then enter, so you can go...

MAN: No, you go first. You want to do it, right? Look—you thieves—not even paying you makes you listen. Let's go, or I'll whip you! [*Pushing her*]

WOMAN: I'm going, pig, what do you think!...I'd be better off killing myself....

MAN: For what you're worth, you may as well have already done it. [*They enter the house, he pushing her forward.*]

—1916

DOROTHY CANFIELD FISHER (1879-1958)

Dorothea Frances Canfield was born in Lawrence, Kansas. Her father, James Hulme Canfield, was a college professor and president of Ohio State University; her mother, Flavia Camp, was an artist and writer. After graduating from Ohio State University, Canfield received a Ph.D. in Romance Languages from Columbia University in 1904, one of the few American women to receive a doctorate in the early years of the century. She married John Redwood Fisher in 1907, the same year that she published her first novel, *Gunhild,* under the name Dorothy Canfield. The first to introduce the Montessori teaching method in the United States, Canfield wrote two books explicitly about Montessori education: *A Montessori Mother* (1912) and *The Montessori Manual* (1913); much of her work for and about children, such as the popular juvenile novel *Understood Betsy* (1917), was influenced by the Montessori theory of early childhood education. Canfield and her husband raised their two children in Vermont, which is a significant subject in much of her fiction. Canfield was the first woman to serve on the Vermont Board of Education; she supervised the first adult education program in the United States; and she was a member of the selection committee of the Book of the Month Club for more than twenty-five years. Eleanor Roosevelt named her one of the ten most influential women in the U.S. In all, Canfield wrote and translated dozens of books, including novels, short fiction, juvenile fiction, nonfiction writing on education and politics, memoir, and literary criticism.

The Biologist and His Son

The older children had gone noisily and cheerfully off to kindergarten and school. Upstairs the baby was making half-grumbling, half-cheerful remarks, giving notice to any ear acquainted with babies that he had now been a long time awake after his nap, that he was feeling blithe and refreshed, but that he would be seriously displeased if one of his servitors did not soon give him some attention.

"What do you say we bring him down for a few minutes?" suggested the mother. "I don't have to start clearing up the table this minute."

With the habitual, only half-conscious gesture of the twentieth-century man, the scientist father glanced at his watch. So the mariner glances at his compass. For the same purpose. To learn the exact spot to which the moment had brought him. The glance reassured him. "Sure," he answered, "I have half an hour before I must start for the laboratory. I'll go get him." He pushed back his chair and went upstairs.

The mother relaxed in her chair. Unheard of, she thought, to have a pause between one and another of the tasks which trod fast on each other's heels, from her waking hour to the falling-into-bed end of her day.

A door opened upstairs. The baby, seeing his father coming towards his crib, cried out joyfully in his own lingo, quite intelligible to both his parents, that he was pleased at the prospect of being picked up by one of the two pickers-up he most approved of.

The mother heard her two menfolks coming down the stairs. She had given her youngest child his bottle just before his nap, not two hours before. But she turned her face towards the door as eagerly as though she had been separated from him for days or months. The baby rode through the door, high in his father's arms. The mother's eyes (only a few years before they had been the shallow pretty eyes of a pretty girl, fixed exclusively on her skin, her lipstick, her hair-do, her boy-friends, her own affairs) shone in a passion of love. She had forgotten how marvelous her little son was, how miraculous it was to have a new baby. The same astonished delight that he and his mother were in the same world brightened the baby's round face to a glow. He opened his mouth in a toothless grimace of joy, grotesque and exquisite.

"Hello there, Toots!" said his American mother, undramatically.

The father sat down at the table, holding his small son on what for a father corresponds to the lap of a mother. The baby was still so young that he could not sit up without support. At the times when he was out of his crib, somebody held him. This procedure is passed by the latest baby-books as psychologically acceptable, so the parents enjoyed without reservations the rich sensuous pleasure given them by this contact with the warm, firming jelly of the small body. The baby liked it too.

But the table was still cluttered with dishes, silver, glass from the luncheon. With that array of glittering and shining objects before him on the table, *within reach,* the baby forgot his mother, he thought no more of his father. He lunged far forward—much farther than any adult seeing his tininess could have dreamed possible—and in a fiercely energetic sweep, gathered towards him an armful of—of everything. Water-glass, plate, spoons, fork, butter-dish, together with a wisp of the tablecloth clutched firmly in one hand. In a commanding gesture of power, he drew it all towards him, tipping over, clattering.

"Mercy on us!" cried the mother, laughing, dismayed. She sprang up with the steel-spring speed and controlled accuracy of her thirty-two years. She pushed all those breakable objects to one side and the other, tucked the tablecloth back out of the baby's reach, and left a bare expanse of wood before him.

But rapid as her action had been, her mind had remembered an axiom of those excellent baby-books: "Don't take away from children things they can't have, without substituting something they can have. No vacuums!"

"I'll get him a pot-lid to play with," she said; "Mitsy used to like pot-lids when she was little. Perhaps he's old enough now for that." She stepped quickly into the kitchen and brought out a tin lid. It was round, with a black knoblike handle in the middle. She laid it on the table in front of the baby, knob down, tilted to one side.

It did not look as interesting to the baby as the glass and china which had been taken away. But he felt too comfortable to resent the affront. His spine braced against his father's warm solid body gave him a delicious sensation of security. He gave the pot-lid an amiable look and put out a fat small hand to see what it felt like.

The lid was balanced unevenly on the knob. It tilted down at one side under the weight of the baby's hand. The tin edge made a little click as it struck the table.

The baby was surprised. He lifted his hand and put it down again on the other side of the lid. The lid tilted again, and clicked more loudly on the table. The baby liked clicks. But he did not understand what made the thing move. He had not told his hand to make it move.

His hand rose again and came down more heavily. His purpose was to make that thing stay put. But it did not stay put. His muscles were, as yet, by no means under the control of his brain. His hand struck the metal circle a slanting wavering blow. Now the lid did not tilt. It spun part way around on its knob—a quarter-turn before coming to rest. At this unexpected circular motion, the little face took on an expression of astonishment, so extreme that the mother began to laugh. He did not notice this. His eyes were fixed, so intently that they crossed a little, on the phenomenon he was exploring. He had handled other objects. But they had all moved to and fro, bang! Or up and down, bang! But not around in this new circular spinning motion.

Visibly and purposefully he took thought, and set his hand tentatively to the lid. It swung part way around a circle, its rim clicking irregularly on the table as the wobbling little hand moved it.

The baby had wanted it to lie flat. The other things he knew, like a block, or a stick, or a spoon, all lay flat. What was this unruly idea of waveringly going around in a circle? The faintly marked eyebrows drew into a straight line, the little mouth clamped shut on the resolve to make the thing do what he wanted it to do, not what it wanted to. He looked much older than he was. For the time between two heartbeats his parents saw to their incredulous astonishment that he looked exactly as his doctor-grandfather, now gray-haired and bespectacled, looked when confronted with a complicated surgical case.

His face was dark with determination. He frowned, focusing his will power on the problem before him. And for the first time in his life, he stretched out both his hands in a co-ordinated gesture.

"Oh–!" cried his mother in surprise and delight.

The scientist had followed the baby's doings with an accurate professional knowledge. It was as though he could look through the gold-down-covered skull at the developing brain and see, visibly enacted, the inner drama of growth, development, increasing mastery of nerve-centers and muscles. He smiled at his wife as proud as he would be when their son graduated from college with high honors.

The scientist's wife thought back and said aloud, "That's much earlier than any one of the others could control both hands at once."

Silently she thought forward, "He is going to be very bright. Very strong. Fine co-ordination." In one leap, her imagination soared years ahead, saw him conquering in football, in hockey. Or perhaps that good muscular co-ordination would make him a world-famous pianist. Or perhaps—foreboding blew coldly across her dream—there may be in him some of Uncle Jerry's moral slipperiness, and this muscular dexterity may tempt him into cheating at cards.

All this at the time-annihilating speed of feeling and thinking, between two breaths, between two heartbeats. She looked back at the baby as he was now. He looked like any other baby. He was not doing anything at all remarkable. His short, short human ability to give his attention to anything had come abruptly to an all too human end. He had forgotten that he had wanted to make that tilting thing lie flat. His interest in it had sprung suddenly to life. It was gone as quickly, like a light snapped off at the switch. He cared no more about it. As idly as a monkey, still bleeding from his fight over a bright piece of tin, lets it fall from his hand to scratch himself and look blankly around with his shallow, hard simian eyes, the baby had forgotten the existence of the pot-lid, challenging his powers. Like the adult voter at the polls, forgetting—what was so agonizingly present to his heart when his son was on the front line in battle—the life-and-death need for a strong international organization to keep the peace, the baby saw no point in making any effort to go on mastering a problem which, a moment before, had passionately interested him.

His face sagged into vacancy. He looked younger than he was, looked as he had when he was a passive, month-old cocoon. He leaned his head, that great human bone-box crammed with the raw material of intelligence, peacefully against his father's chest, and took his ease within the support of his father's encircling arms. He slumped down, he let his hand—antenna of his personality—stray aimlessly over the surface of the pot-lid. He yawned the startlingly human yawn of his age.

His mother gave the modern's look of unquestioning submissiveness at her master, the watch on her wrist. "About time to put his next feeding on to warm," she thought.

In the baby's inattentive tactile exploring of the new object before him, his tiny fingers grasped the edge of the lid. It was a gentle meaningless reflex. From his birth, his fingers had closed on anything they touched. But it happened that at the same moment, the muscles of his arm chanced to contract a little, so that the hand grasping the lid lifted it slightly from the table. Since he did not know he had done this, he let it fall. The resultant noise was no mere click. It was a clash, a metallic bang.

His hand halted dead to ask his brain what this noise was. His eyes, which had begun to float sleepily to and fro, opened wide and focused with a snap on the hand and the lid. He had learned to focus his eyes so many weeks ago that he could now control and give the necessary orders to the complicated set of nerves and innumerable tiny muscles involved, instantly, with as automatic a skill as a master-violinist rips off a two-octave run, or a star batter lines out a home run over the scoreboard. He was trying to bring his brain into a focus as clear. What had happened to his hand? To the lid?

His fingers were still curved around the edge of the lid. He set those muscles, flexed the bigger muscles of his arm and lifted his hand. The tin object rose with it. Why, it wasn't the shape he thought it was! The baby's face took on an expression of epic intentness—so perhaps did Madame Curie's in the laboratory. Or Benjamin Franklin's, when he touched his knuckle to the key.

Up, up, up! When the lid stood straight up, one side towards him, the baby saw it no longer as a round flat object, but tall and thin. How could it be utterly different from what it had been? He gazed at it in a wild surmise—so Columbus may have gazed over the railing of his caravel at the wavering shore light in the night's blackness.

Of course the untutored muscles of his arm could not hold themselves steady more than an instant. They wavered. The lid slid down, knob uppermost this time, and clashed with its whole metal surface on the wood.

Oh, what a glorious sound was that! The baby's ears transmitted the rolling sound waves to his brain as, to ours, comes the clash of cymbals in an orchestra. His nerves, quivering to the stimulation of the clatter, swept him away from those capacities for logic and intellectual deduction which for a single instant had been stirred into dawning life. Deep, primitive, sensory reflexes shook his little being to the core. That mighty crash! Had he himself made it? How? He leaned forward, panting. He would do it again. He had done it once.

But now what was involved was not an old reflex gesture for his hand, like closing around an adult finger. This was new, and there were several parts to it. His fumbling baby-brain tried to bear in mind the several complicated movements to be made. In years to come, learning to check his speed on the beginner's slope of the skier's practice field, he would recite his directions to himself, "Knees bent! Toes turned in equally from both sides! Weight well forward!" trying to think and perform a number of things in the same instant. As manfully he now wrestled with the complex maneuver of tensing some muscles and loosing others.

At his first try he failed. Once he failed. Twice he failed. His smooth round face that had been so bland became savagely taut. Strange to see his little jaw set hard.

His parents watched him intently. They held their breath. He had forgotten that they were in the room with him. He had forgotten that they existed. He was alone with the effort that was to be lifelong with him, as with all his ancestors, all his descendants—to master and direct the forces of the material world around him.

On this he concentrated all that he could control of the forces he found within him.

And then—why, it was easy. His brain perceived which orders to issue to muscles and nerves. As soon as he knew what orders to give, mere brute matter, like tin and wood, became his slave. In a gesture wild and uncertain but not random, using far more energy than was needed, he lifted the lid high from the table and dashed it down. Again that marvelous exciting clatter. And then again. And again. His face blazed. His nerves tingled in delicious spasms as the agitated air waves beat on his eardrums. Bang! Clash! Bang! Clash!

His mouth fell open in animal gratification like that of a primitive man dancing his heart out to the frenzy of rattle and drum. Bang! Clash! He could do it as often as he wanted. Clash! Clash! Bang! On his face sat might and power. Bang! Clash! Clatter! Glory! Glory! Bang!

During his struggle to go beyond what till then had been possible to him, his parents' young faces had been almost as tense as his. Their well-disciplined brains analyzed accurately the meaning of the moment for him. They followed him in thought to the last nerve-center. But their eardrums, like his, had been violently assaulted by the unexpectedly loud clang of metal on wood. For them, as for the baby, this jar had snapped the thread of the effort to understand. It summoned their nerves, as it did his, to a reaction that was purely, wildly sensory. The little boy gloriously clashing a tin pot-lid on the table suddenly seemed to them the funniest thing they had ever seen. They burst into laughter. Tears ran down their cheeks. They laughed like crazy things. They did not look at all like serious young intellectuals. They looked like hilarious children playing with a toy.

But through the rhythmic clang of the little Maenad's[1] cymbal, the kitchen clock now made a remorselessly reasonable sound, striking the half hour. It said but one syllable in a small, self-contained voice. To the parents it was like the stentorian "—'SHUN!" of a drill sergeant. Docile, obedient, unquestioning, they snapped to attention, wheeled and marched as they were ordered.

The mother took the lid away from the baby and went out to the kitchen to put the milk for his next feeding on to warm. The father carried him upstairs to his crib.

The baby made no protest. He was tired. He had lived deeply with all he had. He had adventured forward beyond his age. He had reached out from the simple manageable mechanisms of babyhood to grasp some of the complexity of being human. And he had had enough—for a while. He yawned, rubbed his eyes with his fists, relaxed all his muscles, sagged limply in his father's arms till, as when he had been newborn, his weight seemed twice what it was.

His father laid him down in his crib. His fingers clutched mechanically around the big masculine thumb. But he did not care when his father gently unloosed the five pink petals. He drew in a deep breath and turned his head to one side till he could see the particular wall-lamp which was his landmark for being sure he was in his own bed.

[1] In Greek mythology, a female worshipper of Dionysus.

He had used up an unheard-of sum of nervous, muscular, intellectual energy. He needed food. He slid back to an age far below his own and gazing vacantly at the ceiling, waited with the idiotic simplicity of a one-celled organism for someone to put the food he needed into his mouth.

—1944

MARGARET SANGER (1879-1966)

Margaret Higgins Sanger was born in Corning, New York, to Michael Higgins, a stonecutter, and Anne Purcell Higgins. Sanger's mother bore eleven children, and Sanger later attributed her mother's death in 1896 to the toll taken by these many births. After attending boarding school in Hudson, New York (her older sisters worked to pay for her education), Sanger began training to become a nurse. There, she met William Sanger, an artist and architect eight years her senior. They married in 1902, and within a few years had two sons and a daughter. The Sangers' apartment in New York City became a popular meeting place for radicals, and Sanger became involved in socialist and labor politics while also working as a visiting nurse to help support the family.

Sanger's involvement in radical politics and the exposure she had to the lives of poor women through her work as a visiting nurse led her to a commitment to making birth control information widely available. She founded a paper, the *Woman Rebel,* in 1914, and also wrote pamphlets offering information on specific contraceptive methods. Threatened with prosecution (the 1873 Comstock Act deemed sending such "obscene" information through the mail illegal), she fled to Europe. She returned in 1915, divorced her husband, and in 1916 opened a clinic in Brooklyn—the first birth control clinic in the United States. Arrested within weeks, Sanger founded another publication, the *Birth Control Review,* during her imprisonment. The new publication's motto, "To Breed a Race of Thoroughbreds," marked the shift in Sanger's work from socialism to social Darwinism. In 1922, she married a wealthy businessman, J. Noah Steele, and in 1923 she opened the Birth Control Clinical Research Bureau. Sanger wrote several books, including *Woman and the New Race* (1920), *Happiness in Marriage* (1926), *My Fight for Birth Control* (1931), and an autobiography (1938). In the late 1930s, Sanger began to promote birth control internationally, helping to found the organizations that would become the International Planned Parenthood Federation and the Planned Parenthood Federation in the U.S. Sanger continued to fight for birth control until her retirement from public life in 1962.

The Prevention of Conception

Is there any reason why women should not receive clean, harmless, scientific knowledge on how to prevent conception? Everybody is aware that the old, stupid fallacy that such knowledge will cause a girl to enter into prostitution has long been shattered. Seldom does a prostitute become pregnant. Seldom does the girl practicing promiscuity become pregnant. The woman of the upper middle class have all available knowledge and implements to prevent conception. The woman of the lower middle class is struggling for this knowledge. She tries various methods of prevention, and after a few years of experience plus medical advice succeeds in discovering some method suitable to her individual self. The woman of the people is the only one left in ignorance of this information. Her neighbors, relatives and friends tell her stories of special devices and the success of them all. They tell her also of the blood-sucking men with M.D. after their names who perform operations for the price of so-and-so. But the working woman's purse is thin. It's far cheaper to have a baby, "though God knows what it will do after it gets here." Then, too, all other classes of women live in places where there is at least a semblance of privacy and sanitation. It is easier for them to care for themselves whereas the large majority of the women of the people have no bathing or sanitary conveniences. This accounts too for the fact that the higher the standard of living, the more care can be taken and fewer children result. No plagues, famines or wars could ever frighten the capitalist class so much as the universal practice of the prevention of conception. On the other hand no better method could be utilized for increasing the wages of the workers.

As is well known, a law exists forbidding the imparting of information on this sub-ject, the penalty being several years' imprisonment. Is it not the time to defy this law? And what fitter place could be found than in the pages of the WOMAN REBEL?

—1914

To Comrades and Friends[1]

New York
Oct. 28th 1914

Comrades and Friends

Every paper published should have a message for its readers. It should deliver it and be done. The Woman Rebel had for its aim the imparting of information of the prevention of conception. It was not the intention to labor on for years advocating the idea, but to give the information directly to those who desired it. The March, May, July, August, September and October issues have been suppressed and confiscated by the Post Office. They have been mailed regularly to all subscribers. If you have not received your copies, it has been because the U.S. Post Office has refused to carry them to you.

My work on the nursing field for the past fourteen years has convinced me that the workers desire the knowledge of prevention of conception. My work among women of the working class proved to me sufficiently that it is they who are suffering because of the law which forbids the imparting of this information. To wait for this law to be repealed would be years and years hense. Thousands of unwanted children may be born into the world in the meantime. Thousands of women made miserable and unhappy.

Why should we wait?

Shall we who have heard the cries and seen the agony of dying Women respect the law which has caused their death?

Shall we watch in patience the murdering of 25000 women, who die each year in U.S. from criminal abortion?

Shall we fold our hands and wait until a body of sleek and well fed politicians get ready to abolish the cause of such slaughter?

---

[1] Sanger had been indicted for publishing obscene material in August of 1914 after copies of *The Woman Rebel* were seized by postal authorities; she fled the country fearing conviction in October.

Shall we look upon a piece of parchment as greater than human happiness, greater than human life?

Shall we let it destroy our womanhood, and hold millions of workers in bondage and slavery? Shall we who respond to the throbbing pulse of human needs concern ourselves with indictments, courts and judges, or shall we do our work first and settle with these evils later?

This law has caused the perpetuation of quackery. It has created the fake and quack who benefits by its existence.

Jail has not been my goal. There is special work to be done and I shall do it first. If jail comes after I shall call upon all to assist me. In the meantime I shall attempt to nullify the law by direct action and attend to the consequences later.

Over 100000 working men and women in U.S. shall hear from me.

The Boston Tea Party was a defiant and revolutionary act in the eyes of the English Government, but to the American Revolutionist it was but an act of courage and justice. Yours Fraternally

Margaret H. Sanger

—1914

Why the Woman Rebel?[2]

Because I believe that deep down in woman's nature lies slumbering the spirit of revolt.

Because I believe that woman is enslaved by the world machine, by sex conventions, by motherhood and its present necessary child-rearing, by wage-slavery, by middle-class morality, by customs, laws and superstitions.

Because I believe that woman's freedom depends upon awakening that spirit of revolt within her against these things which enslave her.

Because I believe that these things which enslave woman must be fought openly, fearlessly, consciously.

Because I believe she must consciously disturb and destroy and be fearless in its accomplishment.

Because I believe in freedom, created through individual action.

Because I believe in the offspring of the immigrant, the great majority of whom make up the unorganized working class to-day.

Because I believe that this immigrant with a vision, an ideal of a new world where liberty, freedom, kindness, plenty hold sway, who had courage to leave the certain old for the uncertain new to face a strange new people, new habits, a strange language, for this vision, this ideal, certainly has brought to this country a wholesome spirit of unrest which this generation of Americans has lost through a few generations of prosperity and respectability.

Because I believe that on the courage, vision and idealism of the immigrant and the offspring does the industrial revolution depend.

Because I believe that through the efforts of the industrial revolution will woman's freedom emerge.

---

[2] This article appeared in the first issue of Sanger's paper, *Woman Rebel*.

Because I believe that not until wage slavery is abolished can either woman's or man's freedom be fully attained.

Because I have six months' time to devote to arousing this slumbered spirit in the working woman, and if within this time I shall have succeeded in arousing my own laggard self I shall have succeeded sufficiently to continue this paper until all the slumbered spirits have awakened to its assistance or its destruction.

—1914

ANGELINA WELD GRIMKÉ (1880-1958)

Angelina Weld Grimké was born into a remarkable, biracial family. Her great-aunts were the noted white abolitionists and feminists Sarah Grimké and Angelina Grimké Weld, and her aunt by marriage was the Black writer Charlotte Forten Grimké. Her father, Archibald Grimké, the second Black graduate of Harvard Law School, was a well-known lawyer and publisher who was vice president of the NAACP and who also served as consul to the Domincan Republic for several years. Her mother, Sarah Stanley, came from a white, middle-class family who opposed her marriage. The marriage was short-lived, and Grimké's mother left in 1883, taking three-year-old Angelina with her. In 1887, Sarah returned Angelina to her father, and they only communicated through correspondence after that. After graduating from the Boston Normal School of Gymnastics, Grimké moved to Washington, D.C., where she taught physical education at Armstrong Manual Training School, and English at Dunbar High School. Grimké was part of Georgia Douglas Johnson's important Washington salon, and published her poetry, essays, and short fiction in the major magazines and anthologies of the Harlem Renaissance. Her 1916 play, *Rachel,* depicts a Black woman's refusal to marry and bear children as an act of resistance to the violence of racism. After her father died in 1930, Grimké ceased writing and moved to New York, where she died in 1958. Like many women writers of the Harlem Renaissance, Grimké never published a book. Recent scholarship has focused on the impact of Grimké's hidden lesbianism upon her work, particularly on her poetry.

The Black Finger

I have just seen a most beautiful thing:
     Slim and still,
    Against a gold, gold sky,
    A straight, black cypress
      Sensitive   5
      Exquisite
     A black finger
     Pointing upwards.
Why, beautiful still finger, are you black?
And why are you pointing upwards?

—1923

A Mona Lisa[1]

1.

I should like to creep
Through the long brown grasses
    That are your lashes;
I should like to poise
    On the very brink   5
Of the leaf-brown pools
    That are your shadowed eyes;
I should like to cleave
    Without sound,
Their glimmering waters,   10
    Their unrippled waters;
I should like to sink down
    And down
        And down…
            And deeply drown.   15

2.

Would I be more than a bubble breaking?
    Or an ever-widening circle
    Ceasing at the marge?
Would my white bones
    Be the only white bones   20
Wavering back and forth, back and forth
    In their depths?

—1927

Tenebris

There is a tree by day
That at night
Has a shadow,
A hand huge and black,
With fingers long and black.   5
    All through the dark,
Against the white man's house,
    In the little wind,
The black hand plucks and plucks
    At the bricks.   10
The bricks are the color of blood and very small.
    Is it a black hand,
Or is it a shadow?

—1927

---

[1] 16th century painting by Leonardo da Vinci.

GEORGIA DOUGLAS JOHNSON (CA. 1880-1966)

Georgia Blanche Douglas Camp was born in Atlanta, Georgia; sources date the year of her birth as 1877, 1880, or 1886. The daughter of Laura Jackson, a maid, and George Camp, she was educated at Atlanta University Normal School and the Oberlin Conservatory of Music. In 1903, she married Henry Lincoln Johnson, a lawyer, with whom she had two children. In 1910, the Johnsons moved to Washington, D.C., where Henry took up a political appointment in 1912. Georgia Johnson was the best-published woman poet of the Harlem Renaissance, with four volumes of poetry: *The Heart of a Woman, and Other Poems* (1918), *Bronze: A Book of Verse* (1922), *An Autumn Love Cycle* (1928), and *Share My World* (1962). In addition to poetry, Johnson wrote plays, stories, and an advice column. She was also an important literary hostess; her Washington salon was a critical meeting place for the writers, artists, and intellectuals of the Harlem Renaissance. After her husband died in 1925, Johnson was often short of money; she applied for and was denied many literary awards and fellowships, despite her popularity.

The Heart of a Woman

The heart of a woman goes forth with the dawn
As a lone bird, soft winging, so restlessly on;
Afar o'er life's turrets and vales does it roam
In the wake of those echoes the heart calls home.

The heart of a woman falls back with the night, 5
And enters some alien cage in its plight,
And tires to forget it has dreamed of the stars
While it breaks, breaks, breaks on the sheltering bars.

—1918

Common Dust

And who shall separate the dust
What later we shall be:
Whose keen discerning eye will scan
And solve the mystery?

The high, the low, the rich, the poor, 5
The black, the white, the red,
And all the chromatique between,
Of whom shall it be said

Here lies the dust of Africa;
Here are the sons of Rome; 10
Here lies the one unlabelled,
The world at large his home!

Can one then separate the dust?
Will mankind lie apart,

When life has settled back again   15
The same as from the start?

—1922

Motherhood

Don't knock on my door, little child,
I cannot let you in;
You know not what a world this is
Of cruelty and sin.
Wait in the still eternity   5
Until I come to you.
The world is cruel, cruel, child,
I cannot let you through.

Don't knock at my heart, little one,
I cannot bear the pain   10
Of turning deaf ears to your call,
Time and time again.
You do not know the monster men
Inhabiting the earth.
Be still, be still, my precious child,   15
I cannot give you birth.

—1922

HELEN KELLER (1880-1968)

Author, socialist, and activist Helen Adams Keller was born in Tuscumbia, Alabama, in 1880, the daughter of Captain Arthur H. Keller, who had been an officer in the Confederate Army, and Kate Adams Keller. At the age of nineteen months, Keller was stricken with a fever (possibly scarlet fever or meningitis) that left her blind and deaf. After learning of the education of another deaf-blind girl, Laura Bridgman, the Keller family contacted the Perkins Institute for the Blind, which arranged to send a teacher for Helen, who was six at the time. That teacher, twenty-year-old Anne Sullivan, herself visually impaired, would remain with Keller as her teacher and companion for the next forty-eight years.

Under Sullivan's tutelage, Keller learned to read, write, and speak (although due to her untrained vocal cords, her speech was not generally understood by others). A gifted student, Keller eventually learned to read English, French, German, Greek, and Latin in Braille. Keller published twelve books and many articles in her lifetime, although, due to a plagiarism scandal in 1892 (a story published by the eleven-year-old Keller turned out to be a story that Sullivan had signed to her), she abandoned fiction writing.

From an early age, Keller was determined to go to college. After graduating *cum laude* from Radcliffe in 1904, Keller traveled the world, writing and lecturing on topics including suffrage, socialism, birth control, the rights of the disabled, and pacifism. A member of the International Workers of the World, she also stumped for socialist presidential candidate Eugene V. Debs. Keller established a foundation for the blind and was a tireless fundraiser and activist for the rights of blind people. In 1964, she was awarded the Presidential Medal of Freedom.

Blind Leaders

When Mr. Booth[1] read my essay "Blind Leaders," he said to Mrs. Macy,[2] "It's all right. But people won't believe that Helen Keller wrote it. I have heard men say, 'How can she know about these things? How can one deaf and blind from infancy know about life, about people, about affairs? It is impossible for her to have a first-hand knowledge of what is going on in the world. She is only a mouthpiece for somebody else.'"

I must plead guilty to the charge that I am deaf and blind, although I forget this fact most of the time. Occasionally I come into sharp collision with the stone wall out in my back field, and for a second or two there is not the slightest doubt in my mind that I am blind. When my friends tell me they cannot hear me speak because a freight train is passing, I realize that I'm deaf. But I do not feel so very sorry; for it is not pleasant to have one's thoughts disturbed by the noise of a freight train.

As for the other charges, they are groundless, they are ridiculous. My blindness does not shut me out from a knowledge of what is happening about me. True, I did not witness the recent dreadful wreck at Stamford;[3] neither did most people in the United States. But that did not prevent me, any more than it prevented them, from knowing about it. To be sure, I cannot hear my neighbors discuss the events and questions of the day; but, judging from what is repeated to me of those discussions and all that they say is often repeated conscientiously—I feel that I do not miss much.

I prefer to use the eye and the ear of the world which the printed page makes mine. I prefer to read the opinions of well-informed persons, clear thinkers like Alfred Russell Wallace, William Morris, Bernard Shaw, Sir Oliver Lodge, H. G. Wells, William English Walling, Judge Lindsey, Robert Hunter, Karl Kautsky, Herbert Spencer,[4] Darwin, and Marx. You say, "But what do you know about life that enables you to judge of the competency of such men to give an opinion?" If books are not life, I do not know what they are. In the writings of poets, sages, prophets, is recorded all that men have seen, heard, and felt. Having all this in the grasp of my two hands, my means of observing what is going on in the world is not so very limited, after all. I have all the keys to the doors of knowledge. I am benefited by every observation made by scientist, philosopher, prophet. The eyes of the mind are stronger, more penetrating, and more reliable than our physical eyes. We can see a lot of things with a little common-sense light to aid our perceptions.

I have never been a captain of industry or a strike-breaker or a soldier; neither have most people. But I have studied about them, and I think I understand their relation to society. At all events, I claim my right to discuss them. I also know something about gambling. For I gambled once, in stocks and bonds—once only; for I lost all I had in that one venture. But if I did not win, somebody else did, and I had a good deal of "first-hand experience."

---

[1] A literary advisor and friend of Keller's, according to the original editors.
[2] Anne Sullivan Macy (1866-1936), Keller's teacher and companion.
[3] A train crash in Stamford, CT, in June 1913.
[4] Alfred Russell Wallace (1823-1913), 19th century evolutionist; William Morris (1834-1896), British designer and socialist; George Bernard Shaw (1856-1950), Irish playwright and socialist; Sir Oliver Lodge (1851-1940), British scientist, inventor, and socialist; H.G. Wells (1866-1946), English writer and socialist; William English Walling (1877-1936), American labor reformer and socialist; Benjamin Barr Lindsey (1869-1943), American reformer and jurist; Robert Hunter (1874-1942), American sociologist and socialist; Karl Kautsky (1854-1938), German Marxist theorist; Herbert Spencer (1820-1903), English social philosopher.

I have worked for the blind. I have come into contact with them. I have taken an active part in meetings and spoken before legislatures in their behalf. I have studied their problems, and in order to understand them fully, I found it necessary to study the problems of the seeing among whom the blind live and work. I have found that the needs and difficulties of the sightless are similar to the needs and difficulties of all who are handicapped in the struggle for a livelihood, for education, for equal opportunity. If this work for the blind is not "first-hand experience," I do not know where you or I can get it.

Finally I have visited sweat-shops, factories, crowded slums of New York and Washington. Of course I could not see the squalor; but if I could not see it, I could smell it. With my own hand I could feel pinched, dwarfed children tending their younger brothers and sisters while their mothers tended machines in near-by factories.

Besides the advantages of books and of personal experience, I have the advantage of a mind trained to think. In most people I talk with thought is infantile. In the well educated it is rare. In time their minds become automatic machines. People do not like to think. If one thinks, one must reach conclusions, and conclusions are not always pleasant. They are a thorn in the spirit. But I consider it a priceless gift and a deep responsibility to think. Thought—intelligent thought—gives new eyes to the blind and new ears to the deaf.

I do not doubt that many persons who read what I am going to write will say to themselves: "She is indeed blind. She is so blind she imagines everybody else to be blind." As a matter of fact, I have been thinking for a long time that most of us are afflicted with spiritual blindness. Certainly, very few people open fresh, fearless eyes upon the world they live in. They do not look at anything straight. They have not learned to use their eyes, except in the most rudimentary ways. They will usually see a lamp-post—if it is a large one—and sometimes they are able to read the danger signal on a railway crossing, but not always. Most of the time they expect some one else to see for them. They often pay fabulous sums to lawyers, doctors, ministers, and other "experts" to do their seeing for them; but, unfortunately, it frequently happens that those hired guides and leaders are also blind. Of course they deny that their sight is imperfect. They claim to have extraordinary powers of vision, and many people believe them. Consequently, they are permitted to lead their fellows. But how often do they steer them to their destruction!

When we look about us with seeing eyes, what do we behold? Men and women at our very doors wrung with hard labor, want or the dread of want, needing help and receiving none, toiling for less than a living wage! If we had had penetrating vision, I know that we could not, we would not, have endured what we saw—cruelty, ignorance, poverty, disease—almost all preventable, unnecessary. Our blind leaders whom we have sent away told us that the poverty and misery of mankind were divinely ordained. They taught us that the words, "Ye have the poor always with you," mean that Christ sanctioned poverty as necessary and irremediable.[5] Now we read the Gospel with our own eyes, and we see that Christ meant no such thing.

Much poverty is abominable, unnecessary, a disgrace to our civilization, or rather a denial that we are civilized. Let us try to understand poverty. What is the cause of it? Simply this: that the land, the machinery, the means of life, belong to the few, while

---

[5] Matthew 26:11; Mark 14:7; John 12:8.

the many are born and live with nothing that they can call their own except their hands and their brains. They live by selling their hands and their brains to the few; and all the work they do makes the rich more rich, and gains for the workers a mere livelihood, or less than a livelihood. The ownership of the world by a small class is the main cause of poverty. Strange that we could not see it before, and that when we did see it we accepted it in blind contentment! Our blind guides consoled us by saying that there was much charity, and that the rich were generous and gave to the poor. We now see that what the rich give is only a small part of the money which is made for them by the labor of the poor! They never stop to think that if the workers received an equitable share of their product, there would be no rich, there would be little need of philanthropy. Charity covers a multitude of sins. It does something worse than that. It covers the facts so that they cannot be seen. It covers the fact that the property of the few is made by the labor of the many. The rich are willing to do everything for the poor but to get off their backs.

Our blind leaders used often to blame the poor for their poverty. They declared that the workers did not work enough, were not thrifty enough, squandered their wages. Now we stop and think. We remember that if the workers do not work enough, they do all the work that is done. They make every house that stands, every yard of cloth, every loaf of bread. All that we have we owe to them. If the worker is not thrifty, does not save, it is as often as not because a large part of what he produces goes to some one else, and some one else does the saving. If one man has without producing, it is only because another man produces without having, and that is the trouble in a nutshell.

We never used to ask ourselves why we were well dressed, well housed, why we had time for study and self-improvement, why some of us who talked about the worker's lack of thrift had abundance to squander and waste. Nor did we ask why thousands live in poor houses, eat poor food, wear shabby clothes, and are overworked, and have nothing to look forward to all their lives but monotonous days of toil and poverty. Those two questions answer each other. It is the labor of many poor, ignorant people which makes it possible for us to be refined and comfortable. The employers own what the workers make, and that means that they own the workers. Think of it! The employers own the workers, their time, their strength, their brains, the houses in which they live. They own them really as if they were actual slaves. But the eyes of the owners are veiled. They do not see that to own the worker's tools is to own the worker. In "The Merchant of Venice" Shylock cried, "You take my life when you do take the means."[6] It was a moneylender who said that. A workman can say it with better justice and with warmer appeal to our sympathies. But the masters are blind, they are insensible.

We used to walk through dark, dirty streets; we saw debased men and women, stunted children, blind beggars, brutalized young men, and our curiosity was not aroused to ask the cause of these things. Our blind leaders told us that that was human nature. Poor human nature! When human nature plays with matches and sets fire to our house, shall we sit down and say, "How human!" or shall we try to put out the fire? We want to turn the intelligence and goodness of human nature against the ignorance and evil of human nature. I believe we can do this, and that is why I am not a

---

[6] Act iv, sc. 1.

pessimist. When I talk about poverty and ignorance and misery, I know that I am not drawing a beautiful picture of the world. Yet I am no pessimist. The pessimist— another kind of blind leader—says, "Man lives by darkness and in darkness he shall die." I do not believe it. Man was intended for the light, and he shall not die. In light I would have every one live and see clearly to dispel all darkness. The diagnosis of evil is the beginning of cure. I am no prophet of evil. I find much to love in this world of ours. It is a good world—or it will be when we all use our eyes to make it more as it should be. It is a better world than it was ten centuries ago. It is a better world than it was last year. We lose nothing that man has gained by the sweat of his brow or the genius of his brain. We are every day gaining a little more love, light, and knowledge. We are not becoming blind, we are widening our vision. We are not losing our freedom, because we never had it. Freedom is an ideal. Because it is an ideal I want to make it clear that most of us are not free. If we understand that we are not free, we can work towards our freedom. We cannot be optimists until we have an ideal. We cannot seek intelligently for good until we know evil. We cannot be free until we know the nature of our bondage and examine the chains that bind us.

Our blind leaders used to stand in the high places and harangue about our freedom. The truth is, there never was a free nation, there never was a good government. Since the slaying of Abel there has never been a brother-loving period. We still have to say with Mark Twain:[7] "The brotherhood of man is the most precious thing in the world—what there is of it." From times immemorial men have bowed to the will of masters. Each day they have gone, some to do battle, some to hunt, some to dig and delve, some to spin, all striving to win the bread of life. Ever have the toilers tilled and planted, and been hungry. Ever have the mighty rejoiced and feasted. Never have men labored with glad confidence, glorying in the work of their hands. Ever have some stronger, fiercer brothers robbed them of a portion of their labor.

We remember to have heard our blind leaders say that the people were free men, that if they did not like a "job" they could go wherever they pleased. But where can they go? To some other mill, to some other master. When they stop work, go on strike, society is up in arms against them. Idle workmen make the owners indignant. Why? Because when the workman puts his hands in his pockets the employer's profits are cut off.

Again and again our blind leaders have discoursed on the value of gold and silver. But they never answer the vital question, "Why, after centuries of growth, of education, of intervention, in an age of great plenty, are the majority of men still poor and ignorant?" What a contradiction is this—abundance increasing manifold side by side with increasing poverty, constant improving of labor-saving machinery, but the laborer still without salvation! Worried, puzzled, he knows not how long he shall eat or drink, how he shall stand or sit, wherewithal he shall clothe himself honestly by the work of his hands. But, lo! there is much charity.

From our all-knowing blind leaders we learned that this strange state of things was a result of overproduction. Now let us open our eyes and face this absurdity. How can there be over-production when many men, women, and children are cold and hungry and scantily clothed? The trouble is not over-production or under-production as a whole. As a matter of fact, the worker produces too little for himself and too much for

---

[7] Pseudonym of Samuel Clemens (1835-1910), American writer and Keller's friend.

others. There is enough of everything in the world; but it is not intelligently distributed. Some people are obliged to be idle and have not enough; some people are enabled to be idle and have more than enough. Hundreds of people own more than one house. Thousands of people own no house. Hundreds of people have good incomes, whether or not they contribute one thought or motion of the hand to production. Thousands of men work hard and are underpaid. Women and children are bound to machines in unclean workrooms to eke out the small earnings of the men.

Where, then, is the freedom of the people—I mean, the great majority of the people?

Our blind leaders were wont to vaunt of the great prosperity of the country. They talked so loudly that we failed to hear the protest of the workers. They boasted that "America lifts up the manhood of the poor," that we care for the child and give woman a position of dignity. When we tear away the veil which they so skillfully wrapped about our eyes, what do we see? A dwarfed humanity, stunted in body and mind, at war with each other and with the forces of life; the multitudes of mankind ill fed, ill clothed, living in noisome habitations, working at deadly occupations, dulled to joy and the spirit. Our blind guides wring our hearts with details of the tragic fate of the Titanic. But they never told us about the far greater wreck of human lives in the industrial world, or the heroism of men who grapple with wheel, shuttle, and drill. And yet cotton lint, flint of the quarry, dust of flour, cause more havoc than the slaughter in the Balkans. Gas, steam, deadly vapors, white lead, phosphorus, chlorine from the bleaching-room—these are only a few of the horrors that the workman must face hour after hour every day. When we look into mine and factory for ourselves, what do we see? Little children whose souls are quenched out like a flame in joyless toil—little beings freighted with the bud and sap of divine beginnings bent and stunted, stupid and grown old before their time! Does not all that is kindest in us cry out that they were happiest who went first? For what is there in life for those pinched little ones to grow up for? Sooner or later the giant hands of the machines will seize them and hold them, taking all, giving nothing!

And what about the dignity of womanhood? Only a small part of the millions of workingwomen receive enough pay to maintain a decent home and give their children proper care and education. What dignity do women have as citizens when they may not even elect those who shall decide for them vital questions affecting food, clothing, shelter, education? What do we do to save mothers from the necessity of working at machines until they are unfit to become mothers and they bring feeble children into the world? Eight million women and children are in the factories of this country, and three million men are out of work! Blind indeed must be those who do not see that there must be something wrong when such a state of things exists.

I speak from no personal "grouch" or disappointment. For me life has been one long caress of gentle words and gentle hands. I love all men—rich men, poor men, beggar men, thieves. Millionaires have been among my nearest, kindest friends. Henry Rogers[8] was one of the noblest men that ever lived, in spite of his millions. Kindness and consideration have followed me all the days of my life. But I have seen the exaggerated inequality in the conditions of men, and I have studied the cause of this inequality. I am a child of my generation. I am alive to new forces in the world.

---

[8] Henry Rogers (1840-1909), American businessman and philanthropist who helped to pay for Keller's education at Radcliffe.

Disturbing ideas of dynamic power have penetrated the closed doors to my mind, and awakened in me a social conscience. Not the stream which has passed, but that which is passing, turns the wheel of the mill.

When we inquire why things are as they are, the answer is: The foundation of society is laid upon a basis of individualism, conquest, and exploitation, with a total disregard of the good of the whole. The structure of a society built upon such wrong basic principles is bound to retard the development of all men, even the most successful ones, because it tends to divert man's energies into useless channels and to degrade his character. The result is a false standard of values. Trade and material prosperity are held to be the main objects of pursuit, and consequently the lowest instincts in human natures—love of gain, cunning, and selfishness—are fostered. The output of a cotton mill or a coal mine is considered of greater importance than the production of healthy, happy-hearted, free human beings.

This unmoral state of society will continue as long as we live under a system of universal competition for the means of existence. The workers cannot lift up their heads so long as a small favored class in each generation is allowed to inherit the accumulated labor of all preceding generations, and the many who produce the wealth inherit nothing. (We often forget what wealth is. It is the stored-up labor of men, women, and little children. Money does not create anything. Money is about as productive as a wheel revolving in a void. It has value only in proportion to the toil and sweat of human hands that went into the getting of it.)

During the past century man has gained greater mastery over the forces of nature than he ever had before. Consequently the wealth produced in the world has increased a hundredfold. With the help of the machines he has invented, man can produce enough to provide necessaries, comforts and even some luxuries for every human being. But in spite of this enormously greater productive power the condition of the workers has not essentially improved. Because the industrial system under which we live denies them the fruits of their labor, they have not received their fair share in the products of civilization. As a matter of fact, machinery has widened the gulf between those who own and those who toil. It has become a means of perpetuating man's slavery, because it may be run by unskilled laborers who receive low wages, which of course increases the profits of employers and stockholders. So the workers become part of the machines they manipulate; but the machine is expensive, while human life is cheap. When the workers can no longer live, they go on strike, and what happens? The masters evict them from the hovels that they called home; the police and militia break up their protest-meetings, imprison their leaders, and when they can, drive them out of town. This appalling condition of things exists in many different parts of our county at this moment. For even the Constitution does not safeguard the liberties of the workers when their interests are opposed to those of the capitalist. Our administration of justice, which blind leaders used to tell us was a splendid inheritance from our fathers, is grossly unequal and unjust. It is based on a system of money fees. It is so encumbered at every step with technicalities that it is necessary to employ experts at great cost to explain and interpret the law. Then, too, all petty offenses are punishable by fine or imprisonment. This means that the poor will always be punished, while the rich are usually allowed to go free.

We cannot longer shut our eyes to these glaring evils. They divide the world into economic classes antagonistic to each other. It is because of all these undeniable evils that I am the determined foe of the capitalist system, which denies the workers the rights of human beings. I consider it fundamentally wrong, radically unjust and cruel. It inflicts purposeless misery upon millions of my fellow men and women. It robs little children of the joy of life, embitters motherhood, breaks the bodies of men and degrades their manhood. It must, therefore, be changed, it must be destroyed, and a better, saner, kinder social order established. Competition must give place to co-operation, and class antagonism to brotherhood. "Each for all" is a far more stimulating and effective doctrine than "each for himself." Private ownership of land and the means of production and distribution of the necessaries of life must be replaced by public ownership and democratic management.

Oh, no, it is not human nature that we have to change. Our task is not so difficult as that. All that is necessary to make this world a comfortable abode for man is to abolish the capitalist system. In the words of Sir Oliver Lodge, "we have entered upon the period of conscious evolution, and have begun the adaptation of environment to organism." In other words, we have learned to curb and utilize the forces of nature. The time of blind struggle is drawing to a close. The forces governing the law of the survival of the fittest will continue to operate; but they will be under the conscious, intelligent control of man.

In all my reading I am conscious of a multitudinous discontent. Slowly man is waking up. He is rubbing his eyes and muttering to himself: "There's something wrong with the world. Considering how hard I work I get mighty little in return. I don't see that with a hundred steel plows I get more bread than my forbears who used a wooden plow. I am no better clad, since one machine does the work of a thousand hands, than my ancestors who wore homespun garments. There's a public school in every city and town, but I don't see that my children are the better taught. We have many things that don't count—cheap ornaments, tawdry clothes, patent medicines, and food made to sell, not to eat. This is not reasonable. I will arise and find out why things are as they are." That is what all the "noise" is about. The people—the great "common herd"— are finding out what is wrong with the social, political, and economic structure of the system of which they are a part. The workers—the producers of all the wealth in the world—are chafing at the narrow bounds of their lives. They fret and fume like hounds, and strain at the leash of industrial bondage. They are weary of old trammels, old burdens, creeds outworn, tired of feasting on emptiness and digesting in imagination. The masters find the aroused workman a loud, egotistical animal, a "paid agitator." This is not a time of gentleness, of timid beginnings that steal into life with soft apologies and dainty grace. It is a time of loud-voiced, open speech and fearless thinking, a time of striving and conscious manhood, a time of all that is robust and vehement and bold a time, radiant with new ideals, new hopes of true democracy. I love it, for it thrills me and gives me a feeling that I shall face great and terrible things. I am a child of my generation, and I rejoice that I live in such a splendidly disturbing age. Through the centuries, in spite of hindrances, persecutions, obloquy, "what is to be picks its way" without apology, without fear. Without asking your leave the new order emerges from the old. To the powerful this condition of things is too absurd for patience—the opposition of unreasoning iconoclasts to the traditions of the fathers and the sacred rights of private property; and so they reinforce the police department and call out the militia. In their blindness they think that they can stay the onward march of that dynamic power, silence the voice of God in the land. Those blind ones are but hastening the day when every yoke shall be broken from the necks of men. Crushed, stupefied by terrible poverty, the workers yet demand that they shall have some of the beauty, some of the comforts, some of the luxuries which they have produced. They shall demand, and neither courts, legislatures, nor armies shall prevent the millions from slowly regaining that which the millions have created.

The young generation is beginning to realize this, and new ideas about the workers of the world, about women and children, are "flashing meteor-like through the darkness where we live." Sophistication and greed are instilled characters, and are fortunately not transmitted to offspring by inheritance. The sun of brotherhood is emerging from the eclipse. It is this light that has waked us. It is showing us what we should see in our fellow-men. We are finding out that workmen are not mere machines, they are Men and Women. Imagination, sympathy, and growing knowledge compel us to share in their suffering and in their desires. We are uniting our senses, our hands, and our feelings to end cruel conditions under which millions live, work, and die.

Already thousands of earnest men and women have their faces turned towards this light, and by it they are daily guided in their lives, their thoughts, their work. Steadily, surely, the new light is growing, spreading like the morning upon all lands, broad and broader it glows, and it shall glow until it shines upon all the dark days of humanity. It is a light coming to those who looked for light and found darkness, a life to them who looked for the grave and were bitter in spirit. It shall open all blind hearts, and it shall make evident to every human soul our close dependence upon one another in all the changes, the joys, the sorrows of the world. It is a light which shall banish the cloud of ignorance and the shadow of man-wrought death. At last the deaf, blind, dumb multitude shall find its soul, shall find its tongue! Erect and proud shall all men earn their bread and eat it; for the stigma of labor shall be clotted out forever. The workers shall be no more parts of machines, but masters of them. We shall all stand together; we shall look to each other always for aid and joy, and no one shall be told, "Every man for himself." The hands of all men shall support all men, and we shall dwell in safety. We shall know happiness not bought at the cost of another's misery. We shall be "fellow-workers unto the kingdom of God."[9]

—1913

[9] Colossians 4:11.

JESSIE REDMON FAUSET (1882–1961)

The seventh child of an African Methodist Episcopal minister, Jessie Fauset was born in Camden County, New Jersey, and grew up in Philadelphia, Pennsylvania. Her mother died when she was very young, and her father remarried. The only African-American student in her high school, Fauset tried to attend Bryn Mawr College after graduating, but was rejected because of her race. She went on to study classical languages at Cornell University, graduating in 1905, one of the first African-American women to receive Phi Beta Kappa honors. In her first attempt to teach after graduation (in Philadelphia), Fauset was again denied because of her race, so she moved to Baltimore, where she taught Latin and French at the all-Black

Douglass High School. She later taught French and Latin at M Street High School in Washington, D.C., (which became Dunbar High School in 1916). She decided to continue her education at the University of Pennsylvania, where she graduated with a master's degree, and studied for six months at the Sorbonne in Paris. Eventually taking up residence in New York City, Fauset became literary editor of *The Crisis* magazine, where she discovered and encouraged younger writers such as Langston Hughes, Anne Spencer, and Jean Toomer. Throughout her tenure at *The Crisis*, her short stories, novelettes, poetry, translations, reviews, critiques, and essays were published in the magazine. During this period she also edited *The Brownie's Book*, a magazine for Black children, and traveled abroad while writing news reports and travel narratives. In 1921, Fauset was sponsored by Delta Sigma Theta sorority to attend the second Pan-African Congress in Paris; while in Europe she traveled to London and Brussels, where she lectured on the condition of African-American women in the United States. Fauset traveled to Africa for the first time in 1924; after this visit she returned to Paris, where she continued to write journalistic articles about the condition of Black women. The most prolific woman writer of the Harlem Renaissance, she wrote four novels in the space of a decade: *There Is Confusion* (1924), *Plum Bun* (1929), *The Chinaberry Tree* (1931), and *Comedy: American Style* (1933). She eventually left *The Crisis* in 1926, over a skirmish with W.E.B. DuBois. She went back to teaching French at DeWitt High School in New York, and married Herbert Harris in 1929. Together they eventually settled in Montclair, New Jersey. Fauset died of heart disease in her home town of Philadelphia.

The Sleeper Wakes

Amy recognized the incident as the beginning of one of her phases. Always from a child she had been able to tell when "something was going to happen." She had been standing in Marshall's store, her young, eager gaze intent on the lovely little sample dress which was not from Paris, but quite as dainty as anything that Paris could produce. It was not the lines or even the texture that fascinated Amy so much, it was the grouping of colors—of shades. She knew the combination was just right for her.

"Let me slip it on, Miss," said the saleswoman suddenly. She had nothing to do just then, and the girl was so evidently charmed and so pretty—it was a pleasure to wait on her.

"Oh, no," Amy had stammered. "I haven't time." She had already wasted two hours at the movies, and she knew at home they were waiting for her.

The saleswoman slipped the dress over the girl's pink blouse, and tucked the linen collar under so as to bring the edge of the dress next to her pretty neck. The dress was apricot-color shading into a shell pink and the shell pink shaded off again into the pearl and pink whiteness of Amy's skin. The saleswoman beamed as Amy, entranced, surveyed herself naively in the tall looking-glass.

Then it was that the incident befell. Two men walking idly through the dress-salon stopped and looked—she made an unbelievably pretty picture. One of them with a short, soft brown beard,—"fuzzy" Amy thought to herself as she caught his glance in the mirror—spoke to his companion.

"Jove, how I'd like to paint her!" But it was the look on the other man's face that caught her and thrilled her. "My God! Can't a girl be beautiful!" he said half to himself. The pair passed on.

Amy stepped out of the dress and thanked the saleswoman half absently. She wanted to get home and think, think to herself about that look. She had seen it before in men's eyes, it had been in the eyes of the men in the moving-picture which she had seen that afternoon. But she had not thought *she* could cause it. Shut up in her little room she pondered over it. Her beauty,—she was really good-looking then—she could stir people—men! A girl of seventeen has no psychology, she does not go beneath the surface, she accepts. But she knew she was entering on one of her phases.

She was always living in some sort of story. She had started it when as a child of five she had driven with the tall, proud, white woman to Mrs. Boldin's home. Mrs. Boldin was a bride of one year's standing then. She was slender and very, very comely, with her rich brown skin and her hair that crinkled thick and soft above a low forehead. The house was still redolent of new furniture; Mr. Boldin was spick and span— he, unlike the furniture, remained so for that matter. The white woman had told Amy that this henceforth was to be her home.

Amy was curious, fond of adventure; she did not cry. She did not, of course, realize that she was to stay here indefinitely, but if she had, even at that age she would hardly have shed tears, she was always too eager, too curious to know, to taste what was going to happen next. Still since she had had almost no dealings with colored people and she knew absolutely none of the class to which Mrs. Boldin belonged, she did venture one question.

"Am I going to be colored now?"

The tall white woman had flushed and paled. "You—" she began, but the words choked her. "Yes, you are going to be colored now," she ended finally. She was a proud woman, in a moment she had recovered her usual poise. Amy carried with her for many years the memory of that proud head. She never saw her again.

When she was sixteen she asked Mrs. Boldin the question which in the light of that memory had puzzled her always. "Mrs. Boldin, tell me—am I white or colored?"

And Mrs. Boldin had told her and told her truly that she did not know.

"A—a—mee!" Mrs. Boldin's voice mounted on the last syllable in a shrill crescendo. Amy rose and went downstairs.

Down the comfortable, but rather shabby dining-room which the Boldins used after meals to sit in, Mr. Boldin, a tall black man, with aristocratic features, sat practicing on a cornet, and Mrs. Boldin sat rocking. In all of their eyes was the manifestation of the light that Amy loved, but how truly she loved it, she was not to guess till years later.

"Amy," Mrs. Boldin paused in her rocking, "did you get the braid?" Of course she had not, though that was the thing she had gone to Marshall's for. Amy always forgot essentials. If she went on an errand, and she always went willingly, it was for the pure joy of going. Who knew what angels might meet one unawares?[1] Not that Amy thought in biblical or in literary phrases. She was in the High School it is true, but she was simply passing through, "getting by" she would have said carelessly. The only reading that had ever made any impression on her had been fairy tales read to her in those long remote days when she had lived with the tall proud woman; and descriptions in novels or histories of beautiful, stately palaces tenanted by beautiful, stately women. She could pore over such pages for hours, her face flushed, her eyes eager.

At present she cast about for an excuse. She had so meant to get the braid. "There was a dress—" she began lamely, she was never deliberately dishonest.

Mr. Boldin cleared his throat and nervously fingered his paper. Cornelius ceased his awful playing and blinked at her short-sightedly through his thick glasses. Both of

---

[1] Hebrews 13:2. "Be not forgetful to entertain strangers: for thereby some have entertained angels unaware."

these, the man and the little boy, loved the beautiful, inconsequent creature with her airy, irresponsible ways. But Mrs. Boldin loved her too, and because she loved her she could not scold.

"Of course you forgot," she began chidingly. Then she smiled. "There was a dress that you looked at *perhaps*. But confess, didn't you go to the movies first?"

Yes, Amy confessed she had done just that. "And oh, Mrs. Boldin, it was the most wonderful picture—a girl—such a pretty one—and she was poor, awfully. And somehow she met the most wonderful people and they were so kind to her. And she married a man who was just tremendously rich and he gave her everything. I did so want Cornelius to see it."

"Huh!" said Cornelius who had been listening not because he was interested, but because he wanted to call Amy's attention to his playing as soon as possible. "Huh! I don't want to look at no pretty girl. Did they have anybody looping the loop in an airship?"

"You'd better stop seeing pretty girl pictures, Amy," said Mr. Boldin kindly. "They're not always true to life. Besides, I know where you can see all the pretty girls you want without bothering to pay twenty-five cents for it."

Amy smiled at the implied compliment and went on happily studying her lessons. They were all happy in their own way. Amy because she was sure of their love and admiration, Mr. and Mrs. Boldin because of her beauty and innocence and Cornelius because he knew he had in his foster-sister a listener whom his terrible practicing could never bore. He played brokenly a piece he had found in an old music-book. *"There's an aching void in every heart, brother."*

"Where do you pick up those old things, Neely?" said his mother fretfully. But Amy could not have her favorite's feelings injured.

"I think it's lovely," she announced defensively. "Cornelius, I'll ask Sadie Murray to lend me her brother's book. He's learning the cornet, too, and you can get some new pieces. Oh, isn't it awful to have to go to bed? Good-night, everybody." She smiled her charming, ever ready smile, the mere reflex of youth and beauty and content.

"You do spoil her, Mattie," said Mr. Boldin after she had left the room. "She's only seventeen—here, Cornelius, you go to bed—but it seems to me she ought to be more dependable about errands. Though she is splendid about some things," he defended her. "Look how willingly she goes off to bed. She'll be asleep before she knows it when most girls of her age would want to be up in the street."

But upstairs Amy was far from asleep. She lit one gas-jet and pulled down the shades. Then she stuffed tissue paper in the keyhole and under the doors, and lit the remaining gas-jets. The light thus thrown on the mirror of the ugly oak dresser was perfect. She slipped off the pink blouse and found two scarfs, a soft yellow and a soft pink,—she had had them in a scarf-dance for a school entertainment. She wound them and draped them about her pretty shoulders and loosened her hair. In the mirror she apostrophized the beautiful, glowing vision of herself.

"There," she said, "I'm like the girl in the picture. She had nothing but her beautiful face—and she did so want to be happy." She sat down on the side of the rather lumpy bed and stretched out her arms. "I want to be happy, too." She intoned it earnestly, almost like an incantation. "I want wonderful clothes, and people around me, men adoring me, and the world before me. I want—everything! It will come, it will all come because I want it so." She sat frowning intently as she was apt to do when very much engrossed. "And we'd all be so happy. I'd give Mr. and Mrs. Boldin money! And Cornelius—he'd go to college and learn all about his old airships. Oh, if I only knew how to begin!"

Smiling, she turned off the lights and crept to bed.

II

Quite suddenly she knew she was going to run away. That was in October. By December she had accomplished her purpose. Not that she was the least bit unhappy but because she must get out in the world,—she felt caged, imprisoned. "Trenton is stifling me," she would have told you, in her unconsciously adopted "movie" diction. New York she knew was the place for her. She had her plans all made. She had sewed steadily after school for two months—as she frequently did when she wanted to buy her season's wardrobe, so besides her carfare she had $25. She went immediately to a white Y.W.C.A., stayed there two nights, found and answered an advertisement for clerk and waitress in a small confectionery and bakery-shop, was accepted and there she was launched.

Perhaps it was because of her early experience when as a tiny child she was taken from that so different home and left at Mrs. Boldin's, perhaps it was some fault in her own disposition, concentrated and egotistic as she was, but certainly she felt no pangs of separation, no fear of her future. She was cold too,—unfired though so to speak rather than icy,—and fastidious. This last quality kept her safe where morality or religion, of neither of which had she any conscious endowment, would have availed her nothing. Unbelievably then she lived two years in New York, unspoiled, untouched, going to work on the edge of Greenwich Village early and coming back late, knowing almost no one and yet altogether happy in the expectation of something wonderful, which she knew some day must happen.

It was at the end of the second year that she met Zora Harrison. Zora used to come into lunch with a group of habitués of the place—all of them artists and writers Amy gathered. Mrs. Harrison (for she was married as Amy later learned) appealed to the girl because she knew so well how to afford the contrast to her blonde, golden beauty. Purple, dark and regal, enveloped in velvets and heavy silks, and strange marine blues she wore, and thus made Amy absolutely happy. Singularly enough, the girl, intent as she was on her own life and experiences, had felt up to this time no yearning to know these strange, happy beings who surrounded her. She did miss Cornelius, but otherwise she was never lonely, or if she was she hardly knew it, for she had always lived an inner life to herself. But Mrs. Harrison magnetized her—she could not keep her eyes from her face, from her wonderful clothes. She made conjectures about her.

The wonderful lady came in late one afternoon—an unusual thing for her. She smiled at Amy invitingly, asked some banal questions and their first conversation began. The acquaintance once struck up progressed rapidly—after a few weeks Mrs. Harrison invited the girl to come to see her. Amy accepted quietly, unaware that anything extraordinary was happening. Zora noticed this and liked it. She had an apartment in 12th Street in a house inhabited only by artists—she was by no means one herself. Amy was fascinated by the new world into which she found herself ushered; Zora's surroundings were very beautiful and Zora herself was a study. She opened to the girl's amazed vision fields of thought and conjecture, phases of whose existence Amy, who was a builder of phases, had never dreamed. Zora had been a poor girl of good family. She had wanted to study art, she had deliberately married a rich man and as deliberately obtained in the course of four years a divorce, and she was now living in New York studying by means of her alimony and enjoying to its fullest the life she loved. She took Amy on a footing with herself—the girl's refinement, her beauty, her interest in colors (though this in Amy at that time was purely sporadic, never consciously encouraged), all this gave Zora a figure about which to plan and build a romance. Amy had told her the truth, but not all about her coming to New York. She had grown tired of Trenton—her people were all dead—the folks with whom she lived were kind and good but not "inspiring" (she had borrowed the term from Zora and it was true, the Boldins, when one came to think of it, were not "inspiring"), so she had run away.

Zora had gone into raptures. "What an adventure! My dear, the world is yours. Why, with your looks and your birth, for I suppose you really belong to the Kildares who used to live in Philadelphia, I think there was a son who ran off and married an actress or someone—they disowned him I remember,—you can reach any height. You must marry a wealthy man—perhaps someone who is interested in art and who will let you pursue your studies." She insisted always that Amy had run away in order to study art. "But luck like that comes to few," she sighed, remembering her own plight, for Mr. Harrison had been decidedly unwilling to let her pursue her studies, at least to the extent she wished. "Anyway you must marry wealth,—one can always get a divorce," she ended sagely.

Amy—she came to Zora's every night now—used to listen dazedly at first. She had accepted willingly enough Zora's conjecture about her birth, came to believe it in fact—but she drew back somewhat at such wholesale exploitation of people to suit one's own convenience, still she did not probe too far into this thought—nor did she grasp at all the infamy of exploitation of self. She ventured one or two objections however, but Zora brushed everything aside.

"Everybody is looking out for himself," she said fairly. "I am interested in you, for instance, not for philanthropy's sake, not because I am lonely, and you are charming and pretty and don't get tired of hearing me talk. You'd better come and live with me awhile, my dear, six months or a year. It doesn't cost any more for two than for one, and you can always leave when we get tired of each other. A girl like you can always get a job. If you are worried about being dependent you can pose for me and design my frocks, and oversee Julienne"—her maid-of-all-work—"I'm sure she's a stupendous robber."

Amy came, not at all overwhelmed by the good luck of it—good luck was around the corner more or less for everyone, she supposed. Moreover, she was beginning to absorb some of Zora's doctrine—she, too, must look out for herself. Zora *was* lonely, she *did* need companionship, Julienne *was* careless about change and old blouses and left-over dainties. Amy had her own sense of honor. She carried out faithfully her share of the bargain, cut down waste, renovated Zora's clothes, posed for her, listened to her endlessly and bore with her fitfulness. Zora was truly grateful for this last. She was temperamental but Amy had good nerves and her strong natural inclination to let people do as they wanted stood her in good stead. She was a little stolid, a little unfeeling under her lovely exterior. Her looks at this time belied her—her perfect ivory-pink face, her deep luminous eyes,—very brown they were with purple depths that made one think of pansies—her charming, rather wide mouth, her whole face set in a frame of very soft, very live, brown hair which grew in wisps and tendrils and curls and waves back from her smooth, young forehead. All this made one look for softness and ingenuousness. The ingenuousness was there, but not the softness—except of her fresh, vibrant loveliness.

On the whole then she progressed famously with Zora. Sometimes the latter's callousness shocked her, as when they would go strolling through the streets south of Washington Square. The children, the people all foreign, all dirty, often very artistic, always immensely human, disgusted Zora except for "local color"—she really could reproduce them wonderfully. But she almost hated them for being what they were.

"Br-r-r, dirty little brats!" she would say to Amy. "Don't let them touch me." She was frequently amazed at her protégée's utter indifference to their appearance, for Amy herself was the pink of daintiness. They were turning from MacDougall into Bleecker Street one day and Amy had patted a child—dirty, but lovely—on the head.

"They are all people just like anybody else, just like you and me, Zora," she said in answer to her friend's protest.

"You *are* the true democrat," Zora returned with a shrug. But Amy did not understand her.

Not the least of Amy's services was to come between Zora and the too pressing attention of the men who thronged about her.

"Oh, go and talk to Amy," Zora would say, standing slim and gorgeous in some wonderful evening gown. She was an extraordinarily attractive creature, very white and pink, with great ropes of dazzling gold hair, and that look of no-age which only American women possess. As a matter of fact she was thirty-nine, immensely sophisticated and selfish, even, Amy thought, a little cruel. Her present mode of living just suited her; she could not stand any condition that bound her, anything at all *exigeant.*[2] It was useless for anyone to try to influence her. If she did not want to talk, she would not.

The men used to obey her orders and seek Amy sulkily at first, but afterwards with considerably more interest. She was so lovely to look at. But they really, as Zora knew, preferred to talk to the older woman, for while with Zora indifference was a role, second nature now but still a role—with Amy it was natural and she was also a trifle shallow. She had the admiration she craved, she was comfortable, she asked no more. Moreover she thought the men, with the exception of Stuart James Wynne, rather uninteresting—they were faddists for the most part, crazy not about art or music, but merely about some phase such as cubism or syncopation.

Wynne, who was much older than the other half-dozen men who weekly paid Zora homage—impressed her by his suggestion of power. He was a retired broker, immensely wealthy (Zora, who had known him since childhood, informed her), very set and purposeful and polished. He was perhaps fifty-five, widely traveled, of medium height, very white skin and clear, frosty blue eyes, with sharp, proud features. He liked Amy from the beginning, her childishness touched him. In particular he admired her pliability—not knowing it was really indifference. He had been married twice; one wife had divorced him, the other had died. Both marriages were unsuccessful owing

[2] (Fr.) Exacting.

to his dominant, rather unsympathetic nature. But he had softened considerably with years, though he still had decided views, was glad to see that Amy, in spite of Zora's influence, neither smoked nor drank. He liked her shallowness—she fascinated him.

Zora had told him much—just the kind of romantic story to appeal to the rich, powerful man. Here was beauty forlorn, penniless, of splendid birth,—for Zora once having connected Amy with the Philadelphia Kildares never swerved from that belief. Amy seemed to Wynne everything a girl should be—she was so unspoiled, so untouched. He asked her to marry him. If she had tried she could not have acted more perfectly. She looked at him with her wonderful eyes.

"But I am poor, ignorant—a nobody," she stammered. "I'm afraid I don't love you either," she went on in her pretty troubled voice, "though I do like you very, very much."

He liked her honesty and her self-depreciation, even her coldness. The fact that she was not flattered seemed to him an extra proof of her native superiority. He, himself, was a representative of one of the South's oldest families, though he had lived abroad lately.

"I have money and influence," he told her gravely, "but I count them nothing without you." And as for love—he would teach her that, he ended, his voice shaking a little. Underneath all his chilly, polished exterior he really cared.

"It seems an unworthy thing to say," he told her wistfully, for she seemed very young beside his experienced fifty-five years, "but anything you wanted in this world could be yours. I could give it to you,—clothes, houses and jewels."

"Don't be an idiot," Zora had said when Amy told her. "Of course, marry him. He'll give you a beautiful home and position. He's probably no harder to get along with than anybody else, and if he is, there is always the divorce court."

It seemed to Amy somehow that she was driving a bargain—how infamous a one she could not suspect. But Zora's teachings had sunk deep. Wynne loved her, and he could secure for her what she wanted. "And after all," she said to herself once, "it really is my dream coming true."

She resolved to marry him. There were two weeks of delirious, blissful shopping. Zora was very generous. It seemed to Amy that the whole world was contributing largely to her happiness. She was to have just what she wanted and as her taste was perfect she afforded almost as much pleasure to the people from whom she bought as to herself. In particular she brought rapture to an exclusive modiste in Forty-second Street who exclaimed at her "so perfect taste."

"Mademoiselle is of a marvelous, of an absolute correctness," she said.

Everything whirled by. After the shopping there was the small, impressive wedding. Amy stumbled somehow through the service, struck by its awful solemnity. Then later there was the journey and the big house waiting them in the small town, fifty miles south of Richmond. Wynne was originally from Georgia, but business and social interests had made it necessary for him to be nearer Washington and New York.

Amy was absolute mistress of himself and his home, he said, his voice losing its coldness. "Ah, my dear, you'll never realize what you mean to me—I don't envy any other man in this world. You are so beautiful, so sweet, so different!"

III

From the very beginning *he* was different from what she had supposed. To start with he was far, far wealthier, and he had, too, a tradition, a family-pride which to Amy was inexplicable. Still more inexplicably he had a race-pride. To his wife this was not only strange but foolish. She was as Zora had once suggested, the true democrat. Not that she preferred the company of her maids, though the reason for this did not lie *per se* in the fact that they were maids. There was simply no common ground. But she was uniformly kind, a trait which had she been older would have irritated her husband. As it was, he saw in it only an additional indication of her freshness, her lack of worldliness which seemed to him the attributes of an inherent refinement and goodness untouched by experience.

He, himself, was intolerant of all people of inferior birth or standing and looked with contempt on foreigners, except the French and English. All the rest were variously "guineys," "niggers," and "wops," and all of them he genuinely despised and hated, and talked of them with the huge intolerant carelessness characteristic of occidental civilization. Amy was never able to understand it. People were always first and last, just people to her. Growing up as the average colored American girl does grow up, surrounded by types of every hue, color and facial configuration she had had no absolute ideal. She was not even aware that there was one. Wynne, who in his grim way had a keen sense of humor, used to be vastly amused at the artlessness with which she let him know that she did not consider him to be good-looking. She never wanted him to wear anything but dark blue, or sombre mixtures always.

"They take away from that awful whiteness of your skin," she used to tell him, "and deepen the blue of your eyes."

In the main she made no attempt to understand him, as indeed she made no attempt to understand anything. The result, of course, was that such ideas as seeped into her mind stayed there, took growth and later bore fruit. But just at this period she was like a well-cared for, sleek, house-pet, delicately nurtured, velvety, content to let her days pass by. She thought almost nothing of her art just now except as her sensibilities were jarred by an occasional disharmony. Likewise, even to herself, she never criticized Wynne, except when some act or attitude of his stung. She could never understand why he, so fastidious, so versed in elegance of word and speech, so careful in his surroundings, even down to the last detail of glass and napery, should take such evident pleasure in literature of certain prurient type. He fairly revelled in the realistic novels which to her depicted sheer badness. He would get her to read to him, partly because he liked to be read to, mostly because he enjoyed the realism and in a slighter degree because he enjoyed seeing her shocked. Her point of view amused him.

"What funny people," she would say naively, "to do such things." She would not understand the liaisons and intrigues of women in the society novels, such infamy was stupid and silly. If one starved, it was conceivable that one might steal; if one were intentionally injured, one might hit back, even murder; but deliberate nastiness she could not envisage. The stories, after she had read them to him, passed out of her mind as completely as though they had never existed.

Picture the two of them spending three years together with practically no friction. To his dominance and intolerance she opposed a soft and unobtrusive indifference. What she wanted she had, ease, wealth, adoration, love, too, passionate and imperious, but she had never known any other kind. She was growing cleverer also, her knowledge of French increasing, she was acquiring a knowledge of politics, of commerce and of the big social questions, for Wynne's interests were exhaustive and she did most of his reading for him. Another woman might have yearned for a more youthful companion, but her native coldness kept her content. She did not love him, she had never really loved anybody, but little Cornelius Boldin—he had been such an enchanting, such a darling baby, she remembered,—her heart contracted painfully when she thought as she did very often of his warm softness.

"He must be a big boy now," she would think almost maternally, wondering—once she had been so sure!—if she would ever see him again. But she was very fond of Wynne, and he was crazy over her just as Zora had predicted. He loaded her with gifts, dresses, flowers, jewels—she amused him because none but colored stones appealed to her.

"Diamonds are so hard, so cold, and pearls are dead," she told him.

Nothing ever came between them, but his ugliness, his hatefulness to dependents. It hurt her so, for she was naturally kind in her careless, uncomprehending way. True, she had left Mrs. Boldin without a word, but she did not guess how completely Mrs. Boldin loved her. She would have been aghast had she realized how stricken her flight had left them. At twenty-two, Amy was still as good, as unspoiled, as pure as a child. Of course with all this she was too unquestioning, too selfish, too vain, but they were all faults of her lovely, lovely flesh. Wynne's intolerance finally got on her nerves. She used to blush for his unkindness. All the servants were colored, but she had long since ceased to think that perhaps she, too, was colored, except when he, by insult toward an employee, overt, always at least implied, made her realize his contemptuous dislike and disregard for a dark skin or Negro blood.

"Stuart, how can you say such things?" she would expostulate. "You can't expect a man to stand such language as that." And Wynne would sneer, "A man—you don't consider a nigger a man, do you? Oh, Amy, don't be such a fool. You've got to keep them in their places."

Some innate sense of the fitness of things kept her from condoling outspokenly with the servants, but they knew she was ashamed of her husband's ways. Of course, they left—it seemed to Amy that Peter, the butler, was always getting new "help,"—but most of the upper servants stayed, for Wynne paid handsomely and although his orders were meticulous and insistent the retinue of employees was so large that the individual's work was light.

Most of the servants who did stay on in spite of Wynne's occasional insults had a purpose in view. Callie, the cook, Amy found out, had two children at Howard University—of course she never came in contact with Wynne, the chauffeur had a crippled sister. Rose, Amy's maid and purveyor of much outside information, was the chief support of the family. About Peter, Amy knew nothing: he was a striking, taciturn man, very competent, who had left the Wynnes' service years before and had returned in Amy's third year. Wynne treated him with comparative respect. But Stephen, the new valet, met with entirely different treatment. Amy's heart yearned toward him, he was like Cornelius, with short-sighted, patient eyes, always willing, a little over-eager. Amy recognized him for what he was: a boy of respectable, ambitious parentage, striving for the means for an education; naturally far above his present calling, yet willing to pass through all this as a means to an end. She questioned Rosa about him.

"Oh, Stephen," Rosa told her, "yes'm, he's workin' for fair. He's got a brother at the Howard's and a sister at the Smith's. Yes'm, it do seem a little hard on him, but Stephen, he say, they're both goin' to turn roun' and help him when they get through. That blue silk has a rip in it, Miss Amy, if you was thinkin' of wearin' that. Yes'm, somehow I don't think Steve's very strong, kinda worries like. I guess he's sorta nervous."

Amy told Wynne. "He's such a nice boy, Stuart," she pleaded, "it hurts me to have you so cross with him. Anyway don't call him names." She was both surprised and frightened at the feeling in her that prompted her to interfere. She had held so aloof from other people's interests all these years.

"I *am* colored," she told herself that night. "I feel it inside of me. I must be or I couldn't care so about Stephen. Poor boy, I suppose Cornelius is just like him. I wish Stuart would let him alone. I wonder if all white people are like that. Zora was hard, too, on unfortunate people." She pondered over it a bit. "I wonder what Stuart would say if he knew I was colored?" She lay perfectly still, her smooth brow knitted, thinking hard. "But he loves me," she said to herself still silently. "He'll always love my looks," and she fell to thinking that all the wonderful happenings in her sheltered, pampered life had come to her through her beauty. She reached out an exquisite arm, switched on a light, and picking up a hand-mirror from a dressing-table, fell to studying her face. She was right. It was her chiefest asset. She forgot Stephen and fell asleep.

But in the morning her husband's voice issuing from his dressing-room across the hall, awakened her. She listened drowsily. Stephen, leaving the house the day before, had been met by a boy with a telegram. He had taken it, slipped it into his pocket, (he was just going to the mailbox) and had forgotten to deliver it until now, nearly twenty-four hours later. She could hear Stuart's storm of abuse—it was terrible, made up as it was of oaths and insults to the boy's ancestry. There was a moment's lull. Then she heard him again.

"If your brains are a fair sample of that black wench of a sister of yours—"

She sprang up then thrusting her arms as she ran into her pink dressing-gown. She got there just in time. Stephen, his face quivering, standing looking straight into Wynne's smoldering eyes. In spite of herself, Amy was glad to see the boy's bearing. But he did not notice her.

"You devil!" he was saying. "You white-faced devil! I'll make you pay for that!" He raised his arm. Wynne did not blench.

With a scream she was between them. "Go, Stephen, go,—get out of the house. Where do you think you are? Don't you know you'll be hanged, lynched, tortured?" Her voice shrilled at him.

Wynne tried to thrust aside her arms that clung and twisted. But she held fast till the door slammed behind the fleeing boy.

"God, let me by, Amy!" As suddenly as she had clasped him she let him go, ran to the door, fastened it and threw the key out the window.

He took her by the arm and shook her. "Are you mad? Didn't you hear him threaten me, me,—a nigger threaten me?" His voice broke with nigger, "And you're letting him get away! Why, I'll get him. I'll set bloodhounds on him, I'll have every white man in this town after him! He'll be hanging so high by midnight—" he made for the other door, cursing, half-insane.

How, *how* could she keep him back! She hated her weak arms with their futile beauty! She sprang toward him. "Stuart, wait," she was breathless and sobbing. She said the first thing that came into her head. "Wait, Stuart, you cannot do this thing." She thought of Cornelius—suppose it had been he—"Stephen,—that boy,—he is my brother."

He turned on her. "What!" he said fiercely, then laughed a short laugh of disdain. "You are crazy," he said roughly, "My God, Amy! How can you even in jest associate yourself with these people? Don't you suppose I know a white girl when I see one? There's no use in telling a lie like that."

Well, there was no help for it. There was only one way. He had turned back for a moment, but she must keep him many moments—an hour. Stephen must get out of town.

She caught his arm again. "Yes," she told him, "I did lie. Stephen is not my brother, I never saw him before." The light of relief that crept into his eyes did not escape her, it only nerved her. "But I *am* colored," she ended.

Before he could stop her she had told him all about the tall white woman. "She took me to Mrs. Boldin's and gave me to her to keep. She would never have taken me to her if I had been white. If you lynch this boy, I'll let the world, your world, know that your wife is a colored woman."

He sat down like a man suddenly stricken old, his face ashen. "Tell me about it again," he commanded. And she obeyed, going mercilessly into every damning detail.

IV

Amazingly her beauty availed her nothing. If she had been an older woman, if she had had Zora's age and experience, she would have been able to gauge exactly her influence over Wynne. Though even then in similar circumstances she would have taken the risk and acted in just the same manner. But she was a little bewildered at her utter miscalculation. She had thought he might not want his friends—his world by which he set such store—to know that she was colored, but she had not dreamed it could make any real difference to him. He had chosen her, poor and ignorant, but of a host of women, and had told her countless times of his love. To herself Amy Wynne was in comparison with Zora for instance, stupid and uninteresting. But his constant, unsolicited iterations had made her accept his idea.

She was just the same woman she told herself, she had not changed, she was still beautiful, still charming, still "different." Perhaps, that very difference had its being in the fact of her mixed blood. She had been his wife—there were memories—she could not see how he could give her up. The suddenness of the divorce carried her off her feet. Dazedly she left him—though almost without a pang for she had only liked him. She had been perfectly honest about this, and he, although consumed by the fierceness of his emotion toward her, had gradually forced himself to be content, for at least she had never made him jealous.

She was to live in a small house of his in New York, up town in the 80's. Peter was in charge and there was a new maid and a cook. The servants, of course, knew of the separation, but nobody guessed why. She was living on a much smaller basis than the one to which she had become so accustomed in the last three years. But she was very comfortable. She felt, at any rate she manifested, no qualms at receiving alimony from Wynne. That was the way things happened, she supposed when she thought of it at all. Moreover, it seemed to her perfectly in keeping with Wynne's former attitude toward her; she did not see how he could do less. She expected people to be consistent. That was why she was so amazed that he in spite of his oft iterated love, could let her go. If she had felt half the love for him which he had professed for her, she would not have sent him away if he had been a leper.

"Why I'd stay with him," she told herself, "if he were one, even as I feel now."

She was lonely in New York. Perhaps it was the first time in her life that she had felt so. Zora had gone to Paris the first year of her marriage and had not come back.

The days dragged on emptily. One thing helped her. She had gone one day to the modiste from whom she had bought her trousseau. The woman remembered her perfectly—"The lady with the exquisite taste for colors—ah, madame, but you have the rare gift." Amy was grateful to be taken out of her thoughts. She bought one or two daring but altogether lovely creations and let fall a few suggestions:

"That brown frock, Madame,—you say it has been on your hands a long time? Yes? But no wonder. See, instead of that dead white you should have a shade of ivory, that white cheapens it." Deftly she caught up a bit of ivory satin and worked out her idea. Madame was ravished.

"But yes, Madame Ween is correct,—as always. Oh, what a pity that the Madame is so wealthy. If she were only a poor girl—Mlle. Antoine, with the best eye for color in the place has just left, gone back to France to nurse her brother—this World War is of such a horror! If someone like Madame, now, could be found, to take the little Antoine's place!"

Some obscure impulse drove Amy to accept the half proposal: "Oh! I don't know, I have nothing to do just now. My husband is abroad." Wynne had left her with that impression. "I could contribute the money to the Red Cross or to charity."

The work was the best thing in the world for her. It kept her from becoming too introspective, though even then she did more serious, connected thinking than she had done in all the years of her varied life.

She missed Wynne definitely, chiefly as a guiding influence for she had rarely planned even her own amusements. Her dependence on him had been absolute. She used to picture him to herself as he was before the trouble—and his changing expressions as he looked at her, of amusement, interest, pride, a certain little teasing quality that used to come into his eyes, which always made her adopt her "spoiled child air," as he used to call it. It was the way he liked her best. Then last, there was that look he had given her the morning she had told him she was colored—it had depicted so many emotions, various and yet distinct. There were dismay, disbelief, coldness, a final aloofness.

There was another expression, too, that she thought of sometimes—the look on the face of Mr. Packard, Wynne's lawyer. She, herself, had attempted no defense.

"For God's sake why did you tell him, Mrs. Wynne?" Packard asked her. His curiosity got the better of him. "You couldn't have been in love, with that yellow rascal," he blurted out. "She's too cold really, to love anybody," he told himself. "If you didn't care about the boy why should you have told?"

She defended herself feebly. "He looked so like little Cornelius Boldin," she replied vaguely, "and he couldn't help being colored." A clerk came in then and Packard said no more. But into his eyes had crept a certain reluctant respect. She remembered the look, but could not define it.

She was so sorry about the trouble now, she wished it had never happened. Still if she had it to repeat she would act in the same way again. "There was nothing else for me to do," she used to tell herself.

But she missed Wynne unbelievably.

If it had not been for Peter, her life would have been almost that of a nun. But Peter, who read the papers and kept abreast of times, constantly called her attention, with all due respect, to the meetings, the plays, the sights which she ought to attend or see. She was truly grateful to him. She was very kind to all three of the servants. They had the easiest "places" in New York, the maids used to tell their friends. As she never entertained, and frequently dined out, they had a great deal of time off.

She had been separated from Wynne for ten months before she began to make any definite plans for her future. Of course, she could not go on like this always. It came to her suddenly that probably she would go to Paris and live there—why or how she did not know. Only Zora was there and lately she had begun to think that her life was to be like Zora's. They had been amazingly parallel up to this time. Of course she would have to wait until after the war.

She sat musing about it one day in the big sitting-room which she had had fitted over into a luxurious studio. There was a sewing-room off to the side from which Peter used to wheel into the room waxen figures of all colorings and contours so that she could drape the various fabrics about them to be sure of the best results. But today she was working out a scheme for one of Madame's customers, who was of her own color and size and she was her own lay-figure. She sat in front of the huge pier glass, a wonderful soft yellow silk draped about her radiant loveliness.

"I could do some serious work in Paris," she said half aloud to herself. "I suppose if I really wanted to, I could be very successful along this line."

Somewhere downstairs an electric bell buzzed, at first softly, then after a slight pause, louder, and more insistently.

If Madame sends me that lace today," she was thinking, idly, "I could finish this and start on the pink. I wonder why Peter doesn't answer the bell."

She remembered then that Peter had gone to New Rochelle on business and she had sent Ellen to Altman's to find a certain rare velvet and had allowed Mary to go with her. She would dine out, she told them, so they need not hurry. Evidently she was alone in the house.

Well she could answer the bell. She had done it often enough in the old days at Mrs. Boldin's. Of course it was the lace. She smiled a bit as she went downstairs thinking how surprised the delivery-boy would be to see her arrayed thus early in the afternoon. She hoped he wouldn't go. She could see him through the long, thick panels of glass in the vestibule and front door. He was just turning about as she opened the door.

This was no delivery-boy, this man whose gaze fell on her hungry and avid. This was Wynne. She stood for a second leaning against the doorjamb, a strange figure surely in the sharp November weather. Some leaves—brown, skeleton shapes—rose and swirled unnoticed about her head. A passing letter-carrier looked at them curiously.

"What are you doing answering the door?" Wynne asked her roughly. "Where is Peter? Go in, you'll catch cold."

She was glad to see him. She took him into the drawing room—a wonderful study in browns—and looked at him and looked at him.

"Well," he asked her, his voice eager in spite of the commonplace words, "are you glad to see me? Tell me what you do with yourself."

She could not talk fast enough, her eyes clinging to his face. Once it struck her that he had changed in some indefinable way. Was it a slight coarsening of that refined aristocratic aspect? Even in her subconsciousness she denied it.

He had come back to her.

"So I design for Madame when I feel like it, and send the money to the Red Cross and wonder when you are coming back to me." For the first time in their acquaintanceship she was conscious deliberately of trying to attract, to hold him. She put on her spoiled child air which had once been so successful.

"It took you long enough to get here," she pouted. She was certain of him now. His mere presence assured her.

They sat silent a moment, the late November sun bathing her head in an austere glow of chilly gold. As she sat there in the big brown chair she was, in her yellow dress, like some mysterious emanation, some wraith-like aura developed from the tone of her surroundings.

He rose and came toward her, still silent. She grew nervous, and talked incessantly with sudden unusual gestures. "Oh, Stuart, let me give you tea. It's right there in the pantry off the dining-room. I can wheel the table in." She rose, a lovely creature in her yellow robe. He watched her intently.

"Wait," he bade her.

She paused almost on tiptoe, a dainty golden butterfly.

"You are coming back to live with me?" he asked her hoarsely.

For the first time in her life she loved him.

"Of course I am coming back," she told him softly. "Aren't you glad? Haven't you missed me? I didn't see how you *could* stay away. Oh! Stuart, what a wonderful ring!"

For he had slipped on her finger a heavy dull gold band, with an immense sapphire in an oval setting—a beautiful thing of Italian workmanship.

"It is so like you to remember," she told him gratefully. "I love colored stones." She admired it, turning it around and around on her slender finger.

How silent he was, standing there watching her with his sombre yet eager gaze. It made her troubled, uneasy. She cast about for something to say.

"You can't think how I've improved since I saw you, Stuart. I've read all sorts of books—Oh! I'm learned," she smiled at him. "And Stuart," she went a little closer to him, twisting the button on his perfect coat, "I'm so sorry about it all,—about Stephen, that boy, you know. I just couldn't help interfering. But when we're married again, if you'll just remember how it hurts me to have you so cross—"

He interrupted her. "I wasn't aware that I spoke of our marrying again," he told her, his voice steady, his blue eyes cold.

She thought he was teasing. "Why you just asked me to. You said 'aren't you coming back to live with me—'"

Still she didn't comprehend. "But what do you mean?" she asked bewildered.

"What do you suppose a man means?" he returned deliberately, "when he asks a woman to live with him but not to marry him?"

She sat down heavily in the brown chair, all glowing ivory and yellow against its sombre depths.

"Like the women in those awful novels?" she whispered. "Not like those women!—Oh Stuart! you don't mean it!" Her very heart was numb.

"But you must care a little—" she was amazed at her own depth of feeling. "Why I care—there are all those memories back of us—you must want me really—"

"I do want you," he told her tensely. "I want you damnably. But—well—I might as well out with it—A white man like me simply doesn't marry a colored woman. After all what difference need it make to you? We'll live abroad—you'll travel, have all the things you love. Many a white woman would envy you." He stretched out an eager hand.

She evaded it, holding herself aloof as though his touch were contaminating. Her movement angered him.

"Oh, hell!" he snarled at her roughly. "Why don't you stop posing? What do you think you are anyway? Do you suppose I'd take you for my wife—what do you think can happen to you? What man of your own race could give you what you want? You don't suppose I am going to support you this way forever, do you? The court imposed no alimony. You've got to come to it sooner or later—you're bound to fall to some white man. What's the matter—I'm not rich enough?"

Her face flamed at that—"As though it were *that* that mattered!"

He gave her a deadly look. "Well, isn't it? Ah, my girl, you forget you told me you didn't love me when you married me. You sold yourself to me then. Haven't I reason to suppose you are waiting for a higher bidder?"

At these words something in her died forever, her youth, her illusions, her happy, happy blindness. She saw life leering mercilessly in her face. It seemed to her that she would give all her future to stamp out, to kill the contempt in his frosty insolent eyes. In a sudden rush of savagery she struck him, struck him across his hateful sneering mouth with the hand which wore his ring.

As *she* fell, reeling under the fearful impact of his brutal but involuntary blow, her mind caught at, registered two things. A little thin stream of blood was trickling across his chin. She had cut him with the ring, she realized with a certain savage satisfaction. And there was something else which she must remember, which she *would* remember if only she could fight her way out of this dreadful clinging blackness, which was bearing down upon her—closing her in.

When she came to she sat up holding her bruised, aching head in her palms, trying to recall what it was that had impressed her so.

Oh yes, her very mind ached with the realization. She lay back again on the floor, prone, anything to relieve that intolerable pain. But her memory, her thoughts went on.

"Nigger," he had called her as she fell, "nigger, nigger," and again, "nigger."

"He despised me absolutely," she said to herself wonderingly, "because I was colored. And yet he wanted me."

V

Somehow she reached her room. Long after the servants had come in she lay face downward across her bed, thinking. How she hated Wynne, how she hated herself! And for ten months she had been living off his money although in no way had she a claim on him. Her whole body burned with the shame of it.

In the morning she rang for Peter. She faced him, white and haggard, if the man noticed her condition, he made no sign. He was, if possible, more imperturbable than ever.

"Peter," she told him, her eyes and voice very steady, "I am leaving this house today and shall never come back."

"Yes, Miss."

"And, Peter, I am very poor now and shall have no money besides what I can make for myself."

"Yes, Miss."

Would nothing surprise him, she wondered dully. She went on "I don't know whether you knew it or not, Peter, but I am colored, and hereafter I mean to live among my own people. Do you think you could find a little house or little cottage not too far from New York?"

He had a little place in New Rochelle, he told her, his manner altering not one whit, or better yet his sister had a four-room house in Orange, with a garden, if he remembered correctly. Yes, he was sure there was a garden. It would be just the thing for Mrs. Wynne.

She had four hundred dollars of her very own which she had earned by designing for Madame. She paid the maids a month in advance—they were to stay as long as Peter needed them. She, herself, went to a small hotel in Twenty-eighth Street, and here Peter came for her at the end of ten days, with the acknowledgement of the keys and receipts from Mr. Packard. Then he accompanied her to Orange and installed her in her new home.

"I wish I could afford to keep you, Peter," she said a little wistfully, "But I am very poor. I am heavily in debt and I must get that off my shoulders at once."

Mrs. Wynne was very kind, he was sure; he could think of no one with whom he would prefer to work. Furthermore, he often ran down from New Rochelle to see his sister; he would come in from time to time, and in the spring would plant the garden if she wished.

She hated to see him go, but she did not dwell long on that. Her only thought was to work and work and work and save until she could pay Wynne back. She had not lived very extravagantly during those ten months and Peter was a perfect manager—in spite of her remonstrances he had given her every month an account of his expenses. She had made arrangements with Madame to be her regular designer. The French woman guessing that more than whim was behind this move drove a very shrewd bargain, but even then the pay was excellent. With care, she told herself, she could be free within two years, three at most.

She lived a dull enough existence now, going to work steadily every morning and getting home late at night. Almost it was like those early days when she had first left Mrs. Boldin, except that now she had no high sense of adventure, no expectation of great things to come, which might buoy her up. She no longer thought of phases and the proper setting for her beauty. Once indeed catching sight of her face late one night in the mirror in her tiny work-room in Orange, she stopped and scanned herself, loathing what she saw there.

"You *thing!*" she said to the image in the glass, "if you hadn't been so vain, so shallow!" And she had struck herself violently again and again across the face until her head ached.

But such fits of passion were rare. She had a curious sense of freedom in these days, a feeling that at last her brain, her senses were liberated from some hateful clinging thralldom. Her thoughts were always busy. She used to go over that last scene with Wynne again and again trying to probe the inscrutable mystery which she felt was at the bottom of the affair. She groped her way toward a solution, but always something stopped her. Her impulse to strike, she realized, and his brutal rejoinder had been actuated by something more than mere sex antagonism, there was *race* antagonism there—two elements clashing. That much she could fathom. But that he despising her, hating her for not being white should yet desire her! It seemed to her that his attitude toward her—hate and yet desire, was the attitude in microcosm of the whole white world toward her own, toward that world to which those few possible strains of black blood so tenuously and yet so tenaciously linked her.

Once she got hold of a big thought. Perhaps there *was* some root, some racial distinction woven in with the stuff of which she was formed which made her persistently kind and unexacting. And perhaps in the same way this difference, helplessly, inevitably operated in making Wynne and his kind, cruel or at best indifferent. Her reading for Wynne reacted to her thought—she remembered the grating insolence of white exploiters in foreign lands, the wrecking of African villages, the destruction of homes in Tasmania. She couldn't imagine where Tasmania was but wherever it was, it had been the realest thing in the world to its crude inhabitants.

Gradually she reached a decision. There were two divisions of people in the world—on the one hand insatiable desire for power; keenness, mentality; a vast and cruel pride. On the other there was ambition, it is true, but modified, a certain humble sweetness, too much inclination to trust, an unthinking, unswerving loyalty. All the advantages in the world accrued to the first division. But without bitterness she chose the second. She wanted to be colored, she hoped she was colored. She wished even that she did not have to take advantage of her appearance to earn a living. But that was to meet an end. After all she had contracted her debt with a white man, she would pay him with a white man's money.

The years slipped by—four of them. One day a letter came from Mr. Packard. Mrs. Wynne had sent him the last penny of the sum received from Mr. Wynne from February to November, 1914. Mr. Wynne had refused to touch the money, it was and would be indefinitely at Mrs. Wynne's disposal.

She never even answered the letter. Instead she dismissed the whole incident,—Wynne and all,—from her mind and began to plan for her future. She was free, free! She had paid back her sorry debt with labor, money and anguish. From now on she could do as she pleased. Almost she caught herself saying "something is going to happen." But she checked herself, she hated her old attitude.

But something *was* happening. Insensibly from the moment she knew of her deliverance, her thoughts turned back to a stifled hidden longing, which had lain, it seemed to her, an eternity in her heart. Those days with Mrs. Boldin! At night,—on her way to New York,—in the workrooms,—her mind was busy with little intimate pictures of that happy, wholesome, unpretentious life. She could see Mrs. Boldin, clean and portly, in a lilac chambray dress, upbraiding her for some trifling, yet exasperating fault. And Mr. Boldin, immaculate and slender, with his noticeably polished air—how kind he had always been, she remembered. And lastly, Cornelius: Cornelius in a thousand attitudes and engaged in a thousand occupations, brown and near-sighted and sweet—devoted to his pretty sister, as he used to call her; Cornelius, who used to come to her as a baby as willingly as to his mother; Cornelius spelling out colored letters on his blocks, pointing to them stickily with a brown, perfect finger; Cornelius singing like an angel in his breathy, sexless voice and later murdering everything possible on his terrible cornet. How had she ever been able to leave them all and the dear shabbiness of that home! Nothing, she realized, in all these years had touched her inmost being, had penetrated to the core of her cold heart like the memories of those early, misty scenes.

One day she wrote a letter to Mrs. Boldin. She, the writer, Madame A. Wynne, had come across a young woman, Amy Kildare, who said that as a girl she had run away from home and now she would like to come back. But she was ashamed to write. Madame Wynne had questioned the girl closely and she was quite sure that this Miss Kildare had in no way incurred shame or disgrace. It had been some time since Madame Wynne had seen the girl but if Mrs. Boldin wished, she would try to find her again—perhaps Mrs. Boldin would like to get in touch with her. The letter ended on a tentative note.

The answer came at once.

> My dear Madame Wynne:
> My mother told me to write you this letter. She says even if Amy Kildare had done something terrible, she would want her to come home again. My father says so too. My mother says, please find her as soon as you can and tell her to come back. She still misses her. We all miss her. I was a little boy when she left, but though I am in the High School now and play in the school orchestra, I would rather see her than do anything I know. If you see her, be sure to tell her to come right away. My mother says thank you.
>
> Yours respectfully,
> CORNELIUS BOLDIN

The letter came to the modiste's establishment in New York. Amy read it and went with it to Madame. "I must go away immediately. I can't come back—you may have these last two weeks for nothing." Madame, who had surmised long since the separation, looked curiously at the girl's flushed cheeks, and decided that "Monsieur Ween" had returned. She gave her fatalistic shrug. All Americans were crazy.

"But, yes, Madame, if you must go, absolument."[3]

When she reached the ferry, Amy looked about her searchingly. "I hope I'm seeing you for the last time. I'm going home, home!" Oh, the unbelievable kindness! She had left them without a word and they still wanted her back!

Eventually she got to Orange and to the little house. She sent a message to Peter's sister and set about her packing. But first she sat down in the little house and looked about her. She would go home, home—how she loved the word, she would stay there a while, but always there was life, still beckoning. It would beckon forever she realized to her adventurousness. Afterwards she would set up an establishment of her own,—she reviewed possibilities—in a rich suburb, where white women would pay for her expertness, caring nothing for realities, only for externals.

"As I myself used to care," she sighed. Her thoughts flashed on. "Then some day I'll work and help with colored people—the only ones who have really cared for and wanted me." Her eyes blurred.

---

[3] (Fr.) Absolutely.

She would never make any attempt to find out who or what she was. If she were white, there would always be people urging her to keep up the silliness of racial prestige. How she hated it all!

"Citizen of the world, that's what I'll be. And now I'll go home." Peter's sister's little girl came over to be with the pretty lady whom she adored.

"You sit here, Angel, and watch me pack," Amy said, placing her in a little arm-chair. And the baby sat there in silent observation, one tiny leg crossed over the other, surely the quaintest, gravest bit of bronze, Amy thought, that ever lived.

"Miss Amy cried," the child told her mother afterwards.

Perhaps Amy did cry, but if so she was unaware. Certainly she laughed more happily, more spontaneously than she had done for years. Once she got down on her knees in front of the little arm-chair and buried her face in the baby's tiny bosom.

"Oh Angel, Angel," she whispered, "do you suppose Cornelius still plays on that cornet?"

—1920

MINA LOY (1882-1966)

Painter, poet, and montage artist Mina Loy was called the prototype of the "modern woman" by the *New York Evening Sun* in 1917. Like Djuna Barnes, H.D., Edna St. Vincent Millay, and Dorothy Parker, Loy's life and work reflect the struggle to un-girdle herself from the Victorian garb and attitudes she was raised to assume. She was born in London, England, to Sigmund Lowy, a Hungarian-Jewish tailor with artistic sensibilities, and Julia Bryan, a British Protestant. She studied art in Europe and came under the influence of Futurism, a philosophy of modern artistic experimentation. She objected to its misogyny, but began writing experimental forms of poetry and prose (using the surname Loy) that would appear in American avant garde magazines such as *Camera Work* and *Others*.

In 1916, Loy moved to New York City, where she became a touchstone for European avant garde thinking. She wrote and performed with the Provincetown Players, a group of playwrights that included Susan Glaspell, Edna St. Vincent Millay, and Djuna Barnes. From 1918 to 1923, Loy lived in South America, New York, Florence, and Berlin, before settling in the expatriate community in Paris, where she published *Lunar Baedecker* (1923), her first book of poems, with Robert McAlmon's Contact Press. She managed a shop that featured her artistic designs, and continued to write while visiting Natalie Barney's lesbian salon and Sylvia Beach's Shakespeare & Co. Bookstore, among other expatriate havens. Her first marriage, to the artist Stephen Haweis, ended in divorce; her second husband, boxer Arthur Craven, died at sea. Two of her three children died young. Loy returned to New York prior to World War II, becoming an American citizen in 1946. She continued her writing and other artistic pursuits, and a new edition of her poetry attracted Denise Levertov, Robert Creeley, and others associated with the Black Mountain School of poets. Loy died of pneumonia in 1966, in Aspen, Colorado.

Parturition

I am the centre
Of a circle of pain
Exceeding its boundaries in every direction
The business of the bland sun
Has no affair with me   5
In my congested cosmos of agony
From which there is no escape
On infinitely prolonged nerve-vibrations
Or in contraction
To the pin-point nucleus of being   10

Locate an irritation   without
It is   within
                             Within
It is without
The sensitized area   15
Is identical   with the extensity
Of intension

I am the false quantity
In the harmony of physiological potentiality
To which   20
Gaining self-control
I should be consonant
In time

Pain is no stronger than the resisting force
Pain calls up in me   25
The struggle is equal

The open window is full of a voice
A fashionable portrait-painter
Running up-stairs to a woman's apartment
Sings   30
    "All the girls are tid'ly did'ly
    All the girls are nice
    Whether they wear their hair in curls
    Or—"
At the back of the thoughts to which I permit crystallization   35
The conception   Brute
Why?
        The irresponsibility of the male
Leaves woman her superior Inferiority
He is running up-stairs   40

I am climbing a distorted mountain of agony
Incidentally with the exhaustion of control
I reach the summit
And gradually subside into anticipation of

Repose 45
Which never comes
For another mountain is growing up
Which   goaded by the unavoidable
I must traverse
Traversing myself 50

Something in the delirium of night-hours
Confuses while intensifying sensibility
Blurring spatial contours
So aiding elusion of the circumscribed
That the gurgling of a crucified wild beast 55
Comes from so far away
And the foam on the stretched muscles of a mouth
Is no part of myself
There is a climax in sensibility
When pain surpassing itself 60
Becomes Exotic
And the ego succeeds in unifying the positive and negative poles
    of sensation
Uniting the opposing and resisting forces
In lascivious revelation

Relaxation 65
Negation of myself as a unit
       Vacuum interlude
I should have been emptied of life
Giving life
For consciousness in crises   races 70
Through the subliminal deposits of evolutionary processes
Have I not
Somewhere
Scrutinized
A dead white feathered moth 75
Laying eggs?
A moment
Being realization
Can
Vitalized by cosmic initiation 80
Furnish an adequate apology
For the objective
Agglomeration of activities
Of a life.
LIFE 85
A leap with nature
Into the essence
Of unpredicted Maternity
Against my thigh
Touch of infintesimal motion 90

Scarcely perceptible
Undulation
Warmth   moisture
Stir of incipient life
Precipitating into me   95
The contents of the universe

Mother I am
Identical
With infinite Maternity
    Indivisible   100
    Acutely
    I am absorbed
    Into
The was—is—ever—shall—be
Of cosmic reproductivity   105

Rises from the subconscious
Impression of a cat
With blind kittens
Among her legs
Same undulating life-stir   110
I am that cat

Rises from the sub-conscious
Impression of small animal carcass
Covered with blue-bottles
—Epicurean—   115
And through the insects
Waves that same undulation of living
Death
Life
I am knowing   120
All about
    Unfolding

The next morning
Each woman-of-the-people
Tip-toeing the red pile of the carpet   125
Doing hushed service
Each woman-of-the-people
Wearing a halo
A ludicrous little halo
Of which she is sublimely   unaware   130

I once heard in a church
—Man and woman God made them—
                    Thank God.

                                        —1914

Three Moments in Paris

I. One O'Clock at Night

Though you had never possessed me
I had belonged to you since the beginning of time
And sleepily I sat on your chair beside you
Leaning against your shoulder
And your careless arm across my back   gesticulated   5
As your indisputable male voice   roared
Through my brain and my body
Arguing dynamic decomposition
Of which I was understanding nothing
Sleepily   10
And the only less male voice of your brother pugilist of the intellect
Boomed   as it seemed to me   so sleepy
Across an interval of a thousand miles
An interim of a thousand years
But you who make more noise than any man in the world when you
   clear your throat
Deafening   woke me
And I caught the thread of the argument
Immediately assuming my personal mental attitude
And ceased to be a woman

Beautiful half-hour of being a mere woman   20
The animal woman
Understanding nothing of man
But mastery   and the security of imparted physical heat
Indifferent to cerebral gymnastics
Or regarding them as the self-indulgent play of children   25
Or the thunder of alien gods
But you woke me up
Anyhow   who am I that I should criticize your theories of
   plastic velocity

"Let us go home   she is tired   and wants to go to bed."

II. Café du Néant[1]

Little tapers leaning   lighted diagonally   30
Stuck in coffin tables of the Café du Néant
Leaning to the breath of baited bodies
Like young poplars fringing the Loire

Eyes that are full of love
And eyes that are full of kohl   35
Projecting light across the fulsome ambiente
Trailing the rest of the animal behind them
Telling of tales without words

---

[1] (Fr.) Café of Nothingness.

And lies of no consequence
One way or another   40

The young lovers hermetically buttoned up in black
To black cravat
To the blue powder edge dusting the yellow throat
What color could have been your bodies
When last you put them away   45
Nostalgic youth
Holding your mistress's pricked finger
In the indifferent flame of the taper
Synthetic symbol of   LIFE
In this factitious chamber of   DEATH   50
The woman
As usual
Is smiling   as bravely
As it is given to her to be   brave
While the brandy cherries   55
In winking glasses
Are decomposing
Harmoniously
With the flesh of spectators
And at a given spot   60
There is one
Who
Having the concentric lighting focussed precisely upon her
Prophetically blossoms in perfect putrefaction
Yet   there are cabs outside the door.   65

III. Magasins du Louvre [2]
All the virgin eyes in the world are made of glass

Long lines of boxes
Of dolls
Propped against banisters
Walls and pillars   70
Huddled on shelves
And composite babies with arms extended
Hang from the ceiling
Beckoning
Smiling   75
In a profound silence
Which the shop walker left trailing behind him
When he ambled to the further end of the gallery
To annoy the shop-girl

All the virgin eyes in the world are made of glass   80
They alone have the effrontery to

---

[2] Gift shop in the Louvre.

Stare through the human soul
Seeing nothing
Between parted fringes
One cocotte wears a bowler hat and a sham camellia   85
And one an iridescent boa
For there are two of them
Passing
And the solicitous mouth of one is straight
The other curved to a static smile   90
They see the dolls
And for a moment their eyes relax
To a flicker of elements unconditionally primeval
And now averted
Seek each other's   surreptitiously   95
To know if the other has seen
While mine are inextricably entangled with the pattern of the carpet
As eyes are apt to be
In their shame
Having surprised a gesture that is ultimately intimate   100

All the virgin eyes in the world are made of glass.

—1915

Gertrude Stein

Curie[3]
of the laboratory
of vocabulary
    she crushed
the tonnage   5
of consciousness
congealed to phrases
    to extract
a radium of the word

—1924

---

[3] Marie Sklodowska Curie (1867-1934) and her husband Pierre shared the 1903 Nobel Prize with Henri Becquerrel for their discovery of and work with radioactive elements.

ANNE SPENCER (1882-1975)

Annie Bethel Bannister was born in Virginia, the only child of Joel Cephus Bannister and Sarah Louise Scales. Spencer and her mother moved to Bramwell, West Virignia, after the marriage ended. Though her mother was nearly illiterate, Spencer finished high school and college, graduating from the Virginia Seminary in Lynchburg in 1899. She married classmate Edward Spencer in 1901 and had three children with him. Edward built a house in Lynchburg in 1903, where Spencer lived and maintained an extensive garden until her death—today, the house and its gardens are available for tours. The first Black librarian in Lynchburg, Spencer worked at a segregated Black school and also helped to organize Lynchburg's chapter of the NAACP in 1918. She was a significant figure in the Harlem Renaissance, publishing her poems in anthologies of Black writers and hosting artists, writers, and political leaders, among others, at her home. James Weldon Johnson suggested her pen name, and he also introduced her to a patron of Black writers, H. L. Mencken, who helped Spencer publish her first poem, "Before the Feast at Shushan." Spencer published only one poem after the Harlem Renaissance ended, though she continued to write and to host important African Americans at her home. Because she wrote on scraps of paper, however, much of her late work was lost when she was hospitalized toward the end of her life. Although Spencer never published a volume of her poetry, J. Lee Greene collected forty-two of her poems in a 1977 publication entitled *Time's Unfading Garden: Anne Spencer's Life and Poetry,* which, together with an increased interest in Black women writers in the 1980s, brought her work back into prominence. Many of Spencer's poems also appear in Maureen Honey's collection, *Shadowed Dreams: Women's Poetry of the Harlem Renaissance,* published in 1989.

Before the Feast at Shushan[1]

Garden of Shushan!
After Eden, all terrace, pool, and flower recollect thee:
Ye weaves in saffron and haze and Tyrian purple,
Tell yet what range in color wakes the eye;
Sorcerer, release the dreams born here when   5
Drowsy, shifting palm-shade enspells the brain;
And sound! ye with harp and flute ne'er essay
Before these star-noted birds escaped from paradise awhile to
Stir all dark, and dear, and passionate desire, till mine
Arms go out to be mocked by the softly kissing body of the wind—   10
Slave, send Vashti to her King![2]

The fiery wattles of the sun startle into flame
The marbled towers of Shushan:
So at each day's wane, two peers—the one in
Heaven, the other on earth—welcome with their   15
Splendor the peerless beauty of the Queen.

Cushioned at the Queen's feet and upon her knee
Finding glory for mine head,—still, nearly shamed
Am I, the King, to bend and kiss with sharp

---

[1] Palace of King Ahasuerus of Persia.
[2] Vashti, the wife of Ahasuerus, was commanded to appear before the king and court naked; she refused and was replaced by Esther. See Esther 1.

Breath the olive-pink of sandaled toes between;   20
Or lift me high to the magnet of a gaze, dusky,
Like the pool when but the moon-ray strikes to its depth;
Or closer press to crush a grape 'gainst lips redder
Than the grape, a rose in the night of her hair;
Then—Sharon's Rose[3] in my arms.   25

And I am hard to force the petals wide;
And you are fast to suffer and be sad.
Is any prophet come to teach a new thing
Now in a more apt time?
Have him 'maze how you say love is sacrament;   30
How, says Vashti, love is both bread and wine;
How to the altar may not come to break and drink,
Hulky flesh nor fleshly spirit!

I, thy lord, like not manna for meat as Judahn;
I, thy master, drink, and red wine, plenty, and when   35
I thirst. Eat meat, and full, when I hunger.
I, thy King, teach you and leave you, when I list.
No woman in all Persia sets out strange action
To confuse Persia's lord—
Love is but desire and thy purpose fulfillment;   40
I, thy King, so say!

                                                —1920

At the Carnival

Gay little Girl-of-the-Diving-Tank,
I desire a name for you,
Nice, as a right glove fits;
For you—who amid the malodorous
Mechanics of this unlovely thing,   5
Are darling of spirit and form.
I know you—a glance, and what you are
Sits-by-the-fire in my heart.
My Limousine-Lady knows you, or
Why does the slant-envy of her eye mark   10
Your straight air and radiant inclusive smile?
Guilt pins a fig-leaf; Innocence is its own adorning.
The bull-necked man knows you—this first time
His itching flesh sees form divine and vibrant health,
And thinks not of his avocation.   15
I came incuriously—
Set on no diversion save that my mind
Might safely nurse its brood of misdeeds
In the presence of a blind crowd.

---

[3] Flower mentioned in Song of Solomon 2:1.

The color of life was gray.   20
Everywhere the setting seemed right
For my mood!
Here the sausage and garlic booth
Sent unholy incense skyward;
There a quivering female-thing   25
Gestured assignations, and lied
To call it dancing;
There, too, were games of chance
With chance for none;
But oh! The Girl-of-the-Tank, at last!   30
Gleaming Girl, how intimately pure and free
The gaze you send the crowd,
As though you know the dearth of beauty
In its sordid life.
We need you—my Limousine-Lady,   35
The bull-necked man, and I.
Seeing you here brave and water-clean,
Leaven for the heavy ones of earth,
I am swift to feel that what makes
The plodder glad is good; and   40
Whatever is good is God.
The wonder is that you are here;
I have seen the queer in queer places,
But never before a heaven-fed
Naiad[4] of the Carnival-Tank!   45
Little Diver, Destiny for you,
Like as for me, is shod in silence;
Years may seep into your soul
The bacilli of the usual and the expedient;
I implore Neptune[5] to claim his child to-day!   50

—1923

White Things

Most things are colorful things—the sky, earth, and sea.
    Black men are most men; but the white are free!
White things are rare things; so rare, so rare
They stole from out a silvered world—somewhere.
Finding earth-plains fair plains, save greenly grassed,   5
They strewed white feathers of cowardice, as they passed;
    The golden stars with lances fine,
    The hills all red and darkened pine,
They blanched with their wand of power;
And turned the blood in a ruby rose   10
To a poor white poppy-flower.

[4] Freshwater nymph in Greek mythology.   [5] Roman god of the sea.

They pyred a race of black, black men,
And burned them to ashes white; then,
Laughing, a young one claimed a skull,
For the skull of a black is white, not dull,   15
    But a glistening awful thing
    Made, it seems, for this ghoul to swing
In the face of God with all his might,
And swear by the hell that sired him:
    "Man-maker, make white!"

—1923

Lady, Lady

Lady, Lady, I saw your face,
Dark as night withholding a star…
The chisel fell, or it might have been
You had borne so long the yoke of men.
Lady, Lady, I saw your hands,   5
Twisted, awry, like crumpled roots,
Bleached poor white in a sudsy tub,
Wrinkled and drawn from your rub-a-dub.
Lady, Lady, I saw your heart,
And altared there in its darksome place   10
Were the tongues of flames the ancients knew,
Where the good God sits to spangle through.

—1925

ELEANOR ROOSEVELT (1884-1962)

Born on October 11, 1884, to Anna Hall and Elliott Roosevelt (the younger brother of
Theodore Roosevelt) in New York City, Eleanor Roosevelt had a privileged upbringing
marred by tragedy. Her mother died of diphtheria when Roosevelt was eight and her father
succumbed to complications due to alcoholism shortly thereafter. Roosevelt then lived with
her maternal grandmother, who sent her to Allenswood Academy, a boarding school in
England. There, she became a bright, independent, and self-possessed young woman with a
sense of social responsibility. In 1905, she married her father's fifth cousin, Franklin Delano
Roosevelt, after meeting him at a White House reception. They had six children, one of whom
died in infancy.

As the young wife of a politician, Roosevelt became involved with organizations such as
the New York State League of Women Voters, the Red Cross, the Women's Trade Union
League, and the Women's Division of the New York Democratic State Committee. She was
especially active after her husband was stricken with polio in 1921 and her public work served
as a way of maintaining his political profile. After Franklin Roosevelt was elected president in
1932, she became a promoter of New Deal programs, a peace advocate, and an outspoken

supporter of the needs of minorities, women, and the poor. As First Lady, Roosevelt lectured widely, hosted a weekly radio program, and gave frequent press conferences that were limited to female reporters. She also wrote numerous articles and columns for women's magazines, as well as published her syndicated "My Day" newspaper column, written in a daily diary format, from 1935 until shortly before her death in 1962. Roosevelt turned her focus to human rights after the death of her husband in 1945. She served as the first female delegate to the United Nations, where she was influential in creating the Universal Declaration of Human Rights in 1948. Roosevelt continued to be a public figure—lecturing around the world, campaigning for Democratic candidates, and promoting civil rights—until she died, on November 7, 1962.

A Challenge to American Sportsmanship

I can well understand the bitterness of people who have lost loved ones at the hands of the Japanese military authorities, and we know that the totalitarian philosophy, whether it is in Nazi Germany or in Japan, is one of cruelty and brutality. It is not hard to understand why people living here in hourly anxiety for those they love have difficulty in viewing our Japanese problem objectively, but for the honor of our country, the rest of us must do so.

A decision has been reached to divide the disloyal and disturbing Japanese from the others in the War Relocation centers.[1] One center will be established for the disloyal and will be more heavily guarded and more restricted than those in which these Japanese have been in the past.[2] This separation is taking place now.

All the Japanese in the War Relocation centers have been carefully checked by the personnel in charge of the camps, not only on the basis of their own information but also on the basis of the information supplied by the Federal Bureau of Investigation, by G-2 for the Army, and by the Office of Naval Intelligence for the Navy. We can be assured, therefore, that they are now moving into this segregation center in northern California the people who are loyal to Japan.

Japanese-Americans who are proved completely loyal to the United States will, of course, gradually be absorbed. The others will be sent to Japan after the war.

At present, things are very peaceful in most of the Japanese Relocation centers. The strike that received so much attention in the newspapers last November in Poston, Arizona,[3] and the riot at Manzanar, California, in December[4] were settled effectively, and nothing resembling them has occurred since. It is not difficult to understand that uprooting thousands of people brought on emotional upsets that take time and adjustment to overcome.

Neither all the government people, naturally, nor all of the Japanese were perfect, and many changes in personnel had to be made. It was an entirely new undertaking for us, it had to be done in a hurry, and, considering the number of people involved, I think the whole job of handling our Japanese has, on the whole, been done well.

A good deal has already been written about the problem. One phase of it, however,

---

[1] 110,000 Japanese Americans, both U.S. citizens and resident aliens, were interned at ten War Relocation Centers, following a series of executive orders and military proclamations issued in early 1942.

[2] Internees who answered "no" to a series of complicated and confusing questions intended to evaluate their loyalty to the U.S. were sent to Tule Lake Segregation Center in California.

[3] November 19-24, 1942, strike protesting the arrest of two men by camp administrators.

[4] December 5-6, 1942, prisoners' riot protesting the arrest of a popular union leader.

I do not think has as yet been adequately stressed. To cover it, we must get our whole background straight.

We have in all 127,000 Japanese or Japanese-Americans in the United States. Of these, 112,000 lived on the West Coast. Originally, they were much needed on ranches and on large truck and fruit farms, but, as they came in greater numbers, people began to discover that they were competitors in the labor field.

The people of California began to be afraid of Japanese importation, so the Exclusion Act was passed in 1924.[5] No people of the Oriental race could become citizens of the United States by naturalization, and no quota was given to the Oriental nations in the Pacific.

This happened because, in one part of our country, they were feared as competitors, and the rest of our country knew them so little and cared so little about them that they did not even think about the principle that we in this country believe in: that of equal rights for all human beings.

We granted no citizenship to Orientals, so now we have a group of people (some of whom have been here as long as fifty years) who have not been able to become citizens under our laws. Long before the war, an old Japanese man told me that he had great-grandchildren born in this country and that he had never been back to Japan; all that he cared about was here on the soil of the United States, and yet he could not become a citizen.

The children of these Japanese, born in this country, are citizens, however, and now we have about 47,000 aliens, born in Japan, who are known as Issei, and about 80,000 American-born citizens, known as Nisei. Most of these Japanese-Americans have gone to our American schools and colleges, and have never known any other country or any other life than the life here in the United States.

The large group of Japanese on the West Coast preserved their national traditions, in part because they were discriminated against. Japanese were not always welcome buyers of real estate. They were not always welcome neighbors or participators in community undertakings. As always happens with groups that are discriminated against, they gather together and live as racial groups. The younger ones made friends in school and college, and became part of the community life, and prejudices lessened against them. Their elders were not always sympathetic to the changes thus brought about in manners and customs.

There is a group among the American-born Japanese called the Kibei. These are American citizens who have gone to Japan and returned to the United States. Figures compiled by the War Relocation Authority show that 72 percent of the American citizens have never been to Japan. Technically, the remainder, approximately 28 percent, are Kibei, but they include many young people who made only short visits, perhaps as children with their parents. Usually the term Kibei is used to refer to those who have received a considerable portion of their education in Japan.

While many of the Kibei are loyal to Japan, some of them were revolted by what they learned of Japanese militarism and are loyal to the land of their birth, America.

Enough for the background. Now we come to Pearl Harbor, December 7, 1941. There was no time to investigate families or to adhere strictly to the American rule that a man is innocent until he is proved guilty. These people were not convicted of any

---

[5] Part of the Immigration Act of 1924, specifically aimed at excluding Asians from legal immigration to the U.S., as well as denying them citizenship and property rights.

crime, but emotions ran too high. Too many people wanted to wreak vengeance on Oriental-looking people. Even the Chinese, our allies, were not always safe from insult on the streets. The Japanese had long been watched by the FBI, as were other aliens, and several hundred were apprehended at once on the outbreak of war and sent to detention camps.

Approximately three months after Pearl Harbor, the Western Defense Command ordered all persons of Japanese ancestry excluded from the coastal area, including approximately half of Washington, Oregon and California, and the southern portion of Arizona. Later, the entire state of California was added to the zone from which Japanese were barred.

At first, the evacuation was placed on a voluntary basis; the people were free to go wherever they liked in the interior of the country. But the evacuation on this basis moved very slowly, and furthermore, those who did leave encountered a great deal of difficulty in finding new places to settle. In order to avoid serious incidents, on March 29, 1942, the evacuation was placed on an orderly basis, and was carried out by the Army.

A civilian agency, the War Relocation Authority, was set up to work with the military in the relocation of the people. Because there was so much indication of danger to the Japanese unless they were protected, relocation centers were established where they might live until those whose loyalty could be established could be gradually reabsorbed into the normal life of the nation.

To many young people this must have seemed strange treatment of American citizens, and one cannot be surprised at the reaction that manifested itself, not only in young Japanese-Americans, but in others who had known them well and had been educated with them, and who asked bitterly, "What price American citizenship?"

Nevertheless, most of them realized that this was a safety measure. The Army carried out its evacuation, on the whole, with remarkable skill and kindness. The early situation in the centers was difficult. Many of them were not ready for occupation. The setting up of large communities meant an amount of organization which takes time, but the Japanese, for the most part, proved to be patient, adaptable and courageous.

There were unexpected problems and, one by one, these were discovered and an effort was made to deal with them fairly. For instance, these people had property and they had to dispose of it; often at a loss. Sometimes they could not dispose of it, and it remained unprotected, deteriorating in value as the months went by. Business had to be handled through agents, since the Japanese could not leave the camps.

Understandable bitterness against the Japanese is aggravated by the old-time economic fear on the West Coast and the unreasoning racial feeling which certain people, through ignorance, have always had wherever they came in contact with people who were different from themselves.

This is one reason why many people believe that we should have directed our original immigration more intelligently. We needed people to develop our country, but we should never have allowed any groups to settle as groups where they created little German or Japanese or Scandinavian "islands" and did not melt into our general community pattern. Some of the South American countries have learned from our mistakes and are now planning to scatter their needed immigration.

Gradually, as the opportunities for outside jobs are offered to them, loyal citizens and law-abiding aliens are going out of the relocation centers to start independent and productive lives again. Those not considered reliable, of course, are not permitted to leave. As a taxpayer, regardless of where you live, it is to your advantage, if you find one or two Japanese-American families settled in your neighborhood, to try to regard them as individuals and not to condemn them before they are given a fair chance to prove themselves in the community.

"A Japanese is always a Japanese" is an easily accepted phrase and it has taken hold quite naturally on the West Coast because of some reasonable or unreasonable fear back of it, but it leads nowhere and solves nothing. Japanese-Americans may be no more Japanese than a German-American is German, or an Italian-American is Italian. All of these people, including the Japanese-Americans, have men who are fighting today for the preservation of the democratic way of life and the ideas around which our nation was built.

We have no common race in this country, but we have an ideal to which all of us are loyal. It is our ideal which we want to have live. It is an ideal which can grow with our people, but we cannot progress if we look down upon any group of people among us because of race or religion. Every citizen in this country has a right to our basic freedoms, to justice and to equality of opportunity, and we retain the right to lead our individual lives as we please, but we can only do so if we grant to others the freedoms that we wish for ourselves.

—1943

Freedom: Promise or Fact

If I were a Negro today, I think I would have moments of great bitterness. It would be hard for me to sustain my faith in democracy and to build up a sense of goodwill toward men of other races.

I think, however, that I would realize that if my ancestors had never left Africa, we would be worse off as "natives" today under the rule of any other country than I am in this country where my people were brought as slaves.

In a comparatively short period of time the slaves have become free men—free men, that is, as far as a proclamation can make them so. There now remains much work to be done to see that freedom becomes a fact and not just a promise for my people.

I know, however, that I am not the only group that has to make a similar fight. Even women of the white race still suffer inequalities and injustices, and many groups of white people in my country are slaves of economic conditions. All the world is suffering under a great war brought about because of the lag in our social development against the progress in our economic development.

I would know that I had to work hard and to go on accomplishing the best that was possible under present conditions. Even though I was held back by generations of economic inequality, I would be proud of those of my race who are gradually fighting to the top in whatever occupation they are engaged in.

I would still feel that I ought to participate to the full in the war. When the United Nations win, certain things will be accepted as a result of principles which have been enunciated by the leaders of the United Nations, which never before have been part of the beliefs and practices of the greater part of the world.

I would certainly go on working for complete economic equality and my full rights under a democratic government. I would decide which were the steps that I felt represented my real rights as a citizen and I would work for those first, feeling that other things such as social relationships might well wait until certain people were given time to think them through and decide as individuals what they wished to do.

I would not do too much demanding. I would take every chance that came my way to prove my quality and my ability and if recognition was slow, I would continue to prove myself, knowing that in the end good performance has to be acknowledged.

I would accept every advance that was made in the Army and Navy, though I would not try to bring those advances about any more quickly than they were offered. I would certainly affiliate with the labor movement because there is the greatest opportunity for men to work side by side and find out that it is possible to have similar interests and to stand by each other, regardless of race or color.

I would try to remember that unfair and unkind treatment will not harm me if I do not let it touch my spirit. Evil emotions injure the man or woman who harbors them so I would try to fight down resentment, the desire for revenge and bitterness. I would try to sustain my own faith in myself by counting over my friends and among them there would undoubtedly be some white people.

—1943

The Atomic Bomb

The news which came to us yesterday afternoon of the first use of the atomic bomb in the war with Japan may have surprised a good many people, but scientists—both British and American—have been working feverishly to make this discovery before our enemies, the Germans, could make it and thereby possibly win the war.

This discovery may be of great commercial value some day. If it is wisely used, it may serve the purposes of peace. But for the moment we are chiefly concerned with its destructive power. That power can be multiplied indefinitely, so that not only whole cities but large areas may be destroyed at one fell swoop. If you face this possibility and realize that, having once discovered a principle it is very easy to take further steps to magnify its power, you soon face the unpleasant fact that in the next war whole peoples may be destroyed.

The only safe counter weapon to this new power is the firm decision of mankind that it should be used for constructive purposes only. This discovery must spell the end of the war. We have been paying an ever increasing price for indulging ourselves in this uncivilized way of settling difficulties. We can no longer indulge in the slaughter of young men. The price will be too high and will be paid not just by young men, but by whole populations.

In the past we have given lip service to the desire for peace. Now we meet the test of really working to achieve something basically new in the world. Religious groups have been telling us for a long time that peace could be achieved only by a basic change in the nature of man. I am inclined to think that this is true. But if we give human beings sufficient incentive, they may find good reasons for reshaping their characteristics.

Good will among men was preached by the angels as they announced to the world the birth of the child Jesus. He exemplified it in His life and preached it Himself and sent forth His disciples, who have spread that gospel of love and human understanding throughout the world ever since. Yet the minds and hearts of men seemed closed.

Now, however, an absolute need exists for facing a non-escapable situation. This new discovery cannot be ignored. We have only two alternative choices: destruction and death—or construction and life! If we desire our civilization to survive, then we must accept the responsibility of constructive work and of the wise use of a knowledge greater than any ever achieved by man before.

—1945

SARA TEASDALE (1884-1933)

Sara Teasdale was born in St. Louis, Missouri, on August 8, 1884, to a successful middle-class couple in their forties: John Warren Teasdale, a kind but conservative Baptist, and Mary Elizabeth Willard, a strong woman with Puritan ancestry. In keeping with Victorian notions of feminine submissiveness, Teasdale's parents raised her to be sickly, sensitive, and overly dependent. As a result, Teasdale suffered spells of physical and mental fatigue throughout her life, taking periodic rest cures in Connecticut and elsewhere. Her education was limited to home tutoring and schools close to home. In 1903 she met Williamina Parrish, who organized the Potters, a women's group that was devoted to the arts, particularly female artists such as the Greek poet Sappho and the Italian actress Eleonora Duse. Teasdale gained confidence as a poet through her association with the Potters and their magazine, *The Potter's Wheel.* She published her first poem in the *Mirror,* a St. Louis journal with a growing national reputation, in 1906. The following year, Teasdale's parents paid to have her first book, *Sonnets to Duse and Other Poems,* published by a Boston firm. Teasdale's future collections were underwritten by publishers; four of her books, *Rivers to Sea* (1915), *Love Songs* (1917), *Flame and Shadow* (1920), and *Dark of the Moon* (1926), sold well enough to require multiple printings. In 1918 *Love Songs* won the Columbia University Poetry Society Prize for "best book," a precursor of the Pulitzer Prize for Poetry, which was established in 1922. Although Teasdale's poetry may appear conventional or quaint by current standards, its clearly stated exploration of female emotion was a new development in turn-of-the-century verse. Despite a successful career, Teasdale had relatively little happiness in her personal life. She maintained long flirtations with poets Vachel Lindsay and John Hall Wheelock, but married businessman Ernst Filsinger in 1914. Amid concerns that marriage and children would encroach on her writing, she aborted their child and eventually filed for divorce in 1929. She continued to travel and support herself by writing, but after contracting pneumonia she became severely depressed and committed suicide in 1933.

A Song to Eleonora Duse in "Francesca da Rimini"[1]

Oh would I were the roses, that lie against her hands,
The heavy burning roses she touches as she stands!

---

[1] Eleonora Duse (1858-1924), famous Italian actress who toured with her own company in Europe and the U.S. The play *Francesca da Rimini* was written for her by her lover, Gabriele D' Annunzio (1863-1938).

Dear hands that hold the roses, where mine would love to be,
Oh leave, oh leave the roses, and hold the hands of me!
She draws the heart from out them, she draws away their breath,— 5
Oh would that I might perish and find so sweet a death!

—1907

I Shall Not Care

When I am dead and over me bright April
    Shakes out her rain-drenched hair,
Tho' you should lean above me broken-hearted,
    I shall not care.

I shall have peace, as leafy trees are peaceful 5
    When rain bends down the bough,
And I shall be more silent and cold-hearted
    Than you are now.

—1915

New Year's Dawn—Broadway

When the horns wear thin
And the noise, like a garment outworn,
Falls from the night,
The tattered and shivering night,
That thinks she is gay; 5
When the patient silence comes back,
And retires,
And returns,
Rebuffed by a ribald song,
Wounded by vehement cries, 10
Fleeing again to the stars—
Ashamed of her sister the night;
Oh, then they steal home,
The blinded, the pitiful ones
With their gew-gaws still in their hands, 15
Reeling with odorous breath
And thick, coarse words on their tongues.
They get them to bed, somehow,
And sleep the forgiving,
Comes thru the scattering tumult 20
And closes their eyes.
The stars sink down ashamed
And the dawn awakes,
Like a youth who steals from a brothel,
Dizzy and sick.

—1915

EDNA FERBER (1885-1968)

The second daughter of Hungarian-born, Jewish store owner Jacob Ferber and his Milwaukee-born wife, Julia Neumann Ferber, Edna Ferber was born in Kalamazoo, Michigan. Her father's ill health and encounters with anti-Semitism had the family moving frequently; they settled in Appleton, Wisconsin, when Ferber was twelve. She began work as a reporter after graduating from high school. Her first novel, *Dawn O'Hara, The Girl Who Laughed* (1911), was followed by thirty stories about divorced skirt saleswoman Emma McChesney, published between 1911 and 1915, which gained her national attention. Her first play, *Our Mrs. McChesney,* in 1915, starred Ethel Barrymore. At the height of her popularity in the 1920s and 1930s, critics named Ferber the greatest American woman writer of her day. Ferber's fiction frequently depicts assertive women in difficult circumstances, evidencing her feminist sympathies, and she often addresses racism and bigotry with characters drawn from many different ethnic groups. In addition to being a prolific and popular novelist, Ferber collaborated with George S. Kaufman on plays, including *The Royal Family* (1927), *Dinner at Eight* (1932), and *Stage Door* (1936), and was, with Kaufman and Dorothy Parker, a member of the Algonquin Round Table. She won the Pulitzer Prize in 1924 for *So Big,* which was twice adapted for film. Ferber's novels include *Show Boat* (1926), the basis for the Broadway musical; *Cimarron* (1929), the film version of which won the Academy Award for Best Picture in 1931; and *Giant* (1952), the film version of which was nominated for an Academy Award for Best Picture in 1957. In addition to her many novels, plays, and collections of short stories, Ferber wrote two autobiographies. She died of cancer in her New York home.

Sisters Under Their Skin

Women who know the joys and sorrows of a pay envelope do not speak of girls who work as Working Girls. Neither do they use the term Laboring Class, as one would speak of a distinct and separate race, like the Ethiopian.

Emma McChesney Buck was no exception to this rule. Her fifteen years of man-size work for a man-size salary in the employ of the T. A. Buck Featherloom Petticoat Company, New York, precluded that. In those days, she had been Mrs. Emma McChesney, known from coast to coast as the most successful traveling saleswoman in the business. It was due to her that no feminine clothes-closet was complete without a Featherloom dangling from one hook. During those fifteen years she had educated her son, Jock McChesney, and made a man of him; she had worked, fought, saved, triumphed, smiled under hardship; and she had acquired a broad and deep knowledge of those fascinating and diversified subjects which we lump carelessly under the heading of Human Nature. She was Mrs. T. A. Buck now, wife of the head of the firm, and partner in the most successful skirt manufactory in the country. But the hard-working, clear-thinking, sane-acting habits of those fifteen years still clung.

Perhaps this explained why every machine-girl in the big, bright shop back of the offices raised adoring eyes when Emma entered the workroom. Italian, German, Hungarian, Russian—they lifted their faces toward this source of love and sympathetic understanding as naturally as a plant turns its leaves toward the sun. They glowed under her praise; they confided to her their troubles; they came to her with their joys—and they copied her clothes.

This last caused her some uneasiness. When Mrs. T. A. Buck wore blue serge, an epidemic of blue serge broke out in the workroom. Did Emma's spring hat flaunt flowers, the elevators, at closing time, looked like gardens abloom. If she appeared on Monday morning in severely tailored white-linen blouse, the shop on Tuesday was a Boston seminary in its starched primness.

"It worries me," Emma told her husband-partner. "I can't help thinking of the story of the girl and the pet chameleon. What would happen if I were to forget myself some day and come down to work in black velvet and pearls?"

"They'd manage it somehow," Buck assured her. "I don't know just how; but I'm sure that twenty-four hours later our shop would look like a Buckingham drawing-room when the court is in mourning."

Emma never ceased to marvel at their ingenuity, at their almost uncanny clothes-instinct. Their cheap skirts hung and fitted with an art as perfect as that of a Fifty-seventh Street *modiste*;[1] their blouses, in some miraculous way, were of today's style, down to the last detail of cuff or collar or stitching; their hats were of the shape that the season demanded, set at the angle that the season approved, and finished with just that repression of decoration which is known as "single trimming." They wore their clothes with a *chic* that would make the far-famed Parisian *ouvrière*[2] look dowdy and down at heel in comparison. Upper Fifth Avenue, during the shopping or tea-hour, has been sung, painted, vaunted, boasted. Its furs and millinery, its eyes and figure, its complexion and ankles have flashed out at us from ten thousand magazine covers, have been adjectived in reams of Sunday-supplement stories. Who will picture Lower Fifth Avenue between five and six, when New York's unsung beauties pour into the streets from a thousand loft-buildings? Theirs is no mere empty pink-and-white prettiness. Poverty can make prettiness almost poignantly lovely, for it works with a scalpel. Your Twenty-sixth Street beauty has a certain wistful appeal that your Forty-sixth Street beauty lacks; her very bravado, too, which falls just short of boldness, adds a final piquant touch. In the face of the girl who works, whether she be a spindle-legged errand-girl or a ten-thousand-a-year foreign buyer, you will find both vivacity and depth of expression. What she loses in softness and bloom she gains in a something that peeps from her eyes, that lurks in the corners of her mouth. Emma never tired of studying them—these girls with their firm, slim throats, their lovely faces, their Oriental eyes, and their conscious grace. Often, as she looked, an unaccountable mist of tears would blur her vision.

So that sunny little room whose door was marked "MRS. BUCK" had come to be more than a mere private office for the transaction of business. It was a clearing-house for trouble; it was a shrine, a confessional, and a court of justice. When Carmela Colarossi, her face swollen with weeping, told a story of parental harshness grown unbearable, Emma would put aside business to listen, and six o'clock would find her seated in the dark and smelly Colarossi kitchen, trying, with all her tact and patience and sympathy, to make home life possible again for the flashing-eyed Carmela. When the deft, brown fingers of Otti Markis became clumsy at her machine, and her wage slumped unaccountably from sixteen to six dollars a week, it was in Emma's quiet little office that it became clear why Otti's eyes were shadowed and why Otti's mouth drooped so pathetically. Emma prescribed a love philter made up of common sense, understanding, and world-wisdom. Otti took it, only half comprehending, but sure of its power. In a week, Otti's eyes were shadowless, her lips smiling, her pay-envelope

---

[1] (Fr.) Dressmaker.   [2] (Fr.) Woman worker.

bulging. But it was in Sophy Kumpf that the T. A. Buck Company best exemplified its policy. Sophy Kumpf had come to Buck's thirty years before, slim, pink-cheeked, brown-haired. She was a grandmother now, at forty-six, broad-bosomed, broad-hipped, but still pink of cheek and brown of hair. In those thirty years she had spent just three away from Buck's. She had brought her children into the world; she had fed them and clothed them and sent them to school, had Sophy, and seen them married, and helped them to bring their children into the world in turn. In her round, red, wholesome face shone a great wisdom, much love, and that infinite understanding which is born only of bitter experience. She had come to Buck's when old T. A. was just beginning to make Featherlooms a national institution. She had seen his struggles, his prosperity; she had grieved at his death; she had watched young T. A. take the reins in his unaccustomed hands, and she had gloried in Emma McChesney's rise from office to salesroom, from salesroom to road, from road to private office and recognized authority. Sophy had left her early work far behind. She had her own desk now in the busy workshop, and it was she who allotted the piece-work, marked it in her much-thumbed ledger—that powerful ledger which, at the week's end, decided just how plump or thin each pay-envelope would be. So the shop and office at T. A. Buck's were bound together by many ties of affection and sympathy and loyalty; and these bonds were strongest where, at one end, they touched Emma McChesney Buck, and, at the other, faithful Sophy Kumpf. Each a triumphant example of Woman in Business.

It was at this comfortable stage of Featherloom affairs that the Movement struck the T. A. Buck Company. Emma McChesney Buck had never mingled much in movements. Not that she lacked sympathy with them; she often approved of them, heart and soul. But she had been heard to say that the Movers got on her nerves. Those well-dressed, glib, staccato ladies who spoke with such ease from platforms and whose pictures stared out at one from the woman's page failed, somehow, to convince her. When Emma approved a new movement, it was generally in spite of them, never because of them. She was brazenly unapologetic when she said that she would rather listen to ten minutes of Sophy Kumpf's world-wisdom than to an hour's talk by the most magnetic and silken-clad spellbinder in any cause. For fifteen business years, in the office, on the road, and in the thriving workshop, Emma McChesney had met working women galore. Women in offices, women in stores, women in hotels—chambermaids, clerks, buyers, waitresses, actresses in road companies, women demonstrators, occasional traveling saleswomen, women in factories, scrub-women, stenographers, models—every grade, type and variety of working woman, trained and untrained. She never missed a chance to talk with them. She never failed to learn from them. She had been one of them, and still was. She was in the position of one who is on the inside, looking out. Those other women urging this cause or that were on the outside, striving to peer in.

The Movement struck T. A. Buck's at eleven o'clock Monday morning. Eleven o'clock Monday morning in the middle of a busy fall season is not a propitious moment for idle chit-chat. The three women who stepped out of the lift at the Buck Company's floor looked very much out of place in that hummingly busy establishment and appeared, on the surface, at least, very chit-chatty indeed. So much so, that T. A. Buck, glancing up from the cards which had preceded them, had difficulty in repressing a frown of annoyance. T. A. Buck, during his college-days, and for a lamentably long time after, had been known as "Beau" Buck, because of his faultless clothes and his charming manner. His eyes had something to do with it, too, no doubt. He had lived down the title by sheer force of business ability. No one thought of using the nickname now, though the clothes, the manner, and the eyes were the same. At the entrance of the three women, he had been engrossed in the difficult task of selling a fall line to Mannie Nussbaum, of Portland, Oregon. Mannie was what is known as a temperamental buyer. He couldn't be forced; he couldn't be coaxed; he couldn't be led. But when he liked a line he bought like mad, never cancelled, and T. A. Buck had just got him going. It spoke volumes for his self-control that he could advance toward the waiting three, his manner correct, his expression bland.

"I am Mr. Buck," he said. "Mrs. Buck is very much engaged. I understand your visit has something to do with the girls in the shop. I'm sure our manager will be able to answer any questions—"

The eldest women raised a protesting, white-gloved hand.

"Oh, no—no, indeed! We must see Mrs. Buck." She spoke in the crisp, decisive platform-tones of one who is often addressed as "Madam Chairman."

Buck took a firmer grip on his self-control.

"I'm sorry; Mrs. Buck is in the cutting-room."

"We'll wait," said the lady, brightly. She stepped back a pace. "This is Miss Susan H. Croft"—indicating a rather sparse person of very certain years—"But I need scarcely introduce her."

"Scarcely," murmured Buck, and wondered why.

"This is my daughter, Miss Gladys Orton-Wells."

Buck found himself wondering why this slim, negative creature should have such sad eyes. There came an impatient snort from Mannie Nussbaum. Buck waved a hasty hand in the direction of Emma's office.

"If you'll wait there, I'll send in to Mrs. Buck."

The three turned toward Emma's bright little office. Buck scribbled a hasty word on one of the cards.

Emma McChesney Buck was leaning over the great cutting-table, shears in hand. It might almost be said that she sprawled. Her eyes were very bright, and her cheeks were very pink. Across the table stood a designer and two cutters, and they were watching Emma with an intentness as flattering as it was sincere. They were looking not only at cloth but at an idea.

"Get that?" asked Emma crisply, and tapped the pattern spread before her with the point of her shears. "That gives you the fulness without bunching, d'you see?"

"Sure," assented Koritz, head designer; "but when you get it cut you'll find this piece is wasted, ain't it?" He marked out a triangular section of cloth with one expert forefinger.

"No; that works into the ruffle," explained Emma. "Here, I'll cut it. Then you'll see."

She grasped the shears firmly in her right hand, smoothed the cloth spread before her with a nervous little pat of her left, pushed her bright hair back from her forehead, and prepared to cut. At which critical moment there entered Annie, the errand-girl, with the three bits of white pasteboard.

Emma glanced down at them and waved Annie away.

"Can't see them. Busy."

Annie stood her ground.

"Mr. Buck said you'd see 'em. They're waiting."

Emma picked up one of the cards. On it Buck had scribbled a single word: "Movers."

Mrs. T. A. Buck smiled. A little malicious gleam came into her eyes.

"Show 'em in here, Annie," she commanded, with a wave of the huge shears. "I'll teach 'em to interrupt me when I've got my hands in the bluing-water."

She bent over the table again, measuring with her keen eye. When the three were ushered in a moment later, she looked up briefly and nodded, then bent over the table again. But in that brief moment she had the three marked, indexed and pigeonholed. If one could have looked into that lightning mind of hers, one would have found something like this:

"Hmm! What Ida Tarbell[3] calls 'Restless women.' Money, and always have had it. Those hats were born in one of those exclusive little shops off the Avenue. Rich but somber. They think they're advanced, but they still resent the triumph of the motor-car over the horse. That girl can't call her soul her own. Good eyes, but too sad. He probably didn't suit mother."

What she said was:

"Howdy-do. We're just bringing a new skirt into the world. I thought you might like to be in at the birth."

"How very interesting!" chirped the two older women. The girl said nothing, but a look of anticipation brightened her eyes. It deepened and glowed as Emma McChesney Buck bent to her task and the great jaws of the shears opened and shut on the virgin cloth. Six pairs of eyes followed the fascinating steel before which the cloth rippled and fell away, as water is cleft by the prow of a stanch little boat. Around the curves went the shears, guided by Emma's firm white hands, snipping, slashing, doubling on itself, a very swashbuckler of a shears.

"There!" exclaimed Emma at last, and dropped the shears on the table with a clatter. "Put that together and see whether it makes a skirt or not. Now, ladies!"

The three drew a long breath. It was the sort of sound that comes up from the crowd when a sky-rocket has gone off successfully, with a final shower of stars.

"Do you do that often?" ventured Mrs. Orton-Wells.

"Often enough to keep my hand in," replied Emma, and led the way to her office.

The three followed in silence. They were strangely silent, too, as they seated themselves around Emma Buck's desk. Curiously enough, it was the subdued Miss Orton-Wells who was the first to speak.

"I'll never rest," she said, "until I see that skirt finished and actually ready to wear."

She smiled at Emma. When she did that, you saw that Miss Orton-Wells had her charm. Emma smiled back, and patted the girl's hand just once. At that there came a look into Miss Orton-Wells' eyes, and you saw that most decidedly she had her charm.

Up spoke Mrs. Orton-Wells.

"Gladys is such an enthusiast! That's really her reason for being here. Gladys is very much interested in working girls. In fact, we are all, as you probably know,

---

[3] Ida Tarbell (1857-1944), muckraking journalist.

intensely interested in the working woman."

"Thank you!" said Emma McChesney Buck. "That's very kind. We working women are very grateful to you."

"We!" exclaimed Mrs. Orton-Wells and Miss Susan Croft blankly, and in perfect time.

Emma smiled sweetly.

"Surely you'll admit that I'm a working woman."

Miss Susan H. Croft was not a person to be trifled with. She elucidated acidly.

"We mean women who work with their hands."

"By what power do you think those shears were moved across the cutting-table? We don't cut our patterns with an ouija-board."

Mrs. Orton-Wells rustled protestingly. "But, my dear Mrs. Buck, you know, we mean women of the Laboring Class."

"I'm in this place of business from nine to five, Monday to Saturday, inclusive. If that doesn't make me a member of the laboring class I don't want to belong."

It was here that Mrs. Orton-Wells showed herself a woman not to be trifled with. She moved forward to the edge of her chair, fixed Emma Buck with determined eyes, and swept into midstream, sails spread.

"Don't be frivolous, Mrs. Buck. We are here on a serious errand. It ought to interest you vitally because of the position you occupy in the world of business. We are launching a campaign against the extravagant, ridiculous, and often times indecent dress of the working girl, with especial reference to the girl who works in garment factories. They squander their earnings in costumes absurdly unfitted to their station in life. Our plan is to influence them in the direction of neatness, modesty, and economy in dress. At present each tries to outdo the other in style and variety of costume. Their shoes are high-heeled, cloth-topped, their blouses lacy and collarless, their hats absurd. We propose a costume which shall be neat, becoming, and appropriate. Not exactly a uniform, perhaps, but something with a fixed idea in cut, color, and style. A corps of twelve young ladies belonging to our best families has been chosen to speak to the shop girls at noon meetings on the subject of good taste, health, and morality in women's dress. My daughter Gladys is one of them. In this way, we hope to convince them that simplicity, and practicality, and neatness are the only proper notes in the costume of the working girl. Occupying as you do a position unique in the business world, Mrs. Buck, we expect much from your coöperation with us in this cause."

Emma McChesney Buck had been gazing at Mrs. Orton-Wells with an intentness as flattering as it was unfeigned. But at the close of Mrs. Orton-Wells' speech she was strangely silent. She glanced down at her shoes. Now, Emma McChesney Buck had a weakness for smart shoes which her slim, well-arched foot excused. Hers were what might be called intelligent-looking feet. There was nothing thick, nothing clumsy, nothing awkward about them. And Emma treated them with the consideration they deserved. They were shod now, in a pair of slim, aristocratic, and modish ties above which the grateful eye caught a flashing glimpse of black-silk stocking. Then her eye traveled up her smartly tailored skirt, up the bodice of that well-made and becoming costume until her glance rested on her own shoulder and paused. Then she looked up at Mrs. Orton-Wells. The eyes of Mrs. Orton-Wells, Miss Susan H. Croft, and

Miss Gladys Orton-Wells had, by some strange power of magnetism, followed the path of Emma's eyes. They finished just one second behind her, so that when she raised her eyes it was to encounter theirs.

"I have explained," retorted Mrs. Orton-Wells, tartly, in reply to nothing, seemingly, "that our problem is with the factory girl. She represents a distinct and separate class."

Emma McChesney Buck nodded:

"I understand. Our girls are very young—eighteen, twenty, twenty-two. At eighteen, or thereabouts, practical garments haven't the strong appeal that you might think they have."

"They should have," insisted Mrs. Orton-Wells.

"Maybe," said Emma Buck gently. "But to me it seems just as reasonable to argue that an apple tree has no right to wear pink-and-white blossoms in the spring, so long as it is going to bear sober russets in the autumn."

Miss Susan H. Croft rustled indignantly.

"Then you refuse to work with us? You will not consent to Miss Orton-Wells' speaking to the girls in your shop this noon?"

Emma looked at Gladys Orton-Wells. Gladys was wearing black, and black did not become her. It made her creamy skin sallow. Her suit was severely tailored, and her hat was small and harshly outlined, and her hair was drawn back from her face. All this, in spite of the fact that Miss Orton-Wells was of the limp and fragile type, which demands ruffles, fluffiness, flowing lines and *frou-frou*. Emma's glance at the suppressed Gladys was as fleeting as it was keen, but it sufficed to bring her to a decision. She pressed a buzzer at her desk.

"I shall be happy to have Miss Orton-Wells speak to the girls in our shop this noon, and as often as she cares to speak. If she can convince the girls that a—er—fixed idea in cut, color, and style is the thing to be adopted by shop-workers I am perfectly willing that they be convinced."

Then to Annie, who appeared in answer to the buzzer,

"Will you tell Sophy Kumpf to come here, please?"

Mrs. Orton-Wells beamed. The somber plumes in her correct hat bobbed and dipped to Emma. The austere Miss Susan H. Croft unbent in a nutcracker smile. Only Miss Gladys Orton-Wells remained silent, thoughtful, unenthusiastic. Her eyes were on Emma's face.

A heavy, comfortable step sounded in the hall outside the office door. Emma turned with a smile to the stout, motherly, red-cheeked woman who entered, smoothing her coarse brown hair with work-roughened fingers.

Emma took one of those calloused hands in hers.

"Sophy, we need your advice. This is Mrs. Sophy Kumpf—Mrs. Orton-Wells, Miss Susan H. Croft"—Sophy threw her a keen glance; she knew that name—"and Miss Orton-Wells." Of the four, Sophy was the most at ease.

"Pleased to meet you," said Sophy Kumpf.

The three bowed, but did not commit themselves. Emma, her hand still on Sophy's, elaborated:

"Sophy Kumpf has been with the T. A. Buck Company for thirty years. She could run this business single-handed, if she had to. She knows any machine in the shop, can cut a pattern, keep books, run the entire plant if necessary. If there's anything about petticoats that Sophy doesn't know, it's because it hasn't been invented yet. Sophy was sixteen when she came to Buck's. I've heard she was the prettiest and best dressed girl in the shop."

"Oh, now, Mrs. Buck!" remonstrated Sophy.

Emma tried to frown as she surveyed Sophy's bright eyes, her rosy cheeks, her broad bosom, her ample hips—all that made Sophy an object to comfort and rest the eye.

"Don't dispute, Sophy. Sophy has educated her children, married them off, and welcomed their children. She thinks that excuses her for having been frivolous and extravagant at sixteen. But we know better, don't we? I'm using you as a horrible example, Sophy."

Sophy turned affably to the listening three.

"Don't let her string you," she said, and winked one knowing eye.

Mrs. Orton-Wells stiffened. Miss Susan H. Croft congealed. But Miss Gladys Orton-Wells smiled. And then Emma knew she was right.

"Sophy, who's the prettiest girl in our shop? And the best dressed?"

"Lily Bernstein," Sophy made prompt answer.

"Send her in to us, will you? And give her credit for lost time when she comes back to the shop."

Sophy, with a last beamingly good-natured smile, withdrew. Five minutes later, when Lily Bernstein entered the office, Sophy qualified as a judge of beauty. Lily Bernstein was a tiger-lily—all browns and golds and creams, all graciousness and warmth and lovely curves. As she came into the room, Gladys Orton-Wells seemed as bloodless and pale and ineffectual as a white moth beside a gorgeous tawny butterfly.

Emma presented the girl as formally as she had Sophy Kumpf. And Lily Bernstein smiled upon them, and her teeth were as white and even as one knew they would be before she smiled. Lily had taken off her shop-apron. Her gown was blue serge, cheap in quality, flawless as to cut and fit, and incredibly becoming. Above it, her vivid face glowed like a golden rose.

"Lily," said Emma, "Miss Orton-Wells is going to speak to the girls this noon. I thought you might help by telling her whatever she wants to know about the girls' work and all that, and by making her feel at home."

"Well, sure," said Lily, and smiled again her heart-warming smile. "I'd love to."

"Miss Orton-Wells," went on Emma smoothly, "wants to speak to the girls about clothes."

Lily looked again at Miss Orton-Wells, and she did not mean to be cruel. Then she looked quickly at Emma, to detect a possible joke. But Mrs. Buck's face bore no trace of a smile.

"Clothes!" repeated Lily. And a slow red mounted to Gladys Orton-Wells' pale face. When Lily went out Sunday afternoons, she might have passed for a millionaire's daughter if she hadn't been so well dressed.

"Suppose you take Miss Orton-Wells into the shop," suggested Emma, "so that she may have some idea of the size and character of our family before she speaks to it. How long shall you want to speak?"

Miss Orton-Wells started nervously, stammered a little, stopped.

"Oh, ten minutes," said Mrs. Orton-Wells graciously.

"Five," said Gladys, quickly, and followed Lily Bernstein into the workroom.

Mrs. Orton-Wells and Miss Susan H. Croft gazed after them.

"Rather attractive, that girl, in a coarse way," mused Mrs. Orton-Wells. "If only we can teach them to avoid the cheap and tawdry. If only we can train them to appreciate the finer things in life. Of course, their life is peculiar. Their problems are not our problems; their——"

"Their problems are just exactly our problems," interrupted Emma crisply. "They use garlic instead of onion, and they don't bathe as often as we do; but, then, perhaps we wouldn't either, if we hadn't tubs and showers so handy."

In the shop, queer things were happening to Gladys Orton-Wells. At her entrance into the big workroom, one hundred pairs of eyes had lifted, dropped, and, in that one look, condemned her hat, suit, blouse, veil and *tout ensemble*. When you are on piece-work you squander very little time gazing at uplift visitors in the wrong kind of clothes.

Gladys Orton-Wells looked about the big, bright workroom. The noonday sun streamed in from a dozen great windows. There seemed, somehow, to be a look of content and capableness about those heads bent so busily over the stitching.

"It looks—pleasant," said Gladys Orton-Wells.

"It ain't bad. Of course it's hard sitting all day. But I'd rather do that than stand from eight to six behind a counter. And there's good money in it."

Gladys Orton-Wells turned wistful eyes on friendly little Lily Bernstein.

"I'd like to earn money," she said. "I'd like to work."

"Well, why don't you?" demanded Lily. "Work's all the style this year. They're all doing it. Look at the Vanderbilts and that Morgan girl, and the whole crowd. These days you can't tell whether the girl at the machine next to you lives in the Bronx or on Fifth Avenue."

"It must be wonderful to earn your own clothes."

"Believe me," laughed Lily Bernstein, "it ain't so wonderful when you've had to do it all your life."

She studied the pale girl before her with brows thoughtfully knit. Lily had met too many uplifters to be in awe of them. Besides, a certain warm-hearted friendliness was hers for every one she met. So, like the child she was, she spoke what was in her mind:

"Say, listen, dearie. I wouldn't wear black if I was you. And that plain stuff—it don't suit you. I'm like that, too. There's some things I can wear and others I look fierce in. I'd like you in one of them big flat hats and a full skirt like you see in the ads, with lots of ribbons and tag ends and bows on it. D'you know what I mean?"

"My mother was a Van Cleve," said Gladys drearily, as though that explained everything. So it might have, to any but a Lily Bernstein.

Lily didn't know what a Van Cleve was, but she sensed it as a drawback.

"Don't you care. Everybody's folks have got something the matter with 'em. Especially when you're a girl. But if I was you, I'd go right ahead and do what I wanted to."

In the doorway at the far end of the shop appeared Emma with her two visitors.

Mrs. Orton-Wells stopped and said something to a girl at a machine, and her very posture and smile reeked of an offensive kindliness, a condescending patronage.

Gladys Orton-Wells did a strange thing. She saw her mother coming toward her. She put one hand on Lily Bernstein's arm and she spoke hurriedly and in a little gasping voice.

"Listen! Would you—would you marry a man who hadn't any money to speak of, and no sort of family, if you loved him, even if your mother wouldn't—wouldn't——"

"Would I! Say, you go out to-morrow morning and buy yourself one of them floppy hats and a lace waist over flesh-colored chiffon and get married in it. Don't get it white, with your coloring. Get it kind of cream. You're so grand and thin, this year's things will look lovely on you."

A bell shrilled somewhere in the shop. A hundred machines stopped their whirring. A hundred heads came up with a sigh of relief.

Chairs were pushed back, aprons unbuttoned.

Emma McChesney Buck stepped forward and raised a hand for attention. The noise of a hundred tongues was stilled.

"Girls, Miss Gladys Orton-Wells is going to speak to you for five minutes on the subject of dress. Will you give her your attention, please. The five minutes will be added to your noon hour."

Gladys Orton-Wells looked down at her hands for one terrified moment, then she threw her head up bravely. There was no lack of color in her cheeks now. She stepped to the middle of the room.

"What I have to say won't take five minutes," she said, in her clear, well-bred tones. "You all dress so smartly, and I'm such a dowd, I just want to ask you whether you think I ought to get blue, or that new shade of gray for a traveling-suit."

And the shop, hardened to the eccentricities of noonday speakers, made composed and ready answer:

"Oh, get blue; it's always good."

"Thank you," laughed Gladys Orton-Wells, and was off down the hall and away, with never a backward glance at her gasping and outraged mother.

Emma McChesney Buck took Lily Bernstein's soft cheek between thumb and forefinger and pinched it ever so fondly.

"I knew you'd do it, Judy O'Grady,"[4] she said.

"Judy O'Who?"

"O'Grady—a lady famous in history."

"Oh, now, quit your kiddin', Mrs. Buck!" said Lily Bernstein.

—1915

---

[4] From Rudyard Kipling's (1865-1936) poem "The Ladies" (1896): "For the Colonel's Lady an' Judy O'Grady/Are sisters under their skins!"

ALICE GERSTENBERG (1885-1972)

Alice Gerstenberg was part of the early twentieth century ferment of the arts which gave birth to modernism in American theater and drama. Born in Chicago to first generation, German-American parents, she grew up with the advantages of upper-class life. Her interest in writing began as a child, when she would accompany her parents to see theatrical stars such as Lillian Russell, Maude Adams, and John Drew. Gerstenberg attended Bryn Mawr College while feminist M. Carey Thomas was president, but left at the end of her junior year (in 1906) to begin creating her own works. In 1908, she published *A Little World,* a collection of four plays about the contemporary life of women college students. From there, she joined Maurice Browne's Chicago Little Theatre, one of the earliest influential groups in the little theater movement. Out of that experience came the one-act play "Overtones" (1915), her most famous work. Although Gerstenberg is not as well known as her contemporary Susan Glaspell, she was nevertheless a prolific writer and experimenter, toying with plot and staging ideas. "Overtones" uses two actors to play one character's inner and outer selves, a technique later employed by Eugene O'Neill. Gerstenberg examined women's roles in society from girlhood through middle age; while her work reflects the beliefs of her time that women cannot have both marriage and a career, her dramatic vision allows for alternative and varying versions of women's lives and experiences.

Overtones

CHARACTERS

> HARRIET, a cultured woman
>
> HETTY, her primitive self
>
> MARGARET, a cultured woman
>
> MAGGIE, her primitive self

TIME: *The present.*

SCENE: HARRIET'*s fashionable living-room. The door at the back leads to the hall. In the centre a tea table with a chair either side. At the back a cabinet.*

HARRIET'*s gown is a light, "jealous" green. Her counterpart,* HETTY, *wears a gown of the same design but in a darker shade.* MARGARET *wears a gown of lavender chiffon while her counterpart,* MAGGIE, *wears a gown of the same design in purple, a purple scarf veiling her face. Chiffon is used to give a sheer effect, suggesting a possibility of primitive and cultured selves merging into one woman. The primitive and cultured selves never come into actual physical contact but try to sustain the impression of mental conflict.* HARRIET *never sees* HETTY, *never talks to her but rather thinks aloud looking into space.* HETTY, *however, looks at* HARRIET, *talks intently and shadows her continually. The same is true of* MARGARET *and* MAGGIE. *The voices of the cultured women are affected and lingering, the voices of the primitive impulsive and more or less staccato.*

When the curtain rises HARRIET *is seated right of tea table, busying herself with the tea things.*

HETTY: Harriet. [*There is no answer.*] Harriet, my other self. [*There is no answer.*] My trained self.

HARRIET: [*listens intently*] Yes?

[*From behind* HARRIET'*s chair* HETTY *rises slowly.*]

HETTY: I want to talk to you.

HARRIET: Well?

HETTY: [*looking at* HARRIET *admiringly*] Oh, Harriet, you are beautiful to-day.

HARRIET: Am I presentable, Hetty?

HETTY: Suits me.

HARRIET: I've tried to make the best of the good points.

HETTY: My passions are deeper than yours. I can't keep on the mask as you do. I'm crude and real, you are my appearance in the world.

HARRIET: I am what you wish the world to believe you are.

HETTY: You are the part of me that has been trained.

HARRIET: I am your educated self.

HETTY: I am the rushing river; you are the ice over the current.

HARRIET: I am your subtle overtones.

HETTY: But together we are one woman, the wife of Charles Goodrich.

HARRIET: There I disagree with you, Hetty, I alone am his wife.

HETTY: [*indignantly*] Harriet, how can you say such a thing!

HARRIET: Certainly. I am the one who flatters him. I have to be the one who talks to him. If I gave you a chance you would tell him at once that you dislike him.

HETTY: [*moving away*] I don't love him, that's certain.

HARRIET: You leave all the fibbing to me. He doesn't suspect that my calm, suave manner hides your hatred. Considering the amount of scheming it causes me it can safely be said that he is my husband.

HETTY: Oh, if you love him—

HARRIET: I? I haven't any feelings. It isn't my business to love anybody.

HETTY: Then why need you object to calling him my husband?

HARRIET: I resent your appropriation of a man who is managed only through the cleverness of my artifice.

HETTY: You may be clever enough to deceive him, Harriet, but I am still the one who suffers. I can't forget he is my husband. I can't forget that I might have married John Caldwell.

HARRIET: How foolish of you to remember John, just because we met his wife by chance.

HETTY: That's what I want to talk to you about. She may be here at any moment. I want to advise you about what to say to her this afternoon.

HARRIET: By all means tell me now and don't interrupt while she is here. You have a most annoying habit of talking to me when people are present. Sometimes it is all I can do to keep my poise and appear *not* to be listening to you.

HETTY: Impress her.

HARRIET: Hetty, dear, is it not my custom to impress people?

HETTY: I hate her.

HARRIET: I can't let her see that.

HETTY: I hate her because she married John.

HARRIET: Only after you had refused him.

HETTY: [*turning on* HARRIET] Was it my fault that I refused him?

HARRIET: That's right, blame me.

HETTY: It was your fault. You told me he was too poor and never would be able to do anything in painting. Look at him now, known in Europe, just returned from eight years in Paris, famous.

HARRIET: It was too poor a gamble at the time. It was much safer to accept Charles's money and position.

HETTY: And then John married Margaret within the year.

HARRIET: Out of spite.

HETTY: Freckled, gauky-looking thing she was, too.

HARRIET: [*a little sadly*] Europe improved her. She was stunning the other morning.

HETTY: Make her jealous to-day.

HARRIET: Shall I be haughty or cordial or caustic or—

HETTY: Above all else you must let her know that we are rich.

HARRIET: Oh, yes, I do that quite easily now.

HETTY: You must put it on a bit.

HARRIET: Never fear.

HETTY: Tell her I love my husband.

HARRIET: My husband—

HETTY: Are you going to quarrel with me?

HARRIET: [*moves away*] No, I have no desire to quarrel with you. It is quite too uncomfortable. I couldn't get away from you if I tried.

HETTY: [*stamping her foot and following* HARRIET] You were a stupid fool to make me refuse John, I'll never forgive you—never—

HARRIET: [*stopping and holding up her hand*] Don't get me all excited. I'll be in no condition to meet her properly this afternoon.

HETTY: [*passionately*] I could choke you for robbing me of John.

HARRIET: [*retreating*] Don't muss me!

HETTY: You don't know how you have made me suffer.

HARRIET: [*beginning to feel the strength of* HETTY's *emotion surge through her and trying to conquer it*] It is not my business to have heartaches.

HETTY: You're bloodless. Nothing but sham—sham—while I—

HARRIET: [*emotionally*] Be quiet! I can't let her see that I have been fighting with my inner self.

HETTY: And now after all my suffering you say it has cost you more than it has cost me to be married to Charles. But it's the pain here in my heart—I've paid the price—I've paid—Charles is not your husband!

HARRIET: [*trying to conquer emotion*] He is.

HETTY: [*follows* HARRIET] He isn't.

HARRIET: [*weakly*] He is.

HETTY: [*towering over* HARRIET] He isn't! I'll kill you!

HARRIET: [*overpowered, sinks into a chair*] Don't—don't—you're stronger than I— you're—

HETTY: Say he's mine.

HARRIET: He's ours.

HETTY: [*the telephone rings*] There she is now.

[HETTY *hurries to 'phone but* HARRIET *regains her supremacy.*]

HARRIET: [*authoritatively*] Wait! I can't let the telephone girl down there hear my real self. It isn't proper. [*At 'phone.*] Show Mrs. Caldwell up.

HETTY: I'm so excited, my heart's in my mouth.

HARRIET: [*at the mirror*] A nice state you've put my nerves into.

HETTY: Don't let her see you're nervous.

HARRIET: Quick, put the veil on, or she'll see *you* shining through me.

[HARRIET *takes a scarf of chiffon that has been lying over the back of a chair and drapes it on* HETTY, *covering her face. The chiffon is the same color of their gowns but paler in shade so that it pales* HETTY'*s darker gown to match* HARRIET'*s lighter one. As* HETTY *moves in the following scene the chiffon falls away revealing now and then the gown of deeper dye underneath.*]

HETTY: Tell her Charles is rich and fascinating—boast of our friends, make her feel she needs us.

HARRIET: I'll make her ask John to paint us.

HETTY: That's just my thought—if John paints our portrait—

HARRIET: We can wear an exquisite gown—

HETTY: And make him fall in love again and—

HARRIET: [*schemingly*] Yes.

[MARGARET *parts the portières back centre and extends her hand.* MARGARET *is followed by her counterpart* MAGGIE.]

Oh, Margaret, I'm so glad to see you!

HETTY: [*to* MAGGIE] That's a lie.

MARGARET: [*in superficial voice throughout*] It's enchanting to see you, Harriet.

MAGGIE: [*in emotional voice throughout*] I'd bite you, if I dared.

HARRIET: [*to* MARGARET] Wasn't our meeting a stroke of luck?

MARGARET: [*coming down left of table*] I've thought of you so often, Harriet; and to come back and find you living in New York.

HARRIET: [*coming down right of table*] Mr. Goodrich has many interests here.

MAGGIE: [*to* MARGARET] Flatter her.

MARGARET: I know, Mr. Goodrich is so successful.

HETTY: [*to* HARRIET] Tell her we're rich.

HARRIET: [*to* MARGARET] Won't you sit down?

MARGARET: [*takes a chair*] What a beautiful cabinet!

HARRIET: Do you like it? I'm afraid Charles paid an extravagant price.

MAGGIE: [*to* HETTY] I don't believe it.

MARGARET: [*sitting down. To* HARRIET] I am sure he must have.

HARRIET: [*sitting down*] How well you are looking, Margaret.

HETTY: Yes, you are not. There are circles under your eyes.

MAGGIE: [*to* HETTY] I haven't eaten since breakfast and I'm hungry.

MARGARET: [*to* HARRIET] How well you are looking, too.

MAGGIE: [*to* HETTY] You have hard lines about your lips, are you happy?

HETTY: [*to* HARRIET] Don't let her know that I'm unhappy.

HARRIET: [*to* MARGARET] Why shouldn't I look well? My life is full, happy, complete—

MAGGIE: I wonder.

HETTY: [*in* HARRIET'*s ear*] Tell her we have an automobile.

MARGARET: [*to* HARRIET] My life is complete, too.

MAGGIE: My heart is torn with sorrow; my husband cannot make a living. He will kill himself if he does not get an order for a painting.

MARGARET: [*laughs*] You must come and see us in our studio. John has been doing some excellent portraits. He cannot begin to fill his orders.

HETTY: [*to* HARRIET] Tell her we have an automobile.

HARRIET: [*to* MARGARET] Do you take lemon in your tea?

MAGGIE: Take cream. It's more filling.

MARGARET: [*looking nonchalantly at tea things*] No, cream, if you please. How cozy!

MAGGIE: [*glaring at tea things*] Only cakes! I could eat them all!!

HARRIET: [*to* MARGARET] How many lumps?

MAGGIE: [*to* MARGARET] Sugar is nourishing.

MARGARET: [*to* HARRIET] Three, please. I used to drink very sweet coffee in Turkey and ever since I've—

HETTY: I don't believe you were ever in Turkey.

MAGGIE: I wasn't, but it is none of your business.

HARRIET: [*pouring tea*] Have you been in Turkey, do tell me about it.

MAGGIE: [*to* MARGARET] Change the subject.

MARGARET: [*to* HARRIET] You must go there. You have so much taste in dress you would enjoy seeing their costumes.

MAGGIE: Isn't she going to pass the cake?

MARGARET: [*to* HARRIET] John painted several portraits there.

HETTY: [*to* HARRIET] Why don't you stop her bragging and tell her we have an automobile?

HARRIET: [*offers cake across the table to* MARGARET] Cake?

MAGGIE: [*stands back of* MARGARET, *shadowing her as* HETTY *shadows* HARRIET. MAGGIE *reaches claws out for the cake and groans with joy*] At last! [*But her claws do not touch the cake.*]

MARGARET: [*with a graceful, nonchalant hand places cake upon her plate and bites at it slowly and delicately*] Thank you.

HETTY: [*to* HARRIET] Automobile!

MAGGIE: [*to* MARGARET] Follow up the costumes with the suggestion that she would make a good model for John. It isn't too early to begin getting what you came for.

MARGARET: [*ignoring* MAGGIE] What delicious cake.

HETTY: [*excitedly to* HARRIET] There's your chance for the auto.

HARRIET: [*nonchalantly to* MARGARET] Yes, it is good cake, isn't it? There are always a great many people buying it at Harper's. I sat in my automobile fifteen minutes this morning waiting for my chauffeur to get it.

MAGGIE: [*to* MARGARET] Make her order a portrait.

MARGARET: [*to* HARRIET] If you stopped at Harper's you must have noticed the new gowns at Henderson's. Aren't the shop windows alluring these days?

HARRIET: Even my chauffeur notices them.

MAGGIE: I know you have an automobile, I heard you the first time.

MARGARET: I notice gowns now with an artist's eye as John does. The one you have on, my dear, is very paintable.

HETTY: Don't let her see you're anxious to be painted.

HARRIET: [*nonchalantly*] Oh, it's just a little model.

MAGGIE: [*to* MARGARET] Don't seem anxious to get the order.

MARGARET: [*nonchalantly*] Perhaps it isn't the gown itself but the way you wear it that pleases the eye. Some people can wear anything with grace.

HETTY: Yes, I'm very graceful.

HARRIET: [*to* MARGARET] You flatter me, my dear.

MARGARET: On the contrary, Harriet, I have an intense admiration for you. I remember how beautiful you were—as a girl. In fact, I was quite jealous when John was paying you so much attention.

HETTY: She is gloating because I lost him.

HARRIET: Those were childhood days in a country town.

MAGGIE: [*to* MARGARET] She's trying to make you feel that John was only a country boy.

MARGARET: Most great men have come from the country. There is a fair chance that John will be added to the list.

HETTY: I know it and I am bitterly jealous of you.

HARRIET: Undoubtedly he owes much of his success to you, Margaret, your experience in economy and your ability to endure hardship. Those first few years in Paris must have been a struggle.

MAGGIE: She is sneering at your poverty.

MARGARET: Yes, we did find life difficult at first, not the luxurious start a girl has who marries wealth.

HETTY: [*to* HARRIET] Deny that you married Charles for his money.

[HARRIET *deems it wise to ignore* HETTY'*s advice.*]

MARGARET: But John and I are so congenial in our tastes, that we were impervious to hardship or unhappiness.

HETTY: [*in anguish*] Do you love each other? Is it really true?

HARRIET: [*sweetly*] Did you have all the romance of starving for his art?

MAGGIE: [*to* MARGARET] She's taunting you. Get even with her.

MARGARET: Not for long. Prince Rier soon discovered John's genius, and introduced him royally to wealthy Parisians who gave him many orders.

HETTY: [*to* MAGGIE] Are you telling the truth or are you lying?

HARRIET: If he had so many opportunities there, you must have had great inducements to come back to the States.

MAGGIE: [*to* HETTY] We did, but not the kind you think.

MARGARET: John became the rage among Americans travelling in France, too, and they simply insisted upon his coming here.

HARRIET: Whom is he going to paint here?

MAGGIE: [*frightened*] What names dare I make up?

MARGARET: [*calmly*] Just at present Miss Dorothy Ainsworth of Oregon is posing. You may not know the name, but she is the daughter of a wealthy miner who found gold in Alaska.

HARRIET: I dare say there are many Western people we have never heard of.

MARGARET: You must have found social life in New York very interesting, Harriet, after the simplicity of our home town.

HETTY: [*to* MAGGIE] There's no need to remind us that our beginnings were the same.

HARRIET: Of course Charles's family made everything delightful for me. They are so well connected.

MAGGIE: [*to* MARGARET] Flatter her.

MARGARET: I heard it mentioned yesterday that you had made yourself very popular. Some one said you were very clever!

HARRIET: [*pleased*] Who told you that?

MAGGIE: Nobody!

MARGARET: [*pleasantly*] Oh, confidences should be suspected—respected, I mean. They said, too, that you are gaining some reputation as a critic of art.

HARRIET: I make no pretenses.

MARGARET: Are you and Mr. Goodrich interested in the same things, too?

HETTY: No!

HARRIET: Yes, indeed, Charles and I are inseparable.

MAGGIE: I wonder.

HARRIET: Do have another cake.

MAGGIE: [*in relief*] Oh, yes.

[*Again her claws extend but do not touch the cake.*]

MARGARET: [*takes cake delicately*] I really shouldn't—after my big luncheon. John took me to the Ritz and we are invited to the Bedfords' for dinner—they have such a magnificent house near the drive—I really shouldn't, but the cakes are so good.

MAGGIE: Starving!

HARRIET: [*to* MARGARET] More tea?

MAGGIE: Yes!

MARGARET: No, thank you. How wonderfully life has arranged itself for you. Wealth, position, a happy marriage, every opportunity to enjoy all pleasures; beauty, art—how happy you must be.

HETTY: [*in anguish*] Don't call me happy. I've never been happy since I gave up John. All these years without him—a future without him—no—no—I shall win him back—away from you—away from you—

HARRIET: [*does not see* MAGGIE *pointing to cream and* MARGARET *stealing some*] I sometimes think it is unfair for any one to be as happy as I am. Charles and I are just as much in love now as when we married. To me he is just the dearest man in the world.

MAGGIE: [*passionately*] My John is. I love him so much I could die for him. I'm going through hunger and want to make him great and he loves me. He worships me!

MARGARET: [*leisurely to* HARRIET] I should like to meet Mr. Goodrich. Bring him to our studio. John has some sketches to show. Not many, because all the portraits have been purchased by the subjects. He gets as much as four thousand dollars now.

HETTY: [*to* HARRIET] Don't pay that much.

HARRIET: [*to* MARGARET] As much as that?

MARGARET: It is not really too much when one considers that John is in the foremost rank of artists to-day. A picture painted by him now will double and treble in value.

MAGGIE: It's all a lie. He is growing weak with despair.

HARRIET: Does he paint all day long?

MAGGIE: No, he draws advertisements for our bread.

MARGARET: [*to* HARRIET] When you and your husband come to see us, telephone first—

MAGGIE: Yes, so he can get the advertisements out of the way.

MARGARET: Otherwise you might arrive while he has a sitter, and John refuses to let me disturb him then.

HETTY: Make her ask for an order.

HARRIET: [*to* MARGARET] Le Grange offered to paint me for a thousand.

MARGARET: Louis Le Grange's reputation isn't worth more than that.

HARRIET: Well, I've heard his work well mentioned.

MAGGIE: Yes, he is doing splendid work.

MARGARET: Oh, dear me, no. He is only praised by the masses. He is accepted not at all by artists themselves.

HETTY: [*anxiously*] Must I really pay the full price?

HARRIET: Le Grange thought I would make a good subject.

MAGGIE: [*to* MARGARET] Let her fish for it.

MARGARET: Of course you would. Why don't you let Le Grange paint you, if you *trust* him?

HETTY: She doesn't seem anxious to have John do it.

HARRIET: But if Le Grange isn't accepted by artists, it would be a waste of time to pose for him, wouldn't it?

MARGARET: Yes, I think it would.

MAGGIE: [*passionately to* HETTY *across back of table*] Give us the order. John is so despondent he can't endure much longer. Help us! Help me! Save us!

HETTY: [*to* HARRIET] Don't seem too eager.

HARRIET: And yet if he charges only a thousand one might consider it.

MARGARET: If you really wish to be painted, why don't you give a little more and have a portrait really worth while? John might be induced to do you for a little below his usual price considering that you used to be such good friends.

HETTY: [*in glee*] Hurrah!

HARRIET: [*quietly to* MARGARET] That's very nice of you to suggest—of course I don't know—

MAGGIE: [*in fear*] For God's sake, say yes.

MARGARET: [*quietly to* HARRIET] Of course, I don't know whether John would. He is very peculiar in these matters. He sets his value on his work and thinks it beneath him to discuss price.

HETTY: [*to* MAGGIE] You needn't try to make us feel small.

MARGARET: Still, I might quite delicately mention to him that inasmuch as you have many influential friends you would be very glad to—to—

MAGGIE: [*to* HETTY] Finish what I don't want to say.

HETTY: [*to* HARRIET] Help her out.

HARRIET: Oh, yes, introductions will follow the exhibition of my portrait. No doubt I—

HETTY: [*to* HARRIET] Be patronizing.

HARRIET: No doubt I shall be able to introduce your husband to his advantage.

MAGGIE: [*relieved*] Saved.

MARGARET: If I find John in a propitious mood I shall take pleasure, for your sake, in telling him about your beauty. Just as you are sitting now would be a lovely pose.

MAGGIE: [*to* MARGARET] We can go now.

HETTY: [*to* HARRIET] Don't let her think she is doing us a favor.

HARRIET: It will give me pleasure to add my name to your husband's list of patronesses.

MAGGIE: [*excitedly to* MARGARET] Run home and tell John the good news.

MARGARET: [*leisurely to* HARRIET] I little guessed when I came for a pleasant chat about old times that it would develop into business arrangements. I had no idea, Harriet, that you had any intention of being painted. By Le Grange, too. Well, I came just in time to rescue you.

MAGGIE: [*to* MARGARET] Run home and tell John. Hurry, hurry!

HETTY: [*to* HARRIET] You managed the order very neatly. She doesn't suspect that you wanted it.

HARRIET: Now if I am not satisfied with my portrait I shall blame you, Margaret, dear. I am relying upon your opinion of John's talent.

MAGGIE: [*to* MARGARET] She doesn't suspect what you came for. Run home and tell John!

HARRIET: You always had a brilliant mind, Margaret.

MARGARET: Ah, it is you who flatter, now.

MAGGIE: [*to* MARGARET] You don't have to stay so long. Hurry home!

HARRIET: Ah, one does not flatter when one tells the truth.

MARGARET: [*smiles*] I must be going or you will have me completely under your spell.

HETTY: [*looks at clock*] Yes, do go. I have to dress for dinner.

HARRIET: [*to* MARGARET] Oh, don't hurry.

MAGGIE: [*to* HETTY] I hate you!

MARGARET: [*to* HARRIET] No, really I must, but I hope we shall see each other often at the studio. I find you so stimulating.

HETTY: [*to* MAGGIE] I hate you!

HARRIET: [*to* MARGARET] It is indeed gratifying to find a kindred spirit.

MAGGIE: [*to* HETTY] I came for your gold.

MARGARET: [*to* HARRIET] How delightful it is to know you again.

HETTY: [*to* MAGGIE] I am going to make you and your husband suffer.

HARRIET: My kind regards to John.

MAGGIE: [*to* HETTY] He has forgotten all about you.

MARGARET: [*rises*] He will be so happy to receive them.

HETTY: [*to* MAGGIE] I can hardly wait to talk to him again.

HARRIET: I shall wait, then, until you send me word?

MARGARET: [*offering her hand*] I'll speak to John about it as soon as I can and tell you when to come.

[HARRIET *takes* MARGARET'*s hand affectionately.* HETTY *and* MAGGIE *rush at each other, throw back their veils, and fling their speeches fiercely at each other.*]

HETTY: I love him—I love him—

MAGGIE: He's starving—I'm starving—

HETTY: I'm going to take him away from you—

MAGGIE: I want your money—and your influence.

HETTY and MAGGIE: I'm going to rob you—rob you.

[*There is a cymbal crash, the lights go out and come up again slowly, leaving only* MARGARET *and* HARRIET *visible.*]

MARGARET: [*quietly to* HARRIET] I've had such a delightful afternoon.

HARRIET: [*offering her hand*] It has been a joy to see you.

MARGARET: [*sweetly to* HARRIET] Good-bye.

HARRIET: [*sweetly to* MARGARET *as she kisses her*] Good-bye, my dear.

CURTAIN

—1915

JOVITA IDAR (1885-1946)

Jovita Idar was born in Laredo, Texas, the second of eight children. After earning a teaching degree from the Holding Institute in 1903, she began teaching at a small school in Ojuelos, but following a disappointing effort to improve the poor conditions of her school, Idar resigned and began to work for her family's newspaper, *La Crónica*. The paper's focus was anti-Mexican discrimination, deteriorating economic conditions, decreasing use of the Spanish language, the loss of Mexican culture, the lynching of Latinos, poor social conditions, and support for the Mexican Revolution. In 1911 Idar became the first president of the League of Mexican Women, organizing their campaign to provide education for Spanish-speaking women and children. She traveled to Mexico in 1913 to work as a nurse for wounded revolutionary soldiers, and when she returned to Laredo, she joined the staff of the newspaper *El Progreso*. Following her editorial protesting President Woodrow Wilson's dispatch of U.S. troops to the border, the paper was shut down, and Idar returned to *La Crónica*. When her father died in 1914, she joined her brothers in taking over publication of the paper. After her marriage in 1917 to Bartolo Juarez, Idar moved to San Antonio. There, she and her husband became very active in Democratic Party organizing, and Idar continued working on educational projects involving both women and children, establishing a free kindergarten and teaching courses to women on childcare and hygiene. She also continued her journalistic work as the editor of *El Heraldo Christiana,* a publication of the Rio Grande Conference of the Methodist Church. She died in San Antonio in 1946.

We Should Work

The modern woman, cognizant of and recognizing the need to contribute her quota to aid in the development of erudition among the masses, prepares herself valiantly and invades every field of industry, at all levels, without fear and without laziness. She abandons idleness and inactivity, since in the present age, so full of life opportunities and replete with energy and hope, there is no room for the socially indolent.

Inactivity and laziness are seen as contemptible today and, as such, are undone by all of those things that are considered factors in the development and progress of the people.

The modern woman does not spend her days lounging in a comfortable chair. This, not even the rich woman does, since those flattered by fortune also dedicate themselves to the practice of generosity or other philanthropic work, or to the organization of charitable or recreational clubs. What is desirable is to do something useful for yourself or for your fellow man.

The working-class woman, recognizing her rights, raises her head with pride and confronts the struggle; her period of degradation has passed. She is no longer the slave sold for a few coins, no longer the servant. She is an equal to man, his companion; he is her natural protector and not her master and lord.

Much has dealt with and been written about the feminist movement, but despite the opposition, already in California women can cast their vote as jury and occupy public office.

Those fastidious, superficial and unworthy souls make many mistakes in criticizing this type of woman who, brushing aside social convention, dedicates her energies to work for something beneficial and charitable; these critics do not realize the moral influence that this exerts, because a person dedicated to certain jobs or tasks does not have time to be bothered with futile and prejudicial things. She does more, the steadfast working woman, behind a counter and seated in front of her sewing machine or already an office worker, than the young lady with time to spare who occupies herself with making daily social calls or in going through, one by one, every store, which is a life filled with gossip and vulgar stories.

The single woman, decent and hardworking, does not demand a living at the expense of the head of her family, whether or not it be a father, brother or relative. No. A healthy woman, valiant and strong, dedicates her energy and her intelligence to helping her family, or at least, to providing for her own sustenance.

Just as decent and hardworking men regard unemployed and vagrant men with disdain, so too do working women disparage good-for-nothing and unemployed women.

—1911

MOURNING DOVE (CHRISTINE QUINTASKET) (1885?-1936)

Widely recognized as the first Native American woman novelist, Christine Quintasket was born in Idaho, the daughter of Joseph Quintasket (of Nicola and Okanogan descent) and Lucy Stukin (Colville/Salishan). She received some early education at the Sacred Heart School in Ward, Washington, but she had to return home to care for her younger siblings after the death of her mother in 1902. When her father remarried in 1904, she returned to school, this time enrolling in the Fort Shaw Indian School in Great Falls, Montana. While there, she witnessed the last roundup of wild buffalo in 1908, an event which became a central element of her novel *Co-Ge-We-A, the Half-Blood: A Depiction of the Great Montana Cattle Range* (1927). Quintasket married twice: first in 1909 to Hector McLeod, a Flathead Indian and the owner of a livery stable outside Great Falls (the marriage lasted three years), and then in 1919 to Fred Galler, a Wenatchee Indian from the Colville Indian Reservation in north central Washington.

Quintasket worked as a housekeeper and as a migrant farmworker before achieving literary success. In 1914, she met ethnographer Lucullus Virgil McWhorter, who encouraged her to write and was instrumental in promoting her career. McWhorter's editorial interventions in her novel (such as elevating the language in places and inserting political diatribes) troubled both Quintasket and later critics. McWhorter also encouraged her to gather traditional stories, advice that resulted in the publication of *Coyote Stories* in 1933. Once she achieved success as a writer, Quintasket became very active in tribal affairs. She helped organize the Colville Indian Association, which successfully fought to obtain compensation for timber, mining, and water rights for the tribe, and she was the first woman to be elected to the Colville Tribal Council. At the time of her death in 1936, Quintasket was working on an autobiography (which was published in 1990, edited by anthropologist Jay Miller).

from Coyote Stories

Chapter XII
Coyote Quarrels with Mole

Coyote and his wife, Mole, and their children were living by themselves, away from the winter encampment of the people. The other people did not want Coyote around, he was so lazy and tricky. Coyote and his family were poor that winter. They had only a little food, and that was supplied by the faithful Mole. Each day she would go out and gather herbs and moss and dried and shriveled *sko-qeeu* (rose-hips). She did that to keep the five children from starving. And she carried all the wood and water, while Coyote loafed and practised his war songs.

One sun, as Mole was chopping a rotten stump of firewood, a little fawn jumped out of the stump. The deer family had put it there. The deer felt sorry for Mole. They wanted her to have the fawn for food.

Mole dropped her axe and caught the little deer. She told her oldest boy to run and tell his father to come with a knife and cut the fawn's throat.

"Tell your father to hurry," said Mole, "because I cannot hold this fawn long. My strength will give out."

The boy ran fast to the tepee. He told Coyote what Mole had said.

"Go back to your mother and tell her to hold the fawn while I get my bow and arrows ready," Coyote ordered, and the boy ran back to his mother with the message.

Coyote ran out of the lodge and got a piece of dogwood, from which he made a bow. Then he ran to a service berry bush, where he cut two arrows. Then he ran back to his lodge to finish making his weapons. Taking feathers from his war bonnet, he feathered the arrows and, as he had no sinew for a bowstring, he tore the strings off his moccasins and made a string. Then he was ready to shoot the fawn.

All the while Mole was having a hard time holding the fawn. It struggled and kicked and fought to get away, and Mole's strength was leaving her. Her arms ached. She called to Coyote to hurry. He ran out of the lodge and tramped down the snow so he could kneel and shoot. He told Mole to let loose of the fawn so he could shoot it. Mole let go and Coyote shot his arrow, but the little deer fell just then and the arrow missed it. With his second and last arrow Coyote shot again as the fawn leaped up, and again Coyote missed. The fawn escaped into the woods.

Mole was disgusted and angry. She went back to the tepee. There she discovered that Coyote had eaten all the rose-hips, all the food that was left, while he was making his weapons. When Coyote came in, Mole spoke to him about that. They quarreled, and Coyote stabbed her with his flint knife. Mole ran out. Coyote followed. He meant to kill her. Mole changed herself into a real Mole as Coyote stabbed again. He stabbed the earth, and Mole quickly untied her little pouch of *tul-meen* (red facial paint) and put some of the paint on the point of the knife. Drawing the knife out of the ground, Coyote saw the red paint and thought it was blood. He was satisfied that his wife must be dead from that last blow.

Coyote soon found that he could not take care of his children without Mole's help. They could not live as they had before, so Coyote told the four oldest children to visit their "uncle," Kingfisher—*Z-reece*, who was a good hunter and had plenty of food in his lodge. The four boys started for Kingfisher's home, and Coyote took his youngest and favorite son and went traveling. The youngest boy's name was *Top'-kan*.

They traveled many suns without getting much to eat. They were hungry when they came to a large prairie, where a woman dressed in red-painted buckskin was digging *spit-lum* (bitterroot). Seeing her digging reminded Coyote of his wife, and he wished that Mole were alive to dig roots for him to eat. He took *Top'-kan* off his back, where the little boy rode much of the time to keep from tiring, and told him to wait. Then Coyote went toward the strange woman.

"Tell me a story, tell me news, good woman," said Coyote upon getting near to the digger. But the woman did not take any notice of him. She kept on digging roots and cleaning them as she put them in her basket, which was strapped to her side.

Not so easily discouraged, Coyote walked closer, saying: "Tell me news. I am a traveler from a distant country."

"I will tell you a story," said the woman, and she turned angrily to Coyote. "Coyote deserted his children and killed his wife!"

Then Coyote recognized the woman as his own wife, Mole. She had followed him to watch over little *Top'-kan,* but Coyote had not known that. Grabbing his knife, Coyote ran at his wife. He meant to kill her, but she changed into a real mole and went underground and got away.

Coyote returned to *Top'-kan*. He picked the boy up, put him on his back, and resumed his journey. He sought new lands where his tricks and mischief-making were not known.

Chapter XIV
Why Spider Has Such Long Legs

Tu-pel—Spider, the Spinner—was a handsome warrior and good hunter. He lived with his grandmother, *Spu-wel'-kin*—Topknot, Woodpecker. Because he always brought home plenty of game, the maidens of the nearby villages all wanted to marry him. They would visit his lodge, hoping to win him.

Spider had a smoke-test for the maidens. When one came to see him, Spider would send his grandmother outside to close the smoke-flue. She would lap the ear-flaps so that the smoke could not get out. That would make the smoke thick in the lodge, and it would be hard to breathe in there.

Spider thought that he did not want a wife who could not stay in the smoke as long as he could, and he could stay in it a long time. Many maidens had tried the smoke-test and failed. But Spider always was nice to them. He would send them home with big packs of meat.

Stun'-whu—Beaver—had a very pretty daughter. She wanted to win Spider. She spoke to her father—asked his help. Beaver's medicine was strong. He gave his power to his daughter and told her how to use it. Then he sent her to Spider's lodge.

Spider liked the girl right away. He wanted her to be his wife. He did not care if she could not stand his smoke-test. Sending his grandmother out to close the smoke-flue, Spider pretended to make a smoky fire. But there was only a little smoke, and it was not the eye-stinging kind.

Beaver's daughter laughed. She sat on a spread robe and laughed at the smoke that Spider made, but she said nothing to Spider. With Beaver's medicine she called the blackest smoke, pitch smoke. It filled the lodge.

For most of that sun Beaver-girl and Spider sat in the lodge, on opposite sides of the fire. Spider's eyes finally became smoke-sick, and the pitch-smoke choked him. He spoke to Beaver-girl. She made no answer. Spider tried to think. That was hard, for the smoke blinded him, and his whole head ached. His own medicine could not help him. It was weak against the powerful *shoo'-mesh*[1] of Beaver.

Spider wondered if the girl was still in the lodge. He spoke. No answer. He spoke again and again, many times, calling loudly through the smoke-darkness. Maybe the maiden was dead! Maybe the black smoke had killed her!

Spider felt his way around the fire. His foot struck the girl. She laughed. That made Spider ashamed. A woman was beating him in a trial of strength. He kicked Beaver-girl hard. He kicked her three times, and that made her very angry. She caught hold of one of Spider's legs, and she pulled and pulled, stretching the leg out, making it long. Then she pulled his other legs the same way. Spider could not stop her.

Well, when Woodpecker at last uncovered the smoke-flue and turned back the door-flap she saw a strange-looking grandson standing in the swirl of the outrushing smoke. He no longer was handsome. His body was small and his legs were very long and ugly.

Spu-wel'-kin was sorry for him. She knew that the maidens would not try to win him any more. So she ruled that Beaver-girl become his wife. Beaver's daughter was willing; she knew that *Tu-pel* always would provide plenty of game. And Spider was glad. He liked Beaver-girl even though she had treated him so roughly and spoiled his fine looks, and he forgave her for pulling him all out of shape—for making his legs so long.

—1933

[1] (Salishan) Medicine or power.

ELINOR WYLIE (1885-1928)

Elinor Morton Hoyt was born into a prominent Philadelphia family. Her father, Henry Martyn Hoyt, served as solicitor general under President Theodore Roosevelt and later as an assistant U.S. attorney general under President William McKinley, keeping the family in Washington D.C. for much of Wylie's youth. She attended private schools, graduating from Holton-Arms High School in 1904, but did not attend college. Wylie was expected to marry well and maintain her family's social position just as her mother, Anne McMichael Hoyt, had done. Though she tried to follow this formula, Wylie's two divorces and three marriages left her ostracized from society, and from some family members. In 1905 she married Philip Hichborn, a mentally unstable lawyer, and soon gave birth to a son, Philip. With no family to support a needed divorce, she turned to Horace Wylie, who was also married with children. On December 16, 1910, the two left their families and eloped to England, living together under an assumed name for five years. They returned to the U.S. and, after Hichborn committed suicide, married and tried unsuccessfully to have children.

Wylie began writing poetry, and in 1921 published the poetry collection *Nets to Catch the Wind*. Over the next ten years, she published three more volumes of poetry and four novels. Wylie left her husband and moved to New York after meeting William Rose Benet, whom she would eventually wed. In New York, Wylie became the poetry editor of *Vanity Fair* and continued writing. Like Sara Teasdale, Edna St. Vincent Millay, Dorothy Parker, and Louise Bogan—all of whom admired her—Wylie used formal metrics to explore the difficulties of romantic love for the modern woman. Her status in bohemian and literary circles grew with each book. However, despite her popularity, Wylie's life continued to be difficult: two of her siblings committed suicide, and the criticism directed at her lifestyle continued, making her nervous and prone to headaches. She also suffered from high blood pressure and Bright's disease. Beginning in 1926, she traveled alone to England, where she eventually suffered two strokes and a fall. A third stroke at home killed her after she completed her last book, *Angels and Earthly Creatures* (1929); she was forty-three.

Let No Charitable Hope

Now let no charitable hope
Confuse my mind with images
Of eagle and of antelope:
I am in nature none of these.

I was, being human, born alone;   5
I am, being woman, hard beset;
I live by squeezing from a stone
The little nourishment I get.

In masks outrageous and austere
The years go by in single file;   10
But none has merited my fear,
And none has quite escaped my smile.

—1923

Portrait in Black Paint, with a Very Sparing Use of Whitewash

"She gives herself;" there's a poetic thought;
She gives you comfort sturdy as a reed;
She gives you fifty things you might have bought,
And half a hundred that you'll never need;
She gives you friendship, but it's such a bother   5
You'd fancy influenza from another.
She'd give the shirt from off her back, except that
She doesn't wear a shirt, and most men do;
And often and most bitterly she's wept that
A starving tramp can't eat a silver shoe,   10
Or some poor beggar, slightly alcoholic,
Enjoy with Donne[1] a metaphysical frolic.

---

[1] John Donne (1572-1631), British metaphysical poet and Anglican preacher.

She gives away her darling secret hope
At dinner tables between eight and nine,
And she would give Saint Peter's to the Pope,   15
And coals to men of Newcastle-on-Tyne,[2]
She would arrange a match for Solomon[3]
Or give Casanova[4] an adoptive son.
She does not give advice; that I admit;
Here's her sole virtue, and I'll count it double,   20
Forgiving her some crime because of it,
But she gives tiresome and endless trouble.
If you need rest, she'll straight contrive a racket;
If gaiety, she'll fetch a padded jacket.

And she gives love of the least useful kind   25
At which advanced civilization mocks;
Half, a Platonic passion of the mind,
And half, a mad desire to mend the socks;
She's always wishing to turn back the page
And live with children in a golden age.   30

She gives a false impression that she's pretty
Because she has a soft, deceptive skin
Saved from her childhood; yet it seems a pity
That she should be as vain of this as sin;
Her mind might bloom, she might reform the world   35
In those lost hours while her hair is curled.

She gives a vague impression that she's lazy,
But when she writes she grows intense and thorough;
Gone quietly and ecstatically crazy
Among the sea-blue hills of Peterboro;[5]   40
She'll work within her cool, conventual flat
As self-sufficient as a Persian cat.

And she can live on aspirin and Scotch
Or British ginger beer and bread and butter,
And like them both, and neither very much;   45
And in her infancy she possessed a stutter
Which gives a strong impression that she's shy
When heard today, and this is verity.

But when she clothes herself in gold and silver
In the evening, she gives herself away;   50
Having remained a high, laborious delver
For all the hours of a sunny day,

---

[2] Coal-producing area in England.
[3] Solomon, King of the Jews (mid 10th century B.C.E),
known for his numerous wives and for his wisdom, as
collected in various books of the Bible.

[4] Giovanni Giacomo Casanova (1725-1798), Italian writer,
soldier, spy, and diplomatist, as well as a seducer of
many women.
[5] Town north of London, England.

At night she gives you rather the idea
Of mad Ophelia[6] tutored by Medea.[7]

She gives you nothing worth consideration;   55
The effervescence of enthusiasm
Is trivial stuff; she'll give you adoration
If you belong to her peculiar schism;
As, that a certain English man of letters
Need never call the Trinity his betters.   60
Sometimes she gives her heart; sometimes instead
Her tongue's sharp side. Her will is quick to soften.
She has no strength of purpose in her head
And she gives up entirely too often;
Her manners mingle in disastrous ways   65
"The Lower Depths"[8] and the Court of Louis Seize.[9]

Doubtless, she gives her enemies the creeps
And all her friends a vast amount of worry;
She's given oblivion only when she sleeps;
She says she loves the grave; but she'd be sorry   70
To die, while it is vanity to live;
"She gives herself;" what has she left to give?

She'd give her eyes—but both her eyes are blind—
And her right hand—but both her hands are weak—
To be "Careless to win, unskilled to find,   75
And quick—and quick—to lose what all men seek."[10]
But whether this has truly been her story
She'll never know, this side of purgatory.

—1927

---

[6] Character in Shakespeare's *Hamlet* who goes mad and kills herself.

[7] Mythical Greek mother who kills her children as revenge for her husband Jason's infidelity in Euripides' tragedy *Medea*.

[8] A play about impoverished people by the Russian playwright Maxim Gorky (1868-1936).

[9] Louis XVI (1754-1793), king of France from 1774 to 1792; he was guillotined during the French Revolution. His lavish court contrasted with the poverty of many French citizens.

[10] From the poem "A Garden by the Sea" by British poet and artist William Morris (1834-1896).

ANZIA YEZIERSKA (CA. 1885-1970)

Anzia Yezierska's family emigrated from Russian Poland to the United States in 1901, seeking escape from poverty, discrimination, and the vicious pogroms aimed at Eastern European Jews in the 1880s. Yezierska never knew the year she was born, and chose 1883; most scholars agree on 1885. In New York, Yezierska's scholarly father continued his religious studies and, following traditional practice, left the support of his family to others. As a result, the children toiled in sweatshops. Yezierska learned English and attended school at night, while working in a sweatshop during the day. In 1904, she earned a teaching certificate from Teachers College of Columbia University, and in 1917, she met the philosopher John Dewey at Columbia, who encouraged her literary endeavors. Her short story "Fat of the Land" was included in Edward O'Brien's *Best Short Stories of 1919,* and Goldwyn Studios based a 1922 silent film on her collection *Hungry Hearts* (1920); Yezierska spent a brief time in Hollywood, but returned to New York after finding that she was unable to write outside of her immigrant community.

Yezierska chose to write in English rather than Yiddish, apparently to reach an "American" rather than a specifically immigrant reading public. Her reputation peaked with the appearance of *Salome of the Tenements* (1922), *Children of Loneliness* (1923), and *Bread Givers* (1925). During the Depression, Yezierska worked with the New York unit of the Federal Writers Project, a WPA program designed to provide employment for authors. She continued her own writing as well, but her popularity had diminished and she was unable to publish her work. In 1950 she wrote *Red Ribbon on a White Horse,* and interest in her writing revived somewhat. Her late work focused on problems of the elderly and on Puerto Rican immigrants. Today, Anzia Yezierska is best known for her graphic portrayals of life in the Jewish tenements of New York in the early twentieth century.

America and I

As one of the dumb, voiceless ones I speak. One of the millions of immigrants beating, beating out their hearts at your gates for a breath of understanding.

Ach! America! From the other end of the earth from where I came, America was a land of living hope, woven of dreams, aflame with longing and desire.

Choked for ages in the airless oppression of Russia, the Promised Land rose up— wings for my stifled spirit—sunlight burning through my darkness—freedom singing to me in my prison—deathless songs tuning prison-bars into strings of a beautiful violin.

I arrived in America. My young, strong body, my heart and soul pregnant with the unlived lives of generations clamoring for expression.

What my mother and father and their mother and father never had a chance to give out in Russia, I would give out in America. The hidden sap of centuries would find release; colors that never saw light—songs that died unvoiced—romance that never had a chance to blossom in the black life of the Old World.

In the golden land of flowing opportunity I was to find my work that was denied me in the sterile village of my forefathers. Here I was to be free from the dead   drudgery for bread that held me down in Russia. For the first time in America, I'd cease to be a slave of the belly. I'd be a creator, a giver, a human being! My work would be the living joy of fullest self-expression.

But from my high visions, my golden hopes, I had to put my feet down on earth. I had to have food and shelter. I had to have the money to pay for it.

I was in America, among the Americans, but not of them. No speech, no common language, no way to win a smile of understanding from them, only my young, strong body and my untried faith. Only my eager, empty hands, and my full heart shining from my eyes!

God from the world! Here I was with so much richness in me, but my mind was not wanted without the language. And my body, unskilled, untrained, was not even wanted in the factory. Only one of two chances was left open to me: the kitchen, or minding babies.

My first job was as a servant in an Americanized family. Once, long ago, they came from the same village from where I came. But they were so well-dressed, so well-fed, so successful in America, that they were ashamed to remember their mother tongue.

"What were to be my wages?" I ventured timidly, as I looked up to the well-fed, well-dressed "American" man and woman.

They looked at me with a sudden coldness. What have I said to draw away from me their warmth? Was it so low from me to talk of wages? I shrank back into myself like a low-down bargainer. Maybe they're so high up in well-being they can't any more understand my low thoughts for money.

From his rich height the man preached down to me that I must not be so grabbing for wages. Only just landed from the ship and already thinking about money when I should be thankful to associate with "Americans."

The woman, out of her smooth, smiling fatness assured me that this was my chance for a summer vacation in the country with her two lovely children. My great chance to learn to be a civilized being, to become an American by living with them.

So, made to feel that I was in the hands of American friends, invited to share with them their home, their plenty, their happiness, I pushed out from my head the worry for wages. Here was my first chance to begin my life in the sunshine, after my long darkness. My laugh was all over my face as I said to them: "I'll trust myself to you. What I'm worth you'll give me." And I entered their house like a child by the hand.

The best of me I gave them. Their house cares were my house cares. I got up early. I worked till late. All that my soul hungered to give I put into the passion with which I scrubbed floors, scoured pots, and washed clothes. I was so grateful to mingle with the American people, to hear the music of the American language, that I never knew tiredness.

There was such a freshness in my brains and such a willingness in my heart that I could go on and on—not only with the work of the house, but work with my head— learning new words from the children, the grocer, the butcher, the iceman. I was not even afraid to ask for words from the policeman on the street. And every new word made me see new American things with American eyes. I felt like a Columbus, finding new worlds through every new word.

But words alone were only for the inside of me. The outside of me still branded me for a steerage immigrant. I had to have clothes to forget myself that I'm a stranger yet. And so I had to have money to buy these clothes.

The month was up. I was so happy! Now I'd have money. *My own, earned* money. Money to buy a new shirt on my back—shoes on my feet. Maybe yet an American dress and hat!

Ach! How high rose my dreams! How plainly I saw all that I would do with my visionary wages shining like a light over my head!

In my imagination I already walked in my new American clothes. How beautiful I looked as I saw myself like a picture before my eyes! I saw how I would throw away my immigrant rags tied up in my immigrant shawl. With money to buy—free money in my hands—I'd show them that I could look like an American in a day.

Like a prisoner in his last night in prison, counting the seconds that will free him from his chains, I trembled breathlessly for the minute I'd get the wages in my hand.

Before dawn I rose.

I shined up the house like a jewel-box.

I prepared breakfast and waited with my heart in my mouth for my lady and gentleman to rise. At last I heard them stirring. My eyes were jumping out of my head to them when I saw them coming in and seating themselves by the table.

Like a hungry cat rubbing up to its boss for meat, so I edged and simpered around them as I passed them the food. Without my will, like a beggar, my hand reached out to them.

The breakfast was over. And no word yet from my wages.

"*Gottuniu!*"[1] I thought to myself. "Maybe they're so busy with their own things they forgot it's the day for my wages. Could they who have everything know what I was to do with my first American dollars? How could they, soaking in plenty, how could they feel the longing and the fierce hunger in me, pressing up through each visionary dollar? How could they know the gnawing ache of my avid fingers for the feel of my own, earned dollars? *My* dollars that I could spend like a free person. *My* dollars that would make me feel with everybody alike!"

Breakfast was long past.

Lunch came. Lunch past.

Oi-i weh! Not a word yet about my money.

It was near dinner. And not a word yet about my wages.

I began to set the table. But my head—it swam away from me. I broke a glass. The silver dropped from my nervous fingers. I couldn't stand it any longer. I dropped everything and rushed over to my American lady and gentlemen.

"*Oi-i weh!* The money—my money—my wages!" I cried breathlessly.

Four cold eyes turned on me.

"Wages? Money?" The four eyes turned into hard stone as they looked me up and down. "Haven't you a comfortable bed to sleep, and three good meals a day? You're only a month here. Just came to America. And you already think about money. Wait till you're worth any money. What use are you without knowing English? You should be glad we keep you here. It's like a vacation for you. Other girls pay money yet to be in the country."

It went black for my eyes. I was so choked no words came to my lips. Even the tears went dry in my throat.

I left. Not a dollar for all my work.

For a long, long time my heart ached and ached like a sore wound. If murderers would have robbed me and killed me it wouldn't have hurt me so much. I couldn't think through my pain. The minute I'd see before me how they looked at me, the words they said to me—then everything began to bleed in me. And I was helpless.

For a long, long time the thought of ever working in an "American" family made

[1] (Yid.) Oh God.

me tremble with fear, like the fear of wild wolves. No—never again would I trust myself to an "American" family, no matter how fine their language and how sweet their smile.

It was blotted out in me all trust in friendship from "Americans." But the life in me still burned to live. The hope in me still craved to hope. In darkness, in dirt, in hunger and want, but only to live on!

There had been no end to my day—working for the "American" family.

Now rejecting false friendships from higher ups in America, I turned back to the Ghetto. I worked on a hard bench with my own kind on either side of me. I knew before I began what my wages were to be. I knew what my hours were to be. And I knew the feeling of the end of the day.

From the outside my second job seemed worse than the first. It was in a sweatshop of a Delancy Street basement, kept up by an old, wrinkled woman that looked like a black witch of greed. My work was sewing on buttons. While the morning was still dark I walked into a dark basement. And darkness met me when I turned out of the basement.

Day after day, week after week, all the contact I got with America was handling dead buttons. The money I earned was hardly enough to pay for bread and rent. I didn't have a room to myself. I didn't even have a bed. I slept on a mattress on the floor in a rat-hole of a room occupied by a dozen other immigrants. I was always hungry—oh, so hungry! The scant meals I could afford only sharpened my appetite for real food. But I felt myself better off than working in the "American" family, where I had three good meals a day and a bed to myself. With all the hunger and darkness of the sweat-shop, I had at least the evening to myself. And all night was mine. When all were asleep, I used to creep up on the roof of the tenement and talk out my heart in silence to the stars in the sky.

"Who am I? What am I? What do I want with my life? Where is America? Is there an America? What is this wilderness in which I'm lost?"

I'd hurl my questions and then think and think. And I could not tear it out of me, the feeling that America must be somewhere, somehow—only I couldn't find it—*my America,* where I would work for love and not for a living. I was like a thing following blindly after something far off in the dark!

"Oi weh!" I'd stretch out my hand up in the air. "My head is so lost in America! What's the use of all my working if I'm not in it? Dead buttons is not me."

Then the busy season started in the shop. The mounds of buttons grew and grew. The long day stretched out longer. I had to begin with the buttons earlier and stay with them till later in the night. The old witch turned into a huge greedy maw for wanting more and more buttons.

For a glass of tea, for a slice of herring over black bread, she would buy us up to stay another and another hour, till there seemed no end to her demands.

One day, the light of self-assertion broke into my cellar darkness.

"I don't want the tea. I don't want your herring," I said with terrible boldness. "I only want to go home. I only want the evening to myself!"

"You fresh mouth, you!" cried the old witch. "You learned already too much in America. I want no clock-watchers in my shop. Out you go!"

I was driven out to cold and hunger. I could no longer pay for my mattress on the floor. I no longer could buy the bite in the mouth. I walked the streets. I knew what it is to be alone in a strange city, among strangers.

But I laughed through my tears. So I learned too much already in America because I wanted the whole evening to myself? Well, America has yet to teach me still more: how to get not only the whole evening to myself, but a whole day a week like the American workers.

That sweat-shop was a bitter memory but a good school. It fitted me for a regular factory. I could walk in boldly and say I could work at something, even if it was only sewing on buttons.

Gradually, I became a trained worker. I worked in a light, airy factory, only eight hours a day. My boss was no longer a sweater and a blood-squeezer. The first freshness of the morning was mine. And the whole evening was mine. All day Sunday was mine.

Now I had better food to eat. I slept on a better bed. Now, I even looked dressed up like the American-born. But inside of me I knew that I was not yet an American. I choked with longing when I met an American-born, and I could say nothing.

Something cried dumb in me. I couldn't help it. I didn't know what it was I wanted. I only knew I wanted. I wanted. Like the hunger in the heart that never gets food.

An English class for foreigners started in our factory. The teacher had such a good, friendly face, her eyes looked so understanding, as if she could see right into my heart. So I went to her one day for an advice:

"I don't know what is with me the matter," I began. "I have no rest in me. I never yet done what I want."

"What is it you what to do, child?" she asked me.

"I want to do something with my head, my feelings. All day long, only with my hands I work."

"First you must learn English." She patted me as if I was not yet grown up. "Put your mind on that, and then we'll see."

So for a time I learned the language. I could almost begin to think with English words in my head. But in my heart the emptiness still hurt. I burned to give, to give something, to do something, to be something. The dead work with my hands was killing me. My work left only hard stones on my heart.

Again I went to our factory teacher and cried out to her: "I know already to read and write the English language, but I can't put it into words what I want. What is it in me so different that can't come out?"

She smiled at me down from her calmness as if I were a little bit out of my head. "What *do you want* to do?"

"I feel. I see. I hear. And I want to think it out. But I'm like dumb in me. I only feel I'm different—different from everybody."

She looked at me close and said nothing for a minute. "You ought to join one of the social clubs of the Women's Association," she advised.

"What's the Women's Association?" I implored greedily.

"A group of American women who are trying to help the working-girl find herself. They have a special department for immigrant girls like you."

I joined the Women's Association. On my first evening there they announced a lecture: "The Happy Worker and His Work," by the Welfare director of the United Mills Corporation.

"Is there such a thing as a happy worker at his work?" I wondered. "Happiness is only by working at what you love. And what poor girl can ever find it to work at what she loves?" My old dreams about my America rushed through my mind. Once I thought that in America everybody works for love. Nobody has to worry for a living. Maybe this welfare man came to show me the *real* America that till now I sought in vain.

With a lot of polite words the head lady of the Women's Association introduced a higher-up that looked like the king of kings of business. Never before in my life did I ever see a man with such a sureness in his step, such power in his face, such friendly positiveness in his eye as when he smiled upon us.

"Efficiency is the new religion of business," he began. "In big business houses, even in up-to-date factories, they no longer take the first comer and give him any job that happens to stand empty. Efficiency begins at the employment office. Experts are hired for the one purpose, to find out how best to fit the worker to his work. It's economy for the boss to make the worker happy." And then he talked a lot more on efficiency in educated language that was over my head.

I didn't know exactly what it meant—efficiency—but if it was to make the worker happy at his work, then that's what I had been looking for since I came to America. I only felt from watching him that he was happy by his job. And as I looked on this clean, well-dressed, successful one, who wasn't ashamed to say he rose from an office-boy, it made me feel that I, too, could lift myself up for a person.

He finished his lecture, telling us about the Vocational-Guidance Center that the Women's Association started.

The very next evening I was at the Vocational-Guidance Center. There I found a young, college-looking woman. Smartness and health shining from her eyes! She, too, looked as if she knew her way in America. I could tell at the first glance: here is a person that is happy by what she does.

"I feel you'll understand me," I said right away.

She leaned over with pleasure in her face: "I hope I can."

"I want to work by what's in me. Only, I don't know what's in me. I only feel I'm different."

She gave me a quick, puzzled look from the corner of her eyes. "What are you doing now?"

"I'm the quickest shirtwaist hand on the floor. But my heart wastes away by such work. I think and think, and my thoughts can't come out."

"Why don't you think out your thoughts in shirtwaists? You could learn to be a designer. Earn more money."

"I don't want to look on waists. If my hands are sick from waists, how could my head learn to put beauty into them?"

"But you must earn your living at what you know, and rise slowly from job to job."

I looked at her office sign: "Vocational Guidance." "What's your vocational guidance?" I asked. "How to rise from job to job—how to earn more money?"

The smile went out from her eyes. But she tried to be kind yet. "What *do* you want?" she asked, with a sigh of last patience.

"I want America to want me."

She fell back in her chair, thunderstruck with my boldness. But yet, in a low voice of educated self-control, she tried to reason with me:

"You have to *show* that you have something special for America before America has need of you."

"But I never had a chance to find out what's in me, because I always had to work for a living. Only, I feel it's efficiency for America to find out what's in me so different, so I could give it out by my work."

Her eyes half closed as they bored through me. Her mouth opened to speak, but no words came from her lips. So I flamed up with all that was choking in me like a house on fire:

"America gives free bread and rent to criminals in prison. They got grand houses with sunshine, fresh air, doctors and teachers, even for the crazy ones. Why don't they have free boarding-schools for immigrants—strong people—willing people? Here you see us burning up with something different, and America turns her head away from us."

Her brows lifted and dropped down. She shrugged her shoulders away from me with the look of pity we give to cripples and hopeless lunatics.

"America is no Utopia. First you must become efficient in earning a living before you can indulge in your poetic dreams."

I went away from the vocational-guidance office with all the air out of my lungs. All the light out of my eyes. My feet dragged after me like dead wood.

Till now there had always lingered a rosy veil of hope over my emptiness, a hope that a miracle would happen. I would open up my eyes some day and suddenly find the America of my dreams. As a young girl hungry for love sees always before her eyes the picture of lover's arms around her, so I saw always in my heart the vision of Utopian America.

But now I felt that the America of my dreams never was and never could be. Reality had hit me on the head as with a club. I felt that the America that I sought was nothing but a shadow—an echo—a chimera of lunatics and crazy immigrants.

Stripped of all illusion, I looked about me. The long desert of wasting days of drudgery stared me the face. The drudgery that I had lived through, and the endless drudgery still ahead of me rose over me like a withering wilderness of sand. In vain were all my cryings, in vain were all frantic efforts of my spirit to find the living waters of understanding for my perishing lips. Sand, sand was everywhere. With every seeking, every reaching out I only lost myself deeper and deeper in a vast sea of sand.

I knew now the American language. And I knew now, if I talked to the Americans from morning till night, they could not understand what the Russian soul of me wanted. They could not understand *me* any more than if I talked to them in Chinese. Between my soul and the American soul were worlds of difference that no words could bridge over. What was that difference? What made the Americans so far apart from me?

I began to read the American history. I found from the first pages that America started with a band of Courageous Pilgrims. They had left their native country as I had left mine. They had crossed an unknown ocean and landed in an unknown country, as I.

But the great difference between the first Pilgrims and me was that they expected to make America, build America, create their own world of liberty. I wanted to find it ready made.

I read on. I delved deeper down into the American history. I saw how the Pilgrim

Fathers came to a rocky desert country, surrounded by Indian savages on all sides. But undaunted, they pressed on—through danger—through famine, pestilence, and want—they pressed on. They did not ask the Indians for sympathy, for understanding. They made no demands on anybody, but on their own indomitable spirit of persistence.

And I—I was forever begging a crumb of sympathy, a gleam of understanding from strangers who could not understand.

I, when I encountered a few savage Indian scalpers, like the old witch of the sweat-shop, like my "Americanized" countryman, who cheated me of my wages—I, when I found myself on the lonely, untrodden path through which all seekers of the new world must pass, I lost heart and said: "There is no America!"

Then came a light—a great revelation! I saw America—a big idea—a deathless hope—a world still in the making. I saw that it was the glory of America that it was not yet finished. And I, the last comer, had her share to give, small or great, to the making of America, like those Pilgrims who came in the *Mayflower.*

Fired up by this revealing light, I began to build a bridge of understanding between the American-born and myself. Since their life was shut out from such as me, I began to open up my life and the lives of my people to them. And life draws life. In only writing about the Ghetto I found America.

Great chances have come to me. But in my heart is always a deep sadness. I feel like a man who is sitting down to a secret table of plenty, while his near ones and dear ones are perishing before his eyes. My very joy in doing the work I love hurts me like secret guilt, because all about me I see so many with my longings, my burning eagerness, to do and to be, wasting their days in drudgery they hate, merely to buy bread and pay rent. And America is losing all that richness of the soul.

The Americans of tomorrow, the America that is every day nearer coming to be, will be too wise, too open-hearted, too friendly-handed, to let the least last-comer at their gates knock in vain with his gifts unwanted.

—1923

H.D. (HILDA DOOLITTLE) (1886-1961)

Hilda Doolittle (Ezra Pound later provided the pen name H.D.) was born in 1886 in Bethlehem, Pennsylvania, to Helen Wolle Doolittle, a Moravian teacher of art and music, and Charles Leander Doolittle, an astronomer. During her youth, H.D. was an avid classicist (an interest that would remain strong throughout her life) and a basketball player. She met and fell in love with poet Ezra Pound when she was fifteen and he sixteen, and they were briefly engaged. In 1904 she entered Bryn Mawr; shortly thereafter she met lifelong friends William Carlos Williams and Marianne Moore. She left Bryn Mawr after only one year and attended the University of Pennsylvania. In 1911, she traveled to Europe, settled in London, and never returned to the U.S. to live. In Europe, H.D. became a leader of the Imagist movement in poetry. Her first poems appeared in *Poetry* in January 1913, having been submitted by Pound to the editor, Harriet Monroe. In 1919, H.D. gave birth to her only child, Frances Perdita, named after her mother's lover Frances Gregg and the daughter of Hermione in Shakespeare's *The Winter's Tale.*

In the year before Perdita's birth, H.D. had been ill and she was attended by Annie Winifred Ellerman (Bryher), a fan of her poetry, a friend, and a lifelong romantic companion. Together, H.D. and Bryher went to Paris, where they became involved in the expatriate literary community and where Bryher and one of her husbands, Robert McAlmon, founded Contact Editions, which published Djuna Barnes and Gertrude Stein, among others. It was H.D.'s connection to Bryher and to Kenneth Macpherson (another of Bryher's husbands) that got her involved with the film company POOL Productions; she played roles in all three of POOL's films: *Foothills* (1927), *Wingbeat* (1929), and *Borderline* (1930).

H.D. was a prolific writer, publishing more than fifty books of poetry and prose and writing a number of unpublished books and short stories. Though she is often known for her early Imagist work, the second half of her career was marked by epic works such as *The Trilogy,* which is comprised of *The Walls Do Not Fall* (1944), *Tribute to the Angels* (1945), *The Flowering of the Rod* (1946), and *Helen in Egypt* (1961). The concise and experimental nature of H.D.'s work attracted many followers in the twentieth century. In the late 1940s and early 1950s, the Black Mountain and Beat poets (Robert Duncan, Robert Creeley, Allen Ginsberg, and Denise Levertov) adopted H.D. as a mentor, and poets such as Barbara Guest, Alicia Ostriker, and Carolyn Forché have noted H.D. as an inspiration to their work.

Oread[1]

Whirl up, sea—
whirl your pointed pines,
splash your great pines
on our rocks,
hurl your green over us,   5
cover us with your pools of fir.

—1914

Sheltered Garden

I have had enough.
I gasp for breath.

Every way ends, every road,
every foot-path leads at last
to the hill-crest—   5
then you retrace your steps,
or find the same slope on the other side,
precipitate.

I have had enough—
border-pinks, clove-pinks, wax-lilies,   10
herbs, sweet-cress.

O for some sharp swish of a branch—
there is no scent of resin
in this place,
no taste of bark, of coarse weeds,   15

---

[1] In Greek mythology, a type of nymph.

aromatic, astringent—
only border on border of scented pinks.

Have you seen fruit under cover
that wanted light—
pears wadded in cloth,   20
protected from the frost,
melons, almost ripe,
smothered in straw?

Why not let the pears cling
to the empty branch?   25
All your coaxing will only make
a bitter fruit—
let them cling, ripen of themselves,
test their own worth,
nipped, shrivelled by the frost,   30
to fall at last but fair
with a russet coat.

Or the melon—
let it bleach yellow
in the winter light,   35
even tart to the taste—
it is better to taste of frost—
the exquisite frost—
than of wadding and of dead grass.

For this beauty,   40
beauty without strength,
chokes out life.
I want wind to break,
scatter these pink-stalks,
snap off their spiced heads,   45
fling them about with dead leaves—
spread the paths with twigs,
limbs broken off,
trail great pine branches,
hurled from some far wood   50
right across the melon-patch,
break pear and quince—
leave half-trees, torn, twisted
but showing the fight was valiant.

O to blot out this garden   55
to forget, to find a new beauty
in some terrible
wind-tortured place.

—1916

Fragment Forty

Love...bitter-sweet. —Sappho.

1

Keep love and he wings,
with his bow,
up, mocking us,
keep love and he taunts us
and escapes.   5

Keep love and he sways apart
in another world,
outdistancing us.

Keep love and he mocks,
ah, bitter and sweet,   10
your sweetness is more cruel
than your hurt.

Honey and salt,
fire burst from the rocks
to meet fire   15
spilt from Hesperus.

Fire darted aloft and met fire:
in that moment
love entered us.

2

Could Eros be kept?   20
he were prisoned long since
and sick with imprisonment;
could Eros be kept?
others would have broken
and crushed out his life.   25

Could Eros be kept?
we too sinning, by Kypris,
might have prisoned him outright.

Could Eros be kept?
nay, thank him and the bright goddess   30
that he left us.

3

Ah, love is bitter and sweet,
but which is more sweet,
the sweetness
or the bitterness?   35
none has spoken it.

Love is bitter,

but can salt taint sea-flowers,
grief, happiness?

Is it bitter to give back   40
love to your lover
if he crave it?

Is it bitter to give back
love to your lover
if he wish it   45
for a new favourite?
who can say,
or is it sweet?

Is it sweet
to possess utterly?   50
or is it bitter,
bitter as ash?

4
I had thought myself frail;
a petal,
with light equal   55
on leaf and under-leaf.

I had thought myself frail;
a lamp,
shell, ivory or crust of pearl,
about to fall shattered,   60
with flame spent.

I cried:
"I must perish,
I am deserted,
an outcast, desperate   65
in this darkness,"
(such fire rent me with Hesperus,)
then the day broke.

5
What need of a lamp
when day lightens us,   70
what need to bind love
when love stands
with such radiant wings
over us?

What need—   75
yet to sing love,
love must first shatter us.

Helen[2]

All Greece hates
the still eyes in the white face,
the lustre as of olives
where she stands,
and the white hands.   5

All Greece reviles
the wan face when she smiles,
hating it deeper still
when it grows wan and white,
remembering past enchantments   10
and past ills.

Greece sees unmoved,
God's daughter, born of love,
the beauty of cool feet
and slenderest knees,   15
could love indeed the maid,
only if she were laid,
white ash amid funereal cypresses.

—1924

Sigil[3]

I
Ground
under a maple-tree
breeds parasite,

so I
bear tentacles, as it were,   5
from you, tree-loam;

ground
under a beech
breeds faun-lily, each

tree   10
spreads separate leaf-mould,
whether maple or beech,

whether paper-birch;
I come
as those parasites   15

out of frost almost,
Indian-pipe, hypatica

---

[2] In Greek mythology, Helen was the daughter of Leda
and Zeus. Married to Menalaus of Greece, she was kidnapped by Paris and taken to Troy, which caused the
Trojan War.
[3] A seal or device.

or the spotted snake-cup,

adder-root, blood-root,
or the white, white plaque   20
of the wild dog-wood tree;

each alone,
each separately, I come
separate parasite,

white spear-head   25
with implacable fragile shoot
from black loam.

II
This is my own world,
these can't see;
I hear, "this is my dower,"   30

I fear no man, no woman;
flower does not fear
bird, insect nor adder;

I fear neither the wind
nor viper,   35
familiar sound

bids me raise
frost-nipped, furred head
from winter-ground;

familiar scent   40
makes me say,
"I am awake";

familiar touch
makes me say, "all this was over-done,
much   45

was wasted, blood and bone spent
toward this last
secret

wild,
wild,   50
wild fulfilment."

III
For:
I am not man,
I am not woman;
I crave   55

you

as the sea-fish
the wave.

IV
When you turn to sleep
and love is over,   60
I am your own;

when you want to weep
for some never-found lover,
I come;

when you would think,   65
"what was the use of it,"
you'll remember

something you can't grasp
and you'll wonder
what it was   70

altered your mood;
suddenly, summer grass
and clover

will be spread,
and you'll whisper,   75
"I've forgotten something,

what was it,
what was it,
I wanted to remember?"

V
That will be me,   80
silver
and wild and free;

that will be me
to send a shudder through you,
cold wind   85

through an aspen tree;
that will be me
to bid you recover

every voice,
every sound,   90
every syllable

from grass-blade,
tree-toad,
from every wisp and feather

of fern   95

and moss
and grass,

from every wind-flower,
tethered
by a thread,   100

from every thread-stem
and every thread-root
and acorns half-broken

above ground
and under the ground.   105

VI
Confine
your measure to the boundary of the sky,
take all that, I

am quite content
with fire-fly,   110
with butter-fly;

take everything,
I compensate my soul
with a new rôle;

you're free   115
but you're only a song,
I'm free but I've gone;

I'm not here,
being everywhere
you are.   120

VII
Whether this happened before,
whether this happen again,
it's the same;

there is no magic nor lure,
there is no spell and no power   125
to equalise love's fire;

whether he fasten his car
with the bright doves and afar
threaten great Zeus[4] and the stars;

or whether he cringe at my feet,   130
whether he beat on your eyes,
white wings, white butterflies.

—1931

[4] In Greek mythology, the ruler of the pantheon of gods and goddesses.

GERTRUDE "MA" RAINEY (1886-1939)

Born Gertrude Pridgett, and called "Ma" Rainey after her marriage to Will "Pa" Rainey in 1904, Ma Rainey is often referred to as the "Mother of the Blues." During the first decades of the twentieth century, she performed for the Theater Owners Booking Association (T.O.B.A.), the primary vaudeville circuit for black artists. As a star with the Rabbit Foot Minstrels, Rainey met and befriended the younger performer Bessie Smith.

Rainey began singing the blues after hearing blues music performed in the early 1900s; she later claimed to have invented the term "blues," although the word seems to have been used in a musical context as early as the 1880s. In any case, Rainey was probably the first widely-known blues performer; her Paramount recordings from the 1920s brought the blues to a nationwide audience. Two of her most famous songs from the Paramount period were "C.C. Rider" and "Ma Rainey's Black Bottom." The latter song became the title of August Wilson's 1982 play, which takes a loosely biographical approach to Ma Rainey's life and vaudeville experiences. Wilson's play also "outed" Rainey as a bisexual woman, though her "Prove It on Me Blues" openly describes her love for women.

Cell Bound Blues

Hey, hey, jailer, tell me what have I done
Hey, hey, jailer, tell me what have I done
You've got me all bound in chains, did I kill that woman's son?

All bound in prison, all bound in jail
All bound in prison, all bound in jail   5
Cold iron balls all around me, no one to go my bail

I've got a mother and father, livin' in a cottage by the sea
I've got a mother and father, livin' in a cottage by the sea
Got a sister and brother, wonder do they think of poor me

I walked in my room the other night   10
My man walked in and begin to fight

I took my gun in my right hand,
"Hold him, folks, I don't wanta kill my man."

When I did that, he hit me 'cross my head
First shot I fired, my man fell dead   15

The paper came out and told the news
That's why I said I got the cell bound blues
Hey, hey, jailer, I got the cell bound blues.

—1924

Ma Rainey's Black Bottom

[Spoken]
Unknown man: Now, you've heard the rest. Ah, boys, I'm gonna show you the best. Ma Rainey's gonna show you her black bottom!

[Sung]
Rainey: Way down South in Alabamy
I got a friend they call dancin' Sammy
Who's crazy about all the latest dancin'   5
Black bottom stomps and the new baby prancin'

The other night at a swell affair
Soon as the boys found out that I was there
They said, "Come on, Ma, let's go to the cabaret."
When I got there, you ought to hear me say   10

Want to see the dance you call the black bottom
I wanna learn that dance
Want to see the dance you call your big black bottom
They put you in a trance.

All the boys in the neighborhood   15
They say your black bottom is really good
Come on and show me your black bottom
I want to learn that dance.

I want to see the dance you call the black bottom
I want to learn that dance   20
Come on and show that dance you call your big black bottom
It puts us in a trance.

Early last morning 'bout the break of day
Grandpa told my grandmama, I heard him say
"Get up and show your good old man your black bottom   25
I want to learn that dance."

Now I'm gon' show you all my black bottom
They stay to see that dance
Wait until you see me do my big black bottom
It'll put you in a trance.   30

[Spoken]
Man: Ah, do it, Ma, do it, honey. Look out, now, Ma, you's gettin' kinda
rough there! You bet' be yourself, now, careful now, not too strong, not too
strong, Ma!

[Sung]
Rainey: I done showed y'all my black bottom
You ought to learn that dance.

—1928

Prove It on Me Blues

Went out last night, had a great big fight
Everything seemed to go on wrong
I looked up, to my surprise
The gal I was with was gone

Where she went, I don't know 5
I mean to follow everywhere she goes
Folks say I'm crooked, I didn't know where she took it
I want the whole world to know

They said I do it, ain't nobody caught me
Sure got to prove it on me 10
Went out last night with a crowd of my friends
They must've been women, 'cause I don't like no men

It's true I wear a collar and a tie
Make the wind blow all the while
'Cause they say I do it, ain't nobody caught me 15
They sure got to prove it on me

Say I do it, ain't nobody caught me
Sure got to prove it on me
I went out last night with a crowd of my friends
They must've been women, 'cause I don't like no men 20

Wear my clothes just like a fan
Talk to the gals just like any old man
'Cause they say I do it, ain't nobody caught me
Sure got to prove it on me.

—1928

MARÍA LUISA GARZA (1887-1990)

Journalist, writer, and newspaper editor María Luisa Garza was born in 1887 and lived to be over one hundred years old. Like other immigrant Mexican crónistas (columnists) who wrote for U.S. newspapers, she launched her critiques of contemporary society under a pseudonym. As "Loreley" she wrote the column "Crónicas Femeninas" and contributed regularly to *El Imparcial de Texas*. "The Intelligent Woman" has been archived and preserved by the Recovering the U.S. Hispanic Literary Heritage Project; it was first anthologized in *Herencia: The Anthology of Hispanic Literature of the United States* (2002).

The Intelligent Woman

Much has been said about intelligent women, and intelligent women have been criticized for many things also. In my opinion, this is one of the principal reasons that there are few women writers. From a young age, females hear the interminable little phrase: "Hey…that one over there, she's a bluestocking."

Under these circumstances, beginning in childhood girls are afraid of intelligent women. Instead of reading books, they find it better to dedicate themselves to coquettishness, or they surrender completely to the talons of the fashion world.

There is nothing more misguided than this, because an educated woman is attractive, charming and seductive, from the very minute you meet her.

Napoleon once said that a pretty woman is a charm and a good woman a treasure.

I cannot imagine how goodness can illuminate a dull soul. Goodness is attractive, but only if it is a characteristic of knowledge.

The woman who reads and educates herself, not in the shallow works of Luis de Val, but in vital and informative books—the seeds of fruitful illumination—is the woman who can dare to venture out alone into the raging sea of life.

It is common to observe how many young girls are perverted and fall into prostitution, enticed by nothing more than the lure of silks and the sparkle of jewels. I am sure that these gullible creatures never opened any book other than a fashion magazine.

I met a girl who was born into luxury and wealth but, through some misfortune, came to be enveloped by poverty. She was young and attractive and could have married, but her suitors turned away when they found out that she was poor.

One or another suitor who would continue the courtship was able to recognize the young lady's intelligence, but was not interested in her for such a respectable reason. Like so many naive women, she could have continued to live her lavish life at the cost of her honor, but this woman was smart. She was educated and looked to her erudition for the shield that would protect her from vice.

Once banished, her exceptional intelligence opened the redemptive doors of work to her. When she was thought to have been completely defeated, she was able to ascend the luminous path to success, something that is attained through knowledge.

It is often said: "She is an intellectual…and doesn't know anything about managing her home." Do those women who go dancing, walking or out visiting friends not waste time that should be invested in house work? Is it not true that they actually waste more time than the bookworms, who everyone ridicules? If only these critics would really think about it. If only they would reflect on who wastes more time. Would they conclude that it is the woman who is always at home with her books, or the one constantly out in the streets?

An intelligent woman hates filth and ensures that her house is clean, the garden well-tended, and birds are close by.

Everyone would agree that not even a man could be happy having as his companion a frivolous wife who does not know how to brighten the home with her intelligence. Not even honor can be entrusted to such a woman, for she is capable of selling it in order to buy a suit *à la derniere*[1] or a string of pearls from the Far East.

—1920

[1] (Fr.) Of the latest fashion.

MARIANNE MOORE (1887-1972)

Born November 15, 1887, in Kirkwood, Missouri, Moore never met her father, a victim of a nervous breakdown, but remained close to her mother, Mary Warner Moore, and her brother John throughout her life. The family moved to Carlisle, Pennsylvania, where Moore attended private school; she later attended Bryn Mawr College. After graduating in 1909, she took a business course at Carlisle Commercial College and traveled to Europe with her mother, meanwhile publishing poems in *The Egoist, Others,* and *Poetry,* new but influential literary magazines that launched her reputation as a poet. She taught various business courses at the U.S. Industrial Indian School in Carlisle from 1911 to 1915. Her move, with her mother, to Greenwich Village in 1918 and her job with the New York Public Library brought her into contact with contemporary writers who later became important literary figures, such as H.D. and Bryher. In her work as a poet and editor of *The Dial,* a literary magazine of the 1920s, Moore was a seminal figure in the shaping of literary modernism (she later mentored Elizabeth Bishop). Moore published seven volumes of poetry, as well as several collected editions, translations, letters, and prose. Her work garnered major prizes, including the Bollingen Prize, the National Book Award, and the Pulitzer Prize. Like Edna St. Vincent Millay, Moore was a public literary figure, though later in life. Disabled by a stroke in 1969, she ceased to write, and died on February 5, 1972. Her poems, marked by acute observation, wit, syllabic verse, and a broad range of line lengths and stanza forms, continue to influence contemporary poets.

The Fish

wade
through black jade.
    Of the crow-blue mussel-shells, one keeps
    adjusting the ash heaps;
        opening and shutting itself like   5

an
injured fan.
    The barnacles, which encrust the side
    of the wave cannot hide
        there, for the submerged shafts of the   10

sun,
split like spun
    glass, move themselves with spotlight swiftness
    into the crevices—
        in and out, illuminating   15

the
turquoise sea
    of bodies. The water drives a wedge
    of iron through the iron edge
        of the cliff; whereupon the stars,   20

pink
rice-grains, ink-
    bespattered jellyfish, crabs like green
    lilies, and submarine
        toadstools slide each on the other.   25

All
external
    marks of abuse are present on this
    defiant edifice—
        all the physical features of   30

ac-
cident—lack
    of cornice, dynamite grooves, burns, and
    hatchet strokes, these things stand
        out on it; the chasm side is   35

dead.
Repeated
    evidence has proved that it can live
    on what can not revive
        its youth. The sea grows old in it.

—1921

Marriage[1]

This institution,
perhaps one should say enterprise
out of respect for which
one says one need not change one's mind
about a thing one has believed in,   5
requiring public promises
of one's intention
to fulfill a private obligation:
I wonder what Adam and Eve
think of it by this time,   10
this fire-gilt steel
alive with goldenness;
how bright it shows—
"of circular traditions and impostures,
committing many spoils,"[2]   15
requiring all one's criminal ingenuity
to avoid!
Psychology which explains everything
explains nothing,
and we are still in doubt.   20
Eve: beautiful woman—
I have seen her
when she was so handsome
she gave me a start,
able to write simultaneously   25
in three languages—[3]
English, German, and French—
and talk in the meantime;
equally positive in demanding a commotion

---

[1] An aspect of Moore's technique was to incorporate quotations from a range of sources, not always identified or identifiable. The notes to this poem are adapted from those provided by Moore or quoted directly.

[2] Francis Bacon (1561-1626), English philosopher and essayist.

[3] Refers to a woman writing simultaneously in three languages, reported in "Multiple Consciousness or Reflex Action of Unaccustomed Range" in *Scientific American*, January 1922.

and in stipulating quiet: 30
"*I* should like to be alone";
to which the visitor replies,
"I should like to be alone;
why not be alone together?"
Below the incandescent stars   35
below the incandescent fruit,
the strange experience of beauty;
its existence is too much;
it tears one to pieces
and each fresh wave of consciousness   40
is poison.
"See her, see her in this common world,"[4]
the central flaw
in that first crystal-fine experiment,
this amalgamation which can never be more   45
than an interesting impossibility,
describing it
as "that strange paradise
unlike flesh, stones,
gold or stately buildings,   50
the choicest piece of my life:
the heart rising
in its estate of peace
as a boat rises
with the rising of the water";[5]   55
constrained in speaking of the serpent—
shed snakeskin in the history of politeness
not to be returned to again—
that invaluable accident
exonerating Adam.   60
And he has beauty also;
it's distressing—the O thou
to whom from whom,
without whom nothing—Adam;
"something feline,   65
something colubrine"[6]—how true!
a crouching mythological monster
in that Persian miniature of emerald mines,
raw silk—ivory white, snow white,
oyster white, and six others—   70
that paddock full of leopards and giraffes—
long lemon-yellow bodies
sown with trapezoids of blue.
Alive with words,

[4] Moore attributes this line to "George Shock," possibly a reference to "George Schock," a pseudonym for novelist Katherine Riegel Loose.

[5] Richard Baxter, *The Saints' Everlasting Rest* (Lippincott, 1909).

[6] From a review by Philip Littell of *Poems* by George Santayana (1863-1952) in *New Republic*, March 21, 1923.

vibrating like a cymbal 75
touched before it has been struck,
he has prophesied correctly—
the industrious waterfall,
"the speedy stream
which violently bears all before it, 80
at one time silent as the air
and now powerful as the wind."
"Treading chasms
on the uncertain footing of a spear,"[7]
forgetting that there is in woman 85
a quality of mind
which as an instinctive manifestation
is unsafe,
he goes on speaking
in a formal customary strain, 90
of "past states, the present state,
seals, promises,
the evil one suffered,
the good one enjoys,
hell, heaven, 95
everything convenient
to promote one's joy."[8]
In him a state of mind
perceives what it was not
intended that he should; 100
"he experiences a solemn joy
in seeing that he has become an idol."[9]
Plagued by the nightingale
in the new leaves,
with its silence— 105
not its silence but its silences,
he says of it:
"It clothes me with a shirt of fire."[10]
"He dares not clap his hands
to make it go on 110
lest it should fly off;
if he does nothing, it will sleep;
if he cries out, it will not understand."[11]
Unnerved by the nightingale
and dazzled by the apple, 115
impelled by "the illusion of a fire

---

[7] *Essay on Burke's Style* by William Hazlitt (1778-1830), English essayist and literary critic. Edmund Burke (1729-1797) was an Irish-born English statesman and author sympathetic toward the American colonies and Irish Catholics, but not the French Revolution.

[8] See note 5.

[9] "A Travers Champs" (Across the Fields) from Anatole France's *Filles et Garçons* (Girls and Boys). France (1844-1924) was a French novelist, poet, and critic.

[10] "The Nightingale," a poem in Armenian by Dr. Hagoop Boghossian.

[11] *Feminine Influence on the Poets* (1910) by Edward Thomas (1878-1917), an English poet who died during World War I.

effectual to extinguish fire,"[12]
compared with which
the shining of the earth
is but deformity—a fire   120
"as high as deep
as bright as broad
as long as life itself,"[13]
he stumbles over marriage,
"a very trivial object indeed"[14]   125
to have destroyed the attitude
in which he stood—
the ease of the philosopher
unfathered by a woman.
Unhelpful Hymen!   130
a kind of overgrown cupid[15]
reduced to insignificance
by the mechanical advertising
parading as involuntary comment,
by that experiment of Adam's   135
with ways out but no way in—
the ritual of marriage,
augmenting all its lavishness;
its fiddlehead ferns,
lotus flowers, opuntias, white dromedaries,   140
its hippopotamus—
nose and mouth combined
in one magnificent hopper—
its snake and the potent apple.
He tells us   145
that "for love that will
gaze an eagle blind,
that is with Hercules
climbing the trees
in the garden of the Hesperides,   150
from forty-five to seventy
is the best age,"[16]
commending it
as a fine art, as an experiment,
a duty or as merely recreation.   155
One must not call him ruffian
nor friction a calamity—
the fight to be affectionate:

[12] See note 5.
[13] See note 5.
[14] William Godwin (1756-1836), radical political theorist and novelist in England; his wife was Mary Wollstonecraft (1759-1797), author of *A Vindication of the Rights of Woman* (1792); their daughter, Mary Wollstonecraft Shelley (1797-1851), wrote the gothic novel *Frankenstein, or the Modern Prometheus* (1818).

[15] "Brewer, *Dictionary of Phrase and Fable*." Hymen is the Greek god of marriage.
[16] *Barchester Towers* (1857), by Anthony Trollope (1815-1882), English novelist. Hercules was a Greek hero who slew his wife and children in a fit of madness, and had to perform a penance of twelve tasks, one of which was to steal golden apples given as a wedding gift to Hera, wife of the Greek god Zeus.

"no truth can be fully known
until it has been tried
by the tooth of disputation."[17]   160
The blue panther with blue eyes,
entirely graceful—
one must give them the path—
the black obsidian Diana   165
who "darkeneth her countenance
as a bear doth,"[18]
the spiked hand
that has an affection for one
and proves it to the bone,   170
impatient to assure you
that impatience is the mark of independence,
not of bondage.
"Married people often look that way"—[19]
"seldom and cold, up and down,   175
mixed and malarial
with a good day and a bad."[20]
We Occidentals are so unemotional,
self lost, the irony preserved
in "the Ahasuerus *tête-à-tête* banquet"[21]   180
with its small orchids like snakes' tongues,
with its "good monster, lead the way,"[22]
with little laughter
and munificence of humor
in that quixotic atmosphere of frankness   185
in which "four o'clock does not exist,
but at five o'clock
the ladies in their imperious humility
are ready to receive you";[23]
in which experience attests   190
that men have power
and sometimes one is made to feel it.
He says, "What monarch would not blush
to have a wife
with hair like a shaving brush?"[24]   195
The fact of woman
is "not the sound of the flute
but very poison."[25]
She says, "Men are monopolists

---

[17] Robert de Sorbonne (1201-1274), founder of Sorbonne University in Paris, France.

[18] Ecclesiasticus, "Women: Bad and good—An Essay," *The Modern Reader's Bible* (Macmillan).

[19] C. Bertram Hartman (1892-1960), American painter.

[20] See note 5.

[21] *Expositor's Bible* by George Adam Smith (1856-1942), Scottish biblical scholar. In the book of Esther, Ahasuerus, a Persian king, banishes his wife Vashti for disobeying him. He chooses Esther as his next wife, who, after preparing him a banquet, asks him to spare the Jews.

[22] *The Tempest* (1610-11) by William Shakespeare.

[23] *Femina,* la Comtesse de Noailles, December 1921.

[24] "The Rape of the Lock," a satire in verse by Mary Frances Nearing with suggestions by M. Moore. Nearing is satirizing English poet Alexander Pope's (1688-1744) poem by the same name.

[25] *The Syrian Christ* (1916) by Abraham Mitram Rihbany.

of 'stars, garters, buttons   200
and other shining baubles'—
unfit to be the guardians
of another person's happiness."[26]
He says, "These mummies
must be handled carefully—   205
'the crumbs from a lion's meal,
a couple of shins and the bit of an ear';[27]
turn to the letter M
and you will find
that 'a wife is a coffin,'[28]   210
that severe object
with the pleasing geometry
stipulating space not people,
refusing to be buried
and uniquely disappointing,   215
revengefully wrought in the attitude
of an adoring child
to a distinguished parent."
She says, "This butterfly,
this waterfly, this nomad   220
that has 'proposed
to settle on my hand for life'—[29]
What can one do with it?
There must have been more time
in Shakespeare's day   225
to sit and watch a play.
You know so many artists who are fools."
He says, "You know so many fools
who are not artists."
The fact forgot   230
that "some have merely rights
while some have obligations,"[30]
he loves himself so much,
he can permit himself
no rival in that love.   235
She loves herself so much,
she cannot see herself enough—
a statuette of ivory on ivory,
the logical last touch
to an expansive splendor   240
earned as wages for work done:
one is not rich but poor
when one can always seem so right.

---

[26] Founder's Address, Mount Holyoke College (1821) by M. Carey Thomas, president emeritus of Bryn Mawr College.
[27] Smith.
[28] Quoted by John Cournos from Ezra Pound (1885-1972), American poet, critic, and controversial literary figure.
[29] *Christie Johnstone* (1853) by Charles Reade (1814-1884), English novelist.
[30] Edmund Burke (see note 7).

What can one do for them—
these savages   245
condemned to disaffect
all those who are not visionaries
alert to undertake the silly task
of making people noble?
This model of petrine fidelity   250
who "leaves her peaceful husband
only because she has seen enough of him"—[31]
that orator reminding you,
"I am yours to command."
"Everything to do with love is mystery;   255
it is more than a day's work
to investigate this science."[32]
One sees that it is rare—
that striking grasp of opposites
opposed each to the other, not to unity,   260
which in cycloid inclusiveness
have dwarfed the demonstration
of Columbus with the egg—
a triumph of simplicity—
that charitive Euroclydon   265
of frightening disinterestedness
which the world hates,
admitting:

 "I am such a cow,
 if I had a sorrow
 I should feel it a long time;   270
 I am not one of those
 who have a great sorrow
 in the morning
 and a great joy at noon",[33]   275

which says: "I have encountered it
among those unpretentious
protégés of wisdom,
where seeming to parade
as the debater and the Roman,   280
the statesmanship
of an archaic Daniel Webster
persists to their simplicity of temper
as the essence of the matter:

 'Liberty and union   285
 now and forever';

---

[31] "Simone Puget, advertisement entitled 'Change of Fashion,' *English Review*, June 1914."
[32] "F. C. Tilney, *The Original Fables of La Fontaine*, 'Love and Folly': Book XII, No. 14."
[33] Daniel Webster (1782-1852), American statesman and orator.

the Book on the writing-table;
the hand in the breast-pocket."

—1924

Roses Only

You do not seem to realize that beauty is a liability rather than
    an asset—that in view of the fact that spirit creates form we are justified
                in supposing
    that you must have brains. For you, a symbol of the unit, stiff and
                sharp,   5
    conscious of surpassing by dint of native superiority and liking for
                everything
self-dependent, anything an

ambitious civilization might produce: for you, unaided, to attempt through
    sheer
    reserve to confute presumptions resulting from observation is idle. You 10
                cannot make us
    think you a delightful happen-so. But rose, if you are brilliant, it
is not because your petals are the without-which-nothing of pre-eminence.
                You would look, minus
thorns—like a what-is-this, a mere   15

peculiarity. They are not proof against a storm, the elements, or mildew
    but what about the predatory hand? What is brilliance without
                coordination? Guarding the
    infinitesimal pieces of your mind, compelling audience to
the remark that it is better to be forgotten than to be remembered too 20
                violently,
your thorns are the best part of you.

—1924

FANNIE HURST (1889–1968)

Fannie Hurst was born in Hamilton, Ohio, the daughter of businessman Samuel Hurst and
Rose Koppel, both of whom were first-generation, German-Jewish Americans. Hurst's 1958
autobiography, *Anatomy of Me,* depicts a comfortable, middle-class childhood in St. Louis,
Missouri, but in reality, Hurst's father struggled to support the family, her sister died in an
epidemic of diphtheria, and the family moved frequently. After graduating from Washington
University in 1909, Hurst moved to New York City, where she spent the rest of her life. She
married pianist Jacques Danielson in 1915; the secret marriage, which became public in 1920,
lasted until his death in 1952. In both her fiction and her extensive civic work, Hurst was a
passionate advocate for working women, especially working-class and lower middle-class
women working in urban, sex-segregated areas such as the garment industry. Hurst became
friends with Eleanor Roosevelt in the course of their shared work in support of domestic
workers. She was also a supporter of the NAACP, although Zora Neale Hurston, who worked

as her personal assistant, emphasized Hurst's racism in her own autobiography, *Dust Tracks on a Road* (1942). Hurst was prolific and well paid; she published more than three hundred stories, primarily in women's magazines for an audience of women readers, and she was reported to be the most highly paid woman writer of her day. Some twenty-nine films were made from Hurst's fiction, including *Imitation of Life* (1934, 1959) and *Humoresque* (1946). Hurst wrote eighteen novels, eight collections of stories, and several autobiographical works. Perhaps because of her popularity, and likely because of her work's focus on working women, Hurst is rarely anthologized. *Imitation of Life* remains in print largely for its importance to film scholars; Susan Koppelman edited a collection of Hurst's short fiction for the Feminist Press in 2004.

T.B.

The figurative underworld of a great city has no ventilation, housing or lighting problems. Rooks and crooks who live in the putrid air of crime are not denied the light of day, even though they loathe it. Cadets, social skunks, whose carnivorous eyes love darkness, walk in God's sunshine and breathe God's air. Scarlet women turn over in wide beds and draw closer velvet curtains to shut out the morning. Gamblers curse the dawn.

But what of the literal underworld of the great city? What of the babes who cry in fetid cellars for the light and are denied it? What of the Subway track-walker, purblind from gloom; the coal-stoker, whose fiery tomb is the boiler-room of a skyscraper; sweatshop workers, a flight below the sidewalk level, whose faces are the color of the dead Chinese; six-dollar-a-week salesgirls in the arc-lighted subcellars of six-million-dollar corporations?

This is the literal underworld of the great city, and its sunless streets run literal blood—the blood of the babes who cried in vain; the blood from the lungs of the sweatshop workers whose faces are the color of dead Chinese; the blood from the cheeks of the six-dollar-a-week salesgirls in the arc-lighted subcellars. But these are your problems and my problems and the problems of the men who have found the strength or the fear not to die rich. The babe's mother, who had never known else, could not know that her cellar was fetid; she only cried out in her anguish and hated vaguely in her heart.

Sara Juke, in the bargain basement of the Titanic Department Store, did not know that lint from white goods clogs the lungs, and that the air she breathed was putrefied as from a noxious swamp. Sometimes a pain, sharp as a hat-pin, entered between her shoulder-blades. But what of that? When the heart is young the heart is bold, and Sara could laugh upward with the musical glee of a bird.

There were no seasons, except the spring and fall openings and semi-annual clearing-sales, in the bargain basement of the Titanic Store. On a morning when the white-goods counter was placing long-sleeve, high-necked nightgowns in its bargain bins, and knit underwear was supplanting the reduced muslins, Sara Juke drew her little pink-knitted jacket closer about her narrow shoulders and shivered—shivered, but smiled. "Br-r-r! October never used to get under my skin like this."

Hattie Krakow, room-mate and co-worker, shrugged her bony shoulders and laughed; but not with the upward glee of a bird—downward, rather, until it died in a croak in her throat. But then Hattie Krakow was ten years older than Sara Juke; and ten years in the arc-lighted subcellar of the Titanic Department Store can do much to muffle the ring in a laugh.

"Gee! You're as funny as your own funeral, you are! You keep up the express pace you're going and there won't be another October left on your calendar."

"That's right; cheer me up a bit, dearie. What's the latest style in undertaking?"

"You'll know sooner'n me if—"

"Aw, Hat, cut it! Wasn't I home in bed last night by eleven?"

"I ain't much on higher mathematics."

"Sure I was. I had to shove you over on your side of the bed; that's how hard you was sleeping."

"A girl can't gad round dancing and rough-housing every night and work eight hours on her feet, and put her lunch money on her back, and not pay up for it. I've seen too many blue-eyed dolls like you get broken. I—"

"Amen!"

Sara Juke rolled her blue eyes upward, and they were full of points of light, as though stars were shining in them; and always her lips trembled to laugh.

"There ain't nothing funny, Sara."

"Oh, Hat, with you like a owl!"

"If I was a girl and had a cough like I've seen enough in this basement get; if I was a girl and my skirtband was getting two inches too big, and I had to lie on my left side to breathe right, and my nightie was all soaked round the neck when I got up in the morning—I wouldn't just laugh and laugh. I'd cry a little—I would."

"That's right, Hat; step on the joy bug like it was a spider. Squash it!"

"I wouldn't just laugh and laugh, and put my lunch money on my back instead of eggs and milk inside of me, and run round all hours to dance-halls with every sporty Charley-boy that comes along."

"You leave him alone! You just cut that! Don't you begin on him!"

"I wouldn't get overheated, and not sleep enough; and—"

"For Pete's sake, Hat! Hire a hall!"

"I should worry! It ain't my grave you're digging."

"Aw, Hat!"

"I ain't got your dolly face and your dolly ways with the boys; but I got enough sense to live along decent."

"You're right pretty, I think, Hat."

"Oh, I could daub up, too, and gad with some of that fast gang if I didn't know it don't lead nowheres. It ain't no cinch for a girl to keep her health down here, even when she does live along decent like me, eating regular and sleeping regular, and spending quiet evenings in the room, washing out and mending and pressing and all. It ain't no cinch even then, lemme tell you. Do you think I'd have ever asked a gay bird like you to come over and room with me if I hadn't seen you to begin to fade like a piece of calico, just like my sister Lizzie did?"

"I'm taking that iron-tonic stuff like you want and spoiling my teeth, ain't I, Hat? I know you been swell to me and all."

"You ain't going to let up until somebody whispers T.B. in your shell-pink ear; and maybe them two letters will bring you to your senses."

"T.B.?"

"Yes, T.B."

"Who's he?"

"Gee! You're as smart as a fish on a hook! You oughtta bought a velvet dunce-cap with your lunch money instead of that brown poke-bonnet. T.B. was what I said— T. B."

"Honest, Hat, I dun'no'—"

"For Heaven's sake! *Too Berculosis* is the way the exhibits and the newspapers say it. L-u-n-g-s is another way to spell it. T.B."

"Too Berculosis!" Sara Juke's hand flew to her little breast. "Too Berculosis! Hat, you—you don't—"

"Sure I don't. I ain't saying it's that—only I wanna scare you up a little. I ain't saying it's that; but a girl that lets a cold hang on like you do and runs round half the night, and don't eat right, can make friends with almost anything, from measles to T.B."

Stars came out once more in Sara Juke's eyes, and her lips warmed and curved to their smile. She moistened with her forefinger a yellow spit-curl that lay like a caress on her cheek. "Gee! You oughtta be writing scare heads for the *Evening Gazette!*"

Hattie Krakow ran her hand over her smooth salt-and-pepper hair and sold a marked-down flannelette petticoat.

"I can't throw no scare into you so long as you got him on your mind. Oh, lud! There he starts now—that quickstep dance again!"

A quick red ran up into Miss Juke's hair, and she inclined forward into the attitude of listening.

"The silly! Honest, ain't he the silly? He said he was going to play that for me the first thing this morning. We dance it so swell together and all. Aw, I thought he'd forget. Ain't he the silly—remembering me?"

The red flowed persistently higher.

"Silly ain't no name for him, with his square, Charley-boy face and polished hair; and—"

"You let him alone, Hattie Krakow! What's it to you if—"

"Nothing—except I always say October is my unlucky month, because it was just a year ago that they moved him and the sheet music down to the basement. Honest, I'm going to buy me a pair of earmuffs! I'd hate to tell you how unpopular popular music is with me."

"Huh! You couldn't play on a side-comb, much less play on the piano like Charley does. If I didn't have no more brains than some people—honest, I'd go out and kill a calf for some!"

"You oughtta talk! A girl that 'ain't got no more brains than to gad round every night and every Sunday in foul-smelling, low-ceilinged dance-halls, and wear paper-soled slippers when she oughtta be wearing galoshes, and cheese-cloth waists that ain't even decent, instead of wool undershirts! You oughtta talk about brains—you and Charley Chubb!"

"Yes, I oughtta talk! If you don't like my doings, Hattie Krakow, there ain't no law says we gotta room together. I been shifting for myself ever since I was cash-girl down at Tracy's, and I ain't going to begin being bossed now. If you don't like my keeping steady with Charley Chubb—if you don't like his sheet-music playing—you gotta lump it! I'm a good girl, I am; and if you got anything to in-sinuate, if—"

"Sara Juke, ain't you ashamed!"

"I'm a good girl, I am; and there ain't nobody can cast a reflect on—on—"

Tears trembled in her voice, and she coughed from the deep recesses of her chest, and turned her head away, so that her profile was quivering and her throat swelling with sobs.

"I—I'm a good girl, I am."

"Aw, Sara, don't I know it? Ain't that just where the rub comes? Don't I know it? If you wasn't a good girl would I be caring?"

"I'm a good girl, I am!"

"It's your health, Sara, I'm kicking about. You're getting as pale and skinny as a goop; and for a month already you've been coughing, and never a single evening home to stick your feet in hot water and a mustard plaster on your chest."

"Didn't I take the iron tonic and spoil my teeth?"

"My sister Lizzie—that's the way she started, Sara; right down here in this basement. There never was a prettier little queen down here. Ask any of the old girls. Like you in looks and all; full of vim, too. That's the way she started, Sara. She wouldn't get out in the country on Sundays or get any air in her lungs walking with me evenings. She was all for dance-halls, too, Sara. She—she— 'Ain't I told you about her over and over again? 'Ain't I?"

"'Sh-h-h! Don't cry, Hat. Yes, yes; I know. She was a swell little kid; all the old girls say so. 'Sh-h-h!"

"The—the night she died I—I died, too; I—"

"'Sh-h-h, dearie!"

"I ain't crying, only—only I can't help remembering."

"Listen! That's the new hit Charley's playing—'Up to Snuff!' Say, 'ain't that got some little swing to it? Dum-dum-tum-tee-tum-m-m! Some little quickstep, ain't it? How that boy reads off by sight! Looka, will you? They got them left-over ribbed undervests we sold last season for forty-nine cents out on the grab table for seventy-four. Looka the mob fighting for 'em! Dum-dum-tum-tee-tum-m-m!"

The day's tide came in. Slowly at first, but toward noon surging through aisles and around bins, up-stairs and down-stairs—in, around, and out. Voices straining to be heard; feet shuffling in an agglomeration of discords—the indescribable roar of humanity, which is like an army that approaches but never arrives. And above it all, insistent as a bugle-note, reaching the basement's breadth, from hardware to candy, from human hair to white goods, the tinny voice of the piano—gay, rollicking.

At five o'clock the patch of daylight above the red-lighted exit door turned taupe, as though a gray curtain had been flung across it; and the girls, with shooting pains in their limbs, braced themselves for the last hour. Shoppers, their bags bulging and their shawls awry, fumbled in bins for a last remnant; hatless, sway-backed women, carrying children, fought for mill ends. Sara Juke stood first on one foot and then on the other to alternate the strain; her hands were hot and dry as flannel, but her cheeks were pink—very pink.

At six o'clock Hattie Krakow untied her black alpaca apron, pinned a hat as nondescript as a bird's nest at an unrakish angle, and slid into a warm, gray jacket.

"Ready, Sara?"

"Yes, Hat." But her voice came vaguely, as through fog.

"I'm going to fix us some stew to-night with them onions Lettie brought up to the room when she moved—mutton stew, with a broth for you, Sara."

"Yes, Hat."

Sara's eyes darted out over the emptying aisles; and, even as she pinned on her velveteen poke-bonnet at a too-swagger angle, and fluffed out a few carefully provided curls across her brow, she kept watch and with obvious subterfuge slid into her little unlined silk coat with a deliberation not her own.

"Coming, Sara?"

"Wait, can't you? My—my hat ain't on right."

"Come on; you're dolled up enough."

"My—my gloves—I—I forgot 'em. You—you can go on, Hat." And she burrowed back beneath the counter.

Miss Krakow let out a snort, as fiery with scorn as though flames were curling on her lips. "Hanging round to see whether he's coming, ain't you? To think they shot Lincoln and let him live! Before I'd run after any man living, much less the excuse of a man like him! A shiny-haired, square-faced little rat like him!"

"I ain't, neither, waiting. I guess I have a right to find my gloves. I—I guess I gotta right. He's as good as you are, and better. I—I guess I gotta right." But the raspberry red of confusion dyed her face.

"No, you ain't waiting! No, no; you ain't waiting;" mimicked Miss Krakow, and her voice was like autumn leaves that crackle underfoot. "Well, then, if you ain't waiting here he comes now. I dare you to come on home with me now, like you ought to."

"I—You go on! I gotta tell him something. I guess I'm my own boss. I have to tell him something."

Miss Krakow folded her well-worn hand-bag under one arm and fastened her black cotton gloves.

"Pf-f-f! What's the use of wasting breath?"

She slipped into the flux of the aisle, and the tide swallowed her and carried her out into the bigger tide of the street and the swifter tide of the city—a flower on the current, her blush withered under the arc-light substitution for sunlight, the petals of her youth thrown to the muddy corners of the city streets.

Sara Juke breathed inward, and under her cheaply pretentious lace blouse a heart, as rebellious as the pink in her cheeks and the stars in her eyes, beat a rapid fantasia; and, try as she would, her lips would quiver into a smile.

"Hello, Charley!"

"Hello yourself, Sweetness!" And, draping himself across the white-goods counter in an attitude as intricate as the letter S, behold Mr. Charley Chubb! Sleek, soap-scented, slim—a satire on the satyr and the haberdasher's latest dash. "Hello, Sweetness!"

"How are you, Charley?"

"Here, gimme your little hand. Shake."

She placed her palm in his, quivering.

You of the classes, peering through lorgnettes into the strange world of the masses, spare that shrug. True, when Charley Chubb's hand closed over Sara Juke's she experienced a flash of goose flesh; but, you of the classes, what of the Van Ness ball last night? Your gown was low, so that your neck rose out from it like white ivory. The conservatory, where trained clematis vines met over your heads, were like a bower of stars; music, his hand, the white glove off, over yours; the suffocating sweetness of clematis blossoms; a fountain throwing fine spray; your neck white as ivory, and—what of the Van Ness ball last night?

Only Sara Juke played her poor little game frankly, and the cards of her heart lay on the counter.

"Charley!" Her voice lay in a veil.

"Was you getting sore, Sweetness?"

"All day you didn't come over."

"Couldn't, Sweetness. Did you hear me let up on the new hit for a minute?"

"It's swell, though, Charley; all the girls was humming it. You play it like lightning, too."

"It must have been written for you, Sweetness. That's what you are, Up to Snuff, eh, Queenie?" He leaned closer, and above his tall, narrow collar dull red flowed beneath the sallow, and his long, white teeth and slick-brushed hair shone in the arc-light. "Eh, Queenie?"

"I gotta go now, Charley. Hattie's waiting home for me." She attempted to pass him and to slip into the outgoing stream of the store, but with a hesitation that belied her. "I—I gotta go, Charley."

He laughed, clapped his hat slightly askew on his polished hair, and slid his arm into hers.

"Forget it! But I had you going, didn't I, sister? Thought I'd forgot about to-night, didn't you, and didn't have the nerve to pipe up? Like fun I forgot!"

"I didn't know, Charley; you not coming over all day and all. I thought maybe your friend didn't give you the tickets like he promised."

"Didn't he? Look! See if he didn't!"

He produced a square of pink cardboard from his waistcoat pocket, and she read it, with a sudden lightness underlying her voice:

HIBERNIAN MASQUE AND HOP

SUPPER   WARDROBE FREE

ADMIT GENT AND LADY   FIFTY CENTS

"Oh, gee, Charley! And me such a sight in this old waist and all. I didn't know there was supper, too."

"Sure! Hurry, Sweetness, and we'll catch a Sixth Avenue car. We wanna get in on it while the tamales are hot."

She grasped his arm closer, and straightening her velveteen poke-bonnet so that the curls lay pat, together they wormed through the sidewalk crush; once or twice she coughed, with the hollow resonance of a chain drawn upward from a deep well.

"Gee! I bet there'll be a jam!"

"Sure! There's some live crowd down there."

They were in the street-car, swaying, swinging, clutching; hemmed in by frantic, home-going New York, nose to nose, eye to eye, tooth to tooth. Around Sara Juke's slim waist lay Charley Chubb's saving arm, and with each lurch they laughed immoderately, except when she coughed.

"Gee! ain't it the limit? It's a wonder they wouldn't open a window in this car!"

"Nix on that. Whatta you wanna do—freeze a fellow out?"

Her eyes would betray her. "Any old time I could freeze you, Charley."

"Honest?"

"You're the one that freezes me all the time. You're the one that keeps me guessing and guessing where I stand with you."

A sudden lurch and he caught her as she swayed.

"Come, Sweetness, this is our corner. Quit your coughing, there, hon; this ain't no T.B. hop we're going to."

"No what?"

"Come along; hurry! Look at the crowd already."

"This ain't no—what did you say, Charley?"

But they were pushing, shoving, worming into the great lighted entrance of the hall. More lurching, crowding, jamming.

"I'll meet you inside, kiddo, in five minutes. Pick out a red domino; red's my color."

"A red one? Gee! Looka; mine's got black pompons on it. Five minutes, Charley; five minutes!"

Flags of all nations and all sizes made a galaxy of the Sixth Avenue hall. An orchestra played beneath an arch of them. Supper, consisting of three-inch-thick sandwiches, tamales, steaming and smelling in their buckets, bottles of beer and soda-water, was spread on a long picnic-table running the entire length of the balcony.

The main floor, big as an armory, airless as a tomb, swarmed with dancers.

After supper a red sateen Pierrette, quivering, teeth flashing beneath a saucy half-mask, bowed to a sateen Pierrot,[1] whose face was as slim as a satyr's and whose smile was as upturned as the eye-slits in his mask.

"Gee! Charley, you look just like a devil in that costume—all red, and your mouth squinted like that!"

"And you look just like a little red cherry, ready to burst."

And they were off in the whirl of the dance, except that the close-packed dancers hemmed them in a swaying mob; and once she fell back against his shoulder, faint.

"Ain't there a—a up-stairs somewheres, Charley, where they got air? All this jam and no windows open! Gee! ain't it hot? Let's go outside where it's cool—let's."

"There you go again! No wonder you got a cold on you—always wanting air on you! Come, Sweetness; this ain't hot. Here, lemme show you the dip I get the girls crazy with. One, two, three—dip! One, two, three—dip! Ugh!"

"Gee! ain't it a jam, though?"

"One, two, three!"

"That's swell, Charley! Quit! You mustn't squeeze me like that till—till you've asked me to be engaged, Charley. We—we ain't engaged yet, are we, Charley?"

"Aw, what difference does that make? You girls make me sick—always wanting to know that."

"It—it makes a lot of difference, Charley."

"There you go on that Amen talk again. All right, then; I won't squeeze you no more, stingy!"

Her step was suddenly less elastic and she lagged on his arm. "I—I never said you couldn't, Charley. Gee! ain't you a great one to get mad so quick! Touchy! I only said not till we're engaged."

He skirted the crowd, guiding her skilfully. "Stingy! Stingy! I know 'em that ain't so stingy as you."

"Charley!"

"What?"

---

[1] Pierrette, Pierrot: characters in French pantomime.

"Aw, I'm ashamed to say it."

"Listen! They're playing the new one—'Up to Snuff!' Faster! Don't make me drag you, kiddo. Faster!"

They were suddenly in the center of the maze, as tight-packed as though an army had conspired to close round them. She coughed, and in her effort of repression, coughed again.

"Charley, I—honest, I—I'm going to keel. I—I can't stand it packed in here—like this."

She leaned to him, with the color drained out of her face; and the crowd of black and pink and red dominoes, gnomes gone mad, pressed, batted, surged.

"Look out, Sweetness! Don't you give out in here! They'll crush us out. 'Ain't you got no nerve? Here; don't give out now! Gee! Watch out, there! The lady's sick. Watch out! Here; now sit down a minute and get your wind."

He pressed her shoulders downward and she dropped whitely on a little camp-chair hidden underneath the balcony.

"I gotta get out, Charley; I gotta get out and get air. I feel like I'm going to suffocate in here. It's this old cough takes the breath out of me."

In the foyer she revived a bit and drank gratefully of the water he brought; but the color remained out of her cheeks and the cough would rack her.

"I guess I oughtta go home, Charley."

"Aw, cut it! You ain't the only girl I've seen give out. Sit here and rest a minute and you'll be all right. Great Scott! I came here to dance."

She rose to her feet a bit unsteadily, but smiling. "Fussy! Who said I didn't?"

"That's more like it."

And they were off again to the lilt of the music, but, struggle as she would, the coughing and the dizziness and the heat took hold of her, and at the close of the dance she fainted quietly against his shoulder.

When she finally caught at consciousness, as it passed and repassed her befuddled mind, she was on the floor of the cloak-room, her head pillowed on the skirt of a pink domino.

"There, there, dearie; your young man's waiting outside to take you home."

"I—I'm all right!"

"Certainly you are. The heat done it. Here; lemme help you out of your domino."

"It was the heat done it."

"There; you're all right now. I gotta get back to my dance. You fainted right up against him, dearie; and I seen you keel."

"Gee! ain't I the limit!"

"Here; lemme help on with your coat. Right there he is, waiting."

In the foyer Sara Juke met Charley Chubb shamefacedly. "I spoilt everything, didn't I?"

"I guess you couldn't help it. All right?"

"Yes, Charley." She met the air gratefully, worming her little hand into the curve of his elbow. "Gee! I feel fine now."

"Come; here's a car."

"Let's walk up Sixth Avenue, Charley; the air feels fine."

"All right."

"You ain't sore, are you, Charley? It was so jammed dancing, anyway."

"I ain't sore."

"It was the heat done it."

"Yeh."

"Honest, it's grand to be outdoors, ain't it? The stars and—and chilliness and—and—all!"

"Listen to the garden stuff!"

"Silly!" She squeezed his arm, and drew back, shamefaced.

His spirits rose. "You're a right loving little thing when you wanna be."

They laughed in duet; and before the plate-glass window of a furniture emporium they paused to regard a monthly-payment display, designed to represent the $49.50 completely furnished sitting-room, parlor, and dining-room of the home felicitous—a golden-oak room, with an incandescent fire glowing right merrily in the grate; a lamp redly diffusing the light of home; a plaster-of-Paris Cupid shooting a dart from the mantelpiece; and last, two figures of connubial bliss, smiling and waxen, in rocking-chairs, their waxen infant, block-building on the floor, completing the picture.

"Gee! It looks as snug as a bug in a rug! Looka what it says too: 'You Get the Girl; We'll Do the Rest!' Some little advertisement, ain't it? I got the girl all right—'ain't I, hon?"

"Aw!"

"Look at the papa—slippers and all! And the kid! Look at the kid, Sweetness."

Her confusion nearly choked her and her rapid breath clouded the window-glass. "Yeh, Charley! Looka the little kid! Ain't he cute?"

An Elevated train crashed over their heads, drowning out her words; but her smile, which flickered like light over her face, persisted and her arm crept back into his. At each shop window they lingered, but the glow of the first one remained with her.

"Look, Sweetness—'Red Swag, the Train King! Performance going on now.' Wanna go in?"

"Not to-night. Let's stay outside."

"Anything your little heart de-sires."

They bought hot chestnuts, city harbingers of autumn, from a vender, and let fall the hulls as they walked. They drank strawberry ice-cream soda, pink with foam. Her resuscitation was complete; his spirits did not wane.

"I gotta like a queen pretty much not to get sore at a busted evening like this. It's a good thing the ticket didn't cost me nothing."

"Ain't it, though?"

"Look! What's in there—a exhibit?"

They paused before a white-lighted store-front, and read, laboriously:

FREE TUBERCULOIS EXHIBIT
TO EDUCATE THE PEOPLE HOW TO PREVENT CONSUMPTION

"Oh!" She dragged at his arm.

"Aw, come on, Sweetness; nothing but a lot of T.B.'s."

"Let's—let's go in. See, it's free. Looka! It's all lit up and all; see, pictures and all."

"Say, ain't I enough of a dead one without dragging me in there? Free! I bet they pinch you for something before you get out."

"Come on, Charley. I never did see a place like this."

"Aw, they're all over town."

He followed her in surlily enough and then, with a morbid interest, round a room hung with photographs of victims in various emaciated stages of the white plague.

"Oh! Oh! Ain't it awful? Ain't it awful? Read them symptoms. Almost with nothing it—it begins. Night-sweats and losing weight and coughing, and oh—"

"Look! Little kids and all! Thin as matches."

"Aw, see, a poor little shaver like that! Look! It says sleeping in that dirty room without a window gave it to him. Ugh! that old man! 'Self-indulgence and intemperance.' Looka that girl in the tobacco-factory. Oh! Oh! Ain't it awful! Dirty shops and stores, it says; dirty saloons and dance-halls—weak lungs can't stand them."

"Let's get out of here."

"Aw, look! How pretty she is in this first picture; and look at her here—nothing but a stack of bones on a stretcher. Aw! Aw!"

"Come on!"

"Courage is very important, it says. Consumptives can be helped and many are cured. Courage is—"

"Come on; let's get out of this dump. Say, it's a swell night for a funeral."

She grasped at his coat sleeve, pinching the flesh with it, and he drew away half angrily.

"Come on, I said."

"All right!"

A thin line filed past them, grim-faced, silent. At the far end of the room, statistics in red inch-high type ran columnwise down the wall's length. She read, with a gasp in her throat:

1. Ten thousand people died from tuberculosis in the city
   of New York last year.
2. Two hundred thousand people died from tuberculosis
   in the United States last year.
3. Records of the Health Department show 31,631 living
   cases of tuberculosis in the city of New York.
4. Every three minutes some one in the United States
   dies from consumption.

"Oh, Charley, ain't it awful!"

At a desk a young man, with skin as pink as though a strong wind had whipped it into color, distributed pamphlets to the outgoing visitors—a thin streamlet of them; some cautious, some curious, some afraid.

"Come on; let's hurry out of here, Sweetness. My lung's hurting this minute."

They hurried past the desk; but the young man with the clear, pink skin reached over the heads of an intervening group, waving a long printed booklet toward the pair.

"Circular, missy?"

Sara Juke straightened, with every nerve in her body twanging like a plucked violin-string, and her eyes met the clear eyes of the young clerk.

Like a doll automaton she accepted the booklet from him; like a doll automaton she followed Charley Chubb out into the street, and her limbs were trembling so she could scarcely stand.

"Gotta hand it to you, Sweetness. Even made a hit on the fellow in the lung-shop! He didn't hand me no literachure. Some little hit!"

"I gotta go home now, Charley."

"It's only ten."

"I better go, Charley. It ain't Saturday night."

At the stoop of her rooming-house they lingered. A honey-colored moon hung like a lantern over the block-long row of shabby-fronted houses. On her steps and to her fermenting fancy the shadow of an ash-can sprawled like a prostrate human being.

"Charley!" She clutched his arm.

"Whatcha scared about, Sweetness?"

"Oh, Charley, I—I feel creepy to-night."

"That visit to the morgue was enough to give anybody the blind staggers."

Her pamphlet was tight in her hand. "You ain't mad at me, Charley?"

He stroked her arm, and the taste of tears found its way to her mouth.

"I'm feeling so silly-like to-night, Charley."

"You're all in, kiddo." In the shadow he kissed her.

"Charley, you—you mustn't, unless we're—engaged." But she could not find the strength to unfold herself from his arms. "You mustn't, Charley!"

"Great little girl you are, Sweetness—one great little girl!"

"Aw, Charley!"

"And, to show you that I like you, I'm going to make up for this tomorrow night. A real little Saturday-night blow! And don't forget Sunday afternoon—two o'clock for us, down at Crissey's Hall. Two o'clock."

"Two o'clock."

"Good!"

"Oh, Charley, I—"

"What, Sweetness?"

"Oh, nothing; I—I'm just silly to-night."

Her hand lay on his arm, white in the moonlight and light as a leaf; and he kissed her again, scorching her lips.

"Good night, Sweetness."

"Good night, Charley."

Then up three flights of stairs through musty halls and past closed doors, their white china knobs showing through the darkness, and then up to the fourth-floor rear, and then on tiptoe into a long, narrow room, with the moonlight flowing in.

Clothing lay about in grotesque heaps—a woman's blouse was flung across the back of a chair and hung limply; a pair of shoes stood beside the bed in the attitude of walking—tired-looking shoes, run down at the heels and skinned at the toes. And on the far side of the three-quarter bed the hump of an outstretched figure, face turned from the light, with sparse gray-and-black hair flowing over the pillow.

Carefully, to save the slightest squeak, Sara Juke undressed, folded her little mound of clothing across the room's second chair, groping carefully by the stream of moonlight. Severe as a sibyl in her straight-falling nightdress, her hair spreading over her shoulders, her bare feet pattered on the cool matting. Then she slid into bed lightly, scarcely raising the covers. From the mantelpiece the alarm-clock ticked with emphasis.

An hour she lay there. Once she coughed, and smothered it in her pillow. Two hours. She slipped from under the covers and over to the littered dresser. The pamphlet lay on top of her gloves; she carried it to the window and, with her limbs trembling and sending ripples down her nightrobe, read it. Then again, standing there by the window in the moonlight, she quivered so that her knees bent under her.

After a while she raised the window slowly and without a creak, and a current of cool air rushed in and over her before she could reach the bedside.

On her pillow Hattie Krakow stirred reluctantly, her weary senses battling with the pleasant lethargy of sleep; but a sudden nip in the air stung her nose and found out the warm crevices of the bed. She stirred and half opened her eyes.

"For Gawd's sake, Sara, are you crazy? Put that window down! Tryin' to freeze us out? Opening a window with her cough and all that! Put it down! Put—it—down!"

Sara Juke rose and slammed it shut, slipping back into the cold bed with teeth that clicked. After a while she slept; but lightly, with her mouth open and her face upturned. And after a while she woke to full consciousness all at once, and with a cough on her lips. Her gown at the yoke was wet; and her neck, where she felt it, was damp with cold perspiration.

"Oh—oh—Hattie! Oh—oh!"

She burrowed under her pillow to ease the trembling that seized her. The moon had passed on, and darkness, which is allied to fear, closed her in—the fear of unthinking youth who knows not that the grave is full of peace; the fear of abundant life for senile death; the cold agony that comes in the nightwatches, when the business of the day is but a dream and Reality visits the couch.

Deeper burrowed Sara Juke, trembling with chill and night-sweat.

Drowsily Hattie Krakow turned on her pillow, but her senses were too weary to follow her mind's dictate.

"Sara! 'Smatter, Sara? 'Smat-ter?" Hattie's tired hand crept toward her friend; but her volition would not carry it across and it fell inert across the coverlet. "'Smatter, dearie?"

"N-nothing."

"'Smat-ter, dear-ie?"

"N-nothing."

In the watches of the night a towel flung across the bedpost becomes a gorilla crouching to spring; a tree-branch tapping at the window an armless hand, beckoning. In the watches of the night fear is a panther across the chest, sucking the breath; but his eyes cannot bear the light of day, and by dawn he has shrunk to cat size. The ghastly dreams of Orestes[2] perished with the light; phosphorus is yellowish and waxlike by day.

So Sara Juke found new courage with the day, and in the subbasement of the Titanic Store, the morning following, her laughter was ready enough. But when the midday hour arrived she slipped into her jacket, past the importunities of Hattie Krakow, and out into the sun-lashed noonday swarm of Sixth Avenue.

Down one block—two, three; then a sudden pause before a narrow storefront liberally placarded with invitatory signs to the public, and with a red cross blazoning above the doorway. And Sara Juke, whose heart was full of fear, faltered, entered.

The same thin file passed round the room, halting, sauntering, like grim visitors in a grim gallery. At a front desk a sleek young intern, tiptilted in a swivel chair, read a

---

[2] In Greek mythology, Orestes was mercilessly pursued by the Furies, after murdering his mother and her lover. The Furies ceased when he went to trial.

pink sheet through horn-rimmed glasses.

Toward the rear the young man whose skin was the wind-lashed pink sorted pamphlets and circulars in tall, even piles on his desk.

Round and round the gallery walked Sara Juke; twice she read over the list of symptoms printed in inch-high type; her heart lay within her as though icy dead, and her eyes would blur over with tears. Once, when she passed the rear desk, the young man paused in his stacking and regarded her with a warming glance of recognition.

"Hello!" he said. "You back?"

"Yes." Her voice was the thin cry of quail.

"You must like our little picture-gallery, eh?"

"Oh! Oh!" She caught at the edge of the desk, and tears lay heavy in her eyes.

"Eh?"

"Yes; I—I like it. I wanna buy it for my yacht." Her ghastly simulacrum of a jest died in her throat; and he said, quickly, a big blush suffusing his face:

"I was only fooling, missy. You 'ain't got the scare, have you?"

"The scare?"

"Yes; the bug? You ain't afraid you've ate the germ, are you?"

"I—I dun'no'."

"Pshaw! There's a lot of 'em comes in here more scared than hurt, missy. Never throw a scare till you've had an examination. For all you know, you got hay fever, eh! Hay fever!" And he laughed as though to salve his words.

"I—I got all them things on the red-printed list, I tell you. I—I got 'em all, night-sweats and all. I—I got 'em."

"Sure you got 'em, missy; but that don't need to mean nothing much."

"I got 'em, I tell you."

"Losing weight?"

"Feel."

He inserted two fingers in her waistband. "Huh!"

"You a doctor?"

He performed a great flourish. "I ain't in the profesh, missy. I'm only chief clerk and bottle-washer round here; but—"

"Where is the doctor? That him reading down there? Can I ask him? I— Oh! Ain't I scared!"

He placed his big, cool hand over her wrist and his face had none of its smile. "I know you are, little missy. I seen it in you last night when you and—and—"

"My—my friend."

"—your friend was in here. There's thousands come in here with the scare on, and most of 'em with a reason; but I picked you out last night from the gang. Funny thing, but right away I picked you. 'A pretty little thing like her'—if you'll excuse me for saying it—'a pretty little thing like her,' I says to myself. 'And I bet she 'ain't got nobody to steer her!'"

"Honest, did you?"

"Gee! it ain't none of my put-in; but when I seen you last night—funny thing—but when I seen you, why, you just kinda hit me in the eye; and with all that gang round me, I says to myself: 'Gee! A pretty little thing like her, scared as a gazelle, and so pretty and all; and no one to give her the right steer!'"

"Aw, you seen me?"

"Sure! Wasn't it me reached out the pamphlet to you? You had on that there same cutey little hat and jacket and all."

"Does it cost anything to talk to the doctor down there?"

"Forget it! Go right down and he'll give you a card to the Victoria Clinic. I know them all over there and they'll look you over right, little missy, and steer you. Aw, don't be scared; there ain't nothing much wrong with you—maybe a sore spot, that's all. That cough ain't a double-lunger. You run over to the clinic."

"I gotta go back to the store now."

"After store, then?"

"Free?"

"Sure! Old Doc Strauss is on after five, too. If I ain't too nervy I'm off after six myself. I could meet you after and we could talk over what he tells you—if I ain't too nervy?"

"I—"

"Blaney's my name—Eddie Blaney. Ask anybody round here about me. I—I could meet you, little missy, and—"

"I can't to-night, Mr. Blaney. I gotta go somewheres."

"Aw!"

"I gotta."

"To-morrow? To-morrow's Sunday, little missy. There's a swell lot of country I bet you 'ain't never seen, and Old Doc Strauss is going to tell you to get acquainted with it pretty soon."

"Country?"

"Yes. That's what you need—outdoors; that's what you need. You got a color like all indoors—pretty, but putty."

"You—you don't think there's nothing much the matter with me, do you, Mr. Blaney?"

"Sure I don't. Why, I got a bunch of Don'ts for you up my sleeve that'll color you up like drug-store daub."

Tears and laughter trembled in her voice. "You mean that the outdoor stuff will do it, Mr. Blaney?"

"That's the talk!"

"But you—you ain't the doctor."

"I ain't, but I 'ain't been deaf and dumb and blind round here for three years. I can pick 'em every time. You're taking your stitch in time. You 'ain't even got a wheeze in you. Why, I bet you 'ain't never seen red!"

"No!" she cried, with quick comprehension.

"Sure you 'ain't!"

More tears and laughter in her voice. "I'm going to-night, then—at six, Mr. Blaney."

"Good! And to-morrow? There's a lot of swell country and breathing-space round here I'd like to introduce you to. I bet you don't know whether Ingleside Woods is kindling or a breakfast food. Now do you?"

"No."

"Ever had a chigger on you?"

"Huh?"

"Ever sleep outdoors in a bag?"

"Say, whatta you think I am?"

"Ever seen the sun rise, or took the time to look up and see several dozen or a couple of thousand or so stars glittering all at once?"

"Aw, come off! We ain't doing team-work in vaudeville."

"Gee! Wouldn't I like to take you out and be the first one to make you acquainted with a few of the things that are happening beyond Sixth Avenue—if I ain't too nervy, little missy?"

"I gotta go somewhere at two o'clock to-morrow afternoon, Mr.—Mr. Blaney; but I can go in the morning—if it ain't going to look like I'm a freshie."

"In the morning! Swell! But where—who—" She scribbled on a slip of paper and fluttered it into his hand. "Sara Juke! Some little name. Gee! I know right where you live. I know a lot of cases that come from round there. I used to live near there myself, round on Third Avenue. I'll call round at nine, little missy. I'm going to introduce you to the country, eh?"

"They won't hurt at the clinic, will they, Mr. Blaney? I'm losing my nerve again."

"Shame on a pretty little thing like you losing her nerve! Gee! I've seen 'em come in here all pale round the gills and with nothing but the whooping-cough. There was a little girl in here last week who thought she was ready for Arizona on a canvas bed; and it wasn't nothing but her rubber skirtband had stretched. Shame on you, little missy! Don't you get scared! Wait till you see what I'm going to show you in the country to-morrow—leaves turning red and all. We're going to have a heart-to-heart talk out there—eh? A regular lung-to-lung talk!"

"Aw, Mr. Blaney! Ain't you killing!" She hurried down the room, laughing.

At Sharkey's on Saturday night the entire basement café and dance-hall assumed a hebdomadal[3] air of expectancy; extra marble-topped tables were crowded about the polished square of dancing-space; the odor of hops and sawdust and cookery hung in visible mists over the bar.

Girls, with white faces and red lips and bare throats, sat alone at tables or tête-à-tête with men too old or too young, and ate; but drank with keener appetite.

A self-playing piano performed beneath a large painting of an undraped Psyche;[4] a youth with yellow fingers sang of Love. A woman whose shame was gone acquired a sudden hysteria at her lone table over her milky-green drink, and a waiter hustled her out none too gently.

In the foyer at seven o'clock Sara Juke met Charley Chubb, and he slid up quite frankly behind her and kissed her on the lips. At Sharkey's a miss is as good as her kiss!

"You—you quit! You mustn't!"

She sprang back, quivering, her face cold-looking and blue; and he regarded her with his mouth quirking.

"Huh! Hoity-toity, ain't you? Hoity-toity and white-faced and late, all at once, ain't you? Say, them airs don't get across with me. Come on! I'm hungry."

"I didn't mean to yell, Charley—only you scared me. I thought maybe it was one of them fresh guys that hang round here; all of 'em look so dopey and all. I—You know I never was strong for this place, Charley."

"Beginning to nag, are you?"

"No, no, Charley. No, no!"

---

[3] Weekly.　　　　　　　　　　　　　　[4] Greek goddess, originally a mortal.

They drew up at a small table.

"No fancy keeling act to-night, kiddo. I ain't taking out a hospital ward, you know. Gad! I like you, though, when you're white-looking like this! Why'd you dodge me at noon to-day and to-night after closing? New guy? I won't stand for it, you know, you little white-faced Sweetness, you!"

"I hadda go somewheres, Charley. I came near not coming to-night, neither, Charley."

"What'll you eat?"

"I ain't hungry."

"Thirsty, eh?"

"No."

He regarded her over the rim of the smirchy bill of fare. "What are you, then, you little white-faced, big-eyed devil?"

"Charley, I—I got something to—to tell you. I—"

"Bring me a lamb stew and a beer, light. What'll you have, little white-face?"

"Some milk and—"

"She means with suds on, waiter."

"No—no; milk, I said—milk over toast. Milk toast—I gotta eat it. Why don't you lemme talk, Charley? I gotta tell you."

He was suddenly sober. "What's hurting you? One milk toast, waiter. Tell them in the kitchen the lady's teeth hurt her. What's up, Sweetness?" And he leaned across the table to imprint a fresh kiss on her lips.

"Don't—don't—don't! For Gawd's sake, don't!" She covered her face with her hands; and such a trembling seized her that they fell pitifully away again and showed her features, each distorted. "You mustn't, Charley! Mustn't do that again, not—not for three months—you—you mustn't."

He leaned across the table; his voice was like sleet—cold, thin, cutting: "What's the matter—going to quit?"

"No—no—no!"

"Got another guy you like better?"

"Oh! Oh!"

"A queenie can't quit me first and get away with it, kiddo. I may be a soft-fingered sort of fellow, but a queenie can't quit me first and get away with it. Ask 'em about me round here; they know me. If anybody in this little duet is going to do the quitting act first it ain't going to be you. What's the matter? Out with it!"

"Charley, it ain't that—I swear it ain't that!"

"What's hurting you, then?"

"I gotta tell you. We gotta go easy for a little while. We gotta quit doing the rounds for a while till—only for a little while. Three months he said would fix me. A grand old doc he was!

"I been to the clinic, Charley. I hadda go. The cough—the cough was cutting me in two. It ain't like me to go keeling like I did. I never said much about it; but, nights and all, the sweats and the cough and the shooting pains were cutting me in two. We gotta go easy for a while, Charley; just—"

"You sick, Sara?" His fatty-white face lost a shade of its animation. "Sick?"

"But it ain't, Charley. On his word he promised it ain't! A grand old doc, with whiskers—he promised me that. I—I am just beginning; but the stitch was in time. It ain't a real case yet, Charley. I swear on my mother's curl of hair it ain't."

"Ain't what? Ain't what?"

"It ain't! Air, he said, right living—early hours and all. I gotta get out of the basement. He'll get me a job. A grand old man! Windows open; right living. No—no dancing and all, for a while, Charley. Three months only, Charley; and then—"

"What, I say—"

"It ain't, Charley! I swear it ain't. Just one—the left one—a little sore down at the base—the bottom. Charley, quit looking at me like that! It ain't a real case—it ain't; it ain't!"

"It ain't what?"

"The—the T.B. Just the left one; down at—"

"You—you—" An oath as hot as a live coal dropped from his lips, and he drew back, strangling. "You—you got it, and you're letting me down easy. You got it, and it's catching as hell! You got it, you white devil, and—and you're trying to lie out of it—you—you—"

"Charley! Charley!"

"You got it, and you been letting me eat it off your lips! You devil, you! You devil, you! You devil, you!"

"Charley, I—"

"I could kill you! Lemme wash my mouth! You got it; and if you got it I got it! I got it! I got it! I—I—"

He rushed from the table, strangling, stuttering, staggering; and his face was twisted with fear.

For an hour she sat there, waiting, her hands folded in her lap and her eyes growing larger in her face. The dish of stew took on a thin coating of grease and the beer died in the glass. The waiter snickered. After a while she paid for the meal out of her newly opened wage-envelope and walked out to the air.

Once on the street, she moaned audibly into her handkerchief. There is relief in articulation. Her way lay through dark streets where figures love to slink in the shadows. One threw a taunt at her and she ran. At the stoop of her rooming-house she faltered, half fainting and breathing deep from exhaustion, her head thrown back and her eyes gazing upward.

Over the narrow street stars glittered, dozens and myriads of them.

Literature has little enough to say of the heartaches and the heartburns of the Sara Jukes and the Hattie Krakows and the Eddie Blaneys. Medical science concedes them a hollow organ for keeping up the circulation. Yet Mrs. Van Ness's heartbreak over the death of her Chinese terrier, Wang, claims a first-page column in the morning edition; her heartburn—a complication of midnight terrapin and the strain of her most recent rôle of correspondent—obtains her a *suite de luxe* in a private sanitarium.

Vivisectionists believe the dog is less sensitive to pain than man; so, the social vivisectionists, in problem plays and best sellers, are more concerned with the heartaches and heartburns of the classes. But analysis would show that the sediment of salt in Sara Juke's and Mrs. Van Ness's tears is equal.

Indeed, when Sara Juke stepped out of the streetcar on a golden Sunday morning in October, her heart beat higher and more full of emotion than Mrs. Van Ness could find at that breakfast hour, reclining on her fine linen pillows, an electric massage and a four-dollars-an-hour masseuse forcing her sluggish blood to flow.

Eddie Blaney gently helped Sara to alight, cupping the point of her elbow in his hand; and they stood huddled for a moment by the roadway while the car whizzed past, leaving them in the yellow and ocher, saffron and crimson, countryside.

"Gee! Gee whiz!"

"See! I told you. And you not wanting to come when I called for you this morning—you trying to dodge me and the swellest Indian-summer Sunday on the calendar!"

"Looka!"

"Wait! We 'ain't started yet, if you think this is swell."

"Oh! Let's go over in them woods. Let's." Her lips were apart and pink crept into her cheeks, effacing the dark rims of pain beneath her eyes. "Let's hurry."

"Sure; that's where we're going—right over in there, where the woods look like they're on fire; but, gee! this ain't nothing to the country places I know round here. This ain't nothing. Wait!"

The ardor of the inspired guide was his and with each exclamation from her the joy of his task doubled itself.

"If you think this is great, wait—just you wait. Gee! if you like this, what would you have said to the farm? Wait till we get to the top of the hill."

Fallen leaves, crisp as paper, crackled pleasantly under their feet; and through the haze that is October's veil glowed a reddish sun, vague as an opal. A footpath crawled like a serpent through the woods and they followed it, kicking up the leaves before them, pausing, darting, exclaiming.

"I—Honest, Mr. Blaney, I—"

"Eddie!"

"Eddie, I—I never did feel so—I never was so—so—Aw, I can't say it." Tears sprang to her eyes.

"Sure you never was. I never was, neither, before—before—"

"Before what?"

"Before I had to."

"Had to?"

"Yeh; both of them. Bleeding all the time. Didn't see nothing but red for 'leven months."

"You!"

"Yeh; three years ago. Looked like Arizona on a stretcher for me."

"You—so big and strong and all!"

He smiled at her and his teeth flashed. "Gad! little girl, if you got a right to be scared, whatta you think I had? I seen your card over at the clinic last night, and you 'ain't got no right to have that down-and-out look on you had this morning. If you think you got something to be scared at you looka my old card at the clinic some day; they keep it for show. You oughtta seen the day I quit the shipping-room, right over at the Titanic, too, and then see whether you got something to be scared at."

"You—you used to work there?"

"Six years."

"I—I ain't scared no more, Eddie; honest, I ain't!"

"Gee! I should say not! They ain't even sending you up to the farm."

"No, no! They're going to get me a job. A regular outdoor, on-the-level kind of a job. A grand old doc, with whiskers! I ain't a regular one, Eddie; just the bottom of one lung don't make a regular one."

"Well, I guess not, poor little missy. Well, I guess not."

"Three months, he said, Eddie. Three months of right living like this, and air and all, and I'll be as round as a peach, he said. Said it hisself, without me asking—that's how scared I was. Round as a peach!"

"You can't beat that gang over there at the clinic, little missy. They took me out of the department when all the spring-water I knew about ran out of a keg. Even when they got me out on the farm—a grown-up guy like me—for a week I thought the crow in the rooster was a sidewalk faker. You can't beat that, little missy."

"He's a grand old man, with whiskers, that's going to get me the job. Then in three months I—"

"Three months nothing! That gang won't let you slip back after the three months. They took a extra shine to me because I did the prize-pupil stunt; but they won't let anybody slip back if they give 'em half a chance. When they got me sound again, did they ship me back to the shipping department in the subbasement? Not muchy! Looka me now, little missy! Clerk in their biggest display; in three months a raise to ninety dollars. Can you beat it? Ninety dollars would send all the shipping-clerks of the world off in a faint."

"Gee! it—it's swell!"

"And—"

"Look! Look!"

"Persimmons!" A golden mound of them lay at the base of a tree, piled up against the bole, bursting, brown. "Persimmons! Here; taste one. They're fine."

"Eat 'em?"

"Sure!"

She bit into one gently; then with appetite. "M-m-m! Good!"

"Want another?"

"M-m-m—my mouth! Ouch! My m-mouth!"

"Gee! you cute little thing, you! See, my mouth's the same way, too. Feels like a knot. Gee! you cute little thing, you—all puckered up and all."

And linking her arm in his they crunch-crunched over the brittle leaves and up a hillside to a plateau of rock overlooking the flaming country; and from the valley below smoke from burning mounds of leaves wound in spirals, its pungency drifting to them.

"See that tree there? It's an oak. Look; from a little acorn like this it grew. See, this is a acorn, and in the start that tree wasn't no bigger than this little thing."

"Quit your kidding!" But she smiled and her lips were parted sweetly; and always unformed tears would gloze her eyes.

"Here, sit here, little lady. Wait till I spread this newspaper out. Gee! Don't I wish you didn't have to go back to the city by two o'clock, little lady! We could make a great day of it here, out in the country; lunch at a farm and see the sun set and all. Some day of it we could make if—"

"I—I don't have to go back, Eddie."

His face expanded into his widest smile. "Gee! that's great! That's just great!"

Silence.

"What you thinking of, little lady, sitting there so pretty and all?"

"N-nothing."

"Nothing? Aw, surely something!"

A tear formed and zigzagged down her cheek. "Nothing, honest; only I—I feel right happy."

"That's just how you oughtta feel, little lady."

"In three months, if—Aw, ain't I the nut?"

"It'll be a big Christmas, won't it, little missy, for both of us? A big Christmas for both of us; you as sound and round as a peach again, and me shooting up like a sky-rocket on the pay-roll."

A laugh bubbled to her lips before the tear was dry. "In three months I won't be a T.B., not even a little bit."

"Sh-h-h! On the farm we wasn't allowed to even say that. We wasn't supposed to even know what them letters mean."

"Don't you know what they mean, Eddie?"

"Sure I do!" He leaned toward her and placed his hand lightly over hers. "T.B.— True Blue—that's what they mean, little lady."

She could feel the veins in his palm throbbing.

—1915

KATHERINE ANNE PORTER (1890–1980)

Katherine Anne Porter was the pen name of Callie Russell Porter, born in Indian Creek, Texas, in 1890. When Porter was two years old, her mother died, leaving her to the care of her neglectful father and his parents. She admired her grandmother, and took her name when she began publishing her stories. Success did not come easily for Porter: she received only a sketchy formal education; she eloped with the first of her four husbands when she was sixteen; she nearly died from tuberculosis (1915-17) and influenza (1918); and she spent the 1920s supporting herself doing "hack" (non-literary) writing in Mexico and in New York. Porter's first book, a collection of stories entitled *Flowering Judas* (1930), brought her to the attention of the literary world for the first time. But not until *Pale Horse, Pale Rider* (1939) and *The Leaning Tower and Other Stories* (1944) did she achieve real fame as a writer, and she was not financially secure until her only novel, *Ship of Fools* (1962), became a bestseller and, later, a feature film. After *Ship of Fools* Porter did very little writing, although her *Collected Stories* (1965) won the Pulitzer Prize and the National Book Award in 1966. She received the Gold Medal Award for Fiction from the American Academy of Arts and Letters in 1967.

The Downward Path to Wisdom

In the square bedroom with the big window Mama and Papa were lolling back on their pillows handing each other things from the wide black tray on the small table with crossed legs. They were smiling and they smiled even more when the little boy, with the feeling of sleep still in his skin and hair, came in and walked up to the bed. Leaning against it, his bare toes wriggling in the white fur rug, he went on eating peanuts which he took from his pajama pocket. He was four years old.

"Here's my baby," said Mama. "Lift him up, will you?"

He went limp as a rag for Papa to take him under the arms and swing him up over a broad, tough chest. He sank between his parents like a bear cub in a warm litter, and lay there comfortably. He took another peanut between his teeth, cracked the shell, picked out the nut whole and ate it.

"Running around without his slippers again," said Mama. "His feet are like icicles."

"He crunches like a horse," said Papa. "Eating peanuts before breakfast will ruin his stomach. Where did he get them?"

"You brought them yesterday," said Mama, with exact memory, "in a grisly little cellophane sack. I have asked you dozens of times not to bring him things to eat. Put him out, will you? He's spilling shells all over me."

Almost at once the little boy found himself on the floor again. He moved around to Mama's side of the bed and leaned confidingly near her and began another peanut. As he chewed he gazed solemnly in her eyes.

"Bright-looking specimen, isn't he?" asked Papa, stretching his long legs and reaching for his bathrobe. "I suppose you'll say it's my fault he's dumb as an ox."

"He's my little baby, my only baby," said Mama richly, hugging him, "and he's a dear lamb." His neck and shoulders were quite boneless in her firm embrace. He stopped chewing long enough to receive a kiss on his crumby chin. "He's sweet as clover," said Mama. The baby went on chewing.

"Look at him staring like an owl," said Papa.

Mama said, "He's an angel and I'll never get used to having him."

"We'd be better off if we never *had* had him," said Papa. He was walking about the room and his back was turned when he said that. There was silence for a moment. The little boy stopped eating, and stared deeply at his Mama. She was looking at the back of Papa's head, and her eyes were almost black. "You're going to say that just once too often," she told him in a low voice. "I hate you when you say that."

Papa said, "You spoil him to death. You never correct him for anything. And you don't take care of him. You let him run around eating peanuts before breakfast."

"You gave him the peanuts, remember that," said Mama. She sat up and hugged her only baby once more. He nuzzled softly in the pit of her arm. "Run along, my darling," she told him in her gentlest voice, smiling at him straight in the eyes. "Run along," she said, her arms falling away from him. "Get your breakfast."

The little boy had to pass his father on the way to the door. He shrank into himself when he saw the big hand raised above him. "Yes, get out of here and stay out," said Papa, giving him a little shove toward the door. It was not a hard shove, but it hurt the little boy. He slunk out, and trotted down the hall trying not to look back. He was afraid something was coming after him, he could not imagine what. Something hurt him all over, he did not know why.

He did not want his breakfast; he would not have it. He sat and stirred it round in the yellow bowl, letting it stream off the spoon and spill on the table, on his front, on the chair. He liked seeing it spill. It was hateful stuff, but it looked funny running in white rivulets down his pajamas.

"Now look what you're doing, dirty boy," said Marjory. "You dirty little old boy."

The little boy opened his mouth to speak for the first time.

"You're dirty yourself," he told her.

"That's right," said Marjory, leaning over him and speaking so her voice would not carry. "That's right, just like your papa. Mean," she whispered, "mean."

The little boy took up his yellow bowl full of cream and oatmeal and sugar with both hands and brought it down with a crash on the table. It burst and some of the wreck lay in chunks and some of it ran all over everything. He felt better.

"You see?" said Marjory, dragging him out of the chair and scrubbing him with a napkin. She scrubbed him as roughly as she dared until he cried out. "That's just what I said. That's exactly it." Through his tears he saw her face terribly near, red and frowning under a stiff white band, looking like the face of somebody who came at night and stood over him and scolded him when he could not move or get away. "Just like your papa, *mean*."

The little boy went out into the garden and sat on a green bench dangling his legs. He was clean. His hair was wet and his blue woolly pull-over made his nose itch. His face felt stiff from the soap. He saw Marjory going past a window with the black tray. The curtains were still closed at the window he knew opened into Mama's room. Papa's room. Mommanpoppasroom, the word was pleasant, it made a mumbling snapping noise between his lips; it ran in his mind while his eyes wandered about looking for something to do, something to play with.

Mommanpoppas' voices kept attracting his attention. Mama was being cross with Papa again. He could tell by the sound. That was what Marjory always said when their voices rose and fell and shot up to a point and crashed and rolled like the two tomcats who fought at night. Papa was being cross, too, much crosser than Mama this time. He grew cold and disturbed and sat very still, wanting to go to the bathroom, but it was just next to Mommanpoppasroom; he didn't dare think of it. As the voices grew louder he could hardly hear them any more, he wanted so badly to go to the bathroom. The kitchen door opened suddenly and Marjory ran out, making the motion with her hand that meant he was to come to her. He didn't move. She came to him, her face still red and frowning, but she was not angry; she was scared just as he was. She said, "Come on, honey, we've got to go to your gran'ma's again." She took his hand and pulled him. "Come on quick, your gran'ma is waiting for you." He slid off the bench. His mother's voice rose in a terrible scream, screaming something he could not understand, but she was furious; he had seen her clenching her fists and stamping in one spot, screaming with her eyes shut; he knew how she looked. She was screaming in a tantrum, just as he remembered having heard himself. He stood still, doubled over, and all his body seemed to dissolve, sickly, from the pit of his stomach.

"Oh, my God," said Marjory. "Oh, my God. Now look at you. Oh, my God. I can't stop to clean you up."

He did not know how he got to his grandma's house, but he was there at last, wet and soiled, being handled with disgust in the big bathtub. His grandma was there in long black skirts saying, "Maybe he's sick; maybe we should send for the doctor."

"I don't think so, m'am," said Marjory. "He hasn't et anything; he's just scared."

The little boy couldn't raise his eyes, he was so heavy with shame. "Take this note to his mother," said Grandma.

She sat in a wide chair and ran her hands over his head, combing his hair with her fingers; she lifted his chin and kissed him. "Poor little fellow," she said. "Never you mind. You always have a good time at your grandma's, don't you? You're going to have a nice little visit, just like the last time."

The little boy leaned against the stiff, dry-smelling clothes and felt horribly grieved about something. He began to whimper and said, "I'm hungry. I want something to eat." This reminded him. He began to bellow at the top of his voice; he threw himself upon the carpet and rubbed his nose in a dusty woolly bouquet of roses. "I want my peanuts," he howled. "Somebody took my peanuts."

His grandma knelt beside him and gathered him up so tightly he could hardly move. She called in a calm voice above his howls to Old Janet in the doorway, "Bring me some bread and butter with strawberry jam."

"I want peanuts," yelled the little boy desperately.

"No, you don't, darling," said his grandma. "You don't want horrid old peanuts to make you sick. You're going to have some of grandma's nice fresh bread with good strawberries on it. That's what you're going to have." He sat afterward very quietly and ate and ate. His grandma sat near him and Old Janet stood by, near a tray with a loaf and a glass bowl of jam upon the table at the window. Outside there was a trellis with tube-shaped red flowers clinging all over it, and brown bees singing.

"I hardly know what to do," said Grandma, "it's very…"

"Yes, m'am," said Old Janet, "it certainly is…"

Grandma said, "I can't possibly see the end of it. It's a terrible…"

"It certainly is bad," said Old Janet, "all this upset all the time and him such a baby."

Their voices ran on soothingly. The little boy ate and forgot to listen. He did not know these women, except by name. He could not understand what they were talking about; their hands and their clothes and their voices were dry and far away; they examined him with crinkled eyes without any expression that he could see. He sat there waiting for whatever they would do next with him. He hoped they would let him go out and play in the yard. The room was full of flowers and dark red curtains and big soft chairs, and the windows were open, but it was still dark in there somehow; dark, and a place he did not know, or trust.

"Now drink your milk," said Old Janet, holding out a silver cup.

"I don't want any milk," he said, turning his head away.

"Very well, Janet, he doesn't have to drink it," said Grandma quickly. "Now run out in the garden and play, darling. Janet, get his hoop."

A big strange man came home in the evenings who treated the little boy very confusingly. "Say 'please,' and 'thank you,' young man," he would roar, terrifyingly, when he gave any smallest object to the little boy. "Well, fellow, are you ready for a fight?" he would say, again, doubling up huge, hairy fists and making passes at him. "Come on now, you must learn to box." After the first few times this was fun.

"Don't teach him to be rough," said Grandma. "Time enough for all that."

"Now, Mother, we don't want him to be a sissy," said the big man. "He's got to toughen up early. Come on now, fellow, put up your mitts." The little boy liked this new word for hands. He learned to throw himself upon the strange big man, whose name was Uncle David, and hit him on the chest as hard as he could; the big man would laugh and hit him back with his huge, loose fists. Sometimes, but not often, Uncle David came home in the middle of the day. The little boy missed him on the other days, and would hang on the gate looking down the street for him. One evening he brought a large square package under his arm.

"Come over here, fellow, and see what I've got," he said, pulling off quantities of green paper and string from the box which was full of flat, folded colors. He put something in the little boy's hand. It was limp and silky and bright green with a tube on the end. "Thank you," said the little boy nicely, but not knowing what to do with it.

"Balloons," said Uncle David in triumph. "Now just put your mouth here and blow hard." The little boy blew hard and the green thing began to grow round and thin and silvery.

"Good for your chest," said Uncle David. "Blow some more." The little boy went on blowing and the balloon swelled steadily.

"Stop," said Uncle David, "that's enough." He twisted the tube to keep the air in. "That's the way," he said. "Now I'll blow one, and you blow one, and let's see who can blow up a big balloon the fastest."

They blew and blew, especially Uncle David. He puffed and panted and blew with all his might, but the little boy won. His balloon was perfectly round before Uncle David could even get started. The little boy was so proud he began to dance and shout, "I beat, I beat," and blew in his balloon again. It burst in his face and frightened him so he felt sick. "Ha ha, ho ho ho," whooped Uncle David. "That's the boy. I bet I can't do that. Now let's see." He blew until the beautiful bubble grew and wavered and burst into thin air, and there was only a small colored rag in his hand. This was a fine game. They went on with it until Grandma came in and said, "Time for supper now. No, you can't blow balloons at the table. Tomorrow maybe." And it was all over.

The next day, instead of being given balloons, he was hustled out of bed early, bathed in warm soapy water and given a big breakfast of soft-boiled eggs with toast and jam and milk. His grandma came in to kiss him good morning. "And I hope you'll be a good boy and obey your teacher," she told him.

"What's teacher?" asked the little boy.

"Teacher is at school," said Grandma. "She'll tell you all sorts of things and you must do as she says."

Mama and Papa had talked a great deal about School, and how they must send him there. They had told him it was a fine place with all kinds of toys and other children to play with. He felt he knew about School. "I didn't know it was time, Grandma," he said. "Is it today?"

"It's this very minute," said Grandma. "I told you a week ago." Old Janet came in with her bonnet on. It was a prickly looking bundle held with a black rubber band under her back hair. "Come on," she said. "This is my busy day." She wore a dead cat slung around her neck, its sharp ears bent over under her baggy chin.

The little boy was excited and wanted to run ahead. "Hold to my hand like I told you," said Old Janet. "Don't go running off like that and get yourself killed."

"I'm going to get killed, I'm going to get killed," sang the little boy, making a tune of his own.

"Don't say that, you give me the creeps," said Old Janet. "Hold to my hand now." She bent over and looked at him, not at his face but at something on his clothes. His eyes followed hers.

"I declare," said Old Janet, "I did forget. I was going to sew it up. I might have known. I *told* your grandma it would be that way from now on."

"What?" asked the little boy.

"Just look at yourself," said Old Janet crossly. He looked at himself. There was a little end of him showing through the slit in his short blue flannel trousers. The trousers came halfway to his knees above, and his socks came halfway to his knees below, and all winter long his knees were cold. He remembered now how cold his knees were in cold weather. And how sometimes he would have to put the part of him that came through the slit back again, because he was cold there too. He saw at once what was wrong, and tried to arrange himself, but his mittens got in the way. Janet said, "Stop that, you bad boy," and with a firm thumb she set him in order, at the same time reaching under his belt to pull down and fold his knit undershirt over his front.

"There now," she said, "try not to disgrace yourself today." He felt guilty and red all over, because he had something that showed when he was dressed that was not supposed to show then. The different women who bathed him always wrapped him quickly in towels and hurried him into his clothes, because they saw something about him he could not see for himself. They hurried him so he never had a chance to see whatever it was they saw, and though he looked at himself when his clothes were off, he could not find out what was wrong with him. Outside, in his clothes, he knew he looked like everybody else, but inside his clothes there was something bad the matter with him. It worried him and confused him and he wondered about it. The only people who never seemed to notice there was something wrong with him were Mommanpoppa. They never called him a bad boy, and all summer long they had taken all his clothes off and let him run in the sand beside a big ocean.

"Look at him, isn't he a love?" Mama would say and Papa would look, and say, "He's got a back like a prize fighter." Uncle David was a prize fighter when he doubled up his mitts and said, "Come on, fellow."

Old Janet held him firmly and took long steps under her big rustling skirts. He did not like Old Janet's smell. It made him a little quivery in the stomach; it was just like wet chicken feathers.

School was easy. Teacher was a square-shaped woman with square short hair and short skirts. She got in the way sometimes, but not often. The people around him were his size; he didn't have always to be stretching his neck up to faces bent over him, and he could sit on the chairs without having to climb. All the children had names, like Frances and Evelyn and Agatha and Edward and Martin, and his own name was Stephen. He was not Mama's "Baby," nor Papa's "Old Man"; he was not Uncle David's "Fellow," or Grandma's "Darling," or even Old Janet's "Bad Boy." He was Stephen. He was learning to read, and to sing a tune to some strange-looking letters or marks written in chalk on a blackboard. You talked one kind of lettering, and you sang another. All the children talked and sang in turn, and then all together. Stephen thought it a fine game. He felt awake and happy. They had soft clay and paper and wires and squares of colors in tin boxes to play with, colored blocks to build houses with. Afterward they all danced in a big ring, and then they danced in pairs, boys with girls. Stephen danced with Frances, and Frances kept saying, "Now you just follow me." She was a little taller than he was, and her hair stood up in short, shiny curls, the color of an ash tray on Papa's desk. She would say, "You can't dance." "I can dance too," said Stephen, jumping around holding her hands, "I can, too, dance." He was certain of it. " *You* can't dance," he told Frances, "you can't dance at all."

Then they had to change partners, and when they came round again, Frances said, "I don't *like* the way you dance." This was different. He felt uneasy about it. He didn't jump quite so high when the phonograph record started going dumdiddy dumdiddy again. "Go ahead, Stephen, you're doing fine," said Teacher, waving her hands together very fast. The dance ended, and they all played "relaxing" for five minutes. They relaxed by swinging their arms back and forth, then rolling their heads round and round. When Old Janet came for him he didn't want to go home. At lunch his grandma told him twice to keep his face out of his plate. "Is that what they teach you at school?" she asked. Uncle David was at home. "Here you are, fellow," he said and gave Stephen two balloons. "Thank you," said Stephen. He put the balloons in his pocket and forgot about them. "I told you that boy could learn something," said Uncle David to Grandma. "Hear him say 'thank you'?"

In the afternoon at school Teacher handed out big wads of clay and told the children to make something out of it. Anything they liked. Stephen decided to make a cat, like Mama's Meeow at home. He did not like Meeow, but he thought it would be easy to make a cat. He could not get the clay to work at all. It simply fell into one lump after another. So he stopped, wiped his hands on his pull-over, remembered his balloons and began blowing one.

"Look at Stephen's horse," said Frances. "Just look at it."

"It's not a horse, it's a cat," said Stephen. The other children gathered around. "It looks like a horse, a little," said Martin.

"It is a cat," said Stephen, stamping his foot, feeling his face turning hot. The other children all laughed and exclaimed over Stephen's cat that looked like a horse. Teacher came down among them. She sat usually at the top of the room before a big table covered with papers and playthings. She picked up Stephen's lump of clay and turned it round and examined it with her kind eyes. "Now, children," she said, "everybody has the right to make anything the way he pleases. If Stephen says this is a cat, it *is* a cat. Maybe you were thinking about a horse, Stephen?"

"It's a *cat*," said Stephen. He was aching all over. He knew then he should have said at first, "Yes, it's a horse." Then they would have let him alone. They would never have known he was trying to make a cat. "It's Meeow," he said in a trembling voice, "but I forgot how she looks."

His balloon was perfectly flat. He started blowing it up again, trying not to cry. Then it was time to go home, and Old Janet came looking for him. While Teacher was talking to other grown-up people who came to take other children home, Frances said, "Give me your balloon; I haven't got a balloon." Stephen handed it to her. He was happy to give it. He reached in his pocket and took out the other. Happily, he gave her that one too. Frances took it, then handed it back. "Now you blow up one and I'll blow up the other, and let's have a race," she said. When their balloons were only half filled Old Janet took Stephen by the arm and said, "Come on here, this is my busy day."

Frances ran after them, calling, "Stephen, you give me back my balloon," and snatched it away. Stephen did not know whether he was surprised to find himself going away with Frances' balloon, or whether he was surprised to see her snatching it as if it really belonged to her. He was badly mixed up in his mind, and Old Janet was hauling him along. One thing he knew, he liked Frances, he was going to see her again tomorrow, and he was going to bring her more balloons.

That evening Stephen boxed awhile with his uncle David, and Uncle David gave him a beautiful orange. "Eat that," he said, "it's good for your health."

"Uncle David, may I have some more balloons?" asked Stephen.

"Well, what do you say first?" asked Uncle David, reaching for the box on the top bookshelf.

"Please," said Stephen.

"That's the word," said Uncle David. He brought out two balloons, a red and a yellow one. Stephen noticed for the first time they had letters on them, very small letters that grew taller and wider as the balloon grew rounder. "Now that's all, fellow," said Uncle David. "Don't ask for any more because that's all." He put the box back on the bookshelf, but not before Stephen had seen that the box was almost full of balloons. He didn't say a word, but went on blowing, and Uncle David blew also. Stephen thought it was the nicest game he had ever known.

He had only one left, the next day, but he took it to school and gave it to Frances. "There are a lot," he said, feeling very proud and warm; "I'll bring you a lot of them."

Frances blew it up until it made a beautiful bubble, and said, "Look, I want to show you something." She took a sharp-pointed stick they used in working the clay; she poked the balloon, and it exploded. "Look at that," she said.

"That's nothing," said Stephen, "I'll bring you some more."

After school, before Uncle David came home, while Grandma was resting, when Old Janet had given him his milk and told him to run away and not bother her, Stephen dragged a chair to the bookshelf, stood upon it and reached into the box. He did not take three or four as he believed he intended; once his hands were upon them he seized what they could hold and jumped off the chair, hugging them to him. He stuffed them into his reefer pocket where they folded down and hardly made a lump.

He gave them all to Frances. There were so many, Frances gave most of them away to the other children. Stephen, flushed with his new joy, the lavish pleasure of giving presents, found almost at once still another happiness. Suddenly he was popular among the children; they invited him specially to join whatever games were up; they fell in at once with his own notions for play, and asked him what he would like to do next. They had festivals of blowing up the beautiful globes, fuller and rounder and thinner, changing as they went from deep color to lighter, paler tones, growing glassy thin, bubbly thin, then bursting with a thrilling loud noise like a toy pistol.

For the first time in his life Stephen had almost too much of something he wanted, and his head was so turned he forgot how this fullness came about, and no longer thought of it as a secret. The next day was Saturday, and Frances came to visit him with her nurse. The nurse and Old Janet sat in Old Janet's room drinking coffee and gossiping, and the children sat on the side porch blowing balloons. Stephen chose an apple-colored one and Frances a pale green one. Between them on the bench lay a tumbled heap of delights still to come.

"I once had a silver balloon," said Frances, "a beyootiful silver one, not round like these; it was a long one. But these are even nicer, I think," she added quickly, for she did want to be polite.

"When you get through with that one," said Stephen, gazing up at her with the pure bliss of giving added to loving, "you can blow up a blue one and then a pink one and a yellow one and a purple one." He pushed the heap of limp objects toward her. Her clear-looking eyes, with fine little rays of brown in them like the spokes of a wheel, were full of approval for Stephen. "I wouldn't want to be greedy, though, and blow up all your balloons."

"There'll be plenty more left," said Stephen, and his heart rose under his thin ribs. He felt his ribs with his fingers and discovered with some surprise that they stopped somewhere in front, while Frances sat blowing balloons rather halfheartedly. The truth was, she was tired of balloons. After you blow six or seven your chest gets hollow and your lips feel puckery. She had been blowing balloons steadily for three days now. She had begun to hope they were giving out. "There's boxes and boxes more of them, Frances," said Stephen happily. "Millions more. I guess they'd last and last if we didn't blow too many every day."

Frances said somewhat timidly, "I tell you what. Let's rest awhile and fix some liquish water. Do you like liquish?"

"Yes, I do," said Stephen, "but I haven't got any."

"Couldn't we buy some?" asked Frances. "It's only a cent a stick, the nice rubbery, twisty kind. We can put it in a bottle with some water, and shake it and shake it, and it makes foam on top like soda pop and we can drink it. I'm kind of thirsty," she said in a small, weak voice. "Blowing balloons all the time makes you thirsty, I think."

Stephen, in silence, realized a dreadful truth and a numb feeling crept over him. He did not have a cent to buy licorice for Frances and she was tired of his balloons. This was the first real dismay of his whole life, and he aged at least a year in the next minute, huddled, with his deep, serious blue eyes focused down his nose in intense speculation. What could he do to please Frances that would not cost money? Only yesterday Uncle David had given him a nickel, and he had thrown it away on gumdrops. He regretted that nickel so bitterly his neck and forehead were damp. He was thirsty too.

"I tell you what," he said, brightening with a splendid idea, lamely trailing off on second thought, "I know something we can do, I'll—I…"

"I *am* thirsty," said Frances with gentle persistence. "I think I'm so thirsty maybe I'll have to go home." She did not leave the bench, though, but sat, turning her grieved mouth toward Stephen.

Stephen quivered with the terrors of the adventure before him, but he said boldly, "I'll make some lemonade. I'll get sugar and lemon and some ice and we'll have lemonade."

"Oh, I love lemonade," cried Frances. "I'd rather have lemonade than liquish."

"You stay right here," said Stephen, "and I'll get everything."

He ran around the house, and under Old Janet's window he heard the dry, chattering voices of the two old women whom he must outwit. He sneaked on tiptoe to the pantry, took a lemon lying there by itself, a handful of lump sugar and a china teapot, smooth, round, with flowers and leaves all over it. These he left on the kitchen table while he broke a piece of ice with a sharp metal pick he had been forbidden to touch. He put the ice in the pot, cut the lemon and squeezed it as well as he could—a lemon was tougher and more slippery than he had thought—and mixed sugar and water. He decided there was not enough sugar so he sneaked back and took another handful. He was back on the porch in an astonishingly short time, his face tight, his knees trembling, carrying iced lemonade to thirsty Frances with both his devoted hands.

A pace distant from her he stopped, literally stabbed through with a thought. Here he stood in broad daylight carrying a teapot with lemonade in it, and his grandma or Old Janet might walk through the door at any moment.

"Come on, Frances," he whispered loudly. "Let's go round to the back behind the rose bushes where it's shady." Frances leaped up and ran like a deer beside him, her face wise with knowledge of why they ran; Stephen ran stiffly, cherishing his teapot with clenched hands.

It was shady behind the rose bushes, and much safer. They sat side by side on the dampish ground, legs doubled under, drinking in turn from the splender spout.

Stephen took his just share in large, cool, delicious swallows. When Frances drank she set her round pink mouth daintily to the spout and her throat beat steadily as a heart. Stephen was thinking he had really done something pretty nice for Frances. He did not know where his own happiness was; it was mixed with the sweet-sour taste in his mouth and a cool feeling in his bosom because Frances was there drinking his lemonade which he had got for her with great danger.

Frances said, "My, what big swallows you take," when his turn came next.

"No bigger than yours," he told her downrightly. "You take awfully big swallows."

"Well," said Frances, turning this criticism into an argument for her rightness about things, "that's the way to drink lemonade anyway." She peered into the teapot. There was quite a lot of lemonade left and she was beginning to feel she had enough. "Let's make up a game and see who can take the biggest swallows."

This was such a wonderful notion they grew reckless, tipping the spout into their opened mouths above their heads until lemonade welled up and ran over their chins in rills down their fronts. When they tired of this there was still lemonade left in the pot. They played first at giving the rosebush a drink and ended by baptizing it. "Name father son holygoat," shouted Stephen, pouring. At this sound Old Janet's face appeared over the low hedge, with the tan, disgusted-looking face of Frances' nurse hanging over her shoulder.

"Well, just as I thought," said Old Janet. "Just as I expected." The bag under her chin waggled.

"We were thirsty," he said; "we were awfully thirsty." Frances said nothing, but she gazed steadily at the toes of her shoes.

"Give me that teapot," said Old Janet, taking it with a rude snatch. "Just because you're thirsty is no reason," said Old Janet. "You can ask for things. You don't have to steal."

"We didn't steal," cried Frances suddenly. "We didn't. We didn't!"

"That's enough from you, missy," said her nurse. "Come straight out of there. You have nothing to do with this."

"Oh, I don't know," said Old Janet with a hard stare at Frances' nurse. "*He* never did such a thing before, by himself."

"Come on," said the nurse to Frances, "this is no place for you." She held Frances by the wrist and started walking away so fast Frances had to run to keep up. "Nobody can call *us* thieves and get away with it."

"You don't have to steal, even if others do," said Old Janet to Stephen, in a high carrying voice. "If you so much as pick up a lemon in somebody else's house you're a little thief." She lowered her voice then and said, "Now I'm going to tell your grandma and you'll see what you get."

"He went in the icebox and left it open," Janet told Grandma, "and he got into the lump sugar and spilt it all over the floor. Lumps everywhere underfoot. He dribbled water all over the clean kitchen floor, and he baptized the rose bush, blaspheming. And he took your Spode teapot."

"I didn't either," said Stephen loudly, trying to free his hand from Old Janet's big hard fist.

"Don't tell fibs," said Old Janet; "that's the last straw."

"Oh, dear," said Grandma. "He's not a baby any more." She shut the book she was reading and pulled the wet front of his pull-over toward her. "What's this sticky stuff on him?" she asked and straightened her glasses.

"Lemonade," said Old Janet. "He took the last lemon."

They were in the big dark room with the red curtains. Uncle David walked in from the room with the bookcases, holding a box in his uplifted hand. "Look here," he said to Stephen. "What's become of all my balloons?"

Stephen knew well that Uncle David was not really asking a question.

Stephen, sitting on a footstool at his grandma's knee, felt sleepy. He leaned heavily and wished he could put his head on her lap, but he might go to sleep, and it would be wrong to go to sleep while Uncle David was still talking. Uncle David walked about the room with his hands in his pockets, talking to Grandma. Now and then he would walk over to a lamp and, leaning, peer into the top of the shade, winking in the light, as if he expected to find something there.

"It's simply in the blood, I told her," said Uncle David. "I told her she would simply have to come and get him, and keep him. She asked me if I meant to call him a thief and I said if she could think of a more exact word I'd be glad to hear it."

"You shouldn't have said that," commented Grandma calmly.

"Why not? She might as well know the facts…. I suppose he can't help it," said Uncle David, stopping now in front of Stephen and dropping his chin into his collar, "I shouldn't expect too much of him, but you can't begin too early—"

"The trouble is," said Grandma, and while she spoke she took Stephen by the chin and held it up so that he had to meet her eye; she talked steadily in a mournful tone, but Stephen could not understand. She ended, "It's not just about the balloons, of course."

"It *is* about the balloons," said Uncle David angrily, "because balloons now mean something worse later. But what can you expect? His father—well, it's in the blood. He—"

"That's your sister's husband you're talking about," said Grandma, "and there is no use making things worse. Besides, you don't really *know*."

"I *do* know," said Uncle David. And he talked again very fast, walking up and down. Stephen tried to understand, but the sounds were strange and floating just over his head. They were talking about his father, and they did not like him. Uncle David came over and stood above Stephen and Grandma. He hunched over them with a frowning face, a long, crooked shadow from him falling across them to the wall. To Stephen he looked like his father, and he shrank against his grandma's skirts.

"The question is, what to do with him now?" asked Uncle David. "If we keep him here, he'd just be a—I won't be bothered with him. Why can't they take care of their own child? That house is crazy. Too far gone already, I'm afraid. No training. No example."

"You're right, they must take him and keep him," said Grandma. She ran her hands over Stephen's head; tenderly she pinched the nape of his neck between thumb and forefinger. "You're your Grandma's darling," she told him, "and you've had a nice long visit, and now you're going home. Mama is coming for you in a few minutes. Won't that be nice?"

"I want my mama," said Stephen, whimpering, for his grandma's face frightened him. There was something wrong with her smile.

Uncle David sat down. "Come over here, fellow," he said, wagging a forefinger at Stephen. Stephen went over slowly, and Uncle David drew him between his wide knees in their loose, rough clothes. "You ought to be ashamed of yourself," he said, "stealing Uncle David's balloons when he had already given you so many."

"It wasn't that," said Grandma quickly. "Don't say that. It will make an impression—"

"I hope it does," said Uncle David in a louder voice; "I hope he remembers it all his life. If he belonged to me I'd give him a good thrashing."

Stephen felt his mouth, his chin, his whole face jerking. He opened his mouth to take a breath, and tears and noise burst from him. "Stop that, fellow, stop that," said Uncle David, shaking him gently by the shoulders, but Stephen could not stop. He drew his breath again and it came back in a howl. Old Janet came to the door.

"Bring me some cold water," called Grandma. There was a flurry, a commotion, a breath of cool air from the hall, the door slammed, and Stephen heard his mother's voice. His howl died away, his breath sobbed and fluttered, he turned his dimmed eyes and saw her standing there. His heart turned over within him and he bleated like a lamb, "Maaaaama," running toward her. Uncle David stood back as Mama swooped in and fell on her knees beside Stephen. She gathered him to her and stood up with him in her arms.

"What are you doing to my baby?" she asked Uncle David in a thickened voice. "I should never have let him come here. I should have known better—"

"You always should know better," said Uncle David, "and you never do. And you never will. You haven't got it here," he told her, tapping his forehead.

"David," said Grandma, "that's your—"

"Yes, I know, she's my sister," said Uncle David. "I know it. But if she must run away and marry a—"

"Shut up," said Mama.

"And bring more like him into the world, let her keep them at home. I say let her keep—"

Mama set Stephen on the floor and, holding him by the hand, she said to Grandma all in a rush as if she were reading something, "Good-by, Mother. This is the last time, really the last. I can't bear it any longer. Say good-by to Stephen; you'll never see him again. You let this happen. It's your fault. You know David was a coward and a bully and a self-righteous little beast all his life and you never crossed him in anything. You let him bully me all my life and you let him slander my husband and call my baby a thief, and now this is the end….He calls my baby a thief over a few horrible little balloons because he doesn't like my husband…."

She was panting and staring about from one to the other. They were all standing. Now Grandma said, "Go home, daughter. Go away, David. I'm sick of your quarreling. I've never had a day's peace or comfort from either of you. I'm sick of you both. Now let me alone and stop this noise. Go away," said Grandma in a wavering voice. She took out her handkerchief and wiped first one eye and then the other and said, "All this hate, hate—what is it for?… So this is the way it turns out. Well, let me alone."

"You and your little advertising balloons," said Mama to Uncle David. "The big honest businessman advertises with balloons and if he loses one he'll be ruined. And your beastly little moral notions…"

Grandma went to the door to meet Old Janet, who handed her a glass of water. Grandma drank it all, standing there.

"Is your husband coming for you, or are you going home by yourself?" she asked Mama.

"I'm driving myself," said Mama in a far-away voice as if her mind had wandered. "You know he wouldn't set foot in this house."

"I should think not," said Uncle David.

"Come on, Stephen darling," said Mama. "It's far past his bedtime," she said, to no one in particular. "Imagine keeping a baby up to torture him about a few miserable little bits of colored rubber." She smiled at Uncle David with both rows of teeth as she passed him on the way to the door, keeping between him and Stephen. "Ah, where would we be without high moral standards," she said, and then to Grandma, "Goodnight, Mother," in quite her usual voice. "I'll see you in a day or so."

"Yes, indeed," said Grandma cheerfully, coming out into the hall with Stephen and Mama. "Let me hear from you. Ring me up tomorrow. I hope you'll be feeling better."

"I feel very well now," said Mama brightly, laughing. She bent down and kissed Stephen. "Sleepy, darling? Papa's waiting to see you. Don't go to sleep until you've kissed your papa good night."

Stephen woke with a sharp jerk. He raised his head and put out his chin a little, "I don't want to go home," he said; "I want to go to school. I don't want to see Papa, I don't like him."

Mama laid her palm over his mouth softly. "Darling, don't."

Uncle David put his head out with a kind of snort. "There you are," he said. "There you've got a statement from headquarters."

Mama opened the door and ran, almost carrying Stephen. She ran across the sidewalk, jerking open the car door and dragging Stephen in after her. She spun the car around and dashed forward so sharply Stephen was almost flung out of the seat. He sat braced then with all his might, hands digging into the cushions. The car speeded up and the trees and houses whizzed by all flattened out. Stephen began suddenly to sing to himself, a quiet, inside song so mama would not hear. He sang his new secret; it was a comfortable, sleepy song: "I hate Papa, I hate Mama, I hate Grandma, I hate Uncle David, I hate Old Janet, I hate Marjory, I hate Papa, I hate Mama..."

His head bobbed, leaned, came to rest on Mama's knee, eyes closed. Mama drew him closer and slowed down, driving with one hand.

—1939

FRADEL SCHTOK (1890–CA.1930)

Yiddish writer Fradel Schtok was born in Skala, Galicia (now Skala Podolskaya, Ukraine). She received a good education as a child, and was a gifted musician and writer. Her parents died when she was still quite young, and Schtok emigrated to the United States in 1907. Her first verse was published a few years after her arrival, and was well received. She continued to publish in various Yiddish-American periodicals and, in 1919, a collection of her stories in Yiddish was published under the title *Erzeylungen* (Stories). Her work focuses primarily on the experiences of women in *shtetls* (small Eastern European villages or towns with primarily Jewish populations). She published one novel in English, *Musicians Only* (1927), which received negative reviews. She later fell into a deep depression and was institutionalized in a mental hospital, where she died.

The Veil

The veil was brought into the house along with the myrtle. Manya put out a bowl of water and set the myrtle in it.

Tsirl's daughter Beyle was getting married today. When she was betrothed four weeks earlier, the family had thought it a miracle. Beyle was getting on in years, and no-one expected her to marry.

"True, he is an older man, but on the other hand he has a well-stocked store." That's what Zlate, Manya's mother, had told them.

Manya had not been overjoyed, because she knew that she would not be at the wedding even though they were relatives. Ever since Manya's father Itskhok had disappeared and Zlate was left an *agune,*[1] she didn't allow the children to raise their heads. Never did they go to a wedding, nor hear the *klezmer*[2] play, except from a distance. And Manya loved the *klezmer*. More than once she got up at night, opened the window, and listened as they walked through the town playing and moving further away. They played some sad melody that drifted in through the window keeping people awake half the night. Some sadness would then grip the heart so you wouldn't know what it was you wanted.

Her heart would always tremble. And what made it tremble?—at times the ringing sound of the scythes on a summer evening, or a handsome gentile lad on a hay-wagon, or a song of the oppressed at night behind her window.

She had always wanted to go to a wedding, and her mother had never allowed it. For that matter, where did her mother ever allow her to go? Not even to the circus when it came to town! *She* had to stay home and help her mother sew bed-linen for others. So, of course, she didn't really know how to behave in company, and when on *Shabes*[3] at the pre-wedding party she had reached for another piece of strudel, she was glad that her mother had stepped on her toes.

Sunday morning the bride's mother, Tsirl herself, had come in and burst into tears, pleading with Zlate to allow at least Manya to attend the wedding. No garland-maid had yet been chosen. Zlate's face took on a strange pensiveness. "Maybe." When the younger children had heard that "maybe," they began to beg her. Pesi, the neighbour, and Pesi's daughter Leytshe had also beseeched her. Tsirl kept wiping her eyes. Only Manya had been silent; being the eldest, she understood. Nevertheless, her heart trembled, her face turned pale. At last Zlate looked at Manya and said, "All right. Iron your muslin dress, garland-maid."

The veil and the myrtle had been brought in and the house was turned upside down. Leytshe hugged Manya, telling her that the new flutist would play at the wedding. Who was the new flutist? A student—from Vienna!—who played the flute. He had quarrelled with his father, left for another city and become a *klezmer* to spite his father. And oh did he play....

Manya bent over the bowl to sniff the myrtle. The small green branches had swelled in the bowl, drinking their fill of water. And they released their scent through the house, redolent of bride, white veil, *confiture*[4] and *khupe*.[5]

---

[1] (Yid.) A woman who cannot obtain a divorce because her husband has deserted her or his death is not proven, literally "a chained woman."
[2] (Yid.) Musician.
[3] (Yid.) Sabbath.
[4] (Fr.) Jams or preserves.
[5] (Yid.) Canopy.

Royze, the hairdresser, came to weave the garland. She used grey thread to tie the small branches as she braided, tried it on Manya's head for size and then added more at the forehead so it would look like a crown. Then she took the white veil out of a box and shook it out over the room. The room seemed filled with veil. Manya's heart fluttered—so much veil....

Manya stood stock still, to the tips of her fingers respectful of the whiteness and transparency of the veil. Then she moved the neighbours who had come in into the corners of the room. As Royze shook the veil out across the whole room, she trembled, afraid it would be soiled.

"Royze, you'll dirty the veil. Spread something under it...."

"What shall I use?"

"My muslin dress."

"You're crazy!"

Later the veil lay spread out under the green garland, drops of water dripping onto it from the myrtle.

Manya's heart trembled. "A veil that can cover an entire room, and is so...I don't know...ahhhh."

When the time came to take the garland and veil to the bride's house, Manya carried it as one would a breath of air that could at any moment evaporate into nothingness. And when she put the garland on the bride, she bent her own head so as to catch the drops of water dripping onto it from the myrtle.

The *klezmer* were playing for the bride at her house. Manya, wearing her muslin dress, was standing near a lamp that gave her face a rosy glow. She didn't look at the new flutist, but held her head in such a way that she could observe him looking at her.

She heard no-one, only his flute. Suddenly she began to feel ashamed in the presence of the flute, ashamed that Tsirl—her own relative!—was forever going to the *gmiles khesed*[6] for an interest-free loan for her stall, ashamed that Tsirl was toothless, that Tsirl's husband was associated with the Karlsbad waters affair, and that Tsirl's son had a bandaged neck.

She was ashamed that everyone was crying; to her it seemed like water dripping from a frozen roof when the sun suddenly shines on it.

To her eyes, Leyzer's long face looked as it did on *Rosheshone*[7] at *tashlekh*[8] when she saw him shaking out all his sins into the Zbrukh River to rid himself of the burden and to square things with God.

She looked at the *klezmer*—whose music had buried more than one Jewish bride— and it seemed to her they were smiling behind their moustaches. She sensed the truth of what was said when the wedding trumpet sounds, "This too will be your fate, this too will be your fate..." and the fiddle laments, "Oh, how you will be blighted!" while the bass angrily booms, "Just like this, just like this."

A horse-drawn cab took them to the hall for the wedding meal.

Manya sat near the bride, continually straightening Beyle's garland, spreading the veil over her shoulders, her face, her legs, gathering it at her knees, and she kept wiping each droplet of water that fell from the myrtle on Beyle's forehead. She felt she was

---

[6] (Yid.) Refers both to a loan without interest and the people who make such loans.

[7] (Yid.) New Year.

[8] (Yid.) A rite performed at Rosheshone, the Jewish new year.

carrying the weight of the world. She had never before understood what it meant to be a garland-maid; to care for the bride's garland, attend to the bride's veil!

And inside, again all she heard was his flute. Manya didn't look at him but felt his eyes on her.

When she danced the Lancers, she bowed politely to the flute player.

She had many occasions to approach the *klezmer*—a garland-maid has to make sure that everyone dances. And when unintentionally she did look at him, what she saw was chestnut-brown hair, dark eyes, a thick lower lip—and felt him bow to her close, too close.

"*Fräulein*[9]...you dance divinely...."

Later he whispered in her ear many words, words of passion. He said casually, "*Fräulein,* this is of course sweet madness."

And he began to laugh, straight from the heart, and for Manya this laughter burned in her ears, and they turned crimson.

"It is certainly sweet madness...sweet."

Leytshe called her away. "I have to tell you a secret," she moved her head closer. "He, the flutist...is asking about you, asking 'Who is this girl? Oh, what a fine girl.'"

Manya looked at Leytshe, her black teeth, and thought lovingly just how attractive black teeth could be after all....

She went up to the bride and put her flushed face under the veil, straightening the myrtle on the bride's head.

Suddenly her mother came up to her in her everyday dress to say it was three o'clock, she was to go home. The younger children had been carried home sleeping.

She stopped as if she were in a fog, knew nothing of what was happening to her; even the music seemed strange and distant. Suddenly a man's grey sheepskin coat materialized and Manya slipped her arms into it, letting her mother wrap it tightly round her neck, and it seemed to her that was the worst part—it was her mother tightening it closely round her neck.

Translated by Brina Menachovsky Rose

—1919

[9] (G.) Miss.

ZORA NEALE HURSTON (1891-1960)

Born in Notasulga, Alabama, Zora Neale Hurston moved with her family to the all-Black Eatonville, Florida, about a year later. Her mother died when Hurston was thirteen and her father, a preacher and carpenter, was the town's mayor several times. Hurston attended Howard University, supporting herself as a manicurist, but dropped out after a few years. In January of 1925 she moved to New York City, where she met the artists and writers of the Harlem Renaissance. In addition to short fiction, novels, and folklore, Hurston also wrote drama, including a play co-authored with Langston Hughes. She worked as a secretary to writer Fannie Hurst and studied anthropology under Franz Boas at Barnard College (where she was the only Black student), receiving her B.A. in Anthropology in 1927. That same year, Hurston began researching folklore in Eatonville, sponsored by Charlotte Mason, a noted patroness of Black writers and artists. Hurston worked as a teacher, a drama coach, and an editor during the 1930s, and traveled to the Caribbean on Guggenheim fellowships in 1936 and 1937. Two of Hurston's most important works, the folktale collection *Of Mules and Men* (1935) and the novel *Their Eyes Were Watching God* (1937), date from that decade. Hurston's work fell out of favor in the 1940s and 1950s, and she was unable to find publishers for three of her novels. By the late 1940s, Hurston began to have health problems. Following a stroke in 1959, she lived in a welfare hotel, where she died penniless the following year. Novelist and poet Alice Walker championed the revival of Hurston's work in the 1970s, tracking down her grave in order to erect a headstone on it. Since then, Hurston's work has been widely reprinted and taught. Written in 1925, "Black Death" was never published in Hurston's lifetime.

Black Death

The Negroes in Eatonville know a number of things that the hustling, bustling white man never dreams of. He is a materialist with little ears for overtones.

For instance, if a white person were halted on the streets of Orlando and told that Old Man Morgan, the excessively black Negro hoodoo man, can kill any person indicated and paid for, without ever leaving his house or even seeing his victim, he'd laugh in your face and walk away, wondering how long the Negro will continue to wallow in ignorance and superstition. But no black person in a radius of twenty miles will smile, not much. They *know*.

His achievements are far too numerous to mention singly. Besides many of his curses or "conjures" are kept secret. But everybody knows that he put the loveless curse on Della Lewis. She has been married seven times but none of her husbands have ever remained with her longer than the twenty-eight days that Morgan had prescribed as the limit.

Hiram Lester's left track was brought to him with five dollars and when the new moon came again, Lester was stricken with paralysis while working in his orange grove.

There was the bloody-flux that he put on Lucy Potts; he caused Emma Taylor's teeth to drop out; he put the shed skin of a black snake in Horace Brown's shoes and made him as the Wandering Jew; he put a sprig of Lena Merchant's hair in a bottle, corked it and threw it into a running stream with the neck pointing up stream, and she went crazy; he buried Lillie Wilcox's finger-nails with lizard's feet and dried up her blood.

All of these things and more can easily be proved by the testimony of the villagers. They ought to know.

He lives alone in a two-room hut down by Lake Blue Sink, the bottomless. His eyes are reddish and the large gold hoop ear-rings jangling on either side of his shrunken black face make the children shrink in terror whenever they meet him on the street or in the woods where he goes to dig roots for his medicines.

But the doctor does not spend his time merely making folks ill. He has sold himself to the devil over the powerful black cat's bone that alone will float upstream, and many do what he wills. Life and death are in his hands—he sometimes kills.

He sent Old Lady Grooms to her death in the Lake. She was a rival hoodoo doctor and laid claims to equal power. She came to her death one night. That very morning Morgan had told several that he was tired of her pretenses—he would put an end to it and prove his powers.

That very afternoon near sundown, she went down to the lake to fish, telling her daughter, however, that she did not wish to go, but something seemed to be forcing her. About dusk someone heard her scream and rushed to the Lake. She had fallen in and drowned. The white coroner from Orlando said she met her death by falling into the water during an epileptic fit. But the villagers *knew*. White folks are very stupid about some things. They can think mightily but cannot *feel*.

But the undoing of Beau Diddely is his masterpiece. He had come to Eatonville from up North somewhere. He was a waiter at the Park House Hotel over in Maitland where Docia Boger was a chamber-maid. She had a very pretty brown body and face, sang alto in the Methodist Choir and played the blues on her guitar. Soon Beau Diddely was with her every moment he could spare from his work. He was stuck on her all right, for a time.

They would linger in the shrubbery about Park Lane or go for long walks in the woods on Sunday afternoon to pick violets. They are abundant in the Florida woods in winter.

The Park House always closed in April and Beau was planning to go North with the white tourists. It was then Docia's mother discovered that Beau should have married her daughter weeks before.

"Mist' Diddely," said Mrs. Boger, "Ah'm a widder 'oman an' Deshy's all Ah got, an' Ah know youse gointer do what you orter." She hesitated a moment and studied his face. "'Thout no trouble. Ah doan wanta make no talk 'round town."

In a split second the vivacious, smiling Beau had vanished. A very hard vitriolic stranger occupied his chair.

"Looka heah, Mis' Boger. I'm a man that's travelled a lot—been most everywhere. Don't try to come that stuff over me—What I got to marry Docia for?"

"'Cause—'Cause"—the surprise of his answer threw the old woman into a panic. "Youse the cause of her condition, aintcher?"

Docia, embarrassed, mortified, began to cry.

"Oh, I see the little plot now!" He glanced maliciously toward the girl and back again to her mother. "But I'm none of your down-South-country-suckers. Go try that on some of these clodhoppers. Don't try to lie on *me*—I got money to fight."

"Beau," Docia sobbed, "you ain't callin' me a liah, is you?" And in her misery she started toward the man who through four months' constant association and assurance she had learned to love and trust.

"Yes! You're lying—you sneaking little—oh you're not even good sawdust! Me marry you! Why I could pick up a better woman out of the gutter than you! I'm a married man anyway, so you might as well forget your little scheme!"

Docia fell back stunned.

"But, but Beau, you said you wasn't," Docia wailed.

"Oh," Beau replied with a gesture of dismissal of the whole affair. "What difference does it make? A man will say anything at times. There are certain kinds of women that men always lie to."

In her mind's eye Docia saw things for the first time without her tinted glasses and real terror seized her. She fell upon her knees and clasped the nattily clad legs of her seducer.

"Oh Beau," she went, struggling to hold him, as he, fearing for the creases in his trousers, struggled to free himself—"You made—you—you promised"—

"Oh, well, you ought not to have believed me—you ought to have known I didn't mean it. Anyway I'm not going to marry you, so what're you going to do? Do whatever you feel big enough to try—my shoulders are broad."

He left the house hating the two women bitterly, as we only hate those we have injured.

At the hotel, omitting mention of his shows of affection, his pleas, his solemn promises to Docia, he told the other waiters how that piece of earth's refuse had tried to inveigle, to coerce him into a marriage. He enlarged upon his theme and told them all, in strict confidence, how she had been pursuing him all winter; how she had waited in a bush time and again and dragged him down by the Lake, and well, he was only human. It couldn't have happened with the *right* kind of girl, and he thought too much of himself to marry any other than the country's best.

So the next day Eatonville knew; and the scourge of tongues was added to Docia's woes.

Mrs. Boger and her daughter kept strictly indoors, suffering, weeping, growing bitter.

"Mommer, if he jus' hadn't tried to make me out a bad girl, I could look over the rest in time, Mommer, but—but he tried to make out—ah—"

She broke down weeping again.

Drip, drip, drip, went her daughter's tears on the old woman's heart, each drop calcifying a little the fibers till at the end of four days the petrifying process was complete. Where once had been warm, pulsing flesh was now cold heavy stone, that pulled down pressing out normal life and bowing the head of her. The woman died, and in that heavy cold stone a tiger, a female tiger—was born.

She was ready to answer the questions Beau had flung so scornfully at her old head: "Well, what are you going to do?"

Docia slept, huddled on the bed. A hot salt tear rose to Mrs. Boger's eyes and rolled heavily down the quivering nose. Must Docia awake always to that awful desolation? Robbed of *everything*, even faith. She knew then that the world's greatest crime is not murder—its most terrible punishment is meted to her of too much faith—too great a love.

She turned down the light and stepped into the street.

It was near midnight and the village slept. But she knew of one house where there would be light; one pair of eyes still awake.

As she approached Blue Sink she all but turned back. It was a dark night but the Lake shimmered and glowed like phosphorous near the shore. It seemed that figures moved about on the quiet surface. She remembered that folks said Blue Sink the bottomless, was Morgan's graveyard and all Africa awoke in her blood.

A cold prickly feeling stole over her and stood her hair on end. Her feet grew heavy and her tongue dry and stiff.

In the swamp at the head of the Lake, she saw Jack-O-Lanteren darting here and there and three hundred years of America passed like the mist of morning. Africa reached out its dark hand and claimed its own. Drums, tom, tom, tom, tom, tom, beat her ears. Strange demons seized her. Witch doctors danced before her, laid hands upon her alternately freezing and burning her flesh, until she found herself within the house of Morgan.

She was not permitted to tell her story. She opened her mouth but the old man chewed a camphor leaf or two, spat into a small pail of sand and asked:

"How do yuh wants kill 'im? By water, by sharp edge, or a bullet?"

The old woman almost fell off the chair in amazement that he knew her mind. He merely chuckled a bit and handed her a drinking gourd.

"Dip up a teeny bit of water an' po' hit on de flo',—by dat time you'll know."

She dipped the water out of a wooden pail and poured it upon the rough floor.

"Ah wanta shoot him, but how kin ah' 'thout…?"—

"Looka heah." Morgan directed and pointed to a huge mirror scarred and dusty. He dusted its face carefully. "Look in dis glass 'thout turnin' yo' head an' when he comes, you shoot tuh kill. Take a good aim!"

Both faced about and gazed hard into the mirror that reached from floor to ceiling. Morgan turned once to spit into the pail of sand. The mirror grew misty, darker, near the center, then Mrs. Boger saw Beau walk to the center of the mirror and stand looking at her, glaring and sneering. She all but fainted in superstitious terror.

Morgan thrust the gun into her hand. She saw the expression on Beau Diddely's face change from scorn to fear and she laughed.

"Take good aim," Morgan cautioned. "You cain't shoot but once."

She leveled the gun at the heart of the apparition in the glass and fired. It collapsed; the mirror grew misty again, then cleared.

In horror she flung her money at the old man who seized it greedily, and fled into the darkness, dreading nothing, thinking only of putting distance between her and the house of Morgan.

The next day Eatonville was treated to another thrill.

It seemed that Beau Diddely, the darling of the ladies, was in the hotel yard making love to another chamber-maid. In order that she might fully appreciate what a great victory was here, he was reciting the Conquest of Docia, how she loved him, pursued him, knelt down and kissed his feet, begging him to marry her,—when suddenly he stood up very straight, clasped his hand over his heart, grew rigid, and fell dead.

The coroner's verdict was death from natural causes—heart failure. But they were mystified by what looked like a powder burn directly over the heart.

But the Negroes knew instantly when they saw that mark, but everyone agreed that he got justice. Mrs. Boger and Docia moved to Jacksonville where she married well.

And the white folks never knew and would have laughed had anyone told them,—so why mention it?

—1995

NELLA LARSEN (1891-1963)

Fiction writer Nella Larsen was born in Chicago, the daughter of a Danish domestic, Mary Hanson Walker, and an African American, Peter Walker. Not long after her birth, Mary Walker married Scandinavian Peter Larsen, from whom Nella took her surname. After spending several years in Denmark with her mother's family, Larsen spent a year at Fisk University, a historically Black school in Nashville; she then returned to Denmark. After graduating from the all-Black nursing school at New York's Lincoln Hospital in 1915, Larsen went to work at Booker T. Washington's Tuskegee Institute. After the Spanish Flu pandemic of 1918, she gave up nursing and became a librarian. Larsen married physicist Elmer Samuel Imes in 1919 and moved to Harlem, where she began to write, publishing her first story in 1920 and spending time with the writers and artists of the Harlem Renaissance. *Quicksand,* Larsen's first novel, was published in 1928, and her second, *Passing,* in 1929, both to good reviews. In 1930, Larsen became the first African-American woman to win a Guggenheim Fellowship; that same year, however, she was falsely accused of plagiarizing her short story "Sanctuary." She spent the next three years in Europe working on a third novel, which was never published. After returning to the U.S. in 1933, when her divorce from Imes became final, Larsen returned to nursing. She spent the last thirty years of her life in obscurity.

Freedom

He wondered, as he walked deftly through the impassioned traffic on the Avenue, how she would adjust her life if he were to withdraw from it....How peaceful it would be to have no woman in one's life! These months away took on the appearance of a liberation, a temporary recess from a hateful existence in which he lived in intimacy with someone he did not know and would not now have chosen....He began, again, to speculate on the pattern her life would take without him. Abruptly, it flashed upon him that the vague irritation of many weeks was a feeling of smoldering resentment against her.

The displeasure that this realization caused him increased his ill humor and distaste. He began to dissect her with an acrimomy that astonished himself. Her unanimated beauty seemed now only a thin disguise for an inert mind, and not for the serene beauty of soul which he had attributed to her. He suspected, too, a touch of depravity, perhaps only physical, but more likely mental as well. Reflection convinced him that her appeal for him was bounded by the senses, for witness his disgust and clarity of vision, now that they were separated. How could he have been so blinded? Why, for him she had been the universe; a universe personal and unheedful of outside persons or things. He had adored her in a slavish fashion. He groaned inwardly at his own mental caricature of himself, sitting dumb, staring at her in fatuous worship. What an ass he had been!

His work here was done, but what was there to prevent him from staying away for six months—a year—forever?...Never to see her again!...He stopped, irresolute. What would she do? He tried to construct a representation of her future without him. In his present new hatred, she became a creature irresistibly given to pleasure at no matter what cost. A sybarite! A parasite too!

He was prayerfully thankful that appreciation of his danger had come before she had sapped from him all physical and spiritual vitality. But her future troubled him even while he assured himself that he knew its road, and laughed ruefully at the picture of her flitting from mate to mate.

A feverish impatience gripped him. Somehow, he must contrive to get himself out of the slough into which his amorous folly had precipitated him....Three years. Good God! At the moment, those three years seemed the most precious of his life. And he had foolishly thrown them away. He had drifted pleasantly, peacefully, without landmarks; would be drifting yet but for the death of a friend whose final affairs had brought him away....

He started. Death! Perhaps she would die. How that would simplify matters for him. But no; she would not die. He laughed without amusement. She would not die; she would outlast him, damn her!...An angry resentment, sharp and painful as a whiplash, struck him. Its passing left him calm and determined....

He braced himself and continued to walk. He had decided; he would stay. With this decision, he seemed to be reborn. He felt cool, refreshed, as if he had stepped out from a warm, scented place into a cold, brisk breeze. He was happy. The world had turned to silver and gold, and life again became a magical adventure. Even the placards in the shops shone with the light of paradise upon them. One caught and held his eye. Travel...Yes, he would travel; lose himself in India, China, the South Seas...Radiance from the most battered vehicle and the meanest pedestrian. Gladness flooded him. He was free.

A year, thick with various adventures, had slid by since that spring day on which he had wrenched himself free. He had lived, been happy, and with no woman in his life. The break had been simple: a telegram hinting at prolonged business and indefinite return. There had been no reply. This had annoyed him, but he told himself it was what he had expected. He would not admit that, perhaps, he had missed her letter in his wanderings. He had persuaded himself to believe what he wanted to believe—that she had not cared. Actually, there had been confusion in his mind, a complex of thoughts which made it difficult to know what he really had thought. He had imagined that he shuddered at the idea that she had accepted the most generous offer. He pitied her. There was, too, a touch of sadness, a sense of something lost, which he irritably explained on the score of her beauty. Beauty of any kind always stirred him....Too bad a woman like that couldn't be decent. He was well rid of her.

But what had she done? How had he taken it? His contemptuous mood visualized her at times, laughing merrily at some jest made by his successor, or again sitting silent, staring into the fire. He would be conscious of every detail of her appearance: her hair simply arranged, her soft dark eyes, her delicate chin propped on hands rivaling the perfection of La Gioconda's.[1] Sometimes there would be a reversion to the emotions which had ensnared him, when he ached with yearning, when he longed for her again. Such moments were rare.

✦ ✦ ✦

Another year passed, during which his life had widened, risen, and then crashed....

Dead? How could she be dead? Dead in childbirth, they had told him, both his mistress and the child she had borne him. She had been dead on that spring day when, resentful and angry at her influence in his life, he had reached out toward freedom— to find only a mirage; for he saw quite plainly that now he would never be free. It was

---

[1] The correct title of Leonardo da Vinci's "Mona Lisa."

she who had escaped him. Each time he had cursed and wondered, it had been a dead woman whom he had cursed and about whom he had wondered....He shivered; he seemed always to be cold now....

Well rid of her! How well he had not known, nor how easily. She was dead. And he had cursed her. But one didn't curse the dead....Didn't one? Damn her! Why couldn't she have lived, or why hadn't she died sooner? For long months he had wondered how she had arranged her life, and all the while she had done nothing but to complete it by dying.

The futility of all his speculations exasperated him. His old resentment returned. She *had* spoiled his life; first by living and then by dying. He hated the fact that she had finished with him, rather than he with her. He could not forgive her....Forgive her? She was dead. He felt somehow that, after all, the dead did not care if you forgave them or not.

Gradually, his mind became puppet to a disturbing tension which drove it back and forth between two thoughts: he had left her; she was dead. These two facts became lodged in his mind like burrs pricking at his breaking faculties. As he recalled the manner of his leaving her, it seemed increasingly brutal. She had died loving him, bearing him a child, and he had left her. He tried to shake off the heavy mental dejection which weighed him down, but his former will and determination deserted him. The vitality of the past, forever dragging him down into black depression, frightened him. The mental fog, thick as soot, into which the news of her death had trapped him, appalled him. He must get himself out. A wild anger seized him. He began to think of his own death, self-inflicted, with feeling that defied analysis. His zest for life became swallowed up in the rising tide of sorrow and mental chaos which was engulfing him.

As autumn approached, with faint notice on his part, his anger and resentment retreated, leaving in their wake a gentle stir of regret and remorse. Imperceptibly, he grew physically weary; a strange sensation of loneliness and isolation enveloped him. A species of timidity came upon him; he felt an unhappy remoteness from people, and began to edge away from life.

His deepening sense of isolation drove him more and more back upon his memories. Sunk in his armchair before the fire, he passed the days and sometimes the nights, for he had lost count of these, merged as they were into one another.

His increasing mental haziness had rejected the fact of her death; often she was there with him, just beyond the firelight or the candlelight. She talked and laughed with him. Sometimes, at night, he woke to see her standing over him or sitting in his chair before the dying fire. By some mysterious process, the glory of first love flamed again in him. He forgot that they had ever parted. His twisted memories visioned her with him in places where she had never been. He had forgotten all but the past, and that was brightly distorted.

He sat waiting for her. He seemed to remember that she had promised to come. Outside, the street was quiet. She was late. Why didn't she come? Childish tears fell over his cold cheeks. He sat weeping in front of the sinking fire.

A nameless dread seized him; she would not come! In the agony of his disappointment, he did not see that the fire had died and the candles had sputtered out. He sat wrapped in immeasurable sadness. He knew that she would not come.

Something in this thought fired his disintegrating brain. She would not come; then he must go to her.

He rose, shaking with cold, and groped toward the door. Yes, he would go to her.

The gleam of a streetlight through a French window caught his attention. He stumbled toward it. His cold fingers fumbled a moment with the catch, but he tore it open with a spark of his old determination and power, and stepped out—and down to the pavement a hundred feet below.

—1926

DJUNA BARNES (1892-1982)

Poet, playwright, fiction writer, journalist, and artist Djuna Barnes was born on June 12, 1892, in Cornwall-on-Hudson, New York. Barnes experienced a childhood marked by two extremes: a feminist paternal grandmother (Zadel Barnes Gustafson) and an eccentric father (Wald Barnes), who homeschooled her while raising two families under one roof (one with Djuna Barnes' mother, Elizabeth Chappell, and one with his mistress, Fanny Faulkner). After a brief marriage to Faulkner's brother, Barnes moved to New York City with her mother and siblings after her parents separated. There she launched her writing career, before moving to Paris in 1921, where she became part of the circle of women who frequented Natalie Barney's lesbian literary salon, about which she wrote with satire and affection in *Ladies Almanack* (1928). Barnes was a key figure in the avant garde expatriate movement of the 1920s and 1930s. She knew, interviewed, and wrote about famous artists and writers of the period as a Paris correspondent for *McCalls* magazine. Her literary work often focused on sexuality, violence, and the grotesque, using language ranging from Medieval and Restoration English to modern and pre-postmodern rhythms, structure, and wit. Like Dorothy Parker, she was awarded an O. Henry Prize for one of her stories, "A Night Among the Horses," in 1918. *Nightwood* (1936), a novel inspired by her love affair with Thelma Woods and her most famous work, is firmly established in the canons of lesbian and modernist literature. Barnes returned to the U.S. in 1940, settling in Greenwich Village. Her surrealist play *The Antiphon* was published in 1958, and she wrote sporadically after that, dying on June 18, 1982, at the age of ninety.

A Night Among the Horses

Toward dusk, in the summer of the year, a man in evening dress, carrying a top hat and a cane, crept on hands and knees through the underbrush bordering the pastures of the Buckler estate. His wrists hurt him from holding his weight and he sat down. Sticky ground-vines fanned out all about him; they climbed the trees, the posts of the fence, they were everywhere. He peered through the thickly tangled branches and saw, standing against the darkness, a grove of white birch shimmering like teeth in a skull.

He could hear the gate grating on its hinge as the wind clapped. His heart moved with the movement of the earth. A frog puffed forth its croaking immemoried cry; the man struggled for breath, the air was heavy and hot; he was nested in astonishment.

He wanted to drowse off; instead he placed his hat and cane beside him, straightening his coat tails, lying out on his back, waiting. Something quick was moving the ground. It began to shake with sudden warning and he wondered if it was his heart.

A lamp in the far away window winked as the boughs swung against the wind; the odor of crushed grasses mingling with the faint reassuring smell of dung, fanned up and drawled off to the north; he opened his mouth, drawing in the ends of his moustache.

The tremor lengthened, it ran beneath his body and tumbled away into the earth.

He sat upright. Putting on his hat, he braced his cane against the ground between his out-thrust legs. Now he not only felt the trembling of the earth but caught the muffled horny sound of hooves smacking the turf, as a friend strikes the back of a friend, hard, but without malice. They were on the near side now as they took the curve of the Willow road. He pressed his forehead against the bars of the fence.

The soft menacing sound deepened as heat deepens; the horses, head-on, roared by him, their legs rising and falling like savage needles taking purposeless stitches.

He saw their bellies pitching from side to side, racking the bars of the fence as they swung past. On his side of the barrier he rose up running, following, gasping. His foot caught in the trailing pine and he pitched forward, striking his head on a stump as he went down. Blood trickled from his scalp. Like a red mane it ran into his eyes and he stroked it back with the knuckles of his hand, as he put on his hat. In this position the pounding hoofs shook him like a child on a knee.

Presently he searched for his cane; he found it snared in the fern. A wax Patrick-pipe brushed against his cheek, he ran his tongue over it, snapping it in two. Move as he would, the grass was always under him, crackling with twigs and cones. An acorn fell out of the soft dropping powders of the wood. He took it up, and as he held it between finger and thumb, his mind raced over the scene back there with the mistress of the house, for what else could one call Freda Buckler but "the mistress of the house," that small fiery woman, with a battery for a heart and the body of a toy, who ran everything, who purred, saturated with impudence, with a mechanical buzz that ticked away her humanity.

He blew down his moustache. Freda, with that aggravating floating yellow veil! He told her it was "aggravating," he told her that it was "shameless," and stood for nothing but temptation. He puffed out his cheeks, blowing at her as she passed. She laughed, stroking his arm, throwing her head back, her nostrils scarlet to the pit. They had ended by riding out together, a boot's length apart, she no bigger than a bee on a bonnet. In complete misery he had dug down on his spurs, and she: "Gently, John, gently!" showing the edges of her teeth in the wide distilling mouth. "You can't be ostler *all* your life. Horses!" she snorted. "I like horses, but—" He had lowered his crop. "There are other things. You simply can't go on being a groom forever, not with a waist like that, and you know it. I'll make a gentleman out of you. I'll step you up from being a 'thing.' You will see, you will enjoy it."

He had leaned over and lashed at her boot with his whip. It caught her at the knee, the foot flew up in its stirrup, as though she were dancing.

And the little beast was delighted! They trotted on a way, and they trotted back. He helped her to dismount, and she sailed off, trailing the yellow veil, crying back:

"You'll love it!"

Before they had gone on like this for more than a month (bowling each other over in the spirit, wringing each other this way and that, hunter and hunted) it had become a game without any pleasure; debased lady, debased ostler, on the wings of vertigo.

What was she getting him into? He shouted, bawled, cracked whip—what did she figure she wanted? The kind of woman who can't tell the truth; truth ran out and away from her as though her veins wore pipettes, stuck in by the devil; and drinking, he swelled, and pride had him, it floated him off. He saw her standing behind him in every mirror, she followed him from show-piece to show-piece, she fell in beside him, walked him, hand under elbow.

"You will rise to governor-general—well, to inspector—"

"Inspector!"

"As you like, say master of the regiment—say cavalry officer. Horses, too, leather, whips—"

"O my God."

She almost whinnied as she circled on her heels:

"With a broad, flat, noble chest," she said, "you'll become a pavement of honors…Mass yourself. You will leave affliction—"

"Stop it!" he shouted. "I *like* being common."

"With a quick waist like that, the horns will miss you."

"What horns?"

"The dilemma."

"I *could* stop you, all over, if I wanted to."

She was amused. "Man in a corner?" she said.

She tormented him, she knew it. She tormented him with her objects of "culture." One knee on an ottoman, she would hold up and out, the most delicate miniature, ivories cupped in her palm, tilting them from the sun, saying: "But look, look!"

He put his hands behind his back. She aborted that. She asked him to hold ancient missals, volumes of fairy tales, all with handsome tooling, all bound in corded russet. She spread maps, and with a long hatpin dragging across mountains and ditches, pointed to "just where she had been." Like a dry snail the point wandered the coast, when abruptly, sticking the steel in, she cried *"Borgia!"*[1] and stood there, jangling a circle of ancient keys.

His anxiety increased with curiosity. *If* he married her—after he *had* married her, what then? Where would he be after he had satisfied her crazy whim? What would she make of him in the end; in short, what would she leave of him? Nothing, absolutely nothing, not even his horses. Here'd be a damned fool for you. He wouldn't fit in anywhere after Freda, he'd be neither what he was nor what he had been; he'd be a *thing*, half standing, half crouching, like those figures under the roofs of historic buildings, the halt position of the damned.

He had looked at her often without seeing her; after a while he began to look at her with great attention. Well, well! Really a small mousy woman, with fair pretty hair that fell like an insect's feelers into the nape of her neck, moving when the wind moved. She darted and bobbled about too much, and always with the mindless intensity of a mechanical toy kicking and raking about the floor.

And she was always a step or two ahead of him, or stroking his arm at arm's length, or she came at him in a gust, leaning her sharp little chin on his shoulder, floating away slowly—only to be stumbled over when he turned. On this particular day he had caught her by the wrist, slewing her around. This once, he thought to himself, this once I'll ask her straight out for truth; a direct shot might dislodge her.

"Miss Freda, just a moment. You know I haven't a friend in the world. You know positively that I haven't a person to whom I can go and get an answer to any question

---

[1] A town (also spelled Borja) in Italy; also, a family associated with ruthless papal leadership during the Italian Renaissance.

of any sort. So then, just what *do* you want me for?"

She blushed to the roots of her hair. "Girlish! are you going to be girlish?" She looked as if she were going to scream, her whole frame buzzed, but she controlled herself and drawled with lavish calm:

"Don't be nervous. Be patient. You will get used to everything. You'll even like it. There's nothing so enjoyable as climbing."

"And then?"

"Then everything will slide away, stable and all." She caught the wings of her nose in the pinching folds of a lace handkerchief. "Isn't that a destination?"

The worst of all had been the last night, the evening of the masked ball. She had insisted on his presence. "Come" she said, "just as you are, and be our whipperin."[2] That was the final blow, the unpardonable insult. He had obeyed, except that he did not come "just as he was." He made an elaborate toilet; he dressed for evening, like any ordinary gentleman; he was the only person present therefore who was not "in dress," that is, in the accepted sense.

On arrival he found most of the guests tipsy. Before long he himself was more than a little drunk and horrified to find that he was dancing a minuet, stately, slow, with a great soft puff-paste of a woman, showered with sequins, grunting in cascades of plaited tulle. Out of this embrace he extricated himself, slipping on the bare spots of the rosin-powdered floor, to find Freda coming at him with a tiny glass of cordial which she poured into his open mouth; at that point he was aware that he had been gasping for air.

He came to a sudden stop. He took in the whole room with his frantic glance. There in the corner sat Freda's mother with her cats. She always sat in corners and she always sat with cats. And there was the rest of the cast—cousins, nephews, uncles, aunts. The next moment, the *galliard*.[3] Freda, arms up, hands, palm out, elbows buckled in at the breast, a praying mantis, was all but tooth to tooth with him. Wait! He stepped free, and with the knob end of his cane, he drew a circle in the rosin clear around her, then backward went through the French windows.

He knew nothing after that until he found himself in the shrubbery, sighing, his face close to the fence, peering in. He was with his horses again; he was where he belonged again. He could hear them tearing up the sod, galloping about as though in their own ballroom, and oddest of all, at this dark time of the night.

He began drawing himself under the lowest bar, throwing his hat and cane in before him, panting as he crawled. The black stallion was now in the lead. The horses were taking the curve in the Willow road that ran into the farther pasture, and through the dust they looked faint and enormous.

On the top of the hill, four had drawn apart and were standing, testing the weather. He would catch one, mount one, he would escape! He was no longer afraid. He stood up, waving his hat and cane and shouting.

They did not seem to know him and they swerved past him and away. He stared after them, almost crying. He did not think of his dress, the white shirt front, the top hat, the waving stick, his abrupt rising out of the dark, their excitement. Surely they must know him—in a moment.

---

[2] A British term referring to the huntsman's assistant responsible for keeping the hounds in a pack.

[3] A quick French dance.

Wheeling, manes up, nostrils flaring, blasting out steam as they came on, they passed him in a whinnying flood, and he damned them in horror, but what he shouted was "Bitch!," and found himself swallowing fire from his heart, lying on his face, sobbing, "I *can* do it, damn everything, I can get on with it; I can make my mark!"

The upraised hooves of the first horse missed him, the second did not.

Presently the horses drew apart, nibbling and swishing their tails, avoiding a patch of tall grass.

—1923

EDNA ST. VINCENT MILLAY (1892-1950)

Known initially for her bohemian lifestyle and later for her elegant readings in floor-length, flowing gowns, Edna St. Vincent Millay was an immensely popular poet during the first half of her lifetime. She was born in Rockland, Maine, on February 22, 1892, to Cora and Henry Tolman Millay, who divorced when Millay and her two sisters were very young. Her mother, a frustrated musician turned nurse, struggled to support the family without help from Henry, often leaving the girls home alone. She encouraged them, however, to be strong and creative, and at her urging, Millay submitted her poem "Renascence" to a poetry contest in 1912, where it garnered fourth place and publication in *The Lyric Year*. The poem was a sensation and launched her career.

Millay had virtually no formal education until her twenties, when she attended Barnard, and then Vassar College. There she wrote and performed in plays, took male and female lovers, and developed as a poet. By the time she graduated in 1917, her reputation as a poet was established with the publication of *Renascence and Other Poems* (1917). She moved to Greenwich Village, became involved with the Provincetown Players, wrote satires for magazines such as *Vanity Fair* under the pseudonym Nancy Boyd, and continued to write and publish poetry. Her fourth volume, *The Harp-Weaver and Other Poems* won the Pulitzer Prize in 1923, the same year she married Eugene Boissevain, who devoted himself to her caretaking— Millay was plagued by health issues as well as drug and alcohol excess—and career. They eventually settled at Steeplechase, their farm near Austerlitz, New York. The two practiced an open marriage, and remained together until Boissevain's death in 1949. Millay specialized in the love sonnet and formal verse, but turned her pen toward political verse in the 1930s and 1940s. She died alone in 1950 of heart failure, after publishing ten original volumes of poetry, several collected editions, and more than a half dozen plays.

xli

I, being born a woman and distressed
By all the needs and notions of my kind,
Am urged by your propinquity to find
Your person fair, and feel a certain zest
To bear your body's weight upon my breast: 5
So subtly is the fume of life designed,
To clarify the pulse and cloud the mind,
And leave me once again undone, possessed.
Think not for this, however, the poor treason

Of my stout blood against my staggering brain,   10
I shall remember you with love, or season
My scorn with pity,—let me make it plain:
I find this frenzy insufficient reason
For conversation when we meet again.

—1923

xlii

What lips my lips have kissed, and where, and why,
I have forgotten, and what arms have lain
Under my head till morning; but the rain
Is full of ghosts tonight, that tap and sigh
Upon the glass and listen for reply,   5
And in my heart there stirs a quiet pain
For unremembered lads that not again
Will turn to me at midnight with a cry.
Thus in the winter stands the lonely tree,
Nor knows what birds have vanished one by one,   10
Yet knows its boughs more silent than before:
I cannot say what loves have come and gone,
I only know that summer sang in me
A little while, that in me sings no more.

—1928

Dirge without Music

I am not resigned to the shutting away of loving hearts in the hard ground.
So it is, and so it will be, for so it has been, time out of mind:
Into the darkness they go, the wise and the lovely. Crowned
With lilies and with laurel they go; but I am not resigned.

Lovers and thinkers, into the earth with you.   5
Be one with the dull, the indiscriminate dust.
A fragment of what you felt, of what you knew,
A formula, a phrase remains,—but the best is lost.

The answers quick and keen, the honest look, the laughters, the love,—
They are gone. They are gone to feed the roses. Elegant and curled   10
Is the blossom. Fragant is the blossom. I know. But I do not approve.
More precious was the light in your eyes than all the roses in the world.

Down, down, down into the darkness of the grave
Gently they go, the beautiful, the tender, the kind;
Quietly they go, the intelligent, the witty, the brave.   15
I know. But I do not approve. And I am not resigned.

—1928

xxvi

Women have loved before as I love now;
At least, in lively chronicles of the past—
Of Irish waters by a Cornish prow
Or Trojan waters by a Spartan mast
Much to their cost invaded—here and there,   5
Hunting the amorous line, skimming the rest,
I find some woman bearing as I bear
Love like a burning city in the breast.
I think however that of all alive
I only in such utter, ancient way   10
Do suffer love; in me alone survive
The unregenerate passions of a day
When treacherous queens, with death upon the tread,
Heedless and wilful, took their knights to bed.

—1931

Apostrophe to Man
(on reflecting that the world is ready to go to war again)

Detestable race, continue to expunge yourself, die out.
Breed faster, crowd, encroach, sing hymns, build bombing airplanes;
Make speeches, unveil statutes, issue bonds, parade;
Convert again into explosives the bewildered ammonia and the
    distracted cellulose;
Convert again into putrescent matter drawing flies   5
The hopeful bodies of the young; exhort,
Pray, pull long faces, be earnest, be all but overcome, be photographed;
Confer, perfect your formulae, commercialize
Bacteria harmful to human tissue,
Put death on the market;   10
Breed, crowd, encroach, expand, expunge yourself, die out,
Homo called *sapiens.*[1]

—1934

cxxviii

I too beneath your moon, almighty Sex,
Go forth at nightfall crying like a cat,
Leaving the lofty tower I laboured at
For birds to foul and boys and girls to vex
With tittering chalk; and you, and the long necks   5
Of neighbours sitting where their mothers sat
Are well aware of shadowy this and that
In me, that's neither noble nor complex.

[1] (Lat.) Wise or knowing man; species name for modern humans.

Such as I am, however, I have brought
To what it is, this tower; it is my own;   10
Though it was reared To Beauty, it was wrought
From what I had to build with: honest bone
Is there, and anguish; pride; and burning thought;
And lust is there, and nights not spent alone.

—1939

An Ancient Gesture

I thought, as I wiped my eyes on the corner of my apron:
Penelope[2] did this too.
And more than once: you can't keep weaving all day
And undoing it all through the night;
Your arms get tired, and the back of your neck gets tight;   5
And along towards morning, when you think it will never be light,
And your husband has been gone, and you don't know where, for years,
Suddenly you burst into tears;
There is simply nothing else to do.

And I thought, as I wiped my eyes on the corner of my apron: 10
This is an ancient gesture, authentic, antique,
In the very best tradition, classic, Greek;
Ulysses did this too.
But only as a gesture,—a gesture which implied
To the assembled throng that he was much too moved to speak.   15
He learned it from Penelope...
Penelope, who really cried.

—1954

---

[2] The wife of Odysseus who, while waiting for her husband to return from the Trojan War, postponed marriage proposals by promising to consider them once she finished weaving a tapestry, which she would unravel every night.

BESSIE SMITH (CA. 1892-1937)

Bessie Smith was born to a large, impoverished family in Chattanooga, Tennessee. She began
performing as a street musician to help support her older sister Viola, who was trying to raise
the family after the death of Smith's mother. In 1912, Smith joined her brother Clarence as a
member of Moses Stokes' traveling minstrel show; she was a dancer, however, because Ma
Rainey had a firm hold on the position of singer for the group. After three years with the
Stokes outfit, Smith left to go on the Theater Owners Booking Association (T.O.B.A.) circuit;
she quickly developed a following and became T.O.B.A.'s biggest hit in the 1920s. In 1923
Columbia Records signed Smith for a series of recordings in their "race records" line. Her first
record for Columbia, in which she was accompanied by pianist Clarence Williams, sold over
750,000 copies and established her as the most successful blues singer—and the highest-paid
black entertainer—of her day. Her fame brought her the opportunity to perform alongside

some of the greatest jazz and blues performers of the 1920s, including Louis Armstrong, Charlie Green, and Fletcher Henderson. Smith's raw, direct style had enormous appeal for black and white listeners alike, her lyrics and delivery expressing the anger, passion, and frustration of black experience. The Depression signaled the end of Smith's recording contract with Columbia, and the advent of "talkies" (motion pictures with sound) effectively killed vaudeville. But Smith continued to perform live shows in front of thousands. She transformed her style, and was experimenting with Swing music at the time of her death in an automobile accident in 1937.

Back-Water Blues

When it rained five days, and the skies turned dark as night,
When it rained five days, and the skies turned dark as night,
Then trouble taking place in the lowlands at night.

I woke up this morning, can't even get out of my door.
I woke up this morning, can't even get out of my door.   5
That's enough trouble to make a poor girl wonder where she want to go.

Then they rowed a little boat about five miles 'cross the pond.
Then they rowed a little boat about five miles 'cross the pond.
I packed all my clothes, throwed 'em in, and they rowed me along.

When it thunders and lightning, and the wind begins to blow,   10
When it thunders and lightning, and the wind begins to blow,
There's thousands of people ain't got no place to go.

Then I went and stood upon some high old lonesome hill.
Then I went and stood upon some high old lonesome hill.
Then I looked down on the house where I used to live.   15

Back-water blues done caused me to pack up my things and go,
Back-water blues done caused me to pack up my things and go,
'Cause my house fell down, and I can't live there no more.

Mmmm, I can't move no more.
Mmmm, I can't move no more.   20
There ain't no place for a poor old girl to go.

—1927

Please Help Me Get Him Off My Mind

I've cried and worried, all night I've laid and groaned
I've cried and worried, all night I've laid and groaned
I used to weigh two hundred, now I'm down to skin and bones

It's all about a man who always kicked and dogged me 'round
It's all about a man who always kicked and dogged me 'round   5
And when I try to kill him that's when my love for him comes down

I've come to see you, gypsy, beggin' on my bended knees
I've come to see you, gypsy, beggin' on my bended knees

That man put something on me, oh, take it off of me, please

It starts at my forehead and goes clean down to my toes   10
It starts at my forehead and goes clean down to my toes
Oh, how I'm sufferin', gypsy, nobody but the good Lord knows

Gypsy, don't hurt him, fix him for me one more time
Oh, don't hurt him, gypsy, fix him for me one more time
Just make him love me, but please, ma'am, take him off my mind.

—1928

Poor Man's Blues

Mister rich man, rich man, open up your heart and mind
Mister rich man, rich man, open up your heart and mind
Give the poor man a chance, help stop these hard, hard times

While you're livin' in your mansion, you don't know what hard
    times means
While you're livin' in your mansion, you don't know what hard
    times means   5
Poor working man's wife is starvin', your wife's livin' like a queen

Please, listen to my pleading, 'cause I can't stand these hard times long
Oh, listen to my pleading, can't stand these hard times long
They'll make an honest man do things that you know is wrong

Poor man fought all the battles, poor man would fight again today   10
Poor man fought all the battles, poor man would fight again today
He would do anything you ask him in the name of the U.S.A.

Now the war is over, poor man must live the same as you
Now the war is over, poor man must live the same as you
If it wasn't for the poor man, mister rich man, what would you do?

—1928

DOROTHY PARKER (1893-1967)

Dorothy Rothschild was born two months prematurely on August 22, 1893, to Jacob Henry Rothschild and Annie Eliza Rothschild, who died four years later. Two years after that her father married Eleanor Frances Lewis, to whom Parker was never close. Penniless after her father died in 1913, Parker wrote poetry and prose to support herself, and became one of the key figures of the Algonquin Round Table, a group of mostly male writers and performers who met daily for lunch at the Algonquin Hotel in Manhattan. She published poetry, fiction, plays, and reviews in a variety of magazines as well as in book form, becoming one of the most quotable women in New York. Her story "Big Blonde" won the O. Henry Prize for best short story in 1929.

Parker's work often turns a caustic eye toward social custom and relationships between the sexes, and examines racism, class politics, and the effects of war. Like Edna St. Vincent

Millay, Susan Glaspell, and Lola Ridge, Parker was arrested for protesting against the execution of Nicola Sacco and Bartolomeo Vanzetti, two anarchists found guilty of murder in a trial characterized by questionable procedures. After moving to Hollywood in the 1930s, where she wrote or contributed to scripts for thirty-nine films, she helped create the Screen Writers Guild, raised money for Loyalist Spain and the Scottsboro defendants, wrote about the Spanish Civil War for *New Masses,* and participated in other anti-fascist, pro-communist work. As a result, the FBI kept a file on her, and when she sought to be a World War II correspondent, she was denied a passport. Parker suffered from alcoholism, two unsuccessful marriages (to Edwin Pond Parker and Alan Campbell, twice), several disastrous love affairs, abortions, and suicide attempts, but she outlived many of her contemporaries, dying in 1967 from a heart attack.

The Far-Sighted Muse

Dark though the clouds, they are silver-lined;
    (This is the stuff that they like to read.)
If Winter comes, Spring is right behind;
    (This is the stuff that the people need.)
Smile, and the World will smile back at you;   5
    Aim with a grin, and you cannot miss;
Laugh off your woes, and you won't feel blue.
    (Poetry pays when it's done like this.)

Whatever it is, is completely sweet;
    (This is the stuff that will bring in gold.)   10
Just to be living's a perfect treat;
    (This is the stuff that will knock them cold.)
How could we, any of us, be sad?
    Always our blessings outweighing our ills;
Always there's something to make us glad.   15
    (This is the way you can pay your bills.)

Everything's great, in this good old world;
    (This is the stuff they can always use.)
God's in His heaven, the hill's dew-pearled;
    (This will provide for the baby's shoes.)   20
Hunger and War, do not mean a thing;
    Everything's rosy, where'er we roam;
Hark, how the little birds gaily sing!
    (This is what fetches the bacon home.)

—1922

Résumé

Razors pain you;
Rivers are damp;
Acids stain you;
And drugs cause cramp.
Guns aren't lawful;   5
Nooses give;

Gas smells awful;
You might as well live.

—1926

Penelope[1]

In the pathway of the sun,
In the footsteps of the breeze,
Where the world and sky are one,
 He shall ride the silver seas,
  He shall cut the glittering wave.   5
I shall sit at home, and rock;
Rise, to heed a neighbor's knock;
Brew my tea, and snip my thread;
Bleach the linen for my bed.
  They will call him brave.

—1928

The Waltz

Why, thank you so much. I'd adore to.

I don't want to dance with him. I don't want to dance with anybody. And even if I did, it wouldn't be him. He'd be well down among the last ten. I've seen the way he dances; it looks like something you do on Saint Walpurgis Night.[2] Just think, not a quarter of an hour ago, here I was sitting, feeling so sorry for the poor girl he was dancing with. And now *I'm* going to be the poor girl. Well, well. Isn't it a small world?

And a peach of a world, too. A true little corker. Its events are so fascinatingly unpredictable, are not they? Here I was, minding my own business, not doing a stitch of harm to any living soul. And then he comes into my life, all smiles and city manners, to sue me for the favor of one memorable mazurka. Why, he scarcely knows my name, let alone what it stands for. It stands for Despair, Bewilderment, Futility, Degradation, and Premeditated Murder, but little does he wot. I don't wot his name, either; I haven't any idea what it is. Jukes, would be my guess from the look in his eyes. How do you do, Mr. Jukes? And how is that dear little brother of yours, with the two heads?

Ah, now why did he have to come around me, with his low requests? Why can't he let me lead my own life? I ask so little—just to be left alone in my quiet corner of the table, to do my evening brooding over all my sorrows. And he must come, with his bows and his scrapes and his may-I-have-this-ones. And I had to go and tell him that I'd adore to dance with him. I cannot understand why I wasn't struck right down dead. Yes, and being struck dead would look like a day in the country, compared to struggling out a dance with this boy. But what could I do? Everyone else at the table had got up to dance, except him and me. There was I, trapped. Trapped like a trap in a trap.

---

[1] In Homer's epic *The Odyssey,* Penelope was the wife of Odysseus, who waited for his return from the Trojan War. She is associated with patience, loyalty, weaving, and cleverness.

[2] Saint Walpurgis (ca. 710-779), also known as Walpurga or Walburga, was an English missionary in Germany. The Germanic pagan festival *Walpurgisnacht* became associated with her.

What can you say, when a man asks you to dance with him? I most certainly will *not* dance with you, I'll see you in hell first. Why, thank you, I'd like to awfully, but I'm having labor pains. Oh, yes, *do* let's dance together—it's so nice to meet a man who isn't a scaredy-cat about catching my beri-beri. No. There was nothing for me to do, but say I'd adore to. Well, we might as well get it over with. All right, Cannonball, let's run out on the field. You won the toss; you can lead.

Why, I think it's more of a waltz, really. Isn't it? We might just listen to the music a second. Shall we? Oh, yes, it's a waltz. Mind? Why, I'm simply thrilled. I'd love to waltz with you.

I'd love to waltz with you. I'd love to waltz with you. I'd love to have my tonsils out, I'd love to be in a midnight fire at sea. Well, it's too late now. We're getting under way. *Oh.* Oh, dear. Oh, dear, dear, dear. Oh, this is even worse than I thought it would be. I suppose that's the one dependable law of life—everything is always worse than you thought it was going to be. Oh, if I had any real grasp of what this dance would be like, I'd have held out for sitting it out. Well, it will probably amount to the same thing in the end. We'll be sitting it out on the floor in a minute, if he keeps this up.

I'm so glad I brought it to his attention that this is a waltz they're playing. Heaven knows what might have happened, if he had thought it was something fast; we'd have blown the sides right out of the building. Why does he always want to be somewhere that he isn't? Why can't we stay in one place just long enough to get acclimated? It's this constant rush, rush, rush, that's the curse of American life. That's the reason that we're all of us so—*Ow!* For God's sake, don't *kick,* you idiot; this is only second down. Oh, my shin. My poor, poor shin, that I've had ever since I was a little girl!

Oh, no, no, no. Goodness, no. It didn't hurt the least little bit. And anyway it was my fault. Really it was. Truly. Well, you're just being sweet, to say that. It really was all my fault.

I wonder what I'd better do—kill him this instant, with my naked hands, or wait and let him drop in his traces. Maybe it's best not to make a scene. I guess I'll just lie low, and watch the pace get him. He can't keep this up indefinitely—he's only flesh and blood. Die he must and die he shall, for what he did to me. I don't want to be of the over-sensitive type, but you can't tell me that kick was unpremeditated. Freud[3] says there are no accidents. I've led no cloistered life, I've known dancing partners who have spoiled my slippers and torn my dress; but when it comes to kicking, I am Outraged Womanhood. When you kick me in the shin, *smile.*

Maybe he didn't do it maliciously. Maybe it's just his way of showing his high spirits. I suppose I ought to be glad that one of us is having such a good time. I suppose I ought to think myself lucky if he brings me back alive. Maybe it's captious to demand of a practically strange man that he leave your shins as he found them. After all, the poor boy's doing the best he can. Probably he grew up in the hill country, and never had no larnin'. I bet they had to throw him on his back to get shoes on him.

Yes, it's lovely, isn't it? It's simply lovely. It's the loveliest waltz. Isn't it? Oh, I think it's lovely, too.

Why, I'm getting positively drawn to the Triple Threat here. He's my hero. He has the heart of a lion, and the sinews of a buffalo. Look at him—never a thought of the consequences, never afraid of his face, hurling himself into every scrimmage, eyes shining, cheeks ablaze. And shall it be said that I hung back? No, a thousand times no. What's it to me if I have to spend the next couple of years in a plaster cast? Come on,

[3] Sigmund Freud (1836-1939), Austrian founder of psychoanalysis.

Butch, right through them! Who wants to live forever?

Oh. Oh, dear. Oh, he's all right, thank goodness. For a while I thought they'd have to carry him off the field. Ah, I couldn't bear to have anything happen to him. I love him. I love him better than anybody in the world. Look at the spirit he gets into a dreary, commonplace waltz; how effete the other dancers seem, beside him. He is youth and vigor and courage, he is strength and gaiety and—*Ow!* Get off my instep, you hulking peasant! What do you think I am, anyway—a gangplank? *Ow!*

No, of course it didn't hurt. Why, it didn't a bit. Honestly. And it was all my fault. You see, that little step of yours—well, it's perfectly lovely, but it's just a tiny bit tricky to follow at first. Oh, did you work it up yourself? You really did? Well, aren't you amazing! Oh, now I think I've got it. Oh, I think it's lovely. I was watching you do it when you were dancing before. It's awfully effective when you look at it.

It's awfully effective when you look at it. I bet I'm awfully effective when you look at me. My hair is hanging along my cheeks, my skirt is swaddled about me, I can feel the cold damp of my brow. I must look like something out of "The Fall of the House of Usher."[4] This sort of thing takes a fearful toll of a woman my age. And he worked up his little step himself, he with his degenerate cunning. And it was just a tiny bit tricky at first, but now I think I've got it. Two stumbles, slip, and a twenty-yard dash; yes. I've got it. I've got several other things, too, including a split shin and a bitter heart. I hate this creature I'm chained to. I hated him the moment I saw his leering, bestial face. And here I've been locked in his noxious embrace for the thirty-five years this waltz has lasted. Is that orchestra never going to stop playing? Or must this obscene travesty of a dance go on until hell burns out?

Oh, they're going to play another encore. Oh, goody. Oh, that's lovely. Tired? I should say I'm not tired. I'd like to go on like this forever.

I should say I'm not tired. I'm dead, that's all I am. Dead, and in what a cause! And the music is never going to stop playing, and we're going on like this, Double-Time Charlie and I, throughout eternity. I suppose I won't care any more, after the first hundred thousand years. I suppose nothing will matter then, not heat nor pain nor broken heart nor cruel, aching weariness. Well. It can't come too soon for me.

I wonder why I didn't tell him I was tired. I wonder why I didn't suggest going back to the table. I could have said let's just listen to the music. Yes, and if he would, that would be the first bit of attention he has given it all evening. George Jean Nathan[5] said that the lovely rhythms of the waltz should be listened to in stillness and not be accompanied by strange gyrations of the human body. I think that's what he said. I think it was George Jean Nathan. Anyhow, whatever he said and whoever he was and whatever he's doing now, he's better off than I am. That's safe. Anybody who isn't waltzing with this Mrs. O'Leary's cow[6] I've got here is having a good time.

Still if we were back at the table, I'd probably have to talk to him. Look at him— what could you say to a thing like that! Did you go to the circus this year, what's your favorite kind of ice cream, how do you spell cat? I guess I'm as well off here. As well off as if I were in a cement mixer in full action.

I'm past all feeling now. The only way I can tell when he steps on me is that I can

---

[4] An 1839 short story by U.S. writer Edgar Allen Poe (1809-1849).

[5] George Jean Nathan (1882-1958), U.S. drama critic and editor.

[6] According to folklore, Mrs. O'Leary's cow kicked over a lantern and started the Great Chicago Fire of October 8-10, 1871, which destroyed a portion of the city.

hear the splintering of bones. And all the events of my life are passing before my eyes. There was the time I was in a hurricane in the West Indies, there was the day I got my head cut open in the taxi smash, there was the night the drunken lady threw a bronze ash-tray at her own true love and got me instead, there was that summer that the sailboat kept capsizing. Ah, what an easy, peaceful time was mine, until I fell in with Swifty, here. I didn't know what trouble was, before I got drawn into this *danse macabre.*[7] I think my mind is beginning to wander. It almost seems to me as if the orchestra were stopping. It couldn't be, of course; it could never, never be. And yet in my ears there is a silence like the sound of angel voices....

Oh, they've stopped, the mean things. They're not going to play any more. Oh, darn. Oh, do you think they would? Do you really think so, if you gave them fifty dollars? Oh, that would be lovely. And look, do tell them to play this same thing. I'd simply adore to go on waltzing.

—1933

[7] (Fr.) Dance of death.

GENEVIEVE TAGGARD (1894-1948)

Genevieve Taggard was born in Waitsburg, Washington, and moved two years later with her family to Hawaii, where her parents ran a missionary school that they had established. She remained there off and on until 1914, when she entered the University of California at Berkeley. Taggard helped her mother run a boarding house while in school; during that time she also developed her poetic talents (with the encouragement of Witter Bynner) and embraced socialism, along with Josephine Herbst and other Bay Area artists and radicals. After graduating in 1919, Taggard moved to New York. There, she circulated among Greenwich Village bohemians and her socialist ideals flourished. Her poems appeared in radical journals such as *The Masses, The Liberator,* and *The Nation,* and in 1921 she founded *Measure: A Magazine of Verse* with Padraic Colum and Maxwell Anderson. Her first volume of poetry, *For Eager Lovers,* was published in 1922, and she later edited two anthologies, *May Days: An Anthology of Verse from Masses-Liberator* (1925) and *Circumference, Varieties of Metaphysical Verse, 1456-1928* (1929), inspired in part by Emily Dickinson. Taggard also wrote a biography, *The Life and Mind of Emily Dickinson* (1930, 1934). Nine more volumes of poetry embracing domestic, racial, class, gender, and metaphysical themes, as well as two volumes of her collected verse, were published over the course of her life. Taggard married poet and novelist Robert Wolf in 1921 and gave birth to a daughter the following year. After a period in California, they returned to New York, where Wolf was committed to a mental institution and the couple divorced. Taggard married journalist Kenneth Durant in 1935, bought a farm in Vermont, and taught at Bennington, Mount Holyoke, and Sarah Lawrence. Her work throughout the 1930s and 1940s explored proletarian and feminist issues, and she became a contributing editor to *The New Masses* while devoting time to a number of leftist causes. She died in 1948 of complications from high blood pressure.

With Child

Now I am slow and placid, fond of sun,
Like a sleek beast, or a worn one,
No slim and languid girl—not glad

With the windy trip I once had,
But velvet-footed, musing of my own,   5
Torpid, mellow, stupid as a stone.

You cleft me with your beauty's pulse, and now
Your pulse has taken body. Care not how
The old grace goes, how heavy I am grown,
Big with this loneliness, how you alone   10
Ponder our love. Touch my feet and feel
How earth tingles, teeming at my heel!
Earth's urge, not mine,—my little death, not hers;
And the pure beauty yearns and stirs.

It does not heed our ecstacies, it turns   15
With secrets of its own, its own concerns,
Toward a windy world of its own, toward stark
And solitary places. In the dark
Defiant even now; it tugs and moans
To be untangled from these mother's bones.

—1921

Interior

A middle class fortress in which to hide!
Draw down the curtain as if saying *No,*
While noon's ablaze, ablaze outside.
And outside people work and sweat
And the day clangs by and the hard day ends.   5
And after you doze brush out your hair
And walk like a marmoset to and fro
And look in the mirror at middle-age
And sit and regard yourself stare and stare
And hate your life and your tiresome friends   10
And last night's bridge where you went in debt;
While all around you gathers the rage
Of cheated people.
                        Will we hear your fret
In the rising noise of the streets? *Oh no!*

—1936

Demeter[1]

In your dream you met Demeter
Splendid and severe, who said: Endure.
Study the art of seeds,
The nativity of caves.
Dance your gay body to the poise of waves;   5

---

[1] Greek goddess of fertility and grain, and the mother of Persephone.

Die out of the world to bring forth the obscure
Into blisses, into needs.
In all resources
Belong to love. Bless,
Join, fashion the deep forces,   10
Asserting your nature, priceless and feminine.
Peace, daughter. Find your true kin.
                  —then you felt her kiss.

—1946

IDA COX (1896-1967)

A native of Georgia, Ida Prather developed an interest in music through singing in the choir
of the local African Methodist Church. She got her start on the secular stage when she left
home at the age of fourteen to join White and Clark's Black & Tan Minstrels. She went on to
work with other vaudeville acts, including Rabbit Foot Minstrels, which had launched the
careers of blueswomen Bessie Smith and Gertrude "Ma" Rainey. She started out playing "pickaninny" roles (comical young female characters) but eventually became a headliner singing the
blues. Cox's career as a solo performer took off, and she was given a recording contract in
1923 with Paramount, who touted her as "The Uncrowned Queen of the Blues." She was married three times: to trumpeter Adler Cox, who died in World War I; to Eugene Williams, the
father of her daughter, Helen; and to Jesse Crump, who accompanied her on the piano in
some of her recordings and eventually became her musical director. In 1929, Cox and Crump
formed their own traveling revue, *Raisin' Cain,* which was enormously successful; it was the
first act associated with the Theatre Owner's Booking Circuit to open at the Apollo Theater
in New York. Although she managed to keep performing throughout the Depression years,
Cox's career waned with the declining popularity of vaudeville. She left the music business
altogether in 1945, returning for a brief comeback in 1961. She died of cancer in 1967.

Blues Ain't Nothin' But

Rampart Street in New Orleans town,
Don't claim no one for miles around.
For Creoles it's it, I'm melting fast.
That's the best spot in all the land.

(They must have) a cabaret.   5
They play night into day.
I'm blue from my head down to my feet,
for good ole Rampart Street.

I'm first to go down to torment at sunset.
I want to hear that colored jazz band play.   10
The Cadillac, the Red Onion too,
good little boy and the park bench too.
You can enjoy yourself, down on Rampart Street.

I'm going to go down to torment at sunset.
I want to hear that colored jazz band play.   15
The Cadillac, the Red Onion too,
good little boy and the park bench too.
You can enjoy yourself, down on Rampart Street.

—1924

Wild Women Don't Have the Blues

I hear these women raving about their monkey-man,[1]
About their trifling husbands and their no-good friends.
These poor women sit around all day and moan
Wondering why their wandering papa don't come home.
Now when you got a man don't never be on the square,   5
Because if you do he'll have a woman everywhere.
I never was known to treat no one man right,
I keep them working hard both day and night.

I've got a disposition and a way of my own,
When my man starts to kicking I let him find a new home,   10
I get full of good liquor, walk the street all night,
Go home and put my man out if he don't act right.
Wild women don't worry,
Wild women don't have the blues.

You never get nothing by being an angel child,   15
You'd better change your way an' get real wild.
I wanta' tell you something, I wouldn't tell you no lie,
Wild women are the only kind that ever get by.
Wild women don't worry,
Wild women don't have the blues.   20

—1924

How Can I Miss You When I've Got Dead Aim?

Don't let your man know he can make you blue.
'Cause if you do he'll make a fool outta you.
How can you miss him, honey, when you've got dead aim?

When one man won't, another one will.
But don't stop, girls, until you get your fill.   5
How can you miss him, honey, when you've got dead aim?

If your man quits you don't you wear no black.
Find the gal that ditched you for him and fight her back.
How can you miss him, honey, when you've got dead aim?

---

[1] "Monkey-man" is a somewhat ambivalent term, often used to describe a man who is effeminate or easily dominated by women, but also someone who women find sexually attractive.

If you kill my dog, I'm gonna kill your cat.   10
I'm getting even with the world and there's nothing to that.
How can I miss him, honey, when I've got dead aim?

I've got a man in Georgia, a man in Tennessee.
But the Chicago man has put the thing on me.
How can I miss him, honey, when I've got dead aim?   15

The barhand clappers are all the rage,
But good women and good whiskey improve with age.
How can I miss him, honey, when I've got dead aim?

They say the blues is a habit that eats like rust.
Join the blue Monday crowds and play safety first.   20
How can you miss him, honey, when you've got dead aim?

—1925

DAWN POWELL (1896–1965)

Dawn Powell was born in Mt. Gilead, Ohio, the middle daughter of Roy King Powell and Hattie Sherman Powell, who died in 1903. The family was separated and transient until Powell's father, who had a series of jobs (including traveling salesman), remarried in 1907, and they moved to a farmhouse outside of Cleveland. Powell's stepmother was abusive, and Powell and her sisters eventually ran away from home. In 1910, Powell left to live with her aunt, Orpha May Sherman Steinbrueck, in Shelby. Her aunt encouraged her to write and provided her with music lessons. Powell studied on scholarship at Lake Erie College, where she was a mediocre student but stood out in such extracurricular activities as editing the school paper, and writing and acting in plays. After graduating in 1918, Powell moved first to Pomfret, Connecticut, where she worked on a farm and campaigned for woman suffrage, and then to New York. She met and married Joseph Roebuck Gousha in 1920, and gave birth to Joseph Jr., called "Jojo," in 1921. It may be that Jojo was autistic (though the term did not then exist); he suffered violent rages, was alternately diagnosed as "retarded" and "schizophrenic," and was in and out of hospitals and specialized schools for most of his life. In 1947, Powell was hospitalized after he beat her. Although Powell struggled with her son's condition, her husband's alcoholism, and her own depression and illnesses, she nevertheless wrote over a dozen novels, as well as plays, short fiction, and reviews. Her work was largely set either in Midwestern small towns like the ones where she'd grown up or in her beloved Manhattan. When Powell died in 1965, her writing went out of print and she was largely forgotten. A revival of her work was started by writer Gore Vidal, whose essays on her sparked the reprinting of *Angels on Toast* (1940), *The Wicked Pavilion* (1954), and *The Golden Spur* (1962); in the 1990s, scholar Tim Page continued that trend, editing Powell's diaries and writing a biography. More of Powell's works are in print now than at any time during her life.

The Elopers

In the sunken garden the scarlet geraniums bloomed, and the weeping willows dripped pale green branches along the graveled paths. Trees and grass seemed far greener here than in Manhattan, across the bridge. It was only June, but here on

Ward's Island[1] the summer might have been at its ripest. The lush green lawns, the vine-covered porches of the little gingerbread houses, the blossoming country lanes, so tranquil and remote from the city, seemed, under the great stone bridges, to be a lovely buried village of long, long ago. The stern new buildings on the edge were tall sentries, guarding the hush within.

In the bus shed Alma overheard someone remark on the beauty of the grounds, and a woman's tired voice answered, "It's pretty, all right, but you get so you're afraid of beautiful grounds like this. It's always an orphanage or a poorhouse or a prison. I'll bet the ones who have to stay here would be happier in the heart of the slums or in a factory town. At least there'd be life."

It was long past visiting hours, which meant a long wait for the bus back to 125th Street. At least she wouldn't have to stand. Coming over, the young athletes bound for Randall's Island always grabbed the seats, shoving aside the weary old mothers laden with hampers for the hospital patients. Alma recognized two of the women waiting in the shed, those who had probably stayed, as she had, to confer with the doctors. There was the pretty, dark woman who came over every week to visit her old music teacher, "the Maestro," as she called him.

"Today I sang for the Maestro and he *knew*, he really did," she whispered to Alma. "He said, 'How many times must I tell you to come *up* on that note, not pounce on it?' Just like his old self!"

A small gray woman with her canvas carryall on her lap had been coming here as many years as Alma had, and nodded to her.

"I thought you had taken your son home," Alma said. "Wasn't he discharged?"

"He always has to come back," the woman said with a shrug. "Outside gets too much for him after three, four weeks. He can't understand. No friends anymore, nothing to do, no place to go, and me away all day. My mother's in the apartment, but she's old and keeps at him, do this, do that. So he eloped."

"Eloped?"

The woman smiled.

"They call it eloping, running away from the hospital," she said. "He was always in trouble with the doctors, always trying to elope back to the Bronx. Then they'd catch him and put him in a closed ward. Only this time—it's funny, isn't it?—he eloped back to Ward's instead of away. Some do that. When they can't stand up to something they got to elope."

"Well, at least he made his own decision," Alma consoled her.

"If only he could see it that way," said the other. "Your daughter went to staff, didn't she? Does that mean you're taking her home at last?"

"Her father's bringing her home tomorrow," she said. "She's going to be all right now. Those marvelous new drugs! I just brought a new outfit for her, and she was so thrilled. Full of plans, of course."

"You brought her here the same time I brought Max," the woman remembered. "Six years."

"It's been so long," Alma said. "I'm the one that's scared."

The woman knew.

"I'm telling you," she said.

---

[1] An island in New York City's East River.

The bus came along and the three women climbed on, taking separate seats with their separate problems to solve, their separate canvas bags. The bags told the story. There was a time when Alma would see someone carrying one of those cram-full bags on a summer Sunday and she'd think it meant a picnic, a beach outing. Now, whenever she saw a woman carrying one, she wondered what hospital she was headed for, how far she had come, how many weeks or years she had been carrying it. Her own bag today contained the clothes Deedee had on when they brought her here from Bellevue that sad summer day. A size nine then, she had grown taller and stouter and now looked old for her nineteen years. Her fair hair, newly curled at the island beauty shop where she had been working lately, was still beautiful. Even in her most depressed state Deedee had been vain, brushing her hair all day long. Another good thing: Her eyes were alive again. Some of them never got over the fixed, wide-eyed stare, even when they were well, but Deedee's eyes were warm and alert, clouding up quickly, oh yes, when something puzzled her or something was denied her. There were so many things she had been denied, and now that she was coming out the poor child expected everything to be waiting for her—the skates, the cocker spaniel, the guitar with lessons, the electric sewing machine, the fur skating boots, the chocolate almond cake…. Alma took her memo pad out of her purse and wrote "chocolate cake" on her list.

She looked out over the river, the river that had seemed to her the dividing line between hope and despair. Today it was jeweled with sunset colors and the reflected lights of the highway; even the tugs seemed beautiful, because Deedee was coming home, Deedee was going to be all right.

The old doctor himself had acknowledged that she could have gotten out long ago.

"She was one of the half dozen out of a hundred I could have helped, maybe cured," he had said angrily. "But time is what you have to give them, and in my job here I have to see two hundred patients a day. Time, time is what we need and what do they give us—buildings! None of *their* doing we get these bright young doctors coming over to save somebody once in a while! Your good luck, Mrs. Davis."

It was indeed, Alma admitted. The new young doctor had taken a personal interest in Deedee's painting and dress designs. He had several paintings by patients hanging in his office, and Deedee's, the gleaming white sight-seeing boat steaming up the blue river toward Hell Gate, was his favorite. Alma did not like to look at the other paintings, the one of the huge cavern with jagged gray rocks and pitch-black water below, or the one with the twisted dead tree, its branches hung with blood-red blossoms, black roots curling back up around the trunk instead of going into the ground. There was a haunting self-portrait of a woman, a long greenish-white drowned face with black hair floating off into midnight-blue clouds, long snaky throat drifting on marble-white waves. The eyelids were closed, and when Alma exclaimed about this, the doctor said that schizophrenics invariably painted themselves with closed eyes. But Deedee's pictures were outgoing, joyous, he said. There was every chance for her, he said.

On her memo pad Alma wrote "drawing pad."

The conversation of the two men on the seat behind her came into her consciousness.

"Four years isn't so bad," one was saying. "Me, I've been visiting my wife here for thirty years. Can you take yours home weekends?"

"I can't, even if they'd let me," the other said. "She doesn't know the apartment's gone and I'm in a rooming house. She worries about my mending and getting the right meals, as it is. I tell her the reason I have time to visit her on Wednesdays, too, is that the boss is so understanding. Hell, I lost my job three months ago. Too much on my mind. She's better, though. Helps in the hospital laundry, watches TV, plays bingo. She almost always knows me now."

"I sold our house as soon as we got my wife here," the older man said. "Private doctors had used up all the insurance before that. I've kept my job, but that means I have to pay board for her here till I'm retired, so it doesn't leave me much. I couldn't take her home now even if she was well. Nobody to look after her. Nobody even remembers her."

Alma thought of the miracle in her own life and breathed a sigh of immense gratitude. Her last trip on this fateful bus. No more hearing all around her the voices of strangers telling each other, or maybe only themselves, the way it was, always how there was no one else who cared. No more would her heart flip when the bus left the line of cars from the Triborough Bridge headed for Queens and zoomed down through the underpass to the lost island. It was like a ship taking off for outer space, she always felt. But now Deedee was coming back from the island of the moon.

"You can't skip a visit, no," the older man's voice went on. "No one else ever comes. I guess everybody's got their own problems."

"But not even a pack of cigarettes from her own brother," the other said. "Not even a card."

"You get used to it," said the older man. He had a deep, cheerful voice, and when his companion got off at Second Avenue, Alma turned to look at him. He had iron-gray hair and a trim mustache, with a furrowed, ruddy, good face. Settling back alone in his seat, the warm glow faded from his eyes, and she saw him staring out the window with a look of deep, dark loneliness. At 125th Street he was the first to get off, and she watched him marching toward the subway, his shoulders back, jauntily swinging his blue-plaid bag, pausing at the newsstand to buy a paper. She wondered where…but no, she reminded herself, she no longer needed to wonder about all the others. She was free.

She celebrated her new freedom by taking the Lexington Avenue bus down, instead of the subway, because now there was time; life was beginning again. She even felt a vague pang that she might never see this corner of New York again. She looked about her with her new eyes, good-bye eyes, and felt the old joy of the city, its special magic of transforming the familiar by rain or moon or new street lights. Surely she had taken this same bus a hundred times before, but today, bewitched by the miracle of Deedee, she saw out of her window a new world, foreign and magical. She spelled out the shop signs—*Café, Bodega, Carniceria, Joyeria* [2]—and smiled, wishing Walter were along to be reminded of their Caribbean honeymoon. The dingy, crumbling old brownstone houses along upper Lexington, so wretched by day, blazed open by lamplight in brilliant detail, as if their facades were transparent black veils. On the doorsteps, dark, laughing young men plucked guitars; on the street, older men sat on boxes having their shoes shined and watching the girls go by. Saturday night in Spanish Harlem. Doors swung open on lighted staircases down which dark young girls in pink and blue

---

[2] (Sp.) Café; Grocery; Butcher Shop; Jewelry Store.

lace and gleaming satin, hair decked with jeweled flowers, danced to the street. Alma caught a glimpse of a side street bannered with a rainbow of dresses, toys, balloons, stretching a chain of golden lights westward to the medieval-looking arches of the Grand Central tracks. Like an old Spanish town, she would tell Walter. She strained her eyes to drink in the vivid vignettes among the patches of darkness.

The glaring ceiling lights opened up interiors to her as if by a powerful camera. There were shots of families, standing around a piano, gathered around a card table. It dawned on Alma that in each picture there was a close-up of a young girl standing apart, head lifted defiantly, delivering her declaration of independence. She was going to leave home, she was going to marry Pablo, she was going to have this and have that…. The shadowy faces of the girls blended into one fair, proud little face— Deedee's. As the bus rolled on below 100th Street leaving the gaudy glitter of the foreign world for the hostile, bleak fortresses of "projects" and civilization, Alma came back to the thought of Deedee. Tomorrow night, probably at this very hour, Deedee would be home.

"Get blue satin hair band," Alma jotted down on her list.

Her own room all trimmed in blue, Deedee had asked, her own drawing desk, a blue satin dress with shoes to match, and don't forget the black cocker spaniel. Alma shivered, remembering all the impossible things she had promised, reassuring herself that there must certainly be a day when the money would start coming in again instead of always going out. But now the years were up and Deedee was coming home to collect.

If only the bus ride could last a little longer, Alma thought, she might be able to think of the right thing to do. She got off at 80th Street and walked slowly eastward. The city was hotter than the island, but they were near enough to the river to get a breeze and, even though their basement was dark, it was cooler than their old apartment. She opened the iron gate and went down the steps to their entrance.

Walter was stirring a dish on the "efficiency" unit in the corner of the living room and the room smelled of frankfurters and beans, their traditional Saturday-night supper. He had laid the cloth on the card table with the little shaker of Martinis as centerpiece.

"You're late, so I'm two ahead of you," Walter said. "Take a look at the room: see what you think."

Alma went to the curtained-off alcove where Deedee was to sleep. Walter had been fixing it up for days, building in bookshelves, attaching a wall desk, making a false window out of a mirror, with blue plastic curtains to match the cot. She saw that he had placed a tiny black toy dog in the middle of the cot.

"Deedee will love it!" she said.

Walter poured her a drink and refilled his own glass. He was fair, like Deedee, his hair white now but his face still boyish.

"I hope you braced her for the piano being gone," he said.

"The doctor scolded me for not preparing her enough," Alma admitted. "But, darling, how could I? I couldn't have told her all those years when she couldn't reason! And since she's been getting well, she's had her heart so set on things I couldn't bear to bring her down to earth; I could just hope that we'd have some kind of luck before she got out."

"Everything all set for tomorrow?" he asked.

"All set," Alma said. "She's happy. Wants to go to a lot of movies, see Radio City Music Hall, take a course in dress designing, learn to drive a car."

"I'll take her to the Music Hall the minute she gets in," Walter said. "At least we can do that."

"I'll take her to the museum Tuesday to see the costumes," Alma said. "If she has something different to think about every day, it will give us time to figure out how to manage."

"Oh, it'll work out," Walter said. "The great thing is that she's come through and we're going to have her back home at last."

He poured the last of the shaker into her glass. Alma's eyes strayed to the half-filled bottle put away on the shelf for tomorrow.

"Let's drink tomorrow's now," she said. "The way we always do."

—1963

LOUISE BOGAN (1897-1970)

Louise Bogan was born on August 11, 1897, in Livermore Falls, Maine, the second of three children born to Mary Helen Murphy Shields and Daniel Joseph Bogan, a superintendent in a paper mill. The family lived in a variety of northeastern mill towns during Bogan's child-hood. Unhappy in her marriage, Bogan's mother had numerous affairs and at times would abandon the family and then return, a situation that contributed to Bogan's lifelong battle with depression. When the family moved to Boston in 1909, Bogan attended the Girl's Latin School there, becoming the Class Poet in 1910. She attended Boston University for a year, but dropped out to marry Curt Alexander, a soldier, in 1916. During this brief marriage she gave birth to a daughter, Mathilde (Maidie), published her first two poems professionally in *Others,* and suffered the death of her brother Charles at Baumont Woods, France, during World War I. She eventually left Alexander, who died in 1920.

Leaving Maidie with her parents, Bogan moved to New York in 1919, where she continued writing, began a series of jobs and affairs, and circulated among Genevieve Taggard, Leoni Adams, and Edmund Wilson. She married writer Raymond Holden in 1925 (whom she divorced) and later had a relationship with poet Theodore Roethke. Despite several nervous breakdowns, Bogan produced three more books of original verse, three books of criticism, and translations with May Sarton. She was the poetry critic for *The New Yorker* for thirty-eight years, and she served as Poetry Consultant to the Library of Congress (the present-day equivalent to Poet Laureate) in 1945. Her poetry garnered numerous awards, including two Guggenheim Fellowships (1933 and 1937), the Harriet Monroe Award (1948), and the Bollingen Prize (1955), shared with Leoni Adams. Bogan never considered herself a feminist, nor wished to be identified as a "woman" poet, yet many of her poems explore the contradictions embedded in female experience. She died in 1970.

Women

Women have no wilderness in them,
They are provident instead,
Content in the tight hot cell of their hearts
To eat dusty bread.

They do not see cattle cropping red winter grass,   5
They do not hear
Snow water going down under culverts
Shallow and clear.

They wait, when they should turn to journeys,
They stiffen, when they should bend.   10
They use against themselves that benevolence
To which no man is friend.

They cannot think of so many crops to a field
Or of clean wood cleft by an axe.
Their love is an eager meaninglessness   15
Too tense, or too lax.

They hear in every whisper that speaks to them
A shout and a cry.
As like as not, when they take life over their door-sills
They should let it go by.

—1923

Cassandra[1]

To me, one silly task is like another.
I bare the shambling tricks of lust and pride.
This flesh will never give a child its mother,—
Song, like a wing, tears through my breast, my side,
And madness chooses out my voice again,   5
Again. I am the chosen no hand saves:
The shrieking heaven lifted over men,
Not the dumb earth, wherein they set their graves.

—1929

[1] In Greek mythology, Cassandra had the gift of prophecy, as well as the curse of never being believed.

MARITA BONNER (1898-1971)

Marita Bonner was born in Boston, Massachusetts, one of four children of Joseph Andrew and Mary Anne Noel Bonner. Educated in the public schools in Boston's Brookline suburb, Bonner majored in English and Comparative Literature at Radcliffe College; college rules prohibited Black students from living on campus, so Bonner commuted. She began teaching at a local high school in her last year of college. After college, Bonner taught in the Washington, D.C., area from 1922 until 1930, and joined the literary salon hosted by poet Georgia Douglas Johnson. Bonner's first essay appeared in *Crisis,* the magazine of the NAACP, in 1925. She continued to publish essays, short stories, and experimental plays in both *Crisis* and *Opportunity* (the magazine of the Urban League), two of the major venues for Black writers during the

Harlem Renaissance. *The Purple Flower,* an unproduced play written in 1928, is considered by many critics to be her best work. In 1930, Bonner married accountant William Occomy, and moved to Chicago, where she continued to teach and raised three children. Bonner's last published work appeared in 1941, the same year she joined the Christian Science Church. Like many of the women writers of the Harlem Renaissance, Bonner did not publish a book; her stories were collected in 1987 and published as *Frye Street and Environs: The Collected Stories of Marita Bonner,* edited by Joyce Flynn and Joyce O. Strickland.

One Boy's Story

I'm glad they got me shut up in here. Gee, I'm glad! I used to be afraid to walk in the dark and to stay by myself.

That was when I was ten years old. Now I am eleven.

My mother and I used to live up in the hills right outside of Somerset. Somerset, you know is way up State and there aren't many people there. Just a few rich people in big houses and that's all.

Our house had a nice big yard behind it, beside it and in front of it. I used to play it was my fortress and that the hills beside us were full of Indians. Some days I'd go on scouting parties up and down the hills and fight.

That was in the summer and fall. In the winter and when the spring was rainy, I used to stay in the house and read.

I love to read. I love to lie on the floor and put my elbows down and read and read myself right out of Somerset and of America—out of the world, if I want to.

There was just my mother and I. No brothers—no sisters—no father. My mother was awful pretty. She had a roundish plump, brown face and was all plump and round herself. She had black hair all curled up on the end like a nice autumn leaf.

She used to stay in the house all the time and sew a lot for different ladies who came up from the big houses in Somerset. She used to sew and I would pull the bastings out for her. I did not mind it much. I liked to look at the dresses and talk about the people who were to wear them.

Most people, you see, wear the same kind of dress goods all the time. Mrs. Ragland always wore stiff silk that sounded like icicles on the window. Her husband kept the tea and coffee store in Somerset and everybody said he was a coming man.

I used to wonder where he was coming to.

Mrs. Gregg always had the kind of silk that you had to work carefully for it would ravel into threads. She kept the boarding house down on Forsythe Street. I used to like to go to that house. When you looked at it on the outside and saw all the windows and borders running up against it you thought you were going in a palace. But when you got inside you saw all the little holes in the carpet and the mended spots in the curtains and the faded streaks in the places where the draperies were folded.

The pale soft silk that always made me feel like burying my face in it belonged to Mrs. Swyburne. She was rich—awful rich. Her husband used to be some kind of doctor and he found out something that nobody else had found out, so people used to give him plenty of money just to let him tell them about it. They called him a specialist.

He was a great big man. Nice and tall and he looked like he must have lived on milk and beef-juice and oranges and tomato juice and all the stuff Ma makes me eat to grow. His teeth were white and strong so I guess he chewed his crusts too.

Anyhow, he was big but his wife was all skinny and pale. Even her eyes were almost skinny and pale. They were sad like and she never talked much. My mother used to say that those who did not have any children did not have to talk much anyhow.

She said that to Mrs. Swyburne one time. Mrs. Swyburne had been sitting quiet like she used to, looking at me. She always looked at me anyhow, but that day she looked harder than ever.

Every time I raised up my head and breathed the bastings out of my face, I would see her looking at me.

I always hated to have her look at me. Her eyes were so sad they made me feel as if she wanted something I had.

Not that I had anything to give her because she had all the money and cars and everything and I only had my mother and Cato, my dog, and some toys and books.

But she always looked that way at me and that day she kept looking so long that pretty soon I sat up and looked at her hard.

She sort of smiled then and said, "Do you know, Donald. I was wishing I had a little boy just like you to pull out bastings for me, too."

"You couldn't have one just like me," I said right off quick. Then I quit talking because Ma commenced to frown even though she did not look up at me.

I quit because I was going to say, "Cause I'm colored and you aren't," when Ma frowned.

Mrs. Swyburne still sort of smiled; then she turned her lips away from her teeth the way I do when Ma gives me senna and manna tea.[1]

"No," she said, "I couldn't have a little boy like you, I guess."

Ma spoke right up, "I guess you do not want one like him! You have to talk to him so much."

I knew she meant I talked so much and acted so bad sometimes.

Mrs. Swyburne looked at Ma then. She looked at her hair and face and right down to her feet. Pretty soon she said: "You cannot mind that surely. You seem to have all the things I haven't anyway." Her lips were still held in that lifted, twisted way.

Ma turned around to the machine then and turned the wheel and caught the thread and it broke and the scissors fell and stuck up in the floor. I heard her say "Jesus," to herself like she was praying.

I didn't say anything. I ripped out the bastings. Ma stitched. Mrs. Swyburne sat there. I sort of peeped up at her and I saw a big fat tear sliding down her cheek.

I kind of wiggled over near her and laid my hand on her arm. Then Ma yelled: "Donald, go and get a pound of rice! Go now, I said."

I got scared. She had not said it before and she had a lot of rice in a jar in the closet. But I didn't dare say so. I went out.

I couldn't help but think of Mrs. Swyburne. She ought not to cry so easy. She might not have had a little boy and Ma might have—but she should have been happy. She had a great big house on the swellest street in Somerset and a car all her own and some one to drive it for her. Ma only had me and our house which wasn't so swell, but it was all right.

---

[1] Senna and manna: herbal laxatives.

Then Mrs. Swyburne had her husband and he had such a nice voice. You didn't mind leaning on his knee and talking to him as soon as you saw him. He had eyes that looked so smiling and happy and when you touched his hands they were soft and gentle as Ma's even if they were bigger.

I knew him real well. He and I were friends. He used to come to our house a lot of times and bring me books and talk to Ma while I read.

He knew us real well. He called Ma Louise and me Don. Sometimes he'd stay and eat supper with us and then sit down and talk. I never could see why he'd come way out there to talk to us when he had a whole lot of rich friends down in Somerset and a wife that looked like the only doll I ever had.

A lady gave me that doll once and I thought she was really pretty—all pale and blonde and rosy. I thought she was real pretty at first but by and by she seemed so dumb. She never did anything but look pink and pale and rosy and pretty. She never went out and ran with me like Cato did. So I just took a rock and gave her a rap up beside her head and threw her in the bushes.

Maybe Mrs. Swyburne was pale and pink and dumb like the doll and her husband couldn't rap her with a rock and throw her away.

I don't know.

Anyhow, he used to come and talk to us and he'd talk to Ma a long time after I was in bed. Sometimes I'd wake up and hear them talking. He used to bring me toys until he found out that I could make my own toys and that I liked books.

After that he brought me books. All kinds of books about fairies and Indians and folks in other countries.

Sometimes he and I would talk about the books—especially those I liked. The one I liked most was called "Ten Tales to Inspire Youth."

That sounds kind of funny but the book was great. It had stories in it all about men. All men. I read all of the stories but I liked the one about the fellow named Orestes who went home from the Trojan War and found his mother had married his father's brother so he killed them.[2] I was always sorry for the women with the whips of flame like forked tongues who used to worry him afterwards.[3] I don't see why the fairies pursued him. They knew he did it because he loved his father so much.

Another story I liked was about Oedipus—a Greek too—who put out his eyes to hurt himself because he killed his father and married his mother by mistake.

But after I read "David and Goliath,"[4] I just had to pretend that I was David.

I swiped a half a yard of elastic from Ma and hunted a long time until I found a good forked piece of wood. Then I made a swell slingshot.

The story said that David asked Jehovah (which was God) to let his slingshot shoot good. "Do thou lend thy strength to my arm, Jehovah," he prayed.

I used to say that too just to be like him.

I told Dr. Swyburne I liked these stories.

"Why do you like them?" he asked me.

"Because they are about men," I said.

"Because they are about men! Is that the only reason?"

---

[2] This rendering of the story is not quite accurate: Orestes' father, Agamemnon, returned from the Trojan War and was murdered by Clytemnestra, Orestes' mother, and her lover, Aegisthus. Orestes later killed Aegisthus and Clytemnestra.
[3] The Erinyes or Furies.
[4] 1 Samuel 17.

Then I told him no; that I liked them because the men in the stories were brave and had courage and stuck until they got what they wanted, even if they hurt themselves getting it.

And he laughed and said, to Ma: "Louise he has the blood, all right!"

And Ma said: "Yes! He is a true Gage. They're brave enough to put their eyes out too. That takes courage all right!"

Ma and I are named Gage, so I stuck out my chest and said: "Ma, which one of us Gages put his eyes out?"

"Me," she said—and she was standing there looking right at me!

I thought she was making fun. So I felt funny.

Dr. Swyburne turned red and said: "I meant the other blood, of course. All the Swyburnes are heroes."

I didn't know what he meant. My name is Gage and so is Ma's so he didn't mean me.

Ma threw her head up and looked at him and says: "Oh, are they heroes?" Then she says real quick: "Donald go to bed right now!"

I didn't want to go but I went. I took a long time to take off my clothes and I heard Ma and Dr. Swyburne talking fast like they were fussing.

I couldn't hear exactly what they said but I kept hearing Ma say: "I'm through!"

And I heard Dr. Swyburne say: "You can't be!"

I kind of dozed to sleep. By and by I heard Ma say again: "Well, I'm through!"

And Dr. Swyburne said: "I won't let you be!"

Then I rolled over to think a minute and then go downstairs maybe.

But when I rolled over again, the sun was shining and I had to get up.

Ma never said anything about what happened so I didn't either. She just walked around doing her work fast, holding her head up high like she always does when I make her mad.

So I never said a thing that day.

One day I came home from school. I came in the back way and when I was in the kitchen I could hear a man in the front room talking to Ma. I stood still a minute to see if it was Dr. Swyburne though I knew he never comes in the afternoon.

The voice didn't sound like his so I walked in the hall and passed the door. The man had his back to me so I just looked at him a minute and didn't say anything. He had on leather leggins and a sort of uniform like soldiers wear. He was stooping over the machine talking to Ma and I couldn't see his face.

Just then I stumbled over the little rug in the hall and he stood up and looked at me.

He was a colored man! Colored just like Ma and me. You see, there aren't any other people in Somerset colored like we are, so I was sort of surprised to see him.

"This is my son, Mr. Frazier," Ma said.

I said pleased to meet you and stepped on Ma's feet. But not on purpose. You know I kind of thought he was going to be named Gage and be some relation to us and stay at our house awhile.

I never saw many colored people—no colored men—and I wanted to see some. When Ma called him Frazier it made my feet slippery so I stubbed my toe.

"Hello, son!" he said nice and quiet.

He didn't talk like Ma and me. He talked slower and softer. I liked him straight off so I grinned and said: "Hello yourself."

"How's the books?" he said then.

I didn't know what he meant at first but I guessed he meant school. So I said: "Books aren't good as the fishin'."

He laughed out loud and said I was all right and said he and I were going to be friends and that while he was in Somerset he was going to come to our house often and see us.

Then he went out. Ma told me he was driving some lady's car. She was visiting Somerset from New York and he would be there a little while.

Gee, I was so glad! I made a fishing rod for him that very afternoon out of a piece of willow I had been saving for a long time.

And one day, he and I went down to the lake and fished. We sat still on top a log that went across a little bay like. I felt kind of excited and couldn't say a word. I just kept looking at him every once in a while and smiled. I did not grin. Ma said I grinned too much.

Pretty soon he said: "What are you going to be when you grow up, son?"

"A colored man," I said. I meant to say some more, but he hollered and laughed so loud that Cato had to run up and see what was doing.

"Sure you'll be a colored man! No way to get out of that! But I mean this: What kind of work are you going to do?"

I had to think a minute. I had to think of all the kinds of work men did. Some of the men in Somerset were farmers. Some kept stores. Some swept the streets. Some were rich and did not do anything at home but they went to the city and had their cars driven to the shop and to meet them at the train.

All the conductors and porters make a lot of scramble to get these men on and off the train, even if they looked as if they could take care of themselves.

So I said to Mr. Frazier: "I want to have an office."

"An office?"

"Yes. In the city so's I can go in to it and have my car meet me when I come to Somerset."

"Fat chance a colored man has!" he said.

"I can too have an office!" I said. He made me sore. "I can have one if I want to! I want to have an office and be a specialist like Dr. Swyburne."

Mr. Frazier dropped his pole and had to swear something awful when he reached for it though it wasn't very far from him.

"Why'd you pick him?" he said and looked at me kind of mad like and before I could think of what to say he said: "Say son, does that guy come up to see your mother?"

"Sure he comes to see us both!" I said.

Mr. Frazier laughed again but not out loud. It made me sore all over. I started to hit him with my pole but I thought about something I'd read once that said even a savage will treat you right in his house—so I didn't hit him. Of course, he wasn't in my house exactly but he was sitting on my own log over my fishing places and that's like being in your own house.

Mr. Frazier laughed to himself again and then all of a sudden he took the pole I had made him out of the piece of willow I had been saving for myself and laid it across his knees and broke it in two. Then he said out loud: "Nigger women," and then threw the pole in the water.

I grabbed my pole right out of the water and slammed it across his face. I never thought of the hook until I hit him, but it did not stick in him. It caught in a tree and I broke the string yanking it out.

He looked at me like he was going to knock me in the water and even though I was scared, I was thinking how I'd let myself fall if he did knock me off—so that I could swim out without getting tangled in the roots under the bank.

But he didn't do it. He looked at me a minute and said: "Sorry, son! Sorry! Not your fault."

Then he put his hand on my hair and brushed it back and sort of lifted it up and said: "Like the rest."

I got up and said I was going home and he came too. I was afraid he would come in but when he got to my gate he said: "So long," and walked right on.

I went on in. Ma was sewing. She jumped up when I came in.

"Where is Mr. Frazier?" she asked me. She didn't even say hello to me!

"I hit him," I said.

"You hit him!" she hollered. "You *hit* him! What did you do that for? Are you crazy?"

I told her no. "He said 'nigger women' when I told him that Dr. Swyburne was a friend of ours and came to see us."

Oh Ma looked terrible then. I can't tell you how she did look. Her face sort of slipped around and twisted like the geography says the earth does when the fire inside of it gets too hot.

She never said a word at first. She just sat there. Then she asked me to tell her all about every bit that happened.

I told her. She kept wriggling from side to side like the fire was getting hotter. When I finished, she said: "Poor baby! My baby boy! Not your fault! Not your fault!"

That made me think of Mr. Frazier so I pushed out of her arms and said: "Ma your breast pin hurts my face when you do that!"

She leaned over on the arms of her chair and cried and cried until I cried too.

All that week I'd think of the fire inside of the earth when I looked at Ma. She looked so funny and she kept talking to herself.

On Saturday night we were sitting at the table when I heard a car drive up the road.

"Here's Dr. Swyburne!" I said and I felt so glad I stopped eating.

"He isn't coming here!" Ma said and then she jumped up.

"Sure he's coming," I said. "I know his motor." And I started to get up too.

"You stay where you are!" Ma hollered and she went out and closed the door behind her.

I took another piece of cake and began eating the frosting. I heard Dr. Swyburne come up on the porch.

"Hello, Louise," he said. I could tell he was smiling by his voice.

I couldn't hear what Ma said at first but pretty soon I heard her say: "You can't come here any more!"

That hurt my feelings. I liked Dr. Swyburne. I liked him better than anybody I knew besides Ma.

Ma stayed out a long time and by and by she came in alone and I heard Dr. Swyburne drive away.

She didn't look at me at all. She just leaned back against the door and said: "Dear Jesus! With your help I'll free myself."

I wanted to ask her from what did she want to free herself. It sounded like she was in jail or an animal in a trap in the woods.

I thought about it all during supper but I didn't dare say much. I thought about it and pretended that she was shut up in a prison and I was a time fighter who beat all the keepers and got her out.

Then it came to me that I better get ready to fight to get her out of whatever she was in. I never said anything to her. I carried my air-rifle on my back and my sling-shot in my pocket. I wanted to ask her where her enemy was, but she never talked to me about it; so I had to keep quiet too. You know Ma always got mad if I talked about things first. She likes to talk, then I can talk afterwards.

One Sunday she told me she was going for a walk.

"Can I go?" I asked her.

"No," she said. "You play around the yard."

Then she put her hat on and stood looking in the mirror at herself for a minute. All of a sudden I heard her say to herself: "All I need is strength to fight out of it."

"Ma'am?" I thought she was talking to me at first.

She stopped and hugged my head—like I wish she wouldn't sometimes and then went out.

I stayed still until she got out of the yard. Then I ran and got my rifle and sling-shot and followed her.

I crept behind her in the bushes beside the road. I cut across the fields and came out behind the willow patch the way I always do when I am tracking Indians and wild animals.

By and by she came out in the clearing that is behind Dr. Somerset's. They call it Somerset's Grove and it's named for his folks who used to live there—just as the town was.

She sat down so I lay down in the bushes. A sharp rock was sticking in my knee but I was afraid to move for fear she'd hear me and send me home.

By and by I heard someone walking on the grass and I saw Dr. Swyburne coming up. He started talking before he got to her. "Louise," he said. "Louise! I am not going to give anything up to a nigger."

"Not even a nigger woman whom you took from a nigger?" She lifted her mouth in the senna and manna way.

"Don't say that!" he said. "Don't say that! I wanted a son. I couldn't have taken a woman in my own world—that would have ruined my practice. Elaine couldn't have a child!"

"Yes," Ma said. "It would have ruined you and your profession. What did it do for me? What did it do for Donald?"

"I have told you I will give him the best the world can offer. He is a Swyburne!"

"He is *my* child," Ma hollered. "It isn't his fault he is yours!"

"But I give him everything a father could give his son!"

"He has no name!" Ma said.

"I have too!" I hollered inside of me. "Donald Gage!"

"He has no name," Ma said again, "and neither have I!" And she began to cry.

"He has blood!" said Dr. Swyburne.

"But how did he get it? Oh, I'm through. Stay away from my house and I'll marry one of my own men so Donald can be somebody."

"A nigger's son?"

"Don't say that again," Ma hollered and jumped up.

"Do you think I'll give up a woman of mine to a nigger?"

Ma hollered again and hit him right in his face.

He grabbed her wrists and turned the right one, I guess because she fell away from him on that side.

I couldn't stand any more. I snatched out my slingshot and pulled the stone up that was sticking in my knee.

I started to shoot. Then I remembered what David said first, so I shut my eyes and said it: "Do thou, Jehovah (which is God today), lend strength to my arm."

When I opened my eyes Ma had broken away and was running toward the road. Dr. Swyburne was standing still by the tree looking after her like he was going to catch her. His face was turned sideways to me. I looked at his head where his hair was brushed back from the side of his face.

I took aim and let the stone go. I heard him say: "Oh, my God!" I saw blood on his face and I saw him stagger and fall against the tree.

Then I ran too.

When I got home Ma was sitting in her chair with her hat thrown on the floor beside her and her head was lying back.

I walked up to her: "Ma," I said real loud.

She reached out and grabbed me and hugged my head down to her neck like she always does.

The big breast-pin scratched my mouth. I opened my mouth to speak and something hot and sharp ran into my tongue.

"Ma! Ma!" I tried to holler. "The pin is sticking in my tongue!"

I don't know what I said though. When I tried to talk again, Ma and Dr. Somerset were looking down at me and I was lying in bed. I tried to say something but I could not say anything. My mouth felt like it was full of hot bread and I could not talk around it.

Dr. Somerset poured something in my mouth and it felt like it was on fire.

"They found Shev Swyburne in my thistle grove this afternoon," he said to Ma.

Ma look up quick. "*Found* him! What do you mean?"

"I mean he was lying on the ground—either fell or was struck and fell. He was dead from a blow on the temple."

I tried to holler but my tongue was too thick.

Ma took hold of each side of her face and held to it, then she just stared at Dr. Somerset. He put a lot of things back in his bag.

Then he sat up and looked at Ma. "Louise," he said, "why is all that thistle down on your skirt?"

Ma looked down. So did I. There was thistle down all over the hem of her dress.

"You don't think I killed him, do you?" she cried, "you don't think I did it?" Then she cried something awful.

I tried to get up but I was too dizzy. I crawled across the bed on my stomach and reached out to the chair that had my pants on it. It was hard to do—but I dragged my slingshot out of my pocket, crawled back across the bed and laid it in Dr. Somerset's knees. He looked at me for a minute.

"Are you trying to tell me that you did it, son?" he asked me.

I said yes with my head.

"My God! My God!! His own child!!!"

Dr. Somerset said to Ma: "God isn't dead yet."

Then he patted her on the arm and told her not to tell anybody nothing and they sat down and picked all the thistle down out of the skirt. He took the slingshot and broke it all up and put it all in a paper and carried it downstairs and put it in the stove.

I tried to talk. I wanted to tell him to leave it so I could show my grandchildren what I had used to free Ma like the men do in the books.

I couldn't talk though. My tongue was too thick for my mouth. The next day it burnt worse and things began to float around my eyes and head like pieces of wood in the water.

Sometimes I could see clearly though and once I saw Dr. Somerset talking to another man. Dr. Somerset was saying: "We'll have to operate to save his life. His tongue is poisoned. I am afraid it will take his speech from him."

Ma hollered then: "Thank God! He will not talk! Never! He can't talk! Thank God! Oh God! I thank Thee!" And then she cried like she always does and that time it sounded like she was laughing too.

The other man looked funny and said: "Some of them have no natural feeling of parent for child!"

Dr. Somerset looked at him and said: "You may be fine as a doctor but otherwise you are an awful fool."

Then he told the other man to go out and he began talking to Ma.

"I understand! I understand," he said. "I know all about it. He took you away from somebody and some of these days he might have taken Donald from you. He took Elaine from me once and I told him then God would strip him for it. Now it is all over. Never tell anyone and I will not. The boy knows how to read and write and will be able to live."

So I got a black stump in my mouth. It's shaped like a forked whip.

Some days I pretend I am Orestes with the Furies' whips in my mouth for killing a man.

Some days I pretend I am Oedipus and that I cut it out for killing my own father. That's what makes me sick all over sometimes.

I killed my own father. But I didn't know it was my father. I was freeing Ma.

Still—I shall never write that on my paper to Ma and Dr. Somerset the way I have to talk to them and tell them when things hurt me.

My father said I was a Swyburne and that was why I liked people to be brave and courageous.

Ma says I am a Gage and that is why I am brave and courageous.

But I am both, so I am a whole lot brave, a whole lot courageous. And I am bearing my Furies and my clipped tongue like a Swyburne and a Gage—'cause I am both of them.

—1927

ELSA GIDLOW (1898-1986)

Elsa Gidlow, one of the first writers to publish openly lesbian poetry in the English language, was born in 1898 in Yorkshire, England. When she was six, she moved with her family to the tiny French Canadian village of Tetreauville, Québec. Gidlow wrote poetry from an early age, and in her youth she travelled across Canada by train as a secretary for her father. When she was sixteen, the family settled in Montréal, where she took a typing job, joined a library, and experienced her first romantic friendship with a woman. In Montréal, Gidlow formed a bohemian literary group and edited a "little magazine" that frequently published material with homosexual themes. Through her association with this group, she encountered the writings of Havelock Ellis, Edward Carpenter, Baudelaire, Rimbaud, and Verlaine, as well as Indian classical literature.

In 1920 Gidlow moved to New York City, where she worked as an editor at *Pearson's* magazine, which was often censored because of its progressive politics. Her book *On a Grey Thread,* published in 1923, was the first openly lesbian poetry collection published in the United States. In 1926 she moved to San Francisco. She became a naturalized U.S. citizen in 1938, and around that time purchased a secluded five-acre parcel of land north of San Francisco that she named "Druid Heights." It became a spiritual and literary destination for many luminaries, including Alan Watts, who helped to popularize eastern religious philosophies in the U.S. and was a great influence on the Beat Generation poets. A lifelong feminist, Gidlow was accused of communist sympathies in 1947 and was supported by the American Civil Liberties Union. Among her several self-published collections of poetry are *California Valley With Girls* (1932), *From Alba Hill* (1933), *Letters from Limbo* (1956), and *Makings for Meditation* (1973). The feminist publishing house Diana Press published her collection *Sapphic Songs: Seventeen to Seventy* (1976), which was reissued in 1982 as *Sapphic Songs: Eighteen to Eighty.* Her memoir *Elsa: I Come with My Songs,* probably her most widely read work, was published in 1986, the year she died.

For the Goddess Too Well Known

I have robbed the garrulous streets,
Thieved a fair girl from their blight,
I have stolen her for a sacrifice
That I shall make to this night.

I have brought her, laughing,   5
To my quietly dreaming garden.
For what will be done there
I ask no man pardon.

I brush the rouge from her cheeks,
Clean the black kohl from the rims   10
Of her eyes; loose her hair;
Uncover the glimmering, shy limbs.

I break wild roses, scatter them over her.
The thorns between us sting like love's pain.
Her flesh, bitter and salt to my tongue,   15
I taste with endless kisses and taste again.
At dawn I leave her

Asleep in my wakening garden.
(For what was done there
I ask no man pardon.)

—1919

Invocation to Sappho[1]

Sappho
        Sister-Mother
               free-
souled, fire-hearted
Psappha of Mitylene on   5
sea-lapped Lesbos
miracle of a woman
               (Strabo[2] wrote)
now   now
           let me declare   10
devotion.
Not light years   love years
on how many love years
across fields of the dead
does your fragrance   15
travel to me?

Since maidenhood in brain   blood
by you haunted
in my own armpits I have breathed
sweat of your passion   20
in the burning crotch of the lover
tasted your honey
heard   felt in my pulse
               day long
                     night through   25
lure of your song's beat
insistently echo.

By dust of five-and-twenty centuries
                    not smothered
by book-consuming flames of   30
the hate-filled churchmen
                 unsilenced
your fame only haloed   made
more splendid.

Sappho, little and dark,   35

---

[1] Sappho (ca. 630 B.C.E.-ca. 570 B.C.E.), Greek poet whose work survives only in fragments.
[2] Strabo (ca. 63 B.C.E.-21 C.E.), ancient Greek author of *Geographica*, a 17-volume work describing the history of people and places around the world that were known to the Greeks at that time.

the Beautiful, Plato[3] called you
(though his Republic[4] had
grudging use for poets)
Sappho whose veins ran fire

        whose nerves   40

quivered to loves illicit now

        in your day

honored by the noblest,
Sappho, all roses,
Do we not touch   45
across the censorious years?

        —1965

You Say

You say I am mysterious.
Let me explain myself:
In a land of oranges
I am faithful to apples.

        —1973

---

[3] Plato (ca. 427-347 B.C.E.), Greek philosopher.

[4] Masterpiece of western philosophy written by Plato (ca. 360 B.C.E.).

MAY MILLER (1899-1995)

May Miller was born in Washington, D.C., one of Kelly Miller and Annie Mae Butler's five children. Her father, a prominent sociologist, essayist, and educator, was a professor and dean at Howard University and had close social and political ties to such important African-American figures as W.E.B. DuBois, Booker T. Washington, Mary Church Terrell, Lucy Diggs Slowe, and William Stanley Braithwaite. Miller attended the prestigious M Street School (later Paul Laurence Dunbar High School) where she studied under Mary P. Burril and Angelina Grimke, two of the earliest black American female dramatists of the twentieth century. She earned a B.A. in 1920 from Howard University, and was awarded a prize for her one-act play *Within the Shadows,* the first such honor bestowed on a student at Howard. A member of both the Krigwa Players and Georgia Douglas Johnson's "S Street Salon," Miller is one of the most celebrated women playwrights of the Harlem Renaissance. Her plays deal mainly with social and political issues, questioning the morality and humanity that informed key social constructions. She is also notable for her historical plays, which chronicle the black experience in America. Miller's artistic friends included Jean Toomer, Langston Hughes, Marita Bonner, and Zora Neale Hurston. After a celebrated career as playwright and teacher, Miller turned to poetry and achieved equal success in that field. Her dramatic works include: *Pandora's Box* (1914), *The Bog Guide* (1925), *Riding the Goat* (1925), *Graven Images* (1929), *Scratches* (1929), *Stragglers in the Dust* (written in 1930, published in 1989), *Nails and Thorns* (1933), *Christophe's Daughters* (1935), *Harriet Tubman* (1935), *Samory* (1935), *Sojourner Truth*

(1935) and *Freedom's Children on the March* (1943). In 1986 the National Conference of African-American Theatre at Morgan State University in Baltimore presented Miller with the Mister Brown Award for Excellence in Drama and Poetry (Mr. William Brown was manager of the New York's African Company from 1816 to 1823). Miller died at the age of ninety-six in Washington, D.C.

Stragglers in the Dust

CHARACTERS

MAC, *a watchman in the great cemetery*

NAN, *a Negro charwoman*

LESTER BRADFORD, *a distinguished politician*

THE STRAGGLER

THE GUARD

TIME: EARLY 1920s

[*When the curtain rises,* NAN, *a slender stoop-shouldered woman of about fifty years, is discovered seated on the steps. She is hunched over with her face resting on her hands, and her elbows on her knees. Beside her is her scrub pail with a rag hanging carelessly over the rim.* NAN *has clearly forgotten the pail, a symbol of her drudgery, and is lost in reverie as she gazes past the columns to the marble sepulchre and beyond that to the mist that rises from the lazy Potomac.*[1] *One instinctively thinks of "I dreamed I dwelt in marble halls"*[2] *and realizes that here is a new interpretation. Softly she begins to hum and slowly the humming grows into these words*:]

Keep dis in min' an' all'll go right,
as on yo way you goes,
Be shore you knows 'bout all you tells,
But don't tell all you knows.
      [*Refrain*]
Be shore you knows 'bout all you tells,
But don't tell all you knows.[3]

As she is lost in her reverie again, the words of the song are no longer intelligible, but the air is held by a soft humming. A shadowy figure that one distinguishes to be that of a young man in his twenties moves slowly across the top lift of the stairway. He peers down intently at the huddled figure of NAN *and listens a moment to her song, then tips behind a column from which he looks out again at* NAN. *The face that one sees clearly now is chalky in its paleness and the eyes seem haunted as they stare vacantly about. The face disappears as* MAC, *the watchman, moves steadily toward* NAN. MAC *is a stout man of about sixty. He wears a double-breasted suit fastened with brass buttons. His blue cap is trimmed with a gold cord. In his hand he swings a regular watchman's clock which he consults as he approaches.*]

MAC: Well, Nan, I guess it's about finishing up you be.

NAN: Yes, Mistah Mac, Ah's just 'bout done. Ah's rubb'd and rubb'd all dat brass

---

[1] The Potomac River runs between Washington, D.C., and northern Virginia. Arlington National Cemetery, where the Tomb of the Unknowns is located, is directly across the Potomac from Washington, D.C.

[2] "I dreamt that I dwelt in marble halls": a popular aria from *The Bohemian Girl* (1843) by Michael W. Balfe (1808-1870).

[3] An African-American folk rhyme.

bright 'nough to make heavenly crowns.

MAC: To be sure might nice things look nice Nan, but I doubt if I'd be wantin' any brass crown.

NAN: No Ah guess not, Mistah Mac, there's still some of us what's deservin' of better. We done tasted the brass here on earth. God sartinly must be a savin' de gold. [*She sadly shakes her head and stops to pick up the pail.*]

MAC: That's right, Nan, kinda get your things together. It's six thirty and almost closing time.

NAN: Closin' time so soon! Ah hates tuh see it come.

MAC: Hate the time for leaving to come?

NAN: Ah's always kinda had a hankering after graveyards and now—

MAC: Well it's too bad I don't feel that way since I have to spend most of my time here. As for me seven o'clock can't come soon enough to get home.

NAN: Ahh! you see, sah, dat's de difference. Ah ain't got nothin' at home. All Ah got is heah.

MAC: All you got is here?

NAN: Well yuh see, Mistah Mac, Ah ain't nevah had nobody but mah boy, Jim. Dere's nevah been nobody but jus' him and me. An' since he's been heah Ah jus' kinda likes tuh stay neah.

MAC: But I never heard about your son working here. Which one is he?

NAN: Who mah Jim? Ah no he ain't workin'. Fact is Jim ain't neveah liked tuh work much, but now he can't work no more. [*Pointing to the sepulchre*] Dey put him in dat marble box dere aftah dey fin' him on de field. Flanders,[4] Ah think dey calls it.

MAC: [*Looking bewildered*] You mean you lost your Jim in the war, eh?

NAN: Yeah, ain't yuh hear'd dem talkin' 'bout him de uhda day? Dat grand ol' man stand up dere an' tol' how dey call'd an' how Jim lef me broken hearted tuh go fight for dis country an' den how dem guns got him. An' how dey fin' him finally on dat fiel' in France an' bring him back ober heah an put him in dere. [*She points again to the tomb.*]

MAC: [*In a hesitant manner*] Yes, I heard that, but Nan, they weren't talking 'bout your Jim. Why they don't even know who that soldier is—he's unknown. It wasn't about your Jim they were talking.

NAN: Yeah, Ah know some of dem don' know. But Ah knows an' dat man knows. Didn't he say "Yuh mother dere bow'd in grief." Ah was hidin' be-hin' dis very pillow an' Ah heah'd him, but Ah didn' come out cause Ah know'd dere'd be them dere as wouldn't want Jim tuh stay dere cause he's cullud.

MAC: But Nan, that's foolish, don't you see—

NAN: Ah done right didn't Ah?

MAC: [*Despairing of making* NAN *understand*] Yes, I guess you did right not to say any-thing. [*The haunted face of the stranger appears from behind the last column. He listens intently unseen by the others and then disappears again.*]

NAN: Mistah Mac, but you won' tell nobody will ya 'cause Ah don' wan' em tuh keep movin' him.

MAC: [*As if pacifying a child*] Of course not, Nan.

NAN: Yuh know it's kinda nice dat dey bring all dem wreaths and ribbons to put on

---

[4] Belgian Flanders was a major front of fighting throughout World War I.

him, but somehow Ah wishes dey had lef' him where he was.

MAC: Well of all ridiculous ideas this is just about the worst.

NAN: [*Misinterpreting*] Ah know it is an Ah am proud when Ah look at this temple dat's his'n, and see dat soldiers dat's lookin' out for him day an' night; but den when Ah thinks of Jim an' how he lubbed de woods an' de fields Ah'm jus' a little sorry. He might had rested betta ober dere in France. Dey say de wooden crosses is kinda ugly but dat de big blue sky ober head guards an' blesses 'em an' den too dose poppies grow between de rows an' dat wouldn't have been haf bad 'cause Jim liked red. Maybe it's best as 'tis 'cause ober dere be nobody to watch. [*She sighs as she stoops to pick up pail again.*]

MAC: Watch, watch for what?

NAN: Dat's right Ah guess dere ain't no need ob no guard ober dere.

MAC: As far as need's concerned we don't need any either.

NAN: O! yes we does. Dere's dat creature wid de ghost like face and empty eyes what's been haunting dis place for two days. He sartingly needs watchin'. De first time Ah saw him he couldn't see me for lookin' so hard at dat tomb.

MAC: I don't think we'll have any more trouble with him. I notified the police and any way he seems to be perfectly harmless.

NAN: Ah'm sartin he's moon-duff[5] but Ah ain't worried non now, 'cause Jim's got plenty of pertection.

MAC: I'm afraid the moon's got more than one of us, but if you're certain you're satisfied with that protection you can be leaving now.

NAN: [*Taking her pail and moving through the portal*] Thanks Mistah Mac an' if yuh be aneedin' me again soon ju' sen' for me cause yuh knows Ah like tuh come.

MAC: All right, Nan, good-night. [MAC *follows* NAN *to the left portal and closes it behind her. As he stands there meditatively shaking his head, a tall distinguished looking gray haired man in an elegant dark suit mounts the steps and stands facing pass as he turns.* MAC *is startled*]

LESTOR BRADFORD: I'm very sorry if I startled you.

MAC: It wasn't that exactly but it is an odd feeling to think that you're alone and suddenly face company.

BRADFORD: And, too, it's a little late for visitors isn't it?

MAC: Yes, sir, it is. We close the gates in about fifteen minutes. After dusk there aren't so many that tarry here.

BRADFORD: So I noticed as I came up. I passed only one person—a colored woman.

MAC: That was only Nan. She comes here only once a week to shine the brass.

BRADFORD: But during the day many do visit the tomb, eh? I've been out several times and there were always quite a few.

MAC: Sunday's the day, though when we have a crowd. Sundays there's nothing else much to do but think of the dead. Then hundreds visit the unknown's grave. He seems somehow to belong to each one separately.

BRADFORD: He undoubtedly has had an unexplainable effect on the whole white race.

MAC: No sir, you needn't make it that narrow. Better say on all races. You'd be surprised at the number of Negroes that visit here.

BRADFORD: [*Surprised*] For what? Out of patriotism? [*He smiles at his own irony*].

MAC: No telling how many of them feel like Nan.

---

[5] Probably a variant of moon-daft, or moonstruck.

BRADFORD: [*Wondering*] Nan?

MAC: That colored woman you met as you came up the hill.

BRADFORD: O yes.

MAC: Do you know she really believes that the unknown is actually her boy, Jim, that she lost in the war.

BRADFORD: But how could she think that?

MAC: She kinda misunderstood some of the speeches she's heard out here—took everything to herself.

BRADFORD: Such a thing has never even crossed my mind. Why that isn't even possible.

MAC: Of course not, Nan's just a poor old colored woman with nothing left but her dreams.

BRADFORD: But if it were—what a terrible joke on America!

MAC: But it can't be. We just naturally hear and experience odd things out here in this land of tombstones. Some of the visitors might surprise you a little. Nan was just talking about some poor half dazed boy who's been hanging around here for two days. Real innocent sort but with his ghost-like face, not the one you'd want for company in a place like this.

BRADFORD: [*Greatly interested and speaking hurriedly*] And where is that boy now?

MAC: Hanging 'round here somewhere I guess but there's no telling just where he is. I could have sworn there was nobody in this place except the guard when I locked the gates last night. Yet the first creature I met this morning was that crazy boy. Really no use trying to put your hands on that kind.

BRADFORD: But that's just why I am here.

MAC: Beg pardon, sir?

BRADFORD: There's no time for mincing matters, I am here because I think the boy may be—may be my—my son.

MAC: I am sorry, sir, I didn't understand, but what makes you think so?

BRADFORD: My son is missing and when I notified the police they told me of your report. I asked to come for him alone.

MAC: But you are not certain.

BRADFORD: The description tallies but they didn't say anything of his condition. Did he seem sick?

MAC: God knows he was white enough.

BRADFORD: [*Nervously*] Yes, yes, it's those attacks. They always leave him like that.

MAC: But this might not be your son.

BRADFORD: But it is, I know it is—and you say he has been wandering here for two days—ever since he left home. Each attack gets worse. [*He hesitates for a moment, then clenches his hands. As he speaks he becomes more and more vehement.*] Each attack gets worse—God when will they end? He'd be better off dead—dead, did you hear me? And I can say that of my only son. [BRADFORD *starts and listens as a voice is heard singing off stage in a strained uncanny voice.*] I'm afraid you're a bit nervous too.

MAC: O, sir, there he is now. You had better get your nerves steady to meet him. Let's sit here like we've been chatting; we don't want to startle him. You let me talk to him.

BRADFORD: Yes—yes of course.

[*They have just assumed their position on the steps when the unknown enters. Upon close view one notes that the deathlike pallor of his skin is accompanied by a slight tremor of limbs. One realizes that he's a sick man.* BRADFORD *rises and starts with outstretched arms toward the boy who apparently does not even see him.* MAC *pulls him gently but forcefully back in place shaking his head in admonition.*]

STRAGGLER: [*To* MAC *in a hollow weak voice*] I thought you had gone. Isn't it closing time yet?

MAC: [*Calmly*] Yes just about, but I thought I'd kinda wait for you—thought maybe you'd walk home with me.

STRAGGLER: O no—no I can't go yet—you see I've got to wait for him.

MAC: For your father? Then we can leave now because—

STRAGGLER: No for him—the Nigger.

MAC: What Nigger? No one's coming here this late. I shall close the gates in a few minutes.

STRAGGLER: Locked gates are nothing to him. He comes every evening after you've gone, that's the reason I have to stay here. He's a sly rascal. That guard walks back and forth and never even sees him; he comes so quickly and quietly.

BRADFORD: [*Impatiently*] Who?

STRAGGLER: The Nigger who lives in there.

BRADFORD: Where?

STRAGGLER: In the tomb.

BRADFORD: Nobody but the unknown dead's there.

STRAGGLER: He's dead well enough but he's not unknown. There are at least three if not more that know him.

MAC: It's nobody that knows, they tell me.

STRAGGLER: [*Laughing loud*] I heard that colored woman confess to you. You don't know and—

MAC: Who? Nan? The moon-daft one. She's feebled minded.

STRAGGLER: Maybe she is but she only told you what I've been knowing for months. I didn't know though that he was her son. You see I met him in No man's land.[6] It was just a few minutes after one of those infernal German shells had exploded near me. I was standing there a little dazed when he came to save me—did you hear— to save me, I said. [*He laughs harshly*] He was such a huge black one and it was so easy for him to carry me. We had gone some distance when he missed his gun and went back. A shell got him.

MAC: Poor lad—poor fellow.

STRAGGLER: Lucky lad! Didn't they go right to that spot to get him.

MAC: How would you be knowing that?

STRAGGLER: He told me himself how shocked he was when he saw where they were putting him, because he knew how they felt over here about Niggers.

BRADFORD: But son you said he was dead.

STRAGGLER: Sure he's dead but I've talked to him and even Niggers learn sense after death. He only stays there from evening 'til dawn. The rest of the time he spends at the Capitol. He says it's lots of fun to come back and see what foolish things big men say and do. Isn't it funny they can't change the only thing that counts?

---

[6] What soldiers called the terrain between the trenches of opposing sides during World War I.

MAC: It's bad to be alisten'ning to that lad.

STRAGGLER: From a black Nigger too who stole my place. [*He becomes violent in his expression*] He caught the shell aimed at me. He holds the tomb meant for me! He sleeps there and leaves me to live on a shell of a man, a shadow tagging after him—me Captain Lester Bradford Jr.—and I can't die.

BRADFORD: Son, you do remember then and you know me?

STRAGGLER: [*He stands for a moment bewildered and then a gleam of intelligence suffuses the empty face.*] Certainly dad.

BRADFORD: You've been away from home two days.

STRAGGLER: [*Surprised*] Two days?

BRADFORD: The folks were getting anxious about you.

STRAGGLER: Mother and Zelma?

BRADFORD: I promised them I'd bring you back with me.

STRAGGLER: All right, I'm ready.

BRADFORD: [*Turning quickly to speak to* MAC] I am sorry if we detained you. Thank you for your trouble. [*He is in the act of drawing a bill from his wallet.*]

STRAGGLER: [*Turning back*] I had almost forgotten those things don't make any difference.

BRADFORD: What things?

STRAGGLER: Name—home—those things.

BRADFORD: Maybe not, son, but it's late. Let's go.

STRAGGLER: [*He stares at tomb as he walks away.*] I can't go now. If I wait this time until he comes I may go in the tomb with him. I've missed for two nights but tonight I'll make it.

BRADFORD: Nobody can get in that tomb. This gentleman is waiting to lock the gates, come let's go home.

STRAGGLER: You don't understand yet. He belongs there and when he comes from the Capitol in the evening the side opens for him. I talked to him this morning when he left and he promised that I can go in with him tonight if I get there when the slab slides for him.

BRADFORD: [*Taking his son's arm forcefully*] Come son.

STRAGGLER: [*Breaking away from his father*] It's time for him to start now. [*As a faint fog horn is heard in the distance.*] Hear that's the signal for him. [*He runs to the top of the steps.*]

BRADFORD: [*He goes up the steps after his son.*] I believe I did hear something.

MAC: Only some boat, sir, as she puts into wharf.

STRAGGLER: See there he is. He's standing right on the top of the Capitol dome. Watch him. The light's on him now.

BRADFORD: [*Nodding as if wanting to believe him.*] I see him.

MAC: Surely, sir, 'tis the same statue that's always been there.

STRAGGLER: He's stepping off now. [*In his excitement he puts his arm around his father's shoulders and points with the other hand as if following something.*] Doesn't he stride like a king over the city and they don't even know he's there. Look! See him pause at the water's edge!

BRADFORD: Yes—Yes. I see.

MAC: Indeed, sir, you do not; they're only trying to place the search light from Arlington Tower.

BRADFORD: Didn't he walk the Potomac in a hurry, son?

STRAGGLER: He's coming up the hill now and I must be there. Dad you'll tell the folks where I am, won't you. I'm glad you came because now you understand.

BRADFORD: [*Reluctantly holding his son*] I'm going too, son.

STRAGGLER: No, no, dad, you stay here. He might not let me go in if he sees anybody else.

BRADFORD: But—

STRAGGLER: [*Breaking loose and rushing out to the tomb.*] Bye, dad.

MAC: O, sir, why did you let him loose. [*Starts after boy.*] [BRADFORD *clutches* MAC'*s arm and holds him firmly.*]

MAC: [*Struggling*] I fear your son is sick, sir. See he has fallen. Let me go to him.

BRADFORD: O no! You might keep him from getting in.

MAC: But there's no place to get in, sir.

BRADFORD: Sh! Sh! There he goes. He's quite all right now. [*He frees* MAC *who rushes out to the tomb where the boy has fallen. With the aid of the soldier he turns him over and listens to his heart. The* GUARD *straightens and removes his hat standing at attention.* MAC *arises and returns to the top step where* BRADFORD *remains standing.*]

MAC: I am sorry sir, but I fear that your son is dead.

BRADFORD: [*Undisturbed*] You mean that he went with the Nigger. Yes, I know, I saw him.

MAC: No, No, sir. Of course I shall have to notify the police but I was wondering if you care to give any directions concerning the body.

BRADFORD: [*Wondering*] Body, what body?

MAC: Your son's body over there.

BRADFORD: You are mistaken; that's not my son's body.

MAC: But you called him son when you were just talking to him.

BRADFORD: O yes! That was my son, but he went in the tomb you know. [*He starts down the steps, turns back and thrusts the same bill in* MAC'*s hand.*] Thank you for your trouble. Good-night. I am sorry if I detained you. [*He goes down the steps and off stage.* MAC *stands dazed for a moment and then rushes off stage after him. At the tomb the soldier keeps his silent vigil. A boat's whistle calls shrilly in the distance as the curtain falls.*]

—1930

FLORENCE REECE (1900-1986)

Florence Reece, the daughter of a coal miner, grew up in a coal camp in Fork Ridge, Tennessee. At the age of fifteen she met her future husband, Sam Reece (they wed in 1922), with whom she had eight children. Sam Reece was a coal miner and a union organizer, and he was actively involved in the 1931 United Mine Workers of America strike. After having her house ransacked by deputies in the employ of the mine company as she and her children helplessly looked on, Reece tore a sheet from a wall calendar and composed the song that would become a union anthem in the United States, "Which Side Are You On?" The song, set to the melody of the traditional tune "Lay the Lily Low," was sung widely among mine workers' unions in the thirties. It was brought into national circulation when it was recorded by the Almanac Singers (Pete Seeger, Woody Guthrie, Millard Lampell, and Lee Hays) in 1941. Throughout her long life, Reece was active in workers' struggles, speaking and singing at protests. Reece can be seen singing "Which Side Are You On?" to striking mine workers in the Academy Award-winning documentary, *Harlan County, U.S.A.*, a 1976 film about a coal miners' strike in Brookside, Kentucky. Reece died of a heart attack in 1986 in Knoxville, Tennessee.

Which Side Are You On?

Chorus
Come all of you good workers.
Good news to you I'll tell,
Of how the good old union
has come in here to dwell.
Which side are you on?   5
Which side are you on?

Don't scab for the bosses,
Don't listen to their lies.
Us poor folks haven't got a chance
Unless we organize.   10

[*Chorus*]

They say in Harlan County
There are no neutrals there.
You'll either be a union man
Or a thug for J.H. Blair.[1]

[*Chorus*]

Oh, workers can you stand it?   15
Oh, tell me how you can.
Will you be a lousy scab,
Or will you be a man?

[*Chorus*]

My daddy is a miner,
He's in the air and sun,[2]
But he'll stick with the union   20
Till every battle's won.

—1932

---

[1] Reece, a coal miner's wife, wrote this song during a strike in Harlan County, Kentucky, after Sheriff J.H. Blair came and searched her house with armed "deputies."

[2] Blacklisted.

MALVINA REYNOLDS (1900–1978)

Born and raised in San Francisco, Malvina Milder was refused a diploma by Lowell High School because her Jewish, socialist parents had spoken out against U.S. participation in World War I. She later went on to earn a B.A., M.A., and Ph.D. from the University of California at Berkeley, but the combination of the Depression and the fact that she was female, Jewish, and a socialist prevented her from obtaining an academic position at a university. She married William Reynolds, a carpenter and a communist organizer, in 1934; they had one child, Nancy. After doing social work, writing for *People's World* newspaper, and making bombs on an assembly line during World War II, Reynolds and her husband took over his parents' naval tailor shop in Long Beach, California. It was there that she met folksingers Pete Seeger and Earl Robinson, and began to write music of her own. Reynolds wrote and recorded a number of popular songs; probably the best known of these are "Turn Around" (recorded by Harry Belafonte), "What Have They Done to the Rain" (recorded by the Searchers), and "Little Boxes."

We Don't Need the Men

It says in *Coronet* magazine,
June nineteen fifty six, page ten,
That married women are not as happy
As women who have no men.
Married women are cranky,   5
Frustrated and disgusted,
While single women are bright and gay,
Creative and well adjusted.
We don't need the men,
We don't need the men,   10
We don't need to have them round
Except for now and then.
They can come to see us
When we need to move the piano,
Otherwise they can stay at home   15
And read about the White Sox.
We don't care about them,
We can do without them,
They'll look cute in a bathing suit
On a billboard in Manhattan.   20

We don't need the men,
We don't need the men,
We don't need to have them round
Except for now and then.
They can come to see us   25
When they have tickets for the symphony,
Otherwise they can stay at home
And play a game of pinochle.
We don't care about them,
We can do without them,   30

They'll look cute in a bathing suit
On a billboard in Wisconsin.

We don't need the men,
We don't need the men,
We don't need to have them round   35
Except for now and then.
They can come to see us
When they're feeling pleasant and agreeable,
Otherwise they can stay at home
And holler at the T.V. programs.   40
We don't care about them,
We can do without them,
They'll look cute in a bathing suit
On a billboard in Madagascar.

We don't need the men,   45
We don't need the men,
We don't need to have them round
Except for now and then.
They can come to see us
When they're all dressed up with a suit on,   50
Otherwise they can stay at home
[*Spoken*] And drop towels in their own bathroom.
We don't care about them,
We can do without them,
They'll look cute in a bathing suit   55
On a billboard in Tierra del Fuego.

—1959

Little Boxes

Little boxes on the hillside,
Little boxes made of ticky tacky,
Little boxes on the hillside,
Little boxes all the same.
There's a green one and a pink one   5
And a blue one and a yellow one,
And they're all made out of ticky tacky,
And they all look just the same.

And the people in the houses
All went to the university,   10
Where they were put in boxes
And they came out all the same,
And there's doctors and lawyers,
And business executives,
And they're all made out of ticky tacky,   15
And they all look just the same.

And they all play on the golf course
And drink their martinis dry,
And they all have pretty children
And the children go to school,   20
And the children go to summer camp,
And then to the university
Where they are put in boxes
And they come out all the same.

And the boys go into business   25
And marry and raise a family
In boxes made of ticky tacky
And they all look just the same.
There's a green one and a pink one
And a blue one and a yellow one,   30
And they're all made out of ticky tacky
And they all look just the same.

—1962

LAURA (RIDING) JACKSON (1901-1991)

Poet and critic Laura Reichenthal was born in New York City, the daughter of Nathaniel Reichenthal and his second wife, Sadie Edersheim Reichenthal. While attending Cornell University, she met her first husband, history instructor Louis Gottschalk, whom she married in 1920. They moved first to Urbana, Illinois, and then to Louisville, Kentucky. After she published her first poem in 1923 (under the name Laura Riding Gottschalk) in *The Fugitive,* the literary group the Fugitives (made up of Southern, white, conservative poets and writers initially centered at Vanderbilt University) invited her to join. She divorced Gottschalk in 1925 and moved first to New York and then to London, where she worked with poet and critic Robert Graves on several projects, including a small press, and wrote some twenty books of poems, stories, and criticism over the next thirteen years. In 1927, she changed her name to Laura Riding. She and Graves moved to Mallorca in 1929, but were forced to evacuate in 1936 due to the Spanish Civil War. Following the publication of her *Collected Poems* (1938), Riding renounced poetry altogether. She returned to the U.S., married Schuyler B. Jackson in 1941, and turned her attention to language itself, publishing *Rational Meaning: A New Foundation for the Definition of Words*. In 1980, *Collected Poems* was expanded and republished as *The Poems of Laura Riding*. She was co-recipient of the Bollingen Prize for her lifetime contribution to poetry in 1991.

In conformity with her wishes, Laura (Riding) Jackson's Board of Literary Management asks *The Aunt Lute Anthology* to record that, in 1941, Jackson renounced, on the grounds of linguistic principle, the writing of poetry: she had come to hold that "poetry obstructs general attainment to something better in our linguistic way-of-life than we have." Until July 2005, the Laura (Riding) Jackson Board of Literary Management maintained the author's own policy of refusing permission for the inclusion of her work in women-only compilations. In now granting permission, the Board asks that Jackson's view and policy (1986) be quoted here: "I regard the treatment of literary work as falling into a special category of women's writing as an offence against literature as of a human generalness, and an offence against the human identity of women. I refuse every request made of me to contribute to, participate in, such a trivializing of the issues of literature, and oppose this categorization in public commentary, as I can."

Chloe Or...

Chloe or her modern sister, Lil,
Stepping one day over the fatal sill,
Will say quietly: 'Behold the waiting equipage!'
Or whistle Hello and end an age.

For both these girls have that cold ease   5
Of women overwooed, half-won, hard to please.
Death is one more honour they accept
Quizzically, ladies adept

In hiding what they feel, if they feel at all.
It can scarcely have the importance of a ball,   10
Is less impressive than the least man
Chloe, smiling, turns pale, or Lil tweaks with her fan.

Yet, they have been used so tenderly.
But the embarrassment of the suit will be
Death's not theirs. They will avoid aggression   15
As usual, be saved by self-possession.

Both of them, or most likely, Lil,
No less immortal, will
Refuse to see anything distressing,
Keep Death, like all the others, guessing.

—1938

The Tiger

The tiger in me I know late, not burning bright.
Of such women as I am, they say,
'Woman, many women in one,' winking.
Such women as I say, thinking,
'A procession of one, reiteration   5
Of blinking eyes and disentangled brains
Measuring their length in love.
Each yard of thought is an embrace.
To these I have charms.
Shame, century creature.'   10
To myself, hurrying, I whisper,
'The lechery of time greases their eyes.
Lust, earlier than time,
Unwinds their minds.
The green anatomy of desire   15
Plain as through glass
Quickens as I pass.'

Earlier than lust, not plain,
Behind a darkened face of memory,
My inner animal revives. 20
Beware, that I am tame.
Beware philosophies
Wherein I yield.

They cage me on three sides.
The fourth is glass. 25
Not to be image of the beast in me,
I press the tiger forward.
I crash through.
Now we are two.
One rides. 30

And now I know the tiger late,
And now they pursue:
'A woman in a skin, mad at her heels
With pride, pretending chariot wheels—
Fleeing our learned days, 35
She reassumes the brute.'

The first of the pursuers found me.
With lady-ears I listened.
'Dear face, to find you here
After such tiger-hunt and pressing of 40
Thick forest, to find you here
In high house in a jungle,
To brave as any room
The tiger-cave and as in any room
Find woman in the room 45
With dear face shaking her dress
To wave like any picture queen...'
'Dear pursuer, to find me thus
Belies no tiger. The tiger runs and rides,
But the lady is not venturous. 50
Like any picture queen she hides
And is unhappy in her room,
Covering her eyes against the latest year,
Its learning of old queens,
Its death to queens and pictures, 55
Its lust of century creatures,
And century creatures as one woman,
Such a woman as I,
Mirage of all green forests—
The colour of the season always 60
When hope lives of abolished pleasures.'

So to the first pursuer I prolonged
Woman's histories and shames,

And yielded as became a queen
Picture-dreaming in a room 65
Among silk provinces where pain
Ruined her body without stain—
So white, so out of time, so story-like.
While woman's pride escaped
In tiger stripes. 70

Hymn to the hostage queen
And her debauched provinces.
Down fell her room,
Down fell her high couches.
The first pursuer rose from his hot cloak. 75
'Company,' he cried, 'the tiger made magic
While you slept and I dreamt of ravages.
The queen was dust.'
And Queen, Queen, Queen,
Crowded the Captain's brain. 80
And Queen, Queen, Queen,
Spurred the whole train
With book-thoughts
And exploits of queen's armies
On gold and silver cloth. 85
Until they stumbled on their eyes,
Read the number of the year,
Remembered the fast tiger.

The tiger recalled man's fear
Of beast, in man-sweat they ran back, 90
Opened their books at the correct pages.
The chapter closed with queens and shepherdesses.
'Peace to their dim tresses,'
Chanted the pious sages.

And now the tiger in me I knew late. 95
'O pride,' I comforted, 'rest.
The mischief and the rape
Cannot come through.
We are in the time of never yet
Where bells peal backward, 100
Peal "forget, forget".'

Here am I found forgotten.
The sun is used. The men are in the book.
I, woman, have removed the window
And read in my high house in the dark, 105
Sitting long after reading, as before,
Waiting, as in the book, to hear the bell,
Though long since has fallen away the door,
Long since, when like a tiger I was pursued

And the first pursuer, at such and such a date,   110
Found how the tiger takes the lady
Far away where she is gentle.
In the high forest she is gentle.
She is patient in a high house.
Ah me, ah me, says every lady in the end,   115
Putting the tiger in its cage
Inside her lofty head.
And weeps reading her own story.
And scarcely knows she weeps,
So loud the tiger roars.   120
Or thinks to close her eyes,

Though surely she must be sleeping,
To go on without knowing weeping,
Sleeping or not knowing,
Not knowing weeping,   125
Not knowing sleeping.

—1938

GWENDOLYN BENNETT (1902-1981)

Born in Giddings, Texas, Gwendolyn Bennett was the daughter of Mayme Abernathy and Joshua Robin Bennett, both teachers on Nevada's Paiute Indian reservation. The Bennetts moved to Washington, D.C., in 1906 and divorced in 1910. After the divorce, Bennett's father kidnapped her, and she spent most of the following years in hiding with her father and step-mother, eventually settling in New York, where she attended Brooklyn Girls' High, Columbia University, and the Pratt Institute, from which she graduated in 1924. Bennett published her first poems in *Crisis* and *Opportunity* while she was still in college, and her poetry and short fic-tion appeared in the major magazines and anthologies of the Harlem Renaissance. Bennett was also a visual artist—she designed several covers for various African-American magazines, taught art and design courses at Howard University, and studied art in Paris for a year on scholarship. In 1927, she married Alfred Jackson, a doctor; they lived briefly in the South before moving to Long Island. After Jackson died in 1936, Bennett lived with the sculptor Augusta Savage in New York, working at the Harlem Community Art Center until she was suspended by the House Un-American Activities Committee (HUAC) in 1941 for her politics. Bennett also co-founded and directed Harlem's George Washington Carver Community School, an adult education school for African Americans, which was closed down by HUAC in 1947. She married fellow teacher Richard Crosscup, who was white, in 1941; they retired in 1968 and moved to Pennsylvania, where Bennett died in 1981.

Heritage

I want to see the slim palm-trees,
Pulling at the clouds
With little pointed fingers....

I want to see lithe Negro girls
Etched dark against the sky   5
While sunset lingers.

I want to hear the silent sands,
Singing to the moon
Before the Sphinx-still[1] face....

I want to hear the chanting   10
Around a heathen fire
Of a strange black race.

I want to breathe the Lotus flow'r,
Sighing to the stars
With tendrils drinking at the Nile....   15

I want to feel the surging
Of my sad people's soul,
Hidden by a minstrel-smile.

—1923

To a Dark Girl

I love you for your brownness
And the rounded darkness of your breast.
I love you for the breaking sadness in your voice
And shadows where your wayward eye-lids rest.

Something of old forgotten queens   5
Lurks in the lithe abandon of your walk
And something of the shackled slave
Sobs in the rhythm of your talk.

Oh, little brown girl, born for sorrow's mate,
Keep all you have of queenliness,   10
Forgetting that you once were slave,
And let your full lips laugh at Fate!

—1923

Secret

I shall make a song like your hair...
Gold-woven with shadows green-tinged,
And I shall play with my song
As my fingers might play with your hair.
Deep in my heart   5
I shall play with my song of you,
Gently....

---

[1] Egyptian mythical creature; most famously, the Great Sphinx at Giza.

I shall laugh
At its sensitive lustre....
I shall wrap my song in a blanket,   10
Blue like your eyes are blue
With tiny shots of silver.
I shall wrap it caressingly,
Tenderly...
I shall sing a lullaby   15
To the song I have made
Of your hair and eyes...
And you will never know
That deep in my heart
I shelter a song of you   20
Secretly....

—1927

KAY BOYLE (1902-1992)

Born in St. Paul, Minnesota, Kay Boyle was the daughter of Katherine Evans, a literary and social activist, and Howard Peterson Boyle, an attorney. The family traveled extensively, and Boyle finished her education at the Ohio Mechanics Institute in Cincinnati, where she studied architecture. She moved to New York in 1922 and took a job working for Lola Ridge, the editor of the avant-garde magazine *Broom.* Boyle and her husband Richard Brault, whom she married in 1922, moved to France in 1923. There, she began working on another avant-garde magazine, *This Quarter,* with Ernest Walsh, whose daughter she would have after his death in 1927. Over the next two years, she published short fiction in the magazine *transition.* After her divorce from Brault in 1932, Boyle married Lawrence Vail; they moved to Austria the next year and had three children; during that time Boyle received O'Henry Memorial Awards for her short stories "The White Horses of Vienna" (1934) and "Defeat" (1941). In 1943, Boyle and Vail were divorced, and Boyle married Baron Joseph von Franckenstein, who worked for the U. S. State Department, with whom she had two children. After her husband was fired by the State Department because of her liberal politics, Boyle lost her job as foreign correspondent to the *New Yorker* and was blacklisted. After a nine-year battle against the firing, von Franckenstein was reinstated in 1962 and died soon thereafter. Boyle then took a creative writing faculty position at San Francisco State College (now San Francisco State University), where she taught from 1963 to 1979. During this time, she actively participated in the movement against the Vietnam War; her novel, *The Underground Woman* (1975), fictionalizes her arrest at the Oakland Induction Center and subsequent imprisonment. Boyle published fourteen novels, as well as short story collections, children's books, poetry, and essays.

Winter Night

There is a time of apprehension which begins with the beginning of darkness, and to which only the speech of love can lend security. It is there, in abeyance, at the end of every day, not urgent enough to be given the name of fear but rather of concern for how the hours are to be reprieved from fear, and those who have forgotten how it was when they were children can remember nothing of this. It may begin around five o'clock on a winter afternoon when the light outside is dying in the windows. At that hour the New York apartment in which Felicia lived was filled with shadows, and the little girl would wait alone in the living room, looking out at the winter-stripped trees that stood black in the park against the isolated ovals of unclean snow. Now it was January, and the day had been a cold one; the water of the artificial lake was frozen fast, but because of the cold and the coming darkness, the skaters had ceased to move across its surface. The street that lay between the park and the apartment house was wide, and the two-way streams of cars and busses, some with their headlamps already shining, advanced and halted, halted and poured swiftly on to the tempo of the traffic signals' altering lights. The time of apprehension had set in, and Felicia, who was seven, stood at the window in the evening and waited before she asked the question. When the signals below would change from red to green again, or when the double-decker bus would turn the corner below, she would ask it. The words of it were already there, tentative in her mouth, when the answer came from the far end of the hall.

"Your mother," said the voice among the sound of kitchen things, "she telephoned up before you came in from nursery school. She won't be back in time for supper. I was to tell you a sitter was coming in from the sitting parents' place."

Felicia turned back from the window into the obscurity of the living room, and she looked toward the open door, and into the hall beyond it where the light from the kitchen fell in a clear yellow angle across the wall and onto the strip of carpet. Her hands were cold, and she put them in her jacket pockets as she walked carefully across the living-room rug and stopped at the edge of light.

"Will she be home late?" she said.

For a moment there was the sound of water running in the kitchen, a long way away, and then the sound of the water ceased, and the high, Southern voice went on:

"She'll come home when she gets ready to come home. That's all I have to say. If she wants to spend two dollars and fifty cents and ten cents' carfare on top of that three or four nights out of the week for a sitting parent to come in here and sit, it's her own business. It certainly ain't nothing to do with you or me. She makes her money, just like the rest of us does. She works all day down there in the office, or whatever it is, just like the rest of us works, and she's entitled to spend her money like she wants to spend it. There's no law in the world against buying your own freedom. Your mother and me, we're just buying our own freedom, that's all we're doing. And we're not doing nobody no harm."

"Do you know who she's having supper with?" said Felicia from the edge of dark. There was one more step to take, and then she would be standing in the light that fell on the strip of carpet, but she did not take the step.

"Do I know who she's having supper with?" the voice cried out in what might have been derision, and there was the sound of dishes striking the metal ribs of the drain-board by the sink. "Maybe it's Mr. Van Johnson, or Mr. Frank Sinatra, or maybe it's just the Duke of Wincers[1] for the evening. All I know is you're having soft-boiled egg and spinach and applesauce for supper, and you're going to have it quick now because

---

[1] Actor Van Johnson (b. 1916); singer Frank Sinatra (1915-1998); Prince Edward, Duke of Windsor (1894-1972), British king who abdicated the throne in 1936.

the time is getting away."

The voice from the kitchen had no name. It was as variable as the faces and figures of the women who came and sat in the evenings. Month by month the voice in the kitchen altered to another voice, and the sitting parents were no more than lonely aunts of an evening or two who sometimes returned and sometimes did not to this apartment in which they had sat before. Nobody stayed anywhere very long any more, Felicia's mother told her. It was part of the time in which you lived, and part of the life of the city, but when the fathers came back, all this would be miraculously changed. Perhaps you would live in a house again, a small one, with fir trees on either side of the short brick walk, and Father would drive up every night from the station just after darkness set in. When Felicia thought of this, she stepped quickly into the clear angle of light, and she left the dark of the living room behind her and ran softly down the hall.

The drop-leaf table stood in the kitchen between the refrigerator and the sink, and Felicia sat down at the place that was set. The voice at the sink was speaking still, and while Felicia ate it did not cease to speak until the bell of the front door rang abruptly. The girl walked around the table and went down the hall, wiping her dark palms in her apron, and, from the drop-leaf table, Felicia watched her step from the angle of light into darkness and open the door.

"You put in an early appearance," the girl said, and the woman who had rung the bell came into the hall. The door closed behind her, and the girl showed her into the living room, and lit the lamp on the bookcase, and the shadows were suddenly bleached away. But when the girl turned, the woman turned from the living room too and followed her, humbly and in silence, to the threshold of the kitchen. "Sometimes they keep me standing around waiting after it's time for me to be getting on home, the sitting parents do," the girl said, and she picked up the last two dishes from the table and put them in the sink. The woman who stood in the doorway was a small woman, and when she undid the white silk scarf from around her head, Felicia saw that her hair was black. She wore it parted in the middle, and it had not been cut, but was drawn back loosely into a knot behind her head. She had very clean white gloves on, and her face was pale, and there was a look of sorrow in her soft black eyes. "Sometimes I have to stand out there in the hall with my hat and coat on, waiting for the sitting parents to turn up," the girl said, and, as she turned on the water in the sink, the contempt she had for them hung on the kitchen air. "But you're ahead of time," she said, and she held the dishes, first one and then the other, under the flow of steaming water.

The woman in the doorway wore a neat black coat, not a new-looking coat, and it had no fur on it, but it had a smooth velvet collar and velvet lapels. She did not move, or smile, and she gave no sign that she had heard the girl speaking above the sound of water at the sink. She simply stood looking at Felicia, who sat at the table with the milk in her glass not finished yet.

"Are you the child?" she said at last, and her voice was low, and the pronunciation of the words a little strange.

"Yes, this here's Felicia," the girl said, and the dark hands dried the dishes and put them away. "You drink up your milk quick now, Felicia, so's I can rinse your glass."

"I will wash the glass," said the woman. "I would like to wash the glass for her," and Felicia sat looking across the table at the face in the doorway that was filled with such unspoken grief. "I will wash the glass for her and clean off the table," the woman was saying quietly. "When the child is finished, she will show me where her night things are."

"The others, they wouldn't do anything like that," the girl said, and she hung the dishcloth over the rack. "They wouldn't put their hand to housework, the sitting parents. That's where they got the name for them," she said.

Whenever the front door closed behind the girl in the evening, it would usually be that the sitting parent who was there would take up a book of fairy stories and read aloud for a while to Felicia; or else would settle herself in the big chair in the living room and begin to tell the words of a story in drowsiness to her, while Felicia took off her clothes in the bedroom, and folded them, and put her pajamas on, and brushed her teeth, and did her hair. But this time, that was not the way it happened. Instead, the woman sat down on the other chair at the kitchen table, and she began at once to speak, not of good fairies or bad, or of animals endowed with human speech, but to speak quietly, in spite of the eagerness behind her words, of a thing that seemed of singular importance to her.

"It is strange that I should have been sent here tonight," she said, her eyes moving slowly from feature to feature of Felicia's face, "for you look like a child that I knew once, and this is the anniversary of that child."

"Did she have hair like mine?" Felicia asked quickly, and she did not keep her eyes fixed on the unfinished glass of milk in shyness any more.

"Yes, she did. She had hair like yours," said the woman, and her glance paused for a moment on the locks which fell straight and thick on the shoulders of Felicia's dress. It may have been that she thought to stretch out her hand and touch the ends of Felicia's hair, for her fingers stirred as they lay clasped together on the table, and then they relapsed into passivity again. "But it is not the hair alone, it is the delicacy of your face, too, and your eyes the same, filled with the same spring lilac color," the woman said, pronouncing the words carefully. "She had little coats of golden fur on her arms and legs," she said, "and when we were closed up there, the lot of us in the cold, I used to make her laugh when I told her that the fur that was so pretty, like a little fawn's skin on her arms, would always help to keep her warm."

"And did it keep her warm?" asked Felicia, and she gave a little jerk of laughter as she looked down at her own legs hanging under the table, with the bare calves thin and covered with a down of hair.

"It did not keep her warm enough," the woman said, and now the mask of grief had come back upon her face. "So we used to take everything we could spare from ourselves, and we would sew them into cloaks and other kinds of garments for her and for the other children...."

"Was it a school?" said Felicia when the woman's voice had ceased to speak.

"No," said the woman softly, "it was not a school, but still there were a lot of children there. It was a camp—that was the name the place had; it was a camp. It was a place where they put people until they could decide what was to be done with them." She sat with her hands clasped, silent a moment, looking at Felicia. "That little dress you have on," she said, not saying the words to anybody, scarcely saying them aloud. "Oh, she would have liked that little dress, the little buttons shaped like hearts, and the white collar——"

"I have four school dresses," Felicia said. "I'll show them to you. How many dresses did she have?"

"Well, there, you see, there in the camp," said the woman, "she did not have any dresses except the little skirt and the pullover. That was all she had. She had brought just a handkerchief of her belongings with her, like everybody else—just enough for three days away from home was what they told us, so she did not have enough to last the winter. But she had her ballet slippers," the woman said, and her clasped fingers did not move. "She had brought them because she thought during her three days away from home she would have the time to practice her ballet."

"I've been to the ballet," Felicia said suddenly, and she said it so eagerly that she stuttered a little as the words came out of her mouth. She slipped quickly down from the chair and went around the table to where the woman sat. Then she took one of the woman's hands away from the other that held it fast, and she pulled her toward the door. "Come into the living room and I'll do a pirouette for you," she said, and then she stopped speaking, her eyes halted on the woman's face. "Did she—did the little girl—could she do a pirouette very well?" she said.

"Yes, she could. At first she could," said the woman, and Felicia felt uneasy now at the sound of sorrow in her words. "But after that she was hungry. She was hungry all winter," she said in a low voice. "We were all hungry, but the children were the hungriest. Even now," she said, and her voice went suddenly savage, "when I see milk like that, clean, fresh milk standing in a glass, I want to cry out loud, I want to beat my hands on the table, because it did not have to be…" She had drawn her fingers abruptly away from Felicia now, and Felicia stood before her, cast off, forlorn, alone again in the time of apprehension. "That was three years ago," the woman was saying, and one hand was lifted, as in weariness, to shade her face. "It was somewhere else, it was in another country," she said, and behind her hand her eyes were turned upon the substance of a world in which Felicia had played no part.

"Did—did the little girl cry when she was hungry?" Felicia asked, and the woman shook her head.

"Sometimes she cried," she said, "but not very much. She was very quiet. One night when she heard the other children crying, she said to me, 'You know, they are not crying because they want something to eat. They are crying because their mothers have gone away.'"

"Did the mothers have to go out to supper?" Felicia asked, and she watched the woman's face for the answer.

"No," said the woman. She stood up from her chair, and now that she put her hand on the little girl's shoulder, Felicia was taken into the sphere of love and intimacy again. "Shall we go into the other room, and you will do your pirouette for me?" the woman said, and they went from the kitchen and down the strip of carpet on which the clear light fell. In the front room, they paused hand in hand in the glow of the shaded lamp, and the woman looked about her, at the books, the low tables with the magazines and ash trays on them, the vase of roses on the piano, looking with dark, scarcely seeing eyes at these things that had no reality at all. It was only when she saw the little white clock on the mantelpiece that she gave any sign, and then she said quickly: "What time does your mother put you to bed?"

Felicia waited a moment, and in the interval of waiting the woman lifted one hand and, as if in reverence, touched Felicia's hair.

"What time did the little girl you knew in the other place go to bed?" Felicia asked.

"Ah, God, I do not know, I do not remember," the woman said.

"Was she your little girl?" said Felicia softly, stubbornly.

"No," said the woman. "She was not mine. At least, at first she was not mine. She had a mother, a real mother, but the mother had to go away."

"Did she come back late?" asked Felicia.

"No, ah, no, she could not come back, she never came back," the woman said, and now she turned, her arm around Felicia's shoulders, and she sat down in the low soft chair. "Why am I saying all this to you, why am I doing it?" she cried out in grief, and she held Felicia close against her. "I had thought to speak of the anniversary to you, and that was all, and now I am saying these other things to you. Three years ago today, exactly, the little girl became my little girl because her mother went away. That is all there is to it. There is nothing more."

Felicia waited another moment, held close against the woman, and listening to the swift, strong heartbeats in the woman's breast.

"But the mother," she said then in the small, persistent voice, "did she take a taxi when she went?"

"This is the way it used to happen," said the woman, speaking in hopelessness and bitterness in the softly lighted room. "Every week they used to come into the place where we were and they would read a list of names out. Sometimes it would be the names of children they would read out, and then a little later they would have to go away. And sometimes it would be the grown people's names, the names of the mothers or big sisters, or other women's names. The men were not with us. The fathers were somewhere else, in another place."

"Yes," Felicia said. "I know."

"We had been there only a little while, maybe ten days or maybe not so long," the woman went on, holding Felicia against her still, "when they read the name of the little girl's mother out, and that afternoon they took her away."

"What did the little girl do?" Felicia said.

"She wanted to think up the best way of getting out so that she could go find her mother," said the woman, "but she could not think of anything good enough until the third or fourth day. And then she tied her ballet slippers up in the handkerchief again, and she went up to the guard standing at the door." The woman's voice was gentle, controlled now. "She asked the guard please to open the door so that she could go out. 'This is Thursday,' she said, 'and every Tuesday and Thursday I have my ballet lessons. If I miss a ballet lesson, they do not count the money off, so my mother would be just paying for nothing, and she cannot afford to pay for nothing. I missed my ballet lesson on Tuesday,' she said to the guard, 'and I must not miss it again today.'"

Felicia lifted her head from the woman's shoulder, and she shook her hair back and looked in question and wonder at the woman's face.

"And did the man let her go?" she said.

"No, he did not. He could not do that," said the woman. "He was a soldier and he had to do what he was told. So every evening after her mother went, I used to brush the little girl's hair for her," the woman went on saying. "And while I brushed it, I used to tell her the stories of the ballets. Sometimes I would begin with *Narcissus*," the woman said, and she parted Felicia's locks with her fingers, "so if you will go and get your brush now, I will tell it while I brush your hair."

"Oh, yes," said Felicia, and she made two whirls as she went quickly to the bedroom. On the way back, she stopped and held on to the piano with the fingers of one hand while she went up on her toes. "Did you see me? Did you see me standing on my toes?" she called to the woman, and the woman sat smiling in love and contentment at her.

"Yes, wonderful, really wonderful," she said. "I am sure I have never seen anyone do it so well." Felicia came spinning toward her, whirling in pirouette after pirouette, and she flung herself down in the chair close to her, with her thin bones pressed against the woman's soft, wide hip. The woman took the silver-backed, monogrammed brush and the tortoise-shell comb in her hands, and now she began to brush Felicia's hair. "We did not have any soap at all and not very much water to wash in, so I never could fix her as nicely and prettily as I wanted to," she said, and the brush stroked regularly, carefully down, caressing the shape of Felicia's head.

"If there wasn't very much water, then how did she do her teeth?" Felicia said.

"She did not do her teeth," said the woman, and she drew the comb through Felicia's hair. "There were not any toothbrushes or tooth paste, or anything like that."

Felicia waited a moment, constructing the unfamiliar scene of it in silence, and then she asked the tentative question.

"Do I have to do my teeth tonight?" she said.

"No," said the woman, and she was thinking of something else, "you do not have to do your teeth."

"If I am your little girl tonight, can I pretend there isn't enough water to wash?" said Felicia.

"Yes," said the woman, "you can pretend that if you like. You do not have to wash," she said, and the comb passed lightly through Felicia's hair.

"Will you tell me the story of the ballet?" said Felicia, and the rhythm of the brushing was like the soft, slow rocking of sleep.

"Yes," said the woman. "In the first one, the place is a forest glade with little pale birches growing in it, and they have green veils over their faces and green veils drifting from their fingers, because it is the springtime. There is the music of a flute," said the woman's voice softly, softly, "and creatures of the wood are dancing——"

"But the mother," Felicia said as suddenly as if she had been awaked from sleep. "What did the little girl's mother say when she didn't do her teeth and didn't wash at night?"

"The mother was not there, you remember," said the woman, and the brush moved steadily in her hand. "But she did send one little letter back. Sometimes the people who went away were able to do that. The mother wrote it in a train, standing up in a car that had no seats," she said, and she might have been telling the story of the ballet still, for her voice was gentle and the brush did not falter on Felicia's hair. "There were perhaps a great many other people standing up in the train with her, perhaps all trying to write their little letters on the bits of paper they had managed to hide on them, or that they had found in forgotten corners as they traveled. When they had written their letters, then they must try to slip them out through the boards of the car in which they journeyed, standing up," said the woman, "and these letters fell down on the tracks under the train, or they were blown into the fields or onto the country roads, and if it was a kind person who picked them up, he would seal them in envelopes and send them to where they were addressed to go. So a letter came back like this from the little girl's mother," the woman said, and the brush followed the comb, the comb the brush in steady pursuit through Felicia's hair. "It said good-by to the little girl, and it said please to take care of her. It said: 'Whoever reads this letter in the camp, please take good care of my little girl for me, and please have her tonsils looked at by a doctor if this is possible to do.'"

"And then," said Felicia softly, persistently, "what happened to the little girl?"

"I do not know. I cannot say," the woman said. But now the brush and comb had ceased to move, and in the silence Felicia turned her thin, small body on the chair, and she and the woman suddenly put their arms around each other. "They must all be asleep now, all of them," the woman said, and in the silence that fell on them again, they held each other closer. "They must be quietly asleep somewhere, and not crying all night because they are hungry and because they are cold. For three years I have been saying 'They must all be asleep, and the cold and the hunger and the seasons or night or day or nothing matters to them——'"

It was after midnight when Felicia's mother put her key in the lock of the front door, and pushed it open, and stepped into the hallway. She walked quickly to the living room, and just across the threshold she slipped the three blue foxskins from her shoulders and dropped them, with her little velvet bag, upon the chair. The room was quiet, so quiet that she could hear the sound of breathing in it, and no one spoke to her in greeting as she crossed toward the bedroom door. And then, as startling as a slap across her delicately tinted face, she saw the woman lying sleeping on the divan, and Felicia, in her school dress still, asleep within the woman's arms.

—1946

ANAÏS NIN (1903-1977)

Anaïs Nin was born in Nevilly, France, to Joaquin Nin, a Spanish composer and pianist, and Rosa Culmell, a French-Danish singer. After her parents separated, her mother took Anaïs and her two brothers to New York in 1914, the year that Nin began keeping the diaries that would become her most famous work. After abandoning school for modeling while she was still in her teens, Nin married banker Hugh Parker Guiler in 1923. They returned to Paris in 1925, where Nin wrote and studied psychotherapy. Her first novel, *The House of Incest,* was published in 1936, followed by a collection of novellas, *Winter of Artifice,* in 1939. She and Guiler settled in New York City in 1939, fleeing the war in Europe. Unable to find an American publisher for her work, Nin published another novel and collection of short fiction, *Under a Glass Bell* (1944), under her own imprint, and printed new editions of her first books. She published the five parts of her novel *Cities of the Interior* (1959) through the 40s and 50s. In 1961, Nin moved to Los Angeles, where she published the first of her diaries in 1966. Her erotica, written in the 1940s, was collected in 1977 and 1979 as *The Delta of Venus* and *Little Birds*. Her sixty-year diaries, more than 35,000 pages in all, were sometimes rehearsals for her fiction, often edited and revised. Nin's work became even more controversial after Guiler's death in 1985, as her diaries began to appear in unexpurgated form, revealing the details of her relationships with writer Henry Miller and his wife June, and with her father, with whom she seems to have had an adult incestuous affair. "Hedja" is from *Under a Glass Bell.* In 1974, Nin was elected to the National Institute of Arts and Letters.

Hejda

The unveiling of women is a delicate matter. It will not happen overnight. We are all afraid of what we shall find.

Hejda was, of course, born in the Orient. Before the unveiling she was living in an immense garden, a little city in itself, filled with many servants, many sisters and brothers, many relatives. From the roof of the house one could see all the people passing, vendors, beggars, Arabs going to the mosque.

Hejda was then a little primitive, whose greatest pleasure consisted in inserting her finger inside pregnant hens and breaking the eggs, or filling frogs with gasoline and setting a lighted match to them. She went about without underclothes in the house, without shoes, but once outside she was heavily veiled and there was no telling exactly the contours of her body, which were at an early age those of a full-blown woman, and there was no telling that her smile had that carnivorous air of smiles with large teeth.

In school she had a friend whose great sorrow was her dark color. The darkest skin in the many shaded nuances of the Arabian school. Hejda took her out into the farthest corner of the school garden one day and said to her: "I can make you white if you want me to. Do you trust me?"

"Of course I do."

Hejda brought out a piece of pumice stone. She very gently but very persistently began to pumice a piece of the girl's forehead. Only when the pain became unendurable did she stop. But for a week, every day, she continued enlarging the circle of scraped, scarred skin, and took secret pleasure in the strange scene of the girl's constant lamentations of pain and her own obstinate scraping. Until they were both found out and punished.

At seventeen she left the Orient and the veils, but she retained an air of being veiled. With the most chic and trim French clothes, which molded her figure, she still conveyed the impression of restraint and no one could feel sure of having seen her neck, arms or legs. Even her evening dresses seemed to sheathe her. This feeling of secrecy, which recalled constantly the women of Arabia as they walked in their many yards of white cotton, rolled like silk around a spool, was due in great part to her inarticulateness. Her speech revealed and opened no doors. It was labyrinthian. She merely threw off enough words to invite one into the passageway but no sooner had one started to walk towards the unfinished phrase than one met an impasse, a curve, a barrier. She retreated behind half admissions, half promises, insinuations.

This covering of the body, which was like the covering of the spirit, had created an unshatterable timidity. It had the effect of concentrating the light, the intensity in the eyes. So that one saw Hejda as a mixture of elegance, cosmetics, aesthetic plumage, with only the eyes sending signals and messages. They pierced the European clothes with the stabbing brilliancy of those eyes in the Orient which to reach the man had to pierce through the heavy aura of yards of white cotton.

The passageways that led one to Hejda were as tortuous and intricate as the passageways in the oriental cities in which the pursued women lost themselves, but all through the vanishing, turning streets the eyes continued to signal to strangers like prisoners waving out of windows.

The desire to speak was there, after centuries of confinement and repression, the desire to be invaded and rescued from the secretiveness. The eyes were full of invitations, in great contradiction to the closed folds of the clothes, the many defenses of the silk around the neck, the sleeves around the arms.

Her language was veiled. She had no way to say: look at Hejda who is full of ideas. So she laid out cards and told fortunes like the women of the harem, or she ate sweets like a stunted woman who had been kept a child by close binding with yards of white cotton, as the feet of the Chinese women had been kept small by bandaging. All she could say was: I had a dream last night (because at breakfast time in the Orient, around the first cup of dark coffee, everyone told their dreams). Or she opened a book accidentally when in trouble and placed her finger on a phrase and decided on her next course of action by the words of this phrase. Or she cooked a dish as colorful as an oriental market place.

Her desire to be noticed was always manifested, as in the Orient, by a bit of plumage, a startling jewel, a spangle pasted on her forehead between the eyes (the third eye of the Oriental was a jewel, as if the secret life so long preserved from openness had acquired the fire of precious stones).

No one understood the signals: look at Hejda, the woman of the Orient who wants to be a woman of tomorrow. The plumage and the aesthetic adornment diverted them like decoration on a wall. She was always being thrust back into the harem, on a pillow.

She had arrived in Paris, with all her invisible veils. When she laughed she concealed her mouth as much as possible, because in her small round face the teeth were extraordinarily large. She concealed her voraciousness and her appetites. Her voice was made small, again as the Chinese make their feet small, small and infantile. Her poses were reluctant and reserved. The veil was not in her timidities, her fears, in her manner of dressing, which covered her throat and compressed her overflowing breasts. The veil was in her liking for flowers (which was racial), especially small roses and innocent asexual flowers, in complicated rituals of politeness (also traditional), but above all in evasiveness of speech.

She wanted to be a painter. She joined the Academie Julien. She painted painstakingly on small canvases—the colors of the Orient, a puerile Orient of small flowers, serpentines, confetti and candy colors, the colors of small shops with metallic lace-paper roses and butterflies.

In the same class there was a dark, silent, timid young Roumanian. He had decadent, aristocratic hands, he never smiled, he never talked. Those who approached him felt such a shriveling timidity in him, such a retraction, that they remained at a distance.

The two timidities observed each other. The two silences, the two withdrawals. Both were oriental interiors, without windows on the external world, and all the greenery in the inner patio, all their windows open on the inside of the house.

A certain Gallic playfulness presides in the painting class. The atmosphere is physical, warm, gay. But the two of them remain in their inner patio, listening to birds singing and fountains playing. He thinks: how mysterious she is. And she thinks: how mysterious he is.

Finally one day, as she is leaving, he watches her repainting the black line on the edge of her eyes out of a silver peacock. She nimbly lifts up the head of the peacock and it is a little brush that makes black lines around her oriental eyes.

This image confounds him, ensorcells him. The painter is captivated, stirred. Some memory out of Persian legends now adorns his concept of her.

They marry and take a very small apartment where the only window gives on a garden.

At first they marry to hide together. In the dark caverns of their whisperings, confidences, timidities, what they now elaborate is a stalactitic world shut out from light and air. He initiates her into his aesthetic values. They make love in the dark and in the daytime make their place more beautiful and more refined.

In Molnar's hands she is being remolded, refashioned, stylized. He cannot remold her body. He is critical of her heaviness. He dislikes her breasts and will not let her ever show them. They overwhelm him. He confesses he would like her better without them. This shrinks her within herself and plants the seed of doubt of her feminine value. With these words he has properly subjugated her, given her a doubt which will keep her away from other men. He bound her femininity, and it is now oppressed, bound, even ashamed of its vulgarity, of its expansiveness. This is the reign of aesthetic value, stylization, refinement, art, artifice. He has established his domination in this. At every turn nature must be subjugated. Very soon, with his coldness, he represses her violence. Very soon he polishes her language, her manners, her impulses. He reduces and limits her hospitality, her friendliness, her desire for expansion.

It is her second veiling. It is the aesthetic veils of art and social graces. He designs her dresses. He molds her as far as he can into the stylized figures in his paintings. His women are transparent and lie in hammocks between heaven and earth. Hejda cannot reach this, but she can become an odalisque. She can acquire more silver peacocks, more poetic objects that will speak for her.

Her small canvases look childlike standing beside his. Slowly she becomes more absorbed in his painting than in her own. The flowers and gardens disappear.

He paints a world of stage settings, static ships, frozen trees, crystal fairs, the skeletons of pleasure and color, from which nature is entirely shut off. He proceeds to make Hejda one of the objects in his painting; her nature is more and more castrated by this abstraction of her, the obtrusive breasts more severely veiled. In his painting there is no motion, no nature, and certainly not the Hejda who liked to run about without underwear, to eat herbs and raw vegetables out of the garden.

Her breasts are the only intrusion in their exquisite life. Without them she could be the twin he wanted, and they could accomplish this strange marriage of his feminine qualities and her masculine ones. For it is already clear that he likes to be protected and she likes to protect, and that she has more power in facing the world of reality, more power to sell pictures, to interest the galleries in his work, more courage too. It is she who assumes the active role in contact with the world. Molnar can never earn a living, Hejda can. Molnar cannot give orders (except to her) and she can. Molnar cannot execute, realize, concretize as well as she can, for in execution and action she is not timid.

Finally it is Molnar who paints and draws and it is Hejda who goes out and sells his work.

Molnar grows more and more delicate, more vulnerable, and Hejda stronger. He is behind the scene, and she is in the foreground now.

He permits her love to flow all around him, sustain him, nourish him. In the dark he reconquers his leadership. And not by any sensual prodigality, but on the contrary, by a severe economy of pleasure. She is often left hungry. She never suspects for a moment that it is anything but economy and thinks a great abundance lies behind this aesthetic reserve. There is no delight or joy in their sensual contact. It is a creeping together into a womb.

Their life together is stilted, windowless, facing inward. But the plants and fountains of the patio are all artificial, ephemeral, immobile. A stage setting for a drama that never takes place. There are colonnades, friezes, backgrounds, plush drops but no drama takes place, no evolution, no sparks. His women's figures are always lying down, suspended in space.

But Hejda, Hejda feels compressed. She does not know why. She has never known anything but oppression. She has never been out of a small universe delimited by man. Yet something is expanding in her. A new Hejda is born out of the struggle with reality, to protect the weakness of Molnar. In the outer world she feels larger. When she returns home she feels she must shrink back into submission to Molnar's proportions. The outgoing rhythm must cease. Molnar's whole being is one total negation; negation and rejection of the world, of social life, of other human beings, of success, of movement, of motion, of curiosity, of adventure, of the unknown.

What is he defending, protecting? No consuming passion for one person, but perhaps a secret consuming. He admits no caresses, no invitations to love-making. It is always "no" to her hunger, "no" to her tenderness, "no" to the flow of life. They were close in fear and concealment, but they are not close in flow and development. Molnar is now frozen, fixed. There is no emotion to propel him. And when she seeks to propel him, substitute her élan for his static stagnation, all he can do is break this propeller.

"Your ambitions are vulgar."

(She does not know how to answer: my ambitions are merely the balance to your inertia.)

A part of her wants to expand. A part of her being wants to stay with Molnar. This conflict tears her asunder. The pulling and tearing bring on illness.

Hejda falls.

Hejda is ill.

She cannot move forward because Molnar is tied, and she cannot break with him.

Because he will not move, his being is stagnant and filled with poison. He injects her every day with this poison.

She has taken his paintings into the real world, to sell, and in so doing she has connected with that world and found it larger, freer.

Now he does not let her handle the painting. He even stops painting. Poverty sets in.

Perhaps Molnar will turn about now and protect her. It is the dream of every maternal love: I have filled him with my strength. I have nourished his painting. My painting has passed into his painting. I am broken and weak. Perhaps now he will be strong.

But not at all. Molnar watches her fall, lets her fall. He lets poverty install itself. He watches inertly the sale of their art possessions, the trips to the pawnbroker. He leaves Hejda without care. His passivity and inertia consume the whole house.

It is as if Hejda had been the glue that held the furniture together. Now it breaks. It is as if she had been the cleaning fluid and now the curtains turn gray. The logs in the fireplace now smoke and do not burn: was she the fire in the hearth too? Because she lies ill objects grow rusty. The food turns sour. Even the artificial flowers wilt. The paints dry on the palette. Was she the water, the soap too? Was she the fountain, the visibility of the windows, the gloss of the floors? The creditors buzz like locusts. Was she the fetish of the house who kept them away? Was she the oxygen in the house? Was she the salt now missing from the bread? Was she the delicate feather duster dispelling the webs of decay? Was she the silver polish?

Tired of waiting for her to get well—alone, he goes out.

✦ ✦ ✦

Hejda and Molnar are now separated. She is free. Several people help her to unwind the binding wrapped around her personality first by the family life, then by the husband. Someone falls in love with her ample breasts, and removes the taboo that Molnar had placed upon them. Hejda buys herself a sheer blouse which will reveal her possessions.

When a button falls off she does not sew it on again.

Then she also began to talk.

She talked about her childhood. The same story of going about without underwear as a child which she had told before with a giggle of confusion and as if saying: "what a little primitive I was," was now told with the oblique glance of the strip-teaser, with a slight arrogance, the *agent provocateur* towards the men (for now exhibitionism placed the possibility in the present, not in the past).

She discards small canvases and buys very large ones. She paints larger roses, larger daisies, larger trellises, larger candied clouds, larger taffy seas. But just as the canvases grow larger without their content growing more important, Hejda is swelling up without growing. There is more of her. Her voice grows louder, her language, freed of Molnar's decadent refinement, grows coarser. Her dresses grow shorter. Her blouses looser. There is more flesh around her small body but Molnar is not there to corset it. There is more food on her table. She no longer conceals her teeth. She becomes proud of her appetite. Liberty has filled her to overflowing with a confidence that everything that was once secret and bound was of immense value. Every puerile detail of her childhood, every card dealer's intuition, every dream, becomes magnified.

And the stature of Hejda cannot bear the weight of her ambition. It is as if compression had swung her towards inflation. She is inflated physically and spiritually. And whoever dares to recall her to a sense of proportion, to a realization that there are perhaps other painters of value in the world, other women, becomes the traitor who must be banished instantly. On him she pours torrents of abuse like the abuse of the oriental gypsies to whom one has refused charity—curses and maledictions.

It is not desire or love she brings to the lovers: I have discovered that I am very gifted for love-making!

It is not creativity she brings to her painting: I will show Molnar that I was a better painter!

Her friendships with women are simply one long underground rivalry: to excel in startling dress or behavior. She enters a strained, intense competition. When everything fails she resorts to lifting her dress and arranging her garters.

Where are the veils and labyrinthian evasions?

She is back in the garden of her childhood, back to the native original Hejda, child of nature and succulence and sweets, of pillows and erotic literature.

The frogs leap away in fear of her again.

—1948

AYN RAND (1905-1992)

Fiction writer and philosopher Ayn Rand was born Alissa Rosenbaum, the daughter of a Jewish chemist, in St. Petersburg, Russia. She studied history at the University of Leningrad (now Petrograd) and left the Soviet Union in 1926, after witnessing the Russian Revolution and experiencing post-Revolutionary Soviet education. Renaming herself after the Remington-Rand typewriter she brought with her, Rand worked in Hollywood as a screenwriter and married actor Frank O'Connor in 1926. Her early plays and novels received almost universally bad reviews, but her later novels, *The Fountainhead* (1943) and *Atlas Shrugged* (1957), were widely read and extremely popular, despite their didacticism; *The Fountainhead* was adapted for film and released in 1949, starring Gary Cooper and Patricia Neal. Rand's philosophy of Objectivism developed out of her fiction and, after 1961, she focused on codifying it in works such as *The Virtue of Selfishness* (1963) and *Capitalism: The Unknown Ideal* (1966). Objectivism combined Rand's ferocious anti-Communism (in 1947 she offered to testify against fellow screenwriters to the House Un-American Activities Committee) and her atheism with an insistence that all reality was objectively knowable through reason. Objectivism was institutionalized in the Nathaniel Branden Institute, named for her follower and lover, who she met in 1950 when he wrote her a fan letter; she and her husband later moved to New York where Branden studied psychology. Although both married, Rand and Branden had a fourteen-year affair, which ended when Rand discovered another affair of his and publicly dissociated herself from him. Rand was a witty and charismatic lecturer, and worked to popularize Objectivism in her 1962 *Los Angeles Times* column and her newsletters by demonstrating its applicability to current events.

The Man-Haters

Few errors are as naive and suicidal as the attempts of the "conservatives" to justify capitalism on altruist-collectivist grounds.

Many people believe that altruism means kindness, benevolence or respect for the rights of others. But it means the exact opposite: it teaches self-sacrifice, as well as the sacrifice of others, to any unspecified "public need"; it regards man as a sacrificial animal.

Believing that collectivists are motivated by an authentic concern for the welfare of mankind, capitalism's alleged defenders assure its enemies that capitalism is the practical road to the socialists' goal, the best means to the same end, the best "servant" of public needs.

Then they wonder why they fail—and why the bloody muck of socialization keeps oozing forward over the face of the globe.

They fail, because no one's welfare can be achieved by anyone's sacrifice—and because man's welfare is not the socialists' goal. It is not for its alleged flaws that the altruist-collectivists hate capitalism, but for its virtues.

If you doubt it, consider a few examples.

Many collectivist historians criticize the Constitution of the United States on the ground that its authors were rich landowners who, allegedly, were motivated, not by any political ideals, but only by their own selfish economic interests.

This, of course, is not true. But it is true that capitalism does not require the sacrifice of anyone's interests. And what is significant here is the nature of the morality behind the collectivists' argument.

Prior to the American Revolution, through centuries of feudalism and monarchy, the interests of the rich lay in the expropriation, enslavement and misery of the rest of the people. A society, therefore, where the interests of the rich require general freedom, unrestricted productiveness and the protection of individual rights, should have been hailed as an ideal system by anyone whose goal is man's well-being.

But that is not the collectivists' goal.

A similar criticism is voiced by collectivist ideologists about the American Civil War. The North, they claim disparagingly, was motivated, not by self-sacrificial concern for the plight of the slaves, but by the selfish economic interests of capitalism— which requires a free labor market.

This last clause is true. Capitalism cannot work with slave labor. It was the agrarian, feudal South that maintained slavery. It was the industrial, capitalistic North that wiped it out—as capitalism wiped out slavery and serfdom in the whole civilized world of the 19th century.

What greater virtue can one ascribe to a social system than the fact that it leaves no possibility for any man to serve his own interests by enslaving other men? What nobler system could be desired by anyone whose goal is man's well-being?

But that is not the collectivists' goal.

Capitalism has created the highest standard of living ever known on earth. The evidence is incontrovertible. The contrast between West and East Berlin is the latest demonstration, like a laboratory experiment for all to see.

Yet those who are the loudest in proclaiming their desire to eliminate poverty are loudest in denouncing capitalism. Man's well-being is not their goal.

The "underdeveloped" nations are an alleged problem to the world. Most of them are destitute. Some, like Brazil, loot (or nationalize) the property of foreign investors; others, like the Congo, slaughter foreigners, including women and children; after which, all of them scream for foreign help, for technicians and money.

It is only the indecency of altruistic doctrines that permits them to hope to get away with it.

If those nations were taught to establish capitalism, with full protection of property rights, their problems would vanish. Men who could afford it would invest private capital in the development of natural resources, expecting to earn profits. They would bring the technicians, the funds, the civilizing influence and the employment which those nations need. Everyone would profit, at no one's expense or sacrifice.

But this would be "selfish" and, therefore, evil—according to the altruists' code.

Instead, they prefer to seize men's earnings—through taxation—and pour them down any foreign drain, and watch our own economic growth slow down year by year.

Next time you refuse yourself some necessity you can't afford or some small luxury which would have made the difference between pleasure and drudgery—ask yourself what part of your money has gone to pay for a crumbling road in Cambodia or for the support of those "selfless" little altruists who play the role of big shots in the jungle, at taxpayers' expense.

If you wish to stop it, you must begin by realizing that altruism is not a doctrine of love, but of hatred for man.

Collectivism does not preach sacrifice as a temporary means to some desirable end. Sacrifice is its end—sacrifice as a way of life. It is man's independence, success, prosperity and happiness that collectivists wish to destroy.

Observe the snarling, hysterical hatred with which they greet any suggestion that sacrifice is not necessary, that a non-sacrificial society is possible to men, that it is the only society able to achieve man's well-being.

If capitalism had never existed, any honest humanitarian should have been struggling to invent it. But when you see men struggling to evade its existence, to misrepresent its nature and to destroy its last remnants—you may be sure that whatever their motives, love for man is not one of them.

—1962

"Through Your Most Grievous Fault"

The death of Marilyn Monroe[1] shocked people, with an impact different from their reaction to the death of any other movie star or public figure. All over the world people felt a peculiar sense of personal involvement and of protest, like a universal cry of "Oh, no!"

They felt that her death had some special significance, almost like a warning which they could not decipher—and they felt a nameless apprehension, the sense that something terribly wrong was involved.

They were right to feel it.

Marilyn Monroe, on the screen, was an image of pure, innocent, childlike joy in living. She projected the sense of a person born and reared in some radiant Utopia, untouched by suffering, unable to conceive of ugliness or evil, facing life with the confidence, the benevolence and the joyous self-flaunting of a child or a kitten who is happy to display its own attractiveness as the best gift it can offer the world, and who expects to be admired for it, not hurt.

In real life, Marilyn Monroe's suicide—or worse: a suicide that might have been an accident, suggesting that, to her, the difference did not matter—was a declaration that we live in a world which made it impossible for her kind of spirit, and for the things she represented, to survive.

If there ever was a victim of society, Marilyn Monroe was that victim—of a society that professes dedication to the relief of the suffering, but kills the joyous.

None of the objects of the humanitarians' tender solicitude, the juvenile delinquents, could have had so sordid and horrifying a childhood as did Marilyn Monroe.

To survive it and to preserve the kind of spirit she projected on the screen—the radiantly benevolent sense of life, which cannot be faked—was an almost inconceivable psychological achievement that required a heroism of the highest order. Whatever

[1] Marilyn Monroe (1926-1962), iconic movie star.

scars her past had left were insignificant by comparison.

She preserved her vision of life through a nightmare struggle, fighting her way to the top. What broke her was the discovery, at the top, of as sordid an evil as the one she had left behind—worse, perhaps, because incomprehensible. She had expected to reach the sunlight; she found, instead, a limitless swamp of malice.

It was a malice of a very special kind. If you want to see her groping struggle to understand it, read the magnificent article in a recent issue of *Life* magazine. It is not actually an article, it is a verbatim transcript of her own words—and the most tragically revealing document published in many years. It is a cry for help, which came too late to be answered.

"When you're famous, you kind of run into human nature in a raw kind of way," she said. "It stirs up envy, fame does. People you run into feel that, well, who is she— who does she think she is, Marilyn Monroe? They feel fame gives them some kind of privilege to walk up to you and say anything to you, you know, of any kind of nature—and it won't hurt your feelings—like it's happening to your clothing.... I don't understand why people aren't a little more generous with each other. I don't like to say this, but I'm afraid there is a lot of envy in this business."

"Envy" is the only name she could find for the monstrous thing she faced, but it was much worse than envy: it was the profound hatred of life, of success and of all human values, felt by a certain kind of mediocrity—the kind who feels pleasure on hearing about a stranger's misfortune. It was hatred of the good for being the good— hatred of ability, of beauty, of honesty, of earnestness, of achievement and, above all, of human joy.

Read the *Life* article to see how it worked and what it did to her:

An eager child, who was rebuked for her eagerness—"Sometimes the [foster] families used to worry because I used to laugh so loud and so gay; I guess they felt it was hysterical."

A spectacularly successful star, whose employers kept repeating: "Remember you're not a star," in a determined effort, apparently, not to let her discover her own importance.

A brilliantly talented actress, who was told by the alleged authorities, by Hollywood, by the press, that she could not act.

An actress, dedicated to her art with passionate earnestness—"When I was 5—I think that's when I started wanting to be an actress—I loved to play. I didn't like the world around me because it was kind of grim—but I loved to play house and it was like you could make your own boundaries"—who went through hell to make her own boundaries, to offer people the sunlit universe of her own vision—"It's almost having certain kinds of secrets for yourself that you'll let the whole world in on only for a moment, when you're acting"—but who was ridiculed for her desire to play serious parts.

A woman, the only one, who was able to project the glowingly innocent sexuality of a being from some planet uncorrupted by guilt—who found herself regarded and ballyhooed as a vulgar symbol of obscenity—and who still had the courage to declare: "We are all born sexual creatures, thank God, but it's a pity so many people despise and crush this natural gift."

A happy child who was offering her achievement to the world, with the pride of an authentic greatness and of a kitten depositing a hunting trophy at your feet—who found herself answered by concerted efforts to negate, to degrade, to ridicule, to insult, to destroy her achievement—who was unable to conceive that it was her best she was punished for, not her worst—who could only sense, in helpless terror, that she was facing some unspeakable kind of evil.

How long do you think a human being could stand it?

That hatred of values has always existed in some people, in any age or culture. But a hundred years ago, they would have been expected to hide it. Today, it is all around us; it is the style and fashion of our century.

Where would a sinking spirit find relief from it?

The evil of a cultural atmosphere is made by all those who share it. Anyone who has ever felt resentment against the good for being the good and has given voice to it, is the murderer of Marilyn Monroe.

—1962

The Secular Meaning of Christmas

Yes, of course.[2] A national holiday, in this country, cannot have an exclusively religious meaning. The secular meaning of the Christmas holiday is wider than the tenets of any particular religion: it is good will toward men—a frame of mind which is not the exclusive property (though it is supposed to be part, but is a largely unobserved part) of the Christian religion.

The charming aspect of Christmas is the fact that it expresses good will in a cheerful, happy, benevolent, *non-sacrificial* way. One says: "Merry Christmas"—not "Weep and Repent." And the good will is expressed in a material, *earthly* form—by giving presents to one's friends, or by sending them cards in token of remembrance. (The gift-giving is charming only so long as it is non-sacrificial. O. Henry's famous "The Gift of the Magi" is a sadistic horror story, though he did not intend it as such; that story is a good example of the futility of altruism.)

The best aspect of Christmas is the aspect usually decried by the mystics: the fact that Christmas has been *commercialized*. The gift-buying is good for business and good for the country's economy; but, more importantly in this context, it stimulates an enormous outpouring of ingenuity in the creation of products devoted to a single purpose: to give men pleasure. And the street decorations put up by department stores and other institutions—the Christmas trees, the winking lights, the glittering colors— provide the city with a spectacular display, which only "commercial greed" could afford to give us. One would have to be terribly depressed to resist the wonderful gaiety of that spectacle.

Merry Christmas and Happy New Year to all of you.

—1976

---

[2] Rand is responding to the question of whether atheists should celebrate Christmas.

LILLIAN HELLMAN (1906-1984)

Playwright and memoirist Lillian Florence Hellman was born in New Orleans, Louisiana, to Julia Newhouse and Max Hellman, a traveling salesman. After Max's business failed, Hellman's family divided its time between New Orleans and New York City, which Hellman described in her first memoir, *An Unfinished Woman* (1969). Hellman attended college at New York University and Columbia University, but left to work for the publisher Liveright in 1924. She married writer Arthur Kober in 1925, about the time she began to try her hand at fiction writing. In 1930, after studying at the university in Bonn, Germany, Hellman followed Kober to Hollywood, where she worked summarizing novels for film scenarios. There she met the successful mystery writer Dashiell Hammett, who suggested the material for her first play, *The Children's Hour* (1934), which was a great success. Hellmann and Hammett began a relationship before her divorce, continued it through a series of affairs on both sides, and lived together off and on until Hammett's death in 1961.

Hellman's plays include *The Little Foxes* (1939), *Watch on the Rhine* (1941), and *Another Part of the Forest* (1946). She turned to memoir in the 1960s and 1970s, publishing *Pentimento* in 1973 (a portion of which was adapted into the 1977 Academy Award-winning film *Julia*) and *Scoundrel Time* in 1976, both of which generated controversy. *Scoundrel Time* details Hellman's testimony in 1952 before the House Un-American Activities Committee. Critics of her account claim that she deliberately understated her (and Hammett's) involvement with communist organizations. Hellman died in Martha's Vineyard in 1984.

from Scoundrel Time

May 19, 1952

Honorable John S. Wood[1]
Chairman
House Committee on Un-American Activities
Room 226 Old House Office Building
Washington 25, D.C.

Dear Mr. Wood:

As you know, I am under subpoena to appear before your Committee on May 21, 1952.

I am most willing to answer all questions about myself. I have nothing to hide from your Committee and there is nothing in my life of which I am ashamed. I have been advised by counsel that under the Fifth Amendment I have a constitutional privilege to decline to answer any questions about my political opinions, activities and associations, on the grounds of self-incrimination. I do not wish to claim this privilege. I am ready and willing to testify before the representatives of our Government as to my own opinions and my own actions, regardless of any risks or consequences to myself.

But I am advised by counsel that if I answer the Committee's questions about myself, I must also answer questions about other people and that if I refuse to do so, I can be cited for contempt. My counsel tells me that if I answer questions about myself, I will have waived my rights under the Fifth Amendment and could be forced legally to answer questions about others. This is very difficult for a layman

---

[1] John Stephens Wood (1885-1968), Democratic congressman from Georgia.

to understand. But there is one principle that I do understand: I am not willing, now or in the future, to bring bad trouble to people who, in my past association with them, were completely innocent of any talk or any action that was disloyal or subversive. I do not like subversion or disloyalty in any form and if I had ever seen any I would have considered it my duty to have reported it to the proper authorities. But to hurt innocent people whom I knew many years ago in order to save myself is, to me, inhuman and indecent and dishonorable. I cannot and will not cut my conscience to fit this year's fashions, even though I long ago came to the conclusion that I was not a political person and could have no comfortable place in any political group.

I was raised in an old-fashioned American tradition and there were certain homely things that were taught to me: to try to tell the truth, not to bear false witness, not to harm my neighbor, to be loyal to my country, and so on. In general, I respected these ideals of Christian honor and did as well with them as I knew how. It is my belief that you will agree with these simple rules of human decency and will not expect me to violate the good American tradition from which they spring. I would, therefore, like to come before you and speak of myself.

I am prepared to waive the privilege against self-incrimination and to tell you anything you wish to know about my views or actions if your Committee will agree to refrain from asking me to name other people. If the Committee is unwilling to give me this assurance, I will be forced to plead the privilege of the Fifth Amendment at the hearing.

A reply to this letter would be appreciated.

Sincerely yours,
Lillian Hellman

[…]Rauh,[2] his assistant Daniel Pollitt, and I took a taxi to the Old House Office Building. I remember saying to myself, "Just make sure you come out unashamed. That will be enough."

Joe tapped me on the arm. "If things get too much for you, tell me and I'll tell the Committee you have to go to the ladies' room. You can probably do that only once, so take your time, wash your face, have a cigarette. If you don't need a rest, then keep your eye on the clock and remember that they'll take a lunch break around twelve-thirty. We may be called back, of course, but you'll have at least an hour and a half for a nap or a drink or both. Now this is more important so listen carefully: *don't make jokes.*"

"Make *jokes?* Why would I make jokes?"

"Almost everybody, when they feel insulted by the Committee, makes a joke or acts smart-aleck. It's a kind of embarrassment. Don't do it."

The Committee room was almost empty except for a few elderly, small-faced ladies sitting in the rear. They looked as if they were permanent residents and, since they occasionally spoke to each other, it was not too long a guess that they came as an organized group or club. Clerks came in and out, put papers on the rostrum, and disappeared. I said maybe we had come too early, but Joe said no, it was better that I get used to the room.

Then, I think to make the wait better for me, he said, "Well, I can tell you now that

---

[2] Joseph Louis Rauh, Jr. (1911-1992), noted civil rights attorney who advised Hellman and others being scrutinized by HUAC.

in the early days of seeing you, I was scared that what happened to my friend might happen to me."

He stopped to tell Pollitt that he didn't understand about the press—not one newspaperman had appeared.

I said, "What happened to your friend?"

"He represented a Hollywood writer who told him that he would under no circumstances be a friendly witness. That was why my friend took the case. So they get here, in the same seats we are, sure of his client, and within ten minutes the writer is one of the friendliest witnesses the Committee has had the pleasure of. He throws in every name he can, including his college roommate, childhood friend."

I said, "No, that won't happen and for more solid reasons than your honor or even mine. I told you I can't make quick changes."

Joe told Pollitt that he thought he understood about no press and the half-empty room: the Committee had kept our appearance as quiet as they could. Joe said, "That means they're frightened of us. I don't know whether that's good or bad, but we want the press here and I don't know how to get them."

He didn't have to know. The room suddenly began to fill up behind me and the press people began to push toward their section and were still piling in when Representative Wood began to pound his gavel. I hadn't seen the Committee come in, don't think I had realized that they were to sit on a raised platform, the government having learned from the stage, or maybe the other way around. I was glad I hadn't seen them come in—they made a gloomy picture. Through the noise of the gavel I heard one of the ladies in the rear cough very loudly. She was to cough all through the hearing. Later I heard one of her friends say loudly, "Irma, take your good cough drops."

The opening questions were standard: what was my name, where was I born, what was my occupation, what were the titles of my plays. It didn't take long to get to what really interested them: my time in Hollywood, which studios had I worked for, what periods of what years, with some mysterious emphasis on 1937. (My time in Spain, I thought, but I was wrong.)

Had I met a writer called Martin Berkeley?[3] (I had never, still have never, met Martin Berkeley, although Hammett told me later that I had once sat at a lunch table of sixteen or seventeen people with him in the old Metro-Goldwyn-Mayer commissary.) I said I must refuse to answer that question. Mr. Tavenner[4] said he'd like to ask me again whether I had stated I was abroad in the summer of 1937. I said yes, explained that I had been in New York for several weeks before going to Europe, and got myself ready for what I knew was coming: Martin Berkeley, one of the Committee's most lavish witnesses on the subject of Hollywood, was now going to be put to work. Mr. Tavenner read Berkeley's testimony. Perhaps he is worth quoting, the small details are nicely formed, even about his "old friend Hammett,"[5] who had no more than a bowing acquaintance with him.

MR. TAVENNER: ...I would like you to tell the committee when and where the Hollywood section of the Communist Party was first organized.

---

[3] Screenwriter who testified that 162 people in Hollywood were Communists.

[4] Frank S. Tavenner, Jr., HUAC chief counsel.

[5] Mystery writer Dashiell Hammett (1894-1961), with whom Hellman lived, served four months in prison in 1951 for refusing to name names.

MR. BERKELEY: Well, sir, by a very strange coincidence the section was organized in my house. ...In June of 1937, the middle of June, the meeting was held in my house. My house was picked because I had a large living room and ample parking facilities....And it was a pretty good meeting. We were honored by the presence of many functionaries from downtown, and the spirit was swell....Well, in addition to Jerome and the others I have mentioned before, and there is no sense in me going over the list again and again....Also present was Harry Carlisle, who is now in the process of being deported, for which I am very grateful. He was an English subject. After Stanley Lawrence had stolen what funds there were from the party out here, and to make amends had gone to Spain and gotten himself killed, they sent Harry Carlisle here to conduct Marxist classes....Also at the meeting was Donald Ogden Stewart. His name is spelled Donald Ogden S-t-e-w-a-r-t. Dorothy Parker, also a writer. Her husband Allen Campbell, C-a-m-p-b-e-l-l; my old friend Dashiell Hammett, who is now in jail in New York for his activities; that very excellent playwright, Lillian Hellman...

And so on.

When this nonsense was finished, Mr. Tavenner asked me if it was true. I said that I wanted to refer to the letter I had sent, I would like the Committee to reconsider my offer in the letter.

MR. TAVENNER: In other words, you are asking the committee not to ask you many questions regarding the participation of other persons in the Communist Party activities?

I said I hadn't said that.

Mr. Wood said that in order to clarify the record Mr. Tavenner should put into the record the correspondence between me and the Committee. Mr. Tavenner did just that, and when he had finished Rauh sprang to his feet, picked up a stack of mimeographed copies of my letter, and handed them out to the press section. I was puzzled by this—I hadn't noticed he had the copies—but I did notice that Rauh was looking happy.

Mr. Tavenner was upset, far more than the printed words of my hearing show. Rauh said that Tavenner himself had put the letters in the record, and thus he thought passing out copies was proper. The polite words of each as they read on the page were not polite as spoken. I am convinced that in this section of the testimony, as in several other sections—certainly in Hammett's later testimony before the Senate Internal Security Subcommittee—either the court stenographer missed some of what was said and filled it in later, or the documents were, in part, edited. Having read many examples of the work of court stenographers, I have never once seen a completely accurate report.

Mr. Wood told Mr. Tavenner that the Committee could not be "placed in the attitude of trading with the witnesses as to what they will testify to" and that thus he thought both letters should be read aloud.

Mr. Tavenner did just this, and there was talk I couldn't hear, a kind of rustle, from the press section. Then Mr. Tavenner asked me if I had attended the meeting described by Berkeley, and one of the hardest things I ever did in my life was to swallow the words, "I don't know him, and a little investigation into the time and place would have proved to you that I could not have been at the meeting he talks about." Instead, I said that I must refuse to answer the question. The "must" in that sentence annoyed Mr. Wood—it was to annoy him again and again—and he corrected me: "You might refuse to answer, the question is asked, do you refuse?"

But Wood's correction of me, the irritation in his voice, was making me nervous, and I began to move my right hand as if I had a tic, unexpected, and couldn't stop it. I told myself that if a word irritated him, the insults would begin to come very soon. So I sat up straight, made my left hand hold my right hand, and hoped it would work. But I felt the sweat on my face and arms and knew that something was going to happen to me, something out of control, and I turned to Joe, remembering the suggested toilet intermission. But the clock said we had only been there sixteen minutes, and if it was going to come, the bad time, I had better hang on for a while.

Was I a member of the Communist Party, had I been, what year had I stopped being? How could I harm such people as Martin Berkeley by admitting I had known them, and so on. At times I couldn't follow the reasoning, at times I understood full well that in refusing to answer questions about membership in the Party I had, of course, trapped myself into a seeming admission that I once had been.

But in the middle of one of the questions about my past, something so remarkable happened that I am to this day convinced that the unknown gentleman who spoke had a great deal to do with the rest of my life. A voice from the press gallery had been for at least three or four minutes louder than the other voices. (By this time, I think, the press had finished reading my letter to the Committee and were discussing it.) The loud voice had been answered by a less loud voice, but no words could be distinguished. Suddenly a clear voice said, "Thank God somebody finally had the guts to do it."

It is never wise to say that something is the best minute of your life, you must be forgetting, but I still think that unknown voice made the words that helped to save me. (I had been sure that not only did the elderly ladies in the room disapprove of me, but the press would be antagonistic.) Wood rapped his gavel and said angrily, "If that occurs again, I will clear the press from these chambers."

"You do that, sir," said the same voice.

Mr. Wood spoke to somebody over his shoulder and the somebody moved around to the press section, but that is all that happened. To this day I don't know the name of the man who spoke, but for months later, almost every day I would say to myself, I wish I could tell him that I had really wanted to say to Mr. Wood: "There is no Communist menace in this country and you know it. You have made cowards into liars, an ugly business, and you made me write a letter in which I acknowledged your power. I should have gone into your Committee room, given my name and address, and walked out." Many people have said they liked what I did, but I don't much, and if I hadn't worried about rats in jail, and such....Ah, the bravery you tell yourself was possible when it's all over, the bravery of the staircase.

In the Committee room I heard Mr. Wood say, "Mr. Walter[6] does not desire to ask the witness any further questions. Is there any reason why this witness should not be excused from further attendance before the Committee?"

Mr. Tavenner said, "No, sir."

My hearing was over an hour and seven minutes after it began. I don't think I understood that it was over, but Joe was whispering so loudly and so happily that I jumped from the noise in my ear.

He said, *"Get up. Get up.* Get out of here immediately. Pollitt will take you. Don't stop for any reason, to answer any questions from anybody. Don't run, but walk as

---

[6] Francis Walter, Democrat from Pennsylvania.

fast as you can and just shake your head and keep moving if anybody comes near you."

I am looking at a recent letter from Daniel Pollitt, who is now a distinguished professor of law at the University of North Carolina. He doesn't comment on the run we made out of the building, the fastest I ever made since I was a child late for class. But he remembers that we went to a restaurant for a Scotch and then another and another and waited for Joe, who never came, and that he wondered how with only a dollar fifty in his pocket he could pay the check. He was saved, he said, by a friend of mine from the State Department who came by and paid the bill. But according to my diary, he has mixed that day with one that occurred a few weeks before. Rauh did join us, kissed me, patted Pollitt on the shoulder a couple of times, ordered us sandwiches and said to me, "Well, we did it."

"What did we do? I don't understand why it was over so fast."

Rauh said he didn't know whether they had made a legal mistake in reading my letter into the record, but for the first time they had been put in a spot they didn't like, maybe didn't want to tangle with. They could call me again, but they'd have to find another reason, and so he hadn't sent me to jail after all, and everything had worked just fine.[7]

[...]And so I came back to New York and did nothing for a while. Then, not unexpected, we had no money left. I took a half-day job in a large department store, under another name, arranged by an old friend who worked there. I was in the grocery department and that was not unpleasant, but I kept it a secret because I knew it would worry Hammett. About six months later, an aunt I liked very much died in New Orleans, and left me a larger sum than I ever thought she could have saved in her hardworking life.

I guess I began to write again, although I can't remember what, maybe because it was just practice stuff.

Hammett and I rented a house that summer on Martha's Vineyard and the fine black lady, Helen, came back to work because now we could afford to pay her again. Nothing was as it had been, but because it had been bad, small things seemed better than ever—the occasional rental of a catboat for a day's sail, a canoe for the pond, a secondhand car, grocery bills I didn't have to worry so much about. We had a good summer.

And it was the summer of the Army-McCarthy hearings.[8] For us, of course, they came too late to make much difference and seemed a wild mess. The boozy hospital-patched face of McCarthy, sometimes teasing and gay as in the good days, often

---

[7] [*Author's note.*] Many people through the years have asked me why the Committee did not prosecute me. I could only repeat what Rauh thought the day of the hearing. On the completion of this book, I phoned him to ask if, after all these years, there could be another explanation. He said, "There were three things they wanted. One, names which you wouldn't give. Two, a smear by accusing you of being a 'Fifth Amendment Communist.' They couldn't do that because in your letter you offered to testify about yourself. And three, a prosecution which they couldn't do because they forced us into taking the Fifth Amendment. They had enough

sense to see that they were in a bad spot. We beat them, that's all."

[8] 1954 hearings by the Senate Subcommittee on Investigations, chaired by Senator Joseph McCarthy, occasioned by the Army's allegation that Roy Cohn (1927-1986), chief counsel for the senator, had used improper influence in attempting to get special Army assignments for David Schine (1927-1996), a consultant to McCarthy who was drafted. McCarthy argued that the Army's refusal to commission Schine was part of a larger plan to impede the Subcommittee's investigation into Communist infiltration of the Army.

caught in disbelief that he was where he was, and angry. He and his boys, Roy Cohn and David Schine—the brash but less assured older brothers of Haldeman and Ehrlichman[9]—were, indeed, a threesome: Schine's little-boy college face, Cohn plump of body, pout of sensual mouth, and McCarthy, a group breaking up before our eyes after years of a wild ride. Bonnie, Bonnie and Clyde, shooting at anything that came to hand on the King's horses that rode to battle in official bulletproof armor.

Then Mr. Stevens of the Army,[10] a strangely unsympathetic figure, and the lawyer Joseph Welch,[11] certainly a Boston gentleman, remembered for that highly admired sentence, "Have you no sense of decency, sir?" I thought the sentence funny; had it really taken Welch so long to find that out, or was it a good actor's instinct for proper timing?

Because, of course, McCarthy was finished long before the hearings began. It wasn't because he had become too daring and taken to fooling around the sacred precincts of the Army, it was simply and plainly that most of America was sick of him and his two kiddies.

The editor and critic Philip Rahv,[12] an early anti-Communist and then an early anti-anti-Communist, had said it a year before in one of his least decipherable growls: "Nothing can last in America more than ten years. McCarthy will soon be finished." And that, I think, was the truth, just that and not much more. We were not shocked at the damage McCarthy had done, or the ruin he brought on many people. Nor had we been surprised or angered by Cohn and Schine playing with the law as if it were a batch of fudge they enjoyed after the pleasure of their nightly pillow fight. We were bored with them. That and nothing more.

There were many broken lives along the path the boys had bulldozed, but not so many that people needed to feel guilty if they turned their backs fast enough and told each other, as we were to do again after Watergate, that American justice will always prevail no matter how careless it seems to critical outsiders.

It is not true that when the bell tolls it tolls for thee: if it were true we could not have elected, so few years later, Richard Nixon, a man who had been closely allied with McCarthy.[13] It was no accident that Mr. Nixon brought with him a group of high-powered operators who made Cohn and Schine look like cute little rascals from grammar school. The names and faces had been changed; the stakes were higher, because the prize was the White House. And one year after a presidential scandal of a magnitude still unknown, we have almost forgotten them, too. We are a people who do not want to keep much of the past in our heads. It is considered unhealthy in America to remember mistakes, neurotic to think about them, psychotic to dwell upon them.

Nothing more was to happen to me. I began to write plays again and in 1958 to get movie offers that I no longer wanted; the taste had gone.

It is true, as I have said, that Hammett was never again allowed to have a nickel of

[9] H. R. Haldeman (1926-1993), White House chief of staff to President Richard Nixon, convicted of conspiracy and obstruction of justice for his involvement in the Watergate break-in and cover-up; John Erlichman (1925-1999), White House counsel and domestic advisor to Nixon, also convicted of conspiracy, obstruction of justice, and perjury.
[10] Robert Ten Broek Stevens, Secretary of the Army from 1953 to 1955.
[11] Lead counsel for the Army during the hearings.
[12] Philip Rahv (1908-1973), a founder of the journal *Partisan Review.*
[13] As a member of Congress, Nixon had served on HUAC, and much of his political career was built on his opposition to Communism.

his own money and that the emphysema which had started in the Aleutians was to end in cancer of the lungs. Those last years were not good for him, but he managed them fairly well, with no complaints about what had been done to him, even refusing to call the police on two occasions when people, or official people, fired shots through the window of his cottage. But none of those years were as bad as they could have been and were for many people.

I recovered, maybe even more than that, in the sense of work and money. But I have to end this book almost as I began it: I have only in part recovered from the shock that came, as I guess most shocks do from an unexamined belief that sprang from my own nature, time, and place. I had believed in intellectuals, whether they were my teachers or my friends or strangers whose books I had read. This is inexplicable to a younger generation, who look upon the 1930's radical and the 1930's Red-baiter with equal amusement. I don't much enjoy their amusement, but they have some right to it. As I now have some right to disappointment in what the good children of the Sixties have come to.

Maybe what I still feel is best summed up in an evening I once spent in London with Richard Crossman, then an editor of the *New Statesman and Nation* and a member of Parliament.[14] It was about a month after Hammett had gone to jail and Crossman knew nothing of my connection to Hammett. He had turned to me as the only American in the room, to say that it was a disgrace that not one intellectual had come to Hammett's aid, that if such a case had happened in London he, and many others like him, would have protested immediately on the grounds that it is your right to believe, my obligation to stand by even in disagreement. I remember that Kingsley Martin, the intelligent, cranky editor of the *New Statesman and Nation*,[15] very worried, was trying to tell Crossman of my relation to Hammett. He ignored Kingsley to say that it took an Englishman a long time to fight for a liberty but once he had it nobody could take it away, but that we in America fought fast for liberty and could be deprived of it in an hour.

In every civilized country people have always come forward to defend those in political trouble. (There was once even some honor in being a political prisoner.) And there were a few here who did just that, but not many, and when one reads them now the words seem slightly timid, or at best too reasonable.

And it is now sad to read the anti-Communist writers and intellectuals of those times. But sad is a fake word for me to be using; I am still angry that their reason for disagreeing with McCarthy was too often his crude methods—the standards of the board of governors of a country club. Such people would have right to say that I, and many like me, took too long to see what was going on in the Soviet Union. But whatever our mistakes, I do not believe we did our country any harm. And I think they did. They went to too many respectable conferences that turned out not to be under respectable auspices, contributed to and published too many CIA magazines. The step from such capers was straight into the Vietnam War and the days of Nixon. Many of the anti-Communists were, of course, honest men. But none of them, as far as I know, has stepped forward to admit a mistake. It is not necessary in this country; they too know that we are a people who do not remember much.

---

[14] Richard Crossman (1907-1974).   [15] Kingsley Martin (1897-1969).

I have written here that I have recovered. I mean it only in a worldly sense because I do not believe in recovery. The past, with its pleasures, its rewards, its foolishness, its punishments, is there for each of us forever, and it should be.

As I finish writing about this unpleasant part of my life, I tell myself that was then, and there is now, and the years between then and now, and the then and now are one.

—1976

RUTH RUBIN (1906-2000)

Born Rifke Rosenblatt in Montreal, Canada, Ruth Rubin was the daughter of Jewish parents who had immigrated from Russia. She attended a Protestant school in Montreal, as well as a Jewish secular "shule" in the afternoons. Her father died when she was five years old, and she moved with her family to New York in the early 1920s. She married Harry Rubin in 1932, and they had one son. Rubin had been interested in music as a girl, but once in New York she began the serious study of music, both as a musician and as an ethnomusicologist. Tapping first into her mother's vast knowledge of Yiddish folksongs, and then doing extensive ethnographic research herself, Rubin began what would become a lifelong career as a performer, collector, and scholar of Yiddish music. During World War II, she translated diaries smuggled out of ghettos and Nazi camps; after the war was over and the extent of the Holocaust was known, she redoubled her efforts to preserve Yiddish culture by traveling around and recording immigrants singing traditional songs. She published an anthology of Yiddish folksongs in 1950, and then a book-length study, *Voices of a People: The Story of Yiddish Folk Song,* in 1963 (reprinted with new material by the University of Illinois Press in 2000). In 1976, she received her Ph.D. from Union Graduate School in Cleveland, writing on Jewish women's songs. Rubin continued to lecture and collect until late in her life, dying at the age of ninety-three in New York.

The Ballad of the Triangle Fire[1]

In the heart of New York City near Washington Square,
In nineteen-eleven, March winds were cold and bare.
A fire broke out in a building ten stories high,
And a hundred and forty-six young girls in those flames did die.

On the top floor of that building, ten stories in the air,   5
Those young girls were working in an old sweatshop there.
They were sewing shirtwaists for a very low wage,
So tired and pale and wornout they were at a tender age.

The sweatshop was a stuffy room with but a single door.
The windows they were gray with lint from off that dusty floor.   10
There were no comforts, no fresh air, no light to sew thereby,
And the girls they toiled from early morn 'til darkness filled the sky.

---

[1] On March 25, 1911, a fire started on the eighth floor of the Triangle Shirtwaist Factory, a sweatshop in New York City that employed primarily young immigrant women. Most of the workers on the eighth and tenth floors escaped, but the workers on the ninth floor were trapped.

Then on that fateful day, dear God, most terrible of days!
When that big fire broke out, it grew into a mighty blaze!
In that firetrap away up there, with but a single door   15
So many innocent working girls burned, to live no more.

A hundred thousand mourners, they followed those sad biers,
The streets were filled with people, weeping bitter tears.
Poets, writers everywhere, described that awful pyre—
When those young girls were trapped to die in the Triangle Fire.

—1968

LUISA MORENO (1907-1992)

Luisa Moreno, a labor leader who organized industrial and agricultural workers in New York,
Florida, California, Texas, and Colorado for over two decades, was born Blanca Rosa López
Rodríguez on August 30, 1907, in Guatemala City. In 1916 her wealthy parents sent her to
Oakland, California, to attend an elite parochial school, College of the Holy Names. Upon
returning to Guatemala, she used her privilege to open doors for others, organizing her peers
into the Sociedad Gabriela Mistral, which successfully lobbied for admission of women to
Guatemalan universities. Moreno herself opted not to attend college and moved to Mexico
City to pursue a career in journalism. There she met and married her first husband, with
whom she moved to New York City in 1928. Moreno went to work as a seamstress in Spanish
Harlem, where poor labor conditions spurred her first attempts as a labor organizer. In 1935,
her marriage over, Moreno moved to Florida with her daughter, Mytyl. She accepted a job
with the American Federation of Labor (AFL) in the mid-1930s and organized cigar workers
in Florida. At this time, she changed her name from Blanca ("white") to Moreno ("dark"), a
deliberate rejection of her privileged origins. Disillusioned by the conservatism of the AFL,
however, Moreno joined the radical Congress of Industrial Workers (CIO), becoming a representative of its affiliated United Cannery, Agricultural, Packing, Pacing and Allied Workers
of America (UCAPAWA). She began as the editor of UCAPAWA's Spanish language paper,
and rose through the ranks to become the CIO's International Vice President, and later State
Vice President. From 1938 to 1941, Moreno was a principal organizer (along with Josefina
Fierro de Bright and Eduardo Quevedo) of one the first pan-Latino civil rights organizations,
El Congreso de Pueblos de Habla Española (the Congress of Spanish Speaking Peoples). In
1940, she was asked to speak before the American Committee for the Protection of the Foreign
Born, where she delivered her famous speech, "Caravans of Sorrow," about the plight of the
Mexican-American migrant worker. On November 30, 1950, at the height of Joseph
McCarthy's anti-communist witch hunts, Moreno was deported under the McCarren Walter
Immigration Act for her labor organizing, her defense of the civil rights of minorities, and her
Marxist ideals. Whether or not she was a member of the Communist Party remains uncertain,
though it is believed she joined the party early in her time in New York City.

Caravans of Sorrow: Noncitizen Americans of the Southwest[1]

One hears much today about hemisphere unity. The press sends special corre-
spondents to Latin America, South of the Border songs are wailed by the radio,

---

[1] From an address delivered at the panel of Deportation and Right of Asylum of the Fourth Annual Conference of the
American Committee for Protection of Foreign Born, Washington, DC, March 3, 1940.

educational institutions and literary circles speak the language of cultural cooperation, and, what is more important, labor unions are seeking the road of closer ties with the Latin American working people. The stage is set. A curtain rises. May we ask you to see behind the scenery and visualize a forgotten character in this great theater of the Americas?

Long before the "grapes of wrath" had ripened in California's vineyards a people lived on highways, under trees or tents, in shacks or railroad sections, picking crops—cotton, fruits, vegetables—cultivating sugar beets, building railroads and dams, making a barren land fertile for new crops and greater riches.

The ancestors of some of these migrant and resident workers, whose home is this Southwest, were America's first settlers in New Mexico, Texas and California, and the greater percentage was brought from Mexico by the fruit exchanges, railroad companies, and cotton interests in great need of underpaid labor during the early post-war period. They are the Spanish-speaking workers of the Southwest, citizens and noncitizens working and living under identical conditions, facing hardships and miseries while producing and building for agriculture and industry.

Their story lies unpublicized in university libraries, files of government, welfare and social agencies—a story grimly titled the "Caravans of Sorrow."

And when in 1930 unemployment brought a still greater flood of human distress, trainloads of Mexican families with children born and raised in this country departed voluntarily or were brutally deported. As a result of the repatriation drive of 1933, thousands of American-born youths returned to their homeland, the United States, to live on streets and highways, drifting unattached fragments of humanity. Let the annals of juvenile delinquency in Los Angeles show you the consequences.

Today the Latin Americans of the United States are seriously alarmed by the "antialien" drive fostered by certain un-American elements; for them, the Palmer days[2] have never ended. In recent years while deportations in general have decreased, the number of persons deported to Mexico has constantly increased. During the period of 1933 to 1937, of a total of 55,087 deported, 25,135 were deportations of Mexicans. This is 45.5 percent of the total and does not include an almost equal number of so-called voluntary departures.

Commenting on these figures, the American Committee for Protection of Foreign Born wrote to the Spanish-Speaking Peoples' Congress in 1939: "One conclusion can be drawn, and that is, where there is such a highly organized set-up as to effect deportations of so many thousands, this set-up must be surrounded with a complete system of intimidation and discrimination of that section of the population victimized by the deportation drive."

Confirming the fact of a system of extensive discrimination are university studies by Paul S. Taylor, Emory Bogardus, and many other professors and social workers of the Southwest. Let me state the simple truth. The majority of the Spanish-speaking peoples of the United States are victims of a setup for discrimination, be they descendants of the first white settlers in America or noncitizens.

I will not go into the reasons for this undemocratic practice, but may we state categorically that it is the main reason for the reluctance of Mexican and Latin Americans

[2] General A. Mitchell Palmer (1872-1936) was the U.S. attorney general from 1919 to 1921. In the two years following World War II, he was responsible for initiating mass arrests of left-wing radicals and alleged subversives.

in general to become naturalized. For you must know, discrimination takes very definite forms in unequal wages, unequal opportunities, unequal schooling, and even through a denial of the use of public places in certain towns in Texas, California, Colorado, and other Southwestern states.

Only some 5 or 6 percent of Latin American immigrants have become naturalized. A number of years ago it was stated that in a California community with fifty thousand Mexicans only two hundred had become citizens. An average of one hundred Mexicans out of close to a million become citizens every year. These percentages have increased lately.

Another important factor concerning naturalization is the lack of documentary proof of entry, because entry was not recorded or because the immigrants were brought over en masse by large interests handling transportation from Mexico in their own peculiar way.

Arriving at logical conclusions, the Latin American noncitizens, rooted in this country, are increasingly seeing the importance and need for naturalization. But how will the thousands of migrants establish residence? What possibility have these people had, segregated in "Little Mexicos," to learn English and meet educational requirements? How can they, receiving hunger wages while enriching the stockholders of the Great Western Sugar Company, the Bank of America, and other large interests, pay high naturalization fees? A Mexican family living on relief in Colorado would have to stop eating for two and a half months to pay for the citizenship papers of one member of the family. Is this humanly possible?

But why have "aliens" on relief while the taxpayers "bleed"? Let me ask those who would raise such a question: what would the Imperial Valley, the Rio Grande Valley, and other rich irrigated valleys in the Southwest be without the arduous, self-sacrificing labor of these noncitizen Americans? Read *Factories in the Fields,* by Carey McWilliams to obtain a picture of how important Mexican labor has been for the development of California's crop after the world war. Has anyone counted the miles of railroads built by these same noncitizens? One can hardly imagine how many bales of cotton have passed through the nimble fingers of Mexican men, women, and children. And what conditions have they had to endure to pick that cotton? Once, while holding a conference for a trade union paper in San Antonio, a cotton picker told me how necessary a Spanish paper was to inform the Spanish-speaking workers that FSA [Farm Security Administration] camps were to be established, for she remembered so many nights, under the trees in the rain, when she and her husband held gunny sacks over the shivering bodies of their sleeping children—young Americans. I've heard workers say that they left their shacks under heavy rains to find shelter under trees. You can well imagine in what condition those shacks were.

These people are not aliens. They have contributed their endurance, sacrifices, youth, and labor to the Southwest. Indirectly, they have paid more taxes than all the stockholders of California's industrialized agriculture, the sugar beet companies and the large cotton interests that operate or have operated with the labor of Mexican workers.

Surely the sugar beet growers have not been asked if they want to dispense with the skilled labor cultivating and harvesting their crops season after season. It is only the large interests, their stooges, and some badly misinformed people who claim that Mexicans are no longer wanted.

And let us assume that 1.4 million men, women, and children were no longer wanted, what could be done that would be different from the anti-Semitic persecutions in Europe? A people who have lived twenty and thirty years in this country, tied up by family relations with the early settlers, with American-born children, cannot be uprooted without the complete destruction of the faintest semblance of democracy and human liberties for the whole population.

Some speak of repatriation. Naturally there is interest in repatriation among thousands of Mexican families in Texas and, to a lesser degree, in other states. Organized repatriation has been going on, and the net results in one year has been the establishment of the Colonia "18 de Marzo" in Tamaulipas, Mexico, for two thousand families. There are 1.4 million Mexicans in the United States according to general estimates, probably including a portion of the first generation. Is it possible to move those many people at the present rate, when many of them do not want to be repatriated?

What then may the answer to this specific noncitizen problem be? The Spanish-Speaking Peoples' Congress of the United States proposes legislation that would encourage naturalization of Latin American, West Indian, and Canadian residents of the United States and that would nurture greater friendships among the peoples of the Western Hemisphere.

The question of hemispheric unity will remain an empty phrase while this problem at home remains ignored and is aggravated by the fierce "antialien" drive.

Legislation to facilitate citizenship to all natural-born citizens from the countries of the Western Hemisphere, waiving excessive fees and educational and other requirements of a technical nature, is urgently needed.

A piece of legislation embodying this provision is timely and important. Undoubtedly it would rally the support of the many friends of true hemispheric unity.

You have seen the forgotten character in the present American scene—a scene of the Americas. Let me say that, in the face of greater hardships, the "Caravans of Sorrow" are becoming the "Caravans of Hope." They are organizing in trade unions with other workers in agriculture and industry. The unity of Spanish-speaking citizens and noncitizens is being furthered through the Spanish-Speaking Peoples' Congress of the United States, an organization embracing trade unions and fraternal, civic, and cultural organizations, mainly in California. The purpose of this movement is to seek an improvement of social, economic, and cultural conditions, and for the integration of Spanish-speaking citizens and noncitizens into the American nation. The United Cannery, Agricultural, Packing, and Allied Workers of America, with thousands of Spanish-speaking workers in its membership, and Liga Obrera of New Mexico, were the initiators of the Congress.

This Congress stands with all progressive forces against the badly labeled "antialien" legislation and asks the support of this Conference for democratic legislation to facilitate and encourage naturalization. We hope that this Conference will serve to express the sentiment of the people of this country in condemnation of undemocratic discrimination practiced against any person of foreign birth and that it will rally the American people, native and foreign born, for the defeat of un-American proposals. The Spanish-speaking peoples in the United States extend their fullest support and cooperation to your efforts.

—1940

DOROTHY WEST (1907?-1998)

Fiction writer, editor, and journalist Dorothy West was born in Boston (in 1907, 1909 or 1910) and educated at the Girls' Latin School, from which she graduated in 1923. Her father, who had been born in slavery, owned a fruit business. She began winning fiction contests in her teens, including second prize (shared with Zora Neale Hurston's "Muttsy") for her story "The Typewriter" in a contest sponsored by *Opportunity* magazine in 1926. West, who attended Boston University and Columbia University's School of Journalism, lived with her cousin, the poet Helene Johnson, in Harlem, where they met many of the artists and writers of the Harlem Renaissance. West was one of its youngest writers and, at her death, its last surviving one. West was the founder and editor of *Challenge* and co-founder (with Richard Wright) of *New Challenge,* literary magazines that published the next generation of Black writers, including Margaret Walker, Richard Wright, and Ralph Ellison. After the magazines folded, she took a job with the Federal Writers' Project of the WPA. In the mid-1940s, she moved to Martha's Vineyard, where she wrote her first novel, *The Living Is Easy* (1948), which was reprinted by the Feminist Press in 1982. Her second novel, *The Wedding,* was published in 1995 with the encouragement of Jacqueline Onassis, her neighbor. Like fellow Harlem Renaissance writers Jessie Redmon Fauset and Nella Larsen, West focused on Black middle-class protagonists. West worked as a journalist for some forty years; her collection of short stories and essays, *The Richer, the Poorer: Stories, Sketches, and Reminiscences,* was published in 1995.

The Typewriter

It occurred to him, as he eased past the bulging knees of an Irish wash lady and forced an apologetic passage down the aisle of the crowded car, that more than anything in all the world he wanted not to go home. He began to wish passionately that he had never been born, that he had never been married, that he had never been the means of life's coming into the world. He knew quite suddenly that he hated his flat and his family and his friends. And most of all the incessant thing that would "clatter clatter" until every nerve screamed aloud, and the words of the evening paper danced crazily before him, and the insane desire to crush and kill set his fingers twitching.

He shuffled down the street, an abject little man of fifty-odd years, in an ageless overcoat that flapped in the wind. He was cold, and he hated the North, and particularly Boston, and saw suddenly a barefoot pickaninny sitting on a fence in the hot, Southern sun with a piece of steaming corn bread and a piece of fried salt pork in either grimy hand.

He was tired, and he wanted his supper, but he didn't want the beans, and frankfurters, and light bread that Net would undoubtedly have. That Net had had every Monday night since that regrettable moment fifteen years before when he had told her—innocently—that such a supper tasted "right nice. Kinda change from what we always has."

He mounted the four brick steps leading to his door and pulled at the bell, but there was no answering ring. It was broken again, and in a mental flash he saw himself with a multitude of tools and a box of matches shivering in the vestibule after supper. He began to pound lustily on the door and wondered vaguely if his hand would bleed if he smashed the glass. He hated the sight of blood. It sickened him.

Some one was running down the stairs. Daisy probably. Millie would be at that infernal thing, pounding, pounding....He entered. The chill of the house swept him.

His child was wrapped in a coat. She whispered solemnly, "Poppa, Miz Hicks an' Miz Berry's orful mad. They gointa move if they can't get more heat. The furnace's birnt out all day. Mama couldn't fix it." He said hurriedly, "I'll go right down. I'll go right down." He hoped Mrs. Hicks wouldn't pull open her door and glare at him. She was large and domineering, and her husband was a bully. If her husband ever struck him it would kill him. He hated life, but he didn't want to die. He was afraid of God, and in his wildest flights of fancy couldn't imagine himself an angel. He went softly down the stairs.

He began to shake the furnace fiercely. And he shook into it every wrong, mumbling softly under his breath. He began to think back over his uneventful years, and it came to him as rather a shock that he had never sworn in all his life. He wondered uneasily if he dared say "damn." It was taken for granted that a man swore when he tended a stubborn furnace. And his strongest interjection was "Great balls of fire!"

The cellar began to warm, and he took off his inadequate overcoat that was streaked with dirt. Well, Net would have to clean that. He'd be damned—! It frightened him and thrilled him. He wanted suddenly to rush upstairs and tell Mrs. Hicks if she didn't like the way he was running things, she could get out. But he heaped another shovelful of coal on the fire and sighed. He would never be able to get away from himself and the routine of years.

He thought of that eager Negro lad of seventeen who had come North to seek his fortune. He had walked jauntily down Boylston Street, and even his own kind had laughed at the incongruity of him. But he had thrown up his head and promised himself: "You'll have an office here some day. With plate-glass windows and a real mahogany desk." But, though he didn't know it then, he was not the progressive type. And he became successively, in the years, bell boy, porter, waiter, cook, and finally janitor in a down town office building.

He had married Net when he was thirty-three and a waiter. He had married her partly because—though he might not have admitted it—there was no one to eat the expensive delicacies the generous cook gave him every night to bring home. And partly because he dared hope there might be a son to fulfill his dreams. But Millie had come, and after her twin girls who had died within two weeks, then Daisy, and it was tacitly understood that Net was done with child-bearing.

Life, though flowing monotonously, had flowed peacefully enough until that sucker of sanity became a sitting-room fixture. Intuitively at the very first he had felt its undesirability. He had suggested hesitatingly that they couldn't afford it. Three dollars: food and fuel. Times were hard, and the twenty dollars apiece the respective husbands of Miz Hicks and Miz Berry irregularly paid was only five dollars more than the thirty-five a month he paid his own Hebraic landlord. And the Lord knew his salary was little enough. At which point Net spoke her piece, her voice rising shrill. "God knows I never complain 'bout nothin'. Ain't no other woman got less than me. I bin wearin' this same dress here five years an' I'll wear it another five. But I don't want nothin'. I ain't never wanted nothin'. An' when I does as', it's only for my children. You're a poor sort of father if you can't give that child jes' three dollars a month to rent that typewriter. Ain't 'nother girl in school ain't got one. An' mos' of 'ems bought an' paid for. You know yourself how Millie is. She wouldn't as' me for it till she had to. An' I ain't going to disappoint her. She's goin' to get that typewriter Saturday, mark my words."

On a Monday then it had been installed. And in the months that followed, night after night he listened to the murderous "tack, tack, tack" that was like a vampire slowly drinking his blood. If only he could escape. Bar a door against the sound of it. But tied hand and foot by the economic fact that "Lord knows we can't afford to have fires burnin' an' lights lit all over the flat. You'all gotta set in one room. An' when y'get tired settin' y' c'n go to bed. Gas bill was somep'n scandalous last month."

He heaped a final shovelful of coal on the fire and watched the first blue flames. Then, his overcoat under his arm, he mounted the cellar stairs. Mrs. Hicks was standing in her kitchen door, arms akimbo. "It's warmin'," she volunteered.

"Yeh," he was conscious of his grime-streaked face and hands, "it's warmin'. I'm sorry 'bout all day."

She folded her arms across her ample bosom. "Tending a furnace ain't a woman's work. I don't blame your wife none 'tall."

Unsuspecting he was grateful. "Yeh, it's pretty hard for a woman. I always look after it 'fore I goes to work, but some days it jes' ac's up."

"Y'oughta have a janitor, that's what y'ought," she flung at him. "The same cullud man that tends them apartments would be willin'. Mr. Taylor has him. It takes a man to run a furnace, and when the man's away all day—"

"I know," he interrupted, embarrassed and hurt, "I know. Tha's right, Miz Hicks tha's right. But I ain't in a position to make no improvements. Times is hard."

She surveyed him critically. "Your wife called down 'bout three times while you was in the cellar. I reckon she wants you for supper."

"Thanks," he mumbled and escaped up the back stairs.

He hung up his overcoat in the closet, telling himself, a little lamely, that it wouldn't take him more'n a minute to clean it up himself after supper. After all Net was tired and prob'bly worried what with Miz Hicks and all. And he hated men who made slaves of their women folk. Good old Net.

He tidied up in the bathroom, washing his face and hands carefully and cleanly so as to leave no—or very little—stain on the roller towel. It was hard enough for Net, God knew.

He entered the kitchen. The last spirals of steam were rising from his supper. One thing about Net she served a full plate. He smiled appreciatively at her unresponsive back, bent over the kitchen sink. There was no one could bake beans just like Net's. And no one who could find a market with frankfurters quite so fat.

He sank down at his place. "Evenin', hon?"

He saw her back stiffen. "If your supper's cold, 'tain't my fault. I called and called."

He said hastily, "It's fine, Net, fine. Piping."

She was the usual tired housewife. "Y'oughta et your supper 'fore you fooled with that furnace. I ain't bothered 'bout them niggers. I got all my dishes washed 'cept yours. An' I hate to mess up my kitchen after I once get it straightened up."

He was humble. "I'll give that old furnace an extra lookin' after in the mornin'. It'll las' all day to-morrow, hon."

"An' on top of that," she continued, unheeding him and giving a final wrench to her dish towel, "that confounded bell don't ring. An'—"

"I'll fix it after supper," he interposed hastily.

She hung up her dish towel and came to stand before him looming large and yellow. "An' that old Miz Berry, she claim she was expectin' comp'ny. An' she knows they must'a' come an' gone while she was in her kitchen an' couldn't be at her winder to watch for 'em. Old liar," she brushed back a lock of naturally straight hair. "She wasn't expectin' nobody."

"Well, you know how some folks are—"

"Fools! Half the world," was her vehement answer. "I'm goin' in the front room an' set down a spell. I bin on my feet all day. Leave them dishes on the table. God knows I'm tired, but I'll come back an' wash 'em." But they both knew, of course, that he, very clumsily, would.

At precisely quarter past nine when he, strained at last to the breaking point, uttering an inhuman, strangled cry, flung down his paper, clutched at his throat and sprang to his feet, Millie's surprised young voice, shocking him to normalcy, heralded the first of that series of great moments that every humble little middle-class man eventually experiences.

"What's the matter, poppa? You sick? I wanted you to help me."

He drew out his handkerchief and wiped his hot hands. "I declare I must 'a' fallen asleep an' had a nightmare. No, I ain't sick. What you want, hon?"

"Dictate me a letter, poppa. I c'n do sixty words a minute.—You know, like a business letter. You know, like those men in your building dictate to their stenographers. Don't you hear 'em sometimes?"

"Oh, sure, I know, hon. Poppa'll help you. Sure. I hear that Mr. Browning—Sure."

Net rose. "Guess I'll put this child to bed. Come on now, Daisy, without no fuss.— Then I'll run up to pa's. He ain't bin well all week."

When the door closed behind them, he crossed to his daughter, conjured the image of Mr. Browning in the process of dictating, so arranged himself, and coughed importantly.

"Well, Millie—"

"Oh, poppa, is that what you'd call your stenographer?" she teased. "And anyway pretend I'm really one—and you're really my boss, and this letter's real important."

A light crept into his dull eyes. Vigor through his thin blood. In a brief moment the weight of years fell from him like a cloak. Tired, bent, little old man that he was, he smiled, straightened, tapped impressively against his teeth with a toil-stained finger, and became that enviable emblem of American life: a business man.

"You be Miz Hicks, huh, honey? Course we can't both use the same name. I'll be J. Lucius Jones. J. Lucius. All them real big doin' men use their middle names. Jus' kinda looks big doin', doncha think, hon? Looks like money, huh? J. Lucius." He uttered a sound that was like the proud cluck of a strutting hen. "J. Lucius." It rolled like oil from his tongue.

His daughter twisted impatiently. "Now, poppa—I mean Mr. Jones, sir—please begin. I am ready for dictation, sir."

He was in that office on Boylston Street, looking with visioning eyes through its plate-glass windows, tapping with impatient fingers on its real mahogany desk.

"Ah—Beaker Brothers, Park Square Building, Boston, Mass. Ahw—Gentlemen: In reply to yours at the seventh instant I would state—"

Every night thereafter in the weeks that followed, with Daisy packed off to bed, and Net "gone up to pa's" or nodding inobtrusively in her corner there was the chameleon change of a Court Street janitor to J. Lucius Jones, dealer in stocks and bonds. He would stand, posturing importantly, flicking imaginary dust from his coat lapel, or, his hands locked behind his back, he would stride up and down, earnestly and seriously debating the advisability of buying copper with the market in such a fluctuating state. Once a week, too, he stopped in at Jerry's, and after a preliminary purchase of cheap cigars, bought the latest trade papers, mumbling an embarrassed explanation: "I got a little money. Think I'll invest it in reliable stock."

The letters Millie typed and subsequently discarded, he rummaged for later, and under cover of writing to his brother in the South, laboriously with a great many fancy flourishes, signed each neatly typed sheet with the exalted J. Lucius Jones.

Later, when he mustered the courage he suggested tentatively to Millie that it might be fun—just fun, of course!—to answer his letters. One night—he laughed a good deal louder and longer than necessary—he'd be J. Lucius Jones, and the next night—here he swallowed hard and looked a little frightened—Rockefeller or Vanderbilt or Morgan—just for fun, y'understand! To which Millie gave consent. It mattered little to her one way or the other. It was practice, and that was what she needed. Very soon now she'd be in the hundred class. Then maybe she could get a job!

He was growing very careful of his English. Occasionally—and it must be admitted, ashamedly—he made surreptitious ventures into the dictionary. He had to, of course. J. Lucius Jones would never say "Y'got to" when he meant "It is expedient." And, old brain though he was, he learned quickly and easily, juggling words with amazing facility.

Eventually he bought stamps and envelopes—long, important-looking envelopes—and stammered apologetically to Millie, "Honey, poppa thought it'd help you if you learned to type envelopes, too. Reckon you'll have to do that, too, when y'get a job. Poor old man," he swallowed painfully, "came round selling these envelopes. You know how 'tis. So I had to buy 'em." Which was satisfactory to Millie. If she saw through her father, she gave no sign. After all, it was practice, and Mr. Hennessey had said that—though not in just those words.

He had got in the habit of carrying those self-addressed envelopes in his inner pocket where they bulged impressively. And occasionally he would take them out—on the car usually—and smile upon them. This one might be from J. P. Morgan. This one from Henry Ford. And a million-dollar deal involved in each. That narrow, little spinster, who, upon his sitting down, had drawn herself away from his contact, was shunning J. Lucius Jones!

Once, led by some sudden, strange impulse, as an outgoing car rumbled up out of the subway, he got out a letter, darted a quick, shamed glance about him, dropped it in an adjacent box, and swung aboard the car, feeling, dazedly, as if he had committed a crime. And the next night he sat in the sitting-room quite on edge until Net said suddenly, "Look here, a real important letter come to-day for you, pa. Here 'tis. What you s'pose it says," and he reached out a hand that trembled. He made brief explanation. "Advertisement, hon. Thassal."

They came quite frequently after that, and despite the fact that he knew them by heart, he read them slowly and carefully, rustling the sheet and making inaudible, intelligent comments. He was, in these moments, pathetically earnest.

Monday, as he went about his janitor's duties, he composed in his mind the final letter from J. P. Morgan that would consummate a big business deal. For days now letters had passed between them. J. P. had been at first quite frankly uninterested. He had written tersely and briefly. He wrote glowingly of the advantages of a pact between them. Daringly he argued in terms of billions. And at last J. P. had written his next letter would be decisive. Which next letter, this Monday, as he trailed about the office building, was writing itself on his brain.

That night Millie opened the door for him. Her plain face was transformed. "Poppa—poppa, I got a job! Twelve dollars a week to start with! Isn't that *swell!*"

He was genuinely pleased. "Honey, I'm glad. Right glad," and went up the stairs, unsuspecting.

He ate his supper hastily, went down into the cellar to see about his fire, returned and carefully tidied up, informing his reflection in the bathroom mirror, "Well, J. Lucius, you c'n expect that final letter any day now."

He entered the sitting-room. The phonograph was playing. Daisy was singing lustily. Strange. Net was talking animatedly to—Millie, busy with needle and thread over a neat, little frock. His wild glance darted to the table. The pretty, little center-piece, the bowl and wax flowers all neatly arranged: the typewriter gone from its accustomed place. It seemed an hour before he could speak. He felt himself trembling. Went hot and cold.

"Millie—your typewriter's—gone!"

She made a deft little in and out movement with her needle. "It's the eighth, you know. When the man came to-day for the money, I sent it back. I won't need it no more—now!—The money's on the mantlepiece, poppa."

"Yeh," he muttered. "All right."

He sank down in his chair, fumbled for the paper, found it.

Net said, "Your poppa wants to read. Stop your noise, Daisy."

She obediently stopped both her noise and the phonograph, took up her book, and became absorbed. Millie went on with her sewing in placid anticipation of the morrow. Net immediately began to nod, gave a curious snort, slept.

Silence. That crowded in on him, engulfed him. That blurred his vision, dulled his brain. Vast, white, impenetrable....His ears strained for the old, familiar sound. And silence beat upon them....The words of the evening paper jumbled together. He read: J. P. Morgan goes—

It burst upon him. Blinded him. His hands groped for the bulge beneath his coat. Why this—this was the end! The end of those great moments—the end of everything! Bewildering pain tore through him. He clutched at his heart and felt, almost, the jagged edges drive into his hand. A lethargy swept down upon him. He could not move, nor utter sound. He could not pray, nor curse.

Against the wall of that silence J. Lucius Jones crashed and died.

—1926

HARRIETTE SIMPSON ARNOW (1908-1986)

Harriette Simpson, the daughter of schoolteachers, was born in Wayne County, Kentucky, the second of six children. Encouraged to become a teacher like her mother, she taught in Kentucky schools after her first year of college and again after her graduation. She was educated at Berea College (where she found the fifty-dollar fine for smoking particularly irksome) and graduated from the University of Louisville. Arnow moved to Cincinnati and worked as a waitress to support her writing; her first novel, *Mountain Path,* was published in 1936. In 1938, she published a story in *Esquire* (since *Esquire's* policy was not to publish work written by women, she signed her work H. L. Simpson and sent the magazine a photograph of one of her brothers-in-law). She married Harold Arnow in 1939, and the couple bought a farm in Kentucky, planning to combine writing with subsistence farming. After the birth of their first child in 1941, they moved to Detroit, where Harold worked for the *Detroit Times* and their second child was born. Arnow's most famous novel, *The Dollmaker* (1954), was a bestseller depicting the struggle of Appalachian migrants in Detroit during World War II; it was adapted for film in 1983. Two works of Kentucky social history followed: *Seedtime on the Cumberland* (1960) and *Flowering of the Cumberland* (1963). Arnow and her husband then moved to the outskirts of Ann Arbor, where they lived until her death; Arnow would publish two more novels and another Kentucky history. Sandra L. Ballard and Haeja K. Chung collected and edited Arnow's short stories, both published and unpublished, in 2005.

Blessed—Blessed

"Blessed are the peacemakers for...for..."[1] The words would come no further. Katy's mind was winging away to the cry of the bloodhounds, no longer faint but suddenly loud, eager, sweeping in hot quick waves of sound down the wagon road that ran below the farm.

"Go on, Katy," old Mrs. Fairchild said, and counted three and purled.

Katy squirmed on the low hard footstool, pushed back her brown forelock with sticky restless hands. "For...for..."

Her grandmother exploded with a "Study some more," and handed the Bible back to her. Katy cradled the big book on her knees and wished it were sundown. It would be harder to find a black man in the dark, and by then maybe her grandmother would have forgotten her anger over her mother's gray mare.

Lurie, the hired girl, rested on her iron. "They'll git him, th' blood thirsty nigger," she said, and listened, head tipped above the ironing board to the bloodhounds and the shouts of men, sweeping now below the farm.

Young Mrs. Fairchild bit off the thread from a sock she was darning. "Makes me think of a fox hunt."

Katy peeped up at her mother, remembered her grandmother, and let her head fall lower, so low that only with her lashes lifted could she see her mother's hands. They were little thin brown hands, with the knuckles blue-white against the black socks. And now while the bloodhounds boomed out in a full-throated triumphant cry, the hands did no darning, only clutched the socks and the sock darner. Katy marveled at the voice coming out above the hands, cool and uncaring as her mother's always was, laughing almost, not matching the hands. "I reckon Fiddlin' Turpin's fox-hunted so much in his time he'll take to th' lower creek like a fox an'...."

"Fox huntin'," old Mrs. Fairchild snorted. "That nigger was never any good for anythin' but fiddlin' an' fox huntin' an'...." She stopped to listen as the bloodhounds cried their confusion at the spot where the creek crossed the road.

Lurie took a fresh iron from the stove, tried its heat with spit from the tip of her finger. And to Katy, waiting, listening, arms clenched about her knees, the sound of

---

[1] "Blessed are the peacemakers: for they shall be called the children of God." Matthew 5:9.

the spit sounded loud above the bafflement of the hounds, loud like gunfire. "They're a losin' the scent," Lurie said in a hoarse whisper. "He's took tu th' lower creek jist like a fox."

Then one hound gave a joyous eager cry, and in an instant the pack of four took it up, moving straight across the creek and on up the road. "Scent must be gettin' stronger," old Mrs. Fairchild said with satisfaction, and added as she resumed her knitting, "Just let him try any of his fox tricks, goin' off down th' creek toward th' river.... They'll find him, hid like a fox somewhere down on th' river bluff or in th' lower creek."

Lurie rolled her eyes, and glanced uneasily out the window. "I don't reckon he'd take hit into his head an' come up th' creek into Mr. Fairchild's pasture."

"Not less'n he's a plum fool," old Mrs. Fairchild said. "He couldn't go in water any further than th' spring in th' west pasture where Little Sinkin' Creek begins, an' th' hounds could pick up th' scent soon's he tried tu go above th' spring. An' anyhow what nigger would be a hidin' out on a white man's land, an' th' man a helpin' hunt him?"

"Maybe Fiddlin' Turpin doesn't know Papa's after him, an' that they're goin' to hang him with our plowline. I saw 'em take it out of th' barn an' Mr. Crabtree, I heard him tell papa that...."

"Shut up, Katy, an' get on with your studyin'," old Mrs. Fairchild commanded. "When I was a little girl like you I never spoke out before my elders." She gave a sharp angry sigh above the gray knitted socks. "Th' old people would turn over in their graves to see how th' world's goin'. Here a white storekeeper can't total up his store books without runnin' th' risk a bein' cut up by a nigger." She glanced sharply over her spectacles at her daughter-in-law. "An' when he breaks out a jail there's white people to hold out for such goin's on an' won't lift one finger to see that law an' order's kept."

Young Mrs. Fairchild studied the half darned heel of a sock. "Law, Mother, I never meant it to sound like I was holdin' up for him. I just said that I guessed he broke out of jail...maybe with help...because he was afraid th' McChesneys would get a mob an' storm th' jail. Ever'body knows that that young Judge Montgomery would never ha passed a heavy sentence on him. Sam hit him first an' Fiddlin' Turpin lost his temper, an' cut him a little. An' ever'body knows that Sam McChesney does overcharge th' darkies."

Old Mrs. Fairchild forgot both her knitting and Katy. Katy raised her head, and studied her with intent round blue eyes, while she sputtered. "There you go, Mollie, talkin' on so before your child. She'll be holdin' up for trash an' no good fiddle-playin' niggers an' white people wastin' their time on fox hunts an' God knows what else. She'll be like kin of some I could name, but out of respect to you I won't." Her voice rose while she twitched at the unfinished sock, "You know you didn't do right about not lettin' Mat take Chariot. Her eatin' her head off in th' stable an' sayin' she's not strong enough for a long hard ride, an' her able to out jump any horse in th' country."

Lurie who had been leaning heavily on her iron relaxed and peeped around at young Mrs. Fairchild. Katy remembered she was studying the Beatitudes[2] and bent

---

[2] The beginning of the Sermon on the Mount. Matthew 5:3-12.

quickly over the Bible. Young Mrs. Fairchild turned the sock over and considered it with tilted head. "It didn't seem to me they needed th' mare—looks like twenty men with some a th' best horses an' bloodhounds in th' country ought to be enough without takin' out a mare with a colt that's hardly weaned. Mrs. Fairchild, you heard me tell Mat when he wanted her that I'd leave her in th' stable, so they could come an' get her."

"You might ha knowed that after they'd started they couldn't take time to come back. Why you didn't even know that Fiddlin' Turpin would run up this way at all," old Mrs. Fairchild said, and knit with short jabs of her needles as if the thread were a something she would like to break. Her gray eyes from behind their steel rimmed spectacles sent Lurie bouncing to the stove for a hot iron, but her young grand-daughter studied her unblinkingly. Katy asked, "How many children does Fiddlin' Turpin have?"

"Six, not countin' th' baby," young Mrs. Fairchild said, and the older woman's rocking chair gave an impatient angry squeak, as she said, "Katy, you're not studyin'. You'll disgrace th' family in th' quotation contest. When I was your age I knew th' Ten Commandments, th' Beatitudes, th' Sermon on th' Mount, an' twenty-seven Psalms."

"Long ones?"

"Go on with your studyin'."

And Katy went on. The bloodhounds' call came faintly now, though steadily. They had gone up the road below the pasture and down the other side of the hill. Katy closed her eyes and prayed for a thunderstorm, then remembered that in September thunderstorms with rain enough to wash away the scent of a man's feet were rare. She opened her eyes, and studied her mother's hands. They darned the socks slowly, clumsily, as if they were stiff with cold. Her grandmother's rocking chair gave a warning creak, and Katy's eyes skipped to the cramped black print of the Bible, hunted until they found the words in red—all the red was said by Jesus.

"Blessed are the pure in heart for they shall see God."[3] Katy knew that she would never see God. She was wicked. Less than two weeks ago she had run away and played with Fiddlin' Turpin's youngens, and learned to dance like the two middle-sized girls, and patted her feet and whirled her petticoat and skirt in sin while Fiddlin' Turpin fiddled fit to kill. Maybe it was better to have danced so, than to come face to face with God. She was like her mother's people, old Mrs. Fairchild said, a hillbilly with loose wild ways. She shuddered with wickedness as she remembered that she had decided she didn't want to see God, not her grandmother's God. She stopped, forefinger on one red word, listening, her eyes on her mother's hands. The room was so still, too still for any sound to break through—maybe the noise she thought she heard was the wind in the white pines by the gate.

"The meek shall inherit the earth."[4] Her mother would have the Fairchild farm and all the farms in Somerset County and the whole world. She would live in a brick house with white shutters, older than Fairchild Place, built a thousand years before the battle of Bunker Hill instead of less than fifty. She would—but Fiddlin' Turpin would have nothing. He was not meek like most darkies. Sam McChesney, the storekeeper, laughed about the meekness of darkies. The ones who paid whatever he

---

[3] Matthew 5:8.

[4] "Blessed are the meek: for they shall inherit the earth." Matthew 5:5.

said, they would, along with Mama, inherit the earth, but Fiddlin' Turpin, he would never have even a blade of grass or one of his cold-nosed hounds. "Blessed are the merciful for they shall obtain mercy."[5] Granma would not get mercy, not one little drop. Disappointment hurt. Katy remembered that her grandmother would not need it. She was Elijah Fairchild's widow with Fairchild children and a lifetime right to Fairchild Place. The preachers and the old county judges all came to see her. Katy tried to find a blessing for Fiddlin' Turpin. Blessed...blessed...He was not weak, nor did he mourn, and he nor his children ever looked hungry. His heart could not be pure for he had knifed a white man.

The shadow of the box elder tree was almost touching the paling fence by the garden, and still no more sound from the bloodhounds. Lurie banged more wood into the stove, and rattled down the ashes. Old Mrs. Fairchild was toeing off,[6] and could not talk. Young Mrs. Fairchild almost never talked. "Blessed are they that hunger and thirst,"[7] Katy whispered, and peeped at her mother. She would be blessed in that one too, maybe. She always looked hungry—not like she wanted to eat—but hungry at night when they stood sometimes on the hill together and her mother looked west toward the hills, rising up against the sunset. Her own blood kin was there in the hills, and maybe she was hungry for her fox-huntin' hillbilly kin, that had in the old days never owned slaves or fought under Lee.

Katy puzzled over hunger and mercy—and thought of the plowline, the long brown snakelike length of it dragging out of the barn. She shivered and hugged her knees, squeezed her eyes tight to shut out the plowline, opened them and saw the red words. Blessed...blessed...blessed...somewhere there must be a blessing for Fiddlin' Turpin. Maybe God would give him some since he didn't have much time left to make his own. Maybe they'd found him already, and that was why it was so still. She ran her finger over her throat, held it at the soft curve above her dress, pressed harder. She felt sick, as if she might be going to throw up all over the Bible; Granma would get her then for sure.

Lurie folded the last of the shirts. "Must be gettin' nigh supper time. I think I'll leave off ironin'," she said with a cautious glance at old Mrs. Fairchild.

Old Mrs. Fairchild considered, then twisted about in her chair and frowned at the shadow of the box elder tree. "Better iron on a while longer. Th' men'ull maybe not be in 'fore a good spell. Maybe be gone all night." She glanced angrily at her daughter-in-law. "Mollie, you oughtn't to let that mare stay in th' barn all day—a standin' there when she's better in th' pasture."

Young Mrs. Fairchild pulled two socks together, dropped them into the willow work basket. "I was thinkin' that myself, that maybe I ought to turn her out now."

"An' who'll be takin' her I'd like to know? You can't in your condition. An' you know Lurie can't do a thing with her."

"Lord, yes," Lurie agreed, "she fairly hates th' sight of me."

Katy gave her mother's anxious face one quick glance, then bent over the Bible, whispering with tightly shut eyes, "Please Jesus, let me get away an' turn out th' gray mare."

"I could put a halter on her in th' barn, an' Katy could lead her to th' pasture,"

---

[5] Matthew 5:7.
[6] A knitting term.

[7] "Blessed are they which do hunger and thirst after righteousness: for they shall be filled." Matthew 5:6.

young Mrs. Fairchild said.

Katy opened her eyes and lifted her head with careful slowness, and said in careful disconcern with a finger on a red word, "What did you say, Mama? I was studyin' so."

When her mother had repeated her plans for the gray mare, Katy said, "I wouldn't mind," and was careful to be slow about getting up from the stool and marking her place in the Bible. Old Mrs. Fairchild fumed and fretted, told her daughter-in-law to be careful in the barn, and told Katy to be careful of the gray mare's heels, and ended by flouncing up from the rocker and declaring that they'd better wait until the men got home.

Katy glanced nervously at her mother's face, saw her chin lifted and her eyes blandly blue and not caring, the way they were sometimes, and then no longer concerned with her grandmother's wishes she skipped out the door.

She was by the stable door, stroking the gray mare's nose when her mother came, walking rapidly for her mother. She said nothing but took a halter from a peg on the wall and slipped it over the gray mare's neck. She never seemed to hear when Katy jumped up and down and begged to ride, but hurried the gray mare through the barnyard and up the pasture hill toward the bars that led to the west pasture. They were rushing up under the yellow leafed apple trees when old Mrs. Fairchild's long drawn scream of "Mo-l-l-ie," followed them up from the kitchen door.

They both turned and listened to Lurie's explanation: "Miz Fairchild says ye know ye cain't put that mare in th' west pasture. She'll jump th' fence an' git out, or break her leg in one of them sinks in th' creek."

"She's too hungry to bother," young Mrs. Fairchild said as if she didn't much care whether they heard her or not, then turned sharply up the hill again with no looking back at old Mrs. Fairchild babbling in the kitchen door.

"Won't Chariot get out a th' west pasture like Granma says?" Katy asked.

But her mother only walked a little faster, pulling on the gray mare's rein, until the three of them were almost running up the hill. Young Mrs. Fairchild's breath came short and her cheeks were red when they reached the pasture bars at the top of the hill. They stopped a moment to lay down the bars. As they worked both listened and looked below the west pasture to where the wagon road ran until it lost itself in the woodland that crowned the hill. "It's awful still," Katy whispered.

Young Mrs. Fairchild nodded and laid down the last bar, then straightened her shoulders and looked toward the bottom of the west pasture where Little Sinking Creek began. But though bars of the late red sunlight touched them there on the hill, below the cows grazed in shadow heavy like golden purple smoke. "I thought maybe he'd learned somethin' from th' foxes he's hunted all his days," young Mrs. Fairchild said, and continued to hunt over the bottom of the pasture with her eyes.

Katy studied her, uncertain of whether her mother spoke to her or the gray mare or maybe only to the air. "Can I take off th' gray mare's halter now?" she asked. "She's in a hurry to graze."

Her mother considered without taking her eyes from the field. "Maybe Chariot ought to have a little drink first. Maybe you ought to ride her down over th' hill...to th' spring at th' head of th' creek...an' leave her there to drink."

Katy climbed the rail fence, while the gray mare side stepped and minced and seemed to dance with a rolling of her eyes when she saw what Katy was about. Young Mrs. Fairchild quieted her with gentle strokes on one shoulder. "She'd love a long good run," she said.

"Reckon she'd jump th' fence?" Katy asked, and sat waiting on the top rail.

"Not if she grazes down by the bottom of the pasture and fills herself with a good long drink." She listened, head bent above the bars. "I guess it was only th' cowbells...if she did run away she'd go straight to Brother Joe's in McLeary County."

"I guess Uncle Joe could use a good mare," Katy said.

Her mother shook her head. "Brother Joe has plenty of mules an' horses, but he could use a good strong man about th' place...none of his boys are big enough to help."

Katy stood on the fence, watching for a chance to spring on the gray mare. "Fiddlin' Turpin is a good strong man an' a good worker spite a what Granma says."

"I've thought of that but now—"

"It's the bloodhounds—they're coming back," Katy cried, and stood balanced on tiptoe on the top rail to see if they were coming down the road.

"He did have some sense," young Mrs. Fairchild said, and jerked the gray mare's halter. The gray mare shied and plunged, then was suddenly docile drawing nearer the fence.

Katy leaped and caught her mane, as the hounds cried louder from the stretch of road behind the hill. "You've got to hurry," Mrs. Fairchild said, and Katy heard the trembling in her voice, and a lot of other things behind the words. "Ride her down to th' spring and leave her," she said, "but hurry...an' then come straight back home."

She let loose of the halter and the gray mare, mettlesome from her long stay in the stable, plunged down through the deep yellowing clover. Katy dug her heels into her side and clung, and never looked back and hardly nodded when' her mother called after her, in a voice loud and excited for her mother. "You might think on th' Beatitudes, Katy. Recollect blessed are they that are merciful for...."

But Katy was halfway down the hill, and the thud of the gray mare's hoofs and the wind in her ears drowned out her mother's words. She was doing what she had always wanted to do, giving the gray mare her head and letting her go at her will. She wondered if the gray mare would stop at the spring; maybe she'd race right by, lunge up the hill, leap the fence and go crashing and crackling through the wood on the other side. They'd swim Elk Spring Branch and go galloping into the hills to Uncle Joe's where.... She was flying, rising right up to meet the sky, then her feet were hard in the grass and clover, and she was falling belly downward with clover pushing hard into her face and her hands. Nearby someone was calling in a soft undertone, "Whoa, you gray devil, whoa. Oh, my Lordy," and feet were slithering over the grass to her.

She lifted her head and saw Fiddlin' Turpin with the gray mare's halter rein over his arm, and his eyes wide white and rolling in his black face. "Oh, my Lordy, I've kilt ye for shore," he said, and bent over her. "I heared a horse comin' sudden like an' lickety-split right on top a me here by th' spring. I thought hit was them, an' I started tu run, an' skeered yer—"

"S-h-h," Katy whispered, and listened with her ear near the ground.

"It's them bloodhounds," Fiddlin' Turpin whispered, as if he were too tired to care. "I figgered they'd not git back 'fore dark an' I'd have time tu rest a spell, an' try tu git a head start on 'em through th' woods. I've doubled like a fox till I'm clean winded." He squatted on his heels and stared down the valley to the edge of the pasture where the road ran, hidden now by a screen of persimmon bush.

Katy got up and smoothed her skirt and studied the black man. He looked tired, tireder than one of his fox hounds after a three days' run; there was blood on his face and hands from all the saw briars and barbed wire fence he'd come through, but now while he sat and stared at the road, unmoving as a stone man, he looked somehow as if he wouldn't be running much more, as if all the caring had gone out of him, and he would sit and wait with Chariot's halter over his arm till the bloodhounds came. He never even turned his head when the gray mare jerked on her reins and tried to nibble a mouthful of clover.

"You'd better hold on to that horse," Katy said. "She can jump any fence in th' country. Mama said if she broke out she'd never stop till she got to Uncle Joe's in McLeary County."

Fiddlin' Turpin turned and looked at her, his cracked, puffy lips wide open, as if maybe a thought had come into his mind past the bellowing hounds. "Hit'll not take them hounds long tu foller down th' creek an' then...." He stopped, and for the first time really looked at Chariot, and then he looked at Katy. His mouth was still open, but he didn't look so tired anymore.

Katy pulled a dried clover blossom from her hair. "We'd both better get goin'. Mama said Uncle Joe could use a good strong man," she said, and nodded toward the gray mare.

Afterwards she liked to think that Fiddlin' Turpin had thanked her or said, "God bless you, Katy," or some such thing, but he was gone so quickly—like Elijah in his chariot of fire—that she never knew exactly what it was he said. She stood a moment and watched the gray mare surge up the pasture hill, felt a moment's envy of Fiddlin' Turpin when the two of them cleared the fence with a full foot to spare, and then remembering her mother she ran up the hill and home.

Nothing was changed in the kitchen; old Mrs. Fairchild sat knitting and muttering in her chair, fuming because the gray mare would be certain to jump the west pasture fence and the men would be three weeks getting her home. Katy's mother worked in silence, a look of listening on her face as the bloodhounds cried up from the lower creek. Katy tiptoed to her footstool and picked up the Bible, conscious of her mother's eyes, tight somehow and as troubled as her hands twisting over the socks. Old Mrs. Fairchild laid her knitting on her knee. "Well, I hope after takin' th' gray mare to that pasture where she's bound to get out, you can do a little better learnin' your Bible quotations."

Katy folded her hands over the Bible and looked at her mother and said, "Blessed are the merciful for they shall obtain mercy." She hardly heard her grandmother's angry command to recite the first blessing first, for watching her mother's face and hands.

—1938

MARTHA GELLHORN (1908-1998)

Journalist and fiction writer Martha Gellhorn was born in St. Louis, Missouri, to George Gellhorn, a gynecologist, and Edna Fishel Gellhorn. She was educated at Bryn Mawr College in Pennsylvania, but dropped out before graduating. Determined to become a foreign correspondent, Gellhorn went to France in 1930. She covered most of the major wars of the twentieth century, including the Spanish Civil War (together with Ernest Hemingway, to whom she was briefly married), World War II (she was the first correspondent at the Dachau concentration camp), the war in Vietnam, the Six Day War in the Middle East, several of the civil wars in Central America, and the U.S. invasion of Panama (at the age of eighty-one). Gellhorn adopted a son, Sandy, from an Italian orphanage in 1949, several years after her marriage to Hemingway ended. A second marriage to T. S. Matthews also ended in divorce. She published nearly twenty books of fiction, memoir, travel writing, and journalism. "Miami-New York" was published in *The Atlantic Monthly* in 1948.

Miami–New York

There were five Air Force sergeants and they got in the plane and found seats and began to call to each other across the aisle or over the chair backs, saying, How about it, Joe, I guess this is the way to travel, or saying, Where do they keep the parachutes? or saying, Boy, I've got a pillow, what do you know! They were loud and good-natured for a moment, very young, and young in their new importance of being bomber crews, and they wanted the other people, the civilians, to know that they belonged in a different, fiercer world.

There were a half dozen of the men who seemed always to be going to or coming from Washington, the men with gray suits, hats, hair, skin, and with brown calf brief cases. These have no definite age and curiously similar faces, and are all equally tired and quiet. They always put their hats in the rack above the seat and sit down with their brief cases on their laps. Later they open their brief cases and look at sheets of typed or mimeographed paper, or they go to sleep.

The stewardess was young, with blonde hair hanging to her shoulders. She had a neat body of the right height and weight, and a professionally friendly voice. Fasten your seat belts, please, she said. Would you like some chewing gum? Fasten your seat belt, please, sir. Chewing gum?

A woman who had traveled a great deal in planes, and never trusted them because she understood nothing about them, sat in the double front seat behind the magazine rack. This was the best seat, as she knew, because there was enough room to stretch your legs. Also you could see well from here, if you wanted to see. Now, for a moment she looked out the window and saw that the few palm trees at the far edge of the field were blowing out in heavy plumes against the sky. There was something so wrong about Miami that even a beautiful night, sharp with stars, only seemed a real-estate advertisement. The woman pulled off her earrings and put them carelessly in her coat pocket. She ran her hands through her very short dark upcurling hair, deliberately making herself untidy for the night ahead. She hunched her shoulders to ease the tired stiffness in her neck and slouched down in the chair. She had just leaned her head against the chair back and was thinking of nothing when the man's voice said, Is this place taken? No, she said without looking at him. She moved nearer to the window. Anyhow, she said to herself, only eight or ten hours or whatever it is to New York; even if he snores, he can't snore all the time.

The plane taxied into position, turned, the propellers whirled until in the arc lights of the field they were great silver disks, the motor roared, and the plane started that run down the field that always, no matter how many times you had sat it out, no matter in how many countries, and no matter on how many fields, bad fields, dangerous fields, in whatever weather, always stopped your heart for one moment as you waited to see if this time it would work again; if this time, as all the other times, the enormous machine would rise smoothly into the air where no one really belonged except the birds.

"Made it," the man said softly to himself.

She looked at him then. He had said it as she would have said it, with wonder, with a perpetual amazement that the trick worked.

He turned to her and she could see he wanted to talk. She would only have to say yes, and smile, or say nice take-off, or say, what a lovely night; anything would do. But she was not going to say anything and he was not going to talk to her if she could help it. I have ten hours, she said in her mind to the man, and she said it threateningly, and they are mine and I don't have to talk to anyone and don't try. The man, finding her face closed against him, turned away, pulled a package of cigarettes from his pocket, and made a great distance between them, smoking and looking straight ahead.

She could not ignore him though he did nothing to force her attention. She had seen him without really looking; he was a Navy lieutenant and the braid on his cap, which he still held, was grayish black; his stripes and the active-duty star were tarnished; his uniform looked unpressed, and he had a dark weather-dried sunburn. His hair was a colorless blond, so short that it seemed he must have shaved his head and now the hair was just growing in, a month's growth probably.

With resentment, because she did not want to notice him, she studied him now, not caring if he turned his head and caught her. She looked at him with unfriendly professional eyes, the beady eye of the painter, her husband called it. The man's face, in repose, looked brooding and angry; the whole face was square. His eyebrows lay flat and black above his eyes, his mouth did not curve at all, and his chin seemed to make another straight line. There were three horizontal lines marked one after the other across his face, and blocked in by the hard bones of his jaw. But when he had turned to her, wanting to talk, he had been smiling and his face had been oval then, with all the lines flared gayly upwards. Perhaps the gayety came from his eyes, which were china blue, or was it his mouth, she thought, trying to remember. It was a very interesting face; it belonged to two different men. She wondered where he had picked up this dark, thinking, angry man, who showed on his face now.

Damn, she said to herself, what do I care? Let him have six faces. But it was a fine problem. How could you paint one face and make it at the same time square and oval, gay and longingly friendly, but also shut-in, angry and indifferent.

I wonder what she's sore about, the man thought mildly behind his complicated face. She doesn't look as if she was the type of woman who's sore all the time. Pretty women weren't usually sore all the time. He could place her, in a vague general way, as people of the same nationality can place each other. She had money and she had taste; her clothes were not only expensive and fashionable, which was frequent, they were the right clothes and she wore them without concern. He had not heard her voice but he imagined what it would be; Eastern, he thought, rather English. She would say things like, it's heaven, or he's madly energetic, or what a ghastly bore, saying it all without emphasis. She would be spoiled, as they all were, and at a loose end as they all were too. But her face was better than most. He did not think of women as stupid or not stupid. He simply thought her face was not like everyone's; it was small and pointed and even though she was sore, she could not make her face look dead. It was a lively face and her eyebrows grew in a feather line upwards over very bright, very dark eyes. Her hands were beautiful too, and he noticed, looking at them slantwise and secretly, that the nail varnish was cracking and she had broken or chewed off the nail of her right pointer finger. It was childish and careless to have such nails, and he liked that best about her. Sore as a goat, he thought mildly to himself. Then he forgot her.

He relaxed, behind the angry square of this second face that he had never seen and did not know about. He relaxed and enjoyed himself, thinking of nothing, but simply enjoying being alive and being home or almost home. He had been gone eighteen months, and without ever saying it to himself, because he made no poses, not even practical, realistic poses, he had often doubted that he would get back. Whenever he began almost to think about not ever getting back (and this was different from thinking about dying, there was something like self-pity about not getting back, whereas dying was just a thing that could happen) he would say to himself, grim and mocking, life on a destroyer is a big educational experience; you ought to be grateful.

He had worked briefly in his father's mills before he became an officer on a destroyer, but he did not want to be a businessman again. Or rather he could not remember what it was like, being a man in an office, so he had no interest in it. He did not want anything now except to be happy. He was happy. He rested behind his face and told himself how fine and comfortable the seat was and what a fine time he'd had last night in Miami with Bob Jamison and those two beauties and what a fine time he would have tomorrow and all the other days. Oh boy, he said to himself, and stretched all through his body without moving, and felt the fine time bathing him like soft water and sunlight.

No doubt he has a splendid little wife waiting for him, the woman thought. He is evidently going home and from the looks of him, his face and his clothes, he has been somewhere. He has ribbons sewn to his blue serge chest. Ribbons could mean something or nothing; every man in uniform that she knew had ribbons. They rode nobly and with growing boredom from their homes on the subway down to Church Street and presently they had ribbons. They lived in expensive overcrowdedness in Washington and wandered around the Pentagon building and went to cocktail parties in Georgetown and had ribbons. There were, for instance, those two faintly aging glamour boys, with silver eagles on their shoulders and enough ribbons to trim hats, who had just returned from London. She had always known these two and she was prepared to believe that they knew as much about war as she did, and she was certain that they had never ventured much farther afield than, say, Piccadilly Circus, in case they worked in Grosvenor Square. So what real ribbons were or what they meant, she did not know. However, looking at this man, she thought that his ribbons would mean something. His wife would know about the ribbons at once, if she did not know already, and she would be very proud. Why shouldn't she be, the woman asked herself irritably, what have you got against wives?

Am I not in fact a service wife myself? she thought. Could I not wear a pin with one star on it, a little oblong pin made of enamel if you haven't much money, but you can get it in sapphires, diamonds, and rubies if you feel that way? Have I not just returned from seeing my husband off in Miami? Thomas, she said to herself, is so used to getting what he wants that he believes the emotions will also perform as he wishes. A man is leaving for service overseas; he has forty-eight hours leave; his wife flies to him to say good-bye; they have forty-eight lovely last hours together and the lovely last hours were like being buried alive, though still quite alive so you knew all about it, with a stranger whom you ought to love but there it is, he is a stranger. Fine wife, she told herself, everyone handles this perfectly; all women manage to run their hearts smoothly; patriotism, pride, tenderness, farewell, homesickness. I'm not such a bitch as all that, she thought, defending herself; Thomas is only going to Brazil. I wouldn't mind going to Brazil myself. I should think he'd be enchanted to go to Brazil. As long as you aren't doing your own work, it's far better to be in Brazil than in Miami or Pensacola or the Brooklyn Navy Yard.

Only, if I were a real wife, a good wife, a service wife, I'd have made more of a thing of his going. Why does he want to be fooled, she thought angrily, why does he want to fool himself? Why does he go on about loving me when I am everything he dislikes and distrusts? She could hear Thomas now, and her heart moved with pity despite the anger. I love you more than anything, Kate, you know that; I only want you to be happy. Thomas believed it while he said it, and she felt herself to be cold and hard and ungrateful and somehow hideous, because she did not believe it at all.

She groaned and moved her body as if it were in pain. The man beside her turned, and stared, but he could not see her face. All he saw was the stiff line of her right shoulder, hunched up away from him. The woman was saying to herself, desperately, forget it, forget it. There is nothing to do. It cannot be understood; leave it alone. You cannot know so much about yourself; you cannot know why you thought you loved a man, nor why you think you no longer love him. It is not necessary to know. It's an enormous world, she told herself, with millions of people in it; if you're not even interested in yourself why can't you stop thinking about your own dreary little life? Thomas will be gone months, a year, two years. *Stop thinking about it.*

Suddenly, and without any sort of plan or direction from her brain, she pulled the great square diamond engagement ring and the baguette diamond wedding ring from her left hand, pulling them off brutally as if they would not come unless she forced them, and she thrust the two rings into her coat pocket with her earrings. Then she rubbed her left hand, crushing the bones of the hand together and pulling at the fingers. The man beside her, who had seen all this, said to himself, "Well, for God's sake what goes on here?" She's not sore, he thought, she's nuts. Then he amended that thought; nuts, or in some trouble of her own. He wanted no part of trouble; he did not understand it really. Living had become so simple for him that he understood nothing now except being or staying alive.

The stewardess turned off the overhead lights in the plane and one by one the small reading lights on the walls were turned off and presently the plane was dark.

The bright grayish night gleamed in through the windows. Two of the men from Washington snored weakly and one of the Air Force sergeants snored very loudly as if he enjoyed snoring and was going to do as much of it as he wanted. Then the snoring became a part of the plane sounds, and everything was quiet. The woman with the short, upcurling hair slept in a twisted sideways heap. The lieutenant leaned his head quietly against the chair back and stretched out his legs and settled himself without haste to sleep until morning.

In sleep his face was even more square and brooding. He seemed to be dreaming something that made him cold with anger or despair. He was not dreaming; it could not be a dream because it was always the same when he slept. It was as if he went to a certain place to sleep. This place was an enormous darkness; it moved a little but it was not a darkness made up of air or water: it was a solid darkness like being blind. Only the dark something around him had weight and he was under it; he was all alone, lying or floating, at ease, in no pain, pursued by nothing, but simply lying in absolute aloneness in the weight of the dark. He could not see himself, he could only feel himself there. It was terrible because there seemed no way to get out, and yet he did not struggle. He lay there every night and every night he was trapped in it forever, and every morning when he woke he was grateful and astonished though he did not remember why, as he did not remember the place where he had been sleeping.

This sleeping in a complete empty heavy darkness had come on him, gradually, on the ship. He knew nothing about himself and considered himself an ordinary man, quite lucky, doing all right, with nothing on his mind. Nothing had happened to him that had not happened to hundreds of other men. Even talking, in the ward-room, with others of his kind he recognized himself and knew there was nothing special about him. They talked very badly, without thought and without even knowing how to manage their language. It was almost like sign language the way they talked. But surely he felt what they all did.

When the first destroyer was sunk by a bomb, and he jumped overboard (but not nearly so far as he always imagined it would be—it didn't seem any farther than jumping from the high dive at the country club) and swam around and found a raft, he had first been mindless with fury. He did not know what the fury came from: was it because they were hunted and hurled in the sea, was it rage against their own helplessness, was he furious to lose the ship for which he felt now a strong unexpected love, was it fury for himself alone, fury at this outrageous tampering with life? He was so angry that he could not see or think; he did not remember swimming and he did not know how he had gone to the raft. Then the fear came as he watched the Japanese planes, so close above the water, searching them out where they splashed like driven terrified water beetles or hung together like leeches on a log. The fear was as cold as the water and made him weak and nauseated; then it too went. They were picked up very quickly; nothing had happened to him.

There was another time when he stood behind the forward gun crew and seemed to have nothing to do himself. He watched the sailor firing the Oerlikon[1] and saw his body bucking against the crutch-like supports of the gun, and he saw the faint bright stream of the bullets, but the man behind the Oerlikon seemed terribly slow, everything seemed slow, he himself had never had so much time and so little to do. This

---

[1] A Swiss manufactured anti-aircraft gun.

must have lasted a few seconds, but it was a large quiet piece of time and his mind said clearly: this is crazy, what are we all doing? Then his mind said it much louder: this is crazy. Finally he was not sure he had not shouted it out, because the thought was bursting in his mind. *This is crazy.*

Even that was not very remarkable; most of the other men thought everything was pretty screwy. You had to kill the Japs after they started it all, naturally you couldn't let them get away with it. You had to do it since that was how things were, but it was crazy all the same. If you began to think about it, about yourself and all the men you knew out here in this big god-awful ocean, to hell and gone from anywhere you ever wanted to be, and what you were doing and what everybody was doing everywhere, it was too crazy to think about. Then if you tried to think how it all started and what it was about and what difference it would make afterwards, you went crazy yourself. He had not actually talked this over with anyone but he knew the others felt as he did, Bob Jamison and Truby Bartlett and Joe Parks and the other men he knew well.

They all agreed in a simple easy way: they were the age that was in this war, if they'd been older or younger they wouldn't be, but this was what had happened and this was what they had to do. You made a lot of jokes and longed loudly for tangible things, liquor and a fine room at the Waldorf or the St. Francis, depending on taste, with a handy beauty. You played bridge or poker when you had a chance, for higher stakes than before. Time passed; you were the same man you always were. All you had to do was stay alive if you could.

Yet every night he went to this empty solid darkness and was forever buried in it, without hope or escape or anyone to call to.

The man, who had been asleep, woke suddenly and found his face ten inches from the woman's face. She had turned towards him in her sleep. Her eyes were closed and she looked very pale, tired, and a little ill. Her mouth was wonderfully soft. The man was not quite awake and he looked with surprise at this face he had not expected to see, and thought, she's lonely. He was thinking better than he would have done, had he been awake and protected by a long habit of not noticing and not thinking. She's sick lonely, he thought to himself. Without intending to, he leaned toward those soft lips. There was the face, waiting and needing to be kissed. Then he woke enough to remember where he was, and stopped himself, shocked, and thought, God, if I'd done it, she'd probably have called out and there'd have been a hell of a goings-on. He sighed and turned away from her and let his body relax, and slept again.

The plane skidded a little in the wind; it seemed to be forcing itself powerfully through air as heavy as water. The people in the plane slept or held themselves quietly. The plane began to smell close, smelling of bodies and night and old cigarette smoke.

Suddenly the woman felt a hand on her hair. The hand was not gentle; it pressed down the rumpled curly dark hair and stroked once from the forehead back to the nape of her neck. She woke completely but did not move, being too startled and confused to understand what had happened. The hand now left her hair and with harsh assurance rested on her breast; she could feel it through the thin tweed of her coat. She wondered whether she was dreaming this; it was so unlikely, that she must be dreaming it, and in the dark plane she could not see the hand. She looked over at the man and saw his face, dimly. He was asleep, with that troubled brooding look on his face. The hand was quiet, heavy and certain. The hand held and demanded her. What is he doing, she thought. My God, what is happening here? They certainly come back odd, she thought, with a kind of shaky laugh in her mind.

The hand insisted, and suddenly, to her amazement and to her shame, she knew that she wanted to lie against him, she wanted him to put his arms around her and hold her, with this silent unquestioning ownership. She wanted him to wake and hold her and kiss her. It did not matter who she was or who he was, and the other people in the plane did not matter. They were here together in the night and this incredible thing had happened and she did not want to stop it. She turned to him.

When she moved, the man sighed, still sleeping, and his hand fell from her, rested a moment in her lap, and then slowly dragged back, as if of its own will and apart from the man, and lay flat along his side. She waited, watching him, and presently her eyes woke him. He saw the woman's troubled, sad, somehow questioning face and the soft lips that asked to be kissed. He moved his right arm and pulled her as close to him as he could, but there was something between them though he was too sleepy to notice what it was, and he kissed her. He kissed her as if they had already made love, taking all that went before for granted. Having waked up in other places, and not known exactly what had happened, only knowing there was someone to kiss, he did not feel surprised now. Lovely lips, he thought happily. Then he noticed with real surprise that this thing digging into his side was the arm of the chair and then he knew where he was. The woman had pulled away from him and from his owning arm and his assured possessive mouth.

"I'm Kate Merlin," she whispered idiotically. She sounded panic-stricken.

The man laughed softly. He did not see what anyone's name had to do with it. "I'm John Hanley," he said.

"How do you do?" she said and felt both ridiculous and mad, and suddenly laughed too.

"Let's get rid of this obstruction," he said. The woman was frightened. He took everything so calmly; did he imagine that she always kissed the man sitting next to her on the night plane from Miami? The lieutenant worked at the arm of the chair until he discovered how to get it loose. He laid it on the floor in front of his feet. She was leaning forward and away from him, not knowing what to say in order to explain to him that she really wasn't a woman who could be kissed on planes, in case that happened to be a well-known category of woman.

He said nothing; that was evidently his specialty, she thought. He got everywhere without opening his mouth. His body spoke for him. He collected her, as if she belonged to him and could not have any other idea herself. He brought her close, raised her head so that it was comfortable for him, and kissed her. The harsh and certain hand held her as before.

This is fine, the man thought. It was part of the fine time in Miami and part of the fine time that would follow. He seemed to have a lot of luck—but why not, sometimes you did have luck, and he had felt all along that this leave was going to be wonderful. He had waited for it with such confidence that it could not fail him. Now he would kiss this lovely strange soft woman, and then they would go to sleep. There was nothing else they could do on a plane, which was a pity, but it was foolish to worry about something you couldn't have. Just be very damn grateful, he thought, that it's as fine as it is. You might have been sitting next to the Air Force, he thought with amusement, and what would you have then? She smelled of gardenias and her hair was delicious and like feathers against his cheek. He leaned forward to kiss her again, feeling warm and melted and unhurried and happy.

"How did you know?" the woman said. She seemed to have trouble speaking.

"Know what?"

"That you could kiss me?"

Oh God, he thought, we're going to have to talk about it. Why in hell did she want to talk?

"I didn't know anything." he said. "I didn't plan anything."

"Who are you?" She didn't mean that; she meant, how did it happen?

"Nobody," he said with conviction. "Absolutely nobody. Who are you?"

"I don't know," she said.

"Don't let it worry you," he said. He was beginning to feel impatient of this aimless talk. "Aren't we having a fine time?"

She took in her breath, rigid with distaste. So that was what it was. Just like that; it might have happened with anyone. Come on, baby, give us a kiss, isn't this fun. Oh *Lord,* she thought, what have I got into now? She wanted to say to him, I have never done anything like this in my life, you must not think. She wanted him to appreciate that this was rare and therefore important; it could not have happened any night with any man. It had to be alone of its kind, or she could not accept it.

The man again used silence, which he handled far better than words, and again he simply allowed his body to make what explanations seemed necessary. She felt herself helpless and glad to be helpless. But she could not let him think her only a willing woman; how would she face him in the morning if that was all he understood?

"You see," she began.

He kissed her so that she would not talk and he said, with his lips moving very lightly against hers, "It's all right."

She took that as she needed it, making it mean everything she wanted him to think. She was still amazed but she was full of delight. She felt there had been nothing in her life but talk and reasons, and the talk had been wrong and the reasons proved pointless: here was something that had happened at once, by itself, without a beginning, and it was right because it was like magic.

The man pressed her head against his shoulder, pulled her gently sideways to make her comfortable, leaned his head against the chair back, and prepared to sleep. He felt contented, but if he went on kissing her much longer, since there was nothing further he could do about her now, it might get to be tiresome and thwarted and wearing. It had been good and now it was time to sleep; he was very tired. He kissed the top of her head, remembering her, and said, "Sleep well."

Long ragged gray clouds disordered the sky. The moon was like an illuminated target in a shooting gallery, moving steadily ahead of them. The plane was colder now and one of the Air Force sergeants coughed himself awake, swore, blew his nose, sighed, shifted his position, and went back to sleep. The stewardess wondered whether she ought to make an inspection tour of her passengers and decided they were all right. She was reading a novel about society people in a country house in England, which fascinated her.

The woman lay easily against the lieutenant's shoulder and let her mind float in a smooth warm dream of pleasure. After the months of gnawing unlove, this man sat beside her in a plane in the night, and she no longer needed to dread herself as a creature who loved nothing. She did not love this man but she loved how she felt, she loved this warmth and aliveness and this hope. Now she made plans that were like those faultless daydreams in which one is always beautiful and the heroine and every day is more replete with miracles than the next. He would stay in New York, at her house even, since she was alone. Or would it be better if they went to a hotel so that there would be nothing to remind her of her ordinary life? They would treat New York as if it were a foreign city, Vienna in the spring, she thought. They would find new odd little places to eat, and funny places along Broadway to dance, they would walk in the Park and go to the Aquarium and the Bronx Zoo; they would sight-see and laugh and meet no one they knew and be alone in a strange, wonderful city. Someday he would have to go back where he came from, and she would go back to her work, but they would have this now and it was more than she had ever hoped for or imagined. And she would paint his strange face that was two faces, and he would be fresh and exciting every day and every night, with his silence and his fantastic assurance and his angry and happy look.

The plane circled the field at Washington and seemed to plunge onto the runway. The thump of the wheels striking the cement runway woke the man. He sat up and stared about him.

"Put the chair arm back," the woman whispered. "Good morning." She did not want the stewardess to look at her with a smile or a question. Her hair must be very soft; she would like to touch it, but not now. She looked at him with loving intimate eyes and the man looked at her, quite stupidly, as if he had never seen her before.

"The chair arm," she said again.

The man grinned suddenly and picked up the chair arm and fitted it back into its place. Then he turned to the woman and his face was merry, almost jovial.

"Sleep well?" he said.

"I didn't sleep." She had not imagined his face so gay, as if he were laughing at them both.

"Too bad. Well," he said, "I think I'll go and stretch my legs. Coming?"

"No, thank you," she said, terrified now.

The Air Force sergeants jostled each other getting out of the plane.

One of them called to the stewardess, "Don't leave without us, honey." They all laughed and crossed the cement runway, to the airport building, tugging at their clothes, tightening their belts, as if they had just come out of a wrestling match.

The men with brief cases took their hats and coats from the stewardess and thanked her in gray voices for a pleasant journey, and walked away quickly as if they were afraid of being late to their offices. In the front seat, Kate Merlin sat alone and listened to the stewardess talking with some of the ground crew; their voices were very bright and awake for this hour of the morning. Kate Merlin felt cold and a little sick and dismal, but she would not let herself think about it.

Then he was back beside her and the stewardess was moving down the aisle, like

a trained nurse taking temperatures in a hospital ward, to see that they were all properly strapped in for the take-off.

They fastened their seat belts again and then the plane was high in the mauve-gray
early morning sky.

"Do I remember you said your name was Kate Merlin?"

"Yes."

"Think of that."

How did he say it? she wondered. How? Complacently?

He was evidently not going to say anything more right now. She looked out the
window and her hands were cold. The man was thinking, Well, that's funny. Funny
how things happen. He had remembered the night, clearly, while he was walking up
and down the cement pavement by the airport building in Washington. It had seemed
strange to him, in the morning, but now it seemed less strange. Being an artist, he
told himself, they're all a little queer. He had never met an artist before but he was
ready to believe that they were not like other people. And being so rich too, he
thought, that would make her even queerer. The extremely rich were known to be
unlike other people. Her husband, but his name wasn't Merlin, was terrifically rich.
He'd read about them: their names, like many other names, seemed to be a sort of
tangible asset—like bonds, jewels, or real estate—of the New York columnists. Her
husband had inherited millions and owned a famous stable and plane factories or
some kind of factories. Thomas Sterling Hamilton, that was his name. It seemed
peculiar, her being a successful painter, when her husband was so rich and she didn't
need to.

"I've read about you," he remarked.

I have read nothing about you, she thought. What am I supposed to say: you have
the advantage of me, sir?

"I even remember one," he said in a pleased voice. "It said something about how
your clients, or whatever you call them, were glad to pay thousands for your portraits
because you always made them look dangerous. It said that was probably even more
flattering than looking beautiful. The women, that is. I wonder where I read it."

It was too awful; it was sickening. It must have been some revolting paragraph in
a gossip column. She would surely have been called a society portrait painter and
there would be a bit about Thomas and his money.

"What does a painter do during the war?" he asked.

"Paints," she said. Then it seemed too selfish to her and though she was ashamed
to be justifying herself to the man, she said quickly, "I don't know how to do anything but paint. I give the money to the Russian Relief or the Chinese Relief or the
Red Cross, things like that. It seems the most useful thing I can do, since I'm only
trained as a painter." She stopped, horrified at what she had done. What had made
her go into a whining explanation, currying favor with this man so he would see what
a splendid citizen she really was.

"That's fine." The civilians were all busy as bird dogs for the war, as he knew, and
it was very fine of them and all that but it embarrassed him to hear about it. He felt
they expected him to be personally grateful and he was not grateful, he did not care
what anybody did; he wasn't running this war. Then he thought, This isn't at all like
last night. He looked at the woman and saw that she looked even better in the

morning. It was amazing how a woman could sit up all night in a plane and look so clean and attractive. He felt his beard rough on his face and his eyes were sticky. She looked delicious and then he remembered how soft she had been in his arms and he wondered what to do about it now.

"I imagined Kate Merlin would be older," he said, thinking aloud.

It was only then that she realized how young he was, twenty-four or perhaps even less. His silence and his assurance and his closed dark second face had made him seem older, or else she had not thought about it at all. She was appalled. What am I becoming, she wondered, am I going to be one of those women without husbands who hunt young men?

"I'm old enough," she said curtly.

He turned and smiled at her. His eyes said, I know about you, don't tell me; I know how you are. It was the man of last night again, the certain one, the one whose body spoke for him. This talent he had when he was silent worked on her like a spell.

He seemed to understand this and very easily he reached his hand over and rested it on the back of her neck, where her hair grew up in soft duck feathers. Her body relaxed under this owning hand. "Yes, I am," she said dreamily, as if he had contradicted her, "I'm thirty-five."

"Are you?" he said. She could feel his hand change. It was quite different. It was a hand that had made a mistake and did not know where it was. It was a hand that would soon move away and become polite.

The man was thinking, thirty-five, well, that *is* old enough. That makes it something else again. And being an artist, he said to himself uneasily. It seemed to him that there was a trick somewhere; he had gotten into something he did not understand. She probably knew more than he did. She had perhaps been playing him along. Perhaps she was thinking he was pretty simple and inexperienced and was amused at how he came up for the bait.

The woman felt that something very bad, very painful, was happening but she could not name it and she held on to her plans of last night because they were happy and they were what she wanted. She said, in a tight voice, and mistrusting the words as she spoke them, "Will you be staying in New York?"

"I don't think so," he said. Speaking gave him a chance to take his hand away and light a cigarette. It might be fun in New York, he thought, meeting all those famous people she would know. He could go with her to El Morocco and the Colony and those places and see her kind of people. She would be something he hadn't had before, thirty-five and a celebrity and all. It might be fun. But he felt uneasy about it; this was not his familiar country. This was not how he saw a fine time, exactly. It was complicated, not safe, you would not know what you were doing. And how about her husband?

"Don't you know?" she said. He did not like that. That sounded like giving orders. That sounded as if she meant to take him over. He was suspicious of her at once.

"No," he said. His face wore the shut-in, indifferent look.

"What might you be doing?" she insisted. Oh stop it, she told herself, for God's sake stop it. What are you doing now; do you want to prove it to yourself?

"I'll be going home first," he said. Give it to her, he thought. He didn't like that bossy, demanding way she suddenly had. "Springfield," he added. She would be thinking now that he was a small-town boy from Massachusetts and that was all right with him.

Then he thought with sudden pleasure of Springfield; he would have a fine time there for a while, a fine time that he understood. He might go on to Boston, where he knew his way around, and have a different but still excellent sort of time. Later, at the end, he would go to New York for a few days but by himself, on his own terms. He did not want to get mixed up. He did not want anything that he could not manage. He just wanted to have a good easy time with nothing to worry about. She wasn't in his league; he didn't know about married rich, famous women of thirty-five.

The woman felt so cold that she had to hold herself carefully so that she would not shiver. A middle-aged woman, she told herself with horror, hounding a young man. That was what he thought. She had offered herself to him and he had rejected her. He did not want her. She was too old. If only the plane would move faster; if only they would get there so she could hide from him. If only she did not have to sit beside him, sick with the knowledge of what he thought, and sick with shame for herself. She did not know how to protect herself from the shock of this rejection.

The plane flew north along the East River and in the fresh greenish-blue light the city appeared below them. It looked like a great ancient ruin. The towers were vast pillars, planted in the mist, with sharp splintered tops. The squarish skyscrapers were old white temples or giant forts, and there was no life in the jagged quarry of buildings. It was beautiful enough to rock the heart, and suddenly the woman imagined it would look like this, thousands of years from now, enormous and dead.

The man leaned forward to look out the window. "Pretty, isn't it?" he said.

He had really said that and he meant it. That was all he saw. But then it was all right. Whatever he thought of her did not matter; he was too stupid to care about. But she knew this was a lie; nothing had changed. There was the fact and there was no way to escape it; he could have had her and he simply did not want her.

They were the last people off the plane. The other passengers had seemed to block their way on purpose. The woman sent a porter to find a taxi. She would escape from his presence at least, as quickly as she could. When the man saw the taxi stopping before them he said, "Not taking the airline car?"

"No." She did not offer to give him a lift in town. Oh hurry, she thought. The man started to move her bags to the taxi. "Don't bother," she said, "the porter will manage."

He seemed a little puzzled by this flight. "Good luck," he said, shutting the door behind her, "hope I'll see you again some place." It was a thing to say, that was all.

"Good luck to you," she said, and hoped her voice was light and friendly. She did not actually look at him.

"Where to, Miss?" the taxi driver asked. She gave her address and pretended not to see the man saluting good-bye from the curb.

It might have been fun, the man thought, as he watched the taxi turn and head towards the highway. Oh no, hell, he told himself, complications. It was better this way. He began to feel relieved and then he put the whole business out of his mind; he did not want to clutter up his mind with questions or problems and perhaps spoil some of his leave. He thought about Springfield and his face was oval now, smiling. He was in a hurry to get in town and get started. He would not let himself consider the good time ahead in numbered days; he was thinking, now, now, now. He had erased the woman entirely; she was finished and gone.

After the cab passed the gates of the airport, the woman leaned back and took a deep breath to steady herself and to ease the pain in her throat. She covered her eyes with her hand. It's just that I'm so tired, she told herself. This was what she would have to believe. It's nothing to feel desperate about. It's just that I'm so tired, she thought, forcing herself to believe it. It's only because I've been sitting up all night in a plane.

—1948

ANN PETRY (1908-1997)

Ann Lane was born in Old Saybrook, Connecticut, to middle-class, professional Black parents, a fourth generation New Englander. Her father was a pharmacist who owned a drugstore, her mother a licensed chiropodist, barber, and entrepreneur. Petry began writing in high school, but did not publish her work until later in life. She obtained her Ph.G. from the Connecticut College of Pharmacy in 1931 and worked in her family's drugstores for several years, experiences that would influence both her adult novel, *Country Place* (1947), and her children's book, *The Drugstore Cat* (1949). In 1938, she married George D. Petry and had one daughter. They moved to New York City, where Petry edited the women's page and reported for the Harlem-based *Amsterdam News*, and also worked with an after-school program for Harlem children. In 1943, a story of Petry's in *The Crisis*, the magazine of the NAACP, led to her "discovery" by publisher Houghton Mifflin, who put out her first novel, *The Street*, in 1946. *The Street* drew on Petry's knowledge of Harlem, exploring the raced, classed, and gendered struggles of a young Black single mother during World War II; it was the first national bestseller by an African-American woman. Petry wrote two more novels for adults and a variety of books for children, including *Harriet Tubman: Conductor on the Underground Railroad* (1955) and *Tituba of Salem Village* (1964). Her collection of stories, *Miss Muriel and Other Stories*, appeared in 1971. Petry and her husband moved back to Old Saybrook in 1947, where she lived until her death.

Like a Winding Sheet

He had planned to get up before Mae did and surprise her by fixing breakfast. Instead he went back to sleep and she got out of bed so quietly he didn't know she wasn't there beside him until he woke up and heard the queer soft gurgle of water running out of the sink in the bathroom.

He knew he ought to get up but instead he put his arms across his forehead to shut the afternoon sunlight out of his eyes, pulled his legs up close to his body, testing them to see if the ache was still in them.

Mae had finished in the bathroom. He could tell because she never closed the door when she was in there and now the sweet smell of talcum powder was drifting down the hall and into the bedroom. Then he heard her coming down the hall.

"Hi, babe," she said affectionately.

"Hum," he grunted, and moved his arms away from his head, opened one eye.

"It's a nice morning."

"Yeah." He rolled over and the sheet twisted around him, outlining his thighs, his chest. "You mean afternoon, don't ya?"

Mae looked at the twisted sheet and giggled. "Looks like a winding sheet," she said. "A shroud—" Laughter tangled with her words and she had to pause for a moment before she could continue. "You look like a huckleberry—in a winding sheet—"

"That's no way to talk. Early in the day like this," he protested.

He looked at his arms silhouetted against the white of the sheets. They were inky black by contrast and he had to smile in spite of himself and he lay there smiling and savoring the sweet sound of Mae's giggling.

"Early?" She pointed a finger at the alarm clock on the table near the bed and giggled again. "It's almost four o'clock. And if you don't spring up out of there, you're going to be late again."

"What do you mean 'again'?"

"Twice last week. Three times the week before. And once the week before and—"

"I can't get used to sleeping in the daytime," he said fretfully. He pushed his legs out from under the covers experimentally. Some of the ache had gone out of them but they weren't really rested yet. "It's too light for good sleeping. And all that standing beats the hell out of my legs."

"After two years you oughta be used to it," Mae said.

He watched her as she fixed her hair, powdered her face, slipped into a pair of blue denim overalls. She moved quickly and yet she didn't seem to hurry.

"You look like you'd had plenty of sleep," he said lazily. He had to get up but he kept putting the moment off, not wanting to move, yet he didn't dare let his legs go completely limp because if he did he'd go back to sleep. It was getting later and later but the thought of putting his weight on his legs kept him lying there.

When he finally got up he had to hurry, and he gulped his breakfast so fast that he wondered if his stomach could possibly use food thrown at it at such a rate of speed. He was still wondering about it as he and Mae were putting their coats on in the hall.

Mae paused to look at the calendar. "It's the thirteenth," she said. Then a faint excitement in her voice, "Why, it's Friday the thirteenth." She had one arm in her coat sleeve and she held it there while she stared at the calendar. "I oughta stay home," she said. "I shouldn't go outa the house."

"Aw, don't be a fool," he said. "Today's payday. And payday is a good luck day everywhere, any way you look at it." And as she stood hesitating he said, "Aw, come on."

And he was late for work again because they spent fifteen minutes arguing before he could convince her she ought to go to work just the same. He had to talk persuasively, urging her gently, and it took time. But he couldn't bring himself to talk to her roughly or threaten to strike her like a lot of men might have done. He wasn't made that way.

So when he reached the plant he was late and he had to wait to punch the time clock because the day-shift workers were streaming out in long lines, in groups and bunches that impeded his progress.

Even now just starting his workday his legs ached. He had to force himself to struggle past the outgoing workers, punch the time clock, and get the little cart he pushed around all night, because he kept toying with the idea of going home and getting back in bed.

He pushed the cart out on the concrete floor, thinking that if this was his plant he'd make a lot of changes in it. There were too many standing-up jobs for one thing. He'd figure out some way most of 'em could be done sitting down and he'd put a lot more benches around. And this job he had—this job that forced him to walk ten hours a night, pushing this little cart, well, he'd turn it into a sitting-down job. One of those little trucks they used around railroad stations would be good for a job like this. Guys sat on a seat and the thing moved easily, taking up little room and turning in hardly any space at all, like on a dime.

He pushed the cart near the foreman. He never could remember to refer to her as the forelady even in his mind. It was funny to have a white woman for a boss in a plant like this one.

She was sore about something. He could tell by the way her face was red and her eyes were half-shut until they were slits. Probably been out late and didn't get enough sleep. He avoided looking at her and hurried a little, head down, as he passed her though he couldn't resist stealing a glance at her out of the corner of his eyes. He saw the edge of the light-colored slacks she wore and the tip end of a big tan shoe.

"Hey, Johnson!" the woman said.

The machines had started full blast. The whirr and the grinding made the building shake, made it impossible to hear conversations. The men and women at the machines talked to each other but looking at them from just a little distance away, they appeared to be simply moving their lips because you couldn't hear what they were saying. Yet the woman's voice cut across the machine sounds—harsh, angry.

He turned his head slowly. "Good evenin', Mrs. Scott," he said, and waited.

"You're late again."

"That's right. My legs were bothering me."

The woman's face grew redder, angrier looking. "Half this shift comes in late," she said. "And you're the worst one of all. You're always late. Whatsa matter with ya?"

"It's my legs," he said. "Somehow they don't ever get rested. I don't seem to get used to sleeping days. And I just can't get started."

"Excuses. You guys always got excuses," her anger grew and spread. "Every guy comes in here late always has an excuse. His wife's sick or his grandmother died or somebody in the family had to go to the hospital," she paused, drew a deep breath. "And the niggers is the worse. I don't care what's wrong with your legs. You get in here on time. I'm sick of you niggers—"

"You got the right to get mad," he interrupted softly. "You got the right to cuss me four ways to Sunday but I ain't letting nobody call me a nigger."

He stepped closer to her. His fists were doubled. His lips were drawn back in a thin narrow line. A vein in his forehead stood out swollen, thick.

And the woman backed away from him, not hurriedly but slowly—two, three steps back.

"Aw, forget it," she said. "I didn't mean nothing by it. It slipped out. It was an accident." The red of her face deepened until the small blood vessels in her cheeks were purple. "Go on and get to work," she urged. And she took three more slow backward steps.

He stood motionless for a moment and then turned away from the sight of the red lipstick on her mouth that made him remember that the foreman was a woman. And he couldn't bring himself to hit a woman. He felt a curious tingling in his fingers and he looked down at his hands. They were clenched tight, hard, ready to smash some of those small purple veins in her face.

He pushed the cart ahead of him, walking slowly. When he turned his head, she was staring in his direction, mopping her forehead with a dark blue handkerchief. Their eyes met and then they both looked away.

He didn't glance in her direction again but moved past the long work benches, carefully collecting the finished parts, going slowly and steadily up and down, back and forth the length of the building, and as he walked he forced himself to swallow his anger, get rid of it.

And he succeeded so that he was able to think about what had happened without getting upset about it. An hour went by but the tension stayed in his hands. They were clenched and knotted on the handles of the cart as though ready to aim a blow.

And he thought he should have hit her anyway, smacked her hard in the face, felt the soft flesh of her face give under the hardness of his hands. He tried to make his hands relax by offering them a description of what it would have been like to strike her because he had the queer feeling that his hands were not exactly a part of him anymore—they had developed a separate life of their own over which he had no control. So he dwelt on the pleasure his hands would have felt—both of them cracking at her, first one and then the other. If he had done that his hands would have felt good now—relaxed, rested.

And he decided that even if he'd lost his job for it, he should have let her have it and it would have been a long time, maybe the rest of her life, before she called anybody else a nigger.

The only trouble was he couldn't hit a woman. A woman couldn't hit back the same way a man did. But it would have been a deeply satisfying thing to have cracked her narrow lips wide open with just one blow, beautifully timed and with all his weight in back of it. That way he would have gotten rid of all the energy and tension his anger had created in him. He kept remembering how his heart had started pumping blood so fast he had felt it tingle even in the tips of his fingers.

With the approach of night, fatigue nibbled at him. The corners of his mouth drooped, the frown between his eyes deepened, his shoulders sagged; but his hands stayed tight and tense. As the hours dragged by he noticed that the women workers had started to snap and snarl at each other. He couldn't hear what they said because of the sound of machines but he could see the quick lip movements that sent words tumbling from the sides of their mouths. They gestured irritably with their hands and scowled as their mouths moved.

Their violent jerky motions told him that it was getting close on to quitting time but somehow he felt that the night still stretched ahead of him, composed of endless hours of steady walking on his aching legs. When the whistle finally blew he went on pushing the cart, unable to believe that it had sounded. The whirring of the machines died away to a murmur and he knew then that he'd really heard the whistle. He stood still for a moment, filled with a relief that made him sigh.

Then he moved briskly, putting the cart in the storeroom, hurrying to take his place in the line forming before the paymaster. That was another thing he'd change, he thought. He'd have the pay envelopes handed to the people right at their benches so there wouldn't be ten or fifteen minutes lost waiting for the pay. He always got home about fifteen minutes late on payday. They did it better in the plant where Mae worked, brought the money right to them at their benches.

He stuck his pay envelope in his pants' pocket and followed the line of workers heading for the subway in a slow-moving stream. He glanced up at the sky. It was a nice night, the sky looked packed full to running over with stars. And he thought if he and Mae would go right to bed when they got home from work they'd catch a few hours of darkness for sleeping. But they never did. They fooled around—cooking and eating and listening to the radio and he always stayed in a big chair in the living room and went almost but not quite to sleep and when they finally got to bed it was five or six in the morning and daylight was already seeping around the edges of the sky.

He walked slowly, putting off the moment when he would have to plunge into the crowd hurrying toward the subway. It was a long ride to Harlem and tonight the thought of it appalled him. He paused outside an all-night restaurant to kill time, so that some of the first rush of workers would be gone when he reached the subway.

The lights in the restaurant were brilliant, enticing. There was life and motion inside. And as he looked through the window he thought that everything within range of his eyes gleamed—the long imitation marble counter, the tall stools, the white porcelain-topped tables and especially the big metal coffee urn right near the window. Steam issued from its top and a gas flame flickered under it—a lively, dancing, blue flame.

A lot of the workers from his shift—men and women—were lining up near the coffee urn. He watched them walk to the porcelain-topped tables carrying steaming cups of coffee and he saw that just the smell of the coffee lessened the fatigue lines in their faces. After the first sip their faces softened, they smiled, they began to talk and laugh.

On a sudden impulse he shoved the door open and joined the line in front of the coffee urn. The line moved slowly. And as he stood there the smell of the coffee, the sound of the laughter and of the voices, helped dull the sharp ache in his legs.

He didn't pay any attention to the white girl who was serving the coffee at the urn. He kept looking at the cups in the hands of the men who had been ahead of him. Each time a man stepped out of the line with one of the thick white cups the fragrant steam got in his nostrils. He saw that they walked carefully so as not to spill a single drop. There was a froth of bubbles at the top of each cup and he thought about how he would let the bubbles break against his lips before he actually took a big deep swallow.

Then it was his turn. "A cup of coffee," he said, just as he had heard the others say.

The white girl looked past him, put her hands up to her head and gently lifted her hair away from the back of her neck, tossing her head back a little. "No more coffee for a while," she said.

He wasn't certain he'd heard her correctly and he said, "What?" blankly.

"No more coffee for a while," she repeated.

There was silence behind him and then uneasy movement. He thought someone would say something, ask why or protest, but there was only silence and then a faint shuffling sound as though the men standing behind him had simultaneously shifted their weight from one foot to the other.

He looked at the girl without saying anything. He felt his hands begin to tingle and the tingling went all the way down to his finger tips so that he glanced down at them. They were clenched tight, hard, into fists. Then he looked at the girl again. What he wanted to do was hit her so hard that the scarlet lipstick on her mouth would smear and spread over her nose, her chin, out toward her cheeks, so hard that she would never toss her head again and refuse a man a cup of coffee because he was black.

He estimated the distance across the counter and reached forward, balancing his weight on the balls of his feet, ready to let the blow go. And then his hands fell back down to his sides because he forced himself to lower them, to unclench them and make them dangle loose. The effort took his breath away because his hands fought against him. But he couldn't hit her. He couldn't even now bring himself to hit a woman, not even this one, who had refused him a cup of coffee with a toss of her head. He kept seeing the gesture with which she had lifted the length of her blond hair from the back of her neck as expressive of her contempt for him.

When he went out the door he didn't look back. If he had he would have seen the flickering blue flame under the shiny coffee urn being extinguished. The line of men who had stood behind him lingered a moment to watch the people drinking coffee at the tables and then they left just as he had without having had the coffee they wanted so badly. The girl behind the counter poured water in the urn and swabbed it out and as she waited for the water to run out, she lifted her hair gently from the back of her neck and tossed her head before she began making a fresh lot of coffee.

But he had walked away without a backward look, his head down, his hands in his pockets, raging at himself and whatever it was inside of him that had forced him to stand quiet and still when he wanted to strike out.

The subway was crowded and he had to stand. He tried grasping an overhead strap and his hands were too tense to grip it. So he moved near the train door and stood there swaying back and forth with the rocking of the train. The roar of the train beat inside his head, making it ache and throb, and the pain in his legs clawed up into his groin so that he seemed to be bursting with pain and he told himself that it was due to all that anger-born energy that had piled up in him and not been used and so it had spread through him like a poison—from his feet and legs all the way up to his head.

Mae was in the house before he was. He knew she was home before he put the key in the door of the apartment. The radio was going. She had it tuned up loud and she was singing along with it.

"Hello, babe," she called out, as soon as he opened the door.

He tried to say 'hello' and it came out half grunt and half sigh.

"You sure sound cheerful," she said.

She was in the bedroom and he went and leaned against the doorjamb. The denim overalls she wore to work were carefully draped over the back of a chair by the bed. She was standing in front of the dresser, tying the sash of a yellow housecoat around her waist and chewing gum vigorously as she admired her reflection in the mirror over the dresser.

"Whatsa matter?" she said. "You get bawled out by the boss or somep'n?"

"Just tired," he said slowly. "For God's sake, do you have to crack that gum like that?"

"You don't have to lissen to me," she said complacently. She patted a curl in place near the side of her head and then lifted her hair away from the back of her neck, ducking her head forward and then back.

He winced away from the gesture. "What you got to be always fooling with your hair for?" he protested.

"Say, what's the matter with you anyway?" She turned away from the mirror to face him, put her hands on her hips. "You ain't been in the house two minutes and you're picking on me."

He didn't answer her because her eyes were angry and he didn't want to quarrel with her. They'd been married too long and got along too well and so he walked all the way into the room and sat down in the chair by the bed and stretched his legs out in front of him, putting his weight on the heels of his shoes, leaning way back in the chair, not saying anything.

"Lissen," she said sharply. "I've got to wear those overalls again tomorrow. You're going to get them all wrinkled up leaning against them like that."

He didn't move. He was too tired and his legs were throbbing now that he had sat down. Besides the overalls were already wrinkled and dirty, he thought. They couldn't help but be for she'd worn them all week. He leaned farther back in the chair.

"Come on, get up," she ordered.

"Oh, what the hell," he said wearily, and got up from the chair. "I'd just as soon live in a subway. There'd be just as much place to sit down."

He saw that her sense of humor was struggling with her anger. But her sense of humor won because she giggled.

"Aw, come on and eat," she said. There was a coaxing note in her voice. "You're nothing but an old hungry nigger trying to act tough and—" she paused to giggle and then continued, "You—"

He had always found her giggling pleasant and deliberately said things that might amuse her and then waited, listening for the delicate sound to emerge from her throat. This time he didn't even hear the giggle. He didn't let her finish what she was saying. She was standing close to him and that funny tingling started in his finger tips, went fast up his arms and sent his fist shooting straight for her face.

There was the smacking sound of soft flesh being struck by a hard object and it wasn't until she screamed that he realized he had hit her in the mouth—so hard that the dark red lipstick had blurred and spread over her full lips, reaching up toward the tip of her nose, down toward her chin, out toward her cheeks.

The knowledge that he had struck her seeped through him slowly and he was appalled but he couldn't drag his hands away from her face. He kept striking her and he thought with horror that something inside him was holding him, binding him to this act, wrapping and twisting about him so that he had to continue it. He had lost all control over his hands. And he groped for a phrase, a word, something to describe what this thing was like that was happening to him and he thought it was like being enmeshed in a winding sheet—that was it—like a winding sheet. And even as the thought formed in his mind, his hands reached for her face again and yet again.

—1946

EUDORA WELTY (1909-2001)

Born and raised in Jackson, Mississippi, Eudora Welty was the oldest child of Christian Webb Welty, an insurance executive, and Chestina Andrews Welty, a schoolteacher. Welty attended Mississippi State College for Women from 1925 to 1927, and received her B.A. from the University of Wisconsin in 1929. After studying advertising at Columbia University, Welty returned to Jackson upon her father's death in 1931, and worked for a newspaper and a radio station. She was a publicity agent for the Works Progress Administration (WPA), a Depression-era program to provide jobs; her WPA photographs were later published in *One Time, One Place* (1971). Her first book, *A Curtain of Green, and Other Stories,* was published in 1941 with an introduction by Katherine Anne Porter. Like Flannery O'Connor and Carson McCullers, Welty wrote primarily about the South. She published four collections of stories, five novels, two collections of photographs, three works of nonfiction, and one book for children. Welty's work enjoyed both popular and critical success. She was awarded the Pulitzer Prize for her novel *The Optimist's Daughter* (1972); the American Book Award for her best-selling memoir, *One Writer's Beginnings* (1984); and the National Book Critics Circle Award. Welty was elected to the National Institute of Arts and Letters in 1952; she won its William Dean Howells Medal for *The Ponder Heart* (1954) and its Gold Medal in 1972. She also received the Presidential Medal of Freedom (1980), the National Medal of the Arts (1986), the French Légion d'Honneur (1996), and forty honorary degrees. Her home in Jackson has been preserved.

Written immediately after she learned of the assassination of Civil Rights leader Medgar Evers, "Where Is the Voice Coming From?" was published in the *New Yorker* magazine. In her *Collected Stories* (1980), Welty explained that "Where Is the Voice Coming From?" was revised to avoid legal difficulties, because she had so accurately—too accurately—portrayed Evers' murderer.

Where Is the Voice Coming From?

I says to my wife, "You can reach and turn it off. You don't have to set and look at a black nigger face no longer than you want to, or listen to what you don't want to hear. It's still a free country."

I reckon that's how I give myself the idea.

I says, I could find right exactly where in Thermopylae that nigger's living that's asking for equal time. And without a bit of trouble to me.

And I ain't saying it might not be because that's pretty close to where *I* live. The other hand, there could be reasons you might have yourself for knowing how to get there in the dark. It's where you all go for the thing you want when you want it the most. Ain't that right?

The Branch Bank sign tells you in lights, all night long even, what time it is and how hot. When it was quarter to four, and 92, that was me going by in my brother-in-law's truck. He don't deliver nothing at that hour of the morning.

So you leave Four Corners and head west on Nathan B. Forrest Road, past the Surplus & Salvage, not much beyond the Kum Back Drive-In and Trailer Camp, not as far as where the signs starts saying "Live Bait," "Used Parts," "Fireworks," "Peaches," and "Sister Peebles Reader and Adviser." Turn before you hit the city limits and duck back towards the I.C. tracks. And his street's been paved.

And there was his light on, waiting for me. In his garage, if you please. His car's gone. He's out planning still some other ways to do what we tell 'em they can't. I *thought* I'd beat him home. All I had to do was pick my tree and walk in close behind it.

I didn't come expecting not to wait. But it was so hot, all I did was hope and pray one or the other of us wouldn't melt before it was over.

Now, it wasn't no bargain I'd struck.

I've heard what you've heard about Goat Dykeman, in Mississippi. Sure, everybody knows about Goat Dykeman. Goat he got word to the Governor's Mansion he'd go up yonder and shoot that nigger Meredith[1] clean out of school, if he's let out of the pen to do it. Old Ross[2] turned *that* over in his mind before saying him nay, it stands to reason.

I ain't no Goat Dykeman, I ain't in no pen, and I ain't ask no Governor Barnett to give me one thing. Unless he wants to give me a pat on the back for the trouble I took this morning. But he don't have to if he don't want to. I done what I done for my own pure-D satisfaction.

As soon as I heard wheels, I knowed who was coming. That was him and bound to be him. It was the right nigger heading in a new white car up his driveway towards his garage with the light shining, but stopping before he got there, maybe not to wake 'em. That was him. I knowed it when he cut off the car lights and put his foot out and I knowed him standing dark against the light. I knowed him then like I know me now. I knowed him even by his still, listening back.

Never seen him before, never seen him since, never seen anything of his black face but his picture, never seen his face alive, any time at all, or anywheres, and didn't want to, need to, never hope to see that face and never will. As long as there was no question in my mind.

He had to be the one. He stood right still and waited against the light, his back was fixed, fixed on me like a preacher's eyeballs when he's yelling "Are you saved?" He's the one.

I'd already brought up my rifle, I'd already taken my sights. And I'd already got him, because it was too late then for him or me to turn by one hair.

Something darker than him, like the wings of a bird, spread on his back and pulled him down. He climbed up once, like a man under bad claws, and like just blood could weigh a ton he walked with it on his back to better light. Didn't get no further than his door. And fell to stay.

He was down. He was down, and a ton load of bricks on his back wouldn't have laid any heavier. There on his paved driveway, yes sir.

And it wasn't till the minute before, that the mockingbird had quit singing. He'd been singing up my sassafras tree. Either he was up early, or he hadn't never gone to bed, he was like me. And the mocker he'd stayed right with me, filling the air till come the crack, till I turned loose of my load. I was like him. I was on top of the world myself. For once.

I stepped to the edge of his light there, where he's laying flat. I says, "Roland? There was one way left, for me to be ahead of you and stay ahead of you, by Dad, and I just taken it. Now I'm alive and you ain't. We ain't never now, never going to

---

[1] James Meredith (b. 1933) became the first African-American student admitted to the University of Mississippi in 1962; whites rioted on campus, killing two, and federal troops were called out to protect him.

[2] Ross Barnett (1898-1987), Mississippi governor (1960-1964) and staunch segregationist.

be equals and you know why? One of us is dead. What about that, Roland?" I said. "Well, you seen to it, didn't you?"

I stood a minute—just to see would somebody inside come out long enough to pick him up. And there she comes, the woman. I doubt she'd been to sleep. Because it seemed to me she'd been in there keeping awake all along.

It was mighty green where I skint over the yard getting back. That nigger wife of his, she wanted nice grass! I bet my wife would hate to pay her water bill. And for burning her electricity. And there's my brother-in-law's truck, still waiting with the door open. "No Riders"—that didn't mean me.

There wasn't a thing I been able to think of since would have made it to go any nicer. Except a chair to my back while I was putting in my waiting. But going home, I seen what little time it takes after all to get a thing done like you really want it. It was 4:34, and while I was looking it moved to 35. And the temperature stuck where it was. All that night I guarantee you it had stood without dropping, a good 92.

My wife says, "What? Didn't the skeeters bite you?" She said, "Well, they been asking that—why somebody didn't trouble to load a rifle and get some of these agitators out of Thermopylae. Didn't the fella keep drumming it in, what a good idea? The one that writes a column ever' day?"

I says to my wife, "Find *some* way I don't get the credit."

"He says do it for Thermopylae," she says. "Don't you ever skim the paper?"

I says, "Thermopylae never done nothing for me. And I don't owe nothing to Thermopylae. Didn't do it for you. Hell, any more'n I'd do something or other for them Kennedys! I done it for my own pure-D satisfaction."

"It's going to get him right back on TV," says my wife. "You watch for the funeral."

I says, "You didn't even leave a light burning when you went to bed. So how was I supposed to even get me home or pull Buddy's truck up safe in our front yard?"

"Well, hear another good joke on you," my wife says next. "Didn't you hear the news? The N. double A. C. P. is fixing to send somebody to Thermopylae. Why couldn't you waited? You might could have got you somebody better. Listen and hear 'em say so."

I ain't but one. I reckon you have to tell *somebody*.

"Where's the gun, then?" my wife says. "What did you do with our protection?"

I says, "It was scorching! It was scorching!" I told her, "It's laying out on the ground in rank weeds, trying to cool off, that's what it's doing now."

"You dropped it," she says. "Back there."

And I told her, "Because I'm so tired of ever'thing in the world being just that hot to the touch! The keys to the truck, the doorknob, the bed-sheet, ever'thing, it's all like a stove lid. There just ain't much going that's worth holding on to it no more," I says, "when it's a hundred and two in the shade by day and by night not too much difference. I wish *you'd* laid *your* finger to that gun."

"Trust you to come off and leave it," my wife says.

"Is that how no-'count I am?" she makes me ask. "*You* want to go back and get it?"

"You're the one they'll catch. I say it's so hot that even if you get to sleep you wake up feeling like you cried all night!" says my wife. "Cheer up, here's one more joke before time to get up. Heard what *Caroline* said? Caroline said, 'Daddy, I just can't wait to grow up big, so I can marry *James Meredith*.' I heard that where I work. One rich-bitch to another one, to make her cackle."

"At least I kept some dern teen-ager from North Thermopylae getting there and doing it first," I says. "Driving his own car."

On TV and in the paper, they don't know but half of it. They know who Roland Summers was without knowing who I am. His face was in front of the public before I got rid of him, and after I got rid of him there it is again—the same picture. And none of me. I ain't ever had one made. Not ever! The best that newspaper could do for me was offer a five-hundred-dollar reward for finding out who I am. For as long as they don't know who that is, whoever shot Roland is worth a good deal more right now than Roland is.

But by the time I was moving around uptown, it was hotter still. That pavement in the middle of Main Street was so hot to my feet I might've been walking the barrel of my gun. If the whole world could've just felt Main Street this morning through the soles of my shoes, maybe it would've helped some.

Then the first thing I heard 'em say was the N. double A. C. P. done it themselves, killed Roland Summers, and proved it by saying the shooting was done by a expert (I hope to tell you it was!) and at just the right hour and minute to get the whites in trouble.

You can't win.

"They'll never find him," the old man trying to sell roasted peanuts tells me to my face.

And it's so hot.

It looks like the town's on fire already, whichever ways you turn, ever' street you strike, because there's those trees hanging them pones of bloom like split watermelon. And a thousand cops crowding ever'where you go, half of 'em too young to start shaving, but all streaming sweat alike. I'm getting tired of 'em.

I was already tired of seeing a hundred cops getting us white people nowheres. Back at the beginning, I stood on the corner and I watched them new babyface cops loading nothing but nigger children into the paddy wagon and they come marching out of a little parade and into the paddy wagon singing. And they got in and sat down without providing a speck of trouble, and their hands held little new American flags, and all the cops could do was knock them flagsticks a-loose from their hands, and not let 'em pick 'em up, that was all, and give 'em a free ride. And children can just get 'em more flags.

Everybody: It don't get you nowhere to take nothing from nobody unless you make sure it's for keeps, for good and all, for ever and amen.

I won't be sorry to see them brickbats hail down on us for a change. Pop bottles too, they can come flying whenever they want to. Hundreds, all to smash, like Birmingham. I'm waiting on 'em to bring out them switchblade knives, like Harlem and Chicago. Watch TV long enough and you'll see it all to happen on Deacon Street in Thermopylae. What's holding it back, that's all?—Because it's *in* 'em.

I'm ready myself for that funeral.

Oh, they may find me. May catch me one day in spite of 'em selves. (But I grew up in the country.) May try to railroad me into the electric chair, and what that amounts to is something hotter than yesterday and today put together.

But I advise 'em to go careful. Ain't it about time us taxpayers starts to calling the moves? Starts to telling the teachers *and* the preachers *and* the judges of our so-called courts how far they can go?

Even the President so far, he can't walk in my house without being invited, like he's my daddy, just to say whoa. Not yet!

Once, I run away from my home. And there was a ad for me, come to be printed in our county weekly. My mother paid for it. It was from her. It says: "SON: You are not being hunted for anything but to find you." That time, I come on back home.

But people are dead now.

And it's so hot. Without it even being August yet.

Anyways, I seen him fall. I was evermore the one.

So I reach me down my old guitar off the nail in the wall. 'Cause I've got my guitar, what I've held on to from way back when, and I never dropped that, never lost or forgot it, never hocked it but to get it again, never give it away, and I set in my chair, with nobody home but me, and I start to play, and sing a-Down. And sing a-down, down, down, down. Sing a-down, down, down, down. Down.

—1963

BLUME LEMPEL (1910-1999)

Born in Khorostov, Galicia (now part of Ukraine), Blume Lempel was educated in Hebrew schools, both religious and secular. She emigrated to Paris in 1929 and then to New York in 1939, just ahead of the Second World War. Her first story was published in 1943 in *Der Tag* (The Day), a New York Yiddish newspaper, under the pseudonym Rokhl Halperin. She went on to publish several short stories in various Yiddish journals and newspapers, and published two collections of stories, *A Rege Fun Emes* (A Moment of Truth, 1981) and *Blade fun a Kholem* (Ballad of a Dream, 1986). The selection included here was originally published in *Yidishe kultur* (Yiddish Culture) in 1992 and then translated by Irene Klepfisz for the collection *Found Treasures: Stories by Yiddish Women Writers* (1994, Formana, Raicus, Swartz and Wolfe, eds.). In 1985, Lempel was awarded the Atran Prize for Yiddish Literature.

Correspondents

The moment I finished the letter to the girl with the black hair and hungry eyes, I tore it up.

We had met in a library. She happened to have checked out the very same book I had just returned.

"It'll give you a lot of pleasure," I said suddenly.

"Really? How do you know?" she asked and laughed.

"I don't. I just have a feeling."

We left together and walked through the streets. She told me she wrote poetry, not for publication, "but for myself." I looked at her more closely—very closely—and had the feeling I was seeing myself in the distant past. Something in what she chose and chose not to say resonated like an evening echo in a forest.

Her voice heavy with unfulfilled longing caressed and at the same time repelled me. I felt myself engulfed by a spring breeze heavy with the scent of mint. My clothes suddenly felt tight. The seams burst and released the garment which I had concealed from the outside world as if I were ashamed of who I was.

There was no way I could explain all this in a letter. I also couldn't tell her that I saw her as a rose infested with slithering worms. I felt I first needed to clarify this aversion to myself. Only after I realized that this too was impossible did I tear up the letter and write her another—not about her, but about someone else.

In the letter I told her that a while back I had taken the subway from Brooklyn to New York. I held my little boy in my arms. I don't know where or why I was travelling. It was a summer afternoon. There weren't many passengers in the car. A young man got on one of the stations and took a seat near me. He was carrying a violin, maybe even a violoncello, wrapped in a blue silk cover with a gold zipper. The zipper touched my knee accidentally. I raised my eyes and saw how the violin or the violoncello beneath the blue silk was shaped like a dancer waiting for her cue for her first step. Or perhaps it was the power of the young man's eyes which looked into mine and awakened octaves from a hundred-year sleep. I don't know how long I held his gaze, but when I turned my head towards the window through which the dark tunnel looked in, two hot tears fell from my eyes.

Usually I'm not the type who cries. The last Jewish destruction had sealed the well of my tears. The summer after Liberation, I couldn't talk to people. I shared my sorrow with a felled tree which peered at me over my neighbour's fence. I became close with a cat who had lost her newborn kittens. A murderous tom had gouged their throats and left them on the threshold of her den. The cat didn't shed any tears. She just followed the tracks of the murderer, only sought revenge. She didn't touch the milk I put out for her. When I tried to pet her, she clawed me.

What the cat did to me, I did to my friends. I didn't want, nor could I tolerate, any comfort. I just wanted to remain mute, or to scream the same cries that come from a violin or violoncello....

Seated this way near the young man, the violin between us, I saw another violin under another sky in another time. The symphony of that other violin has remained unfinished.

With his violin under his arm, he stood on the bottom step of the panting Express. The violin wept as we exchanged our last kiss. He kept waving his handkerchief for a long time. The wheels began to turn. A rain beat down. For three days and two nights the train wheels sang the Song of Songs[1] to me: "I love you. I love you." All the way from Lemberg to Paris and the Gare du Nord.

After the *Shoah*,[2] I couldn't conceive of these three words. I avoided all musical sounds. I would stop up my ears against the songs of street singers who milked tears from passersby over their betrayed loves. The love which had forced us to separate was betrayed by the world: the world that knew but pretended it did not know when it burned, systematically exterminated, not hundreds, not thousands, but an entire people to the beat of Beethoven's Ninth.

Music, which had once lifted me to heavenly heights, had fallen, together with the ash of burned bodies, into the abyss where snakes swarm and lizards laugh. For many years, I avoided the sounds of strings. Now, the young man on the seat near me, the one with a violin wrapped in blue silk, filled me with fear. Every time my foot

---

[1] Also called the Song of Solomon, the Song of Songs is a book of the Hebrew bible, or Old Testament.

[2] A Hebrew word for the Holocaust.

accidentally touched the silk, the instrument groaned.

I turned my head away, pressed my forehead against the cold pane. In the black tunnel on the other side of the window, I saw not the young man, but the aristocratic image of Arnove. She was the wife of Dr. Oyerhan, the only woman in our *shtetl*[3] who could play the violin. She had no dealings with our women. She was on friendly terms with the gentry and visited Count Szeminiski's home. She had even been a beauty queen at a strictly Christian aristocratic ball.

Summer evenings we could hear her violin through the open windows of her palace. Her dog stood guard lest, God forbid, anyone would set foot inside the fenced-in flower garden. Dr. Oyerhan would come to *shul*[4] once a year to say *yisker*.[5] She never set foot inside *shul*. People doubted that she was even a Jew. But the murderers without horns, without drums, the descendants of Goethe, Mozart, Kant[6]—they knew better. When they drove the last Jews of the *shtetl* to the market place, she was among them. She didn't cry or scream. True to her self-created personality, she played her role to the bitter end. Her husband the doctor was already dead. She had no children. The gentry with whom she'd been friendly had been exiled by the Soviets. All that she had left was the violin.

She was leaning against the ramp, the violin under her blue silk kimono, her hair loose, her face pale. Her skin was drawn, transparent like that of a porcelain statue. The plush slippers on her bare feet were soiled with the dung of the animals which we brought to the fairs. Suddenly she swept back her hair, raised her head, took up her violin and, posed as if she were getting ready to play, drew closer to the officer with the black swastika on his arm. "Gracious sir," she said in her best Viennese accent, "spare me the shame."

The officer looked her over, up and down. His eyes paused on the violin. "Close your eyes," he ordered. And with one bullet, he granted her wish.

The young man sitting on the seat near me kept his head down. Without looking directly, I observed how his lips moved. I thought that perhaps he was keeping time to the music that emanated from beneath the blue silk cover. His head brushed over the divider between us. I felt his lips on my hand. "Madonna, Madonna," he whispered and drowned the rest in a foreign language.

As soon as the train stopped, I got out. Standing on the other side of the door, I turned my head to the window where he had been sitting. But he was no longer there....

The girl with the black hair and hungry eyes read the letter and answered as follows: "As you know, I write poetry for my own pleasure. For whose benefit are you running around in circles? What are you claiming, that life repeats itself? You take one step forward and immediately you're back in the *shtetl,* back to 'once upon a time.' The whole gamble of life is nothing but one banal repetition. Fortunately not without some variations.

"I am now attached to a young woman. It's an extraordinary experience. Think about it, my dear.

"I'm enclosing the address of our club. It has many lost souls. You're a person

---

[3] (Yid.) A small Jewish community in Eastern Europe.
[4] (Yid.) Synagogue.
[5] A Jewish memorial service for the dead.
[6] Johann Wolfgang von Goethe (1749-1832), German

writer; Wolfgang Amadeus Mozart (1756-1791), Austrian composer; Immanuel Kant (1724-1804), German philosopher.

who makes an impression. I'm certain that you'll find there the right note for this life-performance...."

I tore up her letter. I wanted to burn it on the spot. But the word "burn" awakens in me holy images. So I tore her letter into very tiny, tiny pieces.

Translated by Irena Klepfisz

—1992

LING-AI (GLADYS) LI (CA. 1910-)

Ling-ai (Gladys) Li was born in Honolulu, Hawaii, around 1910, the sixth of nine children. Her parents, who immigrated to Hawaii from China in 1896, both practiced medicine. Li received her B.A. from the University of Hawai'i in 1930. She lived in China for a period after she completed her degree, studying music and Chinese theater, and directing a theater at the Beijing Institute of Fine Arts. Li produced a documentary film entitled *Kukan,* about the Japanese siege of China, that won an Academy Award in 1941; she was then invited to the White House to meet Franklin and Eleanor Roosevelt.

Li, a versatile and talented playwright, poet, novelist, and film and stage director, is perhaps best known for her autobiography *Life Is for a Long Time* (1972), which depicts an atypical Chinese immigrant family's experience in turn of the century Hawaii. Her published plays include *The Submission of Rose Moy* (1925), *The Law of Wu Wei* (1929), and *The White Serpent* (1932). In 1975, she was named Bicentennial Woman of the Year by the National Association of Women Artists of America.

The Submission of Rose Moy

CHARACTERS

ROSE MOY: A Hawaiian-born Chinese college girl who is Western in ideas and ideals—and yet not entirely Western. She wishes to become a leader in China on woman suffrage.

WING MOY: Her father—a Chinese aristocrat of the old school who is thoroughly Oriental in his ideas concerning a woman's place in this world. His relationship to his daughter is that of a typical Chinese gentleman—a mere acquaintance. He thinks that he will insure her future happiness by marrying her off well. He interprets a woman's happiness as home, children, serving her lord, submission—an interpretation of Old China. Hawaii has never influenced him.

KWANG WEI: A rich old Chinese merchant of Honolulu who possesses three concubines in China. His first wife has died and he is out looking for a young modern Chinese girl to take her place. She is to be a creature on whom he would be able to lavish his wealth, but he also expects her to be submissive.

LEN DONALD: A thoroughly American artist who in his contact with Rose Moy, who has been sitting for him as a model for a Chinese painting, has learned of her ambitions, and is helping her in every way to study things that are American and to break away from old Chinese traditions concerning a woman's place in the world. His relation to her is that of a teacher and pupil.

SERVANT: A young man in the service of Wing Moy.

SCENE: *Living room of the Wing Moy residence furnished in typical Chinese fashion—rows of teakwood chairs on each side, ancestor tablets with incense in front. Two tables in the center of the room against the back wall which is hung with tapestries. Two doors on right and one on left at back. The tablets are between the doors.*

TIME: *Early in the morning.*

✦ ✦ ✦

[WING MOY *is receiving* KWANG WEI *as a visitor.* KWANG WEI *has come to ask for the hand of* ROSE MOY. *They are seated on the right of the stage.*]

WING MOY: I am honored, my good brother, by your illustrious presence. [*Turning aside and clapping hand to* SERVANT] Tea! [*Motions* KWANG WEI *to seat.* SERVANT *brings tea and sets it on the table.*]

WING MOY: To your honorable name! [*Lifting teacup*]

KWANG WEI: To your illustrious family! [*Tea ended*]

WING MOY: What good wind blows you here, my brother, that you honor my humble abode with your august presence?

KWANG WEI: My honorable Wing Moy, I am a businessman in America. Therefore I shall be brief in what I have come to say. Our sage, the illustrious Confucius, says that the basis of a government is the family. Since my first wife, the delicate Po Ling, passed on to the "Kingdom of the Gods," leaving me alone with my concubines with no male issue to continue the Kwang family line—to pray before our ancestral tablets when it is my turn to ascend to the "Kingdom of the Gods,"—I have been most miserably lonely.

WING MOY: I thank the gracious Buddha for my child, girl that she may be!

KWANG WEI: And I have come to beg of you the hand of your adorable daughter.

WING MOY: My daughter! But she is young.

KWANG WEI: She will graduate from the University in June.

WING MOY: Yes, but she knows nothing about the world!

KWANG WEI: [*Disdainfully*] What woman knows anything about the world! I am not asking that your daughter become a sing song girl. I desire her for my wife.

WING MOY: You have three concubines! My daughter will never consent.

KWANG WEI: You are her father! Why should she consent? Is not a man the head of his own home?

WING MOY: [*Admonishingly*] You forget that my daughter has been brought up in America.

KWANG WEI: And you forget that she is only a girl. Who will protect her when you go to visit the "World Beyond?" I can offer her silks and satins, and jewels, everything that a woman can care for. Within the four walls of my palatial home, she will lead a calm, peaceful existence, embroidering and singing and raising my men children to perpetuate the great and noble name of Kwang. What more can a woman ask than to live the protected life of her mother, and her mother's mother before her?

WING MOY: I bow. The law of our ancestors is supreme, my honorable Kwang Wei.

[*Hits gong. The* SERVANT *enters.*] Request the presence of your mistress. Tell her that her father desires to speak to her.

ROSE MOY: [*Coming from the right entrance expectantly*] Has Mr. Donald arrived yet?

WING MOY: What! Is Mr. Donald coming again?

ROSE MOY: This will be my last sitting for him. The portrait he is painting of me is done with the exception of the finishing touches.

WING MOY: Hereafter, you will pose for no more artists!

ROSE MOY: Pose no more?!

WING MOY: No more! I sent for you to tell you that tomorrow I announce your betrothal.

ROSE MOY: [*Exceedingly shocked*] My betrothal! But I have my college work to finish yet!

WING MOY: Calm yourself, my daughter. Come bow to the illustrious Kwang Wei, your future husband.

ROSE MOY: [*Pleadingly*] Save me, my dear father! You cannot be in your right mind! Mr. Kwang Wei already possesses three concubines in China!

WING MOY: Yes—the honorable Kwang Wei possesses a great name. Your men children will bear an illustrious name.

ROSE MOY: Name! Name! Would you sacrifice your only daughter to be a fourth concubine for a name?

KWANG WEI: [*In a bribing manner*] Think of the comforts and jewels that I can offer you—the pearls, the diamonds, the jades. I would even buy you a Packard roadster, though none of my other wives has ridden in anything but a Ford. [*In a commanding tone*] I shall go to prepare for the betrothal feast. You will make your daughter consent. [*Bows. Exit—through left entrance.*]

WING MOY: You will lead a protected life if you marry Kwang Wei.

ROSE MOY: Yes, my dear father, but what of my college career? Do you forget so soon the promise you made me last year?

WING MOY: What promise?

ROSE MOY: You said that you would let me go to New York to pursue post-graduate work.

WING MOY: Why must we discuss your life work after graduation now? It is six months from now to June. Be patient, wait till the time comes.

ROSE MOY: [*Impatiently*] But I cannot wait. If I am to be the fourth concubine of Mr. Kwang Wei, I would like to know whether I can finish my studies first.

WING MOY: [*In a consoling tone*] We shall discuss the subject in due time.

ROSE MOY: In due time which may mean never! [*With determination*] We must decide now! Why must you break into my college career with this betrothal?

WING MOY: [*Calmly*] You are a girl. You need a man's protection.

ROSE MOY: But you forget that I am a modern woman. You forget my ambition to become one of the first Chinese educational women leaders Hawaii has ever produced.

WING MOY: [*Grandly*] I do not forget. It is a great honor for you to strive for a higher degree, but the risk for attaining such an end is exceedingly great—yes, exceedingly great. You are only a girl.

ROSE MOY: Yes, I am a girl. But this is America and we are living in the twentieth century.

WING MOY: Nevertheless, you are a girl, the daughter of Wing Moy, whose father before him was Kwong Moy the great mandarin of Ning Po. As a daughter of an illustrious house, you will marry as the women of our noble name have done before you. You will marry another eminent house in order that your sons may perpetuate another great name.

ROSE MOY: Yes, then we would be continually living in the horrible past. The present and the future—that is what counts in America! If you do not consent—

WING MOY: Is this what your college education has done to you? Fool that I was to send you to college!

ROSE MOY: Yes, my education has taught me to think for myself—to rise above the shackles of tradition that have bound our women from time immemorial, and have imprisoned their spirits.

WING MOY: And it has taught you to spurn the protection that an illustrious and noble man offers—to break our venerable traditions. [*Shaking his head regrettingly*] Oh, fool that I was to send you to college!

ROSE MOY: Then you do not consent to my going to New York for post-graduate work?

WING MOY: I do not. You will prepare for your betrothal to Mr. Kwang Wei.

ROSE MOY: Why must my life be governed by such dusty and diabolical traditions? [*Very indignantly*]

WING MOY: For centuries, our women have been kept within their courtyards.

ROSE MOY: Imprisoned! Bound for a mere existence of slavery!

WING MOY: But they were happy and content and our home life has run a course as smooth as the breast of the Nuuanu Stream you see yonder—unrumpled by silly whims and fancies. Their supreme desire was to serve their lords.

ROSE MOY: Like slaves!

WING MOY: They bore men children to perpetuate their family line. They were mothers of men.

ROSE MOY: And nothing else! Oh father, don't you know that this is an age in which women strive for careers other than that of domestic drudgery? Have you not often praised the Island-born Chinese girl for her initiative in earning her own living by teaching?

WING MOY: Yes, my rose blossom, but you are the daughter of Wing Moy. Remember your heritage. The women of our family have always been sheltered and treasured. You cannot break a tradition. You are of the East—you are a Chinese.

ROSE MOY: [*With a determined voice*] I can break and I WILL BREAK a tradition when it is an obstacle to my life's ambition.

WING MOY: [*Quite aggravated*] You cannot break our venerable traditions! You are my daughter!

ROSE MOY: I am your daughter, but I will not become tied down against my will to a mere existence with an old man who already has three concubines. Give me liberty, give me freedom—the right of a higher education—and what I desire the most—to lead a worthy career as a great leader of women!

WING MOY: [*Contradictory tone*] A woman's leader in revolt! [*Commandingly*] I am your father and you are my daughter. I know what is the best plan for your future. I command your marriage to the illustrious Kwang Wei. And verily I say unto you, prepare yourself for the wedding ceremony on the fourth day of the new month! Woe be unto you if you heed not my orders!

ROSE MOY: [*Sadly*] You will be sorry.

WING MOY: Prepare yourself for the betrothal feast tomorrow. Compose yourself within the hour before my return. I go to inform our relatives with the news of your happiness. [*Exit*]

ROSE MOY: [*Bitterly*] Ha! My happiness! [*Kneeling before Kwan Yui, which is posed on table on right side of the stage*] They say you have a merciful heart. Help me now, oh Goddess of my mother. [*Rises and looks discouraged*]

SERVANT: [*Enters*] Mistress, Mr. Donald is here.

ROSE MOY: [*Indifferently*] Mr. Donald? Show him in.

MR. DONALD: [*Full of life*] Well, my rose blossom, just one more sitting and we shall have a prize-winning portrait.

ROSE MOY: I am sorry Mr. Donald, but I am not in the mood to pose for you.

MR. DONALD: [*Surprised*] Not in the mood?

ROSE MOY: No.

MR. DONALD: [*Disdainfully*] Pooh! Surely, there must be some other reason or else you would not disappoint me this way.

ROSE MOY: [*Positively*] There is no other reason. I do not want to pose for you today.

MR. DONALD: But this is the last sitting.

ROSE MOY: [*With aroused emotions*] And I am not in the mood to look pleasant. [*Sadly and slowly*] Mr. Donald, I am betrothed. Do you know it? Betrothed—I say, betrothed!

MR. DONALD: Betrothed! Why, you ought to be overjoyed!

ROSE MOY: [*Bitterly*] Yes, overjoyed when I am to marry Mr. Kwang Wei.

MR. DONALD: [*Very surprised*] What—that old beezer! I am told that he already has three concubines in China!

ROSE MOY: It is the will of my father, and his word is law.

MR. DONALD: The will of your father! Good gracious, girl! Will you let a mere thing like that bind you, ruin your career, bring you drudgery and untold woes? Oh, flee dear girl, flee as you would flee from the snare of a demon!

ROSE MOY: Oh, I know I am a coward. But I am a girl—and yet—

MR. DONALD: Yes, and yet you are an American college girl.

ROSE MOY: [*In a tone of distress*] Oh, if I only had some one to back me up! I have no desire to marry anyone. I want to become a great leader of women someday.

MR. DONALD: [*Suddenly*] I know—and say! I have a plan!

ROSE MOY: What is it? Quick!

MR. DONALD: You sure you want it?

ROSE MOY: Anything as long as it is not marrying anyone!

MR. DONALD: Well—listen! We are going to fool the old beezer. Meet me tonight at twelve o'clock. I will be waiting under your window.

ROSE MOY: How will I know that you will be there?

MR. DONALD: Listen for my whistle. I'll help you catch the Matson boat which sails tomorrow morning for San Francisco.

ROSE MOY: But I don't know anyone there.

MR. DONALD: You can live with my sister in Berkeley, work for her and study at the same time.

ROSE MOY: I'd go if I were sure—

MR. DONALD: They cannot do anything to you if you are away and independent of them financially. Come, spunk up!

ROSE MOY: [*Undecided and yet eager to go*] I wonder—

MR. DONALD: [*In a convincing manner*] Of course you want to go. Think! You surely do not wish to be bound for the rest of your dear life to an asthmatic, crab-figured old man with three concubines. Remember, you want to be a woman leader someday. Remember, you are an American-born Chinese girl.

ROSE MOY: Yes, I do honestly want to be a leader someday.

MR. DONALD: Then you must go away to study. Traditions or no traditions, it is imperative that you leave home!

ROSE MOY: Wait for me tonight, please. I'll go. [MR. DONALD *leaves.*]

ROSE MOY: Yes, I will go! No tradition will fetter me! [*Kneels before ancestral tablets*] Oh, angel mother, help me! Help me, I entreat thee!

[WING MOY *returns from visit. He goes to* ROSE MOY *who is bowing before ancestral tablets.* ROSE MOY *turns to look at him.*]

WING MOY: I have notified all the members of the Moy clan of your coming betrothal. You will prepare for it immediately.

ROSE MOY: My dear father, before I go to prepare myself, may I ask you one question?

WING MOY: Yes, my daughter.

ROSE MOY: What would my rose blossom mother say if she were living and knew of my ambitions and your plans for my betrothal?

WING MOY: [*Thoughtfully*] Your rose blossom mother. [*Goes to ancestral tablets and bows slowly three times. Rises and turns to* ROSE MOY.] Your rose blossom mother, before she passed on to the "Kingdom of the Gods," put into my hands a letter which she bid me to give you on your betrothal eve. [*Goes to treasure box which is on a table on left side of stage, and takes carefully from it a letter in a Chinese envelope of white with a red stripe down center.*] Here is the letter. [*Hands it to* ROSE MOY *who looks at it with an amazed look.*]

ROSE MOY: [*In a dreamy sort of a tone*] A letter from my dear little angel mother!

WING MOY: [*Calmly*] Yes. Read it before the dawn of your betrothal day. I go now to order the delicacies for your betrothal feast. [*Proudly*] Shark fins, and birdnest soup, pickled fish, and roasted duck—such a betrothal feast that the guests whom Wing Moy invites will never forget. [*Exits*]

ROSE MOY: [*Slowly*] My rose blossom mother! I shall read your letter—yes, I shall read it but not on my betrothal eve as you would have it, but on the eve of my departure. [*Exits*]

[*Incense burning in clouds before ancestral tablets. Enter* ROSE MOY, *right entrance carrying a suit case*]

ROSE MOY: No one comes! Now for freedom! If I stay I will have to become the fourth wife of Kwang Wei. If I go, it will mean uncertainty—but the continuance of my education on the other hand—and mayhap a future leader of the Chinese women. I choose to go, and go I shall.

[*Starts to go—when gong strikes twelve times from somewhere back of the stage.* ROSE MOY *pauses, becomes a little excited, looks about her—starts to go again. Then she looks back longingly, makes a startled motion to show that she remembers something. Someone whistles "Yankee Doodle"—back stage.*]

Mr. Donald is waiting!

[ROSE MOY *takes letter from right side pocket of jacket. Opens it and reads aloud*]

"My Dear Rose Blossom Daughter:

I am leaving you to ascend to the 'Kingdom of the Gods.' I cry out to my ancestors to let me stay longer to care for my little rose blossom daughter, but it is their will that I go to the 'Kingdom of the Gods.' Yes, it is their will and their will is my law.

My little one, someday in your precious life, you will understand what the law of your ancestors means. I pray from a mother's heart that when that day comes, you too will bow to the will of your ancestors. It will be difficult for you, I know, for you are reared in America, but remember—you are a child of the East—you are a Chinese.

Remember the voice of your people's gods. May the gods of our ancestors bless you till eternity.

With tears from a mother's heart,

Your Mother."

ROSE MOY: The will of my people! But I want freedom! [*Slowly but with determination*] I want freedom! [*Looking at ancestral tablet*] Little angel mother, I cannot—I cannot stay! My urgent duty calls me thither! [*shaking her head*]—I cannot—I cannot stay! [*Someone whistles "Yankee Doodle" outside.* MR. DONALD *is still waiting.* ROSE MOY *starts to go, then looks back again. The incense rises up in clouds before the ancestral tablets. A gong sounds solemnly and slowly somewhere outside.* ROSE MOY *walks slowly and sadly to ancestral tablets and kneels.*]

ROSE MOY: [*In a trembling voice*] Oh, gods of my ancestors, to thee I cry! Help me! Help me decide what course I should take!

[*She rises, stands pensively for a while, as if listening to a voice somewhere. Then suddenly cries out*]

The gods of my ancestors—the law of my people! [*Bows before the ancestral tablets*] [*Slowly and submissively*] Yes, my rose blossom mother, I am of the East—I bow. I submit to the will of my ancestors!

[*Falls down in a fainting pose before the ancestral tablets. Incense keeps burning.*]

[*Outside a whistling of "Yankee Doodle" is heard.* MR. DONALD *is still waiting, and he waits in vain!*]

CURTAIN

—1925

ELIZABETH BISHOP (1911-1979)

Born in Worcester, Massachusetts, Elizabeth Bishop spent part of her childhood with her Canadian grandparents and part in boarding schools; her father died when she was quite young and her mother spent most of Bishop's childhood committed to a sanitarium in Nova Scotia. Bishop attended Vassar College, where she founded a literary magazine, *Con Spirito*, with her peers Mary McCarthy, Eleanor Clark, and Muriel Rukeyser. She also began a friendship with Marianne Moore (which lasted until Moore's death in 1972) while at Vassar. *North & South* (1946), Bishop's first book of poetry, won the Houghton Mifflin Poetry Award, and her 1956 collection, *Poems: North & South—A Cold Spring*, received the Pulitzer Prize for poetry. Bishop also received a National Book Award, a National Book Critics Circle Award, and was the first American and the first woman to win the Books Abroad/Neustadt Prize for Literature. A consistent contributor to the *New Yorker*, Bishop was also a Chancellor of the Academy of American Poets, a member of the American Academy of Arts and Letters, and was a consultant in poetry to the Library of Congress (a post later re-named Poet Laureate of the United States) in 1949. Bishop, who was independently wealthy, traveled widely and devoted her life to writing poetry. She spent much of her life in Brazil, where she began a fifteen-year lesbian relationship with Lota de Macedo Soares. Brazil was also the setting for much of the work collected in her 1965 book, *Questions of Travel.* In September of 1967, Soares took her own life and Bishop eventually returned to the U.S. and began teaching at Harvard University. She also began a relationship with Alice Methfessel, which lasted until Bishop's death in 1979.

The Fish

I caught a tremendous fish
and held him beside the boat
half out of water, with my hook
fast in a corner of his mouth.
He didn't fight.   5
He hadn't fought at all.
He hung a grunting weight,
battered and venerable
and homely. Here and there
his brown skin hung in strips   10
like ancient wallpaper,
and its pattern of darker brown
was like wallpaper:
shapes like full-blown roses
stained and lost through age.   15
He was speckled with barnacles,
fine rosettes of lime,
and infested
with tiny white sea-lice,
and underneath two or three   20
rags of green weed hung down.
While his gills were breathing in
the terrible oxygen
—the frightening gills,
fresh and crisp with blood,   25
that can cut so badly—
I thought of the coarse white flesh
packed in like feathers,
the big bones and the little bones,
the dramatic reds and blacks   30
of his shiny entrails,
and the pink swim-bladder
like a big peony.
I looked into his eyes
which were far larger than mine   35

but shallower, and yellowed,
the irises backed and packed
with tarnished tinfoil
seen through the lenses
of old scratched isinglass. 40
They shifted a little, but not
to return my stare.
—It was more like the tipping
of an object toward the light.
I admired his sullen face, 45
the mechanism of his jaw,
and then I saw
that from his lower lip
—if you could call it a lip—
grim, wet, and weaponlike, 50
hung five old pieces of fish-line,
or four and a wire leader
with the swivel still attached,
with all their five big hooks
grown firmly in his mouth. 55
A green line, frayed at the end
where he broke it, two heavier lines,
and a fine black thread
still crimped from the strain and snap
when it broke and he got away. 60
Like medals with their ribbons
frayed and wavering,
a five-haired beard of wisdom
trailing from his aching jaw.
I stared and stared 65
and victory filled up
the little rented boat,
from the pool of bilge
where oil had spread a rainbow
around the rusted engine 70
to the bailer rusted orange,
the sun-cracked thwarts,
the oarlocks on their strings,
the gunnels—until everything
was rainbow, rainbow, rainbow! 75
And I let the fish go.

—1946

Invitation to Miss Marianne Moore

From Brooklyn, over the Brooklyn Bridge, on this fine morning,
    please come flying.
In a cloud of fiery pale chemicals,

please come flying,
to the rapid rolling of thousands of small blue drums   5
descending out of the mackerel sky
over the glittering grandstand of harbor-water,
    please come flying.

Whistles, pennants and smoke are blowing. The ships
are signaling cordially with multitudes of flags   10
rising and falling like birds all over the harbor.
Enter: two rivers, gracefully bearing
countless little pellucid jellies
in cut-glass epergnes dragging with silver chains.
The flight is safe; the weather is all arranged.   15
The waves are running in verses this fine morning.
    Please come flying.

Come with the pointed toe of each black shoe
trailing a sapphire highlight,
with a black capeful of butterfly wings and bon-mots,   20
with heaven knows how many angels all riding
on the broad black brim of your hat,
    please come flying.

Bearing a musical inaudible abacus,
a slight censorious frown, and blue ribbons,   25
    please come flying.
Facts and skyscrapers glint in the tide; Manhattan
is all awash with morals this fine morning,
    so please come flying.

Mounting the sky with natural heroism,   30
above the accidents, above the malignant movies,
the taxicabs and injustices at large,
while horns are resounding in your beautiful ears
that simultaneously listen to
a soft uninvented music, fit for the musk deer,   35
    please come flying.

For whom the grim museums will behave
like courteous male bower-birds,
for whom the agreeable lions lie in wait
on the steps of the Public Library,   40
eager to rise and follow through the doors
up into the reading rooms,
    please come flying.
We can sit down and weep; we can go shopping,
or play at a game of constantly being wrong   45
with a priceless set of vocabularies,
or we can bravely deplore, but please
    please come flying.

With dynasties of negative constructions
darkening and dying around you,   50
with grammar that suddenly turns and shines
like flocks of sandpipers flying,
    please come flying.

Come like a light in the white mackerel sky,
come like a daytime comet   55
with a long unnebulous train of words,
from Brooklyn, over the Brooklyn Bridge, on this fine morning,
    please come flying.

—1955

In the Waiting Room

In Worcester, Massachusetts,
I went with Aunt Consuelo
to keep her dentist's appointment
and sat and waited for her
in the dentist's waiting room.   5
It was winter. It got dark
early. The waiting room
was full of grown-up people,
arctics and overcoats,
lamps and magazines.   10
My aunt was inside
what seemed like a long time
and while I waited and read
the *National Geographic*
(I could read) and carefully   15
studied the photographs:
the inside of a volcano,
black, and full of ashes;
then it was spilling over
in rivulets of fire.   20
Osa and Martin Johnson[1]
dressed in riding breeches,
laced boots, and pith helmets.
A dead man slung on a pole
—"Long Pig," the caption said.   25
Babies with pointed heads
wound round and round with string;
black, naked women with necks
wound round and round with wire
like the necks of light bulbs.   30
Their breasts were horrifying.

---

[1] Osa Leighty Johnson (1894-1953) and Martin Elmer Johnson (1884-1937) were naturalists, photographers, and film-makers in the first half of the 20th century.

I read it right straight through.
I was too shy to stop.
And then I looked at the cover:
the yellow margins, the date. 35
Suddenly, from inside,
came an *oh!* of pain
—Aunt Consuelo's voice—
not very loud or long.
I wasn't at all surprised; 40
even then I knew she was
a foolish, timid woman.
I might have been embarrassed,
but wasn't. What took me
completely by surprise 45
was that it was *me:*
my voice, in my mouth.
Without thinking at all
I was my foolish aunt,
I—we—were falling, falling, 50
our eyes glued to the cover
of the *National Geographic,*
February, 1918.

I said to myself: three days
and you'll be seven years old. 55
I was saying it to stop
the sensation of falling off
the round, turning world
into cold, blue-black space.
But I felt: you are an *I,* 60
you are an *Elizabeth,*
you are one of *them.*
Why should you be one, too?
I scarcely dared to look
to see what it was I was. 65
I gave a sidelong glance
—I couldn't look any higher—
at shadowy gray knees,
trousers and skirts and boots
and different pairs of hands 70
lying under the lamps.
I knew that nothing stranger
had ever happened, that nothing
stranger could ever happen.

Why should I be my aunt, 75
or me, or anyone?
What similarities—
boots, hands, the family voice
I felt in my throat, or even

the *National Geographic*   80
and those awful hanging breasts—
held us all together
or made us all just one?
How—I didn't know any
word for it—how "unlikely"…   85
How had I come to be here,
like them, and overhear
a cry of pain that could have
got loud and worse but hadn't?

The waiting room was bright   90
and too hot. It was sliding
beneath a big black wave,
another, and another.

Then I was back in it.
The War was on. Outside,   95
in Worcester, Massachusetts,
were night and slush and cold,
and it was still the fifth
of February, 1918.

—1971

One Art

The art of losing isn't hard to master;
so many things seem filled with the intent
to be lost that their loss is no disaster.

Lose something every day. Accept the fluster
of lost door keys, the hour badly spent.   5
The art of losing isn't hard to master.

Then practice losing farther, losing faster:
places, and names, and where it was you meant
to travel. None of these will bring disaster.

I lost my mother's watch. And look! my last, or   10
next-to-last, of three loved houses went.
The art of losing isn't hard to master.

I lost two cities, lovely ones. And, vaster,
some realms I owned, two rivers, a continent.
I miss them, but it wasn't a disaster.   15

—Even losing you (the joking voice, a gesture
I love) I shan't have lied. It's evident
the art of losing's not too hard to master
though it may look like (*Write* it!) like disaster.

—1976

MARY McCARTHY (1912-1989)

Mary McCarthy was born in Seattle, Washington. Orphaned at the age of six, when both parents died in the influenza epidemic of 1918, she was brought up by wealthy and conservative grandparents. McCarthy graduated from Vassar College, where she studied literature and met two young women who would become significant poets of the twentieth century, Muriel Rukeyser and Elizabeth Bishop. McCarthy's novel *The Group* (1963) was a fictionalized account of her Vassar relationships. During the 1930s McCarthy worked for a number of left-wing organizations and publications. She identified as a Trotskyite and an anti-Stalinist, and established a relationship with *The Partisan Review* as an editor and theater critic that lasted twenty-five years. She moved in and wrote about New York intellectual circles, where she met the second of her four husbands, the writer Edmund Wilson, and later the philosopher Hannah Arendt, who became her close friend. McCarthy's quarter century of correspondence with Arendt chronicles the two women's views on world events from 1949 until Arendt's death in 1975. In contrast with her solid friendship with Arendt, McCarthy feuded for decades with playwright Lillian Hellman, whose support of Stalin she could not forgive. McCarthy won several important awards for her seven novels and for her numerous essays and critical pieces, including the Edward MacDowell Medal (1982), the National Medal of Literature (1984), and the first Rochester Literary Award (1985).

Mlle. Gulliver en Amérique

In January 1947, Simone de Beauvoir, the leading French *femme savante*,[1] alighted from an airplane at LaGuardia Field for a four-months' stay in the United States. In her own eyes, this trip had something fabulous about it, of a balloonist's expedition or a descent in a diving bell. Where to Frenchmen of an earlier generation, America was the incredible country of *les peaux rouges*[2] and the novels of Fenimore Cooper, to Mlle. de Beauvoir America was, very simply, movieland—she came to verify for herself the existence of violence, drugstore stools, boy-meets-girl, that she had seen depicted on the screen. Her impressions, which she set down in journal form for the readers of *Les Temps modernes*,[3] retained therefore the flavor of an eyewitness account, of confirmation of rumor, the object being not so much to assay America as to testify to its reality.

These impressions, collected into a book, made a certain stir in France; now, three years later, they are appearing in translation in Germany. The book has never been published over here; the few snatches excerpted from it in magazine articles provoked wonder and hostility.

On an American leafing through the pages of an old library copy, the book has a strange effect. It is as though an inhabitant of Lilliput or Brobdingnag, coming upon a copy of *Gulliver's Travels*,[4] sat down to read, in a foreign tongue, of his own local customs codified by an observer of a different species: everything is at once familiar and distorted. The landmarks are there, and some of the institutions and personages—Eighth Avenue, Broadway, Hollywood, the Grand Canyon, Harvard, Yale, Vassar, literary celebrities concealed under initials; here are the drugstores and the cafeterias and the buses and the traffic lights—and yet it is all wrong, schematized, rationalized, like

---

[1] (Fr.) Scholarly woman.
[2] (Fr.) "Redskins," referring to American Indians.
[3] (Fr.) Modern Times, a French literary and political review founded in 1945 by de Beauvoir, Jean-Paul

Sartre, and Maurice Merleau-Ponty.
[4] 1726 novel by Jonathan Swift (1667-1745) that is both a satire on human nature and a parody of the "travelers' tales" literary sub-genre.

a scale model under glass. Peering down at himself, the American discovers that he has "no sense of *nuance*," that he is always in a good humor, that "in America the individual is nothing," that all Americans think their native town is the most beautiful town in the world, that an office girl cannot go to work in the same dress two days running, that in hotels "illicit" couples are made to swear that they are married, that it almost never happens here that a professor is also a writer, that the majority of American novelists have never been to college, that the middle class has no hold on the country's economic life and very little influence on its political destiny, that the good American citizen is never sick, that racism and reaction grow more menacing every day, that "the appearance, even, of democracy is vanishing from day to day," and that the country is witnessing "the birth of fascism."

From these pages, he discovers, in short, that his country has become, in the eyes of Existentialists,[5] a future which is, so to speak, already a past, a gelid eternity of drugstores, jukeboxes, smiles, refrigerators, and "fascism," and that he himself is no longer an individual but a sort of Mars man, a projection of science fiction, the man of 1984. Such a futuristic vision of America was already in Mlle. de Beauvoir's head when she descended from the plane as from a spaceship, wearing metaphorical goggles: eager as a little girl to taste the rock-candy delights of this materialistic moon civilization (the orange juice, the ice creams, the jazz, the whiskeys, the martinis, and the lobsters). She knows already, nevertheless, that this world is not "real," but only a half-frightening fantasy daydreamed by the Americans.

She has preserved enough of Marxism to be warned that the spun-sugar façade is a device of the "Pullman class"[6] to mask its exploitation and cruelty: while the soda fountains spout, Truman and Marshall prepare an anti-Communist crusade that brings back memories of the Nazis, and Congress plots the ruin of the trade unions. "The collective future is in the hands of a privileged class, the Pullman class, to which are reserved the joys of large-scale enterprise and creation; the others are just wheels in a big steel world; they lack the power to conceive an individual future for themselves; they have no plan or passion, hope or nostalgia, that carries them beyond the present; they know only the unending repetition of the cycle of seasons and hours."

This image of a people from Oz or out of an expressionist ballet, a robot people obedient to a generalization, corresponds, of course, with no reality, either in the United States or anywhere else; it is the petrifaction of a fear very common in Europe today—a fear of the future. Where, in a more hopeful era, America embodied for Europe a certain millennial promise, now in the Atomic Age it embodies an evil presentiment of a millennium just at hand. To Mlle. de Beauvoir, obsessed with memories of Jules Verne,[7] America is a symbol of a mechanical progress once dreamed of and now repudiated with horror; it is a Judgment on itself and on Europe. No friendly experience with Americans can dispel this deep-lying dread. She does not want to know America but only to ascertain that it is there, just as she had imagined it. She shrinks from involvement in this "big steel world" and makes no attempt to see factories, workers, or political leaders. She prefers the abstraction of "Wall Street."

This recoil from American actuality has the result that might be expected, a result,

---

[5] Existentialism is a philosophical movement in which individual human beings are understood as having full responsibility for creating the meanings of their own lives.

[6] Refers to wealthy travelers who could afford to ride on opulent first-class Pullman train cars.

[7] Jules Verne (1828-1905), French science fiction author, whose novels imagined technological possibilities (space flight, air travel, submarines) long before they became realities.

in fact, so predictable that one might say she willed it. Her book is consistently misinformed in small matters as well as large. She has a gift for visual description which she uses very successfully to evoke certain American phenomena: Hollywood, the Grand Canyon, the Bronx, Chinatown, women's dresses, the stockyards, the Bowery, Golden Gate, auto camps, Hawaiian dinners, etc. Insofar as the US is a vast tourist camp, a vacationland, a Stop-in Serv-Urself, she has caught its essence. But insofar as the United States is something more than a caricature of itself conceived by the mind of an ad man or a western Chamber of Commerce, she has a disinclination to view it. She cannot, for example, take in the names of American writers even when she has their books by her elbow: she speaks repeatedly of James Algee (Agee), of Farrel (Farrell), O'Neil (O'Neill), and of Max Twain—a strange form of compliment to authors whom she professes to like. In the same way, Greenwich Village, which she loves, she speaks of throughout as "Greeniwich," even when she comes to live there.

These are minor distortions. What is more pathetic is her credulity, which amounts to a kind of superstition. She is so eager to appear well informed that she believes anything anybody tells her, especially if it is anti-American and pretends to reveal the inner workings of the capitalist mechanism. The Fifth Avenue shops, she tells us, are "reserved for the capitalist international," and no investigative instinct tempts her to cross the barricade and see for herself. Had she done so, she might have found suburban housewives, file clerks, and stenographers swarming about the racks of Peck & Peck or Best's or Franklin Simon's, and colored girls mingling with white girls at the counters of Saks Fifth Avenue. A Spanish painter assures her that in America you have to hire a press agent to get your paintings shown. An author tells her that in America literary magazines print only favorable reviews. A student tells her that in America private colleges pay better salaries than state universities, so that the best education falls to the privileged classes, who do not want it, and so on. At Vassar, she relates, students are selected "according to their intellectual capacities, family, and fortune." Every item in this catalog is false. (Private colleges do not pay better salaries—on the contrary, with a few exceptions, they pay notoriously worse; family plays no part in the selection of students at Vassar, and fortune only to the extent that the tuition has to be paid by someone—friend, parent, or scholarship donor; you do not have to hire a press agent; some literary magazines make a positive specialty of printing unfavorable reviews.)

Yet Mlle. de Beauvoir, unsuspecting, continues volubly to pass on "the low-down" to her European readers: there is no friendship between the sexes in America; American whites are "stiff" and "cold" American society has lost its mobility; capital is in "certain hands," and the worker's task is "carefully laid out." "True, a few accidental successes give the myth of the self-made man a certain support, but they are illusory and tangential…."

The picture of an America that consists of a small ruling class and a vast inert, regimented mass beneath it is elaborated at every opportunity. She sees the dispersion of goods on counters but draws no conclusion from it as to the structure of the economy. The American worker, to her, is invariably the French worker, a consecrated symbol of oppression. She talks a great deal of American conformity but fails to recognize a thing that Tocqueville[8] saw long ago; that this conformity is the expression of a

---

[8] Alexis de Tocqueville (1805-1859), French author of *Democracy in America* (1835-1840).

predominantly middle-class society; it is the price paid (as yet) for the spread of plenty. Whether the diffusion of television sets is, in itself, a good is another question; the fact is, however, that they *are* diffused; the "Pullman class," for weal or woe, does not have a corner on them, or on the levers of political power.

The outrage of the upper-class minority at the spectacle of television aerials on the shabby houses of Poverty Row, at the thought of the Frigidaires and washing machines in farmhouse and working-class kitchens, at the new cars parked in ranks outside the factories, at the very thought of installment buying, unemployment compensation, social security, trade union benefits, veterans' housing, at General Vaughan,[9] above all at Truman the haberdasher,[10] the symbol of this cocky equality—their outrage is perhaps the most striking phenomenon in American life today. Yet Mlle. de Beauvoir remained unaware of it, and unaware also, for all her journal tells us, of income taxes and inheritance taxes, of the expense account and how it has affected buying habits and given a peculiar rashness and transiency to the daily experience of consumption. It can be argued that certain angry elements in American business do not know their own interests, which lie in the consumers' economy; even so, this ignorance and anger are an immense political fact in America.

The society characterized by Mlle. de Beauvoir as "rigid," "frozen," "closed" is in the process of great change. The mansions are torn down and the real estate "development" takes their place: serried rows of ranch-type houses, painted in pastel colors, each with its picture window and its garden, each equipped with deep freeze, oil furnace, and automatic washer, spring up in the wilderness. Class barriers disappear or become porous; the factory worker is an economic aristocrat in comparison to the middle-class clerk; even segregation is diminishing; consumption replaces acquisition as an incentive. The America invoked by Mlle. de Beauvoir as a country of vast inequalities and dramatic contrasts is rapidly ceasing to exist.

One can guess that it is the new America, rather than the imaginary America of economic royalism, that creates in Mlle. de Beauvoir a feeling of mixed attraction and repulsion. In one half of her sensibility, she is greatly excited by the United States and precisely by its material side. She is fascinated by drugstore displays of soap and dentifrices, by the uniformly regulated traffic, by the "good citizenship" of Americans, by the anonymous camaraderie of the big cities, by jazz and expensive record players and huge collections of records, and above all—to speak frankly—by the orange juice, the martinis, and the whiskey. She speaks elatedly of "my" America, "my" New York; she has a child's greedy possessiveness toward this place which she is in the act of discovering.

Toward the end of the book, as she revises certain early judgments, she finds that she has become "an American." What she means is that she has become somewhat critical of the carnival aspects of American life which at first bewitched her; she is able to make discriminations between different kinds of jazz, different hotels, different nightclubs. Very tentatively, she pushes beyond appearance and perceives that the American is not his possessions, that the American character is, not fleshly but abstract. Yet at bottom she remains disturbed by what she has seen and felt, even marginally, of the American problem. This is not one of inequity, as she would prefer

---

[9] General Harry H. Vaughan (1893-1981), President Truman's military aide from 1945 to 1953.

[10] Harry S. Truman (1884-1972) ran a men's clothing store in Kansas City before becoming president.

to believe, but of its opposite. The problem posed by the United States is, as Tocqueville saw, the problem of equality, its consequences, and what price shall be paid for it. How is wealth to be spread without the spread of uniformity? How create a cushion of plenty without stupefaction of the soul and the senses? It is a dilemma that glares from every picture window and whistles through every breezeway.

If Americans, as Mlle. de Beauvoir thinks, are apathetic politically, it is because they can take neither side with any great conviction—how can one be *against* the abolition of poverty? And how, on the other hand, can one champion a leveling of extremes? For Europeans of egalitarian sympathies, America is the dilemma, relentlessly marching toward them, a future which "works," and which for that very reason they have no wish to face. Hence the desire, so very evident in Mlle. de Beauvoir's impressions and in much journalism of the European left, not to know what America is really like, to identify it with "fascism" or "reaction," not to admit, in short; that it has realized, to a considerable extent, the economic and social goals of President Franklin D. Roosevelt and of progressive thought in general.

—1952

TILLIE OLSEN (1912–2007)

Tillie Lerner was born in Omaha, Nebraska. Her parents, Samuel and Ida Lerner, were impoverished Russian-Jewish immigrants who came to the U.S. after participating in the failed Russian revolution in 1905, for which Samuel was imprisoned. Ida Lerner did not learn to read and write until her twenties. The Lerners were active in socialist politics, and Samuel served as State Secretary of the Nebraska Socialist Party. One of six children, Olsen was working to help support the family at the age of ten, and dropped out of school in the eleventh grade. She joined the Young Communist League in 1931, and moved to San Francisco in 1933 with her first child. She married printer and activist Jack Olsen in 1943 and had three more children. Olsen covered strikes and demonstrations for various left-wing publications, and wrote when she could under the enormous pressures of poverty, working-class jobs, family responsibilities, and a post-war political climate deeply hostile to her politics. Her first published book, *Tell Me a Riddle* (1961), is a collection of stories; the title novella won the O. Henry Award as the best American story published that year, and was adapted for film in 1978. In her nonfiction book *Silences* (1978), Olsen explores not only her own long periods of silence as a writer, but a wide range of social and personal forces that silence writers. In 1974, she published a reworked version of a novel she had set aside forty years earlier: *Yonnondio: From the Thirties*. Olsen served as a consultant to The Feminist Press, and wrote an interpretive essay in the Press' reprint of Rebecca Harding Davis' *Life in the Iron Mills and Other Stories*. She also edited several readers and anthologies about mother-daughter relationships. Olsen died in Oakland, California, just days before her ninety-fourth birthday.

I Stand Here Ironing

I stand here ironing, and what you asked me moves tormented back and forth with the iron.

"I wish you would manage the time to come in and talk with me about your daughter. I'm sure you can help me understand her. She's a youngster who needs help and whom I'm deeply interested in helping."

"Who needs help?" Even if I came what good would it do? You think because I am her mother I have a key, or that in some way you could use me as a key? She has lived for nineteen years. There is all that life that has happened outside of me, beyond me.

And when is there time to remember, to sift, to weigh, to estimate, to total? I will start and there will be an interruption and I will have to gather it all together again. Or I will become engulfed with all I did or did not do, with what should have been and what cannot be helped.

She was a beautiful baby. The first and only one of our five that was beautiful at birth. You do not guess how new and uneasy her tenancy in her now-loveliness. You did not know her all those years she was thought homely, or see her poring over her baby pictures, making me tell her over and over how beautiful she had been—and would be, I would tell her—and was now, to the seeing eye. But the seeing eyes were few or nonexistent. Including mine.

I nursed her. They feel that's important nowadays. I nursed all the children, but with her, with all the fierce rigidity of first motherhood, I did like the books said. Though her cries battered me to trembling and my breasts ached with swollenness, I waited till the clock decreed.

Why do I put that first? I do not even know if it matters, or if it explains anything.

She was a beautiful baby. She blew shining bubbles of sound. She loved motion, loved light, loved color and music and textures. She would lie on the floor in her blue overalls patting the surface so hard in ecstasy her hands and feet would blur. She was a miracle to me, but when she was eight months old I had to leave her daytimes with the woman downstairs to whom she was no miracle at all, for I worked or looked for work and for Emily's father, who "could no longer endure" (he wrote in his good-by note) "sharing want with us."

I was nineteen. It was the pre-relief, pre-WPA[1] world of the depression. I would start running as soon as I got off the streetcar, running up the stairs, the place smelling sour, and awake or asleep to startle awake, when she saw me she would break into a clogged weeping that could not be comforted, a weeping I can yet hear.

After a while I found a job hashing at night so I could be with her days, and it was better. But it came to where I had to bring her to his family and leave her.

It took a long time to raise the money for her fare back. Then she got chicken pox and I had to wait longer. When she finally came, I hardly knew her, walking quick and nervous like her father, looking like her father, thin, and dressed in a shoddy red that yellowed her skin and glared at the pock marks. All the baby loveliness gone.

She was two. Old enough for nursery school they said, and I did not know then what I know now—the fatigue of the long day, and the lacerations of group life in nurseries that are only parking places for children.

Except that it would have made no difference if I had known. It was the only place there was. It was the only way we could be together, the only way I could hold a job.

And even without knowing, I knew. I knew the teacher that was evil because all these years it has curdled into my memory, the little boy hunched in the corner, her rasp, "why aren't you outside, because Alvin hits you? that's no reason, go out coward." I knew Emily hated it even if she did not clutch and implore "don't go Mommy" like the other children, mornings.

[1] The Works Progress Administration (1935-1943) provided jobs for the unemployed.

She always had a reason why we should stay home. Momma, you look sick, Momma. I feel sick. Momma, the teachers aren't there today, they're sick. Momma there was a fire there last night. Momma it's a holiday today, no school, they told me.

But never a direct protest, never rebellion. I think of our others in their three-, four-year-oldness—the explosions, the tempers, the denunciations, the demands—and I feel suddenly ill. I stop the ironing. What in me demanded that goodness in her? And what was the cost, the cost to her of such goodness?

The old man living in the back once said in his gentle way: "You should smile at Emily more when you look at her." What *was* in my face when I looked at her? I loved her. There were all the acts of love.

It was only with the others I remembered what he said, so that it was the face of joy, and not of care or tightness or worry I turned to them—but never to Emily. She does not smile easily, let alone almost always as her brothers and sisters do. Her face is closed and somber, but when she wants, how fluid. You must have seen it in her pantomimes, you spoke of her rare gift for comedy on the stage that rouses a laughter out of the audience so dear they applaud and applaud and do not want to let her go.

Where does it come from, that comedy? There was none of it in her when she came back to me that second time, after I had had to send her away again. She had a new daddy now to learn to love, and I think perhaps it was a better time. Except when we left her alone nights, telling ourselves she was old enough.

"Can't you go some other time Mommy, like tomorrow?" she would ask. "Will it be just a little while you'll be gone?"

The time we came back, the front door open, the clock on the floor in the hall. She rigid awake. "It wasn't just a little while. I didn't cry. I called you a little, just three times, and then I went downstairs to open the door so you could come faster. The clock talked loud, I threw it away, it scared me what it talked."

She said the clock talked loud that night I went to the hospital to have Susan. She was delirious with the fever that comes before red measles, but she was fully conscious all the week I was gone and the week after we were home when she could not come near the baby or me.

She did not get well. She stayed skeleton thin, not wanting to eat, and night after night she had nightmares. She would call for me, and I would sleepily call back, "you're all right, darling, go to sleep, it's just a dream," and if she still called, in a sterner voice, "now go to sleep, Emily, there's nothing to hurt you." Twice, only twice, when I had to get up for Susan anyhow I went in to sit with her.

Now when it is too late (as if she would let me hold and comfort her like I do the others) I get up and go to her at her moan or restless stirring. "Are you awake? Can I get you something?" And the answer is always the same: "No, I'm all right, go back to sleep Mother."

They persuade me at the clinic to send her away to a convalescent home in the country where "she can have the kind of food and care you can't manage for her, and you'll be free to concentrate on the new baby." They still send children to that place. I see pictures on the society page of sleek young women planning affairs to raise money for it, or dancing at the affairs, or decorating Easter eggs or filling Christmas stockings for the children.

They never have a picture of the children so I do not know if they still wear those gigantic red bows and the ravaged looks on the every other Sunday when parents can come to visit "unless otherwise notified"—as we were notified the first six weeks.

Oh it is a handsome place, green lawns and tall trees and fluted flower beds. High up on the balconies of each cottage the children stand, the girls in their red bows and white dresses, the boys in white suits and giant red ties. The parents stand below shrieking up to be heard and the children shriek down to be heard, and between them the invisible wall "Not To Be Contaminated by Parental Germs or Physical Affection."

There was a tiny girl who always stood hand in hand with Emily. Her parents never came. One visit she was gone. "They moved her to Rose Cottage," Emily shouted in explanation. "They don't like you to love anybody here."

She wrote once a week, the labored writing of a seven-year-old. "I am fine. How is the baby. If I write my leter nicly I will have a star. Love." There never was a star. We wrote every other day, letters she could never hold or keep but only hear read—once. "We simply do not have room for children to keep any personal possessions," they patiently explained when we pieced one Sunday's shrieking together to plead how much it would mean to Emily to keep her letters and cards.

Each visit she looked frailer. "She isn't eating," they told us. (They had runny eggs for breakfast or mush with lumps, Emily said later, I'd hold it in my mouth and not swallow. Nothing ever tasted good, just when they had chicken.)

It took us eight months to get her released home, and only the fact that she gained back so little of her seven lost pounds convinced the social worker.

I used to try to hold and love her after she came back, but her body would stay stiff, and after a while she'd push away. She ate little. Food sickened her, and I think much of life too. Oh she had physical lightness and brightness, twinkling by on skates, bouncing like a ball up and down up and down over the jump rope, skimming over the hill; but these were momentary.

She fretted about her appearance, thin and dark and foreign-looking at a time when every little girl was supposed to look or thought she should look a chubby blond replica of Shirley Temple.[2] The doorbell sometimes rang for her, but no one seemed to come and play in the house or be a best friend. Maybe because we moved so much.

There was a boy she loved painfully through two school semesters. Months later she told me how she had taken pennies from my purse to buy him candy. "Licorice was his favorite and I brought him some every day, but he still liked Jennifer better'n me. Why Mommy why?" A question I could never answer.

School was a worry to her. She was not glib or quick in a world where glibness and quickness were easily confused with ability to learn. To her overworked and exasperated teachers she was an overconscientious "slow learner" who kept trying to catch up and was absent entirely too often.

I let her be absent, though sometimes the illness was imaginary. How different from my now-strictness about attendance with the others. I wasn't working. We had a new baby, I was home anyhow. Sometimes, after Susan grew old enough, I would keep her home from school, too, to have them all together.

Mostly Emily had asthma, and her breathing, harsh and labored, would fill the house with a curiously tranquil sound. I would bring the two old dresser mirrors and her boxes of collections to her bed. She would select beads and single earrings, bottle

---

[2] Shirley Temple (b. 1928), blonde and dimpled child actor, a major Hollywood star in the 1930s.

tops and shells, dried flowers and pebbles, old postcards and scraps, all sorts of oddments; then she and Susan would play Kingdom, setting up landscapes and furniture, peopling them with action.

Those were the only times of peaceful companionship between her and Susan. I have edged away from it, that poisonous feeling between them, that terrible balancing of hurts and needs I had to do between the two, and did so badly, those earlier years.

Oh there are conflicts between the others too, each one human, needing, demanding, hurting, taking—but only between Emily and Susan, no, Emily toward Susan that corroding resentment. It seems so obvious on the surface, yet it is not obvious. Susan, the second child, Susan, golden and curly haired and chubby, quick and articulate and assured, everything in appearance and manner Emily was not; Susan, not able to resist Emily's precious things, losing or sometimes clumsily breaking them; Susan telling jokes and riddles to company for applause while Emily sat silent (to say to me later: that was *my* riddle, Mother, I told it to Susan); Susan, who for all the five years' difference in age was just a year behind Emily in developing physically.

I am glad for that slow physical development that widened the difference between her and her contemporaries, though she suffered over it. She was too vulnerable for that terrible world of youthful competition, of preening and parading, of constant measuring of yourself against every other, of envy, "If I had that copper hair," or "If I had that skin…" She tormented herself enough about not looking like the others, there was enough of the unsureness, the having to be conscious of words before you speak, the constant caring—what are they thinking of me? what kind of an impression am I making—there was enough without having it all magnified unendurably by the merciless physical drives.

Ronnie is calling. He is wet and I change him. It is rare there is such a cry now. That time of motherhood is almost behind me when the ear is not one's own but must always be racked and listening for the child cry, the child call. We sit for a while and I hold him, looking out over the city spread in charcoal with its soft aisles of light. "Shuggily" he breathes. A funny word, a family word, inherited from Emily, invented by her to say comfort.

In this and other ways she leaves her seal, I say aloud. And startle at my saying it. What do I mean? What did I start to gather together, to try and make coherent? I was at the terrible, growing years. War years. I do not remember them well. I was working, there were four smaller ones now, there was not time for her. She had to help be a mother, and housekeeper, and shopper. She had to set her seal. Mornings of crisis and near hysteria trying to get lunches packed, hair combed, coats and shoes found, everyone to school or Child Care on time, the baby ready for transportation. And always the paper scribbled on by a smaller one, the book looked at by Susan then mislaid, the homework not done. Running out to that huge school where she was one, she was lost, she was a drop; suffering over the unpreparedness, stammering and unsure in her classes.

There was so little time left at night after the kids were bedded down. She would struggle over books, always eating (it was in those years she developed her enormous appetite that is legendary in our familiy) and I would be ironing, or preparing food for the next day, or writing V-mail[3] to Bill, or tending the baby. Sometimes, to make me

---

[3] A WWII system of correspondence to and from military personnel overseas, written on specific forms and microfilmed to reduce cargo space.

laugh, or out of her despair, she would imitate happenings or types at school.

I think I said once: "Why don't you do something like this in the school amateur show?" One morning she phoned me at work, hardly understandable through the weeping: "Mother, I did it. I won, I won; they gave me first prize; they clapped and clapped and wouldn't let me go."

Now suddenly she was Somebody, and as imprisoned in her difference as in anonymity.

She began to be asked to perform at other high schools, even in colleges, then at city and state-wide affairs. The first one we went to, I only recognized her that first moment when thin, shy, she almost drowned herself into the curtains. Then: Was this Emily? the control, the command, the convulsing and deadly clowning, the spell, then the roaring, stamping audience, unwilling to let this rare and precious laughter out of their lives.

Afterwards: You ought to do something about her with a gift like that—but without money or knowing how, what does one do? We have left it all to her, and the gift has as often eddied inside, clogged and clotted, as been used and growing.

She is coming. She runs up the stairs two at a time with her light graceful step, and I know she is happy tonight. Whatever it was that occasioned your call did not happen today.

"Aren't you ever going to finish the ironing, Mother? Whistler[4] painted his mother in a rocker. I'd have to paint mine standing over an ironing board." This is one of her communicative nights and she tells me everything and nothing as she fixes herself a plate of food out of the icebox.

She is so lovely. Why did you want me to come in at all? Why were you concerned? She will find her way.

She starts up the stairs to bed. "Don't get me up with the rest in the morning." "But I thought you were having midterms." "Oh, those," she comes back in and says quite lightly, "in a couple of years when we'll all be atom-dead they won't matter a bit."

She has said it before. She believes it. But because I have been dredging the past, and all that compounds a human being is so heavy and meaningful in me, I cannot endure it tonight.

I will never total it all now. I will never come in to say: She was a child seldom smiled at. Her father left me before she was a year old. I worked her first six years when there was work, or I sent her home and to his relatives. There were years she had care she hated. She was dark and thin and foreign-looking in a world where the prestige went to blondness and curly hair and dimples, slow where glibness was prized. She was a child of anxious, not proud, love. We were poor and could not afford for her the soil of easy growth. I was a young mother, I was a distracted mother. There were the other children pushing up, demanding. Her younger sister was all that she was not. She did not like me to touch her. She kept too much in herself, her life was such she had to keep too much in herself. My wisdom came too late. She has much in her and probably nothing will come of it. She is a child of her age, of depression, of war, of fear.

Let her be. So all that is in her will not bloom—but in how many does it? There is

---

[4] James Abbott McNeill Whistler (1834-1903), American-born painter whose most famous work is *Arrangement in Grey and Black; Portrait of the Artist's Mother* (1872).

still enough left to live by. Only help her to believe—help make it so there is cause for her to believe that she is more than this dress on the ironing board, helpless before the iron.

—1956

MAY SARTON (1912-1995)

A prolific writer, May Sarton was the author of seventeen books of poetry, nineteen novels, two children's books, a stage play, several screenplays, and ten volumes of memoir and journals. Born in Belgium to wealthy parents, Sarton grew up in Cambridge, Massachusetts, where her father was a historian of science and her mother an artist and designer. She earned a scholarship to Vassar College, but at the last minute decided not to attend, and instead joined Eva Le Gallienne's Civic Repertory Theatre as an actress. She published poetry and formed her own theater company in the 1930s, but the Depression led to the end of her acting career and she turned exclusively to writing. During the 1930s and 1940s Sarton supported herself as a writer by lecturing at colleges throughout the United States. She also made a point of visiting Europe each year; these trips gave her the opportunity to meet writers and artists there, including Virginia Woolf and Elizabeth Bowen. In the 1950s Sarton became increasingly well known. Her novel *Faithful Are the Wounds* (1955) and her book of poetry *In Time Like Air* (1958) earned her a dual National Book Award nomination in 1958. The 1965 publication of *Mrs. Stevens Hears the Mermaids Singing* signaled a change in Sarton's writing life. The book was seen by many as the author's "coming-out novel," and her work was celebrated by feminists, particularly lesbians. Sarton resisted the label "lesbian writer" for herself, however, believing that it limited both her assumed scope of vision and her audience appeal. Sarton continued to write until soon before her death. Her journals from the 1990s represent a powerful and poignant description of continuing to live as the body fails.

In Time Like Air

Consider the mysterious salt:
In water it must disappear.
It has no self. It knows no fault.
Not even sight may apprehend it.
No one may gather it or spend it.   5
It is dissolved and everywhere.

But out of water into air
It must resolve into a presence,
Precise and tangible and here.
Faultlessly pure, faultlessly white,   10
It crystallizes in our sight
And has defined itself to essence.

What element dissolves the soul
So it may be both found and lost,
In what suspended as a whole?   15
What is the element so blest
That there identity can rest
As salt in the clear water cast?

Love in its early transformation,
And only love, may so design it   20
That the self flows in pure sensation,
Is all dissolved and found at last
Without a future or a past,
And a whole life suspended in it.

The faultless crystal of detachment   25
Comes after, cannot be created
Without the first intense attachment.
Even the saints achieve this slowly;
For us, more human and less holy,
In time like air is essence stated.

—1958

All Day I Was with Trees

Across wild country on solitary roads
Within a fugue of parting, I was consoled
By birches' sovereign whiteness in sad woods,
Dark glow of pines, a single elm's distinction—
I was consoled by trees.   5

In February we see the structure change—
Or the light change, and so the way we see it.
Tensile and delicate, the trees stand now
Against the early skies, the frail fresh blue,
In an attentive stillness.   10

Naked, the trees are singularly present,
Although their secret force is still locked in.
Who could believe that the new sap is rising
And soon we shall draw up amazing sweetness
From stark maples?   15

All day I was with trees, a fugue of parting,
All day lived in long cycles, not brief hours.
A tenderness of light before new falls of snow
Lay on the barren landscape like a promise.
Love nourished every vein.

—1972

from I Knew a Phoenix
Sketches for an Autobiography

[...]The two springs of 1936 and 1937 melt into each other for me now; they are woven together into a single web of new friendships that were to nourish and sustain me through all the later years. They were a great burst of life. But I cannot leave them without going back for a moment to evoke the end of my stay at Taviton Street.

Shortly before I was leaving for Belgium, John Summerson, as a farewell present, took me to dinner at Elizabeth Bowen's.[1]

At precisely a quarter to eight on that warm May evening, we set out in a taxi for Clarence Terrace on Regent's Park. If I had imagined that a "Terrace" might turn out to be something like a "Mansion" or a "Garden" this was but another proof of my abysmal ignorance; John soon put me right, and showed me the beauty of the Nash designs, the great windows, the cream-colored façades with their balconies and pillars that look like a long elegant palace, and are really sets of houses. We drew up before one of these. Who was there? What happened that evening? I remember it as a daze of happiness, intensified by the poignance of departure. I remember vividly our entrance into the upstairs drawing room, its great French windows open onto the May night, so the heavy curtains seemed to breathe gently, and one was drawn irresistibly to look out, to look down onto the Park, the silent groves of trees lit up by the street lamps like stage scenery, and a patch of moonlight below shivering the lake. I remember turning back, to the bowl of white peonies on the mantel reflected in a Regency mirror above them, white peonies with a streak of crimson jagged at their centers; I remember Elizabeth Bowen herself, sitting on the immense stiff Regency sofa looking like a Holbein[2] drawing, the fine red hair pulled back from her forehead, speaking in small rushes, and too observant (one guessed) to allow herself any but the most fleeting glances at a shy guest, so she was apt to stare fixedly at a cigarette in her hand; like the peonies on the mantel, she resembled a swan, stately, slightly awkward, beautiful and haunting. And I remember Alan Cameron, her husband, though here again the images merge, for I grew only later to appreciate the acute sensitivity and kindness beneath his slightly Blimpish appearance, and his mask of pretended irascibility. We shared a devotion to all members of the cat family, and went sometimes to the zoo in later years, to look, in the grave and beautiful faces of leopards and lions and even tigers, for the portrait of Elizabeth. I think of a midnight years after that first meeting, when I watched Alan walk up and down that room, a glass in his hand, and recite the first page of *The Death of the Heart,* breaking off to shout in his rather high voice, "That's genius!" But on that first evening my attention was focused on the shy heron, John Summerson, talking with animation, at home in this world where I felt still so strange, and sending Elizabeth Bowen into a ripple of sustained laughter, like a musical accompaniment, something between a purr and a song.

That room must still reverberate with the voices of all the friends who gathered there, and all the "occasions," public and private, when love and wit and grace and passion were floating about in the air, magnetized by the presence of Elizabeth. It was there that I first met Virginia Woolf,[3] and with the evoking of that vanished personification of genius, I shall close this chapter of joys, all undeserved, as the final flower in the bouquet I held in my hands. I had, one day, earlier in that spring of 1937, wrapped a copy of my first book of poems carefully in tissue paper, had stopped in Russell Square to ease its passage with the purchase of a bunch of primroses, and then had walked in fear and trembling to 52 Tavistock Square where Virginia and Leonard Woolf lived at that time.

---

[1] Elizabeth Bowen (1899-1973), Anglo-Irish novelist.
[2] Hans Holbein the Younger (1497-1543), German Northern Renaissance painter.

[3] Virginia Woolf (1882-1941), English feminist novelist.

The door was opened by a kindly old servant in an apron, who received the package, and asked whether I would not like to come up. But one does not batter one's way in to see the gods, and I hastily withdrew. A few days later I received a note in that delicate spidery hand to say that Virginia Woolf thanked me and had not yet had time to read the poems. I was disappointed, of course, for at that time, her word about the beginnings of my work seemed to me, in the intensity of my admiration, the only accolade which could possibly matter. I have since learned how overwhelming are the demands for the "attention" of a recognized author, but I did not know it then, and I felt dashed.

Then Elizabeth Bowen, to whom I had related this story, arranged a little dinner party, and I was formally introduced. Virginia Woolf came into the drawing room at Clarence Terrace, visibly shy, for an instant like a deer or some elegant wild creature dazzled by the lights, and walked straight across the room to stand in one of the long windows, looking out into the Park. She was, as has been sufficiently stated, far more beautiful than any of the photographs show, and perhaps less strange, and that night, in a long green *robe-de-style,*[4] she looked exactly as one had imagined she would look. It was a moment of total recognition and delight. Later on that evening she realized that it was I who had left poems and primroses at her door, and the ice was finally broken. She told me how someone had just presented her with a small Chinese vase, and how improbable it seemed that at that very moment primroses should appear out of thin air, to be placed in it. I was invited to tea the next week.

This time I saw her alone, in the small upstairs drawing room which contained so many patterns and small bright objects it gave the impression of being like the inside of a kaleidoscope: a screen painted by Vanessa Bell, flowered prints on the chairs, a wall of French books in many-colored paper covers, and two hassocks by the fire upon one of which I sat, suffering a crisis of shyness. Virginia Woolf, like the elephant's child in Kipling, was a woman of "insatiable curtiosity," as well as rippling malice. She may have looked like some slightly unreal goddess, transparent to every current of air or wave, the eyes set in the sculptured bone in such a way that their beauty was perfectly defined; her conversation was anything but ethereal. I remember that we laughed hilariously, that she teased me about poetry, and told me that it was easy to write poems and immensely difficult to write novels. But when I stammered out that I was actually at work on a novel at the moment, she looked at me with sudden intensity, and said, "You are writing a novel? Ah, then all this must seem totally unreal to you." *The Years* had just been published; I did not think it the best of her novels, nor, I think, did she. For she spoke of it that day as an immense act of will, to break the mold of *The Waves;* she said that someone had called her on the telephone, a disembodied voice like that of a sybil, and had said, "You are becoming too special, too involved in your own inner world. Come back to us." So she labored at *The Years,* which was, she said, to be "about ordinary people." She had worked at it in a curious way, many scenes at a time, picking out first one and then another like the pieces of a mosaic. So that the horror in this case, as she explained, had been the transitions, the linking passages.

At precisely six Leonard Woolf appeared. I felt at once that his arrival was a signal: it was time for me to leave. I felt this, but I also felt that it would be rude to rush away, and, caught in the dilemma, found myself launching into a glowing description of

[4] A type of women's dress popular in the 1920s, characterized by a dropped waistline and a full skirt.

Whipsnade, of the restaurant and the tigers among the hawthorns;[5] suddenly before I knew it, I had invited the Woolfs to come out for dinner.

I have no illusions about this event: the charms that brought them driving thirty miles out of London were not mine, but the bait of a very good restaurant indeed, and my glowing description of the wonders of the place. Everything went wrong, of course. The sky was heavily overcast, great black clouds rising up over Whipsnade Hill. The Woolfs were late, so that the visit to the animals had to be curtailed, and because it was late, various delights I had held out failed to materialize. We did not see one wallaby with a baby in her pocket. The icy wind blew in our faces, and I feared that I might be responsible for giving one of England's glories an attack of pneumonia. It was a long walk to the tigers, but we did—from far off—hear a strange sad mewing. When we got to the round cages, a little like huge aviaries with trees, grass, hawthorn in flower inside them, there was nothing whatever to be seen, not a single tiger face, or even a paw, not a single round ear behind a bush. I was in a state of acute embarrassment and misery, which was not relieved when we discovered that the great cats had all been put to bed in boxlike cages to one side of their green paradise, and were complaining sadly. However, on the way back, we did have one redeeming pleasure. The sight of the baby giraffe, who had been born only a few weeks before, running gaily up and down his paddock, his short tail flying, and such a ridiculous gamboling air despite his long rocking-horse neck, that we laughed aloud, forgetting the black clouds and the icy wind. Was it then or later, that I saw that Virginia Woolf looked rather like a giraffe—her immense dark eyes, long aristocratic neck, and slightly disdainful, sensitive way of lifting her chin?

Fortunately the restaurant provided an excellent *Filet Mignon* with *sauce béarnaise;* we had a bottle of claret, and the deer did come and stare at us through the plate-glass windows. We had coffee upstairs in my rooms, so that Virginia Woolf could smoke one of her long thin elegant cigars. What did we talk about? I was too overwhelmed with responsibility to register, as depressed as a circus manager whose acts have all failed to perform. I felt I had persuaded them to a long journey only to find some poor miserable tigers mewing in their boxes: a fiasco.

Much later, during the Battle of Britain, I heard that the baby giraffe had died of fright in a bombing, that gay gambol turned into a hideous terrified gallop and failure of the heart. And shortly afterward, when I was in Chicago on a lecture trip, someone quite casually handed me a newspaper clipping. It contained a brief statement that Virginia Woolf early that morning had walked down to the River Ouse and drowned herself. I remember how, in an instant of acute grief and recognition, the two images slid together for me. After a long silence I wrote to Leonard Woolf. "I have very vivid recollection of that evening at Whipsnade," he answered, "which now seems to belong to another world and age. It was June 30, 1937."

—1954

---

[5] The village of Whipsnade, in Bedfordshire, is the home of Whipsnade Tree Cathedral and Whipsnade Wild Animal Park.

MURIEL RUKEYSER (1913-1980)

Biographer, playwright, journalist, and critic Muriel Rukeyser is best known as a poet grounded in a fiercely independent, evolving, and empathic poetics. Her interests ranged from science and flight to the politics of body and mind. She was born in New York City in 1913 to wealthy but unhappily married Jewish parents. After attending the Ethical Cultural School of New York, and withdrawing from Vassar in 1932 to become a full-time writer, she launched what became a three-phase career.

During the Depression she aligned herself with the Communist Party, accepting some but not all of its principles. She reported on the Scottsboro trial and investigated the Union Carbide hydroelectric project in Gauley Bridge, West Virginia, where hundreds of miners died from silicosis. The latter story became the basis of her important poem sequence, "The Book of the Dead," which merges testimony, poetic description, and stock dividends into a lyrical narrative. Between 1935 and 1947, she published five books of poems in addition to numerous articles and other writings. During the next phase of her career, from 1947 to 1962, she raised her son William and taught at Sarah Lawrence College (from 1956 to 1967), writing and publishing less work. Her earlier association with the Communist Party had made her a target of critics and politicians during the conservative post-war era, while editors and critics on the left accused her of selling out. By the mid 1960s, with her son in college and the U.S. in turmoil over civil rights and the Vietnam War, Rukeyser became an active and activist poet again. Putting her commitment to non-violence above national politics, she traveled to North Vietnam with Denise Levertov on an unofficial peace mission and later went to South Korea to protest the jailing of poet Kim Chi-Ha. Although she didn't call herself a feminist, she lent her name to feminist causes and wrote poetry volumes such as *The Speed of Darkness* (1968), *Breaking Open* (1973), and *The Gates* (1976), which helped galvanize the second wave of feminism and inspired many poets who followed her, among them Adrienne Rich, Sharon Olds, and Jane Cooper. After a stroke and several years of bad health, she died in February, 1980. Her work is undergoing a renaissance of new readers today.

The Poem As Mask

Orpheus[1]

When I wrote of the women in their dances and wildness, it was a mask,
on their mountain, gold-hunting, singing, in orgy,
it was a mask; when I wrote of the god,
fragmented, exiled from himself, his life, the love gone down with song,
it was myself, split open, unable to speak, in exile from myself.   5

There is no mountain, there is no god, there is memory
of my torn life, myself split open in sleep, the rescued child
beside me among the doctors, and a word
of rescue from the great eyes.

No more masks! No more mythologies!   10

Now, for the first time, the god lifts his hand,
the fragments join in me with their own music.

—1968

---

[1] In Greek mythology, a poet whose work could charm monsters and gods.

Despisals

In the human cities, never again to
despise the backside of the city, the ghetto,
or build it again as we build the despised
backsides of houses.   Look at your own building.
You are the city.   5

Among our secrecies, not to despise our Jews
(that is, ourselves) or our darkness, our blacks,
or in our sexuality   wherever it takes us
and we now know we are productive
too productive, too reproductive   10
for our present invention   —   never to despise
the homosexual who goes building another
with touch   with touch   (not to despise any touch)
each like himself, like herself each.
You are this.   15
                                  In the body's ghetto
never to go despising the asshole
nor the useful shit that is our clean clue
to what we need.   Never to despise
the clitoris in her least speech.   20

Never to despise in myself what I have been taught
to despise.   Nor to despise the other.
Not to despise the *it*.   To make this relation
with the it :   to know that I am it.

                                        —1973

Flying to Hanoi[2]

I thought I was going to the poets, but I am going to the children.
I thought I was going to the children, but I am going to the women.
I thought I was going to the women, but I am going to the fighters.
I thought I was going to the fighters, but I am going to the men and women
    who are inventing peace.
I thought I was going to the inventors of peace, but I am going to the
    poets.   5
My life is flying to your life.

                                        —1973

Not to Be Printed, Not to Be Said, Not to Be Thought

I'd rather be Muriel
than be dead and be Ariel.[3]

                                      —1976

---

[2] Hanoi was the capital of North Vietnam during the U.S.-Vietnam War (1955-1975). The U.S. sided with South Vietnam.

[3] A magical sprite in Shakespeare's *The Tempest;* also the title of Sylvia Plath's posthumous volume of poems.

JULIA DE BURGOS (1914-1953)

Julia de Burgos was born in Carolina, Puerto Rico. Though she grew up in poverty, the oldest of thirteen children, she graduated from the University of Puerto Rico at the age of nineteen with a certificate in teaching. While teaching in her twenties, she also began publishing her poetry. Her first volume of poetry, *Poemas exactos a mi mismo*, was printed privately in 1937. She promoted her next two volumes, *Poema en veinte surcos* (1938) and *Cancion de la verdad sencilla* (1939), by travelling the island giving book readings. In 1940, she moved to New York and then Cuba, where she stayed for two years writing for newspapers and studying literature and philosophy at the University of Havana, before finally settling in New York.

In 1946 de Burgos, an alchoholic, was diagnosed with cirrhosis of the liver, and her mental health declined after a series of disappointing love affairs. In the late 1940s she was hospitalized for treatment of both her alcoholism and her liver problems. She eventually died in 1953 of a pulmonary condition. Her body was returned to Puerto Rico for burial. Public praise for de Burgos and her work exploded immediately after her death, and several collections of her work have been published posthumously. Modern critics argue that de Burgos' poetry anticipated the work of feminist writers and poets as well as other Latin American artists. Her work grasps connections between history, the body, politics, love, self-negation, and feminism.

To Julia de Burgos

The people are already whispering that I am your enemy
because they say that in my verse I give you to the world.
They lie, Julia De Burgos. They lie, Julia De Burgos.
The one that rises in my verses is not your voice. It's my voice;
because you are the clothing and I am the essence   5
and the deepest abyss lies between the two of us.

You are the cold doll of social lie,
and I the virile spark of human truth.

You, honey of courtesan hypocrisies, not I;
because in all my poems I bare my heart.   10

You are like your world, selfish, not I;
Who gambles all to be what I am.

You are only the prim grand lady;
not I; I am the life, strength, the woman.

You belong to your husband, to your master; not I,   15
I belong to no one, or to all, because to all, to all
in my pure feeling and in my thought, I give myself.

You curl your hair and paint your face; not I;
the wind curls my hair; I'm painted by the sun.

You are lady of the home, resigned, submissive,   20
tied to the prejudices of men; not I:

for I am unbridled, runaway Rocinante[1]
sniffing at horizons for the justice of God.
You do not rule yourself, you are ruled by everyone;
you are ruled by your husband, your parents, your relatives,   25
the priest, the dressmaker, the theater, the casino,
the car, the jewels, the banquet, the champagne,
heaven and hell and the what will society say.

Not I, for I am only ruled by my heart,
only my thoughts; who rules in me is I.   30

You, flower of aristocracy, and I, the flower of the people.
You have everything in you and you owe it to all,
while I, my nothing owe to no one.

You, nailed to the ancestral dividend,
and I, a one in the cipher of the social divisor,   35
we are the duel to death that fatally approaches.

When the multitude in an uproar run
leaving behind the ashes from burned injustices,
and when with the torch of the seven virtues,
chasing the seven sins, the multitudes should run   40
against you, and against everything unfair and inhuman,
I shall go in their midst with the torch in my hand.

—1938

Canto to Martí[2]

With a voice barely begun,
barely gathered, barely made;
with a voice floating between horizons
of longed for liberty, without possessing it,
with a crying voice surrounded   5
by robust uniforms, and by stars;
with a voice that escapes through waves,
from a heavy weariness of chains;
with a wounded voice that drags
itself below the scream of America incomplete,   10
with a voice of anguish unheard
where the soul of my land wanders;
with a voice of exasperated soil,
I come to tell you, Saint, to awaken…

---

[1] The name of Don Quixote's horse in Miguel de Cervantes y Saavedra's novel *Don Quixote* (1605, 1615).
[2] José Martí (1853-1895), legendary Latin American intellectual. A journalist and leader of the Cuban independence movement at the end of the 19th century, Martí died in the Battle of Dos Rios during the third wave of independence wars to liberate Cuba from colonial Spain. Though Martí spent many years in the U.S. as an exile, his most famous essay, "Our America," nevertheless warns of the United States' imperialist ambitions against Latin America.

Awaken from the air of the blossom,   15
from the summit and the sun, and the grasses;
awaken from the lip who sings to you,
and the hymn of love that surrounds you;
awaken from the stirring kiss
and the loyal word that lifts you;   20
awaken on your feet over your marble,
and over all peace that sustains you;
awaken from the cult of martyrs,
and return again to your fight;
awaken from Cuba and go forward   25
to your minor island, Borinquen.[3]
The one that in your blood saw its blood run
when you sank your Spring in Dos Ríos;
that in your wounded voice saw itself wounded
the motherland that on your lips escaped them;   30
that in your arm, saw itself lose its arm,
and defenseless remained on the earth;
that in your heart stopped its impetus,
and was lost from the breast of your America;
that mourning and broken and solitary,   35
surrendered its death to another flag;
that exiling yourself, Saint, from men,
you also exiled your small island.
(Puerto Rico and Martí: thirst of Dos Ríos
the same tombstone houses them.)   40

And yet, you have not died, you only sleep;
the earth requested you like a flag;
the roots wanted to shield you,
and the roses called your path.
But you have not died, no, from your name   45
you preside over life, and sustain it;
your song was higher than the birds,
and your blood was deeper than the idea.
Here, to your name, with your Minor Antille
I tearfully knock at your door   50
on this day of mourning for your children,
on this day of death for my land.
More than one voice that arrives from another edge,
I am an open wound in your very flesh.
More than a weak sob that weeps you   55
I am a scream of blood that awaits you.

At your breast Martí, I knock among tears
in this hour of man and of war,
so you may arrive, at peace, awake,
over the greatest pain of America.   60

—?

[3] Colloquial term for Puerto Rico, which refers to the indigenous origins of the island's inhabitants.

The Voice of the Dead

In Spain

It was in a dawn in Madrid, where I started my passage
through this black earth of darkness and worms.
I remember that upon falling, a fury of blindfolds
snatched my eyes from my defeated eyelids.
Were they also erased, premature and fragile, 5
in the sinister mouth that opened to the countryside?
It was that same demon of the swollen wings
that split me; look at me, profound and fragmented.
It was the same one that humiliates the pupils of heaven;
who is nourished by crime and burned rice fields 10
who steals life and swallows cities;
it is loose—catch it; no more tombs, brothers.
My guitar! My eyes! My songs! My Spain!
Where are you? This blindfold! Assassins! Wicked!
If necessary, in worms I will rise to smile at 15
the infernal malediction of your dead, Oh Franco![4]

In China

Chiang Kai Shek![5] And my bones? And my face without eyes?
And my hands raised in hope and work?
And my feet without paths that once were wings?
And my prints, my blood, my fallen pieces? 20
Where are they? In what fury of carnations do they sleep?
In what sun do they fortify their wet rags?
What mystery is nourished by my profound absence?
A memory, a light, that one day I was human!
I am alone, empty, separate and absent; 25
confused, graveless, I am looking for my trail.
Wasn't there room on earth to bury the crime?
Not even a tomb, miserables, avaricious!
But no; it was a tomb way down in Madrid.
Why am I here without a tomb? Where am I? And my eyelids? 30
Why do I travel with a name flagging the air?
Chiang Kai Shek, in what language do the birds greet you?
It must be a mighty name yours; solemn,
and familiar, and mine; I remember you now, brother;
it wasn't in Spain, nor in a dawning, nor broken 35
how I entered death; it was in China, burned.
And right here, in China, without a sepulchre without bones

---

[4] Francisco Franco (1892-1975), dictator of Spain from 1939 until his death. In 1936, Franco participated in a failed *coup d'etat* against the democratically elected Popular Front government, which evolved into the Spanish Civil War. At the end of the war, Franco emerged as the leader of the victorious right-wing Nationalists. During WWII, Franco assisted the Nazis and fascist Italy, though Spain formally maintained a position of neutrality.

[5] Chiang Kai Shek (1887-1975), military and political leader of the national government of the Republic of China (ROC) from 1928 to 1975. During the Chinese Civil War (1927-1949), Chiang attempted to eradicate the Chinese communists, but ultimately failed, forcing his government to retreat to Taiwan, where he continued serving as the President of the Republic of China and Director-General of the Kuomintang (Nationalist Party) for the remainder of his life.

I will remain in your ranks, General, waiting;
and I offer you, certain, my voice of free dead,
to raise victory satisfied and avenged.   40

On the British Seas

My islands, at a distance, extinguishing in me,
under a sky of bombs and shattered terror.
Can death there be more human and more brief;
can it be clearer and deeper than in this hoarse puddle?
Running, without looking, swamped in blues;   45
between machine gun and wave, silenced in pieces,
not seeing one's ample blood rejuvenating paths;
not feeling one's eyes blanketed with weeping!
Solitude of war, rabid solitude,
located in this oceanic whirlpool   50
humiliated in a tragic sepulchre of currents;
finite and alone in so much bluish infinite!
Oh to not know how to die, keeping awake
when only a few wet bones are left of us!
Can death there be more human and more brief   55
on my English islands, beneath that false sky?

In the Russian Wheatfields

I was in the wheatfields, in the laughter of man,
in the happy factory, in the light of work;
the sun awoke me and the bud roused me,
and in my hands the day was a route of cantos.   60
At my side the stalk flowered daylights,
man reaped justice in his fields,
the truth breathed from the lung of the earth,
and in one sole path my steps were tightened.
I was the universe liberated, simple   65
that was then fearlessly crossing over Russia.
How I remember the soul song of the children,
and the white confidence of the lifted pain!
But one day my sight was populated by tombs;
my happiness became a cannon in my hands;   70
some monster was loose in the woods of man,
and only one phrase imposed itself; flatten it.
With so much open life rising through the furrows,
I preferred a sepulchre to a deal; to die tall;
break into pieces, wound oneself with all the paths,   75
but never bow to the thirst of barbarians.
I was in the wheatfields, in the laughter of man,
in the happy factory, in the light of work.
One day my sight was populated by tombs,
and I, tomb among them, am still planting.   80

In the German Ranks

Let me enter, brothers, through the great cemetery!
I was born, raised, to kill; my eyelids
never smiled with the desire of a child
not one surrendered star of my emotion was white.
Aurora of uniforms; youth of uniforms;   85
twilight of dark uniforms stained;
the vision fixed in fixed landscapes of vengeance;
the reason dead in gloomy macabre appetite.
Desolate, escaped from myself, lost
in a solitude bristling with fright...   90
Thus I fell, exhausted from nothing,
in the tragic death of who was never human.
Thus I fell, in the same machine gun
that forged my passion, oriented to the insane.
Deserter of the ranks that erased my name   95
in an epic leap I forgot my past.
Let me enter brothers, through the great cemetery!
Among the dead, I am the greatest, the most tragic;
Soldiers! Since I never had a world among the living
offer me a world among the dead!   100

The Universal Dead

And who am I? What do I look for at the edge of man?
Where did I fall? Wrapped in what ensign?
And that immense horizon of marching sepulchres?
All the dead want a passage in my steps!
You who are alive, stop your orgy of machine guns;   105
for an instant look at yourself in my face of fright;
I am the most gigantic of the dead who will never
close his eyes until I see you saved.

—1942

Farewell in Welfare Island

    It has to be from here,
right this instance,
my cry into the world.

    Life was somewhere forgotten
and sought refuge in depths of tears   5
       and sorrows
over this vast empire of solitude
       and darkness.

    Where is the voice of freedom,
freedom to laugh,   10
to move
without the heavy phantom of despair?

Where is the form of beauty
unshaken in its veil simple and pure?
Where is the warmth of heaven   15
pouring its dreams of love in broken spirits?

It has to be from here,
right this instance,
my cry into the world.
My cry that is no more mine,   20
but hers and his forever,
the comrades of my silence,
the phantoms of my grave.

It has to be from here,
forgotten but unshaken,   25
among comrades of silence
deep into Welfare Island
my farewell to the world.

> Goldwater Memorial Hospital
> Welfare Island—N.Y.C.
> February 1953

—1953

Poem for My Death

A wish

To die by myself, abandoned and alone,
upon the densest rock of a deserted island.
In that instant, a supreme longing for carnations,
and in the landscape, a tragic horizon of stone.

My eyes all full of sepulchers of stars,   5
and my passion, strewn, exhausted, dispersed.
My fingers like children, watching the cloud get lost
and my reasoning covered by immense altar cloths.

My pale wishes returning to the silence,
—even love, my brother, dissolved along my path.   10
My name untwisting, yellow upon the branches,
and my hands clenching as I yield to the grass.

To rise at the last, the integral minute,
and offer to yield to the fields limpid as a star,
and then to fold the leaf of my delicate flesh,   15
and descend without smile or witness to the stillness.

That no one should profane my death with sobs,
nor should I be forever covered with the innocent soil,
so that at the liberating moment I should be free
to dispose of the one and only freedom in the planet.   20

What a ferocious joy as my bones will begin
to seek small windows through the dark skin,
and I, giving myself, giving myself wild and freely
into the open air and alone, breaking my chains!

Who will be able to detain me with useless dreams   25
when my soul begins to fulfill its task,
of making from my dreams a fertile mass
for the fragile worm that at my door will rap?

Each time smaller my smallness subdued,
each instant much greater and simpler the giving;   30
perhaps my breast may tumble to start a rose bud,
perhaps my lips may go to nourish lilies.

How shall I be called when I am merely left
to be remembered on the rock of a deserted island?
A carnation interposed in the midst of the wind and my shadow,   35
child of mine and death, will call me poet!

—1954

RUTH STONE (1915-   )

Poet Ruth Perkins was born in Roanoke, Virginia, to Roger McDowell Perkins, a drummer, and Ruth Ferguson Perkins. The family moved to Indianapolis, where Perkins grew up amid a close extended family, including her paternal grandfather, a senator. An early marriage took her to Illinois, where she met her second husband, Walter Stone. She followed him to Vassar where he taught, and where she wrote her first book, *In an Iridescent Time* (1959). During a sabbatical, he took the family to England, where he committed suicide, leaving Stone with three daughters to support. While on a two-year Radcliffe fellowship, Stone wrote the poems for her second collection, *Topography and Other Poems* (1971). Other books followed, including *Cheap* (1975), *Second-Hand Coat* (1987), *Who Is the Widow's Muse* (1991), *Simplicity* (1995), *Ordinary Words* (1999), and *The Next Galaxy* (2002), for which she won the National Book Award and the Wallace Stevens Award. Stone combined a long teaching career with her writing—she taught at Indiana University at Bloomington, NYU, and UC Davis before taking a permanent position at SUNY Binghampton. In 2007 Stone was named Poet Laureate of Vermont, where she has resided since 1957.

Topography

Do I dare to think that I alone am
The sum total of every night hand searching in the
Pounding pounding over the universe of veins, sweat,
Dust in the sheets with noses that got in the way?

Yes, I remember the turning and holding,   5
The heavy geography; but map me again, Columbus.[1]

—1970

The Room

The room is the belly of the house.
It is pregnant with you.
It belches you out the door.
It sucks you in like a minnow.

You are a parasite in the room.   5
The room distorts with your ego.
It withholds itself from you.
It looks at you with criminal eyes.

Opinions insinuate from the baseboards.
The molding and ceiling are strange, erudite.   10
They see only the top of your head.
The floor, however, is continuously looking up your skirt.

The room keeps its weapons in a side pocket.
You should be hung in the closet, it says.
You should sweep up your hair, you are shedding.   15
You are spoiling my mattress.

Unable to hold your shape you dissolve in the room.
It fastens itself to your skin like a lamprey.
When you thrust yourself out the door,
it peels from your back and snaps like a rubber stocking.   20
It gathers itself in a corner and waits for you.

—1987

So Be It

Look, this string of words
is coming out of my mouth,
or was. Now it's coming
out of this pen whose ink
came from Chattanooga.   5
Something tells me
Chattanooga was a chief.
He came out of his mother's
body. He pushed down
the long tube that got   10
tighter and tighter until
he split it open and stuck
his head out into a cold

---

[1] Christopher Columbus (1451-1506), Italian explorer.

hollow. Holding his belly
by a bloody string he   15
screamed, "I am me,"
and became a cursive
mark on a notepad that
was a former tree taken
with other trees in the   20
midst of life and mutilated
beyond all remembrance
of the struggle from seed
to cambium; the slow
dying roots feeling for some   25
meaning in the eroded
soil; the stench of decay
sucked into the chitin
of scavengers, becoming
alien to xylem and phloem,   30
the vast vertical system
of reaching up. For there
is nothing that is nothing,
but always becoming
something; flinging itself;   35
leaping from level to level.

—1999

Words

Wallace Stevens[2] says,
"A poet looks at the world
as a man looks at a woman."[3]

I can never know what a man sees
when he looks at a woman.   5

That is a sealed universe.

On the outside of the bubble
everything is stretched to infinity.

Along the blacktop, trees are bearded as old men,
like rows of nodding gray-bearded mandarins.   10
Their secondhand beards were spun by female gypsy moths.

All mandarins are trapped in their images.

A poet looks at the world
as a woman looks at a man.

—1999

---

[2] Wallace Stevens (1879-1955), American poet.   [3] From "Adagia," in *Opus Posthumous* (1957).

MARGARET WALKER (1915–1998)

Margaret Walker was born in Birmingham, Alabama, one of four children of Sigismund Walker, a Methodist minister, and Marion Walker, a musicologist. Her talent was recognized by Langston Hughes, who recommended that Walker, who had been schooled in Mississippi, Alabama, and Louisiana, finish her education somewhere other than the South. She transferred to Northwestern University, where she received her B.A. in 1935. While living in Chicago, Walker was a member of the South-Side Writers' Group, along with Richard Wright; although their friendship ended over a misunderstanding in 1939, Walker wrote a biography of Wright which appeared in 1988. From 1936 to 1939, Walker worked for the Federal Writers' Project under the auspices of the Works Progress Administration, a Depression-era program to provide jobs, where she befriended Gwendolyn Brooks. Walker's M.A. project at the University of Iowa became the volume *For My People* (1942), for which she won the Yale Younger Poets Award, the first African-American writer to do so. Walker married Firnist James Alexander in 1943. The couple moved to Jackson, Mississippi, in 1949, after the birth of three of their four children. Walker taught at Jackson State College for thirty years, where she founded, in 1968, the Institute for the Study of History, Life, and Culture of Black People (now the Margaret Walker Alexander National Research Center). During the 1940s and 1950s Walker worked on a Civil War-era novel, which became her dissertation at the University of Iowa, where she received her Ph.D. in 1965. The novel *Jubilee* was published the following year. Based on her grandmother's memories of slavery and its aftermath, *Jubilee* was read by many critics as a Black response to *Gone With the Wind* and its nostalgic view of slavery. The novel won the Houghton Mifflin Literary Fellowship Award and was translated into seven languages. Walker published three more volumes of poetry in the 1970s and 1980s. The intergenerational *A Poetic Equation: Conversations between Nikki Giovanni and Margaret Walker* was published in 1974. Walker received numerous awards over the course of her career, including a Ford Fellowship (1953), a Fulbright Fellowship to Norway (1971), a National Endowment for the Humanities Fellowship (1972), the Lifetime Achievement Award of the College Language Association (1992), and six honorary degrees. She was inducted into the African American Literary Hall of Fame a month before she died.

For My People

For my people everywhere singing their slave songs
    repeatedly: their dirges and their ditties and their blues
    and jubilees, praying their prayers nightly to an
    unknown god, bending their knees humbly to an
    unseen power;   5

For my people lending their strength to the years, to the
    gone years and the now years and the maybe years,
    washing ironing cooking scrubbing sewing mending
    hoeing plowing digging planting pruning patching
    dragging along never gaining never reaping never   10
    knowing and never understanding;

For my playmates in the clay and dust and sand of Alabama
    backyards playing baptizing and preaching and doctor
    and jail and soldier and school and mama and cooking

and playhouse and concert and store and hair and Miss
    Choomby and company;   15

For the cramped bewildered years we went to school to learn
    to know the reasons why and the answers to and the
    people who and the places where and the days when, in
    memory of the bitter hours when we discovered we   20
    were black and poor and small and different and nobody
    cared and nobody wondered and nobody understood;

For the boys and girls who grew in spite of these things to
    be man and woman, to laugh and dance and sing and
    play and drink their wine and religion and success, to   25
    marry their playmates and bear children and then die
    of consumption and anemia and lynching;

For my people thronging 47th Street in Chicago and Lenox
    Avenue in New York and Rampart Street in New
    Orleans, lost disinherited dispossessed and happy   30
    people filling the cabarets and taverns and other
    people's pockets needing bread and shoes and milk and
    land and money and something—something all our own;

For my people walking blindly spreading joy, losing time
    being lazy, sleeping when hungry, shouting when   35
    burdened, drinking when hopeless, tied, and shackled
    and tangled among ourselves by the unseen creatures
    who tower over us omnisciently and laugh;

For my people blundering and groping and floundering in
    the dark of churches and schools and clubs and   40
    societies, associations and councils and committees and
    conventions, distressed and disturbed and deceived and
    devoured by money-hungry glory-craving leeches,
    preyed on by facile force of state and fad and novelty, by
    false prophet and holy believer;   45

For my people standing staring trying to fashion a better way
    from confusion, from hypocrisy and misunderstanding,
    trying to fashion a world that will hold all the people,
    all the faces, all the adams and eves and their countless
    generations;   50

Let a new earth rise. Let another world be born. Let a
    bloody peace be written in the sky. Let a second
    generation full of courage issue forth; let a people
    loving freedom come to growth. Let a beauty full of
    healing and a strength of final clenching be the pulsing   55
    in our spirits and our blood. Let the martial songs be
    written, let the dirges disappear. Let a race of men now
    rise and take control.

—1942

"JO ALLYN"

"Jo Allyn" is the pseudonym of an anonymous woman who contributed stories and poems to the lesbian monthly journal *The Ladder* in the 1950s. *The Ladder,* which ran from 1956 until 1972, was produced by the women's homophile organization Daughters of Bilitis. The Daughters of Bilitis, along with the gay male Mattachine Society, fought for the acceptance of lesbians and gay men at a time when homosexuality was considered an illness in need of a cure—as well as grounds for dismissal from U.S. government (and other) employment. *The Ladder* included political, psychological, and informational material; it also published original fiction and poetry, such as Jo Allyn's "The Eleventh Hour," which appeared in 1957.

The short stories in *The Ladder* bore a stylistic resemblance to the "pro-lesbian" pulp fiction that was popular in the 1950s and early 1960s. Pulp fiction, so named for the cheap pulp paper upon which it was printed, typically dealt with racy topics and was sold not in bookstores, but in bus stations and drugstores. Most lesbian pulp was pornographic, written by men for a straight male readership, but a "pro-lesbian" pulp strain also existed, written by women for women and depicting lesbians in a more positive light. These books represented a literary lifeline for lesbians otherwise isolated from a community. Lesbian pulp of this type was romantic, implicitly sexy, and middle-class—perhaps even ending with the female couple heading for "happily ever after." Or it might, in the tradition of Radclyffe Hall's blockbuster 1928 lesbian novel *The Well of Loneliness,* end in anguish, madness, or even death.

"The Eleventh Hour" is not pulp fiction in that it is shorter than novel length and did not appear as a paperback original. But a case can be made for its close relationship to pulp style, despite its appearance in a "serious" Daughters of Bilitis publication.

The Eleventh Hour

Hazel leaned against the wall and felt again for the letter in her pocket. The counter was clean and empty; there were only occasional customers this time of the afternoon in the little coffee shop. She brushed short, blonde hair back; it was hot and she was weary after the noon rush.

For the tenth time she pulled the letter from her uniform pocket and read it.

"Wednesday will be our first anniversary," it said, "You know I want you to be with me. Navy life isn't the best thing for marriage, not with me gone as much as I've been lately. But the ship will be tied up in San Diego for ten days and we can spend that time together if you'll come down. I know I haven't been a very good husband, Hazel, but give me this chance to make it up to you. Love, Jim."

Another chance….she sighed. How like Jim. Always wanting another chance to make up for the bad times, the loneliness, the indifference and neglect, the quarrels.

Heaven knew she had given him enough chances. She'd also stayed here in the little college town working, as he wanted her to, instead of following when the ship went to the East Coast last winter.

"Your family is here," he had argued when she suggested going with him. "Besides you've got a good job here. You might not find another one back there that pays as well."

Money meant a lot to Jim. Her wages kept the car payments up, among other things. Jim liked driving the late-model convertible he'd bought in New York, and he liked having plenty of "green stuff" to spend drinking with his sea-going buddies.

On the other hand, settling down to marriage didn't appear to mean so much.

There were problems of adjustment that, after a year of being too seldom together, still remained unsolved. And when they were together, his rough demands and careless neglect left her nervous and unhappy.

She sighed. Still, ten days vacation from the daily eight hours of catering to the crotchety hotel-coffee shop guests would be a relief. Maybe she could get rested up if Jim didn't insist on his usual nightly round of skid-row bars.

There was another reason she wanted to see him. Something had been bothering her lately. Perhaps if she was with him again, the growing friendship between herself and Patricia Blaine would fall into a reasonable, explainable perspective. Perhaps she should stay in San Diego, not see her any more.

It had begun the day her boss's daughter returned from Europe where she'd been bicycling across country on a youth-hostel tour. The big, pleasant looking girl with dark, closely cropped hair was enrolling in a post-graduate course at the college. She had enthusiastically detailed her plans to Hazel over a cup of coffee the first day she was back.

"It's wonderful having someone who is interested in these things to talk to," she said. "Most of the kids I know who graduated last year are gone, or," her brow wrinkled a little, "or married. The ones this year seem so darn young." She looked at Hazel's fair hair and level grey eyes with appreciation. "I hope you don't mind my taking up your time this way," she apologized belatedly.

"Not at all," Hazel reassured her quickly. "It gets pretty lonesome in here between two and five." Pat's loneliness was very appealing to Hazel, who certainly understood it much more than the other girl was aware. The older girl's brown eyes were sad and wistful and trusting, all mixed together with something else….the shy admiration and devotion that Hazel recognized. She knew that Pat's mother was dead and that her father was much too busy to bother about being a companion to his only child. Money spent on her education and in travel was his substitute for parental love. Hazel knew it wasn't enough, and wondered if Pat was aware that she, too, was searching for acceptance….for a niche in someone's heart…………

She wondered, too, what Pat would think if she told her of Tommy. Thomasina, the girl whose devotion had filled all the days of Hazel's young childhood. Tommy, the two years older tomboy whose quiet strength had protected Hazel from teasing boys and spiteful girls. Tommy, who was always her sympathetic confidant and helpful friend. And finally when they were in their teens, whose attachment had seemed naturally, of its own accord to ripen into and demand the fulfillment of love.

How strange that the very naturalness of their devotion had turned their parents' adjoining homes into armed enemy camps. Hazel still couldn't understand her mother's revulsion when she discovered her daughter had a "crush" on the older girl next door. But the memory of her mother's bitter denunciation of Tommy, and the angry words that ensued between the two families still had the power to tear agonizingly through Hazel's mind.

Later Tommy's family had moved away without allowing the girls even to say goodbye. The family pastor had come to pray with Hazel and her parents to exorcise the "wicked and evil" thing that had come into their lives. Perhaps it was that, more than anything else, that had fastened the horrible scars of shame and guilt across Hazel's heart so that never again could she think of love and tenderness without the dreadful remembered sensation of guilty fear.

If only both sets of parents had been less dramatic about it…had treated it as a normal crush, perhaps a reasonable adjustment could have been reached later by Hazel. But their super-dramatics only served to freeze her emotionally into the very pattern her parents feared.

And then again, if only they hadn't made such an issue of things when she met Jim some months later, things might have fallen naturally into a different pattern for her. She might have been able, if they'd let her alone, to respond to the attraction he felt for her, and have fallen in love with him. But, inevitably, as soon as her mother knew that Jim was interested, she began her openly obvious campaign to see that Hazel married him.

"Now is your chance to make something of yourself," her mother nagged. "You're just too young to realize what you and that horrible girl branded yourselves with, carrying on like you did," she sniffed in scorn. "If you get married to Jim, as any decent girl would, you'll be a respectable married woman and we can hold up our heads again…." The pressure only served to mix Hazel up. Still, anything would be preferable to her mother's hounding and watching her every minute.

To add to her grief, Tommy had never written since moving away. Eventually this apparent betrayal had weighted the scales in favor of Jim. It wasn't until after the wedding that her mother confessed contritely that a number of letters from Tommy had been burned "to save Hazel embarrassment." They came from another city.

Perhaps it wasn't Jim's fault that he brought none of the tender glory that Hazel had wistfully hoped for to their marriage. Nor that he couldn't understand and was impatient of her lack of response to his rough demands. But by the time he left for a new duty station two weeks after the wedding, Hazel already knew that the new relationship was empty of meaning for her.

Nor was it too odd that, left alone most of this first year, she should respond to the questioning look in Pat's brown eyes that were so very much like Tommy's.

It wasn't too long before Pat began coming downstairs at seven to walk home with Hazel after her work was done. Often she would invite the lonely girl in to have coffee or a glass of wine. Pat, raised since babyhood in the downtown hotel, appreciatively drank in the homey atmosphere of the little apartment.

Sometimes they went to movies together, and soon, without meaning to, Hazel realized they were spending almost every evening of the week together. There were times when Pat talked of her studies. She was majoring in psychology, and Hazel would listen wide-eyed to the amazing knowledge about interesting things that the older girl was acquiring. There were other times when Hazel told Pat haltingly of her life before her marriage to Jim, of the crowded small home across town, of the father who drank too much, and the mother who nagged. But she never mentioned Tommy.

One night she did admit to Pat that her marriage to Jim was not what she had dreamed it would be. Slowly, haltingly she recounted the reasons reluctantly, wanting to find excuses for Jim while she talked.

"I…I think I've tried," she finished humbly, puzzled at her own defensiveness, feeling disloyal to Jim. Yet she felt better for having confided in the sympathetic girl.

Pat's eyes were patient and understanding as she touched Hazel's arm. "I'm sure you have, my dear," she said. "I think you've made him a good wife, as far as he's allowed you to." She looked away to the rim of hills outside the window. "Better than he deserves," she muttered almost under her breath.

Lately Pat had seemed protective as well as sympathetic and Hazel had come to depend on seeing her every day. What fun it was to listen to her talk of her travels, or of the books she had read. Sometimes they would sit in silent companionship, listening to Pat's collection of classical records. With Pat, in her comfortable slacks and shirt, sitting across the room from her, Hazel felt an odd sense of completion. The big girl's eyes were so understanding, so eager and…and tender. Without realizing how it had come about, Hazel found herself wishing that Pat would stay in the little apartment with her always. And in her dreams, when something unknown frightened her, it was Pat who held her close and reassured her, not Jim.

Now that the letter had come, Hazel knew it would be hard to tell Pat she was leaving to be with him. What she wouldn't…couldn't tell her was that if Jim would agree, she would stay in San Diego, and find work there. It was the only way left to salvage their marriage, she knew that now. Only last night, saying goodnight at the apartment, she had sensed the trembling urgency struggling for release in Pat. And the answering response in her own blood had left her weak and filled with longing. Not by any word between them, but by something electric and unspoken.

Although it would hurt both of them, she knew she must go to Jim, severing the sweet companionship that was becoming increasingly dear to her. The association that was trembling on the threshold of something much, much deeper.

Pat was waiting in the hotel lobby, as usual, when she got off work at seven. Falling naturally into perfect stride as they walked towards the apartment, Hazel told the big girl of her plans to join Jim. She touched Pat's arm as she finished. "I'll write to you, and…and I want very much to hear from you, too."

Pat paused to light a cigarette, and Hazel noticed, dismayed, that her friend's hands were shaking. But when she spoke, her voice was level and flat, as if every emotion had been forcibly ejected from it.

"Of course, Hazel. But…but you won't be gone long?"

Hesitating over her words, she answered, "I…I don't know. M..m..maybe not."

Without speaking again, they resumed their walk, but, miserably, Hazel could feel the tight control that Pat was holding over herself. How could she hurt this wonderful girl who meant so much to her? But she had to. Her duty was to Jim, and he wanted her to join him. Maybe this time it really would be different. Maybe he'd made up his mind to make a success of their marriage after all. To love, honor and cherish her, as their wedding vows had said.

"Here we are," Pat broke into her reverie. "I'll see you up to your door, then I'll be on my way," she said crisply. "You've got your packing to do." But her eyes when they met Hazel's were lost and forsaken.

"Thank you, Pat," Hazel murmured, as they started up the stairs. "I'll…I'll phone you tomorrow before I leave."

But there was a yellow envelope slipped half-way under the locked door when they reached her apartment.

"Just a minute, Pat, don't go yet." Hazel touched her arm lightly and she stayed, her eyes watching warily as Hazel read the contents of the telegram.

It was from Jim, of course.

"RESTRICTED TO SHIP NEXT TEN DAYS. SORRY, TOO MUCH PARTY FIRST NIGHT IN PORT. BETTER NOT COME DOWN. SHIP LEAVES FOR HONOLULU TEN DAYS. SEE YOU IN ABOUT THREE

WEEKS. AS ALWAYS, JIM."

Yes, Jim, as always, at the eleventh hour had let her down. Still, sudden tremendous relief flooded her being. Now she could admit to herself how much she had dreaded seeing Jim, submitting to his temper tirades, his sly brutalities. And what was more, she could admit it at last to Pat, too.

Now she could voice what had been in her mind these past few months. She would tell Pat about Tommy and confess her need to find that lost tenderness again. She had tried marriage and failed…whether it was her own fault or Jim's she was not sure. Perhaps some day she would try again, the Fates would decide. Meanwhile, now, in the magic presence of this girl she had come to care so much for, one door had closed, and another was opening.

Hazel put her arm around Pat's waist and opened the door with her key.

"Come in, darling," she said softly. "I'm not going away after all…ever."

And her eyes told Pat that she was glad.

Then, as she put the coffee pot on the stove, she told the other girl her story, chattering with an abandonment of relief brought about by her new decision. And in her joy at being able at last to confide in her friend, she didn't notice that Pat said nothing in reply, only sat lighting a new cigarette on the embers of the old one. Finally through with her tale, Hazel came to stand in front of her and placed a timid hand on her shoulder.

"But you're not glad…about us…that…that I knew…" she stammered, puzzled and suddenly alarmed.

Pat turned her troubled face away from Hazel's searching look for a long moment, and then she sighed and straightened her back. Her eyes, when they rested on Hazel's, held a new determination.

"I'm glad that you know *why* your marriage was failing, Hazel. And…in a way that I can't explain…I'm glad, too, that there was a Tommy[1] in your life. But," she rose and gripped the smaller girl's shoulders, "There is something I want you to promise me."

"I…I promise…" Hazel stammered, unable to guess what was on Pat's mind.

"If you think that you care for me now, I want you to go to Jim. Stay with him, follow him, be near him and with him for at least six months. Talk to him, try to understand him and help him to understand you, Hazel. If all else fails, go to a marriage counselor. You're still young and you owe it to yourself to make your marriage work. Believe me, I know what I'm talking about."

Hazel's eyes fell and her shoulders drooped. Rejection was the last thing she had expected and she didn't know how to meet it.

Then Pat went on. "But remember this. If, after six months' trial…or even a year's trial, it doesn't work….I'll…I'll be waiting right here." She lifted Hazel's chin gently and gazed deeply into her eyes. "I'd wait forever for you, my dearest."

And Hazel knew she was speaking the truth.

—1957

---

[1] "Tommy" was late Victorian slang for a butch, or mannish lesbian. See, for instance, Willa Cather's story "Tommy, the Unsentimental" in this volume.

SHIRLEY JACKSON (1916-1965)

Born in San Francisco, California, Shirley Jackson was the daughter of Leslie (a successful lithographer) and Geraldine Jackson. She grew up in Burlingame, a well-to-do suburb of San Francisco, until her family relocated to Rochester, New York. Jackson began her literary endeavors as a child, writing journals and poetry. She briefly attended the University of Rochester, but left after one year, and in 1940 she received her B.A. from Syracuse University. That same year, she married Stanley Edgar Hyman, who became an important literary critic. The couple, who had four children, lived for a while in New York City, but ultimately settled in North Bennington, Vermont, when Hyman took a job at Bennington College. Mostly remembered now for her short story "The Lottery" (1948), which has become a staple in literary anthologies and high school curricula, Jackson was a very popular writer in her time. She authored several novels, including *The Haunting of Hill House* (1959), for which she won a National Book Award. Jackson's fiction is noted for its deft and chilling representations of the uglier sides of human nature; her stories and novels often revolve around greed, indifference, selfishness, and intolerance. She was also a comic writer of note, publishing autobiographical essays, later collected into the volume *Life Among the Savages* (1953), about the absurdities of family life (an early, but edgier, precursor to the likes of Erma Bombeck and Jean Kerr). Jackson died of heart failure at the age of forty-eight.

The Friends

Ellen Lansdowne had surely never considered herself a cruel, or an unkind, or a vicious woman. She still retained a tiny sense of sick shame at vaguely remembered schoolgirl injustices (that poor child, so long ago, the one who had that dreadful mother), and whenever possible Ellen Lansdowne made a clear and conscious effort to exhibit generosity and thoughtfulness. When there was literally no one who would volunteer to run the community concerts this year, or *someone* had to collect the articles for the white elephant sale, or the laundress's poor children were going to have an inadequate Christmas, dear Mrs. Lansdowne could always be counted on, cheerful and accommodating, sympathetic.

"I have so *much*," she told herself often. "I've been so *lucky*." The rich fur of her coat, she might remind herself with quiet happiness, the good health and intelligence of her two young sons, her pleasant home, the near probability of a glittering birthday present from Arthur...Ellen Lansdowne could point to a world of treasures to show that she had indeed been greatly favored by life.

Much more so, indeed, than most of her friends; certainly much more so than her dear friend Marjorie, with whom she had gone to school and to luncheons, to church to be married, and to concerts. Marjorie had always been weak, Ellen thought sometimes when she was counting her blessings; Marjorie never had quite enough of anything or the best of what she did have. It was a source of deep satisfaction to Ellen that dear Marjorie, too, had a fur coat—not quite so expensive a fur, certainly, as Ellen's—and an affectionate husband, and children—only little Joan, of course—and a nice home. Perhaps Arthur patronized the Actons a little, understandably, because Charles Acton *was* a bit on the pompous side and hadn't done nearly so well as he might, and Marjorie *did* whine a little about almost everything—well, Ellen would think, sighing, I have been *so* lucky. Arthur, and the boys, and everything I ever wanted. Poor

Marjorie, she thought constantly and unwillingly, poor, lovely Marjorie, always so much prettier than the rest of us, poor Marjorie. And from reflections like this Ellen Lansdowne would usually step briskly out to do some good deed—invite someone's aunt to lunch, perhaps, or volunteer to drive the high school cheering section to the basketball game.

Poor Marjorie, Ellen always thought, poor Marjorie—up to the night of the country club dance when, running upstairs to gather her fur jacket, she absentmindedly opened the door of the cloakroom and then, stunned, backed out into the hall again, her hands trembling and her mind saying over and over, "Why, that was Marjorie, Marjorie and John Forrest. *Marjorie.*" For a minute she stood, bewildered, her hand still shaking against the doorknob, and then she turned and ran back downstairs, thinking only of getting away. A few couples were still dancing, and Arthur came across the dance floor, looking surprised. "Thought you went to get your coat," he said. "Changed your mind?"

No, no, Ellen wanted to say, I just couldn't go in while Marjorie and John—while John and Marjorie—I could hardly just walk right in and say..."I stopped to talk to someone," she said, surprised at the quiet of her own voice. "I'll get it now."

This is silly, she thought, holding up her long dress as she went back up the stairs, making two trips to get my jacket—they should have more sense. The door of the cloakroom was open, and Marjorie, inside, was touching up her lipstick at the mirror. Ellen refused to meet Marjorie's eyes in the mirror, and hoped she was not reddening as she crossed the room quickly to the rack where her jacket hung. "Nearly everyone's leaving," she said, addressing her jacket.

"Did you see us?" Marjorie asked.

"Arthur's waiting for me," Ellen said, and fled. Of course I saw you, you crazy fool, she thought, of course. "Ready?" she said, smiling, to her husband: It must have been going on for a long time, she thought, remembering slight oddnesses of behavior, sudden glances, almost unnoticed disappearances at dances and parties; could anyone else know? Not *her* husband, surely; not mine. Not John's wife.

"Poor Ellen," he said. "You worked so hard arranging everything."

I would like, she thought with the great clarity of weariness, to arrange Marjorie Acton right out of this town. And then she thought, how perfectly *beastly* of her, how foul.

Half a dozen times, during the ride home and after Arthur had come back from taking the sitter home and while they were having a glass of milk companionably together in the cool kitchen and then when they were getting ready for bed, Ellen came close to saying, bluntly and without warning, "Dear, Marjorie and John Forrest—I only *knew*, tonight, but I think I've felt it for a long time—Marjorie and John Forrest—" Each time she deliberately stopped herself from speaking, thinking that she had to be loyal to Marjorie, that Marjorie was her friend, that there was no imaginable word she could bring herself to use to her husband that would describe what she thought about Marjorie.

She did not realize how clearly she knew all the truth of it until the next morning when she met Marjorie in the grocery, and, saying, "Good morning, Marjorie," and hearing Marjorie say, "Ellen, hello," she found herself strongly wanting not to remember, and then saw last night's speculative fear still in Marjorie's eyes.

"How are you this morning?" Marjorie asked, and the words had a special weight, as though they should be translated ("I suppose you told Arthur?") before they could be entirely understood.

"Very well. And you?" ("No, of course not; how could I tell anyone?")

"See you soon," Marjorie said as they separated.

It was, however, a day or two before the complete destructiveness of her knowledge came to Ellen. Here we were, she realized suddenly, sitting one morning at her kitchen table with the coffeepot and the morning paper waiting for her, here we were, a little group of friends, playing bridge, dancing, dining, swimming together, and then two among us fall out of step and introduce a new pattern, frightening and dreadful, into our well-filled lives. Good Lord, Ellen thought. I've known Marjorie for twenty-two years. Always so much prettier than the rest of us, we thought she'd do so well for herself, but *I* got Arthur. I *have* been lucky. Sitting peacefully at her kitchen table in the morning sunlight, she thought, without warning, but could I be wrong? Am I, perhaps, the only one who *hasn't* been in step; is everyone like Marjorie, like John, perhaps laughing at innocent Ellen: has Arthur…? "No, *no*," she said aloud, pushing violently at her coffee cup, "this business has me all upset."

Although she tried to avoid seeing Marjorie, and succeeded, she believed, in largely forgetting that there had been any noticeable break in the deepest foundations of all their lives, she found that she had become an unwilling observer; it was almost as though Marjorie and John, reconciled to her awareness, felt a kind of relief at having one person they need not trouble to deceive. There was an evening not more than a week after the country club dance when Ellen, turning to light a cigarette at a cocktail party, saw John Forrest rise and walk casually out onto the terrace; after a minute Marjorie, meeting Ellen's eyes and even smiling a little, went quietly and without other notice after him. "I enjoyed his first play much more," Ellen said easily without more than a second's pause in the conversation in which she had been engaged. "I think this one is somehow too—pretentious."

"And did you see—" someone went on, and Ellen was thinking, it's as though *I* were doing it; *I* feel guilty. They ought to be punished, she thought.

Then there was a moment when, sitting quietly across a bridge table from her husband, with Charles Acton on her left and Marjorie on her right, safe with her own home around her, Ellen turned politely to Charles, waiting for him to bid, and he said, arranging his cards, "You girls enjoy your lunch today?"

"Lunch?" Ellen said, comprehending almost at once, and angry; she had lunched alone and not agreeably on a bowl of vegetable soup at home. The king of hearts winked at her from her hand; irrepressibly she thought of some private little restaurant, where the waiter was quiet and unobtrusive and perhaps recognized them (the handsome young lovers, they came every week), and Marjorie speaking softly, leaning forward, and music, perhaps, in the background, and the conversation of romance, of undying devotion. "Of course," she said half to herself, and Marjorie at the same time cut in swiftly, speaking ostensibly to Arthur, "Ellen and I went out to lunch together in town today. As though we were a couple of debutantes."

"Two spades," Charles said.

"As though we had no responsibilities at all," Ellen said, looking at Marjorie.

"Good idea," Arthur said, nodding. "Ellen ought to get around more. Always doing something for other people," he told Charles, "all this planning bazaars, and concerts, and whatnot."

"Marjorie, too," Charles said vaguely. "I bid two spades."

"Ellen," Marjorie said with all appearance of sincerity, "you look *so* pretty tonight."

No, no, oh, no, Ellen thought, she can't payoff like that, and, almost without thinking of what she was saying, she said to her husband, "Marjorie has offered to take the boys this weekend so we can go skiing. I thought we might go back to that nice place by the lake."

"But I—" Marjorie began, and Ellen cut in smoothly, "I saw John Forrest for a minute today in the bank," she said to Arthur. "That's what made me think of skiing, actually—he was talking about it. And then when Marjorie offered to take the boys…" She smiled affectionately on Marjorie.

"Two no trump," Marjorie said, her voice sullen, and Charles glanced up reprovingly and said, "Not your turn to bid, dear."

Skiing at the lake was wonderful, and Ellen, who had at the last moment decided to borrow Marjorie's new scarlet snowsuit, had never enjoyed herself more; for two days she successfully forgot the precarious defense she and Marjorie held against catastrophe. Driving home from the lake, luxuriously tired and warm in her fur coat, she leaned her head back against the seat, thinking, I *have* been taking this too seriously, and asked, "Arthur, did you ever love anyone but me?"

"Millions of girls," he said obligingly. "Movie stars, and Oriental princesses, and beautiful international spies, and—"

"What would you do if I fell madly in love with some other man?"

"Make him pay for your birthday present," Arthur said without hesitation. "Why, have you got an offer?"

Ellen laughed happily, and fell asleep.

The boys welcomed them with enthusiasm, and Ellen, thanking Marjorie, found herself speaking and laughing with almost the old friendship. "It was *marvelous*," she said. "You've simply got to—"

"I want to hear all about it," Marjorie said, "at lunch tomorrow." And she glanced briefly past Ellen to Charles, and then back at Ellen again.

Ellen, holding on to a hand of each of her sons, turned toward the door at once and said flatly, "Of course, I'll see you tomorrow."

She was weak with anger and helplessness, seeing how this small fiction had been eased past her; she and Marjorie now lunched together regularly in town because dear Ellen needed more gadding about, and she recognized that her lonely lunch at home might give her more discomfort in deception and guilt than Marjorie's clandestine appointment. She is asking too much of loyalty, Ellen thought; she is charging right ahead and expecting to sweep me before her: she thinks I can be handled easily. "Marjorie," she said on the phone the next morning, "I've decided that you can manage the flower show this year. I've done it for three years and I'm tired of it."

"But I can't manage *anything*—you know I'm not any—"

"But of course you'll do it," Ellen said lightly. "Unless it interferes with your various social entanglements?"

"Ellen, look—"

"Shall we discuss it today at lunch?" Ellen said, and hung up. The flower show would be abominable under Marjorie's management, but then, she thought wryly, Marjorie managed *everything* so badly.

It was more difficult to persuade Marjorie to give up little Joan's dancing class in order to take Ellen's boys into town to a matinee, but Ellen, who disliked unpleasant words and avoided unpleasant scenes, found that by now she and Marjorie had developed a private language where comparatively harmless words substituted for the disagreeable ones the rest of the world was required to use: "Cloakroom," for instance, was a word of such threatening import to Marjorie that it might easily have meant "exposure" or "scandal," and even such a trivial phrase as "lunch in town" had come to mean something close to "liar" or "hypocrite." And yet, even though it was Marjorie whose world was endangered, it was Ellen who seemed to suffer for it; when Marjorie and John, driving together to the Golfers' Dinner at the club, arrived half an hour late, only Ellen came, worried, to meet them at the door. "Did you get lost?" she asked, "Don't tell me the two of you lost your way?"

"We had to stop for gas," John said easily, moving already toward their party in the dining room. "By the way," Ellen said to Marjorie, "I want you to take me to that auction tomorrow, over in East Sundale."

"But tomorrow—" Marjorie began, glancing after John.

"Are you busy tomorrow? Something you can't break?"

"No, of course not," Marjorie said, and turned to follow John, pulling away from Ellen's hand on her arm.

Ellen came up to the long table with them, saying loudly, "Well, here they are, everybody; made it at last."

She slid into her own place next to Charles Acton, and said, "Honestly, how they could get *lost* around *here*," and smiled down the table at Marjorie.

It was not always difficult for Ellen. "I'm going into town to the theater," she told Marjorie one morning over the phone. "With my *own* husband, of course. And I'd like to borrow the pearls Charles gave you last Christmas; will you run over with them later?" Or, lightly at the meat counter in the mornings, "Marjorie, I've such a headache today; suppose *you* could bake the cakes for the club luncheon?" And always, if Marjorie protested, or refused, or looked sulky, Ellen could say with affectionate solicitude, "Poor Marjorie, you *do* look worn out. I'm really tempted to speak to Charles about you—you're doing too much. I'm going to tell that husband of yours that he has to keep more of an eye on you." And, with a gentle laugh, "Why don't you just run over to the florist's for me this afternoon? The flowers for the school, you know. I've got so much else to do…unless *you're* too busy?"

It was finally with a kind of amusement that Ellen recognized Marjorie's decision to give up the humiliating affair. It's a shame, Ellen thought, regarding Marjorie amiably over a cup of tea, always the weakest way; poor Marjorie, she was always so much prettier than the rest of us. "You *do* look exhausted these days," Ellen said, setting down her cup.

Marjorie looked up at her, and then down again. She's afraid of me, Ellen thought, leaning back comfortably, and we've been friends for twenty-two years. They were in Marjorie's living room, alone together of an afternoon for an intimate cup of tea.

Unpleasantly, it occurred to Ellen that John Forrest must often have come here, secretly, afraid of the neighbors, and she made a little face of disgust and sat up, drawing away from the back and arms of the chair. "How beastly you are," she said, and it was the first time since she had known that she had mentioned, directly, her knowledge.

Marjorie looked up again, steadily this time. "I think you're jealous of me," she said.

"Good *Lord*." Ellen laughed, a little shocked laugh. "After all," she said with a gesture of distaste, "don't try to drag *me* down *with* you."

"That's what John says—he says you're only jealous." A little thrill of fury went up Ellen's back at the light, familiar naming of John. "I'd really rather not talk about it, I think," she said.

"There's just one thing you ought to know, though," Marjorie said. "There's not going to be any more. It's all through. Over with."

"Marjorie, my dear." Ellen got up and came across the room to sit down next to her friend. "I'm really glad; you've no idea how *worried* I've been."

"So I'll tell Charles myself," Marjorie said. "You needn't bother."

Ellen gasped. "Marjorie!" she said, almost crying. "Did you think I would tell *Charles? I?* Why, I'm your oldest friend and I—"

"How lucky I am," Marjorie said evenly, "that it was my oldest friend who found out and not," she went on, smiling at Ellen, "one of my enemies."

"Margie," Ellen said, her voice tender, "you *are* taking this hard. Look—put it this way. You got yourself caught up in a kind of romantic adolescent dream, and it just wasn't till you began to see it through my eyes that you realized that it wasn't a great rosy love at all, but just something kind of cheap and nasty. After all," she added, touching Marjorie's cheek gently with one finger, "we've always been pretty honest, you and I."

"More tea?" Marjorie asked. She moved away from Ellen and lifted the teapot.

"Thanks, no," Ellen said, and then, after a minute, "I must rush. Million things to do."

"Incidentally," Marjorie said, rising, "I won't be able to pick up your groceries for you this afternoon. I'll be busy."

The coward, Ellen thought, stamping homeward through the snow: *I* would have fought tooth and nail, and she laughed, walking by herself, at the thought of poor Marjorie scratching and biting. Oh, *poor* Marjorie, she thought, and John thinks I'm jealous.

It was like an entirely new kind of freedom, somehow, knowing that she need no longer watch Marjorie. The sun the next day was bright on the snow, and the thought of spring coming inevitably was exhilarating.

"John," she said, sitting in his banker's office looking up at him prettily, "I've done a *dreadful* thing," and then laughed without being able to help it at the panic that showed immediately in his eyes. "No, no," she said, laughing, "not *that* bad." The man's poor conscience, she thought; outside the broad window of the bank the snow seemed cleaner with the sun on it, and Ellen knew that people passing in the street might look in and see her, a pretty woman, talking and laughing with Mr. Forrest in his private office, her furs thrown back over her chair and her head bent charmingly forward to accept a light for her cigarette. "If you're going to jump at every word I say…" she said, and shook her head sadly. "All I've *really* done is overdraw my account."

He smiled, relieved. "New dress?" he asked.

"Hardly. I'm not as wicked as you *think* I am. No, it's some things I got for my boys—clothes, and a bicycle for Jimmie—and I just didn't realize how it mounted up, and then when I came to figure it out—" She stopped, and made a face. "The thing is, I don't dare tell Arthur," she said. "You know all wives keep *some* things from their husbands."

"How much does it come to?" John asked.

Ellen thought. "Not more than forty dollars, I'm *sure*. Probably even less than that. But say fifty to be sure."

"I see," said John.

"If you could…" She was embarrassed, but she went on bravely. "Well…sort of *cover* it for me, and I could get it to you the first of the month."

"Yes," John said without expression. "Of course."

"I don't usually ask men to lend me money," Ellen said, laughing, "but of course with *you* it's different. That is, I never mind borrowing from a banker."

"It's part of the business of a bank," John said, "lending money."

"Is it part of the business of a banker," she asked, almost flirtatiously, "to take his clients to lunch? I've been waiting for you to ask me."

He looked at her, perplexed, and she went on mockingly. "I wouldn't want to force you into it: perhaps you—"

"Not at all," John said, "I've been waiting for *you* to ask *me*."

They laughed together then, and she said, "But I want you to be sure to figure out the right interest on my loan. This is an honest business transaction."

"Of course," John said, still laughing.

"And," she went on, rising and taking up her gloves and her furs. "I'll surely get it to you on the first of the month. Or, at the very *latest*, the month after." Then, aware that she was a pretty woman and that her half smile made her look even prettier, she turned toward the door and waited for him to open it for her.

—1953

TOYO SUYEMOTO (1916-2003)

Toyo Suyemoto was born in Oroville, California, in 1916. Although her poems are not currently well known, she published some of the most interesting and suggestive poems of the period of Japanese-American internment. Suyemoto's poetic inclinations were influenced by her mother, a poet, and her father, an artist; she credits her mother with teaching her tanka and haiku forms. She uses not only these Japanese poetic forms, but also rhymed quatrains, sonnets, and rondeaus. By the age of seventeen, Suyemoto had already published poetry in local journals, newspapers, and Japanese-American publications. She received a B.A. in

English and Latin from the University of California, Berkeley, in 1937. Suyemoto was relocated and interned with her family in 1942, first to Tanforan Race Track in San Bruno, California, then to the Central Utah Relocation Center, known as "Topaz." There she published several poems in the camp publications *Trek* and *All Aboard.* Two poems, "Retrospect" and "Quince," were published in the *Yale Review* in 1946. Like many Nikkei (Japanese Americans), Suyemoto moved to the midwest after relocation, settling in Cincinnati. In the late 1950s, she participated in writing workshops at the University of Cincinnati led by poets Randall Jarrell and Karl Shapiro. Suyemoto's poetry alludes to images and cycles of nature, which obliquely suggest the challenges faced by Nikkei during relocation.

In Topaz

Can this hard earth break wide
    The stiff stillness of snow
And yield me promise that
    This is not always so?

Surely, the warmth of sun   5
    Can pierce the earth ice-bound,
Until grass comes to life
    Outwitting barren ground!

               —1943

Seagulls

The seagulls came out of nowhere
That morning to the camp, and air
Seemed brighter for their clean white wings,
As music wakes from quiet strings.

Their shrill cries called her to the door,   5
Where she stood still, as on a shore,
To watch them circle, dip and rise
Against the wide, unclouded skies.

Did they not know the desert land
Was alien, unwatered sand?   10
Oh, had they come to cleanse her sight
Of dust with their cool liquid flight?

Shielding her eyes against the sun,
She felt she must escape and run
Beyond the heavy barbed-wire fence,   15
Could wings be hers, strong and intense.

And then, as strings cease to vibrate
And silence palls, the noon seemed late.
The gulls vanished. She turned to go
Indoors, eyes blind, feet leaden-slow.

               —1943

Evacuees

The exiles cannot choose domain
Where hostile eyes forbid the way
And voices ask suspiciously
Whether they go or stay.

The whole wide earth has room enough,   5
And yet their land denies them space
To wander in, or even rest.
For them there is no place.

The wind reechoes taunts and jeers;
The sun withdraws; the atmosphere   10
Grows chill with apprehension yet.
Why should they merit fear?

War-refugees in their own country,
Where can they travel now and put
Aside their doubts; what barren stones   15
Shelter surviving root?

—1945

Retrospect

No other shall have heard,
    When these suns set,
The gentle guarded word
    You may forget.

No other shall have known   5
    How spring decays
Where hostile winds have blown,
    And that doubt stays.

But I remember yet
    Once heart was stirred   10
To song—until I let
    The sounds grow blurred.

And time—still fleet—delays
    While pulse and bone
Take count before the days   15
    Lock me in stone.

—1945

GWENDOLYN BROOKS (1917–2000)

Born in Topeka, Kansas, Gwendolyn Elizabeth Brooks was the daughter of Keziah Wims Brooks and David Anderson Brooks, a janitor. The family moved to Chicago before Brooks was two months old; Black life in the city would be the main subject of Brooks' future work. Brooks, who began publishing her work regularly while she was still in high school, graduated from Wilson Junior College in 1936. She married poet Henry Blakely in 1939, and they had two children. Brooks' first book, *A Street in Bronzeville* (1945), took its title from a Black section of Chicago named "Bronzeville" by the African-American newspaper *The Defender*.

In 1950, Brooks became the first African-American writer to win a Pulitzer Prize (for her second book, *Annie Allen*). Her novel *Maud Martha* was published in 1953, followed by another collection of poems in 1960, *The Bean Eaters*. In 1967, Brooks attended the Second Black Writers' Conference at Fisk University, which became a watershed moment in her work. Challenged and revitalized by the younger generation of writers she met there, Brooks embraced a more specifically nationalist vision for Black writers. She began working with Black children and young adults in poetry workshops and publishing her work with African-American presses. Among the books that followed were *In the Mecca* (1968), *Riot* (1969), *Beckonings* (1975), and an autobiography, *Report from Part I* (1972), along with many books of poems for children. Brooks was the most famous and influential Black writer of her generation: she was appointed Poet Laureate of the state of Illinois in 1968; she was the first Black woman elected to the National Institute of Arts and Letters (1976); she was the first Black woman to be named poetry consultant to the Library of Congress (1985); and she received more than seventy honorary doctorates.

Gay Chaps at the Bar

gay chaps at the bar

> ...and guys I knew in the States, young
> officers, return from the front crying and
> trembling. Gay chaps at the bar in Los
> Angeles, Chicago, New York...   5
> Lieutenant William Couch
> in the South Pacific

We knew how to order. Just the dash
Necessary. The length of gaiety in good taste.
Whether the raillery should be slightly iced   10
And given green, or served up hot and lush.
And we knew beautifully how to give to women
The summer spread, the tropics, of our love.
When to persist, or hold a hunger off.
Knew white speech. How to make a look an omen.   15
But nothing ever taught us to be islands.
And smart, athletic language for this hour
Was not in the curriculum. No stout
Lesson showed how to chat with death. We brought
No brass fortissimo, among our talents,   20
To holler down the lions in this air.

still do I keep my look, my identity...

Each body has its art, its precious prescribed
Pose, that even in passion's droll contortions, waltzes,
Or push of pain—or when a grief has stabbed,   25
Or hatred hacked—is its, and nothing else's.
Each body has its pose. No other stock
That is irrevocable, perpetual
And its to keep. In castle or in shack.
With rags or robes. Through good, nothing, or ill.   30
And even in death a body, like no other
On any hill or plain or crawling cot
Or gentle for the lilyless hasty pall
(Having twisted, gagged, and then sweet-ceased to bother),
Shows the old personal art, the look. Shows what   35
It showed at baseball. What it showed in school.

my dreams, my works, must wait till after hell

I hold my honey and I store my bread
In little jars and cabinets of my will.
I label clearly, and each latch and lid
I bid, Be firm till I return from hell.   40
I am very hungry. I am incomplete.
And none can tell when I may dine again.
No man can give me any word but Wait,
The puny light. I keep eyes pointed in;   45
Hoping that, when the devil days of my hurt
Drag out to their last dregs and I resume
On such legs as are left me, in such heart
As I can manage, remember to go home,
My taste will not have turned insensitive   50
To honey and bread old purity could love.

looking

You have no word for soldiers to enjoy
The feel of, as an apple, and to chew
With masculine satisfaction. Not "good-by!"   55
"Come back!" or "careful!" Look, and let him go.
"Good-by!" is brutal, and "come back!" the raw
Insistence of an idle desperation
Since could he favor he would favor now.
He will be "careful!" if he has permission.   60
Looking is better. At the dissolution
Grab greatly with the eye, crush in a steel
Of study—Even that is vain. Expression,
The touch or look or word, will little avail.
The brawniest will not beat back the storm   65
Nor the heaviest haul your little boy from harm.

piano after war

On a snug evening I shall watch her fingers,
Cleverly ringed, declining to clever pink,
Beg glory from the willing keys. Old hungers 70
Will break their coffins, rise to eat and thank.
And music, warily, like the golden rose
That sometimes after sunset warms the west,
Will warm that room, persuasively suffuse
That room and me, rejuvenate a past. 75
But suddenly, across my climbing fever
Of proud delight—a multiplying cry.
A cry of bitter dead men who will never
Attend a gentle maker of musical joy.
Then my thawed eye will go again to ice. 80
And stone will shove the softness from my face.

mentors

For I am rightful fellow of their band.
My best allegiances are to the dead.
I swear to keep the dead upon my mind, 85
Disdain for all time to be overglad.
Among spring flowers, under summer trees,
By chilling autumn waters, in the frosts
Of supercilious winter—all my days
I'll have as mentors those reproving ghosts. 90
And at that cry, at that remotest whisper,
I'll stop my casual business. Leave the banquet.
Or leave the ball—reluctant to unclasp her
Who may be fragrant as the flower she wears,
Make gallant bows and dim excuses, then quit 95
Light for the midnight that is mine and theirs.

the white troops had their orders but the Negroes looked like men

They had supposed their formula was fixed.
They had obeyed instructions to devise 100
A type of cold, a type of hooded gaze.
But when the Negroes came they were perplexed.
These Negroes looked like men. Besides, it taxed
Time and the temper to remember those
Congenital iniquities that cause 105
Disfavor of the darkness. Such as boxed
Their feelings properly, complete to tags—
A box for dark men and a box for Other—
Would often find the contents had been scrambled.
Or even switched. Who really gave two figs? 110
Neither the earth nor heaven ever trembled.
And there was nothing startling in the weather.

firstly inclined to take what it is told

Thee sacrosanct, Thee sweet, Thee crystalline,
With the full jewel wile of mighty light— 115
With the narcotic milk of peace for men
Who find Thy beautiful center and relate
Thy round command, Thy grand, Thy mystic good—
Thee like the classic quality of a star:
A little way from warmth, a little sad, 120
Delicately lovely to adore—
I had been brightly ready to believe.
For youth is a frail thing, not unafraid.
Firstly inclined to take what it is told.
Firstly inclined to lean. Greedy to give 125
Faith tidy and total. To a total God.
With billowing heartiness no whit withheld.

"God works in a mysterious way"

But often now the youthful eye cuts down its
Own dainty veiling. Or submits to winds. 130
And many an eye that all its age had drawn its
Beam from a Book endures the impudence
Of modern glare that never heard of tact
Or timeliness, or Mystery that shrouds
Immortal joy: it merely can direct 135
Chancing feet across dissembling clods.
Out from Thy shadows, from Thy pleasant meadows,
Quickly, in undiluted light. Be glad, whose
Mansions are bright, to right Thy children's air.
If Thou be more than hate or atmosphere 140
Step forth in splendor, mortify our wolves.
Or we assume a sovereignty ourselves.

love note
I: surely

Surely you stay my certain own, you stay 145
My you. All honest, lofty as a cloud.
Surely I could come now and find you high,
As mine as you ever were; should not be awed.
Surely your word would pop as insolent
As always: "Why, of course I love you, dear." 150
Your gaze, surely, ungauzed as I could want.
Your touches, that never were careful, what they were.
Surely—But I am very off from that.
From surely. From indeed. From the decent arrow
That was my clean naïveté and my faith. 155
This morning men deliver wounds and death.
They will deliver death and wounds tomorrow.
And I doubt all. You. Or a violet.

**love note
II: flags**

Still, it is dear defiance now to carry
Fair flags of you above my indignation,
Top, with a pretty glory and a merry
Softness, the scattered pound of my cold passion.
I pull you down my foxhole. Do you mind?
You burn in bits of saucy color then.
I let you flutter out against the pained
Volleys. Against my power crumpled and wan.
You, and the yellow pert exuberance
Of dandelion days, unmocking sun:
The blowing of clear wind in your gay hair;
Love changeful in you (like a music, or
Like a sweet mournfulness, or like a dance,
Or like the tender struggle of a fan).

the progress

And still we wear our uniforms, follow
The cracked cry of the bugles, comb and brush
Our pride and prejudice, doctor the sallow
Initial ardor, wish to keep it fresh.
Still we applaud the President's voice and face.
Still we remark on patriotism, sing,
Salute the flag, thrill heavily, rejoice
For death of men who too saluted, sang.
But inward grows a soberness, an awe,
A fear, a deepening hollow through the cold.
For even if we come out standing up
How shall we smile, congratulate: and how
Settle in chairs? Listen, listen. The step
Of iron feet again. And again wild.

—1945

the mother

Abortions will not let you forget.
You remember the children you got that you did not get,
The damp small pulps with a little or with no hair,
The singers and workers that never handled the air.
You will never neglect or beat
Them, or silence or buy with a sweet.
You will never wind up the sucking-thumb
Or scuttle off ghosts that come.
You will never leave them, controlling your luscious sigh,
Return for a snack of them, with gobbling mother-eye.
I have heard in the voices of the wind the voices of my dim killed children.

I have contracted. I have eased
My dim dears at the breasts they could never suck.
I have said, Sweets, if I sinned, if I seized
Your luck   15
And your lives from your unfinished reach,
If I stole your births and your names,
Your straight baby tears and your games,
Your stilted or lovely loves, your tumults, your marriages, aches, and
    your deaths,
If I poisoned the beginnings of your breaths,   20
Believe that even in my deliberateness I was not deliberate.
Though why should I whine,
Whine that the crime was other than mine?—
Since anyhow you are dead.
Or rather, or instead,   25
You were never made.
But that too, I am afraid,
Is faulty: oh, what shall I say, how is the truth to be said?
You were born, you had body, you died.
It is just that you never giggled or planned or cried.   30

Believe me, I loved you all.
Believe me, I knew you, though faintly, and I loved, I loved you
All.

—1945

A Bronzeville[1] Mother Loiters in Mississippi. Meanwhile, a Mississippi Mother Burns Bacon.

From the first it had been like a
Ballad. It had the beat inevitable. It had the blood.
A wildness cut up, and tied in little bunches,
Like the four-line stanzas of the ballads she had never quite
Understood—the ballads they had set her to, in school.   5

Herself: the milk-white maid, the "maid mild"
Of the ballad. Pursued
By the Dark Villain. Rescued by the Fine Prince.
The Happiness-Ever-After.
That was worth anything.   10
It was good to be a "maid mild."
That made the breath go fast.

Her bacon burned. She
Hastened to hide it in the step-on can, and
Drew more strips from the meat case. The eggs and sour-milk biscuits   15
Did well. She set out a jar
Of her new quince preserve.

---

[1] Name of a Black neighborhood in Chicago.

...But there was a something about the matter of the Dark Villain.
He should have been older, perhaps.
The hacking down of a villain was more fun to think about   20
When his menace possessed undisputed breadth, undisputed height,
And a harsh kind of vice.
And best of all, when his history was cluttered
With the bones of many eaten knights and princesses.

The fun was disturbed, then all but nullified   25
When the Dark Villain was a blackish child
Of fourteen, with eyes still too young to be dirty,
And a mouth too young to have lost every reminder
Of its infant softness.

That boy must have been surprised! For   30
These were grown-ups. Grown-ups were supposed to be wise.
And the Fine Prince—and that other—so tall, so broad, so
Grown! Perhaps the boy had never guessed
That the trouble with grown-ups was that under the magnificent
   shell of adulthood, just under,
Waited the baby full of tantrums.   35
It occurred to her that there may have been something
Ridiculous in the picture of the Fine Prince
Rushing (rich with the breadth and height and
Mature solidness whose lack, in the Dark Villain, was impressing her,
Confronting her more and more as this first day after the trial   40
And acquittal wore on) rushing
With his heavy companion to hack down (unhorsed)
That little foe.
So much had happened, she could not remember now what that foe
   had done
Against her, or if anything had been done.   45
The one thing in the world that she did know and knew
With terrifying clarity was that her composition
Had disintegrated. That, although the pattern prevailed,
The breaks were everywhere. That she could think
Of no thread capable of the necessary   50
Sew-work.

She made the babies sit in their places at the table.
Then, before calling Him, she hurried
To the mirror with her comb and lipstick. It was necessary
To be more beautiful than ever.   55
The beautiful wife.
For sometimes she fancied he looked at her as though
Measuring her. As if he considered, Had she been worth It?
Had *she* been worth the blood, the cramped cries, the little
   stuttering bravado,
The gradual dulling of those Negro eyes,   60
The sudden, overwhelming *little-boyness* in that barn?

Whatever she might feel or half-feel, the lipstick necessity was
   something apart. He must never conclude
That she had not been worth It.

He sat down, the Fine Prince, and
Began buttering a biscuit. He looked at his hands.   65
He twisted in his chair, he scratched his nose.
He glanced again, almost secretly, at his hands.
More papers were in from the North, he mumbled. More meddling
   headlines.
With their pepper-words, "bestiality," and "barbarism," and
"Shocking."   70
The half-sneers he had mastered for the trial worked across
His sweet and pretty face.

What he'd like to do, he explained, was kill them all.
The time lost. The unwanted fame.
Still, it had been fun to show those intruders   75
A thing or two. To show that snappy-eyed mother,
That sassy, Northern, brown-black—

Nothing could stop Mississippi.
He knew that. Big Fella
Knew that.   80
And, what was so good, Mississippi knew that.
Nothing and nothing could stop Mississippi.
They could send in their petitions, and scar
Their newspapers with bleeding headlines. Their governors
Could appeal to Washington…   85

"What I want," the older baby said, "is 'lasses on my jam."
Whereupon the younger baby
Picked up the molasses pitcher and threw
The molasses in his brother's face. Instantly
The Fine Prince leaned across the table and slapped   90
The small and smiling criminal.

She did not speak. When the Hand
Came down and away, and she could look at her child,
At her baby-child,
She could think only of blood.   95
Surely her baby's cheek
Had disappeared, and in its place, surely,
Hung a heaviness, a lengthening red, a red that had no end.
She shook her head. It was not true, of course.
It was not true at all. The   100
Child's face was as always, the
Color of the paste in her paste-jar.

She left the table, to the tune of the children's lamentations, which
   were shriller

Than ever. She
Looked out of a window. She said not a word. *That*   105
Was one of the new Somethings—
The fear,
Tying her as with iron.

Suddenly she felt his hands upon her. He had followed her
To the window. The children were whimpering now.   110
Such bits of tots. And she, their mother,
Could not protect them. She looked at her shoulders, still
Gripped in the claim of his hands. She tried, but could not resist the idea
That a red ooze was seeping, spreading darkly, thickly, slowly,
Over her white shoulders, her own shoulders,   115
And over all of Earth and Mars.

He whispered something to her, did the Fine Prince, something
About love, something about love and night and intention.
She heard no hoof-beat of the horse and saw no flash of the shining steel.

He pulled her face around to meet   120
His, and there it was, close close,
For the first time in all those days and nights.
His mouth, wet and red,
So very, very, very red,
Closed over hers.   125

Then a sickness heaved within her. The courtroom Coca-Cola,
The courtroom beer and hate and sweat and drone,
Pushed like a wall against her. She wanted to bear it.
But his mouth would not go away and neither would the
Decapitated exclamation points in that Other Woman's eyes.   130

She did not scream.
She stood there.
But a hatred for him burst into glorious flower,
And its perfume enclasped them—big,
Bigger than all magnolias.   135

The last bleak news of the ballad.
The rest of the rugged music.
The last quatrain.

—1960

The Last Quatrain of the Ballad of Emmett Till[2]

after the murder,
after the burial

---

[2] Emmett Till (1941-1955), Black teenager from Chicago who was brutally lynched in Mississippi after allegedly whistling at a white woman. Following a trial that gained international media attention, two white men were acquitted for the murder, to which they later confessed.

Emmet's mother is a pretty-faced thing;
   the tint of pulled taffy.
She sits in a red room,   5
   drinking black coffee.
She kisses her killed boy.
   And she is sorry.
Chaos in windy grays
   through a red prairie.

—1960

CARSON MCCULLERS (1917-1967)

Carson McCullers was born Lula Carson Smith in Columbus, Georgia. She seemed headed for a career as a concert pianist, but lost the money that was to pay her tuition at the prestigious Juilliard School of Music in New York City. She worked menial jobs and studied writing; her first published story, "Wunderkind" (1936), described a failed musical prodigy. Indeed, versions of herself appear in a number of her writings. She married Reeves McCullers in 1937. Their marriage was not a success, in part because both had homosexual affairs. They separated in 1940, divorced in 1941, then remarried in 1945 and remained so until Reeves' suicide in 1953. McCullers' career was foreshortened by ill health. She contracted rheumatic fever as a teenager, which possibly contributed to the crippling strokes that limited her mobility later in life. Her novel *The Heart Is a Lonely Hunter* (1940), her novella *The Ballad of the Sad Café* (1943), her collection of children's verses, *Sweet As a Pickle and Clean As a Pig* (1964), and a number of other writings were all produced during convalescences from severe illness. Populated with tortured, eccentric characters, her work has been described as "Southern Gothic," although nearly all of it was produced after she left the South. McCullers adapted several of her works into dramas. Two of these met with particular success: *The Member of the Wedding* won the New York Drama Critics' Circle Award for the best play of the season in 1950, and *The Heart is a Lonely Hunter* was made into a feature film in 1968.

Like That

Even if Sis is five years older than me and eighteen we used always to be closer and have more fun together than most sisters. It was about the same with us and our brother Dan, too. In the summer we'd all go swimming together. At nights in the wintertime maybe we'd sit around the fire in the living room and play three-handed bridge or Michigan, with everybody putting up a nickel or a dime to the winner. The three of us could have more fun by ourselves than any family I know. That's the way it always was before this.

Not that Sis was playing down to me, either. She's smart as she can be and has read more books than anybody I ever knew—even school teachers. But in High School she never did like to priss up flirty and ride around in cars with girls and pick up the boys and park at the drugstore and all that sort of thing. When she wasn't reading she'd just like to play around with me and Dan. She wasn't too grown up to fuss over a chocolate bar in the refrigerator or to stay awake most of Christmas Eve night either, say, with excitement. In some ways it was like I was heaps older than her. Even when Tuck started coming around last summer I'd sometimes have to tell her she shouldn't wear ankle socks because they might go down town or she ought to pluck out her eyebrows above her nose like the other girls do.

In one more year, next June, Tuck'll be graduated from college. He's a lanky boy with an eager look to his face. At college he's so smart he has a free scholarship. He started coming to see Sis the last summer before this one, riding in his family's car when he could get it, wearing crispy white linen suits. He came a lot last year but this summer he came even more often—before he left he was coming around for Sis every night. Tuck's O.K.

It began getting different between Sis and me a while back, I guess, although I didn't notice it at the time. It was only after a certain night this summer that I had the idea that things maybe were bound to end like they are now.

It was late when I woke up that night. When I opened my eyes I thought for a minute it must be about dawn and I was scared when I saw Sis wasn't on her side of the bed. But it was only the moonlight that shone cool looking and white outside the window and made the oak leaves hanging down over the front yard pitch black and separate seeming. It was around the first of September, but I didn't feel hot looking at the moonlight. I pulled the sheet over me and let my eyes roam around the black shapes of the furniture in our room.

I'd waked up lots of times in the night this summer. You see Sis and I have always had this room together and when she would come in and turn on the light to find her nightgown or something it woke me. I liked it. In the summer when school was out I didn't have to get up early in the morning. We would lie and talk sometimes for a good while. I'd like to hear about the places she and Tuck had been or to laugh over different things. Lots of times before that night she had talked to me privately about Tuck just like I was her age—asking me if I thought she should have said this or that when he called and giving me a hug, maybe, after. Sis was really crazy about Tuck. Once she said to me: "He's so lovely—I never in the world thought I'd know anyone like him—"

We would talk about our brother too. Dan's seventeen years old and was planning to take the co-op course at Tech in the fall. Dan had gotten older by this summer. One night he came in at four o'clock and he'd been drinking. Dad sure had it in for him the next week. So he hiked out to the country and camped with some boys for a few days. He used to talk to me and Sis about diesel motors and going away to South America and all that, but by this summer he was quiet and not saying much to anybody in the family. Dan's real tall and thin as a rail. He has bumps on his face now and is clumsy and not very good looking. At nights sometimes I know he wanders all around by himself, maybe going out beyond the city limits sign into the pine woods.

Thinking about such things I lay in bed wondering what time it was and when Sis would be in. That night after Sis and Dan had left I had gone down to the corner with some of the kids in the neighborhood to chunk rocks at the street light and try to kill a bat up there. At first I had the shivers and imagined it was a smallish bat like the kind in Dracula. When I saw it looked just like a moth I didn't care if they killed it or not. I was just sitting there on the curb drawing with a stick on the dusty street when Sis and Tuck rode by slowly in his car. She was sitting over very close to him. They weren't talking or smiling—just riding slowly down the street, sitting close, looking ahead. When they passed and I saw who it was I hollered to them. "Hey, Sis!" I yelled.

The car just went on slowly and nobody hollered back. I just stood there in the middle of the street feeling sort of silly with all the other kids standing around.

That hateful little old Bubber from down on the other block came up to me. "That your sister?" he asked.

I said yes.

"She sure was sitting up close to her beau," he said.

I was mad all over like I get sometimes. I hauled off and chunked all the rocks in my hand right at him. He's three years younger than me and it wasn't nice, but I couldn't stand him in the first place and he thought he was being so cute about Sis. He started holding his neck and bellering and I walked off and left them and went home and got ready to go to bed.

When I woke up I finally began to think of that too and old Bubber Davis was still in my mind when I heard the sound of a car coming up the block. Our room faces the street with only a short front yard between. You can see and hear everything from the sidewalk and the street. The car was creeping down in front of our walk and the light went slow and white along the walls of the room. It stopped on Sis's writing desk, showed up the books there plainly and half a pack of chewing gum. Then the room was dark and there was only the moonlight outside.

The door of the car didn't open but I could hear them talking. Him, that is. His voice was low and I couldn't catch any words but it was like he was explaining something over and over again. I never heard Sis say a word.

I was still awake when I heard the car door open. I heard her say, "Don't come out." And then the door slammed and there was the sound of her heels clopping up the walk, fast and light like she was running.

Mama met Sis in the hall outside our room. She had heard the front door close. She always listens out for Sis and Dan and never goes to sleep when they're still out. I sometimes wonder how she can just lie there in the dark for hours without going to sleep.

"It's one-thirty, Marian," she said. "You ought to get in before this."

Sis didn't say anything.

"Did you have a nice time?"

That's the way Mama is. I could imagine her standing there with her nightgown blowing out fat around her and her dead white legs and the blue veins showing, looking all messed up. Mama's nicer when she's dressed to go out.

"Yes, we had a grand time," Sis said. Her voice was funny—sort of like a piano in the gym at school, high and sharp on your ear. Funny.

Mama was asking more questions. Where did they go? Did they see anybody they knew? All that sort of stuff. That's the way she is.

"Goodnight," said Sis in that out of tune voice.

She opened the door of our room real quick and closed it. I started to let her know I was awake but changed my mind. Her breathing was quick and loud in the dark and she did not move at all. After a few minutes she felt in the closet for her nightgown and got in the bed. I could hear her crying.

"Did you and Tuck have a fuss?" I asked.

"No," she answered. Then she seemed to change her mind. "Yeah, it was a fuss."

There's one thing that gives me the creeps sure enough—and that's to hear somebody cry. "I wouldn't let it bother me. You'll be making up tomorrow."

The moon was coming in the window and I could see her moving her jaw from one side to the other and staring up at the ceiling. I watched her for a long time. The moonlight was cool looking and there was a wettish wind coming cool from the window. I moved over like I sometimes do to snug up with her, thinking maybe that would stop her from moving her jaw like that and crying.

She was trembling all over. When I got close to her she jumped like I'd pinched her and pushed me over quick and kicked my legs over. "Don't," she said. "Don't."

Maybe Sis had suddenly gone batty, I was thinking. She was crying in a slower and sharper way. I was a little scared and I got up to go to the bathroom a minute. While I was in there I looked out the window, down toward the corner where the street light is. I saw something then that I knew Sis would want to know about.

"You know what?" I asked when I was back in the bed. She was lying over close to the edge as she could get, stiff. She didn't answer.

"Tuck's car is parked down by the street light. Just drawn up to the curb. I could tell because of the box and the two tires on the back. I could see it from the bathroom window."

She didn't even move.

"He must be just sitting out there. What ails you and him?"

She didn't say anything at all.

"I couldn't see him but he's probably just sitting there in the car under the street light. Just sitting there."

It was like she didn't care or had known it all along. She was as far over the edge of the bed as she could get, her legs stretched out stiff and her hands holding tight to the edge and her face on one arm.

She used always to sleep all sprawled over on my side so I'd have to push at her when it was hot and sometimes turn on the light and draw the line down the middle and show her how she really was on my side. I wouldn't have to draw any line that night, I was thinking. I felt bad. I looked out at the moonlight a long time before I could get to sleep again.

The next day was Sunday and Mama and Dad went in the morning to church because it was the anniversary of the day my aunt died. Sis said she didn't feel well and stayed in bed. Dan was out and I was there by myself so naturally I went into our room where Sis was. Her face was white as the pillow and there were circles under her eyes. There was a muscle jumping on one side of her jaw like she was chewing. She hadn't combed her hair and it flopped over the pillow, glinty red and messy and pretty. She was reading with a book held up close to her face. Her eyes didn't move when I came in. I don't think they even moved across the page.

It was roasting hot that morning. The sun made everything blazing outside so that it hurt your eyes to look. Our room was so hot that you could almost touch the air with your finger. But Sis had the sheet pulled up clear to her shoulders.

"Is Tuck coming today?" I asked. I was trying to say something that would make her look more cheerful.

"Gosh! Can't a person have *any* peace in this house?"

She never did used to say mean things like that out of a clear sky. Mean things, maybe, but not grouchy ones.

"Sure," I said. "Nobody's going to notice you."

I sat down and pretended to read. When footsteps passed on the street Sis would hold onto the book tighter and I knew she was listening hard as she could. I can tell between footsteps easy. I can even tell without looking if the person who passes is colored or not. Colored people mostly make a slurry sound between the steps. When the steps would pass Sis would loosen the hold on the book and bite at her mouth. It was the same way with passing cars.

I felt sorry for Sis. I decided then and there that I never would let any fuss with any boy make me feel or look like that. But I wanted Sis and me to get back like we'd always been. Sunday mornings are bad enough without having any other trouble.

"We fuss lots less than most sisters do," I said. "And when we do it's all over quick, isn't it?"

She mumbled and kept staring at the same spot on the book.

"That's one good thing," I said.

She was moving her head slightly from side to side—over and over again, with her face not changing. "We never do have any real long fusses like Bubber Davis's two sisters have—"

"No." She answered like she wasn't thinking about what I'd said.

"Not one real one like that since I can remember."

In a minute she looked up the first time. "I remember one," she said suddenly.

"When?"

Her eyes looked green in the blackness under them and like they were nailing themselves into what they saw. "You had to stay in every afternoon for a week. It was a long time ago."

All of a sudden I remembered. I'd forgotten it for a long time. I hadn't wanted to remember. When she said that it came back to me all complete.

It was really a long time ago—when Sis was about thirteen. If I remember right I was mean and even more hardboiled than I am now. My aunt who I'd liked better than all my other aunts put together had had a dead baby and she had died. After the funeral Mama had told Sis and me about it. Always the things I've learned new and didn't like have made me mad—mad clean through and scared.

That wasn't what Sis was talking about, though. It was a few mornings after that when Sis started with what every big girl has each month, and of course I found out and was scared to death. Mama then explained to me about it and what she had to wear. I felt then like I'd felt about my aunt, only ten times worse. I felt different toward Sis, too, and was so mad I wanted to pitch into people and hit.

I never will forget it. Sis was standing in our room before the dresser mirror. When I remembered her face it was white like Sis's there on the pillow and with the circles under her eyes and the glinty hair to her shoulders—it was only younger.

I was sitting on the bed, biting hard at my knee. "It shows," I said. "It does too!"

She had on a sweater and a blue pleated skirt and she was so skinny all over that it did show a little.

"Anybody can tell. Right off the bat. Just to look at you anybody can tell."

Her face was white in the mirror and did not move.

"It looks terrible. I wouldn't ever ever be like that. It shows and everything."

She started crying then and told Mother and said she wasn't going back to school and such. She cried a long time. That's how ugly and hardboiled I used to be and am still sometimes. That's why I had to stay in the house every afternoon for a week a long time ago…

Tuck came by in his car that Sunday morning before dinner time. Sis got up and dressed in a hurry and didn't even put on any lipstick. She said they were going out to dinner. Nearly every Sunday all of us in the family stay together all day, so that was a little funny. They didn't get home until almost dark. The rest of us were sitting on the front porch drinking ice tea because of the heat when the car drove up again. After they got out of the car Dad, who had been in a very good mood all day, insisted Tuck stay for a glass of tea.

Tuck sat on the swing with Sis and he didn't lean back and his heels didn't rest on the floor—as though he was all ready to get up again. He kept changing the glass from one hand to the other and starting new conversations. He and Sis didn't look at each other except on the sly, and then it wasn't at all like they were crazy about each other. It was a funny look. Almost like they were afraid of something. Tuck left soon.

"Come sit by your Dad a minute, Puss," Dad said. Puss is a nickname he calls Sis when he feels in a specially good mood. He still likes to pet us.

She went and sat on the arm of his chair. She sat stiff like Tuck had, holding herself off a little so Dad's arm hardly went around her waist. Dad smoked his cigar and looked out on the front yard and the trees that were beginning to melt into the early dark.

"How's my big girl getting along these days?" Dad still likes to hug us up when he feels good and treat us, even Sis, like kids.

"O.K.," she said. She twisted a little bit like she wanted to get up and didn't know how to without hurting his feelings.

"You and Tuck have had a nice time together this summer, haven't you, Puss?"

"Yeah," she said. She had begun to see-saw her lower jaw again. I wanted to say something but couldn't think of anything.

Dad said: "He ought to be getting back to Tech about now, oughtn't he? When's he leaving?"

"Less than a week," she said. She got up so quick that she knocked Dad's cigar out of his fingers. She didn't even pick it up but flounced on through the front door. I could hear her half running to our room and the sound the door made when she shut it. I knew she was going to cry.

It was hotter than ever. The lawn was beginning to grow dark and the locusts were droning out so shrill and steady that you wouldn't notice them unless you thought to. The sky was bluish grey and the trees in the vacant lot across the street were dark. I kept on sitting on the front porch with Mama and Papa and hearing their low talk without listening to the words. I wanted to go in our room with Sis but I was afraid to. I wanted to ask her what was really the matter. Was hers and Tuck's fuss so bad as that or was it that she was so crazy about him that she was sad because he was leaving? For a minute I didn't think it was either one of those things. I wanted to know but I was scared to ask. I just sat there with the grown people. I never have been so lonesome as I was that night. If ever I think about being sad I just remember how it was then—sitting there looking at the long bluish shadows across the lawn and feeling like I was the only child left in the family and that Sis and Dan were dead or gone for good.

It's October now and the sun shines bright and a little cool and the sky is the color of my turquoise ring. Dan's gone to Tech. So has Tuck gone. It's not at all like it was last fall, though. I come in from High School (I go there now) and Sis maybe is just sitting by the window reading or writing to Tuck or just looking out. Sis is thinner and sometimes to me she looks in the face like a grown person. Or like, in a way, something has suddenly hurt her hard. We don't do any of the things we used to. It's good weather for fudge or for doing so many things. But no she just sits around or goes for long walks in the chilly late afternoon by herself. Sometimes she'll smile in a way that really gripes—like I was such a kid and all. Sometimes I want to cry or to hit her.

But I'm hardboiled as the next person. I can get along by myself if Sis or anybody else wants to. I'm glad I'm thirteen and still wear socks and can do what I please. I don't want to be any older if I'd get like Sis has. But I wouldn't. I wouldn't like any boy in the world as much as she does Tuck. I'd never let any boy or any thing make me act like she does. I'm not going to waste my time and try to make Sis be like she used to be. I get lonesome—sure—but I don't care. I know there's no way I can make myself stay thirteen all my life, but I know I'd never let anything really change me at all—no matter what it is.

I skate and ride my bike and go to the school football games every Friday. But when one afternoon the kids all got quiet in the gym basement and then started telling certain things—about being married and all—I got up quick so I wouldn't hear and went up and played basketball. And when some of the kids said they were going to start wearing lipstick and stockings I said I wouldn't for a hundred dollars.

You see I'd never be like Sis is now. I wouldn't. Anybody could know that if they knew me. I just wouldn't, that's all. I don't want to grow up—if it's like that.

—1971

MONICA ITOI SONE (1919-)

Monica Sone, born Kazuko Monica Itoi, grew up in Seattle, Washington. Following internment, Sone graduated from Hanover College in Hanover, Indiana. In 1949, she received a master's degree in Clinical Psychology from Case Western Reserve University in Cleveland, Ohio. Sone's autobiography, *Nisei Daughter* (1953), depicts the experience of Japanese-American relocation and internment from the perspective of a child. The book opens with an account of Sone's childhood in Seattle's Japanese-American community, where her parents operated a hotel. Sone then describes the suspicion directed against Japanese Americans after the bombing of Pearl Harbor, her family's internment in Topaz, Idaho, and her resettlement after internment. Critics have commented on the incongruity of tonal lightness and serious subject matter in *Nisei Daughter*. This lightness may be explained in part by the reluctance to alienate a postwar, mainstream American audience who were used to thinking of "Japs" as wartime enemies. Indeed, reviewers praised the book for its humor and lack of bitterness. *Nisei Daughter*, which was reprinted in 1979, is often used in Asian-American Studies classes; both its content and its critical reception provide insights into Asian-American and American cultural history.

from Nisei Daughter

Chapter VIII
Pearl Harbor Echoes in Seattle

On a peaceful Sunday morning, December 7, 1941, Henry, Sumi and I were at choir rehearsal singing ourselves hoarse in preparation for the annual Christmas recital of Handel's "Messiah." Suddenly Chuck Mizuno, a young University of Washington student, burst into the chapel, gasping as if he had sprinted all the way up the stairs.

"Listen, everybody!" he shouted. "Japan just bombed Pearl Harbor...in Hawaii! It's war!"

The terrible words hit like a blockbuster, paralyzing us. Then we smiled feebly at each other, hoping this was one of Chuck's practical jokes. Miss Hara, our music director, rapped her baton impatiently on the music stand and chided him, "Now Chuck, fun's fun, but we have work to do. Please take your place. You're already half an hour late."

But Chuck strode vehemently back to the door, "I mean it, folks, honest! I just heard the news over my car radio. Reporters are talking a blue streak. Come on down and hear it for yourselves."

With that, Chuck swept out of the room, a swirl of young men following in his wake. Henry was one of them. The rest of us stayed, rooted to our places like a row of marionettes. I felt as if a fist had smashed my pleasant little existence, breaking it into jigsaw puzzle pieces. An old wound opened up again, and I found myself shrinking inwardly from my Japanese blood, the blood of an enemy. I knew instinctively that the fact that I was an American by birthright was not going to help me escape the consequences of this unhappy war.

One girl mumbled over and over again, "It can't be, God, it can't be!" Someone else was saying, "What a spot to be in! Do you think we'll be considered Japanese or Americans?"

A boy replied quietly, "We'll be Japs, same as always. But our parents are enemy aliens now, you know."

A shocked silence followed. Henry came for Sumi and me. "Come on, let's go home," he said.

We ran trembling to our car. Usually Henry was a careful driver, but that morning he bore down savagely on the accelerator. Boiling angry, he shot us up Twelfth Avenue, rammed through the busy Jackson Street intersection, and rocketed up the Beacon Hill bridge. We swung violently around to the left of the Marine Hospital and swooped to the top of the hill. Then Henry slammed on the brakes and we rushed helter-skelter up to the house to get to the radio. Asthma skidded away from under our trampling feet.

Mother was sitting limp in the huge armchair as if she had collapsed there, listening dazedly to the turbulent radio. Her face was frozen still, and the only words she could utter were, "*Komatta neh, komatta neh.* How dreadful, how dreadful."

Henry put his arms around her. She told him she first heard about the attack on Pearl Harbor when one of her friends phoned her and told her to turn on the radio.

We pressed close against the radio, listening stiffly to the staccato outbursts of an excited reporter: "The early morning sky of Honolulu was filled with the furious buzzing of Jap Zero planes for nearly three hours, raining death and destruction on the airfields below.… A warship anchored beyond the Harbor was sunk.…"

We were switched to the White House. The fierce clack of teletype machines and the babble of voices surging in and out from the background almost drowned out the speaker's terse announcements.

With every fiber of my being I resented this war. I felt as if I were on fire. "Mama, they should never have done it," I cried. "Why did they do it? Why? Why?"

Mother's face turned paper white. "What do you know about it? Right or wrong, the Japanese have been chafing with resentment for years. It was bound to happen, one time or another. You're young, Ka-chan, you know very little about the ways of nations. It's not as simple as you think, but this is hardly the time to be quarreling about it, is it?"

"No, it's too late, too late!" and I let the tears pour down my face.

Father rushed home from the hotel. He was deceptively calm as he joined us in the living room. Father was a born skeptic, and he believed nothing unless he could see, feel and smell it. He regarded all newspapers and radio news with deep suspicion. He shook his head doubtfully, "It must be propaganda. With the way things are going now between America and Japan, we should expect the most fantastic rumors, and this is one of the wildest I've heard yet." But we noticed that he was firmly glued to the radio. It seemed as if the regular Sunday programs, sounding off relentlessly hour after hour on schedule, were trying to blunt the catastrophe of the morning.

The telephone pealed nervously all day as people searched for comfort from each other. Chris called, and I told her how miserable and confused I felt about the war. Understanding as always, Chris said, "You know how I feel about you and your family, Kaz. Don't, for heaven's sake, feel the war is going to make any difference in our relationship. It's not your fault, nor mine! I wish to God it could have been prevented." Minnie called off her Sunday date with Henry. Her family was upset and they thought she should stay close to home instead of wandering downtown.

Late that night Father got a shortwave broadcast from Japan. Static sputtered, then we caught a faint voice, speaking rapidly in Japanese. Father sat unmoving as a rock, his head cocked. The man was talking about the war between Japan and America. Father bit his lips and Mother whispered to him anxiously, "It's true then, isn't it, Papa? It's true?"

Father was muttering to himself, "So they really did it!" Now having heard the news in their native tongue, the war had become a reality to Father and Mother.

"I suppose from now on, we'll hear about nothing but the humiliating defeats of Japan in the papers here," Mother said, resignedly.

Henry and I glared indignantly at Mother, then Henry shrugged his shoulders and decided to say nothing. Discussion of politics, especially Japan versus America, had become taboo in our family for it sent tempers skyrocketing. Henry and I used to criticize Japan's aggressions in China and Manchuria while Father and Mother condemned Great Britain and America's superior attitude toward Asiatics and their interference with Japan's economic growth. During these arguments, we had eyed each other like strangers, parents against children. They left us with a hollow feeling at the pit of the stomach.

Just then the shrill peel of the telephone cut off the possibility of a family argument.

When I answered, a young girl's voice fluttered through breathily, "Hello, this is Taeko Tanabe. Is my mother there?"

"No, she isn't, Taeko."

"Thank you," and Taeko hung up before I could say another word. Her voice sounded strange. Mrs. Tanabe was one of Mother's poet friends. Taeko called three more times, and each time before I could ask her if anything was wrong, she quickly hung up. The next day we learned that Taeko was trying desperately to locate her mother because FBI agents had swept into their home and arrested Mr. Tanabe, a newspaper editor. The FBI had permitted Taeko to try to locate her mother before they took Mr. Tanabe away while they searched the house for contraband and subversive material, but she was not to let anyone else know what was happening.

Next morning the newspapers fairly exploded in our faces with stories about the Japanese raids on the chain of Pacific islands. We were shocked to read Attorney General Biddle's announcement that 736 Japanese had been picked up in the United States and Hawaii. Then Mrs. Tanabe called Mother about her husband's arrest, and she said at least a hundred others had been taken from our community. Messrs. Okayama, Higashi, Sughira, Mori, Okada—we knew them all.

"But why were they arrested, Papa? They weren't spies, were they?"

Father replied almost curtly, "Of course not! They were probably taken for questioning."

The pressure of war moved in on our little community. The Chinese consul announced that all the Chinese would carry identification cards and wear "China" badges to distinguish them from the Japanese. Then I really felt left standing out in the cold. The government ordered the bank funds of all Japanese nationals frozen. Father could no longer handle financial transactions through his bank accounts, but Henry, fortunately, was of legal age so that business could be negotiated in his name.

In the afternoon President Roosevelt's formal declaration of war against Japan was broadcast throughout the nation. In grave, measured words, he described the attack on Pearl Harbor as shameful, infamous. I writhed involuntarily. I could no more have escaped the stab of self-consciousness than I could have changed my Oriental features.

Monday night a complete blackout was ordered against a possible Japanese air raid on the Puget Sound area. Mother assembled black cloths to cover the windows and set up candles in every room. All radio stations were silenced from seven in the evening till morning, but we gathered around the dead radio anyway, out of sheer habit. We whiled away the evening reading instructions in the newspapers on how to put out incendiary bombs and learning about the best hiding places during bombardments. When the city pulled its switches at blackout hour and plunged us into an ominous dark silence, we went to bed shivering and wondering what tomorrow would bring. All of a sudden there was a wild screech of brakes, followed by the resounding crash of metal slamming into metal. We rushed out on the balcony. In the street below we saw dim shapes of cars piled grotesquely on top of each other, their soft blue headlights staring helplessly up into the sky. Angry men's voices floated up to the house. The men were wearing uniforms and their metal buttons gleamed in the blue lights. Apparently two police cars had collided in the blackout.

Clutching at our bathrobes we lingered there. The damp winter night hung heavy and inert like a wet black veil, and at the bottom of Beacon Hill, we could barely make out the undulating length of Rainier Valley, lying quietly in the somber, brooding silence like a hunted python. A few pinpoints of light pricked the darkness here and there like winking bits of diamonds, betraying the uneasy vigil of a tense city.

It made me positively hivey the way the FBI agents continued their raids into Japanese homes and business places and marched the Issei men away into the old red brick immigration building, systematically and efficiently, as if they were stocking a cellarful of choice bottles of wine. At first we noted that the men arrested were those who had been prominent in community affairs, like Mr. Kato, many times president of the Seattle Japanese Chamber of Commerce, and Mr. Ohashi, the principal of our Japanese language school, or individuals whose business was directly connected with firms in Japan; but as time went on, it became less and less apparent why the others were included in these raids.

We wondered when Father's time would come. We expected momentarily to hear strange footsteps on the porch and the sudden demanding ring of the front doorbell. Our ears became attuned like the sensitive antennas of moths, translating every soft swish of passing cars into the arrival of the FBI squad.

Once when our doorbell rang after curfew hour, I completely lost my Oriental stoicism which I had believed would serve me well under the most trying circumstances. No friend of ours paid visits at night anymore, and I was sure that Father's hour had come. As if hypnotized, I walked woodenly to the door. A mass of black figures stood before me, filling the doorway. I let out a magnificent shriek. Then pandemonium broke loose. The solid rank fell apart into a dozen separate figures which stumbled and leaped pell-mell away from the porch. Watching the mad scramble, I thought I had routed the FBI agents with my cry of distress. Father, Mother, Henry and Sumi rushed out to support my wilting body. When Henry snapped on the porch light, one lone figure crept out from behind the front hedge. It was a newsboy who, standing at a safe distance, called in a quavering voice, "I...I came to collect for...for the *Times.*"

Shaking with laughter, Henry paid him and gave him an extra large tip for the terrible fright he and his bodyguards had suffered at the hands of the Japanese. As he hurried down the walk, boys of all shapes and sizes crawled out from behind trees and bushes and scurried after him.

We heard all kinds of stories about the FBI, most of them from Mr. Yorita, the grocer, who now took twice as long to make his deliveries. The war seemed to have brought out his personality. At least he talked more, and he glowed, in a sinister way. Before the war Mr. Yorita had been uncommunicative. He used to stagger silently through the back door with a huge sack of rice over his shoulders, dump it on the kitchen floor and silently flow out of the door as if he were bored and disgusted with food and the people who ate it. But now Mr. Yorita swaggered in, sent a gallon jug of soy sauce spinning into a corner, and launched into a comprehensive report of the latest rumors he had picked up on his route, all in chronological order. Mr. Yorita looked like an Oriental Dracula, with his triangular eyes and yellow-fanged teeth. He had a mournfully long sallow face and in his excitement his gold-rimmed glasses constantly slipped to the tip of his long nose. He would describe in detail how some man had been awakened in the dead of night, swiftly handcuffed, and dragged from out of his bed by a squad of brutal, tight-lipped men. Mr. Yorita bared his teeth menacingly in his most dramatic moments and we shrank from him instinctively. As he backed out of the kitchen door, he would shake his bony finger at us with a warning of dire things to come. When Mother said, "Yorita-san you must worry about getting a call from the

FBI, too," Mr. Yorita laughed modestly, pushing his glasses back up into place. "They wouldn't be interested in anyone as insignificant as myself!" he assured her.

But he was wrong. The following week a new delivery boy appeared at the back door with an airy explanation, "Yep, they got the old man, too, and don't ask me why! The way I see it, it's subversive to sell soy sauce now."

The Matsuis were visited, too. Shortly after Dick had gone to Japan, Mr. Matsui had died and Mrs. Matsui had sold her house. Now she and her daughter and youngest son lived in the back of their little dry goods store on Jackson Street. One day when Mrs. Matsui was busy with the family laundry, three men entered the shop, nearly ripping off the tiny bell hanging over the door. She hurried out, wiping sudsy, reddened hands on her apron. At best Mrs. Matsui's English was rudimentary, and when she became excited, it deteriorated into Japanese. She hovered on her toes, delighted to see new customers in her humble shop. "Yes, yes, something you want?"

"Where's Mr. Matsui?" a steely-eyed man snapped at her.

Startled, Mrs. Matsui jerked her thumb toward the rear of the store and said, "He not home."

"What? Oh, in there, eh? Come on!" The men tore the faded print curtain aside and rushed into the back room. "Don't see him. Must be hiding."

They jerked open bedroom doors, leaped into the tiny bathroom, flung windows open and peered down into the alley. Tiny birdlike Mrs. Matsui rushed around after them. "No, no! Whatsamalla, whatsamalla!"

"Where's your husband! Where is he?" one man demanded angrily, flinging clothes out of the closet.

"Why you mix 'em all up? He not home, not home." She clawed at the back of the burly men like an angry little sparrow, trying to stop the holocaust in her little home. One man brought his face down close to hers, shouting slowly and clearly, "WHERE IS YOUR HUSBAND? YOU SAID HE WAS IN HERE A MINUTE AGO!"

"Yes, yes, not here. *Mah, wakara nai hito da neh.* Such stupid men."

Mrs. Matsui dove under a table, dragged out a huge album and pointed at a large photograph. She jabbed her gnarled finger up toward the ceiling, saying, "Heben! Heben!"

The men gathered around and looked at a picture of Mr. Matsui's funeral. Mrs. Matsui and her two children were standing by a coffin, their eyes cast down, surrounded by all their friends, all of whom were looking down. The three men's lips formed an "Oh." One of them said, "We're sorry to have disturbed you. Thank you, Mrs. Matsui, and good-by." They departed quickly and quietly.

Having passed through this baptism, Mrs. Matsui became an expert on the FBI, and she stood by us, rallying and coaching us on how to deal with them. She said to Mother, "You must destroy everything and anything Japanese which may incriminate your husband. It doesn't matter what it is, if it's printed or made in Japan, destroy it because the FBI always carries off those items for evidence."

In fact all the women whose husbands had been spirited away said the same thing. Gradually we became uncomfortable with our Japanese books, magazines, wall scrolls and knickknacks. When Father's hotel friends, Messrs. Sakaguchi, Horiuchi, Nishibue and a few others vanished, and their wives called Mother weeping and warning her again about having too many Japanese objects around the house, we finally decided to get rid of some of ours. We knew it was impossible to destroy everything. The FBI would certainly think it strange if they found us sitting in a bare house, totally purged of things Japanese. But it was as if we could no longer stand the tension of waiting, and we just had to do something against the black day. We worked all night, feverishly combing through bookshelves, closets, drawers, and furtively creeping down to the basement furnace for the burning. I gathered together my well-worn Japanese language schoolbooks which I had been saving over a period of ten years with the thought that they might come in handy when I wanted to teach Japanese to my own children. I threw them into the fire and watched them flame and shrivel into black ashes. But when I came face to face with my Japanese doll which Grandmother Nagashima had sent me from Japan, I rebelled. It was a gorgeously costumed Miyazukai figure, typical of the lady in waiting who lived in the royal palace during the feudal era. The doll was gowned in an elegant purple silk kimono with the long, sweeping hemline of its period and sashed with rich-embroidered gold and silver brocade. With its black, shining coiffed head bent a little to one side, its delicate pink-tipped ivory hand holding a red lacquer message box, the doll had an appealing, almost human charm. I decided to ask Chris if she would keep it for me. Chris loved and appreciated beauty in every form and shape, and I knew that in her hands, the doll would be safe and enjoyed.

Henry pulled down from his bedroom wall the toy samurai sword he had brought from Japan and tossed it into the flames. Sumi's contributions to the furnace were books of fairy tales and magazines sent to her by her young cousins in Japan. We sorted out Japanese classic and popular music from a stack of records, shattered them over our knees and fed the pieces to the furnace. Father piled up his translated Japanese volumes of philosophy and religion and carted them reluctantly to the basement. Mother had the most to eliminate, with her scrapbooks of poems cut out from newspapers and magazines, and her private collection of old Japanese classic literature.

It was past midnight when we finally climbed upstairs to bed. Wearily we closed our eyes, filled with an indescribable sense of guilt for having destroyed the things we loved. This night of ravage was to haunt us for years. As I lay struggling to fall asleep, I realized that we hadn't freed ourselves at all from fear. We still lay stiff in our beds, waiting.

Mrs. Matsui kept assuring us that the FBI would get around to us yet. It was just a matter of time and the least Mother could do for Father was to pack a suitcase for him. She said that the men captured who hadn't been prepared had grown long beards, lived and slept in the same clothes for days before they were permitted visits from their families. So Mother dutifully packed a suitcase for Father with toilet articles, warm flannel pajamas, and extra clothes, and placed it in the front hall by the door. It was a personal affront, the way it stood there so frank and unabashedly. Henry and I said that it was practically a confession that Papa was a spy, "So please help yourself to him, Mr. FBI, and God speed you."

Mother was equally loud and firm, "No, don't anyone move it! No one thought that Mr. Kato or the others would be taken, but they're gone now. Why should we think Papa's going to be an exception."

Henry threw his hands up in the air and muttered about the odd ways of the Japanese.

Every day Mrs. Matsui called Mother to check Father in; then we caught the habit and started calling him at the hotel every hour on the hour until he finally exploded,

"Stop this nonsense! I don't know which is more nerve-wracking, being watched by the FBI or by my family!"

When Father returned home from work, a solicitous family eased him into his favorite armchair, arranged pillows behind his back, and brought the evening paper and slippers to him. Mother cooked Father's favorite dishes frenziedly, night after night. It all made Father very uneasy.

We had a family conference to discuss the possibility of Father and Mother's internment. Henry was in graduate school and I was beginning my second year at the university. We agreed to drop out should they be taken and we would manage the hotel during our parents' absence. Every week end Henry and I accompanied Father to the hotel and learned how to keep the hotel books, how to open the office safe, and what kind of linen, paper towels, and soap to order.

Then a new menace appeared on the scene. Cries began to sound up and down the coast that everyone of Japanese ancestry should be taken into custody. For years the professional guardians of the Golden West had wanted to rid their land of the Yellow Peril, and the war provided an opportunity for them to push their program through. As the chain of Pacific islands fell to the Japanese, patriots shrieked for protection from us. A Californian sounded the alarm: "The Japanese are dangerous and they must leave. Remember the destruction and the sabotage perpetrated at Pearl Harbor. Notice how they have infiltrated into the harbor towns and taken our best land."

He and his kind refused to be comforted by Edgar Hoover's[1] special report to the War Department stating that there had not been a single case of sabotage committed by a Japanese living in Hawaii or on the Mainland during the Pearl Harbor attack or after. I began to feel acutely uncomfortable for living on Beacon Hill. The Marine Hospital rose tall and handsome on our hill, and if I stood on the west shoulder of the Hill, I could not help but get an easily photographed view of the Puget Sound Harbor with its ships snuggled against the docks. And Boeing airfield, a few miles south of us, which had never bothered me before, suddenly seemed to have moved right up into my back yard, daring me to take just one spying glance at it.

In February, Executive Order No. 9066 came out, authorizing the War Department to remove the Japanese from such military areas as it saw fit, aliens and citizens alike. Even if a person had a fraction of Japanese blood in him, he must leave on demand.

A pall of gloom settled upon our home. We couldn't believe that the government meant that the Japanese-Americans must go, too. We had heard the clamoring of superpatriots who insisted loudly, "Throw the whole kaboodle out. A Jap's a Jap, no matter how you slice him. You can't make an American out of little Jap Junior just by handing him an American birth certificate." But we had dismissed these remarks as just hot blasts of air from an overheated patriot. We were quite sure that our rights as American citizens would not be violated, and we would not be marched out of our homes on the same basis as enemy aliens.

In anger, Henry and I read and reread the Executive Order. Henry crumpled the newspaper in his hand and threw it against the wall. "Doesn't my citizenship mean a single blessed thing to anyone? Why doesn't somebody make up my mind for me. First they want me in the army. Now they're going to slap an alien 4-C on me because of my ancestry. What the hell!"

---

[1] J. Edgar Hoover (1895-1972), director of the Federal Bureau of Investigation (FBI) from 1924 until his death.

Once more I felt like a despised, pathetic two-headed freak, a Japanese and an American, neither of which seemed to be doing me any good. The Nisei leaders in the community rose above their personal feelings and stated that they would co-operate and comply with the decision of the government as their sacrifice in keeping with the country's war effort, thus proving themselves loyal American citizens. I was too jealous of my recently acquired voting privilege to be gracious about giving in, and I felt most unco-operative. I noticed wryly that the feelings about the Japanese on the Hawaiian Islands were quite different from those on the West Coast. In Hawaii, a strategic military outpost, the Japanese were regarded as essential to the economy of the island and powerful economic forces fought against their removal. General Delos Emmons,[2] in command of Hawaii at the time, lent his authoritative voice to calm the fears of the people on the island and to prevent chaos and upheaval. General Emmons established martial law, but he did not consider evacuation essential for the security of the island.

On the West Coast, General J. L. DeWitt[3] of the Western Defense Command did not think martial law necessary, but he favored mass evacuation of the Japanese and Nisei. We suspected that pressures from economic and political interests who would profit from such a wholesale evacuation influenced this decision.

Events moved rapidly. General DeWitt marked off Western Washington, Oregon, and all of California, and the southern half of Arizona as Military Area No. I, hallowed ground from which we must remove ourselves as rapidly as possible. Unfortunately we could not simply vanish into thin air, and we had no place to go. We had no relatives in the east we could move in on. All our relatives were sitting with us in the forbidden area, themselves wondering where to go. The neighboring states in the line of exit for the Japanese protested violently at the prospect of any mass invasion. They said, very sensibly, that if the Coast didn't want the Japanese hanging around, they didn't either.

A few hardy families in the community liquidated their property, tied suitcases all around their cars, and sallied eastward. They were greeted by signs in front of store windows, "Open season for Japs!" and "We kill rats and Japs here." On state lines, highway troopers swarmed around the objectionable migrants and turned them back under governor's orders.

General DeWitt must have finally realized that if he insisted on voluntary mass evacuation, hundreds and thousands of us would have wandered back and forth, clogging the highways and pitching tents along the roadside, eating and sleeping in colossal disorder. He suddenly called a halt to voluntary movement, although most of the Japanese were not budging an inch. He issued a new order, stating that no Japanese could leave the city, under penalty of arrest. The command had hatched another plan, a better one. The army would move us out as only the army could do it, and march us in neat, orderly fashion into assembly centers. We would stay in these centers only until permanent camps were set up inland to isolate us.

The orders were simple:

---

[2] Delos Emmons (1888-1965), American Air Force general.

[3] John Lesesne DeWitt (1880-1962), American Army general who played a major role in both the enactment and implementation of Japanese internment during World War II.

Dispose of your homes and property. Wind up your business. Register the family. One seabag of bedding, two suitcases of clothing allowed per person. People in District #1 must report at 8th and Lane Street, 8 p.m. on April 28.

I wanted no part of this new order. I had read in the papers that the Japanese from the state of Washington would be taken to a camp in Puyallup, on the state fair-grounds. The article apologetically assured the public that the camp would be tempo-rary and that the Japanese would be removed from the fairgrounds and parking lots in time for the opening of the annual State Fair. It neglected to say where we might be at the time when those fine breeds of Holstein cattle and Yorkshire hogs would be proudly wearing their blue satin ribbons.

We were advised to pack warm, durable clothes. In my mind, I saw our permanent camp sprawled out somewhere deep in a snow-bound forest, an American Siberia. I saw myself plunging chest deep in the snow, hunting for small game to keep us alive. I decided that one of my suitcases was going to hold nothing but vitamins from A to Z. I thought of sewing fur-lined hoods and parkas for the family. I was certain this was going to be a case of sheer animal survival.

One evening Father told us that he would lose the management of the hotel unless he could find someone to operate it for the duration, someone intelligent and efficient enough to impress Bentley Agent and Company. Father said, "Sam, Poe, Peter, they all promised to stay on their jobs, but none of them can read or write well enough to manage the business. I've got to find a responsible party with experience in hotel man-agement, but where?"

Sumi asked, "What happens if we can't find anyone?"

"I lose my business and my livelihood. I'll be saying good-by to a lifetime of labor and all the hopes and plans I had for the family."

We sagged. Father looked at us thoughtfully, "I've never talked much about the hotel business to you children, mainly because so much of it has been an uphill climb of work and waiting for better times. Only recently I was able to clear up the loans I took out years ago to expand the business. I was sure that in the next five or ten years I would be getting returns on my long-range investments, and I would have been able to do a lot of things eventually…. Send you through medical school," Father nodded to Henry, "and let Kazu and Sumi study anything they liked." Father laughed a bit self-consciously as he looked at Mother, "And when all the children had gone off on their own, I had planned to take Mama on her first real vacation, to Europe as well as Japan."

We listened to Father wide-eyed and wistful. It had been a wonderful, wonderful dream.

Mother suddenly hit upon a brilliant idea. She said maybe the Olsens, our old friends who had once managed the Camden Apartments might be willing to run a hotel. The Olsens had sold the apartment and moved to Aberdeen. Mother thought that perhaps Marta's oldest brother, the bachelor of the family, might be available. If he refused, perhaps Marta and her husband might consider the offer. We rushed excit-edly to the telephone to make a long-distance call to the Olsens. After four wrong Olsens, we finally reached Marta.

"Marta? Is this Marta?"

"Yes, this is Marta."

I nearly dove into the mouthpiece, I was so glad to hear her voice. Marta remembered us well and we exchanged news about our families. Marta and her husband had bought a small chicken farm and were doing well. Marta said, "I come from the farm ven I vas young and I like it fine. I feel more like home here. How's everybody over there?"

I told her that we and all the rest of the Japanese were leaving Seattle soon under government order on account of the war. Marta gasped, "Everybody? You mean the Saitos, the Fujinos, Watanabes, and all the rest who were living at the Camden Apartments, too?"

"Yes, they and everyone else on the West Coast."

Bewildered, Marta asked where we were going, what we were going to do, would we ever return to Seattle, and what about Father's hotel. I told her about our business situation and that Father needed a hotel manager for the duration. Would she or any of her brothers be willing to accept such a job? There was a silence at the other end of the line and I said hastily, "This is a very sudden call, Marta. I'm sorry I had to surprise you like this, but we felt this was an emergency and..."

Marta was full of regrets. "Oh, I vish we could do someting to help you folks, but my husband and I can't leave the farm at all. We don't have anyone here to help. We do all the work ourselves. Magnus went to Alaska last year. He has a goot job up there, some kind of war work. My other two brothers have business in town and they have children so they can't help you much."

My heart sank like a broken elevator. When I said, "Oh..." I felt the family sitting behind me sink into a gloomy silence. Our last hope was gone. We finally said good-by, Marta distressed at not being able to help, and I apologizing for trying to hoist our problem on them.

The next week end Marta and Karl paid us a surprise visit. We had not seen them for nearly two years. Marta explained shyly, "It was such a nice day and we don't go novair for a long time, so I tole Karl, 'Let's take a bus into Seattle and visit the Itois.'"

We spent a delightful Sunday afternoon talking about old times. Mother served our guests her best green tea and, as we relaxed, the irritating presence of war vanished. When it was time for them to return home, Marta's sparkling blue eyes suddenly filled, "Karl and I, we feel so bad about the whole ting, the war and everyting, we joost had to come out to see you and say 'good-by.' God bless you. Maybe we vill see you again back home here. Anyvay, we pray for it."

Marta and Karl's warmth and sincerity restored a sense of peace into our home, an atmosphere which had disappeared ever since Pearl Harbor. They served to remind us that in spite of the bitterness war had brought into our lives, we were still bound to our home town. Bit by bit, I remembered our happy past, the fun we had growing up along the colorful brash waterfront, swimming through the white-laced waves of Puget Sound, and lolling luxuriously on the tender green carpet of grass around Lake Washington from where we could see the slick, blue-frosted shoulders of Mount Rainier. There was too much beauty surrounding us. Above all, we must keep friends like Marta and Karl, Christine, Sam, Peter and Joe, all sterling products of many years of associations. We could never turn our faces away and remain aloof forever from Seattle.

—1953

MAY SWENSON (1919-1989)

Born in Logan, Utah, poet May Swenson was the daughter of Swedish immigrants. She graduated from Utah State University in 1934, and worked for a time as a reporter for the *Deseret News* before moving to New York City. In 1959, Swenson became the editor for New Directions Press, but she stopped working in 1966 to devote herself to writing full time. Swenson published several books of poetry, beginning in 1954 with *Another Animal*. She also wrote a number of books of poems for children, in addition to translating the work of the Swedish poet Tomas Tranströmer. Swenson received many awards for her work, including Guggenheim, Ford, Rockefeller, and MacArthur fellowships; a National Endowment of the Arts grant; and prizes from Yale University, the Poetry Society of America, and the National Institute for Arts and Letters. She served as Chancellor of the Academy of American Poets from 1980 to 1989. Several volumes of her work were published posthumously.

The Centaur

The summer that I was ten—
Can it be there was only one
summer that I was ten? It must

have been a long one then—
each day I'd go out to choose   5
a fresh horse from my stable

which was a willow grove
down by the old canal.
I'd go on my two bare feet.

But when, with my brother's jackknife,   10
I had cut me a long limber horse
with a good thick knob for a head,

and peeled him slick and clean
except a few leaves for the tail,
and cinched my brother's belt   15

around his head for a rein,
I'd straddle and canter him fast
up the grass bank to the path,

trot along in the lovely dust
that talcumed over his hoofs,   20
hiding my toes, and turning

his feet to swift half-moons.
The willow knob with the strap
jouncing between my thighs

was the pommel and yet the poll   25
of my nickering pony's head.
My head and my neck were mine,

yet they were shaped like a horse.
My hair flopped to the side
like the mane of a horse in the wind.   30

My forelock swung in my eyes,
my neck arched and I snorted.
I shied and skittered and reared,

stopped and raised my knees,
pawed at the ground and quivered.   35
My teeth bared as we wheeled

and swished through the dust again.
I was the horse and the rider,
and the leather I slapped to his rump

spanked my own behind.   40
Doubled, my two hoofs beat
a gallop along the bank,

the wind twanged in my mane,
my mouth squared to the bit.
And yet I sat on my steed   45

quiet, negligent riding,
my toes standing the stirrups,
my thighs hugging his ribs.

At a walk we drew up to the porch.
I tethered him to a paling.   50
Dismounting, I smoothed my skirt

and entered the dusky hall.
My feet on the clean linoleum
left ghostly toes in the hall.

Where have you been? said my mother.   55
Been riding, I said from the sink,
and filled me a glass of water.

What's that in your pocket? she said.
Just my knife. It weighted my pocket
and stretched my dress awry.   60

Go tie back your hair, said my mother,
and *Why is your mouth all green?*
*Rob Roy, he pulled some clover
as we crossed the field,* I told her.

—1956

Women

Women   Or they
should be   should be
pedestals   little horses
moving   those wooden
pedestals   sweet   5
moving   oldfashioned
to the   painted
motions   rocking
of men   horses

the gladdest things in the toyroom   10

The   feelingly
pegs   and then
of their   unfeelingly
ears   To be
so familiar   joyfully   15
and dear   ridden
to the trusting   rockingly
fists   ridden until
To be chafed   the restored

egos dismount and the legs stride away   20

Immobile   willing
sweetlipped   to be set
sturdy   into motion
and smiling   Women
women   should be   25
should always   pedestals
be waiting   to men

—1968

ALICE CHILDRESS (1920-1994)

Alice Childress was born in Charleston, South Carolina. At the age of nine, after her parents separated, she moved to Harlem to live with her maternal grandmother, and was educated in New York City's public schools. Childress joined the American Negro Theater (ANT) in 1940. In addition to her work with ANT, which she did until 1952, Childress held a variety of jobs in order to make a living, including domestic worker, salesperson, insurance agent, and machinist apprentice. *Florence,* her first play, was produced at ANT in 1949, with Childress as director and principal actor. In 1950, ANT produced her play *Just a Little Simple,* based on *Simple Speaks His Mind* by Langston Hughes. These stories were also a model for her collection of vignettes *Like One of the Family...Conversations from a Domestic's Life* (1956). In 1952, Childress' *Gold through the Trees* was the first professionally-produced play by a Black woman in the United States. *Trouble in Mind,* her first play produced outside Harlem, won the OBIE

Award for Best Play in 1956, making Childress the first woman to win an OBIE for play-writing. Her other plays include *Wedding Band: A Love/Hate Story in Black and White* (1966), *Young Martin Luther King* (which was also produced as *The Freedom Play*) (1969), *String* (1969), *Wine in the Wilderness* (1969), *Mojo: A Black Love Story* (1970), *When the Rattlesnake Sounds* (1975), *Let's Hear It for the Queen* (1976), *Gullah* (1984, first produced as *Sea Island Song* in 1977), and *Moms: A Praise Play for a Black Comedienne* (1987). Childress also wrote four novels for young adults: *A Hero Ain't Nothin' but a Sandwich* (1973), for which she wrote the film screenplay in 1978; *A Short Walk* (1979); *Rainbow Jordan* (1981); and *Those Other People* (1989).

Like One of the Family

Hi Marge! I have had me one hectic day....Well, I had to take out my crystal ball and give Mrs. C...a thorough reading. She's the woman that I took over from Naomi after Naomi got married....Well, she's a pretty nice woman as they go and I have never had too much trouble with her, but from time to time she really gripes me with her ways.

When she has company, for example, she'll holler out to me from the living room to the kitchen: "Mildred dear! Be sure and eat *both* of those lamb chops for your lunch!" Now you know she wasn't doing a thing but tryin' to prove to the company how "good" and "kind" she was to the servant, because she had told me *already* to eat those chops.

Today she had a girl friend of hers over to lunch and I was real busy afterwards clearing the things away and she called me over and introduced me to the woman....Oh no, Marge! I didn't object to that at all. I greeted the lady and then went back to my work....And then it started! I could hear her talkin' just as loud...and she says to her friend, "We *just* love her! She's *like* one of the family and she *just adores* our little Carol! We don't know *what* we'd do without her! We don't think of her as a servant!" And on and on she went...and every time I came in to move a plate off the table both of them would grin at me like chessy cats.[1]

After I couldn't stand it any more, I went in and took the platter off the table and gave 'em both a look that would have frizzled a egg....Well, you might have heard a pin drop and then they started talkin' about something else.

When the guest leaves, I go in the living room and says, "Mrs. C....I want to have a talk with you."

"By all means," she says.

I drew up a chair and read her thusly: "Mrs. C...,you are a pretty nice person to work for, but I wish you would please stop talkin' about me like I was a *cocker spaniel* or a *poll parrot* or a *kitten*....Now you just sit there and hear me out.

"In the first place, you do not *love* me; you may be fond of me, but that is all.... In the second place, I am *not* just like one of the family at all! The family eats in the dining room and I eat in the kitchen. Your mama borrows your lace tablecloth for her company and your son entertains his friends in your parlor, your daughter takes her afternoon nap on the living room couch and the puppy sleeps on your satin spread...and whenever your husband gets tired of something you are talkin' about he says, 'Oh, for Pete's sake, forget it....' So you can see I am not *just* like one of the family.

---

[1] Cheshire cats, as in Lewis Carroll's *Alice in Wonderland.*

"Now for another thing, I do not *just* adore your little Carol. I think she is a likable child, but she is also fresh and sassy. I know you call it 'uninhibited' and that is the way you want your child to be, but *luckily* my mother taught me some inhibitions or else I would smack little Carol once in a while when she's talkin' to you like you're a dog, but as it is I just laugh it off the way you do because she is *your* child and I am *not* like one of the family.

"Now when you say, 'We don't know *what* we'd do without her' this is a polite lie...because I know that if I dropped dead or had a stroke, you would get somebody to replace me.

"You think it is a compliment when you say, 'We don't think of her as a servant....' but after I have worked myself into a sweat cleaning the bathroom and the kitchen...making the beds...cooking the lunch...washing the dishes and ironing Carol's pinafores...I do not feel like no weekend house guest. I feel like a servant, and in the face of that I have been meaning to ask you for a slight raise which will make me feel much better toward everyone here and make me know my work is appreciated.

"Now I hope you will stop talkin' about me in my presence and that we will get along like a good employer and employee should."

Marge! She was almost speechless but she *apologized* and said she'd talk to her husband about the raise....I knew things were progressing because this evening Carol came in the kitchen and she did not say, "I want some bread and jam!" but she did say, "*Please,* Mildred, will you fix me a slice of bread and jam."

I'm going upstairs, Marge. Just look...you done messed up that buttonhole!

—1956

"The Pocket Book Game"

Marge...day's work is an education! Well, I mean workin' in different homes you learn much more than if you was steady in one place....I tell you, it really keeps your mind sharp tryin' to watch for what folks will put over on you.

What?...No, Marge, I do not want to help shell no beans, but I'd be more than glad to stay and have supper with you, and I'll wash the dishes after. Is that all right?...

Who put anything over on who?...Oh yes! It's like this....I been working for Mrs. E....one day a week for several months and I notice that she has some peculiar ways. Well, there was only one thing that really bothered me and that was her pocketbook habit....No, not those little novels....I mean her purse—her handbag.

Marge, she's got a big old pocketbook with two long straps on it...and whenever I'd go there, she'd be propped up in a chair with her handbag double wrapped tight around her wrist, and from room to room she'd roam with that purse hugged to her bosom....Yes, girl! This happens every time! No, there's *nobody* there but me and her....Marge, I couldn't say nothin' to her! It's her purse, ain't it? She can hold onto it if she wants to!

I held my peace for months, tryin' to figure out how I'd make my point....Well, bless Bess! *Today was the day!*...Please, Marge, keep shellin' the beans so we can eat! I know you're listenin', but you listen with your ears, not your hands....Well, anyway, I was almost ready to go home when she steps in the room hangin' onto her bag as usual and says, "Mildred will you ask the super to come up and fix the kitchen faucet?" "Yes, Mrs. E…," I says, "as soon as I leave." "Oh, no," she says, "he may be gone by then. Please go now." "All right," I says, and out the door I went, still wearin' my Hoover apron.

I just went down the hall and stood there a few minutes…and then I rushed back to the door and knocked on it as hard and frantic as I could. She flung open the door sayin', "What's the matter? Did you see the super?"…"No," I says, gaspin' hard for breath, "I was almost downstairs when I remembered…*I left my pocketbook!*"

With that I dashed in, grabbed my purse and then went down to get the super! Later, when I was leavin' she says real timid-like, "Mildred, I hope that you don't think I distrust you because…" I cut her off real quick…. "That's all right, Mrs. E…, I understand. 'Cause if I paid anybody as little as you pay me, I'd hold my pocketbook too!"

Marge, you fool…lookout!…You gonna drop the beans on the floor!

—1956

The A B C's of Life and Learning

Oh well, it's all very fine for us grown-ups to worry and fret all kinds of ways about this desegregation business, but I wonder what it feels like to be a little child goin' to school and gettin' right into the thick of things as it were.

Marge, can you imagine a little seven-year-old colored child goin' off to his first day at a school that's just turnin' democratic? It's so hard to explain everything to the little ones so's they will really understand what's goin' on. They must feel all the uneasiness that's in the air and what with the parents bein' worried and cautionin' them about bein' careful and not walkin' down certain streets and comin' directly home and things like that, their little hearts must be awful burdened and put upon.

Is there any grown person that can put themselves in that child's place without feelin' angry and ashamed that this can be done to children? What does it do to a child when he sees adults throwin' things at him and jeerin' at him? How does it feel to walk in a classroom and have no one say a kind word? What does it feel like to sit in the back of the room all by yourself and try to study your lessons? What does it feel like to eat your lunch all alone and off to one side?

What does it feel like to have to run part of the way home in order not to be beat up or even maybe killed? What does it feel like to have to wait for your mama or papa to call for you and take you home by the long, round-about way? Don't you think these children are wonderin' and thinkin' some big, solemn thoughts?

…Sure, I know there's people who try to give this as the excuse not to have the schools mixed, but I don't go along with that at all, and it seems that you can say the same thing for the children. These brave little people take their lives in hand and walk the pathways leadin' to the schools all over the country. They want to learn, and they don't want to keep goin' to school buildin's that get a second place break on the money deal!

Oh, Marge, we got a lot to feel proud about! I wouldn't take anything for livin' right now in this day and time! I'm glad to my heart to see these brave children marchin' to the schools throughout the land, claimin' their rights and plowin' ahead in the face of mobs and threats and all manner of ugliness. These colored boys and girls got their hands stretched out in friendship to the white boys and girls in this land. And you know one thing? They're gonna clasp hands and walk together and get along and learn from each other and be peaceful and enjoy life in spite of these grown-ups tryin' to spread malice and hate. And one of these days this land is gonna be truly beautiful. Yes mam, every square inch of it!

—1956

AMY CLAMPITT (1920-1994)

Born in the small farming community of New Providence, Iowa, Amy Clampitt was raised in a Quaker family, though she later became a devout Episcopalian. She earned a B.A. from Grinnell College and received a graduate fellowship to Columbia University, but left after one year. Clampitt worked as an advertising copywriter for Oxford University Press, a reference librarian for the National Audobon Society, a freelance writer and researcher, and an editor for E.P. Dutton. Beginning in 1978, she published regularly in the New Yorker, but did not gain significant notice as a poet until her first book, *The Kingfisher*, was published in 1983, when she was sixty-three years old. Clampitt was writer-in-residence at the College of William and Mary from 1984 until 1988; she also served as a visiting writer at Amherst College and Washington University. She published four other books of poetry, *What the Light Was Like* (1985), *Archaic Figure* (1987), *Westward* (1990), and *A Silence Opens* (1994), before her death in 1994 from ovarian cancer. During her lifetime she received many awards for her work, including an Academy of American Poets Fellowship, a MacArthur Award Fellowship, and a Guggenheim Fellowship.

Good Friday

Think of the Serengeti lions looking up,
their bloody faces no more culpable
than the acacia's claw on the horizon
of those yellow plains: think with what
concerted expertise the red-necked,   5
down-ruffed vultures take their turn,
how after them the feasting maggots
hone the flayed wildebeest's ribcage
clean as a crucifix—a thrift tricked out
in ribboned rags, that looks like waste—   10
and wonder what barbed whimper, what embryo
of compunction, first unsealed the long
compact with a limb-from-limb outrage.

Think how the hunting cheetah, from
the lope that whips the petaled garden   15
of her hide into a sandstorm, falters,
doubling back, nagged by a lookout
for the fuzzed runt that can't

keep up, that isn't going to make it,
edged by a niggling in the chromosomes   20
toward these garrulous, uneasy caravans
where, eons notwithstanding, silence
still hands down the final statement.

Think of Charles Darwin[1] mulling over
whether to take out his patent on   25
the way the shape of things can alter,
hearing the whir, in his own household,
of the winnowing fan no system
(it appears) can put a stop to,
winnowing out another little girl,   30
for no good reason other than
the docile accident of the unfit,
before she quite turned seven.

Think of his reluctance to disparage
the Wedgwood pieties he'd married into,   35
his more-than-inkling of the usages
disinterested perception would be put to:
think how, among the hard-nosed, pity
is with stunning eloquence converted
to hard cash: think how Good Friday   40
can, as a therapeutic outlet, serve
to ventilate the sometimes stuffy
Lebensraum[2] of laissez-faire[3] society:

an ampoule of gore, a mithridatic
ounce of horror—sops for the maudlin   45
tendency of women toward extremes
of stance, from virgin blank to harlot
to sanctimonious official mourner—
myrrh and smelling salts, baroque
placebos, erotic tableaux vivants   50
dedicated to the household martyr,
underwriting with her own ex votos
the evolving ordonnance of murder.

—1983

Beach Glass

While you walk the water's edge,
turning over concepts
I can't envision, the honking buoy
serves notice that at any time
the wind may change,   5

---

[1] Charles Darwin (1809-1882), British naturalist. [3] (Fr.) To leave alone.
[2] (G.) Living space.

the reef-bell clatters
its treble monotone, deaf as Cassandra[4]
to any note but warning. The ocean,
cumbered by no business more urgent
than keeping open old accounts   10
that never balanced,
goes on shuffling its millenniums
of quartz, granite, and basalt.
                                        It behaves
toward the permutations of novelty—   15
driftwood and shipwreck, last night's
beer cans, spilt oil, the coughed-up
residue of plastic—with random
impartiality, playing catch or tag
or touch-last like a terrier,   20
turning the same thing over and over,
over and over. For the ocean, nothing
is beneath consideration.
                                    The houses
of so many mussels and periwinkles   25
have been abandoned here, it's hopeless
to know which to salvage. Instead
I keep a lookout for beach glass—
amber of Budweiser, chrysoprase
of Almadén and Gallo, lapis   30
by way of (no getting around it,
I'm afraid) Phillips'
Milk of Magnesia, with now and then a rare
translucent turquoise or blurred amethyst
of no known origin.   35
                            The process
goes on forever: they came from sand,
they go back to gravel,
along with the treasuries
of Murano,[5] the buttressed   40
astonishments of Chartres,[6]
which even now are readying
for being turned over and over as gravely
and gradually as an intellect
engaged in the hazardous   45
redefinition of structures
no one has yet looked at.

                                        —1987

---

[4] A prophet on whom Apollo placed a curse: her prophe-
sies, though true, would not be believed. Greek myth
also identifies Cassandra as Alexandra.

[5] An island suburb of Venice noted for the manufacture of
hand-blown glass.
[6] A well-known cathedral in France.

BARBARA GUEST (1920-2006)

Although part of her career was spent in relative obscurity, Barbara Guest wrote nearly thirty books of poetry, fiction, essays, and plays, as well as an acclaimed but controversial biography of H.D., *Herself Defined* (1984). She was born in Wilmington, North Carolina, on September 6, 1920, to a family constantly on the move. She was sent to live with her aunt and uncle in Los Angeles at the age of eleven, and later graduated from UC Berkeley in 1943. In the early 1940s she moved to New York, where she met H.D.; Stephen, Lord Haden-Guest (one of her three husbands); and the male poets who, along with Guest, would be known as the New York School. This group objected to New Critical literary values as well as the Confessional poetics of their contemporaries, such as Sylvia Plath, Anne Sexton, and Robert Lowell. Like others of the New York School, Guest would be influenced by expressionist painters and surrealism. She first became known as an art critic, publishing her first book of poems, *The Location of Things* (1960) at the age of forty. After her close friend and fellow poet Frank O'Hara died in 1966, she moved away from (or, by some accounts, was excluded from) the male-dominated New York School. She refused to write the overtly political poetry that was popular in the 1960s and 1970s, instead developing a poetics that disallowed subjectivity, letting the reader observe language as it observed the world. She also refused to pursue an academic career that might have kept her work in circulation. However, with the growth since the 1980s of the new experimental poetics, sometimes referred to as Language Poetry, Guest found a new audience. Twelve of her poetry volumes were published in the last twenty years of her life, including *The Red Gaze* (2005), *Miniatures and Other Poems* (2002), and *Defensive Rapture* (1994). She died on February 15, 2006, in Berkeley, California. Among her awards is the Robert Frost Medal for Distinguished Lifetime Achievement from the Poetry Society of America.

The Poetess[1]
after Miró

A dollop is dolloping
her a scoop is pursuing
flee vain ignots   Ho
coriander darks   thimble blues
red okays adorn her   5
buzz green circles in flight
or submergence?   Giddy
mishaps of blackness make
stinging clouds what!
a fraught climate   10
what natural c/o abnormal
loquaciousness the
Poetess riddled
her asterisk is there
genial!   as space

—1973

---

[1] Refers to the title of a 1940 abstract painting by Spanish artist Joan Miró (1893-1983). Also a controversial term used to describe women poets prior to the 20th century.

Noisetone

Each artist embarks on a personal search.
  An artist may take introspective refreshment from green.

Or so they say in Barcelona when air is dry.
  In our country it is a water sprinkler that hints, "rinsed green."
  Colors often break themselves into separate hues   5

of noisetone.   In a Barcelona cabaret when green is overtaken,
it is stirred into the mint color of drink.

The spirit is lifted among primary colors. Nine rows of color.
  The future writ in white spaces.

—2002

Sound and Structure

"Sound leads to structure." Schönberg.[2]

On this dry prepared path walk heavy feet.
This is not "dinner music." This is a power structure,
heavy as eyelids.
Beams are laid. The master cuts music for the future.

Sound lays the structure. Sound leaks into the future.

—2002

---

[2] Arnold Schoenberg (1874-1951), Austrian composer associated with atonality in music. Guest uses the original spelling of his name, which he altered after moving to the U.S. to flee the Nazis.

PATRICIA HIGHSMITH (1921-1995)

Patricia Highsmith was born Mary Patricia Plangman in Fort Worth, Texas, to artist parents who separated before she was born (Highsmith was her stepfather's name). She graduated from Barnard College and worked at a series of jobs—including writing story lines for comic books such as *Captain America*—until she began to make money as a writer. *Strangers on a Train* (1950), her first novel, was a "mutual murder" story with a cynical, even amoral, tone that is typical of much of Highsmith's writing. The book became a bestseller and was made into a popular *film noir* by Alfred Hitchcock. Highsmith followed with *The Talented Mr. Ripley* (1955) and its four sequels, as well as other full-length novels and short stories. Highsmith, a closeted lesbian, wrote a number of books (including *Strangers on a Train* and the Ripley novels) that focus on sexually-charged relationships between men. Under the pseudonym Claire Morgan, she also wrote *The Price of Salt* (1952), which pulp novelist Ann Bannon has described as the first lesbian novel with a happy ending—meaning that the heroines do not die or go mad, and their love is validated at the end of the book.

Though Highsmith was generally accepted as a top-rank writer, she never truly achieved success in the United States. She lived most of her adult life as an expatriate in Europe, where her work was greatly appreciated. Highsmith did win a number of awards for mystery writing, however, including the O. Henry Award (1946), the Edgar Allan Poe Award (1951 and 1956), the French Grand Prix de Littérature Policière (1957), and the Crime Writers Association of England Silver Dagger Award (1964).

The Fully Licensed Whore
or, The Wife

Sarah had always played the field as an amateur, and at twenty she got married, which made her licensed. To top it, the marriage was in a church in full view of family, friends and neighbors, maybe even God as witness, for certainly He was invited. She was all in white, though hardly a virgin, being two months pregnant and not by the man she was marrying, whose name was Sylvester. Now she could become a professional, with protection of the law, approval of society, blessing of the clergy, and financial support guaranteed by her husband.

Sarah lost no time. It was first the gas meter reader, to limber herself up, then the window cleaner, whose job took a varying number of hours, depending on how dirty she told Sylvester the windows had been. Sylvester sometimes had to pay for eight hours' work plus a bit of overtime. Sometimes the window cleaner was there when Sylvester left for work, and still there when he came home in the evening. But these were small fry, and Sarah progressed to their lawyer, which had the advantage of "no fee" for any services performed for the Sylvester Dillon family, now three.

Sylvester was proud of baby son Edmund, and flushed with pleasure at what friends said about Edmund's resemblance to himself. The friends were not lying, only saying what they thought they should say, and what they would have said to any father. After Edmund's birth, Sarah ceased sexual relations with Sylvester (not that they'd ever had much) saying, "One's enough, don't you think?" She could also say, "I'm tired," or "It's too hot." In plain fact, poor Sylvester was good only for his money—he wasn't wealthy but quite comfortably off—and because he was reasonably intelligent and presentable, not aggressive enough to be a nuisance and—Well, that was about all it took to satisfy Sarah. She had a vague idea that she needed a protector and escort. It somehow carried more weight to write "Mrs." at the foot of letters.

She enjoyed three or four years of twiddling about with the lawyer, then their doctor, then a couple of maverick husbands in their social circle, plus a few two-week sprees with the father of Edmund. These men visited the house mainly during the afternoons Monday to Friday. Sarah was most cautious and insisted—her house front being visible to several neighbors—that her lovers ring her when they were already in the vicinity, so she could tell them if the coast was clear enough for them to nip in. One-thirty P.M. was the safest time, when most people were eating lunch. After all, Sarah's bed and board was at stake, and Sylvester was becoming restless, though as yet not at all suspicious.

Sylvester in the fourth year of marriage made a slight fuss. His own advances to his secretary and also to the girl who worked behind the counter in his office supplies shop had been gently but firmly rejected, and his ego was at a low ebb.

"Can't we try again?" was Sylvester's theme.

Sarah counterattacked like a dozen battalions whose guns had been primed for years to fire. One would have thought she was the one to whom injustice had been done. "Haven't I created a lovely home for you? Aren't I a good hostess—the *best* according to all our friends, isn't that true? Have I ever neglected Edmund? Have I ever failed to have a hot meal waiting for you when you come home?"

I wish you would forget the hot meal now and then and think of something else, Sylvester wanted to say, but was too well brought up to get the words out.

"Furthermore I have taste," Sarah added as a final volley. "Our furniture is not only good, it's well cared for. I don't know what more you can expect from me."

The furniture was so well polished, the house looked like a museum. Sylvester was often shy about dirtying ashtrays. He would have liked more disorder and a little more warmth. How could he say this?

"Now come and eat something," Sarah said more sweetly, extending a hand in a burst of contact unprecedented for Sylvester in the past many years. A thought had just crossed her mind, a plan.

Sylvester took her hand gladly, and smiled. He ate second helpings of everything that she pressed upon him. The dinner was as usual good, because Sarah was an excellent and meticulous cook. Sylvester was hoping for a happy end to the evening also, but in this he was disappointed.

Sarah's idea was to kill Sylvester with good food, with kindness in a sense, with wifely *duty*. She was going to cook more and more elaborately. Sylvester already had a paunch, the doctor had cautioned him about overeating, not enough exercise and all that rot, but Sarah knew enough about weight control to know that it was what you ate that counted, not how much exercise you took. And Sylvester loved to eat. The stage was set, she felt, and what had she to lose?

She began to use richer fats, goose fat, olive oil, and to make macaroni and cheese, to butter sandwiches more thickly, to push milk-drinking as a splendid source of calcium for Sylvester's falling hair. He put on twenty pounds in three months. His tailor had to alter all his suits, then make new suits for him.

"Tennis, darling," Sarah said with concern. "What you need is a bit of exercise." She was hoping he'd have a heart attack. He now weighed nearly 225 pounds, and he was not a tall man. He was already breathing hard at the slightest exertion.

Tennis didn't do it. Sylvester was wise enough, or heavy enough, just to stand there on the court and let the ball come to him, and if the ball didn't come to him, he wasn't going to run after it to hit it. So one warm Saturday, when Sarah had accompanied him to the courts as usual, she pretended to faint. She mumbled that she wanted to be taken to the car to go home. Sylvester struggled, panting, as Sarah was no lightweight herself. Unfortunately for Sarah's plans, two chaps came running from the club bar to give assistance, and Sarah was loaded easily into the Jag.

Once at home, with the front door closed, Sarah swooned again, and mumbled in a frantic but waning voice that she had to be taken upstairs to bed. It was their bed, a big double one, and two flights up. Sylvester heaved her into his arms, thinking that he did not present a romantic picture trudging up step by step, gasping and stumbling as he carried his beloved towards bed. At last he had to maneuver her onto one shoulder, and even then he fell on his own face upon reaching the landing on the second floor. Wheezing mightily, he rolled out from under her limp figure, and tried again, this time simply dragging her along the carpeted hall and into the bedroom. He was tempted to let her lie there until he got his own breath back (she wasn't stirring), but he could anticipate her recrimination if she woke up in the next seconds and found he had left her flat on the floor.

Sylvester bent to the task again, put all his will power into it, for certainly he had no physical strength left. His legs ached, his back was killing him, and it amazed him that he could get this burden (over 150 pounds) onto the double bed. "Whoosh-sh!" Sylvester said, and went reeling back, intending to collapse in an armchair, but the armchair had rollers and retreated several inches, causing him to land on the floor with a house-shaking thump. A terrible pain had struck his chest. He pressed a fist against his breast and bared his teeth in agony.

Sarah watched. She lay on the bed. She did nothing. She waited and waited. She almost fell asleep. Sylvester was moaning, calling for help. How lucky, Sarah thought, that Edmund was parked out with a baby-sitter this afternoon, instead of a baby-sitter being in the house. After some fifteen minutes, Sylvester was still. Sarah did fall asleep finally. When she got up, she found that Sylvester was quite dead and becoming cool. Then she telephoned the family doctor.

All went well for Sarah. People said that just weeks before, they'd been amazed at how *well* Sylvester looked, rosy cheeks and all that. Sarah got a tidy sum from the insurance company, her widow's pension, and gushes of sympathy from people who assured her she had given Sylvester the best of herself, had made a lovely home for him, had given him a son, had in short devoted herself utterly to him and made his somewhat short life as happy as a man's life could possibly have been. No one said, "What a perfect murder!" which was Sarah's private opinion, and now she could chuckle over it. Now she could become the Merry Widow. By exacting small favors from her lovers—casually of course—it was going to be easy to live in even better style than when Sylvester had been alive. And she could still write "Mrs." at the foot of letters.

—1975

HISAYE YAMAMOTO (1921-)

Hisaye Yamamoto was born in Redondo Beach, California, and began writing as a teenager, contributing regularly to Japanese-American newspapers. During World War II, Yamamoto and her family were interned for three years at the Arizona Poston Relocation Center. There, she published fiction in the camp's newspaper, the *Poston Chronicle*. Following her release from the camp, Yamamoto worked from 1945 to 1948 at the *L.A. Tribune,* a Black weekly. Her first short story, "The High-Heeled Shoes," was published in the *Partisan Review* in 1948. Yamamoto's short stories typically explore the relationship between Issei men and women (first-generation immigrants from Japan) and between immigrant parents and their children, often employing lighthearted tones and details that ironically uncover more serious family or racial drama. Two of her short stories, "Seventeen Syllables" and "Yoneko's Earthquake," were adapted for an American Playhouse/PBS film entitled *Hot Summer Winds*. Yamamoto has written over fifty short stories, but those she wrote in the 1940s and 1950s are widely regarded as her most important work; of these, "Seventeen Syllables" is perhaps the story that has received the most critical attention. While Yamamoto is best known for her short stories, she has also published poetry. "Et Ego in America VIXI" was published in June 1941 in the Nisei (second-generation immigrants from Japan) magazine *Current Life*. Yamamoto has received the Lifetime Achievement Award from the Before Columbus Foundation.

Et Ego in America VIXI[1]

My skin is sun-gold
My cheekbones are proud
My eyes slant darkly
And my hair is touched
With the dusky bloom of purple plums.   5
The soul of me is enrapt
To see the wisteria in blue-violet cluster,
The heart of me breathless
At the fragile beauty of an ageless vase.
But my heart flows over   10
My throat chokes in reverent wonder
At the unfurled glory of a flag—
    Red as the sun
    White as the almond blossom
    Blue as the clear summer sky.

—1941

Seventeen Syllables

The first Rosie knew that her mother had taken to writing poems was one evening when she finished one and read it aloud for her daughter's approval. It was about cats, and Rosie pretended to understand it thoroughly and appreciate it no end, partly because she hesitated to disillusion her mother about the quantity and quality of Japanese she had learned in all the years now that she had been going to Japanese school every Saturday (and Wednesday, too, in the summer). Even so, her mother must have been skeptical about the depth of Rosie's understanding, because she explained afterwards about the kind of poem she was trying to write.

See, Rosie, she said, it was a *haiku*, a poem in which she must pack all her meaning into seventeen syllables only, which were divided into three lines of five, seven, and five syllables. In the one she had just read, she had tried to capture the charm of a kitten, as well as comment on the superstition that owning a cat of three colors meant good luck.

"Yes, yes, I understand. How utterly lovely," Rosie said, and her mother, either satisfied or seeing through the deception and resigned, went back to composing.

The truth was that Rosie was lazy; English lay ready on the tongue but Japanese had to be searched for and examined, and even then put forth tentatively (probably to meet with laughter). It was so much easier to say yes, yes, even when one meant no, no. Besides, this was what was in her mind to say: I was looking through one of your magazines from Japan last night, Mother, and towards the back I found some *haiku* in English that delighted me. There was one that made me giggle off and on until I fell asleep—

    It is morning, and lo!
    I lie awake, comme il faut,[2]
    sighing for some dough.

---

[1] (Lat.) And I have lived in America.   [2] (Fr.) As is proper.

Now, how to reach her mother, how to communicate the melancholy song? Rosie knew formal Japanese by fits and starts, her mother had even less English, no French. It was much more possible to say yes, yes.

It developed that her mother was writing the *haiku* for a daily newspaper, the *Mainichi Shimbun,* that was published in San Francisco. Los Angeles, to be sure, was closer to the farming community in which the Hayashi family lived and several Japanese vernaculars were printed there, but Rosie's parents said they preferred the tone of the northern paper. Once a week, the *Mainichi* would have a section devoted to *haiku,* and her mother became an extravagant contributor, taking for herself the blossoming pen name, Ume Hanazono.

So Rosie and her father lived for awhile with two women, her mother and Ume Hanazono. Her mother (Tome Hayashi by name) kept house, cooked, washed, and, along with her husband and the Carrascos, the Mexican family hired for the harvest, did her ample share of picking tomatoes out in the sweltering fields and boxing them in tidy strata in the cool packing shed. Ume Hanazono, who came to life after the dinner dishes were done, was an earnest, muttering stranger who often neglected speaking when spoken to and stayed busy at the parlor table as late as midnight scribbling with pencil on scratch paper or carefully copying characters on good paper with her fat, pale green Parker.

The new interest had some repercussions on the household routine. Before, Rosie had been accustomed to her parents and herself taking their hot baths early and going to bed almost immediately afterwards, unless her parents challenged each other to a game of flower cards or unless company dropped in. Now if her father wanted to play cards, he had to resort to solitaire (at which he always cheated fearlessly), and if a group of friends came over, it was bound to contain someone who was also writing *haiku,* and the small assemblage would be split in two, her father entertaining the non-literary members and her mother comparing ecstatic notes with the visiting poet.

If they went out, it was more of the same thing. But Ume Hanazono's life span, even for a poet's, was very brief—perhaps three months at most.

One night they went over to see the Hayano family in the neighboring town to the west, an adventure both painful and attractive to Rosie. It was attractive because there were four Hayano girls, all lovely and each one named after a season of the year (Haru, Natsu, Aki, Fuyu), painful because something had been wrong with Mrs. Hayano ever since the birth of her first child. Rosie would sometimes watch Mrs. Hayano, reputed to have been the belle of her native village, making her way about a room, stooped, slowly shuffling, violently trembling (*always* trembling), and she would be reminded that this woman, in this same condition, had carried and given issue to three babies. She would look wonderingly at Mr. Hayano, handsome, tall, and strong, and she would look at her four pretty friends. But it was not a matter she could come to any decision about.

On this visit, however, Mrs. Hayano sat all evening in the rocker, as motionless and unobtrusive as it was possible for her to be, and Rosie found the greater part of the evening practically anaesthetic. Too, Rosie spent most of it in the girls' room, because Haru, the garrulous one, said almost as soon as the bows and other greetings were over, "Oh, you must see my new coat!"

It was a pale plaid of grey, sand, and blue, with an enormous collar, and Rosie, seeing nothing special in it, said, "Gee, how nice."

"Nice?" said Haru, indignantly. "Is that all you can say about it? It's gorgeous! And so cheap, too. Only seventeen-ninety-eight, because it was a sale. The saleslady said it was twenty-five dollars regular."

"Gee," said Rosie. Natsu, who never said much and when she said anything said it shyly, fingered the coat covetously and Haru pulled it away.

"Mine," she said, putting it on. She minced in the aisle between the two large beds and smiled happily. "Let's see how your mother likes it."

She broke into the front room and the adult conversation and went to stand in front of Rosie's mother, while the rest watched from the door. Rosie's mother was properly envious. "May I inherit it when you're through with it?"

Haru, pleased, giggled and said yes, she could, but Natsu reminded gravely from the door, "You promised me, Haru."

Everyone laughed but Natsu, who shamefacedly retreated into the bedroom. Haru came in laughing, taking off the coat. "We were only kidding, Natsu," she said. "Here, you try it on now."

After Natsu buttoned herself into the coat, inspected herself solemnly in the bureau mirror, and reluctantly shed it, Rosie, Aki, and Fuyu got their turns, and Fuyu, who was eight, drowned in it while her sisters and Rosie doubled up in amusement. They all went into the front room later, because Haru's mother quaveringly called to her to fix the tea and rice cakes and open a can of sliced peaches for everybody. Rosie noticed that her mother and Mr. Hayano were talking together at the little table—they were discussing a *haiku* that Mr. Hayano was planning to send to the *Mainichi*, while her father was sitting at one end of the sofa looking through a copy of *Life*, the new picture magazine. Occasionally, her father would comment on a photograph, holding it toward Mrs. Hayano and speaking to her as he always did—loudly, as though he thought someone such as she must surely be at least a trifle deaf also.

The five girls had their refreshments at the kitchen table, and it was while Rosie was showing the sisters her trick of swallowing peach slices without chewing (she chased each slippery crescent down with a swig of tea) that her father brought his empty teacup and untouched saucer to the sink and said, "Come on, Rosie, we're going home now."

"Already?" asked Rosie.

"Work tomorrow," he said.

He sounded irritated, and Rosie, puzzled, gulped one last yellow slice and stood up to go, while the sisters began protesting, as was their wont.

"We have to get up at five-thirty," he told them, going into the front room quickly, so that they did not have their usual chance to hang onto his hands and plead for an extension of time.

Rosie, following, saw that her mother and Mr. Hayano were sipping tea and still talking together, while Mrs. Hayano concentrated, quivering, on raising the handleless Japanese cup to her lips with both her hands and lowering it back to her lap. Her father, saying nothing, went out the door, onto the bright porch, and down the steps. Her mother looked up and asked, "Where is he going?"

"Where is he going?" Rosie said. "He said we were going home now."

"Going home?" Her mother looked with embarrassment at Mr. Hayano and his absorbed wife and then forced a smile. "He must be tired," she said.

Haru was not giving up yet. "May Rosie stay overnight?" she asked, and Natsu, Aki, and Fuyu came to reinforce their sister's plea by helping her make a circle around Rosie's mother. Rosie, for once having no desire to stay, was relieved when her mother, apologizing to the perturbed Mr. and Mrs. Hayano for her father's abruptness at the same time, managed to shake her head no at the quartet, kindly but adamant, so that they broke their circle and let her go.

Rosie's father looked ahead into the windshield as the two joined him. "I'm sorry," her mother said. "You must be tired." Her father, stepping on the starter, said nothing. "You know how I get when it's *haiku,*" she continued, "I forget what time it is." He only grunted.

As they rode homeward silently, Rosie, sitting between, felt a rush of hate for both—for her mother for begging, for her father for denying her mother. I wish this old Ford would crash, right now, she thought, then immediately, no, no, I wish my father would laugh, but it was too late: already the vision had passed through her mind of the green pick-up crumpled in the dark against one of the mighty eucalyptus trees they were just riding past, of the three contorted, bleeding bodies, one of them hers.

Rosie ran between two patches of tomatoes, her heart working more rambunctiously than she had ever known it to. How lucky it was that Aunt Taka and Uncle Gimpachi had come tonight, though, how very lucky. Otherwise she might not have really kept her half-promise to meet Jesus Carrasco. Jesus was going to be a senior in September at the same school she went to, and his parents were the ones helping with the tomatoes this year. She and Jesus, who hardly remembered seeing each other at Cleveland High where there were so many other people and two whole grades between them, had become great friends this summer—he always had a joke for her when he periodically drove the loaded pick-up up from the fields to the shed where she was usually sorting while her mother and father did the packing, and they laughed a great deal together over infinitesimal repartee during the afternoon break for chilled watermelon or ice cream in the shade of the shed.

What she enjoyed most was racing him to see which could finish picking a double row first. He, who could work faster, would tease her by slowing down until she thought she would surely pass him this time, then speeding up furiously to leave her several sprawling vines behind. Once he had made her screech hideously by crossing over, while her back was turned, to place atop the tomatoes in her green-stained bucket a truly monstrous, pale green worm (it had looked more like an infant snake). And it was when they had finished a contest this morning, after she had pantingly pointed a green finger at the immature tomatoes evident in the lugs at the end of his row and he had returned the accusation (with justice), that he had startlingly brought up the matter of their possibly meeting outside the range of both their parents' dubious eyes.

"What for?" she had asked.

"I've got a secret I want to tell you," he said.

"Tell me now," she demanded.

"It won't be ready till tonight," he said.

She laughed. "Tell me tomorrow then."

"It'll be gone tomorrow," he threatened.

"Well, for seven hakes, what is it?" she had asked, more than twice, and when he had suggested that the packing shed would be an appropriate place to find out, she had cautiously answered maybe. She had not been certain she was going to keep the appointment until the arrival of mother's sister and her husband. Their coming seemed a sort of signal of permission, of grace, and she had definitely made up her mind to lie and leave as she was bowing them welcome.

So as soon as everyone appeared settled back for the evening, she announced loudly that she was going to the privy outside, "I'm going to the *benjo!*" and slipped out the door. And now that she was actually on her way, her heart pumped in such an undisciplined way that she could hear it with her ears. It's because I'm running, she told herself, slowing to a walk. The shed was up ahead, one more patch away, in the middle of the fields. Its bulk, looming in the dimness, took on a sinisterness that was funny when Rosie reminded herself that it was only a wooden frame with a canvas roof and three canvas walls that made a slapping noise on breezy days.

Jesus was sitting on the narrow plank that was the sorting platform and she went around to the other side and jumped backwards to seat herself on the rim of a packing stand. "Well, tell me," she said without greeting, thinking her voice sounded reassuringly familiar.

"I saw you coming out the door," Jesus said. "I heard you running part of the way, too."

"Uh-huh," Rosie said. "Now tell me the secret."

"I was afraid you wouldn't come," he said.

Rosie delved around on the chicken-wire bottom of the stall for number two tomatoes, ripe, which she was sitting beside, and came up with a left-over that felt edible. She bit into it and began sucking out the pulp and seeds. "I'm here," she pointed out.

"Rosie, are you sorry you came?"

"Sorry? What for?" she said. "You said you were going to tell me something."

"I will, I will," Jesus said, but his voice contained disappointment, and Rosie fleetingly felt the older of the two, realizing a brand-new power which vanished without category under her recognition.

"I have to go back in a minute," she said. "My aunt and uncle are here from Wintersburg. I told them I was going to the privy."

Jesus laughed. "You funny thing," he said. "You slay me!"

"Just because you have a bathroom *inside,*" Rosie said. "Come on, tell me."

Chuckling, Jesus came around to lean on the stand facing her. They still could not see each other very clearly, but Rosie noticed that Jesus became very sober again as he took the hollow tomato from her hand and dropped it back into the stall. When he took hold of her empty hand, she could find no words to protest; her vocabulary had become distressingly constricted and she thought desperately that all that remained intact now was yes and no and oh, and even these few sounds would not easily out. Thus, kissed by Jesus, Rosie fell for the first time entirely victim to a helplessness delectable beyond speech. But the terrible, beautiful sensation lasted no more than a second, and the reality of Jesus' lips and tongue and teeth and hands made her pull away with such strength that she nearly tumbled.

Rosie stopped running as she approached the lights from the windows of home. How long since she had left? She could not guess, but gasping yet, she went to the privy in back and locked herself in. Her own breathing deafened her in the dark, close space, and she sat and waited until she could hear at last the nightly calling of the frogs and crickets. Even then, all she could think to say was oh, my, and the pressure of Jesus' face against her face would not leave.

No one had missed her in the parlor, however, and Rosie walked in and through quickly, announcing that she was next going to take a bath. "Your father's in the bathhouse," her mother said, and Rosie, in her room, recalled that she had not seen him when she entered. There had been only Aunt Taka and Uncle Gimpachi with her mother at the table, drinking tea. She got her robe and straw sandals and crossed the parlor again to go outside. Her mother was telling them about the *haiku* competition in the *Mainichi* and the poem she had entered.

Rosie met her father coming out of the bathhouse. "Are you through, Father?" she asked. "I was going to ask you to scrub my back."

"Scrub your own back," he said shortly, going toward the main house.

"What have I done now?" she yelled after him. She suddenly felt like doing a lot of yelling. But he did not answer, and she went into the bathhouse. Turning on the dangling light, she removed her denims and T-shirt and threw them in the big carton for dirty clothes standing next to the washing machine. Her other things she took with her into the bath compartment to wash after her bath. After she had scooped a basin of hot water from the square wooden tub, she sat on the grey cement of the floor and soaped herself at exaggerated leisure, singing "Red Sails in the Sunset" at the top of her voice and using da-da-da where she suspected her words. Then, standing up, still singing, for she was possessed by the notion that any attempt now to analyze would result in spoilage and she believed that the larger her volume the less she would be able to hear herself think, she obtained more hot water and poured it on until she was free of lather. Only then did she allow herself to step into the steaming vat, one leg first, then the remainder of her body inch by inch until the water no longer stung and she could move around at will.

She took a long time soaking, afterwards remembering to go around outside to stoke the embers of the tin-lined fireplace beneath the tub and to throw on a few more sticks so that the water might keep its heat for her mother, and when she finally returned to the parlor, she found her mother still talking *haiku* with her aunt and uncle, the three of them on another round of tea. Her father was nowhere in sight.

At Japanese school the next day (Wednesday, it was), Rosie was grave and giddy by turns. Preoccupied at her desk in the row for students on Book Eight, she made up for it at recess by performing wild mimicry for the benefit of her friend Chizuko. She held her nose and whined a witticism or two in what she considered was the manner of Fred Allen; she assumed intoxication and a British accent to go over the climax of the Rudy Vallee recording of the pub conversation about William Ewart Gladstone;[3] she was the child Shirley Temple piping, "On the Good Ship Lollipop"; she was the gentleman soprano of the Four Inkspots trilling, "If I Didn't Care." And she felt reasonably satisfied when Chizuko wept and gasped, "Oh, Rosie, you ought to be in the movies!"

Her father came after her at noon, bringing her sandwiches of minced ham and two

---

[3] William Ewart Gladstone (1809-1898), four-time prime minister of England (1868-1874, 1880-1885, 1886, and 1892-1894).

nectarines to eat while she rode, so that she could pitch right into the sorting when they got home. The lugs were piling up, he said, and the ripe tomatoes in them would probably have to be taken to the cannery tomorrow if they were not ready for the produce haulers tonight. "This heat's not doing them any good. And we've got no time for a break today."

It *was* hot, probably the hottest day of the year, and Rosie's blouse stuck damply to her back even under the protection of the canvas. But she worked as efficiently as a flawless machine and kept the stalls heaped, with one part of her mind listening in to the parental murmuring about the heat and the tomatoes and with another part planning the exact words she would say to Jesus when he drove up with the first load of the afternoon. But when at last she saw that the pick-up was coming, her hands went berserk and the tomatoes started falling in the wrong stalls, and her father said, "Hey, hey! Rosie, watch what you're doing!"

"Well, I have to go to the *benjo*," she said, hiding panic.

"Go in the weeds over there," he said, only half-joking.

"Oh, Father!" she protested.

"Oh, go on home," her mother said. "We'll make out for awhile."

In the privy Rosie peered through a knothole toward the fields, watching as much as she could of Jesus. Happily she thought she saw him look in the direction of the house from time to time before he finished unloading and went back toward the patch where his mother and father worked. As she was heading for the shed, a very presentable black car purred up the dirt driveway to the house and its driver motioned to her. Was this the Hayashi home, he wanted to know. She nodded. Was she a Hayashi? Yes, she said, thinking that he was a good-looking man. He got out of the car with a huge, flat package and she saw that he warmly wore a business suit. "I have something here for your mother then," he said, in a more elegant Japanese than she was used to.

She told him where her mother was and he came along with her, patting his face with an immaculate white handkerchief and saying something about the coolness of San Francisco. To her surprised mother and father, he bowed and introduced himself as, among other things, the *haiku* editor of the *Mainichi Shimbun,* saying that since he had been coming as far as Los Angeles anyway, he had decided to bring her the first prize she had won in the recent contest.

"First prize?" her mother echoed, believing and not believing, pleased and overwhelmed. Handed the package with a bow, she bobbed her head up and down numerous times to express her utter gratitude.

"It is nothing much," he added, "but I hope it will serve as a token of our great appreciation for your contributions and our great admiration of your considerable talent."

"I am not worthy," she said, falling easily into his style. "It is I who should make some sign of my humble thanks for being permitted to contribute."

"No, no, to the contrary," he said, bowing again.

But Rosie's mother insisted, and then saying that she knew she was being unorthodox, she asked if she might open the package because her curiosity was so great. Certainly she might. In fact, he would like her reaction to it, for personally, it was one of his favorite *Hiroshiges*.

Rosie thought it was a pleasant picture, which looked to have been sketched with delicate quickness. There were pink clouds, containing some graceful calligraphy, and a sea that was a pale blue except at the edges, containing four sampans[4] with indications of people in them. Pines edged the water and on the far-off beach there was a cluster of thatched huts towered over by pine-dotted mountains of grey and blue. The frame was scalloped and gilt.

After Rosie's mother pronounced it without peer and somewhat prodded her father into nodding agreement, she said Mr. Kuroda must at least have a cup of tea after coming all this way, and although Mr. Kuroda did not want to impose, he soon agreed that a cup of tea would be refreshing and went along with her to the house, carrying the picture for her.

"Ha, your mother's crazy!" Rosie's father said, and Rosie laughed uneasily as she resumed judgment on the tomatoes. She had emptied six lugs when he broke into an imaginary conversation with Jesus to tell her to go and remind her mother of the tomatoes, and she went slowly.

Mr. Kuroda was in his shirtsleeves expounding some *haiku* theory as he munched a rice cake, and her mother was rapt. Abashed in the great man's presence, Rosie stood next to her mother's chair until her mother looked up inquiringly, and then she started to whisper the message, but her mother pushed her gently away and reproached, "You are not being very polite to our guest."

"Father says the tomatoes…" Rosie said aloud, smiling foolishly.

"Tell him I shall only be a minute," her mother said, speaking the language of Mr. Kuroda.

When Rosie carried the reply to her father, he did not seem to hear and she said again, "Mother says she'll be back in a minute."

"All right, all right," he nodded, and they worked again in silence. But suddenly, her father uttered an incredible noise, exactly like the cork of a bottle popping, and the next Rosie knew, he was stalking angrily toward the house, almost running in fact, and she chased after him crying, "Father! Father! What are you going to do?"

He stopped long enough to order her back to the shed. "Never mind!" he shouted. "Get on with the sorting!"

And from the place in the fields where she stood, frightened and vacillating, Rosie saw her father enter the house. Soon Mr. Kuroda came out alone, putting on his coat. Mr. Kuroda got into his car and backed out down the driveway onto the highway. Next her father emerged, also alone, something in his arms (it was the picture, she realized), and, going over to the bathhouse woodpile, he threw the picture on the ground and picked up the axe. Smashing the picture, glass and all (she heard the explosion faintly), he reached over for the kerosene that was used to encourage the bath fire and poured it over the wreckage. I am dreaming, Rosie said to herself, I am dreaming, but her father, having made sure that his act of cremation was irrevocable, was even then returning to the fields.

Rosie ran past him and toward the house. What had become of her mother? She burst into the parlor and found her mother at the back window watching the dying fire. They watched together until there remained only a feeble smoke under the blazing sun. Her mother was very calm.

"Do you know why I married your father?" she said without turning.

"No," said Rosie. It was the most frightening question she had ever been called

---

[4] (Chin.) A small wooden boat, usually rigged for sailing.

upon to answer. Don't tell me now, she wanted to say, tell me tomorrow, tell me next week, don't tell me today. But she knew she would be told now, that the telling would combine with the other violence of the hot afternoon to level her life, her world to the very ground.

It was like a story out of the magazines illustrated in sepia, which she had consumed so greedily for a period until the information had somehow reached her that those wretchedly unhappy autobiographies, offered to her as the testimonials of living men and women, were largely inventions: Her mother, at nineteen, had come to America and married her father as an alternative to suicide.

At eighteen she had been in love with the first son of one of the well-to-do families in her village. The two had met whenever and wherever they could, secretly, because it would not have done for his family to see him favor her—her father had no money; he was a drunkard and a gambler besides. She had learned she was with child; an excellent match had already been arranged for her lover. Despised by her family, she had given premature birth to a stillborn son, who would be seventeen now. Her family did not turn her out, but she could no longer project herself in any direction without refreshing in them the memory of her indiscretion. She wrote to Aunt Taka, her favorite sister in America, threatening to kill herself if Aunt Taka would not send for her. Aunt Taka hastily arranged a marriage with a young man of whom she knew, but lately arrived from Japan, a young man of simple mind, it was said, but of kindly heart. The young man was never told why his unseen betrothed was so eager to hasten the day of meeting.

The story was told perfectly, with neither groping for words nor untoward passion. It was as though her mother had memorized it by heart, reciting it to herself so many times over that its nagging vileness had long since gone.

"I had a brother then?" Rosie asked, for this was what seemed to matter now; she would think about the other later, she assured herself, pushing back the illumination which threatened all that darkness that had hitherto been merely mysterious or even glamorous. "A half-brother?"

"Yes."

"I would have liked a brother," she said.

Suddenly, her mother knelt on the floor and took her by the wrists. "Rosie," she said urgently, "Promise me you will never marry!" Shocked more by the request than the revelation, Rosie stared at her mother's face. Jesus, Jesus, she called silently, not certain whether she was invoking the help of the son of the Carrascos or of God, until there returned sweetly the memory of Jesus' hand, how it had touched her and where. Still her mother waited for an answer, holding her wrists so tightly that her hands were going numb. She tried to pull free. Promise, her mother whispered fiercely, promise. Yes, yes, I promise, Rosie said. But for an instant she turned away, and her mother, hearing the familiar glib agreement, released her. Oh, you, you, you, her eyes and twisted mouth said, you fool. Rosie, covering her face, began at last to cry, and the embrace and consoling hand came much later than she expected.

—1949

GRACE PALEY (1922-2007)

The youngest of three children, Grace Paley was born in the Bronx, New York, into a Russian-Jewish immigrant family. Russian, Yiddish, and English were spoken in her family home, and her immigrant neighborhood was very culturally diverse; this background would deeply influence her writing. She attended Hunter College, New York University, and the New School for Social Research (where she studied with W.H. Auden), though she never completed an academic degree. Paley is perhaps as well known for her political activism as she is for her writing. Beginning in the 1950s, she was active in the movement to end nuclear proliferation and U.S. militarization, and she worked with the American Friends Service Committee to establish neighborhood peace groups. She protested the Vietnam War, joining the War Resisters League and participating in a 1969 peace mission to Hanoi. She served as a delegate to the World Peace Conference in 1974 and was one of the "White House Eleven," who unfurled an anti-nuclear banner on the White House lawn. Paley has published three collections of short stories and three collections of poems. She is known for writing about the immigrant experience in the United States, as well as for work with feminist and political content.

A Conversation with My Father

My father is eighty-six years old and in bed. His heart, that bloody motor, is equally old and will not do certain jobs anymore. It still floods his head with brainy light. But it won't let his legs carry the weight of his body around the house. Despite my metaphors, this muscle failure is not due to his old heart, he says, but to a potassium shortage. Sitting on one pillow, leaning on three, he offers last-minute advice and makes a request.

"I would like you to write a simple story just once more," he says, "the kind Maupassant[1] wrote, or Chekhov,[2] the kind you used to write. Just recognizable people and then write down what happened to them next."

I say, "Yes, why not? That's possible." I want to please him, though I don't remember writing that way. I *would* like to try to tell such a story, if he means the kind that begins: "There was a woman..." followed by plot, the absolute line between two points which I've always despised. Not for literary reasons, but because it takes all hope away. Everyone, real or invented, deserves the open destiny of life.

Finally I thought of a story that had been happening for a couple of years right across the street. I wrote it down, then read it aloud. "Pa," I said, "how about this? Do you mean something like this?"

> Once in my time there was a woman and she had a son. They lived nicely, in a small apartment in Manhattan. This boy at about fifteen became a junkie, which is not unusual in our neighborhood. In order to maintain her close friendship with him, she became a junkie too. She said it was part of the youth culture, with which she felt very much at home. After a while, for a number of reasons, the boy gave it all up and left the city and his mother in disgust. Hopeless and alone, she grieved. We all visit her.

---

[1] Guy de Maupassant (1850-1893), French novelist and short story writer.

[2] Anton Pavlovich Chekhov (1860-1904), Russian short story writer and playwright.

"O.K., Pa, that's it," I said, "an unadorned and miserable tale."

"But that's not what I mean," my father said. "You misunderstood me on purpose. You know there's a lot more to it. You know that. You left everything out. Turgenev[3] wouldn't do that. Chekhov wouldn't do that. There are in fact Russian writers you never heard of, you don't have an inkling of, as good as anyone, who can write a plain ordinary story, who would not leave out what you have left out. I object not to facts but to people sitting in trees talking senselessly, voices from who knows where…"

"Forget that one, Pa, what have I left out now? In this one?"

"Her looks, for instance."

"Oh. Quite handsome, I think. Yes."

"Her hair?"

"Dark, with heavy braids, as though she were a girl or a foreigner."

"What were her parents like, her stock? That she became such a person. It's interesting, you know."

"From out of town. Professional people. The first to be divorced in their county. How's that? Enough?" I asked.

"With you, it's all a joke," he said. "What about the boy's father? Why didn't you mention him? Who was he? Or was the boy born out of wedlock?"

"Yes," I said. "He was born out of wedlock."

"For godsakes, doesn't anyone in your stories get married? Doesn't anyone have the time to run down to City Hall before they jump into bed?"

"No," I said. "In real life, yes. But in my stories, no."

"Why do you answer me like that?"

"Oh, Pa, this is a simple story about a smart woman who came to N.Y.C. full of interest love trust excitement very up-to-date, and about her son, what a hard time she had in this world. Married or not, it's of small consequence."

"It is of great consequence," he said.

"O.K.," I said.

"O.K. O.K. yourself," he said, "but listen. I believe you that she's good-looking, but I don't think she was so smart."

"That's true," I said. "Actually that's the trouble with stories. People start out fantastic. You think they're extraordinary, but it turns out as the work goes along, they're just average with a good education. Sometimes the other way around, the person's a kind of dumb innocent, but he outwits you and you can't even think of an ending good enough."

"What do you do then?" he asked. He had been a doctor for a couple of decades and then an artist for a couple of decades and he's still interested in details, craft, technique.

"Well, you just have to let the story lie around till some agreement can be reached between you and the stubborn hero."

"Aren't you talking silly, now?" he asked. "Start again," he said. "It so happens I'm not going out this evening. Tell the story again. See what you can do this time."

---

[3] Ivan Sergeyevich Turgenev (1818-1883), Russian novelist, dramatist, and short story writer.

"O.K.," I said. "But it's not a five-minute job." Second attempt:

Once, across the street from us, there was a fine handsome woman, our neighbor. She had a son whom she loved because she'd known him since birth (in helpless chubby infancy, and in the wrestling, hugging ages, seven to ten, as well as earlier and later). This boy, when he fell into the fist of adolescence, became a junkie. He was not a hopeless one. He was in fact hopeful, an ideologue and successful converter. With his busy brilliance, he wrote persuasive articles for his high-school newspaper. Seeking a wider audience, using important connections, he drummed into Lower Manhattan newsstand distribution a periodical called *Oh! Golden Horse!*

In order to keep him from feeling guilty (because guilt is the stony heart of nine-tenths of all clinically diagnosed cancers in America today, she said), and because she had always believed in giving bad habits room at home where one could keep an eye on them, she too became a junkie. Her kitchen was famous for a while—a center for intellectual addicts who knew what they were doing. A few felt artistic like Coleridge[4] and others were scientific and revolutionary like Leary.[5] Although she was often high herself, certain good mothering reflexes remained, and she saw to it that there was lots of orange juice around and honey and milk and vitamin pills. However, she never cooked anything but chili, and that no more than once a week. She explained, when we talked to her, seriously, with neighborly concern, that it was her part in the youth culture and she would rather be with the young, it was an honor, than with her own generation.

One week, while nodding through an Antonioni[6] film, this boy was severely jabbed by the elbow of a stern and proselytizing girl, sitting beside him. She offered immediate apricots and nuts for his sugar level, spoke to him sharply, and took him home.

She had heard of him and his work and she herself published, edited, and wrote a competitive journal called *Man Does Live by Bread Alone*. In the organic heat of her continuous presence he could not help but become interested once more in his muscles, his arteries and nerve connections. In fact he began to love them, treasure them, praise them with funny little songs in *Man Does Live...*

> *the fingers of my flesh transcend*
> *my transcendental soul*
> *the tightness in my shoulders end*
> *my teeth have made me whole*

To the mouth of his head (that glory of will and determination) he brought hard apples, nuts, wheat germ, and soybean oil. He said to his old-friends, From now on, I guess I'll keep my wits about me. I'm going on the

---

[4] Samuel Taylor Coleridge (1772-1834), English Romantic poet.
[5] Timothy Francis Leary (1920-1996), American psychologist and educator, famous for encouraging people to experiment with hallucinogens in the 1960s.
[6] Michelangelo Antonioni (1912-2007), Italian modernist film director.

natch. He said he was about to begin a spiritual deep-breathing journey. How about you too, Mom? he asked kindly.

His conversion was so radiant, splendid, that neighborhood kids his age began to say that he had never been a real addict at all, only a journalist along for the smell of the story. The mother tried several times to give up what had become without her son and his friends a lonely habit. This effort only brought it to supportable levels. The boy and his girl took their electronic mimeograph and moved to the bushy edge of another borough. They were very strict. They said they would not see her again until she had been off drugs for sixty days.

At home alone in the evening, weeping, the mother read and reread the seven issues of *Oh! Golden Horse!* They seemed to her as truthful as ever. We often crossed the street to visit and console. But if we mentioned any of our children who were at college or in the hospital or dropouts at home, she would cry out, My baby! My baby! and burst into terrible, face-scarring, time-consuming tears. The End.

First my father was silent, then he said, "Number One: You have a nice sense of humor. Number Two: I see you can't tell a plain story. So don't waste time." Then he said sadly, "Number Three: I suppose that means she was alone, she was left like that, his mother. Alone. Probably sick?"

I said, "Yes."

"Poor woman. Poor girl, to be born in a time of fools, to live among fools. The end. The end. You were right to put that down. The end."

I didn't want to argue, but I had to say, "Well, it is not necessarily the end, Pa."

"Yes," he said, "what a tragedy. The end of a person."

"No, Pa," I begged him. "It doesn't have to be. She's only about forty. She could be a hundred different things in this world as time goes on. A teacher or a social worker. An ex-junkie! Sometimes it's better than having a master's in education."

"Jokes," he said. "As a writer that's your main trouble. You don't want to recognize it. Tragedy! Plain tragedy! Historical tragedy! No hope. The end."

"Oh, Pa," I said. "She could change."

"In your own life, too, you have to look it in the face." He took a couple of nitroglycerin. "Turn to five," he said, pointing to the dial on the oxygen tank. He inserted the tubes into his nostrils and breathed deep. He closed his eyes and said, "No."

I had promised the family to always let him have the last word when arguing, but in this case I had a different responsibility. That woman lives across the street. She's my knowledge and my invention. I'm sorry for her. I'm not going to leave her there in that house crying. (Actually neither would Life, which unlike me has no pity.)

Therefore: She did change. Of course her son never came home again. But right now, she's the receptionist in a storefront community clinic in the East Village. Most of the customers are young people, some old friends. The head doctor has said to her, "If we only had three people in this clinic with your experiences…"

"The doctor said that?" My father took the oxygen tubes out of his nostrils and said, "Jokes. Jokes again."

"No, Pa, it could really happen that way, it's a funny world nowadays."

"No," he said. "Truth first. She will slide back. A person must have character. She does not."

"No, Pa," I said. "That's it. She's got a job. Forget it. She's in that storefront working."

"How long will it be?" he asked. "Tragedy! You too. When will you look it in the face?"

—1974

JEAN RITCHIE (1922-)

Jean Ritchie was born in Viper, Kentucky, to a family of musicians. The youngest of the fourteen Ritchie children, she and nine sisters slept in one room of their house. Folklorist Alan Lomax came to Kentucky in the mid-1930s and recorded the "Singing Ritchies" (including teenage Jean) for the Library of Congress project entitled "Archive of Folk Song." In spite of this recognition of their skill and musicianship, not until the late 1940s did the family own a radio and learn that what they were singing had a name—hillbilly music.

Ritchie attended Cumberland Junior College and the University of Kentucky, earning a degree in social work in 1946. After graduation, Ritchie traveled to New York City to work in the Henry Street Settlement House. There, she met folk musicians Pete Seeger, Leadbelly, and others. By 1948 she was singing her "family songs" and playing the mountain dulcimer onstage, as well as recording with Elektra Records. Lomax introduced her to New York publishers, and her book *Singing Family of the Cumberlands* appeared in 1955. Ritchie used a Fulbright grant to collect the more than three hundred songs she knew from her childhood, and to explore the connections between the American versions of those ballads and their British and Irish originals. Ritchie has performed all over the world, and is known by many as the "Mother of Folk Music" for her part in leading the U.S. folk music revival in the 1950s and 1960s.

The L and N[1] Don't Stop Here Anymore

Oh, when I was a curly headed baby,
My daddy set me down upon his knee;
Said, "Son, you go to school and learn your letters.
Don't be no dusty miner like me.

Chorus
For I was born and raised at the mouth of the Hazard Holler,   5
Coal cars roarin' and a-rumblin' past my door;
Now they're standin' rusty, rollin' empty,
And the L and N don't stop here anymore."

---

[1] The Louisville and Nashville Railroad operated from 1850 to 1982, primarily in the Southeast.

I used to think my daddy was a black man
With scrip[2] enough to buy the company store,   10
But now he goes downtown with empty pockets
And his face as white as February snow.
[*Chorus*]

Last night I dreamt I went down to the office
To get my pay just like I done before;
Kudzu vines had covered up the doorway,   15
And there was trees and grass a-growin' through the floor.

[*Chorus*]

I never thought I'd live to love the coal dust;
Never thought I'd pray to hear the tipple roar.
But, Lord, how I wish that grass could change to money,
Them greenbacks fill my pockets once more!   20

[*Chorus*]

—1963

Black Waters[3]

I come from the mountains, Kentucky's my home,
Where the wild deer and the black bear so lately did roam;
By cool rushing waterfalls, the wild flowers dream,
And through every green valley there runs a clear stream.
Now there's scenes of destruction on every hand,   5
And there's only black waters run down through my land

Sad scenes of destruction on every hand;
Black waters, black waters run down through our land.

O the quail, she's a pretty bird, she sings a sweet tongue;
In the roots of tall timbers she nests with her young.   10
But the hillside explodes with the dynamite's roar,
And the voices of the small birds will sound there no more;
And the hillsides come a-sliding so awful and grand,
And the flooding black waters rise over my land

Sad scenes of destruction on every hand;   15
Black waters, black waters run down through our land.

—1967

---

[2] A substitute for legal tender. Ritchie is referring here to the practice of companies issuing scrip to workers as a form of credit (and sometimes as pay), which was then redeemable only at company stores where goods were sold at a high markup.

[3] Water containing coal particles, usually as a result of mining activities, that is detrimental to the environment.

JADE SNOW WONG (1922–2006)

Born in 1922 and raised in San Francisco's Chinatown, Jade Snow Wong was the fifth daughter in a family of six girls and three boys. After graduating with honors from Mills College in Oakland in 1942, Wong worked as a secretary with the War Production Board from 1943 to 1945. Her autobiography, *Fifth Chinese Daughter* (1945), recounts her experiences growing up in a Chinese-American family and community. *Fifth Chinese Daughter* was a bestseller, and the U.S. State Department sponsored Wong on a speaking tour through Asia. The State Department also translated the book into Chinese, Japanese, Thai, German, Urdu, Burmese, and Indonesian. Wong explained that her decision to write about herself in the third person was due to Chinese modesty, for using the first person would seem egocentric. The book has been read by critics of Asian-American literature as an autoethnographic text by a writer positioning herself as cultural informant. Because its rhetoric and content seem designed to present the Chinese-American as a model minority, *Fifth Chinese Daughter* is acknowledged within Asian-American literary studies as a foundational but controversial text. Wong published a second book, *No Chinese Stranger,* in 1975. She received an honorary Doctor of Humane Letters from the Mills College the following year. Wong was also an acclaimed ceramicist; some of her pieces are included in the collections of the Metropolitan Museum of Art and the Museum of Modern Art in New York City.

from Fifth Chinese Daughter

Chapter 15
A Measure of Freedom

So, without much enthusiasm, Jade Snow decided upon junior college. Now it was necessary to inform Mama and Daddy. She chose an evening when the family was at dinner. All of them were in their customary places, and Daddy, typically, was in conversation with Older Brother about the factory:

"Blessing, when do you think Lot Number fifty-one twenty-six will be finished? I want to ask for a check from our jobber so that I can have enough cash for next week's payroll."

To which Older Brother replied, "As soon as Mama is through with the seams in Mrs. Lee's and Mrs. Choy's bundles, the women can finish the hems. Another day, probably."

Mama had not been consulted; therefore she made no comment. Silence descended as the Wongs continued their meal, observing the well-learned precept that talk was not permissible while eating.

Jade Snow considered whether to break the silence. Three times she thought over what she had to say, and still she found it worth saying. This also was according to family precept.

"Daddy," she said, "I have made up my mind to enter junior college here in San Francisco. I will find a steady job to pay my expenses, and by working in the summers I'll try to save enough money to take me through my last two years at the university."

Then she waited. Everyone went on eating. No one said a word. Apparently no one was interested enough to be curious. But at least no one objected. It was settled.

Junior college was at first disappointing in more ways than one. There was none of the glamour usually associated with college because the institution was so young that it had not yet acquired buildings of its own. Classes were held all over the city wherever accommodations were available. The first days were very confusing to Jade Snow, especially when she discovered that she must immediately decide upon a college major.

While waiting to register, she thumbed through the catalogue in search of a clue. English…mathematics…chemistry…. In the last semester of high school she had found chemistry particularly fascinating: so with a feeling of assurance she wrote that as her major on the necessary forms, and went to a sign-up table.

"I wish to take the lecture and laboratory classes for Chemistry lA," she informed the gray-haired man who presided there.

He looked at her, a trifle impatiently she thought.

"Why?"

"Because I like it." To herself she sounded reasonable.

"But you are no longer in high school. Chemistry here is a difficult subject on a university level, planned for those who are majoring in medicine, engineering, or the serious sciences."

Jade Snow set her chin stubbornly. "I still want to take Chemistry lA."

Sharply he questioned: "What courses in mathematics have you had? What were your grades?"

Finally Jade Snow's annoyance rose to the surface. "Straight A's. But why must you ask? Do you think I would want to take a course I couldn't pass? Why don't you sign me up and let the instructor be the judge of my ability?"

"Very well," he replied stiffly. "I'll accept you in the class. And for your information, young lady, I am the instructor!"

With this inauspicious start, Jade Snow began her college career.

To take care of finances, she now needed to look for work. Through a friend she learned that a Mrs. Simpson needed someone to help with household work. "Can you cook?" was Mrs. Simpson's first question.

Jade Snow considered a moment before answering. Certainly she could cook Chinese food, and she remembered a common Chinese saying, "A Chinese can cook foreign food as well as, if not better than, the foreigners, but a foreigner cannot cook Chinese food fit for the Chinese." On this reasoning it seemed safe to say "Yes."

After some further discussion Jade Snow was hired. Cooking, she discovered, included everything from pastries, puddings, meats, steaks, and vegetables, to sandwiches. In addition, she served the meals, washed dishes, kept the house clean, did the light laundry and ironing for Mr. and Mrs. Simpson and their career daughter—and always appeared in uniform, which she thoroughly disliked. In return she received twenty dollars a month. At night, she did her studying at home, and sometimes after a hard day she was so tired that the walk from the Simpson flat to the streetcar on Chestnut Street was a blessed respite, a time to relax and admire the moon if she could find it, and to gather fresh energy for whatever lay ahead.

Desserts, quite ignored in a Chinese household, were of first importance in the Simpson household. One particular Saturday, Jade Snow was told to bake a special meringue sponge cake with a fancy fruit filling of whipped cream and peeled and seeded grapes. Following a very special recipe of Mrs. Simpson's, she mixed it for the first time and preheated the oven. Mrs. Simpson came into the kitchen, checked and approved the prepared cake batter, and said that she would judge when it was done.

Meantime she and her husband and their guests lounged happily in the garden.

Almost an hour passed. The meringue was baking in a slow oven. The recipe said not to open the door, as the cake might fall. An hour and a quarter passed, and the pastry smelled sweetly delicate. Yet Mrs. Simpson did not come. Jade Snow wondered whether or not to call her. But she remembered that her employer disliked being disturbed when entertaining officials of her husband's company.

After an hour and forty-five minutes the cake no longer smelled delicate. Jade Snow was worn out! What could she do? At last, there was a rush of high-heeled footsteps; swish went the kitchen door, and Mrs. Simpson burst in, flushed from the sun or excitement.

"I must look at that meringue cake," she burst out.

The oven door was pulled open, and Jade Snow peered in anxiously over her employer's shoulder. Too late! It had fallen and become a tough, brown mass. Jade Snow was dumb with a crushed heart, inspecting the flattened pancake, mentally reviewing all the processes of whipping, measuring, and sifting that she had gone through for hours to achieve this unpalatable result.

Mrs. Simpson crisply broke through to her anguish, "Well, there's nothing to be done but for you to make another."

That afternoon was a torturous nightmare and a fever of activity—to manage another meringue cake, to get rolls mixed, salad greens cleaned and crisped, vegetables cut, meat broiled, the table set, and all the other details of a "company" dinner attended to. By the time she was at last washing the dishes and tidying the dining room she felt strangely vague. She hadn't taken time to eat her dinner; she was too tired anyway. How she wished that she had been asked to cook a Chinese dinner instead of this interminable American meal, especially that cake!

Of her college courses, Latin was the easiest. This was a surprise, for everyone had told her of its horrors. It was much more logical than French, almost mathematical in its orderliness and precision, and actually a snap after nine years of Chinese.

Chemistry, true to the instructor's promise, was difficult, although the classes were anything but dull. It turned out that he was a very nice person with a keen sense of humor and a gift for enlivening his lectures with stories of his own college days. There were only two girls in a class of more than fifty men—a tense blonde girl from Germany, who always ranked first; and Jade Snow, who usually took second place.

But if Latin was the easiest course and chemistry the most difficult, sociology was the most stimulating. Jade Snow had chosen it without thought, simply to meet a requirement; but that casual decision completely revolutionized her thinking, shattering her Wong-constructed conception of the order of things. This was the way it happened:

After several uneventful weeks during which the class explored the historical origins of the family and examined such terms as "norms," "mores," "folkways," there came a day when the instructor stood before them to discuss the relationship of parents and children. It was a day like many others, with the students listening in varying attitudes of interest or indifference. The instructor was speaking casually of ideas to be accepted as standard. Then suddenly upon Jade Snow's astounded ears there fell this statement:

"There was a period in our American history when parents had children for economic reasons, to put them to work as soon as possible, especially to have them help on the farm. But now we no longer regard children in this way. Today we recognize that children are individuals, and that parents can no longer demand their unquestioning obedience. Parents should do their best to understand their children, because young people also have their rights."

The instructor went on talking, but Jade Snow heard no more, for her mind was echoing and re-echoing this startling thought. "Parents can no longer demand unquestioning obedience from their children. They should do their best to under-stand. Children also have their rights." For the rest of that day, while she was doing her chores at the Simpsons', while she was standing in the streetcar going home, she was busy translating the idea into terms of her own experience.

"My parents demand unquestioning obedience. Older Brother demands unquestioning obedience. By what right? I am an individual besides being a Chinese daughter. I have rights too."

Could it be that Daddy and Mama, although they were living in San Francisco in the year 1938, actually had not left the Chinese world of thirty years ago? Could it be that they were forgetting that Jade Snow would soon become a woman in a new America, not a woman in old China? In short, was it possible that Daddy and Mama could be wrong?

For days Jade Snow gave thought to little but her devastating discovery that her parents might be subject to error. As it was her habit always to act after reaching a conclusion, she wondered what to do about it. Should she tell Daddy and Mama that they needed to change their ways? One moment she thought she should, the next she thought not. At last she decided to overcome her fear in the interests of education and better understanding. She would at least try to open their minds to modern truths. If she succeeded, good! If not, she was prepared to suffer the consequences.

In this spirit of patient martyrdom she waited for an opportunity to speak.

It came, surprisingly, one Saturday. Ordinarily that was a busy day at the Simpsons', a time for entertaining, so that Jade Snow was not free until too late to go anywhere even had she had a place to go. But on this particular Saturday the Simpsons were away for the weekend, and by three in the afternoon Jade Snow was ready to leave the apartment with unplanned hours ahead of her. She didn't want to spend these rare hours of freedom in any usual way. And she didn't want to spend them alone.

"Shall I call Joe?" she wondered. She had never telephoned to a boy before and she debated whether it would be too forward. But she felt too happy and carefree to worry much, and she was confident that Joe would not misunderstand.

Even before reporting to Mama that she was home, she ran downstairs to the telephone booth and gave the operator Joe's number. His mother answered and then went to call him while Jade Snow waited in embarrassment.

"Joe." She was suddenly tongue-tied. "Joe, I'm already home."

That wasn't at all what she wanted to say. What did she want to say?

"Hello! Hello!" Joe boomed back. "What's the matter with you? Are you all right?"

"Oh, yes, I'm fine. Only, only…well, I'm through working for the day." That was really all she had to say, but now it sounded rather pointless.

"Isn't that wonderful? It must have been unexpected." That was what was nice and different about Joe. He always seemed to know without a lot of words. But because his teasing was never far behind his understanding he added quickly, "I suppose you're going to study and go to bed early."

Jade Snow was still not used to teasing and didn't know how to take it. With an effort she swallowed her shyness and disappointment. "I thought we might go for a walk…that is, if you have nothing else to do…if you would care to…if…."

Joe laughed. "I'll go you one better. Suppose I take you to a movie. I'll even get all dressed up for you, and you get dressed up too."

Jade Snow was delighted. Her first movie with Joe! What a wonderful day. In happy anticipation she put on her long silk stockings, lipstick, and the nearest thing to a suit she owned—a hand-me-down jacket and a brown skirt she had made herself. Then with a bright ribbon tying back her long black hair she was ready.

Daddy didn't miss a detail of the preparations as she dashed from room to room. He waited until she was finished before he demanded, "Jade Snow, where are you going?"

"I am going out into the street," she answered.

"Did you ask my permission to go out into the street?"

"No, Daddy."

"Do you have your mother's permission to go out into the street?"

"No, Daddy."

A sudden silence from the kitchen indicated that Mama was listening.

Daddy went on: "Where and when did you learn to be so daring as to leave this house without permission of your parents? You did not learn it under my roof."

It was all very familiar. Jade Snow waited, knowing that Daddy had not finished. In a moment he came to the point.

"And with whom are you going out into the street?"

It took all the courage Jade Snow could muster, remembering her new thinking, to say nothing. It was certain that if she told Daddy that she was going out with a boy whom he did not know, without a chaperone, he would be convinced that she would lose her maidenly purity before the evening was over.

"Very well," Daddy said sharply. "If you will not tell me, I forbid you to go! You are now too old to whip."

That was the moment.

Suppressing all anger, and in a manner that would have done credit to her sociology instructor addressing his freshman class, Jade Snow carefully turned on her mentally rehearsed speech.

"That is something you should think more about. Yes, I am too old to whip. I am too old to be treated as a child. I can now think for myself, and you and Mama should not demand unquestioning obedience from me. You should understand me. There was a time in America when parents raised children to make them work, but now the foreigners regard them as individuals with rights of their own. I have worked too, but now I am an individual besides being your fifth daughter."

It was almost certain that Daddy blinked, but after the briefest pause he gathered himself together.

"Where," he demanded, "did you learn such an unfilial theory?"

Mama had come quietly into the room and slipped into a chair to listen.

"From my teacher," Jade Snow answered triumphantly, "who you taught me is supreme after you, and whose judgment I am not to question."

Daddy was feeling pushed. Thoroughly aroused, he shouted:

"A little learning has gone to your head! How can you permit a foreigner's theory to put aside the practical experience of the Chinese, who for thousands of years have preserved a most superior family pattern? Confucius had already presented an organized philosophy of manners and conduct when the foreigners were unappreciatively persecuting Christ. Who brought you up? Who clothed you, fed you, sheltered you, nursed you? Do you think you were born aged sixteen? You owe honor to us before you satisfy your personal whims."

Daddy thundered on, while Jade Snow kept silent.

"What would happen to the order of this household if each of you four children started to behave like individuals? Would we have one peaceful moment if your personal desires came before your duty? How could we maintain our self-respect if we, your parents, did not know where you were at night and with whom you were keeping company?"

With difficulty Jade Snow kept herself from being swayed by fear and the old familiar arguments. "You can be bad in the daytime as well as at night," she said defensively. "What could happen after eleven that couldn't happen before?"

Daddy was growing more excited. "Do I have to justify my judgment to you? I do not want a daughter of mine to be known as one who walks the streets at night. Have you no thought for our reputations if not for your own? If you start going out with boys, no good man will want to ask you to be his wife. You just do not know as well as we do what is good for you."

Mama fanned Daddy's wrath, "Never having been a mother, you cannot know how much grief it is to bring up a daughter. Of course we will not permit you to run the risk of corrupting your purity before marriage."

"Oh, Mama!" Jade Snow retorted. "This is America, not China. Don't you think I have any judgment? How can you think I would go out with just any man?"

"Men!" Daddy roared. "You don't know a thing about them. I tell you, you can't trust any of them."

Now it was Jade Snow who felt pushed. She delivered the balance of her declaration of independence:

"Both of you should understand that I am growing up to be a woman in a society greatly different from the one you knew in China. You expect me to work my way through college—which would not have been possible in China. You expect me to exercise judgment in choosing my employers and my jobs and in spending my own money in the American world. Then why can't I choose my friends? Of course independence is not safe. But safety isn't the only consideration. You must give me the freedom to find some answers for myself."

Mama found her tongue first. "You think you are too good for us because you have a little foreign book knowledge."

"You will learn the error of your ways after it is too late," Daddy added darkly.

By this Jade Snow knew that her parents had conceded defeat. Hoping to soften the blow, she tried to explain: "If I am to earn my living, I must learn how to get along with many kinds of people, with foreigners as well as Chinese. I intend to start finding out about them now. You must have confidence that I shall remain true to the spirit of your teachings. I shall bring back to you the new knowledge of whatever I learn."

Daddy and Mama did not accept this offer graciously. "It is as useless for you to tell me such ideas as 'The wind blows across a deaf ear.' You have lost your sense of balance," Daddy told her bluntly. "You are shameless. Your skin is yellow. Your features are forever Chinese. We are content with our proven ways. Do not try to force foreign ideas into my home. Go. You will one day tell us sorrowfully that you have been mistaken."

After that there was no further discussion of the matter. Jade Snow came and went without any questions being asked. In spite of her parents' dark predictions, her new freedom in the choice of companions did not result in a rush of undesirables. As a matter of fact, the boys she met at school were more concerned with copying her lecture notes than with anything else.

As for Joe, he remained someone to walk with and talk with. On the evening of Jade Snow's seventeenth birthday he took her up Telegraph Hill and gave her as a remembrance a sparkling grown-up bracelet with a card which read: "Here's to your making Phi Beta Kappa." And there under the stars he gently tilted her face and gave her her first kiss.

Standing straight and awkward in her full-skirted red cotton dress, Jade Snow was caught by surprise and without words. She felt that something should stir and crash within her, in the way books and the movies described, but nothing did. Could it be that she wasn't in love with Joe, in spite of liking and admiring him? After all, he was twenty-three and probably too old for her anyway.

Still she had been kissed at seventeen, which was cause for rejoicing. Laughing happily, they continued their walk.

But while the open rebellion gave Jade Snow a measure of freedom she had not had before, and an outer show of assurance, she was deeply troubled within. It had been simple to have Daddy and Mama tell her what was right and wrong; it was not simple to decide for herself. No matter how critical she was of them, she could not discard all they stood for and accept as a substitute the philosophy of the foreigners. It took very little thought to discover that the foreign philosophy also was subject to criticism, and that for her there had to be a middle way.

In particular, she could not reject the fatalism that was at the core of all Chinese thinking and behavior, the belief that the broad pattern of an individual's life was ordained by fate although within that pattern he was capable of perfecting himself and accumulating a desirable store of good will. Should the individual not benefit by his good works, still the rewards would pass on to his children or his children's children. Epitomized by the proverbs: "I save your life, for your grandson might save mine," and "Heaven does not forget to follow the path a good man walks," this was a fundamental philosophy of Chinese life which Jade Snow found fully as acceptable as some of the so-called scientific reasoning expounded in the sociology class, where heredity and environment were assigned all the responsibility for personal success or failure.

There was good to be gained from both concepts if she could extract and retain her own personally applicable combination. She studied her neighbor in class, Stella Green, for clues. Stella had grown up reading Robert Louis Stevenson, learning to swim and play tennis, developing a taste for roast beef, mashed potatoes, sweets, aspirin tablets, and soda pop, and she looked upon her mother and father as friends. But it was very unlikely that she knew where her great-grandfather was born, or whether or not she was related to another strange Green she might chance to meet.

Jade Snow had grown up reading Confucius, learning to embroider and cook rice, developing a taste for steamed fish and bean sprouts, tea, and herbs, and she thought of her parents as people to be obeyed. She not only knew where her ancestors were born but where they were buried, and how many chickens and roast pigs should be brought annually to their graves to feast their spirits. She knew all of the branches of the Wong family, the relation of each to the other, and understood why Daddy must help support the distant cousins in China who bore the sole responsibility of carrying on the family heritage by periodic visits to the burial grounds in Fragrant Mountains. She knew that one could purchase in a Chinese stationery store the printed record of her family tree relating their Wong line and other Wong lines back to the original Wong ancestors. In such a scheme the individual counted for little weighed against the family, and after sixteen years it was not easy to sever roots.

There were, alas, no books or advisers to guide Jade Snow in her search for balance between the pull from two cultures. If she chose neither to reject nor accept *in toto*, she must sift both and make her decisions alone. It would not be an easy search. But pride and determination, which Daddy had given her, prevented any thought of turning back.

By the end of her first year of junior college, she had been so impressed by her sociology course that she changed her major to the social studies. Four years of college no longer seemed interminable. The highlight of her second year was an English course which used literature as a basis for stimulating individual expression through theme writing. At this time Jade Snow still thought in Chinese, although she was acquiring an English vocabulary. In consequence she was slower than her classmates, but her training in keeping a diary gave her an advantage in analyzing and recording personal experiences. She discovered very soon that her grades were consistently higher when she wrote about Chinatown and the people she had known all her life. For the first time she realized the joy of expressing herself in the written word. It surprised her and also stimulated her. She learned that good writing should improve upon the kind of factual reporting she had done in her diaries; it should be created in a spirit of artistry. After this course, if Jade Snow had not mastered these principles, at least she could never again write without remembering them and trying her best to apply them.

Hand in hand with a growing awareness of herself and her personal world, there was developing in her an awareness of and a feeling for the larger world beyond the familiar pattern. At eighteen, when Jade Snow compared herself with a diary record of herself at sixteen, she could see many points of difference. She was now an extremely serious young person, with a whole set of worries which she donned with her clothes each morning. The two years had made her a little wiser in the ways of the world, a little more realistic, less of a dreamer, and she hoped more of a personality. In the interval she had put aside an earlier Americanized dream of a husband, a home, a garden, a dog, and children, and there had grown in its place a desire for more schooling in preparation for a career of service to those less fortunate than herself. Boys put her down as a snob and a bookworm. Well, let them. She was independent. She was also frank—much too frank for many people's liking. She had acquaintances, but no real friends who shared her interests. Even Joe had stopped seeing her, having left school to begin his career. Their friendship had given her many things, including confidence in herself as a person at a time when she needed it. It had left with her the habit of walking, and in moments of loneliness she found comfort and sometimes the answers to problems by wandering through odd parts of San Francisco, a city she loved with an ever increasing affection.

On this eighteenth birthday, instead of the birthday cake which Americans considered appropriate, Daddy brought home a fresh-killed chicken which Mama cooked their favorite way by plunging it into a covered pot of boiling water, moving it off the flame and letting it stand for one hour, turning it once. Brushed with oil and sprinkled with shredded fresh green onions, it retained its sweet flavor with all its juices, for it was barely cooked and never dry. It was the Wongs usual birthday dish. Naturally, the birthday of a daughter did not call for the honor due a parent. There was a birthday tea ritual calling for elaborate preparation when Mama's and Daddy's anniversaries came around. Still, to be a girl and eighteen was exciting.

The rest of the year rushed to an end. The years at junior college had been rewarding. Now several happy surprises climaxed them. First there was the satisfaction of election to membership in Alpha Gamma Sigma, an honorary state scholastic organization. On the advice of her English instructor, this precipitated an exchange of letters with an executive of the society concerning a possible scholarship to the university.

In the meantime, overtiredness and overwork brought on recurring back pains which confined Jade Snow to bed for several days. Against her will because she could not afford it, she had been driven to see a doctor, who told her to put a board under her mattress for back support, and gave her two prescriptions to be filled for relief of pain. But there was no money for medicine. She asked Daddy and Mama, who said that they could not afford to pay for it either. So Jade Snow went miserably to bed to stay until the pain should end of its own accord.

She had been there two days when Older Brother entered casually and tossed a letter on her bed. It was from the scholarship chairman of Alpha Gamma Sigma, enclosing a check for fifty dollars. It was an award to her as the most outstanding woman student of the junior colleges in California. Jade Snow's emotions were mixed. What she had wanted and needed was a full scholarship. On the other hand, recognition was sweet—a proof that God had not forgotten her.

On the heels of this letter came another from her faculty adviser, inviting her as one of the ten top-ranking students to compete for position as commencement speaker. "If you care to try out," it concluded, "appear at Room 312 on April 11 at ten o'clock."

Should she or should she not? She had never made a speech in public, and the thought was panic. But had she a right to refuse? Might not this be an opportunity to answer effectively all the "Richards" of the world who screamed "Chinky, Chinky, Chinaman" at her and other Chinese? Might it not be further evidence to offer her family that her decision had not been wrong?

It seemed obvious that the right thing to do was to try, and equally obvious that she should talk about what was most familiar to her: the values which she as an American-Chinese had found in two years of junior college.

At the try-out, in a dry voice, she coaxed out her prepared thesis and fled, not knowing whether she had been good or bad, and not caring. She was glad just to be done. A few days later came formal notification that she would be the salutatorian at graduation. She was terrified as she envisioned the stage at the elegant San Francisco War Memorial Opera House, with its tremendous sparkling chandelier and overpowering tiers of seats. Now she wished that she could escape.

The reality was as frightening as the anticipation when on June 7, 1940, she stood before the graduation audience, listening to her own voice coming over the loudspeaker. All her family were there among the neat rows of faces before her. What did they think, hearing her say, "The Junior College has developed our initiative, fair play, and self-expression, and has given us tools for thinking and analyzing. But it seems to me that the most effective application that American-Chinese can make of their education would be in China, which needs all the Chinese talent she can muster."

Thus Jade Snow—shaped by her father's and mother's unceasing loyalty toward their mother country, impressed with China's needs by speakers who visited Chinatown, revolutionized by American ideas, fired with enthusiasm for social service—thought that she had quite independently arrived at the perfect solution for the future of all thinking and conscientious young Chinese, including herself. Did her audience agree with her conclusion?

At last it was over, the speeches and applause, the weeping and excited exchange of congratulations. According to plan, Jade Snow met her family on the steps of the Opera House, where they were joined shortly by her faculty adviser and her English professor. Conversation proceeded haltingly, as Daddy and Mama spoke only Chinese.

Mama took the initiative: "Thank your teachers for me for all the kind assistance they have given you. Ask them to excuse my not being able to speak English."

"Yes, indeed," Daddy added. "A fine teacher is very rare."

When Jade Snow had duly translated the remarks, she took advantage of a pause to inquire casually, "How was my speech?"

Mama was noncommittal. "I can't understand English."

"You talked too fast at first," was Older Brother's opinion.

Daddy was more encouraging: "It could be considered passable. For your first speech, that was about it."

The subject was closed. Daddy had spoken. But there was a surprise in store.

"Will you ask your teachers to join us for late supper at a Chinese restaurant?" Daddy suggested.

"What restaurant?" Jade Snow wanted to know, bewildered.

"Tao-Tao on Jackson Street. I have made reservations and ordered food."

Hardly able to credit her senses, Jade Snow trailed after the party. At first she was apprehensive, feeling it her responsibility to make the guests comfortable and at ease in the strange surroundings. But her fears were unfounded. The guests genuinely enjoyed the novel experience of breaking bread with the Wongs. It was a thoroughly happy and relaxed time for everyone as they sat feasting on delicious stuffed-melon soup, Peking duck, steamed thousand-layer buns, and tasty crisp greens.

The whole day had been remarkable, but most remarkable of all was the fact that for the first time since her break with her parents, Mama and Daddy had granted her a measure of recognition and acceptance. For the first time they had met on common ground with her American associates. It was a sign that they were at last tolerant of her effort to search for her own pattern of life.

—1945

DENISE LEVERTOV (1923-1997)

Raised outside of London, Levertov and her older sister Olga were homeschooled in a household with deep intellectual and spiritual leanings. Her mother was a Welsh Congregationalist, and her father, a Russian Hasidic Jew who converted to Christianity and became an Anglican priest, was a scholarly preacher. Their home was a meeting ground for theologians, artists, and refugees from Nazi Europe. Not surprisingly, many of Levertov's poems explore the border between the sacred and profane, and veer sharply into political activism during the Vietnam War era. Levertov published her first poem at the age of seventeen, then worked as a nurse during World War II. In 1947 she married Mitchell Goodman, an American studying in Europe, and moved to the United States. The marriage ended in divorce, but Levertov remained in the U.S. for the rest of her life. Levertov's development as a poet is marked by many American influences and friendships, among them William Carlos Williams, Robert Duncan, Robert Creeley, H.D., and Muriel Rukeyser. Levertov published twenty-two poetry volumes and four collected editions, four books of prose, and two books of translations. The posthumous publication of her letters is ongoing. Late in life she moved to Seattle, Washington, where she converted to Roman Catholicism.

O Taste and See

The world is
not with us enough.
O taste and see

the subway Bible poster said,
meaning **The Lord**, meaning   5
if anything all that lives
to the imagination's tongue,

grief, mercy, language,
tangerine, weather, to
breathe them, bite,   10
savor, chew, swallow, transform

into our flesh our
deaths, crossing the street, plum, quince,
living in the orchard and being

hungry, and plucking   15
the fruit.

—1964

Song for Ishtar[1]

The moon is a sow
and grunts in my throat
Her great shining shines through me

---

[1] Goddess of war and sexual love in Mesopotamian religion.

so the mud of my hollow gleams
and breaks in silver bubbles   5

She is a sow
and I a pig and a poet

When she opens her white
lips to devour me I bite back
and laughter rocks the moon   10

In the black of desire
we rock and grunt, grunt and
shine

—1964

What Were They Like?

1) Did the people of Viet Nam
   use lanterns of stone?
2) Did they hold ceremonies
   to reverence the opening of buds?
3) Were they inclined to quiet laughter?   5
4) Did they use bone and ivory,
   jade and silver, for ornament?
5) Had they an epic poem?
6) Did they distinguish between speech and singing?

1) Sir, their light hearts turned to stone.   10
   It is not remembered whether in gardens
   stone lanterns illumined pleasant ways.
2) Perhaps they gathered once to delight in blossom,
   but after the children were killed
   there were no more buds.   15
3) Sir, laughter is bitter to the burned mouth.
4) A dream ago, perhaps. Ornament is for joy.
   All the bones were charred.
5) It is not remembered. Remember,
   most were peasants; their life   20
   was in rice and bamboo.
   When peaceful clouds were reflected in the paddies
   and the water buffalo stepped surely along terraces,
   maybe fathers told their sons old tales.
   When bombs smashed those mirrors   25
   there was time only to scream.
6) There is an echo yet
   of their speech which was like a song.
   It was reported their singing resembled
   the flight of moths in moonlight.   30
   Who can say? It is silent now.

—1971

MITSUYE YAMADA (1923-   )

Born in Fukuoka, Japan, while her parents were in the country on an extended visit, Mitsuye Yamada emigrated to the U.S. with her family when she was three and a half, settling in Seattle, Washington. Her father, Jack Yasutake, the president of a Japanese poetry group in Seattle and an interpreter for the U.S. Immigration Service, was arrested as a potential spy immediately after the attack on Pearl Harbor, and the family was incarcerated at a relocation camp in Idaho in 1942. Yamada left the camp two years later to attend college, first at the University of Cincinnati and then at New York University, where she received her B.A. in 1947. She received an M.A. from the University of Chicago in 1953.

Yamada's *Camp Notes and Other Poems* is considered a historically significant book because it consists of poems written during and soon after World War II about the experience of internment. The poems were finally printed and distributed in 1976, after Yamada's colleagues persuaded her to publish them with the feminist publishing company Shameless Hussy Press. Yamada's "Invisibility Is an Unnatural Disaster," published in *This Bridge Called My Back* (1981), was a highly influential essay and an important document of Asian-American feminism during the 1970s and 1980s. *Desert Run: Poems and Stories* (1988) continues to articulate Yamada's concerns with race, racism, and gender. Another recurring theme in her writing is the geography of the desert—a key part of her experience in the internment camp as well as her current life in Southern California. Along with Nellie Wong, Yamada is featured in the 1981 documentary film *Mitsuye and Nellie: Asian American Poets*. Yamada taught literature and creative writing at several universities and colleges before retiring in 1989.

Cincinnati

Freedom at last
in this town aimless
I walked against the rush
hour traffic
My first day   5
in a real city
where

no one knew me.

No one except one
hissing voice that said   10
dirty jap
warm spittle on my right cheek.
I turned and faced
the shop window
and my spittled face   15
spilled onto a hill
of books.
Words on display.

In Government Square
people criss-crossed   20

the street
like the spokes of
a giant wheel.

I lifted my right hand
but it would not obey me.   25
My other hand fumbled
for a hankie.

My tears would not
wash it. They stopped
and parted.   30
My hankie brushed
the forked
tears and spittle
together.
I edged toward the curb   35
loosened my fisthold
and the bleached laced
mother-ironed hankie blossomed in
the gutter atop teeth marked
gum wads and heeled candy wrappers.   40

Everyone knew me.

—1976

The Night Before Good-Bye

Mama is mending
my underwear
while my brothers sleep.
Her husband taken away by the FBI
one son lured away by the Army   5
now another son and daughter
lusting for the free world outside.
She must let go.
The war goes on.
She will take one still small son   10
and join Papa in internment
to make a family.
Still sewing
squinting in the dim light
in room C barrack 4 block 4   15
she whispers
Remember
keep your underwear
in good repair
in case of accident   20

don't bring shame
on us.

—1976

Thirty Years Under

I had packed up
my wounds in a cast
iron box
sealed it
labeled it   5
do not open...
ever...

and traveled blind
for thirty years

until one day I heard   10
a black man with huge bulbous eyes
say
there is nothing more
humiliating
more than beatings   15
more than curses
than being spat on

like a dog.

—1976

Invisibility Is an Unnatural Disaster:
Reflections of an Asian American Woman

Last year for the Asian segment of the Ethnic American Literature course I was
teaching, I selected a new anthology entitled *Aiiieeeee!* compiled by a group of outspoken Asian American writers. During the discussion of the long but thought-provoking
introduction to this anthology, one of my students blurted out that she was offended
by its militant tone and that as a white person she was tired of always being blamed
for the oppression of all the minorities. I noticed several of her classmates' eyes nodding in tacit agreement. A discussion of the "militant" voices in some of the other
writings we had read in the course ensued. Surely, I pointed out, some of these other
writings have been just as, if not more, militant as the words in this introduction? Had
they been offended by those also but failed to express their feelings about them? To
my surprise, they said they were not offended by any of the Black American, Chicano
or Native American writings, but were hard-pressed to explain why when I asked for
an explanation. A little further discussion revealed that they "understood" the anger
expressed by the Black and Chicanos and they "empathized" with the frustrations and
sorrow expressed by the Native American. But the Asian Americans??

Then finally, one student said it for all of them: "It made me angry. *Their* anger made *me* angry, because I didn't even know the Asian Americans felt oppressed. I didn't expect their anger."

At this time I was involved in an academic due process procedure begun as a result of a grievance I had filed the previous semester against the administrators at my college. I had filed a grievance for violation of my rights as a teacher who had worked in the district for almost eleven years. My student's remark "Their anger made me angry...I didn't expect their anger," explained for me the reactions of some of my own colleagues as well as the reactions of the administrators during those previous months. The grievance procedure was a time-consuming and emotionally draining process, but the basic principle was too important for me to ignore. That basic principle was that I, an individual teacher, do have certain rights which are given and my superiors cannot, should not, violate them with impunity. When this was pointed out to them, however, they responded with shocked surprise that I, of all people, would take them to task for violation of what was clearly written policy in our college district. They all seemed to exclaim, "We don't understand this; this is so uncharacteristic of her; she seemed such a nice person, so polite, so obedient, so non-troublemaking." What was even more surprising was once they were forced to acknowledge that I was determined to start the due process action, they assumed I was not doing it on my own. One of the administrators suggested someone must have pushed me into this, undoubtedly some of "those feminists" on our campus, he said wryly.

In this age when women are clearly making themselves visible on all fronts, I, an Asian American woman, am still functioning as a "front for those feminists" and therefore invisible. The realization of this sinks in slowly. Asian Americans as a whole are finally coming to claim their own, demanding that they be included in the multicultural history of our country. I like to think, in spite of my administrator's myopia, that the most stereotyped minority of them all, the Asian American woman, is just now emerging to become part of that group. It took forever. Perhaps it is important to ask ourselves why it took so long. We should ask ourselves this question just when we think we are emerging as a viable minority in the fabric of our society. I should add to my student's words, "because I didn't even know they felt oppressed," that it took this long because we Asian American women have not admitted to ourselves that we *were* oppressed. We, the visible minority that is invisible.

I say this because until a few years ago I have been an Asian American woman working among non-Asians in an educational institution where most of the decision-makers were men;[1] an Asian American woman thriving under the smug illusion that I was *not* the stereotypic image of the Asian woman because I had a career teaching English in a community college. I did not think anything assertive was necessary to make my point. People who know me, I reasoned, the ones who count, know who I am and what I think. Thus, even when what I considered a veiled racist remark was made in a casual social setting, I would "let it go" because it was pointless to argue with people who didn't even know their remark was racist. I had supposed that I was practicing passive resistance while being stereotyped, but it was so passive no one noticed I was resisting; it was so much my expected role that it ultimately rendered me invisible.

---

[1] [*Author's note.*] It is hoped this will change now that a black woman is Chancellor of our college district.

My experience leads me to believe that contrary to what I thought, I had actually been contributing to my own stereotyping. Like the hero in Ralph Ellison's novel *Invisible Man,* I had become invisible to white Americans, and it clung to me like a bad habit. Like most bad habits, this one crept up on me because I took it in minute doses like Mithradates' poison[2] and my mind and body adapted so well to it I hardly noticed it was there.

For the past eleven years I have busied myself with the usual chores of an English teacher, a wife of a research chemist, and a mother of four rapidly growing children. I hadn't even done much to shatter this particular stereotype: the middle class woman happy to be bringing home the extra income and quietly fitting into the man's world of work. When the Asian American woman is lulled into believing that people perceive her as being different from other Asian women (the submissive, subservient, ready-to-please, easy-to-get-along-with Asian woman), she is kept comfortably content with the state of things. She becomes ineffectual in the milieu in which she moves. The seemingly apolitical middle class woman and the apolitical Asian woman constituted a double invisibility.

I had created an underground culture of survival for myself and had become in the eyes of others the person I was trying not to be. Because I was permitted to go to college, permitted to take a stab at a career or two along the way, given "free choice" to marry and have a family, given a "choice" to eventually do both, I had assumed I was more or less free, not realizing that those who are free make and take choices; they do not choose from options proffered by "those out there."

I, personally, had not "emerged" until I was almost fifty years old. Apparently through a long conditioning process, I had learned how *not* to be seen for what I am. A long history of ineffectual activities had been, I realize now, initiation rites toward my eventual invisibility. The training begins in childhood; and for women and minorities, whatever is started in childhood is continued throughout their adult lives. I first recognized just how invisible I was in my first real confrontation with my parents a few years after the outbreak of World War II.

During the early years of the war, my older brother, Mike, and I left the concentration camp in Idaho to work and study at the University of Cincinnati. My parents came to Cincinnati soon after my father's release from Internment Camp (these were POW camps to which many of the Issei[3] men, leaders in their communities, were sent by the FBI), and worked as domestics in the suburbs. I did not see them too often because by this time I had met and was much influenced by a pacifist who was out on a "furlough" from a conscientious objectors' camp in Trenton, North Dakota. When my parents learned about my "boy friend" they were appalled and frightened. After all, this was the period when everyone in the country was expected to be one-hundred percent behind the war effort, and the Nisei[4] boys who had volunteered for the Armed Forces were out there fighting and dying to prove how American we really were. However, during interminable arguments with my father and overheard arguments between my parents, I was devastated to learn they were not so much concerned about my having become a pacifist, but they were more concerned about the possibility of my marrying one. They were understandably frightened (my father's prison years of

---

[2] A Greek king (132 B.C.E.-63 B.C.E.) who took small daily doses of poison to immunize himself against it.

[3] [*Author's note.*] Immigrant Japanese, living in the U.S.

[4] [*Author's note.*] Second generation Japanese, born in the U.S.

course were still fresh on his mind) about repercussions on the rest of the family. In an attempt to make my father understand me, I argued that even if I didn't marry him, I'd still be a pacifist; but my father reassured me that it was "all right" for me to be a pacifist because as a Japanese national and a "girl" *it didn't make any difference to anyone.* In frustration I remember shouting, "But can't you see, *I'm* philosophically committed to the pacifist cause," but he dismissed this with "In my college days we used to call philosophy, foolosophy," and that was the end of that. When they were finally convinced I was not going to marry "my pacifist," the subject was dropped and we never discussed it again.

As if to confirm my father's assessment of the harmlessness of my opinions, my brother Mike, an American citizen, was suddenly expelled from the University of Cincinnati while I, "an enemy alien," was permitted to stay. We assumed that his stand as a pacifist, although he was classified a 4-F because of his health, contributed to his expulsion. We were told the Air Force was conducting sensitive wartime research on campus and requested his removal, but they apparently felt my presence on campus was not as threatening.

I left Cincinnati in 1945, hoping to leave behind this and other unpleasant memories gathered there during the war years, and plunged right into the politically active atmosphere at New York University where students, many of them returning veterans, were continuously promoting one cause or other by making speeches in Washington Square, passing out petitions, or staging demonstrations. On one occasion, I tagged along with a group of students who took a train to Albany to demonstrate on the steps of the State Capitol. I think I was the only Asian in this group of predominantly Jewish students from NYU. People who passed us were amused and shouted "Go home and grow up." I suppose Governor Dewey,[5] who refused to see us, assumed we were a group of adolescents without a cause as most college students were considered to be during those days. It appears they weren't expecting any results from our demonstration. There were no newspersons, no security persons, no police. No one tried to stop us from doing what we were doing. We simply did "our thing" and went back to our studies until next time, and my father's words were again confirmed: it made no difference to anyone, being a young student demonstrator in peacetime, 1947.

Not only the young, but those who feel powerless over their own lives know what it is like not to make a difference on anyone or anything. The poor know it only too well, and we women have known it since we were little girls. The most insidious part of this conditioning process, I realize now, was that we have been trained not to expect a response in ways that mattered. We may be listened to and responded to with placating words and gestures, but our psychological mind set has already told us time and again that we were born into a ready-made world into which we must fit ourselves, and that many of us do it very well.

This mind set is the result of not believing that the political and social forces affecting our lives are determined by some person, or a group of persons, probably sitting behind a desk or around a conference table.

Just recently I read an article about "the remarkable track record of success" of the Nisei in the United States. One Nisei was quoted as saying he attributed our stamina and endurance to our ancestors whose characters had been shaped, he said, by

[5] Thomas Edmund Dewey (1902-1971), governor of New York from 1943 to 1955.

their living in a country which has been constantly besieged by all manner of natural disasters, such as earthquakes and hurricanes. He said the Nisei has inherited a steely will, a will to endure and hence, to survive.

This evolutionary explanation disturbs me, because it equates the "act of God" (i.e. natural disasters) to the "act of man" (i.e., the war, the evacuation). The former is not within our power to alter, but the latter, I should think, is. By putting the "acts of God" on par with the acts of man, we shrug off personal responsibilities.

I have, for too long a period of time accepted the opinion of others (even though they were directly affecting my life) as if they were objective events totally out of my control. Because I separated such opinions from the persons who were making them, I accepted them the way I accepted natural disasters; and I endured them as inevitable. I have tried to cope with people whose points of view alarmed me in the same way that I had adjusted to natural phenomena, such as hurricanes, which plowed into my life from time to time. I would readjust my dismantled feelings in the same way that we repaired the broken shutters after the storm. The Japanese have an all-purpose expression in their language for this attitude of resigned acceptance: "Shikataganai." "It can't be helped." "There's nothing I can do about it." It is said with the shrug of the shoulders and tone of finality, perhaps not unlike the "those-were-my-orders" tone that was used at the Nuremberg trials.[6] With all the sociological studies that have been made about the causes of the evacuations of the Japanese Americans during World War II, we should know by now that "they" knew that the West Coast Japanese Americans would go without too much protest, and of course, "they" were right, for most of us (with the exception of those notable few), resigned to our fate, albeit bewildered and not willingly. We were not perceived by our government as responsive Americans; we were objects that happened to be standing in the path of the storm.

Perhaps this kind of acceptance is a way of coping with the "real" world. One stands against the wind for a time, and then succumbs eventually because there is no point to being stubborn against all odds. The wind will not respond to entreaties anyway, one reasons; one should have sense enough to know that. I'm not ready to accept this evolutionary reasoning. It is too rigid for me; I would like to think that my new awareness is going to make me more visible than ever, and to allow me to make some changes in the "man made disaster" I live in at the present time. Part of being visible is refusing to separate the actors from their actions, and demanding that they be responsible for them.

By now, riding along with the minorities' and women's movements, I think we are making a wedge into the main body of American life, but people are still looking right through and around us, assuming we are simply tagging along. Asian American women still remain in the background and we are heard but not really listened to. Like Musak, they think we are piped into the airwaves by someone else. We must remember that one of the most insidious ways of keeping women and minorities powerless is to let them only talk about harmless and inconsequential subjects, or let them speak freely and not listen to them with serious intent.

We need to raise our voices a little more, even as they say to us "This is so uncharacteristic of you." To finally recognize our own invisibility is to finally be on the path toward visibility. Invisibility is not a natural state for anyone.

—1979

[6] A series of trials (1945-1949) prosecuting leaders of Nazi Germany.

ETEL ADNAN (1925-)

Etel Adnan was born in Beirut in 1925 to a multicultural household in which her Syrian Muslim father and Greek Christian mother spoke both Greek and Turkish. She was educated in France and the U.S., studying philosophy at the Sorbonne, UC Berkeley, and Harvard. She uses both French and English in her writing. As a poet, novelist, essayist, playwright, and painter, Adnan examines questions of multiplicity, location, and language, often in the contexts of women, war, and exploration. Adnan's works include the essay collection *Paris, When It's Naked* (1993), a collection of letters, *Of Cities and Women (Letters to Fawwaz)* (1993), and the widely read essay "To Write in a Foreign Language." Her novel *Sitt Marie Rose,* translated into English from the original French in 1982, is considered a touchstone of contemporary Middle Eastern literature. Adnan currently lives in Lebanon, France, and California.

from Of Cities and Women (Letters to Fawwaz)

AMSTERDAM, Friday November 30, 1990

Dear Fawwaz,[1]

We are in the last days of November, a time that is dear to me because it is the month of my mother's birth (and that of the Day for the dead). The French Sisters at my school on Avenue Clemenceau used to tell us that in November the ground was covered with dead leaves. In Beirut, along the treeless avenues. There weren't any dead leaves! But at school, *everything* they told us was unreal. For us, certainly.

I arrived last night in this city of Amsterdam that is so beautiful, beautiful, true to the way we imagined that European cities were, before the war (World War II, of course!). Amsterdam shimmers with shining lights. At night, the city is black and gold. We are here to attend an opera being conducted by Pierre, Simone's nephew: Monteverdi's *Il ritorno di Ulisse in Patria.*[2]

It's superb work, and it's being performed superbly. The Ulysses character leads me directly to Penelope,[3] that archetypal model that has been offered to women for several millennia.

This happy coincidence thrusts me straight into my subject! In the Opera House I watched a myth become reality, because it remains such a powerful one, that of Penelope conceived as pure waiting. In fact, she does not even wait at a window, since, for women, windows have always been tantamount to a door out of the cage. Penelope lives in the back of her room. Penelope just waits.

Job is patience. Originated in the Jordanian desert, Job waits in a harsh light, and on hard stones. He is not even waiting for his misfortune to cease. He is not waiting to heal. He is waiting for God to make yet another demand upon him. It's a case of pure waiting for the pure divine will.

Penelope is thus to Ulysses what Job is to God: the object that waits, and which, by waiting, "divinizes" Ulysses.

And, ever since, in a collective imagination that is brought to date constantly, the

---

[1] This letter, along with others addressed to Lebanese writer and historian Fawwaz Traboulsi, was written in lieu of an essay on feminism Adnan had promised to Traboulsi for the magazine *Zalawa;* the letters were published together in the volume *Of Cities and Women* (1993).

[2] (It.) *The Return of Ulysses to His Country* (1640), opera by Claudio Monteverdi (1567-1643).

[3] In Greek mythology, Ulysses spent ten years trying to return from the Trojan War to his wife Penelope.

woman is that which waits: she waits to grow up, she waits for puberty, waits for her fiancé, her husband, her child, her old age, and her death. She waits for the children to come and go, for them to grow up, for them to marry, for her husband to go to work in the morning and come home at night. She waits for the water to boil, for the war to be over, for the spring to return. She waits to be kissed, taken, rejected, forgotten. She waits for the moment of love, the moment of vengeance, of oblivion, and again, of death. She is the flower awaiting the bee, and the valley awaiting the storm. She is born practically seated, and Penelope does nothing but sit. She is pure waiting. She weaves and unravels her work. She is the one to be Sisyphus.[4] And for the waiting to be perfect, she must produce nothing lasting with her hands.

There you have, in Monteverdi and his poignant accents, the best exponent of woman's fate.

But with the cynicism we have recently acquired, we could say that Penelope actually never waited, that she was dreading Ulysses' return because it would put an end to her well-concealed pleasures and adventures. How many American soldiers came home from the last war to find their wives already remarried, although they had no proof at all that their husbands had been killed?!

I believe that waiting is an even more insidious weapon. Waiting determines the destiny of the one we wait for. Mallarmé,[5] speaking of Ulysses, compared him to Helios,[6] writing that the sun could not deviate from the course assigned to it, be it during the day or the night. Ulysses cannot therefore not return. He is "programmed" by Penelope's wait. This reverses the whole process: the target does then determine the arrow's path.

Dear Fawwaz, I would like to tell you more on Amsterdam because it's a city that calls for description, or the description of the happiness it provides. Holland is immaterial. Everything is made of water. Reflections are mirrored in reflections. The canals and streams are higher than the land. The sky and water begin to flow into one another and into a kind of osmosis. And one is lightened by this atmosphere; Dutch painting, too, participates in this iridescence. Everything ephemeral is quicker than even our perception of it. One's spirit becomes feast, passage, transparency, flotation.

I strayed into the city's world renowned brothel district (I nearly told you "as usual"). I went to visit my friend Yanny Donker who lives there, with her husband and children, and publishes her own magazine of contemporary dance. I am happy to revisit this neighborhood that had kind of blown my mind about fifteen years ago, with the windows of its "maisons closes"[7] which are anything but closed, where anything is available, especially the women with their flesh as rosy as Rembrandt's Ox,[8] hanging in the Louvre. Women are carefully arranged in the display windows of these shop-dormitories; they display themselves in the atrocious lighting as straightforwardly as merchandise. Yanny knows many of them "Oh, they come from all sort of backgrounds," she tells me. "Some earn plenty of money; some continue to ply this trade even after they marry; others are wrecked, mistreated, beaten by their pimps. Naturally," she adds, "it also involves a lot of drugs and violence. The women are often murdered."

---

[4] In Greek mythology, a king who had been punished by being made to roll a stone up a hill for all eternity.
[5] French poet Stéphane Mallarmé (1842-98).
[6] Greek god of the sun.

[7] (Fr.) Euphemism for brothel.
[8] *The Slaughtered Ox* (1655), painting by Rembrandt van Rijn (1606-69).

"Doesn't that make you sad?" I ask. And she replies, no, not really; she and even her children have gotten used to it. Then she amends: "Not long ago I was talking to one of the girls I know best. She told me how every evening, a man used to walk by the window where she waits, totally nude, on display. This young man never approached her; he just greeted her politely, nicely, and she was delighted to think that she had in him a true friend. And then", continues Yanny, "this woman said to me a few days ago: 'You see, yesterday I was walking in the street, and I met my young man, and he walked by without saying hello or recognizing me, because I was wearing clothes!' Isn't that sad?" says Yanny, "this woman's sorrow has been so great, she's so very sad…but that's how it is."

I have lots of ideas about women, but reality obscures them more than it enlightens them. The problem is that the heart can never be separated from the flesh. How can one ever leave behind these Northern cities, with the cold, the terror, the infinite melancholy which has become encrusted into their beauty?!

I don't know what else to tell you. I wish I could stay more. I'm going back to Paris, and I'll be calling you.

E.

Beirut, August 23rd, 1991

Dear Fawwaz,[9]

The plane landed with such a jolt that I had to wonder if Beirut was not still expressing itself with full violence.

After 12 years of absence, my heart is tight. Brigitte Schehadé, and Emile Attieh who meant so much to me (so long ago) during those years at the Ecole des Lettres were passengers on the same plane. Their presence was an omen.

At five o'clock in the afternoon, when we arrived, the shadows of Beirut had already lengthened. Everything was familiar to me. Everything. I was immediately enveloped in that feeling of relaxed resignation which says that things are the way they are. I was merely a pair of eyes, benevolent ones of course, in the indescribable pleasure of being at home.

I am writing to you from an eleventh-floor apartment with a view of the sea from three sides. I'm reunited with that sea again, the one that I love above all, and, I often fear, more than anything in the world, in particular the bit located along this part of the Corniche[10] and the *Bain Militaire*.[11] I never really left her behind.

The first twilight I witnessed upon my arrival was amazing in its purity: an ethereal blue fading into a pink that was equally ethereal and deep. The soft clarity of the light suffused me with the knowledge that over the fifteen years of war, tortures, crimes, and bombings, there was an impalpable veil of purity that could never wear out because it belongs to the infinite. And this reservoir of innocence, of a future, of an intangible beauty, I had immediately seen, on the way from the airport to my home, in the eyes of many people: those of the porter who carried my bags, those of the office worker from Simone's family's business who met us at the airport…It was quickly apparent that in this city of Lebanon, everything can melt into a transfigured memory.

---

[9] See note 1.
[10] Seaside promenade.

[11] (Fr.) Military Bath, a military swim club.

Last night, I called on Janine Rubeiz, and we went out to dinner together. In Raouche we bought flower necklaces from children who were hardly six years old. Two children were sitting on a low wall; one of them was singing in a voice that might have belonged to someone much older than him. It created in me a lingering grief. Janine scolded the little singer, telling him it was time for children to be home and in bed. A young man passing by followed us to say: "Madam, these two children have no home. They have no one. They belong to the street."

After dinner, the air was still warm, the night was brilliant, and the crowd strolled silently through the noise from damaged music tapes whining out melodies painful to hear. A woman rushed up to us, whimpering, crying: "Help me! Help me! For fear of God, help me!" Then another leaped forth, spun around, shrieking with mental agony, her madness etched into her face like smallpox, terrified by her own despair, her hunger…it sent chills up my spine. This is the work of war I said to myself (as if that could be an answer!). In this crowd of unemployed people, resigned to misfortune, the chances for these two desperate women to be rescued are nil.

I resume my letter. I slept very poorly last night. In the heat, with the window wide open, I listened to the sound of the sea, her breath…I thought of our country, our cultures, this land that has been so mortally destroyed. I must say that Beirut clings to me like hot wax, even in slumber.

People have all sorts of stories to tell me. They insist on praising the heroic feats of a war that shouldn't inspire any pride. But for the stories of women, it's something else. The women have kept contact with the earth, if I may say, in the ancient roles of witnesses and memory keepers. They have surpassed themselves: their strength has overcome their habits and their prejudices. Thus Janine's mother, who is ninety years old, still lives alone in her apartment atop a building full of deserted and half-gutted offices, in the French Embassy quarter, which is now in ruins, abandoned, and off-limits.

You know, this war has had several faces, several "phases" I might dare say, so that the early years are not erased, but replaced by more recent battles…The latter always appearing to have been the hardest. Thus the beginnings are obscured by fog, and no one wants to talk about them.

I look at the sea, as if there had never been anything else to do in this city besides looking at her. But the heart of the city is rotting, burdened with a heavy sorrow, and this entire "western" sector, which used to be charming (as you know) is plagued with cars that are wearier than the people. In the conversations, someone's death is always inevitably announced. This person, that person…struck down in a game of chance.

It sometimes seems to me that this fifteen-year war has been an immense tribute to death. They love death in the East because they love the sacred. Everything is sacralized: the person, the family, the tribe, the clan, the State, money, women…And the sacred is whatever is fixed, unchangeable: hence death. It calls for sacrifice, and we're sealed in a circle.

Do we love death because we don't know how to live? Is it because we would rather lose everything than settle for less? Do we confuse celebration and death, and stage the bloody celebrations that we have seen? Is the belief in an afterlife so strong that people die lightly, out of distraction, negligence, or excess of faith? Excess of life?…

As the building has no electricity, I am writing you by the light of a kerosene lamp. It reminds me of my early childhood, when our bedrooms were lit with this kind of lamp. But this place is the absolute opposite of the house we had.

Today, I made a trip to Hamra to buy myself a bathing suit. It was a pleasant surprise to find so many young women in the stores, working as sales girls and cashiers. This part of the city has become more Arabic: no one feels obligated to say "Bonjour" and "Au revoir",[12] to please a customer. There is a certain authenticity despite poverty and disaster. You know how firmly this city was convinced it was the center of an Orient it had never bothered to know, and now it seems to be outside the interest of the Great Powers. It allows its wounds to show wherever it is unable to conceal them, without recrimination, without tears, without begging. The dignity of the little people is what impresses me the most. Some vestige of ancient virtues has survived, exactly the way some houses have remained intact. To make the connection.

Once again, this evening, I found myself on the Corniche. Simone and I, again, stopped near Dbaibo, to buy a necklace of jasmine (and breathe in the sea). Simone chatted with the little boy, another child, not the one of the other night. She asked him where the flowers had come from, assuming he had picked them in his family's garden. He replied, with an astonished air, "But we live in a single room. There are ten of us." Then he explained that they purchase the flowers and weave the jasmine and "filleh" necklaces at home, and that it's a very expensive operation. "Oh!" he cried spontaneously, "How I wish I could return to the South!" And then he continued, as he looked at the abrupt cliff that drops off in front of La Grotte aux Pigeons: "Many young people commit suicide here," measuring with his eyes the few yards that were between him and the abyss: "They're twenty, twenty-five years old, many, many, kill themselves." And then he said no more. And we went home.

The main event of the summer is, of course, the return of those exiled by the war. Everyone is talking about the sumptuous, outrageous, delirious receptions they have given and are still giving. Not less than 300 guests per "evening"! People's talks are filled with their gowns, the sums they spend, the banquets. This excess itself has a taste of death. It comes from far away, the ancient times when, in this part of the world, every feast contained sacrificial rituals. Yet one has to admit that the care devoted to the preparation of food, which persisted among the poor and rich alike, even as the bombs were falling, during the siege, and even in underground shelters, that this care was the basis for the survival of a people trapped so tragically. The luxurious pastry shops are still magical places, like the restaurants which remained open. Nevertheless, the current wave of opulent parties is somewhat worrisome. (So soon! The peace is so fragile that anxiety is quick to rise in one's heart).

A few beggars can be seen here and there, usually women holding sick or maimed children on their laps, seated on caved-in sidewalks, near trash bins, as if they felt a secret and powerful kinship between their condition and the ruins.

Ruins, ruins, dying buildings whose skeletons are exposed by the destruction, and an obsession with houses, especially among the women.

The big apartments of the very wealthy are repaired quickly as if haste were vital to ward off misfortune. Thus in certain quarters, one would have the illusion that

---

[12] (Fr.) Hello; goodbye.

nothing has happened, but that's a sort of hallucination. The destruction has become the truth.

It is the women who speak of the war. The men tend to be quiet: they may seek to hide the horror out of shame for their group as much as for themselves. What makes it terrible is that on the rare occasions when the men do speak of the war, they blame it on others; they always plead that they were trapped; they practically claim they had nothing at all to do with it. Then who committed the crimes, the massacres, the horrors? And if one was merely a pawn, is one not responsible for having accepted to play the role? In this part of the world there seems to be a huge reality-problem!

The women talk; yes, they are ready to do so, and it is of houses that they talk: they describe with an architect's or a doctor's precision exactly whatever happened to each house, and balcony, the charred walls, the disfigured facades, the gutted rooms. War is enemy to the home.

By their very dimensions great events seem to obliterate themselves. Soon the war will have disappeared from the conversations, it will assume the fleeting consistency of a nightmare. It will be stored in people's memories and will emerge again only as a myth, sacralized in its turn. It will die and be redeemed in the land of the dead. It will become a legend in a land where legends have always been accepted as facts.

The moon is rising this evening, looking like a face in prayer. It slides into the sky from behind the Sannine.[13] It rises from where the sun rose this morning.

But, my dear Fawwaz, all analyzing gets to be useless. When it faces the problems that these people must confront. A bloody celebration has ended, and the people find themselves, the morning after, with the food beginning to rot, the dirty dishes, the half-filled glasses, the garbage, and the hangover. The orgy of violence is over, and now there is amnesia which is setting in and the bill to be paid.

Still, I am comforted by the women's stories about the behavior of other women during the war. Their lucidity seems to have survived intact, and they are stubbornly defiant, as if to say that, having seen the worst, they need no longer fear anything. They carry within themselves a cool courage illustrated by the story about this woman from the Southern suburbs of Beirut to whom was brought the corpse of her son on a night when the bombs were falling, and who received it wordlessly, without a cry, mastering the situation, aware of the need to avoid panicking her other children.

Unfortunately, the contradictions and constraints create new hells. Because the Lebanese feel that riding a bicycle is beneath their dignity, they drive cars that are polluting and falling apart. Since it seems that they are unwilling to admit their new and grinding poverty, they do not go to bed at sundown, or use the old acetylene or oil lamps; instead, they have installed huge electric generators in their dwellings so that they can continue to watch television and give parties. The problem is that the generators make an infernal racket that brings the distress of the city to a saturation point. I wonder if this desire to deny defeat, so praiseworthy in itself, doesn't become disastrous when it is a denial of reality, and has not been one of the major reasons for the terrifying length of this war.

Yes, I contemplate the sea, what else is there to do? To dive in. Sensations of coolness followed by waves of heat rush through the body. There is no separation

---

[13] Mount Sannine, 29 miles from Beirut.

between the sea and a woman and it is futile to look further, in thought or through the experience of others, in order to come close to the essence of what is feminine: water, salt, phosphorus, plankton, all the minerals in liquid form, and the sun covering it all. To come close to the sea, to look into her until nothing else is visible, and finally, for a fraction of a second, to finish in the gaze of this shifting mass that has neither beginning nor end...to look at the sea is to become what one is.

If it weren't for the sea, Beirut would not have survived its devastation. But there is salt on the ground, in our mouths, on our clothes, in our hands; something that resists putrefaction.

Newspapers are in a pitiful state. Their pages are covered with venomous political quarrels and no one is prepared to admit that this war ended in a draw.

But the "street" has changed. A woman alone in the streets has nowhere to stop; the cafés are too few and far between. The city, which is by excellence a woman's place, has become the exclusive domain of men.

That gives the streets an air of safety. Between the blackened buildings, along the broken sidewalks and caved-in streets, the very presence of the masculine world provides a sense of security, says that survival is possible. It's a supreme irony: the ones who instigated all this tragedy must remain as our link with life.

But where are the women? In a few stores, perhaps. In the houses, of course. And, when they are wealthy, in their cars. But the street, this living artery, excludes them. More out of indifference than hostility. The war was men's business. When I walk these streets, I feel disconnected from things, as if I came from another world. I indulge in the belief that if greater numbers of women went outdoors in the damaged neighborhoods (and not merely at the seaside on summer evenings), if they formed a crowd, all these overwrought, exhausted men, barricaded in their shops and businesses, still worried, humiliated, would again find in themselves some power for tenderness, some liberation.

As I move from the city center to Ras-Beirut,[14] where my heart beats and where the sun sets, trying to think about women's condition, I meet the male inhabitants instead, and I feel as though I share their lives and understand them much better: mechanics, pushcart vendors, bums, beggars, and hustlers...they all have eyes, wrinkles, worries, and miseries, that I contemplate the way I contemplate the sea. I am overcome by a profound sense of a homecoming, of a coming to terms in this luminous month of August.

It is impossible to conclude. Every theory is a burial. There is nothing to say. In this place, all banalities die.

I've been to the Downtown area, the mother, the matrix of the city. It is immense, golden, and green. And it is mainly grandiose, as "beautiful" as Baalbek.[15] The Arab East seems to know the art of ruins; these are always more impressive than were the original constructions. They have been shaped, always, by tragic forces. It is thanks to this strange architectural ensemble, which, with its own particular harmony and character, looks like the setting of an opera designed by a god, that we can envision the city as an epic tale, an eternally immobile army, a saga written with stones, an immortal place where mortals can tread.

---

[14] A residential neighborhood near several universities. [15] Bekaa Valley, site of the largest Roman temples ever built.

The Christian militias of East Beirut concentrated their attacks, as if to annihilate the essentially Muslim center of the city which was the beauty—and the memory. They behaved as if they believed that they had to destroy History in order to assert their specificity. But like a man who has murdered the woman he loved, the Lebanese will start and have started to become the mad lovers of old Beirut. They glean every crumb of memory, seal themselves off in a past that stirs our souls like a hurricane, and which we destroyed with our own hands, hands which are now groping for phantoms. Our old Beirut is as remote from us as the Stone Age.

Today, already September 3, and the weather has gotten cooler. Gold and purple vie for possession of the sunset sky. The street is shoddy, but the sky is imperial. Anything is possible!

It's difficult for me to get around in these streets where the women are few: life is hard. You can never let down your guard: holes, tires, filthy water, and pieces of metal scrap are constantly obstructing your way. And the worst, the most painful sight: maimed war victims with unbearable afflictions. Some of them crawl between the lanes of cars that keep on driving as if bound for a funeral. And these strange stares that one attracts, and also that one feels like interrogating in turn: Who did they kill? What unnameable acts did they commit? I have not succeeded in reading them; they're too often opaque to my eyes. Is it madness, crime, or a new order of things?

The battles have ceased, but the violence remains. It is sheathed, but only just barely.

Like a child seeing a soldier, all you think of asking, when you see someone, is "Did you kill anyone?, an innocent one, for sure?!" I wish people would be more willing to talk.

Then suddenly you see a child, or an old man, or a worker doing something, and you're disarmed…Lebanon's other face appears: its populist, civilized, wise, "ancient" side, its capacity to absorb blows without breaking, to allow time to take its time, to wait patiently…

Yes, it does look as though Evil has taken a few wrinkles and that Lebanon will be able to convalesce. Will the country become a gigantic supermarket, a floating casino, or a "real" country? Will the new forms of thought vital to our survival ever emerge? For the moment, everything is wrapped in torpor.

But I feel so much at ease in this shabby apartment, despite the fact that every evening I pant and sweat my way up eleven flights of stairs carrying in my hand a candle that seems to add to the heat, after the glory and splendor of the skies, that I say to myself that one can be happy in Beirut, and that the people, oddly enough, are happy: it could be that the age-old rituals of death have taught us also those of resurrection.

I am unwilling for this letter to end, because its completion will mean it is time for me to leave Beirut, and leave the rest to silence.

I think that I will go now to Greece for ten days, and then will see you in Paris.

Love,

E.

—1993

CAROLYN KIZER (1925-   )

Carolyn Kizer was born in Spokane, Washington. Her father was a lawyer and her mother, who held a doctorate in biology, taught in various universities and was a labor organizer in the Pacific Northwest. Kizer, who was an only child, grew up in a home full of intellectual and social stimulation; the poet Vachel Lindsay was a frequent household guest and Kizer was influenced by his sister, Olive Wakefield, who was a missionary in China. After earning her B.A. from Sarah Lawrence College, Kizer did graduate work at Columbia and then at the University of Washington, Seattle. In 1959 she started the literary journal *Poetry Northwest*, which she edited until 1965. From 1966 to 1970, Kizer was the first director of literary programs for the National Endowment for the Arts, which had just been established. Kizer's poetry, often marked by feminism and a keen political consciousness, has garnered her much recognition. She received the Pulitzer Prize in 1985 for her collection *Yin* (1984), and has also received the American Academy of Arts and Letters Award, the Frost Medal, and the Theodore Roethke Memorial Poetry Award. She has been a visiting writer at numerous universities, and served as a chancellor of the American Academy of Poets from 1995 until 1998, when she and fellow poet Maxine Kumin resigned their positions to protest the absence of minorities on the board.

The Suburbans

Forgetting sounds that we no longer hear—
Nightingale, silent for a century:
How touch that bubbling throat, let it touch us
In cardboard-sided suburbs, where the glades
And birds gave way to lawns, fake weathervanes   5
Topping antennae, or a wrought-iron rooster
Mutely presiding over third class mail?—
We live on ironed land like cemeteries,
Those famous levelers of human contours.

But cemeteries are a green relief;   10
Used-car and drive-in movie lots alike
Enaisle and regulate the gaudy junk
That runs us, in a "Park" that is no park.
Our greens kept up for doomed Executives;
Though golf embalms its land, as libraries   15
Preserve an acre for the mind to play
When, laboring at its trash, the trapped eye leaps,
Beholding greensward, or the written word.

What common symbols dominate our work?
"Perpetual care"; the library steps with lions   20
More free than moving kinsmen in the zoos;
The seagull is our bird, who eats our loot,
Adores our garbage, but can rise above it—
Clean scavenger, picks clean, gets clean away!—
Past bays and rivers of industrial waste,   25
Infected oysters, fish-bloat, belly up
In sloughs of sewage, to the open sea.

So much for Nature, carved and animate!
Step in, a minute….But our ankles, brushed
With that swift, intimate electric shock,   30
Signal the muse: the passing of a cat—
All that remains of tygers, mystery,
Eye-gleam at night, synecdoche for jungle;
We catch her ancient freedom in a cage
Of tidy rhyme. Page the anthologies!   35
A bridge between our Nature and our Time.

Easily she moves from outer life to inner,
While we, nailed to our domesticity
Like Van Gogh to the wall, wild in his frame,
Double in mirrors, that the sinister self   40
Who moves along with us may own at least
His own reverses, duck behind his molding
When our phones jerk us on a leash of noise.
Hence mirror poems, Alice, The Looking Glass,
Those dull and partial couplings with ourselves.   45

Our gold-fish gazes, our transparent nerves!
As we weave above these little colored stones—
Fish-furniture—bob up for dusty food:
"Just heat and serve"; our empty pear-shaped tones!
Home is a picture window, and our globes   50
Are mirrors too: we see ourselves outside.
Afraid to become our neighbors, we revolt
In verse: "This proves I'm not the average man."
Only the average poet, which is worse.

The drooping 19th-century bard in weeds   55
On his stone bench, beside a weedy grave,
Might attitudinize, but his tears were free
And easy. He heard authentic birds.
Nobody hid recordings in his woods,
Or draped his waterfalls with neon gauze.   60
No sign disturbed his orisons, commanding,
"Go to Church this Sunday!" or be damned!
He was comfortably damned when he was born.

But we are saved, from the boring Hell of churches;
We ran to graves for picnics or for peace: 65
Beer cans on headstones, eggshells in the grass,
"Deposit Trash in Baskets." For release
From hells of public and domestic noise,
We sprawl, although we neither pose nor pray,
Compose our stanzas here, like that dead bard,   70
But writing poems on poems. Gravely gay,
Our limited salvation is the word.

—1961

MAXINE KUMIN (1925-)

Born in Philadephia, Maxine Winokur Kumin received both a B.A. and an M.A. from Radcliffe College. Though she wrote some poetry in college, Kumin's career as a poet began in 1957 when she participated in a poetry workshop offered by the Boston Center for Adult Education. That workshop helped Kumin realize her poetic talent, and it afforded her the opportunity to meet poet Anne Sexton. The two remained close friends, critiquing and discussing one another's poetry, until Sexton's suicide in 1974. Kumin and Sexton also wrote several children's books together, and Sexton is referenced in Kumin's poetry.

Kumin has written fourteen books of poetry, five novels, five books of essays and memoirs, and twenty children's books. Among her numerous awards are the Pulitzer Prize (for her 1972 poetry collection *Up Country*), the Aiken Taylor Award for Modern Poetry, an American Academy of Arts and Letters award, a National Endowment for the Arts grant, and fellowships from the Academy of American Poets and the National Council on the Arts. Kumin served as Consultant in Poetry to the Library of Congress (a position later renamed Poet Laureate of the United States) and as Chancellor of the Academy of American Poets, though in 1998 she resigned from that position, along with poet Carolyn Kizer, to protest the absence of people of color from the board of Chancellors. That act is consistent with Kumin's practice as a poet: while her poems focus on day-to-day concerns like women's relationships to their children, lovers, and friends, they are also infused with a politics of conscience.

Purgatory

And suppose the darlings get to Mantua,
suppose they cheat the crypt, what next? Begin
with him, unshaven. Though not, I grant you, a
displeasing cockerel, there's egg yolk on his chin.
His seedy robe's aflap, he's got the rheum.   5
Poor dear, the cooking lard has smoked her eye.
Another Montague[1] is in the womb
although the first babe's bottom's not yet dry.
She scrolls a weekly letter to her Nurse
who dares to send a smock through Balthasar,   10
and once a month, his father posts a purse.
News from Verona? Always news of war.
   Such sour years it takes to right this wrong!
   The fifth act runs unconscionably long.

—1965

After Love

Afterward, the compromise.
Bodies resume their boundaries.

These legs, for instance, mine.
Your arms take you back in.

---

[1] One of the families in Shakespeare's *Romeo and Juliet* (1597).

Spoons of our fingers, lips
admit their ownership. 5

The bedding yawns, a door
blows aimlessly ajar

and overhead, a plane
singsongs coming down. 10

Nothing is changed, except
there was a moment when

the wolf, the mongering wolf
who stands outside the self

lay lightly down, and slept.

—1970

FLANNERY O'CONNOR (1925-1964)

Mary Flannery O'Connor was born in Savannah, Georgia, the only child of Edward Francis O'Connor, Jr., a real estate agent, and Regina Cline O'Connor. The family moved to Atlanta, and then to Milledgeville, Georgia. O'Connor was educated at Georgia State College for Women and the Iowa Writers' Workshop; she lived in New York and Connecticut briefly after she completed her M.F.A. at Iowa in 1947. Her father died of lupus in 1941; when O'Connor began to have symptoms of the disease, she moved back to Georgia and lived with her mother on the family farm outside of Milledgeville from 1951 until her death. Most of her fiction was written at the farm, where O'Connor wrote every morning and raised a wide array of birds, including, famously, the peafowl that often appear in her work. Her illness and its treatment limited her travels, restricted her diet, and required a great deal of her attention; she did travel to read and speak when she was able, and kept up a lively correspondence with other writers. O'Connor wrote two novels, *Wise Blood* (1952), which was adapted for film in 1979, and *The Violent Bear It Away* (1960), and thirty-one short stories, collected in *A Good Man Is Hard to Find* (1955) and *Everything That Rises Must Converge* (1965). Her *Complete Short Stories*, published in 1971, won the National Book Award, and a collection of her letters, *The Habit of Being* (1979), won the National Book Critics Circle Award. O'Connor is often linked with Eudora Welty and Carson McCullers as writers of Southern Gothic—fiction with Southern settings, twisted endings, Gothic and sometimes grotesque touches, and oddball, loser, or misfit characters. A mark of her enduring popularity is that both the O'Connor family farm, Andalusia, and her childhood home in Savannah are open to the public for tours.

Revelation

The doctor's waiting room, which was very small, was almost full when the Turpins entered and Mrs. Turpin, who was very large, made it look even smaller by her presence. She stood looming at the head of the magazine table set in the center of it, a living demonstration that the room was inadequate and ridiculous. Her little bright black eyes took in all the patients as she sized up the seating situation. There was one vacant chair and a place on the sofa occupied by a blond child in a dirty blue romper who should have been told to move over and make room for the lady. He was five or six, but Mrs. Turpin saw at once that no one was going to tell him to move over. He was slumped down in the seat, his arms idle at his sides and his eyes idle in his head; his nose ran unchecked.

Mrs. Turpin put a firm hand on Claud's shoulder and said in a voice that included anyone who wanted to listen, "Claud, you sit in that chair there," and gave him a push down into the vacant one. Claud was florid and bald and sturdy, somewhat shorter than Mrs. Turpin, but he sat down as if he were accustomed to doing what she told him to.

Mrs. Turpin remained standing. The only man in the room besides Claud was a lean stringy old fellow with a rusty hand spread out on each knee, whose eyes were closed as if he were asleep or dead or pretending to be so as not to get up and offer her his seat. Her gaze settled agreeably on a well-dressed gray-haired lady whose eyes met hers and whose expression said: if that child belonged to me, he would have some manners and move over—there's plenty of room there for you and him too.

Claud looked up with a sigh and made as if to rise.

"Sit down," Mrs. Turpin said. "You know you're not supposed to stand on that leg. He has an ulcer on his leg," she explained.

Claud lifted his foot onto the magazine table and rolled his trouser leg up to reveal a purple swelling on a plump marble-white calf.

"My!" the pleasant lady said. "How did you do that?"

"A cow kicked him," Mrs. Turpin said.

"Goodness!" said the lady.

Claud rolled his trouser leg down.

"Maybe the little boy would move over," the lady suggested, but the child did not stir.

"Somebody will be leaving in a minute," Mrs. Turpin said. She could not understand why a doctor—with as much money as they made charging five dollars a day to just stick their head in the hospital door and look at you—couldn't afford a decent-sized waiting room. This one was hardly bigger than a garage. The table was cluttered with limp-looking magazines and at one end of it there was a big green glass ashtray full of cigarette butts and cotton wads with little blood spots on them. If she had anything to do with the running of the place, that would have been emptied every so often. There were no chairs against the wall at the head of the room. It had a rectangular-shaped panel in it that permitted a view of the office where the nurse came and went and the secretary listened to the radio. A plastic fern in a gold pot sat in the opening and trailed its fronds down almost to the floor. The radio was softly playing gospel music.

Just then the inner door opened and a nurse with the highest stack of yellow hair Mrs. Turpin had ever seen put her face in the crack and called for the next patient. The woman sitting beside Claud grasped the two arms of her chair and hoisted herself up; she pulled her dress free from her legs and lumbered through the door where the nurse had disappeared.

Mrs. Turpin eased into the vacant chair, which held her tight as a corset. "I wish I could reduce," she said, and rolled her eyes and gave a comic sigh.

"Oh, *you* aren't fat," the stylish lady said.

"Ooooo I am too," Mrs. Turpin said. "Claud eats all he wants to and never weighs over one hundred and seventy-five pounds, but me I just look at something good to eat and I gain some weight," and her stomach and shoulders shook with laughter. "You can eat all you want to, can't you, Claud?" she asked, turning to him.

Claud only grinned.

"Well, as long as you have such a good disposition," the stylish lady said, "I don't think it makes a bit of difference what size you are. You just can't beat a good disposition."

Next to her was a fat girl of eighteen or nineteen, scowling into a thick blue book which Mrs. Turpin saw was entitled *Human Development*. The girl raised her head and directed her scowl at Mrs. Turpin as if she did not like her looks. She appeared annoyed that anyone should speak while she tried to read. The poor girl's face was blue with acne and Mrs. Turpin thought how pitiful it was to have a face like that at that age. She gave the girl a friendly smile but the girl only scowled the harder. Mrs. Turpin herself was fat but she had always had good skin, and, though she was forty-seven years old, there was not a wrinkle in her face except around her eyes from laughing too much.

Next to the ugly girl was the child, still in exactly the same position, and next to him was a thin leathery old woman in a cotton print dress. She and Claud had three sacks of chicken feed in their pump house that was in the same print. She had seen from the first that the child belonged with the old woman. She could tell by the way they sat—kind of vacant and white-trashy, as if they would sit there until Doomsday if nobody called and told them to get up. And at right angles but next to the well-dressed pleasant lady was a lank-faced woman who was certainly the child's mother. She had on a yellow sweat shirt and wine-colored slacks, both gritty-looking, and the rims of her lips were stained with snuff. Her dirty yellow hair was tied behind with a little piece of red paper ribbon. Worse than niggers any day, Mrs. Turpin thought.

The gospel hymn playing was, "When I looked up and He looked down," and Mrs. Turpin, who knew it, supplied the last line mentally, "And wona these days I know I'll we-eara crown."[1]

Without appearing to, Mrs. Turpin always noticed people's feet. The well-dressed lady had on red and gray suede shoes to match her dress. Mrs. Turpin had on good black patent leather pumps. The ugly girl had on Girl Scout shoes and heavy socks. The old woman had on tennis shoes and the white-trashy mother had on what appeared to be bedroom slippers, black straw with gold braid threaded through them—exactly what you would have expected her to have on.

Sometimes at night when she couldn't go to sleep, Mrs. Turpin would occupy herself with the question of who she would have chosen to be if she couldn't have been herself. If Jesus had said to her before he made her, "There's only two places available for you. You can be a nigger or white-trash," what would she have said? "Please, Jesus, please," she would have said, "just let me wait until there's another place available," and he would have said, "No, you have to go right now and I have only those two places so make up your mind." She would have wiggled and squirmed and begged and pleaded but it would have been no use and finally she would have said, "All right,

---

[1] Gospel song by Albert E. Brumley (1905-1977).

make me a nigger then—but that don't mean a trashy one." And he would have made her a neat clean respectable Negro woman, herself but black.

Next to the child's mother was a red-headed youngish woman, reading one of the magazines and working a piece of chewing gum, hell for leather, as Claud would say. Mrs. Turpin could not see the woman's feet. She was not white-trash, just common. Sometimes Mrs. Turpin occupied herself at night naming the classes of people. On the bottom of the heap were most colored people, not the kind she would have been if she had been one, but most of them; then next to them—not above, just away from—were the white-trash; then above them were the home-owners, and above them the home-and-land owners, to which she and Claud belonged. Above she and Claud were people with a lot of money and much bigger houses and much more land. But here the complexity of it would begin to bear in on her, for some of the people with a lot money were common and ought to be below she and Claud and some of the people who had good blood had lost their money and had to rent and then there were colored people who owned their home and land as well. There was a colored dentist in town who had two red Lincolns and a swimming pool and a farm with registered white-face cattle on it. Usually by the time she had fallen asleep all the classes of people were moiling and roiling around in her head, and she would dream they were all crammed in together in a boxcar, being ridden off to be put in a gas oven.

"That's a beautiful clock," she said and nodded to her right. It was a big wall clock, the face encased in a brass sunburst.

"Yes, it's very pretty," the stylish lady said agreeably. "And right on the dot too," she added, glancing at her watch.

The ugly girl beside her cast an eye upward at the clock, smirked, and then looked directly at Mrs. Turpin and smirked again. Then she returned her eyes to her book. She was obviously the lady's daughter because, although they didn't look anything alike as to disposition, they both had the same shape of face and the same blue eyes. On the lady they sparkled pleasantly but in the girl's seared face they appeared alternately to smolder and to blaze.

What if Jesus had said, "All right, you can be white-trash or a nigger or ugly"!

Mrs. Turpin felt an awful pity for the girl, though she thought it was one thing to be ugly and another to act ugly.

The woman with the snuff-stained lips turned around in her chair and looked up at the clock. Then she turned back and appeared to look a little to the side of Mrs. Turpin. There was a cast in one of her eyes. "You want to know wher you can get you one of themther clocks?" she asked in a loud voice.

"No, I already have a nice clock," Mrs. Turpin said. Once somebody like her got a leg in the conversation, she would be all over it.

"You can get you one with green stamps,"[2] the woman said. "That's most likely wher he got hisn. Save you up enough, you can get you most anythang. I got me some joo'ry."

Ought to have got you a washrag and some soap, Mrs. Turpin thought.

"I get contour sheets with mine," the pleasant lady said.

The daughter slammed her book shut. She looked straight in front of her, directly

---

[2] S&H Green Stamps were offered as a bonus by retailers; consumers collected and redeemed them for merchandise. The program, which dates back to the early 20th century, largely disappeared in the 1970s.

through Mrs. Turpin and on through the yellow curtain and the plate glass window, which made the wall behind her. The girl's eyes seemed lit all of a sudden with a peculiar light, an unnatural light like night road signs give. Mrs. Turpin turned her head to see if there was anything going on outside that she should see, but she could not see anything. Figures passing cast only a pale shadow through the curtain. There was no reason the girl should single her out for her ugly looks.

"Miss Finley," the nurse said, cracking the door. The gum-chewing woman got up and passed in front of her and Claud and went into the office. She had on red high-heeled shoes.

Directly across the table, the ugly girl's eyes were fixed on Mrs. Turpin as if she had some very special reason for disliking her.

"This is wonderful weather, isn't it?" the girl's mother said.

"It's good weather for cotton if you can get the niggers to pick it," Mrs. Turpin said, "but niggers don't want to pick cotton any more. You can't get the white folks to pick it and now you can't get the niggers—because they got to be right up there with the white folks."

"They gonna *try* anyways," the white-trash woman said, leaning forward.

"Do you have one of the cotton-picking machines?" the pleasant lady asked.

"No," Mrs. Turpin said, "they leave half the cotton in the field. We don't have much cotton anyway. If you want to make it farming now, you have to have a little of everything. We got a couple of acres of cotton and a few hogs and chickens and just enough white-face that Claud can look after them himself."

"One thang I don't want," the white-trash woman said, wiping her mouth with the back of her hand. "Hogs. Nasty stinking things, a-gruntin and a-rootin all over the place."

Mrs. Turpin gave her the merest edge of her attention. "Our hogs are not dirty and they don't stink," she said. "They're cleaner than some children I've seen. Their feet never touch the ground. We have a pig-parlor—that's where, you raise them on concrete," she explained to the pleasant lady, "and Claud scoots them down with the hose every afternoon and washes off the floor." Cleaner by far than that child right there, she thought. Poor nasty little thing. He had not moved except to put the thumb of his dirty hand into his mouth.

The woman turned her face away from Mrs. Turpin. "I know I wouldn't scoot down no hog with no hose," she said to the wall.

You wouldn't have no hog to scoot down, Mrs. Turpin said to herself.

"A-gruntin and a-rootin and a-groanin," the woman muttered.

"We got a little of everything," Mrs. Turpin said to the pleasant lady. "It's no use in having more than you can handle yourself with help like it is. We found enough niggers to pick our cotton this year, but Claud he has to go after them and take them home again in the evening. They can't walk that half a mile. No they can't. I tell you," she said and laughed merrily, "I sure am tired of buttering up niggers, but you got to love em if you want em to work for you. When they come in the morning, I run out and I say 'Hi yawl this morning?' and when Claud drives them off to the field I just wave to beat the band and they just wave back." And she waved her hand rapidly to illustrate.

"Like you read out of the same book," the lady said, showing she understood perfectly.

"Child, yes," Mrs. Turpin said. "And when they come in from the field, I run out with a bucket of ice water. That's the way it's going to be from now on," she said. "You may as well face it."

"One thang I know," the white-trash woman said. "Two thangs I ain't going to do: love no niggers or scoot down no hog with no hose." And she let out a bark of contempt.

The look that Mrs. Turpin and the pleasant lady exchanged indicated they both understood that you had to *have* certain things before you could *know* certain things. But every time Mrs. Turpin exchanged a look with the lady, she was aware that the ugly girl's peculiar eyes were still on her, and she had trouble bringing her attention back to the conversation.

"When you got something," she said, "you got to look after it." And when you ain't got a thing but breath and britches, she added to herself, you can afford to come to town every morning and just sit on the Court House coping and spit.

A grotesque revolving shadow passed across the curtain behind her and was thrown palely on the opposite wall. Then a bicycle clattered down against the outside of the building. The door opened and a colored boy glided in with a tray from the drugstore. It had two large red and white paper cups on it with tops on them. He was a tall, very black boy in discolored white pants and a green nylon shirt. He was chewing gum slowly, as if to music. He set the tray down in the office opening next to the fern and stuck his head through to look for the secretary. She was not in there. He rested his arms on the ledge and waited, his narrow bottom stuck out, swaying to the left and right. He raised a hand over his head and scratched the base of his skull.

"You see that button there, boy?" Mrs. Turpin said. "You can punch that and she'll come. She's probably in the back somewhere."

"Is thas right?" the boy said agreeably, as if he had never seen the button before. He leaned to the right and put his finger on it. "She sometime out," he said and twisted around to face his audience, his elbows behind him on the counter. The nurse appeared and he twisted back again. She handed him a dollar and he rooted in his pocket and made the change and counted it out to her. She gave fifteen cents for a tip and he went out with the empty tray. The heavy door swung to slowly and closed at length with the sound of suction. For a moment no one spoke.

"They ought to send all them niggers back to Africa," the white-trash woman said. "That's wher they come from in the first place."

"Oh, I couldn't do without my good colored friends," the pleasant lady said.

"There's a heap of things worse than a nigger," Mrs. Turpin agreed. "It's all kinds of them just like it's all kinds of us."

"Yes, and it takes all kinds to make the world go round," the lady said in her musical voice.

As she said it, the raw-complexioned girl snapped her teeth together. Her lower lip turned downwards and inside out, revealing the pink inside of her mouth. After a second it rolled back up. It was the ugliest face Mrs. Turpin had ever seen anyone make and for a moment she was certain that the girl had made it at her. She was looking at her as if she had known and disliked her all her life—all of Mrs. Turpin's life, it seemed too, not just all the girl's life. Why, girl, I don't even know you, Mrs. Turpin said silently.

She forced her attention back to the discussion. "It wouldn't be practical to send them back to Africa," she said. "They wouldn't want to go. They got it too good here."

"Wouldn't be what they wanted—if I had anythang to do with it," the woman said.

"It wouldn't be a way in the world you could get all the niggers back over there," Mrs. Turpin said. "They'd be hiding out and lying down and turning sick on you and wailing and hollering and raring and pitching. It wouldn't be a way in the world to get them over there."

"They got over here," the trashy woman said. "Get back like they got over."

"It wasn't so many of them then," Mrs. Turpin explained.

The woman looked at Mrs. Turpin as if here was an idiot indeed but Mrs. Turpin was not bothered by the look, considering where it came from.

"Nooo," she said, "they're going to stay here where they can go to New York and marry white folks and improve their color. That's what they all want to do, everyone of them, improve their color."

"You know what comes of that, don't you?" Claud asked.

"No, Claud, what?" Mrs. Turpin said.

Claud's eyes twinkled. "White-faced niggers," he said with never a smile.

Everybody in the office laughed except the white-trash and the ugly girl. The girl gripped the book in her lap with white fingers. The trashy woman looked around her from face to face as if she thought they were all idiots. The old woman in the feed sack dress continued to gaze expressionless across the floor at the high-top shoes of the man opposite her, the one who had been pretending to be asleep when the Turpins came in. He was laughing heartily, his hands still spread out on his knees. The child had fallen to the side and was lying now almost face down in the old woman's lap.

While they recovered from their laughter, the nasal chorus on the radio kept the room from silence.

> *"You go to blank blank*
> *And I'll go to mine*
> *But we'll all blank along*
> *To-geth-ther,*
> *And all along the blank*
> *We'll hep each other out*
> *Smile-ling in any kind of*
> *Weath-ther!"*

Mrs. Turpin didn't catch every word but she caught enough to agree with the spirit of the song and it turned her thoughts sober. To help anybody out that needed it was her philosophy of life. She never spared herself when she found somebody in need, whether they were white or black, trash or decent. And of all she had to be thankful for, she was most thankful that this was so. If Jesus had said, "You can be high society and have all the money you want and be thin and svelte-like, but you can't be a good woman with it," she would have had to say, "Well don't make me that then. Make me a good woman and it don't matter what else, how fat or how ugly or how poor!" Her heart rose. He had not made her a nigger or white-trash or ugly! He had made her herself and given her a little of everything. Jesus, thank you! she said. Thank you thank you thank you! Whenever she counted her blessings she felt as buoyant as if she weighed one hundred and twenty-five pounds instead of one hundred and eighty.

"What's wrong with your little boy?" the pleasant lady asked the white-trashy woman.

"He has a ulcer," the woman said proudly. "He ain't give me a minute's peace since he was born. Him and her are justalike," she said, nodding at the old woman, who was running her leathery fingers through the child's pale hair. "Look like I can't get nothing down them two but Co'Cola and candy."

That's all you try to get down em, Mrs. Turpin said to herself. Too lazy to light the fire. There was nothing you could tell her about people like them that she didn't know already. And it was not just that they didn't have anything. Because if you gave them everything, in two weeks it would all be broken or filthy or they would have chopped it up for lightwood. She knew all this from her own experience. Help them you must, but help them you couldn't.

All at once the ugly girl turned her lips inside out again. Her eyes fixed like two drills on Mrs. Turpin. This time there was no mistaking that there was something urgent behind them.

Girl, Mrs. Turpin exclaimed silently, I haven't done a thing to you! The girl might be confusing her with somebody else. There was no need to sit by and let herself be intimidated. "You must be in college," she said boldly, looking directly at the girl. "I see you reading a book there."

The girl continued to stare and pointedly did not answer.

Her mother blushed at this rudeness. "The lady asked you a question, Mary Grace," she said under her breath.

"I have ears," Mary Grace said.

The poor mother blushed again. "Mary Grace goes to Wellesley College," she explained. She twisted one of the buttons on her dress. "In Massachusetts," she added with a grimace. "And in the summer she just keeps right on studying. Just reads all the time, a real bookworm. She's done real well at Wellesley; she's taking English and Math and History and Psychology and Social Studies," she rattled on, "and I think it's too much. I think she ought to get out and have fun."

The girl looked as if she would like to hurl them all through the plate glass window.

"Way up north," Mrs. Turpin murmured and thought, well, it hasn't done much for her manners.

"I'd almost rather to have him sick," the white-trash woman said, wrenching the attention back to herself. "He's so mean when he ain't, look like some children just take natural to meanness. It's some gets bad when they get sick but he was the opposite. Took sick and turned good. He don't give me no trouble now. It's me waitin to see the doctor," she said.

If I was going to send anybody back to Africa, Mrs. Turpin murmured, it would be your kind, woman. "Yes, indeed," she said aloud, but looking up at the ceiling, "it's a heap of things worse than a nigger." And dirtier than a hog, she added to herself.

"I think people with bad dispositions are more to be pitied than anyone on earth," the pleasant lady said in a voice that was decidedly thin.

"I thank the Lord he has blessed me with a good one," Mrs. Turpin said. "The day has never dawned that I couldn't find something to laugh at."

"Not since she married me anyways," Claud said with a comical straight face.

Everybody laughed except the girl and the white-trash.

Mrs. Turpin's stomach shook. "He's such a caution," she said, "that I can't help but laugh at him."

The girl made a loud ugly noise through her teeth.

Her mother's mouth grew thin and tight. "I think the worst thing in the world," she said, "is an ungrateful person. To have everything and not appreciate it. I know a girl," she said, "who has parents who would give her anything, a little brother who loves her dearly, who is getting a good education, who wears the best clothes, but who can never say a kind word to anyone, who never smiles, just criticizes and complains all day long."

"Is she too old to paddle?" Claud asked.

The girl's face was almost purple.

"Yes," the lady said, "I'm afraid there's nothing to do but leave her to her folly. Some day she'll wake up and it'll be too late."

"It never hurt anyone to smile," Mrs. Turpin said. "It just makes you feel better all over."

"Of course," the lady said sadly, "but there are just some people you can't tell anything to. They can't take criticism."

"If it's one thing I am," Mrs. Turpin said with feeling, "it's grateful. When I think who all I could have been besides myself and what all I got, a little of everything, and a good disposition besides, I just feel like shouting, 'Thank you, Jesus, for making everything the way it is!' It could have been different!" For one thing, somebody else could have got Claud. At the thought of this, she was flooded with gratitude and a terrible pang of joy ran through her. "Oh thank you, Jesus, Jesus, thank you!" she cried aloud.

The book struck her directly over her left eye. It struck almost at the same instant that she realized the girl was about to hurl it. Before she could utter a sound, the raw face came crashing across the table toward her, howling. The girl's fingers sank like clamps into the soft flesh of her neck. She heard the mother cry out and Claud shout, "Whoa!" There was an instant when she was certain that she was about to be in an earthquake.

All at once her vision narrowed and she saw everything as if it were happening in a small room far away, or as if she were looking at it through the wrong end of a telescope. Claud's face crumpled and fell out of sight. The nurse ran in, then out, then in again. Then the gangling figure of the doctor rushed out of the inner door. Magazines flew this way and that as the table turned over. The girl fell with a thud and Mrs. Turpin's vision suddenly reversed itself and she saw everything large instead of small. The eyes of the white-trashy woman were staring hugely at the floor. There the girl, held down on one side by the nurse and on the other by her mother, was wrenching and turning in their grasp. The doctor was kneeling astride her, trying to hold her arm down. He managed after a second to sink a long needle into it.

Mrs. Turpin felt entirely hollow except for her heart which swung from side to side as if it were agitated in a great empty drum of flesh.

"Somebody that's not busy call for the ambulance," the doctor said in the off-hand voice young doctors adopt for terrible occasions.

Mrs. Turpin could not have moved a finger. The old man who had been sitting next to her skipped nimbly into the office and made the call, for the secretary still seemed to be gone.

"Claud!" Mrs. Turpin called.

He was not in his chair. She knew she must jump up and find him but she felt like some one trying to catch a train in a dream, when everything moves in slow motion and the faster you try to run the slower you go.

"Here I am," a suffocated voice, very unlike Claud's, said.

He was doubled up in the corner on the floor, pale as paper, holding his leg. She wanted to get up and go to him but she could not move. Instead, her gaze was drawn slowly downward to the churning face on the floor, which she could see over the doctor's shoulder.

The girl's eyes stopped rolling and focused on her. They seemed a much lighter blue than before, as if a door that had been tightly closed behind them was now open to admit light and air.

Mrs. Turpin's head cleared and her power of motion returned. She leaned forward until she was looking directly into the fierce brilliant eyes. There was no doubt in her mind that the girl did know her, knew her in some intense and personal way, beyond time and place and condition. "What you got to say to me?" she asked hoarsely and held her breath, waiting, as for a revelation.

The girl raised her head. Her gaze locked with Mrs. Turpin's. "Go back to hell where you came from, you old wart hog," she whispered. Her voice was low but clear. Her eyes burned for a moment as if she saw with pleasure that her message had struck its target.

Mrs. Turpin sank back in her chair.

After a moment the girl's eyes closed and she turned her head wearily to the side.

The doctor rose and handed the nurse the empty syringe. He leaned over and put both hands for a moment on the mother's shoulders, which were shaking. She was sitting on the floor, her lips pressed together, holding Mary Grace's hand in her lap. The girl's fingers were gripped like a baby's around her thumb. "Go on to the hospital," he said. "I'll call and make the arrangements."

"Now let's see that neck," he said in a jovial voice to Mrs. Turpin. He began to inspect her neck with his first two fingers. Two little moon-shaped lines like pink fish bones were indented over her windpipe. There was the beginning of an angry red swelling above her eye. His finger passed over this also.

"Lea' me be," she said thickly and shook him off. "See about Claud. She kicked him."

"I'll see about him in a minute," he said and felt her pulse. He was a thin gray-haired man, given to pleasantries. "Go home and have yourself a vacation the rest of the day," he said and patted her on the shoulder.

Quit your pattin me, Mrs. Turpin growled to herself.

"And put an ice pack over that eye," he said. Then he went and squatted down beside Claud and looked at his leg. After a moment he pulled him up and Claud limped after him into the office.

Until the ambulance came, the only sounds in the room were the tremulous moans of the girl's mother, who continued to sit on the floor. The white-trash woman did not take her eyes off the girl. Mrs. Turpin looked straight ahead at nothing. Presently the ambulance drew up, a long dark shadow, behind the curtain. The attendants came in and set the stretcher down beside the girl and lifted her expertly onto it and carried her out. The nurse helped the mother gather up her things. The shadow of the ambulance moved silently away and the nurse came back in the office.

"That ther girl is going to be a lunatic, ain't she?" the white-trash woman asked the nurse, but the nurse kept on to the back and never answered her.

"Yes, she's going to be a lunatic," the white-trash woman said to the rest of them.

"Po' critter." the old woman murmured. The child's face was still in her lap. His eyes looked idly out over her knees. He had not moved during the disturbance except to draw one leg up under him.

"I thank Gawd," the white-trash woman said fervently, "I ain't a lunatic."

Claud came limping out and the Turpins went home.

As their pick-up truck turned into their own dirt road and made the crest of the hill, Mrs. Turpin gripped the window ledge and looked out suspiciously. The land sloped gracefully down through a field dotted with lavender weeds and at the start of the rise their small yellow frame house, with its little flower beds spread out around it like a fancy apron, sat primly in its accustomed place between two giant hickory trees. She would not have been startled to see a burnt wound between two blackened chimneys.

Neither of them felt like eating so they put on their house clothes and lowered the shade in the bedroom and lay down, Claud with his leg on a pillow and herself with a damp washcloth over her eye. The instant she was flat on her back, the image of a razor-backed hog with warts on its face and horns coming out behind its ears snorted into her head. She moaned, a low quiet moan.

"I am not," she said tearfully, "a wart hog. From hell." But the denial had no force. The girl's eyes and her words, even the tone of her voice, low but clear, directed only to her, brooked no repudiation. She had been singled out for the message, though there was trash in the room to whom it might justly have been applied. The full force of this fact struck her only now. There was a woman there who was neglecting her own child but she had been overlooked. The message had been given to Ruby Turpin, a respectable, hard-working, church-going woman. The tears dried. Her eyes began to burn instead with wrath.

She rose on her elbow and the washcloth fell into her hand. Claud was lying on his back, snoring. She wanted to tell him what the girl had said. At the same time, she did not wish to put the image of herself as a wart hog from hell into his mind.

"Hey, Claud," she muttered and pushed his shoulder.

Claud opened one pale baby blue eye.

She looked into it warily. He did not think about anything. He just went his way.

"Wha, whasit?" he said and closed the eye again.

"Nothing," she said. "Does your leg pain you?"

"Hurts like hell," Claud said.

"It'll quit terreckly," she said and lay back down. In a moment Claud was snoring again. For the rest of the afternoon they lay there. Claud slept. She scowled at the ceiling. Occasionally she raised her fist and made a small stabbing motion over her chest as if she was defending her innocence to invisible guests who were like the comforters of Job, reasonable-seeming but wrong.[3]

About five-thirty Claud stirred. "Got to go after those niggers," he sighed, not moving.

She was looking straight up as if there were unintelligible handwriting on the ceiling. The protuberance over her eye had turned a greenish-blue. "Listen here," she said.

"What?"

---

[3] Job 16:2. "Miserable comforters are you all."

"Kiss me."

Claud leaned over and kissed her loudly on the mouth. He pinched her side and their hands interlocked. Her expression of ferocious concentration did not change. Claud got up, groaning and growling, and limped off. She continued to study the ceiling.

She did not get up until she heard the pick-up truck coming back with the Negroes. Then she rose and thrust her feet in her brown oxfords, which she did not bother to lace, and stumped out onto the back porch and got her red plastic bucket. She emptied a tray of ice cubes into it and filled it half full of water and went out into the back yard. Every afternoon after Claud brought the hands in, one of the boys helped him put out hay and the rest waited in the back of the truck until he was ready to take them home. The truck was parked in the shade under one of the hickory trees.

"Hi yawl this evening?" Mrs. Turpin asked grimly, appearing with the bucket and the dipper. There were three women and a boy in the truck.

"Us doin nicely," the oldest woman said. "Hi you doin?" and her gaze stuck immediately on the dark lump on Mrs. Turpin's forehead. "You done fell down, ain't you?" she asked in a solicitous voice. The old woman was dark and almost toothless. She had on an old felt hat of Claud's set back on her head. The other two women were younger and lighter and they both had new bright green sunhats. One of them had hers on her head; the other had taken hers off and the boy was grinning beneath it.

Mrs. Turpin set the bucket down on the floor of the truck. "Yawl hep yourselves," she said. She looked around to make sure Claud had gone. "No, I didn't fall down," she said, folding her arms. "It was something worse than that."

"Ain't nothing bad happen to you!" the old woman said. She said it as if they all knew that Mrs. Turpin was protected in some special way by Divine Providence. "You just had you a little fall."

"We were in town at the doctor's office for where the cow kicked Mr. Turpin," Mrs. Turpin said in a flat tone that indicated they could leave off their foolishness. "And there was this girl there. A big fat girl with her face all broke out. I could look at that girl and tell she was peculiar but I couldn't tell how. And me and her mama was just talking and going along and all of a sudden WHAM! She throws this big book she was reading at me and..."

"Naw!" the old woman cried out.

"And then she jumps over the table and commences to choke me."

"Naw!" they all exclaimed, "naw!"

"Hi come she do that?" the old woman asked. "What ail her?"

Mrs. Turpin only glared in front of her.

"Somethin ail her," the old woman said.

"They carried her off in an ambulance," Mrs. Turpin continued, "but before she went she was rolling on the floor and they were trying to hold her down to give her a shot and she said something to me." She paused. "You know what she said to me?"

"What she say?" they asked.

"She said," Mrs. Turpin began, and stopped, her face very dark and heavy. The sun was getting whiter and whiter, blanching the sky overhead so that the leaves of the hickory tree were black in the face of it. She could not bring forth the words. "Something real ugly," she muttered.

"She sho shouldn't said nothin ugly to you," the old woman said. "You so sweet.

You the sweetest lady I know."

"She pretty too," the one with the hat on said.

"And stout," the other one said. "I never knowed no sweeter white lady."

"That's the truth befo' Jesus," the old woman said. "Amen! You des as sweet and pretty as you can be."

Mrs. Turpin knew exactly how much Negro flattery was worth and it added to her rage. "She said," she began again and finished this time with a fierce rush of breath, "that I was an old wart hog from hell."

There was an astounded silence.

"Where she at?" the youngest woman cried in a piercing voice.

"Lemme see her. I'll kill her!"

"I'll kill her with you!" the other one cried.

"She b'long in the sylum," the old woman said emphatically. "You the sweetest white lady I know."

"She pretty too," the other two said. "Stout as she can be and sweet. Jesus satisfied with her!"

"Deed he is," the old woman declared.

Idiots! Mrs. Turpin growled to herself. You could never say anything intelligent to a nigger. You could talk at them but not with them. "Yawl ain't drunk your water," she said shortly. "Leave the bucket in the truck when you're finished with it. I got more to do than just stand around and pass the time of day," and she moved off and into the house.

She stood for a moment in the middle of the kitchen. The dark protuberance over her eye looked like a miniature tornado cloud, which might any moment sweep across the horizon of her brow. Her lower lip protruded dangerously. She squared her massive shoulders. Then she marched into the front of the house and out the side door and started down the road to the pig parlor. She had the look of a woman going single-handed, weaponless, into battle.

The sun was a deep yellow now like a harvest moon and was riding westward very fast over the far tree line as if it meant to reach the hogs before she did. The road was rutted and she kicked several good-sized stones out of her path as she strode along. The pig parlor was on a little knoll at the end of a lane that ran off from the side of the barn. It was a square of concrete as large as a small room, with a board fence about four feet high around it. The concrete floor sloped slightly so that the hogwash could drain off into a trench where it was carried to the field for fertilizer. Claud was standing on the outside, on the edge of the concrete, hanging onto the top board, hosing down the floor inside. The hose was connected to the faucet of a water trough nearby.

Mrs. Turpin climbed up beside him and glowered down at the hogs inside. There were seven long-snouted bristly shoats in it—tan with liver-colored spots—and an old sow a few weeks off from farrowing. She was lying on her side grunting. The shoats were running about shaking themselves like idiot children, their little slit pig eyes searching the floor for anything left. She had read that pigs were the most intelligent animal. She doubted it. They were supposed to be smarter than dogs. There had even been a pig astronaut. He had performed his assignment perfectly but died of a heart attack afterwards because they left him in his electric suit, sitting upright throughout his examination when naturally a hog should be on all fours.

A-gruntin and a-rootin and a-groanin.

"Gimme that hose," she said, yanking it away from Claud. "Go on and carry them niggers home and then get off that leg."

"You look like you might have swallowed a mad dog," Claud observed, but he got down and limped off. He paid no attention to her humors.

Until he was out of earshot, Mrs. Turpin stood on the side of the pen, holding the hose and pointing the stream of water at the hindquarters of any shoat that looked as if it might try to lie down. When he had had time to get over the hill, she turned her head slightly and her wrathful eyes scanned the path. He was nowhere in sight. She turned back again and seemed to gather herself up. Her shoulders rose and she drew in her breath.

"What do you send me a message like that for?" she said in a low fierce voice, barely above a whisper but with the force of a shout in its concentrated fury. "How am I a hog and me both? How am I saved and from hell too?" Her free fist was knotted and with the other she gripped the hose, blindly pointing the stream of water in and out of the eye of the old sow whose outraged squeal she did not hear.

The pig parlor commanded a view of the back pasture where their twenty beef cows were gathered around the hay-bales Claud and the boy had put out. The freshly cut pasture sloped down to the highway. Across it was their cotton field and beyond that a dark green dusty wood which they owned as well. The sun was behind the wood, very red, looking over the paling of trees like a farmer inspecting his own hogs.

"Why me?" she rumbled. "It's no trash around here, black or white, that I haven't given to. And break my back to the bone every day working. And do for the church."

She appeared to be the right size woman to command the arena before her. "How am I a hog?" she demanded. "Exactly how am I like them?" and she jabbed the stream of water at the shoats. "There was plenty of trash there. It didn't have to be me."

"If you like trash better, go get yourself some trash then," she railed. "You could have made me trash. Or a nigger. If trash is what you wanted why didn't you make me trash?" She shook her fist with the hose in it and a watery snake appeared momentarily in the air. "I could quit working and take it easy and be filthy," she growled. "Lounge about the sidewalks all day drinking root beer. Dip snuff and spit in every puddle and have it all over my face. I could be nasty.

"Or you could have made me a nigger. It's too late for me to be a nigger," she said with deep sarcasm, "but I could act like one. Lay down in the middle of the road and stop traffic. Roll on the ground."

In the deepening light everything was taking on a mysterious hue. The pasture was growing a peculiar glassy green and the streak of highway had turned lavender. She braced herself for a final assault and this time her voice rolled out over the pasture. "Go on," she yelled, "call me a hog! Call me a hog again. From hell. Call me a wart hog from hell. Put that bottom rail on top. There'll still be a top and bottom!"

A garbled echo returned to her.

A final surge of fury shook her and she roared, "Who do you think you are?"

The color of everything, field and crimson sky, burned for a moment with a transparent intensity. The question carried over the pasture and across the highway and the cotton field and returned to her clearly like an answer from beyond the wood.

She opened her mouth but no sound came out of it.

A tiny truck, Claud's, appeared on the highway, heading rapidly out of sight. Its gears scraped thinly. It looked like a child's toy. At any moment a bigger truck might smash into it and scatter Claud's and the niggers' brains all over the road.

Mrs. Turpin stood there, her gaze fixed on the highway, all her muscles rigid, until in five or six minutes the truck reappeared, returning. She waited until it had had time to turn into their own road. Then like a monumental statue coming to life, she bent her head slowly and gazed, as if through the very heart of mystery, down into the pig parlor at the hogs. They had settled all in one corner around the old sow who was grunting softly. A red glow suffused them. They appeared to pant with a secret life.

Until the sun slipped finally behind the tree line, Mrs. Turpin remained there with her gaze bent to them as if she were absorbing some abysmal life-giving knowledge. At last she lifted her head. There was only a purple streak in the sky, cutting through a field of crimson and leading, like an extension of the highway, into the descending dusk. She raised her hands from the side of the pen in a gesture hieratic and profound. A visionary light settled in her eyes. She saw the streak as a vast swinging bridge extending upward from the earth through a field of living fire. Upon it a vast horde of souls were rumbling toward heaven. There were whole companies of white-trash, clean for the first time in their lives, and bands of black niggers in white robes, and battalions of freaks and lunatics shouting and clapping and leaping like frogs. And bringing up the end of the procession was a tribe of people whom she recognized at once as those who, like herself and Claud, had always had a little of everything and the God-given wit to use it right. She leaned forward to observe them closer. They were marching behind the others with great dignity, accountable as they had always been for good order and common sense and respectable behavior. They alone were on key. Yet she could see by their shocked and altered faces that even their virtues were being burned away. She lowered her hands and gripped the rail of the hog pen, her eyes small but fixed unblinkingly on what lay ahead. In a moment the vision faded but she remained where she was, immobile.

At length she got down and turned off the faucet and made her slow way on the darkening path to the house. In the woods around the invisible cricket choruses had struck up, but what she heard were the voices of the souls climbing upward into the starry field shouting hallelujah.

—1964

CHRISTINE JORGENSEN (1926-1989)

Christine Jorgensen was born George William Jorgensen, Jr., to a middle-class family in the Bronx. George experienced a happy, even idyllic, childhood, marred only by some teasing over his "sissified" ways. George never identified as a homosexual; like many in his era, he regarded homosexuality as deviant. During the late 1940s, after serving in the Army near the end of World War II, he began experiencing increased gender dysphoria (a profound sense of mismatch between assigned gender and physical sex). In 1950 Jorgensen traveled to Denmark to meet with Dr. Christian Hamburger, an endocrinologist who was doing sex-change work. Hamburger gave Jorgensen a diagnosis of transsexuality, rather than homosexuality. After a year of hormone therapy, Jorgensen underwent sex-change surgery in Copenhagen, renaming herself Christine, after Dr. Hamburger.

Upon returning to the United States after surgery, Jorgensen found herself to be a celebrity, principally because of the culture's prurient desire to know about her sex life, but also because she was an attractive woman. She was followed by paparazzi everywhere she went, and eventually chose a stage and singing career, at which she experienced some success in the 1950s and 1960s. Jorgensen is an important figure because she put a human face on transsexuality. After attempting to maintain privacy in the first years after her transition, she later abandoned the effort and became an articulate spokeswoman for transsexuals. With considerable sophistication and humor, she fielded questions about her own experience and became a significant resource for gender dysphoric individuals around the world. Her 1967 memoir, *Christine Jorgensen: A Personal Autobiography,* and its 1970 film adaptation, *The Christine Jorgensen Story,* brought even more fame to her and hope to many transsexuals. Jorgensen died of cancer in 1989.

from Christine Jorgensen: A Personal Autobiography

June 8, 1952

My Dearest Mom, Dad, Dolly, and Bill:

I am now faced with the problem of writing a letter, one which for two years has been on my mind. The task is a great one and the two years of thought haven't made it any easier. To begin with, I want you to know that I am happier and healthier than ever before in my life. I want you to keep this in mind during the rest of this letter. I suppose I should begin with a little philosophy about life and we, the complex people who live it. Life is a strange affair and seems to be stranger as we experience more of it. It is often that we think of the individuality of each person and yet, we are all basically the same. Nevertheless, we are different in looks and temperament. Then, Nature, often for some unknown reason, steps in and adds her own peculiarities. Sometimes, something goes wrong and an abnormal child is born. These things are all a part of life, but we do not accept them. We strive, through science, to answer the great question of "Why?" Why did it happen and where did something go wrong? And last but not least, what can we do to prevent the disorder, or cure it if it has already happened? This leads to investigation and, if necessary, medical aid.

We humans are perhaps the greatest chemical reaction in the world, and therefore it is not strange that we are subject to so very many physical ailments.

Among the greatest working parts of our bodies are the glands. Several small, seemingly unimportant glands, and yet our whole body is governed by them. An imbalance in the glandular system puts the body under a strain, in an effort to adjust that imbalance. This strain, though not usually fatal, has a great effect on our well-being, both physically and mentally. Along with many other people, I had such an imbalance. I use the past tense, "had," because the condition has been cleared. Although a long, very slow process, a doctor in Copenhagen[1] has managed this miracle. He is a great man and a most brilliant scientist.

Mine is an unusual case, although the condition is not so rare as the average person would think. It is more a problem of social taboos and the desire not to speak of the subject, because it deals with the great "hush-hush," namely, Sex. It was for this reason that I came to Europe to one of the greatest gland and hormone specialists in the world. This doctor was very willing to take my case, because he doesn't have the

---

[1] Dr. Christian Hamburger, the Danish surgeon who performed Jorgensen's sex-change operations and who supervised her hormone therapy.

chance very often of finding a patient who can give such complete cooperation as I have. This cooperation meant months of daily tests and examinations. I do not know if you know that both men and women have hormones of both sexes in their bodies. Regardless of many outward appearances, it is the quantity of those hormones which determines a person's sex. All sex characteristics are a result of those hormones. Sometimes, a child is born and, to all outward appearances, seems to be of a certain sex. During childhood, nothing is noticed, but at the time of puberty, when the sex hormones come into action, the chemistry of the body seems to take an opposite turn and, chemically, the child is not of the supposed sex, but the opposite one. This may sound rather fantastic and unbelievable, but I think the doctor's words fit: "The body and life itself is the world's strangest thing. Why then, should we be shocked or even surprised by anything that this strange mechanism does?" And how true those words are.

I was one of those people I have just written about. It was not easy to face and had it not been for the happiness it brought me, I should not have had the strength to go through these two years. You see, I was afraid of a much more horrible illness of the mind. One which, although very common, is not as yet accepted as a true illness, with the necessity for great understanding. Right from the beginning, I realized that I was working toward the release of myself, from a life I knew would always be foreign to me. So, you see, the task was not so difficult at that; not nearly so much so as this letter is for me to write. Just how does a child tell its parents such a story as this? And even as I write these words, I have not yet told you the final outcome of the tests and an operation last September.

I do hope that I have built the letter properly so you already know what I am going to say now. I have changed, changed very much, as my photos will show, but I want you to know that I am an extremely happy person and that the real me, not the physical me, has not changed. I am still the same old "Brud." But Nature made a mistake, which I have had corrected, and I am now your daughter.

I do so want you to like me very much and not to be hurt because I did not tell you sooner about why I came over here. I felt, and still do, that it was the right way to do it. It wasn't because I didn't want you to be in on it, but rather it would have done no good for you to have spent all this time worrying about me when I was in no danger, whatsoever. I knew that you must be told and it would have been easier on me if I had told you earlier, but I just knew it to be the best way. Right or wrong, it was my decision and I still stand by it.

Please don't be hurt. Tante Tine can tell you more, for we've had some good talks. She paid me the biggest compliment when she said: "My goodness, you look like both Dolly and Dorothy (a second cousin.)"

I can't write more now. I seem to be all dried up for this time. Waiting at every postal delivery for your letter.

Love,

Chris

('Brud')

—1967

ANNE SEXTON (1928-1974)

Born in Newton, Massachusetts, Anne Sexton led a privileged childhood in large Boston houses staffed by servants. Her father, Ralph Harvey, ran a successful wool-garneting business that thrived during both the Depression and World War II. At nineteen, Sexton eloped with Alfred Muller Sexton (nicknamed Kayo); soon after their marriage he began working in her father's business. Both families were extremely supportive of the young couple and of their children, Linda and Joyce. Sexton's family consistently paid her medical bills (mostly psychiatric) and her mother often acted as surrogate mother to Linda and Joyce. According to literary legend, Sexton began writing when her psychiatrist suggested that she attempt to access and express the deep and troubling feelings that gave rise to her depression and anxiety (her diagnosis was "hysteria"). The result was that she wrote some of the best-known and most frequently studied American confessional poetry. Her work was considered a break with poetic tradition because it dispensed with the notion of authorial distance and transformed what had been considered private and taboo into deeply thoughtful, moving poetry. Along with Sylvia Plath, Adrienne Rich, and other women writing during the 1950s, 1960s, and 1970s, Sexton rejected the idea that the difficulties faced by women trying to live as housewives, mothers, and lovers was not appropriate material for poetry. In all, she wrote seven books of poetry, earning the 1967 Pulitzer Prize (for *Live or Die*) and two nominations for the National Book Award. She also wrote one play, *Mercy Street,* which had a successful off-Broadway run in 1969. Sexton enjoyed a lifelong friendship with Maxine Kumin; they saw each other frequently and collaborated on the editing of galleys for their books. Kumin, in fact, had lunch with Sexton on the day of her 1974 suicide by carbon monoxide poisoning. At one of Sexton's memorial services, though, poets like Rich and Denise Levertov called for an end to the notion that poetic genius and self-destructive behavior are necessarily connected.

Housewife

Some women marry houses.
It's another kind of skin; it has a heart,
a mouth, a liver and bowel movements.
The walls are permanent and pink.
See how she sits on her knees all day,   5
faithfully washing herself down.
Men enter by force, drawn back like Jonah
into their fleshy mothers.
A woman *is* her mother.
That's the main thing.   10

—1962

Wanting to Die

Since you ask, most days I cannot remember.
I walk in my clothing, unmarked by that voyage.
Then the almost unnameable lust returns.

Even then I have nothing against life.
I know well the grass blades you mention,   5
the furniture you have placed under the sun.

But suicides have a special language.
Like carpenters they want to know *which tools*.
They never ask *why build*.

Twice I have so simply declared myself,   10
have possessed the enemy, eaten the enemy,
have taken on his craft, his magic.

In this way, heavy and thoughtful,
warmer than oil or water,
I have rested, drooling at the mouth-hole.   15

I did not think of my body at needle point.
Even the cornea and the leftover urine were gone.
Suicides have already betrayed the body.

Still-born, they don't always die,
but dazzled, they can't forget a drug so sweet   20
that even children would look on and smile.

To thrust all that life under your tongue!—
that, all by itself, becomes a passion.
Death's a sad bone; bruised, you'd say,

and yet she waits for me, year after year,   25
to so delicately undo an old wound,
to empty my breath from its bad prison.

Balanced there, suicides sometimes meet,
raging at the fruit, a pumped-up moon,
leaving the bread they mistook for a kiss,   30

leaving the page of the book carelessly open,
something unsaid, the phone off the hook
and the love, whatever it was, an infection.

—1964

In Celebration of My Uterus

Everyone in me is a bird.
I am beating all my wings.
They wanted to cut you out
but they will not.
They said you were immeasurably empty   5
but you are not.
They said you were sick unto dying
but they were wrong.
You are singing like a school girl.
You are not torn.   10

Sweet weight,
in celebration of the woman I am
and of the soul of the woman I am
and of the central creature and its delight
I sing for you. I dare to live.   15
Hello, spirit. Hello, cup.
Fasten, cover. Cover that does contain.
Hello to the soil of the fields.
Welcome, roots.

Each cell has a life.   20
There is enough here to please a nation.
It is enough that the populace own these goods.
Any person, any commonwealth would say of it,
"It is good this year that we may plant again
and think forward to the harvest.   25
A blight had been forecast and has been cast out."
Many women are singing together of this:
one is in a shoe factory cursing the machine,
one is at the aquarium tending a seal,
one is dull at the wheel of her Ford,   30
one is at the toll gate collecting,
one is tying the cord of a calf in Arizona,
one is straddling a cello in Russia,
one is shifting pots on the stove in Egypt,
one is painting her bedroom walls moon color,   35
one is dying but remembering a breakfast,
one is stretching on her mat in Thailand,
one is wiping the ass of her child,
one is staring out the window of a train
in the middle of Wyoming and one is   40
anywhere and some are everywhere and all
seem to be singing, although some can not
sing a note.

Sweet weight,
in celebration of the woman I am   45
let me carry a ten-foot scarf,
let me drum for the nineteen-year-olds,
let me carry bowls for the offering
(if that is my part).
Let me study the cardiovascular tissue,   50
let me examine the angular distance of meteors,
let me suck on the stems of flowers
(if that is my part).
Let me make certain tribal figures
(if that is my part).   55
For this thing the body needs
let me sing
for the supper,

for the kissing,
for the correct   60
yes.

—1969

Rumpelstiltskin

Inside many of us
is a small old man
who wants to get out.
No bigger than a two-year-old
whom you'd call lamb chop   5
yet this one is old and malformed.
His head is okay
but the rest of him wasn't Sanforized.[1]
He is a monster of despair.
He is all decay.   10
He speaks up as tiny as an earphone
with Truman's asexual voice:
I am your dwarf.
I am the enemy within.
I am the boss of your dreams.   15
No. I am not the law in your mind,
the grandfather of watchfulness.
I am the law of your members,
the kindred of blackness and impulse.
See. Your hand shakes.   20
It is not palsy or booze.
It is your Doppelgänger[2]
trying to get out.
Beware…Beware…

There once was a miller   25
with a daughter as lovely as a grape.
He told the king that she could
spin gold out of common straw.
The king summoned the girl
and locked her in a room full of straw   30
and told her to spin it into gold
or she would die like a criminal.
Poor grape with no one to pick.
Luscious and round and sleek.
Poor thing.   35
To die and never see Brooklyn.

[1] A trademark that textile and garment manufacturers can request to have applied to their 100% cotton or cotton-blend products. The Sanforized label indicates that the material consistently meets specific standards regarding shrinkage.
[2] A person's exact double.

She wept,
of course, huge aquamarine tears.
The door opened and in popped a dwarf.
He was as ugly as a wart.   40
Little thing, what are you? she cried.
With his tiny no-sex voice he replied:
I am a dwarf.
I have been exhibited on Bond Street
and no child will ever call me Papa.   45
I have no private life.
If I'm in my cups
the whole town knows by breakfast
and no child will ever call me Papa.
I am eighteen inches high.   50
I am no bigger than a partridge.
I am your evil eye
and no child will ever call me Papa.
Stop this Papa foolishness,
she cried. Can you perhaps   55
spin straw into gold?
Yes indeed, he said,
that I can do.
He spun the straw into gold
and she gave him her necklace   60
as a small reward.
When the king saw what she had done
he put her in a bigger room of straw
and threatened death once more.
Again she cried.   65
Again the dwarf came.
Again he spun the straw into gold.
She gave him her ring
as a small reward.
The king put her in an even bigger room   70
but this time he promised
to marry her if she succeeded.
Again she cried.
Again the dwarf came.
But she had nothing to give him.   75
Without a reward the dwarf would not spin.
He was on the scent of something bigger.
He was a regular bird dog.
Give me your first-born
and I will spin.   80
She thought: Piffle!
He is a silly little man.
And so she agreed.
So he did the trick.
Gold as good as Fort Knox.   85

The king married her
and within a year
a son was born.
He was like most new babies,
as ugly as an artichoke   90
but the queen thought him a pearl.
She gave him her dumb lactation,
delicate, trembling, hidden,
warm, etc.
And then the dwarf appeared   95
to claim his prize.
Indeed! I have become a papa!
cried the little man.
She offered him all the kingdom
but he wanted only this—   100
a living thing
to call his own.
And being mortal
who can blame him?

The queen cried two pails of sea water.   105
She was as persistent
as a Jehovah's Witness.
And the dwarf took pity.
He said: I will give you
three days to guess my name   110
and if you cannot do it
I will collect your child.
The queen sent messengers
throughout the land to find names
of the most unusual sort.   115
When he appeared the next day
she asked: Melchior?
Balthazar?
But each time the dwarf replied:
No! No! That's not my name.   120
The next day she asked:
Spindleshanks? Spiderlegs?
But it was still no-no.
On the third day the messenger
came back with a strange story.   125
He told her:
As I came around the corner of the wood
where the fox says good night to the hare
I saw a little house with a fire
burning in front of it.   130
Around that fire a ridiculous little man
was leaping on one leg and singing:
Today I bake.

Tomorrow I brew my beer.
The next day the queen's only child will be mine.   135
Not even the census taker knows
that Rumpelstiltskin is my name...
The queen was delighted.
She had the name!
Her breath blew bubbles.   140

When the dwarf returned
she called out:
Is your name by any chance Rumpelstiltskin?
He cried: The devil told you that!
He stamped his right foot into the ground   145
and sank in up to his waist.
Then he tore himself in two.
Somewhat like a split broiler.
He laid his two sides down on the floor,
one part soft as a woman,   150
one part a barbed hook,
one part papa,
one part Doppelgänger.

—1971

After Auschwitz

Anger,
as black as a hook,
overtakes me.
Each day,
each Nazi   5
took, at 8:00 A.M., a baby
and sautéed him for breakfast
in his frying pan.

And death looks on with a casual eye
and picks at the dirt under his fingernail.   10

Man is evil,
I say aloud.
Man is a flower
that should be burnt,
I say aloud.   15
Man
is a bird full of mud,
I say aloud.

And death looks on with a casual eye
and scratches his anus.   20

Man with his small pink toes,
with his miraculous fingers

is not a temple
but an outhouse,
I say aloud.   25
Let man never again raise his teacup.
Let man never again write a book.
Let man never again put on his shoe.
Let man never again raise his eyes,
on a soft July night.   30
Never. Never. Never. Never. Never.
I say these things aloud.

I beg the Lord not to hear.

—1975

URSULA K. LE GUIN (1929-   )

Ursula Kroeber was born in Berkeley, California, the daughter of prominent anthropologist
Alfred L. Kroeber and Theodora Covel Brown Kroeber, a writer. She started writing at a
young age, earning her first rejection from *Amazing Stories* at the age of twelve. She was educated at Radcliffe College, graduating in 1951, and went on to earn her M.A. from Columbia
University, intending to teach. She met and married Charles Le Guin while she was studying
on a Fulbright scholarship in France, and returned to the U.S. with him, settling first in
Atlanta, Georgia, and then in Portland, Oregon. Le Guin has written extensively for both
adults and young adults. Her work is mostly in the genre of science fiction and fantasy, but
she has also published several volumes of poetry. Two fiction series in particular have enjoyed
both popular and critical success: Her Hainish cycle, which explores a universe in which
human life originated on the planet Hain, and her Earthsea trilogy, a series for young adults
that follows the adventures of the wizard Ged in a world made up of a chain of islands. Le
Guin has received numerous awards for her work, including Nebula and Hugo awards for *The
Left Hand of Darkness* (1969, part of the Hainish cycle); The Newbery Silver Medal Award for
The Tombs of Atuan (1971, part of the original Earthsea trilogy); and Nebula Award Grand
Master (2003).

Ether, OR

For the Narrative Americans

Edna

I never go in the Two Blue Moons any more. I thought about that when I was
arranging the grocery window today and saw Corrie go in across the street and open
up. Never did go into a bar alone in my life. Sook came by for a candy bar and I said
that to her, said I wonder if I ought to go have a beer there sometime, see if it tastes
different on your own. Sook said Oh Ma you always been on your own. I said I seldom had a moment to myself and four husbands, and she said You know that don't
count. Sook's fresh. Breath of fresh air. I saw Needless looking at her with that kind
of dog look men get. I was surprised to find it gave me a pang, I don't know what of.
I just never saw Needless look that way. What did I expect, Sook is twenty and the

man is human. He just always seemed like he did fine on his own. Independent. That's why he's restful. Silvia died years and years and years ago, but I never thought of it before as a long time. I wonder if I have mistaken him. All this time working for him. That would be a strange thing. That was what the pang felt like, like when you know you've made some kind of mistake, been stupid, sewn the seam inside out, left the burner on.

They're all strange, men are. I guess if I understood them I wouldn't find them so interesting. But Toby Walker, of them all he was the strangest. The stranger. I never knew where he was coming from. Roger came out of the desert, Ady came out of the ocean, but Toby came from farther. But he was here when I came. A lovely man, dark all through, dark as forests. I lost my way in him. I loved to lose my way in him. How I wish it was then, not now! Seems like I can't get lost any more. There's only one way to go. I have to keep plodding along it. I feel like I was walking across Nevada, like the pioneers, carrying a lot of stuff I need, but as I go along I have to keep dropping off things. I had a piano once but it got swamped at a crossing of the Platte. I had a good frypan but it got too heavy and I left it in the Rockies. I had a couple ovaries but they wore out around the time we were in the Carson Sink. I had a good memory but pieces of it keep dropping off, have to leave them scattered around in the sagebrush, on the sand hills. All the kids are still coming along, but I don't have them. I had them, it's not the same as having them. They aren't with me any more, even Archie and Sook. They're all walking along back where I was years ago. I wonder will they get any nearer than I have to the west side of the mountains, the valleys of the orange groves? They're years behind me. They're still in Iowa. They haven't even thought about the Sierras yet. I didn't either till I got here. Now I begin to think I'm a member of the Donner Party.[1]

Thos. Sunn

The way you can't count on Ether is a hindrance sometimes, like when I got up in the dark this morning to catch the minus tide and stepped out the door in my rubber boots and plaid jacket with my clam spade and bucket, and overnight she'd gone inland again. The damn desert and the damn sagebrush. All you could dig up there with your damn spade would be a God damn fossil. Personally I blame it on the Indians. I do not believe that a fully civilised country would allow these kind of irregularities in a town. However as I have lived here since 1949 and could not sell my house and property for chicken feed, I intend to finish up here, like it or not. That should take a few more years, ten or fifteen most likely. Although you can't count on anything these days anywhere let alone a place like this. But I like to look after myself, and I can do it here. There is not so much Government meddling and interference and general hindering in Ether as you would find in the cities. This may be because it isn't usually where the Government thinks it is, though it is, sometimes.

When I first came here I used to take some interest in a woman, but it is my belief that in the long run a man does better not to. A woman is a worse hindrance to a man than anything else, even the Government.

I have read the term "a crusty old bachelor" and would be willing to say that that

---

[1] The Donner Party was a group of California-bound travelers who, delayed by taking a new route, were trapped in the Sierra Nevada in the winter of 1846-1847. Nearly half of the group died, and some resorted to eating their dead in order to survive.

describes me so long as the crust goes all the way through. I don't like things soft in the center. Softness is no use in this hard world. I am like one of my mother's biscuits.

My mother, Mrs. J. J. Sunn, died in Wichita, KS, in 1944, at the age of 79. She was a fine woman and my experience of women in general does not apply to her in particular.

Since they invented the kind of biscuits that come in a tube which you hit on the edge of the counter and the dough explodes out of it under pressure, that's the kind I buy, and by baking them about one half hour they come out pretty much the way I like them, crust clear through. I used to bake the dough all of a piece, but then discovered that you can break it apart into separate biscuits. I don't hold with reading directions and they are always printed in small, fine print on the damn foil which gets torn when you break open the tube. I use my mother's glasses. They are a good make.

The woman I came here after in 1949 is still here. That was during my brief period of infatuation. Fortunately I can say that she did not get her hooks onto me in the end. Some other men have not been as lucky. She has married or as good as several times and was pregnant and pushing a baby carriage for decades. Sometimes I think everybody under forty in this town is one of Edna's. I had a very narrow escape. I have had a dream about Edna several times. In this dream I am out on the sea fishing for salmon from a small boat, and Edna swims up from the sea waves and tries to climb into the boat. To prevent this I hit her hands with the gutting knife and cut off the fingers, which fall into the water and turn into some kind of little creatures that swim away. I never can tell if they are babies or seals. Then Edna swims after them making a strange noise, and I see that in actuality she is a kind of seal or sea lion, like the big ones in the cave on the south coast, light brown and very large and fat and sleek in the water.

This dream disturbs me, as it is unfair. I am not the kind of man who would do such a thing. It causes me discomfort to remember the strange noise she makes in the dream, when I am in the grocery store and Edna is at the cash register. To make sure she rings it up right and I get the right change, I have to look at her hands opening and shutting the drawers and her fingers working on the keys. What's wrong with women is that you can't count on them. They are not fully civilised.

Roger Hiddenstone

I only come into town sometimes. It's a now and then thing. If the road takes me there, fine, but I don't go hunting for it. I run a two hundred thousand acre cattle ranch, which gives me a good deal to do. I'll look up sometimes and the moon is new that I saw full last night. One summer comes after another like steers through a chute. In the winters, though, sometimes the weeks freeze like the creek water, and things hold still for a while. The air can get still and clear in the winter here in the high desert. I have seen the mountain peaks from Baker and Rainier in the north, Hood and Jefferson, Three-Fingered Jack and the Sisters east of here, on south to Shasta and Lassen, all standing up in the sunlight for eight hundred or a thousand miles. That was when I was flying. From the ground you can't see that much of the ground, though you can see the rest of the universe, nights.

I traded in my two-seater Cessna for a quarterhorse mare, and I generally keep a Ford pickup, though at times I've had a Chevrolet. Any one of them will get me in to town so long as there isn't more than a couple feet of snow on the road. I like to come in now and then and have a Denver omelette at the cafe for breakfast, and a visit with my wife and son. I have a drink at the Two Blue Moons, and spend the night at the motel. By the next morning I'm ready to go back to the ranch to find out what went wrong while I was gone. It's always something.

Edna was only out to the ranch once while we were married. She spent three weeks. We were so busy in the bed I don't recall much else about it, except the time she tried to learn to ride. I put her on Sally, the cutting horse I traded the Cessna plus fifteen hundred dollars for, a highly reliable horse and more intelligent than most Republicans. But Edna had that mare morally corrupted within ten minutes. I was trying to explain how she'd interpret what you did with your knees, when Edna started yipping and raking her like a bronc rider. They lit out of the yard and went halfway to Ontario at a dead run. I was riding the old roan gelding and only met them coming back. Sally was unrepentant, but Edna was sore and delicate that evening. She claimed all the love had been jolted out of her. I guess that this was true, in the larger sense, since it wasn't long after that that she asked to go back to Ether. I thought she had quit her job at the grocery, but she had only asked for a month off, and she said Needless would want her for the extra business at Christmas. We drove back to town, finding it a little west of where we had left it, in a very pretty location near the Ochoco Mountains, and we had a happy Christmas season in Edna's house with the children.

I don't know whether Archie was begotten there or at the ranch. I'd like to think it was at the ranch so that there would be that in him drawing him to come back some day. I don't know who to leave all this to. Charlie Echeverria is good with the stock, but can't think ahead two days and couldn't deal with the buyers, let alone the corporations. I don't want the corporations profiting from this place. The hands are nice young fellows, but they don't stay put, or want to. Cowboys don't want land. Land owns you. You have to give in to that. I feel sometimes like all the stones on two hundred thousand acres were weighing on me, and my mind's gone to rimrock. And the beasts wandering and calling across all that land. The cows stand with their young calves in the wind that blows March snow like frozen sand across the flats. Their patience is a thing I try to understand.

Gracie Fane

I saw that old rancher on Main Street yesterday, Mr. Hiddenstone, was married to Edna once. He acted like he knew where he was going, but when the street ran out onto the sea cliff he sure did look foolish. Turned round and came back in those high-heel boots, long legs, putting his feet down like a cat the way cowboys do. He's a skinny old man. He went into the Two Blue Moons. Going to try to drink his way back to eastern Oregon, I guess. I don't care if this town is east or west. I don't care if it's anywhere. It never is anywhere anyway. I'm going to leave here and go to Portland, to the Intermountain, the big trucking company, and be a truck driver. I learned to drive when I was five on my grandpa's tractor. When I was ten I started driving my dad's Dodge Ram, and I've driven pickups and delivery vans for Mom and Mr. Needless ever since I got my license. Jase gave me lessons on his eighteen-wheeler last summer. I did real good. I'm a natural. Jase said so. I never got to get out onto the I-5 but only once or twice, though. He kept saying I needed more practice pulling over and parking and shifting up and down. I didn't mind practicing, but then when I got her stopped he'd want to get me into this bed thing he fixed up behind the seats and pull my jeans off, and we had to screw some before he'd go on teaching me anything.

My own idea would be to drive a long way and learn a lot and then have some sex and coffee and then drive back a different way, maybe on hills where I'd have to practice braking and stuff. But I guess men have different priorities. Even when I was driving he'd have his arm around my back and be petting my boobs. He has these huge hands can reach right across both boobs at once. It felt good, but it interfered with his concentration teaching me. He would say *Oh baby you're so great* and I would think he meant I was driving great but then he'd start making those sort of groaning noises and I'd have to shift down and find a place to pull out and get in the bed thing again. I used to practice changing gears in my mind when we were screwing and it helped. I could shift him right up and down again. I used to yell *Going eighty!* when I got him really shifted up. *Fuzz on your tail!* And make these siren noises. That's my CB name: Sireen. Jase got his route shifted in August. I made my plans then. I'm driving for the grocery and saving money till I'm seventeen and go to Portland to work for the Intermountain Company. I want to drive the I-5 from Seattle to LA, or get a run to Salt Lake City. Till I can buy my own truck. I got it planned out.

Tobinye Walker

The young people all want to get out of Ether. Young Americans in a small town want to get up and go. And some do, and some come to a time when they stop talking about where they're going to go when they go. They have come to where they are. Their problem, if it's a problem, isn't all that different from mine. We have a window of opportunity; it closes. I used to walk across the years as easy as a child here crosses the street, but I went lame, and had to stop walking. So this is my time, my heyday, my floruit.

When I first knew Edna she said a strange thing to me; we had been talking, I don't remember what about, and she stopped and gazed at me. "You have a look on you like an unborn child," she said. "You look at things like an unborn child." I don't know what I answered, and only later did I wonder how she knew how an unborn child looks, and whether she meant a fetus in the womb or a child that never came to be conceived. Maybe she meant a newborn child. But I think she used the word she meant to use.

When I first stopped by here, before my accident, there was no town, of course, no settlement. Several peoples came through and sometimes encamped for a season, but it was a range without boundary, though it had names. At that time people didn't have the expectation of stability they have now; they knew that so long as a river keeps running it's a river. Nobody but the beavers built dams, then. Ether always covered a lot of territory, and it has retained that property. But its property is not continuous.

The people I used to meet coming through generally said they came down Humbug Creek from the river in the mountains, but Ether itself never has been in the Cascades, to my knowledge. Fairly often you can see them to the west of it, though usually it's west of them, and often west of the Coast Range in the timber or the dairy country, sometimes right on the sea. It has a broken range. It's an unusual place. I'd like to go back to the center to tell about it, but I can't walk any more. I have to do my flourishing here.

J. Needless

People think there are no Californians. Nobody can come from the promise land. You have to be going to it. Die in the desert, grave by the wayside. I come from

California, born there, think about it some. I was born in the Valley of San Arcadio. Orchards. Like a white bay of orange flowers under bare blue-brown mountains. Sunlight like air, like clear water, something you lived in, an element. Our place was a little farmhouse up in the foothills, looking out over the valley. My father was a manager for one of the companies. Oranges flower white, with a sweet, fine scent. Outskirts of Heaven, my mother said once, one morning when she was hanging out the wash. I remember her saying that. We live on the outskirts of Heaven.

She died when I was six and I don't remember a lot but that about her. Now I have come to realise that my wife has been dead so long that I have lost her too. She died when our daughter Corrie was six. Seemed like there was some meaning in it at the time, but if there was I didn't find it.

Ten years ago when Corrie was twenty-one she said she wanted to go to Disneyland for her birthday. With me. Damn if she didn't drag me down there. Spent a good deal to see people dressed up like mice with water on the brain and places made to look like places they weren't. I guess that is the point there. They clean dirt till it is a sanitary substance and spread it out to look like dirt so you don't have to touch dirt. You and Walt are in control there. You can be in any kind of place, space or the ocean or castles in Spain, all sanitary, no dirt. I would have liked it as a boy, when I thought the idea was to run things. Changed my ideas, settled for a grocery.

Corrie wanted to see where I grew up, so we drove over to San Arcadio. It wasn't there, not what I meant by it. Nothing but roofs, houses, streets and houses. Smog so thick it hid the mountains and the sun looked green. God damn, get me out of there, I said, they have changed the color of the sun. Corrie wanted to look for the house but I was serious. Get me out of here, I said, this is the right place but the wrong year. Walt Disney can get rid of the dirt on his property if he likes, but this is going too far. This is my property.

I felt like that. Like I thought it was something I had, but they scraped all the dirt off and underneath was cement and some electronic wiring. I'd as soon not have seen that. People come through here say how can you stand living in a town that doesn't stay in the same place all the time, but have they been to Los Angeles? It's anywhere you want to say it is.

Well, since I don't have California what have I got? A good enough business. Corrie's still here. Good head on her. Talks a lot. Runs that bar like a bar should be run. Runs her husband pretty well too. What do I mean when I say I had a mother, I had a wife? I mean remembering what orange flowers smell like, whiteness, sunlight. I carry that with me. Corinna and Silvia, I carry their names. But what do I have?

What I don't have is right within hand's reach every day. Every day but Sunday. But I can't reach out my hand. Every man in town gave her a child and all I ever gave her was her week's wages. I know she trusts me. That's the trouble. Too late now. Hell, what would she want me in her bed for, the Medicare benefits?

Emma Bodely

Everything is serial killers now. They say everyone is naturally fascinated by a man planning and committing one murder after another without the least reason and not even knowing who he kills personally. There was the man up in the city recently who tortured and tormented three tiny little boys and took photographs of them while he tortured them and of their corpses after he killed them. Authorities are talking now about what they ought to do with these photographs. They could make a lot of money from a book of them. He was apprehended by the police as he lured yet another tiny boy to come with him, as in a nightmare. There were men in California and Texas and I believe Chicago who dismembered and buried innumerably. Then of course it goes back in history to Jack the Ripper who killed poor women and was supposed to be a member of the Royal Family of England, and no doubt before his time there were many other serial killers, many of them members of Royal Families or Emperors and Generals who killed thousands and thousands of people. But in wars they kill people more or less simultaneously, not one by one, so that they are mass murderers, not serial killers, but I'm not sure I see the difference, really. Since for the person being murdered it only happens once.

I should be surprised if we had a serial killer in Ether. Most of the men were soldiers in one of the wars, but they would be mass murderers, unless they had desk jobs. I can't think who here would be a serial killer. No doubt I would be the last to find out. I find being invisible works both ways. Often I don't see as much as I used to when I was visible. Being invisible however I'm less likely to become a serial victim.

It's odd how the natural fascination they talk about doesn't include the serial victims. I suppose it is because I taught young children for thirty-five years, but perhaps I am unnatural, because I think about those three little boys. They were three or four years old. How strange that their whole life was only a few years, like a cat. In their world suddenly instead of their mother there was a man who told them how he was going to hurt them and then did it, so that there was nothing in their life at all but fear and pain. So they died in fear and pain. But all the reporters tell is the nature of the mutilations and how decomposed they were, and that's all about them. They were little boys not men. They are not fascinating. They are just dead. But the serial killer they tell all about over and over and discuss his psychology and how his parents caused him to be so fascinating, and he lives forever, as witness Jack the Ripper and Hitler the Ripper. Everyone around here certainly remembers the name of the man who serially raped and photographed the tortured little boys before he serially murdered them. He was named Westley Dodd[2] but what were their names?

Of course we the people murdered him back. That was what he wanted. He wanted us to murder him. I cannot decide if hanging him was a mass murder or a serial murder. We all did it, like a war, so it is a mass murder, but we each did it, democratically, so I suppose it is serial, too. I would as soon be a serial victim as a serial murderer, but I was not given the choice.

My choices have become less. I never had a great many, as my sexual impulses were not appropriate to my position in life, and no one I fell in love with knew it. I am glad when Ether turns up in a different place as it is kind of like a new choice of where to live, only I didn't have to make it. I am capable only of very small choices. What to eat for breakfast, oatmeal or corn flakes, or perhaps only a piece of fruit? Kiwi fruits were fifteen cents apiece at the grocery and I bought half a dozen. A while ago they were the most exotic thing, from New Zealand I think and a dollar each, and now they raise them all over the Willamette Valley. But then, the Willamette Valley may be quite exotic to a person in New Zealand. I like the way they're cool in your mouth, the same way the flesh of them looks cool, a smooth green you can see into, like jade stone. I

---

2 Westley Allan Dodd (1961-1993), serial killer and child molester from Richland, Washington. He was executed in 1993, the first legal hanging in the U.S. since 1965.

still see things like that perfectly clearly. It's only with people that my eyes are more and more transparent, so that I don't always see what they're doing, and so that they can look right through me as if my eyes were air and say, "Hi, Emma, how's life treating you?"

Life's treating me like a serial victim, thank you.

I wonder if she sees me or sees through me. I don't dare look. She is shy and lost in her crystal dreams. If only I could look after her. She needs looking after. A cup of tea. Herbal tea, echinacea maybe, I think her immune system needs strengthening. She is not a practical person. I am a very practical person. Far below her dreams.

Lo still sees me. Of course Lo is a serial killer as far as birds are concerned, and moles, but although it upsets me when the bird's not dead yet it's not the same as the man taking photographs. Mr. Hiddenstone once told me that cats have the instinct to let a mouse or bird stay alive awhile in order to take it to the kittens and train them to hunt, so what seems to be cruelty is thoughtfulness. Now I know that some tom cats kill kittens, and I don't think any tom ever raised kittens and trained them thoughtfully to hunt. The queen cat does that. A tom cat is the Jack the Ripper of the Royal Family. But Lo is neutered, so he might behave like a queen or at least like a kind of uncle if there were kittens around, and bring them his birds to hunt. I don't know. He doesn't mix with other cats much. He stays pretty close to home, keeping an eye on the birds and moles and me. I know that my invisibility is not universal when I wake up in the middle of the night and Lo is sitting on the bed right beside my pillow purring and looking very intently at me. It's a strange thing to do, a little uncanny. His eyes wake me, I think. But it's a good waking, knowing that he can see me, even in the dark.

Edna

All right now, I want an answer. All my life since I was fourteen I have been making my soul. I don't know what else to call it, that's what I called it then, when I was fourteen and came into the possession of my life and the knowledge of my responsibility. Since then I have not had time to find a better name for it. The word responsible means that you have to answer. You can't not answer. You'd might rather not answer, but you have to. When you answer you are making your soul, so that it has a shape to it, and size, and some staying power. I understood that, I came into that knowledge, when I was thirteen and early fourteen, that long winter in the Siskiyous. All right, so ever since then, more or less, I have worked according to that understanding. And I have worked. I have done what came into my hands to do, and I've done it the best I could and with all the mind and strength I had to give to it. There have been jobs, waitressing and clerking, but first of all and always the ordinary work of raising the children and keeping the house so that people can live decently and in health and some degree of peace of mind. Then there is responding to the needs of men. That seems like it should come first. People might say I never thought of anything but answering what men asked, pleasing men and pleasing myself, and goodness knows such questions are a joy to answer if asked by a pleasant man. But in the order of my mind, the children come before the fathers of the children. Maybe I see it that way because I was the eldest daughter and there were four younger than me and my father had gone off. Well, all right then, those are my responsibilities as I see them, those are the questions I have tried always to answer: can people live in this house, and how does a child grow up rightly, and how to be trustworthy.

But now I have my own question. I never asked questions, I was so busy answering them, but am sixty years old this winter and think I should have time for a question. But it's hard to ask. Here it is. It's like all the time I was working keeping house and raising the kids and making love and earning our keep I thought there was going to come a time or there would be some place where all of it all came together. Like it was words I was saying, all my life, all the kinds of work, just a word here and a word there, but finally all the words would make a sentence, and I could read the sentence. I would have made my soul and know what it was for.

But I have made my soul and I don't know what to do with it. Who wants it? I have lived sixty years. All I'll do from now on is the same as what I have done only less of it, while I get weaker and sicker and smaller all the time, shrinking and shrinking around myself, and die. No matter what I did, or made, or know. The words don't mean anything. I ought to talk with Emma about this. She's the only one who doesn't say stuff like, "You're only as old as you think you are," "Oh Edna you'll never be old," rubbish like that. Toby Walker wouldn't talk that way either, but he doesn't say much at all any more. Keeps his sentence to himself. My kids that still live here, Archie and Sook, they don't want to hear anything about it. Nobody young can afford to believe in getting old.

So is all the responsibility you take only useful then, but no use later—disposable? What's the use, then? All the work you did is just gone. It doesn't make anything. But I may be wrong. I hope so, I would like to have more trust in dying. Maybe it's worth while, like some kind of answering, coming into another place. Like I felt that winter in the Siskiyous, walking on the snow road between black firs under all the stars, that I was the same size as the universe, the same *thing* as the universe. And if I kept on walking ahead there was this glory waiting for me. In time I would come into glory. I knew that. So that's what I made my soul for. I made it for glory.

And I have known a good deal of glory. I'm not ungrateful. But it doesn't last. It doesn't come together to make a place where you can live, a house. It's gone and the years go. What's left? Shrinking and forgetting and thinking about aches and acid indigestion and cancers and pulse rates and bunions until the whole world is a room that smells like urine, is that what all the work comes to, is that the end of the babies' kicking legs, the children's eyes, the loving hands, the wild rides, the light on water, the stars over the snow? Somewhere inside it all there has to still be the glory.

Ervin Muth

I have been watching Mr. "Toby" Walker for a good while, checking up on things, and if I happened to be called upon to I could state with fair certainty that this "Mr. Walker" is *not an American.* My research has taken me considerably farther afield than that. But there are these "gray areas" or some things which many people as a rule are unprepared to accept. It takes training.

My attention was drawn to these kind of matters in the first place by scrutinizing the town records on an entirely different subject of research. Suffice it to say that I was checking the title on the Fane place at the point in time when Mrs. Osey Jean Fane put the property into the hands of Ervin Muth Relaty, of which I am proprietor. There had been a dispute concerning the property line on the east side of the Fane property in 1939 into which, due to being meticulous concerning these kind of detailed responsibilities, I checked. To my surprise I was amazed to discover that the adjoining lot, which had been developed in 1906, had been in the name of Tobinye Walker since that date, 1906! I naturally assumed at that point in time that this "Tobinye Walker" was "Mr. Toby Walker's" father and thought little more about the issue until my researches into another matter, concerning the Essel/Emmer lots, in the town records indicated that the name "Tobinye Walker" was shown as purchaser of a livery stable on that site (on Main St. between Rash St. and Goreman Ave.) in 1880.

While purchasing certain necessaries in the Needless Grocery Store soon after, I encountered Mr. Walker in person. I remarked in a jocular vein that I had been meeting his father and grandfather. This was of course a mere pleasantry. Mr. "Toby" Walker responded in what struck me as a suspicious fashion. There was some taking aback going on. Although with laughter. His exact words, to which I can attest, were the following: "I had no idea that you were capable of travelling in time!"

This was followed by my best efforts to seriously inquire concerning the persons of his same name which my researches in connection with my work as a relator had turned up. These were only met with facetious remarks such as, "I've lived here quite a while, you see," and, "Oh, I remember when Lewis and Clark came through," a statement in reference to the celebrated explorers of the Oregon Trail, who I ascertained later to have been in Oregon in 1806.

Soon after, Mr. Toby Walker *"walked"* away, thus ending the conversation.

I am convinced by evidence that "Mr. Walker" is an illegal immigrant from a foreign country who has assumed the name of a Founding Father of this fine community, that is to wit the Tobinye Walker who purchased the livery stable in 1880. I have my reasons.

My research shows conclusively that the Lewis and Clark Expedition sent by President Thos. Jefferson did not pass through any of the localities which our fine community of Ether has occupied over the course of its history. Ether never got that far north.

If Ether is to progress to fulfill its destiny as a Destination Resort on the beautiful Oregon Coast and Desert as I visualize it with a complete downtown entertainment center and entrepreneurial business community, including hub motels, RV facilities, and a Theme Park, the kind of thing that is represented by "Mr." Walker will have to go. It is the American way to buy and sell houses and properties continually in the course of moving for the sake of upward mobility and self-improvement. Stagnation is the enemy of the American way. The same person owning the same property since 1906 is unnatural and Unamerican. Ether is an American town and moves all the time. That is its destiny. I can call myself an expert.

Starra Walinow Amethyst

I keep practicing love. I was in love with that French actor Gerard but it's really hard to say his last name. Frenchmen attract me. When I watch *Star Trek The Next Generation* reruns I'm in love with Captain Jean-Luc Picard, but I can't stand Commander Riker. I used to be in love with Heathcliff when I was twelve and Miss Freff gave me *Wuthering Heights*[3] to read. And I was in love with Sting for a while before he got weirder. Sometimes I think I am in love with Lieutenant Worf[4] but that is pretty

---

[3] Classic novel by English writer Emily Brontë (1818-1848), published in 1847.

[4] Lieutenant Worf, a character from the American television show *Star Trek: The Next Generation*.

weird, with all those sort of wrinkles and horns on his forehead, since he's a Klingon, but that's not really what's weird. I mean it's just in the TV that he's an alien. Really he is a human named Michael Dorn. That is so weird to me. I mean I never have seen a real black person except in movies and TV. Everybody in Ether is white. So a black person would actually be an alien here. I thought what it would be like if somebody like that came into like the drug store, really tall, with that dark brown skin and dark eyes and those very soft lips that look like they could get hurt so easily, and asked for something in that really, really deep voice. Like, "Where would I find the aspirin?" And I would show him where the aspirin kind of stuff is. He would be standing beside me in front of the shelf, really big and tall and dark, and I'd feel warmth coming out of him like out of an iron woodstove. He'd say to me in a very low voice, "I don't belong in this town," and I'd say back, "I don't either," and he'd say, "Do you want to come with me?" only really really nicely, not like a come-on but like two prisoners whispering how to get out of prison together. I'd nod, and he'd say, "Back of the gas station, at dusk."

At dusk.

I love that word. Dusk. It sounds like his voice.

Sometimes I feel weird thinking about him like this. I mean because he is actually real. If it was just Worf, that's OK, because Worf is just this alien in some old reruns of a show. But there is actually Michael Dorn. So thinking about him in a sort of story that way makes me uncomfortable sometimes, because it's like I was making him a toy, something I can do anything with, like a doll. That seems like it was unfair to him. And it makes me sort of embarrassed when I think about how he actually has his own life with nothing to do with this dumb girl in some hick town he never heard of. So I try to make up somebody else to make that kind of stories about. But it doesn't work.

I really tried this spring to be in love with Morrie Stromberg, but it didn't work. He's really beautiful-looking. It was when I saw him shooting baskets that I thought maybe I could be in love with him. His legs and arms are long and smooth and he moves smooth and looks kind of like a mountain lion, with a low forehead and short dark blond hair, tawny colored. But all he ever does is hang out with Joe's crowd and talk about sport scores and cars, and once in class he was talking with Joe about me so I could hear, like, "Oh yeah Starra, wow, *she* reads *books*," not really mean, but kind of like I was like an alien from another planet, just totally absolutely strange. Like Worf or Michael Dorn would feel here. Like he meant OK, it's OK to be like that only not here. Somewhere else, OK? As if Ether wasn't already somewhere else. I mean, didn't it use to be the Indians that lived here, and now there aren't any of them either? So who belongs here and where does it belong?

About a month ago Mom told me the reason she left my father. I don't remember anything like that. I don't remember any father. I don't remember anything before Ether. She says we were living in Seattle and they had a store where they sold crystals and oils and New Age stuff, and when she got up one night to go to the bathroom he was in my room holding me. She wanted to tell me everything about how he was holding me and stuff, but I just went, "So, like, he was molesting me." And she went, "Yeah," and I said, "So what did you do?" I thought they would have had a big fight. But she said she didn't say anything, because she was afraid of him. She said, "See, to him it was like he owned me and you. And when I didn't go along with that, he would get real crazy." I think they were into a lot of pot and heavy stuff, she talks about that sometimes. So anyway next day when he went to the store she just took some of the crystals and stuff they kept at home, we still have them, and got some money they kept in a can in the kitchen just like she does here, and got on the bus to Portland with me. Somebody she met there gave us a ride here. I don't remember any of that. It's like I was born here. I asked did he ever try to look for her, and she said she didn't know but if he did he'd have a hard time finding her here. She changed her last name to Amethyst, which is her favorite stone. Walinow was her real name. She says it's Polish.

I don't know what his name was. I don't know what he did. I don't care. It's like nothing happened. I'm never going to belong to anybody.

What I know is this, I am going to love people. They will never know it. But I am going to be a great lover. I know how. I have practiced. It isn't when you belong to somebody or they belong to you or stuff. That's like Chelsey getting married to Tim because she wanted to have the wedding and the husband and a no-wax kitchen floor. She wanted stuff to belong to.

I don't want stuff, but I want practice. Like we live in this shack with no kitchen let alone a no-wax floor, and we cook on a trashburner, with a lot of crystals around, and cat pee from the strays Mom takes in, and Mom does stuff like sweeping out for Myrella's beauty parlor, and gets zits because she eats Hostess Twinkies instead of food. Mom needs to get it together. But I need to give it away.

I thought maybe the way to practice love was to have sex so I had sex with Danny last summer. Mom bought us condoms and made me hold hands with her around a bayberry candle and talk about the Passage Into Womanhood. She wanted Danny to be there too but I talked her out of it. The sex was OK but what I was really trying to do was be in love. It didn't work. Maybe it was the wrong way. He just got used to getting sex and so he kept coming around all fall, going "Hey Starra baby you know you need it." He wouldn't even say that it was him that needed it. If I need it, I can do it a lot better myself than he can. I didn't tell him that. Although I nearly did when he kept not letting me alone after I told him to stop. If he hadn't finally started going with Dana I might would have told him.

I don't know anybody else here I can be in love with. I wish I could practice on Archie but what's the use while there's Gracie Fane? It would just be dumb. I thought about asking Archie's father Mr. Hiddenstone if I could work on his ranch, next time we get near it. I could still come see Mom, and maybe there would be like ranch hands or cowboys. Or Archie would come out sometimes and there wouldn't be Gracie. Or actually there's Mr. Hiddenstone. He looks like Archie. Actually handsomer. But I guess is too old. He has a face like the desert. I noticed his eyes are the same color as Mom's turquoise ring. But I don't know if he needs a cook or anything and I suppose fifteen is too young.

J. Needless

Never have figured out where the Hohovars come from. Somebody said White Russia. That figures. They're all big and tall and heavy with hair so blond it's white and those little blue eyes. They don't look at you. Noses like new potatoes. Women don't talk. Kids don't talk. Men talk like, "Vun case yeast peggets, tree case piggle beet." Never say hello, never say goodbye, never say thanks. But honest. Pay right up in cash. When they come in town they're all dressed head to foot, the women in these long dresses with a lot of fancy stuff around the bottom and sleeves, the little girls just the same as the women, even the babies in the same long stiff skirts, all of them with bonnet things that hide their hair. Even the babies don't look up. Men and boys in long pants and shirt and coat even when it's desert here and a hundred and five in July. Something like those ammish folk on the east coast, I guess. Only the Hohovars have buttons. A lot of buttons. The vest things the women wear have about a thousand buttons. Men's flies the same. Must slow 'em down getting to the action. But everybody says buttons are no problem when they get back to their community. Everything off. Strip naked to go to their church. Tom Sunn swears to it, and Corrie says she used to sneak out there more than once on Sunday with a bunch of other kids to see the Hohovars all going over the hill buck naked, singing in their language. That would be some sight, all those tall, heavy-fleshed, white-skinned, big-ass, big-tit women parading over the hill. Barefoot, too. What the hell they do in church I don't know. Tom says they commit fornication but Tom Sunn don't know shit from a hole in the ground. All talk. Nobody I know has ever been over that hill.

Some Sundays you can hear them singing.

Now religion is a curious thing in America. According to the Christians there is only one of anything. On the contrary there seems to me to be one or more of everything. Even here in Ether we have, that I know of, Baptists of course, Methodists, Church of Christ, Lutheran, Presbyterian, Catholic though no church in town, a Quaker, a lapsed Jew, a witch, the Hohovars, and the gurus or whatever that lot in the grange are. This is not counting most people, who have no religious affiliation except on impulse.

That is a considerable variety for a town this size. What's more, they try out each other's churches, switch around. Maybe the nature of the town makes us restless. Anyhow people in Ether generally live a long time, though not as long as Toby Walker. We have time to try out different things. My daughter Corrie has been a Baptist as a teen-ager, a Methodist while in love with Jim Fry, then had a go at the Lutherans. She was married Methodist but is now the Quaker, having read a book. This may change, as lately she has been talking to the witch, Pearl W. Amethyst, and reading another book, called *Crystals and You.*

Edna says the book is all tosh. But Edna has a harder mind than most.

Edna is my religion, I guess. I was converted years ago.

As for the people in the grange, the guru people, they caused some stir when they arrived ten years ago, or is it twenty now. Maybe it was in the sixties. Seems like they've been there a long time when I think about it. My wife was still alive. Anyhow, that's a case of religion mixed up some way with politics, not that it isn't always.

When they came to Ether they had a hell of a lot of money to throw around, though they didn't throw much my way. Bought the old grange and thirty acres of pasture adjacent. Put a fence right round and God damn if they didn't electrify that fence. I don't mean the little jolt you might run in for steers but a kick would kill an elephant. Remodeled the old grange and built on barns and barracks and even a generator. Everybody inside the fence was to share everything in common with everybody else inside the fence. Though from outside the fence it looked like the guru shared a lot more of it than the rest of 'em. That was the political part. Socialism. The bubonic socialism. Rats carry it and there is no vaccine. I tell you people here were upset. Thought the whole population behind the iron curtain plus all the hippies in California were moving in next Tuesday. Talked about bringing in the National Guard to defend the rights of citizens. Personally I'd of preferred the hippies over the National Guard. Hippies were unarmed. They killed by smell alone, as people said. But at the time there was a siege mentality here. A siege inside the grange, with their electric fence and their socialism, and a siege outside the grange, with their rights of citizens to be white and not foreign and not share anything with anybody.

At first the guru people would come into the town in their orange color T-shirts, doing a little shopping, talking politely. Young people got invited into the grange. They were calling it the osh rom by then. Corrie told me about the altar with the marigolds and the big photograph of Guru Jaya Jaya Jaya. But they weren't really friendly people and they didn't get friendly treatment. Pretty soon they never came into town, just drove in and out the road gate in their orange Buicks. Sometime along in there the Guru Jaya Jaya Jaya was supposed to come from India to visit the osh rom. Never did. Went to South America instead and founded an osh rom for old Nazis, they say. Old Nazis probably have more money to share with him than young Oregonians do. Or maybe he came to find his osh rom and it wasn't where they told him.

It has been kind of depressing to see the T-shirts fade and the Buicks break down. I don't guess there's more than two Buicks and ten, fifteen people left in the osh rom. They still grow garden truck, eggplants, all kinds of peppers, greens, squash, tomatoes, corn, beans, blue and rasp and straw and marion berries, melons. Good quality stuff. Raising crops takes some skill here where the climate will change overnight. They do beautiful irrigation and don't use poisons. Seen them out there picking bugs off the plants by hand. Made a deal with them some years ago to supply my produce counter and have not regretted it. Seems like Ether is meant to be a self-sufficient place. Every time I'd get a routine set up with a supplier in Cottage Grove or Prineville, we'd switch. Have to call up and say sorry, we're on the other side of the mountains again this week, cancel those cantaloupes. Dealing with the guru people is easier. They switch along with us.

What they believe in aside from organic gardening I don't know. Seems like the Guru Jaya Jaya Jaya would take some strenuous believing, but people can put their faith in anything, I guess. Hell, I believe in Edna.

Archie Hiddenstone
Dad got stranded in town again last week. He hung around awhile to see if the range would move back east, finally drove his old Ford over to Eugene and up the McKenzie River highway to get back to the ranch. Said he'd like to stay but Charlie Echeverria would be getting into some kind of trouble if he did. He just doesn't like to stay away from the place more than a night or two. It's hard on him when we turn up way over here on the coast like this.

I know he wishes I'd go back with him. I guess I ought to. I ought to live with him. I could see Mama every time Ether was over there. It isn't that. I ought to get it straight in my mind what I want to do. I ought to go to college. I ought to get out of this town. I ought to get away.

I don't think Gracie ever actually has seen me. I don't do anything she can see. I don't drive a semi.

I ought to learn. If I drove a truck she'd see me. I could come through Ether off the I-5 or down from 84, wherever. Like that shit kept coming here last summer she was so crazy about. Used to come into the Seven-Eleven all the time for Gatorade. Called me Boy. Hey boy gimme the change in quarters. She'd be sitting up in his eighteen-wheeler playing with the gears. She never came in. Never even looked. I used to think maybe she was sitting there with her jeans off. Bareass on that truck seat. I don't know why I thought that. Maybe she was.

I don't want to drive a God damn stinking semi or try to feed a bunch of steers in a God damn desert either or sell God damn Hostess Twinkies to crazy women with purple hair either. I ought to go to college. Learn something. Drive a sports car. A Miata. Am I going to sell Gatorade to shits all my life? I ought to be somewhere that is somewhere.

I dreamed the moon was paper and I lit a match and set fire to it. It flared up just like a newspaper and started dropping down fire on the roofs, scraps of burning. Mama came out of the grocery and said, "That'll take the ocean." Then I woke up. I heard the ocean where the sagebrush hills had been.

I wish I could make Dad proud of me anywhere but the ranch. But that's the only place he lives. He won't ever ask me to come live there. He knows I can't. I ought to.

Edna

Oh how my children tug at my soul just as they tugged at my breasts, so that I want to yell Stop! I'm dry! You drank me dry years ago! Poor sweet stupid Archie. What on earth to do for him. His father found the desert he needed. All Archie's found is a tiny little oasis he's scared to leave.

I dreamed the moon was paper, and Archie came out of the house with a box of matches and tried to set it afire, and I was frightened and ran into the sea.

Ady came out of the sea. There were no tracks on that beach that morning except his, coming up towards me from the breaker line. I keep thinking about the men lately. I keep thinking about Needless. I don't know why. I guess because I never married him. Some of them I wonder why I did, how it came about. There's no reason in it. Who'd ever have thought I'd ever sleep with Tom Sunn? But how could I go on saying no to a need like that? His fly bust every time he saw me across the street. Sleeping with him was like sleeping in a cave. Dark, uncomfortable, echoes, bears farther back in. Bones. But a fire burning. Tom's true soul is that fire burning, but he'll never know it. He starves the fire and smothers it with wet ashes, he makes himself the cave where he sits on cold ground gnawing bones. Women's bones.

But Mollie is a brand snatched from his burning. I miss Mollie. Next time we're over east again I'll go up to Pendleton and see her and the grandbabies. She doesn't come. Never did like the way Ether ranges. She's a stayputter. Says all the moving around would make the children insecure. It didn't make her insecure in any harmful way that I can see. It's her Eric that would disapprove. He's a snob. Prison clerk. What a job. Walk out of a place every night where the others are all locked in, how's that for a ball and chain? Sink you if you ever tried to swim.

Where did Ady swim up from I wonder? Somewhere deep. Once he said he was Greek, once he said he worked on a Australian ship, once he said he had lived on an island in the Philippines where they speak a language nobody else anywhere speaks, once he said he was born in a canoe at sea. It could all have been true. Or not. Maybe Archie should go to sea. Join the Navy or the Coast Guard. But no, he'd drown.

Tad knows he'll never drown. He's Ady's son, he can breathe water. I wonder where Tad is now. That is a tugging too, that not knowing, not knowing where the child is, an aching pull you stop noticing because it never stops. But sometimes it turns you, you find you're facing another direction, like your body was caught by the thorn of a blackberry, by an undertow. The way the moon pulls the tides.

I keep thinking about Archie, I keep thinking about Needless. Ever since I saw him look at Sook. I know what it is, it's that other dream I had. Right after the one with Archie. I dreamed something, it's hard to get hold of, something about being on this long long beach, like I was beached, yes, that's it, I was stranded, and I couldn't move. I was drying up and I couldn't get back to the water. Then I saw somebody walking towards me from way far away down the beach. His tracks in the sand were ahead of him. Each time he stepped in one, in the footprint, it was gone when he lifted his foot. He kept coming straight to me and I knew if he got to me I could get back in the water and be all right. When he got close up I saw it was him. It was Needless. That's an odd dream.

If Archie went to sea he'd drown. He's a drylander, like his father.

Sookie, now, Sook is Toby Walker's daughter. She knows it. She told me, once, I didn't tell her. Sook goes her own way. I don't know if he knows it. I don't think so. She has my eyes and hair. And there were some other possibilities. And I never felt it was the right thing to tell a man unless he asked. Toby didn't ask, because of what he believed about himself. But I knew the night, I knew the moment she was conceived. I felt the child to be leap in me like a fish leaping in the sea, a salmon coming up the river, leaping the rocks and rapids, shining. Toby had told me he couldn't have children—"not with any woman born," he said, with a sorrowful look. He came pretty near telling me where he came from, that night. But I didn't ask. Maybe because of what I believe about myself, that I only have the one life and no range, no freedom to walk in the hidden places.

Anyhow, I told him that that didn't matter, because if I felt like it I could conceive by taking thought. And for all I know that's what happened. I thought Sookie and out she came, red as a salmon, quick and shining. She is the most beautiful child, girl, woman. What does she want to stay here in Ether for? Be an old maid teacher like Emma? Pump gas, give perms, clerk in the grocery? Who'll she meet here? Well, God knows I met enough. I like it, she says, I like not knowing where I'll wake up. She's like me. But still there's the tug, the dry longing. Oh, I guess I had too many children. I turn this way, that way, like a compass with forty Norths. Yet always going on the same way in the end. Fitting my feet into my footprints that disappear behind me.

It's a long way down from the mountains. My feet hurt.

Tobinye Walker

Man is the animal that binds time, they say. I wonder. We're bound by time, bounded by it. We move from a place to another place, but from a time to another time only in memory and intention, dream and prophecy. Yet time travels us. Uses us as its road, going on never stopping always in one direction. No exits off this freeway.

I say *we* because I am a naturalized citizen. I didn't use to be a citizen at all. Time once was to me what my back yard is to Emma's cat. No fences mattered, no boundaries. But I was forced to stop, to settle, to join. I am an American. I am a castaway. I came to grief.

I admit I've wondered if it's my doing that Ether ranges, doesn't stay put. An effect of my accident. When I lost the power to walk straight, did I impart a twist to the locality? Did it begin to travel because my travelling had ceased? If so, I can't work out the mechanics of it. It's logical, it's neat, yet I don't think it's the fact. Perhaps I'm just dodging my responsibility. But to the best of my memory, ever since Ether was a town it's always been a real American town, a place that isn't where you left it. Even when you live there it isn't where you think it is. It's missing. It's restless. It's off somewhere over the mountains, making up in one dimension what it lacks in another. If it doesn't keep moving the malls will catch it. Nobody's surprised it's gone. The white man's his own burden. And nowhere to lay it down. You can leave town easy enough, but coming back is tricky. You come back to where you left it and there's nothing but the parking lot for the new mall and a giant yellow grinning clown made of balloons. Is that all there was to it? Better not believe it, or that's all you'll ever have: blacktop and cinderblock and a blurred photograph of a little boy smiling. The child was murdered along with many others. There's more to it than that, there is an old glory in it, but it's hard to locate, except by accident. Only Roger Hiddenstone can come back when he wants to, riding his old Ford or his old horse, because Roger owns nothing but the desert and a true heart. And of course wherever Edna is, it is. It's where she lives.

I'll make my prophecy. When Starra and Roger lie in each other's tender arms, she sixteen he sixty, when Gracie and Archie shake his pickup truck to pieces making love on the mattress in the back on the road out to the Hohovars, when Ervin Muth and Thomas Sunn get drunk with the farmers in the ashram and dance and sing and cry all night, when Emma Bodely and Pearl Amethyst gaze long into each other's shining eyes among the cats, among the crystals—that same night Needless the grocer will come at last to Edna. To him she will bear no child but joy. And orange trees will blossom in the streets of Ether.

—1995

PAULE MARSHALL (1929-   )

A native of Brooklyn, New York, fiction writer Paule Marshall was born to Ada and Sam Burke, who had immigrated separately to the U.S. from Barbados after World War I. She learned the craft of storytelling, as well as the rhythms and cadences of West Indian speech, from her mother and her mother's friends who would gather after their work (mostly as domestics) and trade stories and gossip in her mother's kitchen. She received her B.A. from Brooklyn College in 1953 and, after trying to find work in publishing, took a job as the fashion and food editor for *Our World* (a nationally distributed African-American magazine founded by John Preston Davis in 1946), where she worked from 1953 to 1956. While working there, she started work on her first novel, *Brown Girl, Brownstones* (1959), a coming-of-age story about Selina Boyce, the daughter of Barbadian immigrants living in Brooklyn. Critically well-received, the novel explored questions about identity and community, history and myth, that Marshall has continued to take on and complicate from different angles. Her second novel, *The Chosen Place, The Timeless People* (1969), for instance, looks at how the dynamics of class, race, and gender in a fictional Caribbean island town are shaped both by contemporary struggles over land use and development and the deeply felt communal memory of slavery and rebellion. Marshall is also the author of two collections of short stories, *Soul Clap Hands and Sing* (1961), and *Reena and Other Stories* (1983), as well as three other novels, *Praisesong for the Widow* (1983), *Daughters* (1991), and *The Fisher King* (2000). Marshall has been married twice; first, in 1950, to Kenneth E. Marshall, with whom she had one child before they divorced in 1963, and then, in 1970, to Nourry Menard. In addition to receiving a Before Columbus Foundation American Book Award for *Praisesong for the Widow,* Marshall has been the recipient of numerous grants and awards, including a Guggenheim Fellowship and a grant from the National Endowment for the Arts.

Brooklyn

A summer wind, soaring just before it died, blew the dusk and the first scattered lights of downtown Brooklyn against the shut windows of the classroom, but Professor Max Berman—B.A., 1919, M.A., 1921, New York; Docteur de l'Université, 1930, Paris—alone in the room, did not bother to open the windows to the cooling wind. The heat and airlessness of the room, the perspiration inching its way like an ant around his starched collar were discomforts he enjoyed; they obscured his larger discomfort: the anxiety which chafed his heart and tugged his left eyelid so that he seemed to be winking, roguishly, behind his glasses.

To steady his eye and ease his heart, to fill the time until his students arrived and his first class in years began, he reached for his cigarettes. As always he delayed lighting the cigarette so that his need for it would be greater and, thus, the relief and pleasure it would bring, fuller. For some time he fondled it, his fingers shaping soft, voluptuous gestures, his warped old man's hands looking strangely abandoned on the bare desk and limp as if the bones had been crushed, and so white—except for the tobacco burn on the index and third fingers—it seemed his blood no longer traveled that far.

He lit the cigarette finally and as the smoke swelled his lungs, his eyelid stilled and his lined face lifted, the plume of white hair wafting above his narrow brow; his body—short, blunt, the shoulders slightly bent as if in deference to his sixty-three years—settled back in the chair. Delicately Max Berman crossed his legs and, looking down, examined his shoes for dust. (The shoes were of a very soft, fawn-colored leather and somewhat foppishly pointed at the toe. They had been custom made in France and were his one last indulgence. He wore them in memory of his first wife, a French Jewess from Alsace-Lorraine whom he had met in Paris while lingering over his doctorate and married to avoid returning home. She had been gay, mindless and very excitable—but at night, she had also been capable of a profound stillness as she lay in bed waiting for him to turn to her, and this had always awed and delighted him. She had been a gift—and her death in a car accident had been a judgment on him for never having loved her, for never, indeed, having even allowed her to matter.) Fastidiously Max Berman unbuttoned his jacket and straightened his vest, which had a stain two decades old on the pocket. Through the smoke his veined eyes contemplated other, more pleasurable scenes. With his neatly shod foot swinging and his cigarette at a rakish tilt, he might have been an old *boulevardier*[1] taking the sun and an absinthe before the afternoon's assignation.

A young face, the forehead shiny with earnestness, hung at the half-opened door. "Is this French Lit, fifty-four? Camus and Sartre?"[2]

---

[1] (Fr.) A sophisticated, worldly man; a man about town.

[2] Jean-Paul Sartre (1905-1980) and Albert Camus (1913-1960), Nobel Prize-winning French writers.

Max Berman winced at the rawness of the voice and the flat "a" in Sartre and said formally, "This is Modern French Literature, number fifty-four, yes, but there is some question as to whether we will take up Messieurs Camus and Sartre this session. They might prove hot work for a summer-evening course. We will probably do Gide and Mauriac,[3] who are considerably more temperate. But come in nonetheless...."

He was the gallant, half rising to bow her to a seat. He knew that she would select the one in the front row directly opposite his desk. At the bell her pen would quiver above her blank notebook, ready to commit his first word—indeed, the clearing of his throat—to paper, and her thin buttocks would begin sidling toward the edge of her chair.

His eyelid twitched with solicitude. He wished that he could have drawn the lids over her fitful eyes and pressed a cool hand to her forehead. She reminded him of what he had been several lifetimes ago: a boy with a pale, plump face and harried eyes, running from the occasional taunts at his yamilke along the shrill streets of Brownsville in Brooklyn, impeded by the heavy satchel of books which he always carried as proof of his scholarship. He had been proud of his brilliance at school and the Yeshiva, but at the same time he had been secretly troubled by it and resentful, for he could never believe that he had come by it naturally or that it belonged to him alone. Rather, it was like a heavy medal his father had hung around his neck—the chain bruising his flesh—and constantly exhorted him to wear proudly and use well.

The girl gave him an eager and ingratiating smile and he looked away. During his thirty years of teaching, a face similar to hers had crowded his vision whenever he had looked up from a desk. Perhaps it was fitting, he thought, and lighted another cigarette from the first, that she should be present as he tried again at life, unaware that behind his rimless glasses and within his ancient suit, he had been gutted.

He thought of those who had taken the last of his substance—and smiled tolerantly. "The boys of summer," he called them, his inquisitors, who had flailed him with a single question: "Are you now or have you ever been a member of the Communist party?"[4] Max Berman had never taken their question seriously—perhaps because he had never taken his membership in the party seriously—and he had refused to answer. What had disturbed him, though, even when the investigation was over, was the feeling that he had really been under investigation for some other offense which did matter and of which he was guilty; that behind their accusations and charges had lurked another which had not been political but personal. For had he been disloyal to the government? His denial was a short, hawking laugh. Simply, he had never ceased being religious. When his father's God had become useless and even a little embarrassing, he had sought others: his work for a time, then the party. But he had been middle-aged when he joined and his faith, which had been so full as a boy, had grown thin. He had come, by then, to distrust all pieties, so that when the purges in Russia during the thirties confirmed his distrust, he had withdrawn into a modest cynicism.

But he had been made to answer for that error. Ten years later his inquisitors had flushed him out from the small community college in upstate New York where he had taught his classes from the same neat pack of notes each semester and had led him bound by subpoena to New York and bandied his name at the hearings until he had been dismissed from his job.

---

[3] Andre Gide (1869-1951) and François Mauriac (1885-1970), Nobel Prize-winning French writers.

He remembered looking back at the pyres of burning autumn leaves on the campus his last day and feeling that another lifetime had ended—for he had always thought of his life as divided into many small lives, each with its own beginning and end. Like a hired mute, he had been present at each dying and kept the wake and wept professionally as the bier was lowered into the ground. Because of this feeling, he told himself that his final death would be anticlimactic.

After his dismissal he had continued living in the small house he had built near the college, alone except for an occasional visit from a colleague, idle but for some tutoring in French, content with the income he received from the property his parents had left him in Brooklyn—until the visits and tutoring had tapered off and a silence had begun to choke the house, like weeds springing up around a deserted place. He had begun to wonder then if he were still alive. He would wake at night from the recurrent dream of the hearings, where he was being accused of an unstated crime, to listen for his heart, his hand fumbling among the bedclothes to press the place. During the day he would pass repeatedly in front of the mirror with the pretext that he might have forgotten to shave that morning or that something had blown into his eye. Above all, he had begun to think of his inquisitors with affection and to long for the sound of their voices. They, at least, had assured him of being alive.

As if seeking them out, he had returned to Brooklyn and to the house in Brownsville where he had lived as a boy and had boldly applied for a teaching post without mentioning the investigation. He had finally been offered the class which would begin in five minutes. It wasn't much: a six-week course in the summer evening session of a college without a rating, where classes were held in a converted factory building, a college whose campus took in the bargain department stores, the five-and-dime emporiums and neon-spangled movie houses of downtown Brooklyn.

Through the smoke from his cigarette, Max Berman's eyes—a waning blue that never seemed to focus on any one thing—drifted over the students who had gathered meanwhile. Imbuing them with his own disinterest, he believed that even before the class began, most of them were longing for its end and already anticipating the soft drinks at the soda fountain downstairs and the synthetic dramas at the nearby movie.

They made him sad. He would have liked to lead them like a Pied Piper back to the safety of their childhoods—all of them: the loud girl with the formidable calves of an athlete who reminded him, uncomfortably, of his second wife (a party member who was always shouting political heresy from some picket line and who had promptly divorced him upon discovering his irreverence); the two sallow-faced young men leaning out the window as if searching for the wind that had died; the slender young woman with crimped black hair who sat very still and apart from the others, her face turned toward the night sky as if to a friend.

Her loneliness interested him. He sensed its depth and his eye paused. He saw then that she was a Negro, a very pale mulatto with skin the color of clear, polished amber and a thin, mild face. She was somewhat older than the others in the room—a schoolteacher from the South, probably, who came north each summer to take courses toward a graduate degree. He felt a fleeting discomfort and irritation: discomfort at the thought that although he had been sinned against as a Jew he still shared in the sin against her and suffered from the same vague guilt, irritation that she recalled his own humiliations: the large ones, such as the fact that despite his brilliance he had been unable to get into a medical school as a young man because of the quota on Jews (not that he had wanted to be a doctor; that had been his father's wish) and had changed his studies from medicine to French; the small ones which had worn him thin: an eye widening imperceptibly as he gave his name, the savage glance which sought the Jewishness in his nose, his chin, in the set of his shoulders, the jokes snuffed into silence at his appearance....

Tired suddenly, his eyelid pulsing, he turned and stared out the window at the gaudy constellation of neon lights. He longed for a drink, a quiet place and then sleep. And to bear him gently into sleep, to stay the terror which bound his heart then reminding him of those oleographs[5] of Christ with the thorns binding his exposed heart—fat drops of blood from one so bloodless—to usher him into sleep, some pleasantly erotic image: a nude in a boudoir scattered with her frilled garments and warmed by her frivolous laugh, with the sun like a voyeur at the half-closed shutters. But this time instead of the usual Rubens[6] nude with thighs like twin portals and a belly like a huge alabaster bowl into which he poured himself, he chose Gauguin's Aita Parari,[7] her languorous form in the straight-back chair, her dark, sloping breasts, her eyes like the sun under shadow.

With the image still on his inner eye, he turned to the Negro girl and appraised her through a blind of cigarette smoke. She was still gazing out at the night sky and something about her fixed stare, her hands stiffly arranged in her lap, the nerve fluttering within the curve of her throat, betrayed a vein of tension within the rock of her calm. It was as if she had fled long ago to a remote region within herself, taking with her all that was most valuable and most vulnerable about herself.

She stirred finally, her slight breasts lifting beneath her flowered summer dress as she breathed deeply—and Max Berman thought again of Gauguin's girl with the dark, sloping breasts. What would this girl with the amber-colored skin be like on a couch in a sunlit room, nude in a straight-back chair? And as the question echoed along each nerve and stilled his breathing, it seemed suddenly that life, which had scorned him for so long, held out her hand again—but still a little beyond his reach. Only the girl, he sensed, could bring him close enough to touch it. She alone was the bridge. So that even while he repeated to himself that he was being presumptuous (for she would surely refuse him) and ridiculous (for even if she did not, what could he do—his performance would be a mere scramble and twitch), he vowed at the same time to have her. The challenge eased the tightness around his heart suddenly; it soothed the damaged muscle of his eye and as the bell rang he rose and said briskly, "Ladies and gentlemen, may I have your attention, please. My name is Max Berman. The course is Modern French Literature, number fifty-four. May I suggest that you check your program cards to see whether you are in the right place at the right time."

Her essay on Gide's *The Immoralist* lay on his desk and the note from the administration informing him, first, that his past political activities had been brought to their attention and then dismissing him at the end of the session weighed the inside pocket of his jacket. The two, her paper and the note, were linked in his mind. Her paper reminded him that the vow he had taken was still an empty one, for the term was half over and he had never once spoken to her (as if she understood his intention she was

---

[5] A 19th-century process for color lithography that makes prints look like oil paintings.

[6] Peter Paul Rubens (1577-1640), Flemish artist associated with the Baroque style of painting.

[7] Paul Gauguin (1848-1903), French post-impressionist artist, noted for his interest in the "primitive" and his use of non-European subjects in his work. He painted "Aita Parari" in 1893-94.

always late and disappeared as soon as the closing bell rang, leaving him trapped in a clamorous circle of students around his desk), while the note which wrecked his small attempt to start anew suddenly made that vow more urgent. It gave him the edge of desperation he needed to act finally. So that as soon as the bell rang, he returned all the papers but hers, announced that all questions would have to wait until their next meeting and, waving off the students from his desk, called above their protests, "Miss Williams, if you have a moment, I'd like to speak with you briefly about your paper."

She approached his desk like a child who has been cautioned not to talk to strangers, her fingers touching the backs of the chair as if for support, her gaze following the departing students as though she longed to accompany them.

Her slight apprehensiveness pleased him. It suggested a submissiveness which gave him, as he rose uncertainly, a feeling of certainty and command. Her hesitancy was somehow in keeping with the color of her skin. She seemed to bring not only herself but the host of black women whose bodies had been despoiled to make her. He would not only possess her but them also, he thought (not really thought, for he scarcely allowed these thoughts to form before he snuffed them out). Through their collective suffering, which she contained, his own personal suffering would be eased; he would be pardoned for whatever sin it was he had committed against life.

"I hope you weren't unduly alarmed when I didn't return your paper along with the others," he said, and had to look up as she reached the desk. She was taller close up and her eyes, which he had thought were black, were a strong, flecked brown with very small pupils which seemed to shrink now from the sight of him. "But I found it so interesting I wanted to give it to you privately."

"I didn't know what to think," she said, and her voice—he heard it for the first time for she never recited or answered in class—was low, cautious, Southern.

"It was, to say the least, refreshing. It not only showed some original and mature thinking on your part, but it also proved that you've been listening in class—and after twenty-five years and more of teaching it's encouraging to find that some students do listen. If you have a little time I'd like to tell you, more specifically, what I liked about it...."

Talking easily, reassuring her with his professional tone and a deft gesture with his cigarette, he led her from the room as the next class filed in, his hand cupped at her elbow but not touching it, his manner urbane, courtly, kind. They paused on the landing at the end of the long corridor with the stairs piled in steel tiers above and plunging below them. An intimate silence swept up the stairwell in a warm gust and Max Berman said, "I'm curious. Why did you choose *The Immoralist?*"

She started suspiciously, afraid, it seemed, that her answer might expose and endanger the self she guarded so closely within.

"Well," she said finally, her glance reaching down the stairs to the door marked EXIT at the bottom, "when you said we could use anything by Gide I decided on *The Immoralist,* since it was the first book I read in the original French when I was in undergraduate school. I didn't understand it then because my French was so weak, I guess, but I always thought about it afterward for some odd reason. I was shocked by what I did understand, of course, but something else about it appealed to me, so when you made the assignment I thought I'd try reading it again. I understood it a little better this time. At least I think so...."

"Your paper proves you did."

She smiled absently, intent on some other thought. Then she said cautiously, but with unexpected force, "You see, to me, the book seems to say that the only way you begin to know what you are and how much you are capable of is by daring to try something, by doing something which tests you...."

"Something bold," he said.

"Yes."

"Even sinful."

She paused, questioning this, and then said reluctantly, "Yes, perhaps even sinful."

"The salutary effects of sin, you might say." He gave the little bow.

But she had not heard this; her mind had already leaped ahead. "The only trouble, at least with the character in Gide's book, is that what he finds out about himself is so terrible. He is so unhappy...."

"But at least he knows, poor sinner." And his playful tone went unnoticed.

"Yes," she said with the same startling forcefulness. "And another thing, in finding out what he is, he destroys his wife. It was as if she had to die in order for him to live and know himself. Perhaps in order for a person to live and know himself somebody else must die. Maybe there's always a balancing out....In a way"—and he had to lean close now to hear her—"I believe this."

Max Berman edged back as he glimpsed something move within her abstracted gaze. It was like a strong and restless seed that had taken root in the darkness there and was straining now toward the light. He had not expected so subtle and complex a force beneath her mild exterior and he found it disturbing and dangerous, but fascinating.

"Well, it's a most interesting interpretation," he said. "I don't know if M. Gide would have agreed, but then he's not around to give his opinion. Tell me, where did you do your undergraduate work?"

"At Howard University."

"And you majored in French?"

"Yes."

"Why, if I may ask?" he said gently.

"Well, my mother was from New Orleans and could still speak a little Creole and I got interested in learning how to speak French through her, I guess. I teach it now at a junior high school in Richmond. Only the beginner courses because I don't have my master's. You know, *je vais, tu vas, il va* and *Frère Jacques*.[8] It's not very inspiring."

"You should do something about that then, my dear Miss Williams. Perhaps it's time for you, like our friend in Gide, to try something new and bold."

"I know," she said, and her pale hand sketched a vague, despairing gesture. "I thought maybe if I got my master's...that's why I decided to come north this summer and start taking some courses...."

Max Berman quickly lighted a cigarette to still the flurry inside him, for the moment he had been awaiting had come. He flicked her paper, which he still held. "Well, you've got the makings of a master's thesis right here. If you like I will suggest some ways for you to expand it sometime. A few pointers from an old pro might help."

He had to turn from her astonished and grateful smile—it was like a child's. He said carefully, "The only problem will be to find a place where we can talk quietly.

[8] (Fr.) I go; you go; he goes; Brother Jacques (Jack).

Regrettably, I don't rate an office...."

"Perhaps we could use one of the empty classrooms," she said.

"That would be much too dismal a setting for a pleasant discussion."

He watched the disappointment wilt her smile and when he spoke he made certain that the same disappointment weighed his voice. "Another difficulty is that the term's half over, which gives us little or no time. But let's not give up. Perhaps we can arrange to meet and talk over a weekend. The only hitch there is that I spend weekends at my place in the country. Of course you're perfectly welcome to come up there. It's only about seventy miles from New York, in the heart of what's very appropriately called the Borsch Circuit,[9] even though, thank God, my place is a good distance away from the borsch. That is, it's very quiet and there's never anybody around except with my permission."

She did not move, yet she seemed to start; she made no sound, yet he thought he heard a bewildered cry. And then she did a strange thing, standing there with the breath sucked into the hollow of her throat and her smile, that had opened to him with such trust, dying—her eyes, her hands faltering up begged him to declare himself.

"There's a lake near the house," he said, "so that when you get tired of talking—or better, listening to me talk—you can take a swim, if you like. I would very much enjoy that sight." And as the nerve tugged at his eyelid, he seemed to wink behind his rimless glasses.

Her sudden, blind step back was like a man groping his way through a strange room in the dark, and instinctively Max Berman reached out to break her fall. Her arms, bare to the shoulder because of the heat (he knew the feel of her skin without even touching it—it would be like a rich, fine-textured cloth which would soothe and hide him in its amber warmth), struck out once to drive him off and then fell limp at her side, and her eyes became vivid and convulsive in her numbed face. She strained toward the stairs and the exit door at the bottom, but she could not move. Nor could she speak. She did not even cry. Her eyes remained dry and dull with disbelief. Only her shoulders trembled as though she was silently weeping inside.

It was as though she had never learned the forms and expressions of anger. The outrage of a lifetime, of her history, was trapped inside her. And she stared at Max Berman with this mute, paralyzing rage. Not really at him but to his side, as if she caught sight of others behind him. And remembering how he had imagined a column of dark women trailing her to his desk, he sensed that she glimpsed a legion of old men with sere flesh and lonely eyes flanking him: "old lechers with a love on every wind..."

"I'm sorry, Miss Williams," he said, and would have welcomed her insults, for he would have been able, at least, to distill from them some passion and a kind of intimacy. It would have been, in a way, like touching her. "It was only that you are a very attractive young woman and although I'm no longer young"—and he gave the tragic little laugh which sought to dismiss that fact— "I can still appreciate and even desire an attractive woman. But I was wrong...." His self-disgust, overwhelming him finally, choked off his voice. "And so very crude. Forgive me. I can offer no excuse for my behavior other than my approaching senility."

He could not even manage the little marionette bow this time. Quickly he shoved

---

[9] A region in the Catskills famous for its resorts catering to Jewish clientele, also called the "Borscht Belt." Borscht is a Russian-Jewish beet soup.

the paper on Gide into her lifeless hand, but it fell, the pages separating, and as he hurried past her downstairs and out the door, he heard the pages scattering like dead leaves on the steps.

She remained away until the night of the final examination, which was also the last meeting of the class. By that time Max Berman, believing that she would not return, had almost succeeded in forgetting her. He was no longer even certain of how she looked, for her face had been absorbed into the single, blurred, featureless face of all the women who had ever refused him. So that she startled him as much as a stranger would have when he entered the room that night and found her alone amid a maze of empty chairs, her face turned toward the window as on the first night and her hands serene in her lap. She turned at his footstep and it was as if she had also forgotten all that had passed between them. She waited until he said, "I'm glad you decided to take the examination. I'm sure you won't have any difficulty with it"; then she gave him a nod that was somehow reminiscent of his little bow and turned again to the window.

He was relieved yet puzzled by her composure. It was as if during her three-week absence she had waged and won a decisive contest with herself and was ready now to act. He was wary suddenly and all during the examination he tried to discover what lay behind her strange calm, studying her bent head amid the shifting heads of the other students, her slim hand guiding the pen across the page, her legs—the long bone visible, it seemed, beneath the flesh. Desire flared and quickly died.

"Excuse me, Professor Berman, will you take up Camus and Sartre next semester, maybe?" The girl who sat in front of his desk was standing over him with her earnest smile and finished examination folder.

"That might prove somewhat difficult, since I won't be here."

"No more?"

"No."

"I mean, not even next summer?"

"I doubt it."

"Gee, I'm sorry. I mean, I enjoyed the course and everything."

He bowed his thanks and held his head down until she left. Her compliment, so piteous somehow, brought on the despair he had forced to the dim rear of his mind. He could no longer flee the thought of the exile awaiting him when the class tonight ended. He could either remain in the house in Brooklyn, where the memory of his father's face above the radiance of the Sabbath candles haunted him from the shadows, reminding him of the certainty he had lost and never found again, where the mirrors in his father's room were still shrouded with sheets, as on the day he lay dying and moaning into his beard that his only son was a bad Jew; or he could return to the house in the country, to the silence shrill with loneliness.

The cigarette he was smoking burned his fingers, rousing him, and he saw over the pile of examination folders on his desk that the room was empty except for the Negro girl. She had finished—her pen lay aslant the closed folder on her desk—but she had remained in her seat and she was smiling across the room at him—a set, artificial smile that was both cold and threatening. It utterly denuded him and he was wildly angry suddenly that she had seen him give way to despair; he wanted to remind her (he could not stay the thought; it attacked him like an assailant from a dark turn in his mind) that she was only black after all....His head dropped and he almost wept with shame.

The girl stiffened as if she had seen the thought and then the tiny muscles around her mouth quickly arranged the bland smile. She came up to his desk, placed her folder on top of the others and said pleasantly, her eyes like dark, shattered glass that spared Max Berman his reflection, "I've changed my mind. I think I'd like to spend a day at your place in the country if your invitation still holds."

He thought of refusing her, for her voice held neither promise nor passion, but he could not. Her presence, even if it was only for a day, would make his return easier. And there was still the possibility of passion despite her cold manner and the deliberate smile. He thought of how long it had been since he had had someone, of how badly he needed the sleep which followed love and of awakening certain, for the first time in years, of his existence.

"Of course the invitation still holds. I'm driving up tonight."

"I won't be able to come until Sunday," she said firmly. "Is there a train then?"

"Yes, in the morning," he said, and gave her the schedule.

"You'll meet me at the station?"

"Of course. You can't miss my car. It's a very shabby but venerable Chevy."

She smiled stiffly and left, her heels awakening the silence of the empty corridor, the sound reaching back to tap like a warning finger on Max Berman's temple.

The pale sunlight slanting through the windshield lay like a cat on his knees, and the motor of his old Chevy, turning softly under him could have been the humming of its heart. A little distance from the car a log-cabin station house—the logs blackened by the seasons—stood alone against the hills, and the hills, in turn, lifted softly, still green although the summer was ending, into the vague autumn sky.

The morning mist and pale sun, the green that was still somehow new, made it seem that the season was stirring into life even as it died, and this contradiction pained Max Berman at the same time that it pleased him. For it was his own contradiction after all: his desires which remained those of a young man even as he was dying.

He had been parked for some time in the deserted station, yet his hands were still tensed on the steering wheel and his foot hovered near the accelerator. As soon as he had arrived in the station he had wanted to leave. But like the girl that night on the landing, he was too stiff with tension to move. He could only wait, his eyelid twitching with foreboding, regret, curiosity and hope.

Finally and with no warning the train charged through the fiery green, setting off a tremor underground. Max Berman imagined the girl seated at a window in the train, her hands arranged quietly in her lap and her gaze scanning the hills that were so familiar to him, and yet he could not believe that she was really there. Perhaps her plan had been to disappoint him. She might be in New York or on her way back to Richmond now, laughing at the trick she had played on him. He was convinced of this suddenly, so that even when he saw her walking toward him through the blown steam from under the train, he told himself that she was a mirage created by the steam. Only when she sat beside him in the car, bringing with her, it seemed, an essence she had distilled from the morning air and rubbed into her skin, was he certain of her reality.

"I brought my bathing suit but it's much too cold to swim," she said and gave him the deliberate smile.

He did not see it; he only heard her voice, its warm Southern lilt in the chill, its intimacy in the closed car—and an excitement swept him, cold first and then hot, as if the sun had burst in his blood.

"It's the morning air," he said. "By noon it should be like summer again."

"Is that a promise?"

"Yes."

By noon the cold morning mist had lifted above the hills and below, in the lake valley, the sunlight was a sheer gold net spread out on the grass as if to dry, draped on the trees and flung, glinting, over the lake. Max Berman felt it brush his shoulders gently as he sat by the lake waiting for the girl, who had gone up to the house to change into her swimsuit.

He had spent the morning showing her the fields and small wood near his house. During the long walk he had been careful to keep a little apart from her. He would extend a hand as they climbed a rise or when she stepped uncertainly over a rock, but he would not really touch her. He was afraid that at his touch, no matter how slight and casual, her scream would spiral into the morning calm, or worse, his touch would unleash the threatening thing he sensed behind her even smile.

He had talked of her paper and she had listened politely and occasionally even asked a question or made a comment. But all the while detached, distant, drawn within herself as she had been that first night in the classroom. And then halfway down a slope she had paused and, pointing to the canvas tops of her white sneakers, which had become wet and dark from the dew secreted in the grass, she had laughed. The sound, coming so abruptly in the midst of her tense quiet, joined her, it seemed, to the wood and wide fields, to the hills; she shared their simplicity and held within her the same strong current of life. Max Berman had felt privileged suddenly, and humble. He had stopped questioning her smile. He had told himself then that it would not matter even if she stopped and picking up a rock bludgeoned him from behind.

"There's a lake near my home, but it's not like this," the girl said, coming up behind him. "Yours is so dark and serious-looking."

He nodded and followed her gaze out to the lake, where the ripples were long, smooth welts raised by the wind, and across to the other bank, where a group of birches stepped delicately down to the lake and bending over touched the water with their branches as if testing it before they plunged.

The girl came and stood beside him now—and she was like a pale-gold naiad, the spirit of the lake, her eyes reflecting its somber autumnal tone and her body as supple as the birches. She walked slowly into the water, unaware, it seemed, of the sudden passion in his gaze, or perhaps uncaring; and as she walked she held out her arms in what seemed a gesture of invocation (and Max Berman remembered his father with the fringed shawl draped on his outstretched arms as he invoked their God each Sabbath with the same gesture); her head was bent as if she listened for a voice beneath the water's murmurous surface. When the ground gave way she still seemed to be walking and listening, her arms outstretched. The water reached her waist, her small breasts, her shoulders. She lifted her head once, breathed deeply and disappeared.

She stayed down for a long time and when her white cap finally broke the water some distance out, Max Berman felt strangely stranded and deprived. He understood suddenly the profound cleavage between them and the absurdity of his hope. The water between them became the years which separated them. Her white cap was the sign of her purity, while the silt darkening the lake was the flotsam of his failures.

Above all, their color—her arms a pale, flashing gold in the sunlit water and his bled white and flaccid with the veins like angry blue penciling—marked the final barrier.

He was sad as they climbed toward the house late that afternoon and troubled. A crow cawed derisively in the bracken, heralding the dusk which would not only end their strange day but would also, he felt, unveil her smile, so that he would learn the reason for her coming. And because he was sad, he said wryly, "I think I should tell you that you've been spending the day with something of an outcast."

"Oh," she said and waited.

He told her of the dismissal, punctuating his words with the little hoarse, deprecating laugh and waving aside the pain with his cigarette. She listened, polite but neutral, and because she remained unmoved, he wanted to confess all the more. So that during dinner and afterward when they sat outside on the porch, he told her of the investigation.

"It was very funny once you saw it from the proper perspective, which I did, of course," he said. "I mean here they were accusing me of crimes I couldn't remember committing and asking me for the names of people with whom I had never associated. It was pure farce. But I made a mistake. I should have done something dramatic or something just as farcical. Bared my breast in the public market place or written a tome on my apostasy, naming names. It would have been a far different story then. Instead of my present ignominy I would have been offered a chairmanship at Yale....No? Well, Brandeis then. I would have been draped in honorary degrees...."

"Well, why didn't you confess?" she said impatiently.

"I've often asked myself the same interesting question, but I haven't come up with a satisfactory answer yet. I suspect, though, that I said nothing because none of it really mattered that much."

"What did matter?" she asked sharply.

He sat back, waiting for the witty answer, but none came, because just then the frame upon which his organs were strung seemed to snap and he felt his heart, his lungs, his vital parts fall in a heap within him. Her question had dealt the severing blow, for it was the same question he understood suddenly that the vague forms in his dream asked repeatedly. It had been the plaintive undercurrent to his father's dying moan, the real accusation behind the charges of his inquisitors at the hearing.

For what had mattered? He gazed through his sudden shock at the night squatting on the porch steps, at the hills asleep like gentle beasts in the darkness, at the black screen of the sky where the events of his life passed in a mute, accusing review—and he saw nothing there to which he had given himself or in which he had truly believed since the belief and dedication of his boyhood.

"Did you hear my question?" she asked, and he was glad that he sat within the shadows clinging to the porch screen and could not be seen.

"Yes, I did," he said faintly, and his eyelid twitched. "But I'm afraid it's another one of those I can't answer satisfactorily." And then he struggled for the old flippancy. "You make an excellent examiner, you know. Far better than my inquisitors."

"What will you do now?" Her voice and cold smile did not spare him.

He shrugged and the motion, a slow, eloquent lifting of the shoulders, brought with it suddenly the weight and memory of his boyhood. It was the familiar gesture of the women hawkers in Belmont Market, of the men standing outside the temple on Saturday mornings, each of them reflecting his image of God in their forbidding black coats and with the black, tumbling beards in which he had always imagined he could hide as in a forest. All this had mattered, he called loudly to himself, and said aloud to the girl, "Let me see if I can answer this one at least. What *will* I do?" He paused and swung his leg so that his foot in the fastidious French shoe caught the light from the house. "Grow flowers and write my memoirs. How's that? That would be the proper way for a gentleman and scholar to retire. Or hire one of those hefty housekeepers who will bully me and when I die in my sleep draw the sheet over my face and call my lawyer. That's somewhat European, but how's that?"

When she said nothing for a long time, he added soberly, "But that's not a fair question for me any more. I leave all such considerations to the young. To you, for that matter. What will you do, my dear Miss Williams?"

It was as if she had been expecting the question and had been readying her answer all the time that he had been talking. She leaned forward eagerly and with her face and part of her body fully in the light, she said, "I will do something. I don't know what yet, but something."

Max Berman started back a little. The answer was so unlike her vague, resigned "I know" on the landing that night when he had admonished her to try something new.

He edged back into the darkness and she leaned further into the light, her eyes overwhelming her face and her mouth set in a thin, determined line. "I will do something," she said, bearing down on each word, "because for the first time in my life I feel almost brave."

He glimpsed this new bravery behind her hard gaze and sensed something vital and purposeful, precious, which she had found and guarded like a prize within her center. He wanted it. He would have liked to snatch it and run like a thief. He no longer desired her but it, and starting forward with a sudden envious cry, he caught her arm and drew her close, seeking it.

But he could not get to it. Although she did not pull away her arm, although she made no protest as his face wavered close to hers, he did not really touch her. She held herself and her prize out of his desperate reach and her smile was a knife she pressed to his throat. He saw himself for what he was in her clear, cold gaze: an old man with skin the color and texture of dough that had been kneaded by the years into tragic folds, with faded eyes adrift behind a pair of rimless glasses and the roughened flesh at his throat like a bird's wattles. And as the disgust which he read in her eyes swept him, his hand dropped from her arm. He started to murmur, "Forgive me…" when suddenly she caught hold of his wrist, pulling him close again, and he felt the strength which had borne her swiftly through the water earlier hold him now as she said quietly and without passion, "And do you know why, Dr. Berman, I feel almost brave today? Because ever since I can remember my parents were always telling me, 'Stay away from white folks. Just leave them alone. You mind your business and they'll mind theirs. Don't go near them.' And they made sure I didn't. My father, who was the principal of a colored grade school in Richmond, used to drive me to and from school every day. When I needed something from downtown my mother would take me and if the white saleslady asked me anything she would answer.…

"And my parents were also always telling me, 'Stay away from niggers,' and that meant anybody darker than we were." She held out her arm in the light and Max Berman saw the skin almost as white as his but for the subtle amber shading. Staring at the arm she said tragically, "I was so confused I never really went near anybody.

Even when I went away to college I kept to myself. I didn't marry the man I wanted to because he was dark and I knew my parents would disapprove…." She paused, her wistful gaze searching the darkness for the face of the man she had refused, it seemed, and not finding it she went on sadly, "So after graduation I returned home and started teaching and I was just as confused and frightened and ashamed as always. When my parents died I went on the same way. And I would have gone on like that the rest of my life if it hadn't been for you, Dr. Berman"—and the sarcasm leaped behind her cold smile. "In a way you did me a favor. You let me know how you—and most of the people like you—see me."

"My dear Miss Williams, I assure you I was not attracted to you because you were colored…." And he broke off, remembering just how acutely aware of her color he had been.

"I'm not interested in your reasons!" she said brutally. "What matters is what it meant to me. I thought about this these last three weeks and about my parents—how wrong they had been, how frightened, and the terrible thing they had done to me…And I wasn't confused any longer." Her head lifted, tremulous with her new assurance. "I can do something now! I can begin," she said with her head poised. "Look how I came all the way up here to tell you this to your face. Because how could you harm me? You're so old you're like a cup I could break in my hand." And her hand tightened on his wrist, wrenching the last of his frail life from him, it seemed. Through the quick pain he remembered her saying on the landing that night: "Maybe in order for a person to live someone else must die" and her quiet "I believe this" then. Now her sudden laugh, an infinitely cruel sound in the warm night, confirmed her belief.

Suddenly she was the one who seemed old, indeed ageless. Her touch became mortal and Max Berman saw the darkness that would end his life gathered in her eyes. But even as he sprang back, jerking his arm away, a part of him rushed forward to embrace that darkness, and his cry, wounding the night, held both ecstasy and terror.

"That's all I came for," she said, rising. "You can drive me to the station now."

They drove to the station in silence. Then, just as the girl started from the car, she turned with an ironic, pitiless smile and said, "You know, it's been a nice day, all things considered. It really turned summer again as you said it would. And even though your lake isn't anything like the one near my home, it's almost as nice."

Max Berman bowed to her for the last time, accepting with that gesture his responsibility for her rage, which went deeper than his, and for her anger, which would spur her finally to live. And not only for her, but for all those at last whom he had wronged through his indifference: his father lying in the room of shrouded mirrors, the wives he had never loved, his work which he had never believed in enough and, lastly (even though he knew it was too late and he would not be spared), himself.

Too weary to move, he watched the girl cross to the train which would bear her south, her head lifted as though she carried life as lightly there as if it were a hat made of tulle. When the train departed his numbed eyes followed it until its rear light was like a single firefly in the immense night or the last flickering of his life. Then he drove back through the darkness.

—1961

ADRIENNE RICH (1929-   )

Perhaps the best-known feminist and lesbian poet in the United States, Adrienne Rich was born in 1929 in Baltimore, Maryland. Her father was a professor of medicine and her mother was a pianist. Rich, who is known for work that artfully balances a deep political consciousness with an inspired sense of craft, has published over twenty books of poetry and nonfiction prose. The poems in her first book, *A Change of World* (1951), which was selected for the Yale Series of Younger Poets, were formally traditional and showed the influence of the modernist writers Rich had studied as a child and at Radcliffe College. With the publication of her third volume, *Snapshots of a Daughter-in-Law* (1963), Rich's poetry and prose increasingly reflected her interest in feminism and human rights. Rich's publications include *The Will to Change* (1971), *Diving Into the Wreck* (1973), *Of Woman Born: Motherhood As Experience and Institution* (1976), *The Dream of a Common Language* (1978), *On Lies, Secrets and Silence* (1979), *The Fact of a Doorframe* (1984), *Your Native Land, Your Life* (1986), *Blood, Bread and Poetry* (1986), *An Atlas of the Difficult World* (1991), *Fox* (2001), and *The School Among the Ruins* (2004). Among the many awards Rich has received are the Bollingen Prize, the Lannan Lifetime Achievement Award, the National Book Award, a MacArthur Fellowship, and the Wallace Stevens Award from the Academy of American Poets. Rich turned down a National Medal of Arts in 1997, claiming that "[Art] means nothing if it simply decorates the dinner table of power that holds it hostage." Rich lives with her partner in Northern California.

Aunt Jennifer's Tigers

Aunt Jennifer's tigers prance across a screen,
Bright topaz denizens of a world of green.
They do not fear the men beneath the tree;
They pace in sleek chivalric certainty.

Aunt Jennifer's fingers fluttering through her wool   5
Find even the ivory needle hard to pull.
The massive weight of Uncle's wedding band
Sits heavily upon Aunt Jennifer's hand.

When Aunt is dead, her terrified hands will lie
Still ringed with ordeals she was mastered by.   10
The tigers in the panel that she made
Will go on prancing, proud and unafraid.

—1951

Snapshots of a Daughter-in-law

1.

You, once a belle in Shreveport,[1]
with henna-colored hair, skin like a peachbud,
still have your dresses copied from that time,
and play a Chopin[2] prelude

---

[1] The third largest city in Louisiana and the state's Confederate capital in 1863.

[2] Frédéric François Chopin (1810-1849), Polish-French piano composer.

called by Cortot:[3] *"Delicious recollections*   5
float like perfume through the memory."

Your mind now, moldering like wedding-cake,
heavy with useless experience, rich
with suspicion, rumor, fantasy,
crumbling to pieces under the knife-edge   10
of mere fact. In the prime of your life.

Nervy, glowering, your daughter
wipes the teaspoons, grows another way.

2.

Banging the coffee-pot into the sink
she hears the angels chiding, and looks out   15
past the raked gardens to the sloppy sky.
Only a week since They said: *Have no patience.*

The next time it was: *Be insatiable.*
Then: *Save yourself; others you cannot save.*
Sometimes she's let the tapstream scald her arm,   20
a match burn to her thumbnail,

or held her hand above the kettle's snout
right in the woolly steam. They are probably angels,
since nothing hurts her anymore, except
each morning's grit blowing into her eyes.   25

3.

A thinking woman sleeps with monsters.
The beak that grips her, she becomes. And Nature,
that sprung-lidded, still commodious
steamer-trunk of *tempora*[4] and *mores*
gets stuffed with it all: the mildewed orange-flowers,   30
the female pills, the terrible breasts
of Boadicea[5] beneath flat foxes' heads and orchids.

Two handsome women, gripped in argument,
each proud, acute, subtle, I hear scream
across the cut glass and majolica[6]   35
like Furies[7] cornered from their prey:
The argument *ad feminam,*[8] all the old knives
that have rusted in my back, I drive in yours,
ma semblable, ma soeur![9]

---

[3] Alfred Denis Cortot (1877-1962), French pianist and conductor.
[4] (Lat.) Times.
[5] Boadicea (d. ca. 60 C.E.), Celtic queen who led a major
revolt against the occupying Roman empire.
[6] A type of tin-glazed pottery from Italy.
[7] In Roman mythology, three sisters who personify
vengeance.
[8] (Lat.) Against the woman; a play on *ad hominem* (against
the man), a logical fallacy in which an argument is
considered spurious because of the person making it.
[9] (Fr.) My likeness, my sister. A play on "mon semblable,
mon frere" (my likeness, my brother), a line written by
the French poet Charles Baudelaire (1821-1867).

4.

Knowing themselves too well in one another: 40
their gifts no pure fruition, but a thorn,
the prick filed sharp against a hint of scorn...
Reading while waiting
for the iron to heat,
writing, *My Life had stood—a Loaded Gun—*[10]   45
in that Amherst[11] pantry while the jellies boil and scum,
or, more often,
iron-eyed and beaked and purposed as a bird,
dusting everything on the whatnot every day of life.

5.

Dulce ridens, dulce loquens,[12]   50
she shaves her legs until they gleam
like petrified mammoth-tusk.

6.

When to her lute Corinna[13] sings
neither words nor music are her own;
only the long hair dipping   55
over her cheek, only the song
of silk against her knees
and these
adjusted in reflections of an eye.

Poised, trembling and unsatisfied, before   60
an unlocked door, that cage of cages,
tell us, you bird, you tragical machine—
is this *fertillisante douleur?*[14] Pinned down
by love, for you the only natural action,
are you edged more keen   65
to prise the secrets of the vault? has Nature shown
her household books to you, daughter-in-law,
that her sons never saw?

7.

"To have in this uncertain world some stay
which cannot be undermined, is   70
of the utmost consequence."[15]
                                    Thus wrote
a woman, partly brave and partly good,
who fought with what she partly understood.
Few men about her would or could do more,   75
hence she was labeled harpy, shrew and whore.

---

[10] The first line from Emily Dickinson's (1830-1886) *Complete Poems* #754 (1955).
[11] Emily Dickinson's home town in Massachusetts.
[12] (Lat.) Sweetly laughing, sweetly speaking.
[13] Corinna (ca. 500? B.C.E.), Greek poet whose work remains only in fragments.
[14] (Fr.) Fertilizing suffering or pain.
[15] Mary Wollstonecraft (1759-1797), *Thoughts on the Education of Daughters* (1787).

8.

"You all die at fifteen," said Diderot,[16]
and turn part legend, part convention.
Still, eyes inaccurately dream
behind closed windows blankening with steam.   80
Deliciously, all that we might have been,
all that we were—fire, tears,
wit, taste, martyred ambition—
stirs like the memory of refused adultery
the drained and flagging bosom of our middle years.   85

9.

Not that it is done well, but
that it is done at all?[17] Yes, think
of the odds! or shrug them off forever.
This luxury of the precocious child,
Time's precious chronic invalid,—   90
would we, darlings, resign it if we could?
Our blight has been our sinecure:
mere talent was enough for us—
glitter in fragments and rough drafts.

Sigh no more, ladies.   95
                         Time is male
and in his cups drinks to the fair.
Bemused by gallantry, we hear
our mediocrities over-praised,
indolence read as abnegation,   100
slattern thought styled intuition,
every lapse forgiven, our crime
only to cast too bold a shadow
or smash the mold straight off.

For that, solitary confinement,   105
tear gas, attrition shelling.
Few applicants for that honor.

10.

                         Well,
she's long about her coming, who must be
more merciless to herself than history.   110
Her mind full to the wind, I see her plunge
breasted and glancing through the currents,
taking the light upon her
at least as beautiful as any boy
or helicopter,[18]   115

[16] A quotation from one of Diderot's letters to his lover, Sophie Volland. Denis Diderot (1713-1784) was a French author, playwright, art critic, encyclopedist, and leading materialist philosopher of the Enlightenment.
[17] British writer Samuel Johnson's 1763 quip: "Sir, a woman's preaching is like a dog's walking on his hinder legs. It is not done well; but you are surprised to find it done at all."
[18] An image in Simone de Beauvoir's *The Second Sex* (1949).

poised, still coming,
her fine blades making the air wince

but her cargo
no promise then:
delivered   120
palpable
ours.

—1958-1960
[—1963]

Planetarium

(Thinking of Caroline
Herschel, 1750-1848,
astronomer, sister of
William; and others)[19]

A woman in the shape of a monster
a monster in the shape of a woman
the skies are full of them

a woman   'in the snow
among the Clocks and instruments   5
or measuring the ground with poles'

in her 98 years to discover
8 comets

she whom the moon ruled
like us   10
levitating into the night sky
riding the polished lenses

Galaxies of women, there
doing penance for impetuousness
ribs chilled   15
in those spaces   of the mind

An eye,
          'virile, precise and absolutely certain'[20]
          from the mad webs of Uranisborg[21]
                              encountering the NOVA[22] 20

every impulse of light exploding
from the core
as life flies out of us

---

[19] Born in Germany, Herschel lived and worked with her
brother in England. William (1738-1822) discovered
Uranus.
[20] Danish astronomer Tycho Brahe (1546-1601) described
his work this way.

[21] Brahe built Uranisborg (more commonly, Uraniborg),
an observatory predating the telescope, in 1576.
[22] Brahe discovered a supernova in the constellation
Calliope in 1572.

      Tycho whispering at last
      'Let me not seem to have lived in vain'[23]   25

What we see, we see
and seeing is changing

the light that shrivels a mountain
and leaves a man alive

Heartbeat of the pulsar   30
heart sweating through my body

The radio impulse
pouring in from Taurus

      I am bombarded yet   I stand

I have been standing all my life in the   35
direct path of a battery of signals
the most accurately transmitted most
untranslateable language in the universe
I am a galactic cloud so deep   so invo-
luted that a light wave could take 15   40
years to travel through me   And has
taken   I am an instrument in the shape
of a woman trying to translate pulsations
into images   for the relief of the body
and the reconstruction of the mind.   45

                    —1968
                    [—1971]

Origins and History of Consciousness

I

Night-life. Letters, journals, bourbon
sloshed in the glass. Poems crucified on the wall,
dissected, their bird-wings severed
like trophies. No one lives in this room
without living through some kind of crisis.   5

No one lives in this room
without confronting the whiteness of the wall
behind the poems, planks of books,
photographs of dead heroines.
Without contemplating last and late   10
the true nature of poetry. The drive
to connect. The dream of a common language.

Thinking of lovers, their blind faith, their
experienced crucifixions,

---

[23] Brahe's last words.

my envy is not simple. I have dreamed of going to bed   15
as walking into clear water ringed by a snowy wood
white as cold sheets, thinking, *I'll freeze in there.*
My bare feet are numbed already by the snow
but the water
is mild, I sink and float   20
like a warm amphibious animal
that has broken the net, has run
through fields of snow leaving no print;
this water washes off the scent—
You are clear now   25
of the hunter, the trapper
the wardens of the mind—

yet the warm animal dreams on
of another animal
swimming under the snow-flecked surface of the pool,   30
and wakes, and sleeps again.

No one sleeps in this room without
the dream of a common language.

II

It was simple to meet you, simple to take your eyes
into mine, saying: these are eyes I have known   35
from the first....It was simple to touch you
against the hacked background, the grain of what we
had been, the choices, years....It was even simple
to take each other's lives in our hands, as bodies.

What is not simple: to wake from drowning   40
from where the ocean beat inside us like an afterbirth
into this common, acute particularity
these two selves who walked half a lifetime untouching—
to wake to something deceptively simple: a glass
sweated with dew, a ring of the telephone, a scream   45
of someone beaten up far down in the street
causing each of us to listen to her own inward scream

knowing the mind of the mugger and the mugged
as any woman must who stands to survive this city,
this century, this life...   50
each of us having loved the flesh in its clenched or loosened beauty
better than trees or music (yet loving those too
as if they were flesh—and they are—but the flesh
of beings unfathomed as yet in our roughly literal life).

III

It's simple to wake from sleep with a stranger,   55
dress, go out, drink coffee,
enter a life again. It isn't simple

to wake from sleep into the neighborhood
of one neither strange nor familiar
whom we have chosen to trust. Trusting, untrusting,   60
we lowered ourselves into this, let ourselves
downward hand over hand as on a rope that quivered
over the unsearched....We did this. Conceived
of each other, conceived each other in a darkness
which I remember as drenched in light.   65
                                     I want to call this, life.

But I can't call it life until we start to move
beyond this secret circle of fire
where our bodies are giant shadows flung on a wall
where the night becomes our inner darkness, and sleeps   70
like a dumb beast, head on her paws, in the corner.

                                     —1972-1974
                                      [—1978]

Fox

I needed fox   Badly I needed
a vixen for the long time none had come near me
I needed recognition from a
triangulated face   burnt-yellow eyes
fronting the long body the fierce and sacrificial tail   5
I needed history of fox   briars of legend it was said she had run through
I was in want of fox

And the truth of briars she had to have run through
I craved to feel on her pelt   if my hands could even slide
past or her body slide between them   sharp truth distressing surfaces
    of fur   10
lacerated skin calling legend to account
a vixen's courage in vixen terms

For a human animal to call for help
on another animal
is the most riven the most revolted cry on earth   15
come a long way down
Go back far enough it means tearing and torn   endless and sudden
back far enough it blurts
into the birth-yell of the yet-to-be human child
pushed out of a female   the yet-to-be woman   20
                                     —1998

LORRAINE VIVIAN HANSBERRY (1930-1965)

Born on the Southside of Chicago to Carl Augustus and Nannie Perry Hansberry, Lorraine Hansberry grew up experiencing the racial tensions surrounding a black family's attempts at upward social mobility. Her father's innovation of a small scale kitchenette for one- or two-bedroom apartments made him financially successful during the Great Depression and they moved, when Hansberry was eight, to a house in a white neighborhood. The ensuing tension and violence from the neighborhood forms the basis of her first play, *A Raisin in the Sun*, which beat out plays by Eugene O'Neill and Tennessee Williams in 1959 to win the New York Drama Critics Circle Award for best play, making her the first black writer, the fifth woman, and the youngest American playwright ever to receive the honor. Hansberry attended the University of Wisconsin for two years (1948-1950), but dropped out to pursue her new political and theatrical interests. For the next three years she worked as a staff writer for Paul Robeson's *Freedom* magazine, traveling extensively to cover stories on Africa, women, New York social issues, and the arts. She married Robert Nemiroff, a playwright, songwriter, and activist, in 1953. The two formed a close intellectual relationship and collaborated on many works together. The couple separated in 1957 (later divorcing), as Hansberry began to privately come out as a lesbian. As a playwright, Hansberry is credited with being the first to bring realistic portrayals of urban, working-class African Americans to the American stage. Recent literary criticism has also cited the impressive synthesis of varied artistic trends and genres exhibited in her body of work, beyond the purview of *A Raisin in the Sun,* which is by far her most famous work. Hansberry's oeuvre includes the plays *The Sign in Sidney Brustein's Window* (1964), and *Les Blancs*, which was published posthumously in 1972. Also noteworthy was her public debate in the *Village Voice* with Norman Mailer about race in the early 1960s. Hansberry died of cancer at the age of thirty-four, leaving behind a great number of unfinished projects. Over six hundred people attended her funeral in Harlem that year, which featured personal messages from James Baldwin and the Reverend Martin Luther King, Jr. The selection below, *The Drinking Gourd,* is a teleplay that NBC commissioned Hansberry to write for the Civil War centenary; however, the network got cold feet about its depiction of slavery and never produced it.

The Drinking Gourd
An Original Drama for Television

"Our new government is founded upon the great truth that the Negro is not equal to the white man—that slavery is his natural and normal condition."
—*Alexander H. Stephens, Vice President of the Confederacy*

CAST OF CHARACTERS (IN ORDER OF APPEARANCE)

THE SOLDIER

SLAVES-MEN, WOMEN, CHILDREN

RISSA

SARAH

JOSHUA

HANNIBAL

HIRAM SWEET

MARIA SWEET

TWO MALE HOUSE SERVANTS

EVERETT SWEET

TOMMY

DR. MACON BULLETT

ZEB DUDLEY

ELIZABETH DUDLEY

TWO DUDLEY CHILDREN

THE PREACHER

COFFIN

A DRIVER

Following preliminary production titles: Introduce stark, spirited banjo themes. Main play and title credits.

Fade in: under titles. Exterior. Two shot: HANNIBAL, TOMMY—*bright day.*

[HANNIBAL *is a young slave of about nineteen or twenty.* TOMMY, *about ten, is his master's son. It is* HANNIBAL *who is playing the banjo, the neck of which intrudes into close opening shot frame. Camera moves back to wider angle to show that* TOMMY *is vigorously keeping time by clapping his hands to the beat of the music. They are seated in a tiny wooded enclosure. Sunlight and leaf shadow play on their faces, the expressions of which are animated and happy. If workable, they sing, from top.]*

At completion of titles: Fade out

Act One

FADE IN: EXTERIOR. HIGH-ANGLED PANNING SHOT: AMERICAN EAST COAST—DUSK.

Pan down a great length of coast until a definitive mood is established. Presently the lone figure of a man emerges from the distance. He is tall and narrow-hipped, suggesting a certain idealized American generality. He is not Lincoln, but perhaps Lincolnesque. He wears the side whiskers of the nineteenth century and his hair is long at the neck after the manner of New England or Southern farmers of the period. He is dressed in dark military trousers and boots which are in no way recognizable as to rank or particular army. His shirt is open at the collar and rolled at the sleeves and he carries his dark tunic across his shoulders. He is not battle-scarred or dirty or in any other way suggestive of the disorder of war; but his gait is that of troubled and reflective mediation. When he speaks his voice is markedly free of identifiable regionalism. His imposed generality is to be a symbolic American specificity. He is the narrator. We come down close in his face as he turns to the sea and speaks.

SOLDIER: This is the Atlantic Ocean. [*He gestures easily when he needs to*] Over there, somewhere, is Europe. And over there, down that way, I guess, is Africa. [*Turning and facing inland*] And all of this, for thousands and thousands of miles in all directions, is the New World. [*He bends down and empties a pile of dirt from his handkerchief onto the sand.*] And this—this is soil. Southern soil. [*Opening his fist*] And this is cotton seed. Europe, Africa, the New World and Cotton. They have all gotten mixed up together to make the trouble. [*He begins to walk inland, a wandering gait, full of pauses and gestures.*] You see, this seed and this earth—[*Gesturing now to the land around him*] only have meaning—potency—if you add a third force. That third force is labor.

[*The landscape turns to the Southern countryside. In the distance, shadowed under the incredibly beautiful willows and magnolias, is a large, magnificently columned, white manor house. As he moves close to it, the soft, indescribably sweet sound of the massed voices of the unseen slaves wafts up in one of the most plaintive of the spirituals.*]

VOICES:

"Steal away, steal away,
Steal away to Jesus.
Steal away, steal away home—
I ain't got long to stay here.
My Lord he calls me,
He calls me by the thunder.
The trumpet sounds
within-a my soul—
I ain't got long to stay here.

Steal away, steal away,
Steal away to Jesus.
Steal away, steal away home—
I ain't got long to stay here."

[*Beyond the manor house-cotton fields, rows and rows of cotton fields. And, finally, as the narrator walks on, rows of little white-painted cabins, the slave quarters.*

The quarters are, at the moment, starkly deserted as though he has come upon this place in a dream only. He wanders in to what appears to be the center of the quarters with an easy familiarity at being there.

This plantation, like the matters he is going to tell us about, has no secrets from him. He knows everything we are going to see; he knows how most of us will react to what we see and how we will decide at the end of the play. Therefore, in manner and words he will try to persuade us of nothing; he will only tell us facts and stand aside and let us see for ourselves. Thus, he almost leisurely refreshes himself with a drink from a pail hanging on a nail on one of the cabins. He wanders to the community outdoor fireplace at center and lounges against it and goes on with his telling.]

SOLDIER: Labor so plentiful that, for a while, it might be cheaper to work a man to death and buy another one than to work the first one less harshly.

[*The gentle slave hymn ends, and with its end comes the arbitrarily imposed abrupt darkness of true night. Somewhere in the distance a driver's voice calls: "Quittin' time! Quittin' time!" in accompaniment to a gong or a bell. Silent indications of life begin to stir around the narrator. We become aware of points of light in some of the cabins and a great fire has begun to roar silently in the fireplace where he leans. Numbers of slaves begin to file, also silently, into the quarters; some of them immediately drop to the ground and just sit or lie perfectly still, on their backs, staring into space. Others slowly form a silent line in front of the fireplace, holding makeshift eating utensils. The narrator moves to make room for them when it is necessary and occasionally glances from them out to us, as if to see if we are truly seeing.*

There is, about all of these people, a grim air of fatigue and exhaustion, reflecting the twelve to fourteen hours of almost unrelieved labor they have just completed. The men are dressed in the main in rough trousers of haphazard lengths and coarse shirts. Some have hats. The women wear single-piece shifts, some of them without sleeves or collars. Some wear their hair bound in the traditional bandana of the black slave women of the Americas; others wear or carry the wide straw hats of the cotton fields.]

These people are slaves. They did not come here willingly. Their ancestors were captured, for the most part, on the West Coast of Africa by men who made such enterprise their business.

[*We come in for extreme close-ups of the faces of the people as he talks, moving from men to women to children with lingering intimacy.*]

Few of them could speak to each other. They came from many different peoples and cultures. The slavers were careful about that. Insurrection is very difficult when you cannot even speak to your fellow prisoner.

All of them did not survive the voyage. Some simply died of suffocation; others of disease and still others of suicide. Others were murdered when they mutinied. And when the trade was finally suppressed—sometimes they were just dumped overboard when a British Man-o'-War got after a slave ship. To destroy the evidence.

That trade went on for three centuries. How many were stolen from their homeland? Some scholars say fifteen million. Others fifty million. No one will ever really know.

In any case, today some planters will tell you with pride that the cost of maintaining one of these human beings need not exceed seven dollars and fifty cents—a year. You see, among other things there is no education to pay for—in fact, some of the harshest laws in the slave code are designed to keep the slave from being educated. The penalties are maiming or mutilation—or death. Usually for he who is taught; but very often also for he who might dare to teach—including white men.

There are of course no minimum work hours and no guaranteed minimum wages. No trade unions. And, above all, no wages at all.

[*As he talks a murmur of low conversation begins among the people and there is a more conspicuous stir of life among them as the narrator now prepares, picking up his tunic and putting it across his shoulder once again, to walk out of the scene.*]

Please do not forget that this is the nineteenth century. It is a time when we still allow little children—white children—to labor twelve and thirteen hours in the factories and mines of America. We do not yet believe that women are equal citizens who should have the right to vote. It is a time when we still punish the insane for their madness. It is a time, therefore, when some men can believe and proclaim to the world that this system is the—[*Enunciating carefully but without passion*]—highest form of civilization in the world. [*He turns away from us and faces the now-living scene in the background.*] This system:

[*The camera immediately comes in to exclude him and down to a close-up of a large skillet suspended over the roaring fire which now crackles with live sound. Pieces of bacon and corn pone sizzle on it. A meager portion of both is lifted up and onto a plate by* RISSA, *the cook. She is a woman of late years with an expression of indifference that has already passed resignation. The slave receiving his ration from her casts a slightly hopeful glance at the balance but is waved away by the cook. He gives up easily and moves away and retires and eats his food with relish. A second and a third are similarly served.*

The fourth person in line is a young girl of about nineteen. She is SARAH. *She holds out her plate for service but bends as she does so, in spite of her own weariness, to play with a small boy of about seven or eight,* JOSHUA, *who has been lingering about the cook, clutching at her skirts and getting as much in her way as he can manage.*]

SARAH: Hello, there, Joshua!

JOSHUA: I got a stomick ache.

RISSA: [*Busy with her serving*] You ain't got nothing but the devil ache.

SARAH: [*To the child, with mock and heavily applied sympathy*] Awww, poor little thing! Show

Sarah[1] where it hurt you, honey. [*He points his finger to a random place on his abdomen; clearly delighted to have even insincere attention.*] Here? [*She pokes him—ostensibly to determine the place where the pain is, but in reality only to make him laugh, which they both seem to know.*] Or here? Oh, I know—right here! [*She pokes him very hard with one finger, and he collapses in her arms in a fit of giggling.*]

RISSA: If y'all don't quit that foolin' 'round behind me while I got all this here to do-you better! [*She swings vaguely behind her with the spatula.*] Stop it, I say now! Sarah, you worse than he is.

SARAH: [*A little surreptitiously–to* JOSHUA] Where's your Uncle Hannibal? [*The child shrugs indifferently.*]

RISSA: [*Who overhears everything that is ever spoken on the plantation*] Uh-hunh. I knew we'd get 'round to Mr. Hannibal soon enough.

SARAH: [*To* RISSA] Do you know where he is?

RISSA: How I know where that wild boy of mine is? If he ain't got sense enough to come for his supper, it ain't no care of mine. He's grown now. Move on out the way now. Step up here, Ben!

SARAH: [*Moving around to the other side and standing close*] He was out the fields again this afternoon, Aunt Rissa.

RISSA: [*Softly, suddenly—but without breaking her working rhythm or changing facial expression*] Coffin know?

SARAH: Coffin know everything. Say he goin' to tell Marster Sweet first thing in the mornin'.

RISSA: [*Decision*] See if you can find that boy of mine, child. [SARAH *pushes the last of her food in her mouth and starts off.* RISSA *halts her and hands her a small bundle which has been lying in readiness.*] His supper.

CUT TO: EXTERIOR. MOONLIT WOODS.

SARAH: [*Emerges from the woods into a tiny clearing, bundle in hand. Calling softly*] Hannibal— [*The camera pans to a little hillock in deep grass where a lean, vital young man lies, arms folded under his head, staring up at the stars with bright commanding eyes. At the sound of* SARAH's *voice off-camera we come down in his eyes. He comes alert. She calls again.*] Hannibal— [*He smiles and hides as she approaches.*] Hannibal— [*She whirls about fearfully at the snap of a twig, then reassured crosses in front of his hiding place, searching.*] Hannibal— [*He touches her ankle—she screams. Laughing, he reaches for her. With a sigh of exasperation she throws him his food.*]

HANNIBAL: [*Romantically, wistfully—playing the poet-fool*] And when she come to me, it were the moonrise…[*He holds out his hand*] And when she touch my hand, it were the true stars fallin'. [*He takes her hand and pulls her down in the grass and kisses her. She pulls away with the urgency of her news.*]

SARAH: Coffin noticed you was gone first thing!

HANNIBAL: Well, that old driver finally gettin' to be almost smart as a jackass.

SARAH: Say he gona tell Marster Sweet in the mornin'! You gona catch you another whippin', boy…! [*In a mood to ignore peril,* HANNIBAL *goes on eating his food*] Hannibal, why you have to run off like that all the time?

HANNIBAL: [*Teasing*] Don't run off *all* the time.

---

[1] [*Author's note.*] Invariably pronounced "Say-rah."

SARAH: Oh, Hannibal!

HANNIBAL: [*Finishing the meager supper and reaching out for her playfully*] "Oh, Hannibal. Oh, Hannibal!" Come here. [*He takes hold of her and kisses her once sweetly and lightly*] H'you this evenin', Miss Sarah Mae?

SARAH: You don't know how mad old Coffin was today, boy, or you wouldn't be so smart. He's gona get you in trouble with Marster again.

HANNIBAL: Me and you was *born* in trouble with Marster. [*Suddenly looking up at the sky and pointing to distract her*] Hey, lookathere!—

SARAH: [*Noting him and also looking up*] What—

HANNIBAL: [*Drawing her close*] Lookit that big, old, fat star shinin' away up yonder there!

SARAH: [*Automatically dropping her voice and looking about a bit*] Shhh. Hannibal!

HANNIBAL: [*With his hand, as though he is personally touching the stars*] One, two three, four—they makes up the dipper. That's the Big Dipper, Sarah. The old Drinkin' Gourd pointin' straight to the North Star!

SARAH: [*Knowingly*] Everybody knows that's the Big Dipper and you better hush your mouth for sure now, boy. Trees on this plantation got more ears than leaves!

HANNIBAL: [*Ignoring the caution*] That's the old Drinkin' Gourd herself! [*Releasing the girl's arms and settling down, a little wistfully now.*]

HANNIBAL: Sure is bright tonight. Sure would make good travelin' light tonight…

SARAH: [*With terror, clapping her hand over his mouth*] Stop it!

HANNIBAL: [*Moving her hand*]—up there jes pointin' away…due North!

SARAH: [*Regarding him sadly*] You're sure like your brother, boy. Just like him.

HANNIBAL: [*Ignores her and leans back in the grass in the position of the opening shot of the scene, with his arms tucked under his head. He sings softly to himself*]
"For the old man is a-waitin'
For to carry you to freedom
If you follow the Drinking Gourd.
Follow—follow—follow…
If you follow the Drinking Gourd…"

SARAH: [*Over the song*]—look like him…talk like him…and God knows, you sure think like him. [*Pause*] In time, I reckon—[*Very sadly*]—you be gone like him.

HANNIBAL: [*Sitting bolt upright suddenly and peering into the woods about them*] You think Isaiah got all the way to Canada, Sarah? Mama says it's powerful far. Farther than Ohio! [*This last with true wonder*] Sure he did! I bet you old Isaiah is up there and got hisself a job and is livin' fine. I bet you that! Bet he works in a lumberyard or something and got hisself a wife and maybe even a house and—

SARAH: [*Quietly*] You mean if he's alive, Hannibal.

HANNIBAL: Oh, he's alive, all right! Catchers ain't never caught my brother. [*He whistles through his teeth*] That boy lit out of here in a way somebody go who don't mean to never be caught by nothin'! [*He waits. Then, having assured himself within*] Wherever he is, he's alive. And he's free.

SARAH: I can't see how his runnin' off like that did you much good. Or your mama. Almost broke her heart, that's what. And worst of all, leavin' his poor little baby. Leavin' poor little Joshua who don't have no mother of his own as it is. Seem like your brother just went out his head when Marster sold Joshua's mother. I guess everybody on this plantation knew he wasn't gona be here long then. Even Marster must of known.

HANNIBAL: But Marster couldn't keep him here then! Not all Marster's dogs and drivers and drivers and guns. Nothin'. [*He looks to the woods, remembering*] I met him here that night to bring him the food and a extry pair of shoes. He was standin' right over there, right over there, with the moonlight streamin' down on him and he was breathin' hard—Lord, that boy was breathin' so's you could almost hear him on the other side of the woods. [*A sudden pause and then a rush in the telling*] He didn't say nothin' to me, nothin' at all. But his eyes look like somebody lit a fire in 'em, they was shinin' so in the dark. I jes hand him the parcel and he put it in his shirt and give me a kind of push on the shoulder…[*He touches the place, remembering keenly*]… Here. And then he turned and lit out through them woods like lightnin'. He was bound out this place!

[*He is entirely quiet behind the completion of the narrative.* SARAH *is deeply affected by the implications of what she has heard and suddenly puts her arms around his neck and clings very tightly to him. Then she holds him back from her and looks at him for the truth.*]

SARAH: You aim to go, don't you, Hannibal? [*He does not answer and it is clear because of it that he intends to run off.*] H'you know it's so much better to run off? [*A little desperately, near tears, thinking of the terrors involved*] Even if you make it—h'you know what's up there, what it be like to go wanderin' 'round by yourself in this world?

HANNIBAL: I don't know. Jes know what it is to be a slave!

SARAH: Where would you go—?

HANNIBAL: Jes North, that's all I know. [*Kind of shrugging*] Try to find Isaiah maybe. How I know what I do? [*Throwing up his hands at the difficult question*] There's people up there what helps runaways.

SARAH: You mean them aba-aba-litchinists? I heard Marster Sweet say once that they catches runaways and makes soap out of them.

HANNIBAL: [*Suddenly older and wiser*] That's slave-owner talk, Sarah. Whatever you hear Marster say 'bout slavery—you always believe the opposite. There ain't nothin' hurt slave marster so much—[*Savoring the notion*]—as when his property walk away from him. Guess that's the worst blow of all. Way I look at it, ever' slave ought to run off 'fore he die.

SARAH: [*Looking up suddenly, absorbing the sense of what he has just said*] Oh, Hannibal—*I* couldn't go! [*She starts to shake all over*] I'm too delicate. My breath wouldn't hold out from here to the river…

HANNIBAL: [*Starting to laugh at her*] No, not you—skeerified as you is! [*He looks at her and pulls her to him*] But don't you worry, little Sarah. I'll come back. [*He smoothes her hair and comforts her*] I'll come back and buy you. Mama too, if she's still livin'. [*The girl quivers in his arms and he holds her a little more tightly, looking up once again to his stars.*] I surely do that thing!

CUT TO INTERIOR. THE DINING ROOM OF THE "BIG HOUSE."

HIRAM SWEET *and his wife,* MARIA, *sit at either end of a well-laden table, attended by two male servants. The youngest son,* TOMMY, *about ten, sits near his father and across from his older brother,* EVERETT, *who is approaching thirty. A fifth person, a dinner guest, is seated on* EVERETT's *left. He is* DR. MACON BULLETT. *The meal has just ended, but an animated conversation which characterized it lingers actively.*

EVERETT: —by Heaven, I'll tell you we don't have to take any more of it! [*He hits the table with his fist for emphasis*] I say we can have 600,000 men in the field without even feeling it. The whole thing wouldn't have to last more than six months, Papa. Why can't you see that?

HIRAM: [*A man in his mid-sixties, with an overgenerous physique and a kind, if somewhat overindulged, face*] I see it fine! I see that it's the river of stupidity the South will eventually drown itself in.

BULLETT: [*A man of slightly quieter temperament than the other two men; with an air of deeply ingrained "refinement"*] I don't see that we have much choice, however you look at it, Hiram. They've pushed our backs against the wall. Suddenly every blubber-fronted Yankee industrialist in New England has begun to imagine himself the deliverer of the blacks—at least in public speeches. [*At the epithet,* HIRAM *looks down at his own stomach and then back at his friend with some annoyance.*] The infernal hypocrites! Since all they want is the control of Congress, they ought to call a snake by its name.

EVERETT: Hear, hear, sir!

HIRAM: [*Eating something*] The only thing is—it doesn't make sense to fight a war you know you can't win.

[EVERETT *is so exasperated by the remark that he jumps up from the table. His mother laughs.*]

EVERETT: [*With genuine irritation*] Whatever are you laughing about, Mother?

MARIA: Forgive me, darling. It's just that it always amuses me to see how serious you have become now-a-day. [*To* BULLETT] He was so boyish and playful for so long. [*Innocently*] Right up until his twenty-first birthday he used to love to have me come to him and—

EVERETT: Mother, please. Papa, how can you constantly talk about our not winning when—[*On his fingers*]—we have the finest generals in the country and a labor force of four million who can just go on working undisturbed. Why, don't you see-if we had to, we could put every white man in the South in uniform! Will the North ever be able to boast that? [*Smiling at* BULLETT] What will happen to that great rising industrial center—if its men go off to war? [*He bends close to* BULLETT *so they can laugh together*] Who will run the machines then? New England schoolmarms?

[*They laugh heartily together.* HIRAM *watches them and folds his hands on his stomach.*]

HIRAM: And may I ask something of you, my son? When *you* and the rest of the white men of the South go off to fight your half of the war, who is going to stay home and guard your slaves? Or are they simply going to stop running away because then, for the first time in history, running away will be so easy?

[EVERETT'*s mouth is a little ajar from the question, though it is far from the first time he has heard it. He and* BULLETT *are merely exasperated to hear it asked again. They begin to smile at one another as though a child had once again asked a famous and tiresome riddle.*]

BULLETT: [*Waving his hands at absurdity*] Hiram, you know perfectly well that that is not a real consideration. Abolitionist nonsense that any slaveholder should know better than worry about!

HIRAM: I see. Tell me something, Macon. How many slaves did you lose off your plantation last year?

BULLETT: Why—two. Prime hands, too, blast them!

HIRAM: Two. And Robley hit the jackpot with his new overseer: he lost five. And one from the Davis place. And I lost one. Let's see…two, seven, eight, nine—from this immediate district…in spite of every single precaution that we know how to take…

BULLETT: Oh, come on now, Sweet, everyone knows that the ones who run away are the troublemakers, the malcontents. Usually bad workers…

HIRAM: Mmm-hmm. Of course. Then why are there reward posters up on every other tree in this county? Come, man, you're not talking to a starry-eyed Yankee fool! You're talking to a slave-holder!

BULLETT: I don't follow your point.

HIRAM: You follow my point! We all follow my point! Or else will somebody here stop laughing long enough to tell me why you and me and Robley and all the others waste all that money on armed guards and patrols and rewards and dogs? And, above all, why you and me and every other planter in the cotton South *and* the Border States tried to move heaven and earth to get the fugitive slave laws passed? Was it to try and guarantee the return of property that you are sitting there calmly and happily telling me doesn't run off in the first place!

EVERETT: Well, Papa, of course a few—

HIRAM: A few, my eyelashes! What's the matter with you two! I believe in slavery! But I also understand it! I understand it well enough not to laugh at the very question that might decide this war that you are just dying to start.

EVERETT: You forget, Papa, it's not going to be much of a war. And if it is, then we can always arm the *blacks!*

[HIRAM *puts down his cup with astonishment and even* MACON *looks at* EVERETT *askance for his naïve remark.*]

HIRAM: [*With undiluted sarcasm*] I have to admit that my boy here is as logical as the rest of the leaders of our cause. For what could be more logical than the idea that you can give somebody a gun and make him fight *for* what he's trying like blazes to run away *from* in the first place. [*Dryly*] I salute you, Everett. You belong in Washington—immediately—among your peers.

MARIA: Now, Hiram—

EVERETT: You don't have to be insulting, Papa.

HIRAM: I'll be what I please in this house and you'll mind your manners to me in the face of it!

[EVERETT *looks to his mother in outrage for support.*]

MARIA: Well, dear, you shouldn't sass your father.

EVERETT: Mother, I am not Tommy! I am a grown man. Who, incidentally, any place but this would be running his father's plantation at my age.

HIRAM: You'll run it when I can depend on you to run it in my tradition. And not before.

EVERETT: Your "tradition" is running it to ruin!

MARIA: [*Upset*] Everett, I'll not have it at the table. I simply won't have it at the table. [*To the younger boy to get him away from the argument*] You may excuse yourself and go to your room if you are through, Tommy. Say good night to Dr. Bullett.

TOMMY: Good night, sir. [*He exits*]

HIRAM: [*Immediately*] So I am running it to ruin, am I! You hear that, Macon! This polished little pepper is now one of the new experts of the South. Knows everything. Even how to run a plantation. Studied it in Paris cafés!

BULLETT: At this point, Hiram, I hear only that you must quiet yourself. [*Looking at his watch*] In fact, let's get upstairs and get it over.

HIRAM: I don't feel like going upstairs and I don't feel like being poked all over with your little sticks and tubes.

BULLETT: I came over this evening to examine you, Hiram, and I am going to examine you if we have to do it right here at the table. [*He rises and gets his black bag and*
MARIA *sits nodding her appreciation of his forcefulness with the difficult man*]

MARIA: He's been eating salt again, too, Macon. I declare I can't do a thing with him.

HIRAM: [*To his wife*] Yahhhhhh.

EVERETT: [*Watching his father's antics*] Stubbornness, backwardness, disorder, contempt
for new ways. It's the curse of the past and it is strangling us.

HIRAM: All I can say is that if you are the spirit of the Future, it sure is going to be talk-
ative.

MARIA: Can't you ever talk nicely to him, Hiram?

EVERETT: I don't want him to talk "nice" to me. For the eighty-thousandth time, I am
not a little boy!

HIRAM: [*To* MACON] Isn't there something you are always quoting to me from your
Shakespeare about people protesting too much?[2] [*To* EVERETT] Seems to me, son,
that I haven't done too badly with what you seem to think are my backward ways.
You can testify to that, can't you, Macon? Came into this country with four slaves
and fifty dollars. Four slaves and fifty dollars! [*He becomes mellow and a little grand
whenever he recalls this for the world*] I planted the first seed myself and supervised my
own baling. That was thirty-five years ago and I made this one of the finest—
though I am the first to admit, not one of the biggest—plantations in this district.
So I must know a little something about how to run it.

EVERETT: Maybe you *knew* about running it.

HIRAM: I *know* about running it!

BULLETT: Calm down now, Hiram.

HIRAM: [*To* MACON] You know what HIS idea is of running this place? It's simple. It's
the "modern" way. It's what everybody does. You put the whole thing in the hands
of overseers! That's all! Then you take off for Saratoga or Paris. Those aren't
planters who do that—those are parasites! I'm a cotton grower, and I'll manage my
own plantation until I'm put under. And that I promise God!

EVERETT: Papa, can I ask you a simple unemotional question—when is the last time
our yield came anywhere near ten bales to the hand? When, Papa? You tell me.

HIRAM: Well, the land is just about finished. Five bales to the hand is pretty good for
our land at this point.

EVERETT: [*Looking triumphantly from his father to the other*] And when are we going to buy
new land?

HIRAM: [*Troubled in spite of himself*] Next year, if the crop is good.

EVERETT: And if the crop is poor? Listen close to this circular conversation, Macon.
[*He waves his hand to point up the absurdity*]

HIRAM: Well, we'll borrow.

EVERETT: Yes—and then what?

HIRAM: We'll buy more land.

EVERETT: And who will work the extra land? You going to buy new slaves too?

HIRAM: [*Rubbing his ear*] Well, if those Virginia breeders weren't such bandits we could
take on one or two more prime hands—

---

[2] From *Hamlet* (act iii, sc. 2), by William Shakespeare (1564-1616): "The lady doth protest too much, methinks."

EVERETT: But they *are* bandits, and until such time as we can get some decent legislation in this country to reopen the African slave trade we have to meet their prices. So now what?

HIRAM: Don't goad me!

EVERETT: Don't goad you! What do you expect me to do, sit around and watch you let this place go bankrupt! You don't seem to understand, Papa, we don't have much choice. We have got to up our yield or go under. It's as simple as that. [*To the doctor*] You know what this place is, Macon? A resort for slaves! You know what they put in the fields here? I am ashamed to tell you. Nine and one half hours!

HIRAM: Nine and a half hours is plenty of labor for a hand!

EVERETT: [*Almost shouting*] Not on that cotton-burned land it isn't! [*Then fighting to hold himself in check*] Sure, I know—there was a time when the land was pure and fertile as a dream. You hardly had to do anything but just poke something in it and it grew. But that is over with. It has to be coaxed now, and you have to keep your labor in the fields a decent length of time. Nine and one half hours! Why the drivers stroll around out there as though it were all a game. [*Looking at his father*] And the high-water mark gets higher and higher and higher. But he doesn't care! This is his little farm, run in his little way, by his dear old friends out there who understand him and love him: Fa-la-la-la-la!

MARIA: I think that will do, son.

EVERETT: Yes, that will do! That will do—! [*He jumps up as if to leave the room*]

HIRAM: Where are you going?

EVERETT: I am going to find John Robley and his brother and—

HIRAM: —drink and gamble the night away! Is that the way you would be master here! Sit down!

[EVERETT *halts with his mouth open to speak to his father in outrage.* MACON *interrupts with a deliberately quiet note.*]

BULLETT: [*To* MARIA] Get him to take these four times a day, if you can, Maria. [*To* HIRAM] Not three times and not five times—*four.*

MARIA: [*Taking the bottle and going out with it*] I will try, Macon, I will try. [*To* EVERETT *as she passes him*] Do try not to upset your father so, darling. [*She kisses him lightly and pats his cheek and exits with the bottle*]

[EVERETT *moves to a window and stands looking out at the darkness in irritation.* BULLETT *clearly waits for* MARIA'*s distance and then looks at his patient as he starts to put his things away.*]

BULLETT: Well, Hiram—it's all over. [*From the finality of his tone,* EVERETT *turns slowly to listen and stare at them and* HIRAM, *who also understands the opening remark, at once also winds up for a great and loud protest.*] No, I mean it. There's nothing left to joke about and no more trusting to luck. It's that bad. [HIRAM *stares hard at him and the protest starts to fall away as the gravity of his friend penetrates.*] As much as you hate reading, you have got to buy all the books you can and spend the rest of your life doing very little else. That's all. I absolutely insist that you stay out of the fields.

HIRAM: Well, now, just a minute, Macon—

BULLETT: I'm sorry, Hiram—

HIRAM: Well, your being sorry doesn't help me one bit!

EVERETT: Papa!

BULLETT: That's all right, son.

HIRAM: What do you expect me to do with my plantation? Turn it over to *him* so he can turn it over to a pack of overseers?

BULLETT: Well, I hadn't intended to get into that, Hiram, but since you ask me, I think it would be the best thing that could happen to the Sweet plantation. [*Seeing that the remark has cut the man deeply, he tries to amplify in the most impartial and reasonable tone*] You and I have to face the fact that this is a new era, Hiram. Cotton is a big business in a way it never was before. If you treat it any other way, you're lost. You just have to adjust to that, Hiram. For the good of yourself and for the good of the South.

HIRAM: [*Bitterly*] That's easy talk for a blue blood, Macon! We all know that you came from a long line of lace-hankied Bordeaux wine-sniffers, but I think you forget that I don't.

EVERETT: [*Hating most of all that he should raise the question*] Papa, please!

BULLETT: [*Coolly*] I cannot imagine what makes you think I have forgotten. Certainly not your manners.

EVERETT: [*Obligatory*] Sir, I must remind you this is my father's house.

HIRAM: [*To* EVERETT] Don't you ever hush? I'm sorry, Macon, I was a little insulting and a little—

EVERETT: [*Almost to himself, involuntarily*]—common.

[*This is clearly* EVERETT's *anguish. All three men suffer a moment of extreme discomfort and* MACON *stirs himself for departure.*]

BULLETT: Well, that was an extraordinary meal as usual. That Rissa of yours is an eternal wonder.

HIRAM: Macon, tell me something. Don't you have the gray hours, too?

BULLETT: The what?

HIRAM: The gray hours—you know what I mean, don't sit there looking dumb. I call them the gray hours, you probably call them something else. That doesn't matter. I know perfectly well you have them, whatever you call them. I think every man that draws breath on this earth has those hours when—well—when, by God, he wonders why the stars hang out there and this planet turns and rivers run-and what he's here for.

BULLETT: Yes, I suppose we all do.

HIRAM: Then what happens, Macon, if it's all a lie-the way we live, the things we tell ourselves?

BULLETT: Oh, come now, Hiram...

HIRAM: No, I mean it—what happens if there really is some old geezer sitting up there, white beard and all—

BULLETT: I don't think I'm so unready to meet my Maker, Hiram. I haven't been the worst of men on this earth—

HIRAM: Macon—*you own slaves.*

BULLETT: Well, that's not a sin. It was meant to be that way. That's why He made men different colors.

HIRAM: Is it? I hope so, Macon, I truly hope so.

BULLETT: [*Rising*] Hiram, I really must get on. No, don't call Maria. Harry can see me out. Good night, Everett.

EVERETT: Good night, sir.

BULLETT: [*Touching his friend on his shoulder as he exits*] Books and long afternoon naps. Good night, Hiram.

HIRAM: [*Having become strangely quiet*] Good night, Macon. [*The doctor exits*]

EVERETT: [*Turning on him savagely as soon as the man is out of sight*] Papa, why must you insist upon eternally bringing up your "humble beginnings"—

HIRAM: [*Sighing*] Good night, son. I want to be alone. I am tired.

EVERETT: [*Concerned*] Are—you all right?

HIRAM: Yes. Good night. [EVERETT *does not say another word and exits quietly from the room as the planter sits on. Presently a stir in the shadows behind him makes him turn his head.*] That you, Rissa? You there.

RISSA: [*Coming out of the shadows as all of the servants seem to do when they are called or needed*] Yessah.

HIRAM: [*Himself*] There wasn't enough salt in the greens.

RISSA: There was all you gona get from now on.

HIRAM: Now, Rissa—

RISSA: If you aimin' on killin' yourself, Marster Hiram, don't be askin' Riss' to hep you none 'cause she ain't gona do it.

HIRAM: One thing about always listening to other people's conversations, Rissa, is that you hear a lot of blasted nonsense.

RISSA: I don't have to listen to no other folks' conversations to see h'you ailin'. You sittin' there now, white as cotton, sweatin' like you seen the horseman comin'. [*She stands behind him and forces him to sit back in the chair with comforting gestures*] Lord, you one stubborn man. I 'spect you was allus the most stubborn man I ever come across.

HIRAM: Took a stubborn man to do the things I had to. To come into the wilderness and make a plantation. Came here with four slaves and fifty dollars and made one of the finest plantations in this district.

RISSA: [*Attending to him, gently, patiently, mopping his brow as she stands behind his chair*] Yessah. Jes you and me and old Ezra and Zekial who run off and poor old Leo who died last year.

HIRAM: [*Shaking his head*] You ever expect that Ezekial would run off from me after all those years?

RISSA: Sprise me just as much as you. Reckon I don't know what gets into some folks.

HIRAM: [*Suddenly breaking into laughter*] Remember that time when we were building the old barn and Zeke fell from the loft straight into that vat of molasses you had put in there to cool the day before? By God, he was a sticky boy that day! [*He roars and she does also*]

RISSA: —Come flyin' to me in the kitchen screamin'; "Rissa, Rissa, I'se kilt, I'se kilt!" Me and Ezra had to tie him down to wash him he was so scared. [*A new surge of laughter*] Finally had to shave his head like a egg, 'member?

HIRAM: And the time the wild hogs went after the corn in the south fields and I had to go after them with the gun and Farmer Burns thought I was shooting at him!

RISSA: Do I remember?—Why we had po'k 'round here for months after that!

HIRAM: [*Feeling festive*] Fetch the gun, Rissa, go ahead let's have a look at it—

RISSA: [*Fussing good-naturedly as she obeys, reaching for a key hanging among a dozen or so keys on her belt*] I knew it! Every time you get to thinkin' 'bout them days I have to get out that old gun so's you kin look at it. [*She opens a long drawer and pulls the old weapon out. It is wrapped in a cloth and has been kept in excellent repair.*]

HIRAM: [*Reaching out for it eagerly as she brings it to him*] Ah!...And still shoots true as an arrow...[*He caresses it a little*] My father gave me this gun and I remember feeling—

I was fourteen—I remember feeling, "I'm a man now. A true man. I shall go into the wilderness and not seek my fortune—but *make* it!" Hah! What a cocky boy I was!... [HIRAM *is smiling happily*]

RISSA: [*Clearly getting ready to remind him of something. Placing both fists on her hips*] Speakin' of boys, Marster Sweet, ain't you forgot about a certain promise in the last couple of months?

HIRAM: [*Frowning like a boy being reprimanded*] Oh, Rissa, Maria says she won't have it. She put up a terrible fuss about it...

RISSA: [*Just as childishly—they are, in fact, very much alike*] Marster, a promise is a promise! And you promise me when that boy was born that he wasn't never gona have to be no field hand...

HIRAM: But we need all the hands in the fields we've got and Maria says there is absolutely nothing for another house servant to do around here. [*As he is saying this,* MARIA *has reentered with a single pill and a glass of water. She stands where she is and watches the two of them.*]

RISSA: He kin do a little bit of everything. He kin hep me in the kitchen and Harry some in the house. He's gettin' so unruly, Marster Hiram. And you promised me—

HIRAM: All right, for God's sake! Anything for peace in this house! Soon as pickin's over, Hannibal is a house servant—[RISSA *sees* MARIA *and becomes quite still.* HIRAM *follows her eyes and turns to see* MARIA *as she advances toward him with the medicine and water, her face set in silent anger.* HIRAM *shouts at her suddenly.*] Because I say so, that's why! Because I am master of this plantation and every soul on it. I am master of those fields out there and I am master of this house as well. [*She is silent*] There are some men born into this world who make their own destiny. Men who do not tolerate the rules of other men or other forces. [*He is angry at his illness and goes into a mounting rage as the camera pans away from him to the slightly nodding* RISSA *who is cut of the same cloth in her individualism; to his wife who feels in the moment only clear despair for her husband; across the floor through the open door where* EVERETT *stands listening in half-shadow.*] I will not die curled up with some book! When the Maker wants me, let him come for me in the place where He should know better than all I can be found...[EVERETT'*s face turns intently as if for the first time he is hearing the essence of his father.*] I have asked no man's permission for the life I have lived—and I will not start now!

FADE OUT
END OF ACT ONE

Act Two

FADE IN: INTERIOR. EVERETT'S BEDROOM—AFTERNOON.

He is sitting dejectedly alone. Drinking. The door bursts open and his mother stands there with urgency in her face.

MARIA: You had better come, son!

EVERETT: [*With concern*] An attack?

MARIA: Yes, I've sent for Macon. [*He rushes to her and steadies her.*]

EVERETT: It's all right, Mother. It's going to be all right.

CUT TO: INTERIOR HIRAM'S BEDROOM.

The shades have been pulled and HIRAM *lies stretched out on his back, fully dressed. A male house servant is trying to gently remove his clothes.* EVERETT *and* MARIA *enter and go directly to his bedside.*

MARIA: Hiram, Macon is on his way. Everything is going to be all right.

HIRAM: Saw him that time…old horseman…riding out the swamps…He was smiling at me.

MARIA: [*Taking over from the servant in an effort to make him comfortable*] Just lie still. Don't talk. Macon will be here in a little while and everything will be all right.

EVERETT: [*Aside, to the servant*] When did it happen?

SERVANT: Jes a little while ago, suh. They found him stretched out yonder in the fields. Eben and Jed carried him up here and me and Missus got him on the bed fust thing. I think he's powaful sick this time, suh.

HIRAM: Fifty dollars and four slaves…Planted the first seed myself…

[MARIA *looks at her husband intently in his pain and then rises with a new air of determination and signals for her son to follow her out of the room. He obeys—a little quizzically.*]

MARIA: [*To the* SERVANT *as they go out*] We'll be right here, Harry.

SERVANT: Yes, ma'am.

MARIA: [*In the hall, in half tones and with a more precise spirit than her son has ever seen before*] Do you propose to wait any longer now, son?

EVERETT: [*Confused*] For what—?

MARIA: To become master here.

EVERETT: Oh, mother…

MARIA : Everett, your father is perfectly capable of killing himself. We must become perfectly capable of stopping him from doing it.

EVERETT: You heard him last week—"Some men make their destiny"—Well—

MARIA: [*Sharply*] I am not interested in your bitterness at this moment, Everett. You must take over the running of the plantation—no, listen to me—and you must make him believe you have done no such thing. Every night, if necessary, you must sit with pencil and pad and let him tell you everything he wishes. And then—well, do as you please. You will be master then. But he will think that he is still, which is terrible important. [*With that, she turns to the door*]

EVERETT: You would deceive him like that?

MARIA: [*Only half-turning to reply*] Under the circumstances, Everett, I consider that to be the question of a weak boy, when I have clearly asked you to be a very strong man. [*Looking at him*] Which is the only kind I have ever been able to truly love. [*She turns and goes and the camera lingers with* EVERETT'*s face*]

DISSOLVE TO: EXTERIOR. A SMALL FARM.

A lean farmer stands in a cornfield between rows of feeble burnt-out looking corn. A bushel basket sits at his feet. He reaches out and twists an ear off a stalk, pulls back the green shuck and looks at the ear with anger and despair and throws it roughly into the basket, where other ears like it are collected. He picks up the basket and strides angrily toward his cabin.

CUT TO: INTERIOR. THE CABIN.

His wife is working at the stove. ZEB DUDLEY, *the farmer, kicks the door open roughly with his foot and walks in and slams the basket down with fury. The woman watches him.*

ZEB: That ain't corn. That's sticks! [ELIZABETH *wipes her hands and comes to inspect the corn. She picks up a piece or two and drops them sadly back into the basket*] Ain't nobody going to buy that! Can't hardly get a decent price when it's good. Who's going to buy that?

ELIZABETH: Well, take it in anyhow. We have to try at least, Zeb. [*Two small children stand in a corner watching them, looking as if they might welcome the corn at the moment, no matter what its condition.*]

ZEB: Well then—you try! [*He strides across the floor and gets a jug down from the shelf and uncorks it and drinks deeply from it.*]

ELIZABETH: We ain't got no choice, Zeb.

ZEB: I said all right, you try! [*More quietly*] How's Timmy?

ELIZABETH: [*Looking into the crib in a corner of the room*] He ain't been cryin' at least.

[*The man walks over to his baby's crib and then turns away and takes another drink from the jug, only to discover that it is now empty. He looks at it and suddenly smashes it on the floor. An old man has appeared at the door which* ZEB *has left open.*]

PREACHER: H'dy do. [*He surprises both of them a little.*]

ELIZABETH: Oh, hello, Preacher, come on in.

PREACHER: Thought I'd pay my respects to the Dudleys and mebbe find out why they ain't made it to meetin' in the last month of Sundays. Reckon I could stand a cup of lemonade too, if you got it handy, 'Lizabeth. [*He signals the two older children without interrupting his remarks and gives them each a candy.*] Zeb, you look like a stallion somebody been whippin' with a bullwhip.

[ZEB *strides out of the cabin and makes splashing sounds from a basin outside the door.* ELIZABETH *puts a glass of lemonade before the* PREACHER.] What's the matter with Timmy, there?

ELIZABETH: Got the croup all week. [*Her husband comes back in, stripped to the waist, water dripping from his head. She pours lemonade for him also.*]

PREACHER: Now, that's better. Nothin' to bring temper down off a man like a little coolin' water.

ZEB: I'm clearin', Preacher.

PREACHER: Clearin' where, son?

ZEB: Don't know. The West, mebbe.

PREACHER: Oh, the West?

ZEB: [*Defensively*] Well, a lotta folks been pullin' out goin' West lately.

PREACHER: Lookin' for the Frontier again? I kin remember when this was the Frontier.

ZEB: [*Quickly*] That was a long time ago.

PREACHER: A long time. Before the big plantations started gobblin' up the land and floodin' the country with slaves.

ZEB: I heard me some good things 'bout the West. That if a man got a little get up in him, he still got a chance. Hear there's plenty of land still. Good land.

PREACHER: Seems to be three things the South sends out more than anything else. A steady stream of cotton, runaway slaves and poor white folks. I guess the last two is pretty much lookin' for the same thing and they both runnin' from the first.

ZEB: Not me—! No sir! I ain't runnin' from cotton! I'm lookin' for some place where I kin plant me some, that's what. I know 'bout plantin' and I know how to drive slaves!

PREACHER: And you figger you kin get to be somebody, eh? Like the Sweets, mebbe?

ZEB: If I ever got my chance, I make that Sweet plantation look like a shanty!...Why you laughin' like that?

PREACHER: Allus been a laughin' man, allus loved a good joke.

ZEB: Well, I ain't told none.

PREACHER: Yep, it's a hard life.

ZEB: It's a hard life if you ain't got slaves.

PREACHER: That what you think, Zeb?

ZEB: That's what I know.

PREACHER: Your Pa managed to be a pretty good farmer without slaves, Zeb.

ZEB: My Pa was a fool.

PREACHER: Sure hate to hear good men called fools. He was honest and he worked hard. Didn't call anybody Master and caused none to call him Master. He was a farmer and a good one.

ZEB: And he died eatin' dirt.

[*There is a sound of reining-up outside the cabin.* ELIZABETH *goes to look out.*]

ELIZABETH: Why it's Everett Sweet, Zeb!

ZEB: Who— [*He rises from the table with a quizzical expression and goes to the door and looks out to where* EVERETT *is sitting astride his horse.*]

EVERETT: [*Abruptly*] I'm looking for a good overseer, Zeb Dudley.

ZEB: [*Feeling his way*] Well, what you come here for?

EVERETT: I heard you had some experience driving slaves.

PREACHER: [*Coming and standing behind* ZEB *in the doorway, while* ELIZABETH *looks on with interest in the background*] Well, you musta heard wrong. This boy ain't cut from what makes overseers. He's a farmer.

ZEB: [*Scanning* EVERETT *with his eyes, interested*] I helped out once on the Robley place. I can handle blacks if I have to. But how come you interested? You Pa don't 'low no overseer on his place.

EVERETT: My father is ill in bed. I'm master at our place now and I intend to grow cotton there—a lot of cotton, and I want and need an overseer.

PREACHER: [*To* ZEB] Tell him you don't know nobody 'round here for that kind of work, Zeb.

ZEB: [*Shrugging the* PREACHER'*s hand off his shoulder*] Leave me be, Preacher. [*To* EVERETT] How much you figger to pay?

EVERETT: I'll go as high as fifteen hundred if your work is good. And if you up my yield at the end of the year, I'll give you a bonus.

ZEB: Your word on that, sir?

EVERETT: You heard. But I want cotton.

ZEB: [*Vigorously*] For two thousand dollars—I'll get them slaves of yourn to grow cotton 'tween the rows!

EVERETT: You're on. Be at our place early tomorrow.

ZEB: You got yourself an overseer! [EVERETT *touches his hat to them and rides off.* ZEB *gives a yell and wheels and picks up his wife and whirls her around happily. She too is very happy. The* PREACHER *watches their celebration and sits down in his defeat.*] Two thousand dollars! [*He tousles the hair of his kids and gets to the* PREACHER *at the table*] You a book-learned man, Preacher, help me figger that. Fertilizer, tools on credit, so's mebbe I could put the whole two thousand t'ward two prime hands—

PREACHER: [*Looking at him sadly*] So that's what it's come to 'round here. Man either have to go into slavery some kind of way or pull out the South, eh?

ZEB: Aw, come on, Preacher

PREACHER: You think a man's hands was made to drive slaves?

ZEB: If they have to, Preacher, if they have to…Or mebbe you think they was made to sit idle while he watches his babies turn the color of death?

PREACHER: Zeb, I seen your daddy the day he come ridin' into this here country. Perched up on his pony with a sack of flour and some seed. And he done all right with them two hands of his. He dug in the earth with 'em and he made things grow with 'em. [*He takes* ZEB'*s hands*] Your hands is the same kind, boy.

ZEB: Leave me be, Preacher.

PREACHER: They wasn't meant to crack no whip on no plantation. That ain't fit thing for a man to have to do, Zeb. [*Pointing after* EVERETT] Them people hate our kind. Ain't I heard 'em laughin' and talkin' 'mongst themselves when they see some poor cracker walkin' down the road—about how the negras was clearly put here to serve their betters but how God must of run clear out of ideas when He got to the poor white! Me and you is farmers, Zeb. Cotton and slavery has almost ruined our land. 'N' some of us got to try and hold out 'ginst it. Not go runnin' off to do their biddin' every time they need one of us. Them fields and swamps and pastures yonder was give to us by Him what giveth all gifts—to do right by. And we can't just give it all up to folks what hates the very sight of us—

ZEB: [*Frightened inside by the sense of the speech*] You talk for yourself, Preacher! You go on bein' and thinkin' what you want, but don't be 'cludin' me in on it. 'Cause I ain't *never* found nothin' fine and noble 'bout bein' no dirt-eater. I don't aim to end up no redneck cracker the rest of my life, out there scrapin' on that near-gravel trying to get a little corn to grow. Allus watchin' somebody else's plantation gettin' closer and closer to my land! [*A cry of anguish and a vow: his only claim, his only hope for something better, the one thing he can cling to in this life:*] I'm a white man, Preacher! And I'm goin' to drive slaves for Everett Sweet and he's goin' to pay me for it and this time next year, Zeb Dudley aims to own himself some slaves and be a man—you hear!

PREACHER: Yes...I hear. And I reckon I understand. And all I kin say is—God have mercy on all of us...

CUT TO: INTERIOR RISSA'S CABIN—LATE.

Within, a collection of slaves have formed a play circle around which various individual members of the group sing and perform "Raise a Ruckus."

ALL:

"Come along, little children, come along!
Come where the moon is shining bright!
Get along, little children, get along—
We gona raise a ruckus tonight!"

[*Outside the cabin,* HANNIBAL *and* SARAH *linger a moment before going in.*]

SARAH: [*With a sense of conspiracy*] I seen you this morning, Hannibal.

HANNIBAL: [*Who is tuning his banjo*] Where—?

SARAH: You know where! Boy, you must be crazy!

[HANNIBAL *looks frightened. Then waves it away and smiles at her and takes her by the arm and leads her to join the others.* HANNIBAL *begins to accompany on his banjo.* JOSHUA *is in the center of the singing circle, rendering the verse.*]

JOSHUA:

"My old marster promise me
Mmm Mmm Mmm
That when he died he gona set me free

Mmm Mmm Mmm
Well, he live so long 'til his head got bald
Mmm Mmm Mmm
Then he gave up the notion of dying at all!"

ALL:
"Come along, little children, come along!
Come where the moon is shining bright!
Get on board, little children, get on board—
We're gona raise a ruckus tonight!"

SARAH:
"My old mistress promise me
Mmm Mmm Mmm
[*Mimicking*]
"Say-rah! When I die I'm going to set you free!"
Mmm Mmm Mmm
But a dose of poison kinda helped her along
Mmm Mmm Mmm
And may the devil sing her funeral song!"

[SARAH *pantomimes gleefully helping "Mistress" along to her grave with a shoving motion of her hand. The chorus of the song is repeated by all. A man is now pushed out to the center. He gets the first line out—*]

MAN: "Well, the folks in the Big House all promise me—"

[*His eyes suddenly grow wide as the camera pans to a slave who has just entered the cabin. It is* COFFIN, *the* DRIVER. *The others follow his gaze and the song dwindles down and goes out completely, and the people start to file out of the cabin with disappointment.*]

COFFIN: [*Looking about at them in outrage*] Jes keep it up! That's all I got to say—jes keep on! Oughta be shamed of yourselves. Good as Marster is to y'all, can't trust none of you nary a minute what you ain't 'round singing them songs he done 'spressly f'bid on this here plantation.

[*When the last of the guests are gone, including* SARAH, HANNIBAL *settles in a corner on the floor, and* COFFIN *turns his attention to* RISSA, *who has been sitting apart from the festivity, mending by the light of the fire.*]

RISSA: 'Spect you better get yourself to bed, Joshua. H'you this evenin', Brother Coffin?

COFFIN: There ain't supposed to be no singin' of them kind of songs and you knows it good as me!

RISSA: H'I'm supposed to stop folks from openin' and closin' they mouths, man?

COFFIN: This here your cabin.

RISSA: But it's they mouths. Joshua-lee, I told you to get yourself in the bed. Don't let me have to tell you again.

COFFIN: [*To* HANNIBAL *who has been sitting watching both of them with his own amusement*] Wanna see you, boy.

HANNIBAL: I'm here.

COFFIN: Yes, and it's the only place you been all day where you was supposed to be, too. [HANNIBAL *looks uncomfortably to his mother, but she studiedly does not look up from her mending.*] Jes who you think pick your cotton ever'time you decides to run off?

HANNIBAL: Reckon I don't worry 'bout it gettin' picked.

COFFIN: [*To* RISSA] Why don't you do something 'bout this here boy! I tries to be a good driver for Marster and he the kind what makes it hard for me.

HANNIBAL: And what gon' happen when you show Marster what a good, good driver you is? Marster gon' make you overseer? Maybe you think he'll jes make Coffin marster here—

COFFIN: You betta stop that sassy lip of yours with me boy or—

HANNIBAL: Or what, Coffin—?

COFFIN: You jes betta quit, thas all. I'm—

HANNIBAL: "—one of Marster Sweet's drivers"—

COFFIN: And thas a fact!

HANNIBAL: Get out this cabin 'fore you get smacked upside your head.

RISSA: [*Looking up from her sewing*] I 'spect that'll be enough from you, Mr. Hannibal.

HANNIBAL: I say what I please to a driver, which, as everybody know, next to a over-seer be 'bout the lowest form of life known.

COFFIN: Why? 'Cause I give Marster a day's work fair and square and don't fool 'round. Like you, f'instant, with all your carryin'ons. Draggin' along in the fields like you was dead; pretendin' you sick half the time. Act like you drop dead if you pick your full quota one of these days. I knows your tricks. You ain't nothin'!

HANNIBAL: Coffin, how you get so mixed up in your head? Them ain't my fields yon-der, man! Ain't none of it my cotton what'll rot if I leaves it half-picked. They ain't my tools what I drops and breaks and loses every time I gets a chance. None of it *mine*.

COFFIN: [*To* RISSA, *shaking his head ruefully*] Them was some wild boys you birthed, woman. You gona pay for it one of these days, too.

RISSA: [*Putting down her sewing finally*] What was I supposed to do—send 'em back to the Lord? You better get on back to your cabin now, Coffin. [COFFIN *exchanges various glances of hostility with them and leaves. As soon as he is gone the mother turns on the son.*]

RISSA: Where you run off to all the time, son?

HANNIBAL: That's Hannibal's business.

RISSA: [*With quiet and deadly implications*] Who you think you sassin' now?

HANNIBAL: [*Intimidated by her*] I jes go off sometimes, Mama.

[*She crosses the cabin to his pallet and gets a cloth-wrapped package from under it and returns with it in her hands. She unwraps it as she advances on him: it is a Bible.*]

RISSA: Is that when you does your stealin'? [*He sees that the matter is exposed and is silent.*] What you think the Lord think of somebody who would steal the holy book itself?

HANNIBAL: If he's a just Lord—he'll think more of me than them I stole it from who don't seem to pay nothin' it says no mind.

RISSA: H'long you think Marster Hiram have you 'round his house if he thinks you a thief?

HANNIBAL: He ain't got me 'round his house and I ain't aimin' to be 'round his house!

RISSA: Well, he's aimin' for you to. Said last night that from now on you was to work in the Big House.

HANNIBAL: [*In fury*] You asked him for that, didn't you?

RISSA: He promised me ever since you was a baby that you wouldn't have to work in the fields.

HANNIBAL: And ever since I could talk I done told you I ain't never goin' be no house servant, no matter what! To no master. I ain't, Mama, I ain't!

RISSA: What's the matter with you, Hannibal? The one thing I allus planned on was that you and Isaiah would work in the Big House where you kin get decent food and nice things to wear and learn nice mannas like a real genamun. [*Pleadingly*] Why, right now young Marse' got the most beautiful red broadcloth jacket that I heard him say he was tired of already—and he ain't hardly been in it. [*Touching his shoulders to persuade*] Fit you everywhere 'cept maybe a little in the shoulder on account you a little broader there—

HANNIBAL: [*Almost screaming*] I don't want Marster Everett's bright red jacket and I don't want Marster Sweet's scraps. I don't want nothin' in this whole world but to get off this plantation!

RISSA: [*Standing with arms still outstretched to where his shoulders were*] How come mine all come here this way, Lord? [*She sits, wearily*] I done tol' you so many times, that you a slave, right or not, you a slave. 'N' you alive—you ain't dead like maybe Isaiah is—

HANNIBAL: Isaiah ain't dead!

RISSA: Things jes ain't that bad here. Lord, child, I been in some places [*Closing her eyes at the thought of it*] when I was a young girl which was made up by the devil. I known marsters in my time what come from hell.

HANNIBAL: All marsters come from hell.

RISSA: No, Hannibal, you seen what I seen—you thank the good Lord for Marster Sweet. Much trouble as you been and he ain't hardly never put the whip to you more than a few times.

HANNIBAL: Why he do it at all? Who he to beat me?

RISSA: [*Looking only at her sewing*] He's your marster, and long as he is he got the right, I reckon.

HANNIBAL: Who give it to him?

RISSA: I'm jes tryin' to tell you that life tend to be what a body make it. Some things is the way they is and that's all there is to it. You do your work and do like you tol' and you be all right.

HANNIBAL: And I tell you like I tell Coffin—I am the only kind of slave I could stand to be—a bad one! Every day that come and hour that pass that I got sense to make a half step do for a whole—every day that I can pretend sickness 'stead of health, to be stupid 'stead of smart, lazy 'stead of quick—I aims to do it. And the more pain it give your marster and the more it cost him—the more Hannibal be a man!

RISSA: [*Very quietly from her chair*] I done spoke on the matter, Hannibal. You will work in the Big House. [*There is total quiet for a while.* HANNIBAL *having calmed a little, speaks gently to his mother.*]

HANNIBAL: All right, Mama. [*Another pause*] Mama, you ain't even asked me what I aimed to do with that Bible. [*Smiling at her, wanting to cheer her up*] What you think I could do with a Bible, Mama?

RISSA: [*Sighing*] Sell it like everything else you gets your hands on, to them white-trash peddlers comes through here all the time.

HANNIBAL: [*Gently laughing*] No—I had it a long time. I didn't take it to sell it. [*He waits, then*] Mama, I kin read it. [RISSA *lifts her head slowly and just looks at him.*] I kin. I kin read, Mama. I wasn't goin' tell you yet. [RISSA *is speechless as he gets the book and takes her hand and leads her close to a place in front of the fireplace, opening the Bible.*] Listen—[*Placing one finger on the page and reading painfully because of the poor light and the newness of the ability]* "The—Book of—Jeremiah." [*He halts and looks in her face for the wonder which is waiting there. With the wonder, water has joined the expression in her eyes, and the tears come.*]

RISSA: [*Softly, with incredulity*] You makin' light of your old Mama. You can't make them marks out for real—? You done memorized from prayer meetin'—

HANNIBAL: [*Laughing gently*] No, Mama—[*Finding another page*] "And I said... [*With longing: the words reflect his own aspiration*] "Oh, that I...had wings like...a dove...then would I...fly away...and...be at rest..." [*He closes the book and looks at her*]

RISSA: Lord, Father, bless thy holy name I seen my boy read the words of the Scripture! [*She stares at him in joy, and then suddenly the joy and the wonder are transformed to stark fear in her eyes and she snatches the book from him and hurriedly buries it and runs to the cabin door and looks about. She comes back to him, possessed by terror.*] How you come to know this readin'?

HANNIBAL: [*Smiling still*] It ain't no miracle, Mama. I learned it. It took me a long time and hard work, but I learned.

RISSA: That's where you go all the time—Somebody been learnin' you—[*He hangs his head in the face of the deduction.*] Who—?

HANNIBAL: Mama, that's one of two things I can't tell nobody... I'm learnin' to letter too. Jes started but I kin write a good number of words already.

RISSA: [*Dropping to her knees before him almost involuntarily in profound fear*] Don't you know what they do to you if they finds out? I seen young Marster Everett once tie a man 'tween two saplin's for that. And they run the white man what taught him out the county...

HANNIBAL: [*Angrily*] I took all that into account, Mama.

RISSA: You got to stop. Whoever teachin' you got to stop.

HANNIBAL: [*Tearing free of her*] I thought you would be proud. But it's too late for you, Mama. You ain't fit for nothin' but slavery thinkin' no more. [*He heads for the door*]

RISSA: Where you going?

HANNIBAL: With all my heart I wish I could tell you, Mama. I wish to God I could believe you that much on my side! [*He steps quickly into the night and the camera comes down on* RISSA*'s deeply troubled face.*]

DISSOLVE TO: EXTERIOR. THE FIELDS—MORNING.

Close-up of a pistol in a holster slung about a mounted man's hips. We move back to see that it is ZEB *astride his horse in the fields, surrounded by the drivers. A work song surrounds the dialogue.*

ZEB: [*Shouting a little because he is out of doors and topping the singing*] ...the hands are to be in the fields an hour and a half before regular time and we're cuttin' the noon break in half and we'll hold 'em an hour and a half longer than the usual night quittin' time. [*The drivers look at each other with consternation.*] What's the matter?

DRIVER: Jes that these here people ain't used to them kinda hours, suh. Thas a powaful long set. 'Specially when you figger to cut the midday break like that, suh. The sun bad at midday, suh. They kin get to grumblin' pretty bad, suh, and makin' all kinds of trouble breakin' the tools and all.

ZEB: You gonna be surprised to find out how fast these people kin learn to change their ways. And any hand who don't learn fast enough will learn it fast enough when I get through with 'em.

COFFIN: Yessuh! They sho' will, suh! They got inta some bad habits, though, on accounta the way this here place been run. We got some hands, suh, that jes takes advantage of po' Marster Sweet. Breakin' his tools and runnin' off all the time—

ZEB: [*With incredulity*] Running off—? Who runs off?

COFFIN: Oh, Lord, suh! You don't know the carryin' ons what goes on 'round this here place. Some of these here folks done got so uppity they think Marster Sweet should be out there hoein' for them, that's what. [*Pointing out* HANNIBAL *in a nearby row*] There's one there, suh. Lord, that one! You'll see what I mean soon, suh. Once a week he jes pick hisself up and run off somewhere, big as he please. I done told Marster and told him and it don't do a bit of good.

ZEB: Ain't he been flogged?

COFFIN: Hmmmph. Floggin' such as Marster 'low don't mount to much. That one there, shucks, he jes take his floggin' and go on off next time like befo'. He's a bad one, suh.

ZEB: [*Looking to* HANNIBAL *and calling to him*] Come here, boy.

HANNIBAL: [*Straightening up and looking around as if he is not certain who is being summoned*] Who?

ZEB: WHO?—YOU, that's who! Get yourself over here! [HANNIBAL *puts down his bag with a simmering sullenness and comes to the overseer.*] What's the matter with your cap there? [HANNIBAL *draws off his cap, keeping his eyes cast down to the ground. The other slaves sense trouble and slow down to watch.* ZEB *notices them.*] Who called a holiday around here? Get to work! [*They stir with exaggerated activity for a few minutes and gradually slow down, more interested in the incident.*] Raise your eyes up there, boy! [HANNIBAL *raises his eyes and looks in the other man's eyes.*] What's his name?

COFFIN: This be Rissa's boy, Hannibal. He got a brother who's a runaway. [HANNIBAL *looks at* COFFIN *with overt hostility.*]

ZEB: [*Getting down from his horse, with his whip*] Well, now, is that so? Well, what you doin' still hangin' 'round here? Ain't your brother never come back and bought you and your mama and carried you off to Paradise yet? [*One or two of the drivers giggle.*] Maybe you jus' plannin' to go on off and join him some day? [*He reaches up and with the butt end of his whip turns* HANNIBAL'*s face from side to side to inspect his eyes.*] You carry trouble in your eyes like a flag, boy. [*He brings the whip up with power and lands it across* HANNIBAL'*s face. An involuntary murmur rises from the watching slaves. To them all.*] That's right, for *nothin'!* [HANNIBAL *is doubled up before him, holding his face.*] I hope y'all understand it plain! From now on this here is a plantation where we plant and pick cotton! There ain't goin' to be no more foolin', no more sassin' and no more tool breakin'! This is what kin happen to you when you misbehave. Now, everybody get to work! And let's have a song there!—make noise, I say! [*Singing comes up. He turns to the drivers.*] Keep 'em at a good pace till the break, and for God's sake keep 'em singin'! Keeps down the grumblin'! [*Noticing* HANNIBAL *still clutching at his face*] And that's enough of your playactin' there, boy. Get on back to your work in the rows. [HANNIBAL *obeys and goes to his row. We come down for a medium-close shot of* ZEB *remounted, one hand poised on his hip, surveying the fields before him, gun at his hip, whip still in his fingers, watching the land that is not his.*]

DISSOLVE TO: EXTERIOR. THE VERANDA.

EVERETT *is lounging in a porch chair, sipping a drink.* ZEB *stands before him with his field hat in his hand.*

EVERETT: All the same, it would have been better to have picked another boy. His mother is one of my father's favorite house slaves, and they have a way of getting him to know about everything that goes on in the fields.

ZEB: [*Hotly*] I reckon there's some things have to be left up to me if you want this here plantation run proper, Mister Sweet.

EVERETT: [*Slowly turning his eyes on the man and moving them up the length of his body in inspection which overtly announces his disgust at the sight of him*] And, as you say, "I reckon" you had better reckon on knowing who is master here and who is merely overseer. Let us be very clear. You are only an instrument. Neither more nor less than that. This is my plantation. I alone am responsible, for I alone am master. Is that clear?

ZEB: [*Looking back at his employer with hatred in kind*] Yes, sir, I reckon that's pretty clear.

[*They are interrupted by* COFFIN *coming onto the veranda at a run.*]

COFFIN: 'Scuse me, suhs, 'scuse me, but I got somethin' most pressin' to tell you, Marster.

ZEB: Now what?

COFFIN: He's gone agin, suh. He's out in the fields like I told you he do all the time!

ZEB: HANNIBAL!

COFFIN: Yessuh! Even with what you showed him an' all the other day, he done run off from the fields again t'day. But I fix him t'day, suh! Old Coffin knowed it was time for him to pull something like this again. I followed him, suh, yessuh. Coffin know whar he be—

ZEB: Well, don't stand there like a dumb ape. Fetch him and put him in the shed and strip him and—[*Looking with triumph at his employer*]—I'll attend to him there. [*To* EVERETT, *bitterly again*] That is, with your permission, sir.

COFFIN: [*Truly agitated*] You don't understand. He's with young Marster, suh!

EVERETT: [*Sitting up with interest for the first time*] He is with whom?

COFFIN: Young Marster Tom, suh!

EVERETT: [*With incredulity*] My brother?

COFFIN: Yessuh!

ZEB: Let's go!

EVERETT: [*Rising abruptly*] I'm coming with you.

CUT TO:

HANNIBAL's *clearing in the woods as per opening frame before titles. Simultaneously with a close-up shot of his head framed with a banjo neck are introduced stark, spirited banjo rhythms. Now the camera moves back to show the books and papers lying about where* HANNIBAL *and* TOMMY *sit. He finishes playing with a flourish and hands the instrument to the child, who puts it awkwardly in his lap and carefully begins to finger it in the quite uncertain manner of one who is learning to play. He plucks a few chords as his teacher frowns.*

HANNIBAL: Aw, come on now, Marse Tommy, get yourself a little air under this finger here. You see, if the fat of your finger touch the string, then the sound come out all flat like this. [*He makes an unpleasant sound on the instrument to demonstrate and to make the boy laugh, which he does.*] Okay, now try again. [TOMMY *tries again and the slave nods at the minor improvement.*] That's better. [*Comically cheating*] That's all now, time for *my* lessons.

TOMMY: Play me another tune first, please, Hannibal?

HANNIBAL: [*Boy to boy*] Aw, now, that ain't fair, Marse Tom. Our 'rangement allus been strictly one lesson for one lesson. Ain't that right? [*The child nods grudgingly.*] And ain't a genamum supposed to keep his 'rangement? No matter how bad he wants to do something else?

TOMMY: Oh, all right. [*Holding out his hand*] Did you do the composition like I told you?

HANNIBAL: [*With great animation, reaching into his shirt and bringing up a grimy piece of paper*] Here. I wrote me a story like you said, suh!

TOMMY: [*Unfolding it and reading with enormous difficulty the very crude printing*] "The— Drinking—Gourd." [*He looks at his pupil indifferently*]

HANNIBAL: [*A very proud man*] Yessuh. Go on—read out loud, please.

TOMMY: Why? Don't you know what it says?

HANNIBAL: Yessuh. But I think it make me feel good inside to hear somebody else read it. T'know somebody else kin actually make sense outside of something I wrote and that I made up out my own head.

TOMMY: [*Sighing*] All right—"The Drinking Gourd. When I was a boy I first come to notice"—All you have to say is came, Hannibal—"the Drinking Gourd. I thought"— There is a u and a g in thought—"it was the most beautiful thing in the heavens. I do not know why, but when a man lie on his back and see the stars, there is something that can happen to a man inside that be"—Is, Hannibal—"bigger than whatever a man is." [TOMMY *frowns for the sense of the last*] "Something that makes every man feel like King Jesus on his milk-white horse racing through the world telling him to stand up in the glory which is called—freedom." [HANNIBAL *sits enraptured, listening to his words.*] "That is what happens to me when I lie on my back and look up at the Drinking Gourd." Well—*that's* not a story, Hannibal...

HANNIBAL: [*Genuinely, but less raptured because of the remark*] Nosuh?

TOMMY: No, something has to happen in a story. There has to be a beginning and an end— [*He stops midsentence seeing the legs of three male figures suddenly standing behind* HANNIBAL. HANNIBAL *looks into his eyes and leaps to his feet in immediate terror.*]

EVERETT: [*In an almost inexpressible rage*] Get back to the house, Tommy.

TOMMY: [*Reaching for the banjo*] Everett, you wanna hear how I can play already? I was going to surprise you! Hannibal said we should keep it a secret so I could surprise you!

EVERETT: Get home, at once! [*The child looks quizzically at all the adults and gathers up his books and goes off.* HANNIBAL *backs off almost involuntarily from the men.* EVERETT *turns to* HANNIBAL.] So you told him it would be your little secret.

HANNIBAL: I was jes teachin' him some songs he been after me to learn him, suh! [*Desperately*] He beg me so.

EVERETT: [*Holding the composition*] Did you write this—?

HANNIBAL: What's that, suh?

EVERETT: [*Hauling off and slapping him with all his strength.* ZEB *smiles a little to himself, watching*] THIS!...Don't stand there and try to deceive me, you monkey-faced idiot! Did you write this?

HANNIBAL: Nosuh, I don't know how to write! I swear to you I don't know how to write! Marse Tommy wrote it...

EVERETT: Tommy could print better than this when he was seven! You've had him teach you, haven't you...

HANNIBAL: Jes a few letters, suh. I figger I could be of more use to Marster if I could maybe read my letters and write, suh.

EVERETT: [*Truly outraged*] You have used your master's own son to commit a crime against your master. How long has this been going on? Who else have you taught, boy? Even my father wouldn't like this, Hannibal. [*A close-up shot as* EVERETT's *hand reaches out and takes* HANNIBAL's *cheeks between his fingers and turns his face from silk to side to inspect his eyes.*] There is only one thing I have ever heard of that was proper for an "educated" slave. It is like anything else; when a part is corrupted by disease— [*Suddenly with all his energy* HANNIBAL *breaks for it.*]

ZEB: Get him, Coffin! [*The driver tackles* HANNIBAL *and throws him to the ground, and* ZEB *comes over to help subdue him, while* EVERETT *stands immobile, slapping his leg with his riding crop.*]

EVERETT: …when a part is corrupted by disease—one cuts out the disease. The ability to read in a slave is a disease—

HANNIBAL: [*Screaming at him, at the height of defiance in the face of hopelessness*] You can't do nothing to me to get out my head what I done learned…I kin read! And I kin write! You kin beat me and beat me…but I kin read…[*To* ZEB] I kin read and you can't— [ZEB w*heels in fury and raises his whip.* EVERETT *restrains his arm.*]

EVERETT: He has told the truth. [*To* ZEB, *coldly*] As long as he can see, he can read… [ZEB *arrests his arm slowly and slowly frowns, looking at* EVERETT *with disbelief.*] You understand me perfectly. Do it now. [*Astonished and horrified,* ZEB *looks from the master to the slave.* EVERETT *nods at him to proceed and the man opens his mouth to protest.*] Proceed. [ZEB *looks at the master one more time, takes the butt end of his whip and advances slowly toward the slave, who comprehends what is to be done to him.* EVERETT *turns on his heel away from the scene, and with a traveling shot, we follow his face, as he strides through the woods and as, presently, the tortured screams of an agonized human being surround him…*]

FADE OUT

END OF ACT TWO

Act Three

FADE IN: EXTERIOR. PLANTATION GROUNDS—LATE NIGHT.

The shadow of a man ingeniously strung by all four limbs between two saplings, each of which is bent to the ground away from the other. Two male shadows loom near and a voice says: "All right, guess we might as well cut him down now…gangrene must've set in."

DISSOLVE TO: INTERIOR HIRAM SWEET'S BEDROOM.

He is in bed and conducting a violent tirade. A medicine bottle smashes against the fireplace and we move across to his bed where he is in the midst of an angry denunciation of ZEB *and* EVERETT, *who both stand in the center of the floor affecting various moods of defiance, fear and impatience.* MARIA *stands near her husband's bedside, wringing her hands for fear of what the mood will do to a cardiac.* EVERETT *reaches out in a restraining gesture toward his father.*

HIRAM: Don't you put your murderous hands on me!

EVERETT: [*To his mother quietly*] Who in the name of God told him about it?

MARIA: [*Shrugging*] One of them, of course.[*They look at the one lone house servant in the room, who casts his eyes quickly away.*]

HIRAM: None of your business who told me! Should have been told before of your doings. Should have been told when you hired this—this—GET THIS CREATURE OUT OF MY SIGHT AND OFF MY LAND BEFORE I SHOOT HIM!

ZEB: All I got to say is that I done as I was told, sir. I was just following instructions…

SWEET: Get him out of here!

MARIA: Please leave, Zeb.

ZEB: Yes ma'am—but you got to tell him I just done as I was told.

EVERETT: Oh, get out. [ZEB *exits*]

MARIA: Now, darling, just calm yourself—

HIRAM: [*To his son*] So this is the way you took over the plantation.

SERVANT: Dr. Bullett, suh.

[MACON BULLETT *enters in a jubilant mood, with a newspaper.*]

BULLETT: Have you all heard the news—?

MARIA: Why, Macon, wherever are your manners today—?

BULLETT: I'm so sorry, Maria, my dear. [*He bows to her a little and greets the two men, and then resumes his excitement.*] Have you heard the news?

EVERETT: What news—

BULLETT: Why, my dear friends, the conflict has come to life! Gentlemen, ma'am, we fired on Sumter two days ago. The South is at war!

[*There is total silence for a second, and then* EVERETT *and* MACON *whoop with joy, and* EVERETT *climbs up and pulls a scabbarded sword from above the mantelpiece and begins to wave it about, alternately embracing* MACON.]

MARIA: Son, will you have to go?

EVERETT: Oh, Mother, of course, if I am offered a commission!

MARIA: [*Handkerchief to her eyes*] Oh, my little darling.

[*Then, slowly, all notice* HIRAM, *who has been stricken quiet and sober by the news.*]

HIRAM: [*With great sadness*] You fools…you amazing fools…

MARIA: Now, Hiram—

HIRAM: The South is lost, and you two are jumping around like butterflies in your happiness.

EVERETT: Lost! The South is going to assert itself, Papa. It is going to become a nation among nations of the world—

HIRAM: Don't you know that whoever that idiot was who fired on Sumter set the slaves free? Well, get out the liquor, gentlemen, it's all over. [*Pause*] A way of life is over. The end is here and we might as well drink to what it was.

BULLETT: Now, look here, Hiram—

HIRAM: Look where? What do you want me to see? You look. You step to the window there and look at all those people that you and your kind have just set free.

EVERETT: Oh, Papa, what is all this nonsense?

HIRAM: [*Slowly pulling on his robe*] I give you my word that they already know about it in the quarters. [*Sadly*] They do not know who or how or why this army is coming. They do not know if it is for them or indifferent to them. But they will be with it. They will pour out of the South by the thousands—dirty, ignorant and uncertain what the whole matter is about. But they will be against us. And when those Yankee maniacs up there get up one fine morning feeling heady with abolitionist zeal and military necessity and decide to arm any and every black who comes ambling across the Confederate lines—and they will—because they will have to—because you will put on your uniforms and fight like fiends for our lost cause…But when the Yankees give them guns and blue uniforms, gentlemen, it will be all over.

MARIA: Hiram, what are you doing? Where do you think you are going?

HIRAM: [*Pulling himself fully out of the bed*] I am going out to see Rissa.

BULLETT: As your physician, Hiram, I expressly forbid you to leave that bed.

HIRAM: Macon, shut up. My time is over. I don't think I want to see that which is coming. I believed in slavery. But I understood it; it never fooled me. It's just as well that we die together. Get out of my way now. [BULLETT *stands back and he exits slowly.*]

CUT TO: EXTERIOR RISSA'S CABIN.

HIRAM *stands outside a moment. Somewhere in the distance, a slave sings plaintively.*[3] *He goes into the cabin.* RISSA *is at the fire, boiling something in a pot.* HANNIBAL *lies flat on a bed, his eyes covered by a cloth. One or two slaves file out wordlessly as the master enters. Occasionally* HANNIBAL *cries out softly.* RISSA *methodically tastes an extract she is preparing. She then dips a fresh white cloth in a second pot and wrings it out lightly and starts toward her son. Her eyes discover the master standing clutching at the collar of his robe, himself in panting pain. He is looking down at* HANNIBAL. *She looks at the master with uncompromising indictment and he returns her gaze with one of supplication, and drops his hands in a gesture of futility. She ignores him then and goes to the boy and removes the old cover and replaces it with a fresh one. The song continues.*

HIRAM: I'll send for Dr. Bullett.

RISSA: I doctorin' him.

HIRAM: But fever—

RISSA: I makin' quinine. Be ready soon.

HIRAM: I—are you sure…? I think I should get Bullett.

RISSA: [*Without looking up*] He put his eyes back?

[*Silence.*]

HIRAM: I—I wanted to tell you, Rissa—I wanted to tell you and ask you to believe me that I had nothing to do with this. I—some things do seem to be out of the power of my hands after all… Other men's rules are a part of my life…

RISSA: [*For the first time looking up at him*] Why? Ain't you Marster? How can a man be marster of some men and not at all of others—

HIRAM: [*The question penetrates too deeply and he looks at her with sudden harshness*] You go too far—

RISSA: [*With her own deadly precision*] Oh—? What will you have done to me? Will your overseer gouge out my eyes too? [*Shrugging*] I don't 'spect blindness would matter to me. I done seen all there was worth seein' in this world—and it didn't 'mount to much. [*Turning from him abruptly*] I think this talkin' disturb my boy.

[HIRAM *looks at the face which will not turn to him or comfort him in any way and slowly rises. He starts out and we follow him into the darkness several feet, a dejected, defeated figure, which suddenly collapses. He cries out for help and one by one the lights of the cabins go out and doors close. He crawls a little on the grass, trying to get back to* RISSA's *cabin. Inside, we see her at the table again, preparing another cloth for* HANNIBAL. *She lifts her eyes and looks out the window to see the figure of the man she can distinctly hear crying for help. She lowers her lids without expression and wrings the cloth and returns to* HANNIBAL's *bedside and places it over his eyes and sits back in her chair with her hands folded in her lap. We come down on her face as she starts to rock back and forth as* HIRAM's *cries completely cease.*]

FADE OUT.

---

[3] [*Author's note.*] Perhaps "Lord, How Come Me Here?," "Motherless Child," "I'm Gonna Tell God All of My Troubles."

FADE IN: EXTERIOR. THE VERANDA—EVENING.

MARIA *sits, dressed completely in black, not moving and not looking where she stares.* EVERETT *comes up the steps; he wears a Confederate Officer's uniform and a mourning band.*

EVERETT: Mother… [*His manner with her is that of someone seeking very hard to distract another from grief.*] What would you think if I got the carriage and took you for a nice long ride in the cool, out near the pines—?

MARIA: No, thank you, son.

EVERETT: Oh do—it would be so refreshing and cooling for you, and tomorrow I think you should treat yourself to a nice social call on the Robleys—

MARIA: [*Pulling her shawl about her a bit*] Thank you, Everett, but I find it chilly right here tonight. And your father never cared for the Robleys. [*He starts to argue a little, but looks at her and changes his mind and relaxes back in his chair and lets his eyes scan the darkness in front of him, where his plantation lies stretched out, as a gentle hymn rises up from the quarters, the same one as in the introduction— "Steal Away to Jesus."*]

EVERETT: Yes—you're right. Let's just sit here in the peace and the quiet. The singing is pretty tonight, isn't it?

MARIA : [*Looking dead ahead*] Peaceful? Do you really find it peaceful here, Everett?

EVERETT: Sure it is, Mother. [*Enthusiastically*] Things are going to go well now. Zeb is beginning to understand how I want this place run; the crops are coming along as well as can be expected, and the slaves have settled down nicely into the new routine of the schedule. Everything is very orderly and disciplined. [*Touching her hand gently*] Above all, there is nothing for you to worry about. This thing will be all over soon and I'll be home before you know it and everything will be back to normal. Only better, Mama, only better…

[*The camera starts to pan away from them and moves down the veranda in through the front door, into the foyer and across to the darkened dining room, where it discovers, at low angles which do not show her face,* RISSA's *figure in the darkness standing before the gun cabinet, which she opens with the key which hangs at her waist. She removes the gun with stealth and closes the cabinet carefully and turns as we follow her skirts and rapidly moving bare feet across the dining room into the dark kitchen and out the back way. Waiting in the darkness outside is the boy,* JOSHUA. *Still unseen above her waist she takes him by the hand and they go at a half-run toward and into the woods. We stay with them until they come to* HANNIBAL's *clearing where* SARAH *stands, poised for traveling, and trembling mightily. Just beyond her is the figure of a man, seated, waiting patiently—he blind* HANNIBAL. RISSA *locks the other woman's hand about the child's, thrusts the gun into* SARAH's *other hand, and moves with them to* HANNIBAL, *who rises. There is a swift embrace and the woman and the child and the blind man turn and disappear into the woods.* RISSA *watches after them and the singing of "The Drinking Gourd" goes on as we pan away from her to the quarters where the narrator last left us. Only now, his musket leans against the fireplace. Once again the slaves are gone. He walks into the scene with his coat on now—buttoning it with an air of decided preparation. He looks at us as he completes the attire of a private of the Grand Army of the Republic.*]

SOLDIER: Slavery is beginning to cost this nation a lot. It has become a drag on the great industrial nation we are determined to become; it lags a full century behind the great American notion of one strong federal union which our eighteenth-century founders knew was the only way we could eventually become one of the powerful nations of this world. And, now, in the nineteenth century, we are determined to hold on to that dream. [*Sucking in his breath with simple determination and matter-of-factness*] And so—[*Distinct military treatment of "Battle Cry of Freedom" of the period begins under.*]—we must fight. There is no alternative. It is possible that slavery might destroy itself—but it is more possible that it would destroy these United States first. That it would cost us our political and economic future. [*He puts on his cap and picks up his rifle*] It has already cost us, as a nation, too much of our soul.

FADE OUT

THE END

—1960

ROSARIO MORALES (1930-)

Rosario Morales was born in the Bronx to a family that was originally from Naranjito, Puerto Rico. Morales, a socialist and anti-war activist, identified strongly with the Puerto Rican nationalist movement. She married Richard Levins in 1950, and together they moved to Puerto Rico, where Morales farmed and taught. In 1954, Morales gave birth to her daughter, Aurora Levins Morales, in Indiera. The family then returned to the U.S., where she gave birth to two sons. Between university jobs, Morales continued to write poetry and prose. In 1986 she co-authored *Getting Home Alive,* a collection of poetry and prose exploring the lives of two Puerto Rican women, with her daughter.

Ending Poem
(with Aurora Levins Morales)

I am what I am.
A child of the Americas.
A light-skinned mestiza[1] of the Caribbean.
A child of many diaspora, born into this continent at a crossroads.
I am Puerto Rican. I am U.S. American.   5
I am New York Manhattan and the Bronx.
A mountain-born, country-bred, homegrown jíbara[2] child,
up from the shtetl,[3] a California Puerto Rican Jew
A product of the New York ghettos I have never known.
I am an immigrant   10
and the daughter and granddaughter of immigrants.
We didn't know our forbears' names with a certainty.
They aren't written anywhere.
First names only or mija,[4] negra,[5] ne, honey, sugar, dear

I come from the dirt where the cane was grown.   15
My people didn't go to dinner parties. They weren't invited.
I am caribeña, island grown.

---

[1] (Sp.) A woman of mixed racial ancestry (especially mixed European and Native American ancestry).
[2] (Sp.) Someone from the countryside in Puerto Rico.
[3] (Yid.) Jewish villages in Eastern Europe before the Holocaust.
[4] (Sp.) My daughter (short for *mi hija*).
[5] (Sp.) Black girl.

Spanish is in my flesh, ripples from my tongue, lodges in my hips,
the language of garlic and mangoes.
Boricua.[6] *As Boricuas come from the isle of Manhattan.*   20
I am of latinoamerica, rooted in the history of my continent.
I speak from that body. Just brown and pink and full of drums inside.

I am not African.
Africa waters the roots of my tree, but I cannot return.

I am not Taína.   25
I am a late leaf of that ancient tree,
and my roots reach into the soil of two Americas.
Taíno is in me, but there is no way back.

I am not European, though I have dreamt of those cities.
Each plate is different.   30
wood, clay, papier mâché, metals basketry, a leaf, a coconut shell.
Europe lives in me but I have no home there.

The table has a cloth woven by one, dyed by another,
embroidered by another still.
I am a child of many mothers.   35
They have kept it all going
All the civilizations erected on their backs.
All the dinner parties given with their labor.

We are new.
They gave us life, kept us going,   40
brought us to where we are.
Born at a crossroads.
Come, lay that dishcloth down. Eat, dear, eat.
History made us.
We will not eat ourselves up inside anymore.   45

And we are whole.

—1986

I Am the Reasonable One

   I am the reasonable one. I am the one you can say your spite to, the one you can ask the venomous questions. It's so hard to say your contempt of these loud, dirty, emotional people if you're white, rational, and liberal. Your self-expression is so limited by your self-repression, and what can you do with your bile?

   I am the reasonable one and, best of all, I am your friend. We have sat together, talked together, given and received support, touched hands, touched cheeks. You know me to be kind, to be thoughtful.

   You know me to be reasonable, to be rational. You know me to be almost white, almost middle class, almost acceptable. You can count on me, hopefully, to answer quietly, reasonably, and if I don't, you can say, "Don't take it personally." You can ask,

---

[6] Alternate name for Puerto Rican people.

"You're not angry with me?" You can trust me, nearly, to answer "No."

I am the one Puerto Rican you can ask, "Why don't they learn English?" And what I answer is full of love and understanding of all those people, your ancestors included, who were forced by the acculturated jingoist migrants of a previous generation to abandon their languages—yiddish, irish, chinese, japanese, tagalog, spanish, french, russian, polish, italian, german—to give birth to your acculturated jingoist selves.

I am the one who hears it all. You can speak freely about "them," about the lower classes, about puertoricans, about blacks, about chinese. When you lower your voice to ask about them, to talk about them, you don't lower it to exclude me. You know you can tell me.

I am the one you can say "people like us" to, meaning white middle class women who are fine, who are right, whose ways are the only ways, whose life is the only life.

And if I say, "not me"—oh, and I do say, "not me"—you do not need to listen. Surely! You can pooh-pooh my stubborn clinging to being different. You know me better than I know myself. You know I am white like you, english-speaking like you, right-thinking like you, middle-class-living like you, no matter what I say.

And through this all, I have ever been the reasonable one, never wanting to betray myself, to become before your eyes just exactly what you despise: a loud and angry spik, cockroaches creeping out of my ears, spitty spanish curses spilling out of my wet lips, angry crazy eyes shooting hate at you. All victims of all racist outrages look like that in your eyes, like your own evil personified, the evil you participate in, condone, or allow.

But now I tell you reasonably, for the last time, reasonably, that I am through. That I am not reasonable anymore, that I was always angry, that I am angry now.

That I am puertorican. That under all that crisp english and extensive american vocabulary, I always say *mielda*.[7] I say *ai mami, ai mami*[8] giving birth. That I am not like you in a million ways that I have kept from you but that I will no more.

That I am working class and always eat at the only table, the kitchen table. That taking things is not always stealing; it's sometimes getting your own back, and walking around in my underwear is being at home.

And I am angry. I will shout at you if you ask your venomous questions now, I will call you racist pig, I will refuse your friendship.

I will be loud and vulgar and angry and me. So change your ways or shut your racist mouths. Use your liberal rationality to unlearn your contempt for me and my people, or shut your racist mouths.

I am not going to eat myself up inside anymore. I am not going to eat myself up inside anymore. I am not going to eat myself up inside anymore.

I am going to eat you.

—1986

---

[7] Puerto Rican pronunciation of the Spanish *mierda*, meaning "shit."

[8] Colloquial expression for pleasure or pain.

TONI MORRISON (1931-)

Chloe Anthony Wofford was born in Lorain, Ohio, to a working-class family. She received a B.A. from Howard University in 1953, and an M.A. from Cornell University in 1955 (she changed her name to "Toni" while at Howard). After a brief stint in Texas, she returned to Howard to teach. She was married to Harold Morrison from 1958 to 1964; the couple had two children. Morrison worked as a textbook editor in Ohio and then as a senior editor at Random House in New York City, where she edited books by such important African-American women writers as Toni Cade Bambara, Angela Davis, and Gayl Jones. Her first novel, *The Bluest Eye* (1970), was part of the explosion of Black women's literary work in 1970. Her other novels are *Sula* (1973); *Song of Solomon* (1977); *Tar Baby* (1981); the widely acclaimed *Beloved* (1987), which won the Pulitzer Prize for fiction in 1988 (when the novel did not win the National Book Award, other writers protested); *Jazz* (1992); *Paradise* (1998); and *Love* (2003). Later adapted for film, *Beloved* is loosely based on the true story of a fugitive slave mother who murdered her child rather than see her returned to slavery, a story Morrison returns to in her libretto for the opera *Margaret Garner*.

In 1993, Morrison won the Nobel Prize for Literature, the first Black woman to do so. Her other writings include a collection of lectures, *Playing in the Dark: Whiteness and the Literary Imagination* (1992); a series of books for children; and essays about American racial politics, including an early article on Black feminism in 1970 and a controversial 1998 essay in which she refers to then-President Bill Clinton as "the first Black president." Morrison held a named chair at Princeton University from 1989 to 2006.

Margaret Garner

CAST OF CHARACTERS
PRINCIPAL ROLES

MARGARET GARNER* (Mezzo-Soprano): *a slave in her mid-20s,* ROBERT'*s wife.*

ROBERT GARNER* (Lyric Baritone): *a slave in her mid-30s,* MARGARET'*s wife.*

CILLA* (Dramatic-Soprano): *a slave about 50 years old,* ROBERT'*s mother.*

EDWARD GAINES (Lyric Baritone): *the handsome and charismatic Master of Maplewood Plantation, in his late 30s or early 40s.*

SECONDARY ROLES

CASEY (Dramtic Tenor): *the Foreman of Maplewood Plantation.*

CAROLINE GAINES (Light-Lyric Soprano): *the daughter of* EDWARD GAINES, *engaged to* GEORGE HANCOCK.

GEORGE HANCOCK (Tenor): *engaged to* CAROLINE GAINES

AUCTIONEER (Lyric Tenor): *a Professional Salesman* [doubles as JUDGE I]

16 SLAVE CATCHERS** (8 T; 8-Bar *divisi:* lyric and Verdi baritones)

A FOREMAN/THE HANGMAN (non-singing role)

3 JUDGES* (T, Bar, B): [JUDGE I doubles as AUCTIONEER]

2 MILITIA OFFICERS (non-singing roles)

MARGARET'S 2 CHILDREN* (non-singing roles): *a 5-year-old-girl and a 2-year-old boy.*

THE TOWNSPEOPLE/THE GUESTS (SATB: min. 36 voices): *aka* "WHITE CHORUS"

THE SLAVES* (SATB: min. 36 voices): *aka* "BLACK CHORUS"

*Although much latitude is possible in casting, these roles must be sung by Black performers.

**These roles can be sung by members of the WHITE CHORUS.

Act I
Prologue: Kentucky, April 1856.

The opera begins in total darkness, without any sense of location or time period. Out of the blackness, a large group of slaves gradually becomes visible. They are huddled together on an elevated platform in the center of the stage.

CHORUS: **"No More!"**

THE SLAVES: [SLAVE CHORUS, CILLA, *and* ROBERT]
No, no more.
No more, not more.
Please, God, no more.
No, not more.
Dear God, no more!
[*confidently, with a sense of defiance*]
No, no! No more!
No, no! No more!
MARGARET: Ankles circled with a chain…
SLAVE CHORUS: …No, no. No, no more!
No, no more!
[*tenors and basses*] Please, God, no more!
MARGARET: Skin broken by a cane…
SLAVE CHORUS: …No, no! No more!
No, no. No more!
MARGARET: Bloody pillows…
SLAVE CHORUS: …No, no. No, no more!
No, no, no!
[*basses*] Please God, no more!
MARGARET: Under my head…
SLAVE CHORUS: …No, no, no more!
No, no more.
No, no, no!
[*basses*] Dear God, no more!
MARGARET: Wishing, praying…
SLAVE CHORUS: …No, no!
No, no more!…

[*basses*] Dear God, no more!
MARGARET: …I was dead.
THE SLAVES: [SLAVE CHORUS, CILLA, *and* ROBERT]
No, no. No, no more!
No, no. No more! No, no, no!
Dear God please, no more!
SLAVE CHORUS [*without* CILLA and ROBERT]: Dear God,
No more, not more.
Please, no more.
MARGARET: Bloody pillows under my head;
Wishing, praying I was dead.
THE SLAVES: [SLAVE CHORUS, CILLA, *and* ROBERT] Please God, no more.
MARGARET: Master's brand is following me;
Rope can swing from any old tree.
THE SLAVES: [SLAVE CHORUS, CILLA, *and* ROBERT] Please God, no more.
[*pleading*]
Please God, no more.
Please God, no more.
No more!

Act I
Scene 1

The lights go up, and illuminate the entire stage. The "elevated platform" on which the slaves stood at the beginning of the opera is revealed now to be a trading block situated in the middle of the busy town square at Richwood Station in northern Kentucky. It is April 1856. In preparation for a slave auction, members of slave families are being separated from one another, and grouped according to gender and age.

The local townspeople are gathering eagerly for the auction. They exhibit a small-town mentality: familiar with everyone else's daily life and business, they love to gossip and at times can be judgmental of others. Also in the crowd of onlookers is a handsome, ostensibly genteel man named Edward Gaines, accompanied by his daughter Caroline.

AUCTIONEER: [*freely chanted*]
  By the powers invested
  And by customs ingested
  I hereby declare and allow:

  The sale of all goods
  And cattle and woodland,
  Slaves and planting fields
  Dark with loam.

  I hereby declare and allow
  An old estate rich in history
  Is now on the market
  For a gentleman's pocket;
  A prize in the whole county.

  Your shrewd eyes will light up
  Dollar for dollar,
  Pound for pound,
  The bestest value for miles around.
[*A foreman approaches the slaves. He cracks a bullwhip, and the slaves immediately assume different positions for inspection: they bare their teeth, expose their backs, stretch out their necks, etc.*]
THE TOWNSPEOPLE [*White Chorus*]:
  How much? How much?
  For picknies and mammies and breeders and bucks?
  How much? How much?
  What say? What say?
  For milking and plowing
  And spinning and canning and such.
  O, what a problem to decide.
  O, what a burden on our shoulders:
  For those who have nothing,
  Are nothing, do nothing
  Except for we who clothe them and feed them
  And let them sleep when they are ill.

  We teach them all they will
  ever know,
  All they will ever know
  Of God and work and home!
AUCTIONEER:
  By the powers invested
  And by customs ingested,
  I hereby declare and allow
  This sale to be now open!
TOWNSPEOPLE: What say? What say?
  For milking and plowing
  And spinning and canning and such.
  How much? How much?
  For picknies and mammies and breeders and bucks,
  Who know nothing of God and home!
AUCTIONEER [*bringing forth the first slave for sale*]:
  Now this here is Cilla.
  About fifty, she thinks.
  A cook, a child nurse, laundress and seamstress.
  This bid begins at two hundred dollars.
  Do I hear two forty, two forty, two forty, two forty?
[*A customer raises his hand, thereby upping the bid.*]
TOWNSPEOPLE: [*emphatically*] Two forty!
AUCTIONEER: Yes!
  Two hundred forty.
  Do I hear
  Three hundred, three hundred, three hundred?
  I need three hundred dollars.
TOWNSPEOPLE: [*enthusiastically*]
  Three hundred!
AUCTIONEER: Yes!
  Three hundred dollars.
  Do I hear
  Four hundred, four hundred,
  Four hundred, four hundred dollars…
TOWNSPEOPLE: [*excitedly*]…Four
  hundred, four hundred,

four hundred, four hundred,
four hundred!

EDWARD GAINES: [*impatient, forcefully*]
Hold on! Hold on!
I'm telling you to hold on!

TOWNSPEOPLE: [*startled, a little nervously*]
Who is it? What is it?
Who is it? What is it?

AUCTIONEER: [*polite, but annoyed*]
Excuse me, sir.
Legal business is in progress here.

By the powers invested,
And by customs ingested...

EDWARD: [*interrupting the* AUCTIONEER]
...I beg your pardon!

This farm belonged to my brother.
It can't be sold to another.

AUCTIONEER: It is true.
If a family member calls the claim,
No sale can take place here and now.

EDWARD: I am a Gaines.
Edward Gaines, brother of the
deceased. [*incredulously*] Don't you
remember me?

TOWNSPEOPLE: [*their curiosity aroused*]
Edward Gaines? Who is he?
Did old Gaines have a brother?
Who is he? Edward Gaines?

EDWARD: I was born among you
And now I've returned.
Doesn't anyone remember me?

TOWNSPEOPLE: No. No. No.
Was it a long time ago?

EDWARD: You thought I was lost, didn't
you,
In a rough life of the game.
You were wrong.
(Well, no, you weren't...)
Well, yes, you were!

ARIA: *"I Was Just a Boy"*

EDWARD: I was just a boy
When any of you last saw me.
But I've been happily married
With a daughter we both adored.

Now, I'm a widower, a man of means,
A father with a child to raise.

What my brother owned
I have right of first offer to buy.
Which I do now, friends.
Which I do now.

AUCTIONEER: It is true.
It is the law.

TOWNSPEOPLE: It is true. It is true.
It is true, it is the law.

AUCTIONEER: We must entertain his
right under the law.

TOWNSPEOPLE: Under the law.
Under the law.

AUCTIONEER: What is your pleasure,
Mister Gaines, Sir? [*solicitously*] What
parts interest you?

EDWARD: I want it all.
I'll have it all.
Every box of china tea belongs to me.
Every body, every broom,
Every mule, and every loom.
[*pointing at the slaves*] Keep all the
goods and property together. I'll have it
all.

[*The* AUCTIONEER *and* EDWARD *shake
hands after agreeing on terms for the sale of
Maplewood Plantation. As Edward examines
the legal paperwork, the townspeople begin to
disperse. Several prominent businessmen remain
to witness the transaction, as does* Edward's
daughter Caroline, *who will inherit
Maplewood one day.*]

✦ ✦ ✦

*The slave families, now allowed to stay together
thanks to Edward's generosity, celebrate in
dance and song.*

CHORUS: *"A Little More Time"*

SLAVE CHORUS, CILLA, MARGARET *and*
ROBERT [*clapping as they sing*]:
A little more time
A little more time
More time with the children we
love...

[*Tenors*] ...Time with our brothers.

[*All*] We feel the mercy of our Lord God
   With the grace of a little more time.
CILLA *and* MARGARET: Another season of friendship
   Telling stories, sharing secrets by the fire.
SLAVE CHORUS: We feel the mercy of our Lord God
   With the grace of a little more time.
MARGARET: More nights to curl like a vine
   In our husband's arms.
ROBERT: More days to bask in the light
   Of our lover's eyes.
CILLA *and* MARGARET:
   Our father's graves
   We can still attend with
   Sweet William and Columbine.
SLAVE CHORUS:
   Sweet William and Columbine.
SLAVE CHORUS, CILLA, *and* ROBERT:
   Little more time
   A little more time
   More time with the children we love…

[*Altos*] …Time with our mothers.

[*All*] We feel the mercy of our Lord God
   With the grace of a little more time.
[GAINES *nods in assent to the contract's terms, then turns to the businessman standing next to him and asks for a pen with which to sign the contract.*]

   ARIOSO: *"I Made a Little Play Doll"*

MARGARET: [*tenderly*] I made a little play doll for my baby,
   With button eyes and hair of yarn;
   The lips are made of rose-colored thread.
[*Distracted,* EDWARD *looks up from his paperwork; he turns around and notices* MARGARET, *who is wearing a red scarf. He is captivated, and grateful for his good fortune to have just purchased her.*]
   One day she will love it;
   I am waiting for her to love it

[EDWARD *turns around again, and finishes signing the contract. The businessmen extend handshakes of congratulations to him on the acquisition of Maplewood.*]
   When she is old enough to hold it.
[*When one of the slaves brings in* MARGARET'*s infant daughter, wrapped in a white cloth,* MARGARET *puts the play doll in her pocket in order to cradle the baby tenderly in her arms.*]
   I'm watching this mystery called child.
SLAVE CHORUS, CILLA, *and* ROBERT:
   A little more time
   A little more time
   More time with the children we love…

[*Altos*] …Time with our mothers.
SLAVE CHORUS, CILLA, *and* ROBERT:
   We feel the breath of our Lord God
   With the gift of a little more time.
SLAVE CHORUS: We feel the breath of our Lord God.
CILLA, MARGARET, *and* ROBERT:
   We feel the breath of our Lord God.
SLAVE CHORUS: With the gift of a little more time.
[*The slaves exit slowly;* MARGARET *is the last of the slaves to leave. Having completed the legal transaction with* EDWARD, *the* AUCTIONEER *departs with the businessmen.* CAROLINE *remains, however, cheerfully conversing with their wives.*]

✦ ✦ ✦

[EDWARD *watches the last townspeople leave.*]
EDWARD [*disappointed, somewhat disgusted*]:
   Look at them.
   They were my neighbors once.
   They pretend they don't remember me.
CASEY: It was a long time ago, sir.
   You've been away for twenty years…
EDWARD [*turning back around, facing* CASEY]: …Twenty years. [*to himself*]
   They pretend.
   They lie, and they say they don't remember me.

[*Margaret's scarf, still lying on the ground, catches* EDWARD's *attention; he starts walking over towards it.*]

CASEY [*looking in the opposite direction from* GAINES]: Something in the past, sir?

Something best forgotten?

[EDWARD *picks up* MARGARET's *scarf, and mindlessly puts it in his pocket.*]

EDWARD: I was just a boy.

The trouble I caused was inescapable
For a boy with an appetite.

CASEY: But every boy has an appetite, sir.

EDWARD: I left under a cloud of suspicion.

It was nothing, nothing to raise eye brows.

The girl was so young,
And from such a fine family;
Things got a little out of hand. [*sotto voce*]

So now they pretend
Neither I nor it ever happened.

What a shame.
I remember!
I remember everything.

ARIA: *"I Remember"*

EDWARD [*wistful, yet still optimistic*]:
I remember the curve of every hill
The swans in the pond;
I remember them still.
I remember every tree:
Maple, Birch, Willows and Pine.

I can see them now
Shading the drive,
Shelt'ring me from the heat.
Maple, Birch and the odor of Pine.

I remember every tree
But none of them remembers me.

The well, the creek,

Fishing by the lake.
Evening of laughter
With girls who wanted to play.

I remember every tree
But none of them remembers me.

[EDWARD *catches* CAROLINE's *glance, and motions for her to join him.*]

EDWARD [*sotto voce*]: They won't forget me again!

[EDWARD *exits, with* CAROLINE *at his side.* CASEY *follows them.*]

Act I
Scene 2
Harvest time, about six months later.

The slaves—some of whom are children, barely 10 or 12 years old—return to their quarters after a day of working in the fields. In time with the percussion's strong, syncopated beat, they perform a series of domestic chores: chopping wood, pumping water, beating rags, etc.

CHORUS: *"O Mother,*
O Father, Don't Abandon Me!"

ROBERT: Turn my face to the dying sun
SLAVE CHORUS: Turn my face to the dying sun
ROBERT: Can't straighten my back
Til the work is done.
SLAVE CHORUS: Can't straighten my back
Til the work is done.
ROBERT: Plowed the field, baled the hay
SLAVE CHORUS: Plowed the field, baled the hay
ROBERT: Going to dance
On the lead mule's back someday.
SLAVE CHORUS: Going to dance
On the lead mule's back someday.
ALL: *O Mother, O Father*
Don't abandon me
While my sweat still sweets the rich brown soil
Of dear old Kentucky.

O Mother, O Father
Don't abandon me.

MARGARET: Boss is happy at his plate
SLAVE CHORUS: Long as he gets his fowl;

MARGARET: If I stand at his cooking stove,

SLAVE CHORUS: His supper will be foul!

MARGARET *and* ROBERT [*shouted like gospel singers*]: Believe it!

ALL: *O Mother, O Father*
Don't abandon me
While my blood floods the velvet dirt
Of dear old Kentucky.

O Mother, O Father
Don't abandon me
While my sweat still sweets the rich brown soil
Of dear old Kentucky.

Crack uh back

Crack uh cane

Pull uh mule

Chop uh cotton

Split uh wood

Crack uh back

Cut uh Cane

Pull uh mule

Chop uh cotton

Split uh wood

Crack, cut,
Pull, chop, split;

Crack, cut,
Pull, chop, split;

Crack, cut,
Pull, chop, split!

FEMALE CHORISTERS:

[*Soprano soloist*] Boss is happy in his bed
[*All*] Long as his pillow's downey;
[*Soprano soloist*] If I stood by his sleepy head
[*All*] His face would be as fluffy.

MALE CHORISTERS [*like gospel singers*]: Tell it to me!

ROBERT: Plowed the field, baled the hay

CHORUS: Plowed the field, baled the hay

ROBERT: Going to dance
On the lead mule's back someday.

SLAVE CHORUS: Going to dance
On the lead mule's back someday.

ALL: *O Mother, O Father*
Don't abandon me
While my tears muddy the rich brown soil
Of dear old Kentucky.

MARGARET *and* ROBERT [*shouted like gospel singers*]: Sing it to me!

ALL: *O Mother, O Father*
Don't abandon me
While my blood floods the velvet dirt
Of dear old Kentucky. [*sarcastically*]

Crack uh back

Cut uh cane

Pull uh mule

Chop uh cotton

Split uh wood

Crack uh back

Cut uh cane

Pull uh mule

Chop uh cotton

Split uh wood

Crack, cut,
Pull, chop, split;

Crack, cut,
Pull, chop, split;

Crack, cut,
Pull, chop, split!

[*Upon hearing the bell that signals the day's end, the workers wash up for supper. Cilla is waiting at Margaret and Robert's cabin to welcome them home.*]

CILLA: You left the light behind you.
Did you have a worrisome day?

[CILLA, ROBERT, *and* MARGARET *go inside the cabin, and begin preparing dinner.*]

ROBERT: Every new day is like yesterday.

Work the crops,
Forget about pay.

End each day
Like the one before.
Don't leave the field
Til the light's too poor.

CILLA: This Gaines is not like the last
one.
A mean streak rides his brow.
The other one had a heart—sometimes! [*jokingly*]

MARGARET: No such thing as a boss's
heart.
He can't waste the space.

ROBERT If he could harvest corn in his
chest,

ROBERT *and* MARGARET [*laughing
heartily*]: He would lease out his own
heart's place!

[CILLA *beckons for* ROBERT *and*
MARGARET *to sit down at the dinner table.*]

CILLA: Ease yourselves, ease yourselves.
The table is laid.
The supper is plain but warm.

MARGARET: ...You've got milk and
strawberries too.

[*All three sit down to dinner.*]

"Cilla's Prayer"

CILLA: Dear Lord in heaven,

MARGARET *and* ROBERT:[*interjecting, like
a Responsorial*] [Blessed Lord...]

CILLA: Make us grateful for our food.

MARGARET *and* ROBERT: [Sweet
Jesus...]

CILLA: Keep us well and in your sight.

MARGARET *and* ROBERT: [mmm...]

CILLA: Protect those in danger,

MARGARET *and* ROBERT: [Take my
hand...]

CILLA: And let us be guided by your
heavenly light.

MARGARET *and* ROBERT: [Precious
Lord...mmm]

CILLA: Amen.

+ + +

ROBERT [*exuberantly*]: You are a harvest
time blessing, mama.

MARGARET [*to Cilla*]: How's my baby?
Not crying for me?
How's my sweetness?
Not missing me?

CILLA: She's sleeping, Margaret,
sleeping.
Not a frown on her sugar butter face.

ROBERT [*laughing*]: Did you ever see a
mother like that?
The child supposed to need the
mother;
Now here the mother needs the child
more.

MARGARET: I need to smell her breath.

CILLA: The baby needs her rest.

MARGARET: I need to see her eyes, her
smile.

CILLA [*emphatically, as a warning*]: It's
dangerous, daughter,
To love too much.
The Lord giveth
And the Lord taketh away.
Come to your supper before you
wake her.

MARGARET: She is my supper,
The food of my heart.

ROBERT: And what am I?
The leavings?

MARGARET [*smiling, reaching out to* ROBERT]:
Oh no. Oh no.
You are the pulse.
Without you I have no heart.

ROBERT: And without you I have no
pulse to give.

[*They embrace.*]

CILLA [*interrupting*]: Enough said.
Go get your heart
Before you break mine.

[MARGARET *goes to get the baby. As* CILLA
and ROBERT *eat dinner,* MARGARET *sings
tenderly to the child.*]

"Margaret's Lullaby"

MARGARET: Sad things, far away
   Soft things, come and play

Lovely baby…

Sleep in the meadow,
Sleep in the hay
Baby's got a dreamin' on the way.

Bad things, far away
Pretty things, here to stay

Sweet baby, smile at me
Lovely baby, go to sleep.

Sleep in the meadow,
Sleep in the hay
Baby's gonna dream the night away.
Lovely baby, pretty baby
Baby's gonna dream the night away.
[CASEY *approaches the cabin, armed with a double-barreled shotgun and carrying a satchel. He loiters for a few minutes, passing the time by cleaning his gun.*]
Sleep in the meadow,
Sleep in the hay
Baby's gonna dream…
Baby's gonna dream… [*softer*]
Baby's gonna dream… [*softer still*]
CASEY [*quietly, standing in the doorway*]:
   Not tonight.
   Nobody dreams tonight.
ROBERT: What d'you say?
   What's that *you* say?
[CASEY *enters the cabin abruptly, and confronts* ROBERT.]
CASEY [*sarcastically*]: What's that I say?
   What's that you say?
[CASEY *points his gun at* ROBERT.]
ROBERT: Excuse me, sir.
   Yes, sir.
   What's that you say, sir?
CASEY: Better. Much better.
   What I say is
   No happy darky dreamin' t'night.
   Mister Gaines has other plans…other plans.

CILLA: What plans, Mister Casey?
CASEY: I'm talkin' to your boy, Cilla.
   Not you.
CASEY [*to* ROBERT]:
   You have been rented out, boy.
   Mister Gaines wants you on your way t'night
   [*aggressively*] So you'll be ready for work at sunrise.
ROBERT: Where, sir?
   Where is he sending me?
CASEY: Not your business to know.
   Only your business to go.
[*pointing to the door*]
   The wagon is on the road.
   Hop to it, boy!
MARGARET: I'll get ready.
   Hold the baby, Mama.
CASEY: Hold on, girl.

   You'll get ready all right.
   But you won't need the wagon.

[*Quietly, with innuendo*]
   Mister Gaines wants you in the house,
   His house.

   Ain't that nice?
   No more field work.
   Ain't that nice?

   You can put your feet up
   In his house all day,
   All night, too.

   Ain't that nice?
   Ain't that nice?
[CASEY *pulls a stylish housedress out of his satchel. He waves the dress, like a red flag, in* ROBERT'*s face, then tosses it at* MARGARET.]
   Ain't that nice?
[CASEY *leaves.* ROBERT *and* MARGARET *exchange troubled glances;* CILLA *rocks the baby. As he walks away,* CASEY *sings a parody of* MARGARET'*s "Lullaby."*]
CASEY: La-da-da-da-da
   La-da-da-day
[*He laughs derisively.*]

ROBERT [*sotto voce; trying to contain his emotions*]: Skunk! Snake!

[*erupting in rage*]

Son of a whore!

[ROBERT *paces the room, his anger at the boiling point.*]

CILLA: Please! Don't wake the baby.

ROBERT: Yellowbelly!

That son of a dog!!

MARGARET: Cool down, Robert!

He will hear you.

ROBERT [*angrily*]: I am a man!

Ain't I?

Ain't I a man?

Ain't I?

Ain't I?

MARGARET: Yes!

You are to me.

And to us.

ROBERT [*almost stuttering in frustration*]: ...I know...I know...I know...

What is on his mind.

Bastard!

MARGARET [*lovingly*]: It won't happen.

It won't happen, believe me.

Believe me!

ROBERT: How can you know?

How can you be sure?

You can't control a snake in his own nest.

MARGARET: His daughter lives there too.

He will behave.

CILLA: Believe her, son.

It can't be for too long.

MARGARET: We will find a way.

Stay strong.

[*moving closer to* ROBERT]

He is not the master of me.

Standing downstage center, ROBERT *and* MARGARET *are holding hands. As they sing, they gradually move apart.*

DUET: *"Love is the Only Master"*

MARGARET: Hold me.

ROBERT: Hold on.

MARGARET: Stay, sweet.

ROBERT: Stay strong.

MARGARET: Be my moonrise.

ROBERT: Be my dawn.

MARGARET *and* ROBERT [*together*]: You are my shoulder.

ROBERT: You are my spine.

MARGARET *and* ROBERT [*together*]: You are my courage.

MARGARET: And you are the sign

MARGARET *and* ROBERT [*together*]: That love is the only master

The heart obeys;

Love is the only master

That *my* heart obeys.

[*Evening falls as* ROBERT *leaves.*]

FADE TO BLACK.

Act I

Scene 3

Maplewood Plantation,
in the early summer of 1858.

In the candlelit parlor at Maplewood Plantation, a wedding reception is being held to celebrate the marriage of Caroline Gaines, Edward's daughter, to George Hancock. The guests—the local townspeople whom Edward is very eager to impress—waltz to the accompaniment of a parlor piano, and enjoy generous amounts of freely flowing champagne.

EDWARD [*to the guests*]: Please, may I have your attention?

THE GUESTS: [*gathering around*]: Mister Gaines wants to speak.

Gather 'round our gracious host.

There is nothing so fine as seeing a couple in love!

ARIOSO

EDWARD: I promised Caroline's mother

Two things.

One, that I would stay

A widower;

Two, that I would see

To our daughter's future care.

Caroline has proven

The rightness of those promises.

She will inherit a sound estate—

Which, I might add,
Has grown from modest to grand.
And her choice of husband
Is everything
Her mother would have wished for…
THE GUESTS: …Beautiful words
From our generous host!
EDWARD: A man of stature and learning.
[*The pompous guests blatantly examine the room's furnishings to judge their quality.*]
[THE GUESTS]:
   [And her choice of husband
   Is everything her mother wished for.]
CAROLINE: And you, father? Is he
   what you have wished for me?
EDWARD: Exactly so, precisely so.
   Am I right, George?
GEORGE: I'm not sure
   That I deserve her,
   But I will spend my life
   Trying to serve her
   And earn the devotion
   She squanders on me.
THE GUESTS: There is nothing so wondrous
   As being in love.
   There is nothing so wondrous
   As seeing a marriage for love.
CAROLINE *and* GEORGE: There is nothing so wondrous
   As being in a marriage for love!
FEMALE GUESTS: A marriage for love…
MALE GUESTS: …A marriage for love.
EDWARD:
   Caroline, my adorable Caroline.
   Give your father
   A daughter's embrace.
[CAROLINE *walks across the room to her father, who is waiting with open arms. He embraces her too tightly, however.*]
CAROLINE [*lightheartedly*]: Oh, Father, I cannot breathe.
[CAROLINE *goes to mingle with the guests.*]
EDWARD [*warmly*]: Forgive me, Caroline;
[*Upon hearing her name,* CAROLINE *turns towards her father.*]
   My arms are like my love.

Strong and all-embracing.
CAROLINE [*reassuringly, taking her father's hands in hers*]: Never mind, Father.
   I have prospered
   So much in your arms,
   I can now embrace another.
[CAROLINE *suddenly lets go of her father's hands, and turns away from him to walk towards* GEORGE, *who is downstage, on the other side of the room.* GEORGE *embraces* CAROLINE *tenderly.*]
GEORGE [*sensing that Edward feels somewhat rejected*]: There is no rival here.
   Love does not conquer or dispose;
   It doubles and triples with use.
   The language of love is always confusing.
   It can never be as clear
   As the emotion it tries to convey.

   The language of love…
[EDWARD *puts up his hand to interrupt* GEORGE *in mid-sentence.*]
EDWARD: The language of love
   Is an imposter,
   Hiding in dresses of verse.
GEORGE [*emphatically*]:
   The language of love
   Is a magician,
   Turning roses into doves on the wing.
EDWARD: The language of love
   Is an infant's hand in a father's glove.
GEORGE: A raft in a stormy sea,
   Offering rescue.
THE GUESTS [*eagerly joining in the fray*]:
   The language of love
   Is often hard to explain.
   It may offer true joy,
   But it can end in such pain!
GEORGE: The language of love
   Is a lighthouse
   To guide us over heavy waves.
EDWARD: The language of love
   Is a thief respecting no household,
   Stealing the loved ones away.
THE GUESTS: The language of love
   Is too complex to be known.

What is bought without a price,
Can never be owned!
[EDWARD]: [The language of love
Is an imposter...]
[GEORGE]: [...Is a magician...]
[EDWARD]: [...Is an infant's hand in a
father's glove.]
[GEORGE]: [...Turning roses into doves
on the wing!]
[THE GUESTS]: [The language of love
Is a dangerous art.
It can open your eyes
Or it will tear out your heart!]
[*Embarrassed by the argument that has broken
out between her father and her new husband,*
CAROLINE *walks away. She goes over to the
side table and picks up a crystal champagne
glass.*]
EDWARD [*getting angry*]:
The language of love
Is an imposter.
GEORGE: Is a magician.
EDWARD: It's an infant's hand in a
father's glove...
GEORGE: ...It's a lighthouse to guide
us...
EDWARD [*definitively, ending the discussion*]:
...It's a thief respecting no household,
Stealing the loved ones away!
[CAROLINE *returns and makes a "grand
entrance," holding her champagne glass up
high.*]
CAROLINE [*in a celebratory mood*]:
It's a clipper ship
With room after room
For dancing
And cakes and tea and champagne!
[*The newlyweds* CAROLINE *and* GEORGE
*begin the traditional "first dance;" the others
join in the waltz one couple at a time. Ironically,
only* GAINES *is without a partner; he is forced
to watch the festivities.*]
[MARGARET *enters the room to bring in
another tray of glasses. Although she is dressed
more nicely now, in the uniform befitting a house
servant, she acts in a more subjugated manner.*
GAINES, *standing alone, quietly takes notice of
her arrival.*]
[*The guests gradually conclude dancing.*
GAINES *once again plays the gracious host; he
toasts the newlyweds as* MARGARET *serves the
guests.*]
EDWARD:
Well, that is our answer then.
Champagne heals all wounds
And puts all arguments to bed.
Congratulations, son.
Blessings, daughter.
[MARGARET *starts to leave the room.*]
CAROLINE [*warmly*]:
Margaret, wait a moment.
Come to me.
What do you think?
MARGARET [*somewhat surprised*]:
Excuse me, Ma'am?
CAROLINE: What do you think
About love?
We were discussing
The words to describe it.
EDWARD: Child!
Dear child!
CAROLINE [*to* MARGARET]:
Do they help us to love?
Or hurt us beyond repair?
[*to her father*]
I want to know—I *want* to know—
what she thinks.
EDWARD [*insistent*]: Child!
Please, child, no more!
THE GUESTS [*whispering*]:
What is all this talk about,
Talk about?
What is all this talk about?

Oh dear. Oh dear.
We thought he was quality.

Oh dear. Oh dear.
This is a mistake
Quality folk would never make!

Oh dear. Oh dear.
This is a profound insult.
This is a mistake
Quality folk would never make!

EDWARD: Caroline,
You are too willful.
She can't answer you.
She won't answer you.
CAROLINE: Why not?

ARIOSO

She has loved me
Served me, taught me
In these few years;
Watched over my sleep.
Who knows better than she
How to say what love is?

[Can words do it justice, Margaret?
Encourage its success?
Or, as my father says,
Is the language of love
An imposter?
A thief in the night?]
MARGARET: Begging you pardon, Miss
Caroline.
Mister Gaines is the expert here.
CAROLINE: ...His love is rough,
While yours is tender.
EDWARD [*emphatically*]:
You see?
She has nothing to say
On the matter.
Love is not in her vocabulary.
MARGARET [*thoughtfully*]:
Words of love are moths;
Easy food for flame.
Actions alone
Say what love may be.
EDWARD [*agitated, wild*]:
Enough! Enough!
[*angrily*]
We have all had enough of this non-
sense.
I refuse to hear a slave comment
On things outside her scope.
Our guests are right.
Her views are worthless.
[*to* MARGARET]
You are excused.
Leave us.
[MARGARET *exits.*]

CAROLINE: Father, you shame me.
She is as complete a human as you
are.
GEORGE: Since she is a mother,
Maybe more so.
[*The parlor clock strikes 10 o'clock. A few of
the guests realize that the late hour now gives
them an alibi to leave the party.*]
EDWARD [*to* CAROLINE]:
You disappoint me.
How could love exist in a slave?
Passion, perhaps.
But how would she know the
difference?
CAROLINE [*pleading with him to be reason-
able*]: There are many kinds of love,
father.
CAROLINE *and* GEORGE [*looking into each
other's eyes*]:
And many kinds of lovers.
THE GUESTS: This is too subtle for me.
...*and me, and you*...

Perhaps it is time to say goodnight.
...*good night, good night, and good night*...

Argument chills a party.
...*good night, good night, and good night*...

...Good night!
[*The guests leave, bowing stiffly; they disap-
prove of* GAINES's *behavior and act coolly
towards him. He is angered and annoyed by
their early departure.*]
EDWARD: Fools, idiots.
What do they know about "quality"
folk?
[*to* CAROLINE *and* GEORGE, *with regret*]
This was to be a proud moment.
Now you have given my neighbors
more reason to gossip and despise me.
CAROLINE: I am sorry, father,
If I upset you.
GEORGE: Don't think us ungrateful
For this celebration.
CAROLINE *and* GEORGE [*together*]:
We did not mean to be rude,
Only to say what we believe.

Honesty should not offend you.

EDWARD [*agitated*]:

I am not so weak

As to be offended by innocence.

But I have a reputation to maintain.

CAROLINE: Father, please try…

EDWARD: …My sweet Caroline,

It doesn't matter.

All is well.

Take care of yourselves. [*tenderly
kissing his daughter*] Goodbye. [*shaking
GEORGE's hand*] Take care.

[CAROLINE *and* GEORGE *leave, eager to
depart on their honeymoon.* GAINES *pauses,
and somewhat wistfully watches them walk
away.*]

EDWARD [*regaining his inner strength*]:

It doesn't matter at all.

I have succeeded

Just as I said I would.

Envy is the true price of wealth…

Which I easily, happily pay.

A rich man has many remedies.

[EDWARD *begins to leave, but when he notices*
MARGARET *returning to clear the champagne
glasses, he lingers in a hiding place.*]

[MARGARET *picks up a glass and holds it to
the light, peering into it as if it were a crystal
ball.*]

MARGARET [*looking at a glass*]:

Are there many kinds of love?

Show me each and every one.

You can't, can you?

For there is just one kind.

ARIA: *"A Quality Love"*

MARGARET: Only unharnessed hearts

Can survive a locked-down life.

Like a river rushing from the grip of

its banks,

As light escapes the coldest star;

A quality love—the love of all loves—

will break away.

When sorrow clouds the mind,

The spine grows strong;

No pretty words can soothe or cure

What heavy hands can break.

When sorrow is deep,

The secret soul keeps

Its weapon of choice: the love of all
loves.

No pretty words can ease or cure

What heavy hands can do.

When sorrow is deep,

The secret soul keeps its quality love.

When sorrow is deep,

The secret soul keeps

Its weapon of choice: the love of all
loves!

[EDWARD *slowly emerges from his hiding place
and walks towards* MARGARET, *looking her
over with unmistakable intent. She is momentarily unaware of his presence, however, as she
is looking down at the glass in her hand.*]

EDWARD [*coolly; unintentionally startling*
MARGARET]:

Such fine sentiments.

Too fine, I think

For a slave.

[*He gently takes the glass from her hand.
Assuming an air of gentility,* EDWARD *then
pulls Margaret's red scarf out of his pocket and
slowly ties it around her neck.*]

But I have my remedies.

A man has many remedies.

[MARGARET *resists his advances.*]

MARGARET [*agitated*]:

They can not touch

The secret soul.

EDWARD [*losing control*]:

…Your soul

Is not on my mind.

[MARGARET *begins to struggle vigorously. But*
EDWARD *overpowers her, and throws her
forcibly to the floor.*]

[*The curtain falls slowly.*]

END OF ACT ONE

Act II

Scene 1
Maplewood Plantation
Sunday, February 24, 1861,
in the early evening.

Anticipating a visit from ROBERT, *who has been meeting her secretly on Sunday nights,* MARGARET *goes to* CILLA's *cabin. She is disturbed to find* CASEY *lurking nearby.*

MARGARET: Has he come?

CILLA: Not yet.

MARGARET: Is he here?
  Has he come?

CILLA: Not yet.
  But soon.

[MARGARET *suddenly notices that* CILLA *is packing a carpetbag.*]

MARGARET [*unsettled*]:
  What are you doing?
  Where are the children?

CILLA [*with assurance*]:
  Robert is my son
  And his word is gold.
  Calm yourself.
  Your daughter is with Kate.
  So is the little one.

[MARGARET *begins to search the room for signs of the children. She becomes increasingly anxious when she realizes they are not there.*]

MARGARET [*agitated*]:
  Why are you folding their clothes?
  You're packing them away!
  What aren't you telling me?
  Has Casey been here?
  Is he taking them away?

CILLA: Margaret, you have changed so.
  Each time you visit I see less of you
  And more of a wet hen.
  Don't cut up so.
  The news is good.

MARGARET: What news?
  Please, Cilla.
  What is happening?

ARIOSO
CILLA: It's time, darling girl.

At last,
The time has come.
The plan is set.
That's why your husband is late.
He is making sure
That all is in place.
You're leaving tonight!

MARGARET: Sweet Jesus!

CILLA: Sweeter than syrup
  And right on time.

MARGARET:
  Sleep my babies in the meadow
  Sleep my babies in the hay;
  My babies got some dreamin' to do
  'Cause freedom's on the way.

MARGARET *and* CILLA [*together, with joyful exuberance*]:
  Sleep my babies in the meadow
  Sleep my babies in the hay;
  My babies got some dreamin' to do
  'Cause freedom's on the way.

[ROBERT *arrives, and immediately embraces* MARGARET.]

MARGARET [*feigning anger at* ROBERT] :
  You didn't say a word last Sunday.

ROBERT [*taking her seriously*]:
  I couldn't. I had to be sure.

MARGARET [*teasing*]:
  You ought to tell me
  What you're doing…sometimes!

ROBERT: You need to keep it quiet in here.

MARGARET: Alright.
  When do we leave?

ROBERT: Three hours from now.

MARGARET: O Lord,
  I am gonna cry.

ROBERT: You? Not you!
  My soldier girl's going to cry?

[ROBERT *tries to embrace* MARGARET, *but she pulls away, embarrassed to show her tears.*]
  It's alright.
  It's alright.

ARIETTA: *"Go Cry, Girl"*

ROBERT [*tenderly*]: Go cry, girl
  You have won your tears;

Go cry, girl
Obey your tender years.
The string is cut,
The tale is told.
I know.
Don't think I don't know.

The gate is open,
The way is clear;
The work is done
And the time has come,
I know.
Don't think I don't know.

Go cry, girl.
Girl, go cry.

[MARGARET *feels overwhelmed with love for* ROBERT. *Drawing closer, they kiss.*]

MARGARET [*recovering her composure, but still anxious*]: Where will we go?

ROBERT [*reassuringly*]: It's alright.

MARGARET: Are there others?

ROBERT: It's alright.

MARGARET: Do we have money?
Where will we hide?

ROBERT: It's alright.

ROBERT [*emphatically*]: I am in charge now.
Everything is ready—
[*teasing*] Except you.
Now you help Mama finish packing.
I'm going for the children.

[*He leaves.* CILLA *looks around the room one more time, to make sure that all of* ROBERT *and* MARGARET'*s belongings are packed.*]

CILLA [*locking the last bag*]:
All done.
I'm through.

MARGARET: Where are your things?
I don't see your things, Mama.

CILLA: Darling girl,
I am too old to tread new waters.
I am bound to stay here.

MARGARET: Mama!
You have to come with us.

CILLA: No, I don't.
You know I won't.

[*Briefly overcome by painful emotions,* CILLA *looks away from* MARGARET, *who is attempting to make direct eye contact with her mother-in-law.*]

ACCOMPANIED RECITATIVE

Seeing you,
My son and my grandchildren
Gone from this place,
Away from Satan's breath
Is my blessing.

Don't mourn me.
When my family is safe,
I will be only *near* the cross—
Not on it.

ARIA: *"He Is By"*

CILLA: He is by,
Forever by me.
In his shadow
I will linger on a while
'Til he calls me.

He is by,
Forever by me.
No trumpets or streets of gold.
He will come in silence
And gather me in his arms.

He is by,
Forever by me.
No trumpets or streets of gold.
He will come in silence
And gather me in his arms.

MARGARET: Please don't confine us
To the edge of your mind in shadow.
We don't want trumpets
Or streets of gold.
As we leave in silence,
Give us your arms.

CILLA *and* MARGARET [*together*]: Amen.

MARGARET: It'll break my heart
Knowing that you are still here.
We can't be free
Without you.
Robert will insist.

CILLA: Hush, child.

Hear me now:

Don't waste muscle where none is wanted.

You will need every bone and sinew
Plus your mind
To get away from here.
Follow your husband.
Save your children, Mother!

Rear up, now.
Help Robert with the children.
[*They hear footsteps approaching the cabin.*]
Here he comes.
[MARGARET *and* CILLA *are shocked when* CASEY, *not* ROBERT, *storms into the cabin.* CASEY *glances around the cabin, then picks up one of their carpetbags and throws it across the room.*]
CASEY: Planning a little trip?

Or just cleanin' out the sty?
ROBERT [*calling from outside*]:

The children are coming!

The children are…
[*Upon entering the cabin,* ROBERT *halts abruptly when he sees* CASEY.]
CASEY: Well, I'll be…

Look what crawled out of the woods.
Pappy bear.
Comin' to get Mammy bear
And all the little cubs?
[*to* CILLA]

I guess you must be Goldilocks.
Seems the porridge is all et up.
Let me see what I can offer you.
[*pulling a pistol out of his coat*]

Gunpowder might be a little dry
But Goldilocks got to eat,
Don't she?
[*Pointing the pistol at* CILLA'*s mouth,* CASEY *motions to* ROBERT *and* MARGARET *with his free hand.*]

Let's just line up over there.
[*Impulsively,* ROBERT *attacks* CASEY. *A violent struggle ensues, during which* ROBERT *manages to wrest away* CASEY'*s pistol. He grabs* CASEY *from behind, yet hesitates to shoot him.*]

CASEY: You kill me,

Both of us is dead.
Your family too.
ROBERT [*livid, filled with rage*]:

And if you live, will they?
MARGARET: Don't kill him.

He's already dead.
CASEY [*to* MARGARET]: You black slut!

Don't ya beg for me!
ROBERT [*wildly*]: Dog without teeth!

Remember hell?
Go home to it now!
[ROBERT *strangles* CASEY *to death.*]
CILLA: Lap of God, Robert.

What have you done?
ROBERT: Proved my worth

As a man and your son.
CILLA [*clasping her hands*]:

Forgive him, Father.
This may be the end.
MARGARET: No!

No, we can't change what is done.

Quick! Robert,
You have to run!
ROBERT: I can't leave you all here!
MARGARET: Tell me where to meet you.

Then go!
ROBERT [*agitated*]: The bottom…

By the Mimosa.
The grass is tall there.
When the moon hits
The top of the pines,
The wagon will be there.
CILLA: Hurry, son!

Make tracks, now!
We'll handle God's outcast.
[*She covers* CASEY'*s body.*]
ROBERT: Margaret.

Oh, my sweet, loving woman!
MARGARET: The bottom…

Tall grass…
Mimosa…
ROBERT: Be there when the moon-
light…
ROBERT *and* MARGARET [*together*] :

…touches pine.

ROBERT [*a bit more anxious*]:
 Listen for the...
ROBERT and MARGARET:
 ...Wagon wheels.
ROBERT: Watch for the...
ROBERT *and* MARGARET: ...Moonlight.
 We'll meet you in the moonlight.
[ROBERT *kisses her.*]
MARGARET: Go!
[ROBERT *runs away.*]
 [LIGHTS OUT.]

Act II
Scene 2
*In the Free State of Ohio,
three weeks later.*

*At twilight, on an evening in late March
1861. Three weeks have passed since
ROBERT and MARGARET successfully escaped
from Maplewood, and crossed the frozen Ohio
River on the Kentucky border to reach
Cincinnati, a city in the "Free State" of Ohio.*

*ROBERT is standing underneath a huge elm
tree, near the entrance to an underground shed
where he and MARGARET, now both outlaws,
are hiding with their children in an attempt to
avoid being recaptured and returned to their
masters. Glimmering hot coals can be seen in a
hole in the shed's earthen floor.*

MARGARET [*emerging from the shed*]:
 What else have you heard?
 What are they saying about him?
ROBERT: They say this new President
 Doesn't hiss like a snake;
 That he talks like a man.
MARGARET: What else have you heard?
 What has he said?
ROBERT: That a house divided
 Cannot stand.
 And that the Union is sacred.
MARGARET: That means war...
 You better make your spirit ready,
darling.

 Oh Robert,
 The children are troubled.

They cry in their sleep.
ROBERT: I know, I know...
 But freedom is in our teeth.
MARGARET [*with hope*]: Tell me again:
 What is the name of this place?
ROBERT: Ohio.
 It means "beautiful."
MARGARET: Is it?
 Is it beautiful?
ROBERT: So I hear.
 A beautiful place for a future.
MARGARET: Tell me.
 Tell me what the future will be like.
ROBERT: It will be with you as my wife
 No other man can touch or claim.
 It will be the children
 Seated, not bent.
 Seated in school rooms,
 Not bending through rows of corn.
 It will be me paid for my labor
 With coin of the realm.
MARGARET: Will I plant a garden?
 Mend your shirts by lamplight?
ROBERT: It will be just so.
MARGARET: Will I watch from a window
 Our children tumbling in clover and
rosemary?
ROBERT: Trust me, Margaret.
 It will be just so.
MARGARET: Will they swim in clear
water
 Until their skin glitters like brass?
 Tell me...tell me.
ROBERT: They will.
 It will be just so.
 Look! Do you see this tree?
 How it's lowering its branches
 To protect you
 No matter what the weather brings.
 Imagine...
MARGARET: ...That is how it will always
be...
ROBERT: ...That is how I will always be.
MARGARET *and* ROBERT [*together*]:
 That is how it will always be.
ROBERT [*suddenly coming to his senses*]:
 Come inside.

It's dangerous out here.

Someone might see us.

[*As they walk back to the shed,* ROBERT *puts his arm protectively around* MARGARET. *Once inside the shed,* ROBERT *thinks he hears a group of men approaching, and grabs his pistol.* MARGARET *runs to protect the children, who are sleeping in the corner behind a blanket. Accompanied by several slave catchers,* EDWARD GAINES—*who appears to be somewhat intoxicated—pounds on the shed door.*]

EDWARD *and* SLAVE CATCHERS:

Open up! Open up!

[*No sound is heard from inside the shed.*]

EDWARD: If bloodshed is on your mind,

Don't worry.

I just want what is mine.

EDWARD *and* SLAVE CATCHERS:

Open up! Open up!

EDWARD: No harm.

SLAVE CATCHERS: No harm.

EDWARD: Come softly.

SLAVE CATCHERS: Open up! Open up!

EDWARD: There is nothing you can do.

[GAINES *breaks down the shed door and fires his pistol in the air.* ROBERT *shoots at* GAINES, *but misses his target. Overpowered,* ROBERT *is knocked to the ground and tied up.* MARGARET *emerges from behind the children's blanket. Emotionally spent, she falls to her knees.*]

MARGARET [*grief-stricken*]:

No! No more!

No! No more!

[*getting up from the floor*]

Why can't you leave us be?

Why can't you leave us alone?

EDWARD: Leave murderers be?

I own him!

I own your children!

I own *you*!

MARGARET [*pleading*]:

Somebody help us!

Please, somebody!

Please, no more!

[MARGARET *weeps silently as* EDWARD *removes his hat, overcoat, and gloves.*]

EDWARD: My bed is cold, girl.

It wants warming.

Remember…remember?

[*with increasing vigor and excitement*]

Remember the bed warmer you ran over my sheets?

First you filled it with hot coals as I recall…

MARGARET [*wildly*]:

Here they are!

Take them! Take them!

[*With her bare hands,* MARGARET *grabs some coals out of the smoldering fire and lunges at* GAINES, *attempting to burn him. He manages to grasp her wrists, and forces her to drop the coal. He notices that her hands have been scorched.*]

EDWARD: Pretend to be crazy as much as you like.

[*derisively*] Mangle yourself, I don't care.

Casey was not enough?

Will you kill me too?

Oh no, my little crow.

[*A* SLAVE CATCHER *returns to the shed.*]

SLAVE CATCHER: He's bound and ready, sir.

MARGARET: Damn your marble eyes,

Damn your slithering soul!

Your miserable, putrid heart.

EDWARD [*to the* SLAVE CATCHER]:Take the young ones to the wagon.

Then light the fire.

The night is cold

And promises to be long.

[*In the dim light,* ROBERT *can be seen standing outside on a tall box underneath the tree; a noose is hanging around his neck. One by one, the slave catchers plant their torches in the ground, surrounding the condemned man with fire.*]

ROBERT: Margaret! Margaret!

I love you!

I love…

[GAINES' *pistol shot interrupts* ROBERT's *cry, killing him instantly.*]

MARGARET: Never to be born again into slavery!

OSSIA:[1] *My children will not*
live a life in slavery!

[MARGARET *violently attacks and murders her two children: first slitting the throat of her daughter, then stabbing the younger one. Horrified,* GAINES *and his men surround* MARGARET, *who has collapsed.*]

[LIGHTS OUT.]

ATTACCA[2]

Act II: Intermezzo

Total darkness envelops the stage. Gradually, the image of MARGARET, *alone, becomes visible. Her state of mind is changing; the intense isolation she feels in this moment "out of time" is mirrored by the dislocating blackness that surrounds her.*

MARGARET [*consoling herself, almost like crying*]: Ah...

Like a river rushing
From the grip of its banks.
[*With defiant grandeur,* MARGARET *embraces her life's circumstances.*]

Darkness, I salute you.
Reason has no power here,
Over the disconsolate.
Grief is my pleasure;
Thief of life, my lover now.
[*with quiet acceptance*]

Darkness, I salute you.
[*Fade to black.*]

Act II
Scene 3
In a Courtroom, in early April 1861.

Having followed the trial of Margaret Garner with great interest and curiosity, the townspeople fill the local courtroom in eager anticipation of her sentencing by the three presiding judges. MARGARET *sits in court surrounded*

by militia officers; CAROLINE, GEORGE, *and* EDWARD *deliver final testimony.*

JUDGES: What is the charge?
EDWARD: Theft, your honors.
JUDGES: And the value of the theft?
EDWARD: Hundreds, your honors.
Hundreds of dollars lost.
JUDGES: Have the stolen goods been found?
EDWARD: They have, sirs.
JUDGES: And what is the condition of these goods?
EDWARD [*looking at* MARGARET]: Ruined. Useless.
JUDGES: How did they come to be ruined?
EDWARD: The accused destroyed them, your honors.
JUDGES: By accident or deliberately?
EDWARD: Deliberately.
JUDGES: Describe, please, the destroyed goods.
EDWARD: Children, sirs.
Two children, both mine.
I mean, both my *property.*
CAROLINE [*in an aside to* GAINES]:
Father, this is madness.
EDWARD [*retorting loudly, embarrassing* CAROLINE]:
Madness, yes—
Hers, not mine.
CAROLINE *and* GEORGE [*pleading*]:
All the more reason to spare her.
CAROLINE: Your honors, may I speak?
[*The judges nod their consent.*]
The charge is false.
Not theft, but murder
It should be.
JUDGES: That is a very different matter.
Yet it comes to the same thing.

The issue before us
Is of property.
A financial loss...

---

[1] A musical term meaning "or," here, suggesting an alternative lyric.

[2] A musical term meaning "go on at once."

Not a debate
About the human soul.
CAROLINE *and* GEORGE [*together*]:
Respectfully, we beg to differ.
A mother who *kills* her children
Cannot be said to *steal* them.
EDWARD [*interrupting angrily*]:
They didn't belong to her.
She has no right to them,
Living or dead...
Living or dead.

It is clear in our system
She owns *nothing*—
Least of all my slaves.
TOWNSPEOPLE [*assertively*]: Yes! Yes!
Listen to him.
He is right!
He has the right idea.
JUDGE I [*with authority*]:
Order in the court!...
JUDGE II:...Order in the court!...
JUDGE I: ...Order in the court!...
JUDGE III [*emphatically*]:
...Order in the court;
In the name of the law
Of this country!
[*Silence suddenly fills the courtroom.*]
CAROLINE [*quietly, with respect but also
conviction*]: She bore them, your honors.
They are hers until they come of age.
She is responsible for their lives.
JUDGES [*sarcastically*]:
Where have you been, madam?
On an island in the sea?
You are speaking of a slave,
Not someone like you or me.

The law is clear
In the Bible and here.
[*with townspeople*]
Slavery is not a matter
For a slave to judge.
CAROLINE: Father,
Margaret is of no value to you,
[*looking at* MARGARET] Or anyone.

She was more than a mother to me.

Now her silence screams a grief
We dare not know.
EDWARD [*to himself*]:
I have committed no crime.
CAROLINE: But you can help change the
debate
Raging the land.
JUDGES: The law is clear
In the Bible and here.
EDWARD [*to* CAROLINE *and* GEORGE]:
I have committed no crime.
CAROLINE: Let the charge reflect
Our crimes as well as hers.
EDWARD: I have committed no crime.
JUDGES: He has committed no crime.

The law is clear
In the Bible and here.

We do not make laws
Or forsake laws,
We follow them precisely.

The charge is theft,
The sentence just.
This one will be made ready
For execution.
[*While the* JUDGES *confer with one another,*
CAROLINE *pleads with her father to intervene
and have the verdict overturned.*]
TOWNSPEOPLE: [*relieved*]
Bound and made ready,
Bound and made ready,
Bound and ready for execution.

She is not like you or me!
And she is not...like you...or me!

Bound and made ready,
Bound and made ready,
Bound and ready for execution.
MARGARET [*quietly, to herself*]:
I am *not* like you.
I am me.
TOWNSPEOPLE [*to one another*]:
She is not like you or me...
[MARGARET *suddenly rises from her chair and
glances around the courtroom, glaring at the
onlookers.*]

MARGARET [*emphatically*]:
   I am not like you.
   I am me!
JUDGES [*to* MARGARET]: Silence!
   You have no authority.
MARGARET [*to the* JUDGES, *refusing to sit down*]: You have no authority.
   I am not like you.
   [*defiantly*] I am me!
   I am me! I am!
[*The militia officers restrain* MARGARET.]
TOWNSPEOPLE: Bound and made ready
   Bound and made ready...
JUDGE III [*pointedly, looking directly at* MARGARET]: I order you
   In the name of the law of this land
   To be executed
   By sunrise tomorrow!
[*He bangs his gavel resolutely; the three* JUDGES *immediately recess to their chambers.*]
TOWNSPEOPLE [*reassured*]:
   She is not like you or me...
   She is not like you or me...
[MARGARET *is led away; the* TOWNSPEOPLE *file out of the courtroom.*]
CAROLINE [*dismayed by the verdict*]:
   Father,
   You must urge clemency
   From the court.
   They will hear you.
   They will listen to you.
GEORGE: Don't let her die
   Without dignity.
   Don't let her hang
   For the wrong reason.
EDWARD [*disturbed, yet betraying no sign of emotion*]: She must suffer the consequences
   Of what she has done.
CAROLINE *and* GEORGE:
   And so must you.
EDWARD [*angrily*]:
   Meaning what, exactly?
CAROLINE: *We are so at odds*
   In these past few years.
   Our land will not survive
   This violent test.

EDWARD: Daughter, are you threatening me?
CAROLINE *and* GEORGE: No. No.
   We are begging you.
CAROLINE: Don't fail me.
   It is all in your hands.
[EDWARD *turns away as* CAROLINE *and* GEORGE *start to leave the courtroom.* CAROLINE *looks back at her father, then impulsively runs over to him. She gently takes her father's hands, and presses one against her cheek, kissing his palm.* CAROLINE *and* GEORGE *exit. Alone in the courtroom,* EDWARD *contemplates the course of his life.*]

ARIOSO

EDWARD [*examining his hands*]:
   Nothing. I see nothing at all.
   No wound, no rash.
   Yet they burn.

   What lights the flame?
   Is it Caroline's kiss,
   Or Margaret's coals of fire?
[EDWARD *steps forward a few feet—hereby "leaving" the courtroom—and moves to a dimly-lit area of the stage.*]
[*Dismissing any questions or doubts from his mind*] Damn it to hell!
   I am approved.
   Clearly what the world insists
   I should be.
   Law and custom endorse me.
[*reconsidering*] Yet my only child
   Looks at me with strange eyes:
   Cold appraisal where naked adoration
   Used to live.
[*aggressively*] Am I not a legal man?
   God's blueprint,
   Flawed in merely ordinary ways?
[*assuming an aristocratic air*] Hats still tip,
   Gentlewomen dip their heads courteously
   To me.
[*introspectively*] And yet. And yet.
   They sear like molten lead.

[*inwardly, glancing at his hands*]
    (Look at them. Look at them!)
[*upon reflection*] If the flaw is in the blueprint
    Why must I choose?

If the flaw is in the blueprint—
Then I must choose.
[*The lights dim slowly.*]

ATTACCA

Act II
Scene 4
*In the town square of
Richwood Station, Kentucky;
the next morning, at dawn.*

A group of local citizens—including the town authorities; CAROLINE and GEORGE; and CILLA, as well as some slaves from nearby plantations—processes somberly into the town square at Richwood Station. Great sorrow fills the air, for they are accompanying MARGARET GARNER to her execution. All are sobered by the imminence of death. Seemingly, the only person not in the crowded plaza is EDWARD GAINES.

The hangman brings forth the condemned prisoner. MARGARET's hands, bandaged from the burns she received from the hot coals, have not yet been tied up in preparation for execution.

MARGARET is led up the scaffold steps. When she reaches the top of the platform, the hangman places a noose around her neck and positions her on the gallows' trap door. Scattered about are a number of ropes, which will be used to secure her limbs tightly.

[*EDWARD GAINES runs in, excitedly waving a document.*]
CILLA: Margaret, Margaret, Margaret,
    Dear God, no more!
EDWARD: Hold on! Hold on!
    I'm telling you to hold on.
    The judges have granted clemency…
[*in a pointed aside to GEORGE and CAROLINE*]

Clemency.
[*looking around at the faces in the crowd, seeking some sign of approval or acknowledgement of his beneficence*]
    And if the guilty party repents
    Her monstrous crime,
    She will be remanded
    To my custody.
[*Upon hearing of the stay of execution—which eliminates the need for him to bind the prisoner's body—the hangman leaves MARGARET's side and walks over to the edge of the gallows platform to accept the legal document from EDWARD.*]
CAROLINE and GEORGE [*together*]:
    Thank God. Thank you.
[*Overjoyed and relieved, CAROLINE embraces her father. GEORGE shakes EDWARD's hand.*]
CILLA [*stepping forward, thrilled*]:
    Thank you, sweet Jesus.
[*to MARGARET*] Do you hear that?
    You will live, daughter.
    Praise my maker,
    You will live, my angel.
MARGARET [*in a state of transcendence*]:
    Oh yes. I will live.
    I will live.

    I will live among the cherished.
    It will be just so.
    Side by side in our garden
    It will be just so.

    Ringed by a harvest of love.
    No more brutal days or nights.
[*making eye contact with CILLA in the crowd*]
    Goodbye, Sorrow…
    Death is dead forever.

    I live.
    Oh yes, I live!
[*While the crowd's attention is focused elsewhere, MARGARET deliberately trips the trap door's lever and hangs herself. Startled by the onlooker's screams, the hangman quickly turns around and is shocked to see MARGARET's limp body dangling just inches off the ground. He rushes over in a futile attempt to save her.*]

CILLA: Margaret...no!
Margaret!
Dear God, no more.
[CAROLINE *notices* MARGARET'*s scarf in her*
father's front pocket. She removes it, silently
ascends the scaffold, and reverently ties it
around MARGARET'*s waist.*]
EDWARD [*stunned; looking at his hands*]:
No breeze, no cool stream
Calm these palms.
Unhealed, there is no peace.
[*He walks away.*]

Epilogue
[*The hangman unties the noose around* MAR-
GARET'*s neck, and holds her in his arms before*
the TOWNSPEOPLE *and* SLAVES. *The light*
begins to dim; eventually, all that is visible is
MARGARET'*s body, which seems to float alone*
and above the crowd.]

ALL: Sweet Jesus,
Help us break through the night.
Chastened by thy holy might,
Guided by thy holy light
Into thy blessed sight.
ALL [*but* CILLA]: Have mercy. Have
mercy on us.
Help us break through the night.
CILLA: Soon, soon my bold-hearted girl
I'll be there. I'll be there.
THE SLAVES [*without* CILLA]:
Break through the night,
Break through the night;
Let her linger a while
And ride the light,
And ride the light.
[*The curtain descends slowly.*]

—1995

SYLVIA PLATH (1932-1963)

Born in Jamaica Plain, Massachusetts, Sylvia Plath moved with her family to Winthrop (MA)
during the Depression. It was there that she began her writing career, publishing her first
poem (in the *Boston Herald*) at the age of eight. Later, as a student at Smith College, from
which she graduated *summa cum laude* in 1955, Plath wrote approximately four hundred
poems. While in her junior year at Smith, Plath began her lifelong struggle against depression,
nearly succeeding at a suicide attempt that summer. She returned to Smith in the fall after a
recovery period that included electroshock therapy and psychotherapy, which she later chron-
icled in her fictionalized autobiography, *The Bell Jar* (1963), published under the pseudonym
Victoria Lucas. In 1956 Plath married the English poet Ted Hughes, whom she met while in
England on a Fulbright scholarship. *The Colossus,* her first book of poetry, was published in
1960, the same year that she had her first child, Frieda. Two years later, after the birth of their
son Nicholas, Plath and Hughes separated and Plath moved to a flat in London in a house
that Yeats had lived in. Though she was pleased to have found the house and though she was
writing as prolifically as ever (even during the last week of her life), Plath was troubled by
what she perceived to be negative reviews of *The Bell Jar*. About the same time, she fell into
another of the deep depressions that plagued her during her life. She was also ill with a recurrent sinus infection and experiencing some financial difficulty. All of this probably contributed
to her decision to commit suicide on February 11, 1963. Hughes published four more collections of Plath's poetry after her death: *Ariel* (1965), *Crossing the Water* (1971), *Winter Trees*
(1971), and *The Collected Poems* (1981), which was the first posthumous book to win a Pulitzer
Prize.

Ariel

Stasis in darkness.
Then the substanceless blue
Pour of tor and distances.

God's lioness,
How one we grow,   5
Pivot of heels and knees!—The furrow

Splits and passes, sister to
The brown arc
Of the neck I cannot catch,

Nigger-eye   10
Berries cast dark
Hooks——

Black sweet blood mouthfuls,
Shadows.
Something else   15

Hauls me through air——
Thighs, hair;
Flakes from my heels.

White
Godiva, I unpeel——   20
Dead hands, dead stringencies.

And now I
Foam to wheat, a glitter of seas.
The child's cry

Melts in the wall.   25
And I
Am the arrow,

The dew that flies
Suicidal, at one with the drive
Into the red   30

Eye, the cauldron of morning.

—1965

Cut

For Susan O'Neill Roe

What a thrill——
My thumb instead of an onion.
The top quite gone
Except for a sort of a hinge

Of skin, 5
A flap like a hat,
Dead white.
Then that red plush.

Little pilgrim,
The Indian's axed your scalp. 10
Your turkey wattle
Carpet rolls

Straight from the heart.
I step on it,
Clutching my bottle 15
Of pink fizz.

A celebration, this is.
Out of a gap
A million soldiers run,
Redcoats, every one. 20

Whose side are they on?
O my
Homunculus, I am ill.
I have taken a pill to kill

The thin 25
Papery feeling.
Saboteur,
Kamikaze man——

The stain on your
Gauze Ku Klux Klan 30
Babushka
Darkens and tarnishes and when

The balled
Pulp of your heart
Confronts its small 35
Mill of silence

How you jump——
Trepanned veteran,
Dirty girl,
Thumb stump. 40

—1965

Stings

Bare-handed, I hand the combs.
The man in white smiles, bare-handed,
Our cheesecloth gauntlets neat and sweet,

The throats of our wrists brave lilies.
He and I   5

Have a thousand clean cells between us,
Eight combs of yellow cups,
And the hive itself a teacup,
White with pink flowers on it,
With excessive love I enameled it   10

Thinking 'Sweetness, sweetness'.
Brood cells gray as the fossils of shells
Terrify me, they seem so old.
What am I buying, wormy mahogany?
Is there any queen at all in it?   15

If there is, she is old,
Her wings torn shawls, her long body
Rubbed of its plush——
Poor and bare and unqueenly and even shameful.
I stand in a column   20

Of winged, unmiraculous women,
Honey-drudgers.
I am no drudge
Though for years I have eaten dust
And dried plates with my dense hair.   25

And seen my strangeness evaporate,
Blue dew from dangerous skin.
Will they hate me,
These women who only scurry,
Whose news is the open cherry, the open clover?   30

It is almost over.
I am in control.
Here is my honey-machine,
It will work without thinking,
Opening, in spring, like an industrious virgin   35

To scour the creaming crests
As the moon, for its ivory powders, scours the sea.
A third person is watching.
He has nothing to do with the bee-seller or with me.
Now he is gone   40

In eight great bounds, a great scapegoat.
Here is his slipper, here is another,
And here the square of white linen
He wore instead of a hat.
He was sweet,   45

The sweat of his efforts a rain
Tugging the world to fruit.

The bees found him out,
Molding onto his lips like lies,
Complicating his features.   50

They thought death was worth it, but I
Have a self to recover, a queen.
Is she dead, is she sleeping?
Where has she been,
With her lion-red body, her wings of glass?   55

Now she is flying
More terrible than she ever was, red
Scar in the sky, red comet
Over the engine that killed her——
The mausoleum, the wax house.   60

6 October 1962
[—1965]

Wintering

This is the easy time, there is nothing doing.
I have whirled the midwife's extractor,
I have my honey,
Six jars of it,
Six cat's eyes in the wine cellar,   5

Wintering in a dark without window
At the heart of the house
Next to the last tenant's rancid jam
And the bottles of empty glitters——
Sir So-and-so's gin.   10

This is the room I have never been in.
This is the room I could never breathe in.
The black bunched in there like a bat,
No light
But the torch and its faint   15

Chinese yellow on appalling objects——
Black asininity. Decay.
Possession.
It is they who own me.
Neither cruel nor indifferent,   20

Only ignorant.
This is the time of hanging on for the bees—the bees
So slow I hardly know them,
Filing like soldiers
To the syrup tin   25

To make up for the honey I've taken.

Tate and Lyle keeps them going,
The refined snow.
It is Tate and Lyle they live on, instead of flowers.
They take it. The cold sets in.   30

Now they ball in a mass,
Black
Mind against all that white.
The smile of the snow is white.
It spreads itself out, a mile-long body of Meissen,   35

Into which, on warm days,
They can only carry their dead.
The bees are all women,
Maids and the long royal lady.
They have got rid of the men,   40

The blunt, clumsy stumblers, the boors.
Winter is for women——
The woman, still at her knitting,
At the cradle of Spanish walnut,
Her body a bulb in the cold and too dumb to think.   45

Will the hive survive, will the gladiolas
Succeed in banking their fires
To enter another year?
What will they taste of, the Christmas roses?
The bees are flying. They taste the spring.   50

9 October 1962
[—1965]

NINA SIMONE (1933-2003)

Singer, musician, and songwriter Nina Simone was born Eunice Kathleen Waymon in Tyron, North Carolina. The sixth of eight children, Simone distinguished herself as a prodigious musical talent at a young age. Private music lessons exposed Simone to classical music and inspired her attempt to become America's first African-American concert pianist. After a year at Julliard, however, her aspirations met with defeat when the Curtis Institute of Music in Philadelphia denied her admission, a decision she later came to believe was the result of both racism and sexism. She then started singing in nightclubs, changing her name to Nina Simone because of her mother's disapproval of such places. She recorded her first albums in the late 1950s, earning accolades for her eclectic experimentation with mixtures of gospel, blues, classical, and jazz styles. In the 1960s, she became active in the civil rights movement and her music became increasingly more political. "Mississippi Goddam," one of several important songs of this period, was her response to the assassination of Medgar Evars and the bombing of a church in Alabama that killed four young girls. She also wrote the song "To Be Young, Gifted, and Black" (after Lorainne Hansberry's autobiography of the same title), which the Congress on Racial Equality (CORE) declared to be the Black National Anthem. In the 1970s,

Simone left the U.S. first for Barbados, then Liberia, and finally France. The accumulation of many losses, both political (the waning of the civil rights movement in the wake of the deaths of so many of its leaders) and personal (the dissolution of her ten-year marriage to manager Andy Stroud), led her to this self-imposed exile. She returned to the U.S. for a time in the mid-1980s, reviving her career, but eventually moved back to France in 1993, where she died ten years later.

Mississippi Goddam

The name of this tune is Mississippi Goddam
And I mean every word of it

Alabama's gotten me so upset
Tennessee made me lose my rest
And everybody knows about Mississippi Goddam   5

Alabama's gotten me so upset
Tennessee made me lose my rest
And everybody knows about Mississippi Goddam

Can't you see it
Can't you feel it   10
It's all in the air
I can't stand the pressure much longer
Somebody say a prayer

Alabama's gotten me so upset
Tennessee made me lose my rest   15
And everybody knows about Mississippi Goddam

This is a show tune
But the show hasn't been written for it, yet

Hound dogs on my trail
School children sitting in jail   20
Black cat cross my path
I think every day's gonna be my last

Lord have mercy on this land of mine
We all gonna get it in due time
I don't belong here   25
I don't belong there
I've even stopped believing in prayer

Don't tell me
I tell you
Me and my people just about due   30
I've been there so I know
They keep on saying "Go slow!"

But that's just the trouble
"Do it slow"
Washing the windows   35

"Do it slow"
Picking the cotton
"Do it slow"
You're just plain rotten
"Do it slow"   40
You're too damn lazy
"Do it slow"
The thinking's crazy
"Do it slow"
Where am I going   45
What am I doing
I don't know
I don't know

Just try to do your very best
Stand up be counted with all the rest   50
For everybody knows about Mississippi Goddam

I made you thought I was kiddin' didn't we

Picket lines
School boy cots
They try to say it's a communist plot   55
All I want is equality
For my sister my brother my people and me

Yes you lied to me all these years
You told me to wash and clean my ears
And talk real fine just like a lady   60
And you'd stop calling me Sister Sadie

Oh but this whole country is full of lies
You're all gonna die and die like flies
I don't trust you any more
You keep on saying "Go slow!"   65
"Go slow!"

But that's just the trouble
"Do it slow"
Desegregation
"Do it slow"   70
Mass participation
"Do it slow"
Reunification
"Do it slow"
Do things gradually   75
"Do it slow"
But bring more tragedy
"Do it slow"
Why don't you see it
Why don't you feel it   80

I don't know
I don't know

You don't have to live next to me
Just give me my equality
Everybody knows about Mississippi   85
Everybody knows about Alabama
Everybody knows about Mississippi Goddam

That's it!

—1963

Four Women

My skin is black
My arms are long
My hair is wooly
My back is strong
Strong enough to take the pain   5
Inflicted again and again
What do they call me?
My name is Aunt Sarah
My name is Aunt Sarah

My skin is yellow   10
My hair is long
Between two worlds
I do belong
My father was rich and white
He forced my mother late one night   15
What do they call me?
My name is Siffronia
My name is Siffronia

My skin is tan
My hair is fine   20
My hips invite you
My mouth like wine
Whose little girl am I?
Anyone who has money to buy
What do they call me?   25
My name is Sweet Thing
My name is Sweet Thing

My skin is brown
And my manner is tough
I'll kill the first mother I see   30
My life has been rough
I'm awfully bitter these days
because my parents were slaves

What do they call me?
My name is Peaches

—1966

SUSAN SONTAG (1933-2004)

Born in New York City, the daughter of a schoolteacher mother and a fur trader father, Susan Sontag learned to read by the age of three. Her father died when she was five, and she took her stepfather's last name. Raised in Tucson and Los Angeles, Sontag skipped three grades and graduated from North Hollywood High School at fifteen, going on to study at Berkeley, the University of Chicago, Harvard, and Oxford. A bisexual who did not speak or write publicly about her sexuality, Sontag was married at seventeen and later divorced; her son David Rief is also a writer. After moving to New York at the age of twenty-six, Sontag became known as a writer and activist, and was a towering figure in New York intellectual circles. Deeply involved in international human rights campaigns for decades, she traveled to Hanoi during the Vietnam War, which she opposed, and she famously called the efforts to suppress the Solidarity movement in Poland "fascism with a human face." Sontag served as president of the PEN American Center, defending persecuted and imprisoned writers, and organized U.S. writers in defense of Salman Rushdie after an Iranian cleric issued a fatwa calling for his murder. During the siege of the Bosnian capital Sarajevo, Sontag spent much of her time there, directing a production of Samuel Beckett's *Waiting for Godot* in 1993. She was made an honorary citizen of the city, and a street was named for her after her death. Despite being most widely recognized for her nonfiction—including "Notes on 'Camp'" (1964), *On Photography* (1977), *Illness As Metaphor* (1978), *AIDS and Its Metaphors* (1989), and essays in the *New Yorker* and other magazines—Sontag considered herself primarily a novelist and fiction writer. She published seventeen books, including four novels, a collection of short stories, and several plays, and her work has been translated into thirty-two languages. Her 1992 novel *The Volcano Lover* was a bestseller, and her final novel, *In America* (2000), won the National Book Award. Sontag was diagnosed and treated for breast and uterine cancer in the 1970s and died of leukemia in 2004. She is buried in Montparnasse cemetery in Paris, France.

Debriefing

...Frail long hair, brown with reddish lights in it, artificial-looking hair, actressy hair, the hair she had at twenty-three when I met her (I was nineteen), hair too youthful to need tinting then, but too old now to have exactly the same color; a weary, dainty body with wide wrists, shy chest, broad-bladed shoulders, pelvic bones like gulls' wings; an absent body one might be reluctant to imagine undressed, which may explain why her clothes are never less than affected and are often regal; one husband in dark phallocratic mustache; unexpectedly successful East Side restaurant owner with dim Mafia patronage, separated from and then divorced in fussy stages; two flaxen-haired children, who look as if they have two other parents, safely evacuated to grassy boarding schools. "For the fresh air," she says.

Autumn in Central Park, several years ago. Lounging under a sycamore, our bicycles paired on their sides—Julia's was hers (she had once bicycled regularly), mine was rented—she admitted to finding less time lately for doing: going to an aikido class, cooking a meal, phoning the children, maintaining love affairs. But for wondering there seemed all the time in the world—hours, whole days.

Wondering?

"About…" she said, looking at the ground. "Oh, I might start wondering about the relation of that leaf"—pointing to one—"to that one"—pointing to a neighbor leaf, also yellowing, its frayed tip almost perpendicular to the first one's spine. "Why are they lying there just like that? Why not some other way?"

"I'll play. 'Cause that's how they fell down from the tree."

"But there's a relation, a connection…"

Julia, sister, poor moneyed waif, you're crazy. (A crazy question: one that shouldn't be asked.) But I didn't say that. I said: "You shouldn't ask yourself questions you can't answer." No reply. "Even if you could answer a question like that, you wouldn't know you had."

Look, Julia. Listen, Peter Pan. Instead of leaves—that's crazy—take people. Undoubtedly, between two and five this afternoon, eighty-four embittered Viet veter-ans are standing on line for welfare checks in a windowless downtown office while seventeen women sit in mauve leatherette chairs in a Park Avenue surgeon's lair waiting to be examined for breast cancer. But there's no point in trying to connect these two events.

Or is there?

Julia didn't ask me what I wonder about. Such as:

What Is Wrong

A thick brownish-yellow substance has settled in everyone's lungs—it comes from too much smoking, and from history. A constriction around the chest, nausea that follows each meal.

Julia, naturally lean, has managed lately to lose more weight. She told me last week that only bread and coffee don't make her ill. "Oh, no!" I groaned—we were talking on the phone. That evening I went over to inspect her smelly bare refrigerator. I wanted to throw out the plastic envelope of pale hamburger at the back; she wouldn't let me. "Even chicken isn't cheap any more," she murmured.

She brewed some Nescafé and we sat crosslegged on the living-room tatami; after tales of her current lover, that brute, we passed to debating Lévi-Strauss[1] on the clos-ing off of history. I, pious to the end, defended history. Although she still wears sumptuous caftans and treats her lungs to Balkan Sobranies, the other reason she is not eating is that she's too stingy.

One thickness of pain at a time. Julia may not want to go out "at all," but many people no longer feel like leaving their apartments "often."

This city is neither a jungle nor the moon nor the Grand Hotel. In long shot: a cosmic smudge, a conglomerate of bleeding energies. Close up, it is a fairly legible printed circuit, a transistorized labyrinth of beastly tracks, a data bank for asthmatic

---

[1] Claude Lévi-Strauss (b. 1908), French social anthropologist.

voice-prints. Only some of its citizens have the right to be amplified and become audible.

A black woman in her mid-fifties, wearing a brown cloth coat darker than the brown shopping bag she is carrying, gets into a cab, sighing. "143rd and St. Nicholas." Pause. "Okay?" After the wordless, hairy young driver turns on the meter, she settles the shopping bag between her fat knees and starts crying. On the other side of the scarred plastic partition, Esau can hear her.

With more people, there are more voices to tune out.

It is certainly possible that the black woman is Doris, Julia's maid (every Monday morning), who, a decade ago, while down on St. Nicholas Avenue buying a six-pack and some macaroni salad, lost both of her small children in a fire that partly destroyed their two-room apartment. But if it is Doris, she does not ask herself why they burned up just that much and no more, why the two bodies lay next to each other in front of the TV at exactly that angle. And if it is Doris, it is certainly not Monday, Miz Julia's day, because the brown paper bag holds cast-off clothing from the woman whose seven-room apartment she's just cleaned, and Julia never throws out or gives away any of her clothes.

It's not easy to clothe oneself. Since the Easter bombing in Bloomingdale's third-floor boutique section, shoppers in large department stores are body-searched as they enter. Veined city!

If it is not Doris, Julia's Doris, then perhaps it is Doris II, whose daughter (B.A., Hunter College, 1965), having been bewitched, now lives with a woman the same age as her mother, only fatter, muscularly fat, and rich: Roberta Jorrell, the Queen of the Black Arts; internationally known monologist poet, set designer, filmmaker, voice coach, originator of the Jorrell System of body awareness, movement, and functional coordination; and initiated voodoo priestess third-class. Doris II, also a maid, has not heard from her daughter in seven years, a captivity of biblical length that the girl has been serving as assistant stage manager of the Roberta Jorrell Total Black Theater Institute; bookkeeper for Jorrell real-estate holdings in Dakar, Cap-Haïtien, and Philadelphia; decipherer and typist of the two-volume correspondence between R.J. and Bertrand Russell;[2] and on-call body servant to the woman whom no one, not even her husband, dares address as anything other than Miss Jorrell.

After taking Doris, if she is Doris, to 143rd and St. Nicholas, the taxi driver, stopping for a red light on 131st Street, has a knife set against his throat by three brown boys—two are eleven, one is twelve—and surrenders his money. Off-duty sign blazing, he quickly returns to his garage on West Fifty-fifth Street and unwinds in a corner, on the far side of the Coke machine, with a joint.

However, if it is not Doris but Doris II whom he has dropped at 143rd and St. Nicholas, the driver is not robbed but immediately gets a fare to 173rd and Vyse Avenue. He accepts. But he is afraid of getting lost, of never finding his way back. Writhing, uncontrollable city! In the years since the city stopped offering garbage

---

[2] Bertrand Russell (1872-1970), philosopher and mathematician.

collection to Morrisania and Hunts Point, the dogs that roam the streets have been subtly turning into coyotes.

Julia doesn't bathe enough. Suffering smells.

Several days later, a middle-aged black woman carrying a brown shopping bag climbs out of a subway in Greenwich Village and accosts the first middle-aged white woman who's passing by. "Excuse me, ma'am, but can you tell me the way to the Ladies' House of Detention?" This is Doris III, whose only daughter, age twenty-two, is well into her third ninety-day sentence for being a, etcetera.

We know more than we can use. Look at all this stuff I've got in my head: rockets and Venetian churches, David Bowie and Diderot,[3] nuoc mam[4] and Big Macs, sunglasses and orgasms. How many newspapers and magazines do you read? For me, they're what candy or Quaaludes or scream therapy are for my neighbors. I get my daily ration from the bilious Lincoln Brigade veteran[5] who runs a tobacco shop on 110th Street, not from the blind news agent in the wooden pillbox on Broadway, who's nearer my apartment.

And we don't know nearly enough.

What People Are Trying to Do
All around us, as far as I can see, people are striving to be ordinary. This takes a great deal of effort. Ordinariness, generally considered to be safer, has gotten much rarer than it used to be.

Julia called yesterday to report that, an hour before, she had gone downstairs to take in her laundry. I congratulated her.

People try to be interested in the surface. Men without guns are wearing mascara, glittering, prancing. Everyone's in some kind of moral drag.

People are trying not to mind, not to mind too much. Not to be afraid.

The daughter of Doris II has actually witnessed Roberta Jorrell—stately, unflinching—dip both hands up to the wrists in boiling oil, extract some shreds of cornmeal that she kneaded into a small pancake, and then briefly reimmerse pancake and hands. No pain, no scars. She had herself prepared by twenty hours of nonstop drumming and chanting, curtseying and asyncopated hand clapping; brackish holy water was passed around in a tin cup and sipped; and her limbs were smeared with goat's blood. After the ceremony, Doris II's daughter and four other followers, including Henry, the husband of Roberta Jorrell, escorted her back to the hotel suite in Pétionville. Henry was not allowed to stay on the same floor this trip. Miss Jorrell gave instructions that she would sleep for twenty hours and was not to be awakened for any reason. Doris II's daughter washed out Miss J's bloody robes and stationed herself on a wicker stool outside the bedroom door, waiting.

I try to get Julia to come out and play with me (fifteen years have gone by since we

---

[3] David Bowie (b. 1947), rock star; Denis Diderot (1713-1784), French philosopher.

[4] Vietnamese fish sauce.

[5] U.S. volunteers who fought against the fascists in the Spanish Civil War in the 1930s.

met): see the city. On different days and nights I've offered the roller derby in Brooklyn, a dog show, F. A. O. Schwarz, the Tibetan Museum on Staten Island, a women's march, a new singles' bar, midnight-to-dawn movies at the Elgin, Sunday's La Marqueta on upper Park Avenue, a poetry reading, anything. She invariably refuses. Once I got her to a performance of *Pelléas et Mélisande*[6] at the old Met, but we had to leave at the intermission; Julia was trembling—with boredom, she claimed. Moments after the curtain rose on the Scene One set, a clearing in a dark forest, I knew it was a mistake. "Ne me touchez pas! Ne me touchez pas!"[7] moans the heroine, leaning dangerously into a deep well. Her first words. The well-meaning stranger and would-be rescuer—equally lost—backs off, gazing lasciviously at the heroine's long hair; Julia shudders. Lesson: don't take Mélisande to see *Pelléas et Mélisande*.

After getting out of jail, Doris III's daughter is trying to quit the life. But she can't afford to: everything's gotten so expensive. From chicken, even wings and gizzards, to the Coromandel screen, once owned by a leading couturier of the 1930s, for which Lyle's mother bids $18,000 at a Parke-Bernet auction.

People are economizing. Those who like to eat—a category that includes most people, and excludes Julia—no longer do the week's marketing in an hour at one supermarket, but must give over most of a day, exploring ten stores to assemble a shopping cart's worth of food. They, too, are wandering about the city.

The affluent, having invested in their pocket calculators, are now seeking uses for them.

Unless already in a state of thralldom, like the daughter of Doris II, people are answering ads that magicians and healers place in newspapers. "You don't have to wait for pie in the sky by-and-by when you die.[8] If you want your pie now with ice cream on top, then see and hear Rev. Ike on TV and in person." Rev. Ike's church is not, repeat not, located in Harlem. New churches without buildings are migrating from West to East: people are worshiping the devil. On Fifty-third Street west of the Museum of Modern Art, a blond boy with a shag cut who resembles Lyle tries to interest me in the Process Church of the Final Judgment. "Have you ever heard of the Process?" When I say yes, he goes on as if I'd said no. I'll never get into the 5:30 screening if I stop to talk to him, but I hand over a buck fifty for his magazine; and he keeps up with me, telling me about free breakfast programs the Process runs for poor children, until I spin into the museum's revolving door. Breakfast programs, indeed! I thought they ate little children.

People are video-taping their bedroom feats, tapping their own telephones.

My good deed for November 12: calling Julia after a lapse of three weeks. "Hey, how are you?" "Terrible," she answered, laughing. I laughed back and said, "So am I," which wasn't exactly true. Together we laughed some more; the receiver felt sleek and warm in my hand. "Want to meet?" I asked. "Could you come to my place again? I hate leaving the apartment these days." Dearest Julia, I know that already.

---

[6] 1902 opera by French composer Claude Debussy (1862-1918).

[7] (Fr.) Do not touch me! Do not touch me!

[8] "You'll get pie in the sky when you die," from Joe Hill's 1911 song, "The Preacher and the Slave," a rallying song for the Industrial Workers of the World.

I try not to reproach Julia for throwing away her children.

Lyle, who is nineteen now, called me the other morning from a phone booth at Broadway and Ninety-sixth. I tell him to come up, and he brings me a story he's just completed, the first in years, which I read. It is not as accomplished as the stories that were published when he was eleven, an under grown baby-voiced pale boy, the Mozart of *Partisan Review;*[9] at eleven Lyle hadn't yet taken all that acid, gone temporarily blind, been a groupie on a cross-country Rolling Stones tour, gotten committed twice by his parents, or attempted three suicides—all before finishing his junior year at Bronx Science. Lyle, with my encouragement, agrees not to burn his story.

Taki 183, Pain 145, Turok 137, Charmin 65, Think 160, Snake 128, Hondo II, Stay High 149, Cobra 151, along with several of their friends, are sending insolent messages to Simone Weil[10]—no Jewish-American Princess she. She tells them there is no end to suffering. You think that, they answer, because you had migraines. So do you, she says tartly. Only you don't know you have them.

She also says that the only thing more hateful than a "we" is an "I"—and they go on blazoning their names on the subway cars.

What Relieves, Soothes, Helps

It's a pleasure to share one's memories. Everything remembered is dear, endearing, touching, precious. At least the past is safe—though we didn't know it at the time. We know it now. Because it's in the past; because we have survived.

Doris, Julia's Doris, has decorated her living room with photographs, toys, and clothes of her two dead children, which, each time you visit her, you have to spend the first half hour examining. Dry-eyed, she shows you everything.

A cold wind comes shuddering over the city, the temperature drops. People are cold. But at least it clears off the pollution. From my roof on Riverside Drive, squinting through the acceptable air, I can see—across New Jersey—a rim of the Ramapo hills.

It helps to say no. One evening, when I drop by Julia's apartment to retrieve a book, her psychiatrist father calls. I'm expected to answer the phone: covering the mouthpiece, I whisper, "Cambridge!" and, across the room, she whispers back, "Say I'm not home!" He knows I'm lying. "I know Julia never goes out," he says indignantly. "She would have," I say, "if she'd known you were going to call" Julia grins—heartbreaking, childish grin—and bites into a pomegranate I've brought her.

What helps is having the same feelings for a lifetime. At a fund-raising party on Beekman Place for the New Democratic Coalition's alternate mayoral candidate, I flirt with an elderly Yiddish journalist who doesn't want to talk about quotas and school boycotts in Queens. He tells me about his childhood in a shtetl ten miles from Warsaw ("Of course, you never heard of a shtetl. You're too young. It was a village where the Jews lived"). He had been inseparable from another small boy. "I couldn't live without him. He was more to me than my brothers. But, you know, I didn't like him. I hated him. Whenever we played together, he would make me so mad. Sometimes we

[9] U.S. quarterly journal of politics and culture, 1934-2003.   [10] Simone Weil (1909-1943), French philosopher.

would hurt each other with sticks." Then he goes on to tell me how, last month, a shabby old man with stiff pink ears had come into the *Forward* [11] office, had asked for him, had come over to his desk, had stood there, had said, "Walter Abramson, you know who I am?" And how he'd gazed into the old man's eyes, scrutinized his bald skull and shopping-bag body, and suddenly knew. "You're Isaac." And the old man said, "You're right."

"After fifty years, can you imagine? Honestly, I don't know how I recognized him," said the journalist. "It wasn't something in his eyes. But I did."

What happened? "So we fell into each other's arms. And I asked him about his family, and he told me they were all killed by the Nazis. And he asked me about my family, and I told him they were all killed... And you know what? After fifteen minutes, everything he said infuriated me, I didn't care any more if his whole family had been killed. I didn't care if he was a poor old man. I hated him." He trembled—with vitality. "I wanted to beat him. With a stick."

Sometimes it helps to change your feelings altogether, like getting your blood pumped out and replaced. To become another person. But without magic. There's no moral equivalent to the operation that makes transsexuals happy.

A sense of humor helps. I haven't explained that Julia is funny, droll, witty—that she can make me laugh. I've made her sound like nothing but a burden.

Sometimes it helps to be paranoid. Conspiracies have the merit of making sense. It's a relief to discover your enemies, even if first you have to invent them. Roberta Jorrell, for instance, has humorlessly instructed Doris II's daughter and others on her payroll exactly how to thwart the enemies of her federally funded South Philadelphia Black Redress Center—white bankers, AMA psychiatrists, Black Panthers, cops, Maoists, and the CIA—with powders, with hexes, and with preternaturally smooth flat stones blessed by a Cuban *santera* [12] in Miami Beach. Julia, however, doesn't think she has any enemies—as, when her current lover again refuses to leave his wife, she still doesn't understand that she isn't loved. But when she goes down on the street, which happens less and less frequently, she finds the cars menacingly unpredictable.

Flight is said to help. Dean and Shirley, Lyle's parents, having pulled out of the market last year, have bought into a condominium in Sarasota, Florida, whose City Fathers recently voted, in order to make the city more seductive to tourists, to take out all the parking meters they installed downtown five years ago. Lyle's parents don't know how many weeks a year they can actually spend in the Ringling Brothers' [13] home town; but there's never been a decade when real-estate values haven't gone up, right? And that crazy Quiz Kid, their son, will always have his room there if he wants it.

It helps to feel guiltless about your sexual options, though it's not clear that many people actually manage this. After eventually finding his way back from Hunts Point into the well-lit grid of more familiar predators, the driver who had taken Doris II to 143rd and St. Nicholas picks up a pale, blond boy with a shag cut who also resembles

---

[11] Yiddish-language newspaper.

[12] (Sp.) Priestess of Santeria, a religion combining Yoruban and Roman Catholic elements.

[13] Seven brothers whose circus, formed in 1884, merged with Barnum & Bailey Circus in 1919.

Lyle and who says, as he gets into the cab, "West Street and the trucks, please."

Lately, my sexual life has become very pure. I don't want it to be like a dirty movie. (Having enjoyed a lot of dirty movies, I don't want it to be like that.)

Let's lie down together, love, and hold each other.

Meanwhile, the real Lyle has again skipped his four o'clock class, Comp. Lit. 203 ("Sade[14] and the Anarchist Tradition"), and is sprawled in front of a TV set in the dormitory lounge. He's been watching more and more television lately, with a preference for serials like *Secret Storm* and *As the World Turns*. He has also started showing up at student parties, instead of rebuffing his roommate's kindly, clumsy invitations. A good rule: any party is depressing, if you think about it. But you don't have to think about it.

I'm happy when I dance.

Touch me.

What Is Upsetting

To read *Last Letters from Stalingrad*,[15] and grieve for those lost, all-too-human voices among the most devilish of enemies. No one is a devil if fully heard.

To find everyone crazy—example: both Lyle and his parents. And to find the crazy particularly audible.

To be afraid.

To know that Lyle will be introduced to Roberta Jorrell next week at an elegant SoHo loft party given in her honor after her speech at New York University; be recruited by her; drop out of college; and not be heard from again for at least seven years.

To feel how desperate everyone is. Doris, Julia's Doris, is being evicted from her apartment. She not only has no money to pay a higher rent; she wants to go on living in the place where her children perished.

To learn that the government—using information that the law now requires be recorded on tape and stored indefinitely by banks, the telephone company, airlines, credit-card companies—can know more about me (my more sociable activities, anyway) than I do myself. If necessary, I could list most of the plane trips I've taken; and my old checkbook stubs are in a drawer—somewhere. But I don't remember whom I telephoned exactly four months ago at 11 a.m., and never will. I don't think it was Julia.

To find in myself the desire to stop listening to people's distress.

To be unsure of how to exercise the powers I do possess.

Julia had once fallen under the spell of an ex-ESP researcher, then a specialist in the North American Indian occult, who claimed to know how to help her. Most people

---

[14] Marquis de Sade (1740-1814), French novelist.
[15] Compilation of letters by German soldiers fighting in and around Stalingrad during World War II.

who meet Julia, stunned by her vulnerability, take a crack at helping her; the pleasure of her beauty, which is the only gift Julia has ever been able to make to other people, helps too. The sorceress in question, Martha Wooten, was white, Westchester-born, crisp, a superb tennis player—rather like a gym teacher; I thought, condescendingly, she might be good for Julia, until as part of a program for freeing Julia from her demons, she had her bay at the full moon on all fours. Then I swooped back into Julia's underfurnished life, performed my old rites of counter-exorcism—reason! self-preservation! pessimism of the intellect, optimism of the will![16]—and Martha Wooten vanished, metamorphosed, rather, into one of the Wicked Witches of the West, setting up in Big Sur as Lady Lambda, head of the only Lucifer cult that practices deep breathing and bioenergetic analysis.

Was I right to de-bewitch her?

To be unable to change one's life. Doris III's daughter is back in jail.

To live in bad air. To have an airless life. To feel there's no ground: that there is nothing but air.

Our Prospects

Aleatoric. Repetitious. On a Monday, after taking Doris, Julia's Doris, home from cleaning Julia's apartment, the taxi driver stops to pick up three fourteen-year-old Puerto Ricans on 111th and Second Avenue. If they don't rob him, they will get in the cab, ask to be taken to the juice bar in the alley by the Fifty-ninth Street Bridge, and give him a big tip.

Not good. A hand-lettered sign pasted at eye level on the bare brick wall of a housing project on the corner of Ninetieth and Amsterdam reads, plaintively: Stop Killing. Wounded city!

Although none of the rules for becoming more alive is valid, it is healthy to keep on formulating them.

Here's a solid conservative rule, deposited by Goethe with Eckermann:[17] "Every healthy effort is directed from the inner to the outer world." Put that in your hashish pipe and smoke it.

But let's say, or suppose, we're not up to being healthy. Then there's only one way left to get to the world. We could be glad of the world, if we were flying to it for refuge.

Actually, this world isn't just one world—now. As this city is actually layers of cities. Behind the many thicknesses of pain, try to connect with the single will for pleasure that moves even in the violence of streets and beds, of jails and opera houses.

In the words of Rev. Ike, "You Can Be Happy Now." By an extraordinary coincidence, there is one day when Doris, Doris II, and Doris III—who don't know each other—may all be found under the same roof: in Rev. Ike's United Church and Science of Living Institute, attending a 3 p.m. Sunday Healing and Blessing Meeting. As for their prospects of being happy: none of the three Dorises is convinced.

[16] Slogan of an Italian Communist newspaper edited by Antonio Gramsci (1891-1937).
[17] Johann Wolfgang von Goethe (1749-1832), German writer; Johann Peter Eckermann (1792-1854), German poet of *Conversations with Goethe* and editor of Goethe's posthumous works.

Julia…anybody! Hey, how are you? Terrible, yes. But you laughed.

Some of us will falter, but some of us will be brave. A middle-aged black woman in a brown coat carrying a brown suitcase leaves a bank and gets into a cab. "I'm going to the Port of Authority, please." Doris II is taking the bus to Philadelphia. After seven years, she's going to confront Roberta Jorrell and try to get her daughter back.

Some of us will get more craven. Meanwhile, most of us will never know what's happening.

Let's dig through the past. Let's admire whatever, whenever we can. But people now have such grudging sympathy for the past.

If I come out to dinner in my space suit, will you wear yours? We'll look like Dale and Flash Gordon,[18] maybe, but who cares. What everybody thinks now: one can form an alliance only with the future.

The prospects are for more of the same. As always. But I refuse.

Suppose, just suppose, leaden soul, you would try to lead an exemplary life. To be kind, honorable, helpful, just. On whose authority?

And you'll never know, that way, what you most long to know. Wisdom requires a life that is singular in another way, that's perverse. To know more, you must conjure up all the lives there are, and then leave out whatever fails to please you. Wisdom is a ruthless business.

But what about those I love? Although I don't believe my friends can't get on without me, surviving isn't so easy; and I probably can't survive without them.

If we don't help each other, forlorn demented bricklayers who've forgotten the location of the building we were putting up…

"Taxi!" I hail a cab during the Wednesday afternoon rush hour and ask the driver to get to Julia's address as fast as he can. Something in her voice on the phone lately…But she seems all right when I come in. She'd even been out the day before to take a batik (made last year) to be framed; it will be ready in a week. And when I ask to borrow a back issue of a feminist magazine that I spy, under a pile of old newspapers, on the floor, she mentions three times that I must return it soon. I promise to come by next Monday. Reassured by the evidence of those petty forms that Julia's hold on life often takes, I'm ready to leave. But then she asks me to stay on, just a few minutes more, which means that it's changing; she wants to talk sadness. On cue, like an old vaudevillian, I go into my routines of secular ethical charm. They seem to work. She promises to try.

What I'm Doing

I leave the city often. But I always come back.

I made Lyle give me his story—his only copy, of course—knowing that, despite his promise, if I returned it to him, he'd burn it, as he's burned everything he's written since he was fifteen. I've given it to a magazine editor I know.

I exhort, I interfere. I'm impatient. For God's sake, it isn't *that* hard to live. One of

---

[18] Characters from *Flash Gordon*, a science fiction comic strip, later a serial on film and television.

the pieces of advice I give is: Don't suffer future pain.

And whether or not the other person heeds my advice, at least I've learned something from what was said. I give fairly good advice to myself.

That late Wednesday afternoon I told Julia how stupid it would be if she committed suicide. She agreed. I thought I was convincing. Two days later she left her apartment again and killed herself, showing me that she didn't mind doing something stupid.

I would. Even when I announce to friends that I'm going to do something stupid, I don't really think it is.

I want to save my soul, that timid wind.

Some nights, I dream of dragging Julia back by her long hair, just as she's about to jump into the river. Or I dream she's already in the river: I am standing on my roof, facing New Jersey; I look down and see her floating by, and I leap from the roof, half falling, half swooping like a bird, and seize her by the hair and pull her out.

Julia, darling Julia, you weren't supposed to lean any farther into the well—daring anyone with good intentions to come closer, to save you, to be kind. You were at least supposed to die in a warm bed—mute; surrounded by the guilty, clumsy people who adored you, leaving them frustrated and resentful of you to the end.

I'm not thinking of what the lordly polluted Hudson did to your body before you were found.

Julia, plastic face in the waxy casket, how could you be as old as you were? You're still the twenty-three-year-old who started an absurdly pedantic conversation with me on the steps of Widener Library[19]—so thin; so prettily affected; so electric; so absent; so much younger than I, who was four years younger than you; so tired already; so exasperating; so moving. I want to hit you.

How I groaned under the burden of our friendship. But your death is heavier.

Why you went under while others, equally absent from their lives, survive is a mystery to me.

Say we are all asleep. Do we want to wake up?

Is it fair if I wake up and you, most of you, don't? Fair! you sneer. What's fair got to do with it? It's every soul for itself. But I didn't want to wake up without you.

You're the tears in things, I'm not. You weep for me, I'll weep for you. Help me, I don't want to weep for myself. I'm not giving up.

Sisyphus,[20] I. I cling to my rock, you don't have to chain me. Stand back! I roll it up—up, up. And…down we go. I knew that would happen. See, I'm on my feet again. See, I'm starting to roll it up again. Don't try to talk me out of it. Nothing, nothing could tear me away from this rock.

—1973

---

[19] At Harvard University.
[20] In Greek mythology, Sisyphus was doomed eternally to roll a large stone up a hill, only to have it roll down again.

RADICALESBIANS

> Radicalesbians was an activist collective originally formed as the "Lavender Menace" to protest the omission of lesbian issues from the agenda of the National Organization for Women's (NOW) Second Congress to Unite Women in 1970. Original members, including Rita Mae Brown, Karla Jay, and Martha Shelley, were active in the Gay Liberation Front Women, the Daughters of Bilitis, and the Redstockings. They wrote "The Woman-Identified Woman" in response to a slight from NOW's president Betty Friedan, who referred to lesbianism as the "lavender herring" of the women's liberation movement. The collective presented the manifesto dramatically, cutting the lights to the conference auditorium and commandeering the stage to read aloud to the assembly. Radicalesbians was a strict separatist group with a short lifespan, dissolving over internal differences about hard-line political stances within a year. Known as the group that briefly took over the women's liberation movement, and owning the distinction of being the first post-Stonewall radical lesbian group, Radicalesbians' historical stature exceeds its original size and longevity.

The Woman-Identified Woman

What is a lesbian? A lesbian is the rage of all women condensed to the point of explosion. She is the woman who, often beginning at an extremely early age, acts in accordance with her inner compulsion to be a more complete and freer human being than her society—perhaps then, but certainly later—cares to allow her. These needs and actions, over a period of years, bring her into painful conflict with people, situations, the accepted ways of thinking, feeling and behaving, until she is in a state of continual war with everything around her, and usually with herself. She may not be fully conscious of the political implications of what for her began as personal necessity, but on some level she has not been able to accept the limitations and oppression laid on her by the most basic role of her society—the female role. The turmoil she experiences tends to induce guilt proportional to the degree to which she feels she is not meeting social expectations, and/or eventually drives her to question and analyze what the rest of her society more or less accepts. She is forced to evolve her own life pattern, often living much of her life alone, learning usually much earlier than her "straight" (heterosexual) sisters about the essential aloneness of life (which the myth of marriage obscures) and about the reality of illusions. To the extent that she cannot expel the heavy socialization that goes with being female, she can never truly find peace with herself. For she is caught somewhere between accepting society's view of her—in which case she cannot accept herself—and coming to understand what this sexist society has done to her and why it is functional and necessary for it to do so. Those of us who work that through find ourselves on the other side of a tortuous journey through a night that may have been decades long. The perspective gained from that journey, the liberation of self, the inner peace, the real love of self and of all women, is something to be shared with all women—because we are all women.

It should first be understood that lesbianism, like male homosexuality, is a category of behavior possible only in a sexist society characterized by rigid sex roles and dominated by male supremacy. Those sex roles dehumanize women by defining us as a supportive/serving caste *in relation to* the master caste of men, and emotionally cripple men by demanding that they be alienated from their own bodies and emotions in order to perform their economic/political/military functions effectively. Homosexuality is a by-product of a particular way of setting up roles (or approved patterns of behavior) on the basis of sex; as such it is an inauthentic (not consonant with "reality") category. In a society in which men do not oppress women, and sexual expression is allowed to follow feelings, the categories of homosexuality and heterosexuality would disappear.

But lesbianism is also different from male homosexuality, and serves a different function in the society. "Dyke" is a different kind of put-down from "faggot," although both imply you are not playing your socially assigned sex role...are not therefore a "real woman" or a "real man." The grudging admiration felt for the tomboy, and the queasiness felt around a sissy boy point to the same thing: the contempt in which women—or those who play a female role—are held. And the investment in keeping women in that contemptuous role is very great. Lesbian is the word, the label, the condition that holds women in line. When a woman hears this word tossed her way, she knows she is stepping out of line. She knows that she has crossed the terrible boundary of her sex role. She recoils, she protests, she reshapes her actions to gain approval. Lesbian is a label invented by the Man to throw at any woman who dares to be his equal, who dares to challenge his prerogatives (including that of all women as part of the exchange medium among men), who dares to assert the primacy of her own needs. To have the label applied to people active in women's liberation is just the most recent instance of a long history; older women will recall that not so long ago, any woman who was successful, independent, not orienting her whole life about a man, would hear this word. For in this sexist society, for a woman to be independent means she *can't* be a *woman*—she *must* be a *dyke*. That in itself should tell us where women are at. It says as clearly as can be said: women and person are contradictory terms. For a lesbian is not considered a "real woman." And yet, in popular thinking, there is really only one essential difference between a lesbian and other women: that of sexual orientation—which is to say, when you strip off all the packaging, you must finally realize that the essence of being a "woman" is to get fucked by men.

"Lesbian" is one of the sexual categories by which men have divided up humanity. While all women are dehumanized as sex objects, as the objects of men they are given certain compensations: identification with his power, his ego, his status, his protection (from other males), feeling like a "real woman," finding social acceptance by adhering to her role, etc. Should a woman confront herself by confronting another woman, there are fewer rationalizations, fewer buffers by which to avoid the stark horror of her dehumanized condition. Herein we find the overriding fear of many women towards exploring intimate relationships with other women: the fear of being used as a sexual object by a woman, which not only will bring her no male-connected compensations, but also will reveal the void which is woman's real situation. This dehumanization is expressed when a straight woman learns that a sister is a lesbian; she begins to relate to her lesbian sister as her potential sex object, laying a surrogate male role on the lesbian. This reveals her heterosexual conditioning to make herself into an object when sex is potentially involved in a relationship, and it denies the lesbian her full humanity. For women, especially those in the movement, to perceive their lesbian sisters through this male grid of role definitions is to accept this male cultural conditioning and to oppress their sisters much as they themselves have been oppressed by men. Are we going to continue the male classification system of defining all females in *sexual relation* to some *other* category of people? Affixing the label "lesbian" not only to a woman who aspires to be a person, but also to any situation of real love, real solidarity, real primacy among women is a primary form of divisiveness among women: it is the condition which keeps women within the confines of the feminine role, and it is the debunking/scare term that keeps women from forming any primary attachments, groups, or associations among ourselves.

Women in the movement have in most cases gone to great lengths to avoid discussion and confrontation with the issue of lesbianism. It puts people up-tight. They are hostile, evasive, or try to incorporate it into some "broader issue." They would rather not talk about it. If they have to, they try to dismiss it as a "lavender herring." But it is no side issue. It is absolutely essential to the success and fulfillment of the women's liberation movement that this issue be dealt with. As long as the label "dyke" can be used to frighten a woman into a less militant stand, keep her separate from her sisters, keep her from giving primacy to anything other than men and family—then to that extent she is controlled by the male culture. Until women see in each other the possibility of a primal commitment which includes sexual love, they will be denying themselves the love and value they readily accord to men, thus affirming their second-class status. As long as male acceptability is primary—both to individual women and to the movement as a whole—the term "lesbian" will be used effectively against women. Insofar as women want only more privileges within the system, they do not want to antagonize male power. They instead seek acceptability for women's liberation, and the most crucial aspect of the acceptability is to deny lesbianism—i.e., deny any fundamental challenge to the basis of the female role.

It should also be said that some younger, more radical women have honestly begun to discuss lesbianism, but so far it has been primarily as a sexual "alternative" to men. This, however, is still giving primacy to men, both because the idea of relating more completely to women occurs as a *negative reaction to men,* and because the lesbian relationship is being characterized simply by sex, which is divisive and sexist. On one level, which is both personal and political, women may withdraw emotional and sexual energies from men, and work out various alternatives for those energies in their own lives. On a different political/psychological level, it must be understood that what is crucial is that women begin disengaging from male-defined response patterns. In the privacy of our own psyches, we must cut those cords to the core. For irrespective of where our love and sexual energies flow, if we are male-identified in our heads, we cannot realize our autonomy as human beings.

But why is it that women have related to and through men? By virtue of having been brought up in a male society, we have internalized the male culture's definition of ourselves. That definition views us as relative beings who exist not for ourselves, but for the servicing, maintenance and comfort of men. That definition consigns us to sexual and family functions, and excludes us from defining and shaping the terms of our lives. In exchange for our psychic servicing and for performing society's non-profit-making functions, the man confers on us just one thing: the slave status which makes us legitimate in the eyes of the society in which we live. This is called "femininity" or "being a real woman" in our cultural lingo. We are authentic, legitimate, real to the extent that we are the property of some man whose name we bear. To be a woman who belongs to no man is to be invisible, pathetic, inauthentic, unreal. He confirms his image of us—of what we have to be in order to be acceptable by him—but not our real selves; he confirms our womanhood—as he defines it, in relation to him—

but cannot confirm our personhood, our own selves as absolutes. As long as we are dependent on the male culture for this definition, for this approval, we cannot be free.

The consequence of internalizing this role is an enormous reservoir of self-hate. This is not to say the self-hate is recognized or accepted as such; indeed most women would deny it. It may be experienced as discomfort with her role, as feeling empty, as numbness, as restlessness, a paralyzing anxiety at the center. Alternatively, it may be expressed in shrill defensiveness of the glory and destiny of her role. But it does exist, often beneath the edge of her consciousness, poisoning her existence, keeping her alienated from herself, her own needs, and rendering her a stranger to other women. They try to escape by identifying with the oppressor, living through him, gaining status and identity from his ego, his power, his accomplishments. And by not identifying with other "empty vessels" like themselves. Women resist relating on all levels to other women who will reflect their own oppression, their own secondary status, their own self-hate. For to confront another woman is finally to confront one's self—the self we have gone to such lengths to avoid. And in that mirror we know we cannot really respect and love that which we have been made to be.

As the source of self-hate and the lack of real self are rooted in our male-given identity, we must create a new sense of self. As long as we cling to the idea of "being a woman," we will sense some conflict with that incipient self, that sense of I, that sense of a whole person. It is very difficult to realize and accept that being "feminine" and being a whole person are irreconcilable. Only women can give each other a new sense of self. That identity we have to develop with reference to ourselves, and not in relation to men. This consciousness is the revolutionary force from which all else will follow, for ours is an organic revolution. For this we must be available and supportive to one another, give our commitment and our love, give the emotional support necessary to sustain this movement. Our energies must flow toward our sisters, not backwards toward our oppressors. As long as women's liberation tries to free women without facing the basic heterosexual structure that binds us in one-to-one relationship with our own oppressors, tremendous energies will continue to flow into trying to straighten up each particular relationship with a man, how to get better sex, how to turn his head around—into trying to make the "new man" out of him, in the delusion that this will allow us to be the "new woman." This obviously splits our energies and commitments, leaving us unable to be committed to the construction of the new patterns which will liberate us.

It is the primacy of women relating to women, of women creating a new consciousness of and with each other which is at the heart of women's liberation, and the basis for the cultural revolution. Together we must find, reinforce and validate our authentic selves. As we do this, we confirm in each other that struggling, incipient sense of pride and strength, the divisive barriers begin to melt, we feel this growing solidarity with our sisters. We see ourselves as prime, find our centers inside of ourselves. We find receding the sense of alienation, of being cut off, of being behind a locked window, of being unable to get out what we know is inside. We feel a realness, feel at last we are coinciding with ourselves. With that real self, with that consciousness, we begin a revolution to end the imposition of all coercive identifications, and to achieve maximum autonomy in human expression.

—1970

DIANE DI PRIMA (1934-   )

One of the few women poets associated with the Beat movement of the 1950s, Diane di Prima was born on August 6, 1934, in Brooklyn, New York. Di Prima was greatly influenced by her maternal grandfather, Domenico Mallozzi, a committed anarchist. She left Swarthmore College after a year and a half in order to devote herself to writing, and corresponded with the writers Ezra Pound, Kenneth Patchen, Lawrence Ferlinghetti, and Allen Ginsberg. While living in Manhattan, di Prima co-founded the New York Poets Theatre and founded the Poets Press. She also co-edited (with Amiri Baraka) the literary newsletter *The Floating Bear* (1961-69). Di Prima left Manhattan in 1966 to join Timothy Leary's psychedelic community at Millbrook in upstate New York, later traveling across the U.S. in a Volkswagon bus with two of her children, giving poetry readings, participating in political and social causes, and eventually settling in San Francisco, where she worked with the Diggers, a loosely affiliated political organization. In its form and content, her poetry reflects her self-defined lifestyle, and she has produced more than thirty books of poetry, including her epic *Loba* (1973-78, 1998), a mythological exploration of the feminine.

Poetics

I have deserted my post, I cdnt hold it
rearguard/to preserve the language/lucidity:
let the language fend for itself.
it turned over god knows enough carts in the city streets
its barricades are my nightmares   5

preserve the language!—there are
                    enough fascists &
                    enough socialists
on both sides
so that no one will lose this war   10

the language shall be my element, I plunge in
I suspect that I cannot drown
like a fat brat catfish, smug
                    a hoodlum fish
I move more & more gracefully   15
                    breathe it in,
success written on my mug till the fishpolice
corner me in the coral & I die

                                        —1968

Dream: The Loba Reveals Herself

she came
to hunt me down; carried down-ladder trussed
like game herself. And then set free
the hunted turning hunter. She came

thru stone labyrinths, worn by her steps, came   5

to the awesome thunder & drum of her
Name, the LOBA MANTRA, echoing
thru the flat, flagstone walls
  the footprints
    footsteps of the Loba   10
     the Loba
drumming. She came to hunt, but I did not
stay to be hunted. Instead
wd be gone again. silent
children in tow.   15

she came, she followed, she did not
pursue.
   But walked, patient behind me like some
big, rangy dog. She came to hunt, she strode
    over that worn stone floor   20
tailgating, only a step or two
         behind me.
I turned to confront
   to face
     Her: 25
       ring of fur, setting off
the purity of her head.
she-who-was-to-have-devoured me
stood, strong patient
       recognizably   30
goddess.
   Protectress
great mystic beast of European forest.
green warrior woman, towering.
         kind watchdog I cd   35
leave the children with.
      Mother & sister.
      Myself.

             —1978

The Loba Addresses the Goddess / or
The Poet as Priestess Addresses the Loba-Goddess

Is it not in yr service that I wear myself out
running ragged among these hills, driving children
to forgotten movies? In yr service
broom & pen. The monstrous feasts
we serve the others on the outer porch   5
(within the house there is only rice & salt)
And we wear exhaustion like a painted robe
I & my sisters
    wrestling the good from the niggardly

dying fathers   10
healing each other w/ water & bitter herbs

that when we stand naked in the circle of lamps
(beside the small water, in the inner grove)
we show
no blemish, but also no superfluous beauty.   15
It has burned off in watches of the night.
O Nut, O mantle of stars, we catch at you
    lean   mournful
    ragged   triumphant
       shaggy as grass   20
our skins ache of emergence / dark o' the moon

In whose dream
did she beg forgiveness, in whose
did she die alone

For whom did she bend like weeds   25
under mistral; who found her
crumpled beside the sycamores

Who raised her from the streets, who
bought her on auction block; in whose
vision was she lashed to an empty boat?   30

For whom did she gleam
in elfin cloth / unchristian

Who tore thin wraps or cape, who
taught her shame; who was condemned
to go like her on all fours?

—1978

JOAN DIDION (1934-)

A fifth-generation Californian born in Sacramento, Joan Didion has drawn on her upbringing in California for much of her work as a novelist, essayist, memoirist, and (with her late husband, John Gregory Dunne) screenwriter. While she was an undergraduate at the University of California, Berkeley, Didion won an essay prize sponsored by *Vogue* magazine; as a result, she moved to New York City and worked at the magazine for eight years. She married Dunne in 1964, the same year they moved to California, where they lived for the next twenty-five years. Didion's first essay collections, *Slouching Towards Bethlehem* (1968) and *The White Album* (1979), established her reputation as a nonfiction stylist. She has published five novels: *Run, River* (1963), *Play It As It Lays* (1970), *A Book of Common Prayer* (1977), *Democracy* (1984), and *The Last Thing He Wanted* (1996), as well as several volumes of nonfiction. Her 2005 memoir, *The Year of Magical Thinking*, which explored her grief after her husband's sudden death and her daughter's terminal illness, won the National Book Award. Didion lives in New York City.

Notes from a Native Daughter

It is very easy to sit at the bar in, say, La Scala in Beverly Hills, or Ernie's in San Francisco, and to share in the pervasive delusion that California is only five hours from New York by air. The truth is that La Scala and Ernie's are only five hours from New York by air. California is somewhere else.

Many people in the East (or "back East," as they say in California, although not in La Scala or Ernie's) do not believe this. They have been to Los Angeles or to San Francisco, have driven through a giant redwood and have seen the Pacific glazed by the afternoon sun off Big Sur, and they naturally tend to believe that they have in fact been to California. They have not been, and they probably never will be, for it is a longer and in many ways a more difficult trip than they might want to undertake, one of those trips on which the destination flickers chimerically on the horizon, ever receding, ever diminishing. I happen to know about that trip, because I come from California, come from a family, or a congeries of families, that has always been in the Sacramento Valley.

You might protest that no family has been in the Sacramento Valley for anything approaching "always." But it is characteristic of Californians to speak grandly of the past as if it had simultaneously begun, *tabula rasa,* and reached a happy ending on the day the wagons started west. *Eureka*—"I Have Found It"—as the state motto has it. Such a view of history casts a certain melancholia over those who participate in it; my own childhood was suffused with the conviction that we had long outlived our finest hour. In fact that is what I want to tell you about: what it is like to come from a place like Sacramento. If I could make you understand that, I could make you understand California and perhaps something else besides, for Sacramento *is* California, and California is a place in which a boom mentality and a sense of Chekhovian loss meet in uneasy suspension; in which the mind is troubled by some buried but ineradicable suspicion that things had better work here, because here, beneath that immense bleached sky, is where we run out of continent.

In 1847 Sacramento was no more than an adobe enclosure, Sutter's Fort, standing alone on the prairie; cut off from San Francisco and the sea by the Coast Range and from the rest of the continent by the Sierra Nevada, the Sacramento Valley was then a true sea of grass, grass so high a man riding into it could tie it across his saddle. A year later gold was discovered in the Sierra foothills, and abruptly Sacramento was a town, a town any moviegoer could map tonight in his dreams—a dusty collage of assay offices and wagonmakers and saloons. Call that Phase Two. Then the settlers came—the farmers, the people who for two hundred years had been moving west on the frontier, the peculiar flawed strain who had cleared Virginia, Kentucky, Missouri; they made Sacramento a farm town. Because the land was rich, Sacramento became eventually a rich farm town, which meant houses in town, Cadillac dealers, a country club. In that gentle sleep Sacramento dreamed until perhaps 1950, when something happened. What happened was that Sacramento woke to the fact that the outside world was moving in, fast and hard. At the moment of its waking Sacramento lost, for better or for worse, its character, and that is part of what I want to tell you about.

But the change is not what I remember first. First I remember running a boxer dog of my brother's over the same flat fields that our great-great-grandfather had found virgin and had planted; I remember swimming (albeit nervously, for I was a nervous child, afraid of sinkholes and afraid of snakes, and perhaps that was the beginning of my error) the same rivers we had swum for a century: the Sacramento, so rich with silt that we could barely see our hands a few inches beneath the surface; the American, running clean and fast with melted Sierra snow until July, when it would slow down, and rattlesnakes would sun themselves on its newly exposed rocks. The Sacramento, the American, sometimes the Cosumnes, occasionally the Feather. Incautious children died every day in those rivers; we read about it in the paper, how they had miscalculated a current or stepped into a hole down where the American runs into the Sacramento, how the Berry Brothers had been called in from Yolo County to drag the river but how the bodies remained unrecovered. "They were from away," my grandmother would extrapolate from the newspaper stories. "Their parents had no *business* letting them in the river. They were visitors from Omaha." It was not a bad lesson, although a less than reliable one; children we knew died in the rivers too.

When summer ended—when the State Fair closed and the heat broke, when the last green hop vines had been torn down along the H Street road and the tule fog[1] began rising off the low ground at night—we would go back to memorizing the Products of Our Latin American Neighbors and to visiting the great-aunts on Sunday, dozens of great-aunts, year after year of Sundays. When I think now of those winters I think of yellow elm leaves wadded in the gutters outside the Trinity Episcopal Pro-Cathedral on M Street. There are actually people in Sacramento now who call M Street Capitol Avenue, and Trinity has one of those featureless new buildings, but perhaps children still learn the same things there on Sunday mornings:

Q. In what way does the Holy Land resemble the Sacramento Valley?
A. In the type and diversity of its agricultural products.

And I think of the rivers rising, of listening to the radio to hear at what height they would crest and wondering if and when and where the levees would go. We did not have as many dams in those years. The bypasses would be full, and men would sand-bag all night. Sometimes a levee would go in the night, somewhere upriver; in the morning the rumor would spread that the Army Engineers had dynamited it to relieve the pressure on the city.

After the rains came spring, for ten days or so; the drenched fields would dissolve into a brilliant ephemeral green (it would be yellow and dry as fire in two or three weeks) and the real-estate business would pick up. It was the time of year when people's grandmothers went to Carmel; it was the time of year when girls who could not even get into Stephens or Arizona or Oregon, let alone Stanford or Berkeley, would be sent to Honolulu, on the *Lurline*.[2] I have no recollection of anyone going to New York, with the exception of a cousin who visited there (I cannot imagine why) and reported that the shoe salesmen at Lord & Taylor were "intolerably rude." What happened in New York and Washington and abroad seemed to impinge not at all upon the Sacramento mind. I remember being taken to call upon a very old woman, a

[1] A thick ground fog specific to California's Central Valley.

[2] The flagship of the Matson Line, the *Lurline* sailed weekly from San Francisco to Honolulu from the end of World War II until 1963.

rancher's widow, who was reminiscing (the favored conversational mode in Sacramento) about the son of some contemporaries of hers. "That Johnston boy never did amount to much," she said. Desultorily, my mother protested: Alva Johnston, she said, had won the Pulitzer Prize, when he was working for *The New York Times*. Our hostess looked at us impassively. "He never amounted to anything in Sacramento," she said.

Hers was the true Sacramento voice, and, although I did not realize it then, one not long to be heard, for the war was over and the boom was on and the voice of the aerospace engineer would be heard in the land. VETS NO DOWN! EXECUTIVE LIVING ON LOW FHA!

Later, when I was living in New York, I would make the trip back to Sacramento four and five times a year (the more comfortable the flight, the more obscurely miserable I would be, for it weighs heavily upon my kind that we could perhaps not make it by wagon), trying to prove that I had not meant to leave at all, because in at least one respect California—the California we are talking about—resembles Eden: it is assumed that those who absent themselves from its blessings have been banished, exiled by some perversity of heart. Did not the Donner-Reed Party, after all, eat its own dead to reach Sacramento?[3]

I have said that the trip back is difficult, and it is—difficult in a way that magnifies the ordinary ambiguities of sentimental journeys. Going back to California is not like going back to Vermont, or Chicago; Vermont and Chicago are relative constants, against which one measures one's own change. All that is constant about the California of my childhood is the rate at which it disappears. An instance: on Saint Patrick's Day of 1948 I was taken to see the legislature "in action," a dismal experience; a handful of florid assemblymen, wearing green hats, were reading Pat-and-Mike jokes into the record. I still think of the legislators that way—wearing green hats, or sitting around on the veranda of the Senator Hotel fanning themselves and being entertained by Artie Samish's[4] emissaries. (Samish was the lobbyist who said, "Earl Warren[5] may be the governor of the state, but I'm the governor of the legislature.") In fact there is no longer a veranda at the Senator Hotel—it was turned into an airline ticket office, if you want to embroider the point—and in any case the legislature has largely deserted the Senator for the flashy motels north of town, where the tiki torches flame and the steam rises off the heated swimming pools in the cold Valley night.

It is hard to *find* California now, unsettling to wonder how much of it was merely imagined or improvised; melancholy to realize how much of anyone's memory is no true memory at all but only the traces of someone else's memory, stories handed down on the family network. I have an indelibly vivid "memory," for example, of how Prohibition affected the hop growers around Sacramento: the sister of a grower my family knew brought home a mink coat from San Francisco, and was told to take it back, and sat on the floor of the parlor cradling that coat and crying. Although I was not born until a year after Repeal, that scene is more "real" to me than many I have played myself.

---

[3] California-bound settlers who, caught in the Sierra Nevada during the winter of 1846-1847, resorted to cannibalism.
[4] Arthur Samish (1897-1974), lobbyist known as "the secret boss of California."
[5] Earl Warren (1891-1974), governor of California from 1943 to 1953, and Chief Justice of the U.S. Supreme Court from 1953 to 1969.

I remember one trip home, when I sat alone on a night jet from New York and read over and over some lines from a W. S. Merwin[6] poem I had come across in a magazine, a poem about a man who had been a long time in another country and knew that he must go home:

> ...*But it should be*
> *Soon. Already I defend hotly*
> *Certain of our indefensible faults,*
> *Resent being reminded; already in my mind*
> *Our language becomes freighted with a richness*
> *No common tongue could offer, while the mountains*
> *Are like nowhere on earth, and the wide rivers.*

You see the point. I want to tell you the truth, and already I have told you about the wide rivers.

It should be clear by now that the truth about the place is elusive, and must be tracked with caution. You might go to Sacramento tomorrow and someone (although no one I know) might take you out to Aerojet-General, which has, in the Sacramento phrase, "something to do with rockets." Fifteen thousand people work for Aerojet, almost all of them imported; a Sacramento lawyer's wife told me, as evidence of how Sacramento was opening up, that she believed she had met one of them, at an open house two Decembers ago. ("Couldn't have been nicer, actually," she added enthusiastically. "I think he and his wife bought the house next *door* to Mary and Al, something like that, which of course was how *they* met him.") So you might go to Aerojet and stand in the big vendors' lobby where a couple of thousand components salesmen try every week to sell their wares and you might look up at the electrical wallboard that lists Aerojet personnel, their projects and their location at any given time, and you might wonder if I have been in Sacramento lately. MINUTEMAN, POLARIS, TITAN,[7] the lights flash, and all the coffee tables are littered with airline schedules, very now, very much in touch.

But I could take you a few miles from there into towns where the banks still bear names like The Bank of Alex Brown, into towns where the one hotel still has an octagonal-tile floor in the dining room and dusty potted palms and big ceiling fans; into towns where everything—the seed business, the Harvester franchise, the hotel, the department store and the main street—carries a single name, the name of the man who built the town. A few Sundays ago I was in a town like that, a town smaller than that, really, no hotel, no Harvester franchise, the bank burned out, a river town. It was the golden anniversary of some of my relatives and it was 110° and the guests of honor sat on straight-backed chairs in front of a sheaf of gladioluses in the Rebekah Hall. I mentioned visiting Aerojet-General to a cousin I saw there, who listened to me with interested disbelief. Which is the true California? That is what we all wonder.

Let us try out a few irrefutable statements, on subjects not open to interpretation. Although Sacramento is in many ways the least typical of the Valley towns, it *is* a Valley town, and must be viewed in that context. When you say "the Valley" in Los

---

[6] William Stanley Merwin (b. 1927), American poet and translator.

[7] Missile systems.

Angeles, most people assume that you mean the San Fernando Valley (some people in fact assume that you mean Warner Brothers), but make no mistake: we are talking not about the valley of the sound stages and the ranchettes but about the real Valley, the Central Valley, the fifty thousand square miles drained by the Sacramento and the San Joaquin Rivers and further irrigated by a complex network of sloughs, cutoffs, ditches, and the Delta-Mendota and Friant-Kern Canals.

A hundred miles north of Los Angeles, at the moment when you drop from the Tehachapi Mountains into the outskirts of Bakersfield, you leave Southern California and enter the Valley. "You look up the highway and it is straight for miles, coming at you, with the black line down the center coming at you and at you…and the heat dazzles up from the white slab so that only the black line is clear, coming at you with the whine of the tires, and if you don't quit staring at that line and don't take a few deep breaths and slap yourself hard on the back of the neck you'll hypnotize yourself."

Robert Penn Warren[8] wrote that about another road, but he might have been writing about the Valley road, U.S. 99, three hundred miles from Bakersfield to Sacramento, a highway so straight that when one flies on the most direct pattern from Los Angeles to Sacramento one never loses sight of U.S. 99. The landscape it runs through never, to the untrained eye, varies. The Valley eye can discern the point where miles of cotton seedlings fade into miles of tomato seedlings, or where the great corporation ranches—Kern County Land, what is left of DiGiorgio—give way to private operations (somewhere on the horizon, if the place is private, one sees a house and a stand of scrub oaks), but such distinctions are in the long view irrelevant. All day long, all that moves is the sun, and the big Rainbird sprinklers.

Every so often along 99 between Bakersfield and Sacramento there is a town: Delano, Tulare, Fresno, Madera, Merced, Modesto, Stockton. Some of these towns are pretty big now, but they are all the same at heart, one- and two- and three-story buildings artlessly arranged, so that what appears to be the good dress shop stands beside a W. T. Grant store, so that the big Bank of America faces a Mexican movie house. *Dos Peliculas,*[9] *Bingo Bingo Bingo.* Beyond the downtown (pronounced *down*town, with the Okie accent that now pervades Valley speech patterns) lie blocks of old frame houses—paint peeling, sidewalks cracking, their occasional leaded amber windows overlooking a Foster's Freeze or a five-minute car wash or a State Farm Insurance office; beyond those spread the shopping centers and the miles of tract houses, pastel with redwood siding, the unmistakable signs of cheap building already blossoming on those houses which have survived the first rain. To a stranger driving 99 in an air-conditioned car (he would be on business, I suppose, any stranger driving 99, for 99 would never get a tourist to Big Sur or San Simeon, never get him to the California he came to see), these towns must seem so flat, so impoverished, as to drain the imagination. They hint at evenings spent hanging around gas stations, and suicide pacts sealed in drive-ins.

But remember:

> *Q. In what way does the Holy Land resemble the Sacramento Valley?*
> *A. In the type and diversity of its agricultural products.*

---

[8] Robert Penn Warren (1905-1989), American poet, novelist, and literary critic. [9] (Sp.) Two films.

U.S. 99 in fact passes through the richest and most intensely cultivated agricultural region in the world, a giant outdoor hothouse with a billion-dollar crop. It is when you remember the Valley's wealth that the monochromatic flatness of its towns takes on a curious meaning, suggests a habit of mind some would consider perverse. There is something in the Valley mind that reflects a real indifference to the stranger in his air-conditioned car, a failure to perceive even his presence, let alone his thoughts or wants. An implacable insularity is the seal of these towns. I once met a woman in Dallas, a most charming and attractive woman accustomed to the hospitality and social hypersensitivity of Texas, who told me that during the four war years her husband had been stationed in Modesto, she had never once been invited inside anyone's house. No one in Sacramento would find this story remarkable ("She probably had no *relatives* there," said someone to whom I told it), for the Valley towns understand one another, share a peculiar spirit. They think alike and they look alike. *I* can tell Modesto from Merced, but I have visited there, gone to dances there; besides, there is over the main street of Modesto an arched sign which reads:

> WATER – WEALTH
> CONTENTMENT – HEALTH

There is no such sign in Merced.

I said that Sacramento was the least typical of the Valley towns, and it is—but only because it is bigger and more diverse, only because it has had the rivers and the legislature; its true character remains the Valley character, its virtues the Valley virtues, its sadness the Valley sadness. It is just as hot in the summertime, so hot that the air shimmers and the grass bleaches white and the blinds stay drawn all day, so hot that August comes on not like a month but like an affliction; it is just as flat, so flat that a ranch of my family's with a slight rise on it, perhaps a foot, was known for the hundred-some years which preceded this year as "the hill ranch." (It is known this year as a subdivision in the making, but that is another part of the story.) Above all, in spite of its infusions from outside, Sacramento retains the Valley insularity.

To sense that insularity a visitor need do no more than pick up a copy of either of the two newspapers, the morning *Union* or the afternoon *Bee*. The *Union* happens to be Republican and impoverished and the *Bee* Democratic and powerful ("THE VALLEY OF THE BEES!" as the McClatchys, who own the Fresno, Modesto, and Sacramento *Bees,* used to headline their advertisements in the trade press. "ISOLATED FROM ALL OTHER MEDIA INFLUENCE!"), but they read a good deal alike, and the tone of their chief editorial concerns is strange and wonderful and instructive. The *Union,* in a county heavily and reliably Democratic, frets mainly about the possibility of a local takeover by the John Birch Society;[10] the *Bee,* faithful to the letter of its founder's will, carries on overwrought crusades against phantoms it still calls "the power trusts." Shades of Hiram Johnson,[11] whom the *Bee* helped elect governor in 1910. Shades of Robert La Follette,[12] to whom the *Bee* delivered the Valley in 1924. There is something about the Sacramento papers that does not quite connect with the way Sacramento lives now, something pronouncedly beside the

[10] Far-right U.S. political group formed in 1958.
[11] Hiram Johnson (1866-1945), governor of California from 1911 to 1917.
[12] Robert Marion La Follette (1855-1925), Progressive Party candidate for president in 1924.

point. The aerospace engineers, one learns, read the San Francisco *Chronicle*.

The Sacramento papers, however, simply mirror the Sacramento peculiarity, the Valley fate, which is to be paralyzed by a past no longer relevant. Sacramento is a town which grew up on farming and discovered to its shock that land has more profitable uses. (The chamber of commerce will give you crop figures, but pay them no mind—what matters is the feeling, the knowledge that where the green hops once grew is now Larchmont Riviera, that what used to be the Whitney ranch is now Sunset City, thirty-three thousand houses and a country-club complex.) It is a town in which defense industry and its absentee owners are suddenly the most important facts; a town which has never had more people or more money, but has lost its *raison d'être*. It is a town many of whose most solid citizens sense about themselves a kind of functional obsolescence. The old families still see only one another, but they do not see even one another as much as they once did; they are closing ranks, preparing for the long night, selling their rights-of-way and living on the proceeds. Their children still marry one another, still play bridge and go into the real-estate business together. (There is no other business in Sacramento, no reality other than land—even I, when I was living and working in New York, felt impelled to take a University of California correspondence course in Urban Land Economics.) But late at night when the ice has melted there is always somebody now, some Julian English,[13] whose heart is not quite in it. For out there on the outskirts of town are marshaled the legions of aerospace engineers, who talk their peculiar condescending language and tend their dichondra and plan to stay in the promised land; who are raising a new generation of native Sacramentans and who do not care, really do not care, that they are not asked to join the Sutter Club. It makes one wonder, late at night when the ice is gone; introduces some air into the womb, suggests that the Sutter Club is perhaps not, after all, the Pacific Union or the Bohemian;[14] that Sacramento is not *the city*. In just such self-doubts do small towns lose their character.

I want to tell you a Sacramento story. A few miles out of town is a place, six or seven thousand acres, which belonged in the beginning to a rancher with one daughter. That daughter went abroad and married a title, and when she brought the title home to live on the ranch, her father built them a vast house—music rooms, conservatories, a ballroom. They needed a ballroom because they entertained: people from abroad, people from San Francisco, house parties that lasted weeks and involved special trains. They are long dead, of course, but their only son, aging and unmarried, still lives on the place. He does not live in the house, for the house is no longer there. Over the years it burned, room by room, wing by wing. Only the chimneys of the great house are still standing, and its heir lives in their shadow, lives by himself on the charred site, in a house trailer.

That is a story my generation knows; I doubt that the next will know it, the children of the aerospace engineers. Who would tell it to them? Their grandmothers live in Scarsdale, and they have never met a great-aunt. "Old" Sacramento to them will be something colorful, something they read about in *Sunset*.[15] They will probably think that the Redevelopment has always been there, that the Embarcadero, down along the

---

[13] Self-destructive member of the social elite in *Appointment in Samarra*, a 1934 novel by John O'Hara (1905-1970).

[14] Elite private social clubs in San Francisco.

[15] A magazine founded in 1898 to counter negative images of life in California and the western U.S.

river, with its amusing places to shop and its picturesque fire houses turned into bars, has about it the true flavor of the way it was. There will be no reason for them to know that in homelier days it was called Front Street (the town was not, after all, settled by the Spanish) and was a place of derelicts and missions and itinerant pickers in town for a Saturday-night drunk: VICTORIOUS LIFE MISSION, JESUS SAVES, BEDS 25¢ A NIGHT, CROP INFORMATION HERE. They will have lost the real past and gained a manufactured one, and there will be no way for them to know, no way at all, why a house trailer should stand alone on seven thousand acres outside town.

But perhaps it is presumptuous of me to assume that they will be missing something. Perhaps in retrospect this has been a story not about Sacramento at all, but about the things we lose and the promises we break as we grow older; perhaps I have been playing out unawares the Margaret in the poem:

> *Margaret, are you grieving*
> *Over Goldengrove unleaving?...*
> *It is the blight man was born for,*
> *It is Margaret you mourn for.*[16]

—1965

[16] From "Spring and Fall," by British poet Gerard Manley Hopkins (1844-1889).

AUDRE LORDE (1934-1992)

Audre (Audrey Geraldine) Lorde was born in New York City to parents who had immigrated from Grenada. Lorde attributed her poetic imagery to the unique way in which she saw the world from infancy: she was so nearsighted that she was legally blind, and she did not speak until she learned to read, at the age of four. As a child Lorde recited poems when asked how she felt, and she published her first poem in *Seventeen* magazine as a teenager. She met poet Diane di Prima when they were both students at Hunter High School in New York; di Prima later edited Lorde's first book of poetry, *The First Cities* (1968).

After studying at the National University of Mexico, Lorde returned to New York to earn her bachelor's degree at Hunter College in 1959 and worked odd jobs, including as an x-ray technician, which may have led to the breast cancer that would kill her. She married and had two children before meeting the woman who would become her long-time partner, Francis Clayton, at Tougaloo University in 1968, where Lorde was a writer-in-residence.

Lorde was active in the civil rights, anti-war, and feminist movements beginning in the 1960s. By the 1980s she was well known for her statements of multiple, simultaneous identity, naming herself "Black, lesbian, feminist, warrior, poet, mother" in several essays and speeches, many of which are published in her collection *Sister Outsider* (1984). These essays, such as "The Master's Tools Will Never Dismantle the Master's House," remain influential in feminist theory and politics for their direct, deceptively simple statements of complex concepts. Lorde considered herself a poet rather than a theorist, however, and she published volumes of poetry consistently from the late 1960s until her death. Like her essays, her poems expressed her political views and her multifaceted identity. She was included in Langston Hughes' anthology *New Negro Poets* (1962), and by 1970 she had published her first openly lesbian poem,

"Martha," in her book *Cables to Rage*. Though her 1973 volume *From a Land Where Other People Live* was nominated for the National Book Award, *The Black Unicorn* (1978) is considered by many to be her best work. Its poems span history and geography, invoking traditional west African symbolism to explore themes of gender, race, spirituality, and sexuality.

Lorde was awarded National Endowment for the Arts Fellowships in 1968 and 1981. In 1981 she also received an award from the American Library Association for *The Cancer Journals,* a collection of essays exploring her experience living with breast cancer. Other notable publications include her autobiographical novel *Zami: A New Spelling of My Name* (1982), which she termed a "biomythography;" seven other volumes of poetry (she published a total of eleven during her lifetime); and a third prose work, *A Burst of Light* (1988), which discusses her diagnosis of metastasized liver cancer. Lorde was a co-founder of Kitchen Table: Women of Color Press with Barbara Smith, and was a founding member of the U.S.-based group Sisters in Support of Sisters in South Africa. She was appointed Poet Laureate of the State of New York in 1991, the year before she died in St. Croix, where she lived with her partner Gloria Joseph.

The Brown Menace
or, Poem to the Survival of Roaches

Call me
your deepest urge
toward survival
call me
and my brothers and sisters   5
in the sharp smell of your refusal
call me
roach and presumptious
nightmare on your white pillow
your itch to destroy   10
the indestructible
part of yourself.

Call me
your own determination
in the most detestable shape   15
you can become
friend of your image
within me
I am you
in your most deeply cherished nightmare   20
scuttling through the painted cracks
you create to admit me
into your kitchens
into your fearful midnights
into your values at noon   25
in your most secret places
with hate
you learn to honor me
by imitation

as I alter—   30
through your greedy preoccupations
through your kitchen wars
and your poisonous refusal—
to survive.

To survive.   35
Survive.

—1974

To My Daughter The Junkie On A Train

Children we have not borne
bedevil us by becoming
themselves
painfully sharp and unavoidable
like a needle in our flesh.   5

Coming home on the subway from a PTA meeting
of minds committed like murder
or suicide
to their own private struggle
a long-legged girl with a horse in her brain   10
slumps down beside me
begging to be ridden asleep
for the price of a midnight train
free from desire.
Little girl on the nod   15
if we are measured by the dreams we avoid
then you are the nightmare
of all sleeping mothers
rocking back and forth
the dead weight of your arms   20
locked about our necks
heavier than our habit
of looking for reasons.

My corrupt concern will not replace
what you once needed   25
but I am locked into my own addictions
and offer you my help, one eye
out
for my own station.
Roused and deprived   30
your costly dream explodes
into a terrible technicoloured laughter
at my failure
up and down across the aisle

women avert their eyes   35
as the other mothers who became useless
curse their children who became junk.

—1974

Coal

I
is the total black, being spoken
from the earth's inside.
There are many kinds of open
how a diamond comes into a knot of flame   5
how sound comes into a word, coloured
by who pays what for speaking.

Some words are open like a diamond
on glass windows
singing out within the passing crash of sun   10
Then there are words like stapled wagers
in a perforated book,—buy and sign and tear apart—
and come whatever wills all chances
the stub remains
an ill-pulled tooth with a ragged edge.   15
Some words live in my throat
breeding like adders. Others know sun
seeking like gypsies over my tongue
to explode through my lips
like young sparrows bursting from shell.   20
Some words
bedevil me.

Love is a word, another kind of open.
As the diamond comes into a knot of flame
I am Black because I come from the earth's inside   25
now take my word for jewel in the open light.

—1976

Power

The difference between poetry and rhetoric
is being ready to kill
yourself
instead of your children.

I am trapped on a desert of raw gunshot wounds   5
and a dead child dragging his shattered black
face off the edge of my sleep
blood from his punctured cheeks and shoulders
is the only liquid for miles
and my stomach   10

churns at the imagined taste while
my mouth splits into dry lips
without loyalty or reason
thirsting for the wetness of his blood
as it sinks into the whiteness   15
of the desert where I am lost
without imagery or magic
trying to make power out of hatred and destruction
trying to heal my dying son with kisses
only the sun will bleach his bones quicker.   20

A policeman who shot down a ten year old in Queens
stood over the boy with his cop shoes in childish blood
and a voice said "Die you little motherfucker" and
there are tapes to prove it. At his trial
this policeman said in his own defense   25
"I didn't notice the size nor nothing else
only the color". And
there are tapes to prove that, too.

Today that 37 year old white man
with 13 years of police forcing   30
was set free
by eleven white men who said they were satisfied
justice had been done
and one Black Woman who said
"They convinced me" meaning   35
they had dragged her 4'10" Black Woman's frame
over the hot coals
of four centuries of white male approval
until she let go
the first real power she ever had   40
and lined her own womb with cement
to make a graveyard for our children.

I have not been able to touch the destruction
within me.
But unless I learn to use   45
the difference between poetry and rhetoric
my power too will run corrupt as poisonous mold
or lie limp and useless as an unconnected wire
and one day I will take my teenaged plug
and connect it to the nearest socket   50
raping an 85 year old white woman
who is somebody's mother
and as I beat her senseless and set a torch to her bed
a greek chorus will be singing in 3/4 time
"Poor thing. She never hurt a soul. What beasts they are."

—1976

Afterimages

I

However the image enters
its force remains within
my eyes
rockstrewn caves where dragonfish evolve
wild for life, relentless and acquisitive   5
learning to survive
where there is no food
my eyes are always hungry
and remembering
however the image enters   10
its force remains.
A white woman stands bereft and empty
a black boy hacked into a murderous lesson
recalled in me forever
like a lurch of earth on the edge of sleep   15
etched into my visions
food for dragonfish that learn
to live upon whatever they must eat
fused images beneath my pain.

II

The Pearl River floods through the streets of Jackson   20
A Mississippi summer televised.
Trapped houses kneel like sinners in the rain
a white woman climbs from her roof to a passing boat
her fingers tarry for a moment on the chimney
now awash   25
tearless and no longer young, she holds
a tattered baby's blanket in her arms.
In a flickering afterimage of the nightmare rain
a microphone
thrust up against her flat bewildered words   30
    "we jest come from the bank yestiddy
        borrowing money to pay the income tax
        now everything's gone. I never knew
        it could be so hard."

Despair weighs down her voice like Pearl River mud   35
caked around the edges
her pale eyes scanning the camera for help or explanation
unanswered
she shifts her search across the watered street, dry-eyed
        "hard, but not this hard."   40
Two tow-headed children hurl themselves against her
hanging upon her coat like mirrors
until a man with ham-like hands pulls her aside

snarling "She ain't got nothing more to say!"
and that lie hangs in his mouth   45
like a shred of rotting meat.

III
I inherited Jackson, Mississippi.
For my majority it gave me Emmett Till[1]
his 15 years puffed out like bruises
on plump boy-cheeks   50
his only Mississippi summer
whistling a 21 gun salute to Dixie
as a white girl passed him in the street
and he was baptized my son forever
in the midnight waters of the Pearl.   55

His broken body is the afterimage of my 21st year
when I walked through a northern summer
my eyes averted
from each corner's photographies
newspapers protest posters magazines   60
Police Story, Confidential, True
the avid insistence of detail
pretending insight or information
the length of gash across the dead boy's loins
his grieving mother's lamentation   65
the severed lips, how many burns
his gouged out eyes
sewed shut upon the screaming covers
louder than life
all over   70
the veiled warning, the secret relish
of a black child's mutilated body
fingered by street-corner eyes
bruise upon livid bruise
and wherever I looked that summer   75
I learned to be at home with children's blood
with savored violence
with pictures of black broken flesh
used, crumpled, and discarded
lying amid the sidewalk refuse   80
like a raped woman's face.

A black boy from Chicago
whistled on the streets of Jackson, Mississippi
testing what he'd been taught was a manly thing to do
his teachers   85
ripped his eyes out his sex his tongue

---

[1] Emmett Till (1941-1955), Black teenager from Chicago who was brutally lynched in Mississippi after allegedly whistling at a white woman. Following a trial that gained international media attention, two white men were acquitted for the murder, to which they later confessed.

and flung him to the Pearl weighted with stone
in the name of white womanhood
they took their aroused honor
back to Jackson   90
and celebrated in a whorehouse
the double ritual of white manhood
confirmed.

IV

"If earth and air and water do not judge them
who are we to refuse a crust of bread?"

Emmett Till rides the crest of the Pearl, whistling
24 years his ghost lay like the shade of a raped woman   95
and a white girl has grown older in costly honor
(what did she pay to never know its price?)
now the Pearl River speaks its muddy judgment
and I can withhold my pity and my bread.

       "Hard, but not this hard."   100
Her face is flat with resignation and despair
with ancient and familiar sorrows
a woman surveying her crumpled future
as the white girl besmirched by Emmett's whistle
never allowed her own tongue   105
without power or conclusion
unvoiced
she stands adrift in the ruins of her honor
and a man with an executioner's face
pulls her away.   110

Within my eyes
the flickering afterimages of a nightmare rain
a woman wrings her hands
beneath the weight of agonies remembered
I wade through summer ghosts   115
betrayed by vision
hers and my own
becoming dragonfish to survive
the horrors we are living
with tortured lungs   120
adapting to breathe blood.

A woman measures her life's damage
my eyes are caves, chunks of etched rock
tied to the ghost of a black boy
whistling   125
crying and frightened
her tow-headed children cluster
like little mirrors of despair

their father's hands upon them
and soundlessly   130
a woman begins to weep.

—1981

The Transformation of Silence into Language and Action[2]

I have come to believe over and over again that what is most important to me must
be spoken, made verbal and shared, even at the risk of having it bruised or misunderstood. That the speaking profits me, beyond any other effect. I am standing here
as a Black lesbian poet, and the meaning of all that waits upon the fact that I am still
alive, and might not have been. Less than two months ago I was told by two doctors,
one female and one male, that I would have to have breast surgery, and that there was
a 60 to 80 percent chance that the tumor was malignant. Between that telling and the
actual surgery, there was a three-week period of the agony of an involuntary reorgan-
ization of my entire life. The surgery was completed, and the growth was benign.

But within those three weeks, I was forced to look upon myself and my living with
a harsh and urgent clarity that has left me still shaken but much stronger. This is a
situation faced by many women, by some of you here today. Some of what I
experienced during that time has helped elucidate for me much of what I feel
concerning the transformation of silence into language and action.

In becoming forcibly and essentially aware of my mortality, and of what I wished
and wanted for my life, however short it might be, priorities and omissions became
strongly etched in a merciless light, and what I most regretted were my silences. Of
what had I *ever* been afraid? To question or to speak as I believed could have meant
pain, or death. But we all hurt in so many different ways, all the time, and pain will
either change or end. Death, on the other hand, is the final silence. And that might be
coming quickly, now, without regard for whether I had ever spoken what needed to
be said, or had only betrayed myself into small silences, while I planned someday to
speak, or waited for someone else's words. And I began to recognize a source of power
within myself that comes from the knowledge that while it is most desirable not to be
afraid, learning to put fear into a perspective gave me great strength.

I was going to die, if not sooner then later, whether or not I had ever spoken myself.
My silences had not protected me. Your silence will not protect you. But for every real
word spoken, for every attempt I had ever made to speak those truths for which I am
still seeking, I had made contact with other women while we examined the words to
fit a world in which we all believed, bridging our differences. And it was the concern
and caring of all those women which gave me strength and enabled me to scrutinize
the essentials of my living.

The women who sustained me through that period were Black and white, old and
young, lesbian, bisexual, and heterosexual, and we all shared a war against the tyrannies of silence. They all gave me a strength and concern without which I could not
have survived intact. Within those weeks of acute fear came the knowledge—within
the war we are all waging with the forces of death, subtle and otherwise, conscious or

---

[2] Paper delivered at the Modern Language Association's "Lesbian and Literature Panel," Chicago, Illinois, December 28,
1977.

not—I am not only a casualty, I am also a warrior.

What are the words you do not yet have? What do you need to say? What are the tyrannies you swallow day by day and attempt to make your own, until you will sicken and die of them, still in silence? Perhaps for some of you here today, I am the face of one of your fears. Because I am woman, because I am Black, because I am lesbian, because I am myself—a Black woman warrior poet doing my work—come to ask you, are you doing yours?

And of course I am afraid, because the transformation of silence into language and action is an act of self-revelation, and that always seems fraught with danger. But my daughter, when I told her of our topic and my difficulty with it, said, "Tell them about how you're never really a whole person if you remain silent, because there's always that one little piece inside you that wants to be spoken out, and if you keep ignoring it, it gets madder and madder and hotter and hotter, and if you don't speak it out one day it will just up and punch you in the mouth from the inside."

In the cause of silence, each of us draws the face of her own fear—fear of contempt, of censure, or some judgment, or recognition, of challenge, of annihilation. But most of all, I think, we fear the visibility without which we cannot truly live. Within this country where racial difference creates a constant, if unspoken, distortion of vision, Black women have on one hand always been highly visible, and so, on the other hand, have been rendered invisible through the depersonalization of racism. Even within the women's movement, we have had to fight, and still do, for that very visibility which also renders us most vulnerable, our Blackness. For to survive in the mouth of this dragon we call america, we have had to learn this first and most vital lesson—that we were never meant to survive. Not as human beings. And neither were most of you here today, Black or not. And that visibility which makes us most vulnerable is that which also is the source of our greatest strength. Because the machine will try to grind you into dust anyway, whether or not we speak. We can sit in our corners mute for-ever while our sisters and our selves are wasted, while our children are distorted and destroyed, while our earth is poisoned; we can sit in our safe corners mute as bottles, and we will still be no less afraid.

In my house this year we are celebrating the feast of Kwanza, the African-american festival of harvest which begins the day after Christmas and lasts for seven days. There are seven principals of Kwanza, one for each day. The first principle is Umoja, which means unity, the decision to strive for and maintain unity in self and community. The principle for yesterday, the second day, was Kujichagulia— self-determination—the decision to define ourselves, name ourselves, and speak for ourselves, instead of being defined and spoken for by others. Today is the third day of Kwanza, and the principle for today is Ujima—collective work and responsibility— the decision to build and maintain ourselves and our communities together and to rec-ognize and solve our problems together.

Each of us is here now because in one way or another we share a commitment to language and to the power of language, and to the reclaiming of that language which has been made to work against us. In the transformation of silence into language and action, it is vitally necessary for each one of us to establish or examine her function in that transformation and to recognize her role as vital within that transformation.

For those of us who write, it is necessary to scrutinize not only the truth of what we speak, but the truth of that language by which we speak it. For others, it is to share and spread also those words that are meaningful to us. But primarily for us all, it is necessary to teach by living and speaking those truths which we believe and know beyond understanding. Because in this way alone we can survive, by taking part in a process of life that is creative and continuing, that is growth.

And it is never without fear—of visibility, of the harsh light of scrutiny and perhaps judgment, of pain, of death. But we have lived through all of those already, in silence, except death. And I remind myself all the time now that if I were to have been born mute, or had maintained an oath of silence my whole life long for safety, I would still have suffered, and I would still die. It is very good for establishing perspective.

And where the words of women are crying to be heard, we must each of us recognize our responsibility to seek those words out, to read them and share them and examine them in their pertinence to our lives. That we not hide behind the mockeries of separations that have been imposed upon us and which so often we accept as our own. For instance, "I can't possibly teach Black women's writing—their experience is so different from mine." Yet how many years have you spent teaching Plato and Shakespeare and Proust?[3] Or another, "She's a white woman and what could she possibly have to say to me?" Or, "She's a lesbian, what would my husband say, or my chairman?" Or again, "This woman writes of her sons and I have no children." And all the other endless ways in which we rob ourselves of ourselves and each other.

We can learn to work and speak when we are afraid in the same way we have learned to work and speak when we are tired. For we have been socialized to respect fear more than our own needs for language and definition, and while we wait in silence for that final luxury of fearlessness, the weight of that silence will choke us.

The fact that we are here and that I speak these words is an attempt to break that silence and bridge some of those differences between us, for it is not difference which immobilizes us, but silence. And there are so many silences to be broken.

—1977

[3] Plato (ca. 427-347 B.C.E.), Greek philosopher; William Shakespeare (1564-1616), English playwright and poet; Marcel Proust (1871-1922), French novelist.

RENÉE RICHARDS (1934-   )

Renée Richards was born Richard Raskind, to a psychiatrist mother and orthopedist father. In her autobiography *Second Serve* (1986) she describes her childhood as odd, even pathological, as her cold and overbearing mother, passive and distant father, and sadistic older sister combined to force young Richard into cross-dressing and other uncomfortable sex and gender atypicalities. The Raskinds led a privileged life in New York, and Richard went to Yale University, where he excelled at tennis and academics. After college he became an ophthalmologist, then embarked on a career in the Navy. The compulsion to cross-dress remained with him, and in the 1960s he traveled to Europe dressed as a woman, intending to have sex-change surgery. He lost his nerve, returned to the United States, married, fathered a son, and divorced. Finally, in 1975, he had sex reassignment surgery and changed his name to Renée Richards. After she transitioned, Renée Richards began playing in women's tennis tournaments. In 1976 she was refused permission to play in the U.S. Women's Open because, although she was legally a woman, the chromosome tests required of top-rank athletes still indicated that she was male. Richards sued and won in the New York Supreme Court, later losing her match in the first round of the 1977 Open. She did win one tournament on the women's tour, and briefly served as coach to Martina Navratilova before resuming her ophthalmology practice in New York. Richards had a much more difficult time living as a woman than, for instance, Christine Jorgensen had. She attributes the difficulty to having transitioned after having lived successfully as a man into mid-life. Whereas Jorgensen is thought of as a woman, Richards never got past being considered, as she put it in a 1999 interview, "Transsexual Tennis Player Dr. Renée Richards."

from Second Serve

[...] It was as if someone had slipped me a mood-elevating drug. The world seemed less antagonistic, more supportive; I had a sense of lightness as I moved through it. Dick had always been a presence of great density; many people found him aloof, superior. The burgeoning Renée found herself less inclined to isolation, more interested in the people around her. I suddenly began to feel more personally about people who had heretofore been defined primarily by my formal relations with them. So-and-so was my nurse. So-and-so was my anesthesiologist. My efforts in their behalf (and often I bent over backward) were in the line of duty. I went to the captain's mast[1] to speak up for my corpsmen, not out of humanitarian feeling but because it was my duty; it was dictated by an abstract code of fair play. They did for me, and in return I did for them. It was all very civilized but, at the same time, distant. As treatment progressed, I found myself more and more interested in personal details. In some instances my friendships began to alter. One doctor and his wife who had been longtime associates of mine noticed a peculiar shift in my orientation. For most of our relationship I had treated the wife as a tolerable but fairly uninteresting part of the duo. Her conversation centered primarily around the kids and the intricacies of homemaking. I preferred to discuss medicine and tennis strategies with her husband rather than commiserate with her over her son's inability to master a two-wheeled bike. Slowly though, I began to find myself more able to be concerned with the homey details of housewifery. If the husband left the room to go to the bathroom, on his return he might find me gone. Looked for, I could be found in the kitchen watching his wife do the dishes and savoring her chatty résumé of the day's events. I know that they discussed this between themselves. She was impressed with how much more human I had become. He thought maybe I was planning a seduction. Years later they finally understood.

Such misunderstandings were possible because I told no one about my therapy. I had to be on guard. The personality changes, though noticeable, were fairly easy for me to keep within acceptable bounds, though I did begin having what might be called uncontrollable lapses. These centered around two seemingly opposite activities: laughing and crying. I began to be frequently amused all out of proportion to the stimulus. Someone might make a remark that would elicit chuckles from everyone in the group. After they had stopped chuckling, I would continue—all the while escalating. People would wait politely for me to finish, and this would feed my amusement. The sight of them all looking at me inquisitively would strike me as hilarious. Soon the person who

---

[1] A disciplinary hearing during which the commanding officer of a naval unit studies and disposes of cases against the enlisted personnel in the unit.

made the joke in the first place would be saying, "Oh, come on, Dick. It wasn't that funny!" That, too, was funny. These fits could go on for ten or fifteen minutes, their intensity rising and falling until finally they subsided as I grew exhausted. People quickly observed that the fastest way to get by these laughing episodes was to ignore them.

I also began to have crying jags. More often than not these were private, though I did break down in public sometimes. Ordinarily they would be provoked by a movie, a line of poetry, a news report, or even a casual remark that somehow carried a tragic or pathetic overtone. Imagine my surprise when I burst into tears for the first time in a motion picture theater. Dick Raskind had not cried in public since he was a child. There I was, weeping uncontrollably, smack in the middle of a group of one hundred and fifty movie fans. Heads were turning all over the auditorium. Although I tried to keep it down to a quiet sniffle, it soon scaled up into a series of breathless sobs. Finally, treating myself like an uncontrollable child in a public place, I left.

The strangest thing was that I did not feel at all regretful about these episodes; I only wished they were not an inconvenience to others. As a matter of fact, I really felt good after fifteen or twenty minutes of crying in the privacy of my apartment. I had the sensation of being purged. It was as if the control and repression of a lifetime were finally breaking down. Afterward, that lovely feeling of lightness would be doubly noticeable. I think people who witnessed these incidents thought that I must be under some severe emotional stress, and so they were generally kind and indulgent. I experienced these adjustment problems for about the first two months of my hormone therapy, then my personality leveled out and became more stable though I retained much of my newly discovered emotionality.

The physical changes were harder to explain away. It was about five weeks before I noticed any. You might think that I would be getting up each morning and racing to the mirror to check myself, but I was surprisingly blasé about the progress of my transformation. I found it hard to be clinical. I did not, for example, keep track of my measurements so that I could have a record of where I gained and lost inches. Probably the first thing I noticed was an increase in the sensitivity of my nipples. They had never been a major erogenous zone for me, and I had never given them much thought except to wish that they were more like a woman's. Suddenly they were calling themselves to my attention. My shirt would begin to chafe the newly tender tips, and I would absently reach down and pull the material out so that it no longer touched the nipple. About the fifth time I did this the truth flashed on me. I remembered the itchy young man in Dr. Benjamin's waiting room. A slight twinge of fear invaded me; was this the beginning of some unanticipated oddness that I would have to endure? On closer inspection the problem proved to be simple tenderness; and, really, that was not a problem but part of the solution. Now I would know firsthand what all the hoopla over women's nipples was really all about. In private moments I began to manipulate them experimentally. With practice, the sensation passed from slightly irritating to distinctly erotic. My experience in playing with women's breasts helped me here; I concluded that I had a good touch. The end of the nipple shaft was really a hot spot and seemed to be directly connected to my genital area. I experienced some very pleasurable, though not intense, sensations in my penis and in the area of my groin. You might call them tinglings or little pings of response; and with them came a vague sensation of the neurological connection between the two erogenous zones. I could almost feel it like a thread stretched tightly between nipple and groin. As time went on my nipples became enlarged. The boundary of the areola crept outward, and the shaft thickened to a diameter equal to the tip of my little finger. In general my breasts began to plump out. It was a great pleasure to me to feel that softness and realize that it was a very definite reflection of my growing womanhood. I had to start wearing loose clothes to disguise these new curves.

At about the same time I started noticing the tenderness in my nipples, I also began to see a change in the texture of my skin. One day I was looking in the mirror, and I thought idly, "Boy, my mother really gave me good skin. Everybody comments on it and I can see why." Then I looked more closely as I once again densely made the connection between the hormones and what I was seeing in the mirror. The grain of my skin had tightened up to an impressive degree; little flaws that had been there before were gone. Slight wrinkles and enlarged pores were a thing of the past. I ran my hand experimentally over my forehead and then my cheekbones. They were like glass. In addition, I thought I could feel a change in the tone of the muscles just beneath the skin; they seemed to be softer now. As time passed this became more pronounced, and the shape of my face changed as a result. The firm angularity of my jaw line softened, and the general shape of my face became more rounded. My already high and prominent cheekbones became more accentuated because the muscles in my cheeks smoothed out, leaving less mass to mask them. This trend extended to the rest of the muscles in my body as well. Soon I was able to wear sleeveless dresses without worrying about my muscular arms embarrassing me. The definition between bicep, deltoid, and tricep disappeared. Certain veins, forced into prominence by muscular development, receded into the contours of my arms. The muscles themselves elongated, and that gave me a smoother silhouette. My legs became less knotty as well. My behind, however, increased in size due to the fatty deposits that had begun to form there. Though most women dislike the idea of fat being linked to their asses, these deposits were a source of great satisfaction to me. They rounded me out and, along with my breasts, moved me closer to the feminine ideal.

Soon I felt a difference in my hair as I combed it. The individual shafts were smaller in diameter, resulting in a finer consistency. Luckily, I had abandoned my crew cut for a longer style; the new hair was not stiff enough to stand up properly. Other hair on my body grew finer as well as more sparse. I had never had a lot of hair on my legs anyway, but the fineness and the thinning caused by the hormones made it hardly noticeable. Most dramatic was a change in the pattern of my pubic hair. Males have a sort of inverted triangle of hair with the point running up toward the navel. Even for a man as unhairy as I had been, I had had a trail of hair shooting upward from the main thatch around my genitals. This fell out, leaving me with a neatly defined triangle, point down, very feminine in appearance.

Of course, nestled in the midst of my newly redefined bush were my male genitalia. As the treatment progressed they too began to change. For one thing, they got smaller in every way. Both the diameter and length of my penis diminished. Like all the other changes this was a gradual process. At the end of six months of treatment my penis was about two-thirds the size it had been at the start. My testicles atrophied even more dramatically. Before hormones they were about the size of robin's eggs, but they gradually shrank to the diameter of marbles. Their consistency was altered too. Rather than the tough resiliency that characterizes normal testicles, mine developed a doughy quality. They would slowly spring back to their original shape when squeezed, but they were far more malleable than they had been previously. This change was not accompanied by a lessening of sensitivity; if someone had kicked me in the balls, I would have felt the same excruciating pain as before. I also retained the sensitivity in my penis. Regardless of how small it got, I could still be excited to erection. The major change in that regard was that the erections had lost their rod-like stiffness. They were rubbery, and even at the height of excitement my penis could be bent pretty much into a right angle. I remember standing in the bedroom looking down at my penis which, as an experiment, I had bent radically over to the left. It looked so strange and unnatural that I was half amazed at how calm I was. The fact is that I had not one regret with regard to the little fellow's predicament. [...]

—1983

SONIA SANCHEZ (1934-)

A principal figure in the Black Arts movement of the 1960s, Sonia Sanchez was born Wilsonia Benita Driver in Birmingham, Alabama. After her mother died in childbirth a year later, Sanchez and her sister were raised by their paternal grandmother and other relatives. After their grandmother died, the sisters moved to Harlem to be with their father. Those early experiences of loss, combined with her shyness, her difficulty speaking due to a stutter, and her growing sense of outrage at racial injustice, drew Sanchez toward writing at an early age. Sanchez (who was briefly married to Albert Sanchez, a Puerto Rican immigrant) earned her B.A. in Political Science from Hunter College, and later studied writing as a postgraduate, working with poet Louise Bogan. During the early 1960s, she joined poets Haki R. Mdhubuti, Nikki Giovanni, and Etheridge Knight (whom she later married and divorced) in forming the radical poetry collective the Broadside Quartet. In 1965, she moved to San Francisco to teach at San Francisco State College (now University), where she was instrumental in creating some of the first Black studies courses in the nation. Her first book of poetry, *Homecoming Poems,* was published by the Broadside Press in 1969. In both *Homecoming* and the collection that followed, *We a BaddDDD People* (1970), Sanchez experimented with bringing the Black urban vernacular into poetic form, an innovation for which she is particularly noted. Since then, Sanchez has written several other collections of poetry, including *Homegirls and Handgrenades* (1984), which won an American Book Award from the Before Columbus Foundation, and *Wounded in the House of a Friend* (1995). She has also written several plays, including *Malcolm Man/Don't Live Here No Mo'* (1979) and *I'm Black When I'm Singing, I'm Blue When I Ain't* (1982).

Homecoming

i have been a
way so long
once after college
i returned tourist
style to watch all   5
the niggers killing
themselves with
three-for-oners

with
needles   10
that cd
not support
their stutters.
      now woman
i have returned   15
leaving behind me
all those hide and
seek faces peeling
with freudian dreams.
this is for real.   20
    black
   niggers
    my beauty.
baby.
i have learned it   25
ain't like they say
in the newspapers.

                             —1978

Love Song No. 3

1.

i'm crazy bout that chile but she gotta go.
she don't pay me no mind no mo. guess her
mama was right to put her out cuz she
couldn't do nothin wid her. but she been
mine so long. she been my heart so long.   5
now she breakin it wid her bad habits.
always runnin like a machine out of control;
always lookin like some wild woman trying
to get some place she ain't never been to.
always threatenin me wid her looks.   10
wid them eyes that don't blink no mo.

i'm crazy bout her though, but she got to go.
her legs walkin with death everyday and
one day she gon cross them right in front of
me and one of us will fall.   15
here she cum openin the do. comin in wid
him. searchin the room with them eyes that
usta smile rivers, searchin for sumthin to
pick up sumthin to put her 18 years into.

how can i keep welcomin her into my house? how   20
can i put her out the way her mama did
when she 16 years old and fast as lightnin?
she still got baby fat on her cheeks.

still got that smile that'll charm the drawers
off ya. hee hee hee.   25

2.

it's gittin cold in here. that's a cold
wind she walkin with. that granbaby of mine.
rummagin the house wid her eyes.
rummagin me wid her look.

where you been to girl? been waitin for you   30
to come home. huh. how you be walter?
you looking better today girl. marlene
baby we need to talk. we need to sit
down and talk bout what you doin
wid yo life. i ain't gon be here forever. but   35
this money i give you everyday.
this money you usin to eat up your bones everyday.
this money you need mo of each day is
killin you baby. let me help you outa
this business you done got yo self into.   40
let me take you to the place miz jefferson
took her son to. you too young and pretty
and smart to just spend yo days walkin
in and out of doors.

yes. i has yo money. yes. i be here when   45
you come back. but. but. but. alright. Here's
10 dollars. from now on out jest 10 dollars
outa yo mama's insurance money.
that all you need to waste each day on
that stuff. jest 10 dollars. no. i'm not   50
foolin girl. jest 10 dollars.

3.

what i remember bout her wuz
she was so fat. such a fat baby.
wid smiles. creases. all over her body.
her mama had to work weekends   55
so she stayed wid me and i sang
and played the radio for her and
the smiles multiplied on her body.
jest one big smile she wuz.
harlem ain't no place to raise a   60
child though. the streets promise so
much but they full of detours fo
young girls wid smiles on they
bodies. i usta sit on the stoop and
watch her jump doubledutch. her   65
feet bouncin in and out of that
rope like a ballerinas. i could see

two of her inside that rope she
went so fast. multiplyin herself
on these harlem streets outloud. hee hee hee. 70
she usta run so fast i couldn't get
these old legs of mine to keep up wid her.
i called out: marlene baby. you jest
remember to stop at the corner. you jest
remember to stop fo you git hit by one 75
of them cars. you jest remember to stop.

4.

stop it now girl. i ain't studyin you.
stop shovin me. stop it now. you ain't
gittin no mo money. jest the ten dollars.
you got to have sumthin for when you 80
older. this insurance money your mama
left is you security. yo future.
stop it now girl fo you hurt yoself
help me up offa this floor and put
down that hammer girl. ahahahah. 85
ahahahahahah. don't hit me no mo marlene.
i got to stand up, move
towards her try to touch her wid these
hands that worked in every house in Bklyn
and Longisland to give her them pretty 90
dresses she usta wear. heeheehee.
i got to try to turn toward her babyfat.
stop it. marlene. AHAHAHAH.
holy jesus. jesus it hurts. holy jesus.
she see me cryin now she gon stop. 95
she gon remember when i picked her up from her tricycle
and her head wuz bleedin and i run
her to harlem hospital movin like a madwoman
she gon remember how i held
her tears in my dress. 100
she gon remember how her arms reached out
to me when the doctor gave her them stitches.
i jest gon reach up to her arm with that hammer.
give me you arms again baby. its you granmama.
AHAHAHAHAHAHAHAHAHAHAH 105
ohmyjesuswhyhasyouforsakenus?
huh? nobodygonrememberherwhenimgone.
theyonlygonseeherwhitebonesstretchedout
againsttheskynobodygonrememberher
younglegsrunningdownlenoxavenuelessenido 110
marlenebabygivemeyoarms…ahahah.
nobody gon remember me…

—1995

"Just Don't Never Give Up on Love"

Feeling tired that day, I came to the park with the children. I saw her as I rounded the corner, sitting old as stale beer on the bench, ruminating on some uneventful past. And I thought, "Hell. No rap from the roots today. I need the present. On this day. This Monday. This July day buckling me under her summer wings, I need more than old words for my body to squeeze into."

I sat down at the far end of the bench, draping my legs over the edge, baring my back to time and time unwell spent. I screamed to the children to watch those curves threatening their youth as they rode their 10-speed bikes against midwestern rhythms.

I opened my book and began to write. They were coming again, those words insistent as his hands had been, pounding inside me, demanding their time and place. I relaxed as my hands moved across the paper like one possessed.

I wasn't sure just what it was I heard. At first I thought it was one of the boys calling me so I kept on writing. They knew the routine by now. Emergencies demanded a presence. A facial confrontation. No long-distance screams across trees and space and other children's screams. But the sound pierced the pages and I looked around, and there she was inching her bamboo-creased body toward my back, coughing a beaded sentence off her tongue.

"Guess you think I ain't never loved, huh girl? Hee. Hee. Guess that what you be thinking, huh?"

I turned. Startled by her closeness and impropriety, I stuttered, "I, I, I, whhhaat dooooo you mean?"

"Hee. Hee. Guess you think I been old like this fo'ever, huh?" She leaned toward me, "Huh? I was so pretty that mens brought me breakfast in bed. Wouldn't let me hardly do no work at all."

"That's nice ma'am. I'm glad to hear that." I returned to my book. I didn't want to hear about some ancient love that she carried inside her. I had to finish a review for the journal. I was already late. I hoped she would get the hint and just sit still. I looked at her out of the corner of my eyes.

"He could barely keep hisself in changing clothes. But he was pretty. My first husband looked like the sun. I used to say his name over and over again 'til it hung from my ears like diamonds. Has you ever loved a pretty man, girl?"

I raised my eyes, determined to keep a distance from this woman disturbing my day.

"No ma'am. But I've seen many a pretty man. I don't like them though cuz they keep their love up high in a linen closet and I'm too short to reach it."

Her skin shook with laughter.

"Girl you gots some spunk about you after all. C'mon over here next to me. I wants to see yo' eyes up close. You looks so uneven sittin' over there."

Did she say uneven? Did this old buddha splintering death say uneven? Couldn't she see that I had one eye shorter than the other; that my breath was painted on porcelain; that one breast crocheted keloids under this white blouse?

I moved toward her though. I scooped up the years that had stripped me to the waist and moved toward her. And she called to me to come out, come out wherever you are young woman, playing hide and go seek with scarecrow men. I gathered myself up at the gateway of her confessionals.

"Do you know what it mean to love a pretty man, girl?" She crooned in my ear. "You always running behind a man like that girl while he cradles his privates. Ain't no joy in a pretty yellow man, cuz he always out pleasurin' and givin' pleasure."

I nodded my head as her words sailed in my ears. Here was the pulse of a woman whose black ass shook the world once.

She continued. "A woman crying all the time is pitiful. Pitiful I says. I wuz pitiful sitting by the window every night like a cow in the fields chewin' on cud. I wanted to cry out, but not even God hisself could hear me. I tried to cry out til my mouth wuz split open at the throat. I 'spoze there is a time all womens has to visit the slaughter house. My visit lasted five years."

Touching her hands, I felt the summer splintering in prayer; touching her hands, I felt my bones migrating in red noise. I asked, "When did you see the butterflies again?"

Her eyes wandered like quicksand over my face. Then she smiled, "Girl don't you know yet that you don't never give up on love? Don't you know you has in you the pulse of winds? The noise of dragonflies?" Her eyes squinted close and she said, "One of them mornings he woke up callin' me and I wuz gone. I wuz gone running with the moon over my shoulders. I looked no which way at all. I had inside me 'nough knives and spoons to cut/scoop out the night. I wuz a-tremblin' as I met the morning."

She stirred in her 84-year-old memory. She stirred up her body as she talked. "They's men and mens. Some good. Some bad. Some breathing death. Some breathing life. William wuz my beginnin'. I come to my second husband spittin' metal and he just pick me up and fold me inside him. I wuz christen' with his love."

She began to hum. I didn't recognize the song; it was a prayer. I leaned back and listened to her voice rustling like silk. I heard cathedrals and sonnets; I heard tents and revivals and a black woman spilling black juice among her ruins.

"We all gotta salute death one time or 'nother girl. Death be waitin' outdoors trying to get inside. William died at his job. Death just turned 'round and snatched him right off the street."

Her humming became the only sound in the park. Her voice moved across the bench like a mutilated child. And I cried. For myself. For this woman talkin' about love. For all the women who have ever stretched their bodies out anticipating civilization and finding ruins.

The crashing of the bikes was anticlimactic. I jumped up, rushed toward the accident. Man. Little man. Where you bicycling to so very fast? Man. Second little man. Take it slow. It all passes so fast anyhow.

As I walked the boys and their bikes toward the bench, I smiled at this old woman waiting for our return.

"I want you to meet a great lady, boys."

"Is she a writer, too, ma?"

"No honey. She's a lady who has lived life instead of writing about it."

"After we say hello can we ride a little while longer? Please!"

"Ok. But watch your manners now and your bones afterwards."

"These are my sons, Ma'am."

"How you do sons? I'm Mrs. Rosalie Johnson. Glad to meet you."

The boys shook her hand and listened for a minute to her words. Then they rode off, spinning their wheels on a city neutral with pain.

As I stood watching them race the morning, Mrs. Johnson got up.

"Don't go," I cried. "You didn't finish your story."

"We'll talk by-and-by. I comes out here almost every day. I sits here on the same bench every day. I'll probably die sittin' here one day. As good a place as any I 'magine."

"May I hug you ma'am? You've helped me so much today. You've given me strength to keep on looking."

"No. Don't never go looking for love girl. Just wait. It'll come. Like the rain fallin' from the heaven, it'll come. Just don't never give up on love."

We hugged; then she walked her 84-year-old walk down the street. A black woman. Echoing gold. Carrying couplets from the sky to crease the ground.

—1984

NELLIE WONG (1934-)

One of seven children of Cantonese immigrant parents, Wong was born and raised in Oakland, California. After nearly twenty years of working as a secretary for the Bethlehem Steel Corporation, Wong enrolled in fiction writing classes at the Oakland Adult Evening School. Later, in her mid-thirties, she began studying at San Francisco State University. It was during this period that Wong developed a critical consciousness of race, class, and gender. Her first book of poetry, *Dreams in Harrison Railroad Park* (1977), was an important contribution to the development of Asian-American literature as a distinct cultural formation—specifically, what critic George Uba has termed "Asian Pacific American activist poetry." Wong published the poem "When I Was Growing Up" and the autobiographical essay "In Search of the Self as Hero: Confetti of Voices on New Year's Night" in the groundbreaking anthology *This Bridge Called My Back: Writings by Radical Women of Color* (1981). The poem was an early critique of white-centered standards of beauty and humanity, while her essay explained the importance, for her, of writing as an expression of Asian-American womanhood. Wong has published the poetry collections *The Death of Long Steam Lady* (1986) and *Stolen Moments* (1997) and, along with Mitsuye Yamada, was featured in the 1981 documentary film *Mitsuye and Nellie: Asian American Poets*. She has worked as a San Francisco Bay Area organizer for the Freedom Socialist Party, and has long been active in Radical Women, an international socialist feminist organization.

Dreams in Harrison Railroad Park

We sit on a green bench in Harrison Railroad Park.
As we rest, I notice my mother's thighs
thin as my wrists.
I want to hug her
but I am afraid.   5

A bearded man comes by, asks for a cigarette.
We shake our heads, hold out our empty hands.

He shuffles away and picks up
a half-smoked stub.
His eyes light up.   10
Enclosed by the sun he dreams
temporarily.

Across the street an old woman hobbles by.
My mother tells me: She is unhappy here.
She thinks she would be happier   15
back home.
But she has forgotten.

My mother's neighbor dreams
of warm nights in Shanghai,
of goldfish swimming in a courtyard pond,   20
of having a young maid
anoint her tiny bound feet.

And my mother dreams
of wearing dresses that hang in her closet,
of swallowing soup without pain,   25
of coloring eggs
for an unborn grandson.

I turn and touch my mother's eyes.
They are wet
and I dream   30
and I dream
of embroidering
new skin.

—1977

From a Heart of Rice Straw

Ma, my heart must be made of rice straw,
the kind you fed a fire in Papa's home village
so Grandma could have hot tea upon waking,
so Grandma could wash her sleepy eyes. My heart
knocks as silently as that LeCoultre clock   5
that Papa bought with his birthday money.
It swells like a baby in your stomach.

Your tears have flooded the house, this life.
For Canton? No, you left home forty years ago
for the fortune Papa sought in Gum San.[1]   10
In Gold Mountain you worked side by side
in the lottery with regular pay offs
to the Oakland cops. To feed your six daughters
until one day Papa's cousin shot him.

[1] (Chin.) Gold Mountain.

I expected you to fly into the clouds, wail   15
at Papa's side, but you chased cousin instead.
Like the cops and robbers on the afternoon radio.
It didn't matter that Papa lay bleeding.
It didn't matter that cousin accused Papa
of cheating him. You ran, kicking   20
your silk slippers on the street, chasing
cousin until you caught him, gun still in hand.
My sister and I followed you, crying.

If cousin had shot you, you would have died.
The cops showed up and you told them how cousin   25
gunned Papa down, trusted kin who smoked
Havana cigars after filling his belly with rice
and chicken in our big yellow house.

Papa lay in his hospital bed, his kidney removed.
Three bullets out. They couldn't find the last   30
bullet. A search was made, hands dove into Papa's
shirt pocket. A gold watch saved Papa's life.

Ma, you've told this story one hundred times.
The cops said you were brave. The neighbors said
you were brave. The relatives shook their heads,   35
the bravery of a Gold Mountain woman unknown
in the old home village.

The papers spread the shooting all over town.
One said Papa dueled with his brother like
a bar room brawl. One said it was the beginning   40
of a tong war, but that Occidental law
would prevail. To them, to the outside,
what was another tong war, another dead Chinaman?

But Papa fooled them. He did not die
by his cousin's hand. The lottery closed down.   45
We got food on credit. You wept.
I was five years old.

My heart, once bent and cracked, once
ashamed of your China ways.
Ma, hear me now, tell me your story   50
again and again.

—1977

MARY OLIVER (1935-)

Born in Maple Heights, Ohio, Mary Oliver traveled as a teenager to Steepletop, the home of Edna St. Vincent Millay, where she helped the Millay family organize papers left behind by the deceased poet. Oliver studied at both Ohio State University and Vassar, but did not earn a degree. Often described as one of the premier contemporary American nature poets, Oliver earned the Pulitzer Prize in Poetry for her 1983 collection *American Primitive,* and has also won the National Book Award and the Lannan Literary Award. She has published more than twenty books of poetry and prose, and her poems have been put to music by Anne Kearns, Augusta Read Thomas, Theodore Presser, and Joan Szymko. In general, Oliver's work tends to focus on nature as a source of amazement and intrigue, while poems like "Rage," which are meditations on the sometimes dark and troubling ways humans interact with one another, are less representative than those poems that are oriented toward the natural world and human relationships to it. As Millay had before her, Oliver eventually settled in Provincetown, Massachusetts, where she lived with her life partner, Molly Malone Cook, for over forty years. Cook served as Oliver's literary agent until her death in 2005. Oliver has been a Mather Visiting Professor at Case Western Reserve University, a poet-in-residence at Bucknell University, and a writer-in-residence at Sweet Briar College.

Rage

You are the dark song
of the morning;
serious and slow,
you shave, you dress,
you descend the stairs   5
in your public clothes
and drive away, you become
the wise and powerful one
who makes all the days
possible in the world.   10
But you were also the red song
in the night,
stumbling through the house
to the child's bed,
to the damp rose of her body,   15
leaving your bitter taste.
And forever those nights snarl
the delicate machinery of the days.
When the child's mother smiles
you see on her cheekbones   20
a truth you will never confess;
and you see how the child grows—
timidly, crouching in corners.
Sometimes in the wide night
you hear the most mournful cry,   25
a ravished and terrible moment.
In your dreams she's a tree
that will never come to leaf—

in your dreams she's a watch
you dropped on the dark stones   30
till no one could gather the fragments—
in your dreams you have sullied and murdered,
and dreams do not lie.

—1986

Wild Geese

You do not have to be good.
You do not have to walk on your knees
for a hundred miles through the desert, repenting.
You only have to let the soft animal of your body
    love what it loves.   5
Tell me about despair, yours, and I will tell you mine.
Meanwhile the world goes on.
Meanwhile the sun and the clear pebbles of the rain
are moving across the landscapes,
over the prairies and the deep trees,   10
the mountains and the rivers.
Meanwhile the wild geese, high in the clean blue air,
are heading home again.
Whoever you are, no matter how lonely,
the world offers itself to your imagination,   15
calls to you like the wild geese, harsh and exciting—
over and over announcing your place
  in the family of things.

—1986

PEGGY SEEGER (1935-)

Folksinger Peggy (Margaret) Seeger was born into a musical family: her father, Charles Louis Seeger, was a pioneer of ethnomusicology and an accomplished musician; her mother, Ruth Crawford Seeger, was a pianist and composer, and the first woman ever to be awarded a Guggenheim Fellowship Award for Music; her half-brother Pete Seeger has often been called the father of the American folk music revival; and her brother Mike also wrote and performed music. Seeger early on had a knack for learning instruments, playing piano by the age of seven, and guitar, autoharp, Appalachian dulcimer, English concertina, and 5-string banjo by the age of fifteen. She received her formal education at Radcliffe College in Cambridge, Massachusetts, where she refined her vocal skills. After college, she traveled extensively, but had her U.S. passport withdrawn after she visited communist China. She settled in London, married British singer-songwriter Ewan MacColl (who wrote "The First Time Ever I Saw Your Face" in 1957 as a tribute to Seeger), and eventually became a British subject. Seeger's career as a folksinger and songwriter flourished in the 1960s and 1970s as she wrote and sang socially and politically conscious music rooted in folk traditions. She both collaborated with MacColl and worked on her own. Her most recognized song, "I'm Gonna Be an Engineer," was first recorded in 1970 for the British Festival of Fools. She began working with Irene Scott in 1983, and after MacColl's death in 1989, toured with her for a number of years as the duo No Spring Chickens, eventually forming a romantic partnership with her as well. Seeger settled in the U.S. in 1994 (later joined by Scott) and has continued to release new work as well as major retrospectives throughout the 1990s and into the 2000s. She took a teaching position at Northeastern University in Boston in 2006, and continues to lecture and sing throughout the country.

I'm Gonna Be an Engineer

When I was a little girl I wished I was a boy,
I tagged along behind the gang and wore my corduroys;
Ev'rybody said I only did it to annoy,
But I was gonna be an engineer!

Mama told me, "Can't you be a lady?   5
Your duty is to make me the mother of a pearl;
Wait until you're older, dear,
Then maybe you'll be glad that you're a girl."

Chorus
Dainty as a Dresden statue,
Gentle as a Jersey cow,   10
Smooth as silk, gives creamy milk.
Learn to coo, learn to moo,
That's what to do to be a lady now.

When I went to school I learned to write and how to read,
Some history, geography and home economy,   15
And typing is a skill that every girl is sure to need,
To while away the extra time until the time to breed;
And then they had the nerve to say, "What would you like to be?"
I says, "I'm gonna be an engineer!"

No, you only need to learn to be a lady,   20
The duty isn't yours, for to try and run the world;
An engineer could never have a baby,
Remember, dear, that you're a girl.

[*Chorus*]

So I become a typist and I study on the sly,
Working out the day and night so I can qualify,   25
And every time the boss come in, he pinched me on the thigh,
Says, "I've never had an engineer!"

You owe it to the job to be a lady,
It's the duty of the staff for to give the boss a whirl;
The wages that you get are crummy, maybe,   30

But it's all you get, 'cause you're a girl.

She's smart! (for a woman)
I wonder how she got that way?
You get no choice, you get no voice,
Just stay mum, pretend you're dumb;   35
That's how you come to be a lady today!

[*Chorus*]

Then Jimmy come along and we set up a conjugation,
We were busy every night with loving recreation;
I spent my days at work so he could get his education,
And now he's an engineer!   40

He says, "I know you'll always be a lady,
It's the duty of my darling to love me all my life;
Could an engineer look after or obey me?
Remember, dear, that you're my wife!"

[*Chorus*]

As soon as Jimmy got a job, I studied hard again,   45
Then, busy at the drawing board a year or so, and then,
The morning that the twins were born,
Jimmy says to them, "Kids, your mother was an engineer!"

You owe it to the kids to be a lady,
Dainty as a dish-rag, faithful as a chow,   50
Stay at home; you got to mind the baby;
Remember, you're a mother now.

[*Chorus*]

Every time I turn around there's something else to do,
Cook a meal or mend a sock or sweep a floor or two,
Listen to the morning show—it makes me want to spew;   55
I was gonna be an engineer!

I really wish that I could be a lady,
I could do the lovely things that a lady's s'posed to do;
I wouldn't even mind if only they would pay me,
And I could be a person too.   60

What price—for a woman?
You can buy her for a ring of gold,
To love and obey (without any pay),
You get a cook or a nurse, for better or worse,
You don't need a purse when a lady is sold!   65

[*Chorus*]

But now that times are harder, and my Jimmy's got the sack,
I went down to Delco, they were glad to have me back;

I'm a third-class citizen, my wages tell me that,
But I'm a first-class engineer!
The boss he says, "I pay you as a lady,   70
You only got the job 'cause I can't afford a man;
With you I keep the profits high as may be,
You're just a cheaper pair of hands!"

You got one fault! You're a woman,
You're not worth the equal pay,   75
A bitch or a tart, you're nothing but heart,
Shallow and vain, you got no brain;
Go down the drain like a lady today!

[*Chorus*]

I listened to my mother and I joined a typing pool,
I listened to my lover and I sent him through his school;   80
If I listen to the boss, I'm just a bloody fool,
And an underpaid engineer!

I been a sucker ever since I was a baby,
As a daughter, as a wife, as a mother, and a dear;
But I'll fight them as a woman, not a lady;   85
Yes, I'll fight them as an engineer!

—1976

LUCILLE CLIFTON (1936-   )

Born and raised in Depew, New York, Lucille Clifton entered Howard University in Washington, D.C., when she was sixteen years old. Among her associates at Howard was Cloe Wofford (now Toni Morrison), who later edited Clifton's writings for Random House. Clifton left Howard and entered the Fredonia State Teacher's College in New York, where she joined a group of student intellectuals, among whom was her eventual husband, Fred Clifton. Her first volume of poetry, *Good Times,* which was published when Clifton won the 1969 YW-YMHA Poetry Center Discovery Award, was dubbed one of the "Best Books of 1969" by the *New York Times.* She has published eleven other collections of poetry, as well as over twenty children's books, a number of which focus on protagonist Everett Anderson, a boy living in the inner city; *Everett Anderson's Goodbye* received the Coretta Scott King Award in 1984. Among Clifton's other awards are a Lannon Literary Award, a National Book Award, the Shelley Memorial Award, and an Emmy Award from the American Academy of Television Arts and Sciences. She has also served as Poet Laureate of Maryland and is a Chancellor of the Academy of American Poets. Clifton has been nominated twice for the Pulitzer Prize. In the tradition of poets such as Gwendolyn Brooks, Clifton's poetry transforms the ordinary into the extraordinary as it celebrates such topics as the female form (as in "homage to my hips" and "homage to my hair"), her African-American ancestry, and the complex relationships between parents and children. Clifton is Distinguished Professor of Humanities at St. Mary's College of Maryland.

homage to my hips

these hips are big hips.
they need space to
move around in.
they don't fit into little
petty places. these hips   5
are free hips.
they don't like to be held back.
these hips have never been enslaved,
they go where they want to go
they do what they want to do.   10
these hips are mighty hips.
these hips are magic hips.
i have known them
to put a spell on a man and
spin him like a top!

—1980

homage to my hair

when i feel her jump up and dance
i hear the music! my God
i'm talking about my nappy hair!
she is a challenge to your hand
Black man,   5
she is as tasty on your tongue as good greens
Black man,
she can touch your mind
with her electric fingers and
the grayer she do get, good God,   10
the Blacker she do be!

—1982

shapeshifter poems

1

the legend is whispered
in the women's tent
how the moon when she rises
full
follows some men into themselves   5
and changes them there
the season is short
but dreadful   shapeshifters
they wear strange hands
they walk through the houses   10
at night   their daughters
do not know them

2

who is there to protect her
from the hands of the father
not the windows which see and   15
say nothing   not the moon
that awful eye   not the woman
she will become with her
scarred tongue   who   who   who   the owl
laments into the evening   who   20
will protect her   this   prettylittlegirl

3

if the little girl lies
still enough
shut enough
hard enough   25
shapeshifter may not
walk tonight
the full moon may not
find him here
the hair on him   30
bristling
rising
up

4

the poem at the end of the world
is the poem the little girl breathes   35
into her pillow   the one
she cannot tell   the one
there is no one to hear   this poem
is a political poem   is a war poem   is a
universal poem but is not about   40
these things   this poem
is about one human heart   this poem
is the poem at the end of the world

—1987

JUNE JORDAN (1936-2002)

Poet, writer, educator, and activist June Jordan, the daughter of Jamaican immigrants, was born in Harlem and raised in the Bedford-Stuyvesant neighborhood of Brooklyn. Jordan was educated at a predominantly white Massachusetts prep school and later dropped out of Barnard College because of the lack of course content about African Americans and women. She married a white Columbia University student at a time when interracial marriages were uncommon, and went with him to the University of Chicago, where she studied for a year before returning to Barnard. By the late 1960s, immersed in the civil rights movement, Jordan was also beginning her academic career, which would eventually include teaching positions at the City University of New York, Connecticut College (where she also directed the Search for Education, Elevation and Knowledge [SEEK] program), Sarah Lawrence College, Yale University, City College of New York, SUNY Stony Brook, and UC Berkeley. She began publishing her writing after her divorce in 1965. In 1969 she published her first book, *Who Look At Me,* poetry for young readers written in "Black English." Over the next three decades she published several volumes of poetry, five collections of essays, and seven plays, as well as books for children and young adults, and a memoir. She is best known for her poems, some of which were set to music and recorded by the black feminist a cappella singing group Sweet Honey in the Rock.

Jordan's writing and activism challenge racism, sexism, homophobia, and other forms of oppression. Later in her life she was outspoken about her bisexuality (most notably in her 1993 essay "A New Politics of Sexuality" and in her 1989 poetry collection *Naming Our Destiny*). Jordan combined her writing, activism, and teaching when she founded "Poetry for the People," a poetry workshop/class that began at UC Berkeley but soon spread to neighborhood centers, high schools, and other community settings. It remains a permanent class offering at UC Berkeley. Jordan's many prizes and fellowships included awards from the American Library Association, the National Endowment for the Arts, the Rockefeller Foundation, the National Black Journalists Association, and the Prix de Rome. She died of breast cancer in 2002.

If You Saw a Negro Lady

If you saw a Negro lady
sitting on a Tuesday
near the whirl-sludge doors of
Horn & Hardart[1] on the main drag
of downtown Brooklyn   5

solitary and conspicuous as plain
and neat as walls impossible to
fresco and you watched her self-
conscious features shape about
a Horn & Hardart teaspoon   10
with a pucker from a cartoon

she would not understand
with spine as straight and solid
as her years of bending over floors
allowed   15

skin cleared of interest by a ruthless
soap   nails square and yellowclean
from metal files

sitting in a forty-year-old-flush
of solitude and prickling   20
from the new white cotton blouse
concealing nothing she had ever noticed

---

[1] A chain of automat restaurants.

even when she bathed and never
hummed a bathtub tune nor knew one

If you saw her square   25
above the dirty
mopped-on antiseptic floors
before the rag-wiped table tops

little finger   broad and stiff
in heavy emulation of a cockney   30

mannerism
would you turn her treat
into surprise
observing

happy birthday

—1965

Poem About My Rights

Even tonight and I need to take a walk and clear
my head about this poem about why I can't
go out without changing my clothes my shoes
my body posture my gender identity my age
my status as a woman alone in the evening/   5
alone on the streets/alone not being the point/
the point being that I can't do what I want
to do with my own body because I am the wrong
sex the wrong age the wrong skin and
suppose it was not here in the city but down on the beach/   10
or far into the woods and I wanted to go
there by myself thinking about God/or thinking
about children or thinking about the world/all of it
disclosed by the stars and the silence:
I could not go and I could not think and I could not   15
stay there
alone
as I need to be
alone because I can't do what I want to do with my own
body and   20
who in the hell set things up
like this
and in France they say if the guy penetrates
but does not ejaculate then he did not rape me
and if after stabbing him if after screams if   25
after begging the bastard and if even after smashing
a hammer to his head if even after that if he
and his buddies fuck me after that
then I consented and there was

no rape because finally you understand finally   30
they fucked me over because I was wrong I was
wrong again to be me being me where I was/wrong
to be who I am
which is exactly like South Africa
penetrating into Namibia[2] penetrating into   35
Angola[3] and does that mean I mean how do you know if
Pretoria ejaculates what will the evidence look like the
proof of the monster jackboot ejaculation on Blackland
and if
after Namibia and if after Angola and if after Zimbabwe[4]   40
and if after all of my kinsmen and women resist even to
self-immolation of the villages and if after that
we lose nevertheless what will the big boys say will they
claim my consent:
Do You Follow Me: We are the wrong people of   45
the wrong skin on the wrong continent and what
in the hell is everybody being reasonable about
and according to the *Times* this week
back in 1966 the C.I.A. decided that they had this problem
and the problem was a man named Nkrumah[5] so they   50
killed him and before that it was Patrice Lumumba[6]
and before that it was my father on the campus
of my Ivy League school and my father afraid
to walk into the cafeteria because he said he
was wrong the wrong age the wrong skin the wrong   55
gender identity and he was paying my tuition and
before that
it was my father saying I was wrong saying that
I should have been a boy because he wanted one/a
boy and that I should have been lighter skinned and   60
that I should have had straighter hair and that
I should not be so boy crazy but instead I should
just be one/a boy and before that
it was my mother pleading plastic surgery for
my nose and braces for my teeth and telling me   65
to let the books loose to let them loose in other
words
I am very familiar with the problems of the C.I.A.
and the problems of South Africa and the problems

2 After its mandate to rule Namibia was abolished by the
United Nations in 1966, South Africa continued to
engage in armed struggle with the Namibian liberation
movement, SWAPO, until 1990.
3 After gaining independence in 1975, Angola became a
Cold War battleground as the Soviet Union and Cuba
backed one side and the U.S. and South Africa another
in a civil war that lasted sixteen years.
4 Zimbabwe gained independence in 1980 and then
endured martial law, armed insurrections against the ruling party, and, from 1982 to 1987, a military pacification

campaign estimated to have killed as many as 20,000
civilians.
5 Kwame Nkrumah (1909-1972) helped the Gold Coast
become the independent nation of Ghana; he was
Ghana's first prime minister and then president, until his
government was overthrown in 1966.
6 Patrice Lumumba (1925-1961), first elected prime minister of the Democratic Republic of the Congo; his government was overthrown with the help of the CIA
shortly after independence and he was subsequently
assassinated.

of Exxon Corporation and the problems of white   70
America in general and the problems of the teachers
and the preachers and the F.B.I. and the social
workers and my particular Mom and Dad/I am very
familiar with the problems because the problems
turn out to be   75
me
I am the history of rape
I am the history of the rejection of who I am
I am the history of the terrorized incarceration of
my self   80
I am the history of battery assault and limitless
armies against whatever I want to do with my mind
and my body and my soul and
whether it's about walking out at night
or whether it's about the love that I feel or   85
whether it's about the sanctity of my vagina or
the sanctity of my national boundaries
or the sanctity of my leaders or the sanctity
of each and every desire
that I know from my personal and idiosyncratic   90
and indisputably single and singular heart
I have been raped
be-
cause I have been wrong the wrong sex the wrong age
the wrong skin the wrong nose the wrong hair the   95
wrong need the wrong dream the wrong geographic
the wrong sartorial I
I have been the meaning of rape
I have been the problem everyone seeks to
eliminate by forced   100
penetration with or without the evidence of slime and/
but let this be unmistakable this poem
is not consent I do not consent
to my mother to my father to the teachers to
the F.B.I. to South Africa to Bedford-Stuy   105
to Park Avenue to American Airlines to the hardon
idlers on the corners to the sneaky creeps in
cars
I am not wrong: Wrong is not my name
My name is my own my own my own   110
and I can't tell you who the hell set things up like this
but I can tell you that from now on my resistance
my simple and daily and nightly self-determination
may very well cost you your life

—1989

Poem Because the 1996 U.S. Poet Laureate Told the *San Francisco Chronicle* There Are "Obvious" Poets— All of Them White—and Then There Are "Representative" Poets—None of Them White[7]

So the man said
Let there be obvious people
and representative others.
Let there be obvious poets
and representative   5
others
Let the obvious people be white
Let the others
represent what happens
when   10
you fail to qualify
as obvious

And the representative other
not obvious people or poets
worried a lot about just what should you do   15
if you fall into
such a difficult
such a representative
slot

Except for one representative   20
sista poet
who said, "Mista
Poet Laureate!
Please clarify:
Was Timothy McVeigh[8]   25
was he
obvious?

And what about media experts
certain that the murdering terrorist
must look like somebody, 'Middle   30
Eastern'?
Would you say that expertise was
representative?

And how about the cops trying to stop
then   35

---

[7] The 1996 U.S. Poet Laureate was Robert Hass.
[8] On April 19, 1995, the federal building in Oklahoma City was bombed, killing 168 and wounding over 800.

Timothy McVeigh, a white, Christian-raised, decorated veteran of the U.S. Army, was convicted of the bombing. He was executed on June 11, 2001.

trying to kill
Rodney King? [9]

And Sheriff's deputies
Racing to vilify
and humiliate   40
Twenty-one Mexican men and women wannabe
working for minimum
wages
in America/how
about those   45
deputies who chose
on camera
to vent the venom
of their obvious
territorial assertions over land   50
that (truth to tell)
belongs to Mexico?

How about all histories
of all the deputies
hellbent to freeze inverted boundaries   55
according to some Anglo-Saxon
Christian
English Speaking
Crock of Conquest-As-The-Best
of-Destinies?   60
And Patrick Buchanan! [10]

Is he obvious?
Is he legal?

That no way
alien   65
neo-nazi wannabe
neo-nazi 'über alles' [11]
promising death to 'José'
and to *Niggas Jews* and *Queers*
That obvious   70
clear
leader
for obvious
clear
people   75
would you say

---

[9] Rodney King (b. 1965), victim of a vicious police beating after a high-speed car chase in Los Angeles in 1991.
Caught on videotape by a private citizen, the beating led
to trials for the officers involved. Their acquittal was followed by four days of rioting in Los Angeles.

[10] Patrick Buchanan (b. 1938), highly conservative, three-
time candidate for the Republican nomination for
President.
[11] (G.) Over all; referring to the German national anthem
as it was sung during the Third Reich.

he's the bees' knees'
representative?"

Yes?
No?   80

Not all of us must come and go
by pick-up truck
And you can't yank each one
of us
right off the driver's seat   85
to beat up
on our heads and bloody backs!

And after twisted kicks
and billy sticks
to knock us down to   90
knock us down
to ground
our fathers and our mothers
sanctified/sweat
laboring to escape   95
the leather whip
you label who
illegal
or unqualified?

And dangerous to standards   100
and a way of life
that venerates brutality
and turns around to smirk
with overt
obvious   105
and homicidal
pride
you label who
illegal?

And burrowing under everything you think   110
you know
some of us move slow
like inch worms
softening the earth
to bury you   115

And how I hope the obvious
necessity for me to write
this poem
Translates into Spanish
Mandarin   120
Cantonese

Punjabi
Japanese
Xhosa
Arabic   125

and every African
and every Asian
language

Of every people representative
of people   130
kept unequal
on the planet

Mista
Poet Laureate
I close this disquisition   135
on the obvious
with the words of representative
Poet Hero
Langston Hughes:[12]

"The night is beautiful   140
so the faces of my people

The stars are beautiful
so the eyes of my people

Beautiful, also, is the sun.
Beautiful, also, are the souls   145
      of my people."[13]

dedicated to Laura Serna

—1997

[12] Langston Hughes (1902-1967), African-American poet.
[13] [*Author's note.*] "My People," by Langston Hughes from *Selected Poems,* Langston Hughes, Vintage Books, 1974, p. 13.

MARGE PIERCY (1936-   )

Marge Piercy was born in Detroit, Michigan. Her mother was the daughter of Jewish immigrants; her maternal grandfather was a labor organizer killed while trying to organize bakery workers. Piercy, who attended the University of Michigan and Northwestern University, holds honorary doctorates from Eastern Connecticut State University, Hebrew Union College, Lesley College, and Bridgewater State College. Among her many awards are a Literature Award from the Massachusetts Governor's Commission on the Status of Women, the May Sarton Award from the New England Poetry Club, and the Arthur C. Clarke Award for Best Science Fiction Novel in the United Kingdom. Her work has been translated into more than a dozen languages. In January of 2003, Marge Piercy and other American poets were invited by First Lady Laura Bush to the White House to read at an event to celebrate the poets Langston Hughes, Walt Whitman, and Emily Dickinson. The symposium coincided with the U.S. invasion of Iraq; Piercy and many of the other invited poets began making plans to read poems against the war. Laura Bush eventually rescinded the invitations to the symposium arguing that it would be inappropriate for participants to bring politics into a literary event. Participation in this protest-in-poetry is in keeping with the nature of Piercy's lifetime of work. A prolific writer of poetry and prose, she has been an active participant in the feminist and anti-war movements for most of her life.

The Long Death

for Wendy Teresa Simon (September 25, 1954-August 7, 1979)

Radiation is like oppression,
the average daily kind of subliminal toothache
you get almost used to, the stench
of chlorine in the water, of smog in the wind.

We comprehend the disasters of the moment,   5
the nursing home fire, the river in flood
pouring over the sandbag levee, the airplane
crash with fragments of burnt bodies
scattered among the hunks of twisted metal,
the grenade in the marketplace, the sinking ship.   10

But how to grasp a thing that does not
kill you today or tomorrow
but slowly from the inside in twenty years.
How to feel that a corporate or governmental
choice means we bear twisted genes and our   15
grandchildren will be stillborn if our
children are very lucky.

Slow death can not be photographed for the six
o'clock news. It's all statistical,
the gross national product or the prime   20
lending rate. Yet if our eyes saw
in the right spectrum, how it would shine,
lurid as magenta neon.

If we could smell radiation like seeping
gas, if we could sense it as heat, if we   25
could hear it as a low ominous roar
of the earth shifting, then we would not sit
and be poisoned while industry spokesmen
talk of acceptable millirems and .02
cancer per population thousand.   30

We acquiesce at murder so long as it is slow,
murder from asbestos dust, from tobacco,
from lead in the water, from sulphur in the air,
and fourteen years later statistics are printed

on the rise in leukemia among children.   35
We never see their faces. They never stand,
those poisoned children together in a courtyard,
and are gunned down by men in three-piece suits.

The shipyard workers who built nuclear
submarines, the soldiers who were marched   40
into the Nevada desert to be tested by the H-
bomb, the people who work in power plants,
they die quietly years after in hospital
wards and not on the evening news.

The soft spring rain floats down and the air   45
is perfumed with pine and earth. Seedlings
drink it in, robins sip it in puddles,
you run in it and feel clean and strong,
the spring rain blowing from the irradiated
cloud over the power plant.   50

Radiation is oppression, the daily average
kind, the kind you're almost used to
and live with as the years abrade you,
high blood pressure, ulcers, cramps, migraine,
a hacking cough: you take it inside   55
and it becomes pain and you say, not
They are killing me, but *I am sick now.*

—1980

Poetry Festival Lover

He reads his poem about you,
making sure everyone in town
knows you have been lovers
as if he published his own
tabloid with banner head   5
and passed it out at the door.

He kneels at your feet as you sit
a stuffed duck at autographings
and holds the hand others
wait to have sign their   10
purchased books.

Alone the last night he asks
favors (blurbs, readings,
your name on a folder) but
not your favor: he wants   15
the position but not the work.

His private parts lie quiet
and the public is all

he's hot to screw.
Avoid the poet who tells   20
his love loudly in public;
in private he counts his money.

—1980

ESTELA PORTILLO TRAMBLEY (1936-1999)

Estela Portillo Trambley was born on January 16, 1936, to Frank and Delfina Portillo. She received a B.A. in English from the University of Texas at El Paso in 1957, later returning to earn an M.A. in English in 1977. Trambley taught English at the high school level, served as chair of the English department at the El Paso Technical Institute, was a theater director at the Community College in El Paso from 1970 until 1975, and was a founding member of Los Pobres, the first Hispanic theater in El Paso. She also hosted a radio show and a series of television shows that aired locally. Trambley's plays and short stories present strong female protagonists that assert their individuality and seek liberation from the gender roles ascribed by cultural and religious norms. Controversially, some of these characters escape by resorting to murder. Lesbianism also appears as a theme in her writings. Trambley's collection of short stories, *Rain of Scorpions and Other Writings* (1975), is believed to be the first collection of short stories published by a Chicana author. Her other publications include the plays *The Days of the Swallows* (1971), *Sun Images* (1976), *Sor Juana and Other Plays* (1983), and her only novel, *Trini* (1986).

La Jonfontayn

Alicia was forty-two and worked hard at keeping her weight down. Not hard enough really and this was very frustrating for her—never to quite succeed. She wanted to be pencil-thin like a movie star. She would leaf through movie magazines, imagining herself in the place of the immaculately made-up beauties that stared back at her. But in essence she was a realist and was very much aware of the inevitable body changes as years passed. She often studied her face and body in the mirror, not without fears. The fantasy of glamour and beauty was getting harder and harder to maintain. Getting old was no easy task. Why didn't someone invent some magic pill?…

Sitting naked, defenseless, in a bathtub brimming with pink bubbles, she slid down into the water to make the usual check. She felt for flabbiness along the thighs, her underarms for the suspicious cottage cheese called tired, loose fat. Suddenly she felt the sting of soap in her eye. Carefully she cupped water in her hand to rinse it out. Damn it! Part of her eyelashes were floating in the water. It would take close to an hour to paste new ones on again. Probably Delia's fault. Her girl was getting sloppy. Mamie was a new face at the beauty parlor, anxious to please the regular customers. Maybe she would ask for Mamie next time. No dollar tip for Delia after this. The soapy warmth of her body was almost mesmerizing. In her bubbly pink realm Alicia was immortal, a nymph, sweet-smelling, seductive, capable of anything.

Heck! She had to get out if she had to paste the damned eyelashes on. She stood up, bubbles dripping merrily off her nice, plump body. She had to hurry to be in time for her blind date. She giggled in mindless joy. A blind date! She could hardly believe that she had agreed to a blind date. Agreed? She smiled with great satisfaction and murmured to herself, "You insisted on nothing else, my girl. You wanted him served on a platter and that's the way you're getting him."

Rico was her yard boy, and at Katita's wedding she had seen Rico's uncle, Buti, from afar. Such a ridiculous name for such a gorgeous hunk of man. From that moment on she had been obsessed with the thought of owning him. It was her way, to possess her men. That way she could stay on top—teach them the art of making her happy. "Oh, I have such a capacity for love!" she told herself. Humming a love song, she stepped out of the bathtub and wrapped a towel around her body gracefully, assuming the pose of a queen. A middle-aged queen, the mirror on the bathroom door told her. There are mirrors and there are mirrors, she gloomily observed. She sucked in her stomach, watching her posture. But the extra pounds were still here and there. Time had taken away the solid firmness of youth and replaced it with extra flesh. She turned away from the mirror, summarizing life under her breath, "Shit!"

The next instant she was smiles again, thinking of the long-waist bra that would smooth out her midriff and give her an extra curve. Then there was the green chiffon on her bed, the type of dress that Loretta Young would wear. She visualized herself in the green chiffon, floating towards Buti with outstretched hand. There would be the inevitable twinkle of admiration in his eye. In her bedroom she glanced at the clock on her dresser. It was late. With rapid, expert movements, she took out creams, lipstick, eye shadow, rouge, brushes from her cosmetic drawer. She wrapped a towel around her head and had just opened the moisture cream when she remembered the eyelashes. Did she really need them? She remembered Lana Turner[1] with her head on Clark Gable's[2] shoulder, her eyelashes sweeping against her cheeks. Max Factor's finest, Alicia was sure of that.

Hell! She rummaged hurriedly around the bottom drawer until she found a plaster container with the words Max Factor emblazoned on the cover. Anything Lana did, she could do better. She took out a bottle of glue, then carefully blotted the excess cream from her eyes and began the operation.

"Hey, slow down!" yelled Rico as Buti made a turn on two wheels.

Rico turned around to check the load on the back of the pick-up. They were returning from Ratón where at the Rangers' Station they had gotten permits to pick piñones[3] in the Capitán mountains. Buti had presented the rangers with a letter from Don Rafael Aviña giving him permission to pick piñón from his private lands. Buti had also signed a contract with the Borderfield Company to deliver the piñones at the railroad yards in Ancho, New Mexico, where the nuts would be shipped along with cedar wood to Salt Lake City. His first profitable business venture since he had arrived in the United States. He had a check from Borderfield in his pocket. He was well on his way to becoming what he always wanted to be—a businessman. From there—a capitalist—why not? Everything was possible in the United States of America. He even had enough piñones left to sell to small tienditas[4] around Valverde, and a special box of the best piñones for his blind date, the richest woman in Valverde. Things were coming up money every which way. He had had qualms about letting Rico talk him into the blind date until Rico started listing all the property owned by Alicia Flores—

---

[1] Lana Turner (1921-1995), American actress.
[2] Clark Gable (1901-1960), American actor.
[3] (Sp.) Pine nuts.
[4] (Sp.) Small shops.

two blocks of presidios, ten acres of good river land, an office building. That made him ecstatic. Imagine him dating a pretty widow who owned an office building! There was no question about it—he was about to meet the only woman in the world that he would consider marrying. By all means, she could have him. It was about time he settled down.

All that boozing and all those women were getting to be too much for him. What he needed was the love and affection of one good wealthy woman. Yes, ever since he had met Don Rafael things had gone for the better. Only six months before he had even considered going on welfare. Poker winnings had not been enough, and his Antique Shop was not doing very well. He had resorted to odd jobs around Valverde, a new low for Buti. Then, he had met Don Rafael at El Dedo Gordo in Juárez.

At the Fat Finger everybody knew Buti. That's where he did the important things in his life—play poker, start fights, pick up girls, and most important of all—drink until all hours of the morning. It was his home away from home. His feet on native soil and mariachi music floating through his being—that was happiness. One early dawn when only Elote, the bartender, and Buti were left at the Fat Finger—they were killing off a bottle of tequila before starting for home—who stumbles in but this little fat man with a pink head, drunker than a skunk. He fell face down on the floor soon enough. Buti helped him up, dusted him off, and led him to the table where Elote had already passed out.

"You sit right there. I'll get us another bottle." Buti wove his way between tables and made it to the bar. The little man just sat, staring into space until Buti nudged him with a new bottle of tequila.

"Where am I?" the little man asked, clearing his throat.

"In the land of the brave...." Buti responded with some pride.

"Where's that?"

"The Fat Finger, of course."

The friendship was cemented over the bottle of tequila. The little man had been a good ear. Focusing on the pink head, with tears in his eyes, Buti had unloaded all his woes on the little fat man. Buti recounted—he had tried so hard to become a capitalist in the land of plenty to no avail. He tried to look the little fat man in the eye, asking, "Are you a capitalist?"

"Yes," assured the little man with a thick tongue. "I am that."

"See what I mean? Everybody who goes to the United States becomes a capitalist. Now—look at me. Great mind, good body, what's wrong with me?"

"What you need is luck," advised the little man with some wisdom, as he reeled off his chair. Buti helped him up again and shook his head. "That's easier said than done. I know the principles of good business—contacts, capital and a shrewd mind. But where in the hell do I get the contacts and the capital?"

"Me," assured the little fat man without hesitation. "Me, Don Rafael Aviña will help you. I'm a millionaire."

"That's what they all say." Buti eyed him with some suspicion.

"Don't I look like a millionaire?" demanded the little man, starting to hiccup. The spasmodic closure of the glottis caused his eyes to cross. Buti looked at him, still with some suspicion, but decided that he looked eccentric enough to be a millionaire. "Okay, how're you going to help me?"

"First you must help me," said Don Rafael between hiccups, "find my car."

"Where did you park it?"

"I don't know. You see, I have no sense of direction," confessed Don Rafael, leaning heavily on Buti. "It's a green Cadillac."

That did it. A man who owned a Cadillac did not talk from the wrong side of his mouth. "Can you give me a hint?"

Don Rafael had gone to sleep on his shoulder. Now is the time to be resourceful, Buti told himself. How many green Cadillacs can be parked in the radius of six blocks? Don Rafael could not have wandered off farther than that on his short little legs. It would be a cinch, once he sobered up Don Rafael, enough for him to walk on his own speed.

It took six cups of coffee, but Don Rafael was able to hold on to Buti all the way to Mariscal where Buti spotted a lone green Cadillac parked in front of Sylvia's Place, the best whorehouse in Juarez.

"Hey, Don Rafael," Buti had to shake the little man from his stupor. "Is that the car?"

Don Rafael squinted, leaning forward, then back against Buti. "Is it a green Cadillac?"

"A green Cadillac."

"That's my car." Don Rafael began to feel around for the keys. "Can't find my keys." Buti helped him look through all his pockets, but no keys.

"You could have left them in the ignition."

"That would be dumb." Don Rafael kept on searching until Buti pushed him toward the car to look. Sure enough, the keys were in the ignition.

"There are your keys and your car." Buti gestured with a flourish.

"Then, let's go home."

"Your home?" queried Buti.

"Why not? You can be my guest for as long as you like—if you can stand my sister...."

"What's wrong with your sister?"

"Everything—does everything right, prays all the time, and is still a virgin at fifty."

"See what you mean. You could drop me off at my place in Valverde."

They drove off, and it was not until they were crossing the immigration bridge that they heard the police sirens. A police car with a red flashing light cut right across the green Cadillac. In no time, three policemen pulled Buti and Don Rafael roughly out of the car.

"What is the meaning of this?" demanded Don Rafael, sobering up in a hurry.

"You're under arrest," informed a menacing looking policeman.

"What are you talking about?" Buti asked angrily, shaking himself free from another policeman's hold.

"You stole that car," accused the first policeman.

Don Rafael was indignant. "You're crazy. That's my car!"

"That's the mayor's car. He reported it stolen."

"The mayor's car?" Buti was dumbfounded. He would never believe little fat men with pink heads again.

"I have a green Cadillac," sputtered Don Rafael. "I demand to see my lawyers."

"Tomorrow you can call your lawyer. Tonight you go to jail," the third policeman informed them with great stoicism. All of Don Rafael's screaming did no good. They wouldn't even look at his credentials. So they spent a night in jail. Buti diplomatically offered Don Rafael his coat when he saw the little man shivering with cold, and even let him pillow his pink head on his shoulder to sleep. Buti had decided there was more than one green Cadillac in the world, and that Don Rafael threw his weight around enough to be rich. Don Rafael snuggled close to Buti and snored all night.

They were allowed to leave the next morning after Don Rafael made a phone call and three lawyers showed up to threaten the government of Mexico with a lawsuit for false arrest. Outside the jail stood Don Rafael's green Cadillac from heaven knows where.

On the way home, Don Rafael gave Buti a written permit to pick piñon on his property for free, thus Buti could count on a clear profit. Don Rafael wrung his hand in goodbye, making him promise he would come up to Ratón to visit him and his sister, which Buti promised to do. Yes, Buti promised himself, he would soon go to Ratón for a social visit to thank Don Rafael for the piñon. He was well on his way to becoming a capitalist....

"Hey, Buti," called out Rico, "you just passed your house."

Buti backed the pick-up next to a two-room shack he had built on the edge of his sister's one acre of land. The two-room house sported a red roof and a huge sign over the door that read "Antiques." After the roof and the sign, he had built himself an inside toilet, of which he was very proud. That had been six years before when he had come from Chihuahua to live with his sister and to make a fortune. He had fallen into the antique business by chance. One day he had found an old Victrola in an empty lot. That was the beginning of a huge collection of outlandish discards—old car horns, Kewpie dolls, wagon wheels, a stuffed moose head, an old church altar. At one time he had lugged home a rusty, huge commercial scale he claimed would be a priceless antique someday. The day he brought home the old, broken merry-go-round that boasted one headless horse painted blue, his sister, Trini, had been driven to distraction. She accused him of turning her place into an eyesore and ordered he get rid of all the junk.

"Junk!" exclaimed Buti with great hurt in his voice, "why all these antiques will be worth thousands in a few years."

Rico had to agree with his mother—the place was an eyesore. After parking the pick-up, Rico reminded Buti about his date with Alicia that night.

"Put on a clean shirt and shave, okay, Buti?"

"Baboso, who do you think you're talking to?"

"She's a nice lady, don't blow it," Rico reminded him.

"Sure she is. I'm going to marry her," Buti informed his nephew, who stared at him incredulously.

"She's not the marrying kind, Tío," Rico warned him.

"She's a widow, ain't she? She gave in once."

"That's 'cause she was sixteen," explained Rico.

"How old was he?" Buti inquired.

"Seventy and very rich."

"Smart girl. Never married again, eh? What for?"

"She's had lovers. Two of them."

"Smart girl. What were they like?"

Rico wrinkled his brow trying to remember. "The first one was her gardener. She took him because she claimed he looked like Humphrey Bogart."[5]

"Humf…what?"

"Don't you ever watch the late, late show? He was a movie star."

"What happened to him?"

"Humphrey Bogart? He died.…"

"No, stupid, the gardener."

"He died too. Fell off the roof fixing the television antenna."

Buti wanted all the facts. "What about the second lover?"

"He had a cleft on his chin like Kirk Douglas,"[6] Rico remembered.

"Another movie star? What's this thing with movie stars?"

"That's just the way she is." Rico added reassuringly, "But don't worry, Tío. She says you are the image of Clark Gable."

✦ ✦ ✦

After the dog races, Buti took Alicia to Serafín's. It had become their favorite hangout. For one thing, the orchestra at Serafín's specialized in cumbias, and Buti was at his best dancing cumbias. No woman could resist him then. He could tell that Alicia was passionately in love with him by the way she clung to him and batted those ridiculous lashes. As he held the sweet-smelling plump body against him and expertly did a turn on the floor, she hissed in his ear, "Well, are you going to move in?"

"Haven't changed my mind," he informed her in a cool, collected voice.

"Oh, you're infuriating!" She turned away from him, making her way back to the table. He noticed that the sway of her hips was defiant. Tonight could be the night. She plumped down on the table. "I've had it with you, Buti."

"What do you mean?" He tried to look perplexed.

"Stop playing cat and mouse."

"Am I supposed to be the mouse?" His voice was slightly sarcastic. "I've never been a mouse."

"Let's put our cards on the table." Her voice sounded ominous.

"Okay by me."

"Well then, don't give me that jazz about you loving me too much to live with me in sin. Sin, indeed. When I hear about all those girls you run around with…"

"Used to run around with," corrected Buti, looking into her eyes seductively. "I only want you. You are the world to me. Oh, how I want to make love to you. It tortures me to think about it. But I must be strong."

"There you go again. Come home with me tonight and you can make love to me all you want to." It was her stubborn voice.

"Don't say those things, my love. I would never sully our love by just jumping into bed with you." Buti was proud of the fake sincerity in his voice. "Our love is sacred. It must be sanctified by marriage."

"Marriage be damned!" Alicia hit her fists on the table. She was really angry now. He could tell. She accused him. "You just want my money."

"You're not the only girl with money. But you are the only woman I could ever love." Buti was beginning to believe it himself.

"You liar! All the girls you've had have been penniless, submissive, ignorant

---

[5] Humphrey Bogart (1899-1957), American actor.   [6] Kirk Douglas (b. 1916), American actor.

wetbacks from across the river." Her anger was becoming vicious now.

"Wait a minute." Buti was not playing a game anymore. He looked at the woman across the table, knowing that she was a romantic little fool, passionate, sensuous, selfish, stubborn, domineering, and full of fire. That's the kind of woman he would want to spend the rest of his life with. Nevertheless, he took affront. "What am I? I'm penniless not quite, but almost. You could say I'm a wetback from across the river. And you, in your mindless way, want me to submit. Stop throwing stones. We seem to have the same likes!"

She looked at him with her mouth opened. She had sensed the sincerity in his voice. She could tell this was not a game anymore. She knew she had been ambushed, but she would not give in.

"If you love me, and I believe you do, you'll come live with me, or…"—there was a finality in her voice—"I simply will not see you again."

"I will not be another scalp on your belt." There was finality in his voice too.

+ + +

"Hell!" Alicia slammed the half full can of beer against the porch railing. She hated the smell of honeysuckle, the full moon, and the heavy sense of Spring. She hated everything tonight. And look at her—this was her sixth can of beer—thousands of calories going straight to her waistline. She hated herself most of all. Buti was through with her. He must be, if what Rico had told her was true. He had come over to help her plant some rosebushes and she had casually asked him how Buti was doing these days. According to Rico, he spent a lot of time up in Ratón, New Mexico, visiting his friend, Don Rafael Aviña, and his unmarried sister.

"Is she rich?" Alicia asked nonchalantly.

"Very rich," Rico answered in innocence, setting up the young rosebushes against the fence.

She didn't ask much more, but knowing Buti, she could put two and two together. He had found himself a greener pasture and a new playmate. He loves me. I know he loves me, but I've lost him forever. She couldn't stand it anymore—the moon, the smell of honeysuckle. She went back into the house and turned on the late, late show on television. She threw a shawl over her shoulders and huddled in a corner of the sofa. She sighed deeply, her breasts heaving under the thin negligee.

She recognized the actress on the screen. It was Joan Fontaine[7] with the usual sweet, feminine smile and delicate gestures. She always looked so vulnerable, so helpless. Clark Gable came on the screen. Oh, no—why him? Even his dimples were like Buti's! Damn it all. She wanted to see the movie. They had had some kind of quarrel and Joan Fontaine had come to Clark to ask forgiveness, to say she was wrong. Joan's soft beautiful eyes seem to say—you can do what you wish with me. You are my master…. Alicia began to sniffle, then the tears flowed. Especially when she saw big, strong, powerful Clark become a bowl of jelly. All that feminine submissiveness had won out. Joan Fontaine had won the battle without lifting a finger. Hell, I'm no Joan Fontaine. But Clark was smiling on the screen, and Alicia couldn't stand it any longer. She turned off the set and went out into the night wearing only a negligee, a shawl and slippers. She didn't care who saw her. She was walking—no, running—towards Buti's shack almost a mile away. The princess leaving her castle to go to the stable. It was

[7] Joan Fontaine (b. 1917), British-born actress.

her movie now, her scenario. She was Joan Fontaine running towards the man she loved, Clark Gable. It mustn't be too late. She would throw herself at his feet—offer him all she had. She suddenly realized the night was perfect for all this!

The lights were on. She knocked at the door, one hand against her breast, her eyes wide, beseeching…in the manner of Joan Fontaine.

"What the hell.…" Buti stood in the doorway, half a hero sandwich in his hand.

"May I come in?" There was a soft dignity in her voice. Buti took a bite of his sandwich and stared at her somewhat speechless. She walked past him into the room, and when she heard the door close, she turned around dramatically with outstretched arms. "Darling…"

"You're drunk…," Buti guessed.

"I only had five beers," she protested hotly, then caught herself. "No, my love, I'm here for a very good reason.…" Again, the Fontaine mystique.

Buti took another bite from the sandwich and chewed nervously.

"Don't you understand?" She lifted her chin and smiled sweetly as she had seen Joan Fontaine do it hundreds of times. Buti shook his head unbelievingly. She began to pace the floor gracefully, her voice measured, almost pleading. "I've come to tell you that I was wrong. I want to be forgiven. How could I have doubted you? I'm so ashamed—so ashamed." Words straight from the movie.

Buti finished off the sandwich, then scratched his head. Alicia approached him, her hand posed in the air, gently falling against his cheek. "Do you understand what I'm saying?"

"Hell no. I think you've gone bananas.…"

She held back her disappointment with strained courage. "You're not helping much, you know.…" Then she bit her lip, thinking that Joan Fontaine would never have made an unkind judgment like that. She looked into his eyes with a faint, sweetly twisted smile, then leaned her head against his shoulder. She was getting to him.

There was worry in his voice. "Are you feeling okay?"

She began to cry in a very unlike-Joan-Fontaine way. "Why can't you be more like him?"

"Like who?"

"Like Clark Gable, you lout!" She almost shouted it, regretfully.

Buti's eyes began to shine. She was beginning to sound like the Alicia he knew and loved. "Why should I be like some dumb old movie star?"

"Don't you see?…" she held her breath out of desperation. "It's life.…"

"The late, late show?" He finally caught on—the dame on television.

"You were watching it too!" She accused him, not without surprise.

"Had nothing else to do. They're stupid, you know.…"

"What!" Her dark eyes blazed with anger.

"Those old gushy movies…" He gestured their uselessness.

"That proves to me what a brute you are, you insensitive animal!" She kicked his shin.

"Well, the woman, she was kind of nice.…"

"Joan Fontaine…"

"Jonfontayn?"

"That's her name. You're not going to marry her, are you?" There was real concern in her voice.

"Jonfontayn?" He could not keep up with her madness.

"No—that woman up in Ratón."

"Berta Aviña?" The whole scene came into focus. Buti sighed in relief.

"Rico told me she is very rich."

"Very rich."

"Is she slender and frail and soft-spoken like?..."

"Jonfontayn?" Buti silently congratulated himself on his subtle play.

"Yes...."

Buti thought of Berta Aviña, the square skinny body, the tightlipped smile. He lied. "Oh, yes. Berta is the spitting image of Jonfontayn."

"I knew it. I knew it...." Alicia threw herself into his arms. "Please please, marry me. Oh, I love you so, you beast!"

"Not tonight, baby. We have better things to do...." He pulled her roughly against him, first giving her a Clark Gable smile, then he kissed her for a long, long time. Still relying on his dimples, he picked her up, not without effort, and headed for the bed. She tried to push him away protesting, "Oh, we can't...we mustn't...not before we're married."

He stopped in his tracks, not believing his ears. "What?"

"Well, that's—that's what she would say...." Alicia smiled meekly, batting the Max Factor lashes.

"Who?"

"Joan Fontaine, silly...."

"Frankly, my dear, I don't give a damn."

He threw her on the bed.

—1982

KATHLEEN FRASER (1937-   )

Raised in Oklahoma and Colorado, Kathleen Fraser graduated from Occidental College in 1959, and moved to New York City to work as an editorial associate for *Mademoiselle* magazine. In New York, she studied poetry with Stanley Kunitz at the 92nd Street YMCA Poetry Center, and with Robert Lowell and Kenneth Koch at The New School. There, she was influenced by several avant garde poets, including Frank O'Hara, Barbara Guest, George Oppen, Lorine Niedecker, and Charles Olson. Gertrude Stein, Mina Loy, and other modernist women poets also informed her development as a poet. With the publication of her first book of poems, *Change of Address* (1968), Fraser's career as a poet and teacher was launched; she went on to teach writing at the Iowa Writer's Workshop, Reed College, The Naropa Institute, and San Francisco State University (SFSU). While at SFSU, she published and edited *How(ever)*, a journal of innovative and forgotten writing by women, reincarnated in 1997 as the online journal *How2*. Fraser has published sixteen volumes of poetry, her work evolving from an image-based form with a subjective speaker to one more closely associated with, but not limited to, Language Poetry. Whereas her mentor Barbara Guest eschewed feminist or political poetics, Fraser's poetry at its best subverts the patriarchal influence on form and voice without sacrificing a body that experiences and observes. Her recent volumes include the poetry collections *Discrete Categories Forced into Couplings* (2004), *il cuore: the heart: New & Selected Poems*

(1997), and *When New Time Folds Up* (1993), as well as a collection of essays about experimental women poets, *Translating the Unspeakable: Poetry and the Innovative Necessity* (1999). She spends the spring of each year in Rome with her husband, the philosopher Arthur Bierman, translating and lecturing on Italian women poets.

this. notes.
new year.

Dear other, I address you in sentences. I need your nods and I hear your echoes. There is a forward movement still, as each word is a precedent for what new order. You can hear a distant habit. The sound of a low gas flame discharging. Even a hiss is only soothing because it is dark and nearing the shorter perimeters. When I run into boredom, I shift into another's past.

(She was "in a fury" and she wept in spite of herself. His letter told the usual stories in all the old ways. She swallowed them whole. Then came the nausea. She wanted a "flow" she thought, but in the translation it was corrected, displacing the *o* and substituting *a*. She could give herself to an accident. She was looking out the window.)

This is the Year of Our Lord. Every year we always have these difficulties. The sound of water splatting from the bathroom, heard through the kitchen, the clank of a soap dish. "I'm going to take a shower," David bragged, striding through the room on his twelfth birthday.

I tried to protect myself especially well. I had time to play at domesticity this year. Three-quarters cup of bourbon in the chocolate-covered bourbon balls. There were many occasions and I was there in a different skirt. I went to the sales with her. She believed in that and built up her vocabulary like a wardrobe purchased during ten different years, but only on December 26th.

One man said of another that he was committed to the sentence. I sentence you. I could hear the terseness of his sentences and how seductive it seemed to move the words away towards a drop in the voice. What did it mean to be flat? Was there a principle of denial? Of manipulation? I'm worried. He is embarrassed.

The French workers often raised their voices on the Blvd. des Minimes and along the tiny alleys of the Ile St. Louis. You could hear questions rising to the windows of the sixth floor of the Hôtel St. Louis, although the bathroom, if you wanted to take a tub bath, was on the fourth floor. Voices raised at the ends of sentences, as though all were in question.

It made you want to look out the window. You could sniff the momentous occasion. The bakery opening its door each morning to view of *pain au chocolat*[1] on trays. *Entrez, s'il vous plaît.*[2]

I wanted, suddenly, to speak French because of certain French women thinking about layers, thinking *in* layers, but as yet not translated. They had moved ahead but not in a line. It occurred to me that growing up inside of,

---

[1] (Fr.) Chocolate pastry.   [2] (Fr.) Come in, please.

yet opposing, a tradition peculiarly French and masculine appeared to give them a certain authority because the tradition itself assumed a dialectical plane and invited the next position, while echoing "I baptize thee in the name of the father and the son."

(She questioned the wistful half-truths he gained solace from, using a certain Rapidograph pen with its fine black lines. He gave the boy a drawing pen. He said it was for art. The boy's face broke open and filled with light. Enlightened. Boyish and tender.)

I question these wistful half-truths and why I sink into silence around them. Now that I've made the decision to attempt a separation from their hold on me, I am released into sentences. The gas heater is a constant I could compare.

I change my mind every day. I think of my mother's love. The antique bracelet she gave me with dozens of flowers etched into the tarnished brass. A line from Kunitz surfaces from the year I was twenty-one. "A single color oversweeps the field."[3] That is all my memory provides of it. But to understand truly, you'd need the lines before it, building up to that crescendo that thrilled me. A vast field of scarlet poppies in the south of France…a movement in front of one. As a season. In a second. The forward movement of slow motion. Even then, the field. Of many flowers moving at their own speeds. Not one then two then three. But moving. Split. Second. Rushing into petals.

That was a peculiar passion I do not often encounter in the poetry of the later '70s, but do not want to deny. That urgency we call romantic, but which might actually be, in part, the willingness to be told lies. That rush. How I've wanted it. His romance.

(He tried to deflect her anger. He tried to mystify her by leaving half of everything out. He made her laugh. He knew what she wanted. In her "worst moments" she wanted obsession, obliteration of choice.)

You are against confession, because it's embarrassing. I want to embarrass you. To feel your confusion. Someone's rhythm speaking in again. Sharing a language. The osmosis of rubbing up. Communing.

I'll never make candy again. It is a relief to write this music. Who does it belong to? *"Who can I turn to?"* Las Vegas crooners with their soft, slimy hair styles. Feel the lyric hit, anyway. As soft as sniffing it. Where's the kleenex?

Christmas is over and "I'm glad," I said to David. "It's such a pressure building up." He smiled, being twelve now, and not satisfied, even though we tried to cover all the branches with icicles and double strands of lights. Next year, it's snowing.

—1980

---

[3] The final line of "As Flowers Are" (1958) by U.S. poet Stanley Kunitz (1905-2006).

Medusa's hair was snakes. Was thought, split inward.

For Frances Jaffer

I do not wish to report on Medusa[4] directly, this variation of her
writhing. After she gave that voice a shape, it was the trajectory itself
in which she found her words floundering and pulling apart.

Sometimes we want to talk to someone who can't hear us.
Sometimes we're too far away. So is a shadow
a real shadow.

When he said "red cloud," she imagined *red*
but he thought *cloud* (this dissonance in which she was feeling
trapped, out-of-step, getting from here to there).

Historical continuity
accounts for knowing what dead words point to,

a face staring down through green leaves as the man looks up
from tearing and tearing again at his backyard weeds. His red dog sniffs
at what he's turned over. You know what I mean.
We newer people have children who learn to listen as *we* listen.

M. wanted her own.
Kept saying *red dog. Cloud.*
Someone pointing to it while saying it. Someone discovering stone.

Medusa trying to point with her hair.
That thought turned to venom.
That muscle turning to thought turning
to writhing out.

We try to locate blame, going backwards.
I point with my dog's stiff neck
and will not sit down,
the way that girl points her saxophone at the guitar player
to shed light
upon his next invention. He attends her silences, between keys,
and underscores them with slow referents.

Can she substitute *dog* for *cloud,* if *red* comes first?
Red tomato.
Red strawberry.
As if all this happens on the ocean one afternoon in July,
red sunset soaking into white canvas. The natural world.
And the darkness does eventually come down.
He closes her eye in the palm of his hand.
The sword comes down.

Now her face rides above his sails, her hair her splitting tongues.

---

[4] In Greek mythology, a Gorgon with hair of snakes who turned all who looked at her to stone.

Flashes of light or semaphore waves, the sound
of rules, a regularity from which the clouds drift   40
into their wet embankments.

—1984

SUSAN HOWE (1937-   )

Poet Susan Howe was born in Boston, Massachusetts, the daughter of a Harvard Law School
professor and an Irish playwright and actress. Howe's work is often linked to the Language
Poets, a group of contemporary experimental poets. Her volumes of poems include
Singularities (1990), *The Europe of Trusts: Selected Poems* (1990), *The Nonconformist's Memorial*
(1993), *Frame Structures: Early Poems 1974-1979* (1996), *Pierce-Arrow* (1999), *The Europe of
Trusts* (2002), *Kidnapped* (2002), and *The Midnight* (2003). She has also written two books of
criticism: *The Birth-Mark: Unsettling the Wilderness in American Literary History* (1993) and *My
Emily Dickinson* (1985). Howe was elected to the American Academy of Arts and Sciences in
1999 and became a Chancellor of the Academy of American Poets in 2000. The Before
Columbus Foundation has twice awarded her the American Book Award. She retired from the
Samuel P. Capen Chair of Poetry and the Humanities at the State University of New York at
Buffalo in 2006.

There Are Not Leaves Enough to Crown
to Cover to Crown to Cover

For me there was no silence before armies.

I was born in Boston Massachusetts on June 10th, 1937, to an Irish mother and
an American father. My mother had come to Boston on a short visit two years earlier.
My father had never been to Europe. She is a wit and he was a scholar. They met at
a dinner party when her earring dropped into his soup.

By 1937 the Nazi dictatorship was well-established in Germany. All dissenting polit-
ical parties had been liquidated and Concentration camps had already been set up to
hold political prisoners. The Berlin-Rome axis was a year old. So was the Spanish
Civil War. On April 25th Franco's Lufftwaffe pilots bombed the village of Guernica.[1]
That November Hitler and the leaders of his armed forces made secret plans to invade
Austria, Czechoslovakia, Poland, and Russia.

In the summer of 1938 my mother and I were staying with my grandmother, uncle,
aunt, great-aunts, cousins, and friends in Ireland, and I had just learned to walk, when
Czechoslovakia was dismembered by Hitler, Ribbentrop, Mussolini, Chamberlain,
and Daladier,[2] during the Conference and Agreement at Munich.[3] That October we
sailed home on a ship crowded with refugees fleeing various countries in Europe.

---

[1] Between 250 and 1600 people were killed in this bombing, which was commemorated by Spanish painter Pablo
Picasso (1881-1973) in *Guernica* (1937).
[2] Ulrich Friedrich Wilhelm Joachim von Ribbentrop
(1893-1946), foreign minister of Germany; Benito
Mussolini (1883-1945), fascist dictator of Italy; Neville

Chamberlain (1896-1940), prime minister of the United
Kingdom; Édouard Daladier (1884-1970), prime minis-
ter of France.
[3] In which Germany, Italy, the United Kingdom, and
France agreed to divide Czechoslovakia between
Germany, Poland, and Hungary.

When I was two the German army invaded Poland and World War II began in the West.

The fledgling Republic of Ireland distrusted England with good reason, and remained neutral during the struggle. But there was the Battle of the Atlantic to be won, so we couldn't cross the sea again until after 1945. That half of the family was temporarily cut off.

In Buffalo New York, where we lived at first, we seemed to be safe. We were there when my sister was born and the Japanese bombed Pearl Harbor.

Now there were armies in the west called East.

American fathers marched off into the hot Chronicle of global struggle but mothers were left. Our law-professor father, a man of pure principles, quickly included violence in his principles, put on a soldier suit and disappeared with the others into the thick of the threat to the east called West.

> B u f f a l o
> 12. 7. 41
>
> (Late afternoon light.)
> (Going to meet him in snow.)
> HE
> (Comes through the hall door.)

The research of scholars, lawyers, investigators, judges
Demands!

> SHE
>
> (With her arms around his neck
> whispers.)

Herod had all the little children murdered![4]

It is dark
The floor is ice

they stand on the edge of a hole singing—

In Rama
Rachel weeping for her children[5]

refuses
to be comforted

because they *are* not.

Malice dominates the history of Power and Progress. History is the record of winners. Documents were written by the Masters. But fright is formed by what we see not by what they say.

From 1939 until 1946 in news photographs, day after day I saw signs of culture exploding into murder. Shots of children being herded into trucks by hideous helmeted conquerors—shots of children who were orphaned and lost—shots of the

---

[4] Matthew 2:16. [5] Matthew 2:18.

emaciated bodies of Jews dumped into mass graves on top of more emaciated bodies—nameless numberless men women and children, uprooted in a world almost demented. God had abandoned them to history's sovereign Necessity.

If to see is to *have* at a distance, I had so many dead Innocents distance was abolished. Substance broke loose from the domain of time and obedient intention. I became part of the ruin. In the blank skies over Europe I was Strife represented.

Things overlap in space and are hidden. Those black and white picture shots—moving or fixed—were a subversive generation. "The hawk, with his long claws / Pulled down the stones. / The dove, with her rough bill / Brought me them home."[6]

> Buffalo roam in herds
> up the broad streets connected by boulevards
>
> and fences
>
> their eyes are ancient and a thousand years
> too old
>
> hear murder throng their muting
>
> Old as time in the center of a room
> doubt is spun
>
> and measured
>
> Throned wrath
> I know your worth
>
> a chain of parks encircles the city

Pain is nailed to the landscape in time. Bombs are seeds of Science and the sun.

2,000 years ago the dictator Creon said to Antigone who was the daughter of Oedipus and Jocasta: "Go to the dead and love them."[7]

Life opens into conceptless perspectives. Language surrounds Chaos.

During World War II my father's letters were a sign he was safe. A miniature photographic negative of his handwritten message was reproduced by the army and a microfilm copy forwarded to us. In the top left-hand corner someone always stamped PASSED BY EXAMINER.[8]

This is my historical consciousness. I have no choice in it. In my poetry, time and again, questions of assigning *the cause* of history dictate the sound of what is thought.

> Summary of fleeting summary
> Pseudonym cast across empty
>
> Peak proud heart
>
> Majestic caparisoned cloud cumuli
> East sweeps hewn flank
>
> Scion on a ledge of Constitution

[6] From the nursery rhyme "The Girl and the Birds."
[7] From Sophocles' play *Antigone*.
[8] Victory mail (or V-mail) was used during WWII to reduce the volume of overseas mail.

Wedged sequences of system

Causeway of faint famed city
Human ferocity

Dim mirror Naught formula

archaic hallucinatory laughter

Kneel to intellect in our work
Chaos cast cold intellect back

Poetry brings similitude and representation to configurations waiting from forever to be spoken. North Americans have tended to confuse human fate with their own salvation. In this I am North American. "We are coming Father Abraham, three hundred thousand more,"[9] sang the Union troops at Gettysburg.[10]

I write to break out into perfect primeval Consent. I wish I could tenderly lift from the dark side of history, voices that are anonymous, slighted—inarticulate.

—1990

---

[9] 1862 poem by the American abolitionist James Sloan Gibbons (1810-1892), sung to various tunes.

[10] Site of an 1863 Civil War battle.

DIANE WAKOSKI (1937-)

Born in Whittier, California, Diane Wakoski received a B.A. in English from the University of California, Berkeley. She has published more than forty books of poetry, including her early works *The George Washington Poems* (1967), *The Motorcycle Betrayal Poems* (1971), and *Dancing on the Grave of a Son of a Bitch* (1973). She has also published the essay collections *Form Is an Extension of Content* (1972), *Creating a Personal Mythology* (1975), *Variations on a Theme* (1976), and *Toward a New Poetry* (1980). Her *Emerald Ice: Selected Poems 1962-1987* (1988) won the William Carlos Williams award from the Poetry Society of America. Wakoski is also the author of the series "The Archaeology of Movies and Books," which includes *Medea the Sorceress* (1991), *Jason the Sailor* (1993), *The Emerald City of Las Vegas* (1995), and *Argonaut Rose* (1998). Wakoski has received numerous awards for her writing, among them a Fulbright Fellowship, a Michigan Arts Foundation award, and grants from the Guggenheim Foundation, the Michigan Arts Council, the National Endowment for the Arts, and the New York State Council on the Arts. Since 1976, Wakoski has taught at Michigan State University, where she is currently a Distinguished Professor.

From a Girl in a Mental Institution

The morning wakes me as a broken door vibrating on its
hinges.
We are drifting out to sea this morning. I
can barely feel the motion of the boat as it rocks me.
I must be a gull, sitting on the mast,
else why would I be so high above the world?   5

Yes.
I see everything down there—
children tucked, sleeping, into the waves,
their heads nestled in foam   10
                 AND I DON'T LIKE THE WAVES THEY
                 DISTINCTLY SAY THINGS
                 AGAINST ME.
The wind is blowing my feathers. How good
that feels. If the wind   15
had always blown my feathers, I would
never have cried
when the waves spoke
that way—
taking my brother away, when he dove in and never came   20
back.
                 it was because he loved the seashells
                 too much
                 i know
                 and broken water foams in my hair   25
                 in its new color—the color of my wing
Why don't we hear the fog-horns today?
                 IF I AM TO SIT HERE ALL DAY I MUST
                 HAVE SOMETHING TO LISTEN TO.
The waves have torn the sleeping children to bits. I   30
see them scattered on the crests now.
There—an arm floating by.
                 leave me alone, i have not hurt you
                 Stop pulling my wings,
                 my beak, DON'T YOU HEAR STOP IT.   35
There is nothing more horrible than hands
like ancient crabs, pulling at one. And they cannot
hear because they have no ears.
                 I have no ears.
I am a gull. Birds have no ears. I cannot hear   40
Them
or anyone.
The fingers on the dismembered arm, floating
in the waves,
can point and make signs,   45
but I will not hear
the waves
telling the fingers odious things about me.
I will not watch their obscenities
pointing to the bottom where the children are buried;   50
where he is buried;
where I am buried.

Slam the door as often as you like—you will
not wake me.

I am a gull   55
sitting on the mast, and I feel the ocean rocking
because I can hear nothing
but silent voices the wind carries from the past—
                    gently rocking.
The ocean is as still as a newly made bed,   60
rocking.

—1962

Human History: Its Documents

Sometimes poison
a decoration
in our lives/ or more.
                    Black oily
French Roast   5
coffee beans, ground and brewed,
steaming in a cup/ the day still with no wasted and empty
words
in it,
        thick cream   10
floating on the beverage,
the memory of a silver pot and a silk coverlet
somewhere behind
this desirable poison,

hot from the oven   15
flaky butter dough, a beautiful parchment
croissant,
the fingers covered with a film
of grease,
the flour milled empty of   20
nurture,
appeasing the eye and tongue, like
delicate crumpled stiff letters
in the belly,
the cream which would bloat the stomachs of   25
African children/ we have evolved too far
to digest it,
these poisons ARE TREATS
to start special mornings, as if
I were the woman in   30
the peignoir
on "Sunday Morning,"[1]
listening for the beat of giant bird wings,
pterodactyl,
the big poetic line   35

---

[1] Poem by Wallace Stevens (1879-1955).

I wait for
with these poisons I long for.

Spring coming and I fantasize Hot Cross Buns,
all of civilization summed up
in dough, 40
bean,
viney resins,
and the paper, the ink
which allows us to transmit
our recipes, 45
I, standing in line to do my monthly banking
watch a young pregnant mother lean over to her two-year-old
and stuff into his unwilling mouth
a piece of candy. She is grinning and nodding, as if she were in a
Punch and Judy show.[2] "Good," she is saying, as the child grimaces 50
  and
drools and finally chews his little pellet of poison sugar. She
beams
to us all,
as we stand in line with checks and bills. How good she believes 55
herself to be, having just begun one young child's craving
for poison. Food
that will never nourish
and, in this case, didn't even
please. 60

Yes, how I hated that school teacher's phrase, "You can trap more
  flies
with honey than with vinegar." As if we were all going out there
to read *Song of Myself* and *Howl*[3]
to a large swarm of irritating flies.

—2000

---

[2] A traditional puppet show.

[3] Poems by Walt Whitman (1819-1892) and Allen Ginsberg (1926-1997).

LOURDES CASAL (1938-1981)

Lourdes Casal was born in Havana, Cuba, in 1938, to mixed-race parents. Her father was a physician and a dentist and her mother was an elementary school teacher, which meant that Casal grew up with many of the privileges of the middle class, though she struggled with racial tensions. She graduated from the Catholic University of Villanueva, first studying chemical engineering and then moving toward literature and the social sciences. While still a student, she actively participated in revolutionary activities against the Batista dictatorship, but later became disappointed with Castro's political practices and took up counterrevolutionary activities. After going into exile in 1961, Casal came to New York City, where she pursued graduate studies at the New School for Social Research, earning an M.A. and a Ph.D. in Social Psychology. The civil rights movement sharpened Casal's political consciousness and she became an instrumental part of building cultural relationships between Cuban exiles in the U.S. and Cubans on the island. Casal co-founded several institutions dedicated to the cause: the Institute of Cuban Studies (in 1969) and the journals *Nueva Generación* (1972) and *Areíto* (1974). *El Caso Padilla: Literatura y revolución en Cuba,* her collection documenting the rift between the revolutionary government and Cuban intellectuals, was published in 1971. Casal was invited back to Cuba by the Cuban government in 1973, one of the first exiled Cubans to visit. That same year she published a collection of short stories, *Los fundadores: Alfonso y otros cuentos.* Upon her return from Cuba she helped organize the Antonio Maceo brigade, the Cuban-American student movement that led a group of fifty-five young Cuban Americans on their return to Cuba in 1977. Shortly after her co-authored book of memoirs, *Contra viento y marea,* received the Casa de las Américas Award in 1978, Casal was diagnosed with terminal kidney disease. She returned to Havana in December of 1979, where she died on February 1, 1981. *Palabras juntan revolución,* her collection of poetry, was published posthumously and received the Casa de las Américas Award in 1981. An anthology of Casal's writings entitled *Itinerario Ideológico* was released in 1982.

Armando

And, what stops us from speaking?
What stops us
if I know you continue inspired under the sun,
that you still walk, with mustache and umbrella,
through landscapes which were once ours?   5

I know you whistle pavanes[1] through the streets
that you save your chisels in the same drawer
and that your mouth probably tastes the same
all immune to time and militias.

You   10
make everything possible:
the happiness, the work,
the construction, the evenings,
October's biting breeze,
the leaves that strike my windshield,   15
that Newark suddenly seems a beautiful city to me.
Because all difficulties crumble
against the indescribable reality of your gaze:
from there all possibilities emerge,
your eyes and the Revolution are the same thing.   20

I live in Cuba.
I have always lived in Cuba,
even when I thought I dwelled
very far from the caiman of agony
I have always lived in Cuba.   25

---

[1] Formal Spanish court dances of the 16th century; the name also refers to the music accompanying the dances.

No longer in the simple island
of the violent blues
and the arrogant palms
but in the other,
the one who on which Hatuey's[2] unconquerable breath appeared,   30
the one that grew
through palisades[3] and conspiracies,
the one that pushes and shoves to build socialism,
the one belonging to the heroic nation that lived the seventies
and did not give up   35
but in the dark,
quietly,
has been making history
and remaking itself.

Translated by Armando García

—1981

For Ana Veldford[4]

Never a summertime in Provincetown
and even on this limpid afternoon
(so out of the ordinary for New York)
it is from the window of a bus that I contemplate
the serenity of the grass up and down Riverside Park   5
and the easy freedom of vacationers resting on rumpled blankets,
fooling around on bicycles along the paths.
I remain as foreign behind this protective glass
as I was that winter
—that unexpected weekend—   10
when I first confronted Vermont's snow.
And still New York is my home.
I am ferociously loyal to this acquired *patria chica*.[5]
Because of New York I am a foreigner anywhere else,
fierce pride in the scents that assault us along any West Side street,   15
marijuana and the smell of beer
and the odor of dog urine
and the savage vitality of Santana[6]
descending upon us,
from a speaker that thunders, improbably balanced on a fire escape,   20
the raucous glory of New York in summer,
Central Park and us,

---

2 Hatuey was a Taíno leader from the island of Hispaniola
who fought against the Spanish invaders, specifically
Diego Velazquez, the conquistador of Cuba, in the early
1500s. He was captured and killed in Cuba in 1512.
3 Palisades or "Palenques" were territories constructed
and inhabited by runaway African slaves in slave-hold-
ing Cuba, most existing in the mountains surrounding
major sugar plantations.
4 Anna Veltfort, an acquaintance of Casal's who traveled
in the same artistic circle in New York City during the

1970s. The German-born Veltfort immigrated to the
U.S. with her mother when she was a child; when she
was sixteen, she moved with her mother and stepfather,
a blacklisted engineer, to Cuba. In 1967, Velfort and a
college friend were arrested for lewd behavior after they
were attacked with anti-lesbian jeers and physically
beaten by a group of men. The case was never legally
resolved. In 1972, Veltfort was allowed to leave Cuba.
5 [*Translator's note.*] (Sp.) Hometown or province.
6 Carlos Santana (b. 1947) Mexican-born rock musician.

the poor,
who have inherited the lake of the north side,
and Harlem sails through the slackness of this sluggish afternoon.   25
The bus slips lazily,
down, along Fifth Avenue;
and facing me, the young bearded man
carrying a heap of books from the Public Library,
and it seems as if you could touch summer in the sweaty brow of
    the cyclist   30
who rides holding onto my window.
But New York wasn't the city of my childhood,
it was not here that I acquired my first convictions,
not here the spot where I took my first fall,
nor the piercing whistle that marked the night.   35
This is why I will always remain on the margins,
a stranger among the stones,
even beneath the friendly sun of this summer's day,
just as I will remain forever a foreigner,
even when I return to the city of my childhood   40
I carry this marginality, immune to all turning back,
too *habanera* to be *newyorkina*,[7]
too *newyorkina* to be
—even to become again—
anything else.   45

Translated by David Frye

—1981

From Yeats[8]

Too poor for the purple velvet,
I have laid spread under your feet
the carpet of my dreams.
They are your estates.
Travel them without haste;   5
But every now and then, love,
remember
the fragile rush mat upon which you stroll.
Nobody said it was easy
to walk upon dreams.   10

Today is the first day,
the beginning of the world.
Sparkling constellations burst
from your eyes.
I sink my fingers into the earth: 15
I feel the moist weeds
—with their perfume of harvest,

---

[7] [*Translator's note.*] (Sp.) A person from Havana, Cuba;
New Yorker

[8] This poem refers to "He Wishes for the Cloths of
Heaven" by Irish poet William Butler Yeats (1865-1939).

of spring—
you caress my skin and I tremble.

Today is the first day,   20
the beginning of the world.
Beyond the space that we inhabit
novas disintegrate.
The newspaper throws headlines at me
like a procession of punches.   25
But your arms create a space
from where one can come out to battle,
from where building is made possible.

Love,
so many things pain me   30
and though I'd like to believe that to your bed
I can always return,
as to the space of life,
outside so many things
summon me: 35
Che's[9] cadaver over that table,
the broken glasses and the bloodied hair
of Allende,[10]
or, simply,
the school   40
we still haven't finished building
over there in La Yaya.[11]

Translated by Armando García

—1981

That Tenacious One

The Revolution is that country boy from Victoria de las Tunas
illiterate on the eve
of the January hurricane.[12]
That stubborn man of the fields
who now, under the direction of Department XYZ   5
of such and such Ministry,
struggles with the darkness they left him
not only surrounding
but also, and fundamentally, inside his head.

There are nights like these,   10
San Bartolomés[13] of the word
in which silenced verses

[9] Ernesto "Ché" Guevara (1928-1967), an Argentinian
doctor turned Marxist revolutionary who participated in
the Cuban revolution.

[10] Salvador Allende (1908-1973), democratically elected
Chilean president who died during a military coup.

[11] A city in Cuba.

[12] After several years of conflict, Fidel Castro's forces succeeded in the overthrow of General Fulgencio Batista's
regime in Cuba in January of 1959.

[13] Saint Bartholomew, one of the twelve apostles, a
Christian martyr.

explode with unexpected violence.
Words
assemble 15
revolution.

Translated by Armando García

—1981

ROSARIO FERRÉ (1938-)

Rosario Ferré was born in Ponce, Puerto Rico, in 1938. Her mother, Lorenza Ramírez Ferré, came from an elite land-owning family on the island; her father, Luis A. Ferré, served as governor of Puerto Rico from 1968 to 1972. Ferré earned a B.A. from Manhattanville College, New York, an M.A. from the University of Puerto Rico, Rio Piedras, and a Ph.D. from the University of Maryland, College Park. While a graduate student, Ferré became a supporter of Puerto Rican independence, despite her father's support of an industrial and banking economy financed by American corporations. In 1970 she founded the literary magazine *Zona de carga y descarga,* which gave her a platform to advocate for social reform and allowed her to publish the writings of young Puerto Ricans. Ferré's short stories, novels, poetry, and critical essays, which are credited with inspiring a feminist movement on the island, speak to the colonial status of Puerto Rico and the oppressive roles women play in its society. Her works include the short story collection *Papeles de Pandora* (1976), which won awards from Ateneo Puertorriqueño and Casa de las Américas; a collection of feminist essays, *Sitio a Eros* (1982); and the novel *The House on the Lagoon* (1995), which received a nomination for the National Book Award. Ferré was honored with the "Liberatur Prix" from the Frankfurt Book Fair in 1992, and in 2004 she received a Guggenheim Latin American and Caribbean Fellowship.

Sleeping Beauty

DECEMBER 1, 1973

DEAR DON FELISBERTO:

I KNOW YOU'LL BE SURPRISED TO GET THIS LETTER. I FEEL THE ONLY DECENT THING FOR ME TO DO, IN VIEW OF WHAT'S GOING ON, IS TO WARN YOU. IT SEEMS YOUR WIFE DOESN'T APPRECIATE WHAT YOU'RE WORTH, A HANDSOME MAN AND RICH BESIDES. IT'S ENOUGH TO SATISFY THE MOST DEMANDING WOMAN.

FOR A FEW WEEKS NOW, I'VE WATCHED HER GO BY THE WINDOW OF THE BEAUTY PARLOR WHERE I WORK, ALWAYS AT THE SAME TIME. SHE TAKES THE SERVICE ELEVATOR AND GOES UP TO THE HOTEL. I CAN SEE YOU TURNING THE ENVELOPE AROUND TO SEE IF YOU CAN FIND OUT MY IDENTITY, IF THERE'S A RETURN ADDRESS. BUT YOU'LL NEVER GUESS WHO I AM; THIS CITY IS FULL OF FLEABAG HOTELS WITH BEAUTY PARLORS ON THE LOWER LEVEL. SHE ALWAYS WEARS DARK GLASSES AND COVERS HER HAIR WITH A KERCHIEF, BUT EVEN SO I RECOGNIZED HER EASILY FROM THE PICTURES I'VE SEEN OF HER IN THE

PAPERS. IT'S JUST THAT I'VE ALWAYS ADMIRED HER. BEING A BALLERINA AND AT THE SAME TIME THE WIFE OF A BUSINESS TYCOON IS NO MEAN ACHIEVEMENT. I SAY "ADMIRED" BECAUSE I'M NOT SURE I STILL DO. THAT BUSINESS OF GOING INTO HOTEL SERVICE ELEVATORS DISGUISED AS A MAID SEEMS RATHER SUSPICIOUS TO ME.

IF YOU STILL CARE FOR HER, I SUGGEST YOU FIND OUT WHAT SHE'S UP TO. SHE'S PROBABLY RISKING HER REPUTATION NEEDLESSLY. YOU KNOW THAT A LADY'S REPUTATION IS LIKE A PANE OF GLASS, IT SMUDGES AT THE LIGHTEST TOUCH. A LADY MUSTN'T SIMPLY BE RESPECTABLE, SHE MUST ABOVE ALL APPEAR TO BE.

SINCERELY YOURS,
A FRIEND AND ADMIRER

She folds the letter and puts it in an envelope. Painstakingly, using her left hand, she scrawls an address on it with the same pencil she used for the letter. Then she stretches before the mirror and stands on her toes. She walks to the barre and starts on her daily routine.

+ + +

DECEMBER 18, 1973

DEAR DON FELISBERTO:

I HAVE NO WAY OF KNOWING WHETHER OR NOT MY LAST LETTER REACHED YOU. IF IT DID, YOU DIDN'T TAKE IT SERIOUSLY, BECAUSE YOUR WIFE KEEPS UP HER DAILY VISITS TO THE HOTEL. DON'T YOU LOVE HER? IF YOU DON'T LOVE HER, WHY DID YOU MARRY HER? SHE'S RUNNING AROUND LIKE A BITCH IN HEAT AND IT DOESN'T SEEM TO BOTHER YOU. THE LAST TIME SHE WAS HERE I FOLLOWED HER. NOW I'LL DO MY DUTY AND GIVE YOU THE ROOM NUMBER (7B) AND THE HOTEL: HOTEL ELYSIUM. SHE'S THERE EVERY DAY FROM THREE TO FIVE-THIRTY. BY THE TIME YOU GET THIS LETTER, YOU WON'T BE ABLE TO FIND ME. DON'T BOTHER CHECKING; I QUIT MY JOB AT THE BEAUTY PARLOR AND I'M NOT GOING BACK.

SINCERELY YOURS,
A FRIEND AND ADMIRER

She folds the letter, puts it in an envelope, writes the address and leaves it on the piano. She picks up the chalk and painstakingly dusts the tips of her slippers. Then she gets up, faces the mirror, grasps the barre with her left hand and begins her exercises.

I. Coppelia

SOCIAL COLUMN
MUNDO NUEVO
APRIL 6, 1971

Coppelia, the ballet by the famous French composer Léo Delibes,[1] was marvelously performed here last Sunday by our very own Pavlova dance troupe. For all the

---

[1] Léo Delibes (1836-1891) composed *Coppelia* in 1870.

Beautiful People in attendance (and there really were too many of the *crème de la crème* to mention all by name), people who appreciate quality in art, the *soirée* was proof positive that the BP's cultural life is reaching unsuspected heights. (Even at $100 a ticket there wasn't an empty seat in the house!)

Our beloved María de los Angeles Fernández, daughter of our honorable mayor Don Fabiano Fernández, performed the main role admirably. The ballet was a benefit performance for the many charitable causes supported by CARE. Elizabeth, Don Fabiano's wife, wore one of Fernando Peña's exquisite creations, done in sun-yellow with tiny feathers, which contrasted strikingly with her dark hair. There, too, were Robert Martínez and his Mary (fresh from a skiing trip to Switzerland) as well as George Ramírez and his Martha (Martha was also done up in a Peña original—I love his new look—pearl-gray egret feathers!). We also loved the theater's decorations and the pretty corsages donated by Jorge Rubinstein and his Chiqui. (Would you believe me if I told you their son sleeps in a bed made out of a genuine racing car? That's just one of the many fascinating things to be found in the Rubinsteins' lovely mansion.) Elegant Johnny Paris was there, and his Florence, dressed in jade-colored *quetzal*[2] feathers in a Mojena original inspired by the Aztec *huipil*.[3] (It almost seemed as if the BP's had prearranged it, for the night was all feathers, feathers, and more feathers!)

And, as guest star for the evening, the grand surprise, none other than Liza Minelli,[4] who once fell in love with a question mark-shaped diamond brooch she saw on Elizabeth Taylor[5] and, since she couldn't resist it, has had an identical one made for herself which she wears every night on her show, as a pendant hanging from one ear.

But back to our Coppelia.

Swanhilda is a young village maiden, daughter of the burghermeister, and she is in love with Frantz. Frantz, however, seems uninterested. Each day he goes around the town square to walk by the house of Doctor Coppelius, where a girl sits reading on the balcony. Swanhilda, overcome with jealousy, goes into Doctor Coppelius' house while he is out. She discovers that Coppelia (the girl on the balcony) is just a porcelain doll. She places Coppelia's body on a table and, with a tiny dollmaker's hammer, smashes each and every one of her limbs, leaving only a mound of gleaming dust. She dresses up as Coppelia and hides in the doll's box, stiffening her arms and staring straight ahead.

The brilliant waltz danced by Swanhilda posing as the doll was the high point of the evening. María de los Angeles would bend her arms, moving them in circles as if they were screwed on at the elbows. Her legs went up and down stiffly, pausing slightly before each motion and accelerating until the hinges rotated in a frenzy. Then she began to dance round and round, spinning madly across the room. Both the dancer who played Doctor Coppelius and the one who played Frantz stood looking at her, aghast. It seems María de los Angeles was improvising, and her act did not fall in with her role at all. Finally, she sprang into a monumental *jetté*, leaving the audience breathless. Leaping over the orchestra pit, she pirouetted down the carpeted aisle and, flinging open the theater doors, disappeared down the street like a twirling asterisk.

---

[2] The national bird of Guatemala, the quetzal is a long-tailed, multicolored bird, whose natural habitat is the tropical areas of Central America.

[3] A traditional blouse, usually handwoven and embroidered, worn by Mayan women in villages of southern Mexico and Guatemala.

[4] Liza Minelli (b. 1946), American singer and actress.

[5] Elizabeth Taylor (b. 1932), American actress.

We loved this new interpretation of Coppelia despite the confusion it evidently caused among the rest of the troupe.

The BP's thunderous applause was well-deserved.

✦ ✦ ✦

like a flash, her toes barely touch, barely skim the felt, flight, light, first a yellow then a gray, leaping from tile to tile her name was Carmen Merengue Papa really loved her skipping over cracks, from crack to crack break your mother's back light lightning feet dance dancing is what I love just dancing when she was Papa's lover she was about my age I remember her well Carmen Merengue the trapeze artist hurtling from one trapeze into the flying knife, the human boomerang, the female firecracker, meteorite-red hair going off around her jettisoned through the air hanging by her teeth, going round and round on a silver string, whirling, faster faster till she disappeared, dancing as if nothing mattered, whether she lived or died, pinned to the tent top by reflectors, a multicolored wasp gyrating in the distance, the bulging eyes staring at her from below, the open mouths, the shortness of breath, the sweating brows, ants in the pants of the spectators who moved around in their seats below, when the fair was over she'd visit all the bars in town, she'd stretch her rope from bar to bar, the men would place one finger on her head and Carmen Merengue would spin around, was on my way to Ponce cut through to Humacao, wide-hipped gentlemen cheering, clapping, she was nuts, taking advantage of her, hey lonnie lonnie, right foot horizontal, one foot in front of the other, her body stretched out in an arc, her right arm over her head trying to slow the seconds that slipped by just beyond her tip-toes, concentrating all her strength on the silk cord that

✦ ✦ ✦

April 9, 1971
Academy of the Sacred Heart

Dear Don Fabiano:

I am writing on behalf of our community of sisters of the Sacred Heart of Jesus. Our great love for your daughter, a model student since kindergarten, requires that we write to you today. We cannot ignore the generous help you have provided our institution, and we have always been deeply grateful for your concern. The recent installation of a water heater, which serves both the live-in students and the nuns' cells, is proof of your generosity.

Your daughter's disgraceful spectacle, dancing in a public theater and dressed in a most shameless manner, was all over the social pages of this week's papers. We know that such spectacles are quite common in the world of ballet, but, Señor Fernández, are you prepared to see your daughter become part of a world so full of danger to both body and soul? What good would it do her to gain the world if she lost her soul? Besides, all that tossing of legs in the air, those cleavages down to the waist, all that leaping and legspreading, Sacred Heart of Jesus, where will it lead? I cannot keep from you that we had placed our highest hopes in your daughter. It was understood that, at graduation time, she would be the recipient of our school's highest honor—our Sacred Medallion. Perhaps you are not aware of the great prestige of this prize. It is a holy reliquary, surrounded by tiny sunbeams. Inside the locket is an image of our Divine Husband, covered by a monstrance. On the other side of the locket are inscribed all the names of those students who have received our Sacred Medallion. Many of them have heard the calling; in fact most have entered our convent. Imagine our distress at seeing those photographs of María de los Angeles on the front page.

The damage has already been done and your daughter's reputation will never be the same. But you could at least keep her from persisting down this shameful path. Only if she abandons the Pavlova Company will we see fit to excuse her recent behavior and allow her to continue at our school. We beg you to forgive this saddest of letters; we would have preferred never to have written it.

Most cordially yours, in the
name of Jesus Christ our Lord,
Reverend Mother Martínez

✦ ✦ ✦

like a flash, toes barely touching the suncracked pavement, leaping crack over crack, break your mother's back, Felisberto's my boyfriend, says we'll get married, Carmen Merengue would never marry, no, she'd shake her head, her white face framed by false curls, the circus left without her, she stayed in the tiny room my father rented, didn't want her to be a trapeze artist any more, wanted her to be a lady, forbade her to go to bars, tried to teach her to be a lady but she would lock herself in, practice practice all the time, blind to her surroundings, worn-out cot, chipped porcelain washbasin, one slippered foot in front of the other, lifting her leg slightly to draw circles in the air, touching the surface of a pool of water with her tiptoe, but one day the circus came, she heard the music from afar, her red curls shook, she sat on the cot and covered her ears so as not to hear, but she couldn't not hear, something tugged, tugged at her knees, at her ankles, at the tips of her dance shoes, an irresistible current pulled and pulled, the music pierced the palms of her hands, her eardrums aflame with the clatter of hooves, she rose to look at herself in the shard of mirror she'd hung on the wall, that's what I am, a dancer, face framed by false curls, eyelashes loosened by the heat, thick pancaked cheeks, falsies under my dress, and that very day she went back

✦ ✦ ✦

April 14, 1971

Dear Reverend Mother:

Your letter made Elizabeth and I think long and hard. We both agreed that the best thing would be to withdraw María de los Angeles from the Pavlova Company. The matter of her dancing had gotten a little out of hand lately, and we had already discussed the possibility. As you know, our daughter is a child of artistic sensibilities, and she is also very religious. We've often found her kneeling in her room with that same distant, ecstatic expression that takes hold of her when she is dancing. Our greatest hope for María de los Angeles, however, is to see her someday neither as a ballerina nor as a nun, but rather, surrounded by loving children. That is why we beg you to refrain from stimulating an inordinate piety in her, Mother, at this critical time when she will be most vulnerable.

María de los Angeles will inherit a large fortune as our only child. It truly concerns us that when we have passed away, our daughter might fall into the hands of some heartless scoundrel who's just out for her money. One has to protect one's fortune even after death, as you well know, Mother, for you yourself have to watch over the considerable assets of the Holy Church. You and I both know that money is like water, it flows away to sea, and I'm not about to let some hustler take away what I had to work so hard to get.

Elizabeth and I have always loved María de los Angeles deeply, and no one can say we weren't the happiest couple on the island when she was born. Though boys are, of course, more helpful later on, girls are always such a comfort, and we certainly enjoyed our daughter when she was a little girl. Mother, she was the light of our house, the apple of our eye. Later we tried to teach her how to be both kind and smart, because a loving young lady with a good education is a jewel coveted by any man, but I don't know how well we succeeded! Only when I see María de los Angeles safely married, Mother, as safe in her new home as she was in ours, with a husband to protect and look out for her, will I feel at ease.

Let me point out to you, Mother, that your suggestion that María de los Angeles might someday enter your order was totally out of place. I assure you that if this were the case, we would not be able to avoid feelings of resentment and suspicion, in spite of our sincere devotion to your cause and the affection we feel toward you. The fortune accruing to the convent, in that event, would be no *pecata minuta*.[6]

I beg your forgiveness, Mother, for being brutally honest, but truthfulness usually preserves friendship. Rest assured that, as long as I'm alive, the convent will lack nothing. My concern for God's work is genuine, and you are his sacred workers. Had Elizabeth and I had a son as well as a daughter, you would have met no resistance from us. On the contrary, we would have welcomed the possibility of her joining you in your sacred task of ridding this world of so much sin.

Please accept a most cordial greeting from an old and trusted friend,
Fabiano Fernández

✦ ✦ ✦

April 17, 1971
Academy of the Sacred Heart

Dear Señor Fernández:

Thank you for your recent letter. Your decision to remove María de los Angeles from the harmful environment of ballet was wise. It will be just a matter of time before she forgets the whole thing, which will then seem only a fading dream. As to your suggestion that we divert her from a pious path, with all due respect, Señor Fernández, despite your being the major benefactor of our School, you know we cannot consent to that. The calling is a gift of God; we would never dare interfere with its fulfillment. As our good Lord said in the parable of the vineyard and the works, many will be called but few chosen. If María de los Angeles herself is chosen by our Divine Husband, she must be left free to heed the calling. I understand that your worldly concerns are foremost in your mind. Seeing your daughter join our community would perhaps be heartrending for you. But that wound, Sr. Fernández, would heal in time. We must remember that the Good Lord has us here only on loan; we're in this vale of tears only for a spell. And if you ever come to believe that your daughter was lost to this world, you will have the comfort of knowing that she was found by angels. It seems to me that her given name is surely a sign that Divine Providence has been on our side since the child was born.

Respectfully yours in the
name of Jesus Christ our Lord,
Reverend Mother Martínez

✦ ✦ ✦

---

[6] (It.) Small sin.

April 27, 1971

Dear Reverend Mother:

You cannot imagine the suffering we are going through. The very day we told María de los Angeles about our decision to forbid her dancing, she fell gravely ill. We brought in the best specialists to examine her, but to no avail. I don't want to burden you with our sorrow; I write you these short lines because I know you are her friend and truly care for her. I beg you to pray for her, so the Lord will bring her back to us safe and sound. She's been unconscious for ten days and nights now, on intravenous feeding, without once coming out of her coma.

Your friend,
Fabiano Fernández

II. Sleeping Beauty [7]

it was her birthday, she was all alone, her parents had gone for a ride in the woods on their dappled mares, she thought she'd make a tour of the castle, it was so large, she'd never done that before because something was forbidden and she couldn't remember what, she went through the hallway taking tiny steps tippytoes together in tiny slippers, going up the circular stairs tippytoes together tiny steps through the dark, couldn't see a thing but she could feel something tugging at her shoes, each time more insistently, like Moira Shearer [8] on tippytoes tapping the floor with the tips of her toes, trying to hit the note on the nose that would remind her just what it was she was forbidden to do, but no she couldn't, she bouréed without stopping to rest, she opened door after door as she went up the spiraled steps, it seemed days she was going up and up and she never reached the top, she was tired but she couldn't stop, her shoes wouldn't let her, she finally reached the cobwebbed door at the end of the tunnel, the doorknob went round and round in the palm of her hand, her fingertip pinched, a drop of blood oozed, fell, she felt herself falling, PLAFF! everything slowly dissolving, melting around her, the horses in their stalls, their saddles on their backs, the guards against the door, the lances in their hands, the cooks, the bakers, the pheasants, the quails, the fire in the fireplace, the clock under the cobwebs, everything lay down and went to sleep around her, the palace was a huge ship rigged to set out into the great unknown, a deep wave of sleep swept over her and she slept so long her bones were thin needles floating around inside her, piercing her skin, one day she heard him from afar TATI! TATI! TATI! she recognized his voice, it was Felisberto coming, she tried to get up but the heavy gold of her dress wouldn't let her rise, dance DANCE! that's what was forbidden! Felisberto draws his face closer to mine, he kisses my cheek, is it you my prince, my love, the one I've dreamt of? You've made me wait so long! Her cheeks are warm, take those blankets off, you're stifling her, wake up my love, you'll be able to dance all you want, the hundred years are up, your parents are dead, the social commentators are dead, society ladies and nuns are dead, you'll dance forever now because you'll marry me and I'll take you far away, talk to me, I can see you tiny, as though at the bottom of a well, you're getting bigger, closer, coming up from the depths, my gold dress falls away, I feel it tugging at my toes, I'm free of it now, light, naked, moving towards you, my legs breaking through the surface, kiss me again, Felisberto, she woke up

✦ ✦ ✦

---

[7] 1889 ballet by Russian composer Pyotr Tchaikovsky (1840-1893).

[8] Moira Shearer (1926-2006), Scottish ballerina and actress.

April 29, 1971

Dear Reverend Mother:

Our daughter is safe and sound! Thanks no doubt to Divine Providence, she woke up from that sleep we thought would be fatal. While she was still unconscious, Felisberto Ortiz, a young man we'd never met, paid us a visit. He told us they had been going together for some time and that he loved her deeply. What a wily daughter we have, to be able to keep a secret from us for so long! He was with her for a while, talking to her as though she could hear everything he said. Finally he asked us to remove the heavy woolen shawls we had wrapped her in to keep the little warmth still left in her body. He went on rocking her in his arms until we saw her eyelids flutter. Then he put his face close to hers, kissed her, and Bless the Lord, María de los Angeles woke up! I couldn't believe my eyes.

To sum it all up, Mother, the day's events made us agree to the young couple's plans to be married and set up house as soon as possible. Felisberto comes from a humble background, but he's a sensible young man, with feet firmly planted on the ground. We agreed to their engagement and they'll be married within a month. Of course, it saddens us that now our daughter will never be the recipient of the Sacred Medallion, as you had so wished. But I am sure that, in spite of it all, you will share our happiness, and be genuinely pleased to see María de los Angeles dressed in white.

I am, as always,
your affectionate friend,
Fabiano Fernández

+ + +

Social Column
Mundo Nuevo
January 20, 1972

Dear Beautiful People: without a doubt, the most important social event of the week was the engagement between the lovely María de los Angeles Fernández, daughter of our own Don Fabiano, and Felisberto Ortiz, that handsome young man who holds so much promise as a young executive.

María de los Angeles' parents announced that the wedding would be within a month. They are already sending out invitations, printed—where else?—at Tiffany's. So go right to it, friends, start getting yourselves together, because this promises to be the wedding of the year. It should be very interesting to see the Ten Best Dressed Men competing there with the Ten Most Elegant Ladies. The occasion will bring to the fore the contest that has been going on all year long on our irresistibly exciting little island.

The cultural life of our Beautiful People will reach unheard-of levels on that day, as our beloved Don Fabiano has announced he will lend his dazzling Italian Baroque collection to the Mater Chapel, where the wedding will be held. He has also announced that he is so happy with his daughter's choice (the groom has a Ph.D. in marketing from Boston University) that he will donate a powerful Frigid King ($200,000) to the chapel, so as to free the BP's who will attend the ceremony from those inevitable little drops, as well as suspicious little odors, of perspiration brought about by the terrible heat of our island, a heat that not only ruins good clothing, but also makes elaborate hairdos turn droopy and stringy. That is why so many wedding guests skip the church ceremony these days, despite being devout and even daily churchgoers, opting instead to greet the happy couple at the hotel receiving line, where the air conditioning is usually turned on full blast. This results in a somewhat lackluster religious ceremony. But this wedding will be unique because, for the first time in the island's history, the BP's will be able to enjoy the glitter of our Holy Mother Church wrapped in a delightful Connecticut chill.

Now, the BP's have a new group which calls itself the SAP's (Super Adorable People). They get together every Sunday for brunch to comment on the weekend's parties. Then they go to the beach and tan themselves and sip piña coladas. If you consider yourself "in" and miss these beach parties, careful, because you might just be on your way "out." Oh, I almost forgot to tell you about the most recent "in" thing among BP's who are expecting a call from the stork: you must visit the very popular Lamaze Institute, which promises a painless delivery.

For my darling daughter, so as to herald her entry into the enchanted world of brides.

(Newspaper clippings pasted by María de los Angeles' mother in her daughter's Wedding Album.)

AN IDEA FOR A SHOWER

If you've recently been invited to a shower for an intimate friend or family member and it has been stipulated that presents should be for personal use, here's an idea that will tickle the guests pink: first, buy a small wicker basket, a length of plastic rope for a clothesline and a package of clothespins. Then look for four bra and panty sets in pastel colors, two or three sets of pantyhose, a baby doll set, a pretty and bouffant haircurler coverup and two or more chiffon hairnets. Stretch out the clothesline and pin the various items of clothing to it, alternating color according to taste, until you've filled the entire clothesline. Now, fold it up, clothes and all, and place it in the basket. Wrap the basket in several yards of nylon tulle and tie it with a bow surrounded by artificial flowers. You won't believe what a big hit this novel gift will be at the party.

A BRIDE'S GRACEFUL TABLE

Despite recent changes in lifestyle and decor, brides still generally prefer traditional gifts such as silverware, stemware and china.

China is now being made of very practical and sturdy materials which make it quite resistant to wear. It also comes in all kinds of modern designs. However, these sets are just not as fine as the classic porcelain sets. Elegant china such as Limoges, Bernadot or Bavarian Franconia can be found in homes where they have been handed down from generation to generation.

Silverware comes in different designs and levels of quality, among them sterling silver, silver plate, and stainless steel. Of course, stainless is practical, but for a graceful table there is nothing like sterling.

What is known as silver plate is a special process of dipping in liquid silver. Many brides ask for Reed and Barton, as it is guaranteed for a hundred years. The stemware should match the china, and there are several fine names to choose from in stemware. Brides, depending on their budgets, tend to ask for Fostoria, St. Louis or Baccarat.

A bride who makes out her list requesting these brands will have gifts that last a lifetime. It depends on the means of her guests: they might get together and, piece by piece, get her the china set, for example. If they are of more abundant means, they will probably want to give her sterling trays, vases, pitchers, gravy servers, oil and vinegar sets, etc. These articles are the *sine qua non* of a well-set table.

WHAT MAKES FOR HAPPINESS?

A beautiful house surrounded by a lovely garden, fine furniture, rugs and draperies? Trips abroad? Clothes? Plenty of money? Jewels? Latest model cars? Perhaps you have all these and are still not happy, for happiness is not to be found in worldly goods. If you believe in God and in His word, if you are a good wife and mother, one who knows how to manage the family budget and makes her home a shelter of peace and love, if you are a good neighbor, always willing to help those in need, you will be happy indeed.

From your loving mother,
Elizabeth

(Footnotes to María de los Angeles and Felisberto's Wedding Album, written in by Elizabeth, now mother to both.)

1. Exchanging rings and vowing to love each other in Sickness and in Health.
2. Drinking Holy Wine from the Golden Wedding Chalice during the Nuptial Mass.
3. María de los Angeles in profile, with the veil spilling over her face.
4. Marching down the church aisle! What a scared little girl she was!
5. Married at last! A dream come true!
6. María de los Angeles, front shot. Veil pulled back, she smiles. A married woman!

III. Giselle[9]

dressed in white like Giselle, happy because I'm marrying him I come to you and kneel at your feet, Oh Mater! pure as an Easter lily, to beg you to stand by me this most sacred day, I place my bouquet on the red velvet stool where your foot rests, looking once again at your modest pink dress, at your light blue shawl, the twelve stars fixed in a diamond arc around your head, Mater, the perfect home-maker, here I am all dressed in white, not dressed like you but like Giselle after she buried the dagger in her chest, because she suspected Loys her lover would not go on being a simple peasant as she had thought but was going to turn into a prince with vested interests, she knew Loys would stop loving her because Giselle was very clever, she knew whenever there are vested interests love plays sec-ond fiddle, that is why Giselle killed herself or perhaps she didn't perhaps she just wanted to meet the willis,[10] to reach them she had to go through the clumsy charade of the dagger, bury it in her chest, her back to the audience, hands legs feet thrashing around unhinged, poor Giselle lost her mind, that's what the peasants said, crazy! they cried surrounding her fallen body, but she wasn't there, she hid behind the cross in the graveyard where she put on her white willis dress, she stretched it over her frozen flesh, then she donned her dance shoes never to remove them again because her fate was to dance dance dance through the woods and Mater smiled from heaven because she knew that for her danc-ing and praying were one and the same, her body light as a water clock, the Queen of Death startled to see her dance, she slid her hand through her body, pulled it back covered with tiny drops, Giselle had no body she was made of water, suddenly the willis fled in panic, they heard footsteps it was Loys intent on following Giselle, a tiny voice deep inside her warned be careful Giselle a terrible danger stalks you, Loys always succeeds in his attempts and he's not about to let Giselle get away from him, he's bent on finding her so as to shove a baby into her narrow clepsydra womb, so as to take away her dewdrop lightness, widen her hips and spread out her body so she can never be a willis again, but no, Giselle is mistaken, Loys truly loves her, he won't get her pregnant, he'll put on a condom

---

[9] 1841 ballet by French composer Adolphe Adam (1803-1856).

[10] Nymph-like characters in Slavic mythology.

light and pink he promised next to her deathbed, he takes her by the arm and twirls her round the altar till she faces the guests who fill the church, then he takes her hand in his so as to give her courage, take it easy darling it's almost over, and now as rosy-fingered dawn colors the horizon distant churchbells can be heard and the willis must make their retreat. They're not angels as they had so deceitfully seemed, they're demons, their dresses are filthy crinolines, their gossamer wings are tied to their backs with barbed wire. And what about Giselle, what will she do? Giselle sees the willis slipping through the trees, disappearing like sighs, she hears them calling to her but she knows it's too late, she cannot escape, she feels Felisberto's hand pressing her elbow, marching her down the center of the church aisle

✦ ✦ ✦

SOCIAL COLUMN
MUNDO NUEVO
FEBRUARY 25, 1972

Well, my friends, it seems the social event of the year has come and gone and María de los Angeles' fabulous wedding is now just a luminous memory lingering in the minds of the elegant people of Puerto Rico.

All the BP's showed up at the Mater Chapel to see and be seen in their gala best. The pretty bride marched down an aisle lined with a waterfall of calla lilies. The main aisle of the church, off-limits to all but the bride and groom, was covered with a carpet of pure silk, imported from Thailand for the occasion. The columns of the chapel were draped from ceiling to floor with orange blossoms ingeniously woven with wires so as to give the guests the illusion that they were entering a rustling green forest. The walls were lined with authentic Caravaggios, Riberas and Carlo Dolcis,[11] a visual feast for the BP's eyes, avid as always for the beauty that also educates. Our very own Don Fabiano kept his promise, and María de los Angeles' wedding was no less glorious than those of the Meninas[12] in the Palace of the Prado. Now, after the installation of the air conditioning unit, the nuns will surely never forget to pray for the souls of Don Fabiano and his family. A clever way to gain entry into the kingdom of heaven, if ever there was one!

The reception, held in the private hall of the Caribe Supper Club, was something out of *A Thousand and One Nights*. The décor was entirely Elizabeth's idea, and she is used to making her dreams come true. The theme of the evening was diamonds, and all the decorations in the ballroom were done in silver tones. Three thousand orchids flown in from Venezuela were placed on a rock crystal base imported from Tiffany's. The bridal table was all done in Waterford crystal imported from Ireland; the menus were pear-shaped silver diamonds; and even the ice cubes were diamond shaped, just to give everything the perfect touch. The wedding cake was built in the shape of the Temple of Love. The porcelain bride and groom, strikingly like María de los Angeles and her Felisberto, were placed on a path of mirrors lined with lilies and swans of delicate pastel colors. The top layer was crowned by the temple's pavilion, which had crystal columns and a quartz ceiling. A tiny classic Cupid with wings of sugar revolved around it on tiptoe, aiming his tiny arrow at whoever approached.

The main attraction of the evening was Ivonne Coll,[13] singing hits like "Diamonds

---

[11] Michelangelo Mirisi da Caravaggio (1571-1610), Jusepe de Ribera (1591-1652), and Carlo Dolci (1616-ca.1686): Baroque painters.

[12] *Las Meninas,* 1656 painting by Spanish painter Diego Velazquez (1599-1660).

[13] Ivonne Coll (b. 1947), Puerto Rican-born singer and actress.

are Forever" and "Love is a Many-Splendored Thing."

The bride's gown was out of this world. It was remarkable for the simplicity of its lines. Our BP's should learn a lesson from María de los Angeles, for simplicity is always the better part of elegance.

+ + +

HELLO! I ARRIVED TODAY
NAME: Fabianito Ortiz Fernández
DATE: November 5, 1972
PLACE: Mercy Hospital; Santurce, Puerto Rico
WEIGHT: 8 lbs.
PROUD FATHER: Felisberto Ortiz
HAPPY MOTHER: María de los Angeles de Ortiz

+ + +

December 7, 1972
Academy of the Sacred Heart

Dear Don Fabiano:

The birth announcement for your grandson Fabianito just arrived. My heartfelt congratulations to the new grandfather on this happy event. They certainly didn't waste any time. Right on target, nine months after the wedding! A child's birth is always to be celebrated, so I can well imagine the party you threw for your friends, champagne and cigars all around, right there in the hospital's waiting room. You've been anxious for a grandson for so many years, my friend, I know this must be one of the happiest moments of your life. But don't forget, Don Fabiano, that a birth is also cause for holy rejoicing. I hope to receive an invitation to the christening soon, though my advice is to avoid having one of those pagan Roman fiestas with no holds barred which have lately become fashionable in your milieu. The important thing is that the little cherub not continue a heathen, but that the doors of heaven be opened for him.

As always,
Your devoted friend in
Jesus Christ our Lord,
Reverend Mother Martínez

+ + +

December 13, 1972

Dear Reverend Mother:

Thank you for your caring letter of a week ago. Elizabeth and I are going through a difficult trial; we are both grieved and depressed. It is always a comfort to know that our close friends are standing by us at a time like this.

As one would expect, our grandson's birth was a joyous occasion. Since we thought the christening would be soon, Elizabeth had gone ahead with the arrangements. The party was to take place in the Patio de los Cupidos, in the Condado Hotel's new wing, and of course, all our friends were to have been invited. These social events are very important, Mother, not only because they serve to tighten bonds of personal loyalties, but because they are good for business. Imagine how we felt, Mother, when we got a curt note from María de los Angeles telling us to cancel the party, because she had decided not to baptize her son.

This has been a hard test for us, Mother. María de los Angeles has changed a lot since she got married, she's grown distant and hardly ever calls to say hello. But we'll always have the pleasure of her child. He's a beautiful little urchin with sea-blue eyes. Let's hope they stay that way. We'll take him to the convent one of these days so you can meet him.

Please accept our
affectionate regards,
Fabiano Fernández

✦ ✦ ✦

December 14, 1972
Academy of the Sacred Heart

Dear María de los Angeles:

Your father wrote me of your decision not to baptize your son, and I am deeply shaken. What's wrong with you, my child? I fear you may be unhappy in your marriage and that has greatly saddened me. If you are unhappy, I can understand your trying to get through to your husband, to make him see that something is wrong. But you are being unfair if you are using your own son towards that end. Who are you to play with his salvation? Just think what would become of him if he were to die a pagan! I shudder to think of it. Remember this world is a vale of tears and you have already lived your life. Now your duty is to devote yourself heart and soul to that little cherub the good Lord has sent you. We have to think in practical terms, dear, since the world is full of unavoidable suffering. Why not accept our penance here, so as to better enjoy the life beyond? Leave aside your fancies, María de los Angeles, your ballet world filled with princes and princesses. Come off your cloud and think of your child. This is your only path now. Resign yourself, my child. The Lord will look out for you.

I embrace you, as always,
with deepest affection,
Reverend Mother Martínez

✦ ✦ ✦

DECEMBER 20, 1973

DEAR DON FABIANO:

PLEASE EXCUSE MY LONG LAPSE IN WRITING. MY AFFECTION FOR YOU HAS ALWAYS REMAINED THE SAME, DESPITE MY LONG SILENCES, AS I TRUST YOU KNOW. YOUR GRANDSON IS HANDSOME AS CAN BE AND I TAKE PLEASURE IN HIM DAILY. WITH ALL THE PROBLEMS MARÍA AND MYSELF HAVE BEEN HAVING, THE CHILD HAS BEEN A REAL COMFORT.

DON FABIANO, I BEG YOU TO KEEP WHAT I'M ABOUT TO TELL YOU IN THE STRICTEST CONFIDENCE, OUT OF CONSIDERATION FOR ME AND SYMPATHY FOR HER. NOW I REALIZE WHAT A MISTAKE IT WAS FOR US TO HAVE MOVED TO OUR NEW HOUSE IN THE SUBURBS, A YEAR AFTER FABIANITO WAS BORN. WHEN WE WERE LIVING NEAR YOU, YOU WERE ALWAYS MY ALLY AND MY GUIDE AS TO HOW

TO HANDLE MARÍA DE LOS ANGELES, HOW TO LOVINGLY LEAD HER DOWN THE RIGHT PATH, SO SHE WOULDN'T GUESS IT HAD ALL BEEN PLANNED.

YOU'LL RECALL THAT, BEFORE WE WERE MARRIED, I GAVE YOUR DAUGHTER MY WORD SHE COULD CONTINUE HER CAREER AS A DANCER. THIS WAS HER ONLY CONDITION FOR MARRIAGE, AND I HAVE KEPT MY WORD TO THE LETTER. BUT YOU DON'T KNOW THE REST OF THE STORY. A FEW DAYS AFTER OUR WEDDING, MARÍA DE LOS ANGELES INSISTED THAT MY PROMISE TO LET HER DANCE INCLUDED THE UNDERSTANDING THAT WE WOULD HAVE NO CHILDREN. SHE EXPLAINED THAT ONCE DANCERS GET PREGNANT, THEIR HIPS BROADEN AND THE PSYCHOLOGICAL CHANGE MAKES IT VERY DIFFICULT FOR THEM TO BECOME SUCCESSFUL BALLERINAS.

YOU CAN'T IMAGINE THE TURMOIL THIS THREW ME INTO. LOVING MARÍA DE LOS ANGELES AS I DO, I HAD ALWAYS WANTED HER TO HAVE MY CHILD. I FELT IT WAS THE ONLY WAY TO KEEP HER BY ME, DON FABIANO; PERHAPS BECAUSE I COME FROM SUCH A HUMBLE BACKGROUND, I'VE ALWAYS HAD A TERRIBLE FEAR OF LOSING HER.

I THOUGHT THAT PERHAPS THE REASON SHE DIDN'T WANT MY CHILD WAS BECAUSE I COME FROM A HUMBLE FAMILY, AND THIS SUSPICION HURT ME DEEPLY. BUT I WON'T ALWAYS BE POOR, DON FABIANO, I WON'T ALWAYS BE POOR. COMPARED TO YOU I GUESS I AM POOR, WITH MY MEASLY ONE HUNDRED THOUSAND IN THE BANK. BUT I'VE MADE THAT HUNDRED THOUSAND THE HARD WAY, DON FABIANO, BECAUSE FAR FROM YOUR DAUGHTER'S HAVING BEEN AN ASSET TO ME, SHE'S BEEN A WEIGHT, A DRAWBACK, AN ALBATROSS. DESPITE HER UNBECOMING REPUTATION AS A DANCER, THANKS TO MY FINANCIAL SUCCESS, NO ONE IN THIS TOWN CAN AFFORD TO SNUB US, AND WE GET INVITED TO ALL OF SAN JUAN'S MAJOR SOCIAL EVENTS.

WHEN MARÍA DE LOS ANGELES TOLD ME SHE DIDN'T WANT TO HAVE A CHILD, I REMEMBERED A CONVERSATION YOU AND I HAD HAD A FEW DAYS BEFORE THE WEDDING. YOU SAID YOU WERE GLAD YOUR DAUGHTER WAS GETTING MARRIED, BECAUSE YOU WERE SURE SHE'D FINALLY SETTLE DOWN AND MAKE HER PEACE. AND THEN YOU ADDED WITH A LAUGH THAT YOU HOPED WE WOULDN'T TAKE LONG IN GIVING YOU A GRANDSON, BECAUSE YOU NEEDED AN HEIR TO FIGHT FOR YOUR MONEY WHEN YOU WERE NO LONGER AROUND. BUT I DIDN'T FIND YOUR JOKE THE LEAST BIT FUNNY. I REMEMBER THINKING, "WHO DOES THIS MAN THINK HE'S TALKING TO? A HEALTHY STUD HE CAN MARRY HIS DAUGHTER OFF TO?" LATER I GOT OVER IT, AND I REALIZED IT WAS ALL A JOKE AND THAT YOU REALLY MEANT WELL. AFTER ALL, IT WASN'T SUCH A BAD IDEA, THAT BUSINESS OF AN HEIR; NOT A BAD IDEA AT ALL. BUT IT WOULD BE *MY* HEIR. A FEW DAYS LATER I TRIED TO CONVINCE MARÍA DE LOS ANGELES THAT WE SHOULD HAVE A CHILD. I TOLD HER I LOVED HER AND DIDN'T WANT TO LOSE HER. I WAS CONVINCED THAT A CHILD WAS THE ONLY WAY TO MAKE OUR MARRIAGE LAST. BUT WHEN SHE REFUSED DOGGEDLY, I LOST MY PATIENCE, DON FABIANO—DAMMIT, I GOT HER PREGNANT AGAINST HER WILL.

RATHER THAN BRINGING PEACE TO OUR HOME, FABIANITO WAS A CURSE TO MARÍA DE LOS ANGELES FROM THE START, AND SHE SOON ABANDONED HIM TO THE CARE OF HIS NANNY. DESPITE HER FEARS OF NOT BEING ABLE TO DANCE AGAIN, HER RECOVERY HAS BEEN REMARKABLE SINCE SHE GAVE BIRTH. WE

WENT ON LIKE THIS, KEEPING A PRECARIOUS PEACE, UNTIL TWO WEEKS AGO WHEN, AS THE DEVIL WOULD HAVE IT, I TOOK HER TO SEE A FLYING TRAPEZE SHOW AT THE ASTRODOME. IT HAD JUST COME TO TOWN AND I THOUGHT SINCE SHE HAD BEEN SO DEPRESSED, IT MIGHT CHEER HER UP. THE USUAL JUG-GLERS AND STRONGMEN CAME ON, AND THEN A REDHEADED WOMAN WEAR-ING AN AFRO WALKED INTO THE ARENA. SHE DANCED ON A TIGHTROPE UP HIGH NEAR THE TENT TOP, AND I DON'T KNOW WHY, BUT MARÍA DE LOS ANGELES WAS VERY IMPRESSED, SHE'S BEEN SURPRISINGLY ABSENT, TOTALLY WOUND UP IN HERSELF SINCE THEN. WHEN I SPEAK TO HER SHE DOESN'T ANSWER, AND I HARDLY SEE HER EXCEPT AT DINNER TIME.

TO TOP IT ALL OFF, YESTERDAY—IT'S HARD TO TELL YOU ABOUT IT, DON FABIANO—I GOT AN ANONYMOUS LETTER, THE SECOND ONE IN SEVERAL DAYS; A DISGUSTING NOTE SCRAWLED IN PENCIL. WHOEVER WROTE IT MUST BE SICK. IT IMPLIES THAT MARÍA DE LOS ANGELES MEETS REGULARLY WITH A LOVER IN A HOTEL, WHEN SHE'S SUPPOSED TO BE AT THE STUDIO.

I SUPPOSE I SHOULD BE ANGRY, DON FABIANO, BUT INSTEAD I FEEL TORN TO PIECES. THE TRUTH IS, NO MATTER WHAT SHE DOES, I'LL ALWAYS LOVE HER, I CAN'T LIVE WITHOUT HER.

TOMORROW I'LL GO AND FIND OUT WHAT'S GOING ON IN THAT HOTEL ROOM. I'M SURE IT'S ALL JUST VILE SLANDER. UNHAPPY PEOPLE CAN'T STAND TO SEE OTHER PEOPLE'S HAPPINESS. STILL, I CAN'T AVOID FEELING A SENSE OF FOREBODING. YOU KNOW A MAN CAN TAKE ANYTHING, ABSOLUTELY ANYTHING BUT THIS KIND OF INNUENDO, DON FABIANO. I'M AFRAID OF WHAT MAY HAPPEN, AND YET I FEEL I MUST GO....

Suddenly he stops writing and stares blankly at the wall. He crumples the note he's been writing into a tight wad and tosses it violently into the wastepaper basket.

+ + +

The afternoon sun filters in through the window of room 7B, Hotel Elysium. It lights up the dirty venetian blinds, torn on one side, and falls in strips over the naked bodies on the sofa. The man, lying on the woman, has his head turned away. The woman slowly caresses him, burying the fingers of her left hand in his hair. In her right hand, she holds a prayerbook from which she reads aloud. "María was a virgin in all she said, did and loved." The man stirs and mutters a few indistinct words as if he were about to wake up. The woman goes on reading in a low voice, after adjusting her breast under his ear. "Mater Admirabilis, lily of the valley and flower of the moun-tains, pray for us. Mater Admirabilis purer than..." She shuts the prayerbook and looks fixedly at the termite-ridden woodwork of the ceiling, at the water stains on the wallpaper. She'd finally worked up enough courage to do it, and everything had turned out according to plan. She had picked the man up that very afternoon, on the corner of De Diego and Ponce de León. The Oldsmobile had pulled up and she had seen the stranger stare at her through the windshield, eyebrows arched in silent query. The man had offered her twenty-five dollars and she had accepted. She had specified the hotel and they had driven in silence. She refused to look at his face even once.

Now that it was over she felt like dancing. The man slept soundly, one arm dan-gling to the floor, face turned towards the sofa. She slowly slid out from under the warm body, pulled a nylon rope out of her purse and stretched it taut from the hooks she had previously put into the walls. She slipped on her dancing shoes, tied the ribbons around her ankles and leaped onto the rope. A cloud of chalk from the tips of her slippers hung for a moment in the still air. She was naked except for her exaggerated makeup: thick rouge, meteorite-red hair and huge black eyelashes. She felt now she could be herself for the first time, she could be a dancer; a second or third class dancer, but a dancer nonetheless. She began, placing one foot before the other, feeling the sun cut vainly across her ankles. She didn't even turn around when she heard the door burst open violently, but went on carefully placing one foot before the...

✦ ✦ ✦

December 27, 1974

Dear Reverend Mother Martínez:

Thank you so much for the sympathy card you sent us almost a year ago. Your words, full of comfort and wisdom, were a salve for our pain. I apologize for not finding the courage to answer you until today. To speak of painful things is always to live them over again, with gestures and words which we would like to erase but can't. There are so many things we wish had been different, Mother. Our daughter's marriage, for one. We should have gotten to know her husband better before the wedding; a neurotic and ambitious young man as it turns out, now that it's too late. Perhaps if we had been more careful, María de los Angeles would still be with us.

I apologize, Mother, I know I shouldn't speak that way about Felisberto. He's also dead, and we shouldn't bear grudges against the dead. But try as I may, I just can't bring myself to forgive him. He made María de los Angeles so unhappy, tormenting her about her dancing, throwing at her the fact that she'd never been anything but a mediocre star. And what wakes me up in the middle of the night in a cold sweat, Mother, what makes me shake with anger now that it's too late, is that he was making money on her; that he had bought the Pavlova Company, and that it was paying him good dividends. My daughter, who never needed to work a day in her life, exploited by that heartless monster.

On the day of the accident, she was in her choreographer's hotel room, working on some new dance steps for her next recital, when Felisberto barged in. According to the choreographer, he stood at the door and began to hurl insults at her, threatening to thrash her right there unless she promised she'd stop dancing for good. It had always struck me that Felisberto didn't seem to mind María de los Angeles' dancing, and when he did speak against it, it was only halfheartedly. Of course, it never occurred to me he was making money on her. At the time of the accident, however, he had just received an anonymous letter, which had made him begin to be concerned about public opinion. So that afternoon he set out to teach María de los Angeles a lesson.

The choreographer, who didn't know a thing about what was going on, stood up for María de los Angeles. He tried to force Felisberto out of the room, and Felisberto pulled out a gun. He then tried to grab María de los Angeles but stumbled, accidentally shooting her. The choreographer then struck Felisberto on the head, tragically fracturing his skull.

You can't imagine what we went through, Mother. I keep seeing my daughter on the floor of that hotel dump bleeding to death, away from her mother, away from me, who would gladly have given my life to save her. I think of the uselessness of it all, and a wave of anger chokes me. When the ambulance arrived, she was already dead.

Felisberto was lying next to her on the floor. They took him to Presbyterian Hospital and he was in intensive care for two weeks, but never regained consciousness.

It's been almost a year now, Mother. There seems to be a glass wall between the memory of that image and myself; a wall that tends to fog up if I draw too near. I no longer look for answers to my questions; I've finally stopped asking them. It was God's will. It was a comfort to spare no expense at her funeral. All of high society attended the funeral mass. Elizabeth and I were both touched by such proof of our friends' loyalty. All those Beautiful People and Super Adorable People whom you always refer to a little disdainfully in your letters, Mother, aren't really so bad. Deep down inside, they're decent.

We buried María de los Angeles surrounded by her bridal veil as though by a cloud bank. She looked so beautiful, her newly-washed hair gleaming over the faded satin her wedding dress. Those who had seen her dance remarked that she seemed to be sleeping, performing for the last time her role of Sleeping Beauty. Fabianito, of course, is with us.

If it hadn't been for our daughter's sufferings, Mother, I would almost say it was all divine justice. You remember how Elizabeth and I prayed vainly for a son, so that we could grow old in peace? The ways of God are tortuous and dark, but perhaps this tragedy wasn't all in vain. María de los Angeles was a stubborn, selfish child. She never thought of the suffering she was inflicting upon us, insisting on her career as a dancer. But God, in his infinite mercy, will always be just. He left us our little cherub, to fill the void of our daughter's ingratitude. While we're on the subject, you'll soon get an invitation to his christening. We hope you'll get permission to leave the convent to attend, because we would very much like you to be his godmother.

From now on you can rest assured the convent will want for nothing, Mother. When I die, Fabianito will still be there to look after you.

I remain, as always,
Your true friend,
Fabiano Fernández

+ + +

that ceiling is a mess looks like smashed balls up there I told you dancing was forbidden keep insisting on it and I'll break every bone in your forbidden it's forbidden so just keep on sleep sleep sleep sleep sleep sleep sleep sleep sleep sleep wake up my love I want you to marry me I'll let you dance all you want bar to bar no please not today, you'll make me pregnant I beg you Felisberto I beg you for the sake of a mess that ceiling's a mess dancing Coppelia dancing Sleeping Beauty dancing Mater knitting white cotton booties while she waits for the savior's child to grow in her oh Lord I don't mind dying but I hate to leave my children crying just forget about being a dancer forget about it you will praise him protect him so that later on he'll protect and defend you now and forever more amen now kneel down and repeat this world is a vale of tears it's the next one that counts we must earn it by suffering not with silver trays not with silver goblets not with silver pitchers not with silver slander not with words put in your mouth with a silver spoon say yes my love say you're happy dancing Giselle but this time in smelly torn crinolines with wings tied to your back with barbed wire no I'm not happy Felisberto you betrayed me that's why I've brought you here so you can see for yourself so you can picture it all in detail my whiteface my black eyelashes loosened by sweat my thick pancaked cheeks eastsidewestside onetwothree the stained ceiling the rotting wood the venetian blinds eastsidewestside onetwothree what is money made of one day the circus came to town again and she covered her ears

*so as not to hear but she couldn't help it something was tugging at her ankles at her knees at the tips
of her shoes eastsidewestside onetwothree something was pulling dragging her far away neither safe
nor sweet nor sound María de los Angeles be still with balls sheer balls money's made with sheer balls
neither recant nor resign nor content nor*

✦ ✦ ✦

Translated by Diana L. Vélez and Rosario Ferré

—1979

NICHOLASA MOHR (1938-   )

Nicholasa Golpe Rivera was born in New York City on November 1, 1938, the daughter of a
Puerto Rican mother and a Basque merchant-marine father. The last of seven children (and
the only girl), Nicholasa was named after her mother. Both of Mohr's parents died when she
was young, and she was raised by her aunt. Mohr began her artistic career as a fine arts
painter and illustrator, attending the Art Students League and the Pratt Center for
Printmaking, both in New York City. She is best known, however, for her autobiographical fiction. Among the first generation of Puerto Rican-American authors to write and publish in
English, Mohr helped found the genre of Nuyorican literature, which documents the gritty
experience of growing up Puerto Rican in New York City's various barrios. Mohr represents
her own history of growing up working class and Puerto Rican in unflinching terms, but with
humor and grace, in her first publications for young adults, the novel *Nilda* (1973) and the collection of short stories *El Bronx Remembered* (1972), both of which she illustrated herself. Mohr
is primarily considered the author of books for young adults, but her texts are by no means
innocent. Her young protagonists—pre-adolescent girls coming of age—deal with drug-
addicted siblings, neighborhood violence, and sexual predators. Mohr's *Rituals of Survival: A
Woman's Portfolio* (1985) and *A Matter of Pride and Other Stories* (1997) are both written for an
adult audience, with adult protagonists who take on such themes as feminine sexuality, gendered identity on the "mainland" and the "island," matriarchy, sexual abuse, and violence
against women.

In Another Place in a Different Era

Although I had arrived twenty minutes ahead of time, I fixed my gaze at the
entrance, hoping Joaquín Thomas would come early. Joaquín and I had been living
together for eight months and planned to get married early next year. Tonight we were
having our own private celebration to seal our commitment. The Alsace-Lorrane was
a small restaurant serving French Provincial food, located in the west Forties in
Manhattan. I had already ordered an expensive bottle of champagne, and it sat in a
cooler waiting to be opened.

When she first walked in, I wasn't sure it was Iris, because she wasn't wearing her
thick horn-rimmed glasses. This was curious; just last week I thought I'd spotted her
walking about a couple of yards ahead of me. I was on 57th Street, heading towards
Carnegie Hall to purchase tickets for the following Friday's concert recital by the
soprano Victoria de los Angeles. I couldn't get a clear view even from the back because

the person was under a large black umbrella, yet somehow I was sure that the diminutive frame and brisk walk belonged to Iris Martínez.

Eager to catch up, I rushed after her, carelessly stepping into puddles and soaking my shoes. Fortunately, she was heading in my direction and I followed close behind until we got to Carnegie Hall. Then, all I saw was her black umbrella vanish as she slipped inside.

The lobby was damp and crowded and smelled of clammy bodies. People held their dripping umbrellas while others came in drenched. I searched along the long line of ticket buyers and among those who had come in to avoid the downpour. No one resembled a short, skinny, pale woman wearing thick horn-rimmed glasses. Perhaps I was mistaken. After all, I hadn't gotten a clear look at the person under the umbrella. I gave up and queued at the back of the ticket line.

Now this evening, here she was again. For twelve years I had not laid eyes on Iris, and only this past week it seemed I had spotted her twice. An unusual coincidence, for sure, although she didn't exactly look like the Iris I used to know. I remembered how she would struggle to keep her hair in place by winding hair bands and placing clips all over her head. Yet tufts of her brown hair always stuck out every which way like soft cotton. She usually dressed in baggy shirts or sweaters and loose skirts or jeans, and wore low pumps or sneakers.

Tonight she was not wearing glasses, and since she was terribly nearsighted I assumed she was wearing contact lenses. Her hair was impeccably cropped in a short, becoming afro. Iris wore a simple double-breasted black suit, large gold hoop earrings, a red silk scarf and black suede boots. No matter how chic she looked, there was no way I could mistake that skinny body all of four feet ten inches with the build of an eleven-year old. Even with her high heel boots she looked petite. It definitely was Iris.

Her companion, a distinguished middle-aged white man with gray hair, was dressed in an expensive business suit. Attentively, he took her coat, gave it to the maitre d' to be checked and escorted Iris to her seat.

Their table was placed by the far wall of the dining room near the windows, and she sat at an angle facing away from me. My table was situated in the no-smoking section on the opposite side on the upper floor level, where I could clearly observe them. He was making quite a fuss over Iris, lighting her cigarette and showing interest in her every gesture. Iris had not yet turned in my direction, so I supposed she still hadn't seen me.

Well, we both had changed in twelve years. I was just twenty-two back then and married to Gerry Garza. Iris was about twenty-nine and living with Dennis, Gerry's older brother. The last time I saw her, she was recovering from the worst beating Dennis had ever given her. Sure, he had beat on her before, but Dennis had never been so brutal.

Now I think back and attribute her lack of self-esteem to the persistent abuse she endured. Iris was convinced she was ugly beyond remedy, repulsive without hope of improvement. These feelings were constantly reinforced by the man she adored and whom she supported, Dennis himself.

Of all the many women Dennis had been with, Iris was the best. She was educated, smart and had a heart of gold. If you needed a few dollars, all you had to do was ask. Many of the folks in the neighborhood owed her money. Most paid her back, but she never hassled those who didn't. As my mom said, she was *buena gente*.[1] Iris worked downtown as a paralegal, was finishing college and wanted to become a lawyer. In spite of her reputation for being unkempt and homely, everybody commented on how intelligent Iris was. "Too bad," Gerry used to say, "she might be smart and have a good job, but she don't know how to dress good. And, she's *bien fea*. Ugly...man what a dog."

It was true Iris appeared less than sexy and unattractive, yet there was also something impish and upbeat about her. She had a vitality in her demeanor, as well as a wonderful smile that lit up her face, and I thought all that was downright appealing. I figured those grotesque glasses she wore and the way she dressed contributed to making her appear homely. But whenever I suggested that she wear nicer clothes and use contact lenses, she'd always say no.

"I don't have money to spend on fancy clothes. And I already have contacts, just can't get used to them. They tire my eyes when I read for long periods. Besides, I like it when people say my glasses are bigger than I am and that's how they know it's me who's coming. My horn-rimmed glasses are my trademark."

I speculated that by hiding behind those ostentatious glasses, she was telling the world, "Look, I may not be pretty, but I am intelligent."

It was a surprise to everyone when those two started going together because Dennis Garza usually picked pretty women who were shallow thinkers, witless, and who had little ambition. And, he was also a handsome, handsome guy. At one time I thought he was one of the sexiest men I'd ever met. I wasn't the only one to say so, either.

"There's nothing outstanding about him," my sister Rachel had once said. "Like he ain't real tall or nothing. It's like the way he's put together, all the pieces are perfect, especially that smile."

Dennis stood medium height, had dark, shiny, curly hair, brown eyes with long lashes, smooth light-olive skin and a set of very white straight teeth. When people first met Dennis he appeared affable and gentle. He had a way of cocking his head boyishly, grinning and somehow appearing like a guileless adolescent. Dennis easily pretended to be an interested listener by staring at you wide-eyed, as if impressed by every word you spoke.

Actually, Dennis Garza was neither guileless nor concerned. He was a vain, selfish man capable of great cruelty and violence. In fact, he had gotten a few unfortunate girls pregnant and quickly abandoned them. People said he was the father of several children in the neighborhood whom he refused to acknowledge as his own. He never held down a job, was always in debt and caused his parents a great deal of grief. Dennis was his mother's favorite and he could twist her around his little finger. More than once he had taken her rent money without an ounce of remorse.

"This boy'll be the death of me," she'd say, and no one would contradict her.

Dennis prided himself on the way he could con his way into women's hearts. It was a sport with him. He'd live off his women, take all their money and, when there was nothing more to be gained, he'd dispose of them like worn-out garments. That's why it didn't take long before he began to live exclusively off women.

"It's easy," he bragged, "and comes naturally because I give the broads what they need."

---

[1] (Sp.) Good people.

Up until the age of about fourteen I had a crush on Dennis. So did Rachel and the rest of the girls in my neighborhood. Then one day I was in my bedroom and over-heard him talking to my brother Frankie, who sometimes hung out with Dennis, hoping to make out with one of the women he had discarded. The two of them were in the living room gossiping and bragging.

"Women ain't nothing but cunts, man. All you have to do is say you love them and they fall right into your bed. They don't care if you mean it or not. *Ay, papi, dime que me quieres.*[2]

"Bitches love to be bossed around, too. Just give them a few serious slaps when they don't behave. Then fix them with your magic wand and tell them all that love bullshit they wanna hear. And you got it made, bro."

From that time forward, I had a sincere dislike for Dennis Garza. When I married his brother, Gerry, it was all I could do to tolerate Dennis' presence.

Now, as I recollect, Iris was the smartest woman Dennis ever had. Dennis was crafty and knew how to swindle and get over, but intellectually he was dense. After high school I don't believe he ever read anything but sports, and tits and ass maga-zines. Once, after Iris had endured yet another nasty whipping, I asked her why she accepted his abuse.

"You are so smart, Iris. Why don't you leave that mean bastard?"

"I don't care what people think or say," she told me, wincing in pain. "I got the handsomest guy around. Dennis Garza is my man and he loves me. Me, ugly little Iris."

That was when I understood that his stupidity and reckless abuse didn't matter, because Dennis' deception had convinced her she was loved and that the ugly duck-ling had conquered the beautiful prince. Iris was bewitched.

During their three years together, her entire life revolved around Dennis. In her judgment he could do no wrong. Every two weeks Iris handed him her paycheck and he gave her an allowance. She made a home for him, took care of his clothes, cleaned and cooked for him. He continued to cheat on her with no thought to discretion. When she protested or complained, he beat her. It was common to see her walking around with bruises or a black eye. Yet Iris accepted her physical and emotional wounds and remained loyal.

On occasion when he was in a good mood, Dennis tossed her a compliment in the way one might speak to a pet. "Iris Martínez, you're some homely bitch, ugly as a toad, but you're my baby. I love my toad, my sweet Mami." Iris would smile and bask in his words, grateful for any kindness he offered her.

✦ ✦ ✦

Usually, I kept my distance and wanted nothing to do with them as a couple. Then one day, because of my Aunt Dora's generosity, all four of us spent a weekend together. My Aunt Dora and Uncle Felix had *una casa de campo*[3] and seven wooded acres in upstate New York, near the town of Poughkeepsie. It was about a two-hour drive from the South Bronx where we all lived. All of our family helped my aunt and uncle improve their country cottage by building extensions to accommodate more peo-ple and by planting fruit trees. In the warm months my relatives even raised chickens. Although my Uncle Felix would have preferred to live out his old age in the tropical

---

[2] (Sp.) Hey daddy, tell me you love me.   [3] (Sp.) A country house.

warmth of Fajardo, his hometown in Puerto Rico, this was to be their retirement home. My Aunt Dora insisted that as long as their children and family were in the Bronx, they would remain in New York State. We were all invited to come up and stay for the long Memorial holiday weekend.

"To celebrate the beginning of summer, we're going to roast a whole pig, and your mother is making her wonderful *pasteles* and *arroz con gandules.*[4] There's going to be music, dancing, *una fiesta sabrosa.*[5] Sarita, you gotta be there and you must bring Gerry's brother Dennis and his girlfriend Iris," insisted Aunt Dora. "It's a time for the entire family to get together."

Aunt Dora and my mother loved to cook and see all of their children and grand-children together. In the typical Puerto Rican clan tradition, no one should be excluded. Food and drink was provided in abundance, and the more folks that came to rejoice in sharing, the better.

As I said, personally I didn't mind Iris at all; she was good people, but being with Dennis was not my idea of fun. By the time we drove over to their apartment on Longwood Avenue, Dennis was already drinking. Dennis became mean and nasty when he drank too much. He and Iris loaded their gear in the car trunk and settled in back. It was a Friday evening, and the roads were crowded with traffic heading out of the city. Driving was slow, almost bumper to bumper. Dennis pulled out a fifth of Scotch.

"Here." He shoved the bottle toward Gerry. "Take a drink bro, ease your driving." Gerry glanced my way furtively. I shook my head emphatically.

"No drinking and driving, Dennis," I told him. "Gerry's gotta concentrate. We don't want an accident."

"I ain't talking to you, Sarita. I mean, I respect that you're my brother's wife and all. But excuse me, I'm talking to Gerry. Let him answer. Come on bro, take a small swig..."

"No!" I was furious. "He's driving!"

"Hey! *Qué falta de respeto.*[6] I'm talking to the man here. Show a little respect," Dennis sneered. "Too bad, but my little brother's henpecked," he mocked, and pointed to Gerry. "Look, Iris, my *hermanito* Gerry's wearing *pantaletas!*"[7]

I began to feel uneasy because Gerry and I were always feuding over his claims that I wanted too much freedom. He criticized my option to dress as I pleased, would not allow me to learn how to drive our car and forbade me to ever contradict him in public. All of this had recently become major issues since my enrollment in night school at New York University. Although I didn't know exactly what I wanted to do yet, go into law, history or another specialty, I was definitely going on to higher edu-cation. Gerry worked as a municipal bus and train inspector. A good job with bene-fits, hospitalization, retirement, a job most guys would kill for, he frequently reminded me.

From the start, my attending college had infuriated Gerry. Just that morning he began his harangue about my being out four evenings a week. Why did I have to be better than him? he chided. What was I trying to prove, anyway? Who, he insisted on questioning, was going to wear the pants in his family?

---

[4] (Sp.) Meat pies, rice with green pigeon peas (typical Puerto Rican dishes).

[5] (Sp.) A great party.

[6] (Sp.) What a lack of respect.

[7] (Sp.) Panties.

"I can't believe your old lady won't even let you take a sip of Scotch," Dennis kept goading. "*Bendito,*[8] Iris, are you seeing how sad things are for ole Geraldo?" Whereupon Gerry reached out and Dennis promptly handed him the bottle. He put it to his mouth and took a long pull.

"Not a word," Gerry said, giving me a defiant look. "Don't say shit."

As we drove on, the brothers passed the bottle back and forth, stopping only to ask if either Iris or myself wanted a swig. Each time, we both refused. Traffic was flowing slowly and it looked like the two-hour trip was going to be about twice as long. I glanced back at Iris, who appeared terrified.

Instinctively, I turned on the radio and tuned to a popular salsa music station, hoping to cheer us up. Iris and I began to prattle on about music and what singers and bands we both preferred: Blanca Rosa, La Lupe or Celia Cruz, Tito Puente or Ray Barretto. Our conversation remained idle, yet neither of us wanted to stop. It was as if the sound of our own voices provided some sort of veiled shield against the menacing Garza brothers. After what seemed an interminable amount of time, Dennis gave Iris a violent shove.

"God, what a bunch of gabby hens, right, Gerry?"

As soon as Gerry agreed, Dennis slapped Iris across the back of her head, shouting, "So then shut the fuck up, bitch!"

Iris encased her arms over her head and cowered in the corner.

"Listen, why don't we stop for something to eat," I said, desperate to avoid what I already knew was about to happen. "I'm starving."

At first Gerry was reluctant. He wanted to make driving time, but I also insisted on going to the bathroom. We stopped at a diner, ate some hamburgers and drank coffee. Dennis had a coke, refusing coffee.

I took Iris aside and explained that I planned to ride in back. "He may try to hurt you. But if I'm beside you, he'll back off."

"Dennis is very drunk," she whimpered, and nodded like a frightened child. "They finished the bottle, but Dennis has another fifth of Scotch with him." I told Gerry I was very tired and wanted to sleep. I went in back with Iris while Dennis took my seat up front.

Within a few miles, Dennis was pulling from the second bottle. I was relieved when Gerry refused to join in, claiming he was already high and preferred to concentrate on driving. That was when Dennis started on Iris.

"You are such an ugly bitch. I don't know what I see in a toad like you. Your mother must have been married to that Quasimodo, or Quasifeo. You know, the hunchback of Notre Dame. No, wait...I know, SHE was the hunchback of Notre Dame." His diatribe was unrelenting. "Do you all know that this bitch barks for me when I ask her? Go on, Iris, show 'em. Bark for us, bitch. Bark. Wuff, wuff. Bow, wow...grrr. I whip her skinny butt with my belt; she whines and yelps. Go on, show us how you cry for Daddy. Ouch, geez, ooooh, ouch...gee. Show them, you ugly mongrel..." As Dennis reached in back to slap Iris, I slid in front of her.

"Cut it out!" I shouted. "Gerry, tell him to stop it."

"Stay out of it, Sarita," Gerry warned me. "It's not our business." But he did tell Dennis to stop. "Come on, man, quit it! I'm trying to drive and my old lady's sitting

---

[8] (Sp.) Figure of speech; literally, "blessed," but used as one might use "Jesus" in the U.S. vernacular.

back there. Have some respect."

Dennis would quiet down for a few miles, then he'd turn, grimace at Iris and start his invective. "Do you know that this motherfucking bitch has one tit larger than the other? Imagine having to make love to two different tits on the same skinny body. I'm fucking a freak. She's a freak show…come on, Mami, show them. Take out your tits!" All of this time Iris sat recoiled in a corner, crying silently. Once in a while she wiped her eyes and blew her nose. When I tried to comfort her, she shook her head and gently pushed me away.

"This bitch went and got pregnant on me. I bet nobody knew that, right? Then she wanted to have the kid. No way! She got an abortion because I told her, do you think that kid's gonna come out with my beautiful looks? You too ugly…I can't take no chances on fathering no freak and…" It was then that Iris interrupted Dennis.

"You're a miserable motherfucker," she rasped. "You bastard! Motherfucker, I hope you die! I hope you die!" Dennis turned and, with an incredulous stare frozen on his face, moved his lips but remained mute. After a few moments, he finally bellowed, "You just cursed my mother! Did you hear the bitch, Gerry? She cursed our mother. Nobody in this world curses my mother. Nobody. Shit, my mother's a saint. *Una santa.* A fucking saint!"

The rest of the trip lasted for about another hour, during which time Dennis kept on working himself into a rage, repeating how he was going to whip Iris. "I'm gonna beat your ass so bad, *puta,* that you're gonna wish you was never born. There's gonna be none of you left after I get through with you…"

✦ ✦ ✦

The second I recognized the familiar road leading to Aunt Dora's, I began to plan how to get Iris away from Dennis. I poked Gerry and whispered that we had to do something. "I'll grab Iris and make a run for the house. You deal with Dennis." He nodded and gestured that he was with me.

As we drove up the path, Gerry screeched the car to a halt, jumped out and went over to block Dennis. I swung the door open, grabbed Iris and shouted, "Run to the house!"

Iris stepped out, shoved past me and, swinging an empty bottle of Scotch, ran toward Dennis, who was struggling to free himself from Gerry's hold.

"Bastard, motherfucker, I'll kill you!" Iris screamed as she swung full force, barely grazing Dennis' forehead and smashing the empty bottle against the car fender.

"*Coño,*[9] you cut me, bitch!" Dennis wailed.

I had been trailing behind Iris, yelling that she run for cover, and felt myself showered with bits of flying glass. I looked to see that Gerry had also been struck, because he had stepped aside and was busy brushing off pieces of glass that had gotten stuck in his hair.

It took only seconds before Iris and Dennis charged at each other like wild beasts. She clawed and pounded him with her small fists. But she was a sorry match for Dennis. He pummeled Iris like a punching bag, ripped out her hair and locked his fingers so tightly around her throat that I was sure he would strangle the life out of her. It became impossible to separate them.

By now everyone had rushed outdoors and jumped into the scuffle, trying

---

[9] (Sp.) Cunt.

desperately to pry them apart. A free-for-all of bodies, arms twisting, legs kicking, and flying fists, soared across the ground followed by screams that invaded the quiet country night. My mother and Aunt Dora shrieked the loudest, demanding that Dennis had to be stopped. "*¡Por Dios...no!*[10] He mustn't kill her!"

It took everyone's strength to wrestle him off Iris and to finally disengage her. I had suffered a wallop in my left shoulder, Gerry had a bloody nose, and both of us had tiny cuts and scratches all over our faces and arms. Poor Aunt Dora received a nasty bump on her forehead, and my mom had a long and bloody scratch on her forearm.

But it was Iris who was injured beyond recognition. Her face had disappeared under a thick coat of blood, shattered bones and lacerated skin. All the men, about eight of them, jumped on top of Dennis and held him down while we led Iris, who was reeling helplessly, inside the house. My mother, Aunt Dora and some of the other women cleaned her up, put ice packs and raw steak on her face, neck and arms. Aunt Dora gave Iris some of her painkiller pills that had been prescribed for arthritis. My aunt and uncle gave her their bed. The older women took turns tending to Iris all night long.

I lay awake in bed that night beside Gerry, who slept as soundly as a baby. All I could feel for my husband was a void that sank into my chest. I felt utterly helpless. From the minute we got to Longwood Avenue, I had seen Dennis' brutality emerging. Not only had I felt powerless to stop Dennis' abuse, I wasn't even allowed to walk away. I had to stay and listen, to witness and wait, and be a silent participant as another woman was viciously attacked. When my father was verbally abusive, my mother always backed off, appeasing him and apologizing for whatever he accused her of doing or saying.

"*Ay, mi hijita,*[11] you know how men are. I always keep quiet and let your papa get everything off his chest. That's why he's never laid a hand on me. You have to understand men. They're like little boys who want their own way."

Some little boy, I thought. Dennis almost killed Iris, somebody so small and frail. For the first time in my two years of marriage I understood that I had committed to a man who would never allow me to take charge of my own life.

"No, Mami," I whispered to myself. "I'm not doing it like you. I can't." It was that very night when I first considered a future without Gerry Garza.

The next day I couldn't believe my eyes. Iris' face was puffed up like a balloon and her features were so distorted, it was difficult to figure out where her eyes belonged and if she actually had sockets. Iris' inflamed cheeks and swollen nostrils looked like a pig's snout. Her lips were split open and had the consistency of liver. Several gashes extended from her face down to her neck and arms.

Iris looked so hideous that I burst into tears and began pleading with her to press charges and put Dennis in jail.

"You're a person, a grown woman, not an animal, not his pet slave to abuse and beat!" I was close to hysterics and implored her to have some self-respect. "Have some fucking pride. Stop him from doing this again and send that son of a bitch to jail. I'll testify in court and be a witness. For God's sake, you've got dozens of witnesses." Iris quickly assented that jail was the least he deserved and agreed to go to the police station that very day.

---

[10] (Sp.) Please God, no.   [11] (Sp.) My little daughter.

But, Dennis was a professional abuser of women, and he knew how to survive. He feigned remorse and pleaded his case in public. He pointed to the scratches on his own face and told everybody that the worst scratches were in his broken heart. Dennis even asked my Uncle Felix for permission to speak to Iris in everyone's presence. He wept openly and asserted that it would be unjust for her to leave him or to put him in prison.

Then he got down on his knees, kissed her feet, and begged Iris to forgive him. "Mami, you know you're my life. Without you I'm nothing. I'm nobody without my baby. *Te lo juro,* right here in front of everybody. I swear…don't kill me, Iris, don't do this to me. I love you, please, Mami." Dennis smiled his sweetest smile and donned his most innocent bearing.

He didn't fool me for a moment, but Dennis convinced everyone else. They said it was hard to believe that such a sweet and self-effacing guy could be a wicked monster. He should be allowed to show us his good side, was the consensus.

Iris was swayed, and ultimately agreed to forgive him. My family's generosity allowed them to stay on in the country until she got better. Iris took part of her work vacation in order to recuperate in quiet surroundings with Dennis by her side.

I was stunned and dismayed by Iris' behavior. Somehow I had foolishly believed that my words and sentiments had merit and that I could actually help Iris. But instead I was ashamed of my own vulnerability and became even more disgusted with Iris and with myself. I was no one to be giving advice, I thought, not as long as I was still being intimidated by the same kind of abuse that my grandmother and mother had endured.

The following day when I insisted on returning home, Gerry became furious. "We're already here. Let's enjoy ourselves like everybody else. *¿Qué te pasa, coño?* What the fuck's wrong with you, Sarita?"

By now I was too distressed to be bullied, and was quite prepared, if necessary, to take the train home. In the end, Gerry gave in and we left.

The very next day, I got a phone call from my Aunt Dora, telling me that Iris had hemorrhaged and was in the hospital for a few days. My folks had convinced the doctors that she'd been in a car accident. Luckily, she was out of danger now and getting better. Dennis and Iris would be returning to the city the following week, said Aunt Dora.

✦ ✦ ✦

Three more weeks passed and I went on with my own life, coping with Gerry's moods and trying to hold down a full-time job and carry nine credits at night. Then one day we received a dinner invitation from Iris. At first I refused to go near them, but Gerry was adamant.

"You always get your way with this college business. Now, you give me some slack here. Dennis is my older brother, I said we would go, so don't be making me look bad." I would never hear the end of it if Gerry went alone. Holding back a heap of adverse feeling, I went.

Remarkably, Iris' face looked almost normal, except for some swollen scar tissue where the stitches were still healing. They were both glad to see us, and Dennis was on his best behavior, obviously still somewhat grateful that Iris had not put his ass in jail. After Iris poured our drinks, she led us into their bedroom and pointed toward the ceiling.

There was a gaping hole of about four to five feet in diameter in the ceiling. "It collapsed in huge blocks." She handed me some Polaroid photos. "See?" Large chunks of cement and lumps of plaster were scattered all over the bed and bureau. "Why, I could have been killed!" Iris chuckled. Then both she and Dennis began to laugh uncontrollably. Gerry and I were perplexed. We failed to see what was so funny.

"This happened the weekend we went to your Aunt Dora's," grinned Dennis. "Now, if I had not given my baby here a little ass-whupping, we wouldn't be able to sue the motherfucking landlord."

"You're suing?" I asked, not believing what was happening.

"Damned straight!" nodded Dennis. "We got a doctor who's cooperating and says Iris has got permanent damage to her vision, and you all know she was already blind! She got partial hearing loss…and what else you got, Mami?"

"Enough to sue for a lot of money," she snickered. I wanted to say something to Iris, like, how can you take money for a bogus accident when it's the man beside you who damaged you in such a vile way. But I was dumbstruck. I barely ate my dinner, anxious to get away from them.

Before I left, Iris called me into the bedroom. "Just some girl talk," she called out to Dennis and Gerry. "We'll be out in a minute." She shut the door. "Look, Sarita. I know you're angry with me."

"No," I shrugged, lying. "Not at all, it's your life, Iris. Do what you want, girl!"

"Never mind, I know you're angry. But listen, I heard you, I heard every word you told me when we were upstate. It's all true." When I pressed her to explain, all she said was, "I can't tell you everything now. I just can't talk about it. But, Sarita, just so you know your words didn't fall on deaf ears. OK?" She gave me a long hug and said nothing more.

A few months later, Iris left Dennis. Disappeared, they said, and no one knew where she had gone. People told me that as soon as Iris received a generous out-of-court settlement from the landlord's insurance company, she split. Some said it was on the very day she got her check. Dennis became so infuriated, he got a piece and went looking to shoot Iris. He searched everywhere—at her work place, in night school—and even harassed her family. But it did him no good. No one saw Iris after that. She seemed to have vanished.

✦ ✦ ✦

About a year after she split, I also left Gerry, and two years almost to that day, I got my final divorce papers. I continued my studies, earned a partial scholarship, worked nights and was able to study full-time. Now I'm finishing my doctoral studies at the City University of New York in the History of the Spanish Caribbean. In fact, that's where I met Joaquín Thomas, an associate professor in the Social Sciences Department.

I checked my watch; Joaquín was already ten minutes late. I was tempted to go over to Iris, but felt apprehensive by the sort of greeting I might receive, and decided I'd better not. Instead, I made a quick pit stop in the Ladies Room. As I came out, I heard my name.

"Hi, Sarita." Iris stood before me smiling. "I thought it was you." Shyly, we both hugged. "I told my friend I wanted to speak to you for a few minutes."

She asked if I was alone, I told her about Joaquín, and we chatted at the bar. We spoke briefly about what each of us had been doing for the past twelve years. Iris had become an attorney, and the guy with her was a client who had the hots for her. She wasn't married yet, but she was seeing somebody, another lawyer and it was serious.

"You want to know what happened and why I left Dennis?" she asked as if reading my mind.

I could feel myself blushing and said it wasn't my business. "Dennis killed my baby. You see, Sarita, I didn't have the abortion because I wanted the kid. I thought something that belonged to the both of us would make a difference, would change Dennis. But that night, he beat the child out of me and I had a miscarriage. All the feelings I had for Dennis died with my baby. After that, I couldn't love him any more. It was all over." Iris paused and took a long drag on her cigarette.

"By the time we got back to the Bronx, I had already decided to leave him. And when I saw the damage in the apartment, I asked Dennis to testify that he was there when the ceiling fell on me. You know how good Dennis was at conning people. He used his acting talents well and made a very convincing witness. The insurance company settled out of court. It was wrong to take the money. As a lawyer, I know it's a felony. But I needed to get away, far away from Dennis, and the money gave me a fresh start." She paused and added mischievously, "Anyway, fraud is risky, but Dennis was lethal, right?" We both had a good laugh.

"He thought he was going to get rich from the beating he gave you, so the joke was on him. Dennis deserved far worse for the way he treated you."

"I know..." Iris whispered, then checked her watch and said it was time to get back to her horny client. She asked if I was in the telephone book.

"Yes, I'm living over on West 28th Street now. Call me."

She said she'd do just that. But I knew she would never call.

Reminiscences of beatings and humiliation at a point in time that once linked us both to the Garza brothers were memories neither of us wanted to recall. In these past twelve years we each transformed our lives. Iris and I had traveled on to another place in a different era.

I saw Joaquín enter and headed back to my table. He apologized for being late, then inquired about the person I was speaking to. I told him it was a passing acquaintance from a long time ago. When Joaquín asked what we had talked about, I assured him that it was inconsequential.

"Just girl talk. Now let's order before we open the champagne. I'm starving!" We picked up our menus and proceeded to order dinner.

—1997

JOYCE CAROL OATES (1938-)

Born in rural Lockport, New York, to working-class parents, Joyce Carol Oates was educated on scholarship at Syracuse University. She received her M.A. from the University of Wisconsin-Madison in 1961, and began her teaching career at the University of Detroit. She published her first novel, *With Shuddering Fall,* in 1964, and has gone on to publish over one hundred works, including novels, novellas, short stories, poetry, plays, essays, nonfiction, and books for children and young adults. She has also edited anthologies, and has published (mostly mystery novels) under the names Rosamond Smith and Lauren Kelly.

In her enormous body of work, Oates combines meticulous social observation with Gothic elements and a feminist attention to such themes as domestic violence and racism. Oates has won the National Book Award for *them* (1969), the PEN/Malamud Award for excellence in the short story, and the O. Henry Prize for achievement in the short story form. Three of her novels have been nominated for the Pulitzer Prize. Since 1978, Oates has taught creative writing at Princeton University, where she is the Roger S. Berlind '52 Professor in the Humanities.

6:27 P.M.

7:30 a.m. Squinting in the bathroom mirror. Her eyebrows are growing out coarsely—shouldn't have shaved them—a mistake. She steams her face and plucks her eyebrows. That looks better. A thin, arching curve. She pats pink moisturizer on her face, rubs it into her skin in small deft circles, mechanically, hurrying. Hears Bobby fretting at the table. "Hey Bobby, you finish that cereal yet? Eat that cereal, it's good for you," she calls over her shoulder. She can hear the tinkle of his spoon against the bowl: but is he eating it or not? Her face, seen so close, is enormous like a balloon. After the pink moisturizer comes the liquid make-up—expensive stuff, eight dollars for the medium-sized bottle—which she rubs into her skin quickly, with upward strokes, up toward the outsides of her cheeks—and then her lips outlined with a lipliner, and then her lipstick, then rouge—very lightly on her cheekbones—and then the eye make-up, which will take ten minutes—"Hey Bobby, you're eating that stuff, aren't you? You better eat it all down," she cries. The kid had bad dreams last night and who can blame him, with a father like his? Glenda strokes mascara on her eyelashes, swift upward strokes, frowning into the mirror. Already she is chewing gum—no cigarette this morning—and her jaws are moving constantly, agreeably, as she appraises her face and her high—puffed pink—blond hair, hair like cotton candy. She looks all right.

8:00 a.m. Lets Bobby off at the nursery school. His collar is wrinkled—a mass of wrinkles that look baked solid, how'd she manage that?— "You be good now, y'hear?" she says, and Bobby swings his short legs across the car seat, manages to get the car door open without any help from her. He looks back at her and says, "Is Daddy coming back tonight?" and Glenda feels her face go sour. "I sure as hell hope not," she says with a shudder. Bobby doesn't let on whether this is the answer he wanted or not.

8:15 a.m. Fifteen minutes late. She struggles into the pink uniform—tight around the hips—and snaps on the radio. Coral is fussing around at the counter up front and yells back to Glenda, "Who's this supposed to be at eleven? Looks like "W" something—" "That's Mrs. Wieden," Glenda yells up front, plugging in the hot plate—she's dying for some coffee—and glancing at herself in the mirror. The mirror runs the entire length of the shop, so Glenda has to parade around in front of it all day long. Always strutting in front of mirrors, her mother used to scold—Glenda pauses, thinking of her mother. Gray-faced and sour, the old woman, but not a bad old gal—except she wouldn't do anything for Glenda's wedding, and she paid out a lot for Glenda's kid sister—but she had it rough on that farm, a few acres in Texas, down in the southeast corner. Glenda is staring at herself in the mirror and her gaze becomes vague, watery.

8:30 a.m. Roxanne is doing her first customer, but Glenda's first customer—a regular named Babs—hasn't showed up yet, so Glenda answers the telephone when it rings. "Hello, Coral Hardee's," she says, but there is no one at the other end—must have been a wrong number. She hangs up. Coral, who is going over some bills, looks over at her. "Nobody there?" she says suspiciously. "Must of hung up when I answered," Glenda says. Glenda inspects her fingernails—it's been almost a week since she did them—thick gold lacquer, very attractive, worth the extra dollar. The telephone rings again and she answers it and this time it's her eight o'clock customer, Babs, with an excuse Glenda doesn't believe for one minute. But she says, "Sure, okay, Babs, I'll put you down for eleven-thirty. Sure." She hangs up. Coral says, "That one is always late." Glenda grunts in agreement. She tears the wrapper off a stick of peppermint gum and pops the gum in her mouth, wishing she could smoke a cigarette instead, after the rotten night she had…four or five hours of sleep, maybe less, ruined by the kid's nightmares…then the kid has to go and ask, "Is Daddy coming back tonight?" Jesus Christ.

10:15 a.m. A woman with a northern accent, her hair practically down to her hips, looking at Coral with big blue innocent eyes and asking if it costs more for long hair. "Afraid so, honey," Coral says. The bitch blinks as if she'd never heard of such a thing and Glenda holds her breath, hoping she'll walk out, but she decides to have her hair done anyway. Just Glenda's luck to be free for the next twenty minutes. So she spends ten minutes washing that haystack (inky black hair, probably dyed with a do-it-yourself kit) and ten minutes setting it up, using the biggest rollers in the place, and the woman is watching her in the mirror all the time, sharp—eyed as a lynx, trying to make small talk. Glenda notices a big diamond on her finger. "Are you from Miami?" she asks Glenda. "No, Port Arthur in Texas," says Glenda with a business-like smile. "I'm from Chicago," the woman says, in that harsh whiny accent Glenda can't stand, "and I want to tell you that my husband and I just love it down here…everybody is so friendly down here…." The woman chatters and Glenda nods, barely listening. When she had long hair herself, long wavy blond hair, she sure as hell didn't go to a beauty parlor to have it done; she'd have been sitting under the drier all day. She washed it herself and let it dry loose, running around barefoot, and at five o'clock on the dot she'd stop whatever she was doing and get fixed up for Guy, brushing her hair until it gleamed, putting on fresh make-up, checking herself from every angle. Guy liked her in slacks best. Her white slacks. She'd stand sideways and pose, assessing herself in the mirror critically—a nice trim waist, broad hips, a big bosom—she was all right. They had lived in Pensacola then. "You married, honey?" the woman with the black hair says, as Glenda packs her away for a nice two-hour session under the drier. "Was," Glenda says with a fast, tight smile, to shut her up.

11:35 a.m. Babs finally shows up, wearing a red playsuit, a girl blobbing all over—you'd think she would be ashamed to walk on the street like that, half a mile from any beach. She calls out hello to Coral and Roxanne, has to be friendly to everybody. Glenda is a little put out this morning and deliberately keeps still for the first few minutes, as she brushes out Babs' hair—the set is still stiff from last week, sticky with hairspray—and Babs winces. Glenda begins the washing, notices that the spray is hot, but Babs doesn't complain—probably embarrassed for coming late. Glenda says, grudgingly, "How're you this week?" She gets Babs all toweled up and leads her over to the counter, to her chair. A big orange plastic container of hair rollers and pins is on the counter; it says "Glenda" in nail polish on its side. In the next chair Roxanne—with a new red wig, looking good—is toiling with a little old lady who drifted in from the street; in the other chair Coral herself is doing an old customer, Sally Tuohy, an ex-dancer at one of the clubs, the two of them chatting loudly and smoking so that Glenda's eyes water. She would give anything for a cigarette, herself. But she won't give in, she absolutely will not give in…."You heard from *him* lately?" Babs asks. Glenda, winding a strand of blond hair around a pink roller, wonders who Babs is talking about—then she remembers that she was telling Babs about a new friend of hers, Ronnie Strong, the race-track man…or was it her other, fading friend W.J. Hecht, the mystery man? She doesn't think it was Guy; she doesn't talk about Guy if she can help it. So she says with a little grin, "Can't complain."

12:25 p.m. A guy in baggy shorts and sunglasses leads an elderly woman in—says to Coral, "Can you make her beautiful? Make her beautiful, okay? I'll be back in two hours." Thank God Roxanne is free, so Roxanne gets stuck with this dilly; the poor old woman is so feeble she can hardly walk. Glenda and Roxanne and Coral all glance at each other in the mirror—at the same instant—all thinking the same thing, what hell it is to be old, doddering like that, especially in Miami. Glenda goes across the street to get some sandwiches and coffee for them. When she strides in the restaurant people glance at her. Men glance at her. For some reason this makes her nervous today—maybe because she has been thinking of Guy so often. She dreads running into him. Maybe seeing him in a place like this. He'd be sitting at the counter and waiting, waiting….Guy with his cowboy hat and his denim work-clothes, walking sort of bow-legged, showing off to her or anybody who would watch. Guy with his bleached-out hair and face, looking weathered at the age of thirty-one—reddened skin, a boil on the side of his neck, his looks ruined from too much sun and too much alcohol. Jesus, she thinks in amazement, she was married to that man for six years….She feels a kind of kick in the belly—the memory of a kick from when she was carrying the baby—and the men's eyes up and down the counter make her shiver, they are the same eyes, Guy's eyes, always same. "Hey, Pink Princess," one of the men whispers, referring to the "Pink Princess" stitching on Glenda's collar, but Glenda ignores him. Her uniform is too tight. Should lose a few pounds, or buy another uniform. "Hey, Pink Princess, are you snooty?" the man says, but Glenda pays no attention to him. She waits nervously for the sandwiches and the coffee. She has always liked men to look at her, but today she feels different…today everything seems different….

1:15 p.m. Shelley, the part-time girl, who is a hat-check girl also at one of the clubs, hurries in to pay back the ten dollars she owes Glenda; she is all perfume and clattering heels. Glenda likes Shelley even though the kid is pretty stupid. She's twenty-three and Glenda is a few years older, she's a few decades wiser, but Shelley won't listen to her advice. It's always hurry, hurry, hurry with her. Shelley got out of her marriage without any kids, no threats, no crazy telephone calls, no spying…now she's heading into trouble with a married man, but do you think she'll listen to Glenda? Glenda feels irritated with Shelley's excitement. The girl is always in a hurry, a sweaty erotic daze, her perfect lips curled up into a mindless, pleased smile…. Her eyes catch onto Glenda's in the mirror and she whispers, "Murray says he saw Guy the other night. Is he back in town? Is he bothering you again?" Glenda's heart begins to pound. "No," she says, "No. I got an injunction against him." "Yeah, well, Murray says he's back in town, says to tell you," Shelley says, on her way out. Her white skirt is so short it looks like a slip, nothing more, straining tight against her thighs. Glenda stands staring after her, holding the ten-dollar bill in her fingers.

2:05 p.m. The telephone rings. Glenda is in the middle of brushing out a customer and Coral is out and so Roxanne finally dashes up to the desk at about the tenth ring. Glenda's nerves are on edge. She pauses in her brushing of this woman's hair, her rather square chin contemplative, stern, hoping the telephone isn't...isn't for her....But Roxanne yells, "Hey Glenda, for you!" So Glenda hurries up front, just knowing that it is Mrs. Foss at the nursery, that sorry old bat, with some bad news, or maybe W.J. with some far-out story about why he hadn't called her for two weeks, as if she gave a damn....But when she picks up the receiver the line is dead. Not even a dial tone. "Hello? Hello?" she says sharply. "Hello?" She slams the receiver down, since Coral isn't in. Roxanne, lighting a cigarette, asks her what it was—Glenda shakes her head, nothing, no one—Roxanne says whoever it was was a man, and asked for Glenda in person. "Well, that could be anyone, couldn't it," she says sharply, and goes back to her customer. She hates Roxanne always snooping into her business.

2:15 p.m. One of her regular customers, Mrs. Foster, is being teased and brushed and sprayed. The poor old gal is withered on the bottom and puffed out on the top, her hair a bright burnished red, glowing from the tint—you'd swear she was a kid until she turned around and you saw her face. She always gives Glenda a dollar tip. Coral is back, chatting over the telephone with someone. So the telephone can't ring. Glenda stops herself from thinking of that call—the dead line—stops herself from thinking of Guy, because it never does any good to think about him. That's over. Gone. He has enough sense to leave her alone, since that night in the parking lot when he tried to beat up a boy friend of hers and the police carted him off—he never was stupid—he's got enough sense to leave her alone.

3:05 p.m. Cute little Bonnie from the insurance place down the block comes in for a shampoo and set; Glenda likes her, approves of her petite figure, no more than a size 5—Glenda is a size 12 now, going on 13, she's going to have to lose a few pounds. She approves of Bonnie's long pink fingernails and her golden tan. She's cute, all right, but most of it is make-up...some of it gets on Glenda's fingers when she washes Bonnie's hair. Bonnie is getting married next month. "Ma wants to have three hundred people, isn't that wild?" Bonnie laughs. "How many'd you have to yours?" "Oh, not more than a hundred," says Glenda, adding a few people, and reluctant to think again about that hot Texas afternoon, getting drunk and squabbling all during the reception with one another and with Guy—not wanting to think about the hotel in Houston that stank of insecticide, and the bed with its musty covers and mattress. No, she doesn't want to think about that Saturday, or about how it all ran down to a day last July, also a Saturday, with Guy screaming at her that he was going to kill her. Washing Bonnie's hair, briskly, she rubs a row of very small pimples just at Bonnie's hair-line, and the pimples begin to bleed, just thin trickles of blood mixed in with the water...and while Bonnie is chattering about her wedding gown Glenda is trying to blot the blood with a towel. She leads Bonnie over to the chair, sees that the bleeding seems to have stopped, it looks O.K., tosses away the stained towel, then sprays Bonnie's hair with the bluish hair-set mixture. She puts two rows of pink rollers on Bonnie's head, a back row of green rollers, and pins down the back hair carefully. Sprays it all. The spray stinks—almost chokes Bonnie. God-awful stuff. Glenda reaches down, grunting, to fish out a pair of ear-protectors. They are made of flesh-pink plastic. She fastens them over Bonnie's reddened ears, puts a hair-net over the whole business and draws it tight. Fixed up like this, Bonnie looks small and trivial; her face looks pasty. "There you are," Glenda says, leading Bonnie over to the hair-drier where Angel Laverne is all set to come out.

3:30 p.m. Angel Laverne strolls with Glenda up to the front desk to make next week's appointment. Angel always asks for Glenda. She is a dancer at the Cutless Club and much admired by everyone, for her long trim legs and her expensive clothes. "It looks great," Angel says, admiring her high-stacked orange hair, with the row of stiff curls across the front. It is an open secret that Angel had silicone injected into her breasts and that the operation was a marvelous success; Angel sucks in her breath, glances at herself in the mirror approvingly. Once in a while she tells Glenda, seriously, that Glenda should try out at the club—"you'd make a great dancer," she tells Glenda—and Glenda laughs in embarrassment, not mentioning the fact that she tried out for something like that back in Houston, but with no luck, and she was younger and better-looking then. Angel thanks her again and says goodbye. Glenda goes to the book to see who's next but someone starts shouting—an old biddy under the hair-drier—"Glenda, Glenda, what time is it?" She has a hoarse, froggy voice; her double chins tremble. Glenda tells her the time, though she knows the old girl won't be able to hear—why the hell do they always try to talk under the hair-drier? So Glenda strides over and holds out her arm so that the woman can see her wristwatch. "Oh. Three-thirty," she says stupidly, as if she thought it might be some other time. Glenda feels sorry for her, the old dame is a widow and probably hasn't anywhere to get to; this town is filled with widows. It occurs to Glenda that Coral Hardee's Pink Princess Salon is like the backstage of a theater—the audience is men, made up only of men, who know what they want to see and who are impatient with anything else. She goes back to check the book. God, is she tired, and it's only three-thirty....Three more customers coming up, one right after the other, and the first one wants a permanent....

4:10 p.m. And the call does come from the nursery: a very unconvincing story about Lynda going home early, having to babysit for a neighbor who's had a baby, or some such lying crap, so could Glenda come pick up Bobby early? "No, I cannot," Glenda says in a soft furious voice. "I'm going to report you to the Better Business Bureau if this keeps on!" On the other end Mrs. Foss stammers, no doubt she's been drinking and the kids have been running wild, no doubt, Glenda is fed up with Mrs. Foss's problems and says firmly: "Look, you know I have a job here and I can't leave early. It's your responsibility to take care of those children until the mothers get there—Mrs. Foss—" Mrs. Foss hangs up. Glenda wonders if she should call back, maybe the old bat is passed out, or whether this means she has won. Scaring her with the Better Business Bureau probably did the trick.

4:45 p.m. "Did you read here about Jackie Kennedy and Onassis,[1] what's-his-

---

[1] Jacqueline Bouvier Kennedy Onassis (1929-1994), widow of President John F. Kennedy, who was married to Greek shipping tycoon Aristotle Onassis from 1968 until his death in 1975.

name, they spent twenty million dollars in one year?" Glenda's customer, a woman with thinning brown hair, is tapping a movie magazine angrily on the counter.

Roxanne, standing next to Glenda, says, "He can't be such a geek, or else how could he make all that money? Or is the twenty million just the interest, you know, the interest on the stuff they own?"

"Jesus, twenty million," Glenda says, whistling through her teeth, "that's—that's like more than what all of us make in a year, or in our lives—"

She is backcombing her customer's hair energetically.

"What I feel sorry for is the kids, those two little kids—"

"Yeah, those two little kids."

"Caroline,[2] you know, she has a shrine devoted to her father. It's in their New York apartment. What do you think Onassis thinks about that?"

"If he wants to have any opinion on it, let him get himself assassinated. He's only a guest in this country."

"I wouldn't want his nose—"

"Isn't he ugly?"

"Caroline has a whole staff of servants to occupy her mind, and all the allowance money she wants to occupy the rest of her mind," Roxanne says. "Think of all the clothes and stuff she could buy—"

"How Onassis got started," Glenda's customer explains, "he bought some ships from the United States for ten million dollars. Just bought them. The United States gave up some navy ships, I mean fighting ships—"

"Really?"

"They gave them to him, and he went back to Greece—which is incidentally just about the poorest country in Europe—he went to Greece with them—now, ten million dollars' worth of boats, in a country like that—that's why the United States can't get the money back, That's what was behind all that to-do about Onassis not being allowed in the country."

"Which country?"

"*This* country. He was barred, until he married Jackie Kennedy. That was in the newspapers."

"Well, he can't be such a geek if he made all that money. But I wouldn't want to be married to him!"

"If you can prove you're a blood relative of his, he'll pay you $25,000 a year interest-free for life. That's what they say. But he never gives any money to charity, not one dime."

"I wouldn't want to be related to him," Glenda says with a laugh. "You ever see his sister? Her nose? I wouldn't want that family nose, Christ!"

"Yeah, there's a picture of his sister or somebody in one of these magazines, a few months ago, she's all pock-marked and's got eyes sunk ten miles back in her face, all bags and stuff—I wouldn't want to look like that just to be that guy's sister!"

"Me neither!"

5:00 p.m. Coral has to go to the lawyer's—some fuss about a customer who got her eye poked by one of the part-time girls, the girl stuck her little finger in the woman's eye, just an accident, but Coral has bad luck. Glenda takes over. She tries on

---

[2] Caroline Bouvier Kennedy (b. 1957), daughter of John F. and Jacqueline Kennedy.

a red wiglet, remembers when she was a red-head, smirks at herself, exchanges wiglets with Roxanne—they always fool around when Coral is out of the shop—and wonders if maybe she should invest in a red wig. Only forty dollars with her discount. Maybe. Maybe for a change. But seeing herself in the mirror, that striking face—like a billboard, that face—she feels uneasy, because the red hair will make people look at her, men, men will look at her, men will look at her in that certain way, and does she want this to happen? To happen again?

5:10 p.m. Telephone rings. Coral isn't back yet, so Glenda goes to answer it. Begins to perspire even before she picks up the receiver. She approaches the desk, legs working hard, fast, the muscles of her thighs straining against the tight skirt, she can feel, remember, the football-sized baby inside her, she picks up the pink plastic receiver breezily….

"Hello!"

No answer.

"I said hello. This is Coral Hardee's. Hello…?"

Be calm. Calm.

"Hello…?"

She begins to pick at one of her fingernails. The gold polish is chipping. She says suddenly, "Listen, Guy, if this is you you'd better cut it out. I'm going to call the police—" She can see him suddenly: the grimy cowboy hat crooked on his head, his grin that had nothing to do with his eyes, his wise-guy grin, his little-boy wise-guy grin, the way he'd sit with a toothpick in his mouth and stare at her. At first she liked it, but then after they'd been married for a while she could feel him staring at her even while she was in another room, staring through the walls at her. Sometimes he'd joke with her, slapping her rear, Hey, is all that mine? he'd say. He liked her best in slacks. Out on the street he got mad if other men looked at her, but he liked her to wear slacks, especially that pair of white knitted slacks…."I'm going to call the police!" she says, hanging up. She is about to cry. Roxanne is watching her, hesitating…not knowing if she should say anything or stay out of this….

5:15 p.m. The door opens. A man enters.

Glenda stares at him, frowning. He is short, stocky, wearing neat beige trousers and a shirt and, in spite of the 85 degree temperature, a dark green wool sweater, armless, and a large wristwatch. Glenda feels a dull automatic tug in his direction, wondering how his face will change when he sees her. Their faces always change, always; she shivers with excitement, though the man is homely himself—a swarthy face, too small, a very small receding chin, sunglasses with cheap plastic frames, hair that looks a little kinky.

"Hiya, Jere, that you?" says Coral, who has just come in.

He takes off the sunglasses with a grin, and Glenda, shocked, sees that this isn't a man after all, but that woman—"Jere"—who comes into the Salon every two weeks to have her hair cut.

"Hiya, Coral. How's business?"

"Can't complain."

"I can't complain either."

Jere smiles and waves at Glenda and Roxanne, but shyly: she knows they won't smile back.

Ugh.

Glenda glances at the book to see who's stuck with this character—too bad, Roxanne!—Roxanne is down for 5:15. Last customer of the day. Glenda ignores Jere and starts tidying up her things. Feels sorry for poor Roxanne, but thank God it isn't her. Coral, bustling by with an armful of wigs, winks at Glenda and Glenda winks back.

5:30 p.m. Sits with Coral in the back room, smoking. Her first and only cigarette of the day. "Tomorrow I'm giving it up permanently," she tells Coral, "but today I feel kind of nervous. Real jumpy." Coral chain-smokes and drinks coffee all day long. "How come you're jumpy?" she says. "I don't know," Glenda says slowly, "on account of Guy...." "Oh, hell! Is he back in town again?" says Coral. "That I don't know," says Glenda. She hesitates, wanting to tell Coral about the telephone calls. She can't stop shivering. Coral says with a harsh expulsion of breath, "Listen, kid, frankly I never liked his looks. I mean he's nice-looking and all that, he's a handsome guy, but, you know, he *knows* he's handsome, and...." She glances out to see if the last customer is gone. Yes, Jere is gone and Roxanne is gathering up the towels. "And handsome men, when they go to bed with you, you know, they're going to bed with themselves. I read that."

Glenda stares at her. "They *what?*"

"They're doing it to *themselves.* The woman is just a mirror or something. I read it in a psychiatrist's column in the newspaper."

"I don't get it."

"Well, that's what he said. A good-looking man is apt to be a son of a bitch and the woman doesn't count, I mean he wants a good-looking woman himself, I don't mean that, but whichever one it is doesn't count because, you know, he's doing it to himself and the woman is the mirror he looks into. I read it. It was real convincing."

Glenda shakes her head, confused. "Yeah, well, Guy's handsome and all that...but....Coral, could you maybe come over to my place with me after work? After I pick up Bobby?"

"What? Why?"

"Oh, we could have supper together and then go to a movie, all three of us, you know, like we did that one time....I was just thinking...."

"I don't know, Glenda, I got a lot of work to do tonight."

"Bobby ain't no trouble, is he?"

"Bobby is a real sweet kid. Does he still wet the bed?"

"Not so much now."

"How's that what's-her-name, Foss? She any better?"

"Oh, she's all right," Glenda says nervously. "We could send out for some Chinese food or maybe a pizza...."

Coral lights another cigarette and gets to her feet. "The problem is I got to look through the bills and stuff tonight...start making out some refill orders, you know...."

"Bobby ain't no trouble, he sits real still in the movies."

"Oh, Bobby is sweet, he's a sweetheart," Coral says vaguely. "Oh, hey, Roxanne, don't forget that peroxide thing—"

"I put it away," Roxanne calls back.

"Half-full, did you?"

"Yeah, it's half-full."

"Did you put it down for re-order?"

"Okay, I'll do it now," Roxanne says wearily.

"She always lets things go, it never fails," Coral mutters to Glenda.

Glenda has finished her cigarette and is staring at it, at the dry lipstick stains on it.

"So you can't make it tonight, then?" Glenda says.

"Some other time, maybe…okay?" Coral says.

Glenda puts out her cigarette. For some reason the cigarette made her feel cold.

5:50 p.m. Doubleparks by Mrs. Foss's, and what the hell—there comes Bobby running up the street! "What are you doing out by yourself?" Glenda shouts. Bobby climbs in the car; his mouth is stained with something greenish. He looks a little sick. "What happened, did she kick you kids out on the street?" Glenda cries. Bobby says, vaguely, "She said you was sposed to come at five-thirty and you didn't." Glenda has half a mind to leave her car out on the street here and run up to Mrs. Foss's door and pound on it until the old bitch answers…."Oh, goddam her, goddam everybody," Glenda whispers, so angry she could almost cry, and now somebody is honking his horn behind her…."You gonna cry now?" Bobby asks scornfully, fearfully.

6:05 p.m. The A & P, very crowded, Glenda has picked a cart with wobbling wheels, just her luck. Bobby is muling and whining and pulling at her. She moves as fast as she can up and down the aisles, her stomach jumpy, she buys a barbecued chicken wrapped in greasy cellophane and some potato chips that Bobby starts to eat right away—probably didn't get any decent lunch—probably got slapped around all day. But Glenda has no time to think about Bobby and Mrs. Foss, she has to get this stupid limping cart over in line, she is perspiring with strain or with worry, something seems to be wrong with her nerves today. If she got married again….

But she isn't going to get married again. No.

But if….

The cashier has pink-blond hair, like Glenda's, ringing up the items one-two-three, very efficient and skillful. Glenda notes approvingly the girl's pierced ears and tiny gold earrings, her large, rather sullen red mouth, her red-polished nails. Men would like her looks. She probably does well with men.

6:15 p.m. Parks crooked at the curb, runs into the drugstore for some sleeping pills—a new brand called *Sleepeez,* might as well try something new—and some laxatives, the usual. She feels a little sick, like rocks in her intestines, her stomach is bad again and has been for the last week; on her way out she remembers that she needs some toothpaste, she'll have to get it tomorrow—hell—and her first customer is due in at eight, that fussy skinny bitch with the "sensitive scalp"….

6:25 p.m. Parks behind her apartment building. Bobby groggy, sniffing; what if he's coming down with another cold? She checks his forehead and it seems very warm. She notices that the garbage men haven't come yet to pick up the enormous piles of junk out behind the apartment building, there was talk of a slow-down this week….Hell, she is so tired of slow-downs and strikes and demonstrations…."Bobby, come *on,* carry one of these packages," she says in exasperation, because he is just sitting there, staring. "What are you staring at?" she says. He shakes his head. Nothing. She looks and sees only the back of the building, the dreary back entrance and the stacked boxes and damp, scattered newspapers. There is nothing there. No one there. She lives on the first floor, her apartment is nearby, there is nothing to worry about. "Bobby, come on, please," she says, and this time he rouses himself and starts moving.

—1971

LUISA VALENZUELA (1938-   )

Novelist, journalist, and short story writer Luisa Valenzuela is often recognized as one of the most significant Argentinean literary figures since the Latin American literature "boom" of the 1960s and 1970s. Valenzuela began her writing career in her teenage years, contributing to magazines such as *Esto Es, Atlantida,* and *El Hogar.* Her short stories "Ese Canto" and "Cuidad Ajena" appeared in 1956, and she wrote her first novel, *Hay que sonrier,* in 1959 (though it was not published until 1966, the novel received an award from Argentina's El Fondo Nacional de las Artes in 1964). Valenzuela moved to Paris in 1958 but returned to Buenos Aires in 1961, and continued writing for newspapers and magazines, including *The Nation* and *Revista Crisis.* In 1969, after receiving a Fulbright scholarship, she studied in the International Writers Program at the University of Iowa. Valenzuela left Argentina as an exile in 1979 and began teaching as a writer-in-residence at Columbia University. She was selected as a Guggenheim Fellow in 1983, and began teaching writing courses at New York University in 1985. Valenzuela relocated to Buenos Aires in April of 1989, and continues to offer lectures on her writing in Mexico, Paris, and New York. Among her works that have been translated into English are: *Clara* (1976), *Strange Things Happen Here* (1979), *The Lizard's Tail* (1983), *Other Weapons* (1985), *Open Door* (1988), *The Censors* (1992), *Black Novel (with Argentines)* (1992), *Bedside Manners* (1994), *Symmetries* (1998), and *La travesía/The Journey* (2002).

I'm Your Horse in the Night

The doorbell rang: three short rings and one long one. That was the signal, and I got up, annoyed and a little frightened; it could be them, and then again, maybe not; at these ungodly hours of the night it could be a trap. I opened the door expecting anything except him, face to face, at last.

He came in quickly and locked the door behind him before embracing me. So much in character, so cautious, first and foremost checking his—our—rear guard. Then he took me in his arms without saying a word, not even holding me too tight but letting all the emotions of our new encounter overflow, telling me so much by merely holding me in his arms and kissing me slowly. I think he never had much faith in words, and there he was, as silent as ever, sending me messages in the form of caresses.

We finally stepped back to look at one another from head to foot, not eye to eye, out of focus. And I was able to say Hello showing scarcely any surprise despite all those months when I had no idea where he could have been, and I was able to say

I thought you were fighting up north
I thought you'd been caught
I thought you were in hiding
I thought you'd been tortured and killed
I thought you were theorizing about the revolution in another country

Just one of many ways to tell him I'd been thinking of him I hadn't stopped thinking of him or felt as if I'd been betrayed. And there he was, always so goddamn cautious, so much the master of his actions.

"Quiet, Chiquita.[1] You're much better off not knowing what I've been up to."

Then he pulled out his treasures, potential clues that at the time eluded me: a bottle of cachaça[2] and a Gal Costa[3] record. What had he been up to in Brazil? What was he planning to do next? What had brought him back, risking his life, knowing they were after him? Then I stopped asking myself questions (quiet, Chiquita, he'd say). Come here, Chiquita, he was saying, and I chose to let myself sink into the joy of having him back again, trying not to worry. What would happen to us tomorrow, and the days that followed?

Cachaça's a good drink. It goes down and up and down all the right tracks, and then stops to warm up the corners that need it most. Gal Costa's voice is hot, she envelops us in its sound and half-dancing, half-floating, we reach the bed. We lie down and keep on staring deep into each other's eyes, continue caressing each other without allowing ourselves to give into the pure senses just yet. We continue recognizing, rediscovering each other.

Beto, I say, looking at him. I know that isn't his real name, but it's the only one I can call him out loud. He replies:

"We'll make it some day, Chiquita, but let's not talk now."

It's better that way. Better if he doesn't start talking about how we'll make it someday and ruin the wonder of what we're about to attain right now, the two of us, all alone.

"A noite eu so teu cavalo," Gal Costa suddenly sings from the record player.

"I'm your horse in the night," I translate slowly. And so as to bind him in a spell and stop him from thinking about other things:

"It's a saint's song, like in the *macumba*.[4] Someone who's in a trance says she's the horse of the spirit who's riding her, she's his mount."

"Chiquita, you're always getting carried away with esoteric meanings and witchcraft. You know perfectly well that she isn't talking about spirits. If you're my horse in the night it's because I ride you, like this, see?…Like this…That's all."

It was so long, so deep and so insistent, so charged with affection that we ended up exhausted. I fell asleep with him still on top of me.

I'm your horse in the night.

The goddamn phone pulled me out in waves from a deep well. Making an enormous effort to wake up, I walked over to the receiver, thinking it could be Beto, sure, who was no longer by my side, sure, following his inveterate habit of running away while I'm asleep without a word about where he's gone. To protect me, he says.

---

[1] (Sp.) Little one. A diminutive used as an endearment.
[2] Distilled alcoholic beverage common in Brazil.
[3] Popular female singer in Brazil.

[4] A word used to refer to Afro-Brazilian spiritist religious practices.

From the other end of the line, a voice I thought belonged to Andrés—the one we call Andrés—began to tell me:

"They found Beto dead, floating down the river near the other bank. It looks as if they threw him alive out of a chopper. He's all bloated and decomposed after six days in the water, but I'm almost sure it's him."

"No, it can't be Beto," I shouted carelessly. Suddenly the voice no longer sounded like Andrés: it felt foreign, impersonal.

"You think so?"

"Who is this?" Only then did I think to ask. But that very moment they hung up.

Ten, fifteen minutes? How long must I have stayed there staring at the phone like an idiot until the police arrived? I didn't expect them. But, then again, how could I not? Their hands feeling me, their voices insulting and threatening, the house searched, turned inside out. But I already knew. So what did I care if they broke every breakable object and tore apart my dresser?

They wouldn't find a thing. My only real possession was a dream and they can't deprive me of my dreams just like that. My dream the night before, when Beto was there with me and we loved each other. I'd dreamed it, dreamed every bit of it, I was deeply convinced that I'd dreamed it all in the richest detail, even in full color. And dreams are none of the cops' business.

They want reality, tangible facts, the kind I couldn't even begin to give them.

Where is he, you saw him, he was here with you, where did he go? Speak up, or you'll be sorry. Let's hear you sing, bitch, we know he came to see you, where is he, where is he holed up? He's in the city, come on, spill it, we know he came to get you.

I haven't heard a word from him in months. He abandoned me, I haven't heard from him in months. He ran away, went underground. What do I know, he ran off with someone else, he's in another country. What do I know, he abandoned me, I hate him, I know nothing.

(Go ahead, burn me with your cigarettes, kick me all you wish, threaten, go ahead, stick a mouse in me so it'll eat my insides out, pull my nails out, do as you please. Would I make something up for that? Would I tell you he was here when a thousand years ago he left me forever?)

I'm not about to tell them my dreams. Why should they care? I haven't seen that so-called Beto in more than six months, and I loved him. The man simply vanished. I only run into him in my dreams, and they're bad dreams that often become nightmares.

Beto, you know now, if it's true that they killed you, or wherever you may be, Beto, I'm your horse in the night and you can inhabit me whenever you wish, even if I'm behind bars. Beto, now that I'm in jail I know that I dreamed you that night; it was just a dream. And if by some wild chance there's a Gal Costa record and a half-empty bottle of cachaça in my house, I hope they'll forgive me: I will them out of existence.

—1985

PAULA GUNN ALLEN (1939-   )

Born Paula Marie Francis, Allen grew up in Cubero, New Mexico, a Spanish land-grant town near the Laguna and Acoma reservations. She is of Lebanese descent on her father's side and Laguna Pueblo, Sioux, and Scottish on her mother's side, and grew up in a household where Spanish, English, Arabic, German, and Laguna were spoken with regularity. She attended a convent school for most of her childhood, and went on to receive a B.A. and an M.F.A. from the University of Oregon, and a Ph.D. from the University of New Mexico. Allen has made important contributions to Native American literary tradition as a poet, fiction writer, and scholar, bringing to both her creative and critical work a sensibility informed by the woman-centeredness and orality of Pueblo culture. Allen is the author of several poetry collections, including *The Blind Lion* (1974), *Shadow Country* (1982), *Skins and Bones* (1988), and *Life Is a Fatal Disease: Collected Poems, 1962-1995* (1997); a novel, *The Woman Who Owned the Shadows* (1983); and several works of nonfiction, including *The Sacred Hoop: Recovering the Feminine in American Indian Traditions* (1986) and *Pocahontas: Medicine Woman, Spy, Entrepreneur, Diplomat* (2003). She is also the editor of several collections of Native American literature, including *Spider Woman's Granddaughters* (1989), which won an American Book Award. She has been awarded grants from the National Endowment for the Arts and the Ford Foundation.

Some Like Indians Endure

i have it in my mind that
dykes are indians

they're a lot like indians
they used to live as tribes
they owned tribal land   5
it was called the earth

they were massacred
lots of times
they always came back
like the grass   10
like the clouds
they got massacred again

they thought caringsharing
about the earth and each other
was a good thing   15
they rode horses
and sang to the moon

but i don't know
about what was so longago
and it's now that dykes   20
make me think i'm with indians
when i'm with dykes

because they bear
witness bitterly
because they reach   25

and hold
because they live every day
with despair laughin
in cities and country places
because earth hides them   30
because they know
the moon

because they gather together
enclosing
and spit in the eye of death   35

indian is an idea
some people have
of themselves
dyke is an idea some women
have of themselves   40
the place where we live now
is idea
because whiteman took
all the rest
because daddy   45
took all the rest
but the idea which
once you have it
you can't be taken
for somebody else   50
and have nowhere to go
like indians you can be
stubborn

the idea might move you on,
ponydrag behind   55
taking all your loves and
children maybe downstream
maybe beyond the cliffs
but it hangs in there
an idea   60
like indians
endures

it might even take your
whole village with it
stone by stone   65
or leave the stones
and find more
to build another village
someplace else

like indians   70
dykes have fewer and fewer

someplace elses to go
so it gets important
to know
about ideas and   75
to remember or uncover
the past
and how the people
traveled
all the while remembering   80
the idea they had
about who they were
indians, like dykes
do it all the time

dykes know all about dying   85
and that everything belongs
to the wind
like indians
they do terrible things
to each other   90
out of sheer cussedness
out of forgetting
out of despair

so dykes
are like indians   95
because everybody is related
to everybody
in pain
in terror
in guilt   100
in blood
in shame
in disappearance
that never quite manages
to be disappeared   105
we never go away
even if we're always
leaving

because the only home
is each other   110
they've occupied all
the rest
colonized it: an
idea about ourselves is all
we own   115

and dykes remind me of indians
like indians dykes

are supposed to die out
or forget
or drink all the time   120
or shatter
go away
to nowhere
to remember what will happen
if they don't   125

they don't anyway—even
though the worst happens
they remember and they
stay
because the moon remembers   130
because so does the sun
because the stars
remember
and the persistent stubborn grass
of the earth

—1981

The One Who Skins Cats

She never liked to stay or live where she could not see the mountains, for home she called them. For the unseen spirit dwelt in the hills, and a swift-running creek could preach a better sermon for her than any mortal could have done. Every morning she thanked the spirits for a new day.

She worshipped the white flowers that grew at the snowline on the sides of the tall mountains. She sometimes believed, she said, that they were the spirits of little children who had gone away but who returned every spring to gladden the pathway of those now living.

I was only a boy then but those words sank deep down in my soul. I believed them then, and I believe now that if there is a hereafter, the good Indian's name will be on the right side of the ledger. Sacagawea is gone—but she will never be forgotten.

—Tom Rivington[1]

1.
Sacagawea, Bird Woman[2]

Bird Woman they call me
for I am the wind.
I am legend. I am history.
I come and I go. My tracks
are washed away in certain places.   5

---

[1] Tom Rivington, a western pioneer who, as a young man, knew Sacagawea. This is taken from his correspondence with Grace Hebard, who wrote a popular novel based on Sacagawea's life in 1933.

[2] Sacagawea (ca. 1788-1812?/1884?), from Hidatsa tsakáka wía, meaning "bird woman," the Shoshone woman who accompanied Lewis and Clark on their 1804-1806 exploration of the Louisiana Purchase and Pacific Northwest. Sacagawea's function in the expedition is the subject of debate, some (especially early suffragists) claiming for her a central role as guide and translator, others suggesting her role was more peripheral.

I am Chief Woman, Porivo.[3] I brought
the Sundance to my Shoshone people—I am
grandmother of the Sun.
I am the one who wanders, the one
who speaks, the one who watches,   10
the one who does not wait,
the one who teaches, the one who goes
to see, the one who wears a silver
medallion inscribed with the face
of a president.[4] I am the one who   15
holds my son close within my arms,
the one who marries, the one
who is enslaved, the one who is beaten,
the one who weeps, the one who knows
the way, who beckons, who knows the wilderness.   20
I am the woman who knows the pass and where
the wild food waits to be drawn from the mother's breast.
I am the one who meets,
the one who runs away.
I am Slave Woman, Lost Woman, Grass Woman, Bird Woman.   25
I am Wind Water Woman and White Water Woman, and I come
and go as I please. And the club-footed man
who shelters me is Goat Man, is my son,
is the one who buried me
in the white cemetery so you would not forget me.   30
He took my worth to his grave
for the spirit people to eat.
I am Many Tongue Woman, Sacred Wind Woman,
Bird Woman. I am Mountain Pass
and River Woman. I am free.   35
I know many places, many things.
I know enough to hear the voice
in the running water of the creek,
in the wind, in the sweet, tiny flowers.

2.
Porivo, Chief Woman

Yeah. Sure. Chief Woman, that's   40
what I was called. Bird Woman. Snake
Woman. Among other things. I've had
a lot of names in my time. None of em
fit me very well, but none of em was
my true name anyway,   45
so what's the difference?

---

[3] While some accounts suggest that Sacagawea died in 1812, others believe that she survived into old age living under the name of Porivo ("chief woman") on the Wind River Indian Reservation in Wyoming.

[4] Lewis and Clark carried with them Jefferson Peace Medals, which they gave as tokens of goodwill to the Indian leaders they encountered on their expedition.

Those white women who decided I alone
guided the whiteman's expedition across
the world. What did they know?
Indian maid, they said.   50
Maid. That's me.

But I did pretty good for a maid.
I went wherever I pleased, and
the whiteman paid the way.
I was worth something then. I still am.   55
But not what they say.

There's more than one way
to skin a cat. That's what they say
and it makes me laugh. Imagine me,
Bird Woman, skinning a cat.   60
I did a lot of skinning in my day.

I lived a hundred years or more
but not long enough to see the day
when those suffragettes
made me the most famous squaw in all creation.   65
Me. Snake Woman. Chief.
You know why they did that?
Because they was tired of being nothing
themselves. They wanted to show how nothing
was really something of worth.   70
And that was me. Indian squaw,
pointing the way they wanted to go.
Indian maid, showing them how they oughta be.
What Susan B. Anthony had to say
was exactly right: they couldn't have   75
made it without me.

Even while I was alive, I was worth something.
I carried the proof of it in my wallet
all those years. They saw how I rode the train
all over the West for free. And how I got   80
food from the white folks along the way.
I had papers that said I was Sacagawea,
and a silver medal the president got made for me.

But that's water under the bridge.
I can't complain,   85
even now when so many of my own kind
call me names. Say
I betrayed the Indians
into the whiteman's hand.
They have a point,   90
but only one.

There's more than one way to skin a cat,
is what I always say.

One time I went wandering—
that was years after the first trip west,   95
long after I'd seen the ocean and the whale.
Do you know my people laughed
when I told em about the whale?
Said I lied a lot.
Said I put on airs.   100
Well, what else should a bird woman wear?

But that time I went wandering out west.
I left St. Louis because my squawman, Charbonneau,
beat me. Whipped me so I couldn't walk
It wasn't the first time, but that time I left.   105
Took me two days to get back on my feet.
Then I walked all the way to Comanche country
in Oklahoma, Indian Territory it was then.
I married a Comanche man, a real husband,
one I loved. I stayed there nearly 27 years.   110
I would have stayed there till I died,
but he died first.

After that I went away. Left the kids,
all but one girl I took with me, but
she died along the way—not as strong   115
as she should be, I guess. But
the others, they was Comanche after all,
and I was nothing, nothing at all.
Free as a bird. That's me.

That time I went all the way   120
to see the Apaches, the Havasupai,
all sorts of Indians. I wanted
to see how they were faring. I like
the Apaches, they were good to me.
But I wouldn't stay long. I had fish to fry.   125
Big ones. Big as the whales
they said I didn't see.

Oh, I probably betrayed some Indians.
But I took care of my own Shoshones.
That's what a chief woman does, anyway.   130
And the things my Indian people call me now
they got from the whiteman, or, I should say,
the white women. Because it's them who said
I led the whitemen into the wilderness and back,
and they survived the journey with my care.   135
It's true they came like barbarian hordes
after that, and that us Indians lost our place.

We was losing it anyway.
I didn't lead the whitemen, you know. I just
went along for the ride. And along the way   140
I learned what a chief should know,
and because I did, my own Snake people survived.
But that's another story,
one I'll tell some other time.

This one's about my feathered past,   145
my silver medallion I used to wear to buy my rides
to see where the people lived, waiting for
the end of the world.

And what I learned I used. Used every bit
of the whiteman's pride to make sure   150
my Shoshone people would survive
in the great survival sweepstakes of the day.
Maybe there was a better way to skin that cat,
but I used the blade that was put in my hand—
or my claw, I should say.   155

Anyway, what it all comes down to is this:
The story of Sacagawea, Indian maid,
can be told a lot of different ways.
I can be the guide, the chief.
I can be the traitor, the Snake.   160
I can be the feathers on the wind.
It's not easy skinning cats
when you're a dead woman.
A small brown bird.

—1988

TONI CADE BAMBARA (1939-1995)

Miltona Mirkin Cade, the daughter of Helen Brent Henderson Cade and Walter Cade II, changed her name to Toni as a child, and added "Bambara" in 1970. She and her brother were raised in Harlem and Bedford-Stuyvesant, New York. Bambara received a B.A. from Queens College in 1959 in Theater Arts and English, and an M.A. in Modern American Literature from the City College of New York in 1964. After working as a welfare investigator for two years, she studied in Europe. Her anthology *The Black Woman* (1970) was part of an extraordinary Black women's literary renaissance that included Maya Angelou, Toni Morrison, and Alice Walker; in it, Bambara collected material from a wide range of Black women writers, including her students at City College. In 1971, Bambara published an anthology for children and young adults, *Tales and Stories for Black Folks*. Two collections of stories for adults followed: *Gorilla, My Love* (1972) and *The Sea Birds Are Still Alive* (1977). Her novel *The*

Salt-Eaters (1980) won the American Book Award. Bambara also worked in film, and made a documentary, *The Bombing of Osage Avenue* (1986), about the bombing of the headquarters of a Black activist group in Philadelphia. Diagnosed with colon cancer in 1993, Bambara rushed to complete a novel she'd been working on for twelve years, *Those Bones Are Not My Child,* about a series of child murders in Atlanta in the 1980s. Her friend Toni Morrison edited the novel, and it was published after Bambara's death. "Going Critical" is from Bambara's final collection, *Deep Sightings and Rescue Missions* (1995), which includes fiction, interviews, and essays.

Going Critical

I

One minute, Clara was standing on a wet stone slab slanting over the drop, a breaker coming at her, the tension tingling up the back of her legs as though it were years ago and she would dive from the rocks to meet it. And in the next minute, the picture coming again, brushing behind her eye, insistent since morning but still incomplete. Then the breaker struck the rocks, the icy cold wash lifting her up on her toes, and the picture flashing, still faint, indistinct. Teeth chattering, she flowed with it, tried not to understand it and blur the edges, but understood it beneath words, beneath thought. The brushing as of a feather, the wing-tip arrival of the childhood sea god who had buoyed her up from the deep when she'd been young and reckless in the waters. A feather brushing in the right side of the brain, dulled by three centuries of God-slight neglect, awakened in Clara at the moment of her daughter's conception.

Nineteen eighty, middle-aged woman in dated swimsuit and loose flesh, sliding perilously on moss slime stone, image clustering behind right eye, image-idea emerging from the void, a heresy in one era, a truth in the next, decaying into superstition, then splashing its message before returning to the void. The water sucking at the soles of her feet before sliding out again to sea, she saw it and shivered.

And then she was running, forgetting all her daughter had taught her about jogging. Running, she pushed her chilled body through an opening in the bushes as though heading toward a remembered site—a clearing, a desert nearly, where the bomb test was to be conducted. They'd been told through memos, at briefings, and over the PA system that they were in no danger providing, so long as, on the condition that, and if. No special uniforms or equipment had been issued, not even a shard of smoked glass. They were simply to take up their positions in the designated spots where the NCO rec hall was to be built. Line up, shut up, close the eyes—that was all, once the incomprehensible waivers had been signed.

Cold and damp, Clara plunged through the green, seeing in memory remnants of the ghost bush, seeing the open-mouth Lieutenant Reed, a gospel singer in civilian life, crash through the bush at the last minute, leaving a gaping wound. The twigs and leaves trying to squeeze to, trying to knit closed, trying to lock up before the blast. Their straining prying Clara's eyes open. And in that moment, the deep muffled thunder of the detonation. And the ground broke and the light flared and her teeth shook in the jellied sockets of her gums. Her heart stopped, but her eyes kept on seeing—Lieutenant Bernice Reed a shadow, an X-ray, the twigs and leaves transparent too, showing their bones.

Clara passed through the bushes out of breath and exchanged her swimsuit for a towel, wondering if the bush still quaked on the flats in Utah. Had it ever closed, had it ever healed? And did Bernice Reed still sing in the choir in Moultrie, Georgia, or had she left her voice there in the wounded green?

II

"Ya know, Mama, the really hip part of the fish and loaves miracle?"[1]

Clara watched her daughter squat-walk across the sandy blanket, thinking fishes and loaves, the Piscean age, Golden Calf, the Taurean. Wondering too, would the girl ever get it together and apply her gift in useful ways in the time of the Emptying Vessel?

"There were no dishes to wash, no bottles to sterilize or nipples to scrub. And no garbage to put out, Mama. That was the miracle. Hell, feeding the multitudes ain't no big thing. You and Aunt Ludie and women before and mamas since been doing that season in and season out."

Season in and season out. To feed the people, Clara muttered, pulling her overall strap over her shoulder and hooking it. What crops would be harvested from the contaminated earth?

"But of course, it was probably a classic case of the women doing the cleaning up. So quite naturally all that non-high drama escaped the chronicler's jaundiced eye."

"I knew you were going to say that," Clara said. She stumbled into her clogs, watching Honey bury a lump of potato salad in the sand.

Honey shrugged. "How boring it must be for you to always know what I'm going to say."

"Not always. I don't always know, I mean."

Clara stuffed garbage into a plastic sack while her daughter gathered up the casting stones. The bone white agate Honey always used as the control was slipped into the leather pouch she wore around her neck. The two pebbles she'd found on the beach, the yes and no for the impromptu reading, Honey tossed into the picnic hamper.

"You were able to help them?" Clara knew Honey would merely glance toward the couple she'd read and shrug. The arguments over the proper use of Honey's gifts had been too frequent and too heated of late. Honey could not be lured into a discussion just like that. Clara ignored the press of time and softened her voice all the more. "You saw something for them?"

They had walked right up, the couple, tracking sand onto the blanket, ignored Clara altogether as though she were already gone, and said to Honey that they'd recognized her from the Center and would she read their cards, or read their palms, or throw the cowries, or "Give us some money," the woman had joked not joking, "Cash money in the hand," karate-chopping the air and baring her teeth. And Clara had done a quick aura-scan, first of the couple, swarmy and sparkish, then of her daughter, a steady glow.

"They seemed bad news to me," Clara said, still not expecting an answer, but searching for a point of entry. And saying it for the sake of the phrase "bad news," in preparation for the talk they'd come to the old neighborhood beach for but thus far

---

[1] In the New Testament, Jesus fed a crowd of 5,000 men (and uncounted women and children) with five loaves and two fishes (John 6:1-14, Luke 9:10-17, Mark 6:35-44, Matthew 14:15-21).

had skirted. "Vampires," Clara said flatly. Honey did not take up the challenge, but went right on gathering up their things, her beaded braids clinking against her earrings.

Clara squatted down and folded the towels, wondering if Honey'd had a chance to rest, to recharge after the command-performance reading. She leaned over to dump the towels in the hamper and too to place her hand on her daughter's nerve center.

"Was there anything helpful you could tell them, Honey, about, say budgeting for the future?" Clara heard it catch in her throat, "the future," and felt Honey hearing it in the small of her back.

They both sat silent for a moment, gazing off in the direction of the couple arguing and wrassling their beach chairs as far from the water's edge as they could get.

"But then, what could you tell them? Hard to make ends meet when you've got your ass on your shoulders," Clara said, and was immediately sorry.

"Mama," Honey made no effort to disguise her annoyance, "I will gladly pay you back for the wedding. I will tell Curtis not to bug you any further about a loan. And damnit, I will pay for the parking."

"I didn't mean..." Clara didn't bother to say the rest of it, that she was only trying her hand at a joke. Her ears, her tongue, her heart were stinging.

III

They shook the sand out, then began folding the blanket, remembering how they used to do the laundry together, each backing up till the bedspread or sheet pulled taut—the signal to begin. Sometimes, flapping it flat, they'd dance to meet in the center, doing precise minuet steps, their noses pointed toward the basement ceiling, their lips pursed in imitation of a neighbor lady who complained of their incense, candles, gatherings, "strange" ways. Or, clicking across the ceramic tile of the laundry room, grimacing in tortured Flamenco postures, they'd olé olé till Jake, overhead in his den, hollered down the heat duct to lighten up and hurry up with supper. Sometimes, as part of their put-down of the school PE program, they'd clog, doing the squarest square dance steps they could muster. Yodeling, they'd bring each other the corners of the sheet, their knuckles knocking softly when they met, blind, each hiding behind her side of the raised-high fabric to prepare a face to shock the other with, once Clara, clasping all the corners and twanging in a hillbilly soprano, or Honey, nesting her hands in the folds to get the edges aligned, signaled the other to lower the covers in the laundry basket, their howls drawing stomps from overhead.

In those free times before the lumps appeared and the nightmare hauntings began, Clara would hold on to a funny face remembered from a Galveston carnival mask, while Honey, bending, would smooth the bedspreads down her mother's body to save her time at the ironing board. But then came the days when their signals went awry, when Clara, breathless with worry and impotence, and Honey, not yet reading the streaks in her mother's aura or the netted chains in her palm's mercury line, were both distracted, and the neatly folded tablecloth would wind up a heap on the basement floor. "I thought you had it, damnit. I thought you were going to take it. Shit." And Jake, husband/father, would avoid the loyalty trap by giving both bristling women wide berth for the course of the day.

There were the hot, silent times too, Clara racing feverishly through lists of healers yet to be seen, Honey searching for some kind thing to say now that radium and chemotherapy had snatched huge patches out of Clara's hair and softened her gums, ruining a once handsome jawline. The covers between would get ironed flat by the heat of mother and daughter clinging to the spread, touching through terry cloth or wool or chenille, neither letting go. Overhead, Jake, his face pressed against cold iron, breathing in burnt dust from the grate and cat hairs in the carpet, weeping into the ashes, would pray they'd let go of each other before the time.

"I've got it," Clara said finally, when she could bear it no longer, neither the strain of the silence, the memories, nor her daughter's presence too close and too intense. "Let go, Honey," as though the sun that Honey's young body had soaked up all day were searing her now through the wool. "Let go."

Clara draped the blanket over Honey's outstretched arm, dropped it really, as though it had singed her, as though she wanted to be done with blankets and outings and Honey and all of it quickly and get away, race back to the rocks, to the ice-cold waters that had known her young and fit and with a future.

"Mama, are you alright?"

Her daughter whispering as in a sickroom with shades drawn and carpets muffling; Honey slow-motion bending to lay the blanket in the hamper, slow and quiet as in the presence of the dying. Clara grabbed up one handle of the wicker hamper, and Honey took up her end. And now they could go. There was nothing to keep them there except what was keeping them there. But how to begin? Honey, your ole mama's on her last leg and needs to know, you won't be silly…My darling, please promise not to abuse your gifts…Before I kick off, Sweetie, one last request…? Words tumbled moist and clumsily in Clara's mouth, and she rejected them. For now she wanted to speak of other things—of life, food, fun—wanted to invite her daughter, her friend, for a promenade along the boardwalk on the hunt for shrimp and beer, or quiche and a nice white wine.

"The lunch was lovely, Honey, but I'm hungry for more. For more," she said, veering closer to the subject that held them on the sand. But she could get no further into it and was grateful that Honey chose that moment to turn aside and hook-shoot the garbage sack into the dumpster some three feet away from the arguesome couple. Clara longed to touch her again, to trace with the tip of one finger the part in the back of Honey's head, knowing the scalp would be warm, hot even. Hot Head. Jake had nicknamed her when she was just an infant. And Curtis had revived it of late, preferring it to Khufu, the name his wife was known by at the Center, to Vera, the name on the birth certificate, and to Honey, the name she'd given her daughter to offset the effects of "Hot Head." Honey, a name she gave to give her daughter options.

"Starved? Say no more," Honey said, walking off and yanking Clara along at the other end of the hamper. "Aunt Ludie swears she's going to put her extramean gumbo together tonight. Needless to say, I told her to put our names in the pot."

"We're not staying for the fireworks?" Clara pulled on the handle to make Honey slow up. "I thought we'd eat around here and then see the fireworks. I thought that was the whole point of parking in the lot instead of on the street, so we'd have access to the dunes and…" She felt panic welling up, time running away from her. "Five damn dollars to park just so we'd have a pass to the dunes, Honey."

"Whatchu care about five damn dollars, Mama? You a rich lady," Honey said over her shoulder with a smile Clara knew was not a smile at all. If Honey's lackadaisacal attitude at the Center was a hot issue, then the money was a scorcher. Her daughter had married into a family on Striver's Row, had in-laws with little patience for "community," "the people," "development," and even less tolerance for how their son's mother-in-law, Clara, dispersed her funds and spent her time and tried to influence their son's wife.

"Not yet, I'm not rich. Not yet." Clara stumbled along in the sand and wondered if she'd live long enough to see the money, at least to sign it over to the Center and its works. The suit the former GIs had brought against the Army had dragged on for years. And though the medical reports had grown sharper from "radiation exposure a high-probability factor in the development of malignancies," to "disabilities a direct result of the veterans' involvement with the nuclear test program"—and though the lawyers for the National Association of Atomic Vets were optimistic despite the sorry box score of twenty recognized suits out of hundreds of claims, and though the Board of Veterans' Appeals had overturned earlier VA rulings, the Army was still appealing, denying, holding out.

"It's easier walking along the beach," Honey was saying, shifting direction sharply and wrenching Clara's arm, her thoughts. "And maybe we can find some sandblasted bottles for Daddy's collection."

Nineteen eighty, deadline for probable-future choice imminent, people collecting shells, beer cans, stamps, rally buttons, posters, statistics, snapshots. Middle-aged woman in loose flesh and tight overalls pulled past old men sissy-fishing along sandbar in rolled-up pants. Tips of rods quivering like thin silver needles the Chinese doctor placed along meridian, electricity turned on, mother prayers turned up drowning Muzak out. Line pulled in, fish flopping its last, hook through gills, tail fin lashing at fisherman who's wrecked its life. Life already ruined. Woman on leave from Department of Wildlife recites fish kills typed up daily. Agriculture—insecticides, pesticides; industrial mining, paper, food, metallurgy, petroleum, chemical plants, municipal sewerage system, refuse disposal, swimming pool agents.

"Remember the church fish fries here when I was little? You'd leave me with Aunt Ludie to go visit the tearoom. Remember, Mama?"

Dog River, Alabama; Santa Barbara Harbor, California; Anacostia River, D.C.; Mulatto Bayou, Florida; Salt Bayou, Louisiana.

"Mama, you look beat. Wanna rest?"

Slocum Creek, North Carolina; Radar Creek, Ohio; San Jacinto River, Texas; Snake River, Washington.

"Why don't you sit down on the rocks while I put this stuff in the car."

"Girl, don't you know my sitting days are over? And there's work to do and we need to talk." But she let Honey take the whole of the hamper onto her shoulder and march off with it. So there was nothing for Clara to do but find a dry rock not too far out on the breakwater wall and sit down, be still, be available, wait. She slumped. The weight of the day, of unhealth, relationships, trying to organize for the end, pressed her down onto the rocks, her body yearning to return to the earth—disoriented, detached and unobliged. And then the picture flashed. The bush. A maze of overgrown hedges and thickets, prickly to the eye. She, looking for a path and it suddenly there, bones at the mouth of the passage. On her knees inching through briars. Inching forward to the edge. And nothing there at the drop. No matter which way she turned, the view the same. The world an egg blown clean.

IV

"They say, Honey, that cancer is the disease of new beginnings, the result of a few cells trying to start things up again."

"Your point being?" Honey was picking her teeth, weaving in and out of boardwalk traffic, deliberately allowing, it seemed to Clara, cyclists, skaters, parents pushing baby strollers, to come between them.

"That it's characteristic of these times, Honey. It signals the beginning of the new age. There'll be epidemics. And folks, you know it, are not prepared."

"And so?"

They were side by side now, veering around a "sidewalk" artist down on his knees, pushing a plate of colored chalks along the boards, drawing rapidly fantastic figures that stumped those strollers who paused to look, dripping the ice cream or sweaty cups of beer on the artwork. Together, they walked briskly past the restaurants and bars, the kiddie park, the wax museum, the horror house, finally talking. But Clara was still dissatisfied, had still not gotten said what she'd come to the beach to say to her only child. And she still did not altogether know what it was. When my time comes, Honey, release me 'cause I've work to do yet? Watch yourself and try not be pulled off of the path by your in-laws? Develop the gifts, girl, and try to push at least one life in the direction of resurrection?

"You do understand about the money?" Clara was hugging close as marines, couples, teenagers walking four and five abreast, threatened to shove between them. She felt Honey's arm stiffen as though she meant to pull away.

"Money, money, money. I'm sick of the subject. Curtis, his mother…And his father, you know, has his eye on a liquor store and keeps asking me if…"

An elderly couple clumping along in rubber-tipped walkers separated them. Then an Asian-American family Clara dimly recalled from the old neighborhood streamed between them, the mother spitting watermelon seeds expertly through the cracks in the boardwalk, the father popping kernels from what was evidently a very hot cob of corn, one youngster cracking into a sugar-glazed apple, the other absentmindedly plucking tufts of cotton candy from a paper cone as though it were a petaled daisy.

Liquor store. Clara frowned, her face contorted from the effort to salute her old neighbors, answer Honey, and continue the dialogue on the inside all at the same time. And so she almost missed it, not the Fotomat Honey was pointing toward where summers before they'd horsed around, meeting up with odd characters they never told Jake and, later, Curtis about; posing as sisters or actresses fresh back from madcap adventures on the Orient Express, they would give each other fanciful names and outlandish histories to flirt with. She almost missed the tearoom. Jammed between the tattoo parlor and the bingo hall, looking tinier and tackier than she remembered it, was the tearoom where Clara had watched, under the steady gaze of Great Ma Drew, her work emerge clear and sharp from the dense fog of the crystal ball that good sense had taught her to scoff at till something more powerful than skepticism and something more potent than the markings on her calendar forced Clara's eyes to acknowledge two events: motherhood, and soon (despite all the doctors had had to say about Jake's sluggish sperm and her tilted uterus), and a gift unfolding right now, a gift that would enable Clara to train the child.

Clara linked arms with Honey and steered her toward the tearoom with her hips.

The woman, though, lounging against the Madame Lazar Tearoom sign was neither the seer Drew, nor any of the gypsified Gypsies or non-Gypsies that had taken over the business during Honey's growing-up days. She was a young, mariny woman in a Donna Summer[2] do—a weave job, Clara's expert eye noted—wearing exactly the kind of jewelry and flouncy dress, vèvè-encrusted hem and metallic smocking in the bodice, that Clara always associated with the Ioa Urzulie Frieda.[3] Clara felt Honey resisting, her hard bone pushing through flesh against her.

"Sistuh, are you gifted?" Honey challenged, before Clara could speak, could get her balance, Honey still steeling herself against her.

The woman's eyes slid insolently over them. Clara was about to give in and let Honey steer along to the dunes, but the woman flashed, and Clara felt a reaching-out come in her direction, and then a mind probe, bold, prickly, and not at all gentle.

"She's telepathic," Clara whispered, pulling Honey up short. "But can she see, I wonder. Can she see around the bend and probe the future?" Honey sucked her teeth and stood her ground between the two women. And now the woman smiled and Clara dropped Honey's arm and dropped, too, her shield. At this point in time, Clara mused, I can afford to be open to anything and everything.

"How far can you see?" Clara asked, setting up a chain reaction of questions on the inside for the woman to touch upon. She waited. In an open-bodied position, Clara invited the woman to move in.

"Mama, come on, damnit."

And then Clara felt the woman withdraw. And it was Honey's turn to smile. She was gifted, this new Madame Lazar. She was simpatico. But business is business, no freebies here. The woman slid her eyes over Honey in dismissal, and to Clara she jerked her chin in the direction of the incense-fragrant interior and passed, sashaying in her noisy crinolines and taffetas, through the curtain.

"Oh no, you don't," Honey said, linking arms and shoving her hip hard against Clara's, almost knocking her out of her clogs. "She has a gift alright, Mama, but no principles. Liable to put a hex on you," she grinned, "plus take all your money. Let's go."

"Now wait a minute." Clara tried to disengage her arm and back up for a moment to get her thoughts lined up, but Honey was pulling her along like an irritated parent with an aggravating child. Hex, Clara thought, trying to get it organized. UF_6, the gaseous form of uranium, was called hex and that was something to talk about. Gifts and principles—exactly the topic to get to an appraisal of the Center's work. Money perfect. But Honey would not give her a moment. Who was the mother here anyway? Clara squinched up her toes, trying for traction, trying to dig in. She yanked hard on her daughter.

"Whatcha so mad about, Mama?"

"Well, damnit, what are you so angry about, and all week long too?" They were falling over the chalk artist, causing a pileup in front of the tattoo parlor. "You're mad because I'm leaving you?" She was clutching the lapels of her daughter's shirt, breathing hot breath into her face, her body shuddering. "Oh, girl, don't you know it's the way of things for children to bury their elders?" She barely had the strength to hold on as Honey dropped her face into her shoulders, pressing her beaded braids into

[2] Donna Summer (b. 1948), singer with a series of hits in the 1970s; known as the "Queen of Disco."

[3] Female spirit in the African and Diasporic religion of Vodun who represents love and beauty.

Clara's skin. They stood in the throng, getting bumped and jostled by sailors coming out of the parlor displaying their arms and banging each other on the back in congratulations.

"Please, Honey, you say the words over me, hear? No high-falutin eulogies, OK? Don't let them lie me into the past tense and try to palm me off on God as somebody I'm not, OK? And don't let anybody insult my work by grieving and carrying on, OK? Cause I'm not at all unhappy, and Jake's come to terms with it. I've still my work to do, whatever shape I'm in. I mean whatever form I'm in, you know? So OK, Honey? And don't mess up, damnit."

"You and your precious work," Honey hissed, catching Clara off-balance. And then a smile broke up her frown, the sun coming out, and Clara could bear the pain of the beads' imprint. "Fess up, Mama," grinning mischievously, "you're mostly pissed about the five dollars for parking, aincha?"

Someone on the dunes was singing, the music muted at first by the dark and the ocean breeze. Clara leaned back against Honey's knees and issued progress reports on the boat. Decked out in banners and streamers for the occasion, flying its colors on the mast overhead, it was easing its cargo of fireworks out to the raft where T-shirted lifeguards and parkees in orange safety harnesses and bright helmets waited, eager to begin.

She could feel Honey behind her—her knees softening at intervals, then jerking awake as the singer modulated—going to sleep.

"Take care, Honey, that you keep your eyes sharp and spirit alert," she instructed, her voice sounding to her already flat, lifeless, as if it traveled from a great distance and through a veil, vibrancy gone, her self removed to the very outskirts of her being, suspended over her flesh, over the sand, on the high note now sounding while the slap of the waves, a baby's ball buffeted by the waters, was being sucked under the rocks of the breakwater wall, and bits of conversation from blankets around them and from the boardwalk overhead, and then even the high notes, churned below her.

She was hanging in the music, in the swoop of the notes across the humps of the dunes so like beings rising from the sand, dipping down in sound between the children's pail-castles and grown-ups' plumped pillows, buoyed up again toward the moon, full, red and heavy, till the wail of a child and Honey's jerking pulled her back again inside her skin. Being dragged past them by a mother determined to ignore her son's bedtime tactic, a young child in a Hank Aaron[4] shirt was trickling sand across Clara's toes and bawling, his tiny hand digging up another fistful from a bulging pocket to trail sand across the tufts of dune grass and up the steps to the boardwalk gate, people shoving over as though they recognized this tribal wiseman spreading the time-running-fast message to the heedless, then making sand-paintings on the boards, chalkings, the ritual cure for sleepwalkers.

"It begins," Clara said. But still Honey did not sit up to appreciate the view. The fisherfolk had parked their poles and taken up their perch on the rocks, couples on blankets propped each other up, the boardwalk crowd bunched along the railing, the overflow packed on the top steps, leaning into the mesh of the gate—the vista was wide open for the first whoosh of yellow and pink that careened across the night sky. The ahhhhh from the crowd harmonizing with the singer climbing an octave and the

---

[4] Hank Aaron (b. 1934), member of the African-American Baseball Hall of Fame.

bedtime boy still wailing and wheeling around in the chalk drawings, smearing and stamping. A rocket shot out across the waters and exploded into a shower of red, white and blue that fountained down at the far end of the breakwater wall.

"Don't miss this," she said, her voice hollow again, drawn into the music, into the next burst of colors, pulses of energy like the frenzy of atoms like the buzzing of bees like the comings and goings of innumerable souls immeasurably old and in infinite forms and numerous colors. She was floating up, her edges blurring, her flesh falling away, the high note reachable now coming at her from nine different directions, sailing out with her past the boat's flag, echoing through blue through time. And she was a point of light, a point of consciousness in the dark, looking down on her body accusingly—how could it let her go like that?—but ready to be gone and wanting too to go back and nestle inside her old self intimate and warm, skin holding her in, bone holding her up, blood flowing. Her body summoning not yet. Her daughter a magnet, drawing her back.

A cluster of pinwheels came spinning from the boat deck, and the bedtime boy seemed content to whimper between wails. But the singer held on, leaning into the music, pressing sound into the colors. A salvo of sparklers shot out, streaking across the pinwheel's paths, sizzling.

She'd put sparklers on Honey's birthday cake the year Alvin Ailey's[5] company came into town. Had thought it a brilliant change from pastel candles, but the children were frightened, leapt from the table, overturned the benches, dragged half of the tablecloth away in tatters, knocked over the ruffled cups of raisins and nuts, and the punch bowl too. She tried, as they scooted away bursting balloons which only made it worse, tried to explain, as they tripped entangled in crepe paper streamers and string, raking off to the woods before she could assure them, those children of the old neighborhood who'd never seen Chinese New Year, who'd never celebrated the Fourth of July with anything louder than an elder's grunt "Independence for whom?" or "Freedom, my ass!" or anything noisier than a grease-popping what-the-hell barbecue, who'd never seen a comet or heard the planetarium's version of asteroid, the running children who'd never been ushered from bed to watch the street rebellions on TV or through the window and have explained why things were so— doing the hundred-yard dash to the woods fleeing sparklers, Honey right along with them, leaving her with frosting on her chin and hundreds of lessons still to teach.

"You chuckling, coughing, crying, or what?" Honey's voice was drowsy. And Clara didn't know the answer, but remembered the twenty-five dollars' worth of box-seat tickets to see the Ailey dancers, and the exhausted birthday sprinter falling asleep in the middle of *Revelations,* Jake shaking her by the shoulders to at least watch a few dollars' worth.

"That a human voice or what?" Honey sounded neither irritated nor curious, her way, Clara supposed, of letting her know she was still available for talk. The boy was still crying and the note was still holding as firecrackers went off, sounding powerful enough to launch a getaway spaceship. "Ain't it the way," Jake had said just that morning, huddled over the pale, "they mess up, then cut out to new frontiers to mess up

---

[5] Alvin Ailey (1931-1989), choreographer who founded the American Dance Theater (renamed the Alvin Ailey American Dance Theater after his death) to showcase Black dancers; his masterpiece, *Revelations,* was based on growing up in the South.

again." The singer climbing over the thundering, holding out past the crowd's applause, past the crowd's demand for release, past endurance for even extraordinary lungs, the note drawn thin and taut now like a wire, a siren, the parkees, looking now like civil defense wardens sending up flares from the shoot machines, cannons. And still the singer persisted, piercing, an alarm, step-sitters twisting round in annoyance now, the first wave of anger shaking through the crowd at the railing, a big man shoving through to the gate and to hell with a dune pass, heroic, on the hunt for the irritant to silence it. Then a barrage of firecrackers heading straight across the water, caused many to duck before reminding themselves, embarrassed, that this was Sunday at the beach, holiday entertainment and all's well.

"A jug of wine, a crust of pizza and thou for Crissake," someone was saying. Then the note shuddered to a gasping halt and the bedtime boy's wail was cut short by a resounding slap heard on the dunes. After a faint ripple of applause, attention turned fully to the lifeguards prying open the last crate, the parkees spinning out the remaining pinwheels to hold the audience until the specialty works that would spell out a message, the final event, could be crammed into the cannons and fired off.

"Girl, wake up and watch my money."

Honey, knees wobbled against Clara's back, glanced round and smiled at her efforts to come awake and keep her mother company.

There was no way she could carry her child to the car anymore, lay her down gently in the back seat, cover her over with a dry towel, and depend on tomorrow for what went undone today. Clara turned toward the water and joined the people, attentive to the final event about to light up the sky.

—1995

ANGELA DE HOYOS (1940-)

Angela de Hoyos was born in Coahuila, Mexico. When she was three, she was severely burned by a gas heater, and during her long convalescence she began composing verses in her head. When de Hoyos finally recovered, her family moved to San Antonio, Texas, where she still lives today. Often regarded as a product of the Chicano Movement, particularly of its literary renaissance, de Hoyos' first three poetry collections, *Arise Chicano! And Other Poems, Poems/Poemas,* and *Chicano Poems: for the Barrio,* were all published in 1975. Her later collections include *Selecciones* (1976), *Woman, Woman* (1985), and *Linking Roots* (1993). Her work has been translated into fifteen languages. Among the awards that de Hoyos has received are the 1992 Guadalupe Cultural Arts Center Award for Literature and the 1994 Lifetime Achievement Award from the Texas Commission on the Arts. She has co-edited two collections of Latina literature with Bryce Milligan and Mary Guerrero-Milligan: *Daughters of the Fifth Sun: A Collection of Latina Fiction and Poetry* (1995) and *¡Floricanto Sí! A Collection of Latina Poetry* (1998). De Hoyos is the editor and publisher of M and A Editions and of *Huehuetitlan,* a journal of poetry and Chicano culture.

When Conventional Methods Fail

...bat your eyelashes!

ain't nothing wrong
with using wile

:Eve used an apple
:Cleopatra used a rug   5
:La Malinche?[1] oh she

   used Cortez[2]
   to create
   La Nueva Raza[3]

there's something   10
to be said for a
gal who understands
humanity, and thereby
the secret to success

feminists,   15
take heed:

   no se compliquen
   la vida!![4]

you're going at it
the hard way.

                      —1995

[1] La Malinche, also referred to as Marina or Malintzín Tenepal, was the indigenous translator for Hernán Cortés Pizarro (1485-1547) during his 16th century conquest of Mexico.
[2] Hernán Cortés Pizarro is the conquistador who, in 1519, led the military expedition that initiated the Spanish conquest of Mexico.
[3] (Sp.) The new race.
[4] (Sp.) Don't complicate your life!

JUDY GRAHN (1940-   )

Judy Grahn grew up in a working-class home in New Mexico. Seeking options not available in her small town, she broke away and joined the Air Force, but was later given a "blue discharge" (named for the blue paper on which these letters were printed) because she was a lesbian. This experience galvanized Grahn into public ownership of her lesbianism, the writing of poetry, and the project of publishing lesbian literature. She founded, with artist Wendy Cadden, the Women's Press Collective (WPC) in Oakland, California, in 1969. Using a barrel mimeograph machine, the WPC published the work of lesbians such as Grahn, Pat Parker, and Willyce Kim. Grahn's poetry collections include *Edward the Dyke and Other Poems* (1972), *The Common Woman* (1969), *She Who* (1971-72), *A Woman Is Talking to Death* (1974), *The Queen of Wands* (1982), and *The Queen of Swords* (1987). In addition to poetry, Grahn has written extensively on what it means to be a lesbian and a lesbian writer. In *Another Mother Tongue: Gay Words, Gay Worlds* (1984) she explores queer meanings, while *The Highest Apple: Sappho and the Lesbian Poetic Tradition* (1985) focuses on the ways poetry has served as a vehicle for establishing a lesbian literary tradition. *Really Reading Gertrude Stein* (1989) offers a personal interpretation of Stein intertwined around and among examples of Stein's writing, and *Blood, Bread and Roses: How Menstruation Created the World* (1993) analyzes lesbian self-consciousness. The strength of Grahn's writing comes from her willingness to transcend a narrow lesbian viewpoint in favor of a wider vision of the lives and feelings of "common women." Grahn works at New College of California, where she is the co-director of the M.A. program in Women's Sprituality and Program Director of the M.F.A. program in Creative Inquiry.

The Common Woman

I. Helen, at 9 am, at noon, at 5:15
Her ambition is to be more shiny
and metallic, black and purple as
a thief at midday; trying to make it
in a male form, she's become as
stiff as possible.   5
Wearing trim suits and spike heels,
she says "bust" instead of breast;
somewhere underneath she
misses love and trust, but she feels
that spite and malice are the   10
prices of success. She doesn't realize
yet, that she's missed success, also,
so her smile is sometimes still
genuine. After a while she'll be a real
killer, bitter and more wily, better at   15
pitting the men against each other
and getting the other women fired.
She constantly conspires.
Her grief expresses itself in fits of fury
over details, details take the place of meaning,   20
money takes the place of life.
She believes that people are lice
who eat her, so she bites first; her
thirst increases year by year and by the time
the sheen has disappeared from her black hair,   25
and tension makes her features unmistakably
ugly, she'll go mad. No one in particular
will care. As anyone who's had her for a boss
will know
the common woman is as common   30
as the common crow.

II. <u>Ella, in a square apron, along Highway 80</u>

She's a copperheaded waitress,
tired and sharp-worded, she hides
her bad brown tooth behind a wicked
smile, and flicks her ass   35
out of habit, to fend off the pass
that passes for affection.
She keeps her mind the way men
keep a knife—keen to strip the game
down to her size. She has a thin spine,   40
swallows her eggs cold, and tells lies.
She slaps a wet rag at the truck drivers
if they should complain. She understands
the necessity for pain, turns away
the smaller tips, out of pride, and   45
keeps a flask under the counter. Once,
she shot a lover who misused her child.
Before she got out of jail, the courts had pounced
and given the child away. Like some isolated lake,
her flat blue eyes take care of their own stark   50
bottoms. Her hands are nervous, curled, ready
to scrape.
The common woman is as common
as a rattlesnake.

III. <u>Nadine, resting on her neighbor's stoop</u>

She holds things together, collects bail,   55
makes the landlord patch the largest holes.
At the Sunday social she would spike
every drink, and offer you half of what she knows,
which is plenty. She pokes at the ruins of the city
like an armored tank; but she thinks   60
of herself as a ripsaw cutting through
knots in wood. Her sentences come out
like thick pine shanks
and her big hands fill the air like smoke.
She's a mud-chinked cabin in the slums,   65
sitting on the doorstep counting
rats and raising 15 children,
half of them her own. The neighborhood
would burn itself out without her;
one of these days she'll strike the spark herself.   70
She's made of grease
and metal, with a hard head
that makes the men around her seem frail.
The common woman is as common as
a nail.   75

IV. <u>Carol, in the park, chewing on straws</u>

     She has taken a woman lover
     whatever shall we do
     she has taken a woman lover
     how lucky it wasnt you
And all the day through she smiles and lies   80
and grits her teeth and pretends to be shy,
or weak, or busy. Then she goes home
and pounds her own nails, makes her own
bets, and fixes her own car, with her friend.
She goes as far   85
as women can go without protection
from men.
On weekends, she dreams of becoming a tree;
a tree that dreams it is ground up
and sent to the paper factory, where it   90
lies helpless in sheets, until it dreams
of becoming a paper airplane, and rises
on its own current; where it turns into a
bird, a great coasting bird that dreams of becoming
more free, even, than that—a feather, finally, or   95
a piece of air with lightning in it.
     she has taken a woman lover
     whatever can we say
She walks around all day
quietly, but underneath it   100
she's electric;
angry energy inside a passive form.
The common woman is as common
as a thunderstorm.

V. <u>Detroit Annie, hitchhiking</u>

Her words pour out as if her throat were a broken   105
artery and her mind were cut-glass, carelessly handled.
You imagine her in a huge velvet hat with great
dangling black feathers,
but she shaves her head instead
and goes for three-day midnight walks.   110
Sometimes she goes down to the dock and dances
off the end of it, simply to prove her belief
that people who cannot walk on water
are phonies, or dead.
When she is cruel, she is very, very   115
cool and when she is kind she is lavish.
Fishermen think perhaps she's a fish, but they're all
fools. She figured out that the only way
to keep from being frozen was to
stay in motion, and long ago converted   120
most of her flesh into liquid. Now when she

smells danger, she spills herself all over,
like gasoline, and lights it.
She leaves the taste of salt and iron
under your tongue, but you dont mind.   125
The common woman is as common
as the reddest wine.

VI. <u>Margaret, seen through a picture window</u>

After she finished her first abortion
she stood for hours and watched it spinning in the
toilet, like a pale stool.   130
Some distortion of the rubber
doctors with their simple tubes and
complicated prices,
still makes her feel guilty.
White and yeasty.   135
All her broken bubbles push her down
into a shifting tide, where her own face
floats above her like the whole globe.
She lets her life go off and on
in a slow strobe.   140
At her last job she was fired for making
strikes, and talking out of turn;
now she stays home, a little blue around the edges.
Counting calories and staring at the empty
magazine pages, she hates her shape   145
and calls herself overweight.
Her husband calls her a big baboon.
Lusting for changes, she laughs through her
teeth, and wanders from room to room.
The common woman is as solemn as a monkey   150
or a new moon.

VII. <u>Vera, from my childhood</u>

Solemnly swearing, to swear as an oath to you
who have somehow gotten to be a pale old woman;
swearing, as if an oath could be wrapped around your shoulders
like a new coat: 155
For your 28 dollars a week and the bastard boss
you never let yourself hate;
and the work, all the work you did at home
where you never got paid;
For your mouth that got thinner and thinner   160
until it disappeared as if you had choked on it,
watching the hard liquor break your fine husband down
into a dead joke.
For the strange mole, like a third eye
right in the middle of your forehead;   165
for your religion which insisted that people
are beautiful golden birds and must be preserved;

for your persistent nerve
and plain white talk—
the common woman is as common   170
as good bread
as common as when you couldnt go on
but did.
For all the world we didnt know we held in common
all along   175
the common woman is as common as the best of bread
and will rise
and will become strong—I swear it to you
I swear it to you on my own head
I swear it to you on my common   180
woman's
head

—1971

Helen[1] you always were / the factory

1.

   Spider:

Helen you always were
the factory

Though almost wherever you sat placid,
bent at your creative toil,
someone has built a shed around you   5
with some wheels to oil, some owner
has put you in the shade to weave
or in a great brick box, twelve stories,
twenty, glassed, neonic and with cards
to time your time.   10
Though he has removed you from your homey
cottage industry, and made you
stranger to your own
productions, though he titles you his worker,
and himself your boss, himself "producer"   15

Helen you always were
the factory
Helen you always were producer

Though the loom today be made mechanic,
room-sized, vast, metallic, thundering;   20
though it be electric, electronic,
called a mill—a plant—a complex—
city of industry—

---

[1] In Greek mythology Helen, the daughter of Leda and Zeus, was married to Menalaus of Greece. She was kidnapped by Paris and taken to Troy, which caused the Trojan War.

still it is a loom, simply, still just a frame,
a spindle (your great wand) pistons and rods,   25

heddle bars lifting
so a shuttle can be thrown across the space created
and the new line tapped down into place;
still there is a hot and womblike bucket
somewhere boiling up the stuff of thread   30
in cauldrons, and some expert fingers dancing
whether of aluminum or flesh; still there is
a pattern
actualized, a spirit caught
in some kind of web   35
whether it's called a system
or a network or a double breasted
cordless automatic nylon parachute
still it is a web and
still it comes from you   40
your standing and your wandish
fingers, source, your flash of inspiration,
your support, your faith in it
is still the fateful thread, however it is spun,
of whatever matter made.   45

And still it is the one true cord,
the umbilical line
unwinding into meaning, transformation,
web of thought and caring and connection.

Just as, Helen you dreamed and weaved it   50
eons past, just as your seamy fingers
manufactured so much human culture,
all that encloses, sparks
and clothes the nakedness of flesh and
mind and spirit,   55
Helen, you always were the factory.

2.

   Hannah:

Flames were already eating
at my skirts,
and I heard one of the girls
behind me screaming just how much   60
burning hurts. I could see the
people gathered on the sidewalk.
Eight stories high
I stood on the ledge

of the Triangle building[2]   65
and exclaimed out loud.
Then I took my hat
with its white and yellow flowers
and flung it out, and opening
my purse, I scattered the coins   70
I had earned
to the shocked crowd.
Then, I took Angelina's hand in mine.
I thought we should go down
in style, heads high   75
as we had been during the strike
to end this kind of fire.
I grabbed Ellie's fingers to my right;
her clothes were smoking
like a cigarette, my little sister,   80
so serious, seventeen,
actually gave me a clenched smile
just as we leaped, all three
into the concrete sea.
We fell so far.   85
We're probably falling still.

They say a hundred twenty
thousand workers
marched on our behalf;
they say our eulogy   90
was delivered in a whisper;
they say our bodies
landed under the earth,
so heavy we became,
so weighted as we spun down;   95
they say safety conditions changed
after we were killed.
Because we fell so hard
and caused such pain.
Because we fell so far.   100
We're falling still.

3.

    Spider:

Helen you always were
the one enticed

The one consigned
to leave your pile of clothing   105

---

[2] On March 25, 1911, a fire started on the eighth floor of the Triangle Shirtwaist Factory, a sweatshop in New York City
that employed primarily young immigrant women. Most of the workers on the eighth and tenth floors escaped, but the
workers on the ninth floor were trapped.

by the river while you
bathed your beauty
and were stolen. Always
you are the one thrown over
the shoulder, carried off,   110
forced to enter the car, the plane,
the bed, at swordpoint; lined up,
loaded onto the ships and
shanghaied, tricked
out of your being, shafted,   115
lifted and held hostage,
taken for a ride.
Always you are the one
coerced to sign the bad
contract; ordered to work past sundown;   120
the queen riding the stern
of her once proud ships,
serving two or ten or twenty years
before the mast,
cheated of all pay at last,   125
and thrashed by the birch rod,
the cat-o'-nine tail wand.

Helen you always are
the coals stoked
and taken from the hearth,   130
the precious flama
spilled upon the floor
and blamed and blamed
for the uproar
when the whole house   135
goes up in smoke…

4.

   Nelda:

We were marched to the coast
where the ships waited.
I remember their masts, tossing,
—the pain of loss,   140
of being lost—
like spikes, through our hearts.
On the passage over
we were stacked like logs
below the deck, our fragile   145
and our sick
thrown to the fiery sea.

My whole family died.
My husband, my beloved child;

my village, my past life 150
became a dream.
I barely existed
when I arrived.
For who was "I" to be alive?
Like a lone star 155
through the blue sky
falling netless
to a new world. What
was new about it was our terror.

But we kept our memories. 160
We kept our peoplehood, our past.
And oh good god
we stood. We stood in
water to our knees, to plant the
seeds, we stood in ashy fields 165
and picked the ill-gotten
tobacco and the cotton and
the sugar beets and all the sweet
sweet meats we could never eat.
The sun a dragon. 170

We spread out
a network to Detroit, Chicago,
Newark and LA, all over the land
for the assemblyline work,
getting blistered in the oil-slick 175
city streets, scalded in the kitchens
and the laundries, fired in the
fires of hard times. But we did
much more than just survive; we scarred
and healed and sealed and shared and spieled 180
and blared and smoldered,
joining—however knotty it may be—
our memories
our dreaming and our wand-like hands,
to burn together like a great black 185
brand. A dance of fire.

"Remember dreams, remember Africa,"
we sing, and what we mean
is freedom, wholeness,
that integrity of being 190
that chooses its own time, its
own kings and queens.

5.

Spider:

Helen you always were
the bag of life

You with your carriage,   195
the yoni-weaving basket
with the belly-drag,
the well-used pouch,
the cookie jar indefinitely
filled and emptied.   200

Helen you always were
Santa's fat sack,
full of little worlds
to hang on the great
green tree, so prettily.   205

Helen you always were the belle
of the ball and the ball
of the bell
with the golden heart,
the egg yolk   210
of we human folk.

The singing music box
composing magic children
with their sticky
democratic fingers   215
in your eyes like wands
in water.
The ship's hold stuffed with cargo,
a carving of your image on the bow;
the white sails strung along your arms   220
like everyday laundry.

Helen you always were
the honeycomb
the honey and the honey jar
kept open by the bear's claw   225
and the words, "we need her,"
and sometimes even, in your nightmare,
the harried wasp who hurries
to lay her hungry eggs
before they hatch inside   230
and eat her

Helen you always were
the factory
Helen you always were producer

6.

Nancy:

Do you see the boys lined up   235
to board the ships
to ride the tanks
around the walls?

The flint-faced fathers
with their scanners   240
and their maps,
the saplings on the firing
line, woven in the mat
of war, to be rolled out
on any shore   245
to batter after
every door,
to lie in lifeless lines
across the warehouse floor—
is this the pattern   250
that I labored and I bore,
the blood for blood, the arms
for arms, the heart
torn out
to hurt some more   255

And who am I

if it is me
they say
they do it

for?   260

7.

Spider:

Helen
you always were
the egg laid
by the golden goose,
the full pot, the fat purse,   265
the best bet, the sure horse
the Christmas rush
the bundle he's about to make;
the gold mine, a house of our own
the ship come in, the next stake,   270
the nest egg, the big deal, the steal—
the land of opportunity
the lovely lady being
luck and love and lust
and the last chance   275

for any of us,
the reason that he's living
for, Helen you're always
high card, ace in the hole and
more, the most, the first and best,   280
the sun
burst
goodness   quenching every thirst
the girl of the golden golden golden
West,   285
desire that beats
in every chest

heart of the sky

and some bizarre
dream substance   290
we pave streets with
here in America

8.

   Annie Lee:

Oh hell yes! I stand,
have stood, will stand;
my feet are killing me!   295

This tube of lipstick
is *my* wand,
this pencil and this emery board,
this mascara applicator
brushing black sex magic   300
from a bottle
these long fingernails aflame
with hot red polish, and
these pins, these sharp
spike heels, these chopsticks,   305
this letter opener
this long handled spoon,
this broom, this vacuum
cleaner tube, this spray can
and this mop,   310
all these cleaning tools
for sweeping, for undoing knots,
these spools and needles, all
these plugs and slugs and soldering
irons, these switchboards and   315
earphones and computer boards,
these knitting tools for
putting things together,
these are my wands.

In the parade I'm the one 320
in bangles and short skirt
twirling the rubber-tipped
baton; this is my umbrella,
and my parasol, my fan,
these are my wands 325
and oh hell yes I stand

I am who stands
I am also who sits
who greets   who wipes
who notices, who serves, 330
who takes note
and I am who stoops
who picks and sorts
who cuts and fits
who files and stores 335
who seals and bonds

and I need my wands
and oh hell yes I stand,
have stood, will stand,
in lines, in queues, in rows, 340
in blocks, in crowds, in basic
traffic pattern flows.
I have my wands, my hands,
my ways of understanding
and my family strands. 345

And here in the sunset
is where I like to hear
the singing
of the loom.
The strings of light 350
like fingers and
the fingers like a
web, dancing. It has
all the meaning
we have made of it. 355

9.
    Spider:

And still it is a loom, simply,
still just a frame, a spindle,
heddle bars lifting
so a shuttle can be thrown across
the space created 360
and the new line

tapped down into place;
still there is a hot and womblike bucket
somewhere boiling up the stuff of thread
in cauldrons, and some expert fingers   365
dancing…

Still it is the one true cord,
the umbilical line
unwinding into meaning,
transformation,   370
web of thought and caring and connection.

Just as, Helen you dreamed and weaved it
eons past, just as your seamy fingers
manufactured so much human culture,
all that encloses, sparks   375
and clothes the nakedness of flesh and
mind and spirit,
Helen, you always were the factory.
Helen you always were the factory.
Helen you always were the factory.   380
Helen you always were producer.
Helen you always were
who ever is
the weaving tree
and Mother of the people.

—1982

MAXINE HONG KINGSTON (1940-)

The daughter of Chinese immigrants, Maxine Ting Ting Hong was born in Stockton, California, the third of eight children. A bright young girl whose first language was a dialect of Cantonese, she received multiple scholarships to study at the University of California, Berkeley, earning a B.A. in English and a teaching certificate. Kingston and her husband Earl, an actor, moved to Hawaii in 1967, where they both taught for ten years before returning to the Bay Area, where Kingston began teaching at UC Berkeley. While in Hawaii, Kingston published *The Woman Warrior: Memoirs of a Girlhood Among Ghosts* (1976), the book from which "No Name Woman" is excerpted. An immensely popular, commercial, and critical success— it was rated one of the decade's top ten nonfiction books by *Time* magazine and won the National Book Critics Award for nonfiction—*The Woman Warrior* is considered the first Asian-American "crossover" book of the post-civil rights and second-wave feminist era. However, *The Woman Warrior* also generated controversy within Asian-American cultural critics. Some took issue with the marketing of the book as "nonfiction," charging that many elements of the book are fictionalized, and that the book was marketed as autobiography because of the white public's appetite for stories about the ethnic and exotic "other." Another criticism was Kingston's focus on critiquing Chinese patriarchy and her relative muting of American racism and patriarchy.

Four years after the publication of *The Woman Warrior,* Kingston received another National Book Critics Award for Nonfiction, for *China Men* (1980). The following year, she received a Guggenheim Fellowship. Kingston has since published a collection of essays, *Hawai'i One Summer* (1987); the novel *Tripmaster Monkey: His Fake Book* (1989); a work of non-fiction, *The Fifth Book of Peace* (2003); and a collection of writings by World War II, Vietnam, and Iraq veterans entitled *Veterans of War, Veterans of Peace* (2006). She was awarded a National Humanities Medal in 1997 by then-President Bill Clinton.

No Name Woman

"You must not tell anyone," my mother said, "what I am about to tell you. In China your father had a sister who killed herself. She jumped into the family well. We say that your father has all brothers because it is as if she had never been born.

"In 1924 just a few days after our village celebrated seventeen hurry-up weddings —to make sure that every young man who went 'out on the road' would responsibly come home—your father and his brothers and your grandfather and his brothers and your aunt's new husband sailed for America, the Gold Mountain. It was your grandfather's last trip. Those lucky enough to get contracts waved goodbye from the decks. They fed and guarded the stowaways and helped them off in Cuba, New York, Bali, Hawaii. 'We'll meet in California next year,' they said. All of them sent money home.

"I remember looking at your aunt one day when she and I were dressing; I had not noticed before that she had such a protruding melon of a stomach. But I did not think, 'She's pregnant,' until she began to look like other pregnant women, her shirt pulling and the white tops of her black pants showing. She could not have been pregnant, you see, because her husband had been gone for years. No one said anything. We did not discuss it. In early summer she was ready to have the child, long after the time when it could have been possible.

"The village had also been counting. On the night the baby was to be born the villagers raided our house. Some were crying. Like a great saw, teeth strung with lights, files of people walked zigzag across our land, tearing the rice. Their lanterns doubled in the disturbed black water, which drained away through the broken bunds. As the villagers closed in, we could see that some of them, probably men and women we knew well, wore white masks. The people with long hair hung it over their faces. Women with short hair made it stand up on end. Some had tied white bands around their foreheads, arms, and legs.

"At first they threw mud and rocks at the house. Then they threw eggs and began slaughtering our stock. We could hear the animals scream their deaths—the roosters, the pigs, a last great roar from the ox. Familiar wild heads flared in our night windows; the villagers encircled us. Some of the faces stopped to peer at us, their eyes rushing like searchlights. The hands flattened against the panes, framed heads, and left red prints.

"The villagers broke in the front and the back doors at the same time, even though we had not locked the doors against them. Their knives dripped with the blood of our animals. They smeared blood on the doors and walls. One woman swung a chicken, whose throat she had slit, splattering blood in red arcs about her. We stood together in the middle of our house, in the family hall with the pictures and tables of the ancestors around us, and looked straight ahead.

"At that time the house had only two wings. When the men came back, we would build two more to enclose our courtyard and a third one to begin a second courtyard. The villagers pushed through both wings, even your grandparents' rooms, to find your aunt's, which was also mine until the men returned. From this room a new wing for one of the younger families would grow. They ripped up her clothes and shoes and broke her combs, grinding them underfoot. They tore her work from the loom. They scattered the cooking fire and rolled the new weaving in it. We could hear them in the kitchen breaking our bowls and banging the pots. They overturned the great waist-high earthenware jugs; duck eggs, pickled fruits, vegetables burst out and mixed in acrid torrents. The old woman from the next field swept a broom through the air and loosed the spirits-of-the-broom over our heads. 'Pig.' 'Ghost.' 'Pig,' they sobbed and scolded while they ruined our house.

"When they left, they took sugar and oranges to bless themselves. They cut pieces from the dead animals. Some of them took bowls that were not broken and clothes that were not torn. Afterward we swept up the rice and sewed it back up into sacks. But the smells from the spilled preserves lasted. Your aunt gave birth in the pigsty that night. The next morning when I went for the water, I found her and the baby plugging up the family well.

"Don't let your father know that I told you. He denies her. Now that you have started to menstruate, what happened to her could happen to you. Don't humiliate us. You wouldn't like to be forgotten as if you had never been born. The villagers are watchful."

Whenever she had to warn us about life, my mother told stories that ran like this one, a story to grow up on. She tested our strength to establish realities. Those in the emigrant generations who could not reassert brute survival died young and far from home. Those of us in the first American generations have had to figure out how the invisible world the emigrants built around our childhoods fits in solid America.

The emigrants confused the gods by diverting their curses, misleading them with crooked streets and false names. They must try to confuse their offspring as well, who, I suppose, threaten them in similar ways—always trying to get things straight, always trying to name the unspeakable. The Chinese I know hide their names; sojourners take new names when their lives change and guard their real names with silence.

Chinese-Americans, when you try to understand what things in you are Chinese, how do you separate what is peculiar to childhood, to poverty, insanities, one family, your mother who marked your growing with stories, from what is Chinese? What is Chinese tradition and what is the movies?

If I want to learn what clothes my aunt wore, whether flashy or ordinary, I would have to begin, "Remember Father's drowned-in-the-well sister?" I cannot ask that. My mother has told me once and for all the useful parts. She will add nothing unless powered by Necessity, a riverbank that guides her life. She plants vegetable gardens rather than lawns; she carries the odd-shaped tomatoes home from the fields and eats food left for the gods.

Whenever we did frivolous things, we used up energy; we flew high kites. We children came up off the ground over the melting cones our parents brought home from work and the American movie on New Year's Day—*Oh, You Beautiful Doll* with Betty Grable one year, and *She Wore a Yellow Ribbon* with John Wayne another year. After the one carnival ride each, we paid in guilt; our tired father counted his change on the dark walk home.

Adultery is extravagance. Could people who hatch their own chicks and eat the embryos and the heads for delicacies and boil the feet in vinegar for party food, leaving only the gravel, eating even the gizzard lining—could such people engender a prodigal aunt? To be a woman, to have a daughter in starvation time was a waste enough. My aunt could not have been the lone romantic who gave up everything for sex. Women in the old China did not choose. Some man had commanded her to lie with him and be his secret evil. I wonder whether he masked himself when he joined the raid on her family.

Perhaps she had encountered him in the fields or on the mountain where the daughters-in-law collected fuel. Or perhaps he first noticed her in the marketplace. He was not a stranger because the village housed no strangers. She had to have dealings with him other than sex. Perhaps he worked an adjoining field, or he sold her the cloth for the dress she sewed and wore. His demand must have surprised, then terrified her. She obeyed him; she always did as she was told.

When the family found a young man in the next village to be her husband, she had stood tractably beside the best rooster, his proxy, and promised before they met that she would be his forever. She was lucky that he was her age and she would be the first wife, an advantage secure now. The night she first saw him, he had sex with her. Then he left for America. She had almost forgotten what he looked like. When she tried to envision him, she only saw the black and white face in the group photograph the men had had taken before leaving.

The other man was not, after all, much different from her husband. They both gave orders: she followed. "If you tell your family, I'll beat you. I'll kill you. Be here again next week." No one talked sex, ever. And she might have separated the rapes from the rest of living if only she did not have to buy her oil from him or gather wood in the same forest. I want her fear to have lasted just as long as rape lasted so that the fear could have been contained. No drawn-out fear. But women at sex hazarded birth and hence lifetimes. The fear did not stop but permeated everywhere. She told the man, "I think I'm pregnant." He organized the raid against her.

On nights when my mother and father talked about their life back home, sometimes they mentioned an "outcast table" whose business they still seemed to be settling, their voices tight. In a commensal tradition, where food is precious, the powerful older people made wrongdoers eat alone. Instead of letting them start separate new lives like the Japanese, who could become samurais and geishas, the Chinese family, faces averted but eyes glowering sideways, hung on to the offenders and fed them leftovers. My aunt must have lived in the same house as my parents and eaten at an outcast table. My mother spoke about the raid as if she had seen it, when she and my aunt, a daughter-in-law to a different household, should not have been living together at all. Daughters-in-law lived with their husbands' parents, not their own; a synonym for marriage in Chinese is "taking a daughter-in-law." Her husband's parents could have sold her, mortgaged her, stoned her. But they had sent her back to her own mother and father, a mysterious act hinting at disgraces not told me. Perhaps they had thrown her out to deflect the avengers.

She was the only daughter; her four brothers went with her father, husband, and uncles "out on the road" and for some years became western men. When the goods were divided among the family, three of the brothers took land, and the youngest, my father, chose an education. After my grandparents gave their daughter away to her husband's family, they had dispensed all the adventure and all the property. They expected her alone to keep the traditional ways, which her brothers, now among the barbarians, could fumble without detection. The heavy, deep-rooted women were to maintain the past against the flood, safe for returning. But the rare urge west had fixed upon our family, and so my aunt crossed boundaries not delineated in space.

The work of preservation demands that the feelings playing about in one's guts not be turned into action. Just watch their passing like cherry blossoms. But perhaps my aunt, my forerunner, caught in a slow life, let dreams grow and fade and after some months or years went toward what persisted. Fear at the enormities of the forbidden kept her desires delicate, wire and bone. She looked at a man because she liked the way the hair was tucked behind his ears, or she liked the question-mark line of a long torso curving at the shoulder and straight at the hip. For warm eyes or a soft voice or a slow walk—that's all—a few hairs, a line, a brightness, a sound, a pace, she gave up family. She offered us up for a charm that vanished with tiredness, a pigtail that didn't toss when the wind died. Why, the wrong lighting could erase the dearest thing about him.

It could very well have been, however, that my aunt did not take subtle enjoyment of her friend, but, a wild woman, kept rollicking company. Imagining her free with sex doesn't fit, though. I don't know any women like that, or men either. Unless I see her life branching into mine, she gives me no ancestral help.

To sustain her being in love, she often worked at herself in the mirror, guessing at the colors and shapes that would interest him, changing them frequently in order to hit on the right combination. She wanted him to look back.

On a farm near the sea, a woman who tended her appearance reaped a reputation for eccentricity. All the married women blunt-cut their hair in flaps about their ears or pulled it back in tight buns. No nonsense. Neither style blew easily into heart-catching tangles. And at their weddings they displayed themselves in their long hair for the last time. "It brushed the backs of my knees," my mother tells me. "It was braided, and even so, it brushed the backs of my knees."

At the mirror my aunt combed individuality into her bob. A bun could have been contrived to escape into black streamers blowing in the wind or in quiet wisps about her face, but only the older women in our picture album wear buns. She brushed her hair back from her forehead, tucking the flaps behind her ears. She looped a piece of thread, knotted into a circle between her index fingers and thumbs, and ran the double strand across her forehead. When she closed her fingers as if she were making a pair of shadow geese bite, the string twisted together catching the little hairs. Then she pulled the thread away from her skin, ripping the hairs out neatly, her eyes watering from the needles of pain. Opening her fingers, she cleaned the thread, then rolled it along her hairline and the tops of her eyebrows. My mother did the same to me and my sisters and herself. I used to believe that the expression "caught by the short hairs" meant a captive held with a depilatory string. It especially hurt at the temples, but my mother said we were lucky we didn't have to have our feet bound when we were seven. Sisters used to sit on their beds and cry together, she said, as their mothers or their slaves removed the bandages for a few minutes each night and let the blood gush back into their veins. I hope that the man my aunt loved appreciated a smooth brow, that he wasn't just a tits-and-ass man.

Once my aunt found a freckle on her chin, at a spot that the almanac said predestined her for unhappiness. She dug it out with a hot needle and washed the wound with peroxide.

More attention to her looks than these pullings of hairs and pickings at spots would have caused gossip among the villagers. They owned work clothes and good clothes, and they wore good clothes for feasting the new seasons. But since a woman combing her hair hexes beginnings, my aunt rarely found an occasion to look her best. Women looked like great sea snails—the corded wood, babies, and laundry they carried were the whorls on their backs. The Chinese did not admire a bent back; goddesses and warriors stood straight. Still there must have been a marvelous freeing of beauty when a worker laid down her burden and stretched and arched.

Such commonplace loveliness, however, was not enough for my aunt. She dreamed of a lover for the fifteen days of New Year's, the time for families to exchange visits, money, and food. She plied her secret comb. And sure enough she cursed the year, the family, the village, and herself.

Even as her hair lured her imminent lover, many other men looked at her. Uncles, cousins, nephews, brothers would have looked, too, had they been home between journeys. Perhaps they had already been restraining their curiosity, and they left, fearful that their glances, like a field of nesting birds, might be startled and caught. Poverty hurt, and that was their first reason for leaving. But another, final reason for leaving the crowded house was the never-said.

She may have been unusually beloved, the precious only daughter, spoiled and mirror gazing because of the affection the family lavished on her. When her husband left, they welcomed the chance to take her back from the in-laws; she could live like the little daughter for just a while longer. There are stories that my grandfather was different from other people, "crazy ever since the little Jap bayoneted him in the head." He used to put his naked penis on the dinner table, laughing. And one day he brought home a baby girl, wrapped up inside his brown western-style greatcoat. He had traded one of his sons, probably my father, the youngest, for her. My grandmother made him trade back. When he finally got a daughter of his own, he doted on her. They must have all loved her, except perhaps my father, the only brother who never went back to China, having once been traded for a girl.

Brothers and sisters, newly men and women, had to efface their sexual color and present plain miens. Disturbing hair and eyes, a smile like no other, threatened the ideal of five generations living under one roof. To focus blurs, people shouted face to face and yelled from room to room. The immigrants I know have loud voices, unmodulated to American tones even after years away from the village where they called their friendships out across the fields. I have not been able to stop my mother's screams in public libraries or over telephones. Walking erect (knees straight, toes pointed forward, not pigeon-toed, which is Chinese-feminine) and speaking in an inaudible voice, I have tried to turn myself American-feminine. Chinese communication was loud, public. Only sick people had to whisper. But at the dinner table, where the family members came nearest one another, no one could talk, not the outcasts nor any eaters. Every word that falls from the mouth is a coin lost. Silently they gave and accepted food with both hands. A preoccupied child who took his bowl with one hand got a sideways glare. A complete moment of total attention is due everyone alike. Children and lovers have no singularity here, but my aunt used a secret voice, a separate attentiveness.

She kept the man's name to herself throughout her labor and dying; she did not accuse him that he be punished with her. To save her inseminator's name she gave silent birth.

He may have been somebody in her own household, but intercourse with a man outside the family would have been no less abhorrent. All the village were kinsmen, and the titles shouted in loud country voices never let kinship be forgotten. Any man within visiting distance would have been neutralized as a lover—"brother," "younger brother," "older brother"—one hundred and fifteen relationship titles. Parents researched birth charts probably not so much to assure good fortune as to circumvent incest in a population that has but one hundred surnames. Everybody has eight million relatives. How useless then sexual mannerisms, how dangerous.

As if it came from an atavism deeper than fear, I used to add "brother" silently to boys' names. It hexed the boys, who would or would not ask me to dance, and made them less scary and as familiar and deserving of benevolence as girls.

But, of course, I hexed myself also—no dates. I should have stood up, both arms waving, and shouted out across libraries, "Hey, you! Love me back." I had no idea, though, how to make attraction selective, how to control its direction and magnitude. If I made myself American-pretty so that the five or six Chinese boys in the class fell in love with me, everyone else—the Caucasian, Negro, and Japanese boys—would too. Sisterliness, dignified and honorable, made much more sense.

Attraction eludes control so stubbornly that whole societies designed to organize relationships among people cannot keep order, not even when they bind people to one another from childhood and raise them together. Among the very poor and the wealthy, brothers married their adopted sisters, like doves. Our family allowed some romance, paying adult brides' prices and providing dowries so that their sons and daughters could marry strangers. Marriage promises to turn strangers into friendly relatives—a nation of siblings.

In the village structure, spirits shimmered among the live creatures, balanced and held in equilibrium by time and land. But one human being flaring up into violence could open up a black hole, a maelstrom that pulled in the sky. The frightened villagers, who depended on one another to maintain the real, went to my aunt to show her a personal, physical representation of the break she had made in the "roundness." Misallying couples snapped off the future, which was to be embodied in true offspring. The villagers punished her for acting as if she could have a private life, secret and apart from them.

If my aunt had betrayed the family at a time of large grain yields and peace, when many boys were born, and wings were being built on many houses, perhaps she might have escaped such severe punishment. But the men—hungry, greedy, tired of planting in dry soil—had been forced to leave the village in order to send food-money home. There were ghost plagues, bandit plagues, wars with the Japanese, floods. My Chinese brother and sister had died of an unknown sickness. Adultery, perhaps only a mistake during good times, became a crime when the village needed food.

The round moon cakes and round doorways, the round tables of graduated sizes that fit one roundness inside another, round windows and rice bowls—these talismans had lost their power to warn this family of the law: a family must be whole, faithfully keeping the descent line by having sons to feed the old and the dead, who in turn look after the family. The villagers came to show my aunt and her lover-in-hiding a broken house. The villagers were speeding up the circling of events because she was too shortsighted to see that her infidelity had already harmed the village, that waves of consequences would return unpredictably, sometimes in disguise, as now, to hurt her. This roundness had to be made coin-sized so that she would see its circumference: punish her at the birth of her baby. Awaken her to the inexorable. People who refused fatalism because they could invent small resources insisted on culpability. Deny accidents and wrest fault from the stars.

After the villagers left, their lanterns now scattering in various directions toward home, the family broke their silence and cursed her. "Aiaa, we're going to die. Death is coming. Death is coming. Look what you've done. You've killed us. Ghost! Dead ghost! Ghost! You've never been born." She ran out into the fields, far enough from the house so that she could no longer hear their voices, and pressed herself against the earth, her own land no more. When she felt the birth coming, she thought that she had been hurt. Her body seized together. "They've hurt me too much," she thought. "This is gall, and it will kill me." With forehead and knees against the earth, her body convulsed and then relaxed. She turned on her back, lay on the ground. The black well of sky and stars went out and out and out forever; her body and her complexity seemed to disappear. She was one of the stars, a bright dot in blackness, without home, without a companion, in eternal cold and silence. An agoraphobia rose in her, speeding higher and higher, bigger and bigger; she would not be able to contain it; there would be no end to fear.

Flayed, unprotected against space, she felt pain return, focusing her body. This pain chilled her—a cold, steady kind of surface pain. Inside, spasmodically, the other pain, the pain of the child, heated her. For hours she lay on the ground, alternately body and space. Sometimes a vision of normal comfort obliterated reality: she saw the family in the evening gambling at the dinner table, the young people massaging their elders' backs. She saw them congratulating one another, high joy on the mornings the rice shoots came up. When these pictures burst, the stars drew yet further apart. Black space opened.

She got to her feet to fight better and remembered that old-fashioned women gave birth in their pigsties to fool the jealous, pain-dealing gods, who do not snatch piglets. Before the next spasms could stop her, she ran to the pigsty, each step a rushing out into emptiness. She climbed over the fence and knelt in the dirt. It was good to have a fence enclosing her, a tribal person alone.

Laboring, this woman who had carried her child as a foreign growth that sickened her every day, expelled it at last. She reached down to touch the hot, wet, moving mass, surely smaller than anything human, and could feel that it as human after all—fingers, toes, nails, nose. She pulled it up on to her belly, and it lay curled there, butt in the air, feet precisely tucked one under the other. She opened her loose shirt and buttoned the child inside. After resting, it squirmed and thrashed and she pushed it up to her breast. It turned its head this way and that until it found her nipple. There, it made little snuffling noises. She clenched her teeth at its preciousness, lovely as a young calf, a piglet, a little dog.

She may have gone to the pigsty as a last act of responsibility: she would protect this child as she had protected its father. It would look after her soul, leaving supplies on her grave. But how would this tiny child without family find her grave when there would be no marker for her anywhere, neither in the earth nor the family hall? No one would give her a family hall name. She had taken the child with her into the wastes. At its birth the two of them had felt the same raw pain of separation, a wound that only the family pressing tight could close. A child with no descent line would not soften her life but only trail after her, ghostlike, begging her to give it purpose. At dawn the villagers on their way to the fields would stand around the fence and look.

Full of milk, the little ghost slept. When it awoke, she hardened her breasts against the milk that crying loosens. Toward morning she picked up the baby and walked to the well.

Carrying the baby to the well shows loving. Otherwise abandon it. Turn its face into the mud. Mothers who love their children take them along. It was probably a girl; there is some hope of forgiveness for boys.

"Don't tell anyone you had an aunt. Your father does not want to hear her name. She has never been born." I have believed that sex was unspeakable and words so strong and fathers so frail that "aunt" would do my father mysterious harm. I have thought that my family, having settled among immigrants who had also been their neighbors in the ancestral land, needed to clean their name, and a wrong word would incite the kinspeople even here. But there is more to this silence: they want me to participate in her punishment. And I have.

In the twenty years since I heard this story I have not asked for details nor said my aunt's name; I do not know it. People who can comfort the dead can also chase after them to hurt them further—a reverse ancestor worship. The real punishment was not the raid swiftly inflicted by the villagers, but the family's deliberately forgetting her. Her betrayal so maddened them, they saw to it that she would suffer forever, even after death. Always hungry, always needing, she would have to beg food from other ghosts, snatch and steal it from those whose living descendants give them gifts. She would have to fight the ghosts massed at crossroads for the buns a few thoughtful citizens leave to decoy her away from village and home so that the ancestral spirits could feast unharassed. At peace, they could act like gods, not ghosts, their descent lines providing them with paper suits and dresses, spirit money, paper houses, paper automobiles, chicken, meat, and rice into eternity—essences delivered up in smoke and flames, steam and incense rising from each rice bowl. In an attempt to make the Chinese care for people outside the family, Chairman Mao encourages us now to give our paper replicas to the spirits of outstanding soldiers and workers, no matter whose ancestors they may be. My aunt remains forever hungry. Goods are not distributed evenly among the dead.

My aunt haunts me—her ghost drawn to me because now, after fifty years of neglect, I alone devote pages of paper to her, though not origamied into houses and clothes. I do not think she always means me well. I am telling on her, and she was a spite suicide, drowning herself in the drinking water. The Chinese are always very frightened of the drowned one, whose weeping ghost, wet hair hanging and skin bloated, waits silently by the water to pull down a substitute.

—1975

BHARATI MUKHERJEE (1940-   )

Bharati Mukherjee was born in Calcutta to an upper-middle class Brahmin family. She graduated from Calcutta University in 1959 and attended the University of Iowa Writers'
Workshop, where she received an M.F.A. in 1963. She moved to Canada, where she lived for
almost fifteen years, completing work for a doctorate in English and Comparative Literature
at McGill University in Montreal. In 1980, after publishing her first books, *The Tiger's
Daughter* (1962) and *Wife* (1975), she moved with her family to the United States. Mukherjee
eschews what she considers "hyphenated American" identities and prefers to think of herself
as an "American" writer. Much of her writing enthusiastically embraces America as the site
of a New World where the immigrant subject can make herself over. Although her stories
celebrate the freedom of America, she also shows the violence and brutality that comprise it.
Her writing stresses the mutually transformative dynamic between immigrant and nation. In
1988, Mukherjee was awarded the National Book Critics Circle Award for Fiction for *The
Middleman and Other Stories*. Recent novels include *Jasmine* (1989), *The Holder of the World*
(1993), *Leave it to Me* (1997), and *Desirable Daughters* (2002).

A Wife's Story

Imre says forget it, but I'm going to write David Mamet.[1] So Patels are hard to sell
real estate to. You buy them a beer, whisper Glengarry Glen Ross, and they smell
swamp instead of sun and surf. They work hard, eat cheap, live ten to a room, stash
their savings under futons in Queens, and before you know it they own half of
Hoboken. You say, where's the sweet gullibility that made this nation great?

Polish jokes, Patel jokes: that's not why I want to write Mamet.

Seen their women?

Everybody laughs. Imre laughs. The dozing fat man with the Barnes & Noble sack
between his legs, the woman next to him, the usher, everybody. The theater isn't so
dark that they can't see me. In my red silk sari I'm conspicuous. Plump, gold paisleys
sparkle on my chest.

The actor is just warming up. *Seen their women?* He plays a salesman, he's had a bad
day and now he's in a Chinese restaurant trying to loosen up. His face is pink. His
wool-blend slacks are creased at the crotch. We bought our tickets at half-price, we're
sitting in the front row, but at the edge, and we see things we shouldn't be seeing. At
least I do, or think I do. Spittle, actors goosing each other, little winks, streaks of
makeup.

Maybe they're improvising dialogue too. Maybe Mamet's provided them with
insult kits, Thursdays for Chinese, Wednesdays for Hispanics, today for Indians.
Maybe they get together before curtain time, see an Indian woman settling in the front
row off to the side, and say to each other: "Hey, forget Friday. Let's get *her* today. See
if she cries. See if she walks out." Maybe, like the salesmen they play, they have a
little bet on.

Maybe I shouldn't feel betrayed.

Their women, he goes again. *They look like they've just been fucked by a dead cat.*

The fat man hoots so hard he nudges my elbow off our shared armrest.

"Imre. I'm going home." But Imre's hunched so far forward he doesn't hear.

---

[1] David Mamet (b. 1947), American playwright and filmmaker, author of *Glengarry, Glen Ross* (1984).

English isn't his best language. A refugee from Budapest, he has to listen hard. "I didn't pay eighteen dollars to be insulted."

I don't hate Mamet. It's the tyranny of the American dream that scares me. First, you don't exist. Then you're invisible. Then you're funny. Then you're disgusting. Insult, my American friends will tell me, is a kind of acceptance. No instant dignity here. A play like this, back home, would cause riots. Communal, racist, and antisocial. The actors wouldn't make it off stage. This play, and all these awful feelings, would be safely locked up.

I long, at times, for clear-cut answers. Offer me instant dignity, today, and I'll take it.

"What?" Imre moves toward me without taking his eyes off the actor. "Come again?"

Tears come. I want to stand, scream, make an awful scene. I long for ugly, nasty rage.

The actor is ranting, flinging spittle. *Give me a chance. I'm not finished, I can get back on the board. I tell that asshole, give me a real lead. And what does that asshole give me? Patels. Nothing but Patels.*

This time Imre works an arm around my shoulders. "Panna, what is Patel? Why are you taking it all so personally?"

I shrink from his touch, but I don't walk out. Expensive girls' schools in Lausanne and Bombay have trained me to behave well. My manners are exquisite, my feelings are delicate, my gestures refined, my moods undetectable. They have seen me through riots, uprootings, separation, my son's death.

"I'm not taking it personally."

The fat man looks at us. The woman looks too, and shushes.

I stare back at the two of them. Then I stare, mean and cool, at the man's elbow. Under the bright blue polyester Hawaiian shirt sleeve, the elbow looks soft and runny. "Excuse me," I say. My voice has the effortless meanness of well-bred displaced Third World women, though my rhetoric has been learned elsewhere. "You're exploiting my space."

Startled, the man snatches his arm away from me. He cradles it against his breast. By the time he's ready with comebacks, I've turned my back on him. I've probably ruined the first act for him. I know I've ruined it for Imre.

It's not my fault; it's the *situation*. Old colonies wear down. Patels—the new pioneers—have to be suspicious. Idi Amin's[2] lesson is permanent. AT&T wires move good advice from continent to continent. Keep all assets liquid. Get into 7-11s, get out of condos and motels. I know how both sides feel, that's the trouble. The Patel sniffing out scams, the sad salesmen on the stage: postcolonialism has made me their referee. It's hate I long for; simple, brutish, partisan hate.

After the show Imre and I make our way toward Broadway. Sometimes he holds my hand; it doesn't mean anything more than that crazies and drunks are crouched in doorways. Imre's been here over two years, but he's stayed very old-world, very courtly, openly protective of women. I met him in a seminar on special ed. last semester. His wife is a nurse somewhere in the Hungarian countryside. There are two sons, and miles of petitions for their emigration. My husband manages a mill two hundred

---

[2] Idi Amin (1925-2003), brutal ruler of Uganda in the 1970s.

miles north of Bombay. There are no children.

"You make things tough on yourself," Imre says. He assumed Patel was a Jewish name or maybe Hispanic; everything makes equal sense to him. He found the play tasteless, he worried about the effect of vulgar language on my sensitive ears. "You have to let go a bit." And as though to show me how to let go, he breaks away from me, bounds ahead with his head ducked tight, then dances on amazingly jerky legs. He's a Magyar, he often tells me, and deep down, he's an Asian too. I catch glimpses of it, knife-blade Attila cheekbones, despite the blondish hair. In his faded jeans and leather jacket, he's a rock video star. I watch MTV for hours in the apartment when Charity's working the evening shift at Macy's. I listen to WPLJ on Charity's earphones. Why should I be ashamed? Television in India is so uplifting.

Imre stops as suddenly as he'd started. People walk around us. The summer sidewalk is full of theatergoers in seersucker suits; Imre's year-round jacket is out of place. European. Cops in twos and threes huddle, lightly tap their thighs with night sticks and smile at me with benevolence. I want to wink at them, get us all in trouble, tell them the crazy dancing man is from the Warsaw Pact. I'm too shy to break into dance on Broadway. So I hug Imre instead.

The hug takes him by surprise. He wants me to let go, but he doesn't really expect me to let go. He staggers, though I weigh no more than 104 pounds, and with him, I pitch forward slightly. Then he catches me, and we walk arm in arm to the bus stop. My husband would never dance or hug a woman on Broadway. Nor would my brothers. They aren't stuffy people, but they went to Anglican boarding schools and they have a well-developed sense of what's silly.

"Imre." I squeeze his big, rough hand. "I'm sorry I ruined the evening for you."

"You did nothing of the kind." He sounds tired. "Let's not wait for the bus. Let's splurge and take a cab instead."

Imre always has unexpected funds. The Network, he calls it, Class of '56.

In the back of the cab, without even trying, I feel light, almost free. Memories of Indian destitutes mix with the hordes of New York street people, and they float free, like astronauts, inside my head. I've made it. I'm making something of my life. I've left home, my husband, to get a Ph.D. in special ed. I have a multiple-entry visa and a small scholarship for two years. After that, we'll see. My mother was beaten by her mother-in-law, my grandmother, when she'd registered for French lessons at the Alliance Française. My grandmother, the eldest daughter of a rich zamindar,[3] was illiterate.

Imre and the cabdriver talk away in Russian. I keep my eyes closed. That way I can feel the floaters better. I'll write Mamet tonight. I feel strong, reckless. Maybe I'll write Steven Spielberg[4] too; tell him that Indians don't eat monkey brains.

We've made it. Patels must have made it. Mamet, Spielberg: they're not condescending to us. Maybe they're a little bit afraid.

Charity Chin, my roommate, is sitting on the floor drinking Chablis out of a plastic wineglass. She is five foot six, three inches taller than me, but weighs a kilo and a half less than I do. She is a "hands" model. Orientals are supposed to have a monopoly in the hands-modelling business, she says. She had her eyes fixed eight or

---

[3] (Hindi) Landlord.   [4] Steven Spielberg (b. 1946), American film director.

nine months ago and out of gratitude sleeps with her plastic surgeon every third Wednesday.

"Oh, good," Charity says. "I'm glad you're back early. I need to talk."

She's been writing checks. MCI, Con Ed, Bonwit Teller. Envelopes, already stamped and sealed, form a pyramid between her shapely, knee-socked legs. The checkbook's cover is brown plastic, grained to look like cowhide. Each time Charity flips back the cover, white geese fly over sky-colored checks. She makes good money, but she's extravagant. The difference adds up to this shared, rent-controlled Chelsea one-bedroom.

"All right. Talk."

When I first moved in, she was seeing an analyst. Now she sees a nutritionist.

"Eric called. From Oregon."

"What did he want?"

"He wants me to pay half the rent on his loft for last spring. He asked me to move back, remember? He *begged* me."

Eric is Charity's estranged husband.

"What does your nutritionist say?" Eric now wears a red jumpsuit and tills the soil in Rajneeshpuram.

"You think Phil's a creep too, don't you? What else can he be when creeps are all I attract?"

Phil is a flutist with thinning hair. He's very touchy on the subject of *flautists* versus *flutists*. He's touchy on every subject, from music to books to foods to clothes. He teaches at a small college upstate, and Charity bought a used blue Datsun ("Nissan," Phil insists) last month so she could spend weekends with him. She returns every Sunday night, exhausted and exasperated. Phil and I don't have much to say to each other—he's the only musician I know; the men in my family are lawyers, engineers, or in business—but I like him. Around me, he loosens up. When he visits, he bakes us loaves of pumpernickel bread. He waxes our kitchen floor. Like many men in this country, he seems to me a displaced child, or even a woman, looking for something that passed him by, or for something that he can never have. If he thinks I'm not looking, he sneaks his hands under Charity's sweater, but there isn't too much there. Here, she's a model with high ambitions. In India, she'd be a flat-chested old maid.

I'm shy in front of the lovers. A darkness comes over me when I see them horsing around.

"It isn't the money," Charity says. Oh? I think. "He says he still loves me. Then he turns around and asks me for five hundred."

What's so strange about that, I want to ask. She still loves Eric, and Eric, red jump suit and all, is smart enough to know it. Love is a commodity, hoarded like any other. Mamet knows. But I say, "I'm not the person to ask about love." Charity knows that mine was a traditional Hindu marriage. My parents, with the help of a marriage broker, who was my mother's cousin, picked out a groom. All I had to do was get to know his taste in food.

It'll be a long evening, I'm afraid. Charity likes to confess. I unpleat my silk sari—it no longer looks too showy—wrap it in muslin cloth and put it away in a dresser drawer. Saris are hard to have laundered in Manhattan, though there's a good man in Jackson Heights. My next step will be to brew us a pot of chrysanthemum tea. It's a very special tea from the mainland. Charity's uncle gave it to us. I like him. He's a humpbacked, awkward, terrified man. He runs a gift store on Mott Street, and though he doesn't speak much English, he seems to have done well. Once upon a time he worked for the railways in Chengdu, Szechwan Province, and during the Wuchang Uprising, he was shot at. When I'm down, when I'm lonely for my husband, when I think of our son, or when I need to be held, I think of Charity's uncle. If I hadn't left home, I'd never have heard of the Wuchang Uprising. I've broadened my horizons.

Very late that night my husband calls me from Ahmadabad, a town of textile mills north of Bombay. My husband is a vice president at Lakshmi Cotton Mills. Lakshmi is the goddess of wealth, but LCM (Priv.), Ltd., is doing poorly. Lockouts, strikes, rock-throwings. My husband lives on digitalis, which he calls the food for our *yuga*[5] of discontent.

"We had a bad mishap at the mill today." Then he says nothing for seconds.

The operator comes on. "Do you have the right party, sir? We're trying to reach Mrs. Butt."

"Bhatt," I insist. "*B* for Bombay, *H* for Haryana, *A* for Ahmadabad, double *T* for Tamil Nadu." It's a litany. "This is she."

"One of our lorries was firebombed today. Resulting in three deaths. The driver, old Karamchand, and his two children."

I know how my husband's eyes look this minute, how the eye rims sag and the yellow corneas shine and bulge with pain. He is not an emotional man—the Ahmadabad Institute of Management has trained him to cut losses, to look on the bright side of economic catastrophes—but tonight he's feeling low. I try to remember a driver named Karamchand, but can't. That part of my life is over, the way *trucks* have replaced *lorries* in my vocabulary, the way Charity Chin and her lurid love life have replaced inherited notions of marital duty. Tomorrow he'll come out of it. Soon he'll be eating again. He'll sleep like a baby. He's been trained to believe in turnovers. Every morning he rubs his scalp with cantharidine oil so his hair will grow back again.

"It could be your car next." Affection, love. Who can tell the difference, in a traditional marriage in which a wife still doesn't call her husband by his first name?

"No. They know I'm a flunky, just like them. Well paid, maybe. No need for undue anxiety, please."

Then his voice breaks. He says he needs me, he misses me, he wants me to come to him damp from my evening shower, smelling of sandalwood soap, my braid decorated with jasmines.

"I need you too."

"Not to worry, please," he says. "I am coming in a fortnight's time. I have already made arrangements."

Outside my window, fire trucks whine, up Eighth Avenue. I wonder if he can hear them, what he thinks of a life like mine, led amid disorder.

"I am thinking it'll be like a honeymoon. More or less."

When I was in college, waiting to be married, I imagined honeymoons were only for the more fashionable girls, the girls who came from slightly racy families, smoked Sobranies in the dorm lavatories and put up posters of Kabir Bedi, who was supposed to have made it as a big star in the West. My husband wants us to go to Niagara. I'm not to worry about foreign exchange. He's arranged for extra dollars through the

---

[5] (Sanskrit) Epoch or era.

Gujarati Network, with a cousin in San Jose. And he's bought four hundred more on the black market. "Tell me you need me. Panna, please tell me again."

I change out of the cotton pants and shirt I've been wearing all day and put on a sari to meet my husband at JFK. I don't forget the jewelry; the marriage necklace of *mangalsutra,* gold drop earrings, heavy gold bangles. I don't wear them every day. In this borough of vice and greed, who knows when, or whom, desire will overwhelm.

My husband spots me in the crowd and waves. He has lost weight, and changed his glasses. The arm, uplifted in a cheery wave, is bony, frail, almost opalescent.

In the Carey Coach, we hold hands. He strokes my fingers one by one. "How come you aren't wearing my mother's ring?"

"Because muggers know about Indian women," I say. They know with us it's 24-karat. His mother's ring is showy, in ghastly taste anywhere but India: a blood-red Burma ruby set in a gold frame of floral sprays. My mother-in-law got her guru to bless the ring before I left for the States.

He looks disconcerted. He's used to a different role. He's the knowing, suspicious one in the family. He seems to be sulking, and finally he comes out with it. "You've said nothing about my new glasses." I compliment him on the glasses, how chic and Western-executive they make him look. But I can't help the other things, necessities until he learns the ropes. I handle the money, buy the tickets. I don't know if this makes me unhappy.

+ + +

Charity drives her Nissan upstate, so for two weeks we are to have the apartment to ourselves. This is more privacy than we ever had in India. No parents, no servants, to keep us modest. We play at housekeeping. Imre has lent us a hibachi, and I grill saffron chicken breasts. My husband marvels at the size of the Perdue hens. "They're big like peacocks, no? These Americans, they're really something!" He tries out pizzas, burgers, McNuggets. He chews. He explores. He judges. He loves it all, fears nothing, feels at home in the summer odors, the clutter of Manhattan streets. Since he thinks that the American palate is bland, he carries a bottle of red peppers in his pocket. I wheel a shopping cart down the aisles of the neighborhood Grand Union, and he follows, swiftly, greedily. He picks up hair rinses and high-protein diet powders. There's so much I already take for granted.

One night, Imre stops by. He wants us to go with him to a movie. In his work shirt and red leather tie, he looks arty or strung out. It's only been a week, but I feel as though I am really seeing him for the first time. The yellow hair worn very short at the sides, the wide, narrow lips. He's a good-looking man, but self-conscious, almost arrogant. He's picked the movie we should see. He always tells me what to see, what to read. He buys the *Voice.* He's a natural avant-gardist. For tonight he's chosen *Numéro Deux.*

"Is it a musical?" my husband asks. The Radio City Music Hall is on his list of sights to see. He's read up on the history of the Rockettes. He doesn't catch Imre's sympathetic wink.

Guilt, shame, loyalty. I long to be ungracious, not ingratiate myself with both men. That night my husband calculates in rupees the money we've wasted on Godard.[6]

---

[6] Jean-Luc Godard (b. 1930), French filmmaker.

"That refugee fellow, Nagy, must have a screw loose in his head. I paid very steep price for dollars on the black market."

Some afternoons we go shopping. Back home we hated shopping, but now it is a lovers' project. My husband's shopping list startles me. I feel I am just getting to know him. Maybe, like Imre, freed from the dignities of old-world culture, he too could get drunk and squirt Cheez Whiz on a guest. I watch him dart into stores in his gleaming leather shoes. Jockey shorts on sale in outdoor bins on Broadway entrance him. White tube socks with different bands of color delight him. He looks for microcassettes, for anything small and electronic and smuggleable. He needs a garment bag. He calls it a "wardrobe," and I have to translate.

"All of New York is having sales, no?"

My heart speeds watching him this happy. It's the third week in August, almost the end of summer, and the city smells ripe, it cannot bear more heat, more money, more energy.

"This is so smashing! The prices are so excellent!" Recklessly, my prudent husband signs away traveller's checks. How he intends to smuggle it all back I don't dare ask. With a microwave, he calculates, we could get rid of our cook.

This has to be love, I think. Charity, Eric, Phil: they may be experts on sex. My husband doesn't chase me around the sofa, but he pushes me down on Charity's battered cushions, and the man who has never entered the kitchen of our Ahmadabad house now comes toward me with a dish tub of steamy water to massage away the pavement heat.

Ten days into his vacation my husband checks out brochures for sightseeing tours. Shortline, Grayline, Crossroads: his new vinyl briefcase is full of schedules and pamphlets. While I make pancakes out of a mix, he comparison-shops. Tour number one costs $10.95 and will give us the World Trade Center, Chinatown, and the United Nations. Tour number three would take us both uptown *and* downtown for $14.95, but my husband is absolutely sure he doesn't want to see Harlem. We settle for tour number four: Downtown and the Dame. It's offered by a new tour company with a small, dirty office at Eighth and Forty-eighth.

The sidewalk outside the office is colorful with tourists. My husband sends me in to buy the tickets because he has come to feel Americans don't understand his accent.

The dark man, Lebanese probably, behind the counter comes on too friendly. "Come on, doll, make my day!" He won't say which tour is his. "Number four? Honey, no! Look, you've wrecked me! Say you'll change your mind." He takes two twenties and gives back change. He holds the tickets, forcing me to pull. He leans closer. "I'm off after lunch."

My husband must have been watching me from the sidewalk. "What was the chap saying?" he demands. "I told you not to wear pants. He thinks you are Puerto Rican. He thinks he can treat you with disrespect."

The bus is crowded and we have to sit across the aisle from each other. The tour guide begins his patter on Forty-sixth. He looks like an actor, his hair bleached and blow-dried. Up close he must look middle-aged, but from where I sit his skin is smooth and his cheeks faintly red.

"Welcome to the Big Apple, folks." The guide uses a microphone. "Big Apple. That's what we native Manhattan degenerates call our city. Today we have guests from fifteen foreign countries and six states from this U. S. of A. That makes the Tourist Bureau real happy. And let me assure you that while we may be the richest city in the richest country in the world, it's okay to tip your charming and talented attendant." He laughs. Then he swings his hip out into the aisle and sings a song.

"And it's mighty fancy on old Delancey Street, you know...."

My husband looks irritable. The guide is, as expected, a good singer. "The bloody man should be giving us histories of buildings we are passing, no?" I pat his hand, the mood passes. He cranes his neck. Our window seats have both gone to Japanese. It's the tour of his life. Next to this, the quick business trips to Manchester and Glasgow pale.

"And tell me what street compares to Mott Street, in July...."

The guide wants applause. He manages a derisive laugh from the Americans up front. He's working the aisles now. "I coulda been somebody, right? I coulda been a star!" Two or three of us smile, those of us who recognize the parody. He catches my smile. The sun is on his harsh, bleached hair. "Right, your highness? Look, we gotta maharani[7] with us! Couldn't I have been a star?"

"Right!" I say, my voice coming out a squeal. I've been trained to adapt; what else can I say?

We drive through traffic past landmark office buildings and churches. The guide flips his hands. "Art deco," he keeps saying. I hear him confide to one of the Americans: "Beats me. I went to a cheap guide's school." My husband wants to know more about this Art Deco, but the guide sings another song.

"We made a foolish choice," my husband grumbles. "We are sitting in the bus only. We're not going into famous buildings." He scrutinizes the pamphlets in his jacket pocket. I think, at least it's air-conditioned in here. I could sit here in the cool shadows of the city forever.

Only five of us appear to have opted for the "Downtown and the Dame" tour. The others will ride back uptown past the United Nations after we've been dropped off at the pier for the ferry to the Statue of Liberty.

An elderly European pulls a camera out of his wife's designer tote bag. He takes pictures of the boats in the harbor, the Japanese in kimonos eating popcorn, scavenging pigeons, me. Then, pushing his wife ahead of him, he climbs back on the bus and waves to us. For a second I feel terribly lost. I wish we were on the bus going back to the apartment. I know I'll not be able to describe any of this to Charity, or to Imre. I'm too proud to admit I went on a guided tour.

The view of the city from the Circle Line ferry is seductive, unreal. The skyline wavers out of reach, but never quite vanishes. The summer sun pushes through fluffy clouds and dapples the glass of office towers. My husband looks thrilled, even more than he had on the shopping trips down Broadway. Tourists and dreamers, we have spent our life's savings to see this skyline, this statue.

"Quick, take a picture of me!" my husband yells as he moves toward a gap of railings. A Japanese matron has given up her position in order to change film. "Before the Twin Towers disappear!"

I focus, I wait for a large Oriental family to walk out of my range. My husband holds his pose tight against the railing. He wants to look relaxed, an international

---

[7] (Sanskrit) Queen.

businessman at home in all the financial markets.

A bearded man slides across the bench toward me. "Like this," he says and helps me get my husband in focus. "You want me to take the photo for you?" His name, he says, is Goran. He is Goran from Yugoslavia, as though that were enough for tracking him down. Imre from Hungary. Panna from India. He pulls the old Leica out of my hand, signaling the Orientals to beat it, and clicks away. "I'm a photographer," he says. He could have been a camera thief. That's what my husband would have assumed. Somehow, I trusted. "Get you a beer?" he asks.

"I don't. Drink, I mean. Thank you very much." I say those last words very loud, for everyone's benefit. The odd bottles of Soave with Imre don't count.

"Too bad." Goran gives back the camera.

"Take one more!" my husband shouts from the railing. "Just to be sure!"

The island itself disappoints. The Lady has brutal scaffolding holding her in. The museum is closed. The snack bar is dirty and expensive. My husband reads out the prices to me. He orders two french fries and two Cokes. We sit at picnic tables and wait for the ferry to take us back.

"What was that hippie chap saying?"

As if I could say. A daycare center has brought its kids, at least forty of them, to the island for the day. The kids, all wearing name tags, run around us. I can't help noticing how many are Indian. Even a Patel, probably a Bhatt if I looked hard enough. They toss hamburger bits at pigeons. They kick styrofoam cups. The pigeons are slow, greedy, persistent. I have to shoo one off the table top. I don't think my husband thinks about our son.

"What hippie?"

"The one on the boat. With the beard and the hair."

My husband doesn't look at me. He shakes out his paper napkin and tries to protect his french fries from pigeon feathers.

"Oh, him. He said he was from Dubrovnik." It isn't true, but I don't want trouble.

"What did he say about Dubrovnik?"

I know enough about Dubrovnik to get by. Imre's told me about it. And about Mostar and Zagreb. In Mostar white Muslims sing the call to prayer. I would like to see that before I die: white Muslims. Whole peoples have moved before me; they've adapted. The night Imre told me about Mostar was also the night I saw my first snow in Manhattan. We'd walked down to Chelsea from Columbia. We'd walked and talked and I hadn't felt tired at all.

"You're too innocent," my husband says. He reaches for my hand. "Panna," he cries with pain in his voice, and I am brought back from perfect, floating memories of snow, "I've come to take you back." I have seen how men watch you."

"What?"

"Come back, now. I have tickets. We have all the things we will ever need. I can't live without you."

A little girl with wiry braids kicks a bottle cap at his shoes. The pigeons wheel and scuttle around us. My husband covers his fries with spread-out fingers. "No kicking," he tells the girl. Her name, Beulah, is printed in green ink on a heart-shaped name tag. He forces a smile, and Beulah smiles back. Then she starts to flap her arms. She flaps, she hops. The pigeons go crazy for fries and scraps.

"Special ed. course is two years," I remind him. "I can't go back."

My husband picks up our trays and throws them into the garbage before I can stop him. He's carried disposability a little too far. "We've been taken," he says, moving toward the dock, though the ferry will not arrive for another twenty minutes. "The ferry costs only two dollars round-trip per person. We should have chosen tour number one for $10.95 instead of tour number four for $14.95."

With my Lebanese friend, I think. "But this way we don't have to worry about cabs. The bus will pick us up at the pier and take us back to midtown. Then we can walk home."

"New York is full of cheats and whatnot. Just like Bombay." He is not accusing me of infidelity. I feel dread all the same.

That night, after we've gone to bed, the phone rings. My husband listens, then hands the phone to me. "What is this woman saying?" He turns on the pink Macy's lamp by the bed. "I am not understanding these Negro people's accents."

The operator repeats the message. It's a cable from one of the directors of Lakshmi Cotton Mills. "Massive violent labor confrontation anticipated. Stop. Return posthaste. Stop. Cable flight details. Signed Kantilal Shah."

"It's not your factory," I say. "You're supposed to be on vacation."

"So, you are worrying about me? Yes? You reject my heartfelt wishes but you worry about me?" He pulls me close, slips the straps of my nightdress off my shoulder. "Wait a minute."

I wait, unclothed, for my husband to come back to me. The water is running in the bathroom. In the ten days he has been here he has learned American rites: deodorants, fragrances. Tomorrow morning he'll call Air India; tomorrow evening he'll be on his way back to Bombay. Tonight I should make up to him for my years away, the gutted trucks, the degree I'll never use in India. I want to pretend with him that nothing has changed.

In the mirror that hangs on the bathroom door, I watch my naked body turn, the breasts, the thighs glow. The body's beauty amazes. I stand here shameless, in ways he has never seen me. I am free, afloat, watching somebody else.

—1986

INA CUMPIANO (1941-)

Puerto Rican poet, translator, and children's book author Ina Cumpiano holds master's degrees from The Johns Hopkins University, the University of Northern Colorado, and the Iowa Writers' Workshop, as well as a Ph.D. from the University of California, Santa Cruz. Cumpiano's poetry has appeared in several magazines and journals, including the *Iowa Review*, *Black Warrior Review*, *Seneca Review*, *Five Fingers Review*, and *Americas Review*. She is the recipient of the Jaime Suárez/Editores Salvadoreños Poetry Award and the New Millennium Writings Award, and is currently the Editorial Director of Children's Book Press in San Francisco, California.

Yo, La Malinche

1
Native Tongue

*Tecle,[1] these seven women are for your captains, and this one, who is my niece, is for
you, and she is the señora of towns and vassals.*
—A "fat cacique"[2] to Cortés, as reported by Bernal Díaz del Castillo

I had no one name.
I was Malinalli, Malintzín, Doña Marina de Jaramillo.[3]
Lady of Olutlán, Jilotepec, and Tequipaje.[4]
From Coatzacoalco,[5] my father sold me
as if I were daily cloth,   5
as if I were a clay bowl,
less than the grain of corn that is kept
for the next season, but after
I became
Malinche, *la lengua,*[6]   10
Malinche, the *Tecle*'s voice
Malinche, the tongued serpent pointing to the dismembered
bodies at the battle of Cholula,[7]
Malinche, the traitor,
Malinche, *la chingada,*[8]   15
woman of the *lope luzio,*[9] Cortés' whore,
Malinche, Malinche.

My name for myself is wing.
My name for myself is loud silence.
My name for myself is spring-fed brook.   20
My name for myself is unknowing.
My name is My Name.

Who will speak up for Malinche?
Who will say she spoke as women speak,
in another's language   25
so that even when the eagle Cuauhtémoc[10]
was caged that one last time
she had no words of her own that could warn him.

---

[1] Although the term "tecle" first appears in Bernal del Castillo's *Historia verdadera* and is attributed to a Totonac-speaking Indian, the word is believed to be of Nahuatl origin. It is an honorific with religious connotations, such as that one might use to address a priest.
[2] A *cacique* is a Nahuatl term designating the recognized authority of a town or village.
[3] Malinalli, Malintzín, and Doña Marina de Jaramillo are all alternate names for Malinche, the indigenous translator for Hernán Cortés Pizarro (1485-1547) during his 16th century conquest of Mexico.
[4] Small towns in central and coastal Mexico.
[5] The region of Coatzacoalco is located on the Yucatán peninsula.
[6] (Sp.) Literally "the tongue," but is also another word

for "language."
[7] The battle of Cholula took place in 1519 and was a historic massacre in the conquest of New Spain. Malinche is believed to have warned Cortés of a plot by the Cholulans to ambush and kill the Spanish contingent housed in the holy city. Cortés instead attacked the Cholulans, aided by a contingent of Tlaxclalan allies. Over 3,000 Cholulans, by Cortés' account, were killed, and the city was sacked and razed.
[8] (Sp.) The fucked one.
[9] (Totanac) Prince, great lord.
[10] Cuauhtémoc, the last Aztec emperor, was captured in 1521 after the fall of Tenochtitlán, the Aztec capital. He was executed by Cortés in 1525 in what is today Honduras.

How could she have saved him?
How would you have saved him?
Would you have saved him?
How can we save ourselves?

2
Translating Woman

Everything I say is in a foreign language.
When I say *woman,* whose word is that
if not his?
And even the long howl in the darkness—*¡Ayyy!*—
is a code he has taught me.
Nothing, not *joy,* not *rain,* is my own.

I will make a language from stones.
One stone lifted from wet earth will mean *everything.*
The mark the stone leaves will mean *night.*

3
November 8, 1519[11]

In writing, they say we told the story otherwise:

Moctezuma, knowing the Spanish Army was close at hand, came out to meet it, his Meshico kings and great *señores,* our land's glory, with him. Such a triumph, a luxury of roses. Blanketed in fine cloth, each on a litter shouldered by four lords (Cacama,[12] that little ear of corn, was but one among them), they arrived at Tenochtitlan—the place of wild cactus—and there at the temple of Toco, who is our grandmother, they waited for Cortés.

Moctezuma Xocoyotzin, el Tlatoani, stepped down to meet the Spaniard when he arrived. The four lords covered him with a mantle and with a green feather train embroidered in pearls and the green chalchihuitl stones due such a man. Cortés stepped down from his tall horse and, not knowing any better, tried to embrace the Tlatoani but the four lords stopped him so the best Cortés could do was to hang from Moctezuma's neck a daisy chain made of green stones. Moctezuma awarded *two* necklaces: each adorned with red seashells and eight gold shrimp hanging, long as a hand span.

Later the two spoke in my lord's chambers.

✦ ✦ ✦

I, Miahuaxóchitl, called Corn Blossom, called Tecuihepoch,[13] was there. I was nine. When my father the Tlatoani learned that Cortés approached, making his way with his men along the narrow causeway of Iztapalpa—"the ambassador of a great lord whose vast dominions

---

[11] Motecuhzoma Xocoyotzín (ca. 1466-1520), also known as Moctezuma II, was the Aztec ruler *(huey tlatoani)* of Tenochtitlán (now Mexico City) at the time of the Spanish conquest. According to Bernal Díaz del Castillo, on November 8, 1519, Moctezuma met Cortés outside the city and the leaders exchanged gifts.
[12] Cacama, ruler of Texcoco, was a nephew and ally of Moctezuma II.
[13] According to the author, one of Moctezuma II's daughters; the name Tecuihepoch means "high born."

lay beyond the waters of the sea"—he gathered us, my father gathered us at his gold throne, my mother, his other wives, his other children, his warriors and priests and wise men to meet the Spaniards there.   65

Their captain spoke not. Only the woman, although she looked like us, although our own black eyes looked back at us from her wide face, she spoke.
      —Truly, is it you? Are you truly Moctezuma?
My father's voice was the honey gathered before the clouds arose,   70
before the thunder sundered the trunk of the tree in two.
      —I am he. (Gracious he. Serene he. Our king he.)
And still the captain held his tongue. My mother pulled me to her; I could not see her eyes. The smell of her body changed; it heated the air around her, as lilies do, and marked it, like a warning. Again the   75
woman spoke.
      —Tell the lord Moctezuma not to worry...(My mother pulled
        me closer.), that I love him dearly, that I mean him no harm.
His words, her mouth. Her voice was a gold chain and the Tlatoani was manacled, and his ankles were and his hands, and he was nailed to the   80
spot. Gracious he. Serene he. Our king he. My father.

4
Martín's Birth
Soon, the war party Malinalli followed
would return to the great city;
soon she would seem, almost, to recover her tongue   85
but now, in her time,
Malinalli hid herself in the undergrowth.
Dappled by the fickle light, she was as silent as a doe—
only the sound of small twigs settling and breaking
under her weight.   90
No ancient *ticitl*[14] would midwife this birth;
no neighbor wife would croon—
The child will be a bird called quecholli;
the child will be a bird called zacuán—
over and over, a naming like a prayer.   95
This time no reeds softened in the river for a basket.
no feathers were gathered to line it.
The first painhad been a garter snake that slithered, quick and sharp;
now claws ripped at her belly.
The child will be a bird called quecholli;   100
the child will be a bird called zacuán,
the child, the child.

Soon she would wash the child's bloody white skin in the river.
Soon she would wrap him in the folds of her huipilli.
Soon the soldiers would come to take him to his father.   105
Soon Cortéz would name this cry of hers *Martín*.

---

[14] (Nahuatl) Doctor or healer.

5
My Dream of Ciuacoatl [15]

*According to Sahagún,[16] the Aztec goddess appeared at night,
wailing for her lost children.*

The woman lifts a rock high over her head
and describes
swiftly
the arc of the moon, the egg's curve,   110
as she brings the rock down to shatter
her children's skulls
as if the skulls were eggs, as if the light they gave off
were as insignificant
as the *luciernaga's*[17] pitiful, intermittent glimmer in a glass jar,   115
as if their skulls were as translucent as jars,
as if the jars were in shards already at her feet,
as if she walked through the shards,
as if she had shattered the children's skulls
in order,   120
in order to save them, in order to save herself,
in order to return the children to the dark of her body
or to save her children from the dark of her body,
or in order to free herself from her body,
or in order to free them,
in order to say I never had them,   125
in order to keep them safe,
away from her saying I never had them,
and then
having taken pebbles from the round hollow of her mouth,
and placed them in her shoe, to feel them as she walks,   130
she wanders, she still
keeps to the river bank where the first rock lay
smoothed by the white tongue of water—
her name is what she does:
La llorona.[18]   135

6
Bacalán [19]

When Bacalán said this is my body,
I will do with my body
what I choose,
there was only that one choice…
And when the *adelantado's*[20] soldiers found   140

---

[15] Aztec earth goddess.
[16] Bernardino de Sahagún was a Spanish missionary to
New Spain and an Aztec archeologist who published
twelve manuscripts on Aztec history, art, and language.
[17] (Sp.) Firefly.
[18] La llorona is a figure from Mexican and Chicana/o folklore. The ghost of a mother who has lost her children
and who has drowned herself in the river, la llorona
presumably haunts the night, taking children in lieu

of her own.
[19] Diego de Landa (1524-1579), Bishop of Yucatán, wrote
an account of the Maya, *Relación de las cosas Yucatán* (ca.
1566). In it, he recounts the story of a young Indian
woman from Bacalán who, rather than "having relations" with her Spanish captors, killed herself, after
which her body was thrown to the dogs.
[20] A kind of military governor installed by the Spanish conquerors.

the body
where the stubborn woman left it
(the bitter root still clutched in her hand
as if she had treasured this little bit of stuff
more than   145
life and so her fingers had hung on to it)
they threw the body to the dogs like so much meat—
so that Bacalán's flesh would not speak
for itself any longer.

I am not as brave as you, Bacalán.   150
Daily I give myself away, Bacalán.
Piece by piece, they take me, Bacalán, so that
never again will I be whole
like you, Bacalán.

Bacalán,   155
when de Landa tells your story
in *Relación de las cosas de Yucatán*
he gets it wrong, I think.
He says *She had promised her husband…*
not to have relations with any man other than him   160
and so no persuasion was sufficient…

Was it fidelity, I wonder,
or did you see the chance for once
to call your body back
as a *palomera*[21] might welcome her pigeons   165
to their cote and settle them in
after their too-long flight over the battlefield.

7
Year of the Lord 1541[22]
When, during the battle of Jalisco, a frightened horse
rolled over Pedro de Alvarado—perhaps the same sorrel
he took by force before Tenotchitlán—his men asked   170
what hurt the most.
"Me duele el alma,"[23]
he said, and the words dripped from his mouth
like old blood. As well they should,
after the life he'd led. Back home in Almolonga,   175
a cloudburst,
and his wife, Beatriz,[24] *la sin ventura,*[25] painted

[21] (Sp.) A woman who cares for pigeons.
[22] Pedro de Alvarado (1485-1541), a conquistador and trusted confidant of Cortés who aided in the subjugation of the Aztecs in Tenochtitlán. The woman referred to here as Tecuilhuiatzín was his mistress, one of three hundred women given to Cortés at Tlaxcala. Alvarado went on to lead expeditions against the Mixtecs and Zapotecs, and eventually was installed as governor of Guatemala. He arrived in Jalisco in 1541 to help put down a revolt

by the Zacatecans and died from injuries he received when a horse fell on him as the Spanish were retreating in disarray.
[23] (Sp.) My soul aches.
[24] Beatriz de la Cueva (of the cave), the wife of Pedro de Alvarado, became governor after the death of her husband. She died in 1541 when the volcano the Spanish named "De Agua" (of water) erupted in Guatemala City.
[25] (Sp.) She who had not ventured.

their mansion as black
as the cave that named her,
as that soul, though she said it was sorrow.   180
The heavens knew and the city shook
and from the volcano Hanapu,
named after the twin of anger,
the one the Spaniards, who knew little,
called Water   185
and not Fire, lava rained after the flood,
and mud. And when her body was found,
the hand still clenched a rosary,
a bunch of beads, nothing
in the same crushed, ruined chapel   190
where the *restos*[26] of his other woman lay:
María Luisa, called by her people
Tecuilhuiatzin,
fire that sings. Tecuilhuiatzin, yet another woman
given by her father to Cortés   195
who gave her to the other Spanish lord, she too, she served
and served.
Tecuilhuiatzin, who blazed and then wept stone.
Doomed city, Tecuilhuiatzin.

8
Detroit, 1931-2:
Wife of the Master Mural Painter Dabbles in Art[27]

Not here-not there, she considers   200
the vagaries
of language: that while

frontera is the scar line,
frontier speaks to a whole new life, a whole
new life. On this side,   205

living at the Wardell,
the best home address in Detroit,
while Diego wows them at the Institute,

drives a Ford, dreams "of the new race
of the age of steel," she plays   210
cadavre exquis,[28] miscarries, her mother dies:

this too a border
she must straddle. With no *coyote*[29] to guide her,
no hermaphroditic spirit

---

[26] (Sp.) Remains.
[27] Mexican muralist Diego Rivera (1886-1957) painted a series of twenty-seven murals depicting industry and art for the Detroit Institute of Arts. He was accompanied by his wife and fellow artist, Frida Kahlo (1907-1954).

[28] (Fr.) Exquisite corpse. A Surrealist game Kahlo was known to enjoy, in which images or words are assembled collectively.
[29] A person who aids in an illegal border crossing, especially between the U.S. and Mexico.

to show her how, she must form words in this ugly language,   215
change her name, make her way. But what about "before,"
the left side of that other margin? She paints

a mound of rocks, a death head, a temple like the one at Monte Royal,
male, huge and square, with steps leading
to thunder, above;   220

and under ground: roots and cable cords to jump start
this old and new transition. Going south again,
home from Gringolandia, that Gaul divided,

she'll still need a passport,
a street map, coins in her pockets for change.   225
She'll need a wider brush, a large valise, her bivalve heart.

—1994-2007

DIANE GLANCY (1941-   )

Helen Diane Hall was born in Kansas City, Missouri, the daughter of a Cherokee father and a German and English mother. She received her B.A. in English from the University of Missouri in 1964, the same year that she married Dwayne Glancy (whom she divorced in 1983). She spent a number of years working for the state arts council in Oklahoma, actively promoting education to Native American students throughout the state. She published her first volume of poetry, *Traveling On,* in 1982. The following year she received her M.A. in Creative Writing from Central State University in Edmond, Oklahoma, and later went on to earn an M.F.A. in Scripting from the University of Iowa. Glancy is notable for fusing genres and styles in a way that reflects the hybridity of her own social and cultural location. Her work includes the poetry collections *Brown Wolf Leaves the Res and Other Poems* (1984), *Offering: Aliscolidodi* (1988), *Iron Woman* (1990), and *Primer of the Obsolete* (1998); the short fiction collections *Trigger Dance* (1990), *Firesticks* (1993), *Monkey Secret* (1995), and *The Voice That Was in Travel: Stories* (1999); the essay collection *Claiming Breath* (1992); the play *War Cries* (1994); and the novels *Pushing the Bear: A Novel of the Trail of Tears* (1996), *Fuller Man* (1999), and *Stone Heart: A Novel of Sacajawea* (2003). In addition to being named laureate for the Five Civilized Tribes (1984-1986), Glancy has received numerous awards and honors for her work, including the Pegasus Award for *Brown Wolf Leaves the Res,* a Before Columbus Foundation American Book Award for *Claiming Breath,* an Oklahoma Theater Festival Award for *Segwohi,* and the Juniper Prize for *Primer of the Obsolete.*

The Woman Who Was a Red Deer Dressed for the Deer Dance

In this I try. Well, I try. To combine the overlapping realities of myth, imagination and memory with spaces for the silences. To make a story. The voice speaking in different agencies. Well, I try to move on with the voice in its guises. A young woman and her grandmother in a series of scenelets. Divided by a line of flooring. Shifting between dialogue and monologue. Not with the linear construct of conflict/resolution, but with the story moving like rain on a windshield, between differing and unreliable experiences.

✦ ✦ ✦

GIRL: Have you heard of *Ahw'uste?*

GRANDMOTHER: I have, but I've forgotten.

GIRL: They said they fed her.

GRANDMOTHER: Yes, they did.

GIRL: What was she?

GRANDMOTHER: I don't know.

GIRL: A deer?

GRANDMOTHER: Yes, a deer. A small deer.

GIRL: She lived in the house, didn't she?

GRANDMOTHER: Yes, she did. She was small.

GIRL: They used to talk about her a long time ago, didn't they?

GRANDMOTHER: Yes, they did.

GIRL: Did you ever see one of the deer?

GRANDMOTHER: I saw the head of one once. Through the window. Her head was small, and she had tiny horns.

GIRL: Like a goat?

GRANDMOTHER: Yes, like that.

GIRL: Where did you see her?

GRANDMOTHER: I don't know. Someone had her. I just saw her. That's all.

GIRL: You saw the head?

GRANDMOTHER: Yes, just the head.

GIRL: What did they call her?

GRANDMOTHER: A small deer.

GIRL: Where did you see her?

GRANDMOTHER: What do they call it down there?

GIRL: Deer Creek.

GRANDMOTHER: Yes, that's where I saw her.

GIRL: What did they use her for?

GRANDMOTHER: I don't know. There were bears there, too. And larger deer.

GIRL: Elk maybe?

GRANDMOTHER: Yes, they called them elk.

GIRL: Why did they have them?

GRANDMOTHER: They used them for medicine.

GIRL: How did they use them?

GRANDMOTHER: They used their songs.

GIRL: The deer sang?

GRANDMOTHER: No, they were just there. They made the songs happen.

GIRL: The elk, too?

GRANDMOTHER: Yes, the elk, too.

GIRL: And the moose?

GRANDMOTHER: Yes, the moose.

✦ ✦ ✦

GIRL: It was like talking to myself when I stayed with her. If I asked her something, she answered flat as the table between us.

Open your deer mouth and talk. You never say anything on your own. I could wear a deer dress. I could change into a deer like you. We could deer dance in the woods under the red birds. The blue jay. The finch.

U-da-tlv:da de-s-gi-ne-hv'-si, E-li'-sin

Pass me the cream, Grandmother.

My cup and saucer on the oilcloth.

How can you be a deer? You only have two legs.

GRANDMOTHER: I keep the others under my dress.

+ + +

GIRL: It was a wordless world she gave me. Not silent, but wordless. Oh, she spoke, but her words seemed hollow. I had to listen to her deer noise. I had to think what she meant. It was like having a conversation with myself. I asked. And I answered. Well—I could hear what I wanted.

When I was with her, I talked and never stopped because her silence ate me like buttered toast.

What was she saying? Her words were in my own hearing?

I had to know what she said before I could hear it?

+ + +

GRANDMOTHER: I don't like this world anymore. We're reduced to what can be seen and felt. We're brought from the universe of the head into the kitchen full of heat and cold.

GIRL: She fought to live where we aren't tied to table and fork and knife and chair.

It was her struggle against what happens to us.

Why can't you let me in just once and speak to me as one of your own? You know I have to go into the *seeable*—live away from the world of imagination. You could give me more.

+ + +

GIRL: You work the church soup kitchen before? You slop up the place, and I get to clean up. You night shifts think you're tough shit. But I tell you, you don't know nothing. I think you took my jean jacket. The one with Jesus on the cross in sequins on the back. Look—I see your girl wearing it, I'll have you on the floor.

Don't think I don't know who's taking the commodities—I'm watching those boxes of macaroni and cheese disappear.

I know it was you who lost the key to the storeroom, and I had to pay for the locksmith to change the lock. They kept nearly my whole check. I couldn't pay rent. I only got four payments left on my truck. I'm not losing it.

+ + +

GIRL: She said once, there were wings the deer had when it flew. You couldn't see them, but they were there. They pulled out from the red deer dress. Like leaves opened from the kitchen table—

Like the stories that rode on her silence. You knew they were there. But you had to decide what they meant. Maybe that's what she gave me—the ability to fly when I knew I had no wings. When I was left out of the old world that moved in her head. When I had to go on without her stories.

They get crushed in this *seeable* world.

But they're still there. I hear them in the silence sometimes.

I want to wear a deer dress. I want to deer dance with *Ahw'uste*....

✦ ✦ ✦

GIRL: "What does *Ahw'uste* mean in English?

GRANDMOTHER: I don't know what the English was. But *Ahw'uste* was a spirit animal.

GIRL: What does that mean?

GRANDMOTHER: She was only there for some people to see.

GIRL: She was only there when you thought she was?

GRANDMOTHER: She had wings, too. If you thought she did. She was there to remind us—you think you see something you're not sure of. But you think it's there anyway.

GIRL: Maybe Jesus used wings when he flew to heaven. Ascended right up the air. Into holy Heaven. Floating and unreachable. I heard them stories at church when I worked the soup kitchen.

Or maybe they're wings like the spirits use when they fly between the earth and sky. But when you pick up a spirit on the road, you can't see his wings—he's got them folded into his jacket.

GRANDMOTHER: They say rocket ships go there now.

GIRL: The ancestors?

GRANDMOTHER: Yes, all of them wear red deer dresses.

GIRL: With two legs under their dresses?

GRANDMOTHER: In the afterworld they let them down.

GIRL: A four-legged deer with wings—wearing a red deer dress with shoes and hat? Dancing in the leaves—red maple, I suppose. After they're raked up to the sky? Where they stay red forever only if they think they do?

Sometimes your hooves are impatient inside your shoes. I see them move. You stuff twigs in your shoes to make them fit your hooves. But I know hooves are there.

Why would I want to be a deer like you?

Why would I want to eat without my hands?

Why would I want four feet?

What would I do with a tail? It would make a lump behind my jeans.

Do you know what would happen if I walked down the street in a deer dress? If I looked for a job?

I already know I don't fit anywhere—I don't need to be reminded—I'm at your house, Grandma, with my sleeping bag and old truck—I don't have any place else to go....

✦ ✦ ✦

GIRL [*Angrily*]: OK, dude. Dudo. I pick you up on the road. I take you to the next town to get gas for your van, take you back when it still won't start. I pull you to town 'cause you don't have money for a tow truck. I wait two hours while you wait. Buy you supper. I give you love, what do you want? Hey, dude, your cowboy boots are squeaking, your hat with the beaded band. Your CB's talking to the highway, the truckers, the girls driving by themselves, that's what you look for. You take what we got. While you got one eye on your supper, one eye on your next girl.

I could have thought you were a spirit. You could have been something more than a dude....

+ + +

GRANDMOTHER: The leaves only get to be red for a moment. Just a moment, and then the tree grieves all winter until the leaves come back. But they're green through the summer. The maple waits for the leaves to turn red. All it takes is a few cold mornings. A few days left out of the warmth.

Then the maple tree has red leaves for a short while.

+ + +

GIRL [*Angrily*]: I can't do it your way, Grandma. I have to find my own trail—is that why you won't tell me? Is that why you won't speak? I'm caught? I have no way through? But there'll be a way through—I just can't see it yet. And if I can't find it, it's still there. I speak it through. Therefore, it is. If not now, then later. It's coming—if not for me—then for others.

I have to pass through this world not having a place, but I'll go anyway.

GRANDMOTHER: That's *Ahw'uste*.

GIRL: I'll speak these stories I don't know. I'll speak because I don't know them.

GRANDMOTHER: We're like the tree waiting for the red leaves. We count on what's not there as though it is, because the maple has red leaves—only you can't always see them.

GIRL: You'd rather live with what you can't see—is that the point of your red-leaf story?

GRANDMOTHER: I was trying to help you over the hard places.

GIRL: I can get over them myself.

GRANDMOTHER: I wanted you to look for the red leaves instead of the dudes on the highway.

GIRL: A vision is *not* always enough—

GRANDMOTHER: It's all I had.

GIRL: You had me—is a vision worth more than me?

GRANDMOTHER: I wanted to keep the leaves red for you.

GIRL: I don't want you to do it for me.

GRANDMOTHER: What am I supposed to do?

GIRL: Find someone else to share your silence with.

+ + +

GIRL: I was thinking we could have gone for a drive in my old truck.

GRANDMOTHER: I thought we did.

+ + +

GRANDMOTHER: *Ahw'uste*'s still living. Up there on the hill, straight through [*Indicating*] near Asuwosg' Precinct. A long time ago, I was walking by there, hunting horses. There was a trail that went down the hill. Now there's a highway on that hill up there, but, then, the old road divided. Beyond that, in the valley near Ayohli Amayi, I was hunting horses when I saw them walking and I stopped.

They were this high [*Indicating*], and had horns. They were going that direction. [*Indicating*] It was in the forest, and I wondered where they were going. They were all walking. She was going first, just this high [*Indicating*], and she had little horns.

Her horns were just as my hands are shaped—five points, they call them five points. That's the way it was. Just this high. [*Indicating*] And there was a second one, a third one, and a fourth one. The fifth one was huge, and it also had horns with five points. They stopped a while, and they watched me. I was afraid of the large one! They were turning back, looking at me. They were pawing with their feet, and I was afraid. They were showing their anger then. First they'd go [*Indicates pawing*] with the right hoof and then with the left, and they'd go: *Ti! Ti! Ti! Ti!* They kept looking at me and pawing, and I just stood still.

They started walking again and disappeared away off, and I wondered where they went. I heard my horses over there, and I went as fast as I could. I caught a horse to ride and took the others home.

There was a man named Tseg' Ahl'tadeg, and when I got there, at his house, he asked me: What did you see?

I saw something down there, I told him.

What was it?

A deer. She was just this high [*Indicating*], and she had horns like this [*Indicating*], and she was walking in front. The second one was this high [*Indicating*], and the third one was this high [*Indicating*], and the fourth one [*Indicating*]—then the rest were large.

It was *Ahw'uste,* he said.

GIRL: I thought you said *Ahw'uste* lived in a house in Deer Creek.

GRANDMOTHER: Well, she did, but these were her tribe. She was with them sometimes.

GIRL: She's the only one who lived in a house?

GRANDMOTHER: Yes.

GIRL: In Deer Creek?

GRANDMOTHER: Yes, in Deer Creek.

GIRL: Your deer dress is the way you felt when you saw the deer?

GRANDMOTHER: When I saw *Ahw'uste,* yes. My deer dress is the way I felt, transformed by the power of ceremony. The idea of it in the forest of my head.

✦ ✦ ✦

GIRL: Speak without your stories. Just once. What are you without your deer dress? What are you without your story of *Ahw'uste?*

GRANDMOTHER: We're carriers of our stories and histories. We're nothing without them.

GIRL: We carry ourselves. Who are you besides your stories?

GRANDMOTHER: I don't know—no one ever asked.

✦ ✦ ✦

GIRL: OK, bucko. I find out you're married. But not living with her. *You aren't married in your heart,* you say. *It's the same as not being married.* And you got kids, too? Yeah, several, I'm sure. Probably left more of them behind to take care of themselves than you admit. You think you can dance me backwards around the floor, bucko?

GRANDMOTHER: Why would I want to be like you?

✦ ✦ ✦

GRANDMOTHER: Why can't my granddaughter wait on the spirit? Why is she impatient? It takes a while sometimes. She says, *Hey spirit, what's wrong? Your wings broke down? You need a jumper cable to get them started?*

My granddaughter wants to do what she wants. Anything that rubs against her, well, she bucks. Runs the other way. I'm not going to give her my deer dress to leave in a heap on some dude's floor. It comes from long years from my grand-mother....

I have to live so far away from you. Take me where you are—I feel the pull of the string. [*She touches her breastbone*] Reel me in. Just pull. I want out of here. I want to see you ancestors. Not hear the tacky world. No more.

GIRL: You always got your eye on the next world.

GRANDMOTHER: I sit by the television, watch those stupid programs.

GIRL: What do you want? Weed the garden. Do some beans for supper. Set a trap for the next spirit to pass along the road.

GRANDMOTHER: The spirits push us out so we'll know what it's like to be without them. So we'll struggle all our lives to get back in—

GIRL: Is that what life is for you? No—for me—I get busy with day-to-day stuff until it's over.

I told 'em at church I didn't take the commodities—well not all those boxes—I told 'em—shit—what did it matter?

Have you ever lost one job after another?

GRANDMOTHER: Have you eaten turnips for a week? Because that was all you had in your garden. In your cupboard. Knowing your commodities won't last because you gave them to the next family on the road? They got kids and you can hear them crying.

GIRL: Well, just step right off the earth. That's where you belong. With your four deer feet.

GRANDMOTHER: Better than your two human ones. All you do is walk into trouble.

GIRL: Because I pick up someone now and then? Didn't you know what it was like to want love?

GRANDMOTHER: Love—ha! I didn't think of that. We had children one after another. We were cooking supper or picking up some crying child or brushing the men away. Maybe we did what we didn't want to do. And we did it every day.

GIRL: Well, I want something more for my life.

GRANDMOTHER: A trucker dude or two to sleep with till they move on? Nights in a bar. The jukebox and cowboys rolling you over.

GIRL [*She slaps her*]: What did I do? Slap my grandmother? That felt good!

You deserved it. Sitting there in your smug spirit mode. I don't curl up with stories. I live in the world I see.

I've got to work. Christ—where am I going to find another job?

GRANDMOTHER: You can't live on commods alone.

GIRL: You can't drive around all day in your spirit mobile either.

✦ ✦ ✦

GIRL: I been paying ten years on my truck, bub. You think I need a new transmission? 'Cause I got 180,000 miles on the truck and it's in the garage? You think you can sell me a new one, bubby? My truck'll run another hundred thousand. I don't have it paid for yet. You think you can sell me a used truck? You couldn't sell me mud flaps. Just get it running—try something else or my grandma'll stomp you with her hooves. My truck takes me in a vision. You got a truck that has visions? I don't see it on the list of options, bubby.

+ + +

GRANDMOTHER: *Gu'-s-di i-da-da-dv-hni.* My relatives—I'm making medicine from your songs. Sometimes I feel it. But mostly I have to know it's there without seeing. I go there from the hurts he left me with—all those kids and no way to feed them but by the spirit. Sometimes I think the birds brought us food. Or somehow we weren't always hungry. That's not true. Mostly we were on our own. Damned spirits. Didn't always help out. Let us have it rough sometimes. All my kids are gone. Run off. One of my daughters calls from Little Falls sometimes. Drunk. Drugged. They all have accidents. One got shot.

What was that? *E-li'-sin*—Grandmother?

No, just the blue jay. The finch.

Maybe the ancestors—I hear them sometimes—out there, raking leaves—or I hear them if I think I do.

Hey—quiet out there, my granddaughter would say.

Just reel me in, Grandmother, I say.

+ + +

GIRL: So I told 'em at my first job interview: No, I hadn't worked that kind of machine—but I could learn.

I told 'em at my second interview the same thing....

I told 'em at the third...

At the fourth I told 'em—my grandmother was a deer. I could see her change before my eyes. She caused stories to happen. That's how I knew she could be a deer.

At the fifth I continued—I'm sewing my own red deer dress. It's different than my grandma's. Mine is a dress of words. I see *Ahw'uste* also.

At the rest of the interviews I started right in—let me talk for you, that's what I can do.

My grandma covered her trail. Left me without knowing how to make a deer dress. Left me without covering.

But I make a covering she could have left me if only she knew how.

I think I hear her sometimes—that crevice you see through into the next world. You look again, it's gone.

My heart has red trees. The afterworld must be filling up with leaves.

You know, I've learned she told me more without speaking than she did with her words.

—1998

IRENA KLEPFISZ (1941-)

Jewish lesbian poet Irena Klepfisz was born in the Warsaw ghetto in 1941. She and her mother escaped the ghetto and were sheltered by nuns and peasants until the end of World War II, though her father was killed in the Ghetto Uprising of 1943. Klepfisz and her mother briefly lived in Sweden before settling in New York City in 1949. There, Klepfisz was immersed in secular, socialist Jewish culture. She attended *Arbeiter ring shule,* Workmen's Circle school, where she developed her skills in Yiddish. Klepfisz graduated from the City College of New York with honors in English and Yiddish. After receiving a Ph.D. in English from the University of Chicago, she returned to her Yiddish studies with a post-doctoral fellowship at the Max Weinreich Center for Jewish Studies at the YIVO Institute for Jewish Research, where she was a translator-in-residence in the 1980s.

Klepfisz's first two books, *Periods of Stress* (1975) and *Keeper of Accounts* (1982), include poems about surviving the Holocaust. By the early 1980s Klepfisz had emerged as a leading voice of Jewish lesbian-feminism in an era of multicultural coalition politics in the women's and lesbian movements. She published two essays about living in the U.S. as a Jewish lesbian in the collection *Nice Jewish Girls: A Lesbian Anthology* (1982), and she co-edited *The Tribe of Dina: A Jewish Women's Anthology* (1986) with Melanie Kaye/Kantrowitz. In 1990 Klepfisz published *Dreams of an Insomniac: Jewish Feminist Essays, Speeches, and Diatribes* and *A Few Words in the Mother Tongue: Poems Selected and New (1971-1990),* which include several bilingual poems in English and Yiddish. She was a founding editor of the feminist journal *Conditions* and serves as editorial consultant for Yiddish and Yiddish literature to *Bridges: A Journal for Jewish Feminists and Our Friends.* Klepfisz is the co-founder of the Jewish Women's Committee to End the Occupation of the West Bank and Gaza. She teaches courses on Jewish women in the Women's Studies Program at Barnard College.

Work Sonnets
with Notes and a Monologue about a Dialogue

I: Work Sonnets

i.
iceberg
I dream   yearning
to be fluid.
through how many nights
must it float   cumbersome   5
for how many centuries
of sun   how many
thousands of years
must it wait
so that one morning   10
I'll wake
as water of lake
of ocean
of the drinking well?

and day breaks.   15

ii.

today was another day. first i typed some
letters that had to get out. then i spent
hours xeroxing page after page after page
till it seemed that i was part of the machine
or that it was a living thing like me. its   20
blinking lights   its opening mouth   looked
as if they belonged to some kind of terrible
unthinking beast to whom i would always be bound.
oblivious to my existence   it simply waited
for its due   waited for me to keep it going   25
waited for me to provide page after page after page.
when it overheated   i had to stop while it
readied itself to receive again. so i typed
some letters that had to get out. and he said

he was pleased with the way things were going.   30

iii.

today was my day for feeling bitter. the xerox
broke down completely   and the receptionist
put her foot down   and made it clear to the repairmen
that *we* couldn't afford to keep such a machine
and it was costing *us* extra money every time *we* had   35
to xerox outside. they hemmed and hawed and said
the fuzz from the carpet clogged things up   and
then they worked on it. and she watched over them
and made sure it was going properly when they left.
by then i'd fallen behind and he asked me to stay   40
late   and i said i was tired and really wanted to go
home. so he said it was really important and i could
come in late tomorrow with pay. so i said okay and
stayed. but i didn't feel any better about it.

a morning is not an evening.   45

iv.

volcano
I dream   yearning
to explode.
for how many centuries
of earth   relentless   50
grinding   how many
thousands of unchanged
years   buried
will it take
so that one morning   55
I'll wake as unfettered flame

as liquid rock
as fertile ash?

and day breaks.

v.

today was my day for taking things in stride.   60
i was helpful to the temp in the office next
door   who seemed bewildered and who had definitely
lied about her skills. the dictaphone[1] was
a mystery to her and she did not know how to use
the self-erasing IBM[2] nor the special squeezer   65
to squeeze in words. she was the artist type:
hair all over the place   and dirty fingernails.
i explained everything to her   during her coffee
break   when she had deep creases in her forehead.
i felt on top of things. during lunch   70
i went out and walked around window shopping
feeling nice in the afternoon sun. and then
i returned and crashed through a whole bunch

of letters so i wouldn't have to stay late.

vi.

today was my day for feeling envy. i envied   75
every person who did not have to do what i
had to do. i envied every person who was rich
or even had 25 cents more than me   or worked
even one hour less. i envied every person who
had a different job   even though i didn't want   80
any of them either. i envied poor homeless children
wandering the streets because they were little
and didn't know the difference   or so i told myself.
and i envied the receptionist who'd been there
for years and years and years and is going to retire   85
soon   her hearing impaired from the headpiece she'd
once been forced to wear. for her it was over.
she was getting out. i envied her so much today.

i wanted to be old.

vii.

rock   90
I dream   yearning
to yield.
how many centuries
of water pounding

---

[1] Tape recorder used for transcribing dictation.
[2] International Business Machines (IBM), a common   brand of electric typewriters used for business purposes
before the advent of the personal computer.

for how many thousands 95
of years   will it take
to erode this hardness
so that one morning
I'll wake
as soil 100
as moist clay
as pleasure sand
along the ocean's edge?

and day breaks.

viii.

today we had a party. he said he had gotten a 105
new title and brought in a bottle of wine during
lunch and we all sat around and joked about how
we'd become such important people and drank the
wine. and the receptionist got a little giddy
and they told her to watch it or she would develop 110
a terrible reputation which was not appropriate for
someone her age and maturity. and she laughed and
said "that's all right. i'll risk it." and the temp
from the office next door came in to ask me to go to
lunch. so we gave her some wine and she said she'd 115
been hired permanently and was real happy because
she'd been strung out and getting pretty desperate.
i noticed her hair was tied back and her nails neater.

and then we all got high and he said to everyone
this was a hell of a place. and then he announced 120
he had a surprise for me. he said he was going to
get a new xerox because it was a waste of my time to
be doing that kind of work and he had more important
things for me to do. and everyone applauded and the
receptionist said she hoped this one was better than 125
the last because we sure were losing money on that
old clinker. and he assured her it was. and then he
welcomed the temp to the floor and said "welcome aboard."
and he told her across the hall they treat their people
like we treat our people and their place is one hell 130
of a place to work in as she'd soon discover. and then
he winked over in my direction and said: "ask her.

she knows all about it."

ix.

dust
I dream   yearning 135
to form.
through how much emptiness

                    must it speed
                    for how many centuries
                    of aimless orbits   140
                    how many thousands
                    of light years   must it wait
                    so that one morning
                    I'll wake
                    as cratered moon   145
                    as sea-drenched planet
                    as exploding sun?

                    and day breaks.

                    and day breaks.

II: Notes

Says she's been doing this for 12 years. Her fifth job since she started working at 18. The others were: office of paper box manufacturing company (cold and damp almost all year round); office of dress factory (was told she could also model for buyers; quit because buyers wanted to feel the materials and her; was refused a reference); real estate office; and this, which she considers the best one. Through high school, she worked part time contributing towards household expenses.

Extremely sharp with them. Says: "I'm not a tape recorder. Go through that list again." Or: "It's impossible. I've got too much to do." Two days ago, she told me: "Make *them* set the priorities. Don't make yourself nuts. You're not a machine."

Am surprised, because I always feel intimidated. But she seems instinctively to understand power struggles. Is able to walk the fine line between doing her job well and not knocking herself out beyond what she thinks she is being paid for. And she *is* good. Quick. Extremely accurate. Am always embarrassed when they return things with errors and ask me to do them over again. Never happens to her. She's almost always letter perfect.

I've told her she should demand more. The dictaphone is old and the typewriter is always breaking down. She should make them get her better equipment. It's too frustrating the way it is. She shrugged. Said it really didn't matter to her. Was surprised at her indifference.

Friendly, yet somehow distant. Sometimes I think she's suspicious of me, though I've tried to play down my background. I've said to her: "What's the difference? We're doing exactly the same work, aren't we?" Did not respond. Yet, whenever I've had trouble, she's always been ready to help.

Her inner life: an enigma. Have no idea what preoccupies her. Would be interested in knowing her dreams. Hard for me to imagine. This is a real problem. First person demands such inside knowledge, seems really risky. Am unclear what the overall view would be. What kind of vision presented. How she sees the world. How she sees herself in it. It seems all so limited, so narrow. Third person opens it up. But it would be too distanced, I think. I want to be inside her. Make the reader feel what she feels.

A real dilemma. I feel so outside.

Says she reads, but is never specific what. Likes music, dancing. Smokes. Parties a lot, I think, for she seems tired in the morning and frequently says she did not get much sleep. Lives by herself. Thinks she should get married, but somehow can't bring herself to do it. "I like having the place to myself," she said the other day. Didn't specify what she was protecting.

Attitude towards them remains also unformulated. Never theorizes or distances herself from her experience. She simply responds to the immediate situation. Won't hear of organizing which she considers irrelevant (and also foreign inspired). Yet she's very, very fair and helpful to others and always indignant if someone is being treated unfairly. Whenever a temp arrives, she always shows her what's what. Tells her not to knock herself out. Reminds her to take her coffee break. Once gave up her lunch hour so one of them could go to the dentist for a bad tooth. Did it without hesitation. For a stranger.

Q: Is she unique or representative? The final piece: an individual voice? or a collective one?

I've learned a lot here, I think. It hasn't been as much of a loss as I expected. At least I've gotten some ideas and some material. But thank god I'm leaving next week. Can't imagine spending a whole life doing this.

III: A Monologue about a Dialogue

And she kept saying: "There's more. Believe me, there's more."

And I was kind of surprised because I couldn't imagine what more there could be. And then I began to wonder what she meant by the more, like maybe a bigger apartment or more expensive restaurants.

But she said that wasn't it, not really. "I'm not materialistic," she said and then looked kind of hopeless, as if I could never understand her. "I just want to *do* something," she said, obviously frustrated. And she looked hopeless again. And then she took a big breath, as if she was going to make a real effort at explaining it to me.

"It's just," she said, "it makes no difference whether I'm here or not. *Anyone* can do this. And I've always wanted to do special, important work."

Well, that made me laugh, because I've stopped wanting to do any work at all. All work is bullshit. Everyone knows that. No matter how many telephones and extensions, no matter how many secretaries, no matter how many names in the rolodex.[3] It's all bullshit.

But she disagreed. "No," she said. "There's really important work to be done."

"Like what?" I asked curious, for I've seen enough of these types running around telling me how important it is to do this or that and just because they're telling me it's important they start feeling that they're important and doing important work. So I was curious to see what she'd come up with.

---

[3] Card file for addresses and telephone numbers.

But she was kind of vague, and said something about telling the truth and saying things other people refused to say. And I confess I'd never heard it put that way before.

"I want to be able to say things, to use words," she explained.

"Oh, a writer," I said. I suddenly understood.

"Well, yes. But not like you think. Not romances or anything like that. I want to write about you and how you work and how it should be better for you."

"So that's it," I said, understanding now even more than I had realized at first. "So that's the important work. That certainly sounds good. Good for you, that is. But what about me? Do you think there's more for me? Because I'm not about to become a writer. And I don't know why I should just keep doing this so you have something to write about that's important. So can you think of something more for me? I mean I can't do anything except this."

And I could feel myself getting really mad because I remembered how in school they kept saying: "Stop daydreaming and concentrate!" And they said that your fingertips had to memorize the letters so that it would feel as if they were part of the machine. And at first it seemed so strange, because everything was pulling me away, away from the machine. And I really wanted to think about what was going on outside. There seemed so many things, though I can't recall them now. But they kept pushing me and pushing me: "Stop daydreaming! Concentrate!" And finally I did. And after a while it didn't seem so hard to do. And I won first prize in class. And the teacher said I'd have a real good choice in the jobs I could get because quality is always appreciated in this world and with quality you can get by.

And when I remembered how I'd sat doing those exercises, making my fingertips memorize the letters, I was real mad because she was no different than the others. There's always something more. More for them. But not one notion about something more for me. Except maybe a better machine so that I can do more work more quickly. Or maybe a couple of hours less a week. That's the most that they can ever think of for me.

And I was so furious. I'd heard all this before. And I know that as soon as they tell you they'll fight to get you better working conditions, they go home and announce: "You couldn't pay me enough to do that kind of work." That's what they say behind your back.

And I started to yell at her: "If you got words and know what to say, how come you can't come up with something more for me?"

And she was so startled. I could see it in her eyes. I mean you've got to have nerve. I'm supposed to just stay here while she writes about me and my work.

And then I said: "They're always going to need people to type the final copies. And I can see you'll never waste your time with that once you've thought of all the right words." And she kind of backed up, because I must have looked really mad. And she bumped into the file cabinet and couldn't move back any further. And I said to her: "What's the difference to me? It's all the same. I always end up doing the same thing.

So let's make it clear between us. Whenever you finish whatever it is you're writing about me and my work, don't count on me to help you out in the final stages. Never count on me, no matter how good the working conditions."

—1982

Fradel Schtok

Yiddish writer. B. 1890 in Skale, Galicia. Emigrated to New York in 1907. Became known when she introduced the sonnet form into Yiddish poetry. Author of *Erzeylungen* (Stories) in 1919, a collection in Yiddish. Switched to English and published *For Musicians Only* in 1927. Institutionalized and died in a sanitarium around 1930.

> Language is the only homeland.
> —Czeslow Milosz

They make it sound easy: some disjointed
sentences   a few allusions   to
mankind.   But for me   it was not
so simple   more like   trying
to cover the distance   from here   5
to the corner   or between two sounds.

Think of it: *heym*   and   *home*   the meaning
the same   of course   exactly
but the shift   in vowel   was the ocean
in which I drowned.   10

I tried. I did   try.
First held with Yiddish   but you
know   it's hard. You write   *gas*
and   *street*   echoes back
No resonance.   And—let's face it—   15
memory falters.
You try to keep track of the difference
like *got* and *god*   or *hoyz* and *house*
but they blur   and you start using
alley   when you mean *gesele*   or *avenue*   20
when it's a *bulevar*.

And before you know it
you're on   some alien path
standing   before a brick house
the doorframe   slightly familiar.   25
Still   you can't place it
exactly.   Passers-by   stop.
Concerned   they speak   but you've
heard   all this   before   the vowels
shifting   up and down   the subtle   30
change   in the guttural sounds

and now   it's nothing more
nothing   more   than   babble.
And so   you accept it.
You're lost.   This time   you really   35
don't know   where you are.

Land or sea   the house floats before you.
Perhaps you once sat   at that window
and it was home   and looked out
on that *street* or *gesele*.   Perhaps   40
it was a dead end   perhaps a short cut.
Perhaps not.
A movement by the door.   They stand there
beckoning   mouths open and close:
Come in! Come in!   I understood   it was   45
a welcome.   *A dank! A dank!* [4]
I said   till I heard the lock
snap   behind me.

—1990

---

[4] (Yid.) Thank you.

BUFFY SAINTE-MARIE (1941-   )

Born on the Piapot Cree reservation in the Qu'Appelle Valley of Saskatchewan, Buffy Sainte-Marie was best known during the mid-twentieth century as an activist and singer-songwriter, particularly of protest and love songs. Much has been made of what she calls her "Pocahontas-with-a-guitar" image, but Sainte-Marie is much more accomplished than that characterization might indicate: she is an artist who holds a doctorate in fine arts and was among the pioneers of digital art and music. In 1993, Sainte-Marie was named France's "Best International Artist," and she participated in the United Nations' official proclamation of that year as the International Year of Indigenous Peoples. Sainte-Marie claims that her work was among that which President Lyndon Johnson believed "deserved to be suppressed," and that he wrote letters on White House stationery praising radio stations that refused to play it. After spending five years as a regular on *Sesame Street,* Sainte-Marie founded the Cradleboard Teaching Project, which utilizes distance-education computer technology to "joyfully replace the old inaccuracies" about Native peoples, and produced a multimedia curriculum CD entitled *Science: Through Native American Eyes.* Sainte-Marie continues to appear in concert and as a speaker, though much of her time is now devoted to the Cradleboard Teaching Project.

The Universal Solider

He's five feet two and he's six feet four.
He fights with missiles and with spears.
He's all of thirty-one and he's only seventeen,
He's been a soldier for a thousand years.

He's a Cath'lic, a Hindu, an atheist, a Jain,   5
A Buddhist and a Baptist and a Jew.
And he knows he shouldn't kill
And he knows he always will
Kill you for me my friend and me for you.
And he's war.   10

And he's fighting for Canada, he's fighting for France,
He's fighting for the U.S.A.
And he's fighting for the Russians and he's fighting for Japan
And he thinks we'll put an end to war this way.

And he's fighting for democracy, he's fighting for the Reds.   15
He says it's for the peace of all.
He's the one who must decide who's to live and who's to die
And he never sees the writing on the wall.

But without him how would Hitler have condemned him at Dachau,
Without him Caesar would've stood alone.   20
He's the one who gives his body as a weapon of the war,
And without him all this killin' can't go on.

He's the universal soldier and he really is to blame.
His orders come from far away no more.
They come from here-and-there and you-and-me,   25
And, brothers, can't you see,
This is not the way we put an end to war.

—1963

Bury My Heart At Wounded Knee[1]

Indian legislation on the desk of a do-right Congressman
Now, he don't know much about the issue
so he picks up the phone and he asks advice from the
Senator out in Indian country
A darling of the energy companies who are   5
ripping off what's left of the reservations. Huh.

I learned a safety rule
I don't know who to thank
Don't stand between the reservation
and the corporate bank   10
They send in federal tanks
It isn't nice but it's reality

Chorus
Bury my heart at Wounded Knee
Deep in the Earth

---

[1] Wounded Knee, South Dakota (located on what is now the Pine Ridge Reservation of the Oglala Sioux), the site of an 1890 massacre of Lakota Sioux men, women, and children by U.S. cavalrymen. In 1973, the town of Wounded Knee was seized by members of the American Indian Movement (AIM), and held for 71 days while U.S. marshals laid siege.

Cover me with pretty lies   15
bury my heart at Wounded Knee. Huh.

They got these energy companies that want the land
and they've got churches by the dozen
who want to guide our hands
and sign Mother Earth over to pollution, war and greed   20
Get rich...get rich quick.

[*Chorus*]

We got the federal marshals
We got the covert spies
We got the liars by the fire
We got the FBIs   25
They lie in court and get nailed
and still Peltier goes off to jail[2]

[*Chorus*]

My girlfriend Annie Mae[3] talked about uranium
Her head was filled with bullets and her body dumped
The FBI cut off her hands and told us she'd died of exposure   30
Loo loo loo loo loo

[*Chorus*]

We had the Goldrush Wars
Aw, didn't we learn to crawl and still our history gets
written in a liar's scrawl
They tell ya "Honey, you can still be an Indian   35
down at the 'Y'
on Saturday nights"

Bury my heart at Wounded Knee
Deep in the Earth
Cover me with pretty lies   40
Bury my heart at Wounded Knee. Huh!

—1991

---

[2] Leonard Peltier (b. 1944), Native American activist and member of the American Indian Movement (AIM), convicted of the murder of two federal agents on the Pine Ridge Reservation in 1975. The fairness of his conviction has been the subject of considerable debate.
[3] Anna Mae Pictou Aquash (1945-1975), a prominent activist in the American Indian Movement who was murdered in 1975, though the medical examiner for the Bureau of Indian Affairs initially reported that she had died of exposure. Aquash's hands were cut off and sent to the F.B.I. for fingerprinting.

GLORIA ANZALDÚA (1942-2004)

Gloria Anzaldúa was born in the Rio Grande Valley of Texas, the eldest child of Urbano and Amalia Anzaldúa. Her father supported the family as a sharecropper; Anzaldúa and her three younger siblings helped out by working in the fields. After her father died when she was fifteen years old, they did migrant farm work. Anzaldúa was the only member of her family to attend college, earning a B.A. in English, Art, and Secondary Education at Pan American University and an M.A. in English at the University of Texas. When her dissertation in Chicano feminist studies was rejected at the University of Texas, she transferred to the University of California at Santa Cruz, where she was working on her Ph.D. when she died of complications from diabetes at the age of sixty-two.

A self-described "chicana dyke-feminist, tejana patlache poet, writer, and cultural theorist," Anzaldúa is best known for her work of poetic prose theory, *Borderlands/La Frontera: The New Mestiza* (1987), and the anthology she co-edited with Cherríe Moraga, *This Bridge Called My Back: Writings by Radical Women of Color* (1981). *This Bridge* is the most important collection of writings of the women-of-color movement of the 1980s; Anzaldúa updated it with *Making Face/Making Soul: Haciendo Caras, Creative and Critical Perspectives by Women of Color* (1990) and *This Bridge We Call Home: Radical Visions for Transformation* (co-edited with AnaLouise Keating, 2002). *Borderlands* was named one of the "Best Books of 1987" by *Library Journal,* and it became a central text of both women's studies and border studies in the U.S. academy. In the book's main concept of the "new mestiza," Anzaldúa asserts that the different parts of her identity are indivisible. In her writings she frequently switched between Spanish, English and Nahuatl, including in her three children's books, *Prietita and the Ghost Woman/Prietita y la llorona* (1996), *Friends from the Other Side/Amigos del otro lado* (1993), and *Prietita Has a Friend/Prietita tiene un amigo* (1991). In June 2004, UC Santa Cruz awarded Anzaldúa a posthumous doctoral degree.

A Sea of Cabbages
(for those who have worked in the fields)

On his knees, hands swollen
sweat flowering on his face
his gaze on the high paths
the words in his head twinning cords
tossing them up to catch that bird of the heights.   5
Century after century swimming

with arthritic arms, back and forth
circling, going around and around
a worm in a green sea
life shaken by the wind   10
swinging in a mucilage of hope
caught in the net along with *la paloma.*

At noon on the edge
of the hives of cabbage
in the fields of a *ranchito* in *Tejas*   15
he takes out his chile wrapped in tortillas
drinks water made hot soup by the sun.

Sometimes he curses
his luck, the land, the sun.
His eyes: unquiet birds   20
flying over the high paths
searching for that white dove
and her nest.

Man in a green sea.
His inheritance: thick stained hand   25
rooting in the earth.

His hands tore cabbages from their nests,
ripping the ribbed leaves covering tenderer leaves
encasing leaves yet more pale.
Though bent over, he lived face up,   30
the veins in his eyes
catching the white plumes in the sky.

Century after century flailing,
unleafing himself in a sea of cabbages.
Dizzied   35
body sustained by the lash of the sun.
In his hands the cabbages contort like fish.
Thickened tongue swallowing

the stench.

The sun, a heavy rock on his back,   40
cracks,
the earth shudders, slams his face
spume froths from his mouth spilling over
eyes opened, face up, searching searching.

The whites of his eyes congeal.   45
He hears the wind sweeping the broken shards
then the sound of feathers surging up his throat.
He cannot escape his own snare—
faith: dove made flesh.

—*Translated from the Spanish by the author*

—1987

Cihuatlyotl,[1] Woman Alone

Many years   I have fought off your hands, *Raza*
father mother   church your rage at my desire to be
with myself,   alone.   I have learned
to erect barricades   arch my back against
you   thrust back fingers, sticks   to   5
shriek no   to kick and claw   my way out of

[1] Aztec warrior goddess representing women who die in childbirth.

your heart   And as I grew   you hacked away
at the pieces   of me   that   were   different
attached your tentacles   to my face and breasts
put a lock between my legs.   I had to do it,   10
Raza,   turn my back on your crookening finger
beckoning beckoning   your   soft brown
landscape, tender *nopalitos.*[2]   Oh,   it was hard,
Raza   to cleave flesh from flesh   I risked
us both   bleeding to death.   It took   a long   15
time   but   I learned   to let
your values   roll off   my body   like water
those I swallow to stay alive   become tumors
in my belly.   I refuse   to be taken over   by
things   people   who fear that hollow   20
aloneness   beckoning   beckoning.   No self,
only race *vecindad familia.*[3]   My soul   has always
been yours   one spark   in the roar of your fire.
We Mexicans are   collective animals.   This I
accept   but my life's work   requires autonomy   25
like oxygen.   This lifelong battle has ended,
Raza.   I don't need to flail against   you.
Raza india mexicana norteamericana,   there's nothing more you can chop off   or graft on me that
will change my soul.   I remain who I am, multiple   30
and one   of the herd, yet not of it.   I walk
on the ground of my own being   browned and
hardened by the ages.   I am fully formed   carved
by the hands of the ancients,   drenched with
the stench of today's headlines.   But my own   35
hands whittle   the final work   me.

—1987

How to Tame a Wild Tongue

"We're going to have to control your
tongue," the dentist says, pulling out all the metal from my mouth. Silver bits plop and
tinkle into the basin. My mouth is a motherlode.

The dentist is cleaning out my roots. I get
a whiff of the stench when I gasp. "I can't cap that tooth yet, you're still draining," he
says.

"We're going to have to do something
about your tongue," I hear the anger rising in his voice. My tongue keeps pushing out
the wads of cotton, pushing back the drills, the long thin needles. "I've never seen anything as strong or as stubborn," he says. And I think, how do you tame a wild tongue,
train it to be quiet, how do you bridle and saddle it? How do you make it lie down?

---

[2] (Sp.) A dish made of prickly pear.   [3] (Sp.) Neighborhood family.

"Who is to say that robbing a people of
its language is less violent than war?"
—Ray Gwyn Smith[4]

I remember being caught speaking Spanish at recess—that was good for three licks on the knuckles with a sharp ruler. I remember being sent to the corner of the class-room for "talking back" to the Anglo teacher when all I was trying to do was tell her how to pronounce my name. "If you want to be American, speak 'American.' If you don't like it, go back to Mexico where you belong."

"I want you to speak English. *Pa' hallar buen trabajo tienes que saber hablar el inglés bien. Qué vale toda tu educación si todavía hablas inglés con un* 'accent,'" my mother would say, mortified that I spoke English like a Mexican. At Pan American University, I, and all Chicano students were required to take two speech classes. Their purpose: to get rid of our accents.

Attacks on one's form of expression with the intent to censor are a violation of the First Amendment. *El Anglo con cara de inocente nos arrancó la lengua.* Wild tongues can't be tamed, they can only be cut out.

Overcoming the Tradition of Silence

Ahogadas, escupimos el oscuro.
Peleando con nuestra propia sombra
el silencio nos sepulta.

En boca cerrada no entran moscas. "Flies don't enter a closed mouth" is a saying I kept hearing when I was a child. *Ser habladora* was to be a gossip and a liar, to talk too much. *Muchachitas bien criadas,* well-bred girls don't answer back. *Es una falta de respeto* to talk back to one's mother or father. I remember one of the sins I'd recite to the priest in the confession box the few times I went to confession: talking back to my mother, *hablar pa' 'trás, repelar. Hocicona, repelona, chismosa,* having a big mouth, questioning, car-rying tales are all signs of being *mal criada.* In my culture they are all words that are derogatory if applied to women—I've never heard them applied to men.

The first time I heard two women, a Puerto Rican and a Cuban, say the word *"nosotras,"* I was shocked. I had not known the word existed. Chicanas use *nosotros* whether we're male or female. We are robbed of our female being by the masculine plural. Language is a male discourse.

And our tongues have become
dry   the wilderness has
dried out our tongues   and
we have forgotten speech.
—Irena Klepfisz[5]

Even our own people, other Spanish speakers *nos quieren poner candados en la boca.* They would hold us back with their bag of *reglas de academia.*

---

[4] [*Author's note.*] Ray Gwyn Smith, *Moorland Is Cold Country,* unpublished book.
[5] [*Author's note.*] Irena Klepfisz, "*Di rayze aheym /* The Journey Home," in *The Tribe of Dina: A Jewish Women's*

Anthology, Melanie Kaye/Kantrowitz and Irena Klepfisz, eds. (Montpelier, VT: Sinister Wisdom Books, 1986), 49.

Oyé como ladra: el lenguaje de la frontera

Quien tiene boca se equivoca.
                                                        —Mexican saying

"*Pocho*,[6] cultural traitor, you're speaking the oppressor's language by speaking English, you're ruining the Spanish language," I have been accused by various Latinos and Latinas. Chicano Spanish is considered by the purist and by most Latinos deficient, a mutilation of Spanish.

But Chicano Spanish is a border tongue which developed naturally. Change, *evolución, enriquecimiento de palabras nuevas por invención o adopción* have created variants of Chicano Spanish, *un nuevo lenguaje. Un lenguaje que corresponde a un modo de vivir:* Chicano Spanish is not incorrect, it is a living language.

For a people who are neither Spanish nor live in a country in which Spanish is the first language; for a people who live in a country in which English is the reigning tongue but who are not Anglo; for a people who cannot entirely identify with either standard (formal, Castillian) Spanish nor standard English, what recourse is left to them but to create their own language? A language which they can connect their identity to, one capable of communicating the realities and values true to themselves—a language with terms that are neither *español ni inglés*, but both. We speak a patois, a forked tongue, a variation of two languages.

Chicano Spanish sprang out of the Chicanos' need to identify ourselves as a distinct people. We needed a language with which we could communicate with ourselves, a secret language. For some of us, language is a homeland closer than the Southwest—for many Chicanos today live in the Midwest and the East. And because we are a complex, heterogeneous people, we speak many languages. Some of the languages we speak are:

1. Standard English
2. Working class and slang English
3. Standard Spanish
4. Standard Mexican Spanish
5. North Mexican Spanish dialect
6. Chicano Spanish (Texas, New Mexico, Arizona and California have regional variations)
7. Tex-Mex
8. *Pachuco* (called *caló*)

My "home" tongues are the languages I speak with my sister and brothers, with my friends. They are the last five listed, with 6 and 7 being closest to my heart. From school, the media and job situations, I've picked up standard and working class English. From Mamagrande Locha and from reading Spanish and Mexican literature, I've picked up Standard Spanish and Standard Mexican Spanish. From *los recién llegados*, Mexican immigrants, and *braceros*,[7] I learned the North Mexican dialect. With Mexicans I'll try to speak either Standard Mexican Spanish or the North Mexican dialect. From my parents and Chicanos living in the Valley, I picked up Chicano Texas Spanish, and I speak it with my mom, younger brother (who married a Mexican and who rarely mixes Spanish with English), aunts and older relatives.

---

[6] (Sp.) Anglicized Mexican-American (derogatory).   [7] (Sp.) Farm workers.

With Chicanas from *Nuevo México* or *Arizona* I will speak Chicano Spanish a little, but often they don't understand what I'm saying. With most California Chicanas I speak entirely in English (unless I forget). When I first moved to San Francisco, I'd rattle off something in Spanish, unintentionally embarrassing them. Often it is only with another Chicana *tejana* that I can talk freely.

Words distorted by English are known as anglicisms or *pochismos*. The *pocho* is an anglicized Mexican or American of Mexican origin who speaks Spanish with an accent characteristic of North Americans and who distorts and reconstructs the language according to the influence of English.[8] Tex-Mex, or Spanglish, comes most naturally to me. I may switch back and forth from English to Spanish in the same sentence or in the same word. With my sister and my brother Nune and with Chicano *tejano* contemporaries I speak in Tex-Mex.

From kids and people my own age I picked up *Pachuco*. *Pachuco* (the language of the zoot suiters) is a language of rebellion, both against Standard Spanish and Standard English. It is a secret language. Adults of the culture and outsiders cannot understand it. It is made up of slang words from both English and Spanish. *Ruca* means girl or woman, *vato* means guy or dude, *chale* means no, *simón* means yes, *churo* is sure, talk is *periquiar*, *pigionear* means petting, *que gacho* means how nerdy, *ponte águila* means watch out, death is called *la pelona*. Through lack of practice and not having others who can speak it, I've lost most of the *Pachuco* tongue.

Chicano Spanish

Chicanos, after 250 years of Spanish/Anglo colonization have developed significant differences in the Spanish we speak. We collapse two adjacent vowels into a single syllable and sometimes shift the stress in certain words such as *maíz/maiz, cohete/cuete*. We leave out certain consonants when they appear between vowels: *lado/lao, mojado/mojao*. Chicanos from South Texas pronounced *f* as *j* in *jue (fue)*. Chicanos use "archaisms," words that are no longer in the Spanish language, words that have been evolved out. We say *semos, truje, haiga, ansina*, and *naiden*. We retain the "archaic" *j*, as in *jalar*, that derives from an earlier *h*, (the French *halar* or the Germanic *halon* which was lost to standard Spanish in the 16th century), but which is still found in several regional dialects such as the one spoken in South Texas. (Due to geography, Chicanos from the Valley of South Texas were cut off linguistically from other Spanish speakers. We tend to use words that the Spaniards brought over from Medieval Spain. The majority of the Spanish colonizers in Mexico and the Southwest came from Extremadura[9]—Hernán Cortés[10] was one of them—and Andalucía.[11] Andalucians pronounce *ll* like a *y* and their *d*'s tend to be absorbed by adjacent vowels: *tirado* becomes *tirao*. They brought *el lenguaje popular, dialectos y regionalismos*.)[12]

Chicanos and other Spanish speakers also shift *ll* to *y* and *z* to *s*.[13] We leave out initial syllables, saying *tar* for *estar, toy* for *estoy, hora* for *ahora* (*cubanos* and *puertorriqueños* also leave out initial letters of some words.) We also leave out the final syllable such as

[8] [*Author's note.*] R.C. Ortega, *Dialectología Del Barrio*, trans. Hortencia S. Alwan (Los Angeles, CA: R.C. Ortega Publisher & Bookseller, 1977), 132.
[9] A region in western Spain.
[10] Hernán Cortés (1485-1547), Spanish conquistador who invaded Mexico.
[11] A region in southern Spain.

[12] [*Author's note.*] Eduardo Hernández-Chávez, Andrew D. Cohen, and Anthony F. Beltramo, *El Lenguaje de los Chicanos: Regional and Social Characteristics of Language Used By Mexican Americans* (Arlington, VA: Center for Applied Linguistics, 1975), 39.
[13] [*Author's note.*] Hernández-Chávez, xvii.

pa for *para*. The intervocalic *y*, the *ll* as in *tortilla, ella, botella*, gets replaced by *tortia* or *tortiya, ea, botea*. We add an additional syllable at the beginning of certain words: *atocar* for *tocar*, *agastar* for *gastar*. Sometimes we'll say *lavaste las vacijas*, other times *lavates* (substituting the *ates* verb endings for the *aste*).

We use anglicisms, words borrowed from English: *bola* from ball, *carpeta* from carpet, *máchina de lavar* (instead of *lavadora*) from washing machine. Tex-Mex argot, created by adding a Spanish sound at the beginning or end of an English word such as *cookiar* for cook, *watchar* for watch, *parkiar* for park, and *rapiar* for rape, is the result of the pressures on Spanish speakers to adapt to English.

We don't use the word *vosotros/as* or its accompanying verb form. We don't say *claro* (to mean yes), *imagínate*, or *me emociona*, unless we picked up Spanish from Latinas, out of a book, or in a classroom. Other Spanish-speaking groups are going through the same, or similar, development in their Spanish.

Linguistic Terrorism

> *Deslenguadas. Somos los del español deficiente.* We are your linguistic nightmare, your linguistic aberration, your linguistic *mestizaje*, the subject of your *burla*. Because we speak with tongues of fire we are culturally crucified. Racially, culturally and linguistically *somos huérfanos*—we speak an orphan tongue.

Chicanas who grew up speaking Chicano Spanish have internalized the belief that we speak poor Spanish. It is illegitimate, a bastard language. And because we internalize how our language has been used against us by the dominant culture, we use our language differences against each other.

Chicana feminists often skirt around each other with suspicion and hesitation. For the longest time I couldn't figure it out. Then it dawned on me. To be close to another Chicana is like looking into the mirror. We are afraid of what we'll see there. *Pena*. Shame. Low estimation of self. In childhood we are told that our language is wrong. Repeated attacks on our native tongue diminish our sense of self. The attacks continue throughout our lives.

Chicanas feel uncomfortable talking in Spanish to Latinas, afraid of their censure. Their language was not outlawed in their countries. They had a whole lifetime of being immersed in their native tongue; generations, centuries in which Spanish was a first language, taught in school, heard on radio and TV, and read in the newspaper.

If a person, Chicana or Latina, has a low estimation of my native tongue, she also has a low estimation of me. Often with *mexicanas y latinas* we'll speak English as a neutral language. Even among Chicanas we tend to speak English at parties or conferences. Yet, at the same time, we're afraid the other will think we're *agringadas* because we don't speak Chicano Spanish. We oppress each other trying to out-Chicano each other, vying to be the "real" Chicanas, to speak like Chicanos. There is no one Chicano language just as there is no one Chicano experience. A monolingual Chicana whose first language is English or Spanish is just as much a Chicana as one who speaks several variants of Spanish. A Chicana from Michigan or Chicago or Detroit is just as much a Chicana as one from the Southwest. Chicano Spanish is as diverse linguistically as it is regionally.

By the end of this century, Spanish speakers will comprise the biggest minority group in the U.S., a country where students in high schools and colleges are encouraged to take French classes because French is considered more "cultured." But for a language to remain alive it must be used.[14] By the end of this century English, and not Spanish, will be the mother tongue of most Chicanos and Latinos.

So, if you want to really hurt me, talk badly about my language. Ethnic identity is twin skin to linguistic identity—I am my language. Until I can take pride in my language, I cannot take pride in myself. Until I can accept as legitimate Chicano Texas Spanish, Tex-Mex and all the other languages I speak, I cannot accept the legitimacy of myself. Until I am free to write bilingually and to switch codes without having always to translate, while I still have to speak English or Spanish when I would rather speak Spanglish, and as long as I have to accommodate the English speakers rather than having them accommodate me, my tongue will be illegitimate.

I will no longer be made to feel ashamed of existing. I will have my voice: Indian, Spanish, white. I will have my serpent's tongue—my woman's voice, my sexual voice, my poet's voice. I will overcome the tradition of silence.

> My fingers
> move sly against your palm
> Like women everywhere, we speak in code....
> —Melanie Kaye/Kantrowitz[15]

"Vistas," corridos, y comida: My Native Tongue

In the 1960s, I read my first Chicano novel. It was *City of Night* by John Rechy,[16] a gay Texan, son of a Scottish father and a Mexican mother. For days I walked around in stunned amazement that a Chicano could write and could get published. When I read *I Am Joaquín*[17] I was surprised to see a bilingual book by a Chicano in print. When I saw poetry written in Tex-Mex for the first time, a feeling of pure joy flashed through me. I felt like we really existed as a people. In 1971, when I started teaching High School English to Chicano students, I tried to supplement the required texts with works by Chicanos, only to be reprimanded and forbidden to do so by the principal. He claimed that I was supposed to teach "American" and English literature. At the risk of being fired, I swore my students to secrecy and slipped in Chicano short stories, poems, a play. In graduate school, while working toward a Ph.D., I had to "argue" with one advisor after the other, semester after semester, before I was allowed to make Chicano literature an area of focus.

Even before I read books by Chicanos or Mexicans, it was the Mexican movies I saw at the drive-in—the Thursday night special of $1.00 a carload—that gave me a sense of belonging. "*Vámonos a las vistas,*" my mother would call out and we'd all—grandmother, brothers, sister and cousins—squeeze into the car. We'd wolf down cheese and bologna white bread sandwiches while watching Pedro Infante[18] in

---

[14] [*Author's note.*] Irena Klepfisz, "Secular Jewish Identity: Yidishkayt in America," in *The Tribe of Dina,* Kaye/Kantrowitz and Klepfisz, eds., 43.

[15] [*Author's note.*] Melanie Kaye/Kantrowitz, "Sign," in *We Speak In Code: Poems and Other Writings* (Pittsburgh, PA: Motheroot Publications, Inc., 1980), 85.

[16] John Rechy (b. 1934), gay novelist of Mexican-Scottish descent, author of *City of Night* (1963).

[17] [*Author's note.*] Rodolfo Gonzales, *I Am Joaquín/Yo Soy Joaquín* (New York, NY: Bantam Books, 1972). It was first published in 1967.

[18] Pedro Infante (1917-1957), famous actor and singer of the golden age of Mexican cinema.

melodramatic tear-jerkers like *Nosotros los pobres*, the first "real" Mexican movie (that was not an imitation of European movies). I remember seeing *Cuando los hijos se van* and surmising that all Mexican movies played up the love a mother has for her children and what ungrateful sons and daughters suffer when they are not devoted to their mothers. I remember the singing-type "westerns" of Jorge Negrete[19] and Miguel Aceves Mejía.[20] When watching Mexican movies, I felt a sense of homecoming as well as alienation. People who were to amount to something didn't go to Mexican movies, or *bailes* or tune their radios to *bolero, rancherita,* and *corrido* music.

The whole time I was growing up, there was *norteño* music sometimes called North Mexican border music, or Tex-Mex music, or Chicano music, or *cantina* (bar) music. I grew up listening to *conjuntos*, three or four-piece bands made up of folk musicians playing guitar, *bajo sexto*, drums and button accordion, which Chicanos had borrowed from the German immigrants who had come to Central Texas and Mexico to farm and build breweries. In the Rio Grande Valley, Steve Jordan[21] and Little Joe Hernández[22] were popular, and Flaco Jiménez[23] was the accordion king. The rhythms of Tex Mex music are those of the polka, also adapted from the Germans, who in turn had borrowed the polka from the Czechs and Bohemians.

I remember the hot, sultry evenings when *corridos*—songs of love and death on the Texas-Mexican borderlands—reverberated out of cheap amplifiers from the local *cantinas* and wafted in through my bedroom window.

Corridos first became widely used along the South Texas/Mexican border during the early conflict between Chicanos and Anglos. The *corridos* are usually about Mexican heroes who do valiant deeds against the Anglo oppressors. Pancho Villa's[24] song, *"La cucaracha,"* is the most famous one. *Corridos* of John F. Kennedy[25] and his death are still very popular in the Valley. Older Chicanos remember Lydia Mendoza,[26] one of the great border *corrido* singers who was called *la Gloria de Tejas*. Her *"El tango negro,"* sung during the Great Depression, made her a singer of the people. The everpresent *corridos* narrated one hundred years of border history, bringing news of events as well as entertaining. These folk musicians and folk songs are our chief cultural mythmakers, and they made our hard lives seem bearable.

I grew up feeling ambivalent about our music. Country-western and rock-and-roll had more status. In the 50s and 60s, for the slightly educated and *agringado* Chicanos, there existed a sense of shame at being caught listening to our music. Yet I couldn't stop my feet from thumping to the music, could not stop humming the words, nor hide from myself the exhilaration I felt when I heard it.

There are more subtle ways that we internalize identification, especially in the forms of images and emotions. For me food and certain smells are tied to my identity, to my homeland. Woodsmoke curling up to an immense blue sky; woodsmoke perfuming my grandmother's clothes, her skin. The stench of cow manure and the

---

[19] Jorge Negrete (1911-1953), famous actor and singer of the golden age of Mexican cinema.

[20] Miguel Aceves Mejía (1915-2006), Mexican actor, composer and singer known as "the king of the falsetto."

[21] Esteban "Steve" Jordan (b. 1939), accordion player known for *tejano* and *norteño* music.

[22] José Maria de Leon Hernández (b. 1940), star of *orquesta tejana* style music since the 1950s.

[23] Flaco Jiménez (b. 1939), Grammy Award-winning *tejano conjunto* accordion player.

[24] Pancho Villa (1878-1923), a leader of the Mexican Revolution, primarily in Chihuahua, northern Mexico.

[25] John F. Kennedy (1917-1963), 35th president of the United States.

[26] Lydia Mendoza (b. 1916), singer and guitarist known as "the queen of *tejano* music."

yellow patches on the ground; the crack of a .22 rifle and the reek of cordite. Homemade white cheese sizzling in a pan, melting inside a folded *tortilla*. My sister Hilda's hot, spicy *menudo, chile colorado* making it deep red, pieces of *panza* and hominy floating on top. My brother Carito barbequing *fajitas* in the backyard. Even now and 3,000 miles away, I can see my mother spicing the ground beef, pork and venison with *chile*. My mouth salivates at the thought of the hot steaming *tamales* I would be eating if I were home.

Si le preguntas a mi mamá, "¿Qué eres?"

> "Identity is the essential core of who
> we are as individuals, the conscious
> experience of the self inside."
> —Kaufman[27]

Nosotros los Chicanos straddle the borderlands. On one side of us, we are constantly exposed to the Spanish of the Mexicans, on the other side we hear the Anglos' incessant clamoring so that we forget our language. Among ourselves we don't say *nosotros los americanos, o nosotros los españoles, o nosotros los hispanos.* We say *nosotros los mexicanos* (by *mexicanos* we do not mean citizens of Mexico; we do not mean a national identity, but a racial one). We distinguish between *mexicanos del otro lado* and *mexicanos de este lado.* Deep in our hearts we believe that being Mexican has nothing to do with which country one lives in. Being Mexican is a state of soul—not one of mind, not one of citizenship. Neither eagle nor serpent, but both. And like the ocean, neither animal respects borders.

> *Dime con quien andas y te diré quien eres.*
> (Tell me who your friends are and I'll
> tell you who you are.)
> —Mexican saying

Si le preguntas a mi mamá, "¿Qué eres?" te dirá, *"Soy mexicana."* My brothers and sister say the same. I sometimes will answer *"soy mexicana"* and at others will say *"soy Chicana"* o *"soy tejana."* But I identified as *"Raza"* before I ever identified as *"mexicana"* or "Chicana."

As a culture, we call ourselves Spanish when referring to ourselves as a linguistic group and when copping out. It is then that we forget our predominant Indian genes. We are 70 to 80% Indian.[28] We call ourselves Hispanic[29] or Spanish-American or Latin American or Latin when linking ourselves to other Spanish-speaking peoples of the Western hemisphere and when copping out. We call ourselves Mexican-American[30] to signify we are neither Mexican nor American, but more the noun "American" than the adjective "Mexican" (and when copping out).

---

[27] [*Author's note.*] Kaufman, 68.
[28] [*Author's note.*] Chávez, 88-90.
[29] [*Author's note.*] "Hispanic" is derived from *Hispanis* (*España,* a name given to the Iberian Peninsula in ancient times when it was a part of the Roman Empire)
and is a term designated by the U.S. government to make it easier to handle us on paper.
[30] [*Author's note.*] The treaty of Guadalupe Hidalgo created the Mexican-American in 1848.

Chicanos and other people of color suffer economically for not acculturating. This voluntary (yet forced) alienation makes for psychological conflict, a kind of dual identity—we don't identify with the Anglo-American cultural values and we don't totally identify with the Mexican cultural values. We are a synergy of two cultures with various degrees of Mexicanness or Angloness. I have so internalized the borderland conflict that sometimes I feel like one cancels out the other and we are zero, nothing, no one. *A veces no soy nada ni nadie. Pero hasta cuando no lo soy, lo soy.*

When not copping out, when we know we are more than nothing, we call ourselves Mexican, referring to race and ancestry; *mestizo* when affirming both our Indian and Spanish (but we hardly ever own our Black ancestry); Chicano when referring to a politically aware people born and/or raised in the U.S.; *Raza* when referring to Chicanos; *tejanos* when we are Chicanos from Texas.

Chicanos did not know we were a people until 1965 when Cesar Chavez[31] and the farmworkers united and *I Am Joaquín* was published and *la Raza Unida* party[32] was formed in Texas. With that recognition, we became a distinct people. Something momentous happened to the Chicano soul—we became aware of our reality and acquired a name and a language (Chicano Spanish) that reflected that reality. Now that we had a name, some of the fragmented pieces began to fall together—who we were, what we were, how we had evolved. We began to get glimpses of what we might eventually become.

Yet the struggle of identities continues, the struggle of borders is our reality still. One day the inner struggle will cease and a true integration take place. In the meantime, *tenemos que hacerla lucha. ¿Quién está protegiendo los ranchos de mi gente? ¿Quién está tratando de cerrar la fisura entre la india y el blanco en nuestra sangre? El Chicano, sí, el Chicano que anda como un ladrón en su propia casa.*

Los Chicanos, how patient we seem, how very patient. There is the quiet of the Indian about us.[33] We know how to survive. When other races have given up their tongue, we've kept ours. We know what it is to live under the hammer blow of the dominant *norteamericano* culture. But more than we count the blows, we count the days the weeks the years the centuries the eons until the white laws and commerce and customs will rot in the deserts they've created, lie bleached. *Humildes* yet proud, *quietos* yet wild, *nosotros los mexicanos-*Chicanos will walk by the crumbling ashes as we go about our business. Stubborn, persevering, impenetrable as stone, yet possessing a malleability that renders us unbreakable, we, the *mestizas* and *mestizos,* will remain.

—1987

---

[31] César Chávez (1927-1993), leader of the United Farm Workers, who organized primarily Mexican and Mexican-American laborers.

[32] Political party established in Texas in 1970.

[33] [*Author's note.*] Anglos, in order to alleviate their guilt for dispossessing the Chicano, stressed the Spanish part of us and perpetrated the myth of the Spanish Southwest. We have accepted the fiction that we are Hispanic, that is Spanish, in order to accommodate ourselves to the dominant culture and its abhorrence of Indians. Chávez, 88-91.

MARILYN HACKER (1942–)

Born in New York City, poet Marilyn Hacker was educated at New York University. In 1961, she married science fiction writer Samuel R. Delany; the couple had one child and divorced in 1980. Hacker has identified as a lesbian most of her life. Her volumes of poetry include *Assumptions* (1975), *Separations* (1976), *Taking Notice* (1980), *Love, Death, and the Changing of the Seasons* (1986), *Selected Poems, 1965-1990* (1994), *Squares and Courtyards* (2000), *First Cities: Collected Early Poems 1960-1979* (2003), and *Desesperanto: Poems 1999-2002* (2003). She received a National Book Award for *Presentation Piece* (1974), a Lambda Literary Award for *Going Back to the River* (1990) and another for *Winter Numbers* (1994). She lives in New York City and Paris.

Ballad of Ladies Lost and Found[1]

for Julia Álvarez

Where are the women who, *entre deux guerres*,[2]
came out on college-graduation trips,
came to New York on football scholarships,
came to town meeting in a decorous pair?
Where are the expatriate *salonnières*,[3]   5
the gym teacher, the math-department head?
Do nieces follow where their odd aunts led?
The elephants die off in Cagnes-sur-Mer.
H. D., whose "nature was bisexual,"
and plain old Margaret Fuller died as well.   10

Where are the single-combat champions:
the Chevalier d'Eon with curled peruke,
Big Sweet who ran with Zora in the jook,
open-handed Winifred Ellerman,
Colette, who hedged her bets and always won?   15
Sojourner's sojourned where she need not pack
decades of whitegirl conscience on her back.
The spirit gave up Zora; she lay down
under a weed field miles from Eatonville,
and plain old Margaret Fuller died as well.   20

Where's Stevie, with her pleated schoolgirl dresses,
and Rosa, with her permit to wear pants?
Who snuffed Clara's *mestiza* flamboyance
and bled Frida onto her canvases?
Where are the Niggerati hostesses,   25
the kohl-eyed ivory poets with severe
chignons, the rebels who grew out their hair,
the bulldaggers with marceled processes?

---

[1] In the spirit of Hacker's directive in line 93 to "make your own footnotes," we have opted to leave the pleasure of tracking down the references in this poem to the reader.

[2] (Fr.) Between two wars, referring to the period between World Wars I and II.

[3] (Fr.) Women who hosted salons (literary and intellectual gatherings) in 18th-century France.

Conglomerates co-opted Sugar Hill,
and plain old Margaret Fuller died as well. 30

Anne Hutchinson, called witch, termagant, whore,
fell to the long knives, having tricked the noose.
Carolina María de Jesús'
tale from the slag heaps of the landless poor
ended on a straw mat on a dirt floor. 35
In action thirteen years after fifteen
in prison, Eleanor of Aquitaine
accomplished half of Europe and fourscore
anniversaries for good or ill,
and plain old Margaret Fuller died as well. 40

Has Ida B. persuaded Susan B.
to pool resources for a joint campaign?
(Two Harriets act a pageant by Lorraine,
cheered by the butch drunk on the IRT
who used to watch me watch her watching me.) 45
We've notes by Angelina Grimké Weld
for choral settings drawn from the *Compiled
Poems* of Angelina Weld Grimké.
There's no such tense as Past Conditional,
and plain old Margaret Fuller died as well. 50

Who was Sappho's protégée, and when did
we lose Hrotsvitha, dramaturge and nun?
What did bibulous Suzanne Valadon
think about Artemisia, who tended
to make a life-size murderess look splendid? 55
Where's Aphra, fond of dalliance and the pun?
Where's Jane, who didn't indulge in either one?
Whoever knows how Ende, Pintrix, ended
is not teaching Art History at Yale,
and plain old Margaret Fuller died as well. 60

Is Beruliah upstairs behind the curtain
debating Juana Inés de la Cruz?
Where's savante Anabella, Augusta-Goose,
Fanny, Maude, Lidian, Freda and Caitlin,
"without whom this could never have been written"? 65
Louisa who wrote, scrimped, saved, sewed, and nursed,
Malinche, who's, like all translators, cursed,
Bessie, whose voice was hemp and steel and satin,
outside a segregated hospital,
and plain old Margaret Fuller died as well. 70

Where's Amy, who kept Ada in cigars
and love, requited, both country and courtly,
although quinquagenarian and portly?
Where's Emily? It's very still upstairs.

Where's Billie, whose strange fruit ripened in bars? 75
Where's the street-scavenging Little Sparrow?
Too poor, too mean, too weird, too wide, too narrow:
Marie Curie, examining her scars,
was not particularly beautiful;
and plain old Margaret Fuller died as well. 80

Who was the grandmother of Frankenstein?
The Vindicatrix of the Rights of Woman.
Madame de Sévigné said prayers to summon
the postman just as eloquent as mine,
though my Madame de Grignan's only nine. 85
But Mary Wollstonecraft had never known
that daughter, nor did Paula Modersohn.
The three-day infants blinked in the sunshine.
The mothers turned their faces to the wall;
and plain old Margaret Fuller died as well. 90

Tomorrow night the harvest moon will wane
that's floodlighting the silhouetted wood.
Make your own footnotes; it will do you good.
Emeritae have nothing to explain.
She wasn't very old, or really plain— 95
my age exactly, volumes incomplete.
"The life, the life, will it never be sweet?"
She wrote it once; I quote it once again
midlife at midnight when the moon is full
and I can almost hear the warning bell 100
offshore, sounding through starlight like a stain
on waves that heaved over what she began
and truncated a woman's chronicle,
and plain old Margaret Fuller died as well.

—1985

JANICE MIRIKITANI (1942-   )

Janice Mirikitani was born in Stockton, California. During World War II, she was interned with her family in Rohwer, Arkansas. In the 1960s and 1970s, Mirikitani emerged as a leader in the Third World movement in San Francisco. During this period, she edited several influential anthologies, including *Third World Women* (1973), *Time to Greez! Incantations from the Third World* (1975), and *Ayumi: A Japanese American Anthology* (1980). In 1965, Mirikitani began working at Glide Memorial United Methodist Church in San Francisco, where she is currently the Executive Director of Programs. Mirikitani is known especially for her work with women and youth in San Francisco's low-income Tenderloin district, sometimes using poetry and dance as vehicles of expression and empowerment. In conjunction with this work, she has edited anthologies such as *I Have Something to Say About This Big Trouble: Children of the Tenderloin Speak Out* (1989) and *Watch Out! We're Talking: Speaking Out About Incest and Abuse* (1993). In 2000, Mirikitani was named Poet Laureate of San Francisco. Mirikitani's books of poetry include *Awake in the River* (1978), *Shedding Silence* (1987), *We, the Dangerous* (1995), and *Love Works* (2001). Her poem "Breaking Silence," which partly speaks in the voice of her mother testifying before the Commission on Wartime Relocation and Internment of Japanese American Civilians in 1981, provided the inspiration for the title of the anthology *Breaking Silence* (1983; ed. Joseph Bruchac), one of the first major collections of Asian-American poetry.

We, the Dangerous

I swore
it would not devour me
I swore
it would not humble me
I swore   5
it would not break me.

     And they commanded we dwell in the desert
     Our children be spawn of barbed wire and barracks

We, closer to the earth,
squat, short thighed,   10
knowing the dust better.

     And they would have us make the garden
     Rake the grass to soothe their feet

We, akin to the jungle,
plotting with the snake,   15
tails shedding in civilized America.

     And they would have us skin their fish
     deft hands like blades / sliding back flesh / bloodless

We, who awake in the river
Ocean's child   20
Whale eater.

     And they would have us strange scented women,
     Round shouldered / strong and yellow / like the moon
     to pull the thread to the cloth
     to loosen their backs massaged in myth   25

We, who fill the secret bed,
the sweat shops
the laundries.

     And they would dress us in napalm,
     Skin shred to clothe the earth,   30

Bodies filling pock marked fields.
Dead fish bloating our harbors.
We, the dangerous,
Dwelling in the ocean.
Akin to the jungle.   35
Close to the earth.

Hiroshima
Vietnam
Tule Lake

And yet we were not devoured.   40
And yet we were not humbled
And yet we are not broken.

—1978

Breaking Silence

For my mother's testimony
before Commission on Wartime Relocation and
Internment of Japanese American Civilians[1]

There are miracles that happen
she said.
From the silences
in the glass caves of our ears,
from the crippled tongue,   5
from the mute, wet eyelash,
testimonies waiting like winter.
        We were told
that silence was better
golden like our skin,   10
        useful like
go quietly,
        easier like
don't make waves,
        expedient like   15
horsetails and deserts.

                "Mr. Commissioner...
                ...the U.S. Army Signal Corps confiscated
                our property...it was subjected to vandalism
                and ravage. All improvements we had made   20
                before our incarceration was stolen
                or destroyed...
                I was coerced into signing documents
                giving you authority to take..."
                ...to take   25
                ...to take.

[1] [*Author's note.*] Quoted excerpts from my mother's testimony modified with her permission.

My mother,
soft like tallow,
words peeling from her
like slivers   30
of yellow flame,
her testimony
a vat of boiling water
surging through the coldest
bluest vein.   35
        She, when the land labored
with flowers, their scent
flowing into her pores,
had molded her earth
like a woman   40
with soft breasted slopes
yielding silent mornings
and purple noisy birthings,
yellow hay
and tomatoes throbbing   45
like the sea.
        And then
all was hushed for announcements:
        "Take only what you can carry..."
We were made to believe   50
our faces betrayed us.
Our bodies were loud
with yellow
screaming flesh
needing to be silenced   55
behind barbed wire.

                "Mr. Commissioner...
                ...it seems we were singled out
                from others who were under suspicion.
                Our neighbors were of German and Italian   60
                descent, some of whom were not citizens...
                It seems we were singled out..."

She had worn her sweat
like lemon leaves
shining on the rough edges of work,   65
removed the mirrors
from her rooms
so she would not be tempted
by vanity.
        Her dreams   70
honed the blade of her plow.
The land,
the building of food was

noisy as the opening of irises.
The sounds of work   75
bolted in barracks...
silenced.

        Mr. Commissioner...
        So when you tell me I must limit testimony
        to 5 minutes, when you tell me my time is up,   80
        I tell you this:
        Pride has kept my lips
        pinned by nails
        my rage coffined.
        But I exhume my past   85
        to claim this time.
        My youth is buried in Rohwer,
        Obachan's ghost visits Amache Gate,
        My niece haunts Tule Lake.
        Words are better than tears,   90
        so I spill them.
        I kill this, the silence...

There are miracles that happen,
she said,
and everything is made visible.   95
        We see the cracks and fissures in our soil:
We speak of suicides and intimacies,
of longings lush like wet furrows,
of oceans bearing us toward imagined riches,
of burning humiliations and   100
crimes by the government.
Of self hate and of love that breaks
through silences.
        We are lightning and justice.
        Our souls become transparent like glass   105
revealing tears for war-dead sons
red ashes of Hiroshima
jagged wounds from barbed wire.
        We must recognize ourselves at last
        We are a rainforest of color   110
and noise.
        We hear everything.
        We are unafraid.
                Our language is beautiful.

                     —1987

PAT MORA (1942-)

Pat Mora was born in El Paso, Texas, to parents who immigrated to the U.S. from Mexico during the Mexican Revolution. Mora received a B.A. from Texas Western College in 1963, an M.A. from the University of Texas El Paso in 1967, and an Honorary Doctorate of Letters from the State University of New York (SUNY) Buffalo in 2006. Her publications include books of poetry such as *Chants* (1984) and *Borders* (1986), both of which received the Southwest Book Awards; a family memoir, *House of Houses* (1997), which received the Southwest Book Award and the Premio Aztlán Literature Award; and over twenty-five multi-cultural children's books that evidence her dedication to family literacy and the preservation of Mexican-American heritage, such as *The Rainbow Tulip* (1999), which is based on her mother's childhood of living on the border. Mora has been a teacher, a radio show host (of "Voices: The Mexican American Perspective"), a museum director, and an administrator at the University of Texas, El Paso. Among the honors she has received are the Kellogg National Leadership Fellowship, the National Endowment for the Arts Creative Writing Fellowship in Poetry, and the National Hispanic Cultural Center Literary Award. A supporter of bilingual literacy, Mora is an advocate for Día de Los Niños, Día de Los Libros (Day of Children, Day of Books), a national day of celebration.

Plot

I won't let him hit her. I won't
let him bruise her soft skin, her dark
brown eyes. I'll beg her to use the ring
snapped from a Coke can. That's my wedding
gift for my daughter.   5

My body betrayed me years ago, failed
to yield that drop of blood: proof
of virginity in this village of Mexican fools.

My groom shoved me off the white sheet
at dawn, spat insults. Had he planned to wave   10
the red stain at his drunken friends?
My in-laws' faces sneered *whore* and my neighbors
snickered at my beatings through the years.

I'll arm my daughter with a ring.
She'll slip it under her wedding mattress.   15
When he sleeps, she'll slit her finger,
smear the sheet. She must use the ring.
I don't want to split his throat.

—1984

Hands

The woman walked quickly down the dusty streets of Juarez. Every few seconds she would glance behind her, checking to see that Miguel was not following. It was a foolish fear. Her husband knew that every morning she rose early and left their three small rooms wearing her black *mantilla*,[1] going to the dark church.

She put her cool palms to her cheeks. Feverish.

"What is happening to me?"

She walked faster. She could remember when she had seemed calm, slow, like the river. The women around her would cry often, fight. But not Cuca. The women came to her with their problems, stories of husbands who threw plates, sons who staggered home drunk. And she dispensed wisdom like Solomon. She had prayed often then for humility, had knelt before the heart of flickering candles at church. Yet the secret pride remained.

Now she smiled sadly at the woman she had been. Now it was she seeking help from another woman, if the witch was a woman.

Bruja,[2] the townspeople called her. She lived alone in a small house a half mile from the last city street. The priests warned that her magic was black, evil, smelling of the devil. But when, day after day, Cuca had dug her nails into her palms until her hands ached all night; when night after night Miguel entered her bed smelling of another woman, Cuca decided that she would reach for any help.

For she loved Miguel.

At first, years ago, when she saw him at dances or after church, she had convinced herself that her love was pure. Wasn't she a good Catholic girl seeking a man to reform, seeking a union more spiritual than physical? Before she went to sleep then she would think of how his lips would feel on hers—soft, gentle, undemanding.

She walked faster. She walked faster thinking of the first time he touched her. He had smiled slowly at her quick response, at her soft moans when he kissed her deeply, when he touched her breasts lightly with the palms of his hands.

Through the years the song of Miguel's touch remained. To her neighbors she was an attractive, religious woman. But at night or on Sunday afternoons, she and Miguel wrapped their legs around each other and rocked to their secret music.

But the music had begun to fade. Two months ago Cuca had cried after their lovemaking.

"What?" asked Miguel.

"You don't stroke my body anymore. I bore you." Cuca did not like to discuss sex. The words had caused her pain.

Miguel patted her head, got dressed, left for a few hours. They never spoke of the change again, but the lovemaking became shorter, less often.

Cuca had reached the edge of Juarez. She began down the dirt road to Bruja's house. She had seen this woman at the market. She dressed in black—black blouse, long black skirt, black shawl wrapped around her head. The gossips said Bruja's gray hair reached to her waist and that when she danced alone in the desert, the moonlight did not dare touch the gray strands that spun round and round.

Cuca's palms were damp as she carefully walked up the two steps leading to the small porch. Jars of herbs covered most of the rotting planks. A pungent smell almost frightened Cuca away.

But his hands.

She wanted Miguel's hands back on her body. She wanted to feel his desire warm, under his skin.

---

[1] (Sp.) Veil, typically worn over the head and shoulders.   [2] (Sp.) Witch.

She knocked. Bruja opened the door.

Her eyes were pale blue. They stung Cuca much as the herb smell had stung her nostrils.

Bruja walked to the table in the center of the room. Cuca followed her, darting quick glances at the chipped furniture, the old black stove, the small bedroom adjoining the larger room.

Bruja sat and motioned for Cuca to sit opposite her. Cuca wanted to run.

"I am thirty-eight," she thought. "And I want to run to my mother. But my mother is dead, and the Virgin ignores my prayers."

"What do you want," asked Bruja. Her voice was flat. She began to shred dried herbs into a mayonnaise jar.

"I am embarrassed to be here," said Cuca. "I am embarrassed to have such a weak body."

"You look healthy," said Bruja.

"But I *need*," said Cuca slowly. "I need my husband back."

"He has gone to Texas?" asked Bruja watching Cuca's face with her pale eyes.

"No. No, he is in Juarez. He is in my bed. But I know that when he touches me in his sleep, it is her he wants. He opens his hands wide, reaching for her large breasts."

"You have seen this woman?" asked Bruja still showing no interest or emotion.

Cuca dug her nails into her palms. "Yes," she whispered. "I followed him to her room. I've stood across the street and watched her. I've seen her stand before her mirror admiring her body, remembering his hands pressing on her skin as they once pressed on mine."

Cuca bit her finger. She hated for others to see her weakness. Only Miguel had seen her lose control. "Yes," he would say urgently. "Let go. Let go. I'll bring you back."

Bruja looked out the window for a long time.

"I hear you shrink things," said Cuca.

Bruja looked at her.

"I hear you shrunk a man's private parts."

"Is that what you want me to do to your husband?" asked Bruja with a trace of a smile.

"I want you to shrink her breasts. I want you to make her flat like a boy. I want him to feel bones beneath her skin and to long for my warm softness. And I'll be there waiting. I will take him back. And we will rock wildly in the dark."

Bruja said nothing.

The sound of their breathing filled the room.

Finally Bruja went into the bedroom. She returned with a small jar of brownish powder.

"I can make her breasts disappear," said Bruja. "I can't promise that your man will return."

"I know my Miguel. He will return."

"Ten American dollars," said Bruja.

Cuca was surprised at the amount, although she didn't show it. She had saved carefully this last month. She had known she must either pay to have Masses said or see Bruja. And one didn't ask the Lord to remove a woman's breasts.

"You must sprinkle this powder outside her door every day for a month. Each day the breasts will grow smaller. At the end of the month your husband will feel bones."

Bruja then reached into a large basket. She removed needle, thread, stuffing, and a small, crude cloth figure. Her fingers worked quickly. Soon she handed Cuca the cloth doll.

"Each morning after your husband leaves for work, snip a bit of the breasts from this figure. Guide the magic, but slowly, slowly."

Cuca paid Bruja. She stuffed the powder and doll into her purse and left quickly. She half-ran all the way back to her neighborhood.

The next morning she could hardly wait for Miguel to leave.

"You seem nervous," he said.

As soon as she was sure he'd left the block, she went into the bathroom with a pair of scissors and the cloth figures. She pulled hard at the cloth nipples and snipped a small piece from each. She flushed the cloth away and hid the doll under her slips and gowns.

She then hurried to the woman's small room. She walked by the door, sprinkled the powder carefully, and walked on.

That day she was supremely happy. She smiled at her neighbors and spent hours in her kitchen cooking *chiles rellenos,* and *flan.*

That evening while Miguel was gone she knelt by the bed and said the rosary. Seldom had she felt as devout.

The ritual of snipping, flushing, sprinkling, continued day after day. At the end of the week Cuca was frantic to know if her money had been well spent. She stood, partly hidden, across from the girl's room and waited.

In time the young woman stood before her mirror wearing only a thin lilac gown. She looked in the mirror for a long time, then turned to the side. She cupped her hands to her breasts then slowly looked at her palms.

Cuca smiled. She wanted to throw back her head and laugh. She wanted to dance on the girl's bed. Instead she walked home quickly.

Snip. Flush. Sprinkle.

"You can only go once a week," she said to herself. She bought a low-cut blouse and began wearing it in the evenings, after supper. She would catch Miguel staring at her, and she would smile softly.

She began to sleep facing him again. And she waited for the music to return.

At the end of the second week, she again hid across from the girl's window. Cuca bit her finger as she waited.

In time the girl stood before the mirror, again wearing only a thin gown. The sight of the girl's small breasts caused Cuca to bite so hard she tasted blood.

She walked to the market and bought a bag of milk candy for the neighborhood children. "It is a sweet life, little ones," she said as she returned their smiles of surprise. "Sweet, sweet."

She washed the gown Miguel had always liked most on her. She remembered how she would say, "Poor green gown, you are never left on me long enough to be appreciated."

And Miguel would whisper, "I want to appreciate you."

That night Cuca started yawning early. "You look tired, Miguel. Don't go out."

Miguel frowned. "Business," he said. He returned late, but Cuca was still awake. Waiting. She pulled the bodice of the gown to reveal more of her warm flesh.

Miguel lay staring at the ceiling, Cuca edged closer to him. She licked her lips, slowly.

"Miguel," she finally said softly.

"Yes, Cuca, yes," he said with a sigh, and he rolled her over and began to rub her back slowly, very slowly until he fell asleep.

Cuca began to dig her nails into her palms again. In the morning she wanted to throw Miguel out of the house so that she could pull out the doll. The breasts were almost gone now. A month had almost passed.

Cuca returned to her hiding place behind a large, old tree on the girl's street. This time Cuca did not have to wait at all. The young girl was standing before the mirror wearing a skirt and no blouse. She was naked from the waist up. The girl was running her hands over her hard, flat chest, moving her hands up and down, pressing into the bones. Smiling.

And Cuca remembers that at night now, Miguel would roll her over in his sleep, and rub her back. He would almost hurt her as he stroked the smooth lines slowly, and then more and more quickly, and his breathing would grow heavy.

—1982

SHARON OLDS (1942-)

Born in San Francisco, Sharon Olds grew up in Berkeley and earned her B.A. from Stanford University in 1964. She went on to receive a Ph.D. from Columbia University, after which she worked in various posts teaching poetry in New York and Massachusetts. Although Olds has been writing poetry all her life, she did not publish her first volume of poetry until she was thirty-seven. However, the eight volumes she has published since then have garnered considerable critical attention, and have established her as an important figure in twentieth century American poetry. Her works include *Satan Says* (1980); *The Dead and the Living* (1984), which won a National Book Critics Circle award; *The Father* (1992); *Blood, Tin, Straw* (1999); and *The Unswept Room* (2002). Like Sylvia Plath, Anne Sexton, and a number of other women poets writing in the twentieth century, Olds has been classified as a "confessional" poet. This term has come to describe poetry (mostly written by women) that makes public the complex relationships between the speaker and her "private" world. Olds, however, rejects this label and has diligently maintained her privacy, refusing to answer questions about which aspects of the narratives in her poems are "true," in the sense of being verifiable fact. Olds is a professor of English at New York University, where she has worked since 1992, and she is the founding director of the New York University workshop program at Goldwater Hospital for the severely physically disabled on Roosevelt Island, New York.

What if God

And what if God had been watching, when my mother
came into my room, at night, to lie down on me
and pray and cry? What did He do when her
long adult body rolled on me
like lava from the top of the mountain   5

and the magma popped from her ducts, and my bed
shook from the tremors, the cracking of my nature
across? What was He? Was He a bison
to lower His partly extinct head
and suck His Puritan phallus while we cried 10
and prayed to Him, or was He a squirrel
reaching through her hole in my shell, His arm
up to the elbow in the yolk of my soul
stirring, stirring the gold? Or was He
a kid in Biology, dissecting me 15
while she held my split carapace apart
so He could firk out the eggs, or was He a man
entering me while she pried my spirit
open in the starry dark—
she said that all we did was done in His sight 20
so He must have seen her weep, into my
hair, and slip my soul from between my
ribs like a tiny hotel soap, He
washed His hands of me as I washed my
hands of Him. Is there a God in the house? 25
Is there a God in the house? Then reach down
and take that woman off that child's body,
take that woman by the nape of the neck like a young cat,
and lift her up, and deliver her over to me.

—1987

Japanese-American Farmhouse, California, 1942

Everything has been taken that anyone
thought worth taking. The stairs are tilted,
scattered with sycamore leaves curled
like ammonites in inland rock.
Wood shows through the paint on the frame 5
and the door is open—an empty room,
sunlight on the floor. All that is left
on the porch is the hollow cylinder
of an Alber's Quick Oats cardboard box
and a sewing machine. Its extraterrestrial 10
head is bowed, its scrolled neck
glistens. I was born, that day, near there,
in wartime, of ignorant people.

—1995

Mrs. Krikorian

She saved me. When I arrived in sixth grade,
a known criminal, the new teacher
asked me to stay after school the first day, she said

I've heard about you. She was a tall woman,
with a deep crevice between her breasts,   5
and a large, calm nose. She said,
This is a special library pass.
As soon as you finish your hour's work—
that hour's work that took ten minutes
and then the devil glanced into the room   10
and found me empty, a house standing open—
you can go to the library. Every hour
I'd zip through the work, and slip out of
my seat as if out of God's side and sail
down to the library, down through the empty   15
powerful halls, flash my pass
and stroll over to the dictionary
to look up the most interesting word
I knew, *spank,* dipping two fingers
into the jar of library paste to   20
suck that tart mucilage as I
came to the page with the cocker spaniel's
silks curling up like the fine steam of the body.
After *spank,* and *breast,* I'd move on
to *Abe Lincoln* and *Helen Keller,*   25
safe in their goodness till the bell, thanks
to Mrs. Krikorian, amiable giantess
with the kind eyes. When she asked me to write
a play, and direct it, and it was a flop,
and I hid in the coat-closet, she brought me a candy-cane   30
as you lay a peppermint on the tongue, and the worm
will come up out of the bowel to get it.
And so I was emptied of Lucifer
and filled with school glue and eros and
Amelia Earhart, saved by Mrs. Krikorian.   35
And who had saved Mrs. Krikorian?
When the Turks came across Armenia,
who slid her into the belly of a quilt, who
locked her in a chest, who mailed her to America?
And *that* one, who saved *her,* and *that* one—   40
who saved *her,* to save the one
who saved Mrs. Krikorian, who was
standing there on the sill of sixth grade, a
wide-hipped angel, smokey hair
standing up lightly all around her head?   45
I end up owing my soul to so many,
to the Armenian nation, one more soul someone
jammed behind a stove, drove
deep into a crack in a wall,
shoved under a bed. I would wake   50
up, in the morning, under my bed—not

knowing how I had got there—and lie
in the dusk, the dustballs beside my face
round and ashen, shining slightly
with the eerie comfort of what is neither good nor evil.

—1995

BERNICE JOHNSON REAGON (1942-)

Bernice Johnson Reagon is known for her work as both activist and musician. In 1973, Reagon founded the African-American female a cappella group Sweet Honey in the Rock, which is famous for its rhythmic, complex, and powerful performances of work influenced by the music of the Black church. Reagon, who has a Ph.D. in U.S. History from Howard University, is Professor Emerita of History and Curator Emerita of the Smithsonian Institution, National Museum of American History. She has authored several books, including *We Who Believe in Freedom: Sweet Honey in the Rock—Still on the Journey* (1993) and *If You Don't Go, Don't Hinder Me* (2001), and edited the collection *We'll Understand It Better By and By: Pioneering African-American Gospel Composers* (1992). Reagon once said, "If you're comfortable, you ain't doing no coalescing," a sentiment that has guided groups hoping to work across race and class differences for human rights and social justice. Among the awards she has received for her activism, scholarship, and music are the Heinz Award for the Arts and Humanities (2003), the Leeway National Award for Women in the Arts (2000), the Charles E. Frankel Prize for contribution to public understanding of the humanities (1995), and a MacArthur Fellowship (1989).

I Be Your Water

I woke up mourning in a crowded sick place
Surrounded by evil protected by grace

There were these hands, hundreds beckoning for me
They knew exactly who and what I should be

Each way I turn pulled me stronger than the last   5
How would I choose and how could I pass

Then I heard whispers   *be still be still be still*
From deep inside me   *be still be still be still*
Then I heard whispers   *be still be still be still*
From deep inside me   *be still be still be still*   10

As I gave power to the sound of my own voice
The way broke before me, I followed my choice

I walked along the way other lives had been
Till I came to what seemed like an end

Again these hands reaching beckoning for me   15
They knew exactly who and what I should be

Still I heard whispers   *be still be still be still*
From deep inside me   *be still be still be still*
Save by whispers   *be still be still be still*
Keeping me steady   *be still be still be still*   20

The way before me was mine to make
There was no road no path to take

As I hacked my life through this muddy rocked way
Others toiled beside for a justice new day

Still I have felt lonely most of the time   25
Walking this sweet freedom struggle of mine

Save by whispers   *be still be still be still*
Keeping me steady   *be still be still be still*
Still I hear whispers   *be still be still be still*
From deep inside me   *be still be still be still*   30

Yesterday I stumbled around the bend
I saw you standing, you reached me your hand

I'd seen you before, oh many a times
Why, your life had plowed the row right next to mine

Now you make the sun rise in my sky   35
You rock my cradle honey you make fly
Up keep me company

I be your shelter, I be your land
I be your everything, I be your friend
I be your water, when you're thirsty and dry...

—1987

Greed

I been thinking about how to talk about greed
I been thinking about how to talk about greed
I been wondering if I could talk about greed
Trying to find a way to talk about greed

Greed is a poison rising in this land   5
The soul of the people twisted in its command

It moves like a virus seeking out everyone
Greed never stops, its work is never ever done

Not partial to gender or your sexual desire
All it wants is for you to own, to possess, to buy   10

I been thinking about how to talk about greed
I been thinking about how to talk about greed

I been wondering if I could sing about greed
Trying to find a way to talk about greed

Nothing seems to stop it once it enters your soul   15
Has you buying anything, spending out of control

It moves within the culture touching us all
Greed really isn't picky, it'll make anybody fall

It's been around a long time since before we began
Before this was a nation, greed drove people to this land   20

I been trying to think about how to talk about greed
I been trying to think about how to talk about greed
I been wondering if I could sing about greed
Trying to find a way to talk about greed

Greed is a strain in the American dream   25
Having more than you need is the essential theme

Maybe you don't know exactly what I mean
You don't really want to know about my and your greed

You may wonder whether you're infected by greed
If you have to ask then this song you really need   30

Greed is sneaky hard to detect in myself
I see it so clearly in everybody else

I been trying to find a way to talk about greed
I been trying to find a way to talk about greed
I been wondering if I could sing about it   35
Trying to find a way to talk about greed

I can see it in you
You can see it in me
We can see it in big corporations
All throughout the government   40
See it in the banks
I can see it in the military
See it in the church
I can see it in my neighbor
It all shows up so clearly   45
You and you and your greed

I been trying to find a way to talk about greed
I been trying to find a way to talk about greed
I been wondering if I could sing about greed
Trying to find a way to talk about greed   50
I'm trying to find a way to talk about greed
I'm trying to find a way to talk about greed

—1995

NIKKI GIOVANNI (1943-   )

Yolande Cornelia Giovanni, Jr., was born in Knoxville, Tennessee, and spent the majority of her youth in various suburbs of Cincinnati. As a child she was very successful in school, and she credits her family with sparking her interest in storytelling and the literary arts. In 1960, during her first semester at Fisk University, Giovanni was asked to leave because she visited her grandparents without permission during the Thanksgiving break. After working for a few years and attending classes at the University of Cincinnati, Giovanni re-entered Fisk and became active in literary and political life on campus. She also underwent a political transformation, rejecting her early conservatism and turning toward more revolutionary social and political positions. Following her first volumes of poetry, *Black Feeling, Black Thought* (1968) and *Black Judgement* (1969), which established her place as an important voice in the Black Arts movement, Giovanni went on to publish several other volumes of poetry, including *Re:Creation* (1970), *The Women and the Men* (1975), *Those Who Ride the Night Winds* (1983), and *Blues: For All the Changes* (1999). Her work has consistently reflected a concern for justice and truth-telling, characteristically conveyed within a personal framework, even as her thematic interests have shifted from politics to introspection to concern for more global issues. Giovanni has written several volumes of verse for children, including *Ego-Tripping and Other Poems for Young People* (1973) and *Vacation Time: Poems for Children* (1980), and prose, including *Gemini: An Extended Autobiographical Statement on My First Twenty-five Years of Being a Black Poet* (1971) and *Sacred Cows… and Other Edibles* (1988).

Nikki-Rosa

childhood remembrances are always a drag
if you're Black
you always remember things like living in Woodlawn[1]
with no inside toilet
and if you become famous or something   5
they never talk about how happy you were to have
your mother
all to yourself and
how good the water felt when you got your bath
from one of those   10
big tubs that folk in chicago barbecue in
and somehow when you talk about home
it never gets across how much you
understood their feelings
as the whole family attended meetings about Hollydale[2]   15
and even though you remember
your biographers never understand
your father's pain as he sells his stock
and another dream goes
And though you're poor it isn't poverty that   20
concerns you
and though they fought a lot

---

[1] A suburb of Cincinnati where the Giovanni family lived briefly.
[2] An all-Black housing development where the Giovanni family hoped to build a home but could not do so, due to racist lending practices.

it isn't your father's drinking that makes any difference
but only that everybody is together and you
and your sister have happy birthdays and very good   25
Christmases
and I really hope no white person ever has cause
to write about me
because they never understand
Black love is Black wealth and they'll   30
probably talk about my hard childhood
and never understand that
all the while I was quite happy

—1968

Seduction

one day
you gonna walk in this house
and i'm gonna have on a long African
gown
you'll sit down and say "The Black..."   5
and i'm gonna take one arm out
then you—not noticing me at all—will say "What about
this brother..."
and i'm going to be slipping it over my head
and you'll rap on about "The revolution..."   10
while i rest your hand against my stomach
you'll go on—as you always do—saying
"I just can't dig..."
while i'm moving your hand up and down
and i'll be taking your dashiki off   15
then you'll say "What we really need..."
and i'll be licking your arm
and "The way I see it we ought to..."
and unbuckling your pants
"And what about the situation..."   20
and taking your shorts off
then you'll notice
your state of undress
and knowing you you'll just say
"Nikki,   25
isn't this counterrevolutionary...?"

—1968

Ego Tripping
(there may be a reason why)

I was born in the congo
I walked to the fertile crescent and built

the sphinx
I designed a pyramid so tough that a star
 that only glows every one hundred years falls   5
 into the center giving divine perfect light
I am bad

I sat on the throne
 drinking nectar with allah
I got hot and sent an ice age to europe   10
 to cool my thirst
My oldest daughter is nefertiti
 the tears from my birth pains
 created the nile
I am a beautiful woman   15

I gazed on the forest and burned
 out the sahara desert
 with a packet of goat's meat
and a change of clothes
I crossed it in two hours   20
I am a gazelle so swift
 so swift you can't catch me

 For a birthday present when he was three
I gave my son hannibal an elephant
 He gave me rome for mother's day   25
My strength flows ever on

My son noah built new/ark and
I stood proudly at the helm
 as we sailed on a soft summer day
I turned myself into myself and was   30
 jesus
 men intone my loving name
 All praises All praises
I am the one who would save

I sowed diamonds in my back yard   35
My bowels deliver uranium
 the filings from my fingernails are
 semi-precious jewels
 On a trip north
I caught a cold and blew   40
My nose giving oil to the arab world
I am so hip even my errors are correct
I sailed west to reach east and had to round off
 the earth as I went
 The hair from my head thinned and gold was laid 45
 across three continents

I am so perfect so divine so ethereal so surreal
I cannot be comprehended

except by my permission

I mean...I...can fly   50
like a bird in the sky...

—1970

LOUISE GLÜCK (1943-   )

Louise Glück was born in New York City and grew up in an affluent family on Long Island.
Glück, who attended Sarah Lawrence College and Columbia University, and who holds a law
degree from Williams College, is the author of eleven books of poetry, including *Firstborn*
(1968), *The House of Marshland* (1975), *Ararat* (1990), *Vita Nova* (1999), and *Averno* (2006), and
one book of prose, *Proofs and Theories: Essays on Poetry* (1994). Among her many honors are
the Pulitzer Prize, the National Book Critics Circle Award, the Bollingen Prize in Poetry, and
the Lannan Literary Award for Poetry. She has also received fellowships from the
Guggenheim Foundation, the National Endowment for the Arts, and the Rockefeller
Foundation, and she has served as the Library of Congress's Poet Laureate Consultant in
Poetry (2003-2004). Glück taught at Williams College for twenty years, and now teaches at
Yale University, where she is an Adjunct Professor of English and the Rosencranz Writer-in-
Residence.

Nest

A bird was making its nest.
In the dream, I watched it closely:
in my life, I was trying to be
a witness not a theorist.

The place you begin doesn't determine   5
the place you end: the bird

took what it found in the yard,
its base materials, nervously
scanning the bare yard in early spring;
in debris by the south wall pushing   10
a few twigs with its beak.

Image
of loneliness: the small creature
coming up with nothing. Then
dry twigs. Carrying, one by one,   15
the twigs to the hideout.
Which is all it was then.

It took what there was:
the available material. Spirit
wasn't enough.   20

And then it wove like the first Penelope[1]
but toward a different end.
How did it weave? It weaved,
carefully but hopelessly, the few twigs
with any suppleness, any flexibility,   25
choosing these over the brittle, the recalcitrant.

Early spring, late desolation.
The bird circled the bare yard making
efforts to survive
on what remained to it.   30

It had its task:
to imagine the future. Steadily flying around,
patiently bearing small twigs to the solitude
of the exposed tree in the steady coldness
of the outside world.   35

I had nothing to build with.
It was winter: I couldn't imagine
anything but the past. I couldn't even
imagine the past, if it came to that.

And I didn't know how I came here.   40
Everyone else much farther along.
I was back at the beginning
at a time in life we can't remember beginnings.

The bird
collected twigs in the apple tree, relating   45
each addition to existing mass.
But when was there suddenly *mass?*

It took what it found after the others
were finished.
The same materials—why should it matter   50
to be finished last? The same materials, the same
limited good. Brown twigs,
broken and fallen. And in one,
a length of yellow wool.

Then it was spring and I was inexplicably happy.   55
I knew where I was: on Broadway with my bag of groceries.
Spring fruit in the stores: first
cherries at Formaggio. Forsythia
beginning.

First I was at peace.   60
Then I was contented, satisfied.
And then flashes of joy.

---

[1] Wife of Odysseus, who evaded the proposals of other men while her husband was away at the Trojan War by repeatedly weaving and then unraveling the same piece of cloth.

And the season changed—for all of us,
of course.

And as I peered out my mind grew sharper.   65
And I remember accurately
the sequence of my responses,
my eyes fixing on each thing
from the shelter of the hidden self:

first, *I love it.*   70
Then, *I can use it.*

—1999

October[2]

1.

Is it winter again, is it cold again,
didn't Frank just slip on the ice,
didn't he heal, weren't the spring seeds planted

didn't the night end,
didn't the melting ice   5
flood the narrow gutters

wasn't my body
rescued, wasn't it safe

didn't the scar form, invisible
above the injury   10

terror and cold,
didn't they just end, wasn't the back garden
harrowed and planted—

I remember how the earth felt, red and dense,
in stiff rows, weren't the seeds planted,   15
didn't vines climb the south wall

I can't hear your voice
for the wind's cries, whistling over the bare ground

I no longer care
what sound it makes   20

when was I silenced, when did it first seem
pointless to describe that sound

what it sounds like can't change what it is—
didn't the night end, wasn't the earth
safe when it was planted   25

---

[2] First published in chapbook form in 2004, "October" later became the second poem in Glück's *Averno,* a poetry collection that revisits the myth of Persephone. Abducted by Hades, Persephone was forced to return to the underworld for a season each year thereafter, during which time her mother, the earth goddess Demeter, mourned her absence, thereby causing winter. Averno is a small crater lake in southern Italy that the Romans believed was the entrance to the underworld.

didn't we plant the seeds,
weren't we necessary to the earth,
the vines, were they harvested?

2.
Summer after summer has ended,
balm after violence: 30
it does me no good
to be good to me now;
violence has changed me.

Daybreak. The low hills shine
ochre and fire, even the fields shine.   35
I know what I see; sun that could be
the August sun, returning
everything that was taken away—

You hear this voice? This is my mind's voice;
you can't touch my body now.   40
It has changed once, it has hardened,
don't ask it to respond again.

A day like a day in summer.
Exceptionally still. The long shadows of the maples
nearly mauve on the gravel paths.   45
And in the evening, warmth. Night like a night in summer.

It does me no good; violence has changed me.
My body has grown cold like the stripped fields;
now there is only my mind, cautious and wary,
with the sense it is being tested.   50

Once more, the sun rises as it rose in summer;
bounty, balm after violence.
Balm after the leaves have changed, after the fields
have been harvested and turned.

Tell me this is the future,   55
I won't believe you.
Tell me I'm living,
I won't believe you.

3.
Snow had fallen. I remember
music from an open window.   60

Come to me, said the world.
This is not to say
it spoke in exact sentences
but that I perceived beauty in this manner.

Sunrise. A film of moisture   65
on each living thing. Pools of cold light

formed in the gutters.

I stood
at the doorway,
ridiculous as it now seems.   70

What others found in art,
I found in nature. What others found
in human love, I found in nature.
Very simple. But there was no voice there.

Winter was over. In the thawed dirt,   75
bits of green were showing.

Come to me, said the world. I was standing
in my wool coat at a kind of bright portal—
I can finally say
long ago; it gives me considerable pleasure. Beauty   80

the healer, the teacher—

death cannot harm me
more that you have harmed me,
my beloved life.

4.
The light has changed;   85
middle C is tuned darker now.
And the songs of morning sound over-rehearsed.

This is the light of autumn, not the light of spring.
The light of autumn: *you will not be spared.*

The songs have changed; the unspeakable   90
has entered them.

This is the light of autumn, not the light that says
I am reborn.

Not the spring dawn: *I strained, I suffered, I was delivered.*
This is the present, an allegory of waste.   95

So much has changed. And still, you are fortunate:
the ideal burns in you like a fever.
Or not like a fever, like a second heart.

The songs have changed, but really they are still quite beautiful.
They have been concentrated in a smaller space, the space of the
    mind.   100
They are dark, now, with desolation and anguish.

And yet the notes recur. They hover oddly
in anticipation of silence.
The ear gets used to them.
The eye gets used to disappearances.   105

You will not be spared, nor will what you love be spared.

A wind has come and gone, taking apart the mind;
it has left in its wake a strange lucidity.

How privileged you are, to be still passionately
clinging to what you love;   110
the forfeit of hope has not destroyed you.

Maestoso,[3] *doloroso:*[4]

This is the light of autumn; it has turned on us.
Surely it is a privilege to approach the end
still believing in something.   115

5.
It is true there is not enough beauty in the world.
It is also true that I am not competent to restore it.
Neither is there candor, and here I may be of some use.

I am
at work, though I am silent.   120

The bland

misery of the world
bounds us on either side, an alley

lined with trees; we are

companions here, not speaking,   125
each with his own thoughts;

behind the trees, iron
gates of the private houses,
the shuttered rooms

somehow deserted, abandoned,   130

as though it were the artist's
duty to create
hope, but out of what? what?

the word itself
false, a device to refute   135
perception— At the intersection,

ornamental lights of the season.
I was young here. Riding
the subway with my small book
as though to defend myself against   140

this same world:

---

[3] (It.) Majestically.   [4] (It.) Sorrowfully.

you are not alone,
the poem said,
in the dark tunnel.

6.

The brightness of the day becomes   145
the brightness of the night;
the fire becomes the mirror.

My friend the earth is bitter; I think
sunlight has failed her.
Bitter or weary, it is hard to say.   150

Between herself and the sun,
something has ended.
She wants, now, to be left alone;
I think we must give up
turning to her for affirmation.   155

Above the fields,
above the roofs of the village houses,
the brilliance that made all life possible
becomes the cold stars.

Lie still and watch: 160
they give nothing but ask nothing.

From within the earth's
bitter disgrace, coldness and barrenness

my friend the moon rises:
she is beautiful tonight, but when is she not beautiful?

—2004

SUSAN GRIFFIN (1943-   )

Susan Griffin was born and raised in Los Angeles, California. She received her B.A. (1965) and her M.A. (1973) from San Francisco State College (now University). Known for poetry deeply influenced by feminism, Griffin is also a radical feminist philosopher and playwright. Her works include the poetry collections *Like the Iris of an Eye* (1976), *Unremembered Country* (1987), and *Bending Home* (1998), and the plays *Voices* (1974) and *Thicket* (1992). She has also published several volumes of political and social theory, including *Women and Nature* (1978), *Pornography and Silence* (1981), and *A Chorus of Stones: The Private Life of War* (1992). Griffin has received grants from the National Endowment for the Arts and the Kentucky Foundation for Women; she has also been honored with a Commonwealth Club Silver Medal, an Emmy for *Voices,* and a MacArthur Grant for Peace and International Cooperation. In her poetry and in her essays, Griffin has addressed topics such as war and its devastation, connections between nature and the human (particularly the female) body, and pornography.

I Like to Think of Harriet Tubman[1]

I like to think of Harriet Tubman.
Harriet Tubman who carried a revolver,
who had a scar on her head from a rock thrown
by a slave-master (because she
talked back), and who   5
had a ransom on her head
of thousands of dollars and who
was never caught, and who
had no use for the law
when the law was wrong,   10
who defied the law. I like
to think of her.
I like to think of her especially
when I think of the problem of
feeding children.   15

The legal answer
to the problem of feeding children
is ten free lunches every month,
being equal, in the child's real life,
to eating lunch every other day.   20
Monday but not Tuesday.
I like to think of the President
eating lunch Monday, but not
Tuesday.
And when I think of the President   25
and the law, and the problem of
feeding children, I like to
think of Harriet Tubman
and her revolver.

And then sometimes   30
I think of the President
and other men,
men who practice the law,
who revere the law,
who make the law,   35
who enforce the law
who live behind
and operate through
and feed themselves
at the expense of   40
starving children
because of the law,
men who sit in paneled offices

---

[1] Harriet Tubman (ca. 1820-1913) escaped slavery to guide many others to freedom via the Underground Railroad; Tubman was also an abolitionist speaker, and served as both a scout and a nurse for the Union Army during the Civil War.

and think about vacations
and tell women   45
whose care it is
to feed children
not to be hysterical
not to be hysterical as in the word
hysterikos, the greek for   50
womb suffering,
not to suffer in their
wombs,
not to care,
not to bother the men   55
because they want to think
of other things
and do not want
to take the women seriously.
I want them   60
to take women seriously.
I want them to think about Harriet Tubman,
and remember,
remember she was beat by a white man
and she lived   65
and she lived to redress her grievances,
and she lived in swamps
and wore the clothes of a man
bringing hundreds of fugitives from
slavery, and was never caught,   70
and led an army,
and won a battle,
and defied the laws
because the laws were wrong, I want men
to take us seriously.   75
I am tired wanting them to think
about right and wrong.
I want them to fear.
I want them to feel fear now
as I have felt suffering in the womb, and   80
I want them
to know
that there is always a time
there is always a time to make right
what is wrong,   85
there is always a time
for retribution
and that time
is beginning.

—1970

DOLORES PRIDA (1943-   )

Dolores Prida was born in 1943 in Caibarien, on the northern coast of Cuba. After the 1959 revolution, her father fled to the United States; two years later she and her family followed. As a child, Prida wrote poems and short stories that she mostly kept to herself. Eventually, after taking literature courses in night school at Hunter College, she developed a successful career in journalism writing and editing for New York's Spanish language daily *El Tiempo,* as well as for *Vision* and *Nuestro* magazines and the monthly newsletter of the Association of Hispanic Arts. Her theatrical work flourished in the 1970s when she began working with a collective group in New York's Lower East Side called Teatro Popular. By the 1980s, Prida had written several full-length plays, one-acts, and musicals, and had published poetry as well. During this time she worked with Duo, an experimental theater, as well as the Puerto Rican Traveling Theater. Her plays, which mix English and Spanish, often tackle political, gender, and cultural issues in a lighthearted manner by employing stylistic tools such as humor, music, farce, and satire. Prida's prolific career also includes writing for Spanish language television and film including sitcoms, series pilots, educational films, and documentaries. She has received various playwriting fellowships and residences, conducted workshops at colleges, spoken on conference panels, and has worked as Senior Editor for *Latina* magazine. Two of her most recent works include a play about a group of Latina professionals called *Latinas in Power...Sort Of* (L.I.P.S.), which explores the possibility of a new generation of Latinas with education, consumer power, and successful careers, and a play entitled *Four Guys Named José and Una Mujer Named Maria* (2000), a musical revue organized around the best known Latino songs of the 1940s and 1950s.

Beautiful Señoritas[1]

CHARACTERS

Four BEAUTIFUL SEÑORITAS[2] who also play assorted characters: CATCH WOMEN, MARTYRS, SAINTS, and JUST WOMEN
The MIDWIFE, who also plays the MOTHER
The MAN, who plays all the male roles
The GIRL, who grows up before our eyes

SET

The set is an open space or a series of platforms and a ramp, which becomes the various playing areas as each scene flows into the next.

Act I

As lights go up DON JOSÉ *paces nervously back and forth. He smokes a big cigar, talking to himself.*

DON JOSÉ: Come on, woman. Hurry up. I have waited long enough for this child. Come on, a son. Give me a son...I will start training him right away. To ride horses. To shoot. To drink. As soon as he is old enough I'll take him to La Casa de Luisa. There they'll teach him what to do to women. Ha, ha, ha! If he's anything like his father, in twenty years everyone in this town will be related to each

---

[1] As a bilingual play, *Beautiful Señoritas* is likely to present non-Spanish speaking audiences with some difficulty. While we want to acknowledge that this difficulty is probably an important way to experience the play, we also feel obliged to provide translations for those passages in which the meaning is not made clear from context.

[2] (Sp.) A customary title of courtesy for unmarried, usually young, women.

other! Ha, ha, ha! My name will never die. My son will see to that...

MIDWIFE: [MIDWIFE *enters running, excited.*] Don José! Don José!

DON JOSÉ: ¡Al fin! ¿Qué? Dígame, ¿todo está bien?[3]

MIDWIFE: Yes, everything is fine, Don José! Your wife just gave birth to a healthy...

DON JOSÉ: [*Interrupting excitedly*]. Ha, ha, I knew it! A healthy son!

MIDWIFE: ...It is a girl Don José...

DON JOSÉ: [*Disappointment and disbelief creep onto his face. Then anger. He throws the cigar on the floor with force, then steps on it.*] A girl! ¡No puede ser! ¡Imposible! What do you mean a girl! ¡Cómo puede pasarme esto a mí?[4] The first child that will bear my name and it is a...girl! ¡Una chancleta![5] ¡Carajo![6] [*He storms away, muttering under his breath.*]

MIDWIFE: [*Looks at* DON JOSÉ *as he exits, then addresses the audience. At some point during the following monologue the* GIRL *will appear. She looks at everything as if seeing the world for the first time.*] He's off to drown his disappointment in rum, because another woman is born into this world. The same woman another man's son will covet and pursue and try to rape at the first opportunity. The same woman whose virginity he will protect with a gun. Another woman is born into this world. In Managua, in San Juan, in an Andes mountain town. She'll be put on a pedestal and trampled upon at the same time. She will be made a saint and a whore, crowned queen and exploited and adored. No, she's not just any woman. She will be called upon to...[*The* MIDWIFE *is interrupted by off stage voices.*]

BEAUTIFUL SEÑORITA 1: ¡Cuchi cuchi chi-a-boom!

BEAUTIFUL SEÑORITA 2: ¡Mira caramba oye!

BEAUTIFUL SEÑORITA 3: ¡Rumba pachanga mambo![7]

BEAUTIFUL SEÑORITA 4: ¡Oye papito, ay ayayaiiii![8]

Immediately a rumba is heard. The four BEAUTIFUL SEÑORITAS *enter dancing. They dress as Carmen Miranda, Iris Chacón, Charo and María la O. They sing:*

"THE BEAUTIFUL SEÑORITAS SONG"

WE BEAUTIFUL SEÑORITAS
WITH MARACAS IN OUR SOULS
MIRA PAPI AY CARIÑO[9]
ALWAYS READY FOR AMOR[10]

WE BEAUTIFUL SEÑORITAS
MUCHA SALSA AND SABOR[11]
CUCHI CUCHI LATIN BOMBAS[12]
ALWAYS READY FOR AMOR

AY CARAMBA MIRA OYE[13]
DANCE THE TANGO ALL NIGHT LONG
GUACAMOLE LATIN LOVER
ALWAYS READY FOR AMOR

---

[3] (Sp.) Finally. What? Tell me, is everything okay?
[4] (Sp.) How could this happen to me?
[5] (Sp.) A scandal!
[6] (Sp.) A curse meaning "hell" or "shit."
[7] Three different forms of Latin dance music.
[8] (Sp.) Hey daddy, wheeee!

[9] (Sp.) Look daddy, my sweet.
[10] (Sp.) Love.
[11] (Sp.) Lots of salsa (form of Latin music) and flavor.
[12] (Sp.) Latin bombshells.
[13] (Sp.) Oh caramba (colloquial expression), look, listen.

ONE PAPAYA ONE BANANA
AY SÍ SÍ SÍ SÍ SEÑOR
SIMPÁTICAS MUCHACHITAS[14]
ALWAYS READY FOR AMOR

PIÑA PLÁTANOS CHIQUITAS[15]
OF THE RAINBOW EL COLOR
CUCARACHAS MUY BONITAS[16]
ALWAYS READY FOR AMOR

WE BEAUTIFUL SEÑORITAS
WITH MARACAS IN OUR SOULS
MIRA PAPI AY CARIÑO
ALWAYS READY FOR AMOR

AY SÍ SÍ SÍ SÍ SEÑOR
ALWAYS READY FOR AMOR
AY SÍ SÍ SÍ SÍ SEÑOR
ALWAYS READY FOR AMOR
¡AY SÍ SÍ SÍ SÍ SEÑOR!

The SEÑORITAS *bow and exit.* MARÍA LA O *returns and takes more bows.* MARÍA LA O *bows for the last time. Goes to her dressing room. Sits down and removes her shoes.*

MARÍA LA O: My feet are killing me. These juanetes[17] get worse by the minute. [*She rubs her feet. She appears older and tired, all the glamour gone out of her. She takes her false eye lashes off, examines her face carefully in the mirror, begins to remove makeup.*] Forty lousy bucks a week for all that tit-shaking. But I need the extra money. What am I going to do? A job is a job. And with my artistic inclinations…well…But look at this joint! A dressing room! They have the nerve to call this a dressing room. I have to be careful not to step on a rat. They squeak too loud. The patrons out there may hear, you know. Anyway, I sort of liked dancing since I was a kid. But this! I meant dancing like Alicia Alonso, Margot Fonteyn…and I end up as a cheap Iris Chacón. At least she shook her behind in Radio City Music Hall. Ha! That's one up the Rockettes!

BEAUTY QUEEN: [*She enters, wearing a beauty contest bathing suit.*] María la O, you still here. I thought everyone was gone. You always run out after the show.

MARÍA LA O: No, not tonight. Somebody is taking care of the kid. I'm so tired that I don't feel like moving from here. Estoy muerta, m'ija.[18] [*Looks* BEAUTY QUEEN *up and down.*] And where are *you* going?

BEAUTY QUEEN: To a beauty contest, of course.

MARÍA LA O: Don't you get tired of that, mujer!

BEAUTY QUEEN: Never. I was born to be a beauty queen. I have been a beauty queen ever since I was born. "La reinecita,"[19] they used to call me. My mother entered me in my first contest at the age of two. Then, it was one contest after the other. I have been in a bathing suit ever since. I save a lot in clothes…Anyway, my mother used

---

[14] (Sp.) Oh, yes, yes, yes, mister/Charming young girls.
[15] (Sp.) Pineapple, bananas, chiquitas (slang for young girls).
[16] (Sp.) Beautiful cockroaches.

[17] (Sp.) Bunions.
[18] (Sp.) I'm dead tired, my little one.
[19] (Sp.) The little princess.

to read all those womens magazines—*Vanidades, Cosmopolitan, Claudia, Buenhogar*—where everyone is so beautiful and happy. She, of course, wanted me to be like them...[*Examines herself in the mirror.*] I have won hundreds of contests, you know. I have been Queen of Los Hijos Ausentes Club; Reina El Diario-La Prensa; Queen of Plátano Chips; Queen of the Hispanic Hairdressers Association; Reina de la Alcapurria; Miss Caribbean Sunshine; Señorita Turismo de Staten Island; Queen of the Texas Enchilada...and now of course, I am Miss Banana Republic!

MARÍA LA O: Muchacha, I bet you don't have time for anything else!

BEAUTY QUEEN: Oh, I sure do. I wax my legs every day. I keep in shape. I practice my smile. Because one day, in one of those beauty contests, someone will come up to me and say...

MARÍA LA O: You're on Candid Camera?

BEAUTY QUEEN: ...Where have you been all my life! I'll be discovered, become a movie star, a millionaire, appear on the cover of *People Magazine*...and anyway, even if I don't win, I still make some money.

MARÍA LA O: Money? How much money?

BEAUTY QUEEN: Five hundred. A thousand. A trip here. A trip there. Depends on the contest.

MARÍA LA O: I could sure use some extra chavos...Hey, do you think I could win, be discovered by a movie producer or something...

BEAUTY QUEEN: Weeell...I don't know. They've just re-made "King Kong"...ha, ha!

MARÍA LA O: [MARÍA LA O *doesn't pay attention. She's busily thinking about the money.* BEAUTY QUEEN *turns to go.*] Even if I am only third I still make some extra money. I can send Johnny home for the summer. He's never seen his grandparents. Ya ni habla español.[20] [MARÍA LA O *quickly tries to put eye lashes back on. Grabs her shoes and runs after* BEAUTY QUEEN.] Wait, wait for me! ¡Espérame! I'll go with you to the beauty contest! [*She exits. The* MIDWIFE *enters immediately. She calls after* MARÍA LA O.]

MIDWIFE: And don't forget to smile! Give them your brightest smile! As if your life depended on it!

The GIRL *enters and sits at* MARÍA LA O*'s dressing table. During the following monologue, the* GIRL *will play with the makeup, slowly applying lipstick, mascara, and eye shadow in a very serious, concentrated manner.*

MIDWIFE: Yes. You have to smile to win. A girl with a serious face has no future. But what can you do when a butterfly is trapped in your insides and you cannot smile? How can you smile with a butterfly condemned to beat its ever-changing wings in the pit of your stomach? There it is. Now a flutter. Now a storm. Carried by the winds of emotion, this butterfly transforms the shape, the color, the texture of its wings; the speed and range of its flight. Now it becomes a stained glass butterfly, light shining through its yellow-colored wings, which move ever so slowly, up and down, up and down, sometimes remaining still for a second too long. Then the world stops and takes a plunge, becoming a brief black hole in space. A burned-out star wandering through the galaxies is like a smile meant, but not delivered. And I am so full of undelivered smiles! So pregnant with undetected laughter! Sonrisas, sonrisas, who would exchange a butterfly for a permanent smile! Hear, hear, this butterfly will keep you alive and running, awake and on your toes, speeding along

---

[20] (Sp.) He doesn't even speak Spanish anymore.

the herd of wild horses stampeding through the heart! This butterfly is magic. It changes its size. It becomes big and small. Who will take this wondrous butterfly and give me a simple, lasting smile! A smile for day and night, winter and fall. A smile for all ocassions. A smile to survive…[*With the last line, the* MIDWIFE *turns to the* GIRL, *who by now has her face made up like a clown. They look at each other. The* GIRL *faces the audience. She is not smiling. They freeze. Black out.*]

In the dark we hear a fanfare. Lights go up on the MC. *He wears a velvet tuxedo with a pink ruffled shirt. He combs his hair, twirls his moustache, adjusts his bow tie and smiles. He wields a microphone with a flourish.*

MC: Ladies and gentlemen. Señoras y señores. Tonight. Esta noche. Right here. Aquí mismo. You will have the opportunity to see the most exquisite, sexy, exotic, sandungueras, jacarandosas[21] and most beautiful señoritas of all. You will be the judge of the contest, where beauty will compete with belleza; where women of the tropical Caribbean will battle the señoritas of South America. Ladies and gentlemen, the poets have said it. The composers of boleros have said it. Latin women are the most beautiful, the most passionate, the most virtuous, the best housewives and cooks. And they all know how to dance to salsa, and do the hustle, the mambo, the guaguancó…And they are always ready for amor, señores! What treasures! See for yourselves!…Ladies and gentlemen, señoras y señores…from the sandy beaches of Florida, esbelta as a palm tree, please welcome Miss Little Havana! [*Music from "Cuando salí de Cuba" is heard.* MISS LITTLE HAVANA *enters. She wears a bathing suit, sun glasses and a string of pearls. She sings.*]

CUANDO SALÍ DE CUBA
DEJÉ MI CASA, DEJÉ MI AVIÓN
CUANDO SALÍ DE CUBA
DEJÉ ENTERRADO MEDIO MILLÓN[22]

MC: Oye, chica, what's your name?

MISS LITTLE HAVANA: Fina de la Garza del Vedado y Miramar. From the best families of the Cuba de Ayer.

MC: [*To the audience.*] As you can see, ladies and gentlemen, Fina es muy fina.[23] Really fine, he, he, he. Tell the judges, Fina, what are your best assets?

MISS LITTLE HAVANA: Well, back in the Cuba of Yesterday, I had a house with ten rooms and fifty maids, two cars, un avión[24] and a sugar mill. But Fidel took everything away. So, here in the U.S. of A. my only assets are 36-28-42.

MC: Hmmm! That's what I call a positive attitude. Miss Fina, some day you'll get it all back. Un aplauso[25] for Fina, ladies and gentlemen! [MISS LITTLE HAVANA *steps back and freezes into a doll-like posture, with a fixed smile on her face.*]

MC: Now, from South of the Border, ladies and gentlemen—hold on to your tacos, because here she is…Miss Chili Tamale![26] [*Music begins: "Allá en el Rancho Grande".*] Please, un aplauso! Welcome, welcome chaparrita![27] [MISS CHILI TAMALE *enters. She also wears a bathing suit and a sarape over her shoulder. She sings.*]

---

[21] Two forms of song in which words rhyme.
[22] (Sp.) When I left Cuba/I left my house, I left my airplane/When I left Cuba/I left half a million buried.
[23] (Sp.) Fina is very fine.
[24] (Sp.) An airplane.

[25] (Sp.) A round of applause.
[26] (Sp.) A traditional corn dish that is stuffed with a filling and wrapped in a corn husk.
[27] (Sp.) Shortie.

ALLÁ EN EL RANCHO GRANDE
ALLA DONDE VIVÍA
YO ERA UNA FLACA MORENITA
QUE TRISTE SE QUEJABA
QUE TRISTE SE QUEJAABAAA
NO TENGO NI UN PAR DE CALZONES
NI SIN REMIENDOS DE CUERO
NI DOS HUEVOS RANCHEROS
Y LAS TORTILLAS QUEMADAS[28]

MC: Your name, beautiful señorita?

MISS CHILI TAMALE: Lupe Lupita Guadalupe Viva Zapata y Enchilada, para servirle.[29]

MC: What good manners! Tell us, what's your most fervent desire?

MISS CHILI TAMALE: My most fervent desire is to marry a big, handsome, very rich americano.

MC: Aha! What have we here! You mean you prefer gringos instead of Latin men?

MISS CHILI TAMALE: Oh no, no no. But, you see, I need my green card. La migra[30] is after me.

MC: [*Nervously, the* MC *looks around, then pushes* MISS TAMALE *back. She joins* MISS LITTLE HAVANA *in her doll-like pose.*] Ahem, ahem. Now, ladies and gentlemen, the dream girl of every American male, the most beautiful señorita of all. Created by Madison Avenue exclusively for the United Fruit Company...ladies and gentlemen, please welcome Miss Conchita Banana! [*"Chiquita Banana" music begins.* MISS CONCHITA BANANA *enters. She wears plastic bananas on her head and holds two real ones in her hands. She sings.*]

I'M CONCHITA BANANA
AND I'M HERE TO SAY
THAT BANANAS TASTE THE BEST
IN A CERTAIN WAY
YOU CAN PUT'EM IN YOUR HUM HUM
YOU CAN SLICE'EM IN YOUR HA HA
ANYWAY YOU WANT TO EAT'EM
IT'S IMPOSSIBLE TO BEAT'EM
BUT NEVER, NEVER, NEVER
PUT BANANAS IN THE REFRIGERATOR
NO, NO, NO NO![31]

[*She throws the two real bananas to the audience.*]

MC: Brava, bravissima, Miss Banana! Do you realize you have made our humble fruit, el plátano, very very famous all over the world?

MISS CONCHITA BANANA: Yes, I know. That has been the goal of my whole life.

MC: And we are proud of you, Conchita. But, come here, just between the two of us...tell me the truth, do you really like bananas?

---

[28] (Sp.) There at the big ranch/There where I used to live/I was a skinny little dark girl/So sad, my plaint/So sad, my plaint/I don't even have a pair of underwear/Nor any leather for mending/Nor two ranch-style eggs/And burnt tortillas (A parody of the popular Mexican folk song "Allá en el Rancho Grande").

[29] (Sp.) At your service.

[30] (Sp.) Immigration authority.

[31] A parody of a jingle used to sell Chiquita brand bananas in the 1960s and 1970s.

MISS CONCHITA BANANA: Of course, I do! I eat them all the time. My motto is: a banana a day keeps the doctor away!

MC: [*Motioning to audience to applaud.*] What intelligence! What insight! Un aplauso, ladies and gentlemen…[MISS CONCHITA BANANA *bows and steps back, joining the other doll-like contestants. As each woman says the following lines she becomes human again. The* MC *moves to one side and freezes.*]

WOMAN 1: [*Previously* MISS LITTLE HAVANA.] No one knows me. They see me passing by, but they don't know me. They don't see me. They hear my accent but not my words. If anyone wants to find me, I'll be sitting by the beach.

WOMAN 2: [*Previously* MISS CHILI TAMALE.] My mother, my grandmother, and her mother before her, walked the land with barefeet, as I have done too. We have given birth to our daughters on the bare soil. We have seen them grow and go to market. Now we need permits to walk the land—our land.

WOMAN 3: [*Previously* MISS CONCHITA BANANA.] I have been invented for a photograph. Sometimes I wish to be a person, to exist for my own sake, to stop dancing, to stop smiling. One day I think I will want to cry.

MC: [*We hear a fanfare. The* MC *unfreezes. The contestants become dolls again.*] Ladies and gentlemen…don't go away, because we still have more for you! Now, señoras y señores, from la Isla del Encanto, please welcome Miss Commonwealth! Un aplauso, please! [*We hear music from "Cortaron a Elena."* MISS COMMONWEALTH *enters, giggling and waving. She sings.*]

CORTARON EL BUDGET
CORTARON EL BUDGET
CORTARON EL BUDGET
Y NOS QUEDAMOS
SIN FOOD STAMPS
CORTARON A ELENA
CORTARON A JUANA
CORTARON A LOLA
Y NOS QUEDAMOS
SIN NA' PA' NA'[32]

MC: ¡Qué sabor! Tell us your name, beautiful jibarita…[33]

MISS COMMONWEALTH: Lucy Wisteria Rivera [*Giggles.*]

MC: Let me ask you, what do you think of the political status of the island?

MISS COMMONWEALTH: [*Giggles.*] Oh, I don't know about that. La belleza y la política no se mezclan. Beauty and politics do not mix. [*Giggles.*]

MC: True, true, preciosa-por-ser-un-encanto-por-ser-un-edén.[34] Tell me, what is your goal in life?

MISS COMMONWEALTH: I want to find a boyfriend and get married. I will be a great housewife, cook and mother. I will only live for my husband and my children. [*Giggles.*]

---

[32] (Sp.) They cut the budget/They cut the budget/They cut the budget/And they leave us/Without food stamps/They cut Elena [from the welfare rolls]/They cut Juana/They cut Lola/And they leave us/Nothin' for nothin'.

[33] (Sp.) Country girl.

[34] (Sp.) You're precious for being so enchanting, for being a garden of Eden. (A reference to "Preciosa" by Rafael Hernandez, a popular song about the natural beauty of Puerto Rico.)

MC: Ave María, nena! You are a tesoro![35] Well, Miss Commonwealth, finding a boyfriend should not be difficult for you. You have everything a man wants right there up front. [*Points to her breasts with the microphone.*] I am sure you already have several novios, no?

MISS COMMONWEALTH: Oh no, I don't have a boyfriend yet. My father doesn't let me. And besides, it isn't as easy as you think. To catch a man you must know the rules of the game, the technique, the tricks, the know-how, the how-to, the expertise, the go-get-it, the…works! Let me show you.

[*The MC stands to one side and freezes. The doll-like contestants in the back exit.* MISS COMMONWEALTH *begins to exit. She runs into the* GIRL *as she enters.* MISS COMMONWEALTH'*s crown falls to the floor. She looks at the* GIRL, *who seems to remind her of something far away.*]

WOMAN 4: [*Previously* MISS COMMONWEALTH.] The girl who had never seen the ocean decided one day to see it. Just one startled footprint on the sand and the sea came roaring at her. A thousand waves, an infinite horizon, a storm of salt and two diving birds thrust themselves furiously into her eyes. Today she walks blindly through the smog and the dust of cities and villages. But she travels with a smile, because she carries the ocean in her eyes. [WOMAN 4 *exits. Spot on the* GIRL. *She picks up the crown from the floor and places it on her head. Spot closes in on the crown.*]

As lights go up, the MAN *enters with a chair and places it center stage. He sits on it. The* GIRL *sits on the floor with her back to the audience. The* CATCH WOMEN *enter and take their places around the man. Each* WOMAN *addresses the* GIRL, *as a teacher would.*

CATCH WOMAN 1: There are many ways to catch a man. Watch…[*Walks over to the* MAN.] Hypnotize him. Be a good listener. [*She sits on his knees.*] Laugh at his jokes, even if you heard them before. [*To* MAN.] Honey, tell them the one about the two bartenders…[*The* MAN *mouths words as if telling a joke. She listens and laughs loudly. Gets up.*] Cuá, cuá, cuá! Isn't he a riot! [*She begins to walk away, turns and addresses the* GIRL.] Ah, and don't forget to move your hips.

CATCH WOMAN 2: [CATCH WOMAN 1 *walks moving her hips back to her place.* CATCH WOMAN 2 *steps forward and addresses the* GIRL.] Women can't be too intellectual. He will get bored. [*To* MAN, *in earnest.*] Honey, don't you think nuclear disarmament is our only hope for survival? [*The* MAN *yawns. To* GIRL.] See? When a man goes out with a woman he wants to relax, to have fun, to feel good. He doesn't want to talk about heavy stuff, know what I mean? [CATCH WOMAN 2 *walks back to her place. She flirts with her boa, wrapping it around the man's head. Teasing.*] Toro, toro, torito![36]

CATCH WOMAN 3: [*The* MAN *charges after* CATCH WOMAN 2. CATCH WOMAN 3 *stops him with a hypnotic look. He sits down again.* CATCH WOMAN 3 *addresses the* GIRL.] Looks are a very powerful weapon. Use your eyes, honey. Look at him now and then. Directly. Sideways. Through your eyelashes. From the corner of your eyes. Over your sunglasses. Look at him up and down. But not with too much insistence. And never ever look directly at his crotch. [*She walks away dropping a handkerchief. The* MAN *stops to pick it up.* CATCH WOMAN 4 *places her foot on it. Pushes the* MAN *away.*] Make him suffer. Make him jealous. [*Waves to someone offstage, flirting.*] Hi Johnny! [*To* GIRL.] They like it. It gives them a good excuse to get drunk. Tease him. Find out what he likes. [*To* MAN.] Un masajito, papi?[37] I'll make you a burrito de machaca con

---

[35] (Sp.) Treasure.
[36] (Sp.) Bull, bull, little bull.

[37] (Sp.) Would you like a massage, daddy?

huevo,[38] sí? [*She massages his neck.*] Keep him in suspense. [*To* MAN.] I love you. I don't love you. Te quiero. No te quiero. I love you. I don't love you…[*She walks away.*]

ALL: [*All four* CATCH WOMEN *come forward.*] We do it all for him!

MAN: They do it all for me! [MAN *raps the song, while the* CATCH WOMEN *parade around him.*]

"THEY DO IT ALL FOR ME"

[*Wolf whistles.*]
MIRA MAMI, PSST, COSA LINDA!
OYE MUÑECA, DAME UN POQUITO
AY, MIREN ESO
LO QUE DIOS HA HECHO
PARA NOSOTROS LOS PECADORES[39]
AY MAMÁ, DON'T WALK LIKE THAT
DON'T MOVE LIKE THAT
DON'T LOOK LIKE THAT
'CAUSE YOU GONNA GIVE ME
A HEART ATTACK
THEY DO IT ALL FOR ME
WHAT THEY LEARN IN A MAGAZINE
THEY DO IT ALL FOR ME
'CAUSE YOU KNOW WHAT THEY WANT
AY MAMÁ, TAN PRECIOSA TAN HERMOSA[40]
GIVE ME A PIECE OF THIS
AND A PIECE OF THAT
'CAUSE I KNOW YOU DO IT ALL FOR ME
DON'T YOU DON'T YOU
DON'T YOU DO IT ALL FOR ME

[CATCH WOMAN 2 *throws her boa around his neck, ropes in the* MAN *and exits with him in tow.*]

CATCH WOMAN 1: ¡Mira, esa mosquita muerta ya agarró uno![41]

CATCH WOMAN 3: Look at that, she caught him!

CATCH WOMAN 4: Pero, ¡qué tiene ella que no tenga yo![42]

All exit. The GIRL *stands up, picks up the handkerchief from the floor. Mimes imitations of some of the* WOMEN*'s moves, flirting, listening to jokes, giggling, moving her hips, etc. Church music comes on. The* NUN *enters carrying a bouquet of roses cradled in her arms. She stands in the back and looks up bathed in a sacred light. Her lips move as if praying. She lowers her eyes and sees the* GIRL *imitating more sexy moves. The* NUN*'s eyes widen in disbelief.*

NUN: What are you doing, creature? That is sinful! A woman must be recatada, saintly. Thoughts of the flesh must be banished from your head and your heart. Close your eyes and your pores to desire. The only love there is is the love of the

---

[38] (Sp.) Dried meat with eggs (a breakfast dish associated with cowboys).

[39] (Sp.) Look mami, psst, pretty thing!/Listen doll, give me a little/Oh, Look at that/Look what God has made/For us sinners.

[40] (Sp.) Oh mama, so precious, so beautiful.

[41] (Sp.) Look, that dead mosquito caught one!

[42] (Sp.) But what has she got that I don't have?

Lord. The Lord is the only lover! [*The* GIRL *stops, thoroughly confused. The* NUN *strikes her with the bouquet of roses.*] ¡Arrodíllate! Kneel down on these roses! Let your blood erase your sinful thoughts! You may still be saved. Pray, pray! [*The* GIRL *kneels on the roses, grimacing with pain. The* PRIEST *enters, makes the sign of the cross on the scene. The* NUN *kneels in front of the* PRIEST.] Father, forgive me for I have sinned…[*The* SEÑORITAS *enter with her lines. They wear mantillas and peinetas,[43] holding Spanish fans in their hands, a red carnation between their teeth.*]

SEÑORITA 1: Me too, father!

SEÑORITA 2: ¡Y yo también!

SEÑORITA 3: And me!

SEÑORITA 4: Me too! [*A tango begins. The following lines are integrated into the choreography.*]

SEÑORITA 1: Father, it has been two weeks since my last confession…

PRIEST: Speak, hija mía.[44]

SEÑORITA 2: Padre, my boyfriend used to kiss me on the lips…but it's all over now…

PRIEST: Lord, oh Lord!

SEÑORITA 3: Forgive me father, but I have masturbated three times. Twice mentally, once physically.

PRIEST: Ave María Purísima sin pecado concebida…[45]

SEÑORITA 4: I have sinned, santo padre. Last night I had wet dreams.

PRIEST: Socorro espiritual, Dios mío.[46] Help these lost souls!

SEÑORITA 1: He said, fellatio…I said, cunnilingus!

PRIEST: No, not in a beautiful señorita's mouth! Such evil words, Señor, oh Lord!

SEÑORITA 2: Father, listen. I have sinned. I have really really sinned. I did it, I did it! All the way I did it! [*All the* SEÑORITAS *and the* NUN *turn to* SEÑORITA 2 *and make the sign of the cross. They point at her with the fans.*]

SEÑORITAS 1, 3, 4: She's done it, Dios mío, she's done it! Santísima Virgen, she's done it!

PRIEST: She's done it! She's done it!

SEÑORITA 2: [*Tangoing backwards.*] I did it. yes. Lo hice. I did it, father. Forgive me, for I have fornicated!

PRIEST: She's done it! She's done it! [*The* NUN *faints in the* PRIEST'*s arms.*]

SEÑORITAS 1, 3, 4: Fornication! Copulation! Indigestion! ¡Qué pecado y qué horror! ¡Culpable! ¡Culpable! ¡Culpable![47] [*They exit tangoing. The* PRIEST, *with the fainted* NUN *in his arms looks at the audience bewildered.*]

PRIEST: [*To audience.*] Intermission!

[*Black out*]

Act II

In the dark we hear a fanfare. Spot light on MC.

MC: Welcome back, ladies and gentlemen, señoras y señores. There's more, much much more yet to come. For, you see, our contestants are not only beautiful, but also very talented señoritas. For the benefit of the judges they will sing, they will dance, they will perform the most daring acts on the flying trapeze!

Spot light on WOMAN 3 *swinging on a swing center stage. She sings:*

---

[43] Traditional long veils and hair ornaments associated with Spain.
[44] (Sp.) My daughter.

[45] (Sp.) Holy Mary conceived without sin.
[46] (Sp.) Spiritual succor, my God.
[47] (Sp.) What a sin and horror! Guilty! Guilty! Guilty!

"BOLERO TRAICIONERO"

TAKE ME IN YOUR ARMS
LET'S DANCE AWAY THE NIGHT
WHISPER IN MY EARS
THE SWEETEST WORDS OF LOVE

I'M THE WOMAN IN YOUR LIFE
SAY YOU DIE EVERY TIME
YOU ARE AWAY FROM ME
AND WHISPER IN MY EAR
THE SWEETEST WORDS OF LOVE

PROMISE ME THE SKY
GET ME THE MOON, THE STARS
IF IT IS A LIE
WHISPER IN MY EAR
THE SWEETEST WORDS OF LOVE

DARLING IN A DREAM OF FLOWERS
WE ARE PLAYING ALL THE GREATEST GAMES
LIE TO ME WITH ROMANCE AGAIN
TRAICIÓNAME ASÍ, TRAICIÓNAME MÁS

(Bis)
PROMISE ME THE SKY...

[*During the song lights go up to reveal the other women sitting in various poses waiting to be asked to dance. The* GIRL *is also there, closely watched by the* CHAPERONE, *who also keeps an eye on all the other women. The* MAN *enters wearing a white tuxedo and a Zorro mask. He dances with each one. Gives each a flower, which he pulls out of his pocket like a magician. The* GIRL *wants to dance, the* MAN *comes and asks her, but the* CHAPERONE *doesn't let her. The* MAN *asks another woman to dance. They dance very close. The* CHAPERONE *comes and taps the woman on the shoulder. They stop dancing, The* MAN *goes to the woman singing, pushes the swing back and forth. At the end of the song, the singer leaves with the* MAN. *The other women follow them with their eyes.*]

SEÑORITA 2: I swear I only did it for love! He sang in my ear the sweetest words, the most romantic boleros. Saturdays and Sundays he sat at the bar across the street drinking beer. He kept playing the same record on the juke box over and over. It was a pasodoble about being as lonely as a stray dog. He would send me flowers and candies with the shoeshine boy. My father and brother had sworn to kill him if they saw him near me. But he insisted. He kept saying how much he loved me and he kept getting drunk right at my doorsteps. He serenaded me every weekend. He said I was the most decent woman in the world. Only his mother was more saintly...he said.

SEÑORITA 3: He said the same thing to me. Then he said the same thing to my sister and then to her best friend. My sister was heartbroken. She was so young. She had given him her virginity and he would not marry her. Then three days before Christmas she set herself on fire. She poured gasoline on her dress, put a match to it and then started to run. She ran like a vision of hell through the streets of the town. Her screams awoke all the dead lovers for miles around. Her long hair, her flowing dress were like a banner of fire calling followers to battle. She ran down Main Street—the street that leads directly to the sea. I ran after her trying to catch her to embrace her, to smother the flames with my own body. I ran after her, yelling not to go into the water. She couldn't, she wouldn't hear. She ran into the sea like thunder…Such drama, such fiery spectacle, such pain…It all ended with a half-silent hiss and a thin column of smoke rising up from the water, near the beach where we played as children…

[*We hear the sound of drums. The women join in making mournful sounds. The mournful sounds slowly turn into the "Wedding Song."*]

"THE WEDDING SONG"
("Where Have All the Women Gone")

WOMAN:
THERE, THERE'S JUANA
SEE JUANA JUMP
SEE HOW SHE JUMPS
WHEN HE DOES CALL
THERE, THERE'S ROSA
SEE ROSA CRY
SEE HOW SHE CRIES
WHEN HE DOESN'T CALL

CHORUS:
WHERE HAVE ALL
THE WOMEN GONE

WOMAN:
JUANA ROSA CARMEN GO
NOT WITH A BANG
BUT WITH A WHIMPER
WHERE HAVE THEY GONE
LEAVING THEIR DREAMS
BEHIND
LEAVING THEIR DREAMS
LETTING THEIR LIVES
UNDONE

CHORUS:
[*Wedding March Music.*]
LOOK HOW THEY GO
LOOK AT THEM GO
SIGHING AND CRYING
LOOK AT THEM GO

Towards the end of the song the women will form a line before the CHAPERONE *who is holding a big basket. From it she takes and gives each woman a wig with hairrollers on it. Assisted by the* GIRL, *each woman will put her wig on. Once the song ends, each woman will start miming various housecleaning chores: sweeping, ironing, washing, etc. The* MOTHER *sews. The* GIRL *watches.*

MARTYR 1: Cry my child. Las mujeres nacimos para sufrir.[48] There's no other way but to cry. One is born awake and crying. That's the way God meant it. And who are we to question the ways of the Lord?

MARTYR 2: I don't live for myself. I live for my husband and my children. A woman's work is never done: what to make for lunch, cook the beans, start the rice, and then again, what to make for supper, and the fact that Juanito needs new shoes for school. [*She holds her side in pain.*]

MARTYR 3: What's wrong with you?

MARTYR 2: I have female problems.

MARTYR 3: The menstruation again?

MARTYR 2: No, my husband beat me up again last night. [*The* GIRL *covers her ears, then covers her eyes and begins to play "Put the Tail on the Donkey" all by herself.*]

MARTYR 3: I know what you mean, m'ija. We women were born to suffer. I sacrifice myself for my children. But, do they appreciate it? No. Someday, someday when I'm gone they'll remember me and all I did for them. But then it will be too late. Too late.

MOTHER: Such metaphysics. Women should not worry about philosophical matters. That's for men. [*She returns to her sewing, humming a song of oblivion.*]

MARTYR 3: The Virgin Mary never worried about forced sterilization or torture in Argentina or minimum wages. True, she had housing problems, but I'm sure there was never a quarrel as to who washed the dishes or fed that burro.

MAMA: Such heretic thoughts will not lead to anything good, I tell you. It is better not to have many thoughts. When you do the ironing or the cooking or set your hair in rollers, it is better not to think too much. I know what I'm saying. I know…[*Continues her sewing and humming.*]

MARTYR 1: And this headache. We're born with migraine. And with the nerves on edge. It is so, I know. I remember my mother and her mother before her. They always had jaquecas. I inherited the pain and tazas de tilo, the Valiums and the Libriums…

MAMA: You don't keep busy enough. While your hands are busy…

MARTYR 2:…And your mouth is busy, while you run from bed to stove to shop to work to sink to bed to mirror no one notices the little light shining in your eyes. It is better that way…because I…I don't live for myself. I live for my husband and my children, and it is better that they don't notice that flash in my eyes, that sparkle of a threat, that flickering death wish…[*The* GIRL *tears off the cloth covering her eyes. Looks at the women expecting some action. Mumbling and complaining under their breaths, the women go back to their chores. The* GUERRILLERA *enters. She is self-assured and full of energy. The* GIRL *gives her all her attention.*]

GUERRILLERA: Stop your laments, sisters!

MARTYR 1: Who's she?

GUERRILLERA: Complaining and whining won't help!

MARTYR 3: That's true!

GUERRILLERA: We can change the world and then our lot will improve!

MARTYR 3: It's about time!

GUERRILLERA: Let's fight oppresion!

---

[48] (Sp.) We women are born to suffer.

MARTYR 3: I'm ready! Let's go!

MARTYR 2: I ain't going nowhere. I think she's a lesbian.

GUERRILLERA: We, as third world women…

MARTYR 1: Third world…? I'm from Michoacán…

GUERRILLERA:…Are triply oppressed, so we have to fight three times as hard!

MARTYR 3: That's right!

GUERRILLERA: Come to the meetings!

MARTYR 3: Where? Where? When?

GUERRILLERA:…Have your consciousness raised!

MARTYR 2: What's consciousness?

MARTYR 1: I don't know, but I'm keeping my legs crossed…[*Holds her skirt down on her knees.*]

GUERRILLERA: Come with me and help make the revolution!

MARTYR 3: Let's go, kill'em, kill'em!

GUERRILLERA: Good things will come to pass. Come with me and rebel!

MARTYR 3: Let's go! [*To the others.*] Come on!

MARTYR 2: All right, let's go!

MARTYR 1: Bueno…

ALL: Let's go, vamos! ¡Sí! ¡Arriba! ¡Vamos! Come on come on!

[MARTYR 3 *picks up a broom and rests it on her shoulder like a rifle. The others follow suit. All sing.*]

SI ADELITA SE FUERA CON OTRO
LA SEGUIRÍA POR TIERRA Y POR MAR
SI POR MAR EN UN BUQUE DE GUERRA
SI POR TIERRA EN UN TREN MILITAR[49]

GUERRILLERA: But first…hold it, hold it…but first…we must peel the potatoes, cook the rice, make the menudo[50] and sweep the hall… [*The* WOMEN *groan and lose enthusiasm.*] …because there's gonna be a fund raiser tonight! [*Music begins. The* GUERRILLERA *and* WOMEN *sing.*][51]

GUERRILLERA:
THERE'S GONNA BE A FUND-RAISER
THE BROTHERS WILL SPEAK OF CHANGE

CHORUS:
WE GONNA HAVE BANANA SURPRISE
WE GONNA CUT YAUTÍAS[52] IN SLICE
THERE'S GONNA BE A FUND-RAISER
BUT THEY'LL ASK US TO PEEL AND FRY

GUERRILLERA:
WE SAY OKAY
WE WILL FIGHT NOT CLEAN

---

[49] (Sp.) If Adele leaves with another/I would follow her by land and by sea/If by sea in a war ship/If by land in a military train. (A folk song from the Mexican Revolution written in honor of the many women who participated in the effort and who were referred to as "Adelitas.")

[50] (Sp.) Stew of hominy and tripe.

[51] Based on the words to "Tonight" from the musical *West Side Story*.

[52] (Sp.) Edible tuber, like a yam.

BUT THEY SAY GO DEAR
AND TYPE THE SPEECH

ANITA IS GONNA MAKE IT
SHE'S GONNA MAKE IT

CHORUS:
MARIA WILL SWEEP THE FLOOR
JUANITA IS FAT AND PREGNANT
PREGNANT FOR WHAT
NO MATTER IF WE'RE TIRED
AS LONG LONG LONG LONG
AS LONG AS THEY'RE NOT
TONIGHT TONIGHT
TONIGHT TONIGHT
TONIGHT TONIGHT
TONIGHT TONIGHT

GUERRILLERA:
WON'T BE JUST ANY NIGHT

CHORUS:
TONIGHT TONIGHT
TONIGHT TONIGHT
TONIGHT TONIGHT
TONIGHT TONIGHT

GUERRILLERA:
WE'LL BE NO MORE HARRASSED

CHORUS:
TONIGHT TONIGHT
TONIGHT TONIGHT
TONIGHT TONIGHT
TONIGHT TONIGHT

GUERRILLERA:
I'LL HAVE SOMETHING TO SAY

CHORUS:
TONIGHT TONIGHT

GUERRILLERA:
FOR US A NEW DAY WILL START

CHORUS:
TODAY THE WOMEN
WANT THE HOURS

GUERRILLERA:
HOURS TO BE LOVING

CHORUS:
TODAY THE WOMEN
WANT THE HOURS

GUERRILLERA: CHORUS:
AND STILL THE TIME TO FIGHT   BORING BORING
TO MAKE THIS ENDLESS   BORING BORING
BORING BORING BORING   BORING BORING
BORING BORING BORING   BORING BORING
FLIGHT!   FLIGHT!

[All end the song with mops and brooms upraised. A voice is heard offstage.]
MAN: *[Offstage.]* Is dinner ready! *[The* WOMEN *drop their "weapons" and run away.]*
WOMAN 1: ¡Ay, se me quema el arroz![53]
WOMAN 2: ¡Bendito, las habichuelas![54]
WOMAN 3: ¡Ay, Virgen de Guadalupe, las enchiladas! *[They exit.]*
GUERRILLERA: *[Exiting after them.]* Wait! Wait! What about the revolution!...*[Black out.
    As the lights go up the* MAN *enters dressed as a campesino,[55] with poncho and sombrero. The*
    SOCIAL RESEARCHER *enters right behind. She holds a notebook and a pencil.]*
RESEARCHER: *[With an accent.]* Excuse me señor...buenas tardes. Me llamo Miss
    Smith.[56] I'm from the Peaceful Corps. Could you be so kind to answer some
    questions for me—for our research study?
MAN: Bueno.
RESEARCHER: Have you many children?
MAN: God has not been good to me. Of sixteen children born, only nine live.
RESEARCHER: Does you wife work?
MAN: No. She stays at home.
RESEARCHER: I see. How does she spend the day?
MAN: *[Scratching his head.]* Well, she gets up at four in the morning, fetches water and
    wood, makes the fire and cooks breakfast. Then she goes to the river and washes
    the clothes. After that she goes to town to get the corn ground and buy what we
    need in the market. Then she cooks the midday meal.
RESEARCHER: You come home at midday?
MAN: No, no, she brings the meal to me in the field—about three kilometers from
    home.
RESEARCHER: And after that?
MAN: Well, she takes care of the hens and the pigs...and of course, she looks after the
    children all day...then she prepares supper so it is ready when I come home.
RESEARCHER: Does she go to bed after supper?
MAN: No, I do. She has things to do around the house until about ten o'clock.
RESEARCHER: But, señor, you said your wife doesn't work...
MAN: Of course, she doesn't work. I told you, she stays home!
RESEARCHER: *[Closing notebook.]* Thank you, señor. You have been very helpful. Adiós.
    [She exits. The MAN *follows her.]*
MAN: Hey, psst, señorita...my wife goes to bed at ten o'clock. I can answer more

[53] (Sp.) Oh, I've burned the rice!
[54] (Sp.) Goodness, the beans!
[55] (Sp.) Peasant.
[56] (Sp.) Excuse me, sir...good afternoon. My name is Miss
Smith.

questions for you later…[*Black out.*]

In the dark we hear the beginning of "Dolphins by the Beach." The DAUGHTER 1 *and the* GIRL *enter. They dance to the music. This dance portrays the fantasies of a young woman. It is a dance of freedom and self-realization. A Fanfare is heard, breaking the spell. They run away. The* MC *enters.*

MC: Ladies and gentlemen, señoras y señores …the show goes on and on and on and ON! The beauty, the talent, the endurance of these contestants is, you have to agree, OVERWHELMING. They have gone beyond the call of duty in pursuit of their goal. They have performed unselfishly. They have given their all. And will give even more, for, ladies and gentlemen, señoras y señores, the contest is not over yet. As the excitement mounts—I can feel it in the air!—the question burning in everyone's mind is: who will be the winner? [*As soap opera narrator.*] Who will wear that crown on that pretty little head? What will she do? Will she laugh? Will she cry? Will she faint in my arms?… Stay tuned for the last chapter of Reina for a Day! [MC *exits. All the women enter.*]

DAUGHTER 1: Mamá, may I go out and play? It is such a beautiful day and the tree is full of mangoes. May I get some? Let me go out to the top of the hill. Please. I just want to sit there and look ahead, far away. If I squint my eyes real hard I think I can see the ocean. Mami, please, may I, may I go out?

MOTHER: Niña, what nonsense. Your head is always in the clouds. I can't give you permission to go out. Wait until your father comes home and ask him. [FATHER *enters.*]

DAUGHTER 1: Papá, please, may I go out and play? It is such a beautiful day and…

FATHER: No. Stay home with your mother. Girls belong at home. You are becoming much of a tomboy. Why don't you learn to cook, to sew, to mend my socks…

WIFE: Husband, I would like to buy some flowers for the windows, and that vase I saw yesterday at the shop…

HUSBAND: Flowers, flowers, vases. What luxury! Instead of such fuss about the house, why don't you do something about having a child? I want a son. We've been married two years now and I am tired of waiting. What's the matter with you? People are already talking. It's me they suspect…

MOTHER: Son, I have placed all my hopes on you. I hope you will be better than your father and take care of me…

SON: I'm going off to the war. I have been called to play the game of death. I must leave you now. I must go and kill…

WIDOW: He gave his life for the country in a far away land, killing people he didn't know, people who didn't speak his language. I'm with child. His child. I hope it's a son…he wanted a son so much…

DAUGHTER 2: Mother, I'm pregnant. He doesn't want to get married. I don't want to get married. I don't even know whether I want this child…

MOTHER: Hija…how can you do this to me?! How is it possible. That's not what I taught you! I…your father…your brother…the neighbors…what would people say?

BROTHER: I'll kill him. I know who did it. I'll wring his neck. He'll pay for this! Abusador sin escrúpulos[57]…Dishonoring decent girls…And I thought he was my friend. He'll pay dearly for my sister's virginity. ¡Lo pagará con sangre![58]

DAUGHTER 1: But I read it in *Cosmopolitan*. It said everyone is doing it! And the TV

---

[57] (Sp.) Unscrupulous abuser.   [58] (Sp.) He'll pay with blood!

commercials...and...

MOTHER: Hijo, what's the matter? You look worried...

SON: Mother, my girlfriend is having a baby. My baby. I want to bring her here. You know, I don't have a job, and well, her parents kicked her out of the house...

MOTHER: Just like his father! So young and already spilling his seed around like a generous spring shower. Bring her. Bring your woman to me. I hope she has wide hips and gives you many healthy sons. [MOTHER *and* SON *exit.*]

[*The* WOMEN *make moaning sounds, moving around, grouping and regrouping. Loud Latin music bursts on. The* WOMEN *dance frenetically, then suddenly the music stops.*]

WOMAN 1: Sometimes, while I dance, I hear—behind the rhythmically shuffling feet—the roar of the water cascading down the mountain, thrown against the cliffs by an enraged ocean.

WOMAN 2: ...I hear the sound of water in a shower, splattering against the tiles where a woman lies dead. I hear noises beyond the water, and sometimes they frighten me.

WOMAN 3: Behind the beat of the drums I hear the thud of a young woman's body thrown from a roof. I hear the screeching of wheels from a speeding car and the stifled cries of a young girl lying on the street.

WOMAN 4: Muffled by the brass section I sometimes hear in the distance desperate cries of help from elevators, parking lots and apartment buildings. I hear the echoes in a forest: "please...no...don't..." of a child whimpering.

WOMAN 1: I think I hear my sister cry while we dance.

WOMAN 2: I hear screams. I hear the terrorized sounds of a young girl running naked along the highway.

WOMAN 3: The string section seems to murmur names...

WOMAN 4: To remind me that the woman, the girl who at this very moment is being beaten...

WOMAN 1: raped...

WOMAN 2: murdered...

WOMAN 3: is my sister...

WOMAN 4: my daughter...

WOMAN 1: my mother...

ALL: myself...

[*The* WOMEN *remain on stage, backs turned to the audience. We hear a fanfare. The* MC *enters.*]

MC: Ladies and gentlemen, the choice has been made, the votes have been counted, the results are in...and the winner is...señoras y señores: the queen of queens, Miss Señorita Mañana![59] There she is... [*Music from Miss America's "There She Is...." The* GIRL *enters followed by* MAMA. *The* GIRL *is wearing all the items she has picked from previous scenes: the tinsel crown, the flowers, a mantilla, etc. Her face is still made up as a clown. The* WOMEN *turn around to look. The* GIRL *looks upset, restless with all the manipulation she has endured. The* WOMEN *are distressed by what they see. They surround the* GIRL.]

WOMAN 1: This is not what I meant at all...

WOMAN 2: I meant...

WOMAN 3: I don't know what I meant.

WOMAN 4: I think we goofed. She's a mess. [*They look at* MAMA *reproachfully.* MAMA *looks*

[59] (Sp.) Tomorrow.

apologetic.]

MAMA: I only wanted…

WOMAN 1: [*Pointing to the* MC.] It's all his fault!

MC: Me? I only wanted to make her a queen! Can we go on with the contest? This is a waste of time…

WOMAN 2: You and your fff…contest!

WOMAN 3: Cálmate,[60] chica. Wait.

WOMAN 4: [*To* MC.] Look, we have to discuss this by ourselves. Give us a break, Okay?

MC: [*Mumbling as he exits.*] What do they want? What's the matter with them?…

WOMAN 1: [*To* GIRL.] Ven acá,[61] m'ija. [*The* WOMEN *take off, one by one, all the various items, clean her face, etc.*]

WOMAN 2: Honey, this is not what it is about…

WOMAN 3: I'm not sure yet what it's about…

WOMAN 4: It is about what really makes you a woman.

WOMAN 1: It is not the clothes.

WOMAN 2: Or the hair.

WOMAN 3: Or the lipstick.

WOMAN 4: Or the cooking.

WOMAN 3: But…what is it about?

WOMAN 4: Well…I was 13 when the blood first arrived. My mother locked herself in the bathroom with me, and recited the facts of life, and right then and there, very solemnly, she declared me a woman.

WOMAN 1: I was 18 when, amid pain and pleasure, my virginity floated away in a sea of blood. He held me tight and said "now I have made you a woman."

WOMAN 2: Then, from my insides a child burst forth…crying, bathed in blood and other personal substances. And then someone whispered in my ear: "Now you are a real real woman."

WOMAN 3: In their songs they have given me the body of a mermaid, of a palm tree, of an ample-hipped guitar. In the movies I see myself as a whore, a nymphomaniac, a dumb servant or a third-rate dancer. I look for myself and I can't find me. I only find someone else's idea of me.

MAMA: But think…what a dangerous, deadly adventure being a woman! The harassment of being a woman…So many parts to be played so many parts to be stifled and denied. But look at so many wild, free young things crying, like the fox in the story: "tame me, tame and I'll be yours!"

WOMAN 1: But I'm tired of stories!

WOMAN 2: Yes, enough of "be this," "do that!"

WOMAN 3: "Look like that!" Mira, mira!

WOMAN 4: "Buy this product!"

WOMAN 1: "Lose 10 pounds!"

MAMA: Wait, wait some more, and maybe, just maybe…

WOMAN 1: Tell my daughter that I love her…

WOMAN 2: Tell my daughter I wish I had really taught her the facts of life…

WOMAN 3: Tell my daughter that still there are mysteries…

WOMAN 4: …that the life I gave her doesn't have to be like mine.

---

[60] (Sp.) Calm yourself.   [61] (Sp.) Come here.

THE GIRL:...that there are possibilities. That women that go crazy in the night, that women that die alone and frustrated, that women that exist only in the mind, are only half of the story, because a woman is...

WOMAN 1: A fountain of fire!

WOMAN 2: A river of love!

WOMAN 3: An ocean of strength!

WOMAN 4: Mirror, mirror on the wall...

They look at each other as images on a mirror, discovering themselves in each other. The GIRL *is now one of them. She steps out and sings:*

"DON'T DENY US THE MUSIC"

WOMAN IS A FOUNTAIN OF FIRE
WOMAN IS A RIVER OF LOVE
A LATIN WOMAN IS JUST A WOMAN
WITH THE MUSIC INSIDE

DON'T DENY US THE MUSIC
DON'T IMAGINE MY FACE
I'VE FOUGHT MANY BATTLES
I'VE SUNG MANY SONGS
I AM JUST A WOMAN
WITH THE MUSIC INSIDE

I AM JUST A WOMAN BREAKING
THE LINKS OF A CHAIN
I AM JUST A WOMAN
WITH THE MUSIC INSIDE
FREE THE BUTTERFLY
LET THE OCEANS ROLL IN
FREE THE BUTTERFLY
LET THE OCEANS ROLL IN
I AM ONLY A WOMAN
WITH THE MUSIC INSIDE

—1994

RITA MAE BROWN (1944-   )

Born to a working-class family in Pennsylvania, Rita Mae Brown grew up in Florida. Determined to break out of poverty, she excelled in academics and earned a scholarship to the University of Florida. There she became involved in the civil rights movement; later, at New York University, she joined the feminist and the gay liberation movements. When Betty Friedan, president of the National Organization of Women (NOW), declared that lesbian visibility would hurt the image of the women's movement, calling lesbians the "lavender menace," Brown and others resigned from NOW and formed a lesbian activist group called Lavender Menace. That group, which soon changed its name to Radicalesbians, protested against lesbian invisibility at women's liberation gatherings; it also produced a manifesto entitled "The Woman-Identified Woman" that argued for lesbianism as the locus of meaningful change for women. Brown and a group of activists moved to Washington, D.C., in 1970 and created the Furies collective, a short-lived lesbian-feminist commune, in 1971. In 1973 Brown completed her first novel, *Rubyfruit Jungle,* a semi-autobiographical *Bildungsroman* describing the childhood and young adulthood of Molly Bolt, an irrepressibly self-confident lesbian. *Rubyfruit Jungle* was originally published by Daughters Inc., a feminist press, and attracted a wide alternative readership. When Bantam reissued the novel as a mass-market paperback in 1977, it sold more than a million copies. In the thirty years since her first published work appeared, Brown's writing has evolved from lesbian polemics to popular novels and mysteries "co-authored" with her cat, Sneaky Pie Brown.

> "A case of jam tomorrow and never jam today."
> Alice in Wonderland

The New Lost Feminist
A Triptych[1]

The Center Panel:
In the twilight of the Supreme Court
Wrinkled robed children
Passed judgement on Whistling lollipops and women.
Goliath staggers, his briefcase hemorrhaging with deals.
The Court hears the last appeal   5
For a land where means do not devour ends.

The underground railway smuggles giant blacks and
Glistening women to hidden empires beneath the polar caps.
America's rotting rib cage frames the gallows
Of her putrid goals.   10
How the nation rolls to stand on its feet
An upturned crab as decayed as its prey.
The young vomit and turn away.

Underground stations fill with blacks,
Women and the young   15
Fleeing a Troy that has built its own horse
America becomes a bloated corpse.

The Right Panel:
How this beast follows us
His leprous shadow blending with our own
And we fall to fighting among ourselves   20
Clawing the silk cheeks of other women.

Was there a golden age to remember?

---

[1] A three-paneled work of art, usually with the panels hinged together. The right and left panels are related to the center panel, which is the most important. Also a three-paneled writing tablet.

Was there a time when we knew our name
And called up great cities within us,
Our voices ringing out tidings of future nations? 25
Did we walk past ziggurats[2] then as now
Heads bowed, shameful as a conquered race?
Was there ever a time?

Women, women limping on the edges of the History of Man
Crippled for centuries and dragging the heavy emptiness 30
Past submission and sorrow to forgotten and unknown selves.
It's time to break and run.

The Left Panel:
Incoherent in the midst of men
I bleed at the mouth
Gushing broken participles 35
And teeth cracked on bullet words.
I bleed for want of a single, precious word,
Dying in the network of swollen blue veins
Large with my life force.
How can you turn away and chatter in your small change 40
Of prefixes and suffixes?
A woman is dying for want of a single unrealized word,
Freedom.

—1971

---

[2] Terraced pyramid that served as a temple in ancient Assyrian and Babylonian cultures.

THE COMBAHEE RIVER COLLECTIVE

The Combahee River Collective formed in Boston in 1974 (after the National Black Feminist Organization conference of 1973) as a response to the racism of the predominantly white women's movement and the sexism of the Black Nationalist movement. The group took its name from a river along which Harriet Tubman guided hundreds of people escaping from slavery. Meeting weekly throughout the 1970s, the collective sought to define the particular perspectives that Black women were bringing to feminism, Black activism, and the wider community. The members were active in movements to desegregate Boston schools, stop police brutality in Black neighborhoods, advocate for construction jobs for Black workers, defend Black people unfairly accused of crimes, and to stop violence against women, sterilization abuse, and the death penalty. The collective is best known for two publications: "A Black Feminist Statement" (also known as the "Combahee River Collective Statement") and the pamphlet "Six Black Women: Why Did They Die?," which responded to a series of murders of Black women in Boston in 1979. "A Black Feminist Statement" (1977) is considered an important articulation of identity politics as a simultaneous locus of multiple identities and a basis for the coalition politics that were dominant in the women's movement in the 1980s.

Among the group's members were some of the earliest African-American lesbians to be open about their sexual identity, including Barbara Smith, co-founder of Kitchen Table: Women of Color Press. Other well-known members included the poet Cheryl Clarke and the literary critic Akasha Gloria Hull.

A Black Feminist Statement[1]

We are a collective of Black feminists who have been meeting together since 1974. During that time we have been involved in the process of defining and clarifying our politics, while at the same time doing political work within our own group and in coalition with other progressive organizations and movements. The most general statement of our politics at the present time would be that we are actively committed to struggling against racial, sexual, heterosexual, and class oppression and see as our particular task the development of integrated analysis and practice based upon the fact that the major systems of oppression are interlocking. The synthesis of these oppressions creates the conditions of our lives. As Black women we see Black feminism as the logical political movement to combat the manifold and simultaneous oppressions that all women of color face.

We will discuss four major topics in the paper that follows: (1) the genesis of contemporary Black feminism; (2) what we believe, i.e., the specific province of our politics; (3) the problems in organizing Black feminists, including a brief herstory of our collective; and (4) Black feminist issues and practice.

1. The Genesis of Contemporary Black Feminism

Before looking at the recent development of Black feminism we would like to affirm that we find our origins in the historical reality of Afro-American women's continuous life-and-death struggle for survival and liberation. Black women's extremely negative relationship to the American political system (a system of white male rule) has always been determined by our membership in two oppressed racial and sexual castes. As Angela Davis[2] points out in "Reflections on the Black Woman's Role in the Community of Slaves," Black women have always embodied, if only in their physical manifestation, an adversary stance to white male rule and have actively resisted its inroads upon them and their communities in both dramatic and subtle ways. There have always been Black women activists—some known, like Sojourner Truth, Harriet Tubman, Frances E. W. Harper, Ida B. Wells Barnett, and Mary Church Terrell,[3] and thousands upon thousands unknown—who had a shared awareness of how their sexual identity combined with their racial identity to make their whole life situation and the focus of their political struggles unique. Contemporary Black feminism is the outgrowth of countless generations of personal sacrifice, militancy, and work by our mothers and sisters.

---

[1] [*Authors' note*.] The Combahee River Collective is a Black feminist group in Boston whose name comes from the guerrilla action conceptualized and led by Harriet Tubman on June 2, 1863, in the Port Royal region of South Carolina. This action freed more that 750 slaves and is the only military campaign in American history planned and led by a woman.

[2] Angela Davis (b. 1944), African-American activist, writer, and educator who came to prominence during the Black Power movement of the late 1960s and 1970s.

[3] Sojourner Truth (1797-1883), African-American abolitionist, suffragist, and itinerant preacher, best known for her "Arn't I a Woman" speech; Frances E. W. Harper (1825-1911), African-American writer and abolitionist, author of *Iola Leroy, or Shadows Uplifted* (1892); Ida B. Wells-Barnett (1862-1931), African-American journalist and lecturer who championed the anti-lynching movement and woman's suffrage; Mary Church Terrell (1863-1954), African-American teacher, writer, civil rights activist, and suffragist.

A Black feminist presence has evolved most obviously in connection with the second wave of the American women's movement beginning in the late 1960s. Black, other Third World,[4] and working women have been involved in the feminist movement from its start, but both outside reactionary forces and racism and elitism within the movement itself have served to obscure our participation. In 1973 Black feminists, primarily located in New York, felt the necessity of forming a separate Black feminist group. This became the National Black Feminist Organization (NBFO).

Black feminist politics also have an obvious connection to movements for Black liberation, particularly those of the 1960s and 1970s. Many of us were active in those movements (civil rights, Black nationalism, the Black Panthers), and all of our lives were greatly affected and changed by their ideology, their goals, and the tactics used to achieve their goals. It was our experience and disillusionment within these liberation movements, as well as experience on the periphery of the white male left, that led to the need to develop a politics that was antiracist, unlike those of white women, and antisexist, unlike those of Black and white men.

There is also undeniably a personal genesis for Black feminism, that is, the political realization that comes from the seemingly personal experiences of individual Black women's lives. Black feminists and many more Black women who do not define themselves as feminists have all experienced sexual oppression as a constant factor in our day-to-day existence. As children we realized that we were different from boys and that we were treated differently. For example, we were told in the same breath to be quiet both for the sake of being "ladylike" and to make us less objectionable in the eyes of white people. As we grew older we became aware of the threat of physical and sexual abuse by men. However, we had no way of conceptualizing what was so apparent to us, what we *knew* was really happening.

Black feminists often talk about their feelings of craziness before becoming conscious of the concepts of sexual politics, patriarchal rule, and, most importantly, feminism, the political analysis and practice that we women use to struggle against our oppression. The fact that racial politics and indeed racism are pervasive factors in our lives did not allow us, and still does not allow most Black women, to look more deeply into our own experiences and, from that sharing and growing consciousness, to build a politics that will change our lives and inevitably end our oppression. Our development also must be tied to the contemporary economic and political position of Black people. The post World War II generation of Black youth was the first to be able to minimally partake of certain educational and employment options, previously closed completely to Black people. Although our economic position is still at the very bottom of the American capitalistic economy, a handful of us have been able to gain certain tools as a result of tokenism in education and employment which potentially enable us to more effectively fight our oppression.

A combined antiracist and antisexist position drew us together initially, and as we developed politically we addressed ourselves to hetero-sexism and economic oppression under capitalism.

---

[4] Coined in 1952 by French demographer and economic historian Alfred Sauvy, the term "Third World" refers to countries in the developing world. It was later taken on as a politicized identity by some people of color in the United States in the 1970s.

2. What We Believe

Above all else, our politics initially sprang from the shared belief that Black women are inherently valuable, that our liberation is a necessity not as an adjunct to somebody else's but because of our need as human persons for autonomy. This may seem so obvious as to sound simplistic, but it is apparent that no other ostensibly progressive movement has ever considered our specific oppression a priority or worked seriously for the ending of that oppression. Merely naming the pejorative stereotypes attributed to Black women (e.g. mammy, matriarch, Sapphire, whore, bulldagger), let alone cataloguing the cruel, often murderous, treatment we receive, indicates how little value has been placed upon our lives during four centuries of bondage in the Western hemisphere. We realize that the only people who care enough about us to work consistently for our liberation is us. Our politics evolve from a healthy love for ourselves, our sisters, and our community which allows us to continue our struggle and work.

This focusing upon our own oppression is embodied in the concept of identity politics. We believe that the most profound and potentially the most radical politics come directly out of our own identity, as opposed to working to end somebody else's oppression. In the case of Black women this is a particularly repugnant, dangerous, threatening, and therefore revolutionary concept because it is obvious from looking at all the political movements that have preceded us that anyone is more worthy of liberation than ourselves. We reject pedestals, queenhood, and walking ten paces behind. To be recognized as human, levelly human, is enough.

We believe that sexual politics under patriarchy is as pervasive in Black women's lives as are the politics of class and race. We also often find it difficult to separate race from class from sex oppression because in our lives they are most often experienced simultaneously. We know that there is such a thing as racial-sexual oppression that is neither solely racial nor solely sexual, e.g., the history of rape of Black women by white men as a weapon of political repression.

Although we are feminists and lesbians, we feel solidarity with progressive Black men and do not advocate the fractionalization that white women who are separatists demand. Our situation as Black people necessitates that we have solidarity around the fact of race, which white women of course do not need to have with white men, unless it is their negative solidarity as racial oppressors. We struggle together with Black men against racism, while we also struggle with Black men about sexism.

We realize that the liberation of all oppressed peoples necessitates the destruction of the political-economic systems of capitalism and imperialism as well as patriarchy. We are socialists because we believe the work must be organized for the collective benefit of those who do the work and create the products and not for the profit of the bosses. Material resources must be equally distributed among those who create these resources. We are not convinced, however, that a socialist revolution that is not also a feminist and antiracist revolution will guarantee our liberation. We have arrived at the necessity for developing an understanding of class relationships that takes into account the specific class position of Black women, who are generally marginal in the labor force, while at this particular time some of us are temporarily viewed as doubly desirable tokens at white-collar and professional levels. We need to articulate the real class situation of persons who are not merely raceless, sexless workers, but for whom racial and sexual oppression are significant determinants in their working/economic lives.

Although we are in essential agreement with Marx's[5] theory as it applied to the very specific economic relationships he analyzed, we know that this analysis must be extended further in order for us to understand our specific economic situation as Black women.

A political contribution that we feel we have already made is the expansion of the feminist principle that the personal is political. In our consciousness-raising sessions, for example, we have in many ways gone beyond white women's revelations because we are dealing with the implications of race and class as well as sex. Even our Black women's style of talking/testifying in Black language about what we have experienced has a resonance that is both cultural and political. We have spent a great deal of energy delving into the cultural and experiential nature of our oppression out of necessity because none of these matters have ever been looked at before. No one before has ever examined the multilayered texture of Black women's lives. An example of this kind of revelation/conceptualization occurred at a meeting as we discussed the ways in which our early intellectual interests had been attacked by our peers, particularly Black males. We discovered that all of us, because we were "smart" had also been considered "ugly", *i.e.,* "smart-ugly." "Smart-ugly" crystallized the way in which most of us had been forced to develop our intellects at great cost to our "social" lives. The sanctions in the Black and white communities against Black women thinkers is comparatively much higher than for white women, particularly ones from the educated middle and upper classes.

As we have already stated, we reject the stance of lesbian separatism because it is not a viable political analysis or strategy for us. It leaves out far too much and far too many people, particularly Black men, women, and children. We have a great deal of criticism and loathing for what men have been socialized to be in this society: what they support, how they act, and how they oppress. But we do not have the misguided notion that it is their maleness, per se—i.e., their biological maleness—that makes them what they are. As Black women we find any type of biological determinism a particularly dangerous and reactionary basis upon which to build a politic. We must also question whether lesbian separatism is an adequate and progressive political analysis and strategy, even for those who practice it, since it so completely denies any but the sexual sources of women's oppression, negating the facts of class and race.

3. Problems in Organizing Black Feminists

During our years together as a Black feminist collective we have experienced success and defeat, joy and pain, victory and failure. We have found that it is very difficult to organize around Black feminist issues, difficult even to announce in certain contexts that we *are* Black feminists. We have tried to think about the reasons for our difficulties, particularly since the white women's movement continues to be strong and to grow in many directions. In this section we will discuss some of the general reasons for the organizing problems we face and also talk specifically about the stages in organizing our own collective.

The major source of difficulty in our political work is that we are not just trying to fight oppression on one front or even two, but instead to address a whole range of oppressions. We do not have racial, sexual, heterosexual, or class privilege to rely

---

[5] Karl Marx (1818-1883), German philosopher whose work is the grounding of modern socialism and communism.

upon, nor do we have even the minimal access to resources and power that groups who possess any one of these types of privilege have.

The psychological toll of being a Black woman and the difficulties this presents in reaching political consciousness and doing political work can never be underestimated. There is a very low value placed upon Black women's psyches in this society, which is both racist and sexist. As an early group member once said, "We are all damaged people merely by virtue of being Black women." We are dispossessed psychologically and on every other level, and yet we feel the necessity to struggle to change our condition and the condition of all Black women. In "A Black Feminist's Search for Sisterhood," Michele Wallace[6] arrives at this conclusion:

> We exist as women who are Black who are feminists, each stranded for the moment, working independently because there is not yet an environment in this society remotely congenial to our struggle—because, being on the bottom, we would have to do what no one else has done: we would have to fight the world.

Wallace is pessimistic but realistic in her assessment of Black feminists' position, particularly in her allusion to the nearly classic isolation most of us face. We might use our position at the bottom, however, to make a clear leap into revolutionary action. If Black women were free, it would mean that everyone else would have to be free since our freedom would necessitate the destruction of all the systems of oppression.

Feminism is, nevertheless, very threatening to the majority of Black people because it calls into question some of the most basic assumptions about our existence, i.e., sex should be a determinant of power relationships. Here is the way male and female roles were defined in a Black nationalist pamphlet from the early 1970s.

> We understand that it is and has been traditional that the man is the head of the house. He is the leader of the house/nation because his knowledge of the world is broader, his awareness is greater, his understanding is fuller and his application of this information is wiser.... After all, it is only reasonable that the man be the head of the house because he is able to defend and protect the development of his home....Women cannot do the same things as men—they are made by nature to function differently. Equality of men and women is something that cannot happen even in the abstract world. Men are not equal to other men, i.e. ability, experience or even understanding. The value of men and women can be seen as in the value of gold and silver—they are not equal but both have great value. We must realize that men and women are a complement to each other because there is no house/family without a man and his wife. Both are essential to the development of any life.

The material conditions of most Black women would hardly lead them to upset both economic and sexual arrangements that seem to represent some stability in their lives. Many Black women have a good understanding of both sexism and racism, but because of the everyday constrictions of their lives cannot risk struggling against them both.

The reaction of Black men to feminism has been notoriously negative. They are, of course, even more threatened than Black women by the possibility that Black feminists might organize around our own needs. They realize that they might not only lose valuable and hard-working allies in their struggles, but that they might also be

---

[6] Michele Wallace (b. 1952), African-American writer and academic, best known for her book *Black Macho and the Myth of the Superwoman* (1978).

forced to change their habitually sexist ways of interacting with and oppressing Black women. Accusations that Black feminism divides the Black struggle are powerful deterrents to the growth of an autonomous Black women's movement.

Still, hundreds of women have been active at different times during the three-year existence of our group. And every Black woman who came, came out of a strongly felt need for some level of possibility that did not previously exist in her life.

When we first started meeting early in 1974 after the NBFO first eastern regional conference, we did not have a strategy for organizing, or even a focus. We just wanted to see what we had. After a period of months of not meeting, we began to meet again late in the year and started doing an intense variety of consciousness-raising. The overwhelming feeling that we had is that after years and years we had finally found each other. Although we were not doing political work as a group, individuals continued their involvement in Lesbian politics, sterilization abuse, and abortion rights work, Third World Women's International Women's Day activities, and support activity for the trials of Dr. Kenneth Edelin, Joan Little, and Inéz García.[7] During our first summer, when membership had dropped off considerably, those of us remaining devoted serious discussion to the possibility of opening a refuge for battered women in a Black community. (There was no refuge in Boston at that time.) We also decided around that time to become an independent collective since we had serious disagreements with NBFO's bourgeois-feminist stance and their lack of a clear political focus.

We also were contacted at that time by socialist feminists, with whom we had worked on abortion rights activities, who wanted to encourage us to attend the National Socialist Feminist Conference in Yellow Springs.[8] One of our members did attend and despite the narrowness of the ideology that was promoted at that particular conference, we became more aware of the need for us to understand our own economic situation and to make our own economic analysis.

In the fall, when some members returned, we experienced several months of comparative inactivity and internal disagreements which were first conceptualized as a Lesbian-straight split but which were also the result of class and political differences. During the summer those of us who were still meeting had determined the need to do political work and to move beyond consciousness-raising and serving exclusively as an emotional support group. At the beginning of 1976, when some of the women who had not wanted to do political work and who also had voiced disagreements stopped attending of their own accord, we again looked for a focus. We decided at that time, with the addition of new members, to become a study group. We had always shared our reading with each other, and some of us had written papers on Black feminism for group discussion a few months before this decision was made. We began functioning as a study group and also began discussing the possibility of starting a Black feminist publication. We had a retreat in the late spring, which provided a time for both political discussion and working out interpersonal issues. Currently we are planning to gather together a collection of Black feminist writing. We feel that it is absolutely

---

[7] Dr. Kenneth Edelin (b. 1939) was convicted of performing a surgical abortion in Massachusetts after the U.S. Supreme Court legalized the procedure in the *Roe v. Wade* decision: The conviction was overturned on appeal to the state supreme court in 1976; Joan Little (b. 1953) aka Jo Ann Little, an African-American woman accused in 1974 of killing a white prison guard whom she said had tried to sexually assault her. Her case was taken up by the feminist, civil rights, and anti-death penalty movements; Inéz García (b. 1941), Latina whose case was championed by the women's movement when she was accused of murdering a man who raped her in 1974.

[8] The National Socialist Feminist Conference took place at Antioch College, Ohio, in July 1975.

essential to demonstrate the reality of our politics to other Black women and believe that we can do this through writing and distributing our work. The fact that individual Black feminists are living in isolation all over the country, that our own numbers are small, and that we have some skills in writing, printing, and publishing makes us want to carry out these kinds of projects as a means of organizing Black feminists as we continue to do political work in coalition with other groups.

4. Black Feminist Issues and Projects

During our time together we have identified and worked on many issues of particular relevance to Black women. The inclusiveness of our politics makes us concerned with any situation that impinges upon the lives of women, Third World and working people. We are of course particularly committed to working on those struggles in which race, sex, and class are simultaneous factors in oppression. We might, for example, become involved in workplace organizing at a factory that employs Third World women or picket a hospital that is cutting back on already inadequate health care to a Third World community, or set up a rape crisis center in a Black neighborhood. Organizing around welfare or daycare concerns might also be a focus. The work to be done and the countless issues that this work represents merely reflect the pervasiveness of our oppression.

Issues and projects that collective members have actually worked on are sterilization abuse, abortion rights, battered women, rape and health care. We have also done many workshops and educationals on Black feminism on college campuses, at women's conferences, and most recently for high school women.

One issue that is of major concern to us and that we have begun to publicly address is racism in the white women's movement. As Black feminists we are made constantly and painfully aware of how little effort white women have made to understand and combat their racism, which requires among other things that they have a more than superficial comprehension of race, color, and Black history and culture. Eliminating racism in the white women's movement is by definition work for white women to do, but we will continue to speak to and demand accountability on this issue.

In the practice of our politics we do not believe that the end always justifies the means. Many reactionary and destructive acts have been done in the name of achieving "correct" political goals. As feminists we do not want to mess over people in the name of politics. We believe in collective process and a nonhierarchical distribution of power within our own group and in our vision of a revolutionary society. We are committed to a continual examination of our politics as they develop through criticism and self-criticism as an essential aspect of our practice. In her introduction to *Sisterhood is Powerful* Robin Morgan writes:

> I haven't the faintest notion what possible revolutionary role white heterosexual men could fulfill, since they are the very embodiment of reactionary-vested-interest-power.

As Black feminists and Lesbians we know that we have a very definite revolutionary task to perform, and we are ready for the lifetime of work and struggle before us.

—1977

PAT PARKER (1944-1989)

Born in Houston, Texas, in 1944, Pat Parker was involved with the Black Panther and lesbian-feminist movements in California in the 1960s and 1970s, during which time her career as a writer and activist developed. Parker married playwright and Black Panther activist Ed Bullins in 1962. They were divorced in 1966, the year of a second marriage that also ended in divorce. By the late 1960s, Parker had become one of the first African-American writers to perform lesbian-themed poetry. In the early 1970s she moved with her two daughters to Oakland, California, where she frequently performed with the poet Judy Grahn. Parker and Grahn were among the founders of the Women's Press Collective, and together they recorded their poetry on the album *Where Would I Be Without You?* (1976). Parker worked for over ten years as a medical coordinator for the Oakland Feminist Women's Health Center. Poems from her early chapbooks *Child of Myself* (1972), *Pit Stop* (1974), and *Womanslaughter* (1978) were collected in the volume *Movement in Black* in 1978, which was reissued in 1999. She also contributed to the groundbreaking feminist anthologies *This Bridge Called My Back: Writing by Radical Women of Color* and *Home Girls: A Black Feminist Anthology.* Her long poem "Womanslaughter," about the murder of her sister by an abusive husband, was performed at the first International Tribunal on Crimes Against Women in Brussels, Belgium, in 1976. Parker died of breast cancer in 1989, at the age of forty-five.

WOMANSLAUGHTER

It doesn't hurt as much now—
the thought of you dead
doesn't rip at my innards,
leaves no holes to suck rage.
Now, thoughts of the four   5
daughters of Buster Cooks,
children, survivors
of Texas Hell, survivors
of soul-searing poverty,
survivors of small town   10
mentality, survivors,
now three
doesn't hurt as much now.

I
An Act

I used to be fearful
of phone calls in the night—   15
never in the day.

Death, like the vampire
fears the sun
never in the day—
"Hello Patty"   20
"Hey big sister
what's happening?
How's the kids?"

"For protection—just in case."
"Can you shoot it?"
"Yes, I have learned well." 115

"Hello, Hello Police
I am a woman alone
& I am afraid.
My husband means to kill me."

"Lady, there's nothing we can do 120
until he tries to hurt you.
Go to the judge & he will decree
that your husband leaves you be."
She found an apartment
with a friend. 125
She would begin
a new life again.
Interlocutory Divorce Decree[1] in hand;
The end of the quiet man.
He came to her home 130
& he beat her
Both women were afraid.

"Hello, Hello Police
I am a woman alone
& I am afraid 135
My ex-husband means to kill me."

"Fear not, Lady
He will be sought."
It was *too* late,
when he was caught. 140
One day a quiet man
shot his quiet wife
three times in the back.
He shot her friend as well.
His wife died. 145

The three sisters
of Shirley Jones
came to cremate her—
They were not strong.

III
Somebody's Trial

"It is good, they said 150
that Buster is dead.
He would surely kill

---

[1] Legal ruling granting a divorce that only becomes permanent after a waiting period, designed to give couples the chance to reconcile.

the quiet man."
I was not at the trial.
I was not needed to testify.   155
She slept with other men, he said.
No, said her friends.
No, said her sisters.
That is a lie.

She was Black.   160
You are white.
Why were you there?
We were friends, she said.
I was helping her move
the furniture; the divorce court   165
had given it to her.
Were you alone? they asked.
No two men came with us.
They were gone with a load.
She slept with women, he said.   170
No, said her sisters.
No, said her friends.
We were only friends;
That is a lie.
You lived with this woman?   175
Yes, said her friend.
You slept in the same bed?
Yes, said her friend.
Were you lovers?
No, said her friend.   180
But you slept in the same bed?
Yes, said her friend.

What shall be done with this man?
Is it a murder of the first degree?
No, said the men   185
It is a crime of passion.
He was angry.
Is it a murder of second degree?
Yes, said the men,
but we will not call it that.   190
We must think of his record.
We will call it manslaughter.
The sentence is the same.
What will we do with this man?
His boss, a white man came.   195
This is a quiet Black man, he said.
He works well for me
The men sent the quiet
Black man to jail.
He went to work in the day.   200

He went to jail & slept at night.
In one year, he went home.

IV

Woman-slaughter

"It is good, they said,
that Buster is dead.
He would surely kill   205
the quiet man."

Sister, I do not understand.
I rage & do not understand.
In Texas, he would be freed.
One Black kills another   210
One less Black for Texas.
But this is not Texas.
This is California.
The city of angels.
Was his crime so slight?   215
George Jackson[2] served
years for robbery.
Eldridge Cleaver[3] served
years for rape.
I know of a man in Texas   220
who is serving 40 years
for possession of marijuana.
Was his crime *so* slight?
What was his crime?
He only killed his wife.   225
But a divorce I say.
Not final, they say;
Her things were his
including her life.
Men cannot rape their wives.   230
Men cannot kill their wives.
They passion them to death.

The three sisters
of Shirley Jones
came & cremated her.   235
& they were not strong.
Hear me now—
It is almost three years
& I am again strong.

---

[2] George Jackson (1941-1971), a Black Panther Party militant who was one of the "Soledad Brothers" held in solitary confinement after being accused of killing a prison guard in retaliation for another guard's killing of a Black activist; Jackson was killed during an attempted escape from prison.

[3] Eldridge Cleaver (1935-1998), spokesperson for the Black Panther Party in the late 1960s and author of *Soul on Ice* (1968), a classic of the Black Power movement.

I have gained many sisters. 240
And if one is beaten,
or raped, or killed,
I will not come in mourning black.
I will not pick the right flowers.
I will not celebrate her death 245
& it will matter not
if she's Black or white—
if she loves women or men.
I will come with my many sisters
and decorate the streets 250
with the innards of those
brothers in womenslaughter.
No more, can I dull my rage
in alcohol & deference
to *men's* courts. 255
I will come to my sisters,
not dutiful,
I will come strong.

—1978

ALICE WALKER (1944-)

The eighth child of Willie Lee Walker, a sharecropper, and Minnie Tallulah Grant Walker, who worked as a maid, Alice Walker grew up in Eatonton, Georgia. Her talent as a writer developed both from listening to her parents' storytelling and from her avid reading as a child. She attributes some of the observational skill that she draws on as a writer to a childhood accident that left her blind in one eye and facially scarred: viewing herself as disfigured, she withdrew into herself and started to watch events around her with more intensity. She earned a scholarship to Spelman College in 1961, and while there she became involved in the civil rights movement. (Her second novel, *Meridian* [1976] has often been hailed as the best literary treatment of that era.) Walker left Spelman after two years, accepting a scholarship to Sarah Lawrence College in New York. She spent the summer before her senior year in Africa, an experience that had a profound impact on her. After receiving her B.A., she moved to Mississippi and worked on voter registration and with a Head Start program. There she met and married civil rights lawyer Melvyn Leventhal, with whom she had one child, feminist writer Rebecca Walker. Leventhal and Walker divorced in 1976. Walker has written several volumes of poetry, a number of novels, as well as collections of short stories and essays. Her third novel, *The Color Purple* (1982), an epistolary novel told from the point of view of a young Black girl who has been sexually abused by her stepfather, established her reputation as a major American writer, and won her a Pulitzer Prize. While some critics have objected to her portrayals of Black men as weak or abusive, the critical response to Walker's work has generally been very positive; she has been lauded for her rich characterizations, her use of the Black vernacular (particularly as she combined it with the epistolary mode in *The Color Purple*), and for her work in bringing the lives of Black women to the forefront of literary representation.

Everyday Use
for your grandmama

I will wait for her in the yard that Maggie and I made so clean and wavy yesterday afternoon. A yard like this is more comfortable than most people know. It is not just a yard. It is like an extended living room. When the hard clay is swept clean as a floor and the fine sand around the edges lined with tiny, irregular grooves, anyone can come and sit and look up into the elm tree and wait for the breezes that never come inside the house.

Maggie will be nervous until after her sister goes: she will stand hopelessly in corners, homely and ashamed of the burn scars down her arms and legs, eyeing her sister with a mixture of envy and awe. She thinks her sister has held life always in the palm of one hand, that "no" is a word the world never learned to say to her.

You've no doubt seen those TV shows where the child who has "made it" is confronted, as a surprise, by her own mother and father, tottering in weakly from backstage. (A pleasant surprise, of course: What would they do if parent and child came on the show only to curse out and insult each other?) On TV mother and child embrace and smile into each other's faces. Sometimes the mother and father weep, the child wraps them in her arms and leans across the table to tell how she would not have made it without their help. I have seen these programs.

Sometimes I dream a dream in which Dee and I are suddenly brought together on a TV program of this sort. Out of a dark and soft-seated limousine I am ushered into a bright room filled with many people. There I meet a smiling, gray, sporty man like Johnny Carson[1] who shakes my hand and tells me what a fine girl I have. Then we are on the stage and Dee is embracing me with tears in her eyes. She pins on my dress a large orchid, even though she has told me once that she thinks orchids are tacky flowers.

In real life I am a large, big-boned woman with rough, man-working hands. In the winter I wear flannel nightgowns to bed and overalls during the day. I can kill and clean a hog as mercilessly as a man. My fat keeps me hot in zero weather. I can work outside all day, breaking ice to get water for washing; I can eat pork liver cooked over the open fire minutes after it comes steaming from the hog. One winter I knocked a bull calf straight in the brain between the eyes with a sledge hammer and had the meat hung up to chill before nightfall. But of course all this does not show on television. I am the way my daughter would want me to be: a hundred pounds lighter, my skin like an uncooked barley pancake. My hair glistens in the hot bright lights. Johnny Carson has much to do to keep up with my quick and witty tongue.

But that is a mistake. I know even before I wake up. Who ever knew a Johnson with a quick tongue? Who can even imagine me looking a strange white man in the eye? It seems to me I have talked to them always with one foot raised in flight, with my head turned in whichever way is farthest from them. Dee, though. She would always look anyone in the eye. Hesitation was no part of her nature.

"How do I look, Mama?" Maggie says, showing just enough of her thin body enveloped in pink skirt and red blouse for me to know she's there, almost hidden by

---

[1] John William "Johnny" Carson (1925-2005), American comedian and host of the NBC television program *The Tonight Show* from 1962 to 1992.

the door.

"Come out into the yard," I say.

Have you ever seen a lame animal, perhaps a dog run over by some careless person rich enough to own a car, sidle up to someone who is ignorant enough to be kind to him? That is the way my Maggie walks. She has been like this, chin on chest, eyes on ground, feet in shuffle, ever since the fire that burned the other house to the ground.

Dee is lighter than Maggie, with nicer hair and a fuller figure. She's a woman now, though sometimes I forget. How long ago was it that the other house burned? Ten, twelve years? Sometimes I can still hear the flames and feel Maggie's arms sticking to me, her hair smoking and her dress falling off her in little black papery flakes. Her eyes seemed stretched open, blazed open by the flames reflected in them. And Dee. I see her standing off under the sweet gum tree she used to dig gum out of; a look of concentration on her face as she watched the last dingy gray board of the house fall in toward the red-hot brick chimney. Why don't you do a dance around the ashes? I'd wanted to ask her. She had hated the house that much.

I used to think she hated Maggie, too. But that was before we raised the money, the church and me, to send her to Augusta to school. She used to read to us without pity; forcing words, lies, other folks' habits, whole lives upon us two, sitting trapped and ignorant underneath her voice. She washed us in a river of make-believe, burned us with a lot of knowledge we didn't necessarily need to know. Pressed us to her with the serious way she read, to shove us away at just the moment, like dimwits, we seemed about to understand.

Dee wanted nice things. A yellow organdy dress to wear to her graduation from high school; black pumps to match a green suit she'd made from an old suit somebody gave me. She was determined to stare down any disaster in her efforts. Her eyelids would not flicker for minutes at a time. Often I fought off the temptation to shake her. At sixteen she had a style of her own: and knew what style was.

I never had an education myself. After second grade the school was closed down. Don't ask me why: in 1927 colored asked fewer questions than they do now. Sometimes Maggie reads to me. She stumbles along good-naturedly but can't see well. She knows she is not bright. Like good looks and money, quickness passed her by. She will marry John Thomas (who has mossy teeth in an earnest face) and then I'll be free to sit here and I guess just sing church songs to myself. Although I never was a good singer. Never could carry a tune. I was always better at a man's job. I used to love to milk till I was hooked in the side in '49. Cows are soothing and slow and don't bother you, unless you try to milk them the wrong way.

I have deliberately turned my back on the house. It is three rooms, just like the one that burned, except the roof is tin; they don't make shingle roofs any more. There are no real windows, just some holes cut in the sides, like the portholes in a ship, but not round and not square, with rawhide holding the shutters up on the outside. This house is in a pasture, too, like the other one. No doubt when Dee sees it she will want to tear it down. She wrote me once that no matter where we "choose" to live, she will manage to come see us. But she will never bring her friends. Maggie and I thought about this and Maggie asked me, "Mama, when did Dee ever *have* any friends?"

She had a few. Furtive boys in pink shirts hanging about on washday after school.

Nervous girls who never laughed. Impressed with her they worshipped the well-turned phrase, the cute shape, the scalding humor that erupted like bubbles in lye. She read to them.

When she was courting Jimmy T she didn't have much time to pay to us, but turned all her faultfinding power on him. He *flew* to marry a cheap city girl from a family of ignorant flashy people. She hardly had time to recompose herself.

When she comes I will meet—but there they are!

Maggie attempts to make a dash for the house, in her shuffling way, but I stay her with my hand. "Come back here," I say. And she stops and tries to dig a well in the sand with her toe.

It is hard to see them clearly through the strong sun. But even the first glimpse of leg out of the car tells me it is Dee. Her feet were always neat-looking, as if God himself had shaped them with a certain style. From the other side of the car comes a short, stocky man. Hair is all over his head a foot long and hanging from his chin like a kinky mule tail. I hear Maggie suck in her breath. "Uhnnnh," is what it sounds like. Like when you see the wriggling end of a snake just in front of your foot on the road. "Uhnnnh."

Dee next. A dress down to the ground, in this hot weather. A dress so loud it hurts my eyes. There are yellows and oranges enough to throw back the light of the sun. I feel my whole face warming from the heat waves it throws out. Earrings gold, too, and hanging down to her shoulders. Bracelets dangling and making noises when she moves her arm up to shake the folds of the dress out of her armpits. The dress is loose and flows, and as she walks closer, I like it. I hear Maggie go "Uhnnnh" again. It is her sister's hair. It stands straight up like the wool on a sheep. It is black as night and around the edges are two long pigtails that rope about like small lizards disappearing behind her ears.

"Wa-su-zo-Tean-o!"[2] she says, coming on in that gliding way the dress makes her move. The short stocky fellow with the hair to his navel is all grinning and he follows up with "Asalamalakim,[3] my mother and sister!" He moves to hug Maggie but she falls back, right up against the back of my chair. I feel her trembling there and when I look up I see the perspiration falling off her chin.

"Don't get up," says Dee. Since I am stout it takes something of a push. You can see me trying to move a second or two before I make it. She turns, showing white heels through her sandals, and goes back to the car. Out she peeks next with a Polaroid. She stoops down quickly and lines up picture after picture of me sitting there in front of the house with Maggie cowering behind me. She never takes a shot without making sure the house is included. When a cow comes nibbling around the edge of the yard she snaps it and me and Maggie *and* the house. Then she puts the Polaroid in the back seat of the car, and comes up and kisses me on the forehead.

Meanwhile, Asalamalakim is going through motions with Maggie's hand. Maggie's hand is as limp as a fish, and probably as cold, despite the sweat, and she keeps trying to pull it back. It looks like Asalamalakim wants to shake hands but wants to do it fancy. Or maybe he don't know how people shake hands. Anyhow, he soon gives up on Maggie.

---

[2] Luganda phrase meaning "good morning" (literally, "I hope you have slept well").

[3] (Ar.) Peace be with you.

"Well," I say. "Dee."

"No, Mama," she says. "Not 'Dee,' Wangero Leewanika Kemanjo!"[4]

"What happened to 'Dee'?" I wanted to know.

"She's dead," Wangero said. "I couldn't bear it any longer, being named after the people who oppress me."

"You know as well as me you was named after your aunt Dicie," I said. Dicie is my sister. She named Dee. We called her "Big Dee" after Dee was born.

"But who was *she* named after?" asked Wangero.

"I guess after Grandma Dee," I said.

"And who was she named after?" asked Wangero.

"Her mother," I said, and saw Wangero was getting tired. "That's about as far back as I can trace it," I said. Though, in fact, I probably could have carried it back beyond the Civil War through the branches.

"Well," said Asalamalakim, "there you are."

"Uhnnnh," I heard Maggie say.

"There I was not," I said, "before 'Dicie' cropped up in our family, so why should I try to trace it that far back?"

He just stood there grinning, looking down on me like somebody inspecting a Model A car.[5] Every once in a while he and Wangero sent eye signals over my head.

"How do you pronounce this name?" I asked.

"You don't have to call me by it if you don't want to," said Wangero.

"Why shouldn't I?" I asked. "If that's what you want us to call you, we'll call you."

"I know it might sound awkward at first," said Wangero.

"I'll get used to it," I said. "Ream it out again."

Well, soon we got the name out of the way. Asalamalakim had a name twice as long and three times as hard. After I tripped over it two or three times he told me to just call him Hakim-a-barber. I wanted to ask him was he a barber, but I didn't really think he was, so I didn't ask.

"You must belong to those beef-cattle peoples down the road," I said. They said "Asalamalakim" when they met you, too, but they didn't shake hands. Always too busy: feeding the cattle, fixing the fences, putting up salt-lick shelters, throwing down hay. When the white folks poisoned some of the herd the men stayed up all night with rifles in their hands. I walked a mile and a half just to see the sight.

Hakim-a-barber said, "I accept some of their doctrines, but farming and raising cattle is not my style." (They didn't tell me, and I didn't ask, whether Wangero (Dee) had really gone and married him.)

We sat down to eat and right away he said he didn't eat collards and pork was unclean. Wangero, though, went on through the chitlins and corn bread, the greens and everything else. She talked a blue streak over the sweet potatoes. Everything delighted her. Even the fact that we still used the benches her daddy made for the table when we couldn't afford to buy chairs.

"Oh, Mama!" she cried. Then turned to Hakim-a-barber. "I never knew how lovely these benches are. You can feel the rump prints," she said, running hands underneath

---

[4] According to scholar Helga Hoel, the name Wangero Leewanika Kemanjo is a mixture of misspelled East African names: Wanjiru and Kamenju from Kikuyu (a major language of Kenya), and Lewanika, the name of the king of Barotseland, Zambia, from 1878 to 1916.

[5] The first car produced by the Ford Motor Company in 1903.

her and along the bench. Then she gave a sigh and her hand closed over Grandma Dee's butter dish. "That's it!" she said. "I knew there was something I wanted to ask you if I could have." She jumped up from the table and went over in the corner where the churn stood, the milk in it clabber[6] by now. She looked at the churn and looked at it.

"This churn top is what I need," she said. "Didn't Uncle Buddy whittle it out of a tree you all used to have?"

"Yes," I said.

"Uh huh," she said happily. "And I want the dasher,[7] too."

"Uncle Buddy whittle that, too?" asked the barber.

Dee (Wangero) looked up at me.

"Aunt Dee's first husband whittled the dash," said Maggie so low you almost couldn't hear her. "His name was Henry, but they called him Stash."

"Maggie's brain is like an elephant's," Wangero said, laughing. "I can use the churn top as a centerpiece for the alcove table," she said, sliding a plate over the churn, "and I'll think of something artistic to do with the dasher."

When she finished wrapping the dasher the handle stuck out. I took it for a moment in my hands. You didn't even have to look close to see where hands pushing the dasher up and down to make butter had left a kind of sink in the wood. In fact, there were a lot of small sinks; you could see where thumbs and fingers had sunk into the wood. It was beautiful light yellow wood, from a tree that grew in the yard where Big Dee and Stash had lived.

After dinner Dee (Wangero) went to the trunk at the foot of my bed and started rifling through it. Maggie hung back in the kitchen over the dishpan. Out came Wangero with two quilts. They had been pieced by Grandma Dee and then Big Dee and me had hung them on the quilt frames on the front porch and quilted them. One was in the Lone Star pattern. The other was Walk Around the Mountain. In both of them were scraps of dresses Grandma Dee had worn fifty and more years ago. Bits and pieces of Grandpa Jarrell's Paisley shirts. And one teeny faded blue piece, about the size of a penny matchbox, that was from Great Grandpa Ezra's uniform that he wore in the Civil War.

"Mama," Wangero said sweet as a bird. "Can I have these old quilts?"

I heard something fall in the kitchen, and a minute later the kitchen door slammed.

"Why don't you take one or two of the others?" I asked. "These old things was just done by me and Big Dee from some tops your grandma pieced before she died."

"No," said Wangero. "I don't want those. They are stitched around the borders by machine."

"That'll make them last better," I said.

"That's not the point," said Wangero. "These are all pieces of dresses Grandma used to wear. She did all this stitching by hand. Imagine!" She held the quilts securely in her arms, stroking them.

"Some of the pieces, like those lavender ones, come from old clothes her mother handed down to her," I said, moving up to touch the quilts. Dee (Wangero) moved back just enough so that I couldn't reach the quilts. They already belonged to her.

"Imagine!" she breathed again, clutching them closely to her bosom.

---

[6] Raw milk that has turned sour and thickened.
[7] In the style of butter churn referred to here, the dasher (or dash) is pushed up and down through a hole in the wooden cover of a barrel or stone tub.

"The truth is," I said, "I promised to give them quilts to Maggie, for when she marries John Thomas."

She gasped like a bee had stung her.

"Maggie can't appreciate these quilts!" she said. "She'd probably be backward enough to put them to everyday use."

"I reckon she would," I said. "God knows I been saving 'em for long enough with nobody using 'em. I hope she will!" I didn't want to bring up how I had offered Dee (Wangero) a quilt when she went away to college. Then she had told me they were old-fashioned, out of style.

"But they're *priceless!*" she was saying now, furiously; for she has a temper. "Maggie would put them on the bed and in five years they'd be in rags. Less than that!"

"She can always make some more," I said. "Maggie knows how to quilt."

Dee (Wangero) looked at me with hatred. "You just will not understand. The point is these quilts, *these* quilts!"

"Well," I said, stumped. "What would *you* do with them?"

"Hang them," she said. As if that was the only thing you *could* do with quilts.

Maggie by now was standing in the door. I could almost hear the sound her feet made as they scraped over each other.

"She can have them, Mama," she said, like somebody used to never winning anything, or having anything reserved for her. "I can 'member Grandma Dee without the quilts."

I looked at her hard. She had filled her bottom lip with checkerberry snuff[8] and it gave her face a kind of dopey, hangdog look. It was Grandma Dee and Big Dee who taught her how to quilt herself. She stood there with her scarred hands hidden in the folds of her skirt. She looked at her sister with something like fear but she wasn't mad at her. This was Maggie's portion. This was the way she knew God to work.

When I looked at her like that something hit me in the top of my head and ran down to the soles of my feet. Just like when I'm in church and the spirit of God touches me and I get happy and shout. I did something I never had done before: hugged Maggie to me, then dragged her on into the room, snatched the quilts out of Miss Wangero's hands and dumped them into Maggie's lap. Maggie just sat there on my bed with her mouth open.

"Take one or two of the others," I said to Dee.

But she turned without a word and went out to Hakim-a-barber.

"You just don't understand," she said, as Maggie and I came out to the car.

"What don't I understand?" I wanted to know.

"Your heritage," she said. And then she turned to Maggie, kissed her, and said, "You ought to try to make something of yourself, too, Maggie. It's really a new day for us. But from the way you and Mama still live you'd never know it."

She put on some sunglasses that hid everything above the tip of her nose and her chin.

Maggie smiled; maybe at the sunglasses. But a real smile, not scared. After we watched the car dust settle I asked Maggie to bring me a dip of snuff. And then the two of us sat there just enjoying, until it was time to go in the house and go to bed.

—1973

---

[8] Finely ground tobacco that is placed between the upper or lower lip and the gum.

SHERLEY ANNE WILLIAMS (1944-1999)

Novelist, poet, and scholar Sherley Anne Williams was born in Bakersfield, California, and spent her childhood in the housing projects in Fresno, where the family made a living picking cotton and fruit. Her father, Jesse Winson Williams, died when she was eight, and her mother, Lena-Lelia Marie Siler, when she was sixteen. Williams graduated from Fresno State College (now California State University, Fresno) in 1966, did graduate work at Howard University, and received her M.A. in English from Brown University in 1972, the same year she published a thematic study of African-American fiction, *Give Birth to Brightness*. Her first book of poems, *The Peacock Poems* (1975), was nominated for both the National Book Award and the Pulitzer Prize. Her second collection, *Some One Sweet Angel Chile,* was published in 1982; she turned a portion of that volume into a one-woman play entitled *Letters from a New England Negro*. Her neo-slave narrative *Dessa Rose* was published in 1986 and was adapted for the stage as a musical in 2005. Williams also wrote two novels for children, *Working Cotton* (1992) and *Girls Together* (1999). Williams, the first African-American professor of literature at the University of California, San Diego, died of cancer in 1999.

Any Woman's Blues
every woman is a victim of the feel blues, too.

Soft lamp shinin
      and me alone in the night.
Soft lamp is shinin
      and me alone in the night.
Can't take no one beside me   5
      need mo'n jest some man to set me right.

I left many peoples and places
      tryin not to be alone
Left many a person and places
      I lived my life alone.   10
I need to get myself together.
      Yes, I need to make myself to home.

What's gone can be a window
      a circle in the eye of the sun.
What's gone can be a window   15
      a circle, well, in the eye of the sun.
Take that circle from the world, girl,
      you find the light have gone.

These is old blues
      and I sing em like any woman do.   20
These the old blues
      and I sing em, sing em, sing em. Just like any woman do.
My life ain't done yet.
      Naw. My song ain't through.

—1975

Drivin Wheel
myth story and life

> *I want you to come on, baby,*
> *here's where you get*
> *yo steak, potatoes and tea.*

first story

The darkened bedroom, the double bed,   5
the whispers of the city night,
against it her voice, husky, speaking
past the one soft light.

> I am   through you   wholly woman. You
> say I am cold   am hard   am vain. And   10
> I know I am fool and bitch. And black.
> Like my mother before me and my
> sisters around me. We share the same
> legacy   are women to the same
> degree.   15

And I ain't even touched what's between us.
A sullen, half tearful thought.
Others lay below the surface of her mind,
rushing, gone, finally caught.

> Not circumstance; history   20
> keeps us apart. I'm black. You black. And
> how have niggas proved they men? Fightin
> and fuckin as many women as
> they can. And even when you can do
> all the things a white man do you may   25
> leave fightin behind but fuckin stay
> the same.

> For us it's havin babies and how
> well we treats a man and how long we
> keep him. And how long don't really have   30
> that much to do with how well. I just
> can't be woman to yo kinda man.

second song

> my man is a fine fine man
> the superman of his time   35
>   the black time   big time
> in a mild mannered disguise
> revealed only as needed:
>   the heart steel   heart stone   heart
> and its erratic beating.   40

Inner and outer

rine and heart and running.
Running.   Hanging.   Caught by that powerful joint.
But my man can pull his ownself's coat
come at last to see that dick is just that same old rope.   45

>   Yeah.

>   A mild mannered

disguise: laughing country boy astride
>   a laughing goat.

>   *first fable*   50

We do not tell ourselves all the things we
know or admit, except perhaps in dreams,
oblique reminiscence, in sly yearnings, all
the people we feel ourselves to be.

>   Except   55
perhaps in dreams   the people we
feel…

>   Three. A prideful panther who
stalks a white wolf, a goatish rooster who was lured on
by a grey fox and a head, a body   60
and, lying to one side, a heart.
The head, the heart, the body had always
been apart. The rooster called
them Humpty Dumpty things and urged
the panther to attack. The rooster was accustomed   65
to command, ruling the panther through
words he had taught the panther to
talk; the words only said what he wanted
the panther to know. He would crow
or blow upon his horn   70
and the panther would forget
all the questions he had ever known.
And once in a while, just for show,
the rooster would allow the panther
to have his way.   75
Now, the panther thought it too good
a body to waste, too good a brain to be
forever cut from its source.
>   Let's put them together, man,
he called. You begin with the heart.   80
>   But the rooster
knew that rebuilt Humpty Dumpty men have a
way of taking worlds apart, have new ways of
putting them together again. He lived in the world
of already was and it was all he ever wanted   85

to know.

Not so fast, the rooster cried.

But the panther had already touched the heart
and for the first time he realized
that Not So Fast meant Don't Go. He   90
could feel something new, something
indefinable pumping through him. The rooster's
words failed to sway him. The rooster, angered,
sank his talons into the panther's shoulder.
The panther turned and, instinctively,   95
went upside the rooster's head.
The rooster absorbed the first blow;
he was smart enough to know it was coming.
But the second was a surprise, beyond
his comprehension. He died with the question   100
Why   still unspoken.

...in glancing asides
we are seen, or in oblique reference. And still
left to answer is how we can pull it all together.

fourth life   105

They lie up in the darkened bedroom
and listen to the whispers of the city night;
each waits upon the other
to make the final move to the light
or toward the door. They have met   110
history; it is them. Definitions from the past
—she bitch and fool; he
nigga and therefore jive—seem the last

reality. And, once admitted, mark
the past as them. They are defeated.   115
She moves to strap on her shoes.

You said,

and he speaks.
voice and hand holding her seated,
his head moving into the circle of light.   120

You said we are more than the
sum jiveness, the total foolishness.
You are wholly woman, right? Isn't that
more than bitch?

What do it matter, huh?   125

His hand holds her, holds the wary
wearied question. He speaks, slow:

Matter a helluva lot. We can't
get together less we stay together.

His lips brush her cheek; she buries   130

her fingers in his bush. The question will always
be present, so too the doubt it leaves in its wake.
To question and to answer is to confront. To deal.
History is them; it is also theirs to make.

—1975

LUCHA CORPI (1945-   )

Lucha Corpi was born in a small town in Veracruz, Mexico, and relocated to Berkeley,
California, with her then-husband in 1964. After their divorce in 1970, she decided to continue
her studies, which had been put on hold while her husband pursued his education, and she
enrolled at the University of California, Berkeley. She earned a B.A. in Comparative
Literature from UC Berkeley and an M.A. in World and Comparative Literature from San
Francisco State University. Corpi received a National Endowment for the Arts Creative
Writing Fellowship in 1970, which began her career as a writer. Her poems appeared in
Fireflight: Three Latin American Poets in 1976, followed by her first collection, *Palabras de Medio
Día,* in 1980. A vital point in Corpi's career came in 1990 with the publication of her second
collection of poetry, *Variaciones Sobre Una Tempestad/Variations On a Storm,* when she was
awarded a Creative Arts Fellowship in Fiction by the City of Oakland and was named poet
laureate at Indiana University Northwest. She also published her first novel, *Delia's Song,* that
year. Corpi has written four mystery novels that feature Brown Angel Investigations and
Gloria Damasco, the first Chicana detective in American literature: *Eulogy for a Brown Angel*
(1992), which received the PEN Oakland Josephine Miles Award and the Multicultural
Publishers Exchange's Best Book of Fiction; *Cactus Blood* (1995); *Black Widow's Wardrobe*
(1999); and *Crimson Moon: A Brown Angel Mystery* (2004). She has also written a semi-autobiographical children's book entitled *Where Fireflies Dance/Ahi, Donde Bailan las Luciernagas*
(1997). Corpi has been a teacher in the Oakland Public Schools Neighborhood Centers
Program since 1973.

Dark Romance

A flavor of vanilla drifts
on the Sunday air.

Melancholy of an orange,
clinging still,
brilliant, seductive,   5
past the promise of its blooming.

Guadalupe was bathing in the river
that Sunday, late,

a promise of milk in her breasts,
vanilla scent in her hair,   10
cinnamon flavor in her eyes,

cocoa-flower between her legs,

and in her mouth a daze
of sugarcane.

He came upon her there   15
surrounded by water
in a flood of evening light.

And on the instant cut the flower
wrung blood from the milk

dashed vanilla on the silence   20
of the river bank

drained the burning liquid
of her lips

And then he was gone,
leaving behind him a trail of shadow   25
drooping at the water's edge.

Her mother found her, and at the sight
took a handful of salt from her pouch
to throw over her shoulder.

A few days later, her father   30
accepted the gift of a fine mare.

And Guadalupe...Guadalupe hung her life
from the orange tree in the garden,
and stayed there quietly,
her eyes open to the river.   35

A scent of vanilla drifts
on the evening air.

Ancestral longing
seizes the mind.

An orange clings to the branch   40
the promise lost of its blooming.

—1980

Marina[1] Mother

They made her of the softest clay
and dried her under the rays of the tropical sun.
With the blood of a tender lamb
her name was written by the elders
on the bark of that tree   5
as old as they.

Steeped in tradition, mystic
and mute she was sold—
from hand to hand, night to night,
denied and desecrated, waiting for the dawn   10
and for the owl's song
that would never come;
her womb sacked of its fruit,
her soul thinned to a handful of dust.

You no longer loved her, the elders denied her,   15
and the child who cried out to her "mama!"
grew up and called her "whore."

—1980

---

[1] Marina, also referred to as Malinche and Malintzín Tenepal, was the indigenous translator for Hernán Cortés Pizarro (1485-1547) during his 16th century conquest of Mexico.

MELANIE KAYE/KANTROWITZ (1945-   )

Melanie Kaye (she later reclaimed the name Kantrowitz, which her father had anglicized to Kaye) was born and raised in Brooklyn, New York, the daughter of shopkeepers. She became an activist at an early age, participating in the civil rights movement in Harlem while still a teenager. She graduated with a B.A. from City College/City University of New York in 1966, and then went on to earn her M.A. and Ph.D. in Comparative Literature from UC Berkeley, where she taught one of the first women's studies courses in the nation. Kaye/Kantrowitz has twice been a Visiting Distinguished Professor as the Jane Watson Irwin Chair in Women's Studies at Hamilton College, as well as the Belle Zeller Chair in Public Policy at Brooklyn College/CUNY, and has taught writing at the Bayview Women's Correctional Facility in New York City with the Bard College Prison Initiative as well. She currently teaches Secular Jewish Studies at Queens College/CUNY, under the auspices of the Posen Foundation for Cultural Judaism.

Kaye/Kantrowitz was granted tenure at Vermont College in 1990, a position she left to return to New York City, where she served as the co-chair of the New Jewish Agenda Task Force on Anti-Semitism and Racism, and then as the first director of Jews for Racial and Economic Justice (1992-1995), serving on its board of directors until 2004. Her social and political activism has been recognized with the Union Square Award for Grassroots Activism from the Fund of the City of New York. Kaye/Kantrowitz, who edited *Sinister Wisdom: A*

Multicultural Journal by and for Lesbians from 1983 to 1987, is the author of *We Speak in Code: Poems and Other Writings* (1980), *My Jewish Face & Other Stories* (1990), *The Issue Is Power: Essays on Women, Jews, Violence, and Resistance* (1992), and *The Colors of Jews: Racial Politics and Radical Diasporism* (2007). She also co-edited, with Irena Klepfisz, *The Tribe of Dina: A Jewish Women's Anthology* (1989).

Hanukkah Stones[1]

december when winter grips the planet
the moon turns dark, the shortest day
spins into the longest night

in the pitch of the year the heart
begins to dread   5
or hope

last year children in gaza began
to throw stones

        ✦ ✦ ✦

december birth of a child who rises up
over and over with stones   10
child after child
stone after stone
hanukkah *gelt*[2]   everyone pays

        ✦ ✦ ✦

dark of the moon, pitch of the year
at this time we need hope   15

take down the menorah
burnish with a soft cloth
each night light one more candle:

that no one gives up without a fight
is the miracle   20
brighter than fire
harder than stones

—1988

Casablanca Colorized[3]

you must remember
this: Rick's bar
but in pastels. Bergman's
dress hat match exactly
shimmering blue and all the white people's skin is   5
pink which is to say

[1] [*Author's note.*] In 1988, I wrote this poem to send as a Hanukkah card. The Intifada (Palestinian uprising) was then a year old.

[2] Small amounts of money often distributed to children during Hanukkah.

[3] Set in Morocco during World War II, the black-and-white film *Casablanca* (1942) stars Humphrey Bogart as a cynical American expatriate and Ingrid Bergman as his ex-lover, now the wife of Victor Laszlo, a leader of the European resistance movement.

everyone   except Sam at the piano
black backdrop for white romance or
in this case   pink.

Oh 1942   10
no one says Arab   or Jew
you must remember *here's looking at you kid*
here comes your favorite movie's favorite part
Deutschland Deutschland Uber Alles[4]
oversung as Victor Laslow bursts into   15
Allons enfants de la patrie—[5]

as if Casablanca were a French city
as if the Marseillaise were Morocco's national anthem
everyone joins   *le jour de gloire est arrivé*[6]
swallows the German oath to   20
control everything

you must remember *let's march let's march*
til impure blood waters our fields[7]

here's looking at impure blood
here's looking at you in your eerie blue ensemble   25
pink skin   except for Sam   you must remember
you must remember this

—1994

bad daughters

1.
just before my mother burned down her apartment, i threw my
     paycheck in the garbage
not on purpose, but it was a sign.

i went through the garbage and found it whereas the apartment really
     is gone.

she is alive. no one was hurt. (we think)
then we hear people went to the hospital   5
someone's pet bird died.

then we hear this was the third fire.

2.
the mother who beat us every Saturday while the father was at
     work. sometimes when he came home she'd tell how the girls made
     her beat them, then he would beat us too.

---

[4] (Ger.) Germany, Germany above all. The opening lines
of *"Das Lied der Deutschen"* ("The Song of the
Germans"), the whole or parts of which have been used
as the national anthem of Germany since 1922.
[5] (Fr.) Go children of the motherland. From "La

Marseillaise," the French national anthem.
[6] (Fr.) The day of glory has arrived. From "La
Marseillaise."
[7] Lines from "La Marseillaise."

lighting a cigarette, she drops the match. burns down her apartment.
burns up? down? and sleeps at the neighbor's.

in the morning the red cross comes to take her to an SRO hotel.[8] the
bad daughters will not take her in. the younger daughter thanks god
she has only one bed.   10

aren't you coming to get me? in the middle of the night the mother phones
the older daughter, *aren't you coming to get me? i don't want to go to some
fleabitten hotel.*

ma, you're going where you're going, says the older daughter.

when she repeats this line in the diner around the corner from the
younger daughter's apartment with thank god only one bed, "and i said,
ma, you're going where you're going," the younger daughter raises her fist
go girl.

is she staying with you? everyone asks.

the bad daughters will not take their mother in.   15

3.
lighting a cigarette, she drops the match, burns up/burns down everything.
barefoot, in her nightgown.

i go to the store to buy her clothes. i tell everyone, people i hardly know,
the woman who sells underwear. my mother's apartment, the third fire.

is everything gone? asks one woman, young but wise.
everything, i say, *even her shoes.*

they offer advice. they know someone who knows someone who went
into a nursing home once.   20
they say, *what a tragedy.*

4.
at the hotel at broadway and 77th St., everyone i pass on the stairs is
young and poor.
my mother is lying on the bed lost in a once-shocking-pink tshirt full of
holes. she looks tiny, frail, and poor. what stands between her and
poverty is us, the bad daughters.

my mother looks around brightly, pert as a child, hideously innocent,
beyond mannerism, beyond manipulation. this is real. she is an infant.

i have to get to my commode, she says, then sits, skinny legs mottled with
lumps of once-muscle, blue streaks of veins, waits for her bladder to
release.   25

help me up, she says, eyes beseeching, *let me down gently.*

---

[8] Single Room Occupancy (SRO) hotels provide affordable housing for low income and homeless people.

5.

the bad daughters phone and visit, shop and visit, phone and xerox and
    phone and phone and make lists and visit. once the mother is alone on
    the bed smoking when the younger daughter arrives, and shrieks, *ma, you*
    know you can't smoke alone, don't you get it, you could have been killed. you could
    have killed someone else.

no one was hurt, says the mother, tossing her head pertly.

the impulse to strangle leaps into the bad daughter's hands as words leap
    into her throat, *if you're going to kill yourself jump off a fucking building,*

she doesn't say them out loud but the words   30
bang around inside her skull for hours.

—1997

GAIL TREMBLAY (1945–   )

Poet and visual artist Gail Tremblay was born in Buffalo, New York. She is of mixed
Onondaga/Mic Mac and French-Canadian descent. Tremblay earned her B.A. in Drama from
the University of New Hampshire and her M.F.A. in Creative Writing from the University of
Oregon. Her collection of poetry *Indian Singing in the 20th Century* (1990), later reissued with
new poems as *Indian Singing: Poems* (1998), has been noted for the musicality of its verse, as
well as for its humor and strong thread of cultural critique. Tremblay's visual and mixed-
media art has been widely exhibited across the U.S. She is currently a professor at Evergreen
State College, where she teaches expository and creative writing, Native American literature,
weaving, and Native American Studies.

After the Invasion

On dark nights, the women cry together
washing their faces, the backs of their hands
with tears—talking to their grandmother, Moon,
about the way life got confused. Sorrow
comes through tunnels like the wind and wails   5
inside an empty womb. The need to be cherished,
to be touched by hands that hold sacred objects,
that play the drums and know the holy songs,
rises and moves as certain as the stars.
Women murmur about men who don't sing   10
when women grind the corn. There are too many
mysteries men learn to ignore; they drink together
and make lewd remarks—defeat makes them forget
to see the magic when women dance, the touch of foot

upon the Earth that mothers them and bears 15
their bodies across the wide universe of sky.
Men brag how many touch them, who they use,
forget to help women whose love must feed
children that speak of fathers harder to hold
than distant mountains, fathers as inconstant 20
as the movement of the air. Mothers cook corn
and beans and dream of meat and fish to fill
the storage baskets and the pots. On dark nights,
the women whisper how they love, whisper
how they gave and give until they have no more— 25
the guilt of being empty breaks their hearts.
They weep for sisters who have learned to hate,
who have gone crazy and learned to hurt
the fragile web that makes the people whole.
Together, women struggle to remember how to live, 30
nurture one another, and pray that life will fill
their wombs, that men and women will come
to Earth who know that breath is a sacred gift
before the rising sun and love can change
the world as sure as the magic in any steady song. 35

—1990

Hén; Iáh; Tóka' Nón:Wa.[1]

Death comes drenching me to the bone,
a drop at a time like rain falling
slow and steady; cells swell
and burst; nerves alter, and scars
block pathways to old possibilities 5
as surely as dams keep fish
from going upstream to spawn.
Some days, *kahséhtha' akweriàkon,*[2]
kón:nis[3] invisible that change in sense
that marks the passing of dreams 10
that can never come to be. I refuse
to cry and think it best to act
on the instant, to give each moment
its special weight, notice the way
light shifts defining the movement 15
of minutes that bury what could move
in me. I give up the desire to dance
one more season around the drum;
I grow content to feel its rhythm
move my pulse one beat, then another, 20
while others slap footsoles on the path

---

[1] [*Author's note.*] Yes; no; maybe [Mohawk].
[2] [*Author's note.*] I hide something in my heart [Mohawk].
[3] [*Author's note.*] I make [Mohawk].

I used to keep. You ask me, honestly,
can I face years of this continual loss?
    Hén. Iáh. Tóka' nón:wa.

—1990

Indian Singing in 20th Century America

We wake; we wake the day,
the light rising in us like sun—
our breath a prayer brushing
against the feathers in our hands.
We stumble out into the streets;   5
patterns of wires invented by strangers
are strung between eye and sky,
and we dance in two worlds,
inevitable as seasons in one,
exotic curiosities in the other   10
which rushes headlong down highways,
watches us from car windows, explains
us to its children in words
that no one could ever make
sense of. The image obscures   15
the vision, and we wonder
whether anyone will ever hear
our own names for the things
we do. Light dances in the body,
surrounds all living things—   20
even the stones sing
although their songs are infinitely
slower than the ones we learn
from trees. No human voice lasts
long enough to make such music sound.   25
Earth breath eddies between factories
and office buildings, caresses the surface
of our skin; we go to jobs, the boss
always watching the clock to see
that we're on time. He tries to shut   30
out magic and hopes we'll make
mistakes or disappear. We work
fast and steady and remember
each breath alters the composition
of the air. Change moves relentless,   35
the pattern unfolding despite their planning—
we're always there—singing round dance
songs, remembering what supports
our life—impossible to ignore.

—1990

Laughter Breaks

Laughter breaks like sun rising;
the whole world shimmers and light
shakes as though the belly of Earth
moves with the mirth in one's own gut.
The power to celebrate excess wakes in us;   5
we know enough to joke around, to survive
the agonies of feeling irreversible pain
explode upon the day. We sing of folly
that shapes experience, remember
to act indelicate and play. Coyote,   10
mangy as ever, grins and whispers
our sisters' names; he plots to climb
into the sky and dance with stars
down some eternal day. We giggle
like children, grateful that fool   15
never did learn to behave. Life
carries us down a stream that gurgles
between rocks and sings improbable
songs. Who cares we'll have to paddle
like hell and know panic before we get home.   20
That's how all the good stories were born.

—1990

MEG CHRISTIAN (1946-   )

Meg Christian, one of the founders of the women's record label Olivia Records, was a major force in the lesbian feminist movement of the 1970s, and a regular at the Michigan Womyn's Music Festival. She was born and grew up in Lynchburg, Virginia, and attended the University of North Carolina, majoring in English and Music. As her political consciousness about women's issues developed in the early seventies, she began writing her own music and her repertoire became increasingly woman-centered. Christian's lyrics focus on a wide range of lesbian issues, from love to uncertainty to the experience of bigotry. "Ode to a Gym Teacher," the selection included here, gives humorous voice to a young lesbian's experience; in its time, it was one of the most important songs of the women's music movement. Christian stopped performing in the 1980s.

Ode to a Gym Teacher

She was a big tough woman, the first to come along
That showed me being female meant you still could be strong;
And though graduation meant that we had to part,
She'll always be a player on the ballfield of my heart.

I wrote her name on my note-pad   5
And I inked it on my dress
And I etched it on my locker
And I carved it on my desk
And I painted big red hearts with her initials on my books
And I never knew 'til later why I got those funny looks.   10

Chorus
She was a big tough woman, the first to come along
That showed me being female meant you still could be strong;
And though graduation meant that we had to part,
She'll always be a player on the ballfield of my heart.

Well, in gym class while the others   15
Talked of boys that they loved,
I'd be thinking of new aches and pains
The teacher had to rub.
And when other girls went to the prom,
I languished by the phone,   20
Calling up and hanging up if I found out she was home.

[*Chorus*]   25

I sang her songs by Johnny Mathis,[1]
I gave her everything—
A new chain for her whistle,
And some daisies in the spring,
Some suggestive poems for Christmas   30
By Miss Edna Millay,[2]
And a lacy, lacy, lacy card for Valentine's day.

[*Chorus*]

So you just go to any gym class
And you'll be sure to see
One girl who sticks to teacher
Like a leaf sticks to a tree,   40
One girl who runs the errands
And who chases all the balls,
One girl who may grow up to be the gayest of all.

[*Chorus*]

—1974

---

[1] Johnny Mathis (b. 1935), popular singer and songwriter, famous for his romantic ballads.
[2] Edna St. Vincent Millay (1892-1950), highly regarded lyrical poet who had romantic relationships with both men and women.

CHRYSTOS (1946-   )

Native American poet and activist Chrystos was born in San Francisco, California, to a Menominee father and a French and Lithuanian mother. Largely self-educated as a writer, she identifies herself primarily through her Native roots, and describes herself as an "Urban Indian." Much of her work, often fiercely confrontational, illuminates the ways in which institutionalized forces harm the lives of indigenous people, women, and children. Another important strand of her work is her erotic poetry celebrating lesbian sexuality. Chrystos is the author of several collections, including *Not Vanishing* (1988), *Dream On* (1991), *In Her I Am* (1993), *Fire Power* (1995), and *Fugitive Colors* (1995). She has received several awards for her poetry and her activism, including the Barbara Deming Memorial Grant, a National Endowment for the Arts grant, a Lannan Foundation grant, a Freedom of Expression Award from the Fund for Human Rights (with Minnie Bruce Pratt and Audre Lorde), and a Sappho Award of Distinction from the Astraea National Lesbian Action Foundation.

Ceremony for Completing a Poetry Reading

This is a give away poem
You've come gathering   made a circle with me of the places
I've wandered   I give you   the first daffodil opening
from earth I've sown   I give you warm loaves of bread baked
in soft mounds like breasts   In this circle I pass each of you   5
a shell from our mother sea   Hold it in your spirit   Hear
the stories she'll tell you   I've wrapped your faces
around me   a warm robe   Let me give you ribbonwork leggings
dresses sewn with elk teeth   moccasins woven with red
& sky blue porcupine quills   10
I give you blankets woven of flowers & roots   Come closer
I have more to give   this basket is very large
I've stitched it of your kind words
Here is a necklace of feathers & bones
a sacred meal of chokecherries   15
Take this mask of bark which keeps out the evil ones
This basket is only the beginning
There is something in my arms for all of you
I offer this memory of sunrise seen through ice crystals
Here   an afternoon of looking into the sea from high rocks   20
Here   a red-tailed hawk circles over our heads
One of her feathers drops for your hair
May I give you this round stone which holds an ancient spirit
This stone will soothe you
Within this basket is something you've been looking for   25
all of your life   Come take it   Take as much as you need
I give you seeds of a new way
I give you the moon shining on a fire of singing women
I give you the sound of our feet dancing
I give you the sound of our thoughts flying   30
I give you the sound of peace moving into our faces & sitting down

Come   This is a give away poem
I cannot go home
until you have taken everything & the basket which held it
When my hands are empty   35
I will be full

—1988

No Public Safety

I can't tell you how much
they want to lock her up
She sleeps in their building   It's trespassing   How would you
like to come to work in the morning & have to step over her
See how little she has   compared to you   5
Chronic Paranoid Schizophrenic they say
The law is ambiguous   Can she take care of herself
or not
Obviously not if she thinks the building for Public Safety
means just that   10
There are laws against the literal interpretation of words
She has been taken to Western State Hospital & observed
They say she hallucinates
Join the army   murder a lot of people you don't know   but don't
hallucinate   That's crazy   15
Incompetent to stand trial they say   Would you
let her live in your house   sleep on your porch
keep her bags in your garage   pitch a tipi for her on your lawn
What would the neighbors think
Better lock her up   We don't want to look at failure   scares us   20
isn't safe   They say for her to sleep alone in that building
why anything could happen to her
Let's keep the building warm & lit all night even after
the janitors go home   We like to take better care
of our papers   file cabinets   metal desks   plastic chairs   25
potted plants   posters of trees in Yosemite
than an old woman
Who does she think she is anyway   expecting us to help
to give her safety   Anyone who doesn't take care of themselves
should be locked up   we have lots of places for it   30
We're all terrified   not of growing old   but of being unable
to take care of ourselves
Would you rather sleep in the Public Safety Building
or be locked up on a back ward at Western State Hospital
the food   the drugs   regular & terrible   35
This is her second trial   Keep the lawyers off the streets
They can take care of themselves with a little help
from their wives who clean   buy groceries   take the suits
to the cleaners   change the bed   cook meals   raise

the children   & admire   40
Who admires Anna Mae Peoples besides me
What is shelter   the judge asks rhetorically
you won't catch HIM sleeping under bridges or begging
$40,230 buys a lot of shelter   a king size bed
hot massage shower   wall to wall carpeting or probably   45
oriental rugs   A long time ago Anna Mae Peoples
probably waxed judges' floors
Too old now her back hurts all the time
the cool floor of the Public Safety Building is all she asks
They want to label her gravely disabled   50
they think there's a very good chance they'll win
Nowhere in the six column article
is one word
that Anna Mae Peoples has to say

for Anna Mae Peoples

—1988

Savage Eloquence

     Big Mountain
you old story you old
thing you fighting over nothing everything
how they work us
against one another   They mean to kill us   5
all   Vanishing is no joke   they mean it
We don't fit this machine they've made instead of life   We breathe
spirit   softness of dirt between our toes   No metaphors
Mountains ARE our mothers   Stars our dead
Big Mountain we've heard your story a thousand times   10
We've grown up inside your slaughtered sheep   Move here
move there   die on the way   fences through our hearts
ask permission to gather eagle feathers   no sun dance
take our bundles   shirts   bowls to put in dry empty buildings
walls more walls jails more jails agencies thieves rapists   15
drunken refuge from lives with nothing left
take our children   take our hands hacked from us in death
tell lies to us   about us   lies written spoken lived
death that comes in disease relentless   Vanishing is no metaphor
Big Mountain you are no news   Our savage eloquence is dust   20
between their walls their thousand deaths   We go to funerals
never quite have time to step out of mourning
Everything we have left is in our hearts deeply hidden
No photograph or tape recorder or drawing can touch
the mountain of our spirits   25
They are Still
saying they know
what is best for us

they who know nothing
their white papers decisions empty eyes laws rules stone fences   30
time cut apart with dots
killing animals to hang their heads on walls
We cannot make sense of this
It has nothing   everything
to do with us   35
Big Mountain I've met you before in Menominee County[1]
at Wounded Knee[2]   on Trails of Tears[3]
in the back street bars of every broken city
I could write a list long & thick as the books they call
Indian Law   40
which none of us
wrote
We know you fences death laws death hunger death
This is our skin
you take from us   These were our lives   our patterns   our dawns 45
the lines in our faces
which tell us our songs
Big Mountain you are too big you are too small you are such an old
old story

for Aisha Masakella

—1988

Wings of a Wild Goose

A hen, one who could have brought more geese, a female, a wild one
dead   Shot by an excited ignorant young blond boy, his first
His mother threw the wings in the garbage   I rinsed them
brought them home, hung them spread wide on my studio wall
A reminder of so much, saving what I can't bear to be wasted   5
Wings
I dream of wings which carry me far above human bitterness
human walls   A goose who will have no more tiny pale fluttering
goslings to bring alive   to shelter   to feed   to watch fly
off on new wings   different winds   10
He has a lawn this boy   A pretty face which was recently paid
thousands of dollars to be in a television commercial   I clean
their house every Wednesday morning
2 dogs which no one brushes   flying hair everywhere

---

[1] A county in Wisconsin that is virtually co-extensive with the Menominee Indian Reservation.

[2] Wounded Knee, South Dakota (located on what is now the Pine Ridge Reservation of the Oglala Sioux), the site of an 1890 massacre of Lakota Sioux men, women, and children by U.S. cavalrymen. In 1973, the town of Wounded Knee was seized by members of the American Indian Movement (AIM) and held for 71 days while the U.S. Marshal Service laid siege.

[3] Between 1830 and 1838, the Cherokee, Choctaw, Chickasaw, Seminole, and Creek peoples living in the southeastern U.S. (Mississippi, Georgia, South Carolina, and Alabama) were forcibly removed by the U.S. government and made to walk to reservation lands set aside for them in Oklahoma. Many thousands died on this march, often referred to as the Trail of Tears.

A black rabbit who is almost always out of   15
water   usually in a filthy cage   I've cleaned the cage
out of sympathy a few times although it is not part of what
are called my duties   I check the water as soon as I arrive
This rabbit & those dogs are the boy's pets   He is very lazy
He watches television constantly leaving the sofa in the den   20
littered with food wrappers, soda cans, empty cereal bowls
If I'm still there when he comes home, he is rude to me   If he
has his friends with him, he makes fun of me behind my back
I muse on how he will always think of the woods
as an exciting place to kill   This family of three lives   25
on a five acre farm   They raise no crops   not even their own
vegetables or animals for slaughter   His father is a neurosurgeon
who longs to be a poet   His mother frantically searches
for christian enlightenment   I'm sad for her   though I don't like
her   because I know she won't find any   The boy does nothing   30
around the house to help without being paid   I'm 38 & still
haven't saved the amount of money he has in a passbook found
in the pillows of the couch under gum wrappers   That dead goose
This boy will probably never understand that it is not right
to take without giving   He doesn't know how to give   His mother   35
who cleaned & cooked the goose says she doesn't really like
to do it but can't understand why she should feel any different
about the goose than a chicken or hamburger from the supermarket
I bite my tongue & nod   I could explain to her that meat raised
for slaughter is very different than meat taken from the woods   40
where so few wild beings survive   That her ancestors are
responsible for the emptiness of this land   That lawns feed no
one   that fallow land lined with fences is sinful   That hungry
people need the food they could be growing   That spirituality
is not separate from food or wildness or respect or giving   45
But she already doesn't like me   because she suspects me
of reading her husband's poetry books when no one is around
& she's right   I do   I need the 32 dollars a week tolerating
them provides me   I wait for the wings on my wall to speak to me
guide my hungers   teach me winds I can't reach   I keep   50
these wings because walls are so hard   wildness so rare   because
ignorance must be remembered   because I am female   because I fly
only in my dreams   because I too
will have no young to let go

for Dian Million

—1988

MICHELLE CLIFF (1946-)

Born in Jamaica, Michelle Cliff was raised both there and in the U.S. She was educated in the U.S. and Britain, and holds a Ph.D. in Italian Renaissance from the Warburg Institute of the University of London. Cliff has published three novels: *Abeng* (1984), *No Telephone to Heaven* (1987), and *Free Enterprise* (1993, 2004). Her books of poetry and stories include *Claiming an Identity They Taught Me to Despise* (1980), *The Land of Look Behind: Prose and Poetry* (1985), *Bodies of Water* (1990), and *The Store of a Million Items: Stories* (1998), and she has also edited a collection of writing by social reformer Lillian Smith entitled *The Winner Names the Age* (1978). Cliff lives in California.

Contagious Melancholia

"Did you notice they didn't even have a piece of evergreen tacked to the walls?"
"Poor devils."

My parents, sitting in the front seat of the Vauxhall,[1] are reminiscing about a visit just completed, to the house where an old family friend, Miss Small, and her invalid sister live. We visit them only on Christmas, the most exciting day of the year for the likes of us. We recognize how fortunate we are.

"How the mighty are fallen." In this sliver of the island such language applies.

Almost the same exact exchange takes place year after year, followed by a recitation of the vast holdings once enjoyed by the Smalls, where there are now developments, hotels, alumina operations. And the Smalls realized little profit, the fault of an outsider who mismanaged the properties. There are a thousand such stories on this island; my father seems to know them all.

Miss Small is called by her family (none left but the sister) and friends (which you can count on one hand, so few remain) Girlie. She lives up to her name.

She is tiny in stature, each year growing smaller. At eleven I overwhelm her in height. She is dressed this particular Christmas Day in what looks to be an old school uniform, down to the striped tie and tied-up brown oxfords. She wears tortoiseshell spectacles. The huge, sea-going ancient beasts are an island treasure. We do not worship them, as did the Arawak;[2] but we know they are worth a lot. Their shells are sold for eyeglass frames, their flesh for tinned soup. I drank them once in the Place de l'Odéon in Paris.

Miss Small's chestnut hair is bobbed and turns under at her neckline. The spectacles make her eyes big, two surprised circles, dark brown, against a pallid, lineless skin.

Her girlishness seems intact. She claps her hands in excitement when my father presents her with a tin of Huntley & Palmer's[3] Christmas assortment.

As we enter the house the wireless is tuned to the Queen's message, coming to us live from what my father calls the Untidy Kingdom. He believes this puts them in their place, as when he refers to our neighbor to the north as the Untidy Snakes of America.

We sometimes live in New York City but always return home.

---

[1] British car brand.
[2] Original inhabitants of Haiti and the Dominican

Republic.
[3] British cookie manufacturer.

One return took place a week after Emmett Till's[4] body was found. I heard my mother behind their bedroom door, "I've had enough of this damn-blasted place!"

That's another story.

+ + +

I have never seen Miss Small's sister, Miriam. I have only heard her voice, calling from the room where she is bed-ridden. When I ask what is wrong with her, why doesn't she get up, my mother demurs, muttering something about "disappointment."

"What kind of disappointment?" I ask, hoping for a true-romance response. At best a fiancé killed in a war; at least an outside child.

"In life," my mother sighs.

In a few days, believe it or not, only ninety miles away, on another island, where turtles were also worshipped, the rebel forces are to take Havana.

"Rachel, go into the kitchen with Miss Girlie and see if you can be of help."

I follow my tiny host down the hall to the back of the house, to the kitchen, where my eyes are met with an excitement of roaches, another huge and ancient beast known to us. They scramble across a mound of wet sugar someone has spilled on a counter.

"Bitches," Girlie mutters under her breath. I do not know if she refers to the cockroaches, who know no shame, continuing to scramble over the mound, their feet gloriously crystalline with sugar, even after she has flattened one with a teacup, or does she mean the two women who are visible to me through the slats in the jalousie window.

"Pardon, Miss Girlie?" I say, not quite believing a word she would never utter in the parlor has escaped her mouth in the kitchen.

"Nothing."

The two women are no longer in my line of vision.

The remains of the cockroach cling to the bottom of the teacup in her hand.

The sugar mound appears to be the only food in sight. The safe, as it's called, a screen-fronted cabinet designed to stay flies and roaches, stands before me, apparently empty, not even a tin of sardines. She catches me looking.

"Damn bitches nuh tek all me foodstuff?" She speaks for them to understand.

Cigarette smoke rises outside the jalousie. Someone is listening.

"Listen to de bitch, nuh. Listen to she. Nasty man-woman."

Miss Girlie gives a little shrug and places the teacup on a tray.

"Shouldn't we rinse it off?"

She nods and hands the cup to me. I turn on the tap. Nothing.

"You will have to use the standpipe in the yard. This tap does not function at the moment."

I find an enamel pan to catch water and head out back. I know my entry into the yard will cause comment. We live in an oral society in which everything, every move, motion, eyeflash, is commented upon, catalogued, categorized, approved or disapproved. The members of this society are my writing teachers, but I don't

---

[4] Emmett Till (1941-1955), Black teenager from Chicago who was brutally lynched in Mississippi after allegedly whistling at a white woman. Following a trial that gained international media attention, two white men were acquitted for the murder, to which they later confessed.

know this yet.

The two women wear the dark blue dresses and white aprons usual to Kingston maids. I don't know their names. We visit only once a year, and the personnel is never the same.

"You raise where?" I am immediately spoken to.

"Pardon?"

"Me say is where dem raise you?"

"Why?"

"Far me wish fi know why you nuh wish we a Happy Christmas?"

"Happy Christmas, missis."

"You hear de chile? Is too late fe dat. Better watch de man-woman nuh get she."

I am reddening, which will cause more comment. About the resemblance my skin bears to a pig, for one thing.

I am too young to understand it.

I bend over the standpipe and pray that the trickle soon fills the enamel pan. I have set the teacup to one side.

"Me name Patsy." The second woman is speaking to me.

"Happy Christmas, Patsy."

"Change a come."

I slowly rinse the cockroach shell and guts from the flowered cup.

"Me say change a come. It due."

"Lord Jesus," the woman who is not Patsy is speaking.

"Missis?"

"Is what dat on de teacup?"

"Cockroach."

"Lord Jesus, what a nasty smaddy."[5]

Back in the kitchen Girlie is standing in a corner, her eyes focused on the floor.

"I must make some tea for Miriam, my sister," she says.

"Where is the tea?" I ask her.

"In the safe."

I open the door into the emptiness, and with great care, and certain knowledge my hand is about to encounter something truly dreadful, feel around for Earl Grey or lapsang souchong. Something wet is on my finger; I quickly draw it back. Without looking I wipe my hand on my best clothes. Another foray into the darkness of the safe and I manage to find an envelope with the words "Tower Isle Hotel" stamped on it. Inside there is a handful of miserable leaves.

"Miss Girlie, where is the teapot?"

"In the breakfront in the drawing room. I will fetch it."

I know I must venture again into the yard to fetch water for the tea.

The woman who is not Patsy has left. Patsy has her back against the wall of the house, one leg bent for balance, the foot flat against grayish wood.

She is staring into space.

"I'm just here to get some more water."

"Please yourself."

The yard is the classic design of old-style Kingston houses. A verandah attached

[5] Somebody.

to the kitchen overlooks a rectangular space, across which are the servants' quarters. Invariably thin rooms with one square of window.

I am brought up not to think about such things, to be content with paradise.

There is something about Patsy as she stands against that wall, her foot bent back like a great sea bird. I say this now, describing her image in my brain. But then? Then I was probably glad of the quiet, of the absence of the other woman, her tongue.

The water trickles into the enamel pan, finally filling it. I return to the kitchen.

Miss Girlie awaits, with a flowered teapot, a riot of pansies and forget-me-nots fading with time and the hard water of Kingston. I take the pot from her and put the measly handful of leaves into the stained inside. She puts the water on the kerosene stove.

Who were the Misses Small? For these are real women I have been talking about. Down to their names. They are long gone. Girlhood chums of my great-grandmother, they cluster together in my mind with all the other mad, crazy, eccentric, disappointed, demented, neurasthenic women of my childhood, where Bertha Mason[6] grew on trees. Every family of our ilk, every single one, had such a member. And she was always hidden, and she was always a shame, and she was always the bearer of that which lay behind us.

—1993

[6] Edward Rochester's first wife, a madwoman from the Caribbean, in Charlotte Brontë's *Jane Eyre* (1847).

WANDA COLEMAN (1946-   )

A writer of poetry, fiction, essays, screenplays, and journalism, Wanda Coleman was born in the Watts district of Los Angeles to Lewana (Scott) and George Evans. Following two years of college, she became involved with Studio Watts, a politically infused art group, and later participated in Beat-influenced workshops in Venice, California. Coleman's work uses an avant-garde aesthetic to address political and social realities; language play and intertextuality are often juxtaposed with anger and direct speech. Recurring themes include the intersection of gender, race, and class, and their effects on African Americans, particularly women; historical figures and events; and life in and around Los Angeles. Coleman, who has written since childhood, has held a variety of jobs to support herself, including a staff writing position on the television soap opera *Days of Our Lives* (for which she won an Emmy for best writing in a daytime drama in 1976). The recipient of fellowships from the Guggenheim Foundation and the National Endowment for the Arts, Coleman has published numerous works, including the poetry collections *Bathwater Wine* (1998), which won the 1999 Lenore Marshall Poetry Prize, and *Mercurochrome* (2001), a finalist for the 2001 National Book Award in poetry. She has also issued a solo spoken word CD entitled *High Priestess of Word* (1990). Coleman has three children and lives in Los Angeles.

Wanda Why Aren't You Dead

wanda when are you gonna wear your hair down
wanda. that's a whore's name
wanda why ain't you rich

wanda you know no man in his right mind want a ready-made family
why don't you lose weight   5
wanda why are you so angry
how come your feet are so goddamn big
can't you afford to move out of this hell hole
if i were you were you were you
wanda what is it like being black   10
i hear you don't like black men
tell me you're ac/dc. tell me you're a nympho. tell me you're into chains
wanda i don't think you really mean that
you're joking. girl, you crazy
wanda *what* makes you so angry   15
wanda i think you need this
wanda you have no humor in you you too serious
wanda i didn't know i was hurting you
that was an accident
wanda i know what you're thinking   20
wanda i don't think they'll take that off of you

wanda why are you so angry

i'm sorry i didn't remember that that that
that that that was so important to you

wanda you're ALWAYS on the attack   25

wanda wanda wanda i wonder

why ain't you dead

—1987

Intruder

i have broken and entered poetry's house. where have they
hidden the valuables? there is no safe. the refrigerator
is empty and something covered in green-gray fuzz
stains my eyes and stings my nose. the oven door hangs
off its hinge. the trash of countless meals—eggshells,   5
coffee grounds, half-eaten fruit, old cheese—litters
unmopped floors. an inky foot-deep ring circles the basin
of the white enameled tub. the unflushed toilet is
feces-clogged. clusters of beer bottles and ashtrays erupting
with cigarette butts crowd table and counter tops. the TV   10
buzzes its spill of white noise. the radio persistently whines
those nostalgic rhythms innocence is ever lost by. in the
closet, all coat pockets and elbows are frayed. there is no
safe. in the jewel box, all the diamonds, rubies and pearls
prove paste. i've broken into poetry's house. it smells   15
unclean/unholy. and there is nothing here worthy of theft

—1998

Business As Usual

you saw me when i came in, drawn
by your fire sale sign

i have entered your shop
to spend my slave's wages on goods
you pretend are available to anyone   5

i have behaved like a lady
joined the line and have stood here forever
without complaining even though
my feet are screaming and i'm suffering
from a raging heartache   10

and now it is my turn
to opt for what i want. and you suddenly
do not see me. even though
i'm as black as blazes as tall
as a drink of salt water and wide as two stadiums   15
even though
i am standing within stabbing distance

your eyes see everything around me but me

and then you look straight at the White
person behind me, lean forward   20
and ask, "may i help you?"

at least they have sense enough to squirm
before i clear my throat

—2001

CAROLYN LEI-LANILAU (1946-   )

Of Chinese, Hawaiian, and Portuguese heritage, Carolyn Leilani Yu Zhen Lau was born in Honolulu, Hawai'i. She received an M.A. in English at San Francisco State University, specializing in Chinese poetry, linguistics, and William Blake. She has also done research on Nu Shu, a secret language of women in the Hu Nan province of China. Her first book, *Wode Shuofa: My Way of Speaking* (published under the name Carolyn Lau) received a 1989 American Book Award. Lei-lanilau's next publication was an autobiographically-based collection of essays, entitled *Ono-Ono Girl's Hula* (1997), which transforms both genre and language. The essays, two of which appear below, are written in both "standard" and pidgin English, and include Native Hawaiian, Hakka, Mandarin, French, and Yiddish as well. *Ono-Ono Girl's Hula* was recognized with a Small Press Book Award and a Firecracker Alternative Book Award.

Lei-lanilau's writing has been published in anthologies such as *The Best American Poetry of 1996, Making More Waves: New Writing By Asian American Women,* and *Chinese American Poetry:*

An Anthology, as well as journals such as *Bloomsbury Review, American Poetry Review, Manoa, Yellow Silk, Zyzzyva,* and *Calyx.* She has been a lecturer at the University of Hawai'i at Manoa, West O'ahu, Tianjin Foreign Language Institute in China, and California State University, Hayward. She lives in Oakland, California, and Honolulu, Hawai'i.

The Inner Life of Lani Moo

This is one touchy subject that I cannot objectify. To some folks, "Lani Moo" is merely a matter of phonemes, an abstraction at best. A sound perhaps. Others might confuse Lani Moo[1] with *mu'umu'u.*[2] The go-aheaders consider Lani a relic, a thing of the past to forget. Then, there are the In-betweeners who along with shortie and Suzy *mu'umu'u;* beer-can hats, handmade cloth book covers and slippers, desk calendars with thermometers; going down to Aloha Tower to throw streamers and confetti, leis and money into the water for the divers as the Lurline and Mariposa[3] drifted into fantasyland—the In-betweeners remember. An then, like Elvis fans dead and alive, there are the *pa'a*[4] toughnuts, the underground killerbees *others* like me who derive nirvana from the concept, the riddle and memory of, ice cream parties; the at-Halloween-only chocolate molds of witches and cats and orange custard half-moons and pumpkins packed in break-your-teeth dry ice that you couldn't breathe the same way Aunty Scan instructed when you drove past the mental institution down in Kaneohe—because you could get dumb or crazy like dem. For kids in Hawai'i who hate hate hate stinky smelly toejam cheese, the way the family tells it, it was the brainstorm of my uncle Tong Lee, father of Nelia Beatrice Stanley Flossie and Jimmy; husband of Tai Yi—innovator, he created Lani Moo for Dairyman's because island kids like myself liked only to squish the cheese between the holes in swiss cheese. In those days (as we refer to) only the *haole*[5] ate cheese. The *avant-garde* Lee's were the only relatives who had cheese in their ice box. Locals did not eat cheese—we had much mo bettah food to eat.

We whacked-up *saimin,*[6] portuguese sausage, *kim chee,*[7] *lomi lomi* salmon,[8] *pipi kaula.*[9] Our beloved *poi*[10] and orgasmic rice. Rice with *lup cheong;*[11] rice with egg omelet; rice with canned corned beef and onions. Yummm. Sometimes, after we eat a whole dinner, we eat rice and tea. *Ono,* so good. And, we'd fight for the burnt rice at the bottom of the pot (you need a pot for this and actually, this is not supposed to happen unless you are yakking on the telephone or maybe you fell asleep waiting to turn off the stove in time to avoid having burnt rice). Cheese was like pok and beans—something that only *haole* ate. Proudly, we ate meat. Man, we ate with straight backs/we spoke English. Just like my China husband sez when he describes himself in ESL terms as "the best speaker of English"—we celebrated diagramming sentences. Who needed to eat cheese on top of that! And who could suffer and bury your taste buds in that ugly white pus-sy stuff: milk? You know, Hawaiians know how—to Eat.

But it wasn't eating that my class stayed in for recess too many lectures while I knew it was not me that threw in that whole baby-size container of milk into the rubbish can. I hated that white uky stuff. It looked ugly and didn't taste like food.

---

[1] The cow-mascot of Meadow Gold Dairies, a Hawai'i based dairy company; "lani" means heavenly.
[2] (Hawaiian) A long, loose Hawaiian dress.
[3] Ocean liners.
[4] (Hawaiian) Firm.
[5] (Hawaiian) White people.
[6] Hawaiian noodle soup dish.
[7] Korean dish of fermented vegetables.
[8] Pacific Island salmon and tomato salad.
[9] Hawaiian-style jerky.
[10] Hawaiian staple made from taro.
[11] Chinese-style sausage.

No God, no Miss Whiteface could force me to suck that warm sour "cow milk" during those wet hot days. I don't care if we had graham crackers or crack—I did not and would not drink that thick white medicine. That white drink. That poison. Enter Lani Moo.

Lani—Moo. Remember Lani—moo?

Lani Moo was sacred. She was her own unique version of the sacred Hindi cow, sexy as hell. Cue-tte! Children of the unborn children, *kupuna*,[12] Aunty Lani Moo, *hula* maiden, *tūtū*.[13] Nymph: Lani Moo was centerfold. Just saying the sounds, "Lani" swept me to the heavens where all the *aloha* in the world comes from. Not the classic long Hawaiian name. Lani Moo was *kaona*[14] itself. She is truly revered as our Mother Teresa, our Madonna, Madame Curie, Wonder Woman. Drop dead when you say her name. She was libidinous James Bond in a formidable shape. And the "Moo" piece was genuinely the mystical, meditative, and lovestruck part of Lani's awesome symbolism. Loved by plants and animals; heads of state, past and future. Regaled higher than all *ali'i*[15] and gods, included in the *Kumulipo*[16] creation prayers, Lani Moo with her fresh carnation and plumeria leis internally pumping iron while posing along Kalaniana'ole Hwy in grass. Never ever even laid cowslop while kids stood in line dazed by headache heat desiring to touch her forehead. Patient. Understanding: caressing our pitiful hearts with soothing vowels while forgiving our broken English as we honored her in our island simple manners.

Anthropomorphic that she was, briefly, we had meaning in our disenfranchised lives.

And then, there was the matter of Lani's baby. Hawaiians are crazy about babies. Baby anythings are cute. To us, babies mean chance. Maybe change, but hopefully a chance for change. Every baby born is potentially a Kawaipuna or Pono or Maile or Iwalani or Owana or Moke or Nainoa or Kalanihiapo:[17] every baby born is influenced by passion for that *'āina*.[18] The little *keiki*[19] moo was important in the genealogy but Who remembers the name? Who cared if there was a bull or not? That nut Calvin/Kaleo quipped, "Immaculate Conception Moo, right?" All that mattered was the Unmoved Mover Lani Moo. Sensitive nostrils, galaxy big eyes, vamp orange-brown and white *kīkepa*[20] wrapped around her *'ōpū*.[21] One *wahine*[22] woman, female, mother, island girl, sex. No flies. Never any flies around Ms. Moo. She was an identity: no lunch cans or plastic icons dared replicate her bestial beauty. A milkcover maybe which entitled you to a Lani Moo ice cream feast day where you could get free ice cream, all the milk (urrgh) and cheese (aarph) you wanted, and schmooze with Lani Moo for a second. If politicians ever learn the secret of Lani Moo, we will be in good or bad *kūkae* aka shit!

Then, Lani went *holo holo*.[23] *Pau hana*.[24]

P.S. An den: you know what went happening now! Pogs! Yea, what the hell are *pogs?* Metal replacements for the unique cardboard caps that held the cream and milk together—pogs that cost individually from fifty or one hundred dollars which are now

---

[12] (Hawaiian) Elders and ancestors.
[13] (Hawaiian) Grandma.
[14] (Hawaiian) Multiple layers of meanings.
[15] (Hawaiian) Highest rank in traditional Hawaiian society.
[16] Hawaiian Creation chant.
[17] Prominent Hawaiian families.
[18] (Hawaiian) Land; earth.

[19] (Hawaiian) Child.
[20] (Hawaiian) Wrap.
[21] (Hawaiian) Belly.
[22] (Hawaiian) Woman.
[23] (Hawaiian) To go for a ride without a specific destination.
[24] (Hawaiian) To end work.

used as gambling chips! The New Hawaiian rave sweeping kids, the super markets, *obachan*,[25] and P.R. men into the latest "Go for Broke" mindset, pogs. The ugliest.

The dumbest of the dumb and yet, it is the rage: almost as high as each crane layering on the steel or thick as the layers of cement that protect it. Cann you replace Lani Moo with tofutti? Could you replace milk cover with metal?

Auē koʻu Hawaiʻi Nei![26]

—1997

The Presence of Lite Spam—lingering in my psyche for a long time but oozing out after the (first) Rodney King verdict.

Anyone who is a darky—that is "who lives inside light- or dark-colored skin," poor or both—has eaten the forerunner of *pate*, spam. I wonder how the buggah's[27] name "spam" was born? "Ham" in the "spa"? "Spit" plus "ham"? "the Sp(irit) in the present tense of the verb 'to be,'" communing in the "am"? Or was it just military *cordon bleu cuisine?*

With the advent of Yuppies in Hawaiʻi, a competition was devised among local wannabe yuppies to contest in a spam-diversity competition. Spam *pate,* spam *musubi* (a kind of *sushi*), and delicious rewarding fresh from the can with jelly and cold white lard probably horse meat and flyswappings in the spam staring *and* yuckking-it-up-at-you-in-the-face Third World Spam hands down authentic turn the silver key attached to the can spam incarnate gospel finally becomes Legitimate. The poet sculptor painter activist gardener husband father cook visionaire jokester Imaikalani warned me about his now famous spam stew.

Cringing, I begged, "What the hell you put in it?"

"A lot of potatoes, man!" he smacked.

Those "damn spam" sushi/musubi are enthusiastically bought and sold at every honorable *sushi* stand at home in Kaleponi where everybody, everybody, is calesterol-conscious. At every Hawaiian event, there are the food booths with, of cuss, spam. In 1992, Lite Spam appears first in paper—literature: always the first art to be eliminated—becomes the prize introductory media to premier Lite Spam followed by discretionary late night tv ads. What can this mean to a Naive Native? Aye! what's happening to us now? This is an example of deep counter-culture adverse manipulation assimilation *buffet a la carte* in our butts. This lite spam is the new tool for exchange brokerage—the new nails. After a flash of *hā*[28] and *ʻōlelo*[29] word power, I race to the telephone and dial 808. Know what that is? The area code to Hawaiʻi, man. In trouble, dial 808. On the coconut wireless, I shout the scandal to my chiefs of culture.

We are burned up, mostly we suffer from a kind of ancient pain: (You know Lololo? Tita[30]—One. Da Screamer rattled our McInerny three-piece vested brains and Hawaiʻi Visitors Bureau Hawaiian Telephone operator voices. That Ph.D. said that Someting wass wrong.—I dunno if SHE got da ANSA though.)

Da tightshoe Madison Avenue execs (all kine color) who sell our land, our weather, and get on the plane to *lūʻau* in our backyard ain't factoring in the brahhss and sisstahs

---

[25] (Japanese) Grandma.
[26] (Hawaiian) A phrase of lament for "my Hawaii."
[27] (Hawaiian pidgin) Person or thing; connotation depends on tone.
[28] (Hawaiian) Breath of life.
[29] (Hawaiian) Language.
[30] (Hawaiian pidgin) Tough female.

who put our big feet inside-out college departing with the *palapala*[31]—before and after Civil Rights. No matter, mainstream-kind-scared American—Japan too—no gettum darkies: *akamai*[32]—hip to double- and triple-talk hardcopy assessment deadline net worth. Some of us are white, some of us be village green. We have learned from Chinese to conquer people by marriage. Give you the best singing and sex in your no mo fun lives. Aye Progressive, because we only in our developmental stages of processing bureaucratic white agenda and underneath it all, somewhere, yes sir, yess ma'am, we not logic by your instruments of measure. Some white folks, as much as we love you and you may have children by us: we nevah expect you and intelligent converted colored—yellow, red brown, sage, indigo, florida Hawaiian folks nevah know that we no get the verbs "to be" or "to have" in our wishes.

Means, we no lik compete an cut troat for success. *'a'ole*,[33] NO.

Who asked Captain Cook come Hawai'i an insult us into Victorian habits and uniforms? You know what follows? Syphilis, false eyelashes, shoes, peanut butter and jelly sandwich, Miss Hawaii contest, Ala Moana Shopping Center. The otta day myfren Ivan the psychiatrist went say in pidgin rhythms, "Man, I have been having *angst*." Poorting, needed to say it in Nazi talk what he felt as a star trekking *kanaka*.[34] (The greatest is when I was home and had to report a lost item to who? my favorite, the Honolulu Police.

When the Hertzgirl said that, "All security was involved in something and would be tied up for an hour,"

I said, "What? Somebody was murdered?" The joke did not go over: we all knew the cops were eating dinner and did not want to bother with some tourist who lost something.

Later on, at my mother's, I call the cops and up drives this cute little meter maid cart and in it is a disarming local boy in a cop's costume. When he walks up to the house, I invite him in and he begins to unlace his shoes! Soo cute! [At that moment, I knew someday, I would move home just so that as an "old fut"[35] I could push anyone around. Instead, I offer that he interviews me in the kitchen where he can enter through the back door and therefore leave his shoes on.]) But as far as *kānaka maoli*[36] and our lost kings and queens, before the missionaries and then Mackindly Mckinley screwed us, eh? Thee United States government—man, haole:[37] how did Christians learn from their god to be so *mākonā*—so mean. How come *haole* love to hear our music and love to watch us *hula* but never let us—"forbid" was the word; how come *kānaka* were forbidden to *'ōlelo o Hawai'i*—speak Hawaiian. No wonder we real *da kine*[38] and like beef or cry all da time—try-ing to reach our metaphors, man. When we had *ali'i*, we had *ahupua'a*,[39] system. Oh, it was *some system* and Ka'ahaumanu[40] did her share to create even more complexity to it, but bottom line, it was Hawaiian. We had slaves and human sacrifice: it was not humanistic or maybe not even democratic but it was okay. And, along comes the whitebutts to embarrass our people to wear corsets and girdles around our throats. Exercise and Diets! Those English and those damn wigs? And while I'm *nuha*[41]—**what is it with people who need to conquer** people? Talk

---

[31] (Hawaiian) Document or certificate.
[32] (Hawaiian) Smart.
[33] (Hawaiian) No.
[34] (Hawaiian) Native Hawaiian.
[35] (Hawaiian pidgin) Old fart.
[36] (Hawaiian) Native Hawaiian.

[37] (Hawaiian) White person.
[38] (Hawaiian pidgin) A placeholder word that can refer to anything; meaning is assumed from context.
[39] (Hawaiian) Land division.
[40] A Hawaiian queen.
[41] (Hawaiian) Angry.

about an inferiority complex! Must be someting wrong. Whoa, now, after convincing us that our beloved and adopted spam not good for us, what is next? Words: when I was born, my father—disappointed that I wasn't a boy disguised my name to link with Charlemagne. My Hawaiian name is so common that I never used it before my friend Faye made it sound so pretty and sweet. All my life I have had impossible too much heaven in my body for this earth. Maybe because my Chinese and Hawaiian names both have heaven in them. Best thing that I have learned in life is to make a good life here and not worry about heaven. For a while, I changed my Hawaiian name to "Leilo'i," meaning "flowers in the mud terrace." I kept the *lei* part because it was half the name that my daddy gave me. And I *hanai*,[42] adopted the *lo'i*[43] part because that is where *taro,* our staple food, flourishes. That is where the *'oha* the old root, and the *kalo,* the first *taro,* growing from the planted stalks and the *keiki,* the new shoots, thrive. In the *lo'i,* the *'ohana,* the entire family of water, insects, mud, wind, salt air; the fish that wander in by accident; the hands that come to gather and plant *taro* within the *'aina:* which we are, belong: meaning. We are meaning. We cry, fight, and love each other. More is nevah enough passion. Sometimes we are like the birds and sometimes we are Pele. We like to go barefeet because in Hawai'i even dirt tastes good. Our earth is *Papa;* our mother, sweet. Our water is sweet and soft. In a way, we are kind of like babies. Maybe that is the shadow side of us as our skin wrinkles slowly—now the cosmetics industry doing test on us wondering how *kupuna*[44] no mo wrinkles. We have a here-and-now kind of nature and that, in comparison to NYSE or NASDAQ, just doesn't cut it.

If you want to come see and have fun, *hele mai.*[45] Come look at us. See if you can find the Indians in the puzzle. See if you can tell we are standing in line behind and before you at the Safeway in your hometown. We will not appear in costume, but just let your heart leak a little sweetness or laughter and we will balloon our *kolohe*[46] bodies. If you go to the source of red dirt, however, please, *kokua.*[47] Ask first, and then no steal our bones and put your name on top of *the name* of our most loved *kupuna*. No make shame.

It has been long years to figure out how and who and what race and color go good with my skin and ears. And then you have to throw it to the wind like a fisherman throwing the net out to sea. To catch crab, turtles, shoes, a husband, my kids, my bigbest family in the world or nothing. Maybe tears, maybe laughs. And, then after I wrote testimony for *Ho'okolokolonui,*[48] I changed my name back to Lei-lani and then Lei-lanilau. And then, I made another list of windows to look out or into.

THE LIST (for today)

The Slop Can Man	The Marriage Proposal in Hawaiian
Beatrice's Hernia	My Kona Hat *Manapua*[49] Man on Bicycle

—1997

---

[42] (Hawaiian) Adopt.
[43] (Hawaiian) Taro patch.
[44] (Hawaiian) Elders.
[45] (Hawaiian) Come.
[46] (Hawaiian) Mischievous; rascal.

[47] (Hawaiian) Cooperate.
[48] (Hawaiian) Tribunal; probably referencing the People's International Tribunal in 1993.
[49] (Hawaiian pidgin) Barbecue pork-filled steamed bun; called *char siu bao* in Chinese.

MINNIE BRUCE PRATT (1946-   )

Minnie Bruce Pratt was born September 12, 1946, in Selma, Alabama. After graduating from a segregated high school, she received a B.A from the University of Alabama in Tuscaloosa, and a Ph.D. in English Literature from the University of North Carolina, Chapel Hill. Pratt first gained widespread acclaim as a writer for *Crime Against Nature* (1990), a book of poems about losing custody of her sons after coming out as a lesbian, which was awarded the Lamont Poetry Prize. She was already well known in lesbian-feminist circles for two earlier books of poetry, *The Sound of One Fork* (1981) and *We Say We Love Each Other* (1985), as well as for her 1988 essay "Identity: Skin, Blood, Heart," in which she explores the motivation of a white woman from a Christian background to question her own privilege in order to fight racism and anti-Semitism. In 1990, Pratt (along with Chrystos and Audre Lorde) was targeted by right-wing attacks on the National Endowment for the Arts, which had awarded her a fellowship. A long-time activist for issues ranging from lesbian rights to racism to U.S. imperialism, Pratt has also published the essay collection *Rebellion* (1991) and *S/HE* (1995), a collection of prose poems focused on the fluidity of gender and sexuality inspired by her life partner, transgender activist and writer Leslie Feinberg. Pratt's most recent collections of poetry are *Walking Back Up Depot Street* (1999) and *The Dirt She Ate* (2003).

Crime Against Nature

1

The upraised arm, fist clenched, ready to hit,
fist clenched and cocked, ready to throw a brick,
a rock, a Coke bottle. When you see this on TV,

robbers and cops, or people in some foreign alley,
is the rock in your hand? Do you shift and dodge?   5
Do you watch the story twitch in five kinds of color

while you eat Doritos, drink beer; the day's paper
sprawled at your feet, supplies bought at the 7-11
where no one bothered you? Or maybe he did. All

depends on what you look like, on if you can smile,   10
crawl, keep your mouth shut. Outside the store,
I, as usual, could not believe threat meant me, hated

by four men making up the story of their satiated
hot Saturday night and what they said at any woman
to emerge brash as a goddess from behind smoky glass,   15

how they won, if she would not bend her eyes or laugh,
by one thrusting question, broke her in half,
a bitch in heat, a devil with teeth for a cunt:

What's wrong with you, girl? The grin, gibe, chant.
What's the matter? (Split the concrete under her feet,   20
send her straight to hell, the prison pit fire,

blast her nasty self.) *You some kind of dyke?*

Sweating, damned if I'd give them the last say,
hissing into the mouth of the nearest face, *Yesss,*

hand jumped to car door, metal slam of escape 25
as he raised his hand, green bomb of a bottle,
I flinched, arm over my face, split-second

wait for the crash and shards of glass. His nod
instead, satisfied he'd frightened me back down
into whatever place I'd slid from. Laughter 30

quaked the other men. At me, a she-dog, queer
enough to talk? At him, tricked by a stone-face
drag woman stealing his punch line, astonished

as if a rock'd come to life in his hand and slashed
him? He dropped his hand, smiled like he'd won. 35
Slammed into the car, I drove away, mad, ashamed.

All night I seethed, helpless, the scene replayed,
slow-motion film, until I heard my *Yes,* and the dream
violence cracked with laughter. I was shaken out

on the street where my voice reared up her snout, 40
unlikely as a blacksnake racing from a drain, fire-
spitting, whistling like a siren, one word, *Yes,*

and the men, balanced between terror and surprise,
laugh as the voice rolls like a hoopsnake, tail
in her mouth, obscure spinning blur, quiet howl, 45

a mouth like a conjuring trick, a black hole
that swallows their story and turns it inside out.

For a split second we are all clenched, suspended:
upraised fist, approving hoots, my inverted ending.

2
The ones who fear me think they know who I am. 50
A devil's in me, or my brain's decayed by sickness.
In their hands, the hard shimmer of my life is dimmed.
I become a character to fit into their fictions,
someone predictable, tragic, disgusting, or pitiful.
If I'm not to burn, or crouch in some sort of cell, 55
at the very least I should not be let near children.

With strangers, even one with upraised fisted hand,
I blame this on too much church, or TV sci-fi, me cast
as mutant sexual rampage, Godzilla[1] Satan, basilisk
eyes, scorching phosphorescent skin, a hiss of words 60
deadly if breathed in.

---

[1] Godzilla, classic Japanese horror film monster (1954), is a giant dinosaur that has been irradiated by the fallout from a U.S. hydrogen bomb test.

But what about my mother? Or
the man I lived with, years? How could they be so
certain I was bad and they were not? They knew me: girl
baby-fat and bloody from the womb, woman swollen-   65
stomached with two pregnancies. My next body shift:
Why did it shake them? Breasts full for no use but
a rush of pleasure, skin tightened, loosened, nipples,
genitals gleaming red with unshed blood.

                                        I left   70
certainty for body, place of mystery. They acted
as if I'd gone to stand naked in a dirty room, to spin
my skin completely off, turn and spin, come off skin,
until, under, loomed a thing, scaly sin, needle teeth
like poison knives, a monster in their lives who'd run   75
with the children in her mouth, like a snake steals
eggs.
    I've never gotten used to being their evil,
the woman, the man, who held me naked, little and big.

No explanation except: the one who tells the tale   80
gets to name the monster. In my version, I walk
to where I want to live. They are there winding
time around them like graveclothes, rotten shrouds.
The living dead, winding me into a graveyard future.

Exaggeration, of course. In my anger I turn them   85
into a late-night horror show. I've left out how
I had no job for pay, he worked for rent and groceries,
my mother gave me her old car. But they abhorred me:

my inhuman shimmer, the crime of moving back and forth
between more than one self, more than one end to the story.   90

3
The hatred baffles me: individual, doctrinal, codified.
The way she pulled the statute book down like a novel

off the shelf, flipped to the index, her lacquer-red
lips glib around the words *crime against nature,* and yes,

he had some basis for threat. I've looked it up to read   95
the law since. Should I be glad he only took my children?

That year the punishment was: not less than five nor more
than sixty years. For my methods, indecent and unnatural,

of gratifying a depraved and perverted sexual instinct.
For even the slightest touching of lips or tongue or lips   100

to a woman's genitals. That means any delicate sip,
the tongue trail of saliva like an animal track quick

in the dew, a mysterious path toward the gates, little
and big (or *per anum*[2] and *per os*[3]), a pause at the riddle,

how tongue like a finger rolls grit into a jewel of flesh,   105
how finger is like tongue (another forbidden gesture),

and tongue like a snake (*bestial* is in the statute)
winding through salty walls, the labyrinth, curlicue,

the underground spring, rocks that sing, and the cave
with an oracle yelling at the bottom, certainly depraved.   110

All from the slightest touch of my lips which can
shift me and my lover as easily into a party on the lawn

sipping limeade, special recipe, sprawled silliness,
a little gnawing on the rind. The law when I read it

didn't mention teeth. I'm sure it will some day if   115
one of us gets caught with the other, nipping.

4
No one says *crime against nature* when a man
shotguns one or two or three or four or five
or more of his children, and usually his wife,
and maybe her visiting sister. But of the woman   120
who jumps twelve floors to her death, no I.D.
but a key around her neck, and in the apartment
her cold son in a back room, dead on a blanket:

Some are quick to say she was a fraud hiding
in a woman's body. Some pretend to be judicious   125
and give her as a reason why unmarried sluts
are not fit to raise children. But the truth is
we don't know what happened. Maybe she could not
imagine another ending because she was dirt poor,
alone, had tried everything. Or she was queer   130
and hated herself by her family's name: *crooked*.

Maybe she killed the child because she looked
into the future and saw her past. Or maybe
some man killed the boy and pushed her, splayed,
out the window, no one to grab, nothing to hide   135
but the key between her breasts, so we would find
the child and punish the killer. The iron key
warm, then cooling against her skin. Her memory,
the locked room. She left a clue. We don't know
her secret. She's not here to tell the story.   140

---

[2] (Lat.) By way of the anus.   [3] (Lat.) By mouth.

5

Last time we were together we went down to the river,
the boys and I, wading. In the rocks they saw a yellow-
stripped snake, with a silver fish crossways in its mouth,
just one of the many beautiful terrors of nature,
how one thing can turn into another without warning.   145

When I open my mouth, some people hear snakes slide
out, whispering, to poison my sons' lives. Some fear
I'll turn them into queers, into women, a quick reverse
of uterine fate. There was only that bit of androgen,
that Y, the diversion that altered them from girls.   150

Some fear I've crossed over into capable power
and I'm taking my children with me. My body a snaky
rope, with its twirl, loop, spin, falling escape,
falling, altered, woman to man and back again, animal
to human: And what are the implications for the political   155
system of boy children who watch me like a magic
trick, like I have a key to the locked-room mystery?
(Will they lose all respect for national boundaries,
their father, science, or private property?)

In Joan's picture of that day, black, white, grey   160
gleaming, we three are clambered onto a fist of rock,
edge of the river. You can't see the signs that say
Danger No Wading, or the waterweeds, mud, ruck
of bleached shells from animal feasting, the slimy
trails of periwinkle snails. We are sweaty, smiling   165
in the sun, clinging to keep our balance, glinting
like silver fishes caught in the mouth of the moment.

6

I could have been mentally ill or committed
adultery, yet not been judged unfit. Or criminal
but feminine: prostitution, passing bad checks.   170
Or criminally unnatural with women, and escaped,
but only if I'd repented and pretended
like Susan S., who became a convincing fiction:

Rented a two-bedroom, poolside apartment, nice,
on Country Club Road, sang in the choir at Trinity,   175
got the kids into Scouts, arranged her job to walk
them to school in the morning, meet them at 3:00 p.m.,
a respected, well-dressed, professional woman
with several advanced degrees and correct answers
for the psychiatrist who would declare her *normal,*   180
in the ordinary sense of the word. No boyfriend
for cover, but her impersonation tricked the court.
In six months she got the children back: *custody.*

It's a prison term, isn't it? Someone being guarded.
I did none of that. In the end my children visit me   185
as I am. But I didn't write this story until now when
they are too old for either law or father to seize
or prevent from hearing my words, or from watching
as I advance in the scandalous ancient way of women:

Our assault on enemies, walking forward, skirts lifted,   190
to show the silent mouth, the terrible power, our secret.

—1990

Profits

On the first anniversary of the Montreal massacre,[4] I tell my feminist theory class about the moment when a man with a rifle entered an engineering class at that university. He divided the students up, men to one wall, women to the other. When he had decided who was male and who was female, he shot the women, killing fourteen of them. Later he said he wanted the women dead because they were feminists and were taking jobs away from men. I say that there is no record of how many, if any, of the women considered themselves feminists. Perhaps they were just women who wanted to work in a job designated *male* in this century, on this continent. I say crossing gender boundaries as women does not automatically make us feminists, but the consequences of doing so may, if we live.

During the discussion, a student raises her hand. At a women's music festival last summer, she had met a survivor of the massacre. The woman had lived because the male terrorist had perceived her as male, and put her in the group with the men. Although my student, who herself looks like a teenage boy, doesn't recount how the woman felt watching the other women die, her face is blotched and etched with anguish. I imagine that room: The woman facing a man so sure he knows who is *man* and who is *woman*. His illusion of omniscience spares her, allows her to become an engineer, and then she spends years trying to find work. She gets turned down for jobs as "too masculine" if she is seen as woman, "too effeminate" if seen as man. To the students I say there is no gender boundary that can make us into either one or the other. There is no method, including violence, that can enforce complete conformity to "man," to "woman." I say we know that this man hated women, that he meant to kill women, but what we do not know is how many ways of being human have been hidden in the word *woman*. We don't yet know how large is this *other* that has been made the opposite of the narrow rod of *man*. We don't know who was male or female in that Montreal room, how many genders lived or died. I say that *here* we are trying to end a war on women in which we all get caught in the crossfire.

In this basement classroom, the steam pipes crisscross the ceiling and drip on our heads. Other students on campus bait those who take this women's studies course— the men are called feminine, the women masculine, the men queer, the women dykes. They are seen as crossing sex and gender boundaries simply because they question them. Today we all jump at noises in the hall, imagining that the one we fear stands in the doorway. Perhaps an unknown man, perhaps someone from our family with a

---

[4] On December 6, 1989, Marc Lépine entered an engineering classroom at the Ecole Polytechnique de Montréal, separated the men and the women, and killed fourteen women, claiming that he was "fighting feminism."

cold, murderous stare. The ones who believe the lie that there are only men and women, and that the first should rule the last. The ones who believe we should keep separate, sheep and goats, until judgment day. It is 3:30 P.M., the end of today's class. I assign readings on the origin of the family, private property, women, and the State. I say, "Next time we will talk about gender stratification and corporate profit."

—1995

PATTI SMITH (1946-   )

2007 Rock and Roll Hall of Fame inductee Patti Smith was born in Chicago and raised in New Jersey. Her mother was a waitress and her father a factory worker. The oldest of four children, Smith dropped out of college and moved to New York in 1967. There she met the photographer Robert Mapplethorpe, who later financed her first recording, a single entitled "Piss Factory/Hey Joe." The Patti Smith Group was signed to Arista Records in 1975 and their first album, *Horses,* included reworkings of conventional rock and roll songs as well as Smith's spoken word passages. The Patti Smith Group made three more albums—*Radio Ethiopia* (1976); *Easter* (1978), the most commercially successful; and *Wave* (1979)—before Smith married musician Fred "Sonic" Smith and retired to suburban Detroit to raise their two children. In 1988, the couple released an album together, *Dream of Life.* After Fred Smith died in 1994, she returned to performing, and released *Gone Again* in 1996. Other albums include *Peace and Noise* (1997), *Gung Ho* (2000), and *Trampin'* (2004), along with *Twelve* (2007), a collection of covers. Widely recognized as one of rock and roll's most influential figures for combining punk with poetry, feminist politics, and art, Smith played the final show at New York City's famed punk club CBGB in 2006. Smith has also published several collections of her poems, lyrics, drawings, and photographs.

georgia o'keeffe[1]

great lady painter
what she do now
she goes out with a stick
and kills snakes

georgia o'keeffe   5
all life still
cow skull
bull skull
no bull shit
pyrite pyrite   10
she's no fool
started out pretty
pretty pretty girl

---

[1] Georgia O'Keeffe (1887-1986), American painter.

georgia o'keeffe
until she had her fill   15
painted desert
flower cactus
hawk and head mule
choral water color
red coral reef   20
been around forever
georgia o'keeffe

great lady painter
what she do now
go and beat the desert   25
stir dust bowl
go and beat the desert
snake skin skull
go and beat the desert
all life still   30

—1973-74

babelogue

i haven't fucked w/the past but i've fucked plenty w/the future. over the silk of skin are scars from the splinters of stages and walls i've caressed. each bolt of wood, like the log of helen,[2] was my pleasure. i would measure the success of a night by the amount of piss and seed i could exude over the columns that nestled the P/A. some nights i'd surprise everybody by snapping on a skirt of green net sewed over w/flat metallic circles which dangled and flashed. the lights were violet and white. for a while i had an ornamental veil. but i couldn't bear to use it. when my hair was cropped i craved covering. but now my hair itself is a veil and the scalp of a crazy and sleepy comanche lies beneath the netting of skin.

i wake up. i am lying peacefully and my knees are open to the sun. i desire him and he is absolutely ready to serve me. in house i am moslem. in heart i am an american artist and i have no guilt. i seek pleasure. i seek the nerves under your skin. the narrow archway. the layers. the scroll of ancient lettuce. we worship the flaw. the mole on the belly of an exquisite whore. one who has not sold her soul to god or man nor any other.

—1975-76

[2] Probably a reference to Alexander Trocchi's erotic novel, *Helen and Desire* (1954).

AI (1947-   )

Florence Anthony was born in Albany, Texas, of African, Japanese, German, and Choctaw descent. She chose the name Ai (her legal name), which means "love" in Japanese, to commemorate her Japanese paternity. The author of seven books of poetry, Ai is best known for her poetic dramatic monologues. These poems are often written in the voices of characters who are the victims or perpetrators of trauma and violence (such as Jimmy Hoffa, Ferdinand Marcos, Mary Jo Kopechne, and Jack Ruby), though they do not attempt to "recreate" the characters' voices so much as imagine them. The winner of the National Book Award for *Vice* (1999), the American Book Award for *Sin* (1986), and the Lamont Award for *Killing Floor* (1979), Ai has received fellowships from the Guggenheim Foundation, the National Endowment for the Arts, and Radcliffe College's Bunting Fellowship Program. Ai lives in Tempe, Arizona, and teaches at Oklahoma State University in Stillwater, Oklahoma.

The Cockfighter's Daughter

I found my father,
face down, in his homemade chili
and had to hit the bowl
with a hammer to get it off,
then scrape the pinto beans   5
and chunks of ground beef
off his face with a knife.
Once he was clean
I called the police,
described the dirt road   10
that snaked from the highway
to his trailer beside the river.
The rooster was in the bedroom,
tied to a table leg.
Nearby stood a tin of cloudy water   15
and a few seeds scattered on a piece of wax paper,
the cheap green carpet
stained by gobs of darker green shit.
I was careful not to get too close,
because, though his beak was tied shut,   20
he could still jump for me and claw me
as he had my father.
The scars ran down his arms to a hole
where the rooster had torn the flesh
and run with it,   25
finally spitting it out.
When the old man stopped the bleeding,
the rooster was waiting on top of the pickup,
his red eyes like Pentecostal flames.
That's when Father named him Preacher.   30
He lured him down with a hen
he kept penned in a coop,

fortified with the kind of grille
you find in those New York taxicabs.
It had slots for food and water   35
and a trap door on top,
so he could reach in and pull her out by the neck.
One morning he found her stiff and glassy-eyed
and stood watching
as the rooster attacked her carcass   40
until she was ripped
to bits of bloody flesh and feathers.
I cursed and screamed, but he told me to shut up,
stay inside, what did a girl know about it?
Then he looked at me with desire and disdain.   45
Later, he loaded the truck and left.
I was sixteen and I had a mean streak,
carried a knife
and wore such tight jeans I could hardly walk.
They all talked about me in town,   50
but I didn't care.
My hair was stringy and greasy and I was easy
for the truckers and the bar clowns
that hung around night after night,
fighting sometimes   55
just for the sheer pleasure of it.
I'd quit high school, but I could write my name
and add two plus two without a calculator.
And this time, I got to thinking,
I got to planning, and one morning   60
I hitched a ride
on a semi that was headed for California
in the blaze of a west Texas sunrise.
I remember how he'd sit reading
his schedules of bouts and planning his routes   65
to the heart of a country
he thought he could conquer with only one soldier,
the $1000 cockfight always further down the pike,
or balanced on the knife edge,
but he wanted to deny me even that,   70
wanted me silent and finally wife
to some other unfinished businessman,
but tonight, it's just me and this old rooster,
and when I'm ready, I untie him
and he runs through the trailer,   75
flapping his wings and crowing
like it's daybreak
and maybe it is.
Maybe we've both come our separate ways
to reconciliation,   80
or to placating the patron saint

of roosters and lost children,
and when I go outside, he strolls after me
until I kneel down and we stare at each other
from the cages we were born to,   85
both knowing what it's like
to fly at an enemy's face
and take him down for the final count.
Preacher, I say, I got my GED,
a AA degree in computer science,   90
a husband, and a son named Gerald, who's three.
I've been to L.A., Chicago,
and New York City on a dare, and know what? —
it's shitty everywhere, but at least it's not home.

After the coroner's gone, I clean up the trailer,   95
and later, smoke one of Father's
hand-rolled cigarettes
as I walk by the river,
a quivering way down in my guts,
while Preacher huddles in his cage.   100
A fat frog catches the lit cigarette
and swallows it.
I go back and look at the picture
of my husband and son,
reread the only letter I ever sent   105
and which he did not answer,
then tear it all to shreds.
I hitch the pickup to the trailer
and put Preacher's cage on the seat,
then I aim my car for the river, start it,   110
and jump out just before it hits.
I start the pickup and sit
bent over the steering wheel,
shaking and crying, until I hear Preacher
clawing at the wire,   115
my path clear,
my fear drained from me like blood from a cut
that's still not deep enough
to kill you off, Father,
to spill you out of me for good.   120
What was it that made us kin,
that sends daughters crawling after fathers
who abandon them at the womb's door?
What a great and liberating crowing
comes from your rooster   125
as another sunrise breaks the night apart
with bare hands
and the engine roars
as I press the pedal to the floor

and we shoot forward onto the road. 130
Your schedule of fights,
clipped above the dashboard,
flutters in the breeze.
Barstow, El Centro, then swing back
to Truth or Consequences, New Mexico,[1] 135
and a twenty-minute soak in the hot springs
where Geronimo once bathed,
before we wind back again into Arizona,
then all the way to Idaho by way of Colorado,
the climb, then the slow, inevitable descent 140
toward the unknown
mine now. Mine.

—1991

Flashback
For Norman Fox

I'm on my way to work
at the Tackn' Feed shop
of which I own fifty-five percent,
when I hear sirens behind me
and pull over as three cop cars, 5
an ambulance, unmarked van, and a firetruck zoom past.
Not two minutes later, I start to sweat.
My heart beats rapidly
and I get that old feeling of dislocation
as my truck rocks like a cradle. 10
I grip the steering wheel the way I always do
when the pit bulls of bad memory
threaten to chew off my hands.
I count to twenty and drive on,
but as I pass the abortion clinic, 15
suddenly, I am in country again,
snorting pure heroin.
It's setting off flares in my brain,
tracers and those psychedelic snakes
I hallucinate are crawling all over me, 20
until I jump out of the truck,
which somehow I have driven onto the sidewalk.
I am using the open door for cover,
when Captain Kiss My Ass yells,
"Get down there where Charlie's[2] holed up." 25
Waste the motherfucker. Motherfucker, I think.

---

[1] Resort town in northern New Mexico. The current name was given to the town in 1950 when Ralph Edwards said he would broadcast his "Truth or Consequences" show from the first town that changed its name to match that of the show. Edwards became a yearly visitor to the town.

[2] Victor Charlie (as a stand-in for Viet Cong) was used as military slang during the Vietnam War to refer to the enemy.

I hear Simpson screaming something
and I am screaming too
and running through the elephant grass and bullets.
Someone steps on a land mine,   30
but it's nothing to me.
I am focused on my objective,
which is to wipe out the enemy,
but who is he?
"Bud, Bud, you OK?" I hear a voice call.   35
It's Harley, the guy who works at 7-Eleven.
He says, "Right to Lifers
threatened to blow up the clinic again."
I don't want to know anything about it,
even though I have a personal connection to the place.   40
"Need some help?" he asks.
"No thanks, man, I'm OK," I tell him, but I am shaking,
as if I am still trying to kick back in Saigon.
My girlfriend squeezes tepid water on my face
from a dirty towel and clucks her tongue,   45
as if I'm the one who needs sympathy.
"Save it," I tell her, shoving her hand away.
I don't need anything but a way out.
I had it for a while,
but I could not give myself over to the drug.   50
Even when I was high, I always felt
as if I were above my body watching myself
pretend to descend into my own hell,
which even the Devil had abandoned
for more fertile ground.   55
My hell was just a hole in the ground
at the bottom of which the captain waited.
I hated him, but in an almost loving way,
for like a bad parent, he made me what I was
and what I am, despite my settled life,   60
my wife, kids, a savings account,
and once-a-year vacations to Barbados.
So many men died, because of his ambition.
He'd send us into more dangerous situations
than he had to, so he could make himself   65
a hotshot with the yahoos,
back at headquarters.
He had one eye on the slaughter
and one fixed on war's end,
when he'd use its career boost   70
and ascend the ladder of command.
I was just a grunt, humping my ass,
but I could shoot even better than I could breathe.
He needed me, so most times he left me alone
and focused on some other slob,   75

Simpson, another old-timer and volunteer like me,
Miller, Dean, Johnson, Macafee, Sanchez, or Willoughby,
our latest "FNG." We didn't use his name at first,
but called him Fucking New Guy,
until I said I'd "marry" him   80
and teach him the ropes.
I'd been in country twice and in the bush
more times than I cared to think about.
I can admit now that I liked war,
but I didn't like killing the way Miller did,   85
or that kid who fell on sharpened bamboo poles
hidden in a foliage-covered hole.
One even went through his asshole and ruptured his guts,
which spilled all over the ground,
when we pulled him off the poles.   90
"Like a stuck pig," said Johnson,
as he sat back on his heels,
looking down at the bloodstained bamboo.
Then he used a flamethrower to incinerate them.
"Anybody for barbecue?" he asked.   95
That set off a round of jokes about the Fourth of July
and by the time we got back to base camp,
we were good and hungry.
The CO didn't join in. He never did.
He hid behind his mirrored sunglasses and his commands.   100
He could give you a death sentence
with a smile and a handshake.
He'd say, "Men, make me proud"
and if we didn't, next time he sent us on patrol,
we knew he'd have us taking fire no matter how intense,   105
not caring whether we all went home in body bags,
as long as he survived to receive his medals
from the boardroom generals and jive-ass politicians
who only played at war.

Finally, I get back in my truck,   110
as the unneeded bomb squad, cops, and firemen start to leave.
I should too, but I just sit
only half aware of my surroundings
and watch as a protester is lead to a police car.
I see it is my wife, Pam,   115
who must have violated the court order
to stay one hundred feet
from the entrance of the clinic again.
She notices me and waves,
just as a cop pushes her into the backseat,   120
but I imagine I see Captain Kiss,
waving me on toward the lair of the VC[3]

---

[3] Viet Cong.

who wasted Macafee and Simpson,
who had just become a short-timer.
Since I am the only old salt left,   125
the others look to me for some semblance of reason,
but they also realize I'm itching for a confrontation
and the captain has given me permission
to make the VC pay for every shitty day
I've been in my self-made exile.   130
When Sanchez says, "Waste the sonofabitch"
and Captain Kiss for once is outrunning me,
firing like he really means it,
until maybe he realizes what he is doing
and slows and seeks cover,   135
I can't resist screaming "Yellow dog" at him,
but he doesn't hear me as I run past,
zeroing in on the hole, where the tunnel rat
is dug in with a machine gun
and God knows it's booby-trapped,   140
so even if he dies, he'll take more of us with him.
Suddenly, I slow down, until I come to a full stop.
I'm hit, I think, almost relieved
as I sink to the ground.
I'm ready to die. I want to die,   145
having at last found the peace
that only comes when you cease to struggle
against the inevitable
and intense disintegration of body and soul,
but my survival instinct takes hold   150
and I manage to get up on my knees
and see the captain as he retreats
even farther from the fray.
I can't get to my launcher,
so I throw the grenade as far as I can   155
and remember only the terrific force as it explodes,
but soundless and somehow divorced from time,
while I am outside myself,
just swimming in the amniotic sack of destiny.
When I finally drag myself to where I last saw the captain,   160
there's nothing left but dog tags splashed with blood
and a few shreds of cloth.
I want to cry, but I don't.
I just lie on my back, listening to the eerie quiet
as the bloodshot-eyed afternoon stumbles off   165
and early evening arrives with the fanfare of rats
scurrying through the grass.
I remember the sapper who attacked the transit facility
the night I arrived in Vietnam.
She wasted four men, when she detonated her grenades.   170
I wonder why she chose certain death,

when she could have thrown them and perhaps survived?
Should I have done the same? I wonder,
as I hear someone coming toward me.
It's the VC.   175
I wait for him to take me out,
but he only bends closer and closer,
then he smiles and says, "I see you,"
and raises his arm, pretending to throw.
Then he stabs me with my own K-bar.   180
The rest is insignificant, is just evac and recovery,
is going through the motions back in the world.
Now I use my family like a magic potion
to get me through the memories
that are more real than the life I lead,   185
but nothing really eases my conscience.
Sometimes I even pretend the captain
has come home at last
with the ugly past forgotten
and the present rotten with happiness.   190
Maybe he's a general now too,
or a senator who won't give a guy like me the time of day.
Ain't that the way? I think,
as I choke on the stink of the last twenty-eight years
and have to light a cigarette   195
and suck it really hard.
I start the truck and head downtown,
where I will bail Pam out of jail
and never tell her about the crime I committed,
which at the time seemed necessary,   200
seemed like the very essence of the meaning
of the word, *soldier.*

—1999

MEI-MEI BERSSENBRUGGE (1947-   )

The daughter of a Chinese mother who was a mathematician and a first generation Dutch-American father, Mei-mei Berssenbrugge was born in Beijing and raised in Massachusetts. She attended Barnard College for one year before transferring to Reed College, where she earned her B.A. in 1969. After receiving an M.F.A. from Columbia University, Berssenbrugge moved to rural northern New Mexico and began teaching at the Institute of American Indian Art in Santa Fe, where she co-founded the literary journal *Tyuonyi*. Her frequent travels to New York brought her into contact with the abstract art movement, as well as with New York School and Language poets, which influenced her own poetry.

Berssenbrugge's poems, mainly characterized by stretched-out lines, often begin with concrete images but proceed to suggest the fluidity of boundaries, moving between the abstract and the concrete, and between the philosophical and the experiential. Her volumes of poetry include *The Heat Bird* (1983), *Empathy* (1989), *Sphericity* (1993), *Endocrinology* (1997), *Four Year Old Girl* (1998), *Nest* (2003), and *I Love Artists: New and Selected Poems* (2006). Her collaborations include artist books with her husband, Richard Tuttle, and with Kiki Smith, in addition to theatre projects with Frank Chin, Blondell Cummings, Tan Dun, Chen Shi-Zheng, and Alvin Lucier. She has also been a contributing editor of *Conjunctions Magazine* since 1978. Berssenbrugge has received two NEA Fellowships, two American Book Awards, and awards from the Asian American Writers Workshop and the Western States Art Foundation. She lives in both New Mexico and New York with her husband and daughter.

The Four Year Old Girl

1

The *genotype* is her genetic constitution.

The *phenotype* is the observable expression of the genotype as structural and biochemical traits.

Genetic disease is extreme genetic change, against a background of normal variability.

Within the conventional unit we call subjectivity due to individual particulars, what is happening?

She believes she is herself, which isn't complete madness, it's belief.

The problem is not to turn the subject, the effect of the genes, into an entity.

Between her and the displaced gene is another relation, the effect of meaning.

The meaning she's conscious of is contingent, a surface of water in an uninhabited world, existing as our eyes and ears.

You wouldn't think of her form by thinking about water.

You can go in, if you don't encounter anything.

Though we call heavy sense impressions stress, all impression creates limitation.

I believe opaque inheritance accounts for the limits of her memory.

The mental impulse is a thought and a molecule tied together like sides of a coin.

A girl says sweetly, it's time you begin to look after me, so I may seem loveable to myself.

She's inspired to change the genotype, because the cell's memory outlives the cell.

It's a memory that builds some matter around itself, like time.

2

Feelings of helplessness drove me to fantastic and ridiculous extremes.

Nevertheless, the axis of her helplessness is not the axis I grasp, when I consider it a function of inheritance.

Chromatin fails to condense during mitosis.

A fragile site recombines misaligned genes of the repeated sequence.

She seems a little unformed, gauze stretches across her face, eyelids droop.

When excited, she cries like a cat and fully exhibits the "happy puppet" syndrome.[1]

Note short fingers and hypoplastic painted nails.

Insofar as fate is of real order here, signifying embodiment, the perceived was present in the womb.

---

[1] Another name for Angelman's syndrome, a condition characterized by mental retardation and seizures; affected children laugh often with little provocation.

A gap or cause presents to any apprehension of attachment.

In her case, there's purity untainted by force or cause, like the life force.

Where, generically, function creates the mother, in this case it won't even explain this area.

She screams at her.

A species survives in the form of a girl asking sweetly.

Nevertheless, survival of the species as a whole has meaning.

Each girl is transitory.

3

Her focus extends from in front of her into distance, so she's not involved in what she looks at.

Rhodopsin in the unaffected gene converts photons to retinal impulse, so she sees normally for years.

The image, the effects of energy starting from a real point, is reflected on a surface, lake or area of the occipital lobe.

You don't need the whole surface to be aware of a figure, just for some points of real space to correspond to effect at other points.

There's an image and a struggle to recognize reception of it.

She sees waves and the horizon as if she were water in the water.

The mother's not looking at her daughter from the place from which the daughter sees her.

She doesn't recognize abnormal attributes.

The daughter resolves her image as fire in the woods, red silk.

In the waiting room, she hopes a large dog will walk up to her, be kind and fulfill her wishes.

Between what occurs, as if by chance and, "Mother, can you see I'm dying?" is the same relation we deal with in recurrence.

Is not what emerges from the anxiety of her speech, their most intimate relation, beyond death, which is their chance?

Obedience to one's child is anxious, heartfelt, but not continuous, like a white mote in her eye.

Within the range of deteriorating sight, in which sight will be her memory, disobedience moves toward unconsciousness.

4

Her skull is large and soft to touch. The thoracic cavity small, limbs short, deformed and vertebrae flattened.

All the bones are undermineralized.

Bluish light surrounds her.

This theme concerns her status, since she doesn't place her inheritance in a position of subjectivity, but of an object.

Her X-ray teems with energy, but locked outside material.

One creates a mouse model of human disease by disrupting a normal mouse gene in vitro, then injecting the mutated gene into host embryos.

DNA integrated into the mouse genome is expressed and transmitted to progeny.

Like touch, one cell can initiate therapy.

The phenotype, whose main task is to transform everything into secondary, kinetic energy, pleasure, innocence, won't define every subject.

The mother's genotype makes a parallel reality to her reality, now.

She stands over her and screams.

That the exchange is unreal, not imaginary, doesn't prevent the organ from embodying itself.

By transfering functional copies of the gene to her, he can correct the mutant phenotype, lightly touching the bad mother, before.

5

On her fourth birthday, a rash on the elbow indicated enzyme deficiency.

Her view folded inward.

Ideas about life from experience are no use in the unfolding of a potential, empty and light, though there's still potential for phenomena to be experienced.

A moment of seeing can intervene like a suture between an image and its word.

An act is no longer structured by a real that's not caught up in it.

Instead of denying material, I could symbolize it with this mucus and its trailings.

The moment the imaginary exists, it creates its own setting, but not the same way as form at the intuitive level of her mother's comprehension.

In all comprehension, there's an error, forgetting the creativity of material in its nascent form.

So, you see in her eyes her form of compassion for beings who perceive suffering as a real substrate.

6

Mother must have done something terrible, to be so bereaved.

Ambiguity of a form derives from its representing the girl, full of capability, saturated with love.

If the opposite of possible is real, she defines real as impossible, her real inability to repeat the child's game, over and over.

Parallel woven lines of the blanket extend to water.

Just a hint of childish ferocity gives them weight.

At night, inspiration fell on her like rain, penetrating the subject at the germ line, like a navel.

Joy at birth, a compaction of potential and no potential, is an abstraction that was fully realized.

Reducing a parent to the universality of signifier produces serene detachment in her, abstract as an electron micrograph of protein-deplete human metaphase DNA.

Its materiality is a teletransport of signified protoplasm across lineage or time, avid, muscular and compact, as if pervasive, attached to her, *in* a particular matriarchy of natural disaster, in which the luminosity of a fetal sonogram becomes clairvoyant.

The love has no quantity or value, but only lasts a length of time, different time, across which unfolds her singularity without compromising life as a whole.

—1998

OCTAVIA BUTLER (1947-2006)

Octavia Butler was born in Pasadena, California. Her father was a shoeshine man who died when she was very young, and she was raised by her mother, also named Octavia, who worked as a maid. A shy and bookish child despite her dyslexia, Butler began writing science fiction at the age of twelve, an almost unheard of ambition for an African-American girl. She received an associate's degree from Pasadena City College in 1968 and studied at California State University, Los Angeles, and UCLA. More important as an influence, Butler claimed, were the Open Door writing workshops she attended in 1969-70, sponsored by the Screenwriters Guild of America, West, where she met science fiction writer Harlan Ellison, and the Clarion workshop for science fiction writers in 1970, where she met Samuel R. Delany, perhaps the most renowned Black science fiction writer at that time. When lecturing to students and young writers, Butler often spoke about her own difficult apprenticeship, during which she supported herself by working blue-collar jobs in the day and writing for eight hours at night; she said that she learned to write a novel by writing one after another. Her first novel, *Patternmaster,* was published in 1976, and was followed by four others in the Patternist series. After the publication of the critically acclaimed *Kindred* in 1979, which tackles the legacy of slavery by way of time travel, her work garnered an audience beyond readers of science fiction. Butler published thirteen novels and one collection of short fiction. She received Hugo and Nebula awards for her "Bloodchild" novella, a Hugo for the short story "Speech Sounds," a MacArthur "genius" grant in 1995 (the first science fiction writer to receive one), a Lifetime Achievement in Writing award from PEN, and a Nebula award for the dystopian novel *Parable of the Talents* in 2000. She died in Seattle, where she had lived since 1999.

Bloodchild

My last night of childhood began with a visit home. T'Gatoi's sister had given us two sterile eggs. T'Gatoi gave one to my mother, brother, and sisters. She insisted that I eat the other one alone. It didn't matter. There was still enough to leave everyone feeling good. Almost everyone. My mother wouldn't take any. She sat, watching everyone drifting and dreaming without her. Most of the time she watched me.

I lay against T'Gatoi's long, velvet underside, sipping from my egg now and then, wondering why my mother denied herself such a harmless pleasure. Less of her hair would be gray if she indulged now and then. The eggs prolonged life, prolonged vigor. My father, who had never refused one in his life, had lived more than twice as long as he should have. And toward the end of his life, when he should have been slowing down, he had married my mother and fathered four children.

But my mother seemed content to age before she had to. I saw her turn away as several of T'Gatoi's limbs secured me closer. T'Gatoi liked our body heat and took advantage of it whenever she could. When I was little and at home more, my mother used to try to tell me how to behave with T'Gatoi—how to be respectful and always obedient because T'Gatoi was the Tlic government official in charge of the Preserve, and thus the most important of her kind to deal directly with Terrans. It was an honor, my mother said, that such a person had chosen to come into the family. My mother was at her most formal and severe when she was lying.

I had no idea why she was lying, or even what she was lying about. It *was* an honor to have T'Gatoi in the family, but it was hardly a novelty. T'Gatoi and my mother had been friends all my mother's life, and T'Gatoi was not interested in being honored in the house she considered her second home. She simply came in, climbed onto one of her special couches, and called me over to keep her warm. It was impossible to be formal with her while lying against her and hearing her complain as usual that I was too skinny.

"You're better," she said this time, probing me with six or seven of her limbs. "You're gaining weight finally. Thinness is dangerous." The probing changed subtly, became a series of caresses.

"He's still too thin," my mother said sharply.

T'Gatoi lifted her head and perhaps a meter of her body off the couch as though she were sitting up. She looked at my mother, and my mother, her face lined and old looking, turned away.

"Lien, I would like you to have what's left of Gan's egg."

"The eggs are for the children," my mother said.

"They are for the family. Please take it."

Unwillingly obedient, my mother took it from me and put it to her mouth. There were only a few drops left in the now-shrunken, elastic shell, but she squeezed them out, swallowed them, and after a few moments some of the lines of tension began to smooth from her face.

"It's good," she whispered. "Sometimes I forget how good it is."

"You should take more," T'Gatoi said. "Why are you in such a hurry to be old?"

My mother said nothing.

"I like being able to come here," T'Gatoi said. "This place is a refuge because of you, yet you won't take care of yourself."

T'Gatoi was hounded on the outside. Her people wanted more of us made available. Only she and her political faction stood between us and the hordes who did not understand why there was a Preserve—why any Terran could not be courted, paid, drafted, in some way made available to them. Or they did understand, but in their desperation, they did not care. She parceled us out to the desperate and sold us to the rich and powerful for their political support. Thus, we were necessities, status symbols, and an independent people. She oversaw the joining of families, putting an end to the final remnants of the earlier system of breaking up Terran families to suit impatient Tlic. I had lived outside with her. I had seen the desperate eagerness in the way some people looked at me. It was a little frightening to know that only she stood between us and that desperation that could so easily swallow us. My mother would look at her sometimes and say to me, "Take care of her." And I would remember that she too had been outside, had seen.

Now T'Gatoi used four of her limbs to push me away from her onto the floor. "Go on, Gan," she said. "Sit down there with your sisters and enjoy not being sober. You had most of the egg. Lien, come warm with me."

My mother hesitated for no reason that I could see. One of my earliest memories is of my mother stretched alongside T'Gatoi, talking about things I could not understand, picking me up from the floor and laughing as she sat me on one of T'Gatoi's segments. She ate her share of eggs then. I wondered when she had stopped, and why.

She lay down now against T'Gatoi, and the whole left row of T'Gatoi's limbs closed around her, holding her loosely, but securely. I had always found it comfortable to lie that way, but except for my older sister, no one else in the family liked it. They said it made them feel caged.

T'Gatoi meant to cage my mother. Once she had, she moved her tail slightly, then spoke. "Not enough egg, Lien. You should have taken it when it was passed to you. You need it badly now."

T'Gatoi's tail moved once more, its whip motion so swift I wouldn't have seen it if I hadn't been watching for it. Her sting drew only a single drop of blood from my mother's bare leg.

My mother cried out—probably in surprise. Being stung doesn't hurt. Then she sighed and I could see her body relax. She moved languidly into a more comfortable position within the cage of T'Gatoi's limbs. "Why did you do that?" she asked, sounding half asleep.

"I could not watch you sitting and suffering any longer."

My mother managed to move her shoulders in a small shrug. "Tomorrow," she said.

"Yes. Tomorrow you will resume your suffering—if you must. But just now, just for now, lie here and warm me and let me ease your way a little."

"He's still mine, you know," my mother said suddenly. "Nothing can buy him from me." Sober, she would not have permitted herself to refer to such things.

"Nothing," T'Gatoi agreed, humoring her.

"Did you think I would sell him for eggs? For long life? My son?"

"Not for anything," T'Gatoi said, stroking my mother's shoulders, toying with her long, graying hair.

I would like to have touched my mother, shared that moment with her. She would take my hand if I touched her now. Freed by the egg and the sting, she would smile and perhaps say things long held in. But tomorrow, she would remember all this as a humiliation. I did not want to be part of a remembered humiliation. Best just be still and know she loved me under all the duty and pride and pain.

"Xuan Hoa, take off her shoes," T'Gatoi said. "In a little while I'll sting her again and she can sleep."

My older sister obeyed, swaying drunkenly as she stood up. When she had finished, she sat down beside me and took my hand. We had always been a unit, she and I.

My mother put the back of her head against T'Gatoi's underside and tried from that impossible angle to look up into the broad, round face. "You're going to sting me again?"

"Yes, Lien."

"I'll sleep until tomorrow noon."

"Good. You need it. When did you sleep last?"

My mother made a wordless sound of annoyance. "I should have stepped on you when you were small enough," she muttered.

It was an old joke between them. They had grown up together, sort of, though T'Gatoi had not, in my mother's lifetime, been small enough for any Terran to step on. She was nearly three times my mother's present age, yet would still be young when my mother died of age. But T'Gatoi and my mother had met as T'Gatoi was coming into a period of rapid development—a kind of Tlic adolescence. My mother was only a child, but for a while they developed at the same rate and had no better friends than each other.

T'Gatoi had even introduced my mother to the man who became my father. My parents, pleased with each other in spite of their different ages, married as T'Gatoi was going into her family's business—politics. She and my mother saw each other less. But sometime before my older sister was born, my mother promised T'Gatoi one of her children. She would have to give one of us to someone, and she preferred T'Gatoi to some stranger.

Years passed. T'Gatoi traveled and increased her influence. The Preserve was hers by the time she came back to my mother to collect what she probably saw as her just reward for her hard work. My older sister took an instant liking to her and wanted to be chosen, but my mother was just coming to term with me and T'Gatoi liked the idea of choosing an infant and watching and taking part in all the phases of development. I'm told I was first caged within T'Gatoi's many limbs only three minutes after my birth. A few days later, I was given my first taste of egg. I tell Terrans that when they ask whether I was ever afraid of her. And I tell it to Tlic when T'Gatoi suggests a young Terran child for them and they, anxious and ignorant, demand an adolescent. Even my brother who had somehow grown up to fear and distrust the Tlic could probably have gone smoothly into one of their families if he had been adopted early enough. Sometimes, I think for his sake he should have been. I looked at him, stretched out on the floor across the room, his eyes open, but glazed as he dreamed his egg dream. No matter what he felt toward the Tlic, he always demanded his share of egg.

"Lien, can you stand up?" T'Gatoi asked suddenly.

"Stand?" my mother said. "I thought I was going to sleep."

"Later. Something sounds wrong outside." The cage was abruptly gone.

"What?"

"Up, Lien!"

My mother recognized her tone and got up just in time to avoid being dumped on the floor. T'Gatoi whipped her three meters of body off her couch, toward the door, and out at full speed. She had bones—ribs, a long spine, a skull, four sets of limb bones per segment. But when she moved that way, twisting, hurling herself into controlled falls, landing running, she seemed not only boneless, but aquatic—something swimming through the air as though it were water. I loved watching her move.

I left my sister and started to follow her out the door, though I wasn't very steady on my own feet. It would have been better to sit and dream, better yet to find a girl and share a waking dream with her. Back when the Tlic saw us as not much more than convenient, big, warm-blooded animals, they would pen several of us together, male and female, and feed us only eggs. That way they could be sure of getting another generation of us no matter how we tried to hold out. We were lucky that didn't go on long. A few generations of it and we would have *been* little more than convenient, big animals.

"Hold the door open, Gan," T'Gatoi said. "And tell the family to stay back."

"What is it?" I asked.

"N'Tlic."

I shrank back against the door. "Here? Alone?"

"He was trying to reach a call box, I suppose." She carried the man past me, unconscious, folded like a coat over some of her limbs. He looked young—my brother's age perhaps—and he was thinner than he should have been. What T'Gatoi would have called dangerously thin.

"Gan, go to the call box," she said. She put the man on the floor and began stripping off his clothing.

I did not move.

After a moment, she looked up at me, her sudden stillness a sign of deep impatience.

"Send Qui," I told her. "I'll stay here. Maybe I can help."

She let her limbs begin to move again, lifting the man and pulling his shirt over his head. "You don't want to see this," she said. "It will be hard. I can't help this man the way his Tlic could."

"I know. But send Qui. He won't want to be of any help here. I'm at least willing to try."

She looked at my brother—older, bigger, stronger, certainly more able to help her here. He was sitting up now, braced against the wall, staring at the man on the floor with undisguised fear and revulsion. Even she could see that he would be useless.

"Qui, go!" she said.

He didn't argue. He stood up, swayed briefly, then steadied, frightened sober.

"This man's name is Bram Lomas," she told him, reading from the man's armband. I fingered my own armband in sympathy. "He needs T'Khotgif Teh. Do you hear?"

"Bram Lomas, T'Khotgif Teh," my brother said. "I'm going." He edged around Lomas and ran out the door.

Lomas began to regain consciousness. He only moaned at first and clutched spasmodically at a pair of T'Gatoi's limbs. My younger sister, finally awake from her egg dream, came close to look at him, until my mother pulled her back.

T'Gatoi removed the man's shoes, then his pants, all the while leaving him two of her limbs to grip. Except for the final few, all her limbs were equally dexterous. "I want no argument from you this time, Gan," she said.

I straightened. "What shall I do?"

"Go out and slaughter an animal that is at least half your size."

"Slaughter? But I've never—"

She knocked me across the room. Her tail was an efficient weapon whether she exposed the sting or not.

I got up, feeling stupid for having ignored her warning, and went into the kitchen. Maybe I could kill something with a knife or an ax. My mother raised a few Terran animals for the table and several thousand local ones for their fur. T'Gatoi would probably prefer something local. An achti, perhaps. Some of those were the right size, though they had about three times as many teeth as I did and a real love of using them. My mother, Hoa, and Qui could kill them with knives. I had never killed one at all, had never slaughtered any animal. I had spent most of my time with T'Gatoi while my brother and sisters were learning the family business. T'Gatoi had been right. I should have been the one to go to the call box. At least I could do that.

I went to the corner cabinet where my mother kept her large house and garden tools. At the back of the cabinet there was a pipe that carried off waste water from the kitchen—except that it didn't anymore. My father had rerouted the waste water below before I was born. Now the pipe could be turned so that one half slid around the other and a rifle could be stored inside. This wasn't our only gun, but it was our most easily accessible one. I would have to use it to shoot one of the biggest of the achti. Then T'Gatoi would probably confiscate it. Firearms were illegal in the Preserve. There had been incidents right after the Preserve was established—Terrans shooting Tlic, shooting N'Tlic. This was before the joining of families began, before everyone had a personal stake in keeping the peace. No one had shot a Tlic in my lifetime or my mother's, but the law still stood—for our protection, we were told. There were stories of whole Terran families wiped out in reprisal back during the assassinations.

I went out to the cages and shot the biggest achti I could find. It was a handsome breeding male, and my mother would not be pleased to see me bring it in. But it was the right size, and I was in a hurry.

I put the achti's long, warm body over my shoulder—glad that some of the weight I'd gained was muscle—and took it to the kitchen. There, I put the gun back in its hiding place. If T'Gatoi noticed the achti's wounds and demanded the gun, I would give it to her. Otherwise, let it stay where my father wanted it.

I turned to take the achti to her, then hesitated. For several seconds, I stood in front of the closed door wondering why I was suddenly afraid. I knew what was going to happen. I hadn't seen it before but T'Gatoi had shown me diagrams and drawings. She had made sure I knew the truth as soon as I was old enough to understand it.

Yet I did not want to go into that room. I wasted a little time choosing a knife from the carved, wooden box in which my mother kept them. T'Gatoi might want one, I told myself, for the tough, heavily furred hide of the achti.

"Gan!" T'Gatoi called, her voice harsh with urgency.

I swallowed. I had not imagined a single moving of the feet could be so difficult. I realized I was trembling and that shamed me. Shame impelled me through the door.

I put the achti down near T'Gatoi and saw that Lomas was unconscious again. She, Lomas, and I were alone in the room—my mother and sisters probably sent out so they would not have to watch. I envied them.

But my mother came back into the room as T'Gatoi seized the achti. Ignoring the knife I offered her, she extended claws from several of her limbs and slit the achti from throat to anus. She looked at me, her yellow eyes intent. "Hold this man's shoulders, Gan."

I stared at Lomas in panic, realizing that I did not want to touch him, let alone hold him. This would not be like shooting an animal. Not as quick, not as merciful, and, I hoped, not as final, but there was nothing I wanted less than to be part of it.

My mother came forward. "Gan, you hold his right side," she said. "I'll hold his left." And if he came to, he would throw her off without realizing he had done it. She was a tiny woman. She often wondered aloud how she had produced, as she said, such "huge" children.

"Never mind," I told her, taking the man's shoulders. "I'll do it." She hovered nearby.

"Don't worry," I said. "I won't shame you. You don't have to stay and watch."

She looked at me uncertainly, then touched my face in a rare caress. Finally, she went back to her bedroom.

T'Gatoi lowered her head in relief. "Thank you, Gan," she said with courtesy more Terran than Tlic. "That one…she is always finding new ways for me to make her suffer."

Lomas began to groan and make choked sounds. I had hoped he would stay unconscious. T'Gatoi put her face near his so that he focused on her.

"I've stung you as much as I dare for now," she told him. "When this is over, I'll sting you to sleep and you won't hurt anymore."

"Please," the man begged. "Wait..."

"There's no more time, Bram. I'll sting you as soon as it's over. When T'Khotgif arrives she'll give you eggs to help you heal. It will be over soon."

"T'Khotgif!" the man shouted, straining against my hands.

"Soon, Bram." T'Gatoi glanced at me, then placed a claw against his abdomen slightly to the right of the middle, just below the left rib. There was movement on the right side—tiny, seemingly random pulsations moving his brown flesh, creating a concavity here, a convexity there, over and over until I could see the rhythm of it and knew where the next pulse would be.

Lomas's entire body stiffened under T'Gatoi's claw, though she merely rested it against him as she wound the rear section of her body around his legs. He might break my grip, but he would not break hers. He wept helplessly as she used his pants to tie his hands, then pushed his hands above his head so that I could kneel on the cloth between them and pin them in place. She rolled up his shirt and gave it to him to bite down on.

And she opened him.

His body convulsed with the first cut. He almost tore himself away from me. The sound he made...I had never heard such sounds come from anything human. T'Gatoi seemed to pay no attention as she lengthened and deepened the cut, now and then pausing to lick away blood. His blood vessels contracted, reacting to the chemistry of her saliva, and the bleeding slowed.

I felt as though I were helping her torture him, helping her consume him. I knew I would vomit soon, didn't know why I hadn't already. I couldn't possibly last until she was finished.

She found the first grub. It was fat and deep red with his blood—both inside and out. It had already eaten its own egg case but apparently had not yet begun to eat its host. At this stage, it would eat any flesh except its mother's. Let alone, it would have gone on excreting the poisons that had both sickened and alerted Lomas. Eventually it would have begun to eat. By the time it ate its way out of Lomas's flesh, Lomas would be dead or dying—and unable to take revenge on the thing that was killing him. There was always a grace period between the time the host sickened and the time the grubs began to eat him.

T'Gatoi picked up the writhing grub carefully and looked at it, somehow ignoring the terrible groans of the man.

Abruptly, the man lost consciousness.

"Good," T'Gatoi looked down at him. "I wish you Terrans could do that at will." She felt nothing. And the thing she held...

It was limbless and boneless at this stage, perhaps fifteen centimeters long and two thick, blind and slimy with blood. It was like a large worm. T'Gatoi put it into the belly of the achti, and it began at once to burrow. It would stay there and eat as long as there was anything to eat.

Probing through Lomas's flesh, she found two more, one of them smaller and more vigorous. "A male!" she said happily. He would be dead before I would. He would be through his metamorphosis and screwing everything that would hold still before his sisters even had limbs. He was the only one to make a serious effort to bite T'Gatoi as she placed him in the achti.

Paler worms oozed to visibility in Lomas's flesh. I closed my eyes. It was worse than finding something dead, rotting, and filled with tiny animal grubs. And it was far worse than any drawing or diagram.

"Ah, there are more," T'Gatoi said, plucking out two long, thick grubs. "You may have to kill another animal, Gan. Everything lives inside you Terrans."

I had been told all my life that this was a good and necessary thing Tlic and Terran did together—a kind of birth. I had believed it until now. I knew birth was painful and bloody, no matter what. But this was something else, something worse. And I wasn't ready to see it. Maybe I never would be. Yet I couldn't not see it. Closing my eyes didn't help.

T'Gatoi found a grub still eating its egg case. The remains of the case were still wired into a blood vessel by their own little tube or hook or whatever. That was the way the grubs were anchored and the way they fed. They took only blood until they were ready to emerge. Then they ate their stretched, elastic egg cases. Then they ate their hosts.

T'Gatoi bit away the egg case, licked away the blood. Did she like the taste? Did childhood habits die hard—or not die at all?

The whole procedure was wrong, alien. I wouldn't have thought anything about her could seem alien to me.

"One more, I think," she said. "Perhaps two. A good family. In a host animal these days, we would be happy to find one or two alive." She glanced at me. "Go outside, Gan, and empty your stomach. Go now while the man is unconscious."

I staggered out, barely made it. Beneath the tree just beyond the front door, I vomited until there was nothing left to bring up. Finally, I stood shaking, tears streaming down my face. I did not know why I was crying, but I could not stop. I went further from the house to avoid being seen. Every time I closed my eyes I saw red worms crawling over redder human flesh.

There was a car coming toward the house. Since Terrans were forbidden motorized vehicles except for certain farm equipment, I knew this must be Lomas's Tlic with Qui and perhaps a Terran doctor. I wiped my face on my shirt, struggled for control.

"Gan," Qui called as the car stopped. "What happened?" He crawled out of the low, round, Tlic-convenient car door. Another Terran crawled out the other side and went into the house without speaking to me. The doctor. With his help and a few eggs, Lomas might make it.

"T'Khotgif Teh?" I said.

The Tlic driver surged out of her car, reared up half her length before me. She was paler and smaller than T'Gatoi—probably born from the body of an animal. Tlic from Terran bodies were always larger as well as more numerous.

"Six young," I told her. "Maybe seven, all alive. At least one male."

"Lomas?" she said harshly. I liked her for the question and the concern in her voice when she asked it. The last coherent thing he had said was her name.

"He's alive," I said.

She surged away to the house without another word.

"She's been sick," my brother said, watching her go. "When I called, I could hear people telling her she wasn't well enough to go out even for this."

I said nothing. I had extended courtesy to the Tlic. Now I didn't want to talk to anyone. I hoped he would go in—out of curiosity if nothing else.

"Finally found out more than you wanted to know, eh?"

I looked at him.

"Don't give me one of *her* looks," he said. "You're not her. You're just her property."

One of her looks. Had I picked up even an ability to imitate her expressions?

"What'd you do, puke?" He sniffed the air. "So now you know what you're in for."

I walked away from him. He and I had been close when we were kids. He would let me follow him around when I was home, and sometimes T'Gatoi would let me bring him along when she took me into the city. But something had happened when he reached adolescence. I never knew what. He began keeping out of T'Gatoi's way. Then he began running away until he realized there was no "away." Not in the Preserve. Certainly not outside. After that he concentrated on getting his share of every egg that came into the house and on looking out for me in a way that made me all but hate him—a way that clearly said, as long as I was all right, he was safe from the Tlic.

"How was it, really?" he demanded, following me.

"I killed an achti. The young ate it."

"You didn't run out of the house and puke because they ate an achti."

"I had...never seen a person cut open before." That was true, and enough for him to know. I couldn't talk about the other. Not with him.

"Oh," he said. He glanced at me as though he wanted to say more, but he kept quiet.

We walked, not really headed anywhere. Toward the back, toward the cages, toward the fields.

"Did he say anything?" Qui asked. "Lomas, I mean."

Who else would he mean? "He said 'T'Khotgif.'"

Qui shuddered. "If she had done that to me, she'd be the last person I'd call for."

"You'd call for her. Her sting would ease your pain without killing the grubs in you."

"You think I'd care if they died?"

No. Of course he wouldn't. Would I?

"Shit!" He drew a deep breath. "I've seen what they do. You think this thing with Lomas was bad? It was nothing."

I didn't argue. He didn't know what he was talking about.

"I saw them eat a man," he said.

I turned to face him. "You're lying!"

"I saw them eat a man." He paused. "It was when I was little. I had been to the Hartmund house and I was on my way home. Halfway here, I saw a man and a Tlic and the man was N'Tlic. The ground was hilly. I was able to hide from them and watch. The Tlic wouldn't open the man because she had nothing to feed the grubs. The man couldn't go any further and there were no houses around. He was in so

much pain, he told her to kill him. He begged her to kill him. Finally, she did. She cut his throat. One swipe of one claw. I saw the grubs eat their way out, then burrow in again, still eating."

His words made me see Lomas's flesh again, parasitized, crawling. "Why didn't you tell me that?" I whispered.

He looked startled as though he'd forgotten I was listening. "I don't know."

"You started to run away not long after that, didn't you?"

"Yeah. Stupid. Running inside the Preserve. Running in a cage."

I shook my head, said what I should have said to him long ago. "She wouldn't take you, Qui. You don't have to worry."

"She would...if anything happened to you."

"No. She'd take Xuan Hoa. Hoa...wants it." She wouldn't if she had stayed to watch Lomas.

"They don't take women," he said with contempt.

"They do sometimes." I glanced at him. "Actually, they prefer women. You should be around them when they talk among themselves. They say women have more body fat to protect the grubs. But they usually take men to leave the women free to bear their own young."

"To provide the next generation of host animals," he said, switching from contempt to bitterness.

"It's more than that!" I countered. Was it?

"If it were going to happen to me, I'd want to believe it was more, too."

"It *is* more!" I felt like a kid. Stupid argument.

"Did you think so while T'Gatoi was picking worms out of that guy's guts?"

"It's not supposed to happen that way."

"Sure it is. You weren't supposed to see it, that's all. And his Tlic was supposed to do it. She could sting him unconscious and the operation wouldn't have been as painful. But she'd still open him, pick out the grubs, and if she missed even one, it would poison him and eat him from the inside out."

There was actually a time when my mother told me to show respect for Qui because he was my older brother. I walked away, hating him. In his way, he was gloating. He was safe and I wasn't. I could have hit him, but I didn't think I would be able to stand it when he refused to hit back, when he looked at me with contempt and pity.

He wouldn't let me get away. Longer legged, he swung ahead of me and made me feel as though I were following him.

"I'm sorry," he said.

I strode on, sick and furious.

"Look, it probably won't be that bad with you. T'Gatoi likes you. She'll be careful."

I turned back toward the house, almost running from him.

"Has she done it to you yet?" he asked, keeping up easily. "I mean, you're about the right age for implantation. Has she—"

I hit him. I didn't know I was going to do it, but I think I meant to kill him. If he hadn't been bigger and stronger, I think I would have.

He tried to hold me off, but in the end, had to defend himself. He only hit me a couple of times. That was plenty. I don't remember going down, but when I came to, he was gone. It was worth the pain to be rid of him.

I got up and walked slowly toward the house. The back was dark. No one was in the kitchen. My mother and sisters were sleeping in their bedrooms—or pretending to.

Once I was in the kitchen, I could hear voices—Tlic and Terran from the next room. I couldn't make out what they were saying—didn't want to make it out.

I sat down at my mother's table, waiting for quiet. The table was smooth and worn, heavy and well crafted. My father had made it for her just before he died. I remembered hanging around underfoot when he built it. He didn't mind. Now I sat leaning on it, missing him. I could have talked to him. He had done it three times in his long life. Three clutches of eggs, three times being opened up and sewed up. How had he done it? How did anyone do it?

I got up, took the rifle from its hiding place, and sat down again with it. It needed cleaning, oiling.

All I did was load it.

"Gan?"

She made a lot of little clicking sounds when she walked on bare floor, each limb clicking in succession as it touched down. Waves of little clicks.

She came to the table, raised the front half of her body above it, and surged onto it. Sometimes she moved so smoothly she seemed to flow like water itself. She coiled herself into a small hill in the middle of the table and looked at me.

"That was bad," she said softly. "You should not have seen it. It need not be that way."

"I know."

"T'Khotgif—Ch'Khotgif now—she will die of her disease. She will not live to raise her children. But her sister will provide for them, and for Bram Lomas." Sterile sister. One fertile female in every lot. One to keep the family going. That sister owed Lomas more than she could ever repay.

"He'll live then?"

"Yes."

"I wonder if he would do it again."

"No one would ask him to do that again."

I looked into the yellow eyes, wondering how much I saw and understood there, and how much I only imagined. "No one ever asks us," I said. "You never asked me."

She moved her head slightly. "What's the matter with your face?"

"Nothing. Nothing important." Human eyes probably wouldn't have noticed the swelling in the darkness. The only light was from one of the moons, shining through a window across the room.

"Did you use the rifle to shoot the achti?"

"Yes."

"And do you mean to use it to shoot me?"

I stared at her, outlined in the moonlight—coiled, graceful body. "What does Terran blood taste like to you?"

She said nothing.

"What are you?" I whispered. "What are we to you?"

She lay still, rested her head on her topmost coil. "You know me as no other does," she said softly. "You must decide."

"That's what happened to my face," I told her.

"What?"

"Qui goaded me into deciding to do something. It didn't turn out very well." I moved the gun slightly, brought the barrel up diagonally under my own chin. "At least it was a decision I made."

"As this will be."

"Ask me, Gatoi."

"For my children's lives?"

She would say something like that. She knew how to manipulate people, Terran and Tlic. But not this time.

"I don't want to be a host animal," I said. "Not even yours."

It took her a long time to answer. "We use almost no host animals these days," she said. "You know that."

"You use us."

"We do. We wait long years for you and teach you and join our families to yours." She moved restlessly. "You know you aren't animals to us."

I stared at her, saying nothing.

"The animals we once used began killing most of our eggs after implantation long before your ancestors arrived," she said softly. "You know these things, Gan. Because your people arrived, we are relearning what it means to be a healthy, thriving people. And your ancestors, fleeing from their homeworld, from their own kind who would have killed or enslaved them—they survived because of us. We saw them as people and gave them the Preserve when they still tried to kill us as worms."

At the word "worms," I jumped. I couldn't help it, and she couldn't help noticing it.

"I see," she said quietly. "Would you really rather die than bear my young, Gan?"

I didn't answer.

"Shall I go to Xuan Hoa?"

"Yes!" Hoa wanted it. Let her have it. She hadn't had to watch Lomas. She'd be proud....Not terrified.

T'Gatoi flowed off the table onto the floor, startling me almost too much.

"I'll sleep in Hoa's room tonight," she said. "And sometime tonight or in the morning, I'll tell her."

This was going too fast. My sister Hoa had had almost as much to do with raising me as my mother. I was still close to her—not like Qui. She could want T'Gatoi and still love me.

"Wait! Gatoi!"

She looked back, then raised nearly half her length off the floor and turned to face me. "These are adult things, Gan. This is my life, my family!"

"But she's...my sister."

"I have done what you demanded. I have asked you!"

"But—"

"It will be easier for Hoa. She has always expected to carry other lives inside her."

Human lives. Human young who should someday drink at her breasts, not at her veins.

I shook my head. "Don't do it to her, Gatoi." I was not Qui. It seemed I could become him, though, with no effort at all. I could make Xuan Hoa my shield. Would it be easier to know that red worms were growing in her flesh instead of mine?

"Don't do it to Hoa," I repeated.

She stared at me, utterly still.

I looked away, then back at her. "Do it to me."

I lowered the gun from my throat and she leaned forward to take it.

"No," I told her.

"It's the law," she said.

"Leave it for the family. One of them might use it to save my life someday."

She grasped the rifle barrel, but I wouldn't let go. I was pulled into a standing position over her.

"Leave it here!" I repeated. "If we're not your animals, if these are adult things, accept the risk. There is risk, Gatoi, in dealing with a partner."

It was clearly hard for her to let go of the rifle. A shudder went through her and she made a hissing sound of distress. It occurred to me that she was afraid. She was old enough to have seen what guns could do to people. Now her young and this gun would be together in the same house. She did not know about the other guns. In this dispute, they did not matter.

"I will implant the first egg tonight," she said as I put the gun away. "Do you hear, Gan?"

Why else had I been given a whole egg to eat while the rest of the family was left to share one? Why else had my mother kept looking at me as though I were going away from her, going where she could not follow? Did T'Gatoi imagine I hadn't known?

"I hear."

"Now!" I let her push me out of the kitchen, then walked ahead of her toward my bedroom. The sudden urgency in her voice sounded real. "You would have done it to Hoa tonight!" I accused.

"I must do it to someone tonight."

I stopped in spite of her urgency and stood in her way. "Don't you care who?"

She flowed around me and into my bedroom. I found her waiting on the couch we shared. There was nothing in Hoa's room that she could have used. She would have done it to Hoa on the floor. The thought of her doing it to Hoa at all disturbed me in a different way now, and I was suddenly angry.

Yet I undressed and lay down beside her. I knew what to do, what to expect. I had been told all my life. I felt the familiar sting, narcotic, mildly pleasant. Then the blind probing of her ovipositor. The puncture was painless, easy. So easy going in. She undulated slowly against me, her muscles forcing the egg from her body into mine. I held on to a pair of her limbs until I remembered Lomas holding her that way. Then I let go, moved inadvertently, and hurt her. She gave a low cry of pain and I expected to be caged at once within her limbs. When I wasn't, I held on to her again, feeling oddly ashamed.

"I'm sorry," I whispered.

She rubbed my shoulders with four of her limbs.

"Do you care?" I asked. "Do you care that it's me?"

She did not answer for some time. Finally, "You were the one making the choices tonight, Gan. I made mine long ago."

"Would you have gone to Hoa?"

"Yes. How could I put my children into the care of one who hates them?"

"It wasn't...hate."

"I know what it was."

"I was afraid."

Silence.

"I still am." I could admit it to her here, now.

"But you came to me...to save Hoa."

"Yes." I leaned my forehead against her. She was cool velvet, deceptively soft. "And to keep you for myself," I said. It was so. I didn't understand it, but it was so.

She made a soft hum of contentment. "I couldn't believe I had made such a mistake with you," she said. "I chose you. I believed you had grown to choose me."

"I had, but..."

"Lomas."

"Yes."

"I had never known a Terran to see a birth and take it well. Qui has seen one, hasn't he?"

"Yes."

"Terrans should be protected from seeing."

I didn't like the sound of that—and I doubted that it was possible. "Not protected," I said. "Shown. Shown when we're young kids, and shown more than once. Gatoi, no Terran ever sees a birth that goes right. All we see is N'Tlic—pain and terror and maybe death."

She looked down at me. "It is a private thing. It has always been a private thing."

Her tone kept me from insisting—that and the knowledge that if she changed her mind, I might be the first public example. But I had planted the thought in her mind. Chances were it would grow, and eventually she would experiment.

"You won't see it again," she said. "I don't want you thinking any more about shooting me."

The small amount of fluid that came into me with her egg relaxed me as completely as a sterile egg would have, so that I could remember the rifle in my hands and my feelings of fear and revulsion, anger and despair. I could remember the feelings without reviving them. I could talk about them.

"I wouldn't have shot you," I said. "Not you." She had been taken from my father's flesh when he was my age.

"You could have," she insisted.

"Not you." She stood between us and her own people, protecting, interweaving.

"Would you have destroyed yourself?"

I moved carefully, uncomfortable. "I could have done that. I nearly did. That's Qui's 'away.' I wonder if he knows."

"What?"

I did not answer.

"You will live now."

"Yes." *Take care of her,* my mother used to say. Yes.

"I'm healthy and young," she said. "I won't leave you as Lomas was left—alone, N'Tlic. I'll take care of you."

—1984

ROBERTA HILL (1947-)

Born in Baraboo, Wisconsin, the poet, fiction writer, and scholar Roberta Hill is of Oneida heritage. She received her undergraduate degree from the University of Wisconsin, and briefly pursued a medical career before deciding to focus on her writing instead (she had been writing poetry since she was a child). Hill earned her M.F.A. from the University of Montana in 1973 and went on to earn a Ph.D. in American Studies from the University of Minnesota. Her dissertation was a biography of her grandmother, Dr. Lillie Rosa Minoka-Hill, the second American Indian woman physician. In 1980, Hill married the artist Ernest Whiteman, with whom she had three children. Hill has published two collections of poetry, *Star Quilt* (1984) and *Philadelphia Flowers* (1996). She is a professor of English and American Indian Studies at the University of Wisconsin in Madison.

Leap in the Dark

"The experience of truth is indispensable
for the experience of beauty and the sense
of beauty is guided by a leap in the dark."
Arthur Koestler[1]

I.

Stoplights edged the licorice street with ribbon,
neon embroidering wet sidewalks. She turned

into the driveway and leaped in the dark. A blackbird
perched on the bouncing twig of a maple, heard

her whisper, "Stranger, lover, the lost days are over.   5
While I walk from car to door, something inward opens

like four o'clocks in rain. Earth, cold from autumn,
pulls me. I can't breathe the same

with dirt for marrow and mist for skin,
blurring my vision, my vision's separate self.   10

I stand drunk in this glitter, under the sky's grey shelter.
The city maple, not half so bitter, hurls itself

in two directions, until both tips darken and disappear,
as I darken my reflection in the smoking mirror

of my home. How faint the sound of dry leaves,   15
like the clattering keys of another morning, another world."

II.

She looked out the window at some inward greying door.
The maple held her glance, made ground fog from her cigarette.

---

[1] Arthur Koestler (1905-1983), British novelist.

Beyond uneven stairs, children screamed,
gunned each other down. Then she sealed her nimble dreams   20

with water from a murky bay. "For him I map
this galaxy of dust that turns without an answer.

When it rains, I remember his face in the corridor
of a past apartment and trace the anguish around his mouth,

his wrinkled forehead, unguarded eyes, the foreign fruit   25
of an intricate sadness. With the grace that remains,

I catch a glint around a door I cannot enter.
The clock echoes in dishtowels; I search love's center

and bang pans against the rubble of my day, the lucid
grandeur of wet ground, the strangeness of a fatal sun   30

that makes us mark on the margin of our loss,
trust in the gossamer of touch, trust in the late-plowed field."

III.
When the sun opened clouds and walked into her mongrel soul,
she chopped celery into rocky remnants of the sea,

and heard fat sing up bread, a better dying.   35
The magnet in each seed of the green pepper kept her flying,

floating toward memories that throb like clustered stars:
the dark water laughter of ducks, a tangle of November oaks,

toward sudden music on a wheel of brilliant dust
where like a moon she must leap back and forth   40

from emptiness. "I remember the moon shimmering
loss and discovery along a water edge, and skirting

a slice of carrot, I welcome eternity in that sad eye of autumn.
Rare and real, I dance while vegetables sing in pairs.

I hug my death, my chorus of years, and search   45
and stretch and leap, for I will be apprentice to the blood

in spite of the mood of a world
that keeps rusting, rusting the wild throats of birds."

IV.
In lamplight she saw the smoke of another's dream:
her daughter walk woods where snow weighs down pine,   50

her son cry on a bridge that ends in deep-rooted dark,
her man, stalled on a lonely road, realize his torque

was alcohol and hatred. "Hungry for silence, I listen
to wind, to the sound of water running down mountain,

my own raw breath. Between the sounds, a seaborn god   55
plays his reed in the caverns of my being.

I wear his amethyst, let go my dreams: Millars, Lacewings,
and Junebugs scatter, widen and batter the dark,

brightening this loud dust with the fever of their eyes.
Oh crazy itch that grabs us beyond loss   60

and lets us forgive, so that we can answer birds and deer,
lightning and rain, shadow and hurricane.

Truth waits in the creek, cutting the winter brown hills.
It sings with needles of ice, sings because of its scar."

—1984

Star Quilt

These are notes to lightning in my bedroom.
A star forged from linen thread and patches.
Purple, yellow, red like diamond suckers, children

of the star gleam on sweaty nights. The quilt unfolds
against sheets, moving, warm clouds of Chinook.[2]   5
It covers my cuts, my red birch clusters under pine.

Under it your mouth begins a legend,
and wide as the plain, I hope Wisconsin marshes
promise your caress. The candle locks

us in forest smells, your cheek tattered   10
by shadow. Sweetened by wings, my mothlike heart
flies nightly among geraniums.

We know of land that looks lonely,
but isn't, of beef with hides of velveteen,
of sorrow, an eddy in blood.   15

Star quilt, sewn from dawn light by fingers
of flint, take away those touches
meant for noisier skins,

anoint us with grass and twilight air,
so we may embrace, two bitter roots   20
pushing back into the dust.

—1984

[2] A warm wind.

LINDA HOGAN (1947–)

Born in Denver, Colorado, the poet, fiction writer, and activist Linda Hogan is the daughter of Charles Henderson (Chickasaw) and Cleona Bower Henderson (German American). Although Hogan moved around a good deal in her childhood because her father was in the army, she considers Oklahoma, where much of her father's family lives, to be her home state. Hogan received her B.A. from the University of Colorado at Colorado Springs, and then went on to earn an M.A. in English and Creative Writing at the University of Colorado at Boulder. Much of her work as a writer, feminist, and activist has to do with articulating and fostering the increasingly endangered connection between humans and the natural world, especially the animal world. She is the author of several collections of poetry, including *Calling Myself Home* (1978); *Daughters, I Love You* (1981); *Seeing Through the Sun* (1985), which was awarded both an American Book Award from the Before Columbus Foundation and a Juniper Prize; and *The Book of Medicines: Poems* (1993). She has also published the novels *Mean Spirit* (1990) and *Solar Storms* (1995), and the autobiography *Woman Who Watches Over the World: A Native Memoir,* for which she received a 2002 Wordcraft Circle Writer of the Year award.

Friday Night

Sometimes I see a light in her kitchen
that almost touches mine,
and her shadow falls straight
through trees and peppermint
and lies down at my door   5
like it wants to come in.

Never mind that on Friday nights
she slumps out her own torn screen
and lies down crying on the stoop.
And don't ask about the reasons;   10
she pays her penalties for weeping.
Emergency Room:
Eighty dollars to knock a woman out.
And there are laughing red-faced neighbor men
who put down their hammers   15
to phone the county.
Her crying tries them all.
Don't ask for reasons
why they do not collapse
outside their own tight jawbones   20
or the rooms they build
a tooth and nail at a time.

Never mind she's Mexican
and I'm Indian
and we have both replaced the words   25
to the national anthem with our own.
Or that her house smells of fried tortillas
and mine of Itchko and sassafras.

Tonight she was weeping in the safety of moonlight
and red maples. 30
I took her a cup of peppermint tea,
and honey,
it was fine blue china
with marigolds growing inside the curves.
In the dark, under the praying mimosa 35
we sat smoking little caves of tobacco light,
me and the *Señora of Hysteria,* who said
Peppermint is every bit as good as the ambulance.
And I said, Yes. It is home grown.

—1985

The Truth Is

In my left pocket a Chickasaw hand
rests on the bone of the pelvis.
In my right pocket
a white hand. Don't worry. It's mine
and not some thief's. 5
It belongs to a woman who sleeps in a twin bed
even though she falls in love too easily,
and walks along with hands
in her own empty pockets
even though she has put them in others 10
for love not money.

About the hands, I'd like to say
I am a tree, grafted branches
bearing two kinds of fruit,
apricots maybe and pit cherries. 15
It's not that way. The truth is
we are crowded together
and knock against each other at night.
We want amnesty.

Linda, girl, I keep telling you 20
this is nonsense
about who loved who
and who killed who.

Here I am, taped together
like some old Civilian Conservation Corps[1] 25
passed by from the Great Depression
and my pockets are empty.
It's just as well since they are masks
for the soul, and since coins and keys
both have the sharp teeth of property. 30

---

[1] Depression-era federal work program in rural areas.

Girl, I say,
it is dangerous to be a woman of two countries.
You've got your hands in the dark
of two empty pockets. Even though
you walk and whistle like you aren't afraid   35
you know which pocket the enemy lives in
and you remember how to fight
so you better keep right on walking.
And you remember who killed who.
For this you want amnesty,   40
and there's that knocking on the door
in the middle of the night.

Relax, there are other things to think about.
Shoes for instance.
Now those are the true masks of the soul.   45
The left shoe
and the right one with its white foot.

—1985

Wall Songs

The southern jungle is a green wall.
It grows over the roads
men have hacked away
that they may keep things separate
that they may pass through life   5
and not be lost in it.

There are other walls
to keep the rich and poor apart
and they rise up like teeth out of the land
snapping, Do Not Enter.   10
Do not climb the wire fences
or cross ledges embedded with green
and broken glass.

These walls have terrible songs
that will never stop singing   15
long after the walls have collapsed.

On one side of the wall there is danger.
On the other side
is danger.

There is a song   20
chanting from out of the past,
voices of my evicted grandmothers
walking a death song
a snow song

wrapped in trade cloth   25
out of Mississippi.

Open the cloth
and I fall out.

And the confines of this flesh
were created by my grandfather's song: 30
No Whites May Enter Here.

My own walls are smooth river stones.
They sing at night
with the beat of crickets.
They stand firm at 5 a.m.   35
when the talking world wants to invade
my skin
which is the real life
of love and sorrow.

My skin. Sometimes a lover   40
and I turn our flesh to bridges
and the air between us disappears
like in the jungle
where I am from.
Tropical vines grow together, lovers,   45
over roadways men have slashed,
surviving
the wounds of those lost inside
and the singing of machetes.

May all walls be like those of the jungle,   50
filled with animals
singing into the ears of night.
Let them be
made of the mysteries further in
in the heart, joined with the lives of all,   55
all bridges of flesh,
all singing,
all covering the wounded land
showing again, again
that boundaries are all lies.   60

—1985

Luz Maria Umpierre (1947-)

Luz Maria Umpierre was born in Santurce, Puerto Rico, on October 15, 1947. A poet, literary critic, lesbian activist, and human rights advocate who has combined her professional and artistic career with the pursuit of social justice, Umpierre graduated with honors from the Universidad del Sagrado Corazón in Puerto Rico in 1970 and moved to the United States to pursue graduate study. She received her M.A. and Ph.D. in Spanish and Portuguese Literature from Bryn Mawr College in 1978. A year later, she published her first book of poetry, *Una puertorriqueña en Penna,* in Puerto Rico. An expanded edition quickly followed, entitled *En el pais de las maravillas* (1982), published in the U.S. by Third Women Press. Umpierre's insistence on combining the poetic languages of English and Spanish, as witnessed in her subsequent books of poetry *The Margarita Poems* (1987) and *for Christine* (1995), suggest a refusal to privilege one colonial influence in Puerto Rico over another. From 1978 to 1989, Umpierre was a professor of Spanish and Portuguese at Rutgers University. In 2003, she was awarded the Order of Merit by the U.S. Congress in recognition of her literary achievements and her humanitarian efforts.

In Response

My name is not María Cristina.
I am a Puerto Rican woman born in another barrio.[1]
Our men...they call me pushie
for I speak without a forked tongue
and I do fix the leaks in all faucets.   5

I don't accept their ways,
shed down from macho-men ancestors.
I sleep around whenever it is possible;
no permission needed from dearest *marido*[2]
or kissing-loving papa.   10
I need not poison anyone's belly but my own;
no cooking mama here;
I cook but in a different form.

My name is not María Cristina.
I speak, I think,   15
I express myself in any voice,
in any tone, in any language that conveys
my house within.
The only way to fight oppression is through
       resistance: 20
I do complain
I will complain
I do revise,
I don't conceal,
I will reveal,   25
I will revise.

---

[1] (Sp.) Neighborhood; commonly used to indicate the Puerto Rican neighborhoods of Manhattan.

[2] (Sp.) Husband.

I am not the mother of rapist warriors,
I am the child that was molested.
I teach my students to question all authority,
to have no fears, no nail biting in class,   30
no falling in love with the teacher.

My eyes reflect myself,
the strengths that I am trying to attain,
the passions of a woman who at 35 is 70.
My soul reflects my past,   35
my soul deflects the future.

My name is not María Cristina.
I am a Puerto Rican woman born in another barrio.
Our men…they call me bitchie
for I speak without a twisted tongue   40
and I do fix all leaks in my faucets.

—1985

No Hatchet Job

for Marge Piercy

They would like
to put the tick and flea collar
around her neck and
take her for walks on sunny afternoons
in order to say to the neighbors: 5
"We had domesticated this unruly woman."

They would like
to see her curled up on the corner,
fetal position, hungry, un-nursed
so that they can enter the scene,   10
rock-a-bye her to health
to advertise in the *Woman News* or *Psychology Today:*
"We have saved, we have cured this vulnerable woman."

They would like
to see her unclean,   15
10 days without showers,
in filth and foul urine,
frizzled hair and all,
her business in ruins,
her reputation in shambles,   20
her body repeatedly raped on a billiard board
so that they can say in their minds:
"We have finally reduced this superior woman."

They would like
to have her OD on the carpet,   25

anorexic, bulimic and stiff on her bed
so that they can collect a percentage for burial
from the deadly mortician:
"We have found you this cadaverous woman."

They would like   30
to spread her ashes at sea,
arrange *pompas fúnebres,*[3]
dedicate a wing or a statue in her name
so that their consciences
can finally rest in saying: 35
"We have glorified this poet woman."

But headstrong she is unleashed,
intractable she nourishes her mind,
defiantly she lives on in unity,
obstinately she refuses the limelight, the pomp and the glory.   40
Eternally she breathes
one line after next,
unrestrained, unshielded
   willfully
   WRITER   45
   WOMAN

                      —1987

The Statue

Flower child
twirling around a yellow full moon.
Trinkets crowning her long messy hair,
glossy bead droplets encircling her neck,
magma, chalazas,   5
metal links as insignias,
imprisoning rings.

"Peace," she says.
"Love," the victoria sign on her hands.
Flowered blazer from Saks on her back,   10
loafer shoes mold her feet,
Calvin Klein faded jeans
with the brand name torn out.
Flower child.

At the core of her fabric and emblems: 15
economics, gastronomics, the computer,
the lag of the jet, quintessential histrionics,
flower child.
Twisting faces,
mutilating backs of the dark colored faces.   20

---

[3] (Sp.) Funeral services.

"Whip," she whimpers in silence,
"Chain,"
"Dow Jones,"
"Apartheid."
Flower child, slave making ant   25
in a midnight assembly of forgeries,
transferential concoction:
love to hate
peace to war
"listen, man" to "obey"   30
hip to yup
Black to White
cornucopias to caldrons
Vietnam to El Salvador
esprit to *corps*   35
1960 to 1985.

—1987

SANDRA MARÍA ESTEVES (1948-   )

Sandra María Esteves was born in the Bronx, New York, to a Dominican mother and a Puerto Rican father. Her parents, who had never married, separated before she was born, but Esteves was nevertheless close to her paternal aunts and cousins, and developed a strong identification as a Puerto Rican. Raised in the Huntspoint area of the South Bronx, Esteves attended a strict Catholic boarding school on the Lower East Side, returning to her neighborhood only on weekends. At school, Esteves was chastised for speaking Spanish and she grew anxious over her language skills in both English and Spanish. She retreated into the world of the visual arts, eventually enrolling at the Pratt Institute of Design in Brooklyn, where she pursued a graphic arts degree. Before beginning college, Esteves traveled to Puerto Rico, where she stayed with relatives and experienced a political awakening. When she returned to the U.S. she encountered poetry at the National Black Theater that spoke about people's experiences with racism and sexism, and she began writing her own poetry. Nuyorican poet and playwright Jesús Meléndez took notice of her work and introduced Esteves to the world of Latino artists in New York. Esteves became a principal figure in the Nuyorican Poets movement, which included Miguel Algarín, Tato Laviera, and Miguel Piñero. She was also a member of "El Grupo," a traveling collective of Nuyorican socialist poets, performers, and musicians. Esteves has published six books of poetry to date, including *Yerba Buena* (1980), *Tropical Rain: A Bilingual Down Pour* (1984), *Bluestown Mockingbird Mambo* (1990), and *Finding Your Way* (2001).

A la Mujer Borrinqueña[1]

My name is Maria Christina
I am a Puerto Rican woman born in el barrio[2]

---

[1] An indigenous name for Puerto Rico made popular during the Puerto Rican nationalist social movements of the 1960s and 1970s.

[2] (Sp.) Neighborhood; commonly used to indicate the Puerto Rican neighborhoods of Manhattan.

Our men...they call me negra because they love me
and in turn I teach them to be strong

I respect their ways   5
inherited from our proud ancestors
I do not tease them with eye catching clothes
I do not sleep with their brothers and cousins
although I've been told that this is a liberal society
I do not poison their bellies with instant chemical foods   10
our table holds food from earth and sun

My name is Maria Christina
I speak two languages broken into each other
but my heart speaks the language of people
born in oppression   15

I do not complain about cooking for my family
because abuela[3] taught me that woman is the master of fire
I do not complain about nursing my children
because I determine the direction of their values

I am the mother of a new age of warriors   20
I am the child of a race of slaves
I teach my children how to respect their bodies
so they will not o.d. under the stairway's shadow of shame
I teach my children to read and develop their minds
so they will understand the reality of oppression   25
I teach them with discipline...and love
so they will become strong and full of life

My eyes reflect the pain
of that which has shamelessly raped me
              but my soul reflects the strength of my culture   30
My name is Maria Christina
I am a Puerto Rican woman born in el barrio
Our men...they call me negra because they love me
and in turn I teach them to be strong.

—1980

For South Bronx

I live amidst hills of desolate buildings
rows of despair
crowded together
in a chain of lifeless shells

Every five minutes the echoing roar   5
of the racing elevated train
sears thru the atmosphere
floating low over the horizon

---
[3] (Sp.) Grandmother.

But at every moment
like magic the shells breathe   10
and take on the appearance of second cousins
or sometimes even look like old retired ladies
who have nothing more to do
but ride empty subways from stop to stop

At night   15
hidden away from the city
the youngbloods invade the trainyards
laiden with colors of dreams
crying for existence
on the empty walls of desolation's subway cars   20
for old ladies to read on and on…

—1980

Black Notes and "You Do Something to Me"
for Gerry González and The Fort Apache Band[4]

Jazz—jazzy jass juice,
just so smooth,
so be-bop samba blue to sweet bump black.
So slip slide back to mama black—
to mamaland base black.   5
Don't matter could be bronx born basic street black.
Or white ivory piano coast negro dunes bembé[5] black.
Mezclando manos[6] in polyrhythm sync to fingers,
to keys, to valves, to strings, to sticks,
to bells, to skins, to YEAH black.   10
Bringin' it home black.
The bad Fort Apache tan olive brown beat black.
Bringin' it all the way up fast black.
Flyin' across Miles 'n Sony,
across John, Rhasaan 'n Monk's '81,   15
across Dizzy blue conga Jerry horn,[7]
'n básico Andy mo-jo black.
Across Nicky's campana timbaleando tumbao black.[8]
'N Dalto's multi-octave chords with all those keys black.
Those multifarious dimensional openings   20
playin' loud—soft—hard—cold—slow—'n—suavecito black.

---

[4] The Fort Apache Band is a renowned Latin Jazz band founded in the early 1980s in New York City by Jerry and Andy Gonzalez, and Steve Berrios. Initially a large ensemble featuring up to fifteen pieces, many famous jazz musicians rotated through the ensemble, including Kenny Kirkland, Sonny Fortune, Steve Turre, Jorge Dalto, Frankie Rodriguez, Milton Cardona, Hector Hernandez, and Angel Vazques, some of whom are referenced in the poem.
[5] Bembé refers both to an Afro-Cuban form of music in 6/8 rhythm, as well as to an Bantu-speaking people from Zaire.
[6] (Sp.) Mixing hands.
[7] Miles Davis (1926-1991), Sonny Fortune (b. 1939), John Coltrane (1926-1967), Rahsaan Roland Kirk (1936-1977), Thelonious Monk (1917-1982), and John Birks "Dizzy" Gillespie (1917-1993): legendary jazz musicians.
[8] Jazz percussionist Nicky Marrero (b. 1950), who specializes in the timbales. Tumbao is a basic 1/8 rhythm.

Playin' it runnin'—jumpin'—cookin'—greasin'—'n—smokin' black.
Playin' it mellow, yeah mellow,
makin' it mean somethin' black.
Makin' it move, rockin' round black.   25
Walk with it, talk with it, wake the dead with it black.
Turnin' it out, touchin' the sky with it black.
Shakin' it suave, shakin' it loose,
shakin' it che-ché-que-re black.
Season it, sugar it, lingerin', lullaby black.   30
Livin' it, ALIVE BLACK!
Always lovin' it—Yeah!

Jazz.
How I love your sweet soul sounds.
Yeah,   35
how I love how you love me.
Yeah, how I love that deep black thang...
              ..."You do so well"...

—1990

LINDA FAIGAO-HALL (1948-   )

Born in the Philippines, Linda Faigao-Hall immigrated to the U.S. in 1973. She holds a B.A.
in English from Silliman University, the Philippines, and holds advanced degrees in English
literature and educational theatre from New York University and Bretton Hall College in
England. She has been a full-time computer systems analyst since 1983. Faigao-Hall's work is
notable for introducing Filipino mythologies and folklore to Asian American theatre, while
simultaneously addressing contemporary issues such as third-world poverty, neocolonialism,
hate crimes, and the Filipino experience in America. Her innovations in dramatic structure
often elide the imaginary with the real to test the audience's notion of rational explanations
for the experience of marginalized peoples. Faigao-Hall's produced plays include *Woman from
the Other Side of the World* (1997), *God, Sex, and Blue Water* (1998), *The 7th of October* (1999),
and *Pusong Babae (Heart of a Woman)* (2000), an earlier version of the play included here. She
lives in Brooklyn.

The FeMale Heart *(Pusong Babae)*

CAST, IN ORDER OF APPEARANCE:
  ANGHEL OCON, *a Filipino, late 20s*
  ADELFA, *his sister, early 20s*
  ROSARIO, *mother to* ADELFA *and* ANGHEL, *50s*
  ROGER FLYNN, *Caucasian-American, early to mid-30s*

The action shifts between Manila, Philippines, and Park Slope, Brooklyn, New York, 1992-2001.[1]

---

[1] [*Author's Note.*] Many of the Filipino expressions are not integral to the plot or meaning of the play; they are there to
establish local color and to signal that a character is speaking Tagalog. The letters from the family to Adelfa, however,
are completely devoid of such expressions, because it is understood that they are writing only in Tagalog.

[*There are two spaces: one space is set in the present, in Park Slope, Brooklyn, New York, a well-appointed bedroom with two side tables, a television set, a telephone. The other is the landscape of* ADELFA'*s memory, where the distant past and recent past events come to life. The play's text will clearly indicate whenever action occurs in the present.*]

At Rise: Spring 2001. ADELFA *is in Brooklyn, picking up letters strewn on the bed, one by one, examining each one, and sorting them in date order. As she nears the end of this sorting, she finds a red envelope still unopened. She picks it up and rips it open. A TV dance program is on. A piece of music spills into the space; it reminds her of something; she stares at the screen; a few beats.*]

ADELFA: [*Voiceover*] "Reverend Mother Superior Natividad, Reverend Father Kintanar, my mother and my brother Kuya Anghel, my dearest sisters and brothers in the parish of the Risen Christ—

[*Lights go up on* ANGHEL *in Smokey Mountain; he is seated on a bench, eating purple ice cream, watching* ADELFA, *who is standing in front of him, reading from a sheet of paper.* ANGHEL'*s face has been half-covered by a handkerchief and it is now around his neck. He is wearing plastic gloves and boots and next to him is a hook-shaped metal rod. Once in awhile, there are popping sounds coming from the trash.*]

ADELFA: "…and our honored funders and benefactors at our sister parish in Sydney, Australia. Today, June 15, 1992, I graduate from the parish of the Risen Christ High School in Smokey Mountain in the Philippines."

ANGHEL: [*Clapping his hands.*] Spriketek! 'tang ina! Ang galing mo![2]

ADELFA: That's just the beginning, Kuya. Father Kintanar says he'll help me finish it. [ANGHEL *gives her the rest of his ice cream.*]

ANGHEL: Lola Epang's ube.[3] Today's special.

ADELFA: Thank you, *Kuya.*

ANGHEL: Sikat mo talaga.[4] Making speeches. Just like those politicians on TV!

ADELFA: Father K said he's taping it and sending it to Sydney.

ANGHEL: Sydney? Talaga ba?[5] Have you told Inay?[6] First high school graduate in all of Smokey. And now *baldictatorian!*

ADELFA: *Valedictorian. Hindi naman.*[7] Lola Epang finished high school. Her diploma's hanging outside her window.

ANGHEL: The one she found in the trash?

ADELFA: What?

ANGHEL: She wrote her name on it! So what else are you going to say?

ADELFA: I should thank everybody. My teachers…Mother Superior. God. But I told Father K, *I only want to thank my mother and my brother.* I only want to thank you, Kuya, and Inay.

ANGHEL: Short speech.

ADELFA: Then I'll tell the people of Smokey to get out of here. Leave this place. But the only way they can do that is to let their children stay in school. Not pull them out to pick trash.

ANGHEL: What? Not everyone is a *baledictorian* like you, Adelfa. And it's not too bad. Look how well we're doing. We own the biggest junk shop in all of Smokey,

---

[2] (Tag.) You're good!
[3] (Tag.) Purple yam.
[4] (Tag.) How impressive.

[5] (Tag.) Is that true?
[6] (Tag.) Mother.
[7] (Tag.) Not true.

seventeen jumpers work for us. And I'm their boss. It's not garbage. It's *recycling*. *Waste management, di ba?* Your own words.

ADELFA: Exactly. Garbage. *Basora*.

ANGHEL: *Aba, ang yabang mo.*[8] It takes a man to do this job. And it's honest work. It's better than begging…it's always here. Nobody loses his job. Even Marcos lost his job, *di ba?* And here, in the bottom of the world, there's nowhere to go but up. [*Sweeps his arm around.*] The best part of Smokey. *Basora* from Hyatt. From tourists. And it's ours.

ADELFA: But as soon as I get that high school diploma, I'll get work as a salesgirl at the mall. I'll be wearing a nice clean dress, selling shoes, handbags, RTW's! And the only people who'll touch the garbage will be the janitors. And I can finally get us out of Smokey. Into a rooming house in Baclaran.

ANGHEL: A rooming house in Baclaran. And what will I be doing?

ADELFA: *Siempre*. I'll find something for you at the mall.

ANGHEL: And what will I show them? Lola Epang's diploma? The nearest I ever been to school was picking up trash from La Salle Boys High.

ADELFA: You went to school.

ANGHEL: Until grade five only. That won't even get me a job at Pablo's Pizza Palace.

ADELFA: Nobody human should live like this!

[*Lights change. Spotlight on* ADELFA, *in Smokey, giving her speech.*]

ADELFA: …June 15, 1992, I graduate from the parish of the Risen Christ High School in a community called Smokey Mountain in the Philippines, my home. I was born here. And just like any community in millions of places in my beloved country, it has clinics. Schools. A church. Junk shops, food stalls. Even ice cream.

Except that underneath my feet, is a cement footpath that winds its way through 18 hectares of trash, 750 feet high. To our honored donors at our sister parish in Sydney, Australia, this mountain of garbage is as big as 45 football fields and as high as an eight-story building.

Yet it is home to twenty thousand people who live and work here, searching for scrap metal and other recyclables, enduring the stench, the flies, the toxic waste, and the smoke that gives the mountain its name, the fog and haze that come from the spontaneous combustion of sewage—Smokey Mountain—

[*Slow fade.* ANGHEL *is scavenging.* ADELFA *enters; she looks exhausted, dispirited. She's carrying a cup of coffee. She sits on a stool.* ANGHEL *joins her. She gives him the coffee.* ANGHEL *takes it.*]

ADELFA: *Cuppa Java.* Coffee. Eighty-five pesos!

[ANGHEL *almost drops it.*]

ANGHEL: *"Tangina!"*[9] Eighty-five pesos? What's in it? Imelda's pee?

ADELFA: No. Café latte. Coffee from America. The manager gave it to me.

ANGHEL: What's wrong with instant Nestle?

ADELFA: *Mas masarap ito, Kuya.*[10]

ANGHEL: *O sigi nga.*[11] [*Taking a sip, expecting something different. A beat.*] It's still coffee!

ADELFA: [*Disconsolate.*] And I'm still unemployed. Dunkin' Donuts. Kentucky Fried Chicken. Cuppa Java. Zero.

ANGHEL: Don't be discouraged. One of these days, it will happen. I guarantee it.

---

[8] (Tag.) You're way too proud.
[9] (Tag.) Son of a bitch.

[10] (Tag.) This is better!
[11] (Tag.) Go ahead.

ADELFA: It's been a month! There's just too many of us. And so few jobs. Saleslady. Waitress. Barrista. Nothing.

ANGHEL: Barrista?

ADELFA: They make this coffee. Four thousand pesos a month, Kuya.

ANGHEL: Four thousand a month? Just for making coffee?

ADELFA: I told you. It's not just coffee. Café latte. Cappuccino, espresso. But I'm only a high school grad!

ANGHEL: Don't be sad. [*Peers into his sack and takes out a tight ball of black debris. He peels it with a knife. Underneath is a bar of soap.*] For you. Palmolive.

ADELFA: [*Smelling the soap.*] Ivory, *Kuya.*

ANGHEL: What do you think of Cebu Teacher's College?

ADELFA: Mr. Paredes. Remember him? He went to Cebu Teacher's.

ANGHEL: So you wanna go there?

ADELFA: What?

ANGHEL: Do you wanna go there?

ADELFA: I heard you the first time, Kuya. It's not funny.

ANGHEL: Am I laughing? Don't you have dreams, Adelfa?

ADELFA: I used to.

ANGHEL: Don't you know if you stop dreaming, you die. So you get a job at the mall, we'll be renting a room in Baclaran. You'll have a nice clean job making *kape latti.* And then what? Didn't you say you wanted to be a teacher once?

ADELFA: That was a long time ago, Kuya.

ANGHEL: So how about now? You still want to be a teacher?

ADELFA: Stop playing with me. It's cruel. And I'm tired.

ANGHEL: They don't call me Anghel for nothing. [*Dramatic pause.*] Something miraculous has happened.

ADELFA: What are you talking about?

[ROSARIO *appears from behind a mound, dragging a large sack.*]

ROSARIO: Adelfa, jackpot! Jackpot! Did you tell her? To even dream of a way out…Stinky Mountain. Hopeless Mountain. If your Itay could see us now…

ANGHEL: I'd spit in his face, 'tang ina.

ROSARIO: Remember you wanted to go back to Bicol. But I told you to stay. Stay in Smokey. There's hope here. Where there's garbage, there's life.

ADELFA: Did we win the sweepstakes?

ANGHEL: I sold the junk shop. Lola Epang met our terms. An hour ago.

ADELFA: But she's been trying to buy it for years!

ROSARIO: I know!

ROSARIO: She's no fool, Lola Epang. She thinks there's a future here. All these foreigners sending money.

ANGHEL: The money from the shop will pay for your first year of school. We'll figure out the rest.

ADELFA: But what will you and Inay live on?

ANGHEL: I'm selling everything. Our lots, too. The Hyatt. [*Jumping to another mound, gesturing, like a king.*] Remember this? Tio Berto had this lot since the 50's until Itay inherited it in '74—

ROSARIO: No. 1970.

ANGHEL: 1974, Inay.

ROSARIO: No. Your Itay split in '74.

ADELFA: Stop arguing. I don't understand!

ANGHEL: Adelfa, who's the best dancer in the barrio?

ADELFA: You. Except maybe for Ronald Reagan Rampatanta. But he's getting old. What has this got to do with anything?

[ANGHEL *picks up the cassette tape recorder from DL.*]

ANGHEL: Spare parts from the dump. I put it together myself. A 'demo tape.' Last week I saw someone in Quiapo who's got a dancing school there. I'm going to be a DI!

ADELFA: A DI? A dance instructor!

ANGHEL: Remember the Mother Teresa Hip Hop Jam?

ADELFA: When you won first place?

ANGHEL: He saw me dance. He said if I ever needed a job to look him up. So I did.

ADELFA: [*Breathlessly.*] And?

ANGHEL: [*Shaking her hand.*] Good evening, Ma'am. I'm your D.I. for the evening, Ma'am. My boss taught me how to say it. *Okay, ba?*

ADELFA: Okay? It's perfect!

ROSARIO: I will never sell another piece of junk in my life. This time tomorrow everyone will be envious of us.

ANGHEL: The boss said he'll give me an attaché case, so people will think I'm a lawyer. Then they'll have to call me attorney. That's me, Adelfa. Attorney Anghel Ocon.

ROSARIO: And lonely rich ladies from Green Hills will pay you to dance with them at the Marriott.

ANGHEL: The boss said the best D.I.'s make one thousand five a night. But if I get the American tourists, I'll get paid in dollars. One hundred dollars a night, *daw!* How much is that, Adelfa.

ADELFA: One US dollar is 40 pesos…four thousand pesos. That's how much barristas make a month! One hundred dollars a month. You can make that in one night?

ANGHEL: *Spriketek!* I'll work overtime. Hit all the hotels. I have connections. I know all the garbage people there.

ROSARIO: Then one day you'll meet someone young and beautiful and rich who'll fall in love with you.

ANGHEL: And I'll be honest with her. I'll tell her I used to live in Smokey—

ROSARIO: *Punieta.* Why?

ANGHEL: If she holds it against me that's how I'll know she's not the one, *di ba?*

ADELFA: [*Still stunned.*] Cebu Teacher's College…Nobody from Smokey ever went to college. I'm dreaming. Is it a dream?

[ROSARIO *sits down and opens her sack, peering inside.*]

ROSARIO: My last pick! [*She spots something, takes it out.*] No label? [*Opens it, smelling it.*] Jackpot! Oil of Olay. Tourists. They throw everything away too soon. [*Takes out a baby food glass jar*] Baby food. You know Father Kintanar gives me ten pesos for fifty of these? Candle holders! But Lola Epang said she'll sell it for twenty. *Pambihira.* [*Throwing it back to the lot.*] Americans have food just for babies…

ADELFA: They have food just for dogs.

ROSARIO: What?

ADELFA: For cats, too.

ROSARIO: [*To* ANGHEL.] *Tutuo, ba?*[12]

ANGHEL: This used to be trash from the PX years ago. [*Taking out a printer cartridge from his sack.*] That's nothing. Look. I got a bunch of assholes working for me! They missed this! *A printer cartrid.*

ROSARIO: *Susmariosep.*[13] A *hayteek.*

ADELFA: What's a *hayteek.*

ANGHEL: Spare parts from computers. Cables. Like that.

ADELFA: Oh. 'High tech.' It means high technology. 'High tech.'

ROSARIO: 'High tekology' *daw.*

ANGHEL: 'High tik' is the best thing that ever happened to garbage. See? A Canon. One hundred and fifty pesos…easy.

ROSARIO: Lola Epang will probably sell it for three hundred. [*Beat.*] The hours I spent on my knees praying for this day to come…[*To* ADELFA.] You *are* the ticket.

ADELFA: I promise, Inay. This mountain will never cast its shadow on us again. [*To* ANGHEL.] What changed your mind, Kuya?

ANGHEL: You. Graduation day. On the stage. When they called your name—Maria Adelfa Ocon—*Baledictorian!* And that speech. Proudest moment of my life. I knew then without a doubt—how you're made for bigger things, Adelfa. [*Pause, touching her face.*] You're not going to be a salesgirl. You're going to be a teacher.

[ADELFA *watches wide-eyed as* ANGHEL *jumps from his perch and turns the tape deck on. Dance music spills into the space. Some parts of the music is reminiscent of the music that is heard on television when the play opens.*]

ANGHEL: [*To* ADELFA, *in English.*] Good evening, Ma'am. I'm your DI for the evening. [ADELFA *and* ANGHEL *dance.* ROSARIO *joins in.*]

ROSARIO/ADELFA/ANGHEL: Cha cha!…o…salsa!…tango!…disco! Disco! [*They dance, their bodies moving in perfect harmony as Smokey Mountain casts its long shadow on their happy hopeful faces. Then rap music.*]

ROSARIO: [*Freezing in her tracks.*] *Ano yan?*[14]

ADELFA: Rap, Inay. Rap!

ROSARIO: Rap? [*Making a face.*] *Ang pangit!*[15]

[*Lights change. Two years later. A male dancer in an evening jacket glides into the space, dancing solo waltz-like movements; he is elegant and graceful; he does a few turns…then the music shifts; the waltz morphs into something more contemporary—upbeat—until it explodes like a firecracker—the pounding throb of harsh, deafening disco music. Strobe lights rain on the dancer, as the feel of air takes on the smell of sweat, heat and bodies undulating in the dark.*]

ROSARIO, *carrying a small bag and* ADELFA *enter, watching.*

The dancer is now stripping. A piercing wave of sound, cheers and cat-calls collide with the music. The man is graceful, erotic, sensual. Water from somewhere above him cascades down his body; he caresses himself, his hands leaving swirls of white foam where they slip and glide. This is macho dancing. A spotlight hits the dancer. It is ANGHEL. ADELFA *watches in horror and then flees from the scene followed by* ROSARIO.]

ADELFA: The Angel of Desire? He's the Angel of Desire?

---

[12] (Tag.) Is that true?
[13] Contraction of "Jesus, Mary and Joseph."

[14] (Tag.) What's that?
[15] (Tag.) Sounds ugly.

ROSARIO: He's the club's biggest dancer, Adelfa. They say he's bigger than the star he replaced. Spartacus.

ADELFA: Spartacus. I don't know what you're talking about? How long has he been doing this?

ROSARIO: Right after you left for college.

ADELFA: That was two years ago! Two years ago he was a D.I.

ROSARIO: He was never a D.I.

ADELFA: What?

ROSARIO: Soon after you left, Peaches spotted him outside the club—

ADELFA: Peaches Bodoy? She's a prostitute, Inay. What does she have to do with this?

ROSARIO: You know her mother, Cherry Pie. She used to live in Smokey years ago. Peaches saw him outside the club and she told Lola Epang—

ADELFA: You listen to gossip, Inay?

ROSARIO: And Lola Epang told me. One night I followed him to work—I saw it all. He asked me to keep it from you.

ADELFA: And you agreed? All this time, you knew and you didn't tell me? Is he *bakla?* Is he gay?

ROSARIO: Don't you know your own brother?

ADELFA: Some people say if you do this work long enough, a man will turn gay.

ROSARIO: He's more of a man than your Itay ever was. How do you think we could pay for your school and the rent?

ADELFA: But a macho dancer. A macho dancer!

ROSARIO: Half of those dancers are married. Their wives wait outside the club with food. During the break they have supper together. I wait with them. I bring Angel his change of clothes.

[ANGHEL *enters. At first he doesn't see* ADELFA. *He opens* ROSARIO's *small overnight bag and takes out a T-shirt. Then he sees* ADELFA. *A few beats.*]

ANGHEL: What are you doing here? [*To* ROSARIO, *ferociously.*] What's she doing here, Inay?

ROSARIO: I'm tired of keeping secrets!

ADELFA: You lied to me.

ANGHEL: Yes, I did.

ADELFA: Why?

ANGHEL: From Smokey Mountain to the Hyatt? Did you really believe that? I can't get past the security guard!

ADELFA: I don't get it!

ANGHEL: Packaged sex tours for gay men. What is it you don't get?

ADELFA: You're not even gay!

ANGHEL: It's a business. I'm a professional. Spartacus—it took him a year before they'd let him do the soap and water number. It took me three months. I'm a star, Adelfa. I have repeat customers from all over the world, paying me in dollars, marks, yen. I'm still king of the goddamn mountain.

ADELFA: That day at Smokey. I told you I was going to get us out of there.

ANGHEL: Serving coffee to the rich and stupid? We'd be back in Smokey sooner than you think. Didn't you tell me nobody human should live there?

ADELFA: They closed Smokey down.

ANGHEL: And many more dumps take its place. Same mountain. Same people. There are dogs in Makati that live better. I can't go back, Adelfa. It's too late. I've seen the world. [*He is seized by a spasm of coughs.*]

ANGHEL: I have another show in ten minutes. [*Pause.*] You were ashamed of Smokey. Are you ashamed of this, too? [*He exits.*]

ADELFA: Two years you kept it to yourself!

ROSARIO: He wanted you to finish college.

ADELFA: [*Impetuously.*] So why am I here? There's a boat going back to Cebu in an hour. I have papers to write. Exams next week!

ROSARIO: [*Fiercely.*] Adelfa! *Sasampalin kita.*[16] I'm doing laundry from the apartment building next door, making dresses for the office girls there. But they're going to the mall and buying them off the rack. Those RTW's. Ready to Wears! I'm losing my customers. I can't make enough for him to quit and for you to continue with school.

ADELFA: Quit? Does he want to quit?

ROSARIO: Didn't you see how thin he is?

ADELFA: I'm not blind!

ROSARIO: He's tired all the time. There are days he can't get out of bed; nights, he wakes up sweating; he's cough's gotten worse. Last week, he began complaining of chest pains.

ADELFA: Has he been to the clinic?

ROSARIO: He takes pills. They don't help. That's why I asked you to come. To see for yourself.

ADELFA: Maybe he needs a break. Maybe that's all he needs.

ROSARIO: Then we will continue to be blessed. But what if he's really sick?

[ADELFA *falls quiet.*]

ROSARIO: I've borne this shame in silence. I don't pray anymore. All my prayers come up hard as stones. I didn't even know I could bear the thought of going to hell. But I will not watch my own child die.

ADELFA: Die? Why are you saying that? He's not going to die!

ROSARIO: Someone is already dead. Spartacus. He died. He was complaining of chest pains. I'm afraid to think!

ADELFA: Inay. Inay. Let's not jump to conclusions.

ROSARIO: They're building a new mall. Lola Epang said it's the biggest mall in Asia. Maybe you can get a job there.

ADELFA: You need a college diploma, Inay. And only the very rich go there. I'm not even sure if they'll let me in the door. Salvatore Ferragamo…Versace…Vera Wang…

ROSARIO: You can do it. I know it. I feel it in my bones. You're young and strong—

ADELFA: And hopeful. All I had was hope. And you put it there. A teacher!

ROSARIO: I'm so sorry, *anak*. That dream is over. [*Silence, like a heavy blanket, falls on both of them, muffling all sound.*]

ROSARIO: You understand, don't you?

ADELFA: Wait. Wait. Please. [*The silence continues.* ADELFA *begins to weep.*]

ROSARIO: Are you crying for yourself or for him?

---

[16] (Tag.) I'm going to slap your face!

ADELFA: I don't know where I end and he begins.

ROSARIO: We survived Smokey. We will survive this one.

[*Lights change. A year later.*]

ADELFA: It's Roger's. As he promised, Inay. An airline ticket. And a check.

ROSARIO: Five hundred dollars! Jackpot! Eight months. How quickly God answers all my prayers. No. Better than the jackpot. A miracle. Anghel is safe.

[ANGHEL *walks in on them. Something has gone out of him. He looks sick and frail. Throughout this scene* ANGHEL *coughs into a handkerchief occasionally.*]

ANGHEL: Safe from what?

[ADELFA *shows him the airline ticket.*]

ANGHEL: What's that?

ADELFA: An airplane ticket to America. And a check. Five hundred dollars, Kuya.

ANGHEL: Where did you get it? Who gave it to you?

ADELFA: I went to the library—there's hundreds—maybe, thousands of American men who want Filipino wives.

ANGHEL: What are you talking about?

[ROSARIO *brings out a catalogue and places it on the table.* ANGHEL *peers down at it.*]

ANGHEL: [*Trying to read it.*] Ke—kerry—blossoms?

ADELFA: 'Cherry Blossoms.' They bloom in Japan.

ANGHEL: Never heard of it. So it's a book. What's that to us?

[ROSARIO *opens it to a page.* ANGHEL *looks at it and takes a step back. He looks at* ADELFA.]

ANGHEL: What's your picture doing in it?

ADELFA: It's a business, Kuya. A mail order bride catalogue business. A woman sends her picture to this catalogue, and it's published. A man who's looking for a wife buys the book for fifty dollars, and if he likes her picture he writes to her.

ANGHEL: Pen pals?

ADELFA: No. Cherry Blossoms is only for men looking for wives. Six thousand women, Kuya, in this book alone. Half of them from the Philippines.

ANGHEL: [*He sweeps the book off the table.*] Whose idea was this?

ROSARIO: Mine.

ANGHEL: Inay?

ADELFA: I received ten letters—from Germany, Australia, Canada, the US—

ANGHEL: From all over the world. Just like the men I dance for. So we're two of a kind, Adelfa? There's nothing special about you either?

ADELFA: I told them the truth. I was ready to be any man's wife for three hundred dollars a month. Only one wrote back. An American. Roger Flynn. He's got a real estate business in a place called Brooklyn.

ANGHEL: How do you know he's not black? Or an old man?

ADELFA: [*Gives him a photograph.*] He sent us his picture.

ANGHEL: [*Looks at it.*] But he's very handsome. What's wrong with him? And how do you know it's him?

ADELFA: He fits what they say in the book. [*Opening to a page, reading.*] "Demographic profiles of men—"

ANGHEL: What?

ADELFA: "...seeking mail-order brides...94% white...in their thirties...incomes higher than average..."

ANGHEL: So what?

ADELFA: They need to have money, Kuya. They have to pay for travel. And they're educated. "Only 5% never finished high school, 42% are in professional and managerial positions"—

ROSARIO: And tall! Very tall! Average height, five feet seven!

[ANGHEL *and* ADELFA *look at* ROSARIO. *A beat.*]

ADELFA: And if it doesn't work, the agency will send me home. For the man, there's a money back guarantee.

[ANGHEL *grabs the ticket to rip it up but* ADELFA *and* ROSARIO *struggle with him.* ROSARIO *manages to pull the ticket away from* ANGHEL.]

ANGHEL: How long has this been going on? And behind my back? Don't you have any respect?

ADELFA: Since I quit school.

ANGHEL: Quit? You said you're just taking the year off!

ADELFA: You're sick.

ANGHEL: I feel better everyday. I'm going back to work and you're going back to school! I'm taking the pills they're giving me at the clinic.

ADELFA: St. Joseph's aspirin, Kuya. They're just volunteers. Socialites from Makati. I've tried the mall. But the money would only pay for the rooming house. Inay's laundry—the food. But nothing for a doctor. A real doctor. In a hospital. Three hundred dollars a month will take care of it all.

ANGHEL: But from a salesgirl selling shoes to marrying a man you've never met—how did that happen? It doesn't make sense!

ADELFA: In the beginning I thought of being an OFW. An overseas foreign worker. So I took a test.

ANGHEL: What test?

ADELFA: A government test. It was very easy. Cooking, sewing, baby-sitting. Entertainment skills. They give you a certificate that says you're an artist. They send you overseas. Even arrange the visas.

ROSARIO: At first, they suggested she go to Saudi.

ANGHEL: Do you know how many women come back in body bags from the fucking Middle East?

ADELFA: I know that! So I thought of going to Japan.

ANGHEL: *Japayukis!* [*To* ROSARIO.] I thought you didn't want her to be a whore!

ROSARIO: That's why she's going as a mail-order bride!

ANGHEL: What's the difference?

ROSARIO: *Ingrato ka.*[17] Adelfa will be a wife in the eyes of the law and of God. Married to an American, living in America. How many women in the country would go through hell to get the same chance?

ADELFA: Some marriages turn out right. Here. [*Taking out sheets of paper.*] Copies of letters from women who found husbands. Good husbands. The office clerk gave them to me. It's a risk I'm willing to take.

ANGHEL: Why?

ADELFA: You're sick. And we're poor. We'll always be poor. But I can get you well. It's something I can do. Be someone's wife.

ANGHEL: Aren't you afraid for yourself? I am.

---

[17] (Tag.) Ingrate!

ADELFA: We're more afraid for you.

ANGHEL: Don't you want to fall in love someday? You're giving away your life.

ADELFA: And why not? You've given yours.

ANGHEL: But not my heart. [ANGHEL *is seized by a spasm of deep, racking coughs. He exits.*]

ROSARIO: He's been spitting blood. Take the check and cash it. Marry this man Mr. Flynn. And save your brother's life. God will bless you.

[*Lights change. Four months later.*]

ANGHEL: [*V.O.*] "My dear Adelfa, You said snow looked like dust dancing in the wind. I thought it came down all at once, like a blanket. Splat. And there it is. So did you eat it? Father K says that's how the Chinese invented ice cream. They put sugar in snow. Guy named Marco Polo loved it and gave it to the world. Never heard of him. Is it true? Your loving brother, Kuya Angel…"

ROSARIO: [*V.O.*] "That photo in the Prospect Park. When I saw it, I cried. As if you were inside a Christmas card. Then you said snow has many shades of white? White is white. Then you said Roger had to use a pick axe to break up the frozen black mud. What black mud? So what happened to the white snow? Next time, explain everything, ok? Love, Inay."

[*Lights on* ROGER *in the memoryscape.* ADELFA *is wearing a white cotton dress.*]

ROGER: Your pictures didn't do you justice. We've been married a month, and I still can't keep my eyes off you. [*He gives her an elegantly-wrapped gift. He puts it on the bed.*]

ROGER: Open it.

ADELFA: Another one?

[ADELFA *unwraps it. It is a beautiful piece of batik cloth.*]

ADELFA: It's beautiful.

ROGER: Only the best. Because you're precious. Go ahead. Try it on. Take down your hair, please?

[ADELFA *exits.* ROGER *sits on the bed, waiting in anticipation.*]

ROGER: I've always loved Oriental women. Now I'm married to one…

[ADELFA *comes back in. She has taken down her hair, and has transformed herself into what looks like a 'fantasy' of the 'exotic Oriental.'* ROGER *is stunned by her transformation.*]

ROGER: [*Proudly.*] You must never wear anything else.

[*She starts to take off the batik.*]

ROGER: No. Keep it on. This one fits all my pictures. [*He kisses her. There is something harsh and insistent about his kiss.* ROGER *gets carried away and whacks her behind, sharply.* ADELFA *instinctively pulls back.*]

ADELFA: What's wrong? You're angry with me? I won't wear anything else, I promise!

ROGER: I've been very gentle with you. All this time. Patient.

ADELFA: Yes. You are gentle. Very gentle. So why are you angry now?

ROGER: I'm not angry. [*Laughing sheepishly.*] I'm just playing.

ADELFA: Playing?

ROGER: [*He holds out his arms to her.*] You know you can hit me back.

ADELFA: What?

ROGER: Hit me back. I'm a bad boy…go on. Hit me. I won't get angry. Promise…

[ADELFA *gives him a light slap, playfully, unsure of herself.* ROGER *laughs.* ADELFA *begins to laugh, too. He pulls her tenderly in his arms.*]

ROGER: See? Don't look so scared. I'm harmless. Really. [*Pause.*] Don't hate me, please.

ADELFA: Hate you? I don't know you. How can I hate you?

ROGER: We're married now. You're my wife.

ADELFA: Did I do something wrong?

ROGER: Are you kidding? I fell in love with you just from reading your letters. But seeing you the first time—bringing you here—this past Christmas has been the best I've ever had…I'm the luckiest man in the world. [*Kissing her tenderly.*] I'm gonna take care of you…you and your family. I promised you that.

ADELFA: That was the agreement.

ROGER: Best deal I ever made. Hey, don't cook tonight. You like Italian? Let's go to Cucina.

ADELFA: Pizza? [*Pronouncing it 'pi-cha.'*]

ROGER: No. Not pizza. Fettuccini Alfredo.

[ADELFA *tries to take off her sarong.*]

ROGER: I really like you in it. Always look like that, please?

[*Lights change. The telephone rings.* ADELFA *picks it up.*]

ADELFA: Hello?…Yes. I accept.

ROSARIO: Adelfa? Did I wake you? What time is it there?

ADELFA: It's seven in the evening, Inay. Where are you calling from?

ROSARIO: I'm at the mall. I'm using a phone card!

ADELFA: Is Kuya Angel with you? May I speak with him?

ROSARIO: He's at home, resting. Where's Roger?

ADELFA: He's at work. He should be home soon.

ROSARIO: Send us more pictures, okay, *anak?*

ADELFA: I just sent—

ROSARIO: And the food? Are you finally getting used to the food?

ADELFA: The food? Last night we had—

ROSARIO: You know what we did last night? Angel, Ronald Reagan Rampatanta and I went to Lola Epang's *carenderia* for dinner. We ordered the Special Beefstik. I wore a white dress. It was so clean.

ADELFA: That's nice, Inay.

ROSARIO: We couldn't finish the beefstik. We had it for breakfast the next day and lunch and dinner. Why are you so quiet?

ADELFA: You talk, Inay. I'll listen.

ROSARIO: Anak, I'm so ashamed to bring this up.

ADELFA: *Ano yan,*[18] Inay.

ROSARIO: Adelfa, *anak,* has he started giving you the three hundred?

ADELFA: *Bakit,* Inay?

ROSARIO: We went to PG Hospital for a check-up. But they asked him to stay overnight—so the next day, I was short 2,500 pesos. So the hospital won't release him.

ADELFA: What do you mean, Inay?

ROSARIO: *Sabi daw,* they'll hold him until I can pay in full. *Ang galit ko.* I was so angry. I wanted him to just walk out. But I didn't know where they put him. *Sabi daw* he's in a special room. I tried looking for him but it's like Divisoria—it's crowded and big except they're not shopping. They're all sick.

ADELFA: So what did you do? Where's Roger's five hundred dollars?

[18] (Tag.) What's that?

ROSARIO: That's what happened. I gave it all to a Dr. Valdes, a private specialist. He was able to get him out of there. Okay *ba,* anak?

ADELFA: [*Relieved.*] *Opo,* Inay. Get the best. Do you understand? Get the best.

ROSARIO: Thank you, Adelfa. I'm so confused. Even in Smokey, working twenty years, he's never been sick like this. What did you want to say to Angel?

ADELFA: I just wanted to hear his voice. [*Pause.*] Inay, I'm so—confused.

ROSARIO: Confused? About what?

ADELFA: Being married.

ROSARIO: [*Laughing.*] *Ay, naku.* Just be patient. You'll figure it out soon enough.

ADELFA: I hope so.

ROSARIO: Men are easy, Adelfa. Just do what they say. I have to go, *anak.*

ADELFA: Please call me again tomorrow. I miss you and Kuya Angel! I love you!

[*Lights change. Three months later.*]

ANGHEL: [*V.O.*] What's that you're wearing, a *malong?* Is that the fashion there? Half a year into your marriage and you already look like an American!

ROSARIO: Dr. Valdes wants to do more tests. They're so expensive. I'd put away fifty dollars for a telephone but perhaps next time. So that $300 is almost gone. That picture of you cooking lasagna. Without the meat. Just cheese…how pretty you look…you must be happy…

[*Lights change. Three months later.* ROGER *is in the memoryscape.*]

ROGER: That brownstone on St. John's? Sold! [*He sweeps her off her feet.*] There's nothing I can't sell these days! [*Giving her a playful slap in her rear*] I feel like fun and games tonight.

ADELFA: Fun and games?

ROGER: Yeah. Something really special. [*Beat.*] Ever heard of role-playing?

ADELFA: No.

ROGER: It's like—acting. I'll go to *Lemon Grass* around the corner. Sit at the bar. Then you follow a few minutes later. You see me. You pretend you don't know me. Then you pick me up.

ADELFA: Pick you up?

ROGER: You're from out of town. You feel lonely. Then you see me. You find me— you know, attractive. [*Flustered.*] This is so embarrassing.

ADELFA: A let's pretend game.

ROGER: Yes! You're a quick study! That's good. And then we come back here to play some more.

ADELFA: Like those movies…*Bomba.* Sexy movies.

ROGER: Kind of. But it's—consensual. Harmless, you know.

ADELFA: Like an actress…like this…[*Taking on a sexual pose but not successfully.*] "Hi, Mister… you wanna good time?" Like that? "Twenty-five bucks…"

ROGER: What?

ADELFA: I'm playing…"Twenty-five bucks, Joe…" Joking only, Roger…

ROGER: Wait. Hold on. Would you be more into it if you got something for it?

ADELFA: [*Beat.*] Maybe.

ROGER: Twenty-five…that's not bad.

ADELFA: No?

ROGER: No.

ADELFA: Really. [*Pause.*] Another twenty-five and I'll do anything you want.

ROGER: Hello…

[*Lights change.*]

ROSARIO: [*V.O.*] An extra fifty dollars! God bless you, *anak!* You have no idea how much we need it—especially now. Dr. Valdes said he called you yesterday. Anghel has HIV. You asked him not to tell Anghel because it might upset him. Is that why he told Anghel he's got TB? He's also ordering drugs from Hong Kong. They're more effective. I told him, get the best, *di ba?*

[*And another.*]

ANGHEL: There's something I'm missing. All you do is talk about your chores. You must keep the cleanest house in Brooklyn. What else do you do, Adelfa? You don't mention any friends. It sounds like Kuya Roger keeps you close to home. Thank you for the leather wallet you sent for my birthday. It's so soft. Dr. Valdes said I have TB. When I was in Smokey, almost everybody had that. Why is it I'm getting it only now?

[*Lights change.* ROGER *is unpacking grocery bags.*]

ROGER: [*Shaking his head.*] Adelfa? Honey! I said paper not plastic.

[ADELFA *enters.*]

ADELFA: What?

ROGER: You keep forgetting, Hon. Don't you want to save the planet?

ADELFA: [*Without irony.*] Save the planet? You want me to save the planet?

ROGER: I said *"toilet bowl cleaner,"* not *"shower and tub."* And *"window"* cleaner. Not *glass.*

ADELFA: Dirt is dirt.

[ADELFA *exits, and once in a while peeks into the room.*]

ROGER: No, it's not. In this country, it's a science. And look at all these garbage bags! There must be a dozen boxes in here.

ADELFA: It's for Inay.

ROGER: Rosario?

ADELFA: *Nay* Rosario. *Nay* Rosario. Back home, we never address anyone older by their first names. Kuya Angel calls you *Kuya* Roger.

ROGER: But we're in America. Here everybody's equal. [*Pause.*] Okay. So why are you sending *Nay* Rosario garbage bags?

ADELFA: Smell it.

ROGER: I'm smelling.

ADELFA: Lemon! I wrote her about them. She wouldn't believe me so I sent her a pack. Now she won't use anything else. I even told her about our bathroom.

ROGER: What about the bathroom?

ADELFA: Even our toilet paper smells like potpourri. And I told her about the spray that makes ca-ca smell like vanilla ice cream!

[*Lights change. Three months later.*]

ROSARIO: The medications are working! Anghel is getting better! I go to mass everyday now. Adelfa, I love it where we are. The air is so fresh, the sky is blue. And the stars. When I was in Smokey, I never noticed them before. But here at Baclaran, they look big and bright. Was I dead and now I'm alive?

[*All of a sudden, the sound of glass breaking is heard coming from offstage.*]

ROGER: [*Alarmed.*] Jesus Christ! What's that? Adelfa?

ADELFA: [*Walking into the scene, Down Center.*] An accident. I'm sorry.

[ROGER *seats her on a chair. He kneels in front of her.*]

ROGER: You hurt?

ADELFA: Please don't be angry.

ROGER: I'm not. But what broke?

ADELFA: A flower vase.

ROGER: We have one?

ADELFA: Mrs. Santorini was selling it on her stoop.

ROGER: You're buying Mrs. Santorini's junk now?

ADELFA: It was only 50 cents.

ROGER: You want a flower vase, I'll buy you one from Macy's. Are you sure you're not hurt?

ADELFA: It broke in two pieces. That's all. [*Pause.*] Are you so protective of me, Roger?

ROGER: Of course, I am.

ADELFA: Then why—I don't understand—last night—

ROGER: I know. I'm sorry I got carried away.

ADELFA: You are carrying away all the time! Why can't we make love without the playing.

ROGER: I enjoy our games, don't you?

ADELFA: But you always end up getting mad at me. If you didn't, we can play all you like.

ROGER: But I told you I'm not mad at you. It's not about you. I can't—I need to play. It's a paradox. You understand what that means?

ADELFA: You love and hurt.

ROGER: Sometimes you surprise me. I'm under so much pressure. I can't find listings as fast as I can sell. I need another broker. The one I've got can't keep up!

ADELFA: So it's work that makes you angry?

ROGER: I have rage issues.

ADELFA: What?

ROGER: Sometimes things come up for me. Then I get mad and I lose control. But at least I'm aware of it. That's half the problem licked.

ADELFA: I don't understand!

ROGER: I used to see someone. Sometimes talking helps. You gain some insight about why you do what you do, who you are, where you've been in life.

ADELFA: A girlfriend?

ROGER: [*Laughing.*] That's precious. No. It's called therapy. I paid her a hundred thirty-five bucks an hour. You're not gonna understand it, Adelfa. It's very American.

ADELFA: How many hours, Roger?

ROGER: Let's see…one a week. Five years, give or take.

ADELFA: Five years?

ROGER: Exactly my feeling. All that money and she said squat. My life still sucked. So I quit and thought of doing Anger Management instead.

ADELFA: Anger what?

ROGER: Anger Management. They have an intensive four-week program at the Wellness Institute.

ADELFA: There's a school for this?

ROGER: No. It's just another form of therapy. But then the business took off. I couldn't find the time. So I dropped out. And then I found you. I realized I didn't need Anger Management.

ADELFA: So I am angry manager.

ROGER: No. I told you. I'm not angry with you. Please don't take it personally. [*Beat.*] I have so much garbage in my life!

ADELFA: What garbage?

ROGER: The remains of my past.

ADELFA: That's garbage?

ROGER: Don't you have things in your life you want to get rid of but can't? And every time you think about them you get angry? But I don't want to burden you with them, Adelfa.

ADELFA: Roger, we have a good life. Don't you think it's a good life?

ROGER: There's always something.

ADELFA: No, there isn't always something.

ROGER: That's because you expect so little.

ADELFA: But this is not so little. A beautiful house. A booming business. I'm sending money home every month. Inay's moved out of Baclaran to a bigger apartment. My brother's getting the best care. Life is good.

ROGER: I've had such a hard life, Adelfa.

ADELFA: But you don't have a hard life now.

ROGER: Look, you don't get it. To you, life is simple. Food, clothing and shelter.

ADELFA: You need health. And family. Family is essential.

ROGER: I'm not ready to have a family.

ADELFA: I'm talking about mine.

ROGER: Yours. I envy you and your family. You have no idea how lucky you are. [*Pause.*] But you never talk about your father.

ADELFA: Kuya Anghel said one day he went to buy some salt and never came back.

ROGER: Salt? Salt…How interesting…I wonder what that means. Salt…

ADELFA: Salt. You know, salt…what you put in your food…or tears. Tears taste of salt.

ROGER: How old were you?

ADELFA: I was just born.

ROGER: You never get over things like that. It doesn't matter how old you are.

ADELFA: But if I don't remember, what would I need to get over?

ROGER: Your soul remembers everything.

ADELFA: If that's true, then there's no escape.

ROGER: I used to think so. But that's before I met you. You've never felt despair, have you, Adelfa.

ADELFA: How can you say that?

ROGER: Do you know despair has a sound? The sound of breaking glass… I grew up wearing shoes all the time in the house. Or, else I'd step on shards of glass or china my parents threw at each other in their rages. No matter how hard she tried cleaning up, she could never find them all. Don't you wonder why we only have acrylic? Thank god for acrylic.

ADELFA: I'm sorry, Roger. Maybe you should go back to that woman. The therapy. Or be an Angry Manager. I'll help you. I went to the library yesterday—I'm sure they have books on Anger—

ROGER: You did what?

ADELFA: I saw this book. In the library. Around the corner.

ROGER: You went to the library? Keyfood. St. Francis. Duane Reade. That's it. I told you. I forbid you to go anywhere else.

ADELFA: Roger, why can't I work? I'm not afraid of work.

ROGER: Being my wife. That's your work. And you're doing a great job. I can finally look forward to coming home everyday now.

ADELFA: I have two years of college! Make me your secretary. I'll go to computer class. Learn Word processing. You said you're busy!

ROGER: I've a friend Tony. His wife's from Romania. He sends her to Excel training and next thing you know, she's run off with a classmate from the Ukraine. So he says next time he gets a new wife, he's gonna keep her home and her passport under lock and key.

ADELFA: Don't you trust me?

ROGER: Of course, I trust you. I trust you more than my ex-wife.

ADELFA: [*Pause.*] Ex-wife? Ex-wife! Like me?

ROGER: No way. Nothing like you. You're one in a million, Adelfa.

ADELFA: Six months we write each other. You never told me!

ROGER: What's there to say? That Joanne couldn't put up with my crap? She was so impatient. American women. You have to get it together right here right now. Well, some things take time. They don't know how to suffer.

ADELFA: American women are splendid! We love them in the Philippines.

ROGER: That's the only place to do it. From half-way around the world. Get close enough, and they're all the same—spoiled, ungrateful, too damned independent. Do you know there's a huge market just on Filipino women, Adelfa? Tony says they make the best wives. And he's right. You're understanding. Hard-working. You don't talk too much. And when you do talk, you speak English. You're— perfect! [*Pause.*] Please don't let this change anything between us.

ADELFA: What you're doing for Angel. And Inay. I could never pay you back.

ROGER: Let me make it up to you.

ADELFA: What are you going to do, Roger? Buy me something again? Don't buy me anything, please.

ROGER: I never in my life heard a woman say, "Don't buy me anything." [*Taking a few bills from his billfold.*] A raise. Fifty more a month. You deserve it. And that's another thing. Joanne. She was so fuckin' high maintenance. When she asked for money, it was always for something—a car—the latest model Miata. When you ask, it's so your brother can live another day. You're so grateful. Because you've been poor. Poor people never take anything for granted. There's something to be said for poverty.

ADELFA: There's nothing to be said for poverty.

[*Lights change.*]

ROSARIO: Fifty dollars more a month? You must be making Roger very happy. I'm so proud of you, *anak*. You must tell Roger how grateful we are. Here's a picture of us in front of Kentucky Fried Chicken. Do you like my white dress?

[*Lights change. Three months later.*]

ROGER: So what's with the dress?

ADELFA: It's a Donna Karan. I thought you liked it!

ROGER: No, I don't. It's too short. Too tight. What are you trying to prove.

ADELFA: You bought this for me!

ROGER: Hon, I'm playing?

ADELFA: Oh, okay. [*Pause. Then pushes him back.*] Fuck you! [*They laugh.* ADELFA *hits him hard. He hits her back.*]

ROGER: Oh, yeah? So let's do it. [*Aroused, he pins her down. She struggles.*] Oh, she's feisty tonight! Say the words, Adelfa. Say the words…

ADELFA: No!

ROGER: No?

ADELFA: Make me!

ROGER: Oh, yeah?

[ROGER *pulls her hands and she grabs the headboard as if she were being bound and tied to it. They are breathless with laughter.* ROGER *turns to exit. Then stops.*]

ROGER: Okay, Hon? Ready? You're gonna do it this time?

ADELFA: Yes.

ROGER: Promise?

ADELFA: Okay. Promise.

[ROGER *exits.*]

ADELFA: [*Overcome by giggling.*] Save me.

ROGER: [*Offstage*] I can't hear you!

ADELFA: SAVE ME, WHITE MAN!

[ROGER *runs into the room and "rescues" her, a damsel in distress. They erupt into paroxysms of laughter. A few beats. Then the laughter recedes. They begin kissing each other. They are both aroused. Then* ROGER *pulls out a cord from his back pocket. He pulls* ADELFA'*s hands and begins tying them together to the headboard.*]

ADELFA: What's that? What are you doing, Hon?

ROGER: It's you who need to trust me… will you trust me?

ADELFA: Yes, yes. I trust you. What are you doing? [*He tugs at her, tightly. She winces.*]

ROGER: Please?

ADELFA: Honey, this isn't fun.

ROGER: I'm sorry… [*But he tugs at them some more.*]

ADELFA: No!

ROGER: Please? [*On top of her.*]

ADELFA: [*Ferociously.*] I said NO! GET THE FUCK OFF ME! [*Her fury catches him by surprise.* ROGER *backs off, suddenly self-conscious. He steps back. In the following letter, he unties* ADELFA. ADELFA *bursts into quiet sobbing.*]

ANGHEL: Your letters don't sound like you. Remember the snow? Your first Christmas? I can't hear your voice in my head. And then there are my dreams. Last night you wanted to tell me something but I couldn't make out the words, your face, hidden. What do you want to tell me? Why do I dream such dreams?

ROGER: [*Wiping her tears.*] What I do to you—this is not who I am. I wish I was someone else. I'm so aware of what's wrong with me. But it doesn't keep me from hurting you. I could go back to therapy and talk until I'm blue in the face, but it's still like turning over mud. I have so much love for you. I can feel it—this sweet solid thing that sits in my heart, waiting to be free. Someday… soon… I promise. It's gonna happen. I feel it. But you've got to believe me.

ADELFA: You know what I want? This. This moment now. When I'm crying and you're sorry and I believe you… I feel hopeful. Hope is a wonderful thing. You can see the stars.

ROGER: That's why I love you. Everything amazes you. Stars. Garbage bags. Oprah Winfrey.

ADELFA: Oprah Winfrey is splendid.

ROGER: No. You. *You're* splendid.

ANGHEL: You say you keep seeing me in your dreams. I don't see you in mine. But I know you're there, shrouded in darkness and silence. What does it all mean? You look so different in these pictures. Your clothes are very stylish. But you look thin. And you never smile. Why is that? I must be crying in my sleep. I wake up always, my heart pounding, your face, an after image, and the taste of salt in my mouth. Here's a picture of me. Inay took it the day I left for the sanatorium.

[*Lights change. Three months later.* ROGER *has a piece of paper in her hand.*]

ROGER: They need more? We're already sending them three hundred fifty bucks a month!

ADELFA: It's drug resistant TB.

ROGER: Drug resistant TB? How the hell did he get that?

ADELFA: I don't know! [*Pause.*] The drugs from Hong Kong have stopped working. Dr. Valdes says he's going to try new ones from Australia, but Kuya Angel needs to be monitored closely. He needs to stay in the sanatorium indefinitely.

ROGER: Indefinitely. I don't like the sound of that. Are you sure this doctor's legit?

ADELFA: Inay chose him. I trust her.

ROGER: And Rosario needs an extra 50 for a cell phone?

ADELFA: It's for Kuya Angel.

ROGER: We pay close to 200 bucks a month in long distance calls already.

ADELFA: There's a sign at the pharmacy on Seventh Avenue for a part-time cashier —

ROGER: Out of the question. We've had this talk before. [*Pause.*] Drug-resistant TB. Are you sure Anghel's not faking it? So he doesn't have to work? Don't you think it's suspicious?

ADELFA: Don't you ever say that about Kuya Angel.

ROGER: What do they do? Sit around all day and wait for the check? It's like welfare except that I'm the fucking government.

ADELFA: That's unfair!

ROGER: But it's true!

ADELFA: How dare you judge my family.

ROGER: You're too kind. They're taking advantage of you.

ADELFA: How can my own family take advantage of me? Everything I have is theirs!

ROGER: I'm your family now. I'm looking out for you. You have nothing of your own. It's fucked up.

ADELFA: It's not fucked up! Stop saying that!

ROGER: It's called denial.

ADELFA: And in my country it's called the truth.

ROGER: The truth? Okay. So what's the truth?

ADELFA: [*Pause.*] Never mind.

ROGER: [*Pulling her back, roughly.*] Not never mind. Come on. Tell me. What the fuck is going on?

ADELFA: [*Letting go of his hold.*] Anghel was sick before you and I wrote to each other and he's still sick. That's why I married you. So we could pay his medical bills.

That's why I stay. And wait on you hand and foot. And sometimes—sometimes I hate you so much I stop breathing!

[*She turns to run but* ROGER *catches her, cupping his hand over her mouth, while with his other hand he rips her dress off. He throws her to the bed and heaves himself on to her, kissing her as she thrashes wildly at him. She struggles in vain. He pushes her down, on her stomach.*]

ADELFA: [*Wincing in pain.*] I don't want to play, Roger.

ROGER: [*He climbs on her back and begins entering her from behind.*] Yes, you do.

ADELFA: No, please, Roger.

ROGER: Yes, please Adelfa.

ADELFA: I said I don't want to play!

[ROGER *pulls out a bill from his pants pocket.*]

ROGER: A fifty.

ADELFA: Keep your money!

ROGER: Oh, the bitch wants more! [*Pulling out another bill.*] Twenty.

ADELFA: I said let me go!

ROGER: Easy does it…come, Adelfa…come, baby…I like it…it's good…oh, yes…oh, baby…oh, baby…

[ADELFA *screams. The sound rips the air in two.*]

ANGHEL: You're sending us so much money. The 350 a month. Then there's the fifties—twenties. Are you working outside the home now? Are you keeping some of it for yourself? You seemed so distant last night on the phone. And your letters are short with nothing to say. Even my life seems more interesting than yours and Adelfa, I live in a sanatorium.

ROGER: [*With extreme tenderness*] I'm so sorry…

ADELFA: I told you to stop.

ROGER: [*Inconsolable.*] I don't mean it… I didn't mean it… please…

ADELFA: You've never done anything like that before.

ROGER: I'm not worthy of you… it's so damned hopeless… I'm hopeless… Please don't hate me. Do you really hate me?

ADELFA: No, Roger. I don't hate you. I told you. This you. Now. This I love. I'm in love with this you.

[*Lights out.*]

ROSARIO: "Did I tell you Dr. Valdes is moving Angel to another sanatorium? Dr. Valdes says it's better than the one he's at now. He's got his own room and twenty-four hour care. I'm looking for a house near there, so I can visit him everyday. But they're expensive in this part of the city. But don't worry. I think we can afford it. Happy birthday, *anak*. I'm sending a heart-shaped pouch filled with adelfas I grow in the garden. Dr. Valdes says I've made a *"potpourri."* It's French. Imagine that?

[*Lights up on* ROGER *and* ADELFA *in the memoryscape. A month later.* ROGER *has a piece of paper in his hand.*]

ROGER: Do you know what this is? It's a bank statement. A private checking account!

ADELFA: Give me that!

ROGER: Why do you have your own checking account, Adelfa?

ADELFA: How did you get hold of that?

ROGER: I went to high school with the mailman. We have an arrangement.

ADELFA: An arrangement?

ROGER: Let's just say I make sure I know what goes in and out of this house.

ADELFA: Roger, you yourself told me to have something of mine.

ROGER: Without telling me? I'm hurt! Don't I give you everything you want? What are you planning to do with it?

ADELFA: Save money. Go back to school. I thought if I saved enough of my own, you'd change your mind.

ROGER: You're lying.

ADELFA: I'm not.

ROGER: Dangerous combination, Adelfa. Money and women. A woman gets hold of a little cash and she's out the door. Joanne was smart as a whip. She even went to NYU. I used to like smart women. Until I found out how exhausting they are. They never shut the fuck up! You're not going anywhere. I bought you. I bought your family. I bought your house. And everything in it. Your brother is still alive. Every fuckin' breath he takes, he takes because of me.

ADELFA: You can't pay me enough for what I do for you.

ROGER: What are you gonna do about it?

ADELFA: I quit!

ROGER: Quit? Quit. And go where?

ADELFA: Do you think I care? You'll never see me again. Who'll put up with you then? I'm one in a million, remember? I'll find work. I have skills. I have two years of college.

ROGER: From the Philippines? We eat people like you.

ADELFA: I was wrong. There's something to be said for poverty. Once you survive it, you can survive anything. And besides, it's the easiest country in the world. I've seen the stuff that's thrown away.

ROGER: I've got your papers. Your passport.

ADELFA: I'll get a lawyer.

ROGER: Lawyers cost money.

ADELFA: I'll get a woman. An American woman.

ROGER: You don't know Americans. We like our victims blameless.

ADELFA: It's a big country. I'll find someone who'll understand.

ROGER: Your brother will die.

ADELFA: And you'll be wishing you were dead. Every day—all alone and lonely in this sad, empty house where nothing ever breaks.

ROGER: Stop it! You're scaring me!

ADELFA: Three thousand. A month.

ROGER: What?

ADELFA: A raise. Three thousand a month. Not one penny less! I mean it.

ROGER: You're crazy! You're nuts! [*A beat.*] A thousand.

ADELFA: Twenty-five hundred.

ROGER: Fifteen hundred.

ADELFA: Twenty-two hundred.

ROGER: Two thousand.

ADELFA: I'll take it.

ROGER: But on my own terms.

ADELFA: What are they?

ROGER: Only one phone call a month. And I have to be there. No letters.

[ADELFA *sits down.*]

ROGER: Adelfa—

ADELFA: No. Wait. Wait.

[*A heavy silence descends on them both as if she's listening to something finally break inside her.*]

ADELFA: How did I get here?

ROGER: Do you accept my terms or not?

ADELFA: Yes.

ROGER: And one more thing.

ADELFA: It doesn't matter now.

ROGER: Find it in your heart to love me exactly the way I am.

ADELFA: Give me the money, and I love you already.

[ADELFA *moves Down Left and puts on a new sarong. She takes down her hair. Lights change. A year passes. During the following voiceovers,* ADELFA *enters and exits carrying shopping bags, trying on different shoes, clothes, handbags, each change of accessory, costume, as expensive as the next. She is transformed into an expensively groomed woman, perhaps the kind of woman* ROGER *has referred to as "high maintenance."*]

ROSARIO: What's the IBM computer for? I don't even want to turn it on. I'm scared it would explode. And I can't sleep on that new mattress. It's like sleeping on air. So I'm still sleeping on the floor.

ANGHEL: Dr. Valdes told me you sent him a shopping list. Adelfa, Inay doesn't need a 25-inch Sony TV. Or the AT&T phone. What kind of a telephone is it we have to read a book to call someone? The fridge. She goes to the market every day. She gets everything fresh.

ROSARIO: Mondays, the whole neighborhood comes for the *Bay Watch*. Tuesday, all the women in the *baranggay*[19] watch *Oprah*. Wednesday nobody comes because it's only the *Seinfeld*. We don't understand that show. What's so funny? Last night, Ronnie, Lola and I watched *The Exorcist* on the Toshiba. We all fell asleep.

ANGHEL: My dear Adelfa, don't send any more things. It just confuses Inay. They're just things, Adelfa. Stuff. And it always comes down to this. Someday they'll be garbage.

ROSARIO: The landowner is going to write you a letter. Something about the building. About a condo. What's a condo?

ANGHEL: You've done it, Adelfa. Congratulations. You should be proud of yourself. Roger's check comes regularly every month now straight from the bank.

ROSARIO: Did you hear about Lola Epang? When they closed Smokey Mountain, the government built another garbage dump at Payatas. So she moved there. There was a trash slide on July 20. The garbage fell on the squatters. They all died. Look how this letter is smudged with tears. We are so blessed, Adelfa. God has been so good to us.

ANGHEL: Your letters are few and far between. You don't call anymore. I'd rather hear you lie than not hear from you at all. My nightmares remain silent, shadows without sound. Something is wrong.

ROSARIO: Ronald Reagan Rampatanta asked me to marry him. Ronnie has been a great comfort to me. And he's still a good dancer. He's teaching me the hip hop!

ANGHEL: Your cell phone has been disconnected. I call your home but it's always

---

[19] (Tag.) The smallest unit of a town.

Kuya Roger who answers. I can't share my fears with Inay. I don't want her to worry…So this is what it means losing you— sorrow in my bones, and in my heart, the burden of its weight…

ROSARIO: I catch myself singing all the time. As if I've always lived here in this place…Smokey Mountain…was it all a nightmare?

ANGHEL: I sat up all night waiting for your call. It never came. You didn't even send a card. You've never missed my birthday, Adelfa. How can I say this? That day we danced at Smokey. That was the happiest day of my life…

ROSARIO: Who would have thought we'd own a condo…or I'd fall in love again? At my age? A miracle. My life is full of miracles.

ANGHEL: Last night, you appeared in my dreams again. Your face remained in shadow, but this time, I finally heard you, clear as a bell. "Save me…" You said, "Save me." I woke up, screaming. I'm way past the sadness. Now I'm simply afraid. Something has gone terribly wrong. I know that now. And you've chosen not to tell me.

[*Fragments of letters flood the air, overlapping each other as lights go down gradually.*]

ROSARIO: I can't get hold of you. I keep leaving you messages. Have you changed your number? Why don't you call me? Anghel's condition changed all of a sudden. Even Dr. Valdes doesn't understand…

ANGHEL IS VERY SICK CALL US

ANGHEL IS IN A COMA

ANGHEL DIED LAST NIGHT I HAVE NOT HEARD FROM YOU WHY FUNERAL TOMORROW

[*Blackout. In the darkness, a heart-rending wail. A few beats. Lights go up in the memoryscape.* ADELFA *is holding a telegram in her hand.* ROGER *places a batch of letters on the bed.*]

ADELFA: Dead? Kuya Anghel is dead? No! NO! How? Why? Why didn't I know about it?

[ROGER *tries to comfort her, but she resists.*]

ROGER: Now, Honey, take it easy, okay… please. I—I've got some very good reasons—Honey, please understand.

ADELFA: [*She sees the letters on the bed. She pores over them.*] Letters…telegrams… what are you, a monster?

ROGER: I only wanted to make sure you weren't lying to me! I didn't want to lose you. I'm sorry.

ADELFA: You had me, you son of a bitch!

[ADELFA *tears into him, hitting him.* ROGER *doesn't fight back.*]

ADELFA: Come on! Hit me. Hit me back. I'm going to kill you. Angel is dead!

ROGER: Adelfa, I said I'm sorry.

ADELFA: I'm sick and tired of sorry. It's only a word.

[ADELFA *flings a closet open, takes out a suitcase and starts dumping her clothes into the case.*]

ROGER: Where are you going?

ADELFA: Angel is dead. I want to go home, kneel at his grave and ask for his forgiveness.

ROGER: [*Grabbing the suitcase.*] I am your home. [*He turns to hit her.*]

ADELFA: Go ahead. But you better do a good job. This time tomorrow if I can still walk, I'm gone.

ROGER: [*A beat.*] I'll change. I am changing. I am getting better!

[ROGER *picks out a large red envelope from his attache case and gives it to* ADELFA.]

ROGER: It's for you. You see that? I didn't open it, Honey. It came two days ago. Just before the telegram. I was going to give them both to you today. You've got to believe me—

[*She grabs the envelope from his hand and throws it away.*]

ADELFA: It's too late!

ROGER: No, it isn't. I'll go back to the Institute—find that therapist. I'll take the four-week treatment. Adelfa, give me one more chance!

ADELFA: I have nothing left to give you.

ROGER: I know you're very angry right now. I don't blame you. I understand.

ADELFA: I've heard this shit before!

ROGER: I've made your mother happy. I've done some good. You can't take that away from me.

ADELFA: And I've made you happy. We're even.

ROGER: All right. If you want to split, then split. Just don't do it out of anger. Give yourself time to cool off. The most important decisions in life take time, Adelfa. If I fail this time, I'll—I'll let you go. I'll even give you the money to go back home…

ADELFA: I don't believe you.

ROGER: What if the me you love—what if there's a chance of a lifetime without the demons. There's hope here. And where there's hope, there's stars. That's what you said. [*A long silence.*]

ADELFA: I need time. And peace and quiet. Room to think it over. You understand?

ROGER: Yes.

ADELFA: I need to hear myself think.

ROGER: Take all the time you want. I promise to leave you alone. I'll check into a hotel. The place is yours. [*Pause*] I know your heart… your tender, forgiving heart…

You have no idea how much power you have over me. If you leave me, I'll die.

[*Smokey Mountain, 1985.* ANGHEL *is working the trash. This is the Smokey before* ANGHEL *became its "king." He's carrying a large and heavy bag of trash, metal hook in hand poking, stabbing at hardened mounds of debris, face and head covered with cloth, the grime, the soot, the sewage clinging to his skin, his bare arms and legs, his soul.* ADELFA *is seen Downstage, in the present, in Brooklyn. She speaks her lines from where she is.*]

ANGHEL: [*Reading an empty tin can's label.*] A-L-P-O! Alpo… for dogs…. Beef—bacon—! [*He mulls over this, gets it.*] Pambihira. Food for dogs…?

ADELFA: [*Something in the distance, offstage, has caught her eye.*] Kuya! Kuya, look! Charing! The whole family… where are they going, Kuya?

ANGHEL: [*Aloud. Waving.*] Uy, Charing! Suerteng-suerte mo![20] Aba. Ang yabang.[21] She's not even waving back. [*Another whistle.*] Cherry Pie! Now she's waving back. Punieta.

ADELFA: Cherry Pie? What's that?

ANGHEL: A cocktail waitress.

ADELFA: Why is she wearing white?

ANGHEL: It's the only color you can't wear in Smokey.

[ANGHEL, ADELFA *watch in silence.*]

---

[20] (Tag.) You're so lucky!   [21] (Tag.) So proud!

ANGHEL: A whore. But look. The whole family…She doesn't care what people think. She'll do anything to get her family out of here. Even sacrifice herself. You know why? Because she's got a female heart. *Pusong babae…*[*Putting his hand over her heart.*] This. What you've got—right here—that's what makes you special. *Pusong babae,* Adelfa. A female heart beats only for the people it loves.

ADELFA: Is that why Itay left? Because he was a man?

ANGHEL: *Hindi naman.* A female heart is simply a tender heart. And a man can be just as tender as a woman.

ADELFA: I want to be like Mr. Paredes. Mr. Paredes knows so many things!

ANGHEL: Who put that idea in your head? No one from Smokey ever becomes a teacher!

ADELFA: I don't want to be a whore!

ANGHEL: [*laughs.*] Whores make more money!

ADELFA: [*Bursting into tears.*] I don't want to be Cherry Pie!

ANGHEL: *Aba. Ambitiosa.*[22]

ADELFA: Cherry Pie may not live here anymore but she's still living in Smokey!

[ROSARIO *enters.*]

ROSARIO: Anghel!

ANGHEL: *Ano?*

ROSARIO: That meeting with Father Kintanar? Adelfa. Adelfa. She's a Sydney scholar.

ANGHEL: What's that?

ROSARIO: This Sydney gives money to the best pupils in Adelfa's school. Mr. Paredes recommended her. *Kasi* she's number one in her class. We've got to take her off the garbage.

ANGHEL: No, Inay. We can't! Six hands are better than four.

ROSARIO: Think! Think, Anghel. If she does well, she might even end up going to high school. High school!

ANGHEL: High school? *Talaga ba? Ang suerteng-suerte mo,* Adelfa.

ROSARIO: We'll work harder. We'll pick twice as much for as long as our bodies can take it. Adelfa, you're gonna be a salesgirl. At the mall. You've seen them. They're very clean, wear nice shiny shoes and pretty white dresses. They live with their Itay and Inay in rooming houses in Baclaran. You can do it. You're young and pretty and smart… you're the ticket.

[*Lights change. We are back with* ADELFA *in the present, in Brooklyn, picking up letters strewn on the bed, examining each one, and sorting them in date order. As she nears the end of this sorting, she finds the red envelope* ROGER *had just given her, unopened. She picks it up and rips it open. She gives it a quick scan at first, reading a few phrases aloud.*]

ANGHEL: "Last night I finally saw you clearly…walking in a pool of sunlight…caught a glimpse of your face…that same bold look in your eyes…I know now that what I'm going to do is the right thing. Adelfa, we've wrecked our lives to save ourselves. It has to stop. I know Inay and Itay Ronnie will mourn for me deeply, as you will. But when that mourning is over, I want you to be glad. I've stopped taking the medication."

ADELFA: "…I've stopped taking the medication"?

ANGHEL: "Use my life, my last gift to you…"

[22] (Tag.) How ambitious!

ADELFA: … I've stopped taking the medication!

ANGHEL: You have two choices. You can stay with Roger and work it out. Or you can walk away and not look back. Goodbye, my dearest, Adelfa. *Mahal na mahal kita.*[23] Your loving brother, Kuya Angel.

ADELFA: [*Weeping*] *Pusong babae…*it was you all along. You're the one with the female heart!

[*Lights change.* ADELFA *is taking out other letters from the drawers in the bedside table, gathering them together with the letters she had picked up from the bed, now a neat pack in her hand. She stands over the wastebasket.*]

ADELFA: *Basora.*

[*She drops all the letters into the wastebasket. They make a sound as they fall into it. Then she turns around, giving the room one last look.*]

ADELFA: Goodbye, Roger.

BLACKOUT

END OF PLAY

—2000

---

[23] (Tag.) I love you very, very much.

JEWELLE GOMEZ (1948-)

Jewelle Gomez was born in Boston in 1948. Her father, a bartender, and her mother, a nurse, never married, and Gomez was raised by her extended African-American/Native American family, learning to appreciate history and social activism from her great-grandmother, who was born on a reservation in Iowa. She received her bachelor's degree from Northeastern University in 1971 and went on to earn a master's degree from the Columbia University School of Journalism in 1973. Gomez was active in the anti-war and Black liberation movements of the 1960s, and the lesbian-feminist movement of the 1970s. She was an original staff member of Boston's *Say Brother,* one of the first weekly Black television shows in the U.S. Gomez also worked at the Children's Television Workshop and, in the late 1970s, was a stage manager for off-Broadway theaters. She was a founding board member of the Gay and Lesbian Alliance Against Defamation (GLAAD), an original board member of the Open Meadows Foundation and the Astrea Foundation, and a member of the sex-positive Feminist Anti-Censorship Task Force (FACT), which responded to anti-pornography feminism. Gomez has directed grant programs at the New York State Council on the Arts, the San Francisco Arts Commission, and the Horizons Foundation. Her poetry, fiction, and essays have appeared in the *New York Times,* the *Village Voice, Ms., Essence,* and a number of other publications. Her first books, *The Lipstick Papers* (1980) and *Flamingoes and Bears* (1986), were self-published collections of poetry celebrating lesbian life and sexuality. *The Gilda Stories* (1991), which won Lambda Literary Awards for both fiction and science fiction, is a novel that focuses on race, class, and sexual oppression via the story of a Black lesbian vampire who lives from 1850 to 2050. Gomez is also the author of a book of essays entitled *Forty-Three Septembers* (1993), the short fiction collection *Don't Explain* (1998), and the forthcoming novel, *Televised.* She lives in San Francisco.

Don't Explain

Boston 1959

Letty deposited the hot platters on the table effortlessly. She slid one deep-fried chicken, a club steak with boiled potatoes, and a fried porgy plate down her arm as if removing beaded bracelets. Each one landed with a solid clink on the shiny Formica in its appropriate place. The last barely settled before Letty turned back to the kitchen to get Savannah and Skip their lemonade and extra biscuits. Then to put her feet up. Out of the corner of her eye she saw Tip come in the lounge. His huge shoulders, draped in sharkskin, narrowly cleared the doorframe.

Damn! He's early tonight! she thought, but kept going. Tip was known for his extravagance; that's how he'd gotten his nickname. He always sat at Letty's station because they were both from Virginia, although neither had been back in years.

Letty had come up to Boston in 1946 and been waiting tables in the 411 Lounge since '52. She liked the casual community formed around it. The pimps were not big thinkers but good for a laugh; the musicians who played the small clubs around Boston often ate at the 411, providing some glamour—and now and then a jam session. The "business" girls were usually generous and always willing to embroider a wild story. After Letty's mother died there'd been no family to go back to down in Burkeville.

Letty took her newspaper from the locker behind the kitchen and filled a tall glass with the tart grape juice punch for which the cook, Henrietta, was famous.

"I'm going on break, Henrietta. Delia's takin' my station."

She sat in the back booth nearest the kitchen, beside the large blackboard which displayed the menu. When Delia came out of the bathroom, Letty hissed to get her attention. The reddish-brown of Delia's face was shiny with a country freshness that always made Letty feel a little shy.

"What's up, Miss Letty?" Her voice was soft and saucy.

"Take my tables for twenty minutes. Tip just came in."

The girl's already bright smile widened as she started to thank Letty.

"Go 'head, go 'head. He don't like to wait. You can thank me if he don't run you back and forth fifty times."

Delia hurried away as Letty sank into the coolness of the overstuffed booth and removed her shoes. After a few sips of her punch she rested her head on the back of the seat with her eyes closed. The sounds around her were as familiar as her own breathing: squeaking Red Cross shoes[1] as Delia and Vinnie passed, the click of high heels around the bar, the clatter of dishes in the kitchen, and ice cascading into glasses. The din of conversation rose, leveled, and rose again over the jukebox. Letty had not played her record in days, but the words spun around in her head as if they were on a turntable:

> *Right or wrong don't matter*
> *When you're with me sweet*
> *Hush now, don't explain*
> *You're my joy and pain.*[2]

---

[1] Comfortable shoes worn by nurses, waitresses, etc.

[2] Lyrics to "Don't Explain," a signature song of jazz singer Billie Holiday (1915-1959).

Letty sipped her cool drink; sweat ran down her spine, soaking into the nylon uniform. July weather promised to give no breaks, and fans were working overtime like everybody else.

She saw Delia cross to Tip's table again. In spite of the dyed red hair, no matter how you looked at her, Delia was still a country girl. Long, self-conscious, shy—she was bold only because she didn't know any better. She'd moved up from Anniston with her cousin a year before and landed the job at the 411 immediately. She was full of fun, but that didn't get in the way of her working hard. Sometimes she and Letty shared a cab going uptown after work, when Delia's cousin didn't pick them up in her green Pontiac.

Letty caught Tip eyeing Delia as she strode on tight-muscled legs back to the kitchen. That lounge lizard! Letty thought to herself. Letty had trained Delia how to balance plates, how to make tips, and how to keep the customer's hands on the table. She was certain Delia would have no problem putting Tip in his place. In the year she'd been working at the 411, Delia hadn't gone out with any of the bar flies, though plenty had asked. Letty figured that Delia and her cousin must run with a different crowd. They talked to each other sporadically in the kitchen or during their break, but Letty never felt that wire across her chest like Delia was going to ask her something she couldn't answer.

She closed her eyes again for the few remaining minutes. The song was back in her head, and Letty had to squeeze her lips together to keep from humming aloud. She pushed her thoughts onto something else. But when she did she always stumbled upon Maxine. Letty opened her eyes. When she'd quit working at Salmagundi's and come to the 411 she'd promised herself never to think about any woman like that again. She didn't know why missing Billie so much brought it all back to her.

She heard the bartender, Duke, shout a greeting from behind the bar to the owner as he walked in. Aristotle's glance skimmed his dimly lit domain before he made his way to his stool, the only one at the bar with a back. That was Letty's signal. No matter that it was her break: she knew white people didn't like to see their employees sitting down, especially with their shoes off. By the time he was settled near the door, Letty was up, her glass in hand, and on her way through the kitchen's noisy swinging door.

"You finished your break already?" Delia asked.

"Ari just come in."

"Uh oh, let me git this steak out there. Boy, he sure is nosy!"

"Who, Tip?"

"Yeah. He ask me where I live, who I live with, where I come from, like he supposed to know me!"

"Well, just don't take nothing he say to heart and you'll be fine. And don't take no rides from him!"

"Yeah. He asked if he could take me home after I get off. I told him me and you had something to do." Letty was silent as she sliced the fresh bread and stacked it on plates for the next orders.

"My cousin's coming by, so it ain't a lie, really. She can ride us."

"Yeah," Letty said as Delia giggled and turned away with her platter.

Vinnie burst through the door like she always did, breathless and bossy. "Ari up there, girl! You better get back on station."

Letty drained her glass with deliberation, wiped her hands on her thickly starched white apron, and walked casually past Vinnie as if she'd never spoken. She heard Henrietta's soft chuckle float behind her. She went over to Tip, who was digging into the steak like his life depended on devouring it before the plate got dirty.

"Everything all right tonight?" Letty asked, her ample brown body towering over the table.

"Yeah, baby, it's all right. You ain't working this side no more?"

"I was on break. My feet can't wait for your stomach, you know."

Tip laughed. "*Break.* What you need a break for, big and healthy as you is!"

"We all get old, Tip. But the feet get old first, let me tell you that!"

"Not in my business, baby. Why you don't come on and work for me and you ain't got to worry 'bout your feet."

Letty sucked her teeth loudly, the exaggeration a part of the game they'd played over the years. "Man, I'm too old for that mess!"

"You ain't too old for me."

"Ain't nobody too old for *you*. Or too young, neither, looks like."

"Where you and that gal goin' tonight?"

"To a funeral," Letty responded dryly.

"Aw, woman, get on away from my food!" The gold cap on his front tooth gleamed from behind his greasy lips when he laughed. Letty was pleased. Besides giving away money, Tip liked to hurt people. It was better when he laughed.

The kitchen closed at 11:00. Delia and Letty slipped off their uniforms in the tiny bathroom and were on their way out the door by 11:15. Delia looked even younger in her knife-pleated skirt and white cotton blouse. Letty felt old in her slacks and long-sleeved shirt as she stood on Columbus Avenue in front of the neon 411 sign. The movement of car headlights played across her face, which was set in exhaustion. The dark green car pulled up and they got in quietly, both anticipating Sunday, the last night of their work week.

Delia's cousin was a stocky woman who looked about thirty-five, Letty's age. She never spoke much. Not that she wasn't friendly. She always greeted Letty with a smile and laughed at Delia's stories about the customers. Just close to the chest like me, that's all, Letty often thought. As they pulled up to the corner of Cunard Street, Letty opened the rear door. Delia turned to her and said, "I'm sorry you don't play your record on break no more, Miss Letty. I know you don't want to, but I'm sorry just the same."

Delia's cousin looked back at them with a puzzled expression but said nothing. Letty said goodnight, shut the car door, and turned to climb the short flight of stairs to her apartment. Cunard Street was quiet outside her window, and for once the guy upstairs wasn't blasting his record player. After her bath, Letty lay awake and restless in her bed. The electric fan was pointed at the ceiling, bouncing warm air over her, rustling her sheer nightgown.

Inevitably the strains of Billie Holiday's songs brushed against her, much like the breeze that moved around her. She felt silly when she thought about it, but the melody gripped her like a solid presence. It was more than the music. Billie was her hero. Letty saw Billie as big, like herself, with big hungers and a hard secret she couldn't tell anyone. Two weeks before, when Letty had heard that Lady was dead, sorrow had enveloped her. A door had closed that she could not consciously identify to herself or to anyone. It embarrassed her to think about. Like it did when she remembered how she'd felt about Maxine.

Letty had met Billie soon after she started working at the 411 when the singer had stopped in the club with several musicians on their way back from the Jazz Festival. There the audience, curious to see what a real, live junkie looked like, had sat back waiting for Billie to fall on her face. Instead she'd killed them dead with her liquid voice and rough urgency. Still, in the bar, the young, thin horn player had continued to reassure her: "Billie, you were the show, the whole show!"

Soon the cloud of insecurity receded from her face and it lit up with a center-stage smile. Once convinced, Billie became the show again, loud and commanding. She demanded her food be served up front, at the bar, and sent Henrietta, who insisted on waiting on her personally, back to the kitchen fifteen times. Billie laughed at jokes that Letty could barely hear as she bustled back and forth between the abandoned kitchen and her own tables. The sound of that laugh from the bar penetrated her bones. She'd watched and listened, certain she saw something no one else did. Vulnerability was held at bay, and behind that, a hunger even bigger than the one for food or heroin. Letty found reasons to walk up to the front—to use the telephone, to order a drink she paid for and left in the kitchen—just to catch the scent of her, the scent of sweat and silk emanating from her.

"Hey, baby," Billie said when Letty reached past her to pick up her drink from Duke.

"Henny sure can cook, can't she," Letty responded, hoping to see into Billie's eyes.

"Cook? She in these pots, sister!" the horn player shouted from down the bar, sitting behind his own heaping plateful of food.

Billie laughed, holding a big white napkin in front of her mouth, her eyes watering. Letty enjoyed the sound even though she still sensed something deeper, unreachable.

When Billie finished eating and gathered her entourage to get back on the road, she left a tip, not just for Henrietta but for each of the waitresses and the bartender. Generous just like the "business" girls, Letty was happy to note. She still had the two one-dollar bills in an envelope at the back of her lingerie drawer.

After that, Letty felt even closer to Billie. She played one of the few Lady Day[3] records on the jukebox every night during her break. Everyone at the 411 had learned not to bother her when her song came on. Letty realized, as she lay waiting for sleep, that she'd always felt if she had been able to say or do something that night to make friends with Billie, it might all have been different. The faces of Billie, her former lover Maxine, and Delia blended in her mind in half-sleep. Letty slid her hand along the soft nylon of her gown to rest it between her full thighs. She pressed firmly, as if holding desire inside herself. Letty could have loved her enough to make it better.

Sunday nights at the 411 were generally quiet. Even the pimps and prostitutes used it as a day of rest. Letty came in early to have a drink at the bar and talk with Duke before going to the back to change into her uniform. She saw Delia through the window as the younger woman stepped out of the green Pontiac, looking as if she'd

---

[3] Nickname for Billie Holiday.

just come from Concord Baptist Church. "Satin Doll"[4] played on the jukebox, wrapping the bar in mellow nostalgia for the Sunday dinners they'd serve.

Aristotle let Henrietta close the kitchen early on Sunday, and Letty looked forward to getting done by 9:30 or 10:00 and maybe enjoying some of the evening. When her break time came, she started for the jukebox automatically. She hadn't played anything by Billie in two weeks. Now, looking down at the inviting glare, she knew she still couldn't do it. She punched the buttons that would bring up Jackie Wilson's "Lonely Teardrops" and went to the back booth.

She'd almost dropped off to sleep when she heard Delia whisper her name. Letty opened her eyes and looked up into the girl's smiling face. Her head was haloed in tight, shiny curls.

"Miss Letty, won't you come home with me tonight?"

"What?"

"I'm sorry to bother you, but your break time almost up. I wanted to ask if you'd come over to the house tonight…after work. My cousin'll bring you back home after."

Letty didn't speak. Her puzzled look prompted Delia to start again.

"Sometime on Sunday my cousin's friends from work come over to play cards, listen to music, you know. Nothin' special, just some of the girls from the office building down on Winter Street where she work, cleaning. She, I mean we, thought you might want to come over tonight. Have a drink, play some cards—"

"I don't play cards much."

"Well, not everybody play cards…just talk…sitting around talking. My cousin said you might like to for a change."

Letty wasn't sure she liked the last part—*for a change*—as if they had to entertain an old aunt.

"I really want you to come, Letty. They always her friends, but none of them is my own friends. They all right, I don't mean nothin' against them, but it would be fun to have my own personal friend there, you know?"

Delia was a good girl. Perfect words to describe her, Letty thought, smiling. "Sure, honey. I'd just as soon spend my time with you as lose my money with some fools."

By ten o'clock the kitchen was clean. Once they'd changed out of their uniforms and were out on the street Delia apologized that they had to take a cab uptown. She explained that her cousin and her friends didn't work on Sunday so they were already at home. Letty almost declined, tempted to go home. But she didn't. She stepped into the street and waved down a Red and White cab with brisk, urban efficiency. All the way uptown Delia explained that the evening wasn't a big deal and cautioned Letty not to expect much. "Just a few friends, hanging around, drinking and talking." She was jumpy, and Letty tried to put her at ease. She had not expected her visit would make Delia so anxious.

The apartment was located halfway up Blue Hill Avenue in an area where a few blacks had recently been permitted to rent. They entered a long, carpeted hallway and heard the sounds of laughter and music ringing from the rooms at the far end.

Inside, with the door closed, Delia shed her nervousness. This was clearly her home turf, and Letty couldn't believe she ever really needed an ally to back her up;

---

[4] 1953 hit jazz song, written by Duke Ellington (1899-1974), Billy Strayhorn (1915-1967), and Johnny Mercer (1909-1976).

Delia stepped out of her shoes at the door and walked to the back with her same long-legged gait. They passed a closed door, which Letty assumed to be one of the bedrooms, then came to a kitchen ablaze with light. Food and bottles were strewn across the blue-flecked table top. A counter opened from the kitchen into the dining room, which was the center of activity. Around a large mahogany table sat five women in smoke-filled concentration, playing poker.

Delia's cousin looked up from her cards with the same slight smile she displayed when she picked them up at work. Here it seemed welcoming, not guarded as it did in those brief moments in her car. She wore brown slacks and a matching sweater. The pink, starched points of her shirt collar peeked out at the neck.

Delia crossed to her and kissed her cheek lightly. Letty looked around the table to see if she recognized anyone. The women all seemed familiar in the way that city neighbors can, but Letty was sure she hadn't met any of them before. Delia introduced them, and each acknowledged Letty without diverting her attention from her cards: Karen, a short, round woman with West Indian bangles almost up to her elbow; Betty, who stared intently at her cards through thick eyeglasses encased in blue cat's-eye frames; Irene, a big, dark woman with long black hair and a gold tooth in front. Beside her sat Myrtle, who was wearing army fatigues and a gold Masonic ring on her pinkie finger. She said hello in the softest voice Letty had ever heard. Hovering over her was Clara, a large redbone woman whose hair was bound tightly in a bun at the nape of her neck. She spoke with a delectable Southern accent that drawled her "How're you doin'" into a full paragraph draped around an inquisitive smile.

Letty felt Delia tense again. Then she pulled Letty by the arm toward the French doors behind the players. There was a small den with a desk, some books, and a television set. Through the second set of glass doors was a living room. At the record player was an extremely tall, brown-skinned woman. She bent over the wooden cabinet searching for the next selection, oblivious to the rest of the gathering. Two women sat on the divan in deep conversation punctuated with constrained laughter.

"Maryalice, Sheila, Dolores...this is Letty. She work with me at the 411."

They looked up at her quickly, smiled, then went back to their preoccupations. Two of them resumed their whispered conversation; the other returned to the record collection. Delia directed Letty back toward the foyer and the kitchen.

"Come on, let me get you a drink. You know, I don't even know what you drink!"

"Delia?" Her cousin's voice reached them over the counter, just as they stepped into the kitchen. "Bring a couple of beers back when you come, okay?"

"Sure, babe." Delia went to the refrigerator and pulled out two bottles. "Let me just take these in. I'll be right back."

"Go 'head, I can take care of myself in this department, girl." Letty surveyed the array of bottles on the table. Delia went to the dining room and Letty mixed a Scotch and soda. She poured slowly as the reality settled on her. These women were friends, perhaps lovers, like she and Maxine had been. The name she'd heard for women like these burst inside her head: *bulldagger*. Letty flinched, angry she had let it in, angry that it frightened her. "Ptuh!" She blew through her teeth as if spitting the word back at the air.

She did know these women, Letty thought, as she stood at the counter looking out at the poker game. They were oblivious to her, except for Terry. Letty finally remembered that that was Delia's cousin's name.

As Letty took her first sip, Terry called over to her, "We gonna be finished with this hand in a minute, Letty, then we can talk." This time her face was filled by a large grin.

"Take your time," Letty said. She went out through the foyer door and around to the living room. She walked slowly on the carpet and adjusted her eyes to the light, which was a bit softer. The tall woman, Maryalice, had just put a record on the turntable and sat down on a love seat across from the other two women. Letty stood in the doorway a moment before the tune began:

> *Hush now, don't explain*
> *Just say you'll return*
> *I'm glad you're back*
> *Don't explain…*

Letty was stunned. She realized the song sounded different among these women: Billie sang just to them. Letty watched Maryalice sitting with her long legs stretched out tensely in front of her. She was wrapped in her own thoughts, her eyes closed. She appeared curiously disconnected after what had clearly been a long search for this record. Letty watched her face as she swallowed several times. Then Letty sat beside her. They listened to the music while the other two women spoke in low voices.

Maryalice didn't move when the song was over.

"I met her once," Letty said.

"I beg your pardon?"

"Kinda met her. At the 411 Lounge where me and Delia work."

"Naw!" Maryalice said as she sat up.

"She was just coming back from a gig."

"Honestly?" Maryalice's voice caught with excitement.

"She just had dinner—smothered chicken, potato salad, green beans, side of stewed tomatoes, and an extra side of cornbread."

"Big eater."

"Child, everybody is when Henrietta's cooking. Billie was…," Letty searched for the words, "she was sort of stubborn."

Maryalice laughed. "You know, that's kinda how I pictured her."

"I figure she had to be stubborn to keep going," Letty said. "And not stingy, either!"

"Yeah," Maryalice said, enjoying the confirmation of her image of Billie.

Letty rose from the sofa and went to the record player. Delia stood tentatively watching from the doorway of the living room. Letty picked up the arm of the phonograph and replaced it at the beginning of the record. Letty noticed the drops of moisture on Maryalice's lashes, but she relaxed as Letty settled onto the seat beside her. They listened to Billie together, for the first time.

—1998

WENDY ROSE (1948-)

Born Bronwen Elizabeth Edwards in Oakland, California, to a Hopi father and a mother of European and Miwok descent, poet Wendy Rose had a difficult childhood. Alienated from both of her parents, she dropped out of high school and spent time on the streets as an adolescent. Rose attended various community colleges in the San Francisco Bay Area, eventually receiving an M.A. in Anthropology from the University of California, Berkeley, in 1978, and completing Ph.D. coursework in anthropology. During this period, she also began publishing her poetry. Rose's books include *Hopi Roadrunner Dancing* (1973, published under the pseudonym Chiron Khanshendel), *Long Division: A Tribal History* (1976), *Academic Squaw: Reports to the World from the Ivory Tower* (1977), *Lost Copper* (1980), *What Happened When the Hopi Hit New York* (1982), *The Halfbreed Chronicles & Other Poems* (1985), *Going to War with All My Relations* (1993), *Bone Dance: New and Selected Poems, 1965-1992* (1994), and *Itch Like Crazy* (2002). Several strong themes have emerged over Rose's long career, including autobiographically-inspired grappling with what it means to be a "mixed-blood" woman in a racially divided world and lyrical critiques of the anthropological distortions and exploitations of Native American culture. Rose is also a visual artist, and she has illustrated both her own work and the work of other writers. She has coordinated the American Indian Studies program at Fresno City College since 1984.

Three Thousand Dollar Death Song

Nineteen American Indian skeletons from Nevada...
valued at $3,000.

> *—invoice received at a museum*
> *as normal business, 1975*

Is it in cold hard cash? the kind
that dusts the insides of mens' pockets
laying silver-polished surface along the cloth.
Or in bills? papering the wallets of they
who thread the night with dark words. Or   5
checks? paper promises weighing the same
as words spoken once on the other side
of the mown grass and dammed rivers
of history. However it goes, it goes.
Through my body it goes   10
assessing each nerve, running its edges
along my arteries, planning ahead
for whose hands will rip me
into pieces of dusty red paper,
whose hands will smooth or smatter me   15
into traces of rubble. Invoiced now
it's official how our bones are valued
that stretch out pointing to sunrise
or are flexed into one last fetal bend,
that are removed and tossed about,   20
cataloged, numbered with black ink
on newly-white foreheads.

As we were formed to the white soldier's voice,
so we explode under white students' hands.
Death is a long trail of days   25
in our fleshless prison.
From this distant point
we watch our bones auctioned
with our careful quillwork,
beaded medicine bundles, even the bridles   30
of our shot-down horses. You who have priced us,
you who have removed us—at what cost?
What price the pits
where our bones share
a single bit of memory,   35
how one century has turned
our dead into specimens,
our history into dust,
our survivors into clowns.
Our memory might be catching, you know.   40
Picture the mortars, the arrowheads, the labrets
shaking off their labels like bears suddenly awake
to find the seasons ended while they slept.
Watch them touch each other, measure reality,
march out the museum door!   45
Watch as they lift their faces
and smell about for us. Watch our bones rise
to meet them and mount the horses once again!
The cost then will be paid
for our sweetgrass-smelling having-been   50
in clam-shell beads and steatite, dentalia
and woodpecker scalp, turquoise and copper,
blood and oil, coal and uranium,
children, a universe
of stolen things.   55

—1980

Loo-Wit[1]

The way they do
this old woman
no longer cares
what others think
but spits her black tobacco   5
any which way
stretching full length
from her bumpy bed.
Finally up

---

[1] [*Author's note.*] Cowlitz Indian name for Mount St. Helens in Washington.

she sprinkles   10
ashes on the snow,
cold buttes
promising nothing
but the walk
of winter.   15
Centuries of cedar
have bound her
to earth,
huckleberry ropes
lay prickly   20
on her neck.
Around her
machinery growls,
snarls and ploughs
great patches   25
of her skin.
She crouches
in the north,
her trembling
the source   30
of dawn.
Light appears
with the shudder
of her slopes,
the movement   35
of her arm.
Blackberries unravel,
stones dislodge.
It's not as if
they weren't warned.   40

She was sleeping
but she heard
the boot scrape,
the creaking floor,
felt the pull of the blanket   45
from her thin shoulder.
With one free hand
she finds her weapons
and raises them high;
clearing the twigs   50
from her throat
she sings, she sings,
shaking the sky
like a blanket about her
Loo-Wit sings and sings and sings!

—1983

NTOZAKE SHANGE (1948-   )

Paulette Linda Williams was born in Trenton, New Jersey, the oldest of four children. As a child of relative affluence, she was exposed by her parents to a wide variety of arts and culture, and she grew up with a strong sense of connection to African-American and African cultures. However, she also experienced racial prejudice firsthand when, in 1956, her family moved to St. Louis, Missouri, and she was among the first black children to attend St. Louis' newly desegregated schools, where she encountered a good deal of racial hostility. Shange earned her B.A. from Barnard College in 1970, but her years there were marked with struggle: an early marriage failed and she made several suicide attempts. It was while she was in graduate school at the University of Southern California (where she received her M.A. in 1973) that she took on the name Ntozake Shange, which means "she who comes with her own things and walks like a lion" in the Xhosa dialect of the Zulu language.

Shange achieved a major success with her first full-scale work for the stage, *for colored girls who have considered suicide/when the rainbow is enuf* (1975), a "choreopoem," (the form was invented by Shange) that combines dance, poetry, and elements of traditional dramatic characterization. Both her theatrical work and her poetry are marked by an unwillingness to conform to conventional modes of representation and a drive to invent forms that can give voice to the experience of African-American women. Other plays by Shange include *Boogie Woogie Landscapes* (1978), *Spell #7* (1979), and *Three Views of Mt. Fuji* (1987). She is also the author of three novels and several volumes of poetry, including *Nappy Edges* (1978), *A Daughter's Geography* (1983), and *The Love Space Demands: A Continuing Saga* (1992). Shange has won many awards for her work, including Obie and Outer Critic Circle Awards for *for colored girls....* She was honored as a "Living Legend" by the National Black Theatre Festival in 1993.

About Atlanta[1]

cuz he's black & poor
he's disappeared
the name waz lost   the games werent played
nobody tucks him in at night/ wipes traces
of cornbread & syrup from his fingers   5
the corners of his mouth
cuz he's black & poor/ he's not
just gone
disappeared one day
& his blood soaks up what's awready red   10
in atlanta

no ropes this time   no tar & feathers
werent no parades of sheets fires & crosses
nothing/ no signs

empty bunkbeds   15
mothers who forget & cook too much on sundays
just gone/ disappeared
cuz he's black & poor   he's gone
took a bus/ never heard from again

---

[1] The poem is referring to a series of murders, often referred to as the "Atlanta Child Murders," that occurred in Atlanta, Georgia, from 1979 to 1981.

but somebody heard a child screaming   20
  & went right on ahead
children disappearing/ somewhere in the woods/ decaying
just gone/ disappeared/ in atlanta

mothers are always at the window watching
caint nobody disappear right in fronta yr eyes   25
but who knows what we cd do
when we're black & poor
we aint here no way/ how cd we disappear?
who wd hear us screaming?

say it was a man with a badge & some candy   30
say it was a man with a badge & some money
say it was a maniac
cd be more n sticks n stones
gotta be more than stars n stripes
children caint play war when they in one.   35
caint make believe they dyin/ when they are
caint imagine what they'll be/ cuz they wont
just gone/ disappeared

oh mary dont you weep & dont you moan
oh mary dont you weep & dont you moan   40
HOLLAR i say HOLLAR
cuz we black & poor & we just disappear

we cant find em   jesus cant find em
til they seepin in soil
father reekin in soil   45
they bones bout disappeared
they lives aint never been
bleeding where the earth's awready red
dyin cuz they took a bus
& mama caint see that far out her window   50
the front porch dont go from here to eternity
& they gone
just disappeared

but somebody heard them screaming
somebody crushed them children's bones   55
somebody's walkin who shd be crawling
for killing who aint never been
cuz we black & poor/ we just be gone

no matter how sweet/ no matter how quiet
just gone   60
be right back ma
going to the store mother dear
see ya later nana
call ya when i get there mama

& the soil runs red with our dead in atlanta   65
cuz somebody went right on ahead
crushing them lil bones/ strangling them frail wails
cuz we black & poor
our blood soaks up dirt
while we disappearing   70

mamas keep looking out the door
saying "i wonder where is my child/ i wonder
          where is my child"
she dont turn the bed back cuz she knows
we black & poor   75
& we just disappear/ be gone

oh mary dont you weep & dont you moan
oh mary dont you weep & dont you moan
i wonder where is my child
i wonder where is my child   80

nothing/ no signs
in atlanta

—1983

We Need a God Who Bleeds Now

we need a god who bleeds now
a god whose wounds are not
some small male vengeance
some pitiful concession to humility
a desert swept with dryin marrow in honor of the lord   5

we need a god who bleeds
spreads her lunar vulva & showers us in shades of scarlet
thick & warm like the breath of her
our mothers tearing   to let us   in
this place breaks open   10
like our mothers bleeding
the planet is heaving   mourning our ignorance
the moon tugs the seas
to hold her/ to hold her
embrace swelling hills/ i am   15
not wounded i am bleeding to life

we need a god who bleeds now,
whose wounds are not the end of anything

—1983

LESLIE MARMON SILKO (1948-   )

Leslie Marmon was born in Albuquerque, New Mexico, and grew up on the Laguna Pueblo Reservation in northern New Mexico. Of mixed Laguna, European, and Mexican origin, she attended Bureau of Indian Affairs schools as a child before attending Catholic school in Albuquerque. She went on to earn a B.A. from the University of New Mexico in 1969; while there she married and had her first child. She then studied law briefly, but after she received a National Endowment for the Arts discovery grant for short fiction, she left law school to pursue a career in writing. Her first book was a collection of poetry entitled *Laguna Woman* (1974); however, it was the publication of her first novel, *Ceremony* (1977), that established Silko's literary reputation. Silko's Laguna heritage figures significantly in her writing, as evidenced in her emphasis on traditional stories and modes of storytelling, as well as a woman-centeredness that reflects the matrilineal traditions of the Laguna. Much of Silko's poetry and fiction is concerned with tensions between white and Native cultures, which are embodied in mixed-race characters or characters who experience cultural dislocation and alienation. Those themes are central to both *Ceremony* and Silko's later novel, *Almanac of the Dead* (1991), an epic historical tale that weaves together traditional Native myths with conventional fictional narrative. The recipient of a Pushcart Prize for poetry in 1977 and a MacArthur Foundation grant in 1981, among other awards, Silko is widely recognized as a major figure in Native American literature.

Private Property

All Pueblo Tribes have stories about such a person—a young child, an orphan. Someone has taken the child and has given it a place by the fire to sleep. The child's clothes are whatever the people no longer want. The child empties the ashes and gathers wood. The child is always quiet, sitting in its place tending the fire. They pay little attention to the child as they complain and tell stories about one another. The child listens although it has nothing to gain or lose in anything they say. The child simply listens. Some years go by and great danger stalks the village—in some versions of the story it is a drought and great famine, other times it is a monster in the form of a giant bear. And when all the others have failed and even the priests doubt the prayers, this child, still wearing old clothes, goes out. The child confronts the danger and the village is saved. Among the Pueblo people the child's reliability as a narrator is believed to be perfect.

Etta works with the wind at her back. Sand and dust roll down the road. She feels scattered drops of rain and sometimes flakes of snow. What they have been saying about her all these years is untrue. They are angry because she left. Old leaves and weed stalks lie in gray drifts at the corners of the old fence. Part of an old newspaper is caught in the tumbleweeds; the wind presses it into brittle yellow flakes. She rakes the debris as high as her belly. They continue with stories about her. Going away has changed her. Living with white people has changed her. Fragments of glass blink like animal eyes.

The wind pushes the flames deep into the bones and old manure heaped under the pile of dry weeds. The rake drags out a shriveled work shoe and then the sleeve torn from a child's dress. They burn as dark and thick as hair. The wind pushes her off balance. Flames pour around her and catch the salt bushes. The yard burns bare. The sky is the color of stray smoke. The next morning the wind is gone. The ground is crusted with frost and still the blackened bones smolder.

The horses trot past the house before dawn. The sky and earth are the same color then—dense gray of the night burned down. At the approach of the sun, the east horizon bleeds dark blue. Reyna sits up in her bed suddenly and looks out the window at the horses. She has been dreaming she was stolen by Navajos and was taken away in their wagon. The sound of the horses' hooves outside the window had been the wagon horses of her dreams. The white one trots in the lead, followed by the gray. The little sorrel mare is always last. The gray sneezes at their dust. They are headed for the river. Reyna wants to remember this, and gets up. The sky is milky. Village dogs are barking in the distance. She dresses and finds her black wool cardigan. The dawn air smells like rain but it has been weeks since the last storm. The crickets don't feel the light. The mockingbird is in the pear tree. The bare adobe yard is swept clean. A distance north of the pear tree there is an old wire fence caught on gray cedar posts that lean in different directions. Etta has come back after many years to live in the little stone house.

The sound of the hammer had been Reyna's first warning. She blames herself for leaving the old fence posts and wire. The fence should have been torn down years ago. The old wire had lain half-buried in the sand that had drifted around the posts. Etta was wearing men's gloves that were too large for her. She pulled the strands of wire up and hammered fence staples to hold the wire to the posts. Etta has made the fence the boundary line. She has planted morning glories and hollyhocks all along it. She waters them every morning before it gets hot. Reyna watches her. The morning glories and hollyhocks are all that hold up the fence posts anymore.

Etta is watching Reyna from the kitchen window of the little stone house. She fills the coffee pot without looking at the level of water. Reyna is walking the fence between their yards. She paces the length of the fence as if she can pull the fence down with her walking. They had been married to brothers, but the men died long ago. They don't call each other "sister-in-law" anymore. The fire in the cookstove is cracking like rifle shots. She bought a pickup load of pinon wood from a Navajo. The little house has one room, but the walls are rock and adobe mortar two feet thick. The one who got the big house got the smaller yard. That is how Etta remembers it. Their mother-in-law had been a kind woman. She wanted her sons and daughters-in-law to live happily with each other. She followed the old ways. She believed houses and fields must always be held by the women. There had been no nieces or daughters. The old woman stood by the pear tree with the daughters-in-law and gave them each a house, and the yard to divide. She pointed at the little stone house. She said the one who got the little house got the bigger share of the yard. Etta remembers that.

Cheromiah drives up in his white Ford pick-up. He walks to the gate smiling. He wears his big belly over his Levi's like an apron. Reyna is gathering kindling at the woodpile. The juniper chips are hard and smooth as flint. She rubs her hands together although there is no dust. "They came through this morning before it was even daylight." She points in the direction of the river. "They were going down that way." He frowns, then he smiles. "I've been looking for them all week," he says. The old woman shakes her head. "Well, if you hurry, they might still be there." They are his horses. His father-in-law gave him the white one when it was a colt. Its feet are as big around as pie pans. The gray is the sorrel mare's colt. The horses belong to Cheromiah, but the horses don't know that. "Nobody told them," that's what people say and then they laugh. The white horse leans against corral planks until they give way. It steps over low spots in old stone fences. The gray and little sorrel follow.

"The old lady said to share and love one another. She said we only make use of these things as long as we are here. We don't own them. Nobody owns anything." Juanita nods. She listens to both of her aunts. The two old women are quarreling over a narrow strip of ground between the two houses. The earth is hard-packed. Nothing grows there. Juanita listens to her Aunt Reyna and agrees that her Aunt Etta is wrong. Too many years living in Winslow. Aunt Etta returns and she wants to make the yard "private property" like white people do in Winslow. Juanita visits both of her aunts every day. She visits her Aunt Etta in the afternoon while her Aunt Reyna is resting. Etta and Reyna know their grandniece must visit both her aunts. Juanita has no husband or family to look after. She is the one who looks after the old folks. She is not like her brothers or sister who have wives or a husband. She doesn't forget. She looked after Uncle Joe for ten years until he finally died. He always told her she would have the house because women should have the houses. He didn't have much. Just his wagon horses, the house and a pig. He was the oldest and believed in the old ways. Aunt Reyna was right. If her brother Joe were alive he would talk to Etta. He would remind her that this is the village, not Winslow, Arizona. He would remind Etta how they all must share. Aunt Reyna would have more space for her woodpile then.

Most people die once, but "old man Joe he died twice," that's what people said, and then they laughed. Juanita knew they joked about it, but still she held her head high. She was the only one who even tried to look after the old folks. That November, Uncle Joe had been sick with pneumonia. His house smelled of Vicks and Ben-Gay. She checked on him every morning. He was always up before dawn the way all the old folks were. They greeted the sun and prayed for everybody. He was always up and had a fire in his little pot belly stove to make coffee. But that morning she knocked and there was no answer. Her heart was beating fast because she knew what she would find. The stove was cold. She stood by his bed and watched. He did not move. She touched the hand on top of the blanket and the fingers were as cold as the room. Juanita ran all the way to Aunt Reyna's house with the news. They sent word. The nephews and the clansmen came with picks and shovels. Before they went to dress him for burial, they cooked the big meal always prepared for the gravediggers. Aunt Reyna rolled out the tortillas and cried. Joe had always been so good to her. Joe had always loved her best after their parents died.

Cheromiah came walking by that morning while Juanita was getting more firewood. He was dragging a long rope and leather halter. He asked if she had seen any sign of his horses. She shook her head and then she told him Uncle Joe had passed away that morning. Tears came to her eyes. Cheromiah stood quietly for a moment. "I will miss the old man. He taught me everything I know about horses." Juanita nodded. Her arms were full of juniper wood. She looked away toward the southeast. "I saw your gray horse up in the sandhills the other day." Cheromiah smiled and thanked her. Cheromiah's truck didn't start in cold weather. He didn't feel like walking all the way up to the sand hills that morning. He took the road around the far side of the village to get home. It took him past Uncle Joe's place. The pig was butting its head against the planks of the pen making loud smacking sounds. The wagon horses were eating corn stalks the old man had bundled up after harvest for winter feed. Cheromiah wondered which of the old man's relatives was already looking after the livestock. He heard someone chopping wood on the other side of the house. The old man saw him and waved in the direction of the river. "They were down there last evening grazing in the willows." Cheromiah dropped the halter and rope and gestured with both hands. "Uncle Joe! They told me you died! Everyone thinks you are dead! They already cooked the gravediggers lunch!"

From that time on Uncle Joe didn't get up before dawn like he once did. But he wouldn't let them tease Juanita about her mistake. Behind her back, Juanita's cousins and in-laws were saying that she was in such a hurry to collect her inheritance. They didn't think she should get everything. They thought all of it should be shared equally. The following spring, Uncle Joe's wagon horses went down Paguate Hill too fast and the wagon wheel hit a big rock. He was thrown from the wagon and a sheepherder found him. Uncle Joe was unconscious for two days and then he died. "This time he really *is* dead, poor thing," people would say and then they'd smile.

The trouble over the pig started on the day of the funeral. Juanita caught her brother's wife at the pig pen. The wife held a large pail in both hands. The pail was full of a yellowish liquid. There were bones swimming in it. Corn tassels floated like hair. She looked Juanita in the eye as she dumped the lard pail into the trough. The pig switched its tail and made one push through the liquid with its snout. It looked up at both of them. The snout kept moving. The pig would not eat. Juanita had already fed the pigs scraps from the gravediggers' plates. She didn't want her brothers' wives feeding the pig. They would claim, they had fed the pig more than she had. They would say that whoever fed the pig the most should get the biggest share of meat. At butchering time they would show up to collect half. "It won't eat slop," Juanita said, "don't be feeding it slop."

The stories they told about Etta always came back to the same thing.

While the other girls learn cooking and sewing at the Indian School, Etta works in the greenhouse. In the evenings the teacher sits with her on the sofa. They repeat the names of the flowers. She teaches Etta the parts of the flower. On Saturdays while the dormitory matrons take the others to town, Etta stays with the teacher. Etta kneels beside her in the garden. They press brown dirt over the gladiola bulbs. The teacher runs a hot bath for her. The teacher will not let her return to the dormitory until she has cleaned Etta's fingernails. The other girls tell stories about Etta.

The white gauze curtains are breathing in and out. The hollyhocks bend around the fence posts and lean over the wire. The buds are tight and press between the green lips of the sheath. The seed had been saved in a mason jar. Etta found it in the pantry behind a veil of cobwebs. She planted it the length of the fence to mark the boundary. She had only been a child the first time, but she can still remember the colors—reds and yellows swaying above her head, tiny black ants in the white eyes of pollen. Others were purple and dark red, almost black as dried blood. She planted the seeds the teacher had given her. She saved the seeds from the only year the hollyhocks grew. Etta doesn't eat pork. She is thinking about the row of tamarisk trees she will plant along the fence so people cannot see her yard or house. She does not want to spend her retirement with everyone in the village minding her business the way they always have. Somebody is always fighting over something. The years away taught her differently. She knows better now. The yard is hers. They can't take it just because she had lived away from the village all those years. A person could go away and come back again. The village people don't understand fences. At Indian School she learned fences tell you where you stand. In Winslow, white people built fences around their houses, otherwise something might be lost or stolen. There were rumors about her the whole time she lived in Winslow. The gossip was not true. The teacher had written to her all the years Etta was married. It was a job to go to after her husband died. The teacher was sick and old. Etta went because she loved caring for the flowers. It was only a job, but people like to talk. The teacher was sick for a long time before she died.

"What do you want with those things," the clanswoman scolded, "wasting water on something we can't eat." The old woman mumbled to herself all the way across the garden. Etta started crying. She sat on the ground by the hollyhocks she had planted, and held her face. She pressed her fingers into her eyes. The old woman had taken her in. It was the duty of the clan to accept orphans.

Etta tells her she is not coming back from Indian School in the summer. She has a job at school caring for the flowers. She and the clanswoman are cleaning a sheep stomach, rinsing it under the mulberry tree. The intestines are coiled in a white enamel pan. They are bluish gray, the color of the sky before snow. Strands of tallow branch across them like clouds. "You are not much good to me anyway. I took you because no one else wanted to. I have tried to teach you, but the white people at that school have ruined you. You waste good water growing things we cannot eat."

The first time Etta returned from Winslow for a visit, Reyna confided there was gossip going on in the village. Etta could tell by the details that her sister-in-law was embroidering stories about her too. They did not speak to each other after that. People were jealous of her because she had left. They were certain she preferred white people. But Etta spoke only to the teacher. White people did not see her when she walked on the street.

The heat holds the afternoon motionless. The sun does not move. It has parched all color from the sky and left only the fine ash. The street below is empty. Down the long dim hall there are voices in English and, more distantly, the ticking of a clock. The room is white and narrow. The shade is pulled. It pulses heat the texture of pearls. The water in the basin is the color of garnets. Etta waits in a chair beside the bed. The sheets are soaked with her fever. She murmurs the parts of the flowers—she whispers that the bud is swelling open, but that afternoon was long ago.

Ruthie's husband is seeing that other woman in the cornfield. The cornfield belongs to her and to her sister, Juanita. Their mother left it to both of them. In the morning her husband walks to the fields with the hoe on his shoulder. Not long after, the woman appears with a coal bucket filled with stove ashes. The woman follows the path toward the trash pile, but when she gets to the far corner of the cornfield she stops. When she thinks no one is watching she sets the bucket down. She gathers up the skirt of her dress and steps over the fence where the wire sags.

Ruthie would not have suspected anything if she had not noticed the rocks. He was always hauling rocks to build a new shed or corral. But this time there was something about the colors of the sandstone. The reddish pink and orange yellow looked as if they had been taken from the center of the sky as the sun went down. She had never seen such intense color in sandstone. She had always remembered it being shades of pale yellow or peppered white-colors for walls and fences. But these rocks looked as if rain had just fallen on them. She watched her husband. He was unloading the rocks from the old wagon and stacking them carefully next to the woodpile. When he had finished it was dark and she could not see the colors of the sandstone any longer. She thought about how good-looking he was, the kind of man all the other women chase.

Reyna goes with them. She takes her cane but carries it ready in her hand like a rabbit club. Her grandnieces have asked her to go with them. Ruthie's husband is carrying on with another woman. The same one as before. They are going after them together—the two sisters and the old aunt. Ruthie told Juanita about it first. It was their mother's field and now it is theirs. If Juanita had a husband he would work there too. "The worst thing is them doing it in the cornfield. It makes the corn sickly, it makes the beans stop growing. If they want to do it they can go down to the trash and lie in the tin cans and broken glass with the flies," that's what Reyna says.

They surprise them lying together on the sandy ground in the shade of the tall corn plants. Last time they caught them together they reported them to the woman's grandmother, but the old woman didn't seem to care. They told that woman's husband too. But he has a job in Albuquerque, and men don't bother to look after things. It is up to women to take care of everything. He is supposed to be hoeing weeds in their field, but instead he is rolling around on the ground with that woman, killing off all their melons and beans.

Her breasts are long and brown. They bounce against her like potatoes. She runs with her blue dress in her hand. She leaves her shoes. They are next to his hoe. Ruthie stands between Juanita and Aunt Reyna. They gesture with their arms and yell. They are not scolding him. They don't even look at him. They are scolding the rest of the village over husband-stealing and corn that is sickly. Reyna raps on the fence post with her cane. Juanita calls him a pig. Ruthie cries because the beans won't grow. He kneels to lace his work shoes. He kneels for a long time. His fingers move slowly. They are not talking to him. They are talking about the other woman. The red chili stew she makes is runny and pale. They pay no attention to him. He goes back to hoeing weeds. Their voices sift away in the wind. Occasionally he stops to wipe his forehead on his sleeve. He looks up at the sky or over the sand hills. Off in the distance there is a man on foot. He is crossing the big sand dune above the river. He is dragging a rope. The horses are grazing on yellow rice grass at the foot of the dune. They are down wind from him. He inches along, straining to crouch over his own stomach. The big white horse whirls suddenly, holding its tail high. The gray half-circles and joins it, blowing loudly through its nostrils. The little sorrel mare bolts to the top of the next dune before she turns.

Etta awakens and the yard is full of horses. The gray chews a hollyhock. Red petals stream from its mouth. The sorrel mare watches her come out the door. The white horse charges away, rolling his eyes at her nightgown. Etta throws a piece of juniper from the woodpile. The gray horse presses hard against the white one. They tremble in the corner of the fence, strings of blue morning glories trampled under their hooves. Etta yells and the sorrel mare startles, crowding against the gray. They heave forward against the fence, and the posts make slow cracking sounds. The wire whines and squeaks. It gives way suddenly and the white horse stumbles ahead tangled in wire. The sorrel and the gray bolt past, and for an instant the white horse hesitates, shivering at the wire caught around its forelegs and neck. Then the white horse leaps forward, rusty wire and fence posts trailing behind like a broken necklace.

—1983

DOROTHY ALLISON (1949-)

Dorothy E. Allison was born in Greenville, South Carolina, to an unmarried teen mother. The physical and sexual abuse Allison suffered at the hands of her stepfather, as well as the poverty of the family and the strength of its women, form dominant themes in Allison's writing, notably the short story collection *Trash* (1988), the novels *Bastard Out of Carolina* (1992) and *Cavedweller* (1998), and the memoir *Two or Three Things I Know for Sure* (1995). Allison has also published a volume of poetry, *The Women Who Hate Me* (1983, expanded and reissued in 1991), and a collection of essays, *Skin: Talking About Sex, Class, and Literature* (1994). Allison was the first member of her family to graduate from high school. She then received a bachelor's degree from Florida Presbyterian College in 1971 and studied anthropology at the master's level at the New School for Social Research. While in college she became active in feminist and lesbian political movements, focusing particularly on projects related to domestic violence, child care, and women's health. She began writing for feminist, lesbian, and gay/lesbian newspapers in the 1970s, and over the next decades, she became a leading feminist voice in support of butch/femme and sex-radical politics. Allison has won numerous awards for her writing, including two Lambda Literary Awards, the American Library Association Prize for Lesbian and Gay Writing, and the Robert Penn Warren Award for Fiction. *Bastard Out of Carolina* was a finalist for the National Book Award. Allison lives in Northern California with her partner and their son.

Don't Tell Me You Don't Know

I came out of the bathroom with my hair down wet on my shoulders. My Aunt Alma, my mama's oldest sister, was standing in the middle of Casey's dusty hooked rug looking like she had just flown in on it, her grey hair straggling out of its misshapen bun. For a moment I was so startled I couldn't move. Aunt Alma just stood there looking around at the big bare room with its two church pews bracketing the only other furniture—a massive pool table. I froze while the water ran down from my hair to dampen the collar of the oversized tuxedo shirt I used for a bathrobe.

"Aunt Alma," I stammered, "well...welcome...."

"You really live here?" she breathed, as if, even for me, such a situation was quite past her ability to believe. "Like this?"

I looked around as if I were seeing it for the first time myself, shrugged and tried to grin. "It's big," I offered, "lots of space, four porches, all these windows. We get along well here, might not in a smaller place." I looked back through the kitchen to Terry's room with its thick dark curtains covering a wall of windows. Empty. So was Casey's room on the other side of the kitchen. It was quiet and still, with no one even walking through the rooms overhead.

"Thank God," I whispered to myself. Nobody else was home.

Aunt Alma turned around slowly and stepped over to the mantel with the old fly-spotted mirror over it. She pushed a few of her loose hairs back and then laid her big rattan purse up by a stack of fliers Terry had left there, brushing some of the dust away first.

"My God," she echoed, "dirtier than we ever lived. Didn't think you'd turn out like this."

I shrugged again, embarrassed and angry and trying not to show it. Well hell, what could I do? I hadn't seen her in so long. She hadn't even been around that last year I'd lived with Mama, and I wasn't sure I particularly wanted to see her now. But why was she here anyway? How had she found me?

I closed the last two buttons on my shirt and tried to shake some of the water out of my hair. Aunt Alma watched me through the dark spots of the mirror, her mouth set in an old familiar line. "Well," I said, "I didn't expect to see you." I reached up to push hair back out of my eyes. "You want to sit down?"

Aunt Alma turned around and bumped her hip against the pool table. "Where?" One disdainful glance rendered the pews for what they were—exquisitely uncomfortable even for my hips. Her expression reminded me of my Uncle Jack's jokes about her, about how she refused to go back to church till they put in rocking chairs.

"No rocking chairs here," I laughed, hoping she'd laugh with me. Aunt Alma just leaned forward and rocked one of the balls on the table against another. Her mouth kept its flat, impartial expression. I tried gesturing across the pool table to my room and the big waterbed outlined in sunlight and tree shade from the three windows overlooking it.

"It's cleaner in there," I offered, "it's my room. This is our collective space." I gestured around.

"Collective," my aunt echoed me again, but the way she said the word expressed clearly her opinion of such arrangements. She looked toward my room with its narrow cluttered desk and stacks of books, then turned back to the pool table as by far the more interesting view. She rocked the balls again so that the hollow noise of the thump resounded against the high, dim ceiling.

"Pitiful," she sighed, and gave me a sharp look, her washed-out blue eyes almost angry. Two balls broke loose from the others and rolled idly across the matted green surface of the table. The sunlight reflecting through the oak leaves outside made Aunt Alma's face seem younger than I remembered it, some of the hard edge eased off the square jaw.

"Your mama is worried about you."

"I don't know why." I turned my jaw to her, knowing it would remind her of how much alike we had always been, the people who had said I was more her child than my mama's. "I'm fine. Mama should know that. I spoke to her not too long ago."

"How long ago?"

I frowned, mopped at my head some more. Two months, three, last month? "I'm not sure…Reese's birthday. I think it was Reese's birthday."

"Three months." My aunt rocked one ball back and forth across her palm, a yellow nine ball. The light filtering into the room went a shade darker. The -9- gleamed pale through her fingers. I looked more closely at her. She looked just as she had when I was thirteen, her hair grey in that loose bun, her hands large and swollen, her body straining the seams of the faded print dress. She'd worn her hair short for a while, but it was grown long again now, and the print dress under her coat could have been any dress she'd worn in the last twenty years. She'd gotten old, suddenly, after the birth of her eighth child, but since then she seemed not to change at all. She looked now as if she would go on forever—a worn stubborn woman who didn't care what you saw when you looked at her.

I drew breath in slowly, carefully. I knew from old experience to use caution in dealing with any of my aunts, and this was the oldest and most formidable. I'd seen grown men break down and cry when she'd kept that look on them too long; little children repent and swear to change their ways. But I'd also seen my other aunts stare her right back, and like them I was a grown woman minding my own business. I had a right to look her in the eye, I told myself. I was no wayward child, no half-drunk, silly man. I was her namesake, my mama's daughter. I had to be able to look her in the eye. If I couldn't, I was in trouble, and I didn't want that kind of trouble here, 500 miles and half a lifetime away from my aunts and the power of their eyes.

Slow, slow, the balls rocked one against the other. Aunt Alma looked over at me levelly. I let the water run down between my breasts, looked back at her. My mama's sister. I could feel the tears pushing behind my eyes. It had been so long since I'd seen her or any of them! The last time I'd been to Old Henderson Road had been years back. Aunt Alma had stood on that sagging porch and looked at me, memorizing me, both of us knowing we might not see each other again. She'd moved her mouth and I'd seen the pain there, the shadow of the nephew behind her—yet another one she was raising since her youngest son, another cousin of mine, had run off and left the girl who'd birthed that boy. The pain in her eyes was achingly dear to me, the certain awful knowledge that measured all her children and wrenched her heart.

Something wrong with that boy, my uncles had laughed.

Yeah, something. Dropped on his head one too many times, you think?

I think.

My aunt, like my mama, understood everything, expected nothing, and watched her own life like a terrible fable from a Sunday morning sermon. It was the perspective that all those women shared, the view that I could not, for my life, accept. I believed, I believed with all my soul that death was behind it, that death was the seed and the fruit of that numbed and numbing attitude. More than anything else, it was my anger that had driven me away from them, driven them away from me—my unpredictable, automatic anger. Their anger, their hatred, always seemed shielded, banked and secret, and because of that—shameful. My uncles were sudden, violent, and daunting. My aunts wore you down without ever seeming to fight at all. It was my anger that my aunts thought queer, my wild raging temper they respected in a boy and discouraged in a girl. That I slept with girls was curious, but not dangerous. That I slept with a knife under my pillow and refused to step aside for my uncles was more than queer. It was crazy.

Aunt Alma's left eye twitched, and I swallowed my tears, straightened my head, and looked her full in the face. I could barely hold myself still, barely return her look. Again those twin emotions, the love and the outrage that I'd always felt for my aunt, warred in me. I wanted to put out my hand and close my fingers on her hunched, stubborn shoulder. I wanted to lay my head there and pull tight to her, but I also wanted to hit her, to scream and kick and make her ashamed of herself. Nothing was clean between us, especially not our love.

Between my mama and Aunt Alma there were five other sisters. The most terrible and loved was Bess, the one they swore had always been so smart. From the time I was eight Aunt Bess had a dent in the left side of her head—a shadowed dent that emphasized the twitch of that eye, just like the twitch Aunt Alma has, just like the twitch I sometimes get, the one they tell me is nerves. But Aunt Bess wasn't born with that twitch as we were, just as she wasn't born with that dent. My uncle, her husband, had come up from the deep dust on the road, his boots damp from the river, picking up clumps of dust and making mud, knocking it off on her steps, her screen door, her rug, the back rung of a kitchen chair. She'd shouted at him, "Not on my clean floor!" and he'd swung the bucket, river-stained and heavy with crawfish. He'd hit her in the side of the head—dented her into a lifetime of stupidity and half-blindness. Son of a bitch never even said he was sorry, and all my childhood he'd laughed at her, the way she'd sometimes stop in the middle of a sentence and grope painfully for a word.

None of *them* had told me that story. I had been grown and out of the house before one of the Greenwood cousins had told it so I understood, and as much as I'd hated him then, I'd raged at them more.

"You let him live?" I'd screamed at them. "He did that to her and you did nothing! You did nothing to him, nothing for her."

"What'd you want us to do?"

My Aunt Grace had laughed at me. "You want us to cut him up and feed him to the river? What good would that have done her or her children?"

She'd shaken her head, and they had all stared at me as if I were still a child and didn't understand the way the world was. The cold had gone through me then, as if the river were running up from my bowels. I'd felt my hands curl up and reach, but there was nothing to reach for. I'd taken hold of myself, my insides, and tried desperately to voice the terror that was tearing at me.

"But to leave her with him after he did that, to just let it stand, to let him get away with it." I'd reached and reached, trying to get to them, to make them feel the wave moving up and through me. "It's like all of it, all you let them get away with."

"Them?" My mama had watched my face as if afraid of what she might find there. "Who do you mean? And what do you think we could do?"

I couldn't say it. I'd stared into mama's face, and looked from her to all of them, to those wide, sturdy cheekbones, those high, proud eyebrows, those set and terrible mouths. I had always thought of them as mountains, mountains that everything conspired to grind but never actually broke. The women of my family were all I had ever believed in. What was I if they were not what I had shaped them in my own mind? All I had known was that I had to get away from them—all of them—the men who could do those terrible things and the women who would let it happen to you. I'd never forgiven any of them.

It might have been more than three months since I had talked to Mama on the telephone. It had been far longer than that since I had been able to really talk to any of them. The deepest part of me didn't believe that I would ever be able to do so. I dropped my eyes and pulled myself away from Aunt Alma's steady gaze. I wanted to reach for her, touch her, maybe cry with her, if she'd let me.

"People will hurt you more with pity than with hate," she'd always told me. "I can hate back, or laugh at them, but goddamn the son of a bitch that hands me pity."

No pity. Not allowed. I reached to rock a ball myself.

"Want to play?" I tried looking up into her eyes again. It was too close. Both of us looked away.

"I'll play myself." She set about racking up the balls. Her mouth was still set in that tight line. I dragged a kitchen stool in and sat in the doorway out of her way, telling myself I had to play this casually, play this as family, and wait and see what the point was.

"Where's Uncle Bill?" I was rubbing my head again and trying to make conversation.

"What do you care? I don't think Bill said ten words to you in your whole life." She rolled the rack forward and back, positioning it perfectly for the break. "'Course he didn't say many more to anybody else either." She grinned, not looking at me, talking as if she were pouring tea at her own kitchen table. "Nobody can say I married that man for his conversation."

She leaned into her opening shot, and I leaned forward in appreciation. She had a great stance, her weight centered over her massive thighs. My family runs to heavy women, gravy-fed working women, the kind usually seen in pictures taken at mining disasters. Big women, all of my aunts move under their own power and stalk around telling everybody else what to do. But Aunt Alma was the prototype, the one I had loved most, starting back when she had given us free meals in the roadhouse she'd run for a while. It had been one of those bad times when my stepfather had been out of work and he and Mama were always fighting. Mama would load us all in the Pontiac and crank it up on seventy-five cents worth of gas, just enough to get to Aunt Alma's place on the Eustis Highway. Once there, we'd be fed on chicken gravy and biscuits, and Mama would be fed from the well of her sister's love and outrage.

You tell that bastard to get his ass out on the street. Whining don't make money. Cursing don't get a job…

Bitching don't make the beds and screaming don't get the tomatoes planted. They had laughed together then, speaking a language of old stories and older jokes.

You tell him.

I said.

Now girl, you listen to me.

The power in them, the strength and the heat! How could anybody not love my mama, my aunts? How could my daddy, my uncles, ever stand up to them, dare to raise hand or voice to them? They were a power on the earth.

I breathed deep, watching my aunt rock on her stance, settling her eye on the balls, while I smelled chicken gravy and hot grease, the close thick scent of love and understanding. I used to love to eat at Aunt Alma's house, all those home-cooked dinners at the roadhouse; pinto beans with peppers for fifteen, nine of them hers. Chow-chow[1] on a clean white plate passed around the table while the biscuits passed the other way. My aunt always made biscuits. What else stretched so well? Now those starch meals shadowed her loose shoulders and dimpled her fat white elbows.

She gave me one quick glance and loosed her stroke. The white ball punched the center of the table. The balls flew to the edges. My sixty-year-old aunt gave a grin

---

[1] A spicy Southern relish made with cabbage, peppers, okra, and other vegetables in a vinegar base.

that would have scared piss out of my Uncle Bill, a grin of pure, fierce enjoyment. She rolled the stick in fingers loose as butter on a biscuit, laughed again, and slid her palms down the sides of polished wood, while the anger in her face melted into skill and concentration.

I rocked back on my stool and covered my smile with my wet hair. Goddamn! Aunt Alma pushed back on one ankle, swung the stick to follow one ball, another, dropping them as easily as peas on potatoes. Goddamn! She went after those balls like kids on a dirt yard, catching each lightly and dropping them lovingly. Into the holes, move it! Turning and bracing on ankles thickened with too many years of flour and babies, Aunt Alma blitzed that table like a twenty-year-old hustler, not sparing me another glance.

Not till the eighth stroke did she pause and stop to catch her breath.

"You living like this—not for a man, huh?" she asked, one eyebrow arched and curious.

"No," I shrugged, feeling more friendly and relaxed. Moving like that, aunt of mine I wanted to say, don't tell me you don't understand.

"Your mama said you were working in some photo shop, doing shit work for shit money. Not much to show for that college degree, is that?"

"Work is work. It pays the rent."

"Which ought not to be much here."

"No," I agreed, "not much. I know," I waved my hands lightly, "it's a wreck of a place, but it's home. I'm happy here. Terry, Casey and everybody—they're family."

"Family." Her mouth hardened again. "You have a family, don't you remember? These girls might be close, might be important to you, but they're not family. You know that." Her eyes said more, much more. Her eyes threw the word *family* at me like a spear. All her longing, all her resentment of my abandonment was in that word, and not only hers, but Mama's and my sisters' and all the cousins' I had carefully not given my new address.

"How about a beer?" I asked. I wanted one myself. "I've got a can of Pabst in the icebox."

"A glass of water," she said. She leaned over the table to line up her closing shots.

I brought her a glass of water. "You're good," I told her, wanting her to talk to me about how she had learned to play pool, anything but family and all this stuff I so much did not want to think about.

"Children," she stared at me again. "What about children?" There was something in her face then that waited, as if no question were more important, as if she knew the only answer I could give.

Enough, I told myself, and got up without a word to get myself that can of Pabst. I did not look in her eyes. I walked into the kitchen on feet that felt suddenly unsteady and tender. Behind me, I heard her slide the cue stick along the rim of the table and then draw it back to set up another shot.

Play it out, I cursed to myself, just play it out and leave me alone. Everything is so simple for you, so settled. Make babies. Grow a garden. Handle some man like he's just another child. Let everything come that comes, die that dies; let everything go where it goes. I drank straight from the can and watched her through the doorway. All my uncles were drunks, and I was more like them than I had ever been like my aunts.

Aunt Alma started talking again, walking around the table, measuring shots and not even looking in my direction. "You remember when ya'll lived out on Greenlake Road? Out on that dirt road where that man kept that old egg-busting dog? Your mama couldn't keep a hen to save her life till she emptied a shell and filled it again with chicken shit and baby piss. Took that dog right out of himself when he ate it. Took him right out of the taste for hens and eggs." She stopped to take a deep breath, sweat glittering on her lip. With one hand she wiped it away, the other going white on the pool cue.

"I still had Annie then. Lord, I never think about her anymore."

I remembered then the last child she had borne, a tiny girl with a heart that fluttered with every breath, a baby for whom the doctors said nothing could be done, a baby they swore wouldn't see six months. Aunt Alma had kept her in an okra basket and carried her everywhere, talking to her one minute like a kitten or a doll and the next minute like a grown woman. Annie had lived to be four, never outgrowing the vegetable basket, never talking back, just lying there and smiling like a wise old woman, dying between a smile and a laugh while Aunt Alma never interrupted the story that had almost made Annie laugh.

I sipped my beer and watched my aunt's unchanging face. Very slowly she swung the pool cue up and down, not quite touching the table. After a moment she stepped in again and leaned half her weight on the table. The 5-ball became a bird murdered in flight, dropping suddenly into the far right pocket.

Aunt Alma laughed out loud, delighted. "Never lost it," she crowed. "Four years in the roadhouse with that table set up in the back. Everyone of them sons of mine thought he was going to make money on it. Lord those boys! Never made a cent." She swallowed the rest of her glass of water.

"But me," she wiped the sweat away again. "I never would have done it for money. I just loved it. Never went home without playing myself three or four games. Sometimes I'd set Annie up on the side and we'd pretend we was playing. I'd tell her when I was taking her shots. And she'd shout when I'd sink 'em. I let her win most every time."

She stopped, put both hands on the table, closed her eyes.

"'Course, just after we lost her, we lost the roadhouse." She shook her head, eyes still closed. "Never did have anything fine that I didn't lose."

The room was still, dust glinted in the sunlight past her ears. She opened her eyes and looked directly at me.

"I don't care," she began slowly, softly. "I don't care if you're queer or not. I don't care if you take puppydogs to bed, for that matter, but your mother was all my heart for twenty years when nobody else cared what happened to me. She stood by me. I've stood by her and I always thought to do the same for you and yours. But she's sitting there, did you know that? She's sitting there like nothing's left of her life, like...like she hates her life and won't say shit to nobody about it. She wouldn't tell me. She won't tell me what it is, what has happened."

I sat the can down on the stool, closed my own eyes, dropped my head. I didn't want to see her. I didn't want her to be there. I wanted her to go away, disappear out of my life the way I'd run out of hers. Go away, old woman. Leave me alone. Don't talk to me. Don't tell me your stories. I an't a baby in a basket, and I can't lie still for it.

"You know. You know what it is. The way she is about you. I know it has to be you—something about you. I want to know what it is, and you're going to tell me. Then you're going to come home with me and straighten this out. There's a lot I an't never been able to fix, but this time, this thing, I'm going to see it out. I'm going to see it fixed."

I opened my eyes and she was still standing there, the cue stick shiny in her hand, her face all flushed and tight.

"Go," I said and heard my voice, a scratchy, strangling cry in the big room. "Get out of here."

"What did you tell her? What did you say to your mama?"

"Ask her. Don't ask me. I don't have nothing to say to you."

The pool cue rose slowly, slowly till it touched the right cheek, the fine lines of broken blood vessels, freckles, and patchy skin. She shook her head slowly. My throat pulled tighter and tighter until it drew my mouth down and open. Like a shot the cue swung. The table vibrated with the blow. Her cheeks pulled tight, the teeth all a grimace. The cue split, and broke. White dust rose in a cloud. The echo hurt my ears while her hands rose up as fists, the broken cue in her right hand as jagged as the pain in her face.

"Don't you say that to me. Don't you treat me like that. Don't you know who I am, what I am to you? I didn't have to come up here after you. I could have let it run itself out, let it rest on your head the rest of your life, just let you carry it—your mama's life. YOUR MAMA'S LIFE, GIRL. Don't you understand me? I'm talking about your mama's life."

She threw the stick down, turned away from me, her shoulders heaving and shaking, her hands clutching nothing. "I an't talking about your stepfather. I an't talking about no man at all. I'm talking about your mama sitting at her kitchen table, won't talk to nobody, won't eat, won't listen to nothing. What'd she ever ask from you? Nothing. Just gave you your life and everything she had. Worked herself ugly for you and your sister. Only thing she ever hoped for was to do the same for your children, someday to sit herself back and hold her grandchildren on her lap...."

It was too much. I couldn't stand it.

"GODDAMN YOU!" I was shaking all over. "CHILDREN! All you ever talk about—you and her and all of you. Like that was the end-all and be-all of everything. Never mind what happens to them once they're made. That don't matter. It's only the getting of them. Like some goddamned crazy religion. Get your mother a grandchild and solve all her problems. Get yourself a baby and forget everything else. It's what you were born for, the one thing you can do with no thinking about it at all. Only I can't. To get her a grandchild, I'd have to steal one!"

I was wringing my own hands, twisting them together and pulling them apart. Now I swung them open and slapped down at my belly, making my own hollow noise in the room.

"No babies in there, aunt of mine, and never going to be. I'm sterile as a clean tin can. That's what I told Mama, and not to hurt her. I told her because she wouldn't leave me alone about it. Like you, like all of you, always talking about children, never able to leave it alone." I was walking back and forth now, unable to stop myself from talking. "Never able to hear me when I warned her to leave it be. Going on and on till I thought I'd lose my mind."

I looked her in the eye, loving her and hating her, and not wanting to speak, but hearing the words come out anyway. "Some people never do have babies, you know. Some people get raped at eleven by a stepfather their mama half-hates but can't afford to leave. Some people then have to lie and hide it 'cause it would make so much trouble. So nobody will know, not the law and not the rest of the family. Nobody but the women supposed to be the ones who take care of everything, who know what to do and how to do it, the women who make children who believe in them and trust in them, and sometimes die for it. Some people never go to a doctor and don't find out for ten years that the son of a bitch gave them some goddamned disease."

I looked away, unable to stand how grey her face had gone.

"You know what it does to you when the people you love most in the world, the people you believe in—cannot survive without believing in—when those people do nothing, don't even know something needs to be done? When you cannot hate them but cannot help yourself? The hatred grows. It just takes over everything, eats you up and makes you somebody full of hate."

I stopped. The roar that had been all around me stopped, too. The cold was all through me now. I felt like it would never leave me. I heard her move. I heard her hip bump the pool table and make the balls rock. I heard her turn and gather up her purse. I opened my eyes to see her moving toward the front door. That cold cut me then like a knife in fresh slaughter. I knew certainly that she'd go back and take care of Mama, that she'd never say a word, probably never tell anybody she'd been here. 'Cause then she'd have to talk about the other thing, and I knew as well as she that however much she tried to forget it, she'd really always known. She'd done nothing then. She'd do nothing now. There was no justice. There was no justice in the world.

When I started to cry it wasn't because of that. It wasn't because of babies or no babies, or pain that was so far past I'd made it a source of strength. It wasn't even that I'd hurt her so bad, hurt Mama when I didn't want to. I cried because of the things I hadn't said, didn't know how to say, cried most of all because behind everything else there was no justice for my aunts or my mama. Because each of them to save their lives had tried to be strong, had become, in fact, as strong and determined as life would let them. I and all their children had believed in that strength, had believed in them and their ability to do anything, fix anything, survive anything. None of us had ever been able to forgive ourselves that we and they were not strong enough, that strength itself was not enough.

Who can say where that strength ended, where the world took over and rolled us all around like balls on a pool table? None of us ever would. I brought my hands up to my neck and pulled my hair around until I clenched it in my fists, remembering how my aunt used to pick up Annie to rub that baby's belly beneath her chin—Annie bouncing against her in perfect trust. Annie had never had to forgive her mama anything.

"Aunt Alma, wait. Wait!"

She stopped in the doorway, her back trembling, her hands gripping the doorposts. I could see the veins raised over her knuckles, the cords that stood out in her neck, the flesh as translucent as butter beans cooked until the skins come loose. Talking to my mama over the phone, I had not been able to see her face, her skin, her stunned and haunted eyes. If I had been able to see her, would I have ever said those things to her?

"I'm sorry."

She did not look back. I let my head fall back, rolled my shoulders to ease the painful clutch of my own muscles. My teeth hurt. My ears stung. My breasts felt hot and swollen. I watched the light as it moved on her hair.

"I'm sorry. I would…I would…anything. If I could change things, if I could help…."

I stopped. Tears were running down my face. My aunt turned to me, her wide pale face as wet as mine. "Just come home with me. Come home for a little while. Be with your mama a little while. You don't have to forgive her. You don't have to forgive anybody. You just have to love her the way she loves you. Like I love you. Oh girl, don't you know how we love you!"

I put my hands out, let them fall apart on the pool table. My aunt was suddenly across from me, reaching across the table, taking my hands, sobbing into the cold dirty stillness—an ugly sound, not softened by the least self-consciousness. When I leaned forward, she leaned to me and our heads met, her grey hair against my temple brightened by the sunlight pouring in the windows.

"Oh, girl! Girl, you are our precious girl."

I cried against her cheek, and it was like being five years old again in the road-house, with Annie's basket against my hip, the warmth in the room purely a product of the love that breathed out from my aunt and my mama. If they were not mine, if I was not theirs, who was I? I opened my mouth, put my tongue out, and tasted my aunt's cheek and my own. Butter and salt, dust and beer, sweat and stink, flesh of my flesh.

"Precious," I breathed back to her.

"Precious."

—1988

JANICE GOULD (1949-   )

Janice Gould was born in San Diego, California, and grew up in Berkeley during the civil rights era. Gould, who is of Konkow/Maidu descent, draws on her experiences as a Native lesbian in both her poetry and her scholarly work. She earned her M.A. from the University of California, Berkeley, and her Ph.D. from the University of New Mexico. The author of three poetry collections, *Beneath My Heart: Poetry* (1990), *Earthquake Weather: Poems* (1996), and *Alphabet* (1996), and the co-editor (with Dean Radar) of *Speak to Me Words: Essays on Contemporary American Indian Poetry* (2003), Gould is the recipient of a fellowship from the Ford Foundation, a National Endowment of the Arts literary fellowship, and an Astraea award for poetry from the Lesbian Writers Fund.

My Father

I have tried to understand
what makes me afraid, wondering
what my sisters and I will do
with the body of my father

when he dies. 5
While in his seventies
he changed his sex,
becoming a woman
like us.

As a man, my father was not beautiful. 10
The skin on his chest was fish white,
he was ruddy at the neck,
his muscles were stringy.
The veins showed on the backs of his hands.
Standing, he gave no pose of strength, 15
nothing stern, nothing possessive.
He never wished to take up space.
Of the two, my mother was the angrier:
her curses brought my father to shame.
I remember his response to her, 20
the set line of his mouth,
his lips pressed firmly together.

As a woman, is my father beautiful?
Sometimes in the morning
he calls me long distance. 25
His voice is softer.
I know it's the voice he uses as Cynthia.
He asks how I am.
I want to say, "I am trying
to deal with my fear of you. 30
If it weren't for that,
I'd be fine."

In the letters he wrote me
after my mother died,
he said, "When you last came home, 35
I'm sure you noticed
I've changed. I have been taking hormones
these last few years.
It must be no surprise."

He wrote, "Now that I am a woman 40
I like to go dancing.
One night Eduardo walked me to my car.
As we stood there, Eduardo wanted to hug me.
I allowed him to put his arms around me.
Suddenly he was feeling me up, 45
his hands on my breasts.
It was a strange sensation.
I liked it very much.
I don't know if I want to see him again."

Those letters! 50

I threw them on the floor.
I wanted to stomp on them.
"Your mother," he wrote,
"got the notion when you were young
that you were not normal.   55
Perhaps it was because
you hated to wear dresses.
She took you to the pediatrician one day,
remarking that if he found anything wrong with you
she would kill you,   60
then kill herself. Of course,
after the doctor poked and prodded,
he declared there was absolutely
nothing wrong with you."

"Your mother," he wrote again,   65
"was no saint. Your cousin Elaine
was not your cousin at all
but a half sister by an Indian father,
your mother's lover.
I agreed to raise her as my daughter,   70
but your mother was so hard on the poor girl
she ran away. Your mother would never
acknowledge her as her own."

"Don't tell your sisters any of this,"
he begged. "It must remain a secret."   75

O, my father,
father I never knew,
father who never was
yet was my only father,
who do you imagine I am?   80

Would my father remember the time
I tried to run away from home?
Up as early as him,
my suitcase already packed
and placed on the dark front porch,   85
I caught the first bus downtown.
He never even knew that I left.
Later he found me at the Greyhound station,
bus ticket in hand.
"Let's go home," he said.   90
"She hates me," I said.
"I know," he replied.

Then I wept.
I wanted him to hug me,
but he stood, embarrassed,   95
his arms at his sides.

"Please," he whispered,
"don't make a scene in public."

What will my sisters and I do
on the day of your death? 100
Where will you be?
At home,
or in the apartment you rented
in that city we do not know?
Will someone be with you? 105
You have always been so alone.
Will your death come in the fall
or the spring?
Will it be when the hills
have turned green in California? 110
Will the pear orchards be in blossom?
Will you die on the interstate
near a fallow field
where blackbirds have settled
because it is evening? 115

But I don't want to think about it.
Whom will we tell?
What will we tell them?

"No one will be able to tell the difference,"
my father wrote. "I will be anatomically perfect."

—1996

The Sixties

1.

When the fire hoses were turned
on the Negro citizens
of those southern towns—
on mourners, protesters,
human beings— 5
the spray blew men, women,
and children off their feet.
Bodies rolled helplessly
on the pavement,
while the white men who shot them down 10
laughed. "We'll wash those vermin
down the river and out to sea."
They were pleased with the humiliation.

Miles away in California
I watched on TV, 15
and tasted a pure hatred.
I was nothing

if not passionate.
But I had to be careful
not to show too much,   20
or I risked being taunted
by my mother who called me
"nigger-lover."
I remember seeing on her lips
the spittle of contempt.   25

When the churches were bombed
·and protesters beaten,
when the lynched bodies
were cut from trees,
and the men who did the lynching   30
sat smirking in the knowledge
they would go free,
I tasted pure bile,
the vinegar of muted dissent,
the salt of fugitive tears.   35
A firestorm of rage
built in me
as I watched my mother
take Communion on Sundays
and afterwards leave the church,   40
high and mighty,
like the Indian Princess
she imagined herself to be.

2.
When the conflagrations started
in Detroit and Watts,   45
my mother triumphed.
The towns were in blazes,
the looters shot
through shattered windows
of store-fronts and houses.   50
The damned "niggers,"
so arrogant and lawless,
were getting what they deserved!
How then could I condone those people
who didn't care about rule or order,   55
those thieves, rapists,
welfare artists?

Dr. King[1] had been shot,
Medgar Evers,[2] and Malcolm X.[3]

---

[1] Martin Luther King, Jr. (1929-1968), civil rights leader assassinated in Memphis, Tennessee.
[2] Medgar Evers (1925-1963), civil rights organizer shot in his driveway in Jackson, Mississippi.
[3] Malcolm X (1925-1965), born Malcolm Little, African-American Muslim minister and activist who was assassinated as he was giving a speech at the Audobon Ballroom in Manhattan.

The white men who controlled things   60
were still in power.
In Viet Nam the war was raging.
Every day I was more frightened
as I felt a riotous resistance
fist in my heart,   65
the stench of burning tar
and asphalt pour down my throat.
What are you? she'd ask.
A communist?
A lesbian?   70
A damned subversive?

I endured her hatred,
her contradictions. After church
she wanted to slap me silly
because I was sassy and unrepentant.   75
I said I wanted justice.

When the flames of antipathy
raced down the hall in our house
and beat on the door of my room,
when even self-laceration   80
did nothing to stifle those words
so carefully chosen to destroy me,
I would tip down the brandy
and imagine myself lying in a snowy meadow,
winking back at the pure cold points of fire   85
that greeted me from afar.

—1996

JESSICA HAGEDORN (1949-   )

Jessica Hagedorn was born in the Santa Mesa section of Manila (the Philippines). She moved with her mother to San Francisco at the age of thirteen, where she was influenced by the San Francisco Beat and post-Beat literary scenes, as well as the ethnic arts movements of the 1970s. Hagedorn studied acting at the American Conservatory Theater, but the limited roles available to young women of color led her to writing, which she has called her "salvation." Kenneth Rexroth mentored Hagedorn in her early years as a poet and published her poems in the collection *Four Young Women: Poems* (1973). Hagedorn then published two collections of poetry and fiction: *Dangerous Music* (1975) and *Pet Food and Tropical Apparitions* (1981), which won an American Book Award. During this period, she formed a band called the West Coast Gangster Choir (renamed the Gangster Choir upon her move to New York City in 1978). Her 1990 novel *Dogeaters* was a critical and commercial success, and it is one of the most widely taught Filipino-American texts. She has published two more novels, *The Gangster of Love* (1996) and *Dream Jungle* (2003), and has also created works of poetry, music, performance art, video art, and drama (in 1998 she adapted *Dogeaters* into a play, which was staged at the Joseph Papp Theater in New York City). Hagedorn has collaborated with many performance artists, including Thulani Davis, Ntozake Shange, Laurie Carlos, Robbie McCauley, and Han Ong. Her familiarity with music and performance art can be seen in her poetic style, which has oral, musical, and rhythmic qualities.

Canto de Nada

her name is nada
daughter of ainu[1] and t'boli[2]
igorot[3] and sioux
sister to inca and zulu

born from the mouth of a tree   5
the lullaby of joe loco[4]
and mongo
turquoise eye
the lullaby of pattie labelle
and the bluebells[5]   10
flowers of her smile
the strut   the style

she is the punk
the dancing girl
the brand new bag   15
purple and red
the brand new bag
the sweetness
the lullaby of herself
the riff of a biwa[6]   20
the daughter of a sorceress
the gong
the dragon lady's baby

she is the punk
the dancing girl   25
la cucaracha   who can even
get up from her own o.d.

every night the color
of her hair
she is the song   30
soul sister number one
the brand new bag
her jewels are as loud
as her love

---

[1] An ethnic group on the Japanese island of Hokkaido.
[2] An indigenous group from South Mindanao, Philippines.
[3] People of the Cordillera region on the Philippine island of Luzon.

[4] José Estevez (1921-1988), American pianist who popularized the mambo and other Latin rhythms in the U.S.
[5] 1960s girl group.
[6] A Japanese short-necked, fretted lute.

her name is nada   35
mother to rashid
koumiko   carmen miranda[7]
ylang-ylang   ruby delicious
she is the cocaine princess
with the hundred dollar nose   40
gettin higher because she got
to aim for the stars

she is the star
she is the city
flaunting sequins   45
and butterflies
she is peru   mindanao
shanghai

the divine virgin
waitin for a trick   50
on the borderline
between emeryville
and oakland

at noon on sunday
at noon on monday   55
at noon   hail mary
full of grace

she is nada   all music
she is nothing   all music
she is the punk   all music   60
the dancing girl   all music

she is nada   nothing
she is the real thing

and in her womb
one could sleep   65
                for
                    days

—1972

Sorcery

there are some people i know
whose beauty
is a crime.
who make you so crazy
you don't know   5
whether to throw yourself

---

[7] Carmen Miranda (1909-1955), Brazilian singer and actress.

at them
or kill them.
which makes
for permanent madness.   10
which could be
bad for you.
you better be on the lookout
for such circumstances.

stay away   15
from the night.
they most likely lurk
in corners of the room
where they think
they being inconspicuous   20
but they so beautiful
an aura
gives them away.

stay away
from the day.   25
they most likely
be walking
down the street
when you least
expect it   30
trying to look
ordinary
but they so fine
they break your heart
by making you dream   35
of other possibilities.

stay away
from crazy music.
they most likely
be creating it.   40
cuz when you're that beautiful
you can't help
putting it out there.
everyone knows
how dangerous   45
that can get.

stay away
from magic shows.
especially those
involving words.   50
words are very
tricky things.

everyone knows
words
the most common   55
instruments of
illusion.

they most likely
be saying them,
breathing poems   60
so rhythmic
you can't help
but dance.
and once
you start dancing   65
to words
you might never
stop.

—1975

Ming the Merciless[8]

dancing on the edge / of a razor blade
ming / king of the lionmen
sing / bring us to the planet
of no return…

king of the lionmen   5
come dancing in my tube
sing, ming, sing…
blink sloe-eyed phantasy
and touch me where
there's always hot water   10
in this house

o flying angel
o pterodactyl
your rocket glides
like a bullet   15

you are the asian nightmare
the yellow peril
the domino theory
the current fashion trend

ming, merciless ming,   20
come dancing in my tube
the silver edges of your cloak
slice through my skin
and king vulgar's cardboard wings

---

[8] Villain in the Flash Gordon comics, series, and films.

flap-flap in death   25
(for you)

o ming, merciless ming,
the silver edges of your cloak
cut hearts in two
the blood red dimensions   30
that trace american galaxies

you are the asian nightmare
the yellow peril
the domino theory
the current fashion trend   35

sing, ming, sing…
whistle the final notes
of your serialized abuse
cinema life
cinema death   40
cinema of ethnic prurient interest

o flying angel
o pterodactyl
your rocket glides
like a bullet   45
and touches me where
there's always hot water
in this house

                                                                              —1981

The Song of Bullets

Formalized
by middle age
we avoid crowds
but still
love music.   5

Day after day
with less surprise
we sit
in apartments
and count   10
the dead.

Awake,
my daughter croons
her sudden cries
and growls   15
my new language.
While she sleeps

we memorize
a list of casualties:

The photographer's brother   20
the doctor is missing.
Or I could say:
"Victor's brother Oscar
has been gone for two years…
It's easier for the family   25
to think of him dead."

Victor sends
a Christmas card
from El Salvador:
"Things still the same."   30

And there are others
who don't play
by the rules—
someone else's brother
perhaps mine   35
languishes in a hospital;
everyone's grown tired
of his nightmares
and pretends
he's not there.   40

Someone else's father
perhaps mine
will be executed
when the time comes.
Someone else's mother   45
perhaps mine
telephones incessantly
her husband is absent
her son has gone mad
her lover has committed suicide   50
she's a survivor
who can't appreciate
herself.

The sight
of my daughter's   55
pink and luscious flesh
undoes me.
I fight
my weakening rage
I must remember   60
to commit
those names to memory
and stay angry.

Friends send postcards:
"Alternating between hectic   65
social Manila life & rural wonders
of Sagada…on to Hong Kong and Bangkok—
Love…"

Assassins cruise the streets
in obtrusive limousines   70
sunbathers idle
on the beach

War is predicted
in five years
ten years   75
any day now
I always thought
it was already happening

snipers and poets locked
in a secret embrace   80
the country
my child may never see

a heritage
of women in heat
and men   85
skilled at betrayal

dancing
to the song
of bullets.

—1993

LE LY HAYSLIP (1949-   )

Le Ly Hayslip was born in the village of Ky La, Vietnam, the seventh child in a peasant
farm family. Hayslip's autobiography *When Heaven and Earth Changed Places* (1989; co-written
with Jay Wurts) is perhaps the best-known account of the U.S. war in Vietnam from the
perspective of a Vietnamese writer. Thematizing survival, this autobiography traces Hayslip's
childhood and adolescence in a Vietnamese village torn by war, her move to Da Nang and
Saigon after she is suspected by the Vietcong of betrayal, and her eventual move to the United
States with her American husband. Director Oliver Stone based his 1993 film *Heaven and
Earth* on this autobiography and its sequel, *Child of War, Woman of Peace* (1993). Co-written
with her son James, the second autobiography focuses on her life after her arrival in the U.S.
in 1970, and on the years after her first return to Vietnam. Critics have noted that Hayslip's
message of forgiveness in the autobiographies is appealing to many American readers, as it
represents reconciliation with and absolution from a former "enemy" who is also popularly

understood as a "victim." Hayslip's East Meets West Foundation, which she founded in 1987, also popularizes this message of reconciliation. The Foundation describes its mission as "working together to heal the wounds of war," and is dedicated to helping both Vietnamese and U.S. victims and veterans of the war. The following selection, which recounts Hayslip's experiences as an adolescent in Vietnam during the war, appears in her autobiography framed by the story of her return to Vietnam in 1986, a journey fraught with apprehension about how she would be greeted by Vietnamese officials.

from When Heaven and Earth Changed Places
(with Jay Wurts)
Chapter Three
Open Wounds

[...] When I arrived back at Ky La after my first arrest, Republican and American soldiers were everywhere. Although there had been a few funerals after the bombardment, the Viet Cong warning had saved many lives and the government troops were angry and discouraged at their inability to locate the enemy.

In the absence of fighting, the Republicans and Americans tried harder to "pacify" our village, distributing food and cigarettes, and taking our wounded civilians to GI hospitals. Still, the government soldiers who wandered too far were soon discovered with their throats slashed or with a bullet between their eyes. Whenever they heard gunshots or found more victims, the Republican and American forces would deploy and pepper the area with gunfire, artillery shells, and air strikes. Because the Viet Cong were always low on ammunition and had to make every shot count, they seldom attacked unless they were sure of victory. Because they had so much of everything, the Republican soldiers seldom counted their shots and called most attacks a victory. This pull and tug soon settled into a kind of routine for fighting the war: Viet Cong attack, government counterattack, period of calm, then Viet Cong retribution and another round of fighting.

Unfortunately, this routine came to an end about six months after my return from the district jail—just before the New Year's holiday. Convinced by the enemy's sloppy tactics that the allies were ripe for defeat, the Viet Cong decided to mass for a major attack against Ky La—a "bloody nose" for the government delivered by schoolchildren and militiamen that would be felt all over Vietnam.

First, because everyone went visiting during New Year's, our major holiday of Tet, the Viet Cong used the week of extra traffic to smuggle weapons and troops into the area. Some rode in coffins during fake funerals or right along with the corpse if the funeral was real. Others changed clothes with the pallbearers and sneaked into the village undetected by Republican sentries. Code words were passed by people who pretended to be drunks shouting or singing in the streets. Village girls were told to prepare extra food and bandages because the battle was supposed to last three days and casualties might be high. Old men and women said extra prayers while those few younger men left around made coffins or ran off to join the Viet Cong so that they would not be left out of the victory.

Two girls I grew up with who had gone off with the Viet Cong earlier in the year now came back for the battle. When I saw them just before the fight, I could hardly believe my eyes. They had undergone training in Hanoi and were tough as old army boots. They snapped orders and wore their weapons the way Saigon girls wore jewelry. They said the attack had been planned to the last detail and rehearsed in the jungle using models of the village. Their battle code, as always, was simple: "When the enemy attacks, we withdraw. When he stands, we harass. When he is tired and disorganized, we attack. When he withdraws, we pursue." I tried to talk to them about village things—teenage-girl things, like handsome boys and local gossip—but they were not interested. War, for them, was more than a name on a blackboard or a bottle cap medal for stealing some soldier's watch.

Finally, on the evening when the Republican garrison and their American allies were getting ready to move out—to be replaced by another unit—we got word the attack was coming. My father gave the warning signal from our house—it was a careless poke with his broom at our roof—something the Republican sentries, who were always watching, never suspected. The signal was passed from house to house until everyone knew to take shelter after dark. For us, the trick would be to get into our family bunker without being seen by the soldiers. Because this was not always possible, we knew we might have to pass the night in the tunnel beneath our cookstove, as we had done before, praying—wide-eyed and terrified—while the shooting went on outside.

And as fate or luck or god would have it, the attack began too soon, catching the villagers, as well as the enemy, off-guard. Out of the shadows beyond Ky La, mortar rounds screamed in and exploded on the Republican convoy. Viet Cong fire teams inside the village popped out of their hiding places and raked the streets with bullets while the Viet Cong main force began advancing through the darkened fields.

When the shooting started, I was at a neighbor's house delivering some first aid kits I had hidden in a basket. They were for the Viet Cong riflemen the widow woman let hide in a tunnel underneath her bed. The first explosions knocked us down and when I tried to get up, the woman's bed flew back and knocked me down again as three Viet Cong fighters scrambled up to their positions. In the street outside, the Republicans and Americans dove for cover and began firing blindly, not knowing where the enemy shots were coming from.

The Viet Cong in the room started shooting and the noise from their guns was so loud I saw double. They were supposed to be snipers but it sounded like they were firing at anything and everything that moved—just like their terrified opponents outside. How many allies shot allies and Viet Cong shot Viet Cong we never knew but the melee was murderous and nothing but chaos—a riot of shouts and screams and terrible, ear-crushing thunder. Time and again machine gun bullets ripped through the poor woman's house and covered us with splinters, but miraculously no one was hit. The floor itself vibrated with the rhythm of battle—spent cartridges and pottery shards danced around our heads—and I finally covered my ears with my hands and coiled up like a baby: too terrified to move—to slide to safety in the hole where the Viet Cong had come out—or to even think about doing it. I was too ter-rified even to pray. All I could do was hug my head and curl up like an almost-squashed bug and wait for it all to be over.

Then, as if my unsaid prayers were answered, everything got quiet. When I dropped my shaking hands and raised my head, I saw that the Viet Cong in the room were gone. The door to the house was open, and outside, smoke billowed like an oily black caterpillar down the street. The widow woman beside me looked up too, but she was too shocked or scared to move. I crawled to the door and peeked out. Across the street, an army truck lay on its side against a house which it had set on fire with burning gas. A treasure-trove of government supplies—backpacks, tools, spilled cartons of rations, and bits and pieces of wrecked equipment—lay everywhere on the road, along with several crumpled bodies. In the distance, I could hear gunfire crackle and the steady *whump* of mortars; but here, the battle of Ky La seemed over.

Like a little black cat, I hopped to my bare feet, grabbed a first aid kit, and darted out the door. I crouched on the warm earth for a moment, making sure nobody saw me, then scampered down the street in the direction of my house. All I could think of was finding my parents and returning to the safety of our bunker.

Before I got very far, I came to a half-dozen bodies sprawled in the light of the burning truck. All were villagers or Viet Cong but only one was still alive—I could tell by his groans. I didn't see any Republican or American casualties—there must have been many—but it was their custom to remove their dead and wounded as soon as possible, even in the middle of a fight.

As far as I could see the survivor had two wounds: a big shrapnel tear in one shoulder and a bullet hole in the chest. I put a compress on the shoulder as I had been taught to do in our midnight meetings, but the chest wound was sucking air and, although I timidly poured what little antiseptic I had all over it, I knew from my first aid lessons that the poor man would not live long enough to be tended by a doctor. I tried to cover the bullet hole with a bandage but the man twitched and yelled and coughed blood so badly that I got scared and backed away. I watched him squirm for a minute, deciding what, if anything, I could do, then finally closed the lid of my stolen American first aid kit, crawled back, and said a little Buddhist prayer in his ear, and left him to his ancestors.

Near our house at the edge of the village the battle was raging much closer. The Americans and Republicans were fighting fiercely in the paddies—I could see them leapfrogging to and fro in the failing light. Flares began popping overhead and covered the fields with an eerie blue light while gun muzzles flashed like fireflies in the darkness below the trees. Overhead, helicopters and warplanes began to arrive— traced by their fiery exhaust and the deafening noise of their engines. Explosions from their bombs and rockets began to rip the jungle. Soon the whole field was lost in acrid smoke.

I found my parents hurriedly burying two dead Viet Cong fighters and although their hearts rejoiced at seeing me, we had no time for greeting. As I helped my mother roll one badly mutilated body in a mat, I noticed that the strangely unmarred face staring back at me was the handsome, cocky Viet Cong fighter who had winked at me that night the Viet Cong first came to Ky La. My heart rose to my throat and my arms became like lead.

"What's wrong, Bay Ly?" my mother snapped. "Do you want us to get caught? Hurry—cover him up!"

Hiding my feelings as I had seen the other women do, I gently covered his face and lifted—embraced—the body's head while my mother took the feet. Together, we lowered him into the dark hole my father had dug and covered him up with earth.

The fighting raged for the rest of the night and although the Viet Cong never controlled the village, they claimed later to have killed over fifty enemy soldiers at the cost of only eight. When morning finally came, my mother and father and I climbed out of our bunker to watch the sun rise on our battered, bullet-pocked home. Our mouths were dry as the dusty street but we were too tired to drink—too exhausted even for sleep. Our job now, as it had always been, was to clean up and rebuild our lives with whatever the war had left us.

For the next few days, the Republicans and Americans poured troops and firepower into the jungle around Ky La—a raging elephant stomping on red ants too far down in their holes now to feel the blows. The Viet Cong had planned a three-day battle, but they had underestimated the colossal numbers of men and arms the enemy was willing to commit to prevent Ky La from falling into their hands. Inside the village, soldiers went from house to house, tearing everything apart to find the Viet Cong hideouts. Where anything suspicious was found, the house was burned and its occupants tied up and taken away for interrogation. Two thirds of my village disappeared this way: in smoke and prison trucks during those first days after the battle. So little was left that even the Viet Cong soon lost interest in Ky La as a prize of war. Instead, they turned their attention to the one thing they knew they could gain no matter what: a grip of terror on the survivors.

Despite—or perhaps because of—the terrible battle, the Viet Cong cadremen took even harsher steps to control us. They began by killing those they suspected of spying for the enemy, usually by taking the accused from their houses in the middle of the night and shooting them in the street—leaving the bodies for relatives to discover. Later, when government forces weren't around, the Viet Cong called villagers to special justice meetings—*moi chi di hop*—during which they held kangaroo courts for the accused and shot them afterward. Everybody knew these trials weren't trials at all but warnings to make sure we did what we were told. To us, the trials simply gave the Viet Cong the excuse they needed to kill more and more villagers for smaller and smaller crimes.

Naturally, these trials made us stay on our toes and we were careful not to talk to the wrong person or go to the wrong place at the wrong time. After a while, our fear of the Viet Cong—of false accusation by jealous neighbors or headstrong kids—was almost as strong as our fear of the Republicans. If the Republicans were like elephants trampling our village, the Viet Cong were like snakes who came at us in the night. At least you could see an elephant coming and get out of its way.

One consequence of the increased killing by both sides was the growing number of parentless children. Many of them found homes with relatives, in Ky La or more distant places, but many others were reduced to scavenging in the fields and garbage dumps, begging, or stealing from farmers. They wandered around, alone or with other orphans, looking as miserable as they were. Sometimes they played with the other kids, only to stop when they remembered their situation and move on like little ghosts. Most of the time they just hung around like old people, waiting for something good or bad to happen: for a little food or affection to come their way, or for death—sudden or slow—to release them from their suffering.

The oldest child in each family was responsible for providing for that family once the parents were gone. Sometimes this responsibility included vengeance for the father's death. I think many killings in the war, all over Vietnam, came from this alone. Too few of us were able to leave hurt behind and seek life instead of death. Too many of us were willing to die, and not enough were willing to live, no matter what. I finally began to realize that *this* was what my father meant when he called me a "woman warrior" so many years before. A woman may do many things, but the first thing god equipped her for is to bring forth and nourish life, and to defend it with a warrior's strength. My task, I was beginning to see, was to find life in the midst of death and nourish it like a flower—a lonely flower in the graveyard my country had become.

At times these killings were so frequent—from vendettas against informers or fighting among old rivals, as well as from patrolling soldiers—that anyone nearby, including children or old women, was collared into burying the dead. More than once while working in our fields, I heard gunshots and hit the deck. When it was safe to look up, I would see people running to a dike or to the middle of a paddy where a dead villager would be sprawled in the mud. We would stop our work and drag the person to a space of dry ground and dig an instant grave. We even stopped wondering which side had done the killing. Someone might say, *My ban*—killed by Americans, or simply *dich ban*—killed by the enemy, without taking the time or risk of specifying which enemy it was. As months of this went by, we children gradually lost our appetite for the "game" of liberation. We were, after all, just kids. We could take only so many sleepless nights, endless hours in musty bunkers, unjust beatings at the hands of soldiers, and terror at the Viet Cong trials before all we wanted was for things to return to the way they had been before the new war started. Of course, a child must grow up—she can't stay an infant forever; just as a war, once started, grows from infancy to assume a life of its own—one so terrible that even the parents who spawned it no longer claim it for their own.

When our enthusiasm for resisting got too cool, the Viet Cong simply turned up the heat. By the second year of this new war, we could not go to another town or talk with anyone from outside the area without first getting permission from the cadre. If a stranger came to the village—even someone's long-lost relative or an orphan from another district—everyone wanted to know who it was and how long he or she was going to stay. Life in the village had gone from love and distrust of no one to fear and mistrust of everyone, including our neighbors. It was okay to visit your friends and relatives, but if you stayed too long, the cadre leaders were sure to ask about it later. If you stopped for a ladle of water, they asked why you chose to stop at that particular house and why you lifted the ladle in that particular way. And there was no doubt who was answering those questions—warping every innocent act to make it appear to be a threat: it was the younger children. They had studied the example of older kids like me and wanted to be heroes. They wanted to get their names on the Blackboard of Honor, even if it cost them, now and again, a neighbor, aunt, or sister.

Unlike suspicion, however, food and money were in short supply. Girls were expected to gather wild fruit and firewood and sell it in the market to earn money for Viet Cong clothing, medicine, cigarettes, and anything else the soldiers needed. The Viet Cong also wanted us to keep a record of every animal we slaughtered so that our tithe of rations could be computed. This was especially troublesome during times of feasting for our departed ancestors. We needed permission from the cadre leaders to consume anything more special than our daily fare and permission was not always granted. Finally, my parents decided it was simpler just to eat all our food outside so the neighbors could count what we ate and reassure the Viet Cong we were not feasting in secret. We agreed that nobody should waste food or clothing or have luxuries while our countrymen were suffering to rid us of invaders. But we also knew that the reason they were fighting—the reason they were *supposed* to be fighting—was to preserve our ancient rights and independence. When the Viet Cong began to condemn us for practicing what they claimed to be protecting, we began to suspect—at least in our hearts—that the new war we began with high hopes was over, and that another sort of war had begun.

On a February morning in 1964, shortly after I had been released from the district jail after my first arrest, I was on sentry duty in Ky La. It was unusually chilly and a heavy mist hung in the valleys on three sides of the village. My shift had started at sunrise—about an hour before—and I knew it would be a long day. The older woman, Sau, who was supposed to be my partner, had not shown up. The Viet Cong were very careful about scheduling the teams of sentries upon whom so much depended. Usually, a team consisted of one mature woman and a girl, or two women—but never two girls, for the temptation to daydream or gossip was too strong and there was always the chance that something unusual would happen—something not foreseen by detailed Viet Cong instructions—which would require quick action and good judgment. Occasionally, Viet Cong inspectors would check us if the area seemed safe—Loi and Mau were the fighters detailed most often to my shift, and we had an easy, friendly relationship. But today, even the birds stayed shivering in their nests.

The fog that morning made everything drippy and caused the world to collapse to my feet. To make matters worse, the white air absorbed all sounds from the village and ever since I arrived I had heard a faint moaning and grinding which my predecessors (the sentries from dusk till dawn) had attributed to mountain spirits.

Consequently, I put my bucket (we always carried a pail or basket to avoid suspicion) on a piece of dry ground beneath the big tree that was our station and made myself a fortress against the ghosts: sitting hunched with my arms over my knees; peeking between them and the brim of my useless sun hat at the watery wall of air.

After what seemed like half the morning, the ground gradually opened around me—ten meters, twenty, finally a hundred and more until the fog touched the dikes at the edge of the field and the trees beyond the road to Phe Binh loomed out of the mist like giants. It was then that I saw the teeming mass of soldiers on the road—Republicans, hundreds of them. The moaning had been their voices, muffled by the fog; the grinding, the soldiers' boots on the rocky road.

Panicked, I jumped up—but saw I had no place to go. The troops were already past my station and almost inside the village. If I ran either way—toward Ky La or away toward the Viet Cong—I would surely be cut down. If I stood still, or attempted to hide among the rocks, I would not only let the Viet Cong walk into a trap, but be caught in the crossfire myself. In the blink of an eye, my situation had gone from nervous boredom to one so desperate that only a desperate act would save me. Despite my terror, I forced myself to walk nonchalantly toward the road, right into the soldiers' teeth. Every few paces, I bent to pick up a sweet potato or low-lying berries that grew around the field, and put them in my bucket. When I got close enough to see out of the corner of my eye the soldiers watching me from the corners of their eyes, I hummed a little tune and paused even longer and more often. *Surely, they must think, there is no more loyal Republican than this happy little farm girl out gathering her family's breakfast!*

By good acting or good luck, nobody bothered me and when I was completely past the troops and within a stone's throw of the swamp (the direction from which the Viet Cong usually came), I dropped my bucket and peeled off the top two of the three shirts I always wore. The top shirt—the one I would wear all day if nothing happened—was brown. Any Viet Cong seeing it would know that conditions were clear in my sector. The second shirt was white, which I would show if anything suspicious had happened—like a helicopter loitering in the area or a reconnaissance team passing through. The bottom shirt, the one I wore now, was all black and meant that a major threat was around—a fully armed patrol or convoy of troops headed in my direction.

As it turned out, a woman I recognized as a Viet Cong scout was coming down the road from the direction of Bai Gian carrying a shoulder pole with two buckets. Her presence meant that the Viet Cong were on the move and probably close behind her. If she was doing her job properly, she would be looking for me in the fields, which were now barely visible through the mist. Sure enough, she scanned the horizon as she walked, then stopped when she saw that I was not at my station. Slowly, she looked around until she saw me in my black shirt pretending to pick berries by the road. Quick as a wink, she unshouldered her pole, pretended to have trouble with one of the ropes that held the buckets, and scuttled back in the opposite direction.

My legs went limp with relief. By giving my signal in time, I had prevented a Viet Cong massacre. But there were still hundreds of enemy troops between me and the village. I had no alternative but to continue playing the innocent schoolgirl.

When my bucket had a respectable load of potatoes and berries, I walked back toward Ky La. The Republicans by now were beginning their sweep through the fields and the quarter-mile of road between me and the village was almost clear. The further I went, the faster I walked until I dashed the last few steps to my house. Inside, my father greeted me with a sigh of relief. He had looked for me on the hillside when the fog lifted and, seeing I wasn't there, became frantic. I told him about the soldiers and the close call with the scout and he told me to change my shirt quickly so that, in case of trouble, the soldiers who saw me couldn't identify me as the girl beside the road.

We then got our tools and went out to watch the situation—but we didn't wait long. The Republican and American soldiers were back within hours, angry because their mission had been spoiled. They sent squads through the village rounding up women who fit my description. Although most girls ran away, I just stood there with my father, trusting my new shirt and loyalty act to get me through. Unfortunately, I had already pushed my luck too far that wintry day. A squad surrounded us at once and I was arrested, along with three other girls, and blindfolded. My hands were tied behind my back and as the soldiers led us to a truck, my father tried to convince the sergeant in charge that I had only been out gathering breakfast, but the soldiers pushed him away and threatened him, too, with arrest if he didn't stop interfering.

The ride to Don Thi Tran prison was unpleasantly familiar. I prayed that my old tormentors would not be on duty when I arrived—especially Sergeant Hoa. I hoped I would be kept in the arrival area instead of the awful cages, and that my sister Ba's policeman husband could be summoned from Danang before I was called for interrogation. To my surprise, all my wishes came true.

The holding room was full of prisoners—mostly girls—and because I had not been charged with anything specific, my priority for interrogation was low. Besides, as I had already learned, the questions and answers were always the same: *Why were you arrested?* "I don't know." *How old are you?* "Fifteen—I'm just a little kid." *Have you seen any Viet Cong?* "Yes." *What do they look like?* "They look like you, but with black clothes," and so on. The problem with their questions was that you could answer most of them honestly, even if you were a cadre leader yourself, and not get into trouble. For most of us, including the district police who inherited us as prisoners, the mass arrests after a raid were little more than a game. The worst part was being held captive while a sweep was going on. The troops would herd us together and make us wait in the hot sun without water or permission to go to the toilet—sometimes for most of the day. We often wondered why heavily armed soldiers worried so much about us women and children, but by this time, experience had taught them never to turn their back on a villager—no matter how skinny, little, or harmless she appeared.

Late the next morning, Ba's husband, Chin, arrived on his bicycle and gave the prison commander an order for my release. When I came out from the cell, both the commandant and my brother-in-law scowled at me.

"The logbook shows you've been here before, Phung Thi Le Ly," the commandant said sourly. "Your brother-in-law vouched for you then, but you can't seem to stay out of trouble. Well, I promise you both that if you're picked up again, even a note from the President won't get you out! Now get out of here! *Di ve*—both of you!"

I could see Chin was even more angered by the commandant's chewing out than by the trouble I had caused him. When we were outside, he pulled me up by the shoulders and gave me a good shaking.

"Look, you little troublemaker," he barked, "I'm finished with you and your whole family! I don't care if we're related or if Ba Xuan cries to high heaven about her poor little sister. You tell your mother and father that I'm finished risking my job for you. One day the soldiers will catch you doing something really bad and then we'll *all* go to prison—this policeman's badge won't mean a thing! Do you understand me?"

I nodded yes and he got onto his bicycle and pedaled away, ringing the bell irritably at some people who blocked his path.

It took me an hour to walk home, and when I got there, the soldiers were gone and the village was buzzing about my exploit.

"You're a hero, Bay Ly!" my mother told me. "The Viet Cong are calling a meeting tonight in your honor!"

It was true. Shortly after sundown, the villagers crept out of their houses and went into the swamp where the cadre leaders were already waiting by a roaring fire. When everyone had gathered, the woman with the shoulder pole testified that I had risked my life by walking right through the enemy column to find a place to give my signal. Next, the cadre leader proclaimed that his small band of fighters would probably have been wiped out by the Republican force, which meant that I was indirectly responsible, too, for saving his own life.

"To honor you, Miss Le Ly," he said, grinning in the firelight, "we will do much more than write your name on the blackboard. We will teach all the children in the village to sing the 'Sister Ly' song in your honor."

The original "Sister Ly" was a Viet Cong fighter who killed many enemies and was very famous, although she was eventually arrested and never seen again. It was Viet Cong practice to dedicate such patriotic songs to a hero's namesake when that person distinguished herself—but it had never before happened in Ky La, and the honor, for such a young girl, was unprecedented. The cadremen passed out papers with the following song printed neatly across it:

SONG FOR SISTER LY
Sister Ly, who comes from Go Noi,
Where the Thu Bon[1] washes the trees,
Has defeated the horse-faced enemy.
Her daily rice she could not eat
Without hearing the tortured prisoners.
Although the moon is covered with clouds,
Her glory will shine forever.
One day we heard Sister Ly
Was in prison—tied up hand and foot.
Beaten by day—tortured by night
She sings "Mother don't cry.
While I live, I still struggle."
Comrades, please save your tears,
Sister Ly is still living,
And her struggle will go on forever.

After the cadreman had led the children through a few choruses of this song, he added: "Miss Le Ly is now assigned the honored task of teaching the young children how to serve the fighters who defend them. She will teach them how to resist their captors in jail—as she has done twice herself—so that they may follow in her glorious footsteps."

The villagers all clapped and the little kids, who were always the most enthusiastic at these meetings, cheered with them. My mother beamed proudly and although my father smiled too, I could see by his eyes that he was worried. He realized that my notoriety might very well put me in more danger over the next few months than any of us had bargained for.

During the next few days, I carried my song sheet around with me constantly, even though I had already memorized the words. I diligently taught our neighbors' children all the Viet Cong songs I knew but told them never to practice them at home, where Republicans might be listening. In the fields, we played the "Viet Cong game" and they all ran and hid and I praised those who were hard to find and made those whom I discovered too easily keep practicing until I had to shout for them to come out. It was just like my old war games at school, except now everyone was on the same side.

One afternoon, at a time that was usually quiet, I was resting in a hammock under the shed that housed our water buffalo, humming "Sister Ly" to myself, when I was completely surprised by a Republican patrol that appeared out of nowhere by the roadside. I could tell from their camouflaged uniforms, red scarves, and painted faces, as well as by the crispness and silence of their movements, that these were not ordinary soldiers, but *linh biet dong quan*—South Vietnamese Rangers. These special forces were seldom seen in our area, and when they were, bad trouble always

---

[1] (Vietnamese) River; also, a goddess believed to bless those who earn a living on the river.

followed. Where the regular Republican troops feared to go, these tough, clever fighters walked right in. Whenever I saw them, my mind filled with half-forgotten images of *ma duong rach mac*—the "slash face" legionnaires of my most terrifying childhood memories. Now, these ghosts from my past had materialized for real and their weapons were pointed at me.

I rolled out of my hammock and glanced involuntarily at the hillside, wondering why the danger signal had not been given, but it was too late for heroics. One camouflaged trooper stepped up and grabbed me by the collar. The paper with the Viet Cong song on it fluttered to the ground from under my shirttail.

"What's your name?" the soldier demanded.

I stammered an answer and prayed the paper would go unnoticed.

"Hey, look," the soldier beside him said. "She dropped something!"

The first soldier picked up the paper, studied it a moment, then looked me straight in the eye. "Where did you get this, girl?"

"I—I found it—"

"Where?"

I turned and pointed to the swamp.

"You mean somebody gave it to you?"

"No! I found it blowing in the wind. There were lots of them flying around. Just ask the other kids. They all have one too!"

More soldiers crowded around to look at the paper and I could already feel their fists and rifle butts beating me. I chewed my lip and tried to look innocent even though I wanted to cry.

Finally the first soldier shook the paper in my face and said, "You know what we do when we find trash like this?"

I shook my head, wide-eyed with terror.

"We do this!" He took out his lighter, flipped open the top, and in seconds my little song was reduced to ashes. "Wrap her up," he snapped to a subordinate. "We'll take her into the village."

Again, my hands were tied behind my back and I was shoved down the road to Ky La. As we went, more of these camouflaged, fast-moving troopers darted out of the bushes and from behind trees and dikes into the fields. Moments later gunfire broke out but it did not sound like a battle until I arrived with the rest of the villagers at the holding area behind our house. There we were held at gunpoint while Republican helicopters swarmed overhead and landed beyond the trees. Within the hour, thick smoke rose above the distant jungle. "Bai Gian—" the word passed quietly. "The soldiers are attacking Bai Gian!"

Bai Gian was a peaceful forest hamlet tucked in among coconut, orange, and mangrove trees with freshwater pools and waterfalls that were a haven for animals and birds and the many people who used to go there just to enjoy the scenery. It was also a very wealthy place with big houses and people who bore the honorary surname *Cuu,* which meant "village elder." Because it was so quiet and hard to reach, the Viet Cong often used Bai Gian for recreation, and because the Viet Cong were usually lurking nearby, the Republicans avoided it like the plague. That was before the special forces took an interest in the place. When all was said and done, not only Bai Gian, but its poorer, neighboring suburbs and most of its sister village of Tung Lam would be reduced to ashes.

Near sundown the troops came back and, although the battle was continuing, they apparently felt safe enough to let us go back to our homes. My hands were untied and with my parents I went immediately to our bunker where we lived on emergency rations for two days while troops and tanks and airplanes widened the battle zone around Bai Gian.

On the third day we came out. Although the air was hazy from dust and smoke, the sunshine felt good and we were glad to leave the musty bunker, which now smelled of our collective waste and sweat. Rumor had it that the rangers had trapped a few Viet Cong away from their sanctuaries, but the ordinary troops who came in to press the attack had suffered heavy losses. Consequently, the soldiers mopping up after the battle were in a vengeful mood.

While the other troops withdrew, these soldiers stayed behind to question us for clues to the enemy's sanctuaries. When the temporary camp by my school was too full to admit more prisoners, they set up assembly-line interrogation stations in the street and sometimes openly beat the villagers who didn't give satisfactory answers. This caused us to worry even more because such actions showed the soldiers no longer cared about our good opinion. Ominously, they seemed to talk about us the way we talked about our barnyard animals on the day they ceased to be pets and began to look like supper.

Near sundown, when all but a score of Republicans had withdrawn, the last of the soldiers began shooting at random, hitting people and animals that were unlucky enough to be caught in the streets. Others looted houses near the center of town and set them on fire with lighters and gasoline. By the time they had finished, the fire had spread to outlying buildings and over half of Ky La was in flames.

My father and the other village men spent the rest of the night battling the fires as best they could. My mother went from house to house giving food to survivors and consoling several women who had been raped and beaten by departing troops. For my part, I remained in our house and watched over the little children whose parents could no longer care for them. I dressed burns on tiny hands and put bandages on cut legs and bloody heads. The kids' terrified eyes stared back at me in the light of their own burning homes as if they expected the heroic Miss Ly to bind up their breaking hearts as well as their battered bodies. As much as I wanted to raise their spirits, I couldn't think of anything to say.

One little boy with bad burns on his arm saw that I was distressed. In the saddest, smallest voice I ever heard, he began to sing the "Song for Sister Ly." I knelt beside him and, being careful not to disturb his arm, hugged his head and chest so hard that his song turned into sobs. Within moments, all of Ky La's children were wailing as their village and childhood innocence came crashing down around them. Although I could silence Miss Ly's song—which now seemed to me obscene—I could not silence the children's pain. For the pain itself was a voice; a voice that had risen above Ky La as a chorus of deathly smoke.

For several weeks after the three-day battle, the Republicans bombarded the area around my village—attempting to do with aircraft and artillery what ground troops had failed to accomplish: drive the Viet Cong away or slaughter them in their hiding places. Although the aerial attacks didn't occur every day, they happened often enough and with so little warning that we seldom went into the fields, and even then what we found usually did not make the risk worth taking. The paddies would be littered with rubble—upturned trees, shattered rocks, and charred craters where bombs or artillery rounds went astray. Those crops that weren't pulverized were scorched by the blast and lay withering on stalks like embryos cut from the womb. Dead animals lay rotting in the sun—water buffalo with stiff legs and bodies bloated as big as a car; disemboweled pigs and the remains of jungle animals that had run out of the forest to escape the gunfire only to be ripped apart by the explosions. Every now and then, too, we came across some dead humans—charred like wooden dolls fished from an oven, blackened arms cocked in an eternal embrace with their ancestors.

For the most part, the soldiers ignored civilian and animal casualties and we had to dispose of them as best we could to prevent disease from infecting the living. By the time we cleared our fields of rubble and buried the victims, another attack would usually begin or it would be dark and time to go back to our homes. Like it or not, we had become part of the endless machinery of terror, death, and regeneration.

One afternoon during this long campaign, some families were brought to Ky La from Bai Gian after what was left of that once-beautiful village had been converted to a "strategic hamlet," requiring half of the people to move to a more secure location. Because the bombings and periodic sweeps by Republican and American soldiers had suppressed Viet Cong activity in our area, Ky La was considered a "pacified" village, although government troops seldom spent the night here and when they did, it was always under arms.

Among these refugees reduced to begging was the family of Cuu Loi, the second wealthiest man in Bai Gian and an old friend of my father's. Cuu Loi's number-eight daughter, Thien, was about two years older than I was and a little bit shorter, with the much darker skin typical of people from that area. She was a quiet girl and we always got along well because I loved to talk and, after several years of war, there was a shortage of listeners in the village—the teenagers having gone off with the Viet Cong, the Republicans, or to shallow, premature graves. Thien was also a Viet Cong supporter, but had been arrested more often and (although she wouldn't speak of it) had been tortured more intensely and more frequently than I had. When I saw her again after the destruction of Bai Gian, she had the lackluster eyes of one who had seen and suffered too much. She clung to me for security just as I clung to her for companionship—although I could never make her safe anymore than she could substitute for my own lost brothers and sisters. Anyway, for the time being, we were all that each other had.

Cuu Loi repaired an abandoned house next to Uncle Huong, who lived at the edge of the village. For several weeks things went well—Thien's mother set up a garden and tended some hens that we gave her. Her father worked the land next to ours and we girls spent many pleasant hours together helping each other do chores. One night, however, our unaccustomed good luck ran out. Cuu Loi went out after dark to relieve himself and was shot dead outside his door. To make matters worse, no one could claim or examine the body until daybreak—such were the dangers from the government "cat" while Viet Cong "mice" were around our village.

When I went to Thien's house the next morning, it had already been surrounded by troops. After a few minutes' questioning about her father, Thien was arrested once more and taken away in a truck. When she came back two days later, she had been beaten quite badly and could hardly move or speak. I nursed her at our house because she was my friend and because her mother now had to labor in the fields without a husband. Over the next six weeks, Thien was arrested again and again, and each time returned in worse shape than before. Although she was always quiet, she now said nothing at all, and even my mother—who had never particularly liked Thien's family owing to their wealth and high station—began to pity her. As it turned out, she could have saved her pity for us both.

After one evening of particularly intense bombardment, Thien and I were rousted by soldiers from a roadside trench into which we had jumped to escape the shells. As soon as we climbed out, I knew we were in for trouble. The soldier who shone the flashlight in my face was none other than the Republican ranger who had burned my song a while before.

"Didn't we arrest you on the road a few weeks ago?" the ranger said. "Yes—you're the girl with the filthy VC songbook!"

"No, not me—" I protested.

He shone the light at poor Thien, whose face was still raw from a QC (Quan Canh, the Republican military police) beating administered a few days before. "Then maybe, it was you—"

"No—not her either!" I interrupted. "She's from Bai Gian. She's only been in the village a little while!"

"Bai Gian!" the soldier spat. "That shithole is full of VC! Here"—he called to his corporal—"*bat no Di!* [arrest them both!] Two more Charlie for My Thi."

A pair of rangers quickly put us on the ground, frisked us for weapons, and tied our hands; but cold terror at the very mention of My Thi had already paralyzed us like a punch to the stomach. My Thi torture camp—the maximum security POW prison outside Danang—was run by the army, not the district police. It was a place even the toughest Viet Cong couldn't talk about without wincing. While the rangers hustled us back to the village with the day's haul of prisoners, we were all too terrified even to whisper among ourselves.

For about twenty minutes Thien and I rode down the bumpy, darkened road with a half-dozen others, mostly grown-ups I didn't recognize. Although we were in a walled compound when we got out, I recognized the sounds and smells of China Beach immediately. My Thi was a huge camp containing many American-built shacks—some for prisoners, some for guards, some for purposes I did not want to know. As soon as we were off the truck, QCs descended on us like vultures and hustled us off to different places. I was led to a small bare cell where I would spend the rest of the night alone—listening to guards shuffling up and down the hall and, when they went away, to the roaring surf beyond the brightly lit perimeter.

In the morning, I was awakened by human screams. I got off the plywood board that served as a bed and crouched on the cement floor, covering my head to block the sound. Perhaps, if I looked small and pathetic enough, the guards would leave me alone. Such was the state of reasoning even one night in My Thi produced.

Within an hour two guards came to my cell and pulled me into the corridor. They didn't even wait until I was in the interrogation room to brutalize me, but banged me against the walls and punched me with their fists, shouting threats and accusations as we went. Inside the interrogation room, which was at the end of the same long building as my cell, I was shown a number of implements on a table in front of me. There were some electric wires hooked up to a hand-cranked generator, scissors, razor blades, and knives of various shapes (like the kind a surgeon uses), and buckets of soapy water which I knew were not for washing.

Without even asking me a question, the interrogator ordered: "Put your hands on the table!"

As soon as I did, the guards strapped down my wrists and the interrogator clipped a wire to each thumb. He turned the crank casually a few times and flicked a switch the way someone else might turn on a radio. A jolt of electricity knocked my legs out from under me and the entire room went white. A second later I was hanging from the straps, clambering to stand up. My lips were tingly and I could see my fingers twitching in the harness.

"So—you see we're not playing games!" the interrogator said, leaning on the table. "Tell me quickly: Why were you and the other girl hiding in the trench?"

"We jumped in to escape the explosions—"

"Liar!" The interrogator slammed the table. "There was a battle going on! You are *phu nu can bo*—VC cadre girl! You were carrying supplies! Where is the ammunition hidden?"

"I don't know anything about ammunition!"

"Then what were you doing on the battlefield? How many battles have you been in, eh? What is your rank?"

"Please! I'm just a little girl! I haven't done anything!" His hand hovered near the crank and I instinctively pulled against the straps. But instead of turning on the electricity, he picked up a short-bladed knife.

"Do you know what these are for?" he asked.

"Yes. I've seen them before."

"Has anyone used them on you?"

I hesitated before answering, "No—"

"Good." He put down the knife and stood up quickly. "Release her."

To my amazement, the guards unbuckled the straps. I backed away from the table like a wary animal and rubbed my wrists.

"Go back to your cell. Think about what these things could do to your body. How would your boyfriend or husband or baby like you without nipples, eh? Or, perhaps, I'll cut some skin off your ass for some sandals, or maybe throw a few of your fingers to the guard dogs. You think well about it, Miss Viet Cong hero—then when you're called again, come prepared to tell me everything you know!"

The guards pushed me to the door and down the hall to my cell. I knew it was as useless to worry about the torture the interrogator described as it was to try and figure out ways to outsmart him. If I was to survive, I must play my own game—not his. Experience had taught me that if you answer one way long enough, it ruins your tormentor's game. After all, for most of them, it's just a job (just like my job now was to be a prisoner). No workman wants to work harder than he has to—especially for no reward. Even a sadistic interrogator has better things to do than terrorize dumb schoolgirls when there is nothing left to learn. With my mind reassured by that plan, I had the luxury of stretching out on my small board and thinking about Thien—wondering where she was, what was happening to her, and what would be left of her should she ever be released. How hopeless it must seem to her—to be in a place like this without a father to grieve for you, work for your release, or greet you when you came back.

The next morning the same two guards took me from my cell, but instead of going back to the interrogation room, I was taken with two other girls whom I did not know to an alley between the buildings where a post was set into the ground. We were ordered to stand against the post, each facing a different direction, while one guard tied us fast with a rope. I had no idea what they intended to do with us—we were too close to the buildings to be set on fire and if they intended to rape us, we would not be left clothed with our legs immobilized by rope. I concluded that, with no interrogator present, we three had, for some reason, been singled out for punishment—and that punishment was to stand under the hot sun, without water or toilet, for the afternoon. Compared with the knives and scissors, there were worse ways we could have spent the day. Besides, feeling the other girls' shoulders against my own was comforting, and after a few moments we found our fingers were locked together in mutual support. Unfortunately, the post held other perils besides the sun.

As soon as we were were tied up, one guard brought out a can and began to brush something sticky all over our feet. When I looked down, I saw that the whole area between the buildings was covered with anthills—the small black kind whose bites stung worse than bees. Within minutes, our sticky feet had attracted dozens of them and the girls beside me were screaming and trying to drive them off, but the ropes prevented us from raising our legs. For some reason, I alone had the presence of mind to stand still. *The ants want honey, not me,* I thought, as if it all made perfect sense, *so I will stand still and let them have it.* The more the girls beside me struggled, the more the ants attacked them. The longer I stood still, the higher I could feel the hundreds of little legs on my skin—tickling the fine hair of my body, crawling along my crotch and buttocks and down the backside of my knees—but the fewer times I was bitten. To make matters worse, the guards had gone on about their business and the girls had no one to appeal to with their screams and I had nobody to impress with my self-control. And so we occupied ourselves, shrieking and pulling against the ropes or trying to hold still, while the shadow of the pole crept from one building to the other.

After several hours, our perspiration had carried away most of the honey and we were no more to the ants than what the post had been before. The guards came back and looked us over, smirking at how our legs had become swollen and purple as berries.

"Have our patriotic ants made you girls any smarter?" one of them asked, looking directly at me. "Are you ready to talk now to the interrogator? Huh? Answer me!"

"I'm ready to go *home!*" was the only reply I could think of.

The soldier laughed and went away. A few minutes later he came back with a bucket of water. Gingerly, he rolled up his sleeve, fished around in the bucket and brought out a glistening water snake about half the length of his arm. This he promptly dropped into my shirt, and repeated the act with two more snakes for the other girls. I knew from their appearance that the little snakes weren't poisonous, but their bite was painful and the awful slithering—as they probed my waist, breasts, armpits, and neck trying to find a way back to the water—was, in its own way, worse than the ants. Besides, whatever patience or self-control I could muster had long ago been exhausted. I screamed at the snake, then screamed at the guards, then screamed at the sky until the noon blue turned black and my voice was reduced to a squeak.

After sundown, the guards untied us and threw water all over us to get rid of the honey and ants and to help them recover their snakes. I was taken again to the interrogator's room where the previous day's encounter was repeated. This time, the interrogator tried to trick me by asking the same question several different ways, banging the table whenever my answer was wrong. "Where do the Viet Cong hide?" he would ask. "I don't know," I would answer. "Okay then, if you don't know where they hide, tell me where they come from!" Then, "If you don't know where they come from, tell me where they go!" and so on. Next he asked if I ever stole weapons and ammunition and went down the list of other commonly pilfered items: first aid kits, clothing, and rations. My only defense was to answer all his questions the same way ("No," "I don't know," and "I don't understand") and avoid playing the interrogator's game: giving measured answers to trick questions which would only whet his suspicions and draw me closer toward the deadly instruments he reserved for his final assault. In the end, he just threw up his hands and had me taken to my cell.

When the door slammed shut I found myself in darkness with a hollow heart, sick stomach, and itchy legs. I lay down on my hard little bed and tried to make sense of what was happening. I truly believed this interrogator was at last convinced I had nothing to hide, but his realization of this was no guarantee of a speedy release—now, or ever. The army had many interrogators and one suspect held in prison would be one less Viet Cong to worry about in the bush. Already, in the few times I had been moved around the camp, I recognized several people from the village—people who had disappeared years before and who, very likely, would call My Thi their home until the end of the war, or death, released them.

The next morning, however, I was taken neither to the interrogation room nor to the torture post, but to the front gate where I was escorted through layers of fences, barbed wire, and curling concertina to the sandy headlands and told simply to "Go home!"

Dumbfounded, I could only stand there and watch the soldiers go back into the compound, wondering why and how I had been so miraculously released. It then occurred to me that perhaps Thien had been released too—maybe ahead of me—so I ran as fast as I could for the road to Danang and my sister Ba's house, where I could get cleaned up and eat a meal before beginning the long walk home.

At Ba's house, however, I was surprised to find my mother waiting for me.

"How did you know I would be released?" I asked her. "Nobody gets out of My Thi in three days!"

"Well, you do, little miss hero—and it cost me more than you can count!" She immediately began inspecting me for damage, her face angry, relieved, and sad all at once.

"Chin got me out?" I didn't believe my policeman brother-in-law could have such clout, let alone such a monumental change of heart—as well as character.

"Chin? Don't be silly! He has no influence in a military camp. He wouldn't even handle the bribe for fear of a corruption charge on his record! No, I had to go to my nephew, Uncle Nhu's son—the Republican lieutenant. He couldn't act directly, but he knew someone I could approach. It cost me half your dowry, but I suppose you're worth it—" She took me by the ear and twisted me around, inspecting my backside for wounds. "Well, I can see you're in one piece. Wash up and I'll take you home before anything else can happen."

As it turned out, there was no more dangerous place we could have gone than

Ky La. As soon as we entered the village, I could tell everything had changed. People—even old neighbors—avoided my glance, then stared at me as I passed. That night, the Viet Cong held a rally, but the messenger didn't come to our house. "Just stay at home tonight," my father counseled with a worried look on his face. "It's going to take a while for them to decide what to do."

"Decide about what, Father? Are they angry with me?"

"They're suspicious because nobody gets out of My Thi so quickly—even for a bribe."

"Then why don't we tell them about Uncle Nhu's son?" I asked innocently.

"That would be even worse." My father shook his head. "Then they'd know we had blood ties to the Republicans. Just sit still for a while and let things calm down."

But things didn't calm down—they went from bad to worse. Because the Viet Cong (and because of them, the villagers) didn't trust us, we no longer got warnings about Republican raids or Viet Cong reprisals. When troops appeared, our only defense was to stand still and so we were frequently questioned when Americans and Republicans came to the village—contact that only strengthened the Viet Cong's suspicions. To make things worse, our obvious estrangement from the villagers made us even more trustworthy in Republican eyes, and our house was often spared while the other homes were ransacked. Even my own father, in his attempts to protect me, wound up increasing my danger. He was certain I would not survive another arrest (Thien, in fact, still hadn't come back) and forbade me to go to the fields. Instead, he did all my work himself, even those chores I customarily did for the Viet Cong— delivering rations and making up first aid kits. My absence, however, only convinced them even more that I was cooperating with the Republicans. My father argued that I was sick—first to the Republican soldiers, who remembered me from their patrols, and then to the Viet Cong, when they asked about my absence. Of course, no one believed him, and I could see from his expression each night that the noose around my neck was also tightening around his own. I decided I could not let anything happen to my father because of me.

The next morning, I took my hoe and left the house before my parents, determined to put in a good day's work in front of everyone. On the way, I passed six Republican soldiers, who, having grown more friendly toward me over the last few weeks, only waved. I ignored them, stuck my proud nose higher in the air, and went about my business. Unfortunately, I soon heard their boots on the soil behind me.

The faster I walked, the faster the crunching followed. I forced myself not to look back, but I knew they were behind me. A moment later I heard shouts, followed by the crackle of gunfire, and hit the dirt. But the soldiers weren't firing at me. Instead, they were all shooting furiously into the bushes beside the road. A second later, they charged forward and I heard one yell that they had hit two Viet Cong fighters— killing one and badly wounding the other. Apparently, the Viet Cong were in the process of setting up an ambush and, afraid the soldiers had seen them, tried to run away. Some of them made it, but these two did not.

Now I could hear the Republicans chatter excitedly. They were pleased with their trophies, but wondered if I was a Viet Cong spy sent to lure them to an ambush. One of them started to come after me, then stopped, looked around, and went back to his buddies. Without further delay, they took their prisoner and scuttled down the road the way they came, worried, apparently, that a bigger force of Viet Cong lurked somewhere in the forest.

Now I had no doubt that my days with the Viet Cong were over. Not only had I mysteriously escaped the notorious My Thi prison, but I had just been seen leading a Republican squad toward a Viet Cong position. Nobody would be interested in my side of the story. Nobody would be interested in the truth. The same "facts" were there for everyone to see and truth, in this war, was whatever you wanted to make it. And, as if all this wasn't bad enough, I had brought it on by disobeying my father. I was a disgrace and liability to everyone. I didn't deserve to live.

With tears streaming down my face, I stumbled down the road to our paddy and began working like a robot. As self-inflicted punishment, I would expose myself to whichever side wanted to shoot me first. *Giet toi di*—go ahead! My heart shouted silently, *Kill me! My life is over. What more do I have to lose?*

But no one attacked me that morning in the paddy—nor that afternoon. My father went to work in another field and the villagers ignored me, as usual. At the end of the day I just went home. The winter air seemed chillier than usual and even the setting sun and calling birds held no warmth for me. Workers hurried to stuff a last few bundles of rice into their baskets before the light was gone; the kids, ducks, and chickens all jammed around their houses waiting to be fed. Pigs squealed and dogs barked but their familiar sounds no longer gave me comfort. When I got home my mother asked me where I'd been.

"Working," I told her in a sullen voice, and began sweeping the house while she prepared our evening meal.

"Your father will want to speak to you," she said, and made it clear that she, too, was displeased with my disobedience. I didn't mention the skirmish by the road.

Furiously, I swept a cloud of dust out our front door and onto the feet of two callers who had suddenly appeared in the dusk. I apologized and looked up into the faces of Loi and Mau—the two Viet Cong fighters who had been my supervisors on sentry duty. Normally, I would have been pleased to see them. Now, their hard faces made the broom freeze in my hands.

"Miss Ly," Loi, the oldest, said formally, "*Moi chi di hop*." (You must come to a meeting.)

Because we had been excluded from meetings since my release, my first reaction was one of gratitude: I was being accepted back by my comrades!—or at least was being given a chance to tell my side of the story.

"Who is it?" my mother called.

"Loi and Mau," I replied in an eager voice. "I'm supposed to go to a meeting!"

My mother came to the door with terror in her eyes. She studied the stony Viet Cong faces a moment, then said, "Give me a minute. I'm coming with you—"

"No!" Loi held up his rifle. "Miss Ly comes alone!"

I looked at my mother and a lump of fear rose in my throat. Still, there was no way to argue with Loi's rifle.

"I'll tell your father." My mother hugged me tightly, then gave me up.

As we walked through the darkened street, Loi in front and Mau in the rear—as guards would escort a criminal, not a hero—our neighbors glanced with hate from their windows. "Now you're going to get what you deserve!" their eyes seem to say. "Spy! Now you'll see what we do to traitors!"

"Where are we going?" I asked Loi, trying to keep the panic from my voice.

"*Chi im di!*" (Shut up!) he replied. "The prisoner may not ask questions."

Prisoner! Mo toa oan nhan dan—So I am going to my trial! Of course, the Viet Cong "people's court" followed only one script and had only one ending—I had seen enough of them to know that. As we left the settled area and the gloom of the forest engulfed us, my mind raced for an answer—what to say, what to do, to convince them of my innocence? Somehow, even the cold efficiency of the My Thi torture factory seemed more just than this. At least the government kept you alive in order to give you pain, and where there's life, I had learned, there's always hope.

After marching awhile, I could see we were headed for a thatched cottage near Phe Binh where children's education meetings were often held. My old girlfriend Khinh used to live there—she had a crush on my brother Sau Ban and came around often before the youth corps took him away. Now, seeing the cottage again reminded me of Khinh; and Khinh, of my brother Ban. By the time we got to the clearing, my eyes were so full of tears I could hardly see the front door.

Inside, about twenty people were seated in a circle around the floor. One of the cadre leaders, a strident woman named Tram, was in the middle of a speech. Loi stopped me at the door and I felt Mau grab my hands and begin tying them behind my back. As he did so, I recognized an old family friend—a man highly regarded in the village—get up and leave the meeting. He squeezed past me in the doorway and for a second our eyes met. Oddly, there was no hint of reproach in his glance—not even the kind of fear that would drive a loyal friend to abandon me in my hour of need. Instead, the eyes were friendly—almost joking—as if this were all some kind of prank. I was too stunned by his manner—by the events of the day—to call out for help. And so the only man who might have saved me in what was obviously my trial for life slipped wordlessly into the jungle.

Feeling more helpless than ever I turned my attention to Tram's belligerent speech. I saw at once from her flame-red cheeks and raspy voice that this would not be a prosecution, but a denunciation.

"...So, I ask you, what should we do with a woman who betrays our revolution? What should be done with a woman who spies for the enemy and betrays her comrades in the field? What have we done to such people in the past?"

"Execute her! Kill her!" some voices piped back. "Teach her a lesson all traitors will learn from!"

Two things happened now that were very odd. First, it struck me that Tram never once mentioned my name—only "a woman" who has done this and that. Second, although my hands had been tied and my escort made it clear I was a prisoner, I had not been thrust into the center of the room—the usual place for the condemned at a Viet Cong trial. Did the people at Tram's meeting really know it was Phung Thi Le Ly she was denouncing? Or was this some other meeting to which I had been summoned merely as a warning? Or—worst of all—had Tram and Loi and Mau simply decided to take the people's justice into their own hands?

"There, do you hear that, Miss Ly?" Loi whispered menacingly in my ear. "The sentence is death!"

Tram had stopped speaking now and was staring at me with hard, pitiless eyes. All of a sudden I was pulled backward out of the house and hustled down a narrow path toward Rung Phe Binh—the swamp at the edge of the village. Loi and Mau were moving quickly, as if they were afraid of being followed or of not finishing their mission fast enough. This too was unusual. All executions heretofore had been in front of a crowd. Who would profit from my lesson if my little body simply disappeared into the swamp? Such was the work of gangsters, not the liberation army—but still, I would be just as dead. It was all too confusing and horrifying to think about—and time for thinking, or anything else, was running out.

The hard dirt turned mushy beneath our feet and I felt flying bugs and dangly branches and tall grass brush against me in the dark. Eventually we came to a neck of ground that led to a weedy island in a part of the river that had been dammed for irrigation. It had always been a pleasant, vital place—full of birds and fish and frogs—I had played there many times with my brother Sau Ban and kids from school. Now, the ragged, moonlit brush and scruffy trees bobbed ominously in the wind and the black water, like the gauzy air, was silent and foreboding.

We splashed across the swampy ground and plowed through the brush to a clearing among the trees. In the middle of the clearing was a hole—a grave—with two shovels stuck into the loamy soil. There was no question about where we were headed. All I could think of was my mother and father—had someone from the meeting gone to tell them what was happening? *Maybe they're on their way to save me right now!* How would they take the news of my death? I was the last child in the family—everyone else had been lost to the cities or the war. I knew my father couldn't live without his family around him. The bullet that killed me might just as well pass through his heart. *So this is how I will repay him as a Phung Thi woman—a woman warrior—by lying dead in a swampy grave!*

Loi pulled my tied hands up sharply, buckling my legs, and I fell to my knees beside the grave.

"Well, Miss Ly, you know why we're here," he said, almost casually, as if we were about to go fishing or pick some fruit.

I heard the bolt slide up and down in his rifle, chambering a round. I swayed on my knees, trying to think of something to say—*anything*—that would keep me alive a little longer. While I fretted, another part of my brain wondered what my *ma ruoc hon*—the ancestral ghost who would escort me down to hell—would look like. Would she be beautiful and filmy, like the Christian death-angels I had seen in the Catholic picture books? Or would she be harsh and painted, like the Buddhas that guarded Marble Mountain? I concentrated on my breath—on taking in and letting out the stuff of life. Living things breathe and as long as I could feel my own breath I'd know I was alive. I closed my eyes, took in a deep, quivering, lungful of air, and—

Loi's heavy sandal kicked me over onto my side.

Although the air was cool, the sand on my cheek still held the warmth of day. I lay there relishing the sound of the wind and the croaking frogs and—somewhere far away—a barking dog and wailing baby. I opened my eyes and through the brush I could see the village oil lamps come on across the river: *ngon den treo truoc gio*, I thought—the lamp before the storm—like the light of life, so terribly hard to spark and so easy to put out. If a lamp glowed in my parents' house, it would mean my father was home—banging his head against the wall, raging at his impotence to save his daughter. My mother would be shrieking in his ear, *What are you doing? Do something!* I can hear him answer in a voice that's thick with pain, *"Dap dau vao tuong chet!"* (I cannot, so I must break my head upon the wall!)

Around me, the swamp creatures went about their nightly rituals—spinning webs, setting traps, stalking prey—and I knew I was only one of many beings on this island who would not see the morning sun. Here is where I would stay. My little bones would become a part of this tiny island for the rest of time—my spirit a mournful howl in the wind. With dirt in my eyes and mouth and hair, I was already becoming part of Mother Earth.

Loi's strong hand plucked me out of the sand and I teetered again on my knees. He forced my head out over the yawning grave.

"Do you see that?"

"Yes," I said in a weary voice.

"What is it?" he asked.

"A grave—"

He yanked my hair savagely. "Stupid girl! It's *your* grave!"

"It's my grave—" I repeated tonelessly.

"Do you know that the enemy is with your parents right now?"

"No."

"Do you care about your parents?"

"Yes."

"Okay then. You answer my questions honestly and maybe they'll stay alive. Why did you lead the soldiers to our comrades this morning?"

"I didn't lead them. I was just going into the fields and they followed me. Why won't you believe me?"

"What kind of deal did you make to get out of My Thi prison? Did you promise them some Viet Cong ears for their belts?"

"I don't know what you're talking about. My mother bribed an official—"

"Why did you lead the enemy to our ambush?"

Loi repeated all his questions as if I hadn't answered. I repeated all my answers as if I didn't care. There was no point prolonging things. I was ready to die.

"Bah!" Loi hit the back of my head and I fell over. I closed my eyes and chanted a prayer.

"What's this?" Loi asked sarcastically, "Our hero Miss Ly is afraid to die?" His rifle barrel bit into my temple like a drill, pushing my head further into the sand.

My heart shouted silently into the night, *Why don't you do it—bastard! What are you waiting for?* and I prepared for the shattering explosion that would return my spirit to the well of souls, to come back at another time and place to a better life.

Suddenly, the pressure of the gun barrel went away and Loi turned around. I heard him whispering with Mau, then his moon shadow fell over me again.

"Hey—hero! Do you want to live?"

My heartbeat, reduced to a trickle—no more than the sap in the trees whose roots would soon surround my corpse—began to pound in my head. My eyes flickered open. For a second, I almost resented my body's desperate desire to live after my soul had made its peace with eternity. But I was just a little girl and living flesh, as it must, won out. I prayed that I would find the right words.

"My life is in your hands—"

"What the hell does that mean?"

Before I replied, I thanked god for my extra breath—my extra time. Whatever happened, I knew I must try to calm things down—to keep Loi from jerking the trigger even by accident. In as soft a voice as I could muster, I said, "I mean I won't ever talk to the enemy. I have been shamed enough in the village."

"You hear that, Mau?" Loi turned and I heard Mau laugh like a ghost. Loi's hands wrapped around my ankles, twisted me onto my back, then grabbed my collar and jerked me to my feet like a puppet. He removed his peasant's hat and tossed it to the sand. His rifle was gone, but a knife gleamed evilly in his hand. He looked me up and down the way a butcher eyes a roast.

Now they're going to do it! I thought. *He's going to stab me! He doesn't want to waste a bullet!* Like an alarm, my spirit voice cried to my mother and father, blotting out all sounds in my head except the pounding of my heart. My skin broke out in sweat, clammy as a fish. Leaves rustled at the edge of the clearing and I noticed Mau had disappeared. *What's happening? What are they up to? What—*

Loi knocked me flat on my back. When I opened my eyes, the shadow of Loi's face—inches away, grotesque and distorted, scarcely human—blotted out the stars. I rolled my head from side to side, trying to escape his face and evil breath.

"All right, you fucking traitor—!" His rough hands tore down my pants. His weight went away and he stood astride me in the moonlight, frantically unbuttoning his pants. "But if you tell anybody about this, we're going to kill you for real!"

New terror rose inside me. I wriggled like a crab—flopped like a fish—toward the grave, for the safety of the hole, but with my hands tied behind me and my feet tangled in my pants and Loi's fence-post legs holding me fast, I couldn't move.

"God—*no!*" I shouted "Mother! Father! Please—no!"

Loi's hand covered my mouth, "Shut up, you little bitch—!" The hand went to my neck and stopped me from sliding and what felt like a big, blunt thumb pressed urgently between my legs. A second later it was as if the knife itself had cut my crotch. Loi's hips pumped furiously and his fingers tightened around my throat, choking me till my vision sparkled. I went limp and prayed that when this was over, Loi would at least have the kindness to kill me quickly. What choice would he have now? *None.* In Viet Cong eyes, he was now as much a criminal as me. I prayed my father would find my grave. Certainly, my lingering, shrieking soul would guide him to it like a beacon and I would then have a casket and funeral as I deserved. But not this. *Not this!*

Loi's hand relaxed and breath flowed back in my body. He pulled away, staggered to his feet, and raised his pants. His face, though dim in the moonlight, was still revolting. He hawked up some spittle and spat it over me. I turned my head and rolled to one side, pulling my quivering knees up to my chin. I tried to think but my brain was as numb as my body.

I have been raped—I now knew the horror that every woman dreads. What had been saved a lifetime for my husband had been ripped away in less time than it takes to tell. Most horrible of all was that the act of making life itself had left me feeling dead. The force of Loi's twisted soul had entered me and killed me as surely as his knife. He could shoot me now—I wouldn't even feel the bullet.

Mau was next to me. He untied my hands and gently turned me over. "Le Ly," he whispered, as if afraid to be overheard, "listen to me. If you live, do you promise to never tell anybody about what happened?"

I pulled up my pants and stared into the younger man's face. "I didn't deserve this, Mau," I said bitterly.

He didn't answer. I saw Loi across the clearing, urinating into the bushes. Loi called over his shoulder, "She's going to tell her family, isn't she?"

"No," Mau shouted. "She's too ashamed. Aren't you, Le Ly?"

I didn't say anything. Loi came back and picked up his rifle.

"Okay" he said. "We could've killed you for your crime, but we didn't. Consider yourself lucky. What happens next is up to you. If you ever say anything about this to anyone at all, we'll wipe out your whole family. Do you understand?"

I nodded sullenly.

"Okay," he sniffed loudly. "Now get the hell out of here!"

I started to jump up but Mau held me fast.

"No, wait," Mau said. "She can't go home tonight. Even if she doesn't talk, Tram will skin us for letting her go."

"You're right." Loi thought a moment, then said to me, "Hey, hero! Don't you have an aunt who lives near here?"

He meant my cousin Thum, Uncle Huong's daughter. Thum had two brothers who went to Hanoi and her house was sometimes used by the Viet Cong to hide supplies. "Yes," I said, averting my eyes—I couldn't bear to look at him, "in Tung Lam."

"Okay then, we'll take you there for the night. But say one word to her about about any of this and we'll burn her house down with both of you inside! Now get up. Get moving!"

Painfully, as if I had been on the sand for a thousand years, I got up and straightened my clothes. The grave still lay open beside me, but it was now no more threatening than a post hole or a bunker. What Loi had killed in me could not be buried; yet I already felt its weight—like a shoulder pole or tumor—on my soul. My bottom stung and was wet with my virgin blood and Loi's seed, and as I walked bowlegged toward the old boat used as a ferry on the far side of the island, I felt filthy and wanted only to bathe in the river and pray at the ruined pagoda that loomed darkly above the trees outside Tung Lam.

But there would be time for all that later. In fact, my whole life now seemed burdened with time: time I would not spend with a husband for whom I had been ruined; time free of happy children that I would never bear. Curiously, despite the paralyzing fear I had felt only moments before, I now longed for the bullet that slept in Loi's rifle.

We took one of the canoes the villagers kept tethered to the bank and paddled onto the river. I could easily see the lights of Tung Lam through the trees ahead, and behind and to the east, the lights of Ky La, which was now circled with flares and aircraft.

"The Americans are back," Mau whispered, pointing to the lights.

Loi sniffed the chill air and wouldn't look. Certainly, the allies would return in force after the morning's skirmish and chances were good that Loi and Mau would be in battle again before tomorrow was over. An hour ago I would have felt sorry for them. Now I silently relished the moment of their death.

We tied up the boat on the opposite bank and moved quietly through the brush— no place at night was one hundred percent safe, even for the Viet Cong—and knocked on the door to my cousin's house. It swung open and I saw Thum with a baby in her arms. Loi pushed her aside and went in, rifle cocked and ready. There was nobody home except Thum and her three children.

"Bay Ly!" Thum was surprised to see me, "What are you doing here this time of night?"

"Never mind," Loi answered for me. He pointed the gun at my cousin. "Come inside."

Loi and Mau went in and talked with Thum while I shivered on the porch. A few minutes later the fighters came out and started off for the jungle.

"So remember," Loi said over his shoulder to Thum, "mind your own business and give her a place to sleep. We'll come for her in the morning."

Thum looked me up and down and could see from my pale face, rumpled clothes, and shivering body that I had been through an ordeal. "Come on, Bay Ly," she said softly, "come and sit by the stove. Have you eaten?" She called to Loi, "Don't worry—she'll be fine."

Thum took me inside and poured some water for me to wash. Although she never said so, I could see she thought I had been assaulted by soldiers—beaten up and maybe molested. "Those damned Republicans!" she swore under her breath, confirming what I had already guessed Loi told her. "Damn all of them to hell!" I was too tired and too afraid of Loi's threat—and too ashamed—to contradict her. All I wanted now was sleep.

I wrapped myself in a blanket and lay on the bed while Thum's children did homework around the stove. It was a warm, peaceful scene and my eyelids began to sag. Just as I was about to go to sleep, someone knocked on the door.

Thum answered it and I heard a male voice. I opened my eyes and saw Thum look at me, then step back from the door. Mau came into the room and said, "Miss Ly, you must come with me."

With every joint on fire, I threw back the blanket, got up, and trudged after Mau like a zombie. Just outside the house, I stopped and asked, "Where's Loi? Where are you taking me? What's going on?"

Mau looked back with his little boy's face and motioned me forward, "Come on. Just a little further. I've got something to tell you."

I sighed, but I figured that without Loi around, Mau at least could be trusted. I knew he felt bad about what Loi had done. Maybe he wanted to apologize. Maybe he had already reported Loi to Tram, their hard-nosed lady commandant, and Loi himself had been arrested. Maybe Mau couldn't stand the thought of a comrade so vilely degrading a hero of the liberation—let alone a young girl from their own village—and killed Loi himself and had come now to tell me I could rest easy.

When we were just beyond sight of Thum's house, Mau whirled around and pushed me down on the jungle floor. I squealed and covered my face, expecting him to beat me, but instead he sat on my stomach and aimed his rifle at my head.

"I'm—I'm sorry, Miss Ly"—his voice quivered more than mine—"but this is something I have to do!"

My god—here it comes! I swallowed hard and closed my eyes. I tilted my head upward to give him a better shot. I didn't want him to miss or just wound me. I wanted him to end it—to end all this, to end everything now all at once. This was god's mercy. I would wait for peace no longer.

But Mau didn't fire. Instead, rough male hands again tore down my pants. I opened my eyes to see Mau struggling feverishly with his belt, the rifle crooked absently in his arm. It would have been easy to disarm him—to knock the gun away and crush his testicles with my knee and run back to cousin Thum's—but what then?

I could take the gun and shoot him, but would that save me from Viet Cong retribution? Would hunting down Loi and splattering the sand with his brains restore my lost virginity? Would accusing the two Viet Cong who wronged me make the cadre leaders think I had wronged the Viet Cong any less?

Drugged by too much hate and fear and confusion, I just lay back and let Mau do what he had to do. Unlike Loi, he did not spit on me and curse my womanness when he finished. Rather, he seemed like a sad little boy who, believing he was not a man, settled for the imitation of manhood Loi had shown him. That I was the stage for this poor show made no difference; for by now I knew I was no more than the dirt on which we lay. The war—these men—had finally ground me down to oneness with the soil, from which I could no longer be distinguished as a person. Dishonored, raped, and ruined for any decent man, my soiled little body had become its own grave.

When Mau was done, he got up, buttoned his pants, and offered me his hand. Slowly, dizzily—like falling in a dream—I put on my pants and got up without his help. He walked me back to Thum's house, then ran when she opened the door.

"What happened to you?" Thum asked, looking at the leaves in my hair and the dirt on my just-washed face.

"Nothing." I didn't even give her the courtesy of a decent lie. "Mau had something to tell me."

I went back to bed and Thum put out the lamp. I could hear her children asleep around me like warm puppies. While I began the endless wait for sleep, I tried to plan what to do in the morning, but it all seemed so pointless and futile. Either Loi and Mau would come, or they would not. Either I would be raped again, or I would not. I might be arrested again by the Viet Cong, or perhaps by the Republicans—but what did it matter? The bullets of one would just save bullets for the other. I no longer cared even for vengeance. Both sides in this terrible, endless, *stupid* war had finally found the perfect enemy: a terrified peasant girl who would endlessly and stupidly consent to be their victim—as all Vietnam's peasants had consented to be victims, from creation to the end of time! From now on, I promised myself, I would only flow with the strongest current and drift with the steadiest wind—and not resist. To resist, you have to believe in something. [...]

—1989

JAMAICA KINCAID (1949-   )

Jamaica Kincaid (Elaine Potter Richardson) was born in 1949 in Antigua, the setting of many of her fictional works. Her mother, Annie Richardson, encouraged her to read and write; Kincaid does not talk about her biological father, but she has written about her stepfather, a cabinet maker. With no opportunity to pursue an education in Antigua, Kincaid moved to the U.S. in 1966 to work as an au pair. She studied photography at the New School for Social Research and attended Franconia College in New Hampshire.

Kincaid is well known for the stories she wrote for the *New Yorker,* which began appearing in 1976. By the time she made her first trip home to Antigua in 1986, she had published two books: the short story collection *At the Bottom of the River* (1983) and *Annie John* (1985), an autobiographical novel. Kincaid's nonfiction work *A Small Place* (1988) discusses the colonial past and current tourist presence in Antigua, while *Talk Stories* (2000) collects her "Talk of the Town" essays from the *New Yorker*. Kincaid's short stories and novels—*Lucy* (1990), *Autobiography of My Mother* (1995), and *Mr. Potter* (2002)—all draw on her personal and family stories. She has also written a memoir about her brother's death from complications of AIDS entitled *My Brother* (1997).

from A Small Place

If you go to Antigua[1] as a tourist, this is what you will see. If you come by aeroplane, you will land at the V. C. Bird International Airport. Vere Cornwall (V. C.) Bird is the Prime Minister of Antigua. You may be the sort of tourist who would wonder why a Prime Minister would want an airport named after him—why not a school, why not a hospital, why not some great public monument? You are a tourist and you have not yet seen a school in Antigua, you have not yet seen the hospital in Antigua, you have not yet seen a public monument in Antigua. As your plane descends to land, you might say, What a beautiful island Antigua is—more beautiful than any of the other islands you have seen, and they were very beautiful, in their way, but they were much too green, much too lush with vegetation, which indicated to you, the tourist, that they got quite a bit of rainfall, and rain is the very thing that you, just now, do not want, for you are thinking of the hard and cold and dark and long days you spent working in North America (or, worse, Europe), earning some money so that you could stay in this place (Antigua) where the sun always shines and where the climate is deliciously hot and dry for the four to ten days you are going to be staying there; and since you are on your holiday, since you are a tourist, the thought of what it might be like for someone who had to live day in, day out in a place that suffers constantly from drought, and so has to watch carefully every drop of fresh water used (while at the same time surrounded by a sea and an ocean—the Caribbean Sea on one side, the Atlantic Ocean on the other), must never cross your mind.

You disembark from your plane. You go through customs. Since you are a tourist, a North American or European—to be frank, white—and not an Antiguan black returning to Antigua from Europe or North America with cardboard boxes of much needed cheap clothes and food for relatives, you move through customs swiftly, you move through customs with ease. Your bags are not searched. You emerge from customs into the hot, clean air: immediately you feel cleansed, immediately you feel blessed (which is to say special); you feel free. You see a man, a taxi driver; you ask him to take you to your destination; he quotes you a price. You immediately think that the price is in the local currency, for you are a tourist and you are familiar with these things (rates of exchange) and you feel even more free, for things seem so cheap, but then your driver ends by saying, "In U.S. currency." You may say, "Hmmmm, do you have a formal sheet that lists official prices and destinations?" Your driver obeys the law and shows you the sheet, and he apologises for the incredible mistake he has made in quoting you a price off the top of his head which is so vastly different (favouring him) from the one listed. You are driven to your hotel by this taxi driver in his taxi, a brand-new Japanese-made vehicle. The road on which you are travelling is a very bad

[1] Island nation in the West Indies, formerly a British colony.

road, very much in need of repair. You are feeling wonderful, so you say, "Oh, what a marvellous change these bad roads are from the splendid highways I am used to in North America." (Or, worse, Europe.) Your driver is reckless; he is a dangerous man who drives in the middle of the road when he thinks no other cars are coming in the opposite direction, passes other cars on blind curves that run uphill, drives at sixty miles an hour on narrow, curving roads when the road sign, a rusting, beat-up thing left over from colonial days, says 40 MPH. This might frighten you (you are on your holiday; you are a tourist); this might excite you (you are on your holiday; you are a tourist), though if you are from New York and take taxis you are used to this style of driving: most of the taxi drivers in New York are from places in the world like this. You are looking out the window (because you want to get your money's worth); you notice that all the cars you see are brand-new, or almost brand-new, and that they are all Japanese-made. There are no American cars in Antigua—no new ones, at any rate; none that were manufactured in the last ten years. You continue to look at the cars and you say to yourself, Why, they look brand-new, but they have an awful sound, like an old car—a very old, dilapidated car. How to account for that? Well, possibly it's because they use leaded gasoline in these brand-new cars whose engines were built to use non-leaded gasoline, but you musn't ask the person driving the car if this is so, because he or she has never heard of unleaded gasoline. You look closely at the car; you see that it's a model of a Japanese car that you might hesitate to buy; it's a model that's very expensive; it's a model that's quite impractical for a person who has to work as hard as you do and who watches every penny you earn so that you can afford this holiday you are on. How do they afford such a car? And do they live in a luxurious house to match such a car? Well, no. You will be surprised, then, to see that most likely the person driving this brand-new car filled with the wrong gas lives in a house that, in comparison, is far beneath the status of the car; and if you were to ask why you would be told that the banks are encouraged by the government to make loans available for cars, but loans for houses not so easily available; and if you ask again why, you will be told that the two main car dealerships in Antigua are owned in part or outright by ministers in government. Oh, but you are on holiday and the sight of these brand-new cars driven by people who may or may not have really passed their driving test (there was once a scandal about driving licences for sale) would not really stir up these thoughts in you. You pass a building sitting in a sea of dust and you think, It's some latrines for people just passing by, but when you look again you see the building has written on it PIGOTT'S SCHOOL. You pass the hospital, the Holberton Hospital, and how wrong you are not to think about this, for though you are a tourist on your holiday, what if your heart should miss a few beats? What if a blood vessel in your neck should break? What if one of those people driving those brand-new cars filled with the wrong gas fails to pass safely while going uphill on a curve and you are in the car going in the opposite direction? Will you be comforted to know that the hospital is staffed with doctors that no actual Antiguan trusts; that Antiguans always say about the doctors, "I don't want them near me"; that Antiguans refer to them not as doctors but as "the three men" (there are three of them); that when the Minister of Health himself doesn't feel well he takes the first plane to New York to see a real doctor; that if any one of the ministers in government needs medical care he flies to New York to get it?

It's a good thing that you brought your own books with you, for you couldn't just go to the library and borrow some. Antigua used to have a splendid library, but in The Earthquake (everyone talks about it that way—The Earthquake; we Antiguans, for I am one, have a great sense of things, and the more meaningful the thing, the more meaningless we make it) the library building was damaged. This was in 1974, and soon after that a sign was placed on the front of the building saying, THIS BUILD-ING WAS DAMAGED IN THE EARTHQUAKE OF 1974. REPAIRS ARE PEND-ING. The sign hangs there, and hangs there more than a decade later, with its unful-filled promise of repair, and you might see this as a sort of quaintness on the part of these islanders, these people descended from slaves—what a strange, unusual percep-tion of time they have. REPAIRS ARE PENDING, and here it is many years later, but perhaps in a world that is twelve miles long and nine miles wide (the size of Antigua) twelve years and twelve minutes and twelve days are all the same. The library is one of those splendid old buildings from colonial times, and the sign telling of the repairs is a splendid old sign from colonial times. Not very long after The Earthquake Antigua got its independence from Britain, making Antigua a state in its own right, and Antiguans are so proud of this that each year, to mark the day, they go to church and thank God, a British God, for this. But you should not think of the confusion that must lie in all that and you must not think of the damaged library. You have brought your own books with you, and among them is one of those new books about eco-nomic history, one of those books explaining how the West (meaning Europe and North America after its conquest and settlement by Europeans) got rich: the West got rich not from the free (free—in this case meaning got-for-nothing) and then underval-ued labour, for generations, of the people like me you see walking around you in Antigua but from the ingenuity of small shopkeepers in Sheffield[2] and Yorkshire and Lancashire,[3] or wherever; and what a great part the invention of the wristwatch played in it, for there was nothing noble-minded men could not do when they discovered they could slap time on their wrists just like that (isn't that the last straw; for not only did we have to suffer the unspeakableness of slavery, but the satisfaction to be had from "We made you bastards rich" is taken away, too), and so you needn't let that slightly funny feeling you have from time to time about exploitation, oppression, domination develop into full-fledged unease, discomfort; you could ruin your holiday. They are not responsible for what you have; you owe them nothing; in fact, you did them a big favour, and you can provide one hundred examples. For here you are now, passing by Government House. And here you are now, passing by the Prime Minister's Office and the Parliament Building, and overlooking these, with a splendid view of St. John's Harbour, the American Embassy. If it were not for you, they would not have Government House, and Prime Minister's Office, and Parliament Building and embassy of powerful country. Now you are passing a mansion, an extraordinary house painted the colour of old cow dung, with more aerials and antennas attached to it than you will see even at the American Embassy. The people who live in this house are a merchant family who came to Antigua from the Middle East less than twenty years ago. When this family first came to Antigua, they sold dry goods door to door from suitcases they carried on their backs. Now they own a lot of Antigua; they regularly lend money to the government, they build enormous (for Antigua), ugly (for Antigua), concrete buildings in Antigua's capital, St. John's, which the government then rents for

---

[2] Industrial city in northern England.   [3] Yorkshire and Lancashire: regions of northern England.

huge sums of money; a member of their family is the Antiguan Ambassador to Syria; Antiguans hate them. Not far from this mansion is another mansion, the home of a drug smuggler. Everybody knows he's a drug smuggler, and if just as you were driving by he stepped out of his door your driver might point him out to you as the notorious person that he is, for this drug smuggler is so rich people say he buys cars in tens—ten of this one, ten of that one—and that he bought a house (another mansion) near Five Islands, contents included, with cash he carried in a suitcase: three hundred and fifty thousand American dollars, and, to the surprise of the seller of the house, lots of American dollars were left over. Overlooking the drug smuggler's mansion is yet another mansion, and leading up to it is the best paved road in all of Antigua—even better than the road that was paved for the Queen's visit in 1985 (when the Queen came, all the roads that she would travel on were paved anew, so that the Queen might have been left with the impression that riding in a car in Antigua was a pleasant experience). In this mansion lives a woman sophisticated people in Antigua call Evita. She is a notorious woman. She's young and beautiful and the girlfriend of somebody very high up in the government. Evita is notorious because her relationship with this high government official has made her the owner of boutiques and property and given her a say in cabinet meetings, and all sorts of other privileges such a relationship would bring a beautiful young woman.

Oh, but by now you are tired of all this looking, and you want to reach your destination—your hotel, your room. You long to refresh yourself; you long to eat some nice lobster, some nice local food. You take a bath, you brush your teeth. You get dressed again; as you get dressed, you look out the window. That water—have you ever seen anything like it? Far out, to the horizon, the colour of the water is navy-blue; nearer, the water is the colour of the North American sky. From there to the shore, the water is pale, silvery, clear, so clear that you can see its pinkish-white sand bottom. Oh, what beauty! Oh, what beauty! You have never seen anything like this. You are so excited. You breathe shallow. You breathe deep. You see a beautiful boy skimming the water, godlike, on a Windsurfer. You see an incredibly unattractive, fat, pastrylike-fleshed woman enjoying a walk on the beautiful sand, with a man, an incredibly unattractive, fat, pastrylike-fleshed man; you see the pleasure they're taking in their surroundings. Still standing, looking out the window, you see yourself lying on the beach, enjoying the amazing sun (a sun so powerful and yet so beautiful, the way it is always overhead as if on permanent guard, ready to stamp out any cloud that dares to darken and so empty rain on you and ruin your holiday; a sun that is your personal friend). You see yourself taking a walk on that beach, you see yourself meeting new people (only they are new in a very limited way, for they are people just like you). You see yourself eating some delicious, locally grown food. You see yourself, you see yourself...You must not wonder what exactly happened to the contents of your lavatory when you flushed it. You must not wonder where your bathwater went when you pulled out the stopper. You must not wonder what happened when you brushed your teeth. Oh, it might all end up in the water you are thinking of taking a swim in; the contents of your lavatory might, just might, graze gently against your ankle as you wade carefree in the water, for you see, in Antigua, there is no proper sewage-disposal system. But the Caribbean Sea is very big and the Atlantic Ocean is even bigger; it would amaze even you to know the number of black slaves this ocean has swallowed up. When you sit down to eat your delicious meal, it's better that you don't know that most of what you are eating came off a plane from Miami. And before it got on a plane in Miami, who knows where it came from? A good guess is that it came from a place like Antigua first, where it was grown dirt-cheap, went to Miami, and came back. There is a world of something in this, but I can't go into it right now.

The thing you have always suspected about yourself the minute you become a tourist is true: A tourist is an ugly human being. You are not an ugly person all the time; you are not an ugly person ordinarily; you are not an ugly person day to day. From day to day, you are a nice person. From day to day, all the people who are supposed to love you on the whole do. From day to day, as you walk down a busy street in the large and modern and prosperous city in which you work and live, dismayed, puzzled (a cliché, but only a cliché can explain you) at how alone you feel in this crowd, how awful it is to go unnoticed, how awful it is to go unloved, even as you are surrounded by more people than you could possibly get to know in a lifetime that lasted for millennia, and then out of the corner of your eye you see someone looking at you and absolute pleasure is written all over that person's face, and then you realise that you are not as revolting a presence as you think you are (for that look just told you so). And so, ordinarily, you are a nice person, an attractive person, a person capable of drawing to yourself the affection of other people (people just like you), a person at home in your own skin (sort of; I mean, in a way; I mean, your dismay and puzzlement are natural to you, because people like you just seem to be like that, and so many of the things people like you find admirable about yourselves—the things you think about, the things you think really define you—seem rooted in these feelings): a person at home in your own house (and all its nice house things), with its nice back yard (and its nice back-yard things), at home on your street, your church, in community activities, your job, at home with your family, your relatives, your friends—you are a whole person. But one day, when you are sitting somewhere, alone in that crowd, and that awful feeling of displacedness comes over you, and really, as an ordinary person you are not well equipped to look too far inward and set yourself aright, because being ordinary is already so taxing, and being ordinary takes all you have out of you, and though the words "I must get away" do not actually pass across your lips, you make a leap from being that nice blob just sitting like a boob in your amniotic sac of the modern experience to being a person visiting heaps of death and ruin and feeling alive and inspired at the sight of it; to being a person lying on some faraway beach, your stilled body stinking and glistening in the sand, looking like something first forgotten, then remembered, then not important enough to go back for; to being a person marvelling at the harmony (ordinarily, what you would say is the backwardness) and the union these other people (and they are other people) have with nature. And you look at the things they can do with a piece of ordinary cloth, the things they fashion out of cheap, vulgarly colored (to you) twine, the way they squat down over a hole they have made in the ground, the hole itself is something to marvel at, and since you are being an ugly person this ugly but joyful thought will swell inside you: their ancestors were not clever in the way yours were and not ruthless in the way yours were, for then would it not be you who would be in harmony with nature and backwards in that charming way? An ugly thing, that is what you are when you become a tourist, an ugly, empty thing, a stupid thing, a piece of rubbish pausing here and there to gaze at this and taste that, and it will never occur to you that the people who inhabit the place in which you have just paused cannot stand you, that behind their closed doors they laugh at your strangeness (you do not look the way they look); the physical sight of you does not please them; you have bad manners (it is their custom to eat their food with their hands; you try eating their way, you look silly; you try eating the way you always eat, you look silly); they do not like the way you speak (you have an accent); they collapse helpless from laughter, mimicking the way they imagine you must look as you carry out some everyday bodily function. They do not like you. *They do not like me!* That thought never actually occurs to you. Still, you feel a little uneasy. Still, you feel a little foolish. Still, you feel a little out of place. But the banality of your own life is very real to you; it drove you to this extreme, spending your days and your nights in the company of people who despise you, people you do not like really, people you would not want to have as your actual neighbour. And so you must devote yourself to puzzling out how much of what you are told is really, really true (Is ground-up bottle glass in peanut sauce really a delicacy around here, or will it do just what you think ground-up bottle glass will do? Is this rare, multicoloured, snout-mouthed fish really an aphrodisiac, or will it cause you to fall asleep permanently?). Oh, the hard work all of this is, and is it any wonder, then, that on your return home you feel the need of a long rest, so that you can recover from your life as a tourist?

That the native does not like the tourist is not hard to explain. For every native of every place is a potential tourist, and every tourist is a native of somewhere. Every native everywhere lives a life of overwhelming and crushing banality and boredom and desperation and depression, and every deed, good and bad, is an attempt to forget this. Every native would like to find a way out, every native would like a rest, every native would like a tour. But some natives—most natives in the world—cannot go anywhere. They are too poor. They are too poor to go anywhere. They are too poor to escape the reality of their lives; and they are too poor to live properly in the place where they live, which is the very place you, the tourist, want to go—so when the natives see you, the tourist, they envy you, they envy your ability to leave your own banality and boredom, they envy your ability to turn their own banality and boredom into a source of pleasure for yourself.

—1988

HOLLY NEAR (1949-)

Born in Ukiah, California, and raised in a politically active environment, Holly Near was a major voice of the women's music movement of the 1970s. Not only did she produce many albums of women-centered, politically driven songs, she also controlled the use of this material and created a space for other women artists by founding the Redwood Records label, with which she toured tirelessly for political causes, including an anti-Vietnam War tour of Southeast Asia called "Free the Army." Near has collaborated with many of the major figures of folk music, including Pete Seeger, Ronnie Gilbert, and Mary Travers. In addition to writing lyrics about a range of contemporary issues, Near co-authored the autobiographical book *Fire in the Rain...Singer in the Storm: An Autobiography* (1990), co-authored the play *Fire in the Rain* (1993), and also created the lyrical text for a children's book entitled *The Great Peace March* (1993). She has received several awards for promoting international peace and raising popular awareness of human rights injustices through her music and her work in the women's community, including the Legends of Women's Music Award in 2000, the 1997 California State Governor's Award, and a nomination for the "1000 Women for the Nobel Peace Prize" in 2005. The selection included here, "Hay Una Mujer," was Near's intervention on behalf of *las desaparecidas* in Chile; the text was updated to reflect a wide range of contemporary Latin American concerns.

Hay Una Mujer

Michelle Peña Herrera
Nalvia Rosa Meña Alvarado
Cecelia Castro Salvadores
Ida Amelia Amarza.[1]

Chorus 1
Hay una mujer desaparecida,   5
Hay una mujer desaparecida
En Chile, en Chile, en Chile.[2]

Chorus 2
And the junta, and the junta knows[3]
And the junta knows where she is
And the junta knows where they are   10
Hiding her, she's dying.
Hay una mujer desaparecida.
Hay una mujer desaparecida
En Chile, en Chile, en Chile.

Clara Elena Cantero   15
Elisa del Carmen Escobar
Eliana Maria Espinosa
Rosa Elena Morales

[*Chorus 1 and 2, repeat Chorus 1*]

Missing in Brazil
Missing in Uruguay   20
Missing in Guatemala
Missing in El Salvador

(Hay) un hombre
Hay un niño
O los niños   25
Hay una mujer desaparecida.[4]

A spirit lives in Chile
New lives, new songs

---

[1] These four women, and the four named in the second verse, were among the many thousands of those who "disappeared" *(los desaparacidos)* in Chile under the military dictator Augusto Pinochet (1915-2006).

[2] (Sp.) There is a missing woman/There is a missing woman/In Chile, in Chile, in Chile.

[3] The military coup that overthrew the democratically elected government of Salvador Allende in 1973 resulted in the formation of the Government Junta of Chile, led by Augusto Pinochet.

[4] (Sp.) There is a man/There is a child/O the children/There is a missing woman.

A spirit grows in Chile
New lives, new songs are rising up 30

A spirit sings in Chile
New lives, new songs are rising up
A spirit lives in Chile
New lives, new songs
In Chile!

—1978

C.D. WRIGHT (1949-   )

The Israel J. Kapstein Professor of English at Brown University and a former state poet of
Rhode Island, C.D. Wright was born and raised in the Ozark Mountains of Arkansas. Her
Southern roots no doubt propelled her toward two projects in particular: she curated "a walkin book of Arkansas" exhibition with funding from the Lila Wallace-Reader's Digest
Foundation, and she wrote poetic text to accompany photographs by Deborah Luster for *One
Big Self: Prisoners of Louisiana* (2003). The latter project examines prisoners through their por-
traiture, as well as the concept of incarceration itself. Her ten books of poetry include two
book-length poems: *Deepstep Come Shining* (1998) and *Just Whistle* (1993), another photo-
poetic collaboration with Deborah Luster. *Steal Away: Selected and New Poems* was published in
2002. Although Wright does not consider herself an experimental poet, she uses poetry to
explore a subject from multiple perspectives, expanding the lyric form beyond its conventional
relational frame. Her work has garnered fellowships and awards from the Guggenheim
Foundation, the National Endowment for the Arts, and the Lannan Foundation. In addition
to teaching and writing, Wright edits Lost Roads Publishers with poet Forrest Gander, with
whom she has a son. They live outside of Providence, Rhode Island.

The Secret Life of Musical Instruments

Between midnight and Reno
the world borders on a dune.
The bus does not stop.

The boys in the band have their heads on the rest.
They dream like so-and-sos. 5

The woman smokes
one after another.
She is humming "Strange Fruit."[1]
There is smoke in her clothes, her voice,
but her hair never smells. 10

She blows white petals off her lapel,
tastes salt.
It is a copacetic moon.

[1] Song written by Abel Meeropol and made famous by Billie Holiday.

The instruments do not sleep in their dark cribs.
They keep cool, meditate.   15
They have speech with strangers:

Come all ye faithless
young and crazy victims of love.
Come the lowlife and the highborn
all ye upside-down shitasses.   20

Bring your own light.
Come in. Be lost. Be still.
If you miss us at home
we'll be on our way to the reckoning.

for Claudia Burson

—1982

[Hole of holes]

Hole of holes: world in the world of the os, an ode, unspoken, hole in its
infancy, uncuretted, sealed, not yet yielded, nulliparous mouth, girdle
against growth, inland orifice, capital O, pore, aperture to the aleph, within
which all, the over-stocked pond, entrance to vast funnel of silence, howling os, an idea of beautiful form, original opening, whistling well, first vor-
tex, an idea of form, a beautiful idea, a just idea of form, unplugged,
reamed, scored, plundered, insubduable opening, lightsource, it opens.
This changes everything.

—1993

Dear Prisoner,

    I too love.   Faces.   Hands.   The circumference
Of the oaks.   I confess.   To nothing
You could use.   In a court of law.   I found.
That sickly sweet ambrosia of hope.   Unmendable
Seine of sadness.   Experience taken away.   5
From you.   I would open.   The mystery
Of your birth.   To you.   I know.   We can
Change.   Knowing.   Full well.   Knowing.
                                It is not enough.
    poetry   time   space   death   10
I thought.   I could write.   An exculpatory note.
I cannot.   Yes, it is bitter.   Every bit of it, bitter.
The course taken by blood.   All thinking
Deceives us.   Lead (kindly) light.
Notwithstanding this grave.   Your garden.   15
This cell.   Your dwelling.   Who is unaccountably free.

—2003

JULIA ALVAREZ (1950-   )

Born in New York City, Julia Alvarez and her family returned to the Dominican Republic when she was three months old. She spent the first ten years of her life there, but the family fled in 1960 because of her father's underground political activities against the U.S.-backed dictatorship of General Rafael Trujillo. Alvarez's first novel, *How the Garcia Girls Lost Their Accents* (1991), is a semi-autobiographical account of her family's transition into American life. Alvarez has published several books, collections of essays, and poetry, including three historical novels based on heroic women from the Dominican Republic and Spain. The first of these, *In the Time of the Butterflies* (1994), offers a fictional account of the Mirabal sisters, three women who founded the underground resistance movement in the Dominican Republic and who were brutally murdered by the Trujillo dictatorship shortly after Alvarez's family fled the country. Her second historical novel, *In the Name of Salomé* (2000), centers on the relationship between Salomé Ureña, a renowned nineteenth-century Dominican poet and feminist, and her only daughter, Camila, who taught in the prestigious summer language program at Middlebury College, where Alvarez is a writer-in-residence today.

How I Learned to Sweep

My mother never taught me sweeping...
One afternoon she found me watching
t.v. She eyed the dusty floor
boldly, and put a broom before
me, and said she'd like to be able   5
to eat her dinner off that table,
and nodded at my feet, then left.
I knew right off what she expected
and went at it. I stepped and swept;
the t.v. blared the news; I kept   10
my mind on what I had to do,
until in minutes, I was through.
Her floor was as immaculate
as a just-washed dinner plate.
I waited for her to return   15
and turned to watch the President,
live from the White House, talk of war:
in the Far East our soldiers were
landing in their helicopters
into jungles their propellors   20
swept like weeds seen underwater
while perplexing shots were fired
from those beautiful green gardens
into which these dragonflies
filled with little men descended.   25
I got up and swept again
as they fell out of the sky.
I swept all the harder when
I watched a dozen of them die...
as if their dust fell through the screen   30

upon the floor I had just cleaned.
She came back and turned the dial;
the screen went dark. *That's beautiful,*
she said, and ran her clean hand through
my hair, and on, over the window-   35
sill, coffee table, rocker, desk,
and held it up—I held my breath—
that's beautiful, she said, impressed,
she hadn't found a speck of death.

—1985

On Not Shoplifting Louise Bogan's *The Blue Estuaries*

Connecticut College, fall 1968

Your book surprised me on the bookstore shelf—
swans gliding on a blueblack lake;
no blurbs by the big boys on back;
no sassy, big-haired picture
to complicate the achievement;   5
no mentors musing
over how they had discovered
you had it in you
before you even knew
you had it in you.   10
The swans posed on a placid lake,
your name blurred underwater
sinking to the bottom.

I had begun to haunt
the poetry shelf at the college store—   15
thin books crowded in by texts,
reference tomes and a spread
of magazines for persistent teens
on how to get their boys,
Chaucer-Milton-Shakespeare-Yeats.[1]   20
Your name was not familiar,
I took down the book and read.

Page after page, your poems
were stirring my own poems—
words rose, breaking the surface,   25
shattering an old silence.
I leaned closer to the print
until I could almost feel
the blue waters drawn
into the tip of my pen.   30
I bore down on the page,

---

[1] Geoffrey Chaucer (ca. 1343-1400), English poet; John Milton (1608-1674), English poet; William Shakespeare (1564-1616), English dramatist; William Butler Yeats (1865-1939), Irish poet.

the lake flowed out again,
the swans, the darkening sky.
For a moment I lost my doubts,
my girl's voice, my coming late   35
into this foreign alphabet.
I read and wrote as I read.

I wanted to own this moment.
My breath came quickly, thinking it over—
I had no money, no one was looking.   40
The swans posed on the cover,
their question-mark necks arced
over the dark waters.
I was asking them what to do...

The words they swam over answered.   45
I held the book closed before me
as if it were something else,
a mirror reflecting back
someone I was becoming.
The swans dipped their alphabet necks   50
in the blueblack ink of the lake.
I touched their blank, downy sides, musing,
and I put the book back.

—1995

Making Up the Past

This never happened and yet I want the memory
so much I have made it true, recalling

a fall day our third year (and a month)
in this country: the house recently bought

in a nice neighborhood, my sisters and I paired up   5
in the two immaculate bedrooms that look out

into the sad box of a backyard, a yard
I will wander in all my long adolescence

searching for answers that will never be there
in the tidy oak (my sister says maple)   10

and the scrappy bushes of something
that never did well in the shade.

The memory or rather pseudo memory
is of my mother in a bathrobe at the window

watching my progress down the block   15
and around the corner until I am out of sight,

not knowing (how could she know?)
and knowing (she always knows everything!)

of my terror at setting off by myself
to Hillside to pick up something she needs.   20

I'm pretending to myself and to her that my fear
is really excitement, that I want to be

adrift in America without her,
that if by the time I head back

the ground gives, the streets shift   25
(I am sure this will happen),

and I cannot find her up the hill
of our driveway at the bay of little windows,

why then, I'll survive, an ethnic Dorothy[2]
(my first beloved American movie)   30

who never gets back to her Mami in Kansas
but gets caught up in the rest of her life.

This is how my memory ends my childhood,
with a made-up moment of my mother

in a flowered bathrobe she never owned,   35
the zipper fixed twice already

from my mother's roughhandling
(always in a hurry), her hands lifting

though even with the tints of memory
I can't touch up the gesture as goodbye   40

(she is checking a smudge on the glass),
a memory doublecoded in Spanish

so that I also remember *Mami
acechándome por la ventana.*[3]

What could possess me to invent this?   45
As if we need to stage our losses,

set the lights just so, dress our mothers
like dolls in the clothes we make up for them,

and then rewind to the moment of departure,
the kiss at the door, the query, *Do you have*   50

enough money? the click of the latch, the jingling
of the chain lock sliding back in its groove.

---

[2] Dorothy Gale, the heroine of L. Frank Baum's classic
novel, *The Wonderful Wizard of Oz* (1900).

[3] (Sp.) Mommy spying on me from the window.

Even now when I know half a dozen ways
to get back to that mock Tudor house

on a hillock of landfill, even now   55
I can make myself feel lost all over again,

feel that thirty years have passed in which
all I've been doing is reading street signs

for a way back to a moment that never
(I am sure of it) happened. So be it—   60

this movie we must make of the past
so it doesn't break our hearts,

or worse, leave us, in remembering it,
leave us, untouched and dismissive, turning

the pages of our albums, reading the captions   65
to what we can prove really happened—

which will never be this moment I made up
of my mother's hand lifting, my steady progress

down the block, my shoulders already set
in a posture I assume every time   70

I sit down to write—a feisty, terrified squaring
of the shoulders—my hands fisting

in my pockets and all of me refusing
(for the moment) to turn back and face

what I am leaving behind, what I must know   75
I will keep coming back to all my imagined life.

—for David Huddle

—1996

FRANCES CHUNG (1950-1990)

Frances Chung was born and raised on the border between New York City's Chinatown and
Little Italy. After graduating from Smith College, she returned to the Lower East Side to teach
math in the public schools, often in Spanish. Much of Chung's poetry describes the streets and
neighborhoods she inhabited in a compact, episodic, and imagistic style that is subtle and com-
passionate, yet often somewhat impersonal. Her work is significant for historical reasons as
well, as it captures a particular segment of 1960s and 1970s New York life. Chung's travels in
Central and South America, Europe, Asia, and Africa also informed her writing. Chung was
awarded poetry fellowships by both the New York State Council on the Arts and the New York

Times Company Foundation, and her poetry has been included in several anthologies, including *Ordinary Women/Mujeres Comunes: An Anthology of Poetry by New York City Women* (1978), *American Born and Foreign: An Anthology of Asian American Poetry* (1979), as well as in the journals *Bridge* and *IKON*. When she died in 1990 at the age of forty, Chung left behind assorted manuscripts in various stages. Writer and editor Walter K. Lew collected and published these writings as *Crazy Melon and Chinese Apple: The Poems of Frances Chung* in 2000.

[Neon lights that warm no one. How long]

Neon lights that warm no one. How long
ago have we stopped reading the words
and the colors? On Saturday night,
the streets are so crowded with people
that to walk freely I have to walk in   5
the gutter. The visitors do not hear
you when you say excuse me. They are
so busy taking in the wonders of Chinatown.
People line up to enter the restaurant
(you must know which one). The way   10
the couples hold each other they make
it seem like Coney Island. They are
busy looking for Buddhas and gifts to
take home. Some men are looking for
'Asian chicks.' There is a deficiency   15
of Chinese couples. Windchimes chime on.
Bells ring on. Paperweights sit and
stare as if from under a pond. The
irony reeks.

—CA. 1977

[Yo vivo en el barrio chino]

Yo vivo en el barrio chino
de Nueva York...I live in
New York's Chinatown. Some
call it a ghetto, some call
it a slum, some call it home.   5
Little Italy or Northern
Chinatown, to my mind, the
boundaries have become fluid.
I have two Chinatown moods.
Times when Chinatown is a   10
terrible place to live in.
Times when Chinatown is the
only place to live...

—CA. 1977

Double Ten (10/10 day)[1]

early morning
the Sunday sound of an accordion
a conversation with two Ukrainian women
about calling the plumber
taking baths in our kitchens   5
you like the green stone around my neck
later on the Bowery
black man strutting along
singing a Chinatown ballad
as I sing one of Billie's songs   10
in your kitchen warmer than mine
the strong smell of black mushrooms

—CA. 1977-80

[1] Double Ten Day, the national holiday of the Republic of China, celebrates the Wuchang Uprising of October 10, 1911.

CAROLYN FORCHÉ (1950-   )

Poet, translator, editor, and essayist Carolyn Forché was born in Detroit, Michigan, and holds an M.F.A. from Bowling Green State University. Her first book, *Gathering the Tribes* (1976), was selected for the Yale Series of Younger Poets. Her next volume of poetry, *The Country Between Us* (1981), was a Lamont Poetry Selection and won the Alice Fay di Castagnola Award from the Poetry Society of America. These were followed by *The Angel of History* (1994) and *Blue Hour* (2004). Forché has received numerous awards, including the *Los Angeles Times* Book Award for Poetry, the Edita and Ira Morris Hiroshima Foundation Award for Peace and Culture, and fellowships from the Lannan Foundation and the National Endowment for the Arts. Following her 1983 translation of *Flowers from the Volcano* by Claribel Alegría, a poet who had been exiled from El Salvador by Anastasio Somoza, Forché received a Guggenheim Foundation Fellowship and went to El Salvador, where she was a human rights worker. Known as both an activist and a political poet, Forché edited the anthology *Against Forgetting: 20th Century Poetry of Witness* in 1983. Her review essays and articles have appeared in *The Nation, The New York Times,* and *Mother Jones,* among others. She teaches in the M.F.A. program at George Mason University in Fairfax, Virginia.

The Colonel

What you have heard is true. I was in his house. His wife carried a tray of coffee and sugar. His daughter filed her nails, his son went out for the night. There were daily papers, pet dogs, a pistol on the cushion beside him. The moon swung bare on its black cord over the house. On the television was a cop show. It was in English. Broken bottles were embedded in the walls around the house to scoop the kneecaps from a man's legs or cut his hands to lace. On the windows there were gratings like those in liquor stores. We had dinner, rack of lamb, good wine, a gold bell was on the table for calling the maid. The maid brought green mangoes, salt, a type of bread. I was asked how I enjoyed the country. There was a brief commercial in Spanish. His wife took everything away. There was some talk then of how difficult it had become to govern. The parrot said hello on the terrace. The colonel told it to shut up, and pushed himself from the table. My friend said to me with his eyes: say nothing. The colonel returned with a sack used to bring groceries home. He spilled many human ears on the table. They were like dried peach halves. There is no other way to say this. He took one of them in his hands, shook it in our faces, dropped it into a water glass. It came alive there. I am tired of fooling around he said. As for the rights of anyone, tell your people they can go fuck themselves. He swept the ears to the floor with his arm and held the last of his wine in the air. Something for your poetry, no? he said. Some of the ears on the floor caught this scrap of his voice. Some of the ears on the floor were pressed to the ground.

May 1978

[—1981]

The Garden Shukkei-en[1]

By way of a vanished bridge we cross this river
as a cloud of lifted snow would ascend a mountain.

She has always been afraid to come here.

It is the river she most
remembers, the living   5
and the dead both crying for help.

A world that allowed neither tears nor lamentation.

The *matsu* trees brush her hair as she passes
beneath them, as do the shining strands of barbed wire.

Where this lake is, there was a lake,   10
where these black pine grow, there grew black pine.

Where there is no teahouse I see a wooden teahouse
and the corpses of those who slept in it.

On the opposite bank of the Ota, a weeping willow
etches its memory of their faces into the water.   15

Where light touches the face, the character for heart is written.

She strokes a burnt trunk wrapped in straw:
I was weak and my skin hung from my fingertips like cloth

---

[1] A garden in Hiroshima whose name translates as "the garden of condensed beauty."

Do you think for a moment we were human beings to them?
She comes to the stone angel holding paper cranes.   20
Not an angel, but a woman where she once had been,
who walks through the garden Shukkei-en
calling the carp to the surface by clapping her hands.

Do Americans think of us?

So she began as we squatted over the toilets: 25
If you want, I'll tell you, but nothing I say will be enough.

We tried to dress our burns with vegetable oil.

Her hair is the white froth of rice rising up kettlesides, her mind also.
In the postwar years she thought deeply about how to live.

The common greeting *dozo-yiroshku* is please take care of me.   30
All *hibakusha*[2] still alive were children then.

A cemetery seen from the air is a child's city.

I don't like this particular red flower because
it reminds me of a woman's brain crushed under a roof.

Perhaps my language is too precise, and therefore difficult to
    understand?   35

We have not, all these years, felt what you call happiness.
But at times, with good fortune, we experience something close.
As our life resembles life, and this garden the garden.
And in the silence surrounding what happened to us

it is the bell to awaken God that we've heard ringing.   40

—1994

[2] (Jap.) Bomb victim.

JORIE GRAHAM (1950-   )

Born in New York, Jorie Graham grew up in France and Italy. Her mother was a sculptor and her father was *Newsweek*'s Rome bureau chief. She attended the Sorbonne, from which she was dismissed for her participation in student protests, and she finished her degree at New York University, where she studied film with Martin Scorsese. She went on to complete an M.F.A. at the University of Iowa in 1978. Between 1980 and 2002, she published nine books of poetry. Considered by many to be one of the most innovative of contemporary American poets, Graham has been awarded the Pulitzer Prize, a MacArthur Fellowship, the Morton Dauwen Zabel Award from the American Academy and Institute of Arts and Letters, as well as grants from the National Endowment for the Arts and the Guggenheim Foundation. She was the first woman to be named Boylston Professor of Rhetoric and Oratory at Harvard University.

The Geese

Today as I hang out the wash I see them again, a code
as urgent as elegant,
tapering with goals.
For days they have been crossing. We live beneath these geese

as if beneath the passage of time, or a most perfect heading.   5
Sometimes I fear their relevance.
Closest at hand,
between the lines,

the spiders imitate the paths the geese won't stray from,
imitate them endlessly to no avail: 10
things will not remain connected,
will not heal,

and the world thickens with texture instead of history,
texture instead of place.
Yet the small fear of the spiders   15
binds and binds

the pins to the lines, the lines to the eaves, to the pincushion bush,
as if, at any time, things could fall further apart
and nothing could help them
recover their meaning. And if these spiders had their way,   20

chainlink over the visible world,
would we be in or out? I turn to go back in.
There is a feeling the body gives the mind
of having missed something, a bedrock poverty, like falling

without the sense that you are passing through one world,   25
that you could reach another
anytime. Instead the real
is crossing you,

your body an arrival
you know is false but can't outrun. And somewhere in between   30
these geese forever entering and
these spiders turning back,

this astonishing delay, the everyday, takes place.

—1980

I Was Taught Three

names for the tree facing my window
almost within reach, elastic

with squirrels, memory banks, homes.
Castagno took itself to heart, its pods

like urchins clung to where they landed   5
claiming every bit of shadow

at the hem. *Chassagne,* on windier days,
nervous in taffeta gowns,

whispering, on the verge of being
anarchic, though well bred.   10

And then *chestnut,* whipped pale and clean
by all the inner reservoirs

called upon to do their even share of work.
It was not the kind of tree

got at by default—imagine that—not one   15
in which only the remaining leaf

was loyal. No, this
was all first person, and I

was the stem, holding within myself the whole
bouquet of three,   20

at once given and received: smallest roadmaps
of coincidence. What is the idea

that governs blossoming? The human tree
clothed with its nouns, or this one

just outside my window promising more firmly   25
than can be

that it will reach my sill eventually, the leaves
silent as suppressed desires, and I

a name among them.

—1980

SAPPHIRE (1950-   )

Poet, writer, and performance artist Sapphire was born Ramona Lofton in Fort Ord, California. She spent much of her childhood on Army bases in California and Texas, but moved to Los Angeles when she was sixteen to live with her father after her parents' divorce. She went on to study chemistry and dance at San Francisco's City College before moving to New York, where she earned a degree in dance from City College in Harlem in 1993, followed by an M.F.A. from Brooklyn College, where she received a poetry scholarship from the MacArthur Foundation. Sapphire has published two collections of poetry, *Meditations on the Rainbow* (1987) and *Black Wings & Blind Angels* (1999), and a collection of poetry and prose, *American Dreams* (1994). Her novel *Push* (1996) won numerous awards, including a Book-of-the-Month Club Stephen Crane Award for First Fiction and, in Great Britain, The Mind Book of the Year Award. *Push* was cited as one of the "Best Books of 1996" by both *The Village Voice* and *Timeout New York*. Sapphire's work, which has been translated into several languages and has been adapted for the stage, is often controversial in its focus on issues such as incest, AIDS, and domestic violence; her poem "Wild Thing" was copied and distributed throughout the White House by conservatives working with Jesse Helms to end funding for the National Endowment for the Arts. Sapphire has taught at various colleges and universities, and in 1990 she received an Outstanding Achievement in Teaching Award for her work with literacy students in Harlem and the Bronx. She lives in New York.

American Dreams

Suspended in a sea of blue-gray slate
I can't move from the waist down
which brings visions & obsessions of & with
quadriplegics & paraplegics,
wondering how they live, smell,   5
why they don't just die.
Some people wonder that about blacks,
why they don't just die.
A light-skinned black woman I know
once uttered in amazement about a black black woman   10
"I wanted to know how did she *live*
being as black as she was!"
I don't quite know how to get free
of the karma I've created
but I can see clearly now   15
that I have created my life.
My right ankle has mud in it,
I'm in debt.
I need dental work
& I am alone.   20
Alone if I keep seeing myself
through "Donna Reed"[1] & "Father Knows Best"[2] eyes,
if I don't see the friends,
people who care,
giving as much from their lives as they can.   25
If you live in the red paper valentine of first grade in 1956
then you are alone.
If you live in the world of now
of people struggling free
then you are not.   30

Isolation rises up
like the marble slabs
placed on the front
of cheap concrete high-rises
with apartments that start at 500,000 dollars.   35

---

[1] Family situation comedy that aired from 1958 to 1966.   [2] Family situation comedy that aired from 1954 to 1960.

It all seems so stupid
but I understand it now,
why they have homeless people
sleeping in front of these
artificial-penis-looking buildings.   40
It's so we'll move in,
so such terror will be implanted
in our guts
we'll save our money
& buy a concrete box   45
to live in & be proud
to call it home.
All anybody really wants
is some security,
a chance to live comfortably   50
until the next
unavoidable tragedy
unavoidably hits them
& splices open their chests,
& takes the veins from their legs,   55
& carves up their heart
in the name of surgery
or vicious murder
murder
murderer   60
ha! ha! ha!
murderer.
No one,
nothing
can protect you   65
from the murderer.
Not the police, nuclear weapons, your mother, the
Republicans, mx missiles—
none of that
can protect you   70
from the murderer.
Even if you get all the niggers
out the neighborhood
the murderer might be
a white boy like David Berkowitz[3]   75
baby-faced Jewish boy
who rarely missed a day
of work at the post office.
ha! ha! ha!
you're never safe!   80
Like a crab walking sideways
America hides its belly

---

[3] David Berkowitz (b. 1953), American serial killer known as "Son of Sam."

under an arsenal of radioactive crust,
creeping along with its
long crustacean eyes,   85
stupid & blind
sucking debris from
the ocean floor
till there is no more,
while the giant Cancer breasts   90
get biopsied & amputated
& the crab caves in
under the third world's dreams
& 5 million pounds of concrete.
& the murderer   95
stabs stabs stabs
at the underbelly &
submicroscopic
viruses
fly out   100
in
ejaculate
& claim
your life,
while the powers that don't be   105
join
for a loving circle jerk
& nostalgic reminiscence
of days gone by,
lighting candles for Roy Cohn[4]   110
& J. Edgar Hoover[5]
as they lay a bouquet of cigarettes
on John Wayne's[6] grave
who is clandestinely slipping
into the wax museum   115
to suck Michael Jackson's[7] dick
only to find he has had his penis
surgically reconstructed
to look like Diana Ross's[8] face.
& the Trane[9] flies on   120
like Judy Grahn's[10] wild geese
over a land diseased like cancer
killing flowers by the hour
& a huge hospice
opens up in the sky   125
& the man quietly tells his wife

---

[4] Roy Cohn (1927-1986), lawyer and chief counsel for
Senator Joseph McCarthy.
[5] J. Edgar Hoover (1895-1972), director of the Federal
Bureau of Investigation (FBI) from 1924 until his death.
[6] John Wayne (1907-1979), American actor.

[7] Michael Jackson (b. 1958), American pop star.
[8] Diana Ross (b. 1944), American pop star.
[9] John Coltrane (1926-1967), American jazz musician.
[10] Judy Grahn (b. 1940), American poet.

as he picks up his rifle,
"I'm going people hunting."
& he steps calmly
into McDonald's & picks off 130
20 people
& blood pours red
Big Macs fall flat
to the floor amid
shrieks & screams 135
while a plastic clown
smiles down on the house
additives & the destruction of
the rain forests built.
& you smile for a while 140
feeling ever so American
& in good company
as you eat compulsively.
After all,
the whole country does it. 145
It's just pasta heaven here
till you get your x-ray
or biopsy back.
Making the world safe
for democracy 150
& you can't even evade
heart disease
until you're 40,
& it attacks quietly
walking on those big 155
expensive sneakers
niggers wear
as they shove the pawn shop gun
to your head & say,
"GIMME EVERYTHING YOU GOT!" 160
& for once you are not afraid
cause the nigger has AIDS.
You laugh triumphantly,
finally you've given him
& the world 165
everything you got!

I was at Clark Center for the Performing Arts
getting ready for my morning ballet class
when this old wrinkled-up white faggot
ran up to me, threw his arms around me & grabbed me 170
in a vise-like grip & screamed:
BE MY BLACK MAMMY SAPPHIRE
BE MY BLACK MAMMY
He held on & wouldn't let go.

Finally I thought to turn   175
my hand into a claw
& raked straight down his face
with my fingernails.
He let go.
I'll never forget how   180
hurt & bewildered he looked.
I guess he was just playing.
I was just devastated.

There are no words
for some forms   185
of devastation
though we constantly
try to describe
what America has done
& continues to do to us.   190
We try to describe it
without whining
or quitting
or eating french fries
or snorting coke.   195
It's so hard not
to be an addict in America
when you know numerology
& have x-rayed the inside
of Egyptian mummies 5,000 years old   200
& robbed the graves of Indians
deliberately blinded children
& infected monkeys & rats
with diseases you keep alive
waiting for the right time   205
so you can spring 'em
on anyone who might be making progress.

Well, you're miserable now America.
The fact you put a flag
on the moon   210
doesn't mean you own it.
You can't steal everything
all the time
from everybody.
You can't have the moon, sucker.   215

A peanut farmer
warned
you could not stay number 1;
number 1 being an illusion
in a circle, which is   220
what the world is,

but you still think that
the world is flat
& you can drive out evil
with a pitchfork & pickup truck.   225

One time when I was a little girl living on an army base
I was in the gymnasium & the general walked in.
& the general is like god or the president, if you believe.
The young woman who was supervising
the group of children I was with said,   230
"Stand up everybody! The general's here!"
Everybody stood up except me.
The woman looked at me & hissed,
"Stand up for the general!"
I said, "My father's in the army, not me."   235
& I remained seated.
& throughout 38 years
of bucking & winging
grinning & crawling
brown nosing & begging   240
there has been a quiet
10 year old in me
who has remained seated.
She perhaps is the real American Dream.

—1994

THERESA HAK KYUNG CHA (1951-1982)

An experimental multimedia and performance artist, Theresa Hak Kyung Cha was born in Pusan, Korea, of parents who were exiled in Manchuria during the Japanese occupation of Korea. She moved with her family to San Francisco in 1964, after living briefly in Hawaii. Cha studied comparative literature and art at the University of California, Berkeley, earning two B.A. degrees, an M.A., and an M.F.A. She also attended Centre d'Etudes Américaine du Cinéma in Paris in 1976. Cha traveled to Korea in 1979, returning twice over the next few years. She was murdered in 1982 in New York City, where she had moved in 1980.

Cha is best known for her experimental collage text *Dictee,* which includes such diverse elements as translation exercises, catechism lessons, journals, poetry, photographs, film stills, found letters, historical documents, a map of Korea divided by the Demilitarized Zone, anatomical charts of the human body, and references to Greek mythology, Japanese colonialism, and U.S. citizenship. *Dictee* is considered an important avant-garde, postcolonial Korean-American text. A primary concern of Cha's art is the relationship between geographical dislocation, linguistic dislocation, and psychic dislocation. Her art has been exhibited at the Whitney Museum of American Art and the University Art Museum at the University of California, Berkeley.

from Dictee

Diseuse[1]

She mimicks the speaking. That might resemble speech. (Anything at all.) Bared noise, groan, bits torn from words. Since she hesitates to measure the accuracy, she resorts to mimicking gestures with the mouth. The entire lower lip would lift upwards then sink back to its original place. She would then gather both lips and protrude them in a pout taking in the breath that might utter some thing. (One thing. Just one.) But the breath falls away. With a slight tilting of her head backwards, she would gather the strength in her shoulders and remain in this position.

It murmurs inside. It murmurs. Inside is the pain of speech the pain to say. Larger still. Greater than is the pain not to say. To not say. Says nothing against the pain to speak. It festers inside. The wound, liquid, dust. Must break. Must void.

From the back of her neck she releases her shoulders free. She swallows once more. (Once more. One more time would do.) In preparation. It augments. To such a pitch. Endless drone, refueling itself. Autonomous. Self-generating. Swallows with last efforts last wills against the pain that wishes it to speak.

She allows others. In place of her. Admits others to make full. Make swarm. All barren cavities to make swollen. The others each occupying her. Tumorous layers, expel all excesses until in all cavities she is flesh.

She allows herself caught in their threading, anonymously in their thick motion in the weight of their utterance. When the amplification stops there might be an echo. She might make the attempt then. The echo part. At the pause. When the pause has already soon begun and has rested there still. She waits inside the pause. Inside her. Now. This very moment. Now. She takes rapidly the air, in gulfs, in preparation for the distances to come. The pause ends. The voice wraps another layer. Thicker now even. From the waiting. The wait from pain to say. To not to. Say.

She would take on their punctuation. She waits to service this. Theirs. Punctuation. She would become, herself, demarcations. Absorb it. Spill it. Seize upon the punctuation. Last air. Give her. Her. The relay. Voice. Assign. Hand it. Deliver it. Deliver.

She relays the others. Recitation. Evocation. Offering. Provocation. The begging. Before her. Before them.

Now the weight begins from the uppermost back of her head, pressing downward. It stretches evenly, the entire skull expanding tightly all sides toward the front of her head. She gasps from its pressure, its contracting motion.

Inside her voids. It does not contain further. Rising from the empty below, pebble lumps of gas. Moisture. Begin to flood her. Dissolving her. Slow, slowed to deliberation. Slow and thick.

The above traces from her head moving downward closing her eyes, in the same motion, slower parting her mouth open together with her jaw and throat which the above falls falling just to the end not stopping there but turning her inside out in the same motion, shifting complete the whole weight to elevate upward.

---

[1] (Fr.) Speaker, reciter (feminine).

Begins imperceptibly, near-perceptible. (Just once. Just one time and it will take.) She takes. She takes the pause. Slowly. From the thick. The thickness. From weighted motion upwards. Slowed. To deliberation even when it passed upward through her mouth again. The delivery. She takes it. Slow. The invoking. All the time now. All the time there is. Always. And all times. The pause. Uttering. Hers now. Hers bare. The utter.

—1982

JOY HARJO (1951-)

Joy Harjo, the oldest of four siblings, was born on May 9, 1951, in Tulsa, Oklahoma, to Allen W. Foster, a Creek (Muscogee) who worked as an airplane mechanic, and Wynema Baker Foster, of mixed Cherokee and French-Canadian ancestry. Harjo left home at sixteen to attend high school at the Institute of American Indian Arts in Santa Fe, New Mexico, where she became an actor and dancer in Rosalie Jones' all-Indian dance troupe Deep Roots, Tall Cedar. After receiving a B.A. in Creative Writing from the University of New Mexico, Harjo earned an M.F.A. in Creative Writing from the Iowa Writers' Workshop while raising two children alone. During these difficult years, she took two steps that would help solidify her identity and her poetic voice. She took the surname of her paternal grandmother, Naomi Harjo, an accomplished painter and college graduate who served as a kind of mentor. She also enrolled as a member of the Muscogee tribe of the Creek Indian Nation.

Harjo's poetry has evolved from short, personal lyrics to a more expansive poetry of witness and storytelling. She uses elements of Native American spirituality (trickster figures, nature imagery, chanting, creation stories, shifting boundaries between animate and inanimate worlds, and non-linear time) and jazz and blues rhythms in much of her work. She also has a music career, playing saxophone solo and with her band Poetic Justice, and has combined spoken word and music on two albums, *Letters from the End of the Twentieth Century* (1997) and *Native Joy for Real* (2004). Harjo does not consider herself a feminist, but she calls her work "woman-identified," and the influence of feminist poets such as Adrienne Rich and Audre Lorde is clearly present in poems from her volumes *She Had Some Horses* (1983), *In Mad Love and War* (1990), and *The Woman Who Fell from the Sky* (1994). *In Mad Love and War* won several prizes, among them the William Carlos Williams Prize from the Poetry Society of America. Harjo has received a number of other literary awards, including the New Mexico Governor's Award for Excellence in the Arts, a National Endowment for the Arts Fellowship, and the American Indian Distinguished Achievement Award.

The Book of Myths

When I entered the book of myths
                    in your sandalwood room on the granite island,
    I did not ask for a way out.
This is not the century for false pregnancy
                    in these times when myths   5
                                        have taken to the streets.
There is no more imagination; we are in it now, girl.

We traveled the stolen island of Manhattan
               in a tongue of wind off the Atlantic
        shaking our shells, in our mad skins.   10
I did not tell you when I saw Rabbit sobbing and laughing
                  as he shook his dangerous bag of tricks
       into the mutiny world on that street outside Hunter.
Out came you and I blinking our eyes once more, entwined in our loves
        and hates as we set off to recognize the sweet   15
and bitter gods who walk beside us, whisper madness
in our invisible ears any ordinary day.
      I have fallen in love a thousand times over; every day is a common
miracle of salt roses, of fire in the prophecy wind, and now and then
        I taste the newborn blood in my daughter's   20
          silk hair, as if she were not nearly a woman
     brown and electric in her nearly womanly self.
There is a Helen in every language; in American her name is Marilyn
          but in my subversive country,
     she is dark earth and round and full of names   25
dressed in bodies of women
      who enter and leave the knife wounds of this terrifyingly
beautiful land;
        we call ourselves ripe, and pine tree, and woman.
      In the book of myths that fell open in your room of unicorns 30
I did not imagine the fiery goddess in the middle of the island.
She is a sweet trick of flame,
         had everyone dancing, laughing and telling the stories
that unglue the talking spirit from the pages.
When the dawn light came on through the windows,   35
        I understood how my bones would one day
      stand up, brush off the lovely skin like a satin blouse
and dance with foolish grace to heaven.

                              —1990

For Anna Mae Pictou Aquash,[1] Whose Spirit Is Present Here and in the Dappled Stars (for we remember the story and must tell it again so we may all live)

Beneath a sky blurred with mist and wind,
                   I am amazed as I watch the violet
heads of crocuses erupt from the stiff earth
                after dying for a season,
as I have watched my own dark head   5
          appear each morning after entering

---

[1] [*Author's note.*] In February 1976, an unidentified body of a young woman was found on the Pine Ridge Reservation in South Dakota. The official autopsy attributed death to exposure. The FBI agent present at the autopsy ordered her hands severed and sent to Washington for fingerprinting. John Trudell rightly called this mutilation an act of war. Her unnamed body was buried. When Anna Mae Aquash, a young Micmac woman who was an active American Indian Movement member, was discovered missing by her friends and relatives, a second autopsy was demanded. It was then discovered she had been killed by a bullet fired at close range to the back of her head. Her killer or killers have yet to be identified.

the next world
     to come back to this one,
         amazed.
It is the way in the natural world to understand the place   10
         the ghost dancers[2] named
after the heart/breaking destruction.
        Anna Mae,
        everything and nothing changes.
You are the shimmering young woman   15
       who found her voice,
when you were warned to be silent, or have your body cut away
from you like an elegant weed.
     You are the one whose spirit is present in the dappled stars.
(They prance and lope like colored horses who stay with us 20
     through the streets of these steely cities. And I have seen them
       nuzzling the frozen bodies of tattered drunks
           on the corner.)
This morning when the last star is dimming
        and the buses grind toward 25
the middle of the city, I know it is ten years since they buried you
     the second time in Lakota, a language that could
          free you.
I heard about it in Oklahoma, or New Mexico,
      how the wind howled and pulled everything down 30
   in a righteous anger.
     (It was the women who told me) and we understood wordlessly
the ripe meaning of your murder.
    As I understand ten years later after the slow changing
        of the seasons 35
that we have just begun to touch
     the dazzling whirlwind of our anger,
we have just begun to perceive the amazed world the ghost dancers
   entered
     crazily, beautifully.

             —1990

Reconciliation

A Prayer

I.

We gather at the shore of all knowledge as peoples who were put
here by a god who wanted relatives.

This god was lonely for touch, and imagined herself as a woman,
with children to suckle, to sing with—to continue the web of the
terrifyingly beautiful cosmos of her womb. 5

---

[2] A reference to the "Ghost Dance," a 19th-century Native American spiritual and cultural revival.

This god became a father who wished for others to walk beside him
in the belly of creation.

This god laughed and cried with us as a sister at the sweet tragedy of
our predicament—foolish humans—

Or built a fire, as our brother to keep us warm. 10

This god who grew to love us became our lover, sharing tables of
food enough for everyone in this whole world.

II.

Oh sun, moon, stars, our other relatives peering at us from the inside
of god's house walk with us as we climb into the next century
naked but for the stories we have of each other. Keep us from giving 15
up in this land of nightmares which is also the land of miracles.

We sing our song which we've been promised has no beginning or
end.

III.

All acts of kindness are lights in the war for justice.

IV.

We gather up these strands broken from the web of life. They shiver 20
with our love, as we call them the names of our relatives and carry
them to our home made of the four directions and sing:

Of the south, where we feasted and were given new clothes.

Of the west, where we gave up the best of us to the stars as food
for the battle. 25

Of the north, where we cried because we were forsaken by our
dreams.

Of the east because returned to us is the spirit of all that we love.

for the Audre Lorde Memorial, 1993

—1994

LeAnne Howe (1951-   )

LeAnne Howe is an enrolled member of the Choctaw Nation of Oklahoma. Born and educated in Oklahoma, Howe attended Oklahoma State University as an English major. She
worked as a journalist and a stockbroker before receiving her M.F.A. from Vermont College.
Much of Howe's work is occupied with Choctaw history, particularly as that history illuminates present tribal issues. She is the author of two short story collections, *Coyote Stories* (1984)
and *A Stand Up Reader* (1987), and two novels. The first, *Shell Shaker* (2001), which won a
Before Columbus Foundation American Book Award, explores the connections between

eighteenth-century Choctaw engagements with the French and English colonists and contemporary tribal politics, while *Miko Kings* (2007) is about a turn-of-the-century Indian baseball team. Her 2005 poetry and prose collection *Evidence of Red,* from which "Choctalking on Other Realities" is taken, received the Oklahoma Book Award for Poetry.

Choctalking on Other Realities

There is only one pigeon left in Jerusalem. It could be the weather. Perhaps his more clever relatives took refuge in the cities by the Red Sea where the climate is better. Jerusalem occupies a high plateau in Israel/Palestine. In January 1992, record snows have fallen here. Outside our hotel, ice-covered oranges weigh the trees down like leaded Christmas ornaments.

I've come to Israel as an academic tourist on a university-sponsored tour. We're told that with few natural advantages and no indigenous raw materials, apart from stone, the economy of Jerusalem has always been supported from the outside. They're entirely dependent on peace. If that's true, we want to know why Jews, Muslims, and Christians in Jerusalem have adopted the stance of a "mobilized society." Perhaps it's their heritage. Each of these religious groups has always made great sacrifices to change the status quo. Recall the Jews taking Canaan and greater Israel; the Christians capturing the Roman Empire and the New World; and the Muslims seizing Arabia, Asia and Africa. The wars of heaven.

I leave the National Palace Hotel in east Jerusalem and meander down a narrow street. The pigeon comes and goes. He sails above my head. I pass a park where the benches are vacant and gray. As the afternoon light creeps behind another ragged wall of snow clouds I stop. The bird lands just beyond my reach, and I throw him the remains of my falafel sandwich. A late breakfast. We eye each other until he draws his head back as if his attention is fixed in the distance on something no one else sees. Eventually I see it too. A group of women march toward us chanting slogans in Arabic and the sky cracks open and the pigeon flies away.

They're Palestinians. Seven women. Their arms are linked together in solidarity like a chain of paper dolls. I don't understand what they are saying but I can guess. They want to change the status quo.

I follow the procession. After all this is what I've come for. To see who is doing what to whom. Like peeping toms or UN observers, we academics do very little except tell each other what we've seen. Always in dead earnest.

Soon tourists come out of the shops to see what all the ruckus is about. The women encourage us to join their protest. In a few minutes two blue and white truckloads of soldiers arrive carrying white clubs and tear gas launchers. The women stay together as long as they can until they are broken apart by the soldiers. Many of the tourists become frantic. They run into the soldiers or away from them. People scramble in all directions.

One woman breaks away from the others and runs in the direction of the American Colony Hotel. For some unexplainable reason I run after her.

Suddenly she's behind me. I know her by the sound of her feet running. I run faster across the dirt playground. If she catches me I'll never escape. I hear her panting loudly. Her weight and large frame knocks me down. I can't breathe. Her blonde face blushes red as she yanks me up by my arms.

I twist out of her grasp and run toward a fence made of chicken wire. Beyond it is the WA-HE Café in Bethany, Oklahoma. Indians are inside drinking coffee and gossiping about the weather. If I make it to the WA-HE they'll protect me. But she tackles me again. Hammers my head with her elbow. Sweat pours out of her body and wets my face. I gag trying not to swallow. A second white teacher comes to her aid. Together they carry me toward a small building, the kindergarten school connected to their church. They open the broom closet and shove me inside. The door slams shut.

I am still running.

This Is the Story I Really Wanted to Tell

It was so hot in the kitchen of the Oklahoma City airport café that the plastic clock melted. Time oozed down the wall just like Salvador Dali[1] imagined. The metal pieces of the flimsy clock went, "clink, clank, ting" as they hit the floor. That's because the steaks were burning, the beans were boiling, and Nina the Ukrainian, had pulled a butcher knife on Gretchen the German. There is a war going on. I am in uniform. But I race ahead of myself. This story begins in 1970.

First there are the characters.

Gretchen the German. A Catholic. The blonde cook with the white hairnet pulled down over her ears like a helmet. A Berliner, she escaped Nazi Germany during World War II to come to America and cook wiener schnitzels. That's what she tells all the customers at the airport café.

Susan B. Anthony. The black, six-foot-tall-night-cook-in-charge, Susan B. likes the blues. Speaks choicest Gullah. Cooks like snapping fingers in time. Her great-great-grandmother was a slave. Every night at the airport café she says, "Honey, don't mess with me." And I don't.

Nina. A Russian Jew from the Ukraine, she wears a white cotton uniform with socks held up by rubber bands. Nina's thumb is tattooed and causes people to stare impolitely. She says she escaped the massacre at Babi Yar. Each night she chisels perfect heads of lettuce into identical salads and weighs each portion. She is quite insane.

And me. An Oklahoma Choctaw. The waitress in the yellow uniform at the airport café. I'm a union steward for the International Brotherhood of Hotel, Motel, and Restaurant Workers of America; I'm nineteen years old and have been baptized many times. The Southern Baptists, the Nazarenes, even the Mormons got to me. Finally, I've given up being a religious consumer to become a socialist. The AFL-CIO is going to send me to college.

The Scene.

The airport café. Feeding time. The fall of 1970. Nightshift comes through the looking glass walls of the airport café. Braniff and United Airlines roar out of sight to exotic places. Somewhere a radio blasts Leon Russell's[2] singing, *"...Here comes Uncle Sam again with the same old bag of beans. Local chiefs on the radio, we got some hungry mouths to feed, goin' back to Alcatraz."*

At 6:30 p.m., one hundred Vietnam draftees drag into the Oklahoma City airport café. Afros, pork-chop sideburns, crew cuts, Indian braids. After two years, hairless pimpled faces all look alike. Some smell bad. Some have beautiful teeth.

---

[1] Salvador Dali (1904-1989), Spanish surrealist painter; this is a reference to his 1931 painting, "The Persistence of Memory."

[2] Leon Russell (b. 1942) American singer-songwriter from Oklahoma who wrote and recorded the song "Alcatraz."

It's not news at the airport café that the Vietnam War is being fought disproportionately by the poor. Every Monday through Friday we serve red and yellow, black, and poor white boys their last supper as civilians. They're on their way to boot camp. They clutch their government orders and puke-belch to themselves. Their hands shake. My hands are steady. I want to tell them to run. But don't.

"No one gets hurt if they do what they're told," whispered the white teacher through the door of the broom closet. "Would you like to come out now?"

"Curious," booms a voice across the airport café's dining room. Some of the draftees look toward the kitchen, others continue eating as if they'd heard nothing.

The voice gathers strength and explodes.

"There were no survivors of Babi Yar," roars Gretchen grimly.

I rush through the kitchen door. The steaks are burning, and the beans are boiling over the fire, and Gretchen is scrutinizing Nina in front of the gas grill.

"Your story is certainly unfamiliar to me. You probably branded your own thumb so people won't accuse you. Very clever."

Nina's eyes make a circle of the kitchen. She examines her work; the stainless steel bins of freshly washed lettuce, tomatoes, radish flowers, onions, carrots, and watermelon balls. All are arranged, lined up in neat rows at her workstation. "I do what I am told," she says pushing her head against the walk-in freezer. "The sins of my occupation."

"What a wreck you are. Always building a pile of shadows," says Gretchen grabbing a slice of onion.

Nina's mouth is set in a fold of bitterness. "I know Babi Yar. It's a ravine near Kiev where the Germans murdered 35,000 Jews in September 1941. By 1943, it had become a mass grave for more than 100,000 Jews." She looks at something beyond us then screams. "I WAS THERE!"

"Yes, but what did you do?"

Nina charges Gretchen with a butcher knife in one hand, and a watermelon scoop in the other. Gretchen holds a small toaster oven in front of her like a shield. Together they dance around the room like a couple of marionettes being pulled by the fingers of God.

Eventually Susan B. Anthony interrupts the madness and Gretchen shouts, "SCHWEIG, du Neger!"

This is where I come in. I intercede like a good union steward should. Susan B. Anthony holds a hot pan of grease and is set to attack them both. The World War II survivors are screaming in languages I can't understand and pointing their weapons. They all scare the hell out of me because I'm unarmed.

1970 is a terrible year to be a teenage Indian in Oklahoma City. Vietnam is on television, nightly. World War II is still going on in the kitchen of the airport café, and I'm losing my classmates to mortar fire in Asia. Emmet Tahbone is dead. Blown away, literally. Richard Warrior is MIA, and George Billy has a shrapnel mouth.

This past week there were sit-ins at a downtown department store where blacks are still being refused services at the lunch counter. For almost ten months American Indians have occupied the abandoned prison on Alcatraz Island. The word on the streets of Oklahoma City is that we're fed up with colonialism. American Indians are finally going to change the status quo. Standing in the middle of the kitchen with my palms turned upward, a sign that I carry no weapons, I squint like a mourner who draws the curtains against the light. I feel powerless to change anything.

I look out the window and a moonbeam is crisscrossing a watery plain. It's the Pearl River with its saw grass islands and Cypress knees rising out of the water like hands in prayer to Hashtali, whose eye is the Sun. This light once cut clear across the heavens and down to the Choctaw's ancient mother mound, the Nanih Waiya in the Lower Mississippi Valley. Now it's no longer visible except on special occasions.

I see a Choctaw woman, her daughter, and their relatives. They're being attacked by a swarm of warriors from another tribe. Unfortunately bad weather has driven them into a little bayou. They're exposed from head to foot to their enemies, the Cherokees, who've been following them for days. The Choctaw woman shows her daughter how to be brave. Several times she runs and cuts the powder horns loose from her dead relatives in order to distribute them among the living. Finally the seven warriors, and the mother and daughter, seeing that they can no longer hold their ground rush headlong upon their enemies.

A feminine voice interrupts my vision. *"No one gets hurt if they do what they're told."* I shake my head trying to drive it out of me. *"We fly daily non-stop flights to locations across America, Europe, and Asia,"* continues the recorded message on the airport's loudspeaker.

I turn back to my co-workers who are drowning in a pool of tears. "No one will get hurt if we do what we're supposed to do," I say meekly. For a moment no one moves. Then they begin struggling with their kitchen utensils. Suddenly Nina is composed, Gretchen too, both of them square their shoulders the way soldiers do when called to attention. They promise it will never happen again, but no one believes them.

At midnight the lines on my face have melted like the clock in Salvador Dali's painting. I resemble a sad clown. When Susan B. Anthony and I walk outside to share a smoke we eye one other wearily.

"What happened?" I ask quietly.

"God knows," she says lighting a cigarette.

Together we watch as the lights of a crayon-colored Braniff jet leave a trail of stale dead air, and I think I'll buy a mask and become someone else. The AFL-CIO can't save me now.

Choctalking on Other Realities

I did become someone else. A mother, a teacher, a writer, a wife. When the opportunity came to visit Israel in 1992, I signed up for the two-week trip at the behest of my husband, a geographer and co-leader of the study tour. We are going to Jerusalem to learn about the effects of the Intifada[3] on the region and its peoples. At first, I was hesitant. The very word Jerusalem connotes religion. Three of them: Judaism, Christianity, Islam, birthed in that order. They all look the same to me. They share one God known as Yahweh, Allah, or Jesus. They honor the same prophets. They share many of the same books. Their holidays center around religious and cultural victories over each other. Kind of like Americans celebrating Thanksgiving. Holidays are the masks of conquerors.

But wouldn't you know it. On my first day in Jerusalem I met a Jewish woman who said her great-grandmother was a Cherokee.

She tells me it is a long story—how one side of her family immigrated to America, then re-immigrated to Israel after 1948. I stand motionless and look at the woman

---

[3] (Arabic) Shaking off, uprising. This refers to the First Intifada (1987-1993), a Palestinian uprising against Israeli rule.

across the glass counter of her gift shop. Listen skeptically to the ragged tenderness of her story. The weary but elusive Indian ancestry, the fawning desire to be related to me, at least my Indianness, is something I've experienced before.

I study the shopkeeper's face. We are remarkably alike. Black eyes. Dark hair. About the same age. As the shadows of Jerusalem invade her shop windows I grow nostalgic. The city looms under a delicious haze of smoke from the outdoor falafel stands, and I want to take this woman away with me. To cross time and the ocean together. To place her in our past, to put myself in her beginning, and intertwine our threads of history—for we are nothing without our relationships. That's Choctaw.

I begin my story in the middle. "Choctaws are not originally from Oklahoma. We are immigrants too."

The woman whose ancestor was a Cherokee nods her head as if she understands, and I continue.

"Our ancient homelands are in the Southeastern part of the United States where we were created in the spectacular silken flatness of the delta lands. The earth opened her body and beckoned us to join her above ground so our ancestors tunneled up through her navel into tinges of moist red men and women. We collected our chins, knees, breasts, and sure-footed determination—long before Moses parted the Red Sea, and the God with three heads was born in the Middle East.

"Choctaws were the second largest allied group of peoples in the south east. Our population centers were clustered like wheels around three major rivers: to the east the Tombigbee River; to the west the Pearl River; and in the South the Chickasawhay River. We made trading relationships with other tribes in our regions whenever possible."

She interrupts my story, asks me if I will come to her house for an evening meal. She talks on. Says that she went to school in New York City, and that she misses the company of Americans. Her own mother is dead, since she was a child. All she has left is her father, the one who owns the shop. She looks at me. "You promise to tell me more of your history?"

"What I can."

Her home is west of Jerusalem. Opposite the old city where everyone walks instead of rides. There are great American-style streets full of Mercedes, Peugeots and Perrier bottles. Her place is elegant, an estate on a hill. There's a dark studio with a mahogany desk, Navajo rugs, and an enormous basket made from the skeleton of a Saguaro tree sits near the stone fireplace. She builds a fire against the cold and opens the shutters to let in the city. She says she doesn't feel anything in particular toward the Arabs, no hate, and no repulsion either. I asked her what about the Choctaws? She smiles, not knowing what I mean. She says she is where she has to be. Placed here. Of course she feels a tinge of fear. It's as if this is not only what she expects, but what must happen to her.

She says she pays closest attention to the noise of the city. That the city shouts what is going to happen. The explosions, the bullets, the prayers, the celebratory demonstrations, they're all part of it she says, like messages from God.

She begins telling me some rigmarole about how Jerusalem meets the needs of all its people. Throughout its four-thousand-year history she says the city was meant to be a place of unity. Her father believes that now the Intifada is over there can be peace between the Arabs and Jews.

Behind her a shadow walks into the room. I see the image of a woman in darned socks. I think I recognize her face, but I can't quite make it out, so speak up without waiting for a polite pause in our conversation.

"Then why, every day, do Jews and Arabs try and kill one another?"

"Why did Indians sell Manhattan to the Christians?"

Night comes through the shutters. The din of the streets below grows louder. It's more penetrating than the livid red streetlamps.

We look at each other. Our expressions are suddenly changed. We realize we're on the side of societies that have reduced us to grief.

All the same she rushes to tell me the story of her great-grandfather, a shoemaker, an outcast in North Carolina just like her great-grandmother, the Cherokee. "He was in exile, she was conquered. They fell in love because they had this in common. After World War II my grandfather, the one who was half-Jewish-half-Cherokee, made a pilgrimage to the Holy Land. He never returned to America."

"Indians are not conquered!"

"But your nerve is gone," she says, sadly. "I was a student at New York City University when the Indians surrendered Alcatraz Island in June 1971. We would have never given up."

There is a long silence.

"Who is we?" I ask.

"I've provoked you," she says. "Now I give you the chance to give me a piece of your mind."

There was a trace of something odd in her remark, so I began with a metaphor. "Once a very ancient god came back from everywhere. Arriving at a banquet in his honor with a bundle of keys, he announced that it was closing time, and toilets around the world exploded."

We laugh. It breaks the tension.

"It's from the good book. The missing pages."

"And then what happened?" she asks. "You promised to tell me your history."

"After the war ended between the British and the French in 1763 Indians in the Southeast couldn't make the foreigners do anything. Soldiers went AWOL and married into our tribes. No one wanted to live in Paris or London anymore. That's why so many Choctaws, Creeks, Chickasaws and Cherokees have British and French last names.

"In 1830, after the Treaty of Dancing Rabbit Creek was signed, the Choctaw are the first to be removed from our ancient homelands. Many walked all the way with very little to eat or drink. The road to the Promised Land was terrible. Dead horses and their dead riders littered the way. Dead women lay in the road with babies dried to their breasts, tranquil as if napping. A sacred compost for scavengers."

She stokes the fire to keep it from dying, and I know the more revolting the details, the less she believes me. Finally she says. "You are exaggerating."

"Perhaps. But four thousand Choctaws died immigrating to Oklahoma."

"It is late," she says, ignoring my facts. "Time I returned you to your hotel. I'm sure your husband is waiting for you."

"But you said you wanted to know about my history?"

She gives me a fishy look but agrees. "Very well."

"It's no accident that there are sixty-six Indian Nations headquartered in

Oklahoma. Oklahoma or Indian Territory was a forerunner of Israel. Choctaws were the first to be removed there, other Indian tribes from around country soon followed. We were supposed to live together in peace. Form relationships. It wasn't easy, but for the most part we did it because we do not idealize war. However throughout the nineteenth century more and more whites moved into Indian Territory. Followed by missionaries and lawyers who began converting us, or swindling us."

"Then on April 22, 1889 the American government opened the unassigned lands to the whites. When the trumpet sounded, the Run of 1889 began. It was estimated that twenty thousand immigrants were waiting at the border to stake their claims. Today the Run of 1889 is an annual celebration in Oklahoma. Like a holiday."

"I thought you were going to tell me *your* story."

"I'm coming to it," I answer, pausing to clear my throat. "There was no color in the broom closet. Light edged around the door. There may have been other teachers outside the closet, but I only knew of her by the smell of her sweat.

"The church had started a kindergarten program. She was a missionary. That morning the preacher said we were lucky to have a missionary lead us in a song. *"Red and yellow, black and white we are separate in his sight, Jesus loves the little children of the world."* Then I sang it several times by myself. I was only repeating what I thought I heard. The words had no meaning for me, I was five years old. When she marched toward me shaking her fist, with that mouth of angry nails I panicked and ran outside across the playground and toward a café.

"Down, down, down, the fall crushes me, and I'm mucking around in the dirt. She oozed through my pores that hot afternoon in Bethany Oklahoma, and there she has remained whispering inside my head."

I stare at my host. "It isn't that we lost our nerve. Sometimes we're just overwhelmed."

After I finish my story, a strange quiet grips the Jewish woman whose ancestor was a Cherokee. Her face becomes attentive, as if listening to something that penetrated her soul.

When she drops me off at the National Palace hotel, I watch her drive away. All I can think of is that she's right, that Jerusalem, "the city of peace" is what is meant to happen to her.

There Is No God but God

The next day I rejoin our study tour and we meet some Palestinian women from the Gaza Strip. In 1992 the Gaza Strip is still one of the Occupied Territories of Israel. The Palestinian women tell us their stories through an interpreter. One woman says that the government prohibits them from displaying the colors of the Palestinian flag, which are green, red, black and white. She says her husband has been arrested for having a picture of a watermelon on his desk. Many others show us empty tear-gas canisters that have been shot into their homes by the soldiers. They are plainly marked, "MADE IN USA."

To show concern for the Palestinians some members of our study tour present the women with duffel bags full of used clothes and high heel shoes marked MADE IN USA. I didn't bring any used clothes, so I ask the Christian coordinator from the Council of Middle East Churches if I could give the Palestinian women money instead of used clothes.

"No," she replies. "They'll just come to expect it from us."

The next day when the study tour leaves for a two-day visit for Nazareth, I stay behind at our hotel. I've had enough. I want to be alone, walk the streets of the old city, and eat in the small cafés.

Throughout the day prayers are broadcast over loudspeakers. For Muslims, the first prayer of the day begins at the moment the rays of the sun begin to appear on the horizon. The last prayer in the evening ends at sunset. Devout Jews pray three times a day; devout Muslims pray five times daily. When I hear a man singing the prayers on a mosque's loud speaker system I am sure he is praying to the Sun, just like Choctaws once prayed to Hashtali.

"The prayers are to Allah, not the Sun," says a vendor outside the Al-Aqsa Mosque in Jerusalem.

"It looks like you are praying to the Sun, especially with your palms turned up toward the sky. The Egyptians once worshipped the sun God, RA. Since the Hebrews and the Egyptians once lived together, maybe your religions rubbed off on each other. Everyone in this country says 'Yis-RA-el' for Israel. Maybe there's a relationship?"

He waved me away. "No, no, no, you have been misinformed! There is no God, but the God of us all."

I Am Still Running

Palestinian men from around the community race past me toward the soldiers and meet them head-on. The protest explodes into a riot. Mothers, daughters, and grand-mothers from inside the shops join the women in the streets. The soldiers begin dragging people inside the blue and white paddy wagons, one or two at a time, amidst weeping and bleeding fists.

I run toward the leader crumpled against the stonewall. Suddenly I recognize her. It's Nina from the airport café. I can't believe it, but it's really Nina. She's dressed in her white cotton uniform, her shabby socks still held up with rubber bands. A soldier reaches her before me.

"Don't hurt her, it's Nina. Can't you see? She's a survivor of Babi Yar."

Suddenly I'm on the ground. I cannot breathe. Someone rifles through my purse and pulls out my American passport. He yanks me up by my arms and tells me in English to go home.

"No one gets hurt if they do what they're told."

"No, it's a lie. RUN!" I scream so loud that I frighten the voice out of my head.

Nina gets up and tries to jump the stone fence, but the soldier bashes her in the legs with a club. She falls down and he carries her to the paddy wagon and shoves her inside.

I am back to the dubious place where memory distorts fragments of an indivisible experience and we meet a different self. It wasn't Nina the soldier carried into the government vehicle. She died talking to God that terrible night in the airport café. She collapsed on the floor of the kitchen, not long after the fight with Gretchen, asking God why she had to die, why now that she'd regained her courage. "Very well," was all she whispered.

Standing in the middle of the street in east Jerusalem, I watch the determined faces of the Palestinian women and weep for Nina. I still believe she is with the Palestinian protesters, just as I believe she was at Babi Yar.

An Arab member of the Knesset, the Israeli parliament, finally arrives in a government car and calls for calm. He holds both hands out to the soldiers, a sign that he carries no weapons.

The pigeon returns and lands next to me, as if surveying the waste. The Knesset member sees us, stops, then walks on with his palms facing toward the Sun. I will believe the rest of my life that this is what he prayed for.

"Save her. She is the Jewish women shot to death by the Germans at Babi Yar.

"Save her. She is the Palestinian women shot to death by the Jews at Deir Yassin.

"Save her. She is the Vietnamese women shot to death by the Americans at Mi Lai

"Save her. She is the Mayan women shot to death by the Mexicans in Chiapas.

"Save her. She is the Black women shot to death by the Ku Klux Klan in Alabama.

"Save her. She is The People, our grandmothers, our mothers, our sisters, our ancestors, ourselves.

"Save us."

—2005

KATE RUSHIN (1951-)

Born in Syracuse, New York, Kate Rushin was raised first in Camden, New Jersey, and then in a predominantly Black New Jersey town established by freed slaves. She is best known as a poet, performance artist, and teacher. Rushin credits two of her aunts with helping her develop her love of poetry by giving her *Poetry of the Negro,* edited by Arna Bontemps and Langston Hughes, and *Best Loved Poems of the American People.* Rushin memorized and recited poetry from those anthologies and then began to submit her own poems to her school literary magazine and to newspapers; she published her first poem in a local newspaper, the Camden *Courier-Post.* Rushin attended Oberlin College, where she majored in Communications and Theater, was active in an experimental theater group, and presented her poems publicly. Among the honors that Rushin has received for her work are the Fine Arts Work Center Fellowship in Provincetown, Massachusetts; a residency at the Cummington Community of the Arts; a poet-in-residency at South Boston High School; the Grolier Poetry Prize; and a Massachusetts Artist's Foundation Poetry Fellowship.

The Black Back-Ups

This is dedicated to Merry Clayton, Fontella Bass, Vonetta
Washington, Carolyn Franklin, Yolanda McCullough,
Carolyn Willis, Gwen Guthrie, Helaine Harris, and Darlene
Love. This is for all the Black women who sang back-up for
Elvis Presley, John Denver, James Taylor, Lou Reed.   5
Etc. Etc. Etc.

I said Hey Babe
Take a Walk on the Wild Side
I said Hey Babe
Take a Walk on the Wild Side   10

And the colored girls say
Do dodo do do dodododo
Do dodo do do dodododo
Do dodo do do dodododo ooooo[1]

This is for my Great-Grandmother Esther, my Grandmother   15
Addie, my grandmother called Sister, my Great-Aunt
Rachel, my Aunt Hilda, my Aunt Tine, my Aunt Breda,
my Aunt Gladys, my Aunt Helen, my Aunt Ellie,
my Cousin Barbara, my Cousin Dottie and my Great-Great-
Aunt Vene.   20

This is dedicated to all of the Black women riding on buses
and subways back and forth to the Main Line, Haddonfield,
Cherry Hill and Chevy Chase.[2] This is for the women who
spend their summers in Rockport, Newport, Cape Cod and
Camden, Maine.[3] This is for the women who open those   25
bundles of dirty laundry sent home from those ivy-covered
campuses.

My Great-Aunt Rachel worked for the Carters
Ever since I can remember
There was *The Boy*   30
Whose name I never knew
And there was *The Girl*
Whose name was Jane

Great-Aunt Rachel brought Jane's dresses for me to wear
Perfectly Good Clothes   35
And I should've been glad to get them
Perfectly Good Clothes
No matter they didn't fit quite right
Perfectly Good Clothes
Brought home in a brown paper bag   40
With an air of accomplishment and excitement
Perfectly Good Clothes
Which I hated

At school
In Ohio   45
I swear to Gawd
There was always somebody
Telling me that the only person
In their whole house
Who listened and understood them   50
Despite the money and the lessons
Was the housekeeper

[1] Lyrics from "Walk on the Wild Side" by Lou Reed.
[2] Main Line refers to wealthy suburbs west of
Philadelphia; Haddonfield and Cherry Hill are towns in
New Jersey; Chevy Chase is in Maryland. All of these
neighborhoods are predominantly white and well-to-do.
[3] Rockport, Newport, Cape Cod, and Camden are seaside
resort communities in the Northeast that are visited
primarily by wealthy white people.

And I knew it was true
But what was I supposed to say

I know it's true   55
I watch her getting off the train
Moving slowly toward the Country Squire[4]
With their uniform in their shopping bag
And the closer she gets to the car
The more the two little kids jump and laugh   60
And even the dog is about to
Turn inside out
Because they just can't wait until she gets there
Edna Edna   Wonderful Edna

But Aunt Edna to me, or Gram, or Miz Johnson, or   65
Sister Johnson on Sundays

And the colored girls say
Do dodo do do dodododo
Do dodo do do dodododo
Do dodo do do dodododo ooooo   70

This is for Hattie McDaniels,[5] Butterfly McQueen[6]
Ethel Waters[7]
Sapphire
Saphronia
Ruby Begonia   75
Aunt Jemima[8]
Aunt Jemima on the Pancake Box
Aunt Jemima on the Pancake Box?
AuntJemimaonthepancakebox?
Ainchamamaonthepancakebox?   80
Ain't chure Mama on the pancake box?

Mama Mama
Get off that box
And come home to me

And my Mama leaps off that box   85
She swoops down in her nurse's cape
Which she wears on Sunday
And for Wednesday night prayer meeting
And she wipes my forehead
And she fans my face   90

---

[4] Ford station wagon model (1950-1991).
[5] Hattie McDaniel (1895-1952), who also performed under the name McDaniels, was the first African-American performer to win an Academy Award, for her role as Mammy in *Gone With the Wind* (1939).
[6] Butterfly McQueen (1911-1995), actress most famous for playing Prissy, a house slave, in *Gone With the Wind* (1939).

[7] Ethel Waters (1896-1977), blues singer and actress; the second African American ever nominated for an Academy Award.
[8] A brand of pancake mix; also a stereotype of Black women as nurturing cooks who feed white people.

And she makes me a cup of tea
And it don't do a thing for my real pain
Except she is my mama

Mama Mommy Mammy
Mam-mee Mam-mee   95
I'd Walk a Mill-yon Miles
For one of your smiles[9]

This is for the Black Back-Ups
This is for my mama and your mama
My grandma and your grandma   100
This is for the thousand thousand Black Back-Ups

And the colored girls say
Do   dodo   do do   dodododo
do   dodo
dodo   105
do
do

—1993

The Tired Poem: Last Letter from a Typical Unemployed Black Professional Woman

So it's a gorgeous afternoon in the park
It's so nice you forget your Attitude
The one your mama taught you
The one that says Don't-Mess-With-Me
You forget until you hear all this   5
Whistling and lip smacking
You whip around and say
I ain't no damn dog
It's a young guy
His mouth drops open   10
Excuse me Sister
How you doing
You lie and smile and say
I'm doing good
Everything's cool Brother   15

Then five minutes later
Hey you Sweet Devil
Hey Girl come here
You tense   sigh   calculate
You know the lean boys and bearded men   20

---

[9] Lyrics to "My Mammy," a hit song from the first sound motion picture, *The Jazz Singer* (1930); Al Jolson performed the song in blackface.

Are only cousins and lovers and friends
Sometimes when you say Hey
You get a beautiful surprised smile
Or a good talk

And you've listened to your uncle when he was drunk   25
Talking about how he has to scuffle to get by and
How he'd wanted to be an engineer
And you talk to Joko who wants to be a singer and
Buy some clothes and get a house for his mother
The Soc. and Psych. books say you're domineering   30
And you've been to enough
Sisters-Are-Not-Taking-Care-Of-Business discussions
To know where you went wrong
It's decided it had to be the day you decided to go to school
Still you remember the last time you said hey   35
So you keep on walking
What   you too good to speak
Don't nobody want you no way

You go home   sit on the front steps   listen to
The neighbor boy brag about   40
How many girls he has pregnant
You ask him if he's going to take care of the babies
And what if he gets taken to court
And what are the girls going to do
He has pictures of them all   45
This real cute one was supposed to go to college
Dumb broad knew she could get pregnant
I'll just say it's not mine
On the back of this picture of a girl in a cap and gown
It says something like   50
I love you in my own strange way
Thank you

Then you go in the house
Flip through a magazine and there is
An-Ode-To-My-Black-Queen poem   55
The kind where the Brother
Thanks all of the Sisters Who Endured
Way back when he didn't have his Shit Together
And you have to wonder where they are now
And you know what happens when you try to resist   60
All of this Enduring
And you think how this
Thank-you poem is really
No consolation at all
Unless you believe   65
What the man you met on the train told you

The Black man who worked for the State Department
And had lived in five countries
He said Dear
You were born to suffer   70
Why don't you give me your address
And I'll come visit

So you try to talk to your friend
About the train and the park and everything
And how it all seems somehow connected   75
And he says
You're just a Typical Black Professional Woman
Some sisters know how to deal
Right about here
Your end of the conversation phases out   80
He goes on to say how
Black Professional Women have always had the advantage
You have to stop and think about that one
Maybe you are supposed to be grateful for those sweaty
Beefy-faced white businessmen who try to   85
Pick you up at lunchtime
And you wonder how many times your friend had
Pennies thrown at him
How many times he's been felt up in the subway
How many times he's been cussed out on the street   90
You wonder how many times he's been offered
$10 for a piece of himself
$10 for a piece
So you're waiting for the bus
And you look at this young Black man   95
Asking if you want to make some money
You look at him for a long time
You imagine the little dingy room
It would take twenty minutes or less
You only get $15 for spending all day with thirty kids   100
Nobody is offering you
Any cash for your poems
You remember again how you have the advantage
How you're not taking care of business
How this man is somebody's kid brother or cousin   105
And could be your own
So you try to explain how $10 wouldn't pay for
What you'd have to give up
He pushes a handful of sticky crumpled dollars
Into your face and says   110

Why not
You think I can't pay
Look at that roll
Don't tell me you don't need the money

Cause I know you do   115
I'll give you fifteen
You maintain your sense of humor
You remember a joke you heard
Well no matter what
A Black Woman never has to starve   120
Just as long as there are
Dirty toilets and...
It isn't funny
Then you wonder if he would at least
Give you the money   125
And not beat you up
But you're very cool and say
No thanks
You tell him he should spend his time
Looking for someone he cares about   130
Who cares about him
He waves you off
Get outta my face
I don't have time for that bullshit
You blew it Bitch   135

Then
(Is it suddenly)
Your voice gets loud
And fills the night street
Your voice gets louder and louder   140
Your bus comes
The second-shift people file on
The security guards and nurse's aides
Look at you like you're crazy
Get on the damn bus   145
And remember
You blew it
He turns away
Your bus pulls off
There is no one on the street but you   150

And then
It is
Very
Quiet

—1993

JUDITH ORTIZ COFER (1952–)

Judith Ortiz Cofer was born in Hormingueros, a town in southwest Puerto Rico, to Fanny Morot and Jesús Lugo Ortiz, who was in the U.S. Navy. The family moved between Hormingueros and Paterson, New Jersey, eventually settling in Augusta, Georgia, in 1968. Cofer received her B.A. in English from Augusta College in 1974 and her M.A. in English from Florida Atlantic University in 1977. Her poetry was featured in journals such as the *New Mexico Humanities Review* and *The Bilingual Review,* and the poetry chapbooks *Latin Women Pray* (1980), *The Native Dancer* (1981), and *Among the Ancestors* (1981). In 1986, she published her first poetry collection, *Peregrina,* which was followed by *Reaching for the Mainland* (1987) and *Terms of Survival* (1987). Her first novel, *The Line of the Sun* (1989), was nominated for a Pulitzer Prize. Cofer has also published a book of memoirs, *Silent Dancing* (1990); the prose and poetry collections *The Latin Deli* (1993) and *The Year of Our Revolution* (1998); the novels *The Meaning of Consuelo* (2003) and *Call Me Maria* (2004); a young adult book, *An Island Like You: Stories of the Barrio* (1995); and a collection of essays, *Woman in the Front of the Sun: On Becoming a Writer* (2000). Her most recent poetry collection is *A Love Story Beginning in Spanish* (2005). Cofer teaches at the University of Georgia, where she is the Regent's and Franklin Professor of English and Creative Writing.

Exile

I left my home behind me
but my past clings to my fingers
so that every word I write bears
the mark like a cancelled postage stamp
of my birthplace   5
There was no angel to warn me
of the dangers of looking back.
Like Lot's wife, I would trade
my living blood for one last look
at the house where each window held   10
a face framed as in a family album.
And the place lined with palms
where my friends and I strolled in our pink
and yellow and white Sunday dresses, dreaming
of husbands, houses, and orchards where   15
our children would play in the leisurely summer
of our future. Gladly would I spill
my remaining years like salt upon the ground,
to gaze again on the fishermen of the bay
dragging their catch in nets glittering   20
like pirate gold, to the shore.
Nothing remains of that world, I hear,
but the skeletons of houses, all colors
bled from the fabric of those
who stayed behind   25
inhabiting the dead cities
like the shadows of Hiroshima.

—1987

So Much for Mañana[1]

After twenty years in the mainland
Mother's gone back to the Island
to let her skin
melt from her bones
under her native sun.   5
She no longer wears stockings,
girdles or tight clothing.
Brown as a coconut,
she takes siestas in a hammock,
and writes me letters that say: 10
"Stop chasing your own shadow, niña,[2]
come down here and taste the piña,[3]
put away those heavy books,
don't you worry about your shape,
here on the Island men look   15
for women who can carry a little weight.
On every holy day,
I burn candles and I pray
that your brain won't split
like an avocado pit   20
from all that studying.
What do you say?
Abrazos from your Mamá[4] and a blessing
from that saint, Don Antonio, el cura."[5]
I write back: "Someday I will go back   25
to your Island and get fat,
but not now, Mami, maybe mañana."

—1987

The Latin Deli

Presiding over a formica counter,
plastic Mother and Child magnetized
to the top of an ancient register,
the heady mix of smells from the open bins
of dried codfish, the green plantains   5
hanging in stalks like votive offerings,
she is the Patroness of Exiles,
a woman of no-age who was never pretty,
who spends her days selling canned memories
while listening to the Puerto Ricans complain   10
that it would be cheaper to fly to San Juan
than to buy a pound of Bustelo coffee here,
and to Cubans perfecting their speech

---

[1] (Sp.) Tomorrow.
[2] (Sp.) Little girl.
[3] (Sp.) Pineapple.
[4] (Sp.) Hugs from your mother.
[5] (Sp.) The priest.

of a "glorious return" to Havana—where no one
has been allowed to die and nothing to change until then;   15
to Mexicans who pass through, talking lyrically
of *dólares* to be made in El Norte—
                            all wanting the comfort
of spoken Spanish, to gaze upon the family portrait
of her plain wide face, her ample bosom   20
resting on her plump arms, her look of maternal interest
as they speak to her and each other
of the dreams and their disillusions—
how she smiles understanding,
when they walk down the narrow aisles of her store   25
reading the labels of packages aloud, as if
they were the names of lost lovers: *Suspiros,*
Merengues, the stale candy of everyone's childhood.

                                She spends her days
slicing *jamón y queso* and wrapping it in wax paper   30
tied with string: plain ham and cheese
that would cost less at the A&P, but it would not satisfy
the hunger of the fragile old man lost in the folds
of his winter coat, who brings her lists of items
that he reads to her like poetry, or the others,   35
whose needs she must divine, conjuring up products
from places that now exist only in their hearts—
closed ports she must trade with.

                                       —1993

RITA DOVE (1952-)

Poet, novelist, dramatist, and editor Rita Dove was born to a middle-class African-American family (her father was a chemist and her mother a homemaker) in Akron, Ohio. She attended Miami University of Ohio, where she earned a B.A. *summe cum laude* in 1973, after which she studied at Tübingen University in West Germany on a Fulbright scholarship. In 1977 she received an M.F.A. from the University of Iowa, where she met her future husband, the German novelist and playwright Fred Viebahn. Dove began publishing poetry in 1980, with *The Yellow House on the Corner.* Her third book, *Thomas and Beulah* (1986), a collection of poems based on her grandparents' lives, won the Pulitzer Prize for poetry. Like *Thomas and Beulah,* much of Dove's writing relates to her African-American heritage (though she claims that her characters' race is incidental to the stories they tell).

Dove has received numerous awards for her work, including a National Book Award, a Guggenheim Fellowship, a Rockefeller Foundation Residency, a Mellon Fellowship, a Heniz Award in Arts and Humanities, an Amy Lowell Fellowship, a Shelley Memorial Award, and honorary doctorates from over a dozen universities. She served as U.S. Poet Laureate for two terms (1993-1995), the first African American and the youngest person to do so. Since 1989, Dove has taught at the University of Virginia, where she is currently the Commonwealth Professor of English.

Parsley[1]

1. *The Cane Fields*

There is a parrot imitating spring
in the palace, its feathers parsley green.
Out of the swamp the cane appears

to haunt us, and we cut it down. El General
searches for a word; he is all the world   5
there is. Like a parrot imitating spring,

we lie down screaming as rain punches through
and we come up green. We cannot speak an R—
out of the swamp, the cane appears

and then the mountain we call in whispers *Katalina*.   10
The children gnaw their teeth to arrowheads.
There is a parrot imitating spring.

El General has found his word: *perejil*.
Who says it, lives. He laughs, teeth shining
out of the swamp. The cane appears   15

in our dreams, lashed by wind and streaming.
And we lie down. For every drop of blood
there is a parrot imitating spring.
Out of the swamp the cane appears.

2. *The Palace*

The word the general's chosen is parsley.   20
It is fall, when thoughts turn
to love and death; the general thinks
of his mother, how she died in the fall
and he planted her walking cane at the grave
and it flowered, each spring stolidly forming   25
four-star blossoms. The general

pulls on his boots, he stomps to
her room in the palace, the one without
curtains, the one with a parrot
in a brass ring. As he paces he wonders   30
Who can I kill today. And for a moment
the little knot of screams
is still. The parrot, who has traveled

all the way from Australia in an ivory
cage, is, coy as a widow, practising   35
spring. Ever since the morning
his mother collapsed in the kitchen
while baking skull-shaped candies

---

[1] [*Author's note.*] On October 2, 1957, Rafael Trujillo (1891-1961), dictator of the Dominican Republic, ordered 20,000
blacks killed because they could not pronounce the letter "r" in *perejil,* the Spanish word for parsley.

for the Day of the Dead, the general
has hated sweets. He orders pastries 40
brought up for the bird; they arrive

dusted with sugar on a bed of lace.
The knot in his throat starts to twitch;
he sees his boots the first day in battle
splashed with mud and urine 45
as a soldier falls at his feet amazed—
how stupid he looked!—at the sound
of artillery. *I never thought it would sing*
the soldier said, and died. Now

the general sees the fields of sugar 50
cane, lashed by rain and streaming.
He sees his mother's smile, the teeth
gnawed to arrowheads. He hears
the Haitians sing without R's
as they swing the great machetes: 55
Katalina, they sing, *Katalina,*

mi madle, mi amol en muelte.[2] God knows
his mother was no stupid woman; she
could roll an R like a queen. Even
a parrot can roll an R! In the bare room 60
the bright feathers arch in a parody
of greenery, as the last pale crumbs
disappear under the blackened tongue. Someone

calls out his name in a voice
so like his mother's, a startled tear 65
splashes the tip of his right boot.
My mother, my love in death.
The general remembers the tiny green sprigs
men of his village wore in their capes
to honor the birth of a son. He will 70
order many, this time, to be killed

for a single, beautiful word.

—1983

Dusting[3]

Every day a wilderness—no
shade in sight. Beulah
patient among knicknacks,
the solarium a rage

---

[2] *Mi madre, mi amor en muerte:* (Sp.) My mother, my love
in death. The *l* in place of *r* in *madre, amor,* and *muerte*
signify the unrolled *r*'s used by the Haitians.

[3] This poem is from Dove's book *Thomas and Beulah*
(1986), a series of poems based loosely on the lives of
her maternal grandparents.

of light, a grainstorm   5
as her gray cloth brings
dark wood to life.

Under her hand scrolls
and crests gleam
darker still. What   10
was his name, that
silly boy at the fair with
the rifle booth? And his kiss and
the clear bowl with one bright
fish, rippling   15
wound!

Not Michael—
something finer. Each dust
stroke a deep breath and
the canary in bloom.   20
Wavery memory: home
from a dance, the front door
blown open and the parlor
in snow, she rushed
the bowl to the stove, watched   25
as the locket of ice
dissolved and he
swam free.

That was years before
Father gave her up   30
with her name, years before
her name grew to mean
Promise, then
Desert-in-Peace.
Long before the shadow and   35
sun's accomplice, the tree.

Maurice.

—1986

Canary
for Michael S. Harper

Billie Holiday's[4] burned voice
had as many shadows as lights,
a mournful candelabra against a sleek piano,
the gardenia her signature under that ruined face.

(Now you're cooking, drummer to bass,   5
magic spoon, magic needle.

---

[4] Billie Holiday (1915-1959), American jazz singer.

Take all day if you have to
with your mirror and your bracelet of song.)

Fact is, the invention of women under siege
has been to sharpen love in the service of myth.   10

If you can't be free, be a mystery.

—1987

BELL HOOKS (1952–   )

Feminist scholar and anti-racist cultural critic bell hooks was born Gloria Jean Watkins in
Hopkinsville, Kentucky, one of seven children. Her father, Veodis Watkins, worked as a custodian for the postal service and her mother, Rosa Bell Watkins, worked as a domestic.
Growing up Black in a small, segregated Southern town, hooks developed a reputation for
speaking her mind; it was a quality she shared with her maternal great-grandmother, whose
name she chose to use as a pseudonym when she published her first book. hooks received a
scholarship to attend Stanford University, where she earned her B.A. in 1973. Her experience
there was marked by profound culture shock—the atmosphere was less liberal than she
expected, and not all of her professors were welcoming to Black students. hooks became very
involved with the feminist movement while at Stanford, but was dismayed at the utter lack of
attention to the interests of Black women and to the intersections of sexism with racism and
class politics. She began writing her first book, *Ain't I a Woman: Black Women and Feminism*,
during her second year, and continued to work on it as she pursued her M.A. at the University
of Wisconsin, Madison (1976), and her Ph.D. at the University of California, Santa Cruz
(1983). *Ain't I a Woman* was published in 1981 by South End Press and immediately established hooks' reputation as a major feminist theorist as well as a critic of feminism. hooks has
made many important contributions to the scholarly areas of feminism, critical race theory,
and radical pedagogy, including *Feminist Theory: From Margin to Center* (1984), *Yearning: Race,
Gender, and Cultural Politics* (1990), *Teaching to Transgress: Education As the Practice of Freedom*
(1994), *Killing Rage: Ending Racism* (1995), *Feminism Is for Everybody: Passionate Politics* (2000),
and *Teaching Community: A Pedagogy of Hope* (2003). She has also published poetry, children's
books, essays, and autobiographical writing, including *Bone Black: Memories of Girlhood* (1996),
the volume from which the following selection is taken. In her more recent work, such as *The
Will to Change: Men, Masculinity, and Love* (2004), hooks has turned her attention to a critical
rethinking of masculinity.

from Bone Black
Memories of Girlhood

1

Mama has given me a quilt from her hope chest. It is one her mother's mother
made. It is a quilt of stars—each piece taken from faded-cotton summer dresses—each
piece stitched by hand. She has given me a beaded purse that belonged to my father's

mother Sister Ray. They want to know why she has given it to me since I was not Sister Ray's favorite. They say she is probably turning over in her grave angry that I have something of hers.

Mama tells us—her daughters—that the girls in her family started gathering things for their hope chest when they were very young, gathering all the things that they would carry with them into marriage. The first time she opens hers for us I feel I am witnessing yet another opening of Pandora's box,[1] that the secrets of her youth, the bittersweet memories, will come rushing out like a waterfall and push us back in time. Instead the scent of cedar fills the air. It reminds me of Christmas, of abandoned trees, standing naked in the snow after the celebrations are over. Usually we are not invited to share in the opening of the chest. Even though we stand near her watching, she acts as if we are not there. I see her remembering, clutching tightly in her hand some object, some bit of herself that she has had to part with in order to live in the present. I see her examining each hope to see if it has been fulfilled, if the promises have been kept. I pretend I do not see the tears in her eyes. I am glad she shares the opening of the chest this time with all of us. I am clutching the gifts she hands to me, the quilt, the beaded purse. She knows that I am often hopeless. She stores no treasures for my coming marriage. I do not want to be given away. I cannot contain my dreams until tomorrow. I cannot wait for someone else, a stranger, to take my hand.

That night in my sleep I dream of going away. I am taking the bus. Mama is standing waving good-bye. Later when I return from my journey I come home only to find there has been a fire, nothing remains of our house and I can see no one. There is only the dark and the thick smell of smoke. I stand alone weeping. The sound of my sobbing is like the cry of the peacock. Suddenly they appear with candles, mama and everyone. They say they have heard my sorrow pierce the air like the cry of the peacock, that they have come to comfort me. They give me a candle. Together we search the ashes for bits and pieces, any fragment of our lives that may have survived. We find that the hope chest has not burned through and through. We open it, taking out the charred remains. Someone finds a photo, one face has turned to ash, another is there. We pass around the fragments like bread and wine at communion. The chorus of weeping is our testimony that we are moved.

Louder than our weeping is a voice commanding us to stop our tears. We cannot see who is speaking but we are reminded of the stern sound of our mother's mother's voice. We listen. She tells us to sit close in the night, to make a circle of our bodies, to place the candles at the center of the circle. The candles burn like another fire only this time she says the fire burns to warm our hearts. She says Listen, let me tell you a story. She begins to put together in words all that has been destroyed in the fire. We are all rejoicing when the dream ends.

The next day I want to know what the dream means, who she is, this storyteller who comes in the night. Saru, mama's mother, is the interpreter of dreams. She tells me that I should know the storyteller, that I and she are one, that they are my sisters, family. She says that a part of me is making the story, making the words, making the new fire, that it is my heart burning in the center of the flames.

---

[1] In Greek mythology, Pandora opened her box and released evil into the world.

2

We live in the country. We children do not understand that that means we are among the poor. We do not understand that the outhouses behind many of the houses are still there because running water came here long after they had it in the city. We do not understand that our playmates who are eating laundry starch do so not because the white powder tastes so good but because they are sometimes without necessary food. We do not understand that we wash with the heavy, unsmelling, oddly shaped pieces of homemade lye soap because real soap costs money. We never think about where lye soap comes from. We only know we want to make our skin itch less— that we do not want our mouths to be washed out with it. Because we are poor, because we live in the country, we go to the country school—the little white wood-frame building where all the country kids come. They come from miles and miles away. They come so far because they are black. As they are riding the school buses they pass school after school where children who are white can attend without being bused, without getting up in the wee hours of the morning, sometimes leaving home in the dark.

We are not bused. The school is only a mile or two away from our house. We get to walk. We get to wander aimlessly in the road—until a car comes by. We get to wave at the buses. They are not allowed to stop and give us a ride. We do not understand why. Daddy says the walk to school will be good for us. He tells us again and again in a harsh voice of the miles he walked to school through fields in the snow, without boots or gloves to keep him warm. We are not comforted by the image of the small boy trudging along many miles to school so he can learn to read and be somebody. When we close our eyes he becomes real to us. He looks very sad. Sometimes he cries. We are not at all comforted. And there are still days when we complain about the walk, especially when it is wet and stormy.

School begins with chapel. There we recite the Pledge of Allegiance to the Flag. We have no feeling for the flag but we like the words; said in unison, they sound like a chant. We then listen to a morning prayer. We say the Lord's Prayer. It is the singing that makes morning chapel the happiest moment of the day. It is there I learn to sing "Red River Valley."[2] It is a song about missing and longing. I do not understand all the words, only the feeling—warm wet sorrow, like playing games in spring rain. After chapel we go to classrooms.

In the first grade the teacher gives tasting parties. She brings us different foods to taste so that we can know what they are like because we do not eat them in our homes. All of us eagerly await the Fridays when the tasting part will begin. The day she brings cottage cheese I am not sure I want to try it. She makes me. She makes everyone try a little bit just in case they might really like it. We go home from the tasting parties telling our parents what it was like, telling them to buy this new good food, better food, better than any food we have ever tasted.

Mama tells us that most of that food we taste isn't good to eat all the time, that it is a waste of money. We do not understand money. We do not know that we are all poor. We cannot visit many of the friends we make because they live miles and miles away. We have each other after school. [...]

---

[2] Folk song dating back to the late 19th century.

8

We learn early that it is important for a woman to marry. We are always marrying our dolls to someone. He of course is always invisible, that is until they made the Ken doll to go with Barbie. One of us has been given a Barbie doll for Christmas. Her skin is not white white but almost brown from the tan they have painted on her. We know she is white because of her blond hair. The newest Barbie is bald, with many wigs of all different colors. We spend hours dressing and undressing her, pretending she is going somewhere important. We want to make new clothes for her. We want to buy the outfits made just for her that we see in the store but they are too expensive. Some of them cost as much as real clothes for real people. Barbie is anything but real, that is why we like her. She never does housework, washes dishes, or has children to care for. She is free to spend all day dreaming about the Kens of the world. Mama laughs when we tell her there should be more than one Ken for Barbie, there should be Joe, Sam, Charlie, men in all shapes and sizes. We do not think that Barbie should have a girlfriend. We know that Barbie was born to be alone—that the fantasy woman, the soap opera girl, the girl of *True Confessions,* the Miss America girl was born to be alone. We know that she is not us.

My favorite doll is brown, brown like light milk chocolate. She is a baby doll and I give her a baby doll name, Baby. She is almost the same size as a real baby. She comes with no clothes, only a pink diaper, fastened with tiny gold pins and a plastic bottle. She has a red mouth the color of lipstick slightly open so that we can stick the bottle in it. We fill the bottle with water and wait for it to come through the tiny hole in Baby's bottom. We make her many new diapers, but we are soon bored with changing them. We lose the bottle and Baby can no longer drink. We still love her. She is the only doll we will not destroy. We have lost Barbie. We have broken the leg of another doll. We have cracked open the head of an antique doll to see what makes the crying sound. The little thing inside is not interesting. We are sorry but nothing can be done—not even mama can put the pieces together again. She tells us that if this is the way we intend to treat our babies she hopes we do not have any. She laughs at our careless parenting. Sometimes she takes a minute to show us the right thing to do. She too is terribly fond of Baby. She says that she looks so much like a real newborn. Once she came upstairs, saw Baby under the covers, and wanted to know who had brought the real baby from downstairs.

She loves to tell the story of how Baby was born. She tells us that I, her problem child, decided out of nowhere that I did not want a white doll to play with, I demanded a brown doll, one that would look like me. Only grown-ups think that the things children say come out of nowhere. We know they come from the deepest parts of ourselves. Deep within myself I had begun to worry that all this loving care we gave to the pink and white flesh-colored dolls meant that somewhere left high on the shelves were boxes of unwanted, unloved brown dolls covered in dust. I thought that they would remain there forever, orphaned and alone, unless someone began to want them, to want to give them love and care, to want them more than anything. At first they ignored my wanting. They complained. They pointed out that white dolls were easier to find, cheaper. They never said where they found Baby but I know. She was always there high on the shelf, covered in dust—waiting. [...]

52

We cannot believe we must leave our beloved Crispus Attucks and go to schools in the white neighborhoods. We cannot imagine what it will be like to walk by the principal's office and see a man who will not know our name, who will not care about us. Already the grown-ups are saying it will be nothing but trouble, but they do not protest. Already we feel like the cattle in the stockyard near our house, herded, prodded, pushed. Already we prepare ourselves to go willingly to what will be a kind of slaughter, for parts of ourselves must be severed to make this integration of schools work. We start by leaving behind the pleasure we will feel in going to our all-black school, in seeing friends, in being a part of a school community. Our pleasure is replaced by fear. We must rise early to catch the buses that will take us to the white schools. So early that we must go into the gymnasium and wait for the other students, the white students, to arrive. Again we are herded, prodded, pushed, told not to make trouble in this early morning waiting period.

Sometimes there is protest. Everyone black walks out, except for those whose parents have warned that there will be no walking out of school. I do not walk out. I do not believe that any demands made will be met. We surrendered the right to demand when the windows to Attucks were covered with wood and barred shut, when the doors were locked. Anyhow, mama has warned us about walking out. The walkouts make everything worse. More than ever before we are cattle, to be herded, prodded, pushed. More than ever before we are slaughtered. We can hear the sound of the paddles reverberating in the hallway as black boys are struck by the white principals. The word spreads rapidly when one of us has been sent home not knowing when and if they will be allowed to come back.

Some of us are chosen. We are allowed to sit in the classes with white students. We are told that we are smart. We are the good servants who will be looked to. We are to stand between the white administration and the black student body. We are not surprised that black boys are not in the smart classes, even though we know that many of them are smart. We know that white folks have this thing about black boys sitting in classes with white girls. Now and then a smart black boy is moved into the classes. They have been watching him. He has proved himself. We know that we are all being watched, that we must prove ourselves. We no longer like attending school. We are tired of the long hours spent discussing what can be done to make integration work. We discuss with them knowing all the while that they want us to do something, to change, to make ourselves into carbon copies of them so that they can forget we are here, so that they can forget the injustice of their past. They are not prepared to change.

Although black and white attend the same school, blacks sit with blacks and whites with whites. In the cafeteria there is no racial mixing. When hands reach out to touch across these boundaries whites protest, blacks protest as well. Each one seeing it as a going over to the other side. School is a place where we came face to face with racism. When we walk through the rows of national guardsmen with their uniforms and guns we think that we will be the first to die, to lay our bodies down. We feel despair and long for the days when school was a place where we learned to love and celebrate ourselves, a place where we were number one. [...]

—1996

CHERRÍE MORAGA (1952-   )

Cherríe Moraga is a renowned Chicana feminist essayist, poet, dramatist, and editor. Born in Whittier, California, on September 25, 1952, to a Mexican-American mother and an Anglo-American father, her biracial and bilingual heritage—like her lesbian sexuality—are central themes in her writing. In 1981, she co-edited *This Bridge Called My Back: Writings by Radical Women of Color* with Gloria Anzaldúa. This anthology of prose and poetry marked a turning point in the U.S. feminist movement. In its pages, women of color launched an unflinching critique of the racism and classism inherent in the white feminist movement, as well as a critique of the sexism and homophobia within the various minority nationalist movements of the 1970s. Unable to find a publisher for the collection, Moraga co-founded one of the earliest publishing houses focusing on writing by queer women and women of color in the U.S., Kitchen Table/Women of Color Press. *This Bridge Called My Back,* which won the Before Columbus American Book Award, has become a mainstay of feminist studies courses. Moraga's follow-up book of essays and poetry, *Loving in the War Years* (1983), continued to explore racism within the Anglo and Chicano communities, the relationship between language and sexuality, and the intimate relationship between nationalism and sexism. Moraga's skills as a dramatist have met with similar acclaim, and her plays have been staged in theaters across the country. In 1984, she was selected for a prestigious dramatist-in-residency program at INTAR (Hispanic-American Arts Center) in New York City, which was followed by an artist-in-residency at Brava! Theater Center in San Francisco (1991-1997), sponsored by the California Arts Council and the Theater Communications Group. Currently, Moraga is an artist-in-residence at Stanford University, where she teaches Latino theatre, playwriting, creative writing, and U.S. Latina/o literature for the Drama and the Spanish and Portuguese departments.

La Güera

It requires something more than personal experience to gain a philosophy or point of view from any specific event. It is the quality of our response to the event and our capacity to enter into the lives of others that help us to make their lives and experiences our own.

Emma Goldman[1]

I am the very well-educated daughter of a woman who, by the standards in this country, would be considered largely illiterate. My mother was born in Santa Paula, Southern California, at a time when much of the central valley there was still farm land. Nearly thirty-five years later, in 1948, she was the only daughter of six to marry an anglo, my father.

I remember all of my mother's stories, probably much better than she realizes. She is a fine story-teller, recalling every event of her life with the vividness of the present, noting each detail right down to the cut and color of her dress. I remember stories of her being pulled out of school at the ages of five, seven, nine, and eleven to work in the fields, along with her brothers and sisters; stories of her father drinking away whatever small profit she was able to make for the family; of her going the long way home to avoid meeting him on the street, staggering toward the same destination. I remember stories of my mother lying about her age in order to get a job as a hat-check

---

[1] Emma Goldman (1869-1940), American political activist and writer.

girl at Agua Caliente Racetrack in Tijuana. At fourteen, she was the main support of the family. I can still see her walking home alone at 3 a.m., only to turn all of her salary and tips over to her mother, who was pregnant again.

The stories continue through the war years and on: walnut-cracking factories, the Voit Rubber factory, and then the computer boom. I remember my mother doing piecework for the electronics plant in our neighborhood. In the late evening, she would sit in front of the T.V. set, wrapping copper wires into the backs of circuit boards, talking about "keeping up with the younger girls." By that time, she was already in her mid-fifties.

Meanwhile, I was college-prep in school. After classes, I would go with my mother to fill out job applications for her, or write checks for her at the supermarket. We would have the scenario all worked out ahead of time. My mother would sign the check before we'd get to the store. Then, as we'd approach the checkstand, she would say—within earshot of the cashier—"oh honey, you go 'head and make out the check," as if she couldn't be bothered with such an insignificant detail. No one asked any questions.

I was educated, and wore it with a keen sense of pride and satisfaction, my head propped up with the knowledge, from my mother, that my life would be easier than hers. I was educated; but more than this, I was "la güera": fair-skinned. Born with the features of my Chicana mother, but the skin of my Anglo father, I had it made.

No one ever quite told me this (that light was right), but I knew that being light was something valued in my family (who were all Chicano, with the exception of my father). In fact, everything about my upbringing (at least what occurred on a conscious level) attempted to bleach me of what color I did have. Although my mother was fluent in it, I was never taught much Spanish at home. I picked up what I did learn from school and from over-heard snatches of conversation among my relatives and mother. She often called other lower-income Mexicans "braceros," or "wet-backs," referring to herself and her family as "a different class of people." And yet, the real story was that my family, too, had been poor (some still are) and farmworkers. My mother can remember this in her blood as if it were yesterday. But this is something she would like to forget (and rightfully), for to her, on a basic economic level, being Chicana meant being "less." It was through my mother's desire to protect her children from poverty and illiteracy that we became "anglocized"; the more effectively we could pass in the white world, the better guaranteed our future.

From all of this, I experience, daily, a huge disparity between what I was born into and what I was to grow up to become. Because, (as Goldman suggests) these stories my mother told me crept under my "güera" skin. I had no choice but to enter into the life of my mother. *I had no choice.* I took her life into my heart, but managed to keep a lid on it as long as I feigned being the happy, upwardly mobile heterosexual.

When I finally lifted the lid to my lesbianism, a profound connection with my mother reawakened in me. It wasn't until I acknowledged and confronted my own lesbianism in the flesh, that my heartfelt identification with and empathy for my mother's oppression—due to being poor, uneducated, and Chicana—was realized. My lesbianism is the avenue through which I have learned the most about silence and oppression, and it continues to be the most tactile reminder to me that we are not free human beings.

You see, one follows the other. I had known for years that I was a lesbian, had felt it in my bones, had ached with the knowledge, gone crazed with the knowledge, wallowed in the silence of it. Silence is like starvation. Don't be fooled. It's nothing short of that, and felt most sharply when one has had a full belly most of her life. When we are not physically starving, we have the luxury to realize psychic and emotional starvation. It is from this starvation that other starvations can be recognized—if one is willing to take the risk of making the connection—if one is willing to be responsible to the result of the connection. For me, the connection is an inevitable one.

What I am saying is that the joys of looking like a white girl ain't so great since I realized I could be beaten on the street for being a dyke. If my sister's being beaten because she's Black, it's pretty much the same principle. We're both getting beaten any way you look at it. The connection is blatant; and in the case of my own family, the difference in the privileges attached to looking white instead of brown are merely a generation apart.

In this country, lesbianism is a poverty—as is being brown, as is being a woman, as is being just plain poor. The danger lies in ranking the oppressions. *The danger lies in failing to acknowledge the specificity of the oppression.* The danger lies in attempting to deal with oppression purely from a theoretical base. Without an emotional, heartfelt grappling with the source of our own oppression, without naming the enemy within ourselves and outside of us, no authentic, non-hierarchical connection among oppressed groups can take place.

When the going gets rough, will we abandon our so-called comrades in a flurry of racist/heterosexist/what-have-you panic? To whose camp, then, should the lesbian of color retreat? Her very presence violates the ranking and abstraction of oppression. Do we merely live hand to mouth? Do we merely struggle with the "ism" that's sitting on top of our own heads?

The answer is: yes, I think first we do; and we must do so thoroughly and deeply. But to fail to move out from there will only isolate us in our own oppression—will only insulate, rather than radicalize us.

To illustrate: a gay male friend of mine once confided to me that he continued to feel that, on some level, I didn't trust him because he was male; that he felt, really, if it ever came down to a "battle of the sexes," I might kill him. I admitted that I might very well. He wanted to understand the source of my distrust. I responded, "You're not a woman. Be a woman for a day. Imagine being a woman." He confessed that the thought terrified him because, to him, being a woman meant being raped by men. He *had* felt raped by men; he wanted to forget what that meant. What grew from that discussion was the realization that in order for him to create an authentic alliance with me, he must deal with the primary source of his own sense of oppression. He must, first, emotionally come to terms with what it feels like to be a victim. If he—or anyone—were to truly do this, it would be impossible to discount the oppression of others, except by again forgetting how we have been hurt.

And yet, oppressed groups are forgetting all the time. There are instances of this in the rising Black middle class, and certainly an obvious trend of such "unconsciousness" among white gay men. Because to remember may mean giving up whatever privileges we have managed to squeeze out of this society by virtue of our gender, race, class, or sexuality.

Within the women's movement, the connections among women of different backgrounds and sexual orientations have been fragile, at best. I think this phenomenon is indicative of our failure to seriously address ourselves to some very frightening questions: How have I internalized my own oppression? How have I oppressed? Instead, we have let rhetoric do the job of poetry. Even the word "oppression" has lost its power. We need a new language, better words that can more closely describe women's fear of and resistance to one another; words that will not always come out sounding like dogma.

What prompted me in the first place to work on an anthology by radical women of color was a deep sense that I had a valuable insight to contribute, by virtue of my birthright and background. And yet, I don't really understand first-hand what it feels like being shitted on for being brown. I understand much more about the joys of it— being Chicana and having family are synonymous for me. What I know about loving, singing, crying, telling stories, speaking with my heart and hands, even having a sense of my own soul comes from the love of my mother, aunts, cousins…

But at the age of twenty-seven, it is frightening to acknowledge that I have internalized a racism and classism, where the object of oppression is not only someone outside of my skin, but the someone inside my skin. In fact, to a large degree, the real battle with such oppression, for all of us, begins under the skin. I have had to confront the fact that much of what I value about being Chicana, about my family, has been subverted by anglo culture and my own cooperation with it. This realization did not occur to me overnight. For example, it wasn't until long after my graduation from the private college I'd attended in Los Angeles, that I realized the major reason for my total alienation from and fear of my classmates was rooted in class and culture. CLICK.

Three years after graduation, in an apple-orchard in Sonoma, a friend of mine (who comes from an Italian Irish working-class family) says to me, "Cherríe, no wonder you felt like such a nut in school. Most of the people there were white and rich." It was true. All along I had felt the difference, but not until I had put the words "class" and "color" to the experience, did my feelings make any sense. For years, I had berated myself for not being as "free" as my classmates. I completely bought that they simply had more guts than I did—to rebel against their parents and run around the country hitch-hiking, reading books and studying "art." They had enough privilege to be atheists, for chrissake. There was no one around filling in the disparity for me between their parents, who were Hollywood filmmakers, and my parents, who wouldn't know the name of a filmmaker if their lives depended on it (and precisely because their lives didn't depend on it, they couldn't be bothered). But I knew nothing about "privilege" then. White was right. Period. I could pass. If I got educated enough, there would never be any telling.

Three years after that, another CLICK. In a letter to Barbara Smith,[2] I wrote:

> I went to a concert where Ntozake Shange[3] was reading. There, everything exploded for me. She was speaking a language that I knew—in the deepest parts of me—existed, and that I had ignored in my own feminist studies and even in my own writing. What Ntosake caught in me is the realization that in my development as a poet, I have, in many ways, denied the voice of my brown mother—the brown in me.

---

[2] Barbara Smith (b. 1946), African-American lesbian feminist, teacher, scholar, and activist.

[3] Ntozake Shange (b. 1948), African-American playwright and poet.

I have acclimated to the sound of a white language which, as my father represents it, does not speak to the emotions in my poems—emotions which stem from the love of my mother.

The reading was agitating. Made me uncomfortable. Threw me into a week-long terror of how deeply I was affected. I felt that I had to start all over again. That I turned only to the perceptions of white middle-class women to speak for me and all women. I am shocked by my own ignorance.

Sitting in that auditorium chair was the first time I had realized to the core of me that for years I had disowned the language I knew best—ignored the words and rhythm that were the closest to me. The sounds of my mother and aunts gossiping—half in English, half in Spanish—while drinking cerveza[4] in the kitchen. And the hands—I had cut off the hands in my poems. But not in conversation; still the hands could not be kept down. Still they insisted on moving.

The reading had forced me to remember that I knew things from my roots. But to remember puts me up against what I don't know. Shange's reading agitated me because she spoke with power about a world that is both alien and common to me: "the capacity to enter into the lives of others." But you can't just take the goods and run. I knew that then, sitting in the Oakland auditorium (as I know in my poetry), that the only thing worth writing about is what seems to be unknown and, therefore, fearful.

The "unknown" is often depicted in racist literature as the "darkness" within a person. Similarly, sexist writers will refer to fear in the form of the vagina, calling it "the orifice of death." In contrast, it is a pleasure to read works such as Maxine Hong Kingston's[5] *Woman Warrior,* where fear and alienation are described as "the white ghosts." And yet, the bulk of literature in this country reinforces the myth that what is dark and female is evil. Consequently, each of us—whether dark, female, or both—has in some way *internalized* this oppressive imagery. What the oppressor often succeeds in doing is simply *externalizing* his fears, projecting them into the bodies of women, Asians, gays, disabled folks, whoever seems most "other."

> call me
> roach and presumptuous
> nightmare on your white pillow
> your itch to destroy
> the indestructible
> part of yourself
>
> Audre Lorde[6]

But it is not really difference the oppressor fears so much as similarity. He fears he will discover in himself the same aches, the same longings as those of the people he has shitted on. He fears the immobilization threatened by his own incipient guilt. He fears he will have to change his life once he has seen himself in the bodies of the people he has called different. He fears the hatred, anger, and vengeance of those he has hurt.

This is the oppressor's nightmare, but it is not exclusive to him. We women have a similar nightmare, for each of us in some way has been both oppressed and the oppressor. We are afraid to look at how we have failed each other. We are afraid to see

---

4 (Sp.) Beer.
5 Maxine Hong Kingston (b. 1940), Chinese-American novelist.

6 From "The Brown Menace, or Poem to the Survival of Roaches" (1974), by Audre Lorde (1934-1992), African-American poet and activist.

how we have taken the values of our oppressor into our hearts and turned them against ourselves and one another. We are afraid to admit how deeply "the man's" words have been ingrained in us.

To assess the damage is a dangerous act. I think of how, even as a feminist lesbian, I have so wanted to ignore my own homophobia, my own hatred of myself for being queer. I have not wanted to admit that my deepest personal sense of myself has not quite "caught up" with my "woman-identified" politics. I have been afraid to criticize lesbian writers who choose to "skip over" these issues in the name of feminism. In 1979, we talk of "old gay" and "butch and femme" roles as if they were ancient history. We toss them aside as merely patriarchal notions. And yet, the truth of the matter is that I have sometimes taken society's fear and hatred of lesbians to bed with me. I have sometimes hated my lover for loving me. I have sometimes felt "not woman enough" for her. I have sometimes felt "not man enough." For a lesbian trying to survive in a heterosexist society, there is no easy way around these emotions. Similarly, in a white-dominated world, there is little getting around racism and our own internalization of it. It's always there, embodied in someone we least expect to rub up against.

When we do rub up against this person, *there* then is the challenge. *There* then is the opportunity to look at the nightmare within us. But we usually shrink from such a challenge.

Time and time again, I have observed that the usual response among white women's groups when the "racism issue" comes up is to deny the difference. I have heard comments like, "Well, we're open to *all* women; why don't they (women of color) come? You can only do so much…" But there is seldom any analysis of how the very nature and structure of the group itself may be founded on racist or classist assumptions. More importantly, so often the women seem to feel no loss, no lack, no absence when women of color are not involved; therefore, there is little desire to change the situation. This has hurt me deeply. I have come to believe that the only reason women of a privileged class will dare to look at *how* it is that *they* oppress, is when they've come to know the meaning of their own oppression. And understand that the oppression of others hurts them personally.

The other side of the story is that women of color and working-class women often shrink from challenging white middle-class women. It is much easier to rank oppressions and set up a hierarchy, rather than take responsibility for changing our own lives. We have failed to demand that white women, particularly those who claim to be speaking for all women, be accountable for their racism.

The dialogue has simply not gone deep enough.

I have many times questioned my right to even work on an anthology which is to be written "exclusively by Third World women." I have had to look critically at my claim to color, at a time when, among white feminist ranks, it is a "politically correct" (and sometimes peripherally advantageous) assertion to make. I must acknowledge the fact that, physically, I have had a *choice* about making that claim, in contrast to women who have not had such a choice, and have been abused for their color. I must reckon with the fact that for most of my life, by virtue of the very fact that I am white-looking, I identified with and aspired towards white values, and that I rode the wave of that Southern Californian privilege as far as conscience would let me.

Well, now I feel both bleached and beached. I feel angry about this—the years when I refused to recognize privilege, both when it worked against me, and when I worked it, ignorantly, at the expense of others. These are not settled issues. That is why this work feels so risky to me. It continues to be discovery. It has brought me into contact with women who invariably know a hell of a lot more than I do about racism, as experienced in the flesh, as revealed in the flesh of their writing.

I think: what is my responsibility to my roots—both white and brown, Spanish-speaking and English? I am a woman with a foot in both worlds; and I refuse the split. I feel the necessity for dialogue. Sometimes I feel it urgently.

But one voice is not enough, nor two, although this is where dialogue begins. It is essential that radical feminists confront their fear of and resistance to each other, because without this, there *will* be no bread on the table. Simply, we will not survive. If we could make this connection in our heart of hearts, that if we are serious about a revolution—better—if we seriously believe there should be joy in our lives (real joy, not just "good times"), then we need one another. We women need each other. Because my/your solitary, self-asserting "go-for-the-throat-of-fear" power is not enough. The real power, as you and I well know, is collective. I can't afford to be afraid of you, nor you of me. If it takes head-on collisions, let's do it: this polite timidity is killing us.

As Lorde suggests in the passage I cited earlier, it is in looking to the nightmare that the dream is found. There, the survivor emerges to insist on a future, a vision, yes, born out of what is dark and female. The feminist movement must be a movement of such survivors, a movement with a future.

—1979

NAOMI SHIHAB NYE (1952-   )

Palestinian-American poet and writer Naomi Shihab Nye was born in St. Louis, Missouri. Nye's poetry centers on quotidian imagery from a range of perspectives, especially those of Mexican and Arab Americans, as well as the history and geography of the Southwest through simple, poignant language. Her collections of poetry include *19 Varieties of Gazelle: Poems of the Middle East* (2002), *Red Suitcase* (1994), and *Different Ways to Pray* (1980). Her children's books, which include the autobiographical young adult novel *Habibi* (1997) and an essay collection entitled *Never in a Hurry* (1996), illuminate the perspectives of girls and young women. Nye has won the I.B. Lavan Award from the Academy of American Poets, the Jane Addams Children's Book Award, and four Pushcart Prizes over the span of her career.

The Words Under the Words
(for Sitti Khadra, north of Jerusalem)

My grandmother's hands recognize grapes,
the damp shine of a goat's new skin.
When I was sick they followed me,
I woke from the long fever to find them
covering my head like cool prayers.

5

My grandmother's days are made of bread,
a round pat-pat and the slow baking.
She waits by the oven watching a strange car
circle the streets. Maybe it holds her son,
lost to America. More often, tourists,   10
who kneel and weep at mysterious shrines.
She knows how often mail arrives,
how rarely there is a letter.
When one comes, she announces it, a miracle,
listening to it read again and again   15
in the dim evening light.

My grandmother's voice says nothing can surprise her.
Take her the shotgun wound and the crippled baby.
She knows the spaces we travel through,
the messages we cannot send—our voices are short   20
and would get lost on the journey.
Farewell to the husband's coat,
the ones she has loved and nourished,
who fly from her like seeds into a deep sky.
They will plant themselves. We will all die.   25

My grandmother's eyes say Allah is everywhere, even in death.
When she talks of the orchard and the new olive press,
when she tells the stories of Joha[1] and his foolish wisdoms,
He is her first thought, what she really thinks of is His name.

"Answer if you hear the words under the words—   30
otherwise it is just a world with a lot of rough edges,
difficult to get through, and our pockets full of stones."

—1980

Making a Fist

For the first time, on the road north of Tampico,
I felt the life sliding out of me,
a drum in the desert, harder and harder to hear.
I was seven, I lay in the car
watching palm trees swirl a sickening pattern past the glass.   5
My stomach was a melon split wide inside my skin.

"How do you know if you are going to die?"
I begged my mother.
We had been traveling for days.
With strange confidence she answered,   10
"When you can no longer make a fist."

---

[1] Character in popular Arabic folklore.

Years later I smile to think of that journey,
the borders we must cross separately,
stamped with our unanswerable woes.
I who did not die, who am still living,   15
still lying in the backseat behind all my questions,
clenching and opening one small hand.

—1982

Arabic
(Jordan, 1992)

The man with laughing eyes stopped smiling
to say, "Until you speak Arabic—
—you will not understand pain."

Something to do with the back of the head,
an Arab carries sorrow in the back of the head   5
that only language cracks, the thrum of stones

weeping, grating hinge on an old metal gate.
"Once you know," he whispered, "you can enter the room
whenever you need to. Music you heard from a distance,

the slapped drum of a stranger's wedding,   10
wells up inside your skin, inside rain, a thousand
pulsing tongues. You are changed."

Outside, the snow had finally stopped.
In a land where snow rarely falls,
we had felt our days grow white and still.   15

I thought pain had no tongue. Or every tongue
at once, supreme translator, sieve. I admit my
shame. To live on the brink of Arabic, tugging

its rich threads without understanding
how to weave the rug...I have no gift.   20
The sound, but not the sense.

I kept looking over his shoulder for someone else
to talk to, recalling my dying friend who only scrawled
I can't write. What good would any grammar have been

to her then? I touched his arm, held it hard,   25
which sometimes you don't do in the Middle East, and said
I'll work on it, feeling sad

for his good strict heart, but later in the slick street
hailed a taxi by shouting *Pain!* and it stopped
in every language and opened its doors.   30

—1994

For the 500th Dead Palestinian, Ibtisam Bozieh

Little sister Ibtisam,
our sleep flounders, our sleep tugs
the cord of your name.
Dead at 13, for staring through
the window into a gun barrel   5
which did not know you wanted to be
a doctor.

I would smooth your life in my hands,
pull you back. Had I stayed in your land,
I might have been dead too,   10
for something simple like staring
or shouting what was true
and getting kicked out of school.
I wandered stony afternoons
owning all their vastness.   15

Now I would give them to you,
guiltily, you, not me.
Throwing this ragged grief into the street,
scissoring news stories free from the page
but they live on my desk with letters, not cries.   20

How do we carry the endless surprise
of all our deaths? Becoming doctors
for one another, Arab, Jew,
instead of guarding tumors of pain
as if they hold us upright?   25

People in other countries speak easily
of being early, late.
Some will live to be eighty.
Some who never saw it
will not forget your face.

—1994

ANA CASTILLO (1953–   )

Poet, novelist, short story writer, editor, and essayist Ana Castillo grew up in a working-class Mexican-American family in Chicago. After graduating from a vocational high school, she spent two years at Chicago City College before entering Northeastern Illinois University, where she majored in art and minored in secondary education. Upon graduating in 1975, she moved to Sonoma County, California, where she taught ethnic studies courses, participated in the burgeoning Chicano and feminist movements, and worked on her poetry. Her first collection of poems, *Otro Canto,* was published as a chapbook in 1977. A second chapbook, *The Invitation* (which she later adapted to music for the 1982 New York City Soho Art Festival), appeared in 1979, the same year she earned her M.A. in Latin American and Caribbean Studies from the University of Chicago. Over the next two decades she published three more collections of poems: *Women Are Not Roses* (1984), *My Father Was a Toltec* (1995), and *I Ask the Impossible* (2001).

Since the mid-1980s, Castillo has gained fame as a novelist with a flair for narrative experimentation. Her first novel, *The Mixquiahuala Letters,* was published in 1986 and won the Before Columbus Foundation's American Book Award. Five more novels followed: *Sapogonia: An Anti-Romance in 3/8 Meter* (1990), *So Far from God* (1993), *Peel My Love Like an Onion* (1999), *Watercolor Women, Opaque Men: A Novel in Verse* (2005), and *The Guardians* (2007). She has published a collection of short stories, two plays, and a children's book, and has edited an anthology of essays on the Virgin of Guadalupe. She has also contributed nonfiction pieces to numerous magazines and newspapers. In 1991, Castillo received her Ph.D. in American Studies from the University of Bremen; she later incorporated her dissertation, a series of feminist essays, into *Massacre of the Dreamers: Essays on Xicanisma* (1995). Castillo is the recipient of National Endowment for the Arts fellowships in poetry and fiction; the Sor Juana Achievement Award, bestowed by the Mexican Fine Arts Center Museum in Chicago; the Carl Sandburg Award; the Mountains and Plains Booksellers Award; and the Independent Publisher Story Teller of the Year Award.

1975

talking proletariat talks
over instant coffee
and nicotine.
in better times
there is tea   5
to ease the mind.
talking proletariat talks
during laid-off hours
cussing and cussing
complaining of unpaid bills   10
and bigoted unions
that refuse to let us in.

talking proletariat talks
of pregnant wives
and shoeless kids.   15
no-turkey-thanksgivings.
bare x-mas trees this year.
santa claus is on strike
again.

talking proletariat talks   20
with proletariat friends
and relations who need
a few bucks til the end
of the week
waiting   25
for compensation checks.
talking proletariat talks
of plants closing down

and deportations.
tight immigration   30
busting our brothers again.

talking proletariat talks
of next spring or some
unforeseen vacation
to leave all this behind   35
to forget the winter
in unheated flats
turned off gas and
"ma bell" who serves
the people   40
took the phone away
when we were out
looking for a gig.

talking proletariat talks
of next presidential elections   45
the emperor of chicago
who lives off the fat of the land
and only feeds his sty of pigs.
talking proletariat talks
over rum and schlitz   50
of lottery tickets
on bingo nights at St. Sebastian's.

talking proletariat talks
climbing crime. defenseless
women. unsafe parks and   55
congested highways.
talking proletariat talks
of higher rent two months
behind. landlords who live
on lake shore drive or over   60
where the grass is greener.

talking proletariat talks
talking proletariat talks
talking proletariat talks
until one long   65
awaited day—
we are tired
of talking.

—1984

The Antihero

the antihero
always gets the woman

not in the end
an anticlimax instead
in the end   5
spits on her
stretched out body
a spasmodic carpet
yearning still
washes himself   10

doesn't know why
it is that way searching
not finding finding
not wanting wanting more
or nothing   15
in the end the key is
to leave her yearning lest
she discover that is all

—1984

LUCI TAPAHONSO (1953-   )

Diné (Navajo) poet and short story writer Luci Tapahonso was born in Shiprock, New Mexico, one of eleven children. She was raised on a farm in Dinétah, the largest reservation in the United States, which straddles parts of Arizona, New Mexico, Utah, and Colorado. Although Diné was the primary language spoken in her home, Tapahonso learned English before she started school. She received her early education at the Navajo Methodist Mission Boarding School in Farmington, New Mexico, and went on to earn a B.A. and an M.A. in English from the University of New Mexico; it was there she met Leslie Marmon Silko, who became an important influence on her work. Tapahonso has published several volumes of poetry, including *One More Shiprock Night: Poems* (1981), *Seasonal Woman* (1982), and *A Breeze Swept Through* (1987), as well as *Sáanii Dahataal: The Women Are Singing* (1993) and *Blue Horses Rush In* (1997), collections that mix poetry and stories. Tapahonso's work is particularly noted for its rootedness in the Diné language: because she often writes in Diné and translates her work into English (at times leaving some words in Diné) her poetry and prose in English reflects some of the structures and cadences of the original language. She has won several awards for her work, and was named "Storyteller of the Year" by the Wordcraft Circle of Native American Writers in 1999. Tapahonso is currently Professor of American Indian Studies and English at the University of Arizona.

All the Colors of Sunset

Even after all this time, when I look back at all that happened, I don't know if I would do anything differently. That summer morning seemed like any other. The sun came up over the mountain around seven or so, and when I went to throw the coffee grounds out, I put the pouch of corn pollen in my apron pocket so that I could pray before I came inside.

During the summers, we sleep most nights in the *chaha'oh*, the shadehouse, unless it rains. I remembered early that morning I had heard loud voices yelling and they seemed to come from the north. Whoever it was quieted quickly, and I fell asleep. Right outside the *chaha'oh*, I knew the dogs were alert—their ears erect and eyes glistening. Out here near Rockpoint, where we live, it's so quiet and isolated that we can hear things from a far distance. It's mostly desert and the huge rocks nearby, *tsé ahil ah neeé*, whale rock and the other rocks, seem to bounce noises into the valley. People live far apart and there are no streetlights nearby. The nights are quiet, except for animal and bird noises, and the sky is always so black. In the Navajo way, they say the night sky is made of black jet, and that the folding darkness comes from the north. Sometimes in the evenings, I think of this when the sun is setting, and all the bright colors fall somewhere into the west. Then I let the beauty of the sunset go, and my sadness along with it.

That morning I fixed a second pot of coffee, and peeled potatoes to fry. Just as I finished slicing the potatoes, I thought I heard my grandbaby cry. I went out and looked out toward my daughter's home. She lives across the arroyo a little over a mile away. I shaded my eyes and squinted—the sun was in her direction. Finally, I went inside and finished fixing breakfast. We were going to go into Chinle that afternoon, so I didn't go over to their house.

Later that morning, I was polishing some pieces of jewelry when I heard my daughter crying outside. My heart quickened. I rushed to the door and she practically fell inside the house. She was carrying the baby in her cradleboard and could hardly talk—she was sobbing and screaming so. I grabbed the baby, knowing she was hurt. When I looked at my granddaughter, I knew the terrible thing that had happened. Her little face was so pale and wet from crying. I could not think or speak—somehow I found my way to the south wall of the hooghan and sat down, still holding my sweet baby. My first and only grandchild was gone.

I held her close and nuzzled her soft neck. I sang over and over the little songs that I always sang to her. I unwrapped her and touched slowly, slowly every part of her little smooth body. I wanted to remember every sweet detail and said aloud each name like I had always done, *"Díí nijáád wolyé, sho'wéé."* This is called your leg, my baby. I asked her, *"Nits'iiyah sha'?"* and nuzzled the back of her neck like before. *"Jo ka i."* This time she did not giggle and laugh. I held her and rocked, and sang, and talked to her.

The pollen pouch was still in my pocket, and I put a bit into her mouth as I would have done when her first tooth came in. I put a pinch of pollen on her head as I would have done when she first left for kindergarten. I put a pinch of pollen in her little hands as I would have done when she was given her first lamb, as I would have done when she was given her own colt. This way she would have been gentle and firm with her pets. I brushed her with an eagle feather as I would have done when she graduated from junior high. All this and so much more that could have been swept over me as I sat there leaning over my little grandbaby.

She was almost five months old, and had just started to recognize me. She cried for me to hold her and I tried to keep her with me as much as I could. Sometimes I took her for long walks and showed her everything, and told her little stories about the birds and animals we saw. She would fall asleep on our way home, and still I hummed and sang softly. I couldn't stop singing. For some reason, when she was born, I was given so much time for her. I guess that's how it is with grandparents. I wasn't ever too busy to care for her. When my daughter took her home, my house seemed so empty and quiet.

They said that I kept the baby for four hours that morning. My daughter left and then returned with her husband. They were afraid to bother me in my grief. I don't remember much of it. I didn't know how I acted, or maybe that was the least of what I was conscious of. My daughter said later that I didn't say one word to her. I don't remember.

Finally, I got up and gave the baby to them so they could go to the hospital at Chinle. I followed in my own truck, and there the doctor confirmed her death, and we began talking about what we had to do next. Word spread quickly. When I went to buy some food at Basha's, several people comforted me and helped me with the shopping. My sisters and two aunts were at my home when I returned. They had straightened up the house, and were cooking already. Some of my daughters-in-law were cooking and getting things ready in the *chaha'oh* outside. By that evening, the house and the *chaha'oh* were filled with people—our own relatives, clan relatives, friends from school, church, and the baby's father's kin. People came and held me, comforting me and murmuring their sympathies. They cried with me, and brought me plates of food. I felt like I was in a daze—I hardly spoke. I tried to help cook and serve, but was gently guided back to the armchair that had somehow become "my chair" since that morning.

There were meetings each day, and various people stood up to counsel and advise everyone who was there, including my daughter and her husband. When everything was done, and we had washed our faces and started over again, I couldn't seem to focus on things. Before all this happened, I was very busy each day—cooking, sewing, taking out the horses sometimes, feeding the animals, and often just visiting with people. One of my children or my sisters always came by and we would talk and laugh while I continued my tasks. Last winter was a good year for piñons so I was still cleaning and roasting the many flour sackfuls we had picked. At Many Farms junction, some people from Shiprock had a truckload of the sweetest corn I had ever tasted, so I bought plenty and planned to make *ntsidigodí* and other kinds of cornbread. We would have these tasty delicacies to eat in the winter. We liked to remember summer by the food we had stored and preserved.

When we were little, my mother taught all of us girls to weave, but I hadn't touched a loom in years. When I became a grandmother, I began to think of teaching some of the old things to my baby. Maybe it was my age, but I remembered a lot of the things we were told. Maybe it was that I was alone more than I had ever been—my children were grown. My husband passed on five years ago, and since I was by myself and I had enough on which to live, I stopped working at a paying job.

After all this happened, I resumed my usual tasks and tried to stay busy so that my grandbaby's death wouldn't overwhelm me. I didn't cry or grieve out loud because they say that one can call the dead back by doing that. Yet so much had changed, and it was as if I was far away from everything. Some days I fixed a lunch and took the sheep out for the day and returned as the sun was going down. And when I came back inside, I realized that I hadn't spoken to the animals all day. It seemed strange, and yet I just didn't feel like talking. The dogs would follow me around, wanting attention—for me to throw a stick for them, or talk to them—then after a while they would just lie down and watch me. Once I cleaned and roasted a pan of piñons perfectly without thinking about it. It's a wonder that I didn't burn myself. A few weeks later, we had to brand some colts, and give the horses shots, so everyone got together and we spent the day at the corral in the dust and heat. Usually it was a happy and noisy time, but that day was quieter than usual. At least we had taken care of everything.

Sometimes I dreamt of my grandbaby, and it was as if nothing had happened. In my dreams, I carried her around, singing and talking to her. She smiled and giggled at me. When I awoke, it was as if she had been lying beside me, kicking and reaching around. A small space beside me would be warm, and her scent faint. These dreams seemed so real. I looked forward to sleeping because maybe in sleeping I might see her. On the days following such a dream, I would replay it over and over in my mind, still smiling and humming to her the next morning. By afternoon, the activity and noise had usually worn the dream off.

I heard after the funeral that people were whispering and asking questions about what had happened. It didn't bother me. Nothing anyone said or did would bring my sweet baby back—that was clear. I never asked my daughter how it happened. After the baby's death, she and her husband became very quiet and they were together so much, they seemed like shadows of each other. Her husband worked at different jobs, and she just went with him and waited in the pickup until he was through. He worked with horses, helped build hooghans,[1] corrals, and other construction work. When she came over and spent the afternoon with me, we hardly talked. We both knew we were more comfortable that way. As usual, she hugged me each time before she left. I knew she was in great pain.

Once, when I was at Basha's shopping for groceries, a woman I didn't know said to me, "You have a pretty grandbaby." I smiled and didn't reply. I noticed that she didn't say *"yée"* at the end of *"nitsóíh"* which would have meant "the grandbaby who is no longer alive." That happened at other places, and I didn't respond, except to smile. I thought it was good that people remembered her.

About four months after her death, we were eating at my house when my sisters gathered around me and told me they were very worried about me. They thought I was still too grief-stricken over the baby, and that it was not healthy. "You have to go on," they said, "let her go." They said they wanted the "old me" back, so I agreed to go for help.

We went to a medicine woman near Ganado, and she asked me if I could see the baby sometimes. No, I said, except in dreams.

"Has anyone said they've seen her?" she asked. I said that I didn't think so. Then she said, "Right now, I see the baby beside you." I was so startled that I began looking around for her.

"The baby hasn't left," she said, "she wants to stay with you." I couldn't see my grandbaby. Then I realized that other people could see what the medicine woman had just seen. No wonder, I thought, that sometimes when I woke, I could feel her warm body beside me. She said the baby was wrapped in white.

She couldn't help me herself, but she told me to see another medicine person near Lukaichakai. She said that the ceremony I needed was very old and that she didn't know it herself. The man she recommended was elderly and very knowledgeable and so it was likely that he would know the ceremony, or would at least know of

---

[1] (Diné) Homes.

someone who did.

Early in the morning, we went to his house west of Many Farms—word had already been sent that we were coming. The ceremony lasted for four days and three nights, and parts of songs and prayers had such ancient sacred words I wasn't sure if I understood them. When the old man prayed and sang, sometimes tears streamed down my face as I repeated everything after him—word for word, line for line, late into the night—and we would begin again at daybreak the next morning. I was exhausted and so relieved. I finally realized what my grief had done. I could finally let my grandbaby go.

We were lucky that we had found this old man because the ceremony had not been done in almost eighty years. He had seen it as a little boy and had memorized all the parts of it—the songs, the advice, the prayers, and the literal letting go of the dead spirit. Over time, it has become a rare ceremony, because what I had done in holding and keeping the baby for those hours was not in keeping with the Navajo way. I understood that doing so had upset the balance of life and death. When we left, we were all crying. I thanked the old man for his memory, his life, and his ability to help us when no one else could. I understand now that all of life has ceremonies connected with it, and for us, without our memory, our old people, and our children, we would be like lost people in this world we live in, as well as in the other worlds in which our loved ones are waiting.

—1994

ELMAZ ABINADER (1954-   )

Elmaz Abinader was born to a Lebanese family in rural Pennsylvania in 1954. As a poet, playwright, and performance artist, Abinader explores hypervisibility, displacement, and diaspora in Arab and Arab-American identity. The disparity between the traditions of her Lebanese upbringing and the culture of the rural Pennsylvanian community outside her household became a primary source for Abinader's first text, the autobiographical *Children of Roomje: A Family's Journey from Lebanon* (1991). In 2000 Abinader won the Jospehine Miles/PEN Oakland Award for her poetry collection *In the Country of My Dreams* (1997); that same year she was awarded a Goldies Award for literature by the *San Francisco Bay Guardian*. Abinader and her storytelling troupe, the Country of Origin Band, have performed her play *Country of Origin* (1997) in both the U.S. and the Middle East. Abinader also co-founded the Voices of Our Nations Arts Foundation, which invites authors and performers to teach and collaborate with promising young writers of color. She teaches in the English Department at Mills College in Oakland, California.

Dried Flowers

There are no poor like the poor of Spain.
The old man spits his food and tells me
of the war. His tears have yellowed
over four decades. His battles are waged
eating watermelon in a cafeteria   5

frequented by communists. But they
don't speak of that. I want to clap
my hands over my ears; I want to tell him:
I will not feel guilty this time.
It is not my fault.   10

I watch you as he talks. You agree
about money, art, and education. We listen
differently. You laugh and hold his shoulder
like a comrade. I cringe, faced with a truth
about my ancestors I will carry   15
for life. His memory slices into mine.
I shudder under the quake
of dispossession. Age has come to my face.
Years that say something to me.

Every where we travel, women   20
are singing to Christ. At Tibidabo,
I lean over the tower to watch
the wide city below. The white buildings
aren't moving in the dark.

What do I do about you now? (I have   25
given you a flower.) I walk deep
into the waters of Valencia and think
of you pausing on a hillside in Andorra.
And we move on and on separately.

—1999

Preparing for Occupation

> *This is my place. My territory, Landing*
> *strip of my anxieties. Heaven*
> *upside down. It's my place, and I won't change it*
> *for any other. I fell, and I'm not sorry,*

From *Juicio Final,* by Blas de Otero[1]
translated by Hardie St. Martin

Buy only short books, ones that read quickly with plots
you can keep track of when the pounding starts on the door.
Drive no nails into the wall, no pictures, no pencil sharpener
or mirror. Your face doesn't matter any way. You are no one.

Teach your children at home. Or leave them idle to wander   5
the streets to find a funeral parade; a crowd to join.
Use only votive candles so they can burn out before morning.
Stash your cigarettes in your pocket. Leave nothing
in the cupboards to remind them but a child's toy.

---

[1] Blas de Otero (1916-1979), Spanish poet critical of the Franco regime.

Adopt no pets. Hook up no phones. Print no cards, address   10
labels or stationery. Test your batteries daily.
All your clothes must be light, in similar colors and never need
ironing. Your only family heirlooms are habit, memory, name and
song. Believe that placing your daughter upon your shoulders
will be home enough for her as she feels   15
for something familiar.

Avoid meeting the neighbors unless you've known them
since birth. Be careful of the bird flirting with you in the yard;
one of you may soon fly away.
One of you has migratory patterns.   20

You've been here thousands of years. But aren't your people
nomadic anyway? Can't you pitch your tent in a grove
on the outskirts? Move in with relatives? Cross into another
country, clogging the border with shanty towns, waiting
to return? I've seen you together; you prefer to be together.   25

Because this house bears the prints of your children
upon the wall, because the kitchen is furrowed
from your journeys made to the table from the stove,
the stove to the table, because the floor is pocked
from the weight of your davenport, doesn't mean   30
you can't move on.
The walls have echoed your voices, your sighs floated
up to the ceiling and gathered like clouds in a refugee sky.
Remember the time your son opened the door so quickly
the bulghur flew off the table and around the room?   35
Grains are in the corners still.

You will miss nothing: the window that refuses to open,
the sputtering light of the refrigerator, the leaking pipe
in the girls' room; the cat that crosses the fence in the morning.
He is not your family although you recognize him.   40
This is not your town, although you walked its streets
on your wedding day. Local water mixes with your blood.
This is not your country despite its dust covering
your shoes, the songs you have memorized; the poets
you claim as your own. Don't look down.   45
Look up. When the geese are passing in their vee formation,
join them, tuck your treasures under your wings.
From the refugee sky, you can count the bodies below you,
examine the shipwreck of your home while others pick
through the remains.

—1999

The Volcano
for Geralyn

They tell me you are inside the volcano, camera mounted
on your slight shoulders. Outside, the students in Jakarta
fling their bodies against the gates and get through. And I wonder
why this moment? In any revolution, why now? Not before?
Or later? You cannot distinguish their cries from the rumblings   5
of your big mountain.

I remember you and me and volcanos from many years ago:
your head is on my lap. Your arm is cold flung carelessly
across the side of your head as the road twists us
putting the volcano to my left, then to my right.   10
We are winding our way to a small Guatemalan town
planted in the mountain like tobacco leaves. The highway
shakes the car and throws dust through the open window.
You do not feel the *terremoto*[2] in your sleep—always child
and never child on my right and left, changing so fast,   15
I don't know what to call you. Like the mountain
which has given up its smoke forever, Like myself
who is always standing around the fire; even the quiet ones
waiting for a flame to rise up and begin the rage again.

And there you are now, in Indonesia, gathering the brimstone   20
in your eyes, filling your lungs with smoke. I know how
it has been the same, always the same through years
of eruptions and silences. And how you have twisted
away from me, an insurrection of your own. Going back
and forth, from the child I held to the volcano's fire.   25
I do not wonder why now, or not before, or even later.
The war is ongoing: against dormancy, against sleep,
against silence. You will hold the images
of the volcano: in your film, your history and the blaze
inside you.

—1999

2 (Sp.) Earthquake.

LORNA DEE CERVANTES (1954-   )

Lorna Dee Cervantes was raised in San Jose, California; her autobiographical writings document her experiences as a Chicana living in California with her parents and her brother. Cervantes' poetry weaves her Chicana, feminist, and political ideals together, addressing such topics as genocide, political injustice, romantic love, and the torment of static categories of class and gender. In 1976, she founded the influential literary Chicano small press Mango, and a journal by the same name. Mango was the first press to publish many Chicana/o writers, such as Jimmy Santiago Baca, Sandra Cisneros, and Ray Gonzalez. Cervantes' first published collection of poetry, *Emlumada* (1981), received the American Book Award. In 1982, her mother suffered a brutal death; the mourning that she went through influenced her second published collection, *From the Cables of Genocide: Poems on Love and Hunger* (1991), which earned both the Paterson Prize for Poetry and the Latino Literature Award. Her most recent publication, *Drive: The First Quartet* (2006), is composed of five sections that chronicle her youth and her adult life as an activist. Cervantes, the editor of the poetry journal *Red Dirt,* lives in San Francisco.

Para un Revolucionario[1]

You speak of art
and your soul is like snow,
a soft powder raining from your
mouth,
covering my breasts and hair.   5
You speak of your love of mountains,
freedom,
and your love for a sun
whose warmth is like una liberación[2]
pouring down upon brown bodies.   10
Your books are of the souls of men,
carnales[3] with a spirit
that no army, pig or ciudad[4]
could ever conquer.
you speak of a new way,   15
a new life.

When you speak like this
I could listen forever.

Pero your voice is lost to me, carnal,
in the wail of tus hijos,[5]   20
in the clatter of dishes
and the pucker of beans upon the stove.
Your conversations come to me
de la sala[6] where you sit,
spreading your dream to brothers,   25
where you spread that dream like damp clover
for them to trod upon,
when I stand here reaching
para ti con manos bronces[7] that spring from mi espíritu[8]
(for I too am Raza).[9]   30

Pero, it seems I can only touch you
with my body.

---

[1] (Sp.) For a revolutionary.
[2] (Sp.) A liberation.
[3] (Sp.) Carnal.
[4] (Sp.) City.
[5] (Sp.) Your children.

[6] (Sp.) From the living room.
[7] (Sp.) For you with bronze hands.
[8] (Sp.) My spirit.
[9] (Sp.) Of the race.

You lie with me
and my body es la hamaca[10]
that spans the void between us.   35

Hermano Raza,[11]
I am afraid that you will lie with me
and awaken too late
to find that you have fallen
and my hands will be left groping   40
for you and your dream
in the midst of la revolución.[12]

—1975

Declaration on a Day of Little Inspiration

I pound these streets for poems.
Los viejitos, los vatos, los perros[13]
y los perdidos,[14]
the giant piss-stream of freeway
which covers my barrio,[15]   5
sops my Atlantis;

none of these will own up
and give me the taste
of ripe literature.

I write the same poem everytime   10
about beans and tortillas sin salsa,[16]
about "¿Quién soy yo?"[17]
Flushing this anger is easy

pero el otro[18]
is harder to unfold.   15

It stays shut like a wet piece of paper.
It's a word I don't remember;
an automatic genuflection
that I can't explain.

And it haunts me like an old corrido,[19]   20
this love that has no words,
this love for my Raza[20]
which is a poem.

—1976

---

[10] (Sp.) The hammock.
[11] (Sp.) Brother of the race/brother race.
[12] (Sp.) The revolution.
[13] (Sp.) The old ones; the homeboys; the dogs.
[14] (Sp.) The lost ones.
[15] (Sp.) Neighborhood.

[16] (Sp.) Without hot sauce.
[17] (Sp.) Who am I?
[18] (Sp.) But the other one.
[19] Traditional Mexican ballad, from the border region of northern Mexico and the southwestern United States.
[20] (Sp.) Race.

Crow

She started and shot from the pine,
then brilliantly settled in the west field
and sunned herself purple.

I saw myself: twig and rasp, dry
in breath and ammonia smelling.   5
Women taught me to clean

and then build my own house.
Before men came they whispered,
Know good polished oak.

Learn hammer and Phillips.   10
Learn socket and rivet. I ran
over rocks and gravel they placed

by hand, leaving burly arguments
to fester the bedrooms. With my best jeans,
a twenty and a shepherd pup, I ran   15

flushed and shadowed by no one
alone   I settled   stiff in mouth
with the words women gave me.

—1981

SANDRA CISNEROS (1954-   )

A prominent novelist, short story writer, essayist, and poet, Sandra Cisneros was one of the first Latinas in the U.S. to achieve widespread commercial success as a writer. Cisneros was raised in Chicago, Illinois, in a family of seven children. She received her B.A. from Loyola University in 1976 and her M.F.A. from the University of Iowa Writers' Workshop in 1978. At that time, few of Cisneros' experiences as a Latina were being reflected in mainstream literary culture, and her own writing began to focus on themes such as cultural loyalty, alienation, and poverty. Cisneros' first novel, the critically acclaimed *The House on Mango Street* (1983), is about the hopes, desires, and disillusionments of a young Latina writer, Esperanza, who struggles to make sense of the roles created for women in Latino culture. Cisneros went on to write the short story collection *Woman Hollering Creek and Other Stories* (1991); the poetry collections *My Wicked, Wicked Ways* (1987) and *Loose Woman* (1994); and the novel *Caramelo* (2002). Her books have been translated into over a dozen languages and she has received numerous awards, including a MacArthur Foundation Fellowship (1995). In addition to writing, Cisneros has worked as a teacher and counselor to high school dropouts, a creative writing teacher, an arts administrator, and a visiting writer at a number of universities. She currently lives in San Antonio, Texas.

Never Marry a Mexican

Never marry a Mexican, my ma said once and always. She said this because of my father. She said this though she was Mexican too. But she was born here in the U.S., and he was born there, and it's *not* the same, you know.

I'll *never* marry. Not any man. I've known men too intimately. I've witnessed their infidelities, and I've helped them to it. Unzipped and unhooked and agreed to clandestine maneuvers. I've been accomplice, committed premeditated crimes. I'm guilty of having caused deliberate pain to other women. I'm vindictive and cruel, and I'm capable of anything.

I admit, there was a time when all I wanted was to belong to a man. To wear that gold band on my left hand and be worn on his arm like an expensive jewel brilliant in the light of day. Not the sneaking around I did in different bars that all looked the same, red carpets with a black grillwork design, flocked wallpaper, wooden wagon-wheel light fixtures with hurricane lampshades a sick amber color like the drinking glasses you get for free at gas stations.

Dark bars, dark restaurants then. And if not—my apartment, with his toothbrush firmly planted in the toothbrush holder like a flag on the North Pole. The bed so big because he never stayed the whole night. Of course not.

Borrowed. That's how I've had my men. Just the cream skimmed off the top. Just the sweetest part of the fruit, without the bitter skin that daily living with a spouse can rend. They've come to me when they wanted the sweet meat then.

So, no. I've never married and never will. Not because I couldn't, but because I'm too romantic for marriage. Marriage has failed me, you could say. Not a man exists who hasn't disappointed me, whom I could trust to love the way I've loved. It's because I believe too much in marriage that I don't. Better to not marry than live a lie.

Mexican men, forget it. For a long time the men clearing off the tables or chopping meat behind the butcher counter or driving the bus I rode to school every day, those weren't men. Not men I considered as potential lovers. Mexican, Puerto Rican, Cuban, Chilean, Colombian, Panamanian, Salvadorean, Bolivian, Honduran, Argentine, Dominican, Venezuelan, Guatemalan, Ecuadorean, Nicaraguan, Peruvian, Costa Rican, Paraguayan, Uruguayan, I don't care. I never saw them. My mother did this to me.

I guess she did it to spare me and Ximena the pain she went through. Having married a Mexican man at seventeen. Having had to put up with all the grief a Mexican family can put on a girl because she was from *el otro lado,* the other side, and my father had married down by marrying her. If he had married a white woman from *el otro lado,* that would've been different. That would've been marrying up, even if the white girl was poor. But what could be more ridiculous than a Mexican girl who couldn't even speak Spanish, who didn't know enough to set a separate plate for each course at dinner, nor how to fold cloth napkins, nor how to set the silverware.

In my ma's house the plates were always stacked in the center of the table, the knives and forks and spoons standing in a jar, help yourself. All the dishes chipped or cracked and nothing matched. And no tablecloth, ever. And newspapers set on the table whenever my grandpa sliced watermelons, and how embarrassed she would be when her boyfriend, my father, would come over and there were newspapers all over the kitchen floor and table. And my grandpa, big hardworking Mexican man, saying Come, come and eat, and slicing a big wedge of those dark green watermelons, a big slice, he wasn't stingy with food. Never, even during the Depression. Come, come and eat, to whoever came knocking on the back door. Hobos sitting at the dinner table and the children staring and staring. Because my grandfather always made sure they never went without. Flour and rice, by the barrel and by the sack. Potatoes. Big bags of pinto beans. And watermelons, bought three or four at a time, rolled under his bed and brought out when you least expected. My grandpa had survived three wars, one Mexican, two American, and he knew what living without meant. He knew.

My father, on the other hand, did not. True, when he first came to this country he had worked shelling clams, washing dishes, planting hedges, sat on the back of the bus in Little Rock and had the bus driver shout, You—sit up here, and my father had shrugged sheepishly and said, No speak English.

But he was no economic refugee, no immigrant fleeing a war. My father ran away from home because he was afraid of facing his father after his first-year grades at the university proved he'd spent more time fooling around than studying. He left behind a house in Mexico City that was neither poor nor rich, but thought itself better than both. A boy who would get off a bus when he saw a girl he knew board if he didn't have the money to pay her fare. That was the world my father left behind.

I imagine my father in his *fanfarrón* clothes, because that's what he was, a *fanfarrón*. That's what my mother thought the moment she turned around to the voice that was asking her to dance. A big show-off, she'd say years later. Nothing but a big show-off. But she never said why she married him. My father in his shark-blue suits with the starched handkerchief in the breast pocket, his felt fedora, his tweed topcoat with the big shoulders, and heavy British wing tips with the pin-hole design on the heel and toe. Clothes that cost a lot. Expensive. That's what my father's things said. *Calidad.* Quality.

My father must've found the U.S. Mexicans very strange, so foreign from what he knew at home in Mexico City where the servant served watermelon on a plate with silverware and a cloth napkin, or mangos with their own special prongs. Not like this, eating with your legs wide open in the yard, or in the kitchen hunkered over newspapers. *Come, come and eat.* No, never like this.

+ + +

How I make my living depends. Sometimes I work as a translator. Sometimes I get paid by the word and sometimes by the hour, depending on the job. I do this in the day, and at night I paint. I'd do anything in the day just so I can keep on painting.

I work as a substitute teacher, too, for the San Antonio Independent School District. And that's worse than translating those travel brochures with their tiny print, believe me. I can't stand kids. Not any age. But it pays the rent.

Any way you look at it, what I do to make a living is a form of prostitution. People say, "A painter? How nice," and want to invite me to their parties, have me decorate the lawn like an exotic orchid for hire. But do they buy art?

I'm amphibious. I'm a person who doesn't belong to any class. The rich like to have me around because they envy my creativity; they know they can't buy *that*. The poor don't mind if I live in their neighborhood because they know I'm poor like they are, even if my education and the way I dress keeps us worlds apart. I don't belong to any class. Not to the poor, whose neighborhood I share. Not to the rich, who come to my exhibitions and buy my work. Not to the middle class from which my sister Ximena and I fled.

When I was young, when I first left home and rented that apartment with my sister and her kids right after her husband left, I thought it would be glamorous to be an artist. I wanted to be like Frida or Tina.[1] I was ready to suffer with my camera and my paint brushes in that awful apartment we rented for $150 each because it had high ceilings and those wonderful glass skylights that convinced us we had to have it. Never mind there was no sink in the bathroom, and a tub that looked like a sarcophagus, and floorboards that didn't meet, and a hallway to scare away the dead. But fourteen-foot ceilings was enough for us to write a check for the deposit right then and there. We thought it all romantic. You know the place, the one on Zarzamora on top of the barber shop with the Casasola prints of the Mexican Revolution. Neon BIRRIA TEPATITLÁN sign round the corner, two goats knocking their heads together, and all those Mexican bakeries, Las Brisas for *huevos rancheros* and *carnitas* and *barbacoa* on Sundays, and fresh fruit milk shakes, and mango *paletas,* and more signs in Spanish than in English. We thought it was great, great. The barrio looked cute in the daytime, like Sesame Street. Kids hopscotching on the sidewalk, blessed little boogers. And hardware stores that still sold ostrich-feather dusters, and whole families marching out of Our Lady of Guadalupe Church on Sundays, girls in their swirly-whirly dresses and patent-leather shoes, boys in their dress Stacys and shiny shirts.

But nights, that was nothing like what we knew up on the north side. Pistols going off like the wild, wild West, and me and Ximena and the kids huddled in one bed with the lights off listening to it all, saying, Go to sleep, babies, it's just firecrackers. But we knew better. Ximena would say, Clemencia, maybe we should go home. And I'd say, Shit! Because she knew as well as I did there was no home to go home to. Not with our mother. Not with that man she married. After Daddy died, it was like we didn't matter. Like Ma was so busy feeling sorry for herself, I don't know. I'm not like Ximena. I still haven't worked it out after all this time, even though our mother's dead now. My half brothers living in that house that should've been ours, me and Ximena's. But that's—how do you say it?—water under the damn? I can't ever get the sayings right even though I was born in this country. We didn't say shit like that in our house.

Once Daddy was gone, it was like my ma didn't exist, like if she died, too. I used to have a little finch, twisted one of its tiny red legs between the bars of the cage once, who knows how. The leg just dried up and fell off. My bird lived a long time without it, just a little red stump of a leg. He was fine, really. My mother's memory is like that, like if something already dead dried up and fell off, and I stopped missing where she used to be. Like if I never had a mother. And I'm not ashamed to say it either. When she married that white man, and he and his boys moved into my father's house, it was as if she stopped being my mother. Like I never even had one.

Ma always sick and too busy worrying about her own life, she would've sold us to the Devil if she could. "Because I married so young, *mi'ja,*" she'd say. "Because your father, he was so much older than me, and I never had a chance to be young.

---

[1] Probably Mexican painter Frida Kahlo (1907-1954) and Italian photographer Tina Modotti (1896-1942).

Honey, try to understand…" Then I'd stop listening.

That man she met at work, Owen Lambert, the foreman at the photo-finishing plant, who she was seeing even while my father was sick. Even then. That's what I can't forgive.

When my father was coughing up blood and phlegm in the hospital, half his face frozen, and his tongue so fat he couldn't talk, he looked so small with all those tubes and plastic sacks dangling around him. But what I remember most is the smell, like death was already sitting on his chest. And I remember the doctor scraping the phlegm out of my father's mouth with a white washcloth, and my daddy gagging and I wanted to yell, Stop, you stop that, he's my daddy. Goddamn you. Make him live. Daddy, don't. Not yet, not yet, not yet. And how I couldn't hold myself up, I couldn't hold myself up. Like if they'd beaten me, or pulled my insides out through my nostrils, like if they'd stuffed me with cinnamon and cloves, and I just stood there dry-eyed next to Ximena and my mother, Ximena between us because I wouldn't let her stand next to me. Everyone repeating over and over the Ave Marías and Padre Nuestros.[2] The priest sprinkling holy water, *mundo sin fin, amén.*[3]

+ + +

Drew, remember when you used to call me your Malinalli?[4] It was a joke, a private game between us, because you looked like a Cortez with that beard of yours. My skin dark against yours. Beautiful, you said. You said I was beautiful, and when you said it, Drew, I was.

My Malinalli, Malinche, my courtesan, you said, and yanked my head back by the braid. Calling me that name in between little gulps of breath and the raw kisses you gave, laughing from that black beard of yours.

Before daybreak, you'd be gone, same as always, before I even knew it. And it was as if I'd imagined you, only the teeth marks on my belly and nipples proving me wrong.

Your skin pale, but your hair blacker than a pirate's. Malinalli, you called me, remember? *Mi doradita.*[5] I liked when you spoke to me in my language. I could love myself and think myself worth loving.

Your son. Does he know how much I had to do with his birth? I was the one who convinced you to let him be born. Did you tell him, while his mother lay on her back laboring his birth, I lay in his mother's bed making love to you.

You're nothing without me. I created you from spit and red dust. And I can snuff you between my finger and thumb if I want to. Blow you to kingdom come. You're just a smudge of paint I chose to birth on canvas. And when I made you over, you were no longer a part of her, you were all mine. The landscape of your body taut as a drum. The heart beneath that hide thrumming and thrumming. Not an inch did I give back.

I paint and repaint you the way I see fit, even now. After all these years. Did you know that? Little fool. You think I went hobbling along with my life, whimpering and whining like some twangy country-and-western when you went back to her. But I've

---

[2] (Sp.) Hail Marys and Our Fathers.

[3] (Sp.) World without end, amen.

[4] Malinalli (also referred to as Malinche or Malintzín Tenepal), was the indigenous translator for Hernán

Cortés Pizarro (1485-1547) during his 16th century conquest of Mexico.

[5] (Sp.) My little bronze one.

been waiting. Making the world look at you from my eyes. And if that's not power, what is?

Nights I light all the candles in the house, the ones to La Virgen de Guadalupe, the ones to El Niño Fidencio, Don Pedrito Jaramillo, Santo Niño de Atocha, Nuestra Señora de San Juan de los Lagos, and especially, Santa Lucía, with her beautiful eyes on a plate.[6]

Your eyes are beautiful, you said. You said they were the darkest eyes you'd ever seen and kissed each one as if they were capable of miracles. And after you left, I wanted to scoop them out with a spoon, place them on a plate under these blue blue skies, food for the blackbirds.

The boy, your son. The one with the face of that redheaded woman who is your wife. The boy red-freckled like fish food floating on the skin of water. That boy.

I've been waiting patient as a spider all these years, since I was nineteen and he was just an idea hovering in his mother's head, and I'm the one that gave him permission and made it happen, see.

Because your father wanted to leave your mother and live with me. Your mother whining for a child, at least *that*. And he kept saying, Later, we'll see, later. But all along it was me he wanted to be with, it was me, he said.

I want to tell you this evenings when you come to see me. When you're full of talk about what kind of clothes you're going to buy, and what you used to be like when you started high school and what you're like now that you're almost finished. And how everyone knows you as a rocker, and your band, and your new red guitar that you just got because your mother gave you a choice, a guitar or a car, but you don't need a car, do you, because I drive you everywhere. You could be my son if you weren't so light-skinned.

This happened. A long time ago. Before you were born. When you were a moth inside your mother's heart, I was your father's student, yes, just like you're mine now. And your father painted and painted me, because he said, I was his *doradita,* all golden and sun-baked, and that's the kind of woman he likes best, the ones brown as river sand, yes. And he took me under his wing and in his bed, this man, this teacher, your father. I was honored that he'd done me the favor. I was that young.

All I know is I was sleeping with your father the night you were born. In the same bed where you were conceived. I was sleeping with your father and didn't give a damn about that woman, your mother. If she was a brown woman like me, I might've had a harder time living with myself, but since she's not, I don't care. I was there first, always. I've always been there, in the mirror, under his skin, in the blood, before you were born. And he's been here in my heart before I even knew him. Understand? He's always been here. Always. Dissolving like a hibiscus flower, exploding like a rope into dust. I don't care what's right anymore. I don't care about his wife. She's not *my* sister.

---

[6] The Virgin of Guadalupe, often called *La Virgen Morena* (The Dark Virgin), a highly revered figure among Mexican Catholics, appeared before an indigenous peasant in Mexico in 1523; El Niño Fidencio (1898-1938), a Mexican *curandero*, or faith healer, considered by many to be a saint; Don Pedrito Jaramillo (1829-1907), a *curandero* originally from Mexico, but mostly associated with South Texas; Santo Niño de Atocha, a Roman Catholic image of the infant Jesus, popular in Spain, Mexico, and the U.S. Southwest, associated with helping prisoners and the sick; Nuestra Señora de San Juan de los Lagos, a statue of the Virgin Mary in Jalisco, Mexico, associated with healing the sick; Santa Lucía, 4th century Christian martyr and patron saint of the blind, who either plucked out her own eyes to deflect the attention of a suitor or had them plucked out for refusing to make offerings to Roman gods.

And it's not the last time I've slept with a man the night his wife is birthing a baby. Why do I do that, I wonder? Sleep with a man when his wife is giving life, being suckled by a thing with its eyes still shut. Why do that? It's always given me a bit of crazy joy to be able to kill those women like that, without their knowing it. To know I've had their husbands when they were anchored in blue hospital rooms, their guts yanked inside out, the baby sucking their breasts while their husband sucked mine. All this while their ass stitches were still hurting.

+ + +

Once, drunk on margaritas, I telephoned your father at four in the morning, woke the bitch up. Hello, she chirped. I want to talk to Drew. Just a moment, she said in her most polite drawing-room English. Just a moment. I laughed about that for weeks. What a stupid ass to pass the phone over to the lug asleep beside her. Excuse me, honey, it's for you. When Drew mumbled hello I was laughing so hard I could hardly talk. Drew? That dumb bitch of a wife of yours, I said, and that's all I could manage. That stupid stupid stupid. No Mexican woman would react like that. Excuse me, honey. It cracked me up.

+ + +

He's got the same kind of skin, the boy. All the blue veins pale and clear just like his mama. Skin like roses in December. Pretty boy. Little clone. Little cells split into you and you and you. Tell me, baby, which part of you is your mother. I try to imagine her lips, her jaw, her long long legs that wrapped themselves around this father who took me to his bed.

+ + +

This happened. I'm asleep. Or pretend to be. You're watching me, Drew. I feel your weight when you sit on the corner of the bed, dressed and ready to go, but now you're just watching me sleep. Nothing. Not a word. Not a kiss. Just sitting. You're taking me in, under inspection. What do you think already?

I haven't stopped dreaming you. Did you know that? Do you think it's strange? I never tell, though. I keep it to myself like I do all the thoughts I think of you.

After all these years.

I don't want you looking at me. I don't want you taking me in while I'm asleep. I'll open my eyes and frighten you away.

There. What did I tell you? *Drew? What is it?* Nothing. I'd knew you'd say that.

Let's not talk. We're no good at it. With you I'm useless with words. As if somehow I had to learn to speak all over again, as if the words I needed haven't been invented yet. We're cowards. Come back to bed. At least there I feel I have you for a little. For a moment. For a catch of the breath. You let go. You ache and tug. You rip my skin.

You're almost not a man without your clothes. How do I explain it? You're so much a child in my bed. Nothing but a big boy who needs to be held. I won't let anyone hurt you. My pirate. My slender boy of a man.

After all these years.

I didn't imagine it, did I? A Ganges,[7] an eye of the storm. For a little. When we forgot ourselves, you tugged me, I leapt inside you and split you like an apple.

---

[7] A river running through India and Bangladesh.

Opened for the other to look and not give back. Something wrenched itself loose. Your body doesn't lie. It's not silent like you.

You're nude as a pearl. You've lost your train of smoke. You're tender as rain. If I'd put you in my mouth you'd dissolve like snow.

You were ashamed to be so naked. Pulled back. But I saw you for what you are, when you opened yourself for me. When you were careless and let yourself through. I caught that catch of the breath. I'm not crazy.

When you slept, you tugged me toward you. You sought me in the dark. I didn't sleep. Every cell, every follicle, every nerve, alert. Watching you sigh and roll and turn and hug me closer to you. I didn't sleep. I was taking *you* in that time.

✦ ✦ ✦

Your mother? Only once. Years after your father and I stopped seeing each other. At an art exhibition. A show on the photographs of Eugène Atget.[8] Those images, I could look at them for hours. I'd taken a group of students with me.

It was your father I saw first. And in that instant I felt as if everyone in the room, all the sepia-toned photographs, my students, the men in business suits, the high-heeled women, the security guards, everyone, could see me for what I was. I had to scurry out, lead my kids to another gallery, but some things destiny has cut out for you.

He caught up with us in the coat-check area, arm in arm with a redheaded Barbie doll in a fur coat. One of those scary Dallas types, hair yanked into a ponytail, big shiny face like the women behind the cosmetic counters at Neiman's. That's what I remember. She must've been with him all along, only I swear I never saw her until that second.

You could tell from a slight hesitancy, only slight because he's too suave to hesitate, that he was nervous. Then he's walking toward me, and I didn't know what to do, just stood there dazed like those animals crossing the road at night when the headlights stun them.

And I don't know why, but all of a sudden I looked at my shoes and felt ashamed at how old they looked. And he comes up to me, my love, your father, in that way of his with that grin that makes me want to beat him, makes me want to make love to him, and he says in the most sincere voice you ever heard, "Ah, Clemencia! *This* is Megan." No introduction could've been meaner. *This* is Megan. Just like that.

I grinned like an idiot and held out my paw—"Hello, Megan"—and smiled too much the way you do when you can't stand someone. Then I got the hell out of there, chattering like a monkey all the ride back with my kids. When I got home I had to lie down with a cold washcloth on my forehead and the TV on. All I could hear throbbing under the washcloth in that deep part behind my eyes: *This* is Megan.

And that's how I fell asleep, with the TV on and every light in the house burning. When I woke up it was something like three in the morning. I shut the lights and TV and went to get some aspirin, and the cats, who'd been asleep with me on the couch, got up too and followed me into the bathroom as if they knew what's what. And then they followed me into bed, where they aren't allowed, but this time I just let them, fleas and all.

---

[8] Eugène Atget (1857-1927), French photographer noted for his images of Paris.

+ + +

This happened, too. I swear I'm not making this up. It's all true. It was the last time I was going to be with your father. We had agreed. All for the best. Surely I could see that, couldn't I? My own good. A good sport. A young girl like me. Hadn't I understood…responsibilities. Besides, he could *never* marry *me*. You didn't think…? *Never marry a Mexican. Never marry a Mexican*…No, of course not. I see. I see.

We had the house to ourselves for a few days, who knows how. You and your mother had gone somewhere. Was it Christmas? I don't remember.

I remember the leaded-glass lamp with the milk glass above the dining-room table. I made a mental inventory of everything. The Egyptian lotus design on the hinges of the doors. The narrow, dark hall where your father and I had made love once. The four-clawed tub where he had washed my hair and rinsed it with a tin bowl. This window. That counter. The bedroom with its light in the morning, incredibly soft, like the light from a polished dime.

The house was immaculate, as always, not a stray hair anywhere, not a flake of dandruff or a crumpled towel. Even the roses on the dining-room table held their breath. A kind of airless cleanliness that always made me want to sneeze.

Why was I so curious about this woman he lived with? Every time I went to the bathroom, I found myself opening the medicine cabinet, looking at all the things that were hers. Her Estée Lauder lipsticks. Corals and pinks, of course. Her nail polishes—mauve was as brave as she could wear. Her cotton balls and blond hairpins. A pair of bone-colored sheepskin slippers, as clean as the day she'd bought them. On the door hook—a white robe with a MADE IN ITALY label, and a silky nightshirt with pearl buttons. I touched the fabrics. *Calidad.* Quality.

I don't know how to explain what I did next. While your father was busy in the kitchen, I went over to where I'd left my backpack, and took out a bag of gummy bears I'd bought. And while he was banging pots, I went around the house and left a trail of them in places I was sure she would find them. One in her lucite makeup organizer. One stuffed inside each bottle of nail polish. I untwisted the expensive lipsticks to their full length and smushed a bear on the top before recapping them. I even put a gummy bear in her diaphragm case in the very center of that luminescent rubber moon.

Why bother? Drew could take the blame. Or he could say it was the cleaning woman's Mexican voodoo. I knew that, too. It didn't matter. I got a strange satisfaction wandering about the house leaving them in places only she would look.

And just as Drew was shouting, "Dinner!" I saw it on the desk. One of those wooden babushka dolls Drew had brought her from his trip to Russia. I know. He'd bought one just like it for me.

I just did what I did, uncapped the doll inside a doll inside a doll, until I got to the very center, the tiniest baby inside all the others, and this I replaced with a gummy bear. And then I put the dolls back, just like I'd found them, one inside the other, inside the other. Except for the baby, which I put inside my pocket. All through dinner I kept reaching in the pocket of my jean jacket. When I touched it, it made me feel good.

On the way home, on the bridge over the *arroyo* on Guadalupe Street, I stopped the car, switched on the emergency blinkers, got out, and dropped the wooden toy into that muddy creek where winos piss and rats swim. The Barbie doll's toy stewing there in that muck. It gave me a feeling like nothing before and since.

Then I drove home and slept like the dead.

✦ ✦ ✦

These mornings, I fix coffee for me, milk for the boy. I think of that woman, and I can't see a trace of my lover in this boy, as if she conceived him by immaculate conception.

I sleep with this boy, their son. To make the boy love me the way I love his father. To make him want me, hunger, twist in his sleep, as if he'd swallowed glass. I put him in my mouth. Here, little piece of my *corazón.*[9] Boy with hard thighs and just a bit of down and a small hard downy ass like his father's, and that back like a valentine. Come here, *mi cariñito.*[10] Come to *mamita.*[11] Here's a bit of toast.

I can tell from the way he looks at me, I have him in my power. Come, sparrow. I have the patience of eternity. Come to mamita. My stupid little bird. I don't move. I don't startle him. I let him nibble. All, all for you. Rub his belly. Stroke him. Before I snap my teeth.

✦ ✦ ✦

What is it inside me that makes me so crazy at 2 A.M.? I can't blame it on alcohol in my blood when there isn't any. It's something worse. Something that poisons the blood and tips me when the night swells and I feel as if the whole sky were leaning against my brain.

And if I killed someone on a night like this? And if it was *me* I killed instead, I'd be guilty of getting in the line of crossfire, innocent bystander, isn't it a shame. I'd be walking with my head full of images and my back to the guilty. Suicide? I couldn't say. I didn't see it.

Except it's not me who I want to kill. When the gravity of the planets is just right, it all tilts and upsets the visible balance. And that's when it wants to out from my eyes. That's when I get on the telephone, dangerous as a terrorist. There's nothing to do but let it come.

So. What do you think? Are you convinced now I'm as crazy as a tulip or a taxi? As vagrant as a cloud?

Sometimes the sky is so big and I feel so little at night. That's the problem with being cloud. The sky is so terribly big. Why is it worse at night, when I have such an urge to communicate and no language with which to form the words? Only colors. Pictures. And you know what I have to say isn't always pleasant.

Oh, love, there. I've gone and done it. What good is it? Good or bad, I've done what I had to do and needed to. And you've answered the phone, and startled me away like a bird. And now you're probably swearing under your breath and going back to sleep, with that wife beside you, warm, radiating her own heat, alive under the flannel and down and smelling a bit like milk and hand cream, and that smell familiar and dear to you, oh.

Human beings pass me on the street, and I want to reach out and strum them as if they were guitars. Sometimes all humanity strikes me as lovely. I just want to reach out and stroke someone, and say There, there, it's all right, honey. There, there, there.

—1991

---

[9] (Sp.) Heart.
[10] (Sp.) My dear.

[11] (Sp.) Little mama.

LOUISE ERDRICH (1954-)

Raised in Wahpeton, North Dakota, Louise Erdrich is of Ojibwa (Chippewa) and German heritage, and is a member of the Turtle Mountain band of Objiwe. Both her father, Ralph Louis Erdrich, and her mother, Rita Joanne Gorneau Erdrich, worked for the Bureau of Indian Affairs as teachers, and they encouraged Erdrich's aspiration to be a writer. She earned her B.A. from Darmouth College in 1976 as part of Dartmouth's inaugural class including women, and it was there she met Michael Anthony Dorris, a writer and professor of Native American Studies. After receiving an M.A. from Johns Hopkins University, she returned to Dartmouth in 1981 as a writer-in-residence, and shortly thereafter married Dorris, with whom she collaborated very closely in her writing. He eventually left his academic career to manage her literary career and to start his own. Dorris committed suicide in 1997, two years after the couple split and six years following the death of their oldest adopted son, Reynold Abel, in a car accident.

Erdrich's career as a writer started impressively, with her first published story winning the Nelson Algren fiction competition in 1982. That short story became the basis for *Love Medicine* (1984), a novel-in-stories which received the National Book Critics Circle Award for best work of fiction and the Los Angeles Times Award for best novel, among other honors. In *Love Medicine,* Erdrich introduced readers to a set of Chippewa, German, and Polish characters in North Dakota, to whom she would return in her later works. Her fiction is noted for its inventive narrative structures, its strong women characters, and its multiple protagonists. Erdrich has written several other novels, including *The Beet Queen* (1986), *Tracks* (1988), *The Bingo Palace* (1994), *The Antelope Wife* (1998), and *The Master Butchers Singing Club* (2003). She has also published three volumes of poetry: *Jacklight* (1984), *Baptism of Desire* (1989), and *Original Fire: New and Selected Poems* (2003).

Dear John Wayne[1]

August and the drive-in picture is packed.
We lounge on the hood of the Pontiac
surrounded by the slow-burning spirals they sell
at the window, to vanquish the hordes of mosquitoes.
Nothing works. They break through the smoke screen for blood.   5

Always the lookout spots the Indians first,
spread north to south, barring progress.
The Sioux or some other Plains bunch
in spectacular columns, ICBM missiles,
feathers bristling in the meaningful sunset.   10

The drum breaks. There will be no parlance.
Only the arrows whining, a death-cloud of nerves
swarming down on the settlers
who die beautifully, tumbling like dust weeds
into the history that brought us all here   15
together: this wide screen beneath the sign of the bear.

The sky fills, acres of blue squint and eye
that the crowd cheers. His face moves over us,

---

[1] John Wayne (1907-1979), American film actor best known for Westerns, who died of cancer.

a thick cloud of vengeance, pitted
like the land that was once flesh. Each rut,   20
each scar makes a promise: *It is*
not over, this fight, not as long as you resist.

Everything we see belongs to us.

A few laughing Indians fall over the hood
slipping in the hot spilled butter.   25
The eye sees a lot, John, but the heart is so blind.
Death makes us owners of nothing.
He smiles, a horizon of teeth
the credits reel over, and then the white fields
again blowing in the true-to-life dark.   30
The dark films over everything.
We get into the car
scratching our mosquito bites, speechless and small
as people are when the movie is done.
We are back in our skins.   35

How can we help but keep hearing his voice,
the flip side of the sound track, still playing:
Come on, boys, we got them
where we want them, drunk, running.
They'll give us what we want, what we need.   40
Even his disease was the idea of taking everything.
Those cells, burning, doubling, splitting out of their skins.

—1984

Indian Boarding School: The Runaways

Home's the place we head for in our sleep.
Boxcars stumbling north in dreams
don't wait for us. We catch them on the run.
The rails, old lacerations that we love,
shoot parallel across the face and break   5
just under Turtle Mountains. Riding scars
you can't get lost. Home is the place they cross.

The lame guard strikes a match and makes the dark
less tolerant. We watch through cracks in boards
as the land starts rolling, rolling till it hurts   10
to be here, cold in regulation clothes.
We know the sheriff's waiting at midrun
to take us back. His car is dumb and warm.
The highway doesn't rock, it only hums
like a wing of long insults. The worn-down welts   15
of ancient punishments lead back and forth.

All runaways wear dresses, long green ones,
the color you would think shame was. We scrub

the sidewalks down because it's shameful work.
Our brushes cut the stone in watered arcs   20
and in the soak frail outlines shiver clear
a moment, things us kids pressed on the dark
face before it hardened, pale, remembering
delicate old injuries, the spines of names and leaves.

—1984

Jacklight

The same Chippewa word is used both for flirting and hunting game, while another
Chippewa word connotes both using force in intercourse and also killing a bear with
one's bare hands.

—Dunning 1959

We have come to the edge of the woods,
out of brown grass where we slept, unseen,
out of knotted twigs, out of leaves creaked shut,
out of hiding.

At first the light wavered, glancing over us.   5
Then it clenched to a fist of light that pointed,
searched out, divided us.
Each took the beams like direct blows the heart answers.
Each of us moved forward alone.

We have come to the edge of the woods,   10
drawn out of ourselves by this night sun,
this battery of polarized acids,
that outshines the moon.

We smell them behind it
but they are faceless, invisible.   15
We smell the raw steel of their gun barrels,
mink oil on leather, their tongues of sour barley.
We smell their mother buried chin-deep in wet dirt.

We smell their fathers with scoured knuckles,
teeth cracked from hot marrow.   20
We smell their sisters of crushed dogwood, bruised apples,
of fractured cups and concussions of burnt hooks.

We smell their breath steaming lightly behind the jacklight.
We smell the itch underneath the caked guts on their clothes.
We smell their minds like silver hammers   25
cocked back, held in readiness
for the first of us to step into the open.

We have come to the edge of the woods,
out of brown grass where we slept, unseen,
out of leaves creaked shut, out of our hiding.   30
We have come here too long.

It is their turn now,
their turn to follow us. Listen,
they put down their equipment.
It is useless in the tall brush.   35
And now they take the first steps, not knowing
how deep the woods are and lightless.
How deep the woods are.

—1984

AURORA LEVINS MORALES (1954-   )

An author of both poetry and prose, Aurora Levins Morales is a political activist and feminist
historian; her work is often a mixture of historical writing, storytelling, and political commentary. Born on February 24, 1954, in Indiera, Puerto Rico, to a Jewish father and a Puerto
Rican mother, Levins Morales moved with her family to the United States when she was thirteen. In her writing she actively draws from both sides of her heritage: her father's progressive Jewish politics and her mother's feminist racial politics. A precocious reader—her mother
taught her how to read at the age of five—Levins Morales began writing poetry at a very
young age. She attended Franconia College in New Hampshire before transferring to Mills
College in Oakland, California, where she earned a B.A. in Creative Writing and Ethnic
Studies. She also holds an M.A. and Ph.D. from The Union Institute in Cincinnati, Ohio. In
1981, an essay by Levins Morales was included in groundbreaking anthology *This Bridge
Called My Back: Writings by Radical Women of Color*. Since then, she has published her work in
various magazines, journals, and collections, including *Ms., Americas Review,* and *Revista
Chicano-Riqueña*. Shortly after co-authoring *Getting Home Alive* (1986) with her mother, Rosario
Morales, Levins Morales was in a serious accident and suffered a brain injury from which it
took her many years to recover.

Levins Morales focuses in her writing on the question of mestizaje, the mixture of races,
cultures, and languages that have produced Puerto Rican identity in all its diversity and complexity. Her recent publications include *Medicine Stories: History, Culture and the Politics of
Integrity* (1998), which considers the link between personal healing from sexual abuse and healing from colonial and neocolonial violence, and *Remedios: Stories of Earth and Iron from the
History of Puertorriqueñas* (1998), which mixes historical vignettes about the global, feminist
origins of contemporary Puerto Rican women with herbal remedies and botany. Levins
Morales lives in the San Francisco Bay Area.

Sugar Poem

Poetry
is something refined
in your vocabulary,
taking its place at the table
in a silver bowl: essence   5
of culture.

I come from the earth
where the cane was grown.
I know
the knobbed rooting,   10
green spears, heights of
caña[1]
against the sky,
purple plumed.
I know the backache   15
of the machetero,[2]
the arc of steel
cutting, cutting,
the rhythm of harvest
leaving acres of sharp spikes   20
that wound the feet—
and the sweet smoke
of the llamarada:[3]
rings of red fire burning
dark sugar into the wind.   25

My poems grow from the ground.
I know what they are made of:
heavy, raw and green.

Sugar,
you say, is sweet.   30
One teaspoon in a cup of coffee…
life's not so bad.

Caña, I reply,
yields many things:
molasses   35
for the horses,
rum for the tiredness
of the machetero,
industrial
alcohol to cleanse,   40
distil, to burn
as fuel.

I don't write my poems
for anybody's sweet tooth.

My poems are acetylene torches   45
welding steel.
My poems are flamethrowers
cutting paths through the world.
My poems are bamboo spears

---

[1] (Sp.) Sugar cane.
[2] (Sp.) Cane cutter.
[3] (Sp.) Bonfire.

opening the air.   50
They come from the earth,
common and brown.

—1986

Tita's Poem

Oh, brown skinny girl with eyes like chips of mica
what did we know, straddling the flamboyan branch
hanging dreamy eyed, shivering, in the sun?
What did we know, squatting
over the swollen roots of hillside ginger   5
tipping our wild little animal hips
to catch the stream of water from a roof
right between the legs?
Nothing had a name then.

I remember a photograph in Ladies Home Journal   10
two women, skinny, string haired, gaunt eyed:
"Lesbian Junkie Prostitutes in Jail" said the caption
I never connected that word with us   still
I remembered the picture.
Kiss my mouth you said, and wondered if you'd get pregnant   15
and said you didn't care.

What did we know that we don't know now?
When I come back, I grieved, you'll be married, with babies
and you said *no, no, espera pa' que tu veas, verás que no.*[4]
All that last spring we gathered orchids deep in the rainforest   20
bringing them to our garden,
binding them to the wood with black thread:
green, fresh flowers never meant for the sun,
bouquets of dawn never touched
by the careless brutal burning of noon.   25

In the years since then you've spilled children from you
like wasted blood
half of them dying before you could learn their names.
Still, I imagine you, thin and dear,
gnawing at the rinds of green guavas,   30
tasting each orange to see if it was bitter
or sweet, your dark head bent to my breast.

If I were to find you now, with your thieving husband and three
surviving children   if I were to come to you now in some dark
and stuffy, overcrowded living room in New York   35
where photographs of your wedding and nieces and nephews
crowd the end tables
you sitting on the plastic-covered couch,
with the inner stillness of a girl still moving

---

[4] (Sp.) No, no, wait and you'll see, you'll see that I won't.

in the shadows of trees 40
If I were to come to you now and take you   thin
into my arms   would you remember me
and be wild and daring again, reaching up into the sky
to pluck the sun?

—1986

HELENA MARÍA VIRAMONTES (1954-)

Helena María Viramontes was born and raised in East Los Angeles, California. As a young girl, Viramontes and her eight siblings worked alongside her parents, who were migrant farm laborers (her father also worked in construction). Viramontes attended Garfield High School and Immaculate Heart College, where she received a B.A. in English Literature in 1975. She enrolled in UC Irvine's graduate creative writing program, but left in 1981; she received her M.F.A. in 1994. Viramontes began winning honors for her writing in the late 1970s, after two of her stories were awarded prizes by *Statement Magazine:* "Requiem for the Poor" (1977) and "The Broken Web" (1978). A year later, her short story "The Birthday" won first place in the UC Irvine Chicano Literary Contest. A collection of her short stories, *The Moths and Other Stories,* was published in 1985 by Arte Público Press. In 1989, a National Endowment for the Arts grant enabled Viramontes to attend a Sundance Institute workshop led by Nobel Laureate Gabriel García Márquez. Her experience there contributed to her first novel, *Under the Feet of Jesus* (1995). A second novel, *Their Dogs Came with Them,* was published in 2000. Viramontes has edited two scholarly works with María Herrera-Sobek: *Chicana Creativity and Criticism: Charting New Frontiers in American Literature* (1988) and *Chicana (W)Rites: On Word and Film* (1995). Winner of the Luis Leal Award and the John Dos Passos Award for Literature, Viramontes teaches in the creative writing program at Cornell University.

The Moths

I was fourteen years old when Abuelita[1] requested my help. And it seemed only fair. Abuelita had pulled me through the rages of scarlet fever by placing, removing and replacing potato slices on the temples of my forehead; she had seen me through several whippings, an arm broken by a dare jump off Tío Enrique's toolshed, puberty, and my first lie. Really, I told Amá,[2] it was only fair.

Not that I was her favorite granddaughter or anything special. I wasn't even pretty or nice like my older sisters and I just couldn't do the girl things they could do. My hands were too big to handle the fineries of crocheting or embroidery and I always pricked my fingers or knotted my colored threads time and time again while my sisters laughed and called me bull hands with their cute waterlike voices. So I began keeping a piece of jagged brick in my sock to bash my sisters or anyone who called me bull hands. Once, while we all sat in the bedroom, I hit Teresa on the forehead, right above her eyebrow and she ran to Amá with her mouth open, her hand over her eye while blood seeped between her fingers. I was used to the whippings by then.

[1] (Sp.) Grandmother.   [2] (Sp.) Shortened version of Mama, or mother.

I wasn't respectful either. I even went so far as to doubt the power of Abuelita's slices, the slices she said absorbed my fever. "You're still alive, aren't you?" Abuelita snapped back, her pasty gray eye beaming at me and burning holes in my suspicions. Regretful that I had let secret questions drop out of my mouth, I couldn't look into her eyes. My hands began to fan out, grow like a liar's nose until they hung by my side like low weights. Abuelita made a balm out of dried moth wings and Vicks and rubbed my hands, shaped them back to size and it was the strangest feeling. Like bones melting. Like sun shining through the darkness of your eyelids. I didn't mind helping Abuelita after that, so Amá would always send me over to her.

In the early afternoon Amá would push her hair back, hand me my sweater and shoes, and tell me to go to Mama Luna's. This was to avoid another fight and another whipping, I knew. I would deliver one last shot on Marisela's arm and jump out of our house, the slam of the screen door burying her cries of anger, and I'd gladly go help Abuelita plant her wild lilies or jasmine or heliotrope or cilantro or hierbabuena[3] in red Hills Brothers coffee cans. Abuelita would wait for me at the top step of her porch holding a hammer and nail and empty coffee cans. And although we hardly spoke, hardly looked at each other as we worked over root transplants, I always felt her gray eye on me. It made me feel, in a strange sort of way, safe and guarded and not alone. Like God was supposed to make you feel.

On Abuelita's porch, I would puncture holes in the bottom of the coffee cans with a nail and a precise hit of a hammer. This completed, my job was to fill them with red clay mud from beneath her rose bushes, packing it softly, then making a perfect hole, four fingers round, to nest a sprouting avocado pit, or the spidery sweet potatoes that Abuelita rooted in mayonnaise jars with toothpicks and daily water, or prickly chayotes[4] that produced vines that twisted and wound all over her porch pillars, crawling to the roof, up and over the roof, and down the other side, making her small brick house look like it was cradled within the vines that grew pear-shaped squashes ready for the pick, ready to be steamed with onions and cheese and butter. The roots would burst out of the rusted coffee cans and search for a place to connect. I would then feed the seedlings with water.

But this was a different kind of help, Amá said, because Abuelita was dying. Looking into her gray eye, then into her brown one, the doctor said it was just a matter of days. And so it seemed only fair that these hands she had melted and formed found use in rubbing her caving body with alcohol and marihuana, rubbing her arms and legs, turning her face to the window so that she could watch the Bird of Paradise blooming or smell the scent of clove in the air. I toweled her face frequently and held her hand for hours. Her gray wiry hair hung over the mattress. Since I could remember, she'd kept her long hair in braids. Her mouth was vacant and when she slept, her eyelids never closed all the way. Up close, you could see her gray eye beaming out the window, staring hard as if to remember everything. I never kissed her. I left the window open when I went to the market.

Across the street from Jay's Market there was a chapel. I never knew its denomination, but I went in just the same to search for candles. I sat down on one of the pews because there were none. After I cleaned my fingernails, I looked up at the high ceiling. I had forgotten the vastness of these places, the coolness of the marble pillars and

---

[3] A variety of mint used for both medicinal and cooking purposes in Mexico.

[4] A member of the squash family.

the frozen statues with blank eyes. I was alone. I knew why I had never returned.

That was one of Apá's biggest complaints. He would pound his hands on the table, rocking the sugar dish or spilling a cup of coffee and scream that if I didn't go to mass every Sunday to save my goddamn sinning soul, then I had no reason to go out of the house, period. Punto final. He would grab my arm and dig his nails into me to make sure I understood the importance of catechism. Did he make himself clear? Then he strategically directed his anger at Amá for her lousy ways of bringing up daughters, being disrespectful and unbelieving, and my older sisters would pull me aside and tell me if I didn't get to mass right this minute, they were all going to kick the holy shit out of me. Why am I so selfish? Can't you see what it's doing to Amá, you idiot? So I would wash my feet and stuff them in my black Easter shoes that shone with Vaseline, grab a missal and veil, and wave good-bye to Amá.

I would walk slowly down Lorena to First to Evergreen, counting the cracks on the cement. On Evergreen I would turn left and walk to Abuelita's. I liked her porch because it was shielded by the vines of the chayotes and I could get a good look at the people and car traffic on Evergreen without them knowing. I would jump up the porch steps, knock on the screen door as I wiped my feet and call Abuelita? mi Abuelita? As I opened the door and stuck my head in, I would catch the gagging scent of toasting chile on the placa. When I entered the sala, she would greet me from the kitchen, wringing her hands in her apron. I'd sit at the corner of the table to keep from being in her way. The chiles made my eyes water. Am I crying? No, Mama Luna, I'm sure not crying. I don't like going to mass, but my eyes watered anyway, the tears dropping on the tablecloth like candle wax. Abuelita lifted the burnt chiles from the fire and sprinkled water on them until the skins began to separate. Placing them in front of me, she turned to check the menudo. I peeled the skins off and put the flimsy, limp-looking green and yellow chiles in the molcajete[5] and began to crush and crush and twist and crush the heart out of the tomato, the clove of garlic, the stupid chiles that made me cry, crushed them until they turned into liquid under my bull hand. With a wooden spoon, I scraped hard to destroy the guilt, and my tears were gone. I put the bowl of chile next to a vase filled with freshly cut roses. Abuelita touched my hand and pointed to the bowl of menudo that steamed in front of me. I spooned some chile into the menudo and rolled a corn tortilla thin with the palms of my hands. As I ate, a fine Sunday breeze entered the kitchen and a rose petal calmly feathered down to the table.

I left the chapel without blessing myself and walked to Jay's. Most of the time Jay didn't have much of anything. The tomatoes were always soft and the cans of Campbell soups had rusted spots on them. There was dust on the tops of cereal boxes. I picked up what I needed: rubbing alcohol, five cans of chicken broth, a big bottle of Pine Sol. At first Jay got mad because I thought I had forgotten the money. But it was there all the time, in my back pocket.

When I returned from the market, I heard Amá crying in Abuelita's kitchen. She looked up at me with puffy eyes. I placed the bags of groceries on the table and began putting the cans of soup away. Amá sobbed quietly. I never kissed her. After a while, I patted her on the back for comfort. Finally: "¿Y mi Amá?" she asked in a whisper, then choked again and cried into her apron.

---

[5] (Sp.) Mortar and pestle.

Abuelita fell off the bed twice yesterday, I said, knowing that I shouldn't have said it and wondering why I wanted to say it because it only made Amá cry harder. I guess I became angry and just so tired of the quarrels and beatings and unanswered prayers and my hands just there hanging helplessly by my side. Amá looked at me again, confused, angry, and her eyes were filled with sorrow. I went outside and sat on the porch swing and watched the people pass. I sat there until she left. I dozed off repeating the words to myself like rosary prayers: when do you stop giving when do you start giving when do you…and when my hands fell from my lap, I awoke to catch them. The sun was setting, an orange glow, and I knew Abuelita was hungry.

There comes a time when the sun is defiant. Just about the time when moods change, inevitable seasons of a day, transitions from one color to another, that hour or minute or second when the sun is finally defeated, finally sinks into the realization that it cannot with all its power to heal or burn, exist forever, there comes an illumination where the sun and earth meet, a final burst of burning red orange fury reminding us that although endings are inevitable, they are necessary for rebirths, and when that time came, just when I switched on the light in the kitchen to open Abuelita's can of soup, it was probably then that she died.

The room smelled of Pine Sol and vomit and Abuelita had defecated the remains of her cancerous stomach. She had turned to the window and tried to speak, but her mouth remained open and speechless. I heard you, Abuelita, I said, stroking her cheek, I heard you. I opened the windows of the house and let the soup simmer and overboil on the stove. I turned the stove off and poured the soup down the sink. From the cabinet I got a tin basin, filled it with lukewarm water and carried it carefully to the room. I went to the linen closet and took out some modest bleached white towels. With the sacredness of a priest preparing his vestments, I unfolded the towels one by one on my shoulders. I removed the sheets and blankets from her bed and peeled off her thick flannel nightgown. I toweled her puzzled face, stretching out the wrinkles, removing the coils of her neck, toweled her shoulders and breasts. Then I changed the water. I returned to towel the creases of her stretch-marked stomach, her sporadic vaginal hairs, and her sagging thighs. I removed the lint from between her toes and noticed a mapped birthmark on the fold of her buttock. The scars on her back which were as thin as the life lines on the palms of her hands made me realize how little I really knew of Abuelita. I covered her with a thin blanket and went into the bathroom. I washed my hands, and turned on the tub faucets and watched the water pour into the tub with vitality and steam. When it was full, I turned off the water and undressed. Then, I went to get Abuelita.

She was not as heavy as I thought and when I carried her in my arms, her body fell into a V, and yet my legs were tired, shaky, and I felt as if the distance between the bedroom and bathroom was miles and years away. Amá, where are you?

I stepped into the bathtub one leg first, then the other. I bent my knees slowly to descend into the water slowly so I wouldn't scald her skin. There, there, Abuelita, I said, cradling her, smoothing her as we descended, I heard you. Her hair fell back and spread across the water like eagle's wings. The water in the tub overflowed and poured onto the tile of the floor. Then the moths came. Small, gray ones that came from her soul and out through her mouth fluttering to light, circling the single dull light bulb of the bathroom. Dying is lonely and I wanted to go to where the moths were, stay with her and plant chayotes whose vines would crawl up her fingers and into the clouds; I wanted to rest my head on her chest with her stroking my hair, telling me about the moths that lay within the soul and slowly eat the spirit up; I wanted to return to the waters of the womb with her so that we would never be alone again. I wanted. I wanted my Amá. I removed a few strands of hair from Abuelita's face and held her small light head within the hollow of my neck. The bathroom was filled with moths, and for the first time in a long time I cried, rocking us, crying for her, for me, for Amá, the sobs emerging from the depths of anguish, the misery of feeling half born, sobbing until finally the sobs rippled into circles and circles of sadness and relief. There, there, I said to Abuelita, rocking us gently, there, there.

—1985

TERRY WOLVERTON (1954-　)

The author of fiction, poetry, essays, and drama, Terry Wolverton is among the most prolific contemporary lesbian writers in the United States. Since the early 1970s, Wolverton has been a poet, performance artist, activist, and teacher, though she retired from performance art in 1986 in order to focus on her writing career. The author of the novels *Embers* (2003) and *Bailey's Beads* (1996), the poetry collections *Mystery Bruise* (1999) and *Black Slip* (1992), and the memoir *Insurgent Muse: Life and Art at the Woman's Building* (2002), she has also edited or co-edited twelve anthologies, three of which have won Lambda Literary Awards: *His(2)* (1997), *Hers 3* (1999), and *His 3* (1999). Wolverton, who has taught creative writing at the Women's Building in Los Angeles, the Connexxus Women's Center, and the Gay and Lesbian Community Services Center, operates a management consulting business specializing in non-profit organizations, small businesses, and individuals. Many of Wolverton's poems are autobiographical, and they are written in both inherited forms—sonnets and sestinas, for instance—and in free verse.

As Vulcan[1] Falls from Heaven
for Paul Monette

Odd, that I should think of Vulcan,
soot-caked deity of toil,
heaven's roughest trade, his brutish
biceps lurid in the fire
light as sweat drops kiss the anvil's   5
face. Why couldn't I invoke
Apollo, paragon of male
beauty, tender of the Muse? Or
clever Mercury, intrepid
messenger of gods, a mind with   10

---

[1] God of fire and volcanoes.

wings? But Vulcan's struck the spark in
my imagination, forged a
chain I can't unlink from you: his
early exile from the hallowed
peaks of Mount Olympus, banished   15
from the patriarchal kingdom,
judged grotesque, a deviant,
condemned to dwell in half-light, underground. But he did not stay shadowed;
in his crucible he stoked a   20

blaze that would ignite the world. He
tamed the unrelenting heart of
iron, bent it to his ardor,
fused the fragments of his life and
hammered them to weapons no man   25
could defeat. The blows rang out like
bells, triumphal notes. Soon all
Olympus came to court his skill; none
could deny his valor, nor his
artistry. There are conflicting   30

stories of his fall. Some versions
say he was a child when the
pantheon cast him out, declared him
weak, unfit to live with gods. Still
others hold it was because he   35
challenged the authority of
Jove, who grew enraged and flung the
upstart Vulcan out of heaven. Nine
days and nights he fell, suspended
in the arms of gravity, a   40

slow and shuddering arc toward the
horizon's rim. With each descending
hour he shone brighter, hurtling
into timelessness, this god of
flame, this blazing nebula. He's   45
falling still, a fiery streak that
plummets through the sky. Look up and
witness as he passes by: a
trail of spark, a sailing torch; his
burning is a beacon now to   50
guide us through this unforgiving night.

—1999

Sestina for the End of the Twentieth Century

As the century slogs to its bloody
conclusion, a culture in death rattles
spits its effluvium, exhausted, parched,
the imagination wound down, a clock,
its heartbeat punctured, dark plasma worn thin—   5
none of us feeling very well these days.
Paltry and mean, what remains of our days,
the calendar truncated and bloody.
Time is a blade slicing promises thin,
the tick of our hearts worn to a rattle;   10
faith dissolves beneath the hands of the clock,
prayers beseech a blank sky that remains parched.

Gyrations of love leave us emptied, parched,
its myth too feeble to succor our days.
Sex grinds on, monotonous as a clock,   15
stained with betrayal, cruel and bloody;
flesh rasps against flesh, dry as a rattle,
the tendons of lust now puny and thin.

Memory too is a garden grown thin,
the soil unwatered, untended seeds parched,   20
wind whistles through like the ghost of a rattle,
nothing sprouts in the light of these burnt days.
Digging deeper, the spade comes up bloody,
against our wills it unburies the clock.

Sleep is haunted by the leer of a clock,   25
and even dreams are predictable, thin,
stalked by familiar monsters, bloody
visages that wake us, our clogged throats parched,
swollen with screams unscreamed: another day
of wordless dread, our teeth crazed, rattling.   30

The vision of future that once rattled
our senses, fueled our race against clock,
has collapsed into a stretch of lost days;
lesioned tomorrow, its bones whittled thin,
beckons a skeletal hand, and the parched   35
tear ducts squeeze out a last few drops of blood.

Unimagined days, measured like a clock's
last breath, played on a parched stage; a ratty,
thin curtain descends, the color of blood.

—1999

MARJORIE AGOSÍN (1955-)

Born in Bethesda, Maryland, Marjorie Agosín spent most of her childhood in Santiago, Chile, where her parents, Moises and Frida Agosín, had moved the family when she was three. Following the overthrow of the Chilean government by General Pinochet's military coup, they returned to the U.S. in 1971, settling in Athens, Georgia. Agosín attended the University of Georgia as an undergraduate and received her Ph.D. in Latin American Literature from Indiana University. She has written and edited over forty books, including poetry, fiction and memoir. A passionate writer who celebrates her hybrid identity as a Jewish Chilean-American woman, Agosín is known for her close reflections on her family, her ethnic identity, and her experience as a political exile. In her collection of bilingual poems, *Dear Anne Frank* (1994), she shares a unique and imaginary relationship with a Jewish girl who met her demise in a concentration camp during World War II, while *Uncertain Travelers* (1999) presents stories that chronicle the experiences of her refugee European family in the unfamiliar territories of Chile. In addition to being a writer, Agosín is an activist on behalf of women in Third World countries; she has a notable international reputation and is a critical force in contemporary global politics. She lives in Massachusetts with her husband and two children, where she is a professor at Wellesley College.

Fairy Tales and Something More

The dwarves didn't keep
Snow White as an ornament
she did her chores
mended socks
and who knows   5
how she ended her nights
in a room with seven precocious fellows,
Cinderella cinders,
also no very easy road
washing other people's clothes,   10
always barefoot
until a gentleman
took pity on her
and it seems he gave her one shoe
and the shoe fit her very well   15
and the other thing fit also.
Little Red Riding Hood
had to sleep with a wolf
but all of us women
have slept with wolves that snore   20
and promise us heaven and earth
happy days gathering up
hair from the washbasin
fetching coffee and the newspaper
as tamed mistresses of masters.   25
And the Fairy Tales

rose-colored off-colored
have never had any ever after.

—1984

An Apology[1]

I demand an apology.
You hear me, all of you:
I, a citizen of the
Southern rivers;
I, an involuntary woman immigrant,   5
I demand an apology
from the current and previous
President of the United States,
from the Secretaries of State,
from the CIA agents,   10
from the soldiers,
from the secret police of North America,
from the Georgia teachers who spit on me
the first day of class
and jeered at my height and my language,   15
at my religion,
those who called me a "dirty Jew."

I demand an apology.
From the *New York Times* down to the
smallest local papers   20
of the South, a decorous silence is observed
to soothe the delicate ears of
the democracy.

I demand an apology
because they stole my country from me,   25
my land of shells and fishes,
my haven of mollusks.
My entire childhood sabotaged
because they left me without a country forever;
because I had to leave my dead all by themselves   30
and my living, too;
because I didn't get to be with my cousins.

They stayed behind, waiting for letters.
I traveled on, waiting for letters
and today I am still waiting to hear.   35
I demand an apology
because I had to leave my home and my dolls behind.
I had to leave, an incomplete
fugitive from a borrowed land.

---

[1] Agosín, a political exile who fled Chile as a child with her family following the U.S.-backed coup against the democratically-elected government of President Salvador Allende Gossens, is referring generally to the United States' illegal interventions into the domestic politics of Latin American countries.

I demand an apology because I still   40
haven't finished explaining my origins to everyone,
the color of my hair, the shape of my face,
          the rhythm of my accent.

I demand an apology because I cannot speak
          in Spanish;   45
because I had to learn another language
another way of doing math and making love.

I demand an apology because I always
have to explain why I left,
explain my race, my class,   50
the patio of my house.

I am here
because this North American country
did its little thing in
Guatemala, in the Dominican Republic,   55
in Chile, in Costa Rica,
in Cuba,
across the entire map of hope
that is my America.

I demand an apology   60
however small it may be,
but listen closely now:
I lost what I was.
I no longer am
nor will be.   65
All that I had
faded away like smoke
like mist,
and here I am each day,
marked by the scars of memory,   70
fragile and alone.

Translated by Mary G. Berg

—1998

Once Again

Once again the women linger,
talking about the disappeared:
it must have been for something
isn't it true?
they are no longer in vogue   5
we Chileans
are all friends.
Are you a Chilean?
few died

a few thousand, no more   10
we Chileans
are good about forgetting.

Once again the women linger,
marching in their black widow dresses
they make me nervous seeing them transfigured   15
in the secret circles of death.
It wasn't my fault.
I hid when they came to take them away
in the luxuriant summer nights.

The son of my neighbor is a policeman.   20
I am only the neighbor
of that man.
I knew nothing about the matter.
I heard them.
They were sounds of shrieking birds   25
as if my skin had transformed into another's skin.

And again the lingering women
with their red dresses of death
and sparrows in their hair
do not tire from dancing,   30
they search for sanctuary in the truth
and look for embraces and new children to love.

—1998

MARILYN MEI LING CHIN (1955-   )

Born in Hong Kong and raised in Portland, Oregon, Marilyn Chin received her B.A. in Chinese Language and Literature from the University of Massachusetts at Amherst and her M.F.A. from the University of Iowa. The influence of Chin's formal study of Chinese literature, as well as her work translating Chinese poetry, are evident in her "appropriations" of Chinese poetic forms and style. In tones both ironic and longing, many of Chin's poems explore the themes of exile, loss, desire, betrayal, and art. Her writing is considered innovative in its sharp and witty coupling of Chinese and Western literary forms, resulting in a poetics that is precise and playful. Chin both uses and undermines the conventions of love poetry to comment on colonialism, race, gender, and desire.

Chin's books of poems include *Dwarf Bamboo* (1987), *The Phoenix Gone, The Terrace Empty* (1997), and *Rhapsody in Plain Yellow* (2002). Her work has been featured in a variety of anthologies, including *The Norton Anthology of Modern and Contemporary Poetry, The Norton Introduction to Poetry, The Oxford Anthology of Modern American Poetry,* and *The Best American Poetry of 1996.* Chin has received awards for her poetry from the Radcliffe Institute at Harvard, the Rockefeller Foundation, and the National Endowment for the Arts, among others. She has also won the PEN/Josephine Miles Award, four Pushcart Prizes, and the Paterson Prize. She teaches in the M.F.A. program at San Diego State University.

A Portrait of the Self As Nation, 1990-1991

> Fit in dominata servitus
> In servitude dominatus
> *In mastery there is bondage*
> *In bondage there is mastery*
> —Latin proverb

> *The stranger and the enemy*
> *We have seen him in the mirror.*
> —George Seferis[1]

Forgive me, Head Master,
but you see, I have forgotten
to put on my black lace underwear, and instead
I have hiked my slip up, up to my waist
so that I can enjoy the breeze.   5
It feels good to be *without,*
so good as to be salacious.
The feeling of flesh kissing tweed.
If ecstasy had a color, it would be
yellow and pink, yellow and pink   10
Mongolian skin rubbed raw.
The serrated lining especially fine
like wearing a hair-shirt, inches above the knee.
When was the last time I made love?
The last century? With a wan missionary.   15
Or was it San Wu the Bailiff?
The tax collector who came for my tithes?
The herdboy, the ox, on the bridge of magpies?
It was Roberto, certainly,
high on coke, circling the galaxy.   20
Or my recent vagabond love
driving a reckless chariot, lost
in my feral country. *Country,* Oh I am
so punny, so very, very punny.
Dear Mr. Decorum, don't you agree?   25

It's not so much the length of the song
but the range of the emotions—Fear
has kept me a good pink monk—and poetry
is my nunnery. Here I am alone in my altar,
self-hate, self-love, both self-erotic notions.   30
Eyes closed, listening to that one hand clapping—
not metaphysical trance, but fleshly mutilation—
and loving *it,* myself and that pink womb, my bed.
Reading "Ching Ping Mei"[2] in the "expurgated"
where all the female protagonists were named   35

[1] George Seferis (1900-1971), Greek poet.

[2] [*Author's note.*] Chinese erotic novel, first published in 1610 or 1617; the authorship of this novel is unknown.

Lotus.
Those damned licentious women named us
Modest, Virtue, Cautious, Endearing,
Demure-dewdrop, Plum-aster, Petal-stamen.
They teach us to walk headbent in devotion,   40
to honor the five relations, ten sacraments.
Meanwhile, the feast is brewing elsewhere,
the ox is slaughtered and her entrails are hung
on the branches for the poor. They convince us, yes,
our chastity will save the nation—Oh mothers,   45
all your sweet epithets didn't make us wise!
Orchid by any other name is equally seditious.

Now, where was I, oh yes, now I remember,
the last time I made love, it was to *you.*
I faintly remember your whiskers   50
against my tender nape.
You were a conquering barbarian,
helmeted, halberded,
beneath the gauntleted moon,
whispering Hunnish or English—   55
so-long Oolong went the racist song,
bye-bye little chinky butterfly.
There is no cure for self-pity,
the disease is death,
ennui, disaffection,   60
a roll of flesh-colored tract homes crowding my imagination.
I do hate my loneliness,
sitting cross-legged in my room,
satisfied with a few off-rhymes,
sending off precious haiku to some inconspicuous journal   65
named "Left Leaning Bamboo."
You, my precious reader, O sweet voyeur,
sweaty, balding, bespeckled,
in a rumpled rayon shirt
and a neo-Troubadour chignon,   70
politics mildly centrist,
the *right* fork for the *right* occasions,
matriculant of the best schools—
herewith, my last confession
(with decorous and perfect diction)   75
I loathe to admit. Yet, I shall admit it:
there was no Colonialist coercion;
sadly, we blended together well.
I was poor, starving, war torn,
an empty coffin to be filled,   80
You were a young, ambitious Lieutenant
with dreams of becoming Prince

of a "new world order," Lord
over the League of Nations.

Lover, destroyer, savior!   85
I remember that moment of beguilement,
one hand muffling my mouth,
one hand untying my sash—
On your throat dangled a golden cross.
Your god is jealous, your god is cruel.   90
So, when did you finally return?
And…was there a second coming?
My memory is failing me, perhaps
you came too late
(we were already dead).   95
Perhaps you didn't come at all—
you had a deadline to meet,
another alliance to secure,
another resistance to break.
Or you came too often   100
to my painful dismay.
(Oh, how facile the liberator's hand.)
Often when I was asleep
You would hover over me
with your great silent wingspan   105
and watch me sadly.
This is the way you want me—
asleep, quiescent, almost dead,
sedated by lush immigrant dreams
of global bliss, connubial harmony.   110

Yet, I shall always remember
and deign to forgive
(long before I am satiated,
long before I am spent)
that last pressured cry,   115
"your little death."
Under the halcyon light
you would smoke and contemplate
the sea and debris,
that barbaric keening   120
of what it means to be free.
As if we were ever free,
as if ever we could be.
Said the judge,
"Congratulations,   125
On this day, fifteen of November, 1967,
Marilyn Mei Ling Chin,
application # z-z-z-z-z,
you are an American citizen,
naturalized in the name of God   130

the father, God the son and the Holy Ghost."
Time assuages, and even
the Yellow River becomes clean...

Meanwhile we forget
the power of exclusion[3]   135
what you are walling in or out—
and to whom you must give offence.
The hungry, the slovenly, the convicts
need not apply.
The syphilitic, the consumptive   140
may not moor.
The hookwormed and tracomaed[4]
(and the likewise infested).
The gypsies, the sodomists, the mentally infirm.
The pagans, the heathens, the non-   145
denominational—
The coloreds, the mixed-races and the reds.
The communists, the usurous,
the mutants, the Hibakushas,[5] the hags...

Oh, connoisseurs of gastronomy and *keemun* tea!   150
My foes, my loves,
how eloquent your discrimination,
how precise your poetry.
Last night, in our large, rotund bed,
we witnessed the fall. *Ours*   155
was an "aerial war." Bombs
glittering in the twilight sky
against the Star-Spangled Banner.
Dunes and dunes of sand,
fields and fields of rice.   160
A thousand charred oil wells,
the firebrands of night.
Ecstasy made us tired.

Sir, Master, Dominatrix,
Fall was a glorious season for the hegemonists.   165
We took long melancholy strolls on the beach,
digressed on art and politics
in a quaint warfside café in La Jolla.
The storm grazed our bare arms gently...
History has never failed us.   170
Why save Babylonia or Cathay,
when we can always have Paris?
Darling, if we are to remember at all,

---

[3] [*Author's note.*] Refers to various "exclusion acts" or anti-Chinese legislation that attempted to halt the flow of Chinese immigrants to the U.S.
[4] [*Author's note.*] Two diseases that kept many Chinese detained and quarantined at Angel Island.
[5] [*Author's note.*] Scarred survivors of the atom bomb and their deformed descendants.

Let us remember it well—
We were fierce, yet tender,   175
fierce and tender.

—1994

Blues on Yellow

The canary died in the gold mine, her dreams got lost in the sieve.
The canary died in the gold mine, her dreams got lost in the sieve.
Her husband the crow killed under the railroad, the spokes hath shorn his wings.

Something's cookin' in Chin's kitchen, ten thousand yellow-bellied sapsuckers
*   baked in a pie.*
Something's cookin' in Chin's kitchen, ten thousand yellow-bellied sapsuckers
*   baked in a pie.*   5
Something's cookin' in Chin's kitchen, die die yellow bird, die die.

O crack an egg on the griddle, yellow will ooze into white.
O crack an egg on the griddle, yellow will ooze into white.
Run, run, sweet little Puritan, yellow will ooze into white.

If you cut my yellow wrists, I'll teach my yellow toes to write.   10
If you cut my yellow wrists, I'll teach my yellow toes to write.
If you cut my yellow fists, I'll teach my yellow feet to fight.

Do not be afraid to perish, my mother, Buddha's compassion is nigh.
Do not be afraid to perish, my mother, our boat will sail tonight.
Your babies will reach the promised land, the stars will be their guide.   15

I am so mellow yellow, mellow yellow, Buddha sings in my veins.
I am so mellow yellow, mellow yellow, Buddha sings in my veins.
O take me to the land of the unreborn, there's no life on earth without pain.

—2002

SILVIA CURBELO (1955-   )

Silvia Curbelo was born in Matanzas, Cuba, and immigrated to the United States as a child. She has published three collections of poetry: *The Geography of Leaving* (1991), *The Secret History of Water* (1997), and *Ambush* (2004), which won the Main Street Rag Chapbook Competition. The recipient of a poetry fellowship from the National Endowment for the Arts and three Individual Artist Fellowships from the Florida Division of Cultural Affairs, Curbelo has also been awarded the Jessica Nobel-Maxwell Memorial Poetry Prize from the *American Poetry Review*. Curbelo resides in Tampa, Florida, where she is the editor of *Organica* magazine.

Janis Joplin

There is a song like a light
coming on too fast, the eyes

blink back the static of the road
and in the distance you can almost see
the clean, sweet glow of electric guitars.   5

Call it the music of the rest
of our lives, a stranger's face
peering through a window,
except that face is yours
or mine. Music like backtalk,   10

like wind across your heart,
cigarette smoke and bourbon.
Music our mothers must have held
softly between damp sheets,
before taxes, before lay-offs,   15
before the first door closing,

not piano lessons, not a hymn
or a prayer, or a soft voice
singing you to sleep, but a song
like a green light on summer evenings   20
after a ball game, after rain,
when the fields finally let themselves go
and we'd drive past the Westinghouse plant,
past Vail and Arcadia. Music
of never going back.   25

I'm talking about car radios,
about backseats and hope,
and the jukebox at Pokey's
where the local boys tried
their new luck on anyone   30
and the real history of the world
was going down, nickels and
dimes, the music floating
at the far end of a first kiss,

the first light of the body   35
that isn't love but is stronger than love,
because it must not end,
because it never lasts.

—1993

Between Language and Desire

Imagine the sound of words
landing on a page, not footsteps

along the road, but the road itself,
not a voice but a hunger.

I want to live by word of mouth,⁵
as if what I'm about to say
could become a wall around us,
not stone but the idea

of stone, the bricks
of what sustains us.¹⁰

These hands are not a harvest.
There is no honest metaphor for bread.

—1996

Tourism in the Late 20th Century

Blue boat of morning and already
the window is besieged
by sky. Grace takes no prisoners
in a town like this. Think of the girl
sipping white burgundy⁵
in the local café, her straw hat
with its pale flower, indigenous
and small as the white roll
she's buttering one philosophical
corner at a time. Even the rain¹⁰
that falls some afternoons here
is more conceptual, more a tribute
to rain than actual rain falling
on the tulips, a rumor
the wind carries all the way¹⁵
down the beach.
And would you ask the sea
to explain itself? wrote Kerouac once
in a book about a woman
who was already a metaphor,²⁰
rose fading in its glass bowl.¹
He always knew the world is sentimental,
waving its lacy rags over the face
of the familiar, an architecture
of piano notes and hope.²⁵
Imagine the girl, her hat gone,
her bread finished, holding out
an armful of tulips in the rain.
She knows each road leads
to other roads, to small towns³⁰
with solid names like *Crestview* and
Niceville where even dust has

---

¹ From *The Subterraneans* (1958) by American writer Jack Kerouac (1922-1969), a fictionalized account of his romance with an African-American woman: "Bear with me all lover readers who've suffered pangs, bear with me men who understand that the sea of blackness in a darkeyed woman's eyes is the lonely sea itself and would you go ask the sea to explain itself, or ask woman why she crosseth hands on lap over rose? no–."

a genealogy and an address,
as if there's more forever there.
The tulips long to be metaphysical,   35
closed-mouthed, more faithful
than the rose. Let the windows
take over. Lean out the small
square of the day, past
the rain, past the idea   40
of rain, to where the sky
is snapshot blue, the sea
blue by association.

—1996

KIMIKO HAHN (1955-   )

Kimiko Hahn was born in Mt. Kisco, New York, to a Japanese American mother and a
German-American father, both of whom were artists. Hahn majored in English and East Asian
Studies as an undergraduate at the University of Iowa, and received an M.A. in Japanese
Literature at Columbia University. Her poetry was first collected in book form in *We Stand
Our Ground* (1988), a collaboration with two other women poets. Hahn's other published work
includes *The Narrow Road to the Interior* (2006), *The Artist's Daughter* (2002), *Mosquito and Ant*
(1999), *Volatile* (1998), and *The Unbearable Heart* (1995), which received an American Book
Award. Hahn's poetics are strongly intertextual, often explicitly so. Thematically, her poems
explore the relationship between gender, language, body, desire, and subjectivity. Formally,
her poetics of fragmentation, quotation, and multivocality express various models of gendered
and racialized subjectivity. She has drawn upon forms and techniques used by women writers
in Japan and China, including the *zuihitsu,* or pillow book, and *nu shu,* a nearly extinct script
Chinese women used to correspond with one another.

Hahn is the recipient of fellowships from the National Endowment for the Arts and the
New York Foundation for the Arts, as well as a Lila Wallace-Reader's Digest Writers' Award,
the Theodore Roethke Memorial Poetry Prize, and an Association of Asian American Studies
Literature Award. She is a Distinguished Professor in the English Department at Queens
College/CUNY.

The Hemisphere: Kuchuk Hanem

"Flaubert's[1] encounter with an Egyptian
courtesan produced a widely influential
model of the Oriental woman....
He spoke for and represented her."
[SAID,[2] *ORIENTALISM*, P. 6]

I am four. It is a summer midafternoon, my nap finished. I cannot find her. I hear the
water in the bathroom. Not from the faucet but occasional splashes. I hear something
like the bar of soap fall in. I cannot find her.

---

[1] Gustave Flaubert (1821-1880), French novelist.

[2] Edward Said (1935-2003), Palestinian-American literary
scholar.

Flaubert's encounter, Flaubert's encounter, Flaubert's encounter—

I stand outside the white door. Reflected in the brass knob I see my face framed by a black pixie-cut. More splashes.

I hear humming. It is mother's voice in the bathroom through the closed door and it is midafternoon. No light from beneath the door. I twist the knob and hang my weight to pull it open. In the half-light I see mother sitting in the bath: the white porcelain, gray, the yellow tiles, gray. Her hair is coiled and pinned up.

I see her breasts above the edge of the tub. I have never seen my mother without her clothes. Her nipples.

"[S]he never spoke of herself, she never represented her emotions, presence, or history. [*Flaubert*] spoke for and represented her." [SAID, 6]

Her nipples appear dark and round. They are funny and beautiful. I leave, perhaps to lie down on my pillow or find my bear. What did she say to me? Did she scold? Laugh? Just smile or ignore me? My breasts have never looked like those breasts.

"He was foreign, comparatively wealthy, male and these were historical facts of domination that allowed him not only to possess Kuchuk Hanem physically but to speak for her and tell his readers in what way she was 'typically Oriental.'" [SAID, 6]

In 1850 a woman with skin the color of sand in the shade of the Sphinx, midday, meant little and of course mine was seen more than veiled and I could earn a living "dancing." What I liked best were gifts of chocolate. Usually from a French man thinking I'd consider the evening amorous and reduce the rate. Paris must be lovely but for the French.

Maybe I want a penis. Maybe that's why I love sitting on an outstretched man and, his prick between my legs, rubbing it as if it were mine. Maybe that's why I love to put a cock in my mouth, feel it increase in size with each stroke, each lick, each pulse. Taste the Red Sea. Look over or up and see the man barely able to contain himself, pulling on my nipples or burying a tongue into my Persian Gulf. Also barely able to contain my own sluice. Maybe it's my way to possess a cock. For a moment feel hegemonic and Western.

I have an addiction to silk and chocolate—gold a little. But coins are a necessity. Now chocolates—if there's a plate of chocolate I cannot stop my hand. I tell the Nubian to take it to the kitchen and store it in a cool place. I will sniff it out. Find her fingerprints on the sweaty sweets.

We both use our mouths, professionally.

> "*My heart begins to pound every time I see [a prostitute] in low-cut dresses walking under the lamplight in the rain, just as monks in their corded robes have always excited some deep ascetic corner of my soul....*"

Maybe it's my way to possess a cock. For a moment feel hegemonic and Western.

> "*The idea of prostitution is a meeting of so many elements—lust, bitterness, complete absence of human contact, muscular frenzy, the clink of gold—that to peer into it deeply*

makes one reel. One learns so many things in a brothel, and feels such sadness, and dreams so longingly of love!" [FLAUBERT, 10]

I watch white couples. See how they touch the clitoris. A cat lapping, a cat pawing. Think about betrayal and loss.

The two girls invited their cousin Conrad in the little pool, to see his small penis wobbling about like a party favor.

Playing with the costume jewelry in her mother's drawers then hiding under her vanity, the bathroom door opened, steam poured out and she saw her father naked from the waist down. Swollen balls. Penis dangling. A raw red.

It's true when all is said and done, I am less a dancer than a whore. Men pay me money, stick their cocks in me, laugh, weep, curse, or silently ride my body. And leave. That's what I am, a whore and alone. To be despised by the men because who else would let them come as they come but someone with vagrant morals. Despised by wives, mistresses, and fiancées for my abilities, independence, the peculiar attention that I receive. I am scorned by the religious. By the courts and by my parents. But I do not fear a man's departure. Know that.

And I have made a name for myself that will, Flaubert boasts on his own behalf, not mine, that will cover the globe. Know that. That the image is not my own. My image does not entirely belong to me. And neither does yours, master or slave.

When he writes about Egypt he will write what he has experienced: the adoration of the historical Cleopatra from boyhood lessons, Kuchuk Hanem—my cunt, my dance—the Nile, the squalor, a man slitting his belly and pulling his intestines in and out then bandaging himself with cotton and oils, people fucking animals which I'm told also happens in France but not in the cities. Because there are no animals.

I knew what he wanted. He wanted to fuck me. He guessed I was 16, his sister's age when he last saw her at Christmas while she knelt at Mass, candles lighting her profile. But I was 13. I wore ankle bracelets from Indian shops. Earrings that jingled in the breeze. And a bikini so small I would never wear it before my father. Why would this Portuguese sailor come over to me and in his broken English point to the tatoo of a geisha as if I would identify with it. And I did a little.

He wanted someone who did not resemble his mother or his friends' sisters or wives. The mistress he had dumped before departure. He wanted license. The kind available not even in one's own imagination—but in geographic departure.

> *"The morning we arrived in Egypt…we had scarcely set foot on shore when Max, the old lecher, got excited over a negress who was drawing water at a fountain. He is just as excited by the little negro boys. By whom is he not excited? Or, rather, by what?"*
> [FLAUBERT, 43]

He will think that I am one thing, even as he learns about me. He will believe those things and make them true even while he remembers my eyes, organs no different from his own. Yet what he witnesses on tour and what I see daily are experienced differently. Does no one bugger animals in France? Does no one martyr himself? It is why he adores prostitutes and monks. Adores.

Mother has removed the dish rack and all the dishes, sponges and cleansers from the kitchen sink. She places an old blue towel to the side and fills the basin a little. With one hand she props up the baby who teethes on the faucet. With the other she swirls soap in little circles all over her head and body then pours water over her. The baby looks surprised and angry. She opens her red mouth and cries. She will smell good, like powder, not pee and sour milk, when she falls asleep on the carpet. Mother will read to me.

The air smells of garlic.

I have become a continent.

He liked to fart under a cover then plunge under to smell the gas.
I laughed but it wasn't really funny. Moreover I do not assume all French relish that activity.

A French man who never traveled here, which is to say, never made my acquaintance, wrote a poem about me, Kuchuk Hanem, based on letters written to him by Flaubert. It made Flaubert's mistress, his former mistress, furious. It amuses but does not please me.

> *"This is a great place for contrasts: splendid things gleam in the dust. I performed on a mat that a family of cats had to be shooed off—a strange coitus, looking at each other without being able to exchange a word, and the exchange of looks is all the deeper for the curiosity and surprise. My brain was too stimulated for me to enjoy it much otherwise. These shaved cunts make a strange effect—the flesh is as hard as bronze, and my girl had a splendid arse."* [FLAUBERT, 44]

I have become a continent. I have become half the globe.

She will read from Grimm's Fairy Tales where the youngest daughter is always the prettiest and the stepmother murderous. Her hands smell of garlic from our dinner.

A hemisphere.

After our last hour outside, riding bikes or the tire swing, my sister and I bathe the mud off then slip between white sheets. 1961. The sheets are always white.

> *"Kuchuk Hanem is a tall, splendid creature, lighter in coloring than an Arab…slightly coffee-colored. When she bends, her flesh ripples into bronze ridges…her black hair, wavy, unruly, pulled straight back on each side from a center parting beginning at the forehead; small braids joined together at the nape of the neck. She has one upper incisor, right, which is beginning to go bad."* [FLAUBERT, 114]

What she wanted was to sit on her mother's lap and be small. Smaller than her mother and smaller than her mother's lap. She wanted not to realize the breadth of separation that arrives with growing up, gradual, never complete: crawling, playing hide-and-seek…sneaking a cigarette…a neon-yellow bikini.

With the other hand she swirls soap around in little circles all over her head and body then pours water over her. The baby looks surprised and angry.

curry stains under mother's cuticles—

> *"She asks us if we would like a little entertainment, but Max says that first he would like to entertain himself alone with her, and they go downstairs. After he finished, I go*

*down and follow his example. Groundfloor room, with a divan and a cafas [basket] with
a mattress."* [FLAUBERT, 115]

The hotel salon made an error and not only trimmed my bangs but curled my hair.
For a ten-year-old this excited and threatened. In a bus I feared people might think I
was with my father, a sexual companion, because I do not resemble him unless you
look closely: short knobby fingers, high bridge, gray rings beneath my eyes. Red high-
lights in my jet hair.

A Chinese American man, manager of a clothing chainstore, was astonished by my
daughter's beauty. He could not take his eyes off her as she increased her antics
around the shop mirrors: rock star, beauty pageant queen, Olympic gymnast. He
could not believe a Eurasian mix could produce such a creature. Blue-eyed like an animal. Against dominant genes.

a hemisphere

The female body as imperialists colony is not a new symbol. Sexual impulse as revolutionary impulse? Do women depend upon the sexual metaphor for identity, an
ironic figure of speech? Will I fall into the trap of writing from the imperialists' point
of view? From a patriarchal one? How can we write erotica and not? What would an
anti-imperialist framework look like? Are not women the original keepers of narrative?
Of lineage?

"For Egypt was not just another colony: it was the vindication of Western imperialism;
it was, until its annexation by England, an almost academic example of Oriental backwardness; it was to become the triumph of English knowledge and power." [SAID, 35]

What does a national liberation movement contain for women? Does liberation
encompass history, expression, memory? Can it nurture?

Can I speak for her? For the Turkish, Nubian, the—brown, black, blacker?

The women were in competition for men. For silk, cosmetics, fresh dates, survival.
Dowries, a pale fantasy.

> *"Kuchuk's dance is brutal. She squeezes her bare breasts together with her jacket. She
> puts on a girdle fashioned from a brown shawl with gold stripes, with three tassels hang-
> ing on ribbons...."* [FLAUBERT, 115]

What is contained in the brutality?

If he had loved her enough, needed her in his bones enough, would he have brought
her home? Could he hurt his mother, his friends, his former lovers, his career? With
a black whore? Even such a famous one?

If you are dependent on prostitutes, write about them, dream about them, masturbate
dreaming about them—can you pretend objectivity? Can you kiss your mother or sister without twitching?

> *"Kuchuk dances the Bee...[shedding] her clothing as she danced. Finally she was naked
> except for a fichu which she held in her hands and behind which she pretended to hide,
> and at the end she threw down the fichu. That was the Bee. She danced it very briefly
> and said she does not like to dance that dance."* [FLAUBERT, 117]

> *"Coup with Safia Zugairah—I stain the divan. She is very corrupt and writhing, extremely voluptuous. But the best was the second copulation with Kuchuk. Effect of her necklace between my teeth. Her cunt felt like rolls of velvet as she made me come."*
> **[FLAUBERT, 117]**

Her name, talents, and shaved cunt have outlived her person. We remember her for the dance and the fuck. For the hemisphere created. But what would she have said? Could the words be translated?

What did she say to Gustave or Max?

The way I wish mother to speak up so I can become a woman.

The way I trespass the boundaries of fiction and non-fiction.

The way nothing is ever verbatim.

> *"We went to bed; she insisted on keeping the outside. Lamp: the wick rested in an oval cup with a lip; after some violent play, coup. She falls asleep with her hand in mine. She snores. The lamp, shining feebly, cast a triangular gleam, the color of pale metal, on her beautiful forehead; the rest of her face was in shadow. Her little dog slept on my silk jacket....I dozed off with my fingers passed through her necklace, as though to hold her should she awake....At quarter of three, we wake—another coup, this time very affectionate....I smoke a sheesheh...."* **[FLAUBERT, 118-9]**

> *"She snores."* **[IBID.]**

What is the context? Who hears and records the material?

If you use a language where the subject comes first, where je comes first, can you even pretend objectivity?

Of course there was no agreement: Flaubert fucked her and wrote about her. His words. His worlds.

She opened her red mouth and cried.

Am I seeking an older sister to care for me: show me how to wax my legs, manicure my nails, henna my hair. Walk in stilettos.

To call me a woman.

To teach children a language not to listen and obey, but to engage in narratives.

Is it the story or the story of the story?

> *"We have not yet seen any dancing girls; they are all in exile in Upper Egypt. Good brothels no longer exist in Cairo, either....But we have seen male dancers."*
> **[FLAUBERT, 83]**

Cannot subvert a category without being engaged.

> *"A week ago I saw a monkey in the street jump on a donkey and try to jack him off—the donkey brayed and kicked....[The secretary at the consulate] told me of having seen an ostrich trying to violate a donkey. Max had himself jacked off the other day in a deserted section among some ruins and said it was very good."* **[FLAUBERT, 85-6]**

Three wars have taught military men "about" Asian women. Orientals. Extended by the classifieds.

> *"We are leading a good life, my dear old darling [Mother]. Oh, how sorry I am that you are not here. How you would love it! If you knew what calm surrounds us, and how peaceful are the depths we feel our minds explore—we laze, we loaf, we daydream…."*
> **[FLAUBERT, 105]**

I hear her pour coffee. Open the refrigerator for milk. Walk without shoes to the living room. To a stack of magazines with cakes on the covers.

I hear her pour two cups of coffee.

I am four. It is summer midafternoon, my nap finished. I cannot find her. I hear the water splash in the bathroom. Not from the faucet but occasional splashes. I hear something like the bar of soap fall in. I cannot find her.

I hear her chopping vegetables.

Girls actually fainted. Dozens fell on the tarmac.

The first time I heard of the Beatles I was in third grade, leaning out the police station window on the second floor after baton-twirling class. Christine Van Pelt leaned out with me and told me the Beatles had landed at Idlewild Airport and girls had fainted. I told her I knew though I didn't. Her family moved when she was ten. I heard from an unreliable source that she quit high school and became a prostitute in Boston. I can picture a young woman's large-boned body, full breasted. Black corset and stockings. Blue eyes. What took her to that room? That first john? Was it in part the way she and Mary Jo Murphey, who lived above her Dad's auto parts garage, taunted me because I cried easily? Or was it the way Christine slipped on my mother's tiny wedding slippers, fitting her eight-year-old foot perfectly?

I remember him not for the sex but for the cool shower we took after 3 am. Holding and twisting each other under the hard spray, laughing at the cold. We powder under the fan before I gently push him to the door. To go home. To his wife. If he has one.

I am so hungry. I consume Said's text.

My questions strike a different facet: what does Desire seek? It must become a radical question.

The men want me, Flaubert wanted me, not for the sex but for the experience…especially the sadness he recovers in departure. He knows he will not return once he leaves Esna for Turkey. But I know he will return (that's why he came in the first place, to never leave) perhaps in the sound of rain, invisible in the night. It may not snow in Esna but I know it rains in Paris.

Or the garlic she sliced.

I never receive enough attention. Never. I am jealous of every person, act, article. Is this my inheritance?

What does Desire desire? To be needed absolutely? To fill the other's life not just as a lover but as a mother-symbiotically? To be left alone?

"I thought of my nights in Paris brothels…." [FLAUBERT, 130]

Or the garlic she sliced.

A black girl from the neighborhood wore a t-shirt inscribed: Jewish girls don't swallow. Later I thought, I don't like to either.

Sam wanted to come in my mouth and, if not swallow, transfer it to his. The idea lovely, the reality less appetizing. A real romantic. The best features of that affair: his Rambler's front seat, his cooking with eggplants, his phone messages, his stories about learning to swim which needed to be written down to overcome his writer's block.

She learned to swim in a mossy lake, the fish bumping her ankles like dust. The algae in her hair. A harmless snake by the beach.

A man outside the Love Pharmacy, longish hair pinned back, picked red nail polish off his finger absent-mindedly.

My mother shopped for a bikini with me and I couldn't believe she approved of a very small yellow one that fastened in the front. I could pass for 15. I felt embarrassed showing the bikini to my father. He taught at the Art Institute that summer. From our hotel room I could see over the Lake—see storm clouds floating toward us, lightning beating inside. The dark rain flicking down sharp as razors. I loved Chicago.

My nap is finished. I hear water in the bathroom. Not from the faucet but from occasional splashes. I hear something like the bar of soap fall in. I am four.

My sister and I go to the beach by ourselves. I brought a transistor to connect myself to the rest of the world. One afternoon as I lay on my towel a wiry tanned man in a small aqua bathing suit walked over and asked to sit beside me. He did not speak much English but conveyed that he was a sailor from Portugal. Swarthy. In hindsight probably mid-20s. By way of conversation he pointed to a large tattoo on his arm; an intricately designed geisha after Utamaro. He smiled as if somehow I identified with this. I did a little. He asked if I'd like to board his ship.

In Chicago my knowledge of sex increased rapidly: the call asking if I'd like to model for *Seventeen*…what color my hair, eyes…nipples? pink or brown?…did I know what oral sex was? what? I told the man I couldn't say because my parents were in the room. My father grabbed the phone. I felt like vomiting.

The evening my sister and I ate at Taco Villas' I forgot the money and ran back to the hotel. Around the corner I ran past a man rubbing his protruding cock. Another time a man sitting on a bus, his cock sticking out of his shorts, covered and exposed it with his hat. Pitiful belongings.

Chateaubriand inscribed his name on the Pyramids. [SAID, 175]

The two little girls hold a truce as they abandon Barbies and climb into the tub, giggling as the water rises from their body weight. They hug. They sit on each other's laps. They lay across each other's soapy bodies, gray bubbles ringing the porcelain. Reveal to the other her "penis."

Two cups of coffee.

Even after washing my hands for dinner, after rinsing the dishes—

She could not wash off her patrons but she could wash off their sweat, saliva, cum. The ring of dirt around her neck. The kohl they loved to smear as if blackening her eye. Pour a cup of coffee. Sometimes she felt scattered. Sometimes collected. She wished she could visit her sister.

What would Kuchuk Hanem say if I were to sit beside her in the predawn, tobacco wafting into our hair like the memory of my first husband studying for exams. The fragrance of a coffee as rich as the mud from the Nile that must flood the fields to award farmers a relatively easy season, or predict irrigating with buckets haled from the same, circa 1840. The thick silt coating the land, the throat, the tongue. Sheer caffeine heightening the blue tiles as we turn towards one another. Would she have offered to put on her veil and go out herself to the market for figs or ask her slave to fetch some.

If you are forbidden to dance it's all you want. You might make love instead, you might eat— but it's all to dance. And it's a dance that makes the travelers open their eyes as one does in climax or terror, taste the sea fill the mouth till he swallows it back, and the heart's wings beat bloody, a bird caged in the market, though our Koran prescribes a proper slaughter.

Would she offer me figs and ask me to stay or tell me to get the hell out, what's a married woman doing here—curious? You want lessons? You want me? You looking for someone? It must mean something that our hearts are cut by men like a dress pattern, but sewn by women.

Show me your clitoris.

Do I seek an older sister?

I cannot find her. I hear the water in the bathroom. Occasional splashes. I hear something like the bar of soap fall in.

I hear her chopping vegetables.

They did not know, or maybe could not desecrate "mother's" tit, did not know nipples can glow like the clitoris.

Who is the cartographer? Male or female?

Under what circumstances does a person have choice? Under what circumstances does a woman?

"When it was time to leave I didn't leave…I sucked her furiously—her body was covered with sweat—she was tired after dancing—she was cold…"

The light in Egypt reminded her of the moon—black shade and white sunlight.

"I covered her with my pelisse, and she fell asleep with her fingers in mine. As for me, I scarcely shut my eyes. Watching that beautiful creature asleep (she snored, her head against my arm: I had slipped my forefinger under her necklace), my night was one long, infinitely intense reverie—that was why I stayed. I thought of my nights…."

She "looked like" a lesbian only because she conveyed a sense of not putting up with shit.

> *"...in Paris brothels—a whole series of memories came back—and I thought of her, of her dance, of her voice as she sang songs that for me were without meaning and even without distinguishable words."* [FLAUBERT, 130]

The need to belong overwhelms—to hold my own sister, hold her hand or link arms. Rest a cheek against her neck. To feel in my daughter, my sister. To feel in my mother, my sister. To feel in my sister, my self.

"You know you want it and it's big"…"Sit on my face, China"…"Nice titties"…"Do you want me to teach you some English?"…"Are you from Saigon?"

What is my stake in this?

Woman's role as storyteller included creator and healer. My mother knew this, unconsciously.

After I cook garlic, chop it, dice it, sliver it up, spread it over the crackling oil, I can smell it on my fingers even after I have washed my hands for dinner. Even while I am eating the pasta. Even after eating chocolates.

> *"[Dear Louise,] The oriental woman is no more than a machine: she makes no distinction between one man and another man. Smoking, going to the baths, painting her eyelids and drinking coffee—such is the circle of occupations within which...."*

Even after having washed the children. Even after drinking coffee and throwing out the grounds. Even after cutting my finger on the dog food can. Sucking it. Bandaging my finger. Showering outdoors in the twilight.

> *"...within which her existence is confined. As for physical pleasure, it must be very slight, since the well known button, the seat of same, is sliced off at an early age...."*

Even after television and a bowl of popcorn. After washing the dishes in hot sudsy water. After reading Said's *Orientalism*. After touching every crease and crevice of my husband's body.

> *"...is sliced off at an early age....You tell me that Kuchuk's bedbugs degrade her in your eyes; for me they were the most enchanting touch of all. Their nauseating odor mingled with the scent of her skin which was dripping with sandalwood oil...."* [FLAUBERT, 220]

Even after drifting into sleep my fingers smell of the garlic I sliced for dinner.

> *"[Dear Louis,] At Esna I saw Kuchuk Hanem again; it was sad. I found her changed. She had been sick. I shot my bolt with her only once."* [FLAUBERT, 200]

Even after drifting into sleep my fingers smell of the garlic I sliced for dinner. I am hungry when I wake to the baby's cries at 2 am. My breasts are leaking as well. The milk may also taste of garlic. I drink a glass of water.

I hear a starling stuck in the chimney.

Father sets up a pink and blue folding bassinet, a tube running in to the bathtub.

Mother places my sister into the tepid water. Uses a square, white soap.

We powder by the window before I gently push him to the door. To go home under the stars that vanish if you stare for very long.

No light from beneath the door.

My bad tooth aches.

My mother might have told me this story but she died suddenly a few months ago.

—1995

GISH JEN (1955-)

A second-generation Chinese American born in Scarsdale, New York, Gish Jen often writes about her experiences growing up there. Her second novel, *Mona in the Promised Land* (1996), garnered attention for its adolescent Chinese-American heroine who decides to convert to Judaism. The tone of this novel, like that of Jen's first novel, *Typical American* (1991), was considered unique in its wryly humorous take on ethnically-inflected identities and relationships. Jen's other books include *Who's Irish?* (1999) and *The Love Wife* (2004). Her work has appeared in *The New Yorker, The New Republic,* and *The New York Times,* as well as in a variety of anthologies, including *The Best American Short Stories of the Century* (2000), edited by John Updike. She has received a Lannan Literary Award as well as grants from the Guggenheim Foundation, the Bunting Institute, and the National Endowment for the Arts. Jen, whose first name is Lillian, chose the pen name "Gish" after the silent-screen actress Lillian Gish. She has a degree in English from Harvard University and lives with her family in Cambridge, Massachusetts.

Who's Irish?

In China, people say mixed children are supposed to be smart, and definitely my granddaughter Sophie is smart. But Sophie is wild, Sophie is not like my daughter Natalie, or like me. I am work hard my whole life, and fierce besides. My husband always used to say he is afraid of me, and in our restaurant, busboys and cooks all afraid of me too. Even the gang members come for protection money, they try to talk to my husband. When I am there, they stay away. If they come by mistake, they pretend they are come to eat. They hide behind the menu, they order a lot of food. They talk about their mothers. Oh, my mother have some arthritis, need to take herbal medicine, they say. Oh, my mother getting old, her hair all white now.

I say, Your mother's hair used to be white, but since she dye it, it become black again. Why don't you go home once in a while and take a look? I tell them, Confucius say a filial son knows what color his mother's hair is.

My daughter is fierce too, she is vice president in the bank now. Her new house is big enough for everybody to have their own room, including me. But Sophie take after Natalie's husband's family, their name is Shea. Irish. I always thought Irish people are like Chinese people, work so hard on the railroad, but now I know why the Chinese beat the Irish. Of course, not all Irish are like the Shea family, of course not. My daughter tell me I should not say Irish this, Irish that.

How do you like it when people say the Chinese this, the Chinese that, she say.

You know, the British call the Irish heathen, just like they call the Chinese, she say.

You think the Opium War was bad, how would you like to live right next door to the British, she say.

And that is that. My daughter have a funny habit when she win an argument, she take a sip of something and look away, so the other person is not embarrassed. So I am not embarrassed. I do not call anybody anything either. I just happen to mention about the Shea family, an interesting fact: four brothers in the family, and not one of them work. The mother, Bess, have a job before she got sick, she was executive secretary in a big company. She is handle everything for a big shot, you would be surprised how complicated her job is, not just type this, type that. Now she is a nice woman with a clean house. But her boys, every one of them is on welfare, or so-called severance pay, or so-called disability pay. Something. They say they cannot find work, this is not the economy of the fifties, but I say, Even the black people doing better these days, some of them live so fancy, you'd be surprised. Why the Shea family have so much trouble? They are white people, they speak English. When I come to this country, I have no money and do not speak English. But my husband and I own our restaurant before he die. Free and clear, no mortgage. Of course, I understand I am just lucky, come from a country where the food is popular all over the world. I understand it is not the Shea family's fault they come from a country where everything is boiled. Still, I say.

She's right, we should broaden our horizons, say one brother, Jim, at Thanksgiving. Forget about the car business. Think about egg rolls.

Pad thai, say another brother, Mike. I'm going to make my fortune in pad thai. It's going to be the new pizza.

I say, You people too picky about what you sell. Selling egg rolls not good enough for you, but at least my husband and I can say, We made it. What can you say? Tell me. What can you say?

Everybody chew their tough turkey.

I especially cannot understand my daughter's husband John, who has no job but cannot take care of Sophie either. Because he is a man, he say, and that's the end of the sentence.

Plain boiled food, plain boiled thinking. Even his name is plain boiled: John. Maybe because I grew up with black bean sauce and hoisin sauce and garlic sauce, I always feel something is missing when my son-in-law talk.

But, okay: so my son-in-law can be man, I am baby-sitter. Six hours a day, same as the old sitter, crazy Amy, who quit. This is not so easy, now that I am sixty-eight, Chinese age almost seventy. Still, I try. In China, daughter take care of mother. Here it is the other way around. Mother help daughter, mother ask, Anything else I can do? Otherwise daughter complain mother is not supportive. I tell daughter, We do not have this word in Chinese, *supportive*. But my daughter too busy to listen, she has to go to meeting, she has to write memo while her husband go to the gym to be a man. My daughter say otherwise he will be depressed. Seems like all his life he has this trouble, depression.

No one wants to hire someone who is depressed, she say. It is important for him to keep his spirits up.

Beautiful wife, beautiful daughter, beautiful house, oven can clean itself automatically. No money left over, because only one income, but lucky enough, got the baby-sitter for free. If John lived in China, he would be very happy. But he is not happy. Even at the gym things go wrong. One day, he pull a muscle. Another day, weight room too crowded. Always something.

Until finally, hooray, he has a job. Then he feel pressure.

I need to concentrate, he say. I need to focus.

He is going to work for insurance company. Salesman job. A paycheck, he say, and at least he will wear clothes instead of gym shorts. My daughter buy him some special candy bars from the health-food store. They say THINK! on them, and are supposed to help John think.

John is a good-looking boy, you have to say that, especially now that he shave so you can see his face.

I am an old man in a young man's game, say John.

I will need a new suit, say John.

This time I am not going to shoot myself in the foot, say John.

Good, I say.

She means to be supportive, my daughter say. Don't start the send her back to China thing, because we can't.

✦ ✦ ✦

Sophie is three years old American age, but already I see her nice Chinese side swallowed up by her wild Shea side. She looks like mostly Chinese. Beautiful black hair, beautiful black eyes. Nose perfect size, not so flat looks like something fell down, not so large looks like some big deal got stuck in wrong face. Everything just right, only her skin is a brown surprise to John's family. So brown, they say. Even John say it. She never goes in the sun, still she is that color, he say. Brown. They say, Nothing the matter with brown. They are just surprised. So brown. Nattie is not that brown, they say. They say, It seems like Sophie should be a color in between Nattie and John. Seems funny, a girl named Sophie Shea be brown. But she is brown, maybe her name should be Sophie Brown. She never go in the sun, still she is that color, they say. Nothing the matter with brown. They are just surprised.

The Shea family talk is like this sometimes, going around and around like a Christmas-tree train.

Maybe John is not her father, I say one day, to stop the train. And sure enough, train wreck. None of the brothers ever say the word *brown* to me again.

Instead, John's mother, Bess, say, I hope you are not offended.

She say, I did my best on those boys. But raising four boys with no father is no picnic.

You have a beautiful family, I say.

I'm getting old, she say.

You deserve a rest, I say. Too many boys make you old.

I never had a daughter, she say. You have a daughter.

I have a daughter, I say. Chinese people don't think a daughter is so great, but you're right. I have a daughter.

I was never against the marriage, you know, she say. I never thought John was marrying down. I always thought Nattie was just as good as white.

I was never against the marriage either, I say. I just wonder if they look at the whole problem.

Of course you pointed out the problem, you are a mother, she say. And now we both have a granddaughter. A little brown granddaughter, she is so precious to me.

I laugh. A little brown granddaughter, I say. To tell you the truth, I don't know how she came out so brown.

We laugh some more. These days Bess need a walker to walk. She take so many pills, she need two glasses of water to get them all down. Her favorite TV show is about bloopers, and she love her bird feeder. All day long, she can watch that bird feeder, like a cat.

I can't wait for her to grow up, Bess say. I could use some female company.

Too many boys, I say.

Boys are fine, she say. But they do surround you after a while.

You should take a break, come live with us, I say. Lots of girls at our house.

Be careful what you offer, say Bess with a wink. Where I come from, people mean for you to move in when they say a thing like that.

✦ ✦ ✦

Nothing the matter with Sophie's outside, that's the truth. It is inside that she is like not any Chinese girl I ever see. We go to the park, and this is what she does. She stand up in the stroller. She take off her all her clothes and throw them in the fountain.

Sophie! I say. Stop!

But she just laugh like a crazy person. Before I take over as baby-sitter, Sophie has that crazy-person sitter, Amy the guitar player. My daughter thought this Amy very creative—another word we do not talk about in China. In China, we talk about whether we have difficulty or no difficulty. We talk about whether life is bitter or not bitter. In America, all day long, people talk about creative. Never mind that I cannot even look at this Amy, with her shirt so short that her belly button showing. This Amy think Sophie should love her body. So when Sophie take off her diaper, Amy laugh. When Sophie run around naked, Amy say she wouldn't want to wear a diaper either. When Sophie go *shu-shu* in her lap, Amy laugh and say there are no germs in pee. When Sophie take off her shoes, Amy say bare feet is best, even the pediatrician say so. That is why Sophie now walk around with no shoes like a beggar child. Also why Sophie love to take off her clothes.

Turn around! say the boys in the park. Let's see that ass!

Of course, Sophie does not understand. Sophie clap her hands, I am the only one to say, No! This is not a game.

It has nothing to do with John's family, my daughter say. Amy was too permissive, that's all.

But I think if Sophie was not wild inside, she would not take off her shoes and clothes to begin with.

You never take off your clothes when you were little, I say. All my Chinese friends had babies, I never saw one of them act wild like that.

Look, my daughter say. I have a big presentation tomorrow.

John and my daughter agree Sophie is a problem, but they don't know what to do.

You spank her, she'll stop, I say another day.

But they say, Oh no.

In America, parents not supposed to spank the child.

It gives them low self-esteem, my daughter say. And that leads to problems later, as I happen to know.

My daughter never have big presentation the next day when the subject of spanking come up.

I don't want you to touch Sophie, she say. No spanking, period.

Don't tell me what to do, I say.

I'm not telling you what to do, say my daughter. I'm telling you how I feel.

I am not your servant, I say. Don't you dare talk to me like that.

My daughter have another funny habit when she lose an argument. She spread out all her fingers and look at them, as if she like to make sure they are still there.

My daughter is fierce like me, but she and John think it is better to explain to Sophie that clothes are a good idea. This is not so hard in the cold weather. In the warm weather, it is very hard.

Use your words, my daughter say. That's what we tell Sophie. How about if you set a good example.

As if good example mean anything to Sophie. I am so fierce, the gang members who used to come to the restaurant all afraid of me, but Sophie is not afraid.

I say, Sophie, if you take off your clothes, no snack.

I say, Sophie, if you take off your clothes, no lunch.

I say, Sophie, if you take off your clothes, no park.

Pretty soon we are stay home all day, and by the end of six hours she still did not have one thing to eat. You never saw a child stubborn like that.

I'm hungry! she cry when my daughter come home.

What's the matter, doesn't your grandmother feed you? My daughter laugh.

No! Sophie say. She doesn't feed me anything!

My daughter laugh again. Here you go, she say.

She say to John, Sophie must be growing.

Growing like a weed, I say.

Still Sophie take off her clothes, until one day I spank her. Not too hard, but she cry and cry, and when I tell her if she doesn't put her clothes back on I'll spank her again, she put her clothes back on. Then I tell her she is good girl, and give her some food to eat. The next day we go to the park and, like a nice Chinese girl, she does not take off her clothes.

She stop taking off her clothes, I report. Finally!

How did you do it? my daughter ask.

After twenty-eight years experience with you, I guess I learn something, I say.

It must have been a phase, John say, and his voice is suddenly like an expert.

His voice is like an expert about everything these days, now that he carry a leather briefcase, and wear shiny shoes, and can go shopping for a new car. On the company, he say. The company will pay for it, but he will be able to drive it whenever he want.

A free car, he say. How do you like that.

It's good to see you in the saddle again, my daughter say. Some of your family patterns are scary.

At least I don't drink, he say. He say, And I'm not the only one with scary family patterns.

That's for sure, say my daughter.

✦ ✦ ✦

Everyone is happy. Even I am happy, because there is more trouble with Sophie, but now I think I can help her Chinese side fight against her wild side. I teach her to eat food with fork or spoon or chopsticks, she cannot just grab into the middle of a bowl of noodles. I teach her not to play with garbage cans. Sometimes I spank her, but not too often, and not too hard.

Still, there are problems. Sophie like to climb everything. If there is a railing, she is never next to it. Always she is on top of it. Also, Sophie like to hit the mommies of her friends. She learn this from her playground best friend, Sinbad, who is four. Sinbad wear army clothes every day and like to ambush his mommy. He is the one who dug a big hole under the play structure, a foxhole he call it, all by himself. Very hardworking. Now he wait in the foxhole with a shovel full of wet sand. When his mommy come, he throw it right at her.

Oh, it's all right, his mommy say. You can't get rid of war games, it's part of their imaginative play. All the boys go through it.

Also, he like to kick his mommy, and one day he tell Sophie to kick his mommy too.

I wish this story is not true.

Kick her, kick her! Sinbad say.

Sophie kick her. A little kick, as if she just so happened was swinging her little leg and didn't realize that big mommy leg was in the way. Still I spank Sophie and make Sophie say sorry, and what does the mommy say?

Really, it's all right, she say. It didn't hurt.

After that, Sophie learn she can attack mommies in the playground, and some will say, Stop, but others will say, Oh, she didn't mean it, especially if they realize Sophie will be punished.

✦ ✦ ✦

This is how, one day, bigger trouble come. The bigger trouble start when Sophie hide in the foxhole with that shovel full of sand. She wait, and when I come look for her, she throw it at me. All over my nice clean clothes.

Did you ever see a Chinese girl act this way?

Sophie! I say. Come out of there, say you're sorry.

But she does not come out. Instead, she laugh. Naaah, naah-na, naaa-naaa, she say.

I am not exaggerate: millions of children in China, not one act like this.

Sophie! I say. Now! Come out now!

But she know she is in big trouble. She know if she come out, what will happen next. So she does not come out. I am sixty-eight, Chinese age almost seventy, how can I crawl under there to catch her? Impossible. So I yell, yell, yell, and what happen? Nothing. A Chinese mother would help, but American mothers, they look at you, they shake their head, they go home. And, of course, a Chinese child would give up, but not Sophie.

I hate you! she yell. I hate you, Meanie!

Meanie is my new name these days.

Long time this goes on, long long time. The foxhole is deep, you cannot see too much, you don't know where is the bottom. You cannot hear too much either. If she does not yell, you cannot even know she is still there or not. After a while, getting cold out, getting dark out. No one left in the playground, only us.

Sophie, I say. How did you become stubborn like this? I am go home without you now.

I try to use a stick, chase her out of there, and once or twice I hit her, but still she does not come out. So finally I leave. I go outside the gate.

Bye-bye! I say. I'm go home now.

But still she does not come out and does not come out. Now it is dinnertime, the sky is black. I think I should maybe go get help, but how can I leave a little girl by herself in the playground? A bad man could come. A rat could come. I go back in to see what is happen to Sophie. What if she have a shovel and is making a tunnel to escape?

Sophie! I say.

No answer.

Sophie!

I don't know if she is alive. I don't know if she is fall asleep down there. If she is crying, I cannot hear her.

So I take the stick and poke.

Sophie! I say. I promise I no hit you. If you come out, I give you a lollipop.

No answer. By now I worried. What to do, what to do, what to do? I poke some more, even harder, so that I am poking and poking when my daughter and John suddenly appear.

What are you doing? What is going on? say my daughter.

Put down that stick! say my daughter.

You are crazy! say my daughter.

John wiggle under the structure, into the foxhole, to rescue Sophie.

She fell asleep, say John the expert. She's okay. That is one big hole.

Now Sophie is crying and crying.

Sophia, my daughter say, hugging her. Are you okay, peanut? Are you okay?

She's just scared, say John.

Are you okay? I say too. I don't know what happen, I say.

She's okay, say John. He is not like my daughter, full of questions. He is full of answers until we get home and can see by the lamplight.

Will you look at her? he yell then. What the hell happened?

Bruises all over her brown skin, and a swollen-up eye.

You are crazy! say my daughter. Look at what you did! You are crazy!

I try very hard, I say.

How could you use a stick? I told you to use your words!

She is hard to handle, I say.

She's three years old! You cannot use a stick! say my daughter.

She is not like any Chinese girl I ever saw, I say.

I brush some sand off my clothes. Sophie's clothes are dirty too, but at least she has her clothes on.

Has she done this before? ask my daughter. Has she hit you before?

She hits me all the time, Sophie say, eating ice cream.

Your family, say John.

Believe me, say my daughter.

✦ ✦ ✦

A daughter I have, a beautiful daughter. I took care of her when she could not hold her head up. I took care of her before she could argue with me, when she was a little girl with two pigtails, one of them always crooked. I took care of her when we have to escape from China, I took care of her when suddenly we live in a country with cars everywhere, if you are not careful your little girl get run over. When my husband die, I promise him I will keep the family together, even though it was just two of us, hardly a family at all.

But now my daughter take me around to look at apartments. After all, I can cook, I can clean, there's no reason I cannot live by myself, all I need is a telephone. Of course, she is sorry. Sometimes she cry, I am the one to say everything will be okay. She say she have no choice, she doesn't want to end up divorced. I say divorce is terrible, I don't know who invented this terrible idea. Instead of live with a telephone, though, surprise, I come to live with Bess. Imagine that. Bess make an offer and, sure enough, where she come from, people mean for you to move in when they say things like that. A crazy idea, go to live with someone else's family, but she like to have some female company, not like my daughter, who does not believe in company. These days when my daughter visit, she does not bring Sophie. Bess say we should give Nattie time, we will see Sophie again soon. But seems like my daughter have more presentation than ever before, every time she come she have to leave.

I have a family to support, she say, and her voice is heavy, as if soaking wet. I have a young daughter and a depressed husband and no one to turn to.

When she say no one to turn to, she mean me.

These days my beautiful daughter is so tired she can just sit there in a chair and fall asleep. John lost his job again, already, but still they rather hire a baby-sitter than ask me to help, even they can't afford it. Of course, the new baby-sitter is much younger, can run around. I don't know if Sophie these days is wild or not wild. She call me Meanie, but she like to kiss me too, sometimes. I remember that every time I see a child on TV. Sophie like to grab my hair, a fistful in each hand, and then kiss me smack on the nose. I never see any other child kiss that way.

The satellite TV has so many channels, more channels than I can count, including a Chinese channel from the Mainland and a Chinese channel from Taiwan, but most of the time I watch bloopers with Bess. Also, I watch the bird feeder—so many, many kinds of birds come. The Shea sons hang around all the time, asking when will I go home, but Bess tell them, Get lost.

She's a permanent resident, say Bess. She isn't going anywhere.

Then she wink at me, and switch the channel with the remote control.

Of course, I shouldn't say Irish this, Irish that, especially now I am become honorary Irish myself, according to Bess. Me! Who's Irish? I say, and she laugh. All the same, if I could mention one thing about some of the Irish, not all of them of course, I like to mention this: Their talk just stick. I don't know how Bess Shea learn to use her words, but sometimes I hear what she say a long time later. *Permanent resident. Not going anywhere.* Over and over I hear it, the voice of Bess.

—1998

BARBARA KINGSOLVER (1955-)

Barbara Kingsolver was born in Annapolis, Maryland, where her father was serving as a physician in the U.S. Navy. Both of Kingsolver's parents grew up in Lexington, Kentucky, and had degrees from the University of Kentucky; she was raised in Carlisle, in the eastern part of the state. Kingsolver's father practiced medicine in Africa and the Caribbean in the 1960s, and took the family with him to St. Lucia in 1967. In 1977, Kingsolver graduated from De Pauw University and moved to Tucson to study in the Department of Ecology and Evolutionary Biology at the University of Arizona, where she received an M.S. in Animal Behavior in 1981. Kingsolver's writing, which began with journalism and scientific writing, includes short fiction, novels, nonfiction, essays, and memoir, while her social justice work addresses human rights and environmental issues. Her first novel, *The Bean Trees* (1988), was written during a bout of insomnia during her first pregnancy. It was followed by a nonfiction work, *Holding the Line: Women in the Great Arizona Mine Strike of 1983* (1989), and a collection of short fiction, *Homeland and Other Stories* (1989). Kingsolver's other novels include *Animal Dreams* (1990), *Pigs in Heaven* (1993), *The Poisonwood Bible* (1998), and *Prodigal Summer* (2000). Kingsolver has also published two collections of essays, *High Tide in Tucson* (1995) and *Small Wonder* (2002), as well as the narrative of a year spent eating solely local or self-produced food, *Animal, Vegetable, Miracle* (2007). In 1997, Kingsolver established the Bellwether Prize to honor outstanding literary works of social responsibility. She was awarded National Humanities Medal in 2000.

Why I Am a Danger to the Public

Bueno,[1] if I get backed into a corner I can just about raise up the dead. I'll fight, sure. But I am no lady wrestler. If you could see me you would know this thing is a *joke*— Tony, my oldest, is already taller than me, and he's only eleven. So why are they so scared of me I have to be in jail? I'll tell you.

Number one, this strike. There has never been one that turned so many old friends *chingándose,*[2] not here in Bolton. And you can't get away from it because Ellington don't just run the mine, they own our houses, the water we drink and the dirt in our shoes and pretty much the state of New Mexico as I understand it. So if something is breathing, it's on one side or the other. And in a town like this that matters because everybody you know some way, you go to the same church or they used to babysit your kids, something. Nobody is a stranger.

My sister went down to Las Cruces New Mexico and got a job down there, but me, no. I stayed here and got married to Junior Morales. Junior was my one big mistake. But I like Bolton. From far away Bolton looks like some kind of all-colored junk that got swept up off the street after a big old party and stuffed down in the canyon. Our houses are all exactly alike, company houses, but people paint them yellow, purple, colors you wouldn't think a house could be. If you go down to the Big Dipper and come walking home *loca*[3] you still know which one is yours. The copper mine is at the top of the canyon and the streets run straight uphill; some of them you can't drive up, you got to walk. There's steps. Oliver P. Snapp, that used to be the mailman for the west side, died of a heart attack one time right out there in his blue shorts. So the new

---

[1] (Sp.) Good.
[2] (Sp.) Fucking each other over.
[3] (Sp.) Crazy.

mailman refuses to deliver to those houses; they have to pick up their mail at the P.O.

Now, this business with me and Vonda Fangham, I can't even tell you what got it started. I never had one thing in the world against her, no more than anybody else did. But this was around the fourth or fifth week so everybody knew by then who was striking and who was crossing. It don't take long to tell rats from cheese, and every night there was a big old fight in the Big Dipper. Somebody punching out his brother or his best friend. All that and no paycheck, can you imagine?

So it was a Saturday and there was just me and Corvallis Smith up at the picket line, setting in front of the picket shack passing the time of day. Corvallis is *un tipo*,[4] he is real tall and lifts weights and wears his hair in those corn rows that hang down in the back with little pieces of aluminum foil on the ends. But good-looking in a certain way. I went out with Corvallis one time just so people would have something to talk about, and sure enough, they had me getting ready to have brown and black polka-dotted babies. All you got to do to get pregnant around here is have two beers with somebody in the Dipper, so watch out.

"What do you hear from Junior," he says. That's a joke; everybody says it including my friends. See, when Manuela wasn't hardly even born one minute and Tony still in diapers, Junior says, "Vicki, I can't find a corner to piss in around this town." He said there was jobs in Tucson and he would send a whole lot of money. Ha ha. That's how I got started up at Ellington. I was not going to support my kids in no little short skirt down at the Frosty King. That was eight years ago. I got started on the track gang, laying down rails for the cars that go into the pit, and now I am a crane operator. See, when Junior left I went up the hill and made such a rackus they had to hire me up there, hire me or shoot me, one.

"Oh, I hear from him about the same as I hear from Oliver P. Snapp," I say to Corvallis. That's the rest of the joke.

It was a real slow morning. Cecil Smoot was supposed to be on the picket shift with us but he wasn't there yet. Cecil will show up late when the Angel Gabriel calls the Judgment, saying he had to give his Datsun a lube job.

"Well, looka here," says Corvallis. "Here come the ladies." There is this club called Wives of Working Men, just started since the strike. Meaning Wives of Scabs. About six of them was coming up the hill all cram-packed into Vonda Fangham's daddy's air-condition Lincoln. She pulls the car right up next to where mine is at. My car is a Buick older than both my two kids put together. It gets me where I have to go.

They set and look at us for one or two minutes. Out in that hot sun, sticking to our T-shirts, and me in my work boots—I can't see no point in treating it like a damn tea party—and Corvallis, he's an eyeful anyway. All of a sudden the windows on the Lincoln all slide down. It has those electric windows.

"Isn't this a ni-i-ice day," says one of them, Doreen Carter. Doreen visited her sister in Laurel, Mississippi, for three weeks one time and now she has an accent. "Bein' pay-day an' all," she says. Her husband is the minister of Saint's Grace, which is scab headquarters. I quit going. I was raised up to believe in God and the union, but listen, if it comes to pushing or shoving I know which one of the two is going to keep tires on the car.

"Well, yes, it is a real nice day," another one of them says. They're all fanning theirselves with something paper. I look, and Corvallis looks. They're fanning their-selves with their husbands' paychecks.

I haven't had a paycheck since July. My son couldn't go to Morse with his baseball team Friday night because they had to have three dollars for supper at McDonald's. Three damn dollars.

The windows start to go back up and they're getting ready to drive off, and I say, "Vonda Fangham, *vete al infierno.*" [5]

The windows whoosh back down.

"What did you say?" Vonda wants to know.

"I said, I'm surprised to see you in there with the scab ladies. I didn't know you had went and got married to a yellow-spine scab just so somebody would let you in their club."

Well, Corvallis laughs at that. But Vonda just gives me this look. She has a little sharp nose and yellow hair and teeth too big to fit behind her lips. For some reason she was a big deal in high school, and it's not her personality either. She was the queen of everything. Cheerleaders, drama club, every school play they ever had, I think.

I stare at her right back, ready to make a day out of it if I have to. The heat is ris-ing up off that big blue hood like it's a lake all set to boil over.

"What I said was, Vonda Fangham, you can go to hell."

"I can't hear a word you're saying," she says. "Trash can't talk."

"This trash can go to bed at night and know I haven't cheated nobody out of a liv-ing. You want to see trash, *chica,*[6] you ought to come up here at the shift change and see what kind of shit rolls over that picket line."

Well, that shit I was talking about was their husbands, so up go the windows and off they fly. Vonda just about goes in the ditch trying to get that big car turned around.

To tell you the truth I knew Vonda was engaged to get married to Tommy Jones, a scab. People said, Well, at least now Vonda will be just Vonda Jones. That name Fangham is *feo,*[7] and the family has this whole certain way of showing off. Her dad's store, Fangham Drugs, has the biggest sign in town, as if he has to advertise. As if somebody would forget it was there and drive fifty-one miles over the mountains to Morse to go to another drugstore.

I couldn't care less about Tommy and Vonda getting engaged, I was just hurt when he crossed the line. Tommy was a real good man, I used to think. He was not ashamed like most good-looking guys are to act decent every once in a while. Me and him started out on the same track crew and he saved my butt one time covering the extra weight for me when I sprang my wrist. And he never acted like I owed him for it. Some guys, they would try to put the moves on me out by the slag pile. Shit, that was hell. And then I would be downtown in the drugstore and Carol Finch or somebody would go *huh-hmm,* clear her throat and roll her eyes, like, "Over here is what you want," looking at the condoms. Just because I'm up there with their husbands all day I am supposed to be screwing around. In all that mud, just think about it, in our steel toe boots that weigh around ten pounds, and our hard hats. And then the guys gave me shit too when I started training as a crane operator, saying a woman don't have no business taking up the good-paying jobs. You figure it out.

---

[5] (Sp.) Go to hell.
[6] (Sp.) Girl.

[7] (Sp.) Ugly.

Tommy was different. He was a lone ranger. He didn't grow up here or have family, and in Bolton you can move in here and live for about fifty years and people still call you that fellow from El Paso, or wherever it was you come from. They say that's why he went in, that he was afraid if he lost his job he would lose Vonda too. But we all had something to lose.

✦ ✦ ✦

That same day I come home and found Manuela and Tony in the closet. Like poor little kitties in there setting on the shoes. Tony was okay pretty much but Manuela was crying, screaming. I thought she would dig her eyes out.

Tony kept going, "They was up here looking for you!"

"Who was?" I asked him.

"Scab men," he said. "Clifford Owens and Mr. Alphonso and them police from out of town. The ones with the guns."

"The State Police?" I said. I couldn't believe it. "The State Police was up here? What did they want?"

"They wanted to know where you was at." Tony almost started to cry. "Mama, I didn't tell them."

"He didn't," Manuela said.

"Well, I was just up at the damn picket shack. Anybody could have found me if they wanted to." I could have swore I saw Owens's car go right by the picket shack, anyway.

"They kept on saying where was you at, and we didn't tell them. We said you hadn't done nothing."

"Well, you're right, I haven't done nothing. Why didn't you go over to Uncle Manny's? He's supposed to be watching you guys."

"We was scared to go outside!" Manuela screamed. She was jumping from one foot to the other and hugging herself. "They said they'd get us!"

"Tony, did they say that? Did they threaten you?"

"They said stay away from the picket rallies," Tony said. "The one with the gun said he seen us and took all our pitchers. He said, your mama's got too big a mouth for her own good."

At the last picket rally I was up on Lalo Ruiz's shoulders with a bull horn. I've had almost every office in my local, and sergeant-at-arms twice because the guys say I have no toleration for BS. They got one of those big old trophies down at the union hall that says on it "MEN OF COPPER," and one time Lalo says, "Vicki ain't no Man of Copper, she's a damn stick of *mesquite*. She might break but she sure as hell won't bend."

Well, I want my kids to know what this is about. When school starts, if some kid makes fun of their last-year's blue jeans and calls them trash I want them to hold their heads up. I take them to picket rallies so they'll know that. No law says you can't set up on nobody with a bull horn. They might have took my picture, though. I wouldn't be surprised.

"All I ever done was defend my union," I told the kids. "Even cops have to follow the laws, and it isn't no crime to defend your union. Your grandpapa done it and his papa and now me."

Well, my grandpapa one time got put on a railroad car like a cow, for being a

Wobbly[8] and a Mexican. My kids have heard that story a million times. He got dumped out in the desert someplace with no water or even a cloth for his head, and it took him two months to get back. All that time my granny and Tía Sonia thought he was dead.

I hugged Tony and Manuela and then we went and locked the door. I had to pull up on it while they jimmied the latch because that damn door had not been locked one time in seven years.

+ + +

What we thought about when we wanted to feel better was: What a God-awful mess they got up there in the mine. Most of those scabs was out-of-towners and didn't have no idea what end of the gun to shoot. I heard it took them about one month to figure out how to start the equipment. Before the walkout there was some parts switched around between my crane and a locomotive, but we didn't have to do that because the scabs tied up the cat's back legs all by theirselves. Laying pieces of track backwards, running the conveyors too fast, I hate to think what else.

We even heard that one foreman, Willie Bunford, quit because of all the jackasses on the machinery, that he feared for his life. Willie Bunford used to be my foreman. He made fun of how I said his name, "Wee-lee!" so I called him Mr. Bunford. So I have an accent, so what. When I was first starting on the crane he said, "You aren't going to get PG now, are you, Miss Morales, after I wasted four weeks training you as an operator? I know how you Mexican gals love to have babies." I said, "Mr. Bunford, as far as this job goes you can consider me a man." So I had to stick to that. I couldn't call up and say I'm staying in bed today because of my monthly. Then what does he do but layoff two weeks with so-call whiplash from a car accident on Top Street when I saw the whole story: Winnie Hask backing into his car in front of the Big Dipper and him not in it. If a man can get whiplash from his car getting bashed in while he is drinking beer across the street, well, that's a new one.

So I didn't cry for no Willie Bunford. At least he had the sense to get out of there. None of those scabs knew how to run the oxygen machine, so we were waiting for the whole damn place to blow up. I said to the guys, Let's go sit on Bolt Mountain with some beer and watch the fireworks.

+ + +

The first eviction I heard about was the Frank Mickliffs, up the street from me, and then Joe Gomez on Alameda. Ellington wanted to clear out some company houses for the new hires, but how they decided who to throw out we didn't know. Then Janie Marley found out from her friend that babysits for the sister-in-law of a scab that company men were driving scab wives around town letting them pick out whatever house they wanted. Like they're going shopping and we're the peaches getting squeezed.

Friday of that same week I was out on my front porch thinking about a cold beer, just thinking, though, because of no cash, and here come an Ellington car. They slowed way, way down when they went by, then on up Church Street going about fifteen and then they come back. It was Vonda in there. She nodded her head at my house and the guy put something down on paper. They made a damn picture show out of it.

Oh, I was furious. I have been living in that house almost the whole time I worked

---

for Ellington and it's all the home my kids ever had. It's a real good house. It's yellow. I have a big front porch where you can see just about everything, all of Bolton, and a railing so the kids won't fall over in the gulch, and a big yard. I keep it up nice, and my brother Manny being right next door helps out. I have this mother duck with her babies all lined up that the kids bought me at Fangham's for Mother's Day, and I planted marigolds in a circle around them. No way on this earth was I turning my house over to a scab.

The first thing I did was march over to Manny's house and knock on the door and walk in. "Manny," I say to him, "I don't want you mowing my yard anymore unless you feel like doing a favor for Miss Vonda." Manny is just pulling the pop top off a Coke and his mouth goes open at the same time; he just stares.

"Oh, no," he says.

"Oh, yes."

I went back over to my yard and Manny come hopping out putting on his shoes, to see what I'm going to do, I guess. He's my little brother but Mama always says "*Madre Santa,*[9] Manuel, keep an eye on Vicki!" Well, what I was going to do was my own damn business. I pulled up the ducks, they have those metal things that poke in the ground, and then I pulled up the marigolds and threw them out on the sidewalk. If I had to get the neighbor kids to help make my house the ugliest one, I was ready to do it.

Well. The next morning I was standing in the kitchen drinking coffee, and Manny come through the door with this funny look on his face and says, "The tooth fairy has been to see you."

What in the world. I ran outside and there was *pink* petunias planted right in the circle where I already pulled up the marigolds. To think Vonda could sneak into my yard like a common thief and do a thing like that.

"Get the kids," I said. I went out and started pulling out petunias. I hate pink. And I hate how they smelled, they had these sticky roots. Manny woke up the kids and they come out and helped.

"This is fun, Mom," Tony said. He wiped his cheek and a line of dirt ran across like a scar. They were in their pajamas.

"Son, we're doing it for the union," I said. We threw them out on the sidewalk with the marigolds, to dry up and die.

After that I was scared to look out the window in the morning. God knows what Vonda might put in my yard, more flowers or one of those ugly pink flamingos they sell at Fangham's yard and garden department. I wouldn't put nothing past Vonda.

✦ ✦ ✦

Whatever happened, we thought when the strike was over we would have our jobs. You could put up with high water and heck, thinking of that. It's like having a baby, you just grit your teeth and keep your eyes on the prize. But then Ellington started sending out termination notices saying, You will have no job to come back to whatsoever. They would fire you for any excuse, mainly strike-related misconduct, which means nothing, you looked cross-eyed at a policeman or whatever. People got scared.

The national office of the union was no help; they said, To hell with it, boys, take the pay cut and go on back. I had a fit at the union meeting. I told them it's not the

---

[9] (Sp.) Sainted Mother.

pay cut, it's what all else they would take if we give in. "Ellington would not have hired me in two million years if it wasn't for the union raising a rackus about all people are created equal," I said. "Or half of you either because they don't like cunts or coloreds." I'm not that big of a person but I was standing up in front, and when I cussed, they shut up. "If my papa had been a chickenshit like you guys, I would be down at the Frosty King tonight in a little short skirt," I said. "You bunch of no-goods would be on welfare and your kids pushing drugs to pay the rent." Some of the guys laughed, but some didn't.

Men get pissed off in this certain way, though, where they have to tear something up. Lalo said, "Well, hell, let's drive a truck over the plant gate and shut the damn mine down." And there they go, off and running, making plans to do it. Corvallis had a baseball cap on backwards and was sitting back with his arms crossed like, Honey, don't look at me. I could have killed him.

"Great, you guys, you do something cute like that and we're dead ducks," I said. "We don't have to do but one thing, wait it out."

"Till when?" Lalo wanted to know. "Till hell freezes?" He is kind of a short guy with about twelve tattoos on each arm.

"Till they get fed up with the scabs pissing around and want to get the mine running. If it comes down to busting heads, no way. Do you hear me? They'll have the National Guards in here."

I knew I was right. The Boots in this town, the cops, they're on Ellington payroll. I've seen strikes before. When I was ten years old I saw a cop get a Mexican man down on the ground and kick his face till blood ran out of his ear. You would think I was the only one in that room that was born and raised in Bolton.

✦ ✦ ✦

Ellington was trying to get back up to full production. They had them working twelve-hour shifts and seven-day weeks like Abraham Lincoln had never freed the slaves. We started hearing about people getting hurt, but just rumors; it wasn't going to run in the paper. Ellington owns the paper.

The first I knew about it really was when Vonda come right to my house. I was running the vacuum cleaner and had the radio turned up all the way so I didn't hear her drive up. I just heard a knock on the door, and when I opened it: Vonda. Her skin looked like a flour tortilla. "What in the world," I said.

Her bracelets were going clack-clack-clack, she was shaking so hard. "I never thought I'd be coming to you," she said, like I was Dear Abby. "But something's happened to Tommy."

"Oh," I said. I had heard some real awful things: that a guy was pulled into a smelter furnace, and another guy got his legs run over on the tracks. I could picture Tommy either way, no legs or burnt up. We stood there a long time. Vonda looked like she might pass out. "Okay, come in," I told her. "Set down there and I'll get you a drink of water. Water is all we got around here." I stepped over the vacuum cleaner on the way to the kitchen. I wasn't going to put it away.

When I come back she was looking around the room all nervous, breathing like a bird. I turned down the radio.

"How are the kids?" she wanted to know, of all things.

"The kids are fine. Tell me what happened to Tommy."

"Something serious to do with his foot, that's all I know. Either cut off or half cut off, they won't tell me." She pulled this little hanky out of her purse and blew her nose. "They sent him to Morse in the helicopter ambulance, but they won't say what hospital because I'm not next of kin. He doesn't have any next of kin here, I *told* them that. I informed them I was the fiancée." She blew her nose again. "All they'll tell me is they don't want him in the Bolton hospital. I can't understand why."

"Because they don't want nobody to know about it," I told her. "They're covering up all the accidents."

"Well, why would they want to do that?"

"Vonda, excuse me please, but don't be stupid. They want to do that so we won't know how close we are to winning the strike."

Vonda took a little sip of water. She had on a yellow sun dress and her arms looked so skinny, like just bones with freckles. "Well, I know what you think of me," she finally said, "but for Tommy's sake maybe you can get the union to do something. Have an investigation so he'll at least get his compensation pay. I know you have a lot of influence on the union."

"I don't know if I do or not," I told her. I puffed my breath out and leaned my head back on the sofa. I pulled the bandana off my head and rubbed my hair in a circle. It's so easy to know what's right and so hard to do it.

"Vonda," I said, "I thought a lot of Tommy before all this shit. He helped me one time when I needed it real bad." She looked at me. She probably hated thinking of me and him being friends. "I'm sure Tommy knows he done the wrong thing," I said. "But it gets me how you people treat us like kitchen trash and then come running to the union as soon as you need help."

She picked up her glass and brushed at the water on the coffee table. I forgot napkins. "Yes, I see that now, and I'll try to make up for my mistake," she said.

Give me a break, Vonda, was what I was thinking. "Well, we'll see," I said. "There is a meeting coming up and I'll see what I can do. If you show up on the picket line tomorrow."

Vonda looked like she swallowed one of her ice cubes. She went over to the TV and picked up the kids' pictures one at a time, Manuela then Tony. Put them back down. Went over to the *armario*[10] built by my grandpapa.

"What a nice little statue," she said.

"That's St. Joseph. Saint of people that work with their hands."

She turned around and looked at me. "I'm sorry about the house. I won't take your house. It wouldn't be right."

"I'm glad you feel that way, because I wasn't moving."

"Oh," she said.

"Vonda, I can remember when me and you were little girls and your daddy was already running the drugstore. You used to set up on a stool behind the counter and run the soda-water machine. You had a charm bracelet with everything in the world on it, poodle dogs and hearts and a real little pill box that opened."

Vonda smiled. "I don't have the foggiest idea what ever happened to that bracelet. Would you like it for your girl?"

I stared at her. "But you don't remember me, do you?"

---

[10] (Sp.) Armoire.

"Well, I remember a whole lot of people coming in the store. You in particular, I guess not."

"I guess not," I said. "People my color was not allowed to go in there and set at the soda fountain. We had to get paper cups and take our drinks outside. Remember that? I used to think and *think* about why that was. I thought our germs must be so nasty they wouldn't wash off the glasses."

"Well, things have changed, haven't they?" Vonda said.

"Yeah," I put my feet up on the coffee table. It's my damn table. "Things changed because the UTU[11] and the Machinists and my papa's union the Boilermakers took this whole fucking company town to court in 1973, that's why. This house right here was for whites only. And if there wasn't no union forcing Ellington to abide by the law, it still would be."

She was kind of looking out the window. She probably was thinking about what she was going to cook for supper.

"You think it wouldn't? You think Ellington would build a nice house for every-body if they could still put half of us in those falling-down shacks down by the river like I grew up in?"

"Well, you've been very kind to hear me out," she said. "I'll do what you want, tomorrow. Right now I'd better be on my way."

I went out on the porch and watched her go down the sidewalk—click click, on her little spike heels. Her ankles wobbled.

"Vonda," I yelled out after her, "don't wear high heels on the line tomorrow. For safety's sake."

She never turned around.

✦ ✦ ✦

Next day the guys were making bets on Vonda showing up or not. The odds were not real good in her favor. I had to laugh, but myself I really thought she would. It was a huge picket line for the morning shift change. The Women's Auxiliary thought it would boost up the morale, which needed a kick in the butt or somebody would be busting down the plant gate. Corvallis told me that some guys had a meeting after the real meeting and planned it out. But I knew that if I kept showing up at the union meetings and standing on the table and jumping and hollering, they wouldn't do it. Sometimes guys will listen to a woman.

The sun was just coming up over the canyon and already it was a hot day. Cicada bugs buzzing in the *paloverdes* like damn rattlesnakes. Me and Janie Marley were talk-ing about our kids; she has a boy one size down from Tony and we trade clothes around. All of a sudden Janie grabs my elbow and says, "Look who's here." It was Vonda getting out of the Lincoln. Not in high heels either. She had on a tennis outfit and plastic sunglasses and a baseball bat slung over her shoulder. She stopped a little ways from the line and was looking around, waiting for the Virgin Mary to come down, I guess, and save her. Nobody was collecting any bets.

"Come on, Vonda," I said. I took her by the arm and stood her between me and Janie. "I'm glad you made it." But she wasn't talking, just looking around a lot.

After a while I said, "We're not supposed to have bats up here. I know a guy that got his termination papers for carrying a crescent wrench in his back pocket. He had

---

[11] United Transportation Union.

forgot it was even in there." I looked at Vonda to see if she was paying attention. "It was Rusty Cochran," I said, "you know him. He's up at your dad's every other day for a prescription. They had that baby with the hole in his heart."

But Vonda held on to the bat like it was the last man in the world and she got him. "I'm only doing this for Tommy," she says.

"Well, so what," I said. "I'm doing it for my kids. So they can eat."

She kept squinting her eyes down the highway.

A bunch of people started yelling, "Here come the ladies!" Some of the women from the Auxiliary were even saying it. And here come trouble. They were in Doreen's car, waving signs out the windows: "We Support Our Working Men" and other shit not worth repeating. Doreen was driving. She jerked right dead to a stop, right in front of us. She looked at Vonda and you would think she had broke both her hinges the way her mouth was hanging open, and Vonda looked back at Doreen, and the rest of us couldn't wait to see what was next.

Doreen took a U-turn and almost ran over Cecil Smoot, and they beat it back to town like bats out of hell. Ten minutes later here come her car back up the hill again. Only this time her husband Milton was driving, and three other men from Saint's Grace was all in there besides Doreen. Two of them are cops.

"I don't know what they're up to but we don't need you getting in trouble," I told Vonda. I took the bat away from her and put it over my shoulder. She looked real white, and I patted her arm and said, "Don't worry." I can't believe I did that, now. Looking back.

They pulled up in front of us again but they didn't get out, just all five of them stared and then they drove off, like whatever they come for they got.

+ + +

That was yesterday. Last night I was washing the dishes and somebody come to the house. The kids were watching TV. I heard Tony slide the dead bolt over and then he yelled, "Mom, it's the Boot."

Before I can even put down a plate and get into the living room Larry Trevizo has pushed right by him into the house. I come out wiping my hands and see him there holding up his badge.

"Chief of Police, ma'am," he says, just like that, like I don't know who the hell he is. Like we didn't go through every grade of school together and go see *Suddenly Last Summer*[12] one time in high school.

He says, "Mrs. Morales, I'm serving you with injunction papers."

"Oh, is that a fact," I say. "And may I ask what for?"

Tony already turned off the TV and is standing by me with his arms crossed, the meanest-looking damn eleven-year-old you ever hope to see in your life. All I can think of is the guys in the meeting, how they get so they just want to bust something in.

"Yes you may ask what for," Larry says, and starts to read, not looking any of us in the eye: "For being a danger to the public. Inciting a riot. Strike-related misconduct." And then real low he says something about Vonda Fangham and a baseball bat.

"What was that last thing?"

He clears his throat. "And for kidnapping Vonda Fangham and threatening her with a baseball bat. We got the affidavits."

---

[12] 1959 film based on a play by Tennessee Williams.

"Pa'fuera!"[13] I tell Larry Trevizo. I ordered him out of my house right then, told him if he wanted to see somebody get hurt with a baseball bat he could hang around my living room and find out. I trusted myself but not Tony. Larry got out of there.

The injunction papers said I was not to be in any public gathering of more than five people or I would be arrested. And what do you know, a squad of Boots was already lined up by the picket shack at the crack of dawn this morning with their hands on their sticks, just waiting. They knew I would be up there, I see that. They knew I would do just exactly all the right things. Like the guys say, Vicki might break but she don't bend.

They cuffed me and took me up to the jailhouse, which is in back of the Ellington main office, and took off my belt and my earrings so I wouldn't kill myself or escape. "With an earring?" I said. I was laughing. I could see this old rotten building through the office window; it used to be something or other but now there's chickens living in it. You could dig out of there with an earring, for sure. I said, "What's that over there, the Mexican jail? You better put me in there!"

I thought they would just book me and let me go like they did some other ones, before this. But no, I have to stay put. Five hundred thousand bond. I don't think this whole town could come up with that, not if they signed over every pink, purple, and blue house in Bolton.

It didn't hit me till right then about the guys wanting to tear into the plant. What they might do.

"Look, I got to get out by tonight," I told the cops. I don't know their names, it was some State Police I have never seen, seem like they just come up out of nowhere. I was getting edgy. "I have a union meeting and it's real important. Believe me, you don't want me to miss it."

They smiled. And then I got that terrible feeling you get when you see somebody has been looking you in the eye and smiling and setting a trap, and there you are in it like a damn rat.

What is going to happen I don't know. I'm keeping my ears open. I found out my kids are driving Manny to distraction—Tony told his social-studies class he would rather have a jailbird than a scab mom, and they sent him home with a note that he was causing a dangerous disturbance in class.

I also learned that Tommy Jones was not in any accident. He got called off his shift one day and was took to Morse in a helicopter with no explanation. They put him up at Howard Johnson's over there for five days, his meals and everything, just told him not to call nobody, and today he's back at work. They say he is all in one piece.

Well, I am too.

—1986

---

[13] Short for *para fuera* (Sp.): Get out.

LESLÉA NEWMAN (1955-   )

A native of Brooklyn, New York, Lesléa Newman was first published in *Seventeen* magazine just after graduating from high school. She went on to earn a B.S. in Education from the University of Vermont and a Certificate in Poetics from the Naropa Institute, where she studied under Allen Ginsberg. Newman's best known short story, "A Letter to Harvey Milk" (1988), is typical of her fiction, which brings together Jewish and gay/lesbian themes. Acceptance of one's body is also a frequent theme in Newman's work, in books such as *Good Enough to Eat* (1986), a novel about a girl with bulimia, and the self-help book *Somebody to Love: A Guide to Loving the Body You Have* (1991). In addition to numerous stories published in magazines and anthologies, Newman has published four volumes of poetry, two novels, and several books for children. Her earliest children's books, *Heather Has Two Mommies* (1989) and *Gloria Goes to Gay Pride* (1991), were the target of book-banning attempts because they validated lesbian and gay families.

A Letter to Harvey Milk[1]
for Harvey Milk 1930-1978

I.

The teacher says we should write about our life, everything that happened today. So *nu*,[2] what's there to tell? Why should today be different than any other day? May 5, 1986. I get up, I have myself a coffee, a little cottage cheese, half an English muffin. I get dressed. I straighten up the house a little, nobody should drop by and see I'm such a slob. I go down to the Senior Center and see what's doing. I play a little cards, I have some lunch, a bagel with cheese. I read a sign in the cafeteria, Writing Class 2:00. I think to myself, why not, something to pass the time. So at two o'clock I go in. The teacher says we should write about our life.

Listen, I want to say to this teacher, I.B. Singer[3] I'm not. You think anybody cares what I did all day? Even my own children, may they live and be well, don't call. You think the whole world is waiting to see what Harry Weinberg had for breakfast?

The teacher is young and nice. She says everybody has something important to say. Yeah, sure, when you're young you believe things like that. She has short brown hair and big eyes, a nice figure, *zaftig*[4] like my poor Fannie, may she rest in peace. She's wearing a Star of David[5] around her neck, hanging from a purple string, that's nice. She gave us all notebooks and told us we're gonna write something every day, and if we want we can even write at home. Who'd a thunk it, me—Harry Weinberg, seventy-seven years old—scribbling in a notebook like a schoolgirl. Why not, it passes the time.

So after the class I go to the store, I pick myself up a little orange juice, a few bagels, a nice piece of chicken, I shouldn't starve to death. I go up, I put on my slippers, I eat the chicken, I watch a little TV, I write in this notebook, I get ready for bed. *Nu,* for this somebody should give me a Pulitzer Prize?

---

[1] Harvey Milk (1930-1978), member of the San Francisco Board of Supervisors. The first openly gay elected official in the United States, Milk was assassinated at City Hall in 1978, along with Mayor Dan Moscone, by Dan White, a former city supervisor.

[2] (Yid.) So.

[3] Isaac Bashevis Singer (1904-1991), Nobel Prize-winning Jewish-American author who wrote novels and short stories in Yiddish.

[4] (Yid.) Plump and sexy, literally "juicy."

[5] Six-pointed star that is a symbol of Judaism.

II.

Today the teacher tells us something about herself. She's a Jew, this we know from the *Mogen David* [6] she wears around her neck. She tells us she wants to collect stories from old Jewish people, to preserve our history. *Oy,* [7] such stories that I could tell her, shouldn't be preserved by nobody. She tells us she's learning Yiddish. For what, I wonder. I can't figure this teacher out. She's young, she's pretty, she shouldn't be with the old people so much. I wonder is she married. She doesn't wear a ring. Her grandparents won't tell her stories, she says, and she's worried that the Jews her age won't know nothing about the culture, about life in the *shtetls.* [8] Believe me, life in the *shtetl* is nothing worth knowing about. Hunger and more hunger. Better off we're here in America, the past is past.

Then she gives us our homework, the homework we write in the class, it's a little *meshugeh,* [9] but alright. She wants us to write a letter to somebody from our past, somebody who's no longer with us. She reads us a letter a child wrote to Abraham Lincoln, like an example. Right away I see everybody's getting nervous. So I raise my hand. "Teacher," I say, "you can tell me maybe how to address such a letter? There's a few things I've wanted to ask my wife for a long time." Everybody laughs. Then they start to write.

I sit for a few minutes, thinking about Fannie, thinking about my sister Frieda, my mother, my father, may they all rest in peace. But it's the strangest thing, the one I really want to write to is Harvey.

> Dear Harvey:
>
> You had to go get yourself killed for being a *faygeleh?* [10] You couldn't let somebody else have such a great honor? Alright, alright, so you liked the boys, I wasn't wild about the idea. But I got used to it. I never said you wasn't welcome in my house, did I?
>
> *Nu,* Harvey, you couldn't leave well enough alone? You had your own camera store, your own business, what's bad? You couldn't keep still about the boys, you weren't satisfied until the whole world knew? Harvey Milk, with the big ears and the big ideas, had to go make himself something, a big politician. I know, I know, I said, "Harvey, make something of yourself, don't be an old *shmegeggie* [11] like me, Harry the butcher." So now I'm eating my words, and they stick like a chicken bone in my old throat.
>
> It's a rotten world, Harvey, and rottener still without you in it. You know what happened to that *momzer,* [12] Dan White? [13] They let him out of jail, and he goes and kills himself so nobody else should have the pleasure. Now you know me, Harvey, I'm not a violent man. But this was too much, even for me. In the old country, I saw things you shouldn't know from, things you couldn't imagine one person could do to another. But here in America, a man climbs through the window, kills the Mayor of San Francisco, kills Harvey Milk, and a couple years later he's walking around on the street? This I never thought I'd see in my whole life. But from a country that kills the Rosenbergs, [14] I should expect something different?

---

[6] (Yid.) Star of David.

[7] (Yid.) Oh.

[8] (Yid.) Jewish villages in Eastern Europe before the Holocaust.

[9] (Yid.) Crazy.

[10] (Yid.) Gay man, less pejorative than "faggot."

[11] (Yid.) Idiot; silly fool.

[12] (Yid.) Bastard.

[13] Dan White (1946-1985), former member of the San Francisco Board of Supervisors who assassinated Supervisor Harvey Milk and Mayor Dan Moscone in 1978.

[14] Ethel and Julius Rosenberg were executed in 1953 after being convicted of conspiring to transmit classified information to the Soviet Union; their case was a rallying point for leftist activists in the United States.

Harvey, you should be glad you weren't around for the trial. I read about it in the papers. The lawyer, that son of a bitch, said Dan White ate too many Twinkies the night before he killed you, so his brain wasn't working right. Twinkies, *nu,* I ask you. My kids ate Twinkies when they were little, did they grow up to be murderers, God forbid? And now, do they take the Twinkies down from the shelf, somebody else shouldn't go a little crazy, climb through a window, and shoot somebody? No, they leave them right there next to the cupcakes and the donuts, to torture me every time I go to the store to pick up a few things, I shouldn't starve to death.

Harvey, I think I'm losing my mind. You know what I do every week? Every week I go to the store, I buy a bag of jellybeans for you, you should have something to *nosh*[15] on, I remember what a sweet tooth you have. I put them in a jar on the table, in case you should come in with another crazy petition for me to sign. Sometimes I think you're gonna just walk through my door and tell me it was another *meshugeh* publicity stunt.

Harvey, now I'm gonna tell you something. The night you died the whole city of San Francisco cried for you. Thirty thousand people marched in the street, I saw it on TV. Me, I didn't go down. I'm an old man, I don't walk so good, they said there might be riots. But no, there were no riots. Just people walking in the street, quiet, each one with a candle, until the street looked like the sky all lit up with a million stars. Old people, young people, Black people, white people, Chinese people. You name it, they were there. I remember thinking, Harvey must be so proud, and then I remembered you were dead and such a lump rose in my throat, like a grapefruit it was, and then the tears ran down my face like rain. Can you imagine, Harvey, an old man like me, sitting alone in his apartment, crying and carrying on like a baby? But it's the God's truth. Never did I carry on so in all my life.

And then all of a sudden I got mad. I yelled at the people on TV: for getting shot you made him into such a hero? You couldn't march for him when he was alive, he couldn't *shep* a little *naches?*[16]

But *nu,* what good does getting mad do, it only makes my pressure go up. So I took myself a pill, calmed myself down.

Then they made speeches for you, Harvey. The same people who called you a *shmuck*[17] when you were alive, now you were dead, they were calling you a *mensh.*[18] You were a *mensh,* Harvey, a *mensh* with a heart of gold. You were too good for this rotten world. They just weren't ready for you.

> *Oy Harveleh,*[19] *alav ha-sholom,*[20]
> Harry

III.

Today the teacher asks me to stay for a minute after class. *Oy,* what did I do wrong now, I wonder. Maybe she didn't like my letter to Harvey? Who knows?

After the class she comes and sits down next to me. She's wearing purple pants and a white T-shirt. *"Feh,"*[21] I can just hear Fannie say. "God forbid she should wear a skirt? Show off her figure a little? The girls today dressing like boys and the boys dressing like girls—this I don't understand."

"Mr. Weinberg," the teacher says.

"Call me Harry," I says.

---

[15] (Yid.) Snack.
[16] (Yid.) Get a little pleasure; enjoy.
[17] (Yid.) Dick.
[18] (Yid.) A good man worthy of respect.

[19] (Yid.) Diminutive form of Harvey.
[20] (Yid.) Rest in peace.
[21] (Yid.) An expression of disgust.

"O.K., Harry," she says. "I really liked the letter you wrote to Harvey Milk. It was terrific, really. It meant a lot to me. It even made me cry."

I can't even believe my own ears. My letter to Harvey Milk made the teacher cry?

"You see, Harry," she says, "I'm gay, too. And there aren't many Jewish people your age that are so open-minded. At least that I know. So your letter gave me lots of hope. In fact, I was wondering if you'd consider publishing it."

Publishing my letter? Again I couldn't believe my own ears. Who would want to read a letter from Harry Weinberg to Harvey Milk? No, I tell her. I'm too old for fame and glory. I like the writing class, it passes the time. But what I write is my own business. The teacher looks sad for a moment, like a cloud passes over her eyes. Then she says, "Tell me about Harvey Milk. How did you meet him? What was he like?" *Nu,* Harvey, you were a pain in the ass when you were alive, you're still a pain in the ass now that you're dead. Everybody wants to hear about Harvey.

So I tell her. I tell her how I came into the camera shop one day with a roll of film from when I went to visit the grandchildren. How we started talking, and I said, "Milk, that's not such a common name. Are you related to the Milks in Woodmere?"[22] And so we found out we were practically neighbors forty years ago, when the children were young, before we moved out here. Gracie was almost the same age as Harvey, a couple years older, maybe, but they went to different schools. Still, Harvey leans across the counter and gives me such a hug, like I'm his own father.

I tell her more about Harvey, how he didn't believe there was a good *kosher*[23] butcher in San Francisco, how he came to my store just to see. But all the time I'm talking I'm thinking to myself, no, it can't be true. Such a gorgeous girl like this goes with the girls, not with the boys? Such a *shanda.*[24] Didn't God in His wisdom make a girl a girl and a boy a boy—boom they should meet, boom they should get married, boom they should have babies, and that's the way it is? Harvey I loved like my own son, but this I never could understand. And *nu,* why was the teacher telling me this, it's my business who she sleeps with? She has some sadness in her eyes, this teacher. Believe me I've known such sadness in my life, I can recognize it a hundred miles away. Maybe she's lonely. Maybe after class one day I'll take her out for a coffee, we'll talk a little bit, I'll find out.

IV.

It's 3:00 in the morning, I can't sleep. So *nu,* here I am with this crazy notebook. Who am I kidding, maybe I think I'm Yitzhak Peretz?[25] What would the children think, to see their old father sitting up in his bathrobe with a cup of tea scribbling in his notebook? *Oy, meyn kinder,*[26] they should only live and be well and call their old father once in a while.

Fannie used to keep up with them. She could be such a *nudge,*[27] my Fannie. "What's the matter, you're too good to call your old mother once in a while?" she'd yell into the phone. Then there'd be a pause. "Busy-shmusy," she'd yell even louder. "Was I too busy to change your diapers? Was I too busy to put food into your mouth?" *Oy,* I haven't got the strength, but Fannie could she yell and carry on.

---

[22] The largest Jewish Orthodox community on Long Island, New York.
[23] (Yid.) Acceptable to eat, according to Jewish law.
[24] (Yid.) Shame.

[25] Yitzhak Peretz (1852-1915), Polish-Jewish socialist writer and lawyer.
[26] (Yid.) Oh my children.
[27] (Yid.) Annoying person.

You know sometimes, in the middle of the night, I'll reach across the bed for Fannie's hand. Without even thinking, like my hand got a mind of its own, it creeps across the bed, looking for Fannie's hand. After all this time, fourteen years she's been dead, but still, a man gets used to a few things. Forty-two years, the body doesn't forget. And my little *Faigl*[28] had such hands, little *hentelehs*,[29] tiny like a child's. But strong. Strong from kneading *challah*,[30] from scrubbing clothes, from rubbing the children's backs to put them to sleep. My Fannie, she was so ashamed from those hands. After thirty-five years of marriage when finally, I could afford to buy her a diamond ring, she said no. She said it was too late already, she'd be ashamed. A girl needs nice hands to show off a diamond, her hands were already ruined, better yet buy a new stove.

Ruined? *Feh*. To me her hands were beautiful. Small, with veins running through them like rivers, and cracks in the skin like the desert. A hundred times I've kicked myself for not buying Fannie that ring.

V.

Today in the writing class the teacher read my notebook. Then she says I should make a poem about Fannie. "A poem," I says to her, "now Shakespeare you want I should be?" She says I have a good eye for detail. I says to her, "Excuse me Teacher, you live with a woman for forty-two years, you start to notice a few things."

She helps me. We do it together, we write a poem called "Fannie's Hands":

> Fannie's hands are two little birds
> that fly into her lap.
> Her veins are like rivers.
> Her skin is cracked like the desert.
> Her strong little hands
> baked *challah*, scrubbed clothes,
> rubbed the children's backs.
> Her strong little hands
> and my big clumsy hands
> fit together in the night
> like pieces of a jigsaw puzzle
> made in Heaven, by God.

So *nu*, who says you can't teach an old dog new tricks? I read it to the class and such a fuss they made. "A regular Romeo," one of them says. "If only my husband, may he live and be well, would write such a poem for me," says another. I wish Fannie was still alive, I could read it to her. Even the teacher was happy, I could tell, but still, there was a ring of sadness around her eyes.

After the class I waited till everybody left, they shouldn't get the wrong idea, and I asked the teacher would she like to go get a coffee. "*Nu*, it's enough writing already," I said. "Come, let's have a little treat."

So we take a walk, it's a nice day. We find a diner, nothing fancy, but clean and quiet. I try to buy her a piece of cake, a sandwich maybe, but no, all she wants is coffee.

So we sit and talk a little. She wants to know about my childhood in the old country, she wants to know about the boat ride to America, she wants to know did

---

[28] A Yiddish woman's name.
[29] (Yid.) Small hands.

[30] Braided egg bread eaten for Sabbath and Jewish holidays.

my parents speak Yiddish[31] to me when I was growing up. "Harry," she says to me, "when I hear old people talking Yiddish, it's like a love letter blowing in the wind. I try to run after them, and sometimes I catch a phrase that makes me cry or a word that makes me laugh. Even if I don't understand, it always touches my heart."

Oy, this teacher has some strange ideas. "Why do you want to speak Jewish?" I ask her. "Here in America, everybody speaks English. You don't need it. What's done is done, what's past is past. You shouldn't go with the old people so much. You should go out, make friends, have a good time. You got some troubles you want to talk about? Maybe I shouldn't pry," I say, "but you shouldn't look so sad, a young girl like you. When you're old you got plenty to be sad. You shouldn't think about the old days so much, let the dead rest in peace. What's done is done."

I took a swallow of my coffee, to calm down my nerves. I was getting a little too excited.

"Harry, listen to me," the teacher says. "I'm thirty years old and no one in my family will talk to me because I'm gay. It's all Harvey Milk's fault. He made such an impression on me. You know, when he died, what he said, 'If a bullet enters my brain, let that bullet destroy every closet door.' So when he died, I came out to everyone— the people at work, my parents. I felt it was my duty, so the Dan Whites of the world wouldn't be able to get away with it. I mean, if every single gay person came out—just think of it!—everyone would see they had a gay friend or a gay brother or a gay cousin or a gay teacher. Then they couldn't say things like 'Those gays should be shot.' Because they'd be saying you should shoot my neighbor or my sister or my daughter's best friend."

I never saw the teacher get so excited before. Maybe a politician she should be. She reminded me a little bit of Harvey.

"So *nu,* what's the problem?" I ask.

"The problem is my parents," she says with a sigh, and such a sigh I never heard from a young person before. "My parents haven't spoken to me since I told them I was gay. 'How could you do this to us?' they said. I wasn't doing anything to them. I tried to explain I couldn't help being gay, like I couldn't help being a Jew, but that they didn't want to hear. So I haven't spoken to them in eight years."

"Eight years, *Gottenyu,*"[32] I say to her. This I never heard in my whole life. A father and a mother cut off their own daughter like that. Better they should cut off their own hand. I thought about Gracie, a perfect daughter she's not, but your child is your child. When she married the *Goy,*[33] Fannie threatened to put her head in the oven, but she got over it. Not to see your own daughter for eight years, and such a smart, gorgeous girl, such a good teacher, what a *shanda.*

So what can I do, I ask. Does she want me to talk to them, a letter maybe I could write. Does she want I should adopt her, the hell with them, I make a little joke. She smiles. "Just talking to you makes me feel better," she says. So *nu,* now I'm Harry the social worker. She says that's why she wants the old people's stories so much, she doesn't know nothing from her own family history. She wants to know about her own people, maybe write a book. But it's hard to get the people to talk to her, she says, she doesn't understand.

---

[31] Literally, "Jewish," the language spoken by Jews in Eastern Europe before the Holocaust.

[32] (Yid.) Oh God!

[33] (Yid.) Non-Jewish person.

"Listen, Teacher," I tell her. "These old people have stories you shouldn't know from. What's there to tell? Hunger and more hunger. Suffering and more suffering. I buried my sister over twenty years ago, my mother, my father—all dead. You think I could just start talking about them like I just saw them yesterday? You think I don't think about them every day? Right here I keep them," I say, pointing to my heart. "I try to forget them, I should live in peace, the dead are gone. Talking about them won't bring them back. You want stories, go talk to somebody else. I ain't got no stories."

I sat down then. I didn't even know I was standing up, I got so excited. Everybody in the diner was looking at me, a crazy man shouting at a young girl.

Oy, and now the teacher was crying. "I'm sorry," I says to her. "You want another coffee?"

"No thanks, Harry," she says. "I'm sorry, too."

"Forget it. We can just pretend it never happened," I say, and then we go.

VI.

All this crazy writing has shaken me up inside a little bit. Yesterday I was walking home from the diner, I thought I saw Harvey walking in front of me. No, it can't be, I says to myself, and my heart started to pound so, I got afraid I shouldn't drop dead in the street from a heart attack. But then the man turned around and it wasn't Harvey. It didn't even look like him at all.

I got myself upstairs and took myself a pill, I could feel my pressure was going up. All this talk about the past—Fannie, Harvey, Frieda, my mother, my father—what good does it do? This teacher and her crazy ideas. Did I ever ask my mother, my father, what their childhood was like? What nonsense. Better I shouldn't know.

So today is Saturday, no writing class, but still I'm writing in this crazy notebook. I ask myself, Harry, what can I do to make you feel a little better? And I answer myself, make me a nice chicken soup.

You think an old man like me can't make chicken soup? Let me tell you, on all the holidays it was Harry that made the soup. Every *Pesach*[34] it was Harry skimming the *shmaltz*[35] from the top of the pot, it was Harry making the *kreplach*.[36] I ask you, where is it written that a man shouldn't know from chicken soup?

So I take myself down to the store, I buy myself a nice chicken, some carrots, some celery, some parsley—onions I already got, parsnips I can do without. I'm afraid I shouldn't have a heart attack *shlepping*[37] all that food up the steps, but thank God, I make it alright.

I put up the pot with water, throw everything in one-two-three, and soon the whole house smells from chicken soup.

I remember the time Harvey came to visit and there I was with my apron on, skimming the *shmaltz* from the soup. Did he kid me about that! The only way I could get him to keep still was to invite him to dinner. "Listen, Harvey," I says to him. "Whether you're a man or a woman, it doesn't matter. You gotta learn to cook. When you're old, nobody cares. Nobody will do for you. You gotta learn to do for yourself."

"I won't live past fifty, Har," he says, smearing a piece of rye bread with *shmaltz*.

"Nobody wants to grow old, believe me, I know," I says to him. "But listen, it's not

[34] (Yid. and Hebrew) Passover, the Jewish festival commemorating the liberation of the Jews from slavery in ancient Egypt.

[35] (Yid.) Chicken fat.
[36] (Yid.) Dumplings.
[37] (Yid.) Hauling.

so terrible. What's the alternative? Nobody wants to die young, either." I take off my apron and sit down with him.

"No, I mean it Harry," he says to me with his mouth full. "I won't make it to fifty. I've always known it. I'm a politician. A gay politician. Someone's gonna take a pot shot at me. It's a risk you gotta take."

The way he said it, I tell you, a chill ran down my back like I never felt before. He was forty-seven at the time, just a year before he died.

VII.

Today after the writing class, the teacher tells us she's going away for two days. Everyone makes a big fuss, the class they like so much already. She tells us she's sorry, something came up she has to do. She says we can come have class without her, the room will be open, we can read to each other what we write in our notebooks. Someone asks her what we should write about.

"Write me a letter," she says. "Write a story called 'What I Never Told Anyone.'"

So, after everyone leaves, I ask her does she want to go out, have a coffee, but she says no, she has to go home and pack.

I tell her wherever she's going she should have a good time.

"Thanks, Harry," she says. "You'll be here when I get back?"

"Sure," I tell her. "I like this crazy writing. It passes the time."

She swings a big black bookbag onto her shoulder, a regular Hercules[38] this teacher is, and she smiles at me. "I gotta run, Harry. Have a good week." She turns and walks away and something on her bookbag catches my eye. A big shiny pin that spells out her name all fancy-shmancy in rhinestones: Barbara. And under that, right away I see sewn onto her bookbag an upside-down pink triangle.

I stop in my tracks, stunned. No, it can't be, I says to myself. Maybe it's just a design? Maybe she doesn't know from this? My heart is beating fast now, I know I should go home, take myself a pill, my pressure, I can feel it going up.

But I just stand there. And then I get mad. What, she thinks maybe I'm blind as well as old, I can't see what's right in front of my nose? Or maybe we don't remember such things? What right does she have to walk in here with that, that thing on her bag, to remind us of what we been through? Haven't we seen enough?

Stories she wants. She wants we should cut our hearts open and give her stories so she could write a book. Well, alright, now I'll tell her a story.

This is what I never told anyone. One day, maybe seven, eight years ago—no, maybe longer, I think Harvey was still alive—one day Izzie comes knocking on my door. I open the door and there's Izzie, standing there, his face white as a sheet. I bring him inside, I make him a coffee. "Izzie, what is it," I says to him. "Something happened to the children, to the grandchildren, God forbid?"

He sits down, he doesn't drink his coffee. He looks through me like I'm not even there. Then he says. "Harry, I'm walking down the street, you know I had a little lunch at the Center, and then I come outside, I see a young man, maybe twenty-five, a good-looking guy, walking toward me. He's wearing black pants, a white shirt, and on his shirt he's got a pink triangle."

"So," I says. "A pink triangle, a purple triangle, they wear all kinds of crazy things these days."

---

[38] Roman name for the Greek hero Heracles, who was considered the strongest man who ever lived.

"*Heshel*,"[39] he tells me, "don't you understand? The gays are wearing pink triangles just like the war, just like in the camps."

No, this I can't believe. Why would they do a thing like that? But if Izzie says it, it must be true. Who would make up such a thing?

"He looked a little bit like *Yussl*," Izzie says, and then he begins to cry, and such a cry like I never heard. Like a baby he was, with the tears streaming down his cheeks and his shoulders shaking with great big sobs. Such moans and groans I never heard from a grown man in all my life. I thought maybe he was gonna have a heart attack the way he was carrying on. I didn't know what to do. I was afraid the neighbors would hear, they shouldn't call the police, such sounds he was making. Fifty-eight years old he was, but he looked like a little boy sitting there, sniffling. And who was *Yussl?* Thirty years we'd been friends and I never heard from *Yussl*.

So finally, I put my arms around him, and I held him, I didn't know what else to do. His body was shaking so, I thought his bones would crack from knocking against each other. Soon his body got quiet, but then all of a sudden his mouth got noisy.

"Listen, *Heshel*, I got to tell you something, something I never told nobody in my whole life. I was young in the camps, nineteen, maybe twenty when they took us away." The words poured from his mouth like a flood. "*Yussl* was my best friend in the camps. Already I saw my mother, my father, my Hannah marched off to the ovens. *Yussl* was the only one I had to hold on to.

"One morning, during the selection, they pointed me to the right, *Yussl* to the left. I went a little crazy, I ran after him. 'No, he stays with me, they made a mistake,' I said, and I grabbed him by the hand and dragged him back in line. Why the guard didn't kill us right then, I couldn't tell you. Nothing made sense in that place.

"*Yussl* and I slept together on a wooden bench. That night I couldn't sleep. It happened pretty often in that place. I would close my eyes and see such things that would make me scream in the night, and for that I could get shot. I don't know what was worse, asleep or awake. All I saw was suffering.

"On this night, *Yussl* was awake, too. He didn't move a muscle, but I could tell. Finally he said my name, just a whisper, but something broke in me and I began to cry. He put his arms around me and we cried together, such a close call we'd had.

"And then he began to kiss me. 'You saved my life,' he whispered, and he kissed my eyes, my cheeks, my lips. And Harry, I kissed him back. Harry, I never told nobody this before. I, we…we, you know, that was such a place that hell, I couldn't help it. The warmth of his body was just too much for me and Hannah was dead already and we would soon be dead too, probably, so what did it matter?"

He looked up at me then, the tears streaming from his eyes. "It's O.K., Izzie," I said. "Maybe I would have done the same."

"There's more, Harry," he says, and I got him a tissue, he should blow his nose. What more could there be?

"This went on for a couple of months maybe, just every once in a while when we couldn't sleep. He'd whisper my name and I'd answer with his, and then we'd, you know, we'd touch each other. We were very, very quiet, but who knows, maybe some other boys in the barracks were doing the same."

"To this day I don't know how it happened, but somehow someone found out. One

---

[39] Common man's name; in this case, Yiddish for Harry.

day *Yussl* didn't come back to the barracks at night. I went almost crazy, you can imagine, all the things that went through my mind, the things they might have done to him, those lousy Nazis. I looked everywhere, I asked everyone, three days he was gone. And then on the third day, they lined us up after supper and there they had *Yussl*. I almost collapsed on the ground when I saw him. They had him on his knees with his hands tied behind his back. His face was swollen so, you couldn't even see his eyes. His clothes were stained with blood. And on his uniform they had sewn a pink triangle, big, twice the size of our yellow stars.

"*Oy*, did they beat him but good. 'Who's your friend?' they yelled at him. 'Tell us and we'll let you live.' But no, he wouldn't tell. He knew they were lying, he knew they'd kill us both. They asked him again and again, 'Who's your friend? Tell us which one he is.' And every time he said no, they'd crack him with a whip until the blood ran from him like a river. Such a sight he was, like I've never seen. How he remained conscious I'll never know.

"Everything inside me was broken after that. I wanted to run to his side, but I didn't dare, so afraid I was. At one point he looked at me, right in the eye, as though he was saying, *Izzie, save yourself. Me, I'm finished, but you, you got a chance to live through this and tell the world our story.*

"Right after he looked at me, he collapsed, and they shot him, Harry, right there in front of us. Even after he was dead they kicked him in the head a little bit. They left his body out there for two days, as a warning to us. They whipped us all that night, and from then on we had to sleep with all the lights on and with our hands on top of the blankets. Anyone caught with their hands under the blankets would be shot.

"He died for me, Harry, they killed him for that, was it such a terrible thing? *Oy*, I haven't thought about *Yussl* for twenty-five years maybe, but when I saw that kid on the street today, it was too much." And then he started crying again, and he clung to me like a child.

So what could I do? I was afraid he shouldn't have a heart attack, maybe he was having a nervous breakdown, maybe I should get the doctor. *Vay iss mir*,[40] I never saw anybody so upset in my whole life. And such a story, *Gottenyu*.

"Izzie, come lie down," I says, and I took him by the hand to the bed. I laid him down, I took off his shoes, and still he was crying. So what could I do? I lay down with him, I held him tight. I told him he was safe, he was in America. I don't know what else I said, I don't think he heard me, still he kept crying.

I stroked his head, I held him tight. "Izzie, it's alright," I said. "Izzie, Izzie, *Izzaleh*." I said his name over and over, like a lullaby, until his crying got quiet. He said my name once softly, *Heshel*, or maybe he said *Yussl*, I don't remember, but thank God he finally fell asleep. I tried to get up from the bed, but Izzie held onto me tight. So what could I do? Izzie was my friend for thirty years, for him I would do anything. So I held him all night long, and he slept like a baby.

And this is what I never told nobody, not even Harvey. That there in that bed, where Fannie and I slept together for forty-two years, me and Izzie spent the night. Me, I didn't sleep a wink, such a lump in my throat I had, like the night Harvey died.

Izzie passed on a couple months after that. I saw him a few more times, and he seemed different somehow. How, I couldn't say. We never talked about that night. But

---

[40] (Yid.) Woe is me.

now that he had told someone his deepest secret, he was ready to go, he could die in peace. Maybe now that I told, I can die in peace, too?

VIII.

Dear Teacher:

You said write what you never told nobody, and write you a letter. I always did all my homework, such a student I was. So *nu,* I got to tell you something. I can't write in this notebook no more, I can't come no more to the class. I don't want you should take offense, you're a good teacher and a nice girl. But me, I'm an old man, I don't sleep so good at night, these stories are like a knife in my heart. Harvey, Fannie, Izzie, *Yussl,* my father, my mother, let them all rest in peace. The dead are gone. Better to live for today. What good does remembering do, it doesn't bring back the dead. Let them rest in peace.

But Teacher, I want you should have my notebook. It doesn't have nice stories in it, no love letters, no happy endings for a nice girl like you. A bestseller it ain't, I guarantee. Maybe you'll put it in a book someday, the world shouldn't forget.

Meanwhile, good luck to you, Teacher. May you live and be well and not get shot in the head like poor Harvey, may he rest in peace. Maybe someday we'll go out, have a coffee again, who knows? But me, I'm too old for this crazy writing. I remember too much, the pen is like a knife twisting in my heart.

One more thing, Teacher. Between parents and children, it's not so easy. Believe me, I know. Don't give up on them. One father, one mother, it's all you got. If you were my *tochter,*[41] I'd be proud of you.

Harry

—1998

---

[41] (Yid.) Daughter.

CATHY SONG (1955-)

Cathy Song, who is of Korean and Chinese descent, spent her early childhood in Wahiawa, a former plantation town on the island of Oahu, Hawaii. Her family later moved to Waialae-Kahala, a suburb of Honolulu. She graduated from Wellesley College with a degree in English, then earned an M.F.A. from Boston University. In 1982, Song won the Yale Series of Younger Poets Prize for *Picture Bride* (1983). At the time, this was considered the most prestigious recognition ever received by an Asian-American poet by the "mainstream" poetry establishment. *Picture Bride* begins with a poem that meditates on Song's paternal grandmother's immigration to Hawaii; many of Song's poems feature stories and poetic "pictures" of her family members. Her poems generally center on family and kinship, women's experiences, and the ambivalent emotions associated with home and homecoming. *Picture Bride* was originally titled *From the White Place,* after a painting by Georgia O'Keeffe, whose work (as well as that of Japanese artist Kitagawa Utamaro) inspired the book's poems; O'Keeffe was also the inspiration for the book's organization. Song returned to Hawaii in 1987, where she is active in local literary organizations such as Bamboo Ridge Press. She has taught at the University of Hawaii at Manoa and for the Poets in the Schools program. Other books by Song include *Frameless Windows, Squares of Light* (1988), *School Figures* (1994), and *The Land of Bliss* (2001).

Blue and White Lines after O'Keeffe

1. Black Iris
New York

I climb the stairs
in this skull hotel.
Voices beat at the walls,
railings
fan out like fish bones.   5

The doorman bends the darkness,
his eyes prying under the latch,
admitting nothing
but an infantry of roaches,
lapping up the turpentine.   10

Old woman,
mouth stuffed with socks,
waits outside the door.
Her son, catwalking along the sill,
chips away at the enamel on my sink.   15
He thinks it is hard candy.

His girl friend is the opera singer
who lives inside my pipes.
The radiator hisses in the corner,
drawing warm blood,   20
deflating my tomatoes.

And I, the young painter,
once again,
prepare to dine alone.

I stare into the palette,   25
imagine green in my diet.
Peeling back the tins of sardines,
these silver tubes of paint,
lined like slender bullets:
my ammunition.   30

2. Sunflower for Maggie
Taos, New Mexico

Because you preferred Van Gogh's
mutilations:
that scrawny reproduction
tacked under the kitchen clock,
with its frayed edges   35
curling like the corn skins
we shed all summer long.

I wanted you to remember
the date on the calendar,
your birthday,   40
the way you were smiling in the garden.

3. An Orchid
Makena Beach, Maui

I wear hats now,
like halos,
as I haul my easel into the shade.

    Since the first light,   45
the men have been gone.
I cross myself
with ti leaves:
a gesture they do not understand.

Strung along the beach   50
like cowrie shells,
the island children
squat and brood for hours.
Their eyes are the eyes of old fishermen.

Under the ironwoods,   55
Filipino women chatter,
shredding coconuts for the noon fire.
Their bird language
rises with the smoke
that spirals up in the blue air: 60
arms braceleted with tortoiseshell,
beckoning me to join them.

But here, in my safe shading,
I have all the colors I need
and already, too many clothes.   65
What tropical plants
I cannot eat,
I can use for dyes.
On my side of the beach,
I comb the tide pools for algae,   70
pound the blue organs of jellyfish
into pulps for sea green pastels.
These islands
have swollen my appetite;
still, each fish, fruit and flower   75
diminishes me.

If the bright sun
could only be kinder,
I would crawl out of my sensible shoes
and wear the humid stillness   80

like the young wahine[1]
running to meet the first canoes.
They bear the sweet-sour
odor of mangoes
that rises from welcoming limbs   85

4. Red Poppy

    In Andalusia,
it is the men
who are afraid of the darkness,
charging into the night like bulls—

        dry grain leaping into the wind,   90
        riverbed coughing up stones
                until Gibraltar)

to meet another darkness.
Their fathers instruct them,
holding the blade;   95
while the women sleep,

        the back-bent hills
        hold olive fields.

5. The White Trumpet Flower
Sun Prairie, Wisconsin

"Women are like flowers,"
you said, for years   100
I despised myself
and you—
Mother
and Aunt Winnie in the garden,
arranged like lawn chairs,   105
smiling full of babies and detergent.
The hems of your white dresses,
sprigged with cloves and lavender,
fenced my playground. You were happy then,
happiest when I played   110
with the doll family.
They bored me;
I disliked their fragile bodies
and waxy yellow hair
and none of them looked like my father.   115
But I played with them,
tossing their useless bodies up into the air,
because you were pleased and smiling.
But soon, smiles were not enough.
I discovered my own autonomy then,   120

---

[1] (Hawaiian) Women.

crawling out from your wide skirts
and into your flowerbeds,
where I proceeded to crucify the dolls,
decapitating your crocuses.
You scowled (and I clapped),   125
saying, "Georgia,
you are like the dogwood...
a homely name for a goofy flower.
There's just no potential...."

Dear Mother,   130
you would not like it out here;
in Abiquiu there are no flowers,
not your kind of weather.
I have lived without mirrors and without men
for a long time now—   135
but I can feel my own skin,
how it is parched and crinkled like a lizard's.
And if you looked at my eyes,
you would exclaim, clicking your tongue,
"Crow's feet! So young!"   140
But I like to think of them
as bird tracks, calligraphy in the sand.
Still, you would appear as constricted
as a porcelain flower vase;
claustrophobic in its own skin,   145
in mild-mannered sitting rooms.
Shrinking,
when something wild
like a dog or a young child
comes running and panting through,   150
upsetting its mantelpiece equilibrium.
Yet, I am here, Mother.
I have come to rest at your feet,
to be near the familiar scent of talc,
the ticking of the china clock,   155
another heartbeat.
It has taken me all these years
to realize that this is what I must do
to recognize my life.
When I stretch a canvas   160
to paint the clouds,
it is your spine that declares itself:
arching,
your arms stemming out like tender shoots
to hang sheets in the sky.   165

—1943

Picture Bride

She was a year younger
than I,
twenty-three when she left Korea.
Did she simply close
the door of her father's house   5
and walk away. And
was it a long way
through the tailor shops of Pusan
to the wharf where the boat
waited to take her to an island   10
whose name she had
only recently learned,
on whose shore
a man waited,
turning her photograph   15
to the light when the lanterns
in the camp outside
Waialua Sugar Mill were lit
and the inside of his room
grew luminous   20
from the wings of moths
migrating out of the cane stalks?
What things did my grandmother
take with her? And when
she arrived to look   25
into the face of the stranger
who was her husband,
thirteen years older than she,
did she politely untie
the silk bow of her jacket,   30
her tent-shaped dress
filling with the dry wind
that blew from the surrounding fields
where the men were burning the cane?

—1983

CHITRA BANERJEE DIVAKARUNI (1956-)

Chitra Divakaruni was born in Calcutta, India. After receiving her undergraduate degree from Calcutta University, she moved to the United States and obtained an M.A. in English from Wright State University in Ohio and a Ph.D. in English from UC Berkeley. Divakaruni's earliest published writings were books of poetry: *Dark Like the River* (1987), *The Reason for Nasturtiums* (1990), and *Black Candle* (1991). Divakaruni's writing, which centers on the experiences and relationships of women, especially migrant women, has received numerous awards, including the American Book Award (for *Arranged Marriage,* a collection of short stories published in 1995). Her 1997 novel, *The Mistress of Spices,* was made into a film in 2005, an adaptation with special resonance, as much of her writing responds to visual art forms such as movies, photographs, and paintings. Other works by Divakaruni include *Leaving Yuba City* (1997), *Sister of My Heart* (1999), *The Unknown Errors of Our Lives* (2001), *The Vine of Desire* (2002), *Queen of Dreams* (2004), and several children's books. In addition to writing and teaching, Divakaruni participates in community work; in 1991 she helped found Maitri, a domestic violence hotline providing support for South Asian women in the San Francisco Bay Area. Divakaruni currently lives in Houston with her family and teaches in the English department at the University of Houston.

Indigo
Bengal, 1779-1859[1]

The fields flame with it, endless, blue
as cobra poison. It has entered our blood
and pulses up our veins
like night. There is no other color.
The planter's whip   5
splits open the flesh of our faces,
a blue liquid light trickles
through the fingers. Blue dyes the lungs
when we breathe. Only the obstinate eyes

refuse to forget where once the rice   10
parted the earth's moist skin
and pushed up reed by reed,
green, then rippled gold
like the Arhiyal's waves. Stitched
into our eyelids, the broken dark,   15
the torches of the planter's men, fire
walling like a tidal wave
over our huts, ripe charred grain
that smelled like flesh. And the wind
screaming in the voices of women   20
dragged to the plantation,
feet, hair, torn breasts.

In the worksheds, we dip our hands,
their violent forever blue,

---

[1] [*Author's note.*] The planting of indigo was forced on the farmers of Bengal, India, by the British, who exported it as a cash crop for almost a hundred years until the peasant uprising of 1860, when the plantations were destroyed.

in the dye, pack it in great embossed chests   25
for the East India Company.
Our ankles gleam thin blue from the chains.

After that night
many of the women killed themselves.
Drowning was the easiest.   30
Sometimes the Arhiyal gave us back
the naked, swollen bodies, the faces
eaten by fish. We hold on

to red, the color of their saris,
the marriage mark on their foreheads,   35
we hold it carefully inside
our blue skulls, like a man
in the cold *Paush*² night
holds in his cupped palms a spark,
its welcome scorch,   40
feeds it his foggy breath till he can set it down
in the right place,
to blaze up and burst
like the hot heart of a star
over the whole horizon,   45
a burning so beautiful you want it
to never end.

—1997

Yuba City School

From the black trunk I shake out
my one American skirt, blue serge
that smells of mothballs. Again today
Jagjit came crying from school. All week
the teacher has made him sit   5
in the last row, next to the boy
who drools and mumbles,
picks at the spotted milk-blue skin
of his face, but knows to pinch, sudden-sharp,
when she is not looking.   10

The books are full of black curves,
dots like the eggs the boll-weevil lays
each monsoon in furniture-cracks
in Ludhiana.³ Far up in front the teacher makes word-sounds
Jagjit does not know. They float   15
from her mouth-cave, he says,
in discs, each a different color.

---

² [*Author's note.*] Name of a winter month in the Bengali   ³ A city in Punjab, India.
calendar.

Candy-pink for the girls in their lace dresses,
matching shiny shoes. Silk-yellow for the boys beside them,
crisp blond hair, hands raised   20
in all the right answers. Behind them
the Mexicans, whose older brothers,
he tells me, carry knives,
whose catcalls and whizzing rubber bands clash, mid-air,
with the teacher's voice,   25
its sharp purple edge.

For him, the words are a muddy red,
flying low and heavy,
and always the one he has learned to understand:
idiot idiot idiot.   30

I heat the iron over the stove. Outside
evening blurs the shivering
in the eucalyptus. Jagjit's shadow
disappears into the hole he is hollowing
all afternoon. The earth, he knows, is round,   35
and if he can tunnel all the way through,
he will end up in Punjab,[4]
in his grandfather's mango orchard, his grandmother's songs
lighting on his head, the old words glowing
like summer fireflies.   40

In the playground, Jagjit says, invisible hands
snatch at his turban, expose
his uncut hair,[5] unseen feet trip him from behind,
and when he turns, ghost laughter
all around his bleeding knees.   45
He bites down on his lip to keep in
the crying. They are
waiting for him to open his mouth,
so they can steal his voice.

I test the iron with little drops of water   50
that sizzle and die. Press down
on the wrinkled cloth. The room fills
with a smell like singed flesh.
Tomorrow in my blue skirt I will go
to see the teacher, my tongue   55
a stiff embarrassment in my mouth,
my few English phrases. She will pluck them from me,
nail shut my lips. My son will keep sitting
in the last row
among the red words that drink his voice.   60

—1997

---

[4] A region of India.

[5] [*Author's note.*] The boy in the poem is a Sikh immigrant,
whose religion forbids the cutting of his hair.

Leaving Yuba City

She has been packing all night.

It's taking a long time because she knows she must be very quiet, mustn't wake the family. Father and mother in the big bedroom downstairs, he sharp and angular in his ironed night-pajamas, on the bed-lamp side because he reads the Punjabi newspaper before he sleeps. Her body like a corrugation, a dark apologetic crease on her side of the wide white bed, face turned away from the light, or is it from her husband, *salwar-kameez*[6] smelling faintly of sweat and dinner spices. Brother and his new wife next door, so close that all week bits of noise have been flying through the thin wall at her like sparks. Murmurs, laughter, bed-creaks, small cries, and once a sound like a slap, followed by a sharp in-drawn breath like the startled start of a sob that never found its completion. And directly beneath her bedroom, grandfather, propped up on betel-stained pillows to help him breathe, slipping in and out of nightmares where he calls out in his asthmatic voice hoarse threats in a dialect she does not understand.

She walks on tiptoe like she imagines, from pictures seen in magazines, a ballerina would move. Actually she is more like a stork, that same awkward grace as she balances stiff-legged on the balls of her feet, her for-the-first-time painted toes curling in, then out, splaying fuchsia pink with just a hint of glitter through the crowded half-dark of her bedroom. She moves back and forth between suitcase and dresser, maneuvers her way around the heavy teak furniture that father chose for her. Armchair. Dressing table. Narrow single bed. They loom up in the sad seep of light from her closet like black icebergs. Outside, wind moves through the pepper trees, whispering her name through the humid night. *Sushma, Sushma, Sushma.* She has been holding her breath, not realizing it, until her chest feels like there are hands inside, hot hands with fuchsia-pink nails scraping the lining of her lungs.

Now she lets it out in a rush, shaking her head with a small, embarrassed laugh.

Two weeks back, wandering through the meager cosmetics section of the Golden Temple drugstore, killing time as she waited for grandfather's prescription to be filled, she had seen the fuchsia nail polish. She hadn't been looking for anything. What was the use when mother and especially father believed that nice girls shouldn't wear make-up. But the bottle leaped out at her, so bright and unbelonging in that store with its dusty plastic flowers in fake crystal vases on the counter. *Take me, take me,* it called, a bottle from a book she had read in grade school, what was it, a girl falling through a hole in her garden into magic. But this voice was her own, the voice that cried into her pillow at night. *Take me, take me.* There in the store she had looked up at the faded Christmas streamers wrapped like garlands around the pictures of the *gurus*[7] hanging above the cash register, old holy men in beards and turbans with eyes like opaque water. Her fingers had closed around the fuchsia bottle. That's when she knew she was leaving.

So when at brother's wedding all the relatives said, now it's Sushma's turn, and Aunt Nirmala told her mother she knew just the right boy back in Ludhiana, college

---

[6] (Hindi) Traditional dress worn by women and men in South Asia.

[7] [*Author's note.*] Sikh religious leaders.

graduate, good family, how about sending them Sushma's photo, that one in the pink *salwar-kameez* with her hair double-braided, it was not hard to sit quietly, a smile on her face, tracing the gold-embroidery on her *dupatta,*[8] letting the voices flow around her, *Sushma, Sushma, Sushma,* like the wind in the pepper trees. Because she had already withdrawn her savings, two years salary from working at the Guru Govind grocery, money her mother thought she was keeping for her wedding jewelry. The twenty dollar bills lay folded under her mattress, waiting like wings. Below the bed was the old suitcase she had taken down from the attic one afternoon when no one was home, taken down and dusted and torn off the old Pan Am tag from a forgotten long-ago trip to India. Even her second-hand VW Bug was filled with gas and ready.

Now she pauses with her arms full of satiny *churidars,*[9] *kurtas*[10] with tiny mirrors stitched into them, gauzy *dupattas* in sunset colors. What is she going to do with them in her new life in some rooming house in some downtown she hasn't yet decided on, where she warms a can of soup over a hot plate? But she packs them anyway, because she can't think of what else to do with them. Besides, she has only two pairs of jeans, a few sweaters, and one dress from when she was in high school that she's not sure she can still fit into. Three nightgowns, longsleeved, modest-necked. From old habit she folds them in neat, flat, gift-box rectangles. Comb, toothbrush, paste, vitamin pills. She puts in the bottle of hair oil and lifts it out again. *Nice girls never cut their hair. They let it grow long, braided meekly down their backs.* That's what father and mother had looked for when they arranged brother's marriage. She stands in shadow in front of the mirror with its thick, bulging frame. She pouts her lips like the models on TV, narrows her eyes, imagines something wild and wicked and impossible, short hair swinging against the bare nape of her neck, a frizzy permed mass pinned up on her head. She throws in the bottle of nail polish.

It's time for the letter now, the one she has been writing in her head all week. *I'm leaving,* it says. *I hate you, hate the old ways you're always pushing onto me. Don't look for me. I'm never coming back.* Or, *I'm sorry. I had to go. I was suffocating here. Please understand.* Or perhaps, *Don't worry about me. I'll be fine. I just want to live on my own a while. Will contact you when I'm ready.* She pauses, pen poised over paper. No. None of it is right. The words, the language. How can she write in English to her parents who have never spoken to her in anything but Punjabi, who will have to ask someone to translate the lines and curves, the bewildering black slashes she has left behind?

She walks down the steps in the dark, counting them. *Nineteen, twenty.* The years of her life. She steps lightly on them, as though they have not been cut into her heart, as though she can so easily leave them behind. She puts her hand on the front door, steeling herself for the inevitable creak, for someone to wake and shout, *kaun hai?*[11] For the pepper trees to betray her, *Sushma, Sushma, Sushma.* The suitcase bumps against her knee, bulky, bruising. She bites off a cry and waits. But there is only the sound of the neighbor dog barking. And she knows, suddenly, with the doorknob live and cold under her palm, that it's going to happen, that the car will start like a dream, the engine turning over smooth, smooth, the wind rushing through her open hair, the empty night-streets taking her wherever she wants to go. No one to catch her and drag

---

[8] (Hindi) Long scarf.
[9] (Hindi) Trousers; a variant of the salwar.

[10] (Hindi) Loose shirts.
[11] [*Author's note.*] "Who's there?"

her back to her room and keep her under lock and key like they did with Pimi last year until they married her off. No one to slap her or scream curses at her or, weeping, accuse her of having smeared mud on the family name. And sometime tomorrow, or next week, or next month, when she's far, far away where no one can ever find her, Las Vegas, Los Angeles, she'll pick up a phone and call them. Maybe the words will come to her then, halting but clear, in the language of her parents, the language that she carries with her for it is hers too, no matter where she goes. Maybe she'll be able to say what they've never said to each other all their lives because you don't say those things even when they're true. Maybe she'll say, *I love you.*

—1993

Skin

I woke this morning with a tingling all over my body, not unpleasant, kind of like it feels between your teeth after you've poked at your gum with something for a while, and when I looked I discovered I had no skin. I was disconcerted for a moment, but not really upset, not like someone else would have been. My skin has been nothing but a source of trouble for me ever since the midwife announced to my mother that not only was it a girlchild, but it was colored like a mud road in the monsoon. Mother refused to look, and all through the weeks she had to breastfeed me she kept her head turned away, so all I remember of her is a smooth creamy earlobe with a gold hoop dangling from it.

I spent my childhood learning to blend in with the furniture. This wasn't difficult since the heavy mahogany was a perfect match for my skin, and after my marriage I had ample opportunity to further practice this skill. That I got married at all was a miracle, as I was a far cry from the milk-and-honey shade that in-laws are always advertising for in the matrimonial columns. Relatives ascribed my great good luck to temporary insanity on the part of my in-laws, probably brought about by something my desperate parents slipped into their rose syrup when they came to view me. Or perhaps it was the hefty dowry my father paid—not too unhappily, for as everyone knows, a grown daughter in the house is worse than a firebrand in the grainstacks. My in-laws quickly returned to normal, and the morning after the wedding I was sent to the kitchen. There, camouflaged by the smoke-streaked walls, I cooked enormous breakfasts, lunches and dinners, with tea twice in between, for the family and all their guests that I never saw. I only came to my husband's bedroom after the lights were out so he wouldn't have to look at me, and when he had been satisfied I returned to my quarters. So you can understand why I'm intrigued rather than dismayed as I gingerly touch my arm.

It doesn't hurt, not too much. There's no mirror in the pantry where I sleep, so I can't see my face, but I take a good look at everything else—fingers and elbows, ankles and calves, the soles of my feet. All is a delicate uniform pink, kind of like the inside of a baby's mouth, no, paler, more like the flesh of a *hilsa* fish after you've sliced it open. I'm so fascinated I do something I've never done before—I remove my clothes and examine the forbidden parts—mounds, hollows, slits. I notice the veins and arteries below the surface, red and blue skeins of pulsing silk, the translucent glistening tissues along the curves.

How beautiful I am! I can't wait to share my new body with my family. Surely they will be proud of me, love me at last, a daughter-in-law to brag about, to show off to strangers. I try to imagine the smile on my husband's face—a bit difficult as it's something I've never seen—and on an impulse I rummage in the chest till I find my marriage sari, a lovely deep silk, purple-red. (I'd heard a wedding guest say that it made me look like a brinjal.)[12] But now I arrange it around me with excited fingers. How my skinless body glows against it! How proudly my breasts push against the fabric!

Ready now, I stand tall. I picture myself sweeping into the great hall, the awe on their faces, the adoration. I practice my words of forgiveness, my gracious smile. And then, with my hand stretched out to turn the knob, I notice it. The door is gone. The door to my room is gone.

I look for it everywhere, feeling the cracked, peeling whitewash, the bricks that scrape my new fingertips raw. I move faster, searching, my breath coming in gasps. It's a trick, a new cruel trick, the latest in the series, but I refuse to let it get to me. I throw myself against the wall, hammer at it. Shout. The sound falls back into my ears, small, like a cry from the bottom of a well-shaft. But I won't give up. I *know* it's there, somewhere, my door. I won't be kept from it.

—1997

---

[12] (Hindi) Eggplant.

ACHY OBEJAS (1956-   )

Achy Obejas was born in Havana, Cuba. Like her contemporaries Cristina García and Beatriz Rivera, she is part of the generation of exiled Cuban Americans whose families left Cuba and immigrated to the United States after the Cuban Revolution. She and her parents arrived in Miami in 1963 and, through the efforts of a federal relocation program, resettled in Michigan City, Indiana. Obejas has spent most of her life in the Midwest; she moved to Chicago in 1979, and for the next two decades was employed as a journalist, writing for both mainstream and alternative newspapers such as the *Chicago Sun-Times,* the *Chicago Reader,* the *Windy City Times,* the *Advocate, High Performance,* and the *Village Voice.* In 1991, she joined the *Chicago Tribune;* during her ten-year tenure as a cultural critic, she won several Peter Lisagor awards, the Studs Terkel Journalism Prize, and a 2001 Pulitzer Prize for team explicatory journalism. Obejas has published a collection of short stories, *We Came All the Way from Cuba So You Could Dress Like This?* (1994), and two novels: *Memory Mambo* (1996), winner of the Lambda Lesbian Fiction Award, and *Days of Awe* (2001), named a "Best Book" by both the *Los Angeles Times* and the *Chicago Tribune.* Most recently, she has edited and contributed to the short fiction collection *Havana Noir* (2007). In addition to other honors and distinguished residencies, Obejas has received a National Endowment for the Arts Fellowship in poetry, and was designated the Sor Juana Inés de la Cruz Writer-in-Residence at DePaul University in 2006.

Above All, A Family Man

My name is Tommy Drake, and I'm dying. This is no delusion or attention-getting device; enough doctors have figured it out, and I believe them. I've got the cough, the nausea, the swollen glands—I even have a few of those splotches. Luckily, you can't really see them, although there's one on my neck that's starting to spread. I don't have much in the way of material possessions—an old Pioneer stereo, a few sticks of furniture, and a backpack full of clothes—but I did make out a will leaving it all to a not-for-profit group in Chicago, which is my hometown.

Right now I'm speeding down Interstate 55, stretched flat on the passenger's seat and rubbing my stomach, which is taut on the outside but queasy on the inside. I rub it in a circular motion, with my hand under my shirt, but it doesn't help much. My hand just gets warm, and it feels as primitive and interminable as scratching flint for fire. Nothing happens, except that everything keeps turning inside me.

"You okay?" asks Rogelio, who's driving at rocket speed. I know he's doing more than eighty miles an hour, but every time I say something he tells me he's just a little bit above the speed limit. Even from my reclining position (I'm so low my headrest is bumping the back seat), I can see those big trucks blinking as we zoom past them, but he just tells me to relax.

I try to explain that I'm nauseous and wish he'd slow down, especially around the curves, but my mouth is too dry. My tongue is a beached whale, swollen and sticky. What comes out is a pathetic peep that makes Rogelio laugh. He pats my thigh with rough affection, turns up the radio, and presses his foot on the gas pedal. My body pushes against the car seat from the acceleration.

"Slow down," I finally manage to say.

"What?"

"Goddamn it, slow down!" I'm screaming now, and my throat can't take it; I start to cough, the force of it pitching me from side to side.

"I can't hear you," he says, lowering the volume. He glances at me, then turns back to the road. "What did you say?"

I want to hit him, but all I can do is wipe the drool from my chin. I have my cuffs undone, and my sleeve flaps up to my face, which is now sweaty and red. "Slow down," I say. "Please."

"Okay, okay," he says with exaggerated reassurance. "You take it easy, okay?"

I nod and close my eyes, settling back on the seat and feeling the weight of the car as Rogelio slowly pumps the brake. He reaches across to open my window a little. As he turns the handle, his arm brushes against me, just at my stomach, and I lift my shirt. On its way back to the steering wheel, his hand pats my stomach, which is the wrong thing to do. My insides slosh around, and I swallow. Then I angrily force his hand flat on my abdomen and just hold it there against his will. I don't want to get sick; I don't want to die.

"We're almost in St. Louis," he says, freeing his hand. "You ever been to St. Louis?"

"No," I say. "But I've driven past it."

"You seen the Arch?"

"From the road." I reach up and feel my head for fever, but I'm suddenly fine. "What's in St. Louis besides the Arch?"

"Nothing," Rogelio says with a laugh.

I think he must never stop when he gets behind the wheel. It's just a straight line to him, point A to point B—no bathroom stops, no meals, nothing. "I want to stop in St. Louis," I say.

Rogelio laughs because he thinks I'm kidding. His laugh is almost a giggle, kind of high-pitched. There's a girlishness to it, but if anybody ever pointed it out, he'd probably never laugh again.

"I'm serious, I want to stop in St. Louis."

He's still smiling. "Well, we'll get gas there, okay?"

"No, no, I want to stop, to get off the road."

He does a double-take, but I just grin up at him. "Why? Are you getting sick?" he asks.

"No, actually, I'm feeling okay right now."

"Tommy, we can get to Tulsa tonight, but if we stop in St. Louis, we'll waste time," he says. "Besides, there's nothing in St. Louis. If there was, I would have heard about it by now, don't you think?"

Rogelio is a dark, handsome motherfucker with Indian hair and cheekbones as sharp as a razor. Now he's giving me this insinuating smile, this man-of-the-world macho look.

"I want to get off the road," I say, smiling back. "I want to see the Arch."

"The Arch?" He whines, his face all wrinkled up. "We'll be late. What about your friends in Santa Fe?"

"Rogelio, at the speed you're driving, we'll be in Santa Fe in an hour. Anyway, I can always call them."

My friends are Paul and Ron, these two guys who run a gallery in Santa Fe. It's very Southwest but very gay at the same time. That means they have buffalo skulls like every other Santa Fe gallery, but they also show glossy Mapplethorpe prints of boys in leather. Ron and I were lovers about ten years ago, and we've remained friends. When I told him the news, he and Paul invited me to stay with them, a kindness I'll never get to repay.

Rogelio isn't at all happy. He's actually pouting because of my request. "You'd deny me my *last* chance to see the St. Louis Arch?" I ask. It's a guilt trip, I know, but I do want to get off the road. And it's true, too. If that Arch and I are ever going to get together—not that it would ever have occurred to me before—this is our last chance Texaco.

"No, Tommy, I wouldn't deny you," Rogelio says, and it's with genuine feeling. Because he thinks he's treated me badly, he kind of sinks in the driver's seat. The perk is that his foot lightens up on the gas pedal, and we begin to approach the speed limit.

There is, however, an irony in his response. The fact is that Rogelio denies me pretty routinely. Not pleasures, mind you. He's generous by nature, and he'll do most anything, especially for me. And frankly, it's not because of what I do for him; I'm nothing special. I'm okay. I'm kind of cute, actually. But that has nothing to do with it.

+ + +

Rogelio picked me for no reason other than that I spoke a little Spanish to his kids. He's got four of them, at least that I know of. Two boys, two girls, ages four to twelve. They're little brown butterballs, all of them overweight. At the Montrose Street beach where I met them, they practically bounced around Rogelio. They were playing a loose game of soccer when the oldest boy kicked the ball right into my lap, knocking the newspaper out of my hands. I was pissed off, and ready to say something mean, but then I saw Daddy, and that changed things.

Oh, it wasn't lightning or love at first sight. It was simple fear. Rogelio is as sinewy as tire tread: every ligament is perfectly outlined. And there he was, this little bull ready to charge if I said the wrong thing. So I resurrected some high school Spanish and told his kid to be careful next time, that I'd been sitting in my beach chair all morning in the same spot, and I'd appreciate it if they'd play somewhere else. Rogelio and I never took our eyes off each other, but the look was as much an invitation to murder as to love.

Montrose Beach is a small peninsula that juts out into Lake Michigan. It offers a pretty amazing view of the Loop, Lake Shore Drive snaking north, and the park along the water's edge. But for me, the best part is that Montrose is not a gay beach. That is, it's a respite. The folks there are mostly Latinos and Asians, usually in family groups. The kids play soccer or volleyball; the young men wear long pants and smoke a lot of cigarettes while the women keep an eye on things. For the most part, I'm left alone. I can read, think, just hang out, with very little chance of distraction. If I really want to cruise, all I have to do is walk down to the rocks on Belmont Avenue, and there are boys of all colors everywhere.

So when Rogelio stared back hard, this was a surprise. His roly-poly wife was sitting on a beach towel not too far from us, and I could tell she wasn't happy about any of this. She yelled something at him—I think it was to be careful—and he retreated, kicking the ball back to his kids. I'm sure she meant to say she just didn't want him to get in trouble threatening a white man, but I'd bet her real reasons were different.

"It's okay," I said in her direction, my eyes still fixed on Rogelio but softer now. He smiled shyly, which was so unexpected, I laughed. Then he puffed up, offended, his manhood on the line—it was as if I'd guessed about that high-pitched sound, and he was terrified.

He stomped over. "What's so funny?" he asked, surprising me again. Unlike most of the other people on Montrose Beach, Rogelio speaks English fairly well. He has an accent, but it's slight, more endearing than anything else. "Are you laughing at my wife?"

"No," I said, "I'm laughing at you."

He stepped back. "What?"

"You're making a big deal out of nothing," I said. "Your kids were careless. I told them to be careful, and now your wife is trying to protect you from the big, bad gringo."[1]

"I think you're trying to embarrass me in front of my family," he said quite seriously.

"I think you're crazy," I told him. "I don't even know you."

He winced in the hot sun, jets of black hair breezing around his face. "If you're worried about that," he said, "we can meet here tomorrow morning, at eight o'clock."

His eye contact made it clear this wasn't challenge to a duel, not in the usual sense.

---

[1] (Sp.) A derogatory term for U.S. citizens used throughout Latin America, especially in Mexico. Of uncertain origin, the term connotes a critique of U.S. imperialism in Latin America and U.S. citizens' association with it.

"The beach doesn't open until nine."

"Exactly." His face was stern.

"All right," I said, thinking the whole thing mighty amusing and that I'd never actually meet him.

"Okay," he said, his muscles finally loosening. Then he smiled. "How big are you?"

I looked at him incredulously. I mean, you read about this kind of stuff, but does it ever really happen? "What kind of a question is that?" I asked him. "And in front of your wife."

"Well?"

It was my turn to feel embarrassed. "How big are *you*?"

He didn't hesitate. "Four inches."

I thought he had to be kidding. Who brags about a four-inch cock? I wanted to laugh, not at his size but at his style, until I realized it would devastate him.

"And you?" he asked, now trying to be tough, his hands balled up on his hips.

"You'll see," I managed.

Needless to say, I stood him up. It wasn't a terribly deliberate choice. I was tired, I wasn't in the mood for the lake, and I thought he was kind of weird anyway. But a few days later, he found me in my favorite beach chair, reading. To my surprise, he casually settled on the sand next to me, crossing his legs as if to meditate.

"Hello," he said, a little embarrassed. "Have you got the sports section there?" He nodded at the *Tribune* folded on my lap.

"The Cubs lost," I said as I handed him the paper. I was expecting him to stretch out and start posing for me and everybody else, but he remained Buddha-like, turning the pages with a wet fingertip.

"I don't care about the Cubs," he said, his eyes on the newspaper. "I like football better."

I thought he meant soccer, so I didn't have much to say. "I don't keep up with sports," I told him. He seemed so different now, his face boyish and sweet. "What's the name of our team—The Sting, The Stingers—?"

He looked up at me, amused. "Not *futbol*,"[2] he said. "I mean American football. You know, the contact sport." He winked at me. I took note that his wife and kids were nowhere in sight.

+ + +

I can't really explain how it happened after that, other than to say that suddenly Rogelio was in my orbit. He is no less married, no less a parent—in fact, he is, above all, a family man—and how he manages to juggle it all has always amazed me. Part of it is simple: The man does not consider himself even vaguely homosexual. Instead, he thinks of himself as *sexual,* as capable of sex with a cantaloupe as with a woman or a man. It's a definition that deals in quantity and athleticism and has little, if any, relationship to love or pleasure.

For all of his sexual posturing, however, it was I who taught *him* how to kiss— rather, that it's okay to kiss another man. Before, Rogelio could make love all day without puckering up even once. He is sure, because there are certain things he will not do in bed with a man, and because of—quite literally—his favorite sexual positions, that he's a man in the old fashioned sense of the word.

---

[2] (Sp.) The name used for soccer all over the world, except for the U.S.

We hadn't been friends long when I got sick. It started simply enough—just a cough, a kind of constant fatigue. But Rogelio was astonishingly tender, stopping by with groceries, making thick Mexican bean soups, and actually tucking me in before leaving for the night shift on the South Side. He tried to be nonchalant about it. He said these were all parental skills and that my apartment was on the way to this or that errand.

I'd already concluded that he needed to have these self-delusions, so I didn't bother to point out that I was easily thirty minutes north of his family's home. There are plenty of hardware stores and laundromats in his neighborhood, so all his errands could have been run locally. And his little pit stop at my place meant it took more than an hour for him to get to his factory job. But, hey, I loved his attentions. And as it turned out, he was a fountain of unexpected kindnesses, one after another. It wasn't just the things he did. It was the *way* he did them. There was little mistaking his concern, or even—as strange as this may sound—his devotion. Against all odds, he's always believed I'll get better.

Most of my friends think Rogelio's cute, but pretty transient, too (he's living in the U.S. thanks to a rather dubious green card). We've taken him to a couple of gay bars, but he just stands around, giggling incessantly. He's too shy to dance and too scared to be comfortable. Once, we dragged him to a gay street fair, and even though there were plenty of straight people there—mostly whites—he did seem relaxed. I told him he looked great in the sunshine, with his dark brown skin and all, and a couple of the guys started ribbing me good-naturedly about being a Cha Cha Queen. Surprisingly, even Rogelio joined in.

But for all his involvement with me and his socializing with my friends in New Town, Rogelio always deals with gays as "other." Once, when my friend Stan was over, I put my arm around Rogelio's shoulder, and he violently shook it off. "I'm the man here," he told me. Stan snapped, "Honey, you know what they say…'The butchier the boy, the higher his legs go.'" At first I thought there might be blood on my walls, but Rogelio just giggled. That night, I put him out on the streets.

I've tried to talk to him about this, not out of any particular political conviction, but because I think there's an absurdity in pretending he's so hyper-masculine while he's scratching at my door. Personally, I think he knows better.

Later, I asked him if he understood what Stan had meant, and he made it quite clear that he did. He also said his toes rarely left the sheets. I said that wasn't true, but Rogelio thought the best way to prove his point was just to show me.

+ + +

When my diagnosis came through, I surprised myself by not being devastated. I think I already knew. Three of my former lovers had already died of AIDS, and I've been around the block too many times not to be at risk. But when the social worker at the clinic urged me to tell my sexual partners and encourage them to go for counseling, I did have a moment of panic. How the hell would I tell Rogelio? Not telling him was out of the question—I never doubted the boy's sexual prowess; besides his wife, I was sure there were dozens of others, men and women.

For the record, I've never been around Rogelio without a parachute. In spite of all his efforts to the contrary, we've never engaged in anything but the safest sex. Still, there are so many things that can happen, so there was little question about my responsibility to tell him.

It wasn't easy. I took him out for a beer at a neighborhood bar and explained it as best I could: that I'd had an HIV test which had come back positive, that I'd had the Western blot, and it was positive, too. I told him I was symptomatic, that my swollen glands and fatigue were typical.

"Who gave it to you?" he asked me, his face blank from shock. We were sitting on a pair of stools at the bar, and the neon from behind the register cast an eerie green glow across his features. He looked monstrous, and for the first time since I'd known him, I wanted to get away from him.

"Don't you understand what I just said?"

"Yes, I understand," he said, looking down at his feet. "And I want to know who gave it to you, okay?" His palms rested on his thighs.

"Rogelio, who the fuck knows who gave it to me?"

"Well, you know, don't you?"

"No, I don't; how could I? It could be anybody. And it doesn't matter anyway."

"It doesn't matter?" he asked, amazed. His face contorted with anger. "I want to know who it is, so I can kill the son of a bitch."

"Look, Rogelio, my honor isn't what's at stake here," I said, tired of the school yard bully in him. "It's you—and your family. You've probably been exposed."

"But Tommy," he said, his eyes narrowing into slits. "I'm not going to get this sickness. You, yes—you're a homosexual."

I shrank from him, feeling my fingertips go cold. I wanted to go running down the street, not to believe we'd ever shared an intimate moment or any kind of peace together. This was a monster of a man, the cruel stranger who offered candy from the sedan window. I don't know how it happened, only that suddenly I had my fingers wrapped like rope around his neck. His face disappeared into the black beneath the bar as I screamed at him. It was an awful, primitive howl.

"You and your fucking masculinity!" I shouted, my hands going numb as I tried to strangle him. There were sudden, loud noises in the bar and stools toppling over, men hooking my arms with theirs and pulling, pushing. "You can marry Miss Mexico and have a million little Third World babies, and it won't keep your cock from going up every time you're with a man, motherfucker! I've seen you!"

Somebody else's arm tightened around my throat, pulling me off Rogelio, but I kept screaming and kicking, or trying to, until I was chest-down on the floor. Somebody sat on my shoulders, and somebody else held my hands behind my back. "Calm down, Tommy," said a familiar voice. "Just calm down, baby."

I turned my head enough to see Rogelio being picked up off the floor by a muscular black man who held him as if he were a toy. His face was red, and his nose ran bloody all over his shirt.

"You okay, Tommy?" said the voice on top of me, which I recognized as Stan's. I thought his weight would flatten my lungs. "If I let you up, Tom, are you going to be okay?"

I grunted something that meant yes, and he hopped off me, finally allowing me to breathe. Stan smoothed my hair with one hand and used the other to help me up, but I was dizzy and terrified I was going to pass out.

"Just hold onto me if you need to, Tommy," he said, being gentle and sweet. He kept the circle of men around us at a safe distance. The fight had drawn quite a crowd. I noticed Arthur, the bar owner, staring at me.

"I'm sorry," I mumbled, but Stan just shook his head, telling me it was all right. My knees felt slippery; I had no energy. Stan pushed me against a chair.

"How about a glass of water for Tommy?" he said in Arthur's direction, and one appeared almost instantly. Stan wiped my face with a napkin and smiled. "You almost killed him," he said.

I looked across the room to where Rogelio had buried his face in the black man's shoulder. At first I thought the bastard was necking with him, but then I realized from the way his body shook that he was sobbing, right there in front of everybody.

"You want to tell me about it?" Stan asked.

I sighed. I knew Arthur wouldn't ban me for starting the fight, but the only decent thing would be to leave and not come back for a few weeks. I looked around the room, where most of the other men were relaxing now, the danger having passed. Stan, my healthy, good-looking buddy, was rubbing my shoulders. I hugged him and kissed his ear.

"Come on," he said, pulling back a little. "Tell Auntie Stan."

I chuckled. He can be such a queen sometimes. "It was nothing," I said. "You know…AIDS-related dementia." Then I cried and cried.

✦ ✦ ✦

Rogelio and I wound up speeding down Interstate 55 together for the same reason, I suppose, that desperate people do desperate things. As awful as it can be, there's a strange sense we're all we've got. Of course, I know that's not quite true, and he probably does, too. Right now Rogelio is quietly bitching about having to stop in St. Louis. He's in a hurry to get to Santa Fe only because it's our goal; of course, I'm in no hurry at all. The mountains will still be there, as will Ron and Paul, their leather boys and buffalo skulls.

"There's a sign for the Arch," I say, pointing.

"Okay, okay," Rogelio sighs, resigned to playing tourist. I can tell he thought we might pass it without my noticing. "I see it." He means the Arch itself, which is shimmering just off the highway. Frankly, the Arch is the only thing I've ever noticed about St. Louis—that silver loop rising out of the riverfront. Otherwise, St. Louis seems pretty flat and innocuous; it could be anyone of a million cities.

"Do you know anything about the Arch?" I ask Rogelio, but he just shakes his head. "I wonder what kind of view it has." Then I realize I'm not really thinking of St. Louis, but of Chicago, which is breathtaking from both the Sears Tower and the John Hancock. The panorama is more industrial, more metropolitan and complete from Sears, but I prefer the Hancock, with its strapping steel embrace. From the Hancock's east windows the lake is an endless sheen of blue. As I picture it—the lake dotted with tiny sailboats and specks of people on the shore—I realize I'll never see my hometown again. "Is the Arch a memorial or something?" I ask.

"I don't know, I don't have any idea," Rogelio says as he turns off the interstate and onto a busy city street. He's annoyed.

"Hmmm, does St. Louis have much of a skyline?" I'm determined to ignore his mood.

"I don't think so," Rogelio says. We're now stopped at a light, and the Arch is just to our right. The top of it disappears into the sky. "I don't think St. Louis has much of anything."

"Well, it's got Busch Stadium," I tell him.

"So what?" he says. "St. Louis lost the Cardinals to Phoenix."

"The football team, yeah, but not the baseball team."

We ride alongside the Mississippi River, where the city fathers are trying to develop a mall of sorts. There are a couple of riverboats that look permanently moored and have trendy hand-painted signs advertising authentic river cuisine, whatever that is. Rogelio grunts. He tries to figure out where to park, wanting to avoid the lots nestled under the interstate. We haven't seen a cop anywhere, our car is filled with my things, and Rogelio's silently convinced that leaving the car in the unguarded lot will spell trouble.

"You're the only Latin I know who doesn't care about baseball," I say. We take another turn, and I shade my eyes as I look at the glistening river. I need to buy sunglasses; I'll certainly use them in Santa Fe.

"I think Americans make too much of Latin fascination with baseball," he says, trying to relax.

"There are plenty of Latins at Cubs games," I say.

"Ah, yes, but that has another purpose," Rogelio says, finally emitting a little laugh. "That has to do with psychological identification." He's loose enough now to consider the parking lot, which is empty of all human life.

"Oh really?"

He smiles. "People call the Cubs 'lovable losers,' right?" he asks, while pulling a ticket from the machine at the lot's entrance. He maneuvers the car around the gravel and next to the chain-link fence. We are in the most exposed space in the lot.

"So?"

"Well, it fits in perfectly with the Latin inferiority complex," he explains with a cynical smile. "We're just trying to figure out why people like them, so we can imitate them." He turns off the car, pops his seat belt, and is out before I have a chance to hug him, which I very much want to do.

+ + +

The Arch is just beyond us, on the other side of a well-manicured little park. It looks a lot like the McDonald's arch, only big and made of chrome. When I try to look at it, the reflection is blinding. "God, it's bright," I say. I'm dizzy again.

"Do you want me to help you?" Rogelio's standing above me, watching as I try to get out of the car.

I shake my head. "It'll pass. I just need a minute."

"No problem," he says, but his foot is twitching, almost tapping. The muscles in his arms are tight again.

"You look just like you did that first day," I say, but actually he looks better.

"So do you," he lies, and reaches over to ruffle my hair. His touch is a little rough, but it's kind.

Of course, I look nothing like I did then. I'm pale and wasted, and I know my eyes are sinking into darkness. I wait a few minutes, then push myself off the car seat. I hold the car door for balance and notice Rogelio's worried but impatient look.

"Are you sure you want to do this?" he asks. I nod. "They probably have one of those elevators like at the Sears Tower—you leave your stomach on the ground level. It might make you sick."

I smile at him. "I think I can handle it. Besides, if I get dizzy again, I'll hold on to you." I wink.

"Uh uh," he says, shaking his head, but he's still smiling. "What you need is to get to Santa Fe and relax with your friends."

"Rogelio, I'm not going to get better," I tell him as we step onto the picturesque walkway to the Arch.

"Sure you are."

"Only for a little while," I say, measuring my breath as we walk up the hill. Then I casually reach over to him and touch his fingers. He looks around quickly and obviously, but he doesn't freak out or push me away, as I might have expected. Instead, his hand covers and squeezes mine. I'm just thinking how exhilarating—and amazing—this is, when we hear a voice behind us.

"Excuse me."

Rogelio stiffens, then moves his hand to my elbow as he turns toward me, pretending he's helping me walk. His eyes are panic-stricken and silently pleading with me to cooperate with his charade.

"Excuse me," the voice says again, and Rogelio whirls around, momentarily stumped when he can't find the source. When his eyes finally focus down on two women in wheelchairs trying to get by us, he jumps dramatically out of the way, muttering excuses under his breath.

"My god," he says, panting. "Where did they come from?"

"I think they're racing," I say as the two shiny chairs disappear over the hill.

"Do you think they saw?" he asks.

"Saw what?" I'm disgusted: it wasn't the women who ruined the moment, it was him. He doesn't understand, but he feels badly and tries to make light of the situation by throwing his hands in the air in mock resignation. The problem is, I'm too angry, too disappointed to think it's even a little amusing.

"We don't have a lot of time," I tell him, gasping on the incline.

"Then let's hurry," he says, checking his watch and quickening his step toward the Arch. But he's misunderstood me again.

✦ ✦ ✦

The fact is, I don't really want to deal with the Arch, and I don't really want to go to Santa Fe, which rings in my ears with an unexpected finality. About the only place I want to be is on the front porch of Stan's old house, just a couple of blocks off Broadway back in Chicago. I spent the whole summer of 1978 lounging on that porch, reading about Anita Bryant's antigay crusade in the papers and watching the boys walk by.

I fell in love a million times that season, and each time there would be a triumphant moment when my new lover and I would walk hand in hand down Broadway. I had a real swagger then; I wore satin running shorts and sunglasses at night. At least half the fun came from the stares we got from the Greek restaurant owners and Korean dry cleaners. Gay men were all over Broadway then, even more so than now—we were the guys ordering gyros and bringing in Italian suits to be pressed, so nobody complained. We always said we didn't care what people thought, but we did. And back then we cared even more. Public displays of affection were a statement: No queers had done it before, not like that—right there at high noon, trying desperately to make it seem as commonplace as taking a baby for a stroll.

"Are you okay?" Rogelio asks as we near the Arch. My breathing is labored and my chest feels tight.

I can tell he's afraid I'll get morbid on him; he practically cringes in anticipation. I do want to tell him the truth, but I don't have the energy. As soon as I can, I sit down on the concrete steps just below the Arch, fold my arms on my knees, and put my head down. My legs seem extraordinarily long, and my head feels like a drum.

"Are you all right?" asks a stranger's voice.

I look up enough to make out one of the wheelchair women. "I'm okay," I tell her; she seems totally trustworthy. "I'm just a little dizzy." Her friend is waiting for her, parked about ten yards from us but facing the parking lot. "You already went up?" I ask, surprised that they're ready to leave so soon.

"We can't go up," she says, and her tone is both wry and resigned. "The Arch isn't accessible."

I can tell Rogelio doesn't understand, his eyes scanning mine for meaning. "There aren't any ramps?" I ask the woman, thinking Rogelio and I can help them, but then I realize I'm too weak to push a wheelchair, much less lift one, or two.

She laughs, but it isn't bitter or mean. "Not just that," she says. "The elevators aren't accessible either." Now I'm as confused as Rogelio, but before I have a chance to ask her anything, she's saying good-bye and rolling back to her friend.

✦ ✦ ✦

There's a whole subterranean world under the Arch: a museum, a video show, a couple of souvenir stores. There's also a snake of a line to the elevators. I'm surprised there are so many people, especially because it's a weekday, but then I realize most of the ticket holders are tourists, primarily Asians. Even though the line moves relatively well, I have to squat and lean against the wall. It's getting harder to swallow, too, and I keep seeing little bursts of orange and blue light in front of my eyes.

During all this, Rogelio is a phantom. He stands pale and quiet next to me, but he wants to run. His fingers are folded into tentative fists, and he keeps shifting his eyes from side to side. I know the crowd scares him; there are too many people in uniform. I tell him these are only Arch security people, not covert INS agents. But although he has never gotten so much as a traffic ticket, authority types frighten him, and he won't be reassured.

Me, I resent everything. I hate that with a mouthful of thrush I'm the one having to tell him everything's okay. For once, I want him to do the talking, I want him to be brave, to take my hand, push his way to the front of the line and demand our own elevator. At the top of the Arch, I want us to grope and run our tongues along each other's stubbly chins, right there in front of all the tourist groups and grade-school field trips.

"Tommy?" There's a hand on my cheek. "Tommy?" I lift my eyes and see Rogelio's face emerging from a gray haze. "We should go," he says. "You don't look good." He glances nervously next to me, where a woman with two small children is staring at us.

"Fuck what I look like," I say, my lips sticking to each other. I reach up to undo my mouth, but I can barely feel my fingers.

"Tommy, let's go," Rogelio insists, and he starts to take my elbow.

"No, damn it," I say, standing up and jerking away. "I don't want to go to Santa Fe yet." I think of those ghostly buffalo skulls hung so artfully in Ron and Paul's gallery. "I have a fashionable disease, you know." Rogelio blanches, and I laugh. "Hey, don't worry, you're not going to get it," I add, winking at him. I start to laugh again, but something gets caught in my throat, and I cough instead, my head rocking back and forth. After a minute, I see him through the watery channel in my eyes. He has stepped away a bit, almost as if he's scared of me.

"You look like shit," he says in a whisper.

Soon we're in front of the elevators, and I understand why the wheelchair women were disenfranchised: You have to step up and hunch down to get in the elevators, which aren't elevators at all but tiny little holding pens in which no one can stand. The doors open and shut like a vault. As I watch the tourists get in, I can't help but think of Nazi ovens. A few people refuse to ride these little torture chambers, and I think they look suspiciously Jewish.

"Get in, Tommy," Rogelio orders, and I lift my legs one at a time, but I fall anyway, finally crawling up to a chair. I want to tell Rogelio I don't think we'll survive, but the only thing out of my mouth is air. I finally settle in, wiping my face on my sleeve, which is so wet I could wring it. I feel bruised and weary.

Rogelio says nothing, he just sits quietly across from the two Asians assigned with us to this elevator. They are blank-faced and embarrassed. I supply the soundtrack for the trip, breathing like an iron lung. When the elevator starts moving—not a modern vacuum up some gigantic shaft but a jerky Ferris wheel ride—they're relieved to hear the creaking and groaning of the gears.

I look out the little window and realize we have no view at all. Instead, we're traversing the very bowels of the St. Louis Arch—ancient stairwells, a landing filled with janitorial supplies, a caged room with lockers for maintenance workers. I start to laugh, quietly at first, but then I can't help it, and I slap my thigh hysterically.

Rogelio ignores me at first, then finally reaches over and reluctantly pats my shoulder. "Don't cry, Tommy," he says. But I'm not crying at all. I wipe my nose and brush my hair out of my face. I pull my pants up and dry my eyes. Then I tuck in my shirt, feeling the vast distance between my bones and the waistband.

"I don't ever want to get to Santa Fe," I say after much effort, and Rogelio shakes his head. He can't hear me above the mechanical noises. The Asians across from us shift in their seats, and Rogelio sits as far away from me as space allows. "I don't want to go to Santa Fe," I repeat, but I can't feel my lips move.

+ + +

When the elevator doors part, we tumble out to a steep, narrow stairway. We're all crushed together, the Asians, Rogelio, and me, and traffic keeps going around us. I feel Rogelio's hands on my hips, secretly guiding me up toward the fresh-faced student at the top of the stairs, a red-haired girl with a walkie-talkie strapped to her belt. She's on the lookout for trouble, or troublemakers, and it feels like Rogelio's turning me in. I jerk him loose, pushing my way through the crowd. It's cold up here, and the air feels thin.

At the top, the observation deck is a small room that resembles a space capsule. There are no windows to speak of, just horizontal slits maybe a yard wide and ten inches deep. To get a peek you lean over, resting your body against the incline of the walls. On the east side, there's no lake, just the Mississippi River looking muddy and small. On the west, there's no city, just generic St. Louis. Straight down, I can see the kidney-shaped pond next to the Arch and the walkway to the parking lot. I'm nauseous.

"Rogelio?" I whisper. I don't see him anywhere. A couple of kids are running between adult legs, but none belong to Rogelio. I try to find him by stretching up above the crowd, but I can't seem to muster the strength. I lean my back against the wall and feel my throat with my hand. My fingers seem to be working again, and my glands aren't as tender. I lick my lips, but there's something salty on them. I turn away from the crowd, which keeps brushing against me, and flap my sleeve up to my mouth. My lips feel sore.

It's then I hear unmistakable laughter behind me: high-pitched, kind of girlish. I turn to find it, but whole family groups keep coming and going by me as quickly and enthusiastically as if we were at a political rally. Everybody's got souvenir tee-shirts. There's a grandmother with a Confederate flag sewn on the back of her jacket. Teenage girls cackle with disappointment over the Arch's antiquated futurism. They smack their gum and sigh, barely noticing me. They're so close, I can smell their shampoo and cigarettes.

"St. Louis used to have another baseball team, before the Cardinals," someone is saying; it's a voice I could recognize in the dark. "But the St. Louis Browns left the city and became the Baltimore Orioles in 1954." There's a man with a cowboy hat in front of me, and as the hat dances away, I see Rogelio, cocky, giving away no secrets. He's talking to another man, propped casually against the wall on the other side.

"Well, it's karma then," the man says. He's big and white and wearing a cap with the logo from Rogelio's union local. "You know, Baltimore had a team sneak out on 'em a couple of years ago—the Colts."

"Yes, the football team," Rogelio says. "They're in Indianapolis now."

The man, who's about fifty and graying, hunches forward to look out one of the little windows. I can't keep them in my line of vision because the tourist flow is constant. But I hear them both laugh. Then I see the man slap Rogelio's shoulder in a friendly, manly sort of way. They're obviously friends, and when a small woman in a pair of yellow cotton pants comes up to them, the man goes through a series of introductory motions. Rogelio shakes her hand.

I'm watching from across the way, but he has no idea I'm here. So many people have bumped into me, I feel raw and beaten. I want to leave now; I want to collect my lover and go. "Rogelio," I say, but he doesn't hear me. A girl walking inches in front of me focuses my way. She's not sure if I'm talking to her. "I'm just trying to get my boyfriend's attention," I tell her, nodding in Rogelio's direction. The girl looks frightened, and I feel something wet on my shirt. Someone says something to her over her shoulder, but her eyes are wary and still on me.

I try to get away, but my knees wobble, and I quickly lean back against the wall. I touch my uneasy stomach, rubbing it with my hand. When I reach up to my pounding heart, I find a puddle and follow the trail of saliva up to my chin. I shove my wrist up to my mouth, rubbing my sleeve against it. I turn around slowly, facing the wall, and swallow hard. My forehead throbs. I tell myself it's not a good idea to panic. I remind myself the St. Louis Arch is not accessible, and I'm going to have to walk back to one of those little Nazi elevators. But I don't want to move, I don't want anything to happen now. I want to close my eyes and open them up to the aftermath of a simple dizzy spell in a normal world, where Rogelio comes up from behind me while I'm doing the dishes and wraps me up, nuzzling against my neck.

"Mister, are you all right?"

The red-haired girl with the walkie-talkie is standing next to me. She is all business, and her look is firm. I'd tell her I'm fine, but I'm not. And besides, I could never fool her.

"Do you need help?" she asks, and it's obvious I do. "Here," she says, offering her shoulder as a crutch. She uses a free hand to unhook the walkie-talkie from her belt and gives emergency instructions across the air waves. Then she efficiently snaps it back on her belt and turns to me, holding me with strong, muscular arms. I push slowly off the wall and turn.

The entire observation deck is quiet now, and the crowd has created a space for me. The only sounds are the elevators in the distance and the shuffling of feet. The red-haired girl walks with me, and I hear whispers behind me. As we head toward the stairway, the noise level returns to normal. I hear Rogelio's voice again, and my head jerks toward it. The red-haired girl turns with me.

"Rogelio—"

His back is to us, and he stabs the air with his finger to make a point in an argument. The gray-haired man with whom he's talking sees us and juts his chin our way. Rogelio turns quickly, registering everything with a shiver. Suddenly, he looks just like any other South Side greaser[3]—the too-tight blue jeans and black tee-shirt, his hands rough and calloused. His chest moves up and down with heavy breathing.

My eyelids drop against my will, and the red-haired girl shifts under me. I hear her say something, and Rogelio responds, but when I finally look up all I see is his shoulder turning back to the gray-haired man and the woman in the yellow pants, their voices unnaturally bright. I hear him say something about his son, about football, about his wife. I don't know, I don't know.

I want to throw up. Both Rogelio and I have keys to the car, but I know neither one of us would leave the other. The thing is, I've seen him turn now, and I've heard his voice bob and sink away from me. That means something.

When the red-haired girl leads me away, I look over her shoulder, wanting by sheer force, by the volume of both my love and hatred, to make Rogelio look at me. When he finally does, just this side of the heterosexual couple pretending not to notice our intensity, he's terrified. He sticks his hands in his jeans pockets and balls them up, causing the jeans themselves to hike up an inch or so. He looks at me, then looks away. Then he looks back again, his eyes pleading for understanding. But my heart is pounding its thin walls, and I don't understand. I want to ask him how much he expects me to take.

Special thanks to Gabor and Rex Wockner.

—1994

[3] A derogatory term for Mexicans used throughout the southwest U.S. Dating back to the 19th century, but popularized during the U.S.-Mexican war of 1846, the term was commonly used by soldiers and in dime store novels that were used to propagandize the war. The origin of the term is uncertain, but it may have initially referred to the menial, "greasy" jobs done by Mexicans throughout the southwest.

CAROLINA HOSPITAL (1957-)

Poet, essayist, and fiction writer Carolina Hospital was born in Cuba but left with her parents to seek refuge in the United States. Her poems represent a creative effort to chronicle her search for meaning and identity as a Latina living in the U.S. In addition to co-editing the collection *A Century of Cuban Writers in Florida: Selected Prose and Poetry* (with Jorge Cantera, 1996), she has published *A Little Love* (under the pen name C.C. Medina, 2000) and *The Child of Exile: A Poetry Memoir* (2004), and her writings have appeared in anthologies, newspapers, and literary journals. Hospital, who has an M.A. from the University of Florida, currently lives in Miami, where she teaches writing composition and literature at Miami-Dade Community College.

Freedom
for Belkis Cuza Malé [1]

For twenty years they hid your words
afraid of you,
a young girl from Guantánamo,
the daughter of a cement factory worker.

They silenced poems of   5
cinderellas and silver platters,
frightened by your beautiful people
and portraits of sad poets.

Now, far from your island and
them,   10
your poems shout without restrictions.
But the words remain unheard.
Here, a poem
doesn't upset anyone.

—2004

---

[1] Belkis Cuza Malé (b. 1942), Cuban author and journalist who initially supported the Cuban revolution, but became disillusioned with the Castro government over issues of censorship. She and her husband, Cuban poet Herberto Padilla, were jailed in 1971 for being vocal critics of the regime, an event which drew considerable attention among Latin American intellectuals, many of whom broke with the revolution over it. Cuza Malé was eventually released and in 1979 went into exile in the United States, where she founded a literary review magazine and published several books.

MYUNG MI KIM (1957-)

Myung Mi Kim was born in Seoul, South Korea. When she was nine, her family immigrated to the United States and she spent her teenage years living in Oklahoma, South Dakota, and Ohio. After working as a high school teacher and ESL instructor in New York, Kim attended the Iowa Writers' Workshop, where she received her M.F.A. in 1986. During this period, she published in the avant-garde journal *HOW(ever);* she went on to co-edit the journal in the early 1990s. Kim's first book of poetry, *Under Flag* (1991), met with critical acclaim for its techniques of linguistic defamiliarization to suggest and induce the conditions of multiple-language speakers. *Under Flag* was followed by *The Bounty* (1996), *Dura* (1998), and *Commons* (2002). Kim's poetry interrogates the processes of translation and instruction, compelling her readers to consider how language is formed and deformed by the violences of war and imperialism. In her breaking and re-making of language and its conventions, always informed by a historical consciousness, Kim's writing has been compared to that of Theresa Hak Kyung Cha, especially her work *Dictee* (1982). Yet these texts by Kim and Cha are not "about" historical occurrences in the conventional sense; rather, they enact the impact of history on language, as well as the power of language to make history anew. Kim is on the faculty of the Creative Writing Program at San Francisco State University, where she has taught since 1991.

Body As One As History

Weight of breasts or milk and all blood

This is a tree. It bears fruit.

Ministering to body filling no munificence

This is the body feigning. It is large as I.

Time rage, churn of one part and another   5

Nothing to succor what is dense and fragile at the same time

Inaudible collapse

Given the body's size, size for a grave

Pallid pellucid jar head

Gurgling stomach sack   10

Polyps, cysts, hemorrhages, dribbly discharges, fish stink

Skin, registering bruise or touch

But the body streaked black across a red brick wall

The body large as I, larger

Save the water from rinsing rice for sleek hair   15
This is what the young women are told, then they're told
Cut off this hair that cedar combs combed
Empty straw sacks and hide under them
Enemy soldiers are approaching, are near

And in this way she tried to keep them alive—two dried anchovies   20
for each child and none for herself. The train gathering speed. And
with no words but a thrust of a fist holding out money the soldiers
stroke their penises cup their balls, push stripped plastic dolls
with black ink scratched on between the hard twig legs into her face.

Treadle needle tread thread. Left armhole, right bodice. Cotton   25
rayon nylon dust. The crouch of the mother over machine over
a child's winter coat over a stream rinsing diapers
when night falls while the soldiers ranged while the border loomed
and she crossed it. Over a blouse 3 cents over a skirt 5 cents and
in this way   30

This is the body and we live it. Large as I. Large as

Tips of their fingers touching or not. Women on a clover field where
brown rabbits have just fed. Rise of line of women stretching to the
rise of land. No one moves. Every muscle moves. No one approaches.
In their mouths, more than breath more than each sound buzzed inside 35
the inside of the mouth.

As large as.

—1991

Into Such Assembly

1.
Can you read and write English? Yes____. No____.
Write down the following sentences in English as I dictate them.
         There is a dog in the road.
         It is raining.
Do you renounce allegiance to any other country but this?   5
Now tell me, who is the president of the United States?
You will all stand now. Raise your right hands.

Cable car rides over swan flecked ponds
Red lacquer chests in our slateblue house
Chrysanthemums trailing bloom after bloom   10
Ivory, russet, pale yellow petals crushed
Between fingers, that green smell, if jade would smell
So-Sah's thatched roofs shading miso hung to dry—
Sweet potatoes grow on the rock choked side of the mountain
The other, the pine wet green side of the mountain   15
Hides a lush clearing where we picnic and sing:
         Sung-Bul-Sah, geep eun bahm ae[1]

---

[1] (Kor.) Deep into the night at the Temple of Becoming the Buddha.

Neither, neither

Who is mother tongue, who is father country?

2.

Do they have trees in Korea? Do the children eat out of garbage cans? 20

We had a dalmation
We rode the train on weekends from Seoul to So-Sah where we grew grapes

We ate on the patio surrounded by dahlias

Over there, ass is cheap—those girls live to make you happy

Over there, we had a slateblue house with a flat roof where   25
I made many snowmen, over there

No, "th", "th", put your tongue against the roof of your mouth,
lean slightly against the back of the top teeth, then bring your
bottom teeth up to barely touch your tongue and breathe out, and
you should feel the tongue vibrating, "th", "th", look in the mirror,   30
that's better

And with distance traveled, as part of it

How often when it rains here does it rain there?

One gives over to a language and then

What was given, given over?   35

3.

This rain eats into most anything

        And when we had been scattered over the face of the earth
        We could not speak to one another

The creek rises, the rain-fed current rises

        Color given up, sap given up   40
        Weeds branches groves what they make as one

This rain gouging already gouged valleys
And they fill, fill, flow over

        What gives way losing gulch, mesa, peak, state, nation

Land, ocean dissolving   45
The continent and the peninsula, the peninsula and the continent
Of one piece sweeping

One table laden with one crumb
Every mouthful off a spoon whole

Each drop strewn into such assembly   50

—1991

BEATRIZ RIVERA (1957–   )

Beatriz Rivera was born in Havana, Cuba, to Aida Ruffin and Mario Rivera, owners of an insurance company. In 1960, her family fled the island and relocated to Miami, where Rivera lived until her teens. Her parents' troubled marriage drove her to escape to Switzerland, where she finished high school. After graduating, she moved to Paris and enrolled at the Sorbonne, where she studied philosophy and received her master's degree in 1980. Rivera has been married twice, first to Denis Beneich, a French philosophy student and writer, then to Charles Barnes, a businessman with whom she has two children. Rivera returned to the U.S. with Barnes, seeking an identity as a writer that she was unable to find as a Cuban American living in France. The couple settled in New York before moving to New Jersey; during this time Rivera taught French, worked as a freelance journalist, and wrote fiction. Known for casting a witty and perceptive eye on contemporary Cuban-American culture, Rivera has published a collection of short fiction, *African Passions and Other Stories* (1995), and three novels: *Midnight Sandwiches at the Mariposa Express* (1997), *Playing with Light* (2000), and *Do Not Pass Go* (2006). In 2003, Rivera received her Ph.D. in Spanish Literature from the CUNY Graduate Center in New York City. Currently, she is an assistant professor in the Spanish Department at Penn State Worthington Scranton. "Paloma" first appeared in *The Americas Review*.

Paloma[1]

Her land was green and brown, and rolling and grooved by torrents. It rained almost all year long. It rained harder in September, October, November. It was a tropical rain. It gorged the air and the earth. It made the ground swell. Her village was Indian, Mauresque, Spanish, as colorful, as busy, as warm as a Peruvian blanket. There was an old yellow cathedral, a market place, a flower square. There were several parks staked with statues erected in honor of Spanish heroes some of which were now buried in the graveyard adjacent to the church, a tourist attraction. The oldest headstone was from 1518, but the name was impossible to read; the constant rain had made the stone melt. On some of the other headstones Spanish names such as Grijalva, Jaramillo, and Torquemada could be deciphered; names respected and renowned for having imported to the New World the medieval mysticism, the self-punishment, and the humble submission that her people, because of their wise inborn serenity and survival instinct, had accepted from the very beginning. They hardly had enough to eat, but that was God's will; their ancestors too had lived and survived on half-empty stomachs; they even got fat. There was corruption everywhere, but it was so common that it was confused with normality. Those who weren't satisfied with the system escaped to that paradise called the United States instead of complaining or fighting or trying to alter the deeply rooted ways. They'd been taught that any effort here wasn't really worth making. They'd best save their energy and willpower for America. In truth, corruption was so bad that, in terms of money, it took several years of hard labor for those who had no connections to obtain something as simple as a passport. So the luckier ones who held this precious document didn't even travel. They stayed where they were and took good advantage of their passports. But, whether lucky or unlucky, instead of trying to climb mountains, her people did the best they could to make their way around the mountains.

[1] Though it may be used as a first name, "paloma" means pigeon or dove in Spanish.

Paloma Sánchez stood five feet two inches on her bare feet. She was a tiny little thing with shoulder-length black hair that was curly because of semi-annual permanent waves. From the time they were twelve or thirteen, the women from her village resorted to this kind of hair treatment; their hair was too straight if left natural, and they didn't seem to like it natural. Paloma's skin was ripe olive. She was lean and muscular. Her teeth were shiny white and perfect. She had black almond-shaped eyes and a little-bird quality to her demeanor. And she was pretty. Extremely so. So pretty that a boy of fifteen had claimed her when she was thirteen, and they were married in haste a month later. But that was normal, about as normal as not being able to obtain a passport without money or connections. Even the homely ones married young. Life was so hard that they did everything quickly, perhaps just to be done with it.

But Paloma wasn't normal. She was among the luckier ones in that at age twenty-five, when she went to the market place with her ten, eleven and twelve-year-old sons, she still made heads turn; men thought these boys were her brothers. She hadn't aged quickly like most of the other women. Rodrigo, her husband, always bragged about having married the most beautiful woman in this land. And Rodrigo was the one who came up with the bad idea of having Paloma's picture taken.

If the sleeping dogs had been left to lie, maybe Paloma wouldn't have gone to prison and hers would have been a normal life.

But to commemorate every special occasion in their lives, Rodrigo insisted on dragging Paloma to a little photo studio in the village. At first Paloma didn't want to; she was scared of x-rays and cameras. And the more she went, the more she was humiliated and terrified now. Rodrigo quickly took to repeating the same exact thing after the flash had gone off and Paloma's image had been gulped by the camera. With a loud sigh of relief he'd say that (at last!) her children and future grandchildren would realize how beautiful she had once been. He'd also add that it'd be different this time, that she'd come out looking as spectacular as she was, technology was advancing, practically every day progress was being made with flashes and cameras. Paloma needn't worry. This time she wouldn't be offended by the developed photograph. She'd have a photo she was proud of! This never happened.

These humiliating photo sessions began when Paloma was eighteen. It was in honor of their fifth wedding anniversary. Paloma had already borne three children then, but she had also managed to graduate from high school thanks to the help and cooperation she got from her parents and immediate family. Rodrigo, too, had graduated from high school and they both had excellent jobs. Paloma stayed in her village and worked as a secretary in the administration. Rodrigo was a customs official in the capital. They only saw each other once a month; but this way of life allowed them luxuries such as photo sessions for Christmas, birthdays and anniversaries, meat or fowl every night on their table, decent clothes, a decent dwelling. The clothes were extremely important for Paloma; she was a gentle, sensitive woman with a little vain streak, it happens even to the gentle and the sensitive—and this is precisely why the photo sessions made her life take a turn that nobody had expected.

Neither Paloma nor Rodrigo were disappointed at first. They laughed and blamed it on the flash. So did they the second time. Then it was the photographer. Then it was the camera. Then it was because she was pregnant for the fourth time. They also tried to blame it on the rain. After that, it was her nerves—everybody gets nervous on special occasions. They tried July, that run-of-the-mill month July, when nothing was happening. Still no good. They finally went to the capital. Photographers in the capital were far more competent; they were sure they wouldn't be disappointed.

But they obtained the same puzzling results and this time Paloma overreacted. She cried and swore that she'd never have her picture taken again. She even wondered if she was as ugly as she appeared on a developed photograph. She sobbed and complained that life wasn't worth living if her—she didn't say "beauty"—if her good looks were to disappear one day without leaving a trace. Her perplexed husband tried to comfort her. It was difficult though, for he himself was disappointed, he just couldn't understand. How was it that he had married the most beautiful woman in this land and that she was so homely on a developed photograph? He always bragged about her to his buddies in the airport and had, time after time, promised to bring them a photo of her. But he just couldn't get around to it! How could he show them the image of a common-looking matron after years of bragging?! They'd tell him that love was certainly blind! Rodrigo still had to comfort his wife though, so he put his wounded pride to one side. It wasn't that she actually looked ugly…it was.…What was it? It was that she looked like anybody else. Common! Paloma sobbed even harder. Rodrigo's wife, Paloma. Paloma of all people! Paloma looked common on a photograph! Even the photographer couldn't understand what had happened. He argued that he usually made women look prettier than they really were, he even insisted on taking several other pictures of Paloma who finally gave in after having chanted and chanted "never again" at least fifty times. But the same exact results were obtained again and again. She was as pretty as a bird, but on a photo she looked like anyone. Like everyone. From that day on, Paloma and Rodrigo acted as if she were afflicted by some unknown disease that no doctor could diagnose. For a while they continued running from doctor to doctor, still no result.

One day, Paloma finally dried her tears and said with the resolution of wounded pride, "so be it!" If she was condemned to lose her good looks, if in twenty years' time she wouldn't even be able to produce paper proof of her youth, well, then, she'd start living. Wasn't she, after all, dissatisfied with her life? She'd married too young and that thrill was gone. She had children and she was a loving mother, but the children just couldn't fill the void. What exactly awaited her? More Christmases. More wedding anniversaries. More birthdays. Her children would grow up and marry, and she'd most likely be a grandmother before age thirty, then a great grandmother at forty-five. Then what? She'd wither and die.

Paloma was born strange. She had always wondered about the meaning of life. She was born dissatisfied. Since puberty she had tried to dilute this unpleasantness and swallow it. Like a ghost, it always returned to its haunted house. So if a dull fate was the only thing in store for her, Paloma, who was five feet two inches tall, decided once and for all to walk around it.

She was going to put fine clothes and jewels on her body. She'd have many loves. She'd know the pangs of passion as many times as her spirit could take them without breaking. She'd be married to many, many men. She'd live in sixty different places at the same time. Perhaps she wasn't photogenic. So be it, she'd make the best of it. She knew how to do it. It was a rusty, broken old gift that she'd left behind. At puberty. When she got married and had convinced herself that it was just child's play. Back then it had seemed more important to become an adult, bear children, celebrate Christmas with the family, show your children off, the cute things they say and do, hide behind them, die progressively behind them, give up, be serious. Now she was determined to bring the child Paloma back.

She asked the local photographer to take a small picture of her, the kind you use for passports. A week later, when she went to pick her photo I.D.'s up, the photographer, who knew her well, said, "I think I could sell that exact same photo to any woman who walks in here." Paloma smiled and said, "I know that."

Because she worked in the administration and Rodrigo was a customs official, both she and her husband had certain privileges that the majority of her people wouldn't even dream about. In three months she had her passport. Rodrigo, who was more than content and even proud of his fate, said, "We're not leaving. We're not going to New York." It was absolutely out of the question. Their people suffered there. "Besides, our whole family's here. And the children need their cousins to play with. And Christmas wouldn't be Christmas…" Paloma interrupted him, she said, "Don't worry, I'm staying right here."

Christmas came and went. It barely gave them enough time to try again at the photo studio, to obtain the same offensive results, and to roast a pig at the routine family reunion. Paloma became distant and aloof. Everything saddened her; the food, the festivities, the gifts, the family. She wanted to cry, she wanted to die. The evil depression was gnawing away at her spirit. She tried to cheer up. It was to no avail. Her black eyes were constantly holding back the tears. What was the use of it? One more Christmas. One more wasted year. She was twenty-six, and she felt old and worn-out. She felt her life slipping by, and her youth. She looked in the mirror and noticed thin lines around her eyes. Nothing to look forward to. Nothing but this. While everyone was merry and sentimental, thanking the Lord that they were together, she felt like dying. She didn't consider herself a part of it. She felt trapped. She suddenly wished her husband would leave her, set her free. Sad heart, dirty hands. For the few days that followed she thought she was insane. Why this grief? Would it ever leave her? Christmas was supposed to be a happy season. But why pretend? So insane she must be. She wanted to die, that was all. Couldn't they just leave her alone?

Then came the feast of Saint Sylvester, the new year. Her resolution was to fly, up in the sky, way up high. Yes! She'd fly! And she'd fly before she became a grandmother. She swore to that!

It so happened that her thirteen-year-old son had gotten a nineteen-year-old spinster pregnant. They'd married in haste like everybody else and the baby was due in March. This didn't leave Paloma that much time to fly.

Three Kings Day she fell into a strange torpor. Sons and daughters and nieces and nephews were happily opening their presents. Children were laughing and playing and running and shouting, but Paloma saw and heard nothing. She still remained a loving mother. She continued being the gentle creature she was. But she was just pretending to be there. In reality, she was dreaming. Dreaming. She dreamt she was flying.

The bird was white. It had swallowed many people. You could see half the earth below you. The bird roared and whistled. It was cold in the bird's stomach. Paloma could see its wings of steel breaking the clouds in two. There was a woman sitting next to her. She was small and thin, and looked just like Paloma did on a developed photograph. And she wasn't the only one. All the women inside the bird looked exactly like Paloma's image on paper. "Are you scared?" the woman sitting next to her suddenly asked. Was there anything to be afraid of? Could this bird fall? She laughed and said, "Oh, you poor thing! The bird falling! That's the last thing in the world to be scared of!" Because the bird will land and you have to walk out of it. Into another world where many, many things are magic. But it remains a hard cruel world, a bit like ours, only different. Different because nothing's really obvious. Not even corruption. The truth is masked. Act normal though. Like a tourist. Tell them you're only here for two weeks to visit your family. If you don't convince them, they'll catch you! Don't worry about getting slapped around. They only do that in our land. At least that's what I've been told so far. What they do is catch you and send you back! That's when they hit you, when you get back. And they take you by the elbow. Push you around. You lose the freedom you never had. Have to start over a year later when you finally get out of jail. All those years of hard work to get papers and money to climb into the bird...lost! Lost forever! Have to start all over again. Aren't you scared? Of starting all over again? Yes.

The next day was a Sunday. Paloma woke up early. Her hands were shaking. Word got to her unexpectedly. And she knew where she had to go. She was ready. Rodrigo asked, "Aren't we going to Mass?" Paloma didn't answer. He then wanted her to get back into bed. That same afternoon he was returning to the capital, they wouldn't see each other for a month, shouldn't she get back into bed? Paloma said she never ever wanted to be pregnant again. She slipped her passport into her handbag and walked out of the house. She had nothing to hide.

The bus stopped near the market place. Her destination was an hour away. She went down, down; the hills got higher, greener, browner, the torrents became streams. After having stepped off the bus, she had to walk a while. The earth was soft and the mud ankle-high. There was a woman washing clothes in the river and crying. Her husband had had an accident. His legs were broken. He couldn't leave on Wednesday. The money was wasted. They'd have to start all over again. For years he'd planned this trip to New York. He was to work there and send money home. It was terrible because they'd begun building their house when they were newlyweds fifteen years ago. With cement blocks. Then they ran out of cement blocks. The next door neighbors offered to share one of their walls, but that only gave them a house with three walls. Their house was missing a wall. A plastic canvas had been nailed to that empty side. It worked fine when it didn't rain. The problem was that it rained almost every day and the canvas didn't keep the rain out.

Paloma walked downhill with her, and her house was indeed missing a wall. The house had a door though. They used the door. It was even locked. As if the house had four walls. They'd saved a lot of money. It didn't take long to convince the woman's husband. They gave the money to Paloma and Paloma gave them instructions.

She didn't go to work on Monday. With the intention of spending the newly earned money on herself, she went shopping, but ended up buying clothes and toys for her children instead. She also bought a layette for her grandchild that was due in March. By mid-afternoon the money was gone.

On Wednesday she dreamt she was flying. The bird was going down, down. Underneath her was the American city of Miami. Flat and full of lights, it looked like a gigantic amusement park. There was that same woman sitting beside her. She was afraid they'd catch her, and Paloma, too, was afraid they'd catch her. Those people in uniforms. That was their job. To catch you. They ask all kinds of questions. Even if you're telling the truth it makes you nervous. The bird landed. The stairs moved. The rubber rug moved. The suitcases moved like a serpent in the grass; you had to hurry up and catch them. Imagine your immobile suitcase passing in front of you! You wait, that's all. Then there was a line. The most dangerous part. All her people were nervous. What if they were sent back? English was a strange language. You can't understand it. But you could also hear Spanish. With a different accent. The man in the uniform wanted her passport and the yellow card that she had filled out before the bird put its feet on the ground. The woman sitting next to her had had problems filling it out. She could barely read and write. The man looked at her, then at her passport, then back at her. "What's your name?" he asked. So he repeated it in Spanish. Why did he speak English if he spoke Spanish? Paloma Sánchez. Your name? Paloma Sánchez. Your name? Date of birth? March 26, 1962. Learned all that by heart. Your name? Date of birth? First time you've been here? Open your suitcase! Final destination? New York. Where? Why? Where are you coming from? How long? Why? To visit my family. How long? How much money have you got? By the way, what's your birthdate? Step to the side; some women are coming to search you and ask you your name. And ask you to sign your name several times. Paloma had never been as terrified in her life. She felt the blood gushing up to her head. She thought it would burst. How long would this last? Was it worthwhile? What's your name? Paloma Sánchez. What if they caught her? What if they sent her back? Very well. You may go. Have a nice flight. Was that it?

There were corridors and it was cold. Somebody said it was the air conditioning; nobody could live here without it. And the stairs that went up by themselves. And the rubber mat that went exactly where you were going and took you there. Gate fourteen. Was she free? When the bird landed in New York, would they ask her more questions? That woman again! Waiting to get on the other bird. Maybe she'd know. She seemed to know everything. They were both glad they didn't get caught. Then they started talking about the others. The ones who weren't waiting here with them. That meant they had gotten caught, the woman said. She loved talking about terrible things, and pitying the others. Queens, New York. So many clothes to buy. Beautiful, beautiful stores. The people from this village of Queens are so friendly and helpful. And it's a pretty village. They sell food everywhere. Cheap. The prices don't change, apparently. When it rains, your feet don't get stuck in the mud. Queens is clean. And everybody in Queens seems to own a refrigerator. They put their clothes in machines, wait a while, then their clothes come out clean. Here you don't wash your clothes in the river. A distant cousin of hers who's been here for two years laughed when she asked where the river was. He said that the river here is much dirtier than the clothes will ever get. It's called the East River. Anyway, you can't kneel and wash your clothes in it.

A week later she had a job. They called this town Manhattan. And she kept wondering where New York City was. She wanted to visit New York City. Everybody said it was fabulous. New York City, where was it? And until she learned the truth, she regretted having to work in Manhattan.

One hundred and fifty dollars a week. She was to cook, clean, take care of the children, speak Spanish to the children. Their mother wanted them to be bilingual. What was bilingual? Vacuum? She preferred to sweep. But the mistress was adamant. She had to push that scary machine around. What if it swallowed her? The mistress said you have to vacuum. You have to keep everything very clean. They don't want germs in their apartment. The mistress spoke some Spanish. She said she learned it in Mexico. Every morning, rain or shine, she and her husband would put sport shoes on and go running. Why do people run away from nothing? They said it was to stay in shape. Thin. So that's why the mistress looked like a skeleton. And in spite of all the money they seemed to have, they never put meat or fowl on their table. They said chicken was very, very bad for you. Imagine that! Pork was a bad word. Imagine that! Pork was supposed to be a feast. Now it's bad. Must be the pork here. They ate like rabbits. Maybe they didn't have that much money after all....No sugar allowed either. The mistress said that sugar gave you cancer. What's cancer? Like rabbits, they ate lettuce and raw vegetables. One day they found out that she was giving their children fried food and they got very angry.

She had decided to save every penny she earned and send it home. But the girls wrote to her and said they wanted American clothes. Could she send them some? Reebok sport shoes, stretch jeans, thick socks...So one Saturday when she was in Queens visiting her distant relatives, she asked them to take her shopping. At first she was cautious. She only spent two hundred dollars. But the following weekend she thought that what she'd bought wasn't enough. Might as well buy more and send one big package home. It wasn't long before that was all she could think about. At night when she was lying in bed, she'd think of everything she had to buy on Saturday. The lists got longer and longer. She began needing things she never needed before. Suddenly twenty pairs of underwear weren't enough. She always needed more. And there was always that extra sweater she couldn't live without. And every time she got a new sweater she needed new pants. And the shoes to go with each new outfit. Every Saturday she ended up buying herself a new pair of shoes. There were so many shoes to buy! Then one hundred and fifty dollars weren't enough. She needed more; she needed to buy more. For the first time in her life she wanted, wanted, and suffered for wanting. Her heart ached when her eyes explored that last store window, and her arms were heavy with packages. She'd already spent all her salary. And that last pair of pants there, she wanted them! She began living for Saturday afternoon. That was all she could think about.

Paloma quit her job in the administration. She said she was too tired. With a sarcastic grin on their lips, her brothers, sisters, cousins, aunts, uncles, and even mother and father wondered why in the world she was so tired. After all, she hardly ever did anything in the house. Her daughter-in-law took care of that. The young girl cooked, cleaned, washed dishes, laundered, took care of the children, and gossiped about how Paloma spent her days either staring into blank space, or talking to herself, or telling the youngest children the weirdest stories, supposedly her adventures in America. Lies, all lies! One day her daughter-in-law asked her why she lied like that. Why tell the children stories of stairs that go upstairs by themselves? Why in the world make up stories when there were so many other things to do in life? Paloma replied that she'd already done all the other things in life.

A peaceful harmony, however, reigned in Paloma's house. Although her daughter-in-law loved to gossip about her and to complain about how she had to take care of all the household chores because Paloma wouldn't lift a finger, it so happened that Paloma's psychic retreat and Rodrigo's absence allowed this nineteen-year-old to be the head of the household. All the orders came from her. She ran the place. She took over. There was no clash between the two women; Paloma gave her daughter-in-law total power, and her daughter-in-law enjoyed that. In little or no time she stopped being a passionate pregnant teenager and became a bossy matron.

Word got to Rodrigo that Paloma was acting strange, that she was always tired, and that his daughter-in-law was now the mistress of the house. So Rodrigo decided to check this out and returned home for a four-day visit at the beginning of February. Instead of running to him with outstretched arms and at least ten contained hugs and kisses, Paloma hardly seemed to notice him. She was too busy getting ready to go out. She said she had an errand to run, that it was very important, and that she'd be back in a little while.

She walked in the direction of the market place and took the same bus she had taken before. This time she didn't have to travel as far. In a little village in the plains, two sisters were fighting. They both had long sharp nails and seemed to want to scratch each other's eyes out. They were also screeching like cats. The fight had begun over a lot of land six square feet big on which one of them had planted alfalfa for the pigs and watched the alfalfa grow until her sister had come to claim this portion of earth a bit bigger than a postage stamp. When Paloma arrived, they stopped screeching and fighting. "Which one of you is single?" Paloma asked. One of the she-cats raised her long-nailed hand and said, "I am." Paloma then followed her to her house, took the money, gave her the passport and instructions of what to do once she got to New York; send the passport back and fifty additional dollars a week for the next six months. They shook hands and said good-bye.

Three days later Rodrigo still hadn't left and Paloma dreamt she was flying. But Rodrigo was angry. He wanted his wife. He said he worked hard. He said he deserved what he wanted. He even threatened to abandon Paloma if her attitude didn't change. Paloma, in turn, gently replied that she was too nervous and too tired. The next day she could barely keep track of the time. She wondered whether it was two hours earlier or two hours later and kept asking her sex-starved husband what time it was. She said she was confused. She said she hadn't slept all night. Rodrigo left that day, threatening to return in a month, and that her attitude had better be different by then, or else.

She was in The Bronx. In a small factory. Four rows of sewing machines, side by side, and benches where four could fit but had to take turns lifting their elbows. There were women from every single country she had ever heard of. Bolivia, Colombia, Paraguay. They worked and talked all day, and each had their own transistor radio. They talked about clothes, makeup, men, husbands, and they also talked about themselves. The ones who had children brought their children to work. They ran up and down the narrow aisles between the benches. The men were on the other side of the wall. Everyone got fifteen cents per garment. They talked about birth control and how you had to pray to the moon if you didn't want a baby. They talked about the men on the other side of the wall. Some were worth marrying, others were going to succeed in this country, and like everywhere else there was one particular man that everyone was in love with and wanted. He was ambitious and handsome. He dressed well and smelled fine and even got a manicure every Saturday. His nails were clean and shiny. The women who didn't hate him called him an Adonis. The others hated him and called him the worst son of a whore that ever lived. Adalberto, that's what his name was, had broken some hearts in this factory. Those hearts were angry now. He'd even gotten five women on this side of the wall pregnant and obviously refused to marry each and every one of them. Two of his children often ran up and down the factory aisles.

At break time, one of her new friends pointed to Adalberto and said that that was him, and she fell madly in love the minute she set eyes on him. Besides, she'd heard so much about him that it was as if she'd already known him for two weeks. Suddenly she no longer felt as lonely in this new country. For two weeks it had appeared empty, but now he was here. She started loving every single corner of The Bronx because The Bronx was where he worked and lived.

She in turn lived with three couples and four women in a gloomy, windowless apartment near the factory. Her rent was thirty dollars a week. The rest she began to spend on tight sweaters, high-heeled shoes, tight stretch jeans, fancy dresses, makeup, love witchcraft, anything to attract him. She wondered how she had managed to live without his presence, without him being around. How boring life appeared up to now. So this was love. She hardly ate. She was determined to look like those girls on the covers of magazines. Every day she had to punch in at the factory at six a.m. She woke at four a.m. with a pounding, passionate heart. She was going to see him! Another day of trying to make him notice her! Life was worth living. Not even paradise could have competed with that factory. Without hesitating, she would have turned paradise down. Adalberto. She wanted to be wherever Adalberto was.

Every morning it took her forty-five minutes to get her hair just right and another forty-five minutes to make her face up. Deep green eye shadow and lots of mascara. Her eyes looked mysterious and big and wonderful. She also put lots of foundation and powder on. The last touch was the blush, from her cheekbone all the way up to her eyebrow. At five forty-five a.m., she was ready to go to the factory.

The rest of the day was spent trying to get a glimpse of Adalberto, as well as his attention. At break time, she'd look for him in the crowd, discreetly sneak over to where he was, call a girl friend over, begin a loud show-off conversation about her past and her adventures, and finally burst out laughing, for example, so he'd turn his head toward the laughter, certainly wondering what that laughing was all about. She'd then catch a glimpse of him in the corner of her eye, and look away, or look down, feigning both indifference and difference at the same time. One evening when she was punching out, he walked up to her and said that she had really caught his eye the day she started working here, but that he hadn't dared ask her out before. She was so pretty that she most probably belonged to another man. So if she was engaged or anything, it'd be O.K., he'd understand. He'd always like her though, he even thought he was in love with her. Would she like to go out with him? Of course she would! No, she meant that, yes, she would. She meant it'd be nice.

They went out on Saturday. While they were dancing, he whispered in her ear that she should try being a model or an actress. She was way too pretty to be at the factory. She was the most beautiful woman in the factory. While they were sitting at the bar he said that he loved her dress. It was really sexy on her. He caressed her knee and told her she had spectacular legs. They ordered more beers. He caressed her thigh and told her that he'd noticed men looking at her while they were dancing and that he felt like walking up to them and punching them because he just couldn't stand to have a man setting eyes on her. In the car he continued talking about how jealous he was. He fondled her breasts and drew her closer to him, whispering I'm so jealous, I'm so jealous. I'm so scared that another man will take you away from me. I'll kill him, I swear. She thought she was in heaven. He lifted her skirt. He said the factory was just a stepping stone for him. He had many ideas. He said he was going to start his own business. He slipped her panty hose off, said he wanted to feel her skin, that was all. He said that his business was going to make him rich. In a month. He was going to begin in a month. The factory was just a stepping stone. In this country you have to be intelligent. If you don't have money you're nothing. He took her panties off. He said he had millions of ideas. He said he'd never been in love in his life until he first laid eyes on her. Then he laid down on top of her. There was barely enough room in the car, but there was enough room anyway. While they were making love, he kept begging her to marry him, to be his wife, forever. He said that if she didn't become his wife, he'd either kill himself or die.

The next day she announced her engagement at the factory and also talked about how horribly jealous he was. She loved it! The other women agreed that when you make a man jealous you've got him. She giggled and proudly continued talking about him. One of the jilted women slapped her and she slapped her back.

They spent Sunday together. A friend of Adalberto's lent him a dirty, stinky bachelor's apartment. Adalberto bought imitation champagne and wondered where they should spend their honeymoon. On Monday at the factory she talked about wedding dresses. On Monday night, once again, they made love in Adalberto's car. On Tuesday there was a new girl in the factory. Perhaps she had tighter jeans, higher heels, and tighter sweaters. Perhaps she was seventeen. But the important thing was that she was new. She'd also laugh out loud and pretend Adalberto wasn't around. On Tuesday night in the car, Adalberto told her that the new girl wasn't half as pretty as she was. He then proceeded to slip off her panty hose and panties. On Wednesday she caught him talking to the new girl at break time. She screeched and tried to scratch her face. Adalberto had to separate them. When they were alone, he repeated that she was indeed the love of his life, but they simply had to wait a while before they got married, a man like him needed more room, he had millions of ideas and was going to start a new business next month. Since she didn't get the point, he said he didn't deserve her. He almost cried. Then he cried. She tried to comfort him. Everything would be all right. Adalberto didn't think so. He complained about being too jealous. They made love. Then Adalberto got angry. He accused her of flirting with some other man in the factory. She swore it wasn't true, but he hit her and pushed her around. She cried. On Thursday morning she announced that they'd quarreled. All her co-workers were interested and wanted to hear more about it. She cried and she cried. He started ignoring her. Maybe this was just a lovers' quarrel. He was so jealous! She waited. Then she slowly became friends with the other jilted ones. Two weeks later the new girl was also a jilted girl. She cried. Adalberto had promised to marry her! He'd talked about how jealous he was! Said he'd never had this passionate feeling for a woman in his whole life! He even threatened to commit suicide! She joined the club. They hated all the new girls that came to the factory. At least they hated them until the engagement was called off. They also hated Adalberto. But they continued aching for him. He'd been working there for two years, but the factory was just a stepping stone. Next month he'd start his own business. He said he was intelligent and had millions of ideas.

Paloma told Rodrigo that she never wanted to be with a man again. Men were liars and traitors. Rodrigo pushed her around and hit her and tried to force her. Nothing would do. She said she hated men. He finally left the next day and threatened to return in a month and that her attitude had better be different by then, or else.

Word started getting to Paloma unexpectedly. She even had to turn down some of the women who came to her with their requests. But whenever she had dreamt she was flying, she usually accepted their money. Only cash. Meanwhile, in the capital, Rodrigo was surprised to encounter so many traveling women named Paloma Sánchez. At first it had only happened once a month, then twice a month, now once a week some common-looking Paloma Sánchez would be traveling to New York. And they never returned. Nobody expected them to anyway. They left and disappeared into the American woodwork. So far he had counted fifteen women by the name of Paloma Sánchez. This, combined with the hard time he was having at home, most likely gave him the idea that Paloma Sánchez, his Paloma Sánchez, was probably not the only fish in the sea. There even seemed to be a surplus of her namesakes! So, Rodrigo ended up taking a mistress by the name of Gladys. Perhaps Gladys wasn't as pretty as his Paloma Sánchez, but she was sweet and available and always eager to see him. He had grown weary of his distant wife. Not only that, but Gladys was photogenic. She looked beautiful on a developed photograph, which allowed Rodrigo to satisfy his lifelong dream: everlasting proof of what a woman of his had once been. He even wanted to have children with Gladys. Just so the hypothetical children and grandchildren could admire her photos in the future.

Back home, Paloma could barely keep up. At least the flying didn't make her as nervous anymore. It was even beginning to bore her. The taking off, the landing, those people in uniform with their questions, ready to send you back if you make the slightest mistake, she felt like an expert. She was more than used to landing in New York and disappearing into the woodwork, as they say. At four a.m. she was putting blue eye shadow on her eyelids, at five a.m. she was sleeping in a little bed in a little room, either on Park Avenue, or on Fifth Avenue, or on Central Park South or West, at six a.m. she was mowing lawns in Montauk, Long Island, at seven a.m. she was painting a house in Poughkeepsie, New York, an hour later she was madly in love, rushing to have a cup of coffee with a new love, or she was missing her husband, or she was missing the love she'd left behind to come here and make lots of money. It's terrible to miss someone. The whole country seems empty if that one person isn't around. She'd then be hating her lover and saying terrible things about him and wishing he were sick, old, in a wheelchair, paralyzed. She made friends with all the women who'd loved him and together they'd wonder if he'd ever really marry. By mid-morning she'd be reading letters from her children; she had forty children now and six at her breast, seven on her lap. She was carrying three or four different children in her womb, but she went to a clinic and got rid of one because she had been forced in Brooklyn. This kind of thing never happened in her land, to get rid of a child. Before this she'd never even heard of it. At lunchtime she was either having a meat-less, salt-less, sugar-less, sodium-less, and cholesterol-free meal for her figure, or trying on tight jeans in the stores of Queens, or gossiping about the people who stayed back home, the ones who tried coming to New York and had failed, the ones who had made it and already had a car and a refrigerator, the ones who hadn't made it and had gone to jail, either here or there. Or she was aching for some new man and she was convinced that it was really love this time. Or she was still aching for that same one, who was now engaged for the fifteenth time since she'd arrived. Why was he so handsome? She loved him so and wished he were dead right now. Or perhaps he'd catch that dreadful disease that the buses and the subway and the radio talked about all the time. On Wednesday evening, she was unfaithful to her husband then she missed him terribly because he was such a good man. Then, after having finished painting the house in Poughkeepsie, she started taking the paint off her hair with turpentine. The next day she lost her index finger to a lawnmower. The needle from one of the sewing machines went right through her thumb. On Friday she had a date and she was passionately in love. She bought a party dress and high heels and fancy stockings. And she cleaned offices until twelve midnight. Now she was flying again. Her husband was waiting for her in New York and she hadn't seen him in three years. She was only twenty years old. Then she died. It happened suddenly. After having cleaned the lawyer's office, she was waiting for the train. It happened in the subway. Four men killed her. It hurt. They named her Jane Doe and it was cold in the morgue. Nobody to claim her body. Then she became an alcoholic. Then she was a drug addict. Then she met that horrible man who promised her the world. All she had to do was carry a suitcase from New York to Miami. One day they caught her. The suitcase was full of flour. They put her in prison. Oh, she was so happy the day her husband got his green card! That meant they could lead normal lives. No more fear of getting caught by immigration and sent back. Out of the woodwork. No more hiding.

Paloma's husband left her for Gladys. She hardly noticed he was going. As a matter of fact she was a bit relieved; a peaceful harmony reigned in the house when he was absent. But she didn't even have time to wonder how she felt now that she was an abandoned woman. It was Tuesday. On Tuesdays she rushed to the post office. Her passport always came back on Tuesday.

She asked Rodrigo if she could leave for New York. She said she wanted to start a new life there. Her daughter-in-law had turned out to be an excellent matron, so they didn't need her at home. Paloma even spoke English now. Rodrigo didn't seem to mind, he was too busy admiring and showing everyone the latest photographs of Gladys.

They said good-bye at the airport. Not that he accompanied her there, but that's where he worked. His last words were, "I'll probably never see you again." Paloma boarded an Eastern Airlines flight to Miami. She was thirty years old, three times a grandmother, and as beautiful as ever. She had money, she spoke English, she dressed well. And she knew customs and immigration by heart for having gone through there so so many times. She also knew what the questions would be and how to answer them. They'd ask her to sign her name several times, but that was her signature. Anyway, she had nothing to fear, she had a passport, quite a bit of money, and a visa.

Passport. Your name? How long do you plan to stay? Why? Where? How much money are you bringing? He opened her passport and looked at her photo then looked at her then back at the photo then back at her and smiled. He asked, "Amiga, do you think we're blind?" He called a co-worker of his and exclaimed, "Hey, Joe, look at this! Our amiga here must think we're blind. What do you think?" Joe thought out loud, "I think we've got one here." They both asked her if she really thought they'd fall for that. They had thousands of her kind leaking in through here and they had, what they called, the professional eye. "I can spot them from a mile away," Joe said. "Amiga, it's not that easy to sneak into the United States," the other one added. "Did you really think we'd fall for this?" he asked and slapped the passport. "You're way too pretty."

They showed her to a small waiting area, offered her coffee, then dinner. She waited hours. Some of her people were also in there. Waiting. Waiting for the plane that would take them back. It was hard getting into the United States, they agreed. You couldn't just slip by the customs officials like that. They had the "eye." Even the men cried. They'd be put in jail the minute they got back. But Paloma's eyes remained dry. "Aren't you upset?" someone asked her. "No. There are sixty-seven of me here already," she replied.

—1992

ALICIA GASPAR DE ALBA (1958-)

Born in El Paso, Texas, Alicia Gaspar de Alba holds a B.A. in English and an M.A. in English-Creative Writing from the University of Texas at El Paso, and a Ph.D. from the University of New Mexico, Albuquerque. Her doctoral dissertation, "Mi Casa (No) Es Su Casa: The Cultural Politics of the Chicano Art: Resistance and Affirmation Exhibit, 1965-1985," was awarded the Ralph Henry Gabriel Prize for the best dissertation in American Studies and was later published as *Chicano Art Inside/Outside the Master's House* (1998). Gaspar de Alba has published two works of poetry, *Beggar on the Cordoba Bridge* (a full poetry collection featured in the 1989 anthology *Three Times a Woman: Chicana Poetry*) and *La Llorona on the Longfellow Bridge: Poetry y otras móvidas, 1986-2001* (2003). She has also published a short story collection, *Mystery of Survival and Other Stories* (1993), which won a Premio Aztlán award, and *Sor Juana's Second Dream* (1999), an historical novel celebrating the erotic and literary life of the seventeenth-century Mexican nun Sor Juana Inés de la Cruz. Her second novel, *Desert Blood: The Juárez Murders* (2005), is also grounded in historical fact; it references the unsolved murders of over five hundred female factory workers in Juárez, Mexico, that have taken place since 1993. *Desert Blood* won a Lambda Literary Foundation Award for Best Lesbian Mystery in 2005. Gaspar de Alba, who co-edited the anthology *Velvet Barrios: Popular Culture & Chicana/o Sexualities* (2003), is a founding faculty member of the César E. Chávez Department of Chicana and Chicano Studies at UCLA, where she specializes in interdisciplinary research.

Bamba Basílica[1]

In Oaxaca at the basílica
de la Virgen de la Soledad

a radio blares "La Bamba"[2]
in the faith of an Indian woman,

Zapotec,[3] kneeling her way to the altar.   5
Arms outstretched, she opens

---

[1] (Sp.) Church.
[2] A traditional Mexican folk song made famous in the United States by Mexican-American singer Richie

Valens in the 1950s, when he recorded a rock and roll version of the song.
[3] Oaxacan indigenous people.

her palms to the Virgin's grace,
una poca de gracia y otra cosita.[4]

Her shoulders rise and fall in the dance
of supplication,   10

yo no soy marinero, soy capitán.
Beside her, the other supplicants

stand before la Soledad,
fingers to forehead, mouth, eyelids—

a solar cross suspended   15
over their disbelief—

arriba y arriba y arriba iré.
Now, la india's palms come together,

urgent words pressed between them:
por ti seré, por ti seré.   20

Her head bobs to the rhythm
of a promesa[5]

that Ritchie Valens
never recorded.

—1998

---

[4] Italicized lines are lyrics from "La Bamba" (Sp.): A little bit of grace and something else/I am not a sailor, but a captain/Up, up, up, I'll go/For you I will be, for you I will be.
[5] (Sp.) Promise.

DIANA ABU-JABER (1959-   )

Diana Abu-Jaber was born in Syracuse, New York, to a Jordanian father and an American mother. When she was seven, her family moved from Syracuse to Amman for two years; since then she has lived between the U.S. and Jordan. Abu-Jaber has a B.A. from SUNY-Oswego, an M.A. from the University of Windsor, where she studied with Joyce Carol Oates, and a Ph.D. from SUNY-Binghamton. Her first novel, *Arabian Jazz* (1993), won the Oregon Book Award and her second novel, *Crescent* (2003), won both the PEN Center USA Award for Literary Fiction and the American Book Award from the Before Columbus Foundation. She has also received a Fulbright grant award to do research in Jordan. In addition to her novels, Abu-Jaber has written a thriller, *Origin* (2007), and a memoir, *The Language of Baklava* (2005). She has taught at Iowa State University and the University of Oregon, and is currently a writer-in-residence at Portland State University.

My Elizabeth

I tipped my forehead to the window and watched as we passed another Indian, black-bronze in the sun, thumb in the air.

I was twelve and Uncle Orson was six years older. We'd started our trip in New York City, and I hadn't paid much attention until about two days in, when we began passing long wings of pivot irrigation and the sky started to look like it had been scoured with salt water.

We passed power lines that stood like square-shouldered figures at attention, past grain and silo storage bins, glowing aluminum with pointed tops. At the time I didn't know the names of any of those things; I'd never known that America unraveled as you moved west, until it ran straight as a pulled strand and the trees shrank back into acres of sorghum, beans, corn, and wheat. I stared through the truck window at things mysterious as letters in a foreign language.

My uncle's name had been Omar Bin Nader, but when he first pulled up to my father's apartment on Central Park, he introduced himself to me as Orson. For the rest of the ride out to Wyoming, he cursed his luck, having to transport this newly orphaned niece and all of her father's worldly goods. Then he would stop himself and apologize, saying, nothing personal, and hold my head against his chest.

I slept curled on the wide front seat of the cab. The sound of the engine went on and on. It reminded me of my toy train, an electric engine that had run a two-tiered figure eight around the hall outside our bathroom. It chugged and was painted red with "X & Y Railroad" in white on both sides. I used to watch it with Baba when I'd come home from school and he'd be waiting for me in his bathrobe and slippers and smelling of wrinkle-your-nose. He said to me, "Someday we will climb on to this train and I'll drive us home."

We passed square hay bales, plumes of irrigation water, torn tires, more trucks: Peterbilt, Kenworth, Mack, Fruehauf, Great Dane. Orson pointed out shacks with tires on the roof, sunflowers pointed toward dusk, the road ringing like an anvil.

Near dawn a train horn woke me, mournful and steady. My father had gone away to work on the train; he told me so just before he left. That was why Orson had to come to get me. Baba would be spending his days on the tracks, cross-stitching the same country that Orson and I covered.

New York was not a place to raise children, Umptie Nabila said. Umptie Nabila had become "Great Aunt Winifred" since five Easters ago when we'd last met. What's more, she'd thought it over, and it seemed my name was now Estelle.

"Estelle," I said, turning the name before me. In the following days I often could not remember to answer to it. I put the name on in the morning like a wig. Before long, though, I became accustomed to it. My former name grew faint, then fell from memory.

The land around us was spiced with yellow wildflowers. There were men crawling the construction troughs along the highway, veils of dust and diesel smoke, and grass-lands bearing distant ships of mountains. A sign said, "Welcome to Maybell, pop. 437."

My aunt and cousin lived beside a freight yard; all evening long it rang metal on metal. There were yellow-sided Union Pacific cars, railroad ties, pallets, and stacks of lumber. Past the yard was a field of horses where the colts slept on the ground under their mothers' gazes.

By day, I could look out my window and see the train on the horizon, vanishing into the earth and spilling out the other side. Sometimes the mountains were gray, red lightning scratched the sky. I walked past sandstone hills dusted with sage, rows of snow fences, bikers, vans with MIA/POW bumper stickers. The grass gave way to quills of prairie brush, desert green, and downy cows. It was the top of the world, mountains curling at the edges of basin plains like the ocean.

Aunt Nabila-Winifred, her two-year-old son, and her grown-up nephew—my father—came to America in 1954. My father stayed in New York while she kept traveling, she said, until she felt "at home." She and Orson settled in the Wallabee Acres Trailer Court in a double-wide trailer, three bedrooms and two and a half baths, fourteen hundred square feet.

Now Orson was going to work as a wrangler on a dude ranch thirty miles north of Maybell. Aunt Winifred worked for the oil company, which took her out of the house all day. She fretted over leaving me alone and gave me a lot of advice on how to attract friends, changes involving dress, hair, and speech.

"Never, *ever,* speak Arabic," she told me. "Wipe it out of your brain. It's clutter, you won't need it anymore. And if anyone asks—" she said, then paused a moment, sighing over my brown skin, "—you say you're Mexican—no, no—*Italian,* or Greek, anything but Palestinian."

Wyoming was a perfect place for forgetting. The mountains and snow fences repeated like a four-note melody and chased thoughts from my head.

The week before Orson left he took me driving around in his pickup. My favorite road signs were for the Rifleman Hotel, Bad Boys B.B.Q., Indian Clem's Trading Post, and the Buckaroo Lodge. At a gas station a trucker in a white tee hung his arm out the window and asked, "What kind mileage you get?" From far away the highway glistened like a snail's trail. At Gay Pearson's Stops, a driver said, "Indians told the white man not to build their highway through here, said there were evil spirits laying all over Elk Mountains. But the white man goes on anyway, and sure enough every winter twenty, thirty drivers get dumped in some blizzard."

Outside the Pies & Eats, a black man pulled up with a little boy beside him in the front seat. The man opened his door and swung his legs out to face us, but didn't get out. "Hey bud," he yelled to Orson. "Hey buddy." He was wearing a striped train-conductor cap. Orson walked over to him. "Hey buddy, could you help a guy? I'm out of gas, I got to get to Colorado Springs. Could you help me fill'er up, buddy?"

Orson pulled a dollar and some change from his pocket.

"Aw, buddy, thank you, man," the man said as he took it. "But I don't think that'll fill her. I mean, I don't think that'll do the job."

"That's all I got."

"Well, how many miles *is* it to Colorado Springs?"

"Two-seventy-five," Orson said, his hand on the door handle to the pickup.

"Well, OK then," the man said, got in his car and drove away.

Wallabee Acres Trailer Court and most of the town of Maybell was inside the Sequoya Reservation. On my fifth day there I met Elizabeth Medicine Bow; she was pushing an empty cargo dolly in the freight yard and singing, "Oh the coffee in the army."

Orson and I had seen Indians on the highways and truckstops, their cars pulled over, white rags tied to the antennas. There was something about their eyes which reminded me of the full-hearted Arabs. Elizabeth and I saw each other and started off, "What are you doing?"

"I don't know. What do you want to do?"

Trains pulled away from my window toward south, sometimes coal trains, black as their cargo. Beyond the tracks were green-blanketed pyramids, stone mountains hooked with gaps like piles of skulls, mountains like thunderheads at evening, mountains soft as mirages in morning, sandy-backed, oceans of silty land, cinder fields.

The longer Elizabeth and I knew each other the more certain we felt that we were twins separated at birth. There were many similarities between us: we both had secret names—mine already fading and Elizabeth's used only by her grandmother and great-granny; we both had doubled languages, a public one we spoke in common, and a private language that haunted us. When Elizabeth's mother was angry, she called Elizabeth inside using the other language. Elizabeth always marched in saying, "Speak *American!*"

Also, neither of us knew where our fathers were. We were descended from nations that no map had names or boundaries for.

Elizabeth's mother was twenty-five years old; she was named Shoshona and she looked like a movie star. She worked for the oil company, but unlike my aunt who was higher up, Shoshona said she was always "getting laid off and laid on—like all the fool Indians there."

She would send us out to Bill Dee's—a mile and a half walk into town—for a new tube of lipstick or bottle of nail polish, and always a flask of something called Yippie Tonic that Bill Dee kept behind the counter. On the laid-off days Shoshona and her girlfriends—the girls, Elizabeth called them—sat around the TV, drinking Yippie Tonic out of sewing thimbles.

Elizabeth's grandmother and great-granny preferred the TV reception in the bars downtown, at the Buckaroo. "The girls getting fancy again?" Grandmother said, sticking out her fingers to show how you drink from a thimble. Great-granny was sleeping, stretched out in a booth.

From Elizabeth's window we could see wheat like pink velvet, white floors of grain, and telephone poles going on and on like crucifixes.

"Just wait," she said as we knelt on her bed, elbows propped on her sill. "When we get out of here we'll go where *people* live."

I'd gotten used to the speckled hills and basin. When Elizabeth ran ahead of me through the fields, the sun darkened her skin to eggplant, her hair a whip against the air. In town we played That's-my-father. We would try to be hidden, and pick from the men we saw the gentlest, the sweetest, the tallest, the strongest: a man who inspired us.

The game sometimes made Elizabeth, who'd never seen her own father, very sad. I knew what mine looked like; I knew he was thrumming along the plains, rails singing under the sky, watching from the tracks that would take us back.

Sometimes Elizabeth stayed overnight and shared my bed. Aunt Winifred would tuck us in and give us a cup of tea.

"When I get big I'm gonna go find him," Elizabeth said. "I got a lot of stuff to ask him about. I plan to have money; you'll get equal half. I also plan to get muscles, so nobody will mess with us. After I get my father, we'll go get yours."

"Oh, mine's coming back, though," I said and closed my eyes. The lights were out and we could hear the freight yard; the bed trembled as a boxcar got hitched and rolled out. "Pretty soon. No question about that, dearie," I said.

Elizabeth threw one leg over mine. We were both tall and bony and traded our clothes. She left her toothbrush in our bathroom, and we woke at the same time in the morning.

That year when school started and Elizabeth and I turned thirteen, we began playing That's-your-boyfriend. We chose the most ridiculous boys in the school, poked each other, and said, "That's yours."

We watched the boys in senior high practice football on the field that connected our schools; we thought they looked like soldiers and each claimed one.

The schools were owned by the Sequoya Reservation, seventh to ninth grade and tenth to twelfth, about fifty kids each. The buildings were corrugated aluminum works, "Halleluja! Church of Christ," still fading off the junior high. Elementary school shared with the Grange. Sometimes we heard singing from Grange meetings float beyond the building.

That winter Frank Atchison, a white history teacher at the junior high, took Elizabeth aside and said she had great potential, and he would work on "cultivating" her. She would have to stay after school for lessons. After the first lesson, Elizabeth came rushing home: Mr. Atchison had proclaimed a "great love" for her, and she had decided she was interested. They would see each other as long as his wife didn't find out.

Why, I brooded, had Elizabeth been selected and not me? Mr. Atchison might have preferred Sequoyans, but my skin was so dark that no one seemed to notice my difference. I was jealous that while once we had shared everything, Elizabeth hadn't offered Mr. Atchison. More than anything else, though, I was jealous of Mr. Atchison taking Elizabeth away. As it turned out, Elizabeth didn't go anywhere, and her sharing stopped just short of bringing him to sleep over.

We went to school, cut out after attendance, and walked back to the flat rocks over at the freight yard. Elizabeth told me everything in detail so small and perfect, we could sink into it, the white sun careening past us, the rails flashing like a trail of coins. Listening was like being hypnotized:

> "And then he left me this note—
> "And then we went for this ride—
> "And then he pulled up my shirt—"

It was February and a snowy wind filled the basin, flicking off the sides of the mountains, whirling like the Milky Way. When it got too bad out we went to my trailer and huddled in bed. Elizabeth said she spent most of the time she was with him figuring out how to describe it to me later. I knew about the chip in his incisor, the mole behind his ear, the pressure of his body as he flattened against her. We drifted on stories, Elizabeth floating free while I stayed moored by ordinary life.

After two months of it Elizabeth decided to stop seeing him. Everything ceased as abruptly as it had started. The only reminder was Mr. Atchison staring at Elizabeth in the hall, all the kids grinning. Everybody knew what had happened. "It's time to get on with my life," she said. "I don't have time for these men. The grandmothers need me to come for them after school."

Winter churned into something like spring. Clouds became mountains, steam, and rain. In the freight yard there were boxes of bawling calves again, hissing cargo brakes, and metal wheels heated like branding irons.

In spring assembly we watched *West Side Story*[1] and Elizabeth and I saw that Shoshona looked like Natalie Wood. She was what Natalie Wood might look like if you took a cloth to her and polished her bronze, so her cheekbones and the wings of her nose gleamed like a statue's.

Shoshona taught us about life. She said Elizabeth wouldn't ever have any brothers or sisters as long as it was a so-called free country. The doctor at the clinic where she had Elizabeth gave her what she called her favorite toys:

"I tell the boys, 'you gotta put on your raincoat in heavy weather.' I say to them, 'No glove, no love.'"

Shoshona usually brought one of her men home when the tonic was gone and she was laid off. Elizabeth would come over to spend the night with me. One morning after we decided that Shoshona looked like Natalie Wood, Elizabeth and I walked back to her trailer and found Shoshona sitting at the table with her eyes ringed purple, blue, and black, a crust of blood along one nostril.

"Never let a drunken Indian hit you," she told us as we walked in. "He hits you, you crack him back in the jaw hard as you can." She showed us how to make a fist, with the thumb on the outside of our fingers. She displayed a broken tooth in a baby jar that she'd extracted the evening before, and clenching her hand, showed us how.

"That was Fred Go Slow's. So's this." She showed us a wallet with what looked like a lot of money in it. "The sad thing is when he finally comes to, he won't even remember who did it to him."

About three weeks later, Shoshona walked through Aunt Winifred's door, sat down on the sofa and started crying. Elizabeth and I peeked in from the kitchen door.

"I can't *believe* it. Is this my life? Is this really my life?" she kept saying, while Aunt Winifred tried to get her to drink tea. "*Not* another one! A smelling, snot-nosed, screaming…oh God the screaming. I don't even care about the black eyes, but *this*—those goddamn rubber things *break!*"

That was how we found out Elizabeth was going to get a baby to play with after all.

The school yard was quiet and cows wandered across the playground. We stood behind the school, saw a ripple of antelope, the remains of brushfire, puffs of tumbleweed, a skinned possum, its tongue poking out.

Elizabeth didn't want to go to her trailer much anymore. When Shoshona got through with vomiting in the morning she started taking long pulls on the tonic bottle. The girls, some of whom were also pregnant, kept right up with Shoshona, drinking.

---

[1] 1961 film musical starring Natalie Wood.

Fred Go Slow, who now had a big hole in his teeth, came around the house look-ing guilty and nervous until Shoshona's friends chased him away. He tried to give Elizabeth and me little toys and candies but Elizabeth threw them to the ground, saying, "I'm a woman now, I don't play with baby things."

Summer flared like a match; the freight tracks groaned. Linemen stood against the dusk in overalls, swinging lanterns, coal trains sliding in behind them.

Orson came home from the dude ranch and convinced Aunt Winifred to sell my father's possessions. For a year, furniture, books, and clothing had filled her extra bedroom. Bit by bit, Winifred cleared the room, weeping over every piece she sold, getting remarkable prices in the process. She held back a few things: portraits my father had painted, a sandalwood carving, a brass-topped table, and a small prayer rug. She stored a trunk in my room with a few of my baby toys and some odds and ends.

Elizabeth wanted to investigate the trunk, but it proved disappointing: rigid Barbie dolls, Matchbox racecars, books smelly with dust, and a shotglass with the words "Monticello Raceway." At the bottom, Elizabeth found a big, white cotton square checked with black.

"Oh. Oh yeah," I said. Words and faces I hadn't thought about for a year rushed back. My hands remembered things my mind didn't know about. Elizabeth sat before my bureau mirror and I began arranging the *hutta*[2] around her head and neck. She looked like Elizabeth Taylor in *Cleopatra*.[3]

Aunt Winifred was just back from work. She glanced in the doorway, stopped and said, "Oh, children!" Her eyes were bright and her fist knotted against the base of her throat. Elizabeth looked like royalty.

"Keep it," I said. "It's yours, it was made for you."

"Wait," she said and stood up. First I thought she was going out to show her mother, but minutes later she came running back with something in her hand. A long, tufted feather, deeply colored as the earth, strung on a loop of leather.

"A man who said he was my father gave this to me when I was a kid," she said, the feather covering the palms of both of our hands. "I knew he wasn't any more my father than the rest, but I like to think it came from my real father anyway. He told me it was golden eagle, a warrior's feather. It's for you, my sister Estelle." She slid the leather piece down on my head. It was too big for me and rested on my ears, but the feather glowed like a flame against the black of my hair, brushing my shoulder, lighting my face.

"I love it," I whispered, afraid to move inches to see it. "It's the most beautiful thing."

Elizabeth put her face next to mine. "Remember the Indian girl we saw last week on the late-night movie?"

"Pocahontas,"[4] Aunt Winifred said.

Not long after Elizabeth and I traded headdresses, a woman came to Aunt Winifred's door. She was known around the town as the Social Welfare Lady. She had dark eyebrows and a powdered face. Elizabeth and I spied from the doorway as she talked to Aunt Winifred and rubbed her matchstick legs together. Aunt Winifred

---

[2] A scarf often worn by men in the Middle East.
[3] 1963 film.
[4] Pocahontas (ca. 1595-1617), a Native American woman whose story has been romanticized and retold many times in film.

talked to the woman in a pleading voice, but the woman kept talking straight ahead, with her gray gaze and her rubbing legs. Finally Aunt Winifred turned around to where she knew we were watching, and we saw the lady's eyes lift up, following.

Shoshona had gone drinking the night before. We had heard her outside making the mewing sounds when she wasn't feeling right and the earth was moving beneath her, and she couldn't find her front door key. She'd shown up for work the next morning around the time the lunch whistle was blowing and her boss, Sammy Hudson, who was a cousin of Fred Go Slow, up and reported her to the Bureau.[5] The Bureau had started a new program on the Sequoya Reservation: cash reward for anyone reporting willful endangerment of the unborn through alcohol abuse. All willful endangerers would be imprisoned, length of sentence determined by their due date. They had decided to make an example of Shoshona.

The Welfare Lady said that Elizabeth had to stay with her Aunt Shyela on the other side of the reservation, ten miles away. She led Elizabeth to a big green station wagon and they drove off. That night Elizabeth came back to our trailer on her aunt's bicycle. Her hair was blowing around her face and she looked like a beautiful witch who had climbed out of the sky.

"I promise you, I'm gonna help her escape," Elizabeth whispered as we were falling asleep. "There's no way they're gonna keep my mother in their trap."

"No. I know it," I said.

The train crossed my dreams; I saw my father's eyes, clear as the moon. Voices floated through the dawn, filling me, speaking my other language, words I recognized, forget, don't forget, forget.

Orson drove us to town that day, the air humming with insects. We passed pickups in dust clouds, drivers' fingers off the steering wheels, howdy, rifles shaking in the gunracks. We watched land rising away from us, turning transparent in the light, brown and yellow as the desert.

The day before, Shoshona's pregnancy had looked like nothing more than a held breath, but it seemed to have grown overnight. She was held in a building with the words "Maybell Prison" painted on a water tower on the roof, a small reservation jail. Shoshona sat on a narrow bed in a windowless room, facing away from us. I had never been inside the building before, although we'd passed it plenty of times while searching for grandmothers. Iron bars were a shock. I had imagined a kind of special prison for pregnant women.

"Mom?" Elizabeth said. I had never heard her call her anything but Shoshona. Her voice got inside me, gathering tears behind my eyes, and all I wanted to do was get on my knees and beg Shoshona, come out, come out. Elizabeth and I started crying and Shoshona wouldn't face us. A guard came back and said, "What are you girls doing here? You're not supposed to be back here."

Shoshona stood. "Leave them alone. I'm allowed to have visitors!" Her face was puffy and she was shaking. "Now, kids, be good and go get me some of my medicine tonic," she said in a wobbling voice.

"Sorry, little mama," the man said. "These girls ain't bringing you nothing."

As soon as we got out of the prison we ran to Bill Dee's. Some of the girls were

---

[5] Bureau of Indian Affairs, a federal agency within the Department of the Interior.

inside sitting at the counter, and they quieted fast. Their eyes slid toward us; I heard a whispered mix of languages. Elizabeth refused to look at anyone as we went to the cash register, then we realized neither of us had any money. We stood there, staring at the gun case, as if that was what we'd come in for. Then two of the girls were standing behind us and one of them said, "Bill Dee, we need some Yippie Tonic and we need it on credit and you know what for."

We walked back to the jail, past the Last Chance, "Girls Girls Girls," past scrub, weeds, and alleyways. The guard who'd sent us away was at the front desk. I had a bottle of tonic tucked inside a jacket that was zipped to the neck, though it was already ninety outside. The man fanned himself with a handful of mimeographed sheets and stared at us. We all stood looking at each other, then he sighed and said, "Girls, you know I can't let you back there."

"Please, officer," Elizabeth said, stepping toward him. "I've got to get back there. Maybe—if there's something you want—anything you want—"

He was shaking his head, eyes closed. Elizabeth started to cry, speaking in her other language, blood sounds that made him open his eyes. But he wouldn't stop shaking his head, and then Elizabeth started to scream, and he got up from the desk to grab her. He'd forgotten me—all I had to do was turn down the corridor and find the right bars.

When I got to her, Shoshona was standing, holding the bars. I pulled the bottle out of my jacket and passed it to her. She was shaking so hard she almost dropped it, so I set it on the ground.

"Estelle," she said, her eyes on the bottle, "what's happening to Elizabeth?"

"They won't let her in," I said. "She tried to come in."

Shoshona nodded. "Tell her to keep trying." Then she looked at me and said, "I can kill this baby any time any way I want to. I can hold my breath and starve off its air. I can think evil down into it so it rots before its fifth month. It's my own heart, this baby. They think they can hold onto my heart for me?"

I had to leave before they found me. Shoshona's hot voice echoed up the corridor, "What did I do? Just tell me, who says I did wrong?"

I walked back alone, past bottles of rubbing alcohol, Lysol, cooking spray, past huddles of black-haired men and women outside the plasma donor center, cigarette butts smashed on the sidewalk.

Elizabeth didn't come over that night or the next. Voices began to fill my sleep. I dreamed of the toy train running its figure eight, a man's hands, white as marble, going to it, and I woke gasping.

I didn't look for Elizabeth; I knew if I found her, I would come to the end of our world, that it would be an outdated, useless place. Weeks went by. Aunt Winifred looked at me, but didn't ask about Elizabeth. Orson returned to the dude ranch. A few days later he called to say there was an opening for a chef's assistant—mine, if I wanted it. There was a tutor at the ranch, so I wouldn't need to return to the reservation school.

One week before I was supposed to join Orson, Aunt Winifred came home carrying two bags of groceries and said she had something to tell me. She put down the bags and said, "Your friend Elizabeth has been seen in town. On the arm of a prison officer."

I moved my hands to the edge of the table. "What? Where in town? What officer?"

Aunt Winifred moved some of the cans of food around on the counter. "She's trying to help her mother, I guess," she said. "Poor baby."

I went to the door and Aunt Winifred said, "Estelle, you be careful. You are not to stay out late."

It was mid-August; at five thirty P.M. the reservation was bright and hot as midday. The shadows had barely begun sliding toward evening, things looked blurred, windows and doors shut to the sun. I walked into town, down Main Street, with its line of bars, neon lassos, and dancing girls. Elizabeth and I had gone into all of these places looking for her grandmothers.

I walked to the door of the Tally Ho and tried to will Elizabeth out to me. I slid my hands in my pockets and prayed, oh please come out, Elizabeth, please, please come out.

The door opened, but there was just an old woman with a mouthful of gold teeth and long, red-black hair. I backed up, walking away as quickly as I could. I saw people coming out of the Three Cheers down the block and I walked toward them looking for Elizabeth. It was two men and a woman. They saw me and moved closer.

"Hey, what's this?" one of the men said. "Want to party, youngster?"

"Ain't you Shoshona Medicine Bow's girl?" the woman asked. She stood with her back to the sun, her face in shadows.

"That's my sister. I mean, Elizabeth is," I said, trying to steady my voice. "Have you seen her?"

"No. You want us to help you look?" the other man said in a way that wasn't offering help. I tried to back away, but they moved toward me, so I stood still, arms clasped around my sides.

"She ain't no Indian," one of the men said, reaching out and tipping my face to the sun. "Not much. Look at her, that ain't no kind of Sequoyan *I* know about. What type mixed breed *are* you?"

I remembered Aunt Winifred's warning: never, never tell. I tried to think of other nationalities she'd offered me, but they vanished from my mind. The only countries I could remember were from the unit on Northern Europe we'd done that year: Belgian chocolate and Swiss clocks.

"Swiss," I said. "I'm Swiss."

They started laughing.

"You're Swiss and I'm the Pope's grandfather," the other man said. But they were already losing interest, walking away. I shivered in the heat, wanting to run after them and ask what they knew about Elizabeth.

I heard Shoshona's voice in my dream that night, mixed with other voices, her cry, banging like a hammer, "What did I do, who says I did wrong…" I dreamed cargo doors, Cottonbelt, Union Pacific, Hydro-lite, satellite dishes, tilting trees, the white face of a church minding the plain.

I went into town every evening for a week, becoming bolder, entering bars, asking everyone if they had seen Elizabeth Medicine Bow. I went to the building with the water tower on top; Elizabeth wasn't there. I tried the school, I tried Bill Dee's, I tried at the houses of Elizabeth's family and friends.

I'd worked down the street of bars and by Friday I was back at the Tally Ho again. It was late in the evening, getting dark, and the edge had come off the heat. Maybell hummed with the neon, insects swarming to the lights. I stopped on the sidewalk outside the bar, saying my prayer, please come out, Elizabeth, oh please, please come.

The bar door opened then and a Sequoyan man walked out. He had big rounded shoulders and hair that fell down over his back. I glanced at him and looked away. Then he was beside me suddenly, whispering, "Little one, what are you doing here?"

Then he said, "Elizabeth Medicine Bow lives with her new lover. Why don't you come with me instead?" It was too dark to see him clearly; that might have been why his words were so persuasive. I followed him away from the strip. It was dream-walking, following this bear-quiet figure.

We went through the sleeping neighborhoods, to where the land got steep and sharp. We walked up. At times he took my hand to help me, the rest of the time I followed, listening to the flow of his breath, his foot on the stones. The earth became soft, as if we were walking in powder. Then we stopped and the man was bent over, looking around in the dirt. "I always lose my house key," he said. "So I keep it hidden outside. Then I have to find it again."

He pulled and opened a rectangle of yellow out of the night. It was a small cottage, filled with skins and bones, an old sofa, kitchen table, chamber pot, and freezer. He led me, identifying the skeletons and skulls he had collected. He'd found some bones already sun-washed, others came from carcasses he'd found, and skinned, and sometimes eaten: deer, antelope, tiny bones of raccoon hands, cow and coyote skulls, chicken, cat, dog and the perfect knobs of snake spines. There were various feathers, some small, stitched together, some curling and striped. One, glowing like brown mineral, rested on a pile of books; I touched it. "Golden eagle," I said.

"That's right," he said. "Apparently you know a few things." That was the first time I looked at him directly. He was heavy and strong, and his hair fell all the way down his back, a bed of black, like his eyes.

"See here." He stood at a small nightstand by the bed. "I made these." He showed me a polished comb and brush. "From bear bones and pig bristles. Very valuable, like elk and mountain lions and rattlers."

This was the way he lived, he told me: scavenging, keeping an ear to the ground, sometimes teaching a class in nature appreciation, or sculpture, or taxidermy. Night moved on a slow tide, the house sailing on his voice. We sat on his couch. I picked up his bone brush and began running it down the length of his black hair, over and over, enchanting myself with the repetition, the way it polished. He sat still until I had fallen asleep.

I woke later, drooling a little on his shoulder. His arms were soft around me, his breath deep and regular. I lay still for a few minutes. It was still dark outside, but I could tell morning was coming from the blue sheen in his window and the way my breath made a mist. It must have dropped forty degrees overnight.

He sat up and pulled a knitted shawl off a chair, then lay back and draped it over us. "What did you dream last night?"

"How do you know that I dreamed?"

He propped up on one arm. "You were talking in your sleep, your dreams speaking—"

It came in flashes: Elizabeth running, the blue of her hair melting into black sky. She was telling me, "I've found my father, he's right over there," and I looked, but it was too dark. The little train was running through its circuit on the floor of the trailer house, speeding up and slowing down; the tiny boxcars were trembling; I thought it was an earthquake. Then there were drops of water on me, red drops. I went to turn off the bathtub; it was overflowing, red as velvet, red wine. Then I saw the white shank of my father's leg and his forearm; I tried to ask why he was bathing in wine, but the words wouldn't come.

I realized that I wasn't dreaming anymore, but remembering, and my tongue got thick as if the dream-story was choking me. I stopped speaking and sat opening and closing my eyes slowly. Beyond the window I could see the prairie beneath the hill, divided by tracks, a scroll of light.

"Your dream has more than one meaning," he said.

I was shivering, arms wrapped around myself, trying to press fear back into my ribs. I remembered my father, swallowed by pain, like a drop of bitter wine, his red wrists against the white enamel. Outside the train was passing. I thought, I was weak; I wasn't enough to save him. I put down my head and my tears were light as air.

My friend went into the other room and then returned, giving me the eagle feather. He said, "You won't believe me now, but the feelings you have will dry up after a while. Like everything else, like tears. Your father went where he needed to; some people can't live on this earth. You should prize this pain of yours. This is what will make you human all the way through. Nothing less will do that."

The feather, he told me, was a warrior's prize. At the time, I only cared about my dream, but later I remembered its glow in my hands, softness where he touched me on the face.

I walked down to our trailer later that morning, the path clear in the light. Aunt Winifred was quiet when she saw my changed face. I had decided to join Orson at the dude ranch.

Four years later the owner of the ranch sent me through college, a private school back East. I came back to the reservation for just one Christmas break in all those years. Shoshona and Elizabeth had gone away; their trailer stood empty. I walked through the hills, but couldn't find my friend's cottage.

Not until I'd graduated and was working in New York did my memories become insistent, nudging me in the street or the office, making me wonder what had become of Shoshona and her baby. And of Elizabeth. When I called, Aunt Winifred never talked about the reservation. She said to me, "Your life is *there* now, in New York, out in the world. Forget about what's past."

I took an apartment not far from the one where I'd lived with my father. I imagined my father's ghost waiting there, watching over memories. My walk to work led past the old place, and its brownstone windows moved with shadows.

I began to see Elizabeth too, in stores and restaurants, her blue-black hair in crowds of brown and blond. I would get closer and see it wasn't her. Sometimes I would talk to these women anyway, my wish for her was so strong. Often, they were from other tribes, Iroquois, Tillamuck, Cherokee. Once I stopped someone from the Sioux Pine Reservation who said she knew Elizabeth Medicine Bow. She told me Elizabeth was now Mrs. Jeffrey Harrison, that she had two sons, and lived in South Dakota. Twice

I stopped black-haired women from Korea, once a woman from Bombay, and once a Palestinian.

Orson settled in Denver; Aunt Winifred retired and moved to Florida. Nothing could summon Elizabeth back but imagination.

I'd been in New York for several years when I found a book in the library that described how the American Indian population was being killed off through alcohol abuse. When I finished reading I walked to the fire escape outside my apartment and wanted to shout *Elizabeth,* as loud as I could. I didn't believe the story about her and the South Dakota rancher. My Elizabeth would still be wandering, I thought, pushing open church doors and saloon gates, finding her father.

I stood on the fire escape and noticed how the city hooked itself into crags and canyons, rooftops high enough to snag a singing bird. I went back into the apartment.

I saw the way native people wandered in New York, displaced persons. I thought about the way homes, cities, and whole countries disappeared, the faces of your neighbors and the people you loved, the grass of your home, and the name of the place you lived and played were all gone, incredibly, gone.

My artifacts: a feather or two, a name, the image of a toy train that ran in circles. Sometimes in the mornings before I opened my eyes, a moment and space would come to me, an opening in the past that Elizabeth and I had shared: we are standing together, holding hands, and everywhere we look we see crops of dirt, spouts of smoke and grain, dust-devils, plumes of topsoil, burning crops, and the farmers' hay bales stacked like dominoes. And the land goes on across the wide earth, across our separate lives, our futures silent as the buffalo. We are left with the precious, mysterious past.

—1995

CRISTINA GARCÍA (1959-)

Cristina García was born in Havana, Cuba, and raised in New York. She majored in Political Science at Barnard and received her M.A. in International Relations from the Johns Hopkins School of Advanced International Studies. Upon graduating, García accepted a marketing job with Proctor & Gamble and moved to West Germany, but kept the position only briefly before turning to journalism. She worked at both the *Boston Globe* and the *Knoxville Journal* before beginning at *Time* in 1983, first as a reporter and researcher, then as a correspondent in San Francisco, and, finally, as Bureau Chief in Miami. After seven years at the magazine, García left journalism to pursue her creative writing full time. With the publication of *Dreaming in Cuban* in 1992, she became the first Cuban-American woman to publish a novel written in English. A National Book Award finalist, the novel was inspired by García's 1984 trip to Cuba, her first time back to the island since her family had fled out of anti-Castro sentiment in 1961. García, one of the most commercially successful Latina writers today, is the author of three other novels, *The Agüero Sisters* (1997), *Monkey Hunting* (2003), and *A Handbook to Luck* (2007), as well as an essay on classic American cars that was included in *Cars of Cuba* (1995). She has also edited two Latina/o literary anthologies, *¡Cubanisimo!* (2003) and *Bordering Fires* (2006).

Inés in the Kitchen

Inés Maidique is twelve weeks pregnant and nauseous. Her back hurts, her breasts are swollen, and her feet no longer fit into her dressy shoes. Although she is barely showing, she walks around in sneakers to ease the soreness that has settled in every corner of her body. The eleven pounds she's gained feel like fifty.

When her husband returns home he'll expect her trussed up in a silk dress and pearls and wearing make-up and high heels. It's Friday and Richard likes for her to make a fuss over him at the end of the week. He'll be home in two hours, so Inés busies herself preparing their dinner—a poached loin of lamb with mint chutney, cumin rice, ratatouille, and spiced bananas for dessert.

Richard will question her closely about what she's eaten that day. Inés will avoid telling him about the fudge cookies she devoured that morning in the supermarket parking lot. She hadn't wanted to eat the whole box, but bringing it home was unthinkable. Richard scoured the kitchen cabinets for what he called "illegal foods," and she was in no mood for his usual harangue.

With a long length of string Inés ties together the eye of loin and tenderloin at one-inch intervals, leaving enough string at the ends to suspend the meat from the handles of the kettle. She slits the lamb in several places and inserts slivers of garlic. Then she sets about preparing the stock, skimming the froth as it simmers. Inés thinks about the initial excitement she'd felt when the blood test came back positive. She always knew, or thought she knew, she wanted a child, but now she is less certain.

The mint leaves give off a tart scent that clears her head with each pulse of the food processor. She adds fresh coriander, minced garlic, gingerroot, honey, and a little lemon until the chutney congeals. Then she whisks it together with plain yogurt in a stainless steel bowl. Inés remembers the abortion she'd had the month before her college graduation. She was twenty-one and, like now, twelve weeks pregnant. The baby's father was Cuban, like her, a hematology resident at the hospital where Inés was finishing her practicum. Manolo Espada was not opposed to having the baby, only against getting married. This was unacceptable to Inés. After the abortion, she bled for five days and cramped so hard she passed out. Inés spent the summer working a double shift at an emergency room in Yonkers. Her child would have been eight years old by now. Inés thinks of this often.

Shortly before she was to marry Richard, Inés tracked down her old lover to San Francisco, where he'd been doing AIDS research with an eminent name in the field. Over the phone, Manolo told her he was leaving for Africa the following month on a two-year grant from the Department of Health. Inés abruptly forgot everything she had planned to say. Even if she'd wanted him again, it was too late. She'd already sent out her wedding invitations and Richard had put a down payment on the colonial house across from the riding stables. Manolo was going to Africa. It would have never worked out.

✦ ✦ ✦

Ratatouille is one of Inés's favorite dishes. It's easy to prepare and she cooks big batches of it at a time, then freezes it. The red peppers give the ratatouille a slightly sweetish taste. Inés heats the olive oil in a skillet, then tosses in the garlic and chopped onion. She adds the cubed eggplants and stirs in the remaining ingredients one at a time. On another burner she prepares the rice with chicken broth, cumin seed, and fresh parsley. If she times it right, dinner will be ready just as Richard walks through the door.

Her husband doesn't know about Inés's abortion, and only superficially about Manolo Espada. It is better this way. Richard doesn't like it when Inés's attention is diverted from him in any significant way. How, she wonders, will he get used to having a baby around? Richard was the only boy in a family of older sisters, and accustomed to getting his way. His father died when Richard was eight and his three sisters had worked as secretaries to put him through medical school. Richard had been the great hope of the Roth family. When he told them he was marrying a Catholic, his mother and sisters were devastated. Janice, the oldest, told him point-blank that Inés would ruin his life. Perhaps, Inés thinks, his sister was right.

Inés strains the stock through a fine sieve into an enormous ceramic bowl, discarding the bones and scraps. She pours the liquid back into the kettle and turns on the burner to moderately high. Carefully, she lowers the lamb into the stock without letting it touch the sides or the bottom of the kettle, then she ties the string to the handles and sets the timer for twelve minutes.

Other things concern Inés. She's heard about men running off when their wives become pregnant and she's afraid that Richard, who places such a premium on her looks, will be repelled by her bloating body. As it is, Inés feels that Richard scrutinizes her for nascent imperfections. He abhors cellulite and varicose veins, the corporal trademarks of his mother and sisters, and so Inés works hard to stay fit. She swims, plays tennis, takes aerobics classes and works out twice a week on the Nautilus machines at her gym. Her major weakness is a fondness for sweets. Inés loves chocolate, but Richard glares at her in restaurants if she so much as asks to see the dessert menu. To him a lack of self-discipline on such small matters is indicative of more serious character flaws.

What of her husband's good qualities? Richard takes her to the Bahamas every winter, although he spends most of the time scuba-diving, a sport which Inés does not share. And he is intelligent and well-informed and she believes he is faithful. Also, he isn't a tightwad like so many of her friends' husbands, watching every penny, and he doesn't hang out with the boys or play poker or anything like that. Richard is an adequate lover, too, although he lacks imagination. He likes what he likes, which does not include many of the things that Inés likes. Once, in bed, she asked Richard to pretend he was Henry Kissinger. The request offended him deeply. If Richard rejected so harmless a game, what would he say to the darker, more elaborate rituals she'd engaged in with Manolo?

✦ ✦ ✦

The loin of lamb is medium rare, just the way Richard likes it. Inés lets it cool off on the cutting board for a few minutes before slicing it diagonally into thick, juicy slabs. She sets the table with their wedding linen and china and wedges two white candles into squat crystal holders. Inés thinks back on the five years she worked as a nurse. She was good at what she did and was sought after for the most important cardiology cases. More than one surgeon had jokingly proposed to her after she'd made a life-saving suggestion in the operating room. But like most men, they assumed she was unavailable. Someone so pretty, so self-contained, they thought, must already be spoken for.

When Richard first started working at the hospital, Inés felt drawn to him. There was something about his manner, about his nervous energy that appealed to her. It certainly wasn't his looks. Richard was skinny and tall with fleecy colorless hair, not at all like the mesomorphic Manolo whose skin seemed more of a pelt. For three months she and Richard worked side by side on coronary bypasses, ventricular aneurysm resections, mitral valve replacements. Their manner was always cordial and efficient, with none of the macabre bantering one often hears in operating rooms. One day, Richard looked up at her from a triple bypass and said, "Marry me, Inés." And so she did.

When Inés was a child, her father had predicted wistfully that she would never marry, while her mother seemed to gear her for little else. Inés remembers the beauty pageants she was forced to enter from an early age, the banana curls that hung from her skull like so many sausages. She'd won the "Little Miss Latin New York" pageant in 1964, when she was seven years old. Her mother still considers this to be Inés's greatest achievement. Inés had sung and played the piano to "Putting on the Ritz," which she'd translated to Spanish herself. Gerardo complained to his wife about sharing Inés with an auditorium full of leering strangers, but Haydée would not budge. "This is better than a dowry, Gerardo." But Gerardo preferred to have his daughter, dolled up in her starched Sunday dress and ruffled anklets, all to himself.

Gerardo expected Inés to drop everything to play the piano for him, and for many years she complied. This became more and more difficult as she got older. Her parents separated and her father would call at all hours on the private phone line he'd installed in Inés' bedroom, pleading with her to come play the white baby grand he had rented just for her. Sometimes he would stroke her hair or tickle her spine as she played, tease her about her tiny new breasts or affectionately pat her behind. Inés remembers how the air seemed different during those times, charged and hard to swallow. Now her father is dead. And what, she asks herself, does she really know about him?

+ + +

Inés turns off all the burners and pours herself a glass of whole milk. She is doing all the right things to keep the life inside her thriving. But she accomplishes this without anticipation, only a sense of obligation. Sometimes she has a terrible urge to pour herself a glass of rum, although she hates the taste, and she knows what it would do to the baby. Or to burn holes in the creamy calfskin upholstery of her husband's sports car. Other times, mostly in the early afternoons, she feels like setting fire to the damask curtains that keep their living room in a perpetual dusk. She dreams about blowing up her herb garden with its fragrant basil leaves, then stealing a thoroughbred from the stable across the street and riding it as fast as she can.

Inés finishes the last of her milk. She rinses the glass and leans against the kitchen sink. There is a jingling of keys at the front door. Richard is home.

—1996

DEBORAH MIRANDA (1961–)

Born in Los Angeles, Native American poet Deborah Miranda moved to Washington state as a child. Her father, Alfred Edward Robles Miranda, is Esselen and Chumash, and her mother, Madgel Eleanor, is of French and Jewish ancestry. Together with her parents, Miranda has worked to re-establish connections with and among the members of the Ohlone/Costanoan Esselen Nation, which is currently petitioning for federal recognition.

Miranda, who received her Ph.D. in English from the University of Washington, has authored two poetry collections. The first, *Indian Cartography* (1997), won the Diane Decorah Memorial First Book Award for Poetry from the Native Writers Circle of the Americas; the second, *The Zen of La Llorona* (2005), was nominated for a Lambda Literary Award. Both of these collections center around themes of tribal memory, alienation, and survival. Miranda currently works as an Assistant Professor of English at Washington and Lee University, and lives with her two children and her partner, the poet Margo Solod.

Hunger

You came back for me one day:
drove up in a big white pick-up truck
with a new husband. I left them
behind in an instant—
Uncle Mike, Aunt Sandy,   5
the cousin my age who was so pretty,
so jealous. I climbed into that truck
and we drove away together.
I knew I belonged
only to you.   10

We began again,
in a small house
with my own bedroom
and a huge palm tree out front.
California spring.   15
Nests filled the branches:
robins, pigeons,
or maybe crows, I don't know;
I only remember
the constant cries   20
of hunger waking me each morning,
a rush of wings
as parents came and went
with food. I ran
on tiptoes   25
into the bright kitchen,
found your embrace,
and breakfast waiting for me.
I always wanted
yellow cornflakes in milk.   30

My appetite
came back, *how many bowls?*
you laughed, but you were pleased.
Afterwards while you cleaned

I went outside, dived   35
into the vacant
lot next door, reveling
in orange poppies, grass
tall as me. I tunneled, hid,
made caves of dry stalks alive   40
with grasshoppers,
potato bugs, spiders.
Much later, I emerged
flushed with secrecy,
anxious for lunch.   45
There was tomato soup
with crackers,
cold milk in a thick
glass tumbler. Your hair
was damp and fragrant   50
beneath a silky gold
scarf: pincurls for later.
You'd ask,
can you remember this shopping list?
and all the way to the store,   55
down heated sidewalks,
at intersections
waiting for the walk signal,
our hands
stayed clasped securely   60
as I recited to myself
bread, coffee, cigarettes, milk.

It was like this, then,
when the boys came
with their slingshots, sticks, rocks.   65
I thought the house, the palm tree,
were ours
but we were renters, and new.
The boys showed us
a custom we hadn't heard of: shoot down   70
the nests, watch eggs break
onto dry cut grass or
baby birds split apart,
fragile bellies spilling blue
and red intestines,   75
beaks still gaping
for air, rescue, filling.
I stood frozen

with hatred.
I think I screamed,   80
but did I?
Could I move?
I think I chased the boys, threw my own rocks
but did I only want to?
I remember the aftermath—   85
the boys gone gleefully
into the L.A. streets,
me falling to my knees,
handling the horrific remains,
burying small soft ones   90
in the lot next door, alone:
never telling you.

One day there was a survivor.
It lived through the bursting nest,
the long fall, impact.   95
Struggling in my palm,
trying to get to its feet,
beak an aching **O**
that called to every cell
in my female body: *feed me.*   100
I carried it into the house, to you.
You helped me gather the shoebox,
cotton, grass. We walked
to the store, bought a set
of tiny doll's bottles.   105
All the way home,
I thought I could hear cries
but when we arrived, silence.
We found grayish skin
limp against cotton: 110
dead from fear or shock.
We left the plastic bottles
on the counter.

Mama, I've had you back
all these years   115
and still I awake to the morning
clamor of birds
in trees, a particular cry,
not knowing how to satisfy that
open shape of need,   120
remembering how you tried.

—1999

Indian Cartography

My father opens a map of California—
traces mountain ranges, rivers, county borders
like family bloodlines. Tuolomne,
Salinas, Los Angeles, Paso Robles,
Ventura, Santa Barbara, Saticoy,   5
Tehachapi. Places he was happy,
or where tragedy greeted him
like an old unpleasant relative.

A small blue spot marks
Lake Cachuma, created when they   10
dammed the Santa Ynez, flooded
a valley, divided
my father's boyhood: days
he learned to swim the hard way,
and days he walked across the silver scales,   15
swollen bellies of salmon coming back
to a river that wasn't there.
The government paid those Indians to move away,
he says; *I don't know where they went.*

In my father's dreams   20
after the solace of a six-pack,
he follows a longing, a deepness.
When he comes to the valley
drowned by a displaced river
he swims out, floats on his face   25
with eyes open, looks down into lands not drawn
on any map. Maybe he sees shadows
a people who are fluid,
fluent in dark water, bodies
long and glinting with sharp-edged jewelry,   30
and mouths still opening, closing
on the stories of our home.

—1999

SUSAN POWER (1961-   )

An enrolled member of the Standing Rock Sioux tribe, Susan Power was born in Chicago, Illinois. Her mother, Susan (Dunning) Power, moved to Chicago from the Standing Rock reservation in Fort Yeats, North Dakota, at the age of sixteen, starting out as a housekeeper and ultimately becoming the editor of the *University of Chicago Law Review.* Her father, Carleton Power, a European American originally from Ithaca, New York, worked as a publishing sales representative. Encouraged by both parents to be socially aware and to pursue her education, Power received a B.A. from Radcliffe College, a J.D. from Harvard University

Law School, and, having decided to give up her legal career to pursue writing, an M.F.A from the University of Iowa Writers' Workshop. Her first novel, *The Grass Dancer* (1994), won the Hemingway Foundation/PEN Award for first fiction. *Roofwalker* (2002), the collection of short stories in which "Angry Fish" appears, won the 2002 Milkweed National Fiction Prize.

Angry Fish

The day I met Saint Jude[1] I was thinking impure thoughts about Lena Catches, the one I called *Sinihimaniwinga*—Cold Walking Woman. I was visiting her resale shop, known as Lena's Second Chance, as I did every morning, bringing her one sugar donut and one chaste kiss. I was hoping that the kiss would reach her lips one day, but she was quick; when she saw me moving toward her she tucked her lips in her mouth and thrust one round cheek forward to receive a dry peck. I wanted to tell her that my sandpaper lips would soften to velvet and my mouth would taste like cream if she'd just let down her old lady hair and dust the prim particles off her body. But I thought maybe a confession like that would set me back.

I was taught that it's bad manners to walk with hands in your pockets, but watching Lena, I had to plunge mine in the fabric to keep them still. My fingers wanted to comb through her hair, smudge her face powder, work the zippers and buttons of her confining clothes like little locks to her rooms. Lena always wore pantsuits that were the soft colors of baby clothes. She liked everything to match: her shoes, handbag, eye makeup, even the plastic headband she wore in her hair. She was in her late sixties by then, but her face was unwrinkled, and she rinsed her hair a deep blue black.

"Lena, you are too perfect," I teased her that morning.

"What's that?" She was reading the *National Enquirer*.

"You're perfumed, sprayed, and ironed like those Miss America girls. Spit and polish. I'm waiting for a rainstorm and then you better look out. I'm going to soak you in the rain!"

Lena licked the tip of her finger to turn the page. She wasn't listening. It was just as well because I knew the rain would have more sense than to drench Lena Catches. Even I if carried her out to the street in the middle of a storm I imagined the rain would slide harmlessly off her body as if her skin were not porous, as if her clothes were made of sheet metal.

"Listen to this one, Mitchell," she said. "In a small town near Albuquerque three humanoid aliens interrupted a third grade class to take the children's blood pressure. Here's the quote: 'Mrs. Daily told our reporter that she and her students were in a hypnotic trance. They cooperated fully with the intruders and made no attempts to flee. The aliens were friendly and appeared to communicate through a complicated system of humming. Their medical instruments were unremarkable, possibly borrowed from a local hospital. The visit lasted approximately forty-five minutes.'"

Lena sighed and cut the article out of the paper to include in her UFO scrapbook. I knew that later she would use a red pen to plot the sighting in her *Rand McNally Road Atlas*. States such as Utah and Wyoming were peppered with red dots, even southern Illinois was lightly sprinkled, but so far there weren't any sightings plotted in our Chicago area.

---

[1] Roman Catholic patron saint of lost causes.

"There are hot spots," Lena told me the first time I noticed her special road atlas. "I can't tell you *why,* but I can see a pattern. I'm saving my money and any day now I'll head for one of those active places. It's just a matter of being in the right place at the right time."

Lena had a one-track mind when it came to UFOs and aliens from outer space. I could pick any topic of conversation and she would shift the subject to another sighting, or the discovery of another galaxy. I could understand her single-minded interest. I saw the way it filled her up and kept her mind busy, tumbling and whirring in a way that was healthy. When her husband died of cancer, she hadn't retreated into the bitter arena of memories and regrets, but had secured a small loan from the American Indian Businessman's Association to open her shop. Safely installed amidst her musty merchandise, she had begun to contemplate all the worlds shining beyond our vision.

Lena put down her scissors and returned to the *National Enquirer.* I liked to watch her read. Her round Oneida face puckered in concentration and her pale green eyes— the color of creamy jade—attacked the page as if the act of reading made her angry. It reminded me of the way my father had read newspapers, clenching the paper so tightly in his fists his knuckles turned white. Reading was difficult for him, despite his education at the Carlisle Indian School in Pennsylvania, because Winnebago was his first language. He didn't like to think in English.

"English looks at the world this way," he told me, cutting the air with a flat chop parallel to the ground. "*Hocunkgara*[2] sees the world like this." His hand moved in a circle.

+ + +

My father and my Sioux mother had met at Carlisle but didn't remain there after graduation.

"They taught us to be white," my father told me when I was still too young to understand. "They taught us that way but didn't give us anywhere to take it." He slapped his hands together and fine dust emerged from his flesh; clouds burst from his palms.

"And I'm glad," he whispered, kneeling so his lips grazed my ear. "I'm back in the world now."

We lived near Green Bay in Wisconsin, where my father spent his days tending our small orderly fields of corn, squash, and beans, and his nights deep in the woods at secret medicine lodge meetings. When he returned, I could smell cedar on his clothes, his hair smoky. His scent filled our three rooms like pungent incense.

"You're like a church," my mother told him once, laughing.

I fell asleep to the sound of his voice. It scratched the walls and windows, raw from his prayers and sacred songs. He discussed clan politics with my mother, but I never digested the details. I was too transfixed by the strained quality of his voice. *My father really knows how to pray,* I thought.

My father's hands were hallowed, unlike mine, which have been soiled by steel. I saw him bend flexible reeds into animal figures: dogs, rabbits, hawks. When he breathed on the figure's face it would come to life for several moments and behave like any other of its kind. The hawk would coast above our heads and the dog rub against

---

[2] Ho-chunk, or Hochunk, is the indigenous name and language of the Winnebagos.

my legs. But eventually the creature would come apart, break open to reveal a nest of weeds.

I left Wisconsin because my parents barely scratched out a living from their few crops. I figured I could find a good job in the city and send home half my wages. It was just after World War II, and the government was pushing Relocation, moving Indians from reservations into the cities. Like many other Indians, I went into construction. We liked to work on high-rise buildings, weaving steel girders into solid structures that pierced the sky. We were careless on the catwalks and strolled exposed beams twenty stories high as casually as if we were on the ground. I am at least partially responsible for that Lake Michigan skyline. I thought I was bringing something to life back then, but after my parents died, I wasn't so sure. They succumbed to a virulent flu sweeping the Midwest, and I wondered where they would go. I couldn't see them following their teachers into Christ's jeweled heaven. They would be as uncomfortable there as they'd been at Carlisle.

I stayed in construction, but at night I practiced writing, trying to plot my place in the world as neatly as Lena Catches plotted close encounters on her maps. I wrote a poem for my father that was published twenty years later in *Akwesasne Notes*.[3] This is what I told him on the page:

> *My father is heretic pine,*
> *his ashes grown to needles in Wisconsin woods.*
> *I visited the grave and found him*
> *risen in bark.*
> *I smeared his heart's sap on my fingers.*
> *He will not wash away.*
> *I found God speaking Winnebago,*
> *perched in a silver birch tree.*
> *Tiny birds covered him like a feathered quilt.*
> *He was chewing fronds of fern*
> *to keep his teeth sharp and white.*
> *I saw him tremble like a bear,*
> *freeze like a deer,*
> *withdraw like a turtle into his shiny bones.*
> *Winnebago God blessed me from the tree.*
> *His fists rang on either side of my head*
> *where he shook them like rattles.*
> *City brother, he teased,*
> *welcome to this old universe.*

✦ ✦ ✦

I lived in the uptown area near the Chicago Indian Center, which was where I met Lena and her husband, Ray Catches. I didn't covet her then. It wasn't until Ray died that I noticed her little mouth and striking green eyes. In the five years since my retirement, Lena and I had established a pattern: she ducked my kisses and ate my donuts. In the back room of her shop I sorted through boxes of donated items, separating worthless contents from more promising discards while Lena read the tabloids. Once the contents were sorted, Lena made an inventory list and assigned prices. Sometimes I came across items we squirreled away for ourselves. Lena took possession of pastel

---

[3] A journal devoted to Native American news and issues.

pantsuits, leather purses, and science fiction magazines, while I kept a backgammon set and a huge macrame tapestry of an owl with startled eyes large as dinner plates.

✦ ✦ ✦

The day I discovered Saint Jude—or, as some may prefer to think, he discovered me—I was pawing through a box of business suits which had been worn to a shine. Five unopened boxes were stacked behind me. I was checking the pockets of each suit jacket for money or other valuables when I heard a scraping sound. A box behind me rattled, shook, threatened to fall from the top of the stack. *Somebody probably dumped their pet,* I was thinking as I moved to open the box. It contained cookingware: pots and pans once coated with teflon, plastic spatulas burned into unusual shapes, hand mixers, a garlic press, and underneath the clutter, the lumpy plastic statue of a saint.

"Hey, you," the statue hissed. I would have dropped him back into the box, but his tiny hands caught my sleeve and he dangled from the cuff of my shirt.

"I'm talking to you," the voice continued. "Don't you dare put me back in that box!"

"You can talk," I said stupidly. The figure rolled his eyes and knocked his head against one arm to right the halo, which had slipped down on his forehead.

"Funny how I can converse more capably when I'm not hanging in space."

I quickly caught the plastic saint by the waist, but I must have squeezed too hard because I knocked the breath from his molded body. Finally he pointed to a worktable and I set him down.

"This is not an auspicious introduction," he complained.

I was becoming annoyed with his petulance. "So, who's been introduced?"

The saint smoothed his robes and adjusted his halo. "I am Jude, martyr of my faith. Executed by order of Nero Domitius, fifth emperor of Rome, enemy of the Christian world. Who are you?"

For a moment I thought maybe I had breathed life into this statue the way my father had animated straw. But he was too lively. He scraped his sandaled feet against the pedestal; he bent to scratch his knee.

I finally answered, "I'm Mitchell Black Deer. Half Winnebago and half Sioux. Deer clan on my father's side. Originally from Wisconsin."

I decided I was dreaming. Maybe in bed. Maybe sitting at the worktable in Lena's shop with my head in my arms.

"Deer clan?" The saint shook his head. "We are all of the fish clan, little brother. We are all children of the Holy Fisherman." He held out his small hands and I noticed the outline of a fish traced in each palm.

"Do you want to kiss the hem of my robe?" he asked.

"No," I replied. Jude shrugged his shoulders and picked at the frayed ends of his rope belt. I didn't mean to be rude, but I would not bow my head before his white robe. I would not worship his small white toes and stringy hair. However, I *did* agree to take him home with me when he begged. I offered to pay Lena for the statue, although I didn't mention that he'd spoken to me just moments earlier in the back room.

"Since when did you get religion?" she asked. She sounded suspicious.

"Oh, no. He's just for decoration. A little irony," I lied.

She wouldn't accept any money for the statue. "He hasn't even been painted," she pointed out. It was true. He was pure white, smudged here and there by dirty finger-prints. I carried him out of the store, and because I thought I was dreaming I didn't worry about the unopened boxes I'd left behind, which would be extra work for Lena.

It was well into the night before I decided I was awake. It was a sharply cold October evening and I'd opened the windows in my apartment, hoping to rouse myself. I began to shiver and even the saint quivered on the coffee table.

"You're real," I finally admitted, closing the windows and turning up the thermostat. Jude snapped his eyes. "Why did you come to *me?*" I sat before him on the couch.

"You opened the box. You were just in the right place at the right time. And I'm glad you've come to your senses, because I need your help."

I waited for him to continue.

"I want to write poems," Jude told me. "I need someone to transcribe my poems for posterity. Maybe put together a little chapbook."

He discussed the themes and ideas he planned to articulate. He had no desire to be appended to the Bible, and it was my impression that this was because his words might be critical of the regime; the complex government of spirit in the Christian afterlife, he said, was strictly hierarchal.

"The cliques, the jealousy," he muttered. "Issues of seniority. Who was canonized first. Whose miracles were more imaginative. Those who died a martyr's death versus those who died in their sleep. It's endless. Then, too, today's faithful are barely making it to the celestial level. Standards have been lowered. No one's celibate. No one's taken a vow of poverty. Half the clergy are agnostic and when you try to provide them with concrete evidence, such as a direct visitation, they appeal to psychiatrists."

Jude threw his hands in the air and I wagged my head politely in sympathy.

✦ ✦ ✦

Within a week Saint Jude and I settled into a routine. In the morning he would compose poetry I carefully tapped out on an ancient manual typewriter given to me by my father. He stuttered sometimes, fumbled for the precise word. He had me consult the dictionary time and again, listening with eyes closed to the definitions I read aloud. Jude was critical of his own work. Perhaps one in ten poems would be acceptable. In the afternoon we edited the day's output, and in the evenings Jude meditated while I played Lakota language tapes. I had grown up speaking Winnebago and was now attempting to learn my mother's language.

I don't think Jude realized that he was learning Lakota as well. The tapes played in the background and I often heard him repeat phrases in the measured tone of a mantra:

"*Wicahpi owinza kin lila waste.* The star quilt is very pretty."

"*Wacipi ekta ni kta he?* Are you going to the powwow?"

"*Pispiza kin wanlaka he?* Did you see the prairie dog?"

I never saw Jude sleep or eat, although I offered him whatever I was having. One evening I cooked corn soup and he sniffed the air in a pitiful way.

"Are you hungry?" I asked him.

"I don't need your kind of sustenance," he said, "but I do enjoy the cooking aroma."

"Let's fill you up then." I held Jude over my cast-iron soup kettle. The broth sparkled like liquid gold and its steam warmed our faces. Jude inhaled the cooking breath of corn and venison until his cheeks grew fat. He flapped the long sleeves of his robe to capture more of the steam.

"This is good," he sighed, squirming in my hands like a white bird trying to fly into the soup. "This is so good!" He grew heavy, and when I placed him on the coffee table beside my plate, he loosened his rope belt.

✦ ✦ ✦

I was too busy attending to Jude to worry about Lena. I wasn't sure she would even notice my absence. But two weeks after I brought Jude home, she came by to check on me. She'd never visited my place before, and I think she was surprised at how small it was. I lived in a furnished efficiency, and my kitchen was little more than a closet with burners and a sink. I had taken the owl tapestry off the wall because Jude said it unnerved him, so the walls were bare when Lena entered. She carried a shopping bag full of plastic containers. When she unpacked them in my tiny kitchen I saw she had brought me starchy dishes I associated with Winnebago wakes and feasts: fry bread, potato salad, hominy, and grits.

"Are you sick?" she asked me. For a moment I thought she would check my forehead for a temperature. I shook my head, no.

"You should have a telephone," she scolded. "In case of emergencies."

I invited her to share supper with me, the supper she had cooked, but she waved the offer away with her hand. "I can't stay long. I was just worried about you when you didn't show. I thought maybe aliens had spirited you away, and here I missed it."

She smiled, and I realized it was the first time she'd ever poked fun at her obsession. I noticed that her face was no longer smooth as the porcelain doorknob to my closet, but delicately wrinkled, and silver white strands sprouted from her hairline like a glistening spiderweb combed into her hair. I thought she had never been more beautiful.

"Lena Catches," I murmured, taking her hand in mine. "I have some business to finish, but then I'll turn up again. I'll be seeing you all the time."

She blushed from her throat to the tips of her ears. At the door she put her arms around me and pressed her forehead to my breastbone. Just before pulling away, she tipped her head back and kissed my mouth. It was the light kiss of a young girl, and we laughed, because for one moment all our years fell from us like scales.

✦ ✦ ✦

"Lena missed me," I told Jude. He sulked on the sink drainboard, watching me rinse ears of sweet corn. "Who would've thought it?"

Jude shook his head. "It never fails. A woman beckons, a man follows. From the beginning of time to the end of time. It's so predictable, it's depressing."

"You're jealous," I teased. I expected Jude to laugh. Instead he ran a thumb along the edge of his halo as if testing a knife blade. It was a nervous tic I suspected signalled insecurity.

"Am not," he said.

For the first time since Jude caught my sleeve with his miniature hands, I thought to myself, *We have got a problem.* I never intended to give my life over to Saint Jude. I hadn't thought beyond the completion of his chapbook. Where would he go when the last poem was revised and typed? I was suddenly so preoccupied with Lena I knew there wouldn't be room for him when I courted her in earnest. He was too demanding, too exhausting.

The strategy I devised to prepare him for our eventual separation wasn't very kind. I harped on our cultural incompatibility. I told him his idea of heaven could never be mine. I told him I preferred God sitting in a birch tree chewing grass to God reclining on a golden throne. I showed him photographs of my ancestors: men in buckskin breeches wearing single eagle feathers rising from their deer tail headdresses, women with long silver earrings and thick strands of wampum around their necks wearing silk applique dresses.

"Have you seen them in your afterlife?" I asked him. He studied the pictures and shook his head sadly.

"I didn't think so. They're somewhere else. We are deer, bear, and elk clans,   buffalo, water spirit, and warrior clans, but we are not your fish clan. We have never been your fish clan."

This is how I argued the night before Jude composed his last poem, the one I liked best. He called it "Angry Fish," and when I read it back to him he nodded and wiped his eyes.

"That's how I feel," he said. "That's the song of the martyrs."

It was a long poem, a kind of lament, but the last phrases lodged themselves in my brain so that I remember them even now:

> *In the barrel of God's cupped palm*
> *the fish are angry.*
> *Their faith-hooked flesh*
> *cannot heal in the briny tears*
> *God shed for them too long ago.*
> *They are marred by their infirmities,*
> *fish with serrated scales and spiny ridges*
> *unable to press one against the other*
> *for comfort.*
> *Scraped raw by love,*
> *dipped in wax and held to the flame.*
> *Faith's cold fire chills the heart.*

Saint Jude's manuscript included sixty poems and was eighty-five pages long. I held it for a time in my hands, appreciating its weight and the sharp scent of fresh pages. I packed it in a typing paper box that I bound with twine.

"It's done. Mission accomplished," I told Jude. He nodded, and blessed me with his tiny fingers.

+ + +

Four weeks after we first met, I returned Jude to his people. I wrapped him in a soft piece of buckskin, since it was cold that morning. I hadn't told him where I was taking him because I didn't want to argue. I'd bought a large Easter basket from Woolworth's—cheap, out of season—and wrapped a white ribbon around its handle. This is how I carried the manuscript, and Jude, straddling the box with the buckskin pulled around him like a blanket.

It was so quiet that morning I could hear stoplights change from red to green as I stood beneath them. I walked all the way to Saint Michael's Church, a longer walk than I'd managed in recent years—something like four miles. The rectory was in back;

three wrought-iron steps led to the front door, and an elaborate bell was rigged above the entrance. I placed the basket on the top step, poised to ring the bell.

"Take care, old man," I whispered, but he wouldn't look at me. He seemed stiffer, his arms straight at his sides, his feet still. He stood on the manuscript and stared vacantly ahead, the flap of leather fallen around his ankles.

"This is where you really belong." I felt guilty, but it quickly turned to anger. I had played host long enough. I was tired of Indians playing host until we were pushed out of our own lives. But I didn't tell Saint Jude. I didn't want to hurt his feelings.

I rang the bell and stepped back. As I turned to go I heard a muffled voice. "Good-bye," Jude said. I moved down the steps, and he called, *"Unlowanpi,"* the Lakota phrase for, "We are singing together."

I passed through the courtyard and was on the street when I heard his lonely voice singing a song he must have learned from my powwow tapes. It told the story of two brothers reunited after a battle, delighted to discover that they have both survived. I took up the song while I could still hear Jude's voice and sang it, all the way home.

—1995

LOIS-ANN YAMANAKA (1961-)

The third-generation descendent of Japanese immigrants to Hawaii, Lois-Ann Yamanaka grew up in the plantation town of Pahala, on the Big Island of Hawaii, along with her three sisters. She received a B.A. in Education from the University of Hawaii, Manoa, in 1982, followed by a master's degree in 1986. Yamanaka's writing first came into prominence with the publication of *Saturday Night at the Pahala Theatre* (1993), a volume of poetry that won both the Pushcart Prize and the Association for Asian American Studies Book Award. Her poetry is noteworthy for its use of pidgin, the creole dialect that is the legacy of Hawaii's multiracial plantation worker populations. While other Hawaii-based writers had used pidgin (most notably those affiliated with *Bamboo Ridge,* a journal and writing group), Yamanaka's work is distinctive in its exploration of the brutality and humor of working-class island communities from the perspective of adolescent girls. Yamanaka has been praised for her unflinching portrayals of sexual violence, but she has also been criticized because Filipino-American characters are sometimes portrayed as the site or origin of this violence. Her 1997 novel *Blu's Hanging* ignited a firestorm of controversy because of its portrayal of Filipino-American characters. Yamanaka is the recipient of a 1998 Lannan Literary Award and two Pushcart Prizes. Her books also include *Wild Meat and the Bully Burgers* (1996), *Heads by Harry* (1999), *Father of the Four Passages* (2001), *The Heart's Language* (2005), and *Behold the Many* (2006).

Tita:[1] Boyfriends

Boys no call you yet?
Good for you.
Shit, everybody had at least

---

[1] (Hawaiian pidgin) A tough, usually large, local female.

two boyfriends already.
You neva have even *one* yet? 5
You act dumb, ass why.
All the boys said you just one little kid.
Eh, no need get piss off.

Richard wen' call me around 9:05 last night.
Nah, I talk *real* nice to him. 10
Tink I talk to him the way I talk to you?
You cannot let boys know your true self.
Here, this how I talk.
Hello, Richard. How are you?
Oh, I'm just fine. How's school? 15
My classes are just greeaat.
Oh, really. Uh-huh, uh-huh.
Oh, you're so funny.
Yes, me too, I love C and K.
Kalapana? Uh-huh, uh-huh. 20

He coming down from Kona next week.
He like me meet him up the shopping center.
Why, you like see him?
He one fox with ehu[2] hair.
I know he get ehu hair 25
'cause he wen' send me his picture.
What you said?
Of course he know what I look like.
Eh, what you trying for say?
That I one fuckin' fat cow? 30
Yeah, he get one picture of me.

I wen' send him the one of us by the gym.
The one us made you take for the gang
'cause us neva like you in the picture.
Nah—I was in the back row 35
so I wen' look skinny, eh.
Only had my face.

I get this guy wrap around my finger
'cause of the way I talk on the phone.
I told him I get hazel eyes and I hapa[3]— 40
eh, I pass for hapa ever since I wen' Sun-In my hair.
Lemon juice and peroxide too.
Ass why all orange and gold.
Plus when I glue my eyes and make um double,
my eyes ain't slant no mo 45
and I swear, everybody ask me,
Eh, you hapa?

---

[2] (Hawaiian pidgin) Reddish tinge in hair, specifically in Polynesians.

[3] (Hawaiian pidgin) Mixed-race.

So what if not all true?
How he going know from that picture I gave him?
I was so far in the back.   50
He said he get um in his wallet.
And no be acting all cute when he come.
Just shut your mouth
and let me and him do whatevas.
I warning you now, no get stupid.   55
And no follow us if he like go cruising
'cause something might happen
in the car. I get um.

I get um good.
'Cause I know what boys like do   60
and it ain't hanging around the gym
or swimming laps after school
or sitting around the shopping center eating slush
with fuckin' losers like you,
I tell you that much.   65

So you keep writing Elmer's name
inside your folders and prank calling him,
and dedicating songs to him
and writing him stupid letters signed ano-namous
and shoving um in his locker.   70
Eh, think I stupid?
Everybody know you like Elmer.
And everybody know you the dumb ass
doing all those dumb things.
How they know? 'Cause maybe I told um.   75
Why. You going make something of it?
I would *love* to have to kick your ass right now.

Yeah, I told um. I told um all.
And you like know what?
You better give up all that shit   80
and grow up 'cause everybody,
all the boys think you just one small kid
and no boy going eva be your boyfriend
'cause you dunno how
for make your voice all nice,   85
your face all make-up,
your hair all smooth and ehu,
your clothes all low cut,
and your fingernails all long.
You dunno how for act.   90
And you, you just dunno how for please.

—1993

Tita: Japs

I like see your strawberry musk.
Ho, I wen' put too much.
So what if the teacher look at us.
Just another stupid Jap. You eva wen' notice
that every teacher we had since elementry days   5
was one lady Jap?
Eh, what you trying for say to me?
I ain't one fuckin' Jap like them.
Their eyes mo slant than mine and yeah,
I one Jap, but not that kine,   10

the kine all good and smart and perfect
with their Japan pencil case,
leather saddle bag, smart math book,
muumuu every Friday
that the madda wen' sew, of course,   15
and the fadda drive one Torino.
That kine Jap is what I ain't.

But what you think about David?
Cute for one haole,[4] eh?
But you know what I really think?   20
He like one local to me 'cause he surf.
I wen' ask him how he got his tan.
You blind or what? He get one *good* tan.
I hate talking to dummies like you.
You always acting stupid.   25
Now what I was saying?
Oh yeah, he told me he go surf down Honoli'i.
I wish he would ask me for *go* with him.
Gimme that strawberry musk.

Watch this. Watch me ask Lori for gum.   30
I like gum. Eh, you so tight.
No need give me then.
She got doublemint up her ass at that store.
They get one store, you know.
Shit man, just 'cause she came from the mainland,   35
she think she can rule this class?
Her gramma had cancer, you know.
Ass why they gotta move Honolulu.
She get one skinny ass, yeah?

I wonder if her madda them can order   40
strawberry musk and makeup at the store?
Must be, 'cause Lori get all
the Maybelline Blooming Colors.

---

[4] (Hawaiian) Sometimes derogatory slang for a foreign or white person.

Fuckin' Jap slut. They the worse
'cause they like for act like they no poke.   45
But they do, 'cause can tell
by the way they walk funny. Try watch.
Eh, Lori. Go shahpen my pencil. Please.

Remember I told you Lance wen' try throw me
in the pool at that stupid party?   50
I only went 'cause David went.
You was there, eh? Well, you seen this then?
Why you always gotta act dumb?
Eh, what's your trip?
Just like you *like* hear me talk.   55

I wen' tell Lance, *Try throw me in the pool, fucka.*
My damn glue going come off.
Then I'm gonna have to break your face.
He's such a dick. Think he so hot shit.
Puny ass little Jap.   60

You know how long take me for put glue on my eyelid.
Plus my eye shadow and mascara.
Mo worse that night, I only had little bit glue
left in the tube, 'cause I went Longs
and neva have the white Duo glue.   65
Only had the black.
Ugly you know the black.

So anyways, I had for run to the bathroom all wet.
I wen' dig for one toothpick for put the glue.
Then I wen' pound that sink   70
'cause had only little bit glue left.
So I stay all rush and I line the glue
on my eyelid and paste the skin up,
but eh, my fuckin' face was all wet
so the glue came all bumpy.   75
I had for do um *all over again.*
Took one hour for look normal again.
I wish I had double eye.

I tell you, my next birtday,
when my madda ask me what I like,   80
I going tell her I like go Honolulu
for get one double eye operation.
I no care if all bruise
like Donna's one for six months.
Look Donna now, all nice her eyes,   85
and she no need buy Duo glue
or Scotch tape anymore
for make double eye.
I take the operation any day.

You heard what I told Emi? 90
I wen' tell her, *You fuckin' cow.*
I heard you was talking stink about me.
You like me kick your ass? C'mon, right now,
you stink little Japanee slut.
Nah. She wen' back off. 95
But I already went Penneys
for write her name on the chair.
For a good time, call Emi.
959-3311, the pride of Hilo town.

There. The bell wen' ring. 100
Spahk you tomorrow.
Bring your black nail polish. I like borrow.
The teacher wen' ask me yesterday,
Why do you paint your fingernails black?
I told her, *'Cause I like. Why?* 105
Fuck. Fuck um all.
I no give a shit.

—1993

Tita: On Fat

Eh, what you trying for say?
That I one fat cow? Well, fuck you.
I ain't fat. I just more mature than you guys.
You guys ain't developed yet.
I bet you neva even get your rags yet. 5
All you guys a bunch of small shit Japs.
Anyways, look at you, asshole.
Think you so slim? You fuckin' fat too,
especially in the ass.
Besides, no get wise with me 10
for I tell Craig what Leland told you.
Think I wen' forget, eh?

Rememba, Leland told you Craig get one small dick
'cause he seen um in Mr. Yanagi's P.E. class?
Look like one Vienna sausage 15
and you guys giving him the thumbs up sign
like *Howzit-Craig-what's-up*
when actually you guys teasing his dick size.
So go 'head. Wise up with me, asshole.
I tell him today, right now you like. 20
Okay then. No get wise.

You—you just like Nancy.
You guys think you so skinny

when you guys is so fuckin' fat.
Shit, I like punch you guys' face   25
when I see you acting slim.
You wasn't shame take off your shirt
when us went down Leileiwi for swim or what?
Eh, your bikini was so down-the-road.
What you wanted for do?   30

Act in front of the tourist boys that was there?
You and your damn fat friend, Nancy,
you guys look so stupid
'cause you was the only one
in the whole gang who wen' take off their shirt   35
when all us wen' leave ours on
for jump in the water.
You neva see the tourist boys laughing at you?

Where you got those stupid *greeen* hiphuggas from?
Wigwam? Kress Store? Cheap sale, eh?   40
Shit, pull um up.
Can see your ass crack.
You so damn fat and you trying for wear those pants.
Give it up, girl.
You ain't made for clothes like that, fat ass.   45
Mo worse, you get the nerve for wear halter top.
What—you made that in your Singer sewing class
or your gramma made um with leftover blanket material?
Eh, you look so stupid.
And mo worse, you think you look slick.   50

We go eat lunch. I so damn hungry.
I stay staavving to death.
I only been eating chicken noodle soup
for dinner. 'Cause I on one diet, stupid.
You for ask dumb questions.   55
I getting piss off at you.

Yeah and I piss off at my madda too.
Stink ass witch, I told her I was on one diet
and I wen' ask her for buy me some Campbell soup
but her she neva buy me shit.   60
So I had for drink the juice from my bradda's saimin.
I wanted to shove the noodles
down my throat but no can, eh?
Mo worse, my madda stay telling me,
Eat carrots or celery. Shit,   65
I wanted to tell her for shove that carrots
up her tight ass.

I dunno, I too fuckin' fat.
Eh, no say I not fat,

when I *know* you think I fat,   70
'cause that only makes me *mo*
fuckin' mad.

—1993

ELIZABETH ALEXANDER (1962-   )

Elizabeth Alexander was born in Harlem, New York, and raised in Washington, D.C. She holds a B.A. from Yale University, an M.A. from Boston University, and a doctorate from the University of Pennsylvania. Alexander, who began her career as a newspaper reporter, is a scholar and teacher of African American Studies as well as a poet. She is the author of the essay collection *The Black Interior* (2004), and four volumes of poetry: *The Venus Hottentot* (2004), *Body of Life* (1996), *Antebellum Dream Book* (2001), and *American Sublime* (2005). A 1997 winner of the Quantrell Award for Excellence in Undergraduate Teaching at the University of Chicago, Alexander currently teaches African American Studies at Yale and is a summer faculty member at Cave Canem Poetry Workshop. Her other awards include a National Endowment for the Arts Fellowship, a Guggenheim Fellowship, and two Pushcart Prizes. In 2005, her collection *American Sublime* was a finalist for the Pulitzer Prize in poetry.

Early Cinema

According to Mister Hedges, the custodian
who called upon their parents
after young Otwiner and young Julia
were spotted at the matinee
of Rudolph Valentino in *The Sheik*   5
at the segregated Knickerbocker Theater
in the uncommon Washington December
of 1922, "Your young ladies
were misrepresenting themselves today,"
meaning, of course, that they were passing.   10
After coffee and no cake were finished
and Mister Hedges had buttoned his coat
against the strange evening chill,
choice words were had with Otwiner and Julia,
shame upon the family, shame upon the race.   15

How they'd longed to see Rudolph Valentino,
who was swarthy like a Negro, like the finest Negro man.
In *The Sheik,* they'd heard, he was turbaned,
whisked damsels away in a desert cloud.
They'd heard this from Lucille and Ella   20
who'd put on their fine frocks and French,
claiming to be "of foreign extraction"
to sneak into the Knickerbocker Theater

past the usher who knew their parents
but did not know them.   25
They'd heard this from Mignon and Doris
who'd painted carmine bindis on their foreheads
braided their black hair tight down the back,
and huffed, "We'll have to take this up with the Embassy"
to the squinting ticket taker.   30
Otwiner and Julia were tired of Oscar Michaux,[1]
tired of church, tired of responsibility,
rectitude, posture, grooming, modulation,
tired of homilies each way they turned,
tired of colored right and wrong.   35
They wanted to be whisked away.

The morning after Mister Hedges' visit
the paperboy cried "Extra!" and Papas
shrugged camel's hair topcoats over pressed pajamas,
and Mamas read aloud at the breakfast table,   40
"No Colored Killed When Roof Caves In"
at the Knickerbocker Theater
at the evening show
from a surfeit of snow on the roof.
One hundred others dead.   45

It appeared that God had spoken.
There was no school that day,
no movies for months after.

—2001

"The female seer will burn upon this pyre"

Sylvia Plath is setting my hair
on rollers made from orange-juice cans.
The hairdo is shaped like a pyre.

My locks are improbably long.
A pyramid of lemons somehow   5
balances on the rickety table

where we sit, in the rented kitchen
which smells of singed naps and bergamot.
Sylvia Plath is surprisingly adept

at rolling my unruly hair.   10
She knows to pull it tight.
                              Few words.

Her flat, American belly,

her breasts in a twin sweater set,

---

[1] Oscar Michaux (1893-1951), pioneering African-American filmmaker.

stack of typed poems on her desk,   15
envelopes stamped to go by the door,

a freshly baked poppyseed cake,
kitchen safety matches, black-eyed Susans
in a cobalt jelly jar. She speaks a word,

"immolate," then a single sentence   20
of prophecy. The hairdo done,
the nursery tidy, the floor swept clean

of burnt hair and bumblebee husks.

—2001

ANN PANCAKE (1963-   )

Born in Richmond, Virginia, and raised in Romney, West Virginia, Ann Pancake taught English in Japan, American Samoa, and Thailand before undertaking doctoral studies in English at the University of Washington. Her regional fiction, set in West Virginia, often thematizes characters' separation from mainstream society due to their poverty. Pancake has won numerous awards for her stories, which have been published in journals such as the *Southeast Review, Chattahoochee Review, International Quarterly, Journal of Appalachian Studies,* and *Review of Contemporary Fiction.* Her book of short stories, *Given Ground* (2001), won the Bakeless Prize at the Bread Loaf Writers' Conference, and she published her first novel, *Strange As This Weather Has Been,* in 2007. Pancake teaches literature and creative writing at Pennsylvania State University, Erie.

Crow Season

Seems I dreamed it several times before. Me wandering a hollow,[1] branching into hollow, branching into hollow. Dream my shoulders passing through that up and down land, and the dead leaves, snakeskin-dry and slippery. Ground up over my head (the way you're in land over your head). And the sudden reek of dead animal, but you can't see the carcass except for the crows. Hollow, branching into hollow, branching into hollow. Until it all closes up in a draw, and there are no more hollows.

+ + +

I heard it in Ranson the morning after. What my youngest uncle's youngest boy had done. When I got off work, I ate a can of chili and sat on my porch, deciding. Then I drove down to the homeplace to see if I could help.

+ + +

I call out from the back door, then let myself into a kitchen odored of tuna cans and old smoke. Soiled dishes stacked. My uncle eats from a McDonald's bag, and he is odored, too, unbathed, unshaved. He eats from the bag furtive, as though it is a sin.

---

[1] Common term in Appalachia for a small valley.

—Ravelle never could control that boy.

He speaks of his second wife, the boy's mother, who has left him now. I just nod, like I tend to do.

—I knew he'd done some looting up in there. I found a few bottles. But I didn't know he was selling it to other kids.

I nod again. Through the window behind my uncle, everything's coming up thistle and chicory and Queen Anne's lace, weeds that thrive on a drought. No difference between yard and pasture, no difference between pasture and field. Under a dead apple tree, a big dog feeds from a loose refrigerator drawer. I'm thinking. Although I'm not sure, I figure Vincent'll be in one of two places. Not too many hiding places back in the mountain with any water to speak of in this kind of dry.

—I was never moved to do much about it.

I look from the window back to his face.

—The looting, I mean. Hell, far as I'm concerned, underneath up there will always be ours.

—Underneath Joby Knob, I say.

—Hell, yeah, Joby Knob. He works a piece of gristle out of his teeth. How was I supposed to know how hard those people are? He shakes his head. People hard enough to poison liquor to teach a child thief a lesson.

✦ ✦ ✦

I pick the Heplinger Place first, and I choose to walk. And not only because the truck motor will give Vincent warning and make him run. The deer paths in the hollows have been beaten big as cattle crossings, with the size of the herds now and the terrible drought. I place my feet careful, watching for every stick to move. *Snakes'll come out of the high places in dries like this,* I hear my father. The drought has shrunk all the creeks into a few holes, and the earth around these holes, punched solid with deer tracks.

Most of this land would have been my inheritance, and I grew up hunting it, cutting wood off it, running it. I know it better than anyone still living, including the man who owns it now. Never have I seen it so tired, with the deer paths wide as cattle runs up and down the hollow sides, and acornless ground. And the deer themselves, gaunt and puny and sorrowed. Quivering under their flies.

✦ ✦ ✦

From where I sat in the kitchen, I could see behind the stove a ripped sleeping bag where the dog must stay. Unbaited mousetraps scattered in corners. My father and uncles grew up in this house, their father and grandfather, too. I'd been told there were rooms upstairs now where you could see sky. But I hadn't climbed to the second story in twenty years.

—You know they say the Haslacker boy may or may not live. The one he sold the bottle to.

I nodded.

—Vincent has Knob inside him. It's not a matter of who holds the paper. You know that.

The oven door was open to where I could see burnt cheese all over its bottom. Although my uncle sacrificed the house upkeep to save the land, he had to sell off anyway, including Joby Knob.

—Well, either you know better than any of us it's not a matter of who holds the paper. Or you don't know it at all.

I looked at the man across the table. There was a darkness in my uncle. I used not to fear him when I was younger, but the darkness had come in him, and I feared him now. The anger hardening some place in his body. Where eventually it would crack loose and bolt to his brain.

+ + +

I angle to the right, a hollow branching off the Shingle Hollow, a shortcut to the Heplinger Place. A leaf layer sprouts feet, takes on substance, weight. A fawn flushing. This was a road at one time, but I can only see road if I unfocus my eyes.

The Heplinger Place is a little bigger than the Further House, the other spot Vincent might be. The last people to live here were bark strippers with two daughters, one crippled by a gun, but they all four died of typhoid not long after the turn of the century. At least that's what my father always said. But he was known to make things up. I scout around the rubble of house and barn, find a litter of shotgun shells, a Snickers wrapper from last fall. And then the old stuff, metal and stone. A harness buckle. A barrel stave. No sign Vincent has been through.

Just as I'm about to leave, I hear behind me a peculiar misplaced sound. Wavery, and I stop to listen harder. A cat noise, I'm thinking, but crossed with something wild. I turn slowly in a circle, the dry sky turning overhead, and I understand it comes from the old bad well. I listen. A crow throats from a hickory tree. Typhoid, I remember, and all of them dead, and I know inside me a wrongness and grief out of all proportion to common sense.

I can't see where the well was, buried in dead leaves, but I remember stumbling over it several times in the past. I listen. The well mewls again. A hot dry wind rattles through, a wind doesn't belong here. *A Western wind, I call it.* I hear my father say this so clear I wonder for a second if he's in that well, too. I trace the mewling to the rotty cover. I squat over it, clear away the leaves. Then I break off a soft board and peer inside.

The moment the sun falls through, two eyes flash a flat green. Then they go out. I stare harder, but the creature's shrunk from the light. It does not sound again.

Something curls inside me. The dry has drawn it into the well, and there it starves and won't ever get out. And me the last thing to see it, and I can't even tell what it is.

+ + +

Not many weeks ago, I drove up on Joby Knob myself, ignoring the "Posted." It is a foreign place to me now. The developers renamed it Misty Mountain Estates, acre clearings of new houses built to look old. Each lot is armored with a security system and warning signs, and that Vincent even managed to break into one of these places I can't help but admire. A different kind of hunting. Rows of second homes on a clear-cut ridge, up here where no old-timer would ever build. *Those old-timers built in the bottoms and the hollows* (again, my father), *out of the wind and near water.* As I rode along the smooth-graded gravel road, I squinted to find the good crossing place, where I'd shot a big-bodied eight-point when I was seventeen or so. But near as I could tell, the crossing ran straight through a kit log cabin. And the feel of moving among all those new vacation houses, yet not a soul around. The houses creating an expectation of presence, then their emptiness sucking that expectation inside out. So much emptier on Joby Knob now than when it was just trees.

Back before, we'd drive to the power cut to see off. Now you can see off anywhere, but I went to the power cut that day. I leaned against the grill of my truck and looked up and down the valley, several miles in both directions. The drought-stricken trees turning already, even though it was July.

The darkness in my father, too, would wax and wane. He'd have me convinced he'd finally gone pure mean, then he'd do me something kind. He never let me find my footing there. But I learned. I learned I'd never care about anything so much the loss of it would turn me dark.

I climbed into the bed of my truck where I could get a better view and looked out over the cab. The way the land lays in here looks more like a human body than any land I've ever seen, pictures or real. And I often wonder if that's the reason for the hold it has on us.

✦ ✦ ✦

As I pass back through the Deep Hollow to where I'll pick up the jeep track to the Further House, I hear a truck motor. I stop and wait. It is several minutes, and the flies find me good, before I see my uncle's truck. He leans his head and his arm through the window.

—I got news you can give him that might flush him out.

✦ ✦ ✦

The night before, he'd spoken of my father. Though not directly. He'd talked of the strokes, that family vulnerability: his mother, his brother, his father, mine. He spoke not for the loss of them, I knew, but out of fear for himself. Fear of his own blood drying inside him. Making a seed.

He spoke like a drunk man, and I wish that was so. But didn't none of them drink. They could crazy themselves on air. I watched my uncle scratch the insides of his arms, and I wondered if he felt the clotting under his skin.

✦ ✦ ✦

As I climb the jeep track towards the Further House, I wonder from which house Vincent stole the liquor. I picture Joby Knob in my head. One place has an observatory, of all things, another a swimming pool. And one a burglar alarm so sensitive it goes off every time it thunderstorms and I can hear it all the way down to my house. Then I try to imagine the weekenders who did it. I imagine. To poison your own liquor to catch the boy who stole from you.

I finally come up over the last ridge and creep out on a shale point where I can spy down into the flat. I right away see the boy's tarp rigged in a corner of the stone foundation. I let a little shale spill off the bank under my boots to make him look. His face upturns, sooty, smoky. Peering up at me. Him on his haunches and hands like a dog.

"Vincent. Vincent Keadle," I call. "Come on out of there."

Then I can't see him, but I hear him break away through the brush and scramble up the far bank, his tennis shoes slipping in the barrens. Him, again, I know, on his haunches and hands.

"Vincent," I call after him. "They say the boy is going to live."

+ + +

Let me tell you this. I was a few years older than Vincent Keadle when we lost all but the thirty acres down around the house. My father left with his hunting rifle, and this was late spring, the season for nothing. He took the truck, so I had to walk, but he abandoned it a half mile up the Deep Hollow, and the ground was wet, him easy to track. Hollow branching into hollow, and me mounting up, hollow, into draw, into crease, until I'd top a ridge, catch my breath, slide to the bottom and start again. And, yes, I was thinking, what if he shoots me. But I tell myself (I tell myself) I worried more for him.

When I got close enough to glimpse his red coat, I trailed at a distance until he staggered to a stop. Then I snuck over the leaves, them muted with the wet, and hid in the catface of a fire-scarred oak. There I watched him load it, and I knew it was my place to dart out and wrestle it away. But I did not. I squatted in that catface, pressed so tight against the bark it left scratches in my cheek. Saw my father raise the gun, snug the stock against his shoulder, pause and look around.

Then I watched him fire in the ground. Empty and empty it into lost ground.

+ + +

—Sometimes it's hard to look at you, boy. My uncle balled up his McDonald's bag and pitched it to the end of the table with the other trash, mostly unopened mail. I studied the empty blood-thinner bottles rowed up in the sill.

—I used to think you were weak, he told me. But anymore. Anymore I wonder if you're the only one of all you kids was born with any sense.

He leaned in closer to me. Gouged, his eyes looked, in that beginning-to-get-dark.

—Probably not, he said.

+ + +

I grew up in it. Forever, the mutter and drone. The anxiety, the obsession, the fear, the fights: the farm, the money, the family, the past.

Years ago, I made my decision. I sold off my inheritance except an acre.

+ + +

By the time I get all the way back to the paved road, Vincent sits with his head bowed in his father's truck. I catch my uncle's eye in his side mirror. He nods at me, then looks away, but he doesn't look at Vincent either. I walk a quarter mile of asphalt to where I left my own truck, climb in, and drive the last mile home.

I keep no mirrors in my place. I tell what I look like in others' faces, me make-them-gasp identical. I know that I've grown into a ghost. Carrying in my face, in how my body's hung together, in how I speak and move, the man who died and made me take over the looks of him. But I'm used to my outsides. What scares me is if it's printed on my insides, too.

I wait here on my single acre. I hoe my garden. I water the trees.

—2001

SUZAN-LORI PARKS (1964-)

Widely acknowledged as a powerful voice in contemporary American theatre, Suzan-Lori Parks was born in Kentucky in 1964. The daughter of an officer in the U.S. Army, Parks lived in six different states as a child and spent her teenage years in Germany. She began writing novels when she was five. As a student at Mount Holyoke College (she received a B.A. in English and German literature in 1985), Parks was influenced by James Baldwin, who suggested that she write plays, and by Mary McHenry, an English professor who introduced her to the work of Adrienne Kennedy. Parks' singular voice, dazzling command of English vernacular, innovations in form, and complex renderings of, among other topics, the American experience of race and class, has altered the landscape of the American theatre and has added significantly to the shape of its practices. In 1989 the *New York Times* named her the year's "Most Promising Playwright," following *Imperceptible Mutabilities in the Third Kingdom,* which went on to win an Obie Award in 1990. Parks' other plays include *The Death of the Last Black Man in the Whole World* (1990), *Pickling* (1990), *The America Play* (1994), *Venus* (1996), *In the Blood* (1999), *Fucking A* (2000), and *Topdog/Underdog* (2001), which won the 2002 Pulitzer Prize for Drama, the first time the prize was awarded to an African-American woman. Parks has won numerous other prestigious prizes, including two Obies, two NEA grants, and a 2001 "genius grant" from the MacArthur Foundation. She has written screenplays for Spike Lee, Disney, and Jodie Foster, as well as for the television adaptation of Zora Neale Hurston's *Their Eyes Were Watching God,* and the Broadway adaptation of the film *Ray.* She has also written a novel, *Getting My Mother's Body* (2003). Parks is married to the blues musician Paul Oscher and lives in Los Angeles.

Pickling

PLAYER

MISS MISS

MISS MISS [*Sung*]:
 ...I wiped his brow.
 I. Wiped. His. Brooooooooow.
 He grabbed the frail cloth
 Ripped it roughly in two,
 Gave my half to me—I give his half to you.
 "Farewell! Farewell!" So turns the wheel.—
 ————.

 "Farewell! Farewell!" So turns the wheel—ah-la-la-uh-uh—
 ————.

 "MY MUSCLES WERE LIKE STEEL."
 "MY MUSCLES WERE LIKE STEEE-EEEL."

[*Spoken*] Taut. Taut. Taut. Taut. Taut.—Taut. Huh. Huh. Oh well. Thats thuh way things move, huh? From hot tuh cold? From warm tuh not—warm? Ha!: To *worm.* Sssnatural progression of things: When theyre hot they make their progress from hot tuh cold. No sadness, Miss Miss, no sadness today. Ssonly nature going through thuh motions. Well. Oooh! Sscold. Ha! If I'd taken it straight from the icebox and put tonn thuh table then it would uh gone from cooold tuh—warm. Rum tempachur. Now thereres something. Like flesh tone: What temperature is the room what tone is the flesh? Taut! Taut flesh. —Your icebox, Miss Miss, what has happened to your lovely icebox? Ssgone. And in ssplace Ive something better, whowhowho much much better than old icebox: memory of old icebox: three nuts seven bolts and uh rung from thuh topmost tray! Right here. Right here in thuh cream-colored jar. Rattle em uhroun some. Mm huhnn. Good sounds they make. Nothing like good sounds—memory of the icebox. So much better than thuh real thing mm huhn. Never had uh problem with it. Never broke down. No defrosting. Good sounds. Threenutssevenboltsand—aah— uhrungfromthuhtopmosttray! Hee! Wanted tuh keep thuh door handle—but no. Tuh keep thuh door handle woulda been nice tuh have tuh save but. No. Door handle was soiled! Coulda washed it. But. No. Soiled with mothers milk Miss Miss. Mothers milk never comes clean. Look what happened to—wasshisname—Aresting. Mr. Aresting ha he kills his mother raggedy women follow him around yelling. Mothersmilk. Uh. Nothin like heated milk gone cold to downend thuh spirits huh past cold now now— colder. Colder with thuh surface tightening. Taut surface. Taut. Taut. Little-green- bacteria-family-setting-up-house-on-thuh-side-lines. Uh! Put it away Miss Miss put the milk back in the jar! All that trouble gone to all for naught. Miss Miss put thuh milk away. Pour careful thats it. Pour careful dont waste uh drop. Pour careful. Pour care- ful. Huh. Pour poor careful. Tighten thuh lid dont want it to go bad dont want tuh have tuh toss it out. There are people starving you know. People going without. Right next door. Dont want tuh waste. Put thuh lid on tight and it wont spoil. Put thuh lid on tight and itll keep. Then soon itll go back tuh powder. Powdermilk. Dust. Then for guests we will have to reactivate. Rise up from thuh dead. Thuh right amount of saliva. Stir. Heat. Have hot milk for thuh coffee. Put it in uh greeeaaat biiiguh cup. Cold. Well. Ssgood Ive got everythin I need right here at my fingertips never need to go out outside is overwhelming ssstoo much. Havent been out since. Synce uh comedinlass. Hee! Got it all here. Been saving. Savin it up. For guests. Its time: mmm. This is good. Good sounds. Very—oh! and the applause. Yes. That was from. I had guests. In my home. In here. Home. They come for miles. To see me. I sang! Beautifully. Accompany myself with my jars. Hadnt been done before. Jar accompa- niment. Was new news then. Old news now. *Passé.* Huh. Only French you know Miss Miss. Only need one word. One word in each language: for French: *passé;* German: *tschuß!*—the familiar form of bye bye; all African boils down to *umboogie umwoogie* (Ha!thatswhattheysay); in English: *worm.* Only need one. One word. The rest is— just—lettuce. Not at all like the jars. Each jar has a distinctly different sound. Not just uh sound that differs from their shape but. Well. For example. Thuh milk jar: Mother's—oh: cold. Miss Miss thuh peach cobbler ssgettin rubbery. Lets put it back. Jar-for-thuh-cobbler-where-did-you-roam-tuh-god-damn-yuh?! Cobbler goes away. Cobbler goes back. Back back uhway away. They didnt take cobbler today but they will take tuh my cobbler tuh morrow and it wont do Miss Miss not tuh have you some fresh slices listen tuh that will you? In and out of dialect. Shifty. Huh! Keep it. We will work on it. Save it Miss Miss. Yeah. Yes. And I sang. Oh. And they applauded. Clapped. Hard. Clapped vigorously. Good sounds. Huh! Mother calls it "good clap- ping." "I know when I do well," she says, "When I do well, they give me—good clap- ping." Hee! IsangIsangasongIsangasong. A prell-yude. The song was a prell-yude. One uh them pray-lude songs. Warm up to my performance. My farewell performance. First I sang. So sweetly. With—passions. Not just one but several. Several passions. Simultaneously. Uh huhn. Then I am to perform. A short drama. Uh short drama in ten short pages. My farewell. Ive got it right here. On thuh top shelf. Hasnt spoiled—oh no—see? The lid on this one is very tight. Taut. Charles tautened thuh lid. My farewell dramatic performance. Well wrought. Lots of sighs init. — NoMissMissdontopenit: airll get in and it will spoil! dont want it tuh spoil! dont want it tuh waste there are people right next door going without! put it back Miss Miss put it back! Charles tightened this lid. Such arms he had. Such bicepts. Like steel. Steal away steal away my home is—. Such bicepts. He lived next door. Close. He was uh lifeguard. We met on thuh beach. "Don't go in it's much too cold!": Those were his words. Not mine. Saved my life. Was winter. He worked year round. I saved sand from that day. Uh whole jar full. Had tuh dig under thuh snow tuh get at it. "Dont go in ssmuch too col!": I. Entertain him here. He is my guest. The cup with his lips mark. Here. The sand from his bare feet. In this one. His wind: breath; gas. The prophylactic: our love object. Thuh light likes this one. Our love. Dont open it Miss Miss. People—next—door—going without! Charles! Hee! Such bicepts. Taut. Like Steel! Such bravery. Oh. Clapping. Good Clapping! Charles is clapping good thuh loudest! Oh! We had words he and I. We had us uh x-change uh huhnn. Uhbout we spoke of. And—uhbout thuh great-nigger-queen-bee-who-lives-at-thuh-center-of-Mars. He said "center." I said "Uh little off." We had words he and I. "Breed with thuh queen-bee Charles!" Those were mine. Not his. Thats why theyre checking it out you know. Mars. Always looking for some place to go no place to go but owwwwww. Tuh. Understood thuh nigger-queen but didnt understand thuh jars. Didnt get it. Them. Thuh jars. Showed him mother. What I saved. Her photograph went over well enough. Only show one side of a person the pictures do. Showed her from thuh shoulders up. She had such good collarbones. Went over well. He even laughed. Only showed one side. Thuh funny side. Couldnt see the back of her head. Or her hands. Thuh sad parts. Didnt show her middle age spread either it didn't that was our little secret she was a circle from the shoulders down. Uh greeeaaat biiiig baaaaal. Her spread she spread out went round she spread she spread. Huh. They say that "a woman's mother is what—" thuh womanll bee. She had such loverly collerboans. Picture shows uh part. Sound shows all round he even laughed. I have his laugh. Right here: "Oh oh ha heup: Charles." Uh guuud laugh uh huh: "Oh oh ha heup." Always "oh oh ha" with thuh "heup" at thuh end. Then: "Charles." It was just like that. —Thats how I do it. He of course did it differently. The same but differently. His voice was uh little—higher than mine. Said thuh inside dust clogged my pipes while thuh outside dust tightened his taut. Taut. That was Charles. Such bicepts. Steal away. Thuh laugh. Didnt find fault with her picture but did mind her parts isnt that always thuh way. Huh. Used thuh word—"VOODOO." Oh. "Voodoo?" Hhhh. Mother had red hair. She wasuh red haireduhn. In thuh blue jar. Uhp thaar. In thuh blue jar hair looks vi-o-let. I keep it away from thuh sun. She had uh dye job. Black tuh red. Several. Half her hair was roots when she left us. Half roots—other half—. Steal away—. "Mother, you're in for another rinse!" Those were my words. The roots were faintly embarrassing. Always are. Huh. But no: "I-monmuhwayow. Tuh." She said. On her way out no place to go but out. Well-I-dont-want-to-go-out-I-want-to-stay-in-and-see-the-sights-as-if-there-are-no-sights-to-see-in-of-doors sheeeeehad. The most beautiful smile. Oh.—. In thuh red stained jar I keep it. Kept her red gums too. Pickled em. Red gums gone uh little black now. But they were so much uh real red. Always as if they were red always red ready for something tuh bust from em. Red. Such good sounds they make. Rattlerettle and they say anything you want them to say anything you want: not like when she was around. Not at all like when thuh big ball was uhlive. Livin. In thuh flesh. —. Bread-and-buttered-by-thuh-devil: VOODOO. Oh Charles. Voodoo. Damn right. Oh. What bicepts. He was uh lifeguard. A professional savior. Pulled me from the ice. I was drowning. He said drowning but we know I was sticking. You cant drown on ice. I tried. You flail around then get sweaty and stick. He pulled me out and blew—his lips on my lips—a professional savior. He was. I told him to do it in here. They would close the ocean down on Thursdays so that would give him one evening free: Thursday even-nings. "Did you lock the door behind you?" I would ask him "Did you lock thuh door behind you and did you pocket thuh key?" My tanned and laughing Moses. He would show me thuh key to thuh kingdum. I told him to do it in here. I didnt want to waste it. There are people—people—there are people going without. Something to remember you by? Oh. Such. Arms. Good arms for good clapping. And what of my performance and what of it. Its up there all written out. Cast blocked. Alls thats left is the doing of it. Thuh doinsall thats left. She was on her way out to let out the dog. Dog would go roll in thuh yard sniff grass then squat. Such uh funny face when it would squat. I would watch from here. On her way to let him out. Standing at the threshold with the doorhandle in her hand she just—crumbled—. Puddle of her own pickling surrounds her wig like a halo. Guess she had to go tooo my lips on her lips and blew—hee! Mother: she lies there quietly there thinking about her life until she stops thinking no more life to think about no more: —cold. Oh. Now begin: THE TRUTH! Musttellthuhtruthfirst. The truth: the truth Miss Miss: Ah. He loved you for your beets summers were spent with mother pickling the beets and when mother went out her roots—rowtz embarrassing—there were no empty jars you had your beets thats what you had and you had a full life and your beets and noempty jars but OH! He saw your jars! In rows your vows—no: none: the truth! Only rows of deep red beets saw em through thuh window. Cross thuh air shaft. Spied thuh juicy. Had tuh have him some. Lived next door. Close. Steal away. Gobblin thuh beets on his Thursdays. Smackin lips wipin lips on his wrist. He was sleeveless. Muscle shirt. With arms. On thuh backs of his wrists. Eighteen Thursdays of slobbering beet juice back wrists use a napkin please he had hisself developed uh long red beet smear stain. Emptying my jars. Mines. Something tuh re-member you by. Voodoo? Damn right. Eat one beet uh day. Dont wanna waste nothing. Slip back into thuh river lingo gen-tle-like then from thuh river we float out tuh sea. Nothin tuh carry along. Nothing saved. No mementos. —No saviors—all left. Gone out. Aint nowhere else tuh go but out. Now. Begin: I told him to do it in here. Save it. Now begin: Put it in here. Now begin: Dont want tuh waste none. Now begin: People going. Without. And out. Oh. Like steeel he was. Hee! Begin: Steal uhway. Glide-it uhcross. Oh. Warm steal. Oh. Warm. Warm. Oh: To thuh worms. To thuh worms. To thuh worms

—1988

Mohja Kahf (1967-   )

Born in Damascus, Syria, Mohja Kahf immigrated with her family to the United States as a child, and spent part of her childhood in Indiana. Kahf, who has a Ph.D. in Comparative Literature from Rutgers University, is the author of the poetry collection *E-mails from Scheherazade* (2003); a novel, *The Girl in the Tangerine Scarf* (2006); and a scholarly study, *Western Representations of the Muslim Woman: From Termagant to Odalisque* (1999). She also writes a column entitled "Sex and Ummah [Community]" for the online magazine *Muslim Wake Up!* Kahf is an Associate Professor of English and Comparative Literature at the University of Arkansas.

My Grandmother Washes Her Feet in the Sink of the Bathroom at Sears

My grandmother puts her feet in the sink of the bathroom at Sears
to wash them in the ritual washing for prayer,
wudu,
because she has to pray in the store or miss
the mandatory prayer time for Muslims   5
She does it with great poise, balancing
herself with one plump matronly arm
against the automated hot-air hand dryer,
after having removed her support knee-highs
and laid them aside, folded in thirds,   10
and given me her purse and her packages to hold
so she can accomplish this august ritual
and get back to the ritual of shopping for housewares

Respectable Sears matrons shake their heads and frown
as they notice what my grandmother is doing,   15
an affront to American porcelain,
a contamination of American Standards
by something foreign and unhygienic
requiring civic action and possible use of disinfectant spray
They fluster about and flutter their hands and I can see   20
a clash of civilizations brewing in the Sears bathroom

My grandmother, though she speaks no English,
catches their meaning and her look in the mirror says,
I have washed my feet over Iznik tile in Istanbul
with water from the world's ancient irrigation systems   25
I have washed my feet in the bathhouses of Damascus
over painted bowls imported from China
among the best families of Aleppo
And if you Americans knew anything
about civilization and cleanliness,   30
you'd make wider washbasins, anyway
My grandmother knows one culture—the right one,

as do these matrons of the Middle West. For them,
my grandmother might as well have been squatting
in the mud over a rusty tin in vaguely tropical squalor,   35
Mexican or Middle Eastern, it doesn't matter which,
when she lifts her well-groomed foot and puts it over the edge.
"You can't do that," one of the women protests,
turning to me, "Tell her she can't do that."
"We wash our feet five times a day,"   40
my grandmother declares hotly in Arabic.
"My feet are cleaner than their sink.
Worried about their sink, are they? I
should worry about my feet!"
My grandmother nudges me, "Go on, tell them."   45

Standing between the door and the mirror, I can see
at multiple angles, my grandmother and the other shoppers,
all of them decent and goodhearted women, diligent
in cleanliness, grooming, and decorum
Even now my grandmother, not to be rushed,   50
is delicately drying her pumps with tissues from her purse
For my grandmother always wears well-turned pumps
that match her purse, I think in case someone
from one of the best families of Aleppo
should run into her—here, in front of the Kenmore display   55
I smile at the midwestern women
as if my grandmother has just said something lovely about them
and shrug at my grandmother as if they
had just apologized through me
No one is fooled, but I   60

hold the door open for everyone
and we all emerge on the sales floor
and lose ourselves in the great common ground
of housewares on markdown

—1991

Affirmative Action Sonnet

So you think I play the multiculture card
and sign up for affirmative action verse,
slide into print with poetry that's worse?
So you think I get excused from being good

by throwing in Third-World saffron and some veils?   5
Now is the summer of minority malcontent[1]
They have no Idea of Order in the West—[2]
But I do not insist on difference. Difference pales

---

[1] Cf. the opening scene of Shakespeare's *Richard III.*

[2] Cf. "The Idea of Order at Key West" by Wallace Stevens.

beside the horrors facing our race
—the human one: hunger, HIV, genocide,   10
the unconscionable global marketplace
Where is the slave? We write. We recognize

—we must—each other in millennial glow
or we will die from what we do not know

That's all these smoke-and-mirror poems do   15
I came across the world to write for you

—1998

The Marvelous Women

All women speak two languages:
the language of men
and the language of silent suffering.
Some women speak a third,
the language of queens.   5
They are marvelous
and they are my friends.

My friends give me poetry.
If it were not for them
I'd be a seamstress out of work.   10
They send me their dresses
and I sew together poems,
enormous sails for ocean journeys.

My marvelous friends, these women
who are elegant and fix engines,   15
who teach gynecology and literacy,
and work in jails and sing and sculpt
and paint the ninety-nine names,[3]
who keep each other's secrets
and pass on each other's spirits   20
like small packets of leavening,

it is from you I fashion poetry.
I scoop up, in handfuls, glittering
sequins that fall from your bodies
as you fall in love, marry, divorce,   25
get custody, get cats, enter
supreme courts of justice,
argue with God.

You rescuers on galloping steeds
of the weak and the wounded—   30
Creatures of beauty and passion,

---

[3] According to Islamic tradition, God has 99 names; the 100th name is hidden.

powerful workers in love—
you are the poems.
I am only your stenographer.
I am the hungry transcriber   35
of the conjuring recipes you hoard
in the chests of your great-grandmothers.

My marvelous friends—the women
of brilliance in my life,
who levitate my daughters,   40
you are a coat of many colors
in silk tie-dye so gossamer
it can be crumpled in one hand.
You houris, you mermaids, swimmers
in dangerous waters, defiers of sharks—   45

My marvelous friends,
thirsty Hagars and laughing Sarahs,[4]
you eloquent radio Aishas,[5]
Marys[6] drinking the secret
milkshakes of heaven,   50
slinky Zuleikas[7] of desire,
gay Walladas,[8] Harriets[9]
parting the sea, Esthers[10] in the palace,
Penelopes[11] of patient scheming,

you are the last hope of the shrinking women.   55
You are the last hand to the fallen knights
You are the only epics left in the world

Come with me, come with poetry
Jump on this wild chariot, hurry—
Help me with these wayward, snorting horses   60
Together we will pull across the sky
the sun that will make the earth radiant—

or burn in its terrible brilliance,
and that is a good way to die

—1998

---

[4] Genesis 16.
[5] A wife of the Islamic prophet Muhammed.
[6] Mother of Jesus.
[7] Medieval legend gives this name to Potiphar's wife
(Genesis 39:7-20), although she is not referred to by
name in the Bible.
[8] (994-1091) Arab-Andalusian poet.
[9] Harriet Tubman (ca. 1820-1913), called Moses, was a
runaway slave and Underground Railroad conductor.
See Exodus 14:21.
[10] Wife of Ahasuerus and queen of Persia, who saved the
Jews. See Esther 2-8.
[11] In Greek mythology, wife of Odysseus, who fended off
marriage proposals while her husband was on his long
voyage home from the Trojan War.

JHUMPA LAHIRI (1967–   )

The daughter of Bengali parents, Jhumpa Lahiri was born in London and raised in Rhode Island. She holds a B.A. in English from Barnard College, three M.A.s from Boston University (in English, Creative Writing, and Comparative Studies in Literature and the Arts), and a Ph.D. in Renaissance Studies from Boston University. In 1998, the *New Yorker* published three of her short stories and, the following year, named Lahiri one of the "20 best young fiction writers in America." Her debut story collection, *Interpreter of Maladies* (1999), won the Pulitzer Prize for Fiction in 2000, and the title story was selected for both the O. Henry Award and the annual *Best American Short Stories* (1999). In 2002, Lahiri was awarded a Guggenheim Fellowship; the following year she published a novel, *The Namesake,* which was later turned into a film directed by Mira Nair. Lahiri lives in New York with her husband and their son. Her second collection of short fiction, *Unaccustomed Earth,* was released in 2008.

A Temporary Matter

The notice informed them that it was a temporary matter: for five days their electricity would be cut off for one hour, beginning at eight P.M. A line had gone down in the last snowstorm, and the repairmen were going to take advantage of the milder evenings to set it right. The work would affect only the houses on the quiet tree-lined street, within walking distance of a row of brick-faced stores and a trolley stop, where Shoba and Shukumar had lived for three years.

"It's good of them to warn us," Shoba conceded after reading the notice aloud, more for her own benefit than Shukumar's. She let the strap of her leather satchel, plump with files, slip from her shoulders, and left it in the hallway as she walked into the kitchen. She wore a navy blue poplin raincoat over gray sweatpants and white sneakers, looking, at thirty-three, like the type of woman she'd once claimed she would never resemble.

She'd come from the gym. Her cranberry lipstick was visible only on the outer reaches of her mouth, and her eyeliner had left charcoal patches beneath her lower lashes. She used to look this way sometimes, Shukumar thought, on mornings after a party or a night at a bar, when she'd been too lazy to wash her face, too eager to collapse into his arms. She dropped a sheaf of mail on the table without a glance. Her eyes were still fixed on the notice in her other hand. "But they should do this sort of thing during the day."

"When I'm here, you mean," Shukumar said. He put a glass lid on a pot of lamb, adjusting it so only the slightest bit of steam could escape. Since January he'd been working at home, trying to complete the final chapters of his dissertation on agrarian revolts in India. "When do the repairs start?"

"It says March nineteenth. Is today the nineteenth?" Shoba walked over to the framed corkboard that hung on the wall by the fridge, bare except for a calendar of William Morris wallpaper patterns. She looked at it as if for the first time, studying the wallpaper pattern carefully on the top half before allowing her eyes to fall to the numbered grid on the bottom. A friend had sent the calendar in the mail as a Christmas gift, even though Shoba and Shukumar hadn't celebrated Christmas that year.

"Today then," Shoba announced. "You have a dentist appointment next Friday, by the way."

He ran his tongue over the tops of his teeth; he'd forgotten to brush them that morning. It wasn't the first time. He hadn't left the house at all that day, or the day before. The more Shoba stayed out, the more she began putting in extra hours at work and taking on additional projects, the more he wanted to stay in, not even leaving to get the mail, or to buy fruit or wine at the stores by the trolley stop.

Six months ago, in September, Shukumar was at an academic conference in Baltimore when Shoba went into labor, three weeks before her due date. He hadn't wanted to go to the conference, but she had insisted; it was important to make contacts, and he would be entering the job market next year. She told him that she had his number at the hotel, and a copy of his schedule and flight numbers, and she had arranged with her friend Gillian for a ride to the hospital in the event of an emergency. When the cab pulled away that morning for the airport, Shoba stood waving good-bye in her robe, with one arm resting on the mound of her belly as if it were a perfectly natural part of her body.

Each time he thought of that moment, the last moment he saw Shoba pregnant, it was the cab he remembered most, a station wagon, painted red with blue lettering. It was cavernous compared to their own car. Although Shukumar was six feet tall, with hands too big ever to rest comfortably in the pockets of his jeans, he felt dwarfed in the back seat. As the cab sped down Beacon Street, he imagined a day when he and Shoba might need to buy a station wagon of their own, to cart their children back and forth from music lessons and dentist appointments. He imagined himself gripping the wheel, as Shoba turned around to hand the children juice boxes. Once, these images of parenthood had troubled Shukumar, adding to his anxiety that he was still a student at thirty-five. But that early autumn morning, the trees still heavy with bronze leaves, he welcomed the image for the first time.

A member of the staff had found him somehow among the identical convention rooms and handed him a stiff square of stationery. It was only a telephone number, but Shukumar knew it was the hospital. When he returned to Boston it was over. The baby had been born dead. Shoba was lying on a bed, asleep, in a private room so small there was barely enough space to stand beside her, in a wing of the hospital they hadn't been to on the tour for expectant parents. Her placenta had weakened and she'd had a cesarean, though not quickly enough. The doctor explained that these things happen. He smiled in the kindest way it was possible to smile at people known only professionally. Shoba would be back on her feet in a few weeks. There was nothing to indicate that she would not be able to have children in the future.

These days Shoba was always gone by the time Shukumar woke up. He would open his eyes and see the long black hairs she shed on her pillow and think of her, dressed, sipping her third cup of coffee already, in her office downtown, where she searched for typographical errors in textbooks and marked them, in a code she had once explained to him, with an assortment of colored pencils. She would do the same for his dissertation, she promised, when it was ready. He envied her the specificity of her task, so unlike the elusive nature of his. He was a mediocre student who had a facility for absorbing details without curiosity. Until September he had been diligent if not dedicated, summarizing chapters, outlining arguments on pads of yellow lined paper. But now he would lie in their bed until he grew bored, gazing at his side of the closet which Shoba always left partly open, at the row of the tweed jackets and corduroy trousers he would not have to choose from to teach his classes that semester.

After the baby died it was too late to withdraw from his teaching duties. But his adviser had arranged things so that he had the spring semester to himself. Shukumar was in his sixth year of graduate school. "That and the summer should give you a good push," his adviser had said. "You should be able to wrap things up by next September."

But nothing was pushing Shukumar. Instead he thought of how he and Shoba had become experts at avoiding each other in their three-bedroom house, spending as much time on separate floors as possible. He thought of how he no longer looked forward to weekends, when she sat for hours on the sofa with her colored pencils and her files, so that he feared that putting on a record in his own house might be rude. He thought of how long it had been since she looked into his eyes and smiled, or whispered his name on those rare occasions they still reached for each other's bodies before sleeping.

In the beginning he had believed that it would pass, that he and Shoba would get through it all somehow. She was only thirty-three. She was strong, on her feet again. But it wasn't a consolation. It was often nearly lunchtime when Shukumar would finally pull himself out of bed and head downstairs to the coffeepot, pouring out the extra bit Shoba left for him, along with an empty mug, on the countertop.

Shukumar gathered onion skins in his hands and let them drop into the garbage pail, on top of the ribbons of fat he'd trimmed from the lamb. He ran the water in the sink, soaking the knife and the cutting board, and rubbed a lemon half along his fingertips to get rid of the garlic smell, a trick he'd learned from Shoba. It was seven-thirty. Through the window he saw the sky, like soft black pitch. Uneven banks of snow still lined the sidewalks, though it was warm enough for people to walk about without hats or gloves. Nearly three feet had fallen in the last storm, so that for a week people had to walk single file, in narrow trenches. For a week that was Shukumar's excuse for not leaving the house. But now the trenches were widening, and water drained steadily into grates in the pavement.

"The lamb won't be done by eight," Shukumar said. "We may have to eat in the dark."

"We can light candles," Shoba suggested. She unclipped her hair, coiled neatly at her nape during the days, and pried the sneakers from her feet without untying them. "I'm going to shower before the lights go," she said, heading for the staircase. "I'll be down."

Shukumar moved her satchel and her sneakers to the side of the fridge. She wasn't this way before. She used to put her coat on a hanger, her sneakers in the closet, and she paid bills as soon as they came. But now she treated the house as if it were a hotel. The fact that the yellow chintz armchair in the living room clashed with the blue-and-maroon Turkish carpet no longer bothered her. On the enclosed porch at the back of the house, a crisp white bag still sat on the wicker chaise, filled with lace she had once planned to turn into curtains.

While Shoba showered, Shukumar went into the downstairs bathroom and found a new toothbrush in its box beneath the sink. The cheap, stiff bristles hurt his gums, and he spit some blood into the basin. The spare brush was one of many stored in a metal basket. Shoba had bought them once when they were on sale, in the event that a visitor decided, at the last minute, to spend the night.

It was typical of her. She was the type to prepare for surprises, good and bad. If she found a skirt or a purse she liked she bought two. She kept the bonuses from her job in a separate bank account in her name. It hadn't bothered him. His own mother had fallen to pieces when his father died, abandoning the house he grew up in and moving back to Calcutta, leaving Shukumar to settle it all. He liked that Shoba was different. It astonished him, her capacity to think ahead. When she used to do the shopping, the pantry was always stocked with extra bottles of olive and corn oil, depending on whether they were cooking Italian or Indian. There were endless boxes of pasta in all shapes and colors, zippered sacks of basmati rice, whole sides of lambs and goats from the Muslim butchers at Haymarket, chopped up and frozen in endless plastic bags. Every other Saturday they wound through the maze of stalls Shukumar eventually knew by heart. He watched in disbelief as she bought more food, trailing behind her with canvas bags as she pushed through the crowd, arguing under the morning sun with boys too young to shave but already missing teeth, who twisted up brown paper bags of artichokes, plums, gingerroot, and yams, and dropped them on their scales, and tossed them to Shoba one by one. She didn't mind being jostled, even when she was pregnant. She was tall, and broad-shouldered, with hips that her obstetrician assured her were made for childbearing. During the drive back home, as the car curved along the Charles, they invariably marveled at how much food they'd bought.

It never went to waste. When friends dropped by, Shoba would throw together meals that appeared to have taken half a day to prepare, from things she had frozen and bottled, not cheap things in tins but peppers she had marinated herself with rosemary, and chutneys that she cooked on Sundays, stirring boiling pots of tomatoes and prunes. Her labeled mason jars lined the shelves of the kitchen, in endless sealed pyramids, enough, they'd agreed, to last for their grandchildren to taste. They'd eaten it all by now. Shukumar had been going through their supplies steadily, preparing meals for the two of them, measuring out cupfuls of rice, defrosting bags of meat day after day. He combed through her cookbooks every afternoon, following her penciled instructions to use two teaspoons of ground coriander seeds instead of one, or red lentils instead of yellow. Each of the recipes was dated, telling the first time they had eaten the dish together. April 2, cauliflower with fennel. January 14, chicken with almonds and sultanas. He had no memory of eating those meals, and yet there they were, recorded in her neat proofreader's hand. Shukumar enjoyed cooking now. It was the one thing that made him feel productive. If it weren't for him, he knew, Shoba would eat a bowl of cereal for her dinner.

Tonight, with no lights, they would have to eat together. For months now they'd served themselves from the stove, and he'd taken his plate into his study, letting the meal grow cold on his desk before shoving it into his mouth without pause, while Shoba took her plate to the living room and watched game shows, or proofread files with her arsenal of colored pencils at hand.

At some point in the evening she visited him. When he heard her approach he would put away his novel and begin typing sentences. She would rest her hands on his shoulders and stare with him into the blue glow of the computer screen. "Don't work too hard," she would say after a minute or two, and head off to bed. It was the one time in the day she sought him out, and yet he'd come to dread it. He knew it was something she forced herself to do. She would look around the walls of the room, which they had decorated together last summer with a border of marching ducks and rabbits playing trumpets and drums. By the end of August there was a cherry crib under the window, a white changing table with mint-green knobs, and a rocking chair with checkered cushions. Shukumar had disassembled it all before bringing Shoba back from the hospital, scraping off the rabbits and ducks with a spatula. For some reason the room did not haunt him the way it haunted Shoba. In January, when he stopped working at his carrel in the library, he set up his desk there deliberately, partly because the room soothed him, and partly because it was a place Shoba avoided.

Shukumar returned to the kitchen and began to open drawers. He tried to locate a candle among the scissors, the eggbeaters and whisks, the mortar and pestle she'd bought in a bazaar in Calcutta, and used to pound garlic cloves and cardamom pods, back when she used to cook. He found a flashlight, but no batteries, and a half-empty box of birthday candles. Shoba had thrown him a surprise birthday party last May. One hundred and twenty people had crammed into the house—all the friends and the friends of friends they now systematically avoided. Bottles of vinho verde had nested in a bed of ice in the bathtub. Shoba was in her fifth month, drinking ginger ale from a martini glass. She had made a vanilla cream cake with custard and spun sugar. All night she kept Shukumar's long fingers linked with hers as they walked among the guests at the party.

Since September their only guest had been Shoba's mother. She came from Arizona and stayed with them for two months after Shoba returned from the hospital. She cooked dinner every night, drove herself to the supermarket, washed their clothes, put them away. She was a religious woman. She set up a small shrine, a framed picture of a lavender-faced goddess and a plate of marigold petals, on the bedside table in the guest room, and prayed twice a day for healthy grandchildren in the future. She was polite to Shukumar without being friendly. She folded his sweaters with an expertise she had learned from her job in a department store. She replaced a missing button on his winter coat and knit him a beige and brown scarf, presenting it to him without the least bit of ceremony, as if he had only dropped it and hadn't noticed. She never talked to him about Shoba; once, when he mentioned the baby's death, she looked up from her knitting, and said, "But you weren't even there."

It struck him as odd that there were no real candles in the house. That Shoba hadn't prepared for such an ordinary emergency. He looked now for something to put the birthday candles in and settled on the soil of a potted ivy that normally sat on the windowsill over the sink. Even though the plant was inches from the tap, the soil was so dry that he had to water it first before the candles would stand straight. He pushed aside the things on the kitchen table, the piles of mail, the unread library books. He remembered their first meals there, when they were so thrilled to be married, to be living together in the same house at last, that they would just reach for each other foolishly, more eager to make love than to eat. He put down two embroidered place mats, a wedding gift from an uncle in Lucknow, and set out the plates and wineglasses they usually saved for guests. He put the ivy in the middle, the white-edged, star-shaped leaves girded by ten little candles. He switched on the digital clock radio and tuned it to a jazz station.

"What's all this?" Shoba said when she came downstairs. Her hair was wrapped in a thick white towel. She undid the towel and draped it over a chair, allowing her hair, damp and dark, to fall across her back. As she walked absently toward the stove she took out a few tangles with her fingers. She wore a clean pair of sweatpants, a T-shirt, an old flannel robe. Her stomach was flat again, her waist narrow before the flare of her hips, the belt of the robe tied in a floppy knot.

It was nearly eight. Shukumar put the rice on the table and the lentils from the night before into the microwave oven, punching the numbers on the timer.

"You made *rogan josh,*" Shoba observed, looking through the glass lid at the bright paprika stew.

Shukumar took out a piece of lamb, pinching it quickly between his fingers so as not to scald himself. He prodded a larger piece with a serving spoon to make sure the meat slipped easily from the bone. "It's ready," he announced.

The microwave had just beeped when the lights went out, and the music disappeared.

"Perfect timing," Shoba said.

"All I could find were birthday candles." He lit up the ivy, keeping the rest of the candles and a book of matches by his plate.

"It doesn't matter," she said, running a finger along the stem of her wineglass. "It looks lovely."

In the dimness, he knew how she sat, a bit forward in her chair, ankles crossed against the lowest rung, left elbow on the table. During his search for the candles, Shukumar had found a bottle of wine in a crate he had thought was empty. He clamped the bottle between his knees while he turned in the corkscrew. He worried about spilling, and so he picked up the glasses and held them close to his lap while he filled them. They served themselves, stirring the rice with their forks, squinting as they extracted bay leaves and cloves from the stew. Every few minutes Shukumar lit a few more birthday candles and drove them into the soil of the pot.

"It's like India," Shoba said, watching him tend his makeshift candelabra. "Sometimes the current disappears for hours at a stretch. I once had to attend an entire rice ceremony in the dark. The baby just cried and cried. It must have been so hot."

Their baby had never cried, Shukumar considered. Their baby would never have a rice ceremony, even though Shoba had already made the guest list, and decided on which of her three brothers she was going to ask to feed the child its first taste of solid food, at six months if it was a boy, seven if it was a girl.

"Are you hot?" he asked her. He pushed the blazing ivy pot to the other end of the table, closer to the piles of books and mail, making it even more difficult for them to see each other. He was suddenly irritated that he couldn't go upstairs and sit in front of the computer.

"No. It's delicious," she said, tapping her plate with her fork. "It really is."

He refilled the wine in her glass. She thanked him.

They weren't like this before. Now he had to struggle to say something that interested her, something that made her look up from her plate, or from her proofreading files. Eventually he gave up trying to amuse her. He learned not to mind the silences.

"I remember during power failures at my grandmother's house, we all had to say something," Shoba continued. He could barely see her face, but from her tone he knew her eyes were narrowed, as if trying to focus on a distant object. It was a habit of hers.

"Like what?"

"I don't know. A little poem. A joke. A fact about the world. For some reason my relatives always wanted me to tell them the names of my friends in America. I don't know why the information was so interesting to them. The last time I saw my aunt she asked after four girls I went to elementary school with in Tucson. I barely remember them now."

Shukumar hadn't spent as much time in India as Shoba had. His parents, who settled in New Hampshire, used to go back without him. The first time he'd gone as an infant he'd nearly died of amoebic dysentery. His father, a nervous type, was afraid to take him again, in case something were to happen, and left him with his aunt and uncle in Concord. As a teenager he preferred sailing camp or scooping ice cream during the summers to going to Calcutta. It wasn't until after his father died, in his last year of college, that the country began to interest him, and he studied its history from course books as if it were any other subject. He wished now that he had his own childhood story of India.

"Let's do that," she said suddenly.

"Do what?"

"Say something to each other in the dark."

"Like what? I don't know any jokes."

"No, no jokes." She thought for a minute. "How about telling each other something we've never told before."

"I used to play this game in high school," Shukumar recalled. "When I got drunk."

"You're thinking of truth or dare. This is different. Okay, I'll start." She took a sip of wine. "The first time I was alone in your apartment, I looked in your address book to see if you'd written me in. I think we'd known each other two weeks."

"Where was I?"

"You went to answer the telephone in the other room. It was your mother, and I figured it would be a long call. I wanted to know if you'd promoted me from the margins of your newspaper."

"Had I?" .

"No. But I didn't give up on you. Now it's your turn."

He couldn't think of anything, but Shoba was waiting for him to speak. She hadn't appeared so determined in months. What was there left to say to her? He thought back to their first meeting, four years earlier at a lecture hall in Cambridge, where a group of Bengali poets were giving a recital. They'd ended up side by side, on folding wooden chairs. Shukumar was soon bored; he was unable to decipher the literary diction, and couldn't join the rest of the audience as they sighed and nodded solemnly after certain phrases. Peering at the newspaper folded in his lap, he studied the temperatures of cities around the world. Ninety-one degrees in Singapore yesterday, fifty-one in Stockholm. When he turned his head to the left, he saw a woman next to him making a grocery list on the back of a folder, and was startled to find that she was beautiful.

"Okay," he said, remembering. "The first time we went out to dinner, to the Portuguese place, I forgot to tip the waiter. I went back the next morning, found out his name, left money with the manager."

"You went all the way back to Somerville just to tip a waiter?"

"I took a cab."

"Why did you forget to tip the waiter?"

The birthday candles had burned out, but he pictured her face clearly in the dark, the wide tilting eyes, the full grape-toned lips, the fall at age two from her high chair still visible as a comma on her chin. Each day, Shukumar noticed, her beauty, which had once overwhelmed him, seemed to fade. The cosmetics that had seemed superfluous were necessary now, not to improve her but to define her somehow.

"By the end of the meal I had a funny feeling that I might marry you," he said, admitting it to himself as well as to her for the first time. "It must have distracted me."

The next night Shoba came home earlier than usual. There was lamb left over from the evening before, and Shukumar heated it up so that they were able to eat by seven. He'd gone out that day, through the melting snow, and bought a packet of taper candles from the corner store, and batteries to fit the flashlight. He had the candles ready on the countertop, standing in brass holders shaped like lotuses, but they ate under the glow of the copper-shaded ceiling lamp that hung over the table.

When they had finished eating, Shukumar was surprised to see that Shoba was stacking her plate on top of his, and then carrying them over to the sink. He had assumed she would retreat to the living room, behind her barricade of files.

"Don't worry about the dishes," he said, taking them from her hands.

"It seems silly not to," she replied, pouring a drop of detergent onto a sponge. "It's nearly eight o'clock."

His heart quickened. All day Shukumar had looked forward to the lights going out. He thought about what Shoba had said the night before, about looking in his address book. It felt good to remember her as she was then, how bold yet nervous she'd been when they first met, how hopeful. They stood side by side at the sink, their reflections fitting together in the frame of the window. It made him shy, the way he felt the first time they stood together in a mirror. He couldn't recall the last time they'd been photographed. They had stopped attending parties, went nowhere together. The film in his camera still contained pictures of Shoba, in the yard, when she was pregnant.

After finishing the dishes, they leaned against the counter, drying their hands on either end of a towel. At eight o'clock the house went black. Shukumar lit the wicks of the candles, impressed by their long, steady flames.

"Let's sit outside," Shoba said. "I think it's warm still."

They each took a candle and sat down on the steps. It seemed strange to be sitting outside with patches of snow still on the ground. But everyone was out of their houses tonight, the air fresh enough to make people restless. Screen doors opened and closed. A small parade of neighbors passed by with flashlights.

"We're going to the bookstore to browse," a silver-haired man called out. He was walking with his wife, a thin woman in a windbreaker, and holding a dog on a leash. They were the Bradfords, and they had tucked a sympathy card into Shoba and Shukumar's mailbox back in September. "I hear they've got their power."

"They'd better," Shukumar said. "Or you'll be browsing in the dark."

The woman laughed, slipping her arm through the crook of her husband's elbow. "Want to join us?"

"No thanks," Shoba and Shukumar called out together. It surprised Shukumar that his words matched hers.

He wondered what Shoba would tell him in the dark. The worst possibilities had already run through his head. That she'd had an affair. That she didn't respect him for being thirty-five and still a student. That she blamed him for being in Baltimore the way her mother did. But he knew those things weren't true. She'd been faithful, as had he. She believed in him. It was she who had insisted he go to Baltimore. What didn't they know about each other? He knew she curled her fingers tightly when she slept, that her body twitched during bad dreams. He knew it was honeydew she favored over cantaloupe. He knew that when they returned from the hospital the first thing she did when she walked into the house was pick out objects of theirs and toss them into a pile in the hallway: books from the shelves, plants from the windowsills, paintings from walls, photos from tables, pots and pans that hung from the hooks over the stove. Shukumar had stepped out of her way, watching as she moved methodically from room to room. When she was satisfied, she stood there staring at the pile she'd made, her lips drawn back in such distaste that Shukumar had thought she would spit. Then she'd started to cry.

He began to feel cold as he sat there on the steps. He felt that he needed her to talk first, in order to reciprocate.

"That time when your mother came to visit us," she said finally. "When I said one night that I had to stay late at work, I went out with Gillian and had a martini."

He looked at her profile, the slender nose, the slightly masculine set of her jaw. He remembered that night well; eating with his mother, tired from teaching two classes back to back, wishing Shoba were there to say more of the right things because he came up with only the wrong ones. It had been twelve years since his father had died, and his mother had come to spend two weeks with him and Shoba, so they could honor his father's memory together. Each night his mother cooked something his father had liked, but she was too upset to eat the dishes herself, and her eyes would well up as Shoba stroked her hand. "It's so touching," Shoba had said to him at the time. Now he pictured Shoba with Gillian, in a bar with striped velvet sofas, the one they used to go to after the movies, making sure she got her extra olive, asking Gillian for a cigarette. He imagined her complaining, and Gillian sympathizing about visits from in-laws. It was Gillian who had driven Shoba to the hospital.

"Your turn," she said, stopping his thoughts.

At the end of their street Shukumar heard sounds of a drill and the electricians shouting over it. He looked at the darkened facades of the houses lining the street. Candles glowed in the windows of one. In spite of the warmth, smoke rose from the chimney.

"I cheated on my Oriental Civilization exam in college," he said. "It was my last semester, my last set of exams. My father had died a few months before. I could see the blue book of the guy next to me. He was an American guy, a maniac. He knew Urdu and Sanskrit. I couldn't remember if the verse we had to identify was an example of a ghazal or not. I looked at his answer and copied it down."

It had happened over fifteen years ago. He felt relief now, having told her.

She turned to him, looking not at his face, but at his shoes—old moccasins he wore as if they were slippers, the leather at the back permanently flattened. He wondered if it bothered her, what he'd said. She took his hand and pressed it. "You didn't have to tell me why you did it," she said, moving closer to him.

They sat together until nine o'clock, when the lights came on. They heard some people across the street clapping from their porch, and televisions being turned on. The Bradfords walked back down the street, eating ice-cream cones and waving. Shoba and Shukumar waved back. Then they stood up, his hand still in hers, and went inside.

Somehow, without saying anything, it had turned into this. Into an exchange of confessions—the little ways they'd hurt or disappointed each other, and themselves. The following day Shukumar thought for hours about what to say to her. He was torn between admitting that he once ripped out a photo of a woman in one of the fashion magazines she used to subscribe to and carried it in his books for a week, or saying that he really hadn't lost the sweater-vest she bought him for their third wedding anniversary but had exchanged it for cash at Filene's, and that he had gotten drunk alone in the middle of the day at a hotel bar. For their first anniversary, Shoba had cooked a ten-course dinner just for him. The vest depressed him. "My wife gave me a sweater-vest for our anniversary," he complained to the bartender, his head heavy with cognac. "What do you expect?" the bartender had replied. "You're married."

As for the picture of the woman, he didn't know why he'd ripped it out. She wasn't as pretty as Shoba. She wore a white sequined dress, and had a sullen face and lean, mannish legs. Her bare arms were raised, her fists around her head, as if she were about to punch herself in the ears. It was an advertisement for stockings. Shoba had been pregnant at the time, her stomach suddenly immense, to the point where Shukumar no longer wanted to touch her. The first time he saw the picture he was lying in bed next to her, watching her as she read. When he noticed the magazine in the recycling pile he found the woman and tore out the page as carefully as he could. For about a week he allowed himself a glimpse each day. He felt an intense desire for the woman, but it was a desire that turned to disgust after a minute or two. It was the closest he'd come to infidelity.

He told Shoba about the sweater on the third night, the picture on the fourth. She said nothing as he spoke, expressed no protest or reproach. She simply listened, and then she took his hand, pressing it as she had before. On the third night, she told him that once after a lecture they'd attended, she let him speak to the chairman of his department without telling him that he had a dab of pâté on his chin. She'd been irritated with him for some reason, and so she'd let him go on and on, about securing his fellowship for the following semester, without putting a finger to her own chin as a signal. The fourth night, she said that she never liked the one poem he'd ever published in his life, in a literary magazine in Utah. He'd written the poem after meeting Shoba. She added that she found the poem sentimental.

Something happened when the house was dark. They were able to talk to each other again. The third night after supper they'd sat together on the sofa, and once it was dark he began kissing her awkwardly on her forehead and her face, and though it was dark he closed his eyes, and knew that she did, too. The fourth night they walked carefully upstairs, to bed, feeling together for the final step with their feet before the landing, and making love with a desperation they had forgotten. She wept without sound, and whispered his name, and traced his eyebrows with her finger in the dark. As he made love to her he wondered what he would say to her the next night, and what she would say, the thought of it exciting him. "Hold me," he said, "hold me in your arms." By the time the lights came back on downstairs, they'd fallen asleep.

The morning of the fifth night Shukumar found another notice from the electric company in the mailbox. The line had been repaired ahead of schedule, it said. He was disappointed. He had planned on making shrimp *malai* for Shoba, but when he arrived at the store he didn't feel like cooking anymore. It wasn't the same, he thought, knowing that the lights wouldn't go out. In the store the shrimp looked gray and thin. The coconut milk tin was dusty and overpriced. Still, he bought them, along with a beeswax candle and two bottles of wine.

She came home at seven-thirty. "I suppose this is the end of our game," he said when he saw her reading the notice.

She looked at him. "You can still light candles if you want." She hadn't been to the gym tonight. She wore a suit beneath the raincoat. Her makeup had been retouched recently.

When she went upstairs to change, Shukumar poured himself some wine and put on a record, a Thelonius Monk album he knew she liked.

When she came downstairs they ate together. She didn't thank him or compliment him. They simply ate in a darkened room, in the glow of a beeswax candle. They had survived a difficult time. They finished off the shrimp. They finished off the first bottle of wine and moved on to the second. They sat together until the candle had nearly burned away. She shifted in her chair, and Shukumar thought that she was about to say something. But instead she blew out the candle, stood up, turned on the light switch, and sat down again.

"Shouldn't we keep the lights off?" Shukumar asked.

She set her plate aside and clasped her hands on the table. "I want you to see my face when I tell you this," she said gently.

His heart began to pound. The day she told him she was pregnant, she had used the very same words, saying them in the same gentle way, turning off the basketball game he'd been watching on television. He hadn't been prepared then. Now he was.

Only he didn't want her to be pregnant again. He didn't want to have to pretend to be happy.

"I've been looking for an apartment and I've found one," she said, narrowing her eyes on something, it seemed, behind his left shoulder. It was nobody's fault, she continued. They'd been through enough. She needed some time alone. She had money saved up for a security deposit. The apartment was on Beacon Hill, so she could walk to work. She had signed the lease that night before coming home.

She wouldn't look at him, but he stared at her. It was obvious that she'd rehearsed the lines. All this time she'd been looking for an apartment, testing the water pressure, asking a Realtor if heat and hot water were included in the rent. It sickened Shukumar, knowing that she had spent these past evenings preparing for a life without him. He was relieved and yet he was sickened. This was what she'd been trying to tell him for the past four evenings. This was the point of her game.

Now it was his turn to speak. There was something he'd sworn he would never tell her, and for six months he had done his best to block it from his mind. Before the ultrasound she had asked the doctor not to tell her the sex of their child, and Shukumar had agreed. She had wanted it to be a surprise.

Later, those few times they talked about what had happened, she said at least they'd been spared that knowledge. In a way she almost took pride in her decision, for it enabled her to seek refuge in a mystery. He knew that she assumed it was a mystery for him, too. He'd arrived too late from Baltimore-when it was all over and she was lying on the hospital bed. But he hadn't. He'd arrived early enough to see their baby, and to hold him before they cremated him. At first he had recoiled at the suggestion, but the doctor said holding the baby might help him with the process of grieving. Shoba was asleep. The baby had been cleaned off, his bulbous lids shut tight to the world.

"Our baby was a boy," he said. "His skin was more red than brown. He had black hair on his head. He weighed almost five pounds. His fingers were curled shut, just like yours in the night."

Shoba looked at him now, her face contorted with sorrow. He had cheated on a college exam, ripped a picture of a woman out of a magazine. He had returned a sweater and got drunk in the middle of the day instead. These were the things he had told her. He had held his son, who had known life only within her, against his chest in a darkened room in an unknown wing of the hospital. He had held him until a nurse knocked and took him away, and he promised himself that day that he would never tell Shoba, because he still loved her then, and it was the one thing in her life that she had wanted to be a surprise.

Shukumar stood up and stacked his plate on top of hers. He carried the plates to the sink, but instead of running the tap he looked out the window. Outside the evening was still warm, and the Bradfords were walking arm in arm. As he watched the couple the room went dark, and he spun around. Shoba had turned the lights off. She came back to the table and sat down, and after a moment Shukumar joined her. They wept together, for the things they now knew.

—1998

TRACIE MORRIS (?-   )

Brooklyn native Tracie Morris is a critically acclaimed spoken word poet. In 1993, she was named champion of the Nuyorican Grand Slam as well as the National Haiku Slam. Her hip-hop rhymes have been featured in many anthologies, including *The United States of Poetry* (in both book and video form). Morris, who holds degrees from Hunter College and New York University, has published two collections of poems: *Chap-T-her-Won* (1993) and *Intermission* (1999). An accomplished multi-disciplinary artist, Morris has worked in theater, dance, music, and film. She has collaborated with an extensive range of artists and musicians, including jazz musicians Donald Byrd and Vernon Reid, and has participated in numerous recording projects. Her sound poetry was featured in the 2002 Whitney Biennial. Among the awards that Morris has received are a New York Foundation for the Arts Fellowship, a Creative Capital Fellowship, and an Asian Cultural Council Fellowship. She teaches at Eastern Michigan University.

Writer's Delight

My writer's delight
in meta (1-2-3-) 4.
Score with words.
Activist verbiage rounds
out primordial sounds.

5

My writers display
back in the day,
snake charming
voracious contemplation.

Fade to black smack dab   10
in history.
Mysterious backdraft
liquid consistency.

Word smitherine tongue
curls quilling the silence.   15
Nommo[1] sounds empower their
nether surroundings.

Pounding shores up heartbeat
similie metronome.
Like guaguanco,[2] berimbau[3]   20
gospel sounds and home.

Jambalaya jamming
sounds black to me.
Like a take it higher
in a jazz soliloquy.   25

Rocking rap Fats sang
blue musical thrills.
Void fills Hendrix'[4]
little wing.
Decoy that's willing.   30
Tripping the tip of a cacophonous swill.

Chilling words think
I vampirically drink.
My feast the ink
extending   35
my kind's line.

Binded in mind.
Timeless memories
tick-tock-tick.
Quicksand shifts   40
land mass to see.

Improvising on a
Miles Trane[5] melody.
Nat Duke Turner Cole[6]
freedom rings.   45

---

[1] (Dogon) Ancestral spirits or deities.
[2] Cuban rhumba.
[3] A single-stringed Afro-Brazilian instrument.
[4] Jimi Hendrix (1942-1970), African-American rock star.

[5] Miles Davis (1926-1991) and John Coltrane (1926-1967), African-American jazz musicians.
[6] Nat Turner (1800-1831), leader of a slave rebellion; Duke Ellington (1899-1974), jazz bandleader; Nat King Cole (1919-1965), jazz singer and songwriter.

Swing the shoutout
Soundwaves loud.
Pushing the envelope
while moving through the crowd.

Fiercely proud.   50
Judah lion cuddles cubs.
Words and music big up
Reggae dub.

Pride of crew's rep
liberating in clubs.   55
Wielding weight of
each generation.

Sacrosanct promise of
a hosted nation.
Notions of potent and   60
splendid reflection.

On the strength continuum
links up connections.

Engulfing sonic
revolutionaries   65
eclectic vision.

The rhythm,
The rhythm
The rhythm
must be on   70
a mission.

—1998

MESHELL NDEGEOCELLO (1968-   )

Born Michelle Lynn Johnson in Berlin, Germany, the singer, songwriter, and bassist Meshell Ndegeocello was raised in Washington, D.C. She changed her name to Ndegeocello, which means "free as a bird" in Swahili, when she was a teenager. An openly bisexual, single Black mother, she writes lyrics known for their searching commentary on cultural and social politics, as well as for their intensely personal quality. Her music has been noted for its mix of styles (soul, funk, jazz, hip hop, rock, and reggae). Ndegeocello's debut album, *Plantation Lullabies* (1993), on which "soul on ice" appears, was nominated for three Grammy Awards. Other albums include *Peace Beyond Passion* (1996), *Bitter* (1999), *Cookie: The Anthropological Mixtape* (2002), *Comfort Woman* (2003), *Dance of the Infidel* (2005), and *The World Has Made Me the Man of My Dreams* (2007).

soul on ice[1]

hip hop and the white man's world
goin' into niggafide future shock

visions of her virginal white beauty
dancin' in your head
yeah 5
soul's on ice
soul's on ice
illusions of her virginal white beauty
dancing in your head
you let the sisters go by 10
your soul's on ice

we've been indoctrinated and convinced
by the white racist standard of beauty
the overwhelming popularity
of seeing, better off being, and looking white 15

my brothers attempt to defy the white man's law
and his system of values
defile his white women
but my my,
master's in the slave house again 20

visions of her virginal white beauty
dancin' in your head
soul's on ice
soul's on ice
illusions of her virginal white beauty 25
dancin' in your head
you let my sisters go by
your soul's on ice

brother brother brother
are you suffering from a social infection? 30
mis-direction
excuse me,
does your white woman go better
with your brooks brothers suit?
i have psychotic dreams 35
your jism in a white chalk line
you let my sisters go by

used to be customary
to bow one's eyes at the sight of a white face
sight of a white face 40
konks and fade creams

---

[1] A reference to *Soul on Ice*, the 1968 collection of essays written by Black Panther member Eldridge Cleaver (1935-1998) while he was in prison.

sad passion
deferred dreams

i am
a reflection of you   45
a reflection of you
black and blue
pure as the tears of coal-colored children
crying for acceptance
you can't run from yourself   50
she's just an illusion

visions of her virginal white beauty
dancin' in your head
your soul's on ice
your soul's on ice   55
illusions of her virginal white beauty
dancin' in your head
your soul's on ice baby

it's just an illusion
just an illusion   60
all an illusion
it's just an illusion

black Love anthems play
behind white-skinned affection
new birth stereophonic spanish fly   65
but you no longer burn
for the motherland brown skin
you want blonde-haired, blue-eyed soul
snow white passion without the hot comb

visions of her virginal white beauty   70
dancin' in your head
your soul's on ice
your soul's on ice
illusions of her virginal white beauty
dancin' in your head   75
you let my sisters go by
your soul's on ice

illusions of her virginal white beauty
dancin' in your head
you let the sisters go by   80
your soul's on ice
ice, ice
your soul's on ice

illusions of her virginal white beauty
dancing in your head   85

you let the sisters walk on by
your soul's on ice

mmm mmm mmm, la la la
mmm mmm mmm, la la la
mmm mmm mmm, la la la   90
mmm mmm mmm, la la la

it's just an illusion
it's just an illusion
that open-minded Love thing
and equality thing   95
all an illusion
it's just an illusion
take a look in the mirror
just an illusion

if you don't Love yourself   100
your soul's on ice

we've been indoctrinated
it's just an illusion
and convinced by the white
racist standards of beauty   105
just an illusion
my my,
master's in the slave house again
all an illusion
it's just an illusion   110
yeah
all an illusion
your soul's on ice
all an illusion
it's just an illusion.   115

—1993

dead nigga blvd (pt. 1)

you sell your soul
like you sell a piece of ass
slave to the dead white leaders on paper
and welfare cases
rapists and hoes   5
all reinforced your tv show
exotic and beautiful videos

yeah
a jail's a sanctuary for the walking dead
it fucks with your head   10
when every black leader ends up dead
somebody said

our greatest destiny is to become white
but white is not pure
and hate is not pride   15
and just cuz civil rights is law
doesn't mean that we all abide

tell me are you free?
while we campaign for every
dead nigga blvd   20
so y'all young motherfuckers can
drive down it in your fancy cars
free
you try to hold on to some africa of the past
one must remember   25
it's other africans
that helped enslave your ass
everybody's
just trying to make that dollar
remember what jesse² used to say?   30
i am somebody
no longer do i blame others
for the way that we be
cuz niggas need to redefine
what it means to be free   35

i can't even tell my brothers and sisters
that they're fine
this absence of beauty
in their heart and mind
stopped breastfeeding the child   40
you put 'em on the cow
and now you wonder why they act wild
you see brown folks are the
keepers of the earth
unifiers of the soul and mind   45
not these wannabe-gotti³ pimps and thugs
wearing diamond watches
from african slave mines

perhaps to be free
is to all love those who hate me   50
and die a beautiful death
and make pretty brown babies

you campaign for every
dead nigga blvd
so y'all young motherfuckers can   55

² Prominent civil rights activist and Baptist minister Jesse
Jackson (b. 1941) wrote the free-verse poem "I Am-
Somebody" as part of a program to motivate Black
youth to pursue education. He recited the poem in
call-and-response style with a number of children on
Sesame Street in 1971.
³ John Joseph Gotti (1940-2002), New York crime boss.

drive down it in your fancy cars
you try to hold on to some africa of the past
then one must remember
it's other africans
that helped enslave your ass   60
everybody's trying to make that dollar
remember what jesse used to say?
i am somebody
no longer do i blame others
for the way that we be   65
cuz niggas need to redefine
what it means to be free

you campaign for every
dead nigga blvd
just trying to make that dollar   70
so y'all young motherfuckers can
drive down it in your fancy cars
you try to hold on to some africa of the past
then one must remember
it's other africans   75
that helped enslave your ass
cuz everybody's
trying to make that dollar
remember what jesse used to say?
i am somebody   80
no longer do i blame white folks
for the way that we be
cuz niggas need to redefine
what it means to be
free.

—2002

EDWIDGE DANTICAT (1969-   )

Born in Port-au-Prince, Haiti, Edwidge Danticat was raised largely by her aunt and uncle after her parents went to the U.S. in search of work. Danticat followed when she was twelve. In Haiti, she learned French at school and spoke Creole at home; she learned English in the United States. After attending high school in Brooklyn, she received a B.A. in French Literature from Barnard College and an M.F.A. at Brown University. The author of three adult novels, *Breath, Eyes, Memory* (1994), *The Farming of Bones* (1998), and *The Dew Breaker* (2004), and a collection of stories, *Krik? Krak!* (1995), Danticat writes primarily about Haiti, its history, and Haitian Americans. She has also published a memoir of a visit to Haiti, *After the Dance: A Walk through Carnival in Jacmel, Haiti* (2002); two novels for children, *Behind the Mountains* (2002) and *Anacaona, Golden Flower* (2005); several translations and edited collections; and another nonfiction work, *Brother, I'm Dying* (2007). Her literary prizes include a Pushcart Story Prize, a National Book Award nomination, and an American Book Award for *The Farming of Bones*.

Nineteen Thirty-Seven

My Madonna cried. A miniature teardrop traveled down her white porcelain face, like dew on the tip of early morning grass. When I saw the tear I thought, surely, that my mother had died.

I sat motionless observing the Madonna the whole day. It did not shed another tear. I remained in the rocking chair until it was nightfall, my bones aching from the thought of another trip to the prison in Port-au-Prince. But, of course, I had to go.

The roads to the city were covered with sharp pebbles only half buried in the thick dust. I chose to go barefoot, as my mother had always done on her visits to the Massacre River, the river separating Haiti from the Spanish-speaking country that she had never allowed me to name because I had been born on the night that El Generalissimo, Dios Trujillo, the honorable chief of state, had ordered the massacre of all Haitians living there.[1]

The sun was just rising when I got to the capital. The first city person I saw was an old woman carrying a jar full of leeches. Her gaze was glued to the Madonna tucked under my arm.

"May I see it?" she asked.

I held out the small statue that had been owned by my family ever since it was given to my great-great-great-grandmother Défilé by a French man who had kept her as a slave.

The old woman's index finger trembled as it moved toward the Madonna's head. She closed her eyes at the moment of contact, her wrists shaking.

"Where are you from?" she asked. She had layers of 'respectable' wrinkles on her face, the kind my mother might also have one day, if she has a chance to survive.

"I am from Ville Rose," I said, "the city of painters and poets, the coffee city, with beaches where the sand is either black or white, but never mixed together, where the fields are endless and sometimes the cows are yellow like cornmeal."

The woman put the jar of leeches under her arm to keep them out of the sun.

"You're here to see a prisoner?" she asked.

"Yes."

"I know where you can buy some very good food for this person."

She led me by the hand to a small alley where a girl was selling fried pork and plantains wrapped in brown paper. I bought some meat for my mother after asking the cook to fry it once more and then sprinkle it with spiced cabbage.

The yellow prison building was like a fort, as large and strong as in the days when it was used by the American marines who had built it. The Americans taught us how to build prisons. By the end of the 1915 occupation,[2] the police in the city really knew

---

[1] Rafael Leónidas Trujillo Molina (1891-1961), dictator of the Dominican Republic from 1930 to his assassination in 1961. In 1937, Trujillo ordered the massacre of some 20,000 Haitians living or working in the Dominican Republic.

[2] The U.S. military occupied Haiti from 1915 to 1934.

how to hold human beings trapped in cages, even women like Manman who was accused of having wings of flame.

The prison yard was as quiet as a cave when a young Haitian guard escorted me there to wait. The smell of the fried pork mixed with that of urine and excrement was almost unbearable. I sat on a pile of bricks, trying to keep the Madonna from sliding through my fingers. I dug my buttocks farther into the bricks, hoping perhaps that my body might sink down to the ground and disappear before my mother emerged as a ghost to greet me.

The other prisoners had not yet woken up. All the better, for I did not want to see them, these bone-thin women with shorn heads, carrying clumps of their hair in their bare hands, as they sought the few rays of sunshine that they were allowed each day.

My mother had grown even thinner since the last time I had seen her. Her face looked like the gray of a late evening sky. These days, her skin barely clung to her bones, falling in layers, flaps, on her face and neck. The prison guards watched her more closely because they thought that the wrinkles resulted from her taking off her skin at night and then putting it back on in a hurry, before sunrise. This was why Manman's sentence had been extended to life. And when she died, her remains were to be burnt in the prison yard, to prevent her spirit from wandering into any young innocent bodies.

I held out the fried pork and plantains to her. She uncovered the food and took a peek before grimacing, as though the sight of the meat nauseated her. Still she took it and put it in a deep pocket in a very loose fitting white dress that she had made herself from the cloth that I had brought her on my last visit.

I said nothing. Ever since the morning of her arrest, I had not been able to say anything to her. It was as though I became mute the moment I stepped into the prison yard. Sometimes I wanted to speak, yet I was not able to open my mouth or raise my tongue. I wondered if she saw my struggle in my eyes.

She pointed at the Madonna in my hands, opening her arms to receive it. I quickly handed her the statue. She smiled. Her teeth were a dark red, as though caked with blood from the initial beating during her arrest. At times, she seemed happier to see the Madonna than she was to see me.

She rubbed the space under the Madonna's eyes, then tasted her fingertips, the way a person tests for salt in salt water.

"Has she cried?" Her voice was hoarse from lack of use. With every visit, it seemed to get worse and worse. I was afraid that one day, like me, she would not be able to say anything at all.

I nodded, raising my index finger to show that the Madonna had cried a single tear. She pressed the statue against her chest as if to reward the Madonna and then, suddenly, broke down and began sobbing herself.

I reached over and patted her back, the way one burps a baby. She continued to sob until a guard came and nudged her, poking the barrel of his rifle into her side. She raised her head, keeping the Madonna lodged against her chest as she forced a brave smile.

"They have not treated me badly," she said. She smoothed her hands over her bald head, from her forehead to the back of her neck. The guards shaved her head every week. And before the women went to sleep, the guards made them throw tin cups of cold water at one another so that their bodies would not be able to muster up enough heat to grow those wings made of flames, fly away in the middle of the night, slip into the slumber of innocent children and steal their breath.

Manman pulled the meat and plantains out of her pocket and started eating a piece to fill the silence. Her normal ration of food in the prison was bread and water, which is why she was losing weight so rapidly.

"Sometimes the food you bring me, it lasts for months at a time," she said. "I chew it and swallow my saliva, then I put it away and then chew it again. It lasts a very long time this way."

A few of the other women prisoners walked out into the yard, their chins nearly touching their chests, their shaved heads sunk low on bowed necks. Some had large boils on their heads. One, drawn by the fresh smell of fried pork, came to sit near us and began pulling the scabs from the bruises on her scalp, a line of blood dripping down her back.

All of these women were here for the same reason. They were said to have been seen at night rising from the ground like birds on fire. A loved one, a friend, or a neighbor had accused them of causing the death of a child. A few other people agreeing with these stories was all that was needed to have them arrested. And sometimes even killed.

I remembered so clearly the day Manman was arrested. We were new to the city and had been sleeping on a cot at a friend's house. The friend had a sick baby who was suffering with colic. Every once in a while, Manman would wake up to look after the child when the mother was so tired that she no longer heard her son's cries.

One morning when I woke up, Manman was gone. There was the sound of a crowd outside. When I rushed out I saw a group of people taking my mother away. Her face was bleeding from the pounding blows of rocks and sticks and the fists of strangers. She was being pulled along by two policemen, each tugging at one of her arms as she dragged her feet. The woman we had been staying with carried her dead son by the legs. The policemen made no efforts to stop the mob that was beating my mother.

"*Lougarou*,[3] witch, criminal!" they shouted.

I dashed into the street, trying to free Manman from the crowd. I wasn't even able to get near her.

I followed her cries to the prison. Her face was swollen to three times the size that it had been. She had to drag herself across the clay floor on her belly when I saw her in the prison cell. She was like a snake, someone with no bones left in her body. I was there watching when they shaved her head for the first time. At first I thought they were doing it so that the open gashes on her scalp could heal. Later, when I saw all the other women in the yard, I realized that they wanted to make them look like crows, like men.

Now, Manman sat with the Madonna pressed against her chest, her eyes staring ahead, as though she was looking into the future. She had never talked very much about the future. She had always believed more in the past.

When I was five years old, we went on a pilgrimage to the Massacre River, which I had expected to be still crimson with blood, but which was as clear as any water that I had ever seen. Manman had taken my hand and pushed it into the river, no

---

[3] In Caribbean folklore, a person with the power to shed skin and fly, derived from the French *loup-garou* (werewolf).

farther than my wrist. When we dipped our hands, I thought that the dead would reach out and haul us in, but only our own faces stared back at us, one indistinguishable from the other.

With our hands in the water, Manman spoke to the sun. "Here is my child, Josephine. We were saved from the tomb of this river when she was still in my womb. You spared us both, her and me, from this river where I lost my mother."

My mother had escaped El Generalissimo's soldiers, leaving her own mother behind. From the Haitian side of the river, she could still see the soldiers chopping up *her* mother's body and throwing it into the river along with many others.

We went to the river many times as I was growing up. Every year my mother would invite a few more women who had also lost their mothers there.

Until we moved to the city, we went to the river every year on the first of November. The women would all dress in white. My mother would hold my hand tightly as we walked toward the water. We were all daughters of that river, which had taken our mothers from us. Our mothers were the ashes and we were the light. Our mothers were the embers and we were the sparks. Our mothers were the flames and we were the blaze. We came from the bottom of that river where the blood never stops flowing, where my mother's dive toward life—her swim among all those bodies slaughtered in flight—gave her those wings of flames. The river was the place where it had all begun.

"At least I gave birth to my daughter on the night that my mother was taken from me," she would say. "At least you came out at the right moment to take my mother's place."

✦ ✦ ✦

Now in the prison yard, my mother was trying to avoid the eyes of the guard peering down at her.

"One day I will tell you the secret of how the Madonna cries," she said.

I reached over and touched the scabs on her fingers. She handed me back the Madonna.

I know how the Madonna cries. I have watched from hiding how my mother plans weeks in advance for it to happen. She would put a thin layer of wax and oil in the hollow space of the Madonna's eyes and when the wax melted, the oil would roll down the little face shedding a more perfect tear than either she and I could ever cry.

"You go. Let me watch you leave," she said, sitting stiffly.

I kissed her on the cheek and tried to embrace her, but she quickly pushed me away.

"You will please visit me again soon," she said.

I nodded my head yes.

"Let your flight be joyful," she said, "and mine too."

I nodded and then ran out of the yard, fleeing before I could flood the front of my dress with my tears. There had been too much crying already.

✦ ✦ ✦

Manman had a cough the next time I visited her. She sat in a corner of the yard, and as she trembled in the sun, she clung to the Madonna.

"The sun can no longer warm God's creatures," she said. "What has this world come to when the sun can no longer warm God's creatures?"

I wanted to wrap my body around hers, but I knew she would not let me.

"God only knows what I have got under my skin from being here. I may die of tuberculosis, or perhaps there are worms right now eating me inside."

+ + +

When I went again, I decided that I would talk. Even if the words made no sense, I would try to say something to her. But before I could even say hello, she was crying. When I handed her the Madonna, she did not want to take it. The guard was looking directly at us. Manman still had a fever that made her body tremble. Her eyes had the look of delirium.

"Keep the Madonna when I am gone," she said. "When I am completely gone, maybe you will have someone to take my place. Maybe you will have a person. Maybe you will have some *flesh* to console you. But if you don't, you will always have the Madonna."

"Manman, did you fly?" I asked her.

She did not even blink at my implied accusation.

"Oh, now you talk," she said, "when I am nearly gone. Perhaps you don't remember. All the women who came with us to the river, they could go to the moon and back if that is what they wanted."

+ + +

A week later, almost to the same day, an old woman stopped by my house in Ville Rose on her way to Port-au-Prince. She came in the middle of the night, wearing the same white dress that the women usually wore on their trips to dip their hands in the river.

"Sister," the old woman said from the doorway. "I have come for you."

"I don't know you," I said.

"You *do* know me," she said. "My name is Jacqueline. I have been to the river with you."

I had been by the river with many people. I remembered a Jacqueline who went on the trips with us, but I was not sure this was the same woman. If she were really from the river, she would know. She would know all the things that my mother had said to the sun as we sat with our hands dipped in the water, questioning each other, making up codes and disciplines by which we could always know who the other daughters of the river were.

"Who are you?" I asked her.

"I am a child of that place," she answered. "I come from that long trail of blood."

"Where are you going?"

"I am walking into the dawn."

"Who are you?"

"I am the first daughter of the first star."

"Where do you drink when you're thirsty?"

"I drink the tears from the Madonna's eyes."

"And if not there?"

"I drink the dew."

"And if you can't find dew?"

"I drink from the rain before it falls."

"If you can't drink there?"

"I drink from the turtle's hide."

"How did you find your way to me?"

"By the light of the mermaid's comb."

"Where does your mother come from?"

"Thunderbolts, lightning, and all things that soar."

"Who are you?"

"I am the flame and the spark by which my mother lived."

"Where do you come from?"

"I come from the puddle of that river."

"Speak to me."

"You hear my mother who speaks through me. She is the shadow that follows my shadow. The flame at the tip of my candle. The ripple in the stream where I wash my face. Yes. I will eat my tongue if ever I whisper that name, the name of that place across the river that took my mother from me."

I knew then that she had been with us, for she knew all the answers to the questions I asked.

"I think you do know who I am," she said, staring deeply into the pupils of my eyes. "I know who *you* are. You are Josephine. And your mother knew how to make the Madonna cry."

I let Jacqueline into the house. I offered her a seat in the rocking chair, gave her a piece of hard bread and a cup of cold coffee.

"Sister, I do not want to be the one to tell you," she said, "but your mother is dead. If she is not dead now, then she will be when we get to Port-au-Prince. Her blood calls to me from the ground. Will you go with me to see her? Let us go to see her."

We took a mule for most of the trip. Jacqueline was not strong enough to make the whole journey on foot. I brought the Madonna with me, and Jacqueline took a small bundle with some black rags in it.

When we got to the city, we went directly to the prison gates. Jacqueline whispered Manman's name to a guard and waited for a response.

"She will be ready for burning this afternoon," the guard said.

My blood froze inside me. I lowered my head as the news sank in.

"Surely, it is not that much a surprise," Jacqueline said, stroking my shoulder. She had become rejuvenated, as though strengthened by the correctness of her prediction.

"We only want to visit her cell," Jacqueline said to the guard. "We hope to take her personal things away."

The guard seemed too tired to argue, or perhaps he saw in Jacqueline's face traces of some long-dead female relative whom he had not done enough to please while she was still alive.

He took us to the cell where my mother had spent the last year. Jacqueline entered first, and then I followed. The room felt damp, the clay breaking into small muddy chunks under our feet.

I inhaled deeply to keep my lungs from aching. Jacqueline said nothing as she carefully walked around the women who sat like statues in different corners of the cell. There were six of them. They kept their arms close to their bodies, like angels hiding their wings. In the middle of the cell was an arrangement of sand and pebbles in the shape of a cross for my mother. Each woman was either wearing or holding something that had belonged to her.

One of them clutched a pillow as she stared at the Madonna. The woman was wearing my mother's dress, the large white dress that had become like a tent on Manman.

I walked over to her and asked, "What happened?"

"Beaten down in the middle of the yard," she whispered.

"Like a dog," said another woman.

"Her skin, it was too loose," said the woman wearing my mother's dress. "They said prison could not cure her."

The woman reached inside my mother's dress pocket and pulled out a handful of chewed pork and handed it to me. I motioned her hand away.

"No no, I would rather not."

She then gave me the pillow, my mother's pillow. It was open, half filled with my mother's hair. Each time they shaved her head, my mother had kept the hair for her pillow. I hugged the pillow against my chest, feeling some of the hair rising in clouds of dark dust into my nostrils.

Jacqueline took a long piece of black cloth out of her bundle and wrapped it around her belly.

"Sister," she said, "life is never lost, another one always comes up to replace the last. Will you come watch when they burn the body?"

"What would be the use?" I said.

"They will make these women watch, and we can keep them company."

When Jacqueline took my hand, her fingers felt balmy and warm against the life-lines in my palm. For a brief second, I saw nothing but black. And then I *saw* the crystal glow of the river as we had seen it every year when my mother dipped my hand in it.

"I would go," I said, "if I knew the truth, whether a woman can fly."

"Why did you not ever ask your mother," Jacqueline said, "if she knew how to fly?"

Then the story came back to me as my mother had often told it. On that day so long ago, in the year nineteen hundred and thirty-seven, in the Massacre River, my mother did fly. Weighted down by my body inside hers, she leaped from Dominican soil into the water, and out again on the Haitian side of the river. She glowed red when she came out, blood clinging to her skin, which at that moment looked as though it were in flames.

In the prison yard, I held the Madonna tightly against my chest, so close that I could smell my mother's scent on the statue. When Jacqueline and I stepped out into the yard to wait for the burning, I raised my head toward the sun thinking, One day I may just see my mother there.

"Let her flight be joyful," I said to Jacqueline. "And mine and yours too."

—1995

NATHALIE HANDAL (1969-)

Nathalie Handal is a poet, writer, and playwright whose experiences as an Arab-American woman living in the U.S., Europe, and Latin America have infused her work with an international consciousness. She holds a B.A. (in International Relations) and an M.A. (in English) from Simmons College, an M.F.A. in Creative Writing from Bennington College, and a postgraduate degree in English and Drama from the University of London. Handal is the author of the poetry collections *The Neverfield* (1999) and *The Lives of Rain* (2005), which was shortlisted for the Agnes Lynch Starrett Poetry Prize. She has written, produced and/or directed over twelve film and theatrical productions worldwide, including *Between Our Lips* (2005), *The Details of Silence* (2005), and *La Cosa Dei Sogni* (2006). Currently, she works with the New York Theatre Workshop. Handal, who has released the poetry recordings *Traveling Rooms* (1999) and *Spell* (2006), is the editor of *The Poetry of Arab Women: A Contemporary Anthology* (2002), an Academy of American Poets Bestseller and winner of the Pen Oakland/Josephine Miles Award, and the co-editor (with Tina Chang and Ravi Shankar) of *Language for a New Century: Contemporary Poetry from the Middle East, Asia & Beyond* (2008).

The Sigh

The sea sighs, thieves fly
fleeing the suburbs of gloomy dreams—
and sorrow
wanders in the motions of a farmer
as he ploughs his life   5
in slender pieces—
like bits of wind under the fingernails of childhood...
Why does the darkness invite beggars?
Does treachery lie between
a bird and a butterfly,   10
between the legs of fear—
dreaming
a strange dream—
that the sea sighed and the
quiet steps of light   15
held terror in their throats—
nothing crowds us but to see and the sea
as it sighs and sighs in the mouth of will...

—2000

West Bank

What are we to do without the light of shadows
and the devil in the shadows we've repainted in our history

What are we to do without the screams of our streams
the martyrs and their grandfathers' photographs telling us
to stay, face the enemy inside of us   5

What are we to do when between a stone and a bullet
a life is caught in the yawn of history,
one child after another
ready for heaven or hell
how many times will we have to count   10
our dead and our dead brothers
how many times will we
go through the ridged fields
look at each other in the eyes
want to stop,   15
instead, pass by each other
not knowing what to do

What are we to do
but acknowledge
we cannot exist without the other

—2002

The Warrior

It was Wednesday, I remember. Maybe it was Thursday. I had arrived early, early enough to drink some good wine alone with a man I thought we all should fear and for a second forgot. Then they arrived. Nothing in me had changed, even after the wine, even after I saw a goat and corpse cut open side by side. Some say this place is cursed, every drop of water sinks the earth. Strange the things one thinks about at moments like this— was I a stranger to the lover who saw my curves and scars, kissed them then slept like a deserter? Strange what comes to you in the dream-shadows of God—children you saw once in Nablus or Ramallah, who told you the hour the dates will grow in Palestine. Then they arrived. Announced—she died yesterday, but I heard she died a year ago, later that evening I found out she will die tomorrow. And then I heard him say, *Shut up, there is only one way to fight a war. Become the other.* I cross my legs and take his face apart trying to find a way to remember this moment otherwise.

—2005

MICHELLE TEA (1971-)

Poet and performer Michelle Tea is a co-founder, with Sini Anderson, of the all-girl spoken word performance group Sister Spit. Tea's books, *The Passionate Mistakes and Intricate Corruptions of One Girl in America* (1998), *Valencia* (2000), *The Chelsea Whistle* (2002), *Rent Girl* (2004), *The Beautiful: Collected Poems* (2004), and *Rose of No Man's Land* (2006), often depict her working-class youth in Chelsea, Massachusetts, and her life as a young queer in San Francisco, where she began living in 1993. The prolific Tea, who has also edited the antholo-gies *Without a Net: The Female Experience of Growing Up Working Class* (2003); *Pills, Thrills, Chills, and Heartache: Adventures in the First Person* (2004; co-edited with Clint Catalyst); *Baby Remember My Name: An Anthology of New Queer Girl Writing* (2007); and *It's So You: 35 Women*

Write About Personal Expression Through Fashion and Style (2007), is a frequent contributor to publications such as *Curve,* the *Believer,* the *San Francisco Bay Guardian,* the *Bay Times, Girlfriends, Nerve,* the *Stranger,* and *Lesbian Nation.* She also co-authors a weekly astrology column in the *San Francisco Bay Guardian* and curates the monthly Radar Reading Series in San Francisco. Tea has been honored with the Lambda Award for Best Lesbian Fiction for *Valencia,* which was also named one of the Top Twenty-Five Books of 2000 by the *Village Voice Literary Supplement.* She lives in San Francisco.

Bus Story

listen.
i have a dirty mind.
i was on the bus and
there was this man and
on his lap was a young girl and   5
it was the way his hands touched
her waist, familiar, like a secret exposed,
and then he bounced his knee and he laughed
it was the way he laughed, intimate, i
looked away with a blush, feeling   10
like i had stumbled upon lovers but he
had caught my eye and
his look was defiant, it dared me, and again that
laugh, and the bounce of his knee, and her voice,
the high pitch of a child but straining down, reaching   15
for the lipstick low of a woman's, and my
stomach lurched with the braking of the bus
and i looked back as i left and his eyes caged hers and
his hand was in her ponytail and hers, small, a
pale starfish touching his chest and   20
i cannot do anything, his wet
laugh shoves me from the bus, i stand in a
tornado of exhaust, choking, my imagination
wild, pummeling my dirty mind with scenes i
might remember but won't let myself see, the bus   25
is gone now, the girl is gone and the man's
glare sticks to me like a third eye, there are things
i know that others don't know and there are things
i see that you can't see
my mind   30
a secret decoder an open wound a trap
with jaws that spring on the tender ankles
of young girls, girls i can't save, i turn
down the street and walk i have somewhere to go i
have things i have to do my mind is dirty enough   35
without the dirty hurt of a young girl's secret
i've got my own secrets, do you understand, i've got
my own secrets.

—2004

The Love for a Mother Is a Tough, Tough Love

i talked to my mother today,
her voice was thick with sleep
and cigarettes. i could
almost smell that house
and the smoke that soaked   5
my clothes, the television glow
spilling over worn plaid white trash
couch and coffee table stained
with waxy rings from sweating glasses
of coke, the stale stink of homemade   10
knitted afghans wrapped around
sweaty feet, the shoes, the soft white
nurses' shoes, dirty with hospital germs.
but wait, wrong house, she is
lifting my voice to her ear in a new house   15
without holes in walls, without daughters
without even a room for daughters
should they repent and return,
should the patriarch die.
she wants to know if i'm happy   20
but she does not want to know
what is making me happy.
dark bars where i get drunk on words
i am writing, i say, *i have a new book*
and the line becomes this void filled with her fear,   25
what fucked up thing has happened now
to pull words from my pen, she doesn't want
to know and the line is this void filled
with anger i will never express,
thinking about the woman i loved for a year,   30
we crisscrossed the country three times together.
i've been without her for four months
and my mother, she doesn't ask
she has never even asked.
and *i'm in love,* i tell her,   35
that's why i am happy.
i'm in love every day
every day with someone new
i'm in love with this whole city,
like the love was there first   40
and these women just make me
want to share it, and women,
yes, women, and sometimes it feels
like they could be in love too.
they offer me their tongues   45
tucked in the red velvet boxes of
their mouths and i am in love,

i tell her (leaving out the details).
that's nice, dear.
nights spent in a love   50
that yields her no grandchildren
making as much sense
as a job that yields no pay.
but i'm an activist. *ma,*
it's volunteer work, it feeds my soul.   55
work is drudgery
and she works, she works 7-3
she works 3-11
she works 11-7
till her nose becomes blind to the smell   60
of shit and living too long, she goes home
to her home, the home she owns, she
is a homeowner, with brand new furniture
cheap green velvet, they are for show
and holidays and guests who can sit   65
with their asses tightly clenched.
and all those thick-haired dolls with careful
porcelain faces tucked cutely into curios
and her animals, the cat she tore
the claws from, the dog barking   70
from its fenced in pantry pen.
living things are such a responsibility,
they are so hard to control, but she tries.
and i love her, i love her
i love her like a mother loves a daughter   75
who is moving in the wrong direction,
hanging out with the wrong crowd,
going with a guy you know is just no good.
i love her with a love big enough to hold every hurt
every time she did me wrong,   80
and the betrayal,
the big one like the atom bomb, the one
that worked us into ground zero like
we're living in nevada now, out in the desert
and every time i get too close i fear contamination   85
and i love her, so i weld words into instruments
trying to pry the crack in her heart
but they're too big, clumsy to make her angry
or too small, sliding from my fingers into that place
where she keeps everything she never wants to see   90
(her life). and i love her, she is dying a slow,
slow death that will have taken her whole life to reach
in that house, with her cigarettes, her television,
her hamburger helper and her husband.
and i love her.

—2004

SUHEIR HAMMAD (1973-)

Born in Amman, Jordan, to Palestinian refugee parents, poet Suheir Hammad immigrated with her family to Brooklyn, New York, when she was five. When she was sixteen, the family moved to Staten Island. Hammad's books include the poetry collections *Born Palestinian, Born Black* (1996) and *ZataarDiva* (2006), and the memoir *Drops of This Story* (1996). She has performed on Broadway with Russell Simmons' Def Poetry Jam, and reads and performs her work all over the world.

exotic

don't wanna be your exotic
       some delicate   fragile   colorful bird
       imprisoned   caged
       in a land foreign to the stretch of her wings

don't wanna be your exotic   5
       women everywhere are just like me
       some taller   darker   nicer than me
       but like me but just the same
       women everywhere carry my nose on their faces
       my name on their spirits   10

don't wanna

       don't seduce yourself with
       my otherness   my hair
       wasn't put on top my head to entice
       you into some mysterious black vodou   15
       the beat of my lashes against each other
       ain't some dark desert beat
       it's just a blink
       get over it

don't wanna be your exotic   20
       your lovin of my beauty ain't more than
       funky fornication   plain pink perversion
       in fact   nasty necrophilia
       cause my beauty is dead to you
       i am dead to you   25

not your

    harem girl   geisha doll   banana picker
    pom pom girl   pum pum shorts   coffee maker
    town whore   belly dancer   private dancer
    la malinche[1]   venus hottentot[2]   laundry girl   30
    your immaculate vessel emasculating princess

---

[1] La Malinche, also referred to as Marina or Malintzín Tenepal, was the indigenous translator for Hernán Cortés Pizarro (1485-1547) during his 16th-century conquest of Mexico.

[2] In the early 19th century, Saartjie Baartman, a Khoikoi woman from Southern Africa renamed "Hottentot Venus," was exhibited in Europe as an example of *steatopgia,* enlarged buttocks. Following her death at the age of twenty-six, her remains, including her preserved genitalia, were on display at a French museum until 1974.

don't wanna be
> your erotic
not your exotic

—1996

broken and beirut

no mistakes made here
these murders are precise
mathematical
these people blown apart   burned alive
flesh and blood all mixed together   5
a sight no human being can take

and yet we take and take
desensitized to the sacred defamed
witness youth strap 40 lbs of
dynamite to sore bodies 'cause   10
we always return to what we know
and if that's war
we return over and over to it
sit at it's feet to
remove stone shoes   bones and blues   15

don't know what to do with visions
of blown up babies   so we
lamé nails and lame tongues
which should protest
love those who cannot   20
love us   hate ourselves   and become
obsessed with puzzles

shifting through rubble   we ask
where is the head that goes with this 7-year-old shoulder
shattered   this leg looks like it fits with this hip   25
this dead with that dead   cause they wear twin rings
on bloated purple hands

tired of taking fear and calling it life
being strong and getting
over shit   to prepare for more shit   30

(when my heart was broken i turned to the only dynamic i knew
more hurtful   my father)

we return to what we know
it's 1996[3] and beirut all over again
this time the murdered are those who survived the last time   35

---

[3] Year of the Qana massacre, in which more than 100 Lebanese civilians died when Israel bombed a United Nations compound.

and this time's survivors are preparing for the next time
when fire will rain down on heads bowed in prayer

i want to go home
not only to mama and baba
i want to go home to before me and   40
pain   bombs and war   before
loveless sex   poetry   and chocolate

i want to remember what i've never lived
a home within me   within us
where honey is offered from my belly   45
to sweeten babies' breath   make boys moral
and girls strong

want to return to the belly of my honey
and feed myself earth
before 1996   1982⁴   '73⁵   and '48⁶   50
before tv   race   marriage   and meat

return to what we've forgotten
what hunger has faked
return to the whiteness of black
to the drum   the hum   the sum of my parts   55
to god   the boiling in my belly
touch it taste   name it and
come back to here

come back   and make no mistake
be precise   get back to work   60
shifting through the rubble   mathematically
building a new   day
with offerings of honey and memory

never forgetting
where we come from   65
where we've been
and how sweet honey
on the lips of survivors

—1996

---

⁴ Year of the massacre at Sabra and Shatila Palestinian refugee camps by Lebanese Phalangist militia. Some claim they were assisted by Israeli troops.
⁵ Year Israeli special forces infiltrated the Beirut head-quarters of the Palestinian Liberaton Organization and assassinated members of its leadership.
⁶ Year of the Arab-Israeli war.

ALIX OLSON (1975-   )

Queer activist and spoken word poet Alix Olson grew up in Bethlehem, Pennsylvania. She attended public high school there, and credits her English teachers with inspiring her to develop as a writer and a thinker. She went on to graduate from Wesleyan in 1997 with a B.A. in English. Olson has twice headlined on *Def Poetry Jam* and has appeared on the covers of such magazines as *Ms., The Progressive, The Advocate, Poets & Writers,* and *Curve.* In 2003, Olson (along with Margaret Cho and Nobuko Oyabu) was given the "Visionary Award" by the Washington, D.C., Rape Crisis Center; the following year, *Venus Magazine* named her "Best Activist." Olson's documentary *Left Lane: On the Road with Folk Poet Alix Olson* (directed by her road manager, Samantha Farinella), which provides a glimpse into Olson's life on the road as she travels the country performing, won the Audience Award for Best Documentary at New Zealand's Out Takes 2006: A Reel Queer Festival and was an Editor's Pick in the lesbian magazine *Curve.* Olson lives in Brooklyn, New York.

Dear Mr. President

Dear Mr. President:
I don't wanna be in your military, I don't wanna bury
my own kind
I wanna make up my own mind about who I hate,
not what the national slate   5
has in mind.
you see, the american interest is rarely in mine.
and I've got my own wars to wage,
I don't need to engage in your war for oil overseas,
in-between my lover's legs   10
is slick enough for me. I'm the lesbian minority, see,
so I don't need a major to tell me what to be
or who to do things to
somewhere across the pacific.
my sex is too specific to report to a general.   15
and in general, dykes don't respond to command,
so why do we demand
to be a part of this irrational masculine swarmy
that poses as a national army—
see, I've seen armies   20
seen 'em on picket lines, welfare lines,
seen 'em storming the Capitol,
storming the streets,
demanding justice and peace.
I've heard of armies in history,   25
in Birmingham, in Montgomerey.
but these dressed-to-kill boys
with their made-to-kill toys
these yellow ribbons that choke trees, please,
it's a joke,   30
a sadistic display of militaristic play that ends in
american dreams for the owners of both teams—

and who suffers? who buffers the attack?
who lacks the cash to decline the invitation
to the nation's most expensive party?   35
those hearty boys promised schooling,
then sent on their way
to collect their pay from the grave?
well, I don't mind being war-depraved, honey,
we can fight for more than big boys and their money: 40
I'd rather fight phil knight,[1] bomb all his bonds
I'd rather wage a gay crusade on the pope,
grope my girl in front of his nose.
I'd rather pose a problem to disney,
expose michael eisner[2] as a meiser,   45
mickey mouse as leader of the rat race—
just slice right down that rodent's face.
and it's a disgrace to be a rapist
of developing nations
when we can't stop the rape   50
of developing girls.
I'd rather unfurl an attack
on our money guzzling undercover embezzling enemies—
imprisoning just us with no dollar power
impersonating justice from their donald trump[3] tower   55
with their billion dollars trillion crimes
waging their personal war on the poor
for more power in this world of
ABC NBC CBS—his country runs from
CEO to shining CEO,   60
Sending us across the ocean for the promotion
of their cash-devotion ideology.
well, I don't desire your superstar badge of bravery
for enduring modern-day slavery
in your maniacally economically-driven death trap.   65
anyway, I'd give the U.S. a bad rap,
I'd kiss every fine iraqi dyke on the front line,
fuck national pride,
I'd go to their side—
i prefer crossnational desire to crossfire anyway.   70
and i don't need your fatigue uniform
to perform my battles.
I'm wearing layers of tired just from battling
the liars of our system every day.
and my Dear Mr. President: 75
I'd rather die, lyin' in the heat of a fuck I call mine
than in the fuckin' line of duty
you've made mine.

---

[1] Philip H. Knight (b. 1938), co-founder and former C.E.O. of Nike.

[2] Michael Eisner (b. 1942), former C.E.O. of the Walt Disney Company.

[3] Donald Trump (b. 1946), American real estate developer.

but, fine, it's the new big thing to demand inclusion
in your land-intrusion ethic-free military,   80
to request same-sex affirmative action
to de-factionalize who dies in your
money-for-the-man
C-span cam scam, lost-and-found game
you call war   85
where we get to lose our lives
when you've found what's worth more,
well, when this dyke goes down,
she'll go down
knowing what it's for.   90

—2001

ISHLE YI PARK (1977–   )

Poet, spoken word artist, and singer Ishle Yi Park was born and raised in Queens, New York. The first Korean-American woman to feature on the finals stage at the National Poetry Slam, Park has also won the Grand Slam Championship, the Loudpoet of the Year Award (2000), and was a winner at the Glam Slam at New York's famed Nuyorican Poets' Café. She has appeared on HBO's *Russell Simmons Presents: Def Poetry Jam* numerous times, and was also a touring cast member of the Tony-award winning *Def Poetry Jam*. Her first book, *The Temperature of This Water,* won the Pen America Award for Outstanding Writers of Color, the Members' Choice Award of the Asian American Literary Awards, and an Honorable Mention from the Association of Asian American Studies. Park's other awards include a fiction grant from the New York Foundation for the Arts and a residency from the Hedgebrook Foundation. Her work has appeared in numerous publications, including *New American Writing, Beacon Best Writers of All Colors 2001,* and *The Best American Poetry of 2003.* In 2003 she released a CD, which includes tracks with Korean traditional drums, Spanish guitar, and beatboxing. Park has opened for a range of artists, including KRS-One, Ben Harper, De La Soul, and Saul Williams, and has been featured at literary and music festivals in the U.S. and abroad, including the Singapore Writers' Festival, the New Visions Festival in Seoul & Chejudo, Korea, and the Calabash International Literary Festival in Jamaica. Park has taught creative writing in high schools, colleges, prisons, and community centers across the country. In April 2004, she was named Poet Laureate of Queens, N.Y.

House of Sharing
Comfort Women[1]

I can forget everything when I sing,
when the blood is burnt up.

---

[1] Euphemistic term for women, mostly from Korea and China, coerced into sexual service for the Japanese military during World War II.

Drunk from pots filled
with rice wine, she pulled a quilt
over her mouth to cover her smell,   5
listened to Nam Insoo[2] through the blanket,
stack of song books
piled by the foot of her yoh.[3]

I was 14.

Flash flood melts the road into a river.   10

3 pine trees. My parents thought
they sent me to a good place.
My hands like rubber gloves.
My heart bleeding.

This halmoni,[4] silver-streaked hair   15
marcelled down her neck,
in a hanbok[5] of 5 layers like
a white lotus.

She wipes red-pepper stains
from the concrete windowsill, thin   20
tissue shredding in her fingers.

At the sill, she tells me to keep secrets
from my man, even if he is good. *No one*
should open all your contents. You don't
even know the word for contents? She sucks her teeth   25
and closes the window.

They cut her open
because she was too small.
With rusted scissors. Virgin. Doctor
first to enter her after the operation.   30

She ate rice balls prone on stone bed,
thin mattress, one washcloth to rinse
between soldiers. Beheaded
if she bit down.

I can forget everything when I paint,   35
when the blood is burnt up.

I cannot reconcile this halmoni
with a girl 50 years ago,
lips like a folded heart, neck
long as reed, who never learned to write   40
her own name, this halmoni, bundled thick
in two wool coats, bus ticket to her 882nd rally
clenched tightly in gloved fist, pushing

---

[2] Korean folk singer from the 1930s.
[3] (Kor.) Sleeping mat.

[4] (Kor.) Grandmother.
[5] (Kor.) Traditional Korean dress.

glass-shielded policemen
young enough to be grandsons   45
to be in spitting distance
of the Japanese embassy.

She draws a painting
larger than herself of a soldier
in mustard green, wrapped to a cherry blossom tree   50
with black barbed wire, guns pointed
at his chest from 3 directions, white doves
taking flight from its branches,
white doves taking flight, and she danced like this,

hands flicking, hip jutting,   55
wrinkles filling her eyes,
ash falling from her cigarette,
cup of macculi[6] splashing, upraised,
she danced like this.

—2004

Queen Min Bi

Queen Min was the bomb. Smooth forehead, perfectly
parted thick hair and plum lips at fourteen,
enough to make any pedophile happy.
So the king handpicked her,

orphan Korean girl born in Yuhju,   5
to be a royal marionette—no one guessed
she owned a wooden heart to match any politician's.
Maybe she abused her handservants.

Maybe she pumped into her husband doggy style
with an early Korean bamboo strap-on,   10
and that's why she never had children.
Maybe that made Hwang so happy, even after she died,

throat sliced open by invading Japanese,
he hand-carved her name into a slab of man-sized marble,
honoring a woman who snatched his kingdom   15
without a glance back at history,

what those scrolls dictated for female behavior.
I want to be like her, befriending pale-skinned foreigners,
infuriating her father-in-law enough
for him to conspire towards her death   20
while commoners rested head to stone pillow

and dreamt of her brow-raising power;
16 when she married, 32 when she died—

---

[6] A Korean alcoholic beverage usually made with grain and yeast.

before Japanese flags cloaked our country,
before Korean housewives lay beaten   25

without laws to halfway shield
their swollen faces. Half a world away,
yisei Korean children flinch at the smack of skin
on skin, memorize the hiss of curses like bullets,

and I wish she were more than dust and legend, a sold-out opera   30
at Lincoln Center or part of a wistful poem;
I want to inherit the tiger part of her, the part that had me
tracing the clay walls of her birthplace

with my fingers in the rain, wanting
to construct a woman out of myth.   35
So by Chinese calendar, she's a rabbit, her favorite
drink was macculi, Korea's homemade moonshine,

her left breast slightly heavier than her right,
and maybe she kissed her husband on the forehead
before overtaking his kingdom as Queen Min Bi,   40
so loved by all they called her Mama.

—2004

AIMEE PHAN (1977-   )

Aimee Phan is a Vietnamese-American author, born and raised in Orange County, California. She attended UCLA first as a pre-med student, but graduated with a degree in English. She also holds an M.F.A. from the Iowa Writers' Workshop, where she was awarded the Maytag Fellowship. Her first book, *We Should Never Meet* (2005), was a finalist for the 2005 Asian American Literary Awards and was named a Notable Book by the Kiryama Prize. The interlinked stories that make up *We Should Never Meet* explore how the Vietnam War shaped (and continues to shape) the lives of everyday Vietnamese and Vietnamese Americans. Phan's writing has appeared in *The New York Times*, *The Oregonian*, *USA Today*, and *Virginia Quarterly Review*. Previously an Assistant Professor in English at Washington State University, Phan now teaches at California College of the Arts.

Emancipation

I never knew my father and I barely remember my mother. When I was five years old, I was smuggled on a boat with forty-eight other refugees to escape Vietnam. We spent three weeks on the open sea, nearly starving, until a Norwegian naval ship rescued our leaky, water-rotted boat. I arrived in America with no family, no money, and no home. At the refugee center, I was labeled an unaccompanied minor and put in a foster home. I have been in one since then.

Against sound advice, Mai did not look up. During her twenty minutes at the podium, she spoke clearly, articulately, and kept her head down, her eyes smoothing over the memorized words. Maintaining a comfortable balance between conversation and formal speech, Mai was confident she held most of the audience's attention. People bored by her lack of eye contact and charisma—lower classmen, jocks, snobs— were negligible. Those who were supposed to listen—teachers, faculty, friends—would do so whether or not she raised her head. They were enough.

The immediate environment tightened around her. The static on the microphone. The occasional cough and shifting in the metal foldout chairs. Her shoes rubbing against the sweaty gymnasium floor. Losing her breath and needing to swallow at the end of every other sentence. If she looked up, she would see the audience's faces, realize what they thought, and be unable to finish.

Mai didn't like people looking at her. She excelled in academics, not appearance. When people stared, she assumed she didn't measure up, and Mai hated feeling inadequate, especially for things that were out of her control. She'd given up long ago trying to appear pretty. She reinvested her time and effort for more realistic ambitions.

The award for the school's best college essay was a five-hundred-dollar scholarship and a reading at the senior awards assembly. Mai didn't know about the latter until after she won. Admissions committees reading her personal statement was one thing, exposing it to her senior class was another.

You shouldn't apologize for having a hard life, her AP English teacher Mrs. Ward said, when Mai hesitated about reading. You've overcome a lot at such a young age, and you should be proud of that.

Back in September, Mrs. Ward encouraged the students to choose unique subjects for their personal statement, stories that would distinguish them from the pool of other applicants. Colleges liked essays on triumphing over adversity and learning important values from a life lesson. This was one section of the application that wasn't ruled by numbers or letter grades. They should take advantage of it. Many students had problems coming up with something to write. Mai didn't.

But Mai was dissatisfied with her first version. It initially sounded good on paper: orphaned refugee at five years old, living in foster homes all her life. But the truth was after moving in with Karen and Sherman Reynolds when she was nine, she was allowed a childhood, unlike her former foster brothers and sisters. Ultimately good, but not when you're trying to get into an Ivy League school. Her situation turned out so fortunate that she had nothing to write about. It was strange, realizing her life had to be worse to count for something.

So she played it up. Remembering all the sympathies people had projected on her all her life, Mai wrote of her longing for her dead mother and native land and her resolution to return to Vietnam one day and help her former countrymen. Though difficult at first to exaggerate her emotions in such a way, Mai was soon swept up in the embellishments. Perhaps she really did think this, Mai considered as she admired the finished printout. Mrs. Ward was thrilled after reading it, almost crying, pushing away any doubts Mai had about its integrity.

The applause and sympathetic smiles afterward indicated the audience thought so, too. Mai nodded tightly as Principal Baldwin patted her shoulder. When he had introduced her at the assembly, he proudly listed all the schools she'd already been accepted to, the scholarships they offered, declaring her such a lucky girl with fortunate opportunities. He probably meant to be complimentary, but the words bristled her ego. Lucky. Fortunate. Had he talked to the school counselor? Did he know that Mai was still waiting on Wellesley? Did he think she was being ungrateful? It wasn't luck. Yes, she was once the poor orphan child, but she had earned this. Since middle school, she had worked to ensure a future other children already inherited.

The Reynoldses were easy to find, Sherman, with his long red ponytail, and Karen's frizzy gray hair. The third row in the right section, they waved her over. Mai tried to discourage them from coming. They'd have to take time off from work since it was during the middle of the day. She also wasn't sure how they'd react to the essay. But they insisted, especially since it was such a special occasion. When Mai reached the Reynoldses, Karen immediately splayed her arms out, one hand dangling a tissue.

I had no idea, Karen whispered in Mai's ear as they hugged. That was beautiful.

It's just an essay, Mai said. They were staring at her, amazed at what twenty minutes had revealed that nine years previously hadn't.

We are so proud of you, Sherman said.

Students streamed out of the auditorium, slowly, reluctantly returning to classes. Mai sat in an empty folding chair. Has the mail come? she asked.

Karen shook her head. You know we'd tell you if something arrived.

Of course Mai's top choice was the last school to get back to her. She was currently wait-listed at Wellesley. They said they'd have a decision on admission and financial aid in several weeks. That was two months ago. Since then, Mai had reviewed the application in her head over and over, searching for the flaw that was keeping her admission in this miserable limbo. Although not wealthy, the Reynoldses lived in a good school district, with one of the most competitive high schools in the county. Mai's transcript was impeccable: honors and AP classes, A's and A minuses, with only a few B pluses from the sciences, but she was applying as a humanities major. Her extracurricular activities (student government, yearbook, track and field) were decorated with commendations and awards. Despite being unable to afford expensive SAT prep courses, she scored well above the Wellesley average. The teachers who wrote her letters of recommendation adored her. The only part left was the personal statement.

Let's not think about that today, Sherman said, reaching over to squeeze Mai's arm warmly. All right? It's your birthday. We should celebrate.

It's not that important, Mai said.

Nonsense, he said. Eighteen is a landmark year. Adulthood. You'll never forget it.

When will dinner with your friends be over? Karen asked.

You guys don't have to do anything for me, Mai said.

We know we don't have to, Sherman said, with a grin. But I've already made the cake. It would be rude for you not to indulge us one more time.

It was a Reynolds tradition. There was a homemade cake for every birthday in the house since Mai moved in with them. Mai remembered first meeting the Reynoldses, her shock that they were white and vegetarian. She initially thought the social worker had placed her there because she was mad at her. Mai didn't know what a genuine, safe home felt like.

I'll be home at ten, Mai said. Eleven at the latest.

I can't believe you'll be going off to college soon, Karen marveled.

From across the gymnasium, Mai's friend Tiffany smiled and waved. Tiffany had already been accepted to Wellesley. They were planning to room together.

Me neither, Mai said.

She said good-bye to the Reynoldses in the parking lot. They agreed she'd be home by ten o'clock for cake and presents. Her gaze skimmed over the student parking section, full of SUVs and imports, likely their parents' hand-me-down cars or birthday gifts.

Mai never liked birthdays. She hated attention, the scrutiny and judgment, and that was what birthdays were for. There was an expectation to have fun that she resented. For Mai, to make the day special and glorious was too much pressure, the probability of failure so imminent. Then a person was left with only disappointment. Mai had more important things to think about. She couldn't worry about making one day worthwhile.

+ + +

Across the street from campus, Kim waved to her, casually leaning against a car that wasn't hers. Mai looked around, hoping the car's owner wasn't close by.

Kim still wore her work uniform, her long brown ponytail poking from the rear opening of the baseball cap. Though sweaty and tired, Kim still looked beautiful. Mai caught her own inadequate reflection in the car window and looked away.

You got off early, Mai said.

It wasn't too hard. Kim stared at her. I'm coming in earlier on Saturday. What's wrong?

Nothing.

You sure?

Mai nodded. I was going to come by the restaurant.

I figured. Are you going somewhere?

No.

Want to sit out?

Sure.

They walked in silence to a park several blocks from the school. They sprawled out in the grass, stretching their legs in front of them.

What is it, Mai? Kim said. Just say it.

So Mai tried, but the same thing happened that always did whenever she tried to talk to Kim about her college plans. Kim's eyes wandered, her responses became curt, her obvious disinterest and disdain unapologetically obvious. There was no point. Mai bent forward to fix the laces on her tennis shoes, when Kim leaned over to brush some hair from Mai's eyes.

You used to be so little, Kim said. Not anymore.

I think I'm still growing. Maybe I'll grow taller than you.

I don't think so.

Kim was Mai's oldest friend. They had lived in several foster homes together, sharing a bed when there weren't enough. Two years older, Kim was an older sister to Mai, shielding her from the viciousness of foster siblings and foster parents.

Though Mai eventually found a home with the Reynoldses, Kim never found hers. She never stayed in one place longer than two years. It wasn't supposed to be that way. Kim was meant to be luckier. She came over to the States as part of the Babylift evacuation and was promptly adopted by an American family. But the family had given her back, something about not realizing how difficult it would be to raise a foreign child. Social Services put Kim in a foster home, which is where Mai met her.

Even more than Karen and Sherman, Mai was going to miss Kim when she left for college. Her foster parents would be fine without her, but she wasn't sure about Kim. She'd taken their first separation hard. One of the few times Mai had seen Kim cry was when the social worker, Mrs. Luong, split them up: Kim, Mai, and Vinh, this boy who'd been with them since the beginning. Mai didn't mind separating from Vinh. But she did regret leaving Kim behind.

So did the Reynoldses get you anything?

I don't know.

They will, Kim said. They always have. She looked around the park, her attention drifting to two boys pushing each other on a swing set. Think they're going to miss you?

Miss me?

Yeah.

I guess. Maybe.

I think they will, Kim said.

Well, they're getting another foster kid after I leave.

Really?

Yeah. Mai tugged at a handful of grass. It's not a big deal. They had another kid living there before me, too.

Yeah, but you guys were so close, Kim said. What's that? With her foot, she nudged Mai's misshapen backpack, where the award lay wedged inside.

Nothing, Mai said.

Did you get another prize? Kim sang. C'mon, they're hilarious. Show me.

Mai reluctantly pulled out the award. Kim held it with both hands, smudging her fingerprints over the gold-plated plaque. You never showed me your essay.

Really? Mai took the award from her and shoved it into her backpack. I thought I did.

No. Bring a copy to dinner tonight.

Mai sat up a little. We're having dinner?

Aren't we?

But…we never talked about it.

Kim turned on her side, facing Mai. I thought it was assumed.

I…I didn't know. I sort of already made plans.

Seriously? Kim narrowed her eyes. With who?

Huan and Tiffany. Huan is home for spring break, and they're taking me to dinner.

Oh. Kim returned to lying on her back, staring at cloudless sky.

Kim, Mai said.

She looked at Mai, her chin pointed high, her eyes hard. Mai hated when she did that. Kim had this way of looking at her, making Mai feel either wanted or unnecessary, depending on whim. Mai couldn't even invite Kim along. Kim thought Tiffany giggled too much. And she couldn't stand Huan. Mai had introduced them to each other a few years ago, thinking they'd get along because they were both Babylift orphans. Maybe they'd been on the same plane. But Mai had forgotten a crucial difference. Huan's adoptive parents kept him. Kim would speak in Vietnamese whenever Huan was around, always claiming to forget that he only understood English.

Come on, Mai said, trying to poke Kim in the ribs.

What? Kim said, harshly brushing her hand away. You have plans with your other friends. Okay.

Dinner isn't going to take long. Do you want to do something after?

You don't have to.

I want to.

Are you sure?

Yes.

I know you, Mai. Don't lie to me. No one will ever know you like I do.

I know.

✦ ✦ ✦

Mrs. Luong had warned Mai that the Reynoldses were white.

This is good, she said. Their last foster child was Chinese, and he did well with them. You can practice your English and do better in school.

Already shy, Mai hid behind Mrs. Luong's legs. The green front door opened and their smiling faces peered out, presenting confusion: the man's hair was long, and the woman's hair was short. They looked too young and thin to be foster parents. Mai clutched the social worker's hand instinctively.

Too strange for handshakes and too soon for hugs, they simply smiled and nodded at each other as Mrs. Luong introduced everyone. The Reynoldses stared unabashedly as Mai fidgeted, examined her new surroundings, pulled on her hair, straightened her shirt. Their scrutiny made Mai reconsider her frustrations of being ignored at other foster homes.

Their furniture looked clean and comfortable. She noticed immediately there was no television in the living room. They showed Mai her room, her own private room, with a twin bed and dresser and nightstand and bookshelves. There was already a small set of books stacked neatly on the top shelf. She looked through all of them. They were for her reading age level.

When Mai returned to the living room, she could tell Mrs. Luong had been talking about her. The young couple's smiles were gone, and their gazes, once merely genial, seemed more intense and weighted. Self-conscious, Mai put her hands behind her back, hoping they wouldn't ask to look at her wrists like the social worker did.

Show them you're a good girl, Mrs. Luong had whispered to her before leaving.

There were doubts, of course. She'd never been in a foster home by herself before, let alone with a non-Vietnamese family who ate food unfamiliar to Mai. But there was a sense of security in this home she'd never experienced before, and she realized this was what it was supposed to be like. The past had been the deviant, the wrong, but it was over.

✦ ✦ ✦

Tiffany's parents co-owned a seafood restaurant in Newport Beach that offered a panoramic view of the ocean and Orange County. Mai and her friends sat at a table by the window and toasted champagne glasses full of ginger ale. They split orders of lobster, mahimahi, and shrimp, so they could sample all the dishes. Mai brushed away invisible bread crumbs from the front of her dress, carefully gathering them in her palm to deposit in her napkin.

This time next year we won't be playing grown-up, Tiffany said.

C'mon, Huan said. I'm still living off my parents, and so will you.

But not with them, Tiffany said. We'll be on the other side of the country.

Huan looked at Mai. Have you heard from Wellesley?

Mai shook her head.

There's still a lot of time, Tiffany said. My brother didn't hear from Brown until almost June.

They both smiled at her, their futures secure with Huan attending Brown and Tiffany's acceptance to Wellesley. Huan and Tiffany had attended the same private elementary school before meeting Mai in high school. Mai met Huan first while taking Latin, the only Vietnamese students in their class. Huan and Tiffany didn't even bother filling out FAFSA forms or applying for scholarships. It was so easy for them. They had no idea how much more work it was doing everything by yourself.

When they first began looking at colleges, Huan and Tiffany had convinced Mai to consider the East Coast, not only for the education, but for the opportunity of living elsewhere. Growing up wasn't only about classes, but life experience, and they'd already lived in California. Since her escape from Vietnam, Mai had never left the state. When she told the Reynoldses of her college ambitions, Karen encouraged her to apply to Wellesley. She showed Mai her old college yearbooks, reminiscing about the close attention she received since it was such a small school. Gazing at the slightly faded photographs of smiling young women, Mai easily imagined a home there.

We'll finally get to experience seasons, Tiffany said, reaching over for Mai's plate to fork another shrimp. We should take a road trip to see the leaves change color.

I'll have a car by then, Huan said. I can pick you and Mai up, and we'll drive along the coast.

Her teachers, though, advised her to apply to some safety schools in the state, which Mai did. But she was confident in the private institutions she applied to and the minority scholarships available to finance them. She stacked the college brochures neatly on her desk beside her textbooks, looking at them occasionally as further motivation to continue studying.

When the results came in, Mai knew she should have been more grateful, but she couldn't fight off the disappointment. While she gained admission into top choices like Sarah Lawrence and Cornell, the financial aid packages they offered weren't nearly enough to cover projected costs. Wellesley was her last chance.

My fraternity sponsors a ski trip to Vermont every year, Huan said. They rent out a block of condos for the long weekend. You guys should come.

You've never been in snow, have you? Tiffany said, turning to Mai.

Mai didn't answer, engrossed in squeezing the lemon slice from her water glass. The restaurant was lit with tea candles and torch lights, imbuing the tables with a gauzy orange glow. This was a setting for romantic dinners, not high school birthdays.

When Mai looked up, she caught Huan and Tiffany exchanging glances, perhaps finally noticing how little she'd spoken throughout dinner.

Mai, what is it? Huan asked.

I can't talk about it anymore. I know you guys are excited, but I don't know what's going to happen next year. So I can't really make plans for road trips and ski weekends.

Don't worry, Tiffany said. You'll hear from Wellesley soon.

I might not. And even if I do, I have no idea how I'm going to pay for it.

You'll get a scholarship. And the Reynoldses will help you.

No they won't.

Of course they will.

No. Really. I'm eighteen. I'm officially emancipated. They're no longer obligated by the state to support or even shelter me after today.

Mai had never told them about this before. They knew very little about the foster care system, and she'd always preferred it that way. Tiffany and Huan kept looking at each other. Mai wanted to yell that she could see them, the patronizing eyes they shared.

They're not going to kick you out, are they? Huan asked.

No. But I don't know if I'm coming to their house for my school breaks. There might not be room after they get another foster child. They have no responsibility to me.

It's not about responsibility, Tiffany said. They love you. They'll want you to visit.

Mai looked out the window at the blinking lights of the city. The dark slopes of the hills where the wealthy of Orange County hovered. There would be cake soon, but Mai was too full, she didn't want any. And she especially didn't want to be sung to.

Mrs. Luong had told Mai long ago that the Reynoldses were interested in foster care, not adoption. They wanted to help as many children as they could. Mai understood this, most of the time. But there were other times she thought she could change their minds. She did everything to demonstrate she'd make a nice daughter. She listened to them, never disobeyed house rules, and always respected curfew. The Reynoldses talked about how proud they were of Mai, what a fine person she was. That was where their admiration ended. They had so many years to make her a legitimate part of their family, but the possibility was never even discussed.

And if Wellesley accepted me, they have to take you, Tiffany said.

Why? Mai asked, finally returning her gaze to her friends.

Are you kidding? Huan said. Your grades are even better than mine were. And I read your essay.

Mai remembered Huan's college essay. She still had a copy of it somewhere, used it as inspiration to write hers. He talked about being an orphan. She was shocked when she first read it, since Huan never talked about his feelings about being adopted. His essay's authority stemmed from his sincerity. Hers didn't have that.

It is an advantage that you're an orphan, Tiffany whispered, leaning forward like it was a terrible secret. Even though I know it must have been really, really hard. There's no way they can reject you after what you told them about your childhood.

You need to have faith in yourself, Huan said. And relax.

For dessert, their server set a slice of tiramisu cake with one candle in front of Mai. She gazed at the small, flickering flame as her friends and the waiter sang "Happy Birthday." They told her to make a wish. She blew out the candle.

+ + +

This is good, Mai said when the car slowly approached the curb.

Huan looked at the dark apartment building skeptically. Are you sure? You don't want me to wait until you get in?

No, see right there? Mai pointed to the lit window above. I can tell she's home. She looked at Huan. Want to come with me?

I don't think so, he said. Thanks anyway.

Besides Mai, Huan had no other Vietnamese friends. Mai wondered if they'd even be friends if she hadn't introduced herself during their first class together. Huan got so nervous around other Vietnamese—convinced since he was only half and raised by white parents, he wouldn't know how to talk to them.

Mai hesitated as she reached for the door handle of Huan's jeep. I lied. In the essay.

Huan stared at her for a moment. I don't think so. I know you. I read that essay, and I believe you.

Everyone believed me, but it isn't true. Do you miss your biological mother?

Huan looked out his window. They never talked about it, their shared history as orphans. They were always too busy with plans for the future, their new lives. When he didn't say anything, Mai believed she had her answer.

Well, neither do I. I made it all up. I'm an opportunist. It's pathetic.

I do miss her, Huan said. It's a small part of me, but it's there. I think that part of you wrote the essay.

Mai shook her head. I never think about her.

But you had to, Huan said. You couldn't avoid it. You were writing about her.

Mai didn't respond. It seemed too easy. He was offering her an excuse for her behavior, an honorable and justified explanation. She didn't deserve it.

Give me a call if you can't get a ride home, Huan said, when she opened her door. Even if it's late.

Mai ran up the pathway to the front of the building, pressing the buzzer for the correct apartment. When the gate gave, she entered the building. She heard Huan's car finally drive away.

Mai walked through the neglected courtyard, full of brown bushes and rusty, peeling benches. It was a two-story complex with thin walls, so it could get noisy. This wasn't even Kim's apartment. The lease was with her old foster sister Luan. Kim had moved in a month ago, after leaving Vinh. She was trying to convince Luan to let her stay since Kim couldn't afford her own place.

Mai would stay for a half hour, long enough to be polite. Nothing more. The Reynoldses were expecting her home soon. She didn't want to tell them where she was because they would want to pick her up, and Mai didn't want them to see where Kim lived.

She could hear the music from down the hall. Mai pushed on the door, already slightly open. The living room was full of people. No one turned when she slipped in.

Hey, Kim said, emerging from the crowd. She wore a glittery dark blue halter, slim black pants, and an unusually big smile on her face. It's about time.

I didn't know it was a party. Mai tugged at her lavender dress self-consciously. What seemed appropriate for dinner felt silly and childish now.

It's a big day, Kim said. You're an adult now, you're free.

Oh. Mai didn't recognize half the people in the room.

We're all here to celebrate with you, Kim said, throwing her arms around Mai.

Mai scrutinized her friend as they separated. Kim was never affectionate unless she'd been drinking.

Are you going to be able to drive me home tonight?

Sure. Luan said I could use her car.

But can you?

God, don't lecture me. I just need a couple hours.

They walked into the kitchen where Luan was making drinks. The linoleum floor stuck to Mai's heels from spilled beer.

Here she is, Luan said, looking up briefly to smile at them. What do you want to drink?

Mai shook her head.

Come on, Kim said, leaning over the kitchen counter, kicking her bare feet up behind her. It's your birthday.

Mai smiled politely. I'm fine.

What? Luan's face twisted, confused. She often did this, pretended she couldn't understand Mai's Vietnamese accent.

I said I'm fine, Mai said loudly in English.

That's cool, Luan said. It is a school night for you.

Mai nodded and ducked her head, looking back into the living room. Kim and Luan had lived in a foster home together during high school. While Luan was always nice to her, Mai had the feeling she only tolerated her because of Kim. No matter how many years Mai gained, she'd always feel like a little kid with the two of them, never able to catch up.

Did you bring your essay? Kim asked. When Mai didn't answer, she rolled her eyes. I didn't think so. You know, Mai, I do know how to read, if that's what you're worried about.

I'll give it to you later.

Oh, forget it. I don't care anymore.

Kim introduced her to some people, most of them old foster brothers and sisters. These were Kim's friends, but she presented them like Mai had also grown up with them. Over the loud music, they smiled politely, tipping their beer bottles, some shouting happy birthday. Every few minutes, Mai would look at her watch, then at Kim. It was getting late, but she didn't want to leave until Kim was sober.

The party grew thicker with people, the front door opening and closing to let in more, but no one out. Mai was taking in the room again while Kim talked with Luan, when she recognized a new guest.

Mai pulled on Kim's arm until she looked, too.

Did you invite him? Mai asked.

Nooo, Kim said, shaking her head vigorously.

Mai hadn't seen Vinh in several months. Since then, he'd shaved his head, making him look skinnier than ever. He stood alone, which was strange. He usually never went anywhere without Hung, his older foster brother, another gang punk. Vinh caught Mai looking at him, so she quickly glanced away.

Then why don't you ask him to leave?

I don't know, Kim said, now tipping her head to the beat of the music. He had some fallout with his boys. Really harsh. I don't want to make him feel worse.

Why do you care?

Come on. You don't have to talk to him.

Mai knew that. She just didn't want Kim to. For reasons Mai couldn't understand, Kim liked Vinh, even though he was a bully, a high school dropout, and, best of all, a gang member. Unfortunately, they had dated for years.

Mai tried steering them in Vinh-free areas of the party, but he seemed to inch closer, a patient, diligent stalker. Mai had put it off long enough and finally had to use the bathroom, choosing the one in Luan's room that had less traffic. When she returned to the party, sure enough, Vinh had cornered Kim at the kitchen door. She looked bored as he leaned close, whispering in her ear, but she wasn't moving away either.

Mai walked up to them and waited until Kim finally noticed her.

Can you take me home? Mai asked, looking only at her friend.

Hey, Vinh said, staring Mai up and down. Little girl finally grew up.

You want to leave? Kim asked. You just got here.

Not really, it's almost midnight.

But it's your birthday. No it's more than that, it's your emancipation day. Freedom from this damn state. No more visits or lectures from the social worker. Right, Vinh?

Yeah, he said. You can do whatever you want, whenever. No one hassling you.

That's right! Kim said. You could even move out! Do you want to? We could get a place together. It would be so fun, just like when we were kids.

When Luan walked by, Mai grabbed her arm. Can you take me home?

Luan shook her head. I can't drive.

Mai, I said I'd drive you home, Kim said. Just wait a minute.

I want to leave now, I have a headache.

A headache! Why?

I've got a lot on my mind.

God, are you still obsessing over that school in New York?

Massachusetts.

Oh whatever, it's still far away.

Why do you want to leave OC, Mai? Luan asked, looping her arm around Kim's waist. Their outfits almost matched. There are plenty of schools here.

She thinks she's too smart for them, Kim said.

Mai looked at Kim.

It's true, Kim said. It's what you think, I know it.

She's always been like that, huh? Vinh said.

She wants a life away from here. Kim smiled sweetly at Mai, her face angelic. Mai wants to get away from who she is.

There's nothing wrong with wanting to grow up, Mai said.

Honey, it's not that great, Kim said, leaning on Luan, barely able to stand anymore.

Mai took a breath, suddenly aware of everyone's eyes upon her, waiting for her to crumble. She focused her gaze on Kim. And how would you know?

They stared at each other, the others, everyone else at the party, briefly fading away. Then Kim pointed to the door. Get out. Get out right now.

Hey, Luan said.

You come into my house and talk to me like that? Kim said.

Whose house?

While Kim could appear cold to Mai, she'd never before looked hateful. It didn't feel real, the vicious words that slipped from their mouths so easily and quickly.

Out, Kim said. Her hazel eyes were rimmed in red. Or I will throw you out.

Shhh, Luan said, and turned to Mai, almost smugly. Maybe you should leave.

Without saying anything, Mai walked away. Every step required concerted effort to keep from falling. She found her purse buried underneath a pile of jackets in the living room. As she turned to leave, she saw Kim sitting on the couch, her hands covering her face. Luan and Vinh sat on each side of her.

✦ ✦ ✦

At the pay phone outside, Mai called for a cab. She considered calling Huan, but realized she couldn't face anyone she knew. She sat on the curb, careful to avoid the rotten gummy areas, and waited. Mai realized she was shaking. They'd never fought like that before. She considered going back, apologizing, explaining herself, but she was suddenly afraid of facing all those people inside. She once belonged with them, but not anymore. Mai wouldn't know what to say.

When she heard footsteps on the gravel, she sat up.

Mai looked away when Vinh stood in front of her. I'm not getting in a car with you.

I wasn't offering. He shook his head at her, a thin smile on his face.

Mai stood up and backed a few steps, bumping into the bus stop sign. Go upstairs, she said.

Does it feel good making Kim cry like that?

I didn't mean to upset her.

No, you never mean to.

You know nothing about it.

I don't know why, but Kim always defended you. Even after you left us for those white hippies, she still said you were one of us.

I should have stayed and let you terrorize me?

That's right. You got your American dream family by selling us out. Telling everyone I was beating you.

You were.

Oh, come on. Really, Mai, how could that happen with Kim protecting you all the time?

It did. She glared at him. You found ways, I remember.

Okay. Maybe as kids we fought a little. But do you think a kid smacking you a few times even compares to what Kim's gone through?

It's not a contest.

But you won. Do you think it's fair what happened to Kim and never to you?

You can't blame me for that.

That's no one's fault, right? Just the luck of the draw who your foster parents are. Tell me, what makes you so pure and special?

Who's saying I am? She turned away from him, reminding herself that Vinh was a nobody, an uneducated high school dropout, an idiot gang member who preyed on the weak to feel strong. He thought she was weak, always had, but Mai had to show that she wasn't.

And are you still so clean? He skipped around, standing in front of her, invading her personal space, so she couldn't ignore him. Probably not or you'd be adopted by now. Don't you ever wonder why those hippies never adopted you? Why no one ever wanted to have you?

Mai wiped her eyes with the back of her hand. Vinh kept trying to look at her, so she hung her head low, allowing her hair to shield her eyes.

She would never tell him. How could she tell anyone? She has never been touched, kissed, even out of lust, violence, or pity.

Mai forced herself to lift her head, which felt heavy. Vinh was smirking, triumphant. You know nothing about my life, she said. You have no idea.

You're wrong. You may be smart, little girl. But don't think you're any better. Today, you've been released into the world, just like the rest of us.

I am better than you, Mai said. You're a nobody.

Vinh lunged forward, his hands clenching into fists. Mai twisted around, her arms covering her face.

Don't worry, Vinh said, waving his hands in the air, smiling. There must be a reason no one's touched you. I wouldn't dare.

+ + +

The first time Kim spent the night at the Reynoldses', she gingerly touched everything in the house, as Mai had in the beginning. She was nervous around the Reynoldses, only speaking Vietnamese, even when they asked her questions, so that Mai had to translate.

You're staying, aren't you? Kim whispered, when they were under the covers, supposed to be asleep. For several weeks, Kim believed their separation was only temporary, and Mrs. Luong would find another home for them to be together again.

Mai pressed her face into the fresh pillowcase. I think so.

I guess it's not so bad here, Kim said. They seem okay for white people.

Yeah.

Maybe Mrs. Luong will find me a home like this.

Mai turned over so she faced her friend. You don't like it at the Buis?

I don't know. The woman's okay, she doesn't yell as much as Ba Kanh. But the man's weird.

Why?

He looks at me funny. He's always saying how pretty I am.

Mai didn't answer. Everyone was always telling Kim that. One time at the grocery store, this Vietnamese grandma called Mai pretty, but Mai was sure the old lady said that to every child, even the ugly ones.

And he goes to the bathroom when I'm taking a shower.

Mai wrinkled her nose. Don't you lock the door?

Something's wrong with it. I tried putting the wastebasket against the door, but he knocked it over. Sometimes it's not just to pee, sometimes he craps in the toilet.

Eww!

I know.

Does he leave before you get out?

Kim hesitated. No.

Did you tell Mrs. Luong?

Uh-uh. I don't know, it's so gross.

Yeah.

They were silent. Mai returned to lying on her back. She could feel Kim's deep breaths next to her. She stared at the ceiling of this room, her room, where Karen and

Sherman always knocked before entering. All those homes before, she'd escaped. But Kim had not, and Mai didn't know how to go back for her.

✦ ✦ ✦

The house was dark. The Reynoldses were asleep. Mai dropped her purse on the kitchen counter and stood over the sink. Her headache dug into her temples, the blood roaring in her ears. She could feel the floor turning below her, gliding up the walls. Mai closed her eyes, waiting for the house to settle.

Mai traced her fingers over the clean counter surface. The previous summer, the Reynoldses had spent thousands of dollars renovating the kitchen. They expanded the pantry closet. They replaced the tiles and installed an island stove. They decided on a Provençal blue-and-yellow color scheme. Their next project was the living room.

Heavy footsteps on the stairs. Mai stared at the dark reflection of the kitchen window. Her eyes were swollen. The carefully ironed curls in her hair now appeared limp and flat.

Mai? What happened? Sherman asked, coming into the kitchen. Why are you home so late?

It went later than I expected, Mai said, rubbing her mouth with a dish towel.

We called Tiffany and Huan. They were home hours ago.

I went to see Kim. It was a surprise party.

Well why didn't you call us when you knew that?

The pain seeped into her eyes. Mai curled her fingers over the counter's edge, but couldn't prevent herself from sliding to the floor.

Sherman knelt beside her, a look of concern bruising his face. Are you sick? What did you drink?

Mai shook her head. I didn't drink anything.

It's okay if you did, Mai, it's your birthday, and you wanted to celebrate. Just tell me what—

I said I didn't drink. I'm not lying, okay?

Mai, you're yelling.

And what do you mean it's okay if I drink? What dad says that? You wouldn't say that if I was your real daughter.

Why are you so upset? What happened?

Nothing, okay? Nothing that wasn't supposed to, so don't worry about it. I'm not your responsibility anymore.

Come on. Let's get up. You need some water. He started to put his arms around her to help lift her up, but Mai screamed, slapping his hands away.

Don't touch me! Don't you ever touch me like that.

She sat on the floor, her arms crossed protectively over her chest, and watched, unblinking, as his face slowly began to change. Mai realized she should say something, anything, to keep his face from doing that. But she couldn't. He stood up, looking away, his shoulders stiff.

You should go to sleep. His voice was emotionless and unfamiliar. You have school tomorrow. He turned and walked out of the kitchen.

Mai waited and listened to his footsteps on the stairs and the careful opening and shutting of the master bedroom door. She imagined muffled conversation floating through the ceiling, Sherman shaking Karen awake and telling her what happened, her horror and disbelief, but eventual acceptance and disappointment.

Trying to breathe slowly, deeply, Mai pulled herself off the floor. With gentle steps, she made her way through the kitchen. As she pressed her palm against the light switch, she recognized the neatly arranged presents on the kitchen table. No doubt if she opened the refrigerator, there would be the homemade birthday cake wrapped in aluminum foil. Something on the table caught her eye. She leaned forward, her eyes focusing. A large white envelope posed next to the presents. Wellesley College. Mai pressed the light switch off. She went upstairs to bed.

✦ ✦ ✦

Tell me about her, Kim said. She knew Mai hadn't fallen asleep yet. Tell me again. Exactly.

This was a nightly ritual when they used to live together. Kim was fascinated that Mai had known her mother. Mai would say what she could, trying hard to recall, but she'd been so young. If what Mai remembered wasn't enough to satisfy Kim, she'd make up more details. It didn't matter if the attributes contradicted each other from one night to the next. Kim just wanted a picture in her head, shrouding her, before she went to sleep.

I believe she was beautiful. She looked like what I hope to look like when I grow up. Long, shiny black hair, small shoulders, golden skin, thin, elegant hands. She could have been more than what became of her. She should have lived longer, pursued a higher education than grade school level, seen her daughter grow up, lived in a country that didn't expect suffering, experienced a comfortable bed, clean food, and a day off. Because she never had any of these things, I will take them for her. I will live the way she should have.

—2004

Permissions

Abinader, Elmaz: "Dried Flowers," "Preparing for Occupation," and "The Volcano." From *In the Country of My Dreams* © 1999. Published by Sufi Warrior. Reprinted by permission from the author.

Abu-Jaber, Diana: "My Elizabeth" by Diana Abu-Jaber. Published in the Winter 1995 *Kenyon Review*. Reprinted by permission of the author.

Addams, Jane: "Patriots and Pacifism in War Time." From *The Jane Addams Reader* © 2002. Reprinted by permission of BASIC BOOKS, a member of Perseus Books Group.

Adnan, Etel: "Amsterdam" and "Beirut," Aug 23, 1991, letters. Reprinted with permission from the author.

Agosín, Marjorie: "Once Again" and "An Apology" from *An Absence of Shadows,* translated by Cola Franzen, Celeste Kostopulos-Cooperman, and Mary G. Berg. Copyright © 1998 by Marjorie Agosín. Copyright © 1988,1998 by Cola Franzen. Copyright © 1992, 1998 by Celeste Kostopulos-Cooperman. Copyright © 1998 by Mary G. Berg. Reprinted with the permission of White Pine Press, Buffalo, New York; Marjorie Agosín, "Fairy Tales and Something More" from *Brujas y Algo Mas/Witches and Other Things,* translated by Cola Franzen. Copyright © 1984 by Marjorie Agosín. Translation copyright © 1984 by Cola Franzen. Reprinted with the permission of Latin American Literary Review Press, Pittsburgh, www.lalrp.org.

Ai: "Flashback" and "The Cockfighter's Daughter." Copyright © 1991 by Ai, from VICE: NEW AND SELECTED POEMS by Ai. Copyright © 1999 by Ai. Used by permission of W. W. Norton & Company, Inc.

Alexander, Elizabeth: "Early Cinema" and "The Female Seer Will Burn Upon This Pyre" copyright 2001 by Elizabeth Alexander. Reprinted from *Antebellum Dream Book* with the permission of Graywolf Press, Saint Paul, Minnesota.

Allen, Paula Gunn: "Some Like Indians Endure" and "She Who Skins Cats" from *Life is a Fatal Disease: Collected Poems 1962-1995.* Copyright © 1997 by Paula Gunn Allen. Reprinted with the permission of the author and West End Press, Albuquerque, New Mexico.

Allison, Dorothy: "Don't Tell Me You Don't Know" from TRASH. Copyright © 1988 by Dorothy Allison. Reprinted by permission of The Frances Goldin Literary Agency.

Allyn, Jo: "The Eleventh Hour." From *The Ladder* © 1957. Reprinted with kind permission from the editors of *The Ladder.*

Alvarez, Julia: "How I Learned to Sweep." From HOMECOMING. Copyright © 1984, 1996 by Julia Alvarez. Published by Plume, an imprint of The Penguin Group (USA), and originally published by Grove Press. Reprinted by permission of Susan Bergholz Literary Services, New York, NY, and Lamy, NM. All rights reserved; "Making Up the Past" from THE OTHER SIDE/EL OTRO LADO. Copyright © 1995 by Julia Alvarez. Published by Plume/Penguin, a division of Penguin Group (USA). Reprinted by permission of Susan Bergholz Literary Services, New York, NY, and Lamy, NM. All Rights reserved; "On Not Shoplifting Louise Bogan's 'The Blue Estuaries'" from THE OTHER SIDE/EL OTRO LADO. Copyright © 1995 by Julia Alvarez. Published by Plume/Penguin, a division of Penguin Group (USA). Reprinted by permission of Susan Bergholz Literary Services, New York, NY, and Lamy, NM. All rights reserved.

Anzaldúa, Gloria: "Cihuatlyotl, Woman Alone," "How to Tame a Wild Tongue," and "Mar de repollos/A Sea of Cabbages." From *Borderlands/La Frontera: The New Mestiza* © 1987, 1999. Reprinted with permission from Aunt Lute Books. www.auntlute.com.

Arnow, Harriette Simpson: "Blessed, Blessed." From *The Collected Short Stories of Harriette Simpson Arnow* © 1983. Published by Michigan State University Press. Reprinted with permission from Thomas L. Arnow.

Austin, Mary: "The Man Who Was Loved by Women," from ONE SMOKE STORIES by Mary Austin. Copyright 1934 by Mary Austin; copyright renewed © 1961 by Kenneth M. Chapman and Mary C. Wheelwright. Reprinted by permission of Houghton Mifflin Company. All rights reserved.

Bambara, Toni Cade: "Going Critical," from DEEP SIGHTINGS AND RESCUE MISSIONS by Toni Cade Bambara, copyright © 1996 by The Estate of Toni Cade Bambara. Used by permission of Pantheon Books, a division of Random House, Inc.

Barnes, Djuna: Djuna Barnes "A Night Among the Horses" from *Djuna Barnes: Collected Stories.* Reprinted with the permission of Green Integer Books, www.greeninteger.com.

Berssenbrugge, Mei-mei: The Four Year Old Girl. Permission to reprint poem from: I LOVE ARTIST by Mei-mei Berssenbrugge, © 2006 Mei-mei Berssenbrugge. Published by the University of California Press. Reprinted by permission of the University of California Press.

Bishop, Elizabeth: "The Fish," "In the Waiting Room," "Invitation to Miss Marianne Moore" and "One Art" from THE COMPLETE POEMS 1927-79 by Elizabeth Bishop. Copyright © 1979, 1983 by Alice Helen Methfessel. Reprinted by permission of Farrar, Straus and Giroux, LLC.

WOMAN, published by University of Massachusetts Press. Reprinted by permission of Curtis Brown, Ltd.; "homage to my hips." Copyright © 1999 by Lucille Clifton. First appeared in TWO-HEADED WOMAN, published by University of Massachusetts Press. Reprinted by permission of Curtis Brown, Ltd.; "shapeshifter poems" from *Blessing the Boats: New and Selected Poems 1988-2000.* Copyright © 1988, 2001 by Lucille Clifton. Reprinted with the permission of BOA Editions, Ltd., www.boaeditions.org.

Cofer, Judith Ortiz: "Exile" is reprinted with permission from the publisher of "Terms of Survival" by Judith Ortiz Cofer (© 1995 Arte Público Press-University of Houston); "The Latin Deli" and "So Much for Mañana" by Judith Ortiz Cofer are reprinted with permission from the publisher of *The Americas Review* (© 1987 Arte Público Press-University of Houston).

Coleman, Wanda: "Business as Usual." From <u>Mercurochrome</u>, copyright for Wanda Coleman, 2001; "Intruder" from <u>Bathwater Wine</u>, copyright for Wanda Coleman 1998; "Wanda Why Aren't You Dead?" from <u>Heavy Daughter Blues</u>, Black Sparrow Press, copyright from Wanda Coleman 1987 and featured in Camille Paglia's <u>BREAK BLOW BURN: FORTY-THREE OF THE WORLD'S BEST POEMS</u> (Pantheon, 2005).

Combahee River Collective: "A Black Feminist Statement." Copyright © 1979 by MR Press. Reprinted with permission from the Monthly Review Foundation.

Corpi, Lucha: "Marina Mother" and "Dark Romance" by Lucha Corpi are reprinted with permission from the publisher of *Noon Words* (© 2001 Arte Público Press-University of Houston).

Cox, Ida: "Wild Women Don't Have the Blues" by Ida Cox © 1924, Renewed 1952 Universal Music Corp. All rights administered by Universal Music Corp./ASCAP Used By Permission. All Rights Reserved.

Cumpiano, Ina: "Yo La Malinche" by Ina Cumpiano is reprinted with permission from the publisher of *The Americas Review* (© 1994 Arte Público Press-University of Houston).

Curbelo, Silvia: "Janis Joplin" and "Between Language and Desire" by Silvia Curbelo are reprinted with permission from the publisher of "Little Havana Blues" edited by Virgil Suarez and Delia Poey (© 1996 Arte Público Press-University of Houston); Silvia Curbelo, "Tourism in the Late Twentieth Century." From *The Secret History of Water.* Tallahassee, FL: Anhinga Press. Reprinted with permission from publisher.

Danticat, Edwidge: "Nineteen Thirty-Seven." Copyright © 1995 by Edwidge Danticat, used by permission of Soho Press, Inc.

de Burgos, Julia: "Canto a Martí," "Farewell to Welfare Island," "Poem for My Death," "To Julia de Burgos" and "The Voice of the Dead." Translated by Jack Agüeros. From *Song of the Simple Truth: The Complete Poems of Julia de Burgos* © 1996. Published by Curbstone Press. Reprinted with permission from the publisher.

de Hoyos, Angela: "When Conventional Methods Fail" by Angela de Hoyos is reprinted with permission from the publisher of *The Americas Review* (© 1987 Arte Público Press-University of Houston).

Didion, Joan: "Notes from a Native Daughter" from SLOUCHING TOWARDS BETHLEHEM by Joan Didion. Copyright © 1966, 1968, renewed 1996 by Joan Didion. Reprinted by permission of Farrar, Straus and Giroux, LLC.

di Prima, Diane: "Dream: The Loba Reveals Herself" and "The Loba Addresses the Goddess." From *Loba* © 1998. Published by Penguin Books. Reprinted with permission from the author. "Poetics." From *Pieces of Song: Selected Poems* © 1990. Published by City Lights Books. Reprinted with permission from the author.

Divakaruni, Chitra Banerjee: "Indigo," "Leaving Yuba City," "Skin," and "Yuba City School." From LEAVING YUBA CITY by Chitra Banerjee Divakaruni, copyright © 1997 by Chitra Banerjee Divakaruni. Used by permission of Doubleday, a division of Random House, Inc.

Dove, Rita: "Canary," from GRACE NOTES by Rita Dove. Copyright © 1989 by Rita Dove. Used by permission of the author and W. W. Norton & Company, Inc.; "Dusting" from *Thomas and Beulah,* Carnegie Mellon University Press, © 1986 by Rita Dove. Reprinted by permission of the author; "Parsley" from *Museum,* Carnegie Mellon University Press, © 1983 by Rita Dove. Reprinted by permission of the author.

Erdrich, Louise: "Dear John Wayne," "Indian Boarding School," and "Jacklight." Copyright © 1984 by Louise Erdrich, reprinted with permission of The Wylie Agency.

Esteves, Sandra María: "My Name is Maria Christina" is reprinted with author's permission from *Yerba Buena;* Greenfield Review; Greenfield Center, NY 12833; ISBN 0912678-47-X; 91 pgs; 1980; "For South Bronx" and "Black Notes and 'You Do Something to Me'" are reprinted with permission from the publisher of "Bluestown Mockingbird Mambo" by Sandra María Esteves (© 1990 Arte Público Press-University of Houston).

Faigao-Hall, Linda: The FeMale Heart *(Pusong Babae).* Reprinted by permission of the author.

Ferré, Rosario: "Sleeping Beauty." From *Reclaiming Medusa: Short Stories by Contemporary Puerto Rican Women* © 1988 by Diana Vélez. Reprinted with permission from Aunt Lute Books. www.auntlute.com.

Fisher, Dorothy Canfield: "The Biologist and His Son." From *A Harvest of Stories, From a Half Century of Writings* © 1956. Published by Harcourt, Brace. Reprinted by permission of Vivian S. Hixson.

Forché, Carolyn: All lines from "THE COLONEL" FROM THE COUNTRY BETWEEN US by

Said. (Copyright © 1979 by Edward W. Said).

Hammad, Suheir: "broken and beirut" and "exotic." From *Born Palestinian, Born Black* © 1996. Published by Harlem River Press. Reprinted with permission from the author.

Handal, Nathalie: "The Sigh" and "West Bank." From *The Poetry of Arab Women: A Contemporary Anthology* © 2001. Published by Interlink Books. Reprinted with permission from author. "The Warrior." From *The Lives of Rain* © 2005. Published by Interlink Books. Reprinted with permission from author.

Hansberry, Lorraine: "The Drinking Gourd," from LES BLANCS: THE COLLECTED LAST PLAYS by Lorraine Hansberry, copyright © 1969, 1972 by Robert Nemiroff. Copyright renewed 2000 by Jewell Nemiroff. Used by permission of Random House, Inc.

Harjo, Joy: "Book of Myths" by Joy Harjo from *In Mad Love and War* (Wesleyan University Press, 1990). © 1990 by Joy Harjo and reprinted by permission of Wesleyan University Press; "For Anna May Pictou Aquash…" by Joy Harjo from *In Mad Love and War* (Wesleyan University Press, 1990). © 1990 by Joy Harjo and reprinted by permission of Wesleyan University Press; "Reconciliation: A Prayer," from THE WOMAN WHO FELL FROM THE SKY by Joy Harjo. Copyright © 1994 by Joy Harjo. Used by permission of W. W. Norton & Company, Inc.

Hayslip, Le Ly: "Open Wounds." From WHEN HEAVEN AND EARTH CHANGED PLACES by Le Ly Hayslip, copyright © 1989 by Le Ly Hayslip and Charles Jay Wurts. Used by permission of Doubleday, a division of Random House, Inc.

Hellman, Lillian: "Scoundrel Time." © 1976 by Lillian Hellman. Reprinted with permission from the Estate of Lillian Hellman.

Highsmith, Patricia: "The Fully Licensed Whore, or, the Wife." From LITTLE TALES OF MISOGYNY by Patricia Highsmith. Copyright First published in German as *Kleine Geschichten fur Weiberfeinde* in a translation by W.E. Richartz. 1975 by Diogenes Verlag AG Zurich. Original in English first published in Great Britain 1977. Copyright 1977 by Diogenes Verlag AG Zurich. First published as a Norton paperback 2002. Used by permission of W. W. Norton & Company, Inc.

Hill, Roberta: Roberta Hill Whiteman, "Leap in the Dark" and "Star Quilt" from *Star Quilt*. Copyright © 1984, 2001 by Roberta Hill Whiteman. Reprinted with the permission of Holy Cow! Press, www.holycowpress.org.

Hogan, Linda: "Friday Night," "The Truth Is," and "Wall Songs." From *Seen Through the Sun* © 1985. Reprinted with permission from the author.

hooks, bell: Ch. 1, 2, 8, and 52 from BONE BLACK: Memories of Girlhood by bell hooks. Copyright 1996 by Gloria Watkins. Reprinted by permission of Henry Holt and Company.

Hospital, Carolina: "Freedom" by Carolina Hospital is reprinted with permission from the publisher of *Little Havana Blues,* edited by Virgil Suarez and Delia Poey (©1996 Arte Público Press-University of Houston).

Howe, LeAnne: "Choctalking on Other Realities." First appeared in *Cimarron Review*, 1997, #121, October, Oklahoma State University. Reprinted with permission from the author.

Howe, Susan: "There Are Not Leaves Enough to Crown to Cover to Crown to Cover" by Susan Howe, from EUROPE OF TRUSTS, Copyright © 1990 by Susan Howe. Reprinted by permission of New Directions Publishing Corp.

Hurston, Zora Neale: "Black Death," (pp. 202-8) from THE COMPLETE STORIES by ZORA NEALE HURSTON. Introduction copyright © 1995 by Henry Louis Gates, Jr. and Sieglinde Lemke. Compilation copyright © 1995 by Vivian Bowden, Lois J. Hurston Gaston, Clifford Hurston, Lucy Anne Hurston, Winifred Hurston Clark, Zora Mack Goins, Edgar Hurston, Sr., and Barbara Hurston Lewis. Afterword and Bibliography copyright © 1995 by Henry Louis Gates. Reprinted by permission of HarperCollins Publishers.

Idar, Jovita: "We Should Work" by Jovita Idar is reprinted with permission from the rights holder of *Herencia* © 2001 Oxford University Press (Arte Público Press-University of Houston).

Jackson, Laura (Riding): "Chloe Or" and "The Tiger" by Laura (Riding) Jackson from *Poems of Laura Riding*. Copyright © 1991, 2001 by the Board of Literary Management of the late Laura (Riding) Jackson. Reprinted by permission of the Board of Literary Management of the late Laura (Riding) Jackson and Persea Books, Inc. (New York).

Jackson, Shirley: "The Friends," from JUST AN ORDINARY DAY: THE UNCOLLECTED STORIES by Shirley Jackson, copyright © 1997 by The Estate of Shirley Jackson. Used by permission of Bantam Books, a division of Random House, Inc.

Jen, Gish: "Who's Irish." Copyright © 1998 by Gish Jen. First published in *The New Yorker*. From the collection *Who's Irish?* by Gish Jen published in 1999 by Alfred A. Knopf. Reprinted by permission of the author.

Jordan, June: "If You Saw a Negro Lady," "Poem About My Rights" and "Poem Because the 1996 U.S. Poet Laureate Told the *San Francisco Chronicle* There Are 'Obvious' Poets–All of Them White–and Then There are 'Representative' Poets–None of Them White." Used by permission of the June M. Jordan Literary Estate.

Jorgensen, Christine: Excerpts from *Christine Jorgensen: A Personal Autobiography* © copyright 1967 by Christine Jorgensen and reprinted by permission of Paul S. Eriksson, Publisher.

"xlii" and "xxvi." Copyright © 1923, 1928, 1931, and 1939 by Edna St. Vincent Millay and 1951, 1954, 1955, 1958, 1967 and 1982 by Norma Millay Ellis. Reprinted by Permission of Elizabeth Barnett, Literary Executor, The Millay Society.

Miller, May: "Stragglers in the Dust." From *Plays and Pageants from the Life of the Negro* © 1930. Published by Associated Publishers. Reprinted with permission from Dr. Miller Newman.

Miranda, Deborah: "Hunger" and "Indian Cartography." From *Indian Cartography,* published by The Greenfield Review Press, 1999. Reprinted with permission from The Greenfield Review Press.

Mirikitani, Janice: "Breaking Silence" and "We, the Dangerous." Reprinted from *Shedding Silence, Poetry and Prose* by Janice Mirikitani, 1987. Reprinted with permission from the author.

Mohr, Nicholasa: "In Another Place in a Different Era." From *A Matter of Pride and Other Stories* © 1997. Published by Arte Público Press-University of Houston. Reprinted with permission from the author.

Moore, Marianne: "The Fish" and "Marriage." Reprinted with the permission of Scribner, an imprint of Simon & Schuster Adult Publishing Group, from THE COLLECTED POEMS OF MARIANNE MOORE by Marianne Moore. Copyright © 1935 by Marianne Moore; copyright renewed © 1963 by Marianne Moore & T.S. Eliot. All rights reserved; "Roses Only," from THE POEMS OF MARIANNE MOORE by Marianne Moore, edited by Grace Schulman, copyright © 2003 by Marianne Craig Moore, Executor of the Estate of Marianne Moore. Used by permission of Viking Penguin, a division of Penguin Group (USA) Inc.

Mora, Pat: "Hands" by Pat Mora is reprinted with permission from the publisher of *The Americas Review* (©1982 Arte Público Press-University of Houston); "Plot" is reprinted with permission from the publisher of *Chants* by Pat Mora (©1985 Arte Público Press-University of Houston).

Moraga, Cherríe: "La Güera." From *Loving in the War Years* © 1983, 2000. Published by South End Press. Reprinted with permission from the author.

Morales, Aurora Levins: "Sugar Poem" and "Tita's Poem" by Aurora Levins Morales from Getting Home Alive by Aurora Levins Morales and Rosario Morales, Firebrand Books, Ann Arbor, Michigan. Copyright © 1986.

Morales, Aurora Levins and Rosario Morales: "Ending Poem" by Aurora Levins Morales and Rosario Morales from Getting Home Alive by Aurora Levins Morales and Rosario Morales, Firebrand Books, Ann Arbor, Michigan. Copyright © Aurora Levins Morales and Rosario Morales 1986.

Morales, Rosario: "I Am the Reasonable One" by Aurora Levins Morales from Getting Home Alive by Aurora Levins Morales and Rosario Morales, Firebrand Books, Ann Arbor, Michigan. Copyright © 1986.

Morris, Tracie: "Writer's Delight." From *Intermission* © 1999. Published by Soft Skull Press. Reprinted with permission from the author.

Morrison, Toni: "Margaret Garner." Music by Richard Danielpour. Words by Toni Morrison. Copyright © 2005 by Associated Music Publishers, Inc. (BMI) and G. Schirmer, Inc. (ASCAP). International Copyright Secured. All Rights Reserved. Reprinted by Permission.

Mourning Dove: "Why Spider Has Such Long Legs" and "Coyote Quarrels With Mole." From *Coyote Stories.* Published by University of Nebraska Press in 1933: poems are in public domain.

Mukherjee, Bharati: "A Wife's Story." From MIDDLEMAN AND OTHER STORIES. Copyright © 1988 by Bharati Mukherjee. Used by permission of Grove/Atlantic, Inc.

Ndegeocello, Meshell: "Dead Nigga Blvd Pt. 1" and "Soul on Ice." From *Cookie: the Anthropological Mix Tape* © 2002. Released by Maverick. Reprinted with permission from Errol Wander and the author.

Near, Holly: "Hay Una Mujer Desaparecida," Words and Music by Holly Near, Hereford Music ©1978. Reprinted with permission from Alison de Grassi.

Newman, Lesléa: Newman, Lesléa. A LETTER TO HARVEY MILK. ©. Reprinted by permission of The University of Wisconsin Press.

Nin, Anaïs: "Hejda" from Under a Glass Bell, copyright 1995 by The Anaïs Nin Trust (Rupert Pole, Trustee): Foreward © 1995 by Gunther Stuhlmann. Reprinted with permission from Barbara Stuhlmann, Author's Representative.

Nye, Naomi Shihab: "Arabic," "For the 500th Dead Palestinian," "Making a Fist" and "The Words Under the Words." Reprinted by permission of the author, Naomi Shihab Nye, 2007.

Oates, Joyce Carol: "6:27 P.M." Copyright © by ONTARIO REVIEW, INC., 2007. Reprinted with permission from the author.

Obejas, Achy: "Above All, a Family Man." From WE CAME ALL THE WAY FROM CUBA SO YOU COULD DRESS LIKE THIS?, by Achy Obejas. PUBLISHED BY CLEIS PRESS of San Francisco 1994.

O'Connor, Flannery: "Revelation" from THE COMPLETE STORIES by Flannery O'Connor. Copyright © 1971 by the Estate of Mary Flannery O'Connor. Reprinted by permission of Farrar, Straus and Giroux, LLC.

Olds, Sharon: "Mrs. Krikorian" and "Japanese-American Farmhouse, California, 1942" from THE WELL-SPRING by Sharon Olds, copyright © 1996 by Sharon Olds. Used by permission of Alfred A. Knopf, a division of

LANGUAGE: Poems 1974-1977 by Adrienne Rich. Copyright ©1978 by W. W. Norton & Company, Inc. Used by permission of the author and W. W. Norton & Company, Inc; "Planetarium." Copyright © 2002 by Adrienne Rich. Copyright © 1971 by W. W. Norton & Company, Inc, "Fox." Copyright © 2002, 2001 by Adrienne Rich, "Snapshots of a Daughter-in-Law." Copyright © 2002, 1967, 1963 by Adrienne Rich, "Aunt Jennifer's Tigers." Copyright © 2002, 1951 by Adrienne Rich, from THE FACT OF A DOORFRAME: SELECTED POEMS 1950-2001 by Adrienne Rich. Used by permission of the author and W. W. Norton & Company, Inc.

Richards, Renée: "Second Serve." © Richards, Renée; Second Serve; Stein & Day/ 1983. Reprinted with permission from the author.

Ridge, Lola: "Amy Lowell." From *Red Flag* © 1927. Published by Viking. Reprinted by permission by the Literary Executive of the Estate of Lola Ridge; "Emma Goldman." From *Sun-Up and Other Poems* © 1920. Published by BW Huebsch. Reprinted by permission by the Literary Executive of the Estate of Lola Ridge; "Lullaby." From *The Ghetto and Other Poems* © 1988. Published by BW Huebsch. Reprinted by permission by the Literary Executive of the Estate of Lola Ridge.

Ritchie, Jean: "Black Waters" ©1967, 1971 Jean Ritchie Geordie Music Publishing Co. Reprinted with permission from the publisher; "The L & N Don't Stop Here Anymore" © 1963, 1971 Jean Ritchie Geordie Music Publishing Co. Reprinted with permission from the publisher.

Rivera, Beatriz: "Paloma" by Beatriz Rivera is reprinted with permission from the publisher of *Little Havana Blues*, edited by Virgil Suarez and Delia Poey (© 1996 Arte Público Press-University of Houston).

Roosevelt, Eleanor: "A Challenge to American Sportsmanship," "The Atomic Bomb" and "Freedom: Promise or Fact" from *Courage in a Dangerous World,* by Eleanor Roosevelt/Allida M. Black. Copyright © 1999. Reprinted with permission from Columbia University Press.

Rose, Wendy: "Loo-Wit" from *Bone Dance, New and Selected Poems, 1965-1993* by Wendy Rose.© 1994 Arizona Board of Regents. Reprinted by permission of the University of Arizona Press; "Three Thousand Dollar Death Song." From *Lost Copper.* Published by The Malki Museum, Inc. Reprinted with permission from The Malki Museum, P.O. Box 578 Banning, CA 92220 (ph. [951] 849-7289).

Rukeyser, Muriel: "The Poem As Mask," "Not to Be Printed, Not to Be Said, Not to Be Thought" "Despisals," and "Flying to Hanoi." Copyright © 1968, 1976, 1973, & 1873 by Muriel Rukeyser. From *The Collected Poems of Muriel Rukeyser,* 2005 by University of Pittsburgh Press. Reprinted by permission of International Creative Management, Inc.

Rushin, Kate: "The Black Back-Ups" and "The Tired Poem: Last Letter from a Typical Unemployed Black Professional Woman" by Kate Rushin from THE BLACK BACK-UPS by Kate Rushin, Firebrand Books, Ann Arbor, Michigan. Copyright © Kate Rushin 1993. Reprinted with permission from the publisher.

Sainte-Marie, Buffy: "Bury My Heart at Wounded Knee" by Buffy Sainte-Marie © 1992 Caleb Music Co. All rights administered by Almo Music Corp./ASCAP Used By Permission. All Rights Reserved; Universal Soldier by Buffy Sainte-Marie © 1963, Renewed 1991 Caleb Music Co. All rights administered by Almo Music Corp./ASCAP Used By Permission. All Rights Reserved.

Sanchez, Sonia: "Homecoming." From I'VE BEEN A WOMAN: New and Selected Poems copyright 1978, 1985 by Sonia Sanchez, reprinted by permission of Third World Press Inc., Chicago, Illinois; Sanchez, Sonia: "Just Don't Never Give Up on Love." From *Homegirls and Handgrenades.* Reprinted by permission of Perseus Books Group; "Love Song #3," from *Wounded in the House of a Friend* by Sonia Sanchez. Copyright © 1995 by Sonia Sanchez. Reprinted by permission of Beacon Press, Boston.

Sanger, Margaret: "The Prevention of Conception." and "Why the Women Rebel?." From *Women Rebel* © 1914, 1976. Published by Archives of Social History. Reprinted with permission from Alexander Sanger, Executer of the Estate of Margaret Sanger. "To Comrades and Friends." In box 200 of the Margaret Sanger Papers at the Library of Congress (Microfilm reel 129:2). Reprinted with permission from Alexander Sanger, Executer of the Estate of Margaret Sanger.

Sapphire: "American Dreams." From *American Dreams.* © Serpent's Tail. Reprinted with permission from Serpent's Tail.

Sarton, May: "All Day I Was With Trees." Copyright © 1972 by May Sarton, from COLLECTED POEMS 1930-1993 by May Sarton. Used by permission of W. W. Norton & Company, Inc.; Excerpts from I KNEW A PHEONIX: SKETCHES FOR AN AUTOBIOGRAPHY by May Sarton. Copyright © 1959, 1956, 1954 by May Sarton. Used by permission of W. W. Norton & Company, Inc.; "In Time Like Air." Copyright © 1958 by May Sarton, from COLLECTED POEMS 1930-1993 by May Sarton. Used by permission of W. W. Norton & Company, Inc.; "Moth in the Schoolroom," from SELECTED POEMS OF MAY SARTON by May Sarton, edited by Serena Sue Hilsinger & Lois Brynes. Copyright © 1978 by May Sarton. Used by permission of W. W. Norton & Company, Inc.

Schtok, Fradel: "The Veil" by Fradel Schtok, from *Found Treasures: Stories by Yiddish Writers,* edited by Frieda Forman, Ethel Raicus, Sarah Silberstein Swartz, Margie Wolfe. Printed with permission from Second Story Press,

Editors

Lisa Maria Hogeland is Associate Professor of English and Women's Studies at the University of Cincinnati. Her publications include *Feminism and Its Fictions: The Consciousness-Raising Novel and the Women's Liberation Movement* (Univ. of Pennsylvania, 1998), the essay "Fear of Feminism," and articles on the feminist movement and U. S. women writers. She is the co-editor (with Mary Klages) of *The Aunt Lute Anthology of U.S. Women Writers,* Volume One (2004).

Shay Brawn Ph.D., is the Artistic Director of Aunt Lute Books and a lecturer in the Program in Writing and Rhetoric at Stanford University. She is a specialist in twentieth century multi-ethnic literatures of the U.S., and her scholarship and teaching focus on rhetoric of public history and performative rhetorics.

Juliana Chang is Associate Professor of English at Santa Clara University. She has published several essays on Asian American literature, including journal articles in *MELUS, Contemporary Literature, Meridians,* and *MFS: Modern Fiction Studies.* She is also the editor of *Quiet Fire: A Historical Anthology of Asian American Poetry, 1892-1970* (Asian American Writers Workshop/Temple University Press, 1996). Her current book manuscript is a psychoanalytic study of race, fantasy, and trauma in Asian American literature.

Linda Garber is Associate Professor of English, and Director and Associate Professor of Women's and Gender Studies at Santa Clara University. She is the author of *Identity Poetics: Race, Class, and the Lesbian-Feminist Roots of Queer Theory* (Columbia University Press, 2001) and *Lesbian Sources: A Bibliography of Periodical Articles, 1970-1990* (Garland, 1993), and the editor of *Tilting the Tower: Lesbian/Teaching/Queer Subjects (Routledge, 1994).*

Michelle Gibson is the Director of Undergraduate Studies in the Department of Women's Studies at the University of Cincinnati. Much of her scholarly work applies queer and postmodern identity theories to pedagogical practice and popular culture. She also continues to write and publish poetry. Gibson co-edited (with Deborah Meem) *Femme/Butch: New Considerations of the Way We Want to Go* (2002) and *Lesbian Academic Couples* (2005). With Meem and Jonathan Alexander she is writing *Finding Out: An Introduction to LGBT Studies,* which will be published by SAGE in 2009.

Anahid Kassabian's research and teaching focus on film music and ubiquitous music. She has served on faculties of Women's Studies, Literary Studies, Communication and Media Studies, and Music, and is currently James and Constance Alsop Chair in the School of Music at the University of Liverpool. Kassabian is co-founder of Music, Sound and the Moving Image, and a past chair of the International Association for the Study of Popular Music. She writes, with David Kazanjian, on Armenian diasporan film and has curated Armenian film festivals in San Francisco and New York with Thea Farhadian and Hrayr Anmahouni.

Deborah T. Meem, Professor of English and Women's Studies at the University of Cincinnati, specializes in Victorian literature, lesbian studies, and the nineteenth-century woman's novel. Her edition of Eliza Lynn Linton's 1880 novel *The Rebel of the Family* was published in 2002 (Broadview); she is editing Linton's 1851 novel *Realities* (2009). With Michelle Gibson, she co-edited *Femme/Butch: New Considerations of the Way We Want to Go* (2002) and *Lesbian Academic Couples* (2005). Her co-authored book *Finding Out: An Introduction to LGBT Studies* (with Michelle Gibson and Jonathan Alexander) will appear in 2009.

Rhonda Pettit, Ph.D., is Associate Professor of English and Women's Studies affiliate faculty at the University of Cincinnati Raymond Walters College. She is the author of *A Gendered Collision: Sentimentalism and Modernism in Dorothy Parker's Poetry and Fiction* (2000) and editor of *The Critical Waltz: Essays on the Work of Dorothy Parker* (2005). Pettit received a Hedgebrook Fellowship in 2006, and her poetry has recently appeared in *Seneca Review, Colere, Tipton Poetry Journal, Raven Chronicles,* and *Trivia.*

María Josefina Saldaña-Portillo is Associate Professor in the Department of Social and Cultural Analysis at New York University, where she directs the Latino Studies Program. Professor Saldaña is a member of the editorial board of *Social Text* and a member of the organizing collective for the Tepoztlán Institute for the Transnational History of the Americas. She has published several articles, in English and Spanish, on revolutionary subjectivity, race, and representation in the Americas; U.S. imperialism in Latin America; and subaltern politics. In 2003 she published *The Revolutionary Imagination in the Americas and the Age of Development* (Duke University Press).

Aunt Lute Books is a multicultural women's press that has been committed to publishing high quality, culturally diverse literature since 1982. In 1990, the Aunt Lute Foundation was formed as a nonprofit corporation to publish and distribute books that reflect the complex truths of women's lives and to present voices that are underrepresented in mainstream publishing. We seek work that explores the specificities of the very different histories from which we come, and the possibilities for personal and social change.

Please contact us if you would like a free catalog of our books or if you wish to be on our mailing list for news of future titles. You may buy books from our website, by phoning in a credit card order, or by mailing a check with the catalog order form.

Aunt Lute Books
P.O. Box 410687
San Francisco, CA 94141
415.826.1300
www.auntlute.com
books@auntlute.com

This book would not have been possible without the kind contributions of the Aunt Lute Founding Friends:

Anonymous Donor
Anonymous Donor
Rusty Barcelo
Marian Bremer
Marta Drury
Diane Goldstein
Diana Harris
Phoebe Robins Hunter
James Lee
Diane Mosbacher, M.D., Ph.D.
Sara Paretsky
William Preston, Jr.
Elise Rymer Turner